A Common Life

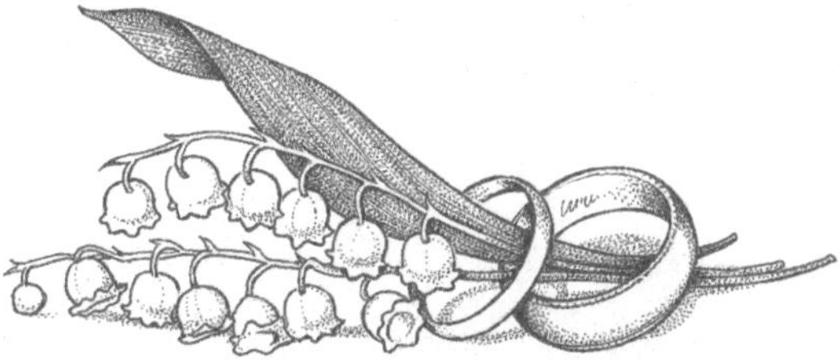

PENGUIN BOOKS

A COMMON LIFE

Jan Karon says she writes "to give readers an extended family, and to applaud the extraordinary beauty of ordinary lives." Other bestselling novels in the Mitford Years series are *At Home in Mitford; A Light in the Window; These High, Green Hills; Out to Canaan; A New Song;* and *In This Mountain.* Her children's books include *Miss Fannie's Hat* and *Jeremy: The Tale of an Honest Bunny.*

THE MITFORD YEARS

A Common Life

The Wedding Story

JAN KARON

PENGUIN BOOKS

PENGUIN BOOKS
Published by the Penguin Group
Penguin Putnam Inc., 375 Hudson Street,
New York, New York 10014, U.S.A.
Penguin Books Ltd, 80 Strand, London WC2R 0RL, England
Penguin Books Australia Ltd, 250 Camberwell Road,
Camberwell, Victoria 3124, Australia
Penguin Books Canada Ltd, 10 Alcorn Avenue, Toronto,
Ontario, Canada M4V 3B2
Penguin Books India (P) Ltd, 11 Community Centre,
Panchsheel Park, New Delhi – 110 017, India
Penguin Books (N.Z.) Ltd, Cnr Rosedale and Airborne Roads,
Albany, Auckland, New Zealand
Penguin Books (South Africa) (Pty) Ltd, 24 Sturdee Avenue,
Rosebank, Johannesburg 2196, South Africa

Penguin Books Ltd, Registered Offices: Harmondsworth, Middlesex, England

First published in the United States of America by Viking Penguin,
a member of Penguin Putnam Inc. 2001
Published in Penguin Books 2002

3 5 7 9 10 8 6 4 2

Illustrations by Laura Hartman Maestro

PUBLISHER'S NOTE
This is a work of fiction. Names, characters, places, and incidents either are the product of the author's imagination or are used fictitiously, and any resemblance to actual persons, living or dead, business establishments, events, or locales is entirely coincidental.

THE LIBRARY OF CONGRESS HAS CATALOGED
THE HARDCOVER EDITION AS FOLLOWS:
Karon, Jan, date.
A common life : the wedding story / Jan Karon.
p. cm.—(The Mitford years)
ISBN 0-670-89437-0 (hc.)
ISBN 0 14 20.0034 5 (pbk.)
1. Weddings—Fiction 2. Mitford (N.C. : Imaginary place)—Fiction.
3. North Carolina—Fiction. 4. City and town life—Fiction I. Title.
PS3561.A678 C6 2001
813'.54—dc21 00-031984

Printed in the United States of America
Set in Fournier MT/Designed by Francesca Belanger

For my much-appreciated
nieces and nephews,
with love

David Craig, Jennifer Craig,
Lisa Knaack, Courtney Setzer, Monica Setzer,
Randy Setzer, and Taja Setzer

Give them wisdom and devotion in the ordering of their common life, that each may be to the other a strength in need, a counselor in perplexity, a comfort in sorrow, and a companion in joy.

Amen.

—*The Book of Common Prayer*

Contents

Acknowledgments

Warm thanks to Viking Penguin Chairman Susan Petersen Kennedy; my agent, Liz Darhansoff; my editor, Carolyn Carlson; Paul Halley; Ruth Bush; Kay Auten; Betty Cox; Bishop Keith Ackerman; Father Charles L. Holt; Father Terry Sweeney; Harvey Karon; Martha J. Marcus; Gail Mayes; James Harris Podgers; Betty Pitts, and the late Hayden Pitts.

Special thanks to Father James Harris, a faithful friend to Mitford; to *Victoria* magazine for excerpts from Mitford fiction that appeared in its pages; and to the lovely Carolyn Clement, our own Hessie Mayhew, who gathered and arranged the wedding flowers which are captured in pastels by Donna Kae Nelson for the jacket of this book.

A Common Life

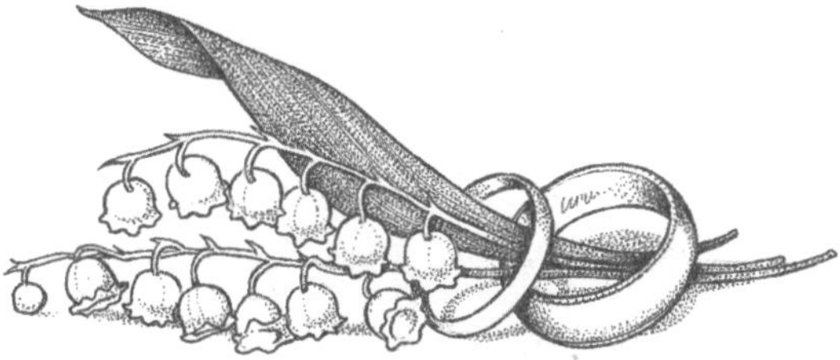

CHAPTER ONE

The Proposal

Father Timothy Kavanagh stood at the stone wall on the ridge above Mitford, watching the deepening blush of a late June sunset.

He conceded that it wasn't the worst way to celebrate a birthday, though he'd secretly hoped to celebrate it with Cynthia. For years, he'd tried to fool himself that his birthday meant very little or nothing, and so, if no cards appeared, or cake or presents, that would be fine.

Indeed, there had been no card from Cynthia, though he'd received a stack from his parishioners, and certainly she'd given no promise of cake or candles that definitively pronounced, *This is it, Timothy, the day you appeared on earth, and though I know you don't really care about such things, we're going to celebrate, anyway, because you're important to me.* He was deeply ashamed to admit that he'd waited for this from her; in truth, had expected it, hoped for it.

He'd known suffering in his thirty-eight years in the priesthood, though nearly always because of someone else's grief or affliction. Now he suffered for himself, for his maddening inability to let his walls down with her, to cast off his armor and simply and utterly love her. He had pled with God to consume his longing and his love, to cast it out as ashes and let nothing interfere with the fulfillment of the vows he'd made years ago as an ordinand. Why should such a flame as this beat up in him now? He was sixty-two years old, he was beyond loving in the flesh! And yet, as desperately as he'd prayed for his longing to be removed, he craved for it to be satisfied.

He remembered the times she had shut herself away from him, guarding her heart. The loss of her ravishing openness had left him cold as a stone, as if a great cloud had gone over the sun.

What if she were to shut herself away from him once and for all? He paced beside the low stone wall, forgetting the sunset over the valley.

He'd never understood much about his feelings toward Cynthia, but he knew and understood this: He didn't want to keep teetering on the edge, afraid to step forward, terrified to turn back.

The weight on his chest was palpable; he'd felt it often since she moved next door and into his life. Yet it wasn't there because he loved her, it was there because he was afraid to love her completely.

Perhaps he would always have such a weight; perhaps there was no true liberation in love. And certainly he could not ask her to accept him as he was—flawed and frightened, not knowing.

He sank to his knees by the stone wall, and looked up and opened his mouth to speak, but instead caught his breath sharply.

A great flow of crimson and gold was spilling across the sky like lava, running molten from west to east. He watched, awestruck, as the pyre consumed the blue haze of the firmament and bathed the heavens with a glory that shook and moved him to his very depths.

"Please!" he whispered.

It was then that he felt a sensation of warmth welling in him, a kind of liquid infilling he'd never experienced before. Something in his soul lifted up, as startling as a covey of quail breaking from the underbrush, and his heart acknowledged, suddenly and finally, that his love for her could not, would not be extinguished. He knew at last that no amount of effort, no amount of pleading with God would enable him to sustain any longer the desperate, wounding battle he had launched against loving her.

In a way he couldn't explain, and in the space of the

merest instant, he knew he'd come fully awake for the first time in his life.

He also knew that he wanted nothing more than to be with her, at her side, and that after all the wasted months, he couldn't afford to waste another moment. But what if he'd waited too long, come to his senses too late?

He sprang to his feet, as relieved as if he'd shaken off an approaching illness; then, animated by a power not his own, he found himself running.

"There comes a time," his cousin Walter had said, "when there's no turning back."

He felt the motion of his legs and the breeze on his skin and the hammering in his temples, as if he might somehow implode, all of it combusting into a sharp inner flame, a durable fire, a thousand hosannas.

Streaming with sweat, he raced down Old Church Lane and into the cool green enclosure of Baxter Park, his body as weightless as a glider borne on wings of ether, though his heart was heavy with dread. She could have gone away as she'd done before . . . and this time, she might never come back.

The dark silhouette of the hedge separating the park from Cynthia's house and the rectory appeared far away, another country, a landmark he might never reach.

As he drew closer, he saw that her house was dark, but his own was aglow with light in every window, as if some wonderful thing might be happening.

He bounded through the hedge; she was standing on his stoop. She held the door open, and the light from the kitchen gleamed behind her.

She stood there as if she'd known the very moment he turned into the park and, sensing the urgency of his heart, felt her own compelled to greet it.

He ran up the steps, his chest heaving, as she stepped back and smiled at him. "Happy birthday!" she said.

"I love you, Cynthia!" His lungs seemed to force the declaration onto the night air as if by their own will. He stood with his mouth open, marveling, while she raised her hand to her cheek in a way that made her appear dubious, somehow, or amused.

Did she think him mad? He felt mad, riotous, he wanted to climb on the roof, baying and whooping—a sixtysomething bachelor priest, mad with love for his next-door neighbor.

He didn't consider the consequences of this wild skidding out of control; it was now or never.

As she backed into the kitchen, he followed. He saw the cake on the breakfast table and the card propped against a vase of flowers, and he fell to one knee beside the table and gathered her hands in his.

"Will you?" he croaked, looking up at her.

"Will I *what,* dearest?"

"You know."

"No, I don't know."

He knew that she knew; why wouldn't she help him with this thing? He was perfectly willing to bring the other knee down if only she would help him.

And why was he crouching here on the linoleum, sweating like a prizefighter, when he might have been dressed in his best suit and doing this in the study, or in the Lord's Chapel garden by the French roses?

He tried to scramble to his feet and run upstairs, where he would take a shower and brush his teeth and get dressed and do this the right way, but his strength failed and he found he couldn't move; he might have been glued to the linoleum, one knee up and one knee down, frozen as a herring.

"Hurry, Timothy!" she said, whispering.

"Will you marry me?"

"Yes! A thousand times yes!"

She was helping him to his feet, and then he was kissing her and she was kissing him back. She drew away and looked at him with a kind of awe; he found her radiance dumbfounding. "I thought you'd never ask," she said.

It was done. He had jumped over the barbed wire.

He buried his face in her hair and held her close and bawled like a baby.

He was a muddle of happiness and confusion, as if his brain had been stirred like so much porridge. He was unable to think straight or put one thought logically after another; he felt the magnitude of the thing he'd done, and knew he should do something to carry through, though he wasn't sure what.

They had sat on his sofa, talking until three in the morning, but not once had they mentioned what they would do today; they had talked only about how they felt and how mindlessly happy and grateful they were that this astonishing benediction should come to them, as a wild bird might come to their outstretched palms.

"To have and to hold," she had murmured.

"'Til death do us part," he had said, nuzzling her hair.

"And no organizing of church suppers or ironing of fair linens, and positively *nothing* to do with the annual Bane and Blessing."

"Right," he said.

"Ever!" she said.

He hadn't a single rule or regulation to foist upon

her; he was chopped liver, he was cooked macaroni; he was dragged into the undertow of the great tsunami of love he'd so long held back.

They had prayed together, at last, and fallen asleep on the sofa, her head on his shoulder, his head against hers, bookends, then waked at five and scrambled to the back door, where Cynthia kissed him and darted through the hedge, devoutly hoping not to be seen.

He'd bounded up the stairs to his room with a vigor that amazed him, murmuring aloud a quote from Wordsworth:

"'Bliss it was in that dawn to be alive, But to be young was very heaven!'"

Bliss, yes, as if he'd suddenly become lighter than air, as if the stone were at last rolled away from the tomb. He thought he might spring upward like a jack-in-the-box. Was any of this familiar to him, had he ever felt it before? Never! Nothing in his supposed love for Peggy Cramer, all those years ago, had prepared him for this.

In a misting summer rain, he headed for the church office at nine o'clock with Barnabas on the red leash.

He should tell Emma, he supposed, who had served him faithfully for nearly thirteen years. And Puny, the best house help a man could ever have, Puny would want to know.

He could see them both, Emma wincing and frowning, then socking him on the arm with approval, and Puny—she would jump up and down and hoot and shout, and great tears would stream down her freckled cheeks. Then she'd go at once and bake a cake of cornbread from which he, due to his blasted diabetes, might have one unbuttered, albeit large, slice.

Aha! And there was Miss Sadie, of course! Wouldn't her eyes sparkle and gleam, and wouldn't she hug his neck for a fare-thee-well?

And wouldn't Louella break out a coconut cake or a chess pie and wouldn't they have a party right there in the kitchen at Fernbank?

On the other hand, wasn't Cynthia supposed to be along when he broke the news to everybody?

He sighed. He was in the very business of life's milestones, including the occasional overseeing of engagements, yet he seemed to have forgotten everything he ever knew— if, indeed, he ever knew anything.

Besides, he wasn't sure he was up for hooting and hollering and being punched in the arm or any of the other stuff that usually came with such tidings.

Then there was J.C. And Mule. And Percy.

Good Lord, he dreaded that encounter like a toothache. All that backslapping and winking and cackling, and the word spreading through the Grill like so much wildfire, and spilling out the door and up Main Street and around the monument to Lew Boyd's Exxon. . . .

He felt his stomach do a kind of dive, as it always did when he took off or landed in a plane.

If Barnabas hadn't suddenly jerked the leash, he would have walked straight into a telephone pole outside the Oxford Antique Shop.

Bottom line, he decided, Dooley Barlowe should be the first to know. And it was clearly right that they tell Dooley together. He was frankly relieved that Dooley had spent the night at Tommy's and hadn't been there to see him skid through the back door and drop to his knee. Not a pretty sight, he was sure of it.

He could just see the face of his thirteen-year-old charge when he heard the news. The boy would flush with embarrassment or relief, or both, then laugh like a hyena. He would very likely exclaim, *Cool!* then race upstairs with a joy that he dare not freely display.

Still, telling anyone at all seemed hotheaded and premature. This was between Cynthia and himself; it was their secret. It was somehow marvelous that it was yet unknown to anyone else in the world.

At the corner, he stopped at a hemlock to let Barnabas lift his leg, and suddenly knew he couldn't contain the secret any longer, he was full to bursting with it.

"Make it snappy," he said to his dog. "I have something to tell you."

Barnabas did as he was told, and when they crossed the street, the rector of the Chapel of our Lord and Savior paused in front of the church office and said under his breath, "I've just decided . . . that is, Cynthia and I are going to get . . ."

His throat tickled. He coughed. A car passed, and he tried again to tell his dog the good news.

But he couldn't say it.

He couldn't say the *m* word, no matter how hard he tried.

As he opened the office door, he realized with complete clarity where he should begin.

His bishop. Of course. How could he have forgotten he had a bishop, and that such a thing as this thing he was going to do would be of utmost importance to Stuart Cullen?

But, of course, he couldn't call Stuart this morning, because Emma Newland would be sitting at her desk cheek-by-jowl with his own.

He greeted his longtime, part-time secretary as

Barnabas collapsed with a sigh onto his rug in the corner.

Desperate to avoid eye contact, he sat down at once and began to scribble something, he knew not what, into his sermon notebook.

Emma stared at him over her half-glasses.

He put his left elbow on the desk and held his head in his hand, as if deeply thoughtful, feeling her hot stare covering him like a cloak.

Blast, he couldn't bear that look. She might have been examining his tonsils or readying him for colon surgery.

"For heaven's sake," he said, swiveling around in his squeaking chair to face the bookcases.

"I'd leave heaven out of this if I were you," she said, sniffing.

"What's that supposed to mean?"

"I mean, I can't imagine heaven wantin' anything to do with you this morning."

Church secretaries had been fired for less, much less, he thought, grinding his teeth. The office was suddenly doing that bizarre thing it sometimes did—it was growing rapidly and infinitely smaller; it was, in fact, becoming the size of a shoe box.

He bolted to his feet and half stood behind his desk, trying to get a deep breath.

"Your collar's too tight," she said.

"How do you know?"

"Your face is red as a beet."

"It's possible that I'm having a heart attack," he snapped.

"I'm telling you it's your collar. Are you wearin' one of those Velcro deals?"

"Yes."

"Let it out a little."

Dadgummit, she was right. He realized he was nearly choking to death. He adjusted the Velcro, disgusted with himself and everybody else.

What had happened to the soft, circumcised heart God had given him only last night? Where had the lighter-than-air spirit of this morning fled? Why was he grumping and grouching when he ought to be leaping and shouting?

Barnabas yawned and rolled on his side.

"I'm getting married!" he blurted uncontrollably. Then he sat down, hard, in his chair.

He would never be able to explain the mysteries surrounding love, only one of which surfaced when he confessed his news to Emma.

By the involuntary utterance of those three amazing words, his frozen Arctic tundra had been transformed into a warm tropical lake. Something in him had actually melted.

In the space of a few moments, he had become jelly. Or possibly custard. Then a foolish smile spread across his face, which seemed destined to remain there for the rest of his life.

When Emma left for the post office, vowing not to say a word to anyone, he prayed at his desk, went to the toilet and did a glucometer check, then positively swaggered to the phone to call his bishop.

Stuart's secretary said he was either in the loo or in a meeting, she wasn't sure which, but she would find out and have him call back.

He slumped in the chair, disappointed.

But wait. *Walter!* Of course, he must call Walter and Katherine at once.

The names of those with special interest in his good fortune were being revealed to him, one by one, in the way some are given inspiration for their Christmas card list.

Since Cynthia had never met Walter, his first cousin

and only known living relative, he supposed he was on his own for spilling the beans to New Jersey.

"Walter!"

"Cousin! We haven't heard from you in the proverbial coon's age."

"Which phone are you on?" asked the rector.

"The kitchen. Why?"

"Is Katherine there?"

"Just blew in from the nursing home, she's teaching them to finger paint. What's up, old fellow?"

"Tell her to get on the phone in the study."

"Katherine!" bellowed Walter. "Pick up in the study! It's clergy!"

"'Lo, Teds, darling, is that really you?" He could see the tall, thin-as-a-stick Katherine draped over the plaid chaise, with the cordless in one hand and her eternal glass of ginger ale in the other.

"Katherine, Walter," he said. "Are you sitting down?"

"Good heavens, what is it?" asked Walter, clearly alarmed.

"Teds . . . those tests you were going to have weeks ago . . . is it . . . ?"

"Dooley, is it Dooley?" asked Walter. "Or Barnabas? We know how you feel about—"

"I'm getting married," he said.

There! Twice in a row, and already it was getting easier.

The other end of the line erupted into a deafening whoop that could have filled Yankee Stadium. He held the receiver away from his ear, laughing for the first time this morning, as Barnabas leapt from the rug and stood barking furiously at the clamor pouring forth from New Jersey.

When Stuart hadn't called back in twenty minutes, he phoned again and was put through to the bishop's office.

"Stuart? Tim Kavanagh here. Are you sitting down?" He was truly concerned that no one go crashing to the floor in a faint.

"For the first time today, actually! What's up?"

"Remember the woman I once brought to visit you and Martha?" That wasn't what he wanted to say. "When we, ah, gave you the bushel of corn? *Cynthia!* You remember. . . ."

"I remember very well, indeed!"

"Well, you see, it's like this. . . ." He swallowed.

He heard his bishop chuckling. "Like what, Timothy?"

"Like . . ."

He was momentarily frozen again, then the custard triumphed.

". . . we're getting married!"

"Alleluia!" shouted his bishop. *"Alleluia!"*

Tears sprang suddenly to his eyes. He had been friends with his bishop since seminary, had confided his heart to him for years. And now came this greatest confidence, this best and most extraordinary of tidings.

"Martha will be thrilled!" said Stuart, sounding as youthful as a curate. "We'll have you for dinner, we'll have you for tea . . . we'll do it up right! This is the best news I've heard in an eon. Good heavens, man, I thought you'd never screw up your courage. How on earth did it happen?"

"It just came to me that . . . well . . ."

"What came to you?"

"That I didn't want to go on without her, that I couldn't."

"Bingo!" said his bishop.

"I, ah, went down on one knee, couldn't help myself."

"You should have done the full kneel, Timothy, she's a prize, a gem, a pearl above price! You dog, you don't deserve such a one!"

"Amen!" He said it the old Baptist way, with a long *a*, the way he was raised to say it.

"Well, now, thanks be to God, what about a date?" asked Stuart.

"We're thinking September, I know that's a busy month for you, but . . ."

"Let's see, I have my calendar right here." Deep sigh, pondering. "Alas, alack." Stuart's fingers drumming on his desktop. "Good heavens, I'd forgotten about that. Hmmm. Ahh." Tuneless, unconscious humming. "No, certainly not then."

If Stuart couldn't do it, they'd get it done somehow, they were definitely not waiting 'til October. . . .

"Oh, yes, look here! I've got September seventh, how's that? Otherwise, I can squeeze you in on—"

"I'm not much on being squeezed in," said the rector.

"Of course not! Will the seventh work for you, then?"

"We're willing to take whatever you have open."

"Then it's done!"

"Perfect!" said the rector.

"Now," said Stuart, "hang up so I can call Martha."

CHAPTER TWO

The Grill

"You goin' to have babies?" asked Dooley.

"Not if I can help it," said Cynthia.

Searching the boy's face, Father Tim felt sure their news was a go, but wanted to hear Dooley declare it. He put his arm around Dooley's shoulders. "So, buddyroe, what do you think about all this?"

"Cool!" said Dooley.

Hallelujah! Dooley Barlowe had been buffeted by every violent wind imaginable before he came to live at the rectory over two years ago. Abandoned by his father and given by his alcoholic mother to his disabled grandfather, the boy had known only upheaval and change.

"Nothing will change," the rector promised. "You'll keep your same room, everything will flow on as usual. The only difference is, Cynthia will live here . . . instead of there." He gestured toward the little yellow house next door.

"I like her hamburgers better'n yours, anyway."

"Yes, but she doesn't have a clue how to fry baloney the way you like it. That's my little secret." He loved the look of this red-haired, earnest boy he'd come to cherish as a son, loved the rare surprise and delight shining in his eyes. Dooley and Cynthia had gotten on famously from the beginning, and Dooley's stamp of approval was more important than that of any bishop.

Not wishing to waste time gaining ground, Dooley gave Cynthia his most soulful look. "Since I'm goin' off t' 'at ol' school pretty soon, I bet *you'll* let me stay up 'til midnight."

Ah, politics! thought the rector, happily observing the two. They're everywhere.

Both Dooley and Emma had promised to keep mum, but truth be told, they were only human.

Before there was a leak, however unintentional, the news must go in Sunday's pew bulletin, thereby giving his parish the dignity of hearing it in church instead of on the street. As this was Friday, he supposed he should tell the guys at the Grill before they heard it from a parishioner. But would they keep it quiet until Lord's Chapel got the news on Sunday?

Then there was Miss Sadie. She definitely wouldn't like reading it in a pew bulletin.

He went home at eleven, changed hurriedly into his running clothes, and jogged up Old Church Lane with Barnabas.

He had just run down this hill to do the thing that resulted in why he was now running up it. Life was a mystery.

Huffing, he zigged to the left on Church Hill Road. Then he zagged to the right and ran up the driveway instead of cutting through the orchard like a common poacher.

Miss Sadie and Louella were sitting on the porch, fanning and rocking.

Each time he came to Fernbank's front porch, the years automatically rolled away. With these two old friends, he felt twelve, or possibly ten. Fernbank was his fountain of youth.

His heart pounding, he sat on the top step and panted. Barnabas lay beside him, doing the same.

"Father," said Miss Sadie, "aren't you too old for this running business?"

"Not by a long shot. I do it to keep young, as a matter of fact."

"Pshaw! Too much is made of running up hill and down dale. I've never done such a thing in my life, and I'm coming up on ninety and healthy as a horse."

Louella rocked. "That's right."

"Is that lemonade?" asked Father Tim, eyeing the pitcher on the wicker table.

"Louella, what's happened to our manners?" asked Miss Sadie.

"I don't know, Miss Sadie. I 'spec' we don' get enough comp'ny t' hardly need manners."

Louella put ice in a glass and handed it to Fernbank's mistress, who, ever conserving, poured the glass half full.

He got up and fetched the lemonade from her, wondering what on earth they would think about his announcement. He'd envisioned them as happy about it, but now he wasn't so sure. He drank the lemonade in two gulps and stood on one foot, then the other.

"You itchy," said Louella.

They could read him like a book.

"Miss Sadie, Louella, are you sitting down?"

The two women looked at each other, puzzled.

Of course they were sitting down, how stupid of him to ask such a thing, it had flown out of his mouth. "Joke!" he said feebly.

"Father, why don't *you* sit down? Get in this chair next to me and start rocking!"

He did as he was told. "Yes, ma'am." Eight years old.

"Louella and I like to rock in harmony, you pay a penny if you get off track."

"Who's leading?"

Miss Sadie looked at him as if he were dumb as a gourd.

"Honey, Miss Sadie always lead."

"Here we go," said Miss Sadie, looking bright and expectant. Since her feet barely touched the floor, this would be no small accomplishment.

After a ragged start, they nailed their synchronization, then worked on building momentum. Miss Sadie was flying in that rocker. . . .

Lord knows he couldn't sit around on porches all day like some jackleg priest, he had things to do, people to see, and besides, he was getting married. . . .

"Miss Sadie, Louella, I have great news."

The two women looked at him eagerly, never missing a beat.

"I'm getting married!" he shouted over the roar of six wooden rockers whipping along on aged white pine.

Miss Sadie's feet hit the floor, Louella's feet hit the

floor. Their rockers came to a dead stop. His was still going.

"To Miss Cynthia?" asked Louella, who was generally suspicious of good news.

"The very one!" he said, feeling a stab of happiness and pride.

Louella whooped and clapped her hands. "Thank you, Jesus! Thank you, *thank* you, Jesus!"

Miss Sadie dug a handkerchief from the sleeve of her dress and pressed it to her eyes. "This is a happy day, Father. I can't tell you how happy we are for you. Cynthia is the loveliest imaginable lady, so bright and positive, just what you need. I hope you've been on your knees thanking the Lord!"

He had, actually.

Louella was beaming. "Miss Sadie, I'm goin' t' cut us all some pie." As she opened the screen door to go inside, she turned and said, "An' remember you owe me five dollars!"

They heard Miss Sadie's longtime companion shuffling down the hall in her slippers. "Why, may I ask, do you owe Louella five dollars?"

She looked at him, barely able to conceal her mirth. "Because, Father, I bet five dollars you didn't have it in you to marry that lovely woman!"

Knowing how dear five dollars was to Sadie Baxter,

he smiled at his favorite parishioner and said, "I suppose I could say I'm sorry you lost."

She patted his arm fondly. "Actually, Father, your good news declares that we've all won."

He typed it on his aged and finicky Royal manual and passed it to Emma, who would do whatever she did to work it into the bulletin:

> ii publish the banns of marriiage between Cynthiia clary Coppersmiith of the pariish of the Chapel of our Lord and Saviior and father Tiimothy andrew Kavanagh, rector of thiis pariish. iif any of you know just cause why they may not be joiined together iin Holy Matriimony, you are biidden to declare iit.

Mitford Muse editor J. C. Hogan slammed his overstuffed briefcase onto the seat in the rear booth and thumped down, huffing.

Mule Skinner, local realtor and longtime Grill regular, slid in beside Father Tim.

"So, what are you roughnecks havin' today?" asked Velma, appearing with her order pad.

Mule jerked his thumb toward the rector. "I'm havin' what he's havin'."

"And what might that be?" This was not her favorite booth; at least two of these turkeys could never make up their minds.

"Chicken salad sandwich," said the rector, always prepared, "hold the mayo, and a side of slaw."

"I don't like slaw," said Mule.

"So sue me," said the rector.

"Make it snappy. You want what he's havin' or not?"

"I don't like slaw," Mule repeated. "I'll have what he's havin', except hold the slaw and give me mayo."

Velma pursed her lips. It was definitely time to retire. Some days, she'd rather work a canning line at the kraut factory than come in here and put up with this mess.

"I'll have th' special," said J.C., wiping his perspiring face with a square of paper towel.

"What special?" asked Mule. "I didn't know there was a special."

"Th' sign's plastered all over th' front door," said Velma, thoroughly disgusted. How Mule Skinner ever sold anybody a house was beyond her.

"So what is it?" asked Mule.

"Raw frog's liver on a bed of mashed turnips."

The rector and the editor roared; the realtor did not.

"I don't like turnips," said Mule.

J.C. rolled his eyes. "Just bring 'im th' frog's liver."

"Dadgummit, give me a BLT and get it over with."

"You might try sayin' please," snapped Velma, who had to talk to some people as if they were children.

"Please," said Mule through clenched teeth.

"White or wheat?" Velma inquired.

"Wheat!" said Mule. "No, make it white."

"Toasted or plain?"

"Ahhh . . ."

"Bring 'im toasted," said J.C.

Velma stomped off and came back with the coffeepot and filled their cups, muttering under her breath.

"What'd she say?" asked Mule.

"You don't want to know," said Father Tim.

He stirred his coffee, though there was nothing in it to stir. Maybe he shouldn't say anything until everyone had eaten lunch and felt . . . happier about life in general. After all, Mule was scowling, and J.C. had his nose stuck in the Wesley newspaper, checking to see if any *Muse* advertisers had defected to the *Telegram*.

He hoped the ensuing discussion wouldn't collapse into a mindless lecture on his advanced age. Age had nothing to do with it, nothing whatever. No one else had bothered to bring it up, and even if they'd thought it, they had the common decency not to mention it.

Then again, why wait to spill the beans? Maybe there was no such thing as the right time with this crowd.

"I've got some great news."

J.C. glanced up and took a sip of coffee. Mule swiveled toward him and looked expectant.

"Cynthia and I are getting married."

The coffee came spewing out of J.C.'s mouth, which was not a pretty sight.

Mule put his hand to his ear. "What's that? I can't always hear out of—"

J.C. wiped his shirtfront with a napkin. "He's gettin' *married.*"

"Don't shout, for heaven's sake!" snapped the rector. He might as well have blared it up and down Main Street from a flatbed truck.

"Who to?" asked Mule.

"Who do you think?" asked J.C., who had apparently appointed himself the rector's official spokesman.

"Cynthia," said Father Tim, wishing to the Lord he'd never mentioned it. "And I have to ask your complete confidence, you're not to tell a soul until it comes out in the pew bulletin on Sunday. I need your word on this," he insisted.

"You want me to swear on th' Bible?" asked Mule.

"No, just promise me. I didn't want you to hear it on the street, I wanted to tell you in person. But I don't want my parish to hear it on the street, either."

"Done," said J.C., shaking hands across the table.

"You've got my word," said Mule.

"Son of a gun. Married." J.C. shook his head. "I thought you had good sense."

"I do have good sense. Look who I'm marrying." His chest actually felt more expansive as he said this.

"Now, that's a fact," agreed J.C. "Cynthia Coppersmith is one fine lady, smart as a whip and good-lookin' into the bargain. What she sees in you is a mystery to me."

"You sure about this?" asked Mule. "Is it a done deal?"

"Done deal. We'll be married in September."

Mule scratched his head. "Seems like you're a little . . . *old* for this, seein' it's the first time and all. I mean, sixty-five—"

"Sixty-two," said the rector. "Sixty-*two*."

J.C. looked grim. "I wouldn't get married if somebody gave me a million bucks. *After* taxes."

"You all are a real encouragement, I must say." The rector heard a positive snarl in his voice.

"Hold on," said Mule. "We're glad for you, cross

my heart an' hope to die. It just shocked me, is all, I'll get over it. See, I'm used to you th' way you *are*. . . ."

"Right. Emerson said it was a bloomin' inconvenience to have to start seeing somebody in a new light. But here's to you, buddyroe." The editor hoisted his coffee cup as Velma delivered their lunch.

She carried a plate in each hand and one in the crook of her right arm. "Take this offa my arm," she said to Mule. He took it.

She set the other two plates down and stomped off.

"I didn't order this," said Mule.

"That's mine," said J.C., snatching the plate.

"If I'd known that's what you were havin,' I'd of had that. Country-style steak is practically my favorite." Mule gazed with remorse at his sandwich, which featured a dill pickle on the side.

"I don't like pickles, you want my pickle?" he asked the rector, who hadn't felt so generally let down since the choir and the organist got the flu simultaneously and the congregation had to sing a cappella.

It was all rushing by in a blur. He didn't want to lose this moment so quickly. He wanted to savor it, rejoice in it, be thankful in it.

He put on his pajamas and pondered what was happening.

It gladdened him that he wanted to see her at the slightest opportunity; he yearned toward his neighbor as if a magnet had been installed in him on the night of his birthday, attracted to some powerful magnet in her.

How he wished the magnet had been installed sooner. He didn't want to think of the time he'd wasted trying to make up his mind. But no, it hadn't been his mind that was slow to make up, it was his heart. His heart had always pulled away when he felt happiness with her; each time the joy came, he had retreated, filled with the fear of losing himself.

He remembered the dream he'd had when she was in New York, when their letters had helped thaw the frozen winter that kept them apart. He dreamed he was swimming toward her in something like a blue lagoon, when his strength failed and he began to sink, slowly, as if with the weight of stones. He felt the water roaring in and the great, bursting heaviness of his head. He had come awake then, gasping for air and crying out.

Now there was the custard feeling, which would terrify most people if they didn't recognize it for what it was—it was love unhindered.

This, too, took his breath away, but by the grace of

God, he was easy with it, not enfeebled or frightened by it.

No wonder he had counseled so many men before their walk down the aisle; the true softening of the heart and spirit toward a woman was usually an alarmingly unfamiliar feeling. How might a man wield a spear and shield, preserve his very life, if he were poured out at her feet like so much pudding?

He turned off the lamp and went to his knees by his bed, praying aloud in the darkened room.

"Father, we bless You and thank You for this miracle, for choosing us to receive it.

"May we treat the love You've given us with gratitude and devotion, humor and astonishment.

"May it be a river of living water to bring delight and encouragement to others, Lord, for we must never hold this rare blessing to ourselves, but pour it out like wine.

"Protect her, Lord, give her courage for whatever lies ahead, and give me, I pray, whatever is required to love her well and steadfastly all the days of our lives."

There was something else, something else to be spoken tonight. He was quiet for a time in the still, dark room where only the sound of his dog's snoring was heard.

Yes. There it was. The old and heavy thing he so often ignored, that needed to be said.

"Father—continue to open me and lay me bare, for I have been selfish and closed, always keeping something back, even from You. Forgive me. . . ."

The clock ticked.

The curtains blew out in a light breeze.

"Through Jesus Christ, our Lord.

"Amen."

CHAPTER THREE

The Fanfare

The tidal wave, the firestorm, the volcanic spew—all the things he'd dreaded had come at last, and all at once.

People were pounding him on the back, kissing him on the cheek, slapping him on the shoulder, pumping his hand. One of his older parishioners, a mite taller than himself, patted his head; another gave him a Cuban cigar, which Barnabas snatched off the kitchen table and ate in the wrapper.

Well-wishers bellowed their felicitations across the street, rang his phone off the hook at home and office, and generally made a commotion over the fact that he had feelings like the rest of the common horde.

Cynthia's phone got a workout, as well. In approximately three days since the news had hit the street, a total of five bridal showers had been booked, not to mention a luncheon at Esther Cunningham's and a tea at

Olivia Harper's. Emma Newland was planning a sit-down dinner with the help of Harold's mother, and the ECW was doing a country club event.

He was stopped on the street by Mike Stovall, the Presbyterian choirmaster, who offered to throw in sixteen voices for the wedding ceremony, which, including the voices at Lord's Chapel, would jack the total to thirty-seven. "A real tabernacle deal!" enthused the choirmaster. "And tell you what, we'll throw in a trumpet! How's that?"

(He'd hardly known what to do about the Anglicans from Wesley, who offered to throw in a handbell choir.)

Had he agreed to Mike Stovall's ridiculous offer? He didn't think so. He might have mumbled something like "Great idea," which it was, but would Mike take that to mean he'd accepted? Thirty-seven people in the choir would barely leave room for the bride and groom to squeeze to the altar.

His head was swimming, his stomach was churning, his palms were sweating, he felt like . . . a rock star. That heady notion was soon squelched, however, when he was forced to dash to the toilet at the church office and throw up. He flushed three times, trying to disguise the wretched indignity of the whole appalling act.

"Something I ate," he said to Emma, who knew a lame excuse when she heard one. He snatched a book off the shelf and sat with his back to her, numb as a pickled herring.

"I'm sorry," he told Cynthia one evening at the rectory.

"Whatever for?"

"For . . . you know . . . the ruckus, the . . . the *tumult*!"

"But dearest, I love this! There's never been such ado over any of my personal decisions. It's wonderful to me!"

"It is?"

"And can't you see how happy this is making everyone? Sometimes I think it really isn't for us, it's for them!"

"Wrong," he said, taking her hand in his. "It's for us."

"Then please relax and enjoy it, darling. Can't you?"

She looked at him so searchingly, with such a poignant hope, that he was weak with a mixture of shame for his current dilapidation and love for her bright spirit.

"Of course. You're right. I'll try. I promise."

"Please. You see, this will only happen to us once."

There! She'd nailed it. What made him uneasy was that it was happening *to* them; he preferred having some say-so, some . . . *control*.

"Let God be in control," she said, smiling. He was

unfailingly astonished that she could read his mind. "After all, He's done a wonderful job so far."

The tension flowed out of him like air from a tire.

"Ahhhh," he said, sitting back on the sofa and unsnapping his collar.

The bishop rang him shortly after dawn.

"Timothy! I know you're an early riser. . . ."

"If I wasn't, I am now."

"Martha and I want the two of you to use our old family camp in Maine, it's on a lake, has a boathouse and two canoes, and an absolutely glorious view! We're thrilled about all this, you must say yes, we'll call at once and make sure it's set aside. . . ."

His bishop was gushing like a schoolgirl.

"And wait 'til you hear the loons, Timothy! Mesmerizing! Magical! Our family has gathered at this house for nearly fifty years, it might have been the set of *On Golden Pond*! Trust me, you'll be thrilled, you'll think you've expired and shot straight up!"

"Thanks, Stuart, let me get back to you on that, we haven't really discussed what we're going to do."

"Don't even think about Cancún, Timothy!"

He hadn't once thought of Cancún.

"And get any notion of southern France out of your head . . ."

He hadn't had any such notion in his head.

". . . it's all the rage, southern France, but you'll like Maine far better! It's where Martha and I spent *our* honeymoon, you know."

He hardly knew what to say to all the offers pouring in; Ron Malcolm had offered the services of a limousine following the wedding, but he'd declined. Why would they need a limo when they were only going a block and a half to spend their wedding night?

Esther Bolick sat in the den that opened off her kitchen and stared blankly at *Wheel of Fortune;* it was nothing more than flickering images, she didn't give a katy what a five-word definition for *show biz* might be.

She glanced irritably at Gene, who was snoring in his recliner after a supper of fresh lima beans, new potatoes, fried squash, coleslaw, and skillet cornbread. They'd also had green onions the size of her fist, which Gene took a fit over. "Sweet as sugar!" he declared. She had never trusted a man who wouldn't eat onions.

She was thinking that she was happy for Father Kavanagh, happy as can be. But it had been *days* since she heard the good news and not *one word* had anybody said to her about baking the wedding cake. She knew Cynthia was very talented; she could do anything in the world except cross-stitch, so she could probably bake her own cake.

Well, then, that was it, she thought with relief. That was why nobody had said doodley-squat about her famous orange marmalade being the center of attraction at one of the most important weddings in Mitford in . . . maybe *decades.*

On the other hand, why would anybody in their right mind take time to bake their own wedding cake when all they had to do was dial Esther Bolick at 8705?

She had designed that cake over and over in her mind. Considering that the color of the icing was white, she might crown the top with calla lilies. Jena Ivey at Mitford Blossoms could order off for callas in a heartbeat. She'd even thought of scattering edible pearls around on the icing; she'd never used edible pearls before, and hoped people's fillings wouldn't crack out and roll around on the parish hall floor.

She also considered wreathing the base of the cake with real cream-colored roses, plus she'd have icing roses tumbling down the sides—after all, she'd seen a few magazines in her time, she was no hick, she knew what was what in today's cake world. And would she dun the father for all that work? Of course not! Not a red cent, though Lord only knows, what they charged for ingredients these days made highway robbery look law-abiding.

Esther pursed her lips and stared, unseeing, at a spot on the wall.

The thing was, it didn't make a bit of sense for somebody to bake their own wedding cake . . .

. . . so, maybe somebody else had been asked to bake the cake.

The thought made her supper turn to a rock in her digestive system. She balled up her fist and rubbed the place between her ribs, feeling the pain all the way to her heart.

How could they ask anybody else to bake the father's wedding cake? He had raved about her orange marmalade for years, had personally told her it was the best cake he had ever put in his mouth, bar none. *Bar none!* So what if two pieces of it had nearly killed him? It was his own blamed fault for stuffing himself!

And how many orange marmalades had she carried to the doors of the downtrodden, the sick, the elderly, and the flat broke? And how many hundreds of miles had she walked from fridge to oven to sink, getting varicose veins and bad knees, not to mention bunions? Well, then—*how many*?

She remembered the rueful time she baked marmalades the livelong day and finally dragged herself to her electric-powered recliner, where she pressed the button on her remote and tilted back to what Gene called "full sprawl." All she lacked of being dead was the news getting out, when, *blam!* the most violent and sudden storm you'd ever want to see hit square over their house and the power went out. There she was, trapped in that plug-in recliner, clutching a dead remote—with no way to haul herself up and Gene Bolick out to a meeting at the Legion hut.

She recalled the shame of having to pitch herself over the side like a sailor jumping ship; landing on the floor had caused her right leg to turn blue as blazes, then black, then brown, not to mention her hip, which, as she'd told the doctor, had given her sporadical pain ever since. And all that for what? For four orange marmalades to help raise money for a new toilet at the library!

Trembling slightly, Esther picked up the TV remote and surfed to a commercial with a talking dog. She and Gene had never had a dog and never would, they were too much trouble, but she liked dogs. She tried to occupy her mind with dogs so she wouldn't think about a shocking idea that suddenly occurred to her. Her attention wandered, however, and there it was, the bald truth, staring her in the face:

Winnie Ivey!

Winnie Ivey was exactly who they'd turned to for this special, once-in-a-lifetime deal—Winnie Ivey, who was a *commercial* baker; Winnie Ivey, who'd never made just *one* of anything in her life!

She sat bolt upright and tried to get her breath. Commercial flour! Commercial butter! And, for all she knew, powdered eggs.

Her blood ran cold.

"Of all th' dadblame things to do!" she said, kicking one of her shoes across the room.

"What?" Gene raised his head and looked around. "Was that you, dollface?"

"Do you know who they've asked to bake the weddin' cake?"

"What weddin' cake?"

"Why, the father's, of course!"

"Who?" asked Gene, genuinely interested.

"Winnie Ivey."

Gene burped happily. "Well, I'll say."

"You'll say what?" she demanded.

When his wife stood up and leaned over his recliner as she was now doing, he thought she looked ten feet tall. "I'll say that was a dirty, low-down trick not to ask you to bake it!"

There. Gene Bolick knew what side his bread was buttered on.

She was stomping into the kitchen, mad as a hornet, when the phone rang.

"Hallo!" she shouted, ready to knock somebody's head off.

"Esther? This is Cynthia Coppersmith, I'm so glad you're home, I thought you and Gene might have gone bowling tonight. Timothy and I agree we'd like nothing better than to have one of your fabulous three-layer marmalades as our wedding cake. We hope you'll be able to do it, Timothy said we'll pay top dollar!"

Cynthia was astounded to hear Esther Bolick burst into tears, followed by a pause in which there was considerable murmuring and shuffling about.

"Hello!" Gene bawled into the phone. "Esther said tell you she'd love to bake your weddin' cake! And no charge, you tell th' father no charge!"

Now his choir was upset because the crowd from down the street had horned in.

Had he actually agreed to such a plan? He remembered only that Mike had brought it up, nothing more. He called Mike Stovall.

"I believe we talked about your choir joining our choir for—"

"Right! And everything's going great, just great! We've got a couple of ideas for the music—"

"The music, of course, is entirely Richard's domain, Richard's and Cynthia's, so—"

"Well!" Mike Stovall sounded annoyed.

"In any case, given the small quarters of our nave and chancel, I think it might be best to—"

"Oh, we've thought that through, Father, here's the deal. Your choir in the chancel, ours in the rear, what do you think?"

He couldn't think. He needed a job foreman, somebody in a hard hat. . . .

"It *will* be September, you know."

Hessie Mayhew—*Mitford Muse* reporter, Presbyterian mover and shaker, and gifted flower arranger—had come to consult with Cynthia in the rectory living room. As Father Tim served them lemonade and shortbread, he couldn't help but listen. After all, wasn't he a gardener? Wasn't he interested in flowers?

He crept to a corner of the room with a glass of lemonade and appeared to be wholly absorbed in scratching his dog behind the ears.

"And in September," said Hessie, "there's precious little that's worth picking." Hessie had staked her reputation on what she foraged from meadow and pasture, roadside and bank. Her loose, informal bouquets were quite the hit at every spring and summer function, and her knowledge of where the laciest wild carrot bloomed and the showiest hydrangeas grew was both extensive and highly secret. However, as autumn drew on and blooms began to vanish, she hedged her bets—by dashing cold water on her clients' heady expectations, she was usually able to come up with something agreeably breathtaking.

"What does this mean?" asked Cynthia, looking worried.

"It means that what we mostly have to deal with is pods."

"Pods?" His fiancée was aghast.

Hessie shrugged. "Pods, seeds, berries," she said, expanding the list of possibilities. "Unless you'd like *mums*." Hessie said this word with undisguised derision.

Mums. He noted that the very word made his neighbor blanch.

Cynthia looked his way, imploring, but he did not make eye contact. No, indeed, he would not get in the middle of a discussion about pods and berries, much less mums.

"Pods and berries *can* be wonderful," Hessie stated, as if she were the full authority, which she was. "Mixed with what's blooming and tied in enormous bunches, they can look very rich hanging on the pew ends. Of course, we'll use wide ribbons, I'd suggest French-wired velvet, possibly in sage and even something the color of the shumake berry." As a bow to tradition, Hessie enjoyed using the mountain pronunciation for sumac.

He stole a glance at Cynthia from the corner of his eye. How had that gone down? She seemed uncertain.

"Why can't we just order dozens of roses and armloads of lilacs and be done with it?"

Hessie sucked in her breath. "Well," she said, "If you want to spend *that* kind of money . . ."

And let the word get out that his bride was a spendthrift? That was Hessie's deeper meaning; he knew Hessie Mayhew like a book. He knew, too, that Hessie considered the ordering of lilacs in September to be something akin to criminal—not only would they cost a royal fortune, they were *out of season in the mountains*!

"Not to mention," said Hessie, pursing her lips, "they're out of season in the mountains."

"Excuse me for living," said his fiancée. "Anyway, we *don't* want to spend that kind of money." In truth, his bride-to-be had the capability to spend whatever she wished, being a successful children's book author and illustrator. Besides, thought the rector, wasn't it her wedding? Wasn't it their money to spend however they liked? He hunkered down in the chair, anonymous, invisible, less than a speck on the wall.

Cynthia heaved a sigh. "So, Hessie, whatever you think. Sage and burgundy . . . or let's call it claret, shall we? Burgundy sounds so . . . *heavy*. Do you think we should intermix the ribbon colors along the aisle or put sage on one side and claret on the other?"

The color deepened in Hessie's ample cheeks. "Sage for the bride's side and claret for the groom's side, is my opinion!"

"Of course, I don't have any family for the bride's side. Only a nephew who isn't really a nephew, and the last I heard, he was in the Congo."

His heart was touched by the small sadness he heard in her voice, and so, apparently, was Hessie's.

"Oh, but you *do* have family!" Hessie threw her head back, eyes flashing. "The entire parish is your family!"

Cynthia pondered this extravagant remark. "Do you really think so?"

"Think so?" boomed Hessie. "I *know* so! Everyone says you're the brightest thing to happen to Lord's Chapel in an *eon,* and you must *not* forget it, my dear!" Mitford's foremost, all-around go-getter patted Cynthia's arm with considerable feeling.

Click! Something wonderful had just taken place. Hessie Mayhew, sensitive to the bone underneath her take-charge manner, had for some reason decided to be his fiancée's shield and buckler from this moment on; and nobody messed with Hessie.

"We'll fill every pew on the bride's side," Hessie predicted. "We'll be falling over ourselves to sit there! It's certainly where *I'm* sitting—no offense, Father."

Cynthia took Hessie's rough hand. "Thank you, Hessie!"

Thank you, Lord, he thought, forsaking his invisibility by bolting from the chair to refill their glasses all around.

"And what," inquired Hessie, "are you planning to do, Father, other than show up?"

Hessie Mayhew was smiling, but he knew she was

dead serious. Hessie believed that every man, woman, and child, including the halt and lame, should participate in all parish-wide events to the fullest.

"I'm doing the usual," he said, casting a grin in the direction of his neighbor. "I'm baking a ham!"

CHAPTER FOUR

The Bishop

"Gone to seed" is how the rector once fondly described his rectory home of more than thirteen years. Puny's eagerness to keep the place fastidious had, he was certain, worn away at least a stratum of walnut on the highboy, a gram or two of wool on the Aubusson, and a millimeter of sterling on the tea service.

She was now feverishly removing another layer from the whole kaboodle, in preparation for any celebration that may be held in the rectory, since, she said, Cynthia's house was too small to cuss a cat, no offense to Violet.

Nearly overcome by the odor of Lemon Pledge, he went to the phone and dialed his neighbor. "Want to bring your notebook and go to the park?"

"I'll race you!" she said.

They sat on the bench and listened for a moment to the birds and a light wind that stirred the leaves in Baxter Park. He kissed her, lingering. She kissed him back, lingering still more. She drew away and fanned herself with the notebook, laughing.

"On to more serious matters!" he exclaimed. "First order of business—pew bulletin or invitations, what do you think?"

"Pew bulletin! That way everyone knows, and those few who aren't in the parish, we'll call. I'll try to reach David, though I can't imagine he'd trek all the way from the Congo to Mitford!"

"Where shall we put Walter and Katherine? Your place or mine?"

"First things first," she said. "We need to know where we're spending our wedding night."

"The rectory?"

"But darling, your bed is so small."

"Yes, but your bed is so *big*." In his view, they could hold a fox hunt on the vast territory she called a bed.

"Draw straws!" she said, leaning from the bench to pluck two tall spears of grass. She fiddled with them a moment, asked him to close his eyes, then presented them in her fist.

"Gambling again," he said.

"Long one, my house, short one, your house."

He drew the short one.

"Rats in a poke!" fumed his neighbor.

"Watch your language, Kavanagh."

"Isn't it a tad early to call me Kavanagh?"

"I'm practicing."

"Anyway, there's your answer. Walter and Katherine spend the night at my house."

"Done!" He checked the topic off his list. "Have you thought any more about flower girls?"

"Amy Larkin and Rebecca Owen!"

"Perfect. Music?"

"Richard and I are just beginning to work on it—let's definitely ask Dooley to sing."

"Splendid. Should have thought of it myself."

"A cappella."

"He doesn't go for a cappella."

"He'll get over it, darling, I promise, and it will be wonderful, a true highlight for everyone. 'O Perfect Love,' what do you think?"

"There won't be a dry eye in the house. By the way, we're scheduled for the bishop on Wednesday at eleven o'clock."

"What are you wearing?" she asked.

"Oh, something casual. A pink curler in my hair, perhaps."

She swatted his arm over this old joke.

"I love you madly," she said.

"I love you madlier."

"Do not!"

"Do, too!"

"Prove it!"

"I shall. I'm serving you dinner tonight, Puny made chicken and dumplings."

"Chicken and dumplings!" she crowed.

"With fresh lima beans."

"I'm your slave!"

"I'll remember that," he said.

He felt the same age he usually felt at Miss Sadie's house.

Here he was in his bishop's office, seated next to his sweetheart, and only minutes away, they'd be talking about sex. He felt the blood surge to his head, coloring his face like a garden tomato. Though he was the priest, presumably competent to discuss a wide variety of personal issues, it was, in fact, Cynthia who felt perfectly at ease talking about anything to anybody, anytime.

They were currently in the touchy area of Financial, always the leading subject on Stuart's program for premarital counseling. Thus far, they were in good shape, having discussed some days ago what Stuart called his bottom-line on the issue:

Consult with the other about significant purchases, be open about your assets and willing to share equally, and agree on a budget that puts God first.

"And how do you feel, Timothy, about having a wife whose income is significantly greater than your own?"

Blast. Why couldn't Stuart have the discretion to avoid this issue? He and Cynthia had discussed it, but he hadn't been completely candid with her. He hesitated, hating this moment for both of them. "Not good," he said at last.

Cynthia looked at him. Did he see hurt or surprise, or both?

"God brought us together," he said. "He knew what He was doing. And if He doesn't mind the inequity in what I bring to the marriage, then I know I'm not to mind it, either. But—sometimes I do.

"Please understand that I don't resent her greater assets, not in the least—Cynthia Coppersmith is the hardest-working, most deserving woman I've ever known. The problem, if there is one, is that . . ." He paused. What *was* the problem? Hadn't he pondered this on several sleepless nights?

"The problem," said Cynthia, "is loss of control! Isn't that it, dearest? You've feared a loss of control all along, from the beginning. And now I'm the one who could buy a new car or take us to Spain—"

"I don't want to go to Spain," he said, feeling suddenly vulnerable, close to tears. He also didn't want a new car; he was perfectly happy with the old one.

Stuart smiled.

"If you're all that God wishes you to be in marriage, you will be one flesh. The money must belong to you equally, Timothy. In your heart you must be able to accept it, not as money you've worked for and earned, but as money God means you to have in stewardship with your wife."

Cynthia leaned over and kissed him on the cheek. Tears sprang instantly to his eyes and escaped to the sides of his nose before he could press them with a handkerchief.

"I think," he said, "that I'm overwhelmed on every side. I still can't think why God should give me this tremendous blessing—a gracious and loving soul who comprehends the depths of my own soul completely—and then to add financial resources beyond my wildest dreams . . .

"In truth, money means very little to me. I've lived simply all my life, and can't imagine doing otherwise."

"You've been exceedingly generous to others," said Stuart. "For example, you've poured your personal revenues into the Children's Hospital for years. Now, Timothy, you must allow someone to be generous with you, if she so chooses."

"I so choose!" Cynthia patted the rector's arm.

Relieved, they all had a sip of water from glasses waiting on a tray.

"Another crucial issue," said Stuart, "is in-laws."

"We won't have any!" exclaimed Cynthia.

Stuart smiled paternally. "In truth, you will."

"We will?"

"According to the Lord's Chapel membership register, there are one hundred and eighty-three of them, which roughly translates to a mere hundred and twenty-five *active* in-laws."

His fiancée appeared vexed, to say the least. "Yes, and there are some who can't bear the sight of me anymore. Everything was just fine until—"

"Until they learned you were getting married," said Stuart. "Then the jealousy flooded in. They were there first—they got his undivided attention for years—now it must be divided."

"Ugh," she said.

"What I hope you'll be able to live with is that his attention to you will also be divided. Like them, you'll have to share your priest. Unlike them, you must also share your beloved, your sweetheart." Stuart looked fondly at Cynthia. "If anyone can do this, you're the one."

"Thank you," she said. "Pray for me."

"Martha and I have prayed for you since the day Timothy brought you to lunch. We both thought you possessed the most extraordinary light, it reflected upon our friend like a beacon. We thank you for that."

The rector noted with a pang of tenderness that his fiancée blushed deeply, something he rarely witnessed.

"I've always felt it takes especially noble character to be a clergy spouse," said Stuart. "In any case, you and they will soon grow accustomed to sharing him; it's all a process—a matter of time and patience and love. I know you're willing."

"Yes!" she said. "Oh, yes!"

The bishop folded his hands across his lean midsection and gazed at his visitors.

Here it comes, thought the rector.

"Do you pray together?" asked Stuart.

"Yes!" they said in unison.

"Every evening," volunteered Father Tim.

"Excellent! I'm reminded of what our friend Oswald Chambers said, that prayer doesn't fit us for the greater work, prayer is the greater work. Praying together affirms you as one flesh, and, among the endless benefits it bestows, it can greatly enhance your sexual communication."

A patch of light danced upon the worn Persian carpet, reflecting the branches of a dogwood tree outside the window.

"The highest form of prayer is one in which we don't beg for ourselves," said Stuart, "but seek to know what we can do for God. This delights God immensely! As you seek to know what you can do for the other, you will surely receive your own inexpressible delight."

The rector took Cynthia's hand.

"To put it simply, making love confirms your spiritual relationship, and your spiritual relationship will deepen your lovemaking. It all moves in a wondrous circle."

The rector and his neighbor drew a deep breath at precisely the same moment and looked at each other, laughing.

"Now!" said Stuart.

"Now, what?" asked Father Tim.

"Conflict resolution."

"Do we have to?" asked Cynthia.

"Have you had any conflicts?"

The two looked at each other. "His car," she said.

"What about my car?" queried the rector.

"Don't you remember? I said it was a gas guzzler, has rust, and the seat covers look like Puny's dishrags."

"And I said I'm perfectly satisfied with it." There! The bishop wanted conflict, he got conflict. The rector felt his collar suddenly tighten.

"And so," Cynthia told Stuart, "when we drive on the Parkway or visit our bishop, we take my car."

"How do you feel about that?"

She wrinkled her nose. She stared briefly at the ceiling. She smiled. "I can live with it."

Stuart chuckled. He had his own opinion of his priest's car, but far be it from him to comment. "It's terrific that you're willing to name the conflict, my dear. This equips us to attack the problem instead of attacking the other person."

Stuart sat back in his chair. "So, Timothy, how do you feel about driving her car instead of yours?"

"Good!" he said, meaning it. "I can live with it." He pressed Cynthia's hand and turned to look at her. She appeared to sparkle in some lovely way he'd never seen before. After his brief moment of righteous indignation, he was custard again.

On the way home in her Mazda, he noticed that she looked at him fondly more than once.

"Sweetie pie," she murmured, patting his knee.

Sweetie pie! As a kid, he was called Slick; Katherine called him Teds; one and all called him Father. He liked this new appellation best of all. Maybe one day—*maybe*—he'd look into trading his Buick for a new model. But certainly nothing *brand*-new, no; no, indeed.

CHAPTER FIVE

The Joke

He drove to the Wesley mall and looked in the jewelry store display cases.

His heart sank like a stone. There was absolutely nothing that measured up to the fire and sparkle, the snap and dazzle of his neighbor.

He would have a ring made, then, fashioned exclusively for Cynthia Coppersmith Kavanagh. He saw their initials somehow entwined inside the band—*ccktak*. But of course he had no earthly idea who to call or where to turn. When someone left a Ross-Simon catalog on the table at the post office, he snatched it up and carried it outside to his car, where he pored over the thing until consciousness returned and he realized he'd sat there with the motor running for a full half hour, steaming in his raincoat like a clam in its shell.

"I'm sorry," he said, looking at her bare ring finger.

"If I'd done things right, I would have given you a ring when I proposed."

"I don't really want an engagement ring, dearest. Just a simple gold band would be perfect."

"You're certain?"

"Yes!" she said. "I love simple gold bands."

The image of his mother's wedding band came instantly to mind. It was in his closet, in a box on the shelf, tied by a slender ribbon. He would take it to the store and have it cleaned and engraved and present it at the altar with unspeakable joy and thanksgiving.

He felt he was at last beginning to get things right.

Uncle Billy Watson brushed the leaves and twigs from last night's storm off the seat of a rusting dinette chair and sat down in the backyard of the Porter house, a.k.a. Mitford's town museum.

He gazed dolefully into the sea of towering grass that extended to the rear of the house and then beyond his view. The town crew was supposed to mow the grass once every twelve days; by his count, it was fourteen going on fifteen, and a man could get lost out here and not be heard from again; it was a disgrace the way the town put every kind of diddledaddle ahead of mowing something as proud and fine as their own museum. If he could do it himself, he would, but his arthritis hardly allowed him to get up and down the steps, much less scour a full acre and a quarter with a rusted push mower. He hoped that when he got to Heaven, the Lord would outfit him with a new body and give him a job that *required* something of a man.

But he hadn't come out here to get his dander up. He'd come out to noodle his noggin about a joke to tell at the preacher's wedding, back in that room where they'd all eat cake and ham after the ceremony. Though nobody had said a word about it, the old man knew the preacher would be expecting a joke, he'd be counting on it, and it was his responsibility, his civic duty to tell the best joke he could come up with.

He would never say this to a soul, but it seemed like the preacher getting married so late in life was sort of a joke in itself. It would be a different thing if the father had been married before and had some practice, but as far as anybody knew, he hadn't had any practice.

But who was he to judge other people's setups? Half the town thought he was crazy as a bedbug for living with Rose Watson; even his uncle—who'd come to see them years ago when Rose was still as pretty as a speckled pup—his uncle had said, "They ain't no way I'm understandin' how you put up with this mess."

Her illness seemed to start right after they married, though he'd witnessed, and ignored, warning signs from the day they met. For years, he'd told himself that it was something he'd done wrong, that he hadn't cherished her like the vows said, and maybe God was punishing them both for his ignorance and neglect. Then the doctors found out about the disease he couldn't spell and could barely pronounce, schizophrenia.

On the worst days, he squeezed his eyes shut and remembered the girl he'd seen in the yard of this very house, more than—what was it?—forty-five, maybe fifty years ago. She was barefooted and had her hair tied back with a ribbon. Ragged and dirty from working in the fields since daylight, he'd come up from the valley with a wagonload of tomatoes and roasting ears, carrying a sack of biscuits and fried side meat for his dinner. He'd gone around the village looking for a spot to park his wagon and sell his produce, and saw her standing in her yard. At first he thought she was a statue. Then she moved and the light fell on her in a certain way and he called out, "Would you let a man park his wagon on your road?" And she'd walked out to him and smiled at him and nodded. "Get on down," she said. He'd always remember her first words to him: *Get on down.* He was ashamed that he wasn't wearing shoes, but then he saw that she wasn't, either. She had hung around, looking at him in a way that made him feel uneasy, then happy, and he'd shared his biscuits and side meat with her and she'd gone in the house and brought out a Mason jar of tea so cold and sweet it hurt his teeth. Between times when customers came and went, she talked about herself more than a little. Her beloved brother, Willard, was dead in the war, buried across the ocean in France, and she was looked after by a woman who paid no attention to her. By early afternoon, he'd sold everything but two tomatoes, which he gave to Rose, who said she'd allow him to park his wagon there next week.

They married eighteen months later, against the wishes of his family in the valley, whom he never went back to visit. And there he was, a rough valley boy with no education to speak of, married to a girl with a big inheritance including the finest house in Mitford, and him caning chairs and making birdhouses and doing whatever else he could to hold up his end of the bargain.

But he wouldn't go back and do it any different. Nossir. He'd loved that long-legged girl with the wild eyes more than anything in this world, and could never forget how she used to cling to him and call him Billy Boy and Sweet William, and kiss him with all the innocence of a woods violet.

His chin dropped to his chest and he jerked awake. Here he was sleeping when he had a job to do.

What was the job? For a moment, he couldn't remember. Then it came to him.

His hand trembled as he propped his cane against the tree. "Lord," he said aloud, "I hope You don't mind me askin' You to provide a good joke for th' preacher, don't you know. . . ."

Mayor Esther Cunningham couldn't help herself. Every time she thought about Father Tim getting married, she thought about the way she and Ray had met and courted, and her eyes misted. She did not like her eyes to mist; she had quit crying years ago when her daddy passed. Whenever she felt like crying, she had learned to turn it inside, where it sometimes felt like a Popsicle melting. She had read an article in a magazine at Fancy Skinner's which said that if you turn sorrow in, it will come out—as cancer or something worse, though she couldn't think of anything worse. The article had gone on to say that intimacy with your husband was good for your health, and no matter what else might happen in this life, she and Ray had that in spades; forty-seven years later, they were still holding hands just like on their first date.

Before Ray, Bobby Prestwood had tried everything to get in her good graces, including making a fool of himself in Sunday School when he stood up one morning and told what he was thankful for. "I'm thankful for my Chevy V-8, my mama and daddy, and Esther Lovell!" She didn't give a katy what Bobby Prestwood was thankful for, and told him so at the picnic, which was where she met Ray. Ray had come late with his cousins, carrying a basket of fried chicken and coleslaw, which he'd made himself. She couldn't believe that anybody that big and tall and good-looking could cook, much less chop cabbage; it just amazed her. She had eyed him up and down to see if he was a sissy, but found no evidence of this. When the cousins invited her to sit with them, she accepted, ate three pieces of Ray's fried chicken with all the trimmings, and took home a wing wrapped in a napkin. Two months later, they were married.

To this day, she'd never met another woman whose husband rubbed her feet, or maybe people just never mentioned it. And not only did Ray rub her feet after she'd worked like a dog all day and half the night in meetings at town hall, he'd have her supper in the oven, which she sometimes took to bed and ate sitting up watching TV, with him lying there patting her leg. "Little darlin'," he might say while he patted.

If she ever had to climb in a bed without Ray Cunningham in it, she would die, she would *go morte,* as Lew Boyd liked to say.

She picked up the phone and dialed home.

"Ray . . ."

She heard Teensy barking in the background. "Hey, sugar babe! It's hot as blazes today, I'll run you up a jar of lemonade in a little bit. What else you need?"

She wouldn't have told him that all she needed was to hear his voice.

Uncle Billy shuffled to the dining room and rifled through stacks of newspaper that the town inspector had threatened to haul off, but had forgotten to do. He was after some copies of *The Farmer's Almanac* that he'd saved for the jokes.

Sweat beaded his forehead and upper lip as he worked through the piles, but not a trace of a *Farmer's Almanac* with its red cover could he find. Dadgummit, he'd hid things in here for years and always managed to find them, and now, not a trace.

He worked his hand around in the pile of *Mitford Muses*, which occupied a space next to the kitchen door, and felt for the familiar shape of an almanac. What was that? He pulled it out and looked. A twenty-dollar bill! He wanted to whoop, but knew better.

If Rose got wind of this twenty, she'd connive every

way in creation to yank it out of him. No, by jing, he'd do something he hardly ever did, but often thought about: he'd walk down to the Grill and get an order of fries and bring Rose a surprise milkshake. Besides, he'd gotten two or three of his best jokes at the Grill—maybe that was where he'd find this one.

Careful to put the twenty in the pants pocket without the hole, he abandoned the search for the almanacs and instituted a hurried quest for any other currency he'd once hidden in the vicinity.

Louella Baxter Marshall sat by the window in the sewing room, now her bedroom at Fernbank, looking at the catalog.

The light was good in here and she could clearly see the picture of the dress she'd be wearing to the wedding.

After two days of praying about it and going back and forth from page 42 to page 47, she had showed Miss Sadie her pick. "Green or lavender?" she asked her lifelong friend and sister in Christ.

Miss Sadie didn't hesitate. "Lavender!" she said. "You always looked good in lavender."

Miss Sadie was a little bit like a mama, for it was Miss Sadie who knew Louella's history, who said things like,

"When you were a baby, you hated apple butter," or "I remember the time I pulled you to town in the wagon—you hopped out and chased Perry Mackey down the street for a lick on his peppermint stick. You nearly scared him to death!"

Louella didn't remember any of the events Miss Sadie liked to recall, but she'd heard them so often, they'd become as good as real memories. She savored the image of chasing a little white boy down the street to lick his candy, and wondered why on earth she loved apple butter now if she hated it then.

"How you know I *always* look good in this color?"

"When you were about six years old, Mama made you a lavender dress with smocking on the bodice. Don't you remember it, with little pearl buttons? It was such a pretty dress I was half jealous!"

She was disgusted with herself for not remembering. "Don' you think this big white collar too fancy for my face?"

"Posh tosh! Your face may be too fancy for that collar!"

They had both laughed and laughed, then they'd zeroed in on the business of Miss Sadie's final choice. Page 36 was too drab; page 37 was too high in the waist; page 40 was not only shapeless, it had three-quarter-length sleeves, which, as anybody knew, were unflattering all the way back to the pharaohs. Page 41, however, showed promise.

"I like the way it's cut," said Miss Sadie, peering at the dress through a magnifying glass, "but I'm too gray-headed for this color."

"Why, listen at that! Gray-headed is what look *good* wit' blue."

"But it's a pale blue, and it might wash me out."

"No, honey, you might wash *it* out!"

They had laughed again, like children, and decided on the pale blue French crepe with smocked bodice.

Louella held the catalog closer to the window and squinted at the picture.

She wished Moses Marshall could see her all dressed up for the father's wedding. He would look at her and be so proud. Oh, how she'd loved that man from the day she laid eyes on him!

She closed her eyes to rest them and held the picture against her heart, and saw her husband-to-be walking into the kitchen of the Atlanta boardinghouse.

She was fifteen years old, with her hair in cornrows and the sense that something wonderful was about to happen.

Moses Marshall flashed a smile that nearly knocked her winding. She had never seen anybody who looked like this when she was growing up in Mitford. The only people of color in Mitford were old and stooped over.

"Who's th' one baked them good biscuits for supper?" he asked.

She'd been scarcely able to speak. "What you want to know for?"

"'Cause th' one baked them good biscuits, that's th' one I'm goin' to marry."

She had looked at old Miss Sally Lou, who had to stand on tiptoe to peer into a pot on the stove. She was so little and dried up, some said she was a hundred, but Louella knew she was only eighty-two, and still the boss cook of three meals a day at the boardinghouse.

She had pointed to Miss Sally Lou, afraid to say the plain truth—that she, Louella Baxter, had baked the biscuits herself, three pans full and not one left begging.

Moses Marshall looked his bright, happy look at Miss Sally Lou and walked over and picked her up and swung her around twice before he set her down like a doll. "Fine biscuits, ma'am. Will you jump th' broom wit' me?"

"Git out of my way 'fore I knock you in th' head!" said Miss Sally Lou. "Marry that 'un yonder, she th' one do biscuits, I does yeast rolls."

She was sixteen when they were married at her grandmother's house in Atlanta, where she'd gone to live after leaving Mitford. Her grandmother had cooked the wedding feast, which was topped off with fresh peach cobbler. "Why eat cake when you can eat cobbler?" was what her grandmother always said.

Her years with Moses had been the happiest years of her life, next to those with Miss Sadie. But the Lord had taken Moses home when he was just thirty-nine, and then He'd taken her precious boy in a terrible wreck, leaving her a grandson living in Los Angeles. . . .

She looked out to the green orchard and nodded her head and smiled. "Moses Marshall," she said, "I invite you to sit wit' me at th' weddin,' an' don' be pinchin' and kissin' on me in front of th' good Lord an' ever'-body. . . ."

Dooley Barlowe was trying to be happy, but he figured he didn't know what that was supposed to mean. He felt around inside himself, around the area of his heart, maybe, and tried to see if he could make things seem good and right about Father Tim and Cynthia getting married. He'd seen what happened when people lived together under the same roof: They yelled and screamed and fought and said terrible things to each other. He'd seen his daddy go at his mama with a butcher knife more than once, and after his daddy ran off, he'd seen his mama leave for two and three days at a time and depend on him to mind the kids and feed them without any money to buy stuff with.

He remembered stealing a pork loin from the grocery store and getting it home and not knowing how to cook it. He had dropped it in a pot of boiling water with oatmeal and let it cook 'til the water boiled out on the stove, then he carved the meat in five chunks and they tried to eat it and got so sick, he thought they'd all die in the night. Once he'd stolen five cans of creamed corn, so they could all have exactly the same thing and not fight over who got what and how much, and the store manager had caught him and jumped on him really bad, but he'd let him have the corn, saying if he ever did it again he'd be sent to the penitentiary. A woman who overheard the commotion had gone and gotten a can of Harvard beets, a loaf of Wonder bread, a pound of M&Ms, and a quart of buttermilk and gave the items to him in a plastic bag. He remembered that he couldn't stomach buttermilk and the kids wouldn't drink it, either, but they couldn't bear to throw it out and it sat in the refrigerator for maybe a year.

He didn't like to think about these things, he wanted to forget everything that had ever happened before he came here, but sometimes he couldn't. He especially wanted to forget about his little sister, Jessie, because thinking of her being gone and nobody knowing where made him want to cry, and he tried to keep his face as hard and tight and straight as possible so nobody would ever be able to tell what he was thinking.

Sometimes, at night especially, he remembered trying to help his mama when she was drunk, and would suddenly feel a great love for her welling up in him. Then he'd be angry with himself for being stupid, and feel the old and shameful desire for her to die.

Things were just fine for him and Father Tim; he felt safe, finally, like things would be all right. But now he didn't know what would happen. He liked Cynthia, but what if she didn't like him, what if she tried to get him to leave or go back to his mother, if anybody could even find his mother? Or what if Cynthia tried to be his mother? His heart felt cold at such a thought. He wanted his own mother, even if he did hate her and wish he would never see her again as long as he lived.

He was glad that Barnabas came to his room and jumped on the foot of his bed, because it felt good to have a friend. Besides, Barnabas would never tell anyone that he was crying and couldn't stop.

CHAPTER SIX

The Letter

His heart was nearly bursting with a kind of longing, though he had no idea why. After all, he was blessed with everything this life could afford, everything and more.

He sat at his desk in the study and looked out the window into the gloaming as it settled over Baxter Park. Cynthia was working on an illustration that had to go out tomorrow by FedEx, or he would have been at her side, as magnetized to her living presence as his grocery list to the refrigerator.

He drummed his fingers on the desktop.

He didn't want to work on his sermon. He didn't want to take a shower and crawl into bed with a well-loved book from his well-stocked shelves, and he most certainly did not want to turn on the TV and have the clamor pour into this quiet place like some foul Niagara.

He was unable to think of anything he wanted to do; there was no seduction in any of the usual pursuits.

Aha. His fingers grew still upon the desktop.

There it was, plain as day:

He wanted to record, somehow, the joy of this breathless thing that had swept him up and overpowered and mesmerized him. Perhaps for most people, people who had been in love again and again, it would not be such a beauteous experience, but it was new to him and dazzling. Yet even in its newness, he felt it slipping away, becoming part of a personal history in which the nuances, the shading, would be lost forever; buried within the consciousness, yes, but paled by time, and then, he feared, vanished altogether.

He opened the desk drawer and took out a writing pad and one of the commercial pens he'd grown to prefer. Though the ink had a noxious odor, he liked the way it flowed onto the page—black, bold, and able.

He knew now what his soul was driving him to. He knew, and he liked the idea immensely.

He would write a poem.

In it, he would tell her everything, he would confess the all of his love, which, by its great and monumental force, had heretofore rendered him dumb as a mackerel.

With her, he experienced a galaxy . . . no, an entire

universe of feelings, yet they continually displayed themselves as the western portion of the state of Rhode Island:

YouarebeautifultomeIshallloveyoueternallywillyou marrymeandmakemethehappiestmanwhoeverdrewbreath, period, end of declaration.

He was amazed at how far he'd gotten with this extraordinary woman by the utterance of the most rudimentary expressions of love, all of them sincere beyond measure, and yet, they were words too simple and words too few; not once had they been equal to the character, the beauty, or the spirit of the one to whom they were addressed.

He knew, now, why people wanted to shout from rooftops, yet he couldn't imagine it to have great effect, in the end. One would clamber onto the roof and, teetering on some gable or chimney pot, bellow until one was hoarse as a bullfrog, "I love! I love!"

And what would people on the street do? They would look up, they would shrug, they would roll their eyes, they would say:

So?

He bounded happily from the chair and went to the kitchen to put the kettle on. Clearly, shouting from the rooftops had been a fleeting thing in the history of the lovestruck, not long enjoyed as a certified expression of ardor. Indeed, what had done the trick each and every time? Poetry! And history had proved it!

"'I love thee,'" he recited as he filled the kettle, "'. . . to the level of every day's Most quiet need, by sun and candlelight . . . I love thee freely, as men strive for Right . . .'"

There! That was getting down to it. The only problem was that E. B. Browning had already written it.

He stood musing by the stove in a kind of fog that made him forget momentarily where he was and what he was up to, until the kettle whistled and he awoke and found himself oddly joyful to be dropping the bags into the teapot and pouring the steaming water therein.

He clamped the lid on the pot and, leaving it to the business of steeping, returned to the study and visited his bookshelves. He couldn't readily put his hand on a volume of love poetry, but surely he'd find something here to spark a thought, to get his blood up. He chose a small blue volume that he'd used a time or two in marital counseling, and opened it at random.

"'I feel sad when I don't see you,'" he read aloud from a letter by a nineteenth-century American suitor. "'Be married, why won't you? And come to live with me. I will make you as happy as I can. You shall not be obliged to work hard, and when you are tired, you may lie in my lap and I will sing you to rest . . .' "

There's a good fellow! he thought.

" '. . . because I love you so well, I will not make you bring in wood and water, or feed the pig, or milk the cow, or go to the neighbors to borrow milk. Will you be married?' "

He shoved the book upon the shelf, took down another, and thumbed through the section on all things marital.

" 'I love you no longer; on the contrary, I detest you . . .' " Napoleon Bonaparte to Josephine, wrong section.

Ah, well, here was one for the books, something Evelyn Waugh had trotted out in a letter of proposal. " 'I can't advise you in my favour because I think it would be beastly for you, but think how nice it would be for me!' "

Would it be beastly for Cynthia? Living with him, an old stick in the mud? He shook the thought away and licked his right forefinger and turned to another page.

" 'You have set a crown of roses on my youth and fortified me against the disaster of our days. Your courageous gaiety has inspired me with joy. Your tender faithfulness has been a rock of security and comfort. I have felt for you all kinds of love at once. I have asked much of you and you have never failed me. You have intensified all colours, heightened all beauty, deepened all delight. . . .'" Duff Cooper, writing to his future wife in the war-dark year of 1918, had known how to get down to brass tacks, all right. Maybe he could do something with the idea of courageous gaiety; he had always thought Cynthia courageous.

He sighed deeply. In truth, this was going nowhere. It was a waste of precious time to try and glean from another man's brain. There'd be no more lollygagging.

He dashed again to the kitchen and poured a mug of tea, then added a little milk and stirred it well, and returned to his desk and sat, gazing at the mug, the pad, and the pen, and the nightfall dark against his window.

He considered that he had written hymns to God, several in his time, but he'd never done anything like this, never! He knew that God was familiar with his very innards and that He perceived the passion of his heart full well; thus he had not sweated greatly over lines that were awkward here or a tad sophomoric there, but this . . .

"*Write!*" he bellowed aloud.

Barnabas bolted from the rug by the sofa and trotted to his master and stood by the desk. The rector turned his head slowly, and for a moment each looked soulfully into the other's eyes.

Dearest love . . ., he wrote at last, *tender one . . . my heart's joy . . .*

He drew a line through the feeble words and began again:

Loveliest angel of light and life . . .

What about something from the Song of Solomon? On second thought, scratch that. The Song still made him blush. Whoever drummed up the notion that it was about Christ and the church . . .

He nibbled his right forefinger and mused upon lines from Shakespeare; he chewed his lower lip and called to mind Keats; he sank his head onto his arms on the desktop and contemplated Robert Browning's fervent avowal, "All my soul follows you, love . . . and I live in being yours."

Blast and double blast. The good stuff had already been written.

He talked to himself with some animation as he trotted up Main Street from Lord's Chapel. What if Shakespeare had never put pen to paper because the good stuff had already been written? In truth, what if he refused one morning to preach because all the good sermons had already been preached?

Ha!

On the other side of the Irish Shop's display window, Minnie Lomax examined the bent head and hunched shoulders of the village priest as he blew past, his mouth moving in what she supposed was prayer.

He didn't look at all like a man besotted with love, not in her view.

Why was he staring at the sidewalk when he might be looking into the heavens, or whistling, or waving to her through the window as he usually did? He was scared of what he'd let himself in for, that's what! Sixty-something and getting married for the *first time*? The very thought gave her the shivers.

She had never married, and never wanted to. Well, not never, exactly. She had wanted to once, and look what happened. She sniffed and smoothed her cardigan over her thin hips and took a Kleenex from her pocket and blew her nose, then turned around to the empty store, wondering what she might do to lure traffic through the door today. Boiled wool had a terrible go of it during the summer; next year she would advise the owner to put in more cotton and linen, for heaven's sake, and get shed of the entire lot of those hideous crocheted caps.

He would choose each word as carefully as his mother had chosen peaches off Lot Stringman's truck. "Let me pick them out for you, Miz Kavanagh." "No, thank you, Mr. Stringman," she would say, "I like the doing of it myself."

Finally despairing that writing a poem was beyond his endowment, he had decided to be content with writing a letter.

Peach by perfect peach, that is how he would choose his words. . . .

Sunday afternoon, four o'clock, a breeze stirring through the open windows

My Own,

Consider how these two small words have the power to move and shake me, and take my breath away! I am raised to a height I have never before known, somewhere above the clouds that hide the mountain-rimmed valleys and present a view of floating peaks. I have been comfortable for years, haplessly rooted in myself like a turnip, and now am not comfortable at all, but stripped of everything that is easeful and familiar, and filled with everything that is tremulous and alive; I am a spring lamb upon new legs. Every nerve is exposed to you, my dearest love, and my thankfulness for this gift from God knows no bounds, no bounds! Indeed, He has saved the best for last, and that He should have saved it at all, set it aside for me, is a miracle. A miracle! Let no one ever say or even think that God does not work miracles, still; every common day, every common life is filled with them, as you know better than anyone I have ever met. You, who see His light and life in the dullest blade of grass, have taught my own eye to look for and find His magnitude abounding everywhere.

Though you are merely steps away, beyond the hedge, I long for you as if you were in Persia, and yet, your presence is with me, your very fragrance clings to the shirt I wear.

I have given my heart completely only once, and that was to Him. Now He has, Himself, set aside in my heart a room for you. It is large and open and suffused with light, with no walls or boundaries to stifle us, and He has graciously fashioned it to give us warmth and shelter and joyous freedom until the end of our days.

May this be only the first of many times I thank you for all you are to me, and for the precious and inimitable gift of your love.

Please know that I shall set a watch upon my-

self—to make every effort to bring you the happiness you so richly deserve, and, by His grace, to place your needs before my own.

May God bless you with His greatest tenderness now and always, my sweetheart, my soon-to-be wife.

Timothy

He sat as if drained; there was nothing left of him, nothing at all, he was parchment through which light might be seen.

"Barnabas," he murmured.

His good dog stirred at his feet.

"I have a mission for you, old friend." He folded the letter, regretting that he'd written it on paper from a mere notepad. Ah, well, what was done was done. He placed the letter in an envelope and thought carefully how he might address it.

In a letter hidden inside an envelope, one might say whatever one wished, but the outside of the envelope was quite another thing, being completely exposed, as it were, to . . . to what? The hedge? The sky?

My love, my blessing, my neighbor, he scrawled with some abandon.

He licked the flap and pressed it down and sat for a moment with it under his hand, then took it to the kitchen and found a length of twine, which he looped around the neck of his patient dog. Lacking a hole punch, he stuck the tip of a steak knife through the corner of the envelope and ran the twine through the hole and tied it in a knot.

"There!" he said aloud.

He walked with Barnabas down the back steps and across the yard to the hedge. "OK, boy, take it to Cynthia!"

Barnabas lifted his leg against a rhododendron.

"Take it to Cynthia!" he said, wagging his finger in the direction of the little yellow house. "Over there! Go see Cynthia!"

Barnabas turned and looked at him with grave indifference.

"Cat!" he hissed. *"Cynthia's house! Cat, cat, cat!"* That ought to do it.

Barnabas sniffed a few twigs that lay in the grass, then sat down and scratched vigorously.

Rats, what a dumb idea. In the old days, a fellow would have sent his valet or his coachman or some such, and here he was trying to send a dog—he deserved what he was getting.

"Go, dadgummit! Go to Cynthia's back door, that's where you love to go when you're not supposed to!"

Barnabas gazed at him for a moment, then turned

and bounded through the hedge and across her yard and up the steps to her stoop, where he sat and pressed his nose against the screen door, peering in.

He suddenly felt ten years old. Why couldn't he think straight for five minutes in a row? His dog might sit at that door 'til kingdom come, with Cynthia having no clue Barnabas was out there. Should he run to the door and knock to alert her, then run away again?

This was suddenly the most ridiculous mess he'd gotten himself into in . . . ever. His face flamed.

"Timothy?" It was Cynthia, calling to him through her studio window. He'd utterly forgotten about her studio window.

"Umm, yes?"

"Why are you hiding behind the hedge?"

He was mortified. *I have no idea,* he wanted to say. "There's a *delivery*"—he fairly thundered the word—"at your back door."

"Oh," she said.

He waited, covering his face with his hands.

"My goodness!" he heard her exclaim as she opened the screen door. "A letter on a string!"

Surely he would regret this.

"'My love, my blessing, my neighbor'!" she crowed.

Did she have to inform the whole neighborhood?

"Go tell your master that I've received his most welcome missive . . . which I can barely get off the string. Ugh! . . . Oh, rats, wait 'til I get the scissors."

His dog waited.

"And further," she said, coming back and snipping the letter off, "do tell him I shall endeavor to respond promptly. However, my dear Barnabas, do not harbor, even for a moment, the *exceedingly* foolish hope that it will be delivered by Violet."

The screen door slapped behind her.

The deed done, his dog arose, shook himself, and came regally down the steps, across the yard, and through the hedge, where, wearing the remains of the twine around his neck, he sat and gazed at his master with a decided air of disdain, if not utter disgust.

CHAPTER SEVEN

The Prayer

She pressed the letter to her heart, wishing the power of its message to enter her very soul and cause her to believe with the writer what an extraordinary benediction had come to them.

Yes, she loved him; in truth, more than life itself. And yet, the fear was beginning to creep in, the fear she had at last grown wise enough to recognize—that she could not please him and give him the joy that he above all others, deserved; the fear that Timothy, like Elliott, would not find her valuable enough for any true purpose; the fear that her priest, her neighbor, and now her betrothed, might discover in her some "terrible lack," as Elliott had called her inability to bear children.

Only weeks earlier, she had wept in despair that Timothy Kavanagh would ever be able to abandon his own raw fear and surrender his heart.

Now she bowed her head and wept because, at last, he had.

She stood at the kitchen sink, spooning an odorous lump of congealed cat food into Violet's dish.

Drawing her breath sharply, she stared at the cat bowl that she had just filled without knowing it.

She felt stricken. What had she done when she accepted his proposal with such unbearable eagerness and joy? Had she rashly agreed to something in which she might prove a bitter disappointment to both Timothy and herself?

And another thing—could she, who had often felt thrown away, be a friend and guide to a thrown-away boy? She thought she could, she knew she wanted to—for Dooley's sake and her own.

She put the bowl on the floor and walked down the hall to her studio and stood at the window, gazing across the hedge to the rectory. There was his stone chimney, his slate roof, his bedroom window beneath the gable. . . .

How often she had found solace in merely looking upon his house, the place where he would be working in his study, snoring by his fire, brushing his dog, commandeering his wayward boy, living his life.

She'd begun by having the most terrific crush on him, like a pathetic schoolgirl; it had been the sort of thing that made her blush at the sight of him, and caused her skin to tingle when she heard his voice. Worse, there had been long lapses in concentration that afflicted her for months on end.

She had plotted ways to meet him on the street, and once thumped onto the bench in front of the Main Street Grill, affecting a turned ankle that delayed her jaunt to The Local. He had, indeed, come by, just as she'd hoped, and sat with her and smiled at her in a way that made her nearly speechless until, finally, she fled the bench, forgetting to limp, and avoided him altogether for several weeks.

She remembered, too, the day she had prayed and marched boldly to his back door. Her heart thundered under her jumper as she asked to borrow a cup of sugar to make a cake. Having no intention of making a cake, she worried whether, in some priestly way, he might see through such guile and find her out. But he had invited her in and fed her from the remains of his own supper and she had seen something in his eyes, some kindness that had nearly broken her heart with its plainness and simplicity. And then his dog, attached to the handle of the silver drawer by a leash, had yanked the drawer out, sending forks, knives, and spoons clattering about the kitchen and skidding into the hallway. They had dropped to their knees as one, hooting with laughter as they collected the errant flatware. Even then, she knew that something had been sealed between them, and that it was laughter that had sealed it

It had been years since Elliott walked out—the divorce papers arrived by certified mail the following day—and in those years, not one soul had made her mouth go dry as cotton and her knees turn to water. Oh, how she had despised the torment of loving like a girl instead of like . . . like a sophisticated woman, whatever that might be.

That early, awkward time had also been irresistibly sweet. But now this—confusion and distress and alarm, and yes, the oddly scary thoughts of the women of Lord's Chapel who for years had stood around him like a hedge of thorns, protecting him as their very own; keeping him, they liked to believe, from foolish stumbles; feeding him meringues and layer cake at every turn; mothering and sistering him as if this were their life's calling. She saw, now, something she'd only glimpsed before, and that was the way an unmarried priest is thought to belong to the matrons of the church, lock, stock, and barrel.

More than once she'd waited at his side, feeling gauche and adolescent, as they clucked over him—inquiring after his blood sugar, flicking an imaginary hair from his lapel, ordering him to take a week off, and coyly insisting he never stray beyond the town limits. They were perfectly harmless, every one, and she despised herself for such cheap and petty thoughts, but they were real thoughts, and now that the word was out, she felt his flock sizing her up in a fresh, even severe way.

Yet, for all their maternal indulgence of their priest, she knew they underestimated him most awfully. She had heard a member of the Altar Guild wondering how anyone "so youthful and sure of herself" could be attracted to their "dear old priest who is going bald as a hen egg and diabetic to boot."

Indeed, he wasn't merely the mild and agreeable man they perceived him to be; he was instead a man of the richest reserves of strength and poise, of the deepest tenderness and most enormous wit and gallantry.

From the beginning, she found him to possess an ardor for his calling that spoke to her heart and mind and soul in such a deep and familiar way, she felt as if he were long-lost kin, returned at last from a distant shore.

He had felt this, too, this connection of some vital force in himself with her own vitality, and he had been knocked back, literally, as if by the thunder-striking power of a summer storm.

She had known she would never again be given such a connection, and she had moved bravely toward it, toward its heat, toward its center, while he had drawn back, shaken.

"'Love bade me welcome,'" he had once quoted from George Herbert, "'but my soul drew back.'" She found a delicate irony in the fact that George Herbert had been a clergyman.

She looked at the handwritten sheet pinned above her drawing board, something she had copied at the Mitford library from an old book by Elizabeth Goudge:

> She had long accepted the fact that happiness is like swallows in spring. It may come and nest under your eaves or it may not. You cannot command it. When you expect to be happy you are not, when you don't expect to be happy there is suddenly Easter in your soul, though it be midwinter. Something, you do not know what, has broken the seal upon that door in the depth of your being that opens upon eternity.

Eternity!

She moved from the window and walked quickly to the kitchen. She would do something that, if only for the briefest hour, had the power to solve everything, to offer certain and absolute consolation.

She would cook.

She removed the chicken from the refrigerator, already rubbed with olive oil and crushed garlic, with half a lemon tucked into its cavity. She misted olive oil into her ancient iron skillet, placed the bird on its back, and ground pepper and sea salt onto its plump flesh. From a glass of water on the windowsill she removed a pungent stalk of fresh rosemary and stuck it under the breast skin. The top of the green stalk waved forth like a feather from a hat band.

She turned the stove dial to 450, where it would remain for thirty minutes before being set at 350 for an hour, and slid the raw feast onto the middle rack.

The wrenching thing, she knew in her heart, was having no one to talk with about it all, and whose fault was that but her own? Had she not worked like a common stevedore since coming to Mitford, making a way for her work instead of making friends? Oh, yes, she was liked well enough, she really was, but there was no trusted friend to whom she might pour her heart out. There was no one, not a soul.

Except . . . she smiled at the thought . . . the priest himself. Her heart warmed suddenly, and lifted up. Hadn't she confessed something to him only yesterday?

"They don't like me," she had said, despising the whine she heard in her voice. "They did, of course, until they learned you were actually going to marry me, but now . . ."

"Nonsense!" he'd said with feeling. "They think the *world* of you!"

That was apparently the most profound compliment a Southerner could pay, to insist that one was thought the "world" of!

She realized she wouldn't finish the illustration as she'd promised her editor; she would finish it tomorrow, instead. She, who was ever loath to break a promise, would break this one.

"Timothy?" she said when he answered the phone. "Can you come over?" Her heart was pounding, and there was a distinct quaver in her voice; she was warbling like a canary.

"I'm scared, dearest, scared to death."

She loved the way he sat with her, not saying anything in particular, not probing, not pushing her, just sitting on her love seat. Perhaps what she liked best was that he always looked comfortable wherever he was, appearing glad to live within his skin and not always jumping out of it like some men, like James, her editor, who was everlastingly clever and eloquent and ablaze with wild ideas that succeeded greatly for him, while with Timothy the thing that succeeded was quietude, something rich and deep and . . . nourishing, a kind of spiritual chicken soup simmering in some far reach of the soul.

"Tell me," he said at last. "Tell me everything. I'm your priest, after all." She thought his smile dazzling, a dazzling thing to come out of quietude. She had pulled a footstool to the love seat and sat close to him.

"I'm terribly afraid I can't make you happy," she said.

"But that was my fear! I finally kicked it out the back door and now it's run over here."

"It's not funny, Timothy."

"I'm not laughing."

He took her hands in his and lightly kissed the tips of her fingers and she caught the scent of him, the innocence of him, and her spirit mounted up again.

"Why don't we pray together?" he said. "Just let our hearts speak to His. . . ."

Sitting at his feet, she bowed her head and closed her

eyes and he stroked her shoulder. Though the clock ticked in the hallway, she supposed that time was standing still, and that she might sit with him in this holy reverie, forever.

"Lord," he said, simply, "here we are."

"Yes, Lord, here we are."

They drew in their breath as one, and let it out in a long sigh, and she realized for a moment how the very act of breathing in His presence was balm.

"Dear God," he said, "deliver Your cherished one from feeling helpless to receive the love You give so freely, so kindly, from the depths of Your being. Help us to be as large as the love You've given us, sometimes it's too great for us, Lord, even painful in its power. Tear away the old fears, the old boundaries that no longer contain anything of worth or importance, and by Your grace, make Cynthia able to seize this bold, fresh freedom. . . ."

"Yes, Lord," she prayed, "the freedom I've never really known before, but which You've faithfully shown me in glimmers, in epiphanies, in wisps as fragile as . . . light from Your new moon!"

He pressed her hand, feeling in it the beating of her pulse.

"Father, deliver me from the fear to love wholly and completely, I who chided this good man for his own fears, his own weakness, while posing, without knowing it a pose, as confident and bold. You've seen through that, Lord, You've . . . You've found me out for what I am . . ."

There was a long silence, filled by the ticking of the clock.

". . . a frightened seven-year-old who stands at the door looking for a father and mother who . . . do not come home.

"Even after years of knowing You as a Father who is always home, I sometimes feel—I feel a prisoner of old and wrenching fears, and I'm ashamed of my fear, and the darkness that prevents me from stepping into the light. . . ."

"You tell us in Your Word," he prayed, "that You do not give us the spirit of fear—"

"But of power and of love and a sound mind!" she whispered, completing the verse from the second letter to Timothy.

"And so, Lord, I rebuke the Enemy who would employ every strategy to deny Your children the blessing of Your grace."

"Yes, Lord!"

"Help us to receive Your peace and courage, Your confidence and power," he said.

"Yes, Lord!"

"Thank you for being with us now, and in the coming weeks and coming years."

"And Father," she said, "please give me the grace to love Dooley as You love him, and the patience to encourage and support and understand him, for I wish with all my heart that we might grow together in harmony, as a true family." She took a deep and satisfying breath. "And now, Lord . . ."

As the prayer neared its end, they spoke in unison as they had recently begun to do in their evening prayers.

". . . create in us a clean heart . . . renew a right spirit within us . . . and fill us with Your Holy Spirit . . . through Christ our Lord . . . amen."

He helped her from the footstool and she sat beside him on the love seat and breathed the peace that settled over them like a shawl.

"There will be many times when fear breaks in," he said, holding her close. "We can never be taken prisoner if we greet it with prayer."

"Yes!" she whispered, feeling a weight rolled away like the stone from the sepulcher.

"I smelled the chicken as I came through the hedge."

"Dinner in twenty minutes?" she murmured.

"I thought you'd never ask," he said.

CHAPTER EIGHT

The Preamble

On the morning of September seventh, in the upstairs guest room of the rectory, Bishop Stuart Cullen checked his vestments for any signs of wrinkles or unwanted creases, found none, then took his miter from the box and set it on the bureau, mindful that his crozier was in the trunk of the car, as were his black, polished shoes and an umbrella in case of rain.

Rummaging about the room in a pair of magenta boxer shorts given him by his suffragan, he hummed snatches of a Johnny Cash tune as Martha Cullen sat up in bed and read an issue of *Country Life* magazine that Puny had placed on the night table three years ago and faithfully dusted ever since. Studying a feature on knot gardens, she was utterly unmindful of the bishop's rendition of "Ring of Fire" as he enjoyed a long, steaming shower that caused water in the shower across the hall to trickle upon the rector's head in a feeble stream.

Under the miserly drizzle, the rector counted his blessings that the bishop would be preaching this morning and he celebrating, a veritable holiday in the Caymans, as far as he was concerned. In truth, he feared that if he opened his mouth to deliver wisdom of any sort, it would pour forth as some uncertified language, resulting not from the baptism of the Holy Spirit but of something akin to panic, or worse. He despaired that the custard had vanished in the night, and fear and trembling had jumped into its place with both feet.

In his room across the hall, Dooley sat on the side of his bed and felt the creeping, lopsided nausea that came with the aroma of baking ham as it rose from the kitchen. He said three four-letter words in a row, and was disappointed when his stomach still felt sick.

He hoped his voice wouldn't crack during the hymn. Though he'd agreed to sing a cappella, he didn't trust a cappella. If you hit a wrong note, there was nothing to cover you. He wished there were trumpets or something really loud behind him, but no, Cynthia wanted "Dooley's pure voice." Gag.

"God," he said aloud, "don't let me sound weird. Amen." He had no idea that God would really hear him or prevent him from sounding weird, but he thought it was a good idea to ask.

He guessed he was feeling better about stuff. Yesterday, Father Tim spent the whole day taking him places, plus they'd run two miles with Barnabas and gone to Sweet Stuff after. Then, Cynthia had given him a hug that nearly squeezed his guts out. "Dooley," she said, "I really care about you."

When he heard that, he felt his face getting hard. He didn't want it to, but it was trained that way. He could tell she really meant it, but she'd have to prove she meant it before he would smile at her; he knew she wanted him to smile. Maybe he would someday, but not now. Now he was trying to keep from puking up his gizzard because he had to sing a song he didn't even like, at a wedding he still wasn't sure of.

In the kitchen of the little yellow house beyond the hedge, Cynthia Coppersmith stood barefoot in her aging chenile robe, her hair in pink foam curlers, eating half a hotdog from the refrigerator and drinking coffee so strong it possessed the consistency of tapioca.

On arriving home last night from the country club dinner party where, out of courtesy, she'd picked at a salad, she had boiled a hotdog and eaten the first half of it in a bun with what she thought was mustard but was, in fact, horseradish, loosely the age of her expiring Boston fern. It was the first true nourishment she'd recently been able to take, except for a rock shrimp and three cherry tomatoes at Friday's bridal luncheon. She ate the remains of the hotdog in two bites and, feeling her lagging appetite suddenly stimulated, foraged in the refrigerator until she found a piece of Wednesday's broiled flounder, which she spritzed with the juice of a geriatric lemon and, standing at the sink, consumed with gusto.

Two blocks south, Esther Bolick peered out her kitchen window as a straggle of rain clouds parted to reveal the sun. "Happy is th' bride th' sun shines on!" she announced with relief.

Going briskly to the oven, she removed three pans of scratch cake layers to a cooling rack, and stood with her hands on her hips in a baby doll nightgown and bedroom shoes with the faces of bunnies. She gazed with satisfaction at the trio of perfect yellow moons, then trotted across the kitchen for another cup of decaf, the black pupils of the bunnies' plastic eyes rolling and clicking like dice.

She would go to Sunday School and the eleven o'clock, then come home and ice the cake and let it sit 'til she carried it to church at four. She and Gene would do what they usually did when hauling around a three-layer—put newspaper on the floor of the cargo area, and while Gene drove, she would sit back there on a stool and hold the cake to keep it from sliding around in its cardboard box. Without a van, there was no way on

God's green earth to follow her calling unless you were making sheet cakes, which she utterly despised and would not be caught dead doing. The icing would go on at home, but she'd put the pearls and lilies on at church in one of the Sunday School rooms. Then she'd take the shelves out of the church fridge and pop the whole thing in 'til just before the thundering horde hit the reception.

She removed the hair net from her head and stuck it in the knife drawer.

Four blocks north, Uncle Billy Watson took the wire hanger from the nail on the wall and squinted at the black wool suit, inherited from his long-dead brother-in-law. Its heaviness had bowed down the arms of the coat hanger, giving the whole thing a dejected appearance.

"Dadgummit," he said under his breath. There was a spot on the right lapel as big as a silver dollar; it looked like paint—or was it vanilla pudding? In his pajamas, he shuffled to the kitchen, where he could see in a better light.

Miss Rose was sitting in her chair by the refrigerator, peeling potatoes with a knife too dull to cut butter. "What are you doing, Bill Watson?"

"Cleanin' my coat."

"You'll not be getting *my* goat!" she said, indignant.

His wife was going deaf as a doorknob, and there

wasn't a thing he could do about it. She wouldn't even discuss hearing aids, let alone ask the county to buy her a pair.

"What are you wearin' to the weddin'?" he shouted.

"What wedding?"

"Th' preacher's weddin' this evenin' at five o'-clock!"

"Five o'clock!" she squawked. "That's suppertime!"

"Well, I cain't help if it is, hit's th' preacher's weddin' an' we're a-goin'." Hadn't he talked about this wedding 'til he was blue in the face, even picked out three dresses she had bitterly rejected? And now this.

He wagged his head and sighed. "Lord have *mercy*."

"What about Percy?" she demanded.

The old man scrubbed at the lapel with a wet dishrag. Some days he could put on a smiley face and go about his business just fine, some days Rose Watson tested his faith, yes, she did. He'd have to trot to church this morning and sit there asking forgiveness for what he was thinking. He'd also be thanking the Lord for the joke. Don't tell him that God Almighty didn't answer foolish prayers!

Four blocks northwest, Hessie Mayhew lay snoring in her double bed with the faded flannel sheets and vintage Sears mattress. She had taken two Benadryl caps last night to dry up her sinuses after a day of messing with lady's-mantle and hydrangeas. Hydrangeas always did something to her sinuses, they had drained like a tap as she plowed through people's yards, taking what she wanted without asking. She'd even ducked behind the Methodist chapel, where a thick hedge of hydrangeas flowered magnificently every year, and took her pick of the huge blooms.

People knew who she was, they knew whose wedding this was; if she'd stopped to ask permission, they'd have said help yourself, take all you want! So why stop and ask, that was her philosophy! People should be proud for her to rogue their flowers, seeing they made so many people happy. *I declare,* she once imagined someone saying, *Hessie Mayhew stripped every peony bush in my yard today, and I'm just* tickled *about it!*

For her money, the hydrangeas were a week shy of the best color, but did people who set wedding dates ever stop and think of such things? Of course not, they just went blindly on. If she lived to marry again, which she sometimes hoped she would, she'd do it in May, when lily of the valley was at it peak.

On her screened porch, a decrepit porcelain bathtub boasted a veritable sea of virgin's bower and hydrangeas.

In her double kitchen sink, Blue Mist spirea, autumn anemone, Queen Anne's lace, artemisia, and knotweed drank thirstily. Inside the back door, buckets of purple coneflowers, autumn clematis, cosmos, and wild aster sat waiting. On the counter above the dishwasher, a soup pot of pink Duet and white Garden Party roses mingled with foxtail grass, Jerusalem artichoke, dog hobble, and panicles of the richly colored pokeberry. A small butterfly that had ridden in, drugged, on a coneflower, came to itself and visited the artemisia.

At seven-thirty, Hessie Mayhew turned on her side, moaning a little due to the pain in her lower back, and though a team of helpers was due to arrive at eight, she slept on.

In her home a half mile from town, Puny Guthrie crumbled two dozen strips of crisp, center-cut bacon into the potato salad and gave it one last, heaving stir. Everybody would be plenty hungry by six or six-thirty, and she'd made enough to feed a corn shuckin', as her granpaw used to say. She had decided to leave out the onions, since it was a wedding reception and very dressy. She'd never thought dressing up and eating onions were compatible; onions were for picnics and eating at home in the privacy of your own family.

Because Cynthia and the father didn't want people

to turn out for the reception and go home hungry, finger foods were banned. They wanted to give everybody a decent supper, even if they would have to eat it sitting on folding chairs from Sunday School. What with the father's ham, Miss Louella's yeast rolls, Miss Olivia's raw vegetables and dip, her potato salad, and Esther Bolick's three-layer orange marmalade, she didn't think they'd have any complaints. Plus, there would be ten gallons of tea, not to mention decaf, and sherry if anybody wanted any, but she couldn't imagine why anybody would. She'd once taken a sip from the father's decanter, and thought it tasted exactly like aluminum foil, though she'd never personally tasted aluminum foil except when it got stuck to a baked potato.

She thought of her own wedding and how she had walked down the aisle on Father Tim's arm. She had felt like a queen, like she was ten feet tall, looking at everything and everybody with completely new eyes. Halfway down the aisle, she nearly burst into tears, then suddenly she soared above tears to something higher, something that took her breath away, and she knew she would never experience anything like it again. Later, when she called Father Tim "Father," she was struck to find she said it as if he really were her father, it wasn't just some religious name that went with a collar. Ever since that moment, she'd felt she was his daughter, in a way that no one except herself could understand. And hadn't he been the one to pray that parade prayer that brought Joe Joe to the back door and into her life forever? She had been cleaning the downstairs rectory toilet when Joe Joe came to the back, because she hadn't heard him knocking at the front. When she saw him, her heart did a somersault, because he was the cutest, most handsome person she'd ever seen outside of a TV show or magazine.

"Father Tim said he might have a candy wrapper in the pocket of his brown pants, if you could send it, please."

She knew immediately that this policeman had been raised right, saying "please." Not too many people said please anymore, much less thank you, she thought it was a shame.

She had invited him in and given him a glass of tea and he perched on the stool where Father Tim sat and read his mail, and she went upstairs and looked in the father's brown pants pockets and there it was, wadded up. Why anybody would want to carry around a wadded-up candy wrapper . . .

"'Scuse my apron," she remembered saying. She would never forget the look in his eyes.

"You look really good in an apron," he said, turning beet red.

She'd never been told such a thing and had no idea what to say. She handed him the candy wrapper and he put it in a little Ziploc bag without taking his eyes off her.

She thought she was going to melt and run down in a puddle. Then he bolted off the stool and was out the door and gone and that was that. Until he came back the very next day when she was cooking lima beans.

"Hey," she said through the screen door as he bounded up the steps. By now, she knew that the whole police force was working on the big jewel theft at Lord's Chapel.

"You're under arrest," he said, blushing again.

For a moment, she was terrified that this might be true, then she saw the big grin on his face.

"What're th' charges?"

"Umm, well . . ." He dropped his head and gazed at his shoes.

She thought it must be awful to be a grown man who blushed like a girl.

He jerked his head up and looked her in the eye. "You're over the legal limit of bein' pretty."

She giggled. "What're you goin' to do about it?" Boy howdy, that had flown right out of her mouth without even thinking.

"Umm, goin' to ask you to a movie in Wesley, how's that?"

"Is it R? I don't see R."

"I don't know," he said, appearing bewildered.

"You could look in the newspaper, or call," she said. She could scarcely get her breath. She had never noticed before that a police uniform looked especially good, it was like he was home on leave from the armed forces.

"Will you see, umm, PG-13?"

"Depending." Why on earth was she being so hard to get along with? Her mouth was acting like it had a mind of its own.

"My grandmother's th' *mayor*!" he exclaimed.

"That's nice," she said. This was going nowhere. She felt she was fluttering around in space and couldn't get her toes on the ground. Suddenly realizing again that she was wearing her apron, she snatched it up and over her head and stood there, feeling dumb as a rock.

"So, just trust me," he said. "We'll find a good movie if we have to go all th' way to . . ." He hesitated, thinking. *"Johnson City!"*

"Thank you," she said, "I'd enjoy goin' to th' movies with you."

After he left, she felt so addled and weak in the knees that she wanted to lie down, but would never do such a thing in the father's house; she didn't even *sit* down on the job, except once in a while to peel peaches or snap string beans.

She walked around the kitchen several times, trying to hold something in, she didn't know what it was. She ended up at the back door, where it suddenly came busting out.

It was a shout.

She put the plastic cover on the potato salad bowl and smiled, remembering that she'd stood at the screen door for a long time, with tears of happiness running down her cheeks.

Having had their flight canceled on Saturday due to weather, Walter and Katherine Kavanagh arrived at the Charlotte airport at 11:35 a.m. Sunday morning, following a mechanical delay of an hour and a half at La Guardia. They stood at the baggage carousel, anxiously seeking her black bag, which contained not only her blue faille suite for the wedding, but the gift they'd taken great pains to schlep instead of ship.

"Gone to Charlottesville, Virginia!" said the baggage claim authority, peering into his monitor. "How about that?"

From her greater height of six feet, Katherine surveyed him with a look capable of icing the wings of a 747.

"Sometimes they go to Charleston!" he announced, refusing to wither under her scorn. He was used to scorn; working in an airline baggage claim department was all about scorn.

Miss Sadie Baxter sat at her dressing table in her slip and robe, near the open window of the bedroom she'd occupied since she was nine years old. The rain clouds had rolled away, the sun was shining, and the birds were singing—what more could any human want or ask for?

She carefully combed the gray hair from her brush, rolled it into a tidy ball, and let it fall soundlessly into the wastebasket that bore the faded decal of a camellia blossom.

Where had the years gone? One day she'd sat here brushing hair the color of chestnuts, and the next time she looked up, she was old and gray. She remembered sitting on this same stool, looking into this same mirror, reading Willard Porter's love letter and believing herself to be beautiful. . . .

"Willard!" she whispered, recalling the letter she had committed to memory, the letter he wrote on her twenty-first birthday:

You may know that I am building a house in the village, on the green where Amos Medford grazed his cows. Each stone that was laid in the foundation was laid with the hope that I might yet express the loving regard I have for you, Sadie.

I am going to give this house a name, trusting that things may eventually be different between us. I will have it engraved on a cedar beam at the highest point in the attic, with the intention that its message may one day give you some joy or pleasure.

Perhaps, God willing, your father will soon see that I have something to offer, and relent. Until then, dear Sadie, I can offer only my fervent love and heartfelt devotion.

Soon afterward, Willard had been killed and buried in France, and many years went by before she learned the name he had engraved on the beam.

"'For lo, the winter is past . . . ,'" she murmured, gazing from her window into the orchard. Learning the name, Winterpast, had indeed given her much joy and pleasure.

"'. . . the rain is over and gone. The flowers appear on the earth; the time of the singing of birds is come. . . .'"

The time of the singing of birds had come for the father and Cynthia.

Miss Sadie looked into the mirror and smiled. Yes, it was their time, now.

At four-fifteen, Cynthia urged Katherine to give her a few minutes alone. So much had gone on in the last days and weeks, she said, that she was quite breathless.

"What if you should fall down the stairs?" Katherine inquired. "And your hair, it's still in curlers!"

Cynthia had known Katherine for just under two hours, but already reckoned her to be a woman who minced no words.

"I'm not going to fall down the stairs," she said. "And the curlers come out in a flash. I must say you look smashing in Olivia's suit, really you do, the color is wonderful on you."

"I've never worn anything this short in my life!" fumed Katherine, peering into the full-length mirror and tugging at her skirt. "I look exactly like Big Bird, I had no *idea* I was so knock-kneed. I'll scandalize the church, your friends will think we're riffraff."

"They'll think no such thing, they've all been dying to meet you." Cynthia urged Katherine toward the door of her bedroom, the bedroom that would, tonight, belong to Walter and Katherine, who currently had no room of their own at all, poor souls.

"I'll take your bouquet out of the parish hall refrigerator," said Katherine, "and see you in the narthex." What could she do with a bride who wanted to be alone? As for herself, she had sprained her ankle twenty minutes before her own wedding and if friends hadn't surrounded her, she might still be lying by the fish pond at that dreadful hotel in the Poconos.

At five 'til five, Father Tim shot his French cuffs and exchanged meaningful glances with Walter and the bishop.

They were cooped into the six-by-eight-foot sacristy like three roosters, he thought, and not a breath of air stirring.

He walked to the door and pushed it open. Avis Packard's cigarette smoke blew in.

"'Scuse me," said Avis, peering into the sacristy at what he considered a sight for sore eyes. There was their pope, dolled up in a long white robe and the oddest-looking headgear he ever laid eyes on, not to mention that long stick with a curve at the end, which was probably for snatching people up by the neck when they dozed off in the pew. Avis took a deep drag off his filtered Pall Mall and threw it in the bushes.

At precisely five o'clock, Father Tim heard the organ. What was going on? Why hadn't anyone come to the outer sacristy door to tell them the bride had arrived?

"Don't go out there!" he nearly shouted, as the bishop's hand went for the door that led to the sanctuary. "Walter, please find Katherine, find out what's going on." Somebody had missed a signal, somehow. He felt oddly uneasy.

At five after five, Walter reappeared, looking mystified. "Katherine can't find Cynthia. She was supposed to meet her in the narthex at five 'til."

Ten minutes late! Cynthia Coppersmith was the very soul of punctuality.

He had a gut feeling, and it wasn't good. "I'll be back," he said, sprinting through the open door.

"I'll come with you!" said Walter.

"No! Stay here!"

He dashed up Old Church Lane, cut through Baxter Park, and hit her back steps running.

"Cynthia!" He was trembling as he opened the unlocked door and ran into the hall. He stood for a moment, panting and bewildered, as Violet rubbed against his pant leg. He wished he could find cats more agreeable.

He took the stairs two at a time and hung a left into her bedroom. "Cynthia!"

"Timothy!"

She was beating on her bathroom door from the inside. "Timothy! I can't get out!"

He spied the blasted doorknob lying on the floor. He picked it up and stuck the stem back in the hole and cranked the knob to the right and the door opened and he saw his bride in her chenile robe and pink curlers, looking agonized.

"Oh, Timothy . . ."

"Don't talk," he said. "Don't even tell me. How can I help you, what can I do?"

She raced to the closet and took out her suit. "I already have my panty hose on, so I'm not starting from scratch. Stand outside and I'll do my best. Pray for me, darling! Oh, I'm so sorry, I should have borrowed something blue for good luck, what a dreadful mess. . . ."

He stood in the hall and checked his watch. Five-seventeen.

Violet rubbed against his ankle. He felt his jaws beginning to lock.

"OK, you can come in now, I have my suit on, where are my shoes, oh, good grief, how did they get there, I can't believe this, Timothy, I couldn't help it, the knob just *fell off,* I yelled out the window and nobody heard, it was awful—"

"Don't talk!" he said, coming into the room. Why was he commanding her not to talk? Let the poor woman talk if she wanted to! Helpless—that's what he felt.

She thumped onto the bench at her dressing table and powdered her face and outlined her lips with a pencil and put on lipstick.

Five-twenty.

Then she did something to her eyebrows and eyelids.

Five-twenty-two.

She sprayed the wisteria scent on her wrists and rubbed them together and touched her wrists to her ears.

He could see Stuart pacing the sacristy, Katherine wringing her hands, Walter going beserk, the entire congregation getting up and walking out, the ham, covered by Saran Wrap, abandoned in the refrigerator. . . .

"Cynthia . . ."

"Oh, dreadful, oh, horrid!" she cried, finishing her mascara with a shaking hand. "And I just remembered, you're not supposed to see the bride before the ceremony!"

"Too late!" he said, eyeing his watch. "Five twenty-four."

"I'm coming, I'm coming!"

She got up and dashed toward him.

"Curlers," he said, his jaws cranking still further into the lock position.

"Rats!"

She plucked curlers from her head like so many feathers from a chicken, and tossed them into the air. They literally rained around the room; he'd never seen anything like it.

"No time to brush!" She looked into the mirror and ran her fingers through her hair. "There! Best I can do. God help me!"

She turned to him now, and he felt a great jolt from heart to spleen. She was so astonishingly beautiful, so radiant, so fresh, it captured his very breath. Thanks be to God, his custard was back. . . .

She grabbed her handbag from the chair. "We can take my car!"

"No place to park!"

"So," she cried, as they headed for the stairs, "race you!"

CHAPTER NINE

The Wedding

In the ninth row of the epistle side, next to the stained-glass window of Christ carrying the lost lamb, Hope Winchester blushed to recall her once-ardent crush on Father Tim. She'd taken every precaution to make certain he knew nothing of it, and now it seemed idiotic to have felt that way about someone twice her age.

She remembered the fluttering of her heart when he came into the bookstore, and all her hard work to learn special words that would intrigue him. She would never admit such a thing to another soul, but she believed herself to be the only person in Mitford who could converse on his level. When she'd learned about Cynthia months ago, she had forced herself to stop thinking such nonsense altogether, and was now truly happy that he and his neighbor had found each other. They seemed perfect together.

Still, on occasion, she missed her old habit of looking for him to pass the shop window and wave, or stop in; and she missed pondering what book she might order that would please and surprise him.

It wasn't that she'd ever wanted to marry him, for heaven's sake, or even be in love with him; it was just that he was so very kind and gentle and made her feel special. Plus he was a lot like herself, deep and sensitive, not to mention a lover of the romantic poets she'd adored since junior high. Early on, she had made it a point to read Wordsworth again, weeping over the Lucy poems, so she could quote passages and dig out morsels to attract his imagination.

"Come in out of the *fretful stir*!" she once said as he popped through the door at Happy Endings.

He had looked up and smiled. "Wordsworth!" he exclaimed, obviously pleased.

How many people would recognize two little words among a poet's thousands? She had felt positively thrilled.

Opening her purse, she examined the contents for the Kleenex she'd stuffed in at the last minute. Though she thought it fatuous to cry at weddings, she deemed it wise to be prepared.

In the fourth row of the epistle side, Gene Bolick wondered what on earth was going on. His watch said five-fifteen. He knew Richard well enough to know he was looking pale after hammering down on the organ all this time with nothing happening.

He glanced again at the bishop's wife, whose head was bowed. Was she praying that the father hadn't chickened out at the last minute? Wouldn't that be a corker if their priest was on a plane bound for the Azores? He didn't know where the Azores were located, but figured it was a distance.

Realizing his fists were clenched and his palms sweaty, he forced his attention to the three-layer orange marmalade sitting in the parish hall refrigerator, looking like a million bucks. He hoped to the Lord the temperature was set right and hadn't accidentally been switched to extra cool, which had once frozen two hundred pimento cheese sandwiches as hard as hockey pucks. He nudged Esther, who appeared to be sleeping under the brim of the hat she wore only to weddings and funerals.

Esther was not sleeping, she was thinking, and ignored the nudge. Didn't she deserve to sit and catch her breath until these people got their act together and got on with it? She was thinking that maybe she'd put in too much sugar, she knew Father Tim didn't like too much sugar, but why, after all these years and hundreds of cakes later, did she still worry and fret over her work as if she'd never baked a cake in her life? The Expert is what some called her, but who could feel like an expert at something as willful and fickle as a cake, cakes having, as she'd always feared, a mind of their own? Use the same ingredients in the same amounts, time after time after time, and were her cakes ever the same? Not as far as she could see.

She'd always depended on Gene to be the judge and he hadn't failed her yet. Gene would take a taste of the batter and his eyes would wander around the room, as if that little taste had transported him on some round of roving thoughts and idle speculation. After a while, he'd come back to himself. "Best yet!" he might say, or, "Couldn't be better!"

Whatever he said, he would have reasoned it out, thought it through, and she could depend on the answer—which was more than most wives could say of their husbands. Now, you take Father Tim, his wife would be able to depend on him—the only question was, was she deserving of such a prize? She thought she was, she hoped she was; she was crazy about Cynthia, but hadn't her senator husband, or was he a congressman, run around with other women? What did that mean? Cynthia didn't look like a cold fish—the opposite, more like it.

Anyway, didn't their rector have enough sense to come in out of the rain and choose who he wanted to spend the rest of his life with? And in the last few months, hadn't she and everybody else in the parish heard him laugh and joke like never before?

Lord help, it must be virgin's bower that was making her eyes burn and her sinuses drain. Virgin's bower mixed with lilies, the bane of her existence, and nobody with the simple courtesy to remove the pollen from the anthers, which means it would be flying around in here like so much snuff, and her with no Sinu-Tabs in her pocketbook and too late to do anything about it.

Pete Jamison made his way into the nave of Lord's chapel, where a robed and expectant choir overflowed from the narthex. Embarrassed at being late, he dodged through the throng to the rear wall and stood, reverent and shaken, feeling at once a stranger here and also oddly at home. He realized his breath was coming in shallow gasps, probably because he'd run more than a block from the Collar Button where he'd parked—or was it from the excitement he felt in being here for the first time since his life had been changed forever?

Two rows from the front, on the gospel side, Miss Sadie sat holding hands with Louella, oblivious of the time and enjoying the music. She felt certain that the emotions stirring in her breast were those of any proud mother.

After all, Father Tim wasn't merely her priest, her

brother in Christ, and one of the dearest friends of this life, he was also like a son. Who else would run up the hill after a hard rain and empty the soup kettle sitting brimful under the leak in her ceiling? And who else would sit for hours listening to her ramble, while appearing to be genuinely interested? God in His Providence had not seen fit to bless her with children, but He'd given her Olivia Harper and Timothy Kavanagh! And, since she'd helped raise Louella from a baby, she could almost count her pewmate as her child—Lord knows, she wasn't but ten years old when she'd begun diapering and dressing that little dark baby as if it were her own!

Miss Sadie wiped a tear with the handkerchief she had carefully chosen for the occasion, a lace-trimmed square of white Irish linen monogrammed with her mother's initial, and turned and smiled proudly at Louella, who looked a perfect blossom in the lavender dress.

Dooley Barlowe swallowed hard. It would have been fine if everything had started when it was supposed to, but here it was twenty minutes after five and who knew where Cynthia and Father Tim were, like maybe they both got scared and ran off, or had a fight and weren't going through with it. He felt foolish sitting here in the front row, all of them tricked into waiting like a bunch of stupid goats, listening to organ music. He was about to die to go to the toilet, but if he tried now to make it to the parish hall, everybody would know where he was going.

He crossed his legs and squeezed his eyes shut and jiggled his foot and went through the verses again.

Reverend Absalom Greer had purposely followed Sadie Eleanor Baxter into the nave, though he tried to appear as if he had no idea she was anywhere around. He followed her so he could sit behind her and look at her again. Who knows when the Lord might call him Home and this would be his last chance on earth to see her face?

The way it fell out was, he was the first to go into the pew behind her, which meant he had to sit all the way to the end, by the window of Jesus washing the disciples' feet. He thought this location was a blessing from above, seeing as he could look at her in profile instead of at the little gray knot on the back of her head.

Absalom felt such a stirring in his breast that he might have been fourteen years old, going up Hogback to see Annie Hawkins, carrying two shot quails and a mess of turnips in a poke. Annie's mama was dead of pneumonia and her daddy not heard of since the flood, and as Annie was left to raise a passel of brothers and sisters, he never went up Hogback without victuals;

once he'd killed a deer and helped her skin it and jerk the meat.

It had taken him three years to get over big-boned, sassy-mouthed Annie Hawkins, but he'd never gotten over Sadie Baxter. Sadie had filled his dreams, his waking hours, his prayers for many a year; he'd earnestly hoped she would forget Willard Porter and marry him. Finally, the burning hope had fizzled into a kind of faint glow that laid on his heart like embers, making him smile occasionally and nod his head and whisper her name. He'd confessed this lingering and soulful love only to the Almighty and never told another, though sometimes his sister, Lottie, suspicioned how he was feeling and derided him with a cool stare.

Reverend Greer settled stiffly into the creaking pew and nodded to those around him and bowed his head and prayed for his dear brother in the Lord, Tim Kavanagh, as fine a man as God ever gave breath to, amen. When he lifted his head and looked at Sadie's profile and the tender smile on her face, the tears sprang instantly to his eyes and he fetched the handkerchief from his pocket, the handkerchief Lottie had starched and ironed 'til it crackled like paper, and thanked the Lord Jesus that he still had eyes to see and tears to wipe, hallelujah.

Pete Jamison, though six-foot-three, eased himself up on the balls of his feet so he could see down front to the gospel side. He found the pew where he sat the day he had wandered, alarmed and desperate, into the darkened church. It had been sometime around Thanksgiving and there was snow on the ground; he remembered noticing his incoming tracks as he left the church a different man, one to whom everything seemed fresh and new.

He'd knelt that day and cried out to God, asking a simple question: *Are you up there?* He wasn't trying to get anything from God, he wasn't begging for money or success, though at the time he urgently needed both, he just wanted to know more desperately than he'd ever wanted to know anything in his life, if God was up there—no more ifs, ands, or buts, just *yes or no*. Now he knew the answer more completely than he could ever have hoped or imagined.

He felt tears smart his eyes, and his heart expand. The music was beginning to enter him; he was beginning to hear it over the pounding of his heart, and was glad to feel the joy of this time and place as if it might, in some small way, belong also to him.

Standing outside the church door in the warm September afternoon, Katherine Kavanagh saw the bride and groom literally galloping down the street, and suppressed a shout of relief. She tugged on her skirt for the umpteenth time and tried to relax her tense shoulders so the jacket would fall below her waistline. In the desperate half hour she'd waited for Cynthia to show up, she had decided what to do. The minute she returned home, she was suing the airline, who had gotten away with their criminal behavior long enough.

Though wanting very much to dash across the churchyard and meet Cynthia, she realized this impetuous behavior would cause her skirt to ride up. She stood, therefore, frozen as a mullet as she watched the bride sprinting into the home stretch.

Next to the aisle on the epistle side, Emma Newland nearly jumped out of her seat as the organ cranked up to a mighty roar. The thirty-seven-voice ecumenical choir was at last processing in, sending a blast of energy through the congregation as if someone had fired a cannon.

The congregation shot to its feet, joining the choir in singing hymn number 410 with great abandon and unmitigated relief:

Praise my Soul the King of Heaven;
To His feet thy tribute bring;
Ransomed, healed, restored, forgiven,
Evermore His praises sing;
Alleluia, alleluia!
Praise the everlasting King!

Dooley Barlowe felt something happen to the top of his head. He had opened his mouth with the rest of the congregation and heard words flow out in a strong and steady voice he scarcely recognized as his own.

Praise Him for His grace and favor;
To His people in distress;
Praise Him still the same as ever,
Slow to chide and swift to bless.
Alleluia, alleluia,
Glorious in His faithfulness.

Dooley thought Father's Tim's voice carried loud and clear from where he stood with the bishop and Walter at the rail. The bishop was decked out in a really weird hat, but looked cool as anything otherwise. As for Father Tim, he'd never seen him in a tuxedo before and thought he looked . . . *different,* maybe sort of handsome.

The tremor in his stomach subsided; he felt suddenly tall and victorious and forgot about having to go to the toilet.

Hessie Mayhew gazed at Stuart Cullen, whom she found exceedingly good-looking, and thought it was a darned good thing that Episcopal clergy were allowed to marry, otherwise it could cause a rumpus. She'd never chased after clergy like some women she knew, but she couldn't dismiss their powerful attraction, either. Anyway, who'd want to tie the knot with a preacher and end up with a whole churchful of people pulling you to pieces day and night? *Head this, chair that!* No, indeed, no clergy for her, thank you very much.

She fluffed her scarf over the odd rash that had appeared on her neck, dismissing it as one of the several hazards of her calling, and hoped the bishop was noticing the flowers and that someone would tell him about Hessie Mayhew, who, even if she was Presbyterian, knew a thing or two about the right and proper way to beautify a church.

Angels, help us to adore Him;
Ye behold Him face to face;
Sun and moon, bow down before Him,
Dwellers in all time and space.
Alleluia, alleluia!
Praise with us the God of grace.

Jena Ivey could not carry a tune in a bucket and preferred to look at the stained-glass window for the duration of the processional hymn. The window was of Christ being baptized while John the Baptist stood onshore in his animal skin outfit. It seemed to her that St.

John could have presented himself better, seeing it was the Lord Jesus who was getting baptized; like it wasn't as if St. John didn't know He was coming, for Pete's sake. Look at the three wise men, who always appeared nicely groomed, though they'd been riding camels for *two years*.

She was startled by the sound of the trumpet only a few feet away, causing, simultaneously, an outbreak of goose bumps and a wild pounding of her heart.

Then, suddenly, there was the matron of honor charging down the aisle; Jena didn't have a clue who this woman might be, she was tall as a giraffe. That's the way it was with weddings, they turned out people you'd never seen before in your life and would never see again.

Emma thought the matron of honor blew past like she was going to a fire, canceling any opportunity to study the skimpy cut of Katherine Kavanagh's suit, or to check out the kind of shoes she had on. She did, however, get a whiff of something that wasn't flowers, it was definitely perfume, possibly from Macy's or some such.

Then came Rebecca Jane Owen and Amy Larkin, wearing velvet hair bows the color of green Baxter apples. As far as Emma could tell, they were fairly smothered with flowers; you'd think Hessie Mayhew would scale down for children, but oh, no, Hessie scaled up, these two infants were fairly tottering under the weight of what looked like full bushes of hydrangeas.

Jabbing Harold to do the same, Emma swiveled her head to see the bride trotting behind the small entourage.

Cynthia Coppersmith was flushed as a girl—her eyes shining, her face expectant, her hair curled damply around her face as if she'd just won a game of tag. Emma thought she looked sixteen years old if she was a day, and her suit was exactly the color of a crayon Emma had favored in first grade, aquamarine. She appeared to be moving fast, but that was all right—hadn't she herself run lickety-split to marry Harold Newland, starved to death for affection after ten years of widowhood and thrilled at the prospect of someone to hug her neck every night?

Emma leaned over the arm of the pew so she could see Father Tim as his bride approached the altar. The look on his face made her want to shut her eyes, as if she'd intruded upon something terribly precious and private.

"Dearly beloved, we have come together in the presence of God to witness and bless the joining together of this man and this woman in Holy Matrimony. The bond and covenant of marriage was established by God in creation, and our Lord Jesus Christ adorned this manner of life by His presence and first miracle at a wedding in

Cana of Galilee. It signifies to us the mystery of the union between Christ and His Church, and Holy Scripture commends it to be honored among all people.

"The union of husband and wife in heart, body, and mind is intended by God for their mutual joy; for the help and comfort given one another in prosperity and adversity; and, when it is God's will, for the procreation of children and their nurture in the knowledge and love of the Lord. Therefore marriage is not to be entered into unadvisedly or lightly, but reverently, deliberately, and in accordance with the purposes for which it was instituted by God.

"Into this holy union, Cynthia Clary Coppersmith and Timothy Andrew Kavanagh now come to be joined. . . ."

Uncle Billy Watson hoped and prayed his wife would not fall asleep and snore; it was all he could do to keep his own eyes open. Sitting with so many people in a close church on a close afternoon was nearabout more than a man could handle. He kept alert by asking himself a simple question: When it came time, would he have mustard on his ham, or eat it plain?

"Cynthia, will you have this man to be your husband; to live together in the covenant of marriage? Will you love him, comfort him, honor and keep him, in sickness and in health; and, forsaking all others, be faithful to him as long as you both shall live?"

Winnie Ivey clasped her hand over her heart and felt tears burn her cheeks. To think that God would give this joy to people as old as herself and no spring chickens . . .

The bride's vow was heard clearly throughout the nave. "I will!"

"Timothy, will you have this woman to be your wife; to live together in the covenant of marriage? Will you love her, comfort her, honor and keep her, in sickness and in health; and, forsaking all others, be faithful to her as long as you both shall live?"

"I will!"

"Will all of you witnessing these promises do all in your power to uphold these two persons in their marriage?"

"*We will!*"

At the congregational response, Dooley Barlowe quickly left the front pew by the sacristy door and took his place in front of the altar rail. As he faced the cross and bowed, one knee trembled slightly, but he locked it in place and drew a deep breath.

Don't let me mess up, he prayed, then opened his mouth and began to sing.

Oh, perfect Love, all human thought transcending,
Lowly we kneel in prayer before Thy throne,
That theirs may be the love which knows no ending,
Whom Thou forevermore dost join in one.

It all sounded lovey-dovey, thought Emma, but she knew one thing—it would never work if Cynthia sat around drawing cats while her husband wanted his dinner! Oh, Lord, she was doing it again, and this time without intending to; she was running down a person who didn't have a mean bone in her body. She closed her eyes and asked forgiveness.

She'd held on to her reservations about Cynthia like a tightwad squeezes a dollar, but she felt something in her heart finally giving way as if floodgates were opening, and she knew at last that she honestly approved of the union that would bind her priest's heart for all eternity. Disgusted with herself for having forgotten to bring a proper handkerchief, Emma mopped her eyes with a balled-up napkin from Pizza Hut.

Oh, perfect Life, be Thou their full assurance
Of tender charity and steadfast faith,
Of patient hope and quiet, brave endurance,
With childlike trust that fears nor pain nor death.

Pete Jamison pondered the words "childlike trust that fears nor pain nor death," and knew that's what he'd been given the day he'd cried out to God in this place and God had answered by sending Father Kavanagh. He remembered distinctly what the father had said: "You may be asking the wrong question. What you may want to ask is, Are You down here?"

He'd prayed a prayer that day with the father, a simple thing, and was transformed forever, able now to stand in this place knowing without any doubt at all that, yes, God is down here and faithfully with us. He remembered the prayer as if he'd uttered it only yesterday. *Thank you, God, for loving me, and for sending Your son to die for my sins. I sincerely repent of my sins, and receive Christ as my personal savior. Now, as Your child, I turn my entire life over to You.* He'd never been one to surrender anything, yet that day, he had surrendered everything. When the church was quiet and the celebration over, he'd go down front and kneel in the same place he'd knelt before, and give thanks.

Gene Bolick wondered how a man Father Tim's age would be able to keep up his husbandly duties. As for himself, all he wanted to do at night was hit his recliner after supper and sleep 'til bedtime. Maybe the father knew something he didn't know. . . .

Louella heard people all around her sniffling and

blowing their noses, it was a regular free-for-all. And Miss Sadie, she was the worst of the whole kaboodle, bawling into her mama's handkerchief to beat the band. Miss Sadie loved that little redheaded, freckle-face white boy because he reminded her of Willard Porter, who came up hard like Dooley and ended up amounting to something.

Louella thought Miss Cynthia looked beautiful in her dressy suit; and that little bit of shimmering thread in the fabric and those jeweled buttons, now, that was something, that was nice, and look there, she wasn't wearing shoes dyed to match, she was wearing black pumps as smart as you please. Louella knew from reading the magazines Miss Olivia brought to Fernbank that shoes dyed to match were out of style

It seemed to her that the sniffling was getting worse by the minute, and no wonder—just *listen* to that boy sing! Louella settled back in the pew, personally proud of Dooley, Miss Cynthia, the father, and the whole shooting match.

Finally deciding on mustard, Uncle Billy abandoned the game. He'd better come up with another way to noodle his noggin or he'd drop off in a sleep so deep they'd have to knock him upside the head with a two-by-four. He determined to mentally practice his main joke, and if that didn't work, he was done for.

Grant them the joy which brightens earthly sorrow,
Grant them the peace which calms all earthly strife,
And to life's day the glorious unknown morrow
That dawns upon eternal love and life.
Amen.

Dooley returned to his pew without feeling the floor beneath his feet. He was surprised to find he was trembling, as if he'd been live-wired. But it wasn't fear, anymore, it was . . . something else.

Father Tim took Cynthia's right hand in his, and carefully spoke the words he had never imagined might be his own.

"In the name of God, I, Timothy, take you, Cynthia, to be my wife, to have and to hold from this day forward, for better for worse, for richer for poorer, in sickness and in health, to love and to cherish, until we are parted by death.

"This is my solemn vow."

They loosed their hands for a moment, a slight movement that caused the candle flames on the altar to tremble. Then she took his right hand in hers.

"In the name of God, I, Cynthia, take you, Timothy,

to be my husband, to have and to hold from this day forward, for better for worse, for richer for poorer, in sickness and in health, to love and to cherish, until we are parted by death.

"This is my solemn vow."

As Walter presented the ring to the groom, the bishop raised his right hand. "Bless, O Lord, these rings to be a sign of the vows by which this man and this woman have bound themselves to each other; through Jesus Christ our Lord, Amen."

"Cynthia, I give you this ring as a symbol of my vow, and with all that I am, and all that I have, I honor you, in the name of the Father, and of the Son, and of the Holy Spirit."

She felt the worn gold ring slipping on her finger; it seemed weightless, a band of silk.

Katherine stepped forward then, delivering the heavy gold band with the minuscule engraving upon its inner circle: *Until heaven and then forever.*

"Timothy . . . I give you this ring as a symbol of my vow, and with all that I am, and all that I have, I honor you, in the name of the Father, and of the Son, and of the Holy Spirit."

Hessie Mahew was convinced the bishop looked right into her eyes as he spoke.

"Now that Cynthia and Timothy have given themselves to each other by solemn vows, with the joining of hands and the giving and receiving of rings, I pronounce that they are husband and wife, in the name of the Father, and of the Son, and of the Holy Spirit.

"Those whom God has joined together . . . let no man put asunder."

Dooley felt the lingering warmth in his face and ears, and heard the pounding of his heart. No, it wasn't fear anymore, it was something else, and he thought he knew what it was.

It was something maybe like . . . happiness.

CHAPTER TEN

The Beginning

Henry Oldman met them at the airport in the Cullen camp car, a 1981 turquoise Chevy Impala that made the rector's Buick look mint condition, showroom.

It was theirs to drive for the week, and they dropped Henry off at his trim cottage with a two-stall cow barn and half-acre garden plot. While Cynthia chatted with Mrs. Oldman, Henry gave him the drill.

"New tires," Henry said, delivering a swift kick to the aforesaid.

"Wonderful!"

"New fan belt."

"Great!"

"Miz Oldman washed y'r seat covers."

"Outstanding. Glad to hear it."

"Mildew."

The handyman who'd served the Cullens for nearly

fifty Maine summers was sizing him up pretty good, he thought; trying to figure whether he'd be a proper steward for such fine amenities.

"You'll be stayin' in th' big house, what they call th' lodge. Miz Oldman put this 'n' that in y'r icebox. Juice an' cereal an' whatnot."

"We thank you."

Henry pulled at his lower lip. "Washin' machine door come off, wouldn't use it much if I was you."

"I suppose not."

"Downstairs toilet handle needs jigglin' or it's bad to run. Ordered th' part t' fix it, but hadn't got it yet."

"We'll remember."

"You got a pretty big hole in y'r floor. Last year or two, we've had more'n one snake come in."

"*Which* floor exactly?"

"Dinin' room. I set a barrel over it, Bishop said it'd be all right 'til I can get somethin' to fix it. Had a rag in th' hole but somethin' chewed it out."

Now we're getting down to it, he thought.

"Got rid of y'r ants, but not much luck with th' mice, mice're smarter'n we give 'em credit for."

His wife didn't need to know this. Not any of this.

Henry kicked the tire again for good measure. "Attic stairs, you pull 'em down, they won't go up ag'in."

The rector shrugged. He'd rather have a root canal without Novocain than stand here another minute.

"Course you know there's no electric at th' Cullen place."

No electric? His blood pressure was shooting up; he could feel the pounding in his temples. "What *lights* the place? *Pine torches?*"

"Only two places hereabout still has gas-lit."

He hadn't fared so badly since trucking off at the age of nine to Camp Mulhaven, where he entertained a double-barreled dose of chiggers and poison ivy. What would Cynthia think? What had he gotten them into? He'd wring his bishop's neck, the old buzzard; his so-called honeymoon cottage was a blasted tumbledown shack! He'd call the moment they arrived and give Stuart Cullen a generous piece of his mind. . . .

"Wouldn't keep any food settin' on th' porch." Henry removed a toothpick from his shirt pocket and pried the circumference of his left molar.

"Why's that?" He couldn't remember ever leaving food on a porch. Why would anyone leave food on a porch?

"Bear."

Bear?

He craned his neck to peer at his wife, standing with

Mrs. Oldman by a flower bed. Thank heaven she hadn't overheard the last pronouncement.

"Well!" said the rector, putting an end to the veritable Niagara of bad news. "We'll see you when we bring the car back."

"You'll see me tomorrow," said Henry. "Bishop called today, asked me to come check th' water, see if it's runnin' muddy. Bishop's daddy, he tried to dig a new well before he passed, but . . ." Henry raised both hands as if he had no responsibility for the failure of this mission, it was some bitter destiny over which he'd lacked any control. "Bishop said bring you some speckled trout, you know how to clean trout?"

"Ahhh," he said, wordless. He'd never cleaned trout in his life.

Henry raised an eyebrow. "I'll have Miz Oldman do it for you."

He could hardly wait to get in the car, if only to sit down.

These were the days of heaven. . . .

He walked out to the porch, loving the feel of old wood, silken with wear, under his bare feet.

The view took his breath away. Early morning mist

hovered above the platinum lake, and just there, near its center, a small island with a cabin on its narrow shore. . . .

Nothing stirred except waterfowl: He saw a merganser and a string of young ply the water with great determination. Next to the lodge, cedar waxwings dived and swooped in the seed-dowered garden.

It would definitely take some getting used to, but he was liking this place better with every passing moment.

He expanded his chest and sucked in his stomach and circled his arms like propellers, awash in happiness, in contentment—in a kind of energized sloth, if there could be such a thing.

Though they'd slept at his house the first night and at hers on the second, last night had somehow marked the true beginning.

At the rectory, his antediluvian mattress had rolled them into the middle of the bed like hotdogs in a bun. At her house, circumstances were considerably improved, though the alarm clock had, oddly, gone off at three a.m. Odder still, the clock wasn't in its usual place on her bedside table. Failing to turn on a lamp, they leapt up to locate the blasted thing and, navigating by moonlight alone, had crashed into each other at the bookcase.

But last night had been everything, everything and more.

He cupped his hands and drew them to his face and smelled her warm scent, now and forever mingled with his own. In truth, he had entered into a realm that had little to do with familiar reason and everything to do with a power and mystery he'd never believed possible. Perhaps for the first time in his life, there was nothing he craved to possess, nothing he felt lacking; he was only waiting for his coffee to perk.

He had schlepped the coffee in his suitcase, for which effort his underwear smelled of decaf Antigua and his socks of full-bore French Roast. Eager to begin their honeymoon on a note of thoughtfulness, if not downright servitude, he had gone to the kitchen to concoct the coffee, to be followed by a breakfast of . . . he opened the cabinets and checked the inventory . . . a breakfast of raisin bran in blue tin bowls.

He'd never messed with gas stoves. While chefs were commonly known to prefer cooking with gas, he'd always feared it might blow his head off. Dangerous stuff, gas, he could smell it in here more strongly than in the rest of the house. If he lit a match, they could be spending their honeymoon in Quebec. . . .

But come on, for Pete's sake, wasn't he up for a little excitement on this incredibly beautiful, endlessly promising day? Wasn't all of this an adventure, a new beginning?

He withdrew a kitchen match from the box and studied it soberly, then walked to the gas-powered refrigerator and retrieved the coffee. Now. Where might the coffee pot be lurking?

Aha. That must be it on the shelf above the stove. Then again, surely not. He took it down and inspected it. Campfires. Many campfires. He lifted the lid. Oh, yes, just like his mother once used, there was the basket on its stick. . . .

Thinking he should try and clean the pot, he removed the basket and peered inside. Hopeless! He rinsed it out under a trickle of cold water. That would have to do; this was not, after all, a military kitchen.

He filled the basket with some satisfaction, thankful he'd brought preground, otherwise they'd be chewing beans. . . .

His wife appeared, looking touseled and teenaged in her nightgown. She slipped her arms around his waist and kissed him. "I love campfire coffee!"

Using the flat of his hand, he hammered down on the lid, which, once round, had somehow become oval with age. "What don't you love, Kavanagh?"

"Ducks that cry all night, beds with creaking springs, and feather pillows with little gnawing things inside."

"My sentiments exactly." He smiled at his bride, set the pot on the stove, and struck the match.

"Stand back!" he warned.

"Those weren't ducks calling last night."

They were rocking on the porch, side by side. He had never felt so far from a vestry in his life. "They're loons."

"*Loons!*" she said, marveling.

The ensuing silence was punctuated with birdsong.

"Related to the auks."

"Who, dearest? The Cullens?"

"The loons."

"Of course."

"They mate for life."

"Lovely! Just like us."

They watched the navigation of yet another duck family, thought they spotted a bald eagle, counted three kingfishers, sipped a second cup of coffee.

He relished their easy quietude this morning; it held a richness to be savored. Surely he was blessed beyond all reckoning to have a highly verbal wife who could also be quiet. He had always valued that in a woman, in a man, in a friend. Though his mother had possessed a sparkling way with people and was bright and eager in conversation on many subjects, she also had a gentle quietude that made her companionship ever agreeable.

"God is mercifully allowing me to forget the dreadful experience of getting here," Cynthia said of yesterday's journey.

"You mean the four-hour mechanical delay, the two-hour layover, and the forty-five minutes on the runway with no air stirring in the cabin?"

"The same!" she said.

"The usual," he said.

He wondered what his dog might be doing at the moment. And how about his boy—how was he faring? He'd call home tonight. On second thought, he could forget calling anybody. His bishop had conveniently forgotten to say there was no phone at Cullen camp.

"I love this place, Timothy. It's so wonderfully simple."

"What would you like to do today?"

"Nothing!"

He was thrilled to hear it.

"Of course," she said, "we might pop down to the village and peek in the shops."

He hated to be the bearer of bad news. "Umm . . ."

"There are no shops!" she said, reading his mind.

"Right. Only a service station, a small grocery store with a post office, and an unused church."

"So we can poke through the graveyard. I love graveyards!"

He grinned. "Of course you love graveyards. But I don't think there's a graveyard at this particular church. Stuart mentioned that the flock was buried elsewhere."

She leaned back in the rocker and turned her head and looked into his eyes, smiling. "Well, then," she murmured.

He took her hand and lightly kissed the tips of her fingers. "Well, then," he said.

Henry had come on Wednesday with fresh trout and a blackberry pie baked by Mrs. Oldman, and on Thursday with a free-range chicken, a quart of green beans, a sack of beets and potatoes, and a providential lump of home-churned butter.

In truth, they were savoring unforgettable meals at an oilcloth-covered table on the porch, lighted in the evening by a kerosene lantern. One evening had been crisp and cold enough for a fire; they'd hauled the table indoors and dined by the hearth on a hearty vegetable stew, sopping their bowls with bread toasted over the fire and slathered with Oldman butter. Each dish they prepared was such a stunning success that he now dreaded going home to four pathetic electric eyes, albeit on a range of more recent vintage.

In the four days since arriving, they'd clung to the porch like moss to a log, celebrating the sunrise, cheering the dazzling sunsets. Their off-porch expeditions had been few—a walk around the lake, twice, and a canoe excursion to the island. Not being water lovers, they made the island foray with considerable temerity. Finding the cabin empty, they picnicked under a fir tree on a threadbare Indian blanket and, setting off for home, found the trip across had so bolstered their confidence that they paddled north for a couple of miles, only to be drenched by a downpour.

Yesterday, they'd climbed through the window of another cabin in the Cullen camp. Sitting on the floor of a room built in 1917, according to the date carved on a rafter, they drank Earl Grey tea from a thermos and told all the jokes they could remember from childhood.

Finding themselves on a roll, she suggested they draw broomstraws to see who'd entertain the other with a retelling of Uncle Billy's wedding joke.

The rector was not pleased to draw the short straw. After all, who but Uncle Billy could tell an Uncle Billy joke? He returned the straw. "Sorry," he said, "but this joke can't be done without a cane."

She got up and went to the fireplace, whipped the broom off the hearth, and handed it over.

"Is there no balm . . . ?" he sighed.

"None!" she said.

Using the hearth for a stage and the broom for a cane, he hunkered down and clasped his right lower back, where he thought he might actually feel an arthritic twinge.

"Wellsir, two fellers was workin' together, don't you know. First'n, he was bright 'n cheerful, th' other'n, he didn't have nothin' to say, seem like he was mad as whiz. First'n said, 'Did you wake up grouchy this mornin'?' Other'n said, 'Nossir, I let 'er wake 'er own self up.'"

Hoots, cheers, general merriment.

"That's just m' warm-up, don't you know, hit ain't m' main joke."

The audience settled down and gazed at him raptly.

"Wellsir, Ol' Adam, he was mopin' 'round th' Garden of Eden feelin' lonesome, don't you know. So, the Lord asked 'im, said, 'Adam, what's ailin' you?' Adam said he didn't have nobody t' talk to. Wellsir, th' Lord tol' 'im He'd make somebody t' keep 'im comp'ny, said hit'd be a woman, said, 'This woman'll rustle up y'r grub an' cook it f'r you, an' when you go t' wearin' clothes, she'll wash 'em f'r you, an' when you make a decision on somethin', she'll agree to it.' Said, 'She'll not nag n'r torment you a single time, an' when you have a fuss, she'll give you a big hug an' say you was right all along.'

"Ol' Adam, he was jist a-marvelin' at this.

"The Lord went on, said, 'She'll never complain of a headache, an' 'll give you love an' passion whenever you call for it, an' when you have young'uns, she'll not ask y' to git up in th' middle of th' night.' Adam's eyes got real big, don't you know, said 'What'll a woman like 'at *cost* a feller?' Th' Lord said, 'A arm an' a leg!'

"Adam pondered a good bit, said, 'What d'you reckon I could git f'r a rib?'"

Generous applause, ending with the whistle his wife learned as a ten-year-old marble player.

Crawling out the way they'd come in, they left the cabin before dusk and trekked to the lodge on an overgrown path.

During these jaunts, he faithfully looked for bear and stayed alert to protect his wife, though he saw nothing more suspicious than a raccoon seeking to purloin Wednesday's chicken bones.

Today, Cynthia had hauled out sketch pads and pencils and abandoned any notion of leaving the porch. She vowed she'd seen a moose swimming in the lake and was not keen to miss further sightings. He, meanwhile, lay in a decrepit hammock and read G. K. Chesterton.

Peace covered them like a shawl; he couldn't remember such a time of prolonged ease. There were, however, moments when Guilt snatched him by the scruff of the neck, determined to persuade him this was a gift he had no right to unwrap and enjoy, and he'd better watch his step or *else*. . . .

"Listen to this," he said. "'An adventure is only an inconvenience rightly considered. An inconvenience is only an adventure wrongly considered.'"

She laughed. "I didn't know G.K. had been to Cullen camp."

"And this: 'The Christian ideal has not been tried and found wanting. It has been found difficult, and left untried.' Does that nail it on the *head*?" He fairly whooped.

"I love seeing you like this," she said.

"Like what?"

"Happy . . . resting . . . at ease. No evening news, no phones, no one pulling you this way and that."

"Stuart knew what he was doing, after all."

"I have a whole new respect for your bishop," she declared.

A loon called, a dragonfly zoomed by the porch rail.

"I heard something in our room last night," she said.

"Something *skittering* across the floor. What do you think it was?"

"Oh, I don't know—maybe a chipmunk?" Right there was proof positive that his brain was still working.

"I love chipmunks!"

He put the Chesterton on the floor beside the hammock and lay dazed and dreaming, complete. "'Blessed be the Lord . . . ,'" he murmured.

"'. . . who daily loadeth us with benefits!'" she exclaimed, finishing the verse from Psalm Sixty-eight.

A wife who could read his mind and finish his Scripture verses. Amazing. . . .

When he awoke, he heard only the faint whisper of her pencils on paper.

"Dearest, could you please zip to the store for us?"

"That car will not *zip* anywhere," he said.

"Yes, but we can't go on like two chicks in the nest, with poor Henry our mother hen. We must have *supplies*."

"I suppose it would be a good thing to keep the battery charged."

"A quart of two-percent milk," she said, without looking up from her sketch pad, "whole wheat English muffins, brown eggs, an onion—we can't make another meal without an onion—and three lemons—"

"Wait!" He hauled himself over the side of the

creaking hammock and trotted into the house for a pen and paper.

She held up the sketch and squinted at it. "Oh, and some grapes!" she called after him. "And bacon! Wouldn't it be lovely to smell bacon frying in the morning? I do love raisin bran, Timothy, but *really*. . . ."

Though the late afternoon temperature felt unseasonably warm when he left the car, it was refreshingly cool as he entered the darkened store.

A man in a green apron was dumping potatoes from a sack into a bin; he looked up and nodded.

The rector nodded back, wondering at his odd sense of liberty in being untethered, yet wondering still more about his desire to hurry back to his wife. This was, after all, the first time they'd been apart since the wedding; he felt . . . barren, somehow, *bereft*. Perhaps it was the sixtysomething years for which, without knowing it, his soul had waited for this inexpressible joy, and he didn't want to miss a single moment of it. Then again, his joy might owe nothing to having waited, and everything to love, and love alone.

He didn't understand these things, perhaps he never

would; all he knew or understood was that he wanted to inhale her, to wear her under his very skin—God's concept of "one flesh" had sprung to life for him in an extraordinary way, it was food, it was nectar; their love seemed the hope of the world, somehow. . . .

He chose a package of thick-sliced market bacon. This was living on the edge, and no two ways about it.

But perhaps he was happiest, in reflection, about the other waiting, the times when the temptation to have it all had been nearly unbearable, but they had drawn back, obeying God's wisdom for their lives. The drawing back had shaken him, yes, and shaken her, for their love had exposed their desire in a way they'd never known before. Yet, His grace had made them able to wait, to concentrate on the approaching feast instead of the present hunger.

He set his basket on the counter.

"You over on the lake?" the man asked.

"We are."

"Looks like you'll have a fine sunset this evenin'."

He peered through the store windows toward the tree line. *Holy smoke!* If he hurried, he could make it back to the lodge in time. . . .

"Anything else I can round up for you?"

"This will do it."

"You sure, now?"

As he took out his wallet, he realized he couldn't stop smiling.

"Thank you, this is all," he said. "I have absolutely everything."

PENGUIN BOOKS

A LIGHT IN THE WINDOW

Jan Karon writes "to give readers an extended family, and to applaud the extraordinary beauty of ordinary lives." She is the author of nine Mitford novels, *At Home in Mitford*; *A Light in the Window*; *These High, Green Hills*; *Out to Canaan*; *A New Song*; *A Common Life*; *In This Mountain*; *Shepherds Abiding*; and *Light from Heaven*, all available from Penguin. She is also the author of *The Mitford Bedside Companion*; *Jan Karon's Mitford Cookbook & Kitchen Reader*; *A Continual Feast: Words of Comfort and Celebration, Collected by Father Tim*; *Patches of Godlight: Father Tim's Favorite Quotes*; *The Mitford Snowmen: A Christmas Story*; *Esther's Gift*; and *The Trellis and the Seed*. Her children's books include *Miss Fannie's Hat*; *Jeremy: The Tale of an Honest Bunny*; and *Violet Comes to Stay*. Coming from Viking in fall 2007 is the first Father Tim Novel, *Home to Holly Springs*.

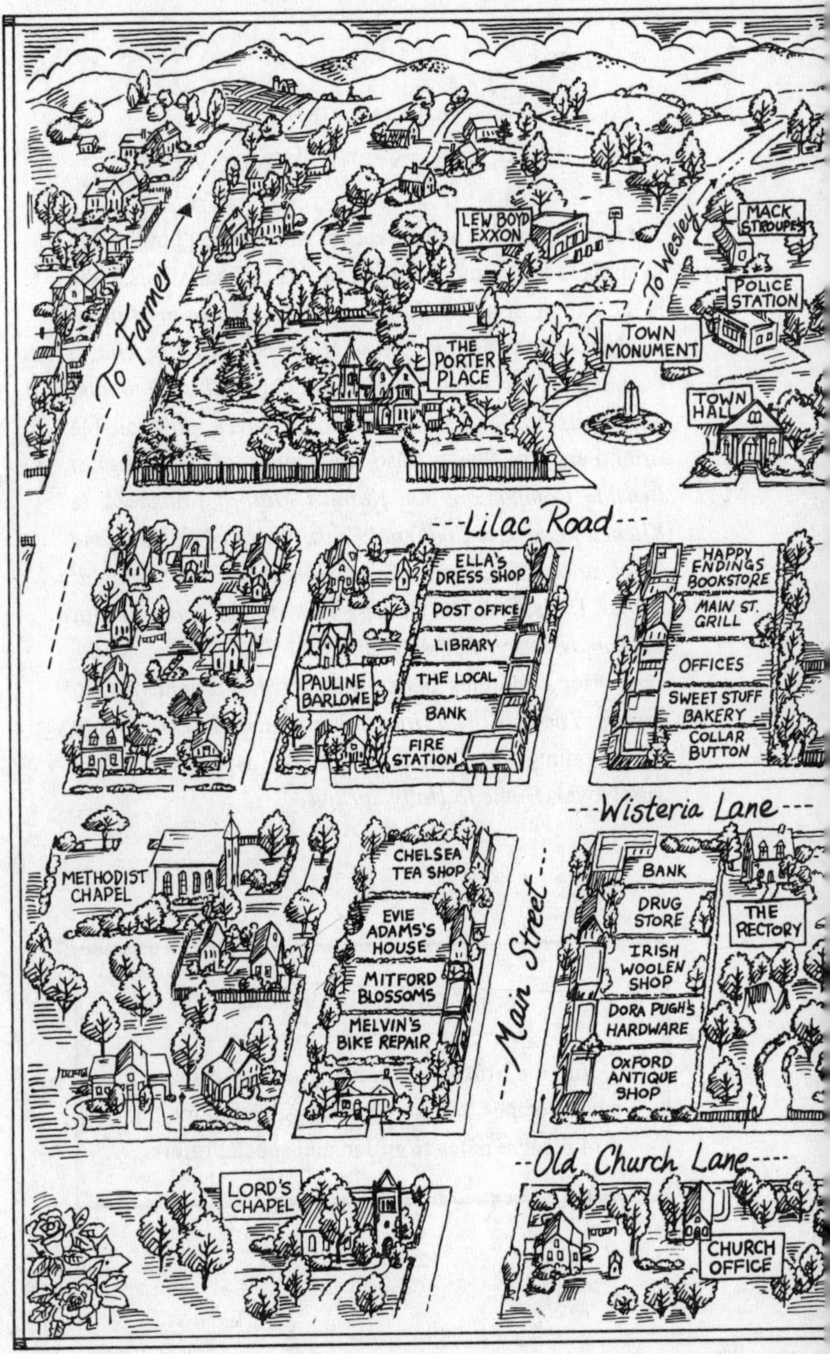
To Farmer
LEW BOYD EXXON
To Wesley
MACK STROUPE'S
POLICE STATION
TOWN MONUMENT
THE PORTER PLACE
TOWN HALL
Lilac Road
ELLA'S DRESS SHOP
POST OFFICE
LIBRARY
THE LOCAL
BANK
FIRE STATION
PAULINE BARLOWE
HAPPY ENDINGS BOOKSTORE
MAIN ST. GRILL
OFFICES
SWEET STUFF BAKERY
COLLAR BUTTON
Wisteria Lane
METHODIST CHAPEL
CHELSEA TEA SHOP
EVIE ADAMS'S HOUSE
MITFORD BLOSSOMS
MELVIN'S BIKE REPAIR
Main Street
BANK
DRUG STORE
IRISH WOOLEN SHOP
DORA PUGH'S HARDWARE
OXFORD ANTIQUE SHOP
THE RECTORY
Old Church Lane
LORD'S CHAPEL
CHURCH OFFICE

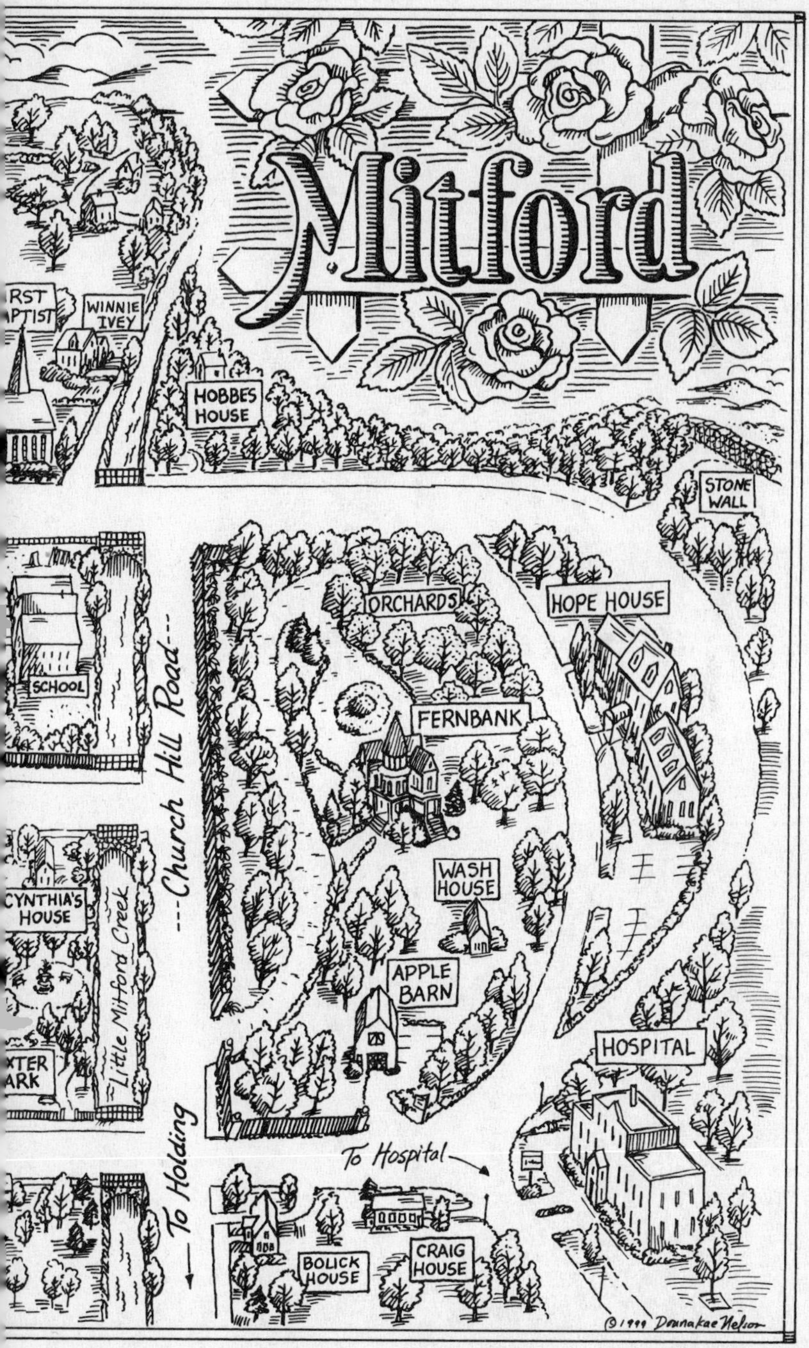
Mitford
RST
PTIST
WINNIE
IVEY
HOBBES
HOUSE
STONE
WALL
ORCHARDS
HOPE HOUSE
SCHOOL
FERNBANK
Church Hill Road
WASH
HOUSE
CYNTHIA'S
HOUSE
Little Mitford Creek
APPLE
BARN
HOSPITAL
XTER
ARK
To Holding
To Hospital
BOLICK
HOUSE
CRAIG
HOUSE
©1999 Donnakae Nelson

Other Mitford Books by Jan Karon

AT HOME IN MITFORD

THESE HIGH, GREEN HILLS

OUT TO CANAAN

A NEW SONG

A COMMON LIFE

Children's Books by Jan Karon

MISS FANNIE'S HAT

JEREMY: THE TALE OF AN HONEST BUNNY

The Mitford Years

A Light in the Window

JAN KARON

PENGUIN BOOKS

PENGUIN BOOKS
Published by the Penguin Group
Penguin Books USA Inc., 375 Hudson Street, New York, New York 10014, U.S.A.
Penguin Books Ltd, 27 Wrights Lane, London W8 5TZ, England
Penguin Books Australia Ltd, Ringwood, Victoria, Australia
Penguin Books Canada Ltd, 10 Alcorn Avenue, Toronto, Ontario, Canada M4V 3B2
Penguin Books (N.Z.) Ltd, 182–190 Wairau Road, Auckland 10, New Zealand

Penguin Books Ltd, Registered Offices: Harmondsworth, Middlesex, England

First published in the United States of America by Lion Publishing, 1995
Published in Penguin Books 1996

39 40 38

PUBLISHER'S NOTE

This is a work of fiction. Names, characters, places, and incidents either are the product of the author's imagination or are used fictitiously, and any resemblance to actual persons, living or dead, events, or locales is entirely coincidental.

LIBRARY OF CONGRESS CATALOGING IN PUBLICATION DATA
Karon, Jan, 1937–
A light in the window/Jan Karon.
p. cm.
Originally published in the series: The Mitford years.
ISBN 0 14 02.5454 4
1. City and town life—United States—Fiction. 2. Christian fiction, American.
3. Domestic fiction, American. I. Title.
II. Series: Karon, Jan, 1937– Mitford years.
PS3561.A678L54 1996
813′.54—dc20 95-35717

Printed in the United States of America
Set in Berkeley Old Style Book
Interior illustrations by George Ulrich
Town map by Donna Kae Nelson

For my mother,
Wanda Setzer,
an encourager

Acknowledgments

My warmest thanks to Buck Waddell; Derald West; Murray Whisnant; Joyce Alexander; Mitford's attending physician, Dr. Bunky Davant; Mitford's attorney, Tony DiSanti; my editor, Dave Toht; my brother and friend, Barry Setzer; my sister and pal, Brenda Furman; my brother, Randy Setzer, who gave me my writing shirt; Father Jack Podsiadlo; Gina and Allan Morehead; Laura Watts; The Singing Boys of Beacon; and all the booksellers whose enthusiasm for Mitford is greatly appreciated. Thanks, also, to my readers, to whom I lovingly give a small town—and a big family—to call your very own.

Contents

A Light in the Window

CHAPTER ONE

Close Encounters

Serious thinking and crossing the street, he once said, shouldn't be attempted simultaneously.

The red pickup truck was nearly upon him when he saw it. The shock of seeing it bear down with such ferocious speed sent him reeling backward to the curb, where he crashed in a sitting position. He caught a fleeting glance of the driver, talking on a telephone, as the truck careened around the corner.

"Father Tim! Are you all right?"

Winnie Ivey's expression was so grieved he felt certain he was badly hurt. He let Winnie help him up, feeling a numb shock where he'd slammed onto the curb.

Winnie's broad face was flushed with anger. "That maniac! Who was that fool, anyway?"

"I don't know. Perhaps I'm the fool for not looking where I was going." He laughed weakly.

"You're no such thing! I saw the light, it was still yellow, you had plenty of time to cross, and here comes this truck roarin' down on you like a freight train, and somebody in it talkin' on a phone."

She turned to the small crowd that had rushed out of the Main Street Grill. "A phone in a truck!" she said with disgust. "Can you believe it? I should have got his license number."

"Thank you, Winnie." He put his arm around the sturdy shoulders of the Sweet Stuff Bakery owner. "You've got a special talent for being in the right place at the right time."

Percy Mosely, who owned the Grill, ran out with his spatula in his hand. "If I was you, I'd ask th' good Lord to kick that feller's butt plumb to Wesley. Them poached eggs you eat are now scrambled."

The rector patted his pockets for the heavy office key and checked his wallet. All there. "No harm done," he assured his friends. The incident had simply been a regrettably dramatic way to begin his first week home from Ireland.

Though he'd spent the summer in Sligo, he found on returning that he hadn't, after all, missed summer in Mitford. His roses bloomed on, the grass lay like velvet under the network of village sprinklers, and parishioners were still leaving baskets of tomatoes on his porch.

As he came up the walk to the rectory, he heard a booming bark from the garage. It was the greeting he had missed every livelong day of his sojourn across the pond.

Since returning home less than a week ago, he had awakened each morning to see Barnabas standing by the bed, staring at him soberly. The inquiry in the eyes of his black Bouvier-cum-sheepdog companion was simple: Are you home to stay, or is this a joke?

He walked through the kitchen and opened the garage door, as Barnabas, who had grown as vast as a bear during his absence, rushed at him with joy. Laying his front paws on the rector's shoulders, he gazed dolefully into the eyes of his master, whose glasses fogged at once.

"Come now, old fellow. Slack off!"

Barnabas leapt backward, danced for a moment on his hind legs, and lunged forward to give the rector a great lick on the face that sent a shower of saliva into his left ear.

The victim dodged toward his parked Buick and crashed onto the hood with his elbow. " 'Sing and make music in your hearts,' " he recited loudly from a psalm, " 'always giving thanks to the Father for everything'!"

Barnabas sat down at once and gazed at him, mopping the garage floor with his tail.

His dog was the only living creature he knew who was unfailingly disciplined by the hearing of the Word. It was a phenomenon that Walter had told over the whole of Ireland's West Country.

"Let's have a treat, pal. And you," he said to Dooley's rabbit, Jack, "will have beet tops." The Flemish giant regarded him with eyes the color of peat.

The house was silent. It wasn't one of Puny's days to work, and Dooley was at football practice. He had missed the boy terribly, reading and rereading the one scrawled message he had received in two long months:

I am fine. Barnabus is fine. Im ridin the hair off that horse.

He had missed the old rectory, too, with its clamor and quiet, its sunshine and shadow. Never before in his life as a rector had he found a home so welcoming or comfortable—a home that seemed, somehow, like a friend.

He spied the thing on his counter at once. It was Edith Mallory's signature blue casserole dish.

He was afraid of that.

Emma had written to Sligo to say that Pat Mallory had died soon after he left for Ireland. Heart attack. No warning. Pat, she said, had felt a wrenching chest pain, had sat down on the top step outside his bedroom, and after dropping dead sitting up, had toppled to the foot of the stairs, where the Mallorys' maid of thirty years had found him just before dinner.

"Oh, Mr. Mallory," she was reported to have said, "you shouldn't have gone and done that. We're havin' lasagna."

Sitting there on the farmhouse window seat, reading Emma's five-page letter, he had known that Edith Mallory would not waste any time when he returned.

Long before Pat's death, he'd been profoundly unsteadied when she had slipped her hand into his or let her fingers run along his arm. At one point, she began winking at him during sermons, which distracted him to such a degree that he resumed his old habit of preaching over the heads of the congregation, literally.

So far, he had escaped her random snares but had once dreamed he was locked with her in the parish-hall coat closet, pounding desperately on the door and pleading with the sexton to let him out.

Now Pat, good soul, was cold in the grave, and Edith's casserole was hot on his counter.

Casseroles! Their seduction had long been used on men of the cloth, often with rewarding results for the cook.

Casseroles, after all, were a gesture that on the surface could not be mistaken for anything other than righteous goodwill. And, once one had consumed and exclaimed over the initial offering, along would come another on its very heels, until the bachelor curate ended up a married curate or the divorced deacon a fellow so skillfully ensnared that he never knew what hit him.

In the language of food, there were casseroles, and there were casseroles. Most were used to comfort the sick or inspire the downhearted. But certain others, in his long experience, were so filled with allure and innuendo that they ceased to be Broccoli Cheese Delight intended for the stomach and became arrows aimed straight for the heart.

In any case, there was always the problem of what to do with the dish. Decent people returned it full of something else. Which meant that the person to whom you returned it would be required, at some point, to give you another food item, all of which produced a cycle that was unimaginably tedious.

Clergy, of course, were never required to fill the dish before returning it, but either way, it had to be returned. And there, clearly, was the rub.

He approached the unwelcome surprise as if a snake might have been coiled inside. His note of thanks, which he would send over tomorrow by Puny, would be short and to the point:

Dear Edith: Suffice it to say that you remain one of the finest cooks in the county. That was no lie; it was undeniably true.

Your way with (blank, blank) is exceeded only by your graciousness. A thousand thanks. In His peace, Fr Tim.

There.

He lifted the lid. Instantly, his mouth began to water, and his heart gave a small leap of joy.

Crab cobbler! One of his favorites. He stared with wonder at the dozen flaky homemade biscuits poised on the bed of fresh crabmeat and fragrant sauce.

Perhaps, he thought with sudden abandon, he should give Edith Mallory a ring this very moment and express his thanks.

As he reached for the phone, he realized what he was doing—he was placing his foot squarely in a bear trap.

He hastily clamped the lid on the steaming dish. "You see?" he muttered darkly. "That's the way it happens."

Where casseroles were concerned, one must constantly be on guard.

"Edith Mallory's lookin' to give you th' big whang-do," said Emma.

Until this inappropriate remark, there had been a resonant peace in the small office. The windows were open to morning air embroidered with birdsong. His sermon notes were going at a pace. And the familiar comfort of his old swivel chair was sheer bliss.

"And what, exactly, is that supposed to mean?

His part-time church secretary glanced up from her ledger. "It means she's going to cook your goose."

He did not like her language. "I am sixty-one years old and a lifelong bachelor. Why anyone would want to give me a whang . . . why anyone would . . . it's unthinkable," he said flatly.

"I can tell she thinks about it all th' time. Besides, remember Father Appel who got married when he was sixty-five, right after his social security kicked in? And that deacon who was fifty-nine, who married th' redheaded woman who owned the taxi company in Wesley? Then, there was that salesman who worked at the Collar Button . . ."

"Spare me the details," he said curtly, opening his drawer and looking for the Wite-Out.

Emma peered at him over her glasses. "Just remember," she muttered.

"Remember what?"

"Forearmed is forewarned."

"No, Emma. Forewarned is forearmed."

"Peedaddle. I never do get that right. But if I were you, I'd duck when I see her comin'."

I've been ducking when I see her coming for twelve years, he thought.

"One thing in her favor," said Emma, recording another check, "is she's a great hostess. As you have surely learned from doin' your parties, a rector needs that. Some preachers' wives don't do pea-turkey, if you ask me. Of course, if anything's goin' to happen with your neighbor, and Lord knows, I hope it will—you ought to just go on and give 'er a nice engagement ring—then Edith would have to jump on somebody else."

"Emma," he said, ripping the cover off the typewriter, "I have finally got a handle on the most important sermon I've written in a year . . ."

"Don't say I didn't warn you," she replied, pressing her lips together in that way he loathed.

At noon, Ron Malcolm appeared at the door, wearing boots caked with dried mud and a red baseball cap.

Being away for two months had given everyone the rector knew, and Mitford as well, a fresh, almost poignant, reality. He had scarcely ever noticed that Ron Malcolm was a man of such cheering vigor. Then again, perhaps it was the retired contractor's involvement in the nursing-home project that had done something for the color in his face and put a gleam in his eyes.

"Well, Father, we're off and running. Jacobs has sent their job superintendent over. He's having a trailer installed on the site today." He shook the rector's hand with great feeling.

"I can hardly believe it's finally happening."

"Five million bucks!" Ron said. "This nursing home is the biggest thing to happen around here since the Wesley furniture factory. Have you met Leeper?"

"Leeper?"

"Buck Leeper. The job superintendent. We talked about him before you left for Ireland. He said he'd try to get by your office."

"I haven't met him. I'll have to walk up—maybe Wednesday afternoon."

Ron sat down on the visitors' bench and removed his cap. "Emma around?"

"Gone to the post office."

"I think it's only fair that I talk to you straight about Buck Leeper. A few months ago, I told you he's hardheaded, rough. I know I don't have to worry about you, but he's the kind who can make you lose your religion."

"Aha."

"His daddy was Fane Leeper, so called because a preacher once said he was the most profane man he'd ever met. Fane Leeper was also the best job superintendent on the East Coast. He made three contractors rich men, and then alcohol got 'im, as they say.

"You need to know that Buck is just like his daddy. He learned contractin', cussin', and drinkin' from Fane, and the only way he could get out from under the shadow of his father was to outdo him in all three categories."

Ron paused, as if to let that information sink in.

"Buck's on this job because he'll save us money—and a lot of grief. He'll bring it in on time and on budget, and you can count on it. Out of respect to you, Father, I talked to Jacobs about sending us another man, but they won't send anybody but Buck on a job this size." He stood up and zipped his jacket. "We'll probably hate Jacobs for this, but before it's over, we'll thank him."

"I trust your judgment."

Ron opened the door and was backing out with his hat in his hand.

"You might look softhearted, Father, but I've seen you operate a time or two, and I know you can handle Buck. Just give 'im his rein."

The rector looked out at the maple across the street, which had taken on a tinge of russet since yesterday. "I can't imagine that Mr. Leeper will be any problem at all," he said.

"Timothy?"

It was Cynthia, his neighbor, peering through the screened door of the kitchen, her hands cupped on either side of her eyes. She was wearing a white blouse and blue denim skirt and a bandanna around her blond hair.

"You look like Heidi!" he said to his neighbor. Though she admitted to being fiftysomething, there were times when she looked like a girl. Again he was struck by the fresh, living way in which he saw people, as if he had lately risen from the dead.

She walked past him, unfurling the faintest scent of wisteria on the air. "You said to think of something we could do to celebrate your return."

She went to the stove and lifted the lid on the pot of soup he was making. "Yum," she said, inhaling. Then, she turned to him and smiled. Her eyes were like sapphires, smoky and deep with that nearly violet hue that always caught him off-guard.

"And have you thought about it?" he asked, afraid he might croak like a frog when he spoke.

"They say walls have ears. I'd better whisper it."

He had completely forgotten how easily she fit into his arms.

Going to a town council meeting was decidedly not what he wanted to do with his evening. After two months away, he hardly knew what was going on. And he was still feeling oddly jet-lagged, shaking his head vigorously on occasion with some hope of clearing it. But he would go; it might put him back in the swing of things, and frankly, he was curious why the mayor, Esther Cunningham, had called an unofficial meeting and why it might concern him.

"Don't eat," Esther told him on the phone. "Ray's bringin' baked beans, cole slaw, and ribs from home. Been cookin' all day."

"Hallelujah," he said with feeling.

There was a quickening in the air of the mayor's office. Ray was setting out his home-cooked supper on the vast desktop, overlooked by pictures of their twenty-three grandchildren at the far end.

"Mayor," said Leonard Bostick, "it's a cryin' shame you cain't cook as good as Ray."

"I've got better things to do," she snapped. "I did the cookin' for forty years. Now it's his turn."

Ray grinned. "You tell 'em, honey."

"Whooee!" said Paul Hartley. "Baby backs! Get over here, Father, and give us a blessin'."

"Come on!" shouted the mayor to the group lingering in the hall. "It's blessin' time!"

Esther Cunningham held out her hands, and the group eagerly formed a circle.

"Our Lord," said the rector, "we're grateful for the gift of friends and neighbors and those willing to lend their hand to the welfare of this place. We thank you for the peace of this village and for your grace to do the work that lies ahead. We thank you, too, for this food and ask a special blessing on the one who prepared it. In Jesus' name."

"Amen!" said the assembly.

The mayor was the first in line. "You're goin' t' get a blessing, all right," she told her husband. "Just look at this sauce! You've done it again, sweet face."

Ray winked at the rector. There, thought the rector, is a happy man if I ever saw one.

"How's your diabetes, Father?"

"It won't tolerate the torque you've put under the hood of that pot, I regret to say."

"Take doubles on m' slaw, then," said Ray, heaping the rector's plate.

"You know what we're here to talk about," said the mayor.

Everybody nodded, except the rector.

"I don't want it to come up in a town meetin', and I don't want it officially voted on, vetoed, or otherwise messed with. We're just goin' to seek agreement here tonight like a family and let it go at that."

She looked at their faces and leaned forward. "Got it?"

Linder Hayes stood up slowly, thin as a strip of baling wire. He placed his hands carefully behind his back, peered at his shoes, and cleared his throat.

"Here goes," said Joe Ivey, nudging the rector.

"Your honor," said Linder.

"You don't have t' 'your honor' me. This is an unofficial meetin'."

"Your honor," said Linder, who was a lawyer and preferred the formalities, "I'd like to speak for the merchants of this town who have to make a livin' out of the day-to-day run of things.

"Now, we know that an old woman dressed up in party hats and gumboots, directin' traffic around the monument, is not a fit sight for tourists, especially with leaf season comin' on.

"You say she's harmless, but that, in fact, is not the point. With her infamous snaggle tooth and those old army decorations, think what she'd look like if she came flyin' out of th' fog wavin' at cars. She'd clean th' tourists out of here so fast it'd make your head swim."

"And good riddance," said the mayor testily.

"Madam Mayor, we've fought this tourist battle for years. We've all moved over to give you plenty of room to do your job, and you've done it. Your faithful defense of what is good and right and true to the character of this town has been a strong deterrent to the rape and plunder of senseless development and reckless growth.

"But . . ." Linder gave a long pause and looked around the room. "Two Model Village awards will not suffice our merchants for cold, hard cash. That ol' woman is enough to make babies squall and grown men tuck tail and run. Clearly, I don't have to make a livin' off tourists, but my wife does—and so, incidentally, do half your grandchildren."

"We're in for it," muttered Joe Ivey. "I should've carried a bed roll and a blanket."

"Linder," said Esther Cunningham, "sit down and take a load off your feet."

"Your honor . . ."

"Thank you, Linder," the mayor said, measuring each word.

Linder appeared to waver for a moment, like a leaf caught in a breeze. Then, he sat down.

"I'd like us to look at a couple of things before we open for a brief discussion," said the mayor. "First, let's look at my platform. There is no such thing in it as a middle plank, a left plank, or a right plank. It's just one straight platform. Period. Joe, why don't you remind us what it is?"

Joe stood up. "Mitford takes care of its own!" He sat down again, flushed with pride.

"Mitford . . . takes . . . care . . . of . . . its . . . own. That's been my platform for fourteen years, and as long as I'm mayor, it will continue to be th' platform. Number one. Miss Rose Watson may be snaggle-toothed and she may be crazy, but she's our own. Number two. Based on that, we're goin' to take care of 'er.

"Number three. Directin' traffic around the monument is the best thing that's happened to her since she was a little girl, as normal as you and me. Uncle Billy says she sleeps like a baby now, instead of ramblin' through that old house all night, and she's turned nice as you please to him. Directin' traffic is a genuine responsibility to her. She takes pride in it."

"She does a real good job," said Ernestine Ivory, who colored beet red at the sound of her own voice.

"What's that, Ernestine?" asked the mayor.

"Miss Rose does a real good job of directing traffic. 'Course that's just me . . ."

"That's just you and a lot of other people who think the same thing. She's very professional. I don't know where in th' world she learned it.

"Now, here's what I propose, and I ask you to consider it in your hearts. Every day from noon to one o'clock, traffic drops off and Mitford eats lunch. My stomach starts growlin' right on th' button, like th' rest of this crowd.

"I propose we let Miss Rose direct traffic five days a week, from noon 'til one, which'll give her just enough cars to keep her happy.

"Now, Linder, I have to hand it to you about those cocktail hats and funny clothes, so I propose we give 'er a uniform. Navy hat, skirt, and jacket from my old days in th' Waves. Be a perfect fit. I was skinny as a rail, wasn't I, doll?"

Ray gave the mayor a thumbs-up.

"Ernestine, I want you to go with me to dress her in th' mornin' at ten o'clock, and Joe, how about you givin' her a nice haircut. We'll bring 'er up to your shop about eleven."

"Be glad to."

"Father, I wish you'd make it your business to pray about this."

"You have my word," he said.

"And Linder, honey, I really appreciate the way you're lookin' after the merchants. God knows, somebody needs to. Any questions?"

Before anyone could respond, the mayor pounded her desk with a gavel. "Meeting adjourned. All in favor say aye."

"I declare," said the rector, walking home with Joe Ivey, "every time I go to a meeting with Esther Cunningham, I feel like somebody's screwed my head around backwards."

You'll be coming home to a new Dooley, Marge had written just before he left Ireland. When he read that, his heart sank. He had managed to grow fond of the old Dooley.

He's actually learning to speak English, his friend wrote from Meadowgate Farm. *Just wait; you'll be thrilled.*

He couldn't say he had been thrilled, exactly, on seeing his twelve-year-old charge again. First, the cowlick had miraculously disappeared. When he left for Sligo in July, it had been shooting up like a geyser; now, it simply wasn't there, and frankly, he missed it. Then, he noticed that Dooley's freckles appeared to be fading, an upshot that he especially regretted.

He also found a new resoluteness in the boy that he'd only fleetingly glimpsed before, not to mention the fact that he was putting the top back on the catsup and the mayonnaise. How could so much change have taken place in two short months?

"I refuse to take credit," Marge told him on the phone from Meadowgate the morning after his return. "It's all that wonderful spade work you'd already done, laced with a strong dose of cow manure and fresh air. Last weekend, he helped Hal deliver a colt, which was like a shot of Miracle-Gro to his self-confidence. Furthermore, I'm crushed to tell you that Rebecca Jane took her first step to . . . guess who? Uncle Dools!"

I have planted, Apollos watered, but God gave the increase, the rector mused as he approached the rectory from the council meeting. Joe Ivey had offered him "a taste of brandy" if he cared to walk up the stairs to the barber shop, but he declined. He could hardly wait to get home and into the old burgundy bathrobe he'd sorely missed in Ireland.

After a quick trip with Barnabas to the Baxter Park hedge, he took a bottle of mineral water from the cabinet, and the two of them climbed the stairs.

"Dooley!"

"Yessir?"

Yessir? He walked down the hall to the boy's room and found him sitting against the head of his bed, reading and absently scratching his big toe. The room seemed remarkably well-ordered.

"How's it going?"

Dooley looked up. "Great."

"Terrific." He stood in the doorway, feeling an awkward joy. "What's the book?"

"Dynamics of Veterinary Medicine."

"Aha."

"See this?" Dooley held the book toward him. "It's a picture of a colt being born. That's jis' the way it happened last weekend. It's the neatest thing I ever done . . . did. I want t' be a vet. Doc Owen said I could be one."

"Of course you can. You can be whatever you want to be." He stepped into the room.

"I never wanted to be anything before."

"Maybe you never saw any choices before."

"I never wanted to be an astronaut or a rock star or anything, like Buster Austin wants t' be."

"That's OK. Why rush into wanting to be something?" He sat down on the bed.

"That's what I thought." Dooley went back to his book, ignoring him but somehow comfortable with the fact that he was there.

"So, how's Buster?" Only months ago, he and Buster Austin had been the darkest adversaries, with Dooley whipping the tar out of him twice.

"Cool. We swapped lunches today. He likes 'at old meatloaf you make. I got 'is baloney."

"Done your homework?"

"Yessir."

Yessir. It rang in his ears like some foreign language. "How's the science project coming? Are we finishing it up Sunday evening?"

"Yep. You'll like it. It's neat."

Since he came home from Ireland, he'd been peering into Dooley's face, searching it out. Something was different. A wound had healed, perhaps; he was looking more like a boy instead of someone who'd grown old before his time.

It had been nearly a year since Russell Jacks, the church sexton and Dooley's grandfather, had come down with pneumonia and was rushed into emergency treatment. The boy had come home with him from the hospital, and he'd been here ever since.

One of the best things he had ever done was bring Dooley Barlowe home. Yes, he'd been trouble and calamity and plenty of it—but worth it and then some.

"I hear you went to see your grandpa every week. Good medicine."

"Yep."

"How is he?"

"That woman that's lookin' after 'im, she says he's doing good, but he ain't had any livermush since you left . . ."

"Uh-oh."

"And he was riled about it."

"We'll take him some. And I'll see you at breakfast. Has Jenny been around?"

"I ain't into 'at ol' poop, n' more."

The rector grinned. There! he thought. There's my old Dooley.

In his room, Barnabas leapt onto the blanket at the foot of the bed, then lay down with a yawn as the rector stepped into the shower. While the raftered room in the Sligo farmhouse had been perfectly comfortable, the long passage down the hall to the finicky shower was another story entirely. As far as he could see, it might be months before the thrill of his own bathroom, *en suite,* began to wane.

He felt as mindless and contented as a steamed clam as he sat on the bed and dialed his neighbor.

"Hello?"

"Hello, yourself."

"Timothy!" said Cynthia. "I was just thinking of you."

"Surely you have something better to do."

"I was thinking that my idea of how to celebrate was too silly."

"Silly, yes, but not too silly," he said. "In fact, I was wondering—when are we going to do it?"

"Ummmm . . ."

"Saturday night?" he asked, hoping.

"Oh, rats. My nephew's coming. I mean, I'm delighted he's coming. You must meet him. He's very dear. Saturday would have been so perfect. Could we do it Monday evening?

"Vestry meeting," he said.

"Tuesday I have to finish an illustration and FedEx it first thing Wednesday morning. Could you do it Wednesday around six-thirty?"

"Building committee at seven."

"Darn."

"I could do it Friday," he said.

"Great!"

"No. No, wait, there's something on Friday," he said, extending the phone cord to the dresser where he opened his black engagement book. "Yes, that's it. The hospital is having a staff dinner for Hoppy, and I'm giving the invocation. Would you come?"

"Dinner in a hospital? That's suicide! Besides, I can't stand hospitals. I nearly died in one, you know."

"No, I didn't know."

"And I don't know how you ever will know these things unless we can figure out a way to see each other. What about Sunday evening? That's usually a relaxing time for you. Sunday might be lovely."

"I'm helping Dooley finish his science project. He has to hand it in Monday morning." A nameless despair was robbing him of any contentment he had just felt.

"I could meet you on the bench by your German roses at six o'clock tomorrow. We could do it there and get it over with."

But he didn't want to do it and get it over with. He wanted to linger over it, to savor it.

"You're sighing," she said.

"It's just that there's so much going on after being away for two months."

"I understand," she said simply.

"You do? Do you really?"

"Of course I do."

"I'll call you tomorrow. Let's not waste it on the garden bench."

"All that lumpy, wet moss," she said, laughing.

"All that cold, damp concrete," he said forlornly.

"I hope you sleep well." He could hear a tenderness in her voice. "Jet lag really does persist for days."

"Yes. Well. So," he said, feeling immeasurably foolish, "blink your bedroom lights good night."

"I will if you will."

"Cynthia?"

"Yes?"

"I . . ." He cleared his throat. "You . . ."

"Spit it out," she said.

He had started to croak; he couldn't have uttered another word if his life depended on it.

"I'm not going to worry anymore about being too silly. It's you, Timothy, who are far too silly!"

His heart pounded as he hung up the phone. He had nearly told her he loved her, that she was wonderful; he had nearly gone over the edge of the cliff, with no ledges to break his fall.

He went to the window and looked down upon her tiny house. He saw the lights blink twice through the windows of her bedroom under the eaves. He raced around the bed and flipped his own light switch off, then on again, and off.

"Good Lord," he said, breathlessly, standing there in the dark. "Who is the twelve-year-old in this house, anyway?"

When he called at noon, her answering machine emitted a long series of beeps followed by a dial tone.

He had just hung up when the phone rang.

"Father!" It was Absalom Greer, the country preacher.

"Brother Greer! I was going to call you this very afternoon."

"Well, sir, how bad a mess did I leave for you to clean up?"

"People are still telling me how much they enjoyed your supply preaching at Lord's Chapel. We caught them off-guard, you know. I hope it didn't go too hard for you in the beginning."

"The first Sunday was mighty lean. Your flock didn't mind you too good about throwin' their support to an old revival preacher. Then the next Sunday, about half-full, I'd say. Third Sunday, full up. On and on like that 'til they were standin' on the steps.

"If you hadn't come home s' soon, we'd have had an altar call. It was all I could do t' hold it back toward the end."

Father Tim laughed. "You're going to be a tough act to follow, my friend."

"I tried to hold back on the brimstone, too, but I didn't always succeed. 'Repent and be saved!' said John. 'Repent and be saved!' said Jesus. There's the gist of it. If you don't repent, you don't get saved. So, you're lookin' at the alternative, and people don't want to hear that nowadays."

"You'd better prepare your crowd for me when I come out to the country."

Absalom laughed heartily. "That might be askin' the impossible!" He could see the faces of his rural Baptist congregation when they got a load of a preacher in a long dress.

"I've got something for you," said the rector. "I'd like to bring it out one day and hear what another man saw from the backside of my pulpit."

"Just let us know when you're comin'. We'll lay on a big feed."

"I'll do it! And God bless you for all the effort you gave us here. It counted for something. Ron Malcolm said you were as plain as the bark on a tree in delivering the Gospel."

"A man has to stand out of the way of the Gospel, and that keeps us plain if we let it."

The rector sat smiling after he hung up. There was nothing, in fact, plain about the old man with the craggy brows and mane of silver hair. His tall, lean frame made a stunning sight in the pulpit, Cynthia said, with his blue eyes blazing like flint striking rock and a sprig of laurel in his buttonhole.

Greer, he wrote on the calendar for the third week of October.

He was walking home from the office in a misting rain when the heavens erupted in a downpour.

Drenched at once, he raced to the wool shop and stood under the awning that was drumming with rain, pondering what to do. Hazel Bailey waved to him from the back of the shop, signaling that he should come in and take refuge. Already soaked, he decided he would make a run for it.

He lifted his newspaper over his head and was ready to dash toward the next awning when he heard a car horn. It was Edith Mallory's black Lincoln, which was approximately the size of a condominium.

The window slipped down as if oiled, and her driver leaned across the seat. "Father Tim," Ed Coffey yelled, "Miz Mallory says get in. We'll carry you home."

The water was already running along the curb in a torrent.

He got in.

Edith Mallory might have been Cleopatra on her barge, for all the swath of silk raincoat that flowed against the cushiony leather and the mahogany bar that appeared from the arm rest.

"Sherry?" she said, smiling in that enigmatic way that made his adrenalin pump. It was, however, his flight adrenalin.

"No, thanks!" he exclaimed, trying to do something with the sodden newspaper. A veritable cloud of perfume hung in the air of the warm interior; he felt instantly woozy, drugged, like a child of four going down for a nap.

That's the way it was with Edith; one's guard weakened when needed most.

"Dreadful weather, and you above all must mind your health . . ."

Why above all, he wondered, irritated.

". . . Because you're our shepherd, of course, and your little flock needs you to take care of us." Edith looked at him with the large brown eyes that overpowered her sharp features, rather like, he thought, one of those urchin children in paintings done on velvet.

"Well, yes, you have a point," he said stiffly. He saw Ed Coffey's eyes in the rearview mirror; the corners appeared to be crinkling, as if he were grinning hugely.

"We want you to stay strong," she crooned, "for all your widows and orphans."

He looked out the window mindlessly, not noticing that they had passed his street. The awning over the Grill had come loose on one corner, and the rain was gushing onto the sidewalk like a waterfall.

"You might have just the weensiest sherry," she said, filling a small glass from a decanter that sat in the mahogany bar like an egg in a nest.

"I really don't think . . . ," he said, feeling the glass already in his hand.

"There, now!" she said. "That will hit the nail on the jackpot!" When she smiled, her wide mouth pushed her cheeks into a series of tiny wrinkles like those in crepe paper. Some people actually found her attractive, he reminded himself—why couldn't he?

He gulped the sherry and returned the glass to her, feeling like a child who had taken his croup medicine.

"Good boy," she said.

Where were they, anyway? The windows were streaming with rain, and the lights of the car didn't penetrate far enough to give him any idea of their whereabouts. They had just passed the Grill, but he couldn't remember turning at the corner. Perhaps they had driven by the monument and were on their way to Wesley.

"Why ah, haven't we gone to the rectory?" He felt a mild panic.

"We're going in just the weensiest minute," she said, blinking at him. He could not believe that her hand snaked across the seat toward his. He remembered the dream about the coat closet, and how he had pounded on the door and shouted for Russell Jacks.

He drew his hand away, quite unobtrusively, he thought, and scratched his nose. The sherry had turned on a small light in a far corner of his mind. Perhaps she imagined he'd be after her money for the Sunday school rooms and willing to do a little hand-holding to get it. It was going to take a cool two hundred thousand to turn that sprawling airstrip of an attic into the Sunday school Josiah Baxter had envisioned. But his own hand would most certainly not milk it forth. On his visitation meeting with the vestry, he had gone over a list of wouldn'ts, so no one would be aggrieved down the road.

He wouldn't, for example, participate in fund-raising efforts outside the pulpit. Period. He would not personally court, cajole, preach to, sweet-talk, or exhort anyone for money to build anything.

"Ah, Timothy," sighed Edith Mallory, rubbing the tweed of his sleeve as if it were a cat, "Ireland has done wonders for you, I can tell." She moved closer. "It's so lonely being a widow," she said, sniffing. "I sometimes just . . . ache all over."

When he was finally delivered to the rectory, nearly soaked to the skin, Puny was getting ready to leave. She stared at him with alarm as she put on her coat.

"You look like you been through somethin' awful!"

"Hell!" he exclaimed.

She was shocked to hear him use such language.

There was a red pickup truck parked in front of the office when he arrived on Monday. Someone inside appeared to be talking on a car phone.

The rector fished the key from his pocket as the man got out of the truck and slammed the door. He flipped a cigarette to the sidewalk and ground it out with a quick turn of his heel.

He was big, beefy, and heavy, wearing chinos stuffed into high boots, a flannel shirt under a quilted vest, and a hard hat.

"You the father?"

"Yes. What can I do for you?"

The man took a package of Lucky Strikes from his shirt pocket, shook a cigarette out, lit it, and inhaled deeply.

"Buck Leeper," he said, walking to the rector and extending his hand. The handshake lasted only an instant, but in that instant, the rector felt an odd shock. The hand seemed hugely swollen and red, as if the flesh might burst suddenly from the skin.

"I'm glad to meet you," he lied, hearing the words automatically form and speak themselves. Yet, in a way, he was glad to meet him; the deed was done. "Come in, Mr. Leeper, and have a cup of coffee."

"No coffee," he said, wedging through the door ahead of the rector. The rector hung his jacket on the peg, noticing how the man's presence had made the room suddenly smaller.

"Malcolm said to ask you about the garden statues."

"Garden statues?"

"Lyin' up there on the site. We dozed 'em up. Maybe a dozen pieces, some broke, some not. I don't have time to mess with it." He exhaled a fume of smoke.

"How extraordinary. Of course. I'll be right up. Give me an hour."

The superintendent took a quick, deep drag off his cigarette. "At fifty smackers an hour for dozers, I don't have an hour."

"Well, then. What would you suggest I do?"

Leeper's tone was insolent and hard. "Tell me I can doze that crap off the side of the mountain."

The rector felt ice water in his veins. "I'd appreciate it," he said evenly, "if you'd put your cigarette out. This small room doesn't tolerate smoke."

The superintendent looked at him for a long moment, dropped his cigarette on the floor, and ground it out with a turn of his heel.

He opened the door. "I don't have time to run errands for your building committee. If you want th' statues, come and get 'em," he said and was gone.

"Good grief," moaned Ron Malcolm, hanging his head.

"Well, I can't say you didn't warn me."

"Yes, but I guess there's no warning that really prepares you for Buck Leeper. I insisted he come down here, say hello, introduce himself, ask you about the statues. I thought you'd want to keep them, but I didn't know. I guess I'm to blame. I should have handled it."

"No. Stop right there. There's no blame now and there's not going to be. If this morning was any indication, we're in for a rough ride. The man is clearly a walking time bomb. All I want to do is stay out of the way and let him get his job done."

"Fine," said Ron.

His building-committee chairman looked so despondent the rector put an arm around his shoulders. "Buck up," he said, without thinking.

They were still laughing when Ron pulled away from the curb in his blue pickup, headed for Lord's Chapel with the load of statuary.

"Whang-do," said Emma sourly, handing him the phone.

"I've invited the building committee to meet here on Wednesday evening." Edith Mallory sounded pleased with herself. "Of course, they loved the idea. Magdolen will do her famous spoonbread, but I'll do the tenderloin."

Tenderloin!

"I know how you enjoy a tenderloin. I've had it sent from New York."

"That's very generous of you. Of course, there's really no need to impose for a dinner meeting . . ."

"But life is so short," she said, sniffing. "Why have a dull meeting when you can have a dinner party?"

He didn't know why. Why, indeed?

"You can see the trump lloyd I had painted in the study. It looks just like old books on a shelf."

"Aha."

"I'll have Ed pick you up at a quarter 'til," she said. He could hear the little sucking noise that came from dragging on that blasted cigarette.

"No!" he nearly shouted. His car was still sitting in the garage with a dead battery. "Ah, no thanks. I'll come with Ron. We have a lot to discuss . . ."

"Of course, but Ron is coming with Tad Sherrill, he said, because his pickup . . . what did he say . . . blew a gasket, I think."

"Well, then, I'll just squeeze in with them. And thank you, Edith. It's more than good of you." He hung up at once, not surprised to find his forehead slightly damp.

"June," said Puny.

"No," sighed the rector.

"The fourteenth."

"But how will I get along without you? I've been dreading this."

"You don't have t' git along without me," she said. "After our honeymoon, I'm comin' back. I told you I would."

"Yes, but shouldn't you and Joe Joe move ahead with having children or . . . something?"

"Not right this minute, if you don't mind," she said archly, setting the mop bucket in the middle of the floor. He thought he had never seen his house help look more enchanting. Her red hair appeared suffused with a kind of glow; her very being radiated happiness. It was like having a wonderful lamp turned on around the place, and he certainly did not want the light to go out.

"Of course," she said, dipping the scrub brush in the soapy water, "we won't leave you hangin'. They'll git somebody else to look after things while I'm gone."

"I don't want anybody else," he said, feeling petulant.

"Oh, poop, eat your carrots. I made 'em th' way my grandpa liked 'em, with butter and a little brown sugar. And that's all the sweets you can have today."

"Thank you, Puny," he said. He couldn't help but notice that when she sassed him these days, she smiled. Looking at her on her hands and knees on the kitchen floor, in that earnest subjection he could hardly bear to see, he thought how he'd learned to love Puny Bradshaw like his own blood.

He wondered if she'd gotten the illustration finished, the one that had to be rushed to her publisher. When he called, he got only the last of her voice recording, ". . . the beep, thanks," and a sort of static that sounded like a transfer truck rolling along the highway.

When he hung up, he sat for a moment, looking at the rain lashing the office windows. He realized he hadn't wanted to talk with her, exactly. It was more like he had a longing to see her.

He skulked toward the rectory in a raincoat and rain hat, vowing to have Lew Boyd come and jump his battery tomorrow morning, first thing. Before going to his own door, he knocked on Cynthia's.

The roof over the shallow back stoop was hardly any protection. The wind and rain gusted around him violently.

"Cynthia!" he called through the roar. She had locked the screen, he knew, to keep the wind from catching it and tearing it off its hinges.

He shouted her name again. Only a dim light glowed in the direction of the stairs.

He rattled the screen door and pounded as hard as he could. He saw Violet leap onto the kitchen counter and peer at him as if he were the garbage collector.

"Madness!" he muttered at last, fleeing through the drenched hedge to the warm kitchen next door.

Magdolen greeted them at Clear Day, the Mallorys' vast contemporary house astride a ridge overlooking the valley. "Oh, good! Here's the father!" she said happily, helping him out of his raincoat. "We're so glad you're back from Ireland. You can never be too sure of your life over there. It's just tragic."

Tad and Ron left their dripping slickers in the foyer and went toward the library, where their hostess was serving canapés.

"We sure missed you during all the . . . well, you know," Magdolen sighed. "Miss Edith took it so hard and no children to comfort her. I thought you might like to see where I found Mr. Pat." She led him to the staircase.

"Right there," she said, pointing to the third step from the bottom. "He had landed there, half sitting up with his back against the banister. When I came into the hall, his eyes were wide open, staring straight at me. I thought he looked kind of off-color. So I said, 'Mr. Pat, I made you a nice, big dish of lasagna, so come and sit down before it gets cold.' "

She shuddered and held tight to his arm. "That's when he . . . rolled down the rest of the way."

"Magdolen!" Edith Mallory said sharply, taking the rector by the other arm and drawing him toward the library. Five damp committee members huddled around a fire that snapped and crackled on the grate.

"Mud and more mud," Ron Malcolm was saying. "Rivers of mud."

Tad Sherrill grunted. "Oceans of mud."

"And more mud coming, if the forecast holds," announced Winona Presley, thumping her secretarial pad with her ballpoint pen.

Warmed by a cabernet from the Mallory cellar, the diners avidly discussed weather disasters they had known.

"I worked on a job in Kentucky one time," said Ron, "where the rain didn't stop for twenty-one days." He was pleased to see he could cut the tenderloin with a fork. "Had four big Cats sittin' in mud up to the cab doors when it was over."

"What I hope I never see again," said Tad, "is a mud slide. Have you ever seen mud slide? It's as bad as lava out of a volcano. I've seen it cover houses above the roof line . . ."

"You know what I like about the French?" asked their hostess.

All eyes turned toward her in the great pause she designed to follow this question.

"When they dine, they talk only of food. The meal in front of them is the topic of their most earnest conversation. They would never think of ruining their digestion by talking of politics, and certainly not . . . mud," she said icily.

"But Edith, honey," said Tad, "mud is one of the things this meetin' is about."

Father Tim thought the look she gave her affable guest was needlessly patronizing. "This," their hostess informed them, "is dinner. The meeting about mud will be held in the library by the fire, with a glass of brandy." She drummed her fingers lightly on the table and smiled.

The rector could not avoid the thought that presented itself for consideration. It was that Pat Mallory probably threw himself down the stairs.

After the dessert of orange mocha cake with fresh cream, which, to the disappointment of their hostess, he feasted on with his eyes only, he excused himself to check his sugar. Diabetes was the sorriest of infirmities to drag to a dinner party.

In the guest powder room, awash with berry-colored chintz and black marble, he did what he had to do, then lowered the commode seat and sat there, wearily. To tell the truth, he would have preferred a meeting in the parish hall, with everyone drinking coffee out of Styrofoam cups.

What if the rain drew on for another week? Worse yet, for another two or three weeks? It had been known to happen in Mitford, which had its own exclusive weather system. Since nothing could go forward on the nursing-home site, did they want to put Buck Leeper's crew to work in the attic?

This would mean a good deal of money up front, entirely separate from the construction budget for Hope House, and so far, not one cent had been raised for that effort. Also, the rain could stop, the crew would go back up the hill, and there the attic job would sit, leaving the sanctuary covered with a fine film of dust.

Beginning on the Sunday school now was untimely, he thought. Yes, his mind was definitely clearing on the issue. Mud was not a sound reason to initiate the attic project.

He got up and went into the hall and headed toward the library. Under the pounding of the rain on the skylights, there was an odd silence in the house.

"Where is everybody?" he asked Edith, who came to meet him.

"They thought they should go before it started pouring again, which of course it did. I told them to go ahead—Ed would take you home."

"I thought we were all going to see your trompe l'oeil in the study."

He felt as if a noose had slipped around his neck. Desperate, he looked for Magdolen. Hadn't she been standing near the dining room door when he came down the hall? If so, she had vanished.

Edith drew him along by the arm. "We'll see it later, just the two of us."

The fire gleamed brightly on the hearth. He saw that someone had pulled the sofa closer to the fire and that the little table where he'd left his notebook now held a silver tray, two glasses, and a crystal decanter.

Dead meat. That's what Dooley would call him.

That she asked for counseling because it was his job was one thing. That she was holding him against his will was another.

As she moved closer to him on the sofa, he leapt to his feet and began pacing the floor. He couldn't emphasize enough, he told her, how some involvement with others would help her regain balance. The Children's Hospital in Wesley might be the best of outlets for her time and energy; he had supported it for years. They were currently anxious for funds to build a cancer unit, and he knew for a fact it was a responsible organization, capable of giving back the truest satisfaction.

But why should she get involved with sick children, she sniffed, which would only make her feel depressed? Besides, where would she find the time? She recited a stunning list of real estate that Pat Mallory had left in her care, including the Shoe Barn and the surrounding property on the highway, not to mention the building that housed the Main Street Grill.

He stood at last in front of the fire, so drowsy and exhausted from the long day, the heavy dinner, Edith's tearful monologue, and the warmth of the room, that he had to steel himself against dropping down prostrate.

At eleven o'clock, Ed Coffey appeared, hat in hand, reporting the car was stalled and it would be awhile before he could get it going. It seemed rain had got under the hood, somehow.

A likely story, he thought miserably. Now it was too late to call Dooley and say he'd been detained. Of course, the boy had the Mallorys' number in case he was worried. But chances were, Dooley was sleeping soundly, emitting that light, whiffling snore that he hoped was not a case of adenoids gone haywire.

The rain was still rattling the skylights as if a full batallion were marching over them. He would be lost out there in the storm, his umbrella ripped out of his hand and tossed into a tree, and no light to see by for miles. If, by grace, he made it to town, he might as well go straight to the hospital and check into the emergency room, as he would shortly be dying of pneumonia.

He sat on the sofa, defeated, only to have Edith grasp his knee. Would this never end?

"Edith," he said firmly, in the voice he knew Emma hated, "it's been a long day, and we both need rest. I think I'll just move to the armchair and have a nap while Ed works on the car."

"Don't you want to see my trump lloyd?" she asked piteously.

In reply, he stalked to the armchair and sat down, folding his arms across his chest as tight as armor plating. Just in case, he also crossed his legs and squeezed his eyes shut.

He deserved this. He had asked for it. He might as well have gotten down on his hands and knees and begged for it. Why hadn't he asked Lew to charge the battery the day after he got home, so he could have driven here under his own steam?

If she laid a hand on him, what could he do besides run for it? Perhaps a coma, if worse came to worst. If he remembered correctly, one simply blanked out and fell down. That, however, could be the most compromising position he could put himself into.

If he ever got out of this one, he would . . . what? He would tell Cynthia he would like to go steady.

There it was. The thought that had been waiting to be revealed, waiting to take him by surprise. And yet, he wasn't surprised.

Instead, he was struck by the irrevocable understanding that Cynthia Coppersmith was a rare find, indeed. Her sweetness, her candor, her joie de vivre and fresh beauty—why had he been so long in appreciating it? And why not enjoy the unexpected gift of happiness that her companionship would surely bring?

He felt a relieved smile spreading over his face and something like freedom in his heart.

Edith sat down on the arm of his chair. "Ummmm," she crooned, "you look cozy."

Enveloped at once by the smell of perfume and stale tobacco, he refused to open his eyes. "I am not cozy," he said through clenched teeth. "I am wanting my bed and a decent night's sleep."

"And you shall soon have it!" she snapped. "When will you ever loosen up?"

He drove toward home with a haggard Ed Coffey at daylight, neither of them speaking. The rain had subsided to a wan drizzle.

What if someone saw him bowling along in Edith Mallory's car at five o'clock in the morning? He slid so far down into the leather that he was sitting on his spine.

What if they passed Percy Mosely, who often arrived at the Grill at five o'clock to do his bookkeeping and load the coffeepots?

Or what if Winnie Ivey spied him on her way to the bakery?

When they pulled to the curb at the rectory, all that could be seen of him was the top of his head, covered by a tweed cap. The five-minute drive had felt like the better part of a day.

Ed turned around as the rector opened the door. The message in the eyes of the exhausted chaffeur was clear: I'm sorry. I didn't mean for this to happen.

He took Ed's hand. "God bless you," he said with feeling.

As he started around the side of the house to the back door, he saw something pink in the hedge. It was Cynthia, in a robe and gown with her hair full of curlers. She stared at him as Ed Coffey pulled quietly away from the curb.

He stared back for one agonizing moment, seeing a certain message in her eyes, as well. She was holding a dripping Violet, who had very likely stayed out all night.

He raised one hand, as if to salute his neighbor, but she turned and dashed through the hedge, the robe flying behind like a coronation mantle. Standing there in the drizzling rain, he heard her back door slam.

His lunch with Miss Sadie and Louella made him feel as if he'd really come home.

He realized he had taken a positive shine to their white bread, and even the processed cheese seemed to possess a certain delicacy.

"I never got Olivia Davenport's hats to her," Miss Sadie confessed. "Two whole months of good intentions and nothing more! But Louella and I are going up to the attic this very week and bring them down, aren't we, Louella?"

Over the pineapple sherbet, his hostess said she wanted to have a meeting with him before too long. Not today, she said, but soon. He remembered other meetings with Miss Sadie and how something major always resulted. In this faded house among the ferns, a bright idea was inevitably taking form.

He told her about the garden statuary, about the moss-covered St. Francis with the missing arm, the seated Virgin with the child, the figure of Jesus carrying a lamb, and the host of wingless cherubs. "Beautiful pieces! A round dozen in all. We'll see to having them restored and put in the church gardens."

"I can't seem to remember them," she said. "We never returned to the churchyard after the fire. It was as if there had been a terrible death, and we never spoke of it. We never even glanced that way when we went down the road.

"But for years, when I looked out my window to the hill where the steeple used to stand against the sky, there was an awful emptiness there, as if something had been stolen from the heavens."

Louella looked at him and shook her head. "Honey, it was mournful."

"Louella, do you think you ought to call the father honey?"

"I think she should," said the rector.

"Well, then," said Miss Sadie. "Papa did everything he could to get the new church going, and we were having services before the roof was even on. Remember, Louella, we used to sit in canvas chairs like you take to a horse event, with just the framing around us. That was a beautiful time, a healing time—the fresh lumber, the new beginning. I remember the way our hymns sounded, out in the open like that, with nothing but grass and trees to catch the music. It was sweet and simple, like the early settlers must have worshiped.

"I remember Absalom came around one Sunday morning. He stood in the back holding his hat and his Bible, and afterward, he walked out front and said to us, 'I'm so sorry.' He was meaning the fire, of course, and everything else.

"You know, Father, I would give anything if I could have fallen in love with Absalom Greer."

Something had to be done, but he couldn't figure out what.

He had called over and over, only to get some odd scrap of message from her answering machine. He had pounded on her door in a thunderstorm but couldn't find her. He had promised to make good on that silly wish but had done absolutely nothing about it. And now, this.

Flowers. He would send flowers.

He couldn't remember sending flowers to anyone before, save his own cut roses. On the other hand, how would it look to tumble out of some woman's car at daylight, only to send flowers to the woman who caught you red-handed? It didn't seem smart.

He would write a note, then. He was fairly decent at penning his thoughts, after all. *Dear Cynthia.*

He stood and stared out the office window.

Dearest Cynthia.

My dear Cynthia.

Cynthia.

He could go on like this for hours. Perhaps even days. Blast!

"You need a haircut," said Emma. He had forgotten she was in the room.

"What else?" he asked sarcastically.

"You need to be seein' more of your neighbor."

He was walking home in a thick fog, wondering when the crisp, blue skies of autumn might appear. He would go to the country, then, perhaps to the very same place he had sat with Cynthia on the quilt, and let Barnabas run until he fell over with joy.

Dearest Cynthia, I remember the day on the quilt . . .

He could feel his face grow warm. That opening seemed too direct. Yet, faint heart never won fair lady.

. . . I remember the day on the quilt, and it's a memory I will always cherish.

How could he not always remember the way she had lain on her back like a girl, looking up at the clouds and seeing Andrew Jackson, and the way she laughed at him when the bull turned and skulked away? And certainly he could never forget the way she had leaned against him, so soft and supple, as he stroked her cheek. They had talked about not letting the path through the hedge grow over; he had said they mustn't let it happen. But how many times had he used that path since he came home a full ten days ago? Just once, as he fled homeward in a downpour.

But he was getting off the point. The point was that he had been remiss and that he was sorry and wanted to make it right. He especially wanted to say that what she'd seen was misleading—he could explain everything.

Dearest Cynthia . . .

He realized he had walked past his corner and was standing helplessly in front of the Main Street Grill. This very thing was only one of the reasons why he had never wanted to lose his heart to anyone.

If Homeless Hobbes had lived in town, the rector was certain he couldn't have confided a word of what he had on his mind. That his friend lived in the woods on Little Mitford Creek, however, was different.

He didn't have the wits to refuse the cup of coffee Homeless brewed at five o'clock in the afternoon. He watched him fill the cup as if he were seeing it happen to someone else.

Homeless was barefoot and wearing a new pair of burgundy pants with galluses. He snapped one brace against his undershirt. "Good as new! Fresh out of th' dumpster."

"That's where Miss Rose does most of her shopping."

"See these pants? I never wanted two pairs, Now I got two pairs. They was layin' right there with th' galluses. I couldn't turn 'em down."

"A new look for fall."

"I hope m' britches don't go to my head."

"I never heard of that particular thing happening to anyone, so I wouldn't worry about it."

"They's somethin' worryin' you, I vow."

The rector raised his cup in a salute. "You've got a good eye."

"I don't know if it's th' eye as much as th' gut. Right here." Homeless thumped himself below the ribs.

"There is something worrying me. I hate to admit it."

"You can admit what you need to back here on the creek."

How in heaven's name was he supposed to talk about it? In all his years as a priest, there had been only one friend to whom he could pour out his innermost conflicts. That friend was now his bishop, and he didn't want to trouble Stuart Cullen with what could seem a triviality.

He sat looking at the steaming black coffee, wondering how long it could keep him awake. Well past Thanksgiving, he decided, taking a reckless swallow.

He was grateful that Homeless didn't urge him on to confession but sat quietly himself. The stove door stood open to reveal a low fire, made with a few sticks of wood to cheer the place against the eternal drumming of rain on the roof.

It wouldn't stay light forever, and walking home along the dark creek in the rain was nothing to look forward to.

He felt as if he were stepping off a cliff when he spoke. "It's a woman," he said.

Homeless looked at him without blinking. "Lord, have mercy."

CHAPTER TWO

Lost

"But who would have sent me a microwave?" he wanted to know.

Puny threw up her hands. "Don't ask me."

"And who am I to ask, for heaven's sake? Weren't you here when it was delivered?"

She shrugged.

"Come on, Puny. Who did this low thing?"

"They was goin' to give you a VCR," she said, "so I told 'em t' send a microwave."

"I won't have it in my kitchen. I knew this would happen someday. It's insidious the way these things take over people's lives."

"How can it take over your dern life if you don't even use it? Who does most of th' cookin' around here, anyway? If I want to heat up some soup for your lunch, I can do it while you're comin' through th' door. If Dooley wants a hamburger, whap, in it goes, out it comes, instead of me slavin' over a hot stove to feed that bottomless pit.

"You don't have to touch it. You don't have to lay a finger on it. I'll cover it with a sheet when I leave of an evenin' if that'll suit you any better."

"Who?" he asked darkly.

"Those vestry people."

"Them again," he said.

"They were jis' tryin' to be helpful."

Helpful! Since when did a vestry have the right to violate a man's kitchen? Was nothing sacred?

"I hope you don't mind my sayin' this . . ."

He knew he would mind.

"You prob'ly ought to take you a laxative."

In all the years of his priesthood, he had pastored the needs of others. Now, he found himself pastoring others to meet his own needs.

He didn't go to encourage Miss Rose in her civic duties because he thought it would be decent of him. He went because he needed what she had to offer, which, although strange, was comforting and familiar.

He walked up the street at noon and stood on the sidewalk while she waved cars around the monument. Well done!

He was astounded by her appearance. No cocktail hat, no military decorations, no trench coat actually worn in the trenches. Just Esther Cunningham's old Waves uniform with a spiffy hat over a new haircut. That she was still sporting her unlaced saddle oxfords hardly mattered. One thing at a time, and be glad for it.

When there was a lull, he called to her and threw up his hand.

She looked at him menacingly.

"I like your uniform!" he said.

"Regulation!" she snapped and turned her back on him.

"Uncle Billy," he said at the Grill, "Miss Rose acted like she didn't know me. I haven't been gone that long, have I?"

"Oh, she knowed you, all right. It's just she don't mix business with pleasure. Keeps 'er mind on 'er work, don't you know. Wants to do 'er best."

The old man was wearing one of his dead brother-in-law's suits, and a tie Father Tim recognized as having been one of his own.

"It's a blessin' if I ever seen it. She's wore out after doin' her job, comes in meek as any lamb, eats her somethin', and sleeps 'til dinner. We have us a nice bite, then we watch the news an' all, an' go to bed. It's th' most peace I can recollect."

"I'm goin' to buy you a hamburger to celebrate."

"If you was to tip in some fries, I'd be much obliged."

Velma wiped off the table. "You ought to get th' special," she advised the rector. "It's a one-day-only deal."

"What is it?" he asked cautiously.

"Beef kidneys."

"Beef kidneys? What got into Percy to cook beef kidneys?"

"Avis had a big run of kidneys and let 'em go cheap. You ought to give 'em a go," she said, poised with her order book.

"Did you give 'em a go?"

"Well . . ."

"Did Percy give 'em a go?"

"He don't eat organ meat."

Uncle Billy looked pale. "You keep talkin' like that, you won't have t' bring me nothin'. I won't be able t' keep it down."

"Bring my friend a hamburger all the way and a large order of fries," said the rector. "I'll have the chicken-salad plate."

"I hope you don't regret it," she said sulkily, walking away. "We'll probably never have these again."

"We dodged a bullet, Uncle Billy."

"Have you seen the drawin's of Willard's statue?"

"No, I haven't. I've got to get by the mayor's office. What do you think?"

"The one a-settin' down is dead-on, if you ask me. Even Rose likes it, but she's stickin' with th' one a-standin', says it makes 'im more dignified."

"You're liking your new apartment? It's good and warm?"

"Oh, it's th' most comfort you'd ever want."

"Nice, dry roof?"

"Not a leak in th' place."

"Well, then, sitting or standing, who cares?"

Uncle Billy laughed, his gold tooth flashing. "Could be a-standin' on 'is head for all I care, when th' hot air comes out of th' vents!"

He was wanting to see Russell Jacks, too, and Betty, and Olivia, and Hoppy. And, of course, Marge and Hal and Rebecca Jane. But most of all, he wanted to see . . .

Dear . . . Dearest Cynthia.

Why could he get no further than this?

When he walked home at four-thirty, he was planning to go to his study, sit down, and force himself to write the letter explaining everything.

Instead, he marched through the hedge and up her back steps and hammered on the door. He knew she was in there; her Mazda was parked in the garage.

Not a sound. He might have been pounding on the door of a tomb.

He felt certain someone was watching him. She was probably looking out the bathroom window, chuckling to herself. Or worse, she'd gone to the club with Andrew Gregory and was doing the tango with the new social director who reputedly looked like Tyrone Power.

Blast!

He stomped through the hedge. Maybe he'd go for a ride on his motor scooter. Maybe he'd open it up on that flat road to Farmer and see, for once, just what it could do. He must remember not to hit the brake too hard; it would lock the rear wheel and lay the bike down. He'd have to hurry if he wanted to get back by six o'clock to feed Dooley who was at football practice.

As he opened the back door, a marvelous aroma greeted him. There was a pot on the stove, a casserole in the oven, and a note on the counter.

Turn the oven off at 5 30, not a minit after. I hope you like it. plese share 1/2 the stew with your neighbor. yours sincerely, Puny.

There it was. A perfect excuse to call and say he was coming over with hot, homemade stew.

"Hello," her answering machine said brightly, "I'm sorry I can't talk to you in person, but Violet and I are in New York for awhile. Please leave a message and I'll get back to you. Thanks!"

His heart pounded as he hung up the receiver.

In New York?

Not right next door, where he might have gone and had a talk with her and arranged a time for them to do the simple thing she asked.

In New York.

He felt an awful emptiness. Even the quality of the afternoon light seemed suddenly flat and dull.

He heard Barnabas in the garage barking to go out, but he sat down on his stool at the counter and stared at the morning mail, not seeing it.

When he stopped in to see the mayor and the renderings of the statue, she looked him up and down.

"You're antsy," she said. "You ought to get you a chew of tobacco to work on. That's what Ray does, an' it helps him every time."

Get a haircut!

See your neighbor!

Loosen up!

Take a laxative!

Chew tobacco!

Women were forever trying to tell him what to do. What he needed was the company of other men. Perhaps he should go hunting. But then, he'd never been hunting in his life.

He saw himself stalking something through the woods, possibly a deer, which made him feel nauseated. Then he saw himself tripping over the gun and blowing his head off.

No, he was not outfitted for stalking anything. And no wonder. His father had not only refused to take him hunting and fishing but refused to let him go with anyone else. He had ended up with his nose stuck in a book when he might have been bagging a few quail with Tommy Noles.

The truth was if he wanted male camaraderie, he'd have to get it in his private club—that finest of institutions known as the Main Street Grill.

In the meantime, he would pour himself into his work as he hadn't done in years. And, he would mind his health with more spirit than ever. No, he was not ready to retire. Stuart had seen all along something he couldn't see. He had many more years left to serve, and that was what he wanted to do, desperately. If nothing else came of his feelings for Cynthia, he had realized, at last, that he wanted to go on, with more stamina and conviction than ever.

He needed to look into Olivia's Bible-reading group, which had become so popular that other churches in the diocese had requested bookings.

He needed to make time for a Youth Choir supper and ferret out his final Bane and Blessing contribution, perhaps that lace cloth bought so long ago for the rectory by the old bishop's wife, which should fetch a nice sum.

There was the visit to Absalom Greer coming up, the final touches required to pull together the Men's Prayer Breakfast, the slide show of his Ireland trip for the ECW and the choir, and the Francis of Assisi observance that would be held in the church gardens. He needed to prepare some remarks for the presentation of the fountain to be installed near the memorial roses.

He needed, also, to get by and see Miss Pattie, and he absolutely had to check on Russell Jacks, their church sexton and Dooley's grandfather.

Though it wasn't on his list of church matters, Dooley Barlowe must have clothes—at once. That meant an evening sorting through Dooley's closet, followed by an afternoon in Wesley.

On top of everything else, of course, were the upcoming sermons. The one he preached on returning from Ireland had been like a crude raft launched upon the ocean; he had nearly swamped himself. That he could have gotten so rusty after two short months was astounding to him.

"Why don't you use one you already done? Did?" Dooley had asked.

Sermons, like manna, he replied, must be fresh. He'd once heard a priest say that he prepared his sermons up to a year in advance! He'd been incredulous.

For him, making a sermon was like getting dressed in the mornings. As the Spirit moved, one put on what one felt like wearing that particular day. After all, who could preach effectively from a prepared sermon on joy when he might be feeling as dull as a post? No, he would not be tempted by prepared sermons any more than he might be tempted by the meatloaf Puny made eight days ago, sitting in the refrigerator in Saran Wrap.

Soon, he wanted to preach on personal, as compared to institutional, salvation. Confessing Christ before others was an act of institutional salvation that most churchgoers had done long ago. He wanted to get at something more compelling, more life-changing—the process of personal confession, of personal relationship with Christ. He also wanted to point out that being a priest no more assured him of heaven than being a chipmunk would assure him of nuts for winter.

He realized he hadn't felt so strong in nearly a year. He would go home, put on his jogging suit, and take Barnabas for a run up Church Hill if the blasted rain would hold off long enough. Yesterday, the sun shone until everything he beheld revealed its dazzle. Then, today, the gray clouds stretched across the heavens like a canopy of steel.

He had turned the corner toward the rectory when he saw it.

A moving van was backed within inches of Cynthia's front door, barely missing the bushes she had so proudly twined last year with strings of Christmas lights.

"Wait up!" he called, running. He reached the van just as two men came out with her drawing board.

"What are you doing?" he asked hoarsely, feeling his heart thunder in his ears.

"We're loadin' this van," said the man with a tattoo on his arm.

"What for? Why are you loading this van when someone lives here? This is a permanent residence!"

"Coppersmith. We're movin' a Coppersmith. And if we're goin' to make time, we gotta haul butt outta here."

"Where? Where are you moving Miss Coppersmith?" He was afraid to hear the answer.

"New York City," they said in unison, disappearing into the van with the drawing board.

"Eat you some grits," said Percy.

"Eat! Eat! Is that all anyone can think of? I'm not here to eat." He came closer to cursing than he had come in years. It was right there, waiting to be spoken, but he turned from it, ashen.

"Dadgum," said Percy quietly.

He sat frozen in the booth, thankful that Emma was out with a toothache. If he had been trapped today in that minuscule office with Emma Newland, he couldn't have hacked it. He felt stripped, exposed, not wanting anyone to speak to him.

Eat. Well, if that's not what he came here to do, what was he doing here? The tea looked insipid to him. He went to the counter and took his mug off the rack.

"I'll have coffee. Half decaf."

Percy filled the mug without a word.

"Sorry."

Percy nodded. He would make it up to him, the rector thought. He had no right to bite the head off one of his staunchest friends. He felt humiliated. Was this what life was going to be like because things hadn't gone to suit him?

The salty old evangelist, Vance Havner, once preached at his mother's church and told a story he'd never forgotten. "How're you?" the preacher had asked one of his congregation. "Oh, pretty good, under the circumstances," was the reply. "What I want to know," said Havner, peering intently at his audience, "is what is a Christian doing under the circumstances?"

What, indeed, was he doing under the circumstances?'

Straighten me out, Lord, he prayed, before I become an embarrassment to you and everybody else.

"Only the mediocre man is always at his best," Somerset Maugham had said.

Aha, he thought, hoping to find some consolation in this.

He did not find any.

"Have you started on the family research?" his cousin Walter wanted to know when he called from New Jersey.

"Haven't touched it," he said. "Too much going on."

"Like what?"

He reeled off his list dutifully, thinking it sounded pretty flat after all. He needed a big wedding, perhaps, or a baptism. He always loved celebrations that filled the church with flowers and relatives and that little hum of excitement and love that gave special witness to the Holy Spirit.

"What about your neighbor?"

"What about her?"

"Blast, Timothy! You know what I mean. Tell all, or I'll put Katherine on. *She'll* be unmerciful."

Lord knows, that was the truth. "She moved to New York."

"What?" Why did his cousin sound so personally affronted? What was it to him that she moved to New York? "Why?"

"I don't have the particulars."

"Well, if you don't have the particulars, who does?"

"Walter . . ."

"You let her slip away, didn't you, old boy? Right through your fingers. As if you could afford such a thing . . ."

"What do you mean, as if I could afford . . ."

"How many men your age, in your income bracket, would be pursued by a good-looking woman with all her wits about her? She sounded like a prize to me, but if you're so hell-bent on growing old alone, with no one to . . ."

"Walter," he said sternly, "put Katherine on."

"Hello, Teds!" She had called him by this silly nickname for twenty years, which she had thankfully shortened from the early version, "Teddy Bear."

"You wicked girl, how are you?"

"Oh, fine, I suppose, as long as Walter goes into the city. But he's been home for days with a runny nose. You'd think it was terminal. I've fetched and carried like a slave."

"There's a good wife."

"Speaking of wife, how's your neighbor?" She had never owned the slightest streak of discretion.

"Moved to New York!" He was surprised to hear himself say this almost gaily, with a certain enthusiasm. There. That was the solution right there. Just toss it off as if it were nothing. A couple of times, and he'd have it down pat.

"Timothy!" she exclaimed. "How could you?"

"Katherine, I refuse to discuss it, and that's that. The whole thing has been beyond me, is beyond me, and promises to stay beyond me. So, please. Back off."

"Back off! Ha! You forget who you're talking to. This is me, Teds, who does not believe that life consists of backing off but of forging ahead! Did you have a fight?"

"We did not. I hardly even saw her after I came home."

"Well, you big dope, that's the problem right there."

He felt weary of all this, as if he'd like to fall prostrate on the carpet and not bother getting up.

The sun had been shining brilliantly for days, and the intense blue sky he'd looked for was there, cloudless, perfect.

Up on the hill, where the ruins of the old church had lain for so many years, something new, something restorative was going on. He could hear engines gunning, hammers ringing, voices shouting back and forth. It was not a clamor. It was, instead, the sound of excitement, even of happiness.

He remembered the summer he and Tommy Noles had hung over the fence surrounding a gaping hole that, in the spring, became the First National Bank. As much as he loved baseball, he had wanted nothing more than to watch the sober gray edifice being constructed, stone upon stone. The sight of an entire building coming together before their very eyes was awesome, better than a movie, better than a hundred movies.

He would have given anything, anything he owned or would ever own, to get in the cab of one of those cranes and muscle something around, something huge, something gigantic.

He would visit Russell and Betty tomorrow, then he'd walk up to the job site and take a look. That he'd steer clear of Leeper went without saying.

Betty Craig looked ten years younger and had lost weight into the bargain.

"Betty! You look like a girl. What's your secret? I demand to be told."

"I don't know!" she said, blushing. "I guess it's that Mr. Jacks is bein' such a help around here. I can't imagine what I ever did without him."

"You can't mean it."

"Oh, but I do! Just look at these shelves he built in the hall."

Putting Russell Jacks into Betty Craig's care had been a brilliant move. It had also kept him from going back to his derelict house in the scrap yard and taking Dooley with him.

Betty took the rector by the arm and led him along the little hallway. "And look here in my room how he made that nice headboard I always wanted and built me a little round table to go by the bed."

Betty's clock radio and a Bible were sitting on the table the old sexton had built. Amazing!

"And see," she said, leading him to the window, "how he's made those nice beds with the pansies for me to look at of a mornin'!"

"A beautiful sight! He's completely well, then, is he?"

"Oh, yes, sir, and I just hate it, I just hate it! Don't tell a soul I said so, but once he goes, they'll want me to nurse Miss Pattie, and I don't believe I'm up to that, oh, Father . . ." Betty was wringing her hands. She had gone from blithe to mournful in only moments.

"Let's cross that bridge when we get to it," he said.

"Do you know the latest on Miss Pattie?"

How could Emma have skipped over that one? "What's the latest?"

"Naked on the roof."

"No."

"Oh, yes. Used to crawl out on the roof in that little pink wrapper, but not anymore. No sirree, now it's her birthday suit."

He put his arm around her shoulder as they walked up the hall.

He was as anxious as Betty for Russell to stay in this sunny home with the starched curtains. Something would have to be done to keep him from going back to the scrap yard, but he didn't know what.

She sighed. "Well, come and see him. He'll want to see you. Oh, dear, you didn't bring the livermush. He's nearly had a fit for livermush since you left."

"I confess I forgot. Two months without livermush is a stretch. Of course, you could have asked Puny to bring some from Wesley. She would have done it gladly."

"Well, he'll be happy to get it when it comes. You know, Father, it's good to do without something that means a lot to you."

"Is it, Betty?" he asked, sincerely wanting to know.

"Oh, yes. Then when you get it again, you appreciate it more."

But he didn't know if he would ever get it again, if he'd ever have the chance to appreciate it more.

"Are you all right?" she asked.

"I am," he said and smiled.

"Got 'er runnin' like a top," said Lew Boyd, wiping his hands on a rag. "You want t' sell 'er, I'll make you an offer."

Lew Boyd no more wanted to buy his Buick than he wanted to go bungee jumping in Wesley. He always said that to his customers. He felt it was part of his service to make them feel good about the vehicle he'd just worked on.

"What would you give me for it, Lew?" He assumed what might be taken for his pulpit look.

"Well," said Lew, "I'd . . . ah, have to think about it."

He tried not to laugh until he got around the monument.

The weather was turning colder, the flame of autumn had torched the red maples along Lilac Road, and now and again he caught the scent of wood smoke. It was his favorite perfume, right up there with horse manure and new-mown hay. And where would he get wood to make his own smoke this year? Parishioners were good about supplying everything from produce for his table to bulbs for his garden, but wood was not something that often came his way. As smart as Avis was about finding a load of corn, surely he'd know where to get a load of wood.

He was barely winded when he turned onto Church Hill Drive from Lilac Road and headed toward Fernbank.

Louella had called and asked him to come. Was Miss Sadie sick? Something worse than sick, Louella said ominously.

When Louella answered the door, she didn't speak but shook her head as if words could not suffice.

In Miss Sadie's upstairs bedroom, he saw hats piled on the bed and hatboxes stacked in the corners and on the dresser. Miss Sadie was sitting in the wing chair where she had told him the last tragic episode of her love story. He was surprised to realize her feet did not touch the floor; she might have been a doll sitting there. Like Louella, she didn't speak.

She handed him a yellowed certificate, and he sat down in the wing chair across from hers.

This certifies that Lydia Anne, child of Father (unknown) and Mother, Rachel Amelia Livingstone, was born in Arbourville, Jackson County, North Carolina, on the 14th day of March, 1901, and that the birth is recorded as Certificate No. 5417.

He looked up slowly to meet her eyes, but she was looking out the window.

He found he didn't wish to speak, either. Three people in one household had been struck dumb by the appearance of a piece of paper, a piece of plain truth. Rachel Livingstone was the maiden name of Miss Sadie's mother.

Clearly, she had sent for him so that he might come and do something, but he could do nothing. He looked at her face in profile, in the unforgiving autumn light, and saw a strange peace. Indeed, the room seemed wrapped in a peace that he began to enter.

They sat for a long time in a silence that he found deeply comforting. He could not remember ever sitting like this with someone, except following a death. Perhaps this hard thing was for her a type of death; the mother whom she had adored as a saint had at last revealed the secret of her illegitimate child. It had been a family of secrets, a life of secrets.

"We went up in the attic yesterday, looking for Mama's hats. I said, 'Louella, let's look in this old dresser. We never really went through Mama's things.' We found the birth certificate folded up in a handkerchief bag with a little pair of socks.

"Last night when I couldn't sleep, I remembered Mama going out with her basket for the poor. Twice a week, every week, she went and always came back so sad, so sad. Finally, I quit begging to go with her. She was going to see my older sister," she said, looking at him in amazement. "Just think . . . I had a sister."

He smiled, sensing an odd happiness welling up in her, even though tears began to roll down her cheeks. She did not try to stop them nor turn her face away but let them come freely.

"All those years I might have known her! Might have skipped rope with her, or let her braid my hair, or told her my dreams! If I might just have seen her or touched her, my own flesh. There she was, all I'd ever wanted, yet God kept her from me . . . and replaced her with China Mae and Louella." She laughed through her tears.

"Two for one," he said gently.

"I have to believe He knew what He was doing."

"You can count on it."

"I had a great aunt in Arbourville. Maybe that's why Mama had the child there. A year and a half later, she married Papa . . . I don't suppose he ever knew . . . In another year and a half, she had me." Her breath caught. "Oh, I so wish I could have known my sister!"

"I so wish she could have known you, Miss Sadie." He stood up and went to her and drew her from the chair and put his arms around her and held her like a child. "I love you," he said simply.

She looked up at him, the tears shining in her eyes. "We're going to make the best of this thing."

She pulled a handkerchief from her pocket and blew her nose. "Now, let's move on to what started all this in the first place. You are going to help me take these hats to Olivia Davenport, aren't you, Father?"

"Absolutely."

"Just think of the joy we'll have when we see her wearing them! You do think she'll wear them, don't you?"

"I haven't the slightest doubt."

"Can we take them this week?"

"I'll have to see about renting a U-Haul," he said, grinning.

"Pshaw! We can get them all in my Plymouth. I have a trunk as big as a bathtub, and you'll do the driving."

"Deal!"

"I'm so glad to have a priest who minds me," she said.

He turned left out of the Fernbank driveway and walked toward the construction site. Church Hill literally vibrated under his feet with the churn and tumult of heavy equipment, which at last had fair weather for operating.

It was a wonder to him that the street wasn't thronged with onlookers, field trips from schools, and chartered buses from every point in the county. For there, under a perfectly blue and cloudless sky, lay an open wound in the earth, with more spectacular vehicles crawling upon it than one could count.

He felt light as air. And no wonder—it was the first time in his life that he'd worn tennis shoes with his tab collar, though that was all the rage with Father Roland and his crowd in New Orleans. He'd been accustomed to running a few years behind the rest of the world, but he was going to make an effort to change that. He was tired of bringing up the rear in the march of civilization.

The equipment crawled over the site like ants on a hill, except for two thundering yellow Cats, stationed at either end of a vast excavation. His attention was instantly riveted by their great maws that dipped into the earth and came up again, overfed with red clay. The arms of the machines swung around and dumped their loads onto a pile.

A man pulled onto the site in a truck, got out, and threw up his hand. It was Ron Malcolm's boy, who had driven from Colorado to work on this job. Though Ed Malcolm was walking hurriedly toward the trailer, the rector caught up with him.

"Ed, how's it going?" They shook hands.

"Great, Father, just great. We're glad to have the good weather."

"And we're glad to have you on this job."

"Thanks, I appreciate that." Ed glanced anxiously at the trailer and then sprinted away. "See you around," he called over his shoulder.

He'd take a look in the hole before he walked to the Grill for lunch. Recalling the plans, he knew the basement would house the kitchen, a composting drum, storage, a ten-bed infirmary, and a small pharmacy.

If he'd worn a hat, he would have removed it respectfully at the rim of the crater. The vast excavation appeared to penetrate Beijing, dug in clay that ranged in layers of color from blood red to purple to black to ochre. Were those layers like the rings of a tree, telling the age of this ancient hill?

"You sonofa . . ." was all he heard as the arm of the machine thundered up from the hole, and he was jerked backward by his left shoulder.

He stumbled, but before he could fall, he was spun around and Buck Leeper grabbed him by his lapel. His face was so close that he could feel the man's spittle when he shouted.

"Do that again, Mister, and you'll *eat* my dirt. Got it? I got enough trouble without some fool lookin' to fall in my excavation. Now, leave my men alone and stay off my site."

Leeper cursed and shoved him roughly away, then stalked toward the trailer.

The rector had felt the man's raw power, as if he were part of the heavy equipment, some extension of it in human form. He stood rooted to the spot, shaken.

"You look like you seen a ghost," said Percy.

"I wish," he muttered. It had been years since anyone had muscled him around like Buck Leeper had just done.

"They's a paper in your booth. J.C. come early and left it for you, said look on page five."

Percy peered intently at him. "Page . . . five . . ." He said this slowly, as if speaking to someone deaf as a stone.

Sitting in the booth, he stirred his unsweetened tea as if it were poison. He couldn't think of anything he detested more than a glass of tea without a few spoonfuls of sugar.

He glanced at the paper on the table but couldn't concentrate. He was remembering Louella's face when she stopped him at the front door.

"We goan tell her 'bout Miss Olivia?"

He had thought for a moment. "No. Something tells me we ought to wait."

"If she fin' out I been knowin' all my days 'bout Miss Olivia bein' her kin, she goan be plenty mad and hurt. Law!" Louella had turned an odd, gray color.

"Let's keep our peace," he had said. "And whatever you do, don't worry. It's going to work out."

Frankly, he wasn't so sure.

He continued to stir his tea, as if there might be something in there to stir.

How would Miss Sadie feel toward Louella, knowing she had hidden that ancient secret about her mother? And what if they told Miss Sadie it was her own great-niece who'd be wearing those hats?

"You seen it yet?"

The *Muse* editor tossed his battered briefcase on the seat and sat down heavily.

"Seen what?"

"Page five. Dadgummit, I told Percy to tell you to look on page five." He stared at the rector, disgruntled, until page five was located.

"You probably know this, already, bein' her neighbor, but I wanted you to see how I wrote it up."

The story appeared under a picture of Fancy Skinner's new beauty shop, the Hair House.

J.C. tapped the headline with his stubby finger. "Right here," he said, "Local Woman Wins Critical Acclaim."

He read the article silently.

> Cynthia Coppersmith, a local author and illustrator of children's books, has been praised by reviewers for her new release, *The Mouse in the Manger*.
>
> Mrs. Coppersmoth, who lives on Wisteria Lane in the house that once belonged to her uncle, Joe Hadleigh, has been writing and drawing since she was ten years old, according to a news report released to the Mitford library.
>
> Mrs. Copermoth's story about a mouse who attended the

birth of the baby Jesus was called "a rare jewel" by one library journal, and another called it "a tiny masterpiece." Our library volunteers say, "This could be another medal winner."

Avette Harris, our local library head, says the book is great for story hour, any time of year. "The only trouble," says Avette, "is that both our copies already have jam or something on the covers and we could do with a new batch."

Mrs. Coppersmitj's book, *Violet Goes Abroad*, won a Davant medal five years ago. It is just one in a series of books about her white cat, Violet, who also lives on Wistoria Lane. According to the titles of the books, this cat has been to school, learned to play a piano and speak French, not to mention has visited the queen. The entire collection is at the library, so hurry on over.

As the rector put the paper down, the editor leaned forward, obviously pleased. "I tried to give it a personal touch. What do you think?"

Think? He couldn't think. His mind felt like it had been stirred with his teaspoon. "Great," he said, feebly. "Terrific. What else did the story at the library say?"

"Said she liked to walk in the rain and eat peanut-butter-and-banana sandwiches. Said somethin' else, too, ah . . . let's see, oh, she likes to dance the rhumba, I thought all that was a little weird, so I left it out."

"Good idea." His heart felt leaden.

"I tried to call her for an interview, but th' machine said she was in . . ."

"New York."

"Right. Well, I gotta get outta here. The Presbyterians have a big story brewin'."

The rector didn't look up.

"Don't you want to know what it is?" asked J.C. wiping his face with the ever-present handkerchief.

"Sure I do."

"They're givin' away a Cadillac," said J.C.

He was dumbfounded. "Doing what?"

"Adios, hasta la vista," said J.C. creaking out of the vinyl seat with his bulging briefcase. "See you in the funny papers."

If there was anything J.C. loved, it was going around town telling half a story to make sure somebody bought his newspaper.

"Don't that beat all?" said Percy, who had heard J.C.'s announcement. "I never knew the Lord was in the car business."

He went at once to the library and gave an astonished Avette Harris two twenty-dollar bills.

"My!" she said, looking at him with admiration.

"This is to replace those *Mouse in the Manger* books," he said.

"I declare, we have tried and tried to clean those book covers. It's something just like jam, but it won't come off. We don't know what it is. You should see the things that happen to children's books, sometimes. We found a dead cricket the other day in *Little Women*, and it looked like lasagna in *The Hungry Caterpillar*."

He nodded.

"Isn't that Miss Coppersmith something? We're so proud of her, we could just bust."

He smiled.

"Of course, this is way too much money. Two little books don't cost forty dollars! Not yet, anyway."

"If there's anything left," he said, "buy a box of candy and pass it around to the volunteers."

He was on the sidewalk, headed toward the post office, when Avette caught up with him.

"Oh, Father, when someone gives a book, we like to put a little book plate in the front that says who it's given by. What would you like yours to say?"

He thought for a moment.

"Just say, 'Given by Miss Coppersmith's neighbor.' "

Peanut-butter-and-banana sandwiches? That had been Tommy Noles's favorite food. Tommy had subsisted on that very fare from fourth grade through high school, with an occasional side of grape jelly. Tommy liked his on white bread, with the bananas mashed flat into the peanut butter. He wondered how she liked hers.

Barnabas stopped to sniff a rock.

The rhumba! What an extraordinary thought. He would have thought the fox trot, if he had ever thought about it at all.

He was struck by the endless number of things he hadn't thought about concerning Cynthia. Why had he never been more curious about her life, about her work? Where had she gone to school, for heaven's sake? And why hadn't he found out why she nearly died in a hospital? He'd even lacked the courtesy to ask lately about her nephew, who was as cherished as a son. It seemed a small thing to wonder, but what was his last name? He didn't even know what kind of work he did.

She had asked him to pose for a wise man in *The Mouse in the Manger*, yet he'd never inquired about the finished book. Worse, he had never once read anything she had written.

He had treated her, he realized, as if she didn't really exist.

That realization was overwhelming to him. He'd believed what his parishioners had told him, that he was caring and nurturing. Yet, it was a lie. He wasn't really either of those things. The truth was, he was unutterably selfish and self-seeking, going his own way, doing his own pious thing. It was disgusting to him.

How had he come this far without seeing himself for what he really was? How had God let him get away with this loathsome deception for so long?

Barnabas lifted his leg against a tulip poplar.

He believed he had never married because he was married to his calling. The truth was, he had a complete lack of the equipment demanded for truly loving.

Perhaps he was like his father, after all, though he'd believed all these years that he had his mother's disposition. He had believed the friends and relatives and old Bishop Slade who had said, "Kind like his mother! Patient like his mother! Easygoing like his mother!"

Yet, underneath all that show of sop and decency was a man utterly fixed on himself, on his own concerns. And underneath some shallow layer of seeming warmth and caring was a cold stratum of granite.

The very last place he wanted to be day after tomorrow was in the pulpit. It was all a joke, and the joke was on him.

CHAPTER THREE

Found

You ought to let fancy give you a haircut," said Mule Skinner over breakfast at the Grill. "Get you somethin' new goin'."

"I've got enough going, thank you," said the rector, who was scheduled for two meetings, a noon invocation at the Rotary Club, a livermush delivery to Russell Jacks, and a visit to the construction site with Ron Malcolm.

"You could take a little more off the sides, if you ask me," said Mule.

"They ain't anybody askin' you," said Percy, handing a plate of toast to J.C.

J.C. grabbed the toast and sopped his egg yolk. "If you promoted your real-estate business like you're promotin' your wife's beauty shop, you'd be a millionaire."

"Besides," said the rector, "I've been with Joe for thirteen going on fourteen years."

"Well, that's the trouble," said Mule. "A man needs a change."

Percy poured another round of coffee. "I hope you can look Joe Ivey in th' eye, th' way you're tryin' to rob 'im of his business."

"Anyway," said J.C., "why would a man want to get a haircut from a woman?"

"I guess you never heard of unisex," said Mule. "Fancy runs a unisex shop. That means she cuts anybody's hair, one sex as well as the other. You ought to let 'er have a go at you, in the meantime."

"Where is she set up?" the rector inquired.

"In th' basement where we had that big blow-out for our twenty-fifth. You ought to see it now—completely redecorated wall to wall, new pink carpet, you name it. Put in two sinks, in case she adds on a stylist."

"Your neighbor still got that dog tied up next door?" Percy called from the grill.

"That dog'll never let anybody near your basement," said J.C. "When it starts lungin' at somebody gettin' out of their car, that'll be enough right there to curl their hair."

"That dog died," said Mule, scowling.

"They'll probably get another one just like it," said J.C. "That's what usually happens."

The rector checked his wristwatch. "Tell Fancy I wish her well. If Joe goes down with the flu this winter, I might consider it. I've got to get out of here. Catch you tomorrow."

"I declare," said Mule as the local priest went out the door, "a little excitement starin' him right in the face, and he won't even spring for it."

"You won't believe this," said Ron Malcolm, "but they've hit rock on the hill. Twelve feet of rock."

"What does that mean?"

"It means Buck Leeper is calling in a dynamite man. This'll set us back. They'll have to drill into the rock and set the dynamite at intervals. It'll be a series of explosions—blam, blam, blam—probably going on for more than a week."

"Not good."

"Once the rock is busted up, they'll have to excavate it out of there with a back hoe and a grab bucket. That's more time."

"And more money."

"By the way," said Ron, as if reading his mind, "Buck is in Wesley today. I guess you won't be brokenhearted."

He had decided not to tell Ron that the superintendent had shoved him around the other day; it was hardly worth repeating.

The architect met them in the trailer. "I've been rethinking a couple of things, Father. I feel the chapel ceiling is too bland, to . . . uninspired. With your blessing, I'd like to enrich the vault. Here's what could happen."

He unrolled a drawing and spread it out on a metal table.

"What if we come in here with a herringbone pattern using V-joint tongue-and-groove fir? Fir is native to these mountains, and the pattern would add to the overall beauty without being a visual distraction. Then we'd come in with a deep fir molding around the base of the vault. What do you think?"

"I like it," said the rector.

"Ditto," said Ron. "And we know a man and his son who could do an outstanding job of it, real native artisans."

"Great! Native workmanship can add a lot of aesthetic value. Terrific."

The architect was clearly excited about the new plan and shook hands gratefully with both men.

"How's Buck working out for you?"

"Couldn't be better," said Ron, eyeing the rector.

"Tough break about striking rock. Well, I'm going to walk over the job and see what's happened since last week. Want to come?"

"You go," said Father Tim. "I've got to make a call."

The two men went out, letting a blast of stinging air into the trailer. He shivered as he sat down at the desk in Buck Leeper's ravaged swivel chair.

"Hello, Avis? I'm running late. Could you put together a few things for me to pick up before you close? A pound of ground sirloin. Right. A gallon of milk. A pack of buns. No, not the whole wheat. Dooley won't eat anything brown." He still felt the blast of cold air along his shoulders.

"While I'm at it, do you know where I can get a load of wood for the winter? Sure, I'll hold."

While Avis laid the receiver down to help a customer, his eyes wandered to the desk blotter that contained a large calendar. He blinked.

In each square that represented the day until today, October the nineteenth, was an exquisite pen-and-ink drawing. Each was intensely thoughtful and rendered with infinite detail. There was a mollusk, an owl, a brick wall, a mountain, a bridge, a chambered nautilus, an ornate staircase, whorls, spirals, hieroglyphs, a pyramid. All so intricate and perfect they might have been mechanically printed.

Nothing was written in any of the squares, no appointments, no schedules, no reminders. The heavy pressure of the pen made each line appear engraved.

There was something jarring about the perfection and precise control, as if these characteristics combined to speak through the drawings with one loud voice. But what was the voice saying?

The thought came to him instantly and clearly. It was saying, Help.

"Right this way," said Mrs. Kershaw. "Miss Olivia has cleared a great big spot in her dressing room."

He could barely see over the stack of hatboxes he was carrying. Trooping behind him like a string of ducks were Miss Sadie, clutching the ribbons of a hatbox in each hand, and Louella, with a hatbox in the crook of each arm.

"Oh, my, I hope that's all," said the housekeeper.

"It certainly is not all," Miss Sadie said. "We'll have to make two more trips to the car!"

They went down the hall to Olivia's bed and dressing room, where she came in from the terrace to greet them. The rector thought she had never looked more beautifully eager and alive, yet only months ago, they had carried her from this room, near death.

"Just put them here for now," she said, rushing to kiss every cheek. "I'm so excited! After lunch, we'll have a hat show. Hoppy is coming over, and we're all going to model!"

"I pass," said Father Tim.

She laughed, giving him a fervent hug. "Oh, I'm so glad to see you all. What a blessing."

"We'll have to make two more trips to the car," Miss Sadie said proudly.

"We'll all help," Olivia insisted. "Lunch is on the terrace, but it's covered, so no bumblebees will land in the salad."

"Ladies, I'm taking charge here. Go sit on the terrace and soak up this unexpected sunshine. I'll fetch the hats."

"But . . ." said Olivia.

"Mind your priest, dear," said Miss Sadie, looking at the large, sunny room with appreciation.

Lunch under an umbrella, in the warm sunshine, surrounded by autumn color and a lawn splashed with the first of the fallen leaves. He was so removed from his daily rounds he felt as if he might be in a foreign country.

Hoppy arrived precisely as Mrs. Kershaw set the dessert tray on the skirted table.

"Wonderful timing, old fellow!" The rector loved the sight of his doctor and friend, who had put on weight and improved in color. Only the wild tangle of his graying hair seemed unchanged. It was a different man who, only a year ago, was still grieving over his dead wife and cursing God.

Hoppy embraced each guest with warmth, saving Olivia until last. He went and stood by her side, his arm around her slender waist. Their happiness was palpable; like the pulsing shimmer of a hummingbird, it seemed to radiate the very air.

He felt an odd piercing of his heart. "My friend, who's your doctor these days? You look positively remade."

"Doctor Davenport is attending me," Hoppy said, grinning. "She's a heart specialist, you know."

When the women went in to get ready for the hat show, Hoppy peered at him intently. "You look a little peaked."

"I'm fine. Top-notch. Stop drumming up business."

"Let me see you next week. I haven't looked at you since Ireland."

"If you insist."

"I saw the story about your neighbor."

The rector gazed at him steadily and smiled.

"So, what's the scoop?" Hoppy asked.

"The scoop? If there's any scoop, J.C. already got it."

"You know what I mean. Are you seeing her?"

"A bit difficult since she's living in New York."

The doctor ran his fingers through his hair. "Rats," he said with feeling.

They heard the first shattering boom on the hill, as if a jet had just broken the sound barrier.

"What an opening!" said Hoppy, as the slender, dark-haired Olivia appeared on the terrace in a swirl of cream-colored chiffon.

"Ta-daaaa!" She was wearing a wide-brimmed hat that tied under her chin with a sash of limp organdy. The hat, once white, had turned a soft ivory color and was adorned with velvet roses. "This fetching number," she announced, "was worn to country picnics and often graced lawn parties at Fernbank."

Hoppy stood and applauded. "Bravo!" he crowed.

"And now," said Olivia, gesturing toward the French doors, "Miss Sadie Baxter, wearing a scarlet felt with leghorn feathers, so perfect for motoring to Wesley in one's town car . . ."

Another thundering boom as Miss Sadie strolled happily onto the terrace, wearing a hat that engulfed her head and left only her mouth and chin visible.

Cheered on by the applause, Miss Sadie bowed low, sending her hat rolling into a perennial border.

"And now," she said in her warbly voice, "Louella, my best friend and lifelong companion, in a smart panama straw, which Mama wore to summer services at Lord's Chapel!"

Louella called loudly from the bedroom, "Miss Sadie, do I have t' do this foolishness?"

"You most certainly do, Louella! It's the entertainment!"

Clutching her handbag, Louella stomped out in a hat smothered with silk lilacs, which were mashed flat with decades of lying in a box.

"Slavery done been over all these years," she grumbled to the rector, "an' some folks act like it still goin' on."

"Poshtosh," said Hoppy. "You should see yourself. You look terrific." He nudged the rector for a comment.

"Sharp as a tack!" he blurted.

"You mean it?"

"Would we lie to you?"

"Well," Louella said thoughtfully and broke into one of her huge smiles.

"More! More!" Hoppy shouted, beating on his tea glass with a spoon. Six more hats were exhibited before the models began to protest and thumped down in chairs in Olivia's bedroom.

After Hoppy left, they sat and talked, the conversation punctuated by explosions on the hill.

"I hope the noise won't be too much for you, Miss Sadie," said the rector. "It's mighty close to Fernbank."

"Oh, no! I like a little something going on for a change." She sighed contentedly. "I don't know when I've had such a good time. Certainly not since Father had his dinner party last spring."

Olivia went to the double closet behind her chaise and pulled out a garment bag.

"While I was rearranging my closets to make room for your mother's wonderful hats, I came across something precious to me, something I'd like to share with just the three of you. It was my grandmother's."

She unzipped the bag and took out a child's red velvet coat with white fur collar and cuffs. A white fur muff, stuffed with tissue paper, was tied around the neck of the padded hanger. Smiling, she held it up for all to see.

An odd sound escaped Miss Sadie; perhaps it was only the word, "Oh."

Louella sank into a chair by the bed, as if her knees had given way.

"Long ago, an aunt told me that my grandmother was born out of wedlock. She never lived with her mother. She grew up in the home of a very kind woman. But her mother visited her each week, never letting it be known who she was. She always brought lovely things, I'm told, and this little coat was one of them. Isn't it beautiful? My aunt said Grandmother treasured it more than anything else.

"I've just finished going through Mother's things, where I found it. So many years have gone by, I feel at peace about sharing this old family secret with friends."

Miss Sadie gave a shuddering sigh, while Louella sat frozen in the chair.

"Miss Sadie, are you all right?" Olivia went to the old woman, who had closed her eyes.

"Father," said Miss Sadie, "could you come and hold my hand?"

He pulled the vanity bench close and did as she asked.

"It's done, now," moaned Louella, who had turned an odd, gray color.

Miss Sadie's eyes remained closed. Then, she spoke slowly, as if something inside were winding down.

"What . . . was your grandmother's name?"

"Lydia Anne. But that's all I know. We've never talked about it in the family all these years. My aunt said I should never discuss it. But it's all so long ago that surely . . ."

Miss Sadie opened her eyes and looked at Olivia. "I've seen that little coat before, my dear. I found it in a box under my mother's bed and thought she had bought it for me. It was a trifle large, and I remember thinking I would grow into it. It was the prettiest thing I ever saw. Several times, I took it out of the box and put it on when Mama was out of the house."

There was a long silence in the room. Olivia looked stricken.

"Christmas came and went," said Miss Sadie, "and the little red coat did not appear. I crawled under her bed to look for it, but it was gone."

The rector held her hand and prayed silently.

"Olivia, dear," said the old woman, "I have every reason to believe your grandmother was my half-sister . . . and that you are my grand-niece."

Olivia sat down beside the rector on the vanity bench, clutching the coat. "I'm so sorry if I said . . . if I did . . ."

Miss Sadie's voice trembled. "I've just learned that my mother had a little girl named Lydia Anne before she married my father. Every week for many years, I watched her go out with her basket for the poor and come home brokenhearted. How strange that I should find this out while collecting her hats to bring to you."

"Oh, Miss Sadie!" Olivia slipped from the bench and knelt by the old woman's knees, weeping with remorse and surprised joy.

Miss Sadie gave Olivia her other hand. "It's all right, my dear. Just wait until you see Mama's picture. You'll think you're looking in a mirror."

"I can't believe the little coat has given me what I long for most—family!"

"Family!" said Miss Sadie, letting her own tears come. "The sweetest treasure on earth. If I hadn't had Louella . . ." Louella came and stood by Miss Sadie, touching her shoulder.

In the room splashed with golden autumn light, they had drawn together, as close as eggs in a nest.

❁

He was no wimp. Instead of writing, he would call her.

That he miserably dreaded the coldness he might hear in her voice was beside the point. The point was to establish contact, to see whether the path through the hedge might be cleared again for passage.

So what if she were cold to him? Hadn't he faced glacial vestries and stony congregations?

He had always managed, somehow, to follow a canonized saint when he was called to a parish, someone who had worn a halo and been surrounded by seraphim, even when walking to the corner for a newspaper.

In his first parish, it had taken a full year to be forgiven his green innocence in the wake of a priest who, mellowed by age, was wise and all-knowing, not to mention full of truth and light.

Though he was again and again the leading choice among the candidates, the frost inevitably came as his congregations sized him up.

One parish had chosen him because he was unmarried but later wished he were married with children.

Another liked him because he was unaffected but decided he needed more charisma.

One search committee thought that being slightly under five feet nine inches in his sock feet was a characteristic that lent spiritual humility but changed their minds and wished he were taller.

What had he to fear, after all?

Absolutely nothing, of course. There was only one problem—he didn't know where to call her.

He walked quickly to the library after lunch and looked up one of the Violet books. He sat down in the reading room and tucked it behind Tuesday's *Wall Street Journal.*

Violet Visits the Queen was filled with watercolors of the irrepressible Violet trying to make friends with garden rabbits under the queen's rosebushes, leaping from a drawing room mantel onto a bird cage, and sending terrified corgis fleeing along dim passageways.

Violet only wanted a friend, read one of the pages in the picture book. *But every time she tried to have one, she did something that chased them away.*

He found the name of the publisher and entered it in his black address book.

He walked to the office, hearing a series of shuddering booms from the hill. His heart beat dully at the very thought of what he was about to do.

He sat in his swivel chair and prayed as simply as he knew how. Lord, if this friendship is not meant to grow, please close the door. If it pleases you, throw the door open wide, and give me the courage to walk through it.

"Bardzvark," someone said at the other end of the line.

"I beg your pardon?"

"Moment, pliz."

He was instantly dumped into the voice mail of someone who suggested he either leave a message or press star for the operator. He had no message to leave and could not, for the life of him, find a star on the telephone keys. He located what appeared to be an asterisk, which produced only an empty silence that he was paying for.

He hung up.

Perhaps he would humiliate himself and Cynthia, to boot. But he would go straight to the publisher, the president, the editor-in-chief, the blasted top.

"Bardzvark."

"The president!" he said, reckless with anxiety.

Pitched into voice mail, he got a recording. "You have reached the office of Helen Boatwright. At the sound of the tone, please leave a message, or dial star for the operator."

He hung up and dialed again.

"Bardzvarkholdpliz."

He was nearly deafened by the music that came pouring out of the telephone. Mozart. Or was it Vivaldi? What a perilous thing it was to try and reach someone in the outside world.

"Who're you holding for, pliz?"

He was glad he had never been troubled with high blood pressure. "The boss of the children's book section, the publisher, the main . . ."

The line seemed to go dead for a moment. "Argonaut."

"May I please speak with the publisher?" he said through his teeth.

"Of which division?"

"Children. Juvenile. Young people."

"This is the children's division."

"I'm trying to find one of your authors."

"I'm sorry, we don't give whereabouts or addresses of our authors. You'll have to write a letter."

"I am this person's neighbor," he said ominously, "and it is imperative that I locate her."

"You may send a letter to our group office and we'll forward it to her. Thank you for calling."

He pounded his fist on the desk. The door appeared not only to have closed but to have slammed in his face.

"How sweet, how passing sweet, is solitude."

"Cowper."

"A man cain't hardly be a hermit n' more," said Homeless.

"Why's that?" the rector asked, moving closer to the glowing wood stove. The door of the stove stood open, and shadows flickered over the walls of a dwelling that was smaller than the rectory kitchen.

"When I moved here a few years ago, I was about th' only one on th' creek. Now th' place is crawlin' with house trailers and squirmin' with little doodad houses. You got dope and alcohol, wife beatin', shootin' and stabbin', you name it. Back along th' creek is th' same as everywhere else . . . namely, th' devil walks to and fro upon the earth . . ."

". . . seeking whom he may devour."

"You know my Wednesday night soup deal has got so it draws upwards of thirty or more at a time. The Local is still givin' me good provender for my pot, an' that bank account from th' reward money I got f'r findin' Barnabas, it squeezes out a pair of shoes here, a pair of britches there. Last week, we got a little kid outfitted with glasses. You ought to seen 'er. She was a doll in them glasses, eyes big as saucers. But you know what we really need in here?"

"What's that?"

"We're gettin' so we need a preacher. You'll not get this bunch to church, no sir, but they need to hear somethin' solid. To my mind, preachin' is like soup. They want a little chunk of meat in it, an' they like it seasoned good. Don't hold back on th' pepper, don't be scant with th' salt, and make sure it ain't watery. They'll turn it down if it's watery, even on an empty stomach."

Father Tim looked into his cocoa. Could this call be for him?

"To tell th' truth, I think you're a mite too educated f'r this bunch. No offense, but that wouldn't be soup, that'd be consommé, if you know what I mean."

The rector nodded.

"We need some gloriously saved sinner that's got the fire of God in 'im, somebody who'd stand on that stump out yonder and say what's what and no bones about it. 'Course, in th' winter, it's goin' to be mighty tight filin' a horde of people through this little shoebox, much less a preacher. Maybe ought to just have summer preachin'."

"Wouldn't hurt to have some music."

"No sir, it wouldn't."

"Let me think about it. Let's pray about it."

"I'll go along with that," said Homeless, taking the lid off a black iron skillet. "Now, how about a dipper of mush?"

"I wouldn't miss it."

"Yeah, but ain't you got some ol' meetin' or somethin'? I seen, saw it on your calendar."

"I won't go to the meeting. There are more important things in life than meetings."

"Really?"

"Really. Are you fellows going to do any good against Wesley?"

Dooley grinned. "We're gonna whip 'em s' bad they'll bawl like sissies."

He looked handsome in his uniform, thought the rector. Very handsome, very healthy, very whole. He put his arm around the boy's padded shoulders. An offensive tackle. A miracle!

"You know what?"

"What's 'at?"

"You're one heck of a guy. I'm proud of you."

Dooley colored slightly and dropped his head.

What he really wanted to say was, "I love you, pal." Why couldn't he say it? He was, after all, in the business of love.

On the way to Absalom Greer's country store, Barnabas sat in the front seat with his eyes fixed on the road, as if he wanted to do a good job of riding in the car.

"I say, old man, you're taking this too seriously. Why don't you loosen up and smudge the windows I've just washed or lean over here and fog my glasses? No, no. Erase that! Too simple. Why not give the collar of my clean shirt a good licking or drool on my jacket?"

Barnabas continued to stare ahead, but one ear flickered.

The rector reached over and put his hand on the dog's neck. Right here was as solid a friend as he'd ever had, with the possible exceptions of Tommy Noles and Stuart Cullen, with Walter thrown in for good measure.

Why didn't he do this more often? Go driving in the country and talk to his dog? It was the simplest of refreshments and didn't cost a dime.

Indian summer was a glad fifth season that didn't come every year. It stepped in without warning, as an inexpressibly welcome bonus, a gift that made limbs lighter, minds clearer, steps quicker.

Absalom Greer bounded from behind the counter of his country store as if all the bonuses of the season resided in him.

They shook hands warmly and embraced. "Preacher Greer has sent his son to greet me," said the rector.

The old man laughed. "You're a fine one to talk, seein' as Ireland knocked a decade or two off your own years."

"What's that wondrous smell? Wait! Don't tell me. Fried chicken!"

"Sure as you're born. Crisp and brown, with a mess of green beans and a bowl of mashed potatoes and gravy. We won't even talk about the biscuits stacked up on our best china platter, already buttered."

"Hallelujah and four amens," said the rector, who refused to consider the lethal consequences of that particular menu on his diabetes.

"Lottie has cooked all morning, and don't be sayin' you wish she hadn't gone to any trouble. It's my sister's joy to go to trouble when the town priest is comin'. Did you bring your dog?"

"I did. In the car."

"Our cat's off on a toot, so bring him in. We'll give him a home-cooked dinner."

Absalom put the handwritten *Closed* sign on the knob of the front door, and all three of them walked the length of the creaking floor to the back rooms. Though the rector had been here but once before, he felt instantly at home.

After the meal the Greers called dinner and the rector called lunch, Lottie went to the garden to clean out the vegetable beds, and Barnabas lay with his head on Absalom's foot.

The rector sipped the strong, black coffee that had been brewed on the stove. "Have they let you retire yet?"

"Law, it's like weanin' babies. They don't want to let me go, but it's got to be done. Next Sunday, I'll be preaching to my last little handful at Sandy Creek, and then it's over—I'll be just a twig broom standin' in the corner."

"I may have a pulpit for you, if the Lord so moves."

Absalom Greer threw back his head and laughed. "You're always looking to put me in the traces! A poor ol' gray-headed country preacher can't get a mite of rest and peace."

"This is a special congregation."

"They're all special."

"This one meets on Wednesday evening, leaving Sunday free to supply one of your little handfuls, if the need arises."

The old man took an apple out of the basket on the table and began to peel it.

"It would be a summer pulpit," the rector said. "You'd be preaching from a hickory stump. Winter along the creek is too hard. You wouldn't be able to get around in there."

"Eighty-nine years old this November, and they won't let me be . . ."

"Of course, the little band at Mitford Creek is very different from the one at Sandy Creek."

"How's that?" He cut a slice of the apple and passed it to the rector on the point of his knife.

"They're not seasoned in the Word of God. They're unchurched. Once a week, they come together to eat a pot of soup made with scraps, but you could give them a banquet, my brother."

"I thought you drove down here in a Buick," said Absalom Greer, "but it looks like you've come drivin' a hard bargain."

"Tasty apple," said the rector.

"I'll talk to th' Lord about it," said the country preacher.

His mail was stacked on the desk in his study.

Dear Father,

They've moved me from the laundry to the mess hall, where I set up and clean up. The boiling temperatures in the laundry took some weight off, so I've been looking like a display in anatomy class. Prison life is not for the fainthearted . . .

He would never forget the look on the faces of his congregation when, just as he was beginning his sermon last spring, the pull-down stairs behind the pulpit lowered. His heart had thundered like a jack hammer when the jewel thief who had hidden for months behind the bells in the church attic came down and confessed his crime.

George Gaynor had been little more than a skeleton even then, living as he had on pilfered coffee-hour provender, Sunday school juice, canned vegetables from the basement, and an occasional carton of half and half. Not to mention, of course, Esther Bolick's marmalade cake, which he had snatched out of its container during a lay readers' meeting.

. . . Thank you for My Utmost for His Highest, *which also is not for the fainthearted. I find it as compelling as anything I've read, apart from the Bible.*

Chambers talks about substituting credal belief for personal belief. He says that's why so many are devoted to causes and so few devoted to Christ. This struck a deep chord with me, and I wish we could sit and talk about it. I grew up on credal belief, and it never worked. It's a dangerous masquerade that's seldom found out until it's too late.

Pete came twice while you were away. A visit with him always has a bonus—it's like a visit with you . . .

He looked up from the letter and realized he was smiling. No, beaming would be a better word for it. While he had prayed that day in the nave with Pete Jamison, George Gaynor had, quite unknown to them, joined them in prayer in his hiding place in the attic.

Two for one, George had called the simple prayer of salvation that had set the lives of both men on vastly different courses.

. . . Please tell Mrs. Bolick that I have dreamed about her marmalade cake on several occasions . . .

He laughed. Esther Bolick's legendary cake had become a warm memory for a convicted criminal, had been devoured at a baptism ceremony in a police station, and had sent him into a diabetic coma that almost took him out. "To die for!" Emma had once said, and hadn't he nearly proved it?

A postcard from Pete Jamison:

My territory has been expanded to six states. I'm praying and it's working. Saw George. Call you soon. God bless.

He didn't recognize the handwriting on the mauve envelope. There was no return address, but the stamps and postmark were Irish. Before opening it, he grudgingly used the microwave to heat a cup of cocoa, then sat at the kitchen counter.

Dear Cousin Timothy,

It was lovely to meet you at Erin Donovan's tea. I had heard for years of the Cousin Tim who was a priest in America and never dreamed we might tip a glass together. I found you terribly clever and charming and so like Great-aunt Fiona that I could scarcely tell the difference except for your trousers.

My scheme is to see your country, as you have seen mine, and to settle for a bit among the people.

It was sweet of you to suggest that I come 'round whenever I'm in America.

Yours very truly,
Meg Patrick

There had been dozens of cousins at Erin Donovan's tea, and he couldn't say that he remembered anyone named Meg Patrick.

There had been Patricks on his grandmother's side, but if there were any left, he didn't know of it. Good of her to write, although he was frankly puzzled by her comparison of his likeness to the famed Great-aunt Fiona, whom he'd always found to be astonishingly attractive in the old photographs in his father's desk.

He glanced up from the letter and studied his reflection in the glass panel of the cabinet door. Perhaps he did have his ancestor's broad forehead and large eyes.

It seemed odd to consider such a connection after so many years of feeling those family connections severed. His father's lifelong reticence about ancestry had caused his paternal side to appear like a nearly blank sheet of paper, with only Walter occupying a space.

The trip, however, had stirred something in him, rather like yeast beginning to work in dough.

He knew little, except for the photographs in his father's desk and a bundle of letters he had read as a child with great avidity in secret. He knew that his grandfather had come over from Ireland at the age of fourteen and went on to make a small fortune as the owner of a box factory. Some rift between his father and grandfather, and later between his father and uncle, had served to slam the door on Ireland.

No wonder he had burrowed so deeply into his mother's small, closely-knit family with their strong Baptist traditions. It had been warm in that burrow, and one always got the straight of things, full force, yet tempered with love.

His mother's family had been shocked at the worst and saddened at the least when he announced his plans to become an Episcopal priest. Perhaps to this day he had never completely understood that decision himself. Though it made no rational sense, he felt it was a way to minister to his Episcopalian father, to his frozen spirit and aloof disdain, though his father would die even before he left seminary.

He had also felt, without being able to express it, that this course could somehow heal their lifelong rift. But more than that, more than anything, he had wanted to serve God and His people—and he had never looked back.

Clearly, Ireland had given him a sense of wholeness he'd longed for, and the mass gatherings at Erin's of near and distant cousins had been a high point. The Irish were known to grumble about the hordes of Americans who stumbled through parish graveyards, rubbing stones, trampling flowers, looking for their roots. But once connected, it was a different story—one was taken in and cosseted like the biblical prodigal.

Yet, if the cousins had been a high point, one event had been higher still—the day he'd taken the rented car with Katherine and Walter and the picnic basket with the rhubarb tart. The landlady had wrapped the tart, hot from the oven, and for miles they salivated as the aroma crept out of the basket and filled the car.

With a sudden screech of tires, Katherine had pulled off the narrow road and looked them dead in the eye. "I can't wait another minute," she said. Excited as children, they peeled the tea towel from around the still-warm delicacy and devoured every crumb.

"There!" Katherine had said, recklessly wiping her mouth on the hem of her dress. "That's how I want to live for the rest of my life!"

He remembered that Katherine had gone up the steep knoll ahead of him, pushing along with the aid of a walking stick. Walter was farther ahead, at the crest of the hill, when they heard his voice echoing off the endless green hills and ancient stone walls, "Look! We've found it! You won't believe it!"

He nearly killed himself climbing to the top to stand there panting with his companions in utter astonishment. "By George!" he had said hoarsely.

The remains of the family castle lay along the top of the facing hill, a shattered toy abandoned to solitude and mist.

Without speaking, he and Walter gazed in wonder at the ruin that bound them together as one blood, until heaven.

Leaning into the wind, he walked to Fernbank for tea, wearing his down jacket for the first time, a muffler, and gloves.

Boom. He could feel the ground shake beneath his feet. According to Ron, the explosions would end today, and he thought how he'd grown accustomed to them.

Much against Miss Sadie's will, Louella had made an effort to remove the crusts from their sandwiches.

"Waste not, want not!" Miss Sadie reminded her friend for the thousandth time in their long life together.

"Miss Sadie, if it's jus' you an' me, don't matter 'bout leavin' on th' crust, but this is *comp'ny.*"

Miss Sadie looked unconvinced.

"This is a *preacher!*" said Louella.

Miss Sadie furrowed her brow.

Louella pulled out her last stop. "Would yo' mama want you servin' san'wiches with *crusts?*" She said the word with such loathing she might have been discussing snakes.

Miss Sadie sniffed and dropped the tea bags into the pot. That was the end of that discussion, thought Louella, who garnished her crustless sandwiches with a stem of parsley.

They sat in Miss Sadie's yellow bedroom, which had lately become a favorite spot to entertain. "It's so she don' have to look at them rain buckets in th' parlor," Louella had told him. "We jus' let 'em get full, then pour it down th' toilet. Miss Sadie call it a free flush."

Louella removed her apron and sat on the vanity bench, as they took their accustomed places in the wing chairs.

His hostess sighed. "I've gone through all Papa's money, you know."

"Yes, I know." She had freely given five million dollars to build Hope House, an ambitious nursing-care facility that promised to be state-of-the-art. Would its benefactor be among its poorest residents? Perhaps he should offer something out of the Lord's Chapel discretionary funds.

"So," she said, brightening, "now we'll start on Mama's money. It's not nearly as much as Papa's, I hate to admit. I could have done so much better, been a much better steward. But when I did so well with Papa's by staying tight as a corset all those years, I decided I'd experiment with Mama's."

"Aha."

She looked at her hands in her lap. "That was a mistake. I conducted a very unfortunate experiment in 1954 and again in 1977." She shook her head, then looked up, smiling again. "But I forgave myself and asked the Lord to do the same. Let bygones be bygones!"

"That's the spirit."

"I'm ashamed to say I'm nearly cleaned out . . ."

"I'm sorry." What a sad irony!

". . . I've got just a little over a million left."

He hoped his face didn't register his shock and amusement, but only the admiration he felt.

"So," she said, "what we need to do is start spending it . . . and I think we should start with Dooley."

"With Dooley?"

"That boy needs to go away to school, Father, to get the kind of education that will make the most of what the good Lord put in him. Mitford School is a fine school, but at best, it can only try to *make up* for his deprivations. We need something that will *overcome* them! Don't you see?"

"Yes. I do see. And you've put it very well."

"Louella and I agree on this a hundred percent."

"Aha."

"He'll be in the eighth grade next year, and if we want to get him in the right school, something needs to be done right away. He may even need tutoring, especially for his English! Now, how do we get started?" There it was again—something he'd seen before; it was the girl in Sadie Baxter.

"I . . . don't exactly know how to start."

"Father," she said a bit sharply, "if I'm going to do my part, you must do yours. It's up to you to find out how to start!"

Boom went the last of the dynamite, rattling the cups on their saucers.

He was sitting at his desk in the study when he happened to glance up and look out the window. There, perched on the window box with her nose glued to the other side of the glass, was Violet. He froze.

Violet studied him like a fish in a tank.

He studied her in return.

He had never noticed that her eyes were so green or that they perfectly matched her collar. She sat like a statue, white against the approaching dusk, unblinking.

Or was it Violet?

Absolutely, he decided. There was something about Violet, after all. And why shouldn't there be? She had been to visit the queen, for Pete's sake, not to mention learned to play the piano.

He didn't want his neighbor's straying cat to be startled and leave. He wanted her to sit right there until he could get his hands on her. Because what he wanted to do, he realized, was find her.

Yes! Violet had run away, but he had found her, and he would return her to her distraught owner, safe and sound, and gain the opening he had hoped for. Perfect.

He moved like a cat, himself, easing out of the chair and gliding across the creaking floor. Violet's eyes followed him as if he were a minnow in a pool.

When he reached the kitchen, he bounded to the back door, threw it open, and looked out at the window box. Violet had vanished.

Blast!

Then he felt something at his ankles.

As he dashed through the hedge with the squirming cat, he saw a red welt on his hand, with blood oozing through. Even better, he thought with satisfaction.

Cynthia opened the door and glared. Somehow, he knew exactly what she was going to say. "Violet, you wretch!"

She grabbed the errant cat from his arms. "I found her!" he exclaimed, displaying his bleeding hand as evidence.

But she closed the door abruptly, and he heard footsteps retreating down the hall.

He was trembling when he reached his back stoop and opened the kitchen door. He was feeling something he didn't like to acknowledge, something he had run from feeling most of his life. It was fury.

How could she close the door in his face without even a thank you or a by-your-leave? What had he done, after all, to deserve her ingratitude and hostility? Nothing!

Hadn't he tried and tried to call her, and pounded on her door in a driving rain, and brought her a Waterford goblet from Ireland even if she hadn't seen it yet, thinking of her always during the entire two months?

Hadn't he written her twice from Sligo?

Hadn't he been perfectly innocent in the Edith Mallory escapade?

Hadn't he rung that blasted publisher's phone off the hook trying to reach her and composed endless letters of contrition in his mind?

He was sick of Dear Cynthia this and Dearest Cynthia that and the whole mess of feelings that erupted in him like a volcano every time he so much as thought of her and which lately had been settling like ash on everyone in his vicinity.

No, he would not write and he would not call. He would not swing this way and that until he was fairly churned to butter over his Pecksniff neighbor. He would march over there right now and pound on her door and demand to be heard. And let the chips fall where they may.

Ulcers! he thought, feeling the wrench in his stomach. He knew that if he backed off for one moment, he would be done for—he would wimp along with her until the cows came home. It was now or never, and the sweat that broke out on his forehead proved it.

There was just one thing he needed:

Prayer.

But where could he turn for it? He dialed Walter. Answering machine. Blast.

Marge Owen. He wouldn't need to say anything more than "Pray for me," and it would be done at once. No answer. Didn't anybody stay home these days?

It came to him so suddenly and with such force, he didn't hesitate. He dialed the phone and when she answered, he said:

"Cynthia, I'm coming over to see you. Pray for me."

He did his own praying as he dodged through the hedge.

The back door was standing open, presumably so he didn't have to be formally greeted.

"Cynthia!"

"I'm in here," she said from the studio. What did he hear in her voice? Iron. Steel. Sheetrock. Knives.

He walked in and saw her sitting on the floor, piling books into a carton. She brushed her hair back and looked at him. He felt he had been slammed across the chest when he saw her eyes. They were the most extraordinary eyes he had ever seen. Why did he always feel he was seeing them for the first time? "Cynthia . . ."

"Timothy." She stared at him, cool and removed.

"Listen to me."

He sat on the floor across from her, and Violet slithered into his lap.

"I'm cursed with an orderly mind," he said, "so let's begin somewhere vaguely at the beginning." There! He was not croaking, and he was not going to croak. He had the voice of Moses on the mount. It might have shattered the glasses in her cupboard.

"I tried to call you again and again, but your machine . . ."

"What about my machine?"

"It made noises like a truck on a highway."

She gave him a stupefying look.

"I knocked one day," he continued, "but it was raining."

"Raining. Oh, my," she said, looking bored.

"And I don't know what you were thinking the morning I came home in Edith Mallory's car . . ."

"Thinking? I didn't think. My mind felt like oat bran stirred with a spoon."

He plunged ahead. "There is absolutely nothing between Edith and me. She held me at her house against my will."

"Really," she said in a voice encrusted with ice.

"It was raining. Tad and Ron went ahead without me. Ed Coffey was going to bring me home, but the car flooded. I slept in a chair. It was a miserable experience."

"Caring about you has been a miserable experience."

He noted the past tense. "Cynthia, I'm sorry. That's what I really came over here to say. If you could know the letters I've written to you . . ."

"I never got them."

"I wrote them in my mind."

"Oh, *those* letters!"

"I tried to call you in New York. I rang your publisher and they wouldn't give me your address." Something was going wrong here. Why was he pleading and explaining?

He tacked into the wind. "Listen," he said firmly, "why didn't you tell me you were moving? Why just go off like that without a word?"

"Without a word? I had hardly had a word from you in months! Two letters that might have been written to a distant relative, and that was all. You said you were going to think about that ridiculous proposition I made to you about going steady and give me an answer on your return. That was your condition, not mine. But of course, you never mentioned it again. And not only did I hardly see you when you came home, but you couldn't even find the time to call me."

"But, Cynthia . . ."

"No 'but Cynthia,' if you please. And it was you who said we mustn't let the path through the hedge grow over. Well, have you seen it? It would take a bush hog to clear it out again!"

"What do you know about bush hogs?" A stupid question, but out it came.

"There are lots of things I know that you'll never know I know, because you'll never ask."

"I just asked."

She looked at him, biting her lip. "I'm either going to punch you in the nose or bawl my brains out," she said.

"I deserve the former, but I'll leave the decision to you."

Great tears loomed in her eyes, and he rose to his knees on the bare floor and took her in his arms.

It was wonderful to sit close to her on the minuscule love seat, to smell the scent of wisteria, to have his arm around her and hear the silken voice he'd longed to hear again. Violet had sprawled across both their laps, purring like the engine of a compact car.

"I've missed you," he said. "I've missed you terribly. It's been like a death, having the little house empty, and no lights on, and not knowing . . ."

"I haven't exactly moved," she said, her eyes red from the storm of weeping. "It's just that I had such a terrific deadline on the new illustrations that my editor said why not take his apartment while he's in Europe for six months, and so I thought, of course, how perfect, and I won't have to bother with . . . with my wretched neighbor!"

He kissed her hair.

"So I moved in there until I'm finished. I had most of my books sent up, and my favorite drawing board, and my bed, which I'm never without—just a few things. Actually, I didn't know what I wanted to do. I felt very foolish, throwing myself at you like that and you backing away from me at sixty miles an hour."

"Forty-five."

"I prayed for you when you called."

"I knew you would." He kissed her temple.

"I thought it was very clever of you to ask me to do that."

"It was the Holy Spirit who had such a wild notion, not me."

She laid her head on his shoulder. What an extraordinary development. An hour ago he had been sitting at his desk in a hard-back chair, laboring over his sermon with an aching heart, and now he was holding someone soft and tender and fragrant and desirable, with a vast furry creature in his lap. He might have sunk to the moss-covered bottom of a clear pond where he was resting like a leaf.

But it was just such false content that had gotten him in trouble before. "Where did you go to school?" he blurted, "and how is your nephew?"

She raised her head and gave him an odd look. "Smith, and he's fine."

"How is *The Mouse in the Manger* doing? Is it selling well? How did I do as a wise man?"

"*Mouse* is selling very well, thank you, and sometimes I think you are not very wise at all."

He had broken the spell, but she mended it with a dazzling smile.

"What do you want in a companion?" he asked.

"Someone to talk with," she said, stroking his cheek. "My husband was too preoccupied to talk. He was too busy making babies with other women . . ."

"Is that why you ended up in the hospital?"

"Yes. I tried to kill myself."

The pain of her confession pierced his heart.

"My parents were well-meaning, but they were always too involved socially to talk. And so, you see, what I want is very simple really."

"What do you want to talk about?"

"Everything and nothing. What you did today, what I did today, what we'll do tomorrow. About God and how He's working in our lives. About my work, about your work, about life, about love, about what's for dinner and how the roses are doing—do they have black spot or beetles . . ."

He kissed the bridge of her nose, smiling.

"Life is short," she said.

"Yes. Yes, it is."

He kissed her mouth, and it was as if he'd been doing it all his life; it was the most natural thing in the world. He felt he was taking a kind of nourishment that would make him strong and fearless.

She wasn't going back until Sunday afternoon. He would wine her and dine her, he would wrap her Waterford goblet in gold paper, he would fulfill that silly and heedless wish of hers, he would buy a dozen roses from Jena, he would buy a new jacket at the Collar Button sale, he would make her a peanut-butter-and-banana sandwich, he would buy a tango album—or was it the rhumba she liked? He would bathe Barnabas, he would give Violet a can of white albacore tuna in spring water, he would ask Dooley to put on his football uniform for her, he would pray for rain and take her walking in it.

He collapsed in bed. It went without saying, he supposed, that the love business could be exhausting.

CHAPTER FOUR

Banana Sandwiches

"I'll come home at Christmas," she said.

They might have been sitting together in just this way, slouching into the disheveled slipcover of his study sofa, since time began.

"I'll string the lights on your bushes to welcome you home."

"What a lovely thing to even *think!* Oh, Timothy, how could you not have loved someone all these years? Loving absolutely seeps from you, like a spring that bubbles up in a meadow."

"Maybe you can convince me of that, but I doubt it. I find myself niggardly and self-seeking, hard as stone somewhere inside. Look how I've treated you."

"Yes, but you could never deceive me into thinking you were hard as stone. You've always betrayed your tenderness to me, something in your face, your eyes, your voice . . ."

"Then I have no cover with you?"

"Very little."

" 'Violet only wanted a friend,' " he quoted, " 'but every time she tried to have one, she did something that chased them away.' "

She looked at him with a kind of joy. "You've read a Violet book!"

"Yes, and learned something about myself, disproving entirely that Violet books are only for ages five through ten. I really try to express my feelings for you, but I always chase you away. It makes me want to give up."

"Please! I can't bear it when someone says that. Remember what Mr. Churchill told a class that was graduating from his old school?"

"I confess I don't remember."

"When Mr. Churchill was a student, the headmaster had told him how hopelessly dumb and trifling he was, and then, years later, when he was prime minister and had written the history of the English-speaking people, for heaven's sake, they invited him back to address a graduating class. They anticipated one of his brilliant and lengthy speeches, and here's the entire text of what he told them:

" 'Young men,' he said, 'nevah, nevah, nevah give up!' And he sat down."

He laughed.

"Nevah," she said soberly.

"I regard that as wise counsel."

"It has counseled me for years."

"Will you have dinner with me on Friday evening?"

She looked into his eyes and smiled. "I would love to have dinner with you on Friday evening."

"How do you like your peanut-butter-and-banana sandwiches?"

"With the bananas cut in thick slices and smashed into the peanut butter."

"Smooth or crunchy?"

"Crunchy."

"White or dark?"

"White."

"With or without crusts?"

"With!"

With such knowledge now his forever, he felt invincible.

"Yellow or red?" asked Jena Ivey at Mitford Blossoms.

"Red," he said.

"Loose or arranged?"

"Loose."

"In a vase or a box?"

"A box."

He needed an assistant, a curate, a gofer, anybody, somebody. Puny had helped him put the tablecloth on and had polished the glasses until the lead crystal sparkled like gems. She had vacuumed the entire house, then cleaned out the rabbit cage in case Cynthia, who loved rabbits, wanted to hold Jack on her lap. She had washed the dining room windows, refilled the bird feeder outside the windows, changed the threadbare mat at the front door, waxed the entrance hall, and done the grocery shopping.

But that only made a dent in what had to be done. At last, and the thought made his heart hammer, he would have to take Walter's advice and let the Holy Spirit come up with Sunday's sermon, because there would be no time for carefully structured notes.

"What can I wrap this goblet in?" he asked Puny. He realized he had been walking around the house in a daze, carrying it in his hand.

"If you aren't the beat," she said, putting her hands on her hips. "I'm wore out jist watchin' you moon around."

"I am not mooning around. I am looking for wrapping paper."

"In th' buffet, don't you remember? That's where you told me you always keep wrappin' paper."

How could he have forgotten? He felt his face grow red. "Did you get the white albacore tuna?"

"I did."

"In spring water?"

"I don't know what it's in."

"I wanted it in spring water. I specifically wrote that on the list."

"Is that what you were talkin' about? I thought you wanted spring water, so I got two gallons."

Why wasn't this more fun? "The Collar Button is having a sale," he said, trying to sound casual. "I thought I might pick up a jacket. What color do you think?"

"What color does she like?"

He should have known there was no hiding from Puny Bradshaw. "Blue. I think she likes blue."

"Perfect! I'm sick of all that brown in your closet. It looks like a pile of dead leaves in there. Besides, it will bring out the color of your eyes."

"Dark or medium?"

"Dark. Get a blazer."

"Thank you," he said, sincerely relieved.

Now if he could get Barnabas bathed and find a rhumba album—or was it the tango?—he would nearly be caught up.

"Here," she said, snatching the goblet from his hand, "let me do that. White tissue paper or red?"

"White," he muttered, feebly.

"Of course!" she said, clearly disgusted.

That he had to drive to the far side of Wesley to find a music store was no surprise. The surprise came when he discovered they had no record albums.

"No record albums?" He was stunned.

"Just compact discs," said the sales clerk, eyeing him as if he'd come from another planet.

No albums! What was the world coming to? Seriously? What did one do, just throw out a perfectly good record player, which was probably not even recyclable? What kind of sense did that make?

He didn't really want to know but thought he should ask. "How do you use a compact disc?"

When he came out of the music store, he went straight to his car and put the box in the trunk. He must not allow Puny Bradshaw to lay her eyes on what he had just purchased. Never. He put the music-store bag containing the rhumba and the tango discs inside the trunk and closed it.

A little excitement was beginning to build, he admitted, but it had not yet risen above the apprehension of where this whole thing might be going and the deep, instinctive fear that he could not, in any case, stop its progress.

"You are far too handsome in blue," she said.

The extraordinary thing about his neighbor is that he knew she really meant this foolish remark. He could see it in her eyes.

"Impossible! I've been plain as a fence post as long as I can remember."

"Well, now that you've started being far too handsome, there's nothing you can do to reverse it." She smiled. "That's the way it works, you see."

He was standing at her back door, having popped through the

hedge to fetch her to the rectory. Not knowing what else to say or do, he handed her the can of tuna. "For Violet."

"How lovely! And in oil, just what she likes best. Thank you!"

The stock market might have taken a radical upturn for the relief he felt.

"And thank you for the roses. Do come and see them!"

He smelled them as he came along the hall. They were in a vase in front of the bay window of her living room, illuminated by the last rays of light through the curtains. "Here," she said, removing a long stem from the vase. "This is for you."

She had taken his breath away when she appeared at the door. Her freshness, her inner vitality were dazzling. Everything about her stood out in the sharpest focus, as if he'd just gotten new glasses. "I . . . ," he said, taking the rose from her hand. He was sinking into her, somehow, and didn't know if he could swim.

He had waited until Dooley went to his room last night before attempting to hook the thing up and put on a disc. He was astonished when music came pouring out, nor had he ever heard anything like it; it was so clear, so lucid, so like the living sound. He confessed he would not miss the riot of static produced by ancient scratches or the scraping of a worn needle.

"It's been years since I danced the tango," he said, holding her close.

She laughed. "The rhumba!"

"Ah, well, I've always been a fox-trot man, to tell the truth."

"Fox-trot men usually have a streak of rhumba in them somewhere. It simply takes some doing to pull it out."

"Could you pull a bit harder then?"

When the dance ended, he stood with her in front of the fire, in front of the table so carefully set with his grandmother's old Haviland and the single rose in a vase.

"Look me in the eye," he said, taking her face in both his hands.

"I'm looking."

"I want to ask you a question."

"I love questions!"

He remembered asking her once, "Is there anything you don't

love?" "Yes," she had said, "garden slugs, stale crackers, and people who're never on time."

"Well, then . . . would you kindly consider the possibility . . . that is to say, the inevitability . . . of going steady?"

She burst into tears.

"Cynthia!"

"I always cry when I'm happy," she wailed.

"Well, answer me, then," he said, giving her the handkerchief from his pocket.

"Yes. I'll consider it!"

"Wait a minute. Will I never get this right? I asked you to consider it, but what I really meant was, will you do it? Starting now?"

"Yes. I'll do it."

He was going to kiss her, but his legs began to buckle under him.

"Timothy!" she said, holding him up. "Sit down before you fall down!"

He sank onto the sofa, laughing. "Hopeless," he said, feeling the trembling in his knees and the pounding of his heart. "Utterly hopeless."

She fairly hooted with laughter. "You'll get over it!" she promised, giving him a hug.

They were still in a frenzy of laughter, tears streaming down their cheeks, when Dooley walked in and looked around. "Mush!" he said, backing out the door.

She would be home for Christmas, which was only two months away, spend a week or ten days, and return to New York until March, when she would come home to the little yellow house for good.

Perfect, he thought, making the sandwiches on Saturday night. Couldn't be better! He would have plenty of time to adjust to what he'd just done, get through the inestimable pressures of the holy days, and be waiting for his bulbs to come up as she flew in.

Dooley had had a big football game this afternoon, which he'd attended while Cynthia packed, and was now spending the night with his friend Tommy. In view of that, he turned on the disc player and listened to the tango music again—or was it the rhumba?

Standing at the kitchen counter, shuffling his feet to the music, he caught himself smiling from ear to ear. For more than sixty years, he had been slogging along in wet concrete; now he felt as if he were swimming in a Caribbean pool.

"What is asked of us," Raymond John Baughan had said, "is that we break open our blocked caves and find each other. Nothing less will heal the anguished spirit or release the heart to act in love."

Break open our blocked caves!

What a lot of battering it had taken to break open his own cave, he thought. Among the many other things she deserved, Cynthia Coppersmith deserved a medal.

With that in mind, he made her peanut-butter-and-banana sandwich extra thick and wrapped it with a note.

"I can't help loving you," she read aloud from his note. "May God bless you and keep you and bring you back safely. Yours, Timothy."

They were sitting in the parking lot of the small commuter airport in Holding, eating their late Sunday lunch out of a paper bag and drinking root beer.

She smiled at him, her eyes the color of blue columbine. "Well, you see, we're just alike, then. I can't help loving you, either. Do you think I would have chased you like I've done if I could help it? Certainly not!" She took a bite of her sandwich. "Yum, yum, and a thousand yums."

"Are the bananas mashed in right?"

"Perfect!"

"I wanted this to be your main course last night, but I hadn't the nerve. I also prayed for rain, but that prayer went unanswered."

"You prayed for rain?"

"So I could take you walking in it. The news release at the library said you like to walk in the rain."

She laughed. He loved the sound of any laughter, but hers was a laughter that ignited something in his spirit.

"Oh, Timothy, there are so many lovely things to do, aren't there? I pray that we have hundreds of rains to walk in. I pray that I find out all your secrets and can do magical things for you, as you have done for me."

"One of my deepest secrets is that I like tapioca," he said, grinning.

"Tapioca? Gross! But I shall set my personal loathing aside, and you'll have all you can eat for Christmas dinner."

"Will you write?"

"Of course, I'll write. And when you write me, will it be one of those notes you'd send to a distant relative, or will it be deeply personal and sexy and delicious?"

"I'll see what I can do," he said, holding her hand.

"I hate to go."

"I hate to see you go."

"I loved your sermon."

"Is there anything you don't love?"

"Crow's feet, age spots, and good-byes."

"Kiss me, then," he said.

He stood on the tarmac and watched her little plane until it became a speck in the sky. He prayed for her safety, her peace, her ability to complete her work, and her joy. "Give her joy," he said aloud, turning back to the terminal.

In the car, he wondered if he should try to find Pauline, Dooley's mother. She had lived in Holding for years, but when Dooley had run away to her last Christmas, and the police had searched for her and him, it had been in vain. She couldn't be found, and not a word from her since. It was just as well; surely it was just as well. What could word from his broken, alcoholic mother do but tear Dooley apart all over again, after he had begun to reconstruct himself?

He wanted to help Pauline, but the way to do that, the only way he had available, was to help Dooley. Had he helped him? Perhaps. Certainly, he had grown to love him, to find even his aggravating ways familiar and comforting. Mush, indeed! His heart had clearly made its own mush for Dooley Barlowe.

An invitation from Edith Mallory arrived the following Wednesday. *Come for Thanksgiving dinner at Clear Day,* she wrote. *I hope I'm asking well in advance of any other demands on your schedule, and rest assured we shall have all your favorites.*

What did she know about his favorites? He would have Emma

reply that he and Dooley would attend the annual All-Church Thanksgiving, which the Presbyterians were hosting this year. Her monogrammed stationery reeked of some musky scent that fairly clung to his fingers after he read it. Why couldn't she leave him in peace?

When he laid the note aside, Emma grabbed it and tossed it in the wastebasket. "Whang-do!" she snorted.

At a quarter 'til twelve, Puny rang. "Are you comin' home for lunch?"

"I thought I'd have a bowl of soup with Percy."

"If I was you, I'd come home," she said mysteriously.

The dozen roses in a box took his breath away. Clearly, they were the finest specimens the zealous Jena Ivey could muster.

Cynthia had handwritten the card before she left: *With love from your neighbor, who misses you dreadfully.*

Dooley helped himself to reading the card that evening. "Double mush," he pronounced.

Two consecutive freezes downed the geraniums but enlivened the pansies in every border. Though mid-November had arrived, the curry-colored leaves of the oak refused to fall, providing a rich background for the remaining gold of the maples.

"A Flemish tapestry!" exclaimed Andrew Gregory, stirring a cup of hot apple cider with a cinnamon stick.

Percy Mosely sat on a stool at the Main Street Grill and declared he was glad to be rid of the tourists, so the locals could have a little peace and quiet. "Gawk an' squawk. That's what they do from May 'til th' leaves drop. Feller in here last week squawked to me about th' coffee, said it was s' weak he had t' help it out of the pot. That," he concluded, darkly, "was a Yankee lie."

"Winter!" grumbled J.C. Hogan, having sausage and eggs in the back booth. "I hate the dadgum thought of it."

"What you need," said police chief Rodney Underwood, "is a good woman to keep you warm."

"I doubt he could find one who'd want th' job," said Mule Skinner. "He was such an ugly young 'un his mama had to tie a pork chop around his neck to get the dogs to play with him."

At the first frost, Miss Rose and Uncle Billy Watson were rumored to have set their brand-new thermostat on seventy-five, and let the chips fall where they may.

Grocery man Avis Packard announced his excitement over the quality of collard greens and turnips he was getting from the valley.

Dooley moved Jack's cage from the unheated garage to his room.

The Chamber of Commerce, who had conducted a woolly worm festival on the school lawn, predicted a bitter winter, while Dora Pugh at the hardware designed a window display with snow shovels and had a plan-ahead sale on kerosene lamps and thermal underwear.

The vase of roses at the old rectory managed to last a very long time, as if defying what was to come. Before their petals fell on the polished walnut of the dining table, Puny decided to tie their stems with a string and hang them upside down to dry, figuring that, one day, they'd make a nice memory for somebody.

"Uncle Billy! How are you?"

"No rest f'r th' wicked, and th' righteous don't need none!" he said, cackling. "Jis' thought I'd call up to chew th' fat, and tell you things is goin' good up here at th' mansion."

"I'm always glad to hear that," said the rector, tucking the receiver under his chin and signing the letter he'd just typed.

"I don't know what you think about preacher jokes . . ."

"What have you got? I could use a good laugh."

"Well, sir, this preacher didn't want to tell 'is wife he was speakin' to th' Rotary on th' evils of adultery. She was mighty prim, don't you know, so he told her he was goin' to talk about boating.

"Well sir, a little later, 'is wife run into a Rotarian who said her husband had give a mighty fine speech.

" 'That's amazin',' she said, 'since he only done it twice. Th' first time he th'owed up and th' second time 'is hat blowed off.' "

He laughed uproariously. "That's a good one, Uncle Billy."

"I can tell that th' livelong winter. It'll do me 'til spring. You're th' first to hear it, next to Rose."

"Where'd you find it?"

"I like to get my jokes off strangers, don't you know, so they're fresh to th' town. Come off a feller down at th' dump, passin' through from Arkansas. He th'ow'd out a whole set of Encyclopaedia Britannica, good as new. We got 'em in th' kitchen. It's a sight f'r sore eyes what they do with drawin's of birds an' all."

"Cynthia tells me she's pushing her publisher to do something with those ink drawings of yours."

"Well, sir, that'd be good. I got more than a thousand dollars in m' mattress off that bunch of pencil drawin's we sold at th' art show. I hated t' take it, since some of my beagles looked like coons."

"What in the world will you do with a bankroll like that?"

"Set Rose up for Christmas, for one thing. It's th' most money I ever put my hands on. She thinks I'm rich. You ought t' see th' way she shines up to me since I got a little somethin' put away. A feller can't make that kind of money canin' chairs and buildin' birdhouses."

"That's a fact."

"We're goin' to have us a Christmas tree, don't you know, for th' first time in more'n thirty years. An' I'm goin' to be Santy and give 'er a dress or two an' some shoes I seen in a catalog—what they call sling-back pumps."

"How about a suit for yourself, my friend?" Uncle Billy had turned himself out in his wife's dead brother's clothes for as long as he had known him.

"Well, sir, I don't know about that."

"You're a good fellow, Uncle Billy."

"I don't think so, m'self, but I thank you, Preacher. Th' same to you."

When they hung up, he found he had a new zeal for his letter-writing. Uncle Billy Watson doeth good like a medicine, he thought, paraphrasing the Scriptures.

The door opened, but even before he saw who was coming in from the street, he felt a nameless dread.

"Hello-o-o," said Edith Mallory, closing the door behind her.

She marched straight to Emma's chair and sat down, as if it were her own. "I'm ravished!" she announced.

Not around here, you won't be, he thought.

"I haven't had a bite all day, except for the teensiest piece of toast for breakfast. Since you can't come for Thanksgiving dinner, there's the cutest new restaurant in Wesley, and I just know you'd love it. I've reserved a table for lunch, on the teensiest chance you can come. They have green tablecloths and green walls—I know how passionately you love green—and can you imagine, their dinner menu features elk and bison!" She peered at him with dauntless expectancy.

He did not love green, and anyone who would stalk and slaughter an elk or bison was a raving lunatic.

"Well? What do you think?" She opened her handbag and removed a compact. Looking into it intently, she twisted her mouth in a manner he found gruesome, then slathered it with a vivid orange lipstick. "Ummm," she said, poking out her tongue and licking her lips. When she crossed her legs, he saw for the first time that her skirt was ridiculously short.

He rose from his chair so suddenly that the silver bud vase on the windowsill above him went flying across the room and skidded to the door.

"Blast!" he said. "I was just leaving. Dooley is feverish, a wound to the knee. Football, you know."

He was stunned at the lie that came rolling out like so many coins from a slot machine. He fled to the peg and grabbed his jacket and was putting it on when she got up and came toward him. In one smooth, swift, gliding motion, she threw her arms around him and pressed her body against his.

"Timothy . . . ," she said, breathing onto his cheek.

He moved away from her, trying to wrench her arms from his neck. "Edith . . ."

"Timothy, I know how you feel about me, how you've always felt. I can see it . . ."

He flung the door open and ran into the street without looking behind him, without observing the careful, lifelong practice of locking up church property, without taking his briefacse, without considering that he might have handled the whole thing far better by meeting her head-on and coming, once and for all, to manly terms with an ungodly circumstance.

He struck the pillow on the study sofa with such force that a welt gaped open, releasing a pouf of white feathers.

The vestry. They could help him. Or should he call Stuart? What could the vestry do, after all? What did you do to provoke it, someone might ask, and well they might. The answer was simple: Nothing! He had done nothing, never, not the slightest thing. He had been kind to her over the years, he had gritted his teeth and been kind, that was all, nothing more than he had been to anyone else in the parish, including her beleaguered dead husband.

Had he passed Ed Coffey when he hurried out of the office and down the sidewalk? Had Ed sat watching him from behind the wheel of the Lincoln, as he fled like a hare before a hound? It was humiliating to think that Ed might even now be shaking his head with pity over the priest who could not hold his own with his employer. Would Ed have to watch him skulk about eternally, fleeing from church offices, trapped in rainstorms, until either he or Edith gave up and gave in?

Certainly, he would never give in.

But he felt a chilling dread that Edith Mallory would not give in, either. There was something indomitable about her; she had had her way with Pat Mallory for more than three decades. She was not used to giving in.

He was not pleased that he felt oddly fearful, like a child in a tale of a wicked stepmother. And why did it suddenly occur to him that her direct approaches were preliminary to something more subtle, something he might not be able to recognize and avoid?

Percy looked at him meaningfully. "That feller you got doin' up your nursin' home . . . ?"

"What about him?"

"He ain't my chew of tobacco."

"Is that right?"

"Started comin' in here two mornin's ago orderin' me around like some ninnyhammer, I like to shoved 'is head in 'is grits."

"Aha."

"Too bad you missed th' last two mornin's, he comes th' same time as your crowd, sits by hisself in th' front booth. Do this, do that, run here, run there. Makes Parrish Guthrie look like a church saint."

"They say he's the best in the business."

"I'll show 'im some business," said Percy.

After he left the Grill, he stopped in front of Happy Endings bookstore. He was looking over new titles in the window when Fancy Skinner got out of her car at the curb. He saw that Fancy had dyed a streak in her blond hair to match her 1982 pink Cadillac, and was wearing an angora sweater of the same hue.

"How you doin'?" she called, waving to him.

"Terrific. How's your new shop?"

"Couldn't be better. My Mister Coffee busted this mornin' and I'm goin' in th' Grill for a coffee to go. By th' way, that bozo of yours up at your nursin' home. . . ."

"Ah, which one is that?"

"Buck Leeper. Came in for a haircut, ordered me around like a slave. When he told me to give 'im his change, I told 'im to bend over. You oughtn't to let him run loose."

"Well." What else could he say?

"You ought let me take a little off your sides. That's kind of a chipmunk look you got there."

"Right."

So now Buck Leeper was *his* bozo, doing up *his* nursing home, and *he* was the one responsible for letting him run loose.

Dearest Cynthia,

Sometimes, if only for a moment, I forget you're away, and am startled to find your bedroom lamp isn't burning, and all the windows are dark. I must always remind myself that you're coming home soon.

I hope your work is going well and that you're able to do it with a light heart. I've never been to New York, and I'm convinced that my opinion of it is a foolish and rustic one. Surely much humor and warmth exist there, and I'll restrain myself from reminding you to hold on to your purse, be careful where you walk, and pray before you get into a taxicab.

I've mulched your perennial beds, and done some pruning in the hedge. I think we'll both find it easier to pop through.

To the news at hand:

On Saturday, Miss Pattie packed a train case with Snickers bars and a jar of Pond's cold cream and ran away from home. She got as far as the town monument before Rodney found her and brought her home in a police car. It appears that riding in a police car was the greatest event of her recent life, and Rodney has promised to come and take her again. Good fellow, Rodney.

I have at last heard Dooley sing in the school chorus, and must tell you he is absolutely splendid. Cold chills ran down my right leg, which is the surest way I have of knowing when something is dead right. Our youth choir, by the way, will have a stunning program ready for your return at Christmas.

Barnabas pulled the leash from my hand yesterday afternoon, and raced into your yard. He sniffed about eternally, before going up your steps and lying down on the stoop. I can only surmise that he misses you greatly, as does yours truly,

Timothy . . .

The Sunday of the Village Advent Walk was bright with sun, yet bitterly cold. He was glad to put on the camel topcoat Puny had brushed and hung on the closet door. He had let it hang there for more than two weeks, eagerly waiting for the weather to turn cold. Winters had become so mild, he had scarcely had it on his back in recent years. Let the hard winter come! he thought, whistling the morning anthem.

At four o'clock, the villagers poured into Lord's Chapel, teeth chattering, to stand expectantly in the pews as the choir processed along the aisle. "O Zion, that bringest good tidings, get thee up to the heights and sing!" Rays of afternoon light poured through the stained glass windows, drenching the sanctuary with splashes of color. It was enough, he thought, if no word were spoken or hymn sung.

After the service, he and Dooley followed the singing procession to the Methodist chapel, where the children's choir met them on the steps. "Hark, the Herald Angels Sing," they warbled, sending puffs of warm breath into the freezing air. People filled the nave and were standing in the churchyard as the ancient story of Christmas was read from Luke, and candles were lighted in every window.

Afterward, they trooped down the alleyway and across Main Street, singing to the tops of their voices in wildly random keys. They were led, at this point, by J.C. Hogan, who was walking backwards at a heedless trot while snapping pictures of the oncoming throng.

The Presbyterians joined them on the corner of Main Street and Lilac Road with ten pieces of brass, and led the frozen, exhilarated regiment across the street to First Baptist, where the the lower grades sang "O Little Town of Bethlehem," accompanied by their preacher on the guitar. They also saw a re-enactment of the manger scene, for which the preacher's wife had made all the costumes.

Then, everyone clattered to the fellowship hall, where the brass band was rattling the cupboards with "Joy to the World!" The women of the church had set out an awesome array of sandwiches, cookies, cake, homemade candy, hot chocolate, and steaming apple cider.

"I think we're about to get our second wind," said the rector to his Presbyterian colleague.

"One more denomination in this town and some of us couldn't make it around. We've just clocked a mile and a quarter."

"I don't think there is another denomination, is there?" asked Miss Pruitt, the Sunday School supervisor.

"Well, let's see. There's the Lutherans!"

Edith Mallory made her way through the crowd, carrying a sloshing cup of cider. There was a certain look in her eye, as if he might be a nail and she a hammer, determined to pound him squarely on the head.

"Lovely service at Lord's Chapel," she said, coolly.

"Yes, I thought so, and how did you like the walk?"

"Walk? I never walk on the Advent Walk, I always ride."

"I see."

He turned away so hastily that he knocked the cider out of Mayor Cunningham's hand, and took refuge in helping someone clean it up. When he got to his feet again in the milling crowd, Edith had disappeared.

Keeping his head down, he found Dooley and left for home, to steam himself like a clam in the shower, and reread the letter that waited by his bed.

Dearest Timothy,

No, scratch that. My dearest neighbor,

I have been riding in taxicabs the livelong day, and have taken your advice. I pray while hailing, as it were, and God has been very gracious to send affable, entertaining, and kindly drivers. One even chased me down the sidewalk to return a scarf I left on the seat. Can you imagine? I look upon this as a true miracle.

O! the shops are brimming with beauteous treasures. I would so love to have you here! I would hold on to your arm for dear life as we looked in the windows and stopped for a warm tea in some lovely hotel with leather banquettes and stuffy waiters. You would overtip to impress me, and I would give you great hugs of gratitude for your coming.

My work is awfully labored just now. Sometimes it has the most wondrous life of its own, it fairly pulls me along—rather like wind surfing! At other times, it drags and mopes, so that I despair of ever writing another word or drawing another picture. I've found that if one keeps pushing along during the mopes, out will flash the most exhilarating thought or idea—a way of doing something that I had never seen before—and then, one is off again, and hold on to your hat!

I am doing the oddest things these days. I brought home a sack of groceries from the deli the other evening and, while thinking of our kisses at the airport, put the carton of ice cream on my bed, and my hat in the freezer.

Worse yet, I'm talking to myself on the street, and that won't do at all! Actually, I'm talking to you, but no one would believe that. "Timothy," I said just the other day when looking in the window at Tiffany's, "I do wish you'd unbutton your caution a bit, and get on an airplane this minute!" How did I know a woman was standing next to me? She looked at me coldly before stomping away. I think it was the part about unbuttoning your caution that did it.

I am thrilled to hear of Dooley's singing, and especially that it ran a fine chill up your leg. As for myself, I know something is right when the top of my head tingles. In any case, I am proud with you, and can barely wait to hear him in chorus when I come home on the 23rd.

A box has been sent to all of you, including my good friend, Barnabas, with a delicious tidbit for Jack, as well. If I were to send you everything that reminds me of you, you should straightaway receive a navy cashmere topcoat, a dove-colored Borsolino hat, a peppered ham and a brace of smoked pheasants, a library table with a hidden drawer, a looking glass with an ivory handle, a 17th-century oil of the 12-year-old Jesus teaching in the temple, a Persian hall runner, a lighted world globe, and a blue bathrobe with your initials on the pocket. There!

Oh, and I haven't forgotten Puny. The truffles are for her, and do keep your mitts off them. They are capable of creating any number of diabetic comas.

Would you please have Mr. Hogan send my Muse *subscription to this address? I suppose I could call him up again, but each time I've tried, there's no answer at his newspaper office. I can't imagine how his news tips come in; he must get them all at the Main Street Grill.*

I will close and go searching for my slippers, which have been missing since yesterday morning. Perhaps I should look in the freezer.

With fondest love to you, and warm hellos to Dooley, Barnabas and Jack . . .

He didn't know how he felt about the Borsolino hat, and he already had a topcoat, but the peppered ham sounded terrific.

Humming "Hark, the Herald Angels Sing," he went downstairs, the folded letter crackling in his robe pocket. After supper with Dooley, he would sit in the study and read it again.

It was only the end of November, and a bit early, in his opinion, for stringing lights.

Mitford, however, had no such qualms—winking lights were strung from one end of Main Street to the other; fresh, beribboned greenery was hung on the light poles; and the merchants had stuffed their windows with everything from a Santa Claus with a moving head to a box of free puppies wearing red collars and mistletoe.

A Christmas tree lot was set up on the edge of Little Mitford Creek, across from Winnie Ivey's cottage, and fairly bristled with Fraser firs from the next county. In fact, everywhere he looked, he saw a tree lashed to the top of a car or truck, and an expectant driver headed home to an evening's festivity.

Carols poured from the music system at Happy Endings, enlivening that end of the street, and the town monument was respectfully draped with garlands of boxwood and holly.

Avis Packard filled the wooden bins in front of The Local with green boughs and mountain apples and ran a special on cider in the jug.

Sitting in the rear booth one morning at breakfast, he watched Percy Mosely lift the door of the hatch behind the grill and carry a box of fruitcakes down the stairs. They would be his holiday dessert special, served with Cool Whip and a cherry. Percy hand-lettered the counter sign, himself: You'll Be Nuts About Our Fruitcake.

The Lord's Chapel service of Lessons and Carols was coming straight ahead, and then, all the services and celebrations would be unleashed full force.

Suddenly, there was the quandry of what to give Cynthia, and what he might give Dooley, and yes, this year, he wanted to take gifts to Fernbank. The thought of it all made his head feel light and oddly empty, so that he had to go searching for sensible thoughts, as one might seek after pillowcases blown from a clothesline by high winds.

Several times, he found himself pacing the study in a circle, like a train on a track. The train! It would need to be brought down from the attic, which was a job for Dooley Barlowe. Delegate! That's what he needed to do. And why agonize over what people might want or like? Why not just ask them? He had never done such a thing, but he'd read an article recently that suggested this strategy was loaded with success.

"A jam box," said Dooley.

"A what?"

"A jam box—to listen to music."

What kind of music, he wanted to ask, but didn't—and how loud?

When he talked to Cynthia that evening, she said, "A neckrub! I've bent over these illustrations for such long hours that my neck is positively stiff as a board. A neckrub would be the loveliest gift imaginable."

A neckrub. He had never given such a thing in his life. How far did one have to unbutton one's caution to give a neckrub?

He heard the strain in her voice. "I'm working very hard to get finished, and with my editor in Europe, I feel all at sixes and sevens when it comes to knowing whether it's really working. There's such comfort in having someone say, Yes, that's lovely, or good heavens, Cynthia, what could you be thinking?

"But that's enough about me. What do you want for Christmas, Timothy?"

"I can't say that I haven't thought about it. I want you and Dooley and Barnabas, and a fire in the study, and a splendid dinner, and peace. The peace of having you home again, of seeing the boy finding his own peace, and feeling your contentment in having a rough task behind you. That, and nothing more."

"How dear you are to me."

"Am I? I wish I could imagine why."

"Perhaps if you could imagine why, it would spoil everything."

That, he admitted, was a thought.

"Isn't there any family left for you, except Walter and Katherine? Are we both so nearly alone in the world?"

"My mother had three sisters, but only one had children."

"Then you have other cousins!" She seemed hopeful for him.

"One of Aunt Lily's kids vanished after a divorce, another died in a train accident. At forty-five, Aunt Martha married a man thirty years her senior, and Aunt Peg was what we used to call a spinster. Immediately after college, she had her linens monogrammed with her own initials, declaring she would never marry."

Cynthia laughed. "What became of her?"

"She grew prize asters and headed up the local D.A.R."

"My!" said Cynthia, not knowing what else to say.

"So there you have it. No kin to speak of, except for that rowdy bunch in Ireland, of course. As I recall, Walter and I were related in some way to almost everyone at the tea party."

"I love the Irish!"

"The Irish would love you," he said.

A neckrub and a jam box made a wildly intriguing start to his gift list, he thought as he dialed Miss Sadie.

"What do I want? Oh, dear, I suppose I should spend more time thinking of my wants instead of my needs. I'd be more interesting, wouldn't I, Father?"

"It would be impossible for you to be more interesting."

"Oh, pshaw! Well, let's see." There was a pause. "I haven't the faintest idea! Let me ask Louella. Louella, what do I want for Christmas?"

"New stockin's, new rouge, and a new slip," came Louella's quick response from the background.

Miss Sadie put her hand over the receiver, but he heard the muffled conversation.

"I can't ask my priest for stockings and a slip!"

"Well, then, ask 'im for rouge, you lookin' white as a sheet."

"Louella says ask for rouge, Father. Not too red and not too pink. Oh, dear, this is embarrassing, maybe just some candy from the drugstore, we like nougats."

He sat back on the sofa, laughing. It had never happened in just this way before, but he was definitely getting the Christmas spirit.

He called Dora Pugh at the hardware and asked her to order a sack of special rabbit food; then he called Avis at The Local, and ordered five pounds of Belgian chocolates—four for the nurses at the hospital, and one for Louella. He asked Avis to put together enough food items to fill a dozen baskets, and to reserve his choice beef bones, starting now.

He had no intention of asking Walter what he might like. No, indeed. Walter would want a cashmere sweater, a blazer from Brooks Brothers, or a Montblanc pen. He might very well ask for a lighted world globe on an antique stand, or a leatherbound atlas, or both.

He ordered a desk calendar for Walter's law office, and a leather frame for Katherine, to hold the photo of the three of them in front of the family castle. They had given a pound note to a passing Irish lad, who used Walter's Nikon with the most amazing results. In the color print, in which they had all appeared to be years younger, one could see the crumbling remains of the castle in the background. Even now, he suspected with wry affection, this priceless photograph was swimming about in one of Katherine's jumbled drawers, getting dog-eared.

He went to the bank and retrieved five crisp one-hundred-dollar bills, and stopped by the drugstore for a compact of rouge,

There. He was nearly done, he thought. He whistled all the way to the Grill.

Grinning, Emma stood in front of his desk, and rattled a bag from Wesley's department store.

"It's your Christmas present," she said. "Guess what it is!" She rattled it some more.

Every year, as much as six weeks before Christmas, she couldn't stand it any longer and gave him his gift. Worse still, she never had gifts of her own to open on Christmas Day, as she always tore into a present the minute she received it.

"I can't guess," he said, dolefully. "A tie?"

"Wrong."

"Shaving lotion!"

"You're not trying."

"A solar calculator."

"Ha! Wrong again." She opened the bag and dumped something on his desk. Her presentation skills had never been noteworthy. "A restaurant guide to New York City!"

He looked at it without speaking.

"I know you've never been there before, so when you go visit your neighbor, you'll know how to do." She was as pleased as if she'd given him a Rolex watch.

"Who says I'm going to New York?"

"You mean you're not?"

"I most certainly am not."

"Not even for a *weekend?*"

"You said it."

"You mean you're going to let her stay in that godforsaken place all by herself, with no relief from home? Have you seen the kind of men they have in the publishing business up there? Handsome! Intelligent! *Tall!*"

She used this last jab for all it was worth.

"And what, may I ask, do you know about the publishing business?"

"I do watch TV, you know, which is more than I can say for some people."

"Aha. So men in the publishing business are often on TV?"

"All the time! Very good-looking and smart as whips."

"From what I've seen in the bookstores lately, they're on TV because they have nothing better to occupy their time. As for myself, Emma, I am presently occupied with five holiday services, a music festival, a youth choir concert, a baptism, a party at the hospital, a discussion topic for the men's prayer breakfast, and an overnight visit from the bishop. Thank you for your gift, and please—I beg you—take the morning off."

He had stumbled around in her basement under a 25-watt bulb, plowing through marked boxes. Though some attempt had been made to stack them in alphabetical order, Christmas Lights were nonetheless on top of Mud Room Odds and Ends.

If there was ever a task that wanted teamwork, it was stringing tree lights. When he got the box upstairs to her living room, he saw that she had put them away like so much cooked vermicelli.

It was a full three hours before the bushes on either side of her front stoop were glowing warmly. Life in the little house, at last! He stood back and blew on his frozen hands. Not a car had been up the street; there was not a soul to see the handiwork that cheered the whole neighborhood and proclaimed something wonderful. If it weren't so late, he'd drag Dooley over to look.

He went inside to her living room, switched off the lights on the bushes, and locked the front door. The house was hollow as a gourd without her, yet everywhere he looked, she had made it her own; it couldn't have belonged to anyone but Cynthia. He moved to the mantle and peered at a picture he hadn't seen before. She must have been sixteen or seventeen, and looked out at him with a poignancy that gripped his heart. Her blond hair was long and free, and her eyes full of hope.

"Cynthia," he said aloud, touching the frame.

There were other pictures on the mantle, one of her nephew, most likely, and one of her parents, her mother wearing a flamboyant shawl with fringe, holding on to the arm of a man who looked like Douglas Fairbanks, Jr., in a double-breasted suit. He saw that they were looking away from each other, and the small girl standing beside them seemed forlorn.

He turned the lights off in the living room and walked down the hall to her studio. It was bare of her drawing board and chair and many of her books, yet a light fragrance of wisteria greeted him.

"Cynthia!" he said, feeling a lump in his throat.

Why shouldn't he go to New York for a day or two, after all? It was not inconceivable. He had been far too hard on Emma, in the tone of his voice, chiding her for a foolish idea. But was it foolish?

He might take Cynthia to dinner at some legendary restaurant like Sardi's or the Stork Club. Was the Stork Club still in existence? If not, they could go to the Plaza, which he knew for a fact was still there; he had read about it in a magazine. Perhaps snow would fall, and they would ride in a carriage in Central Park, bundled under a lap robe. Perhaps they would look in the windows at Tiffany's, and perhaps, who knows, they would go inside and he would buy her something wonderful, something that would make the top of her head tingle.

He didn't want to think of the "men in publishing" who might, in actual fact, be seeking her company for dinner or a play or a concert. But why shouldn't she have the company of suave, dynamic movers and shakers, rather than languish in a strange apartment every evening, struggling to earn her very bread?

He stood by the phone in her studio and inhaled the scent that had become as much a part of her as breathing. He removed a card from his billfold, dialed the number written on the back of it, and charged the call to the rectory.

A man answered. It was such a shock to hear the deep, baritone voice, that he nearly hung up.

"I'd . . . like to speak with Cynthia Coppersmith, please."

"Cynthia? Oh, Cynthia's dressing just now, may I have her ring you tomorrow?"

Tomorrow? The word struck him with an odd force.

"Thank you, no," he said, slowly. "She needn't ring me."

CHAPTER FIVE

The Blizzard

He watched a sheep trot briskly toward the nave, trailed by two spotted cows, a donkey, and a camel. He noticed that the camel's hump had slipped and was bumping along the floor, but it was too late to do anything about it.

The wise men were already processing down the aisle to the altar, where the angel Gabriel and a heavenly host stood precariously on stepladders, gazing at the manger scene.

In the quarter-hour it would take for the children to deliver the pageant, he would just pop back to the parish hall for a drink of water and collect his sermon notes.

How extraordinary, he thought, entering the darkened room. It appears there's an angel in my chair.

Four-year-old Amy Larkin was curled up on the cushion of his favorite armchair, the pale organza wings trembling with her sobs.

"Amy," he said, going down on his knees. "What is it?"

She looked at him with streaming eyes and nose. "Them big angels hurted me! They pushed me and runned in front of me and wouldn't let me in my place! I was in the hall and they runned in front of me and . . . and . . ."

"And?"

"I gotted lost!" she wailed.

He lifted her from the chair and consoled her. He was struck by the happiness that flooded him at merely holding a child.

At the end of the pageant, he walked down the aisle at the rear of the procession, carrying Amy in his arms. As the acolytes settled into their places, he turned to the congregation.

"This small angel got separated from the heavenly host. Margaret Ann? . . ." He searched the pews for her mother.

Amy tightened an arm around his neck and announced in a loud voice, "I was with them big angels, and they runned in front of me and left me and I gotted lost!"

"It occurs to me," he said, "that many of us may be leaving small angels behind. As mature Christians, are we neglecting to help those who would benefit from our love and witness?"

He set Amy down as her mother came quickly along the aisle from a rear pew.

"Just a thought," he said, smiling at his flock.

He couldn't help but notice that Olivia was wearing one of her great-grandmother's hats this morning. On her, it was not merely an antique curiosity but lent a definite mystery to her violet eyes and striking beauty.

He saw from the pulpit that Olivia was holding Miss Sadie's hand, while Hoppy took Olivia's and Miss Sadie held tight to Louella's. A fine kettle of fish, he thought.

Though the facts of their kinship would almost certainly remain a family secret, Miss Sadie had told him her plans. "When Olivia gets married, I want to open the ballroom and give them a grand reception! It will be the first time it's been open in more than twenty years, and it will surely be the last. Do pray, Father, for it will demand a great deal of energy from these old bones. I wish I'd known about my great-niece before I got so decrepit. I could have done so much more!"

After the coffee hour, he was rinsing his cup at the sink when Edith carried in a tray of coffee cups. Though several people still mingled in the parish hall, they were alone in the kitchen.

She talked to him as she put the cups in the dishwasher, but she did not look at him. Her voice was cold and quiet. "Timothy, I know you are a man of passion. I've always seen this in you."

She spoke as if she might be reading aloud from a legal document. A fine chill raced through him.

"You know that I want you, Timothy, and I have every reason to believe you want me. I'm expecting you to get over this silly little game of cat and mouse and show me how you really feel."

"Edith . . ."

"You are behaving as if Pat were still alive. Pat is not alive. He is quite dead."

As he stood there, loathing the way the skin stretched over her face, he felt a sudden, warming sense of power, the conviction that he could face and handle anything. There was even a peculiar sense of being taller.

"Edith, there's something you need to know." He heard the ice in his own voice.

"Whatever it is," she said, continuing to load the dishwasher, "don't bore me with your priestly airs. I can't abide any more of your priestly airs."

"Oh, Father!" Ron Malcolm came into the kitchen, putting on his topcoat. "Before I leave, I need to talk to you about a little problem on the hill. Could we step up the hall a minute?"

He could have hugged his pink-cheeked building chairman on the spot. There was, however, a drawback to this providential escape, which he realized as he walked up the hall.

Standing at the sink, he had felt a surge of complete control; he had total confidence that, once and for all, he could tell Edith Mallory what was on his mind and in no uncertain terms.

He chose to believe he had not missed the moment.

The contents of Cynthia's gift box vanished rapidly. Puny shared the truffles with Joe Joe, Barnabas wolfed down the contents of the deli package inscribed with his name, and Dooley disappeared up the stairs with more than a fair share of cookies, candy, nuts, and chips.

His own portion was put in the cupboard, except for the elaborately boxed cookies that he stashed in his nightstand. Though they were utterly sugarless, he found them addictively delicious. He began to look forward to having one with a cup of tea before bed, while dreading the time they would all be eaten.

Don't think of it that way, he told himself. Think of it this way: When the box is empty, she'll be home.

Stuart Cullen would arrive on Thursday for an overnight at the rectory on his way to a meeting down the mountain.

"Th' pope's comin'," he heard Puny announce to her sister on the phone.

"Stuart's not a pope," he told her, "he's a bishop. It's the Catholics that have a pope."

"My grandpa said he never met a Catholic that knew pea turkey about th' Bible . . ."

"Well, then," he said, heading off a diatribe, "let's do something with the guest room. It's been awhile since we had a guest."

"Never had one, period, since I been here. Needs airin' out, turnin' th' mattress, needs flowers—where'll they come from in th' dead of winter? Holly! We could use holly and save you th' florist bill."

"You're a good one! Let's do it. And let's put a copy of the *Muse* by the bed. Stuart likes a good laugh."

Puny would spend Thursday baking bread and a cake, and he would roast a tenderloin and do the potatoes. When he went by the Local, Avis gave him a bottle of Bordeaux, on the house.

"Seein' as it's th' pope," he said.

Dearest Timothy,

We've had snow flurries all morning and everyone on the street below is bundled in furs and hats and mufflers, looking like a scene from It's a Wonderful Life.

But, oh, it is not a wonderful life to be in this vast city alone!

Sometimes I think I'd like to fling it all away and go somewhere warm and tropical and wear a sarong! I would like to live in my body for awhile instead of in my head!

I've been working far too hard and find it impossible to turn off my thoughts at night. I lie here for hours thinking of you and Mitford and Main Street and the peace of my dear house—and then, the little army of creatures in the new book starts marching in, single file.

I review the tail of the donkey I did this morning, the snout of the pig I'm doing tomorrow, the heavy-lidded eyes of the chicken, wondering—should a chicken look this sexy??!

This can go on for hours, until I've exhausted all the creatures and go back and start at the beginning with the tail of the donkey that I'm afraid looks too much like the tail of a collie. That's when I get up and go to my reference books and find I'm wrong—it looks exactly like the tail of a jersey cow!

This is the price I pay for calling a halt to the Violet books. Yet, I should jump out the window if I had to do another Violet book! She, by the way, lies curled beside me as I write, dreaming of a harrowing escape from the great, black dog who lives next door in her hometown.

I'm thrilled at the thought of coming home and spending my second Christmas in Mitford. It is the truest home I've ever known.

I've looked and looked for a letter from you, and if I don't have one soon, I shall ring you up at the Grill and tell you I'm absolutely mad for you, which will make you blush like crazy while all your cronies look on with amusement.

There! That should compel you to write. I'm sure I'll hear by return mail!

With love, Cynthia

He hadn't wanted not to write, but where was the chance to sit down and begin? It was the busiest time of the year for clergy, not to mention the rest of the human horde. Besides, what was he going to do about the question that kept forcing itself in his mind—namely, Who was the man who answered your phone?

If a man answers, hang up! He never dreamed he would be the butt of such a classic, almost vaudevillian joke. The man had spoken her name with a certain familiarity. "Cynthia," he had said, "is getting dressed."

Getting dressed?

He hated this. It made his stomach churn. Number one, he clearly did not know how to have a romantic relationship; he had no idea what the rules were. And number two, he especially did not relish playing games, second-guessing someone, and generally suffering a gut-wrenching anxiety over what he would absolutely not allow to become jealousy.

He supposed the thing to do was write her at once and just say it:

Dear Cynthia,

Who was the man who answered the phone when I called you on Sunday evening?

Maybe that was the way to handle it. He hadn't the time, however, to figure it out. He would simply dash off a note that made no reference to the incident and forget the whole thing. If Cynthia Coppersmith were nothing else, she was guileless. She was not the sort to say one thing and do another; that was only one of the reasons he loved her.

But, then—did he really love her? Had he merely been swept along by the force of her own impulsive feelings?

Blast!

He slung the notebook against the study wall at the moment Dooley walked in.

"Hey," said Dooley, looking at the notebook.

His face burned. "Hey, yourself."

"When're we gittin' a Christmas tree?"

"Right now," he said. "Put on your jacket, and bring your gloves. I'll get the axe."

The snow began on Thursday afternoon.

He and Dooley had trimmed the tree the night before and he had gone home for lunch, simply to look at it again. Yes! The magic had invaded the rectory. He could smell it as he walked in the door, the permeating fragrance of fir and forest and freedom, which refused to be lost among the smells of baking bread. He felt fairly lifted off the floor.

Barnabas dashed from the rug in front of the study sofa and gave him a resounding wallop on the chest with his paws, followed by a proper licking. What more could he have asked of his life? A job to do, a warm home filled with intoxicating smells, a dog of his own, a growing boy, and all of it covered by the astonishing facts of the nativity.

"Come and see the guest room!" Puny called from the top of the stairs.

The room that was so often shut away and cold, with closed heating vents and a frozen toilet seat, was now warm and inviting. Puny had found extra pillows in the closet and covered them with starched shams. She had stolen a braided rug from the foot of his own bed and a rocking chair from the garage. Bottled water sat on the nightstand with a copy of the *Muse*, a worn copy of *Country Life* magazine, and a chocolate truffle from her own gift box from Cynthia.

She had placed a branch of holly atop the picture frame over the bed.

"You don't reckon it could fall on 'im in the night, do you?" She was clearly concerned.

"It'll be fine."

"Don't be mad about me takin' your rug. He's a bishop, you know, and you're just . . ."

"A lowly preacher."

"No offense."

"None taken!"

He reached in his pocket and handed her an envelope. "Merry Christmas! While I'm but a lowly preacher, you, on the other hand, are an angel. And that's a fact."

Her chin quivered as she opened the envelope and removed the hundred-dollar bill. "I jis' knew it!" she wailed, throwing her arms around his neck. "You'll never know how I needed this. My sister got laid off, and her least one is sick and needs shots, and this is jis' th' best thing in th' world!"

"Well, then, quit crying, if you don't mind."

"I cain't he'p it!" she insisted, wiping her eyes with her sleeve. He handed her his handkerchief.

"I jis' ironed that thing. I'll use toilet paper!" she said, fleeing to the bathroom.

The snow, which had begun as a light sprinkle of small flakes, was falling harder as he headed back to the office. "I'd stay home if I was you," Puny advised. "You know they're callin' for a bad storm."

One of his great failings was paying too little attention to the daily news. And since he had once again missed breakfast at the Grill, it was no wonder he knew nothing of immediate importance.

"I'm leavin' early in case th' roads get slick," she said, handing him his hat and gloves. "Be sure'n take that hall rug out of th' dryer. It's th' last thing I'm washin'."

"Consider it done."

"I'd stay in," she said again.

He opened the door and squinted at the sky. "It probably won't amount to much."

"I'd change my shoes, if I was you."

"Ah, well, Puny, you're not me and be glad of it. Otherwise you wouldn't be marrying Joe Joe come June."

He was surprised to see that everything was already well-covered, including the bushes at Cynthia's front door. Putting his hat on, he set off briskly.

Lay the train tracks after Stuart leaves tomorrow morning. Deliver the baskets. Get enough ribbon to wrap the jam box and tie a bow. Take the car to Lew Boyd. Carry the chocolates to the hospital. Remember to thaw two pounds of Russell's livermush to include in his basket.

Should he decorate Cynthia's mantel, put some greenery on her banisters, a wreath on her door? Surely, it would be no fun coming home to a house barren of Christmas greenery.

Passing Evie Adams's house, he saw Miss Pattie at the window, waving; a mere glance told him that Miss Pattie was excited about Christmas. He grinned, waving back. She would be even more excited if she knew her basket included a dozen Snickers bars.

The snow churned icily into his face as he walked. Beautiful though it was, it was not soft and friendly like some mountain snows; it was the sort one endured until it spent itself.

As he turned the corner toward the office, he saw that Mitford was fast becoming one of those miniature villages in a glass globe, which, when shaken and set on its base, literally teemed with falling flakes.

The mail had come late today. He had seen Harold Newland on Main Street, bowed under the weight of his mailbag and bundled above the ears against the cold.

"I won' send you a Christmas card," Emma had said by way of warning. "I've decided to quit sending Christmas cards, period. It's less for Harold to fool with."

"A noble gesture."

"Every little bit helps," she said, pleased.

He was thrilled to find the cream-colored envelope near the bottom of the pile of greeting cards.

Dear Timothy,

Thank you for the note that might have been written to a great-aunt who once invited you to a tea of toast and kippers.

Yours sincerely,
Cynthia

When he tromped home at three o'clock, barely able to see the green awnings of Main Street, he shucked off his coat and hat and sodden loafers and went at once to the phone, his feet frozen, and dialed her number. Busy.

Stuart Cullen appeared at his door with a hat brim full of snow and a black topcoat frosted across the shoulders like so much Christmas *stöllen.*

"Rough going," he said, stomping snow onto the hall rug and removing his gloves and muffler. "I thought I wasn't going to make it. Windshield started icing up. Cars off the road. Miserable! What smells so good? I'm starved! No time for lunch and running late for dinner! I could eat a table leg."

"Chippendale or federal?"

"A little of both, if it's no trouble."

He had never seen his old friend eat so hungrily, even as a penniless seminarian. "It's great to be at your table, Timothy. Some priests I visit can barely boil water."

They were having dinner in front of the fire, careful to watch the TV screen for a weather report.

"I've got to make it down the mountain in the morning, no fail. I'm praying this thing won't last."

"So far, no good," said the rector, nodding toward the window. The outside lights illumined the steadily falling snow. "But—the town crew is good about keeping the roads clear, and the county will be working the mountain tonight. I think you can relax."

"Relax! That may as well be a word from a foreign language. What does it mean, anyway?"

"I don't suppose you'd like the lecture you gave me several months ago about kicking back, taking it easy, slowing down, letting up?"

"I most certainly would not. I was very tough on you, but it worked. In fact, you look the best I've seen you look in years." Stuart took a sip of the Bordeaux. "By the way, you'll never guess who I saw only a week ago."

"Bill Mutton!"

"No, thanks be to God. Peggy Cramer. I must say she's still very beautiful, but . . ." Stuart stroked his chin and looked vague.

But what? Cancer? Some crippling disease? "But what, for Pete's sake?"

"But boring."

"It could be worse."

"Perhaps. In any case, if you'd seen her, I think you'd be able to thank me for the advice I gave you years ago."

"But I do thank you, you know that. It was completely right. I've never once regretted my decision."

"I must say, Martha never bores me—in fact, it's quite the reverse. She studied my schedule and booked us into a villa in Aruba for a week. Aruba! What an astonishing choice. England, I would have thought, or France—but Aruba? I don't even know where it is. She says I need sun and a place where people aren't so serious about themselves. She says I must stop being a bishop for an entire week."

"Tough call."

"Perhaps the chartreuse swim trunks she bought me will help."

Laughing, they raised their glasses.

"To you, Stuart, your good health."

"And you, Timothy, your long life."

It was all in the past; it seemed as if he had never been in love with the petulant creature who had nearly caused the loss of his senses. Yet, he was tempted to ask more about Peggy Cramer. Was she married? Any children? But no, he wouldn't ask.

"She's married to a brain surgeon. Two kids, five grandchildren. She showed me their pictures. Anything else you'd like to know?" Stuart grinned.

Stuart had always had that odd sixth sense.

"You should know that she asked about you. When I told her you never married, she had that oh-poor-baby look on her face, so I preached her a sermon about your dedication, your devotion, your popularity with your parish, ad infinitum. Thank God, it was all true. She was impressed."

The bishop leaned down to scratch Barnabas behind the ears. "So, what's up? Where's the boy?"

"Reading a veterinary journal in his room. He'll be down to greet you in a bit. Doing pretty well, all things considered. Singing. Playing football. A fine and interesting lad. I believe in him."

"What else?"

"Not much. Terribly pushed right now, but who isn't?"

"Are you going to force me to pry?"

"Into what?"

"Into the women in your life."

"If you must know . . . do you remember Edith Mallory?"

"Yes. She gave a dinner party when Martha and I were here a few years ago. Married to a fellow in plaid pants, as I recall."

"Now dead."

"And something tells me she's after you."

"It's as if you're crossing the street, minding your own business, when suddenly you look up and there's an eighteen-wheeler about to nail you."

"It's serious, then."

"And frightening, somehow. She doesn't take no for an answer. What would you do?"

"Nail her first. Tell her hands off."

"She doesn't hear that. She has the deranged notion I'm lusting for her."

"Classic. You should know that. Clergy attract them like flies."

"That's the prognosis, but what's the cure? Frankly, she calls out something violent in me. I think I understand how a woman feels when a man won't back off."

"You'll have to confront her. I've had to do it in my time and not very long ago, either. Sometimes the problem disappears, like so much summer fog. You say she's a new widow. Maybe time will take care of it."

"I don't think so."

"Well, I trust your instincts. Do it soon, and get it behind you. I can tell it's eating at you."

"A bit, yes. Feels good to talk about it. You know how that is . . ."

"Absolutely."

They looked into the fire. A consoling thing, a fire. But clearly, the wind was getting up. The snow churned and swirled against the windows.

"Wonderful sight," said Stuart, turning his attention to the snow.

"I wish I could relax and enjoy it. But I cannot miss that meeting—it could be worth a million to the diocese. Literally."

"We'll get you out of here. You've got a good vehicle. How about a glass of port? Not as old as your host, but getting on in years, nonetheless."

"Splendid! And then to bed."

He delighted to see Stuart Cullen sitting in front of his fire, scratching his dog's head, drinking his port.

"I'm waiting," the bishop said, his eyes gleaming with mischief.

"For what?"

"Blast it, Timothy, a fellow has to beg on bended knee to get a word out of you."

"But I've talked your arm off, as they say."

"You sly rube. Cynthia! Remember her? Tell me everything, and for heaven's sake, don't tell me there's nothing to tell."

"Well. Where to begin?"

"You're going steady?"

"Yes. I asked her, and she said yes."

"And? So?"

Stuart was leagues ahead of Walter and Katherine when it came to sheer nosiness. But what were bishops and friends for? Why was he holding back at this perfect opportunity to spill it all and perhaps get some decent advice? "So, when I called her apartment in New York, a man answered."

He saw that Stuart nearly burst into laughter but controlled himself. "What did he say?"

"He said, 'Cynthia is getting dressed.' " He felt his face burn and the churning in his stomach. Galling. "He said, 'I'll have her ring you tomorrow.' "

"Did you say who was calling?"

"No."

Stuart drummed the table with his fingers, a habit he had always despised. "Ask her about it," he said at last, stopping the drumming.

"I considered that."

"How long have you considered it?"

"Several days."

"Too long! Call and ask her about it right now, why don't you? Then you can put it out of your mind. We can't be accumulating baggage, you and I, especially this time of year."

"Well, then . . ."

"I'll wait right here. I haven't sat in front of a fire, alone, in a hundred years."

When he went upstairs, he looked into Dooley's room and saw that he'd fallen asleep over his veterinary journal.

The phone rang three times before she answered. "Hello?"

His heart hammered. "Cynthia?"

"Timothy?"

"How are you?" That wouldn't do. She didn't care for casual conversation. She'd want something more direct, more specific, like "I miss you dreadfully." "I miss you dreadfully!" he said, meaning it.

"You do?"

He had no intention of saying what followed, not now, anyway. But out it rolled, like so much change from a vending machine: "Who was the man who answered your phone when I called Sunday before last?"

There was a long silence. It might have been the silence of a tomb. Then the phone went dead. Zero.

He jiggled the buttons on the phone cradle. "Cynthia? Cynthia!" She hadn't hung up; he was sure of it. It was definitely the phone. The wind howled and screeched around the corner of his bedroom. That was the culprit! How many times had he lost his phone service in these mountains, from weather of every known kind?

He slouched into the study, stricken.

"She gave you back your frat pin?"

"I asked her the question, and the phone went dead. The wind probably blew a line down somewhere."

"I prayed for you both as you went up the stairs."

"It's hard, being in love."

"No question. Then again, it's hard not being in love. You know how I feel about that, about finding Martha and what it's meant to me. It's meant everything, literally."

"I envy you. It seemed so easy for the two of you. For me—I don't know, I don't seem to . . . understand the process. From here, it looks like other people do it naturally, with ease and grace, while I fall in a ditch every two or three paces. So, in the end, it all seems a great bother. Too much aggravation."

"I have the sense that you haven't really given yourself up."

"Given myself up?"

"You're holding on to something, guarding yourself—just in case. I call to mind what George Herbert said—you know, the English cleric—'Love bade me welcome, yet my soul drew back.' Am I right?"

He thought about it. This was no time for self-delusion. "You may be right. I haven't . . . surrendered anything."

"So, there's a sense in which you're playing with her feelings?"

"Perhaps."

"I can tell you that a woman will find that out, and she will not like it."

"After the man answered, I felt . . . foolish, somehow. I had pitied her up there alone, never going out in the evenings, without friends. It took days to find the heart to write her. It was only a note, the best I could summon. Here was her answer."

He recited the indignant missive about the kippers and toast.

Stuart roared. "I like this woman! I like her better every time you talk about her. She doesn't beat around the bush, and she doesn't let you get away with anything. My friend, a woman like that is one in a thousand, one in a million. You'd better hunker down and be willing to give yourself, Timothy, or you could lose her."

"I think about the thing with Peggy . . . that was a stunning blow, all of it."

"Right, it was. But it was also more than thirty years ago. Why are you still sporting the bruise from that encounter? Good Lord, man, we've all been knocked around. Wasn't Susan Hathaway my Peggy Cramer?"

"Possibly."

"No possibly about it. I could have taken a dive along with you. Right into the pool, with no water. I can still break a sweat just thinking about it. But I don't hold it against myself, and the Lord has thrown the whole matter as far as the east is from the west."

"Bottom line, Stuart . . ."

"Bottom line? . . ."

"Marriage. That's what it all comes to. At my age, it's all or nothing at all. There's no in-between."

"Quite. But look here, in-between is precisely where you seem to have stationed yourself. Going steady, but no real commitment. Loving, but afraid of the future."

Barnabas yawned and rolled over on his side before the fire.

"Don't kid yourself," Stuart said. "It's not easy for other people, either. Martha and I had our own struggles. I was forty-nine, she was forty-seven, and neither of us had ever been married. But we knew, Timothy. I knew I wanted the shelter of this woman, and God only knows what she wanted in me, but apparently she's found it.

"What do you want, in the long run? To end up tottering around on a walker, muttering to yourself, having missed the bliss and the hell of love?"

"The bliss and the hell. I'm afraid of both those things. I never thought of that before. I've never admitted such a thing in all my life." He felt astonished to discover something so new, and raw, in himself.

"Good! We're getting somewhere. This woman wants a fun-loving, unpredictable relationship, and who does she pick? A serious-minded, rather predictable fellow who, just underneath the zipper, is everything she's looking for."

"But is it all worth . . . unzipping for, if you'll pardon the expression?"

Stuart smiled. "I've found it to be so," he said.

At six o'clock in the morning, the Bronco was fairly buried. Though the streets had been cleared, the plow had knocked an even greater pile of snow onto the vehicle.

The phones were working again. He called Rodney at the police station.

"Any passage down the mountain?"

"If you're goin', better hop to it. Th' roads are pretty clear, but more snow's comin'. They're closin' th' mountain at eight o'clock. I just got a call."

He and Dooley worked with the bishop under the light of a street lamp for a full hour, shoveling the car out. Bundled to the eyes, Stuart got in the Bronco. "Pray for me!" he called before closing the door. Then he turned his car around in the frozen street and disappeared in a cloud of vapor from the exhaust.

White on white, as far as the eye could see. But a million bucks was a million bucks.

They stomped back into the house as a gray dawn broke.

Around noon, the snow started falling again.

Barnabas bounded to the hedge, making a path wide enough for a small sleigh, did his business, and returned at once. White on black, racing through the house, shaking snow from backdoor to front. "Good fellow!"

"Good ol' pooper," said Dooley.

Lord, he prayed, don't let us lose power. There was enough wood in the garage to last two days, maybe less, and no one would be hauling logs in weather like this.

He set the Christmas baskets on the counter, finished filling them, and tied the bows, then looked for the fur-lined boots that laced to his knees. He mustn't sit around mooning, as Puny called it. He needed to move along smartly. No argument could convince Dooley to accompany him.

"Listen, buster," he snapped, "you want Santa Claus, you'll help me take it to others." He was inevitably cross in foul weather. It worked, however. They each carried two baskets, leaving the fifth behind until the weather cleared. There would be no walking along the creekbank to visit Homeless Hobbes today, nor would his Buick get farther than the sidewalk, if he bothered to back it out of the garage.

At Evie Adams's house, he warned Dooley. "We mustn't get Miss Pattie started or we'll be here all day."

Dooley looked daggers at him as Evie opened the door.

"Oh, Father!" she said, bursting into tears. "I'm so glad to see you! And Dooley! How you're growing! Come in, come in. Oh, do come in!" He felt rather like the pope.

There was only one thing to make of her tears. "What's Miss Pattie done now?" he asked. They were standing in a puddle.

"Crawled under the bed and won't come out!"

That ought to be a godsend, he thought.

"Under there, singing to beat the band, and won't come out unless I buy her a baby doll with long, blond hair and a blue pinafore. Where am I going to get a baby doll in weather like this—much less in a blue pinafore?"

"Would you like me to talk to her?"

If looks could kill, Dooley Barlowe would have dropped him right there, dead as a doornail.

At the sagging Porter mansion, he had a word of caution. "Don't eat anything here."

"I'm about t' starve t' death," Dooley said, glaring at the rector.

"You'll live. After all, you're full of baloney."

"Real funny."

"I thought so."

Uncle Billy opened the door. "I'll be et f'r a tater if it ain't th' preacher! Rose, come an' look! It's th' preacher an' th' boy!"

He heard some rustling sounds, and Miss Rose appeared, looking fierce. "The preacher? What's he want?"

"Wants t' give us Santy Claus, looks like."

"Tell him to come in, then."

They dripped a large puddle in the foyer, where a hand-carved banister railing lay on the floor exactly where it had fallen years ago. He looked up at the portrait of the handsome, intense Willard, who was almost certainly turning over in his grave.

Dooley handed them a basket stuffed with fruit, nuts, candy, a tinned ham, and a pecan pie. "Merry Christmas!" he said.

"Looky here, Rose," said the old man, obviously elated. "Ain't this th' beat? Well, come on back to th' warm place. We'll all be froze t' popsicles standin' here. Rose baked a cobbler that'll melt in y'r mouth. You'll have t' set an' have a piece."

"Oh, no, no, Uncle Billy. Can't stay, have to run. They're calling for eight inches tonight and high winds. Have to get along."

"I'm sure this boy would like a piece," said Miss Rose, looking fiercer. "Preachers don't eat like the rest of us. All they like is fried chicken."

"I b'lieve it's th' Methodists as like chicken," said Uncle Billy.

Miss Rose grabbed Dooley by the sleeve. "Come along! Let these men stand an' jaw 'til th' cows come home. We'll have us a bite to eat. I like boys!" She grinned, revealing a frightening display of dental conditions.

Dooley looked back in desperation as she hauled him through the tunnel of newspapers that packed the dining room toward the heated apartment at the rear.

Ah, well, no rest for the wicked and the righteous don't need any, the rector thought, following meekly.

They stomped up the hill to Fernbank, against an increasingly bitter wind, and down the winding driveway that was thigh-deep in snow.

Miss Sadie gave Dooley a set of shoelaces, wrapped in aluminum foil and tied with a ribbon, as they stood in another puddle in another foyer.

"Father, I'm so upset. I ordered you the nicest can of mixed nuts, but if this weather keeps up, UPS will never get through."

"Don't even think about it," he said.

"Louella, why couldn't we just give him a check for the value of the nuts?"

"You askin' th' elf, Miss Sadie. You th' Santy!"

"You wait right here," she said, leaving the room and returning with a check. In her spidery handwriting, she had made out a check for five dollars and thirty-two cents. "Merry Christmas!" she said brightly. "Just in case the nuts don't get through! I didn't include shipping and handling, but I did add state tax."

He literally dragged himself to the door of Betty Craig's snow-bound blue house. It was exhausting to walk through heavy drifts, up-hill and down, hither and yon, and keep a smiling face while crawling under beds and eating cobbler you didn't want.

He had never been so glad to see the rectory, which looked like a cottage on a Christmas card, set as it was into a deep bank of snow with a drift of wind-tossed smoke rising from the chimney.

"I'm give out," Dooley announced at supper, over a fried bologna sandwich. "You can git yourself somebody else next year. That's church stuff. You need to git you some church people t' carry that stuff around."

"My friend, you are church people."

"I wouldn't be if you didn't make me."

"I make you?"

"I reckon you think I'd go if you didn't make me."

"Well, then, I'll quit making you. Why don't you just stop going?"

"I might."

"Nobody should have to go to church against their will." Some-times he had to, but that was beside the point.

At a quarter to seven, Dooley came into the study. "I'm outta here," he said vaguely, putting on his down jacket.

"Out of here to where, may I ask?"

"Church. Choir practice."

"You don't have to go, you know."

"Yeah. Well, bye."

"Bye, yourself."

He went at once to the phone and dialed her number. He was too tired to speak, but it had to be done. No answer.

Nobody but Dooley and Jena Ivey had shown up at the Youth Choir rehearsal.

At eight, Martha Cullen called, distraught. Stuart had not arrived at the meeting, nor had he called home.

"I bought him a car phone, but he said it was too elitist, and it's still in the box. Timothy, I'm beside myself. He always calls."

"He's fine, I'm sure of it. Chances are he's stranded on the side of the mountain. Perhaps there's been an accident. It can back cars up for miles."

"I've protected him so, that I sometimes think of him as a child. I confess this to you, Timothy. I'm not proud of it, but I sometimes treat him like a mindless boy, God forgive me."

"Whatever you're doing, it must be right. You should be a fly on the wall and hear him sing your praises. Don't worry. Please! Call me when you hear."

He got a call from the adult-choir director, who was stranded at the foot of the mountain. Would he contact everyone and cancel the rehearsal?

The head of the Altar Guild phoned to say that forty-four memorial poinsettias had been left by the florist on the church stoop and had frozen solid.

The winds increased. Walter rang.

"We hear you're under three feet of snow, for Pete's sake."

"Nearly. It's losing power that concerns me—there're so many old people in this community . . ."

"Including yourself, of course."

"Ha. There goes your cashmere jacket for Christmas."

"Have you gone through any of the family papers yet?"

"What do you think?"

"You've been too busy, you haven't gotten to it, you apologize for the long delay, but you'll get right on it after the first of the year."

"I couldn't have put it better myself."

"We're off to a party. Keep in touch. Stay warm. Best to Dooley."

"Did the package arrive?"

"Under the tree."

"Great. I love you, you big lout."

"Same here, Cousin. Katherine sends her love. Let's have another trip together in the new year. By the way . . ."

He could hear it coming. To avoid an interrogation about his love life, he put his hand over the phone and yelled, "Be right there!"

"Have to go, Walter. So long. Merry Christmas! God bless you!"

The wind roared around the house, moving the curtains and rattling pictures on the wall.

The evening news reported that major airports across the state were closed, the interstate highways were closing, and the word for the storm was officially "blizzard."

"One of nature's most life-threatening storms is the winter blizzard," said a newscaster, standing hatless in the TV station parking lot, looking bewildered.

The houses of Mitford were frozen like so many ice cubes in a tray. Lights shone from windows onto the drifting snow, as leaden skies made even the daylight seem one long dusk. Everywhere, spirals of chimney smoke were violently snatched by the wind and blown through the streets, so that the stinging drafts of arctic air contained a reassuring myrrh of wood smoke.

The high winds did not cease. In some places, snowdrifts covered doors and windows so completely that people had to be dug out by more fortunate neighbors. Cars that had been abandoned on the street appeared to be the humps of a vast white caterpillar, inching up the hill toward Fernbank.

Percy Mosely lived too far from town to make it to the Grill and open up, but Mule Skinner, who lived only a block away, managed to open the doors at seven on Tuesday morning, brew the coffee extra-strong, and fry every piece of bacon on hand. J.C. Hogan, who was waiting out the storm in his upstairs newspaper office, came down at once. The weary town crew, unable to start the frozen diesel engines of their snowplows, were the only other customers.

Unlike most snows, this one did not bring the children to Baxter Park. The sleds stayed in garages, the biscuit pans shut away in cupboards. This was a different snow, an ominous snow.

Martha called. Stuart was safely ensconced in a motel outside Holding, after being stuck on the mountain behind a brutal wreck for five hours and stranded in a drift on the side of the road for three.

He learned that long-distance calls could not be received because of overloaded circuits, and there was still no answer at Cynthia's apartment.

The winds howled and moaned without letup. He could see the drapes move in the living room but couldn't see across the street for the brilliance of the whirling snow.

He checked the kitchen drawer for candles and matches, the flashlight for batteries, and the lantern for kerosene. He refused to look at the woodpile.

In just two days, she would be home. Surely, the weather would change, she would get through, and she would rush toward him from the little commuter plane, laughing, her eyes blue as cornflowers.

The very last thing to think about was who had answered when he called.

At four o'clock, he discovered the telephone lines were again dead.

Two hours later, he put the kettle on to boil. At the moment he turned the stove dial, the lights went out. It was as if he, himself, had pulled a switch that brought the whole thing down into darkness.

CHAPTER SIX

Water Like a Stone

On Sunday, the alarm rang at five o'clock.

He lay there, frozen as a mullet, listening to the ceaseless roar of the wind. There would be no heat in the church, nor any sensible way for the congregation to get there. He had never before missed a Sunday service because of weather.

In his mind, he counted the logs in the garage. He thought he could count six or seven and not a stick more.

"I'm freezin' m' tail," said Dooley, who appeared in sweatpants and a ski jacket and crawled under the covers. Barnabas yawned and pushed in between them.

"I ain't goin' t' no church," said Dooley. His teeth were chattering.

"Me either."

"What're we goin' t' do?"

If there was anything he didn't like about having a boy in the house, it was feeling he should have all the answers. "Blast if I know," he said, huddling against Barnabas. "What do you think we should do?"

"You could get up an' fry some bacon and baloney."

"How? By rubbing two sticks together?"

"Poop, I done forgot." He soon heard Dooley's whiffling snore.

Hello, Cynthia? Timothy. How's the weather up there? His mind turned once again to what he might say, if only he could reach her.

"Don't start that nonsense," he said aloud. Think, instead, of how Miss Sadie and Louella and Uncle Billy and Miss Rose will be faring on this miserable and wretched morning, and pray, for God's sake, for their welfare.

He crossed himself and prayed silently. Assist us mercifully, O Lord, that among the changes and chances of this violent storm, your people may ever be defended by your gracious and ready help . . . Hello, Cynthia? Timothy. We were cut off the other day, and when I tried to reach you again, there was no answer. Then the lines went down for three days, and so, how are you? . . . O Lord, create in me a clean heart, and renew a right spirit . . . Hello, Cynthia, Timothy. How are you?

There was only one way to knock such idiocy in the head. He got out of bed and fell to his knees on a floor that felt like an ice rink.

The fire was fairly crackling, and he closed his mind to the fact that its cheer would be short-lived.

"This is neat."

"Bologna to die for," he said, picking two thick, browned slices out of the skillet with a fork and putting them on Dooley's toast. "Eat up, my friend, and don't hold back on the mustard." As for himself, he hadn't tasted such bacon since he was a Scout. He looked at their camp mess spread around the hearth. Not a bad way to live, after all.

The wind had cast torrents of snow against the study windows, where it froze solid, shutting out the light. They might have been swaddled in a cocoon, filled with an eerie glow.

He took a swallow of the coffee that he'd brewed over the fire in a saucepan. "Whose name did you draw at school? I've been meaning to ask."

"I drawed ol' Buster's name, but I didn't git 'im nothin'."

"Why not?"

"I traded for somebody else's name."

"Really?"

"Yeah. Jenny's."

"Aha."

"Had t' give ol' Peehead Wilson a dollar and a half to swap."

"Not a bad deal, considering."

"I got 'er a book."

"A book! Terrific. Best gift out there, if you ask me."

"About horses."

"She likes horses?"

"She hates horses."

"I see."

"So I got 'er this book so she can git t' know 'em and like 'em."

"Good thinking, pal."

They drew closer to the brightness of the fire.

"You like ol' Cynthia?"

"Yes. Very much."

"You love 'er?"

"I . . . don't know. I think so."

"How come you don't know?"

He really did dislike feeling that he had to have all the answers. "I don't know why I don't know! Do you love Jenny?"

Dooley looked forlorn. "I don't know."

"One thing's for sure," said the rector, "this is the dumbest conversation I've heard since the vestry made its new ruling on toilet paper."

In some places, the drifts were twenty feet high, and everywhere ice gleamed upon the snow like glaze on a sheet cake.

It was impossible to walk in this glittering ice kingdom, nor was there any standing up on the slick crust that lay over the ground.

Twice, he put on multiple layers of clothing and his warmest boots, determined to check on Miss Rose and Uncle Billy and fight his way up the hill to Fernbank, but the ice turned him back before he was scarcely clear of the garage. Attempting to leave by the front door, he made it down the porch steps but slipped and careened down the bank, slamming into the telephone pole at the sidewalk.

They stuffed towels along the sills of the aged windows and at the base of every door. They kept the faucets open, to delay, at least, the freezing of the pipes. In the garage, they found a ladder-back chair intended for the rummage sale and a set of decrepit pine folding tables.

"We'll use the chair tonight and save the tables for tomorrow," he said, unconsciously looking around his own study for firewood.

He was finding that Dooley Barlowe could go the mile. He might be a complainer when life was soft, but he knew how to be tough when the chips were down.

"You're OK, buddy."

"When's ol' Cynthia comin' home?"

"Day after tomorrow."

"I bet she ain't."

And what gift would he give her if she did come home? As was often the case, he'd left a crucial decision until the last minute, hoping the solution would fall out of the sky.

He thought of his mother as they dozed on the sofa under piles of blankets and the radiant heat of one large dog. She had loved Christmas like a child.

When he went home from seminary, most of the room he slept in would be filled with boxes, wrapping paper, and endless yards of her signature white satin ribbon.

The armoire would be stuffed with gifts she'd been making and buying all year, and the house would smell the way she loved it best—of cinnamon and cloves, oranges and onions, coffee with chickory, and baking bread.

She would expect him to bring his friends and make the house merry, and when they begged her to sit down at the table and stop serving, she would always say, "But it's my joy!"—and really mean it.

Peggy Cramer had been with them for his mother's last Christmas, and Tommy Noles and his fiancée, and Stuart Cullen had called long-distance. He remembered the call because Stuart had spent nearly an hour talking to his mother and making her laugh as she sat by the wall phone in the kitchen.

He automatically loved anyone who made his mother laugh.

He had given her the brooch that year, a lovely thing, costing far more than he could afford, but when he saw it in the jeweler's window, he knew this was the gift that must try to convey his gratitude for the years of encouragement, for the fact that she had believed in him from the beginning, no matter what his father said to the contrary.

One small amethyst brooch with pearls had been required to speak volumes. Above all, he wanted it to say, Thanks for your support when you, more than anyone, wanted me to become a Baptist minister and I did the unthinkable and became an Episcopal priest.

That had been the coldest of affronts to her family and even to her own heart. But she loved him and stood with him, as stalwart as an armed regiment.

"Mother," he had said, "there's no way I can tell you . . ."

"You needn't try," she told him. "I can see it all in your eyes."

He looked at Dooley, asleep under the mountain of covers. It was almost this time last year that he had run away, racing down the mountain in a freezing wind on his Christmas bicycle, desperate to see the face of his own mother.

He prayed for Pauline Barlowe and the children scattered like so many kittens from a box.

"In the bleak midwinter, frosty wind made moan . . ."

He heard the faintest singing somewhere and sat up and listened. Barnabas growled.

"Earth stood hard as iron, water like a stone . . .

"Snow had fallen, snow on snow, snow on snow . . .

"In the bleak midwinter, long ago . . ."

Someone was singing his nearly favorite Christmas hymn, but who? And where was it coming from?

Barnabas bounded off the sofa, barking. "Angels in the garage!" he shouted, slipped his feet into frozen shoes.

A soprano and a baritone from the choir had pulled a sled to his house, wearing hobnail boots that bit into the ice. Lashed to the sled was a load of seasoned oak, and while it was no half-cord, it would give them respite.

They might as well have parked a Mercedes in the garage and presented him with the key. Gleeful, he and Dooley picked a log and split it into kindling.

Next, they chose a second log, as fuel for their supper.

Then they broke the chair into pieces, agreeing to save the folding tables for a Christmas Day blaze.

Things were definitely looking up, though there was no news from the outside world to prove it. The last report, the baritone said, was of helicopters dropping food into the coves and a forecast of freezing rain for tomorrow and the next day.

There was enough oak left to heat the study tomorrow, giving them a chance to write and read, instead of sitting in a frozen stupor, watching their breath vaporize on the air. He could not remember when his heart had felt so full of ease. A load of wood had been delivered and, with it, the spirit of Christmas.

"You know this one," he said to Dooley, who was laying kindling over the crumpled newspaper. "Sing with me! 'What can I give him, poor as I am? If I were a shepherd, I would bring a lamb . . . if I were a wise man, I would do my part . . .' " Hesitantly, Dooley joined in. " 'Yet what can I give him . . . give my heart.' "

He held out hope until the morning she was to arrive. It had rained the day before, and now, at dawn, he heard the relentless freezing rain still rapping sharply against the windows. Flights would be canceled, airports shut down.

He prayed they would be able to go forward with the hanging of the greens and with the afternoon and midnight services on Christmas Eve. After the death of winter had lain upon them like a pall, they needed the breathing life of the Child; they were starving for it.

He continued to pray for Miss Rose and Uncle Billy, Miss Sadie and Louella, and for all who were elderly, sick, or without food or heat. He was bold to ask that angels be sent, and step on it.

He was going to the kitchen door to let Barnabas out when he did an odd thing. Without thinking, and out of sheer habit, he turned on the dial of the burner under the kettle.

The television blared in the study. The light came on in the hall. The kitchen radio announced a Toyota sale.

He shouted, "Hallelujah!" Dooley hollered, "Hot dog!" Barnabas barked wildly. And the washing machine went into a spin cycle in the garage.

He would never bet on it happening again, but he felt he had somehow managed to shut down, and then restore, power to an entire county.

When the phone rang, he jumped as if shot at.

"Father! I just had to talk to somebody . . ."

"Margaret Ann . . . what is it?"

"The most awful thing has happened. I hid all of Amy's Santa Claus at Lisbeth's house, and I was going to pick it up on Christmas Eve. Well, Father, you know that awful hole my sister lives in down by the town cemetery, and now she's frozen in like . . . like . . ."

"A stick in a popsicle."

"Yes! And there's no way I can get my car out of the yard, Father, much less make it to Lisbeth's. What can I do? It's the prettiest little doll you ever saw, it wets like crazy, it cost somethin' awful, and no check from her daddy since Easter. Oh, and there's a little pink wagon with lights on it, and a nurse set, and a blue dress, and socks with lace. Oh, Father!" She was crying. "Amy is *counting* on Santa Claus!"

"I'll see what I can do. Give me a half hour."

Ron Malcolm's son was out, helping the town crew spread salt and slag. Lew Boyd's Esso was closed tight as a clam. The young man who once raked his leaves could not be found.

He called the baritone. "Is there any way I could borrow your hobnail boots for a couple of hours? Terrific. Just leave them inside your porch door." He called the soprano. "What size are your hobnails? Perfect. We won't come in, just set them on the stoop."

"Dooley," he shouted over a TV ball game, "can you come here a minute?"

"I ain't doin' this n' more," said Dooley, whose face was red as a lobster. He stomped along, carrying a doll and a wagon in a sack on his back. The rector's sack contained a dress, socks, and nurse's set, plus the doll carriage Margaret Ann had forgotten to mention.

"You fall and bust your butt," said Dooley, "and you cain't preach. I bust mine, I cain't play football."

"Good thinking." He had to stomp hard on the crust of ice with each step in order to keep from falling. He would pay for this by morning in every aching muscle. "We've only got three more blocks to go. Just keep in mind those steaks sizzling in the skillet . . . those oven-roasted potatoes with all the sour cream you can eat . . . and that triple-chocolate cake, sent by some well-meaning parishioner before the storm, which is currently hidden in the freezer. You can devour the whole thing!"

Dooley grunted.

The Main Street Grill was dead as a doornail, which was a sorry sight to behold.

"Yo, Santy Claus!" called one of the town crew, who was sliding along Main Street, trying to dump salt.

"Bring me a dolly!" hollered another. "Blond hair, blue eyes—and a red pickup with a CD player!"

"Merry Christmas, Father! Merry Christmas, Dooley!" The crew boss grinned and waved. "A package of fifties will suit me just fine, thanks."

"We'll get right on it, boys. Clean your chimneys."

All the reports were in.

Miss Sadie's bedroom had stayed warm as toast with a kerosene stove. Louella slept on the sofa at the foot of Miss Sadie's bed, and they had lived off Nabs, Cheerwine, white bread, Vienna sausages, and cereal. Keeping the gallon of milk cold had been easy—Louella merely raised the window and set it outside on the roof. For recreation, they had looked through Miss Sadie's picture albums and scrapbooks, read the Bible aloud, and sung Christmas carols, seeing who could remember the most words.

"The only thing missing was a hot bath!" said Miss Sadie, "but we're making up for it."

Miss Rose and Uncle Billy had spent a good deal of time in bed. "Th' only trouble, don't you know, is Rose sometimes pees in th' bed, it bein' too cold t' git up an' all. I wouldn't want you to tell that, Preacher."

"Absolutely not."

"We had a big fight about a box of crackers. Rose wanted th' whole thing. Boys howdy, that was a predicament. But I'd saved back a can of sardines, don't you know, and pretty soon we got t' talkin' about it and turned out we split what we each had right down th' middle, so I cain't complain. You don't want t' git low on food with Rose around, no sir."

"I hear you."

"Boys, that basket you delivered over here saved th' day. There it was, a-blowin' like jack outside, and us settin' in bed eatin' honey-baked ham and soppin' th' sauce with yeast rolls. But I'm glad it's over."

"Amen. Stay warm, and don't go out. It's still slick as hog grease on the streets."

"An' bring th' boy back, anytime. Rose likes 'im, wants t' bake 'im a pan of cinnamon stickies."

Since Homeless Hobbes had no phone, he couldn't inquire. But then, he supposed he didn't need to. The richest man in town was probably faring better than anybody, with a wood stove that kept the place like the inside of a toaster and cooking skills that could turn a creekbed rock and a cup of snow into a banquet.

And how had Evie Adams pushed along with Miss Pattie, and Betty Craig with Russell Jacks?

According to Evie, the snow had done wonders for her mother, who bundled up in a rummage-sale ski suit and sat by the window for days counting snowflakes. "One hundred thousand and forty-three!" she announced proudly, showing Evie the totals in her dead husband's sales ledger. "It was like a vacation," said Evie. "I kept a fire going and got to read a detective story all the way through!"

The report on Russell Jacks was not so good. Just when he was considering whether Russell should return in the spring to his house in the junkyard, the sexton had gone out in the snow against Betty Craig's wishes and fallen down while fetching in wood.

"He must have laid out there close to twenty minutes before I missed him!" said his distressed nurse. "I could just kill the old so-and-so!"

He felt immeasurably relieved. Keeping Russell at Betty's was costing Ron Malcolm and himself four hundred dollars a month, but every time he thought of the old man going back to that ramshackle house on the edge of town, he knew Dooley would have to go with him. That would not be good, for more reasons than he cared to consider.

He prayed for Russell's recovery and Betty's sanity.

"The storm of the century," as the media called it, had traveled along the East Coast to New York, where snow accumulation was up to five feet and still piling on. All circuits, he discovered again, were busy.

"Merry Christmas, Timothy!"

Could it be? It was Edith Mallory, sounding different somehow. "I'm sending Ed down with a little something for you and the boy tonight after the five o'clock. Two services on Christmas Eve can be exhausting, and you surely won't want to cook."

"Oh, no, please, we . . ."

"Do let me have this little Christmas joy," she said pleasantly. "I'll be sending baskets around to others down your way, as well."

"It's too good of you, Edith. Why don't you let someone else have ours, someone . . ."

"Less fortunate? Well, perhaps next year! Actually, I'd like to talk with you about the less fortunate. I think I'm ready, Timothy, to do what you recommended!"

"And what's that?"

"I want to help the Children's Hospital in Wesley. I know it's your pride and joy. But we'll talk about it soon. Since the storm, I've been just deluded with calls, people wishing me happy holidays . . ."

"Yes, and let me be one of them. Happy holidays, Edith!"

He felt queasy when he hung up. Was she undergoing some odd conversion? Did he sense she may be willing to back off and leave him in peace?

He had never minded a few empty pews if the people were filled with the Spirit. The faithful remnant that attended on the eve of the Christ child's birth celebrated with joy.

The great joy commingled freely with the smaller joys. A warming trend is predicted! The sun will come back! The roof didn't leak, the pipes didn't burst, we made it through!

He had seldom seen such hugging and kissing, and over it all, the green wreaths adorned with white gypsophila and the candles flickering on the windowsills lent rapt hosannas of their own.

"Joy to the world, the Lord is come . . ."

He prayed that the earth might truly receive her King.

Ed Coffey passed them on their way home from the five o'clock and insisted they get in. With the tire chains lashing the street, Ed drove to the rectory, then walked them to the door, carrying the basket.

As he and Dooley unpacked it on the kitchen counter, he felt compelled to say something positive. Here was a woman, after all, who had sent food still warm from the oven to feed two hungry men on a cold night.

"Mrs. Mallory is . . . very thoughtful to do this," he said, unwrapping a steaming plum pudding.

Dooley looked at him as if he'd lost his mind. "She's a dern witch."

"Is that so?"

"I hate 'er ol' butt."

"Please rephrase that," he said, meaning it.

"I don't like 'er. She seems two-faced t' me, sayin' one thing, doin' another."

"Really?" Roast beef, done to perfection.

"Said she'd give th' Sunday school a barbecue—ain't done it. Said she'd send us t' Grandfather Mountain—ain't done it."

"Hasn't done it."

"Somebody said she was after you. Said she'd like t' git you in th' bed."

"Who said that?"

"I don't know. Somebody. Is 'at right?"

"Let's just say that I have no intention of going to bed—or anywhere else—with Mrs. Mallory."

"Gittin' ahold of her'd be like gittin' ahold of a spider."

"Please. Forget what you heard. And no matter what you think, be respectful when you see her, regardless. Understand?"

He must have understood, for he said something the rector rarely heard: "Yes, sir."

"If this is what it's like to go steady," he muttered, "no wonder I waited so long to do it."

He dialed her number again. The circuits were still busy, as the storm raged through New York state and headed out to the Atlantic.

People thronged to the midnight service, as if the manager were the last way station on earth. Though patches of ice still gleamed lethally throughout the village, Ron Malcolm's son had doused the church walks with salt and sand, giving many the first sure footing they'd had in days.

Deprived of their pre-Christmas concert, the Youth Choir sang with such gleeful energy it fairly rocked the nave.

" 'Go tell it on the mountain, over the hills and everywhere. Go tell it on the mountain, that Jesus Christ is born . . .' "

"Go tell it on *this* mountain—every day, in every way," he said at the close of the service, "and go in peace, to love and serve the Lord."

"Amen!" said the congregation, revived and wide-awake, though it was hours past their bedtime.

Several parishioners had pressed envelopes into his hand. Others had brought cookies, cranberry bread, and a can of his known favorite, mixed nuts, so that he walked home carrying a full paper sack. Not a few had said what his parish was never too shy to say, "We love you!"

In other years, he had often felt a great fatigue after the midnight service. Tonight, he could have shouted through the streets, blown a trumpet, waved a banner. His Christmas adrenaline was up and pumping, and so was Dooley's.

"Well done, old fellow!" he said as they headed toward the rectory. "I heard you hang those high notes in 'Once in Royal David's City.' " He put his arm around the boy's shoulders. Here was another miracle, walking right beside him. "Why don't we open just one present tonight?"

"You ain't goin' t' like what I'm givin' you."

"That's what you said last year, and haven't I carried that glasses case with me everywhere, even to Ireland and back?" When would this boy stop shooting himself in the foot? "I'll tell you one thing—you'll jolly well like what I'm giving you."

Dooley looked up and grinned.

Sitting on the floor in the study, the winking tree lights reflected in every window, he unwrapped the book on veterinary medicine. It was true. He didn't like what Dooley gave him.

"Now you can doctor Barnabas if he gits sick."

"Aha."

"You can doctor ol' Vi'let if she's tryin' t' puke up a mouse."

"I'll let you handle that."

"Looky here. It tells how you can fix up Jack if he gits worms or mange."

"You're the doctor in the house, not me."

"Yeah, but I might not always be here."

"Not always be here? And where might you be?"

"When Grandpa gits well, I guess we'll be goin' back t' 'at ol' house, if it ain't fell in."

He could tell this had been on Dooley's mind for some time, but he hadn't been wise enough to sense it. "We're going to do something about that, but I don't know what exactly. I want you to stay here, for things to stay the way they are."

"Good," said Dooley. "Where's my present?"

He was sitting on the side of the bed, taking his shoes off, when the phone rang. It would be Walter, who often phoned after the late service. "Merry Christmas, potato head."

"Timothy?"

"Cynthia!"

There was an awkward pause.

"Are you all right?" she said. Her voice sounded new to him somehow.

"Yes! Yes, we're fine. A rough go in some places, but fine. I turned your faucets on to drip and put the thermostat at sixty-two . . . shouldn't be any problem. I think the worst is behind us."

"Thank you. I appreciate it."

"I thought you were Walter. That was . . . ah, what I used to call him." He could tell the conversation was having trouble pushing off, like a sled poised at the top of a hill but snared on a rock.

"I hope you're not disappointed that it isn't Walter."

"Why, no. Certainly not! And you—are you all right?"

"I haven't had any spills on icy sidewalks, or power outages, or empty cupboards, if that's what you mean. But my heart is not all right—not in the least," she said coolly.

He felt his own heart pound as the sled pushed off. He sensed that this would be Olympic tobogganing, as opposed to a playful dash down Old Church Lane on a biscuit pan.

"Why don't we start where we ended, all those days ago?" she said. "You were asking me a question."

That question, once so alive in his thoughts, was now a fossil. He was embarrassed even to think how peevish it would sound.

"Yes, well. It's really not worth asking again."

"It must have been worth something—it cost days of trying to figure out the answer.

"The answer, Timothy, is that the man you spoke with on the phone was my editor and friend, James McNeely. He came back from

Europe on business in New York, where he rang the bell of his own apartment, only to find me in a bathrobe, with my face set like papier-mâché in a green mud pack. He needed something in his desk and said that if I'd consider washing my face, he'd take me to dinner.

"It was terribly late, but I was wild to be out of here and have the lovely privilege of talking about my work to somebody who not only understands it but is vastly interested."

"Of course," he said, barely able to speak.

"I didn't even hear the phone ring while I was getting dressed. I had my head stuck so far in the sink trying to dissolve that mask! Days later, I called him in France, wondering if he'd answered my phone, and he said he'd asked whoever it was to leave a message." There was a pause. "So, why didn't you leave a message?"

"I don't know."

He felt as if he had committed a schoolboy crime, like smoking on the bus or putting a frog in the girls' toilet. He fairly squirmed with the agony of having made so much ado about nothing.

He knew he would have to hold on tight and steer. "If I had it to do over, of course, I would insist on speaking with you. 'Haul that woman out of the shower or wherever she is, and put her on the line—at once! This is her neighbor calling!' "

She laughed the breathless, throaty laugh he loved.

"Your laughter is the Christmas music I've been longing to hear. I'm sorry, terribly sorry to have been so petty. Please forgive me."

"Oh, Timothy! How awful it's been, not being able to get home, not hearing from you, getting that dreadful little frozen note that I stuffed in the incinerator, and wondering what was wrong. And all the circuits busy for days, and no way to talk . . . to make contact. And your Christmas present sitting here on the sofa . . . I've felt so alone, so isolated from you . . ."

"I miss you," he said. Without meaning to, he said, "I need you . . ."

"Can you imagine how I love hearing you say that? That is the Christmas music I've longed to hear."

"I have no photograph of you. Sometimes I can't remember what you look like—do you mind my saying it? I want so much to see your face."

"I'll pop into one of those little booths and make dozens of funny faces and send them out as soon as the snow melts."

"Wonderful! And when will you come home? Soon?"

"Not until March. If I could get home now, I wouldn't have but three days. And the ice and rain have begun here, and the work is pressing me so . . ." She sounded anguished.

"What can I do for you. How can I help?"

"Love me! Long for me! Yearn for me! Oh, Timothy, you were jealous, weren't you?"

"Yes. Terribly. It was churning around in me for days, and when you answered the phone, it just popped out. I didn't mean for it to come out that way at all."

"How lovely that you can still surprise yourself. I couldn't love you if you were completely buttoned up. It's that little place you can never quite manage to get closed that makes me love you."

"But it's such a small place. Wouldn't you rather it was a bigger place?"

"Infinitely rather, my dearest."

He felt a kind of thaw, a snow melt. Something was being released and healed, and he sank back on the pillows.

"I love you, Timothy."

"I love you, Cynthia. Truly I do. You are a godsend."

"Do you think God would have me batter through your locked doors?"

"I think that you and only you could do it. I read something the other day—'What is asked of us in our time,' the writer said, 'is that we break open our blocked caves and find each other. Nothing less will heal the anguished spirit, nor release the heart to act in love.' Locked doors, blocked caves, it's all the same. It is so hard to . . ."

"To be real."

"Yes. Terribly hard. Frightening. But there's no other way."

"Ah, you talk tough now, you big galoot, but wait 'til I come home and fling myself into your arms . . . will you run?"

"The very thought takes my breath away," he said, meaning it. "And I don't know if I'll run. I don't want to. But . . ."

"But it could happen?"

"The odd thing is, I don't trust myself with you—yet I trust you. I trust you to be real with me, but I'm afraid that I can't give that back . . ."

"You're giving it back right now."

"Yes. But it's . . . frightening."

"Hold me, Timothy. Just be still with me. Where are you, dearest?"

"Lying on my bed. Can you hear Barnabas snoring?"

"No, but I should like to. I should like to be there with you, only holding you and you holding me."

All the tension of the past weeks, the angry weather, the increased duties of church, the luncheon speeches and invocations, the conflicts of his heart—all had concentrated to feel, somehow, like an inpouring of cement. Now, at last, came the outpouring.

"I need you," he said again, warmed and happy.

"Let's burn 'em ol' tables!" Dooley shouted over the music on his jam box.

"Let's burn 'at ol' jam box!" he shouted back.

Actually, the folding tables made one of the finest fires they'd had all winter.

With the Christmas Day service behind him, he did something he'd nearly forgotten how to do. He undressed and put on his pajamas and robe and made a pot of Darjeeling. He at last sent Dooley to his room, where all he could hear of the music was boom, boom, boom.

There was only one thing for it.

He put the disc on his player in the cabinet and, smiling, fell sound asleep listening to the rhumba—or was it the tango?

Jena Ivey of Mitford Blossoms didn't have the faintest idea which florists in New York would be certain to send roses that didn't drop their heads, but he remembered a magazine article he'd read in the dentist's office that said the Ritz-Carleton was known for its stunning flower arrangements. So he called the hotel manager in New York, was given the name of a florist, and proceeded to order a dozen red roses and a bouquet of fresh lavender, at a price he at first thought was a joke, to be delivered in a box tied with a satin ribbon—and step on it.

CHAPTER SEVEN

More Than Music

My Dearest,

You can't know how the living freshness of roses and lavender has rejoiced my heart. The whole apartment is alive with the sweet familiarity of their company, and I'm not so loath now to come home from the deli, or the newsstand, or the café.

Thus, I'm not thanking you for the roses precisely, which are glorious to look at, nor the fast bundle of lavender that appears to have come from the field only moments ago. I thank you instead for their gracious spirit, which soothes and calms and befriends me.

I tried to call your office after the flowers arrived, but the line was busy again and again. And so, I take this other route, this path made familiar by pen and paper, reflection and time.

What a lovely thing it is to begin to love. I shall not dwell on the fear, which seems always to come with it. I shall write only of victory, for that is what is on my heart tonight.

When I met you, Timothy, I had no thought of loving anyone again. Not for anything would I pay the price of loving! I had shut the door, but God had not.

I remember the evening I came to borrow sugar. Though I did nothing more than gobble up your leftover supper, I felt I'd come home. Imagine my bewilderment, sitting there at your kitchen counter, finding myself smitten.

Over your home was a stillness and peace that spoke to me, and in your eyes was something I hadn't seen before in a man. I supposed it to be kindness—and it was. I later believed it to be compassion, and it was that, also.

Yet, I sensed that God had put these qualities there for your flock and your community, to help you do your job for Him. For a long time, I didn't know whether He might have put something there just for me.

Years ago, I went to Guatemala with Elliott. While he was in meetings, I was on the road with a driver and a sketchbook, slamming along over huge potholes, our teeth rattling. We drove in the jungle for miles, seeing nothing but thick, unremitting forest. The light in that part of the world was strange and unfamiliar to me, and I felt a bit frightened, almost panicked.

Suddenly, we drove into a clearing. Before us lay a vast, volcanic lake that literally took my breath away. The surface was calm and blue and serene, and the light that drenched the clearing seemed to pour directly from heaven.

I shall never forget the suddenness and surprise of finding that hidden and remote lake.

I feel that I have come upon a hidden place in you that is vast and deep and has scarcely been visited by anyone before. It is nearly unbearable to consider the joy this hidden place could hold for us, and yet, tonight, I do.

"Love is like measles," Josh Billings said, ". . . the later in life it occurs, the tougher it gets."

May God have mercy on us, my dearest Timothy!

I close with laughter and tears, the very stuff of life, and race to the drawing board with every hope that I can, at last, make the zebra stop looking like a large dog in striped pajamas!

I kiss you.

Love,
Cynthia

Dearest Cynthia,

At the library today, Hessie Mayhew announced that Latin American dance classes will be held at the Community Club, some-

time in February. I told her I have my own private Latin dance instructor, which she found to be astonishing.

Then I popped into the children's section and talked to Avette about reading Miss Coppersmith.

"Violet Goes to School *and* Violet Plays the Piano *are my two personal favorites," she said, "although* Violet Goes to France *is hilariously funny. What will it be?"*

"The complete works!" I said.

I must tell you that Hessie Mayhew is no dummy. When she saw my selection, she approved. "The Proust of juvenile authors!" were her exact words.

Now I have innumerable photographs of you, though they are all on the backs of book jackets. I am currently displaying the backside of Violet Goes to the Country *on my desk in the study, where I meet your winsome gaze as I sit and write this letter. I'm afraid the author herself looks exceedingly juvenile, and if that's what writing children's books can do, then I'm willing to have a go at it.*

I shall begin this evening at the top of the pile and plunge straight through to the bottom. Never think that I dismiss lightly the hard work and devotion that go into each small volume. I feel privileged to see behind the scenes, if only a little.

Uncle Billy asks about you and says they'd like to have us over when you come home. You and Dooley can go along for the homemade banana pudding he mentioned as a refreshment, and I'll meet you there later.

He was telling me about the money he keeps hidden between his mattress and box spring. He says Miss Rose usually asks him for ten or fifteen dollars on Monday. On Wednesday, she wants twenty, and every Friday she asks for twenty-five.

When I asked him what she does with all that money, he says he doesn't know; he never gives her any.

I believe that's his newest joke, though he didn't say so.

Your letter spoke of victory, and I hesitate to end on a note that is less than uplifting. Yet I can't ignore your allusion to the hidden lake.

Your analogy was extraordinary to me and made me feel at once that I should surely disappoint you. The lake you discovered in Guatemala was tropical and warm. The lake you say you have found in me suffers a climate entirely of my own making—and there is the rub.

Please pray for me in this, my dearest Cynthia. I am well along in years to have such a terrific case of measles. In truth, I am broken out all over and no help for it.

You are ever in my prayers.

Dooley asks after you, as do Emma and Puny. A candle flame has gone out in this winter village, and we count the days until you are safely home.

Love,
Timothy

Dearest Timothy,

It was lovely that you called tonight after reading Violet Goes to the Country. *That is my personal favorite, and I'm so happy it made you smile.*

I'm happy, too, that you read it to Barnabas and that he approved. For one as steeped in Wordsworth as he, I'm not surprised that he could appreciate the pastoral setting, though I'm sorry he was upset when you showed him the picture of Violet chasing the sheepdog.

Violet receives a great swarm of attention wherever we go. I put her in the little carrying case with the top undone, and there she rides, licking her paws. The ladies behind the cosmetic counter at Bergdorf's come crowding into the aisles to give her lots of free samples—both salts for her toilette and mascara for her lashes. They like to spray her with French perfume so that I can hardly bear to be in the taxi with her on the way home!

When James was here, he asked me to do Violet Goes to New York.

He took me to such a vastly expensive restaurant and gave such a persuasive argument that I was fairly undone. I did not tell him I would do it, though I did say I'd think about it. The advance would be the largest amount I've ever received. I will appreciate it if you'd pray for me in this. It's confounding to be asked to do something I said I'd never do again!

Thank you for liking my work and finding the fun in it. I look forward to having the letter you wrote tonight before you called—altogether an embarrassment of riches!

Here are those ridiculous pictures taken in a booth on the street.

In the spring, you could tack them on a post in your garden to keep the crows away!

I've taken stems of lavender from the vase, dried them a wee bit in the toaster oven, and put them under my pillow. Lavender is said to give one sweet dreams, which is what I wish for you tonight.

You are always in my prayers.
With fondest love from—
Your neighbor

Dearest Cynthia,

It is Friday evening, and I've just come from a late meeting. This is only to say hello and that I've switched on the lights in your bushes.

The fog is as thick as lentil soup, and they give a cheering glow. As they were not turned on during the holy days, I hope you won't mind a few hours now, as a send-up of my thoughts of you on this wretched but beautiful winter evening.

God bless you and give you wings for your work. Nay, use them to fly to me here in Mitford. I shall watch for you to glide over the rooftop of your little house and eagerly open my window to let you in.

With loving thoughts,
Timothy

Timothy, dearest,

Violet has been invited out to dinner this evening by Miss Addison, who lives down the hall.

The invitation was delivered by the lady's footman or something—this is a very swanky place—and was for six o'clock, which is when her elderly cat, Palestrina, likes to dine.

Can you imagine?

I have met Miss Addison several times in the hallway or in the foyer, and she is rather old and quite adorable, wrapped from head to toe in furs.

The footman, or whoever he is, came for Violet on the stroke of six, after I'd brushed her until she shone.

But oh, she is wicked! What did she do five minutes before the bell sounded? I was bringing a flowerpot inside when she dashed to the terrace that is forty stories above the street, leapt onto the railing, and stood looking with absorption at the lights of the Chrysler Building.

She will stay until eight, because they are all watching a video after dinner (surely not 101 Dalmatians*?).*

I went to dinner the other evening, quite alone, and confess it was a bit pricey. The waiter finally came over and asked, "And how did you find your steak, Madame?"

"Purely by accident," I said. "I moved the potatoes and the peas, and there it was!"

Oh, Timothy, I'm trying so hard to bloom where God planted me. But I am very homesick. I look forward to our talk on Sunday.

Much love to you and to Barnabas. Do tell Dooley hey for me. I should like to see his frank expression and hear his wonderful way of speaking. When I come home, let's all do something together—like—well, you think of something!

I pray for you.

Warmest regards to Emma and my love to Miss Sadie and Louella.

Sunday eve
Dearest Cynthia,

We've just hung up and it seemed so many things went unsaid. Now that I'm sitting down to write, however, I have no idea at all what they were.

I'm delighted that Violet has made a friend, even though her fancy dinner sent her to the litter box throughout the night. Sautéed quail livers with Madeira sauce are notorious in this regard.

As for us, we had our usual Sunday evening banquet. Fried bologna for Dooley with double mustard, and no sermons about a balanced diet, please. This case is beyond me. Unless I'm mistaken, he has not eaten a vegetable in four or five months, and I'm dashed if I know what to do about it. Any ideas?

I forgot to mention that we had a mild, almost balmy day on Saturday. Miss Rose pulled on galoshes and spent the noon hour directing traffic. After a long confinement, it put the bloom back in her cheeks, Uncle Billy says.

Fancy Skinner has nailed me again about my hair and insists I let her give me a haircut. I hesitate to do this to Joe, who, I'm told, may go with his sister to Tennessee for a week. Possibly I could use his extended absence as an excuse. What do you think?

I've seen Andrew Gregory, who looked smart as all get-out in a cashmere topcoat, and he asked about you. He seems to think that because you're my neighbor, I know all there is to know about you. Yet it occurs to me that I don't even know where you were born.

Well, there you have it. All the urgent things I left unsaid.

Clearly, there's nothing of importance to tell a famous author and illustrator living in New York, whose cat has a more interesting life than most people.

Cynthia, Cynthia—my face grows red when I think of what you said. I hope you will seriously reconsider that outrageous idea, lest I take you up on it.

With something like amazed laughter, and, of course, love,

Timothy

Sunday evening
Timothy!

You rake in a collar! I positively blush like a sophomore when I think of what you said!

You may want to reconsider that outlandish proposal. What if I should take you up on it?

Or was it my idea?

Oh, well, when two hearts beat as one, who knows? And who cares?

I do love you to pieces. You are so funny and wonderful. I knew it the minute I saw that barbecue sauce on your chin, when I came to borrow sugar after just moving in.

Violet has gone down the hall to play with an electronic mouse while Palestrina, who is too old for such nonsense, looks on.

I shall be happy to be home again with people who are ordinary.

Well almost ordinary.

Much love,
Cynthia

My dear neighbor, it was your outlandish idea, not mine, and please do not forget it! I certainly haven't forgotten it. Good grief, I can barely keep my thoughts on my duties. And there's the rub.

I struggle with what old men with measles fear most: not being able to think straight, forgetting their Christian names, wandering in a daze on the street, being late for meetings and early for luncheons, dwelling everlastingly on some woman who only professes to have measles but in truth possesses a case so mild that she can go about her duties as cool and elegant as you please, while the other chap stumbles around trying to locate his shoes or even the very house where he lives.

Cynthia, Cynthia. Be kind.

yrs,
Timothy

Dearest Funny Person,

Your wake-up call this morning—how wonderful it was! It was coffee with brandy, it was eggs Benedict, it was a hot shower and a walk in the park! Words fail me, but not entirely!

So glad you liked the pictures, though I'm sure you were being kind. I can be terribly grave in front of a camera, and that fur-lined hood made me look exactly like an Eskimo woman who has spent the morning chewing a piece of reindeer hide.

Dearest, I really and truly can't come home. I must work some part of each day in order to reach the deadline. If I were to pull up stakes at this point and move home, I should do nothing more than lose time and gain confusion.

Thus far, I've been given God's speed. Now, if I keep going and nevah, nevah give up, I shall come to the finish line on schedule.

And so, I have a question that will make your heart fairly leap into your throat—

Why don't you come to New York?

You could stay here, and while I'm working, you could read or visit the bookshops or pop over to my little café where they've not only adopted me but would take the fondest care of you.

You would have lots of privacy, for this is a very large apartment—and I promise I will not seduce you. Since we've never discussed it, I want to say that I really do believe in doing things the old-fashioned way when it comes to love. I do love you very dearly and want everything to be right and simple and good, and yes, pleasing to God. This is why I'm willing to wait for the kind of intimacy that most people favor having as soon as they've shaken hands.

But enough of what I shall not do, and on to what I shall!

I shall buy fresh bread and fresh fish and vegetables and all the things you love and cook for you right here, and you will save hundreds of dollars on pricey restaurants, which you can give to the children's hospital!

I shall take you to a play with the tickets from my publisher and to the shop with the lighted antique globe, not to mention the Metropolitan Museum and the New York Public Library.

Last but not least, I shall give you as much love and affection and happiness as I am capable of giving. Which, I believe, dearest Timothy, is quite a lot.

There. How can you resist?

Your loving Cynthia

from the office
dearest cynthia,

but i am a rustic, a country bumpkin, a bucolic rube of the worst sort—in a word, a hick.

I can see why you didn't mention this on sunday when we talked—you wanted me to have time to think it over. That indeed is one of the grandest benefits of a letter. it gives one time to reflect, so that one doesn't shout some impulsive, spur-of-the-moment nonsense like yes i'll come to new york and fly in a plane and be stranded in an airport and get lost or maimed, or even killed, not to mention buffeted by throngs on every corner.

Nope. i can't do it. you think i'm kidding, but i am dead serious. I am infamous for my fear of flying—which is chiefly why I hemmed and hawed for twenty years over the trip to Ireland. Large cities are another of my rustic phobias—they literally make me sick—which is the sole reason Kthrn and Wltr and I lodged in the countryside when we went to sligo.

I am willing to take any flailing you dish out—but i cannot come to new york. you're right, the very thought makes my heart leap into my throat. blast, i am sorry,

with love,
Timothy

Dearest Cynthia,

It is Monday evening, and I have read your letter again, feeling like a heel.

Your bright spirit is the light of my life. When I read the gracious things you would do to make me happy, my foolish limitations and fogyisms are humiliating to me.

I can only hope you'll forgive me and know that somehow, in some other way, I shall be forthcoming and good for you.

I, too, hate it that you must be there alone. Emma assures me that men in the publishing field are good-looking, enormously successful, and invariably tall, some of them verging perhaps on nine feet or more.

She went on to suggest that if I don't mind my p's and q's, I will surely lose whatever ground I have gained with you, and you'll be swept away. I would not be surprised if this were true, but I pray it will not be so.

It was consoling to read your brave announcement of what you would not do. No, we have never discussed this, but the time, clearly, was right for you to say it. It is amazing to me that you and I share the same ideal for sexual intimacy, which, needless to say, the world finds exceedingly outdated.

Another consolation is that the world has nothing to do with us in this.

Your openness has widened the door of my own heart, somehow, and I feel a tenderness for you that is nearly overwhelming. I can't think how I could be worth the care you take with me, the effort you expend, and the ceaseless patience you bring to our friendship.

For this alone, I must love you.

My dearest,

You would be amused if you knew how long I have sat and looked at the two words just above, words that I have never written to anyone in my life. Can it have taken more than six decades for these words to form in my spirit, and then, without warning, to appear on the paper before me, with such naturalness and ease?

Even for this alone, I must love you.

I've come across a letter from Robert Browning to EBB, in which he says:

"I would not exchange the sadness of being away from you for any imaginable delight in which you had no part."

To this sentiment, I say Selah.

I also say goodnight, my dearest love. You are ever in my prayers.

Timothy

Timothy,

I understand. I really do. I could feel the intensity behind your typed note. At one moment, your horror of this place makes me laugh. At another, I wonder what on earth I'm doing here myself!

I feel we should go on as we're going and try to enjoy, somehow, this process of working and waiting. I know there is wisdom in that! But it keeps escaping me, like the flea I picked off Violet this morning.

Can you imagine? Forty stories up, in the dead of winter—and a flea? Certainly, she did not get it at Bergdorf's. Which leaves only one consideration.

Palestrina!

I shudder to think what I should do when her next social invitation arrives in the letter box!

I must get something ready for the pickup service that comes at five, so I'll dash,

with love and understanding,
Cynthia

Dearest Timothy,

When I reached into the letter box yesterday morning, I somehow missed your wonderful letter written on Monday evening. How very odd that I didn't feel it in there yesterday, but odder still that I would have looked in there again this morning, knowing that today's mail had not yet arrived.

I so needed your letter with Mr. Browning's words to Elizabeth and the tender things you spoke to me from your heart. Because, though I honestly do understand your refusal to come, it made me sad that you will not.

I had hoped we could be together here, as free as children from everything familiar. Most of all, I wanted to share what I know of this strangely compelling city and take you 'round and show you off!

But you have called me your dearest. And that is worth any window-shopping at Tiffany's or tea we might have sipped at the Plaza.

More than that—it fills me with happiness that you were able, for your own sake, to speak to me so.

It wasn't easy for me to tell you what I shall not do—it was very hard to know when to say it! So, perhaps you can imagine how comforting it was to learn that we agree in this sacred thing—and to find that you are just as silly and old-fashioned as your neighbor.

When Elliott and I were divorced eleven years ago, the first thing my friends did was "fix me up."

Oh, how I hated being "fixed up!"

Practically the first man I went out with said, "Hello, blah, blah, blah, cute nose, I'm wild about your legs, let's check into a hotel."

I wish I could tell you that I poured scalding coffee in his lap! But all I really did was curl up inside in a tinier knot than I'd curled up in before! I refused to go out with anyone again for nearly three years.

The secret truth, dearest, is that I cannot bear dating. I find it absolutely ghastly. I am so glad we have never ever dated and never ever will! You are just the boy next door, which I find to be the most divine providence since France was handed over to Henry the Fifth.

But please don't think our friend Andrew Gregory was anything less than lovely. He is a prince! Yet, among a variety of other sweet incompatibilities, he is too tall. Yes! When he kissed me on the cheek, he had to practically squat down to do it, which made me laugh out loud every time! Poor Andrew. He deserves far better.

You and I, on the other hand, are the perfect size for each other. As we're very nearly the same height, we're just like a pair of bookends.

I close with sleepy wishes for a riveting sermon at Lord's Chapel on Sunday. Please make a photocopy at Happy Endings and send it to me. I shall be sitting on the gospel side at the little church around the corner.

Love and prayers, Cynthia

P.S. My work is simply pouring through. I am thankful beyond telling. James writes from France that my zebras fairly leap with life.

There's not a pair of pajamas in the lot. Pray for me, dearest, I shall be home sooner than we think. Love to Dooley. Here's a bit of a drawing I did of him from memory.

from the office
dear bookend,

i'll have you know i stand 5 feet 9 in my loafers, while you are a mere 5 feet 2. that leaves 7 whole inches waving around in the breeze above your head, and i'll thank you not to forget it.

Dooley laughed at your drawing and must have liked it for he took it to school today. That someone would make a drawing of him was a marvel he did not take lightly. Puny thought it pure genius, and i promised to make her a photocopy when i copy the sermon, which, by the way, was less than riveting, though Miss Rose, to my great surprise, pronounced it stirring.

she refused to wear the sling-back pumps that Uncle billy ordered out of the almanac. She put them on the mantel in the dining room, instead, as a kind of display. She was arrayed in her Christmas finery. Uncle Billy was wearing a new shirt and held himself so stiff and erect i suspect he had left the cardboard in.

Things are back on schedule on the hill and i could hear the hum and buzz of the equipment as i walked in this morning. emma wanted the week off, so i am quite alone here, half-freezing one minute and roasting the next, as the heater has developed a tic and goes on and off at odd moments.

You sounded strong yesterday, so glad Miss Addison invited you for that swell Sunday tea and that you brought home no fleas.

Again, i enjoyed your books more than i can say. i seemed to find all sorts of meaning between the lines.

Love, Timothy

p.s. Dooley says hey

thnx for telling me when you were born, though I forgot, as usual, to ask where. So there'll be no forgetting, i have written your birth date on the wall beside my desk, my first graffiti—except of course for the legend, TOMMY NOLES LOVES PATTY FRANKLIN, that i once chalked on the cafeteria door and which nearly cost my life at the hands of the principal, not to mention Patty Frnkln.

Perhaps you entered the world in maine? or was it massachusetts? You are definitely a Yankee, no doubt about it

Here comes harold

Dearest Timothy,

I've been very sleepless recently. I wish I could call you now, but a ringing phone at such an hour stops the very heart. It would also set Barnabas "to barking" and Dooley "to fussing." So I shall have to be consoled with talking to you in this way.

I've read something wonderful. "Deep in their roots," Roethke said, "all flowers keep the light."

My mind went at once to my tulips, frozen into the black soil of the bed you helped me dig. My imagination burrowed in like a mole and saw, in the center of a frozen bulb, a green place—quick and alive and radiant and indefatigable, the force that survives every winter blast and flies up, in spite of itself, to greet spring.

I am keeping the light, dearest. But sometimes it grows so faint; I'm frightened that I shall lose it entirely.

Why am I not doing the things I should be doing? Going to the library and the bookshops, seeing plays, hearing concerts, looking at great art?

The answer is, there's scarcely anything left of me after bending over the drawing board for hours, and so I send out for Chinese or make the quick walk to the café and am in bed before the late news, only to find I cannot sleep!

I am, however, going faithfully to confirmation class at the little church around the corner, every Thursday evening—and liking it very much.

I pray for us to have long walks together, to dash out into the rain and jump into puddles! Would you jump into puddles with me? I think not, but it's a hope I shall cherish, for it makes me smile to think of it.

Now that I've gotten out of bed, and located the stationery, and rounded up the pen and filled it with ink, and fluffed up the pillows, and adjusted the lamp, and told you I can't sleep, I'm nodding off!

Life is so odd. I can't make heads or tails of it. I'm glad you're a parson and can.

Lovingly yours, C

My dearest C,

Have been pondering our dinner here before you vanished into the sky in that minuscule plane. I can't seem to remember what I fed you, when or how I prepared it, nor even discussing the order with Avis. Though I was sober as a judge, I think I was in a kind of daze—the most I can recall is that we danced, I asked you the question that was so infernally difficult, and you were tender and patient and full of laughter.

This recollection should be more than enough, yet I'm astounded at such a lapse. Something was clearly going on that had little to do with either dinner or dancing and causes me to consider the wisdom of Aiken's poem:

"Music I heard with you was more than music,

"And bread I broke with you was more than bread . . ."

So glad you called last night. It was no disturbance at all, quite the contrary. I hope it's some comfort, however small, that you can call me anytime.

Do you hear? Anytime. Please take this to heart.

I've been in parishes where the phone might ring at any hour, from midnight to morning. Mitford, however, is a reserved parish, and I think the last late-hour call was from Hoppy's wife who was in the agony of dying and wanted prayer—not for herself, but for him.

It occurs to me that I'm not only your neighbor and friend, C, but your parson, as well. All of which seems to make a tight case for your freedom to call me as your heart requires it.

With fondest love to you tonight and prayers for sleeping like an infant,

Timothy

My dear Bookend,

I've had a load of wood carted in and a more splendid fire you've never seen. All this seems to occasion a letter, though I just sent one to you yesterday morning.

A meeting was canceled, thanks be to God. Dooley is spending the night with Tommy, and Barnabas is amused with scratching himself. Wish you were here. It is another night of jollity in our frozen village.

I've just heard from Fr Roland in New Orleans, who complains that my letters to him have dried up like a pond in a drought. Can't imagine why.

Am cooking a pork roast and a pot of navy beans, one more reason I wish you were here. I told Puny I needed to put my hand in again, so she did the shopping with Avis, and I'm handling the rest.

The house is fairly perfumed with a glorious smell, which causes me to remember Mother's kitchen. She always added orange rind to a pork roast and a bit of brandy. Her strong favorite with any roast was angel biscuits, so named for their habit of floating off the plate and hovering above the platter.

I can't help but think how my father never came to the table when called. He would sometimes wait until we were finished or the food had grown cold before sitting down without a word. I remember my mother's disappointment and my own white fury, which often spoiled the meal she had laid.

Later, I could see it was his way of controlling the household, of being the emperor, far above the base need for eating, for loving, for feeling. I remember his refusal of anesthesia when he had an operation on his leg and again a serious abscess on his jaw.

If my mother had not been fashioned of something akin to marzipan, my father's composition of steel would have been my very death.

But why do I waste ink telling you this? It came into the room with the fragrance from the pots and would not let me be.

Sometimes I consider not mailing a letter I've written to you, but you insisted that nothing should be struck through or torn up or unmailed, so there you have it.

Someone has said again that I should work on the book of essays I've long considered. Perhaps when I retire, if I ever do such a thing.

Stuart says I should be making plans for retirement—but his advice mad me want to say, oh, stop being a bishop and let me stumble around and fall in a blasted ditch if that's what it takes.

I am homesick for your spirit.

With love,
Timothy

Darling Timothy,

I've dried the lavender and tied it into small bundles that are tucked everywhere. Here are a few sprigs for your pillow. If that seems too twee, as the English say, perhaps you'll find a place for them in your sock drawer.

I've plucked every petal from every faded rose and have two bowls filled with their lingering fragrance. I cannot let them go! I'm enclosing a handful of petals for you to scatter over the last of the snow.

James says the new book must be a different format than the Violet books and even larger than Mouse in the Manger. *"These creatures must have room to breathe!" he says, and I do agree. I'm going to the publishing house tomorrow afternoon and work with the designer. I shall be thrilled to have someone to talk with, though the lovely people who run the café do make the days go faster. I wish you could meet them.*

The weather is still terrible here. A water main froze and broke in the neighborhood, and the streets have been flooded for two days. I've bought fleece-lined boots after weeks of tripping around in the footwear of a Southern schoolgirl!

I got your letter mailed Saturday a.m. You must have given it wings! Thank you for writing about your father. One day, I shall tell you about mine. Alas, there was no steel in him at all. He was constructed entirely of charm, French cigarettes, and storytelling. He was often sad, utterly defenseless, and I loved him madly. He was thrilled that I was a girl, once saying that he didn't know what he would have done with a little person who wanted to kick around a football or go fly-fishing.

Oh, Timothy! I feel wretched. I cannot look at another zebra, another wildebeest, and certainly no more armadillos! I am so very tired.

I want more than anything to scratch through that last remark or start over, for that is what my mother always said. She always said she was tired, and I vowed never to say it, especially to you. But I am tired, and there you have it. I am exhausted in every bone.

I should love to kiss you over and over. Like at the airport. Our kisses made me feel I was flying, long before I got on the little plane. I am weary of having my feet on the ground, dearest. I should like to poke my head in the clouds!

With inexpressible longings,
Your loving bookend

Dearest Bookend,

Hang in there. i have just this moment heard a male cardinal singing. He is sitting on the branch of an icebound bush outside the office window. It is so reviving to hear his song i had to tell you at once. It has gone on and on, as if he can't bear to end it. His mate swoops and dives about the bush, expressing her own glad joy for the sunshine that is with us at last. Let this be a comfort, somehow, and a hope for us. Am off to Wesley with Dooley to buy a parka, as his was ripped on a fence when we delivered Christmas baskets. Know this comes with tenderest love and fervent prayer, and yes, my own longings.

yrs, timothy

CHAPTER EIGHT

Keeping the Light

He awoke with a start, crying out, and saw Barnabas looking at him with alarm.

In the dream, he'd been standing on the site of Hope House, where Buck Leeper had been seriously hurt. The wound above Buck's knee lay open to the bone; blood soaked his pants and was spreading upward to his shirt.

He rubbed his eyes, trying to wipe away the image of the nearly mortally wounded man whose face he had not seen but whose suffering had been palpable.

He had never been one to try and sort out the meaning of dreams, as a dog might worry a bone. He wanted to put it out of his mind, at once.

It was a half hour before the alarm would go off, but he got out of bed and took a hot shower, scrubbing his head more vigorously than usual, as if to drive out the image of the worst dream he'd had in a very long time.

"I ain't seen you in a month of Sundays," said Percy, who looked up from the grill.

"I'm having breakfast with Dooley these days."

"Th' boy gets you for breakfast, your house help gets you for lunch, an' I ain't open for supper, so there's that." Percy was hurt.

He grinned sheepishly. If ever you got on the good side of Percy Mosely, he would make you feel wanted and needed, no matter how big a scoundrel you turned out to be. Why, indeed, had he stayed away so long when the Grill was his favorite medicine?

"Where's Velma?"

"Waitin' on your buddies over there."

He turned and saw Ron Malcolm and Buck Leeper at the table by the window. The dark pall of the dream settled over him again. He noticed Velma was standing by the table like a stone, her order pad poised.

"Howdy," said J.C., as he slid into the back booth.

"How's it going?"

"You ought to get you some of this gravy," said the *Muse* editor, who had ordered biscuits and gravy, sausage patties, two fried eggs, and grits.

"And have a stroke before I hit the sidewalk? No thanks, pal."

Mule came up to the booth and slapped him on the shoulder. "Where in th' heck you been? Slide over. I been lookin' through th' obituaries to see if I could trace you."

"A lot going on. Glad to see you. How's business?"

"Slow as molasses. How's yours?"

"Steady."

It was a comfort to be back.

He could cook rings around Percy's eggs, but Percy's grits were another matter. While his own grits could be a dash watery, Percy's had a good, firm texture and were yellow with butter. He hadn't recently tasted anything so satisfying. And no wonder. For two mornings in a row, he'd weakened and had fried bologna with Dooley.

"Hope you haven't been eatin' your own cookin' all this time," said Mule, who tucked into an omelet with a side of livermush.

"Bologna two mornings in a row. The obituaries missed me by a hair. What's new?"

"The Presbyterians are raffling off th' Cadillac this month, but they're doin' it at the Legion Hall, to keep it ecumenical," said J.C.

"Aha."

"The school got a new flag, one that flew at the White House, and the Mixed Chorus is going to sing on Thursday while they raise it."

"I heard about that. Dooley's singing."

"Rodney Underwood caught somebody climbin' out th' back window of th' Collar Button. The burglar ran off, but they nabbed two suits of clothes, a sack of underwear, a dress shirt, and a fancy umbrella."

"Keep this up, I won't have to buy a paper on Monday."

"This," said J.C., "is old news. Already run in the paper last week. I figured you hadn't read it. If you're lookin' for new news, buy Monday's *Muse.*"

"A poet and don't know it," said Mule. "Did you hear about ol' Miz Cranford goin' off to visit her daughter and asked Coot Hendrick to watch her house?"

"Didn't hear about that."

"Came back and Coot and his biggest boy had washed it. Top to bottom. Borrowed every ladder they could get hold of."

J.C. was not a pretty sight when he laughed with his mouth full.

"I don't get it," said Father Tim.

"Coot thought she said wash 'er house, not watch it."

"Um," murmured the rector.

"You had to be there," said Mule. "You know Joe Ivey's down sick with th' flu . . ."

"Uh oh. I needed to walk up there this morning and get a haircut."

"You're lookin' a little shaggy, all right. It's hangin' over your collar."

"That bad, is it?"

Mule peered at him over his glasses. "A good time to step over and see Fancy."

The rector ducked his head and buttered his toast.

"She cut J.C. last week."

The rector inspected J.C., who turned red.

"He looks the same to me."

"Well, that's the beauty of it," said Mule. "You go to just any jackleg, and you come out lookin' like a total stranger. Go to a professional and you come out lookin' like yourself."

The rector grinned. "So, you're going the unisex route, J.C.?"

"I hope to God you won't spread it around that I went to a beauty shop. Dadgummit, Mule, I asked you to keep that to yourself."

"All I've told is the preacher, here, hope t' die," said Mule.

Father Tim roared with laughter.

J.C. sopped his plate with the last crust of toast. "I ought t' stop comin' in this place . . ."

"Twenty percent off for clergy," Mule assured him. "That's five more'n what you get in Wesley, plus you burn gas runnin' over there, not to mention th' potholes from all th' bad weather that'll take your hubcaps off, plus your exhaust pipe. About a two hundred dollar run is what you'd have, not includin' th' tip."

"How long can the flu last? I can get by another day or two."

"Yeah, but Joe just took sick. He'll probably be down for a couple of weeks. You know Joe. He won't barber with the flu."

Puny Bradshaw sprang instantly to mind. She was the one for the job. She could trim him up in no time.

"I'll think about it," he lied. Actually, J.C. did look different, after all. He appeared as if he might be wearing bangs.

"Slide in," J.C. said to Ron Malcolm, who walked up to the booth. "I'm leavin'. Some people in this town have to work."

"I'm bustin' out of here, too," said Mule, who stood up and took his meal check. "Listin' a new house. Speakin' of which," he said to the rector, "how's that good-lookin' woman I slipped in next door to you? Haven't seen her around."

"Living in New York for a while."

"I got him a neighbor and a half," Mule told Ron. "Nicest pair of legs you'd ever want t' see."

Mule Skinner had no qualms about taking full credit for an act of providence, thought the rector. All he'd done was handle some paperwork on the little yellow house, which was deeded to Cynthia by her uncle's estate.

Velma came around with the coffeepot. "It's me again," said Ron, looking sheepishly at Percy's wife. "I'll take a fresh cup, if you don't mind."

Velma grunted and stomped away.

"She's sour as milk about Leeper. Any friend of his is an enemy of hers."

"What now?"

"Same old, same old. He's short with her, demanding, kind of high and mighty. She'd like to stab him with a fork."

"I had a horrifying dream about him last night. An accident on the job. Terrible, haunting."

"Worst that ever happened to him is he lost two fingers. One off each hand, a matched set, he says. You ever notice?"

"Our social exchanges have been pretty hasty. No, I didn't notice. What about his family? A wife? Kids?"

"No kids. Three wives. I won't go into what happened with the last one. I promise you don't want to know, and it sure didn't sweeten his temper any."

"Where does he live? What does he find to do around here?"

Velma set Ron's coffee on the table, with two packages of Sweet 'N Low. "There you go," she said tersely.

"Rents the old Tanner cottage, remember it? Go to the end of Church Hill, take the right that goes off in the woods. The cottage sits down in there. Pretty secluded. Beats me what he does. Not much, probably, after the kind of days he puts in. Somebody told me he used to do models, maybe of airplanes, I don't know."

"You said he hits the drinking pretty hard."

"Bottom line, it's not known to interfere with his work. Same way with his daddy for a lot of years, then it got him."

"What's his poison, anyway?"

"Vodka. Straight up."

The rector whistled.

"I have to tell you," said Ron, "there's something about him I like. Nope, I'm not condoning his social behavior, but there's something in the man . . . kind of like that little piece of nut you can't quite get out of the shell, even with a pick. Just that little piece stuck in there, somehow, that's all right."

"How's the job coming?"

"The weather poked a hole in us, but Buck's got it back on line. I tell you, he's the best in the business. If his ol' daddy hadn't kicked his butt so hard when he was a kid . . ."

"There's the rub. How's Wilma?"

"Cuter than a speckled pup." Ron's eyes sparkled with merriment at the mention of his wife of forty years. If there was a man to be turned to and counted on, it was Ron Malcolm, who, in his opinion, occupied the pedestal with Hal Owen. With these men flanking him on either side, he was a rector on whom providence clearly smiled.

"I feel like somethin' th' cat dragged in," said Emma. Her face was blotchy, her hair looked unkempt, and her eyes were swollen.

"What do you think it is?" he asked, truly concerned.

"I ate a whole cheesecake last night."

"You what?"

"Th' whole thing."

"Good Lord!"

"Direct from the freezer," she said, barely moving her lips and appearing to have gone numb in the face.

"How? . . ." He was at a loss.

"Dumped it out of the aluminum pan right on the countertop and busted it into five chunks with a knife handle."

"Good heavens! Where was Harold?"

"Gone. Went off to talk to somebody about plantin' Christmas trees on that four acres behind th' barn. He never leaves me at night. It was th' first time we've been separated in th' evenin' since we got married. Soon as he walked out th' door, somethin' came over me—that cheesecake popped in my mind like it was up on a drive-in theater screen."

"I know the feeling."

"He wasn't hardly out of the driveway 'til I jerked open th' freezer and hauled that cake out of there.

"At least I could have waited for it to thaw, but no sirree, whop, chop, down th' hatch." She sighed deeply, looking mournful. "I could have called in sick, but I knew you needed this report for the buildin' committee."

This was the first time he'd ever seen her too ill to be ill-tempered. She was meek as a lamb, which, regardless of the price she was paying, was not an unwelcome turn of events.

She had a strained look as she peered at him over her glasses. "Knowin' how cheese clogs me up, the worst is not over."

"Well," he said feebly, trying to be helpful, "try not to do it again."

He went up the hill at Miss Sadie's request, for an impromptu lunch of collards, navy beans, hot rolls, and fried chicken.

"Miss Sadie," Louella had said over their early breakfast, "we've crackered and san'wiched that poor preacher half to death. Let's give 'im somethin' can stick to 'is ribs."

Miss Sadie sniffed. "Fried chicken in the daytime is too heavy if you've got work to do. Why not chicken salad?"

"Too much trouble—skinnin', stewin', cuttin' off th' bone. Besides, I feel a cookin' spell comin' on."

"Oh, dear." Miss Sadie drew a deep breath. If Louella was too long discouraged from what she called "real" cooking, she would suddenly take a fit of meal preparation that cost a fortune, the results of which they couldn't possibly eat at one or two sittings. This meant all the leftovers had to be frozen in a veritable stack of containers. She knew for a fact that loading up the freezer made the refrigerator motor work harder, which reflected on the electric bill.

She tried, however, to be reasonable. She didn't mind losing a battle or two if, in the larger issues, she might win the war.

Miss Sadie's eyes were sparkling. "You know why I asked you up for lunch?"

He hardly ever knew why Miss Sadie asked him up for lunch. One thing he did know, however—it would be a surprise; it always was.

"They're going to get married!" she announced.

"Well, now, that's wonderful. Marvelous!" He leaned to her at the dining table and kissed her cheek. "Congratulations! The best news!" He couldn't deny that he felt a dash overlooked that no one had called him.

"Olivia wanted me to be the first to know, and Hoppy was going to tell you second, but he got that awful case of that whole family with food poisoning, and Olivia said I could tell you." He had never seen her look so radiant, as if she, herself, might be a bride. Here was one of the benefits, the bonuses, the perks of being a parson.

He sat back happily in the Queen Anne chair. "I don't know when I've had better news. When will it be?"

"June! Olivia said, 'Aunt Sadie'—oh, if you could know how I love hearing her call me that!—she said, 'Aunt Sadie, we were thinking of May or June. What do you think?' I said, 'Why, June, of course! It's traditional!' And she said, 'But aren't we a bit long in the tooth for that sort of tradition? Isn't that for young brides?' And I said, 'But my dear, you *are* a young bride. Your heart is only a few months old!' And so—June it is. The seventeenth! Oh, Father, I'm beside myself! It's the first family wedding I've ever known.

"How I wish everyone could know that Olivia is my blood kin." As she said that, her eyes lost their dancing light.

"Miss Sadie, you've bossed me around for years, and I've loved every minute of it. Now, I'm going to boss you on something. Forget your disappointment that no one can know. Don't let that rob you of even a moment's joy. You and Olivia have found each other. What a miracle! What grace! And all this joy depending upon a little coat that was spared down the years, so you could at last open this gift of the heart. I'm scolding you, Miss Sadie. Cheer up!"

She smiled and patted his arm. "You're right as rain, Father. You keep after me, you hear? You know I'll keep after you."

"Oh, and it's a privilege to have someone keep after me. I need it."

"Father, I've heard . . . rumors. You know how things get around. There are some who say you might have . . . well, that you might have a special fondness for your neighbor and she for you." Miss Sadie colored slightly. It had taken some courage to ask.

"You've heard right."

"Then, one day, there could be someone besides me to keep after you?"

"There . . . could be." He paused. "Perhaps."

"Father, don't be too cautious. I would never tell anyone to throw caution to the winds, for caution is a good thing." She looked at her hands in her lap for a moment and then looked at him. "But caution can be carried too far."

He shook his head, silent. He had learned to be as comfortable and trusting as a child in Sadie Baxter's company.

"Now," she said. "I have a surprise."

Ah, well, what else was new? Where else did one get genuine surprises these days, if not from Sadie Baxter? Of course, Cynthia Coppersmith was no slacker when it came to surprises . . .

"You're beaming!"

"Weddings," he said. "I like weddings. Baptisms. Confirmations. Even funerals, in a sense. Life events are wondrous."

"I'm going to be cremated, you know."

"Yes, I know."

"I certainly don't want to be laid out in a coffin for everyone to gawk at. Besides, it costs a fortune. Thousands and thousands of dollars, and now they're selling you a liner into the bargain. A liner! That's to go around the casket! As if the casket itself weren't up to the job!"

"Watch your blood pressure," he said, laughing.

"Make sure you put my urn in the rose garden. Don't stick me in that rhododendron grove. It's too shady. Where is Parrish Guthrie, anyway? Is he planted out there? If so, move me across the churchyard!"

"Gosh, I should have brought my notebook to take down all these directions."

She laughed with him. "Isn't it wonderful that we can have such a lively time talking about dying?" She pulled at his arm. "Come, Father, I'm going to show you the ballroom. And I hope you know how privileged you are, for Louella and I are the only ones who have seen it in twenty-four years. Oh, wait. I did let Luther in one day to trap a squirrel."

He walked with her slowly, offering his arm for security. "I'm going to give Olivia and Hoppy the grandest ball you could ever imagine," she said. "I want to give her something she'll remember for the rest of her life."

The ballroom doors were located in the foyer at the foot of the impressive staircase.

"Papa designed the ballroom to go here, so our guests could come sweeping down the stairs in their fine clothes and go right into the festivities. We had friends from all over, 'til Papa's health suffered."

"I've heard," he said gently. "I believe the president visited here."

"President Wilson! I remember he gave me a piece of toffee wrapped in silver paper. I kept it for years. Then, one day I just unwrapped it and ate it! It was still good."

She took the large key out of her pocket and turned it in the lock. "Louella keeps the lock oiled. We use WD-40. What do you use for locks?"

"The very same," he said, feeling excited.

The doors swung open and Miss Sadie stepped over the threshold. "There, now. What do you think?" She looked at him for signs of the admiration this room had always inspired.

"Ah," he said, stricken, needing a place to sit.

"Leaves you speechless, doesn't it, Father?"

"Yes, indeed!" Tattered sheets and blankets were nailed over the windows, furniture of every sort sat moldering along the walls, covered with dust and cobwebs. Great pale splotches appeared on the once-shining parquet floor where water had leaked in and stood in puddles. Some of the parquet tiles had come off their moorings and were scattered about, and the rococo mirrors on every wall needed resilvering, a process of staggering cost, he once learned.

He could have been standing in almost any room of the old Porter place, he thought. How could all this be turned around before June?

"You haven't looked up even once!" Miss Sadie sounded a trifle disgusted.

He looked up, and the sight took his breath away.

"You see! People keep their nose to the ground when they ought to be looking up!"

"A good sermon," he gulped. "Well taken."

Cherubim and seraphim frolicked along the borders of the ceiling and darted among blush-colored clouds. Angels swarmed toward the center of the ceiling in gold-bordered robes of blue and scarlet and purple, their iridescent wings brushed with silver. They bore garlands of roses in their arms, with loose blossoms tumbling down over the borders, so seemingly real that one might rush to catch them as they fell.

"Bravo!" he said quietly, still looking up.

"Papa called it the Heaven Room, after something he'd seen in England in the house of a duke or an earl—I can't remember which."

"It's heavenly, all right." Fortunately, there appeared to be water damage in one area only, which might easily pass for a dark cloud among the shining cumulus variety.

"One day I'll tell you about the time it was painted and who painted it," she said. "Oh, Father, you'll grow weary of my stories."

"Never!" he said, meaning it."

He had laughed today; he had been happy. He didn't know why he had not counted more sunny hours in his life, but he hadn't. God had clearly asked him to, but he was intent on having his own nature, and his own nature could be inward, even melancholy. He didn't like it, but there it was.

At the end of this day, what he wanted more than anything else was the solace of her letters.

A new one had come this morning, and he carried it to his desk, unopened. He put the letter in the drawer, looking forward to sitting down with it after Dooley was upstairs and the little clamor of their supper together was over.

He reminded himself that he needed to have a key made for the desk drawer where he kept her letters. The worn lock was there, but he hadn't inherited the key. Even more than not wanting anyone to discover them, he wanted to protect them for their rarity, for their . . . he couldn't find another word . . . fragility.

As he turned toward the kitchen, the longing he'd felt all day welled up in him again and he went back to the desk. He would read only one line, just the opening, something to sustain him.

My Bookend,

The winter here continues bitter and dark, the work on the book goes poorly, and my heart aches for the consolation of your company. Even so, I am keeping the light . . .

"There's nothing better for the inside of a boy than the outside of a horse," said Hal Owen when he called in the evening. "Let him come for the weekend."

Ah, he'd grown selfish with Dooley. He liked the sound of his tennis shoes on the stairs, the look of astonishment on his face when he ate fried bologna with him for two mornings in a row. He was attached to the bright questions in his eyes, to the occasional breakthrough of a smile or one of those wacky laughs he'd developed with Tommy. He had even made a certain peace with the sound of that blasted jam box thumping above his study.

"He can bring Barnabas," said Hal, sensing the hesitation.

"A boy shouldn't be hanging around the house with a doddering old parson," said the rector.

"Hanging around the house with a parson has saved the day, if you ask me. I'll pick him up after school and you'll get him back after church on Sunday. How's that? I expect you'd like some time to yourself . . ."

No, he thought, he would not like some time to himself. He'd had time to himself for more than sixty years, which was enough for any man. He felt shocked at this odd revelation.

"Timothy? Are you all right?"

"Absolutely. Just a bit jealous of the chicken pie I hear Marge is baking this weekend."

"You know you're invited. It's a standing invitation, has been for twelve years."

"Thirteen, my friend. And thank you. But another time. The boy's backsliding, you know, in the 'ain't' department. I was after him with a stick for a while but slacked off. Marge will send him home talking like a Rhodes scholar."

"I don't suppose there's anything from his mother?"

"Nothing. And Russell is just recovering from the relapse after his fall in the snow."

"What are you going to do about all that?"

"I don't know. I can't seem to come up with a plan that works for anybody, much less everybody. If Russell goes home, Dooley would have to go with him."

"Have to?"

"Hoppy says Russell would need someone to monitor him. If Betty hadn't been around, he could have lain in the snow 'til the buzzards started circling."

"Could you hire somebody to do the monitoring?"

"Who would live in that unheated shack in the middle of a junkyard?"

"True."

"Another thing. If Russell goes out, Miss Pattie goes in. Betty Craig would be done for. She's begged me to protect her from Miss Pattie."

"What about the gardens? Anybody to pitch in there?"

"Not a soul that I can think of. Fortunately, Russell's done such a grand job over the years they won't be that difficult to maintain. But they must be maintained." He heard himself sigh.

"I expect it's costing somebody to keep him at Betty's."

"About four hundred a month, in addition to his social security."

In his opinion, the four hundred covered a lot more than health care for Russell Jacks. Indeed, it was a small price to pay for Betty Craig's sanity, his own peace of mind, and, last but not least, the boy's freedom to keep his mind on his education.

"Considering the circumstances," said the senior warden, who usually got the gist of things, "it sounds like a bargain to me."

The thought came to him as he stopped by the rectory to change jackets for the flag-raising program.

Fun—that thing he was always thinking of having, or feebly attempting to have, or trying awkwardly to figure out how to have—

well, that's what he would have this weekend. He would lighten up and have some fun—he would do something different, something new.

He ran over the list of possibilities. He would, of course, call Cynthia, and he would call whenever the notion struck, whether the rates were down or not. He would go see Homeless who, for all he knew, still hadn't thawed out from the blizzard. He would . . .

He gazed unseeing into the mirror over his chest of drawers, straightening his tie.

"Call Cynthia and visit Homeless" was absolutely as far as he could get with this list. Wasn't there something else he could do, something more innovative, like other people? Didn't people always look forward to the weekend, to eating out or watching a ball game? Well, and there was no place to eat out other than the Grill, except for Mack Stroupe's hot-dog stand next to the Esso station. He was sure it was his imagination, but Mack's hot dogs always tasted like motor oil.

As for watching a ball game, he had never, not even once, been able to follow a game to the end. His mind would wander, he would fall asleep, or he would get up and leave the room, forgetting to come back until after the game was over.

The truth was, he didn't know a blasted thing about having fun. Cynthia, on the other hand, not only seemed to have it, she was very good at making it. In actual fact, they hadn't done much that one could describe as fun, yet they always seemed to have it. With Cynthia, it just naturally happened.

He pulled on his jacket, smiling. Friday afternoon and all day Saturday. That would be his allotment for fun. He would see if he could pull it off. He would call Cynthia tonight and ask her to suggest something.

Not a word had Dooley let slip, not even a hint. And though he'd seen Miss Pearson in front of the bakery the other afternoon, she, too, had kept the secret that Dooley Barlowe was going to sing a solo with the full force of the Mitford School Mixed Chorus behind him.

No wonder the boy had been jumpy as a cat, he realized later. When he wasn't wandering in a daze, he was cussing Barnabas under his breath.

"I heard that," the rector said at breakfast the morning of the flag-raising.

"Heard 'at ol' dog fart is all I heard."

"Dooley . . ."

"All I said was . . ."

"Dooley . . ."

The boy looked at him defiantly. "What are you goin' t' do about it?"

"Same as last time."

Washing someone's mouth out with soap was not a remedy he liked, but it had worked for him when he was a kid. He was sure there were newer techniques, all much smarter and written up in books with deep psychological insights. As for him, he had not asked for this job and was not interested in learning what today's cutting-edge punishment for cussing, if any, might be.

He would, however, make one modern concession.

He let Dooley wash his mouth out himself, as he stood at the bathroom door, recalling the penalty his mother extracted for his own abominable language.

"That ain't so bad," Dooley said, wiping his mouth and looking him squarely in the eye. "It's a whole lot better'n 'at ol' soap in th' kitchen."

Good fellow, he wanted to say, but didn't.

It was what came out of the boy's mouth as the flag was being raised that caused him to catch his breath with unbidden joy. Dooley was doing this? His own Dooley? Why hadn't he thought to invite Puny and Miss Sadie, Percy and Velma, Hal and Marge and Rebecca Jane, Emma—the whole lot? But, of course, he hadn't known about the solo.

He was dashed if he could swallow without choking.

Miss Pearson would need someone to hold her feet on the ground, he could see, or she would float up and over the schoolhouse in a kind of rapture.

They met on the sidewalk after the program, as he and Dooley were leaving for home.

"Good heavens, Miss Pearson!" was all he could find to say.

"Father!" she exclaimed, which was all she could find to say.

There were tears in their eyes as he shook her hand again and again, unable, somehow, to let go.

Jenny passed, carrying her book bag. "You were really great," she murmured softly.

"Mush," said Dooley, bouncing his basketball.

"I can't tell you how terrific that was. It was a glorious thing, hearing God's gift pour out of you like that. And the way your chorus backed you up—strong stuff! I'm proud of you."

"It ain't nothin'."

"No, my friend, it's quite something. I wish Cynthia could have heard you. And your grandfather. And Miss Sadie. Everybody!"

Dooley shrugged. "Jis' ol' school stuff."

"Blast it, Dooley, how did it make you feel to stand up in front of all those people and belt out 'God Bless America'?"

He saw that Dooley couldn't stop the grin that suddenly began spreading across his face. It happened without warning and clearly could not be controlled. "Neat," he said.

"It was, I suppose, the soap that helped do this marvelous thing . . ."

Dooley glared at him. "Yeah, I cain't sing f'r poop usin' 'at ol' stuff in th' kitchen."

Before he turned the corner at Mule's house, he looked up and down the street. If he saw anybody coming, he would stop and examine his fingernails or look more closely at the bark on the tree that had grown through the sidewalk.

He had never been into a beauty shop in his life, nor had a woman other than his mother ever cut his hair. There was absolutely nothing wrong with beauty shops, nor with a woman cutting a man's hair. It's just that it was too strong a dose for him at one sitting after thirteen years with Joe Ivey who, in spite of the brandy he kept sitting in plain view with the hairspray, gel, and setting mousse, knew what the rector liked and how to deliver it.

Another thing—how much would it cost, even with a 20 percent discount? Twice as much as Joe, most likely, to pay for the new sinks she had put in and the carpet, not to mention those color prints of poodles that Mule said cost two hundred dollars to have framed, even without mats.

Double. That's what he should be ready to cough up. If Joe was six bucks, Fancy Skinner would be twelve. He had heard that a tip of ten percent was an insult these days. It was a full twenty or don't bother. That pushed it up to fourteen dollars and forty cents, which he might as well make fifteen, to round it off.

Misery! He would never do this again if his hair grew as long as John the Baptist's. Puny had absolutely refused to do this thing. She claimed it would look butchered, and she wanted no part in giving him an appearance that was beneath his station. He threatened to do it himself, which had not softened her heart.

Thanks be to God, he didn't see a soul when he pushed open the door. But the sight of pink carpet and pink walls gave him a distinct sinking feeling. He would turn around and go home and drive to Wesley as hard as he could go. Losing a hubcap or two was no big deal.

He was starting up the driveway when Fancy yelled from an upstairs window, "Are you my three o'clock? Oh, hey, Father, I thought you were my perm. I'll be right down, don't go away, make yourself at home. You want a glass of tea? It's unsweetened, or I can give you sugar, whichever—you tell me. Maybe you'd like a Coke. I have Classic or Diet, what do you think—you tell me."

If Cynthia Coppersmith had not suggested he go through with this, he would have run and not looked back.

"I like to color-coordinate with my shop," said Fancy, who was wearing pink tights, a pink cashmere tunic, and pink high-heel shoes with ankle straps.

"I'm glad you're here. Cuttin' your hair will put me over th' top this week." She swiveled the chair around, so that he stared at himself in a mirror. At Joe Ivey's, he was able to look out the window at the tops of trees.

"I set a goal every week. Last week I came a bitty bit under. Th' week before that, a bitty bit over. You never know which way it'll go. Now that you walked in, I'll top last week by a hundred dollars!"

His heart sank. Fifteen dollars was clearly a low estimate. Well, let this be a lesson. Let this be a lesson! He felt a wrench in his stomach as she slipped some kind of scarf over his head and around his shoulders. It was such an intense shade of pink it reflected on his face.

"I'll bet you don't put this thing on Buck Leeper."

"Honey, if Buck Leeper ever shows his butt in here again, excuse me, I will personally chase him out with a butcher knife."

"That bad, huh?"

"Have some gum. It's right there on th' magazine. Mule said, 'Fancy, you don't have to cut his hair and take his insults. I'll give you double whatever he spends.' Was that sweet of Mule or what? So, next time Mister High an' Mighty walks through that door, I'm runnin' his tail out of here. *If* he walks through th' door, that is. I iced him so bad when he bossed me, he might never be back. He might cross th' street when he sees me comin'.

"Man, have you got a tight scalp. That's tension. You prob'ly use your brain all th' time. That's what does it. Some people, their scalp just rolls around on their head like baggy pantyhose. You want a little massage? See, that feels better already, right? Oops, these nails. Lord, I nearly poked a hole in you. They're acrylic. Mine won't grow for shoot. I wouldn't drink milk when I was a baby. That's what did it."

"Who's your three o'clock?" he asked darkly. Who in God's name was going to come in here and see him helplessly decked out in this shawl thing?

"Nobody you know, honey. Somebody new from Baltimore. Oh, look at this neck. What a mess. Who does you? Joe Ivey, of course. Joe Ivey has never been to New York City to learn the latest things."

"You go to New York, then?"

"No, but I read the magazines. Th' way he cuts you makes your face look too wide. I'm goin' to just trim it right through here. It's like some kind of *bush.*"

He felt panicked. Why hadn't he brought a hat? He could have brought that old twill garden hat that folded up flat. He could have slipped out of here and been wearing it when he rounded the corner.

"Please," he said, sensing that he was about to croak, "don't do anything different. Like I said, I just want the same thing. Please. Just a trim. Nothing serious." It was as near to pleading as he'd come in years.

"Oh, phoo, that's what they all say. You should've seen J.C. hunker down in this chair like I was goin' to snatch his eyeballs out. You trust me on this, OK?"

She scissored something from above his left ear that fell with a positive thump on his shoulder. He was afraid to speak, and why bother? It was too late.

Not bad, he thought, looking at himself in the mirror at home. He had been too shy to examine himself at the beauty shop. Not bad at all. Yes, his face looked thinner; his jaws looked perfectly hollow. And he could hardly believe she charged only six dollars. He was so grateful he had given her ten. Amazing, he thought, peering intently at his head—he even seemed to have more hair on top. Probably the massage.

He heard the bells toll at Lord's Chapel as he stuffed a canvas bag with a few items from the refrigerator and took a can of water chestnuts from the cabinet.

He missed his dog and his boy. But he was not going to dwell on it. He was going to have supper with Homeless Hobbes. Finally, he was going to have some fun.

CHAPTER NINE

Going On

Winter had been hard; its ravages were revealed in everything from loose roof tiles to crumbling stone walls. With the late-February sunshine predicted to last three days, the town was busy piling up limbs brought down by ice storms, and stomping around on roofs, looking for snow damage.

The sound of hammering drifted down from Fernbank.

According to rumor, this wasn't the much-needed new roof the village had hoped for; this was patching.

When one of the Fernbank roofers named what it would cost to replace "the whole shebang," a hushed reverence moved upon the crowd at the Grill.

They wondered why anyone of Miss Sadie's age and financial security would live in a place that was falling down around her head. It was a comfort to discuss this familiar topic, which had been a town favorite for years. To a man, they were dumbfounded and amazed that she had gone on so long.

"She ain't goin' t' quit, neither," said the roofer, as if he had some confidential information from Miss Sadie herself.

The sound of hammers on the hill and the sight of limbs piled along the curbs seemed to awaken new hope in Mitford. Several people reported hearing a robin sing, and Jena Ivey declared that three purple crocuses had bloomed in her backyard.

"Git over it," said Coot Hendrick. "Winter ain't done yet, and you can take that t' th' bank."

Dearest Timothy,

Miss Addison had a cocktail party, as she calls it, for four cats in the building. Thank goodness, Violet was not able to go, as she has just had a shot and was not feeling sociable. According to the superintendent, who came to fix my faucet, Miss Addison's butler or footman or whatever he is put little heaps of catnip on a silver tray and set the tray on the drawing room floor.

All the cats, it's reported, went absolutely berserk.

They climbed Miss Addison's silk shantung draperies and gave her Louis XIV sofa a good drubbing with their claws. Then they leapt onto the kitchen counter and gobbled up the smoked salmon intended for the horrified people who owned the cats.

It's enough to make one wish for a dog.

Miss Addison said she was told that catnip is a spring tonic and ordered this stuff all the way from a farm in upstate New York. I had entertained the thought of buying some for Violet but have squelched this notion permanently.

Our streets are full of a general sloshiness that lingers and won't go away, as if a glacier is deicing to the north. I forgot to ask on Sunday if anything has poked its head up in my perennial bed. Would you look? I am so homesick I can hardly bear it. I've worked on this stupid book until my eyes are crossing. You won't recognize me. At the airport, you will peer at me and say, "Cynthia?" Then you'll mutter, "No, no, can't be," and walk on.

But oh, this book will be good, I think. I really do believe so. Everyone here seems excited about it, and I pray fervently it will be loved by its readers. Do you know that one of my favorite things is seeing a child reading one of my books? They don't even have to like it. It is merely the sight of a small head bowed over the pages that gives me indescribable joy.

Do you feel the same when your sermons pierce our hearts and convict us of something that must be carried forth or changed in ourselves?

Thank you for sending your typed sermon. I needed to hear all of it. Yes! Intimacy is always about openness, about transparency. Until the Holy Spirit led me into intimacy with Christ, I was as transparent as your iron skillet. It is terribly scary to go around with your very spleen on display, yet, how can He shine through anything that is not made transparent? Well, of course, He could—but well, you understand.

I loved your note confessing that your feelings for me have made you more transparent. Sometimes—well, only once, actually—I've felt a little guilty for falling in love with you. Guilty that I have taken something from you, something very private. I try not to dwell on this.

With much love from
Your bookend

the office

thursday, fog on the heels of sunshine, 56 deg., barnabas snoring, emma making deposit

dear Lord! taken something from me? words cannot express what you have given, do give. that you would love me at all continues to perplex me, i am sorry to say. as we go into Lent ii ponder again and again how the apostles must have felt at losing him, at losing the love that had captured and ennobled and given them something higher than they could have ever known without him. there must have been the deepest despair and disbelief, greater than the ordinary loss of a loved one, until the Holy Spirit arrived on the scene and filled in the blanks. ii have known something of loss, also, in these weeks, these months you have been away, months in which winter has breathed its frost upon our spirits continually. yet i think it is good somehow that we discovered, confessed our feelings for one another and were forced apart to think it through. that at least is true for me, and i am being philosophical about it at the moment. at other moments i could not ask for anything more than to have you here and cook your supper. Afterward, we might sit by the fire and look at the new garden catalogs. there, now, I've run you away with the prospect of such dull evenings, while you might be at the club playing cards or doing the tango.

please do not ever think that you have taken anything from me, but know that you have given me something too precious and amazing to contemplate. and never worry that i won't recognize you. ii would know those blue eyes anywhere, crossed or no.

i kiss you. God bless you and keep you. marge and hal pray for you, as does dooley on occasion.

harold cometh

love, timothy

p.s. nothing poking up, will advise

"He's workin' on his sermon right now, Esther. Can he call you back? He said he has something goin', for a change. He'll call you, or I will. I know it's important. Thirty minutes. Bye."

He could hear her drumming the desktop with her fingers, waiting for him to put the cover on the typewriter.

He swiveled around in his chair. "Well?" he said, pleased with what he had accomplished in less than a half hour. "What did Esther want?"

"You know that big Presbyterian car thing at the Legion Hall on Friday night?"

"Vaguely."

"They asked Esther to do the cakes."

"That was smart," he said, calling up the memory of the cake that had nearly taken him home to glory. Her splendid orange marmalade cake was famed among all the local churches.

"Well, she wants to do something' in the triple chocolate category, for a change, something' called Better Than Sex Cake. But she's nervous as a cat about makin' a change . . . torn, she says."

"Aha."

"She wants to know should she come out with a new cake and throw over the old one that's made her famous? She was wantin' to get your answer by eleven, when she has to start bakin'."

"I have an answer, all right."

"What is it?"

"If it ain't broke, don't fix it."

"Amen!"

"Tell Esther I vote for the orange marmalade, hands down."

"That's what I say! Besides," she said, peering over her glasses, "what could be better than sex?"

He thought he was the last person on earth who should be asked such a question. Nonetheless, he had an opinion. "Certainly not a cake."

"I'll call her back," she said.

He was putting on his jacket to leave when the phone rang.

"Timothy?"

Her voice gave him a fine chill, something like that produced by chalk scraping over a blackboard.

"I'm so glad you're still there," said Edith Mallory.

"What can I do for you, Edith?"

"I think it's what I can do for the Children's Hospital," she said mysteriously.

"And what is that?"

"Remember how you urged me to get involved? Well, you were right, of course. Absolutely right, as always."

"Aha."

"Guess what?"

"I can't."

"Oh, Timothy, do loosen up a weensy bit. I'm calling with good news!"

He couldn't help but notice that when the phone rang, the sun had disappeared behind a cloud. "Fire away."

"I'm going to give ten thousand dollars to the Children's Hospital!"

He wished his heart might have leapt at the thought. Ten thousand would help enormously, but words seemed to fail him.

"Oh, all right!" she said, peeved at his silence. "Fifteen!"

He had never before raised five thousand dollars by keeping his mouth shut. "Wonderful, Edith. You'll never know how desperately it's needed and how thoughtfully it will be used."

"I'd like you to take me there to find out, firsthand."

"You mean, you'd like to look around?"

"Of course, meet the director, talk to the doctors. I'd like some personal contact, after all." She sounded petulant.

"What's your schedule?"

"Could we do it right away? Monday, perhaps? Or Tuesday? Which shall it be? Ed can drive us over. Perhaps we'll have lunch."

The very thought gave him a knot in his stomach. "Monday, I speak at the ECW luncheon about Hope House. There's a long meeting on Tuesday with the building committee. How about Wednesday or even Thursday?"

"Impossible."

"Well, then."

There was a frozen silence. She was waiting, he knew, to be courted and cajoled. Perhaps he should break over a little for the Children's Hospital. Maybe Ron Malcolm could fill in with the ECW.

"Oh, Timothy," she crooned, suddenly thawing. "Why argue over a day or two when children's lives might be in danger? I know how busy, busy, busy you are—of course we can make it Wednesday."

"Thanks for being flexible."

"Flexible? Me? How sweet of you to say that." He heard her take a deep drag on her cigarette.

"Well, then, Wednesday. What time?"

"Ten would be good."

"Let me call the hospital, and I'll get back to you."

"Perfect!" she said.

It wasn't a word he would have chosen.

Ever since Christmas, the thought of the amethyst brooch seemed to hover in his thoughts. Where was it, anyway? He felt a mild distress that he might have lost it. He hadn't seen it in—how long? Had he seen it since he moved here? Yes, he remembered thinking it should be taken to a jeweler and cleaned.

He closed his eyes, trying to visualize where he had put it. Why hadn't he come across it from time to time, if it weren't altogether lost?

He dug through the top left-hand drawer of his chest, where he kept things he didn't need but didn't want to toss out, either. Not there.

He opened his closet door and peered at the top shelves. Maybe. He took the chair that stood by the blanket chest in the hall and set it inside the closet. He took down several of the smaller boxes and put them on the floor by the bed.

Little puffs of dust rose up as he opened them, one by one. Christmas decorations from his last parish. He had searched high and low for these. What were they doing up there?

Buttons. An entire box of buttons. All emptied out of his mother's sewing-machine drawer. He would set them aside for Puny.

Then, the box of his mother's monogrammed handkerchiefs, her silver vanity mirror, a beaded evening bag, a lace collar, a hat pin with filigree work. There, too, was her gold wedding band, with a ribbon slipped through it and tied firmly. She had tied the ribbon herself, he suspected, when she had to remove her ring toward the end.

With the scent of age and mustiness, he also smelled her special smell; perhaps it had been gardenias. So faint, so elusive, it was scarcely there.

"Mother . . ." he said aloud, feeling an odd comfort in the word, the old familiarity of it.

He thought of Miss Sadie coming across the little socks and the certificate. Her departed loved ones seemed bent on speaking to her down the years.

Nearly six decades ago, Willard Porter had carved a message on a crossbeam of the home he hoped to give Sadie Baxter as his bride. Last summer, Miss Sadie had asked her rector to go look at the beam and tell her what was carved there. The legend he found was full of Willard's passionate belief that they would marry and that peace would reign in their lives at last.

Now, Miss Sadie's mother had spoken, helping her find Olivia. In his opinion, Rachel Baxter meant for her daughter to discover the certificate soon after her death. Why would it have been placed so casually in a dressing table, where a daughter would surely look when going through her mother's effects? Clearly, Rachel Baxter had tried to say, Run and find your sister!

What would his own mother say if she could speak to him now? He looked at the lace collar that she had prized, that had been so beautiful on her.

He realized his leg had gone numb, that he'd been sitting among the boxes for a long time. Yet, he hadn't found the brooch. He slid the boxes under the bed and got up, feeling as if his mind had gone away on a short trip and returned to find the surroundings oddly unfamiliar.

He got out of bed on Wednesday morning, feeling the same dread he might feel over an impending root canal. Two root canals.

At the Grill, he was inspired to order a treat that might help him go on with this aggravation.

"Two eggs, scrambled—with bacon and a side of hash browns."

Percy inspected him as if he were a sack of onions. "You sure about this?"

"Dead sure. I'm fed up with eating right."

Percy frowned. "Well, but just this once."

It was a terrible thing when you couldn't watch your own diet without the whole town jumping in to watch it too.

What he'd really like to have was a half-dozen of Winnie's fresh doughnuts, three chocolate-dipped and three glazed, which would leave just enough room to squeak in a napoleon.

"What're you dreamin' about?" Mule slid into the booth, looking dapper in a salmon-colored sport coat, which he had found last summer at Evie Adams's yard sale. Knowing that her dead husband was his exact size, he had appeared at Evie's door at six a.m., well before the crowd, and bought everything Barney had owned, with the exception of his shoes that were triple A's.

"You got your money's worth on that jacket," said the rector.

"Three bucks. You hear about the town museum gettin' started?"

"Esther told me about it yesterday. They're going ahead with fixing up the outside. Hope to have the whole thing operating full-scale in about two years. She said ask around what to put in it, starting with something historic."

"Put Percy's grill in there. That's historic," said J.C., who dropped his loaded briefcase on the seat and slid in. "Or how about his fry grease. That's even more historic."

Percy shook his spatula at the back booth. "Keep talkin' like that, buddyroe, and you'll be history your own self."

"Well," said the rector, "the mayor told me to make a list. What do you think, Mule?"

"Don't ask him," said J.C. "He's so slow it takes him an hour an' a half to watch *60 Minutes.*"

"I got one," Percy called from the grill. "That bench in front of

Lew Boyd's. Been there long as I can remember. A lot of lies been told on that bench."

"Miss Sadie's car," said Mule. "That's about as old a car as you'll find on th' open road. Write that down."

J.C. poured sugar in his coffee and stirred. "Winnie Ivey's oil tank. Nothin' but pure rust, sitting' right on the street in plain view of God an' everybody."

"Somehow, I don't think this is going anywhere," sighed the rector.

"Yeah, well, leave it to Esther. She'll come up with somethin'."

He didn't mention it, but he thought the entire collection of his neighbor's books would be a splendid addition, in case they wanted anything current.

"Oooh," said Edith Mallory.

They arrived at the Wesley Children's Hospital, on a bitterly cold Wednesday, as the sun broke through leaden clouds and shone on the facade of the building. "It's a sign," said Edith, "I just feel it."

All he could feel was a vague gnawing in his stomach, which he reckoned was the beginning of an ulcer.

The meeting in John Brewster's office was worse than he could have imagined. After handing over the check, Edith told the director what color to have his office walls repainted and suggested he get rid of his furniture and start over. "Just because you're a charity," she said, sniffing, "doesn't mean you have to look like one."

John Brewster, whose cheerful personality appeared undaunted, took them to the cafeteria for an early lunch, where Edith cast a withering look at her vegetable plate, telling them how much she hated hospital food.

He was vastly relieved when John winked at him. I can handle this, the wink implied, so relax and eat your tuna sandwich.

There, thought the rector, is a personality trait I desperately need to cultivate. Laissez faire! Easy come, easy go!

The trip through the halls to visit the children, however, could not be taken so lightly. He loathed the way she poked her head in the rooms, looking at the children as if they were so many stuffed sausages. His own heart was breaking.

"Father!" Nine-year-old Gillian Murphy called him from her bed and stretched out her arms.

He stooped and received her hug as if it were a benediction. He was thankful that Edith and John continued down the hall, for tears sprang to his eyes and coursed down his cheeks.

"Blast!" he said, fumbling for the handkerchief he hadn't brought. "See what you've gone and made me do?"

Gillian looked at him almost maternally. "You're sad."

"No," he said, grinning, "I'm happy. You made me happy because you gave me a hug."

"You make me happy," said Gillian, whom he'd visited in this room since he started driving again.

"You look like an angel with that blue ribbon in your hair."

"Nurse Moody put it in. I wanted pink, but she didn't have pink."

"I'll send you a pink ribbon," he promised, having no idea where he'd find one.

Walking up the hill behind Edith in her expensive suit, it occurred to him that, in the language of Coot Hendrick, he'd like to knock the woman upside the head with a two-by-four.

He sat as far away from her in the car as he could. He would have stood on the running board, if cars still had such things. The sliding panel that separated them from Ed Coffey was firmly closed.

Edith studied her fingernails, which he did not take for a good sign. "I certainly don't think your Mr. Brewster was very appreciative."

"I . . ."

"It isn't every day, from the look of things, that someone gives them fifteen thousand dollars."

"You . . ."

"From the look of things, I doubt they know how to use it properly. Perhaps I was too hasty."

Rector Murders Woman in Car, Flees to New Jersey.

He would hide out at Walter's. They'd never find him in that basement room where his cousin kept the paint cans.

"Perhaps so, Edith."

"You know, of course, that I did it for you." She turned and looked at him. "That's what really counts. I did it to give you joy." She smiled then and opened her lizard-skin bag.

Here it comes, he thought.

She took a cigarette from a monogrammed case and held it between her teeth, grinning. Still looking at him, she flicked her lighter and inhaled deeply.

"Ahhh," she said, leaning back. Their compartment filled with blue smoke.

"Thank you, dear, dear Timothy, for the opportunity to do something for . . . for our God."

He could not speak.

"Oh, my," she said, seeing that her skirt had risen well above her knees. "How naughty!" She looked up at him, grinning again. "Do you think I'm naughty, Timothy?"

He would croak if he opened his mouth, so he kept it shut.

She moved closer to him and put her hand on his leg.

"Oh, my dear Timothy, if only you would let me . . . touch you. You would never ever again have even the weensiest doubt about your adoring Edith."

"Edith . . ." he said.

"Timothy."

Her hand moved again as she came closer, and he felt her breath on his cheek.

"Stop!" he cried, lurching forward and banging on the panel. "Pull over at once!"

Ed wheeled into the parking lot of the Shoe Barn, and he leaped from the car while it was still moving.

"I seen you pass th' school in 'at ol' car this mornin'."

"Yes. Well." The walk from the Shoe Barn had been wretched. Twice during the five miles he walked, Ed Coffey pulled the car alongside and called, "Father, Miz Mallory says you shouldn't be walkin' in this cold."

He never once looked around. If he spoke, he would vent the most wicked and abusive language he had ever imagined, much less expressed. No indeed, he would press on in the biting wind and no looking back.

"I thought you said you wouldn't go nowhere with 'at ol' witch."

"I did say that. But circumstances alter cases." He was struggling with an anger so black it made him tremble as he diced the eggs for potato salad. John Brewster would have to take it from here. He was through trying to be accommodating.

"It's m' birthday," said Dooley, looking him in the eye.

"Blast. I forgot. I didn't mean to, I promise."

"I was waitin' t' see if you'd say somethin', but you ain't said nothin', so I'm tellin' you."

"I feel like a heel."

"That's OK. I prob'ly ain't goin' t' remember your birthday, either."

"Please. Don't say ain't. Anything but ain't."

"You know what I want for m' birthday?"

"Let me guess."

"Twenty dollars."

"Really?"

"Jis' one big ol' fat twenty. No fives, no tens, no ones."

"And clearly no small change."

"Nope."

"Where do you expect it to come from?"

"I don't know. It's jis' what I want, that's all. I was jis' tellin' you, like you tol' me you wanted 'at world globe. I ain't—I'm not goin' to get you one, but I reckon it helped you t' tell me you wanted it."

"If you had a twenty, what would you do with it?"

"Carry it in m' pocket, wrap it around them two ones you tell me t' tote. I'd jis' pull it out and ol' Buster, 'is eyes'd pop like a frog's." Dooley made a face so grotesque that the rector nearly fell on the floor laughing.

"So. You want twenty bucks, but just to carry around?"

"That'd be cool."

"In the meantime, what do you want for your birthday dinner? I'll step over to The Local and pick it up. You name it."

"Steak."

"What else?"

"Ice cream."

"Steak and ice cream. No bologna?"

"I'm half-sick of baloney."

"Hallelujah."

"I wouldn't mind t' have some ol' cake or somethin.' If it was chocolate."

"I wouldn't mind to bake you one after we eat."

"Cool," said Dooley. "Can Tommy come for dinner?"

When Tommy left, they walked upstairs.

"Well, buddy, I'd like to congratulate you on becoming thirteen. Shake."

He had folded the twenty three times. Dooley felt it against his palm.

"Man!" he said, unfolding the new bill. "Neat!"

He had become an out-and-out sucker for seeing a smile on that boy's face.

The thought seemed to swim up from some dark grotto in himself, floating to the surface as he picked up the newspaper from the study floor.

His mother's brooch was in the lockbox at the bank.

As he carried it home in his pocket, in the blue velvet pouch, he knew at last why he'd been searching for it, why the thought of it had hovered around him for weeks. The truth was, he wanted Cynthia to have it.

Site of the Mitford
Town Museum

"What do you think?" asked Esther Cunningham.

They were standing in front of the freshly painted sign in Miss Rose's front yard. They might have been looking at Monet's water lilies.

"Beautiful!" said the rector, meaning it.

"Have you ever in your life? Why, they don't even have a town museum in Wesley! You mark my words, this'll bring their TV station runnin'!"

"As well it might. When do we see the statue?"

"Oh, law, that statue! It looks to me like his head's too big. I hope it's just me. But all in all, pretty nice-lookin' and costin' a fortune. Now, listen, Father, I know how you hate to raise money . . ."

"Esther . . ."

"Just this once, you could do somethin'. And I'm not talkin' about bakin' pies. I'm talkin' big money."

"Big money, is it? Why pick on me? What about the Baptists?

What about the Presbyterians? They could auction off another Cadillac."

"Shoot, they didn't raise the price of a used Subaru. All those people just swarmed in there to eat Esther Bolick's cake."

"Aha. Well, about raising money, here's my answer . . ."

Her eyes gleamed.

"I'm not going to do it," he said, standing his ground for dear life.

Esther laughed uproariously. "For a minute there, I thought I had you."

"Your eternal optimism is part of your charm. You persist in thinking you're going to nail me to the wall."

"Oh, and I will," she said, grinning. "One of these days, I will."

Lent would soon be over and the fresh hope of Easter upon them. Cynthia would be home, and the forsythia in Baxter Park would be blooming. He heard the Lord's Chapel bells toll ten o'clock when the phone rang.

"Hello?"

He couldn't precisely identify the sound at the other end.

"Hello?"

There was a long silence, then a sort of squeak. "Tim . . ." It was Cynthia, and she was crying.

"It's OK," he said. "Take your time. I'm right here."

He could hear her muffled sobbing, as if she were holding her hand over the phone.

"I'm right here," he said again, his heart hammering. Was she ill or in some kind of peril? Please, God.

"I . . . ," she said, then another pause. "I can't stop," she said. "I'm OK, it's just that I . . . can't stop." She didn't hold her hand over the phone now but wept unabashedly, as if the weeping were a language of its own and he would understand it.

"I'm so glad . . . you're there," she said. "I just can't do this anymore. It's too hard . . ."

"I understand. I do."

"I think I can't bear it any longer that you're there and I'm here, and all there is, is work, work, work and this . . . this horrid longing. And I know it's going to be over soon, but right now, it seems it will never end. And James absolutely hated the last pages of the book. I'm so angry with him. Why was he so busy careening around Europe if he's so vastly picky about it? Why isn't he here, giving me the kind of direction he's so good at dishing out at the final hour? And I know its wrong to say it, Timothy, but oh, I want to say it, I must say it, Timothy—I'm so very, very angry with you!"

He heard the fresh storm of weeping and knew it was coming from a place he had never touched or known in her. There was an intimacy in the way she bared herself to him, something so oddly intimate that he felt his face grow warm.

"Cynthia . . ."

"Don't . . . don't even speak. I knew I shouldn't have called. I knew I would be hysterical when I heard your voice. I know this is going to take until the end of April now. I won't be able to come home in March.

"Oh, Timothy, why aren't you here? Why aren't you here for even one weekend? Why must you be so tight and controlled and peevish about riding in a taxi or getting mugged or something? I think it is horrid of you, just horrid, horrid, horrid!"

"How long have you worked today?" he asked.

"Twelve or fourteen hours—I don't know."

"Have you eaten?"

"I ate some cottage cheese," she said. He thought she sounded exactly like Gillian Murphy, the day she clung to him and cried because her mother had missed the Sunday visit.

He felt utterly helpless. What could he say, Go wash your face, get some rest, and you'll be fine? He felt the agony of the distance between them in a way he hadn't felt it before. He knew he had denied it. He had never once really faced her absence. He had numbed himself to it. When he missed her, he had simply made himself busy.

"Blast," he said softly.

"What did you say?"

"I said that I love you, though I know you don't believe it."

"No, I don't! I don't believe it at all. I think you like the idea of being in love as long as I'm far away and can't be any trouble to your feelings."

"Cynthia . . ."

"There. I've hurt you. I knew I would somehow hurt you if I made this call."

"I don't know what to say. I . . . am the one who's hurting you, and I regret it."

"Oh, poop! Stop regretting! Don't fall into that bottomless mire of regretting. Just get up and do something, Timothy—I don't know what!" She sounded exhausted.

He didn't know what either.

He put the blue pouch in his breast pocket, though it made a slight lump.

The book Emma gave him for Christmas went in his briefcase, along with a change of socks and underwear and a fresh shirt, nothing more. If he looked like a hick, well then, so be it.

He told Emma he would be away for two days and turned his back on her before the grin even started spreading across her face.

"I'm going to see Walter," he announced to the bookcase, which was true. He would pop into Walter's Manhattan office for precisely five minutes, just to see the look on his cousin's face. He would be only too happy to dial 911 when Walter slumped over in shock, unable to speak.

Of course, he was insane to make the trip. There was absolutely no question at all in his mind, especially with Easter only ten days away and the preparations that had to be made. But how often did he do something insane, after all? The last time was so far in the past that it was no longer considered insane—now, half the population was doing it.

The thought of arriving at the New York airport alone, with only her address on a slip of paper, gave him palpitations. But he must swallow it down like a dose of bitters and get on with it.

"My, my," said Emma, her eyes glittering. She wasn't sure she could put her finger on it exactly, but she felt suddenly proud of her rector. He looked handsome, even taller, and—she had never thought this particular thing before—very distinguished.

He stood at the sink, washing the supper dishes, consumed with plans for her happiness.

He would take her to one of those restaurants in the book, one with four stars, certainly. Yet, if there was anything he couldn't abide, it was a snooty maitre d'—weren't you supposed to give them twenty dollars just for letting you in the door, or was it fifty? The very thought made his knees weak.

He wanted it all to go smoothly, right down to hailing a taxi. When it came to that, he could whistle as well as the next one. Hadn't he and Tommy Noles been world-class whistlers in Holly Springs, able to wake the dead a half-mile away?

He washed the hamburger platter and whistled as loudly as he could, just for practice.

He heard Barnabas hit the study floor running, scattering a braided rug to kingdom come. He skidded to the sink and stood on his hind legs, thrilled to be summoned.

"Here," said the rector, proffering a tea towel, "I'll wash and you dry."

Perhaps he should have let her know; he should have called to say he was coming, but somehow, he couldn't do it. He kept seeing her as she opened the apartment door and the blue surprise in her eyes, and he knew he wanted it this way.

That he made it to her apartment building intact gave him a great sense of triumph. He was trembling inside like a schoolboy as he took the scrap of paper out for the last time and looked at her apartment number, which, though he knew it by heart, he kept forgetting.

"May I help you, Father?"

It was the doorman, he supposed, all gotten up in braid and gold buttons. "I'm seeing someone on your tenth floor. I should have brought flowers . . ." He looked up and down the street, as if flowers might appear at the curb.

"May I ask who you're seeing on our tenth floor?"

"Miss Coppersmith. Miss Cynthia Coppersmith. I'm her . . . priest."

"Very well. I'll buzz you up."

They went into the lobby, where the doorman, inordinately well-dressed to be pushing buzzers, gave 10C a sharp blast.

They waited.

"Must be in the shower," the rector said, helpfully.

"I'm thinking I saw Miss Coppersmith leave early this morning, as I was coming on. I can't be sure."

The doorman pushed again and waited.

"Has the volume up on Mozart, very likely. Do keep ringing."

The doorman gave another long alarm. "I don't believe she's in, sir."

He had what his mother always called "a sinking feeling," as if some vital force went out of him, and he needed to sit down.

"Just once more, if you'd be so kind." He hadn't meant to sound plaintive, but there it was.

The doorman rang again. "Not in, I think. Perhaps having a bit of shopping."

He felt for the brooch, as a child might feel for a blanket. Then, he looked up and saw an elderly woman in a dark fur coat leaving the elevator.

She walked with a cane and was accompanied by a man in a uniform, who carried an aging, long-haired cat of considerable size.

He waited until she nearly passed him.

"Miss . . . Addison?"

She turned and peered at him, squinting. As rustic as he may be, he could tell that Miss Addison had enjoyed a number of face-lifts and was wearing contacts. Close up, she seemed at once forty-five and eighty-three.

"Yes, and who are you?"

"I'm a friend of Cynthia Coppersmith—my neighbor. Ah, your neighbor, to be exact."

"Lovely Southern accent. You're that father she's told me about, I presume."

He felt suddenly daring, expansive. "And what, exactly, did she tell you?"

"Oh, just that you're wonderful, among other things." She smiled a very sophisticated sort of smile, he thought. "I do hope that being wonderful hasn't gone to your head, however."

"Miss Addison, let that be the least of your concerns!" He had to restrain himself from giving her a hug.

"You've come a long way, I should think."

"Yes, very. Up before dawn!"

"Well," she said, leaning on her cane, "I dislike exceedingly having to tell you where she is."

His heart hammered. "Please," he said.

"She's gone home to Mitford."

CHAPTER TEN

Cousins

"Was he expecting you, Father?"

"Not in the least."

"May I give him your name?"

"Just say it's one of his Irish cousins. It's a surprise."

She smiled. "He hates surprises."

"I know."

"But I'll do it for the clergy."

"Thank you."

Walter opened his office door and peered out. "Good God!" he said, freezing in his tracks.

"Ah, and He is good, cousin."

"I can't believe it!"

"I can't believe it myself."

"In New York? Here? A country bumpkin, a bucolic rube . . . ?"

"A hick," he said, grinning.

They embraced heartily, Walter kissing him on both cheeks, which he'd once learned in France and thought a splendid idea. "There was a lot of backslapping and general punching about, like two boys," his secretary later told a friend.

"This, Timothy, is New York!" Walter yelled above the clamor of the restaurant. He held up an enormous deli sandwich as evidence and bit into it with conviction.

"Powerful attorneys eat like this? What happened to nouvelle cuisine?"

"Completely out of fashion! Now, tell me everything. Why are you here? How long are you staying? I'll ring Katherine to take the Christmas ornaments off the guest room bed!"

He didn't have the heart to tell the truth—that he'd flown all the way to a place he never intended to visit, only to discover that the one he'd come to see had passed him in the air, hurtling in the opposite direction.

"It's like this . . ." He couldn't think of a lie if his life had depended on it. "I came to see Cynthia."

"That's the spirit!"

"And she wasn't home."

Walter suspended his garlic pickle in the air. "She let you come all the way to New York—and she wasn't even home?"

"She didn't know I was coming," he said, feeling miserable. "It was supposed to be a surprise."

"And you got the surprise."

Thank heavens, Walter wasn't laughing like a hyena. In fact, his cousin considered this piece of information very soberly.

"She flew to Mitford this morning."

"Rotten luck, old fellow. But Katherine will be thrilled to see you. You're staying the weekend, of course!"

"I'm on my way to the airport, actually."

Walter looked at him and shook his head. "I've known you for fifty-six years, and you never cease to amaze me."

"What's so amazing?"

"That you mustered the courage to come here in the first place—we know how disconcerting this sort of thing is for you. And that you came without telling Cynthia! Quite a romantic piece of business for a country parson."

"Foolish would be the word."

"Actually, I like my word, and I'm sticking with it. You've always been a slow starter, Cousin, but once you get going, stand back."

"There's a rye seed between your front teeth."

"You love her then?"

"What do you think?"

"Just answer my question."

"Yes. She's . . . good for me."

"In what way?"

"Oh, gets me out of myself."

"There's an accomplishment."

"Makes me laugh."

"Go on."

"I trust her. She's real."

"Like Katherine."

"Well . . ."

They both laughed then, with affection for the outspoken, salty-tongued Katherine.

"Not like Katherine, exactly," said the rector, "but in that league."

"The big leagues, then." After nearly thirty years, Walter still thought his wife the most compelling woman he'd ever known. "What are you going to do about all this?"

"I've never understood why people think I should do something about it. Isn't loving her enough?"

"Nope. That's the way it is with feelings like this. You've got to take them somewhere. They can't be allowed to merely dangle around in space. Ask her to marry you."

He felt his heart hammer.

"Either you're blushing or your blood pressure is going out the roof," Walter said.

"Sometimes I'm afraid to move forward, but I'm terrified to turn back."

"There comes a time when there is no turning back. You'll know it when you get there."

"Thanks for your understanding. Sometimes you can be rather . . ."

"A cad," said Walter, finishing his sentence.

"I love you, pal."

"And we love you, Timothy, and want the best for you. You know we pray for that."

"And please don't stop. I've got to get out of here. Which side of the street should I stand on to hail a taxi for the airport?"

"I'll walk you to the best place. Katherine will never believe you've been here. She'll think I'm hallucinating on the antibiotics I'm taking for a sinus infection."

"Is there a store of any kind nearby? A shop?"

"What are you looking for?"

"A pink ribbon," he said, feeling brighter.

When he turned the corner at Wisteria, he saw lights in Dooley's room but could see no lights in the little house next door. He had stood by for more than four hours, which he'd spent dozing in an airport chair, refusing to think of the precious time being wasted.

He felt utterly exhausted. "Lord," he said aloud, which was both an appeal and a thanksgiving.

It started to rain as he pulled the car into the garage. He could hear Barnabas barking wildly in the kitchen.

After receiving a good lathering about the chin, he went with Barnabas to Dooley's room and found him sleeping, the jam box going full blast. He turned it off, covered the boy with the blanket, and went wearily across the hall.

He felt the little bump in his breast pocket and removed the blue pouch and put it on the dresser. Then he unpacked his briefcase.

Why were there no lights next door? Was she sleeping? Was she, in fact, safely home?

He went to the window and looked out at her house. He saw a light come on in her bedroom, just before the Lord's Chapel bells tolled eleven.

He hurriedly splashed water on his face, washed his hands, brushed his teeth, and combed his hair, regretting every moment it took to do it.

The rain had become a downpour as he ran through the hedge and up her back steps, huddling close to the door as he knocked. At last, he opened her never-locked door and shouted, "Cynthia! Are you there?"

"Cynthia!" he called again, going through the kitchen to the stairs.

She appeared on the landing in her bathrobe, her hair bristling with the pink curlers he knew so well.

"Hello," he said, dripping on the carpet. There was a long silence. "You'll never guess where I've been."

"I can't imagine." Her voice was as frozen as the dark side of the moon.

"New York. I've been to New York. I went looking for you."

"You . . . were in New York?" Even in the dim light, he could see the utter astonishment in her eyes.

"It was supposed to be a surprise."

"I don't believe it!"

"Miss Addison invited me to lunch, but I went to a deli with Walter instead."

He saw a thousand fleeting emotions in her face, then she flew down the narrow staircase and into his arms, weeping.

In all his life, he had never had such a hug. It was as if his neighbor poured every power she possessed into it. He became warm all over and full inside. "Cynthia," he murmured, wanting to weep himself, but only for joy.

"I'm so happy to see you!" she said, sobbing. "I can't believe you went to New York, that you really did such a wonderful thing, and then . . ."

"And then you weren't there. I was . . ."

"Devastated! Exactly the way I felt when I came home and you weren't here. Dooley said you had gone away for two days to see your cousin. I had so wanted it to be a surprise! I was going to knock on your door, and you would come padding out from your study, and Barnabas would jump up and lick my face, and you would kiss me, and . . ."

"And I was going to knock on your door, and you would open it and be astounded, and you would know that I really do . . ."

"Do what?"

". . . love you. You would know it, then. I would have somehow . . . proved it. And you could be at peace about it."

She took his face in her hands and looked into his eyes. He thought her curlers had never been more beautiful.

"I'll never forget that you did this thing."

He kissed her. It was a long, slow kiss that penetrated some ancient armor. He felt the top of his head tingle, as if Joe Ivey had applied a lavish dose of Sea Breeze.

They sat on the bottom step, holding each other.

"I think the top of my head just tingled," he said hoarsely.

"I thought you were supposed to get cold chills on your right leg. It's me whose head is supposed to tingle!"

"You mean, it didn't?"

"I cannot tell a lie. It didn't."

He looked so crestfallen that she laughed deliriously. "Goofy!" she said, kissing his cheek. "My goofy, goofy guy!"

He called the office and told Emma he would be late. "Late? I thought you were in New York City!"

"I was in New York, but now I'm in Mitford."

"Well, that explains it," she said airily.

At nine-thirty, Cynthia popped through the hedge to the rectory.

He had laid the table for breakfast in the dining room, something he had done only a few times in thirteen years. On the other side of the window, the birds were at the feeder, and the sun shone warmly on every wet branch from the night's rain.

"Timothy!" she said, with something like wonder. "You've outdone yourself!"

And he had, rather. Grilled sausages from the valley, grits, an omelet with mushrooms and Monterey Jack, Avis Packard's homemade salsa, English muffins with a coarsely-cut orange marmalade, and coffee that was still in the bean only moments ago.

"I love salsa!" she said, helping herself after the blessing. "I love grits!"

His heart swelled at the very look of her; he was thrilled to see her eating like a stevedore.

She dipped into the salsa. "I've decided I'm not going to do *Violet Goes to New York*. James thinks I'm some kind of milk cow, I suppose, made to bring forth whatever strikes his fancy.

"Besides, I'm not going to work myself to death doing a book I don't even want to do. If anything, I'll do *Violet Goes to Mitford!* How's that?"

"Terrific! That's the spirit!"

"Violet Visits the Parson! Violet Takes a Much-Needed Holiday in the South of France! Violet Gets Sick and Tired of Being a Cat and Becomes a Dog!"

"You're on a roll," he said, buttering her muffin. "Best-sellers, every one!"

"Oh," she giggled, leaning back in her chair. "I'm so glad to be home."

"Let's go for a walk after breakfast."

"And see Miss Rose and Uncle Billy?"

"Do we have to? She was threatening cinnamon stickies the last time they invited us, or was it banana pudding? Well, at least we can see the new sign the mayor put up in their yard."

"Let's go shopping at The Local, too, and I'll make dinner for you and Dooley tonight."

"Excellent! I accept. And we can stop off and see the new kneelers at Lord's Chapel. But of course, you'll see them on Sunday."

The light faded from her eyes. "I have to go back tomorrow afternoon."

"No . . ."

"It's the revisions, you see. There's no help for it. This . . . my dearest, is stolen time."

Stolen time.

He took her hand and turned it over to see the small, uplifted palm. He kissed its softness and placed her palm against his cheek.

Stolen time.

He would willingly be the blackest of thieves.

He remembered a speaker at a seminar who had put five large stones in a glass. Those were the important things in life, the speaker said and went on to demonstrate how the small stones, or less important things, could easily be put in and shaken down among the cracks.

However, if the small stones were put in first, it was impossible to add the large stones.

He called Emma. "I won't be in at all, actually."

The last time he hadn't come in at all, she remembered, he'd been deathly sick. He certainly didn't sound sick this time. He sounded like he had never felt better in his life.

They were going out the back door when the phone rang.

"Father?"

"Yes, Evie?"

"Forgive me for calling you at home, Father, but I just had to ask . Can you, would you please come by for a few minutes?"

He could hear Evie trying to suppress the tears that always threatened when she talked with her priest.

"It's nothing really bad this time, it's just . . ." She hesitated for a moment, then wailed, ". . . it's just *general!*"

"I'm on my way," he said.

"What did you get in your stocking?" Miss Pattie wanted to know.

"My stocking?" asked Cynthia, who inspected her legs at once.

"She thinks it's Christmas," said Evie, helping her mother to the sofa, where she sat down, plump and serene as a cherub.

"We baked it all morning!" Miss Pattie exclaimed.

Cynthia joined the old woman on the sofa. "Really?"

"I baked, Evie basted. But we do our cornbread dressing separate. We don't like stuffing." Miss Pattie wrinkled her nose.

"Now, she thinks it's Thanksgiving," said Evie, looking desperate. "She likes holidays."

"Have a drumstick!" Miss Pattie passed a green ashtray to Cynthia, who stared at it, then selected something imaginary from it and took a large bite. The rector noted that she also pretended to chew.

"Delicious!" she said bravely, wiping the corners of her mouth with her fingers. "Just the way I like it! Juicy on the inside, crisp on the outside!"

"Not too dry, is it?" Miss Pattie leaned forward with interest.

"Not one bit!"

"I like the part that goes over the fence last, myself."

"Mama, for Pete's sake!" said Evie.

Miss Pattie turned to the rector. "Have some cranberry sauce, and pass it to your wife." She gave him a copy of *Southern Living* from the lamp table. "It's homemade, you know."

"Thank you," he said, handing the magazine to Cynthia as if it were a hot potato.

"Oh, mercy, I forgot." Miss Pattie lifted the hem of her dress and tucked it into her collar. "Father, would you say the blessing?"

"You're wonderful," he said. They had detoured to a bench in the bookstore garden.

"I am?"

"To eat the drumstick."

She leaned her head to one side and smiled.

"I thought," he said, feeling oddly moved, "that was the most generous thing I've ever seen anyone do."

"Wouldn't you have done the same?" He saw the laughter in her eyes.

"You know I wouldn't, and I'm less the man for it. But for you, it was . . . natural."

"Yes, well, you see, I prefer dark meat."

They laughed so hard that someone passing on Main Street looked suspiciously into the tiny garden.

"To tell the truth, I was frightened to death," she said at last.

"Whatever for?"

"Because I didn't want to embarrass you, or hurt Evie's feelings, or disappoint Miss Pattie. But I couldn't just sit there staring at that ashtray in the shape of a frog. So I ate the drumstick."

"Well done," he said, squeezing her hand.

"It's the first time I've been part of your . . . work. It was an honor, Timothy."

As they walked to The Local, he thought of the relief they'd seen on Evie's face and Miss Pattie sitting upright on the sofa, snoring peacefully. Yet, the visit had been nothing more than a Band-Aid on a gaping wound. He had always wrestled with the frustrating smallness of the things he was able to do. "Let God take care of the big stuff," a seminary friend once said. "It's our job to fill in the cracks. Kind of like caulking."

As they shopped for vegetables at The Local, Miss Pattie's singsong voice came to him: ". . . and pass it to your wife."

When Cynthia glanced up from the artichokes, his face grew suddenly warm, and he could scarcely look her in the eye.

She had made a superb dinner in his own kitchen. Dooley had eaten like a horse and, after washing the dishes at lightning speed, had gone to spend the night with Tommy.

Now they sat together on the sofa, holding hands and listening to one of her Mozart CDs on his player. Tonight was certainly not a night for the tango. Or was it the rhumba?

The smallest of fires crackled on the grate, and he thought how this very thing was what he had wanted all his life. In some unspoken place in himself, in a place he had never regarded or chosen to recognize, had been the longing to sit with someone in this inexplicable peace. He felt oddly complete, as if the final piece of a jigsaw puzzle had been slipped into place.

"How was it for you in New York?" she asked, putting her head on his shoulder. "Were you frightened?"

"Frightened? I was frightened of going, but once I got there, I was . . . almost happy, I think. Flying seems to be the worst of it, the taking off and the landing. But in the end, old fears passed away, and there was the good fellow in the taxi and Miss Addison and Walter. Miss Addison felt woefully sorry for me. She said that very thing had happened to her in Vienna."

"Really? Tell me."

"She went there as a surprise to meet her husband while he was on a business trip, and all the while he was flying to her in Paris."

"Paris to Vienna, New York to Mitford, it's all the same," she murmured against his cheek. "You're my hero."

He had been a lot of things but never ever a hero. He cleared his throat. "I don't think I'd like to do it again." He thought he should say that, just for the record.

"Did you see Palestrina?"

"The Barnabas of the cat kingdom! Large! She had it in for me. I could tell by the look in her eyes. I would not want to be in a closed room with that cat."

"Oh, Palestrina is all bark and no bite."

They laughed uproariously.

Ah, but it felt good to laugh! Why didn't he laugh more often? He had asked himself that very thing a hundred times. Well, and who would he laugh with? Not Emma! And getting a grin out of Dooley Barlowe was like looking for a needle in a haystack.

He drew her close and said, "I have something for you."

"A new joke from Uncle Billy!"

"I haven't had a joke from Uncle Billy in months."

"Well, then, I can't guess."

"I'll be right back," he said, noting that Barnabas helped himself to the warm place he left on the sofa.

When he came down again to the study, she had curled up with his dog, who was fresh from an afternoon bath. "If Violet Coppersmith could see you now . . ." he said.

"Cardiac arrest!"

He passed on to the kitchen, where he took a dog biscuit from the cabinet. "All right, old fellow, off with you!" Barnabas leapt from the sofa and dashed after the biscuit that had skidded under a wing chair.

Why did he have to feel winded from the stairs as he handed her the blue velvet pouch? Why did his knees creak like a garden gate when he sat down beside her? In any case, he thought her face lighted up like the bush he strung outside her door at Christmas.

"May I take my time looking inside?" She drew her bare feet under her and leaned against the cushions.

"There's no hurry."

She held the pouch in both hands, happily feeling the contours of what it contained. "It's the moon, I think!"

"Yes! You've hit it on the head. And the stars are in there somewhere, too—I collected them last night after the rain."

Sudden tears sprang to her eyes.

"Cynthia! Blast!"

"I'm sorry!" she said, laughing and crying at once. "I don't mean to do it. It's just that I love your . . . heart, Timothy."

She reached at last into the pouch and felt the brooch and drew it out.

"It was my mother's," he said. He had intended to say more, had in fact rehearsed a small speech, but it left him.

She held it in her palm and gazed at it, as if stricken, tears streaming down her cheeks. Good grief, he thought, would this never end? She was worse than the man in the attic, who had bawled his head off every time something touched him. Worse than that, weeping was nearly as catching from his neighbor as was laughter—he felt himself choking up.

"Cynthia, stop it this minute!" he said in a voice from the pulpit.

She looked at him then and laughed and touched his face with her hand and leaned to him, kissing his forehead. "Thank you," she said.

Later, he remembered that his mother had done that very thing—kissed his forehead and thanked him and wept.

They walked to her house, passing single file through the gap in the hedge.

"I'll see you tomorrow, then," he said on the porch stoop. "What time shall we leave for the airport?"

"No later than noon."

"Consider it done," he said, tracing her cheek with his finger.

"Bookends," she whispered, putting her arms around his neck.

"You are the most beautiful thing I've ever seen in my life."

She gazed at him, the joy beating in her. "I'm not going to ask you to marry me."

It took a moment for what she said to sink in. He stood very still, as if moving or breathing would expose him, like a rabbit before a hound in the field.

In the glow of the porch light, he saw her eyes turn that mesmerizing shade of periwinkle. She smiled and said, "You'll have to do the thing yourself, my dearest."

"Aha." He thought she looked exactly as Violet might look when sitting at the edge of a fish pond.

Safely through the hedge, he discovered his circulation seemed to have shut down; he felt he had turned to stone. Marriage!

He carried the brooch upstairs, his mind crowded with thoughts. Why was fear always so close upon the heels of his joy, overtaking it every time?

He laid the brooch on the dresser, thinking of her reluctance to leave it with him to be cleaned and the catch repaired. She had at last relented, saying she would wear it always and especially for her confirmation at Lord's Chapel. He went to bed with the image of Stuart Cullen placing his hands on her head at the altar rail.

Lying there, he prayed for deliverance from his fear and confusion, ashamed that he could not do what others appeared able to do every day—take a stand and stick by it.

At midnight, he remembered that he still didn't have a title for his Easter sermon.

He had planned to preach "The Glad Surprise," for that, after all, is what the resurrection had been, coming as it did after the horror of the execution, a hasty funeral, and the loss of hope among the disciples.

On the other hand, "All for Love" contained the entire message of Christ's birth, death, and resurrection in a mere three words. That was the gist of it, the condensed version, the bottom line.

The issue of love, he thought, was surrounding him on all sides.

". . . and pass it to your wife," he heard Miss Pattie say in his dreams. ". . . and pass it to your wife."

After the mournful watch of Maundy Thursday, Mitford awoke to falling snow on Good Friday.

"What'd I tell you?" grinned Coot Hendrick, who was doing his part to steam up the windows of the Main Street Grill.

"Man," groaned J.C. Hogan, who despised snow and especially didn't relish a fulfillment of prophecy by someone with stubs for teeth.

Miss Sadie's extensive roof patching was finished, and the work in the ballroom went at a pace.

"Father," she said, ringing up soon after the ground had turned white, "what do you think of this snow?"

"I'm trying not to think of it at all!" he said with feeling.

"Louella bought a straw hat for Easter, but she declares you can't wear straw in the snow."

"Easter is not about weather. Tell Louella to wear her new straw. We'll be looking for it."

Miss Sadie turned from the phone and warbled into the distance, "He says wear it anyway, he'll be looking for it!"

"How's it coming in the ballroom?"

"Oh, Father! You won't believe how much it's costing. I nearly fainted when I heard what it takes just to scrape the window casings. I had to sit down—the room was spinning every which way. But I'm going through with it! Do you think the Lord will look on this as wrong stewardship, spending so much money on a room we probably won't step foot in again?"

"Miss Sadie, when you consider all those harpists crowding around in heaven, and the mansions and streets of gold, well then—I believe the Lord knows something about big doings, Himself."

"She's my only family, Father."

"Absolutely. I agree one hundred percent. Make that a hundred and twenty."

"I've never had anyone to do for 'til now."

"You can't take it with you, Miss Sadie, and I don't believe Lord's Chapel could bear the blessing of . . . your further generosity."

"Guess who I'm thinking of inviting?"

"I can't guess."

"Absalom!"

"Excellent."

"But his sister won't come. I'm sure of it. Wouldn't you think, Father, that a person who calls themselves a Christian would have forgiven and forgotten after all these years?"

"What makes you think she hasn't?"

"I asked Absalom when he was preaching at Lord's Chapel and you were in Ireland. I said, 'Absalom, has Lottie forgiven me for not marrying you?' I was very direct!"

"The only way to be."

"Absalom just shook his head, and said, 'No, Sadie, I'm afraid not.' I could see it troubled him. And I blurted out something I've been wanting to say for more than sixty years. I said, 'It seems to me she'd be grateful I didn't marry you, so she could keep you for herself!' "

"Strong words," he said, smiling.

"Absalom laughed, but deep in my heart, Father, I felt mean as a snake for saying it."

"Christians hardly ever live up to our expectations, Miss Sadie."

"I think you should know, Father, that I've forgiven her for not forgiving me."

"That's the spirit!"

She sighed, and he heard the rare weariness in it.

"It seems to me you could use a hug."

"A hug?"

"Have you had one since Sunday?"

"Not that I can think of, but the man doing the plasterwork shook my hand."

"I'll be right up," he said.

Miss Sadie leaned on her cane in the rubble of the ballroom and peered at him. "What about Dooley?"

"What about him?"

"Haven't you done your part yet?" she asked tartly. "You're supposed to do your part and be looking into schools."

"Yes, well, how right you are. And I haven't done my part because, to tell the truth, I hate the thought of sending the boy away. Now, don't flog me, Miss Sadie. I'm just telling you the way it is."

"I hope you don't mind my saying so, Father, but that is very selfish thinking."

There was a meaningful silence. "I'll do it," he said at last, feeling as if he had choked down a dose of paregoric.

" 'Love is an actual need, an urgent requirement of the heart,' " he read aloud from an old essay on marriage that he found in his files.

" 'Every properly constituted human being who entertains an appreciation of loneliness . . . and looks forward to happiness and content feels the necessity of loving. Without it, life is unfinished . . .' "

Barnabas dropped his head on his front paws.

Was it true that without love, life is unfinished? Without Christ's love, yes, no doubt, definitely. But the love of another earthly being? He had never thought his bachelor life without love was unfinished, but then, he'd had plenty of love coming from other quarters.

" 'The bosom that does not feel love is cold, the mind that does not conceive it is dull . . .' " His voice trailed off. Still snowing. Dooley studying. Barnabas snoring. The house chilling.

" 'What is to be sought is a companion, a congenial spirit . . . who, under any given combination of circumstances, would be affected, feel, and act as we ourselves would . . .

" 'This is a companion who is already united to us by the ties of spiritual harmony, which union it is the object of courtship to discover.' "

Already united to us by the ties of spiritual harmony . . .

What a man wanted at a time like this was a good pipe, but he didn't smoke. What a man might crave at such an hour was a dram of old whiskey, but he didn't drink. Then, the thing he yearned for most became plain as the nose on his face:

He needed someone to talk to.

Who would it be? Not Walter. Walter had already put in his two cents' worth. Not Katherine, who would give him a proper upbraiding for not having done the thing already.

He thought of Marge Owen, the first friend he had made when he came to Mitford. They had shared many confidences over the years, but he hadn't seen much of her since Rebecca Jane came to Meadowgate and Dooley arrived at the rectory. Besides, he knew precisely what she would say:

"Follow your heart, Timothy."

Blast it, that was the problem. One moment, his heart was filled with longing for Cynthia, and the next moment, the mention of marriage could turn it to stone. His heart was jerking him this way and that, precisely as Barnabas had done when being leash-trained.

What did he want to talk about, anyway? What was his question?

He sat at the desk in the study, staring into the hedge at the rear of Baxter Park, unseeing.

Could he love her fully, freely, without betraying his love for God? Wasn't their love, after all, *from* God? He believed this.

Well, then, how would marriage affect his ministry? What might be lost? No, he thought. That's not the question. Try this: What might be gained?

But he was avoiding the real issue, and he knew it. The issue was not love, nor betrayal, nor even whether his labors might gain or lose meaning.

The real issue was fear.

He tried to name the fear and felt the discomfort of naming it. It was the fear of giving in, of going under, of losing control.

He had made a full surrender once, thinking it the end of surrender. And now, this came, and he had to face it and be just with her and with himself. But was it too late for justice?

If they were to marry, what about his infernal diabetes and his set-in-his-ways sort of life? Could he even share a bed with someone after years of sleeping alone?

Another thing. It was no small matter that she confessed to sleeping with her cat. And did he not sleep with a dog the size of a sofa? And weren't cats and dogs natural enemies from the beginning of time? He could see them now, the whole lot of them, piled on the bed like so many coats at a party. One wrong move . . .

It was one thing to consider the broad view of marriage, as the idealistic essayist had done. It was another to think of the sore details, the nitty-gritty, the way things really were, day to day.

Yet, he knew that he wanted her urgently—her encouraging companionship, her bright candor, her grand good humor. He knew, too, that kissing her and holding her were often excruciating and made all the worse by his holding back and holding in and laboring to keep a wall of defense around himself, so there would be no spilling over like a bursting dam.

Yesterday, he and Dooley had bumped elbows in the kitchen, splashing soda from their glasses onto the floor. As they squatted down to wipe it up, the dark liquid of Dooley's Coke ran into the colorless liquid of his Diet Sprite. You couldn't tell where one began and the other left off. Was he willing to blend into the life of another human being for the rest of his days, and have her blend into his?

That, of course, was the Bible's bottom line on marriage: one flesh. Not separate entities, not two autonomous beings merely coming together at dinnertime or brushing past one another in the hallway, holding on to their singleness, guarding against invasion. One flesh!

If he could do the thing at all, could he stick it through? Would he be of one mind at the church altar and of another mind later? Could he trust himself?

The essay had called the power to love truly and devotedly "a sacred fire, not to be burned before idols."

A sacred fire. And if sacred, then durable? The word held a mild comfort. A durable fire.

Lord, take this fear and dash it. Rebuke the enemy who is the creator of all fear, and give me grace to be the man you've called me to be, no matter what lies in store. If I'm to spend the rest of my life with her, with this lovely . . . this gracious spirit, then open the door wide. Swing it open, I pray! And if this is not pleasing to you, well, then . . .

He could not imagine the other, could not imagine going on without her. Even in prayer, his heart was fickle and deceitful, turning this way and that.

With a bare two hours of daylight left, he fixed Dooley's supper, put it in the oven, snapped the red leash on Barnabas, and headed out to see Homeless Hobbes.

He hadn't talked with Homeless about much of anything, really, but he came away refreshed.

It meant something for a parson to have a place to go where no one judged him or asked anything of him or expected him to be anything special. They had sat together before the wood stove, contented with one another's company, each doing the other some profound good without even trying.

He was headed up to bed when he heard the antiquated blast of the front doorbell.

Barnabas dashed down the stairs and crouched by the mail slot, growling.

He had no earthly idea who the tall, bony, red-haired woman was who stood on the porch stoop, flanked by suitcases, squinting at him through heavy bifocals.

"H'lo, Cousin Timothy," she said in a throaty voice. "It's Cousin Meg from Sligo."

CHAPTER ELEVEN

Meg

Behind the bifocals, her eyes looked like the magnified eyes of a housefly that he'd seen on the cover of Dooley's natural-science book.

"Cousin . . . Meg?" He held Barnabas, who was still growling, by the collar.

"You know," she said, pushing her hair behind her ears, "Cousin Erin's tea party. You invited me for a visit when I came to America."

"Aha," he said, standing awkwardly in the doorway.

"We had a gab by the china dresser. You were drinking sherry."

He remembered Erin Donovan's notable family china dresser, but as for gabbing with anyone by it . . .

"Didn't you get my post a couple of months ago?" She seemed to loom over him.

"A letter?" A letter! On mauve writing paper. "Of course! Please . . . come in . . ."

"Could I borrow a twenty for the driver? Had to be fetched up in a taxi. I'll repay."

"Certainly," he said, digging into his pocket and handing over a twenty.

As she went off to the driver who was parked at the curb, he reached in the foyer closet and brought out the extra leash. He snapped Barnabas to one end and tied the other around the banister.

He picked up the suitcases, which nearly took his arms from their sockets, and set them in the foyer, then watched her walk back to the porch stoop in the glow of the street lamp.

A loping gait, he thought, with something tired in the way she hunched forward. He was reminded of a leggy cosmos.

"Cousin Meg," he said, stepping aside to let her enter, "welcome to Mitford."

She brushed past him in a trench coat that smelled of damp newspapers and peanut butter. "Good heavens, what a dog!" she exclaimed.

He closed the door and turned the lock, completely flabbergasted.

He had lugged the bags to the guest room and set them inside the door, then went downstairs to fix his guest something to eat.

"I'm starved," she said intensely, pushing her hair behind her ears. She sat at the small table under the kitchen window and peered into the empty plate. It might have been a crystal ball forecasting Russian caviar for the hopeful look in her eyes.

"Perhaps it will do 'til morning," he said, serving her a meatloaf sandwich that he'd made extra thick. She peeled back the bread and looked. "I prefer not to eat flesh foods, except on Sunday."

"Aha. Well, I'm dashed if I know what to give you, then. There's soup in the cabinet . . ."

"In a tin?"

"I'm afraid so."

"This will suffice," she said, taking a bite so vast that he turned his back to give her privacy for chewing.

"I'm trying to remember our gab," he said. "Let's see. I suppose we talked about Cousin Erin's china dresser that made its way to America, then miraculously found its way home again."

Clearly, he couldn't stop there, as he heard her still chewing. He stood at the sink and pretended to dry a dish that wasn't wet. "Perhaps you can give me some help on the family tree. We collected a lot of notes and papers in Ireland and stuffed them in a bag, and I'm supposed to make some sense out of it all. Frankly, I haven't opened the bag once and dread it like the toothache."

What else could he say? She wouldn't be interested in the Porter place museum, he didn't think, or the fund-raiser to buy special hymnals for the Youth Choir. He plunged ahead. "We'll have lots to discuss about Sligo, I'm sure. But only when you've rested, of course—I know how jet lag can fog the mind."

He turned around to find her wiping her mouth on her sleeve and having a draught of tea.

"Ah . . . how about another sandwich?"

"Right-o. Splendid. I'm famished."

He gave her the sandwich and hauled himself up to sit on the counter by the sink. "So, tell me, Cousin, how are we related?"

"Your great-grandfather and my great-grandfather were half-brothers, of course."

Clearly, she didn't mind being stared at while she talked with her mouth full.

"And Great-aunt Fiona," he said, "was in there somewhere . . . my grandfather's sister, I believe."

"*My* grandfather's sister," said Meg, gulping down a half glass of tea.

He hated losing Great-aunt Fiona to the other side, straight off.

"Your great-grandfather, Michael, married Glynis Flanagan, and they had Lorna, Fergus, Sybil, Tyrone, Cormac, and Lisbeth. Fergus emigrated to America when he was fourteen and later married Letty Noonan. They had Matthew and Stephen and, of course, Little Betty, who died at birth from the fever."

"Good heavens! How can you contain all that?" Perhaps if she stayed a day or two, she could make short work of the bag that sat on his closet floor.

"Your uncle Stephen married Katie Crain of Pennsylvania, who, they say, was a great beauty. Walter was their issue. Two years earlier, your father had, of course, married Madelaine Howard of Mississippi, whose great-grandfather served in the senate with Mister Jefferson. Matthew and Madelaine had you, and neither you nor Walter ever chose to carry on the family line."

Perhaps he only imagined that she said this coolly.

"My great-grandfather," she said, taking a large bite, "married Gillian Elmurry, who had Reagan, Fiona, Brian, Kevin, Eric, and Inis. Reagan married Deirdre Connors, and they had Allie, Meg, Nolle, Anthony, Stephen, Mary, and . . ." He thought she said Joseph. Clearly, it was a challenge to talk with your mouth full while reciting one's family tree.

"Nolle, as you may recall, flew with Lindbergh on several occasions, before he had Arthur, Allen, Asey, and Abigail.

"Anthony, of course, married Daphne, who had me. I was the only child. In an Irish Catholic family, a laughingstock . . ."

"So we are? . . ."

"Third cousins."

"I see," he said, although he didn't.

Perhaps it was because he had been up since five o'clock and it was now eleven, but he felt as if someone had just read him the entire first Book of Chronicles.

He cautioned Dooley when he came downstairs on Saturday morning. "There's someone sleeping in the guest room."

"I never heard s' much bangin' an' scufflin' around in th' middle of th' night . . . sounded like a dern gang of convicts was let loose in there." His grandfather made over, thought the rector. Dooley Barlowe often woke up as an old man, though he generally went to bed as a boy.

"Who's in there, anyway?"

"A cousin. From Ireland."

"Ireland. 'At's over there in Scotland."

"Try again."

"Somewhere in England, maybe."

"Check it out."

Dooley looked at the world globe on the rector's desk. "I was pretty dern close."

He walked to the office, oddly in step with the throbbing sound of machinery on the hill, and went through his Easter sermon twice. Orating to the rear windows, which showcased the branches of trees in expectant bud, he felt convinced that "All for Love" had been the right theme—he felt the burning fact of its rightness.

He called home at one o'clock and talked to Puny, who had come in to bake an Easter ham. She was shocked to hear there was anyone else in the house.

"She's in the guest room," he said. "Jet lag, more than likely. She'll come down before long, I'm sure."

"You want me to fix 'er somethin' to eat if she does?"

"She ate two meatloaf sandwiches last night and drank a half pitcher of tea, but I'm sure she'll want something before dinner. Oh, yes—she doesn't eat flesh foods except on Sunday."

All he got from the other end was a stunned silence.

At three o'clock, Puny called the office. "You better come home. Your cousin's still up there, and th' floorboards ain't even creaked. I knocked on th' door at two o'clock—that's long enough for anybody to be layin' in bed, if you ask me—but not a peep out of 'er. She must've found that key hangin' on th' wall and locked herself in, 'cause I tried th' knob, thinkin' she might be, you know . . ."

"Mort?"

"Whatever. So maybe you should come home."

Puny was waiting for him at the back door. "She came down right after we talked."

"Oh?"

"Wanted somethin' to eat. I fixed 'er salad and a roll, put it on a tray. She high-tailed it back upstairs, said not to look for 'er at th' dinner table."

"She's pretty trouble-free, I'd say."

Puny appeared thoughtful, or was it his imagination?

At six o'clock, he knocked lightly on her door.

"Cousin Meg?"

Silence.

Must have eaten and gone straight off to sleep. Jet lag could do that, and didn't he know? Arriving home from Ireland, his head had felt stuffed with sheep's wool. For another two days, he hadn't been able to think straight, and finally, it all ended with the odd perception that everything—and everyone—was more poignantly real than he'd ever known, as if a veil had been lifted from his senses.

After midnight, he awoke to a sound he couldn't identify. Barnabas pricked up his ears and growled.

He got up and went to the bedroom door, then stepped into the hall and listened. He would know that sound anywhere. It was coming from the guest room. It was a typewriter, thumping along loudly at sixty miles an hour, as if every key were a mallet pounding the floor.

A Royal manual, he concluded, or he'd eat his hat.

He went back to his room and closed the door. If Dooley could sleep through it, so could he.

All over town, green shoots poked from earth still damp from melting snow, and nearly everyone felt a shiver of delight at a certain fragrance in the air.

Easter morning had "turned off fair," as one villager said, and the various Mitford congregations poured out of church with new hearts.

On the lawn of the Presbyterians stood a wooden cross, massed with blooming vines, fern, galax, and woods moss. Dozens of potted white lilies lined the front walk of Lord's Chapel, and the Baptists draped their wayside pulpit with a banner proclaiming *Hallelujah!* The Methodists had chosen to peal their agreeable chimes at sunrise.

Uncle Billy Watson, according to the rector, had put the whole spirit of the morning in a nutshell. "I'm about t' lift off," the old man announced as he left the churchyard with a sprig of forsythia in his lapel.

Father Tim walked home with Dooley after the eleven o'clock, expecting to see their guest up and about. To that end, he had set the dining room table before the early service, using his grandmother's Haviland.

He found the ham sitting on the counter, loosely covered with foil, minus a vast chunk from one side. He looked under the lid of the green-bean casserole and saw that a full third of it was missing. A pop top from a Coke can lay in the sink.

He went up and knocked on her door. "Cousin Meg?"

No answer.

He knocked more loudly.

"Right-o." He heard the bed creak.

"Happy Easter! Wouldn't you like to have lunch with us?"

"I've had it, if you don't mind."

He stood for a moment, rubbing his chin. Then he went downstairs, wrapped the ham, put it in the refrigerator, and said to Dooley, "Don't take your church clothes off. We're going to Mayor Cunningham's family Easter dinner, then we'll visit your grandpa."

Dooley looked at him approvingly. "It's about time we went somewhere. We never go anywhere."

"There's a first time for everything," he said, admiring the way Dooley had turned himself out this morning.

"Good heavens, Timothy, who answered the phone while you were out? Tallulah Bankhead?"

"My cousin Meg. From Ireland."

"She doesn't sound terribly Irish to me," Cynthia declared.

"Schooled in America."

"Um. There for a visit?"

"Yes. She's a writer."

"Oh, dear!"

"Doing a book on descendants of the Potato Famine emigrants."

"Are you one?"

"No, but she says these mountains are full of them."

"How long will your cousin be with you?"

"I don't know."

"You don't know?"

"No."

"Oh."

"And how is the city?" he asked, changing the subject.

"Grimy. Intoxicating. Tedious. How's Mitford?"

"Quiet. Clean. Comforting. And a dash boring, to tell the blessed truth."

"Boring?"

"Because my neighbor isn't here. I haven't had a good laugh since she left."

She proceeded to tell him a joke so corny that Uncle Billy would have flatly refused it for his own collection.

He laughed, lying back against the sofa cushions, able at last to let go of the week and the intensity of the services and the glory of Easter, which always knocked him winding, somehow.

"There!" she said. "Is that better?"

"Infinitely." He felt the foolish grin on his face.

"At the end of April, I'm moving out, James is moving in, the book will be ready to go to press, and I'm coming home. For good."

"Are you sure?"

"Positive! You won't be able to run me off with a stick. Now—guess who's visiting *me*."

"Palestrina!"

"David. He's helping pack a few things, and I'm taking him to a play this evening. He's so handsome and successful and such a comfort to have with me. I look forward to the day when you meet."

"I look forward to it, also. Have a wonderful evening, and give him my regards."

"I will. And Timothy?"

"Yes?" His heart was full, yet oddly frozen.

"Philippians four-thirteen, for Pete's sake."

"H'lo."

She was standing at the kitchen sink in a faded chenille robe and scuffs, making up a dinner tray. Her mane of red hair was tied back with what appeared to be the sash of her robe. It would be a terrific stretch, but he supposed she could be oddly attractive if she would dress herself and quit hunching over in that defeated way.

"Ah, Cousin. How's it going?" He took his shoes off at the door, so he wouldn't track mud, noting that his radio had been tuned to a country-music station.

"Booming along," she said in her throaty voice. "You've popped home early." There was a Coke can on her tray, but whatever was on her plate couldn't be identified.

"And what did Puny leave us for supper?"

"Stewed chicken and rice."

"And you're having? . . ."

"Rice with raspberry preserve and cottage cheese."

"Aha."

"You may recall that I eat flesh foods only on Sunday."

He thought she looked like a stalk of Evie Adams's Asiatic lilies, which needed staking every summer.

"You'll join us for supper, of course."

She left the kitchen and started down the hallway. "Sorry, but I have momentum on the book."

"I thought you were going 'round and talk with people. Do research, you might say."

She turned and stared at him with her magnified green eyes. "That comes later, of course."

How much later, he couldn't help but wonder, eyeing the pop top she had left in the sink.

"Are you sleeping through it?"

"Sleepin' through what?" Dooley wanted to know.

"All that rumble in the guest room."

"What rumble?"

He supposed that answered his question.

"I hear you've got company," said Emma.

"A cousin. From Ireland."

"Umm. Nobody's seen 'er, includin' your house help. You'd think your house help would see 'er."

"Doesn't get out much, but she's going to. She'll be talking to descendants of Potato Famine emigrants."

Emma peered at him over her half-glasses. "Descendants of *what?*"

"How's Harold?"

"Grouchy."

"Whatever for? His wife is a fine cook with an income-producing job and the housekeeping skills of a barracks sergeant."

"I'm tryin' to make him sleep in pajamas."

"That explains it."

"Says he never will. Baptists are hardheaded, you know. Episcopalians sleep in pajamas, and so do Lutherans. I'm not sure about Methodists."

"You can never tell about Methodists."

"He says he's wearin' his birthday suit, an' that's enough for him."

"Maybe you should concentrate on more important things. What if you won this battle, only to lose the war?"

"Sometimes I don't have a clue what you're talkin' about—win a battle, lose a war . . ."

"Are you putting in a garden this year?"

"Harold is. I told him no more pole beans or I was leavin'. That garden nearly worked me to death last year. Came back from the honeymoon, had to jump in and go to pickin' beans and tomatoes and cucumbers and squash, then put it all up in jars. Harold won't eat anything put up in freezer bags." She sighed deeply.

"That Harold!" he said, in an attempt to be consoling.

At 11:15, the Grill was still quiet. Having had a meeting in lieu of breakfast, he was famished and feeling in the mood to sit at the counter.

"We got two choices on today's lunch menu," Percy told him.

"What is it?"

"Take it . . . or leave it."

"I'll take it."

"Better watch what you're sayin'. It might be liver."

"So give me a tomato sandwich on whole wheat, not much mayonnaise."

"Tomatoes ain't any good yet. Too early. I'd take th' grilled cheese."

"Too much fat. Let me have an omelet with mushrooms."

"All I got today is canned, no fresh."

"Plain omelet, then."

"I'm out of those brown eggs you like. White's all I got. Wait a minute. I might have some brown down th' hatch."

"No, that's OK. Too much trouble."

"Hold your horses. Won't take a minute."

Percy disappeared behind the grill, opened the hatch in the floor, and went down the steps where he stored certain food items. He came back up quickly and lowered the hatch door.

"Nope."

The rector scratched his head. "I'm worn out trying to get a bite to eat around here. How about a hot dog, all the way?" Live a little, he thought.

"My buns ain't come in yet. Be here any minute."

"Plain omelet with white eggs, and make it snappy," he said, feeling his blood sugar plummet.

"I'd sure like to hear a dose of scandal this mornin'," said Percy, taking two eggs out of the refrigerator. "Preachers hear scandal all th' time. What's th' latest?"

"Uncle Billy got a new jacket for Easter. First clothing purchase in thirty years."

"That news is too mild t' mess with. Keep goin'."

"Omer Cunningham's come back to town."

"Shoot, I heard that more'n a week ago. You're about as up t' date as th' *Muse*."

"Here's a good one. Homeless Hobbes has a dog."

Percy rolled his eyes. He could get better gossip out of a brick wall.

"It's a nice little brown and white spotted dog, but it can't bark. He named it Barkless. Homeless and Barkless, how do you like that?"

Percy thought his customer seemed thrilled with his dog story. "I had somethin' more in'erestin' in mind. Like, I hear you were out strollin' with your nice-lookin' neighbor before Easter. Velma told me this mornin' to find out what's goin' on or she'd bust."

The rector stared at the splatter board behind the grill.

"I figured you'd clam up. Here's your omelet. What d'you think?"

"Looks a little dry."

"Have some salsa," said Percy, shoving two jars across the counter. "From Los Angeles to New York City, salsa's th' latest thing."

"Which flavor?"

"Try th' hot. It'll roll your collar back."

He recklessly spooned the stuff onto his plate.

"Lookit this," said Percy, who took a napkin from under the counter and showed it to him. "Don't that beat all?"

He instantly recognized one of Buck Leeper's intricate doodles.

"Buck Leeper done that this mornin'. Looks like it was engraved or somethin'. 'Course, I couldn't tell you what it is if you held a gun t' my head."

"A chambered nautilus."

"Well, anyway," said Percy, "what am I supposed to tell Velma?"

He should have gone home, as originally planned, where the menu was more varied and nobody asked hard questions.

"What about you and your nice neighbor?" inquired Puny when he walked home from the Grill to pick up his checkbook."

"What do you mean?"

"I'm hearin' stuff."

"Stuff?"

"You know."

Barnabas sat down at his feet and peered up at him. Odd, but he thought he saw a questioning look in his eye.

"No, I don't know. Do I pry into your affairs with Joe Joe?"

"It seems to me you'd be proud to talk about it."

"Talk about what?"

"Bein' in love."

"Am I in love?"

"If you ain't, I'll eat your refrigerator."

"That would be a pretty sight," he said, tersely.

"I'm your house help. I ought to be one of th' first to know, don't you think?"

She looked so pretty in her green and white striped apron that he found it hard to refuse her anything. If he ever lost Puny Bradshaw, and the bright light that switched on every time she entered his house, he would be up the creek.

"Ah, Puny." He sat down on the stool at the counter, feeling suddenly deflated.

"I know how you're feelin'," she said.

"You do?"

"Pretty much."

"Well, it's good that somebody does. I hardly know, myself."

"I thought so."

"You did?"

"I'd give you a big hug if you wouldn't take it wrong."

"I wouldn't."

She came and put her arms around him and squeezed. He squeezed back. "You're the best of the best," he said, trying not to croak.

"Same back and ditto. Now, get your chin up off th' floor."

He laughed. "Consider it done."

Walking to the office, he felt that the eighteen-wheeler that had been parked on his shoulders for days had miraculously moved to another parking lot.

He couldn't figure what to do about Meg Patrick.

But why do anything, he wondered, as long as she wasn't a bother? He seldom saw her, and he closed his door at night to the thumping that sounded like a barn dance for field rabbits. Obviously, she was cleaning her own room, for she was no trouble to Puny. She was even doing her own laundry, he supposed.

It was a peculiar circumstance, but why worry about something that clearly wasn't worth it?

Emma answered the phone, then held her hand over the mouthpiece. "Whang-do," she said, looking sour.

"I'm not in," he snapped.

He got up and briefly stepped outside to avoid telling an outright lie.

Edith Mallory came in waves, like the ocean. Roar in, roar out seemed to be her style. If jumping from her moving car had not been a sufficiently eloquent expression of his feelings, what would be?

"She wanted prayer," said Emma, setting her lips like the seal on a Ziploc sandwich bag.

The last person on earth he wanted to pray for . . .

"Said she's got a lump." Emma drummed the desktop with her fingers. "I hope I don't get struck by lightnin' for sayin' this, but I'd like to give 'er a lump."

It was useful that Emma Newland sometimes expressed his true feelings, and he didn't have to take the licking for it.

"Yes. Well. I will pray." And he would. Right after he prayed to be forgiven for the smoldering anger that didn't want to go away.

"I heard you was gittin' married." Grinning, Coot Hendrick stood at the door of Lew Boyd's Esso, which, after all these years, hardly anybody called Exxon.

"Where did you hear that?" he asked, feeling the color drain from his face.

"At th' Grill." Coot was prepared to block the door until he got a satisfactory answer.

"Yes, well, I suppose they also told you that intelligent life has been found on Mars? Not to mention gas is dropping to fifteen cents a gallon."

"No kiddin'," said Coot, wide-eyed.

"I guess you also heard that Elvis Presley was seen shopping at The Local."

"Well, I'll be dadgum."

Coot stood aside, scratching his head, as the rector of Lord's Chapel strode through the door.

He checked Cynthia's perennial beds for signs of life, even though he knew it was too soon. Early April was still a frozen time in Mitford, and spring a full six weeks away.

No local ever put a seed or a plant in the ground before May 15. That date might as well have been engraved in stone, because every time he planted earlier, he paid the price.

Row upon row of impatiens, planted on May 14 three years ago, had ended up as watery mush at the border of his front lawn. A year or two earlier, he had tried to sneak by with planting fifteen cosmos seedlings on May 12, only to find them keeled over the next morning from the hardest freeze they'd had all winter. No, indeed, you did not mess with that date in these mountains.

dear cynthia,

nothing up in your beds, whats up with you? saw miss rose in a t-shirt from presbyterian rummage sale, proclaiming SuPPort WildlifE, Throw a Party. she wore it well. will be glad to see yr new book esp the zebras. all quiet here. dooley warbling like a bird in yth choir, though his voice is beginning to crack a bit and we are definitely in for a change. have started jogging again, as hoppy has come down on me without mercy, feeling stronger for it. are you doing the neck exercises we talked abt, pls do this / everyone asks for you, i pray for you faithfully.

Yrs, timothy

Dear Timothy,

I have received yet another letter addressed to me but clearly written to a distant relative. You are afraid, I can just feel it. You are afraid of your feelings, and if you think you are the only one who is afraid, you are wrong. I am terrified.

Why? Because I love you, and you are not up to it, after all, which makes my heart sink within me and leads me to believe that I have done it all wrong again.

I am closing my eyes and mailing this letter but forcing my heart to remain open.

Yrs
Cynthia

He sat at the desk in the study and put his head in his hands. Why had she insisted on bringing up the subject of marriage? Wasn't the experience of going steady still fresh enough to last for a while, to count for something?

She was a complicated woman, after all, with deep feelings and a sensitive spirit. And, for the moment, he greatly resented that.

Father Roland, the hopeless romantic, wrote to say he was leaving his large New Orleans parish and going off to Canada: *. . . to the wilds, Timothy! Yes, indeed, a parish of a mere one hundred souls, many of them lodging in cabins. Rather the sort of place I imagine Mitford to be. No more stress, Timothy, no more burn-out . . . just the call of wolves in the frozen night, and fresh trout, and time to seek refreshment of the spirit.*

The people are grand in every way. In fact, it is to their credit that I'm willing to take a compensation package that would make you roar with laughter, and which, I can assure you, will keep me humble. Thanks be to God!

A parish in the wilds of Canada. Now, there was an idea, if he ever heard one. And to think he was perfectly free to consider the very same thing.

But, no. Come what may, he was stuck to Mitford like moss on a tree.

"Doing her own laundry, I take it?" He was going through the mail that came to the house, looking for his *Anglican Digest*.

"Must be. Leaves th' washroom jis' like I leave it, clean as a pin. But it's creepy she's been here a whole week an' I ain't laid eyes on 'er. Only way I know she's up there, I hear th' toilet flush."

"That's one way," he said. "Next time you're upstairs, maybe you could bring down the *Country Life* magazine I stuck in the guest room for Stuart during the blizzard. There's an article I'd like to review for a sermon—about basket weavers. There's an intriguing dash of theology in basket weaving."

"I still cain't get in. Her door's locked tight as a drum."

"Aha."

"I hate locked doors. They git my dander up."

"Ummm."

"How's your neighbor? When's she comin' home?"

"End of April," he said, feeling a constriction in his chest.

"I'm prayin' for you," announced Puny, heading toward the dining room with a bottle of lemon oil and a dust rag.

The phone woke him from a light doze on the study sofa.

"Timothy?"

"The very same. How are you, Cousin?"

"Only just recovered from seeing you in New York, to tell the truth. Katherine says you must never do that again—I could have a stroke."

"Tell her not to worry."

"Once was enough, was it?"

"You might say so."

"And how are things with your neighbor? Rotten shame about your planes crossing routes in the air."

"Walter, do you remember meeting Meg Patrick at Erin Donovan's tea? One of the cousins."

"Meg Patrick. Meg Patrick . . ."

"Tall. A Niagara of red hair. Wears bifocals."

"Well, of course, *you* would remember all that, since you were only having sherry. Everyone else was drinking Irish whiskey out of teacups."

"You don't remember, then?"

"How many cousins were there—twenty-four? Thirty-two? No, I draw a blank. Why?"

"She's turned up on my doorstep, out of the blue."

"No warning?"

"Well, there was a letter some weeks ago, thanking me for inviting her. Blast if I can remember doing it. But . . . no matter. How's Katherine?"

"Volunteering four days a week. Singing to the elderly and can't carry a tune in a bucket—they love her. Doing art classes with handicapped kids and can't draw a straight line—they adore her."

He laughed. "Put her on. Then, I'd like to discuss a legal matter."

"Teds!" How many times over the years her voice had cheered him. "How are things with your neighbor . . . with Cynthia? We let you get safely through Easter without calling to find out, but now the jig is up."

"Katherine . . ."

"And don't play your cat-and-mouse game with me! Inquiring minds want to know, Timothy! You would not fly to New York if it weren't terribly serious—either a death in the family . . . or love!"

"Katherine, you're a nuisance."

"I know it, old darling. Now tell me everything."

"I think I hear the phone ringing . . ."

"Timothy, you are *on* the phone."

"Rats," he muttered darkly.

"From the beginning," she said. Hundreds of miles away, in a suburb of New Jersey, he could hear her settling back in the plaid club chair, putting her feet on the ottoman, and clinking the ice in her eternal glass of ginger ale.

He was in for it.

The statue of Willard, which he saw at the sculptor's studio in Wesley, was precisely as the mayor had said—the head was too big. He would never have spoken up if it hadn't been for the fact that Miss Sadie would pass the statue every time she went to shop at The Local.

"The head . . . is too large," he said in what came out as his pulpit voice. He didn't like to pass judgment on a work of art, which was clearly a subjective matter.

The sculptor walked slowly around the clay model as the rector stared at the floor.

"You're right, of course," said the sculptor.

There! What if he hadn't spoken? The size of Willard's head would have rivaled that of a Canadian bull moose. Miss Sadie would have been so disgusted with the whole thing that she would have done her food shopping on the highway, where making a left turn into Cloer's Market would be plain suicide—if she didn't die from eating their produce.

Uncle Billy had gone with him to Wesley but didn't say a word in the artist's studio. On the sidewalk, he took the rector's hand and shook it soberly.

"Rose'll be proud that you're lookin' after things, Preacher. I'll be et f'r a tater if that statue didn't look like a feller with a washtub settin' on his shoulders."

"What did you think," he asked Emma, "of the wedding on Sunday?" As for himself, he thought it fine and beautiful, and it had been grand to see his old parishioners and their daughter, who, though now living in Virginia, still considered Lord's Chapel their home church.

"Did you see that lizard pocketbook sittin' on that little shelf to the left of the altar?"

"Lizard pocketbook?"

"Stuck up there next to th' holy family like a sore thumb. Must've been left there by somebody doin' the flowers. I could not believe my eyes."

"But there was so much else for the believing eye. Sixteen in the wedding party—beautiful young women, handsome young men—and all glowing like so many candles."

"Just stickin' up there like a crow on a limb . . ."

"The trumpet voluntary was outstanding, every bit as good as some recordings I've heard. And the flowers—absolutely the most glorious flowers ever to grace Lord's Chapel, don't you agree?"

"It seems to me the flower people would have stepped back and taken a good look at the whole caboodle before they went rushin' out the door. If they'd done their job, they would have seen a lizard pocketbook sittin' on the shelf."

"The retable never looked more magnificent . . ."

"It's not even the *season* for lizard!"

"Emma, Emma, Emma." What else could he say?

He'd forgotten to take the brooch to the jeweler when he went to Wesley yesterday. He would take it today and pay a visit to the Children's Hospital while he was there.

Remembering that he'd seen a pink ribbon among his mother's things, he got on his knees and fished the box from under the bed. He rolled the ribbon up and put it in his jacket pocket and went to his chest of drawers to collect the brooch.

But it wasn't there.

"It was up there when I dusted," said Puny. "In that little velvet bag."

"Maybe I put it in my coat pocket when I went to Wesley to see the sculptor. What jacket did I wear?"

"Beats me. Try th' blue."

"That's the trouble with having too many clothes," he said sharply. He could remember a year or so ago when he had only two jackets. Now he had five.

Would he have put it in his pants pocket? But those pants went to the cleaners this very morning. Every other Wednesday, Puny Bradshaw bundled up the clothes he had been wearing and, whether they needed it or not, sent them to be cleaned. He argued that the English almost never have their clothing dry-cleaned, and she argued that not only was he not English, but sometimes he sweated, so that was the end of it.

He called the cleaners and begged them to go through his pants pockets the moment the truck drove in. To take his mind off a creeping anxiety, he went through all his suits and jackets, including those he wasn't currently wearing.

If Cynthia had once put her hat in the freezer and a quart of ice cream on the bed, who knows what he might have done while his mind was elsewhere—which it usually was these days.

When Evie Adams called the office at ten, he found himself wishing for a curate, a deacon, anybody. He had two meetings today, recklessly scheduled so as to disallow lunch, a hurried trip to Wesley that included buying two shirts and some poster paper for Dooley, and a visit to the Hope House site to see the progress they'd made in only a few days of good weather. Needless to say, there was plenty of work that needed doing on his sermon.

Evie wanted to know if he could come by as soon as possible, and this time he didn't ask what Miss Pattie had done now. He only wished again for help and then suddenly realized he was wishing for Cynthia. Cynthia would know what to do; she would take care of it and leave Evie with new hope in her heart.

Cynthia could fix things without even trying.

Cynthia could eat the drumstick, and he could not. No matter how hard he tried, he would never be able to eat the drumstick.

CHAPTER TWELVE

Faith Not Feeling

His feeling of panic had passed once before; it would pass again, he told himself. He must go forward on faith, not feeling.

He remembered, too, what Emily Dickinson had said: "The truth must dazzle gradually, or evermore be blind." After the trauma of being asked to go steady, hadn't he settled down and gotten used to the idea? Hadn't he been dazzled, after all, and hadn't it been gradual?

Well, then. He would put his mind to other issues, one of which was sobering in its own right.

No, he could not send Dooley away to school, because, Walter said, he was not Dooley's legal guardian. His heart had leapt up when he heard that.

"However," his cousin advised, "his grandfather can do it. Even though Russell isn't the boy's legal guardian, he is closest of kin, and it can be done on the basis of his verbal consent. It wouldn't hurt to have it in writing, of course."

Getting Russell to go along with such an idea would be one thing. Explaining it to Dooley would be another. And how would the boy fare among affluent kids who had probably never heard the word "ain't" in their lives and who thought "poop" was the latest news in the school paper?

Could he handle the English compositions, the algebra, the science? He felt sure of the algebra, with a little coaching, but the rest of it . . .

On the other hand, he could easily see Dooley scrubbed up and wearing a navy blazer—yes, indeed. And singing in some school chorale and surprising himself on the ball field.

"Be good for him," he said, pumping up for the task.

He called Meadowgate Farm and asked Marge to pray for this crucial thing.

"Ah, Tim. Isn't plain love more valuable than fancy education? But of course, we must let him go, mustn't we?"

"I think so, yes. Such opportunities are once in a lifetime. We're talking twenty thousand a year, here. Certainly nothing I could easily fork over, and clearly, no one else will offer to do it. Sadie Baxter is an angel with wings, a harp, a halo . . ."

"The works!"

He called Cynthia to discuss the school issue. He saw no reason to mention her last note, which boldly stated that he was not up to loving. Perhaps she was right, but he would forge ahead. Faith, not feeling!

"What are you up to today?"

"Taking Miss Addison to lunch at my café. She's never been to a café! She says she wants to drink strong coffee out of a mug and eat something hearty like a plowman's lunch. Why, she's never drunk out of anything less than Baccarat and Sevres in her life!"

"There you are, being a grand influence on yet another neighbor."

"Have I . . . been a grand influence, Timothy?"

"More than I can say." He felt a lump in his throat, for no earthly reason. "I needed your help yesterday."

"You did?" She sounded as if he'd told her some wonderful news.

"Evie Adams called and I went over, but my heart wasn't in it. I thought how you would have made things seem all right."

"But of course, they aren't all right."

"No. And won't be until Hope House is built."

"Do you think it's important to make things seem all right when they aren't?"

"Not always. But in this case, yes, very important."

She was silent for a moment.

He decided not to mention the brooch. It would turn up. Even if the cleaners couldn't find it, it would turn up.

He left the office much later than usual—it was nearly dusk—and saw Buck Leeper walking on the other side of the street, leaning into the strong wind that had been blowing all day. He thought the man looked utterly desolate; perhaps it was something in the slope of his shoulders, but he really couldn't say.

"What will we do? Carry him off kicking and screaming?"

"He wouldn't be the first boy carried to school that way."

"Not meaning any disrespect, Miss Sadie, but what do you know about boys being carried off to school?"

"Father, you do not have to be a villain to act one in a play, nor do you have to be a boy to know that kicking and screaming about private school is more rule than exception."

He pondered this.

She leaned on her cane and gazed at him steadily. "It was Mr. Oliver Wendell Holmes who said that a mind stretched to a new idea never returns to its original shape. That boy needs his mind stretched."

"Why are you so interested in Dooley's development?" He'd been wanting to ask that. At twenty thousand a year, he was curious.

"He's a diamond in the rough, clear as day. My father was, and so was Willard Porter. They both made something of themselves, with no help from anybody. I'd like to see what happens when help comes to a boy who's rough as a cob yet loaded with possibilities."

"Miss Sadie, isn't this like what Uncle Haywood did to you? He convinced your parents to send you to a fancy school in a foreign country, and you hated every minute of it. A fancy school, no matter where it is, will be like a foreign country to Dooley Barlow. Actually, he'll go there speaking a foreign language, if you know what I mean."

"Uncle Haywood thought a fancy school was the right credential for catching a husband," she said crisply. "It had nothing to do with stretching my mind with new ideas!"

More than seventy years later, the very mention of Uncle Haywood was still distasteful to Miss Sadie. She made a face like she'd just eaten a persimmon.

Dooley looked up from his homework at the desk in the study. "I seen that woman today. I come up th' steps and she was in th' hall closet, gittin' an armload of toilet paper."

"Aha."

"Seen me, went back to her room, locked th' door."

"Ummm."

"Got some eyes, ain't she?"

"Green, I think. We need to have a talk."

"When?"

"Oh, soon, I guess." Not now. Not tomorrow. Not necessarily next week or the week after that. But . . . soon.

"What about?" Dooley stared at him, expressionless.

"Oh, this and that."

"I ain't done nothin'."

He sat on the edge of the desk. "Haven't done anything."

"That's what I said."

"Well, then, there's nothing to worry about. Not a thing. Just a talk, that's all."

"Anyway, I ain't smoked but two. Buster Austin sucked down a whole pack."

Rats! He didn't want to know that. "Really?"

"He's th' one stole 'em, not me. Me an' Tommy stood across th' street while he done it."

No, he didn't want to know any of this. But here it was, and he'd have to deal with it, which would result in another kind of talk, entirely.

Dooley dived into the pause to change the subject. "You git me them shirts?"

"I did. No plaid. Just blue."

"Where're they at?"

"Your prepositions dangle terribly," he said, quoting Cynthia Coppersmith.

Those boys in their navy blazers would make chopped liver out of this kid; if he made it through alive, it would be a blasted miracle.

He thought his words had sunk in during their talk at breakfast, but he couldn't be sure.

Hadn't he smoked a few cigarettes in his time? He and Tommy Noles had nearly burned the Noles's barn down, but, thanks be to God, they'd put the fire out by flinging themselves onto the smoldering hay and rolling in it.

They had shoved the blackened hay under the pile in the rear loft, and he'd gone around with singed hair for weeks, his father peering at him in his strangely abstracted way.

Stealing, however, was another thing. Hanging out with a boy who was not only smoking but stealing into the bargain—this was serious business. He hoped he had made his point and that it had been well-taken. Sometimes, talking to Dooley Barlowe was like talking to a fence post.

He was glad it was Emma's day off when Mitford Blossoms made a delivery. Jena Ivey knocked on his office door and stepped inside, carrying a long box.

"Good morning, Father!" He could see the mischief in her eyes as she held it out to him. "Your birthday isn't 'til June, so it must be something really special."

"Aha." He looked at the box as if it contained a set of barbecue tongs.

"They're my best, Father. I know how picky you are about roses."

He should have felt delighted, he thought. Instead, he felt interrupted. "Thanks, Jena. Well, then, see you later. I know how it is when there's no one to mind the store." He held the door open for her.

"Don't you want to peep in before I go?" Jena liked a chance to see the look on people's faces when they received flowers from her shop. " 'Course, you don't have to read the card 'til I leave."

Obliging, he lifted the lid and stared with spontaneous admiration at the dozen roses. They appeared to have come from a country garden only minutes ago—in fact, morning dew still clung to their petals.

"Sprayed with mineral water," Jena said proudly, reading his mind. "What do you think?"

"I think you're the best florist in these mountains—no contest."

She looked disappointed. "Somebody once said the East Coast."

"The East Coast, then! I'm sure of it." He gave her a hug, knowing that his Sunday-school supervisor thrived on hugs.

"Well, enjoy the roses, Father. We're sure loving Dooley's contribution to the choir! Having him, I think we can build something wonderful over the next couple of years."

The next couple of years? He nodded bleakly.

She stepped out to the sidewalk. "Do you need a vase? I can run across the street and bring you one."

"No, thanks. I have just the thing." He called after her as she hurried away, "God bless you! Thank you!"

The roses had already begun to change the very air in the room with their subtle freshness.

He set the box on his desk. All his life, he had been a fool for roses, and she knew it. Perhaps she had been thinking of him as he had been thinking of her, both of them frightened in their own ways, for their own reasons.

He remembered the plaintive way she had said, "Have I been a good influence?"

Well, of course, she had. She deserved a medal for even recognizing his existence. What was he, after all, when you came down to it, but a country parson? Not tall and trim and debonair like Andrew Gregory, who owned a closetful of cashmere jackets, could speak Italian, French, and a bit of Russian, and drove a Mercedes the size of a German tank.

That she would wear a path through their hedge was wonder enough. But to love him into the bargain? That was supernatural.

He put the roses in the vase, stem by stem, and set it on top of the file cabinet, where the morning sun rimmed their petals with a bright glow.

It was as if a light had come on in the room.

He stopped by the rectory after a noon meeting and found a note from Meg Patrick on the kitchen counter: *C Cpersmth rang.*

He put Barnabas on the red leash and hurried to the office, thinking how he didn't deserve the roses, not at all. He didn't deserve anything from her, not even the consolation of her voice.

What was wrong with him, anyway, to have thought he loved her, to have felt the certainty of loving her—only to have this frozen impotence grip him?

He had the image of one of Hal's Guernsey cows going up against the new electrical fencing and stumbling back, dazed. The mention of marriage was for him an electrical fence; it was a barrier with its own raw shock through which he could not force himself to go.

Why was he, after all, fearful of marriage? He trusted her completely not to make a fool of him, or wound his pride, or do some sort of damage that he couldn't foreknow.

The trouble was, he kept making a fool of himself, wounding his own pride, and doing his own damage—which always included disappointing her.

When he talked with Katherine on the phone, he had fought to keep his concerns to himself. But, little by little, like grinding a kernel of corn to a fine powder, she had got it out of him.

"Teds, fear is not of the Lord. You know that."

"I know that."

"So who do you think it's of?"

"The Enemy, of course."

"Bingo! If this weren't right in God's opinion, he would put sensible caution in your heart, not paralyzing fear. But until you have peace about it, it can't be right—no matter how right it all looks on the surface. And believe me, it looks very right . . . at least for you. I don't know about her, of course, but she could probably do a great deal better."

"I don't deserve her honesty," he said.

"Well, of course you don't. You hardly deserve the time of day from her the way you keep yanking her feelings around. But it seems to me this relationship is grace, if it's anything at all, so what's to deserve? The good Lord plunked her down practically on your doorstep, while the single people I've talked with at church go scrambling over hill and dale just to find a dinner companion!"

Katherine could give you an earful, all right.

"I definitely think you should stop moaning about how you don't deserve this or that. Men who're scared silly always say that, thinking they sound gallant or modest. Well, they don't. They sound pompous and artificial."

"Katherine, is this friendly counseling or a bloodletting?"

"You wanted the truth. And the other thing I think is, you need to get out of this retreat mode. Tell her you needed time with the idea of going steady, and you need time with this. Why back off when she's not pushing you? She didn't even ask you to marry her!"

"Yes, well." It was true. Cynthia hadn't asked him, but the implications were . . . numbing.

"Maybe I should go into the city and take her to lunch."

Good grief! "Please," he implored, "don't even think such a thing." If he thought he was in trouble now . . .

Hoping to improve his heart rate before he made the call, he ran in place in front of his desk, causing the old building to rumble on its moorings. He thought it sounded like Meg Patrick composing an index to her book.

Stop saying I don't deserve . . .

Ask for time . . .

But first, thank her for the roses . . .

He had broken a light sweat when he sat down and dialed her number.

"Hello?"

"Cynthia?"

"Timothy?"

"Yes."

"What's . . . up?" she asked.

"Oh, lots of things. A few green leaves on your double hollyhocks . . ."

"I spoke to your cousin earlier."

"Aha."

"She sounds quite . . . settled in."

"Yes."

There was a pause that he wanted to dive into but couldn't.

"You're out of breath," she said.

"I've . . . been running."

"Oh."

". . . to thank you for the roses. They're even lovelier than the ones you sent before. I . . . can't tell you how . . . I hardly know what to say . . ." He desperately wanted to say he didn't deserve them, for that was the complete and utter truth.

"Cynthia, you are . . . so gracious and thoughtful, always . . ." He could hardly bear to go on. Why had he forgotten to pray before he called? He was positively babbling. ". . . and so, I thank you again and again. They have transformed this room . . ."

There was an empty silence on the other end.

"Cynthia? Are you there?"

"Timothy," she said in a voice he hardly recognized. "I didn't send you roses."

"You . . . ?"

"The thought wouldn't have occurred to me," she said in that unfamiliar voice.

He was aware only that his chest hurt.

"Nor will it ever occur to me, Timothy."

After the click and the dial tone, he sat at his desk in an agony he could hardly endure.

The Lord's Chapel bells chimed two o'clock. He had never heard them sound so mournful, as if they were ringing for the dead.

Dazed, he reached into his pocket and removed the small florist's envelope that he'd wanted to save until evening. He drew out the card and read:

Lump benign.
Your prayers worked, as always.
Love, Edith

Dooley had wolfed down his dinner and run upstairs to his homework, leaving the rector to eat alone at the kitchen counter. He hadn't knocked on the guest room door and offered a bite of dinner—frankly, he'd forgotten that anyone else was in the house.

He went to the study and crashed on the sofa, the pain still gripping his chest, when he heard the toilet flush. Immediately afterward, he heard the typewriter.

Thumpetythumpetythumpthumpthump . . .

She was starting early tonight, about five hours early, by his calculations. Perhaps she was coming out of whatever jet lag she had suffered and returning to a normal schedule. Why jet lag would persist for more than two weeks, he didn't have a clue. Perhaps there was a complication because of some medication she was taking.

Thumpetythumpthumpthumpthumpety . . .

Where was the blasted thing sitting, anyway? On the little desk he had inherited with the rectory? Or on the floor? It sounded like she was typing on the floor, which was enough right there to injure someone's back and keep them bedridden for days.

At seven-thirty, Dooley apparently finished his homework and turned on the jam box.

Boomboomboometyboomboomboomthumpetythumpthumpetythump . . .

Barnabas stood at the foot of the stairs, howling, while the rector sat on the sofa, frozen.

His sandwich had turned to a rock in his digestive system.

He stared at the wooden tray in his lap and the stationery on which he'd written two words.

Dear Cynthia . . .

"Cousin Meg!" At nine o'clock, he banged on the door like a federal agent, striving to be heard over the din.

"What is it?" she finally answered.

"Come to the door, please. I'd like to have a word with you."

There was a long pause. "Right-o."

After what seemed an eternity, she opened the door a full two inches and pressed her face to the opening. "What is it?" she said in the voice that slightly resembled the lower octaves of a French horn.

"I must tell you that your typewriter sounds like a construction crew working up here. Could you move it onto another surface, please?"

"Right-o," she said, shutting the door.

"Whoa! Wait up. Open the door!"

She turned the knob and peered through the crack.

"Look here. I think you need to be getting around, getting some fresh air. I've had an idea. I'll wake you at six in the morning and we'll have breakfast at our Grill on Main Street. You'll meet a lot of interesting people, very likely some Potato Famine descendants. No need to dress. It's casual."

He turned on his heel toward the stairs.

"I can't possibly. I have a schedule I must keep to," she called after him.

He didn't turn around. "Haven't we all? I expect you to be dressed and ready at seven—I'll knock at six."

When he knocked, she didn't answer.

"Cousin Meg!" He could wake the dead when he put his mind to it.

He heard the bedsprings creak. "It's six o'clock!" he shouted. "I'll fetch you at seven!"

Silence.

He'd just looked in the refrigerator and found the squash casserole that Puny had made for the weekend. It appeared that a family of raccoons had gotten hold of it. Worse than that, her fresh lemon curd had been reduced to leftovers.

At seven o'clock, he was knocking again.

No answer.

"Cousin Meg! Either you come out or I'm coming in!" Blast if the words didn't roll out of their own accord, and he meant every one of them.

He heard her stomp across the floor as if she were wearing combat boots.

She opened the door and slipped through sideways, then closed it, locked it, and dropped the key in her pocket.

"Good morning, Cousin," she said, pushing her hair behind her ears.

On the sidewalk at the Grill, they met Buck Leeper. "Mr. Leeper, my cousin, Meg Patrick."

"Pleased," she said, thrusting her hands into the pockets of her trench coat.

The Hope House superintendent nodded and flipped his cigarette over the curb. "Miss Patrick."

"Things are looking good on the hill," said the rector.

"Not good enough."

Leeper sauntered through the door ahead of them and went to his table at the window.

The rector greeted the Collar Button and Irish Woolen crowd who were sitting at the counter. He felt every head in the place turn as they walked to the rear booth.

After Velma poured their coffee, Percy came around, wide-eyed with curiosity. "Percy, meet my cousin, Meg Patrick. From Ireland."

"Ireland, is it?" Percy peered into the booth as if into a cage containing a rare panda. "Mule Skinner claims t' be Irish."

"We're distantly related to Skinners," she said, adjusting her bifocals. "Very distantly."

"This one ain't so distant. Here he comes now. How d'you like your eggs?"

"Fried," she said, "and a broiled tomato."

"A what?"

"A broiled tomato." Saying "tomahto" did not cut it with Percy Mosely.

"Grits or hash browns is all we got." Percy appeared to say this through his teeth.

"Are your hash browns freshly peeled and cut, or are they . . . packaged?"

Father Tim stirred his coffee, though there was nothing in it to stir.

"Packaged, like every other hash brown from here t' California."

"Is your cooking oil saturated?"

"You better believe it."

"Just eggs, thank you, and whole-wheat toast. Unbuttered."

"Better have you some of Percy's good sausage t' go with that," said Mule, slipping into the booth.

Please don't say it, thought the rector. But, of course, she did.

"I eat flesh foods only on Sunday."

Percy Mosely would not let him forget this anytime soon.

Puny stopped by the office the next morning to pick up her check. "Here," he said, handing her the vase full of roses, "take these home."

"Law, they're beautiful! Who give you these?"

"Whang-do."

"Whang-*who?*"

He didn't answer.

"Sometimes, I don't know what you're talkin' about."

"You aren't the only one," he said.

She thought she'd never seen such a strange look on his face.

Where was the brooch? The cleaners hadn't turned it up. He had searched the entire room, including the closet, on his hands and knees, not to mention every pocket and drawer.

It was maddening. After all, if something so important could slip away so easily, what else might disappear or run to neglect because of his carelessness? There was the rub.

He was finding scant peace in his own home these days.

Puny was cleaning every blind, curtain, cornice, and shade on the premises, so the rectory could hardly be visited for lunch.

Half the seventh grade was ringing his phone in the evenings to get Dooley's help with their math homework.

And last, but certainly not least, his cousin had turned his home into a hotel, with food vanishing as if into a bottomless pit.

He could remember the time when there was no one here but himself, when the very ticking of the clock could be heard.

Who could hear a clock tick above the din of a Royal manual, a jam box with twin speakers, a vacuum cleaner, a washing machine, a ringing phone, and a toilet that flushed over his head every time he tried catching a nap on the sofa?

It occurred to him that all the people coming and going under his roof, other than himself, were redheads. He wondered if that could have anything to do with it.

"We are not necessarily doubting," said C. S. Lewis, "that God will do the best for us; we are wondering how painful the best will turn out to be."

He had spent an hour on his knees, asking for the best, believing in the best, thanking God in advance for the best. No, he didn't doubt that God would do the best for her and for him. But yes, he was wondering how painful the best might be.

At the office, he typed a note to go out with the morning mail.

Dear cynthia

flowers were thankoffering from parishioner who tho't she might have cancer, asked for prayer, and discovered all is well. sorry for mix-up.

i know this is a distant relative note but am meeting with adult sunday school teachers in five mins. Will write long letter soon.

He stared at what he had written and then typed:

I think of you.

Not knowing what else to say, he took the note from his typewriter and signed it by hand.

With love,
Timothy

He didn't add that no one had ever hung up on him before.

"Knock, knock!" said Puny, pushing the door open. "I had to go to Th' Local to git cornmeal. I'm bakin' you a cake of cornbread tonight."

"Hallelujah!" Puny allowed him this sterling indulgence once a month. Golden brown, steaming on the inside and crying out for butter, Puny Bradshaw's cornbread could win a blue ribbon at the state fair.

"I want to ask you somethin'." She sat on the visitors' bench, holding the grocery bag in her lap.

"Shoot."

"You know I said th' washroom always looks jis' like I leave it? That's 'cause it *is* like I leave it. Your cousin ain't usin' it." She raised her eyebrows and looked at him.

"Ummm."

"The question is, three weeks on th' same sheets? An' how many changes of underwear do you reckon she *has* in there, anyway?" From the look on her face, the thought was appalling.

"Well . . ."

"An' when does she bring 'er dishes down, for another thing?"

"The middle of the night?"

"I suppose you know she shoves 'em in the dishwasher whether th' stuff in there is clean or dirty. I found a clean load settin' in there with a dirty plate an' glass an' silverware."

"Ah," he sighed.

"For another thing, where does she empty 'er wastebasket?"

"Good question. I don't know."

"Not in th' bag under the sink, I can tell you that. An' not in th' garbage cans in th' garage."

She let him ponder that.

"I'm makin' you a nice, lean roast tonight, an' I intend to stay there 'til you git home, or there might not be a bite left, if you git my meanin'."

He hated to say it. "Don't worry. She eats flesh foods only on Sunday."

Puny shook her head, disgusted.

He might have walked into a graveyard for the odd silence that hung over the Grill on Wednesday morning.

Over the years, he'd gotten used to the noise in the place, hardly noticing it. Now, he noticed the lack of it.

He was ready for Percy to give him plenty of heat about his cousin, but Percy looked up from taking an order and didn't even acknowledge that he'd come in.

He sat in the rear booth, strangely anxious. Yesterday morning, he had breakfast with Dooley, skipping the Grill. What had he missed? Was something going on that he hadn't heard about?

He turned around and looked at the door. Where was Mule? Where was J.C.? He heard only forks against plates and shoe leather against bare floors, as if the Grill were observing a wake.

Velma poured his coffee, wordless.

"Has somebody . . . died?"

"I wish," she said curtly, taking the pot to a nearby table.

He might have been a tourist for all they cared.

J.C. slammed into the booth, throwing his briefcase in the corner. He thought how the editor's red face was not a good sign along with sixty pounds of extra weight. "I hope you been on your knees," he growled.

"About what?"

J.C. stared at him, wide-eyed. "You don't know what's goin' on?"

"I don't have a clue."

"Edith Mallory has stuck it to Percy with a hoe handle." He wiped his perspiring face with a much-used handkerchief. "That's who owns this place, in case you didn't know. Kicked up his rent . . ."

"How much?"

"Double, can you believe it? Nobody in this town goes up double."

"What does double mean?"

"Double means highway robbery—better'n two thousand bucks a pop. The only way Percy can swing a rent like that is to raise prices on the menu. You wanna pay four bucks for a poached banty egg on toast? This crowd'll never go for it. Mack Stroupe is circling like a vulture, even as we speak. If Percy moves off Main Street, Mack is fixing to add on to his hot-dog stand and serve breakfast. He'll have grits tastin' like they were cooked in a crankcase."

"Edith Mallory . . ."

"Look," said J.C., "I respect that you're not big on foul language, but I gotta say it. You know what the woman is."

In case he didn't, J.C. told him.

"So if he doesn't come up with the rent, he's out?"

"Big time."

"And if he does, he jacks up his prices and stands to lose his trade . . ."

"You got it."

"I thought somebody had died."

"Yeah, well, somebody could, and it might be Percy. This could kill him. This place is his life. And lest you forget, buddyroe, th' *Muse* is right up those back steps there. Who knows when I'll get *my* little notice in th' mail?"

"Where's Mule?"

"Out lookin' for a place Percy can move into."

The Main Street Grill not on Main Street? It was unthinkable.

"Pat Mallory wouldn't have done a thing like this in a hundred years," said J.C. "He ate his breakfast at the Grill every morning of his life, desperate to get away from that barracuda. He would have paid Percy to keep it open."

Velma stopped to pour J.C.'s coffee.

"Don't worry," the *Muse* editor told Percy's wife. "There's still such a thing as th' power of th' press . . ."

"Whatever that means," said Velma.

Mule slid into the booth. "Let me tell you, it ain't out there."

"No luck?" J.C. said.

"One little old bitty place stuck off behind the Shoe Barn, and she owns that, too."

"Does she really think Percy can cough up the new rent, or is she trying to run him out?" asked the rector.

"Tryin' to run him out is the deal. Has some fancy dress shop from

Florida she wants to bring in, th' kind that would draw customers from Wesley and Holding, all around."

He didn't think he could eat a bite for the churning in his stomach. "How much time do we have?"

"This is the twelfth of April, right? We got to the middle of May and not a day longer. Percy begged for time, but did she give him any? No way."

"There's got to be something we can do." One look at the anguish on Percy's face as he worked the grill was about all he could take.

"There might be somethin' . . ." said Mule. The rector wondered why the realtor was staring a hole through him.

"I could dig up some dirt," said J.C., "and spread it across the front page. First thing you know, she'd come runnin' in here to hand over the deed, forget droppin' the rent . . ."

"Stop talkin' junk and talk sense," snapped Mule.

"See there?" said J.C. "Everybody's got their back up. It's enough to make you sick to your stomach."

Velma appeared and slid J.C.'s order to the end of the table and set down the rector's poached eggs. "You done eat?" she asked Mule.

"Cornflakes at six a.m.," he said. "I could gnaw th' legs offa this booth, but Fancy's got me on a low-fat diet."

"Fancy barks, he jumps," grunted J.C., busting open his egg yolk with his fork.

Mule looked at the rector. "I hear you know Edith Mallory pretty well . . ."

"She's a member of Lord's Chapel."

"You've been carted around in that Lincoln of hers a few times, not to mention you've been seen over in Wesley ridin' around . . ."

"Purely business." His toast suddenly tasted like so much Styrofoam.

"You know what people say . . ."

"No," he said coldly, "I don't know what people say, and furthermore . . ."

"They say she's got you marked off with a red flag . . ."

"I suppose you believe everything you hear?"

"Well, knowin' you as I do, and knowin' her as I wish I didn't, I don't put any stock in what I hear. But what I'm gettin' at is this . . ."

"What you're gettin' at is him suckin' up to a snake," said J.C. "If you ever opened the cover on your Bible, you'd see how that don't work."

Mule put his hand on the rector's shoulder, looking earnest. "One word from you and this whole thing could be turned around. No skin off your nose whatsoever. 'Scuse th' language, but if she's got th' hots for you like people say, you could talk sense to 'er and she'd listen."

"I appreciate that Percy's been driven to the wall, but I won't be thrown on the sacrificial fire. The answer is no."

This was not the usual morning banter. It was serious business; he felt the life-or-death of it. Even so, he despised being made the goat on the altar. He had no intention of humbly submitting to this tactic.

"Nobody's sayin' do anything you'd be *ashamed* of," said Mule, as if the rector's speech had gone in one ear and out the other. "Just take her to a nice dinner over in Wesley. Tell her how th' Grill is one of the oldest businesses in town. Percy's daddy opened it fifty-two years ago. It's a dadgum *historic* landmark . . ."

"Listen. I don't have a lobby with Edith Mallory—I don't give a blast what people say. If she wants two thousand dollars a month, and she can get it, what could I say that would change her mind? You think she's going to turn down twenty-four thousand a year because she thinks I'm . . . I'm . . ."

"Yeah," said J.C.

"Besides," said Mule, "aren't you in that business?"

"What business?"

"Persuadin' people."

"How's it going?" said Ron Malcolm, sliding in beside the *Muse* editor.

"Rotten," growled J.C., which seemed to express the feelings of the entire booth.

Ron took his cap off and looked at the rector. "Father, I've been thinking . . . you know Edith Mallory pretty well. I was wondering if there's anything you could do, anything you might say. I get the feeling she'd listen to you."

If J.C. Hogan had the guts to grin at him, or if Mule Skinner laid on that insipid wink he was famous for, he would puke, plain and simple.

CHAPTER THIRTEEN

A Rock and a Hard Place

They had swarmed over him like so many fire ants.

Then, Percy had joined them when the breakfast crowd thinned out, his eyes filled with some mute pleading that was clearly aimed straight at him.

It was a conspiracy.

Given the ten and a half she was now collecting, what could possibly make Edith Mallory give up an easy twenty-four thousand a year? Nothing that he would be party to.

So what was the use?

On the other hand, what if he got tough and came up with something that would, perhaps, result in only a token rent hike?

Maybe a room in her name at the town museum . . .

Under the circumstances, he thought he could talk Esther Cunningham into it. Sliding it by the town council, however, was another matter.

What about a garden planted in her honor? He and the rest of the Grill regulars would gladly grub the stumps out of the town lot with their own hands.

But he could forget that—the town lot was hidden behind the post office. Edith would want something people could see from Main

Street, with a plaque they could read a block away—lighted at night on both sides, possibly by an eternal flame.

How did he get in a fix like this?

And, come to think of it, how *did* Cousin Meg dispose of her trash?

When the old man called the office, he felt instantly encouraged.

"Uncle Billy, how are you?"

"Pretty Good, considerin' I done fell off a twelve-foot ladder."

"Good Lord! Is anything broken? Why, it's a miracle you survived!"

"Well, sir, t' tell th' truth, I only fell off th' bottom rung."

"Aha."

Uncle Billy sounded disappointed. "That's m' new joke, don't you know."

"I was supposed to laugh?"

"That's th' general thinkin' behind a joke."

"Better get a new joke, Uncle Billy. You scared me with that one."

"You ought t' know I don't git on no ladders, no sir. Th' last 'un I got on, I left it leanin' aginst th' house to rot down. I don't mess with ladders no more."

"A good idea, all around. How's Miss Rose?"

"Sly as a fox."

"How do you mean?"

"Every day she gets in my money and moves a little bit around to her side of th' mattress."

"What are you doing about it?"

"Why, I'm comin' along behind her when she ain't lookin' and movin' a little bit back where it come from."

"Makes sense."

"How's your boy? I seen 'im in church. He's gittin' gangly."

"That's right, he is. He's prospering, I'd say."

"We want you'uns to come up and have cobbler with us this summer when th' berries are on. And bring that nice blond-headed woman what crawled in Rose's playhole and found my ink drawin's."

He remembered Cynthia crawling behind Miss Rose into the dark space under the eaves that had been Miss Rose's childhood playhouse.

"We'll come," he said, meaning it.

"Have you discussed it with him yet?" asked Miss Sadie.

"No, ma'am," he said, feeling despondent.

"Have you come up with anything yet?" Mule wanted to know.

"No, blast it," he said, feeling pressured.

"Have you done anything with those family papers yet?" Walter inquired.

"What do you think?"

"Ah, Timothy. And with an Irishwoman living right under your roof . . ."

"So, sue me," he said.

He had come home early and found her rifling through the shelves in his study. "How's the book coming?" he asked.

"Straight on," she said, burying her nose in a volume of Irish poetry. He thought she looked precisely like a barn owl in a bathrobe.

"I've been wondering . . . how are you disposing of your trash? We did give you a wastebasket, I hope?"

"I'm recycling," she said.

"Aha."

"Paper products in one bag, aluminum cans in another."

"That's terrific. We can take the bags to Wesley next trip, get them out of your way."

"Right-o," she said. "No hurry."

"I'd like you to go with me to the Grill in the morning."

"Ah, no. Too much staring at me just now."

A cattle prod, that would be the thing. But he must be kind. After all, blood was blood. "I'll knock at six, as before. And Cousin . . ."

She pretended not to hear but licked her forefinger and turned the page.

"I'll look for you at the dinner table this evening. Six-thirty."

"I don't think so . . ."

"Sharp," he said, meaning it.

His cousin sat at the kitchen table, glowering.

Where was the Irish wit, he wondered, the droll humor, the unending stories their ancestors were famous for? What was she, anyway—*Scottish?*

He put Puny's low-fat meatloaf on the table, still sizzling from the oven, and went to the stove to dish up the green beans.

"Man!" said Dooley.

He turned around to see that his cousin had helped herself to a vast portion and was going at it, full bore, with her fork and knife. "I ate only grapefruit on Sunday, so this will be my substitute day for flesh . . ."

"We'll wait for the blessing," he said evenly.

Holding her fork in one hand and her knife in the other, she sat hunched forward in her chair. What in heaven's name could he do that might bring a smile to those startled eyes?

At the blessing, he reached for Dooley's hand, but hers was gripping the fork.

How could she eat so heartily and never put an ounce on her bony frame? Metabolism, he supposed. Where in the dickens had he been when the hyperactive metabolisms were passed out?

"How many times have you been to the States? I can't seem to recall if you told me."

"Several times, on and off."

"Staying with cousins, were you?"

"On occasion."

"And where was that?"

"Once in Oregon."

"And where else?"

"Massachusetts."

"Who were you seeing in Massachusetts?"

"No one you know," she said.

"Try me."

"Cousin Riley."

"Umm. That wouldn't be Riley Kavanagh, would it?"

She glared at him. "No, it wouldn't."

He took a deep breath, only to have it end in a sigh. "Dooley, what's going on at school?"

"Nothin'," said Dooley.

Conversing with this crowd was about as reviving as lugging a rock straight uphill. "Well, then, tell us about your book. How does it . . . begin?"

She deftly piled green beans on the back of her fork. "It begins as the horror itself began."

"Aha."

"One morning in 1845, an Irish farmer discovered that something was dreadfully amiss. The book opens with what he had to say, and I quote:

" 'It was a warm day when I saw a thick white fog gradually creeping up the sides of the hills. When I entered it, I was pained with the cold. I at once feared some great disaster. The next morning when I traveled about . . . I found the whole potato crop everywhere blighted. The leaves were blackened and hanging loosely on their stems, and a disagreeable odor filled the air.' "

"Gross," said Dooley.

"Moving," said the rector, knowing how that tragic event had scattered, and nearly destroyed, a nation. Oddly, the longest speech he had heard her make was someone else's.

"When do you expect the book to be finished?"

"It will be done when it is done."

"I see. And how long do you think you . . . might be with us?" Among the Irish, cousins from across the pond were treated with great favor, but he didn't know how much more favor he could fork over.

She pushed her hair behind her ears and gazed at him soberly. "As long as you'll have me, Cousin."

Dear Timothy,

Hanging up on you was a silly and immature thing to do, but I couldn't help it. It just happened. Something came over me.

Your note arrived, telling me about the mix-up, and I've tried to feel remorseful for what I did. Actually, I don't feel one bit remorseful, but I do feel forgiving.

As I thought how you flew to New York to surprise and comfort me, the ice around my heart began to melt and I could not help but love you.

Hasn't our timing, and especially mine, been atrocious? If only I had been here when you arrived, do you think things might have been different? Do you think the ice around your own heart might have melted for eternity?

I've decided I will come home to Mitford at the end of the month and live there always, no matter what the future holds. Nothing can run me away again, not even a neighbor who is kind and loving one moment and distant and indifferent the next.

Somehow, the mention of marriage has strained even the sweet pleasure we found in going steady. It is grieving to think we might throw it all away because we've come to a hard place in the road and cannot cross over it. One would think that two people with brains in their heads could stand in the road and ponder the obstacle and come up with some ingenious way of getting over or round it! I mean, look what Mr. Edison, quite alone, managed to do with the light bulb!

Perhaps we could be friends, Timothy. But it's time for me to quit suggesting what we might do or be together and let it rest in God's hands.

If you think that sounds spiritually noble, it is not. I simply don't know what else to do.

Cynthia

He went to his desk and numbly opened the lower drawer where he kept her letters and laid the envelope on top. He stared into the drawer for a moment, trying to focus his thoughts.

He could have sworn the pile of letters had been deeper, that there had been many more. But then, everything now seemed less than it had been.

Dooley, how would you like to go away to school next fall?

(Suspiciously) Where at?

Virginia, perhaps. Just one state away. You could come home on holidays, and I could come up for special occasions and bring Barnabas.

(Long silence) I wouldn't like it.

You would be given every privilege, not to mention friends for a lifetime—and a chorus to sing with that's twice the size of your group at Mitford School.

(Firmly) I ain't goin'.

That was precisely how the conversation would proceed. It might as well be scripted on a piece of paper.

He was suddenly faced with persuading two people to do

something they had absolutely no intention of doing. Why was a preacher expected to be so all-fired able to accomplish thc impossible when that, clearly, was God's job?

The Lord had never spoken to him in an audible voice, not once. But there were times He had spoken to his heart and in no uncertain terms.

As he labored in prayer on Friday morning, he received a strong but simple message:

Go to Buck Leeper and talk.

This message, which he felt no keen delight to receive, was persistent. Not only did it come when he was on his knees, but again as he washed his hands at the office sink and, later, as he jogged to the hospital.

He knew the consequences of delay when it came to obeying what he'd been asked to do. Oswald Chambers had found this topic of special interest. "It is one thing to choose the disagreeable and another thing to go into the disagreeable by God's engineering. If God puts you there, He is amply sufficient.

". . . There must be no debate," Chambers had gone on to say. "The moment you obey the light, the Son of God presses through you in that particular. . . ."

If a parson could not reach out to the desperate, then who could—or who would?

On the way to the site of Hope House, he made a decision to speak simply. No games, no hidden agendas, no beating around the bush. And let the chips fall where they may.

Buck Leeper was alone in the trailer. He swiveled around in the creaking desk chair and looked up.

"I'd like to talk," said the rector.

"What about?"

"I don't know, to tell the truth. Just talk. Get to know you better."

The superintendent took a long drag off his cigarette and inhaled deeply. "Sit down," he said.

Leeper swung his feet onto the desktop and crossed his legs. In your face, his muddy boots seemed to say, but the rector sat across the desk from them, unflinching.

"You probably need to know I don't like preachers."

"You wouldn't be the first."

"This hill is not a missionary field."

"I'm off-duty." That was a lie, but he told it, anyway.

"My granddaddy was a preacher," Buck said, narrowing his eyes.

"So was mine. Baptist."

"Ditto."

"Did you know your grandfather?"

"Never knew him. Heard about him all my life. Nothin' good." He stubbed his cigarette in the ashtray.

"Your dad's father?"

Leeper toyed with a silver lighter, and the rector saw where his fingers were missing. "Yeah. He turned my old man into the meanest preacher's kid in Mississippi."

"You're from Mississippi?"

"Born and bred."

"Same here."

Leeper barked an expletive. "Small world."

"What part?"

"Northeast. Booneville."

"Holly Springs," said the rector. "Forty miles from Booneville, as the crow flies."

Another expletive and an odd laugh. "Son of a gun."

Leeper glanced at his watch.

"Maybe you'll join us at the rectory for dinner—one of these days."

The superintendent pulled a cigarette from an open pack in his shirt pocket. He lit it with the lighter and inhaled. "I don't think so."

"Drop by the office, then, for a cup of coffee . . . anytime."

Leeper suddenly got to his feet and walked to the door, where he took a jacket and hard hat off the hook. The rector followed him.

"That redheaded kid yours?"

"Dooley?"

"I don't know his name. Tell him if he comes messin' around on this job again, I'll kick his butt. That goes for his sidekick, too."

"They . . ."

"Tell him I mean business. You can get killed out there."

Leeper opened the door. The machinery vibrated the trailer as if it were a toy. "Got to get to th' hole," he said, putting on his hat. "Some people have to work in this town."

Springtime was on its way, no doubt about it.

Hessie Mayhew's gardening column made its annual appearance in the *Muse*, under a photograph of the author taken thirty years ago. The first column of the season always disclosed Lady Spring's current whereabouts.

It seemed she was tarrying on a bed of moss and violets down the mountain, where the temperature was a full ten degrees warmer.

Do not look for her, Hessie cautioned, *for she never arrives until we've given up hope. Once you've sunk into despair over yet another snowfall in April or a hard freeze after planting your beans, she will suddenly appear in a glorious display of Miss Baxter's apple blossoms—not to mention lilacs along south Main Street and wild hyacinths on the creek bank near Winnie Ivey's dear cottage.*

Lest anyone forget what a wild hyacinth looked like, Hessie had done a drawing from memory that J.C. reproduced with startling clarity.

The old sexton was sitting in a chintz-covered armchair, fixing Betty Craig's alarm clock. The contents of the clock were scattered over the top of a lamp table.

"You look comfortable," said his caller, sitting on the side of the bed.

"Dadgum clock's been stuck on high noon since I moved in here. How are you, Father?"

"Fine as frog hair."

Russell Jacks laughed and emitted a racking cough. "Lord have mercy," he said, his eyes watering.

"Might as well tell you straight out, Russell. We've found somebody to look after the gardens. He's not your caliber, not by a long shot. I don't think there are any true gardeners left out there for hire. But we had to have help, and it's going to take time for you to knit. When the doctor gives you a clean bill of health, we'll put you back. How's that?"

"Fair enough. I thought I could hold on t' my job, but I cain't. I'm tryin' to help Miss Betty all I can. How's our boy? Is he troublin' you?"

"No, sir. Not a bit." His heart sank. Here goes, he thought. "Russell, I was wondering if you'd agree to . . . if you'd let us send him off to a fine school next fall, where'd he learn more, think harder . . ."

"Send 'im off?"

"Maybe to Virginia. Close by. You and I could drive up once in a while to see him, and he'd come home for holidays."

Russell studied two small clock springs in the palm of his hand, silent. Finally, he said, "What do you want t' do, Father?"

"I don't want him to go. I'd like to keep him right here in Mitford, but we have an opportunity. Someone is offering to pay his tuition, give him a once-in-a-lifetime chance." He stared at the rug, feeling a chill in the room. "I think we should let him go."

"I want t' do what you want t' do," said Russell.

"I'll bring the papers when the time comes."

His heart felt heavy as a brick when he left Betty Craig's house, and he hadn't even gotten to the hard part yet.

He got no providential word on what to do about Edith Mallory. And he had exhausted every foolish possibility he could think of.

What was the worst scenario?

He could go and talk to her—plead for the continuity, the history, the tradition of the Grill and the place it occupied in the heart of the village. Then he thought of her hand on his leg or being trapped in that blasted car at a speed that did not warrant leaping to safety.

If Percy Mosely and Mule Skinner and J.C. Hogan and Ron Malcolm knew what they'd asked of him, they would never have asked it. After all, they were friends. A man wouldn't ask this of his worst enemy.

Of course, all they expected him to do was give it a shot, just one. Nobody said he should keep going back for punishment.

They tried to puff him up by saying how Edith would listen to anything he said, do anything he wanted. To hear them talk, he might have been the pope. But he saw through it; they didn't fool him. While they had aimed straight for his ego, he'd seen it coming—and ducked.

On Sunday, Ron dragged him to the country club after church, while Dooley begged to go home and make a sandwich and ride bikes with Tommy.

He saw Buck Leeper at a table in the corner, eating with a man in a business suit.

"The honcho," said Ron. "Came to check on the job. They're here as my guests. I figured you wouldn't care to join them."

"I went up to see Mr. Leeper the other day."

"No kidding."

"We were born forty miles apart—in Mississippi."

"I'll be darned. Amazing. What did he think of that?"

The rector repeated what the superintendent had said, expletive and all. "End of quote."

Ron laughed heartily. In fact, he hadn't gouged such a good laugh out of anybody since the opening remarks of a recent sermon on spiritual apathy.

"We'll drop by the table on the way out. You'll like Emil Kettner. Devout. Solid. He's protective of Buck, views him as a real cornerstone of the company."

"What does he think about his drinking . . . about the way he pushes himself?"

"He knows it. He keeps after him—makes it mandatory for him to get a physical every six months."

"The goose that laid the golden egg . . ."

"In a way. But it's more than that. I think Emil loves the son of a gun."

Andrew Gregory stopped to say hello, appearing, as far as the rector could determine, more charming than the last time he'd seen him. His mother's warm Italian blood had clearly fought it out with his father's English reserve and won.

"I have a book you might enjoy looking over. Very early. Splendid engravings, gorgeous binding. Drop by for coffee one morning. Ron, I hope you'll do the same. For you, a book on bridges. German. Eighteenth-century."

"Consider it done," said the rector.

"I'll look forward to it," said the retired building contractor. "Who knows what you might learn from an old book?"

"Our priest and our building-committee chairman!" exclaimed

Edith Mallory. He thought she swooped down at their table like a crow into a cornfield.

"Hello, hello!" she said.

Both men stood. "Edith . . ."

"Timothy, I thought your sermon was excellent. Believe me, I needed to hear all you had to say about fear. I was absolutely eaten up with it for days when I was waiting for the tests to come back. I loved what you said about—what did you call it, the prayer of re . . . re . . ."

"Relinquishment."

"Yes! Just turn it all over. Give it to God."

"How are you feeling!"

"Great! Never better. Can't you tell?" She grasped his hand, and he saw that her blouse was cut considerably lower than he'd noticed at the church door an hour ago.

Seeing Ron Malcolm gaping like a boy, she fingered a diamond pendant at her neck. "A little momentum Pat gave me," she crooned.

"Aha . . ."

"I can tell you're having boy talk, so I'll get back to my veal chop. I'll call you sometime tomorrow, Timothy—just a weensy thing I'd like to get settled before I go to Spain in May. *Hasta vista!*"

Ron shook his head as she walked away. "There for a minute, I thought she was going to have *you* for lunch—forget the veal."

He felt queasy. "That crowd at the Grill is sticking me between a rock and a hard place."

"Don't I know it?" his friend said, grinning.

Buck Leeper had disappeared toward the men's room as they got up to leave. Ron introduced the rector to Emil Kettner and was snared by the club treasurer for a five-minute meeting.

Kettner was a big man, cordial, with steel-gray hair, steel-rimmed glasses, and penetrating blue eyes.

The two men sat over a cup of coffee.

"Well, Father, I hope Buck isn't more than you bargained for."

"He is, actually."

They laughed.

"I like your candor. Of course he is. I don't know how we get away with sending him to certain jobs. But then, we couldn't get away with not sending him. This is a big project, Hope House."

"Agreed."

"I'm here to look it over, check it out. It's a courtesy to your building committee. The job is humming like a top." He paused. "Buck has it in for clergy, you may have noticed."

"I think I noticed, yes."

"His grandfather was a preacher who was brutal to his son. It passed right on down the line. The sins of the fathers are visited upon the children . . ."

". . . unto the third and fourth generation," said the rector, completing the scripture from the Book of Numbers.

"Buck's work is the one place he doesn't fail or mess up. There's not a better man in the business."

"I believe you."

"I make no excuses for him. But something happened to him a long time ago, while he was still in Mississippi. Nobody back here ever got the gist of it, exactly. Some loss, something tragic. He felt responsible. That's all I know."

"Thanks for your candor."

"Thanks for your understanding. I'm going to walk over the job again, then bust out of here to Memphis." He took a business card from his jacket pocket. "I'm at your disposal if you need me."

The superintendent came back to the table, grabbed his jacket off the back of the chair, and nodded curtly to Father Tim.

"Let's hump it," he said to Emil Kettner.

"I've got it," J.C. announced on Monday morning. "I was up 'til two a.m. trying to knock this thing in the head. This is it. This'll work."

Mule caught Percy's attention. "Can you step here a minute, buddyroe? J.C. says he's got it knocked."

Percy came over from the grill. "Make it snappy. I got enough bacon goin' to feed a camp meetin'."

J.C. took out a handkerchief and wiped his face. "Didn't ol' Pat Mallory come draggin' in here every morning of his life after he retired? Didn't he think he'd died and gone to heaven every time he ate Percy's sausage with Velma's biscuits? Didn't he hole up in that first booth and read the paper 'til it fell apart? I was pacin' the floor last night when *boom*—it hit me."

J.C. paused and looked at his listeners. "We change the name to *Pat's* Grill. Anybody's widow would go for that one." He sat back as if he'd divested himself of the brightest idea since sliced bread. "What do you think?"

"Over my dead body," said Percy. He threw his hand towel over his shoulder and stalked back to the bacon.

"Oh, well," said Mule.

"Dadgummit," snorted the editor.

"Good try," said the rector. For a few blissful moments, their eyes had been on J.C. Hogan. Now, every head once again swiveled in his direction.

They waited for the crowd to thin out, so Percy could have a cup of coffee with the rear booth. "Kind of like sittin' up with the dead," said Mule.

"Do you think you'll get a rent hike for upstairs?" Father Tim asked J.C.

"I got the letter yesterday. No rent hike, but I can't run my presses 'til after seven o'clock at night. That burned me. I thought this was th' land of the *free* press."

"Shouldn't be any skin off your nose," said Mule. "You never ran your presses 'til after seven o'clock, anyway. Midnight's more like it."

"Whenever I bloomin' well please should be the big idea here," said J.C. "She also said the stairs to the Grill would be blocked off and I'd have to use the back entrance." He wiped his face with his handkerchief. "Witch on a dadgum broom . . ."

"Who'd want t' walk down th' steps into a shop full of women, anyway?" said Mule.

J.C. looked around the quiet room. "Where's Percy?"

"Down th' hatch," said the rector. "I saw him go down there a minute ago."

"What's this going to do to Velma? We know it'll kill Percy, so that's th' end of that deal," J.C. said.

Mule drained his coffee cup. "Velma said she'd have to go to work. They've got savings, but not much. You know how they've done with their kids, settin' 'em up in college, buyin' one that little house . . ."

"Here he comes," said the rector.

Percy slid in with a coffee mug, looking glum. "On top of everything else, my back's out. Not only that, they shipped me white grits instead of yellow—I can't sell white grits."

"Just want you to know I've been talking with someone who handles real estate," the rector told Percy. "I believe he's got the perfect place for the Grill, whether it's right here . . . or out there."

"Who is it?" Mule scowled.

The rector grinned. "God."

"Oh," said Mule.

"He's th' very one that put my daddy in this buildin' fifty-two years ago," Percy said, brightening. "They claimed my daddy was crazy to go to feedin' people with a war on. But he was a prayin' man, and when th' good Lord opened th' door of opportunity, my daddy walked through it and went to cookin'. Bread was fifteen cents a loaf, tomatoes was four cents a pound, and rent was ten dollars a month."

"Oleo margarine," said Mule, "was white, came in a plastic bag with a little colored capsule in there. You popped that capsule and out oozed this colored stuff and you mashed it all around in that bag 'til it colored your oleo and you thought you had butter."

"Don't think I haven't prayed a time or two myself," Percy said, "especially in '74. There was a whole week when th' single biggest ticket I wrote was for a fried-egg sandwich and a Baby Ruth candy bar."

The conversation slacked off, and they all looked at the rector.

"I've got to get out of here," he said, meaning it.

"When are you goin' to do it?" asked Mule.

"Today."

He planned everything he'd say when she called about the "weensy" matter she mentioned. He also worked out what he'd say when they drove to lunch . . . in *his* car.

He wrote it all down, working on it like a sermon. Then he paced the floor, speaking his lines.

He would plead for a dramatic reduction of the proposed rent hike, stating that the Grill had been a faithful, long-term lessor who had paid its rent on time and never asked for anything more than a little paint and a new toilet. What would a dress shop demand? Everything from wallpaper to carpet, not to mention the repair of the water stain on the ceiling that had been spreading like a storm cloud ever since the blizzard.

If she wouldn't budge on the rent hike, then he'd plead for more time, to the end of June, say, until Percy found another situation.

In case she called, he didn't go out for lunch but drank a Diet Sprite and ate a package of crackers. He dusted his bookshelves, tried writing a note to Cynthia but failed, and wrote notes instead to some of the kids at Children's Hospital. Since he refused to let Emma get call waiting, he made no calls in case Edith tried to get through and was brief with whoever phoned the office.

He wanted to be ready, and he was ready; he was champing at the bit. He even found two positive things he could say to Edith Mallory about herself and wrote them down in case he forgot what they were.

He would ask her to lunch in Wesley, tomorrow, at that place with the green tablecloths—and he'd give it everything he had, once and for all.

As for strategy, he would keep it simple. And—he would stay in control.

There was just one problem.

She never called.

CHAPTER FOURTEEN

Home Again

He waited two days.

When she didn't call, he called her. Magdolen said she'd gone to Florida unexpectedly, something about old business of Mr. Mallory's. No, she didn't know when Miss Edith was coming back, and yes, she was going to Spain in May, the minute that new shop moved into her building on Main Street.

He asked for her number in Florida and carried it around in his pocket like a hot potato.

He also dodged the Grill.

Thumpetythumpetythumpthumpthumpthumpety . . .

He pounded on her door. "Cousin Meg!"

Silence.

"Blast it, move your typewriter off the floor!"

He had turned away from the door when she opened it a crack and glared out at him. "If you don't *mind,*" she said, "I work better on the floor. I cannot *think* in a chair."

A chair isn't the only place you can't think, he said to himself. He turned and looked at her. "Off the floor."

It must be hard to slam a door when it had been opened less than three inches.

He was doing his homework.

He spent several hours on the phone, compiling a list of schools and contacts, including a priest who helped socially and economically disadvantaged boys get into major boarding and prep schools.

Dooley would need testing, along with English, science, and algebra placement. Clearly, he would need tutoring in English. And no, it wouldn't be the way he spoke that could make or break him but the way he pulled an English composition together.

Last but certainly not least, they would need the strong approval and support of two or three current teachers.

At three o'clock, he left the whole exhausting task and, for refreshment, went to make hospital calls.

If making hospital calls was his idea of refreshment, he later realized, he was in trouble.

Joe Ivey was out of town for the day, with a *Closed* sign on his door at the top of the stairs. Feeling like a sneak thief, he called Fancy Skinner who had a cancellation and could take him.

"Good grief! I can't believe what's goin' on with this stuff over your ears. It's that chipmunk look again. I thought I *cured* you of that.

"If I was a man and saw Joe Ivey comin' down th' street, I'd cross to th' other side. What did he use to cut your hair, anyway, a rusty saw blade?

"Do you know how much coffee I've had this mornin'? You won't believe it. A potful! I never drink a pot*ful* of coffee! I declare, it makes me talk a blue streak. Look how my hands are shakin'. I hope I don't cut your ear off or jab a hole in your head. Hold still, for gosh sake. See what I mean about those clumps over your ears? There you go! Look at that. A hundred times better—and I'm not even finished.

"I guess you know what's goin' on at the Grill. Mule is so depressed, you wouldn't believe it. You'd think he was losin' the roof over his head. He said you're goin' to work on changin' her mind. Bein' a preacher and all, you can probably talk her into whatever. I personally don't care if we get a dress shop. I order everything out of catalogs. That is the latest thing, orderin' out of catalogs, which is fine except for shoes. I wouldn't order shoes out of a catalog, would you?

"Oh, no, can you see that little bitty nerve jumpin' in my eye? That is so embarrassin'. I forget that happens if I drink a potful of coffee. Why I did it, I don't know. I don't have the slightest idea. Mule said, 'Don't drink this potful of coffee,' but then he went to the Grill and I drank it. Do you ever do somethin' somebody tells you plainly not to do, and you know they're right, but you can't help yourself?

"Your scalp is tense. You should try to relax. I bet bein' a preacher is hard. I mean, all those people lookin' to see if you're walkin' what you're talkin', right?

"I never did ask if you want a Diet Coke. Or would you like a Sprite? You tell me. I offer cold drinks as a courtesy. I would offer coffee, but it's a mess to clean up—like a fireplace. Mule said, 'Do you want to burn the fireplace this winter?' I said, 'No, it's a mess to clean up.' I bet you burn a fireplace, though. You look like you'd burn a fireplace.

"Oh, mercy, wasn't that some winter we had? Have you *ever?* I am not over that yet. A blizzard! Can you believe it? And snow in April. Or was it March? I don't know. Since I opened this shop, I can't keep up.

"I declare, look at you. You are handsome as all get-out. Do you have a girlfriend? Mule told me somethin' about your neighbor. What was it? Let's see. Oh, yeah. I shouldn't tell that, but what the heck—he said she has great legs. Do you really like her? You don't have to answer—I know that's a personal question. But I hope you do, because people shouldn't live alone. It's not good for your health. Of course, you've got a dog. They say that helps.

"Well! What do you think? See how it slenderizes your face? You ought to let me give you a mask sometime. No, I mean it. Men in Los Angelees and New York do it all the time. It cleans out your pores. Oh, and Italians, they do masks. They even carry handbags, did you know that? Italian men are different. My girlfriend used to date an Italian. He was so macho, you wouldn't believe it. How can you be macho and carry a handbag, I wonder? I don't have the slightest idea.

"Oh, law, this coffee has got me flyin' to the moon. That'll be ten dollars. No, six! I forgot—you're clergy."

He closed the door to the study, then closed his eyes and prayed.

He might as well expect water to flow uphill as to expect this phone call to do any good—but where was his faith?

Ed Coffey answered the phone at Edith's condominium in Boca Raton.

"She's with someone on the patio, Father."

"I can call later."

"Oh, no, sir. I'm sure Miz Mallory would like to talk to you."

He waited an eternity.

"Hello," Edith said, exhaling smoke into the receiver.

"Edith, it's Tim."

"Yes, Timothy." He might have been someone from the IRS for all the enthusiasm he heard in her voice.

"How's the weather down there?"

"Fine."

He pushed on. "Same here. You mentioned you wanted to talk about something before you go off to Spain . . . ?"

"Nothing urgent."

Was she talking through clenched teeth? "Aha. When are you coming home, may I ask?"

"I don't know. But I do know why you're calling me."

"Yes, well, to find out what you wanted to talk about before Spain . . ."

"You're calling because your precious Grill is going to be yanked out from under you, and you think you can talk me out of it."

"Edith . . ."

"I don't know what you men find to love about that tacky hole in the wall. My husband went there every morning of his life. You would have thought they were paying him to open up the place. Magdolen and I begged him to eat something sensible in his own home, but no! He marched right down there and ate God knows what and came home reeking of grease—which, in my opinion, killed him."

"Grease?"

"Gorging himself on sausage and biscuits and grits and every other thing that wrecked havoc with his doctor's orders, and where is he now?"

At peace, he wanted to say. "A double rent hike is . . ."

". . . is the smart thing to do, Timothy. My accountant is here. That's exactly what we've been discussing. Put yourself in my shoes." He heard the familiar whine overtaking her indignation. "If I don't look after Edith, who *will?*"

Her mood was changing. She was batting her eyelashes, he could just feel it. "I'd like to talk with you when you come home," he said.

She breathed into the phone. "I won't let you get away with one single, weensy thing, though I do hope you'll try."

"I don't have a clue," said the mayor, sucking up the last of her Diet Coke through a straw. "If somebody wants to hike rent, they hike rent. It's still a free country, though God knows how long that'll last with th' rabble we've sent to Washington."

"Can't we declare it historic or something?"

"That won't change a thing. Come to think of it, why don't you talk to th' landlord about it? I hear she's taken a shine to you."

He blanched. "Mayor, if you can't help us fight progress around here, who can?"

"Truth is, I'm feelin' too old to fight progress. And if you let on I said that, I'll say you lied. I just want to get in th' Winnebago with Ray and go to Colorado for a little fishin'."

"Take me with you!" he implored.

They had concluded the antiphonal reading of the psalm when he looked up and saw an extraordinary sight.

Barnabas was trotting up the aisle, as a couple of astonished ushers stared after him.

He arrived at the front pew on the gospel side and halted, turning to stare into the face of an alarmed congregant.

Was this a dream? No, it was a nightmare, for Barnabas was now licking a perfect stranger—a visitor, no less—on the right ear.

" 'Let love be genuine,' " said the lay reader, carrying on with the Scripture reading, " 'hate what is evil, hold fast to what is good . . .' "

How had he forgotten to close the garage door? He had never forgotten to close the garage door. He could hear laughter breaking out like measles.

" '. . . *outdo* one another in showing honor. Do not lag in zeal, be *ardent* in spirit . . .' "

Barnabas looked toward the lectern, then gave a sigh and lay down, his head on the visitor's foot. The man wiped his glasses and his ear with a handkerchief and, smiling broadly, gave his rapt attention to the remainder of the reading from Romans.

" 'Do not repay anyone evil for evil, but take thought for what is noble in the sight of all. If it is possible, so far as it depends on you, live peaceably with all. Beloved, never avenge yourselves, but leave room for the wrath of God; for it is written, "Vengeance is mine, I will repay, says the Lord." ' "

That his dog stood for the Nicene Creed and again for the dismissal hymn was, he concluded, something to marvel at.

Dear Cynthia,

It won't be long until lights will burn again in the darkened windows of the little yellow house; bushes will bloom, trees will leaf out, the wrens will build a nest under your eave. So, hurry home, and help these good things to happen.

If you'll let me know when you're arriving, I'd like to fetch you from the airport.

All is well here, only one upset which I'll tell you about. Am investigating schools for Dooley. Thankfully, there are quite a few out there, but must get some tutoring into him before fall. Will likely go on a tour of schools as soon as his classes at Mitford School are over in June.

We will be glad to have you home.

He pondered how to sign it. He might even have agonized over it, but he refused. Did he love her? Of course. That had never been the question.

Love, Timothy

"Where are th' KitKats that was in the kitchen drawer?"

"Where are the KitKats that *were* in the kitchen drawer?"

"Yeah, where're they at?" asked Dooley.

"Where are they."

"I'm askin' you. They ain't in there."

"They aren't in there."

"That's what I said."

He was unable to keep from laughing. "Dooley Barlowe, I'd like to wring your neck."

"You'll have t' catch me," Dooley said, grinning.

"Ask the question in proper English, for Pete's sake. You talk like a Rhodes scholar for Marge Owen. Come on—give me a break."

"Where are the dern KitKats?"

"That's better. And the answer is, I don't know."

"That woman eat 'em is what I think."

"Did you eat them and forget you did it?"

"I don't forget stuff like that. I remember eatin' candy, 'specially since I was savin' those for me and Tommy."

"I'll look into it." he said. Which was worse—the nervous tic that had lately begun to jump in his right cheek or the wrenching in his stomach?

"Cats?" she said, staring at him blankly. "I despise cats."

"No. The candy. The candy that was in the drawer to the left of the sink. That is Dooley's candy drawer."

"I don't know anything about candy," she said with distaste, "as I never touch sweets."

What could he say?

The fog was dense, the afternoon was cold, and her plane was late.

He drank coffee in the terminal café that was the size of his bedroom closet and stared out the window, searching the skies. "Heavy weather in Charlotte," they told him at the flight counter. "It's going to be an hour, maybe two."

He read an abandoned newspaper, checked his urine, jotted sermon notes on the back of a napkin, paced the floor, and observed the reading material of a few desultory air travelers. Grisham, Clancy, and Steel seemed to win, hands down.

The fog had turned to rain when the Fokker commuter descended, two and a half hours behind its scheduled arrival.

He watched her come through the door and down the steps of the plane as an eager airline attendant thrust an umbrella over her head.

He felt that some connection had been broken, as if he might have to start all over again to know her, and that she was walking toward him as if from a very great distance.

Holding on to an airline umbrella with one hand, he helped Cynthia into the front seat, put Violet's crate on the back seat, and piled luggage into the trunk.

His feet were soaked. Who had known the skies were going to give way, when all had been sunshine and birdsong in Mitford at noon?

He returned the umbrella to the desk and dashed to the car.

"Blast," he said, sliding under the steering wheel. The faintest scent of wisteria greeted him.

"Thank you, Timothy."

"For what?"

"For waiting. For coming at all. For getting drenched into the bargain."

"My pleasure." he said, trying to mean it.

As they neared Mitford, she grew silent and rummaged in her purse.

"Oh, no!" she said.

"What is it?"

"My house key! It was on the key ring I left in the apartment. Oh, no."

"Don't worry. I have your key, remember? That's how I got in to find the lights at Christmas."

"Thank heaven!" She sank back against the seat and smiled at him.

He was struck by her warm presence and the way she looked in the purple wool suit the color of hyacinths.

Although their conversation hadn't flowed like wine, he felt better—consoled, somehow.

But he couldn't find her key.

She sat in the kitchen with Violet howling in the crate and Barnabas going berserk in the garage while he searched his bureau drawers. He had meant to put the key on his key ring but had never done it, and he kicked himself for the stupid way in which he managed to lose important things. He wouldn't even think about the brooch, not now, for it was all too much.

He went back to the kitchen. "You're not the only one who can't find your house key. I put it in the bureau drawer, and it's simply not there." He switched on the burner under the tea kettle and sat down across the table from her.

"Oh, dear," she said.

Violet howled. He heard Barnabas lunging against the door from the garage to the hallway.

"Perhaps one of your windows isn't burglar-proof?"

"I never lock the windows on the side toward your house, because I raise them so often in summer."

"Then I could use your stepladder—mine isn't high enough to reach—and we'll have you in your house in no time."

"Wonderful! I shall make all this up to you, somehow."

"Don't even think about it. Let's have a cup of tea first, shall we?"

"I'd love a cup of tea! And do you have a bit of milk for Violet?"

"If Dooley hasn't downed the whole gallon," he said, foraging through the refrigerator.

He left Cynthia with tea and a plate of shortbread, and Violet with a dish of milk, to fetch his slicker that was hanging in the garage.

As he stepped back into the hall, he heard voices in the kitchen.

"H'lo."

"Hello. I'm Cynthia from next door."

"Meg Patrick."

"Yes, well . . ."

He heard the refrigerator door open and shut. His cousin was probably dressed in that moth-eaten chenille robe and those scuffs that were out at the toe. He shuddered to think.

"Are you . . . enjoying your visit?" Cynthia asked.

"Right-o. Very pleasant, all the comforts. And such a thoughtful man, my cousin."

"Yes, he is that. Are you . . . close cousins?"

"Actually not. Third. Although in Ireland, third cousins often become very close, indeed—it's not unusual for them to marry."

"Really?"

"My own mother married her third cousin."

"I see."

"Well, cheerio."

"Cheerio."

He stepped into the kitchen as his cousin stomped up the stairs, and he saw that Cynthia's eyes were wide with a kind of wonder.

He was rummaging in the kitchen handy drawer for a chisel and hammer when the phone rang.

"Would you answer, please? Just tell them I'm busy and I'll call back."

He could hardly wait to lug that blasted stepladder out of her basement and drag it around her house in the pouring rain, looking for a burglar-friendly window.

"Hello?" said Cynthia.

"Hello-o-o, is the man of the house in?"

"He's busy now. May he call you back?"

"Just tell him Edith is home and dying to have the little chat we talked about the other evening. Perhaps over dinner. Why doesn't he ring me later? Tell him I can have my car sent down . . . anytime."

"Oh?"

"You must be the little house help I hear so much about."

Cynthia slammed the receiver on the hook.

"Good heavens," she whispered, turning a scorching shade of red. "I hung up on her. I don't know what came over me."

"Who was it . . . exactly?"

"I don't know what's gotten into me, I . . . I've never hung up on anyone in my life, and now I've done it twice in a row."

He slowly put the hammer in one pocket.

"It was Edith," she said. "That woman in the Lincoln."

He put the chisel in the other pocket.

"They're positively queuing up for you."

There was a very odd look on her face. Was she going to burst into tears or throw something at him? He stood unprotected in the middle of the floor. "Queuing . . . up? he croaked.

"First your so-called cousin who seems to have moved in permanently, and thanks for never telling me she's a raving beauty! And now this . . . this *Edith* who says she'll send her car down for you anytime, so you can have the little chat you're so looking forward to. I'm terribly sorry you had to fetch me from the airport, as it has clearly taken you away from a very demanding social schedule."

She grabbed Violet's crate and flew out the door and down the steps before he could gain any locomotion whatever.

"Cynthia! Where are you going?" he shouted from the back door. The rain was not only steady, it was pouring.

She turned around and glared at him, already drenched. "To a place where people are honest and decent and tell the plain truth instead of lies!"

"I hope this Valhalla isn't next door, because you can't get in."

She looked abashed for a moment. "Then I'll live in my car!" she yelled and dashed toward the hedge.

He had gotten as far as his back stoop when it hit him.

He couldn't use her stepladder to find a point of entry because her stepladder was in the basement and the only way to get to the basement was through a door in her hallway.

If he were a drinking man, he would have a double Scotch. On the rocks, and make it snappy. What was his brain made of these days? He couldn't seem to think straight for five minutes in a row.

The option was to break out a basement window. But could he then get through the door at the top of the basement stairs and into her hallway? If he remembered correctly, she liked to keep that door locked.

Could he even get that leviathan ladder of hers through a basement window, if he managed to crawl through, himself? Didn't he remember seeing the windows when he hauled Violet out of the coal chute, and weren't they unusually narrow?

A locksmith. That was the answer.

But when he called the only advertised locksmith in the area, there was a recording. He left a halfhearted message for the smith to call him back and hung up, feeling mold beginning to form under the slicker.

He splashed through the hedge toward the far side of the little yellow house, passing her garage on the way. He saw the dim outline of her head in the driver's seat of the gray Mazda.

Meg Patrick a raving beauty? The very thought boggled his mind. Had she worked so hard in New York that her eyesight was failing?

The basement windows were not only too narrow to push the ladder through, they were far too small for him to crawl through.

He went into the garage, dripping, and knocked on her car window. She rolled it down halfway.

"Hello, is this Miss Coppersmith's residence?"

"It is," she said, unsmiling.

"Ma'am, we have a problem. I am too large to crawl through your basement window and fetch out your ladder, which is too wide to be fetched out in the first place. So there you have it, and would you care to change your address temporarily and move to the rectory, where a fire and a bowl of soup wouldn't be a bad idea?"

"Don't you have a boy?"

"A boy?"

"Yes, a boy who is small enough to crawl in the basement window."

"We're awfully short on boys right now, ma'am. In any case, the basement door to your hallway may be locked, which means we couldn't gain access to your house even if I rounded up a dozen boys."

She stared straight ahead at a garden hoe hanging on the garage wall and sighed deeply.

"Do you know if the hall door to your basement is locked?"

"I always lock it when I go away, so nothing can . . . crawl up the stairs."

"Quite," he said, sighing also.

"I don't suppose you could crawl up the coal chute?" she said, still not looking at him. Violet howled from her crate in the passenger seat.

"No ma'am, we aren't trained to crawl up coal chutes. It's company policy. We tried it once, but our men kept slipping back and landing where they started."

"A definitive portrait of my relationship with my neighbor," she snapped.

"Why, yes, it is," he said, pleased with himself.

They sat at opposite ends of the study sofa with a box of Kleenex on the middle cushion.

Violet was curled on Cynthia's lap, sleeping, and Barnabas lay on the kitchen rug, leashed to the knob of the back door. The rector had decided he had only a couple of choices: Leave his dog in the garage, feeling punished through no fault of his own, or leash him to the knob where, should Violet get loose, a door torn from its hinges would be the worst that could happen.

The rain lashed the windows, the fire crackled, the clock ticked.

"I love the ticking of a clock," she said, sounding mournful.

He sneezed. "Does anyone else have a key?"

"Bless you. Not a soul, except David, who's traveling on business in the Far East."

He could break the glass pane in her storm door, but he didn't mention that."

She sneezed.

"Bless you," he said.

"You could stand on the back stoop and Dooley could kneel on your shoulders and lean over the railing and pry up the window in the downstairs bathroom," she said.

"That's a thought." He could see such a circus act crashing into the mud below, with only minor fractures as a result. He sneezed.

"Bless you. Maybe the locksmith will call you back."

"Maybe."

She hugged herself. "I'm freezing."

"Why don't you lie down, and I'll stir up the fire?"

"I've been up since four o'clock this morning," she said, looking miserable.

He brought a pillow from the armchair, and she lay down obediently. He covered her with the plaid afghan that was folded over the back of the sofa. "How's that?" he asked, looking at her huddled form.

He could barely hear what she whispered. "Heaven."

He put his hand on her forehead. "Warm," he pronounced, and sneezed.

She spent the night on the sofa, under a pile of quilts, refusing the offer of his bed.

He had brought her a pair of his socks and sat at the end of the sofa with her feet in his lap, sleeping in an upright position until two a.m.

He awoke when Cousin Meg flushed the toilet over his head,

and he added two logs to the fire. Then he crept up the stairs, feeling feverish.

After the locksmith arrived the next morning, he walked her through the hedge, lugging Violet's crate in one hand and her carry-on in the other. He went back to his car for the two suitcases, which were easily as heavy as Meg Patrick's, and popped those through the hedge and up the stairs to her bedroom.

She stood on the soft carpet in the room that he had never before seen and looked at him. He was somehow not surprised that he read his own thoughts and feelings in her eyes, though he had no idea what his thoughts and feelings were.

He took her in his arms and they stood for a moment, wordless.

Then he went down the stairs and home, where he searched for a handkerchief in his upper bureau drawer and found her house key.

❁

He had breakfast with Dooley but stopped by the Grill for coffee.

"Edith Mallory is home," he announced. "I'll talk to her this week."

"Better get a move on," said J.C.

His muscles ached and his head felt the size of a Canadian moose. "For Pete's sake, don't expect miracles." He'd rather take a whipping than see Edith Mallory.

"Percy's decided it's not going to happen," said Mule. "He says somethin's goin' to come up that'll stop it."

J.C. wiped his face. "That's called denial, buddyroe."

"Let me ask you something. Do you think my cousin Meg is . . . good-looking?"

"With those glasses on," said Mule, "she's ugly as homemade sin."

"Without her glasses?"

"I've never seen her without glasses. Probably not bad. Tall, slim, nice legs, great hair. But too weird, you know what I mean?"

Percy came to the booth and sat down. "Yessir, I've lost my last night of sleep over this thing."

Then why, the rector wondered, did Percy's hands shake when he put cream in his coffee?

❁

The crowd at the hospital called to ask if they might drop by before lunch.

He sneezed. Good! He could ride back with them and check into the emergency room.

At eleven, three nurses and Hoppy Harper in a Navy peacoat over a green scrub suit came through his office door with J.C. Hogan.

"Ta-daaa!" said Nurse Kennedy, handing him something.

Several bright flashes went off in rapid succession.

When he could see again, he read what was engraved in brass on the wooden plaque:

For Father Tim—
Beloved friend
and confidant—
For thirteen years,
you have doctored
the gang at
Mitford Hospital
with the best
medicine of all:
love.
We love you, too!

"I wrote it," said Nurse Kennedy, grinning proudly.

"I told her what to say," announced his doctor.

"I corrected their terrible spelling," Nurse Phillips assured him.

Nurse Jennings threw her arms around his neck. "I didn't' do a blessed thing but come up with the whole idea!"

J.C. reloaded his camera as Emma took the plaque out of the rector's hands and looked for a place to hang it. "Sit down and have a cup of coffee. And no offense, but it's fourteen years he's been runnin' up th' hill to th' hospital," said his proud secretary.

"Father, I believe you know who this is."

And he did, more's the pity. It was Dooley's school principal, Myra Hayes.

"This is to inform you that Dooley Barlowe is being suspended for ten school days for the possession of tobacco products and for smoking on school grounds."

There was a deafening silence. The decision might have come

down from a Supreme Court judge, so awesome was Myra Hayes's indignation.

He sneezed and his eyes watered. "When shall I pick him up?"

"Immediately," she said.

And just when they needed the blessing of every teacher they could get their hands on . . .

"Go to your room until I can deal with this thing," he told Dooley. He was shaking with a chill, and all he wanted to do was to lie down.

He managed to get his clothes off and his pajamas on and haul the quilts from the sofa to his bed. Then, he put on the socks Cynthia had worn and crawled between the icy sheets.

He was asleep before he could turn the lamp off.

CHAPTER FIFTEEN

Lady Spring

He couldn't remember being so sick.

For three days, Dooley fetched and carried through the hedge, ran to the drugstore and The Local, heated soup and delivered it upstairs, and generally made himself useful.

Timing is everything, thought the rector, who was getting plenty of mileage out of Dooley Barlowe's recent indiscretion.

A new and virulent strain of flu, complicated by sinus infection, said Hoppy, who made a house call wearing a mask and gloves. His doctor looked down his throat, listened to his breathing through a stethoscope, thumped him like a melon, and darted through the hedge to do the same to his neighbor.

Apparently fearing contamination, his cousin came out only at night, like a cockroach. She was rustling so many books from his shelves that he once heard her make two successive trips downstairs. On the last trip, he groaned loudly, making sure he could be heard beyond his closed door.

Dooley came in the next morning, looking pale. "I heard you hollerin' in here last night like you was dyin'. Are you dyin'?"

"No such luck," he said, feeling his sinuses drain like pipes.

"Well, try t' hold it down in here if you don't mind—you like t' scared me t' death."

"Speaking of being scared to death, wait 'til I get well, buster. You haven't seen anything yet."

Dooley turned paler still. Good! He needed to be scared. Getting himself thrown out of school like so much wastepaper, breaking the blasted law, shooting himself in the foot . . .

"You want ginger ale or tea?"

"Tea, thank you, and ask my dog to come in here while you're at it," he said darkly. "I know he's sleeping on the foot of your bed."

"Cynthia was sick as all get-out when I seen her last night."

"Tell me about it."

"Ol' Vi'let eat a mouse that got in while she was in New York City. Dropped it right on Cynthia's bed. Gross."

"I thought she liked mice."

"Not half eat, she don't," said Dooley, who appeared to know.

"When you bring up the tea, I'd like you sit in the chair under the lamp and read to me."

"What d'you want me to read?"

He might as well reach for the moon. "Shakespeare."

Dooley pointed a finger down his throat. "Gag."

When the boy went downstairs, he dialed her number, but it was busy.

Dooley delivered the *Muse* to his chair in the study, along with a fried bologna sandwich. "You want mustard or catsup?"

"Mustard." This was living. Or it might have been, if he weren't still nearly dying.

There was that blasted photo on the front page, as if nothing else was going on in this town. Why did his nose look like the bulb of a tulip? And that smirk on his face—is that what he looked like when he was smiling? If he never saw another picture of himself, it would be too soon.

"Here," said Dooley, "it's time for your medicine. I hope it makes you better. I'm about give out."

"If you're going to be a vet, you'd better get used to caring for the sick."

"Can I go to Tommy's after school?"

"Are you out of your *mind?*"

Dooley rolled his eyes.

"In case it hasn't occurred to you, you're grounded. Big Time. We'll talk as soon as I can manage it. Now, onto other matters. That was a grand reading from *Hamlet*. We'll have Dickens tonight."

"Who's Dickens?"

"Only one of the finest storytellers in the English language, but long-winded, so eat your Wheaties."

"Man," said Dooley, wishing he were back in school.

"And I'd like to have a look at that English composition you're writing about my dog.

"He ain't . . . isn't . . . just your dog. I live here too, y'know."

"Yes, well, and who feeds and brushes and bathes him?"

"I could brush 'im. An' I could feed him sometime . . ."

"There's a thought. Go to it." Why had he mistakenly assumed that a ten-day suspension was all bad?

He made his usual search for J.C.'s way with words but found only one gem:

Local Man Convicted of Wreckless Driving

He tore the story out to send to Walter.

On page three, Hessie Mayhew continued her annual saga.

Lady Spring has been sighted in our village at last, and skeptics are now convinced that she is here to charm us for the season.

Arriving less discreetly than in times past, she has already covered several banks with fuchsia phlox and tossed bouquets of violets hither as well as yon, showing special favor to the wooded pathways behind the post office.

One always looks for her touch, of course, at Lord's Chapel, where the gardens created by sexton Russell Jacks give pleasure year in and year out. Here, Lady Spring has entreated the redbuds to bloom a dash early, presenting themselves in glorious array behind the old tombstones. Do stroll down and have a look, as they make quite a show.

There's hardly any need to notify you of the great white cloud that is, as we write, settling over Fernbank. As all can see, Miss Baxter's apple trees are once again doing their best to make us the prettiest town in creation.

But take heed: don't plant yet. We've ten days to go, so do try and contain yourself.

Hessie ended with a quote from John Clare:

The snow has left the cottage top;
The thatch-moss grows in brighter green;
And eaves in quick succession drop,
Where grinning icicles have been,
Pit-patting with a pleasant noise
In tubs set by the cottage door;
While ducks and geese, with happy joys,
Plunge in the yard-pond brimming o'er.
The sun peeps through the window pane;
Which children mark with laughing eye,
And in the wet street steal again
To tell each other spring is nigh.

The timeline for planting, May 15, was also the Grill's timeline.

He let the newspaper drop to the floor. How had the days passed so quickly? For there was the shock of hearing the news, which took its own kind of time. Then, the brainstorming sessions and Edith's trip to Florida, and now he was sick.

Unless a miracle happened, they were looking at God knows what—a stroke for Percy, a strange job for Velma, and no way to get a decent cup of coffee, except by standing straight up at a shelf that ran along Winnie Ivey's bakery wall.

It was more than the probable loss of a landmark. It was, he concluded, a violation of ordinary lives made larger by continuity and connections.

He went to the sofa, uttered a brief but loaded petition, and dialed her number.

"Hello-o?"

"Edith?"

"Hello, Timothy. Magdolen has just gone out to The Local, so I'm my own social secretary."

"I'm sick . . ."

"Yes, I've heard. *So* sorry."

"That's why I haven't called sooner . . ."

"Not since your house help hung up in my face . . ."

"Something wrong with the phone lines, no doubt."

"What are you proposing, Timothy? And oh, you may as well know that I have no intention of seeing you while you're contagious, even if you are my priest."

"I should be completely over it in a couple of days. What about lunch in Wesley on Thursday?"

"We'll see," she told him, in a tone that said she had no intention of seeing.

His cousin still refused to accompany them to church. In reply to the note he left under her door, she left a note for him on the kitchen table:

I shan't come with you, though I do appreciate the invitation. Csn Meg

He couldn't help but notice she'd left the lid off the pickles.

"Hello."

"Hello, yourself," he said, noting that the receiver felt like a barbell. "Feeling better?"

"Better than what?"

"Better than if you'd been pushed from a tall building."

"Only slightly. And you?"

"Rotten, if the truth were known."

"The truth is seldom known, Timothy."

He moved quickly. "The truth is, Edith Mallory is involved in something I didn't have a chance to tell you about, which is why she called and invited me to dinner, and if Cousin Meg is a raving beauty, I am Michelangelo's David." There. He hadn't meant to sound so angry about it, but he was angry, he suddenly realized. Why was he having to report his personal life to Cynthia Coppersmith?

Clearly, she didn't want to talk about it. "Thanks for sending Dooley over. You've no idea how it's helped."

"Actually, I do have an idea. He's a boon to me, as well. Couldn't get out of bed the first two days. What did Hoppy say?"

"I have everything you have."

Bookends, he wanted to say, but didn't.

"Everything, that is, except a sinus infection, thanks be to God."

"There is a balm in Gilead."

"I'm making soup with the ounce of energy I got from eating a cracker," she said. "May I send some over?"

"Wonderful! I told Puny not to come in 'til the germs die down, so we're pushing along on our own over here. What time do you want Dooley to make a pickup?"

"Around five," she said, "and I'll leave out the carrots so he'll eat it. Now, with or without a cream base?"

"Without," he said.

"With or without a thin, golden-crusted little morsel of cornbread hot from the oven!"

"With!" he exclaimed, not feeling angry anymore.

Edith Mallory wanted him crawling on his hands and knees. All he was prepared to do, however, was call her again—just as soon as he went to the drugstore for Dooley's prescription.

Dooley had eaten a vast bowl of Cynthia's soup, cleaned up his share of the cornbread, crumbs and all, and fallen on the sofa, unable to move.

"You've done worked me to death," he said, his teeth chattering from the chill that raced through him.

"Tit for tat," replied the rector, covering him with the afghan.

"Timothy, I am not a charity organization." Edith's brown cigarette lay smoldering in the ashtray on the table."

"That's not what I'm saying, Edith."

"Priests are so idealistic—they're like children, really. They know nothing about business."

"I do realize your need to make investments lucrative, to be a wise steward of what you . . ."

"Then do stop nagging me to do what you're asking. A twenty-percent rent increase is not worth bothering about." She stirred sweetener into a glass of tea, while lunch progressed into his digestive system like so much gall.

"The mayor has done everything in her power to stop progress in this town, and while you may think those tacky shops on Main Street are charming, they're an economic liability of the worst sort. Look at that hideous awning on the Grill and that peeling paint."

"May I remind you that hideous awnings and peeling paint are a responsibility of the property owner and not the tenant?"

"Don't mince my words. A fine dress shop from Florida, where people know how to *do,* Timothy, will bring in more shops like it. It will raise rents all along the street. It will . . ."

"It will destroy the character it has taken more than half a century to create. It will erase something central to the core and spirit of the town and demolish a sense of connectedness that is disappearing throughout the country—something we're desperately longing to return to, though in most places it's far too late . . ."

"Oh, for heaven's sake," she said, "stop preaching to me. Save that for the pulpit! I always knew you were old-fashioned, but I never dreamed you were so set in your ways."

"That may be. I'm also saying that doubling the rent is unfair and is clearly a strategy to get the Grill off the street. Another thing. How carefully have you considered the cost of leasing this space to a fine dress shop and the amount of upfitting they'll require of the owner?"

"It has all been considered, and it is all decided. Unless your people can pay the rent I'm asking, which is perfectly legitimate for Main Street, the dress shop will occupy the property on May 16. And no, I can't wait until your people find a new location, if there is such a thing, because the shop owners must occupy on the sixteenth or go elsewhere. Believe me, I'm going to see they don't go elsewhere."

"Waiter," he said, "would you bring the check?"

She crushed out her cigarette. "And don't expect me to pay it, like so many clergy do."

There was one thing he could say for her, but only one:

She hadn't strung him along.

Percy had better be ready to pack up and not look back.

He couldn't separate the anger from the sorrow. "Vent your anger," the bishop had said a few times, "or it turns into depression—then you're down in the mire with half your parish."

He didn't feel up to racing his motor scooter out to Absalom Greer's country store, though the weather was certainly good for it. He was not yet well enough to jog, and smashing glasses into the fireplace was too theatrical.

Instead, he put on a pot of soup, gave Dooley his medicine, read to him from a veterinary book, and brushed Barnabas. Then, while the soup boiled over on the stove, he fell asleep on the sofa, exhausted.

"Are you well, Cousin?" she called through the three-inch opening.

He let out a racking cough and shoved his handkerchief to his face. Then he blew his nose as loudly as he could.

She shut the door.

There, he thought. That ought to hold her for another day or two.

"She's set on it, Percy. I did my best."

Percy looked thinner, and there were dark circles under his eyes. "Thank you, Father. I know you did. I ain't worried about it."

"Percy's cookin' is starting to reflect his mood," said J.C. "Lookit this sausage." To make his point he tried to puncture it with a knife, only to have it skid across his plate.

Mule scowled at Percy. "You got to keep up, buddyroe. You can't let down, especially not here at th' last."

"Depression," said J.C. "That's what it is. That and denial."

"Depression comes from anger," said the rector. "You need to let off steam."

"We could all go to Wesley and get drunk," said Mule.

"Fine," said J.C., "except nobody drinks—besides th' father, that is, who knocks back a little sherry now and then."

"I forgot," said Mule, "that J.C. goes to A.A., I don't drink anything stronger than well water, and Percy was raised Baptist and never touched a drop."

J.C. raked the last of the buttered grits onto his toast. "Bein' raised Baptist can drive you to drink, if you want my opinion."

"So how could Percy let off some steam?" asked the rector. "We need to brainstorm this."

"I'll tell you how,' said J.C. "Let Omer Cunningham fly you

around in that old airplane, upside down and backwards. That'll do it. You'll be so glad to get on th' ground, they could take this place and turn it into a hubcap museum, for all you care."

"Let Fancy give you a face mask," said Mule. "No charge. On the house."

"A what?" asked Percy, looking done in.

"A face mask. It cleans out your pores."

Percy got up and went to the men's room.

"We're makin' him sick," said J.C.

"We've only got eight days to the fifteenth." The rector took off his glasses and rubbed his eyes. "So, what's the answer?"

"There isn't one," said Mule, sounding oddly philosophical.

He had never seen Dooley Barlowe look so haggard and pale. He opened a can of ginger ale and went upstairs and sat on the side of his bed.

"I got you another week of KitKats," he said, holding up the bag. "Thanks for using them as we agreed."

"One every other day, and no cheating," said Dooley, looking feverish. "Leave 'em in here or that woman'll git 'em."

The rector pushed the bag under the bed. "There. Completely out of sight. So how are you feeling?"

"I'd as soon be dead."

"I know the feeling. We'll have a talk when you're better."

"Who's lookin' after ol' Cynthia?"

"I am. The torch has passed to me."

"How's she doin'?"

"Still a bit down."

"Are you goin' to marry her?"

"Well . . ." he said, as if the wind had been knocked out of him.

"Are you or ain't you? I would, if I was you."

"You're not me."

"I'm dern glad of that."

"Why are you glad of that?"

"You ain't no fun."

"Aren't no fun. Come to think of it, you're not exactly a million laughs, yourself. Why would you marry Cynthia if you were me?"

"Because she's neat. She's fun."

"What's so fun about her?"

"She picked 'at ol' mouse up by th' ear and th'ow'd it at me when I laughed at 'er."

"Throwing around a dead mouse is fun?"

"It is if you don't have nothin' else to do," said Dooley.

Dooley's flu hung on longer than his own had done, but then, he had pushed himself. Cynthia was still moping around in her bathrobe and curlers, with scarcely enough energy to bring in the mail.

"It's all right to take your time getting well," he said, having a cup of tea in her workroom. "You've worn yourself out on the book. Allow time to rest. Don't push yourself." He had never been able to take his own advice.

He picked flowers and left them on her kitchen cabinet and brought her a book of quotations from Happy Endings. He stopped by Winnie Ivey's for a napoleon, which he was tempted to step into the bushes and devour on the way home, but delivered it straight to her door.

He sat and read to her one evening while she put her feet on the ottoman and looked pale, and he also endured her infernal sighing.

He even opened some foul-smelling concoction and fed it to Violet, who scratched him on the ankle for his trouble.

If this was what marriage was like, he thought, he was getting a good dose. Cynthia Coppersmith was lapping up his doting attention like cream, without so much as bothering to take the curlers out of her hair.

"That woman left!" Dooley yelled from his bedroom.

He walked to the boy's doorway and looked in. "Left? When?"

"After you went to your office. I seen 'er creepin' down th' stairs."

He went to the guest room door and tried the knob. Locked.

"She'll be back," he told Dooley.

"Poop."

"Tomorrow night is when we'll talk. You'll be well enough and in the nick of time, too. You start back to school on Monday."

Dooley pulled the covers over his head.

“Well! I see you went out. That’s good news.”

“I went out for personal items,” she said, ducking through the kitchen in her trench coat.

“I love you,” he would say, meaning it.

“That’s the first thing I want you to know.”

Then, he would talk about school laws and how they’re designed for the common good, not to mention individual good, which, in this case, had everything to do with health.

Then, he would deal with the issue of wrong friends and once again go over the ramifications of stealing as it affected personal character and spiritual freedom.

He would close with the warning Buck Leeper had commanded him to pass along. Here was yet another infraction of rules, another instance of disregard for set boundaries. He would not allow this sort of behavior to become a pattern, and neither did he want to make any threats he couldn’t keep.

He pondered what Dooley liked best:

Playing with Tommy, singing in the chorus, listening to his jam box, eating hamburgers.

To underscore the ten-day suspension, he could remove everything but the chorus—but should he remove them all at once or in descending order? And for how long? He would call Marge Owen, who had raised two and was sufficiently skilled to be doing it all over again.

This was treacherous ground, and for Dooley’s sake, he didn’t want to step in a hole.

To accommodate two working mothers, the ECW changed their morning meeting to an evening meeting but failed to tell him. As he was the speaker, along with Mayor Cunningham and a Wesley town official, he had to change his own plans and be there.

“We’ll talk when I come home,” he told Dooley, who was well enough to watch TV.

But when he came home, the boy was in bed, snoring, his red hair lying wetly on his forehead.

He looked down at his freckled face and the arm thrown over the covers, grateful for all he had brought into the silent rectory, including the worry and aggravation.

Barnabas, who was sleeping at the foot of Dooley's bed, didn't raise his head but opened one eye.

Right there was some of the best medicine Dooley Barlowe had ever had. His dog could positively cure what ailed you—not to mention the fact that he was an upstanding churchgoer into the bargain.

He looked out his alcove window before getting undressed and gave his neighbor a quick call.

"Hey," he said when she answered the phone.

"Hey, yourself."

"What's going on next door? Do I see your Christmas lights burning?"

"I'm celebrating."

"Alone?"

"I wouldn't be, if you'd come over."

"Well . . . ," he said, uncertain.

"No strings attached."

That was fair enough. He went over.

She invited him to sit on the love seat in her workroom.

"What are you celebrating?" It must be fairly momentous, as she had taken the curlers out of her hair and looked terrific.

"Being alive."

"You were that sick?"

"It has nothing to do with being sick. We breathe, we run around in our underwear, we go to the store, we dig up the tulip bulbs or plan to, we make soup and pay the electric bill, and we never stop to think—we're alive! This is a gift!

"I wasn't even pondering this. I wasn't being poetic or introspective. It's just that I glanced at the floor—right there—this afternoon and saw how the light came through the window and fell on the wood.

"It bowled me over. It took my breath away. I could hardly bear it."

He was silent, looking at her.

"There was so much life in the light on the wood, the way it folded itself gently into the grain. That little spot on the floor radiated with tenderness. And then it was gone."

He couldn't stop looking at her and didn't try.

"Do you know?" she asked softly.

"I know," he said.

"Not everyone knows," she said.

"Yes."

They heard the ticking of her clock in the hallway outside her workroom.

She was perched on the stool at her drawing board. "Why don't you come and sit here?" he said.

She slid off the stool and came to him and sat down, and he took her hand. They were quiet for a time, in a soft pool of light from the lamp.

It occurred to him that he wanted to kiss her, to hold her close, but he didn't deserve it. He didn't deserve even to be sitting here, a man who couldn't make up his mind from one hour to the next.

She leaned her head to one side, in that way of hers. "What are you thinking?"

"That I want to kiss you," he said. "More than anything."

She smiled. "No strings attached?"

"Yes," he said. "No strings attached."

He couldn't help it that Dooley had a mild relapse on Saturday night and that he didn't feel so good himself. Nor did he intend to fall asleep on Sunday after church and nap until the afternoon, which is when Dooley fell asleep and was out like a light until dinnertime. He meant to discuss the whole thing with him that night, before the boy went back to school the following morning, but when he sat on the side of Dooley's bed, it was all he could do to say, "Listen, this can't happen again. Do you hear me?"

Dooley had seemed to hear him, but he couldn't quite forgive himself that he hadn't handled it right. No, he hadn't handled it right at all.

The lilacs bloomed so furiously that not a few of the villagers turned out to view the bushes.

"You've got to walk down behind Lord's Chapel," Hessie Mayhew told Winnie Ivey. "There's a white bush you won't believe! Take a camera!"

"Come and look!" Cynthia called through the hedge one morning. Barnabas nearly pulled him down racing to her yard where an ancient purple bush, half-hidden by the garage, was massed with fragrant blooms.

Andrew Gregory invited two friends from Baltimore to "come for the lilacs" and took them up and down Main Street to meet everybody from the postmaster to Dora Pugh, whose window display at the hardware store had changed to seed packets, bonemeal, garden spades, and wooden trellises.

On Sunday, the rector felt a lightness of spirit like he'd seldom known.

He walked toward home, as if on air, until he saw Percy and Velma driving down Main Street after the Presbyterians let out.

Percy didn't see him, but he saw Percy—and he was shocked at the grief so plainly revealed on his friend's unguarded face, as if it could no longer be hidden.

CHAPTER SIXTEEN

Down the Hatch

"And the name of the slough was despond," said J.C., who couldn't eat a bite.

"Th' last supper," said Mule. "With its own Judas."

They had all seen the sign on the door.

LAST DAY
After lunch,
the Main Street Grill
will be
officially closed.
New location
to be announced.
Thank you for
your business.

J.C. stared into his coffee cup. "I helped pack last night. It was awful."

"I'll help tomorrow," said Mule, "and Fancy's comin' to help Velma. Omer's loadin' this end. Lew Boyd's unloadin' the other end. We got four college kids from Wesley, and Coot and Ron are runnin' their trucks to the warehouse."

"Well done," said the rector. "I'll be here tomorrow at daylight."

J.C. rolled his eyes. "Good luck with what's down th' hatch."

"What's down there?"

"Fifty-two years of bein' in the food business. You got creamed corn in cans big as this booth, not to mention stewed tomatoes and sauerkraut out th' kazoo. You got busted display cases, old counter stools, rusted tin signs, milk crates, and a jukebox that'll take four men to lift it. Did you know this place had a jukebox in 1950? His daddy was trying to loosen up and go after a new demographic. Percy won't throw away a bloomin' thing, so eat your Wheaties."

"You're not packin' tomorrow?" Mule wanted to know.

"I've got a paper to get out."

"How are you going to treat the story?" asked the rector.

"I'm blaring it across the whole front page. Big photo of the sign on the door. Headline says, *Read It and Weep*. We'll run a black border around the front page—which hasn't been done on the *Muse* since World War Two. What do you think?"

"Check your spellin'," said Mule, looking distraught. "This is important. It needs to be respectful."

J.C. wiped his face with his handkerchief. "This is goin' to change my dadgum life. I don't take kindly to things that change my life."

"Get you a hot plate and start cookin'," said Mule. "You bachelors lead a sheltered existence."

"Rave on," said the rector.

J.C. leaned out of the booth and looked toward the front of the Grill. "There's Mack Stroupe with a toothpick stuck in his jaw. He's about to finish roofing that shed he built to snatch Percy's trade.

"There's your Collar Button man. He's shakin' Percy's hand like an undertaker. And there's Esther and Ray, both of 'em bawlin' like babies. Man, this is giving me an ulcerated stomach."

"In two days, they'll be nailin' boards over your stair steps," said Mule.

"I sent her a note, said she better fix th' back steps or I haul my presses out of here."

"I wouldn't get too high-hat with that witch on a broom," said Mule. "You'll be printin' your paper on th' creekbank."

J.C. squinted toward the front. "Velma's breakin' down."

"Let me out," said Father Tim.

He walked with Velma Mosely to the Sweet Stuff Bakery, where

Winnie set her in a chair in the back room and let Velma do something she said she'd been needing to do: cry her eyes out.

A letter from Father Roland in his "rude cabin in the wild":

He'd been taken in a canoe to a parishioner's house, where a meal for fourteen church members consisted of salmon steaks roasted over live coals. He declared he had never tasted anything so fine since his preseminary days in southern France. Clearly, his honeymoon with the rugged north woods of Canada remained in full swing, albeit the pay was minuscule.

A letter from the man in the attic, George Gaynor, who had discovered several prison inmates with whom he was praying and searching the Scriptures:

In this hard place, I have been greatly blessed to find hearts softened by the gospel of Jesus Christ. You're faithfully in my prayers.

A note from Cynthia, faintly reminiscent of wisteria:

Thank you for taking care of me while I was sick. I really was an old poop, but you didn't seem to notice, for which I'm truly thankful.

She had drawn a picture of herself in her bathrobe, looking frazzled, while he sat opposite her in a suit of shining armor, reading aloud from Wordsworth.

Ah, but he liked mail. Always had. One never knew what might turn up in the mail. It was like a lottery in which one could hit the jackpot at any moment.

The letter from Dooley's principal was not the jackpot.

Dear Father:

Dooley has told me that you did not rebuke him in any way for his flagrant conduct, and I am both shocked and disappointed to learn of this.

To cast the full burden for correction upon the school is a gross neglect of moral responsibility, though unfortunately it is a course of behavior almost always chosen by today's new breed of woefully indifferent parents.

You have only to look at the newspaper and watch your television to discover at once where such neglect inevitably leads.

I shall expect you to devise and deliver a proper punishment in the home and report it to me at once.

Myra Hayes

Dear Mrs. Hayes, he might reply, *I have kicked Dooley Barlowe's tail clean across Baxter Park for betraying my moral laxity to your office. For the crime of having smoked cigarettes on school property, I haven't yet come up with a suitable punishment, but when I do, rest assured it will be something that you'll most gleefully approve. Sincerely.*

He woke at five, as usual, and called the hospital to say he wouldn't be around to visit on the wards this morning, but he'd be there tomorrow, without fail.

He read morning prayer and lections and spent time on his knees for Percy and Velma. Then, he asked the Holy Spirit to open his heart for any special prayer for others. Buck Leeper was first in line.

At six, he pulled on an old pair of corduroy workpants and a denim shirt and woke Dooley and their houseguest. He didn't think he was up to looking at his cousin over breakfast, but he knocked anyway.

"Rise and shine!" he shouted, loud enough to be heard to the Presbyterian parking lot and beyond. Two of his dearest friends were being dumped on, and he was plenty mad about it. If his cousin was thinking of ignoring his knock, she had better think again.

When she showed up in the kitchen in her robe and slippers, scowling, he acquainted her with a few rules he should have laid down in the beginning—and in no uncertain terms.

Dooley stared at him with his mouth hanging open.

"And," he informed his charge, "if you think that's something, just wait 'til I get through with you. In other words, my friend, you ain't seen nothin' yet."

Dooley Barlowe didn't say one word during breakfast, nor did his cousin, nor did he.

"Where's Percy?"

Velma's eyes were red and swollen. "Down th' hatch," she said.

The place was a tomb. He could hear his footsteps on the hardwood floor, even though he was wearing tennis shoes.

"You'll open again," he said, meaning it.

Velma didn't reply. She was dumping flatware in a box with egg turners, colanders, and a metal grater. The sound seemed to echo off the walls, which was denuded of its usual array of outdated calendars, prints of covered bridges, and a collection of Cheerwine and Dr. Pepper signs.

The autographed photo of Percy and the former governor was gone, as was the photo of Percy's daddy wrestling an alligator in Florida. The photos of their grandchildren had been peeled off the back of the cash register, and they had stripped off the battered sign that read, *Good Taste, Ample Portions, Quick Service, Low Prices.*

He sighed, not knowing what else to do.

"Mule's runnin' late," said Velma. "Help yourself to coffee."

He poured a cup of coffee and descended broad wooden stairs to the basement.

He'd never been underneath the Grill before, in the room lined with shelves built over earthen walls and lighted by two bare, weak bulbs.

"Percy?"

"Over here," said Percy, appearing from behind the furnace. In the gloom, the pallor of his friend's face was startling.

He'd known priests who could make people laugh in the jaws of disaster, but he wasn't part of that breed. In all his years in the clergy, he'd never been able to think of witty remarks that, even for a moment, might obscure the pain of loss.

"How's it going?" he asked quietly.

Percy looked away from him. "I cain't hardly seem to go on from here."

"Why don't we take a load off our feet before we get started?"

"I thought I'd be able t' handle it," said Percy, sitting with the rector on the bottom step. "But I ain't able, it seems like."

"Thirty-four, thirty-five years. It's a long time."

"Longer'n that. I was ten years old when I stepped behind th' counter. My daddy had a bad toothache and put me in charge of the grill while he went to the dentist."

"How did you do?"

"I stood on a bread crate and fried bacon like a man. I'd never fried bacon in my life, nor anything else. My mama had to drive my daddy. He was in awful pain. She looked back at me as she was goin' out th' door, and said, 'Percy, you can do it.' I'll never forget that."

"She's right. You can do it."

"You mean . . . this?"

"Right. This."

"How come I have to—that's the question. Where's th' Lord when you need 'im is what I'd like to know."

The hot coffee cup warmed his cold hands. "Right here with us, believe it or not."

"You're a preacher. That's easy for you to say."

"Not really. I have times of doubt. I stumble around . . ."

"All that schoolin' you had makes a difference."

"Schooling doesn't count for much in the end. What counts is our personal relationship with God. Period. Bottom line."

"I prayed about this."

"You'll get an answer."

"This ain't any kind of answer."

"I have to tell you that He always answers. And He always shoots straight."

"Well, He's done shot and missed, if you ask me."

The rector looked around at the dark, dismal basement. "Somebody said the brightest diamonds grow in the darkest cavities of the earth . . ."

"Meanin'?"

"In Isaiah, God said, 'I will give you the treasures of darkness, riches stored in secret places, so that you may know that I am the Lord . . .' Times of darkness can be some of the best times."

"My daddy told me for a fact th' Lord helped him start this business. Why would th' Lord be throwin' me out?"

"He may have something different for you now. Something terrific, actually. Maybe it's time, Percy, to look at other options . . ."

"Bein' out of a job at age sixty, with your wife doin' piecework at the glove factory—buddyroe, that ain't an option. Cuttin' and haulin' wood and sellin' it door to door ain't an option either, not with my back. And I can tell you right now that pumpin' gas at Lew Boyd's ain't an option, not now or in the dadgum future. So . . . I ain't got any options."

"Right. Maybe you don't."

Faint rays of daylight shone through the small window that faced the sidewalk on Main Street.

"But maybe God does," the rector said. "Look here. When God takes away the good, He replaces it with something better. Didn't Jesus tell the disciples, 'It's for your good that I'm going away'? And do you think they went for it? No, it plunged them into despair—they felt orphaned and desolate, probably angry into the bargain."

Percy stared at the furnace.

"But when the Holy Spirit came, the disciples had more than Christ in their *midst*—now He was in their hearts." Yes! He felt encouraged just talking about it. He clapped his hand on his friend's shoulder.

"So, Percy—screw up your faith and get ready for something better."

Percy stood and glared at him. "We better screw something up, all right, and get these boxes packed. Start with th' sauerkraut on that top shelf and work down to the pork an' beans. We won't mess with th' jukebox 'til th' college boys get here."

At noon, Mack Stroupe dropped in with a sack of hot dogs all the way, and Winnie Ivey brought a dozen cream horns and napoleons. The Collar Button donated a case of Classic Coke, Coot Hendrick brought a pie his mother had baked, the police chief dropped in with a sack of apples, and Joe Ivey stuck a bottle of brandy under his belt, buttoned his jacket, and walked to the Grill where he passed the bottle around to whoever wanted a taste.

Joe eyed the rector. "If I was you, I wouldn't let your boy cut your hair."

"Dooley?"

"He's made a mess of th' sides," said Joe. "You want a little nip?"

"Thank you, but I pass. I'm a sherry man."

"You can get stumblin' drunk on sherry," Joe told him.

"Man!" said Mule. "This is killer kraut. This is the third box I've heaved up th' steps. Who eats this stuff, anyway?"

"Nobody," said the rector. "That's why he's got a surplus."

Mule looked up as J.C. came down the stairs, wearing his Nikon on a strap around his neck. "I thought you were puttin' out the paper."

"I've said all I've got to say."

"We haven't packed all we've got to pack, so hop to it. Here's a box. There's the stewed okra." Mule kicked an empty box into the light of a sixty-watt bulb.

"I hate stewed okra."

"You don't have to like it to pack it."

"No way, Jose. I did my time. I'll just sit and watch you boys." J.C. scratched himself and sat down on a step.

Fancy appeared at the hatch door, wearing a form-fitting cashmere sweater, pink tights, and white boots with spike heels. "Yoo hoo, Mule honey, Coot's back with the truck. Do y'all have another load ready? If not, we need him to help us clean these floors."

"It'll be awhile, yet."

"Super. Oh, Father, I didn't say one word to Joe Ivey about how you've switched over to me."

He'd switched over?

"I'm about wore out," said Percy. "I wish I dipped or chewed or smoked—somethin'."

"Joe offered you a taste of brandy," said Mule. "You ought to have had a little shooter."

"No sir," said Percy, looking mournful, "I've gone sixty years without it, and I don't intend to start now."

"Liquor gets your kidneys," J.C. announced. "Not to mention dries out your skin, ruins the veins in your nose, gives you palsy, and wrecks your coordination. I've heard that people on gin start walkin' sideways, like crabs."

Mule scratched his head. "They drink an awful lot of gin at the country club, but I never saw anybody walk sideways."

Fancy's spike heels clicked above them like castanets.

"How you 'uns comin'?" Uncle Billy stuck his head in the hatch door and peered into the gloom.

"We need a joke!" said the rector. They had packed seventy-two boxes, all told, not a few of which were breakables that had already been broken.

"How about if I stand right here t' tell it," said Uncle Billy. "Arthur won't let me come down steps, don't you know." Activity subsided as the old man reared back to deliver his contribution to moving day.

"Did you 'uns hear about th' feller lookin' for a good church?"

"No!" chorused his audience.

"Well sir, he searched around and found a little fellowship where th' preacher and th' congregation were readin' out loud. They were sayin', 'We have left undone those things which we ought to have done, and we have done those things which we ought not to have done.'

"Th' feller dropped into th' pew with a big sigh of relief. 'Hallelujah,' he said to hisself, 'I've found my crowd at last.' "

The rector laughed heartily. "It's about time you worked our bunch into your repertoire."

"Hit us again, Uncle Billy," said Mule.

"This feller, he went t' th' doctor and told 'im what all was wrong, so th' doctor give 'im a big load of advice about how to git well. Th' feller started to leave, don't you know, when th' doctor said, 'Hold up. You ain't paid me for my advice.' 'That's right,' th' feller said, 'because I ain't goin' t' take it.' "

"I'll print that one," said J.C., scribbling in his pocket notebook.

"Well, I'll be pushin' off. It's a shame what's happenin' here t' two good friends. Me and Rose, we think th' world of you 'uns. Try not t' take it too hard."

Uncle Billy vanished from the hatch door, and they returned wearily to their work.

Fancy appeared on the top step, where she leaned over and whispered, "Percy, Velma's cryin' again."

"What do you want me to do about it?" Percy snapped. His arms were wrapped around a tub of Crisco.

"Let her cry," said the rector. "It helps."

J.C. cocked his head and listened. "Run for th' hills. It's Lucrezia Borgia."

Mule furrowed his brow. "Who?"

"I'll just duck behind the furnace," said the rector.

Edith Mallory appeared at the hatch door. "Who's down there?" she demanded.

"Mule Skinner, Percy Mosely, and J.C. Hogan," said Mule, peering up the stairs.

"When will you be finished?"

"Before tomorrow."

"What time before tomorrow?"

"We don't have a clue."

"I suggest it be no later than midnight, as agreed. Is Father Tim down there?"

"I don't see him."

"Where do you think he might be?"

"Heaven knows."

"Remember, Mr. Mosely, that the booths come out also. I see they're still attached to the wall. And you'll recall that the stools must be out, as well."

Percy clenched his fists.

"Mr. Coffey will meet their truck in Wesley tomorrow morning. He'll lead the way and they'll proceed. They'll occupy the premises at eight o'clock sharp." Edith stomped away from the hatch door.

"You can come out now," Mule said in the direction of the furnace.

They heaved the last of the boxes up the steps, too weary to speak.

"Give me a flashlight," said the rector. "I'll look around, one last time."

He couldn't remember feeling such exhaustion and soreness of spirit. All he wanted to do was go home and go to bed. Yet, they didn't want to leave behind any valuable items that Percy might be able to turn into cash. The Collar Button man had offered five hundred dollars for the jukebox, if Percy would also let him have the records that included "Sixty-Minute Man," "One Mint Julep," and "Chattanooga Shoeshine Boy." Percy was thinking about it.

Mule had swept the concrete floor and stood the broom in a corner. Strange that nothing but a worn-down broom was left of a family's fifty-two-year history.

He shone the light throughout the eerie space, which had grown colder and damper with nightfall. He had smelled all the sour earth he could stomach and decided that plans for cleaning his own basement could wait a few years.

He pointed the flashlight under the floor joists where raw dirt left only a few feet of interval space. Maybe some of those old advertising signs had been stored in there—the Collar Button man's excitement indicated they were valuable.

That was when he saw it.

CHAPTER SEVENTEEN

Broken Rules

Ron Malcolm whistled.

"The joists are rotten from front to back, but it looks like the worst is smack under the rear booth."

All he could see were Ron's feet sticking out where he'd crawled between the floor joists and the bank of earth.

"For goodness sake, tell Percy to stop jumping around up there."

"Percy!" the rector shouted up the stairs.

"What?"

"Hold it down a minute." He hadn't told Percy what he had seen. Instead, he said he thought Ron Malcolm, being a former builder, might like to see the interesting way the building was supported.

"How fast can you get here?" he said from the phone booth in front of Happy Endings, and Ron had hit the floor beside his bed running.

Ron wriggled out of the space. "After forty years in the construction business, I sure as heck don't want to be crushed under a pile of rubble."

"That bad?"

"You wouldn't believe it. Southern pine, plenty old, and rotten to the core. I've seen it a hundred times. It's a miracle we haven't all been dumped in the basement. Especially the rear booth—it's a real hot seat."

"The new tenants come in tomorrow morning."

"Not in here, they don't. When the town inspector gets a look at this . . ."

"Could we call him, get him to take a look at it . . . now?"

"Now?"

"Edith Mallory needs to hear this, but she probably needs to hear it from a town authority."

"It's eleven o'clock at night . . ."

"How long could it take for repairs?"

Ron looked up and around. "Two months, six months. There's a lot of hidden stuff in a setup like this. Who knows? Minimum, maybe two months. You got to rip out the joists from front to back . . . lay a new floor. . . . Maybe we could salvage some of the old floor. I don't know. I saw this same thing happen in a church once—a few more Sundays and the entire gospel side could have been swallowed up.

"They'll want to check the stairwell that goes to J.C.'s press room, too. That whole area is pretty bouncy, as I recall."

"Let's think this through," said the rector, sitting down on the bottom step.

Edith Mallory looked as if she'd dressed for a bridge luncheon, although it was nearly midnight. She drummed her fingers on the surface of her breakfast counter where they sat on stools. A cigarette smoldered in the ashtray.

"Rotten," said the rector.

"Clear through," said the former builder. "I plan to report it to the town inspector first thing in the morning, because it's a hazardous situation. Somebody could get killed in there."

The muscles in her face appeared to tighten, which made her enormous eyes seem larger. "I have a moving van arriving in Wesley at seven o'clock in the morning."

"When the inspector sees the problem, chances are he'll condemn it."

She uttered an oath.

"It'll take a couple of months, maybe more, to make repairs. Worst case, other problems could be lurking in the structure, as well."

She put the smoldering cigarette out. "I'm flying to Spain day after tomorrow." She sat immobile, frozen. "I don't suppose this is some cooked-up ruse to keep your friend from leaving . . ."

"Keep him from leaving?" said Father Tim. "He's already gone. Midnight, remember?"

She stared at the wall clock, a nerve twitching under her left eye. "How long will you be in Spain?"

"Three months," she snapped. "Then on a world cruise."

"You said the dress shop would have to go elsewhere if they couldn't occupy tomorrow, is that correct?"

"That," she said, turning on him with a kind of seething fury, "is precisely what I said and precisely what they will be forced to do." She drew one of her brown cigarettes out of the package. "That odious place has never been anything but trouble to me."

"Perhaps the space will be attractive to another of your connections . . ."

"I wanted it finalized before I leave." She got up and paced the kitchen floor. "I suppose you think I have time to recruit tenants before Wednesday?"

"I have a tenant for you."

She looked at him condescendingly. "Really?"

"The same tenant who occupied it for thirty-four years."

She sniffed.

"I hear you'll be spending more of your time in your Florida home."

"You heard correctly."

"Sign a lease with Percy and make your repairs. This would put the place in good hands, with no running back and forth to pacify a high-rent lessee. You'd have no fancy carpeting to pay for, no walls and ceilings to restore and paint, no upgraded toilet to install." He paused and plunged ahead. "A five-year-lease with a twenty percent rent increase."

She glared at him. "You must be kidding."

"Five and twenty," he said evenly.

The nerve under her left eye twitched again. "One year at forty percent."

"Five and twenty, and you replace the awning. We'll scrape and paint the front of the building."

"Right," said Ron.

She stood in the middle of the floor, rigid. "One and thirty. Bottom line."

The rector got off the stool. "Have a good trip, Edith." Ron followed him to the door.

He was turning the knob when she came into the foyer behind them. "All right, then. Five and twenty."

He turned around to face her cold rage. Edith hissed a bitter curse, which, for all its foulness, didn't surprise him in the least.

"Not one bit of skin off Percy's nose," said Emma. "He had to move out, anyway, for all that work to get done. Plus, it was in the nick of time, before the whole thing caved in and people raised a stink."

It hadn't been what the scripture from Isaiah had meant, exactly, but God had given Percy a treasure in the darkness. There in that dim basement were the rotten joists—which, oddly, had been worth their weight in gold.

"It's wonderful," said Cynthia. "You're the man of the hour!"

He'd never been the man of any hour. He discovered that he felt taller, even thinner. How that was possible, he had no idea. However, he didn't want to get carried away with such nonsense. And he also didn't want to gloss over the most important of his feelings, which was joy.

A comfortable way of life was being changed—but then, it would soon be restored. Percy would not die, Velma would not cry, he could get a bowl of soup somewhere other than his own kitchen, and life would go on.

He walked to the church and knelt down and prayed, having a good laugh with the Lord as he confessed he had no idea that he'd wind up playing hardball with Edith Mallory—and win.

He would have to do something about Meg Patrick, but he didn't know what.

Also, he needed to contact a few more schools and meet with at least two of Dooley's teachers for the hoped-for recommendations.

Most important, Mitford School would be out in June, which was next month, so he'd better get cracking and have a talk with Dooley Barlowe.

June! he thought, sitting uneasily at his desk. The month in which a tutor would have to be brought in, Puny would be getting married and going away for two weeks, Hoppy and Olivia would be married at Lord's Chapel and feted at Fernbank, and, last but not least, the bishop would come to perform the annual confirmation service—one in which both Dooley and Cynthia would be welcomed into the church. This time, Martha would come with the bishop, and he felt compelled to entertain them.

It seemed that something else was going on in June, but he was relieved that he couldn't remember what.

He took a break and drove to the country to see Brother Greer.

They sat on the porch of the store that looked out to a pasture across the road and slugged down a couple of Cheerwines from the drink box.

Barnabas slept with his head on the old pastor's foot.

"That little handful still needs a preacher," he told Absalom.

"I laid it before the Lord and let it winter over."

"And?"

"I'll do it."

"Splendid! Wonderful!" He felt invigorated by the cheerful light in his friend's eyes.

"How do I get in there and all?"

"Rodney Underwood, our police chief. He said he'd have you picked up and escorted every Wednesday at six o'clock. It's hard to find your way along the creek, and it's rough territory into the bargain. Are you sure you want to do it?"

"The Lord spoke to my heart about what to preach, so I'm set on doing it. 'Behold, now is the accepted time; behold, now is the day of salvation.'

"Lots of folks plan to get around to the Lord tomorrow, but tomorrow never comes. I'm to go on from there with something else Paul said to the Corinthians, 'Therefore, if any man be in Christ, he is a new creation; old things are passed away; behold, all things are become new.' "

"Amen!" said the rector.

"Will you drop in on us now and again?"

"Consider it done," he said, warmed by the old man's fire.

Buck Leeper shouted an oath into the phone and merely said, "Get up here. Now."

He had driven to the office this morning, because it was Saturday and he needed to run errands, but it never occurred to him to drive to the job site. Leaving the office unlocked, he raced up Old Church Lane and headed right on Church Hill, glad for the running shoes he'd worn.

There was something in Buck Leeper's voice that told him everything and nothing. Something was horribly wrong; he could feel it.

His heart pounded as he raced over the brow of the hill and onto the Hope House property. From the direction of the hospital, the shrill whine of the ambulance pierced the air.

He ran toward the group of men standing by a pile of lumber and saw what appeared to be a boy lying on the ground.

Dear God! he prayed, his heart bursting, don't let it be Dooley!

It wasn't Dooley.

"It's Tommy," said Dooley, his face a shocking mask of fear. He was shaking uncontrollably as the rector clasped him to his side.

Buck Leeper loomed over him, cursing so vehemently that he drew back. "Didn't I tell you to keep these kids off my job? I hope to God you like what you see."

What he saw was the boy, lying unconscious on his back. A terrible bruise colored his temple, and his bleeding right leg was gashed from the calf to the thigh, exposing the bone. He had seen this very sight before, in a dream about Buck Leeper. The strangeness of the coincidence was unspeakable.

He instinctively stepped toward Tommy.

"Don't touch him," growled Leeper.

Dooley was sobbing. "We was playin' on that pile of lumber. It started rollin' and Tommy fell down in it. He went on down and hit th' ground. When it started rollin', I jumped off." A deep moan came from Dooley.

The men stood by, shaken, helpless. "We wasn't workin' today. We just drove up to check . . . ," somebody murmured. Then, the ambulance attendants were among them, and the quiet, wounded boy was laid on a gurney and the doors slammed shut and the ambulance was gone up the hill, and they were left there, stunned.

Buck Leeper's presence seemed to consume the very air, so that the rector gasped for breath. He had seen the man angry, but this was something else, something more frightening than anger.

He instinctively looked around for his car, but of course, it wasn't there, and Buck Leeper had turned and headed toward his red pickup.

He looked helplessly to the men.

"Let's go!" They sprinted toward a truck parked at the trailer.

"It's the head I'm worried about, not the leg," said Hoppy. "Wilson's giving the leg a pressure dressing, and we're taking him to Wesley immediately. Must have been a nail—as he fell, the nail kept ripping. It just missed the femoral artery. I could see the artery and the nerve right beside it. Another quarter of an inch and he could have bled to death before we got to him.

"They'll do a CAT scan in Wesley. I've got a call in to Dr. Hadleigh. Good man. Neurosurgeon. There could be blood between the skull and the swelling, a hematoma. He'll need watching."

"Is he still unconscious?"

"Big time. What about his parents?"

"Can't reach them. Got an answering machine."

"Listen," said Hoppy, his face troubled, "I'm praying about this—for whatever it's worth."

"It's worth more than we know," said the rector, who could not stop shaking inside.

They sped to Wesley, trying to keep the ambulance in sight.

He burned with shame and guilt. In all his life, he couldn't remember feeling this terrible nausea of the spirit; he had wounded Tommy by his own hand, by an act of senseless, unforgivable neglect.

He glanced at Dooley, whose face remained a mask of white. The responsibility for Dooley was not only real, it was constant—twenty-four hours a day. He had failed, he had let down, he had only been pulling halftime, when overtime was clearly required.

Five miles out of Mitford, Buck Leeper's truck passed them and held the lead.

He had never felt so worthless, so frightened, and so desperately out of control.

Tommy's stricken parents arrived, responding to the rector's answering-machine message to call him on the third floor at Wesley Hospital.

He wanted nothing more than to say, "I'm sorry, it's all my fault," but could not speak when they came in. A clergyman who couldn't speak in someone's time of need? He felt miserably impotent.

Buck Leeper paced in and out of the smoking room, hovering on the fringes.

"No hematoma," said Dr. Hadleigh, who had just read the X rays. "We don't know how long he'll be unconscious. It could be hours or days. Actually, it could be weeks, but we're hoping against that."

Tommy's mother looked at him and held out her hand. "Go in with us, Father." It was something in her voice, perhaps, but he felt forgiven. He began to weep, unable to control it, and they walked into Tommy's room together.

"I puked," said Dooley, wiping his mouth and getting in the car.

"Good."

"I been wantin' to. Is he goin' to die?"

"No."

"It was my fault," said Dooley, suffering.

"Why?"

"It was my idea. Tommy said we better not go up there n'more. Mr. Leeper told us not to."

He drove in silence. It was nine p.m. They had stayed through the operation that mended the hideous gap in the boy's leg. He felt exhausted, he felt angry, he felt unutterably sad, he felt too much at once.

"Are you mad?" asked Dooley quietly.

"Yes," he said, meaning it.

There was a long pause. "I'm sorry," Dooley whispered.

"Are you?"

"Yeah."

"It seems to me you're in a big hurry lately to mess up your life."

Dooley stared ahead.

"You get thrown out of school and a friend nearly gets killed, all because of breaking the rules. You could have been killed yourself. What is it with you? Talk to me about this."

"I just done it, is all."

"Tell me why you did it."

"It was fun."

"What was fun?"

"Smokin', playin' on 'at ol' lumber pile, messin' around."

"I didn't see you having fun when smoking got you stuck in the house for ten days. How much fun have you had today?"

"I don't know."

"The accident happened about eleven o'clock. How long had you been playing on the lumber?"

"We jis' started. About ten minutes."

"You swapped ten hours of agony for ten minutes of fun."

Dooley was silent.

"Think about it. You're smart enough to know that's stupid."

Sending him off to school could now seem a punishment instead of a privilege. But that's the way it was and no turning back.

"For Tommy, the agony will last more than ten hours. It'll be ten weeks, three months, maybe six months 'til that leg heals up. And when he gets off crutches, he could walk with a limp."

He didn't mention that the boy could lie for weeks in a coma or that serious complications could result from the head injury.

Maybe what Dooley Barlowe needed wasn't talk but a good hiding. Frankly, he couldn't manage giving him one, but perhaps that's why they were in this predicament.

Dooley didn't speak again until they turned into the garage. "Yeah," he said slowly. "It was stupid."

He sat at his kitchen table with Cynthia, having a bowl of her leek soup and talking about what had happened.

He heard the guest room door open. If Meg Patrick came down his stairs and along his hall and into his kitchen where he was trying to sit peacefully with his neighbor, he would dump her in the street, bathrobe and all, followed by her suitcases that approximated the weight of a pair of 1937 Packard sedans.

His cousin must have read his mind, because he heard the door close firmly.

"Nobody's perfect," Cynthia said.

"To roughly paraphrase Paul, why do I do what I don't want to do and don't do what I want to do? I find it one of the most compelling questions in Scripture."

She nodded.

"Why can't I get it right, Cynthia? Right with you, right with Dooley? Blast it, a man's life has to count for more than getting it right in the pulpit once in a blue moon.

"Speaking of which, my sermon for tomorrow is as rough as a cob. I'm going to toss it and ask the Holy Spirit to take over—start to finish. After what I've seen today, it makes the whole thing seem . . . insipid."

He stood up and paced the kitchen. "I'm sick of preaching, anyway."

"Timothy! You can't mean it."

"Oh, but I do mean it. I'm sick of boundaries and twenty-minute sermons and man-made rigmarole. I meant it when I said I want the Holy Spirit to be in control. I don't want to go into the pulpit with anything in my hands . . . 'in my hands no typewritten pages I bring, simply to Thy cross I cling.'

"I'm tired of trying to hold on to the reins and go in this direction or that direction because that's where the propers are leading me, or the congregation is pulling me, or the signs of the times are yanking me. Tomorrow, I'm going to talk about rules—and about breaking them—and what it costs when we choose any means at all to satisfy our own shallow and insatiable longings."

She gazed at him steadily.

"I'm glad you're here," he said, feeling suddenly weak and exhausted.

She came and put her arms around him and held him and patted him gently on the back, and he realized something he hadn't realized before:

Cynthia Coppersmith was his friend.

He wasn't going to wait any longer. He was going to catch up and stay caught up.

After the second service, he would talk with Tommy's parents and confess his neglect in warning Dooley, then commit his help throughout the long ordeal ahead.

Next, he would talk with Dooley and lay out the school proposition. Maybe the time wasn't right, but waiting for the right time had caused this whole tragic episode in the first place.

Finally, he owed an apology to Buck Leeper, plain and simple.

He went into the first service fired with an energy and conviction that lasted through the second, and he delivered a message that made his scalp tingle.

He had prayed for years to find the spiritual gall, the faith, to let go completely of his notes. That prayer had been answered, he knew it. He felt some oppressive weight fly off him.

Tommy's mother said, "Nobody's perfect."

"But if I had come down on Dooley, reinforced the rules . . ."

"It might have worked—we can't be sure. What's done is done, Father. It's hard being a parent."

Truer words were never spoken.

He stood by the bed of the still-unconscious boy and held hands with his parents and prayed. Dooley sat in the waiting room and stared out the window.

"Let him go in for a moment," he implored the nurse. "They're best friends."

When Dooley left Tommy's room, the rector searched the boy's face for information. A place the boy had long and fiercely guarded in himself had somehow been broken into. A process that might have taken years had instead taken minutes.

He sat on Dooley's bed. "There's something you need to know."

Dooley looked up from the veterinary book. "What's 'at?"

"I love you," he said.

He laid it all out, exactly as it was, and told him why going away to school was important and that he believed in him and in his special skills and abilities and so did Miss Sadie and his teachers.

"It's going to be a busy summer. You'll need some tutoring, we'll make a couple of trips to visit schools—and you'll want to spend time with Tommy. He's going to have a tough time adjusting."

He spoke his heart to the boy and waited for the script he had worked out in his mind to be executed: Dooley would say he wasn't going to do it, and a battle of wills would ensue.

Dooley stared at the book in his lap.

Perhaps he might do a little more selling, treat it as a real campaign, but no, he had made it plain and simple and he rested his case.

He leaned over and gave the boy a hug. He didn't flinch or move away.

He went to the house in the woods, finding it at the end of a rough lane, and saw Buck Leeper's truck sitting in the yard.

Except for trips along the creekbank to see Homeless Hobbes, he seldom ventured off the beaten path. He stood for a moment in the yard, looking into the woods and hearing birdsong.

The smell of sour ashes in a cold fireplace carried through the screened door as he stepped onto the porch and knocked.

Buck came down the hallway carrying a glass in his hand. He didn't walk to the door but stopped in the middle of the room. He swayed slightly on his feet. "What do you want?"

"I want to talk to you."

He stood, blocking the light from the other end of the hall, a dark, featureless apparition whose face the rector couldn't read. He swirled the liquid in his glass and swallowed it down. "It's open."

Father Tim opened the door and stepped inside. He still couldn't see Buck's face. "I'd like to apologize."

There was a pause. "Help yourself."

"You asked me to keep the boy off the job site, and I didn't speak to him about it. I meant to, but I didn't. I'm sorry for the turmoil it brought to all concerned. I regret it deeply."

" 'The road to hell is paved with good intentions.' Isn't that the saying? You ought to know."

Buck flicked his cigarette into the fireplace. "Sit down," he said, moving into the light from the windows.

He might have sat in the chair near the door but instinctively walked to the sofa, going deeper into the private territory of a private man. Buck left the room and came back with a bottle, then took a chair opposite him and poured a glass of vodka. He sat hunched over, his elbows on his knees, holding the bottle. "You came to talk? Talk."

He hadn't come to talk; he had come to apologize. "I looked for you at the hospital this afternoon."

Buck drank from the glass. "I was there this morning."

"Right."

There was a long silence. The sour smell of the fireplace ashes permeated the room.

"Drink?" said Buck, tipping the neck of the bottle toward him.

"No, thanks."

"Put hair on your chest." When Buck Leeper laughed, it growled up from him like something boiling on a stove. "Why don't preachers give a crap when it gets down to where the rubber hits the road?"

"What do you mean?"

"You preach eternal life but don't give a crap about this life."

"I do care about this life," he said.

"Not enough to watch out for a couple of stupid kids who're lookin' to get killed." His eyes narrowed. "You should have been all over their butts about it."

"Have you ever meant to do something right and failed?"

Buck drained the glass and cursed.

"Have you? You talk to me."

Buck got up and walked to the windows. Keeping his back to the rector, he looked out into the woods. The silence lasted a long time, then he said, "I got a kid killed."

Through the windows, the rector saw a squirrel leap from one branch to another. He didn't speak.

"It was my first construction job. I was seventeen. I was crazy about those machines. The power in them, even the colors, excited me. My old man turned me loose with a back hoe. He said if I didn't do good, he'd kick my butt all the way to the Mississippi." Buck set his glass on the windowsill and lit a cigarette, cursing his father.

"Then I took th' kid out on the job one night and put him in th' cab, and showed him the hole I'd been digging, and let him dig a bucketful. It had rained for a week, and the ground was mush. I'd pulled the hoe too close to the edge of the hole and when we raised the boom with the dirt on it, the dirt caved away under the stabilizer."

He took a long drag on the cigarette.

"The machine pitched into the hole, and I jumped out. But it . . .

knocked the kid off and pinned him under. When we got the hoe off, he was . . ."

Buck wheeled around from the window and slung the bottle at the fireplace chimney, where it smashed against the rock. Shards of glass rained to the floor and rattled across the hardwood.

Tears coursed down his face. "That kid," Buck said hoarsely, "was my brother."

The violent storm of weeping and cursing went on around him for hours, as he sat it out with the man who had nowhere left to go with his pain.

At one point, Buck picked up a wooden chair and hurled that, too, at the stone of the fireplace, smashing it apart. The rector flinched as a leg careened over the floor and landed at his feet. Any fool, he thought, would run from this violent place, but he could not run.

The bile of bitterness and suffering and impotence and hatred poured from a man who was fighting for his life, as he cursed God, his father, and then, himself.

Yet, as the venom spewed out of Leeper, a deep peace entered into the rector. He didn't try to understand what was happening, and he didn't try to speak. He only sat, praying silently, and went through it with him.

It was ten o'clock when he left Buck Leeper sleeping on the sofa where he had fallen, and went out the door and down the steps to his car.

"You won't believe this," said Emma. "Three guesses what Velma and Percy are goin' to do."

Emma had two infernally favorite games: Three Guesses and Last Go Trade. He despised both.

"Do I have to?"

"Yes," she said, sounding final.

"They're ah . . ." He had never been good at this sort of thing. "They're going to Hawaii!" he said with abandon.

She looked shocked. "How did you guess?"

"You mean they are? Good heavens! I simply picked the most far-fetched thing I could think of."

"That's exactly where they're goin'. You must have ESP. Their kids passed th' hat and collected enough money for a cruise. Velma called me last night. Does that beat all? Velma Mosely has never been outside the county, as far as I know, except to visit her cousin—and then she got carsick."

Percy and Velma in Hawaii? That did, indeed, beat all.

Emma answered the phone.

"Hold on a minute, Evie."

Emma held the receiver against her bosom. "Do you want to talk to Evie?" she whispered.

No, he didn't want to talk to Evie. What could he possibly do? Go by after lunch and watch Miss Pattie stare out the window? Hold Evie's hand and pray, once again? He didn't think he could bear to see any more suffering. No, he didn't want to talk to Evie.

He reached for the phone. "Hello, Evie."

"Hello, Father! For a change, I'm not calling to ask you for anything . . ."

"That's all right," he said, hearing an odd lightness in her voice. "Ask me for something."

"I just wanted to say that Mother had a lucid moment this morning and wanted me to call and give you a message."

"She did?"

"She wanted me to call," said Evie, choking up, "and say that she loves you."

He felt as if he were punched in the chest. "Please tell her I love her, too." He did, of course. He'd merely forgotten it for a moment. "Tell her I'll come by after lunch and give her a hug."

He hung up the phone, beaming.

"What's Miss Pattie done now?" asked Emma.

Percy called to report how lease negotiations had gone with Edith's lawyer. Apparently, the town inspector hadn't found much to be concerned about, outside the rotten joists and flooring. Minor repair was needed to correct the roof leak, and the washroom plumbing would have to be replaced. Bottom line, the Grill was set to reoccupy the premises on August 15.

"I'll bring you one of them wild shirts," said Percy.

"Father?" It was Tommy's mother. "Tommy is trying to talk."

He ran with Barnabas from the office and met Dooley coming out of school alone with his book bag. He thought he had never seen him look so desolate.

"Tommy's trying to talk," he said, swallowing hard.

Dooley's face was transformed. If the rector had never witnessed pure joy, he had now.

With Barnabas straining ahead of them on the leash, they ran all the way home.

CHAPTER EIGHTEEN

The Ceiling

On a scale of one to ten, his energy level was hovering around two and a half.

Age, blast it, and diabetes. And no chocolate cake when a man would give his eyeteeth for a slice.

He thought of taking Cynthia to Wesley for a decent dinner in that place with the green tablecloths, but recalled Edith Mallory's brown cigarette smoldering in the ashtray and didn't think he could stomach it.

Every day after school, he was driving Dooley to the hospital, where Tommy's recovery was brutally slow.

Tommy was stringing words together now, but when he arrived at the end of a sentence, he had forgotten what he said. Blinding headaches accompanied all the repercussions of his accident and the surgery.

The rector sat at his desk in the office, staring through the high windows at the trees. Maybe he should take vitamins.

"Miss Sadie," he said when she answered the phone, "I'm feeling an old, worn-out clergyman. May I walk up and hear the story of the ballroom ceiling? I'll bring lunch."

"Don't bring pizza," she said, "it gives me heartburn!" Apparently, even Miss Sadie had tried the new drive-through pizza franchise on the highway. “Let’s have something plain, like sandwiches on white bread—you bring the filling.”

An hour later, carrying a sack from The Local, he climbed the hill to Fernbank and delivered a bag containing sliced turkey, sliced ham, and a jar of honey mustard into the hands of his hostess.

“We forgot to tell you, Father—we don’t like olive loaf.” She peered into the bag suspiciously. “Is this olive loaf?”

“No, indeed.”

“Good! I said, ‘What if he brings olive loaf?’ and Louella said, ‘We’ll eat it anyway. It’s the right thing to do!’ ”

Throughout lunch, they clinked the ice in their tea glasses, laughed over nothing at all, and Louella called him “honey.”

During dessert, which was a plate of Fig Newtons, he told them how well they were looking, and they, in turn, commented on his jacket and his good color and his trim size, and before he knew it, he wasn’t feeling like an old clergyman anymore; he was feeling like a boy.

Miss Sadie pushed open the door to the ballroom with her cane.

“It’s the first day I haven’t had workmen in here, and I can’t tell you how glad I am for the peace.

“I don’t know how we’re making it through all the uproar, except by the grace of God. Have you ever had your house torn up, Father?”

“I’ve had a washing machine flood the kitchen.”

“Poshtosh! You’ve led a sheltered life.”

She took his arm as they stood and surveyed the scene.

“Sadie Baxter’s folly, that’s what it is. But it’s going to be more beautiful than it was the evening President Wilson danced right over there with my lovely mother.”

He felt the sense of new life, of renovation, that permeated the vast room. There was freshness to it, and hope. “Has Olivia seen what’s going on?”

“Oh, no! And she won’t, until the day of the reception. I pray she’ll think she’s stepped into heaven itself. Oh, Father, in all my life, I’ve never wanted something to be so perfect! What do you think?”

“I think your prayers are being answered,” he said, looking at the freshly restored windows that ran from ceiling to floor and the scaffolding built to lift workmen to the water damage on the ceiling and walls.

A film of sanding dust clung to everything, including the white canvas over the floor and the furniture, so that the whole room was a dreamlike shade of ivory in the early-afternoon light. The only color was on the ceiling, where robed angels burst from clouds and swept among the cherubim with blazing authority.

"Tell me what I can do to help," he said. Somehow, offering to bake a ham didn't seem right.

"Not one thing. The caterer from Charlotte is doing it all—food, flowers, music, chairs. And the cost? Through the ceiling, no pun intended. I just closed my eyes and jumped in."

"I suppose you'll be having a splendid new gown?"

"Certainly not! I'm too old for new gowns. There's not enough time left to wear them out, you see."

He put his arm around her shoulder.

"Let's go to my bedroom, so we can relax while we talk. But first, I want you to take a look at something."

"Yes, ma'am," he said.

She pointed her cane toward the ceiling. "See the angel just over there? That one with the smile—not all angels smile, you know."

"On the far right . . . with the rose in her hand?"

"It's the only single rose on the ceiling. All the other roses are in garlands or swags. Now look how her robe flows behind her—and see her feet peeping out? Aren't they beautiful?"

"Exquisite! In fact, she's my hands-down favorite."

"What do you think of the wings?" she asked.

"One might feel the very air moving through them."

"Carry that in your mind's eye," she said, taking his arm.

Pleased at the prospect of a good story, they went up the stairs as contented as children.

"See down there, Father?"

They peered through her bedroom window, into grounds leading to the orchard.

"That's the old wash house. Our home wasn't even near to being finished when we came to this hill, so we all moved into the wash house like a troop of gypsies.

"China Mae had the room on the back, about the size of the hall cupboard at Lord's Chapel—and not one floorboard was there in any square inch of that little place! Just bare dirt, swept clean and hard as tile.

"It was close living, Father, like sardines in a can, but it was the happiest time I ever knew. After a long day at the lumberyard, Papa would draw up to that big fireplace, and Mama would sit and do her sewing, and I would be making doll clothes as hard as I could go."

She laughed gently and took his arm. "Let's sit down before we fall down."

They sat in the old wing chairs, facing each other, where she had confided so many painful secrets.

"Oh, the smell of cooking that China Mae could stir up in that wash house! If anything ever smelled better than chicken and dumplings, I don't know what it is—unless it's cornbread baked in an iron skillet—or a deep-dish apple pie!"

"Don't even start, Miss Sadie . . ."

"China Mae's little room didn't have a thing but a wood stove and our pots and pans and her cot—there was a Bible, too, even though she couldn't read—and a peg for her clothes and a tin washtub hanging on the wall. We all used the same outhouse—at different times, of course!

"I think living that way got on Mama's nerves something awful, but when our house was finished and we moved in, I cried. I did. I could have gone right on living in the wash house for the rest of my life.

"I remember Papa started talking about his master plan.

"He said the first thing to do was get the orchards planted.

"The second thing to do was get the ballroom ceiling painted.

"And the third thing was have Mr. Woodrow Wilson come for a visit. He didn't want any cabinet members or senators, and nobody from Congress—he wanted the president!"

"Good thinking!"

"When the orchards were under way, Papa started sending letters to Italy. He was writing off for someone to come and paint the ballroom ceiling, you see.

"A man in Asheville wanted to paint it, but Papa saw his drawings and didn't like them at all. He kept saying, 'The artist must be *Italian*.'

"In case someone really came from Italy, I learned three words out of a book. I had no idea what they meant, but I was very proud and made China Mae say them too. *'Tempo è denaro!'* Do you know what that means, Father?"

"I don't have a clue," he said, smiling.

"Good! You'll find out later. Well, now, to make a long story short . . ."

"Don't do that," he said.

She laughed. "All this was a long time ago, and I was too young to pay attention to details. I just know that Papa wrote a lot of letters and got a lot of sample drawings in envelopes with strange stamps. Then he had scaffolding built in the ballroom—just like what's down there now, except it was wood.

"One day two strangers showed up on the porch—a short, dark man with a happy face, and a thin, dark boy with a sad face.

"It was Michelangelo and his son, Leonardo! 'My goodness,' said Mama, 'You send for Italian artists and look who you get!'

"Their last name was Francesca, and they were from Florence. I went around for weeks shouting, 'Michelangelo and Leonardo Francesca from Florence!' I had never heard such words in my life!

"Papa introduced us and I curtsied and said, *'Tempo è denaro!'* And Angelo laughed and laughed, so we had a wonderful start-up, but they could hardly speak a word of English.

"Mama took them to their room down the hall, and China Mae cooked them a wonderful meal, and they rolled up their pants and went right to work.

"Wouldn't you think an artist would roll up his sleeves? But these two always rolled up their pants. I'll never forget it.

"Angelo and Leon did fresco painting. It's like watercolor, but it's done on wet plaster. And you must paint very fast, because when the plaster dries, it won't take color. So they would mix what they might paint in a day, and if any plaster dried before they could paint it, they cut it away.

"I remember they began with the border around the ceiling. They must have worked on that for eight or nine months, every single day except Sunday. On Sunday, they disappeared into their room or packed a knapsack and went walking in the country and sketched in their books.

"I loved to peep into their room, for each had a beautiful cross over his bed, and they always left their room so neat, I could hardly believe my eyes.

"That's where Leon did his studies every evening. Angelo was Leon's tutor, and he was very good at carrying through with his lessons. In the meantime, Mama was teaching Leon English every day after lunch.

"It turned out Leon was sad because his mother had died, and Angelo was always laughing to try and cheer him up. Leon was only twelve years old, but he looked much older because of his sorrow. Dooley reminds me of Leon more than you know, Father.

"Anyway, my mother's gentle way was good for him, and before you know it, he could say, 'I like garden peas!' Or, 'The day is very warm.'

"I know my Mama didn't teach him this, but one day he said, 'Sadie, you are beautiful, *bella.*'

"Can you imagine? I thought I was ugly as a mud fence. But I could tell he meant it. You should have seen his face when he said it."

"Those Italians!" said the rector, grinning.

"Aren't they something, Father? But good gracious, I was only ten and still playing with dolls!

"When they were through with the border, Papa pronounced it excellent. That was high praise from Papa. You had to work like a beaver to get such laurels from him.

"Then the work began on the ceiling itself. Oh, Papa was fussy. He would come home from the lumberyard and stand in the middle of the floor, looking up 'til his neck got a crick in it. He knew just where the angels were to be placed and how the roses were to spill from their hands.

"Slowly but surely, the angels began to fly on the ceiling, and behind them, Leon made the rose-colored clouds appear and painted their robes and their hair. Only twelve years old, Father, and *painting* like an angel!

"They worked so hard that Mama took it on herself to give them a special day off. 'Just go!' she said, 'and I'll deal with Mr. Baxter when he comes home.'

" 'May I go?' I said.

" 'No, they need their rest,' Mama told me, but Angelo said, 'Please!' and for a moment looked so mournful, himself, that I got permission and went!

" 'Til my dying day I'll never forgot the happiness of roaming over the fields and hills with Angelo and Leon. Why, it was one of the loveliest days of my life, until that awful thing happened.

"You can't imagine what was in their knapsack! Colored pencils and sketch pads and a book of verse, not to mention olive oil from Italy and apples and cheese and bread and chicken—and a handful of new potatoes from our garden. They dug a hole in the meadow and built a fire and roasted those little potatoes to a turn, and we broke them open and put coarse salt inside and a bit of the olive oil and—oh, my goodness!"

"Miss Sadie, I can't imagine how Swanson's Chicken Pie ever got to first base with you!"

She laughed. "Nothing ever tastes as good as it did in childhood, does it, Father?"

"Nothing!"

"Even colors were more intense. I remember the purple and aquamarine Leon used to paint some of the robes. I've never seen anything like it again. But it wasn't the tubes of color, Father. It was my childhood eyes—how fresh it all was, what a gift!"

He nodded. Miss Sadie was preaching him a fine sermon without even knowing it. It was splendid to have the shoe on the other foot for a change.

"After we ate, Angelo wanted to lie down in the grass and sleep, and he told Leon to watch after Sadie. Leon always did what his father told him, and so we ran down the hill lickety-split and what did we find? An old orchard!

"I had never seen an old orchard before. Our trees were very small and new, and our orchard floor was raked as clean as a parlor.

"On this orchard floor, there were apples everywhere, a whole carpet of apples, and butterflies by the dozens—you could hardly see the grass! And the smell, Father! It was a perfume I've never forgotten."

She shook her head slowly. "I forget what sweet memories come flooding out if only we open the tap."

He kicked off his loafers, contented.

"Leon chased after a butterfly, and a little further down the hill, I spied an old tree just hanging full of red apples. They were different from those in the orchard, and they looked much redder and sweeter.

"I took off running toward that tree—then, all of a sudden, I started falling and everything went black as ink.

"I had stepped into an old well—the boards over it were rotten and soft as marrow. One minute, I was in an orchard with the sun shining and my heart beating for joy, and the next minute . . ."

"Very much like life in general," he said.

"I was stuffed in there like pimento in an olive. I fell with one leg down and one knee bent against my chest, and there was so much pain I thought I would die. I must have passed out, and when I came to, I was cold. Even though the sun was shining, I was freezing cold.

"I tried to call Leon, but my knee was so tight against my chest, and the pain was so horrible, I could only whisper. Whisper! Who could hear a whisper in a great big orchard on a great big hill?

"I heard Leon calling me. 'Sadie! Sadie!' There was real desperation in his voice because he couldn't find the English words he needed. He called for a long time and finally shouted, 'I like garden peas! Sadie, I like garden peas!'

"Oh, Father, I was so miserable. I wanted to die and get it over with. In a while, I heard Angelo calling too. Their voices would come close, then go far away, and I couldn't move. My arms had gone numb, one leg was completely numb, and I felt like a cube of ice.

"Then the voices stopped, and I felt so alone, and it started raining.

"Believe me, *The Book of Common Prayer* was just words on a page 'til I fell in that hole. You've heard of foxhole religion? I got well-hole religion, and I thank the Lord for it, to this day.

"I'd said 'Now I lay me down to sleep' and 'Our Father who art in Heaven' and 'Give us this day our daily bread' a thousand times. But I'd never once prayed a prayer of my own until then.

"I believe that's when God first started speaking to my heart—the very day I started speaking to His!

"It rained and rained and rained some more. Over the years, the hole had filled with dirt and runoff, but it was still a long way to the bottom. I was stuck about six feet down, and if something didn't happen soon, I knew I'd be six feet under.

"I remember hearing Papa call me, over and over. I would go to sleep, I think, and wake up crying. It was so hard to breathe. It was so horrible I can never express it to you.

"I found out later that the rain had washed away my scent, and the dogs from town couldn't track me. They let them loose, but they just ran every which way and came back to where they started and lay down.

"They searched into the night, Mama said. Leon went to bed about two o'clock in the morning and he couldn't sleep. And he was staring out the window, praying to the Virgin Mother, when he saw a light.

"It was in the air, he said, and it kept growing brighter, but it didn't hurt his eyes. It was a soft light, very soothing. When he told the story later, Mama was able to translate enough to know the light was gentle and loving and reminded him of his mother.

"The light, he said, became an angel, a very beautiful angel like something from the Sistine ceiling. She was dressed in the most beautiful blue robes trimmed with gold, and she was smiling. She beckoned to him through the window, and very fast, he put on his pants and shoes and woke Angelo, and they ran out into the night.

"Angelo never saw the angel, but he believed his son, and he ran with him. And Leon said the angel did not touch the ground but flew above them, slightly in front of them, and the light gleamed from her, showing the way.

"It hadn't occurred to them to bring a lantern, but you see, they didn't need one, for the angel hovered over us, giving light, and Angelo lay down near the hole and stationed his foot behind a big rock and held Leon by the ankles.

"Leon crawled into the hole toward me, and very gently began prying my shoulders up and away from the sides of the well, and slowly but surely he was able to lift me a little.

"The pain just flooded into me, but I remember what a relief it was to be in a different position.

"I could hear Angelo praying very loudly the entire time. I felt we were covered with prayer and with light, just bathed in it.

"Well, Father, somehow they got me up and out, and Angelo was weeping with joy, and he picked me up and they carried me home, and this lovely light covered us all the way."

He was mesmerized.

"I declare," she said, "I'm dry as a bone from that ham. Could you step in my bathroom and get me some water? There's a glass on the sink."

His mind had gone so far away on this celestial ramble that his concerns seemed remote and his heart set free. He returned with the glass of water, proud to have been sent on a mission for Miss Sadie.

She raised the glass with a steady hand and took a sip. "Good, pure well water! Thank you!

"Just think, Father. From the age of four, Leon was taken to the museums and cathedrals of Florence where he saw the work of the Italian masters and was trained to go home and draw the images from memory!

"Angelo said Leon drew and painted the face of the Madonna of the Rock nearly four hundred times before he came to Fernbank. So you see, it's hardly any wonder that he attracted an angel who was properly dressed. You hear a lot about angels these days, but have you noticed how they're usually wearing business suits?"

"A sign of the times," he said, marveling.

"I was awfully bruised and sore and scratched up, but not one thing was broken except two ribs where my knee had cracked against my chest so hard.

"Papa wanted to be angry with Leon for letting me out of his sight and angry with Mama for letting me go off with them. But I preached Papa a sermon, and he changed his mind! I think he did something special for Angelo, but I don't know what.

"Things went on as usual after that. Angelo painted angels and cherubim, and Leon painted clouds and robes and helped with the roses.

"Then something wonderful happened.

"Angelo came to Papa and said in his broken English, 'I know my son was to assist me only with borders and backgrounds and such, but I believe he's ready to paint an angel. Will you trust us, Mr. Baxter? If it doesn't work, we will cut it away and begin again and make up the time on Sunday.'

"For Angelo to offer to work on the Sabbath was shocking. Anyway, what could Papa say? There was Angelo with his happy, expectant face and Leon with his sad, longing face. Papa spoke his first word of Italian. He said, *'Bellisimo!'*

"And so, on the day he turned thirteen, Leon began painting the angel I showed you. He painted the angel who led them to the well in the middle of the night—the only angel on the ceiling who's smiling.

"He wanted to paint the rose in her hand as a tribute to me, but though I was only eleven then, I had enough sense to say he must paint the rose for his mother.

"And so he did."

He sat for a time, silent, as one sits in a movie theater after a film that has stunned the senses. "Words fail me, Miss Sadie."

"That's not one of my handicaps, Father."

They laughed gently, not wishing to break the spell.

"Leon's sorrow went away as he painted the angel. He was done with grieving, somehow, and became the brightest, sweetest boy out of heaven. It broke my heart when they left. I grew to love them so. You don't know how many times I've thought of Leon and yearned to see him again. But he was two years older and must be ancient by now . . . ninety-two, if he's a day."

She closed her eyes and sighed. "Memories give a lot, but they take a lot, too. I'm limp as a dishrag."

"I should have brought you a bag of doughnut holes from Winnie's."

"You could go down to the kitchen for some tea. We've got plenty of unsweetened for you, but I want the sweet!"

"Consider it done," he said happily.

Back at the office, he called the operator and got information on how to do it—including what the time difference was and when the rates were cheaper.

After all, he had never called Italy before.

Tommy had laughed today. It wasn't downright hilarity, by any means, but it had been reviving to hear.

The psalmist had said, "Laughter doeth good like a medicine." Clearly, that was true for the one who heard it, as well as for the one doing the laughing.

He wanted to hear Tommy laugh again and again and see Dooley Barlowe laughing with him.

If he really put his mind to it, perhaps he could think of something funny to do.

Cynthia! There was a brilliant thought. She was funny without even trying to be. He would ask her what to do.

They had walked up the Grill side of Main Street in the balmy spring evening, come back down the post office side, then crossed the street and cut through his backyard to a bench in Baxter Park.

"I think you should wear a gorilla suit," she said.

"Now, Cynthia, be reasonable."

"Timothy, being funny and being reasonable have nothing to do with each other."

"A gorilla suit?"

"I'm serious."

He exploded with laughter. "I can't even imagine such a thing."

"That's the problem," she said, looking cool. "*I* would do it. In fact, I've always wanted to do it."

"Would you do it, then?"

"Certainly not. You're the one who wants to be funny, and I won't be your henchwoman."

He thought she had the most mischievous look in her eye.

"Isn't there something else I could do?"

"Oh, hundreds of things, I'm sure. But wearing a gorilla suit is the best thing of all, so why discuss the others?"

"I wish I hadn't asked, " he said, defeated.

She smiled, looking a trifle superior.

"Will you go with me to the reception at Fernbank for Hoppy and Olivia? In June?"

"Ummm," she said.

"Well?"

"Well, then, yes. I'd love to go."

He was suddenly aware they'd never been out together, officially. This would be something new and different; and it went without saying that everyone would talk.

He felt reckless and expansive and put his arm around her.

"If you were ever . . . ," he began and paused. "That is to say, if you . . ." He thought for a moment. "To put it another way . . ."

"Spit it out," she said.

"Well, then, suppose you actually lived with a clergyman . . ." He thought the pounding of his heart might be heard all the way to the monument.

"*Lived* with a clergyman?"

"You know . . ."

"In *sin?*"

"Certainly not," he said.

"Do you mean, what if I were *married* to a clergyman?"

"Well, yes. If you were ever *that,* what would you do? That is, what sort of . . . how would you spend your time? Just asking, of course." He felt a light perspiration on his forehead. What had happened, anyway? He hadn't meant to stumble into such a conversation.

"I already have a full-time job, as you know. And a clergyman would be another."

"Puny has said that very thing."

"I can't play the piano or the organ."

"Most churches pay someone to do that."

"I can't carry a tune in a bucket."

"Most churches have a full choir, already."

She furrowed her brow and looked at him darkly. "I definitely wouldn't do spaghetti dinners or pancake suppers."

"Good thinking!"

"And I couldn't be bleaching and washing and ironing altar linens."

"There's usually a horde signed up for Altar Guild."

"But," she said, "I can teach Sunday school!"

He saw the warm light in her eyes and the irrepressible hope in her smile.

". . . with a blackboard and colored chalk—the stories of the Bible, illustrated! In fact, I'd like nothing better."

"You're hired!" he said, caught up in the excitement.

"And I can give a tea once a year, with layer cakes and tarts and sorbets and all that. But only once a year, mind you, for it's killing to do it."

"The entire parish will come running." He felt his heart fairly bursting with pride.

"So there," she said "That's it. That's all I'm good for, save an occasional fill-in at lay reading. Oh, and no banners and no needlepoint kneelers."

"Deal," he said, putting his arms around her and kissing her cheek. He liked a woman who knew what she wanted—and didn't want.

"Wait a minute," she said, pulling away, "we're talking what if, not real life, remember?"

"Why, yes," he said, coloring. "Of course we were. I knew that."

The phone rang as he was walking across his bedroom to turn off the light.

"Hey," she said.

"Hey, yourself."

"I've been thinking."

"Umm."

"We were only playing when we talked about being a clergyman's wife . . . right?"

"Oh, yes. Just . . . idle abstraction."

"Well, then, I've something to add to it . . . since we're just playing."

"Do!"

"Yes, I have my own work and I love it and want to continue it, but if I were a clergyman's wife and I truly loved the clergyman, I'd want to do something I failed to mention tonight. More important than teas and teaching, I'd want to take the tenderest care of the clergyman himself."

She was silent for a moment. "That's all," she said softly. "That's all I wanted to say. Good night, Timothy."

After turning off the bedroom light, he went to the alcove window and looked down at the little yellow house with the glow of a lamp burning under the eaves.

"Good night," he whispered, his breath making a vapor on the glass.

"Come home," said Puny, breathless.

"What is it?"

"Come quick as you can," she said.

He went.

CHAPTER NINETEEN

Hasta la Vista

Puny met him at the kitchen door.

"You won't believe this," she said.

"What? What is it?"

She marched down the hall to the stairs. "I've never seen anything to beat it."

He raced behind her up the steps. "What happened?"

"The most disgustin' thing in th' world is what it is."

"What's going on?"

She stopped at the guest room. "I've lived on this earth thirty-four years, and I've never . . . see this little rug? She must of thought she was puttin' th' key in her pocket, and it fell on th' rug, where I found it."

She turned the knob and threw open the door.

Puny was right. He couldn't believe it.

From the unmade bed to the bags of garbage that littered the floor, the room was in complete chaos. Nothing had escaped the disorder—even the pictures hung wildly crooked on the walls.

"Smell that?" demanded his house help. "Nothin' in here's been washed or cleaned for two months. You could get arrested for livin' like this."

He walked slowly into the room.

He saw his books scattered about, many of them open and lying face down. Everywhere, garbage bags spilled forth their contents: KitKat wrappers, old newspapers, scribbled notes, soda bottles, crumpled dinner napkins, tin foil, drink cans.

Clothing lay in a soiled heap in the corner.

"A pigsty!" said Puny, clearly enraged. "And look at this bed." Full of crumbs, he saw. The remains of a sandwich lay on the pillow, and an open bag of potato chips had been shoved under the blanket.

The typewriter sat in the only cleared space on the floor, a sheet of paper rolled into the carriage. What he presumed to be a manuscript lay in sections around the room, the bulk of it scattered across the foot of the bed.

He picked up a page and scanned it. His face burned.

"Good Lord!" This was definitely not about the Potato Famine.

"I read one of them pages, and it shamed me t' death. Her writin' must come straight off th' walls of a public rest room. We ought t' jis' heave it into sacks and burn th' lot of it." Puny was trembling with anger. "And what do you think about that?"

She pointed to an empty milk carton on the dressing table.

No, she was pointing to what lay beside it:

The brooch.

"I found it on the landing," said Meg Patrick, white with fury. "I was going to give it to you, but I forgot. It was right there on the dressing table, in your own house, in plain view—it wasn't as if I'd stolen it, for heaven's sake. And what were you doing in my room? I should think you would respect my privacy as I have unfailingly respected yours."

She stood in the hallway outside the guest room, her hands shoved into the pockets of the belted trench coat, glaring at him.

"I considered asking that you merely clean your room, but I realize that isn't what I want to say, after all."

"What do you want to say, then?" He saw that her magnified pupils had dilated alarmingly.

"I want to say that I'll drive you to the airport in Holding or the bus station in Wesley, whichever you prefer, and we'll leave here this evening at eight o'clock sharp. I'll thank you to pick up my books and stack them properly and take that manuscript out of here before I dispose of it personally."

She didn't slam the door until she had cursed his paternal line all the way back to his great-grandfather.

He lugged the suitcases down the stairs and loaded them in the trunk. His cousin had asked to be dropped at the bus station in Wesley.

"I don't have any money," she said, glowering. "I had thought the heart of a cousin would be generously disposed to a relative who has has traveled all the way from the home country.

"Further, I believed that my needs would be considered as graciously as yours were considered in Sligo, while you lapped up our hospitality like a stoat."

He choked down a retaliation, which would have been futile, and peeled two bills off the money he'd got from the bank only this morning. He handed them to her without a word.

Dooley came along, so they could pay a surprise visit to Tommy.

His houseguest of two months rode to the station without speaking and disappeared into the terminal without a word of good-bye.

"Gross," said Dooley.

His sentiments exactly.

Before Percy let the jukebox go to the Collar Button man, he discovered it was worth more than five hundred dollars—a lot more. Then, before he could run a classified ad in the Wesley paper, Esther Cunningham talked him out of it for the museum, along with a stack of early advertising signs for Camel cigarettes, Dr. Pepper, and Sunbeam bread.

"Just think of the tax deductions," she said, peering at him over a sausage biscuit from Hardee's. "And think of seein' your name on a little sign on the wall next to that jukebox. How about 'Early Wurlitzer, a gift of Percy and Velma Mosely, proprietors of the Main Street Grill, established World War II.' How's that?"

On Wednesday, the mayor called an informal meeting of intimates at her home, hastening to add that Ray would be cooking barbecue with all the trimmings.

The subject was a festival to celebrate the opening of the first room of the museum and the installation of the Willard Porter statue on the lawn.

"Mayor," said the rector, who arrived early with a six-pack of Diet Sprite, "you are hopelessly prone to festivals."

"There's worse things mayors are prone to," she said. The red splotches had appeared on her face and neck, indicating her special enthusiasm for this project.

She stationed him in the family room where he could watch Ray finish making coleslaw. "Take a load off your feet," she said. "I've got to call the hospital an' see if th' new grandbaby is comin' anytime soon."

"Another grandbaby?" he said to Ray with astonishment.

"Number twenty-four!" Ray said, stirring the homemade dressing into the grated cabbage. "Esther likes to be there when it happens, but this one has been hemmin' and hawin' for better than a week."

"Doesn't want to come out here and face the music, I suppose. And no wonder."

Ray shook his head over the vagaries of modern life.

"Can I give you a hand?"

"You can put th' ice in th' glasses. There'll be six of us. Table's set, chairs are pulled to th' table, cornbread's bakin'. We're on go."

"Oh, well," said Esther, blowing into the room, "not a peep. I guess nobody told it that Cunninghams like to jump out and hop to it."

After dinner, the mayor occupied a velveteen swivel rocker in her family room and opened the meeting for discussion.

"I think we ought to have a band for when we unveil the statue," she said. "Do you think the Presbyterians who play the Advent Walk would do it for nothin'—or charge an arm and a leg?"

"I'll call," said Ernestine Ivory, making notes.

"And I think we ought to have the jukebox fixed so we can play it as a demonstration. But it's going to cost money."

"What doesn't?" said Linder Hayes, a local attorney and councilman. "How much?"

"A hundred bucks."

"Are we goin' to charge admission?"

"I should say so! Two dollars a head—man, woman, or child—and no discounts for any faction."

"What are our other expenses?"

"That depends on what we come up with at this meeting. Ernestine, tell them our ideas."

"Well, you see," said the secretary, blushing deeply as all eyes turned to her, "we came up with this list of fun things to do. We'd start the bidding at a certain dollar figure and auction each one to the highest bidder."

"Give us an example," said the rector.

"Well, we thought we could have somebody kiss a pig. We figured the bidding for that ought to start at a hundred dollars."

"If Esther will do it, I'll personally give you a hundred on the spot," said the rector.

The mayor rose to the challenge. "You can't scare me. I like pigs. Put me down for kissin' the pig."

"On the mouth?" inquired Ernestine, her pen poised.

"Make it a hundred and fifty," said Esther.

"Make it five hundred," said Ray. "Think big! After all, it's for a good cause."

"Five hundred," said Ernestine, writing.

"Who in the dickens," said Linder, "can lay out five hundred dollars to see somebody kiss a pig?"

"You've got it all wrong, Linder, honey, which wouldn't be the first time. The money is not to see somebody kiss a pig. It's to help renovate the second room in our one-and-only town museum, which will reflect the culture of this unique place and the history of its people, not to mention provide a valuable document for all time."

"But . . ."

"Kissing a pig is a mere . . ." Esther searched for a word.

"Adornment!" said Ernestine.

Ray attended the meeting from the kitchen, where he had gone to clean up. "By th' time we renovate twenty-two rooms, th' Porter place will be historic all over again."

"Get Percy to do the hula," said Joe Ivey. "That ought to be worth somethin'."

"Write that down," said Esther. "Fifty dollars. If he played a ukulele, we could get seventy-five."

Ray walked into the room carrying a pot and a drying towel. "Tell 'im to wear a grass skirt," he said. "That'll be a crowd pleaser. And another thing. Somebody could push a peanut down Main Street with their nose. I've seen that done. You could get a bundle for that."

"Depends on who you get to push it," said the rector. "For example, Esther doing it might bring five hundred, whereas Coot Hendrick, not being a town bigwig, would bring less."

"Why don't we put you down for that one?" said Esther, peering intently at the rector.

"I pass."

"Eatin' Miss Rose's cookin'—that would be a good one," said Joe Ivey.

"There ain't enough money in the world to get *me* to do that," said Ray, who threw the towel over his shoulder and went back to the kitchen.

"Has any consideration been given to a fund-raiser with more dignity?" asked Linder.

"Dignity?" sniffed the mayor. "You can't raise cash money with dignity. It's hard enough to sell history, much less dignity."

"Just asking," said Linder.

"The peanut deal will definitely draw a crowd," said Ray, not wanting the idea to lose momentum.

"Do you think they ought to push it all th' way down Main Street?" asked Joe. "Lord have mercy, that's a long way. How about from th' bookstore to th' bakery?"

"Fine," said the mayor. "Write that down."

Ernestine raised her hand. "I've got one," she said, coloring furiously. "You could do a demonstration of how the father's dog reacts to Scripture. Nobody's ever seen a thing like that. You could maybe get a hundred."

The rector sighed. "I sincerely hope all this isn't happening in June."

"June twenty-fourth," replied the mayor, looking at the table where Ray was setting out a homemade apple crisp.

On an afternoon jog that took him across Main Street, he met J.C. Hogan.

"Where are you taking nourishment?" he asked, panting from the run.

"On a hot plate. Mule and Fancy gave it to me. I've burned more than I've consumed."

"Come by the rectory one evening, and Dooley and I will set you up to a hamburger."

"How's your cousin? Haven't seen her around."

He wiped his forehead on his sleeve. "Gone. Vamoose. Outta here." He was unable to control the grin that spread across his face.

J.C. emitted one of his rare laughs. *"Hasta la vista?"*

"Right-o. I hear they've started on the Grill."

"I can't think clear enough to write a complete sentence for all the racket goin' on down there."

"Use stringers. I'm sure Hessie Mayhew would fill up a page or two."

"Ha, ha. Have you seen Percy?"

"They're leaving June the tenth. Are you going to publicize the museum festival?"

"What museum festival?"

"Hotfoot it over to the mayor. She'll tell you everything."

J.C. set off at a trot, headed north; the rector sprinted in a southerly direction.

He drove Miss Sadie to see the progress on Hope House. They got out of the car, where she leaned on her cane and gazed across the construction site to the blue swell of mountains.

He looked down at her with affection. "Big things come in little packages, Miss Sadie."

"What do you mean?"

"I mean you," he said, putting his arm around her shoulder.

Buck Leeper left a machine operator and walked over to them.

"Buck Leeper, Miss Sadie Baxter, the generous lady responsible for Hope House."

Buck removed his hard hat. He sheepishly extended his hand, then withdrew it. "Dirt," he said.

"Nothing wrong with dirt," she said brightly.

"Pleased to meet you, Miss Baxter."

"Well, I'm pleased to meet you, Mr. Leeper. I hear wonderful things about your abilities, and I'm proud to have you on this job."

"Thank you," he said, clearing his throat.

He was not imagining it at all. There was something different in Buck Leeper's face, something very different.

"See you at the hospital," he told the rector. Making what was clearly an involuntary bow to Miss Sadie, he said, "Ma'am," then turned and hurried away.

"Shy," she pronounced, looking after the superintendent.

"Twenty-four hundred dollars!" said Cynthia, sitting at his kitchen table, drinking tea.

"Amazing."

"What do you think he'll do with it?"

"I don't know. Stuff it between the matress and box spring, I suppose."

"I wish he wouldn't do that! Life is too short to stuff your money between the matress and box spring."

"Agreed."

"Five of his drawings will appear in the fall. Hardcover. Coffee-table edition! With other art, of course."

"A grand display for the museum." Uncle Billy Watson would be a local celebrity, at the very least.

"Found a tutor yet?"

"Seems there's a Louise Appleshaw around these parts. Spinster. Terribly good at English, but stern."

"Stern. Oh, dear."

"When it comes to English, Dooley Barlowe needs stern. She'd come in the afternoons, three days a week, and take the evening meal with us."

"Always heating up the oven for somebody or other. Not missing your cousin, are you?" She leaned her head to one side and grinned.

"You mean my attractive, terribly good-looking cousin?"

"The same."

"Whatever possessed you to call her good-looking?"

"Oh, but she really is, don't you think? So tall and thin . . . for those of us who're short and dumpy, she seemed . . ."

"You aren't short and dumpy. Short yes, but dumpy, no."

"Thank you," she said sweetly. "I'm not searching for a compliment, I promise, but not only do I feel short and dumpy, I feel vastly old . . ."

"You're a mere child, for heaven's sake. In heart and spirit, quite my junior. Exceedingly my junior."

"Well . . ." she said, gazing at him.

"You look wonderful. Everyone says so."

"They do?"

"Absolutely."

"Who is everyone?"

"Uncle Billy thinks you're a dish. And Mule Skinner still talks about your legs—it's shocking."

"Really? I love this."

"Be glad we're not playing Emma's favorite game, Last Go Trade."

"What's that?"

"I tell you something wonderful I've heard about you, and you, having the last go, had better be prepared to top it. It is a very taxing game."

"I can play that," she said.

"Remember I've just told you some pretty terrific stuff."

"Ha, I can top it all."

"Fire away, then."

"You're sexy, witty, and fun to be with."

"Who said so?"

"I said so."

"It has to be something someone else has said."

She looked blank. "Oh."

"See there? Nobody has said anything worth repeating."

"Avis Packard said you were a good cook."

"That's scraping the bottom of the barrel."

"And Puny once told me you're not hard on shirts."

"Ah. Lovely."

"Let's see . . ." She furrowed her brow in mock concentration.

"Well, enough of that game. I knew I didn't like it." He sipped his tea. "So, I'm all those things you said?"

"What did I say? I forgot."

"You know. Sexy, witty, fun to be with."

"You have your moments. You're not all those things across the board, of course."

"Of course."

She laughed. "I love it when you loosen up."

"What don't you love?" he asked, looking at her intently.

She gazed back at him. "Oh, soggy mittens, chocolate without nuts, and a man who can't find it in himself to hold your hand when it's sticking right out there in plain view."

He took her hand that was resting on the table. "What else?" he said.

"Never being asked out to dinner, not even once."

He got up, still holding her hand. "I have just the place!"

Edith Mallory's smoldering cigarette never entered his mind. He thought only of the soft green walls, the intimate, no-smoking corner table he'd admired, the smiling maitre d', and the menu that, apart from the elk, bison, and reindeer, offered fresh mountain trout.

"You've got something the color of hyacinths . . ." he said.

"I'll wear it! If you'll wear the blue jacket."

"Deal," he said, excited as a boy.

"I think the world of Dooley!" said Miss Pearson, his music teacher. He had crept into her little house like a sneak thief, thinking he'd rather be horse-whipped than spotted by Myra Hayes, who lived only a block away.

"Yes, but he's gotten in a lot of trouble, lately."

"I know," she said, looking forlorn. "But he's working so hard and he's so talented. I believe in him, you see. It would be grand if he could go away to a fine school and have all the privileges."

"Mitford School is itself a privilege, but if we can . . . it will be for the best. Would you write a letter to whom it may concern?"

"Without question," she said, immediately picking up her pen. "I'll do it this minute. And Father . . . ?"

"Yes?"

"Please don't tell Miss Hayes I did this."

"Mum's the word," he said.

Louise Appleshaw would appear at the rectory the first Wednesday after school closed, and tutoring would begin at once.

He had talked with her on the phone, and though she certainly lived up to her reputation for being stern, he put his head down and pushed along.

She was the best, they all said, and he'd better snap her up at once or make do with leftovers.

He wrote a check covering the first three afternoons of tutelage and the books she required, mailed it, and put the whole thing out of his mind, greatly relieved.

Ever since he returned from Ireland, he'd been tripping over the sack of family records in his walk-in closet.

Who else would trip over a sack for better than nine months? The habit of procrastination was something he roundly despised, yet he was, as Coot Hendrick might say, "eat up" with it.

He dragged the sack to the foot of his bed and sat on the floor and opened it.

Postcards, old family letters trustingly lent by Erin Donovan, photographs given him by that dear old neighbor of Erin's whose grandfather had known his . . .

He pored over the dim image of his grandfather as a young man, standing upright and unsmiling in the midst of a field, with a hunting dog at his heels. Was his own face forecast in the face that looked out at him?

He set it aside to show Dooley and Cynthia.

He rifled through the bag, glad to be in touch with all that he'd felt and learned in Sligo, the love that had poured in, and the kindnesses he'd been shown. He caught himself wondering if he'd done the right thing by Meg Patrick, but refused to wonder. Of course he had.

Who had she stayed with in Massachusetts? Riley Kavanagh? He'd always wanted to call Riley, who once sent him a book at Christmas.

Where was the bound document with the family names and addresses in it? At the bottom, of course. He pulled it out and looked up Kavanagh, then looked at his watch. The rates were just going down. Perfect.

He sat on the side of the bed and dialed.

"Hullo?"

"Hello, is this Riley Kavanagh?"

"Speaking."

He introduced himself and reminded his cousin of the Christmas book, and they set off talking at a pace. He gave him the full details of the tea at Erin Donovan's, trying to recall as many names as he could to satisfy Riley's excited curiosity.

"And then of course, Cousin Meg has been here for . . . an extended visit."

Riley let out a whoop of laughter that nearly deafened him, then shouted: "He's got Cousin Meg! He's got Cousin Meg!"

Hysterical laughter erupted in the background. He had never heard such uncontrolled hooting.

"Riley!" he yelled into the phone.

"Oh, heaven help us!" said Riley, gasping for breath. "You do mean the Cousin Meg who eats like a trencherman?"

"The same."

"Room like a pigsty? Eyes like a barn owl?"

"I'm afraid so."

"How long have you had her?"

"Well, I . . . she's just left. Two months."

"Two months!" Riley shouted into the background. "He's had 'er for two months!"

More raucous, knee-slapping laughter, then he heard someone say, "Poor soul. How's 'is blood pressure?"

"Riley . . ."

"Forgive us, Tim. If laughter heals as they say it does, I'm a well man for life. You don't know about Cousin Meg?" Riley blew his nose roundly.

"What's to know?"

"What's to know, he wants to know!" A veritable throng of eavesdroppers broke into convulsions. No wonder Cynthia Coppersmith had developed the habit of hanging up on people. They could be a blasted nuisance.

"God help us!" Riley said, returning at last to the conversation. "Where shall I begin?"

"At the beginning," he said, tersely.

"Cousin Meg is a bloody fraud! She's not even a cousin."

"No!"

"Yes, indeed. Has a hookup with somebody in Sligo who lets her know which poor cousins have been stumbling around the local graveyards looking for their roots, and from all I can gather, she goes from so-called cousin to cousin without a bloody dime in her pocket. She's a professional Irish cousin, you might say. But that's not the worst."

He was afraid to ask. "What's the worst?"

"He wants to know what's the worst!" Riley exploded with laughter yet again, which set off another earsplitting clamor in the background.

He tapped his foot, waiting, his face growing redder and his collar growing tighter. What the deuce . . .

"The worst of it," said Riley, "is she's not even Irish!"

"Not even Irish?"

Something began to bubble up in him. It was the strangest mixture of feelings. What in heaven's name was it? It finally emerged and revealed itself.

It was laughter.

"Never set foot in Ireland, as far as we can learn," said Riley. "Her hookup in Sligo mails those letters that say she's coming, from over the pond. She made the rounds with four of us for seven months. You got off light."

Once he started laughing, he couldn't stop. In fact, he was rolling on the floor, clasping the telephone to his ear, and trying to find the breath to apologize—though, come to think of it, why should he?

CHAPTER TWENTY

June

June.

When he turned the page of the desk calendar and saw that four-letter word emblazoned across the top of the overleaf, he took a deep breath.

Hold on to your hat, he warned himself.

"Jis' say yes," said Puny, beaming.

"Yes," he said, beaming back. "I'll be honored to do it. But must I give you away entirely?"

"I keep tellin' you I'm comin' back!"

"I keep needing reassurance."

"You're a big baby."

He supposed she was right, as usual.

He took the brooch to Wesley for cleaning and repairs.

He waited until the rates went down and called Tiffany's, ordering two wedding gifts and taking the news of the total cost like a man.

He bought a rubber mask of a duck and hid it in his bureau

drawer. As soon as Tommy's headaches subsided, he had every intention of making him laugh like a hyena.

He tried to correct his tendency to procrastinate by jotting down a dinner menu for the bishop and Martha on the evening of the fourteenth, which would follow Puny's afternoon wedding and precede the confirmation service and the bishop's brunch—for which he'd recklessly promised to bake a ham.

He searched for free dates among the jumble of entries on his calendar, then called two schools and arranged visits. It was putting the cart before the horse, since Dooley hadn't done the SATs, but there was no time to waste. He knew the boy could make the cut in math and had to believe the tutoring would bring him around in verbal skills. Getting him in the right school by fall was a seat-of-the-pants, wing-and-a-prayer deal, no two ways about it.

Finally, he apprised Dooley of some social obligations.

"We'll be going to Puny and Joe Joe's wedding and also to the Harper wedding and reception."

"Mush."

"In fact, we're buying you a new jacket this very day. A navy blazer!" he said with pride. "You'll look . . ." He recalled the word the Collar Button man had used to sell him last year's sport coat. "*. . . stunning.*"

"Double mush!" said Dooley.

He was on his way to the Grill for lunch when he remembered there was no Grill.

He fled his office anyway.

At the door of the Oxford Antique Shop, Andrew Gregory was sitting on an early-eighteenth-century bench next to a late-nineteenth-century urn from Sussex.

"Father! Turn in and visit."

"And add another antique to the jumble?"

The handsome Andrew threw back his head and laughed. "I've been waiting for you to come along. I have a glorious art book you'd like to see."

"I'd do well to replace lunch with a feast for the eyes."

"You're looking terrific, actually. In fact, I hear that . . ." Andrew paused discreetly.

"Yes?"

". . . you and your neighbor may be getting married."

"I've heard that very rumor myself. You know how small towns are."

"I'm afraid I do. In any case, if it were true, I wanted to say you're a very lucky man."

He smiled and nodded. "If it were true, I'd have to agree."

"Have a cup of minestrone with me. I fumbled around and made it from a family recipe. You can sit by the window at my prize Georgian dining table and have a go at the book."

How could he refuse?

As the warm June sunlight streamed through the windows of the Oxford, he sat at the mahogany table, contentedly turning the pages of a book on early religious art, unmindful of time.

It was another volume, however, that captured his attention. In a stack of books on one of the dining chairs, he found it.

It was a glorious celebration of the chambered nautilus, from medieval times to the turn of the century. Brilliant scientific drawings and artists' renderings sought to capture the mysterious beauty of the handsomest denizen of the mollusk kingdom.

Excited, he paid Andrew and went on his way, refreshed.

Sixty dollars for lunch! Ah well, he thought, *tempo è denaro,* whatever that meant.

Tommy would be home from the hospital around the time Louise Appleshaw began her afternoon tutoring sessions. That would relieve them of the drive to Wesley and allow Dooley a quick visit to Tommy's house between Miss Appleshaw and dinner.

Dooley felt called to minister to his friend, cheer him on, and tough it out by his side. He was even giving a hand with some light schoolwork. Seeing Tommy's alarming brush with death and feeling the guilt of helping it happen had made Dooley more reflective, less hostile.

Clearly, Tommy's leg was good for Dooley's heart.

He had to miss Louise Appleshaw's first visit because of a three o'clock funeral. Thankfully, her first visit did not stipulate dinner.

When he came home, he found the boy sitting at the study desk, facing a tangle of books and papers and looking disconsolate.

"How'd it go?"

"I'm about t' gag," said Dooley.

"Well, hang in there."

"Have you seen 'er?"

"Who?"

"That ol' teacher that come in here t'day and messed up my mind."

"I have not seen her. We spoke on the phone."

"Here's her picture," said Dooley, who grabbed a felt-tipped pen and angrily drew a long face, a pointed nose, a furrowed brow, and a slash for a mouth.

"That looks like a witch," he said, laughing.

"You got that right."

"Dooley, for Pete's sake, loosen up and learn something new. If you're going to get ahead in this world, you've got to speak and write the King's English. It's that simple." Blast it, he'd already fought this battle.

"I don't want t' go t' that ol' school, no way."

"Anyway! And stop making up your mind ahead of the facts. We're going next week to visit Elmhurst, right after Puny's wedding."

"I don't want t' go t' no mushy weddin', either."

"Go see Tommy," he snapped, "and get back in time for dinner. While you're at it, work on your attitude."

He watched Dooley walk across the backyard and through the hedge to Baxter Park. The little creep, he thought. I love him better every day.

It was amazing. Louise Appleshaw looked exactly like Dooley's drawing. He would have recognized her anywhere.

She looked so stern he thought he'd warm up the introduction. "Louise . . ." he said, extending his hand.

"I don't believe you should call me by my Christian name."

"Of course . . ."

"We wouldn't want your parishioners to talk, since we're both unmarried and thrown together in the intimacy of the home environment."

He felt a positive wrench in his stomach. What was worse, he had to make dinner for this person.

"I got a stomach cramp," said Dooley, whose eyes looked bloodshot.

"Me, too," said the rector. They were still sitting in the kitchen, unable to move since Louise Appleshaw had risen from the table and insisted on seeing herself to the door.

"I hate 'at ol' bat."

"Let me ask you something," he said wearily. "Can you say 'I hate that old bat'? Try it, just like I said it."

"I hate that old bat."

"Well done. Who needs a tutor?"

Dooley looked mournful.

"Tell me you're not going to the hardware store."

"I ain't goin' to th' hardware store."

"Wrong."

"I'm not going to the hardware store," said Dooley.

"Right."

"Why don't you teach me?"

"You don't need teaching as much as you need to shape up and get conscious of the problem. Think before you speak, and you can improve yourself."

"Lots of people say ain't."

"Never mind." He was exhausted. And since Louise Appleshaw was allergic to anything with barley, oats, raisins, nuts, pineapple, white flour, sugar, cow's milk, carob, chocolate, dates, leeks, cabbage, lima beans, beef, pork, and tomatoes, what in the name of heaven was he going to do about dinner on Friday?

He had a word of wisdom so full of meaning that he called the boy on the phone.

"Think of it this way. If you put your head down and give it all you've got, it'll be over before you know it. If you let it get to you, you'll suffer, I'll suffer, Barnabas will suffer. What's the point?"

Dooley was silent, thinking. He had learned when his silences were thoughtful, when they were hostile, and when they were mindless.

"This hurts me worse than it hurts you, pal. I've got to do the cooking. What should we feed her tonight?"

"Rat tonsils, snake bellies, and frog puke."

"OK, that's her menu. What about ours?"

Dooley laughed. Bingo! "Hamburgers all the way and french fries."

"Deal," he said.

No, there was not another English tutor around, except for a student at Wesley college, who, according to one report, was tattooed all over.

He might as well swallow his own advice:

Put your head down, Timothy, and give it all you've got.

The wedding gifts arrived, wrapped in the signature blue paper and simple white ribbon. One detail down and two hundred to go, he thought, taking his dark suit from the closet. He'd lost so much weight since those heedless days before the big D . . .

He tried the suit on and stood before the mirror. Not bad. Slap a boutonniere on the lapel, and it would look good as new.

He went to the alcove window and saw the glow of her bedroom lamp under the eaves.

He wished she were here, sitting in the wing chair. She would know whether the suit needed taking in or whether it would get by with a pressing. Besides, he wanted to show her the picture of his grandfather and ask if she saw any resemblance.

It meant something to him to resemble somebody. He hadn't looked like his mother, who was beautiful, or his father, who was handsome. "Woodpile kid," some unkind neighbor had once been heard to say.

In any case, why did he suddenly need someone to help him make the sort of simple decision he'd made quite alone all his life?

The truth was, he didn't *need* someone to do it; he *wanted* someone do it.

He received that truth as a minor revelation.

"Dooley!" He stood at his bedroom door and called across the hall. The guest room door stood open, thanks be to God, and was not only empty of his fraudulent cousin but clean as a pin. He hoped Puny Bradshaw was not lying in the emergency room at Wesley Hospital from having tackled the nastiest job since the Boer War. He had given her an extra twenty-five dollars, which had made her eyes light up, but only feebly.

"What?" said Dooley, coming into the hall.

"Please step in here a minute. I'd like your advice."

Dooley walked in, glowering.

"What the dickens are you glowering about?"

"You ought t' see th' homework she give me."

"She *what* you?"

"*Gave* me!" said Dooley, raising his voice.

"You don't need to raise your voice to speak proper English," he said grumpily. "What about this suit? Is it too baggy?"

Dooley walked around him as if he were the Willard Porter statue on the lawn of the town museum. "You look huge."

"Huge? Are you sure?"

"You look huge in the waist."

Rats! The last place anyone wanted to look huge. "All right, I'll take it in for alterations. Let me see you again in your blazer."

Dooley didn't waste a minute stepping across the hall to put the new blazer over his striped pajamas.

"Cool," said the rector. "Here's the tie I'm giving you to go with it."

"Tie? I have to wear a tie?"

"You have to wear a tie."

"Gag."

"Gag all you want. You're wearing a tie."

"Puke."

"Gag and puke. What a vocabulary."

"I'm going to bed," said Dooley.

"Good riddance," said the rector, "and say your prayers."

Homeless greeted him at the door.

"Come in! Come in! You must have a nose like a beagle—the' coffee's just perked."

Barnabas bounded into the small room on the red leash, his own nose to the floor. "He's looking for Barkless!" said the rector.

"Over yonder on 'is pallet." Homeless pointed to the short-haired, spotted dog who blinked at them. "He cain't bark, but he can blink. See there—blink, blink, blink. That's how he barks at ol' Barnabas, here."

Barnabas barked back. Then he went to the spotted dog and sniffed it. Barkless didn't flinch.

"Chippy, ain't he?"

"I'll say!" The rector moved to the stove. Though it was a warm day, the fire Homeless had built to perk the coffee was nonetheless inviting. "I'm glad to see you, my friend. It feels like I've come home when I visit the creek."

"You're welcome as th' flowers in May—day or night, hard times or fair."

"I thank you. Tell me how your crowd is taking to Pastor Greer."

"Well, sir, they love 'im, they do. He's one of them. He once fought th' Lord just like they're doin', and so they connect. He's preachin' on th' big stump every Wednesday, and we're drawin' 'em in pretty good."

"How's the soup pot holding out?"

"Now and again, somethin' leaks in. The Baptists sent a hundred last week, and out it went for five pairs of shoes.

"Th' Presbyterians put in fifty back in February. That went for medicine for two sick young 'uns. As for th' Methodists, I've not heard."

"You'll be hearing soon, is my guess. The summer crowd is back. Here's ours." He handed over an envelope.

"I like a preacher that makes house calls," said Homeless, stuffing the envelope under his mattress, "and I thank you mightily. Now, set."

He folded a blanket for his guest and put it in the nearly bottomless ladder-back chair. "M' chair's gettin' bottomless to go with m' dog named Barkless."

Laughing, the rector sat down. As he did, the spotted dog sailed through the air and landed in his lap. He nearly tipped over backward.

"I like a dog with timing!" he exclaimed. Barnabas looked up and growled.

"Hold off, now." Homeless stooped down to give the big dog a good scratching behind the ears. "How're things comin' with your lady friend?"

The rector sighed. Then he smiled. Then he sighed again.

"That's a good place to begin," said Homeless, going to the stove to pour two strong cups of coffee.

He had never before given away a bride.

That the bride was Puny Bradshaw supplied one of the great joys of his life.

He walked down the aisle of First Baptist Church as if on air and could not take his eyes off the lovely creature at his side. Every freckle sparkled, and under the little hat she wore, every curl of red hair seemed to glow.

As he stepped away from her at the altar, he briefly took her hand and felt the shocking roughness of it. This hand had mopped his floors, scrubbed his toilets, ironed his shirts, made his beds, cooked his meals, paired his socks, and fed his dog. He might have sunk to his knees on the spot and kissed it.

"Now we're related!" Esther Cunningham said, loud enough to be heard to the monument.

"Mayor," he said, "we've always been related. Philosophically."

When Puny marched into the reception in her enchanting dress, he had to gulp down his emotions. She flew to where he was standing with the Baptist minister and hugged him warmly.

"Father!" she said.

Father! He heard the name in a way he'd never heard it before.

I may have missed the boat in that department, he thought, but not, thank God, altogether.

When he arrived home from the wedding, Cynthia had everything under control.

The roast was coming along nicely, as were the potatoes. The fresh asparagus was washed and lying in the steamer. The butter was set out to soften, the rolls had risen, the salad greens were clean, the raw vegetables were chopped, the salad dressing was concocted, the Camembert was ripe, and the merlot was open and breathing.

As he came in the back door, she turned around from the stove and smiled.

Good Lord, what had she done to herself? She looked so positively breathtaking that he was stopped in his tracks.

"It's the apron," she said, reading his mind. "Men like seeing women in aprons."

He kissed her tenderly. "Please!" she murmured against his cheek. "One mustn't put dessert first."

"Cynthia, Cynthia." He caressed her shoulders. "What is this happiness?"

"You've been to a wedding," she informed him. "You've seen someone with the bald courage to make a commitment. It's invigorating!"

"Turn around," he said.

"What for?"

"I'm checking you for hair curlers."

They laughed hysterically. Hadn't he taken her to visit the bishop last year, with a maverick curler banging around in her hair? She'd been gravely disinclined to forgive him for not bringing it to her attention—though heaven knows he'd tried.

At dinner, Dooley Barlowe looked a fashion plate, used his manners to a fault, and said 'ain't' only once.

Cynthia Coppersmith made the bishop laugh and caused Martha to exclaim, and as for himself, he was hard-pressed to do anything more than pour the wine, compliment the cook, admire Martha's dress, and ask the blessing. "I'm giving you a break," he told Stuart, who appreciated it.

After Stuart and Martha went up to bed in the scrubbed, polished, disinfected, and thoroughly set-to-rights guest room, he put the blue velvet pouch in his pocket and led Cynthia into the study.

"I've already given you this once, so you don't have to thank me again."

"Good! I'm too tired to enthuse over anything more than the complete success of your dinner party."

"Our dinner party."

She sighed happily. "Whatever."

They sat on the sofa, and he handed her the brooch.

"Thank you," she said, sniffing. "It means more than you know."

"Are you going to cry?"

"Certainly not!"

"Excellent!" He held her hand. "Will you wear it tomorrow?"

"With my bedroom shoes!" she said. He smiled, thinking of the time she met him in the street before church, absentmindedly wearing her embroidered scuffs.

He put his arm around her and looked into her eyes.

"In the morning, the bishop will be confirming you. But you confirm something for me every day."

"What, for heaven's sake?"

"That love is a divine gift and should not be held back. Thank you for not holding back."

She put her head against his chest and he stroked her temple.

The Lord's Chapel bells were chiming eleven o'clock when he discovered she had fallen asleep in his arms.

He felt a great swelling in his heart as he watched them come toward the altar.

His thoughts flashed back to the first time he'd seen Dooley Barlowe—barefoot, unwashed, looking for a place to "take a dump."

Today, he was seeing more than a boy wearing a new blazer and an uncontrollable grin. He was seeing a miracle.

Cynthia came behind Dooley, beaming, wearing the pearl and amethyst brooch. Cynthia! Another miracle in his life.

The candidates for confirmation were presented to the bishop by Hal and Marge Owen, who stood with them throughout the ceremony.

The sight of Stuart Cullen laying his hands on their heads, and praying the centuries-old prayer for God's defense, spoke to him more deeply than he expected.

In fact, the only thing that kept him from bawling like a baby was the sudden realization that he'd forgotten to bring the platter for the ham.

Esther Bolick rang the bell for silence in the parish hall.

"I'm glad," said Stuart Cullen, "that Lord's Chapel hasn't grown too big for us to hold hands around the table."

The excited throng formed a circle, as someone fetched Rebecca Jane Owen from under a folding chair and rescued five-year-old Amy Larkin from the hot pursuit of a mechanical toy run amok from the nursery.

"Give us grateful hearts, our Father, for all thy mercies, and make us mindful of the needs of others; through Jesus Christ our Lord."

"Amen!"

Father Tim joined Stuart and Martha at the head of the buffet line, so the Cullens could eat and get on the road to yet another sermon, a ground breaking, and the installation of a deacon.

"Timothy," Martha said as she helped herself to the string beans, "are you going to marry that lovely woman?"

"Why, yes. Olivia asked me some time ago if I'd officiate."

"Not Olivia! Cynthia!"

He laughed. "Now, Martha . . ."

"Don't 'now Martha' me. Time is running out, dear. I can see she's doing her part. Are you doing yours?"

Martha Cullen was a carbon copy of Katherine when it came to meddling.

"We can't do it all, Timothy. The men must do *something.* When Stuart finally understood that, things fell into place. By the way, is that famous orange marmalade cake here today?"

"I'll have a look," he said, bounding from his place in line, never to return.

He spied Emma Newland, who hadn't darkened the doors of a worship service since she married Harold and "went back to bein' a Baptist."

He saw Miss Sadie, Louella, Hoppy, and Olivia gabbing a mile a minute by the piano.

Dooley and Cynthia were in line with the Owens, and as far as he could tell, the orange marmalade cake had not made it to the reception.

He sliced a piece of homemade coconut, instead, and carried it to Martha's place at the table, fetched the bishop a cup of coffee, picked up Amy Larkin and admired her patent-leather shoes, removed a stuffed bear from the floor, kissed two old parishioners, hugged several of all ages, sat down with Rebecca Jane who bit his nose and chewed on his lapel, fielded an enthusiastic round of congratulations upon Dooley's confirmation, rummaged in the kitchen and found extra flatware for a table of eight who didn't get any, pitched in to serve coffee for the frazzled ECW, and checked the ham to determine its popularity, which, considering the bare bone he found on the tray, was immense.

He packed Stuart and Martha out the side door, waved them off, and went back to join Dooley, Cynthia, the Owens, and Rebecca Jane for the last hoarded pieces of Esther Bolick's coconut cake, served with a pretty good joke from Uncle Billy Watson.

Tommy was asking for Buck Leeper, who had visited the hospital faithfully but hadn't been seen since Tommy came home.

The rector supposed Buck Leeper was far too private a man to invade someone's home. The impersonal ground of the hospital had been a different matter.

Breaking a light sweat, he jogged up the hill to the construction site with the book under his arm. It wasn't every day he could kill two birds with one stone.

Buck Leeper was sitting at the desk with his back to the door.

"Buck?"

The chair creaked as his heavy frame swiveled around to face the door. The superintendent merely nodded.

"Two things . . ."

"Number one," said Buck, stubbing out his cigarette.

"Tommy is asking for you, misses seeing you. I'd be glad to tell you how to find his house, if you'd like to pay a visit."

Buck cleared his throat. "Number two."

"I found something I wanted to give you."

Buck stood up as he handed the book over. He looked at it for a moment before taking it in his hand.

The rector shrugged. "I thought you might like it."

Buck studied the cover silently, drawing a cigarette out of the pack of Lucky Strikes in his shirt pocket. He held it, unlighted, as he laid the book on the desk and opened it. Then he bent over the book and slowly turned a few pages.

The rector wiped his forehead with his sleeve.

The superintendent stayed bent over the book so long, the rector thought he'd forgotten anyone was in the room.

Buck turned, finally, and looked at him. "Thanks."

"You're welcome. Well, I won't keep you."

"Where's th' kid's house?"

He told him, pointing this way and that.

As he was leaving, Buck said, "Something I ought to say to you."

"What's that?"

"Nobody around here knows what I told you the other day."

"Nobody will hear it from me."

Buck lit the cigarette. "I'll go see the boy."

"Good. He'll like that."

Jogging down the hill definitely felt better than going up.

It was a long push to Elmhurst, but if they hustled, they could make it in a day, arriving back home at midnight. His jam-packed calendar wouldn't permit dawdling.

But Dooley Barlowe did not like Elmhurst, which was only one day away from dismissing for the summer.

He did not like the grim look of the brick buildings, he did not like the cool demeanor of the headmaster, he did not like any of the teachers or even one of the boys, he hated the drab, ill-fitting school uniforms, and he refused to eat a bite in the dining room that was morbidly silent.

The boy had judgment, you could say that for him. They were in such a hurry to get out of there that the Buick nosed into the garage an hour and a half ahead of schedule.

As Olivia Davenport walked down the aisle on the arm of Dr. Leo Baldwin, the wedding guests gawked as shamelessly as tourists at a scenic overlook.

No one had ever seen anything like it in Mitford—a successful heart-transplant recipient who looked like a movie star, a famous heart surgeon from Boston, Massachusetts, and a wedding gown that would be the talk of the village for months, even years, to come.

This wedding, as someone rightly said, was "big doings."

If the wedding of Dr. Walter Harper and Olivia Davenport was big doings, the doings that followed at Fernbank were bigger still.

People turned out merely to see the long procession of cars snaking along Main Street and up Old Church Lane.

"Is it a weddin' or a funeral?" Hattie Cloer, who owned Cloer's Market on the highway, was being taken for a Sunday-afternoon drive by her son. Her Chihuahua, Darlene, sat on Hattie's shoulder, with her head stuck out the window.

"Looks like a funeral," said her son. "I seen a long, black deal parked in th' church driveway."

"Oh, law," said Hattie, "I hope it's not old Sadie Baxter who's keeled over. This is her church, you know."

"I hear she had a United States president at her house one time."

"President Jackson, I think it was, or maybe Roosevelt," said Hattie.

Entering Fernbank's ballroom was like entering another world.

No one stepped across the threshold who didn't gasp with amazement or joy or disbelief, so that the reception line was backed up on the porch and down the steps and across the circle drive. No one minded standing on the lawn, some with their heels sinking into the turf, for they'd heard that a marvelous spectacle awaited inside.

Quite a few had never been on the lawn at Fernbank and had only seen the rooftop over the trees. They'd heard for years the place was falling to ruin, but all they saw was some peeling paint here and there, hardly worse than what they had at home.

Not a soul was untouched by the enchantment of it, and the skirted tables on the lawn, and the young, attractive strangers in black bow ties who smiled and poured champagne and served lime-green punch and made them feel like royalty.

Enormous baskets of tuberoses and stephanotis and country roses and stock flanked the porch steps, pouring out their fragrance. And through the open windows, strains of music—Mozart, someone said—declared itself, sweetening the air all the way to the orchards.

Uncle Billy Watson stood near the end of the line and straightened his tie. "Lord have mercy!" he said, deeply moved by the occasion. He gave Miss Rose a final check and discovered he'd missed the label that was turned out of her collar. He turned it in.

Absalom Greer felt an odd beating of his heart. Where had more than sixty years gone since his feet came down those steps and he drove away with Sadie Baxter in her father's town car, believing with all his heart that she would be his bride?

Hessie Mayhew did not wait in line. She marched up the steps and across the porch and slipped in and found a chair and claimed her territory by dumping her pocketbook in it.

Then she took out her notepad and pen. After all, she was not here to have a good time; she was here to work. She had finally talked J.C. Hogan into letting her do something besides the gardening column.

The reception line alone had been an emotional experience for the rector. When he met her, Olivia Davenport had been dying, and he had, with his own eyes, witnessed her agonizing brush with death. Now, to see her beauty and to feel her joy . . . it was another miracle in a string of miracles.

Hoppy Harper clasped his hand and held it for a long moment. Working as a team, they had pitched in and prayed for Olivia, and it would bind them together for life.

But perhaps what he was feeling most deeply of all was this strange, new sense of family as he moved through the line with Cynthia and Dooley. He felt a connection that was beyond his understanding, as if the three of them were bound together like the links of a chain.

It was a new feeling, and he was intoxicated by it even before he got to the champagne.

Esther Bolick had made the wedding cake, which was displayed on a round table, skirted to the floor with ivory tulle and ornamented with calla lilies.

"A masterpiece!" he said, meaning it.

Esther was literally wringing her hands, looking at it. "I declare, I've never done anything this complicated. I was up 'til all hours. Three different cakes, three layers each—it looks like the Empire State Buildin' on that stand the caterers brought."

"What do you think of the other masterpiece in the room?"

"Law, I haven't had a minute to look around. Where?"

"Up there."

Esther looked up and gasped. "Who painted that?"

"Leonardo and Michelangelo."

"You don't mean it!"

"I do mean it!" he said.

Once again, he went to the windows that faced the circle drive and looked out. Planes were always late, weren't they?

And then he saw the taxi coming up the drive, and he went out quickly and hurried down the steps and was there to greet the tall, dark, gentle man who was Leonardo Francesca's grandson.

Sadie Baxter came off the dance floor in her emerald-green dress, on the arm of Leo Baldwin. Leo retrieved her cane and gave it to her as she turned and saw the man walking into the ballroom.

There was an astonished look on her face, and the rector went to her at once, wondering if the shock might . . .

But Miss Sadie regained her composure and held out her hand to the young man and said, wonderingly, "Leonardo?"

Roberto took her hand and kissed it. "I am Roberto, Leonardo's grandson. My grandfather salutes your beauty and grace and deeply regrets that he could not come himself. He has made me the emissary of a very special message to his childhood friend."

The rector was enthralled with the look on her face, as she waited eagerly to hear the message that had come thousands of miles, across nearly eighty years.

"My grandfather has asked me to say—*Tempo è denaro!*"

Roberto smiled and bowed.

No one had ever seen Sadie Baxter laugh like this; it was a regular fit of laughter. People drew round, feeling yet another pulse of excitement in a day of wondrous excitements.

"Does he," she said, wiping her eyes with a lace handkerchief, "still like garden peas?"

"Immensely!" said Roberto.

Miss Sadie reached again for Roberto's hand. "Let's sit down before we fall down. I want to hear everything!"

"Miss Sadie," said the rector, "before you go . . . what does *tempo è denaro* mean, anyway?"

"Didn't I tell you? It means 'time is money'!"

"Is this heaven?" asked Cynthia as they danced.

"Heaven's gates, at the very least."

"Everyone loves you so."

"Everyone?"

"Yes," she whispered against his cheek. "Everyone."

"That's a tough act to follow," he said, his heart hammering.

"You were the one who brought Roberto here."

"Yes. I didn't say anything to you because I wanted to . . . I wasn't sure we could pull it off. I called Florence for his grandfather, who answered but had forgotten all his English. He handed the phone to his son, who knew a bit of English—and then Roberto, whose English is flawless, called me back.

"I said, 'Please, if you could do it, it would give great joy.' And Roberto said, 'My grandfather's life has been spent in giving joy. I will come.'

"I had tickets waiting at the airline counter in Florence, and here, thanks be to God, is Roberto."

"It's the loveliest gift imaginable."

"Miss Sadie is so often on the giving end . . ."

"How long will he be with us?"

"Only a few days. We'll have Andrew step in for a glass of sherry while he's here. They can rattle away in Italian, and we'll do something special for Miss Sadie and Louella. Roberto will occupy my popular guest room. Of course, there's no Puny to give a hand, but we'll manage."

"I'll help you," she said.

He pressed her hand in his. "You always help me."

As the eight-piece orchestra played on, he saw the room revolve around them in a glorious panorama, bathed with afternoon light.

He saw Absalom Greer laughing with Roberto and Miss Sadie.

He saw Andrew Gregory raise a toast to the newlyweds, and Miss Rose standing stiffly with a smiling Uncle Billy, wearing her black suit and a cocktail hat and proper shoes.

He saw Buck Leeper standing awkwardly in the doorway, holding a glass of champagne in his rough hand, and Ron and Wilma Malcolm trying to lure him into the room.

There was Emma wearing a hat, and Harold looking shy, and Esther Bolick sitting down and fanning herself with relief, and Dooley Barlowe walking toward Miss Sadie, who was beaming in his direction.

He saw Winnie Ivey taking something fancy off a passing tray, her cheeks pink with excitement, while J.C. Hogan conferred with Hessie Mayhew next to a potted palm.

And there was Louella, in a handsome dress that brought out the warmth of her coffee-colored skin, dancing with Hal Owen.

The faces of the people in the sun-bathed panorama were suddenly more beautiful to him than heavenly faces on a ceiling could ever be. Let the hosts swarm overhead, shouting hosannas. He wanted to be planted exactly where he was, enveloped in this mist of wisteria.

"Man," said Dooley, as they came toward him off the dance floor, "you were sure dancin' *close.*"

"Not nearly close enough," said Cynthia, looking mischievous.

"Dooley, why don't you dance with Cynthia?" Dooley, who was unable to imagine such a thing, paused blankly. Seizing the moment, Cynthia grabbed Dooley and dragged him at once into the happy maelstrom on the dance floor.

He who hesitates is lost! thought the rector, grinning.

"Mrs. Walter Harper?"

"The very same!"

"May I kiss the bride?"

"I'll be crushed if you don't."

He kissed her on both cheeks and stood holding her hands, fairly smitten with the light in her violet eyes. "You're a great beauty, Mrs. Harper. But there's even greater beauty inside. I won't say that Hoppy is a lucky man, for I don't believe in luck, but grace. May God bless you both with the deepest happiness, always."

"Thank you. May I kiss my priest and friend?"

"I'll be crushed if you don't."

She kissed him on both cheeks, and they laughed. "I've never been so blessed and happy in all my life. A wonderful husband, a loving and doting aunt . . . and this glorious room that I know was done just for us. How can one bear such happiness?"

"Drink deeply. It's richly deserved."

"I hope you'll soon be doing this yourself, Father."

"This?"

"Getting married, sharing your life."

"I don't know if I could . . ."

She looked at him, smiling, but serious. "Don't you remember? Philippians four-thirteen, for Pete's sake!"

CHAPTER TWENTY-ONE

Knowing

Dooley's homeroom teacher wrote in a neat, confined hand:

> *To Whom It May Concern: When it comes to math, Dooley Barlowe is a genius.*

He felt fortified. Now if Louise Appleshaw could pull off a miracle . . .

He said as much. "Miss Appleshaw, I confess I'm expecting a miracle."

"Rector, one does not *expect* miracles. A miracle is, at least partly by definition, something quite *un*expected." She looked down her nose at him.

He became a worm and crawled from the room.

Andrew Gregory stopped in for a glass of Italian wine before meeting friends for dinner at the club.

Roberto had put on the rector's favorite apron, tucked his tie into his shirt front, and was busy creating the most seductive aromas in the rectory's history.

"Osso buco!" Roberto announced, taking the pot lid off with one hand and waving a wooden spoon with the other.

"Ummmm!" cried Cynthia, coming through the back door with an armful of flowers. "Ravishing!"

"Man!" exclaimed Dooley, lured downstairs.

"Oh, my gracious!" gasped Miss Sadie, who arrived with her usual hostess gift of Swanson's Chicken Pie and a Sara Lee pound cake for his freezer.

Louella sniffed the air, appreciatively. "That ain't no collards and pigs' feet!"

The toasts flew as thick as snowflakes during last year's blizzard.

To Leonardo, who lay crippled with rheumatism in Florence.

To Roberto's happiness in Mitford!

To Miss Sadie's good health!

To Louella's quick recovery from an impending knee operation.

To Dooley's prospects for a new school.

To the hospitality of the host!

To the charm and beauty of the hostess!

To Olivia and Hoppy at Brown's Hotel in London!

Avis Packard called to find out if everything was going all right, thrilled with having cut veal for a real Italian who knew what was what.

Roberto showed photos of his wife and three beautiful children, of his grandfather's work in the homes and churches of Florence, and of Leonardo himself, wearing the same boyish smile Miss Sadie remembered from his long-ago visit to Fernbank.

The rector had never seen so much toasting and cooking and pouring of olive oil and peeling of garlic, nor heard so much laughing and joking.

It was as if Roberto were one of their very own and had come home to them all, at last.

Bingo.

Dooley liked the second school they visited. And why not? Cynthia went with them on the journey and kept them laughing all the way.

Better still, she never once let the admissions director believe he was interviewing them but that it was definitely the other way around.

Though the boys were away for the summer and they couldn't tell much about the tone of the place, Dooley warmed up to the affable headmaster who dropped in from his home next door, dressed in khakis, loafers, and a sweatshirt, to give them an enthusiastic tour.

He also liked the science lab with the brain in a jar, and the gym, the track, the football field, and the horse stables where the groom put him on his personal steed and slapped its rump and sent Dooley flying around the ring, barely clinging on.

"Needs polish," said the groom.

The dorm rooms did not measure up.

"Gag," said Dooley.

"Spoiled," said the rector.

"No problem," said Cynthia, who rattled on about paint and curtains.

In all, a satisfying trip, which brought them home at two o'clock in the morning, reeling with exhaustion.

The statue of Captain Willard Porter was definitely the centerpiece of the first—and soon to be annual—Mitford Museum Festival.

It stood on the freshly groomed lawn of the Porter place, mysteriously draped with a tarpaulin and encircled by booths.

Over by the lilac bushes, Joe Ivey had set up a barbering chair and a table displaying the tools of his trade, from tins of talc and bottles of Sea Breeze to a neck brush and a battery-operated shaver. Shaves were three dollars, haircuts were six, and all proceeds would go to the museum.

Across the circle, as far as she could possibly remove herself from the competition, was Fancy Skinner, dressed to the teeth in lime-green pedal pushers and a V-necked sweater. When someone wondered about the shocking departure from her favorite color, she said she was "trying to cut through the clutter and stand out in the crowd, which, as anyone ought to know, is what business is all about."

Fancy was offering manicures for five dollars and lip waxings and pedicures for ten (behind a sheet that was hung on a wire). The only problem with her assigned location, as she later pointed out in a letter to the town council, was that Mack Stroupe was boiling hot dogs right next to her booth, which created both a clamor and a smell that were entirely inappropriate for beauty treatments.

Winnie Ivey manned the Sweet Stuff doughnut stand, which was staked out under the elm tree, in conjunction with her cousin who had made thirty pimento cheese sandwiches, thirty sliced ham and cheese, and forty chicken salad, which she was keeping on ice in a cooler.

On the opposite side of the elm tree, two llamas stood patiently in the shade gazing at the crowd. *Pet the Llamas Fifty Cents,* read the sign tacked to the tree.

"Fifty cents is way too much to pet a llama!" said a young mother, who decided to invest in doughnuts. Her brood of three stood howling at the mere sight of a llama.

There were cakes baked by Esther Bolick, who complained that the Harper wedding and museum festival were far too close together. Her cakes, however, were selling fast, with her prize two-layer orange marmalade waiting to be auctioned to the highest bidder at noon. It sat on review under an open tent, as Percy and Velma Mosely's youngest grandchild waved a fly swatter over it.

Free lemonade was available on the porch, which was the only concession the town council had made in the area of hospitality—except, of course, for the Porta John that leaned alarmingly to the right on a bank next to the cellar door.

Dora Pugh offered a miniature garden shop under a tent, with a box of newly hatched biddies to entertain the children. Ten percent of Dora's sales would go to the museum, while Andrew Gregory was donating all proceeds from the sale of his English Lemon Furniture Wax, which he displayed on an eighteenth-century teak garden bench under the redbud tree.

"Law!" said J.C. Hogan, wiping his face with his handkerchief, "this is a whopper." He had shot four rolls of film in only one hour since the festival officially opened, one of which featured Mayor Cunningham standing on the steps of the Porter place, flanked by Miss Rose and Uncle Billy.

According to Uncle Billy, Miss Rose started the day in one of the worst moods he had ever witnessed and completely refused his offer of help with her wardrobe.

She had turned up at one of the most important events ever staged in Mitford, wearing a cracked-leather bomber jacket from World War II, a black cocktail hat with a mashed-flat silk peony that had come loose and slipped down over one ear, a pair of saddle oxfords, and a flowered dress that had belonged to her mother. She had chosen to carry a handbag made from the cork circles that once appeared in the caps of Pepsi-Cola bottles.

Uncle Billy had been able to make only one inroad on the discouraging situation—his wife had let him tie the laces of her shoes.

As the brass band marched around the lawn playing special selections, the crowd increased. Also, it was the first time anyone could remember the street being roped off, which clearly added to the general excitement.

A list of the day's activities was handwritten on a blackboard, which stood teetering on an easel at the sidewalk facing Lilac Road.

Included in the long list were:

See someone you know push
a peanut with their NOSE!
Watch Percy Mosely do the
HULA DANCE in a grass skirt!

"I ain't doin' any hula dance," said Percy, who had come home from Hawaii with a tan. "I told 'er that plain as day, but Esther Cunningham don't take no for an answer, and now she's got false advertisin' on her hands."

"Aw, Percy," someone cajoled, "go ahead and do it. It's for a good cause."

The band passed by, drowning out Percy's list of indignations.

"I declare," said Chief Rodney Underwood, who was eating a hot dog and talking to the rector, "we go along thinkin' we're a small town. Then we get big doin's like this, and first thing you know, we look like New York City."

Esther Cunningham drew alongside them, wearing a new red linen suit. "Th' tourists are swarmin' over this place like flies," she said with disgust. "You'd think they'd let us alone for five bloomin' minutes."

Rodney wiped the chili off his hand. "It's June, Esther. We always get tourists in June."

She looked down at her jacket. "I hate linen. Would you look at this suit? It's got more wrinkles than Carter has liver pills. I'm packin' up and goin' to Colorado as soon as this thing's over."

She stomped off to get a doughnut.

"I thought this was a festival," said Mule Skinner, arriving fresh from a round of golf, "but it looks like a circus to me."

"Big crowd," said the rector.

"Next year, they better bring in barbecue and sweet-potato pie. Hot dogs won't cut it."

"We'll get Percy to set up a booth."

"When do the events begin, the pig kissin' and all?"

"One o'clock, if there's a soul left alive to watch," said the rector.

"Mack Stroupe?"

The rector nodded, laughing. Two dogs streaked by them, chasing a squirrel. Rodney ran after somebody whose shopping bag had lost its bottom and was spilling a trail of tea towels and bran muffins bought at the Library Ladies booth.

"Are you on for the Scripture Dog act?" said Mule.

"That's me," sighed the rector. "It was that or push a blasted peanut . . ."

"Esther Cunningham makes my army sergeant look like Mother Teresa."

They looked up to see Hattie Cloer charging toward them with Darlene on a leash.

"Duck," hissed Mule, but it was too late.

"Father," said Hattie, "how far gone do you have to be to get last rites?"

"Pretty far," said Mule, helping out with the conversation.

Darlene bared her teeth and growled at the rector.

"I was thinkin' last night of askin' Clyde to call you," said Hattie. "I was layin' there 'til way up in th' morning with somethin' I thought was gas. Oh, law, I was so distended! But it had a worse pain to it than gas, you know. It was something really serious, I could just tell. So I said, 'Clyde, honey, wake up and feel this.' And he rolled over and felt of it and sat straight up and called the ambulance, but he dialed the wrong number and got Charlie's Tavern on the highway. And by the time he was through talkin', I was feelin' better and got up and cooked a pot of string beans that just came in down at th' store. And knowin' how you like string beans, you might want to come over and get you a pound or two. They'll freeze. You know I give a quarter off for clergy. But anyway, it did cause me to wonder about maybe needin' you to come over . . ."

"Call me anytime," he told Hattie, who dragged Darlene away, still growling.

"I'd get an unlisted number if I was you," said Mule.

At one o'clock sharp, the mayor stood on the front porch steps as the brass band played "God Bless America," and everyone crossed their hearts.

The Rotary had loaned a small sea of folding chairs to the festival, which were neatly placed about the lawn in rows near the steps.

Miss Sadie, Louella, Roberto, Father Tim, Cynthia, Dooley, and Andrew Gregory occupied the front row.

The rector glanced anxiously at Miss Sadie. How would she react to seeing the statue of the man she had loved for so many years? She didn't care for public display, to say the least.

The mayor thanked everyone for turning out, reminded them of the free lemonade, and launched into a prepared speech that was ghost-written, as far as he could tell, by Hessie Mayhew.

She thanked Miss Rose and Uncle Billy for their civic generosity in letting their home be overtaken by a museum, and everyone applauded.

Miss Rose stood and bowed, sending her mashed-flat silk peony into the grass.

Then the mayor went on at some length about Willard Porter, his deep roots in Mitford, his fondly remembered generosity to the Presbyterian church, his brilliant contributions to the pharmaceutical profession, and the noble architecture of the house, which, for nearly seventy years, had been the centerpiece of the village. His death in France, she said in closing, had been to the glory of God and America.

Ernestine Ivory stood by the statue, holding the tarpaulin.

Esther Cunningham signaled the band, which struck up at once.

Then she signaled Ernestine, who, blushing furiously, ripped the cover from the statue.

A gasp went up.

Silence ensued.

Then everyone stood and applauded and whistled and cheered. It was the first statue ever erected in Mitford, and public opinion was unanimous—it was a sight to behold.

Willard Porter stood looking toward the blue mountains that swelled beyond the village, his eyes fixed on freedom, his hand over his heart. Nobility was expressed in every feature of his handsome face, in every detail of his officer's uniform. A bed of flowers sprung up at his feet.

"Oh, my," said Miss Sadie, using her handkerchief.

Roberto nodded approvingly.

"Man!" said Dooley.

Some people were still clapping, as the band began to march around the statue.

He thought he had never seen Miss Rose look so wonderful—standing by Uncle Billy, saluting the statue of her brother, and keeping time to the music with her foot.

"Th' deal," announced the mayor from the steps, "is that anytime th' father's dog gets out of hand, all th' father has to do is quote Scripture and his dog . . ."

"Barnabas," said the rector.

"Barnabas . . . shapes up and lies down."

The crowd laughed.

"I'm askin' for fifty dollars for a demonstration," she announced, peering around.

Silence. Birdsong.

"Not twenty-five, so don't even think about it. Fifty! A small price to pay to see somethin' you can't even see on TV! And think what that fifty will do—help add yet another room to this fine museum, the likes of which you'll not see across the whole length of the state . . ."

A hand went up in the back row. "Thirty-five!"

"Get over it!" said Esther. "I'm lookin' for fifty or we move on to th' pig kissin'."

"Fifty!" shouted a voice from the vicinity of the llamas.

"Do I hear fifty-five?"

Silence.

Esther signaled the band, which struck up a drumroll as the rector led Barnabas to the foot of the steps.

He didn't know whether to laugh or cry. How he had ever been talked into this was beyond all understanding.

"One thing you need to know," said Esther. "We do not mean to poke fun at the Word of the good Lord.

"We intend to demonstrate to each and every member present what we should all do when we hear his Word . . . which is to let it have its way with our hearts."

"Amen!" somebody said.

J.C. sank to his knees in the grass and looked through the lens of his camera. Something interesting was bound to happen with this deal.

At that moment, Cynthia Coppersmith rose from her front-row seat, holding what appeared to be a large handbag. As she held it aloft for all to see, Violet's white head emerged. Violet perched there, staring coolly at the crowd.

"That cat is in books at the library," someone said.

Keeping a safe distance, Cynthia turned around and let Barnabas have a look. Violet peered down at him with stunning disdain.

Barnabas nearly toppled the rector as he lunged toward the offending handbag, which Cynthia handed off to Dooley.

His booming bark carried beyond the monument, all the way to Lew Boyd's Esso, and the force of his indignation communicated to every expectant onlooker.

The rector spoke with his full pulpit voice. " 'For brethren, ye have been called unto liberty, only use not liberty for an occasion to the flesh.' "

Barnabas hesitated. His ears stood straight up. He relaxed on the leash.

" '. . . but by love serve one another.' "

The black dog sighed and sprawled on the grass.

" 'For all the law is fulfilled in one word: Thou shalt love thy neighbor as thyself.' "

Barnabas didn't move but raised his eyes and looked dolefully at the front row. Not knowing what else to do, the rector bowed. The crowd applauded heartily.

"A fine passage from Galatians five-thirteen and fourteen!" said the jolly new preacher from First Baptist.

"That was *worth* fifty," said Mule Skinner, pleased to know the dog personally.

As Dooley hurried to take Violet back to her sunny window seat at home, Esther resumed her place on the steps and looked around.

"Ponder that in your hearts," she said.

Somebody heard the pig squeal behind a column on the porch, which encouraged more applause.

Linder Hayes strolled to the foot of the steps and stretched to his full height of six feet, four and a half inches. His courtroom demeanor brought a hush over the assembly.

"Ladies and gentlemen, on this distinguished and momentous occasion, we will now open the bidding that will permit everyone here—with their own eyes—to see a unique and historic event, to see, in other words, the mayor of this fine village . . . kiss . . . a pig."

They gasped. Esther Cunningham would kiss a pig? A great clamor ran through the booths and among the crowd. Coot Hendrick, maybe, but Esther Cunningham?

"Twenty-five dollars!" someone shouted.

Linder held up his hand for silence.

"Surely you jest," he said in the deep baritone that he had honed to reach the hearts of a jury. "This penultimate event will not go for so crass a sum as twenty-five dollars. In fact, no amount of money could fully compensate the priceless act of sacrifice and civic responsibility that . . ."

"Hurry up, dadgum it," hissed Esther.

"The bidding, my friends, will begin at five hundred dollars."

The stunned silence changed into an uproar.

Linder pulled at his chin and looked thoughtful. Esther broke out in a rash.

Someone standing under the elm tree shouted: "Five hundred!"

Linder held up his hand. "Do I hear five twenty-five?"

Silence.

"Going, going, gone for five hundred."

"And dern lucky t' get it, if you ask me," said Percy, who stood under the elm in a shirt printed with chartreuse palm leaves and red monkeys.

"Will someone please bring down the pig?"

A great expectancy hung over the gathering. What kind of pig would it be? A sow? A shoat? What difference did it make?

Ray came down the steps with the pig in his arms. He held it while Esther kissed it.

The crowd cheered as J.C.'s flash went off.

"One more time!" said J.C. "Th' pig moved!"

Esther did it again. More hollering and whistling.

Esther turned to the crowd, who, she knew, would deliver a strong Cunningham vote next election, and raised both arms in triumph.

"I'm about half shot," said Winnie Ivey. "Up at four in th' mornin' to cook all these doughnuts, and here it is way up in the day, and all I've had is half a pimento cheese sandwich."

"Only one more event to go," he said, trying to locate Cynthia in the swirling crowd. "I'll get you some lemonade."

There was Cynthia—trying to pin the errant peony on Miss Rose's bomber jacket. He liked spotting her in the crowd, seeing the blond of her hair and the apple green of her dress. She was wearing tennis shoes, as high heels would only have sunk in the lawn, and looking very much like a girl.

He saw Dooley and Jenny peering at the llamas. Lovely, he thought. And there by Andrew's garden bench was Roberto. Both men gestured happily—speaking Italian, no doubt.

"Father! You're positively radiant!" It was Miss Pearson, Dooley's music teacher, hand in hand with her mother.

Radiance, he was soon to learn, can be exceedingly short-lived.

"I've had about all the fun I can stand, ain't you?" said Uncle Billy.

"One more event," he said, wishing he could rent a hammock and lie down in it.

"I ain't even heard th' jukebox."

"Me, either."

Uncle Billy sighed. "They hooked it up in th' front room. I sure hope it don't cut on in th' middle of th' night and go t' playin'."

He happened to look toward the alley behind the Porter place and saw a red truck slowly driving through. Buck Leeper peered out the window at the throng on the lawn, at their laughter and air of anticipation.

He waved. "Buck!"

Buck threw up his hand and nodded and was gone.

"Dadgum if he didn't wave back," said Mule, who was passing by with lemonade for Fancy. "What's got into him?"

The rector believed it was what had gotten out of him.

Esther was back on the porch steps. If she didn't have laryngitis from the long day's events, it would be a miracle.

"How many of you have ever seen anybody push a peanut down the street with their nose?"

Heads turned. People shrugged. Clearly, no one had ever seen such a thing. Some didn't want to. A few didn't care one way or the other.

"I've seen a sack race!" yelled one of Dooley's classmates.

"That's not the same," snorted the mayor. "This is a hundred times better. That's why we're going to start the bidding high."

The crowd groaned. Some people walked away. Two senior citizens went to sleep sitting up in folding chairs near the lilac bushes.

"To see our brand-new Baptist preacher push a peanut from th' bookstore to th' bakery . . . the bidding will start at five hundred dollars!"

"Not again!" shouted an irate observer.

"That's a dadgum car payment!"

"Lord have mercy, what do you *drive?*

A total stranger stepped forward. As everyone could plainly see, it was a tourist. He was wearing sunglasses, a navy blazer over khakis, and no socks with his loafers.

"I would *not* give five hundred dollars to see only one member of your local clergy fulfill this unique fund-raising proposition . . ."

Several people looked at each other. Not only was this person a tourist, he was a Yankee.

"However, I would most gladly put five hundred into your town coffers to see all your clergy do it—as a team."

"You better jump on that," Linder whispered to the mayor.

The rector could feel Esther, who had eyes like a hawk, boring a hole in him all the way to where he stood with Uncle Billy.

The mayor took a deep breath and bellowed. "Do I hear five hundred to see Reverend Sprouse push the peanut?"

Heads wagged furiously in the negative.

"It's fish or cut bait," hissed Ray.

"Where's th' father?" said Esther, knowing perfectly well where he was. He might have dived under a chair.

"Right here!" hollered Mule.

"Where's Pastor Trollinger from th' Methodists?"

"Over here!" cried the pastor's wife, who couldn't wait to see her husband push a peanut with his nose.

Esther's eyes searched the throng. "That leaves Doctor Browning from over at th' Presbyterians."

"He's not here," said the band leader. "He's doin' a funeral today."

"Where at?" asked Ray.

"Ash Grove."

"Ernestine," said the mayor, "run over there—it's just two miles—and tell 'im to come right after he throws th' dirt in."

"Right," said Ray. "Five hundred bucks is five hundred bucks."

He dragged home at four o'clock, weary of the world.

Dooley and Cynthia trooped down Main Street behind him, laughing like hyenas all the way to the rectory.

"Now, that," declared Cynthia, "was the spirit of ecumenism in a nutshell."

He refused even to crack a smile, though Cynthia, of course, found her odious pun hysterical.

Dooley closed his English book. "I'm not goin' to that school," he said.

"Really?" He wouldn't have uttered another word if his life depended on it. He wasn't fighting battles tonight; he was sitting on his sofa reading his newspaper.

Total silence reigned for some time.

"That ol' brain in that jar—whose do you reckon it is?"

"No idea."

"Th' head guy said they go to Washington on bus trips and all."

"Aha."

"He was cool."

"Umm."

"That groom person said I could ride 'is horse all I wanted to, if I'd help take care of it."

"Sounds like work."

"I wonder what th' football uniforms look like."

"Beats me."

"I like th' school colors."

"Black and gray."

"You got it wrong. Purple and orange."

"Oh."

"We could paint my room and then put posters up. Cynthia has a purple bedspread she'll give me."

Why was he always knocking himself out to convince the boy of something? From now on, maybe he'd keep his mouth shut and let Dooley convince himself.

When the box of monogrammed stationery rolled in from Walter, he realized the worst:

Tomorrow was his birthday.

He had just had a birthday—it seemed only weeks ago. And how old was he, anyway? He could never remember. He had once added a year to his age by mistake, which appalled his friends. Take a couple off, maybe, but *add?*

He did some quick figuring on a piece of paper.

Sixty-two.

Rats.

But what was there to worry about, after all?

At the age of eighty-nine, Arthur Rubinstein had given one of his most enthralling recitals, in Carnegie Hall.

At eighty-two, Chruchill wrote *A History of the English-Speaking People*—in four volumes, no less.

And hadn't Eamon de Valera served as president of Ireland when he was ninety-one? Not to mention Grandma Moses, who was still painting—and getting paid for it—at the age of one hundred.

He stood up from the desk and sucked in his stomach.

"Happy birthday, Father! Ron and I have to go out of town this afternoon, and we didn't want to leave without wishing you the best year ever!"

After Wilma called, so did Evie, who had carefully rehearsed Miss Pattie to say the thing herself. He heard Evie whispering in the background, "Say it, Mama!" "What was it I was supposed to say?" "Happy birthday!" There was a pause, and Miss Pattie spoke into the phone, "I hope you win the lottery!"

He roared with laughter.

Evie grabbed the phone. "She wouldn't say it! I declare, I worked and worked with her . . ."

"Evie," he implored, "don't be disappointed. I loved what Miss Pattie said. It was very original—head and shoulders above the usual greeting."

"Well . . ." He heard the smile creep into her voice.

He didn't think he would ever again have those yearnings to be a milk-truck driver. If he couldn't say another thing about himself, he could say he loved his work.

What Cynthia and Dooley might be plotting, he couldn't imagine.

Roberto had flown home, Andrew Gregory had houseguests, Miss Sadie and Louella were frazzled from all the gaiety and would hardly answer the phone, Esther had carried out her threat and gone fishing with Ray . . .

Then again, maybe Cynthia and Dooley weren't plotting anything at all. Maybe they'd forgotten. Hadn't he forgotten Dooley's birthday? And when was Cynthia's? He felt a moment of panic.

Wait, there was the date—written on the wall next to his desk, his only graffiti since grade school. July 20. He breathed a sigh of relief.

He was convinced they'd forgotten.

At lunch, he saw Cynthia in her backyard, idly pruning a bush. And when he called home at three-thirty to see if Dooley was prepared for Miss Appleshaw, there was nothing in his voice that hinted at anything unusual.

He went home early, carrying the bundle of cards he'd received from the ECW, the Sunday school, Walter and Katherine, Winnie Ivey, Emma, Miss Sadie and Louella, and a dozen others.

As he went in the back door, he saw Cynthia going up her steps with something bulky under her jacket, glancing furtively toward the rectory. When she saw him, she averted her gaze as if he didn't exist.

Had he hurt her feelings after that blasted peanut business, when she laughed at him and he didn't laugh with her? He'd been pretty huffy about it, but why not? He'd gone nonstop for days on end and was flatly exhausted. Run here, run there, do this, do that, and then . . . crawling down the middle of Main Street on his hands and knees into the bargain.

He pricked his finger. He checked his urine. Then he put on his jogging suit and headed across Baxter Park.

Panting, he sat on the old stone wall beyond the Hope House site, at the highest elevation in Mitford. How long had it been since he overlooked this green valley, the Land of Counterpane?

Since he came into the world, he'd seen a lot of changes, but the sight that lay before him had changed little. Over there, a river gleaming in the sunlight. There, a curving road once hewn out for wagons. And there, scattered among the trees, church steeples poking up to be counted.

He heard a distant whistle and saw the little train moving through the valley. Train whistles, crowing roosters, the sound of rain on a tin roof—such simple music had nearly vanished in his life, and he missed it.

But then, life was full of valuable things that somehow managed to vanish.

He was startled to remember the green and sapphire marble that, at the age of twelve, he thought was the most beautiful object he had ever seen.

He had kept it in his pocket, showing it only to his mother, and of course to Tommy Noles, who crossed his heart three times and hoped to die if he ever mentioned its existence to another soul.

Showing it around would have been a violation, somehow. He kept it, instead, a private thing, never using it in a game. But he grew careless with it, he began to take it for granted, and where he had lost or misplaced it, he never knew.

He had grieved over that marble, in a way. Not over the thing itself, but over the loss of its private and remarkable beauty.

Hadn't Cynthia been like that to him? He had enjoyed the warmth and rarity of her nature, but he had never cherished her enough. Over and over, he had carelessly let her go, and only by the grace of God, she had not been taken from him altogether.

He remembered the times she had shut herself away from him, guarding her heart. The loss of her ravishing openness had left him cold as a stone, as if a great cloud had gone over the sun.

What if she were to shut herself away from him, once and for all? He stood up and paced beside the low stone wall, forgetting the scene in the valley.

He'd never understood much about his feelings toward Cynthia, but he knew and understood this:

He didn't want to keep teetering on the edge, afraid to step forward, terrified to turn back.

He felt the weight on his chest, the same weight he'd felt so often since she came into his life and he'd been unable to love her completely.

Perhaps he would always have such a weight; perhaps there was no true liberation in love. And certainly he could not ask her to accept him as he was—flawed and frightened, not knowing.

He turned and looked up and drew in his breath.

A glorious sunset was beginning to spread over the valley, and across the dome of heaven, stars were coming out. He had stood on this hill, wrapped in his selfish fears, while this wondrous thing was shaking the very air around him.

He felt tears on his face and realized the weight had flown off his heart. Every cloud over the valley was infused with a rose-colored light, and great streaks of lavender shot across the upland meadows.

Dear God! he thought if only Cynthia were here.

But Cynthia was there—in the little house just down the hill and through the park. She was there, not in New York or some far-flung corner, but there, sitting on her love seat, or feeding Violet, or putting her hair in those blasted curlers.

The recognition of her closeness to the very spot on which he stood was somehow breathtaking. He remembered the long, cold months of the dark house next door and the strained phone calls and the longing, and then she had come home at last.

The very sight of her had sent him reeling—yet once again, he had closed down his deepest feelings and managed to keep his distance from the only woman, the only human being he had ever known, who would eat the drumstick.

He was amazed to find that he was running; there was nothing but his beating heart and pounding feet. He felt only a great, burning haste to find her and see her face and let her know what he was only beginning to know and could no longer contain.

"There comes a time when there is no turning back," Walter had said.

He pounded on, feeling the motion of his legs and the breeze on his skin, and the hammering in his temples, feeling as if he might somehow implode, all of it combusting into a sharp, inner flame, a durable fire, a thousand hosannas.

Streaming with sweat, he ran past the cool arbors of Old Church Lane and across Baxter Park, desperate to see some sign of life in the little yellow house, to know she was there, waiting, and not gone away from him in her heart.

Her house was dark, but his own was aglow with light in every window, as if some wonderful thing might be happening.

He bounded through the hedge and into his yard and saw her standing at his door. She opened the door for him and held it wide as he came up the steps, and for one fleeting moment suspended in time, he sensed he had come at last to a destination he'd been running toward all his life.

Before the eleven o'clock service began, many of the Lord's Chapel congregation opened their pew bulletins and read the announcements.

There would be a regional Youth Choir performance in the church gardens on August 1. The Men's Prayer Breakfast would begin meeting at seven instead of seven-thirty on Thursdays, and would those who brought dishes to the bishop's brunch please collect their pans and platters from the kitchen.

Directly beneath the names of those who were bequeathing today's memorial flowers, they read the following:

I publish the banns of marriage between
Cynthia Clary Coppersmith
of the parish of the Chapel of Our Lord and Savior
and Father Timothy Andrew Kavanagh,
rector of this parish.
If any of you know just cause
why they may not be joined together in Holy Matrimony,
you are bidden to declare it.

Visit America's favorite small town—
one book at a time
Welcome to the next book,

These High, Green Hills

CHAPTER ONE

Through the Hedge

HE STOOD at the kitchen window and watched her coming through the hedge.

What was she lugging this time? It appeared to be a bowl and pitcher. Or was it a stack of books topped by a vase?

The rector took off his glasses, fogged them, and wiped them with his handkerchief. It was a bowl and pitcher, all right. How the little yellow house next door had contained all the stuff they'd recently muscled into the rectory was beyond him.

"For your dresser," she said, as he held the door open.

"Aha!"

The last thing he wanted was a bowl and pitcher on his dresser. The top of his dresser was his touchstone, his home base, his rock in a sea of change. That was where his car keys resided, his loose coins, his several crosses, his cuff links, his wallet, his checkbook, his school ring, and a small jar of buttons with a needle and thread.

It was also where he kept the mirror in which he occasionally examined the top of his head. Was his hair still thinning, or, by some mysterious and hoped-for reversal, growing in again?

"Cynthia," he said, going upstairs in the wake of his blond and shapely wife, "about that bowl and pitcher . . ."

"The color is wonderful. Look at the blues. It will relieve all your burgundy and brown!"

He did not want his burgundy and brown relieved.

He saw it coming.

Ever since their marriage on September seventh, she had plotted to lug that blasted armoire over for the rectory guest room.

The lugging over was one thing; it was the lugging back that he dreaded. They had, for example, lugged over an oriental rug that was stored in her basement. "Ten by twelve!" she announced, declaring it perfect for the bare floor of the rectory dining room.

After wrestling the table and chairs into the hall, they had unrolled the rug and unrolled the rug—to kingdom come. It might have gone up the walls on all four sides and met at the chandelier over the table.

"This is a rug for a school gym!" he said, wiping the pouring sweat from his brow.

She seemed dumbfounded that it didn't fit, and there they had gone, like pack mules, carting it through the hedge again.

The decision to keep and use both houses had been brilliant, of course. The light in the rectory would never equal that of her studio next door, where she was already set up with books and paints and drawing board. This meant his study could remain unchanged—his books could occupy the same shelves, and his vast store of sermon notebooks in the built-in cabinets could hold their place.

Marrying for the first time at the age of sixtysomething was change enough. It was a blessed luxury to live with so few rearrangements in the scheme of things, and life flowing on as usual. The only real change was the welcome sharing of bed and board.

Over breakfast one morning, he dared to discuss his interest in getting the furniture settled.

"Why can't we keep things as they were . . . in their existing state? It seemed to work. . . ."

"Yes, well, I like that our houses are separate, but I also want them to be the same—sort of an organic whole."

"No organic whole will come of dragging that armoire back and forth through the hedge. It looks like a herd of elephants has passed through there already."

"Oh, Timothy! Stop being stuffy! Your place needs fluffing up, and mine needs a bit more reserve. For example, your Chippendale chairs would give a certain sobriety to my dining table."

"Your dining table is the size of something in our nursery school. My chairs would look gigantic."

She said exactly what he thought she would say. "We could try it and see."

"Cynthia, trust me on this. My chairs will not look right with your table, and neither will that hand-painted magazine rack do anything for my armchair."

"Well, what was the use of getting married, then?"

"I beg your pardon?"

"I mean, if no one is going to change on either side, if we're both just going to be our regular, lifetime selves, what's the use?"

"I think I see what you're getting at. Will nothing do, then, but to cart those chairs to your house? And what about my own table? It will be bereft of chairs. I hardly see the point." He felt like jumping through the window and going at a dead run toward the state line.

"One thing at a time," she said happily. "It's all going to work out perfectly."

deAr stuart,

thanx for your note re: diocesan mtg, and thank martha for the invitation to put my feet under yr table afterward. however, I must leave for home at once, following the mtg—hope you'll understand.

while i'm at it, let me ask you:

why are women always moving things around? at Sunday School, jena iivey just had the youth group move the kindergarten bookcAses to a facing wall.

on the homefront, my househelp has moved a ladderback chair from my bedroom into the hall, never once considering that i hung my trousers over it for 14 years, and put my shoes on the seat so they could be found in an emergency.

last but certainly not least, if C could lift me in my armchair and put it by the window while i'm dozing, she would do it.

without a doubt, you have weightier things to consider, but tell me, how does one deal with this?

i hasten to add that ii've never been happier in my life. to tell the truth, i am confounded that such happiness—in such measure—even exists.

He signed the note, typed on his Royal manual, thankful that Stuart Cullen was not merely his bishop, but his closest personal friend since the halcyon days of seminary.

Fr Timothy Kavanaugh,
The Chapel of Our Lord and Savior
Old Church Lane, Mitford, N.C.

Dear Timothy:

In truth, it is disconcerting when one's househelp, SS supervisor, and wife do this sort of thing all at once.

My advice is: do not fight it. It will wear off.

In His peace,
Stuart

P.S. Martha would add a note, but she is busy moving my chest of drawers to the far side of our bedroom. As I am dealing with an urgent matter with the House of Bishops, I could not be browbeaten to help, and so she has maneuvered it, at last, onto an old bedspread, and I can hear her hauling the whole thing across the floor above me. This particular behavior had lain dormant in her for nearly seven years, and has suddenly broken forth again.

Perhaps it is something in the water.

He could see, early on, that beds were a problem that needed working out.

They had spent their wedding night in his bed at the rectory, where they had rolled down their respective sides and crashed together in the middle.

"What is this *trough* doing in your bed?" she asked.

"It's where I sleep," he said, feeling sheepish.

They had been squeezed together like sardines the livelong night, which he had profoundly enjoyed, but she had not. "Do you think this is what's meant by 'the two shall be one flesh'?" she murmured, her cheek smashed against his.

The following night, he trooped through the hedge with his pajamas and toothpaste in a grocery bag from The Local.

Her bed was a super-king-size, and the largest piece of furniture in her minuscule house.

He found it similar in breadth to the state of Texas, or possibly the province of Saskatchewan. Was that a herd of buffalo racing toward him in the distance, or a team of sled dogs? "Cynthia!" he shouted across the vast expanse, and waited for the echo.

They had ordered a new mattress for the rectory immediately after returning from their honeymoon in Stuart Cullen's summer house. There, on the rocky coast of Maine, they had spent time listening to the cry of the loons, holding hands, walking along the shore, and talking until the small hours of the morning. The sun turned her fair skin a pale toast color that he found fascinating and remarkable; and he watched three freckles emerge on the bridge of her nose, like stars coming out. Whatever simple thing they did together, they knew they were happier than ever before in their lives.

One evening, soon after the new mattress and springs were installed at the rectory, he found her sitting up in bed as he came out of the shower.

"I've had a wonderful idea, Timothy! A fireplace! Right over there where the dresser is."

"What would I do with my dresser?"

She looked at him as if he had toddled in from the church nursery. "Put it in the alcove, of course."

"Then I couldn't see out the window."

"But how much time do you spend staring out the alcove window?"

"When you were parading about with Andrew Gregory, a great deal of time." His face burned to admit it, but yes, he'd been jealous of the handsome antique dealer who had squired her around for several months.

She smiled, leaning her head to one side in that way he could barely resist. "A fireplace would be so romantic."

"Ummm."

"Why must I be the romantic in the family while you hold up the conservative, let's-don't-make-any-changes end?"

He sat down beside her. "How quickly you forget. When we were going steady, you said I was wildly romantic."

She laughed and kissed him on the cheek. "And I was right, of course. I'm sorry, old dearest."

He regretted being anyone's *old* dearest.

"Old dearest, yourself," he said grumpily. "I am, after all, only six years your senior."

"By the calendar," she said imperiously, referring, he supposed, to something decrepit in his overall attitude about life.

In any case, the fireplace issue did not come up again.

In truth, he had no words for his happiness. It grew deeper every day, like the digging of a well, and astounded him by its warmth and power. He seemed to lose control of his very face, which, according to the regulars at the Main Street Grill, displayed a foolish and perpetual grin.

"I love you . . . terribly," he said, struggling to express it.

"I love you terribly, also. It's scary. What if it should end?"

"Cynthia, good grief . . ."

"I know I shouldn't talk of endings when this is a blessed beginning."

"Don't then," he said, meaning it.

That Barnabas had so willingly given up the foot of his master's bed to sleep on a rug in the hall was a gesture he would never forget. Not only did his dog enjoy eighteenth-century poets and submit to his weekly bath without rancor, his dog was a gentleman.

The decisions were made, and both parties were in amicable accord.

They would sleep at the rectory primarily, and on occasion at the little yellow house. Though she would work there, as always, they would treat it much as a second home, using it for refreshment and private retreat.

He promised to have his sermon well under control each Saturday afternoon, with time to relax with her on Saturday evening, and he would continue to make breakfast on Sunday morning.

He showed her where his will was, and promised to have it rewritten. She confessed she didn't have a will, and promised to have one drawn up.

If they should ever, God forbid, have a misunderstanding, neither would dash off to the other house to sulk.

He would continue to have the cheerful and enterprising Puny Guthrie, née Bradshaw, clean the rectory three days a week, and Cynthia would use her services on a fourth day, next door.

They would go on with their separate checking accounts, make some mutual investments, counsel with the other about gift offerings, and never spend more than a certain fixed sum without the other's prior agreement.

He suggested fifty dollars as the fixed sum.

"One hundred!" she countered.

He was glad he had opened the bidding low. "One hundred, then, and I keep that old jacket you earmarked for the Bane and Blessing sale."

"Done!"

They laughed.

They shook hands.

They felt relieved.

Getting a marriage off on the right foot was no small matter.

"I reckon you're gone with th' wind," said Percy Mosely, who rang up his lunch tab at the Main Street Grill.

"How's that?" asked the rector.

"Married an' all, you'll not be comin' in regular, I take it." The proprietor of the Grill felt hurt and betrayed, he could tell.

"You've got that wrong, my friend."

"I do?" said Percy, brightening.

"I'll be coming in as regular as any man could. My wife has a working life of her own, being a well-known children's book writer and illustrator. She will not be trotting out hot vittles for my lunch every day—not by a long shot."

Percy looked suspicious. "What about breakfast?"

"That," said the rector, pocketing the change, "is another matter entirely."

Percy frowned. He liked his regulars to be married to his place of business.

He looked up from his chair in the study. Curlers, again.

"I have to wear curlers," she said, as if reading his mind. "I'm going to Lowell tomorrow."

"Lowell? Whatever for?"

"A school thing. They want me to read *Violet Goes to France* to their French class, and then do a program in the auditorium."

"Must you?"

"Must I what? Read *Violet Goes to France*? That's what they asked me to read."

"No, must you go to Lowell?"

"Well, yes."

He didn't want to say anything so idiotic, but he would miss her, as if she were being dropped off the end of the earth.

A long silence ensued as she curled up on the sofa and opened a magazine. He tried to read, but couldn't concentrate.

He hadn't once thought of her traveling with her work. Uneasy, he tried to let the news sink in. Lowell. Somebody there had been shot on the street in broad daylight.

And another thing—Lowell was a full hundred miles away. Did she have good brakes? Plenty of gas? When had she changed her oil?

"How's your oil?" he asked soberly.

She laughed as if he'd said something hilariously funny. Then she left the sofa and came to him and kissed him on the forehead. He was instantly zapped by the scent of wisteria, and went weak in the knees.

She looked him in the eye. "I love it when you talk like that. My oil is fine, how's yours?"

"Cynthia, Cynthia," he said, pulling her into his lap.

"Guess what?" said Emma, who was taping a photo of her new grandchild on the wall next to her desk.

This was his secretary's favorite game, and one he frankly despised. "What?"

"Guess!"

"Let's see. You're going to quit working for the Episcopalians and go to work for the Baptists." He wished.

"I wish," she said, rolling her eyes. "Try again."

"Blast, Emma, I hate this game."

"It's good for you, it exercises the brain."

"Esther Bolick's orange marmalade cake recipe is coming out in the *New York Times* food section."

"See? You don't even try. You're just talking to hear your head roar. One more guess."

"Give me a clue."

"It has to do with somebody being mad."

"The vestry. It must have something to do with the vestry."

"Wrong. Do you want me to tell you?"

"I beg you."

"Marge Wheeler left her best basket in the kitchen after the bishop's brunch last June, and Flora Lou Wilcox put it in the Bane and Blessing sale. Somebody walked off with it for a hundred dollars! Can you believe a hundred dollars for a basket with a loose handle? Marge is mad as a wet hen, she threatened to sue. But Flora Lou said she doesn't have a leg to stand on, since you're always running notices in the pew bulletin to pick up stuff left in th' kitchen."

"Ummm. Keep me posted."

"It's been four months since the brunch, so I can see Flora Lou's point that Marge should have picked it up and carted it home. Anyway, how could Flora Lou know it was handmade by Navajo Indians in 1920?" Emma sighed. "Of course, I can see Marge's point, too, can't you?"

He could, but he knew better than to intervene unless asked. His job, after all, was Sales and Service.

He rifled through the mail. A note from his cousin, Walter, and wife, Katherine, who had done the Ireland jaunt with him last year.

Dear Timothy,

Since Ireland is now old stomping grounds, why don't you and Cynthia plan to go with us next summer? Thought we'd plant the seed, so it can sprout over the winter.

We shall never forget how handsome you looked on the other side of the pulpit, standing with your beautiful bride. We love her as much as we love you, which is pecks and bushels, as ever,
Katherine

PS, Pls advise if canna and lily bulbs should be separated in the fall, I'm trying to find a hobby that has nothing to do with a pasta machine
Yrs, Walter

He rummaged toward the bottom of the mail stack.

Aha!

A note from Dooley Barlowe, in that fancy prep school for which his eldest parishioner, Miss Sadie Baxter, was shelling out serious bucks.

Hey. I don't like it here. That brain in a jar that we saw is from a medical school. I still don't know whose brain it is. When are you coming back? Bring Barnbus and granpaw and Cynthia. I culd probly use a twenty. Dooley

There! Not one 'ain't,' and complete sentences throughout. Hallelujah!

Who could have imagined that this boy, once barely able to speak the King's English, would end up in a prestigious school in Virginia?

He gazed at the note, shaking his head.

Scarcely more than two years ago, Dooley Barlowe had arrived at the church office, dirty, ragged, and barefoot, looking for a place to "take a dump." His grandfather had been too ill to care for the boy, who was abandoned by a runaway father and alcoholic mother, and Dooley had ended up at the rectory. By grace alone, he and Dooley had managed to live through those perilous times.

"I've been wondering," said Emma, peering at him over her glasses. "Is Cynthia goin' to pitch in and help around the church?"

"She's free to do as much or as little as she pleases."

"I've always thought a preacher's wife should pitch in." She set her mouth in that way he deplored. "If you ask me, which you didn't, the parish will expect it."

Yes, indeed, if he could get the Baptists to take Emma Newland off his hands, he would be a happy man.

"Miss Sadie," he said when she answered the phone at Fernbank, "I've had a note from Dooley. He says he doesn't like it in that fancy school."

"He can like it or lump it," she said pleasantly.

"When you're dishing out twenty thousand a year, you sure can be tough, Miss Sadie."

"If I couldn't be tough, Father, I wouldn't have twenty thousand to dish out."

"You'll be glad to know the headmaster says he's doing all right. A little slow on the uptake, but holding his own with those rich kids. In fact, they're not all rich. Several are there on scholarship, with no more assets than our Dooley."

"Good! You mark my words, he'll be better for it. And don't you go soft on me, Father, and let him talk you into bailing him out in the middle of the night."

"You can count on it," he said.

"Louella and I have nearly recovered from all the doings in June. . . ."

"June was a whopper, all right."

"We're no spring chickens, you know."

"You could have fooled me."

"I'll be ninety my next birthday, but Louella doesn't tell her age. Anyway, we're going to have you and Cynthia up for supper. What did we say we'd have, Louella?"

He heard Louella's mezzo voice boom from a corner of the big kitchen, "Fried chicken, mashed potatoes, gravy, an' cole slaw!"

"Man!" he exclaimed, quoting Dooley.

The announcement rolled on. "Hot biscuits, cooked apples, deviled eggs, bread and butter pickles . . ."

Good Lord! The flare-up from his diabetes would have him in the emergency room before the rest of them pushed back from the table.

"And what did we say for dessert?" Miss Sadie warbled into the distance.

"Homemade coconut cake!"

Ah, well, that was a full coma right there. Hardly any of his parishioners could remember he had this blasted disease. The information seemed to go in one ear and out the other.

"Ask Louella if she'll marry me," he said.

"Louella, the Father wants to know if you'll marry him."

"Tell 'im he got a short mem'ry, he done married Miss Cynthia."

He laughed, contented with the sweetness of this old friendship. "Just name the time," he said. "We'll be there."

Autumn drew on in the mountains.

Here, it set red maples on fire; there, it turned oaks russet and yellow. Fat persimmons became the color of melted gold, waiting for frost to turn their bitter flesh to honey. Sassafras, dogwoods, poplars, redbud—all were torched by autumn's brazen fire, displaying their colorful tapestry along every ridge and hogback, in every cove and gorge.

The line of maples that marched by First Baptist to Winnie Ivey's cottage on Little Mitford Creek was fully ablaze by the eleventh of October.

"The best ever!" said several villagers, who ran with their cameras to document the show.

The local newspaper editor, J. C. Hogan, shot an extravagant total of six rolls of film. For the first time since the nation's bicentennial, readers saw a four-color photograph on the front page of the *Mitford Muse.*

Everywhere, the pace was quickened by the dazzling light that now slanted from the direction of Gabriel Mountain, and the sounds of football practice in the schoolyard.

Avis Packard put a banner over the green awning of The Local: *Fresh Valley Hams Now, Collards Coming.*

Dora Pugh laid on a new window at the hardware store featuring leaf rakes, bicycle pumps, live rabbits, and iron skillets. "What's th' theme of your window?" someone asked. "Life," replied Dora.

The library introduced its fall reading program and invited the author of the *Violet* books to talk about where she got her ideas. "I have no idea where I get my ideas," she told Avette Harris, the librarian. "They just come." "Well, then," said Avette, "do you have any ideas for another topic?"

The village churches agreed to have this year's All-Church Thanksgiving Feast with the Episcopalians, and to get their youth choirs together for a Christmas performance at First Presbyterian.

At Lord's Chapel, the arrangements on the altar became gourds and pumpkins, accented by branches of the fiery red maple. At this time of year, the rector himself liked doing the floral offerings. He admitted it was a favorite season, and his preaching, someone remarked, grew as electrified as the sharp, clean air.

"Take them," he said one Sunday morning, lifting the cup and the Host toward the people, "in remembrance that Christ died for you, and feed on Him in your hearts by faith, with thanksgiving."

Giving his own wife the Host was an act that might never cease to move and amaze him. More than sixty years a bachelor, and now this—seeing her face looking up expectantly, and feeling the warmth of her hand as he placed the bread in her palm. "The body of our Lord Jesus Christ, which was given for you, Cynthia."

He couldn't help but see the patch of colored light that fell on her hair through the stained-glass window by the rail, as if she were being appointed to something divine. Surely there could be no divinity in having to live the rest of her life with him, with his set-in-concrete ways and infernal diabetes.

They walked home together after church, hand in hand, his sermon notebook tucked under his arm. He felt as free as a schoolboy, as light as air. How could he ever have earned God's love, and hers into the bargain?

The point was, he couldn't. It was all grace, and grace alone.

He was sitting in his armchair by the fireplace, reading the newspaper. Barnabas ambled in from the kitchen and sprawled at his feet.

Cynthia, barefoot and in her favorite robe, sat on the sofa and scribbled in a notebook. One of his antiquated towels was wrapped around her damp hair. He still couldn't get over the sight of her on his sofa, looking as comfortable as if she lived here—which, he was often amazed to realize, she did.

"Wasn't it wonderful?" she asked.

"Wasn't what wonderful?"

"Our wedding."

"It was!" She brought the subject up fairly often, and he realized he'd run out of anything new to say about it.

"I love thinking about it," she said, plumping up a needlepoint pillow and putting it behind her head. "A tuxedo and a tab collar are a terrific combination."

"No kidding?" He would remember that.

"I think you should dress that way again at the first possible opportunity."

He laughed. "It doesn't take much for you."

"That's true, dearest, except in the area of my new husband. There, it took quite a lot."

He felt that ridiculous, uncontrollable grin spreading across his face.

"It was a wonderful idea to ask Dooley to sing. He was absolutely masterful. And thank goodness for Ray Cunningham's video camera. I love the frames of you and Stuart in his bishop's regalia, standing in the churchyard . . . and the part where Miss Sadie and Preacher Greer are laughing together."

"Another case of two hearts beating as one."

"Would you like to see it again? I'll make popcorn."

"Maybe in a day or two." Hadn't they watched it only last week?

"It was very sweet and charming, the way you insisted on baking a ham for our reception."

"I always bake a ham for wedding receptions at Lord's Chapel," he said. "I'm stuck in that mode."

"Tell me something . . . ?"

"Anything!" Would he really tell her anything?

"How did you unstick your mode long enough to propose to me? What happened?"

"I realized . . . that is, I . . ." He paused thoughtfully and rubbed his chin. "To tell the truth, I couldn't help myself."

"Ummm," she said, smiling at him across the room. "You know I love that you knelt on one knee."

"Actually, I was prepared to go down on both knees. As soon as I dropped to one, however, you saw what was coming, and seemed so happy about it, I didn't bother to advance to the full kneel."

She laughed uproariously, and held her arms out to him. "Please come over here, dearest. You're so far away over there!"

The evening news was just coming on when the phone rang. It was his doctor and friend, Hoppy Harper, calling from the hospital.

"How fast can you get here?"

"Well . . ."

"I'll explain later. Just get here."

He was out the door in thirty seconds.

Now available from Penguin, the final novel in the beloved Mitford series

Light from Heaven

FATHER TIMOTHY KAVANAGH has never been asked to do the impossible—until now. The retired Episcopal priest takes on the revival of a mountain church that's been closed for forty years. Meanwhile, in Mitford, he's sent on a hunt for hidden treasure, and two beloved friends are called to come up higher. As he meets each new challenge, Father Tim is reminded anew of the most important lesson of all: *It's never too late.*

"Karon saved the best for last." —*The Baltimore Sun*

Includes an excerpt from Jan Karon's next novel, *Home to Holly Springs*, coming from Viking in the fall of 2007

ISBN 0-14-303770-6

For more information about Jan and her books visit www.mitfordbooks.com

NOW AVAILABLE *from* VIKING

The Mitford Bedside Companion

A treasury of favorite Mitford moments, author reflections on the bestselling series, favorite scenes, jokes, prayers, trivia, casts of characters, a crossword puzzle, and lots of personal essays by the author.

0-670-03785-0

NOW AVAILABLE *from* VIKING CHILDREN'S BOOKS

Violet Comes to Stay

Presented by Jan Karon
Story by Melanie Cecka
Illustrated by Emily Arnold McCully

The first in a series of storybooks inspired by Father Tim's wife, Cynthia Coppersmith—with beautiful illustrations by an award-winning artist. Karon searched for three years to find a storytelling voice and art style authentic to Cynthia Coppersmith. She was personally involved in every step of the creation of this book.

0-670-06073-9

Also by Jan Karon from Puffin and Viking Children's Books

Jeremy: The Tale of an Honest Bunny
0-670-88104-X (hc); 0-14-250004-6 (pb)

The Trellis and the Seed
0-670-89289-0 (hc); 0-14-240317-2 (pb)

Miss Fannie's Hat
0-14-056812-3

PENGUIN BOOKS

AT HOME IN MITFORD

Jan Karon writes "to give readers an extended family, and to applaud the extraordinary beauty of ordinary lives." She is the author of nine Mitford novels, *At Home in Mitford*; *A Light in the Window*; *These High, Green Hills*; *Out to Canaan*; *A New Song*; *A Common Life*; *In This Mountain*; *Shepherds Abiding*; and *Light from Heaven*, all available from Penguin. She is also the author of *The Mitford Bedside Companion*; *Jan Karon's Mitford Cookbook & Kitchen Reader*; *A Continual Feast: Words of Comfort and Celebration, Collected by Father Tim*; *Patches of Godlight: Father Tim's Favorite Quotes*; *The Mitford Snowmen: A Christmas Story*; *Esther's Gift*; and *The Trellis and the Seed*. Her children's books include *Miss Fannie's Hat*; *Jeremy: The Tale of an Honest Bunny*; and *Violet Comes to Stay*. Coming from Viking in fall 2007 is the first Father Tim Novel, *Home to Holly Springs*.

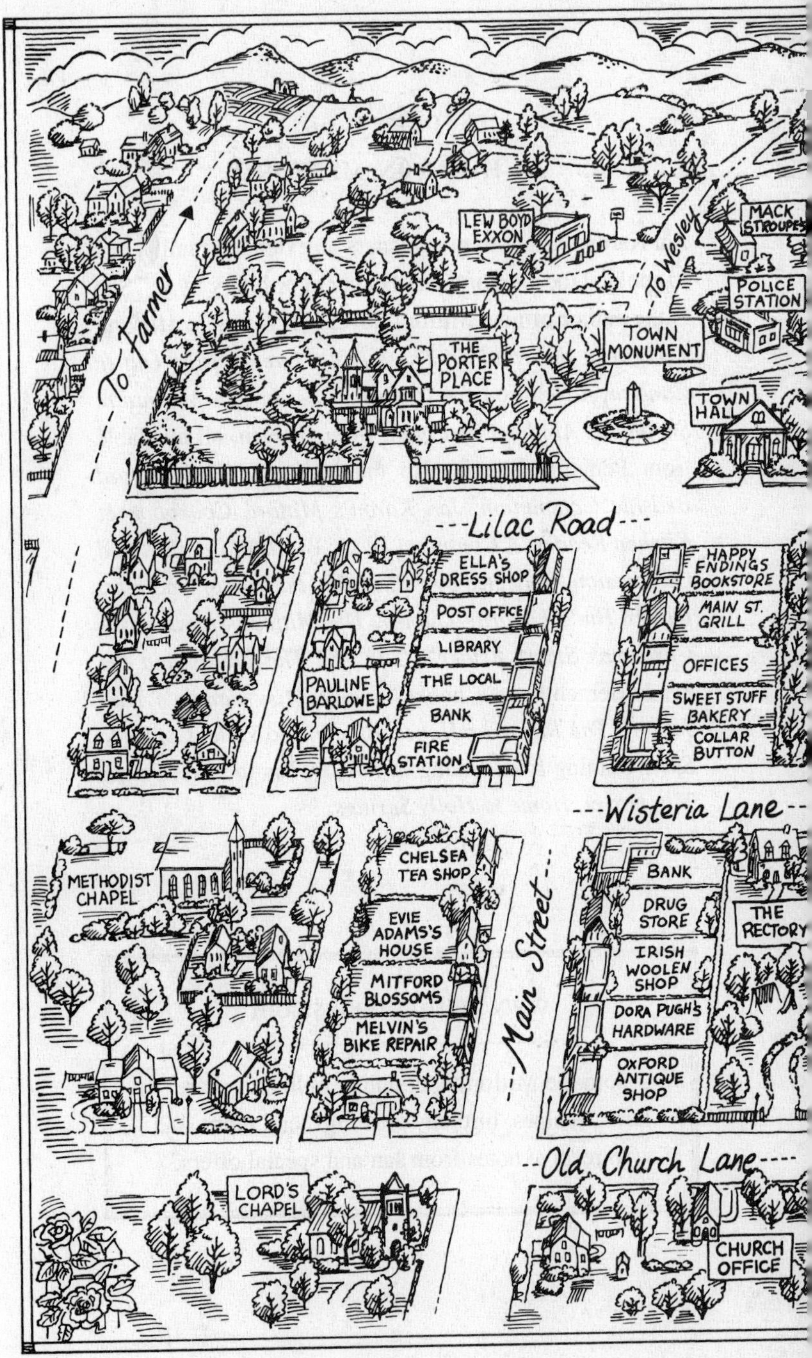

To Farmer
LEW BOYD EXXON
To Wesley
MACK STROUPE'S
POLICE STATION
TOWN MONUMENT
THE PORTER PLACE
TOWN HALL
Lilac Road
ELLA'S DRESS SHOP
POST OFFICE
LIBRARY
THE LOCAL
BANK
FIRE STATION
PAULINE BARLOWE
HAPPY ENDINGS BOOKSTORE
MAIN ST. GRILL
OFFICES
SWEET STUFF BAKERY
COLLAR BUTTON
Wisteria Lane
METHODIST CHAPEL
CHELSEA TEA SHOP
EVIE ADAMS'S HOUSE
MITFORD BLOSSOMS
MELVIN'S BIKE REPAIR
Main Street
BANK
DRUG STORE
IRISH WOOLEN SHOP
DORA PUGH'S HARDWARE
OXFORD ANTIQUE SHOP
THE RECTORY
Old Church Lane
LORD'S CHAPEL
CHURCH OFFICE

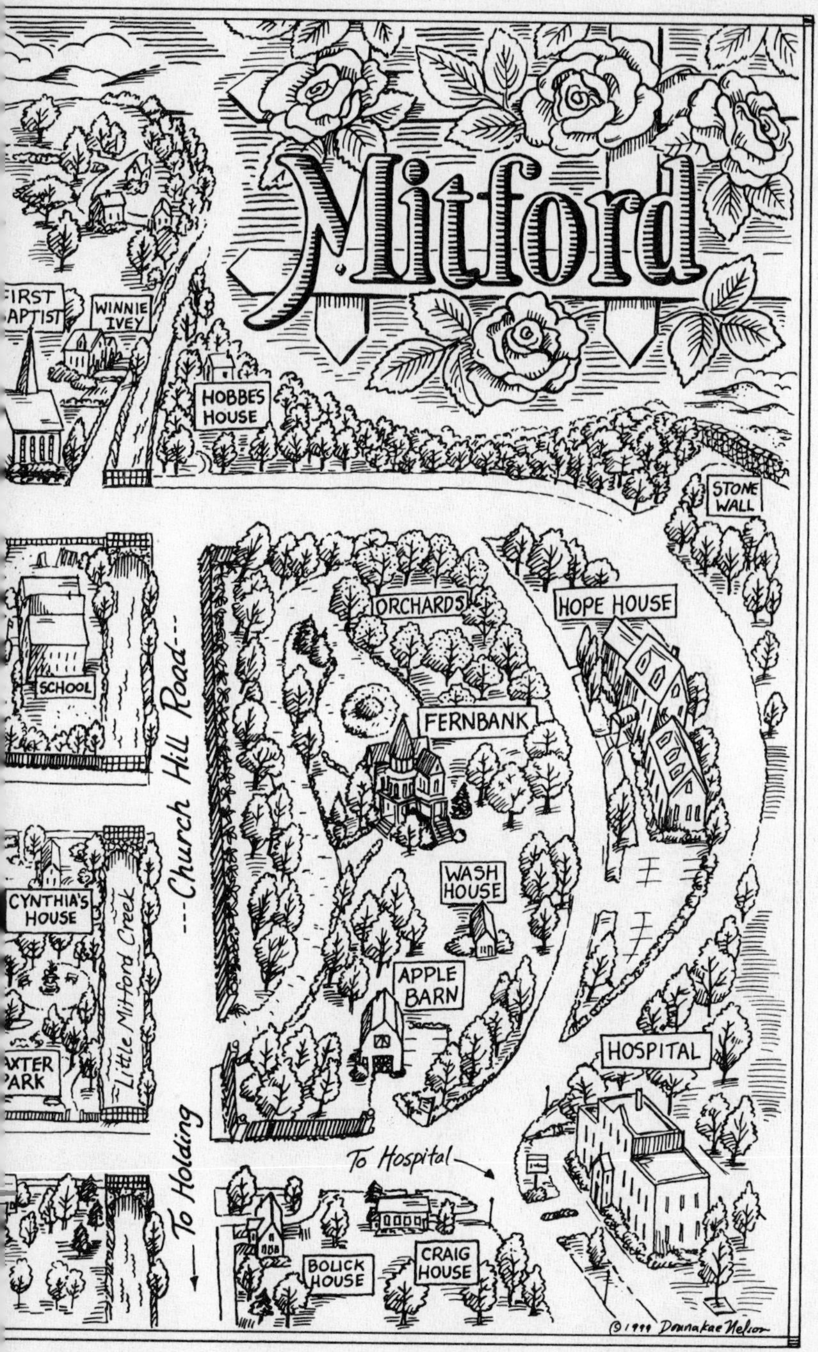

Mitford
FIRST BAPTIST
WINNIE IVEY
HOBBES HOUSE
STONE WALL
ORCHARDS
HOPE HOUSE
SCHOOL
Church Hill Road
FERNBANK
WASH HOUSE
CYNTHIA'S HOUSE
Little Mitford Creek
APPLE BARN
BAXTER PARK
HOSPITAL
To Holding
To Hospital
BOLICK HOUSE
CRAIG HOUSE
©1999 Donnakae Nelson

Other Mitford Books by Jan Karon

A LIGHT IN THE WINDOW
THESE HIGH, GREEN HILLS
OUT TO CANAAN
A NEW SONG
A COMMON LIFE
IN THIS MOUNTAIN
PATCHES OF GODLIGHT

Children's Books by Jan Karon

MISS FANNIE'S HAT
JEREMY: THE TALE OF AN HONEST BUNNY

The Mitford Years

At Home in Mitford

JAN KARON

PENGUIN BOOKS

PENGUIN BOOKS
Published by the Penguin Group
Penguin Group (USA) Inc., 375 Hudson Street, New York, New York 10014, U.S.A.
Penguin Group (Canada), 90 Eglinton Avenue East, Suite 700, Toronto,
Ontario, Canada M4P 2Y3 (a division of Pearson Penguin Canada Inc.)
Penguin Books Ltd, 80 Strand, London WC2R 0RL, England
Penguin Ireland, 25 St Stephen's Green, Dublin 2, Ireland (a division of Penguin Books Ltd)
Penguin Group (Australia), 250 Camberwell Road, Camberwell,
Victoria 3124, Australia (a division of Pearson Australia Group Pty Ltd)
Penguin Books India Pvt Ltd, 11 Community Centre, Panchsheel Park, New Delhi – 110 017, India
Penguin Group (NZ), cnr Airborne and Rosedale Roads,
Albany, Auckland 1310, New Zealand (a division of Pearson New Zealand Ltd)
Penguin Books (South Africa) (Pty) Ltd, 24 Sturdee Avenue,
Rosebank, Johannesburg 2196, South Africa

Penguin Books Ltd, Registered Offices: 80 Strand, London WC2R 0RL, England

First published in the United States of America by Lion Publishing, 1994
Published in Penguin Books 1996

51 53 55 54 52

PUBLISHER'S NOTE

This is a work of fiction. Names, characters, places, and incidents either are the product of the author's imagination or are used fictitiously, and any resemblance to actual persons, living or dead, events, or locales is entirely coincidental.

LIBRARY OF CONGRESS CATALOGING IN PUBLICATION DATA
Karon, Jan, 1937–
At home in Mitford/Jan Karon.
p. cm.—(The Mitford years)
ISBN 0 14 02.5448 X (pbk.)
1. City and town life—United States—Fiction. I. Title. II. Series: Karon, Jan, 1937– Mitford years.
PS3561.A678A92 1996
813′.54—dc20 95-35716

Printed in the United States of America
Set in Berkeley Old Style Book
Designed by Helen Lannis
Illustrations by Donna Kae Nelson

For Candace Freeland,
my daughter and friend

Acknowledgments

Warm thanks to Father James Harris, who inspired and encouraged me; to Jerry Burns, who published this book serially in the best of the small-town newspapers, the *Blowing Rocket;* to my doctor, Charles (Bunky) Davant, III, who also doctors all of Mitford; to Bonnie Setzer, Mary Richardson, and Helen Vennard for their support; to my daughter, who laughed in all the right places; to Mary Tarr and the ladies of our volunteer library; to our local police department; and to everyone who buys this book about a small town that does more than exist in the imagination—it really is out there.

Contents

At Home in Mitford

CHAPTER ONE

Barnabas

He left the coffee-scented warmth of the Main Street Grill and stood for a moment under the green awning.

The honest cold of an early mountain spring stung him sharply.

He often noted the minor miracle of passing through a door into a completely different world, with different smells and attractions. It helped to be aware of the little things in life, he told himself, and he often exhorted his congregation to do the same.

As he headed toward the church office two blocks away, he was delighted to discover that he wasn't walking, at all. He was ambling.

It was a pleasure he seldom allowed himself. After all, it might appear that he had nothing else to do, when in truth he always had something to do.

He decided to surrender himself to the stolen joy of it, as some might eat half a box of chocolates at one sitting, without remorse.

He arrived at the office, uttering the prayer he had offered at its door every morning for twelve years: "Father, make me a blessing to someone today, through Christ our Lord. Amen."

As he took the key from his pocket, he felt something warm and disgustingly wet on his hand.

He looked down into the face of a large, black, mud-caked dog, whose tail began to beat wildly against his pant leg.

"Good grief!" he said, wiping his hand on his windbreaker.

At that, the dog leaped up and licked his face, sending a shower of saliva into his right ear.

"Get away! Be gone!" he shouted. He tried to protect the notebook he was carrying, but the dog gave it a proper licking before he could stuff it in his jacket, then tried to snatch it from him.

He thought of running, but if anyone saw him fleeing before a shaggy, mud-caked dog, everybody in town would know it within the half hour.

"Down!" he commanded sharply, at which the dog leaped up and gave his chin a bath.

He tried to fend the animal off with his elbow, while inserting the key in the office door. If he were a cussing man, he reasoned, this would offer a premier opportunity to indulge himself.

" 'Let no corrupt communication proceed out of your mouth,' " he quoted in a loud voice from Ephesians, " 'but that which is good to the use of edifying . . .' " Suddenly, the dog sat down and looked at his prey with fond admiration.

"Well, now," he said irritably, wiping the notebook on his sleeve. "I hope you've got that nonsense out of your system." At this, the dog leaped up, stood on its hind legs, and put its vast paws on the rector's shoulders.

"Father Tim! Father Tim!" It was his part-time secretary, Emma Garrett.

He stood helpless, his glasses fogged with a typhoon of moist exhalations.

Whop! Emma laid a blow to the dog's head with her pocketbook. Then, *blam,* she hit him again on the rear flank.

"And don't come back!" she shouted, as the yelping dog fled into a hedge of rhododendron and disappeared.

Emma gave him her handkerchief, which was heavily scented with My Sin. "That wasn't a dog," she said with disgust, "that was a Buick!"

In the office, he went directly to the minuscule bathroom and washed his face and hands. Emma called through the door. "I'll have your coffee ready in a jiffy!"

"Blast! Make it a double!" he replied, combing the hairs that remained on the top of his head.

As he walked out of the bathroom, he looked at his secretary for the first time that morning. That he recognized her at all was remarkable. For Emma Garrett, full of the promise of spring, had dyed her gray hair red.

"Emma!" he said, astounded. "Is that you?"

"This," she said with feeling, "is the most me you've seen in years. That ol' gray-headed stuff is not me at all!" She turned her head both ways, so he could get the full effect.

He sighed with a mixture of delight and despair. He had hoped this might be an ordinary morning.

Harold Newland had brought the mail earlier than usual and, since Emma had gone to the bank, put it in a neat pile on the rector's desk. At the bottom of the pile, in reverse order of its importance, was the letter from the bishop.

He had asked the bishop to take his time, not to hurry his reply, and he had not. In fact, it had been a full two months since his own letter had been so thoughtfully written and posted.

He stared at the ivory envelope. There was no return address; this was not official stationery. If one did not know that distinctive, looping handwriting so well, one would never guess the sender.

He dared not open it here. No, he wanted complete privacy in which to read it. Would it be in the bishop's own hand? If so, he would then have a precise sense of how seriously his remarks had been taken.

Years ago, his seminary friend had been moved by the Apostle Paul's comment that the letter he wrote to the Galatians was "by my own hand," as if it were an act of great personal sacrifice. As a young seminarian, Stuart Cullen had taken that to heart. Since his installation as bishop, he was known to personally pen all the letters of real importance to his diocese. How did he have the time, people inevitably wondered. Well, that was the whole point. He didn't. Which, of course, made his handwritten and reflective letters a treasure to anyone who received an example.

No, he would not open it, if only to see whether a secretary had typed it. He would wait until evening and the solitude of the rectory, and the peace of his newly dug garden.

After an early supper, he sat on the stone bench that was half-covered with a fine moss, under the overhanging branches of the rhododendron.

He read the letter, which was, indeed, handwritten in the large, exuberant style that demanded space to gallop across the page.

Dearest Timothy:

It is a good evening to sit in this pleasant room and write a letter. Correspondence is, for me, a luxury which stirs my sensibilities, especially if it be with an old friend.

I believe you'd enjoy the way Martha refurbished my disorderly bookshelves, and put this study into working condition. She has even had your favorite rug repaired, so that when you come again, you won't stumble over the torn patch and go reeling headfirst into the armchair!

You ask if I have ever faced such a thing as you are currently facing. My friend, exhaustion and fatigue are a committed priest's steady companions, and there is no way around it. It is a problem of epidemic proportions, and I ask you to trust that you aren't alone. Sometimes, hidden away in a small parish as you are now—and as I certainly have been—one feels that the things which press in are pointed directly at one's self.

I can assure you this is not the case.

An old friend who was a pastor in Atlanta said this: "I did not have a crisis of faith, but of emotion and energy. It's almost impossible for leaders of a congregation to accept that their pastor needs pastoring. I became beat up, burned out, angry and depressed."

The tone of your letter—and I presume you have been forthright with me, as always—does not indicate depression or anger, thanks be to God. But I'm concerned with you for what might follow if this goes unattended.

A few things to think on: Keep a journal and let off some steam. If that doesn't fit with your affinities, find yourself a godly counselor and let me know the cost, for the diocese will willingly cover it.

Your mother, I believe, left a considerable sum, and perhaps you need to use a bit of it for yourself, for something other than the children's hospital you've been so faithful to all these years. I know you well enough to believe I don't have to exhort you to prayer. You always had enormous stamina in this area, and if that has changed, well, then, Timothy, make it right again.

You may not know that you are one of the strongest, most durable links in this diocesan chain. You are important to me, and firsthand inquiry informs me that you are vitally important to your flock. Do not doubt it.

Martha has come in to tell me it is bedtime. I cannot express how wonderful it is to be sometimes told, rather than always doing the telling!

I really never dreamed I would marry, and no one was more surprised than myself when, at the age of 49, I was ready and willing to take yet another lifetime vow. Others found this extraordinary, but I found it the most natural thing on earth.

I cannot exhort you to go out and marry, Timothy, but I will say that these ten years with Martha have brought an ease to the stress which was plundering my own soul. I can't say that the pace is easier—if anything, it has accelerated—but I find the ability to bear it greatly increased.

As I recall from our days in seminary, you and I were much alike when it came to women. You were fairly smitten with Peggy Cramer, but when your feelings for her began to interfere with your calling, you broke the engagement. Even today, I feel confident in having advised you to do it. Yet I wonder—have you ever entirely reconciled this with your heart?

There she is again, my friend. And believe me, my wife does not enjoy reminding me twice. That she monitors my energy is a good thing. Otherwise, I would spill it all for Him and have nothing left with which to get out of bed in the mornings.

I exhort you to do the monitoring you so sorely need, and hang in there. Give it a year! Or, at most, give it two. If you simply cannot go the distance, Father DeWilde will be coming available in the fall and would be my choice for Lord's Chapel.

Timothy, if you have problems with this one-sided conversation, you know how to ring me up. Please know that you are daily in my prayers.

Ever in His peace,
Stuart

As the light faded, the chill of the stone bench began to creep into his bones.

He stood up and looked around the greening yard, as if seeing it for the first time. There was a certain poignancy in the shadows moving across the rose bed he had double-dug twice, and the borders he'd planted, and the dogwood he had put in himself. He felt at home in Mitford, completely and absolutely. The last thing he wanted to do was leave. Yet, the first thing he wanted to do was make a difference, be productive—and there was the rub.

Nearly every weekday at 6:45 a.m., he made calls at the hospital, then had breakfast at the Grill and walked to the church office. For the rest of the morning, he studied, wrote letters, made telephone calls, and administrated his parish of nearly two hundred.

At noon, he walked to the Grill for lunch or, if it was raining, snowing or sleeting, ate half of Emma's usual egg salad sandwich and shared her Little Debbies.

In the afternoon until four he worked on his sermon, counseled, and generally tidied up the affairs of his calling. "A place for everything and everything in its place," he was known to quote from Mrs. Beeton.

At times, he was saddened by never having married and raised a family of his own. But, he had to admit, being a bachelor left him far more time for his parish family.

On Thursday afternoon, he was going home with a basket that a member of the Altar Guild had delivered, containing home-canned green beans, a jar of pickle relish, and a loaf of banana bread. He put his notebook on top, and covered the whole lot with a draft of Sunday's church bulletin.

"Red Riding Hood," he mused, as he took the key from the peg.

He stepped out and locked the door behind him, dropping the heavy key into his pocket. Then he turned around and stared in disbelief.

Coming toward him at an alarming rate of speed was something he hoped he'd never lay eyes on again.

It was the great leaping, licking, mud-caked dog.

For several days, the dog seemed to appear out of nowhere. Once, when he was walking down Old Church Lane to meet the plumber at Lord's Chapel. Again, when he was planting a border of lavender along the walkway to the rectory. Yet again, when he went to The Local to get milk and sweet potatoes. And on two occasions, as he was leaving the Grill.

The meeting in the church lane had been fairly uneventful. After an enthusiastic hand licking and a vigorous leap that had nearly knocked him to the ground, he'd been able to repulse his attacker with a loud recitation of his laundry list. By the time he got to socks—three pairs white, four pairs black, one pair blue—the dog had wandered into the cemetery at the rear of the churchyard, and disappeared.

The meeting at the lavender bed, however, had been another matter.

He was kneeling in sober concentration on a flagstone, when suddenly he felt two large paws on his shoulders. Instantly, such a drenching bath was administered to his left ear that he nearly fainted with surprise.

"Good Lord!" shouted the rector, who had gone crashing into a flat of seedlings. He had not, however, been thrown clear of his trowel.

He turned around and raised it, as if to strike a fearsome blow, and was surprised to see the dog stand on its hind legs with a look of happy expectation.

Spurred by some odd impulse, he threw the trowel as far as he could. The excited creature bounded after it, giving forth a joyful chorus of barks, and returned to drop the trowel at the rector's feet.

Feeling speechless over the whole incident, he threw the trowel again, and watched the dog fetch it back. He was amazed that he was able to stand there and continue such a foolish thing for twenty minutes. Actually, he realized, he hadn't known what else to do.

At the Grill one morning, he asked around. "Has anybody ever seen that big, black dog before?"

"You mean th' one that's taken a likin' to you?" asked Percy Mosely. "We never laid eyes on 'im 'til a week or two ago. A couple of times, he come by here like a freight train. But anybody tries to catch 'im, he's gone, slick as grease."

"We tried to feed 'im," said Percy's wife, Velma, "but he won't eat Percy's cookin'."

"Ha, ha," said Percy, who was working six orders of hash browns.

"You ought to lay hold of 'im sometime when he's chasin' you, and call th' animal shelter," suggested Velma.

"In the first place," said Father Tim, "it is impossible to lay hold of that particular dog. And in the second place, I have no intention of sending him to what could be his final doom." In the third place, he thought, that dog never chased me. I always stood my ground!

"Well, he's sitting out there waiting for you, right now," observed Hessie Mayhew, who had stopped in on her way to the library, with an armful of overdue books.

The rector raised up from his seat in the booth and looked through the front window. Yes, indeed. He saw the creature, staring soulfully into the Grill.

He couldn't help thinking that it was oddly flattering to have someone waiting for him, even if it was a dog. Emma had said for years that he needed a dog or a cat, or even a bird. But no, not once had he ever considered such a thing.

"We ought to call th' shelter," insisted Percy, who thought that a little action would brighten the morning. "They'll be on 'im before you get down t' your office."

The rector discreetly put a piece of buttered toast in a napkin and slipped it into his pocket. "Let's wait on that, Percy," he said, walking to the door.

He stood there for a moment, composing himself. Then he opened the door and stepped out to the sidewalk.

The village of Mitford was set snugly into what would be called, in the west, a hanging valley. That is, the mountains rose steeply on either side, and then sloped into a hollow between the ridges, rather like a cake that falls in the middle from too much opening of the oven door.

According to a walking parishioner of Lord's Chapel, Mitford's business district was precisely 342 paces from one end to the other.

At the north end, Main Street climbed a slight incline, and circled a town green that was bordered by a hedge of hemlocks and anchored in the center by a World War II memorial. The green also contained four benches facing the memorial and, in the spring, a showy bed of pansies, which one faction claimed was the official town flower.

Directly to the left of the green was the town hall, and next to that, the First Baptist Church. Set into the center of its own display of shrubs and flowers on the front bank was a wayside pulpit permanently bearing the Scripture verse John 3:16, which the members long ago had agreed was the pivotal message of their faith.

To the right of the green, facing Lilac Road, was the once-imposing home of Miss Rose and Uncle Billy Watson, whose overgrown yard currently contained two chrome dinette chairs which they used while watching traffic circle the monument.

Visitors who walked the two-block stretch of the main business district were always surprised to find the shops spaced so far apart, owing to garden plots that flourished between the buildings. In the loamy, neatly edged beds were wooden signs:

Garden Courtesy of Joe's Barber Shop, Upstairs to Right

Take Time to Smell the Roses, Courtesy Oxford Antiques

A Reader's Garden, Courtesy Happy Endings Bookstore

"Mitford," observed a travel feature by a prominent newspaper, "is a village delightfully out of step with contemporary America. Here, where streets are named for flowers, and villagers can seek the shade of a dozen fragrant rose arbors, spring finds most of the citizenry, including merchants, making gardens.

". . . and while Mitford's turn-of-the-century charm and beauty attract visitors like bees to honeysuckle, the town makes a conscious effort to discourage serious tourism.

" 'We want people to come and visit,' says Mayor Esther Cunningham, 'but we're not real interested in having them stick around. The college town of Wesley, just fifteen miles away, is perfect for that. They've got the inns and guest houses and all. Mitford would simply like to be the pause that refreshes.' "

Going south on Main Street to Wisteria Lane were the post office, the library, a bank, the bookstore, Winnie Ivey's Sweet Stuff Bakery, and a new shop for men's furnishings.

There was also a grocery store, so well-known for its fresh poultry and produce from local sources that most people simply called it The Local. For thirty-six years, The Local had provided chickens, rabbits, sausage, hams, butter, cakes, pies, free-range eggs, jams, and jellies from a farming community in the valley, along with vegetables and berries in season. In summer, produce bins on the sidewalk under the green awnings were filled each day with Silver Queen corn in the shuck. And in July, pails of fat blackberries were displayed in the cooler case.

To the left of Main Street, Wisteria Lane meandered past the Episcopal rectory, whose back door looked upon the green seclusion of Baxter Park, and then climbed the hill to the Presbyterians.

To the right of Main, Wisteria led only to Wesley Chapel, a tiny Methodist church that stood along the creek bank in a grove of pink laurel and was known for the sweetness of its pealing bells.

The second and only other business block of Main Street was lined with a hardware store, a tea shop, a florist, an Irish woolen shop, and an antique shop, with gardens in between.

Next, Main was crossed by Old Church Lane, rising steeply on the left to Church Hill Drive, where the ruined foundation of Mitford's first Episcopal church stood in the tall grass of the upland meadow near Miss Sadie Baxter's Fernbank.

At the opposite end of the lane was Lord's Chapel, which stood between two vacant lots. After passing the church, which was noted for its fine Norman tower and showy gardens, the lane narrowed to a few comfortable houses on the bank of a rushing stream, where Indian Pipes were said to grow in profusion.

As the streets and lanes gave way to countryside and sloped toward the deeper valley, the rolling farmland began. Here, pastures were stocked with Herefords and Guernseys; lakes were filled with trout and brim; barnyards succored chattering guineas. And everywhere, in town or out, was the rich, black loam that made the earthworm's toil one of unending satisfaction.

On rare occasions, and for no special reason he could think of, he imagined he was sitting by the fire in the study, in the company of a companionable wife.

He would be reading, and she would be sitting across from him in a wing chair.

In this idyll, he could not see her face, but he knew it had a girlish sweetness, and she was always knitting. Knitting, he thought, was a comfort to the soul. It was regular. It was repetitious. And, in the end, it amounted to something.

In this dream, there was always a delectable surprise on the table next to his chair, and nearly always it was a piece of pie. In his bachelor's heart of hearts, he loved pie with an intensity that alarmed him. Yet, when he was offered seconds, he usually refused. "Wouldn't you like another piece of this nice coconut pie, Father?" he might be asked. "No, I don't believe I'd care for any more," he'd say. An outright lie!

In this imaginary fireside setting, he would not talk much, he thought. But now and then, he might speak of church matters, read Blake or Wordsworth aloud, and try a sermon outline on his companion.

That would be a luxury far greater than any homemade sweet—to have someone listen to his outline and nod encouragement or, even, for heaven's sake, disagree.

Sometimes he shared an outline or argument with his close friend

Hal Owen, the country vet. But in the main, he found that a man must hammer out his theology alone.

He was musing on this one evening, shortly after he'd been to the garage to give the black dog its supper, when he was surprised by a loud, groaning yawn from the vicinity of his own stockinged feet.

He was astounded to see the maverick dog lying next to his chair, gazing up at him.

"Blast!" he exclaimed. "I must have left the garage door open."

The usually gregarious dog not only appeared thoughtfully serene, but looked at him with an air of earnest understanding. How odd that the brown eyes of his companion were not unlike those of an old church warden he'd known as a young priest.

Feeling encouraged, he picked up a volume of Wordsworth from the table by his elbow.

" 'It is a beauteous evening, calm and free,' " he read aloud.

The holy time is quiet as a nun
Breathless with adoration; the broad sun
Is sinking down in its tranquillity;
The gentleness of heaven broods o'er the sea:
Listen! the mighty Being is awake,
And doth with his eternal motion make
A sound like thunder, everlastingly.

The dog appeared to listen with deep interest. And when the rector finished reading the poem Wordsworth wrote for his young daughter, he moved happily along to an essay.

" 'Life and the world,' " it began without pretension, " 'are astonishing things.' "

"No doubt about it," he muttered, as the dog moved closer to his feet.

Barnabas! he thought. That had been the old warden's name. "Barnabas," he said aloud in the still, lamp-lit room.

His companion raised his head, alert and expectant.

"Barnabas?" The dog seemed to blink in agreement, as the rector reached down and patted his head.

"Barnabas, then!" he said, with all the authority of the pulpit. The matter was settled, once and for all.

As he rose to put out the lights in the study, Barnabas got up also, revealing a sight which caused the rector to groan. There, on the worn Aubusson carpet, lay his favorite leather slippers of twenty years, chewed through to the sole.

"A puppy," pronounced Hal Owen, lighting his pipe. "Not fully grown."

"How much bigger, do you think? This much?" Father Tim extended his hands and indicated a small distance between them.

Hal Owen grinned and shook his head.

"This much?" He held his hands even farther apart.

"Umhmm. About that much," said Hal.

Barnabas had settled in the corner by the rector's desk and was happily banging his tail against the floor.

Hal studied him with sober concentration as he puffed on his pipe. "A trace of sheep dog, looks like. A wide streak of Irish wolfhound. But mostly Bouvier, I'd say."

The rector sighed heavily.

"He'll be good for you, Tim. A man needs someone to talk to, someone to entertain his complaints and approve his foolishness. As far as background goes, I like what E. B. White said: 'A really companionable and indispensable dog is an accident of nature. You can't get it by breeding for it and you can't buy it with money. It just happens along.' "

"Well, he does like eighteenth-century poetry."

"See there?" Hal put on his tweed cap. "You bring Barnabas out to Meadowgate, and we'll give him a good run through the fields. Oh, and Marge will bake you a chicken pie. How would that suit you?"

It suited him more than he could express.

"I'm out of here. Have to check the teeth on Tommy McGee's horses and look up the rear of Harold Newland's heifer."

"I wouldn't want to trade callings with you, my friend."

"Nor I with you," said the vet, amiably.

"Ah . . . what exactly shall I feed him?"

"Money," said Hal, without any hesitation. "Just toss it in there twice a day, and he'll burn it like a stove."

"That's what I was afraid of."

"Tell you what. I'll let you have his food in bulk, good stuff. It'll hardly cost you a thing. About like keeping a house cat."

"May the Lord bless you."

"Thank you, Tim, I can use it."

"May he cause his face to shine upon you!" he added with fervor.

"That would be appreciated," said Hal, pulling on his gloves. "I'll even see to his shots in a day or two."

Just then, they heard the sound of Emma Garrett's sensible shoes approaching the office door. And so did Barnabas.

With astonishing agility, he leapt over the rector's desk chair, skidded to the door on the Persian prayer rug, and stood on his hind legs, preparing to greet Emma.

"The Altar Guild is helpin' plant pansies on the town medium today," said Emma, as he came in with Barnabas on a new red leash.

"Median, Emma, median."

"Medium," she said, brightly, "and they wondered if you could come out there after while and direct the colors." It certainly wasn't that the Altar Guild couldn't direct the colors themselves, she thought. But he had gone so far as to win some prizes for his gardening skills and had been written up in a magazine put out by the electric co-op.

He noticed Emma was clearly pretending that Barnabas did not exist, which was hard to do in an office with room for only two desks, two chairs, a visitor's bench, four coat pegs, and a communal wastebasket.

"What do you mean, direct the colors?" he asked, sorting through his phone messages.

"Well, you know. Do the yellow ones go in the middle or around the edges or what? And where do you put the blue? Not next to the purple!" she said with conviction.

"I'll take care of it."

She peered at him over her glasses. "You look handsome with that tan, I must say."

"And thank you for saying it. Compared to a golfer's tan, a gardener's tan is not quite so distinguished, but it has its merits. For example, you do not have to wear chartreuse golf pants in order to get it."

Emma howled with laughter. If there was anything she liked, it was a laugh. And frankly, while he was good for a great many things, her rector was not always good for a laugh.

"You don't look as fagged out as you looked there for a while. I thought we'd have to scrape you off the floor a time or two."

"Spring, Emma. It medicates the bones and revives the spirit."

"Well, let's just hope it lasts," she said, eyeing him as if he were a boiled potato.

She went back to posting Sunday's checks. "It rags me good that Petrey Bostic never catches up his pledge," she grumbled.

"You know I don't want to hear that. I don't want to look out in the congregation and see dollar signs instead of souls."

"You know what I think?"

He didn't know.

"I think you live in an ivory tower. It seems to me you'd want to know the nitty gritty of what goes on. You take the Baptists; they keep up with everything."

Emma liked to talk about the Baptists, having previously been one. "Is that so?" he said mildly.

"What comes in, what goes out, who shot Lizzie. You name it, they like to know it."

"Aha," he said. Ever since she got red hair, she had been living up to it.

He turned to his old Royal manual and typed with his forefingers:

> *Dear Walter, thnx yr letter dated march 12. garden going in, through still cold and much rain. preparations for holy week in full swing.*
>
> *hope yr spirits improved. know that He will lead you to right decision. ps. 32:8 promises: i will instruct you and teach you in the way which you shall go: i will guide you with my eye. never doubt it!*
>
> *ever yr fond cousin.*
>
> *p.s. hope to see you this summer. lv to katherine. i keep you always in my prayers.*

As he looked up from the cryptic message to his first cousin and boyhood friend, he saw it had started to rain. All morning, the fog had hung about the village as thick as soup in a bowl, causing him once again to consider buying one of those orange slickers so he could be seen walking in the fog.

"You don't drive a car?" his former bishop once asked, incredulous. Well, and why should he, after all? The rectory was two minutes from the office and less than three from the church. The hospital was only a few blocks away, and one of the finest grocery stores in existence was right across the street.

The old gospel preacher Vance Havner had written about that very thing: "This is the day of the motorist, and anyone who walks is viewed with suspicion. You see a man coming down the road now, just meditating, and you figure he's either out of his head or out of gas. It's such a rarity that dogs bark as though they'd seen a ghost."

Making his rounds on foot kept him fit and positive, if not altogether trim. And, if push came to shove, he could always get the battery charged on his Buick Riviera, back it out of the garage, and go.

Actually, he'd been thinking seriously of getting a bicycle. Only now, there was Barnabas. And a rector in a clerical collar on a bicycle, leading a great, black dog on a red leash? Well, there was no way to bring it off that he could see.

"Peedaddle!" said Emma, as she made an error in her bookkeeping.

Barnabas leaped up and bounded to her desk, where he put his paws on the ledger, leaned over, and fogged her glasses.

"My God!" she exclaimed.

Why was she always saying My God! in a way that had nothing whatever to do with her God? He caught Barnabas by the collar and dragged him into the corner next to his chair.

"I'm tellin' you the truth," Emma said, squinting as she wiped her glasses, "it's goin' to be either him or me." She grabbed her sandwich bag and put it in her desk, slamming the drawer shut.

"Lie down!" he commanded. Barnabas stood and wagged his tail.

"Stay!" he said, as Barnabas ambled to the door and sniffed it.

"Then, sit!" Barnabas went to his water dish and took a long drink.

"Whatever," he muttered, unable to look at Emma.

He sat down and turned to the Gospel reading for Sunday. As he prepared to practice reading it aloud, which was his custom, he cleared his throat.

Barnabas appeared to take that as a signal to stand by his master's chair and place his front paws on his shoulder, giving a generous lick to the Bible for good measure.

He had just read that ignoring negative behavior and praising the positive could be a fruitful strategy. "Whatever you do," the article had implored, "do not look your dog in the eye if you want to discourage his attentions."

" 'And as Jesus passed by,' " intoned the rector, avoiding the doleful stare, " 'he saw a man which was blind from his birth. And his disciples asked him, saying, "Master, who did sin, this man, or his parents, that he was born blind?" ' "

Barnabas sighed and lay down.

He continued, without glancing into the corner: " 'Jesus answered, "Neither hath this man sinned, nor his parents: but that the works of his God should be made manifest in him." ' "

He read aloud through verse five. Then, he stopped and studied Barnabas with some concentration.

"Well, now," he said at last, "this is extraordinary."

"What's that?" asked Emma.

"This dog appears to be . . . ," he cleared his throat, ". . . ah, controlled by Scripture."

"No way!" she said with disgust. "That dog is not controlled by anything!"

Just then, the door opened, and Miss Sadie Baxter helped prove the odd suspicion.

Before she could speak, Barnabas had bounded across the room to extend his finest greeting, whereupon the rector shouted what came immediately to mind, and what Peter had told the multitude:

" 'Repent and be baptized, every one of you!' "

Barnabas sprawled on the floor and sighed with contentment.

"I *was* baptized, thank you," said Miss Sadie, removing her rain hat.

CHAPTER TWO

A Dubious Gift

Miss Sadie Baxter was the last surviving member of one of Mitford's oldest families.

At the age of eighty-six, she occupied the largest house in the village, with the most sweeping view. And she owned the most land, much of it given over to an aged but productive apple orchard. In fact, the village cooks said that the best pies weren't made of Granny Smiths, but of the firm, slightly tart Sadie Baxters, as they'd come to be called.

As far as anyone knew, Miss Sadie had never given away any of the money her father had earned in his lumber operation in the valley. But she dearly loved to give away apples—by the sack, by the peck, by the bushel. Clearly, the only serious maintenance she'd done around Fernbank in recent years was in the orchards, for as anyone could see from the road, the roof that showed itself above the trees was in urgent need of repair. Some said she sat in her living room, surrounded by a regiment of buckets when it rained, and that the sound of it drumming into the pails was so loud you couldn't hear yourself think.

It was, in fact, pouring when she stopped to visit her rector on Tuesday morning. "Mercy!" she said, shaking out her rain hat. "What a day for ducks!"

Father Tim hurried to help with her raincoat and kiss her damp cheek. "What in heaven's name are you doing out in this deluge?"

"You know weather never keeps me in!" she said in a voice as fresh as a girl's.

It was true. Everyone knew that Sadie Baxter would come down the hill in her 1958 Plymouth in a heartbeat—no matter what the weather. Ice, however, was a different story. "You can't predict it," she'd say, "and I dearly love the predictable." So, on icy days, she read, played the piano, sorted through the family picture albums, or called Louella, her former maid and companion, who now lived with her grandson in Marietta, Georgia.

Father Tim could see that Miss Sadie had driven up on the sidewalk, as usual, and parked her car so close to the steps that if he opened the office door all the way, he'd take the paint off her fender.

"Sit down," Emma said, "and have some coffee."

"You know how I like it," she said, settling in for a visit. "Well! Guess what?"

"I give up," said the rector.

"I weigh exactly the same as my age!"

"No!" exclaimed Emma.

"Yes, indeed. I went to see Hoppy for a checkup and I tip the scales at exactly eighty-six pounds. Have you ever?"

"Never!" said Father Tim.

"And you know what else?" she inquired, sitting on the edge of the visitor's bench like a schoolgirl.

"What's that?" he asked.

"Louella is coming to see me for Easter. Her grandson is driving her up here all the way from Marietta! I certainly wouldn't ask her to do the cooking—she's a guest! So I thought we'd just have frozen chicken pies. Don't you think that would be all right, Emma?"

"Why, sure it would. And maybe some fruit cocktail with Jell-O."

"Good idea! And some tea. I can still make tea. Louella likes it real sweet. And let's see, what else?"

Emma thought, tapping her pen on the typewriter. "Ummm . . ."

"Tell you what," said Father Tim, "I'll bake you a ham."

"You would? Oh, Father, that would be so . . . why, bless your heart."

"Don't even mention it!" he said, feeling his heart blessed already.

"Now that's settled, you'll never guess what else, so I'm going to tell you. Yesterday, I didn't go out of the house at all. Why, I hate to say this, but I never even got dressed, isn't that awful? Just went around in my wrapper all the livelong day, my mama would faint. And first thing you know, I was poking around in the attic, looking for an old baby doll I was thinking about, a baby doll that must be eighty years old if she's a day. But we never threw anything away, so I just knew I'd find it. Oh, the dust! Why, I kicked up a regular dust storm!

"And hats! Oh, mercy, the hats I found, why there was a slew of my mama's beautiful hats. I'm going to bring the whole lot to Sunday school one morning and let the children try them on. Would that be too sacrilegious?"

He laughed. "Certainly not!"

"So, then I got to looking for an old picture of Papa, the one with his handlebar mustache, and I was crawling around in there, back in that place where we always kept pictures standing up in little racks, and I was pulling this one out and that one, and the first thing you know, well . . ." Miss Sadie paused and looked at them intently.

"Well, what?" Emma said, leaning forward.

"Well, there was this old painting of the Blessed Virgin and the baby Jesus, that Papa brought back from overseas."

"Aha!" said Father Tim.

"And I want you to have it for the church, Father," she said, "to hang on the wall."

This could be perilous. He remembered two or three other gifts to the church that had caused the widest consternation. One was a mounted moose head, said by the donor to be one of God's creatures, after all, and therefore fit for the parish house wall, if not the nave.

"Maybe I could come up to Fernbank and look at it one day, and we could just, ah, take it from there."

"Oh, no. No need to do that, Father, I've brought it with me. If you'd just step out to the car . . ."

"It's raining cats and dogs, Miss Sadie."

"Oh, I know, so I wrapped it up in a sheet, and then I wrapped that up in some plastic, and I tied it all with a string!"

He found that he was able to open his office door exactly halfway without scraping it on the green Plymouth. Then he maneuvered an umbrella ahead of him, released it outside the door, moved sideways out of the room, drew the umbrella over his head to the drumming sound of a pouring rain, opened her rear car door, and leaned across the seat to pick the heavy painting up with his right hand while holding the umbrella with his left.

He managed to grasp the painting under his arm, shove the car door closed with the heel of his drenched shoe, push open the office door with the toe of the same shoe, then slip the painting through the door ahead of him, lower the umbrella, squeeze through the narrow opening, and stand dripping on the carpet.

"There!" said Miss Sadie with delight, as if she had just fetched the parcel herself.

He leaned the heavy bundle against the wall, quite spent.

"If you have a scissors, Emma, I'll do the honors." Miss Sadie pushed up the sleeves of her cardigan and addressed herself to cutting through several layers of string, cloth, and plastic.

"All right, now," she said, "you look the other way, and I'll say when."

The rector turned and looked out the window behind his desk, and mopped his rain-soaked face and hands with a handkerchief. Emma stoically faced the door to the bathroom, which displayed a bulletin board of parish notices.

Get a move on, thought Emma, who had to coordinate memorials for Easter flowers.

"Now!" Miss Sadie cried.

He turned around and beheld a sight that stunned him.

The painting, in a wide, gilded frame with elaborate carving, was a rosy-hued depiction of mother and child that fairly glowed, even under years of dirt and grime. A faint halo appeared around the infant's head, and the mother looked upon the child in her arms with a wistful tenderness. In the background, moving away from the blue and gold of her gown, was a landscape with a bright stream flowing through open countryside, and above this, a sky that blushed with the platinum, rose, and lavender of an early morning sun.

"Well, now," he said, feeling a sudden desire to cross himself. "This is quite . . . quite beautiful. I wasn't expecting . . ."

"Then you like it?" Miss Sadie's eyes were dancing.

"Like it? I like it enormously! It's a lovely thing to see."

"I cleaned it up," Miss Sadie told him. "Lemon Pledge."

He squatted down for a closer look. "Any name anywhere? Do we know who did it?"

"No sign of a name. I got out my magnifying glass and went all over it, front and back."

The office door swung open suddenly, bringing in a gust of rain and Harry Nelson in a dripping slicker.

"Occupancy by more than three persons is unlawful," Emma said with ill humor. She could hardly bear the sight of the senior warden, and especially not in a wet slicker that was already soaking the thin carpet.

"If we ever get some real money in this place, we'll knock these walls out and add you a thousand square feet," he said with satisfaction.

Over my dead body, thought the rector, who loved the diminutive stone building that the parish had erected in 1879.

Harry Nelson deposited his slicker in the corner, helped himself to a cup of coffee, and joined Miss Sadie on the visitor's bench.

"Okay, Father, here's the scoop. We've looked into it, and it's goin' to make a bloody mess of the sanctuary to tear that cabinet out of there."

As Father Tim and Harry Nelson talked church matters, Emma and Miss Sadie talked Easter dinner. Emma was actually going to bake cloverleaf yeast rolls from scratch, which she hadn't done since Charlie died ten years ago. And Miss Sadie decided she would serve Louella and her grandson on the sunporch, if the weather turned off nice.

"Well, well, well, what's this?" Harry wanted to know, peering at the painting.

"Miss Sadie is making a gift to Lord's Chapel," Father Tim said proudly.

Harry bent over to look closer. As Emma was seated directly behind him, it afforded her such an intriguing idea that she was nearly breathless.

Harry whistled with appreciation. "This looks mighty like a Vermeer to me," he informed the group.

"Why, Harry Nelson, I didn't know you were familiar with Vermeer," said Miss Sadie.

"Familiar! Why, I reckon I am! Shirley and I've had all kinds of classes in art appreciation. Did you know there's only thirty-five Vermeers in the world, except for some Dutchman in the last century who forged a whole bunch of 'em? Baked 'em in the oven to make 'em look like the real thing."

He took his glasses off and squinted at the painting. "Is there a signature on here anywhere?"

"Not that we've been able to find," the rector said.

"If this isn't the real thing, I'll eat my hat. Shoot, I hear that even the fakes bring a bundle. Tell you what, I have a friend who appraises this stuff, I'll just ask him to drive up from Charlotte and take a look.

He says some of the biggest art finds in history have come out of somebody's attic."

"That's where it came from, all right," Miss Sadie confessed.

"Well, let me get on the road. I've got to go over the mountain to see some customers. Boys howdy, this coffee'll curl your hair."

"Ah, Harry, about that appraiser, I don't know that this is what we need to do just now. I think we should wait on that."

"Wait? Wait was what broke the camel's back!" Harry grabbed his slicker off the peg, threw it over his head, squeezed out the door, and called behind him, "Miss Sadie, you should have just drove this Plymouth on in the door."

For some reason he couldn't explain, the rector found Harry's plan to involve an appraiser oddly unwelcome. Yet, something even less welcome occurred at noon.

While he waited with eager anticipation for his usual rainy-day share of cream-filled Little Debbies from Emma's paper bag lunch, she said nonchalantly, "Little Debbies? I've given 'em up for Lent."

He had just walked in the door and taken off the tweed cap Hal Owen gave him, when Percy Mosely turned around from the grill and winked. Then, he went back to frying his sausage.

That was odd, thought Father Tim, sitting down at his favorite booth and opening his newspaper. "Percy," he said, "I believe I'll have two over easy this morning."

Velma came to the booth and stood there, grinning. "Gonna celebrate, are you? I'd have two eggs myself, if it wasn't for my cholesterol."

Cholesterol, cholesterol, thought Father Tim. He'd heard more than enough about cholesterol. It was as bad as the Hula Hoop craze.

Velma poured his coffee. He had traveled to many conferences, retreats, seminars, and workshops, and right here was the best cup of coffee he'd ever had. "What do you mean, celebrate?"

"Well, celebrate over all that money you'll be gettin' down at th' chapel."

"What money is that?" asked Father Tim, dumbfounded.

"That art money. Why, I heard you had a painting over there worth two hundred thousand dollars."

He had just taken a mouthful of coffee and deeply regretted spitting it down the front of his shirt.

"Now, look at you!" said Velma, helping him clean up.

"Velma, whatever you've heard is absolutely untrue. Someone donated a painting to the church and we haven't even had it appraised. It's just a nice painting, that's all."

"We heard it was a Veneer," said Percy, yelling from the grill.

"Yep, that's what we heard," agreed Mule Skinner, who sold real estate around town.

Blast! he thought, completely losing his appetite.

Miss Sadie had delivered the painting on Tuesday. By the end of the day on Thursday, he had received an unprecedented number of calls. Even Emma, who had the day off, called.

In the Grill at eight o'clock, the figure had been two hundred thousand. By three in the afternoon, he had a call from an architect who wanted to submit plans for an addition to the church, and congratulated him on the million dollars Lord's Chapel would be getting from the sale of the old master. At three-thirty, the village newspaper called for a statement.

By four, his stomach felt painful and empty. Bleeding ulcer! he reasoned darkly.

He put the answering machine on, and left.

At five after four, Walter got this message: "Persevere in prayer, with mind awake and thankful heart. This is the office of The Lord's Chapel. Please leave a message at the sound of the tone."

That evening, Father Tim took the phone off the hook, gave Barnabas what was almost certainly his first bath, made a dinner of broiled chicken and packaged spinach souffle, had a glass of sherry, and went to bed.

What if the painting really were a Vermeer? He didn't know much about art, but he did know the work had a certain power, a vitality he hadn't found in just every depiction of the Blessed Virgin and child.

He also knew the turmoil that would ensue if they were actually in possession of such a priceless work. Hadn't he had enough headaches over the seventeenth-century tapestry hanging in the nave? Just getting it insured had been a process that took months, endless costly phone calls, and sleepless nights. In the end, they'd been forced to keep the church doors locked, a thing he roundly despised.

The bottom line, however, was pretty simple. God would, indeed, be faithful to instruct and guide. As the evening progressed, he grew confident that he'd be led to act in the interest of all concerned.

On the way to the church office the next morning, there was a quickness in his step. Of course, he must never tell a soul. But last night, for the first time in his life, he had allowed a dog to sleep on the foot of his bed. And he'd found it an incomparably satisfactory experience.

"There!" said Emma, plunking a box of Little Debbies on his desk. "You weren't the one who gave these up for Lent. You can have my supply." She wondered what he did give up for Lent, anyway, but didn't think it was proper to ask.

He put the box in his top right desk drawer, "You," he said with feeling, "are a pearl above price."

"What happened?"

"It was a landmark day. Petrey Bostick called to say we ought to use part of the money to put air-conditioning in the church."

Emma rolled her eyes. That old business. What was the point of living at an elevation of 5,000 feet if you had to install air-conditioning? Every year, people got lathered up about air-conditioning.

In the course of the morning, a real estate agent called to suggest they buy the property on either side of the churchyard, which would quietly be made available, if they were interested. The rector was not surprised that the price had gone up fifty percent since the vestry made an inquiry just two years ago.

The newspaper called to ask if they could photograph the painting with Miss Sadie standing on one side and Father Tim on the other. The appraiser called and said he'd be there Monday at 9:30. And, they heard that the vestry had scheduled a meeting to discuss the purchase of a steel columbarium painted to look like walnut, brass collection plates instead of the traditional Lord's Chapel baskets, and a floor-to-ceiling stained-glass window for the narthex.

After two parishioners called to remind him of the hungry around the world, another dropped by to remind him of the hungry here at home.

During a lull, he turned to Emma and said simply, "We must not let this destroy the joy of Easter."

"Amen," she said with conviction.

There was only one problem. He couldn't figure out how to prevent that from happening.

A Canadian cold front was sending streams of icy air along the ridges and into the coves surrounding Mitford.

After walking Barnabas through Baxter Park, attending to his hospital rounds, and counseling a parishioner over breakfast at the Grill, he was profoundly ready for a peaceful time at his desk. Now he needed to catch up the loose strings of the two approaching Easter services. Perhaps he could do this, he thought, after the appraiser's visit at nine-thirty. If he had any lingering anxiety about the outcome of the painting's appraisal, he was blessedly unaware of it.

He saw Winnie Ivey sweeping the sidewalk in front of her Sweet Stuff Bakery, as she did each and every morning. It was one of the sights he liked most to see: someone putting their affairs in order.

"Good morning, Winnie!"

Winnie was bundled warmly. He could see only plump cheeks and bright eyes above her scarf. "Father, I'm glad to catch you! I saved yesterday's napoleons just for you!"

Hoppy had recently warned him, "Stay away from that stuff, pal. Carry raisins in your pocket." Raisins, indeed. Worse yet, he'd recently overheard someone refer to him as "that portly priest at Lord's Chapel."

"Winnie," he said, following her inside and taking a deep breath of the cinnamon-scented air, "Hoppy tells me I've got to go easy on sweets."

"He's been telling me that for years, and I sure do wish I could mind him," she said affably, removing three napoleons from the case.

"Maybe you could give those to Miss Rose and Uncle Billy when they come in."

"Oh, don't you worry about that! They get yesterday's oatmeal cookies. Good fiber, you know."

He wondered why he felt helpless as she handed him the paper bag and patted his arm.

In case Hoppy should drive by on his way to the hospital, he carefully stuffed the bag into his coat pocket. He would not eat one bite, he told himself, not even one. They would go immediately to Emma, who could make her own peace with the seductive charm of Winnie Ivey's napoleons.

As he came within sight of his office, he was startled to see a small group waiting at the door. It appeared to be Harry Nelson, Bud Simmons, and Maude Beatty. Also, two cars were parked at the sidewalk, with their motors running.

He felt a reckless desire to step behind a laurel bush and eat the entire contents of the bag in his pocket.

He was relieved that he'd left Barnabas sleeping in the garage, for the crowd had literally packed the office. He opened the bathroom door, which made room for two, shoved the communal wastebasket under his desk, which made room for another, and let the rest of the group shift for itself.

"Father," Harry said sheepishly, "I know you didn't expect such a big whang-do here this mornin', but we thought the vestry ought to see what this appraiser fellow has to say."

"As you can see, Harry, there's no room left for the appraiser to get in here and say anything."

Harry laughed weakly and stood closer to the wall.

The rector turned on the electric heater, then went about his coffee making. "With patience, forbearing one another in love," he reminded himself. Funny how his morning readings often went out to greet the circumstances of the day.

In a few minutes, the smell of coffee filled the little room and began to warm the hearts of the entire assembly. But since the pot only made four cups, and there were seven people, he proceeded cautiously with the pouring.

Emma opened the front door with a glower and squeezed inside. She did not like cold spring mornings, dimly feeling they were some sort of betrayal.

"Oh, for God's sake!" she said, seeing that Maude Beatty was sitting in her chair like she owned it.

The appraiser arrived at nine-thirty sharp, removed his coat, handed it to Harry Nelson, and went straight to work.

He hummed vaguely to himself and clicked his teeth. No one spoke.

"Hmmmm," he said occasionally.

He took out a magnifying glass and went over every inch of the canvas, which he had propped against a stack of books on the rector's desk.

Then he opened a small black box and removed a pair of pliers and a hammer. "Looking for a signature," he informed the fascinated onlookers.

In a moment, the frame was off, and the appraiser was holding the canvas up to the natural light. "Hmm," he said.

Father Tim thought it a wonderful thing that a man could say only "Hmm," and gain the fixed attention of an entire roomful of people. Even his pithiest sermons failed to accomplish this.

"Use your bathroom?" asked the appraiser. The two vestry members moved out of the minuscule room, which was scarcely the size of a cupboard, and flattened themselves against Harry Nelson.

The appraiser took the canvas under one arm and went in, searching the walls and baseboards. "Got an outlet in here?"

"You'll have to unplug the heater," said Emma, testily. Why in God's name was Bud Simmons sitting on the recipes she'd torn out of *Southern Living* and put on her desk, was he blind?

The appraiser shut the bathroom door, and everyone looked around with faint smiles.

If there was anything Harry Nelson didn't like, it was a nervous silence. "Did you hear the one about the funeral procession?" he wanted to know.

Oh my aching back, thought Emma.

"Well, this funeral procession was goin' up the hill to the church and the back door of the hearse flew open and out shoots the casket and blametty blam, down the hill it goes through the intersection with horns blowin' and people dodgin' out of the way, and it runs on down the street and jumps up on the sidewalk and busts in through the pharmacy door and shoots down the aisle to the druggist and the lid pops up and this guy sits up and says: 'Got anything to stop this coffin?' "

I wouldn't laugh if my life depended on it, Emma thought, as the appraiser came out of the bathroom.

"This may be a Vermeer," he said dryly. A little gasp went up.

"And then again, it may not. I feel reasonably confident that it could have been painted during the mid-to-late seventeenth century, by any one of a dozen people working under Vermeer's influence.

"There is no signature that I can find and no evidence of restoration. I recommend that the canvas be shipped at once to New York, to a team of experts who can research the matter fully and apply more scholarship than I am able to provide."

The appraiser had finished his report. In fact, he didn't even wait for a response from the astonished gathering, but began to repack his tool box and wind up the cord of his black light.

A murmur ran through the group. Bud Simmons got up, scattering recipes to the floor, and spoke in a low voice to Harry Nelson. The others waited.

"We think it ought to be sent to New York," Harry said, considerably louder than was necessary in the small room.

"Agreed!" said Lester Shumaker, looking around for support.

The appraiser produced a sheaf of papers and had Harry Nelson sign every one. Then, he put on his coat and muffler, wrapped the painting in bubble plastic, slipped it into a large sack, picked up his tool box, bowed briefly from the waist, and was gone.

In a few minutes, so were the others.

"Emma," said the rector, with a trace of weariness, "let's have another pot of coffee."

"Great!" said Emma, who, on those rare occasions when he wanted a second pot, considered it a small celebration.

He looked at the visitor's bench. There, propped against the wall just under the coat pegs, was the empty frame.

He squeezed by Emma, who was measuring out the Maxwell House, and took the frame into the bathroom. It fit perfectly behind the shower stall.

"There!" he said with satisfaction. "Out of sight, out of mind."

At eleven o'clock, he had a welcome phone call.

"Tim, Hal here. I heard what's going on with the painting, and in case you're feeling sick and tired of the whole thing, I'd like to give you a prescription."

He didn't know how he felt about receiving medical care from a vet.

"Here it is: be ready at eight o'clock in the morning and I'll pick you and Barnabas up in the truck. We'll spend the day at Meadowgate, chasing rabbits and looking for woodchucks. For supper, Marge'll make a big chicken pie, and I'll bring you back in time to get your beauty sleep for church on Sunday."

If he had gotten a call to say he'd won the lottery, he couldn't have been happier. Thank heaven he'd worked all week on his sermon, thereby giving him the freedom of an entire Saturday.

He drank two full mugs of coffee, which was unusual, with cream, which was even more unusual, and, according to Emma, spent the rest of the morning "chattering like a magpie."

Meadowgate Farm was situated in one of the most beautiful valleys around Mitford. Just ten miles from the village, the land began to roll steeply, looking like the pictures he had seen of Scotland.

A flock of sheep grazed in one green pasture, across the fence from a herd of contented Guernseys. The white blossoms of wild bloodwort gleamed along the roadsides, and here and there the bank of an old farmplace was massed with creeping pink phlox.

You leadeth me beside still waters! he thought happily. You restoreth my soul!

It was a glorious morning, drenched with birdsong, and as they turned into the drive, a horde of farm dogs came bounding toward the red truck. There was Buckwheat, an English foxhound. Bowser, a chow. Baudelaire, a soulful dachshund. Bodacious, a Welsh corgi. And Bonemeal, a mixed-breed foundling who, as a puppy, had dug up the new tulip bulbs in order to eat the fertilizer.

The rector opened his door cautiously, and Barnabas dived into the barking throng. Was it possible his hearing could be permanently impaired? "Let 'em get acquainted," Hal said.

At the back door, Marge gave Father Tim a vigorous hug, which he returned with feeling.

"Tim! You've got your annual planting tan!"

"And you've got your perennial joi de vivre!"

In the center of the kitchen was a large pine table, bleached by age, with benches on either side. A Mason jar of early wildflowers sat in the center, along with a deep-dish apple pie, fresh from the oven. A dazzling beam of light fell through the windows that looked out to the stables.

Their guest stood transfixed. "A foretaste of heaven!" he said, feeling an instant freshness of spirit.

"Sit," said Marge, whose blonde hair was captured in a bandanna the color of her dress. "We'll start with freshly ground coffee and cinnamon stickies. Then, I've packed lunches, because I hear you guys are going tromping in the woods."

" 'Til we drop," promised Hal, lighting his pipe. "Tim has some heavy-duty stress to contend with. Holy Week, two Easter services, a Vermeer, a new dog the size of a Buick, fourteen azaleas to get in the ground, and," he looked at Father Tim, "there must be something else."

"A bone spur in my left heel," he said, cheerfully.

At two-thirty, Marge rang the farm bell, and the men came at a trot across the early spring field with Barnabas, Bowser, and Buckwheat dashing ahead. The bell rang only for an emergency.

"Trissie Steven's pony. Caught in a barbed wire fence. Bleeding badly," Marge said in the telegraphic way she had of communicating urgent news to her husband.

"Want to come or stay, Tim? Your call."

"Oh, stay!" said Marge. "We haven't had a good visit in a hundred years. Besides, you've been talking man talk all day. Let's talk peonies and rose bushes, for heaven's sake."

His breathing was ragged from the trot across the field. "Well," he said, lamely, thinking of downing a glass of Marge's sweetened iced tea.

"I'm off," Hal said, kissing his wife on the cheek.

Marge cleared the remains of the pastry she'd rolled out for the pie, while the chicken simmered on the stove. "Sit down and talk to me while I finish up. The tea's in the pitcher, and fresh peppermint. A few shoots are already out; that tall grass by the garden shed kept it protected over the winter."

He poured the tea, got ice from the refrigerator, and sat down in the rocking chair that had belonged to Marge's father.

It was balm to his soul to sit in this beamed, high-ceilinged room, with its wonderful smells and golden, heart-of-pine floors. At Meadowgate Farm, he mused, nothing terribly dramatic ever seemed to happen. Life appeared to flow along sweetly, without many surprises or obstacles to overcome.

Marge sat down on the window seat, and tucked her hair into the bandanna. He thought she looked unusually bright, radiant.

"Did Hal tell you?"

"Tell me? Tell me what?"

Perhaps their Annie was getting engaged, he thought. Or maybe Hal had finally come across with their much-discussed vacation in France, to celebrate her fiftieth birthday.

"I'm pregnant," she said simply, wiping her hands on her apron.

After dinner, which the rector pronounced "the finest yet," the men washed the dishes. Then they all gathered before a small fire on the kitchen hearth.

Hal and Marge sat on the slouchy, chintz-covered sofa, which the dogs usually favored, and held hands like sweethearts. Bowser and Baudelaire slept peacefully by the fire, and Barnabas slept with his head on his master's feet.

The rector lifted a glass of Hal's oldest port.

"To Marge, the bravest of the brave! May you be blessed with a child who is full of grace and merriment, and endowed with the countenance of its lovely mother."

"Thanks, but I'm not brave, at all. I'm scared silly. I keep thinking Hoppy will call and say, 'Ha, ha, just kidding. You can go back to your real life, now.' "

Barnabas gave a little dream bark.

"Chasing squirrels," said Hal. "You know, I think you've got yourself a fine dog, there. His character appears to reveal the wolfhound in him. There's an old story that says a wolfhound can tell by looking on a man's face whether his intentions are good or evil."

"A trait devoutly to be desired by the rest of us," said the rector, with a new pride in his companion.

"Read to us, Timothy. You'll have to be leaving in an hour or so, and you know how I covet a read before you go." Marge fluffed up the pillow behind her and leaned cozily against her husband's shoulder.

She had put several books on the table next to his chair. "First come, first served," he said cheerfully, and opened a volume at random.

" 'Up! up! my Friend, and quit your books,' " he read from Wordsworth, " 'Or surely you'll grow double: Up! up! my Friend, and clear your looks; Why all this toil and trouble?' "

The sun, above the mountain's head, A freshening lustre mellow
through all the long green fields has spread
His first sweet evening yellow.

Books! 'tis a dull and endless strife: Come, hear the woodland linnet
How sweet his music! on my life, there's more of wisdom in it.

As Father Tim read, Barnabas awoke, yawned, and began to listen with rapt attention.

Sweet is the lore which Nature brings
our meddling intellect/mis-shapes the beauteous forms of things
we murder to dissect.

Enough of Science and of Art
Close up those barren leaves
come forth, and bring with you a heart
That watches and receives.

Barnabas sighed with what appeared to be satisfaction, and gazed at the reader as if waiting for more.

"Remarkable dog," said Hal.

CHAPTER THREE

New Possibilities

Much to his relief, little mention of the painting came to his ears during Holy Week.

Palm Sunday had been a blessing to the congregation, and on Maundy Thursday, he had truly experienced a deep and enriching mournfulness. On Good Friday he fasted, and on Holy Saturday felt much the better for it in every way.

Easter morning dawned bright and clear. "Dazzling to the senses!" said one parishioner. The beautiful old church was full for both services, and the tremor of joy that one always hoped for on this high day was decidedly there.

Perhaps one of the highest points, for him, had been looking out into the eleven o'clock congregation and seeing Miss Sadie sitting with Louella and her grandson. The countenances of all three were radiant, which created a special pool of light on the gospel side.

After church, Louella grabbed him and gave him a bosomy hug.

"That's some good ham you baked," she said. "We got into it las' night, with the Jell-O. An' Miss Sadie goin' to run it by us again today."

Hal and Marge were there, their good news shining in their eyes.

Emma wore a hat with a Bird of Paradise on one side and was proudly showing off her daughter from Atlanta. And Miss Rose and

Uncle Billy, usually partial to the Presbyterians, attended their first service at Lord's Chapel.

He saw faces he'd never seen before, and would never see again, and faces that had become as familiar as his own. It had been a good twelve years in Mitford.

During the days following Easter Sunday, he noticed a certain lassitude of spirit in himself. He would go to his back door and gaze at the azaleas, which he'd left sitting along the bank in their potting cans.

There was still a flat of pansies to be planted, and a dozen rare, pink day lilies.

But the joy he'd felt in gardening, only days before, seemed to have vanished. A letdown was to be expected after the intense activities of high holy days.

He went to the library at noon and sat, idly reading, wanting a nap, forgetting to have lunch. At last, he forced himself to check out the latest Dick Francis, a book on dog breeds, a volume of Voltaire, and Maeterlinck's *Intelligence of the Flowers.* He felt so exhausted from selecting the books that he did something entirely out of the ordinary: he phoned Emma to say he was going home.

"I'm calling Hoppy this minute," she said, alarmed.

"There's nothing to worry about in the least. I'm just a little tired, that's all. I expect to be there bright and early in the morning."

"Well, it's my day off, you know, but I'll come in at ten to check on you. I've found us a new kind of Little Debbies, and I'll bring you a box."

He couldn't summon the energy to argue with her. He also noted, vaguely, that her offer of one of his favorite sweets had no appeal.

By the time he reached the new men's store a block away, he regretted having checked out the books he was carrying, especially the Voltaire, which suddenly felt like the complete works.

Miss Rose and Uncle Billy lived on Mitford's Main Street, in one room of a house that was variously called "a disgrace," "an eyesore," and "a crying shame."

The house had been built in the late 1920s by Miss Rose's brother, Willard Porter, who invented and sold pharmaceuticals.

His biggest seller, a chest rub, had added the second story, the wooden shutters with cut-outs of a dove, a wrap-around porch, and a widow's walk. There was an ornate gazebo, large enough for dances, that had commemorated the success of a flavored lip balm. And four sculptured stone garden benches with carved angels' heads, sitting in what once was a majestic rose garden, had marked the debut of a cough syrup containing mountain herbs.

The house had historically been the pride of the village, sitting as it did on the edge of the old town green, across from the war monument, and displaying the finest architecture of its time.

In recent years, however, all that had changed. The stone benches with carved angels' heads were crumbling to dust. Many of the shutters lay in the grass where they had fallen. And Uncle Billy had nailed a *No Trespassing* sign on the widow's walk.

A decorator from Raleigh had often tried to buy the Porter place for a second home, thinking how spectacular it would be for parties. When all efforts to buy it through Mule Skinner had failed, she took it upon herself personally to visit Miss Rose and Uncle Billy, who were sitting in the backyard in two chrome dinette chairs, at a wooden spool previously used to roll up electrical wiring. They were eating bologna sandwiches and drinking iced tea from jelly glasses.

Miss Rose wiped her mouth on a threadbare t-shirt that said *I surfed Laguna Beach.*

"I'm Susan Parnell Phillips," the intruder informed them, with more eagerness than was necessary.

"This is Rose," said Uncle Billy, "and I'm the thorn."

At that, Uncle Billy grinned broadly, showing all three of his teeth, one of which was "covered with enough gold to reroof the house," as a neighbor once said.

Miss Rose glowered at the visitor. "I'm not selling."

"Selling? But how did you—I mean, what makes you think I'm buying?"

"I can always tell," Miss Rose snapped.

Recently, the new men's store had tried to buy the place. And so had a dozen others over the years. But Miss Rose stood her ground.

"Home is where the heart is," she said to one prospective buyer who knocked on their door in January and found her in a chenille robe, a World War II trench coat, a pair of rubber garden boots, a man's felt hat, and what appeared to be Uncle Billy's flannel pajama bottoms.

As far as the frozen caller could tell, there was no heat in the house.

Being a caring soul, he inquired around and was told that the Presbyterian church had filled up Miss Rose's oil tank in November, and, on last inspection, it was still full.

Most people knew, too, that the old couple walked to Winnie Ivey's bake shop every afternoon, always hand in hand, to pick up what was left over. Winnie, however, was not one to give away the store. She carefully portioned out what she thought they would eat that night and the next morning, and no more. She didn't like the idea of Miss Rose feeding her perfectly good day-old Danish to the birds.

After their visit to the bake shop, Miss Rose and Uncle Billy, walking very slowly due to arthritis and a half-dozen other ailments, dropped by to see what Velma had left at the Main Street Grill.

Usually, it was a few slices of bacon and liver mush from breakfast, or a container of soup and a couple of hamburger rolls from lunch. Occasionally, she might add a little chicken salad that Percy had made, himself, that very morning.

On balance, it was said, Miss Rose and Uncle Billy fared pretty well in Mitford. And many were pleased to see that they provided for their spiritual nourishment, as well, by going to church on Sunday.

Recently, that very thing had been a matter for conversation around the village, since they'd been over to The Chapel of Our Lord and Savior, as it was properly called, four Sundays in a row, including Easter.

"Are you going to visit Miss Rose and Uncle Billy?" Emma asked one morning as Father Tim came in with Barnabas.

He hung his hat on a peg. "Do I need to?"

"Well, you usually do go visit after somebody's been to church a few times."

"Yes, I'll do that. Soon. Remind me to do that."

"Don't eat anything while you're there," she warned. "They say Miss Rose cooks, sometimes."

He was going through the mail that Harold Newland, the postman, had just handed him, since the mailbox was too small to hold this morning's bundle. He spied a letter from Walter.

"Are you pale today?" Emma demanded.

"Pale? Do I look pale?"

"As a ghost."

He slowly opened the letter, stared at what appeared to be a blur, then sat down heavily on the corner of his desk.

"Something . . ." he said vaguely. "Something is . . . not right."

Emma rose to steady him. "Don't move," she said, afraid he might crash to the floor. "I'm bringing the car to the door and we're going to the hospital."

"This," said Dr. Walter Harper, who was known to the village as Hoppy, "is where the rubber hits the road."

"Meaning?"

"Meaning the party's over, pal. You've got to make some changes, big-time."

He sighed. Change! If there was anything he didn't like, that was it, right there in a nutshell.

Emma, who had left her glasses at the office, was squinting at cartoons in an old *New Yorker,* when Hoppy and Father Tim came out to the waiting room.

Hoppy Harper was tall, slim, and even handsome with his piercing green eyes, intense gaze, and determined jaw.

Only last September, his wife of sixteen years had died of cancer, and the grief had aged him noticeably. Those who cared about him enough to look closely, and these were quite a few, saw that grief had also done something else. It had deepened him.

"Emma," he said, "let's have a talk."

Oh, God! Emma thought, using the proper meaning of the phrase, Let everything be all right.

"I've already been over this with Tim. But I think someone close to him should also know the score."

"This is a dark day, Emma," said the rector, managing a weak smile.

"Diabetes," Hoppy said. "That's the bad news. The good news is, it's non-insulin dependent. Which means he won't require regular insulin shots. What he will require is a change of diet. Little Debbies, pies, cakes, candy—outta here.

"We stuck his finger for blood sugar, and it's over 350. Not good. And he's got four-plus sugar in the urine. So, here's the scoop."

There was something in the doctor's green eyes that made Emma concentrate on every word.

"Exercise. Jogging is what I recommend. Three times a week, and no less. Morning, noon, night, whenever. But he's got to do it."

The rector looked anguished.

"Less fat in his diet, juice, a lot of fresh fruit. And no skipping meals."

Hoppy grinned and looked at his patient. "Now, the most important thing of all. And that's changing your schedule. You haven't had a real vacation in twelve years, and you usually work seven days a week. I can't tell you how to change that, but it's got to change. Think about it, pal." Hoppy ran his fingers through his unruly hair. Emma thought he looked tired, and wondered who was taking care of him.

He had a hurried lunch of Percy's soup of the day, with a salad, and went home to say a word to Barnabas. This took him past the new men's store, which he had failed to stop and inspect since it opened with some fanfare before Easter. The Collar Button, it was called.

It had been a long time, indeed, since he'd gone into a clothing store. In the first place, he didn't like to shop. In the second place, the prices for clothes these days were absolutely—yes, he thought he could honestly say it—sinful. And in the third place, what was the going fashion for a rector who didn't wish to appear conspicuously well-dressed?

He slipped his hand into his jacket pocket, and felt his mended gloves, which he still needed from time to time on cold mornings. He must not get carried away in this place, he thought. He would say he was just looking.

The Collar Button was new, but it seemed old. The walls were dark, burnished panels of mahogany, a low fire burned in a grate, and a large golden retriever, lying by the hearth, opened one eye as he came in.

"Good heavens!" he said with earnest appreciation. This was like walking into a study in some far reach of Cambridge, where he had once gone to research a paper on the life and works of C. S. Lewis.

"Father Tim, I believe!" boomed a deep voice, and from behind a wall of brocade curtains stepped the new proprietor, extending his hand to the rector.

"That's right. How did you know?"

"Oh, I've seen you pass now and again, and I thought to myself, there goes a proper candidate for the Collar Button style!"

"And what, ah, style is that, exactly?"

"English gentleman, country squire, village rector, the man of thoughtful reflection and quiet taste."

"Aha."

"What can I show you? Oh, and would you care for a dash of sherry?"

His head was fairly swimming with the unexpected dazzle of the modern shopping experience.

When he left the Collar Button, he was carrying a large bag with two jogging suits and a box with a new spring sport coat.

For the life of him, he couldn't figure out how it had all come about.

He had mentioned jogging and then, before he knew what was happening, he was standing before a mirror in a turquoise jogging outfit, trying to hold his stomach in.

He had to admit he would need something to run in. He certainly could not do it in a jacket, trousers, and shirt with a clerical collar. As he hurried toward home, clutching his packages, he muttered all the excuses he could possibly think of for having spent such a large sum of money on himself.

On Saturday morning, he put on the forest green running suit and a pair of old Nikes that he'd worn for several years in the garden.

Running shoes was a category he dreaded investigating. Someone had recently told him that shoes these days had parts that you literally pumped up. It was an esoteric realm, and so for now, he concluded, it would have to be his old garden shoes or nothing.

He was smitten at once with the comfort of the new outfit he was wearing. In fact, he praised it aloud.

"Why, this feels just like pajamas," he said into the full-length mirror behind the guest room door.

Barnabas barked and leaped backward when he saw the rector come into the hall.

"You'll have to get used to it, old fellow. If I do what the doctor ordered, I'll be looking like this three times a week. So, pipe down."

Barnabas, however, couldn't contain his excitement over something new in the air. He leaped up and put his forepaws on his master's chest and cocked his head to one side.

" 'Jesus said to the disciples, "This is my commandment, that you love one another as I have loved you." ' " The rector looked Barnabas squarely in the eye.

Barnabas sighed heavily and lay down at his master's feet.

"And don't let it happen again," he said, brushing off his new jogging suit.

He knew he didn't want to be seen doing this. First, he wanted to try it out, in a place where there was no traffic. And while he'd seen countless others running heedlessly along Main Street, he felt, somehow, that jogging was an intimate activity, accompanied by snorts, sweating, hawking and spitting, and an inordinate amount of huffing and puffing. Why in the world anyone would want to do that up and down the center of town was beyond him.

He went to the study window at the back of the rectory and peered across his greening yard into Baxter Park. As far as he could see, the coast was clear.

He began in a kind of lope, along the flagstones by his perennial beds, through the space in the hedge and out to Baxter Park, where he turned left and ran close to the hemlock border.

By the time he reached the middle of the park, he was winded. "Take it easy," Hoppy had told him. "Don't try to do Boston the first time out."

He had already broken a light sweat.

A squirrel chattered by one of the ancient park benches. A chipmunk dashed across the grass. And the old fountain, now green with moss and algae, made a sweet, pattering sound.

A bronze plaque on the fountain read: *Given in loving memory of Rachel Livingstone Baxter, 1889–1942.* Miss Sadie's mother, he thought, thankful for such an oasis of peace. He wondered why he hadn't been in this wonderful old park in several years, even though it bordered his yard and he looked into it nearly every day.

Starting again, he jogged over to Old Church Lane. Then, he ran with surprising ease up the hill toward the meadow where the remains of the ruined Lord's Chapel stood.

Panting and soaked with sweat, his heart pounding furiously, he sat on a crumbling stone wall that bordered the old churchyard and saw what lay before him as if for the first time.

It was, he thought, the Land of Counterpane.

The view swept down to a small valley with church spires, orderly farms, and freshly planted fields. Then, the far walls of the valley rose steeply and rolled away to ridge upon ridge, wave upon wave of densely blue, mist-cloaked mountains.

He sat as if stunned for a long moment. Then, he tried to recall when he'd been up here last.

It had been seven or eight years, he figured, since he'd climbed the steep lane with Walter and Katherine and a picnic basket. He wondered who he might share it with now, but could think of no one. Except, of course, Barnabas.

His heart had ceased its thundering, and a light breeze coming up from the valley seemed sweet with the fragrance of earth and manure, leaf mold and blossoming trees.

He got up from the wall, idly wondering how long he had sat there, and began his jog down Old Church Lane.

He was no longer trying to hide himself along the hedges. In fact, he discovered that he was suddenly feeling absolutely "top notch," as Walter might say.

As he ran, he became aware that he was thinking the oddest thoughts. Thoughts of how he might look in his new spring sport coat; about the little girl's pony that had got caught in the barbed wire fence; whether Emma had dyed her hair at home or had it done by Fancy Skinner. Also, he hoped the pink day lilies would not disappoint him and bloom out orange.

He turned out of the bright sun into the cool morning shade of Baxter Park, and paused again to rest at the fountain.

Maybe this jogging business wouldn't be so bad, after all.

New possibilities lay before him, it seemed, though he couldn't yet tell what they were. Perhaps it was time to make some other changes, as well, to do something fresh, something different and unexpected.

The idea came upon him quite suddenly.

He would give a dinner party.

CHAPTER FOUR

Company Stew

In the little village of less than a thousand, everyone's dinner—party or otherwise—began at The Local, unless they wanted to make the fifteen-mile drive to Food Value. Of course, they could go out on the highway to Cloer's Market, but Hattie Cloer was so well-known for telling customers her aches and pains that hardly anyone ever did that.

"See this right here?" she might say, pointing to her shoulder. "Last night somethin' come up there big as a grapefruit. I said, 'Clyde, put your hand right here and feel that. What do you think it is?'

"And Clyde said, 'Why, law, that feels like some kind of a golf ball or somethin' in there,' and don't you know, Darlene took to barkin', and that thing took to hurtin', and I never laid my head on th' pillow 'til way up in the mornin'. Wouldn't you like a pound or two of these nice snap beans?"

Worse than that, according to some, was Darlene, Hattie's Chihuahua, who lay on a sack by the cash register. Every time Hattie rang up a sale, the dog growled and snapped at the customer.

Avis Packard once said that Hattie Cloer had sent more business to The Local than any advertising he'd ever run in the paper.

Two weeks after his first jog up to Church Hill, Father Tim made an early Saturday call at The Local.

Since Barnabas was running with him these days, he found it convenient that The Local had an old bike rack near the front door, where the dog could be tied on a short leash.

He was still out of breath, and Barnabas was panting with some exhaustion himself. The route had by now fallen into place. They ran through Baxter Park and up to Church Hill, then along the quiet road by Miss Sadie's apple orchards, past the Presbyterian Church, three times around the parking lot, down Lilac Road to Main Street, and then to Wisteria Lane where they turned toward home.

"Two miles, right on the money," he discovered with immense satisfaction.

"Mornin', Father," said Avis, who was sitting at the cash register. "How does joggin' compare to workin' up a sermon?"

"Well, Avis, I can't see as there's much difference. I dread both, but once I get started, there's nothing I'd rather be doing."

"We got those fine-lookin' brown eggs you like. And Luther Lovell's boys delivered the nicest bunch of broilers you ever seen. You ought to look at those, and check that pretty batch of calf liver while you're at it."

One thing Father Tim liked about Avis Packard was the way he got excited about his groceries. He could rhapsodize about the first fresh strawberries from the valley in a way that made him a veritable Wordsworth of garden fare. "We got a special today on tenderloin that's so true to the meanin' of th' name, you can cut it with a fork."

"Well, now, I'm not shopping, Avis. I'm looking."

"What're you lookin' for?" Avis cocked his head to one side like he always did when he asked a question.

"Ideas. You see, I've decided to give a dinner party."

"You don't mean it!"

"Oh, I do. But the thing is, I don't know what to cook."

"Well, sir, that's a problem, all right. I'll be thinkin' about it while you look around," Avis assured him.

A little line was forming at the cash register, so the rector moved away, greeting shoppers as he went.

He stopped to talk to everyone, taking note that four people wondered where his collar was, and only one inquired about the painting, for which he was grateful.

At the produce bins, he admitted he was feeling slightly nervous over his idea. First of all, he didn't even have a guest list.

Of course, he was going to ask Emma, and yes, Miss Sadie. He thought she would make a splendid contribution. Besides, he had heard she once went to school in Paris, and he wanted to know more about it.

Hal and Marge, of course. No doubt about that.

Hoppy Harper, now there was a thought, his wife gone and no one to look after him but that old housekeeper. That made six, including himself.

Six. For the life of him, he couldn't think of another soul that would fit in just right with that particular group.

Perhaps he should invite Winnie Ivey, since she was always feeding everybody else. Maybe he would do that.

Avis came down the aisle with a gleam in his eye. "I turned the register over to my boy. I want to help you get your party goin.' What do you think about beef stroganoff, a salad with bibb lettuce, chickory, slices of navel orange and spring onions, and new potatoes roasted with fresh rosemary? 'Course, I'd put a nice bottle of cabernet behind that. 1982."

He sat with Barnabas one evening with a lapful of cookbooks. As much as he appreciated Avis Packard's menu planning, beef stroganoff seemed too ordinary. He wanted something that spoke of spring, that made people feel there was a celebration going on, and that would fill them up without being too heavy.

"This is a lot of work," he confided to Barnabas, who appeared to understand, "and I haven't even started yet."

He wondered why he had waited so long to entertain. It was clear to him that he had gotten completely out of the notion, although once he had loved doing it. He'd had the bishop and his wife for tea three times and twice for dinner, the vestry had come for a light supper on at least four occasions, and, once, he had the courage to give a luncheon for the members of the Altar Guild, who had such a good time they didn't leave until four o'clock.

Not that he was a great cook, of course. Still, he wasn't half bad at barbecued short ribs, an occasional sirloin tip roast that would melt in your mouth, if he did say so himself, and, in the summer, Silver Queen corn, cooked in milk for precisely sixty seconds. Of course, there was always the economical Rector's Meatloaf, as he'd come to call it, which he usually made at least once a week.

He'd even been known to bake his own bread, but the interest these days somehow eluded him. Gardening had taken over. And where once he had sat and read cookbooks, he now read catalogs from Wayside Gardens and White Flower Farms, not to mention Jackson and Perkins.

"And another thing," he said to Barnabas, who raised one ear in response, "is the cost. Do you realize what entertaining costs these day?"

Barnabas yawned.

"Lamb, I think it should be lamb," he mused to himself after going to bed. And he didn't think it should take the form of anything *nouvelle.*

The thought came to him as he laid his head on the pillow. Company Stew! It was an old recipe, nearly forgotten, but one that had always brought raves.

He got out of bed and put on his faded burgundy dressing gown. Noticing that the clock said eleven, he slipped his feet into the chewed leather slippers and went downstairs to look for the recipe.

The search revealed how vagrant his closets had become, so he began rearranging the one in the hall, which, very likely, his guests might see.

When he finished, he was surprised to find that it was two o'clock in the morning, and he'd collected a boxful of odds and ends for the "Bane and Blessing" sale.

It was rather a free feeling, he noticed, prowling about the house at such an odd hour. To explore this strange freedom even further, he went into the kitchen, made himself a meatloaf sandwich with no mayonnaise, and sat at the table reading *Bon Appétit,* which he had bought for ideas and inspiration.

"No wonder I haven't done this sort of thing in years," he muttered. "It's too demanding."

He was feeling the way he'd felt when they asked him to be on the Garden Tour.

Though the tour was to be of gardens only, he'd given the rectory a room-by-room inspection. It was as if he were seeing it for the first time.

To his amazement, every ceiling corner seemed to have a spider web, there was clearly a ring in his bathtub, the shower tiles were mildewed, and the kitchen cabinets were in such a tangle of confusion, it had taken a full half hour to locate his double boiler.

At what point things had fallen into this state, he couldn't say. But fallen they had, and by the time of the tour, he was so exhausted from making both house and garden ready, that he went to Meadowgate Farm for the entire weekend, inviting a retired priest from Wesley to conduct Sunday services.

Now, he found himself compulsively cleaning out drawers his guests would never open and closets they would never see, and polishing silver they would never use. But, he assured himself, it was a perfect time to get caught up. A dinner party provided the most excellent of excuses.

"You need house help," Emma had told him, again and again.

But then, he was often told that he needed one thing or another: a cat, a bird, a gazebo, earmuffs, English garden tools, a word processor, a vacation, a bicycle, a wife, and, until Barnabas, a dog. Several people had even made the unwelcome suggestion that he get himself a microwave.

When he invited Emma on Monday morning, she was inspired at once to submit plans of her own.

"I'll bring the potato salad," she said happily. "And make a batch of yeast rolls."

"No, you won't bring a thing. This is a bona fide party where all you have to do is show up."

"Why not make it a covered dish? You don't need to do all that cookin' by yourself. Marge could bring her chocolate cake they wrote up in the newspaper, and Hoppy Harper's house help could make somethin' for him to bring . . ."

She was doing it again—treating him like a ten year old.

"Emma, no one is to bring anything. And that's final."

It was indeed final, as she could plainly tell.

He washed the slipcover on the sofa in his study, dusted books on the shelves that were low enough for anyone to reach, ordered four pounds of Avis Packard's valley-grown lamb and two bottles of a ridiculously expensive cabernet, asked Winnie Ivey to bake a special triple-chocolate cake with raspberry filling, hung a new bird feeder outside the dining room windows, and pondered washing the study window that overlooked the best part of the garden. At this, however, he balked.

As he might have guessed, everyone in the village seemed to know about the evening, which was now only a few days away. It amazed him that a man couldn't have a simple dinner party without attracting the attention of everybody from the postal clerk to the dry cleaner.

"We hear you're havin' a big blow-out," his barber said, while taking a little more off the sides than they'd discussed. Were people looking at him as if they should have been invited? Couldn't a man have a few friends over without asking the whole blasted town?

Though he still wanted to invite two others, he couldn't decide who they should be. In the meantime, he had ordered for eight and was preparing for eight, and was relieved that everyone not only could come, but seemed pleased at the prospect.

He'd also given some thought to Barnabas. Perhaps he would allow his friend into the study after dinner. Which meant, of course, that Barnabas would need a bath.

At the office one morning, it occurred to him that, instead of bathing Barnabas in the guest room shower stall, he would stop by the hardware store and buy a large tin tub. That way, he could begin the practice of bathing him in the garden and avoid the clean-up in the bathroom.

After a quick lunch with Harry Nelson, who reported that the origin of the painting still hadn't been verified, he went to the hardware.

One of his favorite smells was that of an old hardware store. In fact, it was right up there with the smell of wood smoke, leather-bound books, and leaf mold after a rain. More than that, it unfailingly brought back a rush of memories from his Mississippi boyhood.

As a 4-H rabbit grower for two years, he had often traded at the local hardware for hutch materials and feed. He could even remember the time he picked out six yellow goslings from a box kept warm by a light bulb.

He decided on a tin tub for $22.95, and took it to Dora Pugh at the cash register.

"You want to drive around for this, Father?"

"No, Dora, this is cash and carry."

"I see you walk by here every day and I still forget you don't drive a car. How in the nation do you make out?"

"Not too bad, actually. Nearly everything I could want, and some things I don't, are all right here in these two town blocks."

"I guess you're goin' to tote this tub on your head like in Africa?"

He gave her cash to the penny. "I don't know exactly how I'm going to do it till I get started."

He tried to hold the tub under his arm, but that didn't seem to work, so he took it by one of the handles and was disappointed to note that the rim of it banged against his ankle as he walked to the door.

Turning to say goodbye, he saw that Dora had ducked down behind the pocketknife display case, shaking with laughter.

"Dora, I see you back there laughing! You better quit that and show some respect to the clergy!"

He waved cheerfully and stepped out on the sidewalk, pleased with both his idea and his purchase. He just hoped that people did not think him eccentric. He would far rather be thought ingenious or practical.

By the time he turned the corner at the bank and headed home, he was willing to admit that a car provided something more valuable than convenience. It provided privacy. Otherwise, he reasoned, everyone passing by could stare into your business, which one and all seemed to be doing.

He hurried the last half block to the rectory, set the tub down in a clearing amid some laurel, and unwound the garden hose to make certain it would reach. "Perfect!" he exclaimed, warming to his task on Friday.

On Friday, he left the office early, stopped by The Local, and went home to change into an old t-shirt and khaki pants.

He would get the bath out of the way straight off, he thought, then begin the stew around three, open the wine to breathe at six, and have everything in good order for his guests at seven.

When he opened the door to the garage, Barnabas leaped into the hallway, skidded nearly the length of it on a small Oriental rug, then dashed into the kitchen and hurled himself onto the bar stool, where he began to lick a vinyl placemat on the counter.

The rector put Barnabas on his longest leash. Not only would this give him freedom to thrash about in the bath, it would keep him from bounding into the street if the new setup alarmed him.

Unfortunately, this would prove to be the worst idea he'd had in a very long time.

He was pleased with his location of the tub. The little clearing was shielded from the street by the laurels, and afforded him plenty of elbow room. As soon as Barnabas was bathed, he thought, he'd rub him down with a towel, then lead him into the garage where he could finish drying off and make himself presentable.

Attaching the looped end of the leash to a laurel branch high over his head, he encouraged Barnabas to get into the water, which he'd liberally sudsed with Joy.

Instead, Barnabas hurled himself into the tub with a mighty leap.

Just as quickly as he went in, he came out, diving between the rector's legs. He circled his right leg and plunged back into the water, soaking his master from head to foot.

Then, he leaped out of the tub, raced again between Father Tim's legs, joyfully dashed around his left ankle, and headed for a laurel bush.

It seemed to the rector that it all happened within a matter of seconds. And while his memory searched wildly for a Scripture, nothing came forth.

Barnabas circled the bush at a dead heat, catching the leash in the crotch of a lower limb, and was brought to an abrupt halt.

The tautly drawn leash had run out. Barnabas was trapped on the bush. And each of the rector's ankles was tightly bound.

Shaken, Father Tim observed this set of circumstances from a sitting position, and in the most complete state of shock he could remember.

Miraculously, he was still wearing his glasses.

Barnabas was now lying down, though the leash was caught so tightly in the tree that he could not lower his head. He stared at Father Tim, obviously suffering the misery of remorse. Then, his contrition being so deep that he could not bear to look his master in the eye, he appeared to fall into a deep sleep.

The rector began spontaneously to preach one of the most electrifying sermons of his career.

His deep memory bank of holy Scripture came flooding back, and the power of his impassioned exhortation made the hair fairly bristle on the black dog's neck. In fact, Barnabas opened his eyes and listened intently to every word.

When his oration ended, the rector felt sufficiently relieved to try and figure out what to do.

He could see it now. His guests ringing the doorbell, finally coming inside, searching the house, calling out the back door, and then spying him in this miserable condition, while the stew pot sat cold on the stove.

No wonder so many people these days had heart fibrillations, high blood pressure, and a thousand other stress-related diseases. No doubt all of these people were dog owners.

Lord, be thou my helper, he prayed.

"Father Tim! Is that you back there?"

Avis Packard came crashing through the laurel hedge, looked down at his good customer, and said, without blinking, "I let you get away without your butter. Do you want me to put it in the refrigerator or just leave it right here?"

Fortunately, the washtub incident had put him only an hour off schedule.

The stew was on and simmering, and the fragrance in the rectory was intoxicating. The old walnut dining table gleamed under the chandelier and cast a soft glow over a silver bowl of yellow roses tinged with crimson. The cabernet sparkled in cut-glass decanters, the strains of a Mozart sonata filled the rooms with an air of expectancy, and in the fading afternoon light, the gardens looked fresh and inviting from every window.

He felt rather fresh and inviting, himself, having shaved and showered. Also, he was wearing his new sport coat.

He hadn't come up with two more guests who would perfectly fit in, but he saw this as an advantage. Tonight's little gathering would be relaxed and intimate, like family, and all would get a chance to know each other better.

At 6:45, the bell rang, and while the invitation was for 7:00, he was ready and waiting. He opened the door to see Miss Rose and Uncle Billy, standing on the porch holding hands and dressed in their best finery.

"Preacher," said Uncle Billy, grinning broadly, "we didn't know if you was ever goin' to visit us, so we come t' visit you."

Emma arrived at seven sharp, parking her lilac Oldsmobile in the rectory drive. Hoppy Harper's old Volvo station wagon pulled in behind her.

Emma glanced furtively in the rearview mirror to see whether she was wearing enough eye shadow, as Hoppy walked up to open her door. She thought he looked surprisingly boyish in a cotton sweater and khakis.

When Father Tim greeted them on the porch stoop, Emma was so delighted to see her rector in a new jacket that she gave him a big hug and an air kiss that sounded something like "Ummmwah!"

Then she walked into the living room.

There, seated on the antique Chippendale sofa, were Miss Rose and Uncle Billy Watson, sipping a glass of sherry.

Miss Rose was wearing lisle stockings rolled below her knees, a pair of unlaced saddle oxfords, three World War II decorations on the front of her dress, a great deal of rouge, and a cocktail hat with a veil.

Uncle Billy had on a suit that had belonged to his brother-in-law, with a vest and a gold watch chain. A broad grin revealed his gold tooth, which coordinated handsomely.

"Emma, Hoppy, have a chair," said their host, as serene as a cherub. "And will you have a glass of sherry?"

"Make it a double," said the astounded Emma.

Miss Sadie arrived with Hal and Marge, who had fetched her down from Fernbank.

She carried a small shopping bag that contained several items for her rector's freezer: two Swanson's chicken pies, one package of Sarah Lee fruit turnovers, and a box of Eggos. This was what Miss Sadie considered a proper hostess gift when the Baxter apples were not in season.

Marge was busy hugging one and all, including Miss Rose, who did not relish a hug.

Hal was talking with Hoppy and Uncle Billy about baseball, and Miss Sadie was chattering with Emma.

Why, it's a real celebration already, the rector thought happily, seeing two golden finches dart toward the feeder.

"Miss Sadie, your apple trees have been the prettiest I've ever seen," Marge said, taking a glass of mineral water from her host.

"Do you know car loads of people have driven by the orchards this year? They've been a regular tourist attraction! And somebody from over at Wesley stopped to ask if they could get married under the trees that back up to Church Hill."

"What did you say?"

"I said when do you think it might be, and she said she didn't know, he hadn't asked her yet!"

Their host brought in a tray of cheese and crackers. He refused to serve anything that had to be dipped. He thought dipping at parties was perilous, to say the very least. If you didn't drip dip on yourself, you were likely to drip it on someone else. He'd once had a long conversation with his new bishop, only to look down afterward and discover that his shirt front displayed a regular assortment of the stuff, including bacon and onion.

That he did not serve dip seemed especially convenient for Miss Rose, who took two of everything offered, eating one and putting the other in her dress pocket. Uncle Billy, on the other hand, took two of everything and ate both at once.

As he passed around the mushrooms in puff pastry, Miss Sadie was admiring Miss Rose's military decorations.

He had to admit that he'd never given a party quite like this.

The Company Stew, which had simmered with the peel of an orange and a red onion stuck with cloves, was a rousing success. In fact, he was so delighted with the whole affair that he relented and let Barnabas into the study after dinner.

Marge helped serve coffee and triple-layer cake from the old highboy, as the scent of roses drifted through the open windows.

Barnabas, meanwhile, was a model of decorum and lay next to his master's wing chair, occasionally wagging his tail.

"You must have quoted this dog the whole book of Deuteronomy," said Emma, who still refused to call him by name.

"This dog," he said crisply, "is grounded."

"Uh oh," said Hal. "I guess that means no TV for a week?"

"No TV, no pizza, no talking on the phone."

"Ogre!" said Marge.

"What did the big guy do, anyway?" Hoppy wondered, leaning over to scratch Barnabas behind the ears.

"I'm afraid it's unspeakable, actually."

"Oh, good!" exclaimed Miss Sadie. "Then tell us everything."

Miss Sadie enjoyed the bath story so much, she brought out a lace handkerchief to wipe her eyes.

Miss Rose, however, was not amused. "I leave dogs alone."

"Nope, dogs leave you alone," said her husband.

"Whatever," said Miss Rose, with a wave of her hand.

Hoppy set his dessert plate on the hearth, then leaned back and stretched his long legs. He looked fondly at his elderly patient of nearly a decade. "Uncle Billy, I'd sure like to hear a joke, if you've got one."

Uncle Billy grinned. "Did you hear the one about the skydivin' lessons?"

"I hope you didn't get this from Harry Nelson," said Emma, who didn't like Harry Nelson jokes, not even secondhand.

"Nossir. I got this joke off a feller at the Grill. He was drivin' through from Texas."

Everyone settled back happily, and Miss Rose gave Uncle Billy the go-ahead by jabbing him in the side with her elbow.

"Well, this feller he wanted to learn to sky dive, don't you know. And so he goes to this school and he takes all kind of trainin' and all, and one day comes the time he has to jump out of this airplane, and out he goes, like a ton of bricks, and he gets on down there a little ways and commences to pull th' cord and they don't nothin' happen, don't you know, and so he keeps on droppin' and he switches over and starts pullin' on his emergency cord, and they still don't nothin' happen, an' th' first thing you know, here comes this other feller, a shootin' up from the ground, and the feller goin' down says, 'Hey, Buddy, do you know anything about parachutes?' And the one a comin' up says, 'Nope, do you know anything about gas stoves?' "

Uncle Billy looked around proudly. He would have considered it an understatement to say that everyone roared with laughter.

"I've heard that bloomin' tale forty times," Miss Rose said, removing a slice of cheese from her pocket and having it with her coffee.

Miss Sadie followed her host into the kitchen. "I'm just having the best time in the world, Father!"

"You and me both!" he said, measuring out some more coffee beans.

"I want to have you up to lunch soon. There's something I'd like to talk with you about that's been on my mind for a long while."

It was rare, indeed, for Miss Sadie to have anyone up to Fernbank for anything these days. "It's not another find from your attic, is it?"

"Oh my, no. It's much more important than that!"

"I'll look forward to it," he said, putting his arm around her frail shoulders. "You know, we're supposed to hear something about our painting next week."

"Yes, I know. And I hope you won't think this is awful of me . . ."

"What's that?"

"I dearly hope it's not a Vermeer."

He knew precisely what she meant. Although he'd never said it to a soul, that was his hope as well.

"That was Papa's painting. I remember when he brought it home and we hung it on the wall downstairs. We all stepped back and just stared for hours. It was a real painting from Europe! I'd dearly love to see it on the wall in Lord's Chapel."

"And so would I," he said kindly.

As she went back to the study, Hal joined him, and the two men walked out to the back stoop. The air was balmy, and sweet with springtime.

"Fine dinner, Tim."

"Thanks. It's great to be back in circulation."

"Diabetes seems to be doing you more good than harm." Hal sat on the railing and tamped the tobacco in his pipe. "About that job on the vestry," he said, "let me put it this way: A hundred and seventy acres, a full-time practice, five dogs, two horses, fifteen cows, an old farmhouse that needs a lot of work, and an increasingly pregnant fifty-year-old wife."

"Enough said."

"The timing isn't right . . . and those trips into town at night . . . You know I want to serve, I want to do something more. Just remember that I have in the past and I will in the future."

Father Tim nodded. "When you can, Hal. You know I'd like you to be our senior warden."

Hal puffed on his pipe and nodded thoughtfully. They heard a dog bark in the distance, and a train whistle. "You know that pony that got caught in the fence? We put a saddle on him today."

"Great news! That's been on my mind."

As the coffee finished brewing, they went inside. "You want a good man on the vestry," Hal said with a low chuckle, "recruit Uncle Billy. He'll loosen that crowd up."

Father Tim poured fresh coffee into every cup.

"Miss Sadie," he said, "I've been hoping you'd tell us tonight about your schooling in Paris."

"Oh, do you really want to hear that old stuff?"

"Yes!" said Marge, curling up on the sofa next to Hal. Even Barnabas assumed an air of expectancy. And Emma noticed that Hoppy Harper, who was sitting in Father Tim's wing chair, was as relaxed "as a dishrag," she later said.

"I hardly know where to begin, it's been so long. But, if you're sure . . ."

Everyone was absolutely sure.

"Well, then," she said, sitting even more upright, and squaring her shoulders. "Paris, France, was where I fell in love."

Miss Sadie paused for a moment, her face beaming, and looked around the room. Father Tim saw at once that the truest meaning of the term *captive audience* was being demonstrated right before his eyes.

She sat quietly for a moment, as if she had to summon the memory from a very long distance. "I was sixteen years old when Mama and Papa allowed me to study in Paris," she began.

"Oh, they didn't want me to, not a bit. But Uncle Haywood talked them into it, saying Mitford was just a jumping-off place, that I'd never learn anything worthwhile in Mitford. Wasn't that dreadful of him?

"So off I went with Mama, who was going to take me and spend a month or two near the academy before she came back home. I remember to this day what I was wearing when we left. It was a cream-colored lawn with a georgette bodice worked with seed pearls. And the waist was tied with satin ribbons. Oh, it was lovely!

"Papa took us down to Charleston to catch the boat. Mama and Papa and I all cried the whole way. We just held on to each other and bawled, because my papa was never afraid to shed a tear, he had the tenderest heart, and he was trying so hard to do what was right.

"And so we got on that old boat, and I had the worst sinking feeling. Why, we never even left the dock 'til we were so overcome with homesickness that we nearly threw ourselves overboard."

"Oh, law!" said Uncle Billy, deeply moved.

"But there were such interesting people on that boat! My, what a collection, and they just took on over me, calling me sweet names and inviting us to eat at their table.

"So by the time I reached Paris, I had quit crying, and I just marched into that academy, and started talking the worst old Southern drawl French you ever heard, why, they nearly fell down laughing at me.

"There was one other girl from home, from Virginia, and I stuck to her like bark on a tree. Mama had to live in this house nearby and could only see me on weekends and every Wednesday. She was so lonesome, and she could only say, *'Oui, oui'* and she'd never spent a single night away from Papa.

"Well, I started learning to watercolor, and recite poetry, and play the pianoforte, and do needlework, and study ancient history, and I don't know what all. They just wanted to make me so fancy! And you know, all I dearly wanted to do was be plain.

"Can you imagine a girl with every privilege in the world, just wanting to be plain? I knew it would be a disappointment to Papa, and to Mama, too, and the heck with Uncle Haywood! I wanted to be back in Mitford, picking up walnuts, and playing in my dollhouse at Fernbank, and sewing doll clothes, and helping China Mae in the kitchen, and going barefooted under the apple trees with Louella.

"The very first Wednesday, Mama and I were so glad to have our freedom that we both just went skipping down the lane that led to the pastry shop.

"And while we were in there, Mama let me drink real coffee. Oh, it was the thickest, strongest, blackest stuff you ever could imagine! I just loved it! I thought, if Paris, France, was a taste instead of a city, this would be it!"

Miss Sadie's bright eyes appeared to be looking far away. Marge thought this was like opening an old book and reading a fairy tale with faded watercolor illustrations.

"While we were sitting there, we heard this voice. And we looked up, and there was this . . . this handsome young American man, buying a pastry and a cup of coffee.

" 'Listen to him talk!' said Mama. 'Why, he sounds like he could be from Mitford!'

"He was with another young man, oh, they were so handsome and young and carefree, and they were laughing, and it was just music to our ears.

"Mama never met a stranger in her life, although most people thought she was dignified. She just held out her pretty hand to him and said, 'Young man, where are you from?'

"And he said, 'Mitford, North Carolina, ma'am, United States of America.' "

Miss Sadie's audience murmured with amazement.

"I'll never forget how proudly he said that, just like it was the best place on earth. Which, of course, it is," she said, beaming.

"Amen!" Emma fairly thundered.

"He had just moved to Mitford with his family and baby sister from Tennessee, and he was in Paris to show some of his pharmaceutical inventions. Well, I could go on and on, but he invited Mama and me to have dinner with him that very evening, and he gave us his card and all, and Mama felt sure he was a gentleman.

"Every Wednesday after that, he met us for pastry and coffee, and sent flowers to Mama and me, to her rooms in the little pension."

Miss Rose ate a piece of cubed ham and some Havarti from her pocket. Barnabas had gone to sleep, and the doctor, worn from months of unrelieved strain in his growing practice, snored quietly in the wing chair.

"One day, I said, 'Mama, I don't know how to tell you this, but I just hate this place and everything about it. When I watercolor a dog, it looks exactly like an owl, I am still playing "Three Blind Mice" on the pianoforte, and my French is atrocious. I just want to go home and be plain Sadie.'

"Do you know what my mama said? She said, *'Oui, oui!'*

"When the young man learned we were leaving, he sent a dozen yellow roses to Mama and a dozen red roses to me. There was a note attached to mine, which said: 'Someday when I have made my fortune, I would like to ask you to marry me.'

"So we went home, and Papa met us, and I never spoke another word of French in my life. And to this day," she paused and looked around, "I've never forgotten that handsome young man from Mitford."

Marge leaned forward. "For heaven's sake, Miss Sadie, who was he, anyway?"

Miss Sadie looked straight at Miss Rose Watson, whose cocktail hat had tipped forward at a rakish angle.

"That young man," Miss Sadie said, "was Miss Rose's brother, Willard Porter."

Hal, Marge, and Miss Sadie lingered after the others had gone, eating Belgian chocolates. "I've been very, very good all week in order to do this," Marge explained, looking only slightly sheepish as she took another piece off the tray.

The rector had regained his wing chair and put his feet up. "Miss Sadie, in the years I've known you, you've always been a very private person. Why did you tell us that wonderful version of your Paris story tonight?"

Miss Sadie reflected on this. "When I brought you that painting, it started something. I started thinking about things I'd never thought about before. And I decided I was tired of holding on . . . holding on to my orchard, holding on to my possessions, holding on to my memories.

"I have decided," she said firmly, "to start letting go. And that's one reason I'd like to see you next Thursday for lunch at noon, if you can come, Father."

"I'll be there with bells on."

"Swanson's chicken pie?"

"My favorite!" declared her weary, but enthusiastic host.

At one o'clock in the morning, having refused all offers of help, he put away the last dish and went upstairs, thankful that tomorrow was Saturday.

He felt certain there was more to Miss Sadie's story about Willard Porter, but he was even more certain of something else: Considering this party from beginning to end, from the initial idea to the last dried dish, it had occupied exactly six weeks of his life. And while he'd had a wonderful evening, and so had everyone else, he was certain that he didn't want to do this again for a very long time.

He picked up his open prayer book from the night table.

" 'The Lord grants his loving-kindness in the daytime,' " he read from Psalm 42, " 'In the night season his song is with me.' "

CHAPTER FIVE

The Big Six-O

When the appraiser came the following week, the fog rolled in even heavier than it had on his first visit, which did nothing to improve his temperament.

"Is it always like this in June?" he asked with some sarcasm.

"Not always," Father Tim replied, mildly.

According to the rector's wishes, the vestry was to have only one representative this morning, and it was Harry Nelson. Out of respect, Father Tim had invited Miss Sadie, and he and Emma completed the group who would at last hear the news.

If it is a Vermeer, he reasoned, we'll be in the newspapers, and on TV, and the phone will ring off the hook. He had done a bit of studying on the subject himself and read that a small Vermeer had recently sold at auction for over twenty million dollars.

How the church decided to use the money would, of course, be a topic for the most serious discussion and examination. And, he realized with some regret, at least two of his vestry members would be in deep disagreement over almost any decision.

The little office was fairly bristling with tension and expectation. And, as before, the appraiser did nothing to relieve it.

"Coffee," he said curtly to Emma, removing his jacket and hanging it on a peg.

Just open up your shirt collar, thought Emma, and I'll pour in a whole cup full.

"No cream unless it's the real thing."

Or, she thought, maybe you'd like it in your left ear.

When coffee had been poured all around, the appraiser removed the canvas from its bubble wrap, stacked five books on Anglican church history on the rector's desk, and propped the painting against them.

"This painting has been the subject of grave discussion among the finest Vermeer scholars in America."

"In fact, a paper will be published soon that finely details the depth and distinction of the research it has undergone."

The rector heard himself sigh. Although he'd read that sighing was common to Southern women, he knew for a fact that this unfortunate habit extended also to men.

The appraiser went on for some time, extolling the virtues of the scholarship. Miss Sadie toyed with the diamond cross at her neck. Emma was furious. Harry Nelson could stand it no longer. "Just give us the bottom line!" he blurted.

The appraiser turned to him with a frosty look. "The bottom line?" he asked imperiously.

"That's right," Harry snapped.

"The bottom line is that this painting is not by Vermeer."

"Hallelujah!" shouted Emma.

"Hooray!" said Miss Sadie, clapping her hands.

Father Tim crossed himself, joyfully.

Harry Nelson, however, was devastated. Leaning against the bookcases by the visitor's bench, he brought out a handkerchief and wiped his forehead. Then he sat down, shaking his head. This was a blow. "So who did it and what is it worth?"

"We don't know who did it, but we can safely assume it was done during the time of Vermeer or shortly after his death. It is not one of the famous Vermeer forgeries of the last century.

"As to its market value, we can comfortably expect it to fetch around seven or eight thousand dollars, if properly offered."

"And how much do we owe you for finding this out?" Harry asked, hoarsely.

The appraiser dipped into his jacket pocket and brought forth a crisp envelope, which he handed to the senior warden.

Harry opened it, unfolded the sheet of paper, and read aloud:

"For services of appraisal, as outlined below, four thousand, seven hundred and fifty two dollars and seventy three cents."

"That includes my travel expenses," the appraiser said, adjusting his glasses.

"Thanks be to God!" he exclaimed over and over, as he walked to the Grill the next morning.

He had just come from the hospital, where he had put his arms around a very ill patient, doing for someone else what God had so often done for him. While some priests, he knew, dreaded their hospital visits, he looked forward to his. It was one of the divine mysteries that he came away feeling stronger, and refreshed in spirit. "My hospital visits," he'd been known to say, "are good medicine."

He was surprised, frankly, that he could fit so much into a morning these days. He was dutifully jogging three times a week and now vowed to increase his schedule to four. Would wonders never cease?

Today, he'd even followed his impulses and worn his new sport coat.

"Got you a new neighbor comin' in next door," Mule Skinner said at breakfast. "Be in there in th' fall sometime."

"Terrific."

"Pretty nice lookin'."

"What does he do?"

"It's a she."

"Aha."

"You remember ol' Joe Whattsisname lived there, that was her uncle, the ol' Scrooge."

"Percy's outdone himself on these poached eggs."

"Blonde, blue eyes," said Mule, looking at the rector. "Real nice legs."

"Who? Percy?"

"Your new neighbor."

He had nearly forgotten about the small house next to him, shielded as it was by the rhododendron hedge. Maybe there would be children in the family, he thought. It would be nice to hear the laughter of children.

Later, as he approached his office, he did hear laughter. It sounded like Emma.

He looked at his watch. Too early for Emma, he thought, opening the door and going in.

There, wearing his mailbag and leaning over her desk, was Harold Newland, the postman. And there, too, was Emma, quite frozen with surprise at the sight of her rector, whom she believed to be in a meeting at town hall.

"Preacher, I mean Father, good mornin'," stammered Harold, blushing like a girl.

He looked at Harold's bare legs. Apparently, it was the season for short pants on mail carriers.

"Good morning to you, Harold! Was there too much mail for the box today?"

"That's right, too much mail," said Harold, backing out the door. "Couldn't get it in the box and had to bring it in. Bye, Father. Bye, Emma. Have a good day."

The rector picked up the very slim packet containing only three letters and a copy of the *Anglican Digest.*

"Aha," he said, with hardly any surprise at all.

"I regret to say that lunch isn't chicken pie, Father."

Miss Sadie searched her rector's face for any sign of disappointment. "It's a sandwich with low-salt ham and low-fat cheese."

He felt a bit disappointed, after all.

"With potato chips!" she assured him.

To say that he was happy to be at Fernbank, at the top of Old Church Lane, was an understatement. He felt as if he'd fled to some other country. Up here, the air was drenched with birdsong, the apple orchards were dappled with sunlight, and the broad, cool porch was as consoling as the nave of Lord's Chapel.

From a cut-glass decanter, she poured her guest a glass of sherry, which, he thought, tasted precisely like aluminum foil.

"Three ninety-eight at Cloer's Market!" she announced.

From the porch of Fernbank, he had a commanding view of Mitford. It was a toy village that lay at his feet, like something one would find under a Christmas tree, with an electric train running around it.

There was Main Street, which sliced Mitford neatly in half, and the green circle of the town monument at the north end. And, between the shops, the colorful patches of flower beds made it all appear orderly and safe.

He could see the bell tower of Wesley Chapel, the grand bulk of

First Baptist, and the empty lots, as green as jade, on either side of the tree-enveloped Lord's Chapel. Away to the west, blue mountains rolled like waves.

"Wouldn't it be marvelous, Miss Sadie, if life could be as perfect as it looks from your porch?"

"I've thought that very thing many times. When Hoppy's wife lay dying, I often looked down at his house and thought, we never, ever know what heartache lies under those rooftops."

"I heard a Mississippi preacher say that everybody is trying to swallow something that won't go down."

"Well, he's right about that."

She had put the glass plates on a green wicker table, with a sprinkle of white lace cloth. There were old-fashioned roses in a vase, and a tall pitcher of sweetened tea. They sat down to lunch, and Miss Sadie held her hands out to the rector.

"At Fernbank," she said, "we always hold hands when we say the blessing."

He prayed with a contented heart. "Accept, O Lord, our thanks and praise for all that you've done for us. We thank you for the blessing of family and friends, and for the loving care which surrounds us on every side. Above all, we give you thanks for the great mercies and promises given to us in Christ Jesus our Lord, in whose name we pray."

"Amen!" they said in unison.

He found, with some surprise, that his sandwich looked remarkably inviting, even though it was on white bread.

After lunch, the two sat on the porch, sipping tea. He had wisely cleared his calendar for the afternoon, wanting nothing to interfere.

"We've got chocolate chip ice cream for dessert."

"I hope it's not that low-fat ice milk stuff."

"When we get to dessert at Fernbank, there's no low anything! My mama taught me that dessert should be high."

"I like your style," he said, getting up to help his hostess.

What he was going to hear today, he didn't know. But he felt relieved that he could trust the content. Curiously, some parishioners brought him the most ravishing morsels of slander, as if it were their bounden duty.

He was sitting on the porch railing, finishing his ice cream, when Miss Sadie finally got down to business.

That he nearly fell backward off the railing when he heard her plan was no surprise. In fact, he told Emma later, if he had fallen off, he would have rolled neatly down her steep lawn, through the apple orchards, and across Church Hill Drive.

Then he would have tumbled down the hill toward town and landed on his barber's rooftop, where he would have jumped to his feet and shouted the good news.

The task at hand was to devise an immediate gathering of the vestry and to make it as splendid as humanly possible.

He ran quickly through his list of things to do. A visit by the bishop. Confirmation services. A wedding. A special outing with the Sunday school children. A parishwide barbecue and car wash. Coordinating new artwork for the church letterhead. Two Sunday services. And now this.

It would be enough to make even Father Roland's head swim. If Jeffrey Roland thought he had his hands full out there in his big New Orleans parish, he should be here in Mitford where a mere 200 souls could occupy every waking moment.

He made a phone call. "Miss Sadie, what is your very favorite thing?"

"Well, let's see. Listening to rain on a tin roof!"

He laughed. "I should have been more specific. What is your favorite thing to eat? Besides chicken pie, that is."

"Why, peanut butter and jelly, I believe. Don't you like that, too?"

For the evening at the rectory, he prepared two platters of peanut butter and jelly sandwiches, cut into small squares with no crust. One platter was crunchy. One platter was smooth.

He set out napkins printed with a drawing of Lord's Chapel. He lined up coffee cups, tea glasses, and dessert plates. He filled a small tray with chocolate chip cookies from Winnie Ivey's, and set a fresh lemon pie from The Local on a cake stand.

He cut several blooms from the fragrant Prosperity, and took a handful of blooms as large as peonies from his clove-scented Sarah van Fleet.

Then he put them in a vase, and waited for what would surely be the most dramatic vestry meeting ever held in the history of his parish. Except the one, all those years ago, when the church leaders had to decide what to do after the hideous fire—the fire that had left only a blackened ruin overlooking the green valley.

Miss Sadie sat in a straight-back chair, in front of the fireplace in his study. She was wearing a cut velvet dress of emerald green, with a high neck, and a brooch hand-painted by her mother. That she made a striking figure was an understatement.

"I know you've wondered why I never gave any money to speak of, all these years."

"No, no, certainly not," someone said.

"And don't say you didn't, because I know you did."

There was a profound silence.

"The reason I haven't given as freely as you thought I should is simply this: I've been hoarding Papa's money." She looked slowly around the room, meeting every eye.

"I've earned interest on the capital and invested the interest, and I haven't spent foolishly, or given to every Tom, Dick, and Harry who held his hand out."

There was a variety of supportive murmurs.

"So, what I'm prepared to do this evening is to give Lord's Chapel a special gift, in loving memory of my mama and papa, and in appreciation for the church I've called home since I was nine years old."

She paused for a moment. "This gift is in the amount of five million dollars."

After a collective intake of breath, a cacophony broke out in the rectory study, something like what was usually heard at the Fourth of July parade when the llamas passed by.

"Shush!" said Miss Sadie, "there's more. This money is to be used for one purpose only. And that is to build a nursing home."

She looked around the room. "But I don't mean just any nursing home. This home will have big, sunny rooms, and a greenhouse, and an atrium with real, live birds.

"It will have books and music, and a good Persian rug in the common room, and the prettiest little chapel you ever saw. I want a goldfish pond, and a waterfall running over rocks in the dining room.

"And above every door, there'll be a Bible verse, and this is the verse that will be over the front door: 'Let thy mercy, O Lord, be upon us, according as we hope in thee.' "

Miss Sadie clasped her hands in her lap and leaned forward.

"There, now!" she said, as radiant as a girl. "Isn't that wonderful?"

Of course, it was wonderful. There was no denying, in any way, shape or form, just how wonderful it was.

She appeared to sit even straighter in her chair. "You understand, of course, that this is only half the plan—but it's enough to get us started."

When the meeting broke up at 9:30, those assembled had drunk two pots of coffee and a pitcher of tea, and had eaten every peanut butter and jelly sandwich on the platters. And though no one had said so, the traveling senior warden had not been sorely missed.

In all, it had felt like a very grand party, with Miss Sadie Baxter the center of attention, the belle of the ball.

Emma had told him over and over again that at one o'clock today, no sooner and no later, a printer was coming to pick up a purchase order for the new church letterhead.

The printer, she said, told her to ask him the following:

Did he want the line drawing of Lord's Chapel printed in dark green or burgundy, or would he like purple, which was always a good religious color and, according to the story of the building of Solomon's temple, one of God's favorites?

Also, did he want the address line run under the pen and ink illustration of the church, or at the bottom of the page, like the Presbyterians did theirs? And did he want a Helvetica, a Baskerville, or a Bodoni like the Baptists?

He felt that, among other things this morning, he should look up the meaning of Helvetica, Baskerville, and Bodoni, and made a note to tell the printer that God also requested purple to be used in the temple Moses built.

It was unusually cool for late June, and he savored his short walk to the office, noticing that he was feeling better than he had in years. He had dashed off a note to Walter after his morning prayers, quoting the encouraging message of Hebrews 4:16: "Let us, therefore, come boldly unto the throne of grace, that we may obtain mercy, and find grace to help in time of need."

Boldly! That was the great and powerful key. Preach boldly! Love boldly! Jog boldly! And most crucial of all, do not approach God whining or begging, but boldly—as a child of the King.

"I declare," Emma said as she made coffee, "you're skinny as a rail."

"That's what I hear," he said, with obvious satisfaction.

"What do you mean?"

"They're not calling me 'that portly priest' anymore."

"I can fix that," she said, and opened her bottom desk drawer to reveal several Tupperware containers. The open drawer also contained a glorious fragrance that wafted upward and soon filled the small room.

"Pork roast with gravy, green beans, candied sweet potatoes, cole slaw, and yeast rolls."

"What in the world is this?"

"Lunch!" said Emma. "I figure if we eat early, it'll still be hot."

Just as his clothes were beginning to fit comfortably again, he saw temptation crowding in on every side. He could outrun Winnie Ivey, but in an office barely measuring ten by fourteen, it looked like it was going to be pork roast and gravy, and no turning back.

"Emma, you must not do this again."

"Well, I won't and you can count on it. You've been meek as any lamb to the slaughter, and I thought a square meal would be just what the doctor ordered."

"Not exactly," said her rector, who enjoyed it to the fullest, nonetheless.

After lunch, Emma went head first into the deep bottom drawer, looking for something. She came up with a large bone, wrapped in cellophane.

"For Barnabas," she said, much to his astonishment. That she had called his dog by name was a landmark event. And to have brought him a bone was nearly a miracle.

"I don't know why you're being so good to me," he said, cheerfully.

She glared at him and snapped, "I just told you, for Pete's sake. Weren't you listening?"

For at least two weeks, he'd noticed that her moods were as changeable as the weather.

"Emma, what is it?"

"What do you mean what is it? What is what?" she demanded, then burst into tears, and fled into the bathroom, slamming the door.

By the time she had mumbled an apology, and they'd decided on Baskerville type, burgundy ink, and where to put the address line, it was nearly one o'clock.

"Put your sport coat on," she said.

"What in the world for?"

"Well, just do it, if you don't mind."

"Isn't this the same printer we've been using? He doesn't wear a sport coat."

"Peedaddle! Just trust me on this, and put your sport coat on. You might comb your hair a little, too."

Suddenly, the office had become so minuscule that he wildly imagined Harry Nelson to be right—what they needed to do was knock out the walls, and add a thousand square feet.

As he put on his sport coat, she looked at her watch. "One o'clock," she announced, crisply. She went to the door, threw it open, and shouted, "Here he comes!"

He stared into a veritable sea of smiling faces. And they were all singing "Happy Birthday."

J.C. Hogan jumped in front of him with a camera, as Emma led him, dazed, down the step and onto the sidewalk.

To say that he was surprised would have been totally inaccurate. He was astounded. It had slipped his mind entirely that today, June 28, was his birthday.

He saw Pearly McGee in a wheelchair, with a hospital nurse. There was Hoppy Harper towering over the crowd, grinning, Miss Sadie in a pink straw hat. Hal and Marge, with Barnabas on his red leash. Miss Rose and Uncle Billy, holding hands on the front row. And Percy Mosely, Mule Skinner, Avis Packard, and Winnie Ivey.

He saw Andrew Gregory from the Oxford Antique Shop across the lane, Mayor Esther Cunningham, and more than a dozen others. Who in the dickens was running the town?

"Look up!" said Emma, pointing above his head at the front of the stone office building. He did as he was told and saw a large banner strung above the door. *Happy Birthday, Father Tim, the Big Six-O* was printed in bold, red letters.

"What you thought was a squirrel on the roof this morning was Avis Packard on a ladder, hangin' that thing!"

"Way to go, Avis!" The crowd gave a round of applause.

"See why I told you to wear that dern sport coat?" Emma said as Miss Sadie pinned a rosebud on his jacket. "It's got a lapel!"

J.C. Hogan was already on his second roll of TX 400, declaring that this was better than the turnout for the American Legion barbecue.

Then, Hoppy stepped forward with a handshake and a hug for the honoree. He'd come straight from the hospital and was wearing his white coat, which Emma thought looked romantic. "A young Walter Pidgeon!" she whispered to the mayor.

"According to Avis, who takes note of such things," Hoppy declared, "it's been seven years since you gave up your car for Lent."

"Exactly!" he said, able at last to say anything at all.

"Well, we feel that a man of your distinction should have himself some wheels. But unfortunately, this bunch could afford only two."

He heard a loud, explosive sound behind the hemlock hedge in the lot next door.

"Let 'er rip!" shouted Percy, and from behind the hedge roared what someone later called "a sight for sore eyes."

It was Mule Skinner in a double-knit, chartreuse, yard-sale outfit, weaving wildly back and forth across the lane on a red Vespa motor scooter.

Barnabas led the group in scattering to the sidewalk.

"How do you stop this thing?" Mule yelled.

Hal leaped in front of his pregnant wife. "Turn off the key!"

Mule made a wobbly U-turn, turned off the key, dragged his foot to brake the scooter, and glided smoothly to a stop in front of Father Tim, visibly shaken.

To a loud chorus of "For He's a Jolly Good Fellow," led by Esther Cunningham, the astonished rector got on the scooter, a bit pale beneath his tan, and drove with a mixture of excitement and foreboding to the first rose arbor on the lane, then back again.

By the time he parked it on the sidewalk and put the kickstand down, he noticed that he couldn't stop grinning.

"You don't have to make a speech, since you already make one twice every Sunday," said Mule, slapping him vigorously on the back.

"We know it's not new," said Hoppy, "but it's in great shape. We got it off a little old lady who only drove it on Sundays."

"Nineteen eighty-two, 125 cc, good as new," said Percy, kicking a tire.

"Looky here," Percy said, "you got your horn . . ." He opened up on the horn and everybody clapped.

"You got your high beam and your low beam." He demonstrated, which seemed to be another crowd pleaser.

"And get a load of these turn signals. Ain't that a sight? I rode this thing all the way from Wesley, purred like a kitten."

"Wide open," said Mule, "I followed 'im in th' truck."

Emma cupped her hands to her mouth and made an announcement. "You're all invited in for cake and iced tea. But you'll have to do it in shifts, so step right in and don't tarry. We can take four at th' time."

She had produced a cake from her bottomless bottom drawer, and two gallon jugs of tea with Styrofoam cups.

Hal and Marge filled the cups with ice, and Father Tim cut the cake, as J.C. Hogan shot another roll of black and white, and Esther Cunningham played the kazoo.

The following Monday, the *Mitford Muse* ran two front-page stories on the local Episcopal church community.

A picture of Father Tim on the motor scooter was mistakenly given this bold headline: "Lord's Chapel Rector Receives Gift Worth Five Million Dollars." The story and picture of Miss Sadie giving the rector a cashier's check had no headline at all and referred to the donor as Sudie bixter.

Mule Skinner looked at the front page and sighed.

"Law, law," he said, "J.C.'s done it again."

CHAPTER SIX

Dooley

Hay lay in the fields in fat, round bales.

Blackberries were greening on bushes along the roadside.

Lacy elder flowers bloomed in the meadows.

In his opinion, all was right with the world. Except, of course, for the bitter disappointment of his day lilies. While they had been sold to him as rare and peach colored, they bloomed a fatal orange, just like the commoners in the hedge. In fact, he found them a good deal less attractive, for their color was insipidly pale, compared to the bold hue of their country cousins.

He complained to Emma.

"If *day lilies* were all I had to complain about in this world, I'd be a happy woman."

"What *do* you have to complain about, then?" he asked cheerfully.

She gave him a hard stare, and he noticed that her lower lip trembled. He wisely turned in his swivel chair to face the bookcase, searching, presumably, for a reference work.

That swivel chair was a blessing out of heaven, he mused for the hundredth time. When there was nowhere to go in that infernally small space, one could always swivel in the other direction.

He saw that he was facing a volume on stress in the workplace. He took it off the shelf and opened it at once, daring to hope for a telling insight.

"Well," said Emma, after a considerable silence, "don't you care?" He did not turn around. He was consulting the index.

"Care about what?"

"What I have to complain about."

"I asked you what you have to complain about."

"Yes, but you didn't care."

The rector cleared his throat. He was not accustomed to this sort of thing in his own relationships, although he had seen it in the relationships of countless others.

Slowly, he turned to face his friend and part-time secretary.

"Actually, I am very interested," he said, as kindly as he could.

Tears filled Emma's eyes and splashed down her cheeks.

"Well, then, if you must know," she said, "I'm complaining because I think I'm . . . because I'm falling in love with Harold Newland!"

"Aha," he said, thinking helplessly of Harold Newland's legs in his summer shorts uniform.

"I suppose you're shocked," she said, barely able to speak.

"Not a bit, not one bit. Tell me about it."

She blew her nose on some toilet tissue she'd put in her purse this morning, and composed herself. "Well, whenever I'd get to the office early, he started bringing the mail inside because he saw my car out front.

"Pretty soon, we were talking about this and that, and one evening we went to Wesley to a movie, and then we went to Holding for barbecue, and, well . . . the first think you know, I was . . . I was cooking for him."

Emma inspected her rector's face, and pressed on. "I hate to tell you this, but that big birthday dinner I brought you was leftovers from Harold's supper the night before."

"Two birds with one stone," he said agreeably.

She wiped her eyes. "You know how long Charlie's been gone."

"Ten years."

"Ten *long* years," she said, weeping again.

He waited.

"Harold is such good company. He can fix nearly anything. He even glued three pieces of my good china back together; you can hardly see where. I'd given up ever getting that done! And you know how hard it is to break new ground."

"Oh, I do."

"But he made a little garden out back with nothing but a hoe, and put in a dozen Big Boys."

"That will come in mighty handy around the end of next month."

Emma had warmed to her subject. "And you know those attic stairs that I could never get down? They come down easy as grease, now! Not to mention that he installed new ceiling insulation while he was at it."

"Terrific!" exclaimed her interested listener.

"Plus, he fixed the leak in the basement that mildewed all the clothes I'd saved back for the rummage." Emma wondered if he was getting the point. "You know how things can go down in ten years."

"Around my place, in ten days!"

There was a comfortable silence.

"Does Harold have a church in Mitford?"

"Well, not *right* in. More out. Harold has a farm, you know, eleven acres. He goes to a Baptist church in the country. He said he gave his heart to the Lord when he was a boy."

He had to confess he didn't know much about Harold Newland, since he'd been on their route only a year. Occasionally, if their paths crossed, they'd stop and talk at the mailbox out front.

"Well, then. He goes to church, and knows what for. He owns a farm, he has a job, he's handy around the house, and he likes your cooking. What could you possibly have to complain about?"

Her chin began to quiver. "It's so embarrassing!" she said, wiping fresh tears with the small wad of tissue. "That's why the tomato patch is in the backyard instead of at the side that gets the most sun."

"Whatever can that mean?"

"Well, nobody can see you in the backyard like they can at the side of the house, and I didn't want anybody to see Harold setting out my tomato plants, because . . . well, because . . ."

"Because why, for heaven's sake?"

"Because he's only forty-five!" Emma wailed.

He was quiet for a moment. "Pardon my asking so directly, but how old are *you?*" He thought he remembered that she was two years his junior.

"Fifty-four!"

"Scout's honor."

"Fifty-eight," she said, exhausted by the ordeal of confession.

"I've got an appointment in less than twenty minutes, and I'd like to ask you to think about something."

He looked at her with a gentle franknesss. "As Paul wrote to Timothy, 'God has not given us the spirit of fear, but of power, and of love, and of a sound mind.' "

She blew her nose. "Could you write that down?"

"Who's the secretary around here?" he asked, grinning.

One morning in early August, as he was running on Church Hill Drive, Barnabas came to a sudden halt, which caused him to crash headlong into a ditch filled with the last of the summer sweet peas.

When he limped toward the office later than usual, he was inclined to tell Emma a lie about the whole affair.

"What in God's name have you done to yourself?" she snapped.

He couldn't tell a lie. "We were running. Barnabas stopped, I fell over him. Landed in a ditch."

"Barnabas!" she said, with venom. "From the day you let that creature fool you into taking him home, look what's happened! You got diabetes, your day lilies bloomed out orange, and now here you are black and blue, not to mention half-crippled!"

"It goes without saying that it was not a premeditated act." He eased himself into his swivel chair and felt a sharp pain stab his left knee.

"That does it!"

"Does what?" he asked, not really wanting to know.

"That's it, that's absolutely it!"

If she had a gift, he thought, it was for parable and double-talk. And, while showing off Harold Newland in public had recently sweetened her temperament, he could see a real backsliding under way.

"Do you remember how many times we've all tried to make you get house help?"

"Oh, I remember, all right."

"And how many times you have flatly refused?"

"Over and over again, as I recall."

"Well, that dog has just been the cause of you gettin' it, whether you want it or not!"

"What in the dickens does that mean?"

"That means the vestry had a meeting behind your back, to do something you won't do for yourself! You're on medication, you do your own cooking, you've got a big house and a yard and a busy parish and two services on Sunday, and you won't take a vacation, and now this!

"They said just say when, and we'll hire 'im some help. We'll send 'em on over to the rectory every Wednesday and Friday morning at eight o'clock sharp, but we want you to tell him, because we're scared to do it!"

House help! He felt as if he'd just been delivered a blow to the solar plexus.

He could give himself time to think this over, he reasoned, by swiveling around to face the bookshelves. On the other hand, he could call Harry Nelson at once and attempt to overturn the vestry's decision.

Instead, he did at last what Emma Garrett had so often, in recent weeks, made him feel like doing.

He got up from his desk, walked to the door, and left the office without speaking a word.

He walked briskly to the corner and turned right. At the Oxford Antique Shop, Andrew Gregory invited him in for coffee, but he didn't even slacken his pace. When your vestry goes behind your back and your secretary hates your dog, he thought, there's no place like the Grill to drown your sorrows.

The weather was making it possible for Andrew Gregory to do a thing he liked very much indeed. And that was sit inside the open double doors of the Oxford Antique Shop, on an eighteenth-century bench that was not for sale, and let the breeze drift in while he read from his rare-book collection.

When customers came in, he preferred them to sit on the matching bench as a kind of prelude to the sale, and talk about politics, golf, the gold market, the royal family, Winston Churchill, Italian old masters, and a dozen other subjects that intrigued him.

Without any formal decision to do it, Andrew had become a specialist, not only in old and rare books, but in eighteenth-century partners' desks, English bronzes, hearth fenders, needlepoint chairs, and, for his younger trade, pine farm tables.

He presented these treasures plainly, without even a bowl of potpourri on a table top. Yet, the very soul of elegance pervaded the atmosphere.

The aged, heart-of-pine floors glowed under a regular coat of wax, which he applied himself. And the furnishings got a good rubbing with lemon oil every month, all of which gave the Oxford its seductive signature fragrance.

As a widower, the proprietor of the town's finest antique shop occasioned a good deal of talk. After all, he was attractive, he was trim, he knew how to dress with some flourish, and, because of his early years in Italy, his habits betrayed a certain European gentility.

Also, it did not go unnoticed that he tanned well and was invariably kind to women.

"Five years a widower, and no interest in anybody that we can see. No hope, I'd say," a customer told Winnie Ivey at the bakery.

"There's always hope," said Winnie. Though she was not personally interested, she felt that Andrew Gregory, like her day-old pastries, must not go to waste.

There had once been some talk of Andrew and Emma Garrett, but Emma dismissed it as nonsense.

"Too smart for me!" she said. "And besides, who could live with that ol' dark furniture all over the place?" Emma, who liked sunflower decals on her patio door and kept a vase of artificial tiger lilies on her desk at the office, could not imagine a Georgian highboy in her Danish Modern dining room, or a husband who rattled on about Winston Churchill.

Since he had children in Connecticut, some wondered why he stayed on in Mitford. The truth was, he had grown increasingly happy with his life in the village, and the village was equally happy with him.

It was Andrew Gregory whom the town council sent to visit Myra of Myra's Beauty Bar, to explain why she could not have a shop awning of bubble gum pink instead of the traditional green.

And, when the uproar started over the selling of valley produce through The Local, it was Andrew who was sent to the state capital to set the matter straight.

Still, he was the only Italian in town, and some said, you know how Italians are. They thrive on lots of hugging, kissing, big weddings, and family feasts, hardly any of which was available locally.

Yes, except for those days when he longed for the blue calm of the Mediterranean and a bold sun that made flowers bloom as big as breakfast plates, he was content.

Father Tim was feeling the confusion of too many options in his personal life. For years, he had risen at five, had morning prayer, studied for his sermon, and then made coffee and dressed.

Afterward, he visited the hospital, dropped by the Grill for breakfast, and headed to the office, walking.

It was that simple.

Now, there were decisions to make every new day.

Whether to take Barnabas running if the weather was bad, or leave him at home. Whether to take Barnabas to the office or leave him in the garage. Whether to walk to work or be bold and start riding his motor scooter.

He'd even been considering something he thought would never cross his mind: Whether to start drinking decaf in the mornings.

At his birthday party, Hoppy had reminded him of a tougher decision he needed to make:

When he was going on vacation.

"Go see Walter and Katherine," said his doctor. But he did not want to go to New Jersey, especially in the summer.

"Come out and spend a week with us," said Hal. But he hated to impose for an entire week, with Marge nearly six months pregnant.

He'd never relished planning his own recreation; he simply wasn't good at it. He was prone to turn recreation into something practical, to justify the time and expense, like he'd done with his two-month sojourn in Cambridge. He had intended to make that trip for sheer pleasure, using money from his mother's estate. But he could find no excuse whatever for pleasure alone. So, while he was there, he researched and wrote the paper on C. S. Lewis, which was received with some acclaim.

Recently, he'd heard that the bishop's wife was trying to collect a party to walk a portion of the Appalachian Trail, but since he attracted mosquitos in swarms, this was not an option.

When he arrived at the office earlier than usual, Uncle Billy was sitting on the single step in front of the door, wearing his deceased brother-in-law's finest three-piece suit, and smelling strongly of mothballs.

When he saw Father Tim approaching, he removed his hat.

"Mornin', Preacher."

"Good morning to you, Uncle Billy. You're out mighty early."

"Me and Rose like to get up with the chickens," he said, his gold tooth gleaming.

Uncle Billy looked carefully at the books that lined the office walls, as the rector made coffee.

"I always did want to git educated," he said soberly. "But I lived down in th' valley and couldn't stay with my schoolin', don't you know. I learned to do sums, and I've drawed a few pictures in m' time, but that's about all."

"What kind of pictures?"

"Oh, dogs and th' like. And mountains. And fields and flowers and orchards an' all. Outdoor things, don't you know, that's what I like."

"Well, sir, I'd be pleased to see some of your drawings when the notion strikes."

"Oh, I've got a few here and there, hid back. I'll bring you some, if you're sure you want t' see 'em. They're not much, they're drawed with pencil, and I've not showed 'em off to any but Rose."

Father Tim poured a cup of coffee and handed it to Uncle Billy. "How is Miss Rose?"

"Oh, well, mean as ever, y' might say."

"Is that right?"

"Mean as all get out, don't you know. But that's 'er illness. Sometimes she's good as gold, and those're the times I live for. When I come up from the valley and found Rose and married 'er, I thought I was one lucky man, and I still do. We been married forty-three years now, and I knowed she was sick. Right off, I knowed what I was gettin' into. I've never spent a night away from 'er, don't you know, she's all I've got, and I'm thankful."

Father Tim knew that Miss Rose was schizophrenic and on daily medication.

"I never went back to m' people after I married Rose, I never seen 'em no more. Maybe I should have went back, but I couldn't leave 'er. The first years, we didn't have a car, I done my work at home, don't you know, canin' chairs, makin' bird houses, paintin' signs. Rose, she had plenty of money comin' in from Willard, but she always said, 'Billy, this ain't your'n, it's mine, don't touch it, you git your own.' She kind of scorned me sometimes, but it was 'er illness.

"Some days, she'd come and set on m' lap an' call me 'er Sweet William. She'd laugh an' go on, and dance to th' radio, an' I'd git s' fired up thinkin' she was well, hit was pitiful. Then she'd turn right around and be like a rattler a strikin'. It's grieved me that she never got better, like I thought she might."

"Is there anything we can do to help, Uncle Billy?"

"Well, sir, I don't know what it would be. The Baptists tried, the Presbyterians tried, the Methodists did their part, don't you know. We've gone around to 'em all, but ain't nothin' worked. I wasn't much on comin' over here because of all th' kneelin' and gettin' up and down and all, but we like it."

"I'm glad to hear that. And you know you don't have to kneel. You can stand or you can sit, just as well. Jesus prayed in both those ways."

There was silence as Uncle Billy took a grateful sip of his coffee, and considered this.

"You know, Uncle Billy, our church can't heal Miss Rose any more than the Methodists or the Baptists can. Only God can heal. But we'll do all we can, you have my word."

"I thank you, Preacher."

Father Tim turned the answering machine on, as he usually did when counseling, and sat down in his swivel chair. "Why don't you tell me what's on your mind?"

"Well, you see, all those years ago when Willard, her brother, died, he knowed his baby sister had a illness of some kind, so he left 'er that big ol' house, don't you know, an' all them fine antiques. An' th' way he left it was, it would all go t' the town when she passed.

"Now what's been worryin' me is that if Rose passes before I do, I won't have no place t' call home.

"Sometimes in th' winter, she won't run the furnace and gits awful sick in the chest, but she won't let me git the doctor. That's when I go to thinkin', I'll be on th' state, I'll be on th' welfare, if she takes a bad turn."

"I see."

"All kind of people want to buy that place, nobody knows that the town'll get it, except Rose's old lawyer over in Wesley."

"I'm not much at lawyering," said the rector. "But I believe the town could make a special dispensation, if they cared to. I believe there could be a way for you to go on living there, no matter what they decide to do with the property.

"Why don't you let me look into it, and if you'll come back next week sometime and bring me those drawings of yours, we'll talk it over."

"I'd hate f'r word to git out about th' town endin' up with th' place. Rose never did like to talk about that, don't you know."

"Nobody will hear it from me."

Uncle Billy grinned. "Well, Preacher, you've took a load off my mind, and that's a fact. I've been wrestlin' with this f'r a good while, and I'm just goin' to set it down in th' road and leave it."

"That's a good plan, Uncle Billy. God asks us not to worry about tomorrow."

"That's a hard one, Preacher."

"It sure is. And it takes practice. Just stick with today, is what he recommends. Of course, it helps to stick with him, while we're at it."

"I've been stickin' with him for a good many years. Not like I ought to, but I want t' do better, don't you know."

"Why don't we have a prayer?" He put his arm around Uncle Billy's shoulders.

"Father, we thank you for Bill Watson's faith in you, and for his willingness to let you be in control. We turn this matter over to you now, and ask for the wisdom to proceed, through Christ, our Lord. Amen."

"A-men! Y' know, the Lord always has knowed me as Bill instead of Billy, just like you said!"

When the two men parted, he made a phone call to his cousin, Walter, who was also his attorney.

Then he got down to business with his sermon. Oddly enough, his meeting with Uncle Billy had given him just the insight he needed on a certain difficult point.

"Beggin' your pardon, Father, but there's bats in your belfry." Russell Jacks pushed open the door of the office and peered in.

"Ah, well, Russell! It's been that way since an early age. Come in, come in!"

Russell had been the sexton at the Chapel of Our Lord and Savior for nearly twenty years, but, due to a back ailment, had been living in the valley with his daughter for a year.

"I'm mighty glad to see you, my friend," said Father Tim, wringing Russell's gnarled hand with real feeling. "Welcome home!"

"Soon as we get them bats out of there, I'll scrape up th' droppin's and work 'em in th' flower beds."

Russell Jacks was back and, without missing a beat, ready to get on with his work.

"When in the nation is our bells comin' home?" he wanted to know.

"October, November, around then. All the way from England, at last! It's been a long, dry spell with no bells chiming at Lord's Chapel. And it's been a long, dry spell without you, Russell. Tell me about your back. Is it in good working order?"

"I'd do that, Father, but I've got my little granboy standin' outside." Russell was clasping his hat over his heart, as he usually did in the presence of clergy.

"Let's bring him in, then!" Father Tim stepped to the door and looked out. There, standing at the corner of the stone building, was a barefoot, freckle-faced, red-haired boy in dirty overalls.

I declare, thought the rector. Tom Sawyer!

"His mama's poorly," said Russell, "and cain't half watch after 'im. She kind of looked after me when I was down and out, an' I told her I'd look after him awhile. He's th' oldest of five."

It occurred to the rector that somewhere in his office, though he couldn't recall where, was one last box of Little Debbies. He reached behind a volume of Bonhoeffer's *Life Together*, and pulled out the box of creme-filled cookies.

"What's your grandboy's name?"

"Dooley!" said Russell Jacks with evident pride.

"Dooley!" he called out the door, "Come in and let's have a look at you!"

The boy came and stood on the sidewalk, staring at the rector. Now that he could see him up close, Father Tim was surprised by a certain look in his eyes, a look that made him appear older than his years.

"Ain't this a church place?" the boy asked, skeptically.

"Why, yes, it's a church office."

"I cain't come in, then, I ain't washed."

"You don't have to wash to come in."

"You ain't lyin', I reckon, bein' a preacher an' all."

"No. No, I'm not lying."

The boy bounded up the single step and through the door, searching the room with his quick gaze. "You got any place in here where I can take a dump?"

CHAPTER SEVEN

The One for the Job

It had been a week since Puny Bradshaw had rung his doorbell at precisely eight o'clock in the morning and started taking over his house.

Fortunately, he was just going out the door as she came in, thereby sparing himself the awful trial of having to tell her what to do.

He was humiliated to think that, the night before, he had hidden his laundry in a pillowcase and stuffed it into the back of his closet, like some sneak thief or chicken poacher. What was considerably worse is that she had found it. When he came home around noon to pick up his sermon notebook, she met him in the hall.

"Father," she said, shamelessly holding up the most ragged pair of shorts he owned, "your underwear looks like it's been in a cat fight. How in the world do you preach a sermon in these things?"

He was so stunned by this display that he hadn't been able to reply.

"Don't mind me," she said, seeing that he minded very much. "My granpaw was a preacher, and I waited on 'im hand and foot for years, so you might say I'm cut out for this job. Tell you what, next time I'm at Wal-Mart over in Wesley, I'll get you a dozen pairs, 'cause I'm goin' to use these for cleanin' rags!"

When he arrived home that afternoon at five-thirty, he found a steaming, but spotless, kitchen and a red-cheeked Puny.

"That bushel of tomatoes like to killed me!" she declared. "After I froze that big load of squash, I found some jars in your garage, sterilized 'em in your soup pot, and canned ever' one in th' bushel. Looky here," she said, proudly, pointing to fourteen Mason jars containing vermillion tomatoes.

"Puny," he exclaimed with joyful amazement, "this is a sight for sore eyes."

"Not only that, but I scrubbed your bathroom 'til it shines, and I want to tell you right now, Father, if I'm goin' to stay here—and I dearly need th' work—you're goin' to have to put your toilet seat up when you relieve yourself."

He felt his face burn. A little Emma, her employer thought, darkly. Now I've got one at the office and one at home, a matched set.

He could not, however, dismiss the joy of seeing fourteen jars of tomatoes lined up on his kitchen counter.

On Friday afternoon, he arrived at the rectory to find the house filled with ravishing aromas.

Baked chicken. Squash casserole. Steamed broccoli. Corn on the cob. And frozen yogurt topped with cooked Baxter apples. Oh, ye of little faith, why didst thou doubt? he quoted to himself.

"I know about that old diabetes stuff, my granpaw had it worse'n you," Puny told him with satisfaction. "An' not only can I cook for diabetes, I can cook for high blood pressure, heart trouble, nervous stomach, and constipation."

During the past twelve years, he had sometimes asked in a fit of frustration, "Lord, what have I done to deserve Emma Garrett?" Now, he found himself asking with a full heart, "Lord, what have I done to deserve Puny Bradshaw?"

He chose his best suit, just back from the cleaners in Wesley, and hung it on the hook behind his bedroom door. He laid out a pair of brand-new boxer shorts, which Puny Bradshaw had kindly fetched from Wal-Mart, and a shirt she had ironed to perfection. Then he shined his black loafers, put away the kit, and remembered to get a clean handkerchief from his top drawer.

He had already had morning prayer and studied the challenging message of Luke 12: "Therefore, I tell you, do not be anxious about your life, what you shall eat, nor about your body, what you shall put on. For life is more than food, and the body more than clothing.

"Consider the ravens: they neither sow nor reap, they have neither storehouse nor barn, and yet God feeds them. Of how much more value are you than the birds?"

There was not one man in a thousand who considered these words more than poetical vapor, he thought as he dressed. Don't be anxious? Most mortals considered anxiety, and plenty of it, an absolute requirement for getting the job done. Yet, over and over again, the believer was cautioned to abandon anxiety, and look only to God.

Whatever else that might be, it certainly wasn't common sense.

But "common sense is not faith," Oswald Chambers had written, "and faith is not common sense."

He was entering that part of the week in which his sermon was continually on his mind. "Let me say I believe God will supply all my need," Chambers had written, "and then let me run dry, with no outlook, and see whether I will go through the trial of faith, or . . . sink back to something lower."

He put his handkerchief in his pocket, and looked into the full-length mirror on the back of the guest room door.

There. That would do.

He picked up his sermon notebook, went to the garage to say goodbye to Barnabas, and set out walking to his early meeting with Mayor Cunningham.

In her office at the town hall, Esther Cunningham was eating a sausage biscuit with an order of fries and drinking a Diet Coke, which Father Tim found remarkable, considering that it was only 7:00 a.m.

"Top of the morning!" she said, lifting her cup in a grand salute. "Come in, sit down, take a number!"

There were, indeed, a few places to sit in the mayor's office. When she was first elected fourteen years ago, she had rented a U-Haul truck and brought all her den furniture from home, much to the astonishment of her husband. There was a powder blue sofa, a leather love seat, two club chairs, an ottoman, and a Danish Modern cocktail table. None of which did much to conceal the fact that the walls were slowly mildewing from the effect of a roof leak that no one, in as many years, had been able to locate.

"How do you like that fine snap in the air this morning?" he asked, sitting in a club chair across from Esther.

"There's nothin' I like better! Ray and me are takin' the RV and headin' for the first trout stream we can find. Right after the next granbaby, of course."

The mayor was known for her several beautiful daughters and astonishing number of grandchildren, but he could not recall the latest head count.

"And what number will this be?"

"Twenty-three!" she said. A brass band might have struck up behind her.

"Aha!" he said, looking around for a coffee pot. As far as he could tell, there was not a drop in the place. "Esther, your girls are doing all in their power to raise our taxes."

"Don't complain. So far, you've got two garbage collectors, a postman, a bank teller, a policeman, and a park ranger out of th' deal. Not to mention a fireman and a drove of Sunday school teachers."

"How quickly I forget. Well, shall we get right to business?"

"We'd better. I've got a council meeting at eight o'clock about namin' the town flower. They've chewed on this thing 'til I'm about half sick of it, and now the Wesley paper wants a story, and they won't let us alone 'til we announce it.

"Whichever flower it falls out to be, we're goin' to paint it on signs comin' into town, put a plaque at the monument, set aside a special day with a parade, get the governor to come for the ceremony . . . I never saw such a to-do since the Baxter Apple Bake-Off."

"Don't remind me," said the rector, who had personally baked sixteen deep-dish pies last year to raise money for the library.

"What do you think the town flower should be? You're a gardener." She wadded up her biscuit wrapper and lobbed a fine pass into the wastebasket.

"The pansy vote is mighty strong, of course."

"Well, but look at all the rose arbors up Old Church Lane."

"That's right, but they're out of general view. What do tourists see in the window boxes along Main Street? Pansies! Around the town monument? Pansies every year! And the shop gardens? Full of pansies!"

"Would you want to invite somebody to Pansy Day? I mean, think about it, would you call somebody in Raleigh or Salisbury and say come on up for Pansy Day?"

"Ah, Mayor, you've got a point there. I wouldn't have your job for the world."

"I've had it too long, to tell the truth. I wouldn't want you to spread this, but I'm groomin' one of my grans for the next election."

"Imagine that!"

"Now, while I finish my cholesterol fix, why don't you tell me what's up?"

"What if, upon the event of a death, the town were to be given a large home for civic use, and in that home was left a family member with no place to go? The surviving family member is a good sort, presently of sound mind and body, and no trouble to anyone. Do you think the tone of the council would be agreeable, if this came to pass today, to letting the surviving member stay on? It would be legally sound."

"I don't suppose you'd be willin' to mention any names in this scenario."

" 'Drawing on my fine command of the English language,' " he said, quoting Benchley, " 'I'll say nothing.' "

"So, since none of this has actually happened and I don't know doodley squat about who you're talkin' about—I guess you're lookin' for a gut reaction?"

"That's right."

"I'd say if what you tell me is right, and it always has been, we could work it out. We look after our own here in Mitford, that's been one of my big things all along. You know, for example, that we always make sure Miss Rose and Uncle Billy have oil in their tank."

"Good example."

"So," said the mayor, giving him a broad wink.

"So, what's your vote for the town flower?"

"Johnny Jump-Up!" she said, laughing.

"Tell you what. If you can get anybody to drive all the way from Charlotte or Raleigh for Johnny Jump-Up Day, I'll take you out for a big steak dinner in Wesley."

"I'll hold you to it!" said the mayor, vigorously shaking his hand.

When he got to the office after a visit with the seriously ill Pearly McGee, he found Uncle Billy waiting on the step, holding a package wrapped loosely in yellowed copies of the *Mitford Muse.*

"Mornin', Preacher."

"Good morning, Uncle Billy," he said, helping the old man to his feet.

"That ol' arth'r' is gittin' s' bad, I cain't hardly git down, much less up. Pretty soon, you'uns 'll jis' have to stand me aginst th' wall."

"Maybe use you for a hat rack."

"Maybe put a little birdhouse on top and set me in th' yard." Uncle Billy laughed, showing all three of his teeth. Inside, he eased himself onto the visitor's bench, and carefully laid the package across his knees.

Father Tim plugged in the coffee pot and opened the windows. "To get right to it, Uncle Billy, I've done some checking. My attorney is familiar with cases like yours. Legally, a dispensation could be made that would enable you to live on in the Porter house. And while I never mentioned a name, the mayor thinks the council would cooperate whole-heartedly.

"We both know we can't second-guess what tomorrow will bring, or how the town leadership will change, but it seems to me that you have nothing to worry about."

Uncle Billy lowered his head for a moment. When he looked up, there were tears in his eyes. "Thank you, Preacher."

"No, Uncle Billy, thank you. I believe the Holy Spirit has shown me a sermon in your predicament." The disciples had been repeatedly instructed with one simple word: Ask. Uncle Billy, like much of the rest of humanity, had spent precious years worrying instead of asking.

"I hope that's your drawings you've got there."

"I was about not to bring 'em, don't you know. I got to lookin' at 'em an' said, 'Rose, I cain't drag this ol' stuff over to th' preacher.' Well, she got to fussin' an' sayin' how I never did have much belief in m'self. But that ain't right. I know I can cane chairs and make signs as good as th' next feller, and I ain't too bad with a birdhouse, don't you know. But this here is flat stuff."

"And I've been looking forward to seeing it ever since you mentioned it last week."

The old man stood up slowly and put his package down on the desk. Then he began to peel back the brittle newspapers,

Father Tim saw that the date on the *Mitford Muse* was 1952. And then he saw the first drawing.

In stunned silence, he looked at the finely detailed pencil rendering of a bird dog in a cornfield, a sky alive with quail, and, in the distance, a hunter with upraised shotgun against a background of late autumn trees.

"Good heavens," he said quietly.

On Friday, he did something he'd seldom ever done. He took the day off.

After all, the cleaning truck was coming from Wesley, and he needed to go through the pockets of all his suits, and attach notes about simple alterations. He had to go to the barbershop and get his neck "cleaned up" as Joe Ivey always said, take his shoes to be re-soled, and buy something to remove the beer label from his motor scooter helmet.

Because he made his usual trip to the hospital and the Grill before launching these chores, he wasn't at home when Puny arrived at eight o'clock.

She hoped he would have done something with the bushel of Baxter apples still sitting in the garage, and save her the trouble. But there they sat, drawing flies, as she discovered when she opened the door.

As Barnabas came bounding toward her in a frenzy of delight, Puny recited in a loud voice one of the few Scriptures she'd ever committed to memory:

" 'And this is his commandment, that we should believe on the name of his Son, Jesus Christ, and love one another'!"

Barnabas sprawled at her feet and sighed.

"I've never seen anything to beat you in my whole life," she said with admiration. "They should put you on TV."

Puny picked up the bushel of apples and took it to the kitchen, where she washed the fruit in the sink. Three canning jars were all they had left after she had finished the tomatoes. Which meant just one thing: she'd have to bake pies and dry the rest.

"Lord knows," she muttered to Barnabas, "I'm half give out just gettin' started around here!"

She opened the back door for fresh air, and was startled to see a red-haired boy in ragged overalls standing on the step. From what she'd heard, this would be Russell Jacks's grandson. Barnabas barked joyfully and dashed to the door, yelping to get out. "Hush up and lay down! Philippians four-thirteen, f'r gosh sake!"

The boy looked intently at her through the screen.

Puny didn't know which was more noticeable, his blue eyes or his dirty feet.

"I was jis' goin' to knock," he announced. "Are we kin?"

"Not that I know of. What makes you ask?"

"Freckles same as mine."

"We couldn't be kin. You come from down the mountain!"

"Blood travels," he said soberly.

"What can I do for you?"

"Granpaw told me to come an' git th' preacher."

"Father Tim's not here, he's at the hospital."

"What's the matter with 'im?"

"Nothin's the matter with 'im. He goes and calls on sick people and makes 'em feel better."

He looked down at his feet and spoke in a low voice. "My mama's sick," he said.

"Why don't you come in and wait for him? He'll be here in a little bit." As she pushed open the screen door, Barnabas growled.

"Will 'at ol' dog bite?"

"Not unless he has to," Puny said, catching Barnabas by the collar. "Go set down on that stool."

He ran to the stool and tucked his feet on the top rung. "A dog like t' eat me up, one time."

"Based on your overalls alone, this dog won't mess with you," she said with conviction.

"What's your name?"

"Puny."

"Why'd you git a name like 'at?"

" 'Cause when I was born I was all sickly and puny-like."

"How did you get over bein' puny?"

"Hard work, honey, that's how." She started paring the great mound of apples in the sink. "What's your name?"

"Dooley."

"Dooley? Don't you have a real name like Howard or Buddy or Jack or somethin'?"

"Dooley is a real name!" he said with feeling.

There was a long silence as Puny bent to her task.

"Did you ever try stump water?" Dooley asked.

"Stump water! Shoot, I tried everything, but nothin' ever worked."

"I hear if you lay face down in fresh cow dump, 'at works."

She turned around, still peeling the apple. "Did you try that?"

"Nope."

"Me neither, 'cause I heard you had to lay there awhile for it to take."

"Can I have one of them apples?"

"If you'll say 'May I,' you can have one."

"May I," said Dooley.

He quickly put it in his overalls pocket. "My uncle said if you wash y'r face with the same rag you wash y'r feet with, that'll do it."

"I wouldn't try that, if I was you. Besides, I think we ought to be content with what the good Lord gave us. I don't mess with my freckles no more, and I think you ought to stop wastin' your time, too."

He studied his feet, which he was swinging freely now, since Barnabas had fallen asleep. The kitchen was quiet. Birdsong drifted through the open window and a breeze puffed out the curtains.

Dooley decided to eat his apple. "What else you want t' talk about?"

"How old are you?"

" 'Leven."

Puny peeled furiously. "I'm glad I ain't eleven."

"Why?"

"I didn't like bein' a kid. Somebody was always beatin' on you, pullin' your hair, chasin' you around th' house, throwin' mud on you. I wouldn't be your age for all th' tea in China, much less Japan."

"When I'm twelve, I'm goin' t' whip th' horse hockey out of somebody."

"You better not be usin' that kind of language in this house. Nossir, that won't go around here."

He ate his apple. "When's 'at preacher comin'? My granpaw said make it snappy."

"He'll get here when he gets here. What's the matter with your mama?" Puny started slicing the peeled apples. The room was silent except for the slices dropping into the pot. "Well, cat got your tongue?"

"I ain't tellin' you nothin' about that."

"Why not?"

"Because it ain't none of your stupid business."

She turned and looked at him. His face had hardened, and he looked older, like a little old man perched on the stool.

"Let me tell you somethin', then, buster. Don't come in here in my kitchen with them dirty feet, and think you can go sassin' me. I'll pitch your little butt out on th' porch."

He slid off the stool and headed toward the door. "You ol' fat witch!"

She caught him on the back stoop. "Witch, is it? You know what witches do t' back-talkin' young 'uns?" She held him by his galluses and put her face close to his. "They boil 'em in that big ol' pot in yonder."

"Oh, yeah?"

"Yeah!" She bared her teeth at him ominously. "And then . . ."

"And then what?" asked Father Tim, walking into the yard.

"I was jist about t' cook this young 'un alive," she said, "and you come and spoiled everything."

When Father Tim, Dooley, and Barnabas arrived at the side door of Lord's Chapel, Russell Jacks didn't waste time exchanging pleasantries.

He removed his hat, respectfully. "Lock's been broke."

He felt a sudden chill. In the years he had pastored this parish, there had never once been any vandalism, hardly a beer can thrown onto the front lawn.

"Ain't anything else broke, as I can see."

"Dooley," said Father Tim, "I'd like you to do something for me and keep Barnabas company. Just sit here on the grass and I'll put his leash on the bench leg. That way, you two can get to know each other."

Dooley looked suspiciously at the enormous black dog who had tried to lick his face all the way to the church.

"You do what th' Father tells you," said Russell Jacks, holding the door open for the rector.

He walked home, oddly troubled. In the hour they'd spent searching for any sign of harm, they'd found nothing. The priceless tapestry was unharmed, nothing was taken off the altar, nothing was moved or misplaced that he could see. If someone had broken in looking for money, where would they have looked? Emma always carried the collection home and brought it to the office on Monday.

He had checked the drawers in the sacristy, and found $18.34 in an envelope, about the usual amount that was kept around to pay for brass polish or votive candles.

Why would anyone go to the trouble to force an entry, yet disturb nothing inside? He was making too much of the whole thing. It was only a broken lock, after all, nothing more.

Though he didn't consider himself one to rely greatly upon his feelings, he felt uneasy. Perhaps he should call Rodney Underwood, the young police chief, and see what he thought about it.

Some good, however, had clearly come from the bad.

Out there in the grass by the garden bench, Dooley Barlowe had found himself a friend.

When he got home, he went to the kitchen looking for Puny and saw instead an unusual sight in his backyard.

She had discovered an old screen door in the garage, hosed it down, laid it across two ladderback chairs, and covered the screen with apple slices.

"This is our dryin' rack," she said with authority. "Before I leave today, we'll carry it into the guest room. On sunny days, we'll bring it back out again. I know it's extra trouble, but that's th' price you pay for hot cobblers in winter. Meantime, I've got six pies in the oven and six more to go, and I wish to goodness you'd get that boy to wash his feet."

Father Tim was utterly astonished at what he heard himself say: "Puny, do you have any work on Mondays?"

"No, I don't, and I need some."

"Well, then," he said, "you've got it!"

On Saturday morning, he visited the Oxford Antique Shop, carrying an apple pie in a basket.

"Little Red Riding Hood!" said Andrew Gregory, coming from the back of the store to greet him.

The rector held out the basket. "Homemade apple pie," he said, with some pride.

" 'The best of all physicians is apple pie and cheese'!" exclaimed Andrew, quoting a nineteenth-century poet. "What an excellent treat, my friend. Thank you and come in." He took the basket, delighted as a child. "Why don't we just polish off the whole thing right now and you can carry your basket back?"

The two men laughed.

"I'm afraid I'll have to take my basket back in any case, as there's five more to be delivered in it."

"I don't know how you find time to feed your sheep physically as well as spiritually."

"Andrew, Providence has blessed me with the finest house help a man could ever have. Puny Bradshaw is her name, and she not only baked a dozen pies yesterday, she canned fourteen quarts of tomatoes last week."

"Extraordinary!"

They sat down on the matched loveseats at the shop door.

"Here's something even more extraordinary. I've discovered that Uncle Billy Watson is a splendid artist. Uneducated, grew up in the valley, never had training of any kind. 'Rough as a cob,' as he says. Yet, he draws like a Georgian gentleman."

"You always seem to have a Vermeer of one kind or another on your hands."

"The drawings are in my office, and I'd like your opinion. Perhaps you'll stop over on Monday morning. After all, I've been drinking your coffee for years, now come and have a go at mine."

"I'll look forward to it," said Andrew. "And please don't leave yet. I have something to show you."

Andrew went to the back room and returned with two books.

"Just look at this!" he said. "A first edition of the first volume of Churchill's *History of the English-Speaking Peoples.* Something I've wanted for a very long time." He turned to the opening page and read aloud: " 'Our story centres in an island, not widely sundered from the Continent, and so tilted that its mountains lie all to the west and north, while south and east is a gently undulating landscape of wooded valley, open downs, and slow rivers. It is very accessible to the invader, whether he comes in peace or war, as pirate or merchant, conqueror or missionary.'

"Ah," said Andrew, unashamedly beaming. "A prize! I shall read all the volumes over again. Now, for you," he said, with a twinkle in his eyes, "a prize of your own." He handed the rector an early leather-bound volume of Wordsworth.

The rector was touched by the feeling of the softly worn covers against his palm. It was as if the book had belonged to him all along and had at last come home.

Smiling, he turned the linen-weave pages until he found a favorite passage. "Andrew, if you'll permit me, I also would covet a moment to read aloud."

It was Saturday morning in Mitford. The village was up and stirring, yet a slow, sweet peace reigned, a certain harmony of mood and feeling. In the open door of the shop the two men sat, one reading, one listening, and both, for the passing moment, were content.

He was right. While Miss Sadie had lavishly bestowed bushels of apples upon the village populace, no one had thought to carry her a pie this year.

After lunch, he and Barnabas walked up the steep hill to Fernbank. Though the grand old house was showing its age, it was beautiful still, situated proudly at the crest of a hill massed with wild fern.

Miss Sadie met him at the door. "They've brought me two quarts of apple sauce," she reported, "a quart of apple butter, and a dozen jars of jelly. But, oh my, I'm glad to see this pie!"

She talked him into having a piece with her on the porch, and a glass of cold milk.

"This old place is running down so, I can hardly keep it up. Luther has kept busy in the orchard this year, but he's too old to mow and pick apples to boot. It's just catch as catch can around here." Miss Sadie sighed, something he'd seldom heard her do. "What I need is somebody young and stout!"

The walk up the hill had carried fresh oxygen to his brain. "Dooley Barlowe!" he blurted.

"How's that?"

"Miss Sadie, I know a boy who just might fit the bill. Eleven or twelve, I'd say, old enough to push a mower and prune a bush or two if you'd show him how. Shall I look into it?"

"And be quick about it!" she said, beaming.

"Monday morning, first thing. Now, any considerations about the site for the nursing home? I admit to having my own strong opinion."

"Father," she said soberly, "there isn't but one site to consider."

"And what's that?"

"Right down the road where the old church was."

"Precisely! My thinking exactly!"

"Great minds work alike!" she said, clapping her small hands.

"The view . . ."

"Couldn't be better."

"The proximity . . ."

"Absolutely perfect!" she exclaimed.

"And since the money you so graciously donated also covers the cost of land . . ."

"That means the church gets paid for the land, and Lord's Chapel can have a new roof!"

Barnabas looked up at the odd pair, rocking in unison and laughing like children. He yawned hugely.

"I confess I've been concerned about you, giving away all your father's money. I just hope that . . . well, I hope that you haven't strapped yourself."

She looked at him, he thought, almost coquettishly. "Father, what I gave away was only what belonged to Papa. There's still Mama's money, you know."

On Monday morning, Andrew Gregory left the church office with a large, flat package under his arm, just as Russell Jacks arrived.

"Father," said the sexton, making himself at home on the visitor's bench, "my little granboy cain't be took home to his mama yet, and they say school's a startin'. He don't want t' go, it bein' a strange place an' all. I know it's the law for 'im to go and it's right for 'im to go, but I don't hardly know what to do to git 'im started."

School! Well, of course, it was time for school.

"Russell, he'll need to be registered." And, he thought, scrubbed from one end to the other.

"You mean checked in and all?"

"That's right, and we'll need to find out when and how. I believe sometime next week is the first day."

He picked up the phone and called the school superintendent. Then he called the police department.

"Is it all right for two people to ride on a motor scooter over to Wesley?" he wanted to know.

Extra helmet, he wrote on his notepad, as he hung up.

"You may as well git the police back on the line," said Russell.

"Why's that?"

"Because we ain't reported that broke lock, yet. We're supposed t' report a thing like that, git it on th' record."

Ah, thought Father Tim. Much ado about nothing. "I'll take care of that, Russell. Right now, let's get Dooley in school."

At 10:30, he left the office. He had managed to borrow another helmet, and set out for Wesley with an ecstatic Dooley Barlowe behind him on the Vespa.

At two o'clock, they pulled up at the back door of the rectory, with a large plastic shopping bag strapped into the basket. They marched up the steps and stood looking through the screen at Puny, who was rolling dough for a chicken pie.

"Here's a boy who needs cleaning up," said Father Tim. "And here are some clothes for him to wear." He opened the screen door, let Dooley into the kitchen, and handed her their purchases. "I don't know what to tell you to do, but I know you're the one for the job."

Having said that, he left in some haste, leaving Puny holding the bag.

"So I run a tub of hot water," she said, giving her report, "an' handed 'im a bar of soap and said git in there an' soak.

"Well, he went to sayin' how I wasn't 'is mama and couldn't tell 'im what t' do, so I yanked a knot in 'is tail."

He thought she looked very smug and self-satisfied. "And what did you do to yank this knot exactly?"

"That's for me t' know and you t' find out. Not meanin' any disrespect, of course."

"Certainly not."

"So here's what I done. While he was soakin', I washed 'is overalls, and sent 'im home in 'em. I couldn't see dressin' 'im up in new clothes t' go spillin' somethin' down th' front, or settin' in dog poop. I've seen Mr. Jacks's place and it ain't th' Taj Mahal."

"Well done."

"He was mad as fire about it, but Mr. Jacks is bringin' 'im here in th' mornin' and he's gittin' dressed in 'is new stuff, and you can take 'im up to Miss Sadie's. I've cut off th' tags and pressed everything, an' he can wear 'is new blue jeans with that green plaid shirt."

"You're a marvel," he said, sighing with relief.

"What I am is give out, if you don't mind. I declare, takin' care of a preacher is the hardest work I ever done."

"It is?"

"Trust me on this," she said.

"Miss Sadie, I'd like to present Mister Dooley Barlowe! Then what do you say?"

"I say, how d'you do, pleased t' meet you."

"Flawless!"

The sun had come out, and though Dooley had wanted to go by motor scooter, they agreed to walk to Fernbank.

The boy looked so different in his new jeans and plaid shirt, in his fresh socks and Keds, the rector could hardly believe his eyes. He had personally wet Dooley's hair and brushed it, snipping straggly ends with the kitchen shears.

When they reached Fernbank, Miss Sadie was on the porch, waving. A pitcher of lemonade and a plate of store-bought cookies sat on the wicker table.

"Miss Sadie, I'd like to present Mister Barley Doolowe!"

"You got your part wrong," said Dooley.

In the few days before school opened, Dooley earned $44.00. As agreed, he came by the church office and reported what he'd done.

"I done this an' that."

"What this and what that?"

"I took out 'er ashes from an ol' stove an' put 'em on 'er 'zaleas. I mowed 'er yard, took goin' over twice, it like to killed me, and hit a nest of yellow jackets."

"Aha."

"I got stung two times, pruned some ol' shrubberies, an' hauled stuff to a wash house. Then I run up an' down them stairs carryin' books to th' attic."

"You pruned shrubbery?"

"Granpaw taught me."

"What else?" the rector asked, genuinely interested.

"I eat some chicken pie an' drunk some lemonade an' eat half a pound cake, and pooped in 'er toilet. Doorknob come off 'er toilet door, had t' crawl out 'er window."

"Well done!"

Dooley took the money from his overalls pocket and gave it to the rector, who counted out $40.00 and put it in a box for index cards.

"This will go toward your bicycle. What color did you say you wanted?" He remembered perfectly well.

"Red! Red as a fire engine!"

"Excellent." He took the remaining four dollars and handed it across his desk. "This is for you, just like we talked about. Next week, you can have four dollars again. This after-school work at Miss Sadie's should get that bicycle sooner than we think."

This is too easy, he thought, musing to himself one September evening in his study. For some reason he couldn't explain, he felt like he was waiting for the other shoe to drop.

"Be glad you've never been in love," said Emma.

"Who says I haven't been?"

She stared over her half glasses. "You mean you have?"

"That's for me to know and you to find out."

"I hate it when you talk common." She didn't know which she wanted more, to talk about Harold Newland, or her preacher being in love. She decided to do both. "How bad was it?"

"How bad?"

"Let me put it another way. How good was it, bein' in love?"

"How quickly you forget, Emma. I didn't say I'd been in love."

"I should have known you'd double-talk me blue in the face. He wants me to meet his mother."

"Terrific."

"Terrific? How would you like meeting somebody's mother who's only five years older than you? I could die, I could just die."

"Don't die. Secretary's Day is coming around, and I'm planning to take you to Wesley for dinner."

She brightened. "Really?"

"On my motor scooter."

"I'd give you a good kick if you weren't a priest."

"That never stopped some people," he said.

CHAPTER EIGHT

Golden Days

During the eleven o'clock service, he looked up from the reading in Matthew and found a wife for Hoppy Harper. There, sitting on the gospel side, was one of the loveliest creatures he'd ever seen.

His response was so immediate and overwhelming, he felt certain the inspiration had come from above. What to do about it, however, was not revealed.

From his own observation, matchmaking was more than merely risky, it had proven to be downright disastrous.

Throughout his career as a bachelor priest, people had tried to marry him off. Some parishes had been more intent upon this achievement than others, and the parish of Lord's Chapel had been the worst of the lot.

He had no sooner arrived in Mitford than three vestry members "ganged up," as he called it, and arranged a tea in his honor at the home of a summer resident, Roberta Simpson.

Roberta was so enormously rich that it was beyond his powers of comprehension to imagine the rumored sum.

"You better hook this one," somebody had the gall to say. "You could afford to give up preaching."

After several agonizing meetings, which were manipulated entirely without his knowledge or blessing, Roberta returned to Florida and married her stockbroker. When he met the man the following summer, he could barely resist the impulse to kiss him on both cheeks, after the European fashion.

Then there had been the Becky Nelson Campaign. Becky was a petite and charming widow who played bridge around the clock and thought Wordsworth was a Dallas department store. He didn't like to recall what a fiasco that had been. Talking to Becky Nelson had been precisely like talking to a rock.

It took a full two years for his well-meaning parishioners to throw in the towel. "I give up," he overheard someone declare at a church supper. He had celebrated this good news by eating a second helping of fudge pie.

It was for these reasons, among others, that he refused to play Cupid to any poor, unsuspecting soul, and especially to Hoppy Harper, who had enough worries.

On Monday, Emma was wreathed with smiles. "It worked."

"What worked?"

"Your prayer about me meetin' Harold's mother."

"Never let me say I told you so."

She sat down and put her lunch bag in the bottom desk drawer. "Dottie Newland is a peck of fun. Why, we had such a good time, I think Harold felt left out!"

"Tell me everything."

"We went to Dottie's house and Harold grilled steaks. She made potato salad and deviled eggs and tea and I brought green beans and a pound cake. I washed, Harold dried, and she put up. Guess what?"

"What's that?"

"She's six years older than me, not five."

"I'm glad to hear it."

Emma unlocked her ledger drawer. "Guess what else?"

"Heaven only knows."

"I think I've found Hoppy Harper a wife."

"No!"

"Did you see that new woman sittin' on the gospel side Sunday?

"I don't know, I might have."

"Black hair, fair skin, real pretty. Red suit, little hat, black pumps."

"Aha."

"Widow. Just moved to Lilac Road, to her mother's old summer house. Used to come here as a girl. Married a big engineer, bridges or something, who was rich as cream. Killed in a crash in one of those little planes." She looked determined. "I'm goin' to figure a way to get them together."

"Let me know how it works out," he said pleasantly.

In the afternoon, Russell Jacks swung the office door open and stepped in.

"Got my granboy out workin' them bat droppin's in th' flower beds," he said with evident pride. "We'll be havin' us a second spurt of bloom around here."

Russell stood with his hat over his heart, and inspected his shoes.

"Is there something on your mind, Russell?"

"Well, Father, school's startin' tomorrow, y'know. And I'd be . . ." He cleared his throat. "I'd be much obliged if . . ."

"If what?"

"If you'd go with 'im."

"How do you mean?"

"Well, if you'd go sign the papers and git 'im set and all like that." Russell reached into a pocket on the front of his overalls and pulled out a worn ten-dollar bill. He laid it on the rector's desk.

"There's the money t' do it," he said, as if that were the end of the matter.

On Tuesday, he walked with Dooley up Main Street, crossed over Wisteria Lane, and turned right toward the school.

"I'd rather be dead," Dooley said, grimly.

"Aha."

"Laid out in a casket."

"Is that right?"

"With worms crawlin' on me."

"I don't know why. I always liked school."

"You was a sissy, is why."

"Oh, I don't know about that. I was a pretty tough guy."

"They'll be wantin' t' fight me."

"Who's they?"

"Them ol' dump heads from where Granpaw lives at."

"I wouldn't go expecting it, if I were you. That way, you might get it."

"They like to killed me when I come up here, but me 'n' Granpaw run 'em off. I busted one ol' boy's nose, and they ain't been back."

"Probably won't come back."

"Yeah, but they'll be waitin' to knock th' poop out of me at school."

"I expect those boys will keep busy getting the hang of things. They won't be thinking about Dooley Barlowe."

"Huh! You don't know how mean people do. Preachers don't know real stuff."

"My friend, if that was a fact, I'd be a happy man."

They turned into the driveway of the old brick school, situated in a grove of oak, blue spruce, and maples showing a faint blush of scarlet. Children with bright clothes and book bags chattered along the sidewalks.

"If you don't mind," said Dooley, "I'd thank you to walk up a ways, 'cause I don't want nobody to think I've got a preacher follerin' me around."

"It might do you some good in the matter that's presently concerning you," said the rector.

In his study that evening, he wrote to Father Roland, in his large New Orleans parish.

"just wanted you to know," he typed with his forefingers, "that the sleepy life you insist i'm living is entirely a product of your 18th cent. romanticism. in two short days, i have run eight miles, washed an exceedingly filthy and enormous dog, counseled a woman in love with our postman, washed two grocery sacks full of collard greens, begun next Sunday's sermon outline, prayed with the sick at our little hospital, read the entire lot of Wordsworth's evening voluntaries (which I heartily recommend to you, my friend), attended a vestry meeting about the building site of our new nursing home, personally registered a boy in school, and worked a bucket of bat droppings into my floribunda beds.

"now," he concluded, "do let me know how you're coming on."

"Lord have mercy!" said Puny on Wednesday. "There's always somethin' to cook around here. Some places you go, all you have to do is clean—it's like a vacation. Come over here, and there's a bushel of this, a sack of that, a peck of somethin' or other."

"I thought you liked to cook." He was sitting at the kitchen counter, having a meatloaf sandwich and a glass of tea.

"I like to cook," she said, crossing her arms over her chest like armor plate, "but not for the entire Russian army."

"Aha."

"Besides, these collards 've smelled up the place till it's more'n I can hardly stand."

"Next time, I'll cook the collards and you wash Barnabas. How's that?"

"That dog of yours looks like somethin' the cat drug in. Why you take th' trouble to wash 'im is beyond me, when he just goes out and gets covered with mud again."

"It's the same principle as making the bed. Why do it if you're just going to get in it again? Or, for that matter, why wash the lunch dishes when you're going to use them for supper?"

"That's not the same thing," she said tartly, getting down on her hands and knees with the scrub brush. "Anyway, how did Dooley do on 'is first day?"

"Black eye," he said.

"Oh, law! It's that red hair. I was always pestered for bein' redheaded. Did he whop 'im back?"

"A left to the solar plexus and a right to the nose."

"Hot dog!" she said with evident satisfaction.

"Puny, I know it's none of my business how you conduct your chores here, but I do wish you wouldn't clean the floor on your hands and knees."

"It's the only way to do it right. My mama did it this way, her mama did it this way." She brushed a loose strand of hair out of her eyes. "An' I'm goin' to do it this way."

Little Emma! he thought, finishing his tea.

She looked at him, flushed and beaming. "Did he really get 'im good?"

"I did not press him for the sordid details."

She cocked her head to one side. "Now, Father . . ."

"Oh, well, then, Puny, all right!" He went to the sink and rinsed out his tea glass, so she couldn't see him grinning like an idiot. "Yes! The answer is yes, he got him good."

"I'll bake 'im a cake!" said Puny, scrubbing the worn tiles with renewed vigor.

At the drugstore, he ran into Hoppy Harper, who was buying a bag of jelly beans.

"I overdose on these about twice a week," the doctor said. "I eat the green first."

The rector sighed in mock despair. "You sure cut into my fun. I haven't had a Little Debbie since Easter."

"The trouble with you," said Hoppy, "is that Little Debbies were the only fun you were having."

Hoppy paid for his jelly beans and opened the bag at once, searching for a green. "So when are you going on vacation?"

If Hoppy Harper had asked him that once, he had asked him that a hundred times, he thought. He wasn't proud of the fact that he'd never been good at arranging his own recreation. The trip to Cambridge had been the best of examples.

While the English weather abandoned its usual caprice and offered glorious balm and sunshine, he'd found himself hopelessly plunged into research that confined him for days to the musty, fan-vaulted library.

"There are race horses," a bishop once told him, "and there are plow horses, and the pulpit can make fit use of both kinds."

He didn't try to deceive himself. In his own opinion, he was a plow horse. He set his course at one end of the field, then plowed to the other and back again.

In any case, he felt himself becoming an increasingly dry old crust, and his doctor was profoundly right about his lack of anything even remotely resembling fun.

Autumn drew on in Mitford, and one after another, the golden days were illumined with changing light.

New wildflowers appeared in the hedges and fields. Whole acres were massed with goldenrod and fleabane. Wild phlox, long escaped from neat gardens, perfumed every roadside. And here and there, milkweed put forth its fat pods, laden with a filament as fine as silk.

There were those who were ecstatic with the crisp new days of autumn and the occasional scent of woodsmoke on the air. And there were those who were loathe to let summer go, saying it had been "the sweetest summer out of heaven," or "the best in many years."

But no one could hold on to summer once the stately row of Lilac Road maples began to turn scarlet and gold. The row began its march across the front of the old Porter place, skipped over Main Street and the war monument to the town hall, paraded in front of First Baptist, lined up along the rear of Winnie Ivey's small cottage, and ended in a vibrant blaze of color at Little Mitford Creek.

When this show began, even the summer die-hards, who were by then few enough in number to be counted on the fingers of one hand, gave up and welcomed the great spectacle of a mountain autumn.

"It is quite a treasure trove," Andrew Gregory told the rector. "Primitive, yes, but with great insight, great depth. There's a winsome quality about them, yet they have surprising polish, too. I'd like to show you how they're looking in the frames."

"I'll drop by around noon."

"If arthritis hadn't caught up with him, who knows what he might have done?"

"And who knows what was lost when Miss Rose set fire to his ink sketches, because he ate her portion of the pickle relish?"

Both men shook their heads with regret.

"I'm afraid our parish hall won't hold a great many people. Maybe we should have the showing in the town hall."

"The mildew will keep the crowd away," Andrew wisely reminded him.

"You're right, of course. Well, then, what about the Oxford Antique Shop?"

"Possibly," Andrew said, thoughtfully. "Possibly. With a little mulled wine, sometime in October?"

"Excellent!"

"Of course, we could sell the whole lot without the trouble of hanging them. Miss Sadie loves art, she'd be good for at least one. And Esther Cunningham would very likely take two for the town hall."

"Hoppy Harper, probably two."

"And your veterinarian friend and his wife?"

"One or two, certainly."

"I'll have a half dozen myself, out of that series he did of the valley."

"How many drawings are there? I keep forgetting the number."

"Forty-three, done over a period of maybe fifteen or twenty years. It's fairly easy to put them in sequential order, his early woodcocks look like mourning doves. And I mistook one of his first bird dogs for a deer."

They laughed agreeably. It gave them much satisfaction that Uncle Billy was not merely an affable, rheumatic village indigent, but a gifted artist.

"I'll have one for my study, of course, and one for Walter and Katherine for Christmas."

Andrew's face lighted up with his well-known smile. "We've sat right here and sold a couple of dozen!" He took a small, black book from the breast pocket of his jacket and consulted it. "Well, then! How about Saturday, October twentieth, around four o'clock in the afternoon? At the Oxford! I'll have a new shipment from England, and a container of books from a Northamptonshire manor house. I'm told Beatrix Potter visited there as a child and scribbled throughout two volumes on moles."

The rector laughed. "I'm astounded that two volumes on moles even exist! Though of course, when they tunnel under my back lawn, I have volumes to say on the subject myself."

As Andrew stood up to go, the rector couldn't help but admire his friend's impeccable tailoring. It was safe to say that Andrew Gregory owned more cashmere jackets than anyone who ever lived in Mitford, all of which were cut so cleanly to his form that a weight gain of barely two pounds would have forced him into another wardrobe. Discipline! That's the ticket! thought the rector, chagrined that he'd slacked up on his jogging.

He stood at the door with his neighbor from across the lane. "I hope business is thriving at the Oxford."

"Better than ever! And a curious thing happened. Over the weekend, I sold half the English pieces to an Englishman! Chap's taking the whole lot back to Ipswich! And your business?" Andrew inquired with a twinkle in his blue eyes.

"Oh, up and down," replied the rector, smiling.

He was sitting at the desk in his study when the phone rang.

"Tim, dear!" said a cheerful voice. "We agree that Barnabas is a wonderful dog and boon companion, but how is it that he so easily replaces two old friends?"

"Marge! I think of you daily, and you and Hal are always in my prayers. But you'd never know it, would you? Please forgive me."

"Forgive you, indeed! Your penalty is a Baxter apple pie, which I hear you've frozen in commercial quantities."

He laughed with the first friend he ever made in Mitford.

"Hal will be in on Friday afternoon to do errands," said Marge. "Why don't you come out with Barnabas and spend the night and most of Saturday?"

"Well, I . . ."

"May he fetch you around four?"

"Well . . . ," said Father Tim, thinking of the rose bushes that needed transplanting, and the English ivy that needed digging up and potting, and the carpet stains he'd sworn to Puny he'd try to remove, and the bath that Barnabas must have at once, and the accumulation of papers and magazines on his desk, and the new helmet he had to order, and the perennial beds that needed attention, and the letters that wanted answering.

His gaze fell upon the open Bible at his elbow. "Thine own friend, and thy father's friend, forsake not," began a verse in Proverbs.

"I'll be ready and waiting," he said.

The next morning, he walked across the plush, green churchyard and rounded the east corner of Lord's Chapel, in search of Russell Jacks. He found the old sexton oiling his push mower.

"Russell, how's the world treating you this morning?"

Russell stood up slowly and removed his battered hat. "Well, sir, there's no rest for the wicked, and the righteous don't need none."

"I'll say!"

"Them leaves 're goin' to be comin' down by the wagon load," he said soberly, looking up at the lacy ceiling of oak and maple branches.

"Let me ask you a favor," said Father Tim. "If you wouldn't mind parting with him, I'd like to borrow your grandboy on Friday afternoon and return him Saturday before dark."

"I'd be much obliged!"

"I'm going out to a farm that has a whole raft of cows and horses and dogs, and good trees to climb, and I thought Dooley might enjoy it."

"I'd consider it a blessin', to tell the truth. He's about wore me out. Let's just say he's old enough to want t' drive, but not tall enough to reach the pedals, if you get my meanin'."

"You sure don't look any worse for wear," said the rector, noting a new sparkle in the old man's eyes.

He inspected the mulch Russell was putting on the rhododendrons underneath the windows. Where the mulch hadn't yet been spread, he noticed something unusual.

"Russell, this looks like ashes. Are you putting ashes under the mulch?"

"Nope, I ain't."

He was not of the let's-throw-ashes-around-all-the-shrubs-in-the-garden school. He took a spade out of the green wicker tool basket, and scraped the pile of ashes away from the roots. "Looks like somebody dumped ashes out of an outdoor grill."

"No tellin' what people'll do these days."

"If you see any more of it around, let me know. We haven't used the fireplace in a couple of years; I don't know where that could have come from."

He stood up and wiped his hands on a handkerchief Puny had just ironed. "Well, Russell, keep up the good work. You're the one who's made our grounds a regular showplace, and I want you to know we all appreciate it."

Russell put his hat over his heart. "You reported that broke lock yet?"

"The truth will out—no, I haven't." He could tell Russell believed that negligence in reporting this incident to the police would encourage someone to kick the doors in next time. "You rest up, now, while Dooley's off to the farm."

"I'm goin' to cook me a mess of greens and fry out some side meat, is what I'm goin' to do!" he said eagerly. "I'm about half sick of peanut butter and jelly."

When he went home for lunch on Friday, Puny was ironing the shirt and overalls Dooley had left behind when he dressed for Miss Sadie's interview.

"Great farm clothes!" he said with satisfaction. "I wish you were coming with us, Puny."

"I do not like a farm," she said with unusual emphasis. "You have to watch where you step ever' minute."

"I can safely say you'd like Meadowgate."

"Work, that's what farms are! And no letup! Cain't go off to Asheville or down to Lake Lure nor anywhere else, with all them animals hangin' on your dress tail. Women I've seen livin' on farms looks like their granmaw by the time they git my age. No wonder they all run off t' work in the cannin' plant, even if they do come home smellin' like kraut."

"You don't have to preach me a sermon."

She put her hands on her hips and looked at him steadily. "I'll scrub your floors and wash your drawers and put up your tomatoes and feed your dog, but I'll not scrape your shoes after you been stompin' around a farm."

"You have my word. I am not going out there to jump in a manure pile. I am going out there to walk through the woods, read my new book, and help cook dinner tonight. Now, what's so bad about that?"

"An' I'm not goin' to wash Dooley Barlowe if he comes back with farm mess on 'im."

Little Emma! he thought. "It's a deal," he said.

As they approached the farm gate, the resident dogs ran out to meet the red truck.

"Here they come!" yelled Hal over the din. "Open the door!"

Father Tim threw open the door and Barnabas leaped out to greet Buckwheat, Bowser, Baudelaire, Bodacious, and Bonemeal.

"Don't throw me out there!" yelled Dooley, holding his hands over his ears.

"Throw 'im out there!" Hal shouted, taking Dooley by the shoulder.

"No, no, them ol' dogs'll eat me! Don't throw me out there!"

"Oh, all right, then," Father Tim said, laughing. "We won't throw you out till we get to the barn!"

As the pickup drove through the stable shed, Dooley saw a bay mare looking soulfully over her stall door.

"Throw me out now!" he cried, enthralled at his first sight of Goosedown Owen.

On his list of favorite things to do, "sit in the kitchen at Meadowgate" was clearly among the top five. This afternoon, however, he might have placed it at the very, very top.

A low fire burned on the hearth, warming the autumn air that, by morning, would cause a heavy mist to rise upon the fields.

The dumpling pot was simmering on the black cook stove, and vases brimming with wildflowers stood on the pine table and along the window sills.

However, there was to be no sitting in the Meadowgate kitchen today. Dooley dragged him out to the stable, saying every step of the way, "I want t' ride 'at horse, I got t' git a ride on 'at horse."

"Dooley, have you ever ridden a horse?"

"Nope, but I know how."

"How?"

"You take it over t' th' house, you stand on th' top step of th' porch, and you jis' jump on it an' go."

"What about a saddle?"

"Don't need no saddle."

"Is that a fact?"

"I've thought about it a million times. It'll work."

He thought Dooley's hair seemed redder, his eyes bluer, and his freckles thicker under the bill of his new baseball cap.

Hal came around the side of the stable from his office, carrying his black O.B. bag

"Finally got this bag in order," he said. "Let me set it in the truck and I'll join you boys."

"I'd like t' git a ride on 'at horse," said Dooley, following at the vet's heels.

"I think that might be arranged. Ever been on a horse?"

"Nope, but I done it in my mind over and over 'til I know how."

"To tell the truth, that's how I learned to ride a horse. Goosedown has spirit, but I don't think she'll throw you." Hal put the bag through the open truck window and set it on the front seat. "Course, there's no guarantee, either."

"I can handle it," said Dooley, putting his thumbs in the straps of his overalls.

The first time Hal walked Dooley and Goosedown Owen around the stable yard, Dooley's face went as white as library paste.

"Stick up there!" said Hal.

The second time around, his color had improved.

"Lookin' good!" said Hal.

The third time, Hal ran, still holding the bridle, and Dooley bounced up and down with glee. "Let 'er go!" he hollered.

Hal let her go.

Goosedown Owen cantered to the hog pen, stopped suddenly at the gate, and threw her rider into a trough of fresh slop.

That it was only apple peelings, sour oatmeal, orange rinds, cabbage leaves, sprouted potatoes, and stale soup was no consolation.

"Slop!" sputtered Dooley, rolling out of the trough and into the mud. "I'd like to half kill 'at horse!"

Goosedown Owen had trotted back to the stable and was eyeing the whole scene from the comfort of her stall. Dooley stood up and shook his fist toward the stable. "I'm ridin' you agin, you mule-headed ol' poop!"

Father Tim strolled over to Dooley, who was climbing through the hog pen gate.

"Do you, ah, know what would happen if Puny Bradshaw could see you now?"

He wiped his hair from his eyes with an arm that was smeared to the elbow. "Yep. I'd be dead meat."

Dinner at Meadowgate Farm was always an event, and tonight was no exception. Marge had baked a savory hen stuffed with sausage, bread crumbs, orange peel, and farm onions, which she served with brandied fruit and a pot of dumplings so splendid that the rector recommended entering the recipe in the county fair.

As the men cleared away the dishes, a three-quarter moon rose and shone through the windows that looked toward the meadow.

Dooley sat on the floor with a jumble of dogs. Bodacious and Bonemeal chewed rawhide strips the size of ceiling molding. Barnabas slept on the hearth by the low, simmering fire. Baudelaire curled up on the chintz sofa and looked doleful. Buckwheat chased his tail and barked, and Bowser sat contentedly in Dooley's lap and licked his face.

Marge eased herself into her father's rocking chair. "Dogs!" she said, with mock disgust. "The baby's first words will be 'woof, woof.' "

"Do you think you'll be game for an art showing on the twentieth?" the rector wanted to know. "Andrew Gregory is framing more than forty of Uncle Billy's drawings."

Marge rubbed her sizeable stomach. "I'm not game for much of anything, Tim dear."

"If she can handle it, we'll be there," said Hal. "Like the rest of us, she has her good days and her bad days."

"I know all about that," said the rector, as the phone rang.

Hal reached into a wooden bread bowl filled with winter squash and plucked out a cordless phone. "Hello! Meadowgate here."

He listened ruefully, holding the receiver away from his ear. Even over the din of the dogs, a voice could be heard shouting.

". . . an' you better come quick, for I don't know how long she's been at it, bellerin' her head off, and me down with the pneumonia and cain't leave the house." There followed a series of long, racking coughs, explosive hawking, and general bronchial pyrotechnics that made every dog in the room grow silent and stare at the phone Hal now held above his head.

"Is she in the stall?" Hal shouted.

"In the stall tied to 'er feedbox, and it sounds bad t' me. She's kickin' th' wall to beat the band, and if I lose this 'n on top of losin' Mister Cooley, you'll not see no more of me, it'll put me down like a doornail."

"Hold on, Miss Reba, I'll be there in twenty minutes."

"Tell her to have a cup of hot tea with honey, for goodness sake!"

"My wife says have a cup of hot tea with honey!"

This advice was greeted with a coughing demonstration of such force and magnitude that the audience was mesmerized. Finally, Hal came to himself and simply hung up the phone.

"Reba Cooley," he announced, as if that explained everything.

"Rats!" said Marge, as Hal hurried out of the kitchen and took a jacket off the peg in the hallway.

"I like 'is ol' dog," said Dooley, oblivious to anything but Bowser's devoted attention.

Father Tim dried his hands. "I'd like to come with you."

"You're on, pal. Grab a jacket, it's getting cold tonight."

Hal kissed his wife, tousled Dooley's hair, and was gone, the rector beside him in the moonlight that lay like a platinum sheen over the lawn of Meadowgate Farm.

Hal drove a few miles on the moonlit highway, then turned onto a series of narrow roads that wound steeply along the side of a mountain.

"You should drive along these roads when there's no moon," he said. "It's enough to make a man want a chew of tobacco."

They noticed that the higher they went, the lower the temperature dropped.

"I don't mind telling you that this nursing-home business frightens me," the rector said, pulling on a fleece-lined jacket that smelled strongly of horse linament. "Five million dollars! Sometimes, the enormity of it is overwhelming. It's going to be a huge project to sieve through a little parish.

"It's like that Vermeer fiasco. I was praying it wasn't a valuable painting, as you know, because it would have torn us asunder. I'm not saying we couldn't pull ourselves back together, but I dreaded the . . . well, the violence of the disruption. A small parish is a fragile ecology."

"It is."

"We're close to naming a building committee. And you wouldn't believe the horror stories I've heard about building committees."

Hal tightened his left-hand grip on the wheel. He knew exactly what his rector was working around to. He felt in his pocket for his pipe, which lived in this particular jacket, packed and ready to go during any emergency.

"I'll sit on the committee, of course," Father Tim said, "and I expect Ron Malcolm to be asked . . ."

"A retired contractor," Hal said. "A good man."

"Miss Sadie, of course. Jeb Reynolds." He paused, then plunged ahead. "You know I need you on this committee, even though Marge is only a month away from an event that will change both your lives."

Just then, the truck swung around a bend, and the lights picked out a small farmhouse and barn, an odd assortment of sheds and chicken coops, great rolls of baling wire, a fleet of rusting tractors and hand plows, and three baying coon dogs standing abreast at the side door of the house.

The porch light came on with such fierce wattage that the rector covered his eyes, then the door banged open as if a gale-force wind had caught it. Reba Cooley peered out.

"We're here," called Hal, "and driving on down to the barn. I'll need a bucket of warm water. I'll send the father back for it."

The rector leaned forward and threw up his hand. To say that Reba Cooley presented a striking appearance would have been an understatement of ridiculous proportions. He thought she looked like a vast boulder, dressed in a chenille robe, that someone had rolled to the door. Her hair was cut short, like a man's, so that he said later he would have sworn it was Mr. Cooley, had he not learned the poor fellow now rested in a plot behind the chicken house.

The cow stall was damp and cold, and he was grateful for the jacket. He couldn't remember when he had last heard the bawling of a cow, but suddenly, the smells and sounds brought back memories of his Mississippi boyhood.

His father had been an attorney in their little town of Holly Springs, with a farm that lay just two miles distant from his office. They'd never kept large animals, as the other 4-H families did. But there were rabbits by the dozens, and flocks of chestnut-colored bantams.

He remembered asking, with immeasurable disappointment, why everything on their farm had to be small.

"This is not a working farm," his father had said with finality, and no amount of pleading by his mother had been able to change his mind.

He remembered Harold Johnson, a strapping boy who was held back in seventh grade for three years running, whom he envied for his knowledge of farm life. "Ol' cow calved last night," Harold might say, smugly. "Dropped a big 'un."

Then there was Raymond Lereaux who showed horses and won blue ribbons that he brought to school for Show and Tell.

It had taken awhile to get interested in something as small as rabbits, but when he did get interested, he was fairly consumed, and it was hardly any wonder that he chose to breed Flemish Giants.

Dark-haired Jessica Raney, who dressed in embroidered pinafores and lived on a dairy farm, was wide-eyed with admiration when he started winning ribbons for his sleek show rabbits. And during the year when disease wiped out his entire herd, she sent a card saying she was sorry. Just that, nothing more. And he'd put it in his sock drawer, where it stayed for a very long time.

The death of the herd, and the shock of seeing them sprawled stiffly in the hutches, had not set well with his father.

"No more," he had snapped, walking briskly from the hutches toward the car. He had run after his father with the taste of iron in his mouth, his heart heavy as a stone. "Wait!" he had cried out to his father, who got in the car and roared down the driveway, not looking back.

He would never forget the agony he felt, as if something of himself had perished with the herd. What he hated most was the way their legs had stood stiffly in the air, a humiliating loss of dignity in creatures whom he'd found to be poised and wise.

Hal Owen inspected his patient carefully, then removed most of the contents of his O.B. bag. Anesthetic, syringe, lubricant, gloves, leg chains, hooks, towels. Father Tim warily laid the cow puller, which he'd carried in from the truck, on a shelf. The cow bawled hideously.

"Tim, might as well go to the house for water now, and I'll see what's up. We may be close to the countdown. Make it warm, it's getting cold as blazes. And bring the bucket full."

He zipped his jacket and headed toward the house, where he was greeted by the trio of baying hounds. They leaped against his chest and legs, barking hysterically, and he was not surprised to find that quoting Scripture did nothing to control the onslaught.

He pounded on the storm door, and waited.

When Reba Cooley threw open the door, he couldn't help but notice that she was wearing overalls under her robe.

"Preacher," she said, "I got a job for you."

In the kitchen, she handed him a flashlight and a bucket of warm water.

"Not one real preacher could I lay hold of t' say a word over Mister Cooley." At this, she coughed so hard that the water splashed on his shoes.

"All I could git was a lay preacher, not hardly more'n twenty year old." She reached into a pocket of her overalls. "Here, this is your'n to go over there and do it right. You know I'd go with you, but I'm a sick woman." He laid the money on the table as they walked out to the stoop. The silvery moon that lighted their path at Meadowgate Farm was not shining at the Cooley's.

"Right over yonder," she said, pointing into the inky darkness. "Go around that balin' wire, on past that tractor, take a left by the chicken coop, and you'll step right on 'is grave."

A fine way to put it, he thought, checking the flashlight. It beamed weakly.

"Hit's a little family plot, about a dozen in there. Mister Cooley's is the fresh 'un, you cain't miss it," she said, overcome with another fit of coughing.

He managed to find his way to the baling wire, and set the bucket by the tractor to pick up when his mission was accomplished. The dogs grew bored with his company and ran ahead.

He beamed the flashlight ahead and picked his way around the huge bale of rusted wire. Surely, this would only take a moment. Best to get it out of the way, then go on to the barn and assist Hal.

"Aha!" he said, expecting to see what he was looking for, as the moon broke through leaden clouds.

In the eerie platinum light, he found that he was, indeed, looking at a graveyard, but not the family kind. As far as he could tell, there were three rusted Chevrolets, a 1956 Pontiac with no hood, a Dodge pickup on blocks, and a couple of Studebakers filled with hay.

"Lord," he said, earnestly, "I don't know where this fellow's grave is, and it's too dark to be stumbling around out here looking for it. Surely I don't have to be standing on it to pray over it. So here goes."

He bent his head and prayed on behalf of the departed.

Then he departed, himself, with great haste, only to fall over the bucket he'd left sitting by the tractor, emptying its contents in the grass.

"Left foot's bent backward," Hal said. "Where the dickens have you been?"

"To a funeral," he said, setting the refilled bucket down.

"I washed up under a spigot I found out front. We've got a little job to do here."

It was after two o'clock when they started home in the truck, with the heater going full blast. The moon raced in and out of the clouds, suddenly revealing open meadows and high ridges and cows sleeping under trees in the pastures.

Hal was exhausted, but happy. "Did you see how I turned her to face the calf? Once she licks it, she'll never leave it."

"Tonight ought to be good for at least a couple of sermons."

"Wasn't too much for you, was it? I mean, when I asked you to clean the placental tissue off the calf, you were white as a sheet."

"I beg to differ. When I was doing that, I was merely pale. Turning white as a sheet came when you asked me to help use the cow puller."

"Good, honest work!"

"Let's just say I wouldn't want to swap jobs."

"Me, either, pal. I'd rather reach in a cow's rear end any day than have to deal with a horse's behind."

"Harry Nelson is being transferred to Birmingham," Father Tim said mildly, having saved this *pièce de résistance* for the right moment.

Hal was quiet for a couple of miles.

"Okay," he said, at last. "I'm going to pray about sitting on the building committee, and I want to talk to Marge. I'll let you know next week. Now, lay off, will you?"

Just as he felt a certain warmth in his spirit, he felt the creeping cold in his feet. But it wasn't until later, under the glare of the porch light, that he saw what would have horrified Puny Bradshaw.

Cow manure not only covered his loafers, but the better part of his socks and pants cuffs, as well.

"Lord have mercy!" he said, presumably speaking in the local vernacular, but meaning it quite literally, as well.

He was sitting on the back steps of the farmhouse, a coffee cup beside him, cleaning his shoes. It was a glorious morning, as most mornings had been during this spectacular autumn.

Thy bountiful care, what tongue can recite?
It breathes in the air, it shines in the light!

He sang heedlessly. If there was anywhere on earth he could sing a favorite hymn at the top of his voice, it was here in the sunshine on this very back step.

The screen door slammed. "I want t' ride 'at horse," said Dooley, sitting down beside him.

"You might begin by saying good morning."

"Good mornin', I want t' ride 'at horse."

"Did you know there are cows on this farm? And chickens? And horseshoes and croquet and a grape arbor and apple trees? As I recall, there's even a log cabin down by the creek, built for someone who was once just your age. Would you like to see all that when I finish cleaning these shoes?"

"I would, soon as I ride 'at horse."

"Dooley, you are a man of single purpose, a characteristic which, with proper control, can take you far in this world."

"We're havin' pancakes."

"Wonderful. Who combed your hair?"

"Nobody."

"That's what I thought. What did you do with those clothes covered with slop?"

"I stuffed 'em in a paper sack and put 'em in th' truck. I thought Puny'd wash 'em."

"Ha!" he said, putting the final polish on his loafers.

The two sat in silence for a while, looking toward the barn and away to the steep hill covered with a blaze of autumn maples.

"Do you go t' hollerin' when you preach?"

"Hollering? Oh, not much. Why?"

"Miss Sadie wants me t' go to church with 'er in th' mornin', and if you go t' hollerin', I'll prob'ly go t' runnin'."

"Is that right?"

"I cain't stand a hollerin' preacher."

"Me, either."

"Well, I'll come then."

"Comb your hair first," said the rector.

The morning had continued so fair and golden that, after the service, he greeted his congregation on the lawn. "Did I go to hollerin'?" he asked Dooley.

"A time or two, you had me worried," the boy said.

Miss Sadie gave him the usual bright peck on the cheek. "Louella is coming home to live at Fernbank!" she said, joyfully. "Her grandson's bank has transferred him to Los Angles, and Louella said if she had to live in Los Angeles, she'd kill herself! I'm so happy about this, Father. Could I see you first thing in the morning about some insurance papers? I need your advice."

Harold Newland shook his hand. "If it's all right," he said, blushing, "I'd like to see you sometime in the morning."

The new woman who was sitting on the gospel side these days took his hand and smiled. "Olivia Davenport, Father. I enjoyed the service very much."

"We're glad to have you with us, Olivia. Your hat adds a lovely touch."

"'I'm afraid I'm a bit old-fashioned about wearing hats to church."

"No more old-fashioned than I in liking to see them!" Yes, indeed. A perfect wife for Hoppy Harper.

"Would it be possible to have a visit with you in the morning?"

"I'll look forward to it," he said. "Around ten?"

So far, his Monday morning appointments were stacking up like planes over Atlanta.

CHAPTER NINE

Neighbors

"Father, I've come to ask for Emma's hand in marriage."

Having said that, Harold Newland blushed deeply and squirmed like a schoolboy on the visitor's bench. "You see, there's nobody else to ask, and I believe in askin'."

"I believe in it, myself, Harold. And I'm happy you've come. I'd like to say that I think the world of Emma Garrett. She's as dependable as the day is long and has a spirit of generosity that's practically unequaled in my experience. She's been mighty good for me, and I expect her to be twice as good for you."

" 'Course, I'm not takin' her away from you. She'll want to keep workin', and I thought I might get her a four-wheel drive since we'll be livin' out a ways."

"I can see Emma in a four-wheel drive."

"We'll move into my house and sell her place as soon as we can."

"When do you think the wedding might be?"

"Emma thought we ought to wait 'til spring, but I say the sooner the better. And I was hopin' . . ." Harold hesitated, with obvious discomfort.

"What were you hoping?"

"Hopin' that you might be willin' to join with my preacher for the ceremony."

"Well, I don't see why not. The more the merrier!"

Two down and one to go, he thought, as he flushed the toilet in the office bathroom and got ready for his next caller.

The beautiful, dark-haired Olivia Davenport did an odd thing. Rather than use the visitor's bench like everybody else, she walked to Emma's chair, sat down across from him, crossed her shapely legs, and said:

"Father Tim, I'm dying."

He could only trust that his face didn't convey the shock he felt.

"I'm asking you to help me find something to make the rest of my life worth living.

"Mother left me her winter and summer homes, and I have considerable property of my own. That means I could spend these last months being quite idle and carefree, and, believe me, that's tempting. But I did not come to Mitford to join the club and sit by the pool. There's nothing wrong with that, but it's absolutely wrong for me.

"I came to Mitford to do something that will make a difference. And while I'm not smart enough to know what that something is, I believe with all my heart that you can tell me."

The first time he set eyes on Olivia Davenport, he felt as if the Holy Spirit had spoken to his heart. This time was no different. He sensed at once that Olivia Davenport was the answer to a prayer he'd initiated two years ago.

"Olivia, I'd like to ask you to read something, if you'd be so kind."

He handed her his open Bible, pointed to the twenty-seventh Psalm of David, and in clear, lucid tones, she read:

" 'The Lord is my light and my salvation; whom shall I fear? The Lord is the strength of my life; of whom shall I be afraid? For in the time of trouble he shall hide me in his pavilion; in the secret of his tabernacle shall he hide me; he shall set me upon a rock. Wait on the Lord; be of good courage, and he shall strengthen thine heart. Wait, I say, on the Lord.' "

She let the book rest in her lap.

"If you were ill," he said quietly, "with no one to sit by your bed, to hold your hand when you're lonely, or rejoice with you when you're glad, would there be anything, after all, to live for?"

Olivia looked at him steadily. It was a rhetorical question.

"It would give courage to a lot of people to hear the faith and victory in these words."

She smiled and, without looking at the book in her lap, repeated something she clearly knew well. " 'For in the time of trouble He shall hide me in His pavilion; in the secret of his tabernacle shall He hide me; He shall set me upon a rock.' "

"He has hidden you in His pavilion?"

She smiled, tears shining in her eyes. "And He has set me upon a rock."

"Would you do something to make life worth living for the patients at Mitford Hospital? Would you be willing to read to them each and every morning? It's a big job."

"He's a big God," she said, with something that seemed like excitement.

In the space of precisely seven minutes, which he reckoned to be the full length of her visit, he had been told a terrible truth, discovered an answer to prayer, helped someone find a ministry, and been unutterably refreshed in his own spirit. Perhaps, he thought, we should all live as if we're dying.

The letter arrived, bearing postage stamps with the queen's likeness. The bells would be delayed again. Perhaps by Christmas . . .

He was disappointed. He had hoped the bells would ring at the time of the Owen baby's birth. Ah, well, perhaps for the baptism, he thought as he walked home.

Tonight he would miss seeing Puny, which he was sure she would think he'd planned. After all, there was that bag of Dooley's laundry that he'd set on the washing machine. As far he was personally concerned, his own shoes were shining, he had washed out his manure-soaked socks, and cleaned his own pants cuffs. Enough was enough.

He thought, too, of Olivia Davenport. Olivia didn't want to waste time, for she had none to waste. On Wednesday, they would meet at the hospital at seven, and the first patient they'd visit would be the terminally ill Pearly McGee. Finally, there would be more than a pat and a prayer to be distributed along the halls.

He turned the corner toward home and heard the familiar, booming bark from the garage. He felt spare and light, like the weather, and looked forward to an early supper of Puny's barbecued ribs.

Recently, he'd dared to let Barnabas off the leash, though only in his own backyard. Barnabas would dash to the hedge that separated the rectory from Baxter Park, do his business, and come bounding back, ready for a super-size Milk Bone.

Perhaps, just perhaps, he thought, this could become their bedtime ritual. It would take him out of the house for a breath of air and a look at the stars, provide Barnabas a moment of diversion, and answer any calls of nature, as well. It could even, in a pinch, get him off the hook for the nightly walk to the monument.

It was already dark when he set the dishes in the sink, and turned the radio to a classical station that was more static than Mozart.

He stood at the screen door, assessing his companion's mood. If Barnabas was excitable tonight, he'd put him on a leash, without question. But the dog stood beside him quietly, even reflectively. The strains of a violin obscured the low growl that erupted just as he opened the door.

Barnabas seemed to sail through the air, clearing the steps entirely and landing only inches from a white cat that was streaking across the yard.

Furious with himself, he watched Barnabas disappear through the hedge that bordered the neighboring yard, where he was surprised to see the glimmer of lighted windows.

" 'Blessed be the Lord, who daily loads us with benefits'!" he shouted from a psalm as he raced toward the hedge.

Barnabas, however, could hear nothing above the din of an old-fashioned cat and dog fight.

Father Tim peered into the yard where the humiliated cat was racing up a hemlock tree. "Barnabas!" he yelled.

Barnabas stood at the foot of the tree, his thick fur bristling, filling the night with a bark that seemed to carry to the monument and echo back along the storefronts.

" 'Be filled with the spirit!' " he shouted. " 'Speak to one another in psalms, hymns, and spiritual songs!' " He never knew which Scripture would float to the surface in such emergencies.

"I'll fill you with the spirit!" a voice announced. Suddenly, the beam of a flashlight shone directly into his eyes. "What are you doing in my hedge?"

"I am trying to retrieve my dog from this yard, what else would I be doing?"

"I haven't the faintest idea," the voice said coldly. "Come, then, and get this beast at once."

The flashlight beam was removed from his eyes and, though he found himself momentarily blinded, he proceeded to shout a thundering verse from Jeremiah.

Barnabas crashed obediently through the rhododendron, and sat trembling at his master's feet. Father Tim grabbed him roughly by the collar.

"I'm very sorry, and I apologize," he stated to the hedge, still unable to see who had spoken.

The new neighbor Mule Skinner had promised finally moved into the realm of her porch light, dressed in a robe and pajamas, and carrying a flashlight that she had mercifully put on low beam.

"Is this going to be the usual behavior of your . . . dog?" She said the word with a tinge of loathing.

"Quite possibly, if your cat continues to tear through our yard, dispensing with any shred of caution."

There was an uncomfortable silence.

Then the woman laughed and extended her hand through a bare spot in the foliage.

"Cynthia Coppersmith," she said, "and you must be Father Tim."

"I am. And I'm sorry we've given you such a poor welcome. I promise I'll make it up." Her hand felt as small as a child's, and warm.

"There's no need," she said. "I'm sorry, too. Nerves, you know. Nothing has gone right with this move! Violet is all nerves herself. You know, cats don't like moving, and I saw this man in my hedge, and Violet up a tree, and a dog the size of my refrigerator, and well . . ."

"I got off lightly, then."

"Yes! You did!"

They both laughed.

"The movers broke my table legs, dashed a French mirror, dented my grandmother's tea service, and heaven knows what other carnage I'll discover when the dust settles."

She peered in his direction over a pair of half-glasses. "I do hope you'll stop in when things are calmer."

"And you must stop in, as well," he said, trying to quiet the whimpering creature at his side.

He took Barnabas to the house, holding on to his collar with great authority. Then he put him on a leash and walked with grim determination to the monument and back, muttering the whole way and unashamedly furious.

He had noted, at some point in their desperate conversation through the rhododendron, that his new neighbor was surprisingly attractive, even with a headful of pink curlers. Tomorrow afternoon, he concluded with neighborly zeal, he would bake a meatloaf and take it over. Better yet, he'd put out a Baxter apple pie to thaw. After all, Mitford was still a bastion of old-fashioned hospitality and generous spirit, and he must not fail to demonstrate this whenever the opportunity presented itself.

"A cat!" he said to himself, as he turned off the back porch light. "Of all things to have right next door, a blasted cat!"

The following evening, he heard a light rap at the back door. "I've come borrowing," Cynthia Coppersmith said with a hopeful expression. "You see, my nephew is coming to help put down my toe moldings, and I thought I'd bake a cake."

She extended a measuring cup.

"Oh, indeed! One must have toe moldings. Come right in, come in!" He couldn't help but notice that Mule Skinner had been dead right—her legs were terrific.

Barnabas skidded into the kitchen, galloped toward Cynthia, rose on his hind legs, and put his paws squarely on her shoulders.

"Oh, my," she said, "and how tall are you? I'm five-two!"

He tackled Barnabas, snapped on the leash, and attached him to the handle of the drawer containing the everyday silverware. "I'm sorry. Really I am." Would this creature forever be fogging glasses, mowing people down in their tracks, muddying their clothes?

"Brown sugar or white?" he asked, breathlessly, taking the cup. "White, I suppose, for a cake."

"White would be lovely. But brown would do just as well. Anything!"

He felt an odd mixture of confusion and delight. Having an unexpected knock at the rectory door was unusual, as he had been given a reticent parish who faithfully called before coming.

"Smells good in here!" she exclaimed, sniffing about with curious pleasure.

"Barbecued ribs," he confessed. Barbecued ribs for a clergyman? It was all a trifle self-indulgent, he thought, but a rare treat after endless weeks of Rector's Meatloaf, which Puny now called Old Faithful.

"Do you know I haven't eaten all day long? I meant to go to The Local, but it was one thing and then another, and I looked a fright, too. The water went off, you know. Something at the water main. But I couldn't bathe, or make coffee, or scrub the cabinets. And Violet deposited a mouse on my kitchen rug."

She seemed a bit worn, he thought. She could do with some cheering up. "A cup of tea would be nice. Or how about a glass of sherry?"

"Both, I think!" said his neighbor.

He had his guest sit at the kitchen counter. Talking happily, she sipped a glass of sherry, drank two cups of Darjeeling tea, ate three cold ribs and sopped the sauce with a poppy seed roll, while he stood by the stove, trying not to look at her legs. If Mule had never mentioned them, he probably wouldn't have noticed, he thought; now he had to make a special effort to look her straight in the eye.

He was thankful that he had made a pan of gingerbread to take to the hospital the next morning, and so was his new neighbor, who devoured a large piece with enthusiasm, and afterward licked her fingers. Clearly, this gesture had not removed the last vestige of the gingerbread, for, afterward, as she reached to pat Barnabas on the head and say goodnight, he leaped to the seductive fragrance on her fingers, hauling the silverware drawer onto the floor and scattering its contents throughout the kitchen and into the freshly waxed hall.

A fork sailed on its backside all the way to the front door.

"Bingo!" exclaimed Cynthia.

They were both on their hands and knees for a full twenty minutes, collecting the muddle of twelve place settings, frilled party toothpicks, and a variety of spatulas and wooden spoons.

When he looked into the bathroom mirror that night, he was humiliated to see that there was barbecue sauce smeared on his chin—barbecue sauce that had, without a doubt, been there during Cynthia Coppersmith's entire visit.

He was so stricken with a vain regret, that he had to step outside for a breath of air.

"Of all things!" he said aloud. "Of all things!"

He had finally decided to tell Emma what had been told him in strictest confidence.

"You know, your role at Lord's Chapel has made you privy to quite a few secrets."

"I'll say! And some I wish to goodness I'd never been told."

"Well, this may be another of that very kind. Have you had any bright ideas about how to make Olivia Davenport and Hoppy . . . an item, as they say?"

"You bet I have, but I've been so busy with Harold Newland, I can't hardly see straight."

"You need to know, and it must never be repeated outside this room, that Olivia Davenport is dying."

Emma sat very still and turned pale.

"I didn't want to know that."

"Well, I didn't want to know it either, and I didn't want to tell you. But it appears to me that the very last thing we should do is try and make Hoppy Harper a widower two times in a row."

Emma drummed her fingers on her typewriter. "How bad is it?"

"What do you mean how bad is it? Dying is dying."

"I mean, how long does she have?"

"Months, she said. She referred to months."

"Oh, well. I thought if it was a couple of years, maybe we could still . . ."

"Emma, you are . . . words fail me."

"But they're perfect for each other!" she persisted. "I just hate this! What's she dyin' from?"

"To tell the truth, I have no idea. That wasn't the way the conversation went. In fact, that seemed the most insignificant detail in the world."

"Boys howdy, I'm glad you're not a reporter on the *Muse*."

"No gladder than I."

"Well," she sighed. "I feel terrible about her. I hope I don't go and be too nice to her now, like I know she's dyin'. You know what I mean?"

"Just try to be your usual aggravating, ill-tempered self, and she'll never suspect a thing."

"Ha, ha."

He looked through his phone messages.

"Did Hal say what he wanted?"

"Just said call him, he's ready to tell you something you've been wantin' to hear."

"Thanks be to God! Evie Adams?"

"Said her mother has started puttin' the wet wash in the oven; Miss Pattie thinks it's the dryer. She's about to jump out the window."

"Who, Miss Pattie?"

"No. Evie."

"Miss Sadie's nursing home won't get built a minute too soon. I'll drop over to Evie's after lunch. Do you know what the school principal called about?"

"Well, I wasn't going to say anything, but since you asked . . ."

"I can see I shouldn't have asked."

"Dooley Barlowe beat some boy black and blue."

In his mind, he saw exactly how it would go.

He would pick up the phone and do something that, if nothing else, would at least preserve his sanity.

"Hello, Walter? Please ask Katherine to move the Christmas ornaments off the guest room bed: I'm coming up. For how long? Oh, I don't know, a month or two, maybe more! You and I can go fishing, like we've always talked about. Maybe I'll turn loose some of that money you're always claiming I have, and we'll hop over to Sligo and look up our ancestors.

"Yes, that's right. You heard right. No, Walter, do not call 911. I am of very sound mind.

"So, I'll be there tonight around eleven. No, don't bother, I'll take a taxi. Yes, I know a taxi will cost a fortune, but you see, Walter, I don't care! Walter? Walter! Did I hear something crash to the floor?"

He laughed. If he was half the man he liked to think he was, he would make that very call and get away for a while, just like Hoppy kept insisting he must do.

Well, and he *would* get away for a while. Later.

Right now, he had to do something else. He had to have a talk with Dooley Barlowe about giving Buster Austin two black eyes, a swollen lip, a bloody nose and then, heaven help him, chasing Buster into the principal's office with a baseball bat.

Apparently, Buster Austin had broken in line behind Dooley at the water fountain. While Dooley was bending over for a drink, Buster slammed him behind the knees, so that he sank to the floor, hitting his mouth on the fountain and cutting his lip.

He came up swinging.

"I saw it," said Principal Myra Hayes, standing behind her desk with arms akimbo. "Buster provoked it, but there are rules, after all, and one does not build character by tearing down rules.

"Of course, what Dooley did at the water fountain was only half the story! He then grabbed a softball bat from Willie Bush and chased Buster down the hall into my office, saying that if he didn't tell me whose fault it was right then, he'd meller his head."

"Aha," said Father Tim. Why did she have to frown so? It wasn't the end of the world.

"He'll be severely punished, and so will Buster. And if this sort of thing happens again, we're prepared to take more drastic action. You understand."

"Oh, I do."

He felt she might be considering some special punishment for the offense of even knowing Dooley Barlowe.

At three-fifteen, he met Dooley at the corner and walked with him toward the church, where Russell Jacks was transplanting hydrangeas.

" 'at principal preached me a sermon t'day," said Dooley.

"Good! That'll save me the trouble."

They walked awhile in silence. Leaves had drifted in deep banks of gold and crimson along the curbs and whispered under their feet. Ah, to be as young as Dooley Barlowe, with countless autumns ahead!

"You like Goosedown Owen, don't you?"

"Better'n snuff," he said, using one of Russell Jacks's favorite expressions.

"You got over being thrown in the slop pretty quick."

" 'at ain't nothin'. She was jist playin'. I'm goin' t' ride th' hair off 'at horse next time."

"Let's talk about next time."

They crossed over Old Church Lane and went to the office.

"Got any homework?"

"Just some dumb ol' book t' read."

"Your grandpa will be around for you in an hour." He opened the windows and turned on the fan in his bookcase. The answering machine light was blinking, but that could wait. "I've been thinking," he said, sitting on the corner of his desk. "All of us need a change of scenery now and again, and it occurred to me that some of the best scenery around is at Meadowgate Farm."

The boy's face brightened.

"Let me ask you something. How would you like to learn how it feels to have a horse of your own?"

Dooley was so astounded at this extraordinary thought, he was unable to speak. Instead, his eyes spoke for him.

"Let's say that you and I make it a point to go out there once a month. And that you learn to groom Goosedown, and feed her, and take care of her tack, the whole works. However," he said, as Dooley leaped off the bench, "there's only one way we'll be able to do this."

"What's 'at?"

"You can no longer let Buster Austin or anybody else tempt you to fight." He let that sink in. "Do you understand?"

Dooley looked at the floor. "I reckon."

"Tell me what you think I'm saying to you."

"I can have me a horse, kind of, and take care of 'er an' all, but I cain't whip Buster Austin."

"Nor anybody else."

"N'r anybody else."

"We're going to talk in a little bit about what you can do if Buster . . . or anybody else . . . tries to get you to fight. In the meantime, are you willing to do what it takes to have yourself a horse once a month?"

"I'm willin'."

"Can you do it?"

"I can do it!"

He stood up and took Dooley's money box off the shelf. "Well, then, we'll talk more later. Do you want to work tomorrow? You've got eighty-eight dollars in your bicycle account."

"I don't want t' work tomorrow n'r any other day. I'm tired of haulin' them ashes out of th' basement and cleanin' out all that ol' junk. We filled up Luther's truck three times." Dooley went into the bathroom and slammed the door.

Lord, the rector prayed, I am not very good at this. Thank you for being this boy's Father, and teach me a trick or two, while you're at it.

One thing he needed to do right away, he realized, was get Dooley enrolled in Sunday school, in Jenna Ivey's class.

He heard the toilet flush, and Dooley threw open the door. "You know what was in my poop jis' then?"

"I cannot imagine," he said, gruffly.

"Corn. Big whole pieces of that corn I eat for lunch. That reminded me of what I'm goin' t' do for 'at ol' horse."

"Really."

"I'm goin' to clean out 'er stable. There's no tellin' how long she's been steppin' in 'at stuff."

Esther Cunningham called before he left the office.

"I was goin' to ask you to come by in the mornin' for coffee and a sausage biscuit, but the dern mildew's so bad in here, I'm thinkin' of movin' to the fire depot. Anyway, I've got big news."

"Let me have it before J.C. Hogan gets it crossways and backwards."

"You'll be proud to know you've been elected to officiate at . . . tah dah! . . . The Festival of Roses!"

"What happened to the pansies and the hollyhocks and all that crowd?"

"Outvoted! Here's the deal. We rope off Main Street, put a big garland of roses around the town monument, make speeches—that's where you come in—invite the governor, have house and garden tours—oh, and yours is on, by the way, just say yes—and sell potpourri and rose bushes and have flower arranging, and quilts, and I don't know what all. Not to mention food, of course—box lunches, cakes, pies, Winnie's doughnuts, you name it."

"You people sure don't mind shoveling out a load of work for the rest of us," said the rector.

"Honey, wait'll you hear what some folks are gonna be doin'. You got off light. Now, you're in big with Miss Sadie, and we'd like to use her house for a tour, but not one of us has the guts to ask."

"What makes you think I have?"

"Let's just say I'm countin' on you, Father. Anyhow, it's a long way off, not 'til next summer. Be thinkin' of somethin' good to say in your speech, an' I gotta go, Ray's out here blowin' the horn, got supper cookin' at the house."

One thing he could say for Esther Cunningham. She made people feel almost good about being harassed, talked down to, and generally bossed around.

"You go and get house help and that's the last we see of you," said Percy Moseley, wiping down a booth table. "One of my best reg'lars has fell off to a total stranger."

The rector sighed. "But what's a man to do? When you've got somebody at home three days a week cooking and baking and making a fuss over you, you don't walk home anymore, you run. That is, if you've got the sense God gave a billy goat."

"You missed my latest special. Had it on the menu so long, it's about to go off."

"Bring it."

"But I ain't even told you what it is."

"Surprise me. I need more surprises in my life."

As he sat down and opened his sermon notebook, he heard two women enter the booth behind him.

"Well, of course, I love it here, but there's never anything to do!"

"Do you know this little town has more bachelors than practically Miami Beach?"

"Oh, sure. And where are they? Listed on the war monument?"

"There's J.C. Hogan, you know . . ."

"Too fat!"

"And Andrew Gregory. He's *Italian!*"

"Too old!"

"What about Harold Newland?"

"Too bashful. Besides, he's taken."

"Maybe Avis Packard, then. He could teach you how to flambé something. Or roast a goose."

"Ha! I roasted my own goose when I moved to this hick town."

"Marlene, bein' picky is no way to find somethin' to do around here. What about that rector over at Lord's Chapel? He's kind of cute."

"Too short!"

"OK, OK! I've got it! Here's one to die for. Hoppy Harper!"

"Too handsome."

"Too handsome? Are you *crazy?*"

"Good-looking men are always stuck on themselves."

"Marlene, one of these days, you'll have nothin' to hold on to but your convictions!"

"What in the world are you laughin' at?" asked Percy, setting a plate in front of him.

Father Tim looked down at his meal with genuine alarm.

Liver!

"Why'd you stop laughin'?" Percy wanted to know.

"How do you like your new neighbor?" Emma was putting on her lipstick to meet Harold Newland at the hardware, where they would pick out brass towel rings to give her condo more appeal when they put it on the market.

"Oh, fine, just fine."

"What does she do?"

"Do? I haven't the faintest idea. She has a cat."

"Does she work?"

"I don't know, she didn't say."

"Well, she sure can't be rich, livin' in that little house not big enough for a doll and a tea set. So she must work."

"Like I told you, I don't know."

"What does she look like?"

"Short, I think. Small."

"Short, small, has a cat. You're a fount of information!" She looked in a compact and pressed her lips together. "And you still don't know what's killin' Olivia Davenport?"

"No, I do not. Olivia Davenport is highly involved in living, not dying, and we do not discuss it."

"How's she doin', readin' the Bible to sick people?"

He hadn't felt particularly well this morning, in addition to having some guilt about how slack his running schedule had become.

"Emma," he said crisply, "you are the one who should have a reporter's job on the *Muse.*" And perhaps you'd like to go and inquire about a position this very day, he thought, yanking the cover off his typewriter.

He was following Miss Sadie along the upstairs hall at Fernbank.

"I don't know when I've been so excited!" she said, moving quickly in her tennis shoes. "Having Louella come and live with me will be the best medicine in the world. Did you know they say people who live alone die earlier than people who don't? Now, here, this is the first room I want you to look at and see what you think."

The years had definitely taken their toll on the former glory of Fernbank. The rooms smelled musty and airless, and wallpaper was peeling in great patches. Still, it was hard to dim the beauty of Mitford's grandest house.

"This little room was Mama's sewing room. Look at all the good light it gets, and the view. Don't you love this view? Step right up to the window and you can look down on Mitford. See? There's your office! We could put the bed over there, Dooley could help, and the dresser here. What do you think?"

"How far down the hall is it from your room?"

"Oh, a good ways down."

"Let's look at the room right next to yours," he suggested.

There he found a sitting room with large, airy dimensions, a loveseat and two comfortable chairs, a single bed, a warm rug for winter, and a view of the orchard through the tall windows.

"Miss Sadie, I think you and Louella need to be next door to each other."

"Well, if that's what you think," she said, "that's what we'll do. You know, Father, I've decided to stay right here in Papa's house, no matter what. We'll just fall apart together, and when I die, I'll leave it to the church, like I always planned, and let you fix the roof and patch the walls."

He wondered how much more of Miss Sadie's generosity Lord's Chapel could stand.

"Now I ask you," she said, shaking the dust out of a needlepoint pillow on the loveseat, "how many ladies have a priest who'll come and say which room to put somebody in?"

He laughed. "I try to be versatile."

"Since we're up here, would you like to see another painting Papa bought in Europe?"

"Maybe I should be getting back . . . ," he said, heading for the stairs.

"Now, Father, this is no pretend Vermeer. This is a real Monet!"

He followed Miss Sadie into her bedroom, where he admired a small, vibrant oil that depicted a party of bathers. But what intrigued him more were the old photographs in tarnished silver frames, which sat on a table in front of the windows.

A very striking, dark-haired woman with luminous eyes looked out at him. "Why, how extraordinary! This woman is the very image of Olivia Davenport!"

"That was my mother," said Miss Sadie, "and when I met Olivia Davenport several Sundays ago, I was nearly speechless. I felt as if I were a little child again, looking at my beautiful mother. It was such a queer sensation that I was a bit shaken by it. I think it is the eyes, especially. There's an attitude of . . . of . . ."

"Victorious overcoming!"

"Why, yes. That's the very thing I was trying to say!"

The man in the photograph next to Rachel Livingstone Baxter was strikingly handsome and intense; in his twenties, perhaps.

"May I ask who this is?"

"That was the young man I met in Paris. That was Miss Rose Watson's brother, Willard Porter."

They descended Fernbank's broad staircase, hand in hand.

"I had hoped to walk down these stairs in my bridal gown," she said, "and be taken into the parlor on Papa's arm. I imagined it so clearly, for so long, that years later I would sometimes forget, and think it had really happened.

"In my mind, Willard was standing at the fireplace in the parlor, which Mama and China Mae had decorated with white hydrangeas in silver urns. I liked to imagine that Papa had gotten up on the ladder and strung wild grapevine around the archway, and that I'd twined it with tea roses from the garden."

When they reached the landing, she turned to him.

"In all these years, I've never told anyone my love story. I know that I don't want to die without sharing it with someone. And I've been hoping, Father, that you'd be the one."

"I'd look upon it as a privilege."

"Considering my age, perhaps we shouldn't wait too long," she said, smiling. "So, one day, when you've nothing to do but listen to an old lady ramble, perhaps some rainy day when you've no heart for your chores, well then . . ."

"I'll remember," he said.

"When I've finished telling you my story, you'll be the only other living soul who knows what really happened the night of that terrible fire."

He felt a chill. And though it passed quickly, it was a feeling he didn't like.

CHAPTER TEN

A Grand Feast

"I wish I could make you some cornbread," Puny said, wistfully. "I just crave to do that."

"And you don't know how I appreciate it, and thank you for the thought," he said, eating a tuna sandwich made with whole wheat, and no mayonnaise. "But I can't eat cornbread because of this aggravating diabetes."

"I could leave out th' bacon drippin's, and use vegetable oil. But it wouldn't be no good."

"That's right!"

"If my granpaw didn't git cornbread once a day, he said he couldn't live. I'd bake him a cake at night, he'd eat half of it hot. Then he'd git up in the night and eat what was left, crumbled up in milk."

"Really?"

"Stayed a string bean all his life, too. He said preachin' the word of God kept the fat wore off."

"It has never served me in that particular way, I regret to say."

Puny filled the scrub bucket and went to work with her brush.

Seeing her scrub the floor on her hands and knees continued to be among his least favorite sights. "Puny, may I be so bold to ask why someone with your fine abilities has never married?"

"Th' good Lord ain't sent the right one, is why."

"And your family, is there family?"

She looked up. "My daddy died when I was little, and Mama raised me and my two sisters 'til we was all in junior high. My twin brothers went off to live with my aunt, 'cause she could send 'em to school. After that, Mama took sick and lingered.

"She said she lingered for one reason only, and that was to prepare us for life."

Puny sat back on her heels.

"She knowed she was dyin', and ever' night after we done our schoolwork and got th' supper dishes washed, Mama would call us in to set on her bed.

" 'Tonight I'm goin' to talk to you about hard work,' she might say. 'I've only got one thing to say about it, and that is—don't be afraid of it.'

"That was all the lesson on hard work, and she'd lay back and we'd brush her hair and paint her nails and just kind of play with 'er, like a doll.

"She liked that, and would fall off to sleep that way, with us pettin' 'er. Another night, she might say, 'Girls, I'm goin' to talk to you about men, and here's what I've got to say: Don't let a man pick you. You do the pickin'.'

"You know, if that's all somebody has to say about somethin', you'll think about it more'n if they rattle on and on."

He thought she had a point.

"Mama always told us, 'I don't want to look down from heaven and see my girls makin' fools of theirselves.' "

"Well, I'm sure she's pleased, Puny, for you're a hardworking, good-spirited young woman who'd make any mother proud."

"After Mama died, th' church took my sisters, sent 'em hither an' yon, an' I quit school to go look after granpaw. Lived all by hisself out in th' country, but he had a pretty little place, neat as a pin, wouldn't hardly a leaf fall in th' yard till he was out there sweepin' it up. He was tough as a old turkey gobbler, but I liked 'im. He could preach up a storm! Make the windows rattle!" She looked at him soberly. "How's your preachin'?"

"There's any number of opinions on that subject," he said, laughing. "You'll just have to come and see for yourself."

Puny had left baked chicken and green beans cooked with new potatoes, one of his favorite meals. He laid a tray, and took his supper into the study to watch the news. World events continually reminded him of how blessed he was to live and work in the peace and tranquillity of Mitford. It was only by the grace of God, some said, that their village was still largely unspoiled.

A lot of the credit, of course, belonged to Esther Cunningham. The mayor was like a great, clucking hen, sitting on a nest which was the fragile ecology of their little town, and she was ready to defend it to the death.

Still, development had sprung up around the edges, like weeds encroaching on a garden. Just beyond the big curve from Lew Boyd's Esso was the bright yellow motel with a huge green cactus outlined in neon. There was growing pressure for a shopping center, and a food store chain was pawing the very ground where the town limit sign was erected. It was only a matter of time, was the general consensus at the Grill. "Over my dead body," said Esther, who stood firm on three Churchillian words: Never give up.

After the news, he put the dishes in the sink and went to his desk to make notes on his sermon. He was considering what J. Hudson Taylor, the English missionary to China, had said, in reflecting on the verse from Matthew: "Where could we get enough bread in the wilderness to fill such a great multitude?"

"What God has given us," Taylor had written, "is all we need; we require nothing more. It is not a question of large supplies—it is a question of the presence of the Lord."

That was a sermon that was almost unpreachable in today's world. Why take off along that narrow and difficult path, when wide boulevards were generally more inviting to a congregation?

Barnabas barked gruffly, then leaped across the study floor and into the kitchen, where he put his front paws on the back door and barked again.

He heard a small knock.

"Your sugar!" Cynthia Coppersmith said when he opened the door. He was holding Barnabas firmly by the collar.

"You shouldn't have bothered. Really! I'm just finishing up some notes, and we were going to settle in for a bit of Wordsworth . . ."

"I love Wordsworth!" she exclaimed, handing him the cup of sugar.

He was unable to think of anything to reply, when years of social training came to his rescue. "Won't you come in?" he blurted, much to his surprise.

"Well . . . yes! Yes, I will, if you're sure you don't mind."

Blast! he thought, tucking his shirttail in with one hand and holding Barnabas with the other.

As he almost never had unexpected company in the evening, he hardly knew how to proceed. A drink? Didn't people offer drinks? Well, he didn't have any to offer. It would have to be sherry, perhaps, or tea, and a plate of . . . what? Shortbread.

Giving himself time to think it through, he took Barnabas to the rear hedge, leaving his neighbor happily inspecting his bookshelves.

When he returned, she was sitting on the study sofa, poring over a book of lectures by Oswald Chambers and appearing oddly at home among the jumble of worn needlepoint pillows.

She looked up, quoting the Scottish teacher who happened to be one of his favorite writers. " 'Faith by its very nature must be tried,' he says. Do you agree?"

He sat down in his wing chair, suddenly feeling more at home with his company. "Absolutely!"

"I've never been one for physical exercise," she said, "but what God does with our faith must be something like workouts. He sees to it that our faith gets pushed and pulled, stretched, and pounded, taken to its limits so its limits can expand."

He liked that—taken to its limits so its limits can expand. Yes!

"If it doesn't get exercised," she said thoughtfully, "it becomes like a weak muscle that fails us when we need it."

He felt himself smiling foolishly, though his question was serious. "Would you agree that we must be willing to thank God for every trial of our faith, no matter how severe, for the greater strength it produces?"

"I'm perfectly willing to say it, but I'm continually unable to do it."

"There's the rub!"

When he went to the kitchen to make a second pot of tea, he was astounded to find that it was eleven o'clock. That hardly anyone in Mitford stayed up until eleven o'clock was common knowledge.

At noon, he walked briskly from the church office to Lord's Chapel, with Barnabas on his red leash.

He had a pile of correspondence to tend to and another visit to make to the hospital in the afternoon. That's why he'd brought a sandwich made from last night's chicken, which he'd put in the parish hall refrigerator early this morning.

The sky was darkly overcast, but he hardly noticed the weather. He was thinking of last night's unexpected caller and the visit that ensued.

He turned the key in the lock, and went in the side door of the old parish hall. Though it was barely large enough for a party of fifty, they often squeezed in seventy-five or more for coffee after the late service.

Three walls displayed a collection of framed needlepoint that had been worked by parishoners since 1896, and included embellished crosses, a view from the ruined church on the hill (the first Lord's Chapel), a crown of thorns, and his personal favorite: a mass of roses framing the Scripture from Psalm 68: "Blessed be the Lord, who daily loadeth us with benefits."

The fourth wall contained a series of mullioned windows that looked out to the finest of the Lord's Chapel gardens. As he passed the windows, he saw the rain begin.

He opened the refrigerator, but didn't see his lunch bag. "Odd," he said aloud to Barnabas, "I put it right here with the wine." With some bewilderment, he noted that the sacramental wine was also missing, a fact that was easy to establish since there was nothing in the refrigerator but two containers of half-and-half, and a jar of Sunday school apple juice.

"Did I dream we walked over here this morning and left that sandwich?" Barnabas yawned hugely and lay down by the kitchen worktable. "That's the darndest thing. What in the world . . ."

Perhaps the Altar Guild had come in and cleaned out the refrigerator. But it was already clean. Feeling stupid, he looked in the broom closet, and inspected the contents of the drawers. After all, he had once put a package of butter in the oven while wrestling with the idea of a sermon on greed.

The lunch bag was nowhere to be found. "Well, then," he said, irritated. "We'll give our business to Percy."

As he locked the door, he thought he heard the barest whisper of singing, a mere wisp of last Sunday's anthem. He listened, but heard nothing more.

"Angels!" he said, as they set out in a light autumn rain.

"I've found out all about your neighbor," Emma announced.

"Really?"

"She's an artist and a writer. Paints watercolors for th' children's books she writes. That white cat she has? That's the star of her Violet books. *Violet Comes to Stay, Violet Grows Up, Violet Has Kittens, Violet Goes to England.* You name it, that cat has done it." She paused, hoping for some response, but got none.

She selected another choice piece of information, as one might poke through the caramels to find a chocolate. "She used to be married to somebody important."

"Is that right?"

"A senator," she said grandly.

"Aha."

"Her uncle gave 'er that little house. Remember him? The old scrooge!"

He remembered well enough. He'd tried to be friendly, and had even regularly prayed for his unkind neighbor, seeing that he needed it. Nothing he'd done, including the delivery of an apple pie, had softened the old man's heart toward him. Then, two years ago, his neighbor had died, leaving the little house empty and unkempt.

"It wasn't actually the uncle who gave it to her," said Emma. "It was her uncle's daughter. Called her up, said she didn't want it, thought Cynthia should have it. Said Cynthia was the only one her old daddy ever liked."

"Um," he said, looking through his phone messages.

"Never had any kids. Kind of adopted her husband's nephew."

She waited, having gone nearly to the bottom of her information barrel. "Drives a Mazda!" she said at last.

"With such vast reportorial skills, you might talk to J.C. Hogan about working at the *Muse.*"

"That's more than you'd ever find out in a hundred years!"

"You're right, as usual," he said, dryly. "I think it's especially fascinating to know what kind of car she drives."

Emma pursed her lips. Down deep, she could tell he was thrilled she'd found out all this stuff.

He finished putting his phone messages in order. "And how did you learn all this, exactly?"

"I did what anybody would do. I asked her!"

He queried the sexton when he came by to collect his check. "Russell, did you go in the church yesterday?"

"Nossir, Father, I didn't. I was goin' to heat up some soup in th' kitchen, but th' rain looked like it was settin' in for th' day, so I went home and fried me some livermush. Dooley come home on th' bus."

"The Altar Guild wasn't in there, either. It's a mystery, all right."

"How's that?"

"Yesterday morning, I put a sandwich in the refrigerator, and when I went to look for it, it was gone. along with a bottle of sacramental wine."

Russell scratched his head. "I was in th' churchyard 'til around noon or so, when I seen you leave out to Main Street. I didn't lay eyes on another soul."

The rector shook his head. "Ah, well! Do you think you can get to those broken flagstones before winter?"

"I'm workin' on it, Father," he said, as the phone rang.

"Father," said Oliva Davenport, "Pearly McGee just died."

"I'll be right there," he said.

As he hung up the phone, it rang again.

Marge Owen had delivered a healthy baby girl. Seven pounds, eight ounces. Rebecca Jane!

Sorrow and joy, he thought, so inextricably entwined that he could scarcely tell where one left off and the other began.

He had taken particular pains about dressing for the art show at the Oxford. For one thing, he felt it would demonstrate respect for Uncle Billy. Here he was, dressed in his second new jacket purchase of the year, a circumstance he found just short of miraculous. If there had ever been a year in which he'd bought two jackets, he couldn't remember it.

Of course, there was no way he could have resisted this particular jacket. Not only was it a color that Emma told him would be flattering, but it was comfortable, fit perfectly, would go with everything, and was on sale. So, what was he to do?

"English Copper!" the Collar Button owner said, grandly describing the color. "It will look stunning with your black clericals."

Stunning? He wasn't at all certain that this was how he wanted to look.

The Oxford was wearing its signature fragrance of floor wax, lemon oil, old wood, and worn leather. Andrew had even gone to some pains to buy flowers at Mitford Blossoms and arrange them himself in an ancient silver wine bucket, which he placed on a hunt table newly arrived from Cumbria.

Fortunately, there was one thing a host could count on in Mitford. Villagers arrived early or on time, and everyone, to a person, left at a decent hour.

When he appeared at five minutes after the specified four o'clock, the tea table was already surrounded.

He greeted Esther Cunningham, who was enjoying a large slice of Brie, and shook hands with her husband, Ray. Then, as he turned to look at the drawings, he observed quite another show. It was Miss Rose Watson, dressed to the tee in a green taffeta evening gown, a moth-eaten plaid velvet cummerbund, elbow-length satin gloves, a World War II officer's cape, and saddle oxfords without laces.

She held several tea sandwiches in one gloved hand, while graciously extending the other. "How do you do," she said to the rector, who no longer felt conspicuous in his new jacket, much less overdressed.

The beautifully framed drawings hung in a long, chronological line along the left wall, beginning with Uncle Billy's rendering of three deer in a copse of spruce, drinking from the basin of a waterfall. Seeing them framed and hanging was unexpectedly impressive.

"Eloquent, aren't they?"

Cynthia Coppersmith was standing by his side, dressed in a sweater and skirt the color of periwinkles, and holding a cracker on a napkin.

"Indeed!" he said. "I knew they were well done, but this, well this is . . ."

"Extraordinary!" she said helpfully.

"Emma tells me you're an artist and writer."

"I earn part of my way with a brush, yes. But I don't call myself a true artist. I can't draw people, you see. I'm best at animals, and especially cats."

Someone slapped him on the back so hard, he nearly went reeling into a drawing of a quail on her nest.

"I see you're learnin' to love your neighbor as yourself!" said Harry Nelson. "This is the last I'll be seein' of you. Shirley and I have the car packed and we're headed out behind the movin' van."

"Don't take any wooden Vermeers," said Mule Skinner, who had joined the group.

Uncle Billy was seated in a Chippendale wing chair, balancing a plate of cheese and grapes on his lap, with a paper napkin stuck into his shirt collar.

J.C. Hogan was writing in a notebook with his left hand, and mopping his forehead with his right. "When did you say you started drawin'?"

"Oh, when I was about ten or twelve, m' uncle was a railroad man and ever' time he come through the valley, he'd blow th' whistle startin' up around Elk Grove, and by th' time he got over t' Isinglass, don't you know, I was standin' by the track, and he'd th'ow somethin' out t' me.

"Sometimes, it was a sack of licorice candy, or horehound, and one time it was a little ol' pack of pencils, real wide pencils with a soft lead, don't you know. My daddy said that was a foolish thing to give a boy who couldn't write, so I took to drawin'."

"Did you ever use ink?" J.C. asked.

"Well, sir, I used it some, but I eat up a jar of pickle relish Rose said was hers, and she burned th' whole stack of m' ink pictures."

"No!" exclaimed Winnie Ivey, nearly moved to tears.

"I'd a clapped 'er upside th' head," said Percy Mosely, with feeling.

Miss Rose rustled by in her taffeta gown. "Don't be tellin' that ol' tacky story, Bill Watson! I've heard it a hundred times, and it's a lie."

"No, it ain't," said Uncle Billy, grinning.

"It most certainly is. It was not pickle relish. It was chow chow." As she turned on her heel and walked away, the rector couldn't help but notice the Ritz cracker that fell out of her cummerbund and rolled under a chair.

"I hear you've quit drawin'," said J.C. "Why's that?"

"Arthur," said Uncle Billy.

"Arthur who?"

"Arthur-itis. But that ain't hurt my joke tellin' any. Let me give y' one t' go in th' paper."

"We don't print jokes in the *Muse*," J.C. snapped.

"If that ain't a lie!" said Percy Mosely, who was thoroughly dissatisfied with a recent editorial.

At the food table, he visited with Rodney Underwood, who was Mitford's young new police chief and a deacon at First Baptist.

"My granddaddy and my daddy both were police chiefs in this town. An' bad as I always wanted to work at th' post office, I couldn't do it. No way. After four years of bein' a deputy over in Wesley, I give up an' let th' town council hog-tie me."

"Well, I imagine it's a good life. I hardly ever see any crime reported in the *Muse*."

"It's around, though, don't kid yourself. You don't know what goes on behind these rose arbors . . ."

No, indeed, he thought, moving away. And I don't want to know, either.

"Hello again, Father," said Cynthia, holding what appeared to be the same cracker on the same napkin. "I've been meaning to say you look stunning in that copper-colored jacket."

He felt the color rise to his face. Stunning! He knew he should have bought the navy blue.

"Well, what do you think?"

Andrew Gregory sat on one of the Queen Anne dining chairs that someone had placed in a neat circle around Uncle Billy.

"A smashing success!" said the rector. "Undeniably! How many have we sold?"

Andrew's pleasure was visible. "Twenty-seven!"

He saw Hoppy Harper come through the door with Olivia Davenport. There was a flush in her cheeks, and her violet eyes sparkled. From what he could see, Hoppy looked more rested than he'd looked in months. Green jelly beans! he thought. That'll do it every time.

"Well, I must be off," said Andrew. "Miss Rose and the mayor have eaten all the Brie and I have to dash to The Local and replace it with cheddar!"

Cynthia Coppersmith sat down where Andrew had gotten up. "This is my first social occasion in the village. Except, of course, for visits to the rectory."

He could not think of one word to say.

"Violet ran away today," Cynthia said matter-of-factly.

"She did?"

"But she came back."

"Good! I hear you write and illustrate books about your cat."

"Yes. *Violet Comes to Stay, Violet Goes to the Country* . . . oh, and *Violet Has Kittens*, of course. To name only a few!"

"What a full life! How old is Violet, anyway?"

"Just two."

"Two! And she's done all that?"

"Well, you see, this is Violet Number Three. I have to keep replacing my Violets. The original Violet was seven when I got her, and I painted her for two years before she died of a liver infection.

"Then there was a very haughty Violet, which I found through an ad. Oh, she was lovely to look at, but unaccountably demanding. There were three books with that Violet, before she took off with a yellow tom."

"Aha."

"I was sent scurrying, as you can imagine. A contract for a seventh book, and no model!"

"Couldn't you use a cat of another color, and just, ah, paint it white in your illustrations?"

"No, no. I really must have a Violet to do the job. And not every white cat is one, of course."

"Of course."

"So, we were all looking for another Violet, and the newspaper got wind of it and the first thing you know, fifty-seven white cats turned up."

He had a vision of Barnabas set free in the midst of fifty-seven white cats.

"Then, the eighth Violet story won a book award—the Davant Medal. It's the most coveted award in children's literature, and the whole thing absolutely took my breath away! Suddenly, all the books started selling like . . ."

"Pancakes?" he asked. Blast! He'd meant to say hotcakes.

"Yes! And now I have my own true home after years of apartments, and a bit of money, too. It's a miracle!" she said in the earnest way that made her eyes seem bluer still. "But I must admit I'm weary of Violet books. Perhaps next time, I'll do something with . . . oh, maybe with moles!"

His worst enemy! Why, every blessed spring in Mitford, a man could step into a hole up to his knee. If there were any more detestable creatures in the animal kingdom, he could not think what they might be.

"If it's moles you're after, you can find all you'll ever want right next door. In my lawn."

"You're fun when you laugh," she said, smiling frankly.

"Thank you. I'll have to laugh more often."

"You've been so kind to me, I was hoping you might be able to come for dinner next week. I think I'll be settled by then."

He stood up. "Well . . ."

"Good!" she said. "I'll let you know more."

Andrew Gregory approached, buttoning the cashmere jacket across his trim midsection, and looking even more tanned and vigorous than he had an hour ago.

"Twenty-nine!" he said expansively to Father Tim, and then turned to Cynthia. "If you're ready, I'd like you to see the books Miss Potter is said to have made notes in."

As they walked away, the rector suddenly felt short, pale, overweight, and oddly suspicious that his jacket contained more polyester than wool.

"Why haven't you told me about this woman?" Hoppy wanted to know, as they stood outside Andrew's rear office and waited for the rest room.

"What was there to tell?"

"That she's lovely, new in town, goes to Lord's Chapel, I don't know. I'm walking down the hall last week, and I see this angel sitting by Pearly's bed, reading from the Psalms. I'll never forget it. 'Thou art my hiding place and my shield. I hope in thy word,' she said. It struck me to the very marrow."

And no wonder, thought the rector, whose own marrow had been struck by the depth of her feeling.

"I've been away from church so long . . . so long away from . . . believing." Hoppy leaned against the wall, avoiding the rector's gaze. "I've been very angry with God."

"I understand."

"He operated without anesthetic."

He looked at the man who had lost his wife of sixteen years, and saw the sure mark that bitterness and overwork had left. Yet, something tonight was easier in him.

Percy Mosely came out of the rest room. "You better watch it," he said, "there's a real loud odor in that pink soap."

He insisted that Hoppy go ahead of him and wandered into Andrew's comfortably untidy office. He sat in a wing back chair next to Andrew's desk and looked at the collection of paintings on the walls, at the jumble of books and magazines spilling from baskets and shelves. He idly turned his attention to a fragment of newspaper, protruding from beneath a leather blotter on the desk.

"Jewels Missing from Museum Exhibition," he read silently, without any special interest. "Last night, as the fund-raising gala got under way in the new wing of the Sonningham, an armed guard discovered that a priceless array of antique royal jewels had been stolen while he stood within feet of the glass case.

" 'I stepped away for perhaps a minute and a half, to see what was making a rattling noise in the skylight,' said Nigel Hadleigh, 62, of Armed Forces, Inc., a private security firm. 'When I looked back at the case, the jewels were gone.'

"Investigators so far have no clue to the theft, nor any suspects. There were no fingerprints on the case, which, until 9:30 p.m. on the first night of the museum's fund-raising effort, contained rare jewels from all of the British Isles, including a necklace once worn by Princess Louise.

" 'We're dreadfully embarrassed,' said Museum Director Wilfred Cappman. 'Whatever will we say to the queen?' "

Ah, there's the rub! thought the rector.

Hoppy came out of the rest room and peered into the office. "I need to talk to you pretty soon. But this time," he said, "I'll let you write the prescription."

Strike while the iron is hot! he thought. "How about Thursday at the Grill? That's Percy's day for salmon croquettes."

"Don't be late," warned the village doctor, grinning.

As he finished washing his hands, he heard laughter on the other side of the rest room wall. It was Cynthia Coppersmith. Obviously, she found moles very, very amusing, which was the oddest mark of character he had recently observed.

When he came home, he discovered one of his pie plates on the back step, and in it, a square envelope.

It contained a watercolor of Barnabas, which was so lifelike it might have barked. A note tucked into the envelope read, "Thanks so much for the kindness you've shown a stranger in your midst. Cynthia."

"Truly amazing," he said, looking at the watercolor with rapt fascination.

"Your sermon was real good yesterday," Emma said on Monday morning.

There's obviously no accounting for tastes, thought the rector, who recalled that a baby cried throughout the service, a squirrel chewed something behind the wall, and a lens from his glasses had dropped into the Bible as he read the gospel message.

"I saw you at the art show," she said, "but when I finally got over to where you were standin', you'd up and left."

"Yes, well . . . how's Harold?"

"Work, work, work. Do this, do that. Fix the roof. Paint the porch. Change the oil. Mulch up his corncobs. That's the way the Baptists do, you know."

"Is that right?"

"You don't ever see Episcopalians mulching up their corncobs."

"Don't have any to mulch up."

"I guess."

Emma took her ledger out of the top drawer, along with a locked box containing Sunday's offering.

"Seems to me your new neighbor was on your heels at the art show."

"My neighbor . . . oh, yes, you mean Miss Coppersmith."

"I do mean her, that's right. Everywhere you turned, she turned. It was like ice dancin'."

"Didn't you have anything better to do than watchdog your preacher?"

"First thing you know, there'll be more of those cat books in the stores. Like, *Violet Goes to Church, Violet Visits the Rector . . .*"

"Emma, don't push your luck."

"Didn't Miss Rose look tarted up?"

"Quite."

"And Uncle Billy, what's he goin' to do with all that money?"

"Hard telling."

A sudden wind moaned around the little stone building, rattling the windows. They looked at each other.

"They're calling for snow tonight," he announced.

"Maybe I should marry Harold before spring, after all," she said.

Before Pearly McGee died, she had given him a check for $1,456.00.

"Use it to make somebody happy," she had told him. "That's what I want, is somebody to be happy."

He thought it would make one Dooley Barlowe very happy, indeed, if his red bicycle could be sitting under the Christmas tree.

Dooley had earned a hundred and eight dollars, and needed that much again to pay the layaway balance on the red mountain bike.

Perhaps what he should do, he mused, is give fifty-four dollars of his own money and match it with fifty-four from Pearly's "discretionary fund."

He mentioned it to Emma.

"I don't know about that. Maybe he ought to work for the whole thing."

"Why?"

She shrugged. "He's hot-headed. Workin' for it might cool 'im off."

After Emma left, he called the bicycle store in Wesley. Yes, they could make a delivery to Mitford before Christmas.

When he told Puny that the red bicycle would be coming to hide in the garage, he thought she'd be delighted. She wasn't. "I hope you know what you're doin'," she said, flatly.

On Tuesday, he had breakfast with Olivia Davenport, and allowed her to drive him to the office in a rain so heavy they could scarcely see the lights of oncoming cars along Main Street.

"Did you hear what happened at the lay readers meeting last night?" Emma asked as he removed his raincoat.

"Esther Bolick did her impersonation of the bishop?"

"Worse than that. Somebody stole her famous orange marmalade cake out of the parish hall fridge."

"Stole it?"

"Just cracked open that cake carrier and cleaned it out, crumbs an' all."

"I don't understand."

"Everybody brought a little somethin' for refreshments. After meetin' in the nursery where it was warm, they went to the kitchen to pour tea, and the cake was gone. Hilda Lassister said she'd been waitin' two years for a taste of that marmalade cake, and when they couldn't find it, she said she like to cried."

He scratched his head. "I don't understand why they couldn't find it."

"The point," she said impatiently, "is that it wasn't in the refrigerator where Esther left it. It was gone. Kaput. Zip. Outta there."

"They put the cake in the refrigerator and went back after the meeting and it was gone?"

"That's what I'm tryin' to tell you. But whoever stole it didn't even touch Marge Houck's pineapple upside down."

"Now there's something I can understand," he said.

On Wednesday evening, he took a shower and dressed, and prepared to visit his new neighbor in her tiny house next door. Cynthia Coppersmith had done as promised and invited him to dinner. And the invitation, it seemed to him, was perfectly timed.

The last of his Rector's Meatloaf was gone, and good riddance. To his chagrin, he'd used more oatmeal than before, which resulted in the most unsavory concoction he'd tasted in years. But he had soldiered on and eaten the entire loaf over a period of several days. He was so ashamed of it, he had hidden it at the back of the refrigerator, where he hoped Puny wouldn't find it.

Every light in the small house glowed warmly through the heavy mist that lay upon the village.

"Pleasant!" he said, aloud. "A small house for a small person." He lifted the old brass knocker and rapped three times.

There was no answer to his knock, so he tried again.

Nothing.

Since callers occasionally had to go to the back door of the rectory to rouse him from his study, he thought the same might apply in this case. He stumbled around the side of the house, over broken flagstones, toward a light shining above the back door.

He knocked and waited. Not a sound.

He cautiously opened the door and peered into a minuscule but inviting kitchen.

A broiling pan sat on the stove, containing a blackened roast. Next to it, a pot had boiled over, and a tray of unbaked rolls sat disconsolately on the countertop. "Hello!" he called.

A white cat leaped onto the breakfast table, looked at him curiously, and began cleaning her paws. "Violet, I presume?" He had never been fond of cats.

He heard her coming down the stairs, then she appeared at the kitchen door, her eyes red from crying.

"I've done it again," she said, sniffing. "I can never get it right. I sat down at my drawing table for just one minute. One minute! An hour later, I looked up, and the rice had boiled over and the roast had burned, and well, there you have it."

" 'Whatever your hand finds to do, do it with all your might'!" he quoted cheerfully from Ecclesiastes. "You must have been doing something you liked."

She sighed. "I was drawing moles."

Moles again! That explains it, thought her caller. "Look here," he said, "if you don't mind, let me experiment with this." He made a broad gesture toward the ruined dinner.

"It will take a miracle," she said flatly.

"I'd be very open to a good miracle. Where's your carving knife?"

He drew the sharp knife across the end of the roast, and a thick slice peeled away neatly. "Well, now! Just the way I like it. Overdone on the outside and rare in the middle." He carved a sliver and handed it to his hostess on the point of the blade. "See what you think."

Cynthia eyed it suspiciously, then did as he suggested. "Delicious!" she declared with feeling. "It *is* a miracle!"

He lifted the lid on the pot that had boiled over on the burner, and stirred the contents with a wooden spoon. "It's stuck on the bottom, but I think it's just right. Yes, indeed. Wild rice. A favorite!"

"You really are infernally kind," she said tartly.

"Not kind. Famished. I ran today and missed lunch entirely."

"Well," she said, the color coming back into her cheeks, "I did make a crab-meat casserole for the first course. That worked! And there are glazed onions with rosemary and honey that appear edible." She took two fragrant, steaming dishes out of the oven and set them on the counter.

"I hear you like a drop of sherry now and then," she said, and poured from a bottle with a distinguished label. She handed him a glass, and poured one for herself.

"You've prepared a grand feast!" exclaimed her guest.

"Cheers!" said his relieved hostess.

CHAPTER ELEVEN

A White Thanksgiving

Thanksgiving came to the village, along with a deep and unexpected blanket of snow.

"A white Thanksgiving comes to Mitford," wrote *Muse* editor J.C. Hogan, "and a lot of turkeys have been careening down Baxter Hill on biscuit pans."

Winnie Ivey, wearing last year's Christmas muffler, walked with a heavy basket and a light heart to her brother's rooms over the barbershop.

Miss Rose and Uncle Billy put on their boots and went to the All-Church Feast, with Miss Rose carrying quantities of wax paper in her pockets, for wrapping take-outs.

Miss Sadie, fearing there might be ice under the snow, chose to stay home, eat a Swanson's chicken pie, and make a list of things to do for Louella's arrival the week after Christmas.

Puny Bradshaw roasted a turkey and went to visit her sisters.

And Russell Jacks baked a hen, cooked a mess of collard greens, and made a cake of cornbread. When villagers saw smoke boiling out of the Jacks chimney, and his scrap-metal graveyard obscured by a mantle of fresh snow, they were fairly enchanted.

Before attending the All-Church Feast, held this year at First

Baptist, Father Tim put two pies and a pan of Puny's sausage dressing into a basket and walked with Barnabas to Little Mitford Creek.

When he reached Winnie Ivey's cottage by the bridge, he turned left and headed far along the creek, into the snow-silent woods.

Here and there, limbs fell with a soft thud onto the white crust of the forest floor, which caused Barnabas to leap with a mixture of joy and alarm at the end of his red leash.

What, he wondered, had he ever done without Barnabas? Without the long, companionable walks, the pleasure and the aggravation of a living creature to care for, the growing empathy between them, and yes, the delight?

"Son of consolation" was the meaning given to the name Barnabas in the fourth chapter of Acts, and he was all that and more.

Barnabas had even done for him what nothing else had ever done. This great, black, maverick dog had somehow made him feel twenty years younger.

They followed fresh tracks to a low point on the creek bank and crossed the creek on a series of large boulders. On the other side, the tracks led to the door of a ramshackle house, sitting near a derelict bridge.

The chimney sent up billows of fragrant wood smoke, and from inside the dwelling, which was scarcely bigger than a tool shed, came the sound of laughter.

"Come in, come in!" said Samuel K. Hobbes, as he opened the door and limped aside on his crutch. "Come in and warm yourselves by th' fire!"

Barnabas bounded in to shake his wet fur on all assembled, then lay down by the glowing wood stove. The rector was pleased to see that every church denomination in town was represented in that small room, and each had come with a bag or basket for Homeless Hobbes.

Homeless moved nimbly on his battered crutch, pouring coffee for every guest.

"You could use another chair in this place," suggested a Methodist deacon who was standing in a corner.

"Nossir, I couldn't," said Homeless, setting the empty pot on a shelf. "Mr. Thoreau himself had two and often regretted it. Fact is, m' two pairs of pants is one too many."

Father Tim unwound the wool muffler from around his neck. "What about these two pumpkin pies? You want me to take one back?"

"No, my good Father, I do not. Pants and pies is two different things."

"You got that right!" said Rodney Underwood, who had brought a pie himself.

Homeless hitched up his suspenders and surveyed the little table. "Lookit this bounty! Two, three, four, five . . . seven pies. Scandalous! Far too many pies for ol' Homeless. And a big, fat hen, and a sack of ham biscuits, and a quart of collards, and a fine mess of sweet potatoes . . ."

"Don't forget th' bag of grits and a ham hock for soup," said Rodney, who was a stickler for accuracy.

"And Puny Bradshaw's sausage dressing," said the rector.

Homeless surveyed the gathering. "Well, boys, much as I 'preciate all this, I've got to tell you the gospel truth."

"What's that?" the deacon asked, suspiciously.

"I'm goin' to give the best portion of these eats to folks who're worse off than me."

"I didn't know there was anybody worse off than you," said young Jack Teague from the Presbyterians.

"That's what you think, son. You head up the hill from this creek, and all back in there, you'll find 'em worse off than me. With little young 'uns, too."

"Do what you want to with it," said Rodney. "It's yours in th' name of the Lord."

"And I thank you for it," said Homeless.

Rodney passed a basket of ham biscuits his mother had sent. "Let's bless these ham biscuits, boys," he said, and launched into a prayer covering world hunger, food stamps, stray animals, firewood, the Baptist conference, Little Mitford Creek, Big Mitford Creek, the sick, the unsaved, an unwelcome forecast for more snow, the town council's decision on sidewalks for Lilac Road, the president, the Congress, the Senate, the House of Representatives, and the local fire and police departments.

"Amen!" said Homeless. "That ought t' last me 'til this time next year."

"Mr. Hobbes," said Jack Teague, "I hear tell you used to live in New York City."

"That's a fact. Had a big, fancy office on Madison Avenue, and an apartment right on the Hudson River."

"No kidding!" said Jack, shaking his head in amazement. "And how long have you been homeless . . . sir?"

"My friend, as you can plainly see, I am not homeless in the least." He indicated the wood stove, a rickety table covered with oilcloth, two shelves, a kerosene lamp, a chair, a cot, a sink, and a toilet that was partially hidden by a red gingham tablecloth looped over a wire.

"The way I'm able to live today is not only one hundred percent stress-proof, it is guaranteed recession-proof. No matter which way the economy goes, it don't affect me one way or th' other.

"To tell th' plain truth, this is th' finest home I ever had, and I've lived in high style from New York City to Dallas, Texas, not to mention one stint in Los Angelees, California."

"Wow! What business were you in?"

"Advertisin', my boy!" said Homeless, with a wicked grin. "Advertisin'!"

On Saturday morning, Mitford woke to a second blanket of snow, so Father Tim canceled his trip with Dooley to Meadowgate Farm. Instead, he had lunch at the Grill and went shopping with Uncle Billy.

"Rose needs somethin' to wear," said his friend, who had decided to spend some of the proceeds from his art show. "I'm not a proud man, Preacher, but that ol' army stuff she drags out'n the closet nearly shames me t' death.

"Th' dress she wore t' the drawin' show, she hauled that out'n th' dumpster on Forks Road—seen th' tail of it hangin' over th' side, don't you know, when we was th'owin' out some dinette chairs."

"I don't know how much good I can do you, Uncle Billy. I've never in my life shopped for women's clothes. It's all I can do to shop for myself."

"Well, but you're a preacher, and you know what's right for Sunday morning." Uncle Billy flashed his gold tooth in a winning smile. "I'd be beholden to you."

"Done, then!" said the rector, and they set off in heavy boots and coats toward the dress shop across from the war monument.

He was deep in thought as he walked with Barnabas on Saturday afternoon to Lord's Chapel. His shopping trip with Uncle Billy had been a thorough success, and he could hardly wait to see Miss Rose on Sunday, decked out in the black suit that was forty percent off, and a fuchsia wool coat they landed for half price.

The only trouble was, there was no ladies' shoe store in Mitford. That meant that Miss Rose might very well show up in her brother's army boots with the heavy latches.

The second snowfall had muffled the everyday sounds of the village, so that all he heard as they walked was the crunch of their footsteps in the untracked blanket that covered the sidewalk.

Along the way, Barnabas felt compelled to melt the snow in several places, after which he dashed on eagerly, pleased with the accomplishment.

"Recession-proof!" he muttered aloud, thinking of Homeless Hobbes's comment about his bare-bones existence. If only the rest of Mitford could claim that privilege. In recent months, he had not had to turn on the news to learn the deepening impact of the recession—he could read it in the faces of the town merchants.

As he came by the drugstore, he hoped to wave at Sparks through the window, but saw Hoppy Harper instead. Getting his green jelly bean fix, he thought. It pleased him immeasurably that Hoppy had done more than agree to be on the building committee. He said he'd be taking part, once again, in the life of the church.

Passing the window, he saw Olivia Davenport, muffled in fur, approach Hoppy with a radiant smile.

Like an image caught by the click of a camera shutter, the scene flashed upon his consciousness and was gone. Yet, he'd clearly seen something that troubled him. He'd seen a look of unmistakable happiness on his friend's face, a look of tenderness as he gazed down upon Olivia Davenport, who was dying.

At the church, he found the door unlocked and, coming inside in his snow-encrusted boots, was greeted by the lush, alluring fragrance of flowers. Their fresh scent spoke at once to his heart and lightened his sober thoughts.

He looped the red leash around a chair leg and took off his boots as Barnabas lay down contentedly. Apparently, the Altar Guild had been in to arrange the flowers and had forgotten to lock the side door. He must speak to them about it, of course.

Not that he didn't like an unlocked church. No, indeed; he preferred it. If there was anything disheartening, it was to seek out a church for prayer and refreshment and find its doors barred.

But the Mortlake tapestry, woven in 1675 and now hanging behind the altar, was of such extraordinary rarity that the insurance company not only demanded a darkened room and locked doors, it stipulated the type of locks.

It was unusual for him to visit Lord's Chapel on Saturday, but today he was seeking special refreshment of his own. Who was there, after all, to counsel the counselor? He crossed himself. "Revive me, O Lord," he prayed, "according to thy word."

For days, he had felt weighted and heavy, but not from the holiday turkey and dressing. If anything, he had been more careful of his diet than ever. It was his spirit that was heavy, at a time when church events were in full force and Advent preparations were hurling him madly toward Christmas.

Yet it wasn't the escalating rush of daily life that concerned him. What concerned him were his sermons.

In recent weeks, they had been tepid and controlled. Barren, somehow. It was as if the Holy Spirit had taken his hands off and was standing back, observing, watchful.

He sighed as he opened the door into the nave, and noted that he must stop doing that. Sighing was not becoming to anyone, much less to a rector. Perhaps he could put the burden on Emma, saying, "Emma, I have this bothersome habit of sighing, as you no doubt have noticed. From now on, tell me when I do it, and I'll put a dollar in the thank offering box."

A dollar! he thought. The very stiffness of the penalty should resolve the problem.

Before he prayed, however, he wanted to complete a chore. It had always been his habit to do a chore when he came to the church on Saturday.

Today he would pay some overdue attention to the columbarium, where six ash-filled urns were hidden away in a closet on the parish hall corridor.

He located the key on the top of the door frame, unlocked, and turned on the light.

It wasn't much of a final resting place, he thought. His own wish was to be buried in the old-fashioned way, with birds singing and roses blooming over him.

He moved the 1928 prayer books that someone had piled onto the shelf next to the urns, and partially filled a wastebasket with the glass ashtrays they'd used in the parish hall before the blessed relief of the smoking ban. Rummage sale!

He dumped two arrangements of plastic poinsettias into the wastebasket, lest anyone should find them and use them again, and followed that with a stack of hymnals so badly worn that the covers were off. Recycling bin!

Feeling warmly satisfied with the results of twenty minutes' effort, he went to the kitchen for cleaning rags and returned to dust off the remains of Parkinson Hamrick.

"Gone to Glory!" he said with a smile, remembering the kind man who had sung like an angel.

Parkinson's ashes rattled dully as he set the urn down. Though he had never looked into one of these morbid containers, he'd been told by Father Roland that bits of charred bone were mixed with the ashes, which caused the rattle.

"Lydia Newton," he murmured aloud, lifting her urn. Lydia Newton, herself widowed, had come with her widowed mother-in-law to Mitford, where the two had lived happily for years. "Where thou diest," Ruth had said to Naomi in the Bible story, "will I die, and there will I be buried; the Lord do so to me, and more also, if anything but death part thee and me." It was one of the loveliest passages in Scripture, mistakenly used, he thought, in Protestant weddings.

The musty little closet was, in a sense, coming alive. And he was feeling better already. Then he picked up the next urn.

While the other urns had rattled dully, he found that the remains of Parrish Guthrie rattled differently. Again, he held up the bronze urn and shook it.

Odd. Not at all like the sound of the others. There was a brighter rattle, as of something small and hard, like pebbles.

He was curious. After all, he'd never seen inside one of these things. He looked up at the dim, bare bulb, and decided to move the urn into the kitchen by the big window over the sink.

He took a tea towel from the rack by the sink and applied some pressure to the top of the urn. It wouldn't budge. Need one of those rubber things that unscrews jars, he thought, trying again. The urn rattled brightly. Seashells, he thought, remembering his time as a child at the gulf shore. It sounds like a jar of small seashells.

Then, the top of the urn gave way and unscrewed as if it had been oiled.

He turned the open mouth of the urn toward the light and peered in. Something gleamed.

"I hope that's not the old boy's gold tooth!" he said aloud.

He spread the tea towel on the counter top, then turned the urn on its side and shook it gently. Something loosely wrapped in cloth appeared, and tumbled onto the towel.

When he untied the string, the bright, faceted gems came rolling out like so many peas.

"Good Lord!" he croaked, hearing his voice fail.

The winter light coming through the window struck the stones at playful random. Some, shaped like tiny globes, radiated a scarlet glow that was utterly bewitching. Others, the shape of teardrops, seemed to burn with a green and living fire. Still others were as darkly blue as distant mountains.

He stood by the sink, unaware that he was holding his breath. He could see that the jar contained more of the loosely wrapped parcels, and he was seized with such anxiety that he felt a heaviness in his chest.

"Father, something is out of order here. I need your wisdom. Help me think this through . . ." He let out his breath, and sat down on the stool by the telephone. His knees were weak.

Trouble! What he was looking at was trouble. Before he even began to think it through, he was convinced of that.

He had personally attended these urns about three years ago; the date would be in his journal on the shelf at the office. At that time, Parrish Guthrie's rattle had been no different from the rest. So, the jewels had been put into the urn since then.

Scarcely anyone ever went near that closet. Someone would occasionally open the door, throw in a bit of rubbish and depart. Once, a Sunday school class had been shown the closet, in a teaching about death. "Gross!" said a ten-year-old. If there was a neglected, seldom-used part of the church, the closet was it. A perfect place, then, for someone to hide what he'd just found.

But had he found anything of real importance? Were these the genuine article? He knew nothing about jewels. As payment of a legal fee, his attorney father had once come into possession of some uncut diamonds, which he'd considered dull, gray, and uninteresting. But once they were cut, they flashed like fire. What a marvel!

No, he had no knowledge of jewels. But something told him that these were the real thing. He had seen that same vibrant, indescribable fire in the cut diamonds.

Now what? He moved off the stool and paced the kitchen.

The proper thing, he thought, was to call Rodney Underwood, who would conduct endless questions, investigations, and fingerprinting, just like on TV.

Rodney, always overzealous, would have his small force swarming—yes, swarming—over the place, and here it was nearly Christmas, with new music for the choir to practice, and the special musicale and concert reading coming up within the week, and the Festival of Lessons and Carols. Clearly, the beauty and holiness of a time already fractured by stress and distractions would be further eroded.

Then there was J.C. Hogan to consider.

J.C. would run a front-page story, colored by the usual inaccuracies. He'd very likely have an interview with Emma Garrett, Russell Jacks, the vestry, and whoever had an opinion at the Grill, which was everybody.

Worse than that, J.C. would camp out at Lord's Chapel and the rector's office for days on end, looking for a "scoop" and eating countless bags of M&Ms, a great number of which would end up on the floor, smashed underfoot.

The other course, then, was to let sleeping dogs lie, and wait until after Christmas to call Rodney Underwood.

He didn't think twice about what he did next.

He put the jewels back into the cloth, tied the string and placed the parcel in the urn, screwed the top on, folded the tea towel and replaced it on the rack, walked down the hall and put the urn on the closet shelf exactly where it had been, dusted the other three urns, turned off the light, carried out the full wastebasket and the dust rags, locked the door, put the dust rags under the kitchen sink, stored the wastebasket in the rummage room, and checked on Barnabas before he went to the nave to do what he had, after all, come to do:

Pray about his anemic sermons.

As he paused to let his eyes adjust to the dimness of the nave, he heard a strange sound. Then, toward the front, on the gospel side, he saw a man kneeling in a pew. Suddenly, he leaned back and uttered such a desperate cry that the rector's heart fairly thundered.

Give me wisdom, he prayed for the second time that morning. Then he stood waiting. He didn't know for what.

"If you're up there, prove it! Show me! If you're God, you can prove it!" In the visitor's voice was a combination of anger, despair, and odd hope.

"I'll never ask you this again," the man said coldly, and then, with a fury that chilled his listener, he shouted again, "Are . . . you . . . up . . . there?"

With what appeared to be utter exhaustion, he put his head in his hands as the question reverberated in the nave.

Father Tim slid into the pew across the aisle and knelt on the worn cushion. "You may be asking the wrong question," he said, quietly.

Startled, the man raised his head.

"I believe the question you may want to ask is not, 'Are you up there?' but, 'Are you down here?' "

"What kind of joke is that?"

"It isn't a joke."

The man took a handkerchief from his suit pocket and wiped his face. He was neatly dressed, the rector observed, and his suit and tie appeared to be expensive. A businessman, obviously. Successful, quite likely. Not from Mitford, certainly.

"God wouldn't be God if He were only up there. In fact, another name for Him is Immanuel, which means God with us.' " He was amazed at the casual tone of his voice, as if they'd met here to chat for a while. "He's with us right now, in this room."

The man looked at him. "I'd like to believe that, but I can't. I can't feel Him at all."

"There's a reason . . ."

"The things I've done," the man said flatly.

"Have you asked Him to forgive the things you've done?"

"I assure you that God would not want to do that."

"Believe it or not, I can promise that He would. In fact, He promises that He will."

The man looked at his watch. "I've got a meeting," he said, yet he made no move to leave. He remained on his knees.

"What business are you in?" It was one of those questions from a cocktail party or Rotary meeting, but out it came.

"Shoes. We make men's shoes. I was on my way to a sales meeting in Wesley when I saw this place and I came in. I didn't mean to do it, I just couldn't help it. I had to come in. And now I don't know what I'm doing here. I need to get on the road."

Still, he made no move to rise from his knees.

It was an odd thought, but the rector pursued it. "Let's say you need to move into another factory building. Trouble is, it's crowded with useless, out-of-date equipment. Until you clear out the rubbish and get the right equipment installed, you're paralyzed, you can't produce."

"How did you know we're looking for a new factory?"

"I didn't know. A divine coincidence."

There was a long silence. A squirrel ran across the attic floor.

"You can keep the factory shut down and unproductive, or you can clear it out and get to work. Is your life working?"

"Not in years."

Somewhere in the dark church, the floor creaked. "There's no other way I can think of to put it—but when you let Him move into your life, the garbage moves out. The anger starts to go, and the resentment, and the fear. That's when He can help get your equipment up and running, you might say."

"Look, I don't want to wallow around in this God stuff like a pig in slop. I just want some answers, that's all."

"What are the questions you want answered?"

"Bottom line, is He up there, is He real?"

"Bottom line, He's down here, He's with us right now."

"Prove it."

"I can't. I don't even want to try."

"Jesus," the man said, shaking his head.

This was like flying blind, the rector thought, with the windshield iced over. "I get the feeling you really want God to be real, perhaps you even want to be close to Him, but . . . but you're holding on to something, holding on to one of those sins you don't think God can forgive, and you don't want to let it go."

The man's voice was cold. "I'd like to kill someone, I think of killing him all the time. I would never do it, but he deserves it and thinking about it helps me. I like thinking about it."

The rector felt suddenly weakened, as if the anger had seeped into his own bones, his own spirit. He wanted the windshield to defrost; where was this going?

"Do you like the fall of the year?"

The man gave an odd laugh. "Why?"

"One of the things that makes a dead leaf fall to the ground is the bud of the new leaf that pushes it off the limb. When you let God fill you with His love and forgiveness, the things you think you desperately want to hold on to start falling away . . . and we hardly notice their passing."

The man looked at his watch and made a move to rise from his knees. His agitation was palpable.

"Let me ask you something," said the rector. "Would you like to ask Christ into your life?"

The stranger stared into the darkened sanctuary. "I can't do it, I've tried."

"It isn't a test you have to pass. It doesn't require discipline and intelligence . . . not even strength and perseverance. It only requires faith."

"I don't think I've got that." There was a long silence. "But I'd be willing to try it . . . one more time."

"Will you pray a simple prayer with me . . . on faith?"

He looked up. "What do I have to lose?"

"Nothing, actually." Father Tim rose stiffly from the kneeler and took the short step across the aisle, where he laid his hands on the man's head.

"If you could repeat this," he said. "Thank you, God, for loving me, and for sending your Son to die for my sins. I sincerely repent of my sins, and receive Christ as my personal savior. Now, as your child, I turn my entire life over to you. Amen."

The man repeated the prayer, and they were silent.

"Is that all?" he asked finally.

"That's all."

"I don't know . . . what I'm supposed to feel."

"Whatever you feel is exactly what you're supposed to feel."

The man was suddenly embarrassed, awkward. "I've got to get out of here. I was on my way to a meeting in Wesley, and I saw this old church and I . . . things have been, I've been . . . I've got to get out of here. Look, thanks. Thank you," he said, shaking the rector's hand.

"Please . . . stay in touch."

He stood at the door for a moment and watched him go. There was so much he hadn't said, so much he'd left out. But the Holy Spirit would fill in the blanks.

As they were leaving the church, Barnabas looked up, sniffed the air, and began to bark wildly at the ceiling. His booming voice filled the small nave like the bass of an organ.

With some difficulty, he unglued his charge from the narthex floor, and pulled him along on the leash.

It seemed years ago that he'd come in this door, he thought. Yet his watch told him he'd been at Lord's Chapel only a little more than two hours.

He felt strangely at peace, following the man's footprints along the snowy path to the street.

As Christmas drew nearer, sleep became more elusive. For hours, he'd lie awake while Barnabas snored at his feet. He had tried without success to put the jewels completely out of his mind.

Catching himself pondering the imponderable, he'd toss this way and that, until the bed was a scramble of sheets and blankets and Barnabas had gone to the kitchen for a snack, which he crunched loudly enough to wake the neighbors.

He wondered briefly how his neighbor was doing, anyway. He thought he'd seen Andrew Gregory's gray Mercedes parked in front of her house recently, but he couldn't be sure, as he'd never been good at identifying cars.

Was she going out with Andrew Gregory? Was he coming over for dinners of blackened roasts and burned rolls? He remembered Cynthia's silvery laugh behind the rest room wall, and his odd sense of feeling fat, short, and boring, compared to Andrew. He had not liked that feeling.

He sat up on the side of the bed.

It had just occurred to him that there were no ashes in Parrish Guthrie's urn. No ashes had spilled onto the white tea towel, and, clearly, no ashes had marred the sparkle of the jewels, which had been only loosely contained in the porous cloth. Well, then, where were the ashes of the departed?

Ashes. Ashes. Something dimly tried to get through to him, but he couldn't summon it. Also, he seemed to remember reading about stolen jewels.

He got up and walked to the window and looked down on Cynthia Coppersmith's house. He wondered how she was getting on, she and Violet, and if she was happy in Mitford. There were lights on, though it must easily be midnight. And he saw the tiny white lights she'd strung for Christmas, winking on the bushes by her front steps. A comfort to have someone in that house!

He sat down in his wing chair and picked up the *Observer*, but couldn't read it. Stolen jewels. He'd read something somewhere. . . .

The newspaper article, sticking out from under the ink blotter on Andrew Gregory's desk! Jewels! Stolen from under the guard's nose. Something about the queen being upset.

No, he thought, those were necklaces that royalty had worn, not loose stones. Ah, well.

Ashes, he thought, again. But almost immediately, he dozed off in his chair.

Olivia Davenport opened the office door and said brightly, "Knock, knock!"

She was wearing an emerald-colored suit with black trim, and carrying a Bible under her arm. All in all, he thought, a lovely sight.

"Sit down, Olivia, and bring me up to date."

"I'm excited, Father! We're organizing a reading at the hospital. Isaiah. Ruth. Psalms. Portions of the Gospel of John. I'm hoping you'll join us, be a reader. Will you? You have such a beautiful voice. Oh, and then we're taking it to Wesley, to the hospital there."

Olivia's cheeks were flushed, and her violet eyes sparkled. Whatever her illness may be, her new mission was obviously good medicine.

"Count me in!" he said. "Just give me the schedule and I'll try and work it out."

"Wonderful," she said, getting up to go. "I was just dashing to The Local . . ."

"Olivia . . . ?"

"Yes?"

"Would you mind staying a moment?"

She smiled and sat down again.

He didn't want to do it, but it had to be done. "Olivia, what exactly . . . is going on?"

Her violet eyes were perplexed. "What . . . exactly do you mean?"

"Something tells me, and it isn't Hoppy, I assure you, that he's growing . . . shall I say . . . fond of you."

She stared at him, unspeaking.

"This troubles me," he said simply.

"It troubles me as well."

"Does he know?"

"He does not."

"I'd be grateful if you would tell me everything. It goes without saying that it will be held in the strictest confidence.

"You say you're dying. But why are you dying? Why do you appear so very healthy? What course will this . . . illness . . . take? Are you suffering?" He paused. "These are serious issues. But perhaps, for me, the issue is this: If you're dying, I can't bear to watch a friend who was lately grief stricken by his wife's death form an attachment that—"

Olivia stood up. "Please! I understand." She looked suddenly drawn and pale. "I'm going to tell you everything. You really should know, and I apologize. It's just that, when I moved here, I wanted to try and forget it. I wanted to . . . live without thinking of dying."

She was silent for a moment. "Before I say more, I'd like to ask you to do something for me."

"Consider it done," he said impulsively.

"When I've explained it all to you, I'd like you to tell him everything."

He was silent.

"I tried once," she said, "but, after all, he has said nothing to me of his feelings. It may seem shameful, but I'm too proud to say, 'Look, you appear to be falling in love with me, and you mustn't.' What if he isn't falling in love with me, what if I've guessed wrong, and we're both humiliated?"

"You haven't guessed wrong."

"You'll tell him, then?"

"I will. But I'd like you to do something for me, as well."

"Anything," she said with sincerity.

"This will be his second Christmas alone, and I feel he still has some sorrow to work through. To tell him now would . . . complicate things unduly. You'll probably see him at church, of course, and even at the hospital. But I'd like you to avoid him as graciously as you can. Then, after the holidays, I'll tell him."

"I can do that," she said slowly. "I care for him very much. He's a wonderful man."

"He is, indeed."

"Well, then," she said, sitting down, again. "I suppose I can't put this off any longer."

After Olivia Davenport left, he sat in silence, staring at the door. Then, he cleaned off his desk and typed an overdue letter to Walter, in which he quoted Romans 8:28: " 'We know that all things (*all* things, Walter!) work together for good to them that love God, to them who are called according to His purpose.' Please bear with Katherine on this."

He was typing with more than usual dexterity when Russell Jacks pushed open the door.

"Russell! Come in and sit. Have some coffee." He got up and poured a cup for the old man who, he thought, looked gaunt and tired. "How are you pushing along, Russell?"

The sexton launched into a racking cough. "No rest for th' wicked," he said, grinning.

"How's Dooley doing? We missed our trip to Meadowgate because of the snow, and with Christmas on us, it'll be January before we get out there."

"Well, Father," said Russell, rolling his hat between his palms, "mournful is the word for that boy."

"Mournful? Dooley?"

"Yes, sir. That's th' word."

"What's the trouble?"

Russell hesitated, looking at the floor. "Well, Father, it's 'is mama. He's bad homesick."

"Can't he go home to visit? I've been meaning to ask that."

"I reckon he could . . ."

Father Tim waited.

"But t' tell th' truth, I reckon he cain't . . ."

Another silence.

"What is it, Russell? You need to share the truth with mc, if you will. What exactly is wrong with your daughter?"

"Nerves," Russell mumbled.

"Nerves?"

The old man looked up. His face was sad. "Liquor, t' tell th' truth. His mama lays drunk."

"I'm sorry."

"She let all 'er young 'uns go, all five. Jus' give 'em out like candy. I'd 've took two, if I could, but . . ." He shrugged, then coughed again. "Th' boy was th' oldest, been takin' care of them little 'uns all 'is life, nearly. They were snatched up like a bunch of kittens in a box, one give here, another give yonder, it's an awful bad thing for th' boy."

"I'm sorry. I didn't know." He felt immeasurably sad for Dooley.

Russell held his hat over his mouth as another fit of coughing overcame him. When it was over, his face was ashen.

"What are you doing for that cough, Russell?"

"A little of this an' a little of that, you might say."

"How's your Christmas looking?"

"Oh, we'll get by, me 'n th' boy."

"I'd like to see you do more than get by." He pulled out his upper right-hand desk drawer and felt for the packet of bills. He had banked a thousand dollars of Pearly's "happiness" money and kept some cash for times like these.

He handed Russell a crisp hundred-dollar bill.

"In the name of the Lord, Russell, get the boy a tree, and string some lights, if you can."

"I thank you, Father," Russell said, looking embarrassed and relieved. "Do you reckon th' Lord would mind if we had a nice ham out of th' change?"

"Mind? Why, I think He'd mind if you didn't! And here, this is for that cough." He took a twenty-dollar bill out of his pocket.

The sexton folded the bills respectfully and tucked them into his overalls pocket. "I thank you, Father. We finished mulchin' them rhododendrons before it snowed, I thought you orght t' know."

Rhododendrons. Mulch. Ashes!

He remembered the fall day he'd gone around to the side door where Russell was mulching. He'd found ashes that looked like somebody had cleaned out their barbecue grill. He remembered asking Russell where the ashes came from, and then he'd borrowed Russell's gloves and worked the ashes into the soil.

Suddenly, he knew it just as sure as he was sitting there. He'd buried the remains of the double-dealing Parrish Guthrie in the church rhododendron bed.

In the fall, somebody had emptied the ashes out the side door. Then, he reasoned, they'd put the jewels in the clean urn, where they thought they'd be safe. In most churches, columbariums were not often moved about, and their own had not been touched in fully three years.

He was horrified to think it was a parishioner. Yet, who else but a parishioner would know about the closet, and know that the door was scarcely ever opened. He found he was going over and over the list of members, questioning each name. It was a process that left him angrily depressed. The discovery of those stones had been a wicked intrusion that had robbed him of peace and tranquillity during a season in which both were greatly longed for.

The concert reading and musicale drew a packed house, and the choir had, in his opinion, reached a new pinnacle of praise. After the event at church, the choir proceeded out the church doors and along Main Street, caroling in the chill evening air, carrying lanterns. They made a glowing procession along the old street, stopping here and there in an open shop for hot cider and cookies.

A tenor and a baritone broke away from the choir and went along the dark, cold creek bank, to the little house of Homeless Hobbes, where they warmed themselves by the wood stove and lustily sang, together with their host, as many carols as they had strength left to deliver.

The rector had the caroling choir finish up at the rectory, where he laid a fire in the study and spread out a feast that Puny had spent days preparing. Curried shrimp, honey-glazed ham, hot biscuits, cranberry salad, fried chicken, roasted potatoes with rosemary, and brandied fruit were set out in generous quantities.

The little group gathered around the roaring fire and, as the last carol of the evening, sang something they knew to be their rector's great favorite.

"In the bleak mid-winter," ran the first lines of Christina Rossetti's hymn, "icy wind made moan, earth as hard as iron, water like a stone . . ."

Then, the poignant last verse: "What shall I give him, poor as I am? If I were a shepherd, I would bring a lamb; if I were a wise man, I would do my part; yet what I can I give him . . . give my heart."

That's the key! he thought, as they pulled on heavy coats and gloves, mufflers and boots. Then, with much laughter and warm hugs, they trooped out the door and into the biting wind

"The Lord be with you!" he called, his breath forming gray puffs on the stinging air.

"And also with you!"

For a long time afterward, he sat by the fire, feeling the joy of Christmas, and knowing with unsearchable happiness that Christ did, indeed, live in his heart. Not because he was a "preacher." Not because he was, after a fashion, "good." But because, long ago, he had asked Him to.

He was working on his homily, which he intended to deliver on Christmas morning, glad to be by the study fire instead of out in the howling wind. He was glad, too, for the soup Puny had left simmering on the back burner, for it gave the house not only a mouth-watering fragrance, but a certain cheer.

When his mind wandered from the homily, he admired the tall spruce, garlanded with strings of colored lights like he remembered from his childhood in Holly Springs, and hung with ornaments that, somehow, had made it through dozens of Christmases past.

There was such a quantity of gifts stacked under the tree that he was mildly embarrassed.

Walter and Katherine had sent what he foolishly believed to be an electric train. Miss Sadie had given him a very large package tied with a red bow. Dooley had made him a present in school. Winnie Ivey wrote on hers: *I didn't bake this, but I hope you enjoy it anyway.*

Emma, who always liked to reveal the identity of her presents, had given him a gift certificate from the Collar Button, with which he planned to buy the first new pajamas he'd owned in years.

On and on, the presents went. And who was there to open them with him? There was the rub for a bachelor.

Occasionally, he would go to the garage and stand looking at the red bicycle. None of the presents under his tree inspired the excitement he felt in helping give Dooley Barlowe the desire of his heart.

He had tied a huge bow on the handlebars and made a card which read: *To Dooley from Dooley, and also from his friend, the preacher. When you see this, please don't go to hollerin'.*

When he heard the knock, he thought it was Barnabas scratching.

Then, he heard it again.

Dooley Barlowe stood at the back door, out of breath and shivering in a thin jacket.

"Granpaw's bad off sick," he said, looking desperate. "You got t' come."

He gave the boy a down jacket, gloves, and a wool hat, and, with the icy wind scorching their faces, the two sped off on the motor scooter toward Russell Jacks's house.

This time next year, he thought, I'll be driving my car again. It is eight long years since I gave it up for Lent, and that's long enough.

"Pneumonia," said Hoppy.

The rector wasn't surprised.

When he and Dooley arrived at Russell's house, they had found the old man in bed, scarcely able to breathe and with a frightening rattle in his chest. He had stoked up the embers in the stove, covered the sexton with blankets from Dooley's cot, and, because there was no telephone, rode to the hospital where he ordered the ambulance to fetch his friend, along with the frightened boy.

Hoppy had come on the run from his house three blocks away. "We've got our work cut out for us," he said. "He's in bad shape. Has the boy got a place to go?"

Father Tim looked at Dooley, whose face was ashen. "He'll come home with me."

"Are you two on that bloody motor scooter?"

"We are."

"Park it in the hospital garage, for God's sake. I'll send you home with Nurse Herman."

"You really don't . . ."

"Oh, but I really do! It's twenty degrees and dropping, and if I'm going to be a church regular, I'd like to have a live preacher in the pulpit."

When they came home from the hospital, Barnabas bounded to the back door, put his front paws on Dooley's shoulders and licked his face with happy abandon.

" 'is ol' dog's got bad breath."

"He spoke well of you," replied Father Tim, helping Dooley out of the down jacket.

"Is granpaw goin' t' die?"

"I don't think so."

Dooley took off his hat and gloves, dropped them on the floor, and walked away.

"Dooley . . ."

He looked up at the rector.

The rector looked down at the hat and gloves.

A long moment passed before the boy sighed heavily and picked them up. "Stayin' around here ain't goin' t' be any fun," he muttered.

"If I were you, I wouldn't make that decision just yet. Put your hat and gloves right here in the bin. Hang your coat on this peg. Then I've got something to show you."

When they stepped into the study, which was still warm from the fire on the hearth, Dooley saw the fragrant spruce that reached all the way to the beamed ceiling. It twinkled with hundreds of colored lights, and underneath were presents, dozen upon dozen. "Maybe stayin' around here ain't goin' t' be 'at bad," he said.

Dooley stepped into Father Tim's pajama pants, pulled the drawstring tight, and rolled the legs above his ankles. Then he buttoned the top over his undershirt, and pulled on a pair of green socks. Over this, he put a burgundy terry cloth robe which just touched the floor, and tied it with a sash.

"Well, what do you think?" asked the rector, who had also changed into a robe and pajamas, and was filling soup bowls at the counter.

"It's good you're short," said Dooley, pointing to the hem of the robe. " 'is ol' thing's jis' right on me."

The phone rang.

"Looks like viral pneumonia," said Hoppy. "That's a tough one, because it doesn't respond to treatment with antibiotics. We're giving him oxygen, and we've removed a piece of lung tissue, so we'll know more tomorrow. I'll call you."

"You're in my prayers."

"That's a good place to be," said Hoppy, hanging up.

"Is granpaw goin' t' die?"

"I don't think so."

"Let's eat, then," said Dooley.

Sometime in the early morning, he woke up. While Barnabas snored, he stared at the ceiling, praying for Russell Jacks and Hoppy Harper, for Cynthia Coppersmith and Homeless Hobbes, and anyone else the Holy Spirit called to mind.

At times like these, his mind let down its daytime defenses, and the names of people whom he hadn't remembered in months or even years came before him.

Suddenly, he sat straight up.

The red bicycle!

It was standing in the garage, in plain view of anyone who cared to look.

He crept out of bed, slid his feet into the old leather slippers, and quietly put on his robe. "Stay," he said to Barnabas, who opened one eye, closed it again, and beat the bed with his tail. He did not want an alarmed Barnabas barking his head off and waking Dooley.

The street lamp shone through the wide hall window and was the only light he ever used to go downstairs at odd hours.

He padded softly down the steps and along the hall, then opened the garage door and turned on the light.

The bicycle stood next to his long-unused car. With its vast red ribbon and handmade card, it had transformed the garage into something quite magical.

What if the boy had seen it standing there in broad daylight? All those carefully laid plans—dashed!

He took several blankets from a storage cabinet and wrapped them around the bicycle. Then he gently laid the bicycle on its side, in the corner, and out of sight from the study door. On top of this bundle, he placed stacks of the *Mitford Muse.*

"Excellent!" he said, standing back to survey his camouflage.

He turned off the light, walked quietly to the stairs, and started up. He had nearly reached the landing when he felt a sudden and violent explosion in his head.

As he reeled backward in a half-circle and slammed against the stair railing, he saw a blinding light that was followed by a shooting pain in his temples, and then, everything went black.

When he came to, he was sitting on the stairs.

Dooley Barlowe was crying and staring urgently into his face. Barnabas was licking his ear.

"What in God's name . . ." he began, weakly.

"I didn't know it was you!" Dooley sobbed. "I thought it was a dern burglar tryin' to git me!

He felt exactly as if a train had struck him, but it was only Dooley's tennis shoe, one of the very pair, ironically, that he had bought the boy before school started.

"One time, a burglar broke in my mama's house and it was jis' us young 'uns by ourselves, an' you sounded jis' like 'im, a creepin' up the stairs in th' dark." Dooley's fear suddenly gave way to a rising anger.

"How come you t' creep up your own dern stairs, anyway? How come you couldn't jis' walk up 'em, like anybody else, so this wouldn't 've happened?"

Later, drifting toward a restless sleep, he murmured a deep truth. "It's different having a boy in the house."

Tell Rodney about jewels—after Christmas.

Talk to Hoppy about Olivia—after Christmas.

On his list of things to do, these delicate issues hung suspended like icicles from a limb.

The day following the incident on the stairs, Mitford was enclosed by a thick blanket of fog and rain. And since his parishioners were obviously busy with other affairs, he left the office early and went home. Even with the Tylenol, his head pounded furiously.

"Dadgum!" Percy said with admiration, when he stopped at the Grill to pick up a cup of soup. "Somebody busted you good."

"I'll say."

He paid $1.69 for the soup, which he thought was outrageous, and left without giving Percy the details. As he passed the window, he saw Percy standing at the cash register with a hurt look. If there was anything Percy thrived on, he mused, it was details.

At four o'clock, he helped Dooley with his homework and put a cold washcloth on the enlarging bump that was slowly turning black, blue, and chartreuse.

"I'm sorry," Dooley said, miserably.

"No sorrier than I. But all in all, I think you were brave."

"You do?"

"Indeed I do. I have only one complaint."

"What's 'at?"

"You might have looked before you struck. There was, after all, some light on the stairs, so you could have seen the top of my head shine."

"I seen it shine! But you ain't th' only man in the world gittin' bald-headed, y' know. Burglars git bald-headed, too."

At nine o'clock, they had a report on Russell Jacks. Not faring well, but resting. Age was against viral pneumonia, Hoppy said. While Dooley took a bath, the rector made two calls asking for prayer, and gave Miss Sadie an update.

Then he stretched out before the flickering fire and closed his eyes. Puny hadn't come today, which always made an astonishing difference. He was growing to depend on her, he knew that. And a dependable one she was.

He would slip a crisp hundred-dollar bill into her Christmas envelope. And it would be out of his own happiness fund, not Pearly McGee's. He realized that, in the space of a few days, he would have given out two bills of that stellar denomination, and decided he liked doing it. Very much.

Dooley came into the room, smelling of soap, with Barnabas at his side.

He looked at the pair, feeling a certain contentment. "Are you taking over my dog?"

" 'is ol' dog follers me ever' where I go. It ain't my fault he likes me."

"Well, go up to bed and read your book. I'll come in a bit and say goodnight."

"I'm about give out," Dooley said, sighing.

"You and me both, pal."

At the door, Dooley turned around and looked back. "When you come up them steps tonight . . . ?"

"What about it?"

"Don't creep. I cain't stand creepin'."

That boy needs a lot of teaching, he thought, putting his feet up. Starting tomorrow, we're going back to something I hardly ever hear these days. We're going back to "yes, sir" and "no, sir," not to mention "thank you" and "please." Driving that home ought to be at least as much fun as pulling teeth.

He thought he might lie down and enjoy looking at the tree lights. But then, he'd be fast asleep in minutes, with Dooley waiting upstairs. He went into the kitchen instead, and turned the burner on under the tea kettle.

There was a small, delicate rapping at the door.

No rest for the wicked, he thought, quoting Russell Jacks.

It was his neighbor, dressed in a yellow slicker streaming with rain.

"Just one minute," she said, "that's all it will take. May I come in?"

"Well, absolutely! Do come in."

"Here, I'll just stand right here on the mat, so I won't drip all over the kitchen. I just wanted to give you your Christmas present!" She had one hand tucked inside her slicker.

"You shouldn't have!" he exclaimed, truly meaning it. For heaven's sake, why had he impulsively sent all those Belgian chocolates to the nurses at the hospital, when he might have kept a pound or two at home for emergencies? "I was just going to have a cup of tea, and I hope you'll join me."

"Oh, I'd love that," she said, with unabashed enthusiasm, "but I can't. I finished your present a few minutes ago, and I couldn't wait to give it to you." He saw that earnest look in her blue eyes. "I hope you'll open it tonight."

"Well, yes," he said, feeling a bit rattled, "but wouldn't you like to come in by the fire, and I'll open it while . . ."

"I promise I can't. I must run. Here!" She withdrew her hand from the wet slicker, and gave him a flat manila envelope. "Oh, good!" she said, looking at the envelope. "Dry as a bone!"

She turned and bolted out the door. In the glow of the porch light, he saw her dash across the yard and through the hedge, water splashing around her boots.

"Merry Christmas!" he called. But she was gone. And she hadn't even mentioned the gruesome, multi-colored bump on his head.

CHAPTER TWELVE

An Empty Vessel

The news from the hospital was not good. Russell Jacks was stable, but not improving.

"Pneumonia takes a lot of forms," said Hoppy. "For a man Russell's age, this is the worst form. We're doing all we can, and there's still hope, but it's like swimming upstream."

Russell's name was listed on the prayers of the people at Lord's Chapel and put on a community-wide prayer chain. Father Tim wasn't surprised to see the concern of his parishioners. They cared about the taciturn old man whose tender heart was revealed only in the showy perennials, elaborate paths, and manicured borders of the church gardens.

Food poured into the rectory, to assist with the unexpected duty of having a boy to feed.

"Growin' boys is bottomless pits," said Percy, who sent fresh potato salad and pimiento cheese.

Winnie Ivey delivered doughnuts, cream horns, and a coconut cake.

Miss Sadie had Luther drive over with a bag of Swanson's chicken pies and a Sara Lee pound cake, and the Altar Guild brought a roasted turkey.

"I ain't never seen nothin' like 'is," confessed Dooley, who was able to choose from more than a dozen lunch options.

"I ain't . . . I've never seen anything like it myself, and that's a fact," said Father Tim, as they sat at the kitchen counter.

Soon, he would have to deal with Dooley's English, but as he'd just begun dealing with "please" and "thank you," he didn't want to push his luck.

His eye fell on the manila envelope that Cynthia Coppersmith had delivered several evenings ago in a drenching rain, and which he'd tucked among the books he kept on the counter.

"I hope you'll open it tonight!" she had said. He was deeply ashamed that he'd forgotten. How could he have forgotten? He had stuck it between a couple of books on the shelf so he wouldn't spill tea on it, thinking he'd take it up to bed. Then, he'd forgotten it completely. Whatever might be inside, he clearly didn't deserve it.

He slipped the gift from the envelope and removed the wrapping paper so it wouldn't tear. "You know how I could tell I was getting old?" his mother once said. "I began to save used wrapping paper."

It was a matted watercolor of a furry creature dressed in a dark suit with a clerical collar, and horn-rimmed glasses perched on the end of its nose. The little creature had small toes on its furry feet, a very large smile, and a pair of engaging eyes.

"Father Talpidae," read the caption at the bottom.

" 'at's funny," said Dooley, peering over his shoulder.

The rector thought it was the most charming creature he'd seen in years; better, even, than Beatrix Potter might have imagined.

"Father Talpidae," read a legend on the back, "is the good rector of a small parish, located under the green grass of Father Tim's rectory garden in Mitford. Fr. Talpidae says he's happy to announce that his congregation is growing, and that he has absolutely no plans to retire."

"Mole," Webster informed him, or "L., talpidae." He laughed as heartily as he'd laughed in a long time.

"It ain't that funny," said Dooley.

"That's your opinion."

"I like it when you laugh," said Dooley. "It makes it more fun around here."

"Then I'll try to laugh more often," he said, still chuckling. Hadn't he recently promised Cynthia Coppersmith that very thing?

That evening, he and Dooley walked Barnabas to the monument and looked in all the shop windows. Boxwood wreaths hung on the doors, and windows were garlanded with tiny, winking lights.

Mitford at Christmas was a fairyland. If only their Christmas snow hadn't fallen at Thanksgiving!

Dooley examined the displays in every window, from cuff links and sports jackets at The Collar Button to iron skillets, fishing tackle, and tree stands at the hardware.

As they turned the corner and headed home, he was sure he saw Andrew Gregory's gray Mercedes parked in front of the little house next door.

"Hot chocolate?" he asked Dooley, when they'd taken off their coats. He felt oddly absentminded, unable to concentrate. He'd recently seen Andrew's car parked in that precise spot at least five times.

"No."

Maybe six, he thought, setting the saucepan on the stove. "No, thank you. Milk and fruitcake?"

"No."

"No, thank you. What, then?"

"Nothin'."

Dooley had recently turned mournful, as Russell called it. "You know what I'd do?" Puny had said on Wednesday. "I'd give 'im a swift kick. Just say bend over, honey, and whop, you'd see a diff'rent young 'un. My granpaw wouldn't n' more let me git away with bein' ill to him than he could fly. Blam, he'd yank me up and preach me a sermon that'd scorch the hair off my head."

"I have great respect for that approach, but it's not one I could administer effectively."

"You'd git along better if you was part Baptist."

"You may be interested to know that I'm precisely one-half Baptist."

She looked at him suspiciously.

"My mother was a fervent Baptist, and my father was . . . a lukewarm Episcopalian."

"Lukewarm! I don't even like my dishwater lukewarm!"

"Puny, what if Russell Jacks doesn't make it? What would we do with Dooley?"

"Did you ever find out what's th' matter with 'is mama?"

"Alcohol. I don't know the whole story. She let all five of her children go."

Puny was silent for a long time, as she cleaned the silver and put it in soapy water. "Well," she said, "maybe he don't need a kick in the tail, after all."

"Oh?"

"Maybe what he needs is jist . . . a whole lot of . . . lovin'."

Now, there! he thought. There's an idea I can get my teeth into, in a manner of speaking. "Puny," he said, "that is splendid thinking. So splendid, in fact, it deserves special recognition. Please dry your hands."

He went into the study and took the cream-colored envelope from his desk drawer, and gave it to her at the sink.

"Merry Christmas!"

She looked in the envelope, saw the hundred-dollar bill, and burst into tears, just as Dooley came in with Barnabas.

"Poop on 'at ol' puzzle you're makin' me do," he said, glaring at Puny.

Father Tim saw the color rise in her cheeks.

" 'at's th' stupidest thing I ever seen," said Dooley. "I th'ow'd it in th' trash."

"You know what I'm goin' to do to you?" she snapped.

"What's 'at?"

"I'm goin' to jerk a knot in your tail!" She moved toward him, with fire behind the fresh tears in her eyes.

Dooley backed into Barnabas, who yelped and fled down the hall.

"But you know what I'm goin' to do, first?" She grinned wickedly at Dooley, whose eyes were wide with alarm. "I'm goin' to grab you and give you a great big hug!"

"Oh, no you ain't!"

As he pounded up the stairs, Puny turned to the rector. "There," she said, looking triumphant. "That'll fix 'im for a while."

On the afternoon of Christmas Eve, Father Tim and Dooley planned to visit Russell, who was sitting up and no longer needed oxygen.

"Let's drop by Mitford Blossoms," said Father Tim, "and take Russell a gloxinia."

On the way, they stopped at the drugstore, where he bought a bag of jelly beans for Hoppy and a Reese's Cup for Dooley.

When they walked in the florist shop, he was surprised to see Hoppy standing at the counter, dressed in a hospital scrub suit, his navy pea jacket, boots lined with sheepskin, a worn khaki raincoat, and a cap with ear flaps.

"Left the hospital on the run," he said, grinning.

"My friend, it looks like you were dressed by Miss Rose Watson."

Hoppy laughed. A glorious laugh, thought Father Tim, and one he hadn't heard in far too long.

"These are the best we have," said Jena Ivey, as she came out of the cooler with a bucket of roses. "Hello, Father! Merry Christmas! Merry Christmas, Dooley!"

" 'at's my Sunday school teacher," Dooley whispered to the doctor.

Jena proudly set the bucket on the counter.

"What do you think, pal?" asked Hoppy. "You're the rosarian."

Jena's roses were grown in Holland, a fact that made them considerably more expensive, but they never drooped their heads after a day in the vase, and they always smelled like roses. He nodded his strong approval.

"Two dozen!" Hoppy said, taking out his wallet. "And, Jena, please deliver them right away. You know the house."

As Jena arranged the stems in a long, pink box, he turned to the rector. "She's practically quit speaking to me," he said.

"She?"

"You know, Olivia."

"Aha."

"From cool to freezing."

Father Tim felt his heart beat dully. He had an impulse to take Hoppy across the street to the church office, and tell him the truth at once. But no, he had made a promise, and the promise was to tell him after Christmas—after the joy and trepidation of sending two dozen splendid roses, after Olivia's delight and sorrow in receiving them. Good Lord, why did this have to happen to two of the finest people he knew?

"You're mighty quiet. Do you know something I don't know?" asked Hoppy.

The rector reached into his jacket pocket. "All I know is, this bag contains at least eleven green jelly beans, as I counted every one I could see through the wrapper. Merry Christmas!"

Hoppy laughed as he opened the bag. "Are you going to see Russell?"

"We are."

"My car's out front, I'll give you a lift."

As they were leaving with the purple gloxinia, Dooley tugged at Father Tim's sleeve. "Wait a minute," he said, and went back to the counter where he handed Jena Ivey his Reese's Cup.

At the hospital, they stood outside Russell's open door, and talked.

"It's a bit of a miracle," said Hoppy. "I think he may pull out of it, but there's another problem."

"What's that?"

"He could be down for months. The best way to recover from this is to get plenty of bed rest. That means he won't be able to care for the boy. In fact, he's going to need some care himself."

"Well," said Father Tim, at a loss for words.

Dooley stood by the bed, looking anxiously at his grandfather. The old man was weak and spoke with his eyes closed.

"Dooley, are you behavin' yourself?"

"Nope."

"Don't shame me, boy. You hear?"

"All right, Granpaw, I won't."

Before he left, Dooley took his grandfather's hand. "Granpaw," he said, "don't die!"

Russell Jacks opened his eyes and looked at his grandson with a faint smile. "All right, boy, I won't."

According to parishioners, the Christmas Eve masses at Lord's Chapel were more beautiful, more powerful, more stirring than ever before.

Candles burned on the window sills, among fragrant boughs of spruce and pine. Fresh garlands wrapped the high cedar beams over the nave. A glorious tree from Meadowgate Farm stood near the pulpit, and a lush garden of creme-colored poinsettias sprang up around its feet.

In the midnight service especially, there was an expectant hush that went beyond the usual reverent silence before the service, and someone said that, for the first time in her life, she had felt the sweet savor of the Christ child in her heart.

"Once in royal David's city stood a lowly cattle shed, where a mother laid her baby in a manger for his bed . . ."

Someone who was out walking in the balmy air heard a great wealth of music pouring from the little stone church, music with a poignant clarity and purpose.

". . . This child, this little helpless boy, shall be our confidence and joy . . ."

"Hark! the herald angels sing, glory to the newborn King!"

Miss Rose came on the arm of Uncle Billy, wearing her new black suit and fuchsia coat, and a pair of red and navy argyles with unlaced saddle oxfords.

"We're gittin' there," Uncle Billy said to Father Tim after the service. "You might say we got a pretty good ways past the head, but we ain't made it to th' toe."

As he headed home with Dooley at nearly one-thirty in the morning, he felt deeply grateful, but uncommonly fatigued.

He had never been able to decide when to open his gifts. He could hardly do it on Christmas Eve, when he arrived home past 1:00 a.m. after preaching two services. And on Christmas morning, conducting two masses kept him at Lord's Chapel until well past noon.

"I play it by ear," he once told Emma, who couldn't imagine not opening presents anytime she felt like it, starting on or before December 15.

At nearly two o'clock in the morning, they sat on the floor with hot chocolate and Winnie's doughnuts, and he gave Dooley his presents from Miss Sadie, Puny, Emma, and one from himself: a wool scarf from the Collar Button.

Miss Sadie had sent two pocket handkerchiefs, a pair of shoe laces, and a five-dollar bill wrapped in aluminum foil and tied with a red ribbon. Puny had given him a yellow windbreaker, and there were two dozen Reese's Cups from Emma.

Dooley sat mournfully in the midst of his gifts. "I wanted 'at ol' bicycle."

"The way your earnings are piling up, you'll have it before long. Now, I'd like to open your present to me."

"Wait 'til mornin'. You ain't goin' t' like it, anyway."

"I'd appreciate making that decision myself."

"Wait 'til morning. I'm give out," Dooley said, irritably.

It was two-thirty when the pair trudged upstairs, well behind Barnabas, who was already sprawled at the foot of the bed and snoring.

On the landing, he put his hand on Dooley's shoulder. "I'll be awake before daylight, preparing for two services, and you may definitely expect to hear some creeping on the stairs. But if I catch you coming after me with a shoe . . ."

"I'll be dead meat."

"Precisely!"

At six-thirty, he and Barnabas woke Dooley.

"I don't want t' git up!" he wailed. "You done wore me out goin' t' church. I ain't never been t' s' much church in my life. I didn't know they was that much church in th' whole dern world."

"My friend, you will pleased to know that Santa Claus visited this humble rectory last night and left something in the study for one Dooley Barlowe."

"They ain't no Santy. I don't believe 'at old poop."

"Well, then, lie there and believe what you like. I'm going downstairs and have my famous Christmas morning casserole."

Barnabas leaped on Dooley's bed and began licking his ear.

" 'is ol' dog is th' hatefulest thing I ever seen!" Dooley moaned, turning his face to the wall.

"Come, Barnabas. Leave him be."

Barnabas lay resolutely on Dooley's bed and stared at his master.

Barnabas, at least, was determined to execute Puny's good idea.

He set two places at the counter and took the bubbling sausage casserole from the oven. There would be no diet this day. Then, he turned on the record player and heard the familiar, if scratchy, strains of the *Messiah*.

Dooley appeared at the kitchen door, dressed in the burgundy robe. "Sounds like a' army's moved in down here."

"My friend, you have hit the nail on the head. It is an army of the most glorious voices in recent history, singing one of the most majestic musical works ever written!"

Dooley rolled his eyes.

"I believe you've been asked to sit with Jena Ivey and your Sunday school friends this morning, is that correct?"

"Yeah."

"Yes, sir."

No response.

Directly after Christmas, he would deal with this pigheaded behavior to the fullest.

"I ain't feelin' too good."

"Is that right? What's the trouble?"

"I puked up somethin' green."

"Really?"

"It had a lot of brown in it, too."

"The walk to church will revive you. You've been going pretty strong, keeping to a rector's schedule. Why don't you look in the study and find out what Barnabas is up to?"

He followed the boy into the study, to see what he'd been imagining for weeks:

The look of joyful astonishment on Dooley Barlowe's face.

Dooley really hadn't seemed well, he concluded, as he walked home from church. He'd promised to stay right there on the study sofa, looking at his new bicycle and drinking 7-Up.

Though he'd received three invitations to Christmas dinner with parishioners, he wanted nothing more than to go home and crash. Later, if Dooley felt up to it, they'd take the new bike to the school yard and over to the Presbyterian parking lot.

There was only one problem with that plan.

Dooley could not be found in the study, nor anywhere else in the house. And neither could the new red bicycle.

The down jacket was missing from the peg, and the gloves weren't in the bin. And while he easily located the handkerchiefs and shoe strings from Miss Sadie, the windbreaker, the five-dollar bill, and the Reese's Cups had vanished.

Nurse Herman said she hadn't seen Dooley, and no, she wouldn't mention this call to Russell.

He drove the motor scooter through the school playground and then to the Presbyterian parking lot.

He rode up and down Main Street twice, circled the war monument and checked the lot behind the post office. There was hardly a soul to be seen on the streets, though Christmas lights in the shop windows winked cheerfully. He slowed at the corner of Old Church Lane, then turned left at his office and headed up the hill to Fernbank. Perhaps the boy had taken the bike to show Miss Sadie, he thought, but there was no sign of a visitor at the silent white mansion, nor even Miss Sadie's car.

Coasting down the hill in the increasingly chill wind, he came to a single, desperate conclusion: Dooley Barlowe had run away.

Rodney Underwood answered the phone over the uproarious giggles of his three small daughters. "Aw, he's just gone out for a little spin," said the police chief. "Maybe he went out to Farmer on all them dirt roads."

The rector was convinced that Dooley Barlowe would not take his new red bike on a dirt road. The boy was gone. He could feel it in his bones, and he knew he could trust the feeling.

Rodney said he'd personally file a missing persons report and send an officer out in a cruise car. "Don't you worry, Father. You can't lose a red-headed boy on a red bicycle. We'll find 'im."

After he talked to Rodney, he went to the hospital, where Russell Jacks was sitting up and, with some effort, eating a bowl of soup.

"Dooley wanted to come, Russell, but early this morning, he . . . ah, threw up."

"Puked, did he?" the old man asked, with evident pride.

The heat in the small room was stifling. Father Tim removed his jacket and sat down by the bed. "You know, Russell, I've been wondering about his mother. Has she had any help?"

"Gits food stamps an' all, and I've tried to help."

"I understand. But help with her drinking . . ."

"Went off to Broughton one time t' dry out. Come back, started up again." His hand shook, so that soup spilled down the front of his hospital gown. Father Tim felt miserably guilty about asking such questions on a day when the sick needed special cheering.

"What is your daughter's name, by the way, and where does she live?"

" 'er name's Pauline, married a fella Barlowe worked on the new highways they put through there. Give 'er five little young 'uns in a row, got them highways built, then jumped on one and went. Didn't come back."

He had never ceased to be astonished by the weight of sorrow in the world. "A vale of tears," the poet had called it, and rightly so.

"And she's still down in Holding?"

"I hope t' God she is."

"Has a warm place to live, I expect."

"Ol' trailer over behind Shoney's. She worked there awhile 'til they run 'er off for drinkin' on th' job."

There. That was enough to go on. He'd call Rodney from the phone in the waiting room.

"Russell," said the rector, brightening his tone and changing the subject, "if you could have just one Christmas wish, what might it be?"

Russell pushed the soup bowl away and wiped his mouth with a trembling hand. He lay back on the pillow and closed his eyes, so that Father Tim thought for a moment he hadn't heard the question.

Then he said, "I wish Ida was still livin'; she'd be a blessin' to th' boy . . . an' I wish th' rhododendrons would set their buds real good so we git a nice show of bloom, come spring."

He liked it to be where he could reach for it and find it immediately. Yet he could not find his small, worn, leather-bound Bible with his name stamped on the cover.

He turned on the lights above the pulpit and, once again, searched the empty shelf.

He walked angrily back to the office. That Bible contained marginal notes and special references that were irreplaceable. Who would have been so thoughtless to move it, and where did they move it, and why?

"Missin' Bibles, missin' cakes, missin' boys," Emma said, as if she were filing a report.

"Has Rodney called?"

"Not since he talked to you at ten o'clock."

On Christmas afternoon, Rodney had notified the Holding police, giving them Pauline Barlowe's name and the location of the trailer. Holding had called back to say the trailer had been moved, and they were continuing to investigate.

We're going into the third day, he thought anxiously.

Emma fielded the phone calls. "No, we don't know a thing, yet.

Thank you for calling, we appreciate it, we have no idea. Yes, we'll let you know."

He noticed she'd begun dabbing at her eyes with that wad of toilet tissue she always carried.

"Are you all right?" he asked.

That was when she finally said it:

"That poor little orphan, gettin' somethin' he wasn't responsible enough to own! I hate to say I told you so!"

He turned and blurted angrily, "Then for God's sake, don't say it!"

When he went home for lunch, Puny was back from her holiday with a sister. He told her about Dooley.

Her face went white. "I could've told you so," she said.

Ah, the everlasting smugness of people! He might have sighed, but thought of the thanks box which now contained eleven dollars' worth of his infernal sighing.

"Dadgummit," said Puny, as he left for the office, "I'm worried sick about that little poop-head!" She burst into tears and ran down the hall to the kitchen.

According to Puny, who later saw Emma at The Local, he had "picked at his lunch like a bird, and looked kind of gray-colored."

"Humph," snorted Emma, who was still nettled from her brush with the rector. "If you ask me, he's actin' exactly like he did before he got diabetes."

"Well he cain't be gittin' it again if he's already got it."

"So maybe he's gettin' somethin' else," Emma said, airily.

"Nothing is more wearying," Agatha Christie had said, "than going over things you have written and trying to arrange them in proper sequence or turn them the other way round."

He couldn't agree more, he thought, as he struggled with his sermon. Directly after the meeting with the stranger in the nave, his sermons had seen a definite upturn; he was nearly jubilant afterward. Then, suddenly, he felt that he was right back where he started.

"The trouble with you," Walter had said in a recent phone conversation, "is that you're too prepared. You don't give the Holy Spirit room to do wondrous things. You need to take risks now and then—that's what makes life snap, crackle, and pop."

Snap, crackle, and pop? Not only did people love saying they told you so, they were infernally full of advice.

He looked at the calendar clock on his desk. If the boy didn't turn up in the next few hours, he and Miss Sadie had agreed to drive to Holding, where they'd go over the town with a fine-tooth comb.

"I've got new tennis shoes," she told him. "I'll go up one side of the street and you go up the other!"

"Listen to this," the rector said to Barnabas, who was sprawled at his feet. As he read the first draft of his sermon, Barnabas listened with sincere interest.

Actually, he found his dog more attentive than many of his congregation. On the other hand, none of the congregation ever openly engaged in vigorous scratching. So it was a wash.

He got up and walked to the tall spruce with its twinkling lights, and looked at the array of gifts still lying beneath it. He had lost the heart to finish opening them, somehow, though he'd torn right into his cousin's gift and discovered that it was, indeed, an electric train. As soon as Dooley comes back, he thought, we'll set it up. Surely, Dooley would be coming back.

Suddenly, he remembered the present Dooley had made for him and found it lying near Winnie's bulky gift.

He opened it eagerly.

A glasses case, made at school. Two pieces of leather, glued together on three sides, and monogrammed with the aid of a stencil. *FT* was printed on one side, *DB* on the other. "I put my initials on it," Dooley had scrawled on a piece of notebook paper, "so you won't firgit me."

Forget Dooley Barlowe? Never!

Many boys who'd been raised like Dooley, he reasoned, would be good for nothing. Dooley, he was convinced, was extraordinarily good for something. It only remained to be seen what it was.

He wished he had someone in the house to talk to about this disturbing turn of events. Like Walter, with whom he'd shared nearly every confidence since he was a boy.

He put the glasses case in his shirt pocket, and walked back to his desk. "Talk to Hoppy. Tell Rodney. Thank Cynthia" were scrawled across the top of his desk calendar.

He decided to work his list backward.

Cynthia, he thought, did not have much trouble making herself at home. When he'd called to thank her for the mole watercolor, she'd suggested tea, and he said he had just put the kettle on. In barely two minutes, she had "popped through the hedge," as she liked to say, and curled up on his study sofa, helping herself to a piece of shortbread. He was intrigued to see that another of her pink curlers, obviously overlooked, adorned the back of her head.

"I'm so sorry," she said, when told about Dooley. "I always thought runaway boys come straight home when they got hungry."

"Yes, well, that is complicated by the fact that this is not his home."

"Has anyone seen him?"

"Rodney says he was seen by three different people on his way down the mountain. They remembered the red bicycle."

"Did they say anything else?"

"They said he was . . . ah, flying."

"Flying! Oh, dear."

There was a thoughtful silence.

"I've never raised a boy," said Cynthia.

"That makes two of us."

"But I do try to understand their feelings. I always pretend I'm a child when I write Violet books, and then I write exactly what I want to hear."

Is that the way he should write his sermons? Saying exactly what he would like to hear?

"A publisher who looked at the first manuscript said, 'Oh, we can't print this, it's far too silly.' But the next publisher understood, and there have been eight since then. All silly!"

"And all successful, I believe."

"Well, yes, and then the Davant Medal was announced, and we went into second and third printings of everything. But my point was, let's try and put ourselves in his shoes, even if it seems silly. It might work! Let's see . . . if I were a boy with a new bicycle, where would I go?" She stared intently at the fire, wrinkling her forehead.

"We think he's gone to his mother, but we can't trace her."

"Where does she live?"

"She had a trailer down in Holding, but it's been moved."

"We could go and ask around the neighborhood where she lived. Somebody would know something."

"The police are doing that. They haven't turned up anything."

"I hate this," she said.

"I hate it more."

How, he wondered, could he be sitting here by a warm fire, when a fatherless boy was out there somewhere, almost certainly cold and hungry?

There was a knock at the back door. His heart pounded as Barnabas leaped from his place in front of the fire and skidded into the kitchen. Rodney! Surely it would be Rodney with some news.

When he opened the door, Dooley Barlowe looked him straight in the eye. "My mama tol' me to come back."

"Come in," the rector said, hoarsely.

There was an ugly welt on the boy's face. Barnabas licked it while Dooley silently removed his gloves, the down jacket, and the yellow windbreaker. He dropped the gloves in the bin and hung the jackets on the peg.

"Come and say hello to Miss Coppersmith."

Dooley met Cynthia's gaze without wavering. "Hey," he said.

"Hey, yourself."

His face was red from pedaling in a chill wind, and he trembled slightly from the cold.

"It might be good if I made some hot chocolate to warm you up," said the rector.

But Dooley was headed toward the stairs, Barnabas hard on his heels. "I cain't stand here talkin'," he said over his shoulder, "I got t' take a dump."

The rector looked at his neighbor, coloring furiously.

"Don't look at me," she said. "I never raised a boy!"

Before he called Rodney about the jewels, he called Walter.

"You're in possession of stolen goods," said Walter.

"Good Lord!"

"I doubt if Rodney will press any charges, but you ought to know where you stand by failing to report what you found."

"I knew I should have reported it. It's just that the choir was rehearsing three different performances, and I was busy with Lessons and Carols, and Rodney would have conducted a lengthy investigation, and . . ."

"Believe me, I understand. But it was still a damnfool thing to do," Walter said.

He sat for a moment after talking with Walter, with his head in his hands. Then he called Rodney.

"I've got something I want to show you. How about this morning, at Lord's Chapel?"

"Let me stop by the Grill and get a coffee to go, and I'll be right over."

He felt sick. In possession of stolen goods! A fine thing for a man of the cloth, for heaven's sake. If there were any punishment, it was the nauseating humiliation he felt, which was surely punishment enough.

"You look like somethin' the cat drug in," said Emma, coming through the door.

"That's a fine greeting."

She sighed. "Dooley Barlowe is doin' you about as much good as a case of diabetes, if you ask me."

"He came back last night."

"What a relief! I wish you'd called me!"

"I did. No answer."

"Oh, yes, well . . . I was at Harold's mama's and we worked on my suit."

"Your suit?"

"That I'm gettin' married in. Red. Black buttons. Peplum. High neck."

"I see."

"Black patent shoes. Black hose. Pearl earrings. Where was he?"

"His mother's, like we thought. She sent him back, told him she couldn't care for him."

"Breaks my heart," said Emma.

That's encouraging, he thought.

"But mostly, it makes me mad."

Aha! Here it comes.

"You get house help, change your diet, get you a nice dog for company, start feelin' better, and what happens?"

He was so astounded to hear Emma refer to Barnabas as a nice dog that he was speechless.

"What happens is, you get a boy who runs you down, wears you out, and worries you half to death, and you're right back where you started. I declare, I've seen diabetes make you look better than you look this mornin'." She caught her breath and plunged ahead. "Do you know how old you are?"

Remind me! he thought, enduring her assault.

"Not twenty-five! Not thirty-two! Sixty! You're too old to be takin' on a boy, plus do your preachin', and go to the hospital, and visit the elderly, and go to meetin's, and read in that program with Olivia Davenport, not to mention the bells comin' in, and the nursin' home startin' up, and that old mangy dog to wash . . ."

Now his nice dog was old and mangy.

As she continued her oratorical massacre, he came to a sober realization. He would certainly never tell her so, but he had to admit one thing:

She was right.

"Dark in here," said Rodney. "But it smells good."

"It's the old wood, and years of incense and beeswax and flowers and lemon oil and dried hydrangeas. It's a wonderful smell!" he agreed as he switched on the lights. "Come down this way. What I want to show you is where we keep the ashes of the departed."

They walked down the hall and stopped at the closet, where he removed the key from above the door.

Rodney adjusted his holster. "Is somethin' goin' to jump out of there?"

"I fervently hope not."

He opened the door and turned on the light, relieved to find that everything was as orderly as he'd left it. No one had tossed in any plastic flowers or worn hymnals.

"Now," he said, carefully picking up the bronze urn which was sitting third from the left, "this is Parrish Guthrie. Remember him?"

"Ha! How could I forget th' old so-and-so? I wasn't th' only one that got a deep breath when he went to his grave . . . or whatever that thing is."

"This is an urn. After the body is cremated, the ashes—which are mostly bits of bone—are interred here."

"Bits of bone!" Rodney said, shuddering. "I like th' old-fashioned way—pushin' up daisies."

"Let's take this urn and walk on back to the kitchen." His heart was pounding. Oh, how he hated to tell the bitter truth about his wrong behavior.

He stood at the sink and unscrewed the cap of the bronze urn, which came off more readily than before. "I'm going to show you something very . . . what is the word? Something that grieves me."

With his other hand, he took the white tea towel from the rack and spread it on the drain board. Then he gently shook the urn, so that the contents would spill out.

Nothing tumbled to the mouth of the urn.

He shook it again, and turned the urn nearly upside down. There was no rattle, as of seashells in a jar, and nothing came rolling onto the towel. He realized there was a good explanation for this:

The bronze urn was empty.

He felt strangely light-headed and confused. "I don't understand," he began.

"What's the deal?"

The rector shook the urn. "I don't know. I'm . . ."

"Somethin' was supposed to be in that jar. Right?"

"Jewels," he said weakly. "Jewels that I found in this very urn sometime before Christmas."

"I don't get it."

"Let's sit down."

Rodney sat on the stool by the wall phone. Father Tim sat on the old pine table in the center of the room.

"Before Christmas," he confessed, "I was cleaning up that closet, throwing things out. I picked up Parrish's urn and it rattled strangely. I remembered I'd never seen the contents of an urn, so, out of curiosity, I brought it back here to the kitchen, and opened it. There were little cloth sacks full of jewels in there, cut jewels."

"Maybe it was another jar you brought back here."

"No. It was definitely Parrish."

Rodney rested his hand on the butt of his pistol. "So, why didn't you report it?"

There! There was the question he was dreading.

As he explained why, Rodney took off his hat and scratched his head.

"I don't know," said the chief, "I never run up against anything like this. When you found 'em th' first time and didn't report it, you were in possession of stolen goods, I know that."

"So I'm told by my cousin, who's an attorney."

"But now that there's nothin' here, well, there's nothin' I can see to charge you with. Maybe we ought to look in th' other jars."

The rector shrugged. He didn't think it would do any good.

"This is creepy," said Rodney, peering into the urns and stirring their contents with a bread knife from the silverware drawer. "I wish to th' Lord I'd brought me a chew of Red Man."

When they finished an hour later, they'd found nothing amiss. "I'm just goin' to write up a report, and then you sign it, and I'll file it."

"Where? Where will you file it?"

"In my right-hand drawer over at th' station."

"Aha! I thought you might file a report with J.C. Hogan."

"Not, by dern, if I can help it," said Rodney.

He felt faint with relief.

He had thanked his neighbor for her imaginative gift.

He had confessed his unfortunate discovery and equally unfortunate behavior to Rodney.

And now there was only one thing left to do on his list, and that was to talk with Hoppy Harper.

He felt like calling the airline immediately and flying nonstop to Shannon, then renting a car and driving to Sligo. There, he'd spend at least four weeks in a remote inn, riding a bicycle along narrow lanes, and tapping his foot to fiddle music played in thatched cottages.

Instead of calling the airline, he called Hoppy.

"Harper."

"Your good rector here," he said, not feeling very good at all. "How's Russell?"

"It's amazing the way the infection is reversing. Not typical in cases like this. How're you? Are you running?"

"Slacked off."

"I've got three words to say to you, pal: Just do it."

"OK. You're right, and I will. Let me ask you something. I need to talk with you about . . . an important matter. Your place or mine?"

"Mine, if it's OK with you. Everybody from here to Wesley and back has upper respiratory infections. I can't leave."

"Say when."

"Around six."

"I'll be there."

He put the phone down. It was the first time he'd had a moment to catch his breath, and the jewels came instantly to mind.

Why were they gone from the urn? Why would they have been

moved? Did someone know he'd found them? He felt an odd chill, and he did not like the feeling.

"Viral myocarditis!" Hoppy looked as if he'd been struck. "Good God," he said quietly, and sat back in his chair.

Father Tim looked at the notes he'd taken while Olivia told her story. The condition was complex, and he'd tried to assemble the facts accurately.

The doctor leaned forward. "Tell me everything she said."

"It began with what she thought was flu, about two years ago."

"No energy," said Hoppy. "Shortness of breath, chest discomfort."

"That's right. She said she felt like she was falling apart. She went to the doctor, took antibiotics, accelerated her vitamins, got plenty of rest, but nothing worked. They gave her a battery of blood tests and didn't find anything."

"Typical."

"Finally, they did an EKG and saw some abnormalities. Then an echocardiogram, which showed an enlarged heart."

"Then the biopsy," said Hoppy.

"Right. Viral myocarditis."

The doctor looked ashen.

"The symptoms waxed and waned. She would have perfectly normal times, just like she's had since coming to Mitford, then severe flare-ups when she could hardly breathe, and scarcely walk for the edema in her legs."

"The flare-ups are totally unpredictable. Who's her doctor?"

"A man from your old alma mater, Mass General."

"Leo Baldwin, I hope."

He checked his notes. "Exactly! Leo Baldwin."

"The best. I know him. Stunning credentials. What happened when she had the tissue biopsy?"

"Cocksackie B, she said. They tried medication, but the side effects were gruesome. Affected her blood count."

"You've seen termites in action?" Hoppy asked.

"Yes. Right under my back steps, more's the pity."

"Cocksackie eats away like that, at the heart muscle. Vile, insidious, incurable. Why hasn't she had a transplant?"

"You understand the chances of finding a donor with a normal blood type."

"Seventy-five, a hundred to one."

"Add to that the chance of finding a donor with B blood type."

"Thousands to one."

"And then the chances of getting the heart to the patient with the right kind of timing."

Hoppy removed his glasses and rubbed his eyes. "Crap," he said softly.

He called Walter.

"Not there? You mean just . . . vanished?"

"The urn was empty."

"Look, Timothy, you've been pressing hard. You haven't had a vacation in years and—"

"No, I am not seeing things, and it was not my imagination. The jewels were there before Christmas. I only opened one little sack, there must have been fifteen or twenty stones in it, and I could see there were others, other little cheesecloth sacks just like it." He sighed. "There is, however, one comfort in all this."

"Which is . . . ?"

"I'm no longer in possession of stolen goods."

CHAPTER THIRTEEN

Issues of the Heart

"He's hardly speaking to me," said Olivia.

Percy came over to their booth, wiping his hands on the worn apron. "I don't b'lieve I've had th' pleasure," he said to Olivia.

"Meet Olivia Davenport," said Father Tim. "Olivia Davenport, Percy Mosely, the owner of this venerable establishment. When we were in for breakfast, he was out with the flu."

She smiled and extended her hand. "I hear your calf's liver with onions is four-star."

"She didn't hear it from me," said the rector.

"Well, th' Father here don't like it, n'r Miss Rose, but th' rest of us ain't so hard to satisfy."

"I look forward to deciding for myself."

"For you," said Percy, obviously enchanted, "we can have it back on th' specials by Tuesday."

"Well, then, look for me at noon on Tuesday!"

Percy went away in such ecstasy that the rector feared for his angina condition.

"Barely speaking?" asked her rector.

"I know what it is, of course. He's afraid."

"Yes, of course. And he's ashamed."

"What do you mean?"

"I mean that he wants very much to be brave, to let his feelings for you grow. But, as well as fearing the pain, I believe he's ashamed of the fear."

Olivia's brow furrowed as she considered that. "Yes. Yes, I understand that."

"Also, I feel that Hoppy is . . ."

"Is what?" she asked eagerly.

"Is thinking."

"Thinking?"

"He knows your doctor."

"No! Leo? He knows Leo?" She was obviously thrilled with this news.

"Hoppy interned at Mass General."

Olivia laughed with unbridled warmth. The sparkle danced again in her eyes. "Mass General is like home! I've spent so much of my life there, why, just talking about it makes me suddenly . . . almost homesick. And Hoppy . . . he interned there, and knows Leo." She said this softly, as if it gave her great comfort.

"I believe Hoppy may be thinking of how you could . . . that is, what he might do if . . ."

"A transplant? No. It's too much. I've given up. The chances, the risks . . . nothing is in my favor. Father, I promise you—I can't do it."

"Well, Olivia, all I can say to that is: Philippians four-thirteen."

She laughed easily. "I love it when you talk like that!"

Emma handed him the phone, looking tentative. "Harold's preacher," she said.

"My good brother," said the voice on the line, "this is Absalom Greer—orchard keeper, general-store operator, pastor of three little churches, and all-around worker in the vineyards of the Lord."

"Pastor Greer!" said the rector, instantly attracted to the tone of his caller's voice. "What can I do for you this morning?"

"Well, my friend, since we're to perform a ceremony together, I'd be beholden to you if we could have a mite of fellowship!"

"Consider it done," he said with warm anticipation. "Consider it done!"

"I declare," he told Puny on Wednesday, "if Dooley and I don't get out to Meadowgate soon, Rebecca Jane will be in college."

"When's the baptizin'?"

"Two weeks hence. The weather has been so variable, with rain or snow nearly every Sunday, that I've never laid eyes on her."

"I'd like to hold a baby," Puny said wistfully.

"Well, then, young lady, go find yourself a husband."

"Ha! There's not a soul out there I'd pick."

"How can you know that when you've limited the picking to Mitford and Wesley?" That was a good question, he thought.

"Mama said you don't go huntin', you let 'em kind of go by you in a parade."

"Yes, well, that may be. But have you seen any parades going by lately?"

She sighed. "What d' you want for supper?"

"You're asking me?"

"Well, for a change I thought I'd ask, instead of leavin' a surprise."

"Puny, please do not try to fix a thing that ain't broke."

She stared at him. "What kind of talk is that?"

"I mean that I fervently beseech you to keep doing exactly what you're doing. Your surprises are my unending delight."

She smiled gratefully, but a little weakly, he thought, as she paired his clean socks.

"Puny," he said, "I faithfully pray for you each day. But I believe I'm going to add something to that prayer. I'm going ask the Lord to start the parade!"

Puny blushed, and lowered her eyes. He was astounded to see a tear creep down her freckled cheek.

Without knowing why, it touched him so deeply that he turned away. He heard her blow her nose.

"Cornbread!" she suddenly said, with great feeling.

"Cornbread?"

She flew to the stove drawer. "I'm goin' to make you a cake of cornbread, I don't care what your doctor says! And I'm puttin' salt in it, and bacon drippin's, and fryin' it in Crisco, 'cause I'm tired of holdin' back on my good cornbread."

"Well, then!" he said, with admiration. "Just do it!"

The weather on Thursday morning was grim. He'd been aware of rain all night long, and sometime around four o'clock, Dooley crept into his bedroom. On hearing a noise, he and Barnabas sat straight up, seeing only a silhouette in the doorway. Barnabas growled darkly.

"Oh, shut up!" said Dooley, "I ain't no burglar. I come t' say I'm freezin' m' tailbone in there."

He got up and turned the thermostat to sixty, and Dooley stomped back to bed. The floor was like ice, and the rain beat against the windows in sheets.

At five, just before he was to get up for morning prayer and study, the wind began. It lashed the trees outside his bedroom window, groaned around the rectory, and made him recall the ominous forecast that ice would coat the streets like glass by midmorning. He remembered, too, that this was the day Louella was to arrive in Mitford and begin life again at Fernbank.

He went to the window and looked down at the little house next door. A lamp burned in an upstairs window, a pool of warm light in the dark and pouring rain.

"Well, then, Lord," he said aloud as he stood there. "Is this another memo from you about taking my car to Lew Boyd, so I can start driving again? How will the boy get to school in all this? And how can I make it to the hospital in this downpour?"

He heard a sound behind him.

"Is that you talkin' in here?"

"It is."

"Well, it sounds creepy with this ol' storm a blowin' and you settin' in here in th' dark, yammerin' to yourself."

"Yammerin', is it?"

"It jis' kind of sounds like yammer, yammer, yammer, yammer."

He looked down at the boy's anxious face, and put his arm around his shoulders.

"Dooley?"

Dooley hesitated. Then he said it. "Yes, sir?"

"What if we do something different today?"

"What's 'at?"

"What if we stay home and play with that train my cousin sent?"

Dooley hollered so loud that Barnabas leaped off the bed and ran into the hallway, barking at his shadow on the wall.

" 'at's a great idea! Boy, 'at's a great idea!"

"Would you be willing to admit, then, that preachers can occasionally have a great idea?"

"Yeah! Yes, sir! Boys howdy!"

"And while we're at it, why don't we have some of our favorite things, like hot chocolate with three marshmallows, and chili, and—"

"Popcorn, an' apple pie with ice cream—"

"And a bit of Wordsworth . . ."

"Yuck!"

"And stay in our robes and pajamas."

"Cool!"

"At eight-thirty, I am going to call your school and say, 'Dooley Barlowe is not sick today, but if he came out in this weather, he would surely get sick, so look for him tomorrow.' "

Without a word, Dooley took the rector's hand and shook it vigorously.

Early the following morning, the leaden skies cleared, the sun came out, and the village stirred briskly. After his hospital visit, he made a phone call to Lew Boyd, who agreed to do whatever it took to get his car running.

Then, he drove to Wesley on his motor scooter, took the drivers' license test, and, by grace alone, he later said, passed it.

Lew Boyd was looking out the window when he saw the rector walking past the war monument, toward the station. "Here 'e comes, boys," he said, cutting himself a plug of tobacco.

"Been twenty year since he's drove a car," announced Coot Hendrick.

"No, it hain't," said Bailey Coffey. "Hit's been fourteen, maybe fifteen."

"Ain't none of you got it right," said Lew. "Th' last time he drove that Buick was eight years ago. I looked up where I drained th' fluids."

"Time flies," said Coot, dumping a pack of peanuts in his bottled Coke.

"Boys," said Father Tim, coming in the front door, "she looks good."

Lew went down his list. "We washed 'er, waxed 'er, put on y'r radials, put in y'r fluids, give you a batt'ry, vacuumed 'er out, spot cleaned y'r front seat, warshed y'r mats, filled 'er up, run 'er around th' block, honked th' horn, and tried out th' radio."

"I heard my fav'rite song," said Coot, " 'If You Don't Stand F'r Somethin', You'll Fall F'r Anything.' "

"We just all piled in and rode around, if you want to know th' truth," Bailey Coffey confessed.

"Here's th' bill," said Lew, "and I don't mind tellin' you it's a whopper."

Coot patted the dinette chair next to his. "You better set down, is all I can say."

"Four hundred eighty-six dollars and seventy-eight cents?" the rector asked.

"That includes y'r Peaches an' Cream deod'rant spray."

"A bargain!" he declared, and shook Lew's hand with enthusiasm.

They followed him to the car. "Boys," said Lew, as the rector started the ignition, "since he ain't drove in a good while, I'd step back if I was you."

They stood watching as the car cruised around the monument and disappeared down Main Street, where several people turned and stared in complete disbelief at the sight of the local priest driving a car, apparently absorbed in his own thoughts, but actually listening intently to the country-and-western station on his radio, which was playing a number called "I Bought the Shoes That Just Walked Out on Me."

During the service the following Sunday, he asked the congregation if anyone had seen his Bible, which he described in minute detail.

Black. Embossed with his name in gold. Leather. Worn. Small. Red-letter edition. Marked in the margins.

Not a soul raised a hand, stood up, confessed, or otherwise gave any indication of its whereabouts.

He didn't know why such a thought occurred to him, but he felt he should search the church. The basement, the attic, that sort of thing. Too many things were missing; something felt oddly out of place, like a picture hanging crooked on the wall.

It was after dark when he walked to Lord's Chapel, noticing the sign on the front door of the Oxford as he passed. "Away," it read, which was Andrew's unique language for "Closed." He'd heard that

Andrew had left last week on his biannual trip to England to buy antiques and meet with a society that collected Churchill memorabilia. The gray Mercedes would not be parked at the curb for a while, which gave him a puzzling sense of relief.

Arriving at the church, he turned on all the lights and went first to the basement. He searched the sprawling, unfinished room thoroughly, even looking into the surplus food cabinets where they stored canned goods for church suppers. On the few occasions he'd looked in this cabinet, he'd seen it full, as Esther Bolick was the major-domo of all kitchen activities and a real crackerjack at keeping supplies on hand.

This time, it was nearly empty; they were even low on toilet paper. "Have you ever tried to go to the johnny over at the Baptists'?" Esther once said. "They never have any toilet paper. You have to use the Kleenex in your pocketbook, if you're lucky enough to have any!" It had been a particular ambition of Esther's never to run out of this commodity at Lord's Chapel.

On entering the parish hall, he was surprised to smell the unmistakable odor of chicken noodle soup. He would know that smell anywhere, having lived off that particular soup during his early years in the priesthood.

There was no indication that anyone had been in the church. No meetings were scheduled. Altar Guild never worked on Sunday, having a tradition of cleaning up on Monday. And Russell lay sick in the hospital.

He felt a sudden foreboding. Something was wrong, very wrong. He could sense it, and he didn't like it.

At the left of the altar, he reached up and pulled the chain that brought down the attic stairs.

Why in heaven's name anyone would have put attic stairs near the altar was beyond him. However, the chain did make a fine place to attach a flower basket during spring and summer services.

Chicken noodle soup! As he turned on the attic lights and climbed the creaking steps, he smelled it more distinctly than before.

In his twelve years at Lord's Chapel, he had been in the attic only once, and found it as large as the loft of a New England barn. According to Miss Sadie, they had built the church with room for growth of the Sunday school. As his eyes came level with the floor of the loft, he saw nothing but a vast, empty space filled with shadows.

It was strangely restful to stand in this place, without the fret and clutter of "things."

He noticed something lying near the window in the corner. But when he walked over to it, he saw that it was only a candy wrapper. Almond Joy. One of his favorites.

He picked it up. He could smell the tiniest scent of chocolate on the wrapper.

He put the wrapper in his pants pocket and walked to the door that opened into the nearly empty belfry. Three of the enormous bells were gone from their oak mountings. The fourth, the great and solemn "death bell," as it was called, stood silent in the corner of the Norman tower.

What was he looking for, anyway? he asked himself. Perhaps he hoped the jewels would turn up again somewhere on the premises, and Rodney Underwood would take them away, and the whole incident would be off his mind and out of his hands. After all, wasn't it possible that whoever put them in the urn might have moved them to another hiding place in the church?

If nothing else, he was able to see the pristine condition of the old building, even in the poor light from naked bulbs.

He closed the door to the belfry, and walked to the stairs.

Very likely, he thought, the theft of Esther Bolick's marmalade cake had been an inside job, a practical joke by one of the many fervent admirers of that famous cake. And his Bible would turn up in some unexpected place that, after all, would make perfect sense.

The jewels, however, were another matter. He had hoped to come up from the basement or down from the attic feeling some sort of peace. But the matter of the jewels would give him no peace at all.

When he went home from the office on Monday, Puny was standing at the door, waiting. He could see the fire in her eyes before he opened the screen.

"This is a pleasant surprise," he said, seeing that it wasn't going to be pleasant at all. "You're usually gone when I get home."

"Are you still prayin' that parade prayer?" she demanded, as he came in with a quart of milk and a loaf of bread.

"Parade prayer?"

"You know, th' one that asks th' Lord to let th' parade begin?"

"Aha! Well, yes. Yes, I am."

She glowered at him. "If you don't mind, I'd appreciate it if you'd tell th' Lord to stop th' parade!"

"Well, now," he said, putting the grocery bag down and sitting on his counter stool. "What's going on?"

"Th' very day we talked, I went to th' Local to get those nectarines Avis was ravin' about, and I'm standin' there by the produce, and this ol' coot walks up t' me an' goes, 'Well, little lady, where you bin at all my life?'

"He had his jaw stuck s' full of tobacco, it would've gagged a billy goat. He follered me around till I had to nearly smack 'im to get 'im to leave me alone.

"Th' very next day," Puny continued, quite red in the face, "I was mindin' my own business at th' mall, tryin' to buy you some wash rags, and this big galoot slithers up t' me like a snake and says, 'Want t' go git some chicken fingers at th' arcade?'

"Chicken fingers! I showed 'im chicken fingers!"

"Puny," he said, "when you go to a parade, do you like every float that passes?"

"I like some better'n others," she said grudgingly.

"Well, then."

"I don't know. I think you should pray some other prayer. This'n scares me t' death."

"You wait," he said, mildly. "This is only the start-up. We haven't got to the drum and bugle corps yet, much less to the marching bands!"

"Whatever that's supposed to mean," she said, thoroughly disgusted.

That evening before dinner, he built a fire. Dooley made popcorn, and Barnabas did his business at the hedge with great expediency. He was as glad as a child for the comfort of home, and rest, and peace.

For what he estimated to be the fourth or fifth time, he picked up the *Mitford Muse*, which by now was four days old, and tried to read Esther Cunningham's editorial on the July Festival of Roses. J.C. had done it again. "Festival of Ropes Will Transform Main Street," said the headline.

Dooley answered the ringing phone in the kitchen. "Rec'try. Yep, he's here, but he don't want t' talk t' nobody."

Dooley put his hand over the receiver and yelled, "It's y'r doctor!"

"Hang up," he said, and lifted the cordless by the sofa. "Got anything for exhaustion, sleeplessness, and general aggravation?" he asked.

"I was calling to ask you the same thing."

"The blind leading the blind. How are you, my friend?"

"This place is eating me alive. I've got to get out of here for a while, and the kitchen said they'd make me a plate. I wondered if I could bring it to your place. Dining out, it's called."

"Of course!" he said, trying to conceal the weariness in his voice.

"I'll bring you a plate, too."

"I don't know," said the rector, with some caution. "What do you . . . ah, think it might be?"

"God only knows."

"I've had that a few times. Bring it on, then. I need more surprises in my life."

"Yuck," said Dooley, "don't give me any of that stuff. I eat somethin' off granpaw's plate th' other day at th' hospital, an' it like t' gagged me."

"Thanks for reminding me."

"I'll jis' have me some popcorn, peanut butter an' jelly, an' fried baloney."

"Yuck," said the rector.

"When in heaven's name are you going to get some help?" he asked his doctor. They were sitting by the fire with trays on their laps.

"Soon."

"That's what you always say. And soon never comes. Here you are, a Harvard medical school graduate who could practice anywhere in the country, and you've chosen our obscure little village and the work of three men."

"A man from Wesley will be spending a couple of afternoons with me, starting soon. Good doctor. Wilson. You'll like him. Young."

"A lamb to the slaughter."

Hoppy grinned. "So, what do you think of the cuisine?"

"Well, now . . . words fail me."

"Come on. We're talking Chicken Cordon Bleu here."

He laughed. "If that's what you're talking, my friend, we are clearly speaking two different languages."

Hoppy gulped down his food, a habit encouraged by overwork and understaffing, and leaned back in the wing chair. "I need you to check me on something," he said, looking into the fire.

"Proceed."

"I don't know where I'm going with this. Maybe nowhere." He was silent for some time, as the fire crackled. Barnabas got up from his master's feet and went and lay next to Hoppy's. This act of simple consolation was only one of the reasons Father Tim admired his dog's character.

"When Carol was dying, there was nothing I could do. All I could do was control the pain. It was . . . hopeless."

"Yes. It was. It was hopeless."

Hoppy turned from the fire. "Severe myocarditis isn't hopeless!" he said, with feeling.

"Keep going."

"Which means I'm not helpless!"

"I hear you."

Hoppy stood up and paced the floor. "I'm scared out of my mind. I hardly know this woman. We spent some time at the art show, I see her at church, we've had coffee in the staff room. And of course, I see what she's doing for my patients. She's the best medicine we've got up there."

Father Tim heard Dooley running his bath water upstairs.

"Track me here, and see if I'm making sense."

"I'm with you."

"Severe myocarditis is not hopeless for one reason only—transplants. But this option is complicated by her blood type. Who knows whether we could find a compatible donor in a hundred years? And when we found one, would she be in stable enough condition to receive the heart? Another thing, it can't be just anybody with her blood type, it will take someone who's about her same weight. It's scary business, but what I'm saying is this . . ."

He stood in front of the fire, his tall, lanky frame cast into shadow. "I hardly know this woman, but . . . I feel something for her that's so strong, so . . . compelling . . . that I want to help her. I want to stick my neck out and help her. I want her to have a heart that works. I want . . ."

"What do you want?"

"I want her to live," Hoppy said softly.

"I want that with you."

"Get behind me in prayer, will you?"

"I will."

"You'll think I'm crazy, but I've been running down all the scenarios. I've got a friend in Wesley who's a pilot. He's not always easy to find, but we're twenty minutes to his plane. And if I can't find Millard, there's a little charter service at the same strip, with a couple of Cessnas.

"Wherever they harvest the heart, it could be put on ice until we arrive. Or, it could be packed in ice and flown to Boston. I'm going to talk to Leo Baldwin at Mass General."

Father Tim felt strangely shaken and joyful.

"We can get her on a national waiting list, and if her blood type comes up, we'd have to move immediately. She'll have to wear a beeper, and . . . I'd like you to have one, too. When that thing goes off, pal, we're talking on your knees."

He felt the sobering impact of such a plan. It would mean they would all have to be accessible, every hour of every day.

"The call could come anytime, from anywhere," said Hoppy. "We may even be able to keep the donor alive, keep the heart pumping until we get her wherever we have to go."

"Would that be desirable?"

"The longer it's in the physiological state, the better."

"I see."

Hoppy rubbed his eyes and sat down again, wearily.

"What do I tell her?" he asked his concerned host. "That I'm willing to go out of my way, complicate my life, turn my practice upside down for God knows how long, just because I'm a nice guy? How do I keep . . . what would she think my reasons are for getting involved like this?"

Father Tim sat forward on the sofa. "I suggest you don't concern yourself with what she thinks. You're a doctor. Your business is saving lives."

"But according to you, she's turned off the transplant idea completely. Leo Baldwin has probably walked her through all these scenarios; she's considered them seriously, and dumped the option. Period. So, who's going to sell her?"

"Probably not me, probably not you."

"Who, then?"

"God," he said, simply.

"Tell me more."

"If we're going to be a team, my friend, we must think like a team. And to do that, we need to agree in prayer."

"Count me in."

"Neither you nor I may be able to convince her about this transplant, but if God thinks it's best for her, it's just a matter of time."

"Let's go for it," Hoppy said.

The two men bowed their heads, and Barnabas rested his on the doctor's foot.

After his friend left, he sat for a while on the sofa. Then he went upstairs, said goodnight to Dooley, and took a hot shower. But an hour after getting into bed, the adrenaline was pumping so fast and furiously, that he lay sleepless until three o'clock. At four, he awoke exhausted, and lay staring at his moonlit window until dawn.

He wondered about his recent, creeping fatigue. His running had been sporadic, and he'd let a few taboo foods slip back into his diet. But his indiscretions had been minor in that regard, no more than a piece of cornbread, a sliver of chocolate.

Dear God, what a hideous feeling to go down for the count, when he'd spent most of his life in glowing good health. He wondered, as he lay there, about the helplessness of the elderly, about people who couldn't move their limbs, or walk to the barbershop, or get up and go to the toilet.

He had devoted his life to intercessory prayer, asking little for himself, trusting in God's provisions, and seeing that trust confirmed on every side. But he lay, now, feeling that his very essence was somehow draining away, and prayed fervently for his own strength, for wisdom, and renewal.

The baptism was truly a blessed event. When he held her in his arms and said, "Rebecca Jane, you are sealed by the Holy Spirit in baptism and marked as Christ's own forever," a great warmth flowed through him, and the infant stirred in his arms and looked into his eyes.

At the reception in the parish hall, they were standing in line to hold the amiable Rebecca Jane, whose green eyes, stand-up strawberry hair, and dimpled chin were melting hearts by the score.

Though Dooley didn't attempt to hold her, he stayed by the side of anyone who did, looking at her intently, and marveling

"I like 'is baby," he told Father Tim. "I like 'is baby better'n' . . ."

"Better than snuff, I suppose?"

"Nope. Better'n Goosedown Owen!"

"That's quite a compliment."

"But 'er hair's funny. It looks kind of like a stump full of gran'-daddy spiders."

"Every baby is special," the rector told Marge, who had finally reclaimed her daughter from the eager parishioners. "But there's something quite different about Rebecca Jane. I sense a spirit that's very rich with God's promise."

"I sense that, too," she said, kissing her baby's downy head.

It was inspiring to see Louella's broad, mahogany face smiling at him these days from the gospel side. Her presence brought something nourishing to the spirit of the congregation, like raisins added to bread.

She also made an addition with her fruity, mezzo voice, which she lifted with surprising strength in the Anglican hymns, learned as a girl in this very church.

"She makes me feel young," said Miss Sadie, when Father Tim visited Fernbank for lunch. "When I'm around Louella, it's like being close to Mama, all over again!"

"Did you know Miss Sadie rock' me in her arms when I was a baby?" Louella said, proudly. "So, when I'm aroun' Miss Sadie, I feel young myself!"

"We don't know who raised who!" said the mistress of Fernbank.

A very nice kettle of fish, thought the pleased rector.

On Thursday evening, it occurred to him that he had never invited his neighbor to attend a service at Lord's Chapel. What kind of hospitality was that, he asked himself, as he dialed her number.

"I don't mind telling you," he confessed, "that I've been wanting to invite you to a church service, but, well, I keep forgetting to do it. And I apologize!"

"Do you soak your beans?" asked Cynthia.

"Why, yes. Yes, I do," he said, taken aback.

"I just love to cook a pot of beans. But you will never guess what I did a few days ago, speaking of forgetting."

"I can't imagine," he said, which was the truth if he'd ever told it.

"I was soaking a big pot of beans, and I put the lid on the pot, and set them on the stove, and a week later, there was this horrible smell, I thought something had died in my kitchen, that Violet had, well, you know . . ."

"Killed a mouse?"

"Exactly! But guess what it was? It was those beans! I'd simply forgotten they were in the pot, and they'd just . . . well . . ."

"Spoiled."

"Exactly! So, don't feel bad if you can't remember to ask me to church."

"Well, then, I won't feel a bit bad. But whenever you'd like to come, please know you'll be welcomed by one and all."

"I've been going to the Presbyterians," she said, "but yes, I will come soon!"

After the invitation to his neighbor, he called the hospital to check on Russell.

Nurse Herman said he had sent his dinner back, barely touched, insisting that he could have cooked it better himself, so she figured he was improving, and could the rector please bring a pound of livermush the next time he came to the hospital, as it wasn't something they ordinarily bought, and Russell said he would give a war pension for some.

"He also insisted," reported Nurse Herman, "that he would go down to the kitchen and personally fry it himself, and Dr. Harper said fine, fry him some too. Can you imagine?"

"LIVERMUSH," Father Tim wrote on his list of things to do.

After a useless and frustrating meeting on Friday afternoon, he decided to take Barnabas on a long walk. When Dooley left on his bicycle to do Fernbank chores, he headed toward Little Mitford Creek with Barnabas straining at the leash.

The wet winter promised a glorious spring, and here and there, pushing through sodden leaf mold, were furtive shoots of green that gladdened his heart. He loved the smell of the woods, and the damp alluvial soil that covered these mountains like a blanket.

Smoke was boiling out of the chimney, the great aluminum tub that Homeless used for bathing was hanging on the side of the house, and a colorful wash was on the line. Homeless answered the door, leaning on his crutch and swaddled head to foot in a worn Indian blanket.

"Well, sir, if it ain't the clergy! Come in, come in, make yourself at home!"

The rector and his dog discovered a roaring fire in the old stove, a soup pot simmering on top, and a book open on the little table where an oil lamp burned against the fading afternoon light. In the corner stood the neatly made cot, with two worn quilts folded at the foot.

"I declare, Homeless, I could move in here and be happy as a clam."

"Happy as a hog in slop, is what I am. Set down right here," he said, offering his only chair to the rector, who took it, knowing that it pleased his host to offer him the best seat in the house.

Homeless settled on the wood box between the table and the stove.

"My friend," said the rector, "I'm feeling the ills of the world these days. I thought I'd come and visit a man with some plain sense."

"You're visitin' a man s' plain, he's settin' here with no britches on. One pair is hangin' on th' clothesline, and I give th' other pair away. Fella lives up th' creek yonder was too ragged t' look for work, so I stepped out of m' pants, an' he put 'em on and headed to town. You prob'ly don't want to get that plain, yourself."

"No. No, I don't. You're right. That's too plain for me."

"Sometimes you have to gag on fancy before you can appreciate plain, th' way I see it. For too many years, I ate fancy, I dressed fancy, I talked fancy. A while back, I decided to start talkin' th' way I was raised t' talk, and for th' first time in forty years, I can understand what I'm sayin'."

They laughed easily.

"Right here is the way I talked for a lot of years," said Homeless. "You might have thought I had a degree from some fine college. It was a real paste-up job, you might say." He grinned. "Well, that's the end of my demonstration on talking fancy . . ."

"I'd find it interesting to know what you did all those years in advertising." Leaning against the wall in a straight-back chair gave the rector an odd sense of relief, as if he'd run away to the creek and left his worries behind.

"I was what you call an account man. Toothpaste, beer, and automotive was my categories, with a little stint on bankin' and breakfast cereals. It was when I went on breakfast cereals that liquor got me. If I'd've been around when that oat bran thing hit, somethin' worse than liquor might've got me."

Homeless stood up and opened the stove door, and poked the logs with a stick. The blanket shifted and slipped toward the floor but he grabbed it, adjusted it, and sat back down, grinning broadly. "There's every temptation in th' world for me to get another pair of pants, but I'm fightin' it."

Father Tim laughed heartily.

"Th' bottom line is, I was drunk for thirty years. Thirty years! It astounds me to this very day. I signed contracts, made presentations, drove cars, flew planes, directed meetin's, and stayed half-shot th' whole time.

"I lost three wives, nine jobs, four houses, two kids, and one foot. Th' only thing I didn't lose was m' self-respect, and that's because I didn't have any."

Barnabas listened intently.

"You might say I did everything I could to earn th' name Homeless and live up to it. And now that things are diff'rent and I've been sober for nine years, I don't try to dodge m' name. It reminds me of what I was. Homeless! Sick! Slobberin' in th' gutter! God A'mighty."

"What brought you back here?"

"I asked myself where I'd been th' happiest, and it was right here, back home where I was raised. They were hard times when I was comin' up, but they were good times. And I'd got to th' place where I'd seen it all. I'd made the big money, had th' big expense accounts, th' whole nine yards. I turned myself in to dry out, and I stayed dry. I sold everything, paid my debts, and turned up in Wesley with sixty bucks in m' pocket."

"Did you ever look back?"

"I never looked back."

The fire crackled in the stove.

"I don't mind telling you I'm curious about the kind of terms you're on with God."

"We talk," said Homeless. "We're definitely on speakin' terms. I'm no all-out pagan, by a long shot. I was raised in th' church, and baptized as a boy. But there's somethin' lackin' and I don't know what it is. It's like somethin's itchin' me, won't let me be. I cain't name it, and t' tell you th' truth, I don't want to think about it.

"You know how th' town churches do, bringin' me this t' eat and that t' eat, tryin' to get me in a pew. You people come back in here to th' creek, an' make me feel like a frog you're tryin' to gig."

The rector had fished a stick out of the wood basket. It was a comfort to turn it in his hand, to look at the knots and the grain. He felt the urge to whittle on it with a knife, but no urge to speak. Homeless was right.

"Now that's a hateful thing for a man t' say, but I can talk to you, I can level with you."

"I appreciate that, my friend. Once in a while, I need to talk to somebody I can level with, myself."

"You can level with me any time. But right now," said Homeless, picking up his crutch, "I'm goin' to jump in here and lay on some supper, and give *you* somethin' t' eat, for a change!"

He lifted the lid on the soup pot, and out of it wafted a fragrance so heavenly that his guest was transfixed.

"I'm afraid I won't be able to stay. I've got a boy who'll be wanting his dinner."

"I've got a nice, big ham bone down in here for ol' Barnabas," said their host, stirring the soup with a long-handled spoon.

Barnabas beat the floor with his tail.

"You don't know how we'd like to stay, but the boy . . ."

"How old's this boy?" asked Homeless, setting a cast iron griddle on the stove top.

"Dooley's eleven."

"When I was eleven, my daddy had a big farm th' other side of Wesley. From th' time m' mama died, I got up at four ever' mornin', made breakfast for three little young 'uns, milked th' cows, cleaned up th' kitchen, and walked t' school. If that boy can't make hisself a jam san'wich . . ."

"Set me a place," said Father Tim.

"I got a deal with Avis," Homeless confided, ladling a second helping into his guest's bowl. "All he throws out, I go through. But don't worry that y'r soup's not sanitary. I brought th' cabbage home and washed it good. I cleaned th' potatoes with a scrub brush, cut the soft spots off th' onion, gored a bad place out of th' rutabaga, and put it all on t' boil after I took m' bath and done m' washin'. I keep busy. I'm not one t' lollygag."

The rector thought this might be the best soup he'd ever put in his mouth, and he didn't even like rutabagas.

Homeless waved his hand over their supper, which included mugs of steaming coffee, and the hot, day-old bread he'd toasted on the griddle and buttered. "I paid for th' coffee and th' butter, but not another morsel. There's prob'ly less 'n twenty-five cents in this whole deal!"

"That's a deal, all right."

"Come spring, I won't even be payin' for th' coffee. I'm goin' t' dig a mess of chick'ry, roast th' roots, and grind 'em up. You boil that of a mornin' and drink it, and it'll set y'r feet on th' floor."

"All things considered, my friend, I count you among the richest folks in Mitford."

Homeless winked and laughed his rasping laugh. "That man is th' richest whose pleasures are th' cheapest!"

"Thoreau," said Father Tim.

"Dead right," beamed his host.

When he and Barnabas came out into Lilac Road at Winnie Ivey's cottage, he felt as if he'd been away on vacation.

"Why pay a fortune to fly to Sligo for a month," he asked aloud in the gathering dusk, "when I can spend an hour or two on Mitford Creek?"

He hardly noticed the car that drove slowly toward them across the narrow bridge, its lights on low beam, but Barnabas did. He barked viciously, lunging with all his might as the car slowed down and seemed about to stop.

Just then, one of Rodney Underwood's men came down Lilac Road in a patrol car.

He could barely control the furious energy straining at the leash, as the rusted Impala gunned the engine and shot past them, belching fumes of noxious exhaust.

CHAPTER FOURTEEN

Absalom, My Son

When he arrived at church the following Sunday, he found his missing Bible lying open on the pulpit. He was flooded with relief, as if a picture hanging crooked on the wall had been set nearly straight again.

Rodney Underwood called on Monday afternoon.

"I've just read an in'erestin' article, says a ring of English antique dealers has been shippin' jewels over here in holler table legs and secret desk drawers. Says, ah, let's see, says three English dealers are currently under suspicion of shippin' rare stolen gems and antique jewelry in furniture transported by ship in sealed containers. So far, authorities have not been able to seize a shipment, as those destined recently for America were diverted to other, unknown ports.

"You don't reckon your jewels could have anything to do with this, do you?"

Please don't call them my jewels! he thought. "I don't think so. Fact is, I just searched the church, thinking that . . . well, in any case, I didn't find anything. Nothing but a lone candy wrapper, to tell the truth."

"Candy wrapper? What kind of candy wrapper?"

"Almond Joy."

"Where'd you find it?"

"In the loft. It was absolutely the only thing up there, as we never use that space at all."

"What would it be doin' up there?"

"I haven't the vaguest idea." He felt a creeping alarm that Rodney might deploy fingerprinting crews over the entire church grounds, on account of a harmless candy wrapper.

"You better let me look at that wrapper," Rodney said.

"If you want to run by the house and ask Puny to look in my brown pants pocket, I think that's where I put it."

"I'll send over a cruise car," said Rodney, seemingly pleased with this turn of events.

The police chief called back in an hour. "You sure you searched th' church good? Did you look in behind things?"

"I went over it with a fine-tooth comb. Of course, I didn't pry up any floorboards or look behind the bookcases."

"We got th' wrapper, and th' candy on it's still fresh. You say nobody ever goes in th' attic?"

"Nobody."

"Well, th' wrapper's covered with prints. But since you handled it, we'll have to come and take a set of your prints to see what's what and who's who."

Here we go, he thought.

"Nobody's prints but yours," said Rodney, when he called the rectory in the evening. "But I'll tell you one thing."

"What's that?" he asked, sitting down on his study sofa with the cordless phone.

"No other fingerprints means that whoever eat that Almond Joy was wearin' gloves. Y'see what I mean?" he asked the rector, who clearly didn't. "Anybody wearin' gloves to eat a candy bar is up t' no good."

"Aha."

"What I'm sayin' is, I believe I better come down there tomorrow with th' boys and go over th' place."

Well, and why not? Perhaps the whole thing could be laid to rest.

"Come ahead," he said.

When he arrived at the office the next morning, the phone was ringing.

"Father!" said the caller, "Pete Jamison."

"Pete Jamison?"

"You know, Father, the man you saved."

The stranger in the nave! "Let me say at once that it was not I who saved you, Pete—that power belongs only to God. How are you, my friend?"

"Coming along, I think. When I get your way again, I'd like to drop by and see you. Right now, I'm calling from a coffee shop in Duluth, Minnesota. I just wanted to say thank you. Thank you for being there. May I call you again?"

"I'll be disappointed if you don't," said the rector, who heard an unmistakable difference in Pete Jamison's voice.

Throughout the day, Rodney, Joe Joe Guthrie, and another officer searched Lord's Chapel. They looked for floorboards that might have been freshly pried up. They pounded on walls, searching for unexpected hollows. They peered under rugs in the nursery, examined the ceilings for loose tiles, removed the covers of heating vents, and generally raised a cloud of dust that caused the rector to cough and sneeze throughout the day.

They looked in the gardens for any sign that might indicate the planting of something other than bulbs. They put on gloves and masks to remove strips of insulation in the loft. They shone flashlights into the belfry, searched under the kitchen sink of the parish hall, and peered behind the doors of the retable.

Their search, however, revealed nothing more than a long-lost prayer book that had belonged to Wilma Malcolm's grandmother, a box of Palm Sunday bulletins from 1947, and several squirrel nests containing a store of pecans from trees at the rear of the church yard.

"Dadgummit!" said Rodney, with considerable feeling.

Toward the end of the afternoon, the rector felt like walking to The Local and buying a box of Little Debbies, any variety, and devouring the entire contents in the privacy of his kitchen. Nor would he wait for the kettle to boil for tea.

In the fading afternoon light, Absalom Greer's slim frame might have been that of a twenty-year-old as he hurried down the steps of the old general store.

"Welcome to God's country!" he said, opening the door of the Buick. "Get out and come in, Father!"

The rector was astonished to see that the face of his eighty-six-year-old host was remarkably unlined, and, what was more astounding, he had a full head of hair.

"I was looking for an elderly gentleman to greet me. Pastor Greer must have sent his son!"

The old man laughed heartily. "I can still hear an ant crawling in the grass," he said with satisfaction, "but there's not a tooth in my head I can call my own."

The country preacher led the village rector up the steps and into the dim interior of the oldest store in several counties.

Father Tim felt as if he'd walked into a Rembrandt painting, for the last of the sunlight had turned the color of churned butter, casting a golden glow upon the chestnut walls and heart-of-pine floors.

"My daddy built this store when I was six years old. It's got the first nails I ever drove. It sold out of the family in 1974, but I bought it back and intend to keep it, though it don't do much toward keeping me.

"Let me give you a little country cocktail," said his host, who was dressed in a neat gray suit and starched shirt. He selected a cold drink from an ice box behind the cash register, opened it, and handed it to the rector.

"You're looking at where I do my best preaching," he said, slapping the worn wood of the old counter. "Right here is where the rubber hits the road.

"Like the Greeks said to Philip, 'Sir, we would see Christ.' If they don't see him behind this counter six days a week, we might as well throw my Sunday preaching out the window. Where is your weekday pulpit, my friend?"

"Main Street."

"That's a good place. Some soldiers set around and smell the coffee and watch the bacon frying, but the battle is waged on your feet."

"Absalom," said a quiet voice from the back of the store, "Supper's ready. You can come anytime."

A door closed softly.

"My sister, Lottie," the old man said with evident pride. "She lives with me and does the cooking and housekeeping. I can assure you that I never did anything to deserve her ministry to me. She is an angel of the Lord!"

His host turned the sign on the front door to read "Closed," and they walked the length of the narrow store on creaking floorboards, passing bins of seeds and nails, rows of canned goods, sacks of feed, thread, buttons, iron skillets, and aluminum wash tubs.

Absalom Greer pushed open a door and the rector stood on the threshold in happy amazement. Before him was a room with ancient, leaded windows gleaming with the last rays of sunlight. In the center of the room stood a large table laid with a white cloth and a variety of steaming dishes, and on it burned an oil lamp.

In the corner of the room, a fire crackled in the grate, and books lined the walls behind a pair of comfortable reading chairs. A worn black Bible lay on the table next to one of the chairs, and an orange cat curled peacefully on the deep windowsill.

He thought he'd never entered a home so peaceable in spirit.

A tall, slender woman moved into the room from the kitchen, wearing an apron. Her blue dress became her graying hair, which was pulled back simply and tied with a ribbon. She smiled shyly and extended her hand. "Father Tim," said Absalom Greer, "Lottie Miller! My joy and my crown, my earthly shield and buckler, and my widowed sister."

"It's my great pleasure," said the rector, feeling as if he had gone to another country to visit.

"My sister is shy as a deer, Father. We don't get much company in here, as I do all my pastoring at church or in the store. Why don't you set where you can see the little fire on the hearth, it's always a consolation."

After washing up in a tidy bathroom, Father Tim sat down at the table, finding that even the hard-back chair seemed comforting.

"I left school when I was twelve," said Absalom Greer over dinner, "to help my daddy in the store, and I got along pretty good teaching myself at night. One evenin', along about the age of fourteen—I was back here in this very room, studyin' a book—the wind got to howling and blowing as bad as you ever heard.

"Lottie was a baby in my mother's arms. I can see them now, my mother sitting by the fire, rocking Lottie, and humming a tune, and I was settin' right there on a little bed.

"My eyes were as wide open as they are now, when suddenly I saw a great band of angels. This room was filled with the brightness of angels!

"They were pure white, with color only in their wings, color like a prism casts when the sun shines through it. I never saw anything so beautiful in my life, before or since. I couldn't speak a word, and my mother went on rocking and humming, with her eyes closed, and there were angels standing over her, and all around us was this shining, heavenly host.

"Then, it seemed as if a golden stair let down there by the door, and the angels turned and swarmed up that staircase, and were gone. I remember I went to sobbing, but my mother didn't hear it. And I reached up to wipe my tears, but there weren't any there.

"I've thought about it many a time over the years, and I think it was my spirit that was weeping with joy."

Lottie Miller had not spoken, but had passed each dish and platter, it seemed to the rector, at just the right time. He had a second helping of potatoes that had been sliced and fried with rock salt and chives, and another helping of roasted lamb, which was as fine as any lamb he'd tasted in a very long time.

"It's a mystery how I could have done it, but I completely forgot that heavenly vision," said the preacher, who was buttering a biscuit.

"Along about sixteen, I got to feeling I had no soul at all. They'd take me to hear a preaching, and I couldn't hear. They'd take me to see a healing and I couldn't see. My daddy said it was the name they'd put on me—Absalom! A wicked, rebellious, ungodly character if there ever was one, but my mother was young when I was born, and heedless, and she liked the sound of it, and I was stuck with it. Later on, when I got to reading the Word, I got to understanding Absalom and his daddy, and that pitiful relationship, and the name got to be a blessing to me instead of a curse, and, praise God, some of my best preaching has come out of my name.

"Well, along about twenty, I kissed my mother and daddy goodbye, and my baby sister, and I walked to Wesley and took the train and I went out West carrying a cardboard box tied with twine.

"Times were so hard, I couldn't get a job. I ended up putting the cardboard from that box in the bottoms of my shoes. A fella told me the bottom of one foot said Cream of Wheat, and the other said This Side Up.

"I walked on that box for three months 'til I got work in a silver mine. Way down in that mine, in that deep, dark pit, I heard the Lord call me. 'Absalom, my son,' He said as clear as day, 'go home. Go home and preach my Word to your people.'

"Well sir, I didn't know his Word to preach it. But I up and started home, took the train back across this great land, got off at Wesley, walked twelve miles to Farmer in the middle of the night with a full moon shining, and I got to my mother's and daddy's door right out there, and I laid down with the dogs and went to sleep on a flour sack.

"I remember I told myself I'd never heard the Lord call me in that mine, that I'd just been lonesome and was looking for an excuse to come home.

"I went on like that for a year or two, went to church to look at the girls, helped my daddy in the store. But that wasn't enough, something was sorely missing. One day, I commenced to read everything theological I could get my hands on.

"I drenched myself in Spurgeon, and plowed through Calvin, I soaked up Whitefield and gorged on Matthew Henry, as hard as I could go. But I was fightin' my calling, and my heart was like a stone.

"One day I was settin' in the orchard I planted as a boy, and the Lord spoke again. 'Absalom, my son,' He said, clear as day, 'spread my Word to your people.'

"It made the hair stand up on my head. But in five minutes, I had laid down in the sunshine and gone to sleep like a lizard.

"I went on that way for about three years, not listening to God, 'til one night He woke me up, I thought I'd been hit a blow on the head with a two-by-four.

"It was like a bolt of lightning knocked me out of bed and threw me to the floor. Blam! 'Absalom, my son,' said the Lord, 'go preach my Word to your people, and be quick about it.' "

"I got up off that floor, I ran in here where it was cold enough to preserve a corpse, I wrapped up in a blanket and lit an oil lamp, and I got to reading the Good Book and for two years I did not stop.

"Everybody who knew me thought I'd gone soft.

" 'Absalom Greer has got religion,' they said, but they were only partly right. It was religion that had got me, it was God Himself who had me at last, and it was the most thrilling time of my life.

"The words would jump off the page, I would understand things I had never understood before. I could take a verse my tongue had glibbed over in church, and see in it wondrous and thrilling meanings that kept the hair standing up on my head.

"I would go out to work at the lumber company and take it with me. I would set on the toilet and read it. I would walk to town reading, and I'd be so transported I would fall in the ditch and get up and go again, turning the page.

"I felt God spoke to me continuously for two transcendent years. Glory, glory, glory!" said the old preacher, with shining eyes.

"One Sunday morning, I was settin' in that little church about three miles down the road there and Joshua Hoover was pastoring then. I remember I was settin' there in that sweet little church, and Pastor Hoover come down the aisle and he was white as a ghost.

"He said, 'Absalom, God has asked me to let you preach the service this morning.'

"I like to dropped down dead at his feet.

"He said, 'I don't know about this, it makes me uneasy, but it's what the Lord told me to do.'

"When I stood up, my legs gave out under me, I like to fainted like a girl."

Lottie Miller laughed softly.

"I recalled something Billy Sunday said. He said if you want milk and honey on your bread, you have to go into the land of giants. So, I went into that pulpit and I prayed, and the congregation, they prayed, and the first thing you know, the Holy Ghost got to moving in that place, and I got to preaching the Word of God, and pretty soon, it was just like a mill wheel got to turning, and we all went to grinding corn!"

"Bliss!" said the rector, filled with understanding.

"Bliss, my friend, indeed! There is nothing like it on earth when the spirit of God comes pouring through, and he has poured through me in fair weather and foul, for sixty-four years."

"Have there been dry spells?"

The preacher pushed his plate away and Lottie rose to clear the table. Father Tim smelled the kind of coffee he remembered from Mississippi—strong and black and brewed on the stove.

"My brother, dry is not the word. There was a time I went down like a stone in a pond and sank clear to the bottom. I lay on the bottom of that pond for two miserable years, and I thought I'd never see the light of day in my soul again."

"I can't say my current tribulation is anything like that. But in an odd way, it's something almost worse."

"What's that?" Absalom Greer asked kindly.

"When it comes to feeding his sheep, I'm afraid my sermons are about as nourishing as cardboard."

"Are you resting?"

"Resting?"

"Resting. Sometimes we get so worn out with being useful that we get useless. I'll ask you what another preacher once asked: Are you too exhausted to run and too scared to rest?"

Too scared to rest! He'd never thought of it that way. "When in God's name are you going to take a vacation?" Hoppy had asked again, only the other day. He hadn't known the truth then, but he felt he knew it now—yes, he was too scared to rest.

The old preacher's eyes were as clear as gemstones. "My brother, I would urge you to search the heart of God on this matter, for it was this very thing that sank me to the bottom of the pond."

They looked at one another with grave understanding. "I'll covet your prayers," said Father Tim.

As the two men sat by the fire and discussed the Newland wedding, Lottie Miller shyly drew up an armchair and joined them. She sat with her eyes lowered to the knitting in her lap.

"Miss Lottie," said Father Tim, "that was as fine a meal as I've enjoyed in a very long time. I thank you for the beauty and the goodness of it."

"Thank you for being here," she said with obvious effort. "Absalom and I don't have supper company often, and I'm proud for my brother to have an educated man to talk with. It's a blessing to him."

An educated man! thought Father Tim. It is Absalom Greer who is educating me!

"Take home a peck of our apples." Lottie handed him a basket of what appeared to be Rome Beauties.

"If you like 'em," said her brother, "we'll give you a bushel when you come again!"

"I'm deeply obliged. We have quite an orchard in Mitford, as you may know. Miss Sadie Baxter is the grower of what we've come to call the Baxter apple."

A strange look crossed Lottie Miller's face.

"Miss Sadie Baxter," Absalom said quietly. "I once made a proposal of marriage to that fine lady."

Rain again! he thought, as he put the tea kettle on. But every drop that fell contained the promise of another leaf, another blossom, another blade of grass in the spring. Better still, it would help make Russell Jacks's wish come true, for the buds forming on the rhododendron were as large as old-fashioned Christmas tree lights.

Though it was fairly warm, he had laid a fire, thinking that he and Dooley might have supper in the study. But when he looked in the refrigerator, he found little to inspire him.

"Scraps!" he said, as the phone rang.

"Hello, Father!" said his neighbor. "I remembered that Puny isn't there on Thursdays, and I've made a bouillabaisse with fresh shrimp and mussels from The Local. May I bring you a potful?"

Providence! he thought. And one of his favorite dishes, to boot. "Well, now . . ."

"Oh, and crab meat. I used crab meat, and I promise it isn't scorched or burned."

He laughed.

"I could just pop through the hedge," she said.

"Indeed, not. I'll ask Dooley to come for it. And I have two lemon pies here that Puny baked yesterday. I'll send one over."

"I love lemon pies!" she said.

"Of course, we'd be very glad to have you join us here. Dooley will be getting his science project done on the floor of the study, so if you wouldn't mind a bit of a muddle . . ."

"Oh, but you should see the muddle here! I'd be glad to exchange my muddle for yours!"

"All right, then, fish stew and lemon pie it is! Give us an hour, if you will."

"I will! And I look forward to it," she said.

He couldn't help thinking that his neighbor sounded like a very young girl who'd just been invited to a tea party.

While he was shaving, the phone rang.

Dooley appeared at the bathroom door, and handed him the cordless. "It's a woman," he said, and sat down on the closed lid of the toilet seat to listen.

Father Tim held the phone away from the lather on his face. "Hello?"

"Father, this is Olivia."

"Olivia! You've been much on my mind."

"I could feel it. I've strongly felt your prayers. Something odd seems to be happening."

"I'm all ears." And all lather, he thought, noting that he'd gotten a great deal of it on the phone.

"I feel I'm being released from the fear of seeking a transplant, it has just . . . I feel the fear is being lifted, somehow. You know I've pored over every possibility, every hazard, I've done my homework—it doesn't make sense to consider a transplant, even Leo finally agreed with that. I thought it was all settled, and now . . . and this is the oddest thing of all, there's a sense in which I'm afraid of losing the fear."

"Fear is one of the Enemy's deadliest strategies. Fight this fear, Olivia."

Dooley watched him.

"But how strange that I might be having . . . a change of heart," she said.

"Have you told this to the one who wants to hear it even more than I?"

"No," she said, "I just don't feel sure enough, I feel confused. Will you pray for me to have wisdom in this? I don't want to die, Father. I thought I was resigned to it, but I'm not. I'm not!"

"You know I love it when you talk like this," he said.

"Pray for me," she said, and the lightness of her voice touched him.

"You sure git a lot of calls from women," Dooley said sullenly, taking the phone. The rector noticed that the boy's cowlick was standing straight up.

"My friend, a priest gets a lot of calls from everybody. In fact, there are times when I'd like nothing better than to open the window and throw the phone in the yard!"

"I could tell 'em you ain't here."

"Aren't here."

No response.

"That, however, would be a lie, wouldn't it?"

"I reckon."

"No reckon about it. It would be a lie, and a lie is a hateful thing."

"Why?"

"For one thing, telling a lie is like eating peanuts. One leads to another. In no time at all, you've gone through a bag full."

He rinsed the razor under the tap. "Worst of all, you become a slave to something that isn't real."

"We been readin' about slaves. I wouldn't want t' be one."

"Let me say again that lying will make you a slave, for whoever tells a lie is the servant of that lie. I hope you'll hide that in your heart, son." He put his hand on the boy's shoulder. "Now, why don't we do something with that cowlick before company comes?"

Cynthia arrived, wearing a pair of blue oven mitts and carrying a large stew pot.

She set the pot on the stove and handed Dooley the book that was tucked under her arm. "This is for you. It's my latest book, and it has a boy with red hair in it."

Dooley looked at the cover. " 'is ol' Vi'let stuff's f'r babies," he said, offended.

"It most certainly is not! It's for readers up to ten years old!"

"I'm eleven," said Dooley, "but I'm grown for my age."

A likely story! thought the rector.

"Okay, do this," said Cynthia. "Read it. And if you don't like it, you never have to read another Violet book as long as you live."

"Dooley has been known to make up his mind in advance of the facts."

"I understand perfectly. I was afflicted with that very trait for years on end."

"Are we havin' hot chocolate tonight?" Dooley asked.

"We are, as soon as you've finished your science project. Double marshmallows for you. While I'm in the kitchen, why don't you poke up the fire for Miss Coppersmith?"

"Call me Cynthia," she said to Dooley.

"Would you like to see our train?" asked Dooley.

"Oh, I would! I love trains."

Was there anything his neighbor didn't love, he wondered.

"What's 'at smell?"

Father Tim took the lid off the steaming pot, and the aroma lifted from it like a fragrant cloud. "This, my friend, is a delicacy of the rarest sort. In plain language, fish stew."

"Yuck! I'm not eatin' 'at stuff."

"Thanks be to God! There'll be more for the rest of us."

"You don't know what you're missing," said their neighbor with some asperity. "There's octopus in here."

Dooley looked at the pot with alarm.

"Not to mention good old scrod."

"Scrod?"

"And fish eyes. Mmmmm. Delicious! My favorite! So tender."

"Yuck! Gag!" said Dooley, fleeing to the study.

Cynthia laughed with delight. "I hope you'll forgive an innocent lie."

"Well," he said, grinning, "but just this once."

"I done read half of that book," said Dooley, who had finished eating his fried bologna sandwich and was working on his science project. "I read it while you all was in th' kitchen."

"And what did you think?" asked Cynthia.

"Cool."

"Thank you," she said, obviously pleased.

The table had been moved from the bookcase to the fireplace, and covered with a damask cloth that had come with the rectory. Dooley had lighted a green Christmas candle and set it in a saucer and, overall, the effect was so festive that they lingered over the lemon pie and coffee.

"Again, your bouillabaisse was outstanding."

"I'm glad you liked it." She smiled, almost shyly.

"Gross!" said Dooley.

"By the way," said his neighbor, "if you catch any moles this spring, I'd truly like to have one."

The idea was so grisly that Barnabas, who was lying by the fire, caught the sense of it and growled.

A dead mole! He'd never had such an odd and unwholesome request in his life.

"I'm about t' puke," said Dooley, vanishing into the kitchen.

"I suppose you think Beatrix Potter drew her creatures from imagination, or from one fleeting glance at something scampering across the path?"

"You mean she didn't?"

"Of course not! She drew from life. Or death, if you will."

"You're by far the most unusual, that is to say, unique person I've had the privilege of meeting in years."

"You're only too kind to call me unusual. I've been called worse!"

He smiled. "You don't say!"

"Peculiar . . ."

"No!"

"Curious . . ."

"Certainly not."

"And even eccentric . . ."

"Entirely inaccurate!"

She sighed.

"There are those," he said, "who call me odd, as well, so I understand. I was without a car for nearly eight years, and took up with a maverick dog who's disciplined only by the recitation of Scripture."

"How I wish that all of us might be disciplined that way."

There, he thought. What a grand thing to say.

"How did you become an artist?"

"My mother was artistic, my father too. And I was an only child. They taught me to see. Yes, I think that's the very best way to put it. I didn't just look at a painting or a picture, I looked at every single facet of it. And a tiny flower that most people tread underfoot, well, we'd look at it very closely, and find such extraordinary detail."

" 'To see the world in a grain of sand, and heaven in a wild flower,' " he quoted from Blake.

" 'Hold infinity in the palm of your hand, and eternity in an hour,' " she replied.

"For that alone, you deserve a mole. I can't bring myself to make any promises, but I'll see what I can do."

She laughed. "I've learned not to live on any promises other than God's, actually."

"That's wisdom, indeed. The kind one usually comes by the hard way."

"It was hard, all right. I was married for many years to a man who became . . . an important public figure. I'm perhaps the least public person on earth. That's a terrible kind of division to have in a marriage. And he wanted children, he was desperate for children, and I couldn't give them to him. I learned he had at least three, all by different women."

Her eyes, which he always found so vividly blue, appeared oddly gray.

His mother's death had been the keenest pain in his memory, and his conflict with his father had refused to give him any lasting peace. Yet, compared to the grief and heartache revealed to him by others, he felt he had lived a nearly idyllic existence.

"I must tell you," she said, "that I never dreamed I'd be sitting here now—alive. And happier than I've ever been or ever dreamed of being. Successful in my work, with my own home and no mortgage, and a gracious neighbor who's gone out of his way to make me feel welcome."

"I must admit something."

"What's that?"

"I haven't gone out of my way in the least."

"Oh, rats!" she said, laughing. "I was hoping you had!" Her eyes were blue again. "But what about you? Have you ever had a broken heart?"

One thing he could say for his neighbor. She caught one off-guard. While several had asked if he'd ever been in love, no one had ever directly inquired after his heart.

"Dooley," he called to the kitchen, without taking his eyes from Cynthia, "isn't it about time for hot chocolate?"

He made the hot chocolate with milk, put three mugs on a tray, and walked back to the study, where he found his neighbor on her hands and knees with Dooley, waiting for the train to come through the tunnel.

Rain pattered on the roof, the boy looked happy and confident, there was laughter in his home, and, as he set the tray on the table, the fire crackled invitingly.

He wasn't unaware that it all combined to give him a feeling of unutterable pleasure.

A renewed running schedule had increased his energy. He had finished his Lenten homilies, and Dooley Barlowe had said "thank you" all of four times.

Evie Adams's mother had stopped putting the wet wash in the oven. And the nursing-home building committee had chosen an architect. What did it matter that the bells were once again delayed, when so many other things were chiming along nicely?

On Sunday morning, as he and Dooley were starting out for the eight o'clock service, he saw his neighbor walking briskly up the sidewalk. She was wearing a small hat and navy suit and looking, he thought, quite a picture.

"Good morning!" he called out.

"Good morning to you! Hi, Dooley! You look terrific in suspenders! I thought I'd just pop over to your early service and see what's up with the Anglicans before I go along to the Presbyterians."

"We'll be thrilled to have you."

"Thanks! It's such a beautiful morning, I thought I'd get there a bit early and enjoy the calm."

As she said that, he, for some unexplainable reason, looked down at her shapely legs, which brought her feet into view.

Seeing what must have been a bewildered look on his face, she also looked down. She was still wearing her terry cloth bedroom shoes with the embroidered violets.

"Oh, no," she said, miserably. Without another word, she turned and fled into the little house.

" 'at was funny," said Dooley.

He hated even to think it, but he could understand perfectly why she should never have been a senator's wife.

"Peedaddle!" said Emma, attempting to total the first quarter's offerings. "We didn't collect a hundred and *eighty* thousand! It was only *eighteen* thousand!"

"Decimals can be tricky," he said. "However, that's not bad, considering the recession."

"What recession?"

"I know you've been busy with your wedding plans, but do you mean to say you didn't know we're in a recession?"

"All I know is, the post office has cut back so far, Harold has to bring his own toilet tissue to work."

"No!"

"Yes, can you believe it? And with stamps gone up, to boot."

The phone rang, and Emma listened patiently to the caller before handing the receiver to Father Tim. "Evie Adams," she whispered.

"Hello, Evie. How are you?"

That, thought Emma, is not a good question to ask Evie Adams.

"Is that right? You don't say! Aha. I understand. I'm sorry. Well, then . . . I'll come by right after lunch. Yes, of course, I'll pray for you."

He hung up and shook his head. "Last week, Miss Pattie took her bath while holding an open umbrella over her head."

"No!"

"Well, there *was* a drip in the shower nozzle."

"That explains it," said Emma.

"And when Evie had a bridge luncheon yesterday, Miss Pattie made a centerpiece out of Evie's red pumps and filled them with daffodils."

"That sounds kinda cute. I wouldn't mind tryin' that."

"Well, we'll see what your new husband would think of such a thing."

"My new husband!" Emma said, almost rapturously. "Do you know he begged me last night to do it at the courthouse, he's so bashful about this big weddin'. Dottie told him no way am I wearin' that red suit with the black trim to the courthouse. We have slaved over that outfit."

"I can imagine."

"I saw your neighbor comin' out of the early service on Sunday."

"Really?"

"And I saw Hoppy Harper drive off with Olivia Davenport after the eleven o'clock."

"Is that right?"

"Is she still dyin'?"

"She is still living. Which is more than I can say for most people."

"Well, you don't have to get huffy about it," she replied.

He opened a letter containing photos of a former parishioner's new grandchild. Amazing! The infant looked precisely like Dick Satterfield, wearing a crocheted hat.

"You know what you ought to do?" Emma asked suddenly.

"I can't imagine."

"You ought to get out more. Take Dooley to a movie in Wesley. Boys like movies."

He continued to read the letter that came with the photos.

"Or," she said, peering at him over her glasses, "take your neighbor."

He swiveled in his chair to face the bookcase.

"Harold and Dottie and I saw a great movie the other night. The, ah, something, something, something was th' name. You know, everybody's talkin' about it."

"Is that right?"

"Oh, peedaddle! I can't think of th' name to save my life. You know what it is. Th' something, something, something."

"Who's in it?" he asked, tepidly.

"Oh, ah, what's his name. You know."

He did not know and did not want to know.

"Can't you think?" she asked. "It was all over TV, sayin' it was comin' to a theater near you." She furrowed her brow. "Seems like it starts with a B. Th' something, something, B-something."

"Aha."

"This just drives me crazy. Don't you know all those clips of it on TV, there's this woman with long, black hair, kind of like Loretta Young, and this man that looks like Caesar Romero but it's not. I know you know who I mean, kind of tall."

Dear God, thought Father Tim, when You made Emma Garrett, You broke the mold.

"Well, anyway," she said, "you ought to go see it. It's at th' Avon over in Wesley. It's that new place over around the Farmer's Market. You know. You make a turn somewhere around there, I can't remember if it's left or right, and then there's a tire store maybe on the corner.

"Oh no, I think that's a launderette. Well, anyway, you can't make a U-turn there, so I'd go on down to the post office and turn around in their parking lot—that's what Harold does.

"I think it's the post office—it might be the library—and then in a block or two, you're there. Can't miss it."

Is there no balm in Gilead? he wondered.

He still wasn't sleeping soundly. Recently, he not only had trouble falling asleep, but staying asleep. In the night watches, as the psalmist had called them, he found himself wondering again and again about Andrew Gregory and the hollow table legs Rodney had mentioned and the newspaper clipping he'd seen at the Oxford.

He was relieved to discover that he couldn't imagine Andrew doing such a thing as trafficking in stolen goods, jewels or otherwise. Andrew Gregory breaking into the church and hiding jewels in a closet he very likely knew nothing about? Andrew Gregory in his beautiful suits and cashmere jackets, stumbling around in the dark like a common thief? No. It wouldn't work. Never! Andrew Gregory could not possibly be involved, thanks be to God.

After such thoughts, which he went over again and again, he would drift off to sleep, only to awaken with fresh concerns.

While the stolen jewels mentioned in the clipping had been in necklaces and such, couldn't those same jewels have been taken from their mountings, to prevent a link to the museum theft? And could it be that those very jewels were put into the leg of an English farm table, perhaps, and shipped to Andrew in one of those vast containers he received twice a year? And if the authorities had linked the thefts to antique dealers, wouldn't he have removed the jewels from his own premises at once? And possibly into a church, where no one would ever think of looking?

For God is not the author of confusion, but of peace, he reminded himself more than once, as Paul had reminded Corinth. Confusion was ungodly, the hour was ungodly, and Barnabas had lately begun to snore in an alternate bass and baritone.

He would drift off to sleep again, only to wake and look at the clock. Andrew Gregory, the very soul of graciousness, a lover of rare books—of Wordsworth, for heaven's sake? No, not Andrew. Never.

On Saturday, after Dooley went to Meadowgate for the weekend, he turned off the telephone and lay down on the study sofa where he slept for ten hours under the crocheted afghan Winnie had given him for Christmas. He was awakened by barking in the garage and was bewildered to see that it was nighttime.

After taking Barnabas to the hedge and feeding him, he lay down again in the study, exhausted, and waited for the eleven o'clock news.

He should have visited Russell Jacks today, gone to see Olivia, bathed Barnabas, cleaned up the garage, vacuumed his car, shined his shoes, bundled up the newspapers for recycling. How very odd, he thought, to have slept through an entire day, something he couldn't remember ever doing before. He felt strangely disoriented and feebly guilty, and for a moment could not remember the crux of his sermon for tomorrow.

At a quarter of eleven, the phone rang.

"Father," said Hoppy Harper, "Olivia is in trouble."

At Olivia's home on Lilac Road, Hoppy opened the door. "You're not going to like this," he said.

"What won't I like?"

"The way she looks. You'll be . . ."

"Shocked?"

"Very likely."

"I've been shocked before, my friend."

Hoppy ran his fingers through his disheveled hair. "I've talked to Leo Baldwin. Last week, I took a risk and put her on the national waiting list. She doesn't know I did that."

"Good! The nick of time," he said, observing his friend's anguished look. As they walked down the hall, he laid his hand on Hoppy's shoulder. "Whatever we do, let's remember who's in control here."

Olivia's housekeeper, Mrs. Kershaw, stood outside the bedroom door, wiping her red eyes with a handkerchief and lustily blowing her nose.

As they went into Olivia's bedroom, he saw only a large, high-ceilinged room with softly colored walls and a deep carpet. Silk draperies began at the ceiling and cascaded to the floor. Lamps glowed here and there in the room, creating pools of warm light. Even in view of the circumstances, he sensed that he'd stepped into a treasury of calm and peace.

"Hello . . . Father," a voice said breathlessly. He turned and saw Olivia in a silk dressing gown, sitting in a chair. Tears sprang at once to his eyes, and he was glad for the dimness of the light. For all his priestly experience with sorrow and with shock, nothing had prepared him for this.

"Father . . . ," she said, lifting her hand slightly from her lap. She was so swollen that he wouldn't have recognized her. And her alabaster skin, always such a stunning foil for her violet eyes, was an alarming shade of yellow. He called upon every professional strategy he knew to appear composed.

"Olivia," he said, simply, taking her hand. He didn't recognize his own voice.

"Shock . . . ing," she said, gasping for the breath to say it.

He looked at her feet, which were propped on a footstool. They were more than twice their normal size. He couldn't help but notice that a pair of bedroom slippers beside the footstool looked foolishly small.

"It's the congestion," Hoppy said. "It's backing up from around her heart and enlarging the liver. I'm putting her in intensive care for a couple of weeks, using some IV drugs to move the fluid around. Mrs. Kershaw, have you packed her things?"

Mrs. Kershaw was now weeping openly, without the formality of a handkerchief. She picked up the blue suitcase standing by the bedroom door and carried it into the foyer.

Olivia's desperate struggle for breath created the most agonizing sound the rector had heard since his mother's harsh illness.

He dropped to his knees by her feet, and taking her hands in his, began to pray.

"Socks," Hoppy said. "Is there a pair of socks she can wear?"

"Socks?" asked Mrs. Kershaw with dignity. "Miss Olivia does not wear socks!"

Mrs. Kershaw tenderly wrapped her mistress's feet in scarves, and took a dark mink coat from the closet, as insulation against the night air.

Hoppy bent over and put one arm behind Olivia's shoulders and another under her knees. Carefully, he picked her up from the chair. "She can't lie down in the ambulance because of her breathing, and there's nothing they can do for her. We'll take her in my car."

It was precisely twelve midnight when the doors swung open to the emergency hall, and Hoppy carried his patient inside.

The doctor came swiftly along the corridor, carrying a woman wrapped in scarves and fur, whose dark, unbound hair swept over his arm like a mantilla.

"Get the drips started," he said to a nurse, who was wheeling a stretcher toward them. "Oxygen. EKG. The works."

As he laid her on the stretcher with pillows under her head, Olivia looked at the rector. She was fighting for air like a fish stranded on the beach. "Philipp . . . ians four . . . thirteen, for . . . Pete's sake," she said, and smiled.

"Hook her up," said the doctor.

"How did she get so . . . stricken?" the rector asked, as they stood outside Olivia's room in the Intensive Care Unit. "I knew she wasn't feeling her best, but she assured me it was nothing. I saw her only days ago."

"It flares up without warning, and she couldn't face that it was happening. She's been well-compensated for several months, and she let herself believe . . . the unbelievable. When the relapse came, she let it go too long. Mrs. Kershaw was under strict orders not to call me."

"What next?"

"God knows. She could arrest at any time."

"What does that mean exactly?"

"She could die." Hoppy snapped his fingers. "Just like that."

"I see."

"Pray for me when I tell her I've put her on the list."

"That prayer may already be answered. She's been considering that, but didn't want you to know until she came to a firm decision. Where do we go from here?"

"I'll keep her a couple of weeks, at least, then we can let her go home . . . if all goes well."

"It will go well," Father Tim said, with unusual conviction.

Hoppy took off his glasses and rubbed his eyes. "You need to know that a third of the patients on the waiting list will die while waiting."

"That means," the rector replied, evenly, "that two-thirds of them will not die while waiting."

Hoppy looked at him for a long moment. "You're a good guy," he said.

When he arrived home at two o'clock, after looking in on Russell Jacks, he hurried to Dooley's room to see if he was sleeping soundly, then remembered the boy was at Meadowgate.

He sat on the side of his bed in a daze until nearly two-thirty, when he finally undressed and lay down, taking care to set the alarm for five.

He was surprised and dismayed that he did something he hadn't done since childhood:

He wept until he fell asleep.

CHAPTER FIFTEEN

The Finest Sermon

On Sunday morning, he made entries in the loose-leaf book provided for prayers of the people. Under prayers for the sick, he wrote the names of Olivia Davenport and Russell Jacks, Miss Sadie who had a sore throat, Rebecca Jane who had the colic, Harold Newland who had cut his hand on a saw blade, the Baptist kindergarten who was having a measles epidemic, and Dooley Barlowe who had come home from Meadowgate this morning with a fever.

Lord, he had prayed on the way to the church at seven o'clock, keep that boy in bed and out of mischief.

While he ordinarily trained his eyes on Miss Sadie's painting at the rear of the nave, he allowed himself a quick search of the congregation. Hal, with his pipe sticking out of his jacket pocket. Emma in a leopard-skin hat. Louella with Esther Bolick. And yes, there was his neighbor, sitting on the gospel side, looking happy and expectant.

As he offered the prayer before the sermon, he heard a harsh, grating noise somewhere behind him in the sanctuary. When the prayer ended, he saw the entire congregation sitting with open mouths and astonished faces, gazing toward the ceiling.

It was, perhaps, his dysfunctional sleep pattern that caused such an odd storm of feeling. He turned around with a pounding heart, to see that the attic stairs had been let down and that someone in bare feet was descending.

He heard a single intake of breath from the congregation, a communal gasp. As the man reached the floor and stood beside the altar, he turned and gazed out at them.

He was tall and very thin, with a reddish beard and shoulder-length hair. His clothing fit loosely, as if it had been bought for someone else.

Yet, the single most remarkable thing about the incident, the rector would later say, wasn't the circumstances of the man's sudden appearance, but the unmistakable radiance of his face.

Hal Owen stood frozen by his pew on the epistle side.

"I have a confession to make to you," the man said to the congregation in a voice so clear, it seemed to lift weightlessly toward the rafters. He looked at the rector, "If you'd give me the privilege, Father."

As Hal Owen looked to the pulpit, Father Tim raised his hand. Let him speak, the signal said.

The man walked out in front of the communion rail and stood on the steps. "My name," he said, "is George Gaynor. For the last several months, your church has been my home—and my prison. You see, I've been living behind the death bell in your attic."

There was a perfect silence in the nave.

"Until recently, this was profoundly symbolic of my life, for it was, in fact . . . a life of death.

"When I was a kid, I went to a church like this. An Episcopal church in Vermont where my uncle was the rector. I even thought about becoming a priest, but I learned the money was terrible. And, you see, I liked money. My father and mother liked money.

"We gave a lot of it to the church. We added a wing, we put on a shake roof, we gave the rector a Cadillac.

"It took awhile to figure out what my uncle and my father were doing. My father would give thousands to the church and write it off, my uncle would keep a percentage and put the remainder in my father's Swiss bank account. Six hundred thousand dollars flowed through the alms basin into my uncle's cassock.

"When I was twelve, I began carrying on the family tradition.

"The first thing I stole was a skateboard. Later, I stole a car, and I had no regrets. My father knew everybody from the police chief to the governor. I was covered, right down the line.

"I went to the university and did pretty well. For me, getting knowledge was like getting money, getting things. It made me strong, it made me powerful. I got a Ph.D. in economics, and when I was thirty-three, I had tenure at one of the best colleges in the country.

"Then, I was in a plane crash. It was a small plane that belonged to a friend. I lay in the wreckage with the pilot who was killed instantly, and my mother and father, who would die . . . hours later. I was pinned in the cockpit in freezing temperatures for three days, unable to move."

George Gaynor paused and cleared his throat. He waited for a long moment before he continued.

"Both legs were broken, my skull was fractured, the radio was demolished. Maybe you can guess what I did—I made a deal with God.

"Get me out of here, I said, and I'll clean up my act, I'll make up for what my father, my uncle, all of us, had done.

"Last summer, a friend of mine, an antique dealer, had too much to drink. He took me to his warehouse and pulled an eighteenth-century table out of the corner, and unscrewed one of its legs."

Father Tim's heart pounded dully. He could feel it beating in his temples.

"What he pulled out of that table leg was roughly two and a half million dollars' worth of rare gems, which were stolen from a museum in England, in the Berkshires.

"I'd just gotten a divorce after two years of marriage, and I'd forgotten any deal I'd made with God in the cockpit of that Cessna.

"The bottom line was that nothing mattered to me anymore."

George Gaynor sat down on the top step leading to the communion rail. He might have been talking to a few intimate friends in his home.

"I discovered that thinking about the jewels mattered a great deal. I was consumed with the thought of having them, and more like them.

"The British authorities had gotten wind of the stuff going out of England in shipments of antiques, and my friend couldn't fence the jewels because of the FBI.

"One night, I emptied a ninety-dollar bottle of cognac into him. He told me he had hidden the jewels in one of his antique cars. I stole his keys and went to his warehouse with a hex-head wrench. I lay down under a 1937 Packard and removed the oil pan, and took the jewels home in a bag.

"I packed a few things, then I walked out on the street and stole a car. I changed the tag, and started driving. I headed south."

He paused and looked down. He looked down for a long time. A child whimpered in the back row.

He stood again, his hands in the pockets of the loose, brown trousers. "I hadn't spoken to God in years. To tell the truth, I'd never really spoken to God but once in my life. Yet, I remembered some of the language from the prayer book.

" 'Bless the Lord who forgiveth all our sins. His mercy endureth forever.' That's what came to me as I drove. I pulled off the road at a rest stop and put my head down on the steering wheel and prayed for mercy and forgiveness.

"I'd like to tell you that a great peace came over me, but I can't tell you that. I just started the car and drove on.

"There was no peace, but there was direction. I began to have a sense of where I was going, like I was attached to a fishing line, and somebody at the other end was reeling me in.

"I stopped and bought a box of canned goods and crackers . . . candy bars, Gatorade, beef jerky, so I wouldn't have to stop so often to eat and risk being seen.

"One morning about two, I hit the Blue Ridge Parkway and stayed on it until I saw an exit sign that said Mitford. I took the exit, and drove straight up Main Street, and saw this church."

His voice broke.

"I felt I'd . . . come home. I had never felt that before in my life. I couldn't have resisted the pull God put on me, even if I'd tried. I broke the side door lock, Father."

The rector nodded.

George wiped his eyes with the sleeve of his shirt.

"I brought my things in . . . a change of clothes, a flashlight, a blanket, and my box from 7-Eleven. Then I parked the car several blocks away and removed the tag. No one was on the street. I walked back here and started looking for . . . a place to rest, to hide for a few days."

George Gaynor moved to the lectern, and gestured toward the attic stairs. "I've got to tell you, that's a strange place to put stairs."

Welcoming the relief, the congregation laughed. The placement of the stairs had been a parish joke for years.

"That's how I came to live behind the death bell, on the platform where it's mounted. I didn't have any idea why I was in this particular place, as if I'd been ordered to come. But just before Thanksgiving, I found out.

"I kept my things behind the bell, where they couldn't be seen. But I put the jewels in an urn in your hall closet. The closet looked unused, I figured nobody went in there, and I didn't want them on me, in case I was discovered.

"During the day, I lived in the loft over the parish hall. I exercised, sat in the sun by the windows—I even learned a few hymns, to keep my mind occupied. On Sunday, I could hear every word and every note very clearly, as if we were all sitting in the same room.

"At night, I roamed downstairs, used the toilet, looked in the refrigerator, found the food supplies in the basement. And I always wore gloves. Just in case.

"One day in December, my shoes fell off the platform and landed at the bottom of the bell tower." Grinning, he looked at his feet, then at the congregation. "Every time a box came in for the rummage sale, I was downstairs with my flashlight. But I've yet to find a pair of size elevens."

A murmur of laughter ran through the congregation. Hal Owen continued to stand by his pew, watching, cautious.

"One afternoon, I was sitting in the loft, desperate beyond anything I'd ever known. It made no sense to be here when I could have been in France or South America. But I couldn't leave this place. I was powerless to leave.

"I heard the front door open, and in a few minutes, a man yelled, 'Are you up there?'

"I was paralyzed with fear. This is it, I thought. Then, the call came again. But this time, I knew the question wasn't directed to me. It was directed to God.

"There was something in the voice that I recognized—the same desperation of my own soul. I told you the sound from down here carries up there, and I heard you, Father, speak to that man.

"You said the question isn't whether He's up there, but whether He's down here."

Father Tim nodded.

"He told you that he couldn't believe, that he felt nothing. You said it isn't a matter of feeling, it's a matter of faith. Finally, you prayed a simple prayer together."

Remembering, the rector crossed himself. A stir ran through the congregation, a certain hum of excitement, of wonder.

"That was a real two-for-one deal, Father, because I prayed that prayer with you. You threw out the line for one, and God reeled in two."

The congregation broke into spontaneous applause. The rector noticed that Cynthia Coppersmith was letting her tears fall without shame.

George Gaynor came down the altar steps and walked into the aisle. "After I prayed that prayer with two people I had never seen, to a God I didn't know, I came down, Father, and stole your Bible."

He looked plaintively at the rector, who smiled at him, and nodded.

"As I read during the next few weeks, I began to find the most amazing peace. Even more amazing was the intimacy I was finding with God—one-on-one, moment by moment."

The man from the attic moved to the first pew on the gospel side and leaned on the arm rest.

"I come to you this morning, urging you to discover that intimacy, if you have not.

"I also come to thank you for your hospitality, and to say to whoever made that orange cake—that was the finest cake I ever ate in my life."

Esther Bolick flushed beet red and put her prayer book in front of her face, as every head in the congregation turned to look where she sat in the third row from the organ.

"Father," said George Gaynor, "thank you for calling someone to take me in."

The rector looked at his senior warden. "Hal, go over to First Baptist and get Rodney Underwood." Then he looked at his congregation.

"Let us stand, and affirm our faith," he said, "with the reading of the Nicene creed."

After the confession of sin, Father Tim saw Hal, Rodney, and two officers walk in and wait at the rear of the nave. The rector knew his senior warden would not come forward with the police until the signal was given. How grand to have a man like Hal Owen by his side, he thought. Harry Nelson would have had the entire force storming the aisles with cocked revolvers.

During the final hymn, he went to George Gaynor, who was sitting in the front pew, and took his hand. Together, they walked down the aisle behind the crucifix, toward the rear of the church.

Ron Malcolm, head of the nursing-home building committee, stepped out of the pew in his sock feet and handed George Gaynor his shoes.

A look passed between the two men as George took the loafers. He put them on without a word. They appeared to fit perfectly.

At the rear of the nave, the rector turned and proclaimed: "Go in peace, to love and serve the Lord!"

"Thanks be to God!" chorused his amazed congregation.

While Father Tim, Hal Owen, and one of the officers drove George Gaynor to the Mitford jail, Rodney and another officer collected his things from the bell tower, including a Gatorade jug containing the jewels.

J.C. Hogan, who heard the news from a breathless Lord's Chapel member at Lew Boyd's Esso, rushed to the church, but found it was already locked. He arrived at the jail as lunch was being served.

"Is that him?" J.C. asked Joe Joe Guthrie. J.C. had one eye on the prisoner, who was sitting in a cell with Father Tim, and one eye on the rolling cart that contained Sunday lunch.

"That's him, all right."

"Fried chicken?" asked J.C.

"Fried eggplant," said Joe Joe.

J.C. took out his handkerchief and wiped his face. "I was goin' to see if you had extras today, but I just got over it."

"Eggplant's all right if you soak it," said Joe Joe, who was leaning against the wall in a straight-back chair the department had bought at a library yard sale.

"I hear this guy's been hidin' in the church attic over at Lord's Chapel."

"Had a big job in economics. Turned hisself in during church service, preached 'em a good sermon."

"What's th' deal?" asked J.C. "I hear he stole some jewels worth th' moon."

"Four or five million is what I hear," said Joe Joe, taking a meal off the cart as it passed. He took the plate with both hands, held it under his nose and smelled it, then looked it over carefully. "Checkin' t' see if there's any onions in this deal. I'm goin' out tonight."

"Who with?" asked J.C.

"That's for me t' know and you t' find out, buddy."

Rodney came down the hall, adjusting his holster. "J.C., how can I he'p you?"

"I'd like to talk to your prisoner, if it's all right with you."

"Well, it ain't all right with me, number one. Number two, this is a federal offense, and he's not in my jurisdiction. Go talk t' somebody who was at Lord's Chapel this mornin', that's a whopper of a story right there."

"Maybe I'll just wait for the father."

"I wouldn't do that if I was you," said Rodney, without explanation. "If I was you, I'd talk to Ron Malcolm. He gave th' prisoner th' shoes off his own feet. That's a human-interest angle."

"This town is full of human-interest angles. I'm lookin' for hard news," said J.C., who turned on his heel and left, slamming the door.

"I'd like to give 'im some hard news," said Joe Joe.

He was sitting with the prisoner in a small cell that was spotlessly clean, containing a bed, a chair, a floor lamp, a sink, a toilet, a hooked rug, and a table with an orderly stack of *Southern Living* magazines.

"I didn't know you'd found the jewels in the urn. I kept moving them around, just in case. But the day you came up to the attic, I could sense trouble.

"I'd been sitting in the loft, reading your Bible, when I heard you pull the stairs down. I was scrambling for my place behind the bell, and the wrapper dropped out of my pocket. When I got to the door of the tower, I turned and looked back, and there was the wrapper in the middle of the floor. It looked as big as a football."

"I like Almond Joy, myself," the rector said, agreeably.

"A lot of the time up there, I was starved for a decent meal. The box from 7-Eleven emptied fast, then I found the canned stuff in the basement. All those stewed tomatoes got to me after awhile. Then, around Christmas, your coffee hour picked up for about a month. I remember coming down one Saturday night and sliding the top layer of pimento cheese sandwiches right off the platter, clean as a whistle.

"For Thanksgiving, I ate a jar of pickles and a can of stewed okra. For dessert, I mixed a pint of half-and-half with Sweet 'n Low. I came down from your attic with a new heart and a cast iron stomach."

The rector laughed. "A priceless combination in today's world."

"I have a great feeling for Lord's Chapel. Strange as it seems, it was a true home to me, in many ways. Since I could hear what went on in the church and parish hall through the heating vents, I began to feel close to the people. It was like family."

"The Holy Spirit moved and worked through you in a wonderful way this morning. It was the finest sermon He's delivered to Lord's Chapel in a long time."

"Will I see you tomorrow?"

"Tomorrow and the next day and the next. For as long as you're with us."

"I'd like to be baptized."

He embraced the man from the attic. "Consider it done," he said.

"Where you been at?" A glowering Dooley Barlowe was sitting on the study sofa, wrapped in a blanket.

"At the jail."

" 'is ol' phone's rang off th' hook. I like to th'owed it out th' window."

"Help yourself."

"I ain't had a bite t' eat."

"Feed a cold, starve a fever is what I've been told."

" 'at's easy f'r you t' say."

He took off his jacket and sat on the sofa. Barnabas sprawled at his feet. "Who called?"

"Y'r doc."

"What did he want?"

"Said come up there when you can."

"Who else?"

"Walter."

"And?"

"Said call 'im up tonight after some ol' TV show."

"*60 Minutes.* What else?"

"Y'r neighbor. Cynthia."

"What did she say?"

"Call 'er up. Ol' cat's stuck in th' basement."

Come here. Go there. Do this, do that.

"What do you want to eat?"

"Baloney."

"Baloney, yourself," said Father Tim, getting up from the sofa.

On Monday, he made breakfast, got Dooley off to school with a bag lunch and thirty-five cents for juice, and greeted Puny, who appeared to be all smiles. He gave her a quick recap of Sunday's great drama, and, since he had seen nearly all of the hospital patients on the previous afternoon, he walked quickly toward the office with Barnabas on his red leash.

At the Oxford Antique shop, Andrew Gregory was just opening up.

"Andrew, my friend!" said the rector, with unmistakable joy. He proceeded to give the antique dealer a great slapping on the back and a vigorous, interminable handshake. "I can't tell you how glad I am to see you! You will never, ever know how glad."

What a homecoming! thought a pleased Andrew, as the welcome fragrance of his shop greeted him at the door.

He had seldom been happier to lock up the office.

The phone hadn't stopped ringing the livelong day. J.C. Hogan had dropped by twice, and the Associated Press had called after a parishioner had given the story to the editor of the Wesley *Weekly*. The Wesley TV station had prowled around the village all day, asked him to open the church for tape footage, and trained glaring lights on the Mortlake tapestry.

Puny had called to say the sink had stopped up and Dooley was "ill as a hornet."

He had visited George at the jail, Olivia and Russell at the hospital, and feebly attempted to work on his sermon.

For a change in their routine, he and Barnabas crossed the street and walked past Mitford Blossoms in the deepening gloom. As they approached the corner, the street lights came on. Easily an hour early, he thought, looking at the overcast sky.

Suddenly, Barnabas growled viciously and lunged at a car that had slowed down in the lane next to them. It was the only car on the street, and they were the only pedestrians.

Before he could take it all in, someone opened the back door of the car and grabbed Barnabas by his collar, yanking the leash from his hand. "That'll learn you to steal our dog, Preacher Man!"

An arm shot through an open window and struck him in the

chest. He reeled away as Barnabas was dragged into the back seat and muzzled.

He grabbed for the door handle, but he was shoved again, so violently that he crashed against the lamppost and fell to the sidewalk.

"VAT," he read on the license plate, as the car roared away. He tried to rise, but the breath had been knocked from him.

CHAPTER SIXTEEN

A Sure Reward

The rector nodded to the police chief, who hitched up his holster belt and took a deep breath. "I present George Gaynor," he said in a loud voice, "to receive the sacrament of baptism."

"Do you desire to be baptized?" the rector asked the freshly shaven prisoner.

"I do."

"Do you renounce Satan and all the spiritual forces of wickedness that rebel against God?"

"I renounce them."

"Do you renounce the evil powers of this world which corrupt and destroy the creatures of God?"

"I renounce them."

"Do you renounce all sinful desires that draw you from the love of God?"

"I renounce them."

"Do you turn to Jesus Christ and accept Him as your Savior?"

"I do."

"Do you put your whole trust in His grace and love?"

"I do."

"Do you promise to follow and obey Him as your Lord?"

"I do."

Father Tim turned to the police chief, Joe Joe Guthrie, and two other officers. "Will you who witness these vows do all in your power to support this person in his life in Christ?"

"We will!"

After the thanksgiving over the water, George dropped to his knees on a braided rug.

Father Tim cupped his left hand and filled it with water from a pitcher. "George Gaynor," he said, spilling the water over the prisoner's head, "I baptize you in the name of the Father, and of the Son, and of the Holy Spirit. Amen."

"Amen!" chorused the Mitford police force.

Following the prayer, the rector came to the part of the service that, in all his years in the priesthood, had never failed to move him deeply.

Placing one hand on the prisoner's head, and, with the other, marking his forehead with the sign of the cross, he said, "George Gaynor, you are sealed by the Holy Spirit in baptism and marked as Christ's own forever. Amen."

Marked! Forever. He felt the certainty of it.

After baptism, the prisoner received the Eucharist. Then, he received Esther Bolick's cake.

"Looky here," said Rodney. "Miz Bolick done brought you her knockdown, drag-out cake."

Joe Joe Guthrie stepped forward with a box from the Collar Button. "Me 'n the boys went in and got you a shirt and a pair of pants. Fifty percent off. We don't want any thanks."

Another officer pulled a pair of socks from his pants pocket. "Here," he said, shyly, "they're not new, but my wife washed 'em, seein' as you needed 'em."

George stood in the middle of floor, speechless, tears splashing down his cheeks.

"This feller," Rodney said to the rector, "is bad to bawl. He's about had me doin' it a time or two."

"The Holy Spirit tenderizes the heart."

"You know I don't want to mess with the work of the Holy Spirit," said Rodney, "but we ought to get this cake cut."

Before he left the jail, he placed a cross on a silver chain around the new communicant's neck.

"I'm sorry about your dog," said George.

My dog! He'd been able to forget this sorrow during the baptism service. He instantly felt the pain around his heart. "Pray for me," he said simply.

Rodney met him in the hallway. "We're doin' everything we can. You cain't lose a black dog th' size of a Buick like you could one of them little bitty Chihuahuas. He'll turn up, and you can mark my word."

Barnabas missing! It was unthinkable. He still couldn't believe it. It was a fact that simply would not take hold, except at night, when the foot of his bed felt empty as a tomb.

In recent months, it seemed that a lot of important things had ended up missing. But there was one comfort he clung to: Everything that had ended up missing—jewels, Bible, Dooley—all had come back, all had been restored. It was this thought, and this alone, that kept him going.

Joe Joe Guthrie ran ahead of him to open the door.

"We're real sorry to hear about your dog, Father."

"I appreciate that, Joe Joe."

"My grandmother thinks th' world of you."

"And I think the world of the mayor. She's the finest."

"Yes, sir," said Joe Joe, grinning.

J.C. Hogan caught up with him as he crossed the street at the Collar Button. "Find out anything?" J.C. asked. The editor's briefcase came open suddenly, spilling papers onto the sidewalk.

"The prisoner has been baptized," he said, kneeling down to help pick up the jumble of papers.

J.C. stuffed the papers back in the case and took out his handkerchief. "I cain't go on that," he said, wiping his face. "I got to have more."

The two men walked on. "The only more is that Esther Bolick brought him a marmalade cake and the men on the force gave him a new shirt and pants."

"What else?" said J.C., keeping to the rector's brisk pace.

"Not another crumb or scrap that I can think of."

"I'd like to get out of th' newspaper business," snapped J.C.

They walked on in silence. "What about your dog?" J.C. asked, with sudden enthusiasm. "You want me to run a picture?"

"Excellent! Thank you for thinking of it, my friend."

"Get a picture up to the office today and I'll run it Monday."

He realized he didn't have a picture. He hadn't owned a camera in years.

"I don't have a picture. Could you describe him, instead? You know, you could create a wonderful description of Barnabas. You're a fine writer when you put your mind to it."

"My mind is currently elsewhere," J.C. said, huffily, as he left Father Tim and crossed the street.

There, thought the rector, goes a man who's standing in the need of prayer.

"And what are you still doing here, young lady?" he asked Puny when he came home at five o'clock.

"Fluffin' up this place," she said, grinning. "I never saw a place to need so much fluffin' up."

"What exactly do you call fluffing?"

"Air th' pillows, wash th' mattress covers, soak your seeds . . ."

"Soak my seeds?"

"If you want tomatoes th' size of dinner plates, like you been sayin', you have to soak th' seeds an' then plant 'em in indoor pots."

"Is that right?"

"I hope you don't think you just set them little seeds out in th' ground to make it on their own."

"I never thought about it. I never raised tomatoes before."

"I've raised bushels!" she said happily.

The rector opened the refrigerator. "What's this?"

"Cinnamon chicken salad, out of that diabetes book. I tasted it, and it's delicious, has almonds in it, and grapes."

"What would I do without you, I wonder?"

She giggled. "I don't wonder. I know!"

He shut the door. "Do I detect something . . . different about you? Anything like . . . oh, maybe there's been a parade by here recently?"

"Ha!" she said, blushing.

He raised his eyebrows and smiled. "Well, well."

"Well, well, yourself!"

"I don't suppose you'd care to tell me what's going on?" he asked casually, washing off a carrot at the sink.

"Not meanin' any disrespect," she said, "but that's for me t' know and you t' find out."

"What can I do?" asked Cynthia, who was standing on the other side of the screen door. "I know there must be something I can do."

"About . . . ?"

"Why, about Barnabas, of course! Are you putting it in the paper?"

"J.C. said he would run a picture, but I don't have a picture."

"Why, you most certainly do!" she said, offended. "I gave you one in that pie plate, remember?"

Of course! A watercolor of Barnabas that was so realistic, so natural, that it might have barked.

"Cynthia, you are . . . ," he searched for a word, "terrific."

Her eyes seemed very blue as she laughed. "Whenever possible, I like to work ahead of the need," she said.

"I need me some shoes," said Dooley, coming in the door and slamming his books on the kitchen counter.

He looked up from the counter, where he was working on his sermon. "That," he said evenly, "was no way to speak to me. At any time or in any place."

Dooley met his gaze with defiance. "I still need me some damn shoes."

He felt the wrenching impact of Dooley's hostility, and it was a feeling he did not like. Boys, unfortunately, did not come with owner's manuals, and to fairly address the issues this particular boy raised would be equal to rebuilding the motor of his Buick. In fact, though he had never done more than raise the hood and stare impotently underneath, he believed he could more easily rebuild a motor than instill respect and obedience in Dooley Barlowe.

"Dooley," he said, "there's something in your voice that makes me feel . . . indifferent to your need. Perhaps you could go out and come in again."

Dooley stared at him blankly. In a family of five children, with no money and no stable center, there were a lot of ways to get attention, hostility being only one of them. That this strategy would not work here was a point he must drive home, at all costs.

There was a cold silence.

"Actually, I do recommend that very thing. Why don't you go out the door and come in again? You might say something like, 'Hello' or, 'What's up?' Anything civil.

"Then you might like to come and tell me all about the shoes you need. You can be assured," he said, looking into the boy's eyes, "that I will listen intently."

Father Tim could feel the undercurrent in Dooley's hesitation. He knew he was considering what he was hearing. And he knew he was also considering the alternative.

Dooley stepped back and cursed with such vehemence that the rector stared in disbelief. Then the boy ran up the stairs and slammed his bedroom door.

Good Lord! He felt his heart seized with a sudden, thundering fury. He forced himself to sit where he was, until the feeling passed.

He shut his sermon notebook, removed his glasses, and rubbed his eyes. There was Dooley's own notebook which had skidded across the counter. He saw that the boy had written his name many times on the cover, over and over. Trying to make himself real, thought the rector.

He picked up the notebook and held it next to his own. Two notebooks. Two people trying to make sense out of life.

An odd thought occurred to him. The boy had lived here for weeks without uttering such words. Given his background, wasn't that, after all, an extraordinary accomplishment?

He spoke aloud to himself: "Think on the accomplishment, Timothy. Then act on what just happened."

A Scripture from the Psalms came to him: "I will instruct you and teach you in the way which you shall go. I will guide you with my eye."

He felt the peace of that promise, and went upstairs.

He knocked, but there was no answer. "Dooley?"

Silence. Of course, there would be silence.

He opened the door.

Dooley sat on the side of the bed, sobbing. His whole body seemed given to grief, frustration, and rage.

My heart, thought the rector, feeling it wrench with sorrow. I have never had so many sensations of the heart in one short span of time.

He sat down beside Dooley Barlowe and held him. He held him tightly, as if to say, Hang on, hang on. I won't let go.

"I want me some onions, don't you?" asked Dooley, whose face, though red from weeping, was relieved. It was among the few times the rector had seen Dooley looking only eleven years old.

The hamburgers sizzled in the black iron skillet. "Indeed, I do. Mayonnaise?"

"Mayonnaise, ketchup, mustard, relish, pickles, th' works."

"The works, is it?" He didn't know when he'd heard the boy call for the works on anything. "Somebody needs to tell you, by the way, that crying is a good thing. I hope you will never let anyone convince you otherwise." He moved to the stove to turn over the hamburgers.

Dooley said nothing, but the rector knew he was listening.

"Gives you a fresh start, you might say. And speaking of fresh starts, I want you to know that I appreciate and accept your apology. That apology gives you and me a fresh start."

Dooley was setting plates and silverware on the counter. "D' you cry?"

"Sometimes."

"Did you cry about y'r ol' dog gittin' stole?"

"Not yet, but I've felt like it."

"I did. I cried about 'at ol' dog. I miss 'at ol' dog, even if he has got bad breath. I don't care if 'e's got bad breath. It don't matter none t' me, I wish 'e'd come back, I'd give 'im a big ol' bone or . . . or my hamburger, even."

The rector swallowed hard.

"Can I ask you somethin' else?"

"Ask away."

"If you're a preacher, how can you git away with lyin'?"

"Well, first of all, no one ever really gets away with lying, preacher or no preacher. What have I lied about?"

"About me an' Goosedown Owen. You said we was goin' out there ever' month, and Goosedown could be kind of like mine if I wouldn't git in fights. You an' me ain't bin out there any, and I jis' bin one time. So, that was a dern lie."

It was and it wasn't. Circumstances alter cases, his Uncle Chester always said.

"When I told you that, I meant it sincerely. Then, for weeks on end, the weather was bad on Saturday, and there was no use to go to the country to sit around in the house. Then Christmas came, and there was the baptizing, and then the Owens had company, and . . . well, and you ran away. So, you see, circumstances alter cases."

Dooley furrowed his brow. He was wearing a red shirt and clean blue jeans, and his cowlick was lying down. "It seemed like a lie."

"I understand. And so I won't make any more promises. I'll just take you when I can. How's that?"

"This weekend?"

"If we can get your grandfather settled in with his nurse, that could be. Let me look at my calendar. But right now, let's look at some hamburgers."

"Cool," said Dooley, as the rector set the hot platter on the counter.

"I've got to take Dooley out to the Shoe Barn at four o'clock." He was putting the change from his pockets into the blue thanks offering box.

"Now what?" demanded Emma. "You just got him shoes."

"Boys are hard on shoes."

"What kind are you gettin'?"

"Pumps," said the rector, feeling foolish.

"Pumps!"

"That's what they're wearing these days."

"Pumps?" Emma was astounded.

"Yes, and I'm thinking of getting a pair for myself while I'm at it." There. It was done. Hadn't the bishop said he should do something special for himself?

"I'm speechless," said Emma.

Alleluia, thought the rector.

"You know, you don't look so good to me. Are you takin' your medication?"

"I have to get it refilled. I'll do that today."

"Are you, ah, seein' much of your neighbor?"

He could hardly believe what came out of his mouth. "Not nearly enough!" Where had such a remark come from? His words seemed to hang frozen in the air. He swiveled to the bookcase, feeling his face flush.

"You could fix that," Emma said reasonably, much to his surprise. "I hear she cooks, she ought to have you over." There was a meaningful pause. "Or, since you cook, why don't you have her over?"

It gave him some pleasure, however small, to know that Emma Garrett was considerably behind the times.

When he made his now-daily visit to the Mitford jail, he noticed a stack of boxes near the front door.

"Shoes," said Rodney. "We've had shoes pourin' in here from all over th' county. Old shoes, new shoes, black shoes, blue shoes. We're run over with shoes. Th' FBI's goin' to have t' take George back t' Connecticut with a U-Haul."

"Tell 'im about the casseroles," said Joe Joe.

"Seven casseroles," said Rodney, reading from a list, "two blueberry pies, a pound of sliced turkey because he missed 'is Thanksgivin' dinner, and a box of bridge mix from th' drugstore. Let's see, we've got cream horns and doughnuts from Winnie, a coconut cake from the help up at Miss Sadie's, and a Bible from ah . . . what's that name, Joe Joe?"

"Looks like Cynthia . . . Coppersmith."

"We need a check-in counter," said Rodney.

A clean-shaven George Gaynor was dressed in his new shirt and pants, sitting on the cot, writing. He stood up and smiled at the rector.

"How do you like that shave an' haircut I give 'im?" asked Rodney, who was unlocking the cell door.

"You could put Joe Ivey clean out of business."

"I'm glad to see you," said George, who shook the rector's hand with both of his own. He was looking very different from the gaunt, bearded man who had come down from the attic. "Any word on your dog?"

"Not a word."

"I'd like to put up a reward, if Rodney will let me have my money. I had about two hundred dollars in my wallet."

"Thank you, George. Thank you."

"Make that two twenty-five," said Joe Joe Guthrie, taking out his billfold.

"Why don't we just get up a big reward fund, and I'll keep it in my drawer," said the police chief, hitching up his holster. "Money talks, you know."

Before he made a visit to The Local, he made a call.

"Ron, we need to take care of Russell Jacks. Betty Craig has offered to nurse him in her home, which is good, and I expect he'll need attention for at least three or four months. Whatever you can send, I'll match."

"You've done your share of matching," said Ron Malcolm. "Let me know what it takes, and you'll have it."

"You're a prince, my friend. Thank God for you! When do we look at renderings?"

"Could be summer before we see anything. The architect meets with Miss Sadie on Tuesday. Sometime in July, we ought to get a rough idea of square footage, how it'll be sited, that kind of thing. Before it goes fast, Father, it always goes slow."

"My love to Wilma," said the rector.

On the way to The Local, he stopped by the Grill. "We're gettin' up a reward," said Mule Skinner, who was sitting at the counter, counting. "Sixty-five, seventy-five, ninety-five, a hundred. . . ."

Esther Cunningham, who was having a cup of coffee and a piece of lemon pie at a table, raked through a large knitting bag for her checkbook. She gave Mule a check for fifty dollars. "In Mitford, we take care of our own," she said proudly, reciting her long-established platform.

"You might as well put your money back in your pocket," said one of the loan officers from the bank across the street. "That dog is long gone over the state line, if you want my thinkin'."

"I personally don't want it," snapped Percy. He turned to Father Tim. "We're goin' to get ol' Barnabas back, you just wait'n see."

He found Avis Packard behind the meat counter, wearing a butcher's apron that read *The World Famous Local: Fine Wines and Premium Meats.*

"Avis, how's that duckling you told me about at Uncle Billy's art show?"

"You're lookin' at it," said Avis, who reached into his meat case and held up a duckling. "Less grease, more flavor, corn fed, no chemicals. And there's a big, fine liver in here to make you a pâté as smooth as silk."

The bard of foodstuff, that was Avis Packard.

"Four point two pounds. Just right for two people. And if I was you," said Avis, speaking confidentially, "I'd put a nice, crisp champagne behind this dinner."

"Wrap it up," said the rector, who felt dimly troubled that he hadn't yet extended his proposed invitation for Saturday evening.

He'd seen Olivia, who was sitting up and looking nearly herself again. The swelling had gone down, and Hoppy was ready to send her home on Sunday. Though still lacking energy, she would be able, he said, to walk around the house, and even go shopping for an hour or two with Mrs. Kershaw.

An enormous relief, he thought. And so was his visit to Russell Jacks, who would be moving to Betty Craig's trim, small house above the hospital, sometime next week. Two triumphs. Two victories.

He'd had a call from Marge Owen, who wanted Dooley for the weekend. Perfect timing, in more ways than one, for that meant he could concentrate more fully on his Easter sermon, two Sundays hence. A call to Rodney assured him that George might be allowed to sit between a couple of officers in the eleven o'clock Easter congregation, assuming the FBI had not yet picked him up. "I reckon they think we've took 'im to raise," said Rodney, who could not fathom the red tape of federal bureaus.

At five o'clock on Friday, as Dooley was packing for Meadowgate, Miss Sadie called.

"Are your ears burning?" she asked, brightly.

"Well, let's see. No, I don't believe so."

"Well, they should be! Louella and I have talked about you the livelong day."

"Miss Sadie, I'm shocked that you can't find anything better to talk about."

"You know what we decided?"

"To string Japanese lanterns around the lawn at Fernbank and have a spring gala."

She laughed with delight. "Guess again."

"Let's see . . . to hire a chauffeur and drive to Charlotte for a day of shopping."

"Never!" said Miss Sadie. "One more guess."

"This is too hard. Wait a minute. You've decided to have me up for lunch."

"Exactly. But you'd never guess the best part."

"Please don't make me try."

"We're going to give Rodney Underwood a little something for the reward fund."

"Well, now . . ."

"A thousand dollars!"

"Miss Sadie!"

"Yes, indeed, and don't even thank me for it. Louella prayed and I prayed and we both got the same message."

"Are you sure about the sum? You're sure he didn't say a hundred? Decimals can be tricky."

"We're sure. With all our hearts, we want you to have your Barnabas back. We're just broken-hearted about this hideous crime. To think this could happen in Mitford, and in broad daylight."

"I'm grateful for your concern . . . more than I can say."

"Then you'll come for lunch on Easter, you and Dooley?"

"Consider it done!" he told his oldest parishioner.

After Dooley had gone, he found the ecru lace cloth that a former bishop's wife had given Lord's Chapel. He would use that over the rose-colored damask that Puny had laundered after Christmas.

He would call Jena at Mitford Blossoms first thing in the morning and order . . . what? Roses, of course.

He polished the brass candlesticks that Walter and Katherine had given him for his fortieth birthday. Forty! He could scarcely remember anything about that turning point, except that he thought he was getting old. Now, he knew the truth. Forty was not old, not in the least. It was sixty that was old, and sixty-one was coming straight at him. He decided not to think further on this sore subject.

He would make something simple to serve before dinner. Perhaps the pâté. But he did not, at all costs, want to seem . . . what was it he did not want to seem? Forward, perhaps, as if the evening had been too carefully arranged.

He put the tablecloths on, and set out his grandmother's Haviland china, and the napkins. Then he went to his study to plan the rest of the meal. For dessert, he thought, maybe pears. Poached in a sauce of coffee and sugar, brandy, and chocolate.

When should he call? Or, should he knock on her door and invite her in person? He got up and paced the floor, feeling a burning sensation in his stomach. An ulcer, surely! And right before having company for dinner.

Why should he do anything more than simply pick up the phone and call his neighbor? He had certainly done it in the past, without thinking twice. This was not a good sign.

He walked into the kitchen and looked around vaguely. Then he went upstairs and peered down upon Cynthia's small house. He saw Violet sitting on the roof.

Divine intervention!

He went downstairs to his desk. "Cynthia," he said, when she answered the phone, "I've just seen Violet sitting on your roof."

"No!"

"Yes. And licking her paws."

"Oh, how horrid. First the basement, now the roof. I can't keep up with her for a minute. And licking her paws! It sounds like she's killed a bird. I'm telling you the truth, I wish I had a dog!"

That's a thought. "Shall I bring her down for you?"

"No! She can just sit up there till the cows come home. I mean, yes, would you?"

"I'll be right over," he said.

She met him at the back door.

That she looked stunning, he saw at once, would be an understatement. Her dress was the color of a clematis he'd once had, so blue it was nearly purple. He found that it did something extraordinary to her eyes.

"Hello!" she said, smiling. "You're so wonderful to come. I just hate that you'll have to drag my old wooden ladder out, it's heavy as a truck."

There was no way he could not notice her perfume. Like wisteria, something from a garden.

"It's no problem at all. I know right where it is, from the time Violet got caught in the heating vent."

"Where was she when you looked?"

"When last spotted, she was somewhere over your bedroom."

"Do you think it would help to try coaxing her down? I just opened a can of her favorite dinner."

"We could try that."

She dashed into the kitchen and brought out a malodorous brown lump in a dish. Even so, something caught at his heart, for it was supper time for Barnabas, as well.

"Ugh, it's liver," she said, waving it above her head and calling, "Kitty, kitty, kitty."

"I don't believe you have to hold it up," said the rector, taking the dish from her, "I believe the odor will, ah, rise of itself."

"Oh, dear," said Cynthia, straightening her dress and consulting her watch. "Violet, you wretch," she called toward the roof, "come down at once!"

He could say something like, Cynthia, I was thinking you might pop over to dinner tomorrow evening. Of course, it would have to be an early evening, because of services on Sunday. . . .

"Six-thirty!" said Cynthia with exasperation, looking again at her watch. "Oh, dear. I've been invited to the country club tonight."

"Well, then, let me take care of this, and you go ahead."

"That would be perfect, just perfect! How kind of you, how very good. I'll do something for you, I promise."

"But you already have. In fact, I was wondering if you might come to—"

"There's the bell. Would you like to say hello to Andrew Gregory?"

Andrew Gregory!

"Ah, no," he said, hoarsely, "I'll just carry on with the rescue."

"You're so lovely, Father. Just toss her in the back door, I never lock it. Well, then, bye," she said, blowing a kiss his way, and going quickly down the hall to her front door.

He went as quickly to the basement and found the heavy ladder. There was no need to spend precious time calling a vagrant cat.

He carried the ladder to the porch, climbed to the roof, and at once saw Violet curled happily next to the chimney.

He heard the Mercedes engine start and the car pull slowly away from the curb. From where he was standing, he saw Cynthia looking up anxiously, but she didn't see him.

His heart beat dully.

"Violet, you wretch," he said.

There were many things he did not like to feel. But feeling foolish was at the very top of the list. No question.

It had all happened too suddenly. There had been Emma's unexpected comment, and the surprising realization that he missed seeing

Cynthia. Then he'd impulsively raced to The Local, for no sensible reason whatsoever, and had ended up doing the whole thing backwards. Clearly, he should have invited first, and planned second. In any case, that was hardly the point. The point was Andrew Gregory. Tall, suave, handsome Andrew Gregory.

After tossing Violet in the back door, as suggested, he went home to a house that felt hollow as a tomb. No maverick dog to leap up with joy at his arrival. No boy with a cowlick that needed wetting down, or hot chocolate to fix, or homework to check.

He would never admit it to Avis, but he put the duck in the freezer. Freezing a fresh, local, corn-fed duckling would verge on being a type of moral crime, he supposed.

He paced the living room and looked blankly out the door, then wandered through the dining room and stared at the table, which looked forlorn, somehow, for all the old lace and rose damask.

The cold wind that blew in with flurries of snow on Maundy Thursday made the bare, stripped altar seem even more appalling to the spirit. The congregation left the evening service in silence, not speaking until they passed through the lych-gates facing Old Church Lane.

Father Tim found this service the most dismal in church liturgy, but he also found it to be one of the most crucial. The business of soaking up the joys of Easter without any consideration of the pain of the cross was spiritually risky business, at best.

On Sunday, the wind still blew, but the sun shone brightly. And many of the parishioners at Lord's Chapel felt they had come, at last, through a dark tunnel into new life.

That George Gaynor could kneel at the communion rail on Easter morning added greatly to the rector's personal joy. Rodney and Joe Joe stood behind the prisoner with official solemnity as he took the wafer and cup, then escorted him back to his seat on the gospel side.

FBI agents were to arrive in Mitford on Wednesday, but hardly anyone wanted to see the man from the attic go. The entire village had taken an odd liking to this highly uncommon thief, and the school children had caught the sense of it as well. Letters and cards poured into the jail, with crayon and watercolor drawings that the prisoner taped to the walls of his cell.

Except for clergy, no visitors were allowed, and Cleo had been stationed at the door to discourage the villagers' good intentions.

"Dadgum, I hate to say it," the police chief said, "but I'll be glad to see this brother go. If the feds weren't comin' Wednesday, I'd have to hire on more help."

"How long do you think he'll . . . get?"

"I don't know about these big, fancy jewel jobs," said Rodney, hitching up his holster belt. "My guess is twenty years, more'n likely."

Twenty years, thought the rector. Twenty years out of his new friend's life. On the other hand, he had gained eternity.

The rector said goodbye in the cell, where the two men embraced with some feeling. When George stood back, his face was streaming with tears.

"How long," he asked, laughing, "can I expect this to last?"

The rector could barely speak. "This what, my friend?"

"This . . . bawling."

"May it last always," replied the rector, who knew the worse consequences of a hard heart.

He walked quickly away from the jail, thinking to go home and do some spading around his rose bushes for an hour. But Percy and his crowd of ten o'clock regulars were standing on the sidewalk, waiting for the FBI car to pass on its way out of town.

"I've said my goodbyes," he told Percy.

"Aw, come on and stand with us, it'll swell th' crowd," urged Mule Skinner.

He noticed that people had come out of the shops and were lining the sidewalks on either side of the street.

They saw the car moving toward them, just as Cynthia Coppersmith dashed across from The Local with a string shopping bag. She stood breathlessly beside the rector.

Up and down the street, the onlookers waved silently as the car moved past, its contents kept secret behind dark windows.

Cynthia took the rector's hand, pressed it, then hurried away, as the gray car with the official tag drove slowly around the monument and disappeared from view.

The total collected reward money was $2,400 until Winnie and Joe Ivey came forward with a hundred. At that, the reward committee, composed of Rodney Underwood and Percy Mosely, undertook to have posters printed at the highway Quik Copy, which were soon seen all over town.

"Twenty-five hundred smackeroos," said Mule Skinner. "If that don't flush out those dirty, low-life scumheads, nothin' will."

Rumor had it that Miss Rose Watson was looking for Barnabas herself, as were many other villagers, including Coot Hendrick, who stuck two packs of peanuts in his overalls and headed toward Farmer with his pickup window rolled down, whistling and calling.

"Mayor," said the rector in an early morning phone call, "a thought occurs to me.

"You said the town might keep Uncle Billy in the Porter place if Miss Rose dies. What if Miss Rose deeded the place to the town now, and held a life estate in, say, two rooms and a bath? Would the council consider taking care of them both?"

Two comfortable, well-heated rooms, maintained by the town. Cool in summer, warm in winter, with a good roof and a solid floor, and a commode that flushed every time. In addition, a renovated Porter place, shining on its green lawn across from the monument, and second only in splendor to Fernbank. If someone didn't get to it soon, it would be too late. The whole thing seemed to him the best idea he'd recently generated.

"I'll look into it," said Esther Cunningham, "and get back to you. Have you thought about your speech yet?"

"What speech?"

"Your Festival of Roses speech, of course."

"How's this: 'Roses: I like 'em. Plant some today. Amen.' "

"You can be foolish," she said in her rasping laugh.

"I hope so."

"Joe Joe's been tellin' me all th' excitement about th' man in the attic. I suppose that was a trick you pulled to increase attendance?"

"You're right, as usual. You ought to see the Baptists we raked in the following Sunday."

"Ha, well, you'd do mighty good to get us Baptists singin' those depressin' hymns over at your place."

"Mayor, those hymns are not depressing, they are ancient. There's a difference."

She snorted. "Well, you take Ray, he's ancient *and* depressin'. You know how long we've been married at four o'clock tomorrow?"

"Too long?"

"You got it! Forty-eight years."

"The only thing I've ever done for forty-eight years straight is draw a breath."

"We're havin' a cookout on Saturday and we'd like it if you'd come. All the kids and grans will be there, and th' greatgrans, you name it."

"Why, that's half the town. There won't be a soul left on the street!"

"Well, just come on and don't talk about it," she said.

"I'll give it some thought. Dooley might like that."

"I need you one more minute. I suppose you know about Joe Joe and your Puny."

Aha! No, he didn't. But now he did. "Well, yes," he said, smiling with delight.

"I wouldn't mind knowin' just what you think of her, her bein' an orphan an' all."

"Here's exactly what I think of Puny Bradshaw. She is the finest, hardest-working, most forthright and decent girl on the face of the earth."

"Well!" said the mayor, approvingly. "You know, of course, that Joe Joe was my first gran, and I wouldn't want anybody who isn't . . ."

"Now, Mayor, this sort of thing works both ways. What about *Joe Joe's* credentials?"

"Joe Joe," she said with fervor, "is a Cunningham!"

In the mayor's view, that explained everything. It had never ceased to amaze him, and others as well, that, of the five beautiful Cunningham daughters and more than twenty grandchildren, there was not a black sheep in the lot. Except for Omer.

"We all remember what Omer did," she said crisply, "but he's over it."

"Let's just say that my stake in this goes nearly as deep as yours," suggested the rector. "I happen to like Joe Joe exceedingly, as a matter of fact. And if this were to take shape, he would be the luckiest man alive. Next to Ray, of course."

"Father," said the mayor, "flattery has never ceased to ring my bell."

"You know what they call me out at th' farm?"

"What's that?"

"Uncle Dools."

The rector, who was on his knees in a perennial bed, looked up and laughed. "Uncle Dools, is it?"

Dooley was standing with his arms crossed and his cowlick shooting up like a geyser. A few days of sun had increased his freckles, and his eyes seemed bluer than ever.

"Yeah, an' ol' Goosedown, she tried that bonehead trick agin of th'owin' me in th' slop, but I stuck on 'er good'n tight and I like to rode th' hair off 'at horse."

"Well, I'll say."

There was a long pause. A bird sang. The rector's heart felt at peace.

"I held 'at baby three times."

"Did you, now?"

"She was grinnin' at me an' all."

He flung the dandelions into a pile as he worked.

"Then she called m' name."

The rector stopped weeding and stood up, feeling the stiffness in his knees. He had a sudden sense that Dooley was sharing a deep confidence. "You don't mean it!"

"Yeah, she did, said, 'Doo-oo-ools,' jis' like 'at. I like t' fell out. She ain't hardly six month old, ain't even got teeth."

"Good gracious," said the rector.

"Nobody heard it but me," the boy told him, wondering if he was free to trust his own ears.

"I believe you, son."

Dooley nodded soberly. Something important had just transpired between them. Father Tim could feel it.

"Spring," said the local gardening column in the *Muse*, "is slowly climbing the mountain to Mitford, wearing a frock of morning mist, and carrying an armful of forsythia. She is shod with ivy and dandelion, and her hair is entwined with sprigs of wolf bane. Unfortunately, she is easily distracted and often interrupts her journey to tarry upon a bed of moss, where she sleeps for days on end."

Laughing, Father Tim put the newspaper down and walked to his open bedroom window. Hessie Mayhew had been reading Coleridge again!

He saw the gray Mercedes parked at the curb in front of his neighbor's house. Good Lord, didn't the man have a home of his own?

He tied the sash of his robe and leaned his elbows on the sill. The air was balmy, inviting, and the sound of the rain as gentle as the whisper of moth wings.

He breathed deeply. Much to do tomorrow. Visit Winnie Ivey who was recovering from a gallbladder operation. Take a copy of the New Testament and Psalms to Homeless. Carry a pound of Jenkins's livermush to Russell, out of the freezer. That brand could only be found in Wesley, and who could ask Betty Craig to make such a trek when she had more important things to do for her cantankerous patient?

Finally, write a demanding letter about the bells. The bells! Now, there was an act of the Almighty.

Had the bells arrived while George Gaynor was living in the attic, he would surely have been discovered and arrested, and God's plan would not have been carried out. Perhaps he should write the English restoration firm and praise them for their endless delay! "Gentlemen, Thanks to your inexcusable delinquency, someone has found new life behind our death bell!"

At noon, go to school and have lunch with Dooley in the cafeteria, as tomorrow was the day parents were invited to share this nostalgic ritual.

Get his medication refilled. Or had he already done that? He couldn't recall. He looked at his watch. Ten o'clock. Time, and then some, for evening prayers.

He realized he had gone over this interminable list to keep his mind off something far more important. What was happening over there, anyway?

He heard his neighbor's front door open and Cynthia's mole laughter, recognized first at Uncle Billy's art show. He felt frozen to the spot.

"Well, do think about it," Andrew Gregory said.

"Oh, but I already have thought about it," Cynthia responded.

Their voices carried to his room as clearly as if they'd been standing in it. With what seemed enormous effort, he pulled the window down.

I have no claim on her, none at all, nor any reason to be interested in her activities. What's going on here? It was a question that not only had to be asked, it was a question that had to be answered.

"Just tell me one thing," said his neighbor, standing on the other side of his screen door. "Why are you mad at me?"

He was stunned by her sudden appearance, her extraordinary question, and even more, by the astonishing gleam of her eyes. Since he had seen her eyes many times, why was he always so forcibly struck by the intensity of their color?

"Well?" she said, with an openness that disarmed him completely.

"I don't . . ."

"You can tell me," she said, looking at him quizzically.

"But what makes you . . . ?"

"I can just feel it," she said.

"Why don't you come in?"

"Why don't you come out? We could sit on your garden bench. I've been longing to sit on your old bench." She tilted her head and gazed at him with a half smile.

"Well . . ." His heart hammered, which was a feeling he did not like at all, not in the least. Years of not having such a feeling, perfectly content not to have such a feeling, and now this. He felt his throat constrict, so that he croaked when he tried to talk. There was only one thing to do, he decided, until this desperate condition passed, and that was to keep quiet.

In his opinion, it was far too cool to sit on a moss-covered stone bench, but he followed her around to the side of the rectory.

Very likely, he concluded, this was not happening at all. Possibly, he had dozed off on the study sofa, and this was what his subconscious had concocted.

"Just beautiful," murmured Cynthia, sitting down. He was certain that the damp moss would stain her skirt, but that was not for him to say.

"I'd like to draw this little hidden-away spot," she confided. "I can see it from my bedroom window, and even in winter, it has magic."

He nodded, dumbly.

"Please sit," she said, looking up at him and patting the bench.

He sat.

"Aren't we fortunate to have hours like these, when everyone else is working away under some fluorescent ceiling, with no windows to gaze out, and no Carolina junco to come swooping by?"

The little gray bird landed on a branch of rhododendron and preened itself.

"Ummm," he said, still not trusting his voice.

She turned her head and looked at him. "You see, it's nothing you've said or done, really. It's just that I feel things are not . . . the same between us. Perhaps I really shouldn't mention it, but I . . . well, you see, it's important to me." She stared at him frankly. "I'd love to put it right."

He felt he might be able to leap over the hedge and hit the ground, running, in Baxter Park.

"There isn't anything . . ." he began, and was aghast to find he was still croaking.

She gazed at him steadily, trying not to laugh. He felt his face redden.

"You're so funny," she said. "You're like a boy, really."

"Arrested development!" he exclaimed. There! His voice was back, thanks be to God.

A chill breeze moved her skirt against his legs.

"Wouldn't you like to go inside?" he asked, feeling the moss under him like a sodden pew cushion.

"No, let's just sit out here and freeze together." The junco flew in and out among the branches, singing. "Let's see," she said, closing her eyes, "you're mad at me because you had to go up on the roof and fetch Violet."

"Not at all. It gave me a different perspective."

"Then you're furious because when I made fish stew last week, you could smell it cooking and I didn't offer you any."

"I had a cold," he said, sniffing, "and could not possibly have smelled a thing."

Cynthia laughed uproariously. He hadn't thought it a bit amusing. Would this visit never end?

"Timothy," she said, "I have inquired discreetly and was told it's no form of disrespect for a friend to call a priest by his first name."

"That is absolutely correct."

"Only one thing remains to be decided, then."

"And what's that?" he asked, knowing full well that the dampness from the moss had seeped into the seat of his pants.

"Are we friends?"

He thought she looked surprisingly anxious.

"Of course, we're friends. Would I have hauled that ox cart ladder of yours up from anyone else's basement? Or climbed to the roof, reeling with vertigo, if we weren't friends?"

"Oh, Timothy, it's so hard to know how to do in this life. Why, I was terrified to come to your door and demand to know why you were mad at me."

"Why were you terrified?"

"Because I thought you might tell me, you see! But of course, it's obvious that you're not going to tell me anything. Which is fine. Because now it feels better. It feels like it was before."

"Then why don't we have a cup of tea?" he inquired.

"Perfect!" she exclaimed. "I just love having a cup of tea."

"Andrew!" he said, seeing the antique dealer unlocking the door to the Oxford.

"Father, good morning! You're looking well." Andrew greeted him with a vigorous handshake. "And thin, I must say."

"Fit is what I'd like to be, but for now, thin will do nicely, thank you. How are you, my friend?"

"Couldn't be better, actually. Trying to get away for a quick trip to Florida before the spring deluge."

Andrew swung open one of the heavy double doors to his shop and the fragrance of old wood and lemon oil wafted out like incense.

"Come in and have coffee with me. It's been months since we've talked, there's catching up to do! And God knows, I'd like to hear every detail about the man in the attic."

"Not today, I'm afraid. Too many duties call. But soon," he said.

"I'll consider that a promise," said Andrew, dropping the keys into the pocket of his jacket.

"Getting away for a bit of golf?" asked the rector.

"Yes, I think I'll keep the shop open and let one of the Cunningham daughters look after things. Just three or four days, meeting one of my children down there, and taking part in a tournament. Hoping to get your neighbor to go along with me for company; my son and his wife would be taking us in."

"Aha!"

The phone rang in Andrew's office at the rear of the shop.

"Soon, then," said the proprietor, waving goodbye and stepping quickly inside.

When he dropped into the Oxford on Thursday to look at an old book on roses that had been dedicated to Queen Victoria, he found Marcie Guthrie in charge.

That she looked like a carbon copy of her mother from behind was no surprise. It was when she turned around that the surprise came, for the mayor's eldest daughter was astonishingly beautiful. And though she, like the mayor, wore a size twenty dress, she swept along in it with admirable grace.

"Mama says you're goin' to make a speech at the festival."

"I am, that, God willing, but what I'm going to say is quite another matter. Do you think they'd sit still for a warmed-over sermon on sloth?"

"Nope," she laughed, showing her dazzling teeth.

"Well, then, what about plain laziness, the very worst enemy of the rose gardener?"

"I thought Japanese beetles were," said Marcie, wrinkling her brow.

"Is your proprietor off to the links?"

"Left yesterday."

"Drove down with a friend, I hope. It's quite a distance."

"Oh, no. No, he went by himself. And just as well. He was in a stew about something. I'd never seen him like that! Fussy, you might say, like a baby with colic."

The rector felt suddenly joyful. "Speaking of babies, aren't you a grandmother again?"

"I thought you'd never ask!" said a radiant Marcie, who whipped out an accordion-fold photo album that displayed all seven of her grandchildren. "Now, if we could just find someone for Joe Joe," she said wistfully. "He's the only single one I've got left."

Father Tim sat down at a walnut tea table, and with earnest delight looked carefully at every smiling face.

CHAPTER SEVENTEEN

A Surprising Question

While Dooley was getting his homework done on Thursday night, the rector walked out to the back stoop and sat on the railing. Surely, there would be freezing nights to come, and the balm of these last few evenings was to be savored.

He saw lights in Cynthia's house. He wondered what she did with her time in the evenings when she was not going out to the country club. He, too, might have had a membership at the club; the vestry offered him one upon arrival. But no, he wasn't a golfer, he wasn't a swimmer, and when he entertained, he liked very much to do it at home. So, he'd requested that the funds available for club membership be given instead to a children's hunger fund that he knew to be stable in its financial ethics. He had never once regretted doing this, nor had anyone been piqued with him for doing it.

He heard his neighbor's back door slam.

"Violet!" Cynthia hissed. "Violet, you miserable, witless creature, come back here this minute!"

The rector then heard a deafening cacophony of sound, which he recognized as an all-out, three-alarm cat fight.

"Violet!" shouted her mistress, "I will positively murder you for this!"

If only Barnabas were here, he chuckled to himself, those cats would have an instant parting of the ways.

He walked to the hedge. "Cynthia!" he called. "Do you need help?"

Cynthia flew to her side of the hedge in a robe and slippers, her head bristling with the familiar pink rollers.

"Timothy! Violet got out and two toms are killing each other! I've got to get her back inside. She's in heat!"

Good grief, thought the rector, who grabbed the rake propped against the porch and stumbled through the dark hedge.

"You were wonderful," said a wide-eyed Cynthia, sitting in her workroom on what appeared to be a doll-size love seat. "Just wonderful. First, you ran off those marauding toms and then you crawled down the coal shaft to rescue Violet. You will never, ever know how I appreciate this. No, never!" she said, fiercely.

She had poured two glasses of the stunning sherry she appeared to keep just for him.

"You should see yourself!" she said, marveling at the coal dust that covered him from head to foot.

Ha, she should see *herself!* he thought, in those odd slippers and that old robe and curlers sticking up like chimney pots this way and that.

He laughed. "We're a pair, I'm sure. And here I thought you might be . . . traveling this weekend."

"Traveling?" she asked, looking at him intently. "Oh." A pause. "Traveling. Well," she said, obviously flustered, "as you can see, I am not traveling, I am right here at home, where I am perfectly, perfectly happy."

"Aha."

He looked around her small studio. Every inch of wall space was covered with some cheerful drawing or watercolor, or picture cut from a magazine. She had lettered a scripture from the sixteenth chapter of Proverbs that was push-pinned over her drawing table: "Commit thy works unto the Lord and thy thoughts shall be established."

"That," he said, "is a commendable way to do it."

"For me, it's the only way. I don't work at all without committing it to God first. I've done it the other way, and giving it to Him makes all the difference."

Period! The rector smiled. He liked Cynthia's practical relationship with God. It had none of the boldness of Olivia Davenport's glorious faith. It was simple and easy. Cynthia, it appeared, was definitely down to earth about heavenly things.

"Well, then," he said, setting his empty glass on a shelf brimming with children's books, "I must go to my young scholar. He's studying for a test tomorrow, and I'll give him a hand if he needs it."

She smiled and tilted her head to one side. "You're lovely," she said.

"And so are you," he heard himself reply.

"What are you grinnin' all over yourself about?" Dooley asked, his eyes bleary with approaching sleep.

"I am not grinning all over myself." He sat on the side of the bed. "Did your studying go well? Did you need me to help?"

"Naw, I got 'at ol' mess figgered out."

"I'll be praying for you tomorrow at one o'clock when your test begins."

"Prayin' ain't goin' t' knock 'at ol' test in th' head."

"You're right about that, my friend. However, praying will help *you* knock it in the head."

Dooley yawned and turned over. " 'night," he said.

" 'night," said the rector, putting his hand on the boy's shoulder.

Father, he prayed silently, thank you for sending this boy into my life. Thank you for the joy and the sorrow he brings. Be with him always, to surround him with right influences, and when tests of any kind must come, give him wisdom and strength to act according to your will. Look over his mother, also, and the other children, wherever they are. Feed and clothe them, keep them from harm, and bring them one day into a full relationship with your Son.

He sat for a long time with his hand on the sleeping boy's shoulder, feeling his heart moved with tenderness.

Then he went downstairs and picked up the phone. "Cynthia, I just remembered something."

"What's that?" she asked brightly.

"I'd like you to come for dinner tomorrow evening . . . if you don't have other plans."

"Why, no," she said. "I'd love to come!"

As he went to the refrigerator, he was surprised to find that his forehead had broken out in a light sweat.

He opened the freezer door and removed the duckling.

When he came home for lunch on Friday, Puny had steamed up the kitchen windows with her cooking projects.

"I'm leavin' you a stewed hen and some p'tato salad for the weekend."

"A million thanks."

He sat down at the counter and peered beneath the top slice of bread on his sandwich. Tofu!

"I never thought to see the day I'd touch that stuff," said Puny, who was watching him out of the corner of her eye, "but I read where it's good for people like you, so eat hearty! You wouldn't believe how it feels when you slice it. Ooooh." She shuddered with disgust.

"I would infinitely prefer a cake of your fried cornbread."

"You can infinitely all you want to, I'm not makin' you any more cornbread for a whole month. I marked th' calendar."

He ate his sandwich with some alarm, but said nothing.

"I seen your dinin' table, it looks like Charles and Diana are comin'. Who're you havin'?"

With some difficulty, the rector swallowed the last of his sandwich and wiped his mouth. "That, Miss Bradshaw," he said with unconcealed delight, "is for me to know and you to find out."

After settling Dooley into his room with a model airplane, he went to the refrigerator. The timing would be perfect for dinner at seven.

To say that he was astounded at what he discovered would be an understatement. Puny Bradshaw had mistaken his prize duckling for a chicken, and stewed it.

"Only if it's decaf," said Cynthia. "Otherwise, I'd be awake till Thanksgiving!"

"We wouldn't want that," said her host, who summarily brought in a silver tray with a pot of coffee, cups, and two dishes of poached pears.

"Oh! I just love pears."

"Cynthia," he inquired, "what *don't* you love?"

She thought for a moment as he poured a fragrant cup of coffee.

"Ummm. People who are never on time. It's so thoughtless, the way they rob us of the hours we spend waiting."

"I couldn't agree more."

"Let's see what else. Garden slugs!"

"Aha."

"Artificial flowers!"

"Ditto."

"Loud music. Stale crackers. Cursing. Complaining."

He laughed.

"You'll be relieved to know that I won't ask you such a silly question," she said. "I'd much rather ask you something else."

"Which is . . . ?"

"What were your parents like?"

He poured his own coffee and handed her a dish of pears.

"My mother was a beautiful woman with a loving spirit. She could also be obstinate, strict, and cold at times, but, usually, only toward my father, who was *always* obstinate, strict, and cold." He looked at her with a wry smile.

"My mother was a Baptist, the granddaughter of a great Mississippi preacher. She was well-read in the Scriptures, had a mind of her own and an arresting wit, into the bargain. When I was an infant, she gave me to the Lord, as Hannah gave Samuel.

"She raised me on Scripture, and the extraordinary thing is, she caused me to love it. Some who're raised that way end up reviling it, because it's taught in the wrong spirit. But who could not love what my mother taught? She was adored by everyone. Everyone except, I regret to say, my father."

His guest stirred cream into her coffee, listening intently.

"My mother, brimming with passion, with love for God and for people—my father, remote, arrogant, handsome, disliked. I remember what my Uncle Gus once said: 'A high-falutin', half-frozen Episcopalian and a hidebound, Bible-totin' Baptist. The North Pole and the South Pole, under the same roof!' Why did they marry? I believe my mother saw in him something tender and felt she could change him."

"Oh, dear," said Cynthia, with feeling.

"At the age of ten or so, I had learned one of the most crucial verses on marriage." He laughed, remembering his mother's frequent allusion to it. " 'Be not unequally yoked together with unbelievers . . . for what communion hath light with darkness?' My father did have a dark spirit, and her brightness seemed to drive him even further into the darkness.

"The church was a terrific issue for years. Mother attended Father's church until, as she liked to say, she was overcome by frostbite. Finally, he quit the church entirely, and Mother returned to her Baptist roots. With me in tow."

He took a sip of coffee from the Haviland cup. His guest, who was herself a storyteller, seemed transfixed. "What did you think of that?" she wanted to know.

"I liked it. It was like drawing your chair up to the hearth. Church suppers, hymn sings, a sense of family. A great sense of family. I found there something I never found with my father: a kind of unconditional love. But unconditional love with salt, for there was a real honor of God's bottom line. Walnut Grove was a simple church, and it caused me to treasure simplicity. It was also where I very likely developed my early desire to be a pastor.

"I never wanted to rise to bishop. I only wanted to pastor a small congregation, and to weave myself into the life of a parish in . . . in an intimate way."

"I see that you've done that, with wonderful results."

"I don't know. I very often don't know."

"Well, of course, you don't! That's not unusual. I very often don't know if a watercolor is right. I wish I had someone to run to, to say look at this, what do you think? That's terrific, they might say, keep doing it. Or, haven't you made all the heads too big?"

He laughed.

"These pears," she said, "are ravishing, to put it plainly."

He laughed. "One of the qualities I like in you is that you put things plainly."

"What else do you like about me?" she asked, unashamedly licking the sauce off her spoon.

"Now, Cynthia . . ." He felt a mild panic.

"Oh, just say! And then I'll tell you what I like about you."

To think that he might have been sitting here in perfect peace, in his burgundy dressing gown and old slippers, reading or dozing. . . . "Well, then. Are the rules complete candor? Or shall we shade the truth and flatter one another?"

"Complete truth!"

" 'These are the things that ye shall do,' " he quoted from the book of Zechariah. " 'Speak every man truth to his neighbor.' "

"You see!" she said, laughing.

He sat back on the old sofa with the haphazard slipcover. "One of the things I like about you is that you are . . ." He relished a very long pause, as her eyes grew wide with mock expectancy. ". . . fun," he said, smiling.

"Oh, lovely!"

"One of the things I like about you," he continued, warming to his subject, "is . . . your enthusiasm."

"Really?"

"Yet another thing I like about you is your courage."

"My courage?"

"Yes. You haven't told me any stories of your valor, but it's something I sense, nonetheless. Of course, the thing I like most about you is that you're far too kind to make me continue this list. That is, until I get to know you better."

"Done!" she said, scraping the last of the sauce from the bottom of her dish, and licking the spoon a final time. She set the dish on the coffee table and pushed up her sleeves. "Now, to you."

"Do be kind," he implored.

Cynthia made herself comfortable in the corner of the sofa. "One of the things I like about you is . . . you're romantic."

He felt his face flush. "I dare say I've never once thought of myself as romantic."

"But how could you escape thinking it? It's as plain as the nose on your face. Look at the way you love the old writers, especially Wordsworth. And your roses, and the gardens at Lord's Chapel. And the way you set a table with family china, and attend to the needs of your friends . . . and, oh, and go without a car for years on end!"

"That's romantic?" he asked, perplexed.

"Terribly!"

Certainly this sort of evening beat dining at the country club. Why, he might have been talked into playing a rubber of bridge by now, which he utterly despised, or worse yet, doing the fox trot with Hessie Mayhew. There was, however, a price to pay for an evening with Cynthia Coppersmith: He found that he kept feeling his collar grow tighter.

"I could go on," she announced, tilting her head and gazing at him.

"Please don't!" he said. Please do, he thought.

"Why don't we take a walk, then?" His neighbor got up and fluffed her silk dress which he found to be the color of raspberries crushed in a bowl of cream. "What a splendid dinner! I'm fairly stupefied."

He grinned. "That's one way to put it."

They strolled toward the monument, feeling a light chill in the air. He couldn't avoid seeing the reward posters in every shop window they passed, with Cynthia's bold likeness of Barnabas staring dolefully toward the street.

As they went around the monument and walked by the Porter place, he saw that Miss Rose and Uncle Billy had come out and settled themselves in the chrome dinette chairs that held a permanent position at the edge of their neglected lawn. "Well, looky here, Rose, it's th' Preacher!"

"I can plainly see that," snapped Miss Rose, who was attired in rubber overshoes, a chenille robe, a cotton house dress, pajama pants, and a golf hat. Father Tim was frankly amazed at the style she could bring to such odd apparel.

"Miss Rose, Uncle Billy, I believe you know my neighbor."

"Cynthia Coppersmith!" said Cynthia, extending her hand. "We've met at church. So nice to see you again. I admire your home."

"Don't try to buy it," warned Miss Rose, darkly.

"Preacher, why don't you 'uns come in? Come in an' have a sip of tea Rose made today. You've never seen our place."

"*My* place," said Miss Rose, jabbing him sharply with her elbow.

"Rose, don't act up, now. We got comp'ny."

"Uncle Billy, I don't believe . . ."

"Aw, Preacher, come on and visit a spell. It'd be a blessin'."

The rector looked at his neighbor, who nodded with enthusiasm. "Let's do it! I love old houses."

As they walked up the broken flagstones in the dark, he took Cynthia's arm and whispered: "You might be careful of the refreshments."

She laughed with delight. He knew instinctively that she considered this a grand adventure. How exciting, after all, to go where one must be careful of the refreshments.

Uncle Billy turned on the hall light as they entered the front door, and a great chandelier shone weakly through a layer of grime and dust. "Missin' some bulbs," said their host apologetically.

He heard Cynthia's astonished murmur. They were in a broad foyer with a ceiling that soared two stories high and was ornamented on either side by staircases that, even in the ghostly light, were clearly extraordinary in their design. Faded murals swept up the walls, depicting elaborate gardens and statuary, exotic birds and urns overflowing with fruit. Carved balustrades were missing, with several appearing to lie on the floor where they'd fallen.

In an odd sense, it was a privilege to be in the Porter place, as few had ever been invited and hardly anyone, of late, wished to be asked.

"This is the front hall," Miss Rose said, glowering at her guests.

"Glorious!" said Cynthia. "Absolutely glorious. Who built your home?"

"My brother, Willard," said Miss Rose, in whom the ice suddenly began to melt. "My brother, Willard James Porter. There's his picture." She pointed up the stairs on the right, where a large, wide-framed portrait hung. Even in the dim light, Father Tim recognized the strikingly handsome face of the intense young man in Miss Sadie's silver frame.

"Terribly good looking!" said his neighbor.

In a surprising burst of cordiality, Miss Rose asked if they'd like a piece of pound cake.

"I love pound cake!" said Cynthia.

Now we're in for it, he thought.

"You 'uns go on ahead through th' dinin' room," said Uncle Billy, opening the French doors on their right. "Rose an' me'll bring up th' rear."

Father Tim peered into a vast, dark room with a narrow pathway bordered on either side by towering mounds of musty newspapers.

"You go first," said Cynthia.

He took his neighbor's hand and plunged into the darkness toward a light shining under a distant door.

He saw that she ate the pound cake as if she hadn't had a bite all evening, and did so without inspecting her plate or her fork. As for himself, he broke an infinitesimal piece from the corner of the thin slice, and covered the remainder with his napkin. It was one thing to blindly exercise good manners, he observed, and quite another to exercise reasonable caution.

He saw that the vast kitchen was large enough for an entire studio apartment, especially since it led down a hall to a bathroom. With considerable fixing up, it would make as fine a home as anyone could want.

"My brother," Miss Rose was saying in a loud voice to Cynthia, "nearly married, you know."

"Really?"

"Oh, yes. It would have been the most dreadful thing he ever did, of course."

"I see."

"Caused an uproar."

"Umm."

"Made a fine mess!"

"Oh, dear."

"Nearly broke his faith."

"Oh, no!"

"Set the backbiters on us."

"My, my." Cynthia looked around for help from the rector.

"You 'uns want t' see th' rest of th' place?" Uncle Billy asked.

"We do!" cried Cynthia, jumping up so quickly she nearly upset the table.

His neighbor held on to his hand throughout much of the tour. There were, after all, stacks of newspapers in every room, old pictures, broken furniture, a mirror that had fallen off the wall and scattered glass across the carpet, and even a dozen silver candelabra, black with neglect, sitting squarely in the middle of the floor of an otherwise empty room where the wallpaper was peeling off in sheets.

The young Willard Porter had surely walked through these rooms, admiring their high ceilings and elaborate millwork, the stained glass in every bathroom, the carved balustrades and hardwood floors. He was beginning to wish they hadn't come in to witness the morbid decline of his showplace.

At the end of an upstairs hallway, Cynthia made a discovery. "What is this?" she cried, pointing to a blue door. It was a very small door that appeared to have been put there for children.

"That's my playroom!" said Miss Rose, who had taken off one rubber overshoe because it hurt her corn and was limping down the hall. "My dear brother put that little room up here for his baby sister. Not another living soul could go in there but me."

"Has anyone else *ever* been in there?"

Miss Rose looked fiercely at Uncle Billy. "Bill Watson, have you ever?"

"Nossir, I ain't," declared her stricken husband. "Nossiree bob!"

"Well, we'll just see. I could tell in a heartbeat if anybody's stepped foot in my playroom."

"You ain't stepped foot in there yourself in a hundred years!"

Miss Rose bent down and found a small, rusty key under a broken flower pot by the door, and inserted it into the lock.

The rector heard a soft click, and the little blue door swung open easily.

"You have to get on your hands and knees," instructed Miss Rose, dropping down on all fours, "and crawl in." Cynthia did as she was told.

"Cynthia," said the rector, "are you going in there?"

"Why, of course, I'm going in there! How could I not?"

How could she not, indeed, when it appeared to be a small, black hole in the wall, devoid of any ventilation or light.

"There!" said a satisfied Miss Rose, who reached inside and pulled a chain, illuminating the small space with surprising warmth. "Let's go."

Without any regard for her silk dress, Cynthia wriggled through the little doorway and disappeared.

"Jist foller that overshoe and that stockin' foot," called Uncle Billy.

There were screeches of pleasure, endless sneezes, and uproarious giggles from inside the wall. "Timothy, if I meet the White Rabbit, please take good care of Violet!"

The rector looked wonderingly at his host.

"Ain't that somethin', two growed women carryin' on like that? Don't that beat all!"

"Oh, Timothy, there's a tea set in here! Haviland, just like your grandmother's china! You must come in!"

In the space of a week, he had been on a rooftop and down a coal chute for Cynthia Coppersmith, and that was quite enough for him. He pulled up a battered Morris chair, and sat outside the little door like a cat awaiting a mouse. "You'll have to bring it out here, Cynthia," he called, leaning back and winking at Uncle Billy.

"That's right, Preacher!"

"We can't come out for hours, I'm afraid."

"And Bill Watson," shouted Miss Rose, "don't you dare come in!"

Her husband laughed. "She don't have t' worry about that."

"Uncle Billy, I don't know how you've lasted with Miss Rose all these years."

"Well, I give 'er my word, don't you know."

There. That was the bottom line. The line that hardly mattered to anyone, anymore.

Uncle Billy shook his head. "Y' know, Preacher, th' more things you own, th' more you're owned by things. Rose was always owned by this ol' house and no way out of it, couldn't sell it because of th' way 'er brother fixed it with th' lawyer, and it so big an' drafty, livin' in two rooms, don't you know, lettin' th' oil set in th' tank half th' time, as she don't want t' take charity by burnin' it, but not thinkin' a thing of beggin' food on th' street. . . ."

They heard Miss Rose let out a squawk of delight.

"Th' times I've seen 'er crawl in there, her arthritis jist disappears, she gits like a girl agin."

"We may have your problem taken care of. It's possible that Miss Rose could go ahead and deed the house to the town, with a life estate in a room or two, and one day or another, they'll turn the rest of it into a museum and maybe a concert hall. Your portion would be well-heated, with a good roof, and a nice, modern kitchen and bath. How do you think we can approach her on that?"

"Law, I don't know. She holds on to it like a life raft, and hit's fallin' down on our heads. Th' last time I could git up on a ladder was s' long ago, th' ladder's done half-rotted where I left it."

"Well, my friend, it's something we need to get on with."

"Y' know, Rose has talked about puttin' a statue of Willard in the front yard. If you could git th' town t' do that, it might jist ring 'er bell."

"Aha!"

"But I'd hate t' see a statue of Willard standin' up, it seems too proud. If you was to have 'im settin' down, now, that might work."

"Uncle Billy, you're a thinker!"

"Timothy!"

He peered down at the little door, as his bedraggled neighbor crawled out with something under her arm.

"Look, Timothy! Uncle Billy! It's your ink drawings! A whole stack of them! Miss Rose meant to burn them and forgot!"

"What an adventure," said Cynthia, as they walked home along a deserted Main Street. He was carrying the dust-laden bundle of drawings under his arm, as Miss Rose had insisted that they must reside with Cynthia for the time being. "Hit's f'r th' best," Uncle Billy had said, barely able to contain his joy.

"I'm quite exhausted from having so much fun," sighed his neighbor.

The rector laughed. "We hardly ever hear such a statement in Mitford." He, too, felt a distinct refreshment of spirit.

At the door of her cottage, he handed her the drawings. "I must get to my boy," he said. "Thank you for your company. Tonight has reminded me of yet another thing I like about you."

"What's that?" she asked, smiling at him.

"You're simple."

"I'm perhaps the only woman alive who would be flattered by that remark."

He laughed. "I knew you'd understand," he said, taking her hand.

"Timothy?"

"Yes?"

"Would you be interested in going steady?"

He felt as if the entire front stoop had given away under him, but discovered it was merely his knees. He dared not speak, knowing instinctively that he was in a croaking mode.

"Oh, don't answer now," she said, gazing at him with amusement. "Just think about it."

She leaned forward and brushed his cheek with hers. Wisteria!

Then she turned and went inside. "Goodnight," she said, closing the door.

He didn't know how long he sat on her steps, quite unable to walk the few yards to his back porch.

CHAPTER EIGHTEEN

Something to Think About

When Betty Craig opened the door, she looked worried.

"Father," she said, receiving his weekly delivery of a pound of livermush, "I'm glad you're here. His livermush always cheers him up for a day or two."

"How is he?"

"Ornery."

"Aha."

They walked into Betty's tidy kitchen, wallpapered with geese in blue bonnets. The windowsill was brimming with African violets, and outside the window he saw dozens of bird feeders made from plastic milk containers.

"What has Russell been doing?"

"Sit down, Father, and let me tell you."

Betty, who was one of the most positive people he knew, looked desolate. They sat at her round table, in captain's chairs with blue cushions.

"He gets up in the morning fussing, and he goes to bed fussing. Ida would have done this, Ida would have done that. He hates my cooking and won't take his medicine, and shaves his toenails on the hooked rug. He chased my cat down the hall with an umbrella and . . ."

She looked down at her hands, which she was obviously wringing.

"And what?"

"And peed in the bed twice, for pure meanness!"

"No!"

"Yes, sir," said Betty, whose lower lip had begun to tremble.

"Betty Craig, you are the finest nurse in these mountains. You are caring, sensitive, brave, and persevering. And you are also something else."

"What's that?" she asked meekly.

"Tough! Why, you've nursed men as big as Buicks, and cleaned enough bed pans to sink a ship. How on earth did an old goat like Russell Jacks put you in a shape like this?"

She looked at him fiercely. "I don't know."

"Well, think about it. You nursed Parrish Guthrie in his last days, did you not?"

"I did!"

"Then you can handle a dozen like Russell Jacks, and then some."

She sighed deeply. "I did go off my vitamins about a month ago."

"There! That's it! Take those vitamins, Betty. Tote that barge! Lift that bale!"

"What on earth has got into you, Father?"

"Tell you what I'll do. I'll talk to Russell. I'll tell him exactly what's what, that you'll set him out on the stoop with his suitcase if he doesn't straighten up at once."

Betty looked relieved. "You do that!" she said, blinking back a tear. "And I hope it helps. Because if Mr. Jacks leaves," she said with alarm, "they want me to take in Miss Pattie!"

Russell lay sleeping in a room filled with sunlight and ruffled curtains, with *All My Children* blaring on the TV. The rector quietly turned it off. His last two visits had been hurried. Today, he would spend a full hour.

He sat in a wing chair by the bed and prayed for the old man. With the right opportunities, he could have been another Capability Brown.

"I ain't asleep," said Russell, without opening his eyes.

"Is that right?"

"Nope. I cain't sleep around here."

An old Dooley Barlowe, if he ever saw one!

"Why is that?"

"Noise. Constant goin' an' comin, cat slitherin' around my ankles, phone ringin', neighbors bangin' on th' door."

If he had learned anything in the diocesan counseling workshops, it was that sympathy can be deadly. He changed the subject.

"Russell, I've been meaning to ask . . . do you know if the boy was ever baptized?"

"Nossir. That's th' kind of thing Ida would've knowed. She kept a Bible with such things in it, our married date, when th' kids was born, like that. Ida was a churchwoman and I hate t' think th' times she begged me t' go with 'er."

The old man was silent for a long time, and turned his head away. When he looked at the rector, he was weeping. "I'd give anything on this green earth t' go t' church with Ida now. But I waited 'til it's too late."

How many times had he heard those words from sorrowing parishioners? Too late! Too late to love. Too late to help. Too late to listen. too late to discipline. Too late to say I'm sorry.

"Russell, it's too late to do what Ida wanted, but it's not too late to do what Betty wants." He heard himself speak with unusual severity.

Russell heaved a sigh. "You're right, Father, you're dead right, an' I know it. I'm th' roughest ol' cob you ever seen when it comes t' mindin.' That's why I've fought th' Lord s' long, it meant mindin' 'im if I was t' foller 'im. It's about wore me out, fightin' 'im. Not t' say I don't respect 'im, I do. But I don't want t' mind 'im."

The uneducated Russell Jacks, thought the rector, had just put the taproot cause of the world's ills into a few precise words.

"Well, Russell, when we replace you . . ."

The old man sat up with great force. "You're hirin' somebody else t' do m' work?"

"We'll have to, you know. The way things are going with Betty means you'll probably have to pack up and live at your place. Being without a nurse could set you back a few months, could even send you back to the hospital. All in all, I don't believe the gardens can be let go that long."

Russell threw off the covers and sat up on the side of the bed, which launched a racking cough.

"A mess is what it'll be," he said, breathlessly, "all them bulbs bloomed out and them stems an' leaves dyin' off, and th' weeds comin' in, an' y'r fish pond settin' there all scummed up . . ."

"And you over here wasting energy chasing Betty's cat, when you could be gaining strength." Father Tim looked at him steadily.

There was a long silence, during which Russell Jacks studied his feet.

"Will you hold m' job, Father?"

"Will you hold your temper?"

Russell considered the question. "I'll do it," he said.

"I'll expect it," replied the rector.

Another silence.

"You ought t' git th' boy t' help out in th' church yard when he can. He's gifted at it."

"You know what I'd really like, Russell? I'd like to see that boy laugh."

"He don't laugh. Always was th' soberest little thing you ever seen. 'Course, he was th' oldest, you know, and he's had th' weight of th' world on 'im, lookin' after th' little young 'uns s' much."

See Dooley laugh! On his mental list of things to do, that particular ambition had just gone straight to the top.

Betty Craig knocked lightly on the open door, and came in with a tray. "Time for your medicine!" she said, looking to the rector for a sign of hope.

"*You're* the best medicine this ol' feller could ever have," replied an affable Russell Jacks.

Think about it, she'd told him. Think about it! As if he could forget it for a moment. He urgently wished to call Walter, but could not make himself pick up the phone. Would Walter be shocked? Probably not. Amused? Not especially. What Walter would be was skeptical.

"You're like a' ol' cat," Dooley complained.

"You're laughin' one minute and bitin' my head off the next," snapped Emma.

"Are you takin' your medicine?" Puny demanded to know. Well, no, he wasn't. He'd been meaning to, and he definitely would. He'd do it that very night.

"Grievin' about that dog, are you?" said Joe Ivey, as he trimmed the rector's neck.

It seemed everybody had some comment to make on his behavior these days.

Go steady? At his age? Except for the eleven months he had courted Peggy Cramer, he had never gone steady in his life. What did it mean to go steady, anyway? How in God's name could he know it was something he might like to do, if he hadn't the foggiest notion of what it meant?

And how had all this happened, anyway? He hadn't really meant for anything to "happen." Just dinner occasionally, with the sound of her laughter, and the way she expressed herself so openly, without guile.

The truth of the matter was that he liked her. There! That was it. Nothing more than that. Nothing more than that was needed. Wasn't that extraordinary enough in itself?

He felt oddly excited. So—he liked Cynthia. What was unusual about that? Hadn't he known that? Perhaps. But he had never clearly stated it to himself. The statement of that simple fact felt liberating. He was suddenly relieved.

The relief, however, didn't endure. His everlasting practicality caused him to wonder what he should *do* about liking Cynthia. On the other hand, he reasoned, why couldn't he simply like her, without feeling compelled to do something about it?

When he found that he was pacing the floor of his study like a windup toy, he went to his room and changed into a jogging suit.

As he headed toward Baxter Park, he glanced through her hedge and saw her sitting on the back stoop, holding Violet. She looked his way.

His heart hammered, and he did something he could not remember doing to anyone in recent years.

He turned his head as if he had not seen her at all, and set off through the park at a dead run.

It was J.C. Hogan who was ringing his office phone at eight-thirty on Monday morning. "I got a letter to the editor I need to answer," said J.C.

"How can I help you, my friend?"

"This kid read my story about the man in the attic, about the prayer you prayed with the guy in the pew, and how you got two birds with one stone, you might say. Wrote me this letter."

J.C. cleared his throat. " 'Dear Editor, What exactly was the prayer the preacher prayed when the man in the attic got saved? My daddy wants to know, and I do too. Thank you.' "

"Do you want me to write it down and drop it by, or just tell you on the phone?"

"Phone's fine," said J.C., breathing heavily into the receiver.

"Well, then. Here it is. 'Thank you, God, for loving me, and for sending your Son to die for my sins . . ."

"Got it," said J.C.

"I repent of my sins and receive Jesus Christ as my personal savior."

"Got it."

"And now, as your child . . ."

"As your what?"

"As your child."

"Got it."

"I turn my entire life over to you. Amen."

"What's the big deal with this prayer? It looks like some little ol' Sunday school thing to me. It's too simple."

"It's the very soul of simplicity. Yet, it can transform a life completely when it's prayed with the right spirit."

"I was lookin' for something with a little more pizzazz."

"My friend, the one who prays that prayer and means it will get all the pizzazz he can handle."

"Heard anything from th' man in the attic?"

"Not yet. But I expect to."

"Let me know if you do. I wouldn't mind printin' his letters. They'd be a crowd pleaser."

"Consider it done."

"See you at th' Grill."

He had no sooner hung up than the phone rang again. It was Louella.

"Miss Sadie ain't feelin' too good. Now, I ain't sayin' it's her las' breath, but I thought you might ask Jesus to hang on real tight, like He hung on to Hezekiah. You 'member 'bout Hezekiah, don't you, Father?"

"Indeed, I do. He was sick and cried out to the Lord, who said 'I have heard thy prayer, I have seen thy tears; behold, I will heal thee,' and He added fifteen years to the old king's life."

"I hope to th' good Lord He do Miss Sadie like that."

"Tell her she's in my prayers and I'll be up to see her tomorrow. You think she feels like company?"

"Round here, comp'ny's always good medicine. And Father . . . ?"

"Yes?"

"She bin talkin' day an' night 'bout tellin' you her love story. I don' like that talk, like she got to hurry up 'fore she passes."

"Well, then, tell her I'll be up to hear it, and she can count on it."

The phone rang again, immediately. Some days were like this.

"Father?"

"Olivia!"

"I just wanted to say good morning, that I'm thinking of you and hope to be in church next Sunday."

"Thank God!"

"Thank you, as well, for bringing the Eucharist, and being so faithful."

"What does Hoppy say about your progress?"

"I appear to be in a holding pattern. I look a fright most of the time, as you have clearly seen, but my spirits are strong. I believe the heart will come, I just feel it!"

"And how is . . . ah, your doctor's heart?"

Olivia laughed with delight. "Very tender," she said. "And exceedingly large."

"A diagnosis that even I might have made!"

"Keep us in your prayers."

"You're never out."

"You seem worried about something, Father," said Ron Malcolm, who had been a prominent contractor in the area for many years. "It must be the loss of your dog. I know how much he meant to you."

Frankly, he hadn't had time to think of Barnabas, which some would call a blessing. But suddenly, this fact made him feel desperately guilty. Dear Stuart, he saw himself typing, I have given it better than a year, and believe it would be best if I offered my formal resignation right away . . .

"Well, I believe that's all I had to report," said Ron, standing up and looking at him with some concern.

"Thank you, my friend," said the rector, shaking hands. "Give my love to Wilma."

When he was alone, he sat down and put his head on his desk, like a schoolboy. What had Ron come to see him about? He felt as if his mind had been away on some vague errand during the entire visit.

He breathed a sigh of relief as he saw the papers Ron had left in his in-basket. Of course! The architect and Miss Sadie had come to loggerheads about the placement of the dining room. She wanted it to overlook the valley; the architect considered it more feasible to overlook the village. "How could we go wrong?" the rector asked aloud, thinking of the breathtaking beauty of both views.

As he attempted to study copies of the preliminary drawings, he couldn't bring them into focus. They were a blur, and he was shocked to see that his hand trembled as he held them.

"I ain't eatin' n'more of that slop," said Dooley, who was sitting at the counter while the rector cooked dinner.

"Exactly what slop do you mean?"

"That ol' slop at school. Today, they give us meat loaf an' cherry pie."

His all-time school cafeteria favorite! What was wrong with people these days?

"Ever'body packs a lunch, sissies eat slop."

The rector shrugged. "So, pack a lunch."

"Me?"

"You."

Dooley scratched his head.

"Tell Puny what you need, she'll get it at The Local, and you're on your own. In any case, school will be out so soon, you'll hardly have time to fry up your bologna." School out! What on earth would he do with Dooley Barlowe for an entire summer?

Dooley was silent for some time, sitting on the counter stool and swinging his legs. "I got me a friend," he said at last.

"Aha! Tell me more."

"Name's Tommy."

"Tommy! I once had a friend named Tommy. Tommy Noles. Small world."

" 'e's got five birds, eleven ducks, one pig, and three dogs."

"No!"

"I told 'im he could come over here and spend th' night."

"You spoke hastily, but we can discuss it," said Father Tim, sautéing onions for the hamburgers. "What's Tommy like?"

Dooley thought hard. " 'e's got black hair."

"I can just picture him."

"Yoo hoo," someone called through the screen door. His heart galloped. It was his neighbor, carrying a dish covered with a tea towel. "Guess what?"

"Come in and we'll both guess," he said, opening the screen door.

"Hey," said Dooley.

"Hey, yourself," she replied. It had become their standard greeting. "I've changed my mind," she said, turning to the rector. "You don't need to bring me a mole if you catch one. Now, they've turned up in my lawn, the little beasts, and any passion I ever had for moles is over."

"Thanks be to God!" he said, laughing.

"Do you know how many moles Beatrix Potter drew?"

Nobody knew.

"One! Just one! Diggory Diggory Delvet. It seems perfectly clear that one can't build a career on moles."

"Indeed not."

"And while I've decided I can't possibly draw a mole, I did decide to cook one." She handed him the hot dish.

Dooley looked at her with alarm. " 'at's a ol' *mole* in 'at dish?"

"It certainly is! I found it under a bush, with its hideous little fossorial feet sticking up. Waste not, want not, is my motto."

"Cynthia, you wouldn't . . ."

"Oh, I probably wouldn't. But then again, I might." She tilted her head to one side and laughed.

"Let me see 'at ol' mole," said Dooley.

"You wouldn't know a mole if you met it in the street," said the rector, removing the tea towel. Inside the dish was a steaming gingerbread mole, with whiskers, tiny eyes, and little teeth, all made of lemon frosting. He was, of course, wearing a tab collar.

" 'at's funny," said Dooley, laughing. " 'at's pretty funny. Look at 'is ol' feet, ain't they funny!" Dooley threw his head back and laughed uproariously.

Dooley laughing!

Cynthia understood without being told, and her eyes gleamed.

Dooley laughing! His prayer had been answered so quickly, the rector felt his head fairly swim. "Have a glass of tea," he encouraged his neighbor.

"I'd love one," she said. "Dooley, you'd never guess what I did today."

"I don' know."

"Guess!"

"I cain't."

"Of course, you can. Guesses don't have to be right, they just have to be guesses."

Dooley looked at the floor and scraped the toe of his pumps. "Yanked a knot in ol' Vi'let's tail?"

"Nope. Although she certainly deserves it. Two more guesses. It's something I got that I've never had before. And both of them are brown."

"I hate 'is ol' guessin' poop."

"Men usually do, of course," she sighed. "So, I'll tell you. I've got two brown rabbits!"

"You ain't!"

"I have!"

"What'd you git 'em for?"

"To draw! I told Violet that she'd have to start looking for other employment. I cannot draw another Violet book to save my life, and I'm under contract for two more books this year!"

"Where're they at?"

"Dooley, your prepositions dangle terribly. They're at my house."

"Let's go see 'em."

She looked inquiringly at the rector. "I'll just put the lid on, and come with you," he said, happily. Rabbits! He felt as excited as a child.

"I can assure you," the principal had said, folding her arms across her chest, "that if school were not letting out, Dooley Barlowe would be expelled." She glowered at the rector, to make certain her point had been driven home. This was a solemn matter, and he should not, for one moment, forget it.

He hurried to the rectory from Mitford School, as if a dragon were breathing on his heels.

Buster Austin again. This time, in the cafeteria. Not a good, solid licking on the school ground. Oh, no. Nothing that simple and uncomplicated from Dooley Barlowe. It was an out-and-out dog fight in the cafeteria, with black eyes, a bloody nose, and mashed potatoes thrown in for good measure. "And," the principal had said, darkly, "after he threw the potatoes, he followed them with gravy."

What, exactly, had precipitated this brawl? The principal seemed to relish telling him that Buster Austin had called Father Tim a nerd.

Since Dooley had been sent home earlier, and was in his room behind a closed door, the rector decided to take his time about the matter. The day-to-day relationship with the boy was hard enough, much less the crises that arose without any warning whatsoever.

First things first, he thought, dialing the phone in his study.

"Cynthia," he said, "I'm calling because I think you have some wisdom about children, which I lack entirely. My question is this: What, exactly, is a nerd?" He listened intently. "Aha. Well. That's what I needed to know. You've been a great help, as ever. Yes, I'd love to see your rabbit drawings. I'll ring you soon. Yes. Thanks."

So that's what it meant! To tell the truth, he wouldn't mind giving Buster Austin a good hiding himself.

What was he to do about this, after all? Of course, a boy couldn't go around busting noses and slinging mashed potatoes, yet he'd already given him his walking papers once, and now, he'd clearly be required to give them again. The original walking papers had obviously lacked persuasion, but he had no idea what else to do. Hal Owen, perhaps? He'd raised a boy!

He was doing it again. He was pacing the floor in a circle.

Hello, Walter, he said in his ongoing imaginary conversation, Timothy here, I'm leaving in an hour, and I'll see you at the Shannon Airport as we discussed. I hope you've packed your walking stick. When am I planning to return? Walter, I am not planning to return. No, not at all. You see, there's a boy here who's driving me berserk, and a woman who's learned the trick of making my heart pound, and my dog has been violently snatched from me, and the list goes on. No, indeed, I am buying a small cottage, possibly with a thatch. Of course, I've heard that thatch attracts mice. . . .

Blast! He remembered Emma's wedding on Saturday, for which he'd rashly promised to bake a ham and oversee the flowers. For all his high talk and fancy education, he'd never learned to say one simple word: No.

There was a small knock at the door. He most assuredly did not want to see his neighbor. It came again, which made him oddly angry.

He opened the back door, and saw a girl with blond hair and large, gray eyes peering at him through the screen.

"Can Dooley come out?" she asked, wearing an expression of concern.

"I'm sorry, he can't," the rector replied.

"Thank you," she said, and went down the steps and through the hedge to Baxter Park.

Emma's wedding. Miss Sadie's love story. Cynthia's alarming proposal. And now a pretty visitor for Dooley. Was there some sort of epidemic?

He felt a sudden, burning thirst and drank a glass of water. Then he felt too fatigued to stand. He sat on the study sofa for some time. He simply didn't know what to do about Dooley's behavior. He would pray about it, leave it entirely to God, and trust him to control the outcome.

It was dusk when he climbed the stairs and knocked on Dooley's door.

"Yeah," said Dooley. He went in.

"We've got a lot of talking to do to smooth things out. But before that happens, there's something I'd like to say."

The boy looked up. His face was freshly bruised, but it was the old bruise in his spirit that the rector saw and felt.

"Dooley," he said simply, "I'd like to thank you for standing up for me today."

CHAPTER NINETEEN

A Love Story

"Come in, honey, we glad to see a young face aroun' this ol' folks home."

He hugged Louella with one arm, holding on to the gloxinia he'd picked up at Mitford Blossoms.

"What I got t' do wit' that?" asked Louella, who had just lost a finicky Boston fern.

"Set it in Miss Sadie's window, and water it once a week."

"I could jes' set it right here and let it get its own water. See yonder?"

He looked up to peeling paint and a dark stain on the ceiling. "That doesn't look good."

"That leak done filled two dishpans and a Dutch oven. Miss Sadie say let it pour, she don' care, long as we catch it in a bucket. Don' you think if she was plannin' to live awhile she'd be gettin' her a new roof?"

"Well . . ."

"An' if she was plannin' to keep livin', would she be in any hurry to tell you her love story?" Louella shook her head. "This whole thing got me worried."

Miss Sadie was sitting up in bed, against flowered cushions from her divan, looking bright and expectant in a satin bed jacket.

"Father! You've brought your famous gloxinia. Louella, if Father ever brings you a gloxinia, you are officially sick."

"Miss Sadie, you ain't officially sick."

"Oh, well, whatever. Sit down right here, Father." She patted the arm of a chair that had been pulled up to the bed. He put the flower pot on her sunny windowsill and happily did as he was told.

"Well, now, tell me," he said, unbuttoning his jacket, "*are* you sick?"

"Not one bit. I'm just tired. Some people get sick confused with tired. But I know tired when I see it, and that's what I am."

"All those years of eatin' froze' pies and white bread will make you tired," said Louella, putting her hands on her hips. "I'm goin' down and get lunch ready, and it's goin' to be greens cooked with a nice piece of side meat. Greens is full of iron, even if they do smell up the place, and they'll be good for what ails you, ain't that right, Father?"

She winked at the rector and left the room, closing the door behind her.

"She's the most encouragement in the world to me," said Miss Sadie, with satisfaction. "I'd been rattling around in this old house like a seed in a gourd. Now when I sneeze, there's always someone to say 'Bless you'!"

Someone to say bless you, thought the rector. There's a sermon title!

"I'm going to get out of this bed in a day or two and be good as new. But tell me about you. Are you missing your dog?"

"Terribly," he said. "I would never have dreamed. . . ." He cleared his throat, and they were silent for a moment. "I would never have dreamed that an animal could come to mean so much. Perhaps this sounds foolish, but Barnabas really did have a reflective soul. He was companionable in every way."

She looked at him intently. "You say he *was* companionable, and he *did* have a reflective soul. That is past tense." She held her hand out to him. "Life is so short, let's think in the present tense, shall we? I believe with all my heart you'll get your Barnabas back."

She smiled and pressed his hand, which he found immeasurably comforting.

"Thank you, Miss Sadie. You know I've come to hear your love story, if you're in the mood to tell it. All I have to do today is see Evie Adams, so we've plenty of time."

"Evie? What's Miss Pattie done now?"

"Gave the angel birdbath away."

"Oh, dear, that landmark birdbath! The last I heard, Miss Pattie had climbed out on the roof and was singing 'Amazing Grace' in her wrapper. I hope I never get old!"

"I believe you passed up the chance some time ago."

"The nursing home will make a difference, won't it, Father?"

"More than we can know."

"It's wonderful what comes to mind when you really stop and think. Lying here these last few days has helped me settle things. One is, I don't want to call it a nursing home. I know it will be a home, and the people in it will have to be nursed. But the whole thing has such a sad ring to it, we're going to call ours something else. Would you help me think of a name?"

"I will."

A breeze stirred through the open windows of the bedroom, with its high ceilings and cool, hardwood floors. On Miss Sadie's dressing table, Father Tim saw again the old photos in the silver frames. There was the face of the woman so eerily identical to Olivia Davenport. And the brooding, intense gaze of the young man named Willard Porter, whose grand house had been brought to ruin in full view of the whole village.

Miss Sadie took a deep breath.

"Father," she said, "what I'm about to tell you has never been spoken to another soul. I trust you will carry it to your grave."

"Consider it done," he said, solemnly, sitting back in the slipcovered chair, and finding it exceedingly comfortable.

"I've thought many times about where to begin," she said, folding her small hands and looking toward the open windows. "And while it doesn't have much to do with the rest of the story, my mind keeps going back to when I was a little girl playing in these apple orchards.

"You'll never know how I loved the orchards then, and the way the apples would fall on the grass and burst open in the sun. Then the bees would come, and butterflies by the hundreds, and the fragrance that rose from the orchard floor was one of the sweetest thrills of my life."

She lay back against the pillows and closed her eyes, smiling. "Do you mind if I ramble a bit?"

"I'd be disappointed if you didn't."

"I used to carry my dolls out under the trees. If you walk down the back steps and go straight past the gate and the old wash house and then turn right—that was my favorite place. Louella's mother, China Mae, loved to go with me! Why, she played with dolls as if she were a little girl, herself. She was the most fun, so full of life. I was nine when we moved here from Wesley, into the new house Papa built, and China Mae was twenty. She was my very best friend on earth.

"She was so black, Father! I liked to turn her head in my hands to see the light play on her face, to see the blue in the black!

"She used to call me Little Toad. I have no idea why, I'd love to know. But I'll just have to find that out when I see her in heaven."

"I hope you're not planning to find that out anytime soon."

"Of course not! I'm going to live for ages and ages. I have things to do, you know."

The clock ticked on the dresser.

"Back then, there was a big house in Mitford, right where the Baptist church stands today. It's long gone, now, but it was named Boxwood, and oh, it was a pretty place. Miss Lureen Thompson owned that house, she was like me, an only child; her parents both died in a fall from a rock when they were out on a picnic. Their chauffeur was waiting in the car for them to come back, and they didn't come and didn't come, and when he went to look . . ." Miss Sadie shivered. "It was an awful thing, they say, Miss Lureen was so stricken. You know how she tried to get over it?"

He didn't know.

"Parties! There was always something fine and big going on at Miss Lureen's. And China Mae and I were always invited to come by and sample the sweets before a party. Her cook was as big as the stove, and her cream puffs were the best you ever tasted, not to mention her ambrosia. I have dreamed about that ambrosia several times. She used to make enough to fill a dishpan, because people took such a fit over it.

"Miss Lureen liked to say, 'The firefly only shines when on the wing. So it is with us—when we stop, we darken.' I never forgot that.

"Oh, we all loved Boxwood! It had so many servants hurrying about, and they all seemed so happy in their work. Miss Lureen was good to her people. Why, when her Packard wore out, do you know who she gave it to? Her chauffeur! He fixed it up good as new and drove it back to Charleston when she died.

"His name was Soot Tobin. Black as soot, they said. He was a big, strapping man with a stutter so bad he scarcely ever spoke, but when he did, people listened, colored and white, for his voice was as deep as the bass on a church organ. He made China Mae fairly giddy. 'Most everything he'd say, she'd just giggle and go on, to beat the band. You know, China Mae was not all . . . well, she never grew up, exactly, which is one reason I loved her so. She was just like me!

"One day I came home from school and I could not believe my eyes what had happened.

"China Mae would never have to play with my baby dolls again, for she had one of her own, just her color. It was lying asleep in the bed with her, and had on a little white gown. My mama was standing by the bed looking at that baby, with tears just streaming down her face.

" 'Sadie,' she said to me, 'This is Louella. God has sent her to live with us.' "

Miss Sadie shook her head and smiled at the rector. "Isn't that a surprise? To come home from school one day, and there's your second best friend of life, sent down from heaven?"

He laughed happily. If there was anything more amazing and wonderful than almost anyone's life story, he couldn't think what it was.

"Well, I took after that baby somethin' awful. I rocked her, I bathed her, I pulled her around in a little wagon, I sewed dresses for her, I was as happy as anything to have her to play with and love, and Mama was, too.

"When she got weaned, I started taking her to town. I'd dress her up myself, and they'd say, 'Here comes Sadie Baxter with that little nigger.'

"I never did like to hear that, even as a child. I wanted Louella to be my sister, I played like she was my sister, and then when I'd go to town, they'd say that. So, I stopped going.

"We stayed home and played and I never did miss going to town. Mama hired a tutor for me, anyway. Mr. Kingsley. I declare, he had the worst bad breath in the world, but he taught the prettiest cursive you ever saw, and was real good at history. Mama ordered off for all my clothes and shoes, and China Mae cut my hair, and we went to the doctor and dentist at Papa's lumber yard down in the valley. Or, sometimes, the doctors would drive up the mountain to give us our checkups, and Mama would put on a big spread like the president was coming.

"We called it 'Doctor Day,' and I didn't take to it one bit. I would grab Louella and we would run off and hide in the orchard."

Miss Sadie laughed to herself, with her eyes closed. Father Tim could see that she was watching a movie in which she was both the star and the director. He closed his eyes, too, and quietly slipped his feet out of his loafers.

"When Louella was about three, Mama said she was tired of going off and leaving her and China Mae at home when we marched off to Lord's Chapel. There were only a dozen or so colored people in Mitford, not enough for a church, I suppose. So, Mama said that from now on, we were all going together, that was what God gave us churches for.

"Papa didn't like this one bit, but Mama would not let up on him. She got down the Bible and the prayer book and without a shadow of a doubt, she showed him what was what.

"So, China Mae and Louella and Papa and Mama and me would walk down the road to the old Lord's Chapel that stood on the hill. And we would all sit in the same pew.

"If anybody ever once said 'nigger,' I don't know who it was, for they were scared of Papa. I mean, they respected him, not to mention that he gave a lot of money.

"In a little while, it seemed like nobody noticed anymore, it was just the most natural thing on earth. What they said outside the lychgates, I don't know, but if China Mae missed a Sunday from being sick, lots of ladies would ask about her.

"Life was better in those days, Father, it really was. When China Mae did the wash in the wash house, and we put the fire under that big iron pot, why, it was an exciting event. China Mae had joy over making the clothes come clean, while people today would think it was drudgery. We kind of celebrated on wash day. Mama would make a pineapple upside-down cake, and Louella and I would make stickies out of biscuit dough and cinnamon and sugar, and after that big load of work was done, we all sat down and had a tea party."

A bird called outside the open windows, and a breeze filled the fragile marquisette curtains. Father Tim caught himself nodding off and sat upright at once.

"You know how the Bible is always talking about the poor? Twice every week, Mama went to see the poor. She would pack a big basket of the best things in the world and put her blue shawl on her head and go off walking to see the poor.

"She never let me go with her, not once, but she taught me some verses from Proverbs, the thirty-first chapter, 'She stretcheth out her hand to the poor; yea, she reacheth forth her hands to the needy. . .

She looketh well to the ways of her household, and eateth not the bread of idleness.' That was her favorite in the whole Bible; she said it was her model.

"Those golden days passed so quickly. I wanted to stay a child forever, but before I felt like I was awake real good, I was sixteen, and it was time to go abroad. Abroad! What a hateful word. I came to despise it. So many girls would have given anything to 'go abroad.'

"When I heard that Uncle Haywood had talked Papa into sending me, I was shocked, I felt betrayed. How could he send me away to another country? Mama was horrified, too, but she said it was for the best. I know I'd complained about Mr. Kingsley's bad breath a hundred times, but I didn't see that as a reason to change my schooling to the other side of the world!"

Miss Sadie opened her eyes. She was silent for a moment, gazing at the faded yellow roses on the wallpaper.

"I can just see Papa now. Right before we were ready to go down to Charleston to take the boat, he came in the front door. I remember all the luggage, the big trunks and the hat boxes, was stacked in the hall, and Papa came storming in and threw his hat on the table. He was burning mad, I had never seen him so mad. The veins stood out on his neck, and the top of his head was red as fire where the hair had thinned.

" 'Cur!' is what he said over and over. He was shouting. I thought a dog had bitten him! But oh, it was so much worse than that.

"Mama tried to make him sit down and drink a lemonade, it was so hot his shirt was sticking to him, it was August. But he wouldn't, and he started up again, saying things like 'scoundrel' and 'scum of the earth.'

"It turns out he'd been driving up from the lumber yard in the valley, and somebody had come speeding by him so fast, that Papa had run his Buick town car into a ditch, causing considerable damage to the beautiful grillework and the fenders."

Miss Sadie looked at the rector. "My papa was a good man, but he was not the kind of man you want to run off the road, and especially not into a ditch. You know, Father, times were different, then, and it was considered almost honorable for a man to hold a grudge against an injustice."

She sighed. "I don't suppose I have to tell you who it was that ran him off the road."

No. No, she did not. Father Tim glanced across the room at

the photo of the handsome young Willard Porter, whose dark gaze seemed to pierce the room so forcibly that he might have been present, listening.

"Papa had to borrow a car to drive to Charleston, and in those days, people did not care to loan their cars, so that upset Papa even more. On the way, he talked about what had happened on Lumber Road. He just couldn't seem to get over it. He didn't know who had done it, he hadn't recognized the car, it was a new car, and fancy. And the more he talked about it, the less he acted like himself. Of course, he tried not to talk about me going away, because every time he did, he would cry a little.

"He'd never spent a night away from Mama since they were married, and it was a big sacrifice to give us both up at one time, for she was going with me—to stay 'til I got settled.

"You could have floated that big ol' boat on our tears!" Miss Sadie said, laughing. "And to think—buying all those fancy clothes and hats and steamer trunks, and going to Charleston in August, of all things, and taking that long trip across the ocean in that big storm that broke a freighter in two, and all those tear-stained, homesick letters—just to turn around and come home again, lickety split, in two months!"

"But look what it's given you to remember all these years."

With the only irony he had ever heard in her voice, she said, "Yes. But look what it did to my heart."

Suddenly, an alarm sounded so loudly that it caused his own heart to thunder. "Good Lord!" he exclaimed, thrusting his feet into his shoes and standing up at once.

"That's just Louella," she said, brightly. "Lunch must be ready. Father, dear, would you kindly turn your head and look toward the door?"

He did so, his ears ringing, as she got out of bed and put on her slippers and robe.

"Now you can look!" she said, going to the wall opposite her bed and grasping what appeared to be a drawer pull under a painting. A little door opened in the wall and Miss Sadie stuck her head inside. "Yes, Louella?"

"Miss Sadie!" he heard Louella's mezzo voice boom up the shaft, "Do th' Father want vinegar on his greens?"

"Father, do you want vinegar on your greens?"

"I think not. A little butter, perhaps."

"Louella, he won't have vinegar, he'll have butter."

"Butter! I never heard of butterin' greens. Miss Sadie, y'all want your tea hot or cold?"

"Which is easier?"

"Cold's done fixed."

"Send cold," said Miss Sadie with some pleasure. "And remember he likes his plenty sweet."

"Ah, not anymore," said the rector, fidgeting.

"Louella, not anymore," his hostess shouted.

"What'd you say?"

"He doesn't like his tea too sweet anymore."

"No sugar," he said, feeling as miserable as if he had just delivered an elegy.

"No sugar in his tea, Louella. Are you coming up?"

"I'm eatin' right here in this kitchen. Do y'all want chow chow for your beans?"

"Yes, indeed," said the rector, pacing the floor.

"Chow chow, Louella, and plenty of it. Don't sound the alarm again, it nearly made him faint. Just knock twice with the broom handle and send it up."

He found that the discussion over lunch particulars had given him an odd twinge in his stomach, but the tea, when it came up on the silent butler, revived his spirits.

"Father," said Miss Sadie, who was sitting up in bed, having finished her lunch, "you can't imagine how wonderful it is to have someone listen to me ramble. Did you ever think that just when people grow old and have so much to tell, that's when people want them to hush? I hope when you grow old, there'll be someone to listen to you ramble."

"I feel blessed to have people listen to me ramble every Sunday of my life," he said happily, folding his napkin and putting it on the tray.

"Oh, pshaw, you're so modest. You never give yourself enough credit, in my opinion. You don't ramble at all, you get right to the point, and it's always God's point, as far as I can see. But, do you know what I appreciate more than your sermons?"

"What's that?"

"The fact that you love us. Yes, that's enough for me, that you love us." She closed her eyes and let out a lingering breath. "Ahhh, the peace. What a blessing. Father, will you come again tomorrow? While

I've got the hook in the water, you might say. I don't believe I have the strength to go to the end, today."

"I will. Right after lunch. Don't fix for me tomorrow. I'll bring you a doughnut from Winnie's."

"Just plain," murmured Miss Sadie. "Not fancy."

He went as quietly as he could across the creaking floor, and closed the door behind him.

Miss Sadie was sitting in a slip-covered wing chair by the window, with an afghan over her knees. "I've been thinking all night," she said, "and I don't want to waste a minute."

He sat in the wing chair opposite her and unbuttoned his jacket. "I have until three o'clock, Miss Sadie. My time is yours."

"When Mama and I met Willard in Paris, we would never have dreamed he was the one who made Papa run off the road. He was so nice, so considerate, so genuine. He had just moved to Mitford from Tennessee, and we learned from his conversation that his family had nothing to speak of. He was a boy who was trying to make the most of his God-given talents, and he was busy inventing things in the pharmaceutical field.

"One thing he'd invented was Formula R, which stood for Rose. Formula R was good to put on burns or wounds. It was an antiseptic, it just worked wonders, but it stung like fire.

"We had the sweetest times together in Paris. My mama was a wonderful judge of character, and while she had a soft heart, she couldn't be fooled. She thought Willard was a fine person. But when we got home, and we started telling Papa about the Mitford boy who befriended us in that faraway place, why, I thought he would have a stroke.

"I couldn't believe the horrible anger that welled up in him, something I had never seen before in my life. He said Willard Porter was trash, the lowest kind, an uneducated, penniless, heathen boy with no future and no breeding, and we were never to mention his name in our house again. He was so mean to Mama, as if she had betrayed him.

"I found out Papa had dealt with Willard after Willard came home from Paris, because, when I saw Willard driving around the monument one day, he acted as if he hadn't seen me.

"All the way over on the boat, I had dreamed of seeing him again, the fact that he lived in my hometown was . . . it was just too joyful for words. And then, to come home to that cold anger and rage, and a papa who hardly seemed the same person. . . .

"One day, China Mae brought me a note. It was folded up little bitty, and hidden in her dress. It was from Willard, and when I saw the handwriting, the same handwriting on the notes that came with the roses in Paris, I remember that my heart beat so wildly, I had to sit down.

"China Mae said, 'Don't you dare faint, faintin' is too white for words.'

"I still have the little note. It said: 'I have made the very worst mistake of my life. The incident on the road was inexcusable, and completely unintentional. I deeply regret that I have caused this strife, and am willing to do anything within my power to remove the memory of it. I have apologized to your father with heartfelt sincerity, but he will not hear me. I do not know what more can be done at this time. Please forgive me. Your faithful servant, Willard James Porter.'

" 'Mama,' I said, 'I think I love Willard.'

"She said, 'Don't even speak of it, don't let your heart think such a thing, it is impossible. This has changed your father in a way I don't understand.'

"Just like when I was a little girl, I stopped going to town. We ordered off for my clothes, just like always, and I didn't even cut my hair. Mama helped me study, and I played the piano and did needlepoint, and read books, and went to church every evening and lit a candle and knelt down and talked to God.

"You would have thought the heavens had been barricaded against me, as if God had said, 'Nail everything up good and tight, in case Sadie Baxter tries to get through.'

"It seemed a long time later that China Mae said someone was building a big house over in town, a big showplace, all white with porches and gables and even a widow's walk, though there was no ocean for hundreds of miles.

"Everybody at church was talking about it, and talking about Willard, how he had sold some of his pharmaceutical inventions, and how he was getting rich.

"Something awful happened to Papa when his name was mentioned at church, or wherever. You would think that the years would soften his heart toward a foolish, unfortunate incident, but it did not.

"You know, Father, looking back, Papa was a lot like Willard. He came from nothing, he had no special education, he was a rough man in many ways, but he refined himself and taught himself to speak well and read good books and travel in polite society, just like Willard.

"China Mae came home now and again, all excited. 'I seen 'im, Miss Sadie,' she'd say, 'I seen your Willard and he jus' th' han'-somest man you ever laid eyes on.' He opened up a pharmacy on Main Street where Happy Endings is now. And one in Wesley, and two in Holding.

"I received a letter from him one day, out of the blue. I'd like to show this one to you. Would you be so kind, Father, to step to the dresser and look in the top drawer on the right?"

He opened the drawer and was struck by the scent of lavender that rushed out at him. He found the ivory envelope just where she said it was, and took it back to his chair by the window.

He removed the brittle stationery, unfolded it, and saw that the date at the top was June 13, 1927. He read aloud:

" 'My dear Sadie, I saw you go by yesterday, and though you did not see me, I was very touched by your sweetness and grace. I know it is risky to write to you, and have firmly emphasized to China Mae that you must burn this letter after reading it. I implore you to do so, as I take this liberty with the greatest concern for your happiness.

" 'I once said that when you grow up, I should like to marry you. Today, you are twenty-one, and I believe that is considered by all to be grown up.

" 'As for myself, I am twenty-six, my business is at last going well, and I am beginning to make a place for myself, my mother, and my little sister. For the first time, it is possible for me to marry, and yet it is impossible for me to marry the one I love devotedly and think about night and day.

" 'I do not know your feelings for me, except what China Mae has confided—please, I beg you, do not punish her for speaking out of turn.

" 'I have tried again and again to think of a way to change your father's mind toward me, but I come each time to the same bitter conclusion. He despises me, and anything I might try to do to win your hand would only bring turmoil and despair to you and to your mother.

" 'You may know that I am building a house in the village, on the green where Amos Medford grazed his cows. Each stone that was laid in the foundation was laid with the hope that I might yet express the loving regard I have for you, Sadie.

" 'It is bold to write you so, but I am filled with a longing on this, your twenty-first birthday, that is nearly inexpressible.

" 'I am going to give this house a name, trusting that things may eventually be different between us. I will have it engraved on a cedar beam at the highest point in the attic, with the intention that its message may one day give you some joy or pleasure.

" 'Perhaps, God willing, your father will soon see that I have something to offer, and relent. Until then, dear Sadie, I can offer only my fervent love and heartfelt devotion.' "

Father Tim sat for a time, silently, and then put the letter back into the ivory envelope.

She turned her head and looked out the window. It was a warm, bright spring day. "Such a waste," she said simply.

He waited.

"I prayed for Papa, for God to give him a new heart, like He gave Saul. But He did not. In those days, twenty-one was an old maid, and I believe Papa was sometimes sorry that no one courted me. But there was no one, you see, there was only Willard. And then . . . two or three years later, there was Absalom Greer."

Miss Sadie's eyes twinkled. "Absalom Greer! Another uneducated man! I never could get it right. Which, of course, is why Uncle Haywood wanted me to go off to Paris, France, and then debut in Atlanta where I'd meet all those fancy boys. He told Papa if I stayed in Mitford I would wind up an old maid—or with dishpan hands, married to a farmer!

"I never did like Uncle Haywood," she said, flatly. "By the way, did you bring my doughnut?"

"Your doughnut!" said the rector, patting his jacket pocket and bringing out a bag that had mashed rather flat. "I'm sorry to say Winnie was out of doughnuts, all she had left was the holes, so I brought you four!"

"Four doughnut holes," said Miss Sadie, solemnly, peering down into the bag. "They can't be very filling, can they?"

She laughed suddenly, and for the first time, he saw the girl she had been. It lasted only a moment, the face of the girl, but it was there, and something in him connected with the young Sadie.

"Absalom Greer worked for Papa at the lumber yard. Of course, I never went down there much, but when I did, I liked it. I had taken to sitting rather gloomily around the house, just to show Papa how wicked he'd been, and how I hadn't forgotten what he'd done.

"He said that what I needed was fresh air and hard work. So, he took me down to the lumber yard, and put me in his office and opened all the windows, and that was the fresh air.

"Then he sat me down with an adding machine and ledgers, and that was the hard work!

"I have made Papa sound like a mean man. But oh, I loved him, and he could be such fun. Some days, he would just relax and laugh and pet me to beat the band. But no matter how hard he tried, he could not teach me to keep those hateful books.

"One day, a young man knocked on the office door and I opened it and there he was—a big, tall boy, as slim as a bean pole, wearing a cap and carrying a Bible. There was a kind of electricity about him. He looked down at me and said, 'Miss Sadie Baxter, are you saved?'

"Why, I declare I didn't know what on earth he was talking about! I looked straight up at him and said, 'Well, I'm not lost!'

"He was the cutest thing, so tall and jovial, he had the heartiest laugh and the nicest smile, and knew how to talk plain talk. I just felt so at home with him, like I had a brother, and he was so excited about the Lord and about the Bible. Once, Papa came in and Absalom was sitting there reading me a Bible story on his dinner break. He didn't miss a beat, he just raised his voice and read louder.

"Papa went and sat down at his desk, he was amazed. I don't think he knew what to do about it, so he didn't do anything. It kind of made me nervous, but Absalom read all the way to the end of Second Samuel, then got up, put his Bible under his arm, tipped his cap, and went back to work."

Father Tim laughed with delight. That was another picture of the boy who had been delirious with God, the one who had come home from the silver mine and been knocked out of bed one night with a "two-by-four," and had gotten up, at last, to answer God's call.

"Every day at dinnertime—we called it dinner, then, you know—Papa was usually out on the yard, and Absalom would come in and read to me. What a beautiful voice he had, and how hard he tried to polish his diction and improve his speech! It was a wonderful thing to watch, someone with so little schooling, and so much yearning.

"Then came the day he asked if he could court me. 'Ask Papa,' I said, with fear and trembling. I had never been courted in my life, and

I was nearly twenty-five years old. My father was the richest man in Mitford or Wesley, and a laborer out of his lumber yard was asking to court me. I didn't see one ray of hope in it.

"I remember I was so excited and upset, I ran to the back door and heaved up, if you'll pardon the expression, Father.

"The next morning, on the way to the yard, Papa was looking straight ahead at the road and he said, 'Sadie, Absalom Greer has asked if he can court you. What do you think about it?'

"I couldn't believe my ears that Papa was asking me what I thought about something. I said, 'Papa, I have prayed about it, and I would like to be courted by Absalom Greer.' My heart beat so hard I thought I would pass out, but I always remembered that China Mae thought fainting was too white for words, so I never did it.

" 'Well, then,' Papa said, 'I am going to give him my permission.'

" 'Papa,' I said, 'thank you for your permission, but what I would covet is your blessing.'

"He must have given it to us, for Absalom was allowed to come to our house, he ate Sunday supper with us before he preached in the evenings, and often, I'd go with him and sit on the front row. We were allowed to drive Papa's town car on special occasions, and once, Papa gave Absalom a beautiful suit that was cut too slim, and it fit Absalom like it was made for him! I'll never forget what Mama said, she said, 'My! You look like a Philadelphia lawyer!' That pleased Absalom so much.

"You should have heard him preach, Father! Why, he'd take the fuzz off a peach. Lord's Chapel hadn't had a fine preacher for a long time, and I was starved nearly to death to hear such wondrous things—about salvation and redemption and Christ's suffering for me.

"Absalom made it all so personal, as you often do, and under his preaching, the Bible came alive for me. He was the one who tried to teach me the great meaning of Philippians four-thirteen."

A banner verse, he thought, smiling.

"But Absalom was like a brother . . . I still loved Willard. Now that I was getting out and about more, I would often see Willard, and the pain of that was very deep. His house was finished, of course, and the most beautiful sight in town—it was more wonderful than Boxwood.

"They said Willard worked all the time; even though he joined the new country club, all he did was work. He joined the Presbyterian church, and he worked over there, too. Why, he helped them raise enough money for a new building in a little over a year, and in those days, that was something to crow about.

"All this time, Rose wasn't doing well. They didn't know much about her disease, and they still don't, I'm told. But he took such good care of her, and then his mother passed away, and it was just the two of them in that grand house, a lonely man and a confused girl. Father, there were times when my heart was so broken for him that I wanted nothing more than to knock on his door and go in to him, and never leave.

"But something happened after a while, after two or three years of courting Absalom. It wasn't that I no longer cared for Willard, but the caring had worn me out. I was very tired from caring so much and loving so much and hoping."

She took a sip of water from a glass on the window sill.

"Papa and Mama had come to like Absalom, and even though he had no money, and probably never would, they were happy with things, and all the hurt and the anguish seemed . . . in the past. I would not have wanted to upset that delicate balance for anything in the world.

"When I'd see Willard, he would tip his hat to me, though rumor had it that Papa had threatened to kill him if he ever spoke to me. It's a hard thing to have to change your opinion of someone you love, and my opinion of Papa was changing, no matter how hard I tried to hold it back. It was like trying to hold back the ocean.

"The lumber business got awful bad, and I don't think our finances had ever recovered from the money that was spent on Fernbank. You've never seen the little ballroom with the painted ceiling, it's been closed up all these years, but that alone cost a fortune. The man who painted it came from Italy and lived here thirty-four months. And of course, just look at all this millwork. Nobody in western North Carolina had finer, except Mr. Vanderbilt, of course.

"Father, you know how word gets around in a small town, and the word got around about our circumstances, and Willard heard it, and he approached Papa and offered to buy him out. I know why Willard did that, it was one way of saying, here, let me give you a good price for your business and save your face, and make things right after all these years.

"But Papa didn't take it that way. It made him so angry, thinking that Willard pitied him, that we thought he was going to have a heart attack.

"Mama said, 'I am sick and tired of this hateful, evil battle between you and a man who made a foolish mistake and lived to regret it and said so. I will no longer tolerate the dark spirit it brings into this house and into my husband, and into the heart of my child, and I beg you in the name of all that's holy to meet with Willard Porter and face him like a gentleman and settle your differences and ask God to forgive you.'

"That was the single boldest thing I ever heard my mother say.

"Do you know that my father bowed his head and wept? Mama went and stood beside him and put her arm around him and I dropped down at his feet and clasped my arms around his legs, and we all cried together. China Mae was standing outside the door and tears were streaming down her face, and she was praying and thanking God."

Miss Sadie drew a handkerchief from her robe pocket and touched her eyes.

"It's all as clear to me as if it happened yesterday. I remember the fire was crackling in the fireplace, and Papa said we'd need more wood, they were calling for a big drop in the temperature, it was January. He stood up and hugged us both, and Mama said, 'Why not see if you can meet with Mr. Porter now, while your resolve is fresh, and come home to the night's sleep you've been needing for so long.'

" 'I'll do it,' he said, and I remember that I trembled as he rang the operator and asked for Willard Porter.

"He told Willard he had to go to church to take care of something, he was the senior warden, and it would be a fitting place to settle their differences, if he'd care to meet him there.

"It was awkward for Papa, I could tell. Mama was standing beside me, holding onto my arm for dear life, I don't think she drew a breath 'til that phone call was ended.

"I don't know why, but I was very troubled. Mama went to her room to pray and asked me to pray, and I did, I got on my knees beside my bed. Then, I got up and put on my alpaca cape with the hood, and my fur gloves—it was very cold—and I let myself out the front door.

"I just started walking to the church. And even though it was pitch dark, it was nearly like walking from my dining room to the kitchen, it was all so familiar to me. I don't know what I expected, or why I went, I just seemed pulled along. I remember how loud my heart was beating in my ears.

"Ice had formed all along the road, in some places it was slippery and dangerous, and I just kept walking in that bitter cold and grave darkness.

"You know where the old steps are in the stone wall along Church Hill Drive? Well, I went up those icy steps, holding on to the railing, and I could see that Papa's and Willard's cars were parked in the back of the church, because the moon came out all at once."

Miss Sadie pulled the afghan up around her shoulders, and shivered slightly. Father Tim was suddenly aware that she looked very old, something he'd never seemed to notice before.

"When I reached the door, I heard their voices, and they were not the peaceful voices I had longed to hear, they were angry and shouting. Papa was accusing Willard of trying to humiliate him in front of the town, and Willard said he had come to make peace, and he didn't care to hear any more insults and lies.

"The door was standing open and I could see them so clearly. Papa had lit an oil lamp, it was sitting on the little table at the back of the nave, and I remember a strong smell of linseed oil that came off the floors; they'd just been done for a wedding the next Sunday.

"Papa was standing on one side of the table, and Willard was standing on the other. I wanted to rush in and stop them from arguing, but I felt frozen to the spot. I knew that Papa had left the house with the truest of intentions in his heart, but somehow the Enemy had snared him along the way.

"Papa swung his fist at Willard, and Willard stepped back. Papa's arm sent the oil lamp reeling off the table, and it dashed against the floor, and an awful flame leaped up. It was all so sudden, and so horrible, I cannot tell you how quickly that sheet of flame raced across the oiled floor. I felt that the very soul of evil had been unleashed. And still I could not move, though I remember I heard myself screaming.

"I turned and ran home as fast as I could, falling on the ice, and trying to keep to the sides of the road where it wasn't so slick.

"I turned around and looked back once, and I saw the church lighted up inside. It was so horrible, I shall never forget that sight as long as I live. For years I prayed I might die, so that the memory of it would be erased.

"I crept into the house and went upstairs and looked out my window. The flames were already leaping around the wooden walls, and it seemed the fields were lighted up for miles around.

"They said that when the fire truck came, the water was frozen, and there was no way to do anything but watch it burn. Water everywhere was hard as stone, and there was only that searing flame licking the frozen hilltop."

Miss Sadie closed her eyes, and let out a shuddering sigh. " 'They have cast fire into thy sanctuary,' " she quoted slowly from the Seventy-fourth Psalm, " 'they have defiled by casting down the dwelling place of thy name to the ground.' " She rested her head against the cushion of the chair.

The clock ticked in the room, and the rector felt his heart beat dully. How had this small woman contained this large secret for so long?

"My father," she said, keeping her eyes closed, "told the firemen he had gone to church to check the pipes because of the freezing temperatures, and when he arrived, he found it already burning. Willard Porter had left the scene and no one knew he'd been there.

"They suspected arson.

"The grief that I suffered was nearly unendurable, I could not get out of bed. In fact, it was this very bed in this very room. I kept the draperies closed and lived as if in a dream. I felt invalid, and frail; I began to creep about like an old woman. I couldn't confide to China Mae, my best friend, and certainly not to Louella, nor say a word to Mama, whose worry over me nearly drove her to the breaking point. I refused to see Absalom, yet one day, he delivered a note to the house, asking me to marry him.

"Marry!" Miss Sadie shook her head. "I knew at last, full well, that I would never marry.

"My father never revealed the truth to anyone, and he was so gravely stricken with guilt and shame that I thought he might die. The doctor drove up the mountain to Fernbank regularly, we were all so ravaged by our secrets and our sorrows. For me, it wasn't just all that I'd seen, and the knowledge of Papa's deceit, there was also an awful sadness over the loss of Lord's Chapel, the sweetest church in Mitford.

"It was a very long time until I learned that Papa had commanded Willard to leave the scene of the fire, and Willard, for all those years, was willing to protect Papa. He never said a word. He took the truth to his grave in France.

"It seemed that Satan himself had come against us. I thought Louella would never get over the horror of that time. Our faith did not shine through, Father, even my mother was broken by the burden of what she could not understand."

She reached for the glass on the window sill and took another sip of water.

"Papa's business regained its footing, and he rallied to raise the money to build Lord's Chapel on Old Church Lane. He bought your little stone office, which had been an ice house, and gave it to the parish. The rectory was already owned by the church, and standing where it is today. When the time came, Papa gave the pews and the organ, and put the roof on the nave and sanctuary, that was before the parish hall. And he had the gardens dug and planted.

"I feel that Papa would have let me marry Willard, at last, but it was too late. Oh, it was so late. When the war started, of course, Willard went away to serve, and he was killed in France and buried there." She paused, gazing out the window. "And Absalom? Well, I scarcely ever saw him again. I know that his sister, Lottie, could not find it in her heart to forgive me, for I hurt him, and she loved him so.

"When Papa and Mama died, I did perhaps the only independent thing I had ever done in my life." She looked at him and smiled weakly. "I moved across the aisle and started sitting on the gospel side."

She slumped a little in the chair. He leaned forward and reached for her hand, which felt small and cold.

"That's my love story, Father. I'm sorry it did not have a happier ending. The nursing home will give it a happy ending. The building will be given in honor of Mama and Papa. The beautiful fountain out front will be in memory of Captain Willard James Porter. It will be a place of solace and peace, a place for healing."

Father Tim got up from his chair and placed a hand on her fragile shoulder. "Father," he prayed, "I ask you to heal any vestige of bitter hurt in your child, Sadie, and by the power of your Holy Spirit, bring to her mind and heart, now and forever, only those memories which serve to restore, refresh, and delight. Through Jesus Christ, your Son our Lord, Amen."

"Amen!" she said, reaching up to put her hand on his.

"Y'all been talkin' so long, you mus' be dry as two bones."

Louella set a tray on the foot of the bed and handed out tall glasses of tea with bright circles of lemon.

"Thank you, Louella, please sit down. The deed is done."

"Thank you, Jesus!" said Louella, and sat down on Miss Sadie's blue silk vanity bench.

"Have a doughnut hole, Louella," said Miss Sadie, extending the bakery bag. "Father?" she said, offering him one also.

How much harm could the hole of a doughnut do? he wondered, reaching into the bag.

"That," Miss Sadie exclaimed happily, "leaves two for me!" The rector noticed that her color was returning. "Oh, Father, something I've been meaning to ask you. You know that lovely woman who looks like Mama? Olivia Davenport, I think her name is. I'd like to give her Mama's hats; she wears a hat with such style. You know, there's no family to pass them on to, and there are just so many beautiful hats up in the attic, going to waste. Do you think it would be an insult?"

"Why, no. No, I don't. I think Olivia might be very glad to have those hats. Perhaps you could call her and talk to her. I believe she'd welcome hearing from you, she's rather shut in, you know."

"She's going to get a new heart, isn't she?"

"God willing. She's on a waiting list, but she has a rare blood type, and the heart could come from anywhere in the world. The trick is getting it to her—or her to it—in time."

"A new heart! How thrilling! I will pray for her, Father, and I'll call her in the next day or two. Could you run them over to her, if she's interested? Would you mind? I could get Luther to take them in the pickup, but he hurt his back and can't drive."

"We'll most certainly work it out," he said, draining the tea glass and standing. He bent down and kissed Miss Sadie on the forehead.

"Take good care of one another," he said. "I'll be in touch."

Louella followed him out the door and closed it behind her.

She walked with him to the foot of the stairs. "Father," she said, speaking in a low voice, "Miss Sadie ain't th' only one got a secret t' carry to th' grave. I got one of my own, and somethin' tells me I better let you have it, jus' in case."

Good heavens, thought the rector. No wonder he had never felt the need to devour mystery and suspense stories. Nearly every day he encountered mysteries and suspense galore.

"If I was you, I wouldn't let Miss Olivia and Miss Sadie get too thick. You know how folks always say 'who was yo' mama and yo' granmaw and where was you born at,' an' all. One thing might lead to another, and 'fore you know it, Miss Sadie might fin' out somethin' that would put her down, for sure."

He was afraid to ask. "And what is that?"

"That her mama done had a little baby 'fore she married Miss

Sadie's daddy. And that little baby growed up and was the granmaw of Miss Olivia."

Louella peered closely at the rector's face.

"Now, don't take me wrong, Miss Sadie's mama, she was a saint, she used to go roun' to th' poor just like th' Bible axe us to. An' th' poor she was mostly goin' roun' to was that little girl, who didn't live too far from Fernbank, kep' by a lady from Alabama. That little girl had th' name of Miss Lydia. Well, she growed up and had Miss Caroline and Miss Caroline done had Miss Olivia, an' far as I know, don' nobody know nothin,' they smoothed it out so. You know what's sad?"

"What's that?" asked the rector, who had heard so much of sadness today.

"Miss Sadie always talkin' 'bout how she got no kin, when her own kin livin' right down th' hill—and Miss Olivia thinkin' she got no kin, either!"

"Louella, thank you for telling me this. Will you agree with me in prayer?"

"Honey, you know I will!"

"The psalmist tells us that God 'setteth the solitary in families.' Let's pray that it might please God to make these two a family, in His own way."

"Cast yo' bread on th' waters . . ." said Louella, grinning broadly.

"And sometimes," replied the rector, "it comes back buttered toast."

He drove along Church Hill Drive, beside the stone wall that led to the ruined church. He would never again be able to look at that hilltop without a kind of sorrow. His particular job sometimes revealed more to him than he wanted to know.

There, he thought, as he made the right-hand turn into Old Church Lane, was where he'd first come panting up the hill in his new jogging suit from the Collar Button. That innocent time seemed long ago.

He felt a keen anguish over Barnabas, as he drove slowly down the hill, but reminded himself that, after all, Barnabas was only a dog.

Only a dog? Instantly, he realized where this perverse thought had come from. He'd stood by the cages with his father, surveying in frozen alarm the dead bodies of his entire herd. "There's no use to grieve," his father had said, coldly, "they're only rabbits."

He'd learned that one obstacle to childlike faith in a heavenly father was bitter disappointment in earthly fathers. No, not everyone had that obstacle to faith, which was clearly a favorite of the Enemy, but Miss Sadie had had it, and he had had it and come to terms with it, and forgiven his father, long years ago.

His research for the paper on Lewis revealed this had been a major obstacle for the apologist. One commentator had said, "For years, Lewis had not been able to forgive himself for his failure to love his father, nor had he been able to appropriate God's forgiveness for this sin. But when finally enabled, he was almost incredulous of the peace and the ease he experienced."

He glanced vaguely at the rose arbors that had come into bloom along Old Church Lane. The Rose Festival! He still had no inkling of what to talk about.

The War of the Roses? No, there was enough talk of war in this world.

He would think about it all later, perhaps in the evening when Dooley was asleep. Of course, what he really needed to think about was what to do with Dooley for the summer. And then, there was always what Cynthia had asked him to think about.

He felt oddly relieved to arrive at the office and have the peace of it to himself.

He checked his phone messages and calendar. Meet with the Altar Guild at three o'clock about designs for needlepoint kneelers to replace the ancient leather-covered cushions. Dinner at Wilma and Ron Malcolm's, with Dooley in tow, tomorrow evening. Drop by The Local and pick up a ham to bake for the Newland reception on Saturday. Should he have warned Miss Sadie, who was hoping to be there, that Absalom Greer would be there also?

A note from Emma said: "Winnie expecting you. Olivia fine. Russell behaving. Rabbit food on sale."

As he took the cover off his Royal manual, to type a quick note to Stuart Cullen, he heard a thunderous sound out front, and felt the building shake. There was the explosive whooshing of air brakes, and, in a moment, a loud rap on the door. He opened it to see a truck as vast as an auditorium parked in the street.

"Yes?" he inquired of a large, bearded man with a cut of tobacco in his jaw.

"Bells," said the driver, handing him a clipboard with a delivery slip.

CHAPTER TWENTY

Baxter Park

Puny had set up the ironing board in his bedroom, so she could press the drapes that had been folded over a hanger for two years. Dooley had promised to help her hang them in the afternoon. "I seen that big mess in th' churchyard," she said. "What *is* all that stuff, anyway?"

"Bells. Bells under a tarp, delivered without warning, and nobody to put them in the tower 'til next Wednesday."

"I thought Emma was gittin' married Saturday. That don't look too good with a weddin' goin' on."

"No kidding." He was going through his pants pockets and making a pile for the dry-cleaning truck.

"That ham you got is a whopper. You want me to bake it Friday?"

"I'd be beholden to you if you would."

"I'll use my pineapple glaze that Joe Joe . . . I mean, ah . . . oh well." She flushed beet red.

"Joe Joe, is it?"

"Shoot!" she said, "I didn't mean to let that out."

"And why not? Have you forgotten who prayed for a parade, out of the goodness of his heart?" He was so pleased with her unintentional confession that he could scarcely contain his smug delight.

"I don't think it's right to talk about things like that 'til you know what's goin' on with somebody. That's what Mama said. She courted our daddy a whole year before she talked about it." Frowning, she pulled the heavy, lined drapery panel off the ironing board. "I wish you'd help me put this thing over the chair back, it weighs a ton."

"I've never understood exactly how you keep something like that under cover," he said. He took one end and helped her spread it over the other panels.

"Oh, come on, now," she said, winking hugely at him, "you do know, too. I mean, look at you!"

"What do you mean, look at me?"

"I mean your neighbor is what I mean, ha, ha."

"Ha, ha, yourself," he said, feeling the color steal into his face.

"Somebody said y'all were out walkin' th' other night, right on Main Street."

"Walking on Main Street is hardly keeping anything under cover. Can't two people go for a stroll without causing tongues to wag?"

Puny laughed. "Tongue waggin's 'bout th' only action y'all git over here in Mitford!"

"Now, now. Don't be pulling any of your Wesley high-hat on me, young lady."

"Anyway, I think she's real cute. I like 'er. She's different."

"I agree."

"With what? That she's real cute or that she's different?" Puny's eyes gleamed with mischief.

"I sincerely hope you don't persecute Joe Joe this way," he said, finding two quarters and a dime in a pants pocket. "And speaking of parades, do you find Joe Joe to be a drum and bugle corp, a marching band, or the fire engines?"

"Joe Joe," she said rapturously, "is the Santy Claus at the end, with a big sack of presents, throwin' candy to th' kids."

He was on his hands and knees, searching under the dresser for the dime that rolled across the floor. "That's as lavish a compliment as I've ever heard, I believe."

"He's nice, he's got manners, an' he's got a job. Not to mention good-lookin'."

He stood up, smiling at her. "I agree with all that, and then some. You have my blessing without even asking for it."

"And you," she said, grinning, "have mine."

"Father," said the caller, "Pete Jamison."

"Pete! I'm glad to hear your voice."

"Just wanted to call and check in. I'm in St. Paul. How are you?"

"Good! Can't complain. And you?"

"Not bad. They just gave me an award for the most sales in the first quarter. Considering that this time last year, I had the fewest sales . . ."

"Pete, congratulations. You can't know how I like hearing that."

"Well, Father, you probably won't like hearing this. You know the four things you told me to do when I left that day?"

"Pray. Read your Bible. Be baptized. Go to church."

"Well, I'm going to church. But I've got to tell you that it's full of hypocrites."

Father Tim laughed. If there was ever a popular refrain in modern Christendom, that might be it.

"My friend, if you keep your eyes on Christians, you will be disappointed every day of your life. Your hope is to keep your eyes on Christ."

"Yes, well . . ."

"I will disappoint you, Pete, they will disappoint you, but He will never disappoint you."

"I was about to say to heck with it."

"Don't quit! Are you reading your Bible?"

"Ah, well . . . I was."

"And then you quit."

"You got it."

"Then you can expect to be weak on one of your flanks, and that's precisely where the Enemy will come after you with a vengeance."

"I hear you."

"When are you coming back this way?"

"Soon, I hope. My territory's so big, it's stretching me like a rubber band."

"Keep your faith and you won't snap," said the rector, as Harold Newland walked in with the morning mail and handed him the day's packet. "Excuse me, Pete. Thank you, Harold, see you Saturday." Harold blushed deeply. Right on top, a letter from the man in the attic, with the return address of a federal prison.

"Pete," said Father Tim, "do you have a brother?"

"No, sir. Always wanted one, though."

"You've got one, now. Let me tell you a story."

"Well," Dooley said, slamming his book bag on the kitchen counter, " 'at's 'at."

"That's what?"

"Dern school's out."

"Of course! I'd clean forgotten."

"I tol' Tommy he could spen' th' night t'night."

"We were going to talk about that first. Why did you invite him without talking about it first?"

"I forgot."

Forgot! Well, and so had he. After all these weeks of lamely trying to figure what to do about Dooley when school was out, he'd completely forgotten that, this very day, it was out, period. And here he sat, reading the *Anglican Digest.*

It was enough to make him squirm with guilt, if he'd been so minded. Didn't everybody else have something clearly mapped out for their charges for the summer? Positive things like jobs, and earning money, and opening savings accounts, and sticking to a reading program, and maybe going to camp. Camp! He was astounded that the most obvious thing of all had only at this moment occurred to him. Would he never get this right?

"Put your things away, and we'll have a snack. Then we'll walk up and see your grandfather, take him his livermush."

He heard Dooley bound up the stairs. His face had not shown it, but surely he must be nearly ecstatic with his new freedom. He remembered some of his own ecstasy at the letting out of school and yes, it had to do with friends. Certainly Tommy could come.

Friends, however, could not solve the entire problem of what to do with a summer. For him, those years ago in Holly Springs, there had always been something to look forward to, a project, perhaps, something definite.

He picked up the phone. "Dora," he said to his friend at the hardware, "got any rabbits on hand?"

He had brought home the cage containing one sleek, curious black and white Flemish Giant, and put it on the back porch stoop, when the phone rang.

"Father?" said Miss Sadie. "I've been thinking. School was out yesterday, and I was wondering if Dooley would like a job for the summer? You know there's lots to do at this old place."

"Miss Sadie," he said, "let me talk to him about that. I may put him to work in the church gardens."

When he saw Cynthia at The Local, they stopped to visit by the produce bins. She'd been asked to read from her books at the library, as part of a summer cultural program, and was radiant at the prospect.

Before they went along their separate aisles, she said, "I've been thinking. My basement could use a good clean up. Do you think Dooley would be interested? And we could dig some flower beds in the back, Uncle left it a jungle out there. Oh, and maybe the two of us could build a rabbit hutch. I'd pay him, of course, and teach him to watercolor!"

"Watercolor? Dooley?"

"Well, and why not?"

Why not, indeed?

Later, Hal Owen dropped by the rectory.

"Came to town to pick up a package of serum, hadn't seen you in a while, since we've been skipping the coffee hour. How are you, Tim?"

"Not bad, considering."

"Considering what?"

"Considering that I have a boy who needs proper guidance, wisdom, direction, instruction, discipline, and last but not least, something to do for the summer."

"That's why I came," said Hal, grinning, and taking out his pipe. "We thought you might let Uncle Dools spend a few weeks at Meadowgate."

When the rector walked back to the hardware to pick up the rabbit food he'd left sitting on the counter, he ran into Dooley's teacher.

"Miss Powell, how did we do this year?"

"I've seen some positive changes in Dooley," she said, smiling. "But he has a way to go."

"And, ah, which way do you think he might be going?"

"Oh, I clearly see an outstanding ability in math, if you'll help him stick with it. He also proved to be a pretty tough slugger on the ball field. And then, there's his singing."

"Singing?"

"Why, yes. We coaxed him into mixed chorus a few weeks ago, I've been meaning to tell you that. He has a marvelous voice, and great timing. It may be a gift."

Dooley singing! How extraordinary.

"Jena," he said, calling his Sunday school supervisor at home, "have we ever thought of forming a young people's choir?"

"Well, we've thought of it, but somehow, it just hasn't happened."

"Would you be kind enough to make it happen?" he asked.

He saw Barnabas at the opposite end of the field, running toward him. "Come on, boy," he yelled. "Come on, fella!" But though Barnabas ran and ran, he remained at the opposite end of the field. He tried to run himself to the great, black, barking dog, but felt as if he were trapped, waist high, in Mississippi mud. In an agony of frustrated longing, he exerted a shuddering effort that seemed to force his very heart to burst.

When he awoke, bathed in sweat, Dooley was standing over his bed, looking stricken. "Why'd you go t' hollerin' f'r 'at ol' dog? 'at ol' dog's gone!" he said severely.

"That old dog is *not* gone!" he exclaimed, with sudden anger.

"You like t' scared th' poop outta me."

"The poop is precisely what you *need* to have scared out of you," he declared, unbuttoning his pajama top. He hated those dreams in which he found himself bound like a mummy, unable to move, his heart pounding like a hammer. "Go back to bed," he told the boy, who was still trying to peer into his face.

"I ain't, 'til you quit hollerin'."

"I've quit, for heaven's sake. Haven't you ever had a nightmare?"

"I've had plenty of them ol' things," said the boy, climbing into bed with him.

"Well, then, you understand." He lay back against the pillows, and glanced at the clock. Four a.m.

"I had one of them dreams th' other night at th' farm. I was dreamin' m' little brother Kenny had fell in th' creek and turned into a fish an' I was runnin' after 'im along th' bank, hollerin', 'Kenny, Kenny, come back, don't be a fish, don't leave me!' an' Miz Owen said I woke up Rebecca Jane, but that was all right, she come in and talked t' me."

"Do you miss your brother?"

"Yeah. He was my best friend."

Dear God! Five children wrenched apart like a litter of cats or dogs. "Tell me about your brothers and sisters."

"There's Jessie, she's th' baby, still poopin' in 'er britches, and Sammy, he's five, he stutters. Then, there's ol' Poobaw . . ."

"What does Poobaw mean?"

"Means he took after a pool ball my mama brought home, had a eight on it, she said it was a keepsake. Poobaw hauled 'at ol' thing around, went t' sleepin' with it, an' that's where 'is name come from, it used t' be Henry."

"What's Henry like?"

"Wets 'is bed, 'e's seven."

He dreaded this. "Do you know where they are?"

"Mama said she'd never tell nobody, or th' state would come git 'em. I was th' last'n t' go." There was a long silence.

If it wrenched his own heart to hear this, how must Dooley's heart be faring? "Have you ever prayed for your brothers and your baby sister?"

"Nope."

"Prayer is a way to stay close to them. You can't see them, but you can pray for them, and God will hear that prayer. It's the best thing you can do for them right now."

"How d'you do it?"

"You just jump in and do it. Something like this. You can say it with me. Our Father . . ."

"Our Father . . ."

"Be with my brother Kenny and help him . . ."

"Be 'ith m' brother, Kenny, an' he'p him . . ."

"To be strong, to be brave, to love you and love me . . ."

"T' be strong, t' be brave, t' love you an' love me . . ."

"No matter what the circumstances . . ."

"No matter what th' circumstances."

"And please, God . . ."

"An' please, God . . ."

"Be with those whose names Dooley will bring you right now . . ."

He heard something hard and determined in the boy's voice. "Mama. Granpaw. Jessie an' Sammy an' Poobaw. Miz Ivey at church, an' Tommy . . . 'at ol' dog . . . m' rabbit . . . Miz Coppersmith an' ol' Vi'let an' all." He buried his face in the pillow and pulled it around his ears.

The clock ticked. Somewhere, through the open alcove window, he heard the rooster crow, the rooster whose whereabouts he couldn't identify, but whose call often gave him a certain poignant joy. Dooley moved closer to him, and in minutes, he heard a light, whiffling snore. He sat up and pulled the blanket over the boy's sleeping form.

He didn't know why he felt this would be a splendid summer for Dooley Barlowe.

When his neighbor came over to see the new rabbit, they sat on the top step of the back stoop. The air was warm and balmy, and a light breeze stirred in the trees.

"Thanks for coming to the library to hear me," she said.

"What makes you think I came to hear you? Didn't you see that I was there to read the *Journal?*"

"Ha!" she said, "you never turned a single page!"

He laughed. "Is that a fact?"

"It is, and you know it."

"Then, while we're into this thanking business, let me say that I appreciate it when you come to hear me, and give the Presbyterians the nod."

"My pleasure," she said, looking directly into his eyes, and smiling. "I suppose I need to be making a decision, soon, about where to join."

"It would be a blessing to look out and see your face."

Dooley came through the back door, slamming the screen behind him. "Hey," he said to Cynthia.

"Hey, yourself."

"They ain't no lettuce n'r any carrots n'r nothin' in there!"

The rector pulled a ten-dollar bill out of his wallet. "Go see Avis and load up."

Cynthia looked after the red bicycle as it disappeared around the corner of the rectory. "Can't we do something about his English?"

"Or his negative attitude? Or his table manners? Or his murderous temper? Or his pain? There are so many things to do something about."

"Overwhelming, is it?"

"Very."

"Let me encourage you, Timothy. I think you've done wonders with him."

"Combed his cowlick, bought him some tennis shoes. It's hard to believe I've done any more than that, really. Trust is the foundational problem, he trusts no one. Jena's doing a good job with him in Sunday school, he's getting some of the basics. I'm just waiting to see where to go from here."

"What about the summer?"

"Overnight, he has a full dance card. I feel the best thing is to send him to Meadowgate for three or four weeks, there's a lot of love for him out there, and farm life will do him good. Then, I'll bring him home to work with me in the church gardens, and try to get your basement cleaned up. As for your flower beds, I can dig those. I've been digging beds for twenty years, so my credentials are solid."

"Excuse me." It was the girl who had come looking for Dooley once before. "Is Dooley home?"

"You've just missed him," said the rector. "But he'll be back in a flash, why don't you stay and wait for him?"

"Thank you," she said, softly.

Cynthia patted the step next to her. "Come. Sit on the steps with us. I've just popped over to see the new rabbit."

"I like rabbits," the girl said, sitting down. She was wearing a sleeveless dress that bared her brown arms, and her blond hair was in French braids. A pretty girl who looked straight out of a Nordic fairy tale, observed the rector.

"What's your name?" Cynthia wanted to know.

"Jenny. See that red roof over there? That's my house."

Another neighbor! And another pair of luminous eyes.

"I'm Cynthia, and this is Father Tim."

"Pleased to meet you," she said. "What's the bunny's name?"

Cynthia laughed. "I wanted them to name him Clarence, but they won't listen to me. Can't you just see him with a little pair of horn-rimmed glasses and tweed knickers? Anyway, he doesn't have a name, yet. As soon as Dooley gets back, we're going to give him one. I have two bunnies."

"Do they have names?"

"Flopsy and Mopsy. It was a busy day and I didn't have the wits to be original."

"This one could be Cottontail."

"It could," said Cynthia, "but I don't think they'll go for it."

When the red bicycle tore around the side of the rectory, Dooley, who was carrying a grocery bag in one arm and steering with the other, looked with amazement at the visitor, and, without slowing down, crashed headlong into the sycamore tree.

The bells continued to sit under a tarp on the lawn at Lord's Chapel, though he tried almost daily to get the crew to install them. They were all working, it seemed, on the golf resort in Wesley. "Putting golf before God!" he said to Ron Malcolm. "Now there's a sermon title, and I ought to be man enough to preach it!"

The earliest they could get to it, they said, was Friday, June 28. They'd get right on it at eight a.m. and by noon, the bells should be chiming.

He noted the date on his calendar. June 28? Why did that have a familiar ring, no pun intended?

He wouldn't put more roses in his own garden this year, but he would certainly put a new bed in the church gardens. He had ordered the memorial plaque from a catalog, and was pleased with the bold, Gothic lettering.

The Souvenir de la Malmaison, with its five-inch pink blooms, had been named in honor of the Empress Josephine's famous gardens, and he'd been intimidated for years by its reputation for being difficult and hard to establish. Well, then, no use to hold back any longer, he told himself, it's now or never.

He also ordered several Madame Isaac Pereire, reputed to be far less temperamental, to climb up the east wall. Even more aromatic than Malmaison, they were said to smell like crushed raspberries. What an extraordinary thing, a rose! He was beginning to feel some inspiration for his talk at the festival.

"Y'ought t' make 'at hole bigger," said Dooley, who was helping him install the roses before he went off to Meadowgate. " 'at hole ain't near big enough."

"How do you know it isn't?"

"I jis' know, is all."

When they were putting the rotted manure in the holes, the rector realized he'd forgotten to bring a second pair of gloves.

"I ain't scared of no cow poop," said the boy, working it deftly into the soil with his hands.

"Good fellow. And what did Jenny have to say the other day?"

"Said she was sorry I got in trouble f'r knockin' Buster Austin's lights out. Said he was askin' for it, he's always goin' aroun' askin' for it."

"Yes, but do you always have to be the one to give him what he asks for?"

"I ain't goin' to, n'more."

"Thanks be to God. And why is that?"

" 'cause."

"Because why, may I ask?"

Dooley took a deep breath. There was a long silence, and then he spoke carefully. "Jis' 'cause," he said.

"Here's the deal," said Walter, who called before the evening news. "Katherine and I have it all worked out. We meet you at the Shannon Airport on July 21. We take a bus to the train in Limerick City, and go up to Sligo, where we stay three weeks in a marvelous old farmhouse near Lough Gill. Then we take a car down to Claremorris and Roscommon, perhaps all the way to Ballinasloe. Margaret says we'll find a few family archives at an abbey in Ballinasloe, but you know how she varnishes the plain truth."

"There's no way under heaven I can do this now, there are too many . . ."

"Timothy, for God's sake! You've been making excuses about this trip for fifteen years! Come now, old fellow, if you wait until you have time, you'll never set foot outside Mitford."

"That's true. I agree with you completely."

"Then, let's do it! Katherine and I could go on our own, of course, but we'd much rather go with you in tow. You know how we've talked about splitting up in three directions during the day, to pursue the family secrets, then coming together every evening at dinner to put it all in one pot. What ground we could cover! It would be an experience of a lifetime, following those crooked turns back to our ancestral castle. Timothy, this is the year for it! Trust me on this."

"Walter, I have a boy now, you know, with a long summer stretching ahead of him like a jet runway. He needs someone to hold down the fort. And his grandfather, recovering from pneumonia, and a parishioner who's waiting for a heart transplant, and a five million dollar nursing home on the drawing board. What's more, I just put in a dozen vastly expensive roses, which will need looking after. You must understand, I simply can't do it. Perhaps next year . . ."

"Cousin, you deceive yourself. There will always be a boy and a nursing home and a case of pneumonia, in a manner of speaking."

He noticed that Walter sounded genuinely disappointed.

"I despise saying no, again and again, to this wonderful dream . . ." His voice trailed off. He was miserably disappointed in his own everlasting inability to get up and go, to take strong action and seize control, and do all the things that other people seemed able to do, and which the world admired so much.

There were times when he felt the Ireland trip was the most possible thing in life, and his heart would lift up and he'd begin to plan and read and even daydream about it. Then, suddenly, it seemed ridiculously impossible, a trivial pursuit in a world of so much suffering and pain. It was vain to go gadding after one's thoroughly dead ancestors and a vague ruin of a castle.

"And another thing," he said, having a sudden revival of energy, "Barnabas is missing, and if that twenty-five-hundred-dollar reward works—as a lot of people think it will—who would be here to welcome him back?" There! That was something Walter could not knock down, not in the least.

"Well, of course," his cousin said, reasonably. "You're right. Katherine will be disappointed, but perhaps we'll screw up our enthusiasm and go anyway, just the two of us. We'll bring the research home and see what *you* can make of it."

"Yes!" he said, immeasurably relieved, "That's a terrific idea. You do the footwork, I'll pore over the papers and the dates and try to make sense of everything, and then, perhaps, we could all go later and fill in the holes." Why did he have to say that? He could never leave well enough alone.

On June 13, remembering the date at the top of Willard Porter's letter, he took Miss Sadie a birthday card. The walk up the hill warmed him considerably, and he wished for his running clothes, which he hadn't donned in weeks. He must call Hoppy, but fervently disliked telling the truth about the neglect of his exercise and diet program.

He had done so well, for so long, and then he had lost control. A few days off his medication here, a few taboo foods on his plate there, and the first thing he knew, he was again overweight, fatigued, low in spirits, and generally aggravated by the aggressive takeover agenda of his hateful disorder.

When Louella offered him a piece of coconut birthday cake, he responded with such severity that she was taken aback.

"Sorry, Louella, I was snapping at myself, not at you. Please forgive me."

Miss Sadie was breezing about the bedroom, rouging her cheeks, and getting ready to drive to town with Louella to pick up Q-Tips at the drugstore.

"I'm glad to see you got over being tired. Happy birthday!" He kissed her forehead. "May there be many more to come."

"I want all God can give me!" she said brightly. "Oh, and I'm thrilled to say that Olivia Davenport would love to have Mama's hats. But when I told her there were thirty-two of them, she was kind of shocked, I think."

"I'll see that's taken care of in the next few days. Now, what may I do for you on your birthday? I have a half hour or so." He thought she might like a piece of furniture moved, perhaps, or something carried to the basement.

"You've done more than enough, already. More than enough! But if you could spare the time, one day soon, I'd dearly love to know what's carved on that beam in Willard's attic."

He had an odd, sinking feeling when Dooley went to his room to pack for Meadowgate. He could feel it coming; the house already seemed forlorn. What had he done all those years with no dog and no boy, just the everlasting monotony of his own company? He supposed he hadn't noticed very much that he was alone, proving the old adage that "you can't miss what you never had."

He paced the floor of his study, thinking, It's only for three or four weeks, imagine what you can get done around here with no interruptions, no bologna to fry, no hamburgers to fix, no jeans to wash, no homework to help with. He tried to imagine himself sitting with his feet up, reading Archbishop Carey's book, but somehow that didn't seem very interesting, at all.

He heard Dooley thumping down the stairs, dragging a suitcase that was evidently filled with lead.

"What are you taking in that thing, anyway?"

"Jis' some ol' poop f'r Rebecca Jane."

"And what might that be?"

"Jis' a baseball and a dump truck an' stuff like 'at."

"Hal will be here any minute. I pray you'll remember what we discussed."

"Say please and thank you, don't cuss, wash m' hands, don't sass Miz Owen, change m' underwear, make m' bed. That's all, ain't it?"

"No, that ain't all," said the rector.

"An' say m' prayers?"

"Right. Good fellow. And I'll call you twice a week, and try to get out there before too long." He was astounded that he'd just heard himself say 'ain't,' as if it were the most natural thing in the world. It was good that Dooley Barlowe was going away for a while, as he'd begun talking exactly like him.

He'd been right, of course. The house seemed hollow as a gourd. He heard his footsteps echo dully in the hall.

He took two carrots out of the refrigerator and walked to the garage. "Well, Jack," he said, stooping down and putting the carrots in the rabbit cage, "it's just you and me, old boy."

He walked back to the study, and looked at the clock on the mantle. Five-fifteen. Maybe he should run. Puny hadn't come today, so maybe he'd walk to The Local and get something for dinner. He felt ravenous, as he'd skipped lunch, quite without meaning to. He'd worked on his sermon until twelve-thirty, and then the phone had started ringing, and somehow the afternoon had slipped away and he'd come home to say goodbye to Dooley, and here he was, standing in the middle of the floor as bereft as if he'd lost his last friend.

He gazed out on Baxter Park, half-hidden from view behind the rhododendron hedge. The light had stolen softly across the wide, open park bordered on all sides by darkly green hedges. What a treasure, that park, and yet he never used it, nor even encouraged Dooley to go there. A perfect place to sit and read. To sit and think. To have a picnic.

A picnic?

He looked in the refrigerator and found four lemons and made a jar of lemonade. He found cold chicken, and then, a fine wedge of Brie and French rolls. There were berries left from breakfast, and Puny's banana bread that hadn't even been cut.

He put it all into a picnic basket with damask napkins and fetched a starched tablecloth out of the bottom drawer of the buffet.

He stopped suddenly and shook his head. Once again, he had put the cart before the horse.

"Cynthia?" he said, when she answered the phone, "would you like to go on a picnic?" He feared the worst. She was probably off to the country club, perhaps to a dinner dance with a full orchestra.

"You would?" He had certainly not meant to sound so joyful.

Cynthia sat on the tablecloth in her denim skirt and chambray blouse, with a large napkin across her lap. She held her palms up. "Surely it's not raining?"

"No, indeed. That was dew off the leaves. We're not having rain." He poured the lemonade into crystal glasses. How happy he was with his idea, with an idea that was quite unlike his usual ideas. Perhaps he wasn't as thoroughly dull, after all, as he'd felt when talking with Walter.

"Cynthia," he said, raising his glass, "here's to your next book, and all your future books! To your illustrations, may they come alive on the page! To your happiness, to your health, and to your prosperity!"

They drank.

"My!" she said, "that was a toast and a half. Goodness!"

"A picnic, Cynthia, think of it! How long has it been since you were on a picnic?"

"Shall I tell you the truth?"

"Of course. Always."

"Yesterday," she said simply.

He was fairly devastated. To think he'd imagined he was clever and original, and then, to learn it was all merely humdrum and everyday. Andrew Gregory, he supposed, feeling a slow drip on his pants from the perspiring glass.

"Violet and I found a mossy bank on Little Mitford Creek and had deviled eggs and popcorn and tuna on toast."

He was so relieved, he might have shouted. A roller coaster. Being with Cynthia was like being on a roller coaster, his feelings dipped and soared so uncontrollably.

"I sketched ladybugs and moss, it was wonderful. Violet slept in the sun and a butterfly lighted on her ear. Can you imagine?"

He could, but only with some effort. He leaned against the bench, which they'd spread the cloth beside. Surely he'd reached the very gates of heaven, where he found a balmy breeze, a place far removed from the fret of getting and spending, and best of all, someone agreeable to talk with.

They lingered on in the twilight, the evening birdsong loud and vibrant in the hedges.

He knew he would ask her, sooner or later, but each time he thought of it, his heart pounded. "Cynthia," he said, at last, glad for the fading light, "what does going steady mean . . . exactly?"

"Well, it's one of those wonderful things that means just what it says. You *go* with someone. Steadily! And you don't go out with anybody else."

"I already don't go out with anybody else."

"Yes, but I do. Or did! Or, even might again" She tilted her head to one side, smiling.

"What's wrong with things as they are?" He felt slightly annoyed.

"Things as they are so . . . unofficial. I never know when I might see you. It would be lovely to have something to look forward to with you, like going out to a movie or having you in for dinner more often, just simple things."

"I don't understand why we have to go steady to do those things."

"Well, of course, we don't have to. It would just be nicer, to know that someone was special, set apart."

He cleared his throat. "You've . . . been seeing Andrew Gregory, I believe."

"Andrew is lovely, really he is. Very gracious and lots of fun. But it's Churchill this and Churchill that, and I can't bear Churchill! He was horrid to his wife, rude to his guests, and cursed like a sailor. And every time we went to the club, I got a terrible knot in my stomach, I'm just not good at that sort of thing. Besides, he likes bridge, and I positively loathe it!" She gazed at him intently.

"You're clearly the most interesting woman I've ever known."

"Do you really mean that?"

"I do. You're easy to be with, you're thoughtful and amusing, you're enormously talented, and yes, very lovely to look at." There. He'd said everything.

Why was this so difficult? She had, after all, asked a simple yes or no question: Would you like to go steady? Yet, he felt as if he needed to write a full sermon in reply.

"The truth is," he said, "I'm fearful of anything that might interfere with my . . ."

"With your work."

"Yes."

"Typical."

"What do you mean, typical?"

"Men are always afraid that someone might interfere with their work." Now, she seemed annoyed. "You could try looking at it as something to enhance your work, as a welcome diversion that may help you along in your work."

A fresh way of looking at it, he thought, with some surprise.

"You know, the knot that comes with a party at the country club is mild to what I'm feeling right now."

"What are you feeling?"

"So nervous I could throw up. I have never in my life argued for anything like this. It never occurred to me that a simple question would turn into a Platonic debate. After all, Timothy, I did *not* ask you to marry me!" She stood up suddenly, and he rose, also, catching her arm.

"Please! Don't be upset. It was a wonderful question, I should be flattered and grateful beyond words that you asked me. I'm sorry."

Without thinking, he put his arms around her, and drew her close, entering that territory of wisteria which infused even the faint warmth of her breath on his cheek. Her softness was a shock to him, to the place where he kept his heart orderly and guarded, and he realized it wasn't hammering at all, it was completely at peace.

They heard it before they felt it. "Rain!" they cried, in unison, and, grabbing up the hamper and cloth, fled across the park as it came down in a sudden torrent.

The peace was still there, he thought, lying awake at three o'clock in the morning, listening to the murmur of the rain. It was a palpable thing, this feeling, undefiled by concern or doubt. He prayed for Cynthia, admiring her courage to speak up. "Come boldly to the throne of Grace," Paul had written to the Hebrews. He liked her boldness!

He was filled with a certain excited expectation for the summer, as if his own school had been let out.

It felt as if thunder were vibrating through the bed.

Horrified, he sat up and saw lights flashing wildly around the room. In the sound that filled the air like another presence, he heard an oddly familiar rhythm: cut, cut, cut, cut, cut.

He sprang out of bed and went to the alcove window, but could see nothing more than the flashing light that seemed to be swinging rapidly in circles, like a beacon. Without switching on the hall light, he raced down the stairs to the kitchen window.

A helicopter! In Baxter Park. And people running, and there, just as the light flashed across it, Hoppy's blue Volvo.

Good Lord! Olivia!

He slipped his feet into his garden shoes by the door, and ran toward the hedge and through it, blinded by the light and sickened by the deafening roar.

He saw Hoppy and two others taking Olivia from the car.

"I'm here!" he shouted, fighting the storm of feeling that rose in him.

"Pray!" yelled Hoppy, who had lifted her in his arms. Olivia looked at him and reached out. He was able to touch only her fingertips as Hoppy rushed her to the helicopter door and handed her in to waiting hands. Then, the doctor climbed in, and the door closed.

Someone backed the car across the park, deeply trenching the rain-soaked grass, and almost immediately, the helicopter was lifting, lifting, was in the air, and vanishing over the tops of the trees.

"Philippians four-thirteen, for Pete's sake," he whispered hoarsely to the sudden darkness.

"What a horrid nightmare! What was it all about?" Cynthia came through her hedge with a flashlight.

"It's Olivia. I don't know what the mission is. I pray to God she's flying to her heart." Flying to her heart! A miracle of miracles.

Cynthia took his hand, dropping the flashlight by her side. It beamed on his feet. "Oh, dear," she said, looking down. He had lost one of his untied tennis shoes, the other was covered with mud, his pajama legs were soaked nearly to the knees, and Violet was nuzzling his ankle.

He put his arms around Cynthia, and held her. How good it was to hold someone, especially after the shock of that alarming mission in the park. "So lovely," she murmured against his shoulder, stroking his cheek. "Two dear hugs in one night. It's almost as good as . . ."

"As going steady?"

"Umhmm."

He laughed a little. "Almost, perhaps. But surely, not quite."

It was four-thirty in the morning when he fell to his knees by his bed and began to pray intensely. When he arose from the rug, creaking in his joints and assailed by a burning thirst, he was amazed to see it was six o'clock.

All day, he felt derailed, cut loose from his moorings. The loss of sleep, the accumulating fatigue, maybe it was his age, after all. He had forgotten to call Hoppy, but that was just as well, in view of things. He would see him next week, without fail, assuming Hoppy had returned from wherever he'd gone. If he hadn't returned, he most assuredly did not want to see the new doctor, Wilson, who seemed wet behind the ears.

In the office mailbox, a card from Emma.

"Having wonderful time, do not wish you were here, ha, ha. You should have seen Harold talking to Mickey Mouse, I got a whole roll of snaps. Much love, Emma."

He dropped by the Grill for a late breakfast, comforted by the familiar surroundings and Percy's dependable nosiness.

"I heard that copter set down in th' park last night, it like t' scared Velma to death. Truth is, you look like *you* been scared t' death, you're white as a sheet."

"I come in here to be cheered up, and instead, I get brought down. Do I really look white as a sheet?"

"Warshed out. Gray, like. Sickly . . ."

"That's enough, thank you very much."

"Don't mention it."

He sat in the booth and buttered his toast. Just when he should be gaining a second wind, he was crashing and burning. It seemed a good time to write Stuart Cullen, perhaps even a good time to go see him in person. But he hated the thought of the long drive. Perhaps he would take Cynthia along. There! A brilliant idea. She and Martha would get on famously, and wouldn't Stuart be fairly astounded?

"It's like this . . ." he would explain. It's like what? Well, of course, he didn't know, exactly, so he'd just let Stuart figure it out, and then tell *him*.

J.C. Hogan slipped into the booth with his bulging, half-open briefcase. "When you goin' to have a letter from the man in the attic? I need to fill up some space, advertisin's dropped off."

"A letter from George Gaynor isn't exactly filler. But I just got a letter and you can have it next week."

"Too late. I'd like to get it today, for Monday's paper."

"Let me finish my breakfast. I just came from the office, but I'll go back again."

J.C. got up, jolting the table, and nearly dumping the rector's breakfast in his lap. "Just run it upstairs where I'll be layin' out the center spread."

"I'll see to it," Father Tim said, crisply.

Coot Hendrick slipped into the booth, wearing a red cap from the hardware. "I wish t' God a feller could git 'im a plate of gizzards in this place."

"Gizzards, is it?"

"I was raised on gizzards, like 'em better'n white meat."

"You won't be gettin' no gizzard plate around here," yelled Percy, who could overhear the back booth from the grill.

"Heard anything 'bout y'r dog?" Coot wanted to know.

He dipped his toast in the poached egg. "Not a word."

"I don't think y'r goin' to."

"Is that right?"

"If hit was anybody aroun' here that stoled 'im, they'd've jumped on that money like a beagle on a rabbit. Nossir, I think that dog's long gone."

Percy threw his spatula down and walked over. "Lemme tell you somethin', buddyroe, you say one more word to th' Father 'bout that dog bein' long gone, and you're th' one's gonna be long gone, you hear?"

"You don't have t' git s' bent out of shape," said Coot. "It ain't nothin' but a dog."

"Th' only fella I ever th'owed out of here was Parrish Guthrie. I said that'd be th' only one, and I wouldn't want t' break my promise. Why don't you go on over yonder and set by th' window?"

Coot got up without taking his eyes off the owner and stomped over to the table by the window.

"Don't pay no attention to him," growled Percy. "He ain't got a lick of sense."

"Percy, you didn't have to do that, but I thank you for it. Coot's all right, he didn't mean any harm."

Just then, the door opened with some force, and Homeless Hobbes stumbled in on his crutch. "Father Tim!" he shouted. "Are you in here? I've found your dog! I've found Barnabas!"

The rector bolted from his seat in the booth and stood frozen by the counter.

"He's way up th' hill behind th' creek. They had 'im tied out, I saw 'im with my own eyes. I went up there t' take food t' a sick feller, ol' Barnabas got a load of me and like to barked his head off. Some pretty rough characters come out of that house and dragged him inside."

"How'd he look?"

"I hate t' tell you, he looked starved-like, pore."

"I'm callin' Rodney," said Percy, taking the receiver off the wall phone.

"I asked around about th' jack legs that's livin' there—they say they're bad news, drugs or somethin' else lowdown. One feller said they might be armed. I'd want Rodney t' be plenty careful."

As the few early lunch customers fixed their mute attention on the unfolding drama, Percy held the phone to Father Tim. "He's on th' line."

"Hello, Rodney! Something wonderful has happened. Homeless says he's seen Barnabas at a house up the creek. Yes, yes. A little starved looking, he says. I see. Well, I'll ask him.

"Can you tell Rodney where the house is?"

"I don't think you can get there from here. I'd have t' ride with 'im t' show 'im."

"Rodney, he'd have to ride with you, it's up the hill behind the creek. He says he hears they might be armed, drugs could be involved. Yes. Fine. We'll be at the Grill."

"Anybody wants a doughnut," Percy said to his customers, "it's on th' house!"

He shook hands with Homeless and Rodney. "I'll be at home, then. The Lord be with you."

As the two men left, Percy stared after them. "I know ol' Homeless comes t' town Tuesday nights to go through Avis's garbage, but that's th' only time I ever seen 'im in broad daylight."

It was nearly three o'clock before he saw the police car pull up to the curb, and he was standing at the door as Rodney came up the walk. He saw at once that the mission had not been successful.

"Nothin'," said the police chief. "We got s' dern lost tryin' to find th' way in there, Homeless had walked in before, and when we finally come up on that house, it was tight as a drum. Nobody at home, no dog barkin', nothin'. I hated t' come tell you." Rodney stood with one foot on the top step, looking downcast.

"Well, then."

"We seen two old vehicles on th' place, a car under a tarp, and a van they'd kind of pushed off in th' bushes."

"Did you look at the license plate on the car?"

"I did. Wrote it down on my report. Hang on," he said, going to the curb and taking a clipboard from the front seat. He walked back to the porch stoop, slowly, looking at the report. "Let's see, here. VAT 7841."

"That's it! That was on the license plate of the car that took Barnabas. I forgot all about it 'til this very moment. VAT!"

"Well, all I can do is keep an eye on th' place. I'll send Joe Joe back in th' evenin' and again tomorrow. We'll turn up somethin'. Since you had 'im more'n three days, state law says you own 'im, so they've kidnapped 'im, pure an' simple, and looks like abuse into the bargain. They don't have a snowball's chance."

He felt torn between elation and disappointment. "Thank you, my friend. Keep me posted."

He went into the study and sat on the sofa, feeling a desperate fatigue. He also felt an aching thirst again, which he knew was a warning, but he was too tired to get off the sofa and get a glass of water. "In a minute," he murmured aloud, leaning his head back. "I'll do it in a minute."

On Saturday evening, the phone rang. "Father Tim, it's me. Joe Joe."

"Joe Joe!"

"I went over there and looked around, but I didn't find anything. I tried knockin' on a few doors along the road, but all I could scare up was an old woman and two little kids, they didn't know much. It's spooky back in there, that's where all the liquor used to be made. But don't you worry, I'm goin' again tomorrow, right after church."

Church! He had completely forgotten the crux of his sermon.

"Thank you, Joe Joe, God bless you," he said, going at once to his desk.

There! It was "Tough Times, Tender Hearts," typed rather more neatly than usual, and appearing to be in good order. He turned out the lights and went upstairs. A good night's sleep and the press of Sunday off his shoulders, and he'd be as good as new. Next week, maybe he'd ask Cynthia to go to a movie.

"Nothin'," said Rodney, when he called after church. "Joe Joe went up there and come back empty handed. Th' cars hadn't moved, and there was no sign of a dog except a few piles of poop under a tree, I guess where they'd tied 'im up. I tell you what, my instincts got to workin' on this, an' Tuesday, I'm goin' to stake a man out in th' woods around there.

"Maybe us prowlin' around in a police car has run 'em off, but anyway, I smell a rat."

"Smelling rats is your job, and you're mighty good at it. Remember how you jumped on that candy wrapper?"

"You got to look for th' little things," Rodney said, with dignified authority.

He had no sooner put the phone on the hook than it rang again.

"You comin' out here t'day?"

"Dooley! Well, no, no, I'm not. Not today."

"I thought you might be comin' out."

"I want to get out next Sunday, but not today, we've had a lot of excitement. We think we may have found Barnabas."

"You ain't!"

"Oh, I think we have. We'll see. Rodney's going to stake a man out in the woods to observe the place, it's up on the hill above the creek. Homeless carried food to somebody up there and saw him. Barnabas barked at him, he said."

" 'at's super," said Dooley. " 'at's great!"

"I'll keep you posted. Doing all right, are you?"

"Yep, but Rebecca Jane sleeps all th' time, looks like. I done played 'ith them ol' dogs and rode 'at ol' horse and all."

"Well, let's keep in touch. Are you doing what we talked about?"

"I forgot t' change m' underwear last night."

"Well, then, tonight you get another chance."

"Tell Granpaw hey."

"I will."

"Tell Cynthia hey, and ol' Vi'let and Jack an' all."

"Oh, I will."

"Well, bye," said Dooley, hanging up.

With a warm rush of feeling, he realized that Dooley Barlowe was homesick.

He was getting ready to take a hot shower when the phone rang by his bed.

"Father?" His doctor's voice told him the whole story.

"She's through it! Everything looks good, she's resting. Leo Baldwin is a master. Thank God for Leo. They washed up at eight o'clock last night. I would have called you earlier, but I couldn't, I dropped down on a bed in Leo's office and I was outta here. Today has been hectic, this . . ." His voice broke slightly. "This is a great answer to prayer, Father, thank you, thank you."

He had never heard his friend sound this way, and he was swept up in the joy of it. "Tell me everything, if you have the strength."

"We took the copter to Charlotte, put her on a Lear, and flew to Boston. An ambulance was waiting, we were at Mass General in a little under three hours. The donor was a boy, eighteen years old, motorcycle, no helmet, closed head injury. Rotten business. They had hooked him to a respirator at the scene, brought him in, did brain scans, there was no blood flow to the brain.

"The emergency room doctor called Leo, Leo talked to the parents, they consented, and Leo called me. What an uncanny, unbelievable miracle! Thousands to one, you know." Hoppy was silent for a moment, and cleared his throat.

"She'll be at Mass till we find out whether she's rejecting, probably a couple of weeks, then Leo wants her here in Boston for four to six months."

"That's the bad news."

"I'll fly up whenever I can. Thank God for Wilson, I got him in the nick of time."

"God's timing is always perfect."

"I'm beginning to see that, even about . . . Carol."

"Get the names of the parents who gave their consent; I'd like to pray for them."

"I'll do that."

"When are you coming home?"

"In the morning, the ol' red-eye special. Wilson has probably croaked by now, but he's young, he can handle it. Keep those prayers coming, pal."

"Consider it done," he said, knowing that was one prescription he wouldn't forget to refill.

CHAPTER TWENTY-ONE

The Bells

On Monday, he refilled his medication after a visit to the hospital and breakfast at the Grill, and hurried to the office. Perhaps he should start taking Monday off, like a lot of clergy. But the thought of losing a full day seemed disorienting.

He began his list of calls. "Miss Sadie?"

"Good morning, Father!"

"Remember you asked me to think about a name for the nursing home? I believe the Scripture you want engraved over the front door is Psalm thirty-three, verse twenty-two, 'Let thy mercy, O Lord, be upon us, according as we hope in thee.' "

"You have the best memory! But, of course, you're young."

"Well, then. What do you think of the name Hope House?"

"Hope House? Perfect! Absolutely perfect, Father, I knew I could count on you. Instead of somebody saying their poor mother has gone to a nursing home, they can say she's living at Hope House!"

"The other matter, the matter of the beam in the attic, well, I haven't gotten to it, yet, but I shall. Now, to the good news. We think we've found Barnabas."

After calling a disgruntled J.C. Hogan to say he'd deliver George Gaynor's letter at lunch time, he called Cynthia.

"What are you up to?" he asked.

"No good!" she said brightly. "Trying to make the crossover from a Violet book to another kind of book is hair-raising. I mean, what if I can't do it? What if I'm meant to do cats for the rest of my life? So, I'm forcing myself along, and I'm drawing a . . . ah, well, to tell the truth, a mouse!"

"From memory, I devoutly hope."

"From life. It's in a cage on my drawing board. I plan to reward it with gouda and let it go in the hedge."

"Cynthia, Cynthia."

"Here's the scoop. The story is about a mouse who lived in the stables where Jesus was born. It's about looking at life from down under, as it were, a mere mouse observing the high drama of a lowly birth."

"I like it."

"It's for children four to eight, so I've even lowered the age of my reading audience. Timothy, I'm scared."

"Don't be. Philippians four-thirteen, for Pete's sake."

She laughed. "I needed that."

"How are the rabbits?"

"Wonderful! They help me so much, I've sketched pages and pages. I really wanted to do a rabbit book, I think, but I feel strongly led to do this."

"Follow your heart," he said. "And speaking of hearts, Olivia came through the surgery splendidly. She's resting."

"Wonderful!"

"Thank you for your prayers. I also called to say I think we've found Barnabas."

"Timothy!"

"We'll see. So far, a bit of a hold-up, but I'll keep you posted. And I think Dooley's homesick."

"Will wonders never cease?"

"Let's hope not. How about a movie this week?"

"You're really asking me to a movie?" she said, with amazement. "That's instant proof that wonders never cease!"

On Wednesday, a postcard: "I've got a suntan you won't believe. Harold's legs are fried. See you in the funny papers, ha ha. Love, Emma."

From Stuart:

"Thanks for your note. As always, it was good to have word from you. Of course, you may come for a visit and bring Cynthia Coppersmith. Next Tuesday is a conflict, as I shall be away then. Can you come the following Tuesday, perhaps? Martha insists on having you here for lunch, though I have gallantly offered a pricey restaurant. I count my blessings!

"Just give Norma a ring, so it can go on my calendar at the office. Ever yours in His peace."

Rodney called at eleven.

"They're as good as nailed. They're runnin' drugs in and out of there by th' shipload. They keep Barnabas for a watchdog, and when they don't want 'im barkin', they muzzle 'im. Might be a pretty sophisticated operation. Anyway, it's worse than just a bunch of good ol' boys bein' bad."

"What are you going to do?"

"We're goin' in after 'em, that's what. Th' trick is, we got to go in when there's a load of dope settin' in there. Last night, they drove out with th' van, Joe Joe run down to 'is car and called us on th' radio, and by th' time we got th' call in to th' state, they'd disappeared. They may be drivin' it to a truck somewhere right around here, and loadin' it on. I'm goin' to keep Joe Joe out there."

"Be careful, Rodney. I don't like the sound of this."

"Me, either. That's why I'm countin' on you to do one of th' main things th' Lord hired you to do—pray."

What was going on wouldn't bear thinking about, there was no use in it. Instead, he would keep busy, he would call Dooley. He felt rotten that he'd packed him off somewhere, just as he'd begun to set down roots.

How could I have been so thoughtless? he wondered, staring out the window. Very likely, he's staring out his own window right now, marking time until he comes home to Mitford.

"Hello, Marge? Tim here. How's our girl?"

"Beautiful. Precious. Too wonderful for words."

"And how's our boy?"

"Why don't you ask him that, and then we'll talk before you hang up."

"Dooley!" he heard Marge call. "It's for you!"

He heard someone stomping to the phone. "Hey."

"Hey, yourself. What are you up to?"

"I cain't talk, I'm goin' out with Doc Owen. Bye!"

"Well," Marge said, "I guess I'll have to fill you in. He's busy from morning 'til night, riding Goosedown, shooting baskets with the boy from McGuire Farm, playing with Rebecca Jane, taking off with Hal. I think they're going to deliver a calf this very moment."

"Then he's not . . . homesick?"

"Homesick? Dooley? Maybe for the first five minutes, but he got over it."

A note from Father Roland:

"I must tell you that the pressure here is unrelenting. You say I'm young and it's good for me, but this will surely make me old before my time. How I'd like to come and visit you in that sleepy little village, where I can just see you strolling along Main Street, going your rounds, taking your time. That's surely how God would have us live! My friend, count your blessings, and remember me in your prayers, that I might learn how to better appropriate His peace for labor in the stressful turmoil of a city vineyard."

Hah! And double hah! thought the rector. Going my rounds, taking my time . . . and what sleepy little village? The last time he'd had a decent night's sleep in this village was too long ago to remember.

What if this movie was one of those steamy marathons that would cause them both to be paralyzed with embarrassment? And should he wear his clerical collar or a sport shirt? He had not gone to a movie in well over ten years, and why should he? The last time he had gone, with friends from the parish, he was so astounded at the vile language, casual sex, and equally casual bloodshed that he had left with a pounding headache, declaring, "Never again."

"Cynthia," he said when she answered the phone, "do you think I should wear my clerical collar or a sport shirt?"

"I think you should wear your clerical collar. After all, your job isn't nine to five, it's twenty-four hours a day, isn't it?"

He felt oddly relieved and happy.

"Ah . . . what movie are we seeing?" he asked.

"A Walt Disney," she said, "I hope you don't mind."

Mind? He was thrilled.

The moment he entered the dark theater, he felt the years dropping away. He was certainly twelve, this was the old Delta Theater, *Flying Tigers* would be coming on the screen at any moment, and the girl with him was Elizabeth Mooney, whose parents were waiting at the diner across the street, drinking coffee. He remembered how badly he'd felt that anyone had to drink coffee for an hour and a half in order to accommodate him in some way.

"Where do you want to sit?" he whispered to Cynthia.

"I like the gospel side," she whispered back. "Toward the front."

If he sat too close to the front, it made him, quite literally, throw up—and how would he explain that?

He steered her just slightly forward of the middle, and they went into the empty row with a box of popcorn, a Diet Sprite, a Coke, and a box of Milk Duds. He had completely forgotten about Milk Duds, his childhood favorite, and though he wouldn't eat a single one, of course, he thought it might be nice to have them, just for nostalgia's sake. He put them in his jacket pocket.

Cynthia settled happily into the plush seat, which, to his surprise, rocked. "Where are the Milk Duds?" she whispered. "Didn't I see you get Milk Duds?"

There was the scent of wisteria, as if it were blown in on a garden breeze, and her warm laughter at the very places he found amusing, so it was no surprise that he considered reaching over and holding her hand. He discovered, however, that he was incapable of actually doing it.

Lord, he prayed, I'm not used to this "going out" business. Some might tell me to follow my instincts, but I've spent so many years trying to follow yours that I've nearly lost the hang of following mine. So, thank you for being in on this and handling it to please yourself.

There! That put the burden squarely on the Lord, he thought.

At some point during the movie, they looked at each other while laughing at a funny scene, and when he looked back at the screen, he was amazed to find that he was holding her hand.

He couldn't help but notice how perfectly happy she seemed while eating the last of his Milk Duds.

He was saying goodnight on her front porch when a police car pulled up in front of the rectory and someone got out.

Father Tim walked quickly down the steps to the sidewalk. "Hello! Are you looking for me?"

It was Rodney's new man. "Yessir, you're Father Tim?"

"I am."

"I just got it on my radio from Chief Underwood. He thought you'd want to know that Joe Joe's been shot."

The new officer looked as if he were barely out of junior high. "I don't know what happened, sir," he said as they drove to the hospital, "all I got was the report he'd been shot. The chief's up there bustin' that drug house. He took the whole force, just locked up the jail and left."

He heard a certain wistfulness in the young officer, that he was out here chauffeuring a preacher while his peers were risking their lives.

"How is he?" he asked young Nurse Kennedy, who was Joe Joe's first cousin.

"It could have been worse, Father. It only nicked his left kidney, but it lodged in his abdomen. Dr. Wilson is operating now."

"And where, may I ask, is Dr. Harper?"

"In his office."

In his office? Why in God's name wasn't he in the operating room? Obviously, Hoppy was giving far too much responsibility to someone lacking in practical experience. He felt a sudden anger.

"How is he?" Marcie Guthrie burst through the swinging doors that led to an emergency waiting room, wearing a seersucker housecoat and clutching a pink leather Bible.

"He's with Dr. Wilson, Aunt Marcie, but I think he's fine, I really do." Nurse Kennedy gave her stricken aunt a consoling hug.

"I've been afraid of this for years. And Boyd on the road, somewhere in South Carolina! How did it happen?" Marcie wiped her red eyes with a handkerchief.

"I don't know," said Nurse Kennedy, "they just brought him in and left, nobody told me anything about how it happened. They did say something about drugs and a dog."

The rector's heart pounded. "What did they say about the dog?"

"Just that Joe Joe heard it barking."

J.C. Hogan came through the swinging doors, looking grim. "What happened?" he snapped, directing his question to the rector.

"This probably isn't the best time to get the story. Maybe you should talk to Rodney when he gets through at the creek."

"What's he doin' at the creek?"

"I'm told he's over there with his men, doing a drug bust."

J.C. glared at him. "If I'd wanted a story about a drug bust, I would've asked for it. I'm here to get a story on a shooting."

If there was ever anyone whose lights I'd like to punch out, he thought, this is the guy. He could just see the headline in Monday's *Muse*, but it was, of course, misspelled.

"The only one who knows that story is currently in surgery and isn't able to tell it right now."

Red-faced, J.C. looked at Marcie and the rector, then stormed through the swinging doors.

"That hateful devil," said Marcie. "I ought to sic Mama on him."

Long after midnight, Joe Joe's preacher, Esther and Ray Cunningham, three cousins, two aunts, and an uncle were waiting with the rector in the hallway outside the emergency room. Thinking he heard a familiar voice, Father Tim got up and looked through the glass in the swinging doors, and was nearly knocked against the wall as Puny Bradshaw swept in, followed by an outraged Nurse Herman. "Young lady, to wait in this section, you must be family or clergy. Are you his wife?"

"No, I'm not," snapped Puny, "but I've got a good chance of bein', and that ought t' be enough for anybody who's askin'."

Stopping suddenly, she peered into the faces of a significant portion of the Cunningham clan. "Oh, law," she said, blushing furiously.

Mayor Cunningham rose from the folding chair with all the dignity of her imposing size. "Puny Bradshaw?"

Puny looked so frightened that the rector had to restrain himself from rushing to her side.

"Yes, ma'am?"

The concern of the hour had given the mayor an unusually serious countenance. In addition, she was wearing half glasses, which caused her to look down on the rector's house help with some asperity. "We've heard a lot about you," said the mayor.

"You have?" asked Puny, with a quaking voice.

"And I think it's high time we all met." The mayor's face broke into a big smile as she gave Puny a vigorous hug. Marcie Guthrie followed suit, as did the remainder of the group, including Joe Joe's preacher, who was still in his Little League coach's uniform.

"I can see you're already celebrating," Hoppy said, coming down the hall. "You'll be glad to know the surgery was successful and he's in recovery."

"Praise God!" shouted Marcie.

"The bullet entered the lower left back, went through his ribs, nicked his kidney, and lodged in the abdomen. There were a number of perforations in the small intestine, of course, so it was a tough one, but he had a tough doctor." He stepped aside as Dr. Wilson appeared. The entire group applauded spontaneously.

I'm getting more like Dooley Barlowe every day, thought the rector, seeing the smile that shone on the exhausted young doctor's face. I've been making up my mind ahead of the facts.

Rodney burst through the swinging doors with Cleo. "How bad is it?" The chief's face was scratched and bleeding, and he was walking with a limp. There was a hushed silence.

"Bullet's out, .25 caliber automatic. He's fine," said Dr. Wilson. "You look like you could use some attention yourself."

Everyone stared intently as the chief hitched up his holster and cleared his throat. "They got away," he said, trying manfully to control his feelings. "We surrounded th' house and called 'em t' come out . . ."

"But they won't nothin' in there but warm beer and cold pizza," said Cleo, shaking his head.

"The way it was," said Joe Joe, when the rector visited his hospital room the following day, "was th' chief sent me over to your place to pick up that Almond Joy wrapper and th' truth is, sir, I found somethin' sweeter than candy." He grinned at Puny, who was standing by the bed, and took her hand.

Father Tim laughed. "I've been trying to gouge that out of her for a long time."

"It's hard to talk with this dern thing up my nose," said Joe Joe, "but I want you to know I'm sorry about your dog, Father. Bustin' those low-down snakes was real important to me, but more than anything, I was hopin' you'd get your dog back."

He knew he wouldn't be able to speak, so he said nothing.

"I heard 'im barkin' in there before I went up to th' house. I shouldn't have gone so close to th' house with no backup, but they were bringin' in stuff out of th' van, and I knew if I could get a good look at what it was, I could radio in to th' chief and we could nail 'em. Well, it was cocaine, all right, just like I thought. They were cuttin' it down and puttin' it in little bags for th' street. But somebody turned a light on at th' side of th' house, an' when they saw me, I started runnin' and they started pumpin' that automatic in behind me."

Joe Joe shook his head and sighed. "I managed to get back to my car and call th' station. Cleo came after me, but by th' time th' chief an' th' boys got up there, they'd escaped. I feel real bad about it, Father. You don't know how bad."

The rector nodded. "You made the decision you thought was best, and what you learned will come in handy at another time and place."

"He always has somethin' upliftin' to say," Puny informed Joe Joe, with evident pride.

"No, not always. But I hope I can find something uplifting to say to our police chief."

Puny nodded, soberly. "Anybody who shot a tree stump thinkin' it was a man, and then fell in a hole up to his neck will need some upliftin'."

When he awoke at five, the air had been balmy and soft. Now, at barely ten o'clock, it was so cold, he thought of putting on the heater in the bathroom. Not only that, but a dense fog was rolling in that practically shielded the Oxford Antique shop from his view.

He had made a "catch up" list, but lacked any enthusiasm for the project at the top of it. Frankly, he had no earthly ambition to see what was on that beam in the Porter place attic. He did not care to go swimming through towers of ancient newspapers, mounds of broken glass, decades of dust, and a jumble of derelict furniture, especially on a cold, foggy day. However, the bells were to be installed on Monday, and that would not only tie him up, but put him behind, so he supposed that now was as good a time as any.

As he glanced through his desk drawer for a stamp, he saw the extra reward posters he'd stored there, and hastily looked away.

No, he thought, pulling on his windbreaker, I've done my grieving. I'll give the memory of Barnabas to the One who sent him in the first place and be glad of the pleasure of having known that good fellow. Just last night, he'd come across a splendid thing by Shaw. "I like a bit of a mongrel myself, whether man or beast. They're the best for everyday."

When it came to comfortable, everyday companionship, Barnabas had, indeed, been the best. He'd possessed the noblest characteristics of all the breeds he appeared to descend from: the loyalty and intelligence of the Irish wolfhound, the gentle spirit of the Bouvier, and the happy persistence of the sheep dog. If that was what mongrels were all about, then thanks be to God.

There, he thought, putting on his cap. I've made my peace with this cruel thing.

He had his hand on the doorknob when he stopped suddenly, and leaned his head against the door frame, trying to swallow the terrible knot in his throat. He stood there a long time, only to be sorely disappointed with himself that he was, at last, "cryin' over 'at ol' dog."

He followed Uncle Billy to a room that was divided in half by curtains on a clothesline. "That's my side," he said, "an' that's her'n. She went in there a little bit ago, and won't come out 'til supper, most likely. Rose, th' preacher's here."

"I'm indisposed," she said, haughtily.

"He wants to' know can he go up in th' attic and look around?"

"In the attic?" squawked Miss Rose. "Why does he want to go in th' attic?"

Uncle Billy looked at him. "What was it you was goin' up there for? I plumb forgot."

"Well, I've heard so much about how this place was built, I'd like to take a look at how Willard girded those exceptional gables." Underneath the cap, which he'd forgotten to remove, a mild perspiration stood out on his head. He had escaped without telling a total lie.

"Tell 'im to go on, then, but don't stir up the dust."

Uncle Billy grinned, revealing his gold tooth. "Don't stir up th' dust, Rose says."

Looking up into the vast, black hole made his skin crawl. Where was Cynthia when he needed her? Undoubtedly, she would have bounded up these stairs, two at a time, fully expecting to make some thrilling discovery.

"Dear God!" he exclaimed, involuntarily.

"Prayin' about it, are you?" said Uncle Billy.

"Where's the light?"

"Oh, th' light. It's around here somewhere. Yessir, right there it is." A lone bulb switched on and shone dimly against a vast sprawl of gloomy ceiling. "When you come down," said the old man, "I wouldn't mind if you'd cut my corns off for me; Rose has a shaky hand with th' razor. I'll soak 'em good first."

At the top of the stairs, he unashamedly looked back to see if Uncle Billy was still standing at the door. He was not.

The attic was so filled with an odd jumble of debris that he could barely make passage. Why had he not brought a flashlight or asked for one downstairs? There was the beam, exactly where it should be, precisely at the center of the pitch. Surely it was divine intervention, for the bulb cast its light into the vault of the ceiling and shone directly onto the engraved letters.

"W!" he shouted, and heard something scurry across the floor. The *W,* rendered in what appeared to be old English lettering, was followed by an *i,* then an *n.* "Win," he said aloud, squinting into the dimly illumined space. If only he had a stepladder, anything to draw him nearer.

He managed to climb onto the seat of a broken chair set precariously on two steamer trunks that were seated together.

"Winter!" he exclaimed, able to see the lettering more clearly. As the chair wobbled under him, he fervently hoped J.C. Hogan would not allow Hessie Mayhew to write his obituary.

"Winterpast," he whispered, slowly.

Below this word was inscribed "Song of Solomon."

He cautiously descended his makeshift ladder and hurried down the stairs with a sense of excitement. "Uncle Billy!" he called, "bring me your Bible!"

Finding no one to greet him, he wandered along the musty hallway until he came to the kitchen. Uncle Billy was sitting beside the table, soaking his feet in a dishpan.

"Well, Preacher, I'm ready for m' corn operation when you are."

The old man looked at him with such an expectant grin that the rector rolled up his sleeves and surrendered to the task ahead. Quite suddenly, he remembered hearing about a place where milk truck drivers could still find employment. Unfortunately, it was in Nova Scotia.

The weather was currently doing one of the one hundred and thirty-six things Mark Twain had given it credit for.

The sun was shining gloriously, and the sky was as blue as the egg of a robin, as he set out across Baxter Park in his running clothes. He couldn't remember any recent mission that had pleased him more.

"Miss Sadie," he said, out of breath, finding her on the porch with Louella, "I've been to the attic."

"Come and tell us about it!" she said eagerly, patting the green rocker next to hers.

"Well, then, may I trouble you ladies for a Bible?" he asked, taking his reading glasses out of the pocket of his sweatpants.

"We got one right here," said a beaming Louella, who just happened to have a worn, leather-bound edition lying open in her lap. " 'Course, if you lookin' for some newfangled Bible, you won't find it aroun' here. We jus' keep th' King James."

"My lifelong favorite," he said, taking it from her and sitting down in a rocker.

"Miss Sadie, Willard's letter said he hoped things would be different for the two of you someday, and that his inscription on the beam would signify his trust in a happier time. I believe he intended for you to stand with him where I stood today, as he revealed the name of the house he hoped to share with you as his wife."

She nodded, and he couldn't help but notice that her cheeks had taken on color.

"The name of the house, Miss Sadie, is . . . Winterpast."

She looked at him for a long moment. "Winterpast," she repeated slowly. "Why, that's a lovely name."

"Willard left a further inscription for you, which leads us to the Song of Solomon." He put his reading glasses on, turned the pages, and read:

" 'For lo, the winter is past, the rain is over and gone. The flowers appear on the earth; the time of the singing of birds has come.' "

Miss Sadie folded her hands in her lap, and looked away. The only sound was, in fact, the singing of birds. She was silent for a while, then she spoke. "It's good to have hope. I'm so glad Willard had hope."

"Many waters, Miss Sadie, cannot quench love. Neither can the floods drown it. That, too, is from the Song."

She looked at him with a small light in her eyes.

"So be it," she said.

How could he have considered taking Monday off? Monday was the diving board poised over the rest of the week. One walked out on the board, reviewed the situation, planned one's strategy, bounced a few times to get the feel of things, and then made a clean dive. Without Monday, one simply bombed into the water, belly first, and hoped for the best.

To his astonishment, the bell crew met him in the churchyard promptly at eight, and it didn't take long for his worst fear to be realized. The velvety lawn, which had lain under a persistent drizzle for two days, was so thoroughly mucked about with the heaving and hauling of three vast bells that it soon looked like a battlefield.

At a little after one o'clock, the bells were chiming.

"Let them ring!" he told the foreman. "Let them ring!" What a wildly tender thing it stirred in his heart to hear those glorious bells.

A small crowd gathered, staring with wonder at the Norman tower that was pealing with music. Andrew Gregory walked briskly down the lane to offer his congratulations. "I say," he told the rector, "it's been a bit dry around here without your bells."

J.C. Hogan heard the pealing and came on the run, and was given an elaborate story of their history, manufacture, and recent long sojourn in their homeland.

It was two-fifteen before he went to his office for the first time that day and picked up the mail from the box, noting that the bundle seemed uncommonly fat. The phone was ringing as he unlocked and went in. "Timothy! How grand of you to ring the bells on your birthday!" said Cynthia.

"My what?"

"I think that's just the boldest, most unrepressed thing to do."

"You do?"

"I'd never have thought you'd have the . . . I've always thought you were so everlastingly modest! What a surprise!"

His birthday! How extraordinary that he'd forgotten. But, of course, there had been no one around to remind him, and Walter never said a word before the fact, always letting a package from

Tiffany's stationery department send his greetings, which usually followed the actual date by several days.

He laughed. "Well, then, now you know the truth. It's my birthday, but you got the surprise."

"There's a surprise for you, too. But only if you come for dinner this evening."

"I'd like that very much. How did you know it was my birthday?"

"It's on the church list I picked up last Sunday in the narthex."

"Ah, well, is nothing sacred?"

He saw that the fat bundle was largely made up of birthday cards, two of which also extended a dinner invitation. There was one from Jena Ivey, which said, "Father Tim, you are dearer to us with each passing year." And one from Meadowgate, signed by Hal, Marge, Dooley, Rebecca Jane, Goosedown, and the six farm dogs, who were all, according to the message, expecting him for an early supper on Sunday.

Emma sent a card with a watercolor of roses, and a Polaroid of Harold and herself on the beach, presumably taken by some stranger she'd snared to do the job. He put it on the bathroom door with a thumbtack, noting that Emma had picked up a jot of weight, while Harold looked a bit spindly.

There was a handwritten note from Stuart, with warm best wishes for a glad heart and good health.

He sat before the stack of cards, feeling a certain comfort.

Then he turned on the answering machine and listened to a lengthy series of well-wishers. "Father," said Winnie Ivey, "I just hate to talk on this thing, but I wanted to tell you how much you mean to everyone. I don't see how in the world any of us could get along without you . . ." He heard Winnie sniffing. "So . . . so, well . . . goodbye!"

What a pleasant lot of activity around an event he'd entirely forgotten!

After dinner, they strolled into Baxter Park and sat on the old bench across from Rachel Baxter's memorial fountain.

"Tell me how you're feeling about Barnabas," she said.

"Terrible, and I think I've finally stopped trying to do anything about feeling that way. It will run its course. You know, if he'd died of old age, that would be one thing. But to have him taken so violently . . . I fear for such dark influences on his spirit."

"But think of the bright influences he found with you. Why, that dog knows more Scripture than most people!"

He laughed, just as the bells at Lord's Chapel pealed the ninth hour.

"Let's suppose the scales weigh heavier on the side of light than dark, and that Barnabas is generously fortified to contend with his present circumstances." She looked at him eagerly. "Like, well, like water lasting a long time in a camel."

He thought about this. It helped a little, and he was thankful. He rested his arm along the back of the bench and touched her shoulder. "Thank you," he said.

They sat silently for a time. In the fading light, the green of the hedges was as dark as jade. How blessed they were to sit here in this peace, shielded from the suffering of the outside world. "I do hope," Father Roland once wrote, "that you aren't hiding your head in the sand, and sparing yourself the challenge and passion of serving on the cutting edge."

Perhaps, in a small parish, he was spared the passion, but he didn't feel spared the challenge. He was feeling more surely than ever that he was exactly where God meant him to be. All he really needed, he knew, was the endurance to be there with stamina and zeal.

"Do you think you'll stay in Mitford, Timothy?"

"Funny you should ask. I want to. But I feel . . . worn, somehow. Thin soup. I can't seem to do at least one of the things that would help renew my energies."

"And what's that?"

"Take a break. I'm afraid Pastor Greer nailed me one evening. He asked if I was too tired to run and too afraid to rest. And the answer is, yes. Yes, and I'm confused and ashamed about that, about my seeming inability to take charge of my own life."

"I understand."

"You do?"

"Oh, yes," she said, without elaborating.

It occurred to him that he hadn't heard anyone say "I understand" in a very long time. He was suddenly aware of the warmth of her shoulder through the silk shirt.

"Will you drive over with me next Tuesday to see the bishop and his wife? We're going to talk about this very thing, and I'd enjoy your company." The truth was, she'd make the long drive seem a grand holiday.

She looked at him in the frank way he found so appealing. "Next Tuesday? I don't know. I'm trying to get the first draft of the new book out to my agent, to see what she thinks. If you'll pray for me, then of course, I can get it all finished, and in the mail, and go see the bishop with you."

"Consider it done," he said, feeling a surge of happiness.

CHAPTER TWENTY-TWO

A High Command

Viewed from the site of the burned church, where Hope House would be built, the valley spread below like an emerald carpet, dotted with gardens that stocked the coolers of The Local twice a week.

Already, the Silver Queen corn had started coming up the mountain every Tuesday and Friday, to be unloaded into the wooden bins. And, as always, the villagers could be counted on to clean out the entire truckload in a single day, so that everybody knew what everybody else was having for dinner.

He was happy to stand in line at the sidewalk corn bins holding his paper bag, though, inevitably, someone offered him their place toward the front of the queue. No, he did not want to move through the corn line quickly, he wanted to savor the little hum of excitement that always came, and the fellowship, and the laughter.

He wanted time to get a good look at Avis Packard's face as he peeled back shuck and tassel to display seed-pearl kernels. "Ain't a worm in 'em. You find a worm, you got yourself a free ear."

Miss Rose came, intently looking for worms, while uncle Billy sat on the bench by the street lamp and told his latest joke to a captive audience. Winnie Ivey closed the bakery and filled a sack for herself and her brother.

While Louella hunted for a dozen perfect ears, Miss Sadie sat in the car, which she had pulled onto the sidewalk in front of the library next door, and Percy Mosely walked across the street in his apron to pick up the bushel Avis had earmarked for the Grill.

A tourist once asked a local, "Is there a festival in town?"

"Nope, it's just that th' corn's come in."

"How quaint! Perhaps I should get some."

"Don't know if I'd do that," the local cautioned, darkly. "They say it sours if it travels in a car." Mitford did not like to sell its early corn to outsiders, who, they said, would only overcook it, and couldn't appreciate it, anyway.

Having picked up a bushel for the bishop's wife, he drove around the monument with his neighbor, who looked dazzling in a dress the color of jonquils, and headed toward Wesley as the bells chimed nine o'clock.

"Once you go around the monument," he said, "it's another world."

"I'm excited! Do you know I've hardly been outside the town limits since I came here last fall?"

He laughed. "That happens to some of us. I've hardly been outside the town limits since I came here more than twelve years ago."

"Perhaps this is the day that will start to change."

"I'd like to think so. Old age and creeping provincialism are a dire combination."

"Did I tell you how much I liked your sermon on Sunday?"

"You did not, or I would have remembered it."

"Well, it was glorious. You were very bold, I thought, to preach on sin. Hardly anyone wants to hear sin preached."

"Mainstream Christianity glosses over the fact that it isn't just a question of giving up sin, but of doing something far more difficult—giving up our right to ourselves."

He made the turn onto the busy highway toward Wesley, which always, somehow, seemed a shock to his senses. "The sin life in us must be transformed into the spiritual life."

"How?"

"Through sacrifice and obedience."

She smiled ironically. "How do you think that will be received by those of us who come to sit in a comfortable pew, and find a hot seat instead?

"They'll just have to go across the street until I've finished preaching on that particular subject."

She laughed with delight. "You're different these days."

He laughed with her. "I pray so," he said.

"Timothy!" Stuart Cullen came down the steps with his arms outstretched.

"Stuart, old friend!" said the rector, as they embraced.

"You've come a long way, and relief is on the table," the bishop assured him. "And who is this beautiful woman?"

Cynthia took his outstretched hand.

"This is my neighbor, Cynthia Coppersmith. Cynthia, Bishop Cullen, my seminary confidant, esteemed friend, and—thanks be to God—my bishop."

Cynthia curtsied a little. "Oops, I'm sorry. That was involuntary."

He laughed. "You're a century or so off, Cynthia, but I appreciate it, nonetheless." Still holding her hand, he drew her toward the front door.

The rector saw that Stuart's sandy hair was beginning to mingle more freely with gray, and there were furrows in his brow that he hadn't noticed when they met some months ago. Even so, he was still surprisingly trim and boyish, with an unaffected charm that never seemed to diminish. He felt a great warmth toward this man who had been an ongoing part of his life.

"Come inside, please. We've laid on the family silver, and Martha's rolls are just coming out of the oven. Your timing has always been excellent, Timothy."

As they entered the foyer, the rector saw something he hadn't been able to see as Cynthia sat on the passenger side. It was one of those infernal pink curlers, bobbing jauntily behind her right ear, as she greeted the bishop's wife.

During lunch, he did everything he could think of to apprise her of the curler, to no avail.

He decided he wasn't very good at sending nonverbal signals, and gave up halfway through the veal chops. He remembered his father had been made responsible for telling his mother whether her slip was showing before they set out for church. Any runs in her stockings? Too much rouge? Any labels protruding in unsightly places?

He recalled that his father had taken this job rather seriously, and seemed to enjoy it, though he had no earthly idea why.

In the study, Stuart Cullen sat in a leather wing chair and looked at the rector with his warmly direct gaze.

"Tell me everything, Timothy."

"I've tried to organize my thinking, so I could spare your time."

"Please. Let that be my concern. I've set all else aside until a meeting in my office at six."

"Well, then. Things haven't changed dramatically since my letter more than a year and a half ago. I seem to be paralyzed at times with such fits of exhaustion, that I end up merely plodding on, and my sermons reflect it. I should say my spirit reflects it, and it's carried out into my preaching.

"I'm reminded of the time the vestry was invited to the home of a new parishioner, someone fairly wealthy, by most standards.

"Most of us were pretty excited about the banquet that would likely be spread." He laughed. "Well, we sat around till nine in the evening eating stale crackers and a cheddar so hard it broke the cheese knife."

When the bishop smiled, fine lines crept around his eyes.

"I feel that's what I'm serving. On every side, God's people look for—and deserve—a banquet, but they're getting thin rations. 'Feed my sheep,' he said. That's a direct commission.

"The love of the people at Lord's Chapel is clearly there for me. The church is growing, our obligations are settled on time, and soon we'll build one of the finest nursing homes anywhere. Looking at it from the outside, it seems everything is all right."

He was silent for a moment. "I think what I want to say, Stuart, is that I want it to be more than all right. It must be more than just . . . all right. That's where I am. And I don't know where to go from here."

"Cynthia seems to think your sermon on Sunday was a great deal more than thin rations. Even on first meeting, I trust her judgment. She appears to have a lively faith."

"Yes, well . . ."

"Surely you don't expect your sermons to be preached from the mountain every time? You know as well as I that we must also preach from the valley."

"I do know that. But the times on the mountain have been too few. I have, in many ways, disappointed myself, and if that's so, then surely

I'm disappointing others. It's hard to put it clearly, Stuart, but I feel . . . flat."

"That's putting it clearly."

"Somehow, things seem to have taken a turn about the time of the diabetes."

"Diabetes? You never told me you have diabetes."

"Oh, well," he said, shrugging, "it's the non-insulin-dependent variety, nothing to worry about. I didn't want to trouble you with something unimportant."

"Martha's sister is diabetic. And believe me, it's not unimportant. It's a critical dysfunction."

"Oh, but nothing that diet and exercise can't address. Martha's sister is probably insulin dependent."

"She is now," Stuart said, "but she was once precisely where you are. It erupted suddenly into something far more serious. This concerns me."

The last thing he wanted to do was give his bishop any grave concern. That was not why he had come.

"Are you completely fastidious about taking your medication, about your exercise and diet?"

He couldn't tell a lie. "No. I'm not."

"Timothy. For God's sake."

"I'm feeling as miserably guilty as I should, and I want to promise you that I'll become fastidious again—at once. What I don't want to do is let us confuse this issue with the deeper issue."

"I'm not convinced that this issue isn't part of the deeper issue. Bodily fatigue, which nearly always accompanies this hateful malady, can wear down the spirit. And how can the Holy Spirit work with a vessel that's leaking as fast as he can fill it?

"If I know you," the bishop continued, kindly, "you are not resting. You are not recreating. You haven't been on vacation in a very long time, as I recall."

"Yes. That's right."

"What have you been facing recently? Let's look at the last few months."

"A boy, I've been given a boy, he's nearly twelve. Dooley." He missed Dooley, he realized suddenly. "That's been . . ."

"Rough."

"Yes. For an old bachelor like me. Then, the jewels, of course. All that was morbidly unnerving, though the results, as I told you on the phone, were glorious.

"And Barnabas—my dog—was snatched from me on the street, and a man has been shot over the whole affair."

"I'm sorry . . ."

"Not to mention a parishioner and friend who's just had a heart transplant against some very dire odds."

"So. No recreation of any sort, and a series of stressful circumstances superimposed over your usual round of duties and the symptoms of diabetes. Has sleeping been a problem?"

"The worst."

"Seen your doctor lately?"

"Not lately. He's been very caught up with the transplant logistics."

"Lousy excuse. No good! See your doctor immediately."

He nodded. "You have my word."

"Now, I want to exercise my authority as your bishop and ask you to do something else. I want you to go away for two months."

"But there's the boy, and—"

"I'm not interested in the boy, or in any other condition or circumstance that presently exists in your life. That sounds cold and hard, but it's neither. You are my interest, not because you're my friend, but because you're exceedingly valuable to this diocese, and I very much want to keep it that way.

"You've always known how to take care of everybody and everything but yourself. I can say that freely because I'm afflicted with the identical weakness, and, trust me, it is a weakness. I'm blessed with a wife who monitors me, but you have no monitor. If you're going to extend your life in the body of Christ, Timothy, you must act at once to restore, to revive, to refresh your energies.

"You tell me you've gone stale, but the sound health of your parish disproves it. 'Wherefore, by their fruits ye shall know them,' Christ said. That's how I know you, my friend, by your fruits. You haven't let Him down, you haven't let me down, and you haven't let your parish down. But you've been letting yourself down—shamefully."

He was suddenly chilled and peevish. He wished he had never come. Why hadn't he kept his own counsel, made his own determinations? To be scolded like a child was a rude shock, and he felt his skin grow damp with a disagreeable sweat.

"Do you think I like to speak to you this way?" Stuart asked. "I do not. But it must be done. If you need money to go away, that will be taken care of at once."

"It isn't money."

"I recall that your mother left you a considerable sum, if you haven't given it all away."

"Not all," he said, coloring.

The bishop waited a moment. "Tell me . . . what about Cynthia? Does she mean something to you?"

"Yes. I think so."

"You seem uncertain."

"I'm not uncertain about whether she means something to me; I'm uncertain about what that implies."

"You mean whether it could imply marriage?"

"Yes. And if so, is that what would be right and good at this stage of my life, and good for her . . ."

"I think she feels tenderly toward you."

He realized it felt better to discuss Cynthia than to hammer away at his backsliding. "She asked me to . . ." he cleared his throat, "to go steady."

Stuart laughed heartily. " Why, that's wonderful! That's terrific!"

He waited, impatiently, for the laughter to stop. Blast! Why had he brought it up?

"That must have taken some courage on her behalf."

"She said as much."

"What was your answer?"

"She asked me to think about it—and I'm still thinking."

Stuart eyes shone with happy amusement. "When you've thought it through, I hope you'll let me now the outcome. I like her, she's tonic. And that is, after all, what you seem to be needing."

They had veered off course, and it was clearly up to him to veer back. "Are you suggesting that I carry on? That I take a break and carry on?"

"I am. Since your letter a few months ago, you haven't done anything differently. It's time to do something differently, to rest, to seek God's heart on this matter with a fresh mind. I'd like to see you settle your affairs quickly, and be off. We can put Father John in your pulpit, if that's agreeable. He'd be like a hand slipping into a glove, and you can trust him not to turn the place upside down in your absence."

"Very well," he said, smiling. "You've pushed me to the brink once again."

The bishop chuckled as the two men stood and embraced. "But I only do it once every thirty-five years!"

So it had been thirty-five years since his friend had helped him make the decision about Peggy Cramer.

"Stuart," he said, as they stood for a moment at the door of the study, "I'd like to do something rather unorthodox."

"I trust your orthodoxy enough to trust your unorthodoxy."

"I'd like to put an old Baptist preacher in my pulpit now and again. He has a lot to say to us, I believe, and I trust him. He's self-taught and has pastored several country churches for many years. His theology is sound as a dollar, and his spirit is fervent in the Lord. I believe the very oddity of it would cause many to listen who haven't had ears to hear."

"Do it, then."

"Thank you. Now, where do you and Martha want the corn?"

He was relieved that Cynthia didn't look at him, but at the dashboard of the car, which she addressed with great feeling. "I cannot—no matter how hard I try—believe that you did not tell me that stupid curler was banging around back there. I could have died when I found it! There we sat, civilized as you please, and that stupid curler sticking in there. What's worse, it was on the side next to the bishop!"

"It was only Stuart," he said, mildly.

"But why didn't you say something?" wailed Cynthia.

"I tried to. I did! I kept pointing to my head, I thought that might . . ."

"I thought you were scratching your ear, for heaven's sake!"

"I have never been fluent in body language."

"When you were in the study, Martha just reached over said, 'Do you know, that's exactly where I always forget and leave one, myself,' which was the most dreadful lie, since she's never rolled her hair in her life, it's straight as a stick!"

If he dared even glance at her from the corner of his eye, he would howl with laughter.

"Timothy, you're laughing at me, I can tell! Your stomach is jiggling! Why not come right out with it, and laugh your head off, then? Go on, you're most cordially invited!"

He cleared his throat, unable to speak.

"I mean, what if your fly had been open?"

"I beg your pardon?"

"Well, think about it! If your fly was standing open in broad daylight, don't you think I'd have informed you?"

He had to admit that was a sobering thought. "Cynthia," he said, still looking attentively at the road, "I'm sorry. I'm truly sorry. I did try to tell you. Forgive me."

A long silence. "Oh, poop! I do forgive you." She sat back in the seat, as if exhausted. "Will I never get it right?"

"I think you have it far righter than most people, as a matter of fact."

"You do?"

"Indeed, I do. And so does the bishop. He says you're tonic. Tonic! Is that the cruel judgment of a man who was appalled by the sight of a mere hair curler?"

Though he wasn't inclined to be careless at the wheel of a car, he reached over and took her hand.

"Well . . ." she said, brightening.

He awoke in the night and found himself drenched with sweat, his pajamas clinging wetly to his legs. Water! That's what he wanted. He was burning with thirst.

With great effort, he sat up, then forced himself to go to the bathroom and fill his empty glass. Dear God, he felt strangely weak and bereft.

Tomorrow, he would begin the medication with a vengeance and would be up and running by six. It would be good to get on schedule again. He recalled how terrific he'd felt during those early months of running, seeing Mitford from a new perspective. Life changing!

He put on another pair of pajamas and went back to bed, speaking aloud from the Psalms, to the still room: "Withhold not they tender mercies from me, O Lord; be pleased, O Lord, to deliver me . . ."

An image of Cynthia in the dazzling yellow dress came to him just before he slept.

He stopped by the hospital in his running clothes, and spent a half hour with Joe Joe, who was eager to come home. Then he ran by to see Russell and Betty Craig, who appeared to have struck a happy truce. After a light breakfast at the rectory and a brief visit with Puny, he went to the office to do what the bishop had asked him to do.

"I'm sorry, Father," said the nurse when he called, "but Dr. Harper is out of town for a week. Dr. Wilson would be happy to see you, I could work you in . . ."

"No, that's all right. I'll wait for Dr. Harper. Better put me down right after he returns."

"Let's see. I don't have anything the week after he gets back, but if we have a cancellation, I could call you."

"Excellent! Do that," he said.

There. He had a full prescription on hand, he had taken his medication, he had run, he had eaten a sensible breakfast and cut back on caffeine, and he had called the nurse. All that was easy enough. It was the other, the planning of the two-month sabbatical that he dreaded.

As odious as the prospect seemed, he was, however, grateful. Another sort of bishop might have trusted him to take care of the problem on his own. But Stuart had used his authority to issue a command, and he had been absolutely right. His bishop had done what he hadn't the gall to do himself. That feeling of being stuck to this place like moss on a tree, like lichen on a stump, would have to be gotten over.

"Hello, Walter? Timothy. Is this a good time? Well, then, if it isn't too late to get in on the trip with you and Katherine, I'd like to come along." There was a stunned silence. "Walter? Walter! Hello?"

Had the Enemy tricked him all these years into believing no one could do without him?

Wasn't Russell in the best of circumstances? Didn't Olivia have a new heart, and wasn't she improving daily, with no signs of rejection?

Wasn't Lord's Chapel enjoying an especially smooth state of affairs just now, with as little wrangling and backbiting as he'd witnessed in years?

Wasn't the Sunday school gaining momentum and fulfilling a need? Wasn't the new youth choir gearing up for a full program in the fall?

And wasn't Miss Sadie in better shape than ever, with the secret off her heart and Louella under her roof?

He searched his conscience for anyone who might need him. In a day or two, he would approach Miss Rose about the life estate and whether they could move ahead at once—after resolving, of course, the statue of Willard.

There would be no final drawings of Hope House for some time, and, when they came, Ron Malcolm was infinitely able to judge them fairly and make interim decisions with the vestry.

Emma would be back any day and could handle things without him. Father John would be an agreeable fellow, if a bit lazy. Cynthia would take the rabbit in, surely. Puny would continue to cook and clean on the two days the vestry paid for, very likely causing Father John to think he'd died and gone to heaven.

Perhaps, just perhaps, if he promised to bring her a Waterford goblet, Hessie Mayhew would chip in to turn the sprinkler on the roses in the memorial garden.

But what about Dooley? The last thing he wanted was for Dooley to feel uprooted and pulled apart.

"I'd like to have a boy," said Cynthia, looking brave. "I could . . ."

"You could what?"

"Draw him!"

"Aha," he said, unconvinced.

"I've had a boy in my life, my husband's nephew. His mother died, and Elliott and I took him in while he was in college. David and I got to be the fastest of friends and comrades, he was such a blessing to me when Elliott was away for weeks and months at a time. You've never met him, but you shall."

"I appreciate your offer, but God hasn't yet shown me what to do about Dooley."

"He will show you, of course, so just relax, why don't you?"

Relax? Yes. Well, that was a good idea.

The door to the office swung open.

"They got 'em," Rodney said, proudly. "Down in Holding is where they nailed th' scumheads. Th' law down there had up a roadblock, checkin' licenses. This little ol' boy on th' force remembered hearin' th' statewide when it went out, and recognized 'em. They'd painted their van an' all, but he was on to 'em. Pulled 'em over for a dead headlight, radioed in without 'em knowin' it, and three cars of Holding's best jumped over there like blue ticks on a coon. Dadgum!" said Rodney with considerable joy, hitching up his holster. "That was the biggest bust Holding ever did, a whole vanload of dope."

"Barnabas. What about . . . ?"

"Nope. Sorry. That's th' bad news," said Rodney, taking off his hat. "No sign of your dog. I tell you, Father, that might be just as well, if you know what I mean."

He didn't know, exactly, and probably didn't want to.

"Hey," said Dooley, coming to the phone.

"Hey, yourself. How's it going?"

"Great."

"Tell me about it."

"Me'n ol' Kenny Mcguire rode th' hair off 'em horses this mornin.' Then we played softball with 'em boys down at th' pond, and whipped 'em s' bad they was about t' bawl. You comin' agin Sunday?"

"I wouldn't miss it."

"I want you t' see me ride Goosedown. I got 'er t' likin' me s' good, she's jist like a little ol' baby or somethin'."

"Speaking of which, how is Rebecca Jane?"

"Cryin' after me s' bad, I have t' git out of th' house. Dools this, Dools that. You know how 'at is."

"Oh, I do, I do," said the rector.

To some, he thought as he hung up, that might have sounded like an ordinary conversation. But in fact, it was music, yes, music to his ears.

During the announcements at the eleven o'clock service, he drew attention to the meeting of the Altar Guild and the meeting of the lay readers, and issued another plea for youth choir recruits.

He tried to drum up business for the Baptists, who were having a lawn sale for foreign missions, and the Presbyterians, who were having a bake sale for hymnals.

"Are there any other announcements?" he asked.

"Why, yes," said Hal Owen, coming to the steps in front of the altar with something in his hand, "I'd like to announce, on behalf of the entire congregation, that we're sorry to have taken so long to celebrate your birthday."

He felt his face grow warm.

"You see, we had to wait for everybody to get their Frequent Flyer points together, so we could give you this envelope. It will take you nearly anywhere you care to go . . . and we'd appreciate it if you'd come back."

As he took the envelope, the congregation applauded enthusiastically. "I don't know what to say," he blurted.

Hal grinned. "Oh, just anything that comes to mind will do."

"Hallelujah!" he exclaimed, through the lump in his throat.

"I don't know how to tell you this," said Emma, who had gotten a tan, stepped up the amount of henna in her rinse, and was wearing earrings that looked like small hands of bananas.

"Just start at the beginning," he advised.

"I'm goin' back to bein' a Baptist," she declared flatly.

"Emma, you definitely got too much sun. Baptists quite often become Episcopalians, but Episcopalians seldom ever become Baptists. You will be going against the tide."

"Peedaddle on th' tide. Harold and I talked it over and we decided it was foolish for him to head off in one direction on Sunday and me to head off in another. Because the truth is, Harold will never be an Episcopalian."

"True, Emma, true."

"He said for me not to mention this to you, but if he had to keep singin' that ol' stuff in our hymnbook, he'd jump out the window."

"That would be a sight for sore eyes. Headfirst, I take it."

"Now you want to hear the good news?"

"I'm always ready to hear good news."

"I'm going' to keep workin' just like I've been doin', keepin' the same hours and all. That part won't change a bit."

Blast.

"And I'm goin' to report to you on how the Baptists do things. It will be a big help around here. For example, do you ever see First Baptist hurt for money? No way! That's because they don't have any of this 'tithe on the net or tithe on the gross' business. Baptists do it on the gross, just like the Bible says, period."

Perhaps he would jump out the window, headfirst.

"Anyway, Esther will take the collection home on Sunday and bring it to me on Monday. In the winter, I told her to carry the money bag under her coat, and in the summer, stick it in a book bag under some library books. You never know, these days."

"Absolutely!"

She leaned over her typewriter and peered at him. "Are you all right? You look pale. When's the last time Joe gave you a trim? Have you been seein' your neighbor? Oh, and how's her cat—don't cats make you sneeze? I drove by your house this morning and saw her yard. You should offer to mow it."

Very likely, Emma Garrett was the penance he'd been ordained to pay for the delight of employing Puny Bradshaw.

"So Rose said t' me, she said, 'Bill Watson, I'm goin' t' give you a piece of my mind,' and I said, 'Just a small helpin', please.' " He grinned broadly at the rector.

"Yessir, I told Rose what you said about givin' th' house to th' town, an' them givin' her a nice, modern place all fixed up in th' back, and she said th' only way she'd do it was if the statue was like Sherman or Grant or one of them, don't you know. That's when I said he ought t' be settin' down, and she like to th'owed a fit."

Uncle Billy chuckled. "Preacher, I took Rose f'r better or worse, but I declare, she's s' much worse than I took 'er for!

"Maybe we ought t' let 'er have that statue standin' up. I dread another winter, don't you know with th' wind a blowin' through th' cracks, and th' oil a settin' in th' tank."

The rector doubted that Miss Sadie would be able to drive past such a statue without a shudder, but that was not the issue. "It might be possible to have at least one room modernized by winter, with a bath to go with it, if we can agree on this matter right away."

"Law," said the old man, "I'd dearly love to have me a hot bath, if arthur'll let me set in a tub."

"Why don't we move forward with the standing version. If we carry on too long about whether he sits or stands, you might go out of here lying down."

"You hit the nail on th' head. Why don't you do th' talkin' and I'll do th' duckin'?"

"We can move ahead on the Porter place," he said to Esther Cunningham when he dropped by her office. "If I were you, I'd have some renderings done right away, so Miss Rose can feel involved, or she could change her mind on the whole thing. The D.A.R. crowd ought to know about statues and monuments and who does that sort of thing. Of course, we'll need to talk with her attorney at once, and I'd hope we could have them in a snug room and bath by winter."

"We'll start by dumpin' all th' Rose Festival proceeds in the restoration fund." The mayor's face had started to blotch with red spots, as it usually did when she was excited. "This thing's goin' to cost a king's ransom; we'll have to depend on some big shots around here to help get it done. How about if you. . . ."

"Don't go appointing me to raise any money. I can see it in your eyes."

The mayor laughed heartily. "You're quick."

"I have to be quick to dodge the bullets you'd fire if I gave you half a chance."

"Speakin' of—our boy's lookin' good, wanted mashed potatoes and gravy for supper last night. Puny carried him a bowlful."

"What do you think about that girl?"

"She calls herself a Bradshaw, but she's Cunningham through and through. We love 'er to death. Ray says he wouldn't take a war pension for the way she cuts up and sasses him."

"Well, maybe now that she's got Ray, she'll leave off sassing me."

"I wouldn't hold y'r breath," said the mayor.

It was Olivia.

"Father, I just called to say I love you."

"You did? Why, what a wonderful thing to hear." He felt as if someone had poured a bucket of warm water over him. Love! Sometimes, the very sound of that word conjured the feeling itself.

"I'm missing your sermons. Hoppy gives me a report when we talk, but sometimes he forgets the point!"

He laughed happily. "Let me mail you my sermons each week, shall I? The Holy Spirit often sends more than you'll find typed out, but at least, it will be something from home."

"Thank you! I have a proposition."

"Don't keep me waiting."

"How would you like to fly to Boston with Hoppy and spend a few days? It would be such good medicine to see you. And you could meet Leo. You'd enjoy each other so much. It would be lovely!"

After nearly thirteen years of staying put, it was suddenly "Come to Ireland!" "Come to Boston!" Feast or famine.

CHAPTER TWENTY-THREE

Homecoming

Are you in the mood to have your bed dug?" he asked through the screen door.

"Why, yes!" she said, turning around from the stove.

"Good, because I'm in the mood to dig it."

"Come in and have a cup of tea, the kettle's hot, and I'll get dressed. My, you're an early riser. For heaven's sake, stop looking at me," Cynthia said, fleeing from the kitchen in her bathrobe.

He took a spoonful of tea out of the canister, put it in the silver caddy, poured boiling water into the mug, and sat down on the stool by the wall phone. It was nice to have a change of scenery, to get up and sit in someone else's kitchen and look out someone else's back door. For another change, he'd rested well, and, since it was Saturday, hadn't set the alarm. Then he had run along Church Hill by the orchards, and looked down upon the village in its spring finery. He had felt such a tenderness of heart for the little town tucked so neatly at the foot of the hill, that he had stopped to sit on the stone wall.

Sitting on a stone wall, idly gazing, scarcely thinking. Stuart Cullen would have been proud.

"There!" said Cynthia, who had caught her blond hair in a yellow bow, and was wearing blue jeans, a sweatshirt, and sneakers. He thought she didn't look a day over twenty.

"Any word from your agent?"

"She called last night. She'd like to see more people in it, not just animals. So, I was thinking. Would you be a wise man?"

"Me being a wise man would be a foolish contradiction. Is this drawing to be from life . . . or the other?"

She laughed. "It depends. If you'll go to a party at the Sturgeons' with me, it will be from life. If you refuse to go, it will be from . . . the other."

Digging a bed was no job for the fainthearted, he thought, especially when it was a king-size bed.

"Just dig around here," she said, walking it off in her sneakers, "and then come around like this." She paced the circumference of what might have been a small ballfield.

"Cynthia," he said, wiping his brow, "that is not a bed, that is your entire backyard."

She pushed her glasses up on her nose and peered around.

"A job for a backhoe!" he exclaimed, hoping to make his point. "A John Deere tractor! A team of mules!"

"Oh, well, whatever you think, then," she said, cheerfully.

He dug the long, narrow bed near the sidewalk, away from the shade of the oak tree. "Do you have something we can break up the clods with, and then rake it fine?"

She came back with a motley assortment of her dead uncle's garden tools, which, he reasoned, should be in grand condition, since he'd never used them. She plunked them down proudly at the edge of the bed.

"Well, then," he said, unable to identify little more than an ancient bulb planter. "Let's just break up the clods with our hands, I see you've got good gloves. Then we'll rake it. How's that?"

"Perfect!" she said, with redeeming eagerness.

"What are you going to put in?" he asked, as they knelt side by side and went to work.

"Canterbury bells. Delphinium. Foxglove. Cosmos. And in the fall, double hollyhocks. Gobs and gobs of things!"

Just then, he heard an oddly familiar sound, somewhere. What was it? Still on his knees, he raised his head to listen.

It was the great and booming bark, as deep as the bass of the organ at Lord's Chapel.

Before he could rise or turn around, he was knocked sprawling into the loam of his neighbor's perennial bed, and a warm and lavish bath was administered at once to his left ear.

Barnabas had come home.

He rolled on his back, shouting with joy and trying to get up, but Barnabas immediately stood on his stomach, finding it a good base from which to administer a bath to Cynthia's face. "Timothy!" she shrieked. "Say a Scripture and step on it!"

" 'And we know that all things work together for good to them that love God!' " he shouted.

Barnabas sat on the rector's stomach and sighed.

There he lay in the dirt, with an enormous, mud-caked dog sitting on top of him, while his astonished neighbor was thrashed by a wagging tail the size of a kitchen broom. He laughed until the tears came.

"I'd like t' have a Kodak picture of this deal," said a voice overhead.

He looked up into the face of Homeless Hobbes.

"This critter was at my door at daylight this mornin.' He was s' starved, I give 'im half a cake of cornbread and it was gone in one bite. Then I poured up last night's soup and he eat that. I give 'im two Moonpies and he chased 'em down with a bucket of water. I was doin' m' wash and had t' wait f'r my shirt t' dry, so I put a rope around his neck and staked 'im to my' cot. In a little bit, we come on up here, an' when he heard you talkin', he like t' pulled me down, so I let 'im go."

Father Tim got to his feet and embraced his friend from the creek, as Barnabas collapsed into the dirt with a contented moan. "Homeless, meet my neighbor, Cynthia Coppersmith. Cynthia, meet Samuel K. Hobbes."

"Mr. Hobbes," she said, throwing her arms around him, "you will surely get a blessing for this!"

"I believe I just got my blessin'."

Father Tim examined Barnabas as well as he could through the muddy coat. "Looks like he's been on the road for a while. See here, his feet have been bleeding, not to mention he's a bag of bones under all this hair. I'll have to get him to Hal this afternoon."

Barnabas home! How unbelievable, how extraordinary. He felt as if some part of him had been returned, like an arm, perhaps, or a leg. He felt strangely, suddenly whole. What was needed was something to suit the occasion—shouting, maybe, or anything loud and recklessly fervent!

Just then, Violet strolled around the side of Cynthia's house, and Barnabas shot away from him like an arrow to its mark. The blur of white raced across the grass and disappeared down the coal chute as Barnabas filled the air with sufficient noise to suit the occasion.

Homeless sat at the kitchen counter while the rector brewed a pot of coffee and an exhausted Barnabas lay sleeping by his food bowl at the door.

"It's a treat to have you in my kitchen, for a change," he told his friend from the creek. "You know, you've brought me something I thought I'd never find again."

"That brings up m' own point," said Homeless. "Somethin' I lost has been found, too."

"And what's that?" asked the rector, leaning against the sink.

"My faith. It looks like it's come back. An' t' tell th' truth, it's a whole lot stronger than it was when it left."

"I'm glad to hear it. You don't know how glad."

"Well, I took down th' New Testament you brought me, an' I said, I b'lieve I'll just crack this open f'r a minute—I knew I didn't want t' go gettin' no religion out of it, nossir.

"So I baited me a hook and I put it on my' fishin' line and went 'n' sat on th' creek bank, an' done somethin' I hadn't done since I was a boy—I tied th' line on m' big toe. You know, that makes sense, you don't have t' mess with a pole. That way, when you get a bite, you know it, and all y' have t' do is just pull 'er in. Time savin'!

"So I was settin' there an' I commenced t' read, and first thing you know, I was dead into it. I'd catch me a crappie, take it off th' hook, bait up again, and go back t' readin'. I done that all day, and by th' time I'd fried me some fish and eat a good dinner, it come to me plain as day that m' faith was back. God Almighty had put his hand on me again after all these years. You know what I figure?"

"What's that?"

"I figure what can y' lose? Jesus said, 'Verily, I say unto you, he that believeth on me hath everlasting life.'

"Well sir, what if that's a lie? If it's a lie, then you live in sin, and die in sin, and the worms consume y'r flesh, anyway. But if it's th' God's truth, like he says it is, you win. Y'r sins are forgiven, you get a clean start, and when you die, you live for eternity.

"It seems t' me that's a deal a man cain't pass up. Number one, it's free. Number two, you cain't lose." Homeless grinned happily. "It's a good feelin'. Kind of like I've found a home."

"Your heart is saying you're not homeless, anymore."

" 'Course, I don't know what I'm goin' t' do about it, yet."

"Just enjoy it!" said the rector. "You'll know soon enough. And when you're ready, we'll talk about it, if you'd like."

"Dandy!"

He poured coffee into a mug for his guest. "I don't have a drop of cream, but there's sugar."

"I give up cream when I give up likker. No connection, that's just th' way it fell out."

"You know, they'll be wanting to present you with that twenty-five hundred dollars right away."

"Well, I ain't takin' it," Homeless said, blowing on the steaming coffee. "But I've got a idea."

"Keep talking."

"Up on th' hill behind th' creek is a lot of folks who need it worse'n I do. There's little bitty babies in there that don't get fed right, an' old people that needs medicine and a hot meal. They're people that slip through th' cracks, somehow or 'nother. I'd like t' see that money go in an emergency fund t' help th' ones that need it th' most.

"Give ol' Fred money t' buy 'is own britches instead of wearin' mine to look f'r work. Buy that little ol' Pritchard baby somethin' t' wear, instead of it runnin' around naked. Get ol' woman Harmon a pair of shoes, she's been half-barefooted f'r two winters. Maybe have a free supper once a week, I'll do th' cookin'."

"I guess I thought there'd be social service agencies in there."

"There's this kind of social service and that kind of social service, if y' know what I'm sayin'."

"I know."

"So, if th' reward money's goin' t' be doled out anyway, I'd like t' see it go in a special fund, somethin' we could get to without a lot of flimflam. Maybe we could call this fund th' Creek Bank."

"What a grand idea, in every way!" Barnabas looked up when he heard his master laugh. "See there, old fellow, what you've done? You've helped buy Fred a new pair of pants."

"Homeless man refuses check for $2,500," read the *Muse* headline on Monday.

That the story touched hearts throughout the newspaper's circulation base was no surprise. The surprise was the additional money that poured in, bringing the total to $3,800 in just one week.

The front-page headline on the following Monday gave an update: "Creek Bank Overflows."

"Right there," said Mule Skinner, "is th' single best headline J.C. Hogan ever wrote."

He was doing everything right, including using the food exchange system, which he found to be the very soul of aggravation. But somehow, he didn't feel right. He noticed that his hand shook on several mornings as he read the paper, that his vision blurred occasionally, and his thirst was more pronounced. While all of that had happened before, with no dire consequence, he was relieved that Hoppy would check it out in just two days.

Perhaps the time when he felt most stable and at peace was when he'd wake in the middle of the night and feel Barnabas at the foot of the bed. The comfort of that was so great, that it seemed to alleviate some of the other, milder disorders. Lying awake, he often wondered how a vacation in a foreign country, sleeping in strange beds, and eating strange food, could possibly make one feel better.

He wrote George Gaynor and gave him a complete update on all church doings, including one death and two new members of the nursery.

"Who're you writing?" asked Emma.

"The man in the attic."

"Do you think I ought to send him some fudge?"

"That's a splendid thought."

"I'm makin' Harold a big batch tonight, he's so skinny I have to shake th' sheets to find him. I'll just make a double batch, and mail it tomorrow. Do you think they'll X-ray it for files or razor blades or whatever?"

"Probably."

"If they're doin' their job, they will," she said with authority. "Do you know what we sang Sunday?"

"What's that?" he muttered, looking in his desk drawer for some glue to repair his bookend.

" 'Amazing Grace.' "

"Aha."

"If Episcopalians would sing that more, instead of all that stuff with no tune, you'd be amazed how people would flock in."

"Is that a fact? I suppose you think a Baptist wrote that hymn."

"Well, of course a Baptist wrote it, they sing it all th' time."

"My dear Emma," he said with obvious impatience, "that hymn was written by an Episcopal clergyman."

"He was prob'ly raised Baptist," she said, huffily.

Esther Bolick was standing at the front door of the rectory, with a cake carrier. Instantly, he knew that he must not, at all costs, let her give him whatever it contained.

"Father?"

"Esther, come in!"

"Oh, I can't," she said. "I've left the car running, and Gene's home waiting for his supper, but I was baking today, and I know how you like my orange marmalade cake, and so I baked one for Gene's birthday tomorrow, and one for you, and oh, I do hope you like it, because I think it's the best I've ever made!"

There. That did it. Looking into those bright and expectant eyes, he knew that he could no more refuse that cake than he could run along Church Hill Drive stark naked.

He paced in front of the refrigerator for a full ten minutes after Esther had gone, finally deciding he must get it out of the house at once.

There was no answer at Cynthia's. Russell? Russell and Betty! No, no. He was going to Meadowgate day after tomorrow, and he'd take it out there. Knowing that cake as he did, he recalled that it would only get better with time.

"Well, then," he said, weakly, staring at the refrigerator.

Barnabas had not gotten through that hateful experience without scars, he concluded. When he dropped a book on the hardwood floor of the study, the dog shot from beneath his wing chair, trembling with fear, and bounded up the stairs to hide under the bed.

He called Meadowgate. "He'll get over it," said Hal. "Give him six months or so for his nervous system to heal, and just keep doing what you're doing. Is he taking the vitamins?"

"Like candy."

"He's been through a tough time, very likely made his way from

Holding all the way to Mitford, which was no picnic. Got any plans for your Frequent Flyer points?"

"That's something I need to talk with you and Marge about on Wednesday."

"If you want to leave the boy with us while you take a break, you know you can. He's starting to be pretty responsible around here. He fed the dogs this morning, helped me clean out the kennels, and ran an errand for Marge. He's a neat kid."

"I was going to wait until I got there to tell you, but I'm planning a trip to Ireland."

"Will wonders never cease? You've been talking about that for years."

"Time to put up or shut up. But I want you to know that other arrangements could be made for Dooley. This may be for a couple of months . . ."

"Umm, well . . . he's got some roots going down here. I don't believe I'd disturb them, Tim."

"I don't want to say anything to the boy, yet."

"Come on out, then. I've got a sick horse on the next farm and it doesn't look too good—colic. I may have Dools with me, but we'll catch you around supper time."

"Thank you, my friend. Thank you."

"Don't mention it," said Hal Owen.

He was suffering from his usual evening exhaustion, which he had recently begun to identify as "old age." Perhaps he needed to join Barnabas in a vitamin program.

At a little after nine, the phone rang. It was Stuart.

"Am I interrupting anything?"

"Absolutely nothing of consequence, I'm sorry to say." He was, in fact, very sorry to say it. He would prefer to announce that he'd been reading Archbishop Carey's book or doing sit-ups, something profitable.

"I've just spoken with Father John. His mother died late last night. Quite sudden, the family is devastated. He's going home in the morning to spend some time with his father, who isn't well. I'm sorry about this for many reasons, not the least of which is the jumble it may make of your trip. You *are* planning a trip?"

"Oh, indeed! The congregation has given me a vast store of Frequent Flyer points and I'm planning to go to Ireland with Walter and Katherine."

"Bravo! Well done! It will just take a jot of time to work out plan B."

"Father Douglas? Would he be available?"

"Father Douglas is writing a book and won't budge from his PC."

"Aha."

"Let me think through this, and I'll get back to you. How's Cynthia?"

"I must call and find out. I've been meaning to do that."

"Yes, please do that, Timothy," said the bishop. "He who hesitates is lost, especially where women are concerned. By the way, I'm thankful to have your news about Barnabas."

When he hung up, he noticed that the receiver seemed heavy, like a barbell.

He turned out the lights in the study, then went to the kitchen and opened the refrigerator door.

There was that blasted cake carrier. Thank God, it wasn't a see-through carrier. One glimpse of that cake, and he'd be dead meat. This way, it might contain a lump of coal, for all he knew.

Barnabas was already sleeping at the foot of the bed when he came upstairs.

As he took his socks off, he noticed his feet and ankles were oddly swollen, something he'd never noticed before. Had he been on his feet a lot today? No more than any other day. He remembered going with a parish group on an intensive three-day bus tour of gardens in Vermont. His ankles had swelled exactly like this. "It's the walking," said his curate. "It's the sitting," said the choir director.

"I don't like it," Hoppy told him on Tuesday afternoon, and proceeded to run a series of uncomfortable tests. The rector decided he'd wait to hear the results on Wednesday morning, then head to Meadowgate. The bulletins would be done, the Evensong posters had just been reprinted, and he, as well as Barnabas, could do with the country air.

He returned to the office after seeing Hoppy, and sat staring at the door. He made an effort to pay attention to his calendar, and saw the dreaded words "Rose Festival," which he'd marked in for this coming Friday and Saturday. Had he prepared anything to say? If his life had depended on it, he couldn't be certain whether he had or not.

He looked at the book-lined walls, which seemed to be closing in on him, and then at Barnabas, snoring in the corner.

No, it wasn't Barnabas he heard snoring, it was the sound of his own breath coming in short, hollow gasps. He sat there, praying. Then, with the only ounce of energy he could summon, he left the office, forgetting to lock the door, and walked home.

He saw Cynthia in her yard as he came around the corner of the rectory.

"Hello!" she said, cheerfully, popping through the hedge in a denim smock and jeans. "I'm looking forward to this evening. Around six-thirty, they said, I hope that's OK. You'll like the Sturgeons, I promise."

Those fish people. Six-thirty? What was she saying?

"You look a bit fagged out, Timothy. Would you like a cup of tea or a sherry?"

"No," he said, curtly.

"Well, then," she murmured, backing away with a bewildered look, "I'll just see you at my house around six-fifteen?"

"I'll be there" he said vaguely, going up his back steps. Be there for what? He would find out later. Right now, he wanted a glass of tea, water, anything, something cold.

He let the leash drop and heard Barnabas dash into the hall and bound up the steps with it clattering behind him.

He saw the tea container in the refrigerator door, but the sight of the cake carrier was suddenly so compelling that he couldn't take his eyes off it. Something cold! The cake would be cold. And sweet. Dear God, he was wrenched with a craving for something sweet, if only one bite. Surely one small bite couldn't hurt.

He took the carrier out gingerly, as if trying to prevent an alarm from going off and announcing his indiscretion to the neighborhood.

His hand shook as he snapped off the top and stood staring at what Esther Bolick had done in an act of innocent generosity. Then, without thinking about it any further, he cut a large slice, ate it standing over the sink, and went back for another piece.

At four o'clock, feeling somehow revived, he sat in his wing chair in the bedroom. He was trying to get dressed for the evening, but something was wrong, he told himself, looking at his feet. Possibly, it was his shoes. He seemed to be wearing one black loafer and one brown loafer. Was that it? He wasn't sure. Perhaps it was something worse, something more grave than shoes.

He studied the situation, keeping his eye on the clock, and was finally interested to see that he had not put his trousers on. He was sitting there in his shorts. He knew this was true because he could see his legs quite plainly.

"Pants,"he said aloud. He looked in his closet and found something that felt like pants. It was not a jacket, it was definitely pants, folded over a hanger.

Water. He had meant to drink water, but had somehow forgotten. First, he must get his pants on, though he couldn't understand how it might be done. They seemed to be upside down. He saw that he couldn't stuff his feet in through the cuffs, that wasn't right, he knew that wasn't right. He would sit down and think about it, he decided, dragging the pants behind him and going to the chest of drawers.

He would need . . . what would he need? Cuff links? The Spurgeons just might dress up for this affair. Charles Spurgeon had said, "Christianity rests upon the fact that Christ is risen from the dead, His sovereignty depends upon His resurrection."

He was thrilled that they'd be visiting the Spurgeons. In fact, Spurgeon was among the saints he had wanted most to meet in heaven.

The room seemed still as a tomb, suspended in time. He knew at last that he could not keep running, he was getting out of breath, he was hurrying too fast, it was all too much, he could not go on.

He felt for the foot of the bed and worked his way around to the side. Then he pulled the covers back and got in, still wearing his shoes and clutching his pants, and breathing the Invitation, "The gifts of God for the people of God, take them in remembrance that Christ died for you, and feed on Him in your hearts by faith, with thanksgiving."

He was not surprised to see that the Spurgeons were having fish for dinner. But he was surprised to see the Lord sitting at the table when they walked into the high-ceilinged room. He felt his heart hammer in his breast.

"Timothy, I have a purpose for this time in your life."

"Yes, Lord," he replied, and at once the hammering ceased and a sweet peace invaded him, and he was floating.

He lifted up through the roof of the rectory and over the village, and saw the monument that anchored the little town, and Lew Boyd's Esso, where Coot and Lew were looking up and waving to him as he passed.

He saw that he had great wings, the wings of a butterfly, that they were an iridescent yellow and purple, and as smooth as velvet. The air rushed under him like a caress, he was buoyed along without effort, and found that the movement of his wings wasn't for the sake of keeping him aloft, but was for joy's sake alone.

He passed over the town, over the green and rolling countryside, and in the distance saw a ribbon gleaming in the light. It was a river, a broad, winding river, and on the other side, there was a small church.

He flew down, attracted to a single flower in the churchyard, and lighted there.

Then the procession came, with everyone dressed in white, led by a man who was bearing a wooden cross.

He placed the cross in a newly dug hole near the church door, and dirt was cast into the hole, and the children brought flowers and pressed their roots into the damp earth around it.

Then the man lifted his hands and prayed, thanking God for new life and for hope. The butterfly flew to the cross, and lighted there.

"As He left the shroud of death," said the man, "and rose to new life, so this butterfly, which was once trapped in a cocoon, has become free. Go in new life with Christ. Go, and be as the butterfly."

The butterfly lifted its wings and flew. It soared above the church, in the sunshine. It saw the river again, and a cool, sudden breeze, the kind found in the brewing of a storm, moved in from the west.

The butterfly passed over the town anchored by the monument, and over Fernbank sitting on the hill in the orchards. Then there was the red roof of the little house next door, and the slate roof of the rectory.

His head felt thick, as if he had been drugged, or struck a blow. Uneasily, he rolled over and saw someone sitting in the glow of his bedside lamp, looking at him.

Cynthia put her hand on his forehead. He could not speak, nor could he understand her when she spoke. "Timothy," she said, "I'm here."

CHAPTER TWENTY-FOUR

In New Life

"Profound dehydration," said Hoppy. He had pried the rector's jaws open and was looking at his tongue and mouth. "He's not responding. He may have had a stroke."

"No," Cynthia said softly. She heard a siren somewhere.

"Or his sugar may have dropped off the cliff. I'm going to give him a little dextrose now. I told the ambulance to follow me, just in case. Go down and make sure they find us; it's a new driver."

When she came back up the stairs with the ambulance attendants, she was shocked again to see the eyes which could not see her.

"His dextrostick was off the top of the scale. I think I know what's going on," Hoppy told Nurse Kennedy, coming along the hall behind the stretcher. "I want those lab results immediately."

"But, Doctor, there's nobody—"

"I don't want to hear 'nobody,' " he snapped. "You do what has to be done. Pronto."

"Yessir."

"I'm praying," said Cynthia.

He turned to the older nurse, who was waiting calmly for his directions. "Herman, he needs fluid and lots of it. Run a liter of half-normal saline wide open, then cut it back to 500 cc's 'til we get the report."

"Yes, Doctor."

He was walking up a flight of stairs. They seemed to narrow to a point, with an opening at the end as small as the eye of a needle. A brilliant light shone beyond the opening. He didn't know whether he could make it through. . . .

"Well, pal."

He opened his eyes and stared at the doctor's face, finding it an unutterably welcome sight.

"Well, what?" he croaked, glad for the sound of his own voice.

"You took a dive."

"No kidding."

"You've gone and gotten yourself the real thing."

"Meaning?"

"The Big One. You'll have to start giving yourself shots and peeing on a strip of paper. The nurses will be teaching you how to give yourself insulin, and I've ordered a glucometer so you can follow your blood sugar."

"Bad news."

"The good news is, you're alive. Not always the usual after several hours in nonketotic hyperglycemic coma."

With some effort, he realized that the good news was—he wouldn't have to make a speech at that blasted Rose Festival.

Though he was feeling fine, he was strictly forbidden to have visitors.

"Except your neighbor," said the doctor, without further comment.

He learned, to his surprise, that he would be up and around and better than new in only a few days, so there was no obstacle, after all, to his trip. There would be certain inconveniences, yes, like a daily shot that he'd have to administer himself, extreme caution with his diet, and plenty of exercise, none of which promised to enrich foreign travel.

In the meantime, Father Douglas was found to be willing to stir from his PC after all, and agreed to deliver both sermons for the coming Sunday. Father Lewis in Wesley had cheerfully offered to celebrate.

By the second day, he'd received seven arrangements, a gloxinia, and a topiary, giving him the pleasure of knowing that Jena Ivey, at least, was profiting from his condition.

Cynthia came, wearing something emerald-colored and flowing. "A bedtime story," she said, opening a manila envelope containing her new manuscript. "See what you think." She made herself comfortable on the foot of his bed and read aloud the story of the mouse in the manger.

What did he think? Merely that it was beautifully written, thought-provoking, and charming, not to mention touching, funny, and destined for certain recognition.

"All that?"

"All that and more."

"I've heard that sickness softens the heart, but it's made yours positively expansive!"

"Thank you for being there," he said, taking her hand.

"When you didn't come to fetch me for the Sturgeons, I thought you'd stood me up. I knew you hadn't been thrilled about going anyway. So I waited and waited and you didn't come, and finally, I popped through the hedge and knocked on your door and there was no answer, but Barnabas was in the kitchen, barking his head off. I called, but couldn't find you. I looked in the study, the garage, all over. And then I went upstairs, and found you in bed clutching a pair of pants in your hand."

"You did?"

"And with your shoes on!"

"The usual, then."

She laughed. "But I could tell you weren't sleeping. You looked so odd, and you were sweating and your mouth was moving, though nothing was coming out. I called the hospital and Hoppy wasn't there, and I said it was an emergency, so they found him and sent him to your house, thanks be to God!"

He pressed her hand tightly. "I can't remember anything at all. Nothing. The last thing I remember was eating Esther's cake."

"Esther's cake?"

He looked at her helplessly. "I hope you won't say anything to Hoppy."

He saw the concern in her eyes. "I promise. But let it be a lesson to you, for Pete's sake."

"Will you come again tomorrow?"

"Yes," she said, leaning down to brush his cheek with her lips. At the door, she turned around and waved. He thought she looked for a moment like a wistful child. "Sweet dreams," she said, tilting her head to one side.

The faint scent of wisteria on his pillow was a comfort.

"I wouldn't be kissin' any Blarney Stone, if I was you," said Puny, plumping up the cushions on the sofa. "When you think of how many folks has put their mouth on that thing, it gives me th' shivers."

"I have no intention of hanging over some precipice to kiss a rock," said the rector, who was taking his prescribed midday rest in the study. "Instead, I will devote that time to shopping for one Puny Bradshaw and shipping her a surprise."

"As if I didn't have enough surprises," she said tartly, dusting the mantle.

"Like what?"

"Like Joe Joe gittin' shot, and you gittin' in a coma and half dyin'. That's been keepin' me plenty surprised, thank you, not t' mention busy."

"Speaking of busy, would you keep doing the splendid things you do, for the priest who takes my place while I'm in Ireland?"

"I might" she said cautiously. "I'd have t' check 'im out. I don't work for gripers, complainers, or hypocrites, not to mention bossy, mean, or stingy people."

"A good policy. I wish I could say the same. If I'm still away when school starts, would you be able to live here and take care of Dooley 'til I get back?"

"Well . . ."

"Just think, Joe Joe wouldn't have to drive all the way to Wesley to court you, he could just walk down the street."

She flushed.

"Think about it. It would nearly double your salary, and all you'd need to cook for the boy would be bologna, which, if the priest is young enough, he'd probably like, too."

She sighed. "I wonder why th' Lord is always dishin' out preachers t' me."

Dear Friends:

When I left Mitford several weeks ago, you couldn't see me, but I could see you. Thank you for coming out to wave goodbye.

Especially, I want to thank the kids who cared, and sent those wonderful drawings to the jail. I've been allowed to put a few of them up in my cell, and you'd be surprised to see how much they mean to the other inmates. In this grim and oppressive place, the bright colors stand out vividly, but more than anything, it's a joy to see the freedom in your drawings. They are spontaneous and genuine, and seem to give a certain hope to people who are clearly destitute of hope.

I'm pretty isolated from contact with the other inmates, as I work in the laundry with just five other men. The exercise yard is about the size of the grassy area around your town monument. I go every evening after supper and try to keep myself in shape. Mostly, it's good for clearing my head, as I often feel a real panic about being here.

They told me I'd have to keep an eye on my watch and my shaving kit, but that nobody would steal my Bible. If they could imagine the riches to be found in it, they'd all be after it, and that's what I'm praying for.

I don't know what I can say in this letter, I don't know what is being censored, but I feel pretty certain they will let me say this:

I found something in Mitford that I never believed existed. After I prayed that prayer with Father Tim and my new brother, Pete Jamison, God changed my life. Then He demonstrated His love through you.

Thanks for the shoes. The casseroles. The cakes. The pies. And your prayers. Please write me if you can.

Sincerely, George Gaynor

The rector lowered the latest edition of the *Muse* into his lap. The mail clerks at that prison had their work cut out for them.

"It's Mr. Gregory," announced Puny, wiping her hands on her apron.

He knew he should have shaved this morning. "Ask him to come in!"

He heard Andrew's footsteps coming briskly down the hallway. "A bachelor's paradise!" he said, seeing the book-lined study, the view of Baxter Park, and the bright face of Puny Bradshaw. He inhaled deeply, enjoying a fragrance that clearly had its source in the kitchen.

The rector got up and gave his favorite antiquarian a forceful embrace. "Sit down at once, my friend, and tell me everything. I haven't seen you in . . . when have I seen you? You'd think that since we're across the street from each other, we'd meet more often."

"Life, Father, life," said Andrew, sitting down in a wing chair and unbuttoning his jacket. "It is far too hurried."

"Even in Mitford."

"Particularly in Mitford, I sometimes believe. How are you feeling? Are you going to push along all right?"

"Oh, I think so. A bitter inconvenience, nothing more."

"Would y'all like a cup of coffee or a glass of tea?" asked Puny. The rector thought she looked a picture in her new apron and dress, and her red hair caught up with a green ribbon.

"Tea!" Andrew responded eagerly. "No sugar, if you please."

"I'll have the same," said the rector. He was tenderly amused to see that Puny, who appeared to be in awe of their handsome visitor, curtsied slightly as she left the room.

"Where on earth did you find such a gem?"

"Sent from heaven!"

"Speaking of heaven, I have a new shipment of books from a priory in Northamptonshire. Very rare. Exceptional. One day they won't allow such treasures out of the country. There's a very early *Imitation of Christ.* I thought you'd like to come and have a look."

"I shall. It's a good thing books aren't bad for this aggravating condition, or I'd be a dead man. Any more sales on Uncle Billy's drawings?"

"Why, yes. Four more, and I took him an envelope only yesterday. He likes cash, you know, not checks, and I fear he may be keeping it under his mattress."

"Not a bad move, considering the times."

Andrew laughed. "I read George Gaynor's letter in the paper. And only yesterday, I heard that two of the three British-side dealers have been arrested in Norwich. Fascinating circumstances, really; I've tried to keep up with the account in the newspapers. Inspected all my table legs, but not one is worth a farthing!"

"What can you tell me about Ireland?"

"Ireland? Only a bit. Hopeless Anglophile, you know. Of course, there's been a big trend to Irish antiques, but they're not my cup of tea. Too primitive. Why do you ask?"

"I'm going in a matter of days. Thought you might have some suggestions. We'll be staying in Sligo."

"Ah! rough country. Undeveloped. But spectacularly beautiful, I'm told. Take a raincoat, mud boots, a waterproof watch . . ."

Blast, he thought, why bother to go to such a place, at all?

"Your tea, sir," said Puny, who had put the rectory's best damask napkins on the tray and used their finest cut-glass water goblets.

Andrew took a sip of tea and pressed his mouth with the starched napkin. "I haven't seen much of your neighbor. Is she still about?"

"Oh, very much about."

"Clever lady."

"Yes. Yes, she is."

"Terribly attractive."

"Rather pretty, yes."

"Funny, actually."

"I agree."

"I can't seem to make any headway with her, however. I suspect you know her a bit, being next door. Any suggestions?"

Tall, suave, trim, urbane Andrew Gregory was asking *him?*

He thought for a moment.

"Oh, she'd probably enjoy being invited to more of those fancy country club affairs, perhaps to play bridge, that sort of thing," he lied. Forgive me, Lord, he prayed, I promise I won't do it again.

As Puny saw Andrew to the door, the phone rang.

"Hello," he said. He heard someone breathing. "Hello?"

"I prayed that prayer," said a hoarse voice, and hung up.

"Was that by any chance Joe Joe?" Puny asked, eagerly, hurrying into the study.

"No, it wasn't. I'm not sure who it was." The voice had been oddly familiar, but no . . . no, it couldn't have been who he was thinking.

"You don't know who it was?"

"I didn't recognize the voice, exactly, and then they hung up."

"Wrong number!" said Puny, setting the glasses on the tray and taking it into the kitchen.

Absalom Greer looked at him steadily. "My brother, if I step into your pulpit, some of your flock will be gone when you return."

"So be it."

They were sitting on the steps of the country store, on a day so hot that both had taken their jackets off and rolled their shirt sleeves up.

"You know I'll preach on sin."

"Preach on it, then."

"I'll preach a personal relationship with Jesus Christ."

"I fervently hope so."

"And I'll preach the cross."

"That's what we all need to hear. May God bless you, my friend."

"And may he bless you, Timothy. I didn't know when I quit my little churches last week to get a rest, that th' Lord would hitch me up again before he let th' traces fall." The old pastor laughed, happily. "I'll see that Lottie dresses me proper and I'll keep my shoes shined and a handkerchief in my pocket."

"That's more than I usually manage. How thankful I am that your schedule allows this. It was a sudden inspiration in the middle of the night. I believe the Holy Spirit put it on my heart. Can you hold out for two months?"

"When it comes to preachin', I'd a lot rather hold out than hold it in. I'll answer this call at your place, then I'll quit."

They stood up, and Father Tim clasped the pastor's hand with both of his. "We'll go through the order of service until you get the hang of it, and the bishop will provide someone to celebrate."

"This is pretty unorthodox, you know," Absalom said.

"I trust the orthodoxy of it enough to trust the unorthodoxy," replied the rector, returning his gaze and smiling.

The trip to the airport had become a dilemma. Joe Ivey, Mule Skinner, Ron Malcolm, and Hal Owen had all volunteered to drive.

Emma, however, had insisted, which settled that consequential matter.

"Well, of course, you must leave Barnabas with us," said Marge, when they talked on the phone.

"But you've done—you're doing—so much already." he protested, sincerely.

"Just think of all you do for us, Timothy!"

Frankly, he couldn't think of anything at all.

In his last sermon, he made every effort to prepare the congregation.

"Pastor Greer warns me that some of my flock will have leaped over the wall by the time I return. But I challenge you to remain in the fold, and to hear what he has to say, and to ponder it in your hearts. I haven't made this decision lightly, nor has the bishop been casual in giving his blessing. There will be some awkward moments, very likely, for Pastor Greer doesn't know our order of service, but I want you to pray for him, and give him the right hand of fellowship, and keep a strong hedge around yourselves until I return."

Some of his flock looked at him quizzically as he greeted them on the church lawn. No one liked change, and why in heaven's name couldn't he have brought in Father Douglas, whom they at least knew? What did it matter if his sermons were largely tepid? He was comfortable, they were comfortable, and surely any bishop worth his salt could have talked him into leaving his book, which probably wasn't going to be very exciting, anyway. Or Father Randall, now there was someone who'd pep the place up and make a contribution, though there was always the question of his unfortunate preference for guitar music at the eleven o'clock. And what about this preacher being a Baptist, for heaven's sake? They only hoped he would not raise his voice and shout, or worse yet, issue an altar call.

In the cool of the evening, he walked to Fernbank with Barnabas, taking his time on the hill, and found Miss Sadie and Louella sitting on the porch, fanning.

"Ladies, what's up?"

"What's up is that we're looking for company," Miss Sadie told him. "Louella and I were just talking about how nobody visits on Sundays like they used to. What on earth do you think people *do* if they don't visit?"

"They go to the mall," said the rector, out of breath. He sat on the steps with Barnabas, who was glad for the cool steps on the east side of the house.

"Surely not!"

"However, the old customs haven't vanished entirely. After all, here I am."

"Let Barnabas come up with us," said Miss Sadie, who was still in her church clothes.

Louella drew away from Barnabas. "Thass th' biggest dog I ever seen. I lived in houses ain't as big as that dog."

Barnabas collapsed at Miss Sadie's feet and yawned contentedly.

"There now! What a treat! Louella, do you suppose we ought to get a dog?"

"Oh, law!" Louella was speechless.

"Well, Father, you should know that we're all in a dither about Absalom Greer coming to supply us while you're gone. I think that was a very odd thing to do, but I'm excited about it."

"You're right. It was a very odd thing to do. But I think the oddity of it will have its effects. Will you give me a report on how things are going now and then? I'll leave you an itinerary, with addresses and phone numbers. And I wanted to say I'll write you ladies every week. That's a promise."

"You've spoiled us, Father. You really have. Nearly thirteen years and barely missing a Sunday except for special meetings of the diocese, and that awful winter when the flu kept you down."

"You know to call Hal or Ron if you need anything, and Esther Bolick and Emma will look out for you. Why, after a day or so, you'll be saying, 'Father who?' "

"A likely story!"

"You know Olivia will be coming home soon," he said. "Perhaps you'd care to call her."

"Oh, we bin talkin' 'bout that!" said Louella. "Miss Sadie goan have her up to try on all those fine hats, and I'm goin' t' fry her some chicken that will melt in her pretty mouth, yessir."

"And we'll sit at the dining table, won't we, and use Mama's china?"

"Aw, let's just set in th' kitchen where it's comfortable, and not put on airs for Miss Olivia. Let's just treat her like family!"

"Why, Louella, that's a perfect idea. What will we have with the chicken?"

Father Tim got up and went to Miss Sadie's rocking chair. He leaned down and kissed his eldest parishioner on the forehead, then turned and gave Louella a kiss on her warm cheek. "Keep up the good work," he said. "Remember I'll write you every week."

He hurried down the steps with Barnabas, and out into the drive, where he stopped and looked back, grinning. "Stay out of trouble!" he said.

"Let's have a romantic dinner by candlelight," suggested Cynthia, who had dropped by his office on her way to The Local.

"That sounds good. But I had another suggestion, if you're interested."

"Try me!" she said, tilting her head and looking pleased with life.

"Why don't we take a drive in the country?"

"I love to drive in the country!"

"On my motor scooter."

"On your motor scooter? That little red thing?"

"The very same. We can take a picnic."

"Where would we put it?"

"Well, I don't know. I haven't thought it through."

"Obviously not."

"But I will, I will think it through. I'll devise a plan, and you'll be stunned by the brilliance, the wit, the . . . foolishness of it!"

She laughed with delight. "I love it when you talk like that! The minute you devise your plan, let me know more. Anything I can pick up for you at The Local?"

"Nothing, thanks," he said, seeing her to the door.

She was on the sidewalk when he called to her. "Cynthia?"

"Yes?" She turned around and smiled.

"I'll miss you," he said.

He was dreading it, dreading it all. He had not been on an airplane in nine years, and to fly across the ocean was suddenly unthinkable. Travel always sounded wonderful when one considered the end, but to consider the means was quite another story. Walter and Katherine had gleefully reported that the farmhouse had featherbeds, but as he recalled from boyhood days at his grandfather's, featherbeds contained more than feathers. He recalled hearing faint chewing sounds that lasted the livelong night.

Then there was the issue of where the bathrooms were. They believed both rooms had baths *en suite,* but then again, one of the baths—and guess whose it would be?—just might be a step or two down the hall.

He sat in his chair in the bedroom and looked at the results of his feeble packing effort. He wouldn't leave for four days yet, but he thought it best to start working on that aggravating project now.

"Timothy," he said aloud, causing Barnabas to look around curiously, "you have a rotten attitude about this trip. Back up and start over! Thank you, Lord, for the opportunity to go to this wonderful part of your world, thank you for making provision through the sacrifices of so many people, and for bringing it all together in a way that is clear evidence of your grace.

"Thank you for a good home for Dooley and Barnabas, may you bless the Owens exceedingly for their care for us. Forgive me for being dark-spirited about what is certainly a privilege, and enable me to take care of every need before I go. And, Lord, show me what to pack."

"Leave this packin' alone!" said Puny. "You are makin' a mess. You have two pairs of underwear in here and nine handkerchiefs. You have three pairs of cuff links and no French cuff shirts." He was alarmed to see how she was undoing what he had so carefully done.

"You jis' go on and let me handle this. I packed for my grandpaw all th' time when he was travelin' with a revival tent. He was neat as a pin. He said he got compliments all th' time about the way he turned hisself out. What's this?"

"That," he said, irritably, "is my diabetes case."

"Ugh," she said, looking inside. "Needles! What's this?"

"Those are the strips to dip in my urine, to test blood-sugar levels."

"Do you have something to pee in?"

"Puny . . ."

"Well, think about it. You might need a little jar. You could git over there in that foreign country, and you don't know what you might have to pee in."

"Put in a jar, then," he said.

"I'm so glad you got Mr. Greer, an' another preacher ain't movin' in here. I hope you don't mind that I prayed about it."

They had parked the car on the dirt road, climbed through a barbed wire fence, crossed a meadow brimming with daisies, and climbed a green knoll dotted with buttercups. They spread the quilt where pines and blue spruce cast a cool shade.

He lay down, put his hands behind his head and looked up at a sky filled with vast, cumulus clouds. He felt as if he might have been journeying to this very place for the duration of his sixty-one years. Surely, this was destination enough. Could Ireland be any greener? Its hills any nobler?

"Is this heaven?" inquired Cynthia, who was also lying on her back, looking up at the clouds. "Well, of course it is! Just look over there to the right, you see that chariot with an angel driving it? Look, Timothy, do you see?"

One thing he liked about his neighbor. It didn't take much to entertain her.

"I was looking at the face of Beethoven, myself."

"Where?" she asked eagerly.

"Straight up. See that wild mane of hair?"

"Why, that's not Beethoven at all," she said with urgent sincerity. "That's Andrew Jackson!"

He surprised himself by laughing so hard he couldn't stop. Nor did he want to. Being joined by his neighbor in this foolish collapse made it even better.

When the spasm had passed, Cynthia fetched a handkerchief out of her skirt pocket and blew her nose with some abandon. "Doesn't it feel grand to laugh over nothing?" she wondered. "Why don't we laugh more?"

"I think we forget," he said, wiping his eyes.

"How can we possibly forget to laugh, when it feels so good, and cures so much? How can we possibly?"

He had no answers. Ever since he was a child, he had been prone to forget about laughing.

"When I was a girl, I used to get tickled in chapel. I must tell you that it was the most delicious laughter I ever enjoyed in my life, because it was so forbidden. But oh, it was terribly painful, too. I would laugh 'til I hurt, and the tears would be streaming down my cheeks, but I had to keep all the rest of it inside, because if one single little bit of laughing slipped out, well, you know."

"Sudden death!"

"Dear Cynthia, they said, she sits in chapel and cries, what a tender heart! Oh, dear."

He smiled. How good to lie on his back and talk of nearly nothing, and feel the breeze now and then, and hear the bawling of a calf, and the song of the juncos in the hedges. He could not remember when he had been so supremely contented.

He reached over and took her hand, and turned his head to look at her. He thought that if he dared kiss her, he would devour her. He would kiss her lovely cheek and the tip of her nose, her forehead and her hair, he would not be responsible, he would come undone. It seemed dangerous merely to breathe.

"Timothy, look at that funny cow staring at us."

He raised his head slightly, and froze. "Do not move," he said. "That is a bull."

"Oh, for heaven's sake," she whispered, "this happens in comic books, not real life. Will we be gored?"

He did not feel confident about sitting up, but he felt less confident about lying down. So he continued to hold his head up, gazing at the bull somewhere over its left flank, feeling that the eye contact was not advisable.

"I think that what I should do is stand up slowly, and then you should run for the woods."

"I'll take the basket," she volunteered in a low voice. "I will not share my raspberry tart with that oaf."

He forced himself into a sitting position. How would J.C. handle this story? In the obituaries or on the front page?

The bull looked at him with consuming interest, as he managed to stand, albeit unsteadily. His knees had nearly gone out. "OK, run," he said evenly to his neighbor. He heard her do that very thing.

Were frequent flyer points refundable? he wondered.

The bull gazed at him steadily. Then, it lowered its head and turned to lumber down the hill to a shade tree at the edge of the meadow, without looking back.

The rector picked up the quilt and trudged to the edge of the woods to meet Cynthia, who was standing by a pine tree, shaking with laughter.

"It's stressful in the country," he said, grinning.

"I vote that the best picnic lunch of my life!" she declared. "The best cold chicken, the best French bread, the best cheese, the best raspberry tart!"

"I agree with all of that!" he said, trying to ignore his increasing appetite for holding her in her arms.

She took a small sketchbook out of her skirt pocket, and a box of pencils. "I don't suppose you'd care to put one corner of the quilt over your head?"

"Not particularly. Why, for heaven's sake?"

"I'm starting on the wise men, and this is my very last chance at you, you know. All you have to do is sit over there and pull the quilt up around your head, like this."

"That's all? How long will it take?"

"Five minutes! I'll hurry. Then, when I get to my drawing board, I'll use the sketch as a model for the watercolor." She peered at him. "Actually, if you get on your knees, it will be easier."

"For who?"

"For me, I think. Here, get on your knees, and I'll fix the quilt like a burnoose, sort of." She took the raffia that he'd used to keep the napkin wrapped around the bread, put the quilt over his head, and tied it.

"There!" she said approvingly, "You look just like you've come from afar!"

He was relieved that the ordeal was nearly over, when he looked up to see an old man and woman coming along the path leading from the woods to the knoll. They were carrying burlap sacks filled with newly dug ferns, an occupation pursued by a number of locals.

As oddly stricken as if he'd been caught thieving chickens, he could not seem to budge from his knees, nor remove his burnoose. "Good afternoon!" he called, weakly. They paused, looked at him quizzically, then turned and hurried back into the woods.

"An' that feller's a preacher!' he heard the man say to his wife.

They sat on the grassy knoll until the shadows lengthened over the quilt. They had found peace here today, and laughter, and he was thankful.

"Cynthia," he said, quietly, holding both of her hands, "I've thought about it."

She tilted her head and gazed at him. There was a happy light in her eyes which spoke her own thoughts.

He had decided to be simple and direct. "I can't make that decision yet," he said. "I'd like to think about it while I'm away. But if that's asking too much, then you've only to . . . deny me the privilege of thinking about it anymore, at all."

She listened without speaking, but her hands clasped his tightly.

"I won't try to kid you. I honestly don't know what I want to do. All I know is that I want the decision to be right and good. If I were younger, it would be an easier decision. But I've been so one-track minded, for so long, that I don't know if I can run on two tracks without causing a collision."

She smiled, nodding.

"I care very much for you, Cynthia." He had a sudden foreboding that he might begin to croak, so he was silent for a while, simply looking at her.

He saw in her spirit such a tender willingness that he was touched. She had a gift for touching him—with laughter, with delight, with deep feeling, with hope.

"At first," she said, quietly, "I was hurt that you didn't answer right away. But I think I've come to understand you better just recently, and I feel good about what you're saying. Yet, there's something in me that says, you fool, you've been pushy and presumptuous, he doesn't care for you any more than all the other people he's so lovely to, and you'll frighten him off if you don't back away, and then . . . and then the path through the hedge will grow over . . ."

The path through the hedge will grow over.

Hadn't she been the one with the courage to blaze that path in the first place?

He took her into his arms and held her close, and kissed her hair. They were silent for a time. Then he kissed her cheek and the bridge of her nose. "We must not let the path through the hedge grow over," he said with feeling.

"Good mornin', good mornin', good mornin'," said Mule Skinner, coming through the door in an orange and turquoise shirt with an Indian blanket motif.

"I follered that shirt in th' door," said Rodney, who was behind him, "and you're under arrest."

"What for?" said Mule.

"For disturbin' th' peace."

"You want to arrest somebody, pick on that feller right there," said Mule, pointing to J.C. Hogan in the back booth with Father Tim.

"What'd he do?"

"Forgot t' run my ad this week, an' it a half page."

J.C. was sopping his toast in sausage gravy. "I'll run it next week, and give you a free one th' followin' week."

"That's no more'n anybody at the Wesley paper would do," said

Mule, who had often threatened to take his real estate advertising elsewhere.

"So, how about if I give you two free ads?"

There was a stunned silence.

"Go for it!" said Rodney.

"Deal," said Mule, incredulous.

"Quarter pagers," said J.C.

The rector grinned. How accustomed he'd grown to the simple familiarity of friends in this small place on the map. Mitford had given him an extended family, with cousins galore, and no two alike.

"The usual," Mule told Percy, "an' squeeze th' grease out."

"I'll squeeze you some grease—on your bald head."

What would he find in Sligo? Considering that half of Mitford had Irish blood, with a liberal dose of Scottish thrift, what he'd find might not be so different, after all. He hoped there would be a warm place like the Grill, in the village near the farmhouse.

"Percy," said J.C., "there's somethin' unusual about these grits."

"Oh, yeah?" Percy said suspiciously.

"They're real good 'n' thick an' got plenty of butter, th' way I like 'em."

Percy beamed. "I never used t' eat grits, but now that I've started eatin' 'em of a mornin', I make 'em th' way they taste good t' me."

Was something different about J.C.? Father Tim wondered. Maybe so, but he couldn't put his finger on it.

"Th' only thing is," said J.C., "this gravy's got lumps the size of banty eggs."

The rector finished his coffee and got up from the booth. "Boys, I've got more to do than I can shake a stick at, and Emma's picking me up at the crack of dawn tomorrow. Hold it in the road 'til I get back."

They all got out of the booth and stood up. It wasn't every day that one of their own went off to a foreign country.

Mule slapped him on the back. "Don't take any wooden nickels, buddyroe."

"Drop us a line," said J.C., "but keep it short and axe th' big words."

Rodney shook his hand. "Take it easy, Father. I'll miss all th' business you've been givin' me lately."

"God bless you," said Percy, choking up. "And put y'r money back in y'r pocket, it's on th' house."

There, he thought, untying Barnabas from the bench leg on the sidewalk. It's official. I'm really going to go through with this thing.

They walked down to see the place where Dooley was currently catching his fish bait, down into the cool, sweet-scented woods where the only sounds were birdcalls and running water. How thankful he was that Dooley Barlowe could have this golden time in his life. It would provide nourishment the rest of his days.

"So, I wanted to come out and say goodbye," he said, squatting down on the creek bank beside the boy.

"Goodbye, y'rself," said Dooley, slapping the water with a stick.

"I'm going because I need to, son, not necessarily because I want to. And I want to say that I'll miss you." He tousled the boy's hair.

"You don't need t' miss me," said Dooley, looking at him frankly. "I got plenty t' do. I prob'ly won't miss you."

"Well, heck. I was kind of hoping you would."

"Oh, I might, once in a while, y' know, if I don't have nothin' else t' do."

"That's fair enough. Hal and Marge say you're doing all right out here, keeping up your end. They're old friends, and they mean a lot to me, so I thank you for helping them."

"They need help," Dooley said, flatly. " 'at ol' Rebecca Jane, she cries a lot an' all, and crawls around eatin' dog food outta Bonemeal's dish, and peein' in 'er pants, an' Doc Owen, he don't have nobody t' help 'im clean out th' horse poop, 'n' look after th' kennel. He even gits me t' help 'im deliver calves."

He had never seen Dooley looking so proud. And he could have sworn he'd grown an inch or two just since he saw him ten days ago.

"You'll learn something from Hal Owen."

"You know what 'e told me?"

"What's that?"

"He said I could be anything I want to be."

"That's true. You can."

Dooley slapped the water with the stick. "Anything?"

"Anything."

There was long silence, broken by the call of a cardinal seeking its mate.

"The Owens will take you in to visit your grandpaw. You're good medicine for him, you know. And I'm hoping you'll keep an eye on Barnabas."

"When you comin' back?"

"In September. School will have started, and Puny's coming to live with you. I'll be back by the time you've made your first A in math."

"I like ol' Puny."

"Puny likes you."

"Has Jenny bin around, lookin' f'r me?"

"No, not that I know of. She's a pretty girl."

"Yeah." He jabbed the stick into the moss on the bank.

"Something on your mind, Dooley?"

He hesitated. "I bin prayin'."

"You have? Tell me about it."

"Is it all right to ask for dumb stuff?"

"I sure hope so, I ask for a lot of dumb stuff."

"I mean, like, help me do it right when Doc Owen asks me t' do somethin' in th' barn, or hand 'im somethin' when a calf is comin' . . ."

"That's not dumb stuff. God wants us to ask Him for help. And speaking of how to do something right, you know what God has to say to you, Dooley?"

Dooley looked startled. "What's 'at?"

"In the Thirty-second Psalm, He says, 'I will instruct you, Dooley, and teach you in the way which you should go. I will guide you with my eye.' "

"Did he put my name in like 'at?"

"He did. Just like He put my name in, and the Owens' name, and Cynthia's name. The Bible speaks to everyone who trusts Him."

"I cain't set here jabberin'," Dooley said, leaping to his feet. "I got t' feed 'em ol' dogs. You want t' come?"

"I'm right behind you."

The boy set off at a trot, up the winding path that led to the barn and the kennels. Then, he heard a booming bark, and saw Barnabas race to Dooley, who threw his arms around the black dog and rolled to the ground with him, shouting his name and laughing.

One thing he could say for his secretary. If he'd had any reservations about this trip, any dread of going, the ride down the mountain to Holding with Emma Garrett had made him positively ecstatic about getting on the plane—and the sooner, the better. She had queried him so relentlessly about what he had packed or forgotten to pack, that he finally admitted that he didn't know any of the answers, that Puny Bradshaw had packed absolutely everything—with his blessing. She was mortified that he'd allow anyone else to do something so personal. How could he be sure what he'd end up with over there across the ocean, and no running home to get it?

When he saw that the first leg of his journey would be on a small aircraft that looked like a bathtub, and was patently made of tin, he did not flinch. Never mind that he had heard horror stories about small planes crashing into people's bedrooms, or that they could be as airless as bread boxes.

He took his luggage out of the trunk of Emma's lilac Oldsmobile and, staggering under the weight of the suitcase and the suit bag, gave her a kiss on a cheek wet with tears, and vanished into the terminal building.

He sat looking out at the runway, which was baking in a fierce summer sun. He was the one who was leaving; why did he feel rejected, somehow? Why had they all let him go? Now, here he was, forced to do this thing, to travel thousands of miles away, across an entire ocean, and have an adventure—whether he wanted one or not.

The little plane took off with a rattle and groan so ferocious, he felt the whole thing would come apart under him. If this was the so-called, much-touted technological age, how had they failed so miserably to make a plane that didn't do its job any better than this?

He held on to the leather briefcase in his lap, the one the vestry had given him years ago for Christmas. What had he forgotten, after all? He was mildly alarmed that everything seemed to be taken care of, that there were no loose ends. And why on earth should that be alarming? For the simple reason that it happened so seldom in one's life that it encouraged suspicion, that's why.

He opened his briefcase and pulled out a folder with a legal pad and a pen, and began to make notes about a sermon topic that had occurred to him only yesterday. There. That felt better. Next, he'd make a list of things to write home about, like how had the Rose Festival done? He'd forgotten to ask. And would someone make sure the new bathtub at the Porter place had a rail to hold on to? And when Cynthia heard from her agent about Uncle Billy's ink drawings, would she let him know at once? And had he put the premium increase notice on the Mortlake tapestry in his desk drawer, or given it to Ron for the next vestry meeting? He was surprised at the list he could make if he just put his mind to it.

He happened to look out the window.

They were flying over lush, rolling countryside, with his own blue mountains to the right. He thought it might be the most beautiful thing he had seen in a very long time.

There was a peaceful farm with acres of green crops laid out in neat parcels, and a tractor moving along the road. There was a lake that mirrored the clouds, and the blue sky, and the shadow of the little plane as it passed overhead.

Away toward the mountains, there was a ribbon of water flung out on the land, glittering in the sunlight, and beyond the river, a small, white church with a steeple catching the brilliance of the sun.

He closed the folder in his lap.

"Go in new life," came unbidden to his mind.

He felt as if he were emerging from a long, narrow hallway, from a cocoon, perhaps. He felt a weight lifting off his shoulders as the little plane lifted its gleaming wings over the fields.

Go in new life with Christ, he said silently, wondering at the strangely familiar thought.

Go, and be as the butterfly.

Visit America's favorite small town—
one book at a time

Welcome to the next book,

A Light in the Window

CHAPTER ONE

Close Encounters

Serious thinking and crossing the street, he once said, shouldn't be attempted simultaneously.

The red pickup truck was nearly upon him when he saw it. The shock of seeing it bear down with such ferocious speed sent him reeling backward to the curb, where he crashed in a sitting position. He caught a fleeting glance of the driver, talking on a telephone, as the truck careened around the corner.

"Father Tim! Are you all right?"

Winnie Ivey's expression was so grieved he felt certain he was badly hurt. He let Winnie help him up, feeling a numb shock where he'd slammed onto the curb.

Winnie's broad face was flushed with anger. "That maniac! Who was that fool, anyway?"

"I don't know. Perhaps I'm the fool for not looking where I was going." He laughed weakly.

"You're no such thing! I saw the light, it was still yellow, you had plenty of time to cross, and here comes this truck roarin' down on you like a freight train, and somebody in it talkin' on a phone."

She turned to the small crowd that had rushed out of the Main Street Grill. "A phone in a truck!" she said with disgust. "Can you believe it? I should have got his license number."

"Thank you, Winnie." He put his arm around the sturdy shoulders of the Sweet Stuff Bakery owner. "You've got a special talent for being in the right place at the right time."

Percy Mosely, who owned the Grill, ran out with his spatula in his hand. "If I was you, I'd ask th' good Lord to kick that feller's butt plumb to Wesley. Them poached eggs you eat are now scrambled."

The rector patted his pockets for the heavy office key and checked his wallet. All there. "No harm done," he assured his friends. The incident had simply been a regrettably dramatic way to begin his first week home from Ireland.

Though he'd spent the summer in Sligo, he found on returning that he hadn't, after all, missed summer in Mitford. His roses bloomed on, the grass lay like velvet under the network of village sprinklers, and parishioners were still leaving baskets of tomatoes on his porch.

As he came up the walk to the rectory, he heard a booming bark from the garage. It was the greeting he had missed every livelong day of his sojourn across the pond.

Since returning home less than a week ago, he had awakened each morning to see Barnabas standing by the bed, staring at him soberly. The inquiry in the eyes of his black Bouvier-cum-sheepdog companion was simple: Are you home to stay, or is this a joke?

He walked through the kitchen and opened the garage door, as Barnabas, who had grown as vast as a bear during his absence, rushed at him with joy. Laying his front paws on the rector's shoulders, he gazed dolefully into the eyes of his master, whose glasses fogged at once.

"Come now, old fellow. Slack off!"

Barnabas leapt backward, danced for a moment on his hind legs, and lunged forward to give the rector a great lick on the face that sent a shower of saliva into his left ear.

The victim dodged toward his parked Buick and crashed onto the hood with his elbow. " 'Sing and make music in your hearts,' " he recited loudly from a psalm, " 'always giving thanks to the Father for everything'!"

Barnabas sat down at once and gazed at him, mopping the garage floor with his tail.

His dog was the only living creature he knew who was unfailingly disciplined by the hearing of the Word. It was a phenomenon that Walter had told over the whole of Ireland's West Country.

"Let's have a treat, pal. And you," he said to Dooley's rabbit, Jack, "will have beet tops." The Flemish giant regarded him with eyes the color of peat.

The house was silent. It wasn't one of Puny's days to work, and Dooley was at football practice. He had missed the boy terribly, reading and rereading the one scrawled message he had received in two long months:

I am fine. Barnabus is fine. Im ridin the hair off that horse.

He had missed the old rectory, too, with its clamor and quiet, its sunshine and shadow. Never before in his life as a rector had he found a home so welcoming or comfortable—a home that seemed, somehow, like a friend.

He spied the thing on his counter at once. It was Edith Mallory's signature blue casserole dish.

He was afraid of that.

Emma had written to Sligo to say that Pat Mallory had died soon after he left for Ireland. Heart attack. No warning. Pat, she said, had felt a wrenching chest pain, had sat down on the top step outside his bedroom, and after dropping dead sitting up, had toppled to the foot of the stairs, where the Mallorys' maid of thirty years had found him just before dinner.

"Oh, Mr. Mallory," she was reported to have said, "you shouldn't have gone and done that. We're havin' lasagna."

Sitting there on the farmhouse window seat, reading Emma's five-page letter, he had known that Edith Mallory would not waste any time when he returned.

Long before Pat's death, he'd been profoundly unsteadied when she had slipped her hand into his or let her fingers run along his arm. At one point, she began winking at him during sermons, which distracted him to such a degree that he resumed his old habit of preaching over the heads of the congregation, literally.

So far, he had escaped her random snares but had once dreamed he was locked with her in the parish-hall coat closet, pounding desperately on the door and pleading with the sexton to let him out.

Now Pat, good soul, was cold in the grave, and Edith's casserole was hot on his counter.

Casseroles! Their seduction had long been used on men of the cloth, often with rewarding results for the cook.

Casseroles, after all, were a gesture that on the surface could not be mistaken for anything other than righteous goodwill. And, once one had consumed and exclaimed over the initial offering, along would come another on its very heels, until the bachelor curate ended up a married curate or the divorced deacon a fellow so skillfully ensnared that he never knew what hit him.

In the language of food, there were casseroles, and there were casseroles. Most were used to comfort the sick or inspire the downhearted. But certain others, in his long experience, were so filled with allure and innuendo that they ceased to be Broccoli Cheese Delight intended for the stomach and became arrows aimed straight for the heart.

In any case, there was always the problem of what to do with the dish. Decent people returned it full of something else. Which meant that the person to whom you returned it would be required, at some point, to give you another food item, all of which produced a cycle that was unimaginably tedious.

Clergy, of course, were never required to fill the dish before returning it, but either way, it had to be returned. And there, clearly, was the rub.

He approached the unwelcome surprise as if a snake might have been coiled inside. His note of thanks, which he would send over tomorrow by Puny, would be short and to the point:

Dear Edith: Suffice it to say that you remain one of the finest cooks in the county. That was no lie; it was undeniably true.

Your way with (blank, blank) is exceeded only by your graciousness. A thousand thanks. In His peace, Fr Tim.

There.

He lifted the lid. Instantly, his mouth began to water, and his heart gave a small leap of joy.

Crab cobbler! One of his favorites. He stared with wonder at the dozen flaky homemade biscuits poised on the bed of fresh crabmeat and fragrant sauce.

Perhaps, he thought with sudden abandon, he should give Edith Mallory a ring this very moment and express his thanks.

As he reached for the phone, he realized what he was doing—he was placing his foot squarely in a bear trap.

He hastily clamped the lid on the steaming dish. "You see?" he muttered darkly. "That's the way it happens."

Where casseroles were concerned, one must constantly be on guard.

"Edith Mallory's lookin' to give you th' big whang-do," said Emma.

Until this inappropriate remark, there had been a resonant peace in the small office. The windows were open to morning air embroidered with birdsong. His sermon notes were going at a pace. And the familiar comfort of his old swivel chair was sheer bliss.

"And what, exactly, is that supposed to mean?

His part-time church secretary glanced up from her ledger. "It means she's going to cook your goose."

He did not like her language. "I am sixty-one years old and a lifelong bachelor. Why anyone would want to give me a whang . . . why anyone would . . . it's unthinkable," he said flatly.

"I can tell she thinks about it all th' time. Besides, remember Father Appel who got married when he was sixty-five, right after his social security kicked in? And that deacon who was fifty-nine, who married th' redheaded woman who owned the taxi company in Wesley? Then, there was that salesman who worked at the Collar Button . . ."

"Spare me the details," he said curtly, opening his drawer and looking for the Wite-Out.

Emma peered at him over her glasses. "Just remember," she muttered.

"Remember what?"

"Forearmed is forewarned."

"No, Emma. Forewarned is forearmed."

"Peedaddle. I never do get that right. But if I were you, I'd duck when I see her comin'."

I've been ducking when I see her coming for twelve years, he thought.

"One thing in her favor," said Emma, recording another check, "is she's a great hostess. As you have surely learned from doin' your parties, a rector needs that. Some preachers' wives don't do pea-turkey, if you ask me. Of course, if anything's goin' to happen with your neighbor, and Lord knows, I hope it will—you ought to just go on and give 'er a nice engagement ring—then Edith would have to jump on somebody else."

"Emma," he said, ripping the cover off the typewriter, "I have finally got a handle on the most important sermon I've written in a year . . ."

"Don't say I didn't warn you," she replied, pressing her lips together in that way he loathed.

At noon, Ron Malcolm appeared at the door, wearing boots caked with dried mud and a red baseball cap.

Being away for two months had given everyone the rector knew, and Mitford as well, a fresh, almost poignant, reality. He had scarcely ever noticed that Ron Malcolm was a man of such cheering vigor. Then again, perhaps it was the retired contractor's involvement in the nursing-home project that had done something for the color in his face and put a gleam in his eyes.

"Well, Father, we're off and running. Jacobs has sent their job superintendent over. He's having a trailer installed on the site today." He shook the rector's hand with great feeling.

"I can hardly believe it's finally happening."

"Five million bucks!" Ron said. "This nursing home is the biggest thing to happen around here since the Wesley furniture factory. Have you met Leeper?"

"Leeper?"

"Buck Leeper. The job superintendent. We talked about him before you left for Ireland. He said he'd try to get by your office."

"I haven't met him. I'll have to walk up—maybe Wednesday afternoon."

Ron sat down on the visitors' bench and removed his cap. "Emma around?"

"Gone to the post office."

"I think it's only fair that I talk to you straight about Buck Leeper. A few months ago, I told you he's hardheaded, rough. I know I don't have to worry about you, but he's the kind who can make you lose your religion."

"Aha."

"His daddy was Fane Leeper, so called because a preacher once said he was the most profane man he'd ever met. Fane Leeper was also the best job superintendent on the East Coast. He made three contractors rich men, and then alcohol got 'im, as they say.

"You need to know that Buck is just like his daddy. He learned contractin', cussin', and drinkin' from Fane, and the only way he could get out from under the shadow of his father was to outdo him in all three categories."

Ron paused, as if to let that information sink in.

"Buck's on this job because he'll save us money—and a lot of grief. He'll bring it in on time and on budget, and you can count on it. Out of respect to you, Father, I talked to Jacobs about sending us another man, but they won't send anybody but Buck on a job this size." He stood up and zipped his jacket. "We'll probably hate Jacobs for this, but before it's over, we'll thank him."

"I trust your judgment."

Ron opened the door and was backing out with his hat in his hand. "You might look softhearted, Father, but I've seen you operate a time or two, and I know you can handle Buck. Just give 'im his rein."

The rector looked out at the maple across the street, which had taken on a tinge of russet since yesterday. "I can't imagine that Mr. Leeper will be any problem at all," he said.

"Timothy?"

It was Cynthia, his neighbor, peering through the screened door of the kitchen, her hands cupped on either side of her eyes. She was wearing a white blouse and blue denim skirt and a bandanna around her blond hair.

"You look like Heidi!" he said to his neighbor. Though she admitted to being fiftysomething, there were times when she looked like a girl. Again he was struck by the fresh, living way in which he saw people, as if he had lately risen from the dead.

She walked past him, unfurling the faintest scent of wisteria on the air. "You said to think of something we could do to celebrate your return."

She went to the stove and lifted the lid on the pot of soup he was making. "Yum," she said, inhaling. Then, she turned to him and smiled. Her eyes were like sapphires, smoky and deep with that nearly violet hue that always caught him off-guard.

"And have you thought about it?" he asked, afraid he might croak like a frog when he spoke.

"They say walls have ears. I'd better whisper it."

He had completely forgotten how easily she fit into his arms.

Going to a town council meeting was decidedly not what he wanted to do with his evening. After two months away, he hardly knew what was going on. And he was still feeling oddly jet-lagged, shaking his head vigorously on occasion with some hope of clearing it. But he would go; it might put him back in the swing of things, and frankly, he was curious why the mayor, Esther Cunningham, had called an unofficial meeting and why it might concern him.

"Don't eat," Esther told him on the phone. "Ray's bringin' baked beans, cole slaw, and ribs from home. Been cookin' all day."

"Hallelujah," he said with feeling.

There was a quickening in the air of the mayor's office. Ray was setting out his home-cooked supper on the vast desktop, overlooked by pictures of their twenty-three grandchildren at the far end.

"Mayor," said Leonard Bostick, "it's a cryin' shame you cain't cook as good as Ray."

"I've got better things to do," she snapped. "I did the cookin' for forty years. Now it's his turn."

Ray grinned. "You tell 'em, honey."

"Whooee!" said Paul Hartley. "Baby backs! Get over here, Father, and give us a blessin'."

"Come on!" shouted the mayor to the group lingering in the hall. "It's blessin' time!"

Esther Cunningham held out her hands, and the group eagerly formed a circle.

"Our Lord," said the rector, "we're grateful for the gift of friends and neighbors and those willing to lend their hand to the welfare of this place. We thank you for the peace of this village and for your grace to do the work that lies ahead. We thank you, too, for this food and ask a special blessing on the one who prepared it. In Jesus' name."

"Amen!" said the assembly.

The mayor was the first in line. "You're goin' t' get a blessing, all right," she told her husband. "Just look at this sauce! You've done it again, sweet face."

Ray winked at the rector. There, thought the rector, is a happy man if I ever saw one.

"How's your diabetes, Father?"

"It won't tolerate the torque you've put under the hood of that pot, I regret to say."

"Take doubles on m' slaw, then," said Ray, heaping the rector's plate.

"You know what we're here to talk about," said the mayor.

Everybody nodded, except the rector.

"I don't want it to come up in a town meetin', and I don't want it officially voted on, vetoed, or otherwise messed with. We're just goin' to seek agreement here tonight like a family and let it go at that."

She looked at their faces and leaned forward. "Got it?"

Linder Hayes stood up slowly, thin as a strip of baling wire. He placed his hands carefully behind his back, peered at his shoes, and cleared his throat.

"Here goes," said Joe Ivey, nudging the rector.

"Your honor," said Linder.

"You don't have t' 'your honor' me. This is an unofficial meetin'."

"Your honor," said Linder, who was a lawyer and preferred the formalities, "I'd like to speak for the merchants of this town who have to make a livin' out of the day-to-day run of things.

"Now, we know that an old woman dressed up in party hats and gumboots, directin' traffic around the monument, is not a fit sight for tourists, especially with leaf season comin' on.

"You say she's harmless, but that, in fact, is not the point. With her infamous snaggle tooth and those old army decorations, think what she'd look like if she came flyin' out of th' fog wavin' at cars. She'd clean th' tourists out of here so fast it'd make your head swim."

"And good riddance," said the mayor testily.

"Madam Mayor, we've fought this tourist battle for years. We've all moved over to give you plenty of room to do your job, and you've done it. Your faithful defense of what is good and right and true to the character of this town has been a strong deterrent to the rape and plunder of senseless development and reckless growth.

"But . . ." Linder gave a long pause and looked around the room. "Two Model Village awards will not suffice our merchants for cold, hard cash. That ol' woman is enough to make babies squall and grown men tuck tail and run. Clearly, I don't have to make a livin' off tourists, but my wife does—and so, incidentally, do half your grandchildren."

"We're in for it," muttered Joe Ivey. "I should've carried a bed roll and a blanket."

"Linder," said Esther Cunningham, "sit down and take a load off your feet."

"Your honor . . ."

"Thank you, Linder," the mayor said, measuring each word.

Linder appeared to waver for a moment, like a leaf caught in a breeze. Then, he sat down.

"I'd like us to look at a couple of things before we open for a brief discussion," said the mayor. "First, let's look at my platform. There is no such thing in it as a middle plank, a left plank, or a right plank. It's just one straight platform. Period. Joe, why don't you remind us what it is?"

Joe stood up. "Mitford takes care of its own!" He sat down again, flushed with pride.

"Mitford . . . takes . . . care . . . of . . . its . . . own. That's been my platform for fourteen years, and as long as I'm mayor, it will continue to be th' platform. Number one. Miss Rose Watson may be snaggle-toothed and she may be crazy, but she's our own. Number two. Based on that, we're goin' to take care of 'er.

"Number three. Directin' traffic around the monument is the best thing that's happened to her since she was a little girl, as normal as you and me. Uncle Billy says she sleeps like a baby now, instead of ramblin' through that old house all night, and she's turned nice as you please to him. Directin' traffic is a genuine responsibility to her. She takes pride in it."

"She does a real good job," said Ernestine Ivory, who colored beet red at the sound of her own voice.

"What's that, Ernestine?" asked the mayor.

"Miss Rose does a real good job of directing traffic. 'Course that's just me . . ."

"That's just you and a lot of other people who think the same thing. She's very professional. I don't know where in th' world she learned it.

"Now, here's what I propose, and I ask you to consider it in your hearts. Every day from noon to one o'clock, traffic drops off and Mitford eats lunch. My stomach starts growlin' right on th' button, like th' rest of this crowd.

"I propose we let Miss Rose direct traffic five days a week, from noon 'til one, which'll give her just enough cars to keep her happy.

"Now, Linder, I have to hand it to you about those cocktail hats and funny clothes, so I propose we give 'er a uniform. Navy hat, skirt, and jacket from my old days in th' Waves. Be a perfect fit. I was skinny as a rail, wasn't I, doll?"

Ray gave the mayor a thumbs-up.

"Ernestine, I want you to go with me to dress her in th' mornin' at ten o'clock, and Joe, how about you givin' her a nice haircut. We'll bring 'er up to your shop about eleven."

"Be glad to."

"Father, I wish you'd make it your business to pray about this."

"You have my word," he said.

"And Linder, honey, I really appreciate the way you're lookin' after the merchants. God knows, somebody needs to. Any questions?"

Before anyone could respond, the mayor pounded her desk with a gavel. "Meeting adjourned. All in favor say aye."

"I declare," said the rector, walking home with Joe Ivey, "every time I go to a meeting with Esther Cunningham, I feel like somebody's screwed my head around backwards."

You'll be coming home to a new Dooley, Marge had written just before he left Ireland. When he read that, his heart sank. He had managed to grow fond of the old Dooley.

He's actually learning to speak English, his friend wrote from Meadowgate Farm. *Just wait; you'll be thrilled.*

He couldn't say he had been thrilled, exactly, on seeing his twelve-year-old charge again. First, the cowlick had miraculously disappeared. When he left for Sligo in July, it had been shooting up like a geyser; now, it simply wasn't there, and frankly, he missed it. Then, he noticed that Dooley's freckles appeared to be fading, an upshot that he especially regretted.

He also found a new resoluteness in the boy that he'd only fleetingly glimpsed before, not to mention the fact that he was putting the top back on the catsup and the mayonnaise. How could so much change have taken place in two short months?

"I refuse to take credit," Marge told him on the phone from Meadowgate the morning after his return. "It's all that wonderful spade work you'd already done, laced with a strong dose of cow manure and fresh air. Last weekend, he helped Hal deliver a colt, which was like a shot of Miracle-Gro to his self-confidence. Furthermore, I'm crushed to tell you that Rebecca Jane took her first step to . . . guess who? Uncle Dools!"

I have planted, Apollos watered, but God gave the increase, the rector mused as he approached the rectory from the council meeting. Joe Ivey had offered him "a taste of brandy" if he cared to walk up the stairs to the barber shop, but he declined. He could hardly wait to get home and into the old burgundy bathrobe he'd sorely missed in Ireland.

After a quick trip with Barnabas to the Baxter Park hedge, he took a bottle of mineral water from the cabinet, and the two of them climbed the stairs.

"Dooley!"

"Yessir?"

Yessir? He walked down the hall to the boy's room and found him sitting against the head of his bed, reading and absently scratching his big toe. The room seemed remarkably well-ordered.

"How's it going?"

Dooley looked up. "Great."

"Terrific." He stood in the doorway, feeling an awkward joy. "What's the book?"

"*Dynamics of Veterinary Medicine.*"

"Aha."

"See this?" Dooley held the book toward him. "It's a picture of a colt being born. That's jis' the way it happened last weekend. It's the neatest thing I ever done . . . did. I want t' be a vet. Doc Owen said I could be one."

"Of course you can. You can be whatever you want to be." He stepped into the room.

"I never wanted to be anything before."

"Maybe you never saw any choices before."

"I never wanted to be an astronaut or a rock star or anything, like Buster Austin wants t' be."

"That's OK. Why rush into wanting to be something?" He sat down on the bed.

"That's what I thought." Dooley went back to his book, ignoring him but somehow comfortable with the fact that he was there.

"So, how's Buster?" Only months ago, he and Buster Austin had been the darkest adversaries, with Dooley whipping the tar out of him twice.

"Cool. We swapped lunches today. He likes 'at old meatloaf you make. I got 'is baloney."

"Done your homework?"

"Yessir."

Yessir. It rang in his ears like some foreign language. "How's the science project coming? Are we finishing it up Sunday evening?"

"Yep. You'll like it. It's neat."

Since he came home from Ireland, he'd been peering into Dooley's face, searching it out. Something was different. A wound had healed, perhaps; he was looking more like a boy instead of someone who'd grown old before his time.

It had been nearly a year since Russell Jacks, the church sexton and Dooley's grandfather, had come down with pneumonia and was rushed into emergency treatment. The boy had come home with him from the hospital, and he'd been here ever since.

One of the best things he had ever done was bring Dooley Barlowe home. Yes, he'd been trouble and calamity and plenty of it—but worth it and then some.

"I hear you went to see your grandpa every week. Good medicine."

"Yep."

"How is he?"

"That woman that's lookin' after 'im, she says he's doing good, but he ain't had any livermush since you left . . ."

"Uh-oh."

"And he was riled about it."

"We'll take him some. And I'll see you at breakfast. Has Jenny been around?"

"I ain't into 'at ol' poop, n' more."

The rector grinned. There! he thought. There's my old Dooley.

In his room, Barnabas leapt onto the blanket at the foot of the bed, then lay down with a yawn as the rector stepped into the shower. While the raftered room in the Sligo farmhouse had been perfectly comfortable, the long passage down the hall to the finicky shower was another story entirely. As far as he could see, it might be months before the thrill of his own bathroom, *en suite,* began to wane.

He felt as mindless and contented as a steamed clam as he sat on the bed and dialed his neighbor.

"Hello?"

"Hello, yourself."

"Timothy!" said Cynthia. "I was just thinking of you."

"Surely you have something better to do."

"I was thinking that my idea of how to celebrate was too silly."

"Silly, yes, but not too silly," he said. "In fact, I was wondering—when are we going to do it?"

"Ummmm . . ."

"Saturday night?" he asked, hoping.

"Oh, rats. My nephew's coming. I mean, I'm delighted he's coming. You must meet him. He's very dear. Saturday would have been so perfect. Could we do it Monday evening?

"Vestry meeting," he said.

"Tuesday I have to finish an illustration and FedEx it first thing Wednesday morning. Could you do it Wednesday around six-thirty?"

"Building committee at seven."

"Darn."

"I could do it Friday," he said.

"Great!"

"No. No, wait, there's something on Friday," he said, extending the phone cord to the dresser where he opened his black engagement book. "Yes, that's it. The hospital is having a staff dinner for Hoppy, and I'm giving the invocation. Would you come?"

"Dinner in a hospital? That's suicide! Besides, I can't stand hospitals. I nearly died in one, you know."

"No, I didn't know."

"And I don't know how you ever will know these things unless we can figure out a way to see each other. What about Sunday evening? That's usually a relaxing time for you. Sunday might be lovely."

"I'm helping Dooley finish his science project. He has to hand it in Monday morning." A nameless despair was robbing him of any contentment he had just felt.

"I could meet you on the bench by your German roses at six o'clock tomorrow. We could do it there and get it over with."

But he didn't want to do it and get it over with. He wanted to linger over it, to savor it.

"You're sighing," she said.

"It's just that there's so much going on after being away for two months."

"I understand," she said simply.

"You do? Do you really?"

"Of course I do."

"I'll call you tomorrow. Let's not waste it on the garden bench."

"All that lumpy, wet moss," she said, laughing.

"All that cold, damp concrete," he said forlornly.

"I hope you sleep well." He could hear a tenderness in her voice. "Jet lag really does persist for days."

"Yes. Well. So," he said, feeling immeasurably foolish, "blink your bedroom lights good night."

"I will if you will."

"Cynthia?"

"Yes?"

"I . . ." He cleared his throat. "You . . ."

"Spit it out," she said.

He had started to croak; he couldn't have uttered another word if his life depended on it.

"I'm not going to worry anymore about being too silly. It's you, Timothy, who are far too silly!"

His heart pounded as he hung up the phone. He had nearly told her he loved her, that she was wonderful; he had nearly gone over the edge of the cliff, with no ledges to break his fall.

He went to the window and looked down upon her tiny house. He saw the lights blink twice through the windows of her bedroom under the eaves. He raced around the bed and flipped his own light switch off, then on again, and off.

"Good Lord," he said, breathlessly, standing there in the dark. "Who is the twelve-year-old in this house, anyway?"

A PENGUIN READERS GUIDE TO

THE MITFORD YEARS

Jan Karon

An Introduction to *The Mitford Years Series*

Come away to Mitford, the small town that takes care of its own. Nestled in the Blue Ridge mountains, Mitford is a crazy quilt of saints and sinners, lovable eccentrics all. Seen through the eyes of Father Tim, the long-suffering village rector, Mitford abounds in both mysteries and miracles, compelling readers to return again and again to this beloved series.

As only she can, author Jan Karon brilliantly captures the foibles and delights of a hilarious cast of characters.

Book I: In *At Home in Mitford*, Father Tim finds himself running on empty. Even after twelve years of shepherding his flock, he finds that Emma, his secretary, persists in treating him like a ten-year-old. Barnabas, a huge black dog, adopts him, and a hostile mountain boy, Dooley, is thrust into his care. To add to his confusion, a growing friendship with Cynthia Coppersmith, his new neighbor, stirs emotions he hasn't felt in years.

Book II: In *A Light in the Window*, Father Tim is in love and running scared. Cynthia has won his heart, but he is set in his ways and afraid of letting go. To complicate things, a wealthy and powerful widow pursues Father Tim, plying him with crab cobbler and old sherry. In the ensuing comedy of errors, he just can't set his foot right. Somehow the antidote to this confusion rests in the history of his oldest and dearest parishioner, Miss Sadie, and the discovery of family she didn't know she had.

Book III: In *These High, Green Hills*, Father Tim fulfills Cynthia's conviction that deep down he is a man of romance, panache, and daring. Though his cup of joy overflows, his heart goes out to those around him who so badly need the healing aid of a loving heart. Chief among these is Dooley, his teenage ward, whose rough edges grate against the boarding school he both loves and hates. Can Father Tim face the much deeper needs of Dooley's mother, Pauline, and the battered girl, Lace, whose childhood has been a horror story of neglect?

Book IV: In *Out to Canaan*, Father Tim grapples with his sixty-fourth birthday and his decision to announce his retirement. A mayoral election threatens to divide the town. Old friends are retiring, even moving away. Change seems to be the only constant, and when Mule Skinner, a regular at the Main Street Grill, grimly asserts, "I despise change," Father Tim wholeheartedly agrees. Is it unreasonable to hope that all Father Tim holds precious might somehow be preserved? Or is transformation the real way of things?

Book V: In *A New Song*, Father Tim and Cynthia begin the wrenching process of leaving Mitford, if only for a brief period. They take an interim pastorship on the coastal island of Whitecap. Warmly welcomed, they enjoy the novelties of deep-sea fishing and oceanside picnicking but quickly discover their new church is torn by bitterness and discord. As they get to know the colorful personalities of the island, their answering machine keeps them in touch with what's going on in Mitford (plenty). Father Tim finds himself torn by the needs of two communities. On the island, a wayward choir director has abandoned his young family, leaving hurt and resentment in his wake, and a reclusive neighbor violently rebuffs Father Tim's attempts to get acquainted. Back in Mitford, Dooley lands in jail, a new mayor tries to fill Esther Cunningham's shoes, and a mysterious French piano teacher claims to be an heir to part of Miss Sadie's fortune, jeopardizing the future of the Hope

House nursing home. Father Tim finds his heart torn by situations beyond his power to repair. It takes a tumultuous storm that shakes Whitecap to its foundations to begin the process of healing and new life.

About Jan Karon

Jan Karon was born in Lenoir, North Carolina, in 1937 ("A great year for the Packard automobile," she says). Her creative skills first came alive when her family moved to a farm. "On the farm there is time to muse and dream," she says. "I am endlessly grateful I was reared in the country. As a young girl I couldn't wait to get off that farm, to go to Hollywood or New York. But living in those confined, bucolic circumstances was one of the best things that ever happened to me."

Jan knew that she wanted to be a writer, and even wrote a novel at the age of ten. Her first real opportunity as a writer came at age eighteen when she took a job as a receptionist at an ad agency. She kept leaving her writing on her boss's desk until he noticed her ability. Soon she was launched on a thirty-year career in advertising. She won assignments in New York and San Francisco, numerous awards, and finally an executive position with a national agency.

Leaving advertising to write books, Jan moved to Blowing Rock, North Carolina, a tiny town of 1,800 perched at 5,000 feet in the Blue Ridge mountains. "I immediately responded to the culture of village life," says Jan. "And I must say the people welcomed me. I have never felt so at home." Blowing Rock is the model for Mitford, and the similarities are strong. "None of the people in Mitford is actually based upon anyone here," says Jan. "Yet, the spirit of my characters is found throughout this real-life village. You can walk into Sonny's Grill in Blowing Rock and find the same kind of guys who hang around Mitford's Main Street Grill."

Jan is quick to assert that there are Mitfords all over the country, those hundreds of towns where readers of Jan's books cherish their own cast of eccentric and beloved characters. For relaxation, Jan enjoys Georgian architecture and history, and one day hopes to write a book about the building of an eighteenth-century Georgian manor house.

Jan has a daughter, Candace Freeland, a photojournalist and musician. "My daughter is a vibrant, life-loving woman," Jan says. "Right now she's in Hawaii learning how to play the marimba. A children's book I wrote for her is available from Viking."

Living in the Thick of It

A Conversation with Jan Karon

Q: You write about the small town of Mitford, yet haven't you spent most of your life in cities?

A: Until I was twelve I lived in the country, then I spent many years in cities. I think that I was born with a kind of deep affinity for the rural, the rustic. In addition, I'm very drawn to the pastoral novels of the English genre—the village novel in which a small group is used to paint a picture of a larger society.

Q: Can you find Mitford even in a large city?

A: Mitford is everywhere. I was in a large city recently and while waiting for my car, I was sitting at the door of a department store and I noticed over and over again people extending themselves to help someone. Two elderly men rushed to help a woman in a wheelchair get in her car. Later, a young mother with a baby in one arm and a stroller in the other was trying to get the door open. Before I could get up to help, a man came and opened the door and helped her through. People were simply helping and then they went on their way. It was the most natural thing in the world.

Q: In *A New Song*, Father Tim and Cynthia leave Mitford for the island of Whitecap. Where is Whitecap?

A: I don't write about any place that is modeled directly on another because then it makes everybody mad. I'm not trying to create a real place—this is fiction. It's loosely modeled on an island which might conceivably exist in the Outer Banks chain off the coast of North Carolina.

Q: Father Tim's world is packed with delightful characters. Where do they all come from?

A: Darned if I know. My characters walk in and introduce themselves to me and I'm stuck with them. When I first moved to Blowing Rock to write a book, I struggled hard to write according to the outline I came here with, but the book never worked. The characters never got off the page. That was a real defeat for me. "Woman's dream turns to nightmare," I thought. "I don't know how to write a book!"

Then one night in my mind's eye I saw an Episcopal priest walking down the street. I decided to follow him and see where he went. Well, he went to a dog named Barnabas, they went to a boy named Dooley, and the story unfolded before me. Instead of me driving the story, the story began to drive me! I got interested, wrote a couple of chapters, and there you have it.

Q: Are you very much like Father Tim?

A: Father Tim's personality is far more conservative than mine, but like Father Tim, I don't know a great deal about having fun. If I get dragged into it, I can always enjoy it, but it's hard for me to go out and find it on my own. And of course we both share a faith.

My books are formed on my connection to God. That's the seasoning in the stew.

Q: How would you describe the nature of that faith?

A: In my books I try to depict not a glorious faith with celestial fireworks, but a daily faith, a routine faith, a seven-days-a-week faith. Father Tim's faith is part of his everyday life. He has simple prayers, not polished, pious prayers. He follows the Apostle Paul's command that we pray without ceasing. I try to depict how our faith may be woven into our daily life, like brandy poured into coffee. I believe that spirituality needs to be basic, common, everyday.

Q: Is it an aspect of faith that we are sometimes led to do apparently foolish things? For example, in *A New Song*, Father Tim feels that God is telling him to walk around the wall of Morris Love's house.

A: This wall was a constant in Father Tim's new life at Whitecap: he heard about it from Ernie, he saw it across the side street from his house, then he started going up and over it to chase his dog. Like the Jericho wall that completely surrounded the city in the Bible story, it seemed impenetrable. What an odd thing God called Joshua to do. We would say, "God, are you kidding me? March around the city walls?"

I'd like people to understand that God will ask us to do some things that are hard to understand and he expects us to obey him—outside of our human reason. We see Father Tim's obedience. One of the wonderful things about Father Tim is that with all of his faults and flaws and weaknesses, he is willing to obey God.

Q: Where do you write?

A: My studio stretches across the back of my little house. It has eight windows that look out on a copse of trees. I can see the blue outline of the mountains in the distance. Where I write is exceedingly important to me. I am never comfortable unless I'm in a room that pleases me. I need the pictures on the wall to be hanging straight. I have to do my housekeeping before I can sit down at the computer. Things need to be in order in my mind and in the place where I write.

Recently my life has been topsy-turvy. I have learned to write with utter chaos all around me. I turn to my book with great intensity. Sometimes I may write twelve hours a day. Sometimes I can write only two hours a day.

Q: Do you have a conscious technique that so effectively makes Mitford come alive for people?

A: I grew up in the era of radio. When you turned on the radio, you heard the voices and you filled in all the blanks. Radio helped me become a writer. With radio you have to color in everything yourself. What I need to do for readers is give them as much free rein as they can take. Let them participate in the story by building their own imagery.

Q: Has it been difficult adjusting to the popularity of the Mitford books?

A: It is extremely gratifying, and I absolutely love speaking to people. It's almost right up there with writing, but I can't do it endlessly. I must fight all the time to make room for the work which is the most important thing of all. Robert Frost said, "All an author ever gets is a moment here and a moment there."

Q: You seem to have a lot of lovable eccentrics in your books. Are you attracted to unusual people?

A: I see everyone as unusual. Most everyone seems to have an extraordinary life story. "I just love people," was my grandmother's saying. Casting the writer's light on ordinary people reveals their extra-ordinariness.

Q: What is the next Mitford book?

A: The next Mitford book will be called *A Common Life: The Wedding Story*. It is the story of Father Tim and Cynthia's wedding, and it never fails to make me smile. (When Esther Bolick's recliner remote loses power and she has to heave herself over the side, I laugh out loud!)

Questions for Discussion

The Mitford Years Book I

At Home in Mitford

1. What role does Barnabas play in Father Tim's life? What other characters invade Father Tim's busy life, only later to prove enriching elements? Are there any that are a permanent drag on his spirits? How does Father Tim come to terms with them?

2. Dooley appears on the scene untamed and uninvited. What is it that makes Father Tim and Dooley aware that they need each other? How does Dooley contribute to Father Tim's life? Have you had Dooleys in your own life?

3. Which characters did you dislike at first, only to later come to appreciate or at least understand them? What characters in the book react that way to someone new?

4. Compare Miss Sadie and Miss Rose. They are very different characters, but both make a powerful contribution to the books.

What makes them such vivid characters? What would Mitford be like without them? What unique contribution do they make?

5. Priests seldom have people they can confide in. Who are Father Tim's confidants? What secrets does he entrust to them? What role does prayer play in giving Father Tim a chance to truly vent his feelings?

6. Mitford takes care of its own, says Mayor Cunningham. How does this happen in the book? Is this limited only to small towns? What other types of communities can it take place in?

The Mitford Years Book II
A Light in the Window

1. Why do Father Tim's deepening feelings for Cynthia frighten him so? What are Father Tim's fears about marrying? How might Father Tim's marriage to Cynthia enhance his role as a priest? How might it detract from it?

2. Minor characters are an important part of the Mitford books. Can you name four minor characters? What does one minor character contribute to the fabric of village life in Mitford?

3. Many people don't like to talk about their faith. Why? Why do you think it is socially permissible to discuss sexual behavior, income, politics, and other highly personal matters, yet discussing one's faith is often discouraged?

4. Compare Miss Sadie's gift of money to build the nursing home with Edith Mallory's promise of donations to the children's hospital. What is each looking for in return for her gift?

5. Have you ever had company like Cousin Meg? How could Father Tim have handled her presence in his house better? How can guests enrich your life? What kind of strain does having guests put on your life?

The Mitford Years Book III
These High, Green Hills

1. How has Father Tim's marriage influenced or changed his life? How have his relationships with Barnabas, Dooley, and Miss Sadie changed him?

2. Do Jan Karon's characters remind you of people you know? Have you ever lived next door to a Mitford character? Are you kin to any Mitford characters?

3. Faith in God is clearly a significant part of Father Tim's makeup. How would you describe his faith? What role does prayer play in Father Tim's faith?

4. The Seven Virtues are: Faith, Hope, Charity, Prudence, Temperance, Fortitude, and Justice. Choose a character that exemplifies one of these virtues. For example, what virtue do you feel Uncle Billy exemplifies? What about Miss Sadie? Olivia?

5. What did Father Tim and Cynthia learn about themselves when they were lost in the cave? What did they learn about each other? What did Father Tim learn about his relationship with God? How did understanding and forgiving his father change him?

The Mitford Years Book IV
Out to Canaan

1. In times of crisis, Father Tim and Cynthia pray "the prayer that never fails." What prayer are they referring to? Why is it a prayer that never fails?

2. Pauline's growth and redemption is a gradual, step-by-step process. Who helps her? Where does Pauline succeed? Where does she fail?

3. Father Tim's home is transformed from staid bachelor quarters into a topsy-turvy household. Lace quizzes Harley on his schoolwork in the basement, Dooley pounds up the stairs, Puny cleans with her twins underfoot, Violet the cat balefully eyes Barnabas from atop the refrigerator. How does Father Tim's household compare with your own? Do Jan Karon's descriptions make you view the chaos in your life differently?

4. The construction boss, Buck Leeper, is a diamond in the rough. In *Out to Canaan*, what is Buck Leeper feeling? How does he view himself? How do you think he may view others?

5. Do you have a Main Street Grill? What function does a place like the Grill fill in a town? Where do you get your own town news? Where are you likely to meet friends and neighbors?

6. Esther Bolick's orange marmalade cake plays a role in each book. What is the specialty in your region? What food item makes an annual event special? Festive? What other object can fill this role?

The Mitford Years Book V
A New Song

1. Father Tim and Cynthia's good-bye to their friends in Mitford is long and painful. Have you experienced a similar good-bye? What have you learned that can lessen the pain? What can be done to ease the transition?

2. Ernie Fulcher said the yellow line down the center of the floor of his and Mona's building has helped save their marriage. Is having separate areas a good idea for a couple? How might it affect customers? Friends? In what other ways do people define their space? How do children sharing a bedroom define "my side"?

3. Junior Bryson advertises for a bride. How would you write the personal ad for Junior? Should he have been so honest about himself? How would you describe yourself in an ad?

4. Father Tim met his neighbor, Morris Love, when Barnabas dove under his fence. Father Tim was hot, angry, and feeling foolish. Have you met someone in your life in an unusual way? How do you feel about meeting people when you don't look your best?

5. What elements contributed to helping Father Tim see the suffering soul behind Morris Love's infirmity? Have you ever had such an experience?

6. Should Father Tim have welcomed the wayward ex-choirmaster, Jeffrey Tolson, back to St. John's? Should he have consulted with his parishioners or was it his responsibility to decide? Was repentance a fair requirement?

7. Was it wise for Father Tim and Cynthia to take Jonathan Tolson into their home? Did caring for a toddler help or hinder their work? Was Father Tim's concern about Cynthia's emotional attachment warranted?

8. How did the storm change the landscape of Whitecap? How did it change people's lives?

9. Was Helene Pringle right to come to Mitford? Was Father Tim right to give her his angel? Whom do you think it belonged to? What was he given in its place?

10. How does Father Tim react to the glowing praise of Mitford's new rector? Have you ever been in such a situation? How did you react?

Make Your Mitford Reading Group Special

- For several Mitford residents there is a particular verse in the Bible that resonates in their lives. Have members share their favorite Bible verse and discuss its meaning to them.

- No Mitford get-together would be complete without orange marmalade cake, but anything homemade will make your gathering special. Members can take turns making and sharing their favorite family recipes.

- Introduce Mitford to the next generation—what a wonderful way to spend time with your teenager and see Mitford from a whole new perspective!

- Everyone has a favorite Mitford character. Ask members to dress up as theirs and see whom everyone responds to and why.

- Miss Sadie's hat collection is legendary. Raid the closet (or the attic) and show off your favorite.

- Celebrate the spirit of Mitford by sharing your gathering with someone who may be lonely (a new neighbor etc.). After all, that's what Mitford is really about.

For information about other Penguin Readers Guides, please call the Penguin Marketing Department at (800) 778-6425, E-mail at reading@penguinputnam.com, or write to us at:

Penguin Marketing Department CC
Readers Guides
375 Hudson Street
New York, NY 10014-3657

Please allow 4–6 weeks for delivery.
To access Penguin Readers Guides on-line, visit Club PPI on our Web site at: http://www.penguinputnam.com.

Now available from Penguin, the final novel in the beloved Mitford series

Light from Heaven

FATHER TIMOTHY KAVANAGH has never been asked to do the impossible—until now. The retired Episcopal priest takes on the revival of a mountain church that's been closed for forty years. Meanwhile, in Mitford, he's sent on a hunt for hidden treasure, and two beloved friends are called to come up higher. As he meets each new challenge, Father Tim is reminded anew of the most important lesson of all: *It's never too late.*

"Karon saved the best for last." —*The Baltimore Sun*

Includes an excerpt from Jan Karon's next novel, *Home to Holly Springs*, coming from Viking in the fall of 2007

ISBN 0-14-303770-6

For more information about Jan and her books visit www.mitfordbooks.com

NOW AVAILABLE *from* VIKING

The Mitford Bedside Companion

A treasury of favorite Mitford moments, author reflections on the bestselling series, favorite scenes, jokes, prayers, trivia, casts of characters, a crossword puzzle, and lots of personal essays by the author.

0-670-03785-0

NOW AVAILABLE *from* VIKING CHILDREN'S BOOKS

Violet Comes to Stay

Presented by Jan Karon
Story by Melanie Cecka
Illustrated by Emily Arnold McCully

The first in a series of storybooks inspired by Father Tim's wife, Cynthia Coppersmith—with beautiful illustrations by an award-winning artist. Karon searched for three years to find a storytelling voice and art style authentic to Cynthia Coppersmith. She was personally involved in every step of the creation of this book.

0-670-06073-9

Also by Jan Karon from Puffin and Viking Children's Books

Jeremy: The Tale of an Honest Bunny

0-670-88104-X (hc); 0-14-250004-6 (pb)

The Trellis and the Seed

0-670-89289-0 (hc); 0-14-240317-2 (pb)

Miss Fannie's Hat

0-14-056812-3

PENGUIN BOOKS

A NEW SONG

Jan Karon writes "to give readers an extended family, and to applaud the extraordinary beauty of ordinary lives." She is the author of nine Mitford novels, *At Home in Mitford*; *A Light in the Window*; *These High, Green Hills*; *Out to Canaan*; *A New Song*; *A Common Life*; *In This Mountain*; *Shepherds Abiding*; and *Light from Heaven*, all available from Penguin. She is also the author of *The Mitford Bedside Companion*; *Jan Karon's Mitford Cookbook & Kitchen Reader*; *A Continual Feast: Words of Comfort and Celebration, Collected by Father Tim*; *Patches of Godlight: Father Tim's Favorite Quotes*; *The Mitford Snowmen: A Christmas Story*; *Esther's Gift*; and *The Trellis and the Seed*. Her children's books include *Miss Fannie's Hat*; *Jeremy: The Tale of an Honest Bunny*; and *Violet Comes to Stay*. Coming from Viking in fall 2007 is the first Father Tim Novel, *Home to Holly Springs*.

Other Mitford Books by Jan Karon

AT HOME IN MITFORD

A LIGHT IN THE WINDOW

THESE HIGH, GREEN HILLS

OUT TO CANAAN

A COMMON LIFE

Children's Books by Jan Karon

MISS FANNIE'S HAT

JEREMY: THE TALE OF AN HONEST BUNNY

The Mitford Years

A New Song

JAN KARON

PENGUIN BOOKS

PENGUIN BOOKS
Published by the Penguin Group
Penguin Putnam Inc., 375 Hudson Street,
New York, New York 10014, U.S.A.
Penguin Books Ltd, 27 Wrights Lane, London W8 5TZ, England
Penguin Books Australia Ltd, Ringwood, Victoria, Australia
Penguin Books Canada Ltd, 10 Alcorn Avenue,
Toronto, Ontario, Canada M4V 3B2
Penguin Books (N.Z.) Ltd, 182–190 Wairau Road,
Auckland 10, New Zealand

Penguin Books Ltd, Registered Offices:
Harmondsworth, Middlesex, England

First published in the United States of America by Viking Penguin,
a member of Penguin Putnam Inc. 1999
Published in Penguin Books 2000

10

Illustrations by Donna Kae Nelson

Grateful acknowledgment is made for permission to reprint excerpts from the following copyrighted works: "If Once You Have Slept on an Island" from *Taxis and Toadstools* by Rachel Field. Copyright 1926 by The Century Company. Used by permission of Random House Children's Books, a division of Random House, Inc. "God's Way" by Kao Chung-Ming, appearing in *Your Will be Done*, Youth Desk of Christian Conference of Asia, 1986. By permission of the author.

THE LIBRARY OF CONGRESS HAS CATALOGED THE HARDCOVER EDITION AS FOLLOWS:
Karon, Jan, date.
A new song/ Jan Karon.
p. cm.
ISBN 0-670-87810-3 (hc.)
ISBN 0 14 02.7059 0 (pbk.)
1. Mitford (N.C.: Imaginary place)—Fiction. 2. City and town life—North Carolina—Fiction. 3. Clergy—North Carolina—Fiction. 4. Christian fiction, American.
5. Domestic fiction, American.
I. Title.
PS3561.A678N49 1999
813'.54—dc21 98-55141

Printed in the United States of America
Set in Adobe Garamond
Designed by Francesca Belanger

In memory of my aunt,

Helen Coyner Cloer,

who, when I was ten years old,
typed my first manuscript.

October 4, 1917–October 12, 1998

". . . we shall be like Him . . ."

1 John 3:2

Sing unto the Lord a new song, and His praise from the end of the earth, ye that go down to the sea, and all that is therein, the isles and the inhabitants thereof.

Isaiah 42:10, KJV

Acknowledgments

Gentle Reader,

In the Mitford books, there are nearly as many acknowledgments as there are characters in the story. That's because I try to thank absolutely everyone who helps make the story more authentic. Sometimes I toss in a name out of sheer sentiment, like that of my sixth-grade teacher, Etta Phillips, who comes to my book signings and looks as youthful as ever. Many readers enjoy these acknowledgments because they occasionally find the name of an old school chum, friend, or family member.

Sometimes, they even find themselves.

Warm thanks to:

Brother Francis Andrews, BSG; Rev. Roy M. King; Flyin' George Ronan; John Ed McConnell; Ralph Emery; Dr. Carl Hurley; Loyal Jones and Billy Edd Wheeler; Bonnie Setzer; Mary Richardson; Fr. John Mangrum; Fr. Jeffrey Scott Miller; Dr. George Grant; Austin Gragg; Roger David Craig; Frank Gilbert and his Mustang convertible; the Mitford Appreciation Society; Gwynne Crosley; Rev. Gale Cooper; Sue Yates; Dr. David Ludwig; Dan Blair; Linda Foster; Will Lankenau; William McDonald Parker; Blowing Rock police chief, Owen Tolbert; Officer Dennis Swanson; Bishop Christopher Fitz-Simons Allison; James F. Carlisle, Sr.; Betsy Barnes; Rayburn and

Sheila Farmer; Fr. Scott Oxford; Bishop William C. Frey; Bishop Keith Ackerman; Rev. Stephen J. Hines; Larry Powell; Barry Hubert; Derald West; Sandy McNabb; Donna Kae Nelson for her outstanding cover illustrations for the Mitford series; Captain Weyland Baum, early keeper of the Currituck Light; Billy McCaskill; Major John Coffindaffer; "Bee" Baum; Drs. Melanie and Greg Hawthorne; John L. Beard; Greg and Kathy Fishel; Frank LePore; Garry Oliver; my first-grade teacher, Mrs. Downs; my fifth-grade teacher, Mrs. Sherrill; Dr. Michael C. Ain; Captain Mike Clarkin of *Fishin' Frenzy*; First Mate Matthew Winchester; Dr. Sue P. Frye; Ross and Linda Dodington; Fr. Richard B. Bass; Colonel Ron and Cathey Fallows; Murray Whisnant; Robert Williams; Chris Williams; Michael Freeland; Rabbi David and Barbara Kline; Officer Kris Merithew; Bruce Luke; Johnny Lentz; Judith Burns; Wonderland Books; Tom Enterline; J.W.D.; Loretta Cornejo; Tex Harrison; Jerry Gregg; Officer Tracy Toler; Jeff Cobb; Walter Green; and Anita Chappell.

Special thanks to:

Dr. Bunky Davant, medical counsel to Mitford and Whitecap; Tony DiSanti, legal counsel to Mitford; Grace Episcopal Church, the lovely architectural model for St. John's in the Grove; Fr. Charles Gill, rector of St. Andrews by the Sea; Fr. James Harris, friend and helper; Judy Bistany South, for her warm encouragement over the years; my valued assistant, Laura Watts; Captain Horace Whitfield, master of the *Elizabeth II*; hardworking booksellers everywhere; and, as always, my devoted readers.

Contents

A New Song

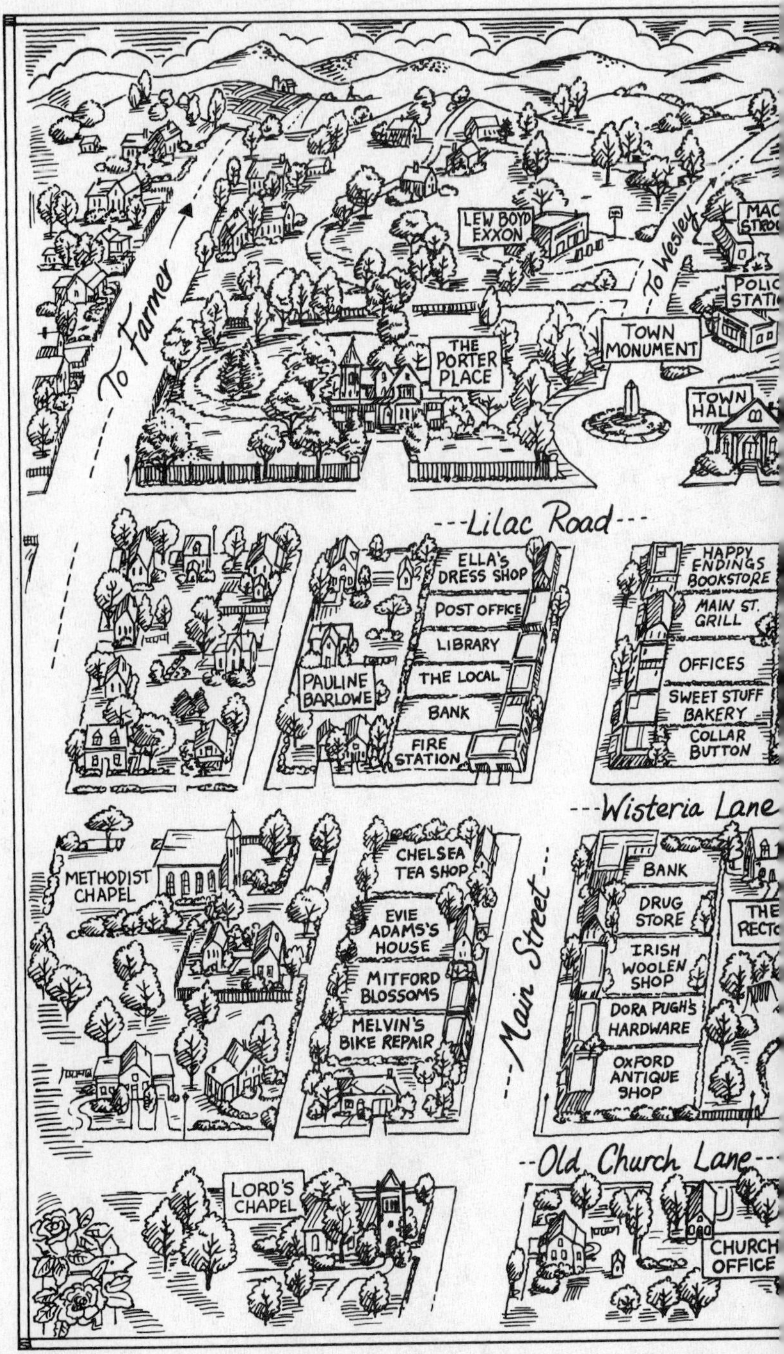

To Farmer
LEW BOYD EXXON
To Wesley
THE PORTER PLACE
TOWN MONUMENT
TOWN HALL
Lilac Road
ELLA'S DRESS SHOP
POST OFFICE
LIBRARY
THE LOCAL
BANK
FIRE STATION
PAULINE BARLOWE
HAPPY ENDINGS BOOKSTORE
MAIN ST. GRILL
OFFICES
SWEET STUFF BAKERY
COLLAR BUTTON
Wisteria Lane
METHODIST CHAPEL
CHELSEA TEA SHOP
EVIE ADAMS'S HOUSE
MITFORD BLOSSOMS
MELVIN'S BIKE REPAIR
Main Street
BANK
DRUG STORE
IRISH WOOLEN SHOP
DORA PUGH'S HARDWARE
OXFORD ANTIQUE SHOP
Old Church Lane
LORD'S CHAPEL
CHURCH OFFICE

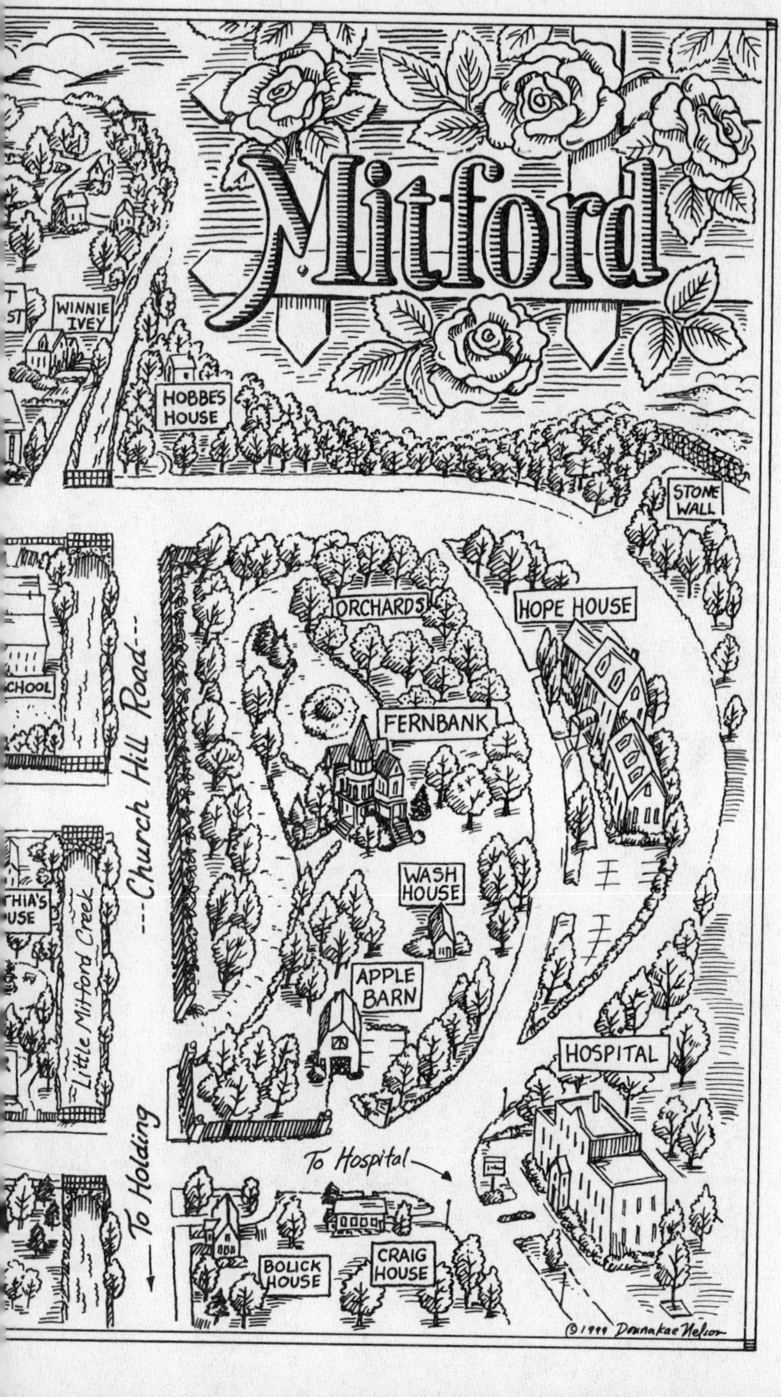
Mitford
WINNIE IVEY
HOBBES HOUSE
STONE WALL
ORCHARDS
HOPE HOUSE
FERNBANK
SCHOOL
Church Hill Road
WASH HOUSE
Little Mitford Creek
APPLE BARN
HOSPITAL
To Holding
To Hospital
BOLICK HOUSE
CRAIG HOUSE
©1999 Donnakae Nelson

CHAPTER ONE

Angel of Light

Dappled by its movement among the branches of a Japanese cherry, the afternoon light entered the study unhindered by draperies or shades.

It spilled through the long bank of windows behind the newly slip-covered sofa, warming the oak floor and quickening the air with the scent of freshly milled wood.

Under the spell of the June light, a certain luster and radiance appeared to emerge from every surface.

The tall chest, once belonging to Father Tim's clergyman great-grandfather, had undergone a kind of rebirth. Beneath a sheen of lemon oil, the dense grain of old walnut, long invisible in the dark rectory hallway next door, became sharply defined. Even the awkward inscription of the letter M, carved by a pocketknife, could now be discovered near one of the original drawer pulls.

But it was the movement and play of the light, beyond its searching incandescence, that caused Father Tim to anticipate its daily arrival as others might look for a sunrise or sunset.

He came eagerly to this large, new room, as if long deprived of light or air, still incredulous that such a bright space might exist, and especially that it might exist for his own pursuits since retiring six months ago from Lord's Chapel.

As the rector of Mitford's Episcopal parish, he had lived next door in the former rectory for sixteen years. Now he was a rector no more, yet he owned the rectory; it had been bought and paid for with cash from his mother's estate, and he and Cynthia were living in the little yellow house.

Of course—he kept forgetting—this house wasn't so little anymore; he and his visionary wife had added 1,270 square feet to its diminutive proportions.

Only one thing remained constant. The house was still yellow, though freshly painted with Cynthia's longtime favorite, Wild Forsythia, and trimmed with a glossy coat of the dark green Highland Hemlock.

"Cheers!" said his wife, appearing in jeans and a denim shirt, toting glasses of lemonade on a tray. They had recently made it a ritual to meet here every afternoon, for what they called the Changing of the Light.

He chuckled. "We mustn't tell anyone what we do for fun."

"You can count on it! Besides, who'd ever believe that we sit around watching the light change?" She set the tray on the table, next to a packet of mail.

"We could do worse."

They thumped onto the sofa, which had been carted through the hedge from the rectory.

"One more week," he said, disbelieving.

"Ugh. Heaven help us!" She put her head back and closed her eyes. "How daunting to move to a place we've never seen . . . for an unknown length of time . . . behind a priest who's got them used to the guitar!"

He took her hand, laughing. "If anyone can do it, you can. How many cartons of books are we shipping down there, anyway?"

"Fourteen, so far."

"And not a shelf to put them on."

"We're mad as hatters!" she said with feeling. During the past week, his wife had worked like a Trojan to close up the yellow house, do most of the packing, and leave their financial affairs in order. He, on the other hand, had been allowed to troop around town saying his goodbyes, sipping tea like a country squire and trying to keep his mitts off the cookies and cakes that were proffered at every turn.

He had even dropped into Happy Endings Bookstore and bought two new books to take to Whitecap, a fact that he would never, even on penalty of death, reveal to Cynthia Kavanagh.

She looked at him and smiled. "I've prayed to see you sit and relax like this, without rushing to beat out a thousand fires. Just think how the refreshment of the last few weeks will help you, dearest, when we do the interim on the island. Who knows, after all, what lies ahead and what strength you may need?"

He gulped his lemonade. Who knew, indeed?

"The jig, however, is definitely up," she said, meaning it. "Next week . . ."

"I know. Change the furnace filter next door, weed the perennial beds, fix the basement step, pack my clothes . . . I've got the entire, unexpurgated list written down."

"Have your suit pressed," she said, "buy two knit shirts—nothing with an alligator, I fervently hope—and find the bicycle pump for Dooley."

"Right!" He was actually looking forward to the adrenaline of their last week in Mitford.

"By the way," she said, "I've been thinking. Instead of loading the car in bits and pieces, just pile everything by the garage door. That way, I can check it twice, and we'll load at the last minute."

"But it would be simpler to—"

"Trust me," she said, smiling.

Barnabas would occupy the rear seat, with Violet's cage on the floor, left side. They'd load the right side with linens and towels, the trunk would be filled to the max, and they'd lash on top whatever remained.

"Oh, yes, Timothy, one more thing . . . stay out of the bookstore!"

She peered at him with that no-nonsense gleam in her sapphire eyes, a gleam that, for all its supposed authority, stirred a fire in him. As a man with a decidedly old-shoe nature, he had looked forward to the old-shoe stage of their marriage. So far, however, it hadn't arrived. His blond and sensible wife had an unpredictable streak that kept the issues of life from settling into humdrum patterns.

"Anything wonderful in the mail?" she asked.

"I don't know, I just fetched it in. Why don't you have a look?"

His wife's fascination with mail was greater even than his own, which was considerable. William James, in his opinion, had hit the nail on the head. "As long as there are postmen," James declared, "life will have zest."

"Oh, look! Lovely! A letter from Whitecap, and it's to *me*!"

He watched her rip open the envelope.

"My goodness, listen to this. . . .

" '*Dear Mrs. Kavanagh, We are looking forward with great enthusiasm to your interim stay in our small island parish, and trust that all is going smoothly as you prepare to join us at the end of June.*

" '*Our ECW has been very busy readying Dove Cottage for your stay at Whitecap, and all you need to bring is bed linens for the two bedrooms, as we discussed, and any towels and pillows which will make you feel at home.*

" '*We have supplied the kitchen cupboards with new pots, and several of us have lent things of our own, so that you and Father Kavanagh may come without much disruption to your household in Mitford. Sam has fixed the electric can opener, but I hear you are a fine cook and probably won't need it, ha ha.*

" '*Oh, yes. Marjorie Lamb and I have done a bit of work in the cottage gardens, which were looking woefully forlorn after years of neglect. We found a dear old-fashioned rose, which I hear your husband enjoys, and liberated it from the brambles. It is now climbing up your trellis instead of running into the street! We expect the hydrangeas and crepe myrtle to be in full glory for your arrival, though the magnolias in the churchyard will, alas, be out of bloom.*

" '*Complete directions are enclosed, which Marjorie's husband, Leonard, assures me should take you from Mitford straight to the door of Dove Cottage without a snare. (Leonard once traveled on the road selling plumbing supplies.)*

" '*Please notice the red arrow I have drawn on the map. You must be very careful at this point to watch for the street sign, as it is hidden by a dreadful hedge which the property owner refuses to trim. I have thought of trimming it myself, but Sam says that would be meddling.*

" '*We hope you will not object to a rather gregarious greeting committee, who are bent on giving you a parish-wide luau the day following your arrival. I believe I have talked them out of wearing grass skirts, but that embarrassing notion could possibly break forth again.*

" '*When Father Morgan joined us several years ago, he, too, came in the summer and was expecting a nice holiday at the beach. I'm sure you've been warned that summer is our busiest time, what with the tourists who swell our little church to bursting and push us to two services! We all take our rest in the winter when one must hunker down and live off the nuts we've gathered!*

" '*Bishop Harvey was thrilled to learn from Bishop Cullen how greatly you and Father Kavanagh were appreciated by your parish in Mitford! We shall all do our utmost to make you feel as welcome as the flowers in May, as my dear mother used to say.*

" '*Goodness! I hope you'll forgive the length of this letter! Since childhood, I have loved the feel of a pen flowing over paper, and often get carried away.*

" '*We wish you and Father Timothy safe travel.*

" '*Yours sincerely,*

" '*Marion Fieldwalker, vestry member of St. John's in the Grove, and Pres. Episcopal Church Women*

" '*P.S. I am the librarian of Whitecap Island Community Library (35 years) and do pray you might be willing to give a reading this fall from one of your famous Violet books. Your little books stay checked out, and I believe every child on the island has read them at least twice!*' "

His wife flushed with approval. "There! How uplifting! Marion sounds lovely! And just think, dearest—trellises and old roses!"

"Not to mention new saucepans," he said, admiring the effort of his future parishioners.

She drank from her perspiring glass and continued to sort through the pile. "Timothy, look at his handwriting. He's finally stopped printing and gone to cursive!"

"Let me see. . . ."

Definitely a new look in the handwriting department, and a distinct credit to Dooley Barlowe's Virginia prep schooling. Miss Sadie's big bucks, forked over annually, albeit posthumously, were continuing to put spit and polish on the red-haired mountain boy who'd come to live with him at the rectory five years ago.

" '*Hey,*' " he read aloud from Dooley's letter, " '*I have thought about it a lot and I would like to stay in Mitford and work for Avis this summer and make money to get a car and play softball with the Reds.*

" '*I don't want to go to the beach.*

" '*Don't be mad or upset or anything. I can live in the basement with*

Harley like you said, and we will be fine. Puny could maybe come and do the laundry or we could do stuff ourselves and eat in Wesley or at the Grill or Harley could cook.

" *'I will come down to that island for either Thanksgiving or Christmas like we talked about.*

" *'Thanks for letting me go home from school with Jimmy Duncan, I am having a great time, he drives a Wrangler. His mom drives a Range Rover and his dad has a BMW 850. That's what I would like to have. A Wrangler, I mean. I'll get home before you leave, Mr. Duncan is driving me on his way to a big meeting. Say hey to Barnabas and Violet. Thanks for the money. Love, Dooley.'* "

"Oh, well," said his wife, looking disappointed. "I'm sure he wanted to be close to his friends. . . ."

"Right. And his brother and sister. . . ."

She sighed. "Pretty much what we expected."

He felt disappointed, himself, that the boy wouldn't be coming to Whitecap for the summer, but they'd given him a choice and the choice had been made. Besides, he learned a couple of years ago not to let Dooley Barlowe's summer pursuits wreck his own enjoyment of that fleeting season.

It was the business about cars that concerned him. . . . Dooley had turned sixteen last February, and would hit Mitford in less than three days, packing a bona fide driver's license.

"Knock, knock!" Emma Newland blew down the hall and into the study. "Don't get up," she said, commandeering the room. "You'll never believe this!"

His former part-time church secretary, who had retired when he retired, had clearly been unable to let go of her old job. She made it her business to visit twice a week and help out for a couple of hours, whether he needed it or not.

"I do it for th' Lord," she had stated flatly, refusing any thanks. Though Cynthia usually fled the room when she arrived, he rather looked forward to Emma's visits, and to the link she represented to Lord's Chapel, which was now under the leadership of its own interim priest.

Emma stood with her hands on her hips and peered over her glasses. "Y'all won't believe what I found on th' Internet. Three guesses!"

"Excuse me!" said Cynthia, bolting from the sofa. "I'll just bring you a lemonade, Emma, and get back to work. I've *gobs* of books to pack."

"Guess!" Emma insisted, playing a game that he found both mindless and desperately aggravating.

"A recipe for mixing your own house paint?"

"Oh, *please*," she said, looking disgusted. "You're not trying."

"The complete works of Fulgentius of Ruspe!"

"*Who?*"

"I give up," he said, meaning it.

"I found another Mitford! It's in England, and it has a church as old as mud, not to mention a castle!" She looked triumphant, as if she'd just squelched an invasion of Moors.

"Really? Terrific! I suppose it's where those writing Mitfords came from—"

"No connection. They were from th' Cotswolds, this place is up north somewhere. I had a stack of stuff I printed out, but Snickers sat on th' whole bloomin' mess after playin' in the creek, and I have to print it out again."

"Aha."

"OK, guess what else!"

"Dadgummit, Emma. You know I hate this."

She said what she always said. "It's good for you, keeps your brain active."

As far as she was concerned, he'd gone soft in the head since retiring six months ago.

"Just tell me and get it over with."

"Oh, come on! Try at least one guess. Here's a clue. It's about the election in November."

"Esther's stepping down and Andrew Gregory's going to run."

She frowned. "How'd you know that?"

"I haven't gone deaf and blind, for Pete's sake. I do get around."

"I suppose you also know," said Emma, hoping he didn't, "that the restaurant at Fernbank is openin' the night before you leave."

"Right. We've been invited."

She thumped into the slipcovered wing chair and peered at him as if he were a beetle on a pin. Though she'd certainly never say such a thing, she believed he was existing in a kind of purgatory between the inarguable heaven of Lord's Chapel and the hell of a strange parish in a strange place where the temperature was a hundred and five in the shade.

"Will you have a secretary down there?" she asked, suspicious.

"I don't think so. Small parish, you know."

"How small can it be?"

"Oh, fifty, sixty people."

"I thought Bishop Cullen was your *friend*," she sniffed. She'd never say so, but in her heart of hearts, she had hoped her boss of sixteen years would be given a big church in a big city, and make a comeback for himself. As it was, he trotted up the hill to Hope House and the hospital every livelong morning, appearing so cheerful about the whole thing that she recognized it at once as a cover-up.

Cynthia returned with a glass of lemonade and a plate of shortbread, which she put on the table next to Emma. "I'll be in the studio if anyone needs me. With all the books we're taking, we may sink the island!"

"A regular Atlantis," said Father Tim.

"Speakin' of books," Emma said to his wife, "are you doin' a new one?"

"Not if I can help it!"

He laughed as Cynthia trotted down the hall. "She usually can't help it." He expected a new children's book to break forth from his energetic wife any day now. Indeed, didn't she have a history of starting one when life was upside down and backward?

Emma munched on a piece of shortbread, showering crumbs in her lap. "Do you have those letters ready for me to do on th' computer?"

"Not quite. I wasn't expecting you 'til in the morning."

"I'm coming in th' morning, I just wanted to run by and tell you all th' late-breakin' news. But," she said, arching one eyebrow, "I haven't told you everything, I saved th' best 'til last."

His dog wandered into the study and crashed at his master's feet, panting.

"If you say you already know this, I'll never tell you another thing as long as I live. On my way here, I saw Mule Skinner, he said he's finally rented your house."

She drew herself up, pleased, and gulped the lemonade.

"Terrific! Great timing!" He might have done a jig.

"He said there hadn't been time to call you, he'll call you tonight, but it's not a family with kids like Cynthia wanted."

"Oh, well . . ." He was thrilled that someone had finally stepped forward to occupy the rectory. He and Harley had worked hard over the last few months to make it a strong rental property, putting new vinyl flooring in the kitchen, replacing the stair runners, installing a new toilet in the master bath and a new threshold at the front door . . . the list had been endless. And costly.

"It's a woman."

"I can't imagine what one person would want with all that house to rattle around in."

"How quickly you forget! *You* certainly rattled around in there for a hundred years."

"True. Well. I'll get the whole story from Mule."

"He said she didn't mind a bit that Harley would be livin' in the basement, she just wanted to know if he plays loud rock music."

Emma rattled the ice in her glass, gulped the last draught, and got up to leave. "Before I forget, you won't believe what else I found on th' Internet—church bulletins! You ought to read some of th' foolishness they put out there for God an' everybody to see."

She fished a piece of paper from her handbag. " 'Next Sunday,' " she read, " 'a special collection will be taken to defray the cost of a new carpet. All those wishin' to do somethin' on the new carpet will come forward and do so.' "

He hooted with laughter.

"How 'bout this number: 'Don't let worry kill you, let th' church help.' "

He threw his head back and laughed some more. Emma's life in cyberspace definitely had an upside.

"By th' way, are you takin' Barnabas down there?" She enunciated "down there" as if it were a region beneath the crust of the earth.

"We are."

"I don't know how you could do that to an animal. Look at all that fur, enough to stuff a mattress."

Barnabas yawned hugely and thumped his tail on the floor.

"You won't even be able to *see* those horrible sandspurs that will jump in there by th' hundreds, not to mention *lodge in his paws.*"

Emma waited for an argument, a rationale—something. Did he have no conscience? "And th' *heat* down there, you'll have to shave 'im bald."

Father Tim strolled across the room to walk her to the door.

"Thanks for coming, Emma. Tell Harold hello. I'll see you in the morning."

His unofficial secretary stumped down the hallway and he followed.

He was holding the front door open and biting his tongue when she turned and looked at him. Her eyes were suddenly red and filled with tears.

"I'll miss you!" she blurted.

"You *will*?"

She hurried down the front steps, sniffing, searching her bag for a Hardee's napkin she knew was in there someplace.

He felt stricken. "Emma! We'll . . . we'll have jelly doughnuts in the morning!"

"*I'll* have jelly doughnuts, *you'll* have dry toast! We don't want to ship you down there in a coma!"

She got in her car at the curb, slammed the door, gunned the motor, and roared up Wisteria Lane.

For one fleeting moment, he'd completely forgotten his blasted diabetes.

"I'm out of here," he said, kissing his wife.

"Get him to leave something for the island breezes to flow through, darling. Don't let him cut it all off."

"You always say that."

"Yes, well, you come home looking like a skinned rabbit. I don't know what Joe Ivey *does* to you."

Considering what Fancy Skinner had done to him time and time again, Joe Ivey could do anything he wanted.

"Leavin' us, are you?" Joe ran a comb through the hair over Father Tim's left ear and snipped.

"Afraid so."

"Leavin' us in th' lurch is more like it."

"Now, Joe. Did I preach to you when you went off to Graceland and left me high and dry?"

Joe cackled. "Thank God I come to m' senses and quit that fool job. An' in th' nick of time, too. I'm finally about t' clean up what

Fancy Skinner done to people's heads around here, which in your case looked like she lowered your ears a foot an' a half."

"My wife says don't cut it too short."

"If I listened to what wives say, I'd of been out of business forty years ago. Do you know how hot it gits down there?"

If he'd been asked that once, he'd been asked it a thousand times. There was hardly anything mountain people despised more than a "hot" place.

"I'm an old Mississippi boy, you know."

"An th' mosquitos . . . !" Joe whistled. "Man alive!"

"Right there," he said, as Joe started working around his collar. "Just clean it up a little right there, don't cut it—"

Joe proceeded to cut it. Oh, well. Joe Ivey had always done exactly as he pleased with Father Tim's hair, just like Fancy Skinner. What was the matter with people who serviced hair, anyway? He had never, in all his years, been able to figure it out.

"I hear it's a ten-hour trot t' get there," said Joe, clearly fixated on the inconvenience of it all.

"Closer to twelve, if you stop for gas and lunch."

"You could go t' New York City in less'n that. Prob'ly run up an' back."

"There's a thought."

Joe trimmed around his customer's right ear. "I'm gettin' t' where I'd like t' talk . . ."—Joe cleared his throat—"about what happened up at Graceland."

"Aha."

"I ain't told this to a soul, not even Winnie."

There was a long pause.

Father Tim waited, inhaling the fragrance from Sweet Stuff Bakery, just beyond the thin wall. Joe's sister, Winnie, and her husband, Thomas, were baking baklava, and he was starting to salivate.

"You couldn't ever mention this to anybody," said Joe. "You'd have to swear on a stack of Bibles."

"I can't do that, but I give you my word."

Joe let his breath out in a long sigh. "Well, sir, there towards th' end, I got to where I thought Elvis might be . . ."

"Might be what?"

"You know. *Alive.*"

"No!"

"I ain't proud t' admit it. Thing is, I was gettin' in th' brandy pretty heavy when I went up there. My sister's husband, he was laid off and things was pretty tight. Plus, their house ain't exactly th' Biltmore Estate when it comes to room, so ever' once in a while, I'd ride around after supper t' give Vern and my sister a little time to theirselves."

"That was thoughtful."

"I took to lookin' for Elvis ever'where I went, 'specially at th' barbecue place, they all said he was a fool for barbecue. My sister, when she heard I was lookin' to sight Elvis, she started pourin' my brandy down th' toilet. A man can't hardly live with somebody as pours 'is brandy down th' toilet."

"That would create tension, all right." Heaven knows, he'd tried for years to get Joe to quit sucking down alcohol, but Joe had told him to mind his own business. Something, however, had happened in Memphis that sent his barber home dry as a bone.

"Then one night I was drivin' around, I said to myself, I said, Joe, Elvis wouldn't be cruisin' through a drive-in pickin' up a chopped pork with hot sauce, he'd *send* somebody. So I said, if *I* was Elvis, where would I be at?

"Seem like somethin' told me to go back to Graceland, it was about eleven o'clock at night, so I drove on over there and parked across th' street with my lights off. I hate to tell you, but I had a pint in the glove department, and I was takin' a little pull now and again."

Joe took a bottle off the cabinet and held it above his customer's head. "You want Sea Breeze?"

"Is the Pope a Catholic?"

"First thing you know, I seen somethin' at th' top of the yard. There's this big yard, you know, that spreads out behind th' gate an' all. It was somethin' white, and it . . ."—Joe cleared his throat—"it was movin' around."

"Aha."

Joe blasted his scalp with Sea Breeze and vigorously rubbed it in. "You ain't goin' to believe this."

"Try me."

Joe's hands stopped massaging his head. In the mirror, Father Tim could see his barber's chin quivering.

"It was Elvis . . . in a white suit."

"Come on!"

"Mowin' 'is yard."

"No way!"

"I said you wouldn't believe it."

"Why would he mow his yard when he could pay somebody else to do it? And why would he do it in a suit, much less a *white* suit? And why would he do it at *night*?"

Joe's eyes were misty. He shook his head, marveling. "I never have figured it out."

"Well, well." What could he say?

"I set there watchin'. He'd mow a strip one way, then mow a strip th' other way."

"Gas or push?"

"Push."

"How could he see?" Father Tim asked, mildly impatient.

"There was this . . . *glow* all around him."

"Aha."

"Then, first thing you know . . ."—Joe's voice grew hushed—"he th'owed up 'is hand and waved at me."

Father Tim was speechless.

"Here I'd been lookin' to see 'im for I don't know how long, and it scared me s' bad when I finally done it, I slung th' bottle in th' bushes and quit drinkin' on th' spot."

His barber drew a deep breath and stood tall. "I ain't touched a drop since, and ain't wanted to."

Father Tim was convinced this was the gospel truth. Still, he had a question.

"So, Joe, what's that, ah . . . bottle sitting over there by the hair tonic?"

"I keep that for my customers. You don't want a little snort, do you?"

"I pass. But tell me this . . . any regrets about coming back to Mitford?"

"Not ary one, as my daddy used to say. It's been a year, now, since I hauled out of Memphis and come home to Mitford, and my old trade has flocked back like a drove of guineas. Winnie gave me this nice room to set my chair in, and th' Lord's give me back my health."

Joe took the cape from his customer's shoulders and shook it out. "Yessir, you're lookin' at a happy man."

"And so are you!" said Father Tim. "So are you!"

After all, didn't he have a new haircut, a new parish, and a whole new life just waiting to begin?

He couldn't help himself.

As the bells at Lord's Chapel pealed three o'clock, he turned into Happy Endings Bookstore as if on automatic pilot. He had five whole minutes to kill before jumping in the car and roaring off to Wesley for a bicycle pump, since Dooley's had turned up missing.

"Just looking," he told Hope Winchester. Hope's ginger-colored cat, Margaret, peered at him suspiciously as he raced through General Fiction, hung a right at Philosophy, and skidded left into Religion, where the enterprising Hope had recently installed a shelf of rare books.

He knew for a fact that the only bookstore on Whitecap Island was in the rear of a bait and tackle shop. They would never in a hundred years have Arthur Quiller-Couch's *On the Art of Reading*, which he had eyed for a full week. It was now or never.

His hand shot out to the hard-to-find Quiller-Couch volume, but was instantly drawn back. No, a thousand times no. If his wife knew he was buying more books to schlepp to Whitecap, he'd be dead meat.

He sighed.

"Better to take it now than call long-distance and have me ship it down there for three dollars."

Hope appeared next to him, looking wise in new tortoiseshell glasses.

No doubt about it, Hope had his number.

He raked the book off the shelf, and snatched Jonathan Edwards's *The Freedom of the Will* from another. He noted that his forehead broke out in a light sweat.

Oh, well, while he was at it . . .

He grabbed a copy of Lewis's *Great Divorce*, which had wandered from his own shelves, never to be seen again, and went at a trot to the cash register.

"I'm sure you're excited about your party!" Hope said, ringing the sale. Margaret jumped onto the counter and glowered at him. Why did cats hate his guts? What had he ever done to cats? Didn't he buy his wife's cat only the finest, most ridiculously priced chicken niblets in a fancy tinfoil container?

"Party? What party?"

"Why, the party Uncle Billy and Miss Rose are giving you and Cynthia!"

"I don't know anything about a party." Had someone told him and he'd forgotten?

"It's the biggest thing in the world to them. They've never given a party in their whole lives, but they want to do this because they hold you in the most edacious regard."

"Well!" He was nearly speechless. "When is it supposed to be?"

"Tomorrow night, of course." She looked at him oddly.

Tomorrow night they were working a list as long as his arm, not to mention shopping for groceries to feed Dooley Barlowe a welcome-home dinner of steak, fries, and chocolate pie.

He mopped his forehead with a handkerchief. He'd be glad to leave town and get his life in order again.

"I'll look into it," he muttered, shelling out cash for the forbidden books. "And if you don't mind, that is, if you happen to see Cynthia, you might not mention that, ah . . ."

Hope Winchester smiled. She would never say a word to the priest's wife about his buying more books. Just as she certainly wouldn't mention to him that Cynthia had dashed in only this morning to buy copies of Celia Thaxter's *My Island Garden*, and the hardback of *Ira Sleeps Over*.

He knocked on the screen door of the small, life-estate apartment in the rear of the town musuem.

"Uncle Billy! Miss Rose! Anybody home?"

He couldn't imagine the old couple giving a party; his mind was perfectly boggled by the notion. Rose Watson had been diagnosed as schizophrenic decades ago, and although on daily medication, her mood swings were fierce and unpredictable. To make matters worse for her long-suffering husband, she was quickly going deaf as a stone, but refused to wear hearing aids. "There's aids enough in this world," she said menacingly.

He put his nose against the screen and saw Uncle Billy sleeping in a chair next to an electric fan, his cane between his legs. Father Tim hated to wake him, but what was he to do? He knocked again.

Uncle Billy opened his eyes and looked around the kitchen, startled.

"It's me, Uncle Billy!"

"Lord if hit ain't th' preacher!" The old man grinned toward the door, his gold tooth gleaming. "Rose!" he shouted. "Hit's th' preacher!"

"He's not supposed to be here 'til tomorrow!" Miss Rose bellowed from the worn armchair by the refrigerator.

Uncle Billy grabbed his cane and slowly pulled himself to a standing position. "If I set too long, m' knees lock up, don't you know. But I'm a-comin'."

"Tell him he's a day early!" commanded Miss Rose.

"Don't you mind Rose a bit. You're welcome any time of th' day or night." Uncle Billy opened the screen and he stepped into the kitchen. The Watsons had cooked cabbage for lunch, no two ways about it.

"Uncle Billy, I hear you're giving . . . well, someone said you're giving Cynthia and me . . . a *party*?"

The old man looked vastly pleased. "Got a whole flock of people comin' to see you! Got three new jokes t' tell, you're goin' t' like 'em, and Rose is makin' banana puddin'."

Father Tim scratched his head, feeling foolish.

"Y' see, th' church give you 'uns a nice, big party an' all, but hit seemed mighty official, hit was anybody an' ever'body, kind of a free-for-all. I said, 'Rose, we ought t' give th' preacher an' 'is missus a little send-off with 'is *friends*!' " The old man leaned on his cane, grinning triumphantly. "So we're a-doin' it, and glad t' be a-doin' it!"

"Well, now—"

"Hit's goin' to be in th' museum part of th' house, so we can play th' jukebox, don't you know."

"Why, that's wonderful, it really is, but—"

"An' me an' Rose took a good bath in th' *tub*!"

He had seen the time when Uncle Billy and Miss Rose could empty two or three pews around their own. . . .

Miss Rose, in a chenille robe and unlaced saddle oxfords, stood up from her chair and looked him dead in the eye. He instantly wished for the protection of his wife.

"I hope you didn't come expecting to eat a day in advance," she snapped.

"Oh, law," said her mortified husband. "Now, Rose—"

She turned to Uncle Billy. "I haven't even *made* the banana pudding yet, so how can we feed him?"

"Oh, I didn't come to eat. I just came to find out—"

"You march home," said Miss Rose, "and come back tomorrow at the right time."

Uncle Billy put his hands over his eyes, as if to deny the terrible scene taking place in front of him.

"And what time might that *be*?" shouted Father Tim.

"Six-thirty sharp!" said the old woman, looking considerably vexed.

His wife went pale.

He felt like putting his hands over his own eyes, as Uncle Billy had done.

"I'm sorry," he said. "I didn't know how to say no. Uncle Billy is so excited. . . . They've never given a party before."

"Why in heaven's name didn't they let us *know*?"

"I think they invited everybody else and forgot to invite us."

"Lord have *mercy*!" said his overworked wife, conveniently quoting the prayer book.

They had collapsed on the study sofa for the Changing of the Light, having gone nonstop since five-thirty that morning. He had made the lemonade on this occasion, and served it with two slices of bread, each curled hastily around a filling of Puny's homemade pimiento cheese.

"I can't even *think* about a party," she said, stuffing the bread and cheese into her mouth. "My blood sugar has dropped through the soles of my tennis shoes."

Ah, the peace of this room, he thought, unbuttoning his shirt. And here they were, leaving it. They built it, and now they were leaving it. Such was life in a collar.

"Timothy, are you really excited about going to Whitecap?"

"It comes and goes in waves. One moment, I'm excited—"

"And the next, you're scared to death?"

"Well . . ."

"Me, too," she confessed. "I hate to leave Mitford. I thought it would be fun, invigorating, a great adventure." She lay down, putting her head on one of the faded needlepoint pillows that had also made it through the hedge. "But now . . ." Her voice trailed off.

"We're pretty worn out, Kavanagh. This is a stressful thing we're doing, pulling up stakes. I've hardly been out of Mitford in sixteen years. But we'll get there and it will be terrific, wait and see. You'll love it. The freedom of an island . . ."

"The wind in our hair . . ."

"Gulls wheeling above us . . ."

"The smell of salt air . . ."

It was a litany they'd recited antiphonally over the last couple of months. It always seemed to console them.

He pulled her feet into his lap. "How about a nap? We've got a tight schedule ahead."

"Tonight," she said, "Puny helps us clean out all the cabinets. . . . Dooley comes tomorrow evening just before the Watson party, and will have supper with his mother. Then a day of shopping with our threadbare boy and moving him in with Harley, followed by your meeting with the new tenant, and Dooley's steak dinner. Then, of course, there's the grand opening at Lucera on Thursday night after we finish packing the car, and on Friday morning we're off. I don't think," she said, breathless, "that we'll have time to celebrate your birthday."

His birthday! Blast! This year, he would be sixty-six, and just think—in four short years, he would be seventy. And then eighty. And then . . . dead, he supposed. Oh, well.

"Don't be depressed," she scolded. "And for heaven's sake, dearest, relax. You're sitting there like a statue in a park."

"Right," he said, guzzling the lemonade.

He had noted over the last few days that the late June light reached its pinnacle when it fell upon the brass angel. Because of the exterior overhang of the room, the direct light moved no higher than the mantel, where the angel stood firm on its heavy base of green marble.

He had found the angel in the attic at Fernbank, Miss Sadie's rambling house at the top of the hill, now owned by Andrew and Anna Gregory. Only months before she died in her ninetieth year, Sadie Baxter had written a letter about the disposition of her family home and its contents. One thing she asked him to do was take something for his own, anything he liked.

As Cynthia rambled through Fernbank seeking her portion of the legacy, he had found the angel in a box, a box with a faded French postmark. Though the attic was filled with a bountiful assortment of inarguable treasures, he had known as surely as if someone had engraved his name upon it that the angel in a box belonged to him.

The light moved now to the angel, to its outspread wings and supplicating hands. It shone, also, on the vase of pink flowering almond next to the old books, and the small silhouette of his mother, which Cynthia had reframed and hung above the mantel.

As long as he could remember, he'd been afraid to sit still, to listen, to wait. As a priest, he'd been glad of every needy soul to tend to; every potluck supper to sit to; even of every illness to run to—thankful for the fray and haste. He'd been frightened of any tendency to sit and let his mind wander like a goat untethered from a chain, free to crop any grass it pleased.

He was beginning to realize, however, that he was less and less afraid to do what appeared to be nothing.

In the end, he wasn't really afraid of moving to Whitecap, either; he'd given his wife the wrong notion. He had prayed that God would send him wherever He pleased, and when his bishop presented the idea of Whitecap, he knew it wasn't his bishop's bright idea at all, but God's. He had learned years ago to read God's answer to any troubling decision by looking to his heart, his spirit, for an imprimatur of peace. That peace had come; otherwise, he would not go.

He inhaled the freshness of the breeze that stole through the open window, and the fragrance of oak and cherry that pervaded the room like incense.

Then, lulled by the sight of his dozing wife, he put his head back and closed his eyes, and slept.

CHAPTER TWO

Social Graces

Rose Watson set out what most people would call an outrageous assortment of cracked, chipped, and broken china, including mismatched cups and saucers that teetered atop a tower of salad plates anchored on a turkey platter.

After standing back and gazing at the curious pile with some satisfaction, she decided to flank the arrangement with a medley of soup bowls.

The large plastic container of banana pudding sat on the electric range, bristling with two serving spoons jabbed into its yellow center. For napkins, Uncle Billy supplied a roll of paper towels, which he stood on one end next to the pudding.

"Don't set paper on a *stove*!" Miss Rose snatched the roll and moved it like a pawn on a chessboard to the kitchen table.

"What about spoons?" shouted her husband. He was fairly benumbed with the idea of having a swarm of people descend on their living quarters, though it had been his notion in the first place.

"Pull out the drawer! They can help themselves."

He did as he was told, thinking that his wife sometimes had a good idea, and wasn't half as crazy as most people thought. Mean-spirited, maybe, but that was her disease.

He had tried to read about schizophrenia in the Mitford library, one of the few times he had ever stepped foot in the place. He had looked for the oldest volunteer he could find, thinking she would be the boss, and asked her to lead him to a volume on a disease whose name he could not spell. He had then taken the book to a table and sat and asked the Lord to give him some kind of wisdom about what was so terribly, horribly wrong with his wife, but he couldn't understand anything the book had said, nothing.

"That's good thinkin'!" he shouted.

"You say somethin's *stinkin'*?" She turned and looked at him.

"Dadgummit, Rose, I said—"

"It might be your upper lip, Bill Watson." She suddenly burst into laughter.

There it was! The laughter he heard so seldom, had almost forgotten, rushing out like a bird freed from a cage, the laughter of the girl he'd known all those years ago. . . .

He stood, stunned and happy, tears springing to his eyes as suddenly as her laughter had come.

Father Tim found the china assortment fascinating. He could spot several pieces of French Haviland in a pattern his grandmother had owned, and not a few pieces of Sevres.

At least he thought it was Sevres. He picked up a bread-and-butter plate and peered discreetly at the bottom. Meissen. What did he know?

He certainly didn't know what to do about the banana pudding. Everyone except themselves had been asked to bring a covered dish, so there was plenty to choose from. Miss Rose, however, stood like a sentinel by the stove, making sure that all comers had a hefty dose of what had taken her a full afternoon to create.

All those cracks in the china, he thought, all those chips and chinks . . . weren't they a known hideout for germs, a breeding ground? And hadn't he sat by the hospital bed of a woman who had put her feet under Rose Watson's table and barely lived to tell about it?

He could remember the story plainly. "Lord knows, I hadn't hardly got home before my stomach started rumblin' and carryin' on, you never heard such a racket. Well, Preacher, I hate to tell you such a thing, but you've heard it all, anyhow—five minutes later, I was settin' on th' toilet, throwin' up on my shoes."

He had not forgotten the mental image of that good lady throwing up on her shoes. He certainly hadn't forgotten her dark warning never to eat a bite or drink a drop at Rose Watson's house.

"Fill y'r plates and march into th' front room!" Their host's gold tooth gleamed. "Some's already in there, waitin' for th' blessin'."

Cynthia served herself from the pudding bowl as if she hadn't eaten a bite since Rogation Sunday.

"Fall to, darling," she said, happy as a child.

Oh, the everlasting gusto of his spouse! He sighed, peering around for the ham biscuits.

He found that everyone was oddly excited about being in a place as prominent as the town museum. It was a little awkward, however, given that not a single chair could be found, and they all had to mill around with their plates in their hands, setting their tea glasses on windowsills and stair steps.

The jukebox boomed out what he thought was "Chattanooga Shoeshine Boy," and laid a steady rhythm into the bare floorboards.

He and Cynthia made a quick tour of the exhibits, which he'd never, for some reason, taken time to study.

There was a copy of Willard Porter's deed to what had been the Mitford Pharmacy and was now Happy Endings Bookstore. There was also a handwritten list of pharmaceuticals that Willard had invented and patented, including Rose Cough Syrup, named for his then-ten-year-old sister, and their hostess for the evening.

There was the framed certificate declaring the Wurlitzer to be a gift to the town from the owner of the Main Street Grill, where it was unplugged on June 26, 1951. It had been fully restored to mint condition, thanks to the generosity of Mayor Esther Cunningham.

He examined the daguerreotype of Coot Hendrick's great-great-grandfather sitting in a straight-back chair with a rifle across his knees.

It had been Coot's bearded ancestor, Hezikiah, who settled Mitford, riding horseback up the mountain along an Indian trading path, with his new English bride, Mary Jane, clinging on behind. According to legend, his wife was so homesick that Mr. Hendrick had the generosity of spirit to give the town her maiden name of Mitford, instead of Hendricksville or Hendricksburg, which a man might have preferred to call a place settled by dint of his own hard labors.

" 'At's my great-*great*-granpaw," said Coot Hendrick, coming alongside the preacher and his wife. He'd been waiting to catch someone looking at that picture. For years, it had knocked around in a drawer at his mama's house, and he'd hardly paid any attention to it at all. Then somebody wanted it for the town museum and it had taken on a whole new luster.

"He looks fearless!" said Cynthia.

"Had twelve young 'uns!" Coot grinned from ear to ear, which was not a pretty sight, given his dental condition. "Stubs!" Mule Skinner had said, marveling at how he'd seen people's teeth fall out, but never wear down in such a way.

"Six lived, six died, all buried over yonder on Miz Mallory's ridge. Her house sets right next to where him and my great-great-granmaw built their little cabin."

"Well!" said Father Tim.

"Hit was a fine place to sight Yankees from," said Coot.

"I'll bet so."

"There probably weren't many Yankees prowling around up here," said Cynthia, who'd read that, barely a hundred and fifty years ago, an Anglican bishop had called the area "wild and uninhabitable."

"You'd be surprised," said Coot, tucking his thumbs in the straps of his overalls. "They say my great-great-granpaw shot five and give ever' one of 'em a solemn burial."

"I didn't know there were any battles fought around Mitford," said Cynthia, who appeared deeply interested in this new wrinkle of local history.

"They won't. Th' Yankees was runaways from their regiment."

Spying Esther and Gene Bolick making a beeline in their direction, they excused themselves and met the Bolicks halfway.

"We just hate this!" said Esther. Overcome, she grabbed his hand and kissed it, then, mortified at such behavior, dropped it like a hot potato. "Gene and I have run th' gambit of emotions, and we still just hate to see y'all go!"

"We hate to go," he said simply.

"I baked you a two-layer orange marmalade and froze it. You can carry it down there in your cooler." There was nothing else she could do to keep her former priest in Mitford where she was certain he belonged—she had prayed, she had lost, she had cried, and in the end, she had baked.

Her husband, Gene, sighed and looked glum.

This, thought Father Tim, is precisely where a going-away party turns into a blasted wake unless somebody puts on a funny hat or slides down the banister, *something*. . . .

He turned to his wife, who shrugged and smiled and sought greener pastures.

"Gene's not been feelin' too good," said Esther.

"What is it?" asked Father Tim.

"Don't know exactly," Gene said, as Miss Rose strode up. "But I talked to Hoppy and went and got th' shots."

"Got the *trots*?" shouted Miss Rose. Everyone peered at them.

Gene flushed. "No, ma'am. The *shots*."

"Bill had the trots last week," she said, frowning. "It could be something going around." Their hostess, who was monitoring everyone's plate to see whether her pudding had gotten its rightful reception, moved on to the next circle of guests.

"We reckon you know how hot it gets down there," said Gene.

"Honey, *hot*'s not th' word for it!" Fancy Skinner appeared in her signature outfit of pink Capri pants, V-neck sweater, and spike-heel shoes. "You will be boiled, steamed, roasted, baked, and fried."

"Not to mention sautéed," said Avis Packard, who owned the grocery store on Main Street, and liked to cook.

Fancy popped her sugarless gum. "Then there's stewed and broiled."

"Please," said Father Tim.

"Barbecued!" contributed Gene, feeling pleased with himself. "You forgot barbecued."

Fancy, who was the owner of Mitford's only unisex salon, hooted with laughter.

"Did you consider maybe goin' to *Vermont*?" Gene wondered if their former rector had thought through this island business.

"Because if you think your hair's curlin' around your ears *now*," said Fancy, "wait'll all that humidity hits it, we're talkin' a Shirley Temple–Little Richard combo. That's why I liked to keep your hair *flat* around your ears when *I* was doin' it, now it's these chipmunk *pooches* again." Fancy reached out to forcibly slick his vagrant pooches down with her fingers, but restrained herself.

He looked anxiously around the room for Cynthia, who was laughing with the mayor and Hope Winchester.

Omer Cunningham trotted in from the kitchen with a plate piled to overflowing, wearing his usual piano-key grin. Father Tim vowed he'd never seen so many big white teeth as the mayor's brother-in-law had in his head. It was enough for a regular Debussy concerto.

"Lord, at th' traffic I've run into today!"

"On Main Street?"

"I mean air traffic," said the proud owner of a ragwing taildragger. "I been buzzin' th' gorge. You never seen th' like of deer that's rootin' around in there. Seems like ever'body and his brother was flyin' today."

Father Tim had instant and vivid recall of his times in the ragwing with Omer. Once to Virginia to hear Dooley in a concert, with his stomach lagging some distance behind the plane. Then again when they flew over Edith Mallory's sprawling house on the ridge above Mitford, trying to see what kind of dirty deal was behind the last mayoral race.

"I spotted a Piper Cherokee, a Cessna 182, and a Beechcraft Bonanza."

"Kind of like bird-watching."

"That Bonanza costs half a million smackers. You don't see many of those."

"I'll bet you don't."

"Listen, now," said Omer, ripping the meat off a drumstick with his teeth, "you let me know if I can ever buzz down to where you're at to help you out or anything. My little ragwing is yours any time of th' day or night, you hear?"

"Thank you, Omer, that's mighty thoughtful!"

Omer's chewing seemed unusually efficient. "I've flew over them little islands where you're goin' any number of times. Landed on many a beach. If you stay out of th' bad thunderstorms they have down there, it's as calm an' peaceful as you'd ever want t' see."

Omer picked up a ham biscuit and eyed it. "I don't like ham in a cathead biscuit," he said. "Have to dig too far for th' ham."

It was his fault. He was the one who casually mentioned it to Mule Skinner.

In nothing flat, the word of Dooley Barlowe's driver's license had replaced the party buzz about Avis Packard's decision to buy a panel truck for grocery delivery, and the huge addition to Edith Mallory's already enormous house.

Did he imagine it, or were they all peering at him as if to inquire when he was trotting out a car to go with Dooley's license?

Absolutely not. He had no intention of buying a car for a sixteen-year-old boy, then running off and leaving him to his own devices. Fortunately, Dooley had agreed to ride his red bicycle this summer, but he knew the notion of a car was definitely in the boy's mind. After all, didn't everybody's father in that fancy school toss around snappy convertibles and upscale four-wheel drives like so much confetti?

While it was obvious that Dooley couldn't earn enough money for a car by bagging groceries, Father Tim thought a summer of trying would hardly damage the boy's character.

In truth, there was an even more serious concern than Dooley's automobile hormones. And that was the fact he'd have nearly ten weeks to come and go as he pleased. Harley Welch would make a dependable, principled guardian, but Dooley could outwit Harley.

He muddled his spoon in the banana pudding.

As if reading Father Tim's mind, Mule said, "We'll all watch after 'im."

"Right," said Gene, "we'll keep an eye on 'im."

Adele Hogan, Mitford's only female police officer and nearly-new wife of the newspaper editor, caught up with him at the jukebox, as her husband snapped pictures for Monday's edition of the *Muse*.

"Just wanted you to know," said Adele, "we've got cars cruisin' around the clock. We'll keep our eyes open for your little guy while you're gone."

The truth was, there'd be a veritable woof of men to look after the boy, not to mention a fine warp of women, including Puny, and Dooley's mother, and now Adele.

"Thank you!" he said, meaning it.

Adele stood with her thumbs tucked into her belt, appearing for a moment to be hired security. She had come straight from the station in her uniform, wearing a Glock nine-millimeter on her hip. The sight of Adele, who was the new hotshot coach of the Mitford Reds and also the grandmother of three, never failed to astonish and impress him.

"Don't worry about a thing," said Adele.

He was almost inclined not to.

"Right!" agreed Avis. "I'm th' only one that'll drive my delivery truck, except for Lew Boyd's cousin, who's fillin' in on Saturdays. Anyway, I'm goin' to work your boy's butt off this summer. He won't have time to get in trouble." In a spontaneous burst of camaraderie, Avis slapped him on the shoulder.

The mayor barged up and slapped him on the other shoulder. He nearly pitched into the Wurlitzer, which was now playing "One Mint Julep."

"Run out on us, then," said Esther Cunningham. "See if I care."

"You don't need me anymore. After praying you into office eight times in a row, you're hanging it up and going off with Ray in the RV."

Esther narrowed her eyes and peered at him. "I guess you know about th' hurricanes they get down there."

"I do."

"And th' heat . . ."

Would they *never* hush . . . ?

A muscle twitched in the mayor's jaw. "We'll miss you."

"We'll miss you back," he said, putting his arm around his old friend's well-cushioned shoulders. He hated this goodbye business. He'd rather be home yanking a tooth out by a string on a doorknob, anything. "Are you laying off the sausage biscuits?"

"Curiosity killed the cat," she said.

Esther cupped her hands to her mouth and shouted, "Somebody unplug th' box!"

Omer squatted by the Wurlitzer, which couldn't be shut off manually, and pulled the plug.

"Must be Uncle Billy's joke," said Gene Bolick, getting up from the stair step where he was sitting with Mule.

Mule sighed. "I hope it's not that deal about th' gas stove! I've heard that more times than Carter has liver pills."

"Here's one for you," said Gene. "What's a Presbyterian?"

"Beats me."

"A Methodist with a drinkin' problem who can't afford to be Episcopalian."

Mule scratched his head. He had never understood jokes about Episcopalians.

"Come on, everybody!" yelled the mayor, her voice echoing in the vaulted room. "Joke time!"

Uncle Billy stood as straight as he was able, holding on to his cane and looking soberly at the little throng, who gave forth a murmur of coughing and throat-clearing.

"Wellsir!" he exclaimed, by way of introduction. "A farmer was haulin' manure, don't you know, an' 'is truck broke down in front of a mental institution. One of th' patients, he leaned over th' fence, said, 'What're you goin' t' do with y'r manure?'

"Farmer said, 'I'm goin' t' put it on m' strawberries.'

"Feller said, 'We might be crazy, but we put whipped cream on our'n.' "

Uncle Billy grinned at the cackle of laughter he heard.

"Keep goin'!" someone said.

"Wellsir, this old feller an' 'is wife was settin' on th' porch, an' she said, 'Guess what I'd like t' have?'

"He said, 'What's that?'

"She said, 'A great big bowl of vaniller ice cream with choc'late sauce and nuts on top!'

"He says, 'Boys howdy, that'd be good. I'll go down to th' store and git us some.'

"Wife said, 'Now, that's vaniller ice cream with choc'late sauce and nuts. Better write it down.'

"He said, 'Don't need t' write it down, I can remember.'

"Little while later, he come back. Had two ham san'wiches. Give one t' her. She looked at that san'wich, lifted th' top off, said, 'You mulehead, I told you t' write it down, I wanted mustard on mine!' "

Loving the sound of laughter in the cavernous room, Uncle Billy nodded to the left, then to the right.

"One more," he said, trembling a little from the excitement of the evening.

"Hit it!" crowed the mayor, hoping to remember the punch line to the vanilla ice-cream story.

"Wellsir, this census taker, he went to a house an' knocked, don't you know. A woman come out, 'e said, 'How many children you got, an' what're their ages?'

"She said, 'Let's see, there's th' twins Sally and Billy, they're eighteen. And th' twins Seth an' Beth, they're sixteen. And th' twins Penny an' Jenny, they're fourteen—'

"Feller said, 'Hold on! Did you git twins ever' time?'

"Woman said, 'Law, no, they was hundreds of times we didn't git nothin'.' "

The old man heard the sound of applause overtaking the laughter, and leaned forward slightly, cupping his hand to his left ear to better take it in. The applause was giving him courage, somehow, to keep on in life, to get out of bed in the mornings and see what was what.

Uncle Billy and Miss Rose looked considerably exhausted from their social endeavors; the old man's hands trembled as they stood on the cool front porch.

"I'd like to pray for you," said Father Tim.

"We'd be beholden to you, Preacher, if you would," said Uncle Billy, "but seems like we ought t' pray f'r you, don't you know."

Hardly anyone ever did that, he thought, moved by the gesture. "I'd thank you for doing it."

Cynthia slipped into the circle and they joined hands.

"Now, Lord . . ."—the old man drew a deep breath—"I ain't used t' doin' this out loud an' all, but I felt You call me t' do it, an' I'm expectin' You t' help me, don't you know.

"Lord Jesus, I'm askin' You t' watch over th' preacher an' 'is missus. Don't let 'em git drownded down there, or come up ag'in' meanness of any kind. You tell 'em whichaway to go when they need it."

Uncle Billy paused. "An' I 'preciate it. F'r Christ's sake, a-men!"

"Amen!"

Father Tim clasped his arms around his old friend. "Uncle Billy—"

"I hope they give you plenty of fried chicken down there!" squawked Miss Rose. She'd always heard preachers liked fried chicken.

He didn't know how many more goodbyes he could bear.

It wasn't that he and Cynthia hadn't wanted to go to Whitecap to see and be seen. They had carefully planned to go for five days in March, but the weather had turned foul, with lashing rains and high winds that persisted for days along the eastern shoreline.

He had then tried to set a date for April, but most of the Whitecap vestry, who were key players in any approval process, would be away for one reason or another.

"Don't sweat it," Stuart Cullen had said in a phone call. Stuart was not only his current bishop, but a close friend since seminary days. "They know all about you. They're thrilled you'll do the interim. Bishop Harvey agrees it's a match made in heaven, so don't worry about getting down there for the usual preview."

"It's a little on the pig-in-a-poke side, if you ask me."

Stuart laughed. "Believe me, Timothy, they need exactly what you've got to offer. Besides, if you don't like each other, Bill Harvey and I will give you your money back."

"How about telling me the downside of this parish? All Bill Harvey talks about is the church being so attractive, it ends up on postcards."

"Right," agreed Stuart. "He also vows he hears the nickering of wild ponies through the open windows of the nave, though I don't think Whitecap has wild ponies these days."

"What I'd rather know is, who's likely to stab the interim in the back? And who's plotting to run off with the choir director?"

He was joking, of course, but equally serious. He wanted to know what was what in Whitecap, and nobody was telling him.

"Ah, well, Timothy, there isn't a choir director." His bishop sounded strained.

"Really? Why not?"

"Well . . ."

"Stuart!"

"Because the choir director ran off with the organist."

"Is this a joke?"

"I wish."

"Surely you can come up with something slicker than that. Good heavens, man, we had a jewel thief living in the attic at Lord's Chapel, not to mention a parishioner who tried to buy the last mayoral election. Tell me something I can get my teeth into."

"Sorry. But I've just given you the plain, unvarnished truth."

There was a long silence. "What else do I need to know?"

The bishop told him. In fact, he told him a great deal more than he needed to know.

He stepped into the downstairs bathroom and took his glucometer kit from the medicine cabinet. With all the hoopla going on, and the radical changes in his diet, he figured he should check his sugar more often.

Once or twice, he'd felt so low, he could have crawled under a snake's belly wearing a top hat. Other times, his adrenaline was pumping like an oil derrick.

He shot the lance into the tip of his left forefinger and spilled the drop of blood onto a test strip. Then he slid the strip into the glucometer and waited for the readout. 130.

Excellent. He didn't need any bad news from his body. Not now, not ever.

"Thank you, Lord," he murmured, zipping the case shut.

He and Dooley loped across Baxter Park with Barnabas on the red leash, then turned left and headed up Old Church Lane.

They ran side by side until the hospital turnoff, where Dooley suddenly looked at him, grinned, and shot forward like a hare.

As he watched the boy pull away toward the crest of the steep hill, he saw at once the reason for his greater speed. Dooley Barlowe's legs were six feet long.

He huffed behind, regretting the way he'd let his running schedule go. Oh, well. Whitecap would be another matter entirely. All that fresh salt air and ocean breeze, and a clean, wide beach that went on for miles . . .

He would even walk to his office, conveniently located in the basement of the church, only two blocks from Dove Cottage. Nor was he the only one whose physical fitness would take an upturn. Cynthia was sending her old blue Schwinn down with their household shipment, and would leave her Mazda in Mitford. For an island only eleven miles long and four miles wide, who needed a car? Even many of the locals were said to navigate on two-wheelers.

"Better watch your step down there," Omer had advised. "Them bicycles'll mow you down, they ride 'em ever' whichaway."

"Wait up!" he shouted to Dooley.

Dooley turned around, laughing, and for a crisp, quick moment, he saw the way the sun glinted on the boy's red hair, and the look in his blue eyes. It was a look of triumph, of exultation, a look he had never, even once, seen before on Dooley Barlowe's face.

He didn't know whether to whoop, which he felt like doing, or weep, which he dismissed at once. Instead, he lunged ahead, closing the gap between them, and threw his arm around the boy's shoulder and told him what must be spoken now, immediately, and not a moment later.

"I love you, buddy," he said, panting and laughing at once. "Blast if I don't."

They sat on the cool stone wall, looking into the valley, into the Land of Counterpane. There beyond the trees was the church spire, and over there, the tiniest glint of railroad tracks . . . and just there, the pond next to the apple orchard where he knew ducks were swimming. Above it all, ranging along the other side of the valley, the high, green hills outlined themselves against a blue and cloudless sky. It was his favorite view in the whole of the earth, he thought.

"There's something I'd like you to know," he told Dooley. "I believe we'll find Sammy and Kenny."

Father Tim had gone into the Creek with Lace Turner and retrieved Dooley's younger brother, Poobaw. Later, he'd driven to Florida on little more than a hunch, and located Dooley's little sister, Jessie. Now two of the five Barlowe children were still missing. Their mother, Pauline, recovering from years of hard drinking, had no idea where they might be. As far as he could discover, there were no clues, no trail, no nothing. But he had hope—the kind that comes from a higher place than reason or common sense.

"Will you believe that with me?" he asked Dooley.

A muscle moved in Dooley's jaw. "You did pretty good with Poo and Jessie."

Barnabas crashed into the grass at Dooley's feet.

"I believe we're closer to deciding on some colleges to start thinking about."

"Yep. Maybe Cornell."

"You've got a while before you have to make any decisions."

"Maybe University of Georgia."

"Maybe. Their specialty is large animals; that's what interests you. Anyway, that's all down the road. For now, just check things out, think about it, pray about it."

"Right."

"We're mighty proud of you, son. You'll make a fine vet. You've come—we've all come—a long way together."

There was an awkward silence between them.

"What's on your mind?" asked Father Tim.

"Nothing."

"Let's talk about it."

Dooley turned to him, glad for the invitation. "It looks like you could let me borrow the money and I'll pay you back. Working six days a week at five dollars an hour, I'll have sixteen hundred dollars. Plus I figure three yards a week at an average of twenty apiece, I'm countin' it seven hundred bucks because some people will give me a tip. Last year, I saved five hundred, so that's two thousand eight hundred."

He had the sudden sense of being squeezed between a rock and a hard place. . . .

"Nearly three thousand," said Dooley, enunciating clearly. "I could prob'ly make it an even three if I cleaned out people's attics and basements."

Aha. He hadn't counted on three thousand bucks being a factor in the car equation. He gazed out to the view, unseeing.

"This just isn't the summer for it. We can't be here, and that's a very crucial factor. Besides, you know we agreed you'd have a car next summer. If we're still at Whitecap, you'll come there, and everything will be fine." He looked at Dooley. "Call me hard if you like, but it's not going to happen."

Dooley turned away and said something under his breath.

"Tell you what we'll do. Cynthia and I will match everything you make this summer." It was a rash decision, but why not? He still had more than sixty thousand dollars of his mother's money, and was a homeowner with no mortgage. It was the right thing to do.

Dooley stared straight ahead, kicking the stone wall with his heels.

If Dooley Barlowe only knew what he knew—that Sadie Baxter had left the boy a cool million-and-a-quarter bucks in her will, to be his when he turned twenty-one. He knew that part of Miss Sadie's letter by heart: *I am depending on you never to mention this to him until he is old enough to bear it with dignity.*

"Look. We gave you a choice between staying in Mitford and a summer at the beach. That's a pretty important liberty. We didn't force you to do anything you didn't want to do. Give us credit for that. The car is a different matter. We're not going to be around to—"

"Harley's going to be around all the time, he's going to let me drive his truck, what's the difference if I have my own car?"

Well, blast it, what *was* the difference? "But only once a week, as you well know, with a curfew of eleven o'clock."

Father Tim stood up, agitated. He never dreamed he'd be raising a teenager. When he was Dooley's age in Holly Springs, Mississippi, nobody he knew had a car when they were sixteen. Today, boys were given cars as casually as they were handed a burger through a fast-food window. And in fact, a vast number of them ended up decorating the grille of an eighteen-wheeler, not critically injured, but dead. He was too old to have a teenager, too old to figure this out the way other people, other parents, seemed to do.

"Look," he said, pacing alongside the stone wall, "we talked about this before, starting a few months ago. You were perfectly fine with no car this summer; we agreed on it. You even asked me to hunt down your bicycle pump so you could put air in the tires."

He knew exactly what had happened. It was that dadblamed Wrangler. "Is Tommy getting a car this summer?"

"No. He's working to raise money so he can have one next year. He's only saved eight hundred dollars."

This was definitely an encouragement. "So, look here. Harley was going to mow our two yards once a week, but why don't I give you the job? I'll pay twenty bucks a shot for both houses."

"If Buster Austin did it, he'd charge fifteen apiece, that's thirty. I'll do both for twenty-five."

"Deal!"

He looked at the boy he loved, the boy he'd do anything for.

Almost.

It rained throughout the night, a slow, pattering rain that spoke more eloquently of summer to him than any sunshine. He listened through the open bedroom window until well after midnight, sleepless but not discontented. They would make it through all this upheaval, all this tearing up and nailing down, and life would go on.

He found his wife's light, whiffling snore a kind of anchor in a sea of change.

Bolting down Main Street the next morning at seven o'clock, he saw Evie Adams in her rain-soaked yard, dressed in a terry robe and armed with a salt shaker.

"Forty two!" she shouted in greeting.

He knew she meant snail casualties. Evie had been at war with snails ever since they gnawed her entire stand of blue hostas down to nubs. Some years had passed since this unusually aggressive assault, but Evie had not forgotten. He pumped his fist into the air in a salute of brotherhood.

After all, he had hostas, too. . . .

"If I have to say goodbye to you one more time, I'll puke," said Mule.

Actually, Mule was moved nearly to bawling that his old buddy had come by the Grill at all. Father Tim could have been loading his car, or turning off the water at the street, or changing his address at the post office—whatever people did who were leaving for God knows how long.

"Livermush straight up," Father Tim told Percy as he slid into the booth. "And make it a double."

"Livermush? You ain't ordered livermush in ten, maybe twelve years."

"Right. But that's what I'm having." He grinned at the dumfounded Percy. "And make it snappy."

It was reckless to eat livermush, especially a double order, but he was feeling reckless.

Percy set his mouth in a fine line as he cut two slices from the loaf of livermush. He did not approve of long-term Grill customers moving elsewhere. Number one, the Father had been coming to the Grill for sixteen, seventeen years; he was established. To just up and run off, flinging his lunch and breakfast trade to total strangers, was . . . he couldn't even find a word for what it was.

Number two, why anybody would want to leave Mitford in the

first place was beyond him. He had personally left it only twice—when Velma was pregnant and they went to see cousins in Avery County, and when he and Velma went on that bloomin' cruise to Hawaii, which his children had sent them on whether he wanted to go or not.

But worse than the Father leaving Mitford, he was leaving it for a location that had once *broken off from the mainland*, for Pete's sake, and could not be trusted as ground you'd want under your feet. So here was somebody he'd thought to be sensible and wise, clearly proving himself to be otherwise.

As he laid two thick slices on the sizzling grill, Percy shook his head. Every time he thought he'd gained a little understanding of human nature, something like this came up and he had to start over.

J. C. Hogan thumped into the booth. "Man!" he said, mopping his face with a rumpled handkerchief. "It's hot as a depot stove today. I hope you know how hot it gets *down there.*"

Father Tim put his hands over his ears and shut his eyes.

"Lookit," said J.C. He tossed the *Muse*, still smelling of ink, on the table. "You made today's front page."

"What for?"

Mule snatched the eight-page edition to his side of the table and adjusted his glasses. "Let me read it. Let's see. Here we go." The realtor cleared his throat and read aloud.

" *'Around Town by Vanita Bentley . . .'*

"Blah, blah, blah, OK, here's th' meat of it. *'Father Kavanagh treated everybody as if equal in intelligence and accomplishment, making his real church the homes, sidewalks and businesses of Mitford. . . .*

" *'Whether we had faith or not, he loved us all.'* "

Father Tim felt his face grow hot. "Give me that," he said, snatching the newspaper.

"What's the matter?" said J.C. "Don't you like it?"

He didn't know if he liked it. What he knew was that it sounded like . . . an obituary.

He was hunkering down now, trying to cover all the bases.

Thanks be to God, it was nearly over, they were nearly on their way. He'd been going at this thing of leaving as if it were life or death, when in fact it was more like a year to sixteen months, and then he'd be back in Mitford, with half the population not realizing he'd left.

He screeched into Louella's room at Hope House, breathing hard. Miss Sadie's will had provided her lifelong companion with Room Number One, which was the finest room in the entire place.

Louella plucked the remote from her capacious lap and muted *All My Children*.

"You look like you been yanked up by th' roots!" she said, concerned.

"Ah . . . ," he replied, unable to muster anything else.

"An' it yo' *birthday*!" she scolded.

"It is?"

"You sixty-six today!"

"Louella, do I remind you of your age?"

"Honey," she said, looking smug, "you don' know my age."

He'd been coming to see Louella every day since Miss Sadie died. Sometimes they played checkers, but more often they sang hymns. The thought of leaving her made him feel like a common criminal. . . .

"How's your knee?" he asked, kissing her warm, chocolate-colored cheek. "How's your bladder infection? Have you started the potting class yet?"

"Set down on yo' stool," she said. He always sat on her footstool, which made him feel nine years old. A feeling, by the way, he rather liked.

"Now," she said, beaming, "we ain' goan talk about knees an' bladders, an' far as pottin' classes goes, I decided I ain't messin' wit' no clay. What I'm wantin' to do is *sing*, and ain't hardly anybody roun' here can carry a tune in a bucket."

"I'll go a round or two with you," he said, feeling better at once.

"I take th' first verse, you take th' second, an' we'll chime in together on number three."

Louella closed her eyes and raised her hands and began to lift her rich, mezzo voice in song. She rocked a little in her chair.

> *"The King of love my shepherd is,*
> *Whose goodness faileth never;*
> *I nothing lack if I am his,*
> *And he is mine forever."*

He waited two beats and picked up the second verse, not caring if they heard him all the way to the monument.

"Where streams of living water flow,
My ransomed soul he leadeth,
And where the verdant pastures grow,
With food celestial feedeth."

Two nurses stuck their heads in the door, grinning, as he joined his voice with Louella's on the third verse.

"Perverse and foolish oft I strayed,
But yet in love he sought me,
And on his shoulder gently laid,
And home, rejoicing, brought me."

They were silent for a moment. "Now," said Louella, "that feels better, don't it?"

He nodded, sensing the tears lurking in him, some kind of sorrow that he'd noticed for a week or more.

"You pushin' too hard," she said.

"You have to push, Louella." Out there in the world, he wanted to say, it was all about push.

"Maybe you done stepped aroun' th' Lord an' tryin' to lead th' way."

He stood up and looked out the window, into the green valley he called the Land of Counterpane. Maybe she was right.

Louella didn't often get out of her chair these days, but now she rose and stood by him, and put her hand on his shoulder.

"You know I pray for you and Miss Cynthia every mornin' an' every night, and I ain' goin' to stop. Anytime you get in a tight place down yonder, you just think, Louella's prayin' for me, and go on 'bout your business."

As he left Room Number One, he found himself humming. He couldn't remember doing that in a very long time.

"Where streams of living water flow, my ransomed soul he leadeth. . . ."

Maybe the real issue wasn't how Louella would manage without him, but how would he manage without Louella?

He cantered down the hall and found Pauline finishing up in the dining room.

"Pauline?"

"Father!"

He gave her a hug. "What do you hear from Buck?"

"He'll be home the fifteenth of October."

"And we'll roar in on the twenty-fifth, after which I'll personally see to it that you become Mrs. Buck Leeper."

She smiled and looked at her hands. He'd never seen her more beautiful. In fact, the miracle of watching Pauline Barlowe become whole wasn't unlike watching the slow unfolding of the petals on his Souvenir de la Malmaison.

"That is what you want, isn't it?"

"More'n anything. Yes, sir, I do."

"You've waited, and I admire that. How's his job in Alaska?"

"Real good. He says he'll bring it in on time."

"He always does," he said, feeling proud with her. "And Jessie and Poo? How're they feeling about all that's ahead?"

"Excited." She hesitated, then dared to use a word she had never trusted in her life. "Happy!"

He nodded, pleased. "Dooley will be in safe hands with Harley, and I know he'll be coming around to your place often. You might want to . . ." *Watch over him,* he wanted to say.

"I will," she replied, knowing.

He was halfway along the hall when she called after him. "Father!"

He turned around. "Yes?"

"We hate to see you go."

"I'll be back before you know I'm gone."

She smiled and waved, and he saw Dooley in her for a fleeting moment, something about the way she held her head, and the thrust of her chin. . . .

"Law, help!" said Puny, looking exhausted. "I'll be glad to see y'all *go*!"

There! The truth from somebody, at last.

"You never seen th' like of mess Dooley'd squirreled away in his room that we had to drag to th' basement. Harley said if we kept on haulin' stuff down there, he'd have to go to livin' out of his truck." The freckled Puny hooted with laughter.

"Where are my grandbabies?" he wondered. Puny sometimes fetched the twins from church school a little early. Sissy and Sassy even kept a stash of toys at the yellow house, consisting of a red wagon, several dolls, stuffed monkeys, crayons, and other paraphernalia.

"They're dead asleep in th' front room, Miz Hart said they fussed all day."

"Uh-oh."

"But they'll be glad to see their granpaw." Puny smiled hugely. The poor soul standing in front of her would never have had the joy of grandchildren if it hadn't been for her generosity. She'd given him her babies as free-handed as you please, and he'd taken to them like a duck to water. The truth was, Sissy was crazy about her granpaw and often kissed a framed picture of him that Puny had proudly placed in her home.

He patted his pocket. "I'm ready when they are."

"You'll make their little teeth fall out with that candy."

"Once a week, two small pieces? I hardly think so. Besides," he said, "they're going to fall out, anyway."

She shook her head, tsking, happy that someone she loved also loved her twin three-year-olds. It would be different around here with the Father gone, and Cynthia, who was always so bright and helpful. . . .

Every last scrap of Dooley's tack had made it to Harley's basement apartment, and Father Tim had helped Dooley clean his room at the rectory, top to bottom. In addition, all the books for Whitecap were packed, sealed, and ready for the shipper to pick up tomorrow.

Before he dragged himself upstairs to take a shower, he'd just lie down and put his head on the arm of the sofa, but only for a moment, of course.

If there was ever a birthday when he had no time or energy to read St. Paul's letters to Timothy, this was it. Ever since seminary, he'd made a point of reading the letters on, or adjacent to, the date of his nativity. Perhaps his yearly pondering of these Scriptures was one way of taking stock.

" 'To Timothy, my dearly beloved son,' " he murmured, quoting at random from the familiar Second Epistle. " 'Grace, mercy, and peace, from God the Father and Christ Jesus our Lord . . . watch thou in all things, endure afflictions, do the work of an evangelist, make full proof of thy ministry.' "

He was sinking into the sofa. " 'The cloke that I left at Troas with Carpus,' " he whispered—this was a favorite part—" 'when thou comest, bring with thee, and the books, but especially the parchments—' "

"Timothy!"

It was his wife, calling from the front hall.

"Can you come here a moment?"

He forced himself off the sofa and trotted along the hall, obedient as any pup.

"You rang?" he asked, rubbing his eyes.

She smiled. "Walk out to the porch with me."

"Why?" he asked, peevish.

"Why not?" she said, taking his hand. It occurred to him that she looked unusually . . . expectant, somehow, on the verge of something.

When they stepped to the porch, he noticed it at once. A slick-looking red convertible was parked at the curb, with the top down. Hardly anybody ever parked in front of their house. . . .

"I wonder who *that* belongs to."

"I'm looking at him," said Cynthia.

His wife was lit up like a Christmas tree.

"What do you mean you're—"

"Happy birthday, dearest!" She was suddenly kissing his face—both cheeks, his nose, his mouth.

"But you can't possibly—"

"It's *yours*! To you from me, for our trip to Whitecap, for zooming around like feckless youths in the rain, in the sunshine, in the *snow*, what the heck!"

"But . . ."

Without meaning to, exactly, he sat down hard on the top step.

She laughed and sat with him. "What do you think?"

He stared at it, aghast, unable to think. "But," he said lamely, "it's red."

"So? Red is good!"

"But I'm a priest!"

"All the better!" she crowed. "Now, darling, don't get stuffy on me."

He saw that he might easily wound her to the very depths.

"But the Buick . . ."

"What about it?"

"It's . . . it's still perfectly *good*."

She raised one eyebrow.

He suddenly had another thought, this one worse than the others. "The new priest rolling into town like a rock star . . . what will people think?"

"I never mind what people think—ever! We didn't sleep together 'til we were married, and yet, imagine how the tongues wagged when we were seen sneaking back and forth through the hedge."

"I never sneaked," he said, indignant.

"Timothy. How quickly you forget."

But surely she hadn't *bought* it. "It's a rental! Right?"

"Darling, remember me? I'm Cynthia, I don't do rentals. It's yours. Here's the key." She shoved it into his hand.

She was tired of fooling around, he could tell. He started to stand up, but sat again, weak-kneed.

"I can't believe it," he said, feeling contrite. "Please forgive me. God knows, I thank you. But I mean, the *expense* . . ." Why couldn't he quit babbling about the negatives? What did these things cost, anyway? It was horrifying to contemplate. . . .

She patted him on the knee. "It's not nice to talk about the cost of a gift. Besides, if you really must know, it's three years old and the radio isn't working."

"It looks brand-new!"

"Yet bought with old money. Royalties from *Violet Goes to the Country* and *Violet Goes to School,* tucked into a money market fund long ago. I've worked very hard, Timothy, and been conservative as a church mouse—I wanted to do this."

He was ashamed to ask what make it was. He'd never been able to identify cars, unlike Tommy Noles, who knew Packards from Oldsmobiles and Fords from Chevrolets. Actually, a Studebaker was the only car he'd ever been able to guess, dead-on.

Maybe a Jaguar. . . .

"It's a Mustang GT," said his wife, looking mischievous.

He put his arm around her and drew her close and nuzzled his face into her hair. "You astound me, you have always astounded me, I need to sit here and just look at it for a minute. Thank you for being patient." He felt wild laughter rising in him, as he'd felt the tears earlier. What kind of roller coaster was he on, anyway?

"I don't deserve it," he said. There. He'd finally gotten down to the bottom line.

She lifted her hand to his cheek. "Deserve? Since when is love about deserving?"

"Right," he said. He felt his heart beginning to hammer at the sight of it sitting there so coolly parked at the curb, as if it owned the house and the people in it.

He realized he'd come within a hair of hurting her by persisting in his fogy ways. No, he'd never have believed he'd be driving a red convertible, not in a million years, but he knew it was absolutely crucial that he begin believing it—at once.

He felt the grin spreading across his face, and didn't think he could stop the laughter that was lurking in him.

"Wait'll Dooley sees this!" he said, as they trotted toward the curb.

CHAPTER THREE

Going, Going, Gone

"Timothy!"

His wife was calling him constantly these days. From the top of the stairs, from the depths of the basement, from the far reaches of the new garage.

It was Timothy here, Timothy there, Timothy everywhere.

"Yes?" he bellowed from the study.

"Do we really need this cast-iron Dutch oven?" she yelled from the hallway, where the items to be packed in the car were being severely thinned.

"How else can I make a pork roast?" he shouted.

"I don't think people at the beach *eat* pork roast!" she shouted back.

He hated shouting.

Cynthia appeared in the study, her hair in a bandanna, wearing shorts and a T-shirt. She might have been a twelfth-grade student from Mitford School. Why was his wife looking increasingly younger as he grew increasingly older? It wasn't fair.

"I think," she said, wiping perspiration from her face, "that beach people eat ocean perch or broiled tuna or . . ." She shrugged. "You know."

He took the heavy pot from her, feeling grumpy. "Leave it," he said, toting it to the kitchen.

"And do you really think," she hooted from the study, "that we need those Wellington boots you garden in?"

He stepped back to the study. "What did you say?"

"Those huge green boots. Those Wellingtons."

"What about them?"

"I mean, there's no mud at the beach!"

He sighed.

"Besides, we can't lash anything on top of the car. . ."—she grinned, bouncing on the balls of her feet like a kid—"because we'll have the top *down.*"

"Axe the boots."

"And the Coleman stove. Why would we need a Coleman *stove*? We won't be camping out, you know."

If he didn't watch her every minute, they would be roaring down the highway with nothing but a change of underwear and a box of watercolors. Besides, he had thought of maybe cooking out one night on the beach, under the stars, with a blanket. . . .

He blushed, just thinking about it.

"We're taking the stove," he said.

He made a quick sweep of the rectory, looking once more in the kitchen drawers, feeling along the top shelves of the study bookcases, peering into the medicine cabinets.

Clean as a whistle.

Their tenant was moving in tomorrow with what she called "light furnishings," a grand piano, and a cat, and he didn't want any of his jumble lying around to welcome her. Ever since he moved in behind Father Bellwether in Alabama, he was careful to clean up any rectory he was vacating.

Father Bellwether had left behind a 1956 Ford on blocks, several leaf bags filled with old shirts and sweaters, a set of mangled golf clubs, three room-size rugs chewed by dogs, an assortment of cooking gear, several doors without knobs, a vast collection of paperback mysteries, and other litter that couldn't be completely identified. Determined not to whine to the vestry who had called him, Father Tim remembered using a shovel and a hired truck to clean the place out while the movers huffed his own things in.

His footsteps echoed along the hallway to the basement door. He opened it and called down the stairs.

"Harley, are you there?"

Lace Turner appeared at the bottom of the steps, her blond hair in French braids.

"Harley's taking a test," she said.

He thought that each time he saw the fifteen-year-old Lace Turner, she had grown more beautiful, more confident. The hard look he'd once seen on her face had softened.

"But you can come down," she said. "He's almost through."

"What's the test on?" he inquired, trotting to meet her in the basement hallway.

"History. It's his favorite subject."

"Hit ain't no such of a thing!" Harley called from the parlor.

Harley was sitting on the sofa with a sheaf of papers in his lap, using a hardcover book as a writing surface. A fan moved slowly left, then right, on a table next to the sofa.

"It was your favorite last week," she said patiently, as they came into the room.

"Rev'rend, she's got me studyin' Lewis 'n' Clark, how they explored th' Missouri River and found half a dadblame nation. . . ."

"Sounds interesting."

"Oh, hit's in'erestin', all right, but this question she's wrote down here is how many falls is in th' Great Falls of th' Missouri. They won't a soul ever ask me that, I don't *need* t' know it, hit won't *pay* t' know it—"

"Harley . . . ," said Lace, looking stern.

"Two falls!" said Harley.

"No. We talked about it yesterday."

"Six!"

Lace shook her head. "Think about it," she advised. "You don't like to think, Harley."

"Didn't I make eighty-nine on my numbers test you give me?" Harley grinned, displaying pink gums perfectly lacking in teeth.

"Yes, and you can make a hundred on this one if you'll just think back to what you read yesterday."

Father Tim quietly hunkered into a chair.

"I don't give a katy how many falls make up th' Great Falls. I quit, by jing." Harley laid his pencil on the arm of the sofa and put his papers to one side. "I'm goin' to pour th' rev'rend a glass of tea. You can mark up m' score on what I done."

Harley marched to the kitchen, looking as determined as his instructor. He turned at the kitchen door. "An' say some of y'r big words for th' rev'rend."

Lace gazed at Father Tim, her amber eyes luminous and intense. "He's learned an awful lot," she said, defending her practice of coming regularly to educate the man who protected her as she was growing up. It had been Harley who often fed Lace, and hid her from a violent, abusive father. To Lace, it was no small matter that Harley had sometimes risked his life for her well-being.

Lace was now living with Hoppy and Olivia Harper, and adoption procedures were under way. Father Tim considered that her privileged life with the Harpers might have turned the girl's affinities in other directions. But, no. Lace visited Harley often, frequently cooked to encourage his finicky appetite, and protected him fiercely. As for her desire that Harley become a learned man, the Education of Harley Welch was entering its third year.

Lace picked up the test papers and examined them. Her eyes glanced quickly over the pages, and she alternately sighed or nodded.

Father Tim gazed at her, profoundly moved. When he had first met Lace Turner, she was living in the dirt under her ramschackle house on the Creek, foraging for food like a dog. Her transformation was a miracle he'd been privileged to witness with his own eyes.

"Ninety," she pronounced, making a mark with the pencil.

"Why, that's terrific!"

"He spelled the Willamette River correctly."

"Good! I hope you'll give him a couple of extra points for that."

Lace smiled one of her rare smiles. He was dazzled, and no help for it.

"Ninety-two, then!" she said, looking pleased.

"So, how many falls?" he asked.

"Five."

"Aha."

"I'm sorry you're leaving," she said.

"Thank you, Lace. Of course, we won't be gone forever, it's an interim situation."

"What's a interim situation?" asked Harley, coming in with two glasses of tea. "This 'uns your'n," he said to Father Tim, "no sugar."

"It means a time between," said Lace.

"Between what?" Harley wondered.

"Between what I've been doing and what I'm going to do later," said Father Tim, laughing.

Lace held up the test paper. "Harley, you made ninety-two on your test."

Harley's eyes widened. "How'd I git two odd points in there?"

"You spelled Willamette right."

"I got it wrote on m' hand. Naw, I'm jis' kiddin', I ain't." He handed her the tea. "Here's your'n."

"Yours," she said. "And thank you."

Harley grinned. "She's like th' *po'*lice, on you at ever' turn." Harley's days in liquor hauling, not to mention car racing, had taught him about police. "Boys, she can go like whiz readin' a book, says words you never heerd of. Did you say one of them big words for th' rev'rend?"

"Omnipresent," said Lace quietly.

"What'n th' nation does that mean?"

"Everywhere at one time."

"That describes my wife's mama near perfect. She had eyes in th' back of 'er head. That woman was a chicken hawk if I ever seen one. Say another'n."

She flushed and lowered her eyes. "No, Harley."

"Look what I done f'r *you.*"

"You didn't do it for me, you did it for you."

Harley nodded, sober. "Jis tell th' rev'rend one more, an' I'll not ask ag'in."

"Mussitation."

"Aha."

Lace hurriedly drank the tea, then collected her books. "It's nice to see you, sir. Harley, eat your supper tonight, and thank you for a good job on your test."

"Thank you f'r teachin' me."

"Well done, Lace!" Father Tim called, as she left by the door to the driveway.

Harley glowed with unashamed pride. "Ain't she somethin'? I've knowed 'er since she was knee-high to a duck. She agg'avates me near t' death, but I think th' world of that young 'un."

Father Tim wished his dictionary weren't packed, as he didn't have a clue as to the meaning of "mussitation."

He sat with Harley next to the fan that turned left, then right.

"Lord, at th' rust they've got down there," sighed Harley, shaking his head. "I don't know but what I'd park your new ride in th' garage and drive th' Buick."

"I don't think so."

In the escalating temperature of an official heat wave, the two men spoke as if in a dream. Harley leaned toward Father Tim, to better catch the stream of air on the left; Father Tim leaned closer to Harley to catch the right stream.

Both had their elbows on their knees, their heads nearly touching, gazing at the floor.

"Think you can keep up with our boy?"

"Rev'rend, don't you worry 'bout a thing. Y'r boy'll be workin', I'll be watchin,' an' th' Lord 'n' Master'll be in charge of th' whole deal."

"I don't know, Harley. . . ."

"Well, if *you* don't, who does?"

"Seems like I can trust Him with everything but a teenager."

"That's what you got t' trust 'im with th' most, if you ask me."

Father Tim felt a trickle of sweat between his shoulder blades.

"Don't let Dooley forget to take the livermush to his granpaw."

"Nossir."

"Every other week is how Russell likes to get it."

Harley nodded. "I'll git them hornets' nestes off th' garage come Friday."

"Good. I thank you."

"I ain't goin' t' rake y'r leaves b'fore winter, if you don't mind, hit'll be good f'r th' grass."

"Fine."

"I'll mulch 'em so they'll rot easy. An' I'll mulch up around y'r plants come October."

"And the roses . . ."

"I'll prune 'em back, jis' like you said."

"I wrote the numbers down by your phone in the kitchen; I gave you the church office and home. Call us any time of the day or night, I don't care how late it is or how early."

"I'll do it. And I'll have Cynthia's little scooter runnin' like a top when you come home f'r the' weddin'. In case she gits wore out ridin' that bicycle, she can drive it back."

"Good. But don't soup it up."

"Ain't nothin' t' soup in a Mazda."

He remembered that Harley had once fiddled around with his Buick so it ran like a scalded dog; he had shot by the local police chief in a blur—twice. Not good.

They sat quiet for a time, Father Tim cupping his chin in his hands.

"And don't let Dooley play loud music down here, or we'll run our tenant off."

Harley sighed. "Lord knows I ain't a miracle worker."

He went out into the night, damp with perspiration, leaving his wife sleeping like a child.

Ten to eleven. No moon. Only a humid darkness that sharply revealed its stars as he looked up.

They weren't used to heat like this in the mountains. Mitford was legendary for its cool summers, which brought flatlanders racing up the slopes every May through October, exulting in the town's leafy shade and gentle breezes.

He walked with Barnabas around the backyard of the yellow house, stopping by the maple and hearing the stream of urine hiss into the grass.

The path through the hedge, he saw in the light from the study windows, had nearly grown over. Harley usually came around to the front door these days, and it had been three years or more since he courted his next-door neighbor.

He smiled, remembering the quote from Chesterton: "We make our friends, we make our enemies, but God makes our next-door neighbor."

Once, the depth of their feeling for one another might easily have been judged by the smooth wear on the path through the rhododendrons. Now the branches on either side of the weed-covered path had nearly grown together; one would have to duck to dash through.

As he stepped under the tulip poplar. he felt a sudden coolness, as if a barrier had been formed around the tree, forbidding the day's heat to collect beneath its limbs.

He thumped onto the sparse grass under the poplar, and Barnabas lay at his feet, panting.

Another party tomorrow night. He was weary of parties, of the endless goodbyes that stretched behind him since last December's retirement party in the parish hall. He remembered feeling his head grow light as a feather, and could not imagine the occasion to be anything but an odd and disturbing dream. Then he found himself gone from Lord's Chapel, the parish that had both succored and tormented him, and made him happier than ever before in his life.

Retiring had been precisely what he wanted to do, and yet, when he did it, it had felt awkward and unreal, as it must feel to walk for the first time with a wooden leg.

He rubbed his dog's ear; it might have been a piece of velvet, or a child's blanket that gave forth consolation, as he stared across the hedge at the rectory's double chimneys rising in silhouette against the light of the street lamp.

It seemed an eternity since he'd lived there, quite another person than the one sitting here in the damp night grass.

For many years in that house, he had made it a practice to do what he'd learned in seminary, and that was spend an hour in study for every minute of his sermon. More than twenty hours he had faithfully spent; then fifteen, and later, starting a couple of years ago, ten. Where had the quiet center of his life gone? It seemed he was racing faster and faster around the tree, turning into butter.

On the other hand, wasn't his life now richer and deeper and more solid than ever before? Yes! Absolutely yes. He would not turn back for anything.

God had, indeed, put Cynthia Coppersmith right next door, and given her to him. But marriage, with all its delight and aggravation, seemed to swell like a dry sponge dipped into water, and occupy the largest, most fervent part of his life. Surely that was why some priests never took a spouse, and remained married to their calling.

Barnabas rolled on his side and smacked his lips, happy for the cool night air under the tree.

He loved Cynthia Kavanagh; she'd become the very life of his heart, and no, he would never turn back from her laughter and tears and winsome ways. But tonight, looking at the chimneys against the glow of the streetlight, he mourned that time of utter freedom, when nobody expected him home or cared whether he arrived, when he could sit with a book in his lap, snoring in the wing chair, a fire turning to embers on the hearth. . . .

He raised his hand to the rectory in a type of salute, and nodded to himself and closed his eyes, as the bells of Lord's Chapel began their last peal of the day.

Bong . . .

"Lord," he said aloud, as if He were there beneath the tree, "Your will be done in our lives."

Bong . . .

"Guard me from self-righteousness, and from any looking to myself in this journey."

Bong . . .

"I believe Whitecap is where You want us, and we know that You have riches for us there."

Bong . . .

"Prepare our hearts for this parish, and theirs to receive us."

Bong . . .

"Thank You for the blessing of my wife, and Dooley; for this place and this time, and yes, Lord, even for this change. . . ."

Bong . . .

Bong . . .

The bells pealed twice before he acknowledged and named the fear in his heart.

"Forgive this fear in me which I haven't confessed to You until now."

Bong . . .

"You tell us that You do not give us the spirit of fear, but of power, and of love, and of a sound mind."

Bong . . .

"Gracious God . . ." He paused.

"I surrender myself to You completely . . . again."

Bong . . .

He took a deep breath and held it, then let it out slowly, and realized he felt the peace, the peace that didn't always come, but came now.

Bong . . .

The tenant was a surprise, somehow. A small woman in her late forties, overweight and mild-mannered, she appeared to try to shrink into herself, in order to occupy less space. He supposed her accent to be French, but wasn't very good at nailing that sort of thing.

They met in the late afternoon in the rectory parlor, now furnished sparingly with her own sofa and two chairs, and a Baldwin grand piano by the window.

The cherry pie he had brought from Sweet Stuff Bakery had been placed on the table in front of the sofa where she sat, her feet scarcely touching the floor. After a day of moving into a strange house in a strange town, he thought she might have been utterly exhausted; to the contrary, she looked as fresh as if she'd risen from a long nap.

". . . very interested in old homes, Father," she was saying.

"Well, you'll certainly be living in one. The rectory was built in 1884, and wasn't dramatically altered until a bishop lived here in the fifties. He closed the fireplace in the kitchen and rebuilt the fireplace in the study—a definite comfort during our long winters. I hope you don't mind long winters."

"Oh, no. We have those in Boston with dismaying frequency."

"Mr. Skinner has shown you around—the attic, the basement?"

"Top to bottom."

"You know you may call him at any time. He'll be looking after everything for us—and for you."

"Thank you, Father, and again, thank you for allowing me to lease for such a short time. It's always good to test the waters, *n'est-ce pas?*"

"Of course."

"Mr. Skinner mentioned that you and Miss Sadie Baxter were dear friends."

"Yes, Miss Sadie meant the world to me. Did you know her?"

"Oh, no. I saw her lovely old home from Main Street and inquired about it. I'm sure she must have left you some very beautiful things."

"I might have taken anything I liked, but I took almost nothing, really. My wife found some needlepoint chair covers she's thrilled with, and so . . ."

He raised his hands, palms up, and smiled. At that moment, a large cat leaped into his lap from out of nowhere, its collar bell jingling.

"Holy smoke!" he exclaimed.

"That's Barbizon," said Hélène Pringle, unperturbed.

He sat frozen as a mullet. Barbizon had taken over his lap entirely, and was licking his white paws for a fare-thee-well. The odor of tinned fish rose in a noxious vapor to his nostrils.

His tenant peered at him. "Barbizon's no bother, I hope."

"Oh, no. Not a bit. Cats don't usually like me."

"Barbizon likes all sorts of people other cats care nothing for."

"I see."

"He was named for my mother's birthplace in France, just south of Paris. I spent my childhood there."

"Well, well."

"Do you speak French, Father?"

"Pathetically."

"I imagine Mr. Skinner told you I'll be giving piano lessons. . . ."

"That's wonderful!" he said. "We need more music in Mitford."

"He's checking to see if I might hang out a sign."

"Aha."

"Only a very small sign, of course."

"Not too small, I hope. We want people to see it!"

" 'Hélène Pringle, Lessons for the Piano, Inquire Within.' " She recited the language of her sign with some wistfulness, he thought.

"Excellent!" He glanced at his watch discreetly, and tried to rise from the chair, thinking the longhaired creature with yellow eyes would pop off to the floor. But no, it clung on with its claws, for which reason Father Tim regained his seat with a strained smile. "I must go. We've a great many things to settle at the last minute, you understand."

Hélène Pringle nodded. "*Parfaitement!* No one could understand better."

"Well, then . . ." He tried to detach the cat from his lap by picking it up, but a single claw was entrenched in his fly. Blast.

"Naughty fellow!" scolded Hélène Pringle, who rose from the sofa and came to him and took the cat, which relaxed its claws at once. He saw, then, the weariness in his tenant's eyes, in her pinched face.

She set the great animal down and it disappeared beneath the Chippendale sofa. "Cats don't like moving, you know."

He sighed agreeably. "Who does?"

"I wish you well on your journey, Father."

"And I wish you well on yours, Miss Pringle. May God bless you, and give you many happy hours here."

"Happy hours . . . ," she said, her voice trailing away.

"Oh, I nearly forgot. The key!" Harley had opened the house for their tenant and the movers.

He placed the key in her hand, and found himself staring at it, lying in her palm. She looked at it, also, and for the briefest moment, something passed between them. He could never have said what, exactly, but he would wonder at the feeling for a long time to come.

He hesitated to put the top down for the haul up the hill to Lucera, thinking it would only agitate Dooley's car lust.

"Put it down, darling!" urged his wife. "That's what it's *for*!"

Oh, well. It *was* a warm June night, and Dooley would just have to grow up and take it like a man. . . .

"Hey, let me drive," Dooley said as they walked to the car he'd been ogling all day. Father Tim thought their charge looked like something out of a magazine in his school blazer, a tie, and tan pants.

"You look great, like something out of a magazine," said Father Tim, rushing around to the driver's side.

"Let me drive," repeated Dooley, staying focused. "It's just up the hill."

Cynthia took her husband's arm and steered him to the passenger side. "Why not let him drive, Timothy? It's just up the hill. But I can't sit in the back, it'll ruin my hair."

Two against one.

What was left of his own hair was flying forty ways from Sunday as they roared up Fernbank's driveway and saw lights blazing from every window in the grand house. He was still combing when they went up the steps and through the open front door.

He blinked. Then he blinked again.

"Wow!" said Cynthia.

"Man!" exclaimed Dooley.

Father Tim remembered flushing Miss Sadie's toilets more than once with rainwater that had leaked from this very ceiling into soup pots and a turkey roaster.

"No way," Dooley muttered, shaking his head in disbelief.

Fernbank's cavernous entry hall had become . . . what? Miraculously warm. Smaller, somehow. Intimate. He fairly shivered with excitement. Was this a dream?

And the music—by jove, it was opera, it was Puccini, he couldn't believe his ears. The last time he'd heard opera was months ago, through the static of his car radio.

"Garlic!" rhapsodized his wife, inhaling deeply.

Along the walls in wooden bins were fresh tomatoes and crusty loaves of bread, bundles of fragrant herbs and great bunches of grapes, yellow globes of cheese and bottles of olive oil. The contents of the bottles gleamed like molten gold in the candlelight.

"Timothy, look! The walls!"

Good grief, there were some of those walls his wife had created in the rectory kitchen a couple of years ago—pockmarked, smoky, primitive—not Miss Sadie's walls at all. Miss Sadie would be in a huff over this, and no two ways about it.

"Father! Cynthia! Dooley! Welcome!"

It was the hospitable Andrew Gregory, coming through the door of the dining room in a pale linen suit.

He felt positively heady with the rush of aromas and sounds, and the sight of Mitford's favorite antiques dealer transformed into a tanned and happy maître d'.

Mule and Fancy dropped by the table where the Kavanaghs and Dooley were seated with the Harpers and Lace Turner.

"How do you say th' name of this place?" Fancy asked in a whisper. "I can't remember for shoot!"

"Lu-*chair*-ah!" crowed Cynthia, glad to be of help.

Fancy stared around the room, disbelieving. "There's people here I never laid eyes on before."

Mule sighed. "This is gonna be a deep-pocket deal," he muttered, following Fancy to their corner table.

Father Tim was fairly smitten with his dinner companions, it all seemed so lively and . . . *fun*, a thing he was always seeking to understand and claim for his own.

Olivia hadn't aged an iota since he married her to the town doctor a few years ago; he remembered dancing at their reception in the ballroom, across the hall from this very table. Her dark hair was pulled into French braids, such as she eagerly wove each day for Lace, and her violet eyes still pierced his heart with appealing candor.

Hoppy grinned at his wife and took her hand. "Where *are* we, anyway?"

"Certainly not in Mitford!" she said, laughing.

"I think we're . . . in a dream," said Lace, so softly that only he and perhaps Dooley could hear.

Enthralled, that was the word. They were all enthralled.

The large dining room, where he'd once eaten cornbread and beans with Miss Sadie and Louella, was crowded with people from Wesley and Holding, with the occasional familiar face thrown in, as it were, for good measure.

There was Hope Winchester waving across the room, and a couple of tables away were the mayor and Ray with at least two of their attractive, deluxe-size daughters, sitting where Miss Sadie's Georgian highboy used to stand, and over in the far corner . . .

His heart pumped wildly, taking his breath away. Edith Mallory. Just as he spotted her, she looked up and gazed directly into his eyes.

He turned away quickly. Any contact at all with his former parishioner was akin to a sting from a scorpion. He had foolishly believed she would somehow drop out of sight, and he'd never be forced to lay eyes on her again. She'd been a thorn in his flesh for years—seeking to manipulate and seduce him, trying to buy the last mayoral race, treating the villagers like pond scum. . . .

Cynthia peered at him. "What is it, dearest? You're white as a sheet."

"Starving," he mumbled, grabbing a chunk of bread.

A couple of years ago, Lace Turner had helped Dooley save Barnabas from bleeding to death when hit by a car. When minutes counted, Dooley and Lace had pitched in to get the job done, and a bond formed between them where only enmity had existed.

But time and distance had strained that bond, and they were now two new and different people.

Father Tim hadn't missed Dooley's fervent appraisal of Lace Turner as she studied her hand-printed menu. He found it more telling, however, that Dooley feigned indifference each time Lace spoke, which wasn't often. Further, he observed, the boy who was known for his appetite picked at his food, laughed nervously, eternally twisted the knot in his tie, and knocked over his water glass.

No doubt about it, Dooley Barlowe was interested in more than cars.

They had feasted on risotto and scallopini, on lamb shank and fresh mussels, on chicken roasted with rosemary from the Fernbank gardens, and on Anna Gregory's freshly made pasta stuffed with ricotta and bathed in a sultry marinara from local greenhouse tomatoes; they had ordered gallons of sparkling water, Coke, and a bottle of Chianti from Lucera, and had all placed their order for Tony's tiramisu.

Hoppy Harper sat back and looked fondly at Lace, who was seated next to him and across from Dooley. "Lace, why don't you tell everyone your good news?"

Lace gazed around the table slowly, half shyly.

Father Tim observed that Dooley pretended to be more interested in drumming his fingers on the table than hearing what Lace had to say.

"I'm going away to school in September."

The fingers stopped drumming.

"Lovely!" said Cynthia. "Where?"

"Virginia. Mrs. Hemingway's." Fresh color stole into the girl's tanned cheeks.

"Oh, man," said Dooley, rolling his eyes. "Gross."

Father Tim bristled. "I beg your pardon?"

"Mrs. Hemingway has geeky girls."

Father Tim could have shaken the boy until his teeth rattled. "Apologize for that at once."

Dooley colored furiously, undecided about whether to stick up for what he had just said, or do as he was told.

He stuck up for what he had just said. "They hardly ever get invited to our school for parties, they're so . . . *smart.*" He said the last word with derision.

"Lace has just told us good news," Father Tim said quietly. "You have just shown us bad behavior. I ask once more that you apologize to Lace."

Dooley tried to raise his eyes to his dinner partner, but could not. "Sorry," he said, meditating on his water glass.

Hoppy slipped his arm around Lace's shoulders. "Dooley's right, actually. The girls at Mrs. Hemingway's are very smart, indeed. Gifted, as well. Lace and several of her classmates will spend next summer in Tuscany, studying classical literature and watercolor—on scholarships. We're very proud of Lace."

Father Tim saw on the girl's face the kind of look he'd seen when he caught her stealing Miss Sadie's ferns—the softness had disappeared, the hardness had returned.

Lace sat straight as a ramrod in the chair, staring over the head of the miserable and hapless wretch opposite her.

Dooley Barlowe had stepped in it, big-time.

While Cynthia trotted off with Dooley to bring the car around, Father Tim went in search of Andrew, seeking the whereabouts of their check.

Andrew Gregory still looked as fresh and unwrinkled as if he'd sauntered through the park, not opened a restaurant and catered to the whims of more than fifty people. He was the only man Father Tim knew who didn't wrinkle linen.

His mind couldn't avoid a momentary flashback to Andrew's earnest courtship of Cynthia. He'd watched their comings and goings from his bedroom window at the rectory, feeling miserable, to say the least. He remembered once thinking of the tall, slender Andrew as a cedar of Lebanon, and of himself, a lowly country parson, as mere scrub pine.

But who had won fair maid?

"I've had quite a visit with your new tenant," Andrew said. "She stayed in Wesley the last few days, waiting for the movers, and came several times to the shop. Very inquisitive about Fernbank, it seems. Wanted to know what was sold out of the house, and so on. Said she had a great interest in old homes."

"Yes, she mentioned that to me."

"She asked me to name the pieces I bought from you, and was eager to learn whether anything was left in the attic. I told her no, it had all been cleaned out and given away. She asked whether relatives had taken anything, and I said I didn't really know."

"Curious."

"I thought so," said Andrew. "And by the way, your money doesn't spend here."

Andrew's wife joined them from the kitchen, looking flushed and happy.

"Put away, put back," said Anna, indicating his wallet. He thought Andrew's Italian bride of two years, who had come from the village of Lucera, bore a breathtaking resemblance to Sophia Loren.

"But . . ."

"It's our gift to you, our farewell present," Andrew insisted.

"Well, then. Thank you. Thank you so much! You've made a great contribution to Mitford, Miss Sadie would be proud to see Fernbank filled with light and laughter. Anna, Andrew—'til we meet again."

"Ciao!" cried Anna, throwing her arms around him and kissing both his cheeks. He loved Italians. "Go with God!"

"Father!" It was Tony, Anna's younger brother and Lucera's chef, running from the kitchen in his white hat and splattered apron. "*Grazie al cielo!* I thought I'd missed you!"

Tony embraced him vigorously, kissed both cheeks, then stood back and gripped his shoulders. Father Tim didn't know when he'd seen a handsomer fellow in Mitford. *"Ciao!"* said Tony, his dark eyes bright with feeling. "God be with you!"

"And also with you, my friend."

"Ciao!" they shouted from the car to Andrew and Anna, who came out to the porch as they drove away from Fernbank, away from the grand old house with the grand new life.

He was driving on the Parkway with the top down, when he looked in the rearview mirror and saw his Buick pulling up behind him.

Who was the driver? It was Dooley, with Barnabas sitting in the seat beside him, looking straight ahead.

Dooley was grinning from ear to ear; he could see him distinctly. Yet, when he looked again, the car was gone, vanished.

He woke up, peering into the darkness.

Two a.m., according to the clock by their bed. He sighed.

"Are you awake?" asked Cynthia.

"I had a dream."

"About what?"

"Dooley. He was driving my Buick."

"Oh. I can't sleep, I can never sleep before a long trip." She sighed, and he reached over and patted her shoulder.

"Maybe I could give Dooley the Buick next year. He could pay something for it, two or three thousand. . . ."

"Umm," she said.

Suddenly he had a brilliant idea. Not everybody could wake in the middle of the night and think so cleverly.

"Tell you what. Why don't I give *you* the Buick, and you let Dooley pay you a few thousand for the Mazda. I think he'd like your car better. It's newer, has more . . . youthful styling."

"Not on your life," she said. "I may be a preacher's wife, but I did *not* take a vow of poverty."

"Cynthia, the Buick drives like a dream."

"Dream on," she said. His wife was stubborn as a mule.

"It never needs any work."

"It is fourteen years old, the paint is faded, and there's rust on the right fender. The upholstery on the driver's side is smithereens, a church fan works better than the air conditioner, and it reeks of mildew."

He sighed. "Other than that, Mrs. Lincoln, how did you like the play?"

She giggled.

He rolled over to her and they assumed their easy spoon position, which someone had called "the staple consolation of the marriage bed." She felt warm and easy in his arms.

"Listen," he said.

"To what?"

"I heard something just then. Music, I think."

They lay very still. The lightest notes from a piano floated through the window.

"A piano," he said.

"Chopin," she murmured.

Moments later, he heard her whiffling snore, found it calming, and fell asleep.

Hammer and tong.

That's how they were going at it in the yellow house.

The plan was to get on the road by eight o'clock, which was when Dooley reported to The Local.

Excited about the idea that had come to him in the dream, Father Tim asked Dooley to help tote the last of the cargo to the curb, where Violet was already in her cage on the rear floor of the Mustang.

The top was down, the day was bright and promising, and Barnabas had been walked around the monument at a trot.

"Ah!" Father Tim inhaled the summer morning air, then turned to Dooley, grinning.

"You're pretty happy," said Dooley.

"I'm happy to tell you that next summer, with only a modest outlay of funds on your part, Cynthia and I would like to make you the proud owner of . . . the Buick."

Dooley looked stunned.

"I ain't drivin' that thing!" he said, reverting to local vernacular and obviously highly insulted.

They were standing on the sidewalk as the Lord's Chapel bells chimed eight.

Puny and the twins were first in line, and he was up to bat.

"Say bye-bye to Granpaw," urged Puny.

"Bye-bye, Ba," said Sissy. She reached out to him, nearly sprawling out of Puny's arms.

He plucked her from her mother and held her, kissing her forehead. "God be with you, Sissy."

Her green eyes brimmed with tears. "Come back, Ba."

He set her down on chubby legs, wondering how he could go through with this. . . .

He hoisted the plump, sober Sassy, who was chewing a piece of toast, and kissed the damp tousle of red hair. "God's blessings, Sassy." Barnabas, who was sitting patiently on the sidewalk, licked Sissy's face.

Puny was openly bawling. Blast. He took it like a man and gave her a hug, feeling her great steadfastness, smelling the starch in her blouse, loving her goodness to him over the years. "You're always in our prayers," he told her, hoarse with feeling.

Puny wiped her nose with the hem of her apron. "We'll miss you."

"We'll be back before you know it."

Puny and the children fled into the yellow house, as Cynthia stood on tiptoe and gave Dooley a hug. "Take care of yourself, you big lug."

"I will."

"And write. Or call. A lot!"

"I will."

Father Tim clasped the boy to him, then stood back and gazed at him intently. "I'm counting on you to help Harley hold things together around here."

"Yes, sir. I will."

"We love you."

"I love you back." Dooley said it fair and square, looking them in the eye. Then he turned and ran to his red bicycle, leaped on it, and pedaled toward Main Street. Before he reached the corner, he stopped, looked back, and waved. " 'Bye, Cynthia, 'bye, Dad!"

They waved as Dooley disappeared around the rhododendron bush.

Father Tim jingled the keys in his hand. "Harley, reckon you can sell the Buick for me?"

Harley looked skeptical, scratched his head, and gazed at the sidewalk.

"Would you . . . like to drive it while I'm gone?"

"Rev'rend, I 'preciate th' offer, but I'll stick to m' truck."

"Aha." Clearly, he had a vehicle he couldn't even give away, much less sell.

"Well, Harley . . ." He put his arm around the shoulders of the small, frail man who was now holding down the fort.

"Rev'rend, Cynthia . . . th' Lord go with you." Harley's chin trembled, and he wiped his eyes with his sleeve.

" 'Bye, Harley," said Cynthia. "We love you."

Father Tim opened the passenger door and put the seat forward. "Come on, fellow, get in."

Barnabas leaped onto the leather seat, sniffed Violet's cage, and lay down, looking doleful.

"Don't even think about crying," he told his wife as they climbed in the car.

"The wind in our hair . . . ," she said, laughing through the tears.

He started the engine. "The cry of gulls wheeling above us . . ."

"The smell of salt air!"

He turned around in a driveway at the end of Wisteria Lane. Man alive, he liked the way this thing handled, and the seat . . . the seat felt like an easy chair.

They waved to Harley, who was rooted to the spot and waving back.

After hooking a right on Main Street, he drove slowly, as if they were a parade car. J. C. Hogan was just trotting into the Grill.

Father Tim hammered down on the horn and J.C. looked up, dumbstruck, as they waved.

Then he stepped on the gas and whipped around the monument, consciously avoiding a glance in the rearview mirror.

CHAPTER FOUR

The Smell of Salt Air

He was loving this.

"You're loving this!" crowed his wife.

He couldn't remember ever having such a sense of perfect freedom; he felt light as air, quick as mercury, transparent as glass.

And hot as blazes.

He looked into the rearview mirror. Barnabas, currently sitting up with his head riveted into the scorching wind, was attracting the attention of all westbound traffic.

"You must stop and get a hat!" his wife declared over the roar of an eighteen-wheeler. "Your head is turning pink!"

"Lunch and a hat, coming up," he said, reluctant to delay their journey, even if it was into the unknown.

They were barreling toward Williamston, through open tobacco country.

"Flat," said Cynthia, peering at the landscape.

"Hard to have an ocean where it isn't flat."

"Hot," she said, reduced to telegraphic speech.

"Don't say we weren't warned. Want to put the top up?"

"Not yet, I'm trying to get the look of an island native." His wife was wearing shorts and a tank top, sunglasses and a Mitford Reds ball cap. All exposed areas were slathered with oil, and she was frying.

"I think we need to get Barnabas under cover before long. We'll put it up at Williamston."

Whoosh. A tractor-trailer nearly sucked them out of the car. He reached up and clamped his new hat to his head.

"Did Miss Pringle say why she left Boston to live in Mitford?"

"No. Didn't say."

"And you didn't ask?"

"Never thought to."

"Why on earth would she pick Mitford? And for only six months! Can you imagine hauling a piano from Boston for only six months? Does she have friends or relatives in Mitford?"

"I don't think so, but I'm not sure."

"Darling, how can you ever *know* things about people if you don't ask?"

As a priest, he usually managed to find out more than he wanted to know, though hardly ever through asking.

She sat thinking, with Violet asleep at her feet on the floorboard.

"Remember that chicken salad we had for lunch?" she inquired.

"Only vaguely."

"It's becoming a distant memory to me, too. I'm starved. Actually, during the entire lunch, I was dreaming of something finer."

"Oh?"

"Esther's cake."

"Aha."

"In the cooler. . . ."

"Umm."

"I've been thinking how moist it is, how cold and sweet, how velveteen its texture. . . ."

"That's Esther's cake, all right."

"And those discreet little morsels of bittersweet rind that burst in your mouth like . . . like sunshine!"

"You're a regular Cowper of cake."

"Don't you think we should have some?" she asked.

"Now you're talking."

"Did you bring your pocketknife?"

"Always," he said, producing it from his pocket.

She got on her knees in her seat and foraged around on the floorboard in back, cranking off the cooler top and fetching out the foil-wrapped mound.

"Oh, lovely. Nice and cold on my legs. Well, now. How shall we do this?" she asked, peeling back layers of foil. "This is the cake that nearly sent you to heaven in your prime. You probably shouldn't have a whole slice."

"If you recall," he said, "it was *two* slices that nearly sent me packing. I'll have one slice, and would appreciate not being able to see through it."

She carefully carved a small piece and put it on a napkin from the glove compartment. "Don't keel over on me," she said, meaning it.

Driving to the beach in a red convertible, eating Esther's cake—how many men wouldn't crave to be in his shoes? The sweetness and delicacy of the vanishing morsel in his hands were literally intoxicating. *Priest Found Drunk on Layer Cake . . .*

"Darling, you talked in your sleep last night."

"Uh-oh."

"You said 'slick' several times; you were very restless."

"Slick?"

"Yes, and once I think you said 'Tommy.' "

"Aha!" The dream flooded back to him instantly. His boyhood friend, Tommy Noles, and that miserable experience that earned him his nickname, a nickname he'd never mentioned to his wife. . . .

"Who is Tommy?" she queried.

"Tommy Noles, my old friend from Holly Springs."

"The one who always knew the make and model of cars."

"Right."

"What were you dreaming?"

As usual, his inquisitive wife wanted to know everything. Should he tell her?

"Well, let's see. I was dreaming about . . . well, about the time when . . ."

"When what?"

Weren't couples supposed to tell each other their fondest wishes, their deepest secrets, their blackest fears? He'd never thought much of that scheme, but so far, it had worked. In fact, he'd found that for every one of his deepest secrets, Cynthia Kavanagh would pour forth two or three of her own; it was like winning at slots.

". . . when I got my nickname."

"Are you blushing or is that the sun?"

"The sun," he said.

"What about when you got your nickname? I never knew you had one."

Tommy Noles had lived right up the road, next to his attorney father's gentleman's farm. Mr. Noles was a history teacher and a packrat. He hauled every imaginable oddity to his seven acres, and parked it around the property as if it were outdoor sculpture. A rusting haymow, an antique tractor, a gas tank from a service station, a prairie schooner, a large advertising sign for tobacco . . .

Mr. Noles mowed around these objects regularly and with great respect, but neglected to trim the grass that grew directly against them, so that each was sheathed in a colorful nest of sedge and wildflowers, which, as a boy, the young Tim had found enhancing.

His father found none of it enhancing, his father who idolized perfection above all else, and no son of his would be allowed to play with Tommy Noles.

But he had, in fact, played with Tommy Noles, wading in the creek, building a fort in the woods, constructing a tree house, fishing for crappie, searching for arrowheads in the fields.

Tommy Noles had wanted to be a fighter pilot in a terrible war, and he, Timothy Kavanagh, wanted to be a boxer or an animal trainer or, oddly enough, a bookbinder, for hadn't he been outrageously smitten with the smell and the look of his grandfather's books?

He remembered training Tommy's dog, Jeff, to catch sticks in midair, and to roll over and play dead. It had been deeply satisfying to finagle another living creature into doing anything at all, and he longed for a dog of his own, but his father wouldn't allow it. Dogs had fleas, dogs scratched, dogs defecated.

He grew uneasy thinking about how it had happened.

Tommy Noles, urged by the others and unbeknownst to him, had put dog poop just inside the double doors of the schoolhouse, two piles of it.

Bust in through those doors, runnin', Tommy said to him, *and we'll give you a nickel.*

Why? he asked. The teachers were in a meeting in the gym, and he smelled trouble brewing.

Just because, just for nothin', just run up th' steps, bust through th' doors, and run down th' hall all th' way to th' water fountain, and we'll give you a In'ian head nickel.

He still didn't know why he did it, he didn't remember wanting the money especially, perhaps he did it because he was the scrawny one, the geek, the one who loved to read and write and think and ponder words and meanings.

Without caring, he just did it; he burst through the doors running, and hit the piles and skidded down the hall as if he'd connected with a patch of crankcase oil. Just outside Miss McNolty's classroom, he lost his balance and crashed to the floor.

He heard the boys screaming with laughter at the front door as he got up, stinking, and tried to scrape the slimy stuff off his shoes. It was slick as grease. . . .

He walked toward them, his heart thundering. He had never picked a fight or been in one; he would have run first, not looking back.

But this was different. His friend had betrayed him.

They watched him coming toward them and backed down the steps.

Hey, Slick! somebody yelled. Three boys who were laughing and holding their noses suddenly turned and ran to the oak tree, where they stopped and peered from behind it. Lee Adderholt and Tommy Noles stood fast near the bottom of the steps, looking awed, mesmerized.

What had they seen on his face? He would never know.

I . . . I'm sorry, Tim, Tommy said.

He felt something building in himself, something . . . towering. He seemed to be suddenly six feet tall, and growing.

I really am! wailed Tommy.

He never remembered what happened, exactly, he just knew that he plowed into Tommy Noles without fear, without trembling, and beat the living crap out of him.

Then he was sitting in the principal's office—thank God it was Mr. Lewis, who was too tenderhearted to whip anybody. Mr. Lewis had looked at him for what seemed a long time, with what appeared to be kindness in his face, but the young Kavanagh couldn't be sure.

He knew, sitting there, that he had liked beating the tar out of

Tommy Noles. But most of all, he had liked making him cry in front of the people who had hooted and laughed, holding their noses.

Your father will never hear this from me, Mr. Lewis said. *But if anyone tells him and he asks, I will, of course, be required to . . .*

For the first time in his life, he had been glad, thrilled, that everyone he knew, his classmates and friends, were terrified of his father, and wouldn't dare speak to him, much less reveal the dark transgression of his son brawling in a fistfight.

What happened, Timothy? asked his mother.

He dropped his head. He had never lied to his mother.

I beat up Tommy Noles.

She studied him. *I'm sure he asked for it,* she said, simply.

Yes, ma'am.

But don't ever do this again.

No, ma'am.

He hadn't ever done it again; he hadn't needed to. It had been the fight of his life, the Grand Inquisition. In his rage, he had taken on the very world with his two hands, and somehow, oddly, won.

The scrawny kid with the scrawny arms and the penchant for reading large books and making straight A's had been suffused with a new aura. They gave him a wide berth when they called him Slick, for they had seen his rage, and witnessed his consuming power, and hadn't understood it and never would. He was Timothy Kavanagh, not to be messed with.

Period.

He grinned, pulling around an RV from Texas. After that incident, Tommy Noles had become the best friend he had in the world, even if he had failed to hand over the nickel. Sometime, when he had nothing else to do, he'd calculate what Tommy would owe him today, given fifty-six years of accumulated interest on a nickel.

"I'm growing older," said his eager wife, "just waiting to hear your nickname."

"Slick," he said, looking straight ahead.

He wasn't surprised that she nearly doubled over with laughter. "Slick! *Slick?*" Clearly, that was the funniest thing she'd ever heard in her life.

"Slick! That's *too* wonderful! I can't *believe* it!"

Ha, ha, ha, on and on. He would nip this in the bud. "So what was *your* nickname, Kavanagh?"

She stopped laughing.

Bingo, he thought.

"Must you know?"

"Cynthia, Cynthia . . . need you ask?"

"You won't laugh?"

"Laugh? I'll kill myself laughing. So tell me."

She sighed deeply and tucked a strand of blond hair under the ball cap. "Tubs."

"Tubs?" Marriage was a wonderful thing. It produced all sorts of ways to get even with somebody without necessarily going to jail. But seeing the look on her face, he couldn't laugh.

"Tubby to begin, then shortened to Tubs. Fatter than fat, that was me."

He couldn't imagine it.

"You couldn't even imagine," she said. "When I was ten years old . . . do you remember those photographers who traveled around with a pony?"

He remembered.

"One took my picture and I waited for weeks for it to come in the mail. When we opened the envelope, I couldn't believe my eyes, nor could anyone else. They all said I was . . . they said I was bigger than the pony."

"No."

"Oh, yes, they raved about it 'til kingdom come, Tubs this and Tubs that. My mother and father loved having their picture taken, so they'd dashed in the house and come out looking like Ginger Rogers and Fred Astaire. I, on the other hand, had been popped onto that sulking pony in a hideous dress, looking precisely like W. C. Fields."

She peered at him. "If you ever mention that hideous name to a soul, I'll murder you."

"If you ever mention mine, same back."

"Deal," she said, shaking his hand.

"Deal," he said, seeing a sign that said *Williamston, 10 miles.*

He was looking at his watch when a raindrop hit the crystal face.

Two-thirty, they should be there around six-thirty or seven o'clock, with plenty of daylight to unload the car and check out their new home.

The suddenness of the downpour was shocking. Without warning, a sheet of wind-driven rain was upon them, thundering out of darkened skies. He veered off the road and careened to a stop, the engine running. Dear God, he knew how to put the top *down* on this thing, but Dooley had been the one who put it up. He fumbled with the button on the console, but nothing happened.

"Timothy!" His wife was drenched, sopping.

"What do we do?" he shouted.

"I don't know!" The wind carried her voice away.

He lunged to the right and felt in the glove compartment for the owner's manual, as Barnabas, quaking with fear, leaped into Cynthia's lap, which was already occupied by Violet.

"Back! Go back!" She was almost wholly concealed by his mass of streaming fur. Barnabas went back.

The force of the rain was unbelievable. It thudded against their skin and heads like so many small mallets. He shoved the manual under the dashboard on Cynthia's side, his glasses running with rain. Index, page 391, not under "Top," not under . . . there it was. "Convertible," page 213. He managed to see the words *Engage the parking brake* before the book absorbed water like a sponge and the instructions ran together in a blur.

He pulled the brake, then pressed the button repeatedly, to no avail. *Dear God, help. . . .*

"The boot!" Cynthia cried.

He leaped out, dangerously close to the highway on which cars were still racing, and fumbled to remove the side edges of the boot clip from under the side belt moldings. It took an eternity, and they were drowning.

Back in the car, he pressed the button, and the top began rising. They were taking on water like a bottomless canoe.

The top rose midway and, like a sail on a boat, was instantly filled with wind and driving rain. The top appeared to freeze in midair.

"We'll have to do it manually!" he shouted above the roar. "Get out!"

Help us, Lord, he prayed, as they hauled the thing over, straining against the terrible force of the wind, then brought it down and opened the doors and sloshed into the brimming seats. They turned the levers and secured the top, and sat back, panting, daunted now by the deafening thunder on the roof.

"The towels!" she shouted. "In the back!"

He strained around and reached behind her seat and found the wrapped bundle of a dozen terry towels, which had been cunningly advertised as "thirsty." They were sodden.

Violet howled in Cynthia's lap.

"If we wring them out, we can mop our seats!"

They wrung the water onto the floorboard at their feet, afraid to open the windows, and swabbed the leather seats. It sounded as if the pounding rain would tear through the canvas and swamp them utterly.

Then the lightning began, cracking over their heads.

Barnabas returned to the front in a single leap, and landed in Father Tim's lap, trembling.

The windows were fogged completely, his glasses were useless. He took them off and put them in his shirt pocket. As he held on to his dog, all he could see from their red submarine were the stabbing streaks of lightning.

The rain that began so violently at two-thirty stopped at three o'clock, then returned around three-thirty to pummel the car with renewed energy, as lightning cracked around them with a vengeance.

Sitting on the shoulder since the last downpour began, they briefly considered trying to get back on the highway and drive to a service station, a bridge, anything, but visibility was zero.

Pouring sweat in the tropical humidity of the car, they found the air-conditioning was no relief. Its extreme efficiency made them feel frozen as cods in their wet clothing.

If only they were driving the Buick, he thought. The feeble air-conditioning his wife had so freely lambasted would be exactly right for their circumstances. In fact, his Buick would be the perfect security against a storm that threatened to rip a frivolous rag from over their heads and fling it into some outlying tobacco field.

The temperature in the car was easily ninety degrees. He remembered paying ten pounds for an hour's worth of this very misery in an English hotel sauna, without, of course, the disagreeable odor of steaming dog and cat fur.

"When life gives you lemons . . . ," he muttered darkly.

". . . make lemonade," said his wife, stroking her drenched cat.

"Four o'clock," he said, pulling onto the highway. "We've lost nearly two hours. That means we'll get into Whitecap around dark."

"Ah, well, dearest, not to worry. This can't go on forever."

He hoped such weather would at least put a crimp in the ridiculous notion of wearing grass skirts tomorrow night.

The aftermath of the storm was not a pretty sight. Apparently, they'd missed the worst of it.

Here and there, billboards were blown down, a metal sign lying in the middle of the highway advertised night crawlers and boiled peanuts, and most crops stood partially immersed.

"Our baptism into a new life," he said, looking at the dazzling light breaking over the fields.

At a little after seven o'clock, the rain returned and the wind with it. No lightning this time, but a heavy, insistent pounding over their heads that clearly meant business.

He stopped and did a glucometer check to make sure he wasn't in a nonketotic hyperglycemic coma, thanks to Esther's cake, and was fairly pleased with the reading.

"What do you think?" he asked, parked by the pump at an Amoco station. "Should we look for supper or keep moving?" When he was tired, he still referred to the evening meal as "supper," as he had in childhood.

"It's a wasteland out there. Where would we find supper unless we catch it off a bank?"

"Now, now, Kavanagh. You were thinking wild asparagus with spring lamb, while I was thinking hot dogs all the way."

"I don't know, darling, I feel we should get there and settle in. After all, we have to make the bed when we arrive, and here we are, hours away, and I'm already dying to be *in* one!"

"No supper, then?"

"Maybe a pack of Nabs or some peanuts while we're here. I mean, look what you've got to drive through for who knows how long."

The Mustang shuddered in a violent crosswind.

"You're right," he said, getting out of the car.

He trudged into the neon light of the service station, feeling like a garden slug in his still-damp clothes.

"This is endless," she said as they crept through the several blinkers of a business district that they presumed to be Roper—or was it Scuppernong? The blinkers danced wildly in the wind, on electric wires strung above the street.

It seemed the wind and rain would hit them for twenty or thirty minutes, slack off or let up altogether, then hit them again with another wallop.

Violet snored in Cynthia's lap, Barnabas snored on the backseat.

Father Tim hunkered over the wheel, staring down the oncoming lights. "Marry a preacher, Kavanagh, and life ceases to be boring."

"I'd give an arm and a leg for a boring life," she said grimly, then suddenly laughed. "But only for five minutes!"

There was a long silence as he navigated through the downpour.

"Dearest, what exactly did you *say* to God in your discussions about what to do in retirement?"

"I said I was willing to go anywhere He sent me."

"Do you recall if He said anything back?"

"He said, 'That's what I like to hear.' Not in an audible voice, of course. He put it on my heart."

"Aha," she said, quoting her husband.

"Look," he said, "there's a sign for Columbia. Do we go on to Columbia, or make a turn somewhere?"

"On to Columbia," she said, squinting at the map.

His wife had never professed to be much of a navigator; he hoped they didn't end up in Morehead City.

When they reached the bridge to Whitecap, the wind and rain had stopped; there was an innocent peace in the air.

A sign stood at the entrance to the bridge, which had been closed off with a heavy chain and a soldierly row of orange cones.

BRIDGE OUT
FERRY 2 Blocks
& Left **$10**
No Ferry
After 10 P.M.

"Good heavens," said his wife, "isn't it after ten o'clock?"

"Five 'til," he said, backing up. He made the turn and hammered down on the accelerator.

"That's *one* block . . . ," she said.

Going this fast on wet pavement didn't exactly demonstrate the wisdom of the ages. "This is two," he counted.

"Now turn left here. I'm praying they'll be open."

He turned left. Nothing but yawning darkness. Then, a dim light a few yards ahead, swinging.

They inched along, not knowing what lay in their path. A sign propped against a sawhorse revealed itself in the glare of the headlights.

Ferry to Whitecap
Have Your $ Ready

A lantern bobbed from the corner of what appeared to be a small building perched at the edge of the water.

He'd read somewhere about blowing your horn for a ferry, and gave it a long blast.

"Lord, is this a joke?" his wife inquired aloud of her Maker.

A light went on in the building and a man came out, wearing a cap, an undershirt, and buttoning his pants.

Father Tim eased the window down a few inches.

"Done closed."

"Two minutes," said Father Tim, pointing to his watch. "Two whole minutes before ten. You've got to take us across." He nearly said, *I'm clergy,* but stopped himself.

"You live across?"

"We're moving to Whitecap."

"Don't know as you'd want to go across tonight," said the man, still buttoning. " 'Lectricity's off. Black as a witch's liver."

Father Tim turned to Cynthia. "What do you think?"

"Where would we stay over here?"

"Have t' turn back fourteen miles."

Cynthia looked at her husband. "We're going across!"

"Twenty dollars," said the man, unsmiling.

"Done," said Whitecap's new priest.

Leaving the tropical confines of the car and clinging to the rail of the ferry, they looked across the black water, and up to clouds racing over the face of the moon. They were leaving the vast continent behind, and going to what looked like mere flotsam on the breast of the sea.

The ferry rocked and labored along its passage, belching oily fumes. Yet, quite apart from the noxious smell, Cynthia detected something finer, "There it is, Timothy! The smell of salt air!"

"Gulls wheeling above us," he muttered lamely, noting that a few gulls followed the ferry, even in the dead of night.

She leaned against his shoulder, and he put his arm around her and took off her cap and nuzzled her hair. She was his rock in an ocean of change, no pun intended.

"Look at the stars coming out, my dearest. The sky is as fresh and new as the fourth day of Creation. It's going to be wonderful, Timothy, our new life. We're going to feel freer, somehow, I promise."

That was a very nice speech, he noted, as only his wife could make. "Absolutely!" he said, trying to mean it.

Their car had been unchained from its moorings, and the ramp to Whitecap cranked down. The ferry pilot stood by the ramp, a cigarette in his mouth, holding the gas lantern and signaling them off.

"Would you look at our map?" Father Tim leaned out the window. "We're trying to get . . . here." He pointed to the location of Dove Cottage, marked by a red arrow. "Since we're not approaching from the bridge . . ."

The lantern was lifted to light the hand-drawn map. "No problem," said the pilot, leaving the cigarette in place. "I've been around in there a few times. Go off th' ramp, take a left, drive about a mile and a half, turn right on Tern Avenue, go straight for about a mile, then take a left on Hastings. Looks like your place is on th' corner . . . right there."

"Left off the ramp, a mile and a half . . ." Father Tim repeated the litany. "Any idea when the power might be restored?"

"By mornin', most likely. Worst out was three days, back in '89. What line of business you in?"

"New priest at St. John's in the Grove."

The pilot took a heavy drag on his cigarette and pitched it over the rail. Then he reached in his pants pocket, withdrew a ten-dollar bill, and handed it through the window.

"Oh, but—"

"Godspeed," said the ferry pilot, walking away.

A waxing moon drifted above them as they drove along the narrow road.

"They all look alike," Cynthia said, peering at the darkened houses. "White, with picket fences. Some on stilts. Goodness, do you think all these people are really sleeping?"

"I saw something that looked like candles in one window."

"Did we bring candles?"

"What do you think?"

"I think we brought candles! I'm thrilled to be married to such a predictable stick-in-the-mud. I hope you brought extra blades for my razor."

"If I didn't, which I did, you could find them at a store. Whitecap isn't the Australian Outback."

"You know one reason I love you?" she asked.

"I haven't the foggiest."

"Because," she said, "you're steady. So very steady."

A former bishop had once said something like that, calling him a "plow horse." The bishop made it clear, however, that it was the race-horse that clambered to the top of the church ladder and made a fine stall for himself.

Barnabas thrust his head out the window, sniffing. New smells were everywhere, there was nothing known or expected about the smells in these parts.

"Hastings Avenue should be coming up," he said. "There! Do you hear it?"

"The ocean! Yes! Oh, stop—just for a moment."

He slowed to a stop, and realized the great roar was out there somewhere, that just over the high dunes was a beach, and, lying beyond, a vast rink of platinum shimmering under the moon.

" 'Listen!' " he whispered, quoting Wordsworth. " 'The Mighty Being is awake, and doth with His eternal motion make, a sound like thunder, everlastingly.' "

"Lovely!" she breathed.

They moved on slowly, as if already obeying some island impulse, some new metabolism. With only the moon, stars, and headlights to illumine their way in the endless darkness, they might have been the last creatures on earth.

"Let's put the top down!" crowed Cynthia.

"Fat chance," he said, turning off Tern.

He walked back to the car with the flashlight.

"I don't see the half-hidden street sign Marion Fieldwalker talked about. . . ."

"I can't understand it," she said, studying the map under the map light. "We turned right on Tern, we went left on Hastings to the corner. This must be it."

"The overgrown hedges are definitely there."

"Maybe the sign blew away in the storm. Should we . . . retrace our steps and try again, or do you think . . . ?"

It had all become a blasted nuisance as far as he was concerned. And he would never say so to his wife, but it was spooky out here, stumbling around on some godforsaken jut of land in the pitch-dark, miles from home and reeling from what had become a fifteen-hour trip with nothing but a pack of blasted peanuts to . . .

"We did exactly as the map said. I don't think trying to do it all over again would help us. Why don't we investigate?"

He helped her out of the car and shone the flashlight onto the porch. It was an older beach cottage, with a line of rocking chairs turned upside down to keep the wind from blowing them into the yard. A derelict shutter leaned against the shingled wall.

"Gosh," she said, otherwise speechless.

"I don't see a rosebush climbing up anything," He'd been looking forward to that rosebush.

"Maybe the storm . . . ," she suggested.

". . . blew it down," he said.

They went up the creaking steps to the door.

"Look, Timothy, up there."

A sign hung lopsided above the door, dangling from a single nail.

OVE

OTTAGE

"Oh, my," she said quietly.

Surely this wasn't . . . surely not, he thought.

"They said it would be unlocked," whispered his wife. "Should we . . . try the door?"

The door swung open easily. He was afraid to look.

"Aha."

The furnishings sat oddly jumbled in the large, paneled room. A slipcovered sofa faced away from two club chairs, card tables blocked the entrance to what appeared to be a dining room, a faded Persian carpet covered one side of the floor, but was rolled up on the other.

They went in carefully, as if walking on eggs.

Cynthia hugged herself and stared around in disbelief. "How could this *possibly* . . . ?"

He passed the light across one of the tables and saw a half-assembled jigsaw image of the Grand Canyon.

"Look at that lovely old fireplace," she said. "Marion never mentioned a fireplace. . . ."

"Mildew," he said. "Do you smell it?"

"Yes, but how odd. Marion said they'd worked like slaves to clean everything up. Timothy, this can't be Dove Cottage."

"It's certainly where her map led us, and the sign above the door said . . ." He sighed, dumbfounded.

"Let's try a lamp. Maybe the power's back on." It wasn't.

Barnabas sniffed the rugs and the sofa, with special interest in an unseen trail that led to the hallway. They followed him, numb with disappointment and fatigue.

In the kitchen, the refrigerator door stood ajar, as did several cabinet doors.

"Ugh!" she said. "I can't believe they'd do this to us. Surely they didn't think we were coming next week. Remember we originally told them it would be next week. Maybe somehow they got confused and

the cleaning hasn't been done, yet. . . ." Her voice trailed off.

She was trying, but he wasn't buying. He wouldn't live in this dump if they sent the cleaning crew from the Ritz-Carlton in Paris, France. Just wait 'til he got hold of the senior warden. He'd had a round or two with senior wardens in his time; he was no babe in the woods when it came to what's what with senior wardens. . . .

"The phone, there must be a phone around here. We can call the Fieldwalkers, shine the light around."

They found a wall phone on the other side of the cabinets, but the line was dead.

"The bedrooms," she said, desperate.

At the end of the hallway, which was covered by a Persian runner, they found a cavernous bedroom, and surveyed it with the flashlight. Closet doors standing agape . . . windows open . . . curtains blowing . . . the bed made, but sopping wet.

"This can't be right, they wouldn't *do* this to us." He could tell his wife was teetering on the edge of hysteria. "Wait 'til I get my hands on that fine bishop of yours who would send you out to some . . . uninhabited wasteland, after the years of faithful service you've given him.

"That . . . that vainglorious *dog*!"

"Nothing personal," he told Barnabas, who was sniffing the closets.

Because they hadn't known what else to do at nearly midnight on a strange, dark island with no lights and no phone, they made the double bed in the guest room and got in it, Barnabas on the floor on one side and Violet in her open crate on the other, where his inconsolable wife sighed and fumed herself to sleep as he lay staring at the pale circle cast by the flashlight onto the ceiling, muttering words and thinking thoughts he never dreamed he would say or think, and feeling distinctly waterlogged even in a perfectly dry pair of pajamas from his bureau in Mitford, thanks be to God for small favors.

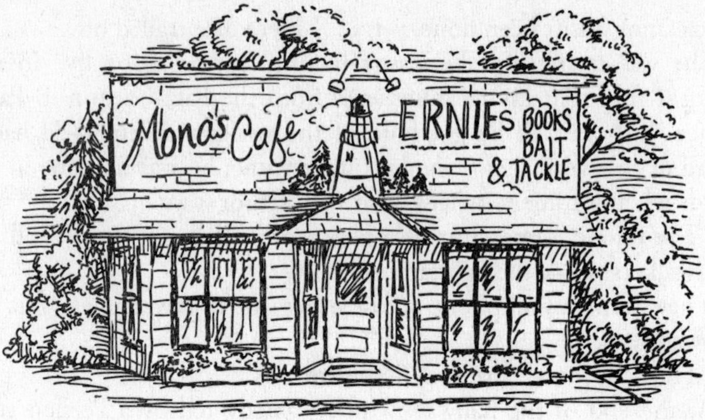

CHAPTER FIVE

A Patch of Blue

He sat up in bed, dazed.

Where in heaven's name . . . ?

Barnabas barked wildly, and someone was knocking on a door. As the room came into focus, he remembered the predicament they were in, and counted it odd that one should wake to, rather than from, a nightmare.

He glanced at his watch—seven o'clock—and bolted into the hallway without robe or slippers. He padded through the dark, paneled living room and opened the door, feeling anger rise in him again.

"Father? Father Kavanagh?"

"Yes!" he snapped, buttoning his pajama top.

"Sam Fieldwalker, sir, your senior warden." The tall, gentle-looking man appeared deeply puzzled.

"Sam . . ." He shook hands as Barnabas sniffed the stranger's shoes.

"We saw your car out front, and . . . well, you see, we waited for you and Mrs. Kavanagh 'til eleven o'clock last night—"

"Waited? Where?"

"In your cottage. Over there." He pointed off the porch.

"You mean . . . this isn't our cottage?"

"Well, no. I'm terribly sorry, I don't know how . . . it must have been the storm and no lights to see by . . ."

"The wrong cottage!" shouted his wife, peering around the hall door in her nightgown. "Thank heaven!"

Sam let Barnabas sniff his hand. "There you are, old fellow, smelling our little Bitsy. My gracious, Father, you all have a dog and a half there!"

"But that sign . . . ," said Cynthia, "that sign above the door . . ."

Sam glanced up, adjusting his glasses. "Oh, my goodness. Of course. Well, you see, this is one of the old *Love* Cottages. . . ."

Cynthia looked fierce. "It certainly doesn't live up to its name!"

"It's owned by the Redmon Love family, who started coming here in the forties. Gracious sakes, Father, Mrs. Kavanagh, I can't begin to tell you how *sorry* . . ."

Father Tim thought Sam Fieldwalker might burst into tears.

"Oh, no, please," he said. "I don't know how we could have thought for a moment . . . well, you see, it was dark as pitch, and we couldn't find the street sign in the hedge, the one Marion told us to look for. . . ."

"Ah, now I'm getting a clear picture!" Sam brightened considerably. "You turned into Love's old driveway, which is wide enough to look like a street—property wasn't so dear in the forties—and, of course, there's a shabby hedge bordering their property, as well. Oh, my, I'm sure Marion never thought of that."

"No harm done! We're glad the mystery is solved. But do the Loves always leave their house unlocked?"

"Hardly anyone on Whitecap locks their doors. And, of course, the Love children and their kids come and go during the summer, though not so much anymore."

"Aha." The sunlight was dazzling, his glasses were by the bed, and he was squinting like a monk at vespers.

"Let me help you move your things, Father. Marion's waiting at Dove Cottage to show you around and cook your breakfast. She's baking biscuits. . . ."

He felt covered with shame. How could he have mistrusted this kind person, believing even for a moment that this was the right cottage? *Lord, forgive me.*

". . . and," Sam continued, looking earnest, "she's found some nice, fresh perch, if . . . if that's all right."

At that moment, Father Tim heard his stomach rumble, and, at the thought of Marion Fieldwalker's fresh perch and biscuits, felt close to tears himself.

Marion met them on the porch of Dove Cottage, a tall, large-boned woman in an apron, with a pleasant face and snow-white hair like her husband.

"In case you'd taken the ferry," said Marion, "we waited 'til eleven. Then, when you didn't come, we thought the storm had held you up and you'd stayed somewhere for the night."

"When we found the bridge was out, we thought it too far to turn back for a place to sleep," Cynthia said.

"And we nearly missed the ferry!" exclaimed Father Tim, oddly enjoying the account of their travail. "We made it with two minutes to spare."

"Oh, my poor souls! That bridge goes out if you hold your mouth wrong. You know the state bigwigs don't pay much attention to little specks of islands like they pay to big cities. Well, we're thrilled you're here, and I hope you like perch."

"We *love* perch!" they exclaimed in unison.

" 'Where two or more are gathered together in one accord . . .' " quoted the senior warden, laughing. Sam liked both the looks and the spirit of this pair.

In truth, he was vastly relieved that his prayers had been answered, and, as far as he could see, St. John's hadn't been delivered two pigs in a poke.

"Before we go inside," said Marion, "take a look at your rose."

"Ah!" said Cynthia.

They rushed to the trellis and buried their noses in the mass of blooms. "Lovely!" murmured his wife.

"It was running toward the street when we found it, and terribly trampled by the men who worked on the floors. But we loved it along and fed it, and came and watered it every day, and *now* . . ."

"What is it, do you think?"

"I have no idea. Marjorie Lamb and I searched our catalogs and rose books, but we can't identify it to save our lives."

"I believe I know exactly what it is," he said, adjusting his glasses and inspecting the petal formation.

"You *do*?"

"Yes. It's the Marion Climber."

"Oh, Father! Go on!"

"It is, I'd recognize it anywhere."

"The Marion Climber!" crowed Cynthia. "I never thought I'd live to see one. They're rare, you know."

"Oh, you two!" said Marion, flushed with delight.

"What do you think about your kitchen?" asked Sam.

Father Tim was a tad embarrassed to see tears brimming in his wife's eyes. "It's too beautiful for words!" she said.

"We couldn't like it better!"

If last night had been a nightmare, this was a dream come true. The sun streamed through a sparkling bay window and splashed across the broad window seat. Bare hardwood floors shone under a fresh coat of wax.

"One of our parishioners bought this cottage a few months ago and had it completely redone," said Sam. "Otis Bragg—you'll meet him tonight—Otis and his wife offered it to the parish for the new interim."

"You see just there?" Marion pointed out the window. "That patch of blue between the dunes? That's the ocean!" She proclaimed this as if the ocean belonged to her personally, and she was thrilled to share it.

"Come and have your breakfast," said Sam, holding the chair for Cynthia.

On a round table laid with a neat cloth, they saw a blue vase of watermelon-colored crepe myrtle, and the result of Marion Fieldwalker's labors:

Fried perch, crisp and hot, on a platter. A pot of coffee, strong and fragrant. A pitcher of fresh orange juice. Cantaloupe, cut into thick, ripe slices. Biscuits mounded in a basket next to a golden round of cheese and a saucer of butter, with a school of jellies and preserves on the side.

"Homemade fig preserve," said Marion, pointing to the jam pots. "Raspberry jelly. Blueberry jam. And orange marmalade."

"Dearest, do you think it possible that yesterday in that brutal storm we somehow died, and are now in heaven?"

"Not only possible, but very likely!"

He'd faced it time and again in his years as a priest—how do you pour out a heart full of thanksgiving in a way that even dimly expresses your joy?

He reached for the hands of the Fieldwalkers and bowed his head.

"Father, You're so good. So good to bring us out of the storm into the light of this blessed new day, and into the company of these blessed new friends.

"Touch, Lord, the hands and heart and spirit of Marion, who prepared this food for us when she might have done something more important.

"Bless this good man for looking out for us, and waiting up for us, and gathering the workers who labored to make this a bright and shining home.

"Lord, we could be here all morning only thanking You, but we intend to press forward and enjoy the pleasures of this glorious feast which You have, by Your grace, put before us. We thank You again for Your goodness and mercy, and for tending to the needs of those less fortunate, in Jesus' name."

"Amen!"

Marion Fieldwalker smiled at him, her eyes shining. "Father, when you were talking to the Lord about me doing this instead of something more important, I think you should know . . . there was nothing more important!"

Their hostess passed the platter of fried perch to Cynthia, as Sam passed the hot biscuits to his new priest.

Oh, the ineffable holiness of small things, he thought, crossing himself.

Marion insisted on cleaning up the kitchen while they sat around the table, idle as jackdaws.

"You're welcome at the library anytime," she said, pouring everyone a last cup of coffee, "as long as it's Monday, Wednesday, or Saturday from nine 'til four!"

"We'll drop in next week," said Father Tim. "And that reminds me, how's the bookstore? I hear you have a small bookstore on the island."

Marion laughed. "It's mostly used paperbacks of Ernie's favorite author, Louis L'Amour!"

"Ernie doesn't sell anything he hasn't read first and totally approved." Sam's eyes twinkled. "I hope you like westerns."

"We've got fourteen boxes of books arriving on Monday," Cynthia announced. "We can open our own bookstore!"

"By the way," said Sam, "Ernie also offers a notary service and UPS pickup, and rents canes and crutches on the side."

"Diversified!"

"Actually, you'll pass Ernie's every morning as you walk to church. It's right up the road."

"Sounds like the place to be."

"Ernie has his quarters on one side of the building, Mona has hers on the other. In fact, they've got a yellow line painted down the center of the hall between their enterprises, and neither one steps over it except to conduct business."

"Aha."

Sam stirred cream into his coffee, chuckling. "Ernie likes to say that yellow line saved their marriage."

Marion looked at the kitchen clock. "Oh, my! We'd better show you how your coffers are stocked, and get a move on!"

She took off her apron and tucked it in her handbag, then opened the refrigerator door as if raising a curtain on a stage.

"Half a low-fat ham, a baked chicken, and three loaves of Ralph Gaskell's good whole wheat . . . Lovey Hackett's bread-and-butter pickles, she's very proud of her pickles, it's her great aunt's recipe . . . then there's juice and eggs and butter, to get you started, the eggs are free-range from Marshall and Penny Duncan—he's Sam's junior warden.

"And last but not least . . ."—Marion indicated a large container on the bottom shelf—"Marjorie Lamb's apple spice cake. It's won an award at our little fair every year for ten years!"

Father Tim groaned inwardly. The endless temptations of the mortal flesh . . .

"What a generous parish you are, and God bless you for it!"

"We've always tried to spoil our priests," said Marion, smiling. "But not all of them deserved it."

Sam blinked his blue eyes. "Now, Marion, good gracious . . ."

"Just being frank," Marion said pleasantly.

"Dearest, I think we should be frank, too."

"In, ah, what way?" inquired Father Tim.

"About your diabetes. My husband likes to think that St. Paul's controversial thorn was, without doubt, diabetes."

"Oh, dear!" said Marion. "That means . . ."

"What that generally means is, I can't eat all the cakes and pies and so on that most folks like to feed a priest."

"But I can!" crowed his wife.

"It helps to get the word out early," he said, feeling foolish. "Cuts down on hurt feelings when . . ."

Sam nodded sympathetically. "Oh, we understand, Father, and we'll pass it on. Well, we ought to be pushing off, Marion. We've kept these good people far too long."

"Everybody's having a fit to get a look at you," Marion said proudly. "We hope you'll rest up this afternoon, and we'll come for you at six. It looks like we've got lovely weather on our side for the luau."

"Is the, ah, grass skirt deal still on?" asked Father Tim.

Marion laughed. "We nixed that. We didn't want to run you off before you get started!"

"Well done! And how do we get to St. John's? I'm longing to have a look."

"Good gracious alive!" said Sam, digging in his pockets. "I nearly forgot, I've got a key here for you."

He fetched out the key and handed it over. "Go out to the front gate, take a left, and two blocks straight ahead. You can't miss it. Oh, and Father, there are a couple of envelopes on the table in your sitting room. From two of our . . . most outspoken parishioners. They wanted to get to you before anyone else does . . ."—Sam cleared his throat—"if you understand."

"Oh, I do," he said.

"If I were you, Father," Marion warned, "I'd visit the church and take a nice nap before you go reading those letters. To put it plainly, they're all about bickering. We hate to tell you, but our little church has been bickering about everything from the prayer book to the pew bulletins for months on end. I've heard enough bickering to last a lifetime!"

They walked out to the porch, into the shimmering light. For mountain people accustomed to trees, it seemed the world had become nothing but a vast blue sky, across which cumulus clouds sailed with sovereign dignity.

"Thank you a thousand times for all you've done for us," Cynthia said.

"It's our privilege and delight. You know, we Whitecappers aren't much on hugging, but I think you could both use one!"

Sam and Marion hugged them and they hugged back, grateful.

The senior warden looked fondly at his new priest. "We'll help you all we can, Father, you can count on it."

He had the feeling that he would, indeed, be counting on it.

His wife notwithstanding, he had eagerly obeyed only a few people in his life—his mother, most of his bishops, Miss Sadie, and Louella. He thought Marion Fieldwalker might be a very good one to mind, so he lay down with Cynthia and took a nap, feeling the warmth of the sun through the large window, loving the clean smell of the softly worn matelassé spread, and thanking God.

Setting off to his new church with his good dog made him feel reborn. But he wouldn't go another step before he toured the garden, enclosed by a picket fence with rear and front gates leading to the streets.

Along the pickets to the right of the porch, a stout grove of cannas and a stand of oleander . . .

By the front gate, roses gone out of bloom, but doing nicely, and on the fence, trumpet vine. Several trees of some sort, enough for a good bit of shade, and over there, a profusion of lacecap hydrangea . . .

He walked around to the side of the house, where petunias and verbena encircled a sundial, and trotted to the backyard. An oval herb garden, enclosed by smaller pickets, a bird feeder hanging by the back steps . . .

He made a quick calculation regarding the grass. Twenty minutes, max, with the push mower Sam had sharpened, oiled, and left in the storage shed.

A light breeze stole off the water, and the purity of the storm-cleansed air was tonic, invigorating. He thought he heard someone whistling as he went out the rear gate, and was amazed to find it was himself.

Zip-a-dee-doo-dah, zip-a-dee-ay . . .

They cantered along the narrow lane, spying the much-talked-about street sign at the corner of the high fence. The fence was thickly massed with flowering vines and overhung by trees he couldn't identify.

It was wonderful to see things he couldn't identify—why hadn't he been more of a traveler in his life, why had he clung to Mitford like moss to a log, denying himself the singular pleasures of the unfamiliar?

He had the odd sense he was being watched. He stopped in the middle of the street and looked around. Not a bicycle, not a car, not a soul, only a gull swooping above them. They might have been dropped into Eden, as lone as Adam.

Ernie's and Mona's, he discovered, sat close to the street, with a dozen or so vehicles parallel-parked in front. Cars and pickups lined the side of the road.

Mona's Cafe
Three Square Meals
Six Days A Week
Closed Sunday

Ernie's Books, Bait & Tackle
Six 'Til Six
NO SUNDAYS

Twelve-thirty, according to his watch, and more than five whole hours of freedom lying ahead. Hallelujah!

He tied the red leash to a bench, and Barnabas crawled under it, panting.

As the screen door slapped behind him, he saw the painted yellow line running from front to back of the center hallway. A sign on an easel displayed two arrows—one pointed left to Mona's, one pointed right to Ernie's.

He read the handwritten message posted next to the café's screen door:

Don't even think about cussing in here.

Should he follow the seductive aromas wafting from Mona's kitchen, or buy a *Whitecap Reader* and see what was what?

He hooked a right, where the bait and tackle shop had posted its own message by the door:

A fishing rod is a stick with a hook at one end and a fool at the other.
—Samuel Johnson

"What can I do for you?" A large, genial-looking man in a ball cap sat behind the cash register.

"Looking for a copy of the *Whitecap Reader*," Father Tim said, taking change from his pocket.

"We prob'ly got one around here somewhere. You wouldn't want to pay good money today since a new one comes out Monday. Roanoke, we got a paper over there?"

Roanoke looked up, squinting. "Junior's got it, he took it to th' toilet with 'im."

"That's OK," said Father Tim. "I'll pay for one. How much?"

"Fifty cents. You can get it out of the rack at th' door."

He doled out two quarters.

"We thank you. This your first time on Whitecap?"

"My wife and I just moved here."

"Well, now!" The man extended a large hand across the counter. "Ernie Fulcher. I run this joint."

"Tim Kavanagh."

"What business're you in?"

"New priest at St. John's."

"I never set eyes on th' old one," said Ernie. "I think Roanoke ran into 'im a time or two."

Roanoke nodded, unsmiling. He thought Roanoke's weathered, wrinkled face resembled an apple that had lain too long in the sun.

"Well, thanks. See you again."

"Right. Stop in anytime. You fish?"

"Not much."

"Need any shrimp, finger mullet, squid, bloodworms, chum . . . let me know."

"I'll do it."

"Plus we're th' UPS station for th' whole island, not to mention we rent crutches—"

"Good, good."

"And loan out jigsaws, no charge."

"I'd like to look at your books sometime."

Ernie jerked his thumb toward a room with a handprinted sign over the open door: *Books, Books and More Books.* "I got a deal on right now—buy five, get one free."

"Aha."

"Can't beat that."

"Probably not. Well, see you around."

He was unhooking the leash from the bench leg as two men walked out of Mona's, smelling of fried fish.

"What kind of dog is that?" one asked, popping a toothpick in his mouth.

"*Big,*" said his friend.

He loved it at once.

St. John's in the Grove sat on a hummock in a bosk of live oaks that cast a cool, impenetrable shade over the churchyard and dappled the green front doors.

The original St. John's had been destroyed by fire during the Revolutionary War, and rebuilt in the late nineteenth century in Carpenter Gothic style. Sam Fieldwalker said the Love family purchased the contiguous property in the forties and gave it to St. John's, so the small building sat on a tract of thirty-five acres of virgin maritime forest, bordered on the cemetery side by the Atlantic.

Father Tim stood at the foot of the steps inhaling the new smells of his new church, set like a gem into the heart of his new parish. St. John's winsome charm and grace made him feel right at home, expectant as a child.

He crossed himself and prayed, aloud, spontaneous in his thanksgiving.

"Thank You, Lord! What a blessing . . . and what a challenge. Give me patience, Father, for all that lies ahead, and especially I ask for Your healing grace in the body of St. John's."

He walked up the steps and inserted the key into the lock. It turned smoothly, which was a credit to the junior warden. Then he put his hand on the knob and opened the door.

Though heavy, it swung open easily. He liked a well-oiled church door—no creaking and groaning for him, thank you.

The fragrance of St. John's spoke to him at once. Old wood and lemon oil . . . the living breath of last Sunday's flowers still sitting on the altar . . . years of incense and beeswax. . . .

To his right, a flight of narrow, uncovered stairs to the choir loft and organ. To his left, an open registry on a stand with a ballpoint pen attached by a string. He turned to the first entry in the thick book, its pages rustling like dry leaves. *Myra and Lewis Phillips, Bluefield, Kentucky, July 20, 1975 . . . we love your little church!!*

He looked above the stand to the framed sign, patiently hand-lettered and illumined with fading watercolors.

> *Let the peace of this place surround you as you sit or kneel quietly. Let the hurry and worry of your life fall away. You are God's child. He loves you and cares for you, and is here with you now and always. Speak to Him thoughtfully, give yourself time for Him to bring things to mind.*

Oh, the balm, he thought, of a cool, quiet church full of years.

He walked into the center aisle, which revealed bare heart-of-pine floorboards. They were more than a handbreadth wide, and creaked pleasantly under his tread. Creaking doors, no, he thought, but floorboards are another matter. He'd never lived in a house in which at least two or three floorboards didn't give forth a companionable creak.

On either side of the broad aisle, eight long oak pews seating . . . three, four, five, six, seven, eight, and four short pews seating four. Here and there, a cushion lay crumpled in a pew, reserving that site as someone's rightful, possibly long-term, territory.

His eye followed the aisle to the sanctuary, where a cross made of ship's timbers hung beneath an impressive stained glass.

In the dimly illumined glass, the figure of Christ stood alone with His hands outstretched to whoever might walk this aisle. Behind Him, a cerulean sea. Above, an azure sky and a white gull. The simplicity and earnestness of the image took his breath away.

" 'Come unto me . . .' " he read aloud from the familiar Scripture etched on the window in Old English script, " 'all ye that labor and are heavy laden, and I will give you rest.' "

These were his first spoken words in his new church, words that Paul Tillich had chosen from all of Scripture to best express his personal understanding of his faith.

Suddenly feeling the weariness under the joy, he slipped into a pew on the gospel side and sank to his knees, giving thanks.

Barnabas strained ahead, his nose to the ground; St. John's new priest-in-charge allowed himself to be pulled hither and yon, as free as a leaf caught in a breeze.

They walked around the church and out to the cemetery, where he pondered the headstones and gazed beyond the copse of yaupon to yet another distant patch of blue. He cupped his hand to his ear and listened, hoping to hear the sweetly distant roar, but heard only a gull instead.

Shading his eyes, he turned and searched toward the Sound, across the open breast of the hummock and into the trees, wondering whether the wild ponies were mythic or actually out there. He hoped they were out there.

Before he and Barnabas headed home, he stood for a moment by the grave site of the Redmon Love family, which was guarded by an iron fence and a tall, elaborately formed angel clothed in lichen. Redmon, his wife, Mary, and a son, Nathan, were the only occupants.

Next to the Love plot was a grave headed by a simple, engraved tablet, which he stopped to read.

A loved one from us has gone,
A voice we love is stilled.
A place is vacant in our home,
Which never will be filled.

Estelle Woodhouse, 1898–1987

He took a deep breath and stroked the head of his good dog who sat contentedly at his feet.

All will be well and very well, he thought. He felt it surely.

Dear Father Kavanagh:

I have been baptized, confirmed, and married at St. John's.

I have served on the Altar Guild, sung in the choir, and taught Sunday School (except for the years I was away on the mainland, getting my schooling).

I have ushered, been secretary and treasurer of the ECW for five terms, read the propers each Sunday for seven years, and in 1975, headed the fund-raising drive for the complete restoration of our organ.

The only thing I haven't done in the Episcopal Church is attend my own funeral.

My point is that I know what I am talking about, and what I am talking about is all those people who refuse to do the things of the church with respect and dignity, wishing only to satisfy their whims and confuse our young people.

Would you agree, Father, that you do not list cars for sale in the pew bulletins? Would you agree that you do not switch back and forth from the 1928 prayer book to the 1979, willy-nilly and harum-scarum, on whatever notion happens to strike? Would you agree that holy communion is a time best savored and appreciated in quietude, rather than with the blare and clamor of every odd instrument conceivable, including the harmonica?

I earnestly hope and pray that Father Morgan's favorite instrument, the guitar, will not be making any surprise appearances during your term as interim.

It grieves me that you should come into such a jumble as we've created at St. John's, but Bishop Harvey guarantees that you are without a doubt the one to save us from ourselves.

I fervently hope you will not allow such behavior to continue, and will remind one and all in no uncertain terms how the venerable traditions of the church are to be properly maintained.

Respectfully yours,
Jean Ballenger

He couldn't help but chuckle. If that was the worst squabbling he'd face as interim, he'd be a happy man.

His wife could be heard puttering about in bare feet, humming snatches of tunes, and boiling water to make iced tea. He sat back in his chair and sighed, deciding that he liked this room very much.

Two club chairs, slipcovered in striped duckcloth, flanked a painted green table topped by a reading lamp.

An old parson's table stood against the facing wall, beneath framed watercolors of a country lane, a lake bordered by trees in autumn foliage, ducks on a pond, a small blue and red boat on the open sea, and an elderly man and woman at prayer over an evening meal. An oddly pleasing combination, he thought, nodding approval.

Their books would arrive on Monday, and he would go foraging for bricks and lumber straightaway. By Tuesday evening, if all went well, they would have bookcases in their sitting room, along the now-barren end wall.

The only doubt he entertained about the room was a print of the Roman Colosseum, which had faded, overall, to pale green.

He felt the weariness of recent days in his very bones. Thanks be to God, he wouldn't be preaching in the morning; however, on the following Sunday, it would be fish or cut bait.

He eyed the other letter, propped against the base of the lamp.

Dear Father,

Avery Plummer is a harlot.

Look up the true meaning of this word if you don't already know it which you probably do. Several months ago, she ran off with another woman's husband and God have mercy on the children in this mess, much less the church that helped them do it.

You ask how a church could help anybody commit a sin, and I say the church helps by seeing what is going on and turning its head the other way when certain steps might be taken that would solve the matter once and for all. Read Matthew 18 if you don't already know it which you probably do.

Somebody said that Jeffrey Tolson, our former choir director and the scoundrel that cares for nothing but himself, wants to come back to St. John's because it is where he grew up, and this is to let you know that if he ever sets foot in our narthex again my husband and I will be gone and so will a lot of other people. What this means is that more than half the annual church budget will walk straight out the door and never look back.

We are looking forward to meeting you at the luau at our home this evening.

Regards to you and Mrs. Kavanagh and I hope you have a successful time in Whitecap.

Yours truly,
Marlene Bragg

"Here's what you do," said Otis Bragg, waving his fork as he spoke. "If a hurricane's gonna hit, everybody shows up at th' church basement. Built like a oil tanker down there. Everybody in th' parish knows about it, we even got a little stash of canned goods and coffee."

"Thinking ahead," said Father Tim.

"We don't have coffee down there anymore," said Marjorie Lamb. "We ran out for the bishop's brunch last spring and had to use it."

Otis grinned. "Have t' bring your own, then." Otis Bragg was short, thickset, and balding, with a fondness for Cuban cigars. Father Tim noticed he didn't light the cigars, he chewed them.

They were sitting at picnic tables in the Braggs' backyard, behind a rambling house that looked more like a resort hotel than a residence. The water in the kidney-shaped pool danced and glinted in the sunlight.

Cynthia furrowed her brow. "Has a hurricane ever hit Whitecap?"

"You better believe it," said Otis. "*Whop,* got one in '72, *blam,* got a big 'un in '84."

"How bad?" she asked.

"Bad. Dumped my gravel trucks upside down, tore the roof off of my storage buildin's."

Leonard Lamb looked thoughtful. "I believe it was Hurricane Herman that took your roof off, but it was Darlene that set Sam Fieldwalker's RV in his neighbor's yard and creamed half the village."

"Nobody on Whitecap's had any kids named Herman or Darlene in a real long time," said Otis. "By th' way, I hear th' Love cottage over by where you're stayin' has a good basement; same thing at Redmon Love's old place. Hard to dig a good basement around here, but that part of the island's on a ridge just like St. John's. You have t' have a ridge to dig a basement."

Father Tim peered at his wife and knew it was definitely time to change the subject. "Do we get home mail delivery, by any chance?"

Otis helped his plate to more coleslaw and another slab of fresh barbecue. "You mountain people have it soft, Father, we have t' haul to th' post office over by QuikPik." Otis dumped hot sauce on the barbecue. "Th' mail usually comes in about two o'clock, just watch for th' sign they stick in th' window, says 'Mail In.' Course, if th' bridge is out, th' ferry runs it over."

"Is the bridge fixed yet?"

"Prob'ly, don't usually take long. It's one thing or another 'til a man could puke, either the rain causes a short, or the roadbed and bridge expand in th' heat, or the relay switch goes out. I remember th' good old days when my business didn't depend on anybody's bridge, we made our livin' right here."

"What's your business?"

"Commercial haulin'—gravel, sand, crushed oyster shell, you name it. Plus we offer ready-mix cement for all your concrete needs—be it residential or commercial."

"Aha!"

"Today, you've got a Bragg's on Whitecap and Manteo, not to mention five locations on th' mainland."

"Cornered the market!"

"You got it!" said Otis, flushing with pride.

Marlene Bragg was an intense woman with long, fuchsia nails, a serious tan, and a great mane of blond hair with dark roots.

"We're real glad to have you and your wife—and you brought your cool weather with you!"

Father Tim smiled at their hostess, who had just toured him through her home. "Actually," he said, "I believe I did feel a mountain breeze this morning!"

"It's usually awful hot this time of year."

"I've heard that," he said.

"But I know you'll love it on Whitecap, just like we do."

"Have you been on Whitecap long?"

"Seventeen years, we're from Morehead City. My husband has worked very hard, Father, to make a name for himself in this area." She pursed her mouth. "He's been mighty generous with the diocese, not to mention St. John's."

"I'm sure."

She smiled. "We'd like to keep it that way."

"I'm sure," he said. Too bad he'd just said that.

Jean Ballenger was a small woman with bangs that appeared plastered to her forehead. At the dessert table, she looked deeply into his eyes and pressed his hand.

"Thank you for your wise consideration of all the matters contained in my letter," she said.

"You're welcome," he replied.

“Who in the world is *this*?” asked Father Tim. A child who appeared to be around three years old was making a beeline toward him with no adult in hot pursuit.

“This is Jonathan Tolson!” said Marjorie Lamb, beaming.

Jonathan fell against Father Tim’s legs and clasped them tight, gazing up as if they were old acquaintances.

He squatted and took the youngster’s hands in his. “Hey, buddyroe!”

The blond toddler sucked his lower lip and gazed steadily at Father Tim with blue, inquisitive eyes. Then he turned and raced back the way he’d come.

“He just wanted to tell you hello,” piped Marjorie, looking pleased as punch.

The message light on their answering machine was blinking.

“Hey,” said Dooley. “I hate answerin’ machines. I hope you got there OK. I mowed a yard after work and got fifteen dollars. Avis’s truck is cool, it came today.

“Well . . .” Deep sigh. “Harley got the hornet nests down.” Long pause. “I miss ol’ Barnabas. Talk to you later. ’Bye.”

Click. Beep.

“I heard there was a terrible storm down there,” said Emma. “I hope it didn’t blow you in a ditch. You hadn’t hardly left town ’til Gene Bolick keeled over and they had to carry him to th’ hospital. I called Esther and th’ doctor said he’s keepin’ him awhile for tests.”

Crackling sounds, as if Emma had her hand in a potato chip bag.

“I hear that young interim at Lord’s Chapel has been passin’ out *song sheets*, they’re not even usin’ a *book*, plus they say two or three people lifted up their hands while they were singin’, I bet I can guess who.” She snorted. “I hear your old choir director’s lower lip is stuck out so far he could trip over it.”

Emma crunched down on a couple of chips.

“I saw that woman tenant of yours the other day, she was scurryin’ along like a mouse, oh, an’ I saw Dooley at Avis’s, he looks even better than when you’re here, so don’t worry about a thing.”

Chewing and swallowing, followed by slurping through a straw.

"Snickers has ear mites, I hope Barnabas is doin' fine in all those sandspurs, I hope to th' Lord you'll check his paws on a regular basis."

Emma was running her straw around the bottom of the cup and sucking with great expectation, but not finding much. He turned the volume down on the answering machine.

"Oh, by th' way, Harold got a real raise, the first one in a hundred years, I wish th' post office would get its act together. Well, got to run, this is costin' a war pension."

Click. Beep.

"Timothy! Bill Harvey here. How do you like the pounding surf? I know you're going to love every minute with the fine people at St. John's. You'll be just what the doctor ordered. All they're looking for is Rite Two, a sermon that doesn't rock the boat, and a little trek across the bridge to Cap'n Willie's Sunday brunch.

"I'll be there on the eighth to plug you in. Barbara's not coming—the grandkids are here from Connecticut—she sends her regrets. I'll bunk in with Otis Bragg and Marlene, as usual.

"Well, listen, call me if you need me, you hear? And be sure and eat plenty of spot and pompano, they're probably running pretty good right now. But I wouldn't eat anything *fried* if I were you; broiled is how I like it, better for the heart. Oh, be sure and do right by Otis, now. He and Marlene are mighty generous donors, wouldn't want to lose *them*, ha ha. Well! Felicitations to your beautiful bride! See you on the eighth."

Click. Beep.

"Let's go find the beach," he said, after returning Dooley's call.

"Now?"

"It's only ten o'clock."

"Nearly everyone in Mitford is sound asleep," said his wife.

"This isn't Mitford." He put his arms around her and drew her close and nuzzled her hair.

"But I'm already in my nightgown."

"Wear it. Nobody's looking."

"And barefoot."

"Perfect," he said.

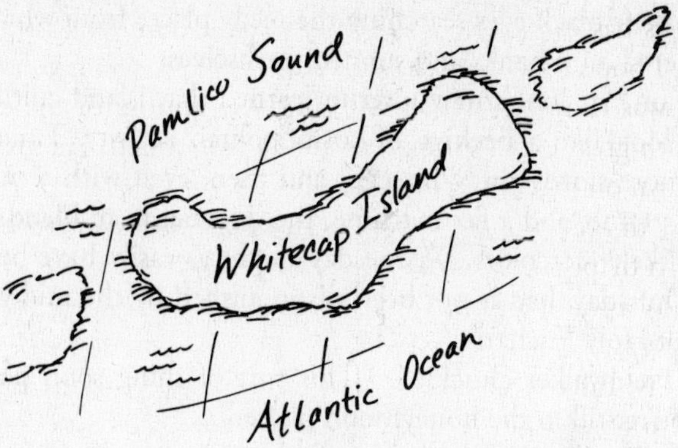

CHAPTER SIX

The Long Shining

Whitecap Island loosely duplicated the shape of a Christmas stocking with a toe full of nuts and candy.

In the toe, Otis Bragg had stationed an extensive system of gravel, rock, and crushed oyster shell inventories, custom cement facilities, and sprawling hangars of grading and construction equipment.

In the heel, the lighthouse stood comfortably surrounded by a hedge of yaupons, an abandoned corral for wild ponies, and a small museum. The remainder of the island was chiefly comprised of high dunes, white beaches, canals and marshes, maritime forest, and a small village of homes, shops, inns, and restaurants, woven together by narrow lanes. The acreage on which St. John's in the Grove sat was located in the top of the stocking.

Increasingly, Whitecap attracted tourists from as far away as Canada and California, swelling the ranks of island churches every summer. While many churches on the mainland cranked down, the churches on Whitecap cranked up, both in numbers and activities.

Even so, a carefree sense of remoteness insinuated itself almost everywhere.

Sandy lanes wound under the heavy shade of live oaks, past summer cottages with picket fences and pleasantly unkempt yards.

Egrets could be seen standing in the marshes, as poised as garden statuary, their black eyes searching the reedy places from which alligators slithered onto banks and sunned themselves.

Early on, St. John's new interim learned that island culture made Mitford look like a beehive of cosmopolitan activity. Time seemed to pass more slowly on Whitecap, and then, even with a calendar, a watch, a phone, and a fax machine, the days began to blend into one another like watercolors. Wednesday might as easily have been Tuesday or Thursday, had it not been distinguished by the midweek celebration of Holy Eucharist.

Sam Fieldwalker chuckled. "This sort of thing soon passes," he said. "You're still in the honeymoon phase."

Father Tim laughed with his affable senior warden. "It all seems like a holiday, somehow, a vacation!"

"You've been going pretty hard, Father, I wouldn't call your first few weeks here a vacation. Truth is, I recommend you take a day off."

Sam looked at his watch. "Good gracious! Got to run by the *Reader* and hand in a story on the Fall Fair, then go across with Marion to the eye doctor and take my fax machine to be fixed. Hope I can get back in time for the planning meeting on the fair."

Even on a small, peaceful island, thought the new priest-in-charge, everybody was going at a trot.

"By the way," said Sam, "glad to hear you're working with Reverend Harmon. The Baptists sure do their part to make the fair the biggest event on the island. We raise a lot of money for needy people."

He went with Sam to the office door that led to the churchyard. "Speaking of needy people," said Father Tim, "I've been counseling Janette Tolson."

"Glad to hear it. When Jeff walked out, Janette didn't feel she could go to Father Morgan, because he was friendly with Jeff. She's gone through the worst of this thing with no priest to turn to."

"She's suffering badly, as you know."

"This has come against us all in a hard way. Not to mention how the choir has fallen into disarray."

Recently, their best tenor had stepped forward to direct the choir and, profoundly disliking such a wrinkle, the lead soprano had quit in disgust and was now teaching Sunday School.

"It'll come right." It was what his mother always said of a rotten situation. "The first thing we need to do is stop thinking of it as a performance choir, and be pleased with how well they lead the congregational singing."

Sam nodded. "Good point."

"You know we're auditioning an organist next week."

"I dislike the thought of a paid organist at St. John's. The Lord has always provided us with somebody in the congregation."

"It may be for the best, Sam. No ties to the church, no axe to grind . . . that's how we handled it at Lord's Chapel for the last few years, and it worked."

"Well, brother . . ."—Sam shook his hand—"hold down the fort while we're across. Oh, my goodness! I forgot the banana bread. I'll just run out to the car. Marion wouldn't be pleased if I come home with it still sliding around in the backseat."

Early on, Father Tim had learned that Marion Fieldwalker was right—the parish really did like to spoil their priests.

He and Cynthia had been treated to brunch at Cap'n Willie's every Sunday, and to dinner at Mona's Café with the Lambs and Fieldwalkers.

They'd received a bushel of hard crabs and clams from the Braggs, and were regularly inundated with bread still warm from parishioners' ovens, not to mention sacks of snap beans and tomatoes.

For performing a baptism, he'd been given a free-range chicken and a pound of butter from the Duncans' little farm, while a wedding ceremony he conducted under the oaks had swelled the Dove Cottage larders with a honey-baked ham.

Thank goodness he was running three days a week, and Cynthia was riding her Schwinn from the post office to the dry cleaner's to the grocery store. She might have been a tanned schoolgirl, wheeling along with carrot tops poking from the grocery sack in her bike basket.

The light on the answering machine blinked as he came in from a meeting with Stanley Harmon at Whitecap Baptist.

"Hey, this is Puny, how y'all doin'? Ever'thing's goin' jis' great up here, hope it's th' same with you. Th' girls wanted to say hey . . . Sissy, come back this minute, come back and say hey to Miss Cynthia and Ba!"

Sounds of small feet storming up the hall, amid shrieks and laughter.

"And there goes Sassy, oh, mercy! Hold on, y'all, 'scuse me. . . ."

Sounds of Puny chasing the girls into another room of her small house. "No, no! Put that down! Ba and Miss Cynthia are waitin' for you to say hey! Oh, Lord help, I can't believe this, come out from under there, Sissy!

"All right, then, I'll let *Sassy* say hey. What a good girl your *sister* is! Come here, Sassy."

Clattering noises along the hallway to the phone.

"Here, now *say hey* to Ba and Miss Cynthia."

Heavy breathing.

"You *wanted* to say hey, you *cried* to say hey . . . now *say hey*!" spluttered a frustrated Puny.

"Kitty?" said Sassy.

"Sassy, honey, stay right there and talk to Ba while I get Sissy! *Sissy!* I see what you're doin', get your hands out of th' toilet this minute!"

Bawling from the bathroom. Heavy breathing on the phone. Puny's footsteps hurrying along the hall.

"Did you say hey yet?"

"Dog!" said Sassy.

"Here, f'r pity's sake, give me th' phone. Well, y'all . . ."

Loud wailing. "Want to say hey! Want to say hey!"

"Not 'til you say somethin' else first," commanded Puny.

"Ple-e-ease!!!"

"All right, here's the phone, say hey and get it over with!"

Deep breath. "Hey, Ba!" Giggling.

"Now go find your cookie! Ba, I mean, Father, I saw your tenant yesterday, she was standin' on 'er tiptoes lookin' in your study window on th' hedge side. I guess I scared her half t' death. I wadn't supposed to go to your house yesterday, but I needed to take in your mail an' all. She said she was lookin' for her cat that run off, and just took a little peek in your window to see how nice it was, said she didn't think y'all'd mind. Well, anyway, Joe Joe says t' tell you hey, and Winnie at Sweet Stuff—

"Sissy, put th' mop down *this minute*! Oh, *law* . . ."

Click. Beep.

The next message was clearly from a dog, who was barking furiously.

"Hush *up*!" shouted Emma. "Go get your sock!

"I guess you know your phone call meant th' world to poor Esther.

I've never seen her like this, practically wringin' her hands, and she's not th' hand-wringin' type, but they still can't find out what's wrong with Gene. They're goin' to run more tests on Monday, you ought to see 'im, he looks bad to me, I hope you're prayin' is all I can say.

"Snickers! Get away from there! Snickers is tryin' to eat th' meatloaf I just made! Oh, shoot, hold on a minute. . . ."

Growling, huffing, rattling of pots and pans.

"I had to set it on the counter, plus check my beans, I'm havin' string beans and . . . *go get your sock and lie down* . . . mashed potatoes with I Can't Believe It's Not Butter.

"Listen to this. Who just jumped in th' mayor's race against Andrew Gregory? You will *not* believe it. Three guesses! Call me and tell me who you think it is, OK? You will keel over.

"By th' way, I heard it's not even hot where y'all are, they say it's strange th' way th' weather's so cool at th' beaches this year. Oh, I just remembered you got a big box of somethin' from Florida at th' post office, I think somebody sent you grapefruit, do you want me to ship it down there or haul it home with me? Harold loves grapefruit, it would save payin' postage all th' way to that island you're on.

"Speakin' of Harold, here he comes, he does *not* like me talkin' on long-distance."

Click. Beep.

"Father? Otis Bragg here. Wanted to send you a little present by one of my boys. You like bourbon? Scotch? You name it. How 'bout a little Wild Turkey? Somebody said you like sherry, but I must've heard wrong.

"Call my secretary on th' mainland, two-eight-two-four, and let 'er know, OK?"

Click. Beep.

"Hmmm," said his wife, puzzling over who had jumped into Mitford's mayoral race.

"Lew Boyd!" he said. "That's who I'd guess. Either Lew or Mule Skinner. Mule's mentioned doing it for years."

Cynthia furrowed her brow. "Would *you* like to see Fancy Skinner as first lady of Mitford?"

"It might add a certain . . ." He was at a loss for words.

"I don't know, I don't have a clue," said his wife, who was usually up for guessing games.

"What do you think about . . . no, no way . . . let's see . . ."

"Or maybe . . . ," said Cynthia, pondering deeply.

"Then again . . . but I don't think so."

"Oh, poop! If you don't call Emma back, I will!"

They raced into the sitting room and took their chairs. He dialed Emma's number.

"Who?" he inquired, when she answered the phone.

"Is this an owl?" asked Emma.

"I guess Lew Boyd!"

"Two more guesses."

He hated that she always made him do three guesses.

"Mule Skinner!"

"Wrong."

"J. C. Hogan!" shouted Cynthia, in a burst of supernatural insight.

"Is it J.C.?" asked Father Tim.

"Are you sittin' down?" inquired his erstwhile secretary.

"We are. Get on with it."

"Coot Hendrick!"

"Coot Hendrick?"

"He says his great-grandaddy founded th' whole town, and it's time he did something that carries on th' family tradition."

"I'll be darned."

"I personally couldn't vote for anybody who has stubs for teeth, but he says he's goin' to work hard to win."

"It's just as well we aren't there. I don't think I could go through another mayor's race," he said, still not fully over the last one.

While he cooked dinner, his wife sat in the kitchen window seat, looking out but not seeing. She was busy twisting a strand of hair around one finger and humming.

He didn't have to be as wise as Solomon to know that every time she got that glazed-over look and twisted her hair and hummed, something was up.

The fresh croaker sizzled in the skillet. "Cynthia?"

No reply. Still humming.

Blast. She definitely had that conjuring-up-a-book look. All of which meant she would soon stop riding her bicycle and lash herself to the drawing board for months on end, getting a crick in her neck and feeling grumpy. When people did what they profess to absolutely love, why didn't they smile and laugh and be carefree and upbeat?

Salt, pepper, a spritz of lemon . . .

Another book would mean this whole beach experience, which might have been relaxing for his overworked wife, would, in fact, be just another nose-to-the-grindstone deal. . . .

"Timothy," she said, "I've been thinking."

He sighed and flipped the croaker, without breaking it apart. He was getting good at this.

"You know how lovely everyone's been to us," she said.

"They have."

"How they've loved us. . . ."

"Right."

"We must do something that loves them back."

"Aha."

She turned to face him, looking fierce. "But *not* a Primrose Tea!" His wife had worked her fingers to the very bone doing two enormous and successful Primrose Teas in Mitford.

"I don't think there's a primrose within two hundred miles of here."

"Absolutely, *positively* not a Primrose Tea!" she said.

"I *hear* you, Kavanagh!"

"It's killing, you know."

"No Primrose Tea."

"Anyway, I'm not sure beach people *drink* tea. Hot tea, I mean, to go with things like scones or shortbread."

"I never thought much about it."

"It seems beach people would be more interested in . . . something *cold*, like lemonade, or a lovely punch with an ice ring of lime sherbet . . . and maybe lots of fresh fruit in a vast, icy watermelon carved with its own handle, to which we could attach a bouquet of flowers from our little garden. . . ."

"There you go!" Out of the pan, onto the plate, and done to perfection.

"And a beautiful cake, three or four layers with white icing—and wedding cookies, don't you think? Except they're so messy, all that powdered sugar falling on your shoes . . ."

"My mouth is watering." He spooned new potatoes onto the dinner plates, cheek by jowl with the fish. Now a dollop of butter, a sprinkle of fresh parsley . . .

"I think we should have everyone here, not at the parish hall," she said. "Parishioners like seeing how their priest lives."

"I'll help. You can count on me."

. . . and a dash of paprika, for color. He felt like a heel for thinking his wife was plotting to write a new book and get a crick in her neck when she was, in fact, intent on doing something exceedingly generous for others. Thank goodness he hadn't opened his big mouth and put his foot in it.

"And I'll probably try something wonderful with peaches, too, I don't know what yet, maybe tarts, very small like this." She made a circle with her thumb and forefinger. "I hear the peaches are lovely this year!"

"Dinner is served," he announced, setting the plates on the table. "Come and get it."

She stared at the plates with surprise. "You *angel*!" She apparently hadn't noticed he was making dinner. "Croaker! And new potatoes and fresh asparagus! Oh, Timothy, I'm so glad you can cook."

"I'm even gladder that you can cook. You have kitchen duty for the next four evenings, I hope you recall."

"Four? Why four?"

"Meetings," he said "Choir practice. The Whitecap Fair Planning Commission. The vestry . . ."

"Umm," she said.

"Umm what?"

"Well, dearest, I've been thinking that maybe . . ."

"Yes?"

"It's so beautiful here, and so liberating, even Violet loves it, have you noticed?"

"I have."

She looked at him in that way he could never resist, with her head tilted slightly to one side and her sapphire eyes gleaming. "I thought I might begin right away . . . working on a new book."

"Let's bow in prayer," he said.

He dialed a number he easily remembered by heart.

"Esther? Is that you?" Esther Bolick didn't sound like herself.

"What's *left* of me."

His heart ached for his old friends; worse, he felt guilty that he wasn't there to go the mile with them.

"How's Gene?"

"Not good." He heard Esther sigh. He couldn't bear it when Esther sighed; Esther was not a sigher, she was a doer.

"We're praying," he said, "and believing Gene's going to be well and strong again. Now tell me about you, Esther, how're *you* doing?"

"I went yesterday to pick out my casket."

"You *what*?"

"It had to be done sometime. All this with Gene reminded me."

"Do you think this is the right time, I mean . . . ?"

"When Louise Parker went to Wesley to pick hers out, Reverend Sprouse went with her."

"Aha."

"There was nobody to go with me."

He felt very uncomfortable. It was the guilt again. "What about your interim? Couldn't he go?"

"Father Hayden? Lord *help*! He's so wet behind the ears, he's still on strained peas and applesauce!"

Father Hayden was forty-five if he was a day. "So what did you pick?" Might as well be upbeat about it.

"Do you know it costs four thousand dollars to get buried in Mitford? Can you believe it? I was goin' to be cremated, but there's nothin' to look at in a jar. I remember when we buried Mama, it was a *comfort* to see her in th' casket."

"Closure," he said.

"So I picked somethin' with a nice iv'ry satin lining. I always looked good in iv'ry."

"I seem to recall that." He honestly did.

"Then you think you're through with th' whole mess, and what happens?"

"What?" He was interested.

"They want to sell you a *liner*! Some bloomin' metal thing you drop th' casket down in, to keep it protected from *dirt.*" Esther snorted.

Miss Sadie had been very upset about liners, he remembered.

"Anyway, so I got th' dadblame thing, and now it's all taken care of and if I kick before Gene, everything's done, he can put his feet up! I even filled th' freezer in case I go first."

He didn't like this at all. Clearly, Esther was in denial about Gene's uncertain future; to avoid thinking of his, she was concentrating on her own.

"Lasagna, chicken divan, squash casserole—"

"Esther . . ."

"There's only only one problem," said his former parishioner.

"What's that?"

"I can't decide what to be buried in. Mama had her outfit hangin' in th' closet, ready to go, even panty hose. Course, it hung there so long, th' dress rotted off th' hanger and we had to dive in and come up with another outfit at th' last minute."

"Umhmm."

"So yesterday, Hessie came over and helped me go through th' closet. I laid out my royal blue suit, do you remember my royal blue suit?"

"I think so." He really did think so.

"But Hessie says it's too plain. So I laid out my pink dress with the chiffon sleeves. Do you remember my pink dress with the chiffon sleeves?"

"Ah . . . let's see . . ."

"I wore it to Fancy and Mule's anniversary party in their basement. It's Gene's favorite."

"Right." He felt like dropping onto the floor prostrate, and giving up the ghost.

"Well, that's what we finally decided on. But after Hessie left, it hit me—what if I die in th' winter?"

He hesitated. "I don't understand."

Esther sighed heavily, "Pink is a *summer* color!"

He gave her what was his only word of wisdom in the entire conversation.

"I recommend you surrender all this to the Lord, Esther. He'll be glad to take care of everything when the time comes."

She kissed him goodbye, one of those lingering kisses that he feared might come to a grinding halt when her book began. Seizing the moment, he kissed her back.

"Darling," she said, brushing his face with the tips of her fingers, "I think you need to take a day off."

"Why? We just got here!"

"We just got here six weeks ago, and you've been working nonstop. I mean, racing across to the hospital twice a week, and teaching adult Sunday School, and setting up the men's fall prayer breakfast, and working with Reverend Harmon . . ."

"But it all seems like a vacation, somehow."

"Trust me. You need to take a day off." She kissed him again, drawing him close in that protective way she sometimes had of making him feel both a man and a child.

He sighed. "I can't do it today."

"Rats!"

"But maybe tomorrow. . . ."

"I'll count on it, dearest."

Headed for St. John's, he ran down the steps of the cottage with Barnabas on the red leash.

Another glorious day! If they ever had to pay a price for the ambrosial weather they continually enjoyed, he shuddered to think how steep the cost might be.

Taking out his pocketknife, he stopped at their bed of cosmos and cut several stems for his office bookshelf.

Glory! He gazed at the cumulus clouds scudding overhead, and took a deep breath. The flowers, the everlasting gulls, the patch of blue beyond the dunes—it hit a man in the solar plexus, between the eyes, in the soul.

It was vastly different, this place, from the protected feeling he had in the mountains. There, summer was one long green embrace. Here, it was one long shining, and the sense of endless freedom.

Barnabas suddenly growled, then barked.

Father Tim glanced around for a stray dog or someone walking by. Nothing.

He quickly snipped two more blooms and put the small bouquet in his shirt pocket.

Trotting through the gate and into the narrow lane, he had the strange sense that someone was watching him. He turned to see if Cynthia might be standing on the porch, but she was not.

His parishioners had given him an earful about the uncaring, self-centered, musically gifted choir director who had abandoned his wife and children for St. John's married organist. Speaking of Jeffrey Tolson, a parishioner had quoted John Ruskin: "When a man's wrapped up in himself, he makes a pretty small package."

He had frequently prayed for Jeffrey Tolson, but was unable to dismiss the hardness of heart he often felt when doing it. And, though he'd never laid eyes on St. John's former choir director, he knew precisely who it was when the tall, blond Scandanavian walked into the church office from the side door.

"Jeffrey Tolson," said his caller. He stood by the desk, arms crossed.

He couldn't help but notice that his caller wore leather clogs, and a full-sleeved white shirt in the manner of eighteenth-century poets.

"Jeffrey." *Lord, give me the words, the wisdom, the heart for this, Your will be done. . . .*

"I won't take much of your time."

He wanted to say, *My time is yours,* but could not. It was what he always liked to say to parishioners, no matter what the time constraints.

Jeffrey Tolson removed his billfold from a rear pocket. "I'm back in Whitecap for a few days. I wanted Janette to have this." He withdrew a hundred-dollar bill and handed it to Father Tim.

"You can't give it to her yourself?"

"She's in no mood to deal with me."

He looked at the money and had a fleeting vision of punching Jeffrey Tolson in the nose—squarely, no holds barred. Gone eight months and this was the only offering?

"I'll see that she gets it."

"I know you think hard of me, most people do. But Janette was no angel to live with. Moody, depressed, demanding. I'm a sensitive man, Father. It was like living with a wet blanket."

"How was it living with those children of yours?"

Jeffrey Tolson's face was suddenly hard. "Don't preach to me."

"Far from it, Mr. Tolson."

His heart was pounding, his mouth dry as he stood facing the man who had brought hurt and anger into the midst of St. John's.

Jeffrey Tolson turned and stomped from the office. He jerked open the door to the outside steps, then slammed it behind him.

He awoke to find Barnabas standing by the bed, his black nose barely an inch from his face.

"Don't let him kid you, Timothy, I've already taken him out to the garden."

He rolled over and put his arm around his wife.

A day off! He'd have to swallow down the guilt before he could get up and enjoy it.

"Timothy . . ." He knew that tone of voice; she could read him like a book.

"Umm?"

"I hear your wheels turning already, clickety-clack! You're going over all the things you should be doing today at church."

"Right. You see, we're working with Marion and her staff to organize and catalog St. John's library, which means—"

"I'm hoping you'll rent a bike and go riding with me today."

Barnabas licked him on the ear and wagged his tail, urgent. His dog was never completely satisfied with Cynthia's idea of a morning constitutional.

"But first," she said, "I think you should walk down to Ernie's after morning prayer and look over his books. You've been wanting to do it ever since we came."

"Ernie's . . . I don't know."

"It's six-thirty. You could have breakfast at Mona's and maybe read the paper like you used to do at the Grill . . ."

He *had* missed that sort of thing.

". . . then, meet me back here at nine and we'll go to Mike's Bikes and—"

"I thought I'd make your breakfast," he said.

"You're always looking for something to do for someone." She stroked his cheek. "It might be good if you spent a little time doing . . . whatever it is that men do."

What did men do? He'd never figured it out.

He yawned. "The next thing I know, you'll be packing me off for a day of deep-sea fishing."

She looked at him and burst into laughter. "How did you guess? I can't *believe* it! I just bought you a ticket on Captain Willie's charter boat!"

CHAPTER SEVEN

A Little Night Music

At seven a.m., the day was already sultry; forecasts were for ninety-nine degrees by noon.

He broke a sweat before he reached Mona's, where he found Ernie paying for a sausage biscuit and a cup of coffee at his wife's cash register.

"I'm only allowed over th' yellow line as a payin' customer," said the genial proprietor from next door. "Get your order and come over to my side—chew th' fat awhile."

"Well . . . ," he said, pleased to be asked, "don't mind if I do."

"That'll be two bucks." Mona extended her hand to her husband, who shelled out the tab, mostly in change.

"I'll have what he's having," said Father Tim.

The red-haired Mona had a no-nonsense look behind a pair of glasses with brightly painted frames. "So you're hangin' with the guys this mornin'?"

He nodded, feeling suddenly shy and excited about having someone to hang with.

"They get too rough for you," said Mona, "come on back to where it's civilized."

"Right," he said.

"This yellow line . . . ," said Father Tim, stepping over it, "it must be a real conversation piece."

"Thing was, Mona kept nosin' around my side sayin' old books wouldn't pay th' light bill. Then I'd go over to her side raisin' Cain because she hadn't hiked her prices in four years. We nearly ended up in divorce court."

"Aha."

"We had to learn to mind our own business, you might say. Thing is, I've come to believe all married people ought t' have a yellow line of some kind or another."

Ernie held the screen door open to Books, Bait & Tackle.

"Welcome to where th' elite meet to eat. Boys, watch your language, Preacher Kavanagh's goin' to join us this mornin'."

"Tim," said the preacher, nodding to the assembly. "Call me Tim."

Ernie set his bag on one of the scarred tables by the drink machines. "You remember Roanoke, he don't much like preachers. But he's harmless."

Roanoke nodded curtly and poured a packet of sugar into a Styrofoam cup.

"That's Roger Templeton over there, an' his dog, Lucas. Lucas is blind. Roger's his Seein' Eye human."

"Tim, nice to meet you," said Roger, who was holding what appeared to be a block of wood in his lap. Roger was a tall, slender man, probably in his sixties, with a pleasant face. The filmy eyes of his brown Labrador appeared to rest on the newcomer with some interest.

"Set your sack down," said Ernie, "and pull up a chair. It's not fancy, but it's all we got. Junior, come out here and meet Preacher Kavanagh."

A sandy-haired, bearded young man came through the door of the book room. He wiped his hand on his work pants and extended it with solemn courtesy.

"How you do, sir, glad to meet you."

"Glad to meet you, Junior."

"Junior's off work today, he hauls for Otis Bragg. You know Otis, I reckon."

"Oh, yes. Otis is a member at St. John's."

Roanoke snorted.

Ernie launched into his sausage biscuit with considerable gusto. "Well, boys, we got a lot of work to do to get Junior's ad in before th' deadline. Tim, we're glad you're here, because you're an educated man and know how to put things. Course, Roger's pretty educated hisself. He was runnin' a billion-dollar corporation before him and his wife retired to Whitecap."

Roger smiled as he deftly used a pencil to make marks on the block of wood. "Half a billion."

"Don't sound as good to say half a billion." Ernie gulped his coffee. "Junior, you got your notepad?"

"Right here," said Junior. He removed a ballpoint pen and notepad from his shirt pocket, which was machine-embroidered with the name *Junior Bryson.*

"What's your ad about?" asked Father Tim.

Junior looked at Ernie.

"*You* tell 'im." Ernie said to Junior.

"Well, sir, I'm tryin' to find a wife." Junior's face colored.

"Aha."

"So, me an' Roanoke an' Ernie an' Roger come up with this idea to advertise."

"That's been known to work," said Father Tim, unwrapping his sausage biscuit.

"We recommended advertising off the island," said Roger.

"Right," said Ernie. "Everybody on Whitecap knows Junior, and he knows everybody."

"Does that mean there aren't any candidates on Whitecap?"

"Not to speak of," said Ernie. "Besides, our advice is, get a woman you have to go *across* to see, makes it more . . . more . . ."

"Romantic," said Roger.

Junior beamed and nodded.

"If I was you," said Roanoke, "I'd run me a big ad with a border around it." He drew a cigarette from a pack of Marlboros in his shirt pocket.

"That'd cost more," said Ernie.

Roanoke struck a match. "Might be worth more."

"Read what you have so far," said Roger.

"White male, thirty-six, five foot eleven an' a half . . ."

Roanoke sipped his coffee. "I'd say six foot."

"Right," said Ernie. "Sounds better."

"That'd be a lie," said Junior.

"Put a lift in your shoes," said Roanoke.

"I ain't goin' to lie. Five foot eleven an' a half with kep' beard—"

Ernie shook his head. "I wouldn't mention a beard. Some women don't like face hair a'tall."

"Might as well git things out in th' open," said Junior.

"Keep readin'," said Roanoke.

"Five foot eleven an' a half with kep' beard, likes country music, fishin', and Scrabble, drives late-model Bronco."

Roanoke leaned forward. "What'd you say Scrabble for? You ought t' say poker or gin rummy."

Ernie frowned. "It's th' Bronco I wouldn't say anything about. I'd say more like a . . . like a . . ."

"A Mustang convertible!" suggested Roanoke, unsmiling. "Maybe you could borry the preacher's car."

"Yessir," said Junior, grinning. "I've seen your car around, it's a real sharp ride."

"Thank you."

"We got to hurry up," said Ernie, checking his watch. "If this is goin' to run in th' *Diplomat,* Junior's got t' call it across in thirty minutes."

"Read it again," said Roanoke. He wadded up his biscuit wrapper and lobbed it into a box beside the Pepsi machine.

Junior cleared his throat and ran a hand through his thinning hair. "White male, thirty-six, five foot eleven an' a half with kep' beard, likes country music, fishin', and Scrabble, drives late-model Bronco . . . plus, I'm addin' this . . . lookin' for serious relationship, send photo."

"I wouldn't put nothin' in there about a serious relationship," said Roanoke. "That'll scare 'em off."

Junior gazed helplessly at his advisors. Then he zeroed in on Father Tim. "What do *you* think, sir?"

In truth, he'd hardly been thinking at all. "Well . . ."

Junior's pen was poised above the notepad.

"Actually, I like your idea about getting things out in the open."

Junior nodded, looking relieved. "Well, good! It's wrote, then."

The sweat was trickling down his back as he made a quick sweep through the book room, finding a ragged copy of Conrad Richter's *The Trees.* He knew he'd never read it again, but he recalled his early fondness for it with such reverence that he couldn't resist. Especially not for fifty cents.

He found a cat asleep in one of the numerous book-filled boxes stationed around the room, and nearly leaped out of his running shorts when it sprang up and hissed at him.

"That's Elmo th' Book Cat," said Ernie, standing in the doorway. "He's older'n dirt. That's his sleepin' box, it's full of Zane Grey paperbacks. You ever read Zane Grey?"

"Tried," he said, his eyes roving the shelves. "Couldn't."

"Ever read Louis L'Amour?"

"Never have."

"That's my main man. Listen to this." Ernie grabbed a book off the shelf, thumbed through the pages, and adjusted his glasses.

" 'We are, finally, all wanderers in search of knowledge. Most of us hold the dream of becoming something better than we are, something larger, richer, in some way more important to the world and ourselves. Too often, the way taken is the wrong way, with too much emphasis on what we want to have, rather than what we wish to become.' "

Ernie looked up. "A world of truth in that."

Father Tim nodded. "I'll say."

"This is his autobiography. Looky here." Ernie turned to the back of the book and displayed a long list. "That's some of th' books he read. He read thousands of books and kep' account of every one. Plus he traveled and wandered all over th' world an', with no education to speak of, turned around an' wrote hundreds of books his own self."

Ernie scratched his head. "I guess if I could, I'd just read books and not strike a lick at a snake."

"Sounds good to me!"

The proprietor took a paperback off the shelf. "Here you go, I'm givin' this to you. Take it an' read it, and tell me what you think."

"I'll do it."

"To my way of thinkin', *Last of the Breed* was L'Amour's best book, and if it don't keep you on th' edge of your pew, nothin' will."

"I thank you, Ernie. Thank you!"

"I take you for a big reader, yourself."

"I guess you could say Wordsworth is my main man."

"Wordsworth, Wordsworth . . . ," said Ernie, trying to place the name.

"I'll bring you something, see what you think."

"Good deal," said Ernie, looking pleased.

At the cash register, Father Tim fetched a dollar and change out of his shorts pocket for the Richter book and the eight-page *Whitecap Reader.*

"Seen your neighbor yet?" asked Ernie. "Guess I ought to say heard 'im, is more like it."

"What neighbor is that?"

"Th' one behind th' hedge."

"Didn't know there was one behind the hedge."

"You didn't?" Ernie looked incredulous.

"Should I have?"

"Seems like somebody would've told you."

He waited for Ernie to elaborate, but he didn't. "Maybe you could tell me."

"Well . . . it's what's left of th' Love family, is what it is."

He thought Ernie looked pained, as if regretting that he'd introduced the subject.

"Aha."

"See, there was a whole clan of Loves at one time. Redmon Love, th' grandaddy, bought that big trac' of land up th' road where you are, built him a fine home in there and put a wall around it. Then planted a hedge both sides of th' wall. It's grown up like a jungle th' last twenty years or so."

Father Tim looked at his watch. If he was going to ride bikes this morning, not to mention walk his dog, he'd better get a move on.

"Th' Love house was th' finest thing on any of these islands, a real mansion, but you can't see it's back there 'less you're lookin' for it."

"I'll be darned."

"Mr. Redmon had somebody come in from upstate New York and make him a tropical garden, had palm trees and monkeys an' I don't know what all."

"Monkeys?"

"Well, there ain't any monkeys in there now, but used to be. I used to hear 'em when I was a kid." Ernie paused and gave a loud rendition of what, it might be supposed, was the call of a monkey.

"Like that," said Ernie.

Father Tim nodded, impressed.

"Used to be macaws in there, too, an' some said elephants, but I never went for that."

"Pretty far-fetched," agreed Father Tim, rolling up his newspaper and putting it under his arm.

"Anyway, th' whole clan built around th' mansion. You're livin' up from th' place his second grandson used 'til, oh, I don't know, maybe two or three years ago, then they pretty much stopped comin'."

"Right. So who lives behind the wall?"

Ernie looked at him soberly. "I wouldn't say nothin' to your wife."

"Really?"

"No use to make 'er worry."

"Who?"

The screen door slammed behind two fisherman. While one examined sinkers and knives, the other ordered bait.

"We need a half pound of shrimp, a dozen bloodworms, and a pound of squid. Better make that a pound and a half."

"Catch you later, Tim," said Ernie. "Come again anytime, you hear?"

He dropped by St. John's to see how the organization of the church library was developing. Marion Fieldwalker and her volunteers were cataloging, dusting, shelving, and generally making sense of books that had been stacked in a room off the narthex since the time of the early prophets. He cheered them on and made a pot of coffee as his contribution to the effort.

There was no reason at all, of course, for his wife to know he'd taken this little detour. . . .

He was zooming by his desk as the phone rang.

"Hello?"

"Hey!" said Dooley.

"Hey, yourself, buddy! What's going on?"

"The Reds whipped th' poop out of th' Blues last night!"

"Hallelujah! Tell me everything!" He thumped into his groaning swivel chair and leaned back.

"You should of seen ol' Mule, he come t' bat four times with runners on base, got a base hit ever' time!"

Ah, it was music to his ears when Dooley lapsed into the old vernacular.

"I scored four runs on 'is hits. We whipped 'em by seven runs."

"Man alive!" he said, rejoicing with his boy. "Well done!"

"Waxin' th' Blues was great, we cleaned their plows. You should of been there."

He should have, it was true. "Good crowd?"

"Ever'body, nearly. Ol' Coot Hendrick, he was there shakin' hands like he was President of the United States. Ol' Mayor Cunningham, she throwed out th' first ball."

"How are Poo and Jessie and your mom?"

"Great. I had supper with 'em Saturday. Poo's gettin' really tall, Jessie's quit suckin' her thumb."

"Have you seen Lace?"

Silence. "A couple of times."

"Really? You took her to a movie?"

"Are you kidding? She hardly looks at me. Anyway, she's not allowed to go out with guys 'til next year. She's still fifteen."

"Aha." He noted that Dooley's speech had returned to the prep school mode.

"But I saw her with some friends a couple of times, like when I took Jenny to a movie."

He rubbed his chin and frowned. That wouldn't have been his agenda for Dooley's summer, but who was he to judge? Jenny was their pretty, soft-spoken neighbor who'd regularly come looking for Dooley, knocking on the back door year after year, summer after summer. What if his own neighbor, his very wife, had not come knocking on the rectory door?

"Is Lace still tutoring Harley?"

"She comes when I'm working, she gave him A-plus on something. I don't know what it was, but he was pretty excited, I think it was math."

"Are you ready to go back to school?"

"I don't want to go back."

"If you're going to be a vet, you have to go to school," he said, stating the obvious.

"Yeah, right. So I'm goin' back, but I'd rather stay home."

"You've got eight days, make the most of it. As we discussed, the Barnhardts will swing by with Joseph to return you to academe."

"Where?"

"By the way, Harley says you're doing great with your curfew."

"He said he'd whip my tail if I messed up." Dooley cackled. The thought of the thin, toothless Harley whipping him was clearly a great amusement.

"What are you guys eating these days?"

"Harley made pizza last night, it was great."

"With everything?" He loved the details.

"No anchovies, no onions, tons of sausage and cheese. He could get a franchise."

"How's our tenant?"

"She asked me twice if I'd show her your house, said she wanted to see what y'all did, the addition and all. I said maybe when you come in October, you'd show it to her. Why would she care anything about the addition? She's not going to do one."

"I have no idea."

"Anyway, I think Lace is taking lessons over there before she goes off to school, she leaves in a week. She'll hate that school."

"Please. Keep your opinions on that school to yourself."

"I promise you those girls are weird. They write and draw and read and wear totally weird clothes like lace-up shoes and glasses with wire rims. I mean, they can't even dance, they step all over you."

"How's your bank account?"

"Huge."

"How huge?"

"I made six hundred dollars so far."

"I owe you six to match it, that makes twelve, what's the total?"

"With what I saved last year, that makes seventeen hundred, even."

"You can buy a sharp little ride for what you'll have by the end of summer."

"I don't want an old car, I told you over and over."

"We'll both be old as the hills if we wait 'til you earn enough for a new one."

Dooley sighed.

"Look," he said, feeling guilty, repressed, and prehistoric. "Cynthia and I will kick in another five hundred, that brings you up to twenty-two hundred."

"Thanks! Hey, really! Thanks, Dad."

"You're welcome. Now stay out of trouble."

"I'm stayin' out."

"Good. Well done. If we're still here, you're going to love this place next summer."

"Why?"

"Sand. Water. Girls. Shrimp and hush puppies. I don't know, good stuff."

"And I'll have a car."

"You'll have a car. Right."

"Look, I've got to go."

"Tell Harley hello."

"I miss ol' Barnabas. Tell Cynthia hey, is she OK?"

"She misses you, she looks great, she has a tan and a half."

"Well, I got to go."

"Love you, buddy."

"Love you back."

He sat for a moment at the desk, nodding to himself and smiling. He was proud of that boy. Though there was only about sixty thousand left of the inheritance from his mother, he should have kicked in an extra hundred.

Hot. Hotter than hot.

He walked into Dove Cottage, thankful for the fan whirring in the living room, and was greeted by his dog bounding down the hallway, pursued by a youngster.

"Look who's here!" he said.

"Jon'than!" said Jonathan Tolson.

Cynthia appeared from the kitchen. "Jonathan's come to spend the day with us. I didn't think you'd mind having company. We can go bike riding Saturday."

"Right!"

"Your dog," said Jonathan, hugging Barnabas around the neck. "My dog."

"Right. Any dog of mine is a dog of yours." He squatted down and met the blue-eyed gaze of their blond-haired visitor.

"I went to visit Jonathan's mommy this morning and she wasn't feeling well, so . . ." Cynthia lifted her palms, smiling.

"So, we'll have an adventure," said Father Tim. "We'll take a walk on the beach, then we'll go eat hotdogs, and ice cream after. How's that?"

"Not hotdogs," said Jonathan, wrinkling his nose.

"Pizza, then! Or french fries. I'm easy."

Jonathan nodded eagerly, his curls bobbing. "French fries."

"You're lots more fun with kids around," announced his wife.

"Your big dog can go?" asked Jonathan.

"Absolutely. He loves ice cream."

Cynthia took her husband's hand and pulled him along the hall to the kitchen.

"Janette's terribly depressed," she said in a low voice. "She doesn't want to get out of bed. I went to check on her this morning—I'm not sure Jonathan had been fed recently. He just devoured a whole plate of cheese and crackers, thank heaven I had milk. . . ."

"What about the other children?"

"Gone across to cousins. She said they didn't have room for Jonathan. Apparently, Janette hasn't been working for some time. She takes in sewing, you know."

"Dear Lord," he murmured. He'd recommended medical help for Janette Tolson, but she refused, assuring him she'd be fine. He'd seen the emptiness in her gaze, heard it in her voice, and knew she was in trouble.

"I'll be back," he said, kissing his wife.

"The children . . . ," he said, sitting by Janette's bed.

"I don't . . . care," she whispered.

He remembered Miss Sadie talking about her love for Willard Porter, about caring so much for so long that all caring was at last exhausted.

"God cares. He's with you in this."

She turned her head slowly and looked at him, disbelieving.

He put his right palm on her damp forehead. He remembered his mother's cool hand on his forehead when he was sick, and how much that simple gesture had counted to him.

"I promise," he told her.

She closed her eyes and the tears seeped from under her lashes.

The average view of the Christian life, Oswald Chambers had said, is that it means deliverance from trouble. Father Tim agreed with Chambers that, in fact, it means deliverance *in* trouble. That alone and nothing more, and nothing more required. But the child of God had to face the strain before the strength could be provided. Janette Tolson could not face the strain.

"Let me pray for you," he said.

He kept his palm against her forehead, and with his other hand, held hers.

"I *not* stay," said Jonathan, frowning.

"We'll have pancakes for breakfast," he implored. It was a lame strategy, but the best he could do.

Jonathan shook his head and stomped one foot. *"No!* I want to go *home."*

"In the shape of ducks!"

"No."

"Babette and Jason are having fun with cousins. Don't you want to spend the night and have fun with Barnabas?"

They couldn't take him home; his mother was in no condition to look after him. He had called Jean Ballenger, who, eager to please her new priest, had agreed to spend the night with Janette. Tomorrow, following the counsel of Hoppy Harper, he would talk with Janette's own doctor, whom she had avoided for months, and take Janette across to the hospital. He dreaded the prospect.

He looked to his wife, who, of all people, should be able to come up with something to entice a three-year-old.

"I don't know how to get little boys to spend the night in a strange house," she said.

Jonathan's eyes were filling with tears.

Hand shadows! He suddenly recalled a family friend in Holly Springs who had kept him engrossed for hours with a kerosene lamp, a bare wall, and two dexterous hands.

"Turn off the lights in the study," he said, feeling desperate.

"Whatever for?"

"Trust me."

"I want to go *home*!" said Jonathan, meaning it.

"Light the big candle in the hurricane globe," he said. Scalpel, sutures . . . "Put it on the table between our chairs."

Cynthia looked at him as if he'd lost his mind and hurried off to the study.

"Movies!" he said to Jonathan. "Picture show!" He thought he could make a dog. At least a pig. He was certain he could make an eagle; he'd made one on his study wall in Mitford only months ago.

"Popcorn?" asked the boy.

"Now you're talking! Cynthia!" he shouted. "Popcorn, and plenty of butter!"

Cynthia appeared from the study.

"Turn off the lights, light the candle, popcorn with plenty of butter . . . where's the division of labor so popular in modern marriage?"

"My dear, I am the *entertainment*, I can't do it all, this takes teamwork!"

"My mommy, my mommy makes popcorn!" said Jonathan, running behind Cynthia to the kitchen.

Lying awake after midnight, he felt the humidity weighing upon them like a blanket. He also felt what he'd dismissed for weeks:

He was homesick.

He was homesick for Mitford and his boy and Harley, for all the countless components that made his mountain village home.

Whitecap had its charms, of course. There was a great deal to be said for the smaller parish, not to mention the general ease induced by sunshine, salt air, and surf. In times past, hadn't doctors prescribed the seashore as a cure-all for nearly anything that ailed?

But he wasn't ailing, and he didn't need curing.

He believed he was making progress in putting the parish into less quarrelsome order. Several rifts had been healed, and he had ignored the petty issues that, he wasn't surprised, were fading away for want of being nursed.

Better still, he saw his wife finding some repose and freedom of spirit after years of toiling like a Trojan. Yes, she'd begun the new book, but overall, he saw her rested, tanned, and vibrant, and flourishing like a kid at summer camp.

Last and certainly not least, St. John's had fallen in love with Cynthia Kavanagh and freely said as much. She stood with him in the churchyard every Sunday after services, giving and receiving handshakes and hugs, and serving in several parish trenches, including the nursery, like paid help.

"But I love doing it!" she'd said only last week, when he thanked her again.

"What don't you love?" he asked.

"Fading eyesight, creeping forgetfulness, and . . . and calendars with no room to enter all the day's events!"

His wife could derail a train of thought in a heartbeat, jump to another track, and run on it with all engines smoking.

Hot.

He drew the sheet off, eased out of bed, and walked down the hall, floorboards creaking.

In the living room, Barnabas left his blanket in the corner and stretched, then came and stood with him at the screen door, looking into the moon-silvered night.

He unlatched the screen and stepped onto the porch. The full moon cast its image on the distant patch of water.

The sight of two moons, voluptuous and shimmering between two sleeping cottages, caused him to shiver in the heat.

What a different world, this immense expanse of sand and shelf that had heaved itself up from the deeps. . . .

He sat on the top step and gazed at the vast dome above, at what James Joyce had called "the heaventree of stars, hung with humid nightblue fruit."

Great beauty was something he had to work up to, he had to take it in slowly, not gulping, but sipping. He put his hands over his eyes and saw the stars dancing behind his hands, another double image in this deep and silent night.

In Mitford, he'd felt tethered; tethered to Lord's Chapel, tethered to the rectory, tethered to the little yellow house. Here, he felt as if he were falling into space, tethered only to God.

He got up and walked down the steps to the garden, restless and excited, like a child who wakes in the night, filled with fervent dreams.

Barnabas lifted his leg against a favorite spot at the picket fence.

If he could, he'd call home and talk with Dooley again. He'd talk even longer than he'd done today, then ask Dooley to pass the phone to Harley. Next, he'd call Esther and check on Gene, even though they'd spoken on Wednesday, and after that, he might ring Louella and they would sing a hymn, right on the phone. . . .

Truth be known, he'd like nothing better than to call Miss Sadie and hear the bright voice that had always made him listen up and step more smartly.

"Miss Sadie," he said aloud to his still-favorite parishioner, "this is a toll-free call. I hope you like it up there and aren't getting in trouble for bossing the angels around. . . ."

He saw the shooting star plummet toward the silhouette of an oceanfront cottage and vanish.

Then he heard the music.

He turned, thinking that somehow a radio had come on in the house.

But the music wasn't coming from the house.

It was Karg-Elert's "Now Thank We All Our God," and it was coming from . . . across the street.

He stood, frozen and alert.

Someone was playing their stereo full blast. It was an extraordinary rendition of one of his sworn favorites for the organ—mighty, dramatic, charged with power.

He walked to the picket fence and looked across the street at the high-grown, moonlit hedge.

Though distant, he could hear each note clearly and, perhaps because the piece was familiar, he was free to hear beneath the notes the terrible urgency of the music behind the wall, under the full and looming moon.

He crept back to bed, thinking of Hélène Pringle and the faint piano music that had floated out on Mitford's night air.

He shivered in the breeze that came suddenly from the water and blew through their open windows.

Sometime before dawn, he felt the bed move near his feet and thought it was Barnabas.

It was Jonathan Tolson. The boy crept toward the head of the bed, silent, and found a place between them. Father Tim heard him sigh and then, in a moment, heard the boy's rhythmic breathing and smelled his damp, tousled hair.

He prayed for Janette and for today's mission before he drifted again to sleep.

On the way to St. John's, he stopped by Mona's for a coffee to go, and ducked into the bait and tackle shop.

"Here's th' latest," said Ernie. "Th' *Democrat* hit th' street last night, Junior's already had an answer to his ad."

"And?" This was pretty exciting stuff, looking for a wife.

"And it was a guy."

"Aha."

"Wanted to know if Junior'd be interested in sellin' his Bronco."

"That's *it*?"

Ernie shook his head, looking gloomy. "I think we need to doctor that ad."

"Maybe so. By the way, you were going to tell me who lives behind the wall."

"Oh, yeah. Right. Well, that's Morris Love that lives back there."

"Morris Love." He searched Ernie's face. "Tell me more."

"Well, Morris is, you know . . ." Ernie pointed to his head and made a circle with his forefinger.

"Like the rest of us," said Father Tim, looking on the positive side.

"Nothin' to worry about. Morris keeps to hisself, never leaves th' place, except he's bad to holler at people sometimes. Kind of hides behind th' wall and hollers crazy stuff. But tell your missus not to worry, he's harmless."

"Why doesn't he leave the place?"

"Don't want anybody to look at 'im."

"Why's that?"

"Well, see, he's got this . . . handicap. There's a woman takes care of him, comes every day or so, does his cookin' an' all, an' th' organ tuner, he comes in his panel truck from Virginia. Not enough traffic in and out of there to keep th' grass off th' driveway."

"Well, well."

"See, there was a big organ put in there by his grandaddy, they say it was world-class in its time, and ol' Morris, he can play th' hair off that thing, but I ain't heard much about him playin' lately. We all take Morris for granted. Most people don't hardly remember he's in there."

"I'll be darned."

"But don't you worry about a thing. He's harmless, just a little mean streak like 'is grandaddy, is all."

"Aha. So, here's the book I promised you."

"Holy smoke! I gave you a used paperback, and this sucker is *leather.*"

"Take that and keep it, and I hope you like it."

"You got th' wrong end of th' stick, if you ask me, but I appreciate it." Ernie opened the book, squinted at a random page, and read aloud, slowly:

"On his morning rounds th' Master
Goes to learn how all things fare;
Searches pasture after pasture,
Sheep and cattle eyes with care;
And, for silence or for talk,
He hath comrades in his walk;
Four dogs, each pair of different breed,
Distinguished two for scent, and two for speed.

"See a hare before him started!
—Off they fly in earnest chase;
Every dog is eager-hearted,
All th' four are in th' race. . . ."

Ernie looked up, grinning. "Got a good bit of action to it."

As he left the tackle shop, he glanced in the front window, pleased to see the proprietor giving rapt attention to the little book of pastoral ruminations.

Janette Tolson wept all the way across the bridge to the hospital fourteen miles away. He sat with her through the admission to the psychiatric floor, explaining to the clerk there was no insurance, and giving his word the bill would be taken care of. How, he didn't know; that would be God's job. He waited until her doctor arrived and she was settled in a shared room.

Reluctantly, she let go of his hand as he left. "Jonathan . . ."

"Don't worry," he said.

He clung to Cynthia before leaving for the vestry meeting at St. John's.

Oh, the blessed softness of a wife in a hard world . . .

He kissed her, his hands at her waist. Even with all the bike riding, there was a pleasant little roll there.

He winked. "See you later, Tubs."

She jerked away from him, glaring.

No doubt about it, he thought as he raced for the door, he had stepped over his wife's yellow line.

CHAPTER EIGHT

The Spark in the Flax

The rain began in the night, drumming steadily on the red roof of Dove Cottage.

At six a.m., he tried to think of one good reason to spend a full day at the church office, but couldn't. Didn't clergy usually take two days every single week, and hadn't he taken only one since arriving? He would go in after lunch, that was the ticket.

"Wonderful, darling, you can help me feed Jonathan!" His wife had a positively wicked gleam in her eye.

"No! I don't like it!" Jonathan shook his head vigorously when a bowl of cereal was set before him.

Cynthia proffered buttered toast.

"No!" said Jonathan. "No toast!"

"What if we put jelly on it?" asked Father Tim.

"I've tried that," she said. "It doesn't work. We go through this every morning while you trot happily down the street, whistling." She sighed. "I don't know how to make children eat things they don't like."

"Hasn't he given you any clues?"

"I've tried oatmeal, Froot Loops, buttered grits, bacon, not to mention eggs scrambled and boiled. Nothing will do. He always ends up in tears with crackers and cheese."

"We could call someone," he said brightly, "and *ask* what he likes for breakfast."

"Who could we call?"

"Let's see. Jean Ballenger! She knows the family!" What a great solution. He was a regular Sherlock.

"I got to pee-pee," said Jonathan.

"You just pee-pee'd," said Cynthia, looking frazzled.

Jonathan tumbled from the chair and headed toward the bathroom at a trot.

"Your turn to go with him," said his wife. "And please put the seat down afterward."

"I have no idea!" exclaimed Jean when he rang her small cottage next to the library. "I never saw anyone eat anything while I was at the Tolsons'."

After the useless phone inquiry, Cynthia pulled him into the study. "I don't suppose Jean would like to keep Jonathan for a little while?"

"Jean Ballenger? I can't imagine such a thing!" Jean, a fastidious spinster with crocheted antimacassars on her armchairs, would hardly be up for tending a strong-willed three-year-old.

"What are we going to do?" asked Cynthia. "I think he's adorable, truly he is. But he's running me ragged. I'm too *old* for this!"

"I'll be here 'til one o'clock. Go to your drawing board, relax, everything is under control."

So why did she peer at him like that, with one eyebrow up and one down?

"Eureka!" he shouted, running along the hall to her studio. "I've found it!"

"Found what?" she asked, not looking up from a watercolor of Violet under a yellow and blue beach umbrella.

"What he likes for breakfast!" He was positively triumphant; he might have located the very Grail.

"I'll never guess, so tell me." She couldn't help grinning at her husband, who looked as if he'd been run through a food processor.

"Guess!" he insisted, playing the mean trick Emma always played on him.

"M&M's?"

"Not even close. Two more."

"Reese's peanut butter cups! That would certainly be *my* preference for breakfast every morning!"

"Cynthia . . ."

"All right, I'm not trying. Here goes, and I'm quite serious this time." She looked out the window. She curled a strand of hair around one finger. She sighed.

"I don't have a clue," she said.

"Spaghetti."

"No."

"Yes!"

"Al dente, I presume."

"A little respect, please. I've just made an important discovery here."

"Yes, dear, and thank you. Plain or with marinara?"

"With butter. No fork, no spoon. Just dump it in a bowl and set it in front of him. Of course, you'll have to bathe him after it's all over."

"Bathe him?" There went that eyebrow again.

"All right, *I'll* bathe him. But just this once."

Why did children keep turning up on his doorstep? Not that he was complaining, but wasn't it odd that he'd lived a full six decades with hardly a youngster in his life except those he encountered in Sunday School? But then, look what it had gained him, after all—Dooley Barlowe. One of the greatest gifts, most of the time, that had ever "come down from the Father of lights," as St. James had put it.

In any case, this was a picnic compared to Father Tracey, who, with his good wife, had adopted fourteen children. Fourteen! It boggled the mind. And then there was Father Moultrie, who had passed into legend, though still living as far he knew. This good fellow had collected twenty-one children of various ages and backgrounds and had managed, so it was said, to keep the lot in good order, though the addition he built to his suburban home had literally fallen down one night after a communal pillow fight; thanks be to God no one was badly hurt.

"And darling . . . ," said his smiling wife as he turned to leave the room.

"Yes?"

"Thank you for mopping the floor under his chair when you've finished."

"No problem," he said, trying to mean it.

He looked out the study window at the incessant rain, then checked his watch.

A quarter 'til twelve.

Mule and J.C. would just be trooping into the rear booth.

He knew it was a busy time at the Grill, but he was missing those guys, and how much trouble could it be for Velma to call somebody to the phone?

He listened as the red phone on the wall beside the grill rang twice. Four times. Six. Seven . . .

He was ready to hang up when Velma answered.

"Velma, it's Tim Kavanagh!"

"Who?"

"Tim Kavanagh."

"What can I do for you, we've got a lunch trade here to take care of."

"Right. Could you, ah, call Mule to the phone? Or J.C.?"

"Hold on."

He heard the receiver being laid on top of the wall unit, then heard it fall, swinging on the cord and knocking against the wall, *blam . . . blam . . . blam.* He held his own receiver away from his ear.

The babble in the Grill sounded a continent away, all the clatter and uproar that had been so familiar for so long seemed so . . . distant. His heart sank.

"I don't serve grits after nine o'clock!" That was Percy.

Clink. Clank. Thunk.

"Dagummit!" Percy again. Must have dropped his spatula.

"Lord help! Lookit what th' President's done now." Sounded like Leonard Stanley, who always sat at the counter opposite the phone. "Oh, boy! *Un*believable."

"I don't read th' paper, makes my stomach wrench. Except for th' funnies, I've plumb quit." Coot Hendrick. "But I like those fliers that come with th' paper—you know, Wal-Mart, Ken's Auto Parts, discount coupons for Domino's Pizza, like that."

Whop. Sizzle.

"We ain't got a special today!" yelled Percy. "I'm over offerin' specials, have t' take it straight off th' menu!"

"So, what'd th' President do?"

"Trust me, you don't want to know. I wonder if there's any Alka-Seltzer in this place." *Rustle, crackle.* Leonard must have sprung for a big newspaper like thc *Atlanta Constitution,* considering the racket it made as he turned the pages.

"Can you *believe* it?" He heard Velma stomp by the phone. "Th' front booth wants a 'BLT without lettuce or tomato!' I said right to 'is face, 'How can you have a BLT without *L* an' *T?'* an' he said, *'What?'* That's th' same fool ordered a cheeseburger th' other day an' asked me to hold th' *cheese.*"

"I'd take early retirement if I was you," said Coot.

It was clear that in the lunch-hour rush, Velma had forgotten his phone call.

He yelled into the mouthpiece. "Velma! Percy! *Hello!*"

He heard the front door open and slam, the hiss of a pop-top soda being opened.

"Hello! Somebody! *Anybody!*"

"What's this phone doin' hangin' by th' cord?" asked Percy. "Must have got knocked off th' hook."

Click.

Jonathan poked a chubby finger at the television screen in the guest room. "I want to watch a movie," he said.

"Ah. A movie."

"In a box," said the three-year-old.

He looked at his watch. "In a box." Fifty-seven minutes to go.

"Peter Pan."

"Peter Pan. Right."

"You like Peter Pan?"

"Oh, yes. Very much!"

Jonathan poked his finger at Father Tim's leg. "So, let's watch it then!"

"We could tell a story. I could read to you, how's that?"

"Watch a movie in a box!"

In a box, in a box. He had a box left over from the books. He dashed to the back porch and hauled it in.

"I one time had a *Li'n King* movie," said Jonathan, "an' my daddy, my daddy, my daddy wouldn't let me watch it." Jonathan furrowed his brow.

He set the boy in the cardboard box and turned on the TV. Good grief! He couldn't believe his eyes, and in broad daylight, too. He surfed. Fifty minutes to go.

"Peter Pan!" yelled Jonathan. "In a *box*!"

He trucked to the studio. "For Pete's sake, Kavanagh, what is a movie in a box?"

"A video, dear. We don't have any."

"Why not?"

"We don't have a VCR."

"We don't even have a microwave," he said, perplexed.

He dashed back to the guest room and pulled Jonathan out of the box. "We're going for a walk."

"I don't want to walk!"

"In this life, my boy, you'll be forced to do many things you'd rather not do, so consider this a rehearsal."

He marched Jonathan into the kitchen and dragged Barnabas from under the table. He snapped the red leash on his dog's collar as the phone rang.

He glanced out the kitchen window as he snatched up the cordless from the window seat. Blast! They couldn't go for a walk, he'd forgotten it was raining cats and dogs.

"Hello!" he barked.

"Father? Is that *you*?"

"Esther!"

"You didn't sound like yourself," said Esther, who didn't sound like herself, either. "I've got to talk to you about Gene."

"Shoot!" he said, cantering down the hall after Jonathan, who was making a beeline for the front door.

"He's actin' so strange, I hardly know him. I'm tellin' you, he's just not my Gene, he could be somebody named Hubert or Pete or Lord knows who, he's actin' so peculiar."

"What's he doing?" he asked, grabbing the boy before he dove off the porch.

He carried him back into the house under one arm. "Down!" yelled the boy, squirming and kicking.

"Who in the world is that?" asked Esther.

"That's Jonathan. Tell me what Gene's doing."

"He's counting things. He stares at me and says, 'Seven.' And I say, 'Seven what?' And he says, 'That's seven times you opened the cabinet door over the stove.'"

"Down!" said Jonathan, wriggling out of Father Tim's grasp.

"Aha. I'm listening, Esther, keep talking. You opened the cabinet door seven times . . ."

Johnathan had dropped to all fours and was drinking water from the dog bowl. He transferred the cordless to his left hand and removed the red leash from Barnabas's collar with his right. He snapped the leash to the boy's romper strap and looped the other end over the back of a kitchen chair.

"He looked at me last night, said, 'Eighteen.' I said, 'Eighteen what?' He said, 'Curlers.' We're goin' up to bed, he said, 'Fourteen.' Lord knows, my nerves are shot by this time, he'd been doin' it all day, I didn't even ask fourteen what, an' he said, 'Steps.' I can tell you right now I do not like it, he has been pullin' this dumb trick for months, but it's gettin' worse by th' minute.

"To tell th' gospel truth, I could knock him in th' head. Can you imagine livin' with somebody who walks around goin' '*Sixty-six!* That's sixty-six window panes.' Or, '*Nineteen!* That's nineteen knobs on th' cabinet doors.' The other day I thought, wonder why there's just nineteen knobs and not twenty, and th' first thing you know, I was countin' knobs *myself.*"

"I'll be darned."

"I'm on th' hall phone, but I can hear him, he's countin' squares in th' kitchen linoleum as we speak!"

"Oh, boy."

"For the umpteenth time!" Esther lowered her voice. "Father, do you reckon he's . . . crazy? It scares th' daylights out of me to even think a word like that."

"Does Hoppy know what's going on?"

"We had all those tests run, you'd think somethin' mental would show up in th' blood work."

"I feel you should talk to Hoppy. When are you seeing him again?"

"Two weeks."

"You may want to give him a ring."

"I can't, he's on vacation. You know he never took one for years, so I reckon he deserves it."

"Talk to his associate, talk to Dr. Wilson."

"Are you kiddin' me? He's green as tasselin' corn."

"I'd talk to Dr. Wilson, Esther."

Esther had started to cry and was trying to hide it. "Only one thing hasn't changed."

"What's that?"

Jonathan was dragging the chair across the kitchen, as Barnabas sat under the table, bewildered.

"He still pats me on the cheek and says, 'Goodnight, Dollface,' just like he's done for forty-two years."

"Horsie!" shouted Jonathan.

"I wish you were here," sobbed Esther.

"I wish I were, too," he said, meaning it.

He put socks on the kitchen chair legs and let Jonathan pull the darned thing all over the house. Cynthia shut her door—in fact, it sounded like she locked it—and Barnabas hid in the corner of the study by the bookshelves. As for himself, he sat in the living room like a country squire, and perused the *Whitecap Reader*.

> Some members of the Wadamo tribe of the Zambezi Valley in Zimbabwe are born with only two toes on each foot, which is an inherited trait. However, these people can walk as well as anyone with five toes on each foot.
>
> **This Space for Rent**
>
> Get Geared Up! Your One Stop Fishing Gear and Auto Supply Store, Whitecap Fishing Gear And Auto Parts
>
> Custom Modular homes, Affordable Quality, Tozier Builders (across from Bragg's in the Toe)
>
> Trivia: Which night precedes May Day? Which island separates the Canadian part of Niagara Falls from the American? Whose army were canned foods developed to feed?
>
> SHEAR CREATIONS: Hairstyling for the entire family, fish sandwiches and pasta to go . . .

> Laugh for the week: "I don't mind her being born again, but did she have to come back as herself?"

He sighed. The *Reader* was the only newspaper he'd ever seen that made the *Muse* look like the *Philadelphia Inquirer*.

He allowed the boy to exhaust himself until, on the dot of one, he went down for a nap without a whimper. "Hallelujah!" Father Tim whispered to his dog as he tiptoed from the guest room and closed the door.

He got into his car at the rear gate and drew the dripping umbrella in with him. As he turned the key in the ignition, he noticed a panel truck parked at Morris Love's entrance. He adjusted his glasses.

L. L. Mansfield, Tuning for Fine Organs.

A driver got out of the truck and went to the iron gate, swung it open, came back to the truck, and drove through.

He sat for a moment, curious at the first sign of coming and going he'd seen across the road. He watched the driver trot back and lock the gate behind him.

Fort Knox! he thought, driving away.

I tell thee what I would have thee do . . .

He sat in the church office, hearing rain peck the windowpanes like chickens after corn, and read from a sermon of Charles Spurgeon, delivered at Newington on March 9, 1873.

> *Go to Him without fear or trembling; ere yon sun goes down and ends this day of mercy, go and tell Him thou hast broken the Father's laws—tell Him that thou art lost, and thou needest to be saved; tell Him that He is a man, and appeal to His manly heart, and to His brotherly sympathies.*
>
> *Pour out thy broken heart at His feet: let thy soul flow over in His presence, and I tell thee He cannot cast thee away . . .*

He jotted in his sermon notebook: *Not that He will not turn a deaf ear, but that He cannot. Press this truth.* Spurgeon had put into a nutshell what he wanted to preach on Sunday to the body at St. John's.

> *. . . though thy prayer be feeble as the spark in the flax, He will not quench it; and though thy heart be bruised like a reed, He will not break it.*
>
> *May the Holy Spirit bless you with a desire to go to God through Jesus Christ; and encourage you to do so by showing that He is meek and lowly of heart, gentle, and tender, full of pity.*

Bottom line, he would tell his congregation what Nike had told the world:

Just do it.

He finished typing up the pew bulletin and rang the hospital. Janette was down the hall. "Tell her I'll be there tomorrow," he said to the nurse. "Tell her Jonathan's having a wonderful time."

He fished the umbrella from the stand by the downstairs door and prepared to head into the downpour.

"Father Kavanagh, is that you?"

He spun around. "Good heavens!"

"I frightened you, Father, I'm sorry as can be!"

"Mercy!" he said, not knowing what else to say. A tall, thin, stooped woman in a dripping hat and raincoat stood before him, her glasses sliding off her wet nose.

"I came in through the front door and couldn't find a soul, so I helped myself to these stairs. I'm Ella Bridgewater, come to audition!"

He was addled. "But I thought tomorrow . . ."

"I wrote down today in my appointment book, Father, I am very precise about such things, and besides, I couldn't have done it tomorrow, for I'm going across to my niece. I always do that on Saturday, so I would never have—"

"Of course. My mistake, I'm sure." He was very precise about such things, as well. But why quibble?

"Well, Miss Bridgewater, glad to see you!" He took her wet hand and shook it heartily, noting that she appeared considerably older than her letter had stated.

She patted her chest. "I have the music under my coat!"

"Excellent. We'll just pop upstairs and have at it. Thanks for coming out in the deluge."

He followed her up the stairs to the sacristy. She was certainly agile, he thought.

"I've always loved this church, Father. I think I wrote in my letter to you that I played for yoked parishes for many years in these islands."

"Yes. Wonderful!"

"So I certainly know the churches in these parts, though I never stepped foot in St. John's 'til this day." She looked around the sanctuary and nave with some wonder.

"You don't mean it!"

"Not once. Too busy playing elsewhere!"

"I wish you could see it in the sunlight, the way the stained glass pours color into the nave."

Wiry gray curls sprung up as she removed her rain hat. "I believe I *will* see it in the sunlight!"

Mighty perky lady, he thought. And seventy if she was a day. Her letter, however, had said sixty-two, and added "in vibrant good health."

"There's the choir loft, as you can see. I believe you'll find our old Hammond in fine working order. Well, then, let me help you off with your coat, and you can pop up the stairs there. Would you like a cup of coffee? Or tea? Won't take but a moment."

"No, thank you, Father, I'm ready to get on with it. I've been practicing like all get-out for days—you know they say if you fail to prepare, you prepare to fail."

"Perfect line for a wayside pulpit!"

"That's where I got it," she said, with a burst of laughter. "Well, here goes."

She walked briskly up the aisle, clutching her manila envelope, and made short work of the stairs to the loft.

There was a moment's rustling in the loft and, he thought, a mite of hard breathing.

"Great day in the morning!" she shouted down. "This organ is old as Methuselah."

"Manufactured the year of my fourth birthday!"

"Which was a good year, I'm sure. Now . . ."—he heard her clear her throat and heave a sigh—"sit and close your eyes. I'll give you a prelude and fugue, followed by a hymn. Then you're allowed to make one personal request."

"Thank you, Miss Bridgewater." He was glad he didn't mind being told what to do by women; he'd never lacked for direction in that department.

"My, my," he heard her say. "Oh, yes." She fiddled with the stops, pressed the pedals, hummed a little. "Well, then!"

The old organ nearly blasted him out of the pew. Aha! It was Bach's Little Prelude and Fugue in C Major, and she was giving it everything she had. This woman had eaten her Wheaties, and no doubt about it.

At the end, she called in a loud voice, "How was that, Father?"

"Why . . . play on!" he said. Very perky.

"For All the Saints" boomed up to the rafters. Ah. Good to have the organ going in this place, a benediction.

He listened carefully, unable to restrain himself from whispering the words under his breath.

" 'For all the saints, who from their labors rest, who thee by faith before the world confessed, thy Name O Jesus, be forever blessed. Alleluia, alleluia . . .' "

Not especially thrilling, as the rendition of it certainly could be, but better than he might have expected, to tell the truth. He patted his foot and attended each note, keeping an open mind to the very end.

Agreeably workmanlike, he concluded.

"How was that?" she trumpeted.

"Well done!"

"Thank you, Father, honesty is the best policy, and I don't mind saying that all my priests have liked my playing."

Rain blew against the windows, *peck, peck, peck.*

"Miss Bridgewater, is it time for my personal request?"

"It is, and I must say I'm filled with curiosity."

"What about 'Strengthen for Service, Lord'?" A communion hymn worth its salt and then some!

"Excellent, Father! Two-oh-one in the old hymnal, three-twelve in the new. Here we go."

He chuckled. He hadn't encountered such bravado since the last meeting of the youth group.

" 'Strengthen for service, Lord,' " he whispered as she played, " 'the hands that holy things have taken; let ears that now have heard thy songs, to clamor never waken . . .' " *To clamor never waken.* His favorite line.

He looked around the walls and up to the ceiling as if the music were painting the very timbers, bathing them, somehow, and making them stand more firmly.

He was drinking it all in as if starved, and then the audition was over.

He stood and faced the loft and clapped with some enthusiasm.

Huffing slightly and clutching her envelope, she was down the stairs, along the aisle, and standing by his pew in a trice. Her long nose and stooped shoulders gave her the appearance, he thought, of an Oriental crane.

"Well done!" he said again.

"Thank you, Father. I have a confession." She held her envelope like a shield against her chest, looking pained but confident.

"Shall we . . . go to the altar?" he asked.

"Don't trouble yourself, I'll just spit it out right here."

"Sit down," he said. He sat, himself, and scooted over.

She thumped into the oak pew. "I lied about my age."

"Oh?"

"I turned seventy-four last month. I didn't think you'd hire me if I told the truth, and I want you to know I'm sorry. As I was playing your request, the Lord convicted my heart and I asked Him to forgive me. Perhaps you'll do the same."

She looked exceedingly pained.

"Why, certainly, Miss Bridgewater. Of course. And may I say you don't look seventy-four."

She brightened considerably. "Why, thank you, Father. You see, I believe the Lord called me to St. John's. When I heard you had a need, I asked Him about it at once, and He said, 'Ella Jean'—the Lord always uses my middle name—'march over there and ask for that job, they need you.' "

"Aha."

"He doesn't speak to me in an audible voice."

"I understand."

"He puts it in my mind, you might say. As you well know, Father, you have to be quiet before the Lord and keep your trap shut for Him to get a word in edgewise, that's my experience."

"Miss Bridgewater—"

"Call me Ella," she said.

"Ella, if we can agree on your compensation, I think you may be just the ticket for St. John's."

Tears sprang to her eyes. "Do you really think so?"

"I do."

"But," she said, regaining her composure, "you'll have to run it by the vestry."

"Right. I intend to."

"When might that be?"

"Wednesday. I'll get back to you right after the meeting. Shouldn't be any problem. Do you have family?"

"I lived with my mother for many years, she went to heaven last March."

"I'm sorry to hear it. Or glad, as the case may be." Heaven! The ultimate place to escape the clamor . . .

"I'm an old maid," she said, bobbing her head and smiling. "But not the sort of dried-up old maid you see in cartoons."

"Oh?" A priest never knew what he might be told. He shifted uneasily on the pew.

"No, indeed. I fell head over heels in love when I was forty-seven, and truth be told, have never gotten over it. They say you came late to love, yourself."

"Late, yes," he said, smiling. "But not too late."

"Minor was a young explorer with Admiral Byrd, and spent his last years as a maker of hot-air balloons."

"You don't say!"

"Oh, yes. And I went up in one!" Her eyes were bright with feeling. "We sailed up the coast and across Virginia and landed in a cow pasture, where we picnicked on cheese and figs. It was the single grandest thing I ever did."

"I'm happy to hear it," he said. And he was.

Miss Bridgewater adjusted her glasses and peered at him. "And when would I begin if . . . if . . ."

"Sunday after next, I should think."

"Well!" she said, sitting back and beaming. "Well!"

The everlasting rain was still going strong at four-thirty, when he pulled into Ernie's for a gallon of milk.

Roger Templeton sat in the corner by a small pile of wood shavings, and looked up when he came in.

"Tim! Glad to see you! How's your weather?"

"You mean my own, apart from the elements? I'd say . . . sunny!" Hadn't God just delivered an organist to St. John's?

He scratched Lucas behind the ears, then pulled up a chair next to Roger, peering into Roger's lap at what had been a block of wood. The rough form of a duck, though headless, had emerged, its right wing beginning to assume feathers.

"Amazing! May I have a look?"

"Help yourself," said Roger, pleased to be asked.

He took the duck and examined it closely. In principle, at least, this was how David had escaped from Michelangelo's block of marble.

"That's tupelo wood," said Roger. "I get it from up around Albemarle Sound. With tupelo, you can cut across the grain, with the grain, or against the grain."

"It's beautiful!" he said. How had Roger known the wood contained a duck just waiting to get out?

"That's a green-winged teal. It's not much to look at yet; I've rough-edged it with a band saw and now I'm carving in the feather groupings."

"How did you know you could do this?"

Roger took a knife from an old cigar box next to his chair. "I didn't. I'd never done anything with my hands."

"Except make money," said Ernie, walking in from the book room. He thumped down at the table.

"I used to go on hunting trips with my colleagues . . . Alaska, Canada, the eastern shore of Maryland around St. Michael's and Easton. I recall the day I dropped a green-winged teal into the river. When the Lab brought it to me, I saw for the first time the great beauty of it. My eyes were opened in a new way, and I wondered how I'd managed to . . . do what I'd been doing."

"Aha."

"Oh, I'm not preaching a sermon against hunting, Tim. Let a man hunt! I also have a special fondness for a boy learning to hunt. But I quit right there at the river, I said if God Almighty could make just one feather, not to mention a whole duck, as intricate and beautiful as that, who am I to bring it down?"

"He still fishes," said Ernie.

"Why did you start carving?"

Roger shrugged. “I wanted to see how close I could come to the real thing. I thought I’d try to make just one and then quit.”

“I see.”

“But I never seem to come very close to the real thing, so I keep trying.”

Father Tim had never done much with his hands, either, except turn the pages of a book or plant a rosebush. “How long does it take to make one?”

“Oh, five or six weeks, sometimes longer.”

“He works on ’is ducks in my place, exclusive,” said Ernie, as if that lent a special distinction to Ernie’s Books, Bait & Tackle.

“Do you also work at home?”

Roger colored slightly. “I paint at home, but my wife doesn’t allow carving.”

He’d heard of not being allowed to smoke cigars at home, but he’d never heard of a ban on duck carving.

“Roger, my wife has bought me a chair on Captain Willie’s fishing boat. You ever go deep-sea fishing?”

“Does a hog love slop?” asked Ernie, who didn’t care to be out of the loop in any conversation.

“Captain Willie has taken me out to the Gulf Stream many times.”

“I don’t mind telling you I’m no fisherman. I’ve never spent much time around water.”

“That’s no liability. Sport fishing is all about relaxing and having fun. It’s an adventure.”

An adventure! He’d always wanted to have an adventure, but wasn’t good at figuring out how to get from A to B. Leave it to his wife to figure it out for him.

“I hear a lot about spending the day with your head over the side.”

Roger and Ernie laughed. “Don’t listen to that mess,” said Ernie. “You stay sober the night before and get a good night’s sleep and you’ll be fine.”

“And don’t eat a greasy breakfast,” said Roger. “Besides, if it’s any comfort, statistics say only twelve percent get seasick.”

He was encouraged.

“What’ll we see out there?”

“Out in the Gulf,” said Ernie, “you’ll see your blue marlin, your white marlin, your sailfish, your dolphin—”

"There's wahoo," said Roger, "and yellow tuna—"

"Plus your black tuna and albacore tuna. . . ."

"Man. Big stuff!" He was feeling twelve years old.

Roger whittled. "You can see everything from a thousand-pound blue marlin to a two-pound mahimahi."

"No kidding? But what kind of fish can you actually *catch*?"

"Whatever God grants you that day," said Roger. "Of course, we always release marlin."

"Fair enough. What sort of boat would we go in?"

"Captain Willie runs a Carolina hull built over on Roanoke Island. About fifty-three feet long—"

"—an' eight hundred and fifty horsepower!" Ernie appeared to take personal pride in this fact. "What you might call a glorified speedboat."

"Eight hundred and fifty horsepower? Man!" He was losing his vocabulary, fast.

Roger adjusted his glasses and looked at Father Tim. "Just show up ready to have a good time. That's what I'd recommend."

"And be sure an' take a bucket of fried chicken," said Ernie.

He cooked the requisite bowl of spaghetti while Jonathan sat in the window seat and colored a batch of Cynthia's hasty sketches. Something baking in the oven made his heart beat faster.

"Cassoulet!" said his creative wife. Though she'd never attempted such a thing, she had every confidence it would be sensational. "Fearless in the kitchen" was how she once described herself.

"It's all in the crust, the way the crust forms on top," she told him, allowing a peek into the oven. "I know it's too hot to have the oven going, but I couldn't resist."

"Where on earth did you find duck?"

"At the little market. It was lying right by the mahimahi. Isn't that wonderful?"

He certainly wouldn't mention it to Roger.

Jonathan had clambered down from the window seat. "Watch a movie!" he said, giving a tug on Father Tim's pants leg.

"Timothy, we've got to get a VCR. Could you possibly go across tomorrow, to whatever store carries these things? I don't think I can make it 'til Monday without in-house entertainment!"

"Do we just plug it in?" He'd never been on friendly terms with high technology, which was always accompanied by manuals printed in Croatian.

"Beats me," she said. "That's your job. I'm the stay-at-home mommy."

He put his arms around her and traced the line of her cheek with his nose. "Thank you for being the best deacon in the entire Anglican communion."

Jonathan had wanted his mother tonight; his tears called up a few of Father Tim's very own.

He thought it must be agony to be small and helpless, with no mother, no father, no brother or sister to be found. He held Jonathan against his chest, over his heart, and let the boy sob until he exhausted his tears.

He walked with him through the house in a five-room circle, crooning snatches of hymns, small prayers and benedictions, fragments of stories about Pooh and Toad and that pesky rabbit, Peter. He didn't know what to do with a child who was crying out of bewilderment and loss, except to be with him in it.

He covered the sleeping boy with a light blanket, praying silently. Then he closed the door and tiptoed down the hall and out to the porch where Cynthia sat waiting, a rain-drugged Violet slumbering in her lap.

Barnabas followed and sprawled at his feet.

What peace to retire into the cool August evening, after a dinner that might have been served in the Languedoc.

For the first time today, he liked the rain, it was friend and shelter to him, enclosing the porch with a gossamer veil.

They watched the distant patch of gray Atlantic turn to platinum in the lingering dusk.

"Weary, darling?" she asked, taking his hand.

"I am. Don't know why, though. Haven't done much today."

"You do more than you realize. Up at dawn, morning prayer, feed and bathe the boy, help the wife, write the pew bulletin, work on your sermon, hire an organist . . ."

He took her hand and kissed it. Of all the earthly consolations, he loved understanding best. Not sympathy, no, that could be deadly. But understanding. It was balm to him, and he had sucked it up like a toad, often denying it to her.

"Your book—how are you feeling about it?" he asked.

"I guess I don't know why I'm doing another book when I might have the lovely freedom to do nothing. I suppose I got excited about being in a new place, the way the light changes, and the coming and going of the tide. It spoke to me and I couldn't help myself." She smiled at him. "I think I make books because I don't know what else to do."

"You know how to make a ravishing cassoulet."

"Yes, but cassoulet has its limitations. Little books do not."

He nodded.

"Do you think we'll ever just loll about?" she asked.

"I don't think we're very good at lolling."

She put her head back and closed her eyes. "Thank God for this peace."

He heard it first, even through the loud whisper of rain. It was the organ music of their neighbor. He sat up, alert, and cupped his hand to his ear.

"What is it, Timothy?"

"It's Morris Love, in the house behind the wall. Listen."

They sat silent for long moments.

"Wondrous," she said quietly.

The rain seemed to abate out of respect for the music, and they began to hear the notes more clearly.

"Name that tune," she said.

" 'Jesus My Joy.' A Bach chorale prelude." He couldn't help but hear the urgency—in truth, a kind of fury—underlying the music. He told her what he knew about Morris Love, leaving out the part about him shouting through the hedge.

"Is Mr. Love a concert organist?"

"Not unless you consider this a private concert for the Kavanaghs."

"What a lovely thought," she said, pleased.

When the phone rang, he fumbled for it. For a moment, he was at home in Mitford and expected to find it next to the bed. But blast, he was in Whitecap, and the phone was across the room.

It rang again; he bumped into the chair and tried to figure what time it was. The rain had stopped, and a stiff breeze blew through the windows.

As the phone continued to ring, he picked up his watch and glanced at the glowing dial. Twelve-forty. Not good. *Lord, have mercy. . . .*

"Hello!"

"I have a collect call from Harley Welch," said an operator. "Will you pay for the call?"

"Yes!"

"Rev'rend?"

"Harley?" His heart hammered.

"Rev'rend, I hate t' tell you this . . ."

CHAPTER NINE

Home Far Away

"They got Dooley in jail."

"What?"

"But he's all right, he ain't hurt or nothin. . . ."

Cynthia sat up. "What is it, Timothy?"

He switched on the lamp. "Dooley."

"Dear God!" she said.

"Tell me, Harley." He once prayed he'd never live to hear what he was hearing now.

"Well, he was comin' home on time, goin' to be here right on th' nickel. . . ."

"And?" His mouth was dry, his stomach churning. *Christ, have mercy. . . .*

"An' he picked up Buster Austin standin' out on th' road. You remember Buster."

Indeed, he did. Buster had called yours truly a "nerd," for which Dooley had mopped the floor of the school cafeteria with him. The last run-in was when Buster stole a pack of cigarettes and talked Dooley into smoking on school grounds. School principal Myra Hayes had nearly eaten one hapless priest alive for "allowing" such a thing to happen, and suspended Dooley for ten days.

"Buster said he needed a ride to git 'is clothes at somebody's house, would Dooley take 'im, an' Dooley said he would but make it snappy. Dooley set in th' truck while Buster took in a empty duffel bag and come out a good bit later. Seems like th' boys was goin' down th' road when two officers drove up behind 'em in a squad car. Pulled 'em over, hauled 'em off to th' station for breakin,' enterin,' an' larceny."

"Larceny?" This was a bad dream.

"You know that empty duffel bag Buster carried in? Hit was full when Buster come out of th' house. Had jewelry, a CD player, money, liquor, I don't know what all in there."

"No!"

"Police said th' house had a silent alarm on it, an' they was on th' boys before they got out of th' driveway good. But Dooley didn't do nothin'."

"I believe that."

"Nossir, he didn't, he was doin' th' drivin' is all, but the police says 'til they know better, he's locked up."

"What can I do?" His legs were turned to water; he sank into the chair by the lamp.

"If I was you, Rev'rend, I'd do what preachers do."

"Pray."

"That's right. I'm down at th' station, an' soon as I hear somethin', I'll call you. I know Dooley don't want you worried an' all. He would of called, but he's upset about worryin' you."

"How is he, Harley? Tell me straight."

"Well, he's scared. He's innocent, but hit's scary bein' th'owed in a cell like that an' locked up."

"Is Rodney there?"

"Last I heard, th' chief was puttin' on 'is britches an' bustin' over here."

"Thank God for you, Harley."

"Now, don't you worry, Rev'rend."

He hung up, trembling, feeling the immutable reality of six hundred miles between Mitford and his racing heart.

At one-thirty, he could bear it no longer and called the Mitford police station.

Rodney Underwood was questioning Dooley and Buster. No, they didn't know when the chief would be through, but he would call when he was.

Jonathan trotted in and clambered onto their bed.

"I think I read somewhere that children aren't supposed to sleep with their parents," he said.

"We're not his parents," explained his wife.

Jonathan bounced down beside Cynthia, looking hopeful. "Watch a movie!"

Cynthia was not amused. "Jonathan, if you so much as utter the M word again, I will jump in the ocean!"

He nodded his head vigorously. "I can swim!"

"Good! Go to sleep."

He poked his chubby finger into Cynthia's arm. "You go to sleep, too."

Father Tim paced the floor, checking his watch.

"I'm hungry," said Jonathan.

"People don't eat during the night."

Jonathan held out both hands. "Give me candy, then?"

Cynthia leaned toward him, shaking her head. "If you weren't so utterly adorable . . ."

"You got bad breath," said Jonathan, wrinkling his nose.

"When I go to the library tomorrow," she told her husband, "I'll see if they have a book on what to do with children."

The phone rang at two o'clock.

"Buster Austin's been askin' for trouble for years," said Rodney. "Now he's gone and stepped in it."

"What about Dooley?"

"Dooley says he rode Buster over to the house and sat in the truck, said he didn't have nothin' to do with it, but Buster says he did. Soon as th' paperwork's done, I'll drive th' boys over to Wesley and take 'em before th' magistrate."

"Good Lord, Rodney. What does that mean?"

"Th' magistrate's th' one signs th' arrest warrant, then I'll serve it. I'm goin' to tell 'im I think Dooley's innocent, he's never been in any trouble, and we'll see where we go from there. He'll set bond, and you'll have to talk to a bondsman if you want Dooley out of jail."

"Right. I know the bondsman in Wesley. Call me the minute you know something. What kind of bond do you think we're talking about?"

"Breakin' and enterin' and larceny is serious business. You might get off for twenty thousand, maybe ten. Th' Austins will probably post a property bond, Buster don't come from fancy circumstances."

He couldn't believe this was happening. It was a nightmare. It was also the ruination of his boy's summer, his last precious days at home. . . . He felt sick in his very gut.

"Where do we go from there?" he asked.

"Th' magistrate will set a court date, two weeks to thirty days away."

"Let me talk with Dooley, if I may." He felt like a Mack truck was sitting on his chest.

"Hey," said Dooley.

"Hey, yourself," he replied, drawing thin comfort from their old greeting.

"I didn't do it."

"I believe you."

"Buster Austin's still th' same lyin', cheatin' geek he always was. I should've known better. I picked 'im up 'cause I thought he was in trouble, I thought maybe his ol' car was broke down an' I was tryin' to help. I could kill 'im, maybe I will."

"I think you did the right thing."

"You do?"

"I do. It was someone you knew, you thought he needed help, and you stopped."

"So how come it turned out like this?" He could hear the barely controlled rage in the boy's voice.

"Sometimes we do good and it turns out badly. I don't know why. But it definitely doesn't mean we're to stop doing the right thing."

"Yeah, well, wait'll Lace an' ever'body hears about it."

"I thought you weren't seeing much of Lace."

"I don't care what she thinks, anyway, but what about ever'body else, like Avis? And what if it gets back to school? I mean, some of th' guys will think it's cool, but th' headmaster, he'll . . . he'll freak."

"If it comes up, tell the truth."

"I want to go home," said Dooley. He sounded exhausted. "I got to work tomorrow."

"Rodney will take you home as soon as the bail issue is settled."

"Did you know I'll have to go to court for this stupid mess?"

"Yes."

"I'll have to come home from school, but I ain't tellin' this to Mr. Fleming, no way. You can say I've got to have an operation or somethin'. Maybe on my kidneys or tonsils or . . . on my brain or spine."

"We'll cross that bridge when we get to it. I'm sorry this happened, I wish we were there. God bless you, everything's going to be fine. I'll call the bondsman as soon I hear back from Rodney, don't be afraid, we love you." He tried to cover all the bases, but his heart felt empty as a gourd.

Rodney called at three a.m.

He'd done everything he could to convince the magistrate that Dooley was a good kid with no previous offenses, emphasizing that his daddy was a clergyman. The magistrate said he was a preacher's kid himself, and based on that alone had a notion to set bail at forty thousand. Bottom line, the magistrate was releasing Dooley on a secured five-thousand-dollar bond, and Rodney was driving him home as soon as the bondsman could get over to the Wesley jail. Buster Austin's parents had refused to post bond, and Buster would not be going home.

He found Ray Porter's number in his black book, and woke him up.

"Ray, Tim Kavanagh. My boy's in the Wesley jail and he's innocent. He's under a five-thousand-dollar secured bond. How fast can you get him out of there?"

"Let me jump in my clothes," said Ray. "I'll have him out in twenty, thirty minutes. Y'all still down at th' coast?"

"Afraid so. How shall I send the fee?"

"Put a check in the mail. You got my address?"

"I have it somewhere."

"Post office box six twenty-one."

"God bless you."

"I've got two boys," said Ray Porter, considering that sufficient empathy.

He was buttering Jonathan's breakfast spaghetti when the phone rang. His hand was on the receiver before it rang again.

"Hello?"

"I hate to tell you this . . . ," said Emma.

"I already know," he said.

"How'd you know?"

"Harley called me last night."

"How'd he know?" she asked, sounding irritable.

"He was *there.*"

"I don't know what you're talkin' about," she said, "but I'm talkin' about Gene Bolick havin' a brain tumor."

"What?"

"He keeled over again yesterday, they sent him down to Baptist Hospital and did a MRI scan. That's why he's been actin' so peculiar, it was that tumor pressin' on his brain."

"Dear Lord!"

"Here, I wrote down what it is, I have to spell it. M-e-n-i-n-g-i-o-m-a. It's way down deep towards th' base of his brain."

"Is it operable?" He realized he was holding his breath.

"Let's see. Where'd I write that down? Here it is on my shoppin' list. No, they can't operate, it's too far down in there. The doctor said unless it gets bigger, leave it alone."

"Do you know anything else?"

"Nothing except I hear Esther's a basket case. Ray Cunningham drove 'em down to Baptist and called back to give th' report. I know it's none of my business, but . . ."

"But what?"

"Like I say, it's none of my business, but I think you ought to come home."

Come home. Come home.

It went around in his head like a liturgical chant.

But how could he go home? As far as he could figure, there wasn't a soul who could take Jonathan in. Everybody was working, away for the summer, or too old to trot after a three-year-old. And there was Janette, who needed him, or so he believed, and Cynthia's parish tea coming up at Dove Cottage in three weeks, and the vestry meeting, and the Ella Bridgewater issue, and his responsibilities to the Whitecap Fair Planning Commission. . . .

"This is home!" he said aloud. But he couldn't force himself to believe it. *Bloom where you're planted,* he'd read on a plaque at Mona's. And wasn't he trying?

In truth, he was longing for Mitford. Longing to see his boy and encourage him and cheer him on and help him pack for school and tuck a few Kit Kats in his suitcase, and sit with Gene and Esther and pray about this terrible thing that had come against them. . . .

He wanted to lay his head on his pillow in the yellow house and walk Barnabas down Main Street and pop into the Grill and surprise everybody. He wanted to dash up to Fernbank and discover what new tricks Anna and Tony were doing with garlic, and visit Uncle Billy and Esther Cunningham, and see his rosebushes, some of which would be more fragrant and richly colored now than in June. . . .

Sleep-deprived and numb with exhaustion, he drove south to the Toe in heat that was ninety degrees and rising.

He didn't know what he expected, but Otis Bragg's office was definitely nothing to write home about. It was, in fact, smaller than his own office in the church basement, and covered with a film of dust from the gravel operation next door. An air conditioner hummed and rattled in the window.

"Well, now!" said Otis. He removed a large cigar butt from his mouth and spit into a wastebasket. "I'd say it's either money or politics that brings you runnin' to th' Toe."

"I didn't know money and politics were necessarily two separate entities."

Otis growled with laughter. "I like a priest with a sense of humor. Seems like the church is a callin' that turns a man sour if he don't watch out."

Father Tim sat down without being asked. "I have come about money."

A strange sadness crossed his parishioner's face. "That's what always sends clergy to my door."

He looked at the short, round man before him, and was oddly moved. He would come back again when he didn't have his hand out; he'd come back just to visit, to say hello.

Otis leaned forward and squinted at him. "What can I do for you, Father? You look like you wrassled alligators half the night."

"There are plenty of alligators out there, only one of which has put Janette Tolson in the hospital with severe depression."

"We heard that. We hear you've got her boy."

"She's having a rough go of it. And there's no insurance in the family. I thought if you'd be willing, I'll see that St. John's matches what you feel led to give."

Otis rolled the cigar butt between his fingers.

"How do you figure St. John's to be dolin' out money for a thing like this?"

"Janette's one of the body, we're her church family. I figure we can put on a fund-raiser, even do something special at the fair—I don't know, but we'll match what you give."

"What if I gave, say, five thousand bucks? Think you could match that?" Otis clamped the cigar in his mouth, narrowing his eyes.

"Well." He was startled. He had expected some largesse, but . . .

"I don't know if we can raise five thousand. I suppose I was hoping for . . . I don't know, maybe a thousand, tops."

"Father, you goin' to rise in this world, you got to think big."

His bishop, Stuart Cullen, firmly held that philosophy; why couldn't he?

"Thanks, Otis. God bless you! Five thousand is more than generous, it will go a long way in helping Janette's children recover their mother."

"I hope I don't ever run across th'—I'll watch my language, out of respect—th' son of a gun. I despised him from the minute I laid eyes on 'im." Otis spit furiously into the wastebasket. "Always struttin' around preenin' hisself, makin' th' choir sing those mid'eval hymns that go back a hundred years."

"Well, there's some good news, Otis. I think we've found our organist."

"Fine, fine, glad to hear it. You just keep up th' good work, you hear?" Otis punched a button on his phone. "Agnes, write th' preacher a check for five thousand, make it to St. John's." He pitched the unlit butt in the wastebasket and stood up. "Now you're in th' Toe, let me show you around my little operation."

Father Tim wanted to decline, but thought better of it. Maybe it wouldn't hurt to see the results of what it means to think big.

"Miz Tolson is not sleeping," said the nurse, clearly displeased. "She just likes to keep her eyes closed." He wanted nothing more than to crash and sleep, himself.

At the door of the room, the nurse whispered, "I hope you'll speak to her about cooperating. She's been acting like she swallows her pills, but we just found out she spits them in her pajama drawer!"

"I'll do my best," he said.

He sat quietly for a time, saying only, "I'm here, Janette." She had her back to him, and didn't move or acknowledge his presence.

His head fell forward twice as he dozed off, then recovered himself. He was here for a purpose, and he'd better get to it. "Janette?"

No answer. Well, then, he would speak to her as if she were listening; he would speak to her heart, her spirit, and let the chips fall where they may. He'd learned a few things about depression, his own as well as that of others. He'd learned that even when the soul seems fallow, there's a vulnerable spot that can be seeded. Whether the seed flourishes was God's job. "I have planted, Apollos watered, but God gave the increase," St. Paul had written to Corinth.

He took the Book of Psalms from the bag.

"I brought you something. You may not be able to read it for a while, but keep it near. It's King David's songs—they're about joy and praise, loss and gain, about his battles with the mortal enemy, and his battles with depression.

"Let me read to you. . . ."

As a child, the most comforting thing he knew was being read to. He figured it worked for everybody.

" 'The Lord is my light and my salvation; whom shall I fear? The Lord is the strength of my life; of whom shall I be afraid?

" 'When the wicked, even mine enemies and my foes, came upon me to eat up my flesh, they stumbled and fell.

" 'Though an host should encamp against me, my heart shall not fear; though war should rise against me, in this will I be confident.' "

He sat silent for a moment.

"David had many foes, Janette, the human kind as well as the foes that have come against you: anger, bitterness, fear, maybe even resentment toward God.

"When I read the psalms, I read them as personal prayers, naming the enemies that come against my own soul.

" 'For in the time of trouble,' " David says, " 'he will hide me in his pavilion: in the secret of his tabernacle shall he hide me: he shall set me upon a rock.'

"Let Him hide you, Janette, until you gain strength. He will set you upon a rock. Please know that."

He listened to her quiet, regular breathing. Maybe she really was asleep. He prayed silently for the seeds to fall on fertile ground.

"I've marked this psalm for you, the thirtieth. Hear this with your very soul, Janette. 'Weeping may endure for a night, but joy comes in the morning.' "

Without turning in the bed, she raised her hand slightly, and he stood, and held it.

He had gone deep into his pockets with the Wesley bondsman, but Dooley was at home with Harley, and that's what counted.

"People look at me different," said Dooley when they talked the following evening. "While I was baggin' their groceries, I could feel their eyes borin' a hole in me."

Dooley's vernacular always returned when he was angry, tired, or frustrated.

"Maybe. Maybe not. Even in a small town, word doesn't travel that fast. Just be yourself. You didn't do anything wrong and you have nothing to apologize for." Couldn't he say something wiser, more profound than that? "Keep smiling!" he said, sounding lame and feeling worse.

"Lace's mama just died," Dooley said.

"I'm sorry to hear it." Lace's mother, ill and failing for years, had never given loving support to her daughter, but had demanded it, instead, for herself. "Have you called Lace?"

"She hates my guts."

"Call her, send her a card, something. She's lost her mother and this will be a blow, no matter what the circumstances were. I'll do the same."

"I wish . . ." Dooley hesitated.

"Wish what?"

"I wish you an' Cynthia would come home. Well, I got to go."

Click.

"Man alive! What's *this*?"

"It's my new iced tea recipe," said his wife. "Do you like it?"

He raised his glass in a salute. "It's the best I ever tasted. I didn't know you could do this."

"I didn't, either. I never knew how to make good iced tea. So, with our parish party coming up, I asked the Lord to give me the perfect recipe."

"That's the spirit!"

"Do you honestly like it?"

"I never tasted better!" he exclaimed, stealing no thunder from his mother, whose tea represented the southern ideal—heavy on sugar, and blasted with the juice of fresh lemons.

"I woke up yesterday morning and was bursting with all these new ideas about tea. It was very exciting."

"Hmm," he said, gulping draughts of the cold, fruity liquid. "Tropical. Exotic." He swigged it down to the last drop. "Two thumbs up," he said. "But I'm not sure everybody would understand where the recipe came from."

She shrugged. "If He gave William Blake those drawings, why couldn't He give me a simple tea recipe?"

"Good point. What's in it?"

"I can't tell you."

"You can't tell me?"

"No, darling, I've decided to do something very southern—which is to possess at least one secret recipe." She looked pleased with herself.

"But you can tell *me*."

"Not on your life!"

"Why not? I'm your husband!"

"Some well-intentioned parishioner would yank it out of you just like that." She snapped her fingers.

"No!"

"Yes. And then I'd be in the same boat with poor Esther, whose once-secret orange marmalade cake recipe is circulating through Mitford like a virus."

"If that's the way you feel," he said, slightly miffed.

"Suicidal," the doctor had said, adding that he had no good idea when she'd be ready to come home.

Father Tim dialed Janette's cousin, long-distance. No, they really couldn't take Jonathan, it was all they could do to squeeze in Babette and Jason, they were sorry and hoped he understood, which he did.

He was definitely into the fray of Whitecap, with back-to-back meetings, hospital treks, home visitation, and a series of three talks to Busy Fingers, the needlework arm of the ECW. He was even pitching in once a week with Cynthia to help tour visitors through the church and grounds.

Because of the hither and yon-ness of it all, he usually took the Mustang. This morning, however, he was walking to church, leaving his dog behind to amuse Jonathan. He heard Jonathan's loud cries from the guest room; the boy definitely wanted his mother.

"I have story hour at the library this morning. It will take his mind off things." Cynthia nudged him down the steps. "He'll be fine, dear, just go!"

He went, not knowing what else to do.

As he passed through the gate into the street, he had the sense, once again, that someone was watching him. He shaded his eyes and peered toward the hedgebound, chest-high wall that surrounded his neighbor's house.

On impulse, he stepped closer to the hedge and called, "Mr. Love! Are you there?"

About two yards to his left, the foliage moved, shook slightly, and was still. What could he lose? If Morris Love was not there, then he was standing here talking to himself. If Morris Love was there, then he was merely being neighborly.

"If you're there, Mr. Love, I'd just like to say that we—my wife and I—enjoy your music very much."

"Out! Out!"

The sudden shout through the hedge was loud, hoarse, and furious.

Father Tim stepped back, startled.

"Out!" The command was repeated with even greater ferocity.

The voice sent chills up his spine. Yes, indeed, he'd done the wrong thing in trying to be neighborly.

He trotted quickly down the lane toward Ernie's, without looking back.

"Junior's got mail!" Ernie proudly announced.

"Off and running, then!" Father Tim sat down at the table with Junior.

"Lookit," said Junior, pushing a stack of letters his way. "You can read 'em if you want to."

He removed the lid from his coffee cup. "Anything promising?"

"See this one?" Junior pointed to the pink envelope that crowned the batch. "It's th' best, I'd read that."

"You sure you want me to read it?"

"Sure!" said Junior. "And I'll let you see her picture when you've read th' letter. You ain't goin' to believe it."

Ernie thumped down at the table, grinning. "Read it out loud. I'd like to hear that one again."

"Yes, sir," said Junior, "read it out loud, that's what I did."

"Here goes." He cleared his throat. " 'Dear—' "

The screen door slapped behind Roanoke. "How y'all?" he queried the general assembly.

"Fine," said Ernie. "Set down, th' preacher's readin' Junior's love letters."

Roanoke pulled up a chair and sat, taking the lid off his coffee. He had a cigarette stuck behind his ear. "I hope they ain't too mushy," he said.

Ernie punched Junior on the arm. "We're lookin' for mushy, right, Junior? Go ahead an' read, Tim."

" '*Dear Serious: I couldn't believe my eyes when I saw your ad. I truly love Scrabble and fishing better than anything! But I personally don't like a whole lot of country music except for Loretta Lynn. I have been looking for somebody to go fishing with and have played Scrabble since I was nine years old. It is my favorite. Are you a Christian? This is real important to me. If you are you ought to say so in your ad it could help somebody decide whether to answer or not.*

" '*If you are and if you are really serious like your ad says you will have to meet my daddy before you can take me out. I am not interested in dirty jokes or cussing. Here's my picture. I am named for Ava Gardner the movie star who was born in Smithfield the same town as my mother who died four years ago with cancer.*

" '*Why am I writing a perfect stranger? My sister said to do it especially as Daddy will meet you first. Before it goes that far though send me your picture to the Box Number if you are interested. I am 29 and was married when I was 17 but my husband was killed driving a tractor trailer which lost its brakes on a bad curve in West Virginia. I have my own business and believe in hard work.*

" '*I also believe that honesty is the best policy.*

" '*Sincerely yours,*

" '*Ava Goodnight.*' "

"Nice letter," said Father Tim. "Very neat handwriting."

"Now lookit," said Junior, taking a photograph out of his shirt pocket.

Father Tim gazed at the photo of a young woman with chestnut hair and a dazzling smile. "I'll be darned. Beautiful!"

"Where's she live at?" asked Roanoke.

"Swanquarter," said Junior, seeming especially proud of this fact.

"That'll be some mighty long distance courtin'."

Junior shrugged as Roanoke peered over Father Tim's shoulder at the photograph. "Looks like you got th' brass ring."

"I don't know. She has her own business an' all, plus she's really . . . nice-lookin'."

"*Good*-lookin' is what I'd say," said Ernie.

"Right. So she prob'ly wouldn't be interested in . . . you know . . . me, or anything."

"Wrong attitude!" said Ernie. "You were rarin' to go 'til you started gettin' feedback, now you want to crawl off an' quit."

"Well, not quit, exactly," said Junior, looking uneasy.

Roanoke blew on his coffee. "With women, you got t' fish or cut bait."

"Right," said Ernie. "Idn't that right, Tim?"

"That's right." Didn't he know? Hadn't he learned? He had cut bait 'til he nearly lost Cynthia Coppersmith for all eternity.

"Write her back," said Ernie. "You don't cuss too bad, and I never heard you tell a dirty joke, so you got that covered. Plus you're both dead set on bein' honest."

"*Are* you a Christian?" asked Roanoke, taking the cigarette from behind his ear. "Seem like that's pretty major in her opinion."

"Well . . ." Junior thought about it. "I guess. I mean, my mama went to church an' all, 'til she died, and I went pretty regular 'til a few years ago."

Roanoke lit his cigarette and inhaled deeply. "That don't necessarily cut it," he said. "I don't know much, but I do know that."

"Anyway," said Junior, "I don't have a picture."

"You got a camera?"

"Somewhere I got a camera I won at the fair."

"Bring it in tomorrow mornin' on your way to the Toe and I'll snap you one or two shots," said Ernie. "I got film over there, we'll use a roll of two-hundred if th' light's not good."

"Should I wear a tie?"

"I wouldn't do that. What you got on'll be fine."

"Maybe I should wear a cap." Junior smoothed his hair, which was thinning in front.

"Honesty is the best policy," said Ernie. "Don't wear a cap. But hold your stomach in an' all."

"I don't think I should wear what I got on, these are my work clothes."

Roanoke blew a smoke ring. "She said she believes in hard work."

Junior was looking increasingly frustrated. Suddenly he turned to Father Tim. "What do you think, sir?"

"Maybe . . . maybe a pair of jeans with a denim shirt and a jacket?"

Junior sighed. "I'll have to wash m' jeans and iron a shirt."

"So?" said Ernie. "Big deal. It ought to be worth a little effort, gettin' a letter like that from a nice girl. Just remember what some of those other letters said."

Junior blushed.

The light on his office answering machine was blinking.

Emma, as usual, did not stand on ceremony.

"Seems like things are fallin' apart up here since you left. I just heard Louella fell and broke her hip, just like Miss Sadie, and she's in th' hospital and Hoppy says it's a good thing she's well padded because it could have been worse. But if you ask me, practically every old person I hear about who breaks a hip . . . well, I don't want to say it, but you know what I mean—

"Snickers, stop that this minute! Hold on, he's chewin' Harold's church shoes." The phone clattered onto the countertop. General mumbling, barking, and door-slamming.

"By th' way, I been meanin' to tell you that Uncle Billy's havin' knee surgery. I think that's what he said, my phone has an awful lot of static since th' storm last week. . . ."

They said their prayers in the darkened room and held each other, talking in low voices lest Jonathan wake up and make his usual midnight invasion.

"I feel we need to run home to Mitford," he said.

"Run home to Mitford? Darling, you don't just *run home* when it's twelve hundred miles round trip and a hundred degrees in the shade. Dooley will be fine, I promise."

"It's not just Dooley. It's also Esther and Gene and Louella and Lace and . . ." He sighed. "I feel helpless."

"You want to help everybody and fix everything. But Timothy, you just can't."

"I've never been able to swallow that down."

"Remember the sign I have over my drawing board at home? 'Don't feel totally, personally, irrevocably responsible for everything. That's my job. Signed, God.' "

"Ummm."

She kissed his cheek. "I love you to pieces," she said.

"I love you to pieces back," he replied, smiling in the dark. He would be in a ditch without Cynthia Kavanagh.

"Listen," she whispered, "you run home to Mitford and I'll hold down the fort, OK? I've got at least two and a half tons of cookies to bake and freeze, not to mention a hundred miniature quiches and six loaves of bread with sun-dried tomatoes."

"You're doing it again, you're not letting anyone help with the party."

"Who can help? Marion is at the library practically every day, poor Jean Ballenger couldn't cook if her life depended on it, Marlene Bragg's fingernails are so long she can barely get ice out of a tray, and everyone else works."

"Who's doing flowers? I know you'll want them in all the rooms."

She sighed. "I'd give my French watercolors for a Hessie Mayhew in this parish. But alas, I suppose I'm doing them myself."

"I'll order flowers for you, have them delivered."

"How sweet, but no, I'll cut what's left in the garden and plunder

Marion's little plot—you know I love that tousled look for flowers, nothing arranged. Anyway, darling, we're getting off the point. Run home to Mitford and see Dooley and make your rounds and come back to me."

"Are you sure?"

"Of course. Go to sleep."

She patted his cheek and turned on her side and he listened for her breathing to become regular, rhythmic. But it did not. He could feel her lying awake, just as he was doing.

"What is it, Kavanagh? Can't sleep?" He reached out and touched her shoulder.

"Cynthia?" Good heavens, she was crying.

He pulled her against him and she turned in his arms and wept quietly.

"My girl, my dearest love, what is it?"

"I'm homesick for Mitford, too, but I've tried and tried to be brave about it and not let you know. I see you wanting to go and take care of things, and, well, so do I. I mean, I like it here, actually I love it here, but I miss Mitford, I miss our home."

"I understand."

"I'm so sorry you've caught me out, Timothy. I feel like a criminal, hiding this from you."

"Thank goodness it's hidden no more. You'll come with me, then, we'll leave first thing next Thursday morning. I'll get Father Jack to supply, I'm sure he'll do it, and we'll head back here on Sunday."

He might have gotten up and danced a jig.

"Best of all," he declared, "we'll have two days with Dooley before he goes off to school."

"Lovely!" she said, forgetting to whisper. "I can't wait to see the big lug. What a dreadful thing he's going through. Of course, we'll have to take Jonathan. . . ."

"Of course! They'll love him in Mitford."

"He can watch a movie, Dooley has a VCR!"

"Thank You, Lord!" he exclaimed, feeling a slow flush happiness.

"Yes, thank You, Lord!" she said, blowing her nose.

CHAPTER TEN

If Wishes Were Horses

He regretted being unable to introduce their new organist around on Sunday, but Sam and Marion said they'd do it for him.

He called Jack Ferguson.

"Happy to!" exclaimed the retired priest, who was fond of peppering his sermons with ecclesiastical jokes. "I'll just pop up with Earlene. Maybe you'll let us stay at your place Saturday night."

"Absolutely! We'll leave the keys under the potted geranium by the front door. You know where the church is . . ."

"Oh, yes, I've supplied St. John's several times, always a pleasure!"

". . . and I'll fax the directions to Dove Cottage."

"Super!" said Father Jack. "By the way, have you heard that Ron Cowper is leaving St. Michael's?"

"I'll be darned. I thought he was rooted in there like a turnip."

"One of the parish told him, said, 'Father Ron, I'm so sorry you're going, we never knew what sin was 'til you came.' "

He chuckled. "Jack, Jack."

"All true, Timothy. And did you hear about Bishop Harvey's big trip to Uganda?"

"Briefly, when he was here in July."

"At the end of a worship service, Bill had a notion to give the blessing in the language of the region. He picked up the printed sheet, made the sign of the cross, then very slowly and solemnly read in Luganda, 'Do not take away the service bulletin.' "

Father Tim laughed heartily. "Thank heaven you don't know anything to tell on me."

"Oh," said Father Jack, "I'll think of something."

There was a new spring in his step; he felt a fresh excitement both at home and at church.

"You're mighty perky," said a member of the Altar Guild, who was trimming candlewicks in the vesting room.

"Darling, you're positively glowing!" said his wife, who appeared to be unusually sunny herself.

"Hit'll be good t' clap eyes on you 'uns," said Harley. "I'll make us a pan of brownies."

"I'm really glad you're comin'," said Dooley.

In the grand anticipation of it all, he made a long-distance "house call" to Uncle Billy.

"I'll be et f'r a tater if it ain't th' preacher!" exclaimed the old man, obviously delighted.

"Just checking on your knee, Uncle Billy."

"My knee? Hit's th' same as ever, ol' arthur's got it, don't you know."

"I thought Emma said you were having knee surgery."

"Nossir, what I had was *tree* surgery."

"Aha. Well. Tell me about it."

"Hit was a big to-do, don't you know, th' town sent a crew t' doctor them old trees out back, they was rotted in some places and about t' fall over. Wellsir, they was there all day Wednesday, then come back again and was there all day Thursday, had a big crane an' all. Hit was like a tent meetin' th' way people turned out t' watch, we could of went t' sellin' corn dogs. Wish you'd been here."

"We'll be there late Thursday for a short visit. I'll get by and see you and Miss Rose on Saturday."

"Hit'll be a treat an' a half t' see you 'uns, I'll ask Rose t' whip up a banana puddin'."

"Don't go to any trouble," said Father Tim, meaning it. "In fact, don't even *think* about it!"

“We’re going home, old buddy,” he said to Barnabas as they loped toward Ernie’s. “We’re going to see Dooley, remember Dooley?”

Of course his dog remembered Dooley. Any dog with a penchant for Wordsworth, Cowper, and Keats was a smart dog.

Just four days and he’d be good as new, ready to pour himself back into St. John’s and no need to run home again until October for Buck’s and Pauline’s wedding, which he’d cleared with his bishop early on.

He felt positively on holiday. He would put in five hours at St. John’s, and dash home to pack and take Cynthia and Jonathan out for an early dinner. Then, at six-thirty tomorrow morning, they were out of here.

Janette’s doctor reported only mild response to the medication. It would take time, he said, for her to feel any meaningful effects; meanwhile, they were monitoring her closely.

He called Janette’s room. No answer. He thought he should have her approval to take Jonathan all the way to the other end of the state, but he dreaded the possibility of upsetting her. What if she felt bereft, knowing that her priest and children were all off the island? He recalled that even her doctor was leaving on Friday to play golf in Beaufort.

Marion agreed to go to the hospital after church on Sunday. He caught Jean Ballenger leaving a Busy Fingers class, and asked her to visit Janette on Thursday, Friday, and Saturday.

“Oh, yes!” she said. “I’ll go. I enjoy the sick.”

“Here,” he said, taking out his wallet and giving her five dollars. “If you don’t mind, please buy her some oranges, or . . .”

Jean took the bill. “Would you like them maybe in a basket with a little bow on the handle?”

“I’d be much obliged,” he said.

“I could put in a pot of African violets for another five,” she said, eyeing his wallet.

He had celebrated Holy Eucharist with seven of the faithful remnant and four tourists from Canada, cleared his desk, returned his calls, thoroughly discussed Sunday's music with Ella Bridgewater by phone, and alerted the choir to be on their best behavior. He had also shown a couple from Delaware around the cemetery, typed the pew bulletin, emptied his wastebasket, and stamped the mail.

He was walking out the door when the phone rang.

"St. John's in the Grove!" he said. Then, feeling suddenly inspired to elaborate, he quoted the psalmist. " 'This is the day the Lord has made!' "

There was a brief silence on the other end. "Timothy?"

Sounded like Bill Harvey.

"Speaking."

"That was a very upbeat phone greeting." It was Bill Harvey, all right.

"I'm feeling upbeat, Bishop, how are you?"

"Wanting to have a little talk with you about something." Bill Harvey was not speaking in his let's-go-fishing voice; this was his high-church, gospel-side *vox populi.*

"Shoot!" He may as well walk straight into the wind, head down and hunkered over.

"It comes to my attention that you're making a little trip to Mitford."

"Why . . . yes." He cleared his throat. "Just four days."

"To attend, I believe, to the needs of several former parishioners . . ."

"Well . . . yes." He'd mentioned to one or two people why he was going away, but had said nothing about Dooley.

". . . and dismissing, I presume, your sworn duty to attend to the needs of your current parishioners?"

"I hadn't thought of it that way, Bishop." His stomach did a small turn.

"It's time you thought of it that way, Timothy. You know very well the policy of the church, and that is to be strictly hands-off the old parish while you go about the business of the new. Surely it doesn't escape your memory that Lord's Chapel has a priest of its own to attend these people."

"Certainly." He heard his voice come near to croaking. He didn't think it would help matters to say his boy had been in jail and might like a little cheering up before he went off to school.

Then again, the bishop was right, he wasn't supposed to meddle in the business of Mitford's new priest. But these people were his friends. . . .

"But they're my *friends*," he said, knowing it would avail him nothing.

"Of course they're your friends, you served them for sixteen years."

"It was my wish to . . . I only wished to—"

"If wishes were horses, Timothy, beggars would ride. Let us stick to the point. I believe you're going to Mitford in October to conduct a wedding."

"Yes."

"I strongly caution you against this current jaunt."

Suddenly out of breath, he thumped into his desk chair and stared unseeing at the wall.

His wife gave the entire episcopate a fine tongue-lashing, mincing no words, and got over the whole incident in a trice. While he enjoyed her stinging barbs, they did little to soothe his sense of injury. It was true that, in principle, Bill Harvey was right, but he'd found his tone of voice, his corporate indifference, rude beyond measure. He was accustomed to a bishop whose kindness extended throughout his diocese, with seeming affection for all his deacons and priests; indeed, he was proud to have in Stuart Cullen a bishop who actually wrote important letters "in his own hand," as St. Paul himself had been pleased to do.

"Blast!" he said, looking out the kitchen window. "Double blast!"

"That's right, darling, let it all out!" encouraged his wife, who was buttering Jonathan's spaghetti.

"Blast!" said Jonathan, smacking the table with both hands.

Why hadn't he kept his big mouth shut about going home? He felt like a traitor, a heel, disappointing everyone. And now he had to go back over all the ground he'd plowed, calling everyone and making excuses. . . .

"You need something . . . *vigorous* to do," she suggested.

"I'll take Barnabas and go running," he said testily.

"Isn't your fishing trip coming up soon?"

Fishing trip! The very last thing he wanted to do was go on a fishing trip. A fine spectacle he'd make, knowing almost nothing about a rod and reel, and even less about sliding around on the deck of a boat with an eight hundred and fifty horsepower engine throbbing under his tennis shoes. Didn't he make a fool of himself every Sunday morning of his life? Why do it all over again on a trip that was costing his wife a cool two hundred bucks, not including a bucket of chicken?

Miss Rose answered the phone with a positive shout. *"Hello!"*

"Miss Rose? This is Father Tim."

"Are you here?"

"No, ma'am, I'm *here*," he shouted back. "You see, something's . . . *come up.*"

"What's that? *Bum luck?*"

"Well, yes, in a way. May I speak with Uncle Billy?"

She turned from the phone and squawked, "Bill! Bill Watson! It's our old preacher!"

He thought she might have put it another way.

There was a long silence.

"I'm sorry, son."

Dooley sighed. "I know. It's OK. Really."

"I'm going to try and have the court date set during the time I'm home for the wedding. You'll be home then, too, so I believe everything's going to work out just fine."

"Great," said Dooley, sounding relieved.

"Have fun these last days. How are Poo and Jessie?"

"Really good!"

He heard the sudden tenderness in the boy's voice.

"And your mother?"

"She's really good, too, she got a raise at Hope House."

"Glad news! You're always in our prayers, buddy. God cares about your needs."

"OK, 'bye." said Dooley. "Wait. That woman upstairs . . ."

"What about her?"

"She plays the dern piano mighty loud. Me'n Harley are thinkin' about knockin' on th' ceiling with a broom handle."

And he'd been worried about Dooley's music aggravating his tenant. "I wouldn't do that. Hang in there."

"I got Lace a card."

"Great! I did, too."

"It was hard as heck to pick out, there are millions of cards."

"True. What did it say?"

"Nothin.' It was blank."

"Aha."

"I just wrote in it, 'I'm sorry.' "

"Couldn't be better."

"I signed my whole name, in case she knows anybody else named Dooley."

"Probably not."

"Well, I got to go, Avis wants me to clean out th' butcher case. *Gross.* I told him I'll pick up anything but liver, he has to do that. I mean, you can feel liver all the way through those weird gloves we have to wear."

"Please!" he said, bilious at the thought.

It wrenched his heart to say goodbye. But what were hearts for, in the end? A little wrenching now and then was far, far better than no wrenching at all.

He was trying to forgive Bill Harvey. In the scheme of things, the bishop's attitude was hardly worth his concern. Why couldn't he blow by it, forgive and forget? Of no small concern, however, was the hardness that would come in if he didn't forgive this slight. He was to drag it into the light and expose it before God and get it over with.

He dropped to his knees in the study and prayed silently. The early morning breeze pushed through open windows and puffed the curtains into the room.

There was a tap on his shoulder.

"What are you doin'?" asked Jonathan, standing next to him in rumpled blue pajamas.

He rose from his knees and picked the boy up. They thumped into the chair, Jonathan in his lap. "I was praying."

"Why?" Jonathan snuggled against him.

"That I might find God's grace to forgive someone."

"Why?"

"Because if I don't forgive this person, it will be unhealthy for me, and God won't think much of it, either."

He loved the chunky, vibrant feel of the boy on his lap, the warm, solid weight against his chest. Exactly the way God wants us to come to Him, he thought, his spirits suddenly brightening.

"I don't want p'sketti no more. No p'sketti."

"Good! Hallelujah! What do you want?"

Jonathan pondered this, then looked up at him. "I don't know."

"Well, if you don't, who does?"

Jonathan poked him in the chest with a chubby finger. "You find somethin'."

"Please."

"Please."

"Consider it done."

He and Cynthia had been transplanted, that was all. He knew from years of digging around in the dirt and moving perennials from one corner of the yard to another what transplanting was about. First came the wilt, then the gradual settling in, then the growth spurt. That simple. What had Gertrude Jekyll said to the gardener squeamish about moving a plant or bush? "Hoick it!"

God had hoicked him and he'd better get over the wilt and get busy putting down roots.

He went out to the porch, whistling. Glorious day—his fair wife sitting contentedly in a rocker, Jonathan rigged with a straw hat and playing in the garden with his dog, and an afternoon romp in the ocean on the family agenda.

He sat in one of the white rockers and kicked off his loafers. "Ahhhh!" he sighed.

"Timothy, you have that wilderness look again."

"What wilderness look?" he asked, as if he didn't know.

"That John the Baptist look."

He had been in denial about it for some time, now, until his hair had fanned out over his clerical collar like the tail of a turkey gobbler. He just didn't seem to have what it took to break in a new barber.

"I hear there's a little shop next to the post office, Linda's or Libbie's or Lola's . . . something like that."

"Aha." No, indeed. He'd cut it himself with an oyster knife before he'd put his head in the hands of another Fancy Skinner.

"I'll hold out for a barber, thank you," he said, feeling imperious.

He checked the answering machine when they came in from the grocery store.

"Father? It's me, Puny."

Puny didn't sound like herself.

"I don't know how to tell you this."

This was definitely his least favorite way for a phone call to begin.

"I just got to your house and realized I'd left th' door unlocked for four days!"

"Speak to Ba!" one of the twins pleaded.

"How in th' world I did a dumb thing like that, I don't know, I'm jis' so sorry. But I've looked and looked, and nothin' seems missin', so I think it's all right, but I know how you count on me to take care of things, and I jis' hate lettin' you down on anything."

"It's OK!" he said aloud to the machine. He loved that girl like his own flesh. "Don't worry about it!"

"I know you sometimes don't lock your doors, but I always do because I'm responsible for things here, and I jis' hope that . . . anyway, we're real sorry you aren't comin', we all looked forward to it a lot, and I hope you'll not think hard of me for leavin' your door unlocked."

"Speak to Ba, speak to Ba!"

"Oh, for Pete's sake, Sissy, you'll wake up Sassy, *here*!"

"Ba! Come home, we got puppies. Come home, Ba!"

"Say 'bye, now. Tell 'im you love 'im."

"Love you, Ba."

"Tell 'im you love Miss Cynthia."

"Love Miss Cynthy."

"That was Sissy. Sassy's still asleep," said his industrious house help. "We've got an awful mess of puppies in th' garage, four little speckled things, I don't know what they are, oh, mercy, I'm prob'ly usin' up all your tape, now here's th' good news! Joe Joe's been promoted to lieutenant! That's right under th' chief. How d'you like that?"

He liked it very much indeed.

"We thought you was goin' home," said Roanoke.

"Change of plans. Where's Ernie this morning?"

"Him an' Roger's gone fishin'."

"Captain Willie?"

"Nope. Over to th' Sound."

"You're minding the store?"

"You got it," said Roanoke. Father Tim thought he'd never seen so many wrinkles in one face. Roanoke Clark, it might be said, looked like he'd been hung out to dry and left on the line.

He didn't exactly relish the idea of spending one-on-one time with a man who didn't like preachers. Then again, it was only six-thirty in the morning, and not a darned thing to do at the church office, since he'd already done it all for the trip to Mitford.

What the heck. He thumped down at a table, unwrapped his egg biscuit, and took the lid off his coffee.

"So . . . how's business?"

"We had a big run this mornin', it slacked off just before you come in."

He ate his biscuit while Roanoke read the paper and smoked.

"What about a good barber on the island? Know anybody?"

"Don't have an official barber on th' island. Have t' go across."

"Seems a waste of time to be running back and forth to the mainland just to get your hair trimmed."

Roanoke appeared to be talking to the newspaper he was holding in front of him. "Lola up by th' post office, she'll give you a trim. You won't need t' go back 'til Christmas."

"Who's Lola?"

"Lola sells fish san'wiches, cuts hair, you name it."

He shivered. "Is that where you get your hair cut?"

"Once every two months, whether I need it or not."

He examined Roanoke's haircut. No way.

"So, ah, where do Ernie and Roger get their hair cut?"

"I do it."

"You do it?"

"Keep my barber tools in th' book room over there." Roanoke indicated the book room with a wave of his hand.

"Aha."

"Six bucks a pop," said Roanoke, laying the paper on the table. "Six bucks and fifteen minutes, that's my motto."

"Did you . . . ever cut hair for a living?"

"I cut hair for truckers. When I was haulin' sheet metal, I had a stopover in Concord twice a month; I set up in th' back room of a barbecue joint. They rolled in there from New York City, Des Moines, Iowa, Los Alamos, Calfornia, you name it, they lined up from here to yonder." Roanoke looked proud of this fact, installing a fresh cigarette behind his ear.

"You might say I've cut hair from sea t' shinin' sea."

"I'll be darned." Now what was he going to do? His egg biscuit began to petrify in his stomach.

"You'll have t' set out here, since I got t' watch th' register, but I'll take care of it for you. I didn't want t' say nothin', but I wondered when you was goin' to get it off your collar. I thought maybe that was your religion."

Father Tim laughed uneasily and clapped his hip. He'd paid for his biscuit with pocket change; maybe he'd left his wallet at home. Sometimes he did. He hoped he did.

"You can pay me anytime. I run a little tab for Roger 'n' Ernie."

Oh, well, how bad could it be? He didn't recall that Ernie or Roger looked too butchered; pretty normal, to tell the truth.

"Fine," he said. "Fifteen minutes?"

Roanoke dragged the battered stool from behind the cash register and set it by the front window.

"Couldn't we, ah, move the stool back a little?" He didn't want to be on display for every passing car and truck on the island.

"I need th' light," said Roanoke, squinting at his hair.

Though he'd spent considerable time at morning prayer in his study, he prayed again as he clambered onto the stool.

Roanoke brought a box from the book room, followed by Elmo the Book Cat. It was the first time he'd seen Elmo out in general society. The elderly, longhaired cat sat on the cement floor, flicked its tail, and stared at him, as Roanoke laid his barbering paraphernalia on the window seat.

"Here you go," said Roanoke, throwing a torn sheet around Father Tim's shoulders. The sheet smelled of fish. Maybe that was why the cat was staring at him.

"Back when I was drivin'," said Roanoke, leaning into his work, "I run thirty-seven states and two provinces of Canada. One time I was caught in a tornada, it blowed me over an embankment and totaled my truck, but I walked away without a scratch, which was th' closest I ever come to believin' in God."

Father Tim felt the scissors snipping away, saw the hair thump onto the cement. The cat watched, still flicking its tail.

"I hauled a lot of orange juice outa Florida in my time. If I was haulin' fresh, a load would run around fifty-five hundred gallons. Concentrate, that'd weigh in around forty-seven hundred." *Snip, snip.*

Barbering certainly loosened the tongue of the usually taciturn Roanoke; he'd turned into a regular jabbermouth. Come to think of it, Father Tim had noticed the same phenomenon in Fancy Skinner and Joe Ivey. Clearly, nonstop discourse was very closely related to messing with hair.

"I even hauled chocolate syrup outa Pennsylvania, a lot of chocolate comes outa Pennsylvania, but I never hauled poultry or anything livin', nossir, I wouldn't haul anything livin'."

"Good idea."

"I never got pulled but one time. Now, there's some drivers, they can be wild, they'll run their rigs hard as they can run 'em to git up th' next hill. Regulations say you cain't drive but ten hours a day, but cowboys, that's what we called 'em, they'll go up t' eighteen, twenty hours, drivin' illegal.

"Cowboys is only about two percent of th' drivers out there today, but they give th' rest of us a bad name, you know what I mean?"

"I do!"

Snip, thump. "I do a little roofin' now, a little house paintin', cut a little hair, a man can make a livin' if he's got ambition."

"I agree!"

"Got rid of my car, ride a bicycle now, it's amazin' how much money you can put back when you shuck a car."

"I'll bet."

"I was raised in a Christian home, but I fell away. See, my first wife run off with a travelin' preacher, I brought 'im home, give 'im a good, warm bed an' a hot meal, an' first thing you know, they hightailed it."

"Aha." So that was why Roanoke was never especially thrilled to see him; he'd been tarred with the same brush. He had a sudden, vivid recall of van Gogh's self-portrait in which he sported only one ear. *Please, Lord . . .*

Elmo yawned and lay down, without removing his gaze from the customer on the stool.

"Now, you take me, I never run around on my second wife, an' they was plenty of chances to do it. Lot lizards is what we called 'em, they'll pester a man nearly to death. But I stayed true to my wife an' I'm glad I did, because you never know what you'll pick up on th' road an' bring home to innocent people."

"Right."

"I never did pills, neither, nossir, th' strongest thing I ever done when I was drivin' was Sun-drop, it'll knock your block off if you ain't used to much caffeine in your system. You want a Sun-drop, we got 'em in th' cooler."

"That's OK, I don't believe so. Maybe another time." Boy howdy, this was an education and a half.

Thump, thump, snip.

"But things is changed. It'd bring a tear to a glass eye to hear what a owner-operator pays these days to run a big rig."

"How much?"

"More'n sixty cent a mile. You have to be tough to make a livin' with truckin'."

"I'll bet so."

"I'm goin' to clean your neck up now. How's our time runnin'?"

Father Tim looked at his watch. "You've got a little under one minute."

"We're goin' to bring you in right on th' dot," said Roanoke, flipping the switch on his electric shaver.

Cynthia waved from the porch. Jonathan and Barnabas were waiting at the gate.

"Look at me!" said the boy, jumping up and down.

"I'm looking. That's a new shirt!"

"And new pants!"

He opened the gate. "Where did those snappy new clothes come from, buddyroe?"

"UPS!"

"Dearest, where's your hair?" called his wife from the porch.

"In a Dumpster behind Ernie's! What do you think?"

"I love it!" she said, sitting down on the top step. "We've got a surprise for you!"

His wife was herself wearing something new and boggling. Red shorts, which were plenty short, a strapless white top, and espadrilles.

He scratched behind his dog's ears and fairly bounded up the steps.

His sermon was finished and walked through, thought for thought, precept upon precept. In the study, Jonathan had paced to the bookcase at his heels, then to the wall with the painting of the Roman Colosseum. Exhausted at last, Jonathan fell asleep on the rug, where Father Tim stepped over him without missing a beat.

The rest of the day lay ahead, shimmering like silk. They would swim in the ocean, they would go out to dinner in their new duds, and tomorrow they'd hear the organ raising its mighty voice to the timbers.

He felt as young as a curate, as bold as a lion.

"Having a little boy is different," said his wife, drying her hair after their frolic in the ocean. "We're going out to dinner and it's only five-thirty."

"Like a bunch of farmhands," he agreed, pulling on his brand-new shorts and golf shirt. One thing he could say about golf, which he'd never played and never would, he sure liked the shirts.

"I sketched Jonathan today," she said.

"Aha!"

"For the new Violet book. I think he'll weave into it beautifully, just what I've been needing to . . . round it out, I think."

He heard someone knocking, and Barnabas flew at once to the door, his bark as throaty as the bass of St. John's organ.

He zipped his shorts and padded down the hall barefoot, stunned to see Father Jack and Earlene peering through the screen.

Good Lord! He'd completely forgotten to tell Jack Ferguson they weren't going home to Mitford!

Beet-red with embarrassment, he let the eager but surprised couple into the living room, and braced himself for the inept explanations he'd be forced to deliver, not only to the Fergusons but to his *wife*.

Dadgummit, now Father Jack would have a story to tell on him, which would spread through the diocese like fleas in August.

"Welcome to Dove Cottage," he said, trying to mean it.

They had gone to Mona's and eaten fried perch, hard crabs, broiled shrimp, yellowfin tuna fresh off the boat, hush puppies, french fries, and buckets of coleslaw. They had slathered on tartar sauce and downed quarts of tea as sweet as syrup, then staggered home in the heat with Jonathan drugged and half asleep on Father Tim's back.

As they walked, Cynthia did her part to deliver after-dinner entertainment, loudly reciting a poem by someone named Rachel Field.

"If once you have slept on an island
You'll never be quite the same;
You may look as you looked the day before
And go by the same old name.
You may bustle about the street or shop;
You may sit at home and sew,
But you'll see blue water and wheeling gulls
Wherever your feet may go."

"I declare!" said Earlene. "You're clever as anything to remember all that. I wonder if it's the truth."

"What?"

"That part about never being quite the same."

"I don't know," said Cynthia. "We'll have to wait and see."

They sat on the porch and watched the gathering sunset through the trellis, where the Marion Climber had put forth several new blooms.

"Now, Jack," he said, "don't go home and tell this story on me."

"I make no promises." Father Jack chuckled.

He gave a mock sigh. "Is there no balm in Gilead?"

"Not as long as Jack's around," said his wife.

He wondered if Jack had discussed his Mitford trip with the bishop. Very likely they'd talked and Jack had mentioned it, a casual thing.

"Talked to the bishop lately?" he asked.

"Nope. Not a word. Saw him at the convention a while back. He's put on a good bit of weight."

"Who hasn't?" asked Father Tim, feeling relieved.

"I guess you heard what happened at Holy Cross over in Manteo."

"All I know about this diocese is what you tell me, Jack."

"More's the pity. Anyway, Bishop Harvey was making his annual visitation at Holy Cross, got there and saw about eight people sitting in the congregation. He was pretty hot about it, as you can imagine. He got vested, kept looking for somebody else to arrive, they didn't, so he asked Luke Castor, said, 'Father, didn't you tell them I was coming?'

"Luke said, 'No, but obviously they found out somehow.' "

"You have to take Jack with a grain of salt as big as your head," said Earlene.

The sunset delivered a great, slow wash of color above the beachfront cottages and turned the patch of blue to violet, then scarlet, then gold.

"Oh, the blessing of a porch," sighed Earlene. "When Jack and I walk out our front door, we just drop off in the yard like heathens."

"That's one way to put it," said her husband.

Earlene gave her hostess a profound look. "Don't let anybody talk you into a retirement home!"

"Never fear!" exclaimed Cynthia.

"It's not that bad, Earlene," said Father Jack. "You may not have a porch, but somebody else does the cooking three meals a day."

"You've got a point, dear," said Earlene, feeling better about lacking a porch. "And after supper in the dining room, some of us play gin rummy, or sometimes pinochle."

"Lovely!" said Cynthia.

Father Tim peered at his wife, thinking she was holding up gamely, though she appeared to be gripping the arms of her rocker with some force.

Earlene Ferguson did not care for silences in conversation, and was doing her level best to caulk every chink and crack, so he didn't know how long the music had been drifting across the street.

"Listen!" hc said, during a chink.

"What's that?" asked Father Jack.

"Just listen." César Franck . . .

There was a brief silence on the porch.

"Goodness!" said Earlene. "Somebody's sure playing their radio loud. That's a problem we have at the retirement home, with so many being half deaf, plus, of course, our walls are thin as paper—"

"Hush, Earlene," said Father Jack.

He'd never quite appreciated the wisdom of having a king-size bed until his wife introduced him to its luxuries on the second night of their marriage. As a bachelor, he'd spent several decades rolled into the middle of a sagging mattress like a hotdog in a bun.

Now, with the addition of a three-year-old in their lives, the chiefest virtues of a large bed were amply demonstrated. He looked in on Jonathan, who was sprawled across Cynthia's pillow, and went to the guest room and tapped on the door.

"Jack? We're going to step down to the beach for a few minutes."

Jack came to the door and cracked it. "How long have you been married?" he asked, grinning.

"Not too long," said Father Tim.

He unrolled the blanket and they spread it on the sand.

"Full moon, my dear, and no extra charge."

"Heaven," she breathed, kneeling on the blanket. "Heaven!"

"Didn't I tell you I'd give you the moon and stars?" He sat next to her and smelled the faintest scent of wisteria lifted to him on the breeze. He would go for months, used to her scent and immune to its seduction, then, suddenly, it was new to him again, compelling.

"How are you holding up being married to a parson?"

"I love being married to my parson."

"The Fergusons didn't throw you too badly?"

"Goodness, Timothy, what kind of wimp do you think I am? I don't know much, but I do know that the wife of a priest must be ready for anything."

"That's the spirit!"

She lay back on the blanket, and he lay beside her, loving her nearness, loving the sense that sometimes, if only for a moment, he couldn't tell where she left off and he began.

Lulled by the background roar and lap of the waves, he gazed up into the onyx bowl spangled with life and light, and took her hand. " 'Bright star,' " he quoted to her from Keats, " 'would I were steadfast as thou art . . .' "

"You've always thought me steadfast," she said, "but I'm not, I'm not at all, Timothy. I'm sometimes like so much Silly Putty."

"You're always there for me, sending off for new clothes, taking in children, drumming up the parish tea, standing with me at the church door. I don't deserve this, you know, it scares me."

"You're all I have," she murmured, drawing him close, "and all I ever wanted. So stop being scared!"

"Yes," he said. "I'll try."

The windows and front doors were thrown open to a fickle breeze, the creaking ceiling fans circled at full throttle. Here and there, an occasional pew bulletin lifted on a draft of moving air and went sailing.

Peering loftward through a glass pane in the sacristy door, he couldn't help but notice that the soprano had returned to the fold and was cooling herself with a battery-operated fan. He also saw that every pew in St. John's was filled to bursting.

Air-conditioning! he thought, running his finger around his collar. Next year's budget, and no two ways about it.

Standing next to him in the tiny sacristy, Marshall Duncan pulled the bell rope eleven times.

. . . bong . . . bong . . .

On the heel of the eleventh bell, Ella Bridgewater, fully rehearsed and mildly fibrillating with excitement, hammered down on the opening hymn as if all creation depended on it.

Marshall opened the sacristy door and crossed himself reverently as the crucifer led the procession into the nave.

Glorious! His congregation was standing bolt upright, and singing as lustily as any crowd of Baptists he'd ever seen or heard tell of.

"Lift high the cross
the love of Christ proclaim . . ."

He threw his head back and, with his flock, gave himself wholly to the utterance of joy on this morning of mornings.

". . . till all the world adore
his sacred Name.
Led on their way by
this triumphant sign
the hosts of God in
conquering ranks combine."

The organ music soared and swirled above their heads like a great incoming tide; surely he only imagined seeing the chandeliers tremble.

"Blessed be God," he proclaimed at the end of the mighty *Amen.* "Father, Son, and Holy Spirit!"

The eager congregational response made his scalp tingle. "And blessed be his kingdom, now and forever!"

He lifted his hands to heaven, and prayed.

"Almighty God, to You all hearts are open, all desires known, and from You no secrets are hid: Cleanse the thoughts of our hearts by the inspiration of Your Holy Spirit, that we may perfectly love You, and worthily magnify Your holy Name; through Christ our Lord."

"Amen!" they said as one.

He didn't sense it every time, no; if only he could. But this morning, the Holy Spirit was moving in the music and among the people of St. John's; He was about the place in a way that left them dazzled and wondering, unable to ken the extravagant mystery of it.

For this moment, this blessed hour, heaven was breathing its perfume on their little handful in the church on the island in the vast blue sea, and they were honored and thankful and amazed.

CHAPTER ELEVEN

Worms to Butterflies

"Father?"

"Puny!"

"Th' most awful thing has happened, I don't know how to tell you. . . ."

He sank into the office chair. "Just tell me," he said, feeling suddenly weary.

"Your angel . . ." Weeping, nose blowing.

"My angel?"

"Th' one on th' mantel! I was runnin' th' dust rag downstairs, you know I run th' dust rag every time I come because of th' work goin' on in th' street, you knew they was relayin' pipes, didn't you?"

"No, I didn't know."

"Well, I was runnin' th' dust rag an' . . ." More nose blowing.

"It's all right. Whatever you're going to tell me is all right." She was dusting and the angel toppled off the mantel and fell to the floor and a wing broke off, or an arm. How bad could it be?

"Well, th' angel . . . it's not *there* anymore, it's gone!"

"Gone?"

"Today I was dustin' downstairs because I dusted upstairs last week, and when I come to th' mantel, I couldn't believe my eyes. It was jis' this empty place where it used to set!"

"Well, now . . ."

"I mean, th' other day when I called you about th' door bein' unlocked, I looked all around an' didn't see nothin' missin', I mean, I thought somethin' seemed different about your study, but I couldn't figure out what it was, I didn't notice anything bein' *gone*, so what I'm sayin' is, maybe it was gone last week, I don't know!"

"Have you talked with Harley? And Puny, stop crying, it's all right. Just sit down, take a deep breath, and tell me everything."

"I talked to Harley, he said he hadn't seen nothin' goin' on at your house, 'cept me goin' in an' out."

"Was anything else missing, anything moved around?"

"No, sir, an' I promise you I really looked, I've went over th' whole house with a fine-tooth comb, even th' closets, an' checked th' windows an' basement door, they're locked tight as a drum. I feel terrible about this, Father, I'll pay for th' angel, whatever it cost, me an' Joe will pay ever' cent."

"This is a mystery. I remember having a fifty-dollar bill and a credit card in my desk drawer. I wonder—"

"I'll go look!" she said.

Very odd, he mused.

"Your money and credit card's in th' drawer on th' left-hand side."

Odder than odd. "I wonder if Dooley would know anything."

"I don't think Dooley was in th' house a single time."

"I'll call him at school and ask. I don't know, Puny, I'm as baffled by this as you are."

"I'm real sorry."

"It's OK, I promise. We'll figure it out, don't worry. Just . . . lock up good when you leave."

He sat at his desk for some time, occasionally nodding his head, speaking half sentences aloud and, in general, feeling befuddled.

Harley Welch sounded down and out.

"M'bunk mate's gone, and Lace has went off to school." He sighed deeply. "Hit's a graveyard around here."

"I believe it."

"Seem like I wadn't hardly ready f'r 'em to go off."

"We never are."

"You know, some of th' stuff Lace taught me, it's stickin'! I set here last night and wrote five pages of things that was goin' around in m' noggin."

"Great! Terrific! I'm proud of you!"

"I got to thinkin' about them great falls of th' Missouri, five of 'em, and how ol' Lewis an' Clark must've felt when they seen such a sight as that."

"Lace is a grand teacher. You're a genuine help and consolation to each other."

But Harley didn't sound consoled. "Both of 'em gone, an' not a soul t' set down an' eat a bite with, hit's jis' mope aroun' an' listen t' y'r head roar. . . ."

"Anytime you feel lonesome, walk up to the Grill, order the special, talk to people. It'll do you good." Heaven knows, that had saved his own sanity a time or two.

"I'm tearin' th' engine out of th' mayor's RV in th' mornin', I ain't got time t' lollygag."

"Puny says you haven't seen anybody around the house, nothing suspicious. . . ."

"Nossir. Course that door bein' unlocked an' all, an' that gang workin' on th' street . . ."

"Seems like they'd have taken something else, though. Well, listen, Harley, you hang in there. We'll be home in October. I'm going to hold you to that pan of brownies."

Harley cackled, sounding like himself again. "I practice on them brownies once ever' week, I'm about t' git it right."

They sat on the porch in the gathering twilight, and watched Jonathan play with a sand bucket and shovel in their end-of-summer garden. The Louis L'Amour paperback lay on the table beside him; Barnabas sprawled at their feet.

His wife knew absolutely nothing about the angel and was as dumbfounded as he. It was bizarre, it was unreal, it was—

"I'll get it," Cynthia said, when the phone rang.

She dashed inside and came back with the cordless.

"Those eggs you gave us last week are wonderful, the yolks are a lovely shade of yellow!"

Covering the mouthpiece, she whispered, "Penny Duncan."

"Oh, really?" She listened intently. "That's wonderful! How good of you, Penny, how thoughtful."

She gazed into the yard at Jonathan. "Oh, he's a handful, all right, but no, thank you so much, we love having him, we're all quite happy together. Yes, I'm sure, but thank you again, you're very dear, Penny. Really? I'd love it if you'd help at the tea. Could you possibly make an ice mold? What a good idea, yes, fresh peppermint would be perfect. Well, then—love to Marshall. See you in church!"

She laid the phone on the arm of the rocker and smiled at him.

"You had an offer for help with Jonathan and turned it down?"

"She has ten days of vacation and offered to keep him, but . . ." She shrugged.

"But what?"

"But I declined."

"Why?" he asked.

She shrugged again. "Because."

"You won't believe this," said Dooley, calling from the hall phone in his dorm.

"Try me."

"Guess what girl's school our first dance is with."

"Mrs. Hemingway's." Who else?

"Can you believe it?"

He thought he discerned a kind of . . . what? Expectation, perhaps, under Dooley's evident disgust.

"I hope you'll ask Lace to dance."

"Not if she's wearing those weird shoes an' all."

"Come on, what do shoes have to do with anything?"

"Plenty," said Dooley, with feeling.

He had pulled whatever strings a clergyman can call to hand, and the court date would fall the day after Buck's and Pauline's wedding, after which Harley would drive Dooley back to school. He gave Dooley the scoop.

"Great! Cool." The boy sounded relieved.

No, Dooley hadn't been in the yellow house, he didn't know anything about the angel, and had never once seen anybody go in or out except Puny.

"Give me a report on the dance," he said.

"May I read you something?"

"I like it when you read," Janette whispered. She sat with him in the cramped space of her semiprivate room, looking toward the wall.

"I asked the Lord
for a bunch of fresh flowers
but instead he gave me an ugly cactus
with many thorns.
I asked the Lord
for some beautiful butterflies
but instead he gave me
many ugly and dreadful worms.
I was threatened.
I was disappointed.
I mourned.
But after many days,
suddenly,
I saw the cactus bloom
with many beautiful flowers
and those worms became
beautiful butterflies
flying in the wind.
God's way is the best way."

Earlier in the visit, he'd been encouraged to see light returning to her eyes, though it was a light that sparked, then waned, like a weak flame in damp wood.

Now she turned her head and looked at him and he searched for the flame, but it wasn't there.

"Someone named Chung-Ming Kao wrote this," he said. "From prison."

She closed her eyes, and he felt the despair of his own helplessness.

In truth, he had no solutions to offer Janette Tolson, not even a burning homily.

In the end, all he had to offer was hope.

"Father—Buck Leeper."

"Buck!" He rejoiced to hear Buck's rough baritone voice. As badly as the superintendent of the Hope House project had once treated him, he now remembered only that night in the rectory, the night Buck had knocked on his door, saying, "I'm ready to do whatever it takes."

What it took, in Buck's case, was a broken spirit and a willing heart. That Christmas Eve night, Buck Leeper prayed a simple prayer and asked Christ to be his Savior and Lord.

They had stood there by the fire, their arms around one another—two old boys from Mississippi, bawling like babies.

He sat forward in his office chair, doubly excited, given that he'd never had a phone call from Alaska.

"How are you, buddy?"

"Scared," said Buck.

"I know. I've been there."

"Yeah, but when you tied th' knot, it was your first time. I've been there three times and messed up."

Buck's three marriages had all ended tragically. His first wife had died of an undiagnosed blood disease, his second wife had committed suicide, and, twelve years ago, his third wife left with his foreman and sued for divorce.

"In those three marriages, you didn't know Him, you didn't have a clue who He really is. St. Paul says that when we give our lives to Christ, we become new creatures. 'If anyone is in Christ, he is a new creation; old things have passed away; behold, all things have become new.' "

There was a grateful silence at the other end.

"I'm praying for you and Pauline and the children. You'll need His grace on this side of the cross as much as you needed it on the other. Pray for His grace, Buck, to carry you and Pauline from strength to strength as you build this new life together."

He listened to static on the line as his friend in Alaska struggled to speak.

"Thanks," said Buck, standing in a phone booth in Juneau, and feeling that a D-8 Cat had just rolled off his chest.

Hoppy Harper called the church office to say that Louella's break was bad, though nothing like Miss Sadie's had been. Louella would be down for the count for a while, but the prognosis looked good.

Gene Bolick's medication was helping, he'd counted the stairs to bed only twice in five nights, and Esther seemed more like her old self. She had, in fact, brought an orange marmalade cake to Hoppy's office.

Hoppy went on to say that a new priest had been called to Lord's Chapel. The interim would finish up the end of October, and the new man, Father Talbot, would be installed on All Saints' Day. Both agreed the call had come pretty quickly; some parishes took up to two years to replace a priest.

He hoofed along the lane toward the Baptist church and the big meeting with the Fall Fair committee.

Thank God things were on the mend in Mitford. He had fish to fry in Whitecap—not the least of which was getting his act together for his wedding anniversary, only three days ahead.

"Father, it's . . . Pauline Barlowe."

"Pauline!"

"I've found something."

He understood at once; she had found some clue, some trail to Kenny and Sammy. He literally held his breath.

"I was gettin' ready to throw out an old pocketbook I hadn't carried in years, and for some reason I looked through it real good, and in th' linin' . . ."

"Yes?"

"In th' linin' I found this little piece of paper, it said . . . Ed Sikes."

"Ed Sikes?"

"Yes. I must have written it down after I gave Kenny . . ." She hesitated, unable to speak the thought. "Th' man that took 'im was named Ed Sikes, that's all I know. I was . . . I was drunk, and didn't ever know where he worked or lived or . . . anything."

He felt the pain under her confession, the pain that might

never heal completely, though Pauline Barlowe had come to know the Healer.

"I'd give anything if you could . . ." She didn't finish.

"I know this man gave you alcohol, but was there any other reason you let Kenny go with him?"

"I don't know . . . he seemed nice, I guess. It seems like I thought he could probably treat Kenny better than I did."

"I'll look into this and let you know if anything turns up. What about Buck? How is he?"

"He just called us, he's doin' real good, he's comin' th' end of September. We're all . . . real excited."

"Dwell on that," he told Dooley's mother.

"Emma, remember when you helped find Jessie Barlowe?"

Emma liked being reminded of the role she played in bringing Dooley's little sister home to Mitford. Emma had gone on-line and nailed the whereabouts of the woman who'd bolted to Florida with Jessie.

On a hunch, he'd piled Cynthia and Pauline into the Buick and driven sixteen hours to Lakeland, Florida, where they miraculously recovered the five-year-old Jessie, now living with her mother and older brother, Poo.

"I'd like you to get on the Internet and look for Ed Sikes. S-i-k-e-s. That could be Edward, Edmund, Edwin—"

"Edisto, even! I had an uncle Edisto we called Ed."

"Whatever. Whatever you can think of."

"Is this about one of Dooley's brothers?" she asked.

"It is."

"I'll get right on it," said his erstwhile secretary, "and I'll pray. Sometimes I pray while I surf."

He slid the Mustang into the gravel area by the church as the heavens burst open in a deluge.

He raced down the basement steps with the *Mitford Muse* under his arm and, sopping wet, trotted to the men's room to dry himself off with paper towels.

"Is that you, Father?" Marion called from the sink at the end of the hall.

"It is! How are you, Marion?"

"Spry! I just made coffee, want a cup?"

"I do!"

A violent clap of thunder crashed overhead as he punched thc play button on his office answering machine.

"Father Timothy? Cap'n Willie. We've got a bad storm warnin' for Thursday, and we're cancelin' th' trip. We're right in th' heart of hurricane season, so I guess it's no surprise. I'll make good on your trip anytime, just call to reschedule, four-oh-two-eight." There was an awkward pause. "Thank you for your business, and good fishin' to you."

Hotdog and Hallelujah!

He took the sodden newspaper apart and draped the three double sheets over Sunday School chairs to dry. Another clap of thunder rolled above them. It was comforting, he thought, to be snug in the basement of the old church, the smell of coffee wafting along the hallway, someone nearby to call to, the rain pelting the windows. . . .

Marion bustled in with a mug in either hand.

"There's sugar cookies left from Sunday School," she said, "but I don't suppose you can have any."

"Not a crumb."

Marion settled into the chair by his desk. "Ella Bridgewater's all the talk," she said, nodding her approval. "You did a fine job rounding her up."

"I didn't do the rounding up. Ella was heaven-sent."

Marion smiled. "You and Cynthia were heaven-sent, is what Sam and I think."

He felt his face grow warm. "Now, Marion . . ."

"Well, it's true. How are you all doing, now that you've dug in? Are you happy in Whitecap?" Marion possessed one of his mother's most desirable characteristics—a frank simplicity that invited the truth.

"We are. There are good people at St. John's, we feel very blessed."

"We've got our downside, but I suppose we're no worse than the rest of the lot. You'vc helped us settle some of our petty squabbles."

"At least the pew bulletin is no longer running classifieds," he said, smiling.

Marion laughed. "And just think—that's where I found my carpet sweeper for nine dollars! In any case, I hope parenting isn't proving too much for you. Goodness, after our grandchildren used to leave, we were pooped for a month of Sundays. And that's when they were old enough to feed and dress themselves!"

"He's a handful, all right."

"Janette's not doing so well, is she? She hardly spoke on Sunday, bless her heart."

"The doctor says the downward spiral has been going on for a long time. The upward spiral takes time, too."

She blew on the steaming coffee. "Thank the Lord I never had trouble with depression. Complaining, that's been my thorn."

"I hadn't noticed," he said.

"I don't suppose most people confide their thorns. Saint Paul only said he had one. I wish he'd gone ahead and told us what it was!"

He laughed. "You'll never hear mine from me!" Self-righteousness, he thought, and no two ways about it.

He enjoyed Marion's company. There was a decided comfort to being in her presence.

"Did you know Janette sews like an angel?" she asked.

"I only know she takes in sewing."

"She sews every bit as well as Jeffrey Tolson sings," Marion said with feeling. "Made all our choir robes and banners, makes all her children's clothes, plus earns a living with it. I guess she'll have to depend on her calling for support 'til she takes him to court. *If* she takes him to court." Marion sipped her coffee, looking concerned. "I saw Jeffrey Tolson the other day."

"Aha."

"I think he's living on the island."

He shook his head. What could he say?

"He thinks this is his church, that it belongs to him because his father and grandfather were members here, as if half the congregation couldn't say the very same thing." She gave a mild shudder. "Oh, how I'd hate to see him come back. Some predict he'll try. It would put us through the wringer."

"Once through the wringer seems quite enough to me," he said, meeting her gaze.

"They say the business with Avery Plummer didn't work out, she left him and went to her mother in Goldsboro." Marion sighed. "I always felt sorry for Janette, being so plain and her husband so handsome. Some people, I won't say who, called her Church Mouse. The boy has his mother's sweet spirit, but looks the spit image of his father, don't you think?"

"I agree."

"Jeffrey always reminded me of an apple I took my sixth-grade teacher, Miss Fox. I'll never forget that apple. I was so proud of it, I polished it on my dress all the way to school; it was the prettiest thing in our orchard. I stood right by her desk and watched her bite into it. I thought she'd say, *Why, Marion Lewis, this is the best apple I ever tasted!* Well! When she bit into it, she had the oddest look on her face."

"Really?"

"Rotten inside! I was embarrassed to death, just mortified."

"Aha."

"We're all excited about the tea," she said, changing a sore subject. "I'm taking a day off from the library to help Cynthia, and Sam and I will loan you our nice canvas folding chairs for the garden. At the ECW meeting, we prayed for sunshine. I don't think that's too pushy, do you?"

" 'Come boldly to the throne of grace!' " he quoted from Hebrews.

"Well, no rest for the weary!" she exclaimed, rising from the chair. "I've got to clean up under the sink, you never saw such a mess of old vases, there's enough oasis under there to capsize a ship. Speaking of ship, when are you going on your big fishing trip with Cap'n Willie?"

"Postponed!"

"Oh, I'm sorry."

"Don't be," he said.

It was nagging him, reminding him of the time years ago when he'd found the lock broken on the church door. He'd found nothing stolen, nothing amiss, and he didn't report it. Then he'd discovered the burial urn filled with precious stones, sitting innocently on the shelf of the makeshift columbarium in the church closet. . . .

"Rodney? Tim Kavanagh, how's business?"

"Slow, thank th' Lord," said Mitford's police chief. "How you doin' down there at th' end of th' world?"

"Pretty well, thanks. Listen, Rodney—an odd thing . . . Puny Guthrie, Joe Joe's wife, you know she's our housekeeper . . ."

"Right."

"She tells me something is missing from our house next door to the old rectory. Just disappeared off the mantel."

"What's th' missin' item?"

"A bronze angel on a green marble base, probably about eighteen inches high, maybe twenty."

"What's th' value?"

"I don't know. But it's a fine piece, very fine. I'd estimate three thousand, at least. Old bronzes aren't cheap."

"What else is missin'?"

"Nothing. And nothing out of place. But Puny had left the door unlocked by mistake, and there's work being done on the street out front, so . . ."

"Any suspects?"

"No, and nobody was seen going in or out. No one even knew the door was unlocked."

"I don't know what we can do but file a report. No suspects, nothin' else missin', no vandalism. That don't leave much to go on. What we probably need to do is go down and take fingerprints."

He remembered that Rodney Underwood loved taking fingerprints.

"Wouldn't it cause an uproar to have your men crawling all over the house? Besides, this was maybe a week or so ago, and Puny dusts pretty faithfully, wouldn't that remove fingerprints?"

"Don't you worry about a thing, you let me take care of it! Now, how do we get in?"

Given the excitement in Rodney's voice, he might have handed the chief the keys to a Harley hog. "Talk to Puny," he said, half regretting he'd brought it up in the first place.

With the newspaper sufficiently dry, he reassembled it and carried it to his desk.

He was surprised to see the gated, well-secluded mountain lodge of Edith Mallory in a photograph. A white arrow pointed to a grove of trees next to Edith's rambling house.

Mallory Property Sight of Tension Over Town History

When the great-great-grandfather of Mitford native and mayoral candidate, Coot Hendrick, settled our town in

1853, he built a dog-trot cabin on Lookout Ridge, and a small trading depot where Happy Endings Bookstore now stands.

Later, as the family of Hezikiah Hendrick grew, our town founder built a spring house, barn, and corncrib on his forty-acre ridge property.

The cabin and outbuildings are long gone, but the stone foundations remains, according to Dr. Lyle Carpenter of Wesley College in our neighboring township. There is also a family graveyard and the graves of five Union soldiers reputed to exist on the property.

"What we discovered on the ridge is a classic example of how our early mountain settlers lived," says Carpenter. "We wish to see this valuable site preserved, perhaps with an eventual replication of buildings, so that residents and visitors can understand and enjoy our mountain frontier heritage."

Dr. Carpenter reports that the Hendrick family dump sight, allegedly located only yards from where the cabin stood, may contain pottery shards, milk buckets, plow shares and other remnants of early highland life.

There is a rub, however. The Hendrick property is now owned by Mrs. Edith Mallory, whose 95-acre ridge-top estate, Clear Day, includes the old homesite. In fact, her house is reported to sit but forty-six feet from the south-facing foundation of the Hendrick cabin.

Mrs. Mallory currently has a town permit to construct an additional 3,000 square feet of residential space, which will intrude on part of the historic sight. She is reported to say she has no intention of halting construction, which is scheduled to begin in September, and has issued a no trespassing warning.

"This is a crucial moment in our local history," says Dr. Carpenter. "We must find a way to preserve this important property, which my colleagues and I have only recently discovered, thanks to the fine work of the Mitford town museum and its archives."

Coot Hendrick, the great-great-grandson of Mitford's founder, says he will fight for the old homeplace to be designated a historic sight.

Dr. Carpenter said that a walking path to the sight from the town, and a nature trail identifying the abundant flora, would also be a fine idea.

The town council is appealing to the State Department of History and Archives for counsel in the matter.

Mrs. Mallory could not be reached for comment.

Edith Mallory, he thought, had the ominous persistence of leaking propane. Just when he thought she had vanished forever in Spain or Florida, she reappeared, and always with malice.

Surely there was some way she could come to terms with the town over this thing.

In the end, had she ever done anything for the benefit of Mitford? Never once, as far as he could remember. Her multimillion-dollar home sprawled along the ridge above the village, looking down on a community of souls who'd been through one tough scrape after another, yet she'd never been forthcoming, even to the library when it was struggling for its very existence.

And hadn't he been sent knocking on her door when the town museum was trying to pull itself together, and hadn't she made her usual seductive, albeit fruitless, overtures and sent him packing? The annual Bane and Blessing had long ago given up asking for contributions, not to mention the volunteer fire department.

Of course, she had given fifteen thousand to add beds to the Children's Hospital, his favorite charity. He'd quickly learned, however, that it was all part of a plan to get him into a bed of her own.

His very skin crawled at the thought of how she'd trapped him in that blasted Lincoln, forcing him to leap from the thing while it was still moving.

He folded the *Muse* and threw it in the wastebasket. As far as he was concerned, the only good news was that J. C. Hogan had evidently installed software with a spell check. Too bad there was no software out there for grammar.

In truth, he was tired of knowing what was going on in Mitford. He didn't want to hear another peep from that realm for a while.

He was going to do what Mona's sign said, and bloom where he was planted.

Somehow, he'd managed to turn the ringer off and didn't hear the phone while he was washing his cup at the sink down the hall.

"I don't know why I keep missin' you," said Emma, when he punched the play button.

"I thought you'd want to know the scoop on Father Talbot, it's what everybody's talkin' about. I didn't lay eyes on him when he was here tryin' out, but Esther Bolick says he's good-lookin' as anything, and *tall. Very* tall. Oh, and thin, she thinks he exercises, maybe with weights. Esther Cunningham said he walked up the street to her office when he was here, said he just wanted to meet the mayor of such a fine town, wanted to shake her hand, wadn't that nice?

"He's comin' in November, is what they're sayin', has a wife that could be th' twin of Meg Ryan, and two kids, both on th' honor roll. Anyway, people are real excited about finally gettin' somebody permanent down at Lord's Chapel, and from a big church, too, I think it was Chicago. They say they saw him on a video and he preaches up a storm and is funny as heck, he had everybody rollin' in th' aisles.

"Let's see, what else . . . somebody, I forget who, said he sings great an' has real white teeth an' looks terrific in . . . whatever it is, maybe his hassock."

Wears a halo, he thought, has wings . . .

"Oh, Lord, here comes Harold back, he must've forgotten his bag lunch."

Click. Beep.

"Timothy?"

"Walter!" His only living cousin, as far as he knew, and lifelong best friend into the bargain. "It's been a coon's age."

"I thought I'd ring down to the boondocks while I'm waiting for a client to show up. How's the fishing?"

"I have no idea."

"Swimming? Doing any swimming?"

"Nope. No swimming."

"Clamming? Crabbing? Duck hunting? *Anything?*"

"Just the same old stick-in-the-mud you've always known me to be." Darn Walter, he was always looking for some big story, some action. So far, the most exciting thing he'd ever done was marry Cynthia Coppersmith. That was such a big one, it got him off the hook with

Walter for a couple of years, but now his attorney cousin was at it again.

"Listen, Potato Head, I've got a new parish to take care of and a yard to mow. That's all the action I can handle right now. How's Katherine?"

"Mean as a snake, skinny as a rail."

"The usual, then!" They laughed easily together. They were both pretty fond of Walter's wide-open wife, her dazzling laughter and unstoppable generosity of spirit.

"And Cynthia?"

"Busy. Doing another book, reading at the library, tending a three-year-old."

"You've taken in another one?"

"Only briefly, his mother's in the hospital."

"How do you like your new parish?"

"I like it. Good people. We're happy here. When can you and Katherine come down? You haven't been my way in years, I was there last, you owe me."

"After you finish this interim, we'll drive down to Mitford for a week, how's that? Slog around in our bathrobes and eat you out of house and home."

"You can't scare me, pal."

"Speaking of scare," said Walter, "we had a little break-in the other night. They took our TVs and my Rolex. We're surprised it wasn't worse."

"We've just had an odd thing happen. Remember the angel I once mentioned, the one from Miss Sadie's attic? It disappeared off the mantel in Mitford. Nothing else was disturbed in the house, no sign of entry, nothing. Just gone, vanished. Very queer."

"Valuable?"

"Probably three thousand or so, maybe more. Bronze. On a heavy marble base. French, I think."

"Life has always been too mysterious to suit my tastes. Well, Cousin, here comes my erstwhile client. It's good to touch base. Love to Cynthia, love to Dooley—how is he?"

"Great!"

"Good. I've got a stock tip for you, so call me, you dog, and let's catch up."

"Consider it done," he said.

He'd written it everywhere but on his hand to make sure he didn't forget. No, indeed, forgetting birthdays and anniversaries did not cut it at his house—nor at any other house, as far as he could tell from his years in clergy counseling.

Headed for the town grocer with the windshield wipers on high, he mulled over the coming event.

They'd already gone to the beach and taken a blanket, but they hadn't gone to the beach and taken a blanket and a Coleman stove.

Just down the strand from the old Miller cottage with the red roof, he would set everything up in their favorite spot.

They would watch the sunset and he would grill fresh mahimahi and corn in the shuck.

He would cut a ripe, sweet melon—he didn't think it was too late in the season to find one—and pour a well-chilled champagne. He noted that he'd have to go across to find a decent label, but while he was there, maybe he could also find something to drink it from, since all they had in the cabinet were what appeared to be top-of-the-line jelly glasses.

For dessert, of course, he'd make her sworn favorite—poached pears—the very thing he'd served Cynthia Coppersmith the first time she came to dinner at the rectory.

All in all, pretty creative thinking for a country parson . . .

As for entertainment, they could search the night sky for Arcturus and Andromeda, maybe Pegasus. He'd bought a book at Ernie's that told very plainly how to find something other than the Big and Little Dippers, which, he'd been disappointed to learn, weren't even constellations.

He went over the list again.

Leonard and Marjorie Lamb had offered to babysit, and were scheduled to arrive at Dove Cottage at six-thirty. . . .

What had he forgotten?

He realized he was holding his breath, and exhaled. All bases covered. Consider the thing done!

Had it been four years ago when he'd raced through the sacristy into the nave of Lord's Chapel, trembling like a leaf in the wind, late for his wedding through no fault of his own, and spied his bride, also late and flushed from running, who appeared like a vision in the aisle?

If ever he'd known the definition of a waking dream, that had been it.

He remembered standing there, terrified that he'd burst into tears with half the congregation, and noted that he'd never seen so many handkerchiefs waving in the breeze. Under the swell of the organ music, there had been a veritable concerto of sniffing and nose-blowing by men and women alike.

And then, there she was, standing with him. He later admitted to his cousin, Walter, that the earth had moved at that moment. He felt it as surely as if the long-inactive fault running from somewhere in the Blue Ridge Mountains to Charleston, South Carolina, had suddenly heaved apart.

He remembered thinking, with a glad and expectant heart, I'm in for it now.

They were out of Jonathan's favorite milk at the grocer's, so back he schlepped to Ernie's, clobbered by rain.

"We had doubles developed," said Ernie, showing him three-by-five glossies of Junior. "These are th' two that went off Friday, what do you think?"

In the first snapshot, Junior had a pained expression, as if he were sitting on a carpet tack. The other was of a red-eyed Junior standing like a statue in front of the drink boxes. He didn't believe Junior had gotten around to ironing his shirt, after all.

"What about these red eyes?" he asked, concerned for the outcome of the whole deal.

"I don't know what that is. Seems like Junior's camera wadn't too swift."

"Well . . ."

"It's been five or six days an' he hadn't heard back."

This didn't look promising. . . .

"Tell me about Junior," he said. "He seems a good fellow. Any family?"

"Junior lost his mama when he was pretty young, and his daddy's not much account. Me an' Roger and Roanoke try to see after him, kind of help raise him."

"Doesn't seem like he'd need much raising at the age of thirty-six."

"Well, but th' thing is," said Ernie, lowering his voice, "Junior's not the sharpest knife in the drawer."

"Who is?"

"We'd like to see him settle down, get married, have a family. He's a hard worker, got money saved, has a little house, and there's not a bigger heart on Whitecap. Helps look after his next-door neighbor, she's blind as a bat. . . ."

"Good fellow!"

Ernie removed his glasses and squinted at Father Tim. "Roanoke told me he barbered you."

"Even my wife was pleased," he said, taking a gallon of milk from the cooler.

"We got a bad storm comin' Thursday."

"I hope it clears out by Friday evening."

Ernie opened the register and gave him change. "Big doin's on Friday?"

"Yep. Fourth anniversary."

"I got one comin' up here sometime, I can't recall when."

"Let it pass and you'll be stepping over something worse than a yellow line."

"You got a point," said Ernie. "By th' way, I'm readin' that Wadsworth book."

"How do you like it?"

"He sure does a lot of runnin' up hill an' down dale. Seems like he takes notice of every little thing, keeps his eyes an' ears peeled. . . ."

"Just like Louis L'Amour!"

"I wouldn't have thought of that," said Ernie, looking pleased.

He hauled the thing from the box.

"A VCR!" His wife was beaming.

He fetched something from a bag. "Not to mention . . ."

"Peter Pan!" she whooped. "Thanks be to God!"

He fetched something else from the bag.

"*Babe!* I've always wanted to see that."

"Now I've made two people happy," he said, feeling like a hero.

Jonathan flew ahead of them, running at sandpipers, shouting at gulls, squatting to examine a shell.

The sun had looked out an hour ago, and they agreed they should take advantage of it. Barefoot and holding hands on the wide sweep of rain-soaked beach, he knew that what he'd told Marion and Walter was true—they were happy in Whitecap.

He stooped and picked up an old Frisbee and threw it for Barnabas, who loped along the sand in pursuit. Watching the boy and Barnabas tumble for the Frisbee, something came swimming back to him across time. He was nine years old in Pass Christian, Mississippi, and in love with a dog. He'd completely forgotten, and the sudden memory of that summer took his breath away.

"I can feel your wheels turning," declared his wife.

"Pass Christian," he said, as if in a dream. "We drove all the way from Holly Springs to the beach at Pass Christian, it's on the gulf near Gulfport and Biloxi. A wonderful place."

"Tell me everything!" she implored.

"It was the year my father decided I should invite a friend on our summer trek; he thought I was too studious, too much a loner. I wanted to take Tommy Noles, but . . ."

"But the Great Ogre refused."

"Oh, yes. He picked the friend I should take."

"Who was it?"

"Drew Merritt, the son of my father's colleague at his law office."

His wife never liked stories about his father. He should probably keep his mouth shut, but he wanted to talk, he wanted to let go of the constraints he felt he was eternally placing on his memories, on his feelings. If he couldn't talk freely here by the ocean, which lay perfectly open to the sun and the sky . . .

"Drew wasn't someone I wanted to spend two weeks with. He was selfish, short-tempered, demanding. I remember we took a jigsaw puzzle of the nation's Capitol . . . he insisted I do the cherry blossoms and he'd work on the Capitol building. Instead of piece by piece, we worked on it section by section. I didn't want to do cherry blossoms."

"But you did them," she said, "because you're nice."

"Nice has its advantages," he said.

She squeezed his hand. "I love you."

"I love you back."

"Finally, after we'd been there a few days, Drew found a crowd to hang with, and I started wandering off on my own. It was a safe place, of course, plenty of kids came and went, reporting in to parents during the course of an afternoon. We stayed at an old hotel, I wish I could remember the name. Anyway, one day I went down to the beach and met . . . a dog."

She smiled, loving even the simplest of his stories.

"It was a red setter, and he didn't seem to belong to anyone, though he was certainly no maverick. I remember his coat was long and silky, it shone when it blew in the wind. He was like something from heaven, we connected instantly. *Click*—just like that, he was mine and I was his."

"I wouldn't let Barnabas hear you talking this way."

He put his arm around her shoulder, laughing.

"No, Jonathan, don't touch it!" Cynthia cried. The heavy rain had helped the sea disgorge flotsam of great variety.

"We started meeting in the afternoons, I never saw him in the morning. I took a little red ball with me every day and threw it to him. He always brought it back." He was able to recall his sense of freedom, and the unutterable joy of having, at last, the dog that had long been forbidden at home.

"I named him . . . Mick," he said, suddenly uneasy with the confession of a time he'd never mentioned to anyone.

"Mick!" she said. "I love that name!"

"I remember the morning we left to go back to Holly Springs." More than five decades later, his heart could recall the grief of that morning.

"My father decided we should leave a day early, and I . . . hadn't said goodbye. I took a napkin full of biscuits down to the old house where we usually met, but of course he wasn't there, it was too early in the day, so I left the biscuits under the steps."

"I love that you did that."

"Ah, Kavanagh, what don't you love?"

"Husbands who can't talk about their feelings, sand in the bed, and maps that won't refold properly."

"Let's go fold into a rocker on our porch," he said.

"Yes, let's!" She turned and gazed at him, then put her hand to his cheek.

"I'd like to remember you just this way . . . every line of your dear face at this moment."

To his amazement, tears stood in her eyes, and she put her arms around him and kissed him with an odd tenderness.

Jonathan tugged at Cynthia's shorts.

"I got to poo-poo!" said the boy, looking urgent.

The tropical depression moved north from the Caribbean, hung a left toward the Outer Banks of North Carolina, migrated across Whitecap, and dumped six inches of rain inland to Smithfield. Not a hurricane, thanks be to God, but with severe high winds. On Friday morning, it seemed to relish pausing directly over Dove Cottage and unleashing itself for a full two hours.

He padded around the house in his robe the entire morning, working on his sermon, looking over the music for Sunday, scribbling in his quote notebook, reading whatever came to hand. As thunder rolled and wind howled, Barnabas and Violet hid themselves at various points under chairs and beds. Miraculously, Jonathan slept through much of it, while his wife worked at the end of the hall on her new book.

Oh, the ineffable peace of a house darkened by a storm, and the sound of rain at its windows. Though quite unknown to his Irish genealogy, he thought he must have a wide streak of Scot in him somewhere.

So what if his plans for the evening were dashed? Didn't all the world lie before them with, God willing, time to celebrate on the beach even without a special occasion?

He sat in his chair in the study and listened to the rain and wind and the beating of his heart.

Bottom line, wasn't life itself a special occasion?

When the storm abated around six-thirty, they had their anniversary dinner in the kitchen.

Then the entire troop piled onto their bed, Barnabas and Violet at the foot, and Jonathan next to Cynthia, who was propped like a czarina against down pillows.

"And now," he announced, "a movie . . . *in a box*!"

He held the video box aloft for all to see.

"*Peter Pan!*" exulted Jonathan, clapping his hands.

He gave Cynthia a profound look. "You'll never know what you missed tonight."

"It's OK, darling," murmured his contented wife. "I love *Peter Pan*!"

They blew through *Peter Pan* and plugged in *Babe*, adrenaline up and pumping.

"I'm crazy about this movie!" crowed his wife. "But *ugh,* I despise that cat."

"Bad cat!" said Jonathan.

Actually, the cat reminded him of someone. Who was it?

Of course. That cat reminded him of Edith Mallory.

He awoke at two in the morning and listened for the rain. Silence. The storm had passed over, and the room was close and humid.

He went to the window and cranked it open.

The music came in with the sweet, cool breeze that whispered against his bare skin.

CHAPTER TWELVE

Over the Wall

Answering the loud knock, he looked through the screen door and saw Otis Bragg.

Otis was carrying what appeared to be a half bushel of shrimp in a lined basket. "Cain't have a party without shrimp!" Otis said, grinning. His unlit cigar appeared to be fresh for the occasion.

"Otis! What a surprise!" Surprise, indeed. His wife would not take kindly to cooking shrimp fifteen minutes before her big tea, and he wasn't excited about it, either.

"Already cooked, ready to trot. A man over on th' Sound does these for me, all we do is peel and eat. Where you want 'em set?"

"Thanks, Otis. This is mighty generous of you." He hastily cleared one end of the table they'd brought out to the porch and draped with a blue cloth.

"Marlene'll be comin' along in a minute or two with somethin' to dip 'em in." Otis wiped his forehead with a handkerchief. "Maybe I could get a little shooter at th' bar?"

"The bar? Oh, the *bar*! We don't have a bar. But there's tea!"

"Tea." Otis chewed the cigar reflectively.

"Or sherry."

"Sherry," said Otis with a blank stare.

"Good label. Spain, I think." He recalled that Otis had sent him a bottle of something expensive, but couldn't remember where it was. . . .

"Oh, well, what th' hey, I pass. Father Morgan always set out a little bourbon, gin, scotch . . . you know."

"Aha."

Otis squinted at him. "You raised Baptist?"

"I was, actually."

"Me, too," said Otis. "But I got over it."

"Let me get you a glass of tea. Wait 'til you taste it. You'll like it, you have my word." He certainly wouldn't mention where the recipe came from.

The soprano, no worse for wear from her brief career in Sunday School, shook hands vigorously. "Gorgeous day, Father!

"Glorious!" said Sam Fieldwalker. "Good gracious alive, what a day!"

"The best all summer!" crowed Marion, exchanging a hug with her priest.

Also receiving rave reviews were the flowers, the table, the refreshments, the hostess, and even the straggling garden in which he'd labored the livelong morning.

His dog's great size garnered a good share of cautious interest, and Jonathan, dressed in a new sailor suit, was busy eluding all prospects of being dandled on knees or pressed to bosoms.

Father Tim had to admit there was a magical air about Dove Cottage this afternoon; he felt as expansive as a country squire. His wife floated around in something lavender, leaving the scent of wisteria on the breeze and making the whole shebang look totally effortless. The truth was, she'd been up since five a.m., cutting flowers and baking final batches of lemon squares while he installed new lace panels in the living room.

"Lace *belongs* there," she told him. "It filters the morning light and makes patterns on the floor." He had nothing but respect for the miracles wrought via UPS.

Cynthia's workroom was of great interest to the parish children who showed up; eager tour groups processed through the minuscule space, once a large closet, pointing at walls adorned with drawings, book jackets, and—a particular favorite—rough sketches of Violet beneath a beach umbrella. The real Violet positioned herself atop the refrigerator, glowering at anyone who sought her celebrity.

Ella Bridgewater arrived, dressed entirely in black, and looking, he thought, even more like a crane adorning an Oriental screen. She was what his mother would have called "a sight for sore eyes," coming through the cottage gate with a bright rouge spot on either cheek.

Cynthia trotted their new organist around to various groups convened in the garden. "Penny, I don't believe you've met Ella Bridgewater. Ella, meet Penny Duncan. You'll have to see the lovely ice mold she made with fresh peppermint."

"Penny used to be a hippie!" said Jean Ballenger. She proclaimed this as if announcing a former background in brokerage services or marketing. "She grows all their vegetables, raises chickens, and makes goat cheese!"

"Heavenly *days*!" Ella wagged her head in disbelief. "The cleverest thing I ever made was a cranberry rope for the Christmas tree!"

"Penny once made her own shoes," Jean continued, causing everyone to look at Penny's feet, which were shod in pumps for the occasion. "And," said Jean, ending on a triumphal note, "all her children say yes, ma'am!"

He moved away to join Leonard and Marjorie, who had thumped into two of Marion's folding chairs by the crepe myrtle and were busily shucking shrimp and tossing shells into the bushes.

If Violet knew what was going on out here . . .

"Seen anything of your neighbor?" asked Leonard.

"I've seen precisely nothing of my neighbor! But I certainly hear a good deal of him."

"We hope he doesn't make too much racket," said Marjorie.

"Racket! We enjoy it, actually. He's an outstanding musician."

Leonard dunked a shrimp into the sauce that appeared to be setting his lemon square afloat. "Some say he could have been a concert organist. I believe he was schooled at Juilliard. But he never liked the spotlight, as you can imagine. He's a real hermit. I haven't laid eyes on him in years."

"His grandaddy once got in Walter Winchell's column!" said Marjorie. "You remember Walter Winchell?"

"Oh, yes," said Father Tim, feeling suddenly antiquated. "What did he get in there for?"

"Going out with chorus girls in New York City!"

"Aha."

"Joan Crawford came to Whitecap to visit the Loves," Marjorie told him. "And Betty Grable, too, or let's see . . . maybe it was Irene Dunne!"

"It was Celeste Holm!" Jean Ballenger, who enjoyed moving from group to group, plunked into a chair.

"I never much cared for Celeste Holm, Father, did you?" asked Marjorie.

"I don't believe I remember Celeste Holm."

"You see," said Jean, "I told you Father Tim was younger than we thought."

He sucked in his stomach. "What age had you thought . . . exactly?"

"Marjorie said going on seventy."

Seventy!

"Why, Jean Ballenger! I said no such thing! I said with all your wonderful background and experience, Father, you *could* be going on seventy, but in the end, I guessed you to be sixty!"

"Thank you!" he said.

"Who else used to come down here and visit Redmon Love?" wondered Leonard.

Jean smoothed her bangs, which were going haywire in the humidity. "Somebody said Winston Churchill, but I never believed it for a minute. Mr. Churchill certainly had no time to be lollygagging around Whitecap, what with winning Nobel Prizes and putting out wars all over the place."

Leonard licked his thumb. "Well, anyway, we heard the family hid Morris whenever the bigwigs came around. They say Morris spent a lot of time in the attic as a boy. Redmon built him a room up there and put an organ in it, a small version of the big one downstairs. Morris was never allowed to play his music when guests were in the house. I guess they didn't want anybody to know he existed."

"The terrible meanness of people!" said Jean, pursing her lips. "They ought to have been horsewhipped. But, 'Vengeance is mine, saith the Lord.' "

"Did his grandparents raise him, then?" asked Father Tim.

"Pretty much. His parents stayed in Europe most of the time. I went to school with Morris in the fifth or sixth grade, but the kids made it so tough on him, he never lasted to junior high. I'm sure they must have gotten him a tutor."

"What exactly . . . is his problem?"

"You mean you don't know?" asked Leonard.

"Not at all."

"Well, you see—"

"Father!" exclaimed Ella Bridgewater, joining the group. "As I've just said to your wife—your party is delightful, and this tea is *heavenly.*" She clinked the ice in her glass, looking appreciative.

"Well, thank you! As for the tea, I couldn't have said it better myself."

Marjorie squinted up at the new arrival. "Miss Bridgewater—"

"Call me Ella!"

"Ella, we hear you live on Dorchester Island." Marion, like the natives, pronounced it *Dorster.* "Lovely over there, quite remote."

"Remote isn't the word for it! I drive ten miles from my little coop by the sea, go over the causeway, come down Highway 20 for fifteen miles, take the bridge to Whitecap, and drive to St. John's at the north end. It's a trek and a half."

"And we thank you for doing it!" said Marjorie. "You nearly took the roof off Sunday. It's been ages since we heard our old organ give forth such a noise!"

"A *joyful* noise," said their priest, wanting no misunderstanding.

"Do come to Dorchester, Father, and bring Cynthia. I'd like nothing better than to behold your faces at my door!"

For the first time, he noticed Ella's gold brooch—it was in the shape of a hot-air balloon.

"We'd like that. We haven't seen much of the area since we came."

"I know how busy your schedule must be with the summer people to shoehorn in, so just pop up whenever—except, of course, Wednesday, that's when I get my hair washed down at Edna's. Louise and I would love seeing you."

"Louise?"

"Louise is my canary. You should hear her sing, Father, you won't believe your ears!"

"I'm sure!"

"Louise is full of years, as they say in the Old Testament. But the older she gets, the sweeter her voicc."

"Aha."

"I'll show you around little Dorchester, it's like going back in time. You'll see the oldest live oak on any of these islands, it's right by my house, and we'll visit Christ Chapel, it's hardly big enough to hold the three of us, it has the most glorious rose window above the altar! Then we'll walk over to the graveyard where Mother is resting. Did I tell you how we buried Mother?"

"I don't believe so."

"Holding the 1928 prayer book clasped to her heart."

"A fine way to go."

"You must come for lunch!" Ella's rouge spots appeared to brighten. "Are you fond of sea bass?"

"Fond is an understatement. One of my great favorites!"

"Miss Child taught me how to poach sea bass on TV. I miss Miss Child, don't you? I loved the way she dropped things on the floor and picked them up and went right on, a good lesson for us all, I think!"

"Indeed!"

Sam Fieldwalker joined them as St. John's organist drew herself up to her full height, which was impressive. "I'm a good hand at plum wine, into the bargain!"

He chuckled. "Yet another incentive to visit. Sam, Ella's asked us to Dorchester."

"Oh, my gracious, we love Dorchester. They do a good bit of fishing business up there. It's nice and quiet, without the tourism we get on Whitecap."

"I think you'll like my little house, Father, it's quite historic. Built in 1902 of timbers that washed up from shipwrecks. I like to say I live in a house that once sailed the sea!"

"When you go over to Miss Bridgewater's," Sam suggested, "that could be a good time to visit Cap'n Larkin. He's the old fellow I told you about who was a longtime member at St. John's. He lives with his twin brother now, on Dorchester."

"Their house is just a skip and a jump from mine," said Ella. "They keep an old pickup truck parked at the front door, that's where their dog sleeps."

"You could take him communion," said Sam. "That would thrill him. Father Morgan never . . . got around to doing that."

"Consider it done! Of course, if we come anytime soon, Ella, you may have to entertain a three-year-old, as well. How would that be?"

Ella eyed Jonathan clattering across the porch tailed by two self-appointed Youth Group baby-sitters.

"I have a little garden plot fenced with pickets," she said. "We could stake him out there!"

He saw a group gathered to the right of the porch and walked over to see what was what. Cynthia stood by a lacecap hydrangea, holding Jonathan on her hip and peering into a variety of cameras. "Smile, Jonathan!" she urged.

"I declare," Jean Ballenger said, "that child looks enough like your wife to be her own! Do you see the resemblance?"

He did, actually. Two pairs of cornflower eyes. Two winning smiles. Two heads the color of ripe corn.

"I hope Janette can come home soon."

"It's going to be a while yet. It's . . . a hard thing." It hurt him to think about it. He could scarcely bear to witness deep depression; he had seen it in his father for years.

"Step over there," said Sam Fieldwalker, "and let's get one of you, too!"

Cynthia put her hand over her eyes and squinted in his direction. "Yes, dear, come and let them record your tan."

He hated photos of himself; in a picture in the new church album, he looked as if he'd been dug up by the roots.

Sheepishly, he put his arm around his wife, adjusted his glasses, and peered at the cameras.

"You better smile!" crowed Jonathan.

"First to come, last to go!" Otis Bragg shook his host's hand with vigor. "Look here, they cleaned us out."

Father Tim peered into the depths of the empty shrimp basket. "A grand contribution, Otis. Thank you again and again."

"My pleasure!" he said. "Good to see th' parish turnin' out like this. It's what makes us family."

"I agree. Come back anytime, you and Marlene."

Like the rest of the common horde, his landlord and parishioner definitely had some traits that were unlikable. Yet he was growing to appreciate Otis; he had the odd feeling that if the chips were ever down, he could count on Otis Bragg.

"We ought to go on a little run with Cap'n Willie one of these days." Otis took the cigar from his mouth and eyed it fondly. "You do any fishin'?"

"I hardly know a hook from a sinker, but my good wife has bought me a chair on Captain Willie's boat, and looks like I'll be forced to go before it's over."

Otis pounded him on the back. "Do you good! Clergy has a tendency to think too much, you need a little fun in your life. Nothin' like a good, hard fight with a blue marlin to get a man's blood up!" Otis pounded him again. "Give me a call when you set a date, I'll try to go out with you."

"Well . . . ," he said, not knowing what else to say.

"I'll bring us a bucket of chicken," declared Otis, spitting shreds of Cuban tobacco into the border of cosmos.

While he took a cleanup shift in the kitchen, Cynthia carried Jonathan, now overtired and overwrought, through the house and out to the back stoop.

"Mommy! I want my mommy!" he sobbed.

Father Tim stood at the kitchen window and watched them approach the bird feeder in the backyard, his wife struggling to console and distract the weeping boy.

"I want Babette an' Jason!"

"There, Jonathan, it's all right. You'll see Mommy soon, and Babette and Jason, too, I promise. Oh, look at the bird on the fence, I wonder what it is. . . ."

He watched her holding the boy close, patting his back, and saw him lay his head on her shoulder. When she turned to look toward the house, he could see tears in her eyes, as well. His wife had a natural gift for "rejoicing with them that do rejoice and weeping with them that weep," as St. Paul commanded the Romans to do.

He lifted his hand and waved awkwardly as they passed from view.

Cynthia was growing attached to the boy, no doubt about it. She'd never been able to have children of her own; in fact, her former husband had spent most of his time, she said, "making babies with other women." The barrenness had been a deep hurt to her, a thorn.

He finished washing up as Cynthia carried Jonathan once more around the route they usually traveled when the boy was crying for family. He heard her murmuring softly to him, crooning bits of stories and songs.

This was torture for all alike, he thought, as Cynthia trudged up the porch steps, looking weary. Surely next week Babette and Jason would be back from visiting another set of family in Beaufort, and they could borrow them for an afternoon. . . .

He stood at the door as Cynthia eased the boy onto his bed and Barnabas leaped up and lay at his feet.

He watched her smooth Jonathan's damp blond hair from his forehead, and saw the infinite tenderness in her eyes.

"What a good boy," she whispered. Then she turned and patted Barnabas.

"And what a good dog!" she said.

Feeling an unexpected weariness of his own, he sat by the phone in the study and dialed Emma's number. "Found anything?"

"Oh, law, there's hundreds, maybe *thousands* of Ed Sikeses out there, it's like lookin' for Bob Jones or John Smith! There's two Ed Sikeses right over in Wesley, one Edmund an' one Edward, but Harold knows 'em both and says they couldn't possibly have run off with anybody's kid, one's a deacon at First Presbyterian and th' other one goes frog giggin' with Harold's brother.

"Plus, you don't even want to *know* how many different names Ed stands for."

"How many?"

"I looked it up on th' Internet and found thirteen—Edison, Eddrick, Edgar, Edwin, Eduardo, to name only a few. You know you can find anything you're lookin' for on th' Internet, you ought to be on th' Internet, it would help with your sermons, it seems like preachin' Sunday after Sunday, you'd be *desperately* lookin' for new material. . . ."

Emma Newland had been into the Little Debbies again, he knew sugar-induced hysteria when he heard it.

"So . . . ," he said, seeking an escape.

"So you'll have to come up with another gimmick this time," she announced.

He called Pauline.

"I forgot to tell you somethin'," she said. "He was from Oregon, or he maybe was goin' to Oregon."

"Excellent! Wonderful!"

"Father . . ."

"Yes?"

"I've been . . . I'm really scared about somethin'."

"What scares you?"

"Well . . . you see, I don't feel like I deserve . . . all this."

"All this what?"

She took a deep breath. "This . . . happiness. It don't seem right for me to have it."

"Grace isn't about deserving, Pauline. We can't earn God's grace, there's no way on earth we can earn it. Grace is free, and I believe as sure as I am sitting here that He brought the two of you together. Do you love Buck?"

"More'n anything. Just . . . more'n I can say. He's so good to me and th' children, he's . . . nobody sees it, but he's tenderhearted, you know."

"I know."

"I just pray everything's going to be all right. I've told the Lord I'll work real hard."

"You'll need to," he said. Why not speak the truth?

"Thank you, Father. It always helps when we talk. I feel better."

"Can you think of anything else? Anything else about Ed Sikes?"

"I've been prayin' to think of somethin' else, but there's only one other thing I remember. . . ."

"Yes?" He sat forward in the chair.

"He was losin' his hair in front."

Who isn't? he thought.

He rang Emma again.

"Oregon," he said. "Look up Ed Sikes in Oregon. We may be on to something."

"You should get your church to set you up on the Internet," she said, sounding grumpy. "Especially since they don't give you a secretary, it seems they could at least—"

"Emma, remember how you helped find Jessie? If it hadn't been for you, Dooley's little sister might still be missing."

"That's true!" she said, sounding brighter. "All right, I'll get to it soon as Harold and I go to Atlanta, we're goin' to borrow Avis Packard's RV, you know he never uses it, it just sits in his driveway losin' air in th' tires because he works all the time, he's th' only man I know who's more interested in rump roast than women.

"You and Cynthia ought to get an RV, it would do you good to throw your cares to the wind, after all, you *are* retired. When Harold retires from th' post office, we're goin' to do as we please and not kowtow to another living soul, he's got six years to go, then we might hit Hawaii or Alaska, maybe even Dollywood, have you ever listened to her sing, I mean really *listened*? She is very talented, I know you like Bach and Mozart, but you could at least *try* tunin' in to the real world once in a while, you have no idea what you might be missin'. . . ."

Roughly speaking, he figured the sugar content in a box of Little Debbie fudge rounds possessed the power to jolt the human system for a full eight hours, minimum.

Why the angel?

He was beyond trying to figure out who had entered the yellow house, and wondered only why they would have taken the angel and nothing more.

If he'd been the thief, he would have stolen the books. Books, however, didn't seem to be a popular item with thieves. They liked silver, TV sets, and jewelry, yet none of those items had been touched.

Boggling. Each time he thought about it, he felt as if someone had removed the top of his head and poured in cooked oatmeal.

No word from Rodney, but he didn't want to call and stir that pot any more than he had already.

He looked at his watch. Six-fifteen, and the sun was setting. He didn't feel like running—maybe a long walk with Barnabas instead. If they'd held on to one of the babysitters, he might have talked his wife into coming along. . . .

He trotted down the steps in shorts and a golf shirt, amazed how all evidence of the merriment had vanished, that a lovely moment in the lives of forty-two people had become history—with scarcely a mark in the garden from the folding chairs.

He latched the gate behind him and hunkered into an easy lope, with Barnabas on the red leash. Maybe a trek past Ernie's, hang a left this side of St. John's, another left at the little gray house, and circle back by Morris Love's front gate.

Seventy, indeed, he thought, huffing up the lane.

They were circling toward home when the fattest, sleekest squirrel he'd seen on Whitecap made a dash across the road. The leash was fairly torn from his hand as Barnabas leaped after the creature, leash flying.

"Barnabas!"

His dog was doing sixty miles an hour and barking like thunder as he raced toward Morris Love's rusted iron gate, and, in a flash, slithered under it.

"Barnabas! *Come!*"

Deaf as a doorknob, like any dog chasing a squirrel . . .

He huffed to the gate and examined it. Locked. Not to mention rusted. "Barnabas! Come *now*!"

He wiped the sweat from his eyes and saw his dog disappear into a thicket—no, a kind of loggia to the left of the house, which was barely visible through the trees. The furious barking continued unabated.

He whistled loudly. Dadgummit, his wife was a better whistler than he was. She could shake green apples from the tree.

More barking. More whistling.

What if Barnabas crossed the Love property, went under the fence on the other side, and into the street? He didn't keep his dog on a leash at all times for no good reason. Hadn't Barnabas been stolen by the vilest drug-dealing Creek scum, and kept staked and half starved for weeks on end?

Grasping the top of the wall with his hands, he gained a foothold against the rough surface and managed to heave himself up and over, landing beside the overgrown driveway with a thud.

He stood for a moment, still winded, and looked around.

He had entered another world.

Though he was mere inches beyond the gate, a few feet from the street, and only yards from Dove Cottage—he was no longer in Whitecap.

It was a jungle in here, literally.

The grounds had the density of a rain forest, with trees and vegetation he'd never seen before, save for one enormous live oak, damaged by an old storm. He wouldn't be surprised to hear monkeys and macaws, the trumpet call of an elephant. . . .

He stood still, as if frozen to the spot. Cool in here, and quiet, strangely quiet. He heard his own hard breathing, and remembered his maverick dog.

"Barnabas!"

In reply, there was crashing through the underbrush to his left, and a revived fit of barking.

"*Come!* Come, old fella!"

Barnabas bolted into the driveway through a vine-entangled hedge, gave him an odd look, then turned and raced toward the house.

He ran, too, pounding along the weed-grown driveway, until the house came fully into view.

Spanish. Stucco. Tile roof. Moss growing in wide, lush patches on the walls of the loggia or portico; vines covering half the house; the smooth, worn roots of a huge tree gnarling up through a stone semicircle at the front door.

He looked at the windows, which returned only a blank and curtainless stare.

"Barnabas!" he hissed.

Dadgummit, there he came around the right side of the house, galloping like a horse after yet another squirrel, which was fleeing for its life through yet another iron gate on some kind of outbuilding that was nearly obscured by undergrowth.

Enough was enough, by heaven. The party was over.

He dashed after his dog as the squirrel ran through the partially open gate, and Barnabas followed, his long hair catching on the rusted iron and slamming the gate behind him.

As it clanged shut, Father Tim stood for a moment, swallowing down his anger.

It was some kind of ancient, stuccoed enclosure, an old dog run, perhaps, grown up with straggling shrubs and weeds. The squirrel was over the rear wall and gone from sight, leaving Barnabas stranded at the end of the run, barking with impotent fury.

Father Tim jiggled the gate, which appeared to have locked. He'd never seen such an odd contrivance to latch a gate; the rust didn't make it work any better, either. Blast! He hit the thing with the palm of his hand, smarting the flesh and drawing blood.

He could fairly throttle his dog, who now turned toward him with a look of sheepish regret. "Come," he said through clenched teeth.

Barnabas, clearly on the downside of his adrenaline rush, walked slowly toward the gate, head down.

His master punched the gate again, repeated the favorite expletive of his school buddy, Tommy Noles, then gave the blasted thing a stiff kick for good measure.

"Out!"

He heard the bellow as if it were projected on a loudspeaker.

"Out!"

His skin prickled. "Mr. Love," he shouted into thin air, "my dog is locked in your run, and I don't have a clue how to get him . . . *out.*"

"You're a fool to let him *in,*" growled Morris Love.

Father Tim looked to an upstairs window where he thought the voice originated, but saw no one.

"I didn't let him in. He ran in on his own, chasing a squirrel!" He was fairly trembling with the frustration of this escapade, and suddenly angry at the man who refused to show himself, much less proffer a grain of human hospitality.

"Take the pin out," Morris Love yelled.

He slid the pin out. Whoever put this thing together ought to have his head examined. . . .

"Turn the latch to the right!"

He cranked it to the right. Nothing. Dead. Not to mention that something was eating his legs alive.

He was furious. He felt as if he could dismantle the gate with his bare hands, like Samson, and pitch it into the weeds. His blood pressure was probably halfway to the moon.

"It doesn't work!" he shouted, slapping at his bitten legs.

"It works, Father, it has always worked. *Don't push it when you turn it to the right!"*

Morris Love could wake the dead with that huge bellow, as if he were speaking through the pipes of his organ. Father Tim tried again, without pushing. The gate opened as easily as if it had just rolled off the assembly line.

He breathed a sigh of relief and wiped his forehead with the tail of his T-shirt. Blast, what a commotion.

His dog's tail was between his legs as they marched toward the house.

"Thank you!" he shouted to the open upstairs window. "We'll try not to trouble you again."

Silence.

As they swung left into the driveway, he gave one of the gnarled roots an impatient kick.

"Goodbye and good riddance," he muttered under his breath.

Now the duck possessed a portion of its other wing.

He handled it carefully, admiring the lifelike beauty of the emerging creature.

"Do you . . . sell these?" he asked Roger.

"Oh, yes. I haven't kept one for myself in a good while."

"What kind of money do they go for?" Four, maybe five hundred, he thought, and well worth it!

Roger's brown eyes sparkled, as they often did when he spoke of his craft. "I'll probably ask around fifteen hundred for this one."

With what he hoped wasn't obvious haste, he handed it back to Roger.

Ernie thumped into a chair at their table. "Junior's been turned down flat," he said, looking crestfallen.

"How? Who?"

"Ava. She won't go out with 'im, won't even let 'im meet 'er daddy."

"I hate to hear it."

"If you ask me," said Ernie, "it was those pictures that did 'im in. Junior's better lookin' than those pictures."

Roanoke took a cigarette from behind his ear. "His fish done wiggled off th' hook."

Ernie sighed. "We could take 'em again with a better camera. I could get one from th' *Whitecap Reader*, I think they use Nikes."

"Nikons," said Roger, not looking up from his work.

"He ought to start over an' run another ad," said Roanoke. "Leave out th' Bronco business, leave out th' Scrabble business, keep in th' fishin' part, axe th' stuff about a serious relationship—"

"He don't want to run another ad," said Ernie. "He don't want to start over, he wants to meet Ava."

"What did he say in his letter to her? Maybe that's the key."

"Beats me. I tried to tell him what to say, but who knows?" Ernie shrugged, looking disconsolate.

For a while, the only sound was Roger's knife against the tupelo wood.

He threw his cup in the wastebasket by the Pepsi machine and fished around in his shorts pocket for fifty-cents, which he gave Ernie for the *Reader.*

Roanoke had pedaled away on his bicycle, Roger was walking Lucas, and Father Tim figured this was as good a chance as he'd get.

"Ernie," he said, "tell me everything you know about Morris Love."

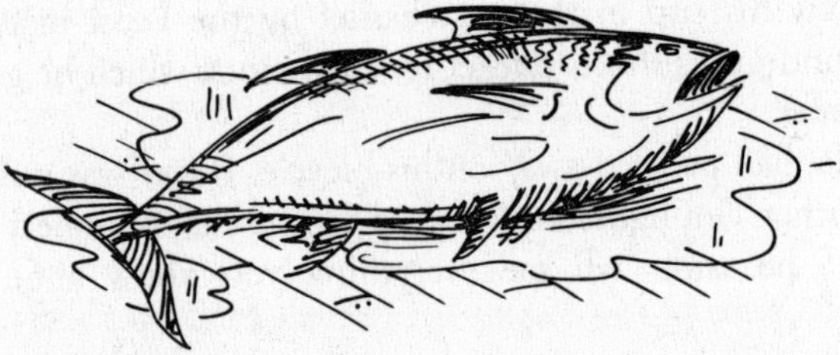

CHAPTER THIRTEEN

Mighty Waters

He was awake ten minutes before the alarm went off, and heard at once the light patter of rain through the open window.

"Timothy?"

"Yes?"

"Is it four o'clock?"

"Ten 'til. Go back to sleep."

"You'll have a great time, I just know you will."

"I'm sure of it. And remember—don't cook dinner. I'm bringing it home."

"Right, darling. I'm excited. . . ."

She was no such thing; she was already snoring again. He kissed her shoulder and crept out of bed.

He was accustomed to rising early, but four o'clock was ridiculous, not to mention he couldn't get pumped up for this jaunt no matter how hard he tried.

He'd entertained every fishing yarn anyone cared to tell, trying to mask his blank stare with a look of genuine interest. Ah, well, surely the whole business would pleasantly surprise him—he'd return home with a cooler full of tuna, tanned and vigorous from a day on the water, whistling a sea chantey.

Chances were—and this was not a perk to be taken lightly—it could even blow a fresh breeze through his preaching, not to mention make him feel more one-in-spirit with his parish. After all, he'd been on their turf for three months and practically the only thing he'd done that he couldn't have done in Mitford was slap a few mosquitoes and pick sandspurs from his dog's paws.

He dressed hurriedly in the bathroom, brushed his teeth, splashed water on his face, and raced to the kitchen to gulp down a cup of coffee he'd set in the refrigerator last night, figuring cold caffeine to be better than no caffeine at all.

He packed the canvas bag with his lunch, having entirely dismissed the notion of fried chicken. Where on earth anybody would find fried chicken at four in the morning was beyond him. He stuffed in plenty of bottled water and a couple of citrus drinks. No time to eat, he'd do that on the boat, he was out of here.

His dog followed him along the hall, thumped down by the front door, and yawned mightily. "Guard the house, old fellow."

Dark as pitch. He turned the lock, shut the door behind him, and patted his jacket pockets for the rolled-up canvas hat and bottle of sunscreen. All there.

He stood on the porch and drew in a deep draught of the cool morning air; it was scented with rain and salt, with something mysteriously beyond his ken. He didn't think he'd ever again take the ocean for granted. He daily sensed the power and presence of it in this new world in which they were living.

All those years ago when he was a young clergyman in a little coastal parish, the water had meant nothing to him; it had hardly entered his mind. He might have lived in the Midwest for all the interest he took in the things of the sea, except for the several bushels of shrimp and clams he'd surely consumed during his curacy. His mind, his heart had been elsewhere, in the clouds, perhaps; but now it was different. Though he wasn't one for swimming in the ocean or broiling on the beach, he was making a connection this time, something he couldn't quite articulate and why bother, anyway?

The light rain cooled his head as he trotted down the front steps, opened the gate, and got into the Mustang parked by the street.

Goin' fishin'! he thought as he buckled the seat belt. The way he'd worried about this excursion had made it seem like a trek to Outer

Mongolia, but so far, so good. And just think—there were thousands, probably millions of people out there who'd give anything to be in his shoes.

It was still dark when he found the marina where the charter boats were tied to the dock like horses waiting to be saddled.

He pulled into the nearly full parking lot, took his gear from the trunk and locked up, then stood by the Mustang, peering into the murky light. People were huffing coolers as big as coffins out of vans and cars, muttering, calling to each other, laughing, slamming doors.

More than once, he'd heard charter boats called party boats, and fervently hoped this was not one of those deals.

Raining a little harder now, but nothing serious. He wiped his head with his hat and put it back in his pocket, checking his watch. Five o'clock sharp.

He hefted the cooler and started walking, looking for *Blue Heaven* and trying to get over the feeling he was still asleep and this was a dream.

Someone materialized out of the gray mist, smelling intensely of tobacco and shaving lotion.

"Mornin', Father! Let's go fishin'!"

"Otis? Is that you?"

"Cap'n Willie told me you were on board today. I didn't want you goin' off by yourself and havin' too much fun."

Otis was schlepping a cooler with a fluorescent label that was readable even in the predawn light: *Bragg's for All Your Cement Needs.*

A bronzed, bearded Captain Willie stood on the deck wearing shorts and a T-shirt, booming out a welcome.

"Father Timothy! Good mornin' to you, we're glad to have you!" He found himself shaking a hand as big as a ham and hard as a rock. "Step over lightly, now, let me take that, there you go, welcome to *Blue Heaven.*"

"Good morning, Captain. How's the weather looking?" It seemed the boat was lurching around in the water pretty good, and they hadn't even gone anywhere yet.

"Goin' to fair off and be good fishin'." Captain Willie's genial smile displayed a couple of gold teeth. "Meet my first mate, Pete Brady."

He shook hands with a muscular fellow of about thirty. "Good to see you, Pete."

"Yessir, welcome aboard."

"This your first time?" asked the captain.

"First ever."

"Well, you're fishin' with a pro, here." He pounded Otis on the back. "Go on in th' cabin, set your stuff down, make yourself at home. And Father . . ."

"Yes?"

"Would you favor us with blessin' th' fleet this mornin'?"

"Ah . . . how does that work, exactly?"

"All th' boats'll head out about th' same time, then after the sun rises, you'll come up to th' bridge an' ask th' Lord for safe passage and good fishin'. Th' other boats can hear you over th' radio."

"Consider it done!" he said, feeling a surge of excitement.

"We'll have prayer requests for you, like, the last few days, we've all been prayin' for Cap'n Tucker's daughter, she's got leukemia."

"I'm sorry. I'd feel honored and blessed to do it."

"We thank you. Now go in there and introduce yourselves around, get comfortable."

Father Tim stuck his head in the cabin.

Ernie Fulcher, sitting with a green cooler between his feet, threw up his hand and grinned from ear to ear. "Didn't want you runnin' out th' first time all by your lonesome."

"Right," said Roger, looking shy about butting in. "We didn't think you'd mind a little company."

Madge Parrott and her friend Sybil Huffman appeared to be dressed for a cruise in the Bahamas. They were clearly proud to announce they were from Rome, Georgia, and this was their first time on a fishing charter. They were out for marlin, would settle for tuna if necessary, but no dolphin, thank you, they'd heard dolphins could sing and had feelings like people.

Both were widows whose husbands had been great fishermen. this trip was about making a connection with the departed, as they'd heard Chuck and Roy talk about deep-sea fishing like it was the best thing since sliced bread. Madge confessed that even though she and Sybil didn't drink beer, they didn't see why they couldn't catch fish like anybody else.

He noted that the group shared a need to explain what they had in their coolers, some even lifting the lids and displaying the contents, and issuing hearty invitations to dip in, at any time, to whatever they'd brought along.

"You run out of drinks, me'n Roger got all you want right here," said Ernie, patting a cooler as big as a Buick. "Got Sun-drop, Mello Yello, Sprite, just help yourself."

"And there's ham and turkey on rye," said Roger. "I made two extra, just in case, plus fried chicken."

Everybody nodded their thanks, as the engines began to throb and hum. Father Tim was mum about the contents of his own cooler—two banana sandwiches on white bread with low-fat mayo.

"Y'all need any sunscreen," said Madge, "we're loaded with sunscreen. It's right here in my jacket pocket." She indicated a blue jacket folded on the seat, so that one and all might note its whereabouts in an emergency.

"And I've got Bonine," said Sybil, "if anybody feels seasick." She held up her package and rattled the contents.

"Have you ever been seasick?" Madge asked Father Tim.

"Never!" he said. Truth was, he'd never been on the sea but a couple of times, and always in sight of shore, so there was no way he could have been seasick. And for today, he'd done what Ernie and Roger so heartily recommended—he'd stayed sober, gotten a good night's sleep, and didn't eat a greasy breakfast.

"Only twelve percent of people get seasick," Roger said, quoting his most encouraging piece of information on the subject.

Ernie lifted the lid of his cooler. "Oh, an' anybody wants Snickers bars, they're right here on top of th' ice. There's nothin' like a Snickers iced down good'n cold."

Madge and Sybil admitted they'd never heard of icing down a Snickers bar, but thought it would be real tasty, especially on a hot day. Sybil pledged to try one before the trip was over.

Otis announced that anybody who wanted to help themselves to his Kentucky Fried, they knew where it was at. He also had cigars, Johnnie Walker Black, and boiled peanuts, for whoever took a notion.

It was the most instant formation of community Father Tim had ever witnessed. He felt momentarily inspired to stand and lead a hymn.

Captain Willie gunned the engines, and the stern of *Blue Heaven* dug low into the water as they moved away from the dock at what seemed like full speed. Father Tim realized he didn't know how he felt about riding backward, not to mention that the water seemed mighty rough.

Very dadgum blasted rough, he thought as they plowed farther out in an unceasing rain. He looked around the hull of the small cabin, where everyone appeared totally sophisticated about being tossed around like dice in a cup. They were all holding on for dear life to whatever they could grab, and yelling over the roar of eight hundred and fifty horses running wide open.

Otis Bragg was clearly tickled pink to have two women on board who didn't know fishing from frog's legs. He'd already begun a seminar on how to keep your thumb on the fishing line, how to hold the rod, how to hold your mouth, and how to position your feet when reeling in a big one. Father Tim listened as attentively as he could, then finally slumped against the back of the padded bench and peered through the door of the cabin.

Out there, it was rain, churning waters, and diesel smoke. In here, it was earsplitting racket and the worst ride he'd had since Tommy Noles had shoved him down a rocky hillside in a red wagon without a tongue.

The sun was emerging from the water, staining the silver sea with patches of light and color.

Pete Brady came into the cabin, holding a dripping ballyhoo in one hand. "You'll want to go up to the bridge now, sir. Better put your jacket on."

"Right!" he said. He was glad to leave the cabin; only a moment ago, he'd had the odd sensation of smothering. . . .

He stood, holding on to the table that was bolted to the deck, then made his way to the door, praying he wouldn't pitch into Madge Parrott's lap.

"You tell th' Lord we're wantin' 'em to weigh fifty pounds and up, if He don't mind." Otis chewed his cigar and grinned.

Father Tim clung to the doorjamb. "How do I get to the bridge?" he asked Pete.

The first mate, who appeared to be squeezing the guts from a bait fish, jerked his thumb toward the side of the cabin. "Right up the ladder there."

He peered around and saw the ladder. The rungs were immediately over the water, and went straight up. Three, four, five . . .

"*That* ladder?"

"Yessir, be sure'n hold on tight."

He peered into the black and churning sea, and made a couple of quick steps to a chair that was bolted to the cockpit deck. Pete was bustling around without any difficulty in keeping his footing, but Father Tim had the certain feeling that if he let go of the chair, he'd end up at the Currituck Light.

He turned and lunged for the bottom rung of the ladder, but miscalculated and bounced onto the rail. Too startled to grab hold, he reeled against the cabin wall, finally managing to grip the lower rung. Thanks be to God, Pete was baiting a hook and facing seaward, and his cabin mates were oblivious to his afflictions.

Lord Jesus, I've never done this before. You were plenty good around water, and I'm counting on You to help me accomplish this thing.

He reached to an upper rung and got a firm grip.

The spray was flying, the waves were churning, the sun was rising . . . it was now or never. He swung himself onto the ladder and went up, trying in vain to curl his tennis shoes around the rungs like buns around frankfurters.

He hauled himself to the bridge, grabbed the support rail for the hard top, and stood for a moment, awed. The view from the bridge literally took his breath away.

How could anyone doubt the living truth of what the psalmist said? *"The heavens declare the glory of God, the skies proclaim the work of his hands!"* He wanted to shout in unabashed praise.

His shirt whipped against his body like a flag; his knees trembled. This boat was flying, no two ways about it, and beneath their feet, the endless, racking, turbulent sea, and a sunrise advancing up the sky like tongues of fire.

Surely this was the habitation of angels, and life in the cabin a thing to be pitied.

He lurched to the helm, where Captain Willie was holding a microphone, and grabbed the back of the helm chair.

"We're glad to have you with us, Father! Greetings to you from th' whole fleet on this beautiful September day!"

His stomach did an odd turn as he opened his mouth to speak, so he closed it again.

The captain winked. "Got a little chop this mornin'."

He nodded.

"A real sharp head sea."

He felt sweat on his brow as the captain spoke into the microphone. "We're mighty happy to have Father Tim Kavanagh to lead us in prayer this mornin'. He's from over at Whitecap, where Toby Rider has his boat shop. Anybody with a prayer request, let's hear it now."

The VHF blared. "Father, my little boy fell off a ladder on Sunday, he's, ah, in the hospital, looks like he's goin' to be fine, but . . . his name's Danny. We thank you."

"Please pray for Romaine, he had his leg tore up by a tractor fell on 'im. Thank you."

"Just like to ask for . . . forgiveness for somethin' I done, there's no use to go into what, I'd appreciate it."

Several other requests came in as he bent his head and listened intently, gripping the helm chair for all he was worth.

"That it? Anybody else?"

He fished in his pocket for his hat. Though the rain had stopped, he put it on and pulled it down snugly above his ears. Then he took the microphone, surprised that it felt as heavy as a lug wrench.

"We'd like to pray for th' owner of th' marina and his wife, Angie, too," said Captain Willie. "She's got breast cancer. And Cap'n Tucker's daughter, we don't want to forget her, name's Sarah, then there's Toby Rider, lost his daddy and we feel real bad about it. Course we'd like to ask God's mercy for every family back home and every soul on board. . . ."

Captain Willie turned to the helm, grabbed the red knob, and cranked the engines back to idle.

In the sudden quiet, the waves slammed against the hull, dulling the gurgling sound of the exhaust. They seemed to be wallowing now in the choppy sea; they might have been so much laundry tossing in a washing machine.

His heart was hammering as if he'd run a race. But it wasn't his heart, exactly, that bothered him, it was his stomach. It seemed strangely disoriented, as if it had moved to a new location and he couldn't figure out where.

"Our Father, we thank You mightily for the beauty of the sunrise over this vast sea, and for the awe and wonder in all the gifts of Your creation. We ask Your generous blessings upon every captain and mate aboard every vessel in this fleet, and pray that each of us be made able, by Your grace, to know Your guidance, love, and mercy throughout the day. . . ."

The names of the people, and their needs, what were they? His mind seemed desperately blank, as if every shred of thought and reason had been blown away like chaff on the wind.

Lord! Help!

"For Sarah, we ask Your tender mercies, that You would keep her daily in Your healing care, giving wisdom to those attending her, and providing strength and encouragement. . . ."

More than three decades of intercessory prayer experience notwithstanding, he found it miraculous that the names came to him, one by one. He leaned into the prayer with intensity, feeling something of the genuine weight and burden, the urgency, of the needs for which he prayed.

He wiped the sweat from his forehead. "Oh, Lord, who maketh a way in the sea, and a path in the mighty waters, we thank You for hearing our prayers, in the blessed name of Your Son, our Savior, Jesus Christ. Amen."

The captain took the microphone and keyed it, thanking him.

He noted what appeared to be a look of compassion on the captain's face as they shook hands.

"*Blue Heaven, Salty Dog,* come back."

"*Blue Heaven,* go ahead, *Salty Dog.*"

"Just want to say we really appreciate Father Kavanagh's prayers, and sure hope he doesn't succumb to the torments of a rough sea. OK, *Salty Dog* back to eighty."

"*Blue Heaven* standin' by on eighty."

As the captain gunned the engines, Father Tim careened to the rail and leaned over.

The goodwill and fond hope of *Salty Dog* had come too late.

Twice over the rail should nip this thing in the bud. Already his ribs hurt from the retching; it was probably over now and he could go down the ladder and have something to drink, maybe even a bite to eat—that was the problem, going out on rough seas with an empty stomach. . . .

He was amazed at his agility on the ladder, as if by the earlier practice shot he'd become a seasoned sailor. No big deal, he thought, looking down at the waves hammering the boat.

Good grief! He scrambled off the ladder and leaned over the rail, the bile spewing in a flume from his very core, hot, bitter, and fathomless.

It was his head. He seemed to have lost his head the last time over the rail. He reached up feebly and felt around. No, it was his hat he'd lost. It had slithered off and dropped into the sea, and his scalp was parching like a Georgia peanut.

"Let 'im set there, we ain't findin' any fish," he heard Otis say. He opened his eyes and realized he was sitting in the privileged fighting chair. The fighting chair. What a joke.

"Hat," he said. "Hat."

Nobody heard him, because he found he couldn't speak above a whisper. He had no energy to force audible words through cracked lips.

Fine. He'd just sit here until they dumped him overboard, which he wished they'd do sooner rather than later. He'd never known such suffering in his life, not from mayonnaise that had nearly taken him out at a parish picnic, not from the diabetic coma brought on by Esther Bolick's orange marmalade cake, not from the raging fever he had as a child when he saw his mother as a circus performer who made lions jump through hoops.

"What I don't like about th' Baptists," Otis was saying, "is they won't speak to you at th' liquor store."

Laughing, shuffling around, general merriment—people living their lives as if he weren't there, as if he were invisible, a bump on a log.

"That's th' way it is, some days," said Pete. "You're either a hero or a zero. Yesterday, we were haulin' 'em in faster than I could bait th' hooks; today, I don't know where they are."

"You got to pump 'em," said Ernie. "Like, say you're reelin' in a fifty-pound tuna, you got to raise the rod up real slow, then drop down quick and *crank*."

Conversations came and went; it was all a kind of hive hum, he thought, as when bees returned from working a stand of sourwoods.

"Now, you take tarpon," said Otis. "I was down in th' Keys where they grow too big to mount on your wall. Tarpon you just jump a few times and then break 'em off before you wear 'em out, you wear 'em out too bad, th' sharks eat 'em."

"I never fished any tarpon," said Ernie.

He opened his eyes and shut them fast. Pete was showing Madge and Sybil how he prepped the bait.

"See, you pop th' eyes out like this . . . then you break up th' backbone . . ."

"Oooh," said Madge.

"Don't make 'er faint," said Otis.

"I have no intention of fainting, thank you!"

"Then you squeeze their guts out, see. . . ."

"Lord help," said Sybil.

"Thing is, th' more they wiggle in th' water, th' better they catch."

"Clever!" said Madge. "That is *really* clever."

Without realizing how he got there, he was at the rail again, on his knees.

"On his knees at th' rail," said Madge. "That is very Episcopalian."

"Or Luth'ran," said Sybil. "Can't that be Luth'ran?"

He didn't know who it was, maybe Otis or Ernie, but someone held his head while he spewed up his insides and watched the vomitus carried away on the lashing water.

"We been out every day for forty-one days straight," said Pete, who was currently varying the bait, trying anything.

"Sometimes you just pray for a nor'easter so you can get a break, but if th' weather's good, you have to go."

The weather today is not *good,* he tried to say, but couldn't. Why in blazes did we go today if you don't go when the weather's not good? *Answer that!* Plus, *plus* . . . he wished he could discuss this with Roger . . . his math told him that, discounting the crew, he represented more than any twelve blasted percent.

He declined the fighting chair in case anyone got a strike, and sat feebly in an adjacent chair.

"What do you think the winds are right now?" asked Roger.

"Oh, fifteen, sixteen miles an hour. This ain't nothin'. I know somebody was out all night last night in forty-mile winds."

General, respectful silence. Diesel fumes.

"We need to think positive," said Madge. "Smoked loin of tuna! That's how *I'm* thinkin'!"

"Must be lunchtime," said Otis. "Believe I'll have me a little shooter. Want one?"

"Maybe later."

"Thank you, you go on, but I wouldn't mind shuckin' a few peanuts with you."

He was baking, he was broiling, he was frying, he was cooked. Sunscreen. He remembered the sunscreen in his jacket pocket, but he wasn't wearing his jacket. Someone had helped him remove it earlier.

"Look," said Sybil. "Th' poor man needs something."

"What?" said Madge. "Oh, mercy, look at his head, it's red as a poker. Where's his hat?"

"He went to the rail and came back without it."

"Here you go," Otis was patting sunscreen on his head and followed it with a hat

"Bless you," he managed to whisper.

"What'd he say?"

"He said bless me." He thought Otis sounded touched. "Father, you want some water or Coke? Coke might be good."

"Nossir," said Ernie, "what he needs is ginger ale. Anybody got ginger ale?"

"Fruit juice," said Madge, "that's what I'd give somebody with upset stomach."

"No deal with th' fruit juice," said Pete. "Too much acid."

"How about a piece of ice to just hold in his mouth?"

"I don't know about that. They say when you're real hot you shouldn't swallow somethin' real cold, it can give you a heart attack or maybe a stroke."

"He's moving his lips. What's he saying?"

Otis leaned down and listened. "He's praying," said Otis.

They had veered east, then south, but weren't finding any fish. Neither was the rest of the fleet. Occasionally a boat would get a couple of strikes, radio the news, and everybody would head in that direction. But so far, *Blue Heaven* had taken only two dolphins, and thrown back a few catches that were too small to gaff.

They were currently idling the boat several miles south of Virginia, and trolling a spreader bar. The chop was as bad as, or worse than, before; they were wallowing like a bear in cornshucks. He thought of looking at his watch, but why bother? The misery was interminable. There was no hope that anyone would turn back to shore for a sick man, much less send a helicopter. He was in this scrape to the bitter end.

He denied to himself that he had to urinate, as doing that would require going through the cabin where this thing first snared and suffocated him. He wouldn't go back in that cabin if they tried to drag him in with a team of mules.

Occasionally, a kind soul visited his chair and stood for a moment in silent commiseration.

"Sorry, Tim."

"You're going to make it, buddy."

Even the captain came down from the bridge and laid a hand on his shoulder. "Hang in there, Father." Their concern was a comfort, he had to admit, though he was hard-pressed to get over the humiliation he felt.

At one point, someone assured him he wasn't going to die, which he found altogether lacking in comfort, since he didn't much care either way.

"Did you hear about th' guy got dragged off th' boat reelin' in a marlin?"

"No way."

"It was in th' paper, said th' marlin was four hundred pounds, said it pulled th' guy over th' stern."

"He would've been sucked into th' backwash."

"Wadn't. Somebody went in after 'im, saved 'im. But that's not th' half of it. He got th' marlin."

"Bull. That never happened in this lifetime."

"I'm tellin' you it's th' truth, it was in th' paper."

"I've heard of fish takin' first mates over," said Pete.

"There is no way I want to listen to this mess," said Madge.

He was shocked to find himself kneeling at the rail again, with no power over this thing, none at all. He felt completely out of control, which frightened him utterly; he might have been a piece of bait himself, without will or reason to alter his circumstances.

"Number five," somebody said. "That's th' fifth time."

"Seven. He heaved over th' bridge rail twice."

"You ready to eat? I'm half starved."

"I've been thinkin' about what I made last night. Tuna salad. On French bread! Oh, and there's late tomatoes out of my neighbor's garden. Delicious!" said Madge. "I'll cut 'em up so we can all have a bite."

"Tuna out of a *can*?" asked Otis. "That'd be sacrilegious."

"Are we goin' to just leave 'im out here?" wondered Sybil.

"Father? *Father!*"

Why did people think the sick automatically went deaf?

What? He couldn't say it audibly, so he thought it, which should be sufficient.

"Do you want to go inside?"

"Don't take him inside," said the first mate. "You lose th' horizon when you do that. That's usually what makes people seasick, is losin' th' horizon."

"But he's been sittin' out here since it quit rainin'. I think we should at least put sunscreen on his arms. Look at his arms."

He felt several people pawing over him, and tried to express his gratitude.

"Lookit. He doesn't have socks on. Rub some on his ankles."

"Th' back of his neck," said Ernie. "That's a real tender place, slather some on there."

"He's an *awful* color," said Madge.

He realized he should have been more specific in his will; now it was too late to say that he did *not* want an open casket.

He slept, or thought he might be sleeping. Perhaps he'd slipped into a state of unconsciousness, his mind vacant as a hollow gourd. If there was anything he distrusted, it was an empty mind. He forced himself to open his eyes and saw only glare, a shining that moved and heaved and shuddered and danced and tried to force entry to his stomach. In truth, he'd never been especially aware of his stomach. When it was empty, he put something in it; when it was full, he was happy. Now he felt it as a raw and flaccid thing that swung in him like a sheep's bladder with every swell that tossed the boat.

He wanted his wife. Lacking that consolation, he pulled his jacket around him and squeezed his eyes shut and dreamed a dream as vacant as mist.

Thank God! He might actually be feeling better.

His eyes seemed clear, some strength was returning; but he didn't want to count his chickens, no, indeed. He rubbed Chap Stick on his lips and hunkered down under Otis's hat, wondering about his sugar, which must have dropped straight to the floor of the Gulf Stream. He wished he'd brought his tachometer . . . no, that wasn't it. What was it, anyway? Could he possibly have suffered brain damage from this terrible assault? *Glu*cometer, that's what it was.

Weak . . . terribly weak. He realized he was thinking of Ernie's Snickers bars, iced down cold. A small flicker, a flame of hope rose in his breast. *Thank You, Lord. . . .*

He looked out upon the restless water and saw other boats on the horizon—one there, two there, like family.

"We had the worst nest of yellow jackets in our church wall-l-l!" said Sybil.

"What'd y'all do about it?"

"Swatted 'em with our hymnals and bulletins."

"Why didn't you kill 'em?"

"They only flare up once a year, late April or May, and only on th' side where hardly anybody sits, anyway."

"Yesterday a hero, today a zero," muttered Pete, hauling up bait that looked like a glorified Christmas tree.

Father Tim waved his hand to Ernie, who came over and squatted by the chair.

"What can I do for you, buddy?"

"Snickers," he said, hoarse as a bullfrog.

"Snickers?"

He nodded, feeble but encouraged.

"We got us one!" yelled Ernie. "Otis! Where's Otis?"

"In th' head. You take it!"

Father Tim had heard of total pandemonium, but he'd never seen it 'til now. Six people erupted into a full horde, and swarmed around him like the armies of Solomon.

"We got a fish here! Yee-hah!"

"Got another one right here. Take it, Madge!"

He looked at the throbbing lines crisscrossed over and around the stern like freeways through L.A.

"That's a keeper!" Pete gaffed something and pulled it in.

"Way to go, Roger!"

He saw the rainbow of color that shimmered on the big fish as it went into the box, where it thrashed like a horse kicking a stall. Pete pulled out the gaff and hosed blood from the deck.

The captain was fishing off the bridge; everybody was fishing. He heaved himself from the chair, out of the fray, and huddled against the cabin.

In the fighting chair, Madge was crouched into the labor of hauling in something big.

Otis had his thumb on her line, helping her raise and lower the rod. "You got to pump 'im, now," he said, clenching his cigar in his teeth.

"Oh, law! This must be an eighteen-wheeler I've got on here!"

"Keep crankin'!"

Captain Willie called over the speaker, "Please tend to the left-hand corner, Pete, tend to the left-hand corner, we got a mess over there."

"A fishin' frenzy," muttered Pete, streaking by in a blur.

Madge cranked the reel, blowing like a prizefighter. "This fish is killin' me. Somebody come and take this bloomin' rod!"

"Don't quit!" yelled Sybil, aiming a point-and-shoot at the action. "Keep goin', Chuck would be proud!"

"That ain't nothin' but solid tuna," said Otis. He helped Madge lift the rod as the fish drew closer to the boat.

Father Tim rubberlegged it to the stern and looked over. The black water of the morning had changed to blue-green, and the fish moved beneath the aqua surface, luminous and quick.

He thought it one of the most beautiful sights he'd ever seen.

"Here it comes!"

He stepped back as Pete darted to the right of the fighting chair, lowered the gaff, and hauled the tuna onto the deck.

"Way to go, Madge!"

"Beautiful! *Beautiful!*"

Whistles, cheers, applause.

"That'll weigh in seventy, seventy-five pounds," Otis said, as Madge staggered out of the chair, grinning into Sybil's camera.

The captain was catching fish, Ernie was catching fish, Roger was catching fish.

"Got a fish on th' line!" yelled Pete. "Who'll take it?"

"I'll take it!" As Father Tim thumped into the fighting chair, hoots of encouragement went up from the entire assembly.

He was back from the dead, he was among the living, he was ready to do this thing.

"How was it, darling?"

"Terrific!" he said, kissing her. "Wonderful fellowship, *great* fellowship—fellows in a ship, get it?"

"Got it. And the weather?"

He shrugged. "A little rough, but not too bad."

"What's for supper?" she asked, eyeing the cooler he was lugging.

"Yellowfin tuna and dolphin! Let's fire up the grill," he said, trotting down the hall, "and I'll tell you all about it!" By the time he hit the kitchen, he was whistling.

She hurried after her husband, feeling pleased. He'd come home looking considerably thinner, definitely tanner, and clearly more relaxed. She'd known all along that buying him a chair with Captain Willie was a brilliant idea.

CHAPTER FOURTEEN

Letting Go

"Turn around a minute and don't look," Roger said.

Father Tim turned and faced the book room, where Elmo sat on the windowsill, licking his paws after a meal of thawed finger mullet.

"OK, you can look now."

Roger had positioned the carved head on the body of the green-winged teal; the duck was gazing at him in a way he found positively soulful.

"Aha," he whispered.

"I set the eyes a while back and forgot to show you."

"It'll be as close to th' real thing as you'll ever see in this life!" Ernie Fulcher was grinning as if he were personally responsible for the whole deal. "Fact is, you can compare it to th' real thing right now, if you want to. We got one we keep in th' freezer for when he needs somethin' to go by."

"That's OK," said Father Tim, not eager to see a dead duck in a Ziploc bag.

"Until I set the eyes," said Roger, "it didn't have any character at all, there was no personality. The eyes lying on the worktable are nothing, but set them in place and this piece of wood becomes a duck."

"Amazing! Just amazing."

"I've got to burn all the feathers, now they've been chiseled, then I'll gesso everything and start to paint. See these speculum feathers on the wing? They'll be green, and the under-tail coverts here, they'll be a champagne color."

Roger passed his handiwork to Father Tim, who took it, feeling oddly reverent.

Though he didn't know why, and he certainly didn't know how . . . this was his duck.

He was getting ready to leave when Junior Bryson came in, looking as if he'd lost his last friend.

Lucas's tail thumped the floor in greeting.

"I done it," Junior said.

"Done what?" asked Ernie.

"Talked to Ava's daddy."

"Come and sit down," said Ernie, pulling out a chair. "You want a Pepsi, have a Pepsi! Or get you a root beer."

Junior shook his head at Ernie's offer and thumped down at the table, looking, thought Father Tim, considerably pale around the gills. He changed his mind about leaving and sat down with Junior.

Roger placed the duck in its carry-box.

Roanoke lit a Marlboro.

Silence.

"Well?" said Ernie.

Junior sighed. "Well, I finally worked up th' nerve to call 'er daddy, so I got th' phone book that has Swanquarter, and found a Goodnight listed in it."

"Smart!" said Ernie.

"It wadn't too smart," said Junior. "I was thinkin' her daddy's name would be Goodnight, but then, when th' phone started ringin', it hit me that Goodnight was prob'ly her married name an' she might answer th' phone."

"Right!" said Ernie, hoping for the best.

"I was about to hang up, when a man answered. That kind of th'owed me. I thought it might be, like, you know, a boyfriend. But it was her daddy, Mr. Taylor. He lives at Ava's."

Roanoke blew a smoke ring. Lucas's yawn sounded like a squeak from a door hinge.

"Well, I'd practiced what I wanted to say, but when he answered, I forgot everything."

"Right," said Ernie. "It usually works that way."

"So, anyhow, I said, 'This is Junior Bryson from over at Whitecap, Ava might of mentioned me.' "

"That was a good start."

"He said, 'Are you th' fella plays Scrabble and fishes?' " Junior's face brightened momentarily. "I said, 'Yessir.' He said, I like a fella says yessir, most people've forgot about sayin' yessir.' "

"And what'd you say?"

"I said 'Yessir, you're right about that.' "

"Common ground!" exclaimed Ernie. Roger and Father Tim nodded their agreement.

"So I said I was hopin' Ava might go out with me, I do Sound an' ocean fishin' both, an' have a little boat I take crabbin' an' all, I could offer her a variety of fishin' options."

"That should of done it right there!"

"I said I'm pretty sharp at Scrabble and could prob'ly give her a good run for th' money."

"An' what'd he say?"

"He said she beats th' stuffin' out of him all th' time, not to mention beats her sister an' some of th' neighbors."

Ernie whistled through his teeth.

"I told him about my job, how I was Employee of th' Month back in April an' all. . . ."

"What else?"

"I told him I own my own house an' keep my truck washed an' waxed, that I change th' oil myself an' just put on a new set of Michelins." Junior looked exhausted.

"That's all your cards right there," said Ernie. "You laid 'em on th' table, that's all a man can do. So what'd he say?"

Junior looked at his hands. "He said I sounded pretty decent an' responsible."

Ernie beamed. "Then what?"

"So then I told him I hadn't heard back from Ava, an' wondered if he'd be willin' to give his permission for me to take 'er out an' all."

Father Tim glanced around. Roanoke was cleaning his fingernails with a pocketknife. Roger was pondering the situation intently. Ernie looked nervous.

"So he said, 'Well, son, I like what you're sayin', I really do, and I thought those snapshots showed a fine-lookin' fella, but your letter failed to convince Ava that you're a Christian, and that's a requirement of hers as well as mine.' Then he said she wrote me a note a day or two ago and he guessed I hadn't got it yet."

Ernie looked disgusted. "Shoot, maybe you don't want to go out with somebody that could whip your butt at Scrabble. You thought of that?"

"Just because she whips her daddy don't mean she can whip me."

"So, what can we do here to move things along?" asked Roger.

It appeared that Roger's CEO mode was kicking in.

Junior's gaze searched every face for an answer to this probing question, and at last zeroed in on Father Tim, who knew Junior's look very well.

"Would you like to have a talk?"

Junior nodded.

"Anytime, just let me know."

Junior appeared suddenly hopeful. "How about right now? We could go set in my truck."

Roger and Ernie gave the clergy an approving nod.

"Consider it done," he said.

"If you need air-conditionin', we can roll th' windows up."

Father Tim noticed Junior's hands were trembling. A talk with the clergy sometimes did that to people.

"Not for me. But you might pull over in the shade," he said. *Lord, give me wisdom here. May Your Holy Spirit be with us.* . . . His heart was moved for Junior Bryson.

As Junior started the motor, a shattering blast of country music erupted from speakers the size of drink crates. Junior hit the off button, embarrassed. "I'm really sorry 'bout that."

"No problem," said his passenger, barely able to speak for the adrenaline pumping into his system.

Junior eased the truck under the leafy branches of a nearby tree. "We could ride around if you'd rather do that," said Junior.

"This is fine, we can sit right here. I think we're getting a little breeze."

Junior switched off the ignition and was silent for a moment, looking anguished. "I hate to tell you this, sir."

"What's that?"

"I all of a sudden have to go to th' toilet."

"Go right ahead. I understand."

Junior swung down from the cab and loped across the parking lot.

Junior's uneasiness reminded him, somehow, of himself, as he met with his first bishop all those years ago.

"Why did you decide to become a priest, Timothy?"

"I was called, sir."

"Who called you?"

"God."

The tall, angular Bishop Quayle sat quietly in the leather chair, holding his hands upright before him with all his fingertips touching. Father Tim remembered noting that his fingers formed a sort of steeple, which he thought becoming to a bishop.

"You will have times of doubt."

"Yes, sir."

"Which you can't imagine now, of course."

"No, sir."

"Do you genuinely love Christ with all your heart?"

"Yes, sir, I do."

"What is the chief reason you love Him?"

"Because He loves me."

Their visit had been short, but rewarding. Bishop Quayle prayed with him and made the sign of the cross on his forehead. "I think you'll do, Timothy," he said, smiling. The young priest marked the extraordinary light shining in the bishop's eyes; it was this light that had encouraged him most.

Junior opened the door and slid into the seat looking contrite but refreshed. "I'm sorry, Father. I'm . . . kind of nervous."

"I understand."

"Well," said Junior. "I was hopin' you could help me with what to do about Ava."

"Aha."

"I've got 'er picture right here . . ."—Junior fished it from his shirt pocket, looking proud—"so you could remember what she looks like." He balanced it in a standing position on the volume knob of the radio.

"Here's what I told her in th' letter. I said I went to church when my mama was livin' an' got baptized when I was fourteen. I reckon that makes me a Christian."

He smiled. "*Did* it make you a Christian?"

"I don't know. I mean, seem like bein' baptized was a big deal, th' way I remember it."

"It is a big deal. A very big deal. But it's what happens in our hearts, in our spirits, that's a much bigger deal. What was going on in your heart when you were baptized, do you remember?"

"Nothin' much. Me'n some other people went out to th' creek, th' preacher laid us back in th' water, I come up and dried off, and we all went an' ate catfish at Cap'n Willie's."

"When we ask Jesus to come into our hearts and save us—and if we really mean it—something always happens. Something powerful. Sometimes we sense it the moment we ask, sometimes later. But it never fails to happen."

Junior shrugged and shifted in the seat, which caused his elbow to hit the horn. They both jumped. " 'Scuse me," he said. A few drops of perspiration appeared on his forehead.

"I don't know what Ava's thinking," said Father Tim, indicating the photograph. "Maybe you'll learn more from her letter. But she may be looking for someone who has a personal relationship with Christ."

"I don't see how'n th' world you can have a *personal* relationship with 'im. That don't seem possible to me. That don't seem . . . *possible.*"

"That's a hard one to understand, how a God so powerful can be so personal. Yet, when you ask the Son of God to come into your heart, something incredible happens."

"What?"

"He actually comes in."

Junior looked blank.

"He comes in and quickens our spirits so that we're truly alive for the first time. We see with new eyes, we hear with new ears, we're able to receive His love." He thought it was moments like this that he lived for. "The relationship becomes deeply personal, one-on-one."

"I'm sorry, sir, but . . . I just don't get it."

"That's OK. I'll pray for you to get it."

Junior sighed. "What am I goin' to do about Ava?"

"Keep being honest, just as she will be, I'm sure. Whatever happens, honesty is always the best policy."

Junior stared into the vacant lot next door.

"God certainly loves our honesty. You can tell Him anything, Junior, anything!"

"I wouldn't want t' tell 'im *anything.*"

He grinned. "Might as well. He knows it anyway."

Junior blushed.

"He not only wants to be your Savior and Lord, He wants to be your best friend. Pretty hard to imagine, but true. Anyway, I think that because you and Ava both admire honesty, everything's going to turn out just fine."

"You think so?"

"I do."

"Thank you, Father. I really thank you."

"Anytime you have questions, anytime you want to just sit and talk, call me or drop by St. John's."

"Yessir, I will. Can I carry you down to church?"

"I'd appreciate it."

Junior removed the photograph from the knob, gave it a furtive glance, and put it back in his pocket. As they wheeled out of the lot, Father Tim couldn't help but see Roger and Ernie peering through the window.

Mother hens! he thought, waving.

The phone on his desk rang twice.

"St. John's in the Grove! Father Kavanagh speaking."

"Hey!" said Dooley.

"Hey, yourself, buddy!" He loved hearing the boy's voice, he could even hear the grin in it. "What's up?"

"I've got . . . like, you know, like a girlfriend."

Whoa. "A girlfriend? Tell me everything."

"Her name's Caroline."

His heart sank. But what business was it of his? "Where did you meet her?"

"I met her at a dance at her school, and we've been writing. You know. Calling each other."

"Aha. What school?"

"It doesn't matter, I mean . . ."

"No, I'd like to know. What school?"

Dooley sounded a little ticked at having it gouged out of him. "Mrs. Hemingway's."

That school where all the girls are geeks, and wear weird shoes and funny glasses? *That* school? "Smart, I suppose . . ."

"Totally smart, straight A's. And really . . . like, you know . . ."

He knew. "Great-looking? Beautiful?"

"Umm, yeah. Yessir. Totally."

He was thrilled that Dooley could confide in him. Who wouldn't be? That pleasure, however, was considerably diminished by wondering what Lace Turner would think of this.

He'd never ask, of course; no, indeed, not for anything.

"Father?" It was Janette's doctor, speaking in his low-country drawl. "I've got a little slip of paper around here somewhere. Janette asked me to give you a message. Let's see, I can't read my own handwriting, I suppose that's no news. . . ."

Father Tim laughed.

"Here it is. Let's see. 'The cactus is beginning to bloom.' "

Tears misted his eyes. "She's coming along, then?"

"Improving. Yes, definitely."

"When do you think she might be coming home?"

"Ten days, maybe two weeks. We want to be absolutely certain the suicidal stuff is behind us."

"Will she be able to care for the children?"

"Yes, we think so. It might help to give her a day or two to settle in, if possible. I understand her cousin is having a time of it, four children in a one-bedroom apartment. . . ."

"We'll do whatever it takes on our end."

"Excellent. Let's just say two weeks, maximum."

"Thanks be to God!" He felt a weight move off his heart. "Thank you, Doctor. Well done!"

"Father Tim?"

"Speaking. Is that you, Rodney?"

"All we could turn up on th' back door an' th' knob was Puny's prints. Then we dusted your mantel and your desk and so on, but didn't find anything. She's rubbed a good bit of lemon oil around in there."

"Right."

"Course we found some of your prints on th' desk drawers, you remember we took your prints a few years ago."

"I do."

"Sorry to be so long gettin' back to you."

Ah, well. He'd done his duty, they'd done theirs, and that was that.

Had Emma Newland vanished from the face of the earth? Whenever she called, he fervently wished she hadn't. When she didn't, he wished she would. Go figure.

Maybe they were still in Atlanta. Maybe Harold had seen the phone bill and laid down the law. Maybe she didn't care anymore what happened to her old boss—out of sight, out of mind.

He dialed her number and charged the call to Dove Cottage.

"Hello!"

"Emma?"

"Is that *you?*"

"It's me, all right. What's up in Mitford? Tell me everything, it's my nickel."

"After we went to Atlanta and saw Jean, we went to New Orleans, Harold had three weeks piled up with th' post office. The food in New Orleans was great, it was unbelievable, you'd never in a hundred *years* believe how much we ate, I think I have gout."

"Gout?"

"From eating all that French food, they say it'll give you gout."

"Does your big toe hurt?"

"My big toe? What does that have to do with anything?"

"With gout, that's usually what's affected. Very painful."

"My toe is fine and dandy, so it must be somethin' else."

"Where did you eat?"

"Sometimes we got carry-out Cajun and ate in th' RV, th' rest of th' time we ate in th' restaurant in th' motel. Meals came with the room, and all for only eighty-eight dollars a day. For *two*!"

"You definitely don't have gout," he said.

"Have they gotten you any help yet? Even *Harold* has help."

"Everybody pitches in." He wondered why on earth he'd called.

"I haven't checked Ed Sikes in Oregon, if that's why you called. We just got in a few days ago, and I'm up to my ears in laundry, plus

Snickers has fleas and they're so bad they're jumpin' on th' counter, I thought I'd spilled pepper. Th' termite man is on his way right now, you wouldn't *believe* what it's goin' to cost and I have to be out of th' house for three hours while they do it, and then come home and *vacuum* for five straight *days*, it's all that rain we had, I'm sure Barnabas is *covered* with fleas. . . ."

"Not that I've seen."

"Well, I don't know why he *doesn't* have fleas, the way th' weather's been, fleas *breed* in weather like we've had."

His erstwhile secretary was positively hopping mad that his dog didn't have fleas.

"Speakin' of fleas, did you hear what Rodney Underwood just got to hunt criminals, you'd never guess."

"True. I wouldn't."

"A rockwilder! You should see people scatterin' when it trots down th' street, Adele Hogan walks it every morning and it drags Joe Joe Guthrie around every evening, I'd hate to be a criminal in this town! Speakin' of criminal, have you heard what Miss Pattie's done now?"

Miss Pattie was a Hope House resident whose mind had been lost some years ago and was found only on the rarest of occasions. Her antics had long been of particular interest to Emma.

"Miss Pattie's too old to get into mischief, I should think."

"Well, think again, she steals everything she can get her hands on in Mr. Berman's room, then goes and throws it out her window."

"No!"

"His money, his bedroom shoes, his good leather belt, you name it. He got undressed the other night and looked around for his pajamas and they weren't there, so he draped himself in a blanket like a red Indian and called the nurse and told her if Miss Pattie didn't stop this mess, his son will sue for a million dollars."

"Can't the staff *do* something?"

"They locked her window, that's the best they can do, they say she's going through a phase."

"What does Mr. Berman say?"

"He says she has a terrible crush on him."

"That makes sense," he said, recalling that Mr. Berman was a very handsome old man.

"Speakin' of crazy people, Coot Hendrick actually believes he's going to win th' election. Can you *imagine* havin' a mayor who's two san'wiches short of a full picnic?"

He suddenly realized that Emma's sluice gate had opened and he was being swept along as if by a raging torrent.

"So, Emma, glad to hear you had a great time in New Orleans. Let me know what you find out about Ed Sikes."

He hung up and wiped his face with his handkerchief.

The search committee was meeting regularly, chatting each other up in the churchyard, whispering among themselves in the parish hall, polling the congregation for general opinion, and basically going about the task of replacement as if eager to unload their interim.

When he laughed with Sam Fieldwalker about their apparent urgency, his senior warden insisted that quite the opposite was true. The committee was hastening to do their job, yes, but in fact, several parishioners had expressed a desire to have their interim remain full-time. Besides, Father Tim was too young to retire. Hadn't Father Grace served St. John's until he was eighty-seven?

Not every interim was urged by the parish to stay on. In fact, many were viewed with suspicion and some with utter disregard. He remembered what one of his early bishops was fond of saying—that the interim who didn't make enemies was a man who wasn't doing his job. The job, it was popularly supposed, was to stir things up, to throw out the old and make way for the new.

Who could, after all, forget Father Harry?

Father Harry, who was seventy-one when his life as an interim began, thoroughly relished the task of disrupting the comfort level of a parish. His style was to barge in and take command before they knew what hit them.

If the congregation was attached to Rite Two, he celebrated Rite One. If they were stubbornly fond of traditional music, he switched them to praise songs. If they venerated their choir and organ, he had them sing a cappella for weeks on end. If they believed children should be seen and not heard, he invited the small fry to take up collection and read simpler Epistles. If their former priest had avoided the very mention of mammon, Father Harry talked about it at considerable length, with special emphasis on tithing. Further, he enjoyed reinstituting the observance of Morning Prayer, which, if not entirely forgotten by most parishes, was thought to be quaintly antique.

When the incoming priest was finally in place, the congregants were so relieved to be done with the old troublemaker, they went for almost anything the newcomer cooked up.

Father Harry could get the job done, all right. As for himself, Father Tim leaned rather more to what C. S. Lewis had said about worship procedures in *Letters to Malcolm.*

"A good shoe is a shoe you don't notice. . . . The perfect church service would be one we were almost unaware of; our attention would have been on God. But every novelty prevents this. It fixes our attention on the service itself, and thinking about worship is a different thing from worshipping."

He relished a note left on his desk by nine-year-old Margaret Wheeler.

Deer Father Tim when we get a new priest I hope he is just like you. Love, Margaret   PS But I hope he has kids!!!

Mayoral Candidate Agrees with Opponent

Andrew Gregory, one of two mayoral candidates for the election on November 3, says he agrees with his opponent, local native Coot Hendrick.

"Mr. Hendrick is absolutely right to fight for the preservation of early Mitford history, though the hope of winning this particular battle appears lost. If elected, I shall do everything in my power to preserve what is good and positive about Mitford. One of my first projects will be to encourage owners of several local buildings to seek listings on our National Register, and receive federal funding assistance for much-needed restoration.

"For nearly two decades, our incumbent mayor, Esther Cunningham, has set an example of community service that raised the standard of this office for all time. It will be a privilege to try and carry on her remarkable vision."

Gregory said that, if elected, he would also work to bring "sensitive, balanced growth to Mitford, which includes increased lodging, food and retail opportunities."

Gregory, his wife, Anna, and his brother-in-law, Anthony Nocelli, are owners of the popular Lucera Restaurant, located in their private residence known to one and all as Fernbank. Mr. Gregory is also the owner/proprietor of Oxford Antique Shop, a Main Street landmark.

Town Council Meeting Turns Musical

Mrs. Beulah Mae Hendrick, 92-year-old mother of Mitford mayoral candidate, Coot Hendrick, was a surprise visitor at last Monday's meeting of the town council.

Mrs. Hendrick was allowed to open the meeting with a song learned from her grandfather, who was the son of Mitford's founder, Hezikiah Hendrick. Local legend has it that Hezikiah Hendrick shot five Union soldiers running from their regiment, and buried them on what is now property belonging to Ms. Edith Mallory.

State law rules that property containing grave sights can not be be disturbed or developed. Ms. Mallory contends there is no proof or evidence that such graves exist on her 90-acre property. Ms. Mallory is currently beginning construction on a 3,000 sq. ft. extension of her home, Clear Day, near or on the sight of the stone foundations of the old Hendrick cabin.

Mrs. Hendrick, who stood beside her wheelchair to sing the song, said afterward, "It will prove we're right!" A written copy of the lyrics was sent to Ms. Mallory by certified mail last Tuesday morning.

Shot five Yankees
a-runnin' from th' war
Caught 'em in a cornfield
Sleepin' by a f'ar
Now they'll not run no more, oh
They'll not run no more!

Dug five graves
With a mattock and a hoe
Buried 'em in th' ground
Before th' first snow

Now they'll not run no more, oh
They'll not run no more!

Mr. Coot Hendrick said, "Mama has known and sung this song all her life, which right there ought to be proof the graves exist."

At press time, a spokesman reported that the town council has received a letter from Ms. Mallory's lawyer in Florida, stating that no proof of graves exists, and the matter is officially closed. He also said nobody could dig five graves with a mattock and a hoe, and that folk songs do not document real life.

A town council spokesman said, "I think it's a low-down shame to shoot people in their sleep, even if they are Yankees."

Ms. Mallory has issued a firm restriction against any digging or trespassing on her property, and has posted signs to that effect.

New Name, Location For Hair House

Ms. Fancy Skinner, proprietor of Mitford's popular Hair House, is moving her beauty Salon uptown and changing its name.

Ms. Skinner, who currently operates Hair House in her basement off Lilac Road, stated, "It's time to go Main Street!!

"I and my customers agree this calls for a more uptown name. The new name will be A Cut Above."

Ms. Skinner is moving in over the Sweet Stuff Bakery, which means that all hair work in Mitford will now be concentrated in one building, as Joe Ivey barbers on the street level behind the Sweet Stuff Bakery kitchen.

A Cut Above will feature all hair services for both sexes, with cuts starting at $12 and up. Fancy's Face Food, a specialty skincare line with organic ingredients, will be available. "But don't even think about using it," says Ms. Skinner, "unless you want to look and feel ten to fifteen years younger and make an all-around better showing for yourself."

A grand opening will held on Tuesday, beginning at nine a.m. with sugar-free gum for all, and a door prize of acrylic nails.

Congratulations to A cut Above!!!!

Local Laughs
—by Anonymous

Seen the new sign in Percy Mosely's window?

"Shoes are required to eat in the Main Street Grill. Socks can eat anyplace they want to."

Then there's the sign on the door of the labor room at Mitford Hospital:

"Push, push, push."

I guess by now everybody's heard about Evie Adams's midnight snail hunt. Seems she was out with a salt shaker and flashlight hunting down snails in her flowerbed, when one of Chief Rodney Underwood's officers rode by her house on South Main and saw this light bobbing around in her yard. The officer who shall be nameless parked up the street and tiptoed down to Evie's with his pistol cocked. He said the moon was out and he thought it was pretty odd that the burglar was wearing a chenille robe and hair curlers.

After he nearly scared the daylights out of her, Evie handed him an extra salt shaker and made him help finish the flower bed, all of which is to say Evie got the last laugh.

Well, that's it for now!! See you back here next week and don't take any wooden nickels.

Displaying her skills with the ability to fax directly from her computer, he found Emma's note at the office.

<To: Father Tim
<From: Emma Newland
<Date: Monday
<Memo: There is no Ed Sikes in Oregon.

<See you at the wedding. Do you want me to bake a ham so you don't have to?

<Love to all.

He couldn't believe this was happening.

As he approached Morris Love's place on an afternoon walk, his dog suddenly lurched forward with all the power and muscle of a horse. The leash jerked from his unsuspecting hand and Barnabas dove under the gate in a flash. Déjà vu!

His anger erupted with such violence, he was astounded.

"Barnabas!" he thundered.

Was he so dim-witted he couldn't have prepared for this, anticipated it, *expected* it to happen? He would never walk this way again, Barnabas was confined to the yard and the back porch 'til doomsday. He'd been treated like a king for years and was now exercising royal privileges. Father Tim couldn't believe the stubborn, willful, selfish disobedience of a dog he'd done everything for. . . .

"Barnabas! *Come now!*" He hardly recognized his own voice; it gave him a positive chill. If he were a dog, he'd either flee the county at the sound of it or slink back to face the music and get it over with.

Hearing the booming bark fade deeper into the Love jungle, he scaled the wall and dropped down on the other side, breathing hard. He didn't want to go through this nonsense again, he really didn't. He certainly didn't want his churlish neighbor ranting at him as if he were some rum-nosed chicken poacher. So what if Morris Love had had a hard time of it? Hadn't plenty of other people, and was that any excuse for refusing to exercise at least a modicum of human kindness toward a neighbor?

He was huffing and blowing as if he'd done the Nags Head Wood Run instead of a mile-long lap through the neighborhood.

He hadn't, for some time, been forced to use Holy Scripture on his dog, a ploy that worked best to keep Barnabas from leaping into the arms of the unsuspecting, or giving their ears and noses a good licking. Though he had no precedent for the current circumstances, it was worth a try.

" 'I delight to do thy will, O my God, *yea*, thy law is within my *heart*!' " He fairly bellowed the line from the psalmist; he thought he'd made the leaves tremble on a bush.

Silence. He felt like a maniac.

Ah, well.

What if he simply gave up and went home? Barnabas would follow eventually; he'd be lying outside their front door in no time flat, looking doleful. But what would that solve? It would only give his dog the dumb notion he could do it again anytime he liked. No, indeed, he was going in after his dog and dragging him home by the collar, and no treats for a week, maybe a *month*. . . .

He stormed down the driveway as if going to a fire, whistling and calling right and left. There was an occasional thrashing in the bushes. Birds started up and flew above him, chattering. A squirrel dashed across his path as he came upon the house.

Beside the drive as it curved toward the front door was something he hadn't noticed before. It was an antiquated verdigris plaque set into a concrete slab and nearly taken by ivy. A house marker, he supposed. He stooped and squinted at the engraving: *Nouvelle Chanson, 1947.*

He wasn't eager to disturb his neighbor, no, indeed, but what could he do? He stood up and let it fly. *"Barnabas!"*

"Is that you again?" Morris Love shouted from an upstairs window.

"Yes, dadgummit, Mr. Love, it is."

"Out! *Out!*"

Please, no more of that drivel. "I can't go out 'til I find my dog. My *dog,* Mr. Love! I'm sorry, for heaven's sake." He stomped through the undergrowth at the side of the house, where he thought he heard a commotion.

"Barnabas! *Come!*" Now there was furious barking at what could be the rear of the house. He suddenly felt the insects chewing on his legs, and if that weren't enough, it was steaming in here. Until he came over the wall, he hadn't noticed the humidity, nor had he realized his desperate thirst.

"Your dog has treed a squirrel off the west side!" Morris Love's hoarse announcement was matter-of-fact.

Father Tim darted into grass that grew to his waist; Lord only knows what was lurking on the ground. He needed a machete, a sling, a hay baler, to get through this stuff. Slogging to the rear of the house, he stumbled over a pile of bricks that had toppled from a chimney and lay hidden in the grass. He fell onto a jagged piece of mortar and hauled himself up. Stubbed toes, skinned knees, cut hands, chewed legs . . . he was biting his tongue.

He forged along the endless rear of the house and rounded the corner, dripping with sweat. Aha, by George, there he was, the impudent beast, sitting on his rear end at the foot of a tree and gazing heavenward as if in prayer.

His dog turned his head and gave him the sort of look that precedes the guillotine.

Speechless, his master pointed to his feet, shod in running shoes. Barnabas thoughtfully considered this gesture for some moments, then arose slowly and, head down, walked toward his master and sat a couple of yards away. Father Tim made the pointing gesture again. Barnabas arose, plodded over, and sat by his master's right foot.

He reached down and plucked the leash from the grass.

"Forgiveness," he said aloud to his dog, "is giving up my right to hurt you because you have hurt me." He didn't know where that particular wisdom had come from, but there it was.

Barnabas sat, looking stoic.

He put his hand through the loop and wrapped the leash around his arm twice. Then, giving his eaten legs a vigorous, overall slapping, he turned to get the heck out of here.

He heard Morris Love laughing behind one of the many shuttered windows on the second floor. It was an odd laughter, to say the least, composed of short explosions of sound.

"Mr. Love," he yelled. "I hope we're entertaining you sufficiently."

"More than sufficiently." Morris Love quit laughing, and the coldness in his voice returned. "You know the way out, Father."

"Yes, indeed, it's becoming all too familiar." His own tone of voice wasn't exactly the one used in greeting people at the church door.

Blast. That high wall ahead must be the back of another wing, though there were no windows. Or perhaps it was the rear of the loggia he'd glimpsed earlier. From the look of things, this meant a longer distance to the front, through a deeper, yet denser thicket.

He had stumbled into some kind of brier patch, or tangle of vines that scratched like a cat. Extracting himself from the snare of this blasted stuff was no easy job. Maybe he shouldn't forge ahead, but retrace his steps. This was maddening, alarming. He felt a moment of panic.

"Go back the way you came." Morris Love was speaking directly above his head.

He tore himself from the vines that snarled about his clothes and stomped back the way he'd come.

Fleas. Emma's suspicion was being confirmed. He yanked up his pants legs and was relieved to find they weren't fleas after all, though something probably worse. He went at a trot, trying to avoid the pile of rubble, and finally made it to the driveway, where he stood and wiped his dripping face with the tail of his T-shirt.

"There's water in the faucet behind you."

Water! He turned and saw the spigot attached to a pipe standing about knee level. He cranked open the tap, letting the sediment flow out, then washed the cut on his hand and splashed his face and head. Cupping his hands, he drank deeply and let Barnabas drink, then drew off his shirt and dried himself and slipped it on again. Good Lord, what a refreshment. He was revived, restored; holy water, indeed!

"God bless you!" he shouted, spontaneous and thankful.

"I don't believe in God." Morris Love's voice contained a positive snarl.

"God believes in you!"

"Then why did He give me such a body?"

"Why did He give you such musical genius?"

"I assure you I think very little of answering a question with a question."

"Sometimes a question is the only answer I have, Mr. Love."

He saw a rusted ornamental lawn chair a few feet to his right, just below the upstairs window where he presumed Morris Love to be standing. He hadn't noticed the chair on his previous safari, nor had he been aware, until now, of his extreme weariness.

He walked to the chair and sat, glad for the chance to catch his breath. What could the lord of the manor do to him anyway—dump a flowerpot on his head?

"I'm sitting down for a moment," he announced, too spent to shout. "I hope you don't object."

He gazed at the view before him, the way the light slanted into the dense tangle of trees and was lost in the foliage. A jungle, indeed. Yet this place had surely been beautiful once, a tropical island within an island, so exotic and unfamiliar that the thought of busy lives just over the wall seemed preposterous.

"Let me ask you, Father, how do you find the conscience to go about practicing the sham of belief?"

He was stunned by the question.

"I don't get your meaning," he said, and he didn't.

"The meaning seems clear enough. You wear a collar, you recite a creed, you speak of God, and yet, as a man whom I presume to be more than nominally intelligent, you cannot possibly believe there is a loving God, or any God at all."

"Quite the contrary, Mr. Love. I find it impossible not to believe in a loving God."

"I see it is useless to discuss a high truth with you."

"Then you see blindly." Though he didn't wish to be harsh, he had every desire to be plain.

"Blindness, you may be certain, has never been one of my handicaps."

"Do you consider your physical condition a handicap?"

"You speak as a fool. Of course I do."

"Many do not, Mr. Love. For example, there are currently several practicing and highly successful physicians with your precise physical condition."

"Not my precise condition at all. You deceive yourself grossly, Father, by presuming to know me. You do not know me now, nor will you ever."

"We're both being presumptuous, Mr. Love. You presume me to be covertly faithless, I presume you to be more physically proficient than you think you're able to be. Tit for tat, as my grandmother used to say. Now let's be done with it, shall we?"

"Out! *Out!*" bellowed Morris Love.

"Yes, indeed, and thank you for your hospitality." He set off at a trot down the driveway, his dog loping ahead on the leash.

The shouting continued in his wake. "Out! *Out!*"

"Out and away, and never to return!" he muttered, breaking into a run as he neared the gate.

In the last couple of days, the air had been miraculously devoid of humidity, and was instead filled with snap and sparkle. Light slanted, sound intensified, clouds vanished from a sky so cerulean it appeared enameled.

He was on his knees, weeding and adding fresh pine straw to the beds, glad to feel his hands in the dirt.

He couldn't, however, ignore the sense of conflict in his spirit—of loving the new season and at the same time feeling the sorrow it brought. It had taken years to name the sorrow and, at last, to face it down.

His father had died on October twelfth, more than forty years ago, and every autumn the heaviness surfaced again. During that dark time in the cave, he'd been able to forgive his father once and for all, which had worked wonders in his spirit, in his whole outlook. Yet something of the suffering remained, like a tea stain on linen, and returned each autumn in the changing light, to remind him.

The conflicting feelings experienced at his father's death were so intricately entwined that he'd never been able to disentangle them, and saw no useful purpose in trying again.

Indeed, perhaps it was time to forgive himself—for having felt relief at his father's passing, for anguishing, even now, over never having pleased him, for continuing to wonder, when he could not know, about his father's soul. Oh, how he'd longed to lead Matthew Kavanagh to Christ, to see the hellish torment of his father's spirit transformed by peace and certainty. But it hadn't happened; it was as if his father, in a last effort to thwart his son, had determined to hold himself away from God for all eternity.

Yes! he thought, thrusting the trowel into the dirt. It's time to let go of it, all of it. . . .

He would surrender this thing right now, completely, though he may be tempted again and again to snatch it back.

He sat in the grass like a child, his legs in a V in front of him, and prayed.

When he lifted his head, he knew at once that he was being watched. He looked through the pickets to Morris Love's hedge and, without thinking, threw up his hand and waved.

He'd broken a few lacy tendrils from the sweet autumn clematis, and was coming into the kitchen to wash up and find a vase when he saw Cynthia in the window seat. She was joggling Jonathan on her knee, as the boy laughed and clapped his hands. Seeing the look on her face, he felt a stab of something he couldn't name.

"Hello, darling!" said his wife.

CHAPTER FIFTEEN

Lock and Key

On his way home from a visit with Janette, he stopped by Ernie's.

Roger looked up and nodded, absorbed in burning the speculum feathers of his duck. Roanoke hoisted a forefinger.

"Junior's got good news!" said Ernie. "He got that letter said she wouldn't go out with 'im, but said she was comin' with her sister to see a girlfriend that lives here, an' she's goin' to drop by and say hello. October twenty-second!" Ernie announced the date as if it were right up there with the day the English landed on Whitecap.

"Said she'n her sister would meet Junior for coffee somewhere, so he wrote back and said Mona's, nine-thirty!"

"Bingo!" Father Tim exclaimed, pulling up a chair. "I'm glad to hear it." He liked the smell of Roger's burning wood, it made the place seem positively cozy.

"Junior's goin' to quit drinkin' beer 'til then, see if he can drop ten pounds."

"Aha."

"Yeah, an' goin' to massage his scalp, try to grow some hair," said Roanoke. "But there ain't no way that's goin' to happen."

"If it works, let me know," said Father Tim.

"Plus," said Ernie, "*plus* I sold Elmo's bed—lock, stock, and barrel."

"The Zane Greys?"

"Th' whole shootin' match. Man come in yesterday, bought a couple sinkers, wandered off in there, come back with th' box in his hands. He said how much, I said fifty bucks, he said I'll take it."

"Where did Elmo wind up sleeping last night?" he asked.

"A box of mixed westerns is where I found 'im this mornin'."

Roger didn't look up from his work. "Tell him about *The Last of the Plainsmen*."

"Fella gave me cash, sat down right over yonder, went through th' whole box one by one, an' found it—a signed hardback first edition! Didn't even know it was there. Worth a fortune, prob'ly two hundred, easy. He said I ain't payin' any more for this, I said I ain't askin' any more, a deal is a deal. But I got to tell you, it broke my heart. Two hundred *bucks*!"

"It'd bring a tear to a glass eye," said Roanoke, tapping a Marlboro from the pack.

Elmo appeared at the door of the book room, looking frazzled and disgusted.

"So, Elmo," said Father Tim, "how are you liking mixed westerns?"

He didn't go home from the office; he went to the beach.

At the bottom of the dune, he took off his socks and stuffed them into his shoes, then rolled up his pants legs and started to walk. No wife, no toddler, no dog, no nothing.

There was a fierceness in him that he didn't completely understand. Maybe he could walk it off, walk it out; maybe it would vaporize over the ocean and descend on Argentina as a minor typhoon. He felt angry at a lot of people for a lot of reasons—at Jeffrey Tolson for being cruel, at Janette Tolson for being passive, at Cynthia Kavanagh for losing her heart to someone else's child, at Morris Love for being imprisoned when he might be free. He was even angry with himself, but for what?

A gull started up from a tidal pool and circled above him, crying. He realized, then, that he was running, running for the way it felt to his bones, his beating heart. He heard the sand churning away from his feet, *chuff, chuff, chuff,* and realized he was the only soul on the beach.

All this vast world, all this great ocean, all this infinite sky, he thought—and Morris Love imprisoned behind a wall in a body he hated.

But, thought Father Tim, hadn't he, too, lived in a prison of his own for years on end, alternately fearing and despising and secretly rebuking his father? As a believer, his freedom in Christ had been severely handicapped for wont of letting go of the old bondage; of the old Adamic bitterness he'd unwittingly nurtured. Chances are, Morris Love's father had been much like Matthew Kavanagh—disappointed and indignant, betrayed by the issue from his own flesh.

And who was praying for Morris Love? Who remembered him at all, except in island legend? Instead of a living, breathing, feeling soul, he'd become apocryphal in the minds of everyone but a housekeeper, an organ tuner, and a retired clergyman who, but for the grace of the living God, would himself be a soul under the Enemy's lock and key.

And another thing—if Morris Love so renounced God, why did he play so much of His music?

Chuff, chuff, chuff . . .

He wondered why he hadn't been praying for Morris Love. How could he continue shirking a mission that had, literally, been dumped in his own backyard?

He muttered aloud as he ran, panting and huffing in a chill breeze coming off the water. That was precisely why he was feeling aggravated with himself: God had found him out for a shirker.

He looked up from the kitchen sink where he was washing tomatoes. His wife, on an errand to pick the last of the basil from the herb bed, suddenly hooted, threw her basket into the air, and began hopping on one foot.

"Ow! Ow! Rats, darn! Hoo! Hoo! *Ha!*"

His wife was a veritable rain dancer, complete with tribal language. What in the world . . . ?

"Timothy! Timothy! *Help!* Oh, ow, ow, *ugh*!"

"Cynthia?" He flew out the back door. *Please, God, not a snake or a terrible cut from broken glass. . . .*

"Yellow jackets!" she shouted, still hopping.

"Here," he said, taking her arm, "I'll help you in."

"I can't put my foot down, Timothy, it's dreadful, it's excruciating, I can't walk!"

"Climb on, then," he said, bending his knees. She threw her arms around his neck and clambered onto his back and he hauled her to the kitchen and thumped her in the window seat like a sack of onions.

"Let's have a look," he said, squatting down. "Aha, two stings, and right between the toes."

"Do something, Timothy, you can't *imagine* how it hurts!" His wife was not a complainer, he knew she meant business.

"Tobacco!" he said. He'd heard that tobacco draws the sting out. He'd seen a cigar butt just the other day. Where was it? "I'll be back!"

Exactly where Otis had thrown it into the bushes when he came by last Tuesday. . . .

He shredded the short stub and mixed it into a paste with water. "Here!" he said, rushing to present it in one of his grandmother's soup bowls. "Put your foot in this."

She did as she was told, shutting her eyes and grimacing. "Ugh! My toes feel exactly like they're being amputated with a handsaw by a doctor in the wilds of Montana, sometime around 1864."

"Really, now." His wife could go a tad over the top.

"It's true, Timothy, that's *exactly* the way it feels."

Jonathan, fully awake from a nap, was pounding him on the back as he squatted by the soup bowl. "You stop!" he shouted. "You stop makin' her cry!"

Truth be told, he was a mite weary of surrogate parenting.

"Look," said his stricken wife, "my toes are swelling up and turning red. How hideous."

"Give it time," he said of his home remedy. "I'll get you a couple of aspirin, then I'll call Marion and see what she recommends."

She drew her breath in sharply and winced. "Have you ever been stung?"

"Not once," he said. "Not a single time."

Even in her suffering, his wife was able to summon an imperious look. "What kind of American boyhood could you possibly have *had*, Timothy?"

He always enjoyed that moment when he could gaze out to his congregation and, as it were, take its pulse. Did it appear eager? Resigned? Grumpy?

Every Sunday, he discovered a different climate of affections, a brand-new meshing of personalities and spiritual longings, all of which assisted in the feeling that what he did was never the same old thing.

There was his buddy, Stanley Harmon, on vacation from the Baptists and seeing what the Anglicans were up to. Stanley would supply St. John's on the twenty-seventh while Father Tim married Pauline and Buck in Mitford.

His wife was beaming at him from the second row of the gospel side, where she sat with Sam and Marion . . .

. . . and there were the Duncans, with their children lined up like so many goslings. Once a month, according to family tradition, the whole lot skipped Sunday School and joined in the service. One, two, three, four hair bows bobbed on dark curls, as the two boys busily colored pew bulletins.

He was dropping his eyes to the opening hymn when he glanced to the rear of the church and saw a face as coldly immobile as if it were carved in stone.

His heart pounded as his gaze locked briefly with Jeffrey Tolson's, in whose countenance he saw anger and arrogance and, yes, defiance.

" 'Ye who do truly and earnestly repent you of your sins, and are in love and charity with your neighbors . . .' "

Because he had long ago committed these words to memory, he wasn't looking at the prayer book, but at his congregation. He noted that some swiveled in their pews and glared at the man in the back row.

" '. . . and intend to lead a new life, following the commandments of God, and walking from henceforth in his holy ways, draw near with faith, and make your humble confession to Almighty God, devoutly kneeling.' "

The parishioners sank to their knees as one, producing a corporate sound of rushing water. Jeffrey Tolson stood and looked for a moment toward the altar, then turned and walked quickly from the nave.

He dreaded his time in the churchyard today, as people poured out into the sunshine. Oliver Hughes withheld his hand, muttering, ". . . to let him come back in here, ransackin' th' church, takin' th' women out one by one like a fox in a henhouse . . ."

". . . carryin' 'em off to his den!" said Millie Hughes, stomping away in disgust.

Marion Fieldwalker gave him a wordless hug. Sam murmured, "My goodness gracious," and laid his hand on his priest's shoulder.

Otis stopped and looked him in the eye, saying only, "We want you to fix this."

Jean Ballenger shook his hand, as usual, but said nothing. Her mouth, which was set in a distinct grimace, said it all.

His wife, who was walking with a temporary limp, came to him and slipped her hand in his.

There were more eloquent ways to express it, but his grandmother's way covered it sufficiently:

When it rains, it pours.

They were leaving for Mitford in a matter of days, and in the meantime, he must find and talk with Jeffrey Tolson, speak with Stanley Harmon and inform him of the circumstances, and confirm Father Jack as the celebrant when Stanley preached. He also needed to oversee loose ends for the Fall Fair on November ninth, and meet with the indomitable Busy Fingers group who were going hammer and tong to complete nearly a thousand dollars' worth of items for the fair, including aprons, embroidered pillowcases, oven mitts, and an ambitious needlepoint of the Last Supper. Most important, he must get up to Dorchester, with the Eucharist for the captain and his visit with Ella.

Possibly the Dorchester trip could wait, but no, his heart exhorted him otherwise. The old captain had waited long enough—no more excuses, this must be done. And how was he to find Jeffrey Tolson, who, some said, was living on the island, but was as elusive as a trout in a pool?

Worse, what would his parishioners think about their priest vanishing to Mitford in the face of a highly disturbing situation?

He dreaded still more a final thing he must do. Before baring his concerns, however, he imagined their conversation. Perhaps he'd bring it up as they lay in bed.

"Cynthia," he might say.

"Yes?"

"You're growing . . . attached to Jonathan." A simple observation, not a criticism.

"Really? Am I?"

"Yes."

He'd considered the whole issue very carefully and knew it wasn't jealousy. It was fear, fear for her feelings, which ran as deep as the ledges of the continental shelf.

"What is your point, exactly?"

"I see how much you care for him. And you know he'll be going home soon."

"Well, yes, Timothy. Of course. Is there some reason I shouldn't care for him?"

What might he say, then? That he thought it best for her to start letting go, to prepare herself in some way he couldn't fully suggest or understand? Though Jonathan had come to them only weeks ago, his wife had bonded with the boy as if he were her own. But then, hadn't he grown to love Dooley in the very same way? He remembered his dark fears that someone would snatch the boy from him. . . .

In the end, he decided to say nothing at all. Jonathan would be going home, and that would be the end of it.

He was relieved, terribly relieved, that he hadn't brought it up; that he would even think of doing such a thing seemed strange and insensitive.

"Banana bread!" crowed his wife, dumping a panful onto the counter.

"My mommy, my mommy, she makes bread," said Jonathan, nodding in the affirmative.

"One loaf for us, one loaf for the neighbors," she announced. "But wait, I forgot—we don't know the neighbors."

It was true. A couple of times, they'd waved to the people in the gray house, who seemed to come and go randomly, and the family next door hadn't shown up for the summer at all; one of the shutters on the side facing Dove Cottage had banged in the wind for a month.

Neighbors, he mused. It was an odd thought, one that made his brain feel like it had eaten a pickle.

He heard the music as he stepped off the porch into the backyard.

No idea what it might be. But one thing was certain: it was strong stuff. . . .

He listened intently as he trotted to his good deed. The steady advance of the brooding pedal tones appeared to form the basis of a harmonic progress that he found strangely disturbing. Above this, an elusive melody wove its way through a scattering of high-pitched notes that evoked images of birds agitated by an impending storm.

The effect, he thought as he heaved himself up and over the wall, was confused, almost disjointed, yet the music seemed to produce an essential unity. . . .

Clutching the bread in a Ziploc bag, he stood at the foot of the window from which his neighbor usually conducted his audiences, and listened as the music moved toward its climax.

He might be one crazy preacher, but he didn't think so. In fact, he'd come over the wall as if it were the most natural way in the world to go visiting. He was feeling pretty upbeat about his impetuous mission—after all, this was his neighbor for whom he was now praying, and besides, who could refuse a loaf of bread still warm from the oven?

When the music ended, he shouted, "Well done! Well done, Mr. Love!"

Floorboards creaked in the room above. "Father Kavanagh . . ."

"One and the same!"

"Your dog isn't here," snapped Morris Love.

"Yes, and what a relief! I brought you some banana bread. My wife baked it, it's still warm from the oven, I think you'll like it."

Silence.

If his neighbor didn't go for the bread, he'd just eat the whole thing on the way home.

"She said to tell you it's a token of our appreciation for your music."

Silence.

"What was that piece, anyway? It was very interesting. I don't think I've heard it before." He was a regular chatterbox.

Silence.

He began to as feel as irritable as a child. He'd come over here with a smile on his face and bread in his hand, and what did he get for his trouble? Exactly what he should have expected.

"Mr. Love, for Pete's sake, what shall I do with your *bread*?"

"Leave it in the chair," said Morris Love.

"Do what?"

"Leave it in the chair!" he roared.

He considered this for a moment, then determinedly walked over and sat down. He was tired of darting away from his irate neighbor like a hare before the hound. Wasn't the trip over worth a moment of small talk, of mere civility? He'd give it a quick go, then he'd be gone.

"Mr. Love, I couldn't help but notice the sign, *Nouvelle Chanson*. How did the house come by that name?"

"My grandmother gave the house its name. She sang with the Met, and counted Rose Bampton and Lily Pons among her friends. Melchior was my grandfather's close acquaintance."

"Aha."

"When my grandparents built this house in 1947 as a summer home, she hoped for a new beginning for their marriage—a new song, if you will." Morris Love's manner was impatient, though decidedly less hostile. "But it didn't work that way."

Father Tim waited a moment. "How *did* it work?"

"My grandparents could only live the old song."

"The old song . . ."

"Little acts of unspoken violence, Father, and bitter hatred towards one another."

Morris Love was actually talking with him. He realized he'd been holding his breath, and released it carefully. "Who taught you to play the organ?"

"My grandfather. Once he had made his fortune, he began to study the organ. In the forties and fifties, several great organ masters spent summers here, instructing him. By the time I came along, he was respectably accomplished and began to teach me at an early age."

"Someone said he had an organ built especially for you. . . ."

"Yes. When I was six years old."

"Is that the organ you play today?"

"That was a toy, Father, a mere toy. I play my grandfather's custom-built Casavant, which was further customized for me."

"I've never seen a Casavant, though I may have heard one without knowing it. It's among the finest in the world, of course."

"More accurately, it is the most magnificent of instruments. Casavant came here to do an acoustical analysis, and worked with the architect to complete this room. My grandfather was a man of exacting preferences."

"I suppose the key covers are of an exotic wood?" It was a small thing, but he'd always been interested in the key covers on old keyboard instruments.

"Only the sharps, which are ebony. The naturals are purest ivory, and of exceeding beauty in their age."

This was pretty heady stuff; he could imagine the splendid hulk of it reigning over the room above. He dove in headfirst. "I'd like very much to see it sometime, and hear you play . . . without walls between us."

He listened to the beating of his heart in the long pause that followed. He'd stepped in it now, he'd pushed too far, and just when he was getting started.

"That would be . . . inappropriate." There was something wistful in Morris Love's voice, he was sure of it. *Lord, speak to his heart.*

"Mr. Love, may I call you Morris? And please—call me Tim."

"I have never addressed a priest by his first name. I find it a repugnant modern custom."

"You've known priests, then? You went to St. John's?"

"Only for baptism. The priests at St. John's often came here, some to pray over me, others to drink my grandfather's French wines. The only joy I ever found in those visits was their occasional gifts of sheet music purloined from the church."

"Your mother and father . . . were they—"

"Out! *Out!*"

He jumped. The shock of hearing the inevitable made his scalp prickle. The tone and repetition of that furious decree were nearly more than he could tolerate. Feeling an invasive weariness in his spirit, and not knowing what else to say or do, he stood to leave.

"Father . . ."

"Yes?"

"You may call me Morris."

"Morris," he said, suddenly hoarse with feeling. "Please don't let the squirrels get your bread. I hope you like it. Try warming it in the oven for breakfast, that's what we do."

He examined an odd intuition, then addressed a question to the window. "Tourette's?"

"Yes. A mild form."

"I'll come again," he said. But there was no reply.

Marion Fieldwalker looked up from the checkout desk.

"Why, Father Tim! We're tickled to see you!"

"I'm looking for a medical encyclopedia, Marion. Something comprehensive." Given the cost per pound for shipping, he'd decided against dispatching his own to Whitecap.

"You've come to the right place. One of our retirees studied at Harvard Medical School, and gave us a wonderful one. It takes a crane to lift it!"

"Bingo!" he said.

While he was here, he wanted to take a look at Dostoyevsky's *Notes from the Underground*, the memory of which resonated profoundly with what he was learning about his neighbor.

It was a work that made him squirm for its dark despair, yet he flipped through it diligently, sneezing from the dust and mold. Out of curiosity, he turned to the card at the back. Aha! One other reader had visited these pages before him, twelve years ago.

Amused, he inscribed his name on the card, *Timothy A. Kavanagh.* For posterity!

"I am a sick man," wrote Dostoyevsky's fictional diarist. "I am a spiteful man. I am an unattractive man. . . .

"The more conscious I was of goodness and of all that was sublime and beautiful, the more deeply I sank into my mire and the more ready I was to sink in it altogether . . . in despair there are the most intense enjoyments, especially when one is very acutely conscious of the hopelessness of one's position. . . .

"I was rude and took pleasure in being so. . . .

"I might . . . be genuinely touched, though probably I should grind my teeth at myself afterward and lie awake at night with shame for months. . . .

"Now I am living out my life in my corner, taunting myself with the spiteful and useless consolation that an intelligent man cannot become anything seriously, and it is only the fool who becomes anything."

Not light summertime reading. He closed the musty book, relieved to look through the window to the bright and cloudless day.

Seated at the antiquated library table, he ran his finger quickly along the text.

". . . characterized by rapid, repetitive, involuntary muscular movements called 'tics,' and involuntary vocalizations . . .

"Phonic tics are diverse and consist of syllables, words (e.g., 'okay'), short phrases (e.g., 'shut up', 'no, no'), and full sentences. Tics are sudden, involuntary, repetitive. . . .

"Tics intensify during periods of stress and anxiety and are frequently misinterpreted as 'nervous habits.' . . .

"Many suffer depression . . . often become withdrawn and even suicidal . . .

". . . evidence that Tourette's syndrome is not an emotional or psychological problem, but a chronic, hereditary neurological disorder."

"I'd like to check this out," he said, toting the large tome to the desk.

"Oh, my goodness, that doesn't check out. It's reference."

Marion must have noted the disappointed look on his face.

"But we'll make a special exception for clergy," she said, smiling. "Would you like a wheelbarrow to help you carry it to the car?"

He didn't have to go looking for Jeffrey Tolson. Shortly after he unlocked the church on Tuesday morning, Jeffrey Tolson came looking for him.

It wasn't stone from which his face had been carved, thought Father Tim, it was ice. He noted that Jeffrey wore the open-necked white shirt with full sleeves that he'd worn on his earlier visit.

He felt the towering wall between them as they sat in the office. He had no sermon to preach. He'd let Jeffrey Tolson do the talking he'd come to do, then he'd lay his cards on the table, plain and simple.

"I intend to come back to my church," said Jeffrey Tolson. A muscle twitched in his jaw.

"Your church?"

"My grandfather's church, my father's church, and my church. Yes."

"Being born into this church body confers no special distinctions or ownership. You've hurt a great many people here, Jeffrey."

"There is such a thing as forgiveness, Father."

"Are you asking forgiveness from the people of St. John's?"

Jeffrey crossed his legs and moved his left foot rapidly back and forth. "If that's what it takes."

"Then you're admitting you sinned?"

"No. I'm admitting I made a mistake."

Father Tim looked carefully at the man before him. "There's a bottom line to asking forgiveness. And it's something I don't see or sense in you in the least."

"A bottom line?"

"Repentance. Forgiveness isn't some cheap thing to be gotten on a whim. It's purchased with a deep desire to please God. It's about renouncing. . . ."

"I have renounced. We aren't living together anymore."

"You're speaking of the flesh; I'm speaking of the heart."

Jeffrey Tolson's face blanched. "As choirmaster here for fourteen years, I've heard a good deal of Scripture. You aren't the only one equipped with the so-called truth. I seem to recall that St. Paul said, 'Forgive one another as God in Christ forgave you.' "

"Do you believe Christ is the divine Son of God?"

Jeffrey Tolson shrugged. "I suppose so. Not necessarily."

"We're told that everyone who believes in and relies on Him receives forgiveness of sins through His name. It's not really about asking me or the vestry or anyone at St. John's; it's about hammering it out with Him."

Jeffrey drummed the desktop with the fingers of his right hand.

"To repent means to turn, to turn from whatever binds or enslaves you. What, for example, do you intend to do about your family?

"Janette has the house and the car, she has a successful sewing business, and as soon I get work on the island, I'll see that she gets a check every week."

"As soon as you get work?"

"You're not from Whitecap, so it probably never occurred to you that getting work on the island is either difficult or impossible."

He heard the sneer in his visitor's voice, and made every effort to keep his own voice even as he spoke. "You could go across to work, like half the population here."

"I'd prefer to work on the island. Commuting is expensive and inconvenient."

"Let's see if I have this right, Jeffrey. You abandoned your wife and children to enter into an adulterous relationship with a married woman, left the island for several months during which your contribution to your family was a grand total of one hundred dollars; you grieved everyone in the church and your choir in particular, and now you state that you don't necessarily believe Christ to be the Son of God, yet you wish His forgiveness."

Jeffrey Tolson opened his mouth to speak, but Father Tim raised his hand. "In addition, you wish to wait 'til you find work that's convenient, while your wife, currently hospitalized and without income, soldiers on with the fallout as you trot back to God's house, whistling Dixie." He was livid. "When you can return to this place with a humble spirit, confessing your sins and longing for His gift of forgiveness, you'll find a willing heart to hear you." He stood from his desk, shaken.

Jeffrey Tolson stood also, his face white with anger. "I'll come for my son tonight. Have his things ready."

"You'll come for your son? I don't think so. Jonathan was given into our care by Janette. It is Janette who directs his coming and going, and that, you may rest assured, will hold up in a court of law." While he didn't know for certain that it would, it certainly seemed that it should.

He thought he might be punched out on the spot, but didn't care; he felt reckless, invincible.

"You can't stop me from attending St. John's."

"You're absolutely correct, I cannot. But I don't advise it."

Jeffrey Tolson uttered an oath. "Father Morgan, unlike yourself, was a peacemaker. You're no Father Morgan."

"Thanks be to God!" he said, holding his office door open.

"Father, before you take your days off, wouldn't you like to put in your order for a new sport coat?"

He looked at Jean Ballenger's newly trimmed bangs, which were curling upward like the lashes of a film star. "A new sport coat?"

"For Janette, to help her get started back in business when she comes home. I'm going to order a paisley shirtwaist; Marion's ordering a red dress, she says she wears too much navy; and we thought you might like to order a sport coat."

"Well . . ."

"Something blue would be good on you."

He had three blue sport coats, but he didn't say anything.

"Penny Duncan is ordering a wrap skirt, even though she doesn't have gobs of money to throw around and sews like a dream herself! Don't you think that's sacrificial?"

"I do."

"And Cynthia could order a suit in linen or piqué, maybe something with a nice peplum, I think she'd look stunning in a peplum."

"How much is a sport coat?"

"I don't have any idea."

"Why don't you get back to me on that?"

"Oh, I will!" she said, making a note on her pad. "I just think it would be the Christian thing to do, don't you?"

He grinned at the earnest Jean Ballenger trotting down the hall to solicit orders from the Busy Fingers group, which was currently living up to their name, big-time.

It was rather a nice thought, actually, that he'd soon be looking into the nave and seeing his entire congregation turned out in new duds, whether they needed them or not.

The encounter with Jeffrey Tolson had shaken him badly. He sat in the study at Dove Cottage with his head in his hand for longer than his wife liked.

"Timothy, dear, what *is* it?" she demanded on a third inquiry.

"Ahhh," he said, lacking the energy to tell the sordid thing. Besides, did this mean Jeffrey Tolson might be hanging about to forcibly take Jonathan while Cynthia and the boy were alone? He despised even thinking this.

He was just getting into bed when he heard the knock.

What time was it, anyway? He peered at the clock on the nightstand. Past ten.

Through the glass panels in the front door, he saw what appeared to be a flashlight bobbing on the porch. He switched on the porch light and threw open the door.

It was someone in uniform, and someone plenty big, to boot.

"Would you identify yourself, sir?"

"Tim Kavanagh. Why do you ask?"

"I have a civil paper to serve you. You're being sued."

"I beg your pardon?"

"Are you the Reverend Timothy *A.* Kavanagh?"

"I am, yes." His heart was hammering.

"I'm Bill Deal, th' sheriff of this county." Bill Deal pocketed his flashlight and brought out his wallet to display a badge. "I hate to do this to you, I believe you fish with Cap'n Willie."

Speechless, he opened the screen door, took an envelope from the man, and gazed at it, dumbfounded. The sheriff cleared his throat and stepped to the edge of the porch, looking at the sky.

"Prob'ly goin' to get us some rain before long. Well, you take it easy, Reverend." The sheriff lumbered down the steps, walked to the front gate, and got in the car.

He stood there in the chill October air as if mesmerized.

Cynthia called from the hallway. "Timothy, what's going on?"

"I have no idea, I don't know."

Nor did he want to know.

CHAPTER SIXTEEN

Dorchester Island

It wasn't that he couldn't understand the general intent of the papers he'd been served—he could. It was that he wasn't able to make it all come together in any sensible order; each time he read them, it was as if his mind split like an atom. He knew only one thing for certain—he was deeply alarmed.

He went to the study and took his quote book from the shelf, the quote book he'd made entries in for fifteen years. He wanted something St. Francis de Sales had said; he'd copied it into the book just the other day. . . .

> Do not look forward to what may happen tomorrow; the same everlasting Father who cares for you today will take care of you tomorrow and every day. Either He will shield you from suffering, or He will give you unfailing strength to bear it. Be at peace, then, put aside all anxious thoughts and imaginations, and say continually: "The Lord is my strength and my shield; my heart has trusted in Him and I am helped. He is not only with me but in me and I in Him."

It was after eleven o'clock when he dressed and drove to St. John's, went down the cement steps by the light of the moon, and faxed the papers to his cousin's home in New Jersey. The fax machine was located in Walter's study where he'd be sure to find the papers the following morning, before he left for his law office in Manhattan.

Father Tim scribbled a cover sheet with St. John's phone number and a brief message:

Please call me the moment you look this over. I'll be at the church office by six a.m.

He didn't want to have the conversation with his attorney cousin at home, where his wife was already in a state of trepidation over this ghastly turn of events.

He left Dove Cottage at five forty-five, bundled into a sweater and jacket.

"Layspeak, Walter, layspeak."

He sat at his desk in the chill basement office, drinking a tepid cup of coffee from home and scribbling on a legal pad. "Start at the beginning. I'm writing everything down." *Put aside all anxious thoughts and imaginations. . . .*

"Hélène Pringle is suing you, as trustee, for one-third of the escrow funds of Hope House."

"Right." His voice sounded like the croaking of a frog, and he realized he was again holding his head in his hand.

"She claims to be the illegitimate daughter of Josiah Baxter. . . ."

Miss Sadie's father. This claim seemed so bizarre and extraordinary, his mind couldn't contain it; the whole notion kept flying out of his head, even as he tried to poke it back in.

"But why now, after all these years . . . ?"

"I've no idea. Apparently they're basing the suit on Baxter's holographic will, in which he decreed that a third of his estate would go to Hélène Pringle's mother, Françoise, upon his death. When did Baxter die, anyway?"

He'd tried to work this out in his mind last night. The date was on the urn in the columbarium at Lord's Chapel. He'd seen it numerous times, but couldn't remember exactly. "Sometime in the late forties."

"How old was he at the time of death?"

"Miss Sadie told me once . . . in his seventies, I think. In fact, I believe she said he died soon after an extended trip to France." He knew Miss Sadie's mother had died in 1942, so Josiah Baxter must have been a widower when . . .

"Of course, the domestic statute of limitations has run out by several decades," said Walter.

"Then they don't really have a case?"

"Unfortunately, the suit is based on French law, involving an obscure treaty between France and the U.S., which was adopted at the end of World War II. I don't know much about it, probably something that spun off the problem of occupation troops and paternity issues."

He thought the whole thing a veritable hash of mystery and confusion.

"Looks like Pringle's attorney is French—Louis d'Anjou of d'Anjou and Pichot—and both Pringle and her mother are French citizens. Let me look into it; I know almost nothing about French law. You've got thirty days to file a written response to the allegations."

He shook his head as if to wake himself from a bad dream.

"I'll call her attorney and see what's what, and get back to you in a couple of days—right now, I'm in court on a big one."

"Anything," he said. "Anything you can do . . ."

He hung up, as winded as if he'd run a mile on the beach.

Ava Goodnight was coming day after tomorrow, the day of the Dorchester trip. He'd have breakfast at Mona's, let Roanoke give him a trim around seven-thirty, tend to a couple of things at St. John's, then go back to Ernie's no later than nine-thirty to meet Ava and her sister. So . . . if he and Cynthia and Jonathan left shortly before eleven, they'd arrive at Ella's around noon. They'd visit with Ella, then he'd administer the sacraments to Captain Larkin and they'd head home. Considering all they had to do before Mitford, he'd suggest they tromp through the graveyard another day; heaven knows, the dead weren't going anywhere.

"Our trek to Dorchester is coming up day after tomorrow," he said over the last of their lunch. "We'll try to keep it short. I know you have plenty to do."

"Jonathan may not be able to go," she said. "He has a miserable cough and his nose is dripping like a faucet."

"Allergies?"

"I don't think so, and besides, Timothy, I hear there's a storm front moving in."

"If we had to drop everything each time a storm came our way, we'd get absolutely nothing done around here!"

She looked bleak. "A lawsuit, a sick boy, a ten-hour drive, and a storm front . . ."

"When it rains, it pours," he said. "No pun intended."

Jonathan ran into the kitchen and clambered onto Cynthia's lap. *"Heavens!"* she exclaimed, wiping his nose with the lunch napkin. "Now, *blow*!"

"We're looking forward to seeing you, buddy."

"Me, too. Mama said Buck came in the other day, he's bunkin' with Harley, she says he lost weight an' all for th' wedding. Poo's wearin' a suit, I can't believe Poo in a suit."

"What are you wearing?"

"Umm," said Dooley. "A suit."

"Don't forget your shirt and tie—or, you could borrow one of my ties."

"Your ties are too . . ."

"Too what?"

"Boring."

For someone who was usually in a collar, he'd never thought much about ties. Maybe he needed to buy something . . . upbeat! Something Italian! "What time are you rolling into Mitford?"

" 'Bout eleven Friday morning."

"How are you feeling about the appearance before the judge?"

"Not too good."

"It'll go well, don't worry. And how are you feeling about Caroline?"

Dooley was shrugging; he could practically hear it. The boy was blushing; he could sense it.

"Ah . . ."

"Pretty good?"

"Well, yeah, she's really neat, really interesting. She does these great watercolors, like Cynthia. You should see the one she did of the mountains behind her school, it was exactly like real life, except better."

"I'll be darned."

"She's got this cool laugh, too, sort of like . . . like this." Dooley made an odd sound, something between a snort and a cackle. "That's not right, it's more like . . . I don't know!"

"I can kind of guess."

"Plus she's really funny."

Dooley Barlowe was a goner, as far as he could tell.

"We can't go, dearest, he's burning with fever. I hope it's only the flu. Nearly everyone in story group was croupy and sick on Wednesday; I'd never have taken him if I'd known. I have a call in to his doctor."

He felt the boy's head, he looked at his red eyes and runny nose, he listened to his labored breathing. Convinced that hauling Jonathan to Dorchester would only make things worse, he finally told her. "Jeffrey Tolson may be hanging about. I don't think he's dangerous, but there's no telling what he might do."

"He can do nothing here!" she said, looking fierce. "We'll keep the doors locked and you'll only be away in broad daylight, so there's no use at all to worry. I'll send Ella the lasagna I froze the other day. Single women almost never make lasagna!"

His wife could convince him of anything. Feeling mildly relieved, he went to the study and closed the door and sat in the chair and prayed about it. He had written Captain Larkin the other day to say he was coming, and the last thing he wanted to do was disappoint. Should he go, or move the trip to a later date?

After he prayed, he listened.

God would have him go. He felt certain of it.

The sky was gunmetal from horizon to horizon; it seemed as if a leaden weight had been clamped over Whitecap like a lid on a turkey roaster.

He paced the front porch, unable to think clearly, anxious about leaving tomorrow. Maybe he should skip the Ava business and leave early, but Ernie was as excited about this little gathering as any parent, a fact he didn't feel like treating lightly. Besides, he wanted to see Ava Goodnight, who, let's face it, had accumulated some pretty heavy mystique without even trying.

Cynthia would be fine, she'd insisted on it, and he'd call her from Ella's house at least once, maybe twice.

While he was thinking of it, why didn't he have a car phone? Everyone else seemed to be zooming around at top speed, yammering into one as if their lives depended on it. Yet there was nothing in the thought of a car phone that attracted him. Wouldn't people break into his car and steal it, or did they steal phones anymore? Maybe car phones were now so cheap and run-of-the-mill that no one wanted the hassle of smashing a window. Anyway, if he had one, wouldn't he have to keep the top up on the Mustang? Otherwise, they could just reach in and yank it off its hinge or whatever.

Why was he thinking such nonsense? He was thinking nonsense because he dreaded thinking the real thing; he was trying desperately to hide from the reality of the lawsuit.

He zipped his jacket and sat in his favorite rocker, looking into the gathering dusk.

The lawsuit dogged him like a dark cloud. What on earth could be the possible meaning behind it all? Thank God, Walter was more than a cousin who happened to practice law. Walter was a tough, no-nonsense attorney with a decent reputation and several heavyweight clients; surely he could help him hammer this thing through.

He realized he was wringing his hands, something he'd hardly ever caught himself doing, and stopped it at once.

Yet, even more than the fret and worry of being slammed with a lawsuit was the possibility of losing a third of the escrow, which included part of what Andrew Gregory had paid for Miss Sadie's antiques, and a third of what the money had earned in mutual funds, making Hélène Pringle the possible recipient of around a hundred and fifty thousand dollars. Miss Sadie had trusted him to be a good steward of all she left behind, and he'd never begrudged this enormous responsibility, not for a moment. Now he felt the full weight of it squarely on his shoulders, with no one to turn to but someone he'd known since childhood as Potato Head.

God hadn't given him much family, but God *had* given him Walter; perhaps, just as Mordecai said in the Book of Esther, for such a time as this.

So—he had excellent legal counsel, and he and Cynthia were praying the prayer that never fails. What more could be done, after all?

Aha! His neighbor was at it again, though he didn't recognize the music.

He walked to the north side of the porch and cupped his hands to his ears. Interesting. Very interesting.

He squatted, then sat on the end of the porch, swinging his legs over the side.

Yes! That's it, Morris! What you're doing with the bass, keep it up, great, beautiful, have at it. . . .

He slipped off the porch, trotted to the rear gate and unlatched it, then went into the twilit street, where he stood for a moment, listening.

His wife would not like him pulling a disappearing act, no, indeed, but he'd be gone only five, maybe ten minutes, she'd never miss him; his dog, however, was another matter. If Barnabas knew he'd gone on a joyride without him . . .

He dropped to the ground on the other side of the wall, and found himself jogging along the driveway.

When he reached the house, he thumped into his chair under the window, and listened.

He alternately nodded enthusiastically and wagged his head. He wagged his head at the foreboding passages in the music, though he knew they gave greater light to the passages of illumination.

Man alive, that Casavant was blowing the roof off.

When the music ended, he felt tears on his cheeks. He waited a few moments.

"Morris?" he shouted.

"It's you, Father."

"Yes."

There was a long, oddly comfortable silence.

"I'm going away for a few days and I came to say . . ." There was a sudden lump in his throat. "I came to say I think the music is . . ." The music is what? Moving? Powerful? How did critics manage to make a living with a language that must often fail them?

"Wonderful!" he shouted. Full of wonder! That was the best he could do for the moment.

"Perhaps you'd like to come in . . . and see the Casavant."

Had he heard right? He wiped his eyes on his shirtsleeve. "Why, yes, thank you, I'd like that." His wife would be frantic, but this was an extraordinary invitation. He was stunned. . . .

"The door is open. Take the stairs. I'll meet you on the landing."

He bolted from the chair, careful not to stumble over the uprooted bricks that once paved the entranceway.

The heavy front door opened easily, and he stepped into a dimly lit foyer. The light appeared to come from a single bulb in a wall sconce, though a large chandelier loomed above his head.

There was definitely a musty smell, but everything looked clean and orderly. Ornately carved armchairs stood on either side of a heavy mirror in which he was startled to see himself. On the floor, a pattern of black and white tiles, and to the right, a curving stairwell and a vast, lighted oil painting on the high wall. The painting was of rolling countryside, somewhere in Europe, perhaps, with a church spire and a procession of people in a lane.

"Father."

He looked toward the landing and saw Morris standing at the rail.

"Morris!"

"Come up."

He went up, as if in a dream. There was absolutely no sense of reality about where he suddenly found himself. He knew only that he needed to be here, was supposed to be here. . . .

Morris held his hands behind his back, apparently declining a handshake, as Father Tim looked directly into his eyes. He noted Morris's prominent forehead and the deep, vertical furrow between his heavy brows.

"You are not surprised," Morris said flatly.

"No, not at all."

"Come with me," said his host.

He was surprised, however, to see that Morris walked with such difficulty. As if sensing his curiosity, Morris turned and said, "Spinal stenosis, aggravated by arthritis. It is not uncommon to my condition. We're in here." Morris stood aside so that he might enter first.

As he stepped over the threshold, he drew in his breath. There, in a room illumined by lamplight, stood the Casavant, regal beneath the rank of elaborately stenciled facade pipes. With its ornamented mahogany casework, he thought the organ possessed the aura of a great throne.

He might have gaped interminably, but turned his gaze to the room itself, which was paneled with walnut. His eyes moved along the intricately detailed dentil moldings and carved inlays, to the open window where Morris must stand when talking with him; it was free of draperies, with only a simple pelmet above, perhaps to enhance the acoustics of the room.

Floor-to-ceiling bookcases, a bare, polished floor, velvet-covered chairs sagging with use, a love seat in a far corner . . .

"Beautiful!" he said, gawking unashamedly. Yet, a prison, nonetheless. He felt the awful weight of the room on his spirit, as if the only thing that ever stirred the air might be the music.

He sensed Morris's eyes on him. "Thank you for asking me in. I'm grateful to be here."

"My housekeeper comes every other day—Mamie has been with me since childhood—and my organ tuner comes as needed. I'm not completely without social intercourse."

"I'm glad. It's one of the things that keeps us soldiering on in this life."

"We strive to keep up appearances in this part of the house, but the grounds are without hope. My grandfather planted a jungle. It cannot be beaten back, and we long ago gave up trying."

Morris's head suddenly wrenched toward his right shoulder, jerking in a manner that seemed uncontrollable. "Out!" he growled. *"Out!"*

Father Tim walked to the organ, making a conscious effort to appear oblivious to what he'd just seen. "The pedals . . ."

"Yes," said Morris, as the tic passed. "Casavant provided a second pedal board for me, elevated one position above the standard pedal board.

"I've considered what I might play for you . . . the Widor Toccata, perhaps. You may know that the Casavant is designed for French voicing. The company founders spent a great deal of time in France, and scaled the pipes to play French repertoire especially well."

Morris slid stiffly onto the bench and pulled the chain of a green-shaded lamp over the keyboards. "You'll find this piece quite vibrant. It demonstrates all the tonal colors of the instrument. Listen to the reed stops, if you will. They're very distinctive, and altogether different from the more mellow English reed stops."

Father Tim stood by the organ, enthralled.

"Please sit," said Morris.

Father Tim hurried to a slipcovered armchair and sat, closing his eyes as the music began. Flashy and flamboyant, upbeat and positive, Widor made the hair stand up along his right arm and leg. Ah, the difference in being in the room with the music rather than sitting outside as a lowly trespasser!

The music so filled him with a nervous and exuberant energy that it flowed out at the climax as laughter.

"Wonderful!" Couldn't he come up with something less tiresome, for heaven's sake? "Marvelous! Bravo!"

Morris reflected for a moment. "And now, perhaps Bach's Great Prelude and Fugue in G Minor. . . ."

As the fugue subject unfolded, he wondered, as he always did when he heard this favorite composition, how a theme in a minor key could express such confident joy and abiding faith. The music soared around the room like a bird set loose from its cage, causing his scalp to prickle.

"Thank you," he said afterward, supremely happy.

Morris labored to rise from the bench, and stood by his instrument. "Thank you for listening, Father. You have an attentive and sympathetic ear."

Father Tim rose from the chair, which gave off the faint odor of old tobacco. "How I wish you might share your gift with . . ." It was hardly out of his mouth before he knew he'd said the wrong thing.

Morris's face grew hard. "Never speak of that again."

"I'm sorry," he said. "You have my word, I'll never speak of it again."

"The wine cellars were depleted years ago. I have nothing to offer you."

"You've given me more than I could possibly wish. Thank you, Morris, thank you. I'll go along, now. My dog will be furious that I've come without him."

Morris did not smile. "I'll walk you to the landing."

At the landing, he had a sudden urge to throw his arms around the man, shake his hand, make the sign of the cross over him—something, anything, to express his deep feeling. "You're faithfully in my prayers," he said.

His host's head jerked toward his shoulder. "Out! *Out!*"

Father Tim's heart pounded as he moved quickly down the stairs, angry with himself for failing to say the right thing, for the terrible alarm those words always ignited in his breast.

In the foyer, he turned briefly to look at Morris, then opened the door of Nouvelle Chanson and stepped into the October night.

He went at a trot—down the dark driveway under a hidden moon, over the wall, across the street, through the gate, up the steps to the back porch, and into the kitchen, panting. She probably had that sheriff out searching for him. He dreaded facing her. How could he have been so thoughtless and insensitive?

"Is that you, dearest?" Cynthia came into the kitchen, rubbing her eyes. "I hope you weren't waiting for me on the porch all this time. I started a new illustration and, well, you know how it is, I forgot." She looked at the kitchen clock. "Good heavens! Eight-thirty! I hope you haven't felt neglected."

"Oh, no, no! Don't even mention it," he said.

Jonathan was on antibiotics delivered from the pharmacy, and Cynthia would spend the day doctoring him for tomorrow's journey to Mitford.

He rose at six a.m., dressed more warmly than usual, and set off for Mona's.

It had definitely been a while since he'd had breakfast like he used to have at the Grill. It gave him a positive thrill to place his order.

"Two medium poached, whole wheat toast, hold the butter, and a side of grits."

"Do you want coffee?" asked the shy waitress, whom he hadn't seen before.

"The hard stuff, no cream, no sugar. Are you new?"

"Yessir, this is my first day. I'm kind of . . . nervous."

"I certainly didn't notice! I'm Father Kavanagh, glad to see you."

"I'm Misty Summers. My name tag says Missy, they got it wrong and have to do it over. Glad to meet you."

"Misty Summers! Now, there's a name for you. Very pretty name."

"Thank you," she said, blushing. "Would you like water? I can get you filtered, Mona serves filtered to special customers, I'm sure you must be special."

"Why on earth would you think so?"

"Your . . ." She indicated his neck. "You know."

"Ah. My collar."

"I've hardly ever met any Catholics."

"I'm Episcopalian."

"Oh," she said. "Well, I'll be right out with your water and your coffee."

"Thank you," he said, pleased to be here with a newspaper and the respite to read it. He really didn't want to make the Dorchester trek, but intended to get this day behind him, no matter what. Besides, when he called last night to say Cynthia and the boy weren't coming, Ella told him she was breaking out the damask tablecloth, which she hadn't used since her mother died and all the neighbors brought food and sat with her.

"There you go!" said Misty, setting a steaming mug before him. She looked like a milkmaid from a storybook, he thought. No makeup, long, chestnut hair caught in a ponytail, and a simple skirt and blouse under the café's signature green apron.

"Where are you from, Misty? Whitecap?"

"Oh, no, sir, Ocracoke. I just moved here two days ago, and was real blessed to get this job right off."

"I'm sure you'll do well. I believe you'll like Whitecap."

"Yessir," she said, pouring his coffee. He couldn't help but notice that her hand shook slightly.

"Try not to worry about getting everything right today," he said.

She lifted her gaze and he noticed her eyes for the first time. Warm. Trusting.

"I'll pray for you."

"Thank you, I really appreciate it. We'll have your order right out. Did you want ketchup?"

"Ketchup?"

"For your hash browns."

"Hash browns?"

She clapped her hand to her mouth. "Oh, gosh, I forgot, you're having grits!"

She fled to the kitchen, flustered.

As relaxed as if he had the whole day in which to do nothing, he opened his newspaper to the editorial page and settled happily into the green vinyl-covered seat of Mona's rear booth.

"Look here!" said Roanoke.

"Look here what?"

"Your hair's growed a good bit more'n I'd expect."

"Olive oil," said Father Tim, propped on the stool like a schoolboy.

"You rub olive oil on your head? I never heard of that one."

"Eat a lot of it on salads."

"Seems like God would've let a man have some say in where 'is hair grows, don't it? I mean, here you got all this hangin' down in back, an' not that much on top."

"Tell me about it."

Snip, snip.

"They say we'll prob'ly get a bad storm tonight," said Roanoke.

"I'm running up to Dor'ster. I hope it holds off 'til I get back."

"Temperature's droppin' pretty steady, too."

There was Elmo, sitting in the doorway to the book room and scowling at him as if he were a mangy hound. "Yo, Elmo!" he said.

At 9:25, according to the clock over Ernie's cash register, the entire room erupted into a bedlam of laughter, fish stories, and adrenaline-driven babble. He figured they wanted Ava and her sister to think this was a busy, prosperous enterprise, not some pokey little deal on a backwater island. Adding to the general vibration was the fact that Roger was nearly through burning, and would soon begin painting.

Father Tim had to admit that Junior was looking good. Instead of washing or ironing anything, however, he'd run across and bought new jeans, a shirt and jacket, and a new cap that read *Go, Bulls.*

"I'd take that off," said Roanoke.

"Why? She's seen my pictures, she knows my hair's a little . . . you know."

"That's not what I mean. I mean she might not like th' Bulls."

Junior looked stubborn. "I don't want to take it off," he said. "It's brand-new."

"Yeah, but what if she likes Carolina? You'd sure wish you was wearin' one that says *Go, Heels.*"

Glowering, Junior snatched the hat off his head and threw it in the corner.

"Now, don't go upsettin' him!" said Ernie, picking up the hat. "If you feel good wearin' th' thing, put it back on."

Junior crammed the hat back on his head and sat stiffly, looking miserable.

"Tim, you ought to tell Junior how you caught that big yellowfin tuna, take everybody's mind off—"

The screen door slammed as Ava Goodnight walked in and stared anxiously at the roomful of men.

The silence was sudden, complete, and absolute.

Ernie appeared turned to stone, Roanoke's hand froze at his shirt pocket where he was reaching for a Marlboro, and Junior's mouth was hanging open.

"You must be Ava!" said Father Tim, walking over and shaking her hand.

"And you must be Father Tim," she said, smiling. "Betty will be here in a minute, Betty's my sister, she's next door in the ladies room." Ava caught her breath and looked as if she might change her mind and run out the way she'd come in.

"And this is Junior. Junior Bryson." As the only one still able to function around here, he guessed the social stuff was up to him.

Junior rose slowly from the table and walked toward Ava as if in a trance. Father Tim wished to heaven that Junior would close his mouth.

"How're you?" asked Junior.

Ava extended her hand. "I'm just fine. How're you?"

"Just fine, an' how 'bout you?"

"And this," he said, pushing on, "is Roanoke Clark. He's a friend of Junior's."

Roanoke grinned and touched his forehead, a remnant gesture, Father Tim supposed, from the days men tipped their hats to women. "Pleasure."

"That's Roger Templeton. . . ."

"How do you do?" said Roger, standing respectfully.

"And I'm Ernie," said Ernie, recovering his speech and bounding over to shake Ava's hand. "We're glad to have you, nice to see you, come and sit down! We know you're goin' next door for coffee, but I could pour you a little somethin' in a cup, like a Cheerwine or a Dr Pepper, but you probably drink Coke, I could open you a Coke, how's that? On th' house!" Ernie was still shaking Ava's hand.

"Oh, no," said Ava, "I don't need a thing. But thanks a lot."

Father Tim figured somebody better make a move or Ava was out of here. "Ava, we're sorry we're a roomful of men. My wife would have come to meet you this morning, but we have a sick boy at home."

"I'm sorry," she said, appearing to mean it.

"Come and sit with us a minute," he said. "Roger, show Ava your duck."

Roger shyly held up his green-winged teal.

"Isn't that a marvel?" asked Father Tim, who was beginning to feel like the Perle Mesta of the Outer Banks.

Ava glanced at the door, looking for Betty. "Really nice! Really pretty!"

"We'd like you to feel welcome on Whitecap," said Father Tim. "Have you been here before?"

"No, sir, I never have. But my friend who lives on Tern Avenue—we've been meaning to get together for a long time."

Junior was currently grinning from ear to ear. He expanded his chest and adjusted his jacket sleeves, which Father Tim judged to be a mite on the short side.

"Oh, law!" said Betty, barging through the screen door. "Are we runnin' late, my watch has stopped, hey, y'all, I'm Ava's sister, her much *old*er sister, who're you?"

"I'm Tim Kavanagh. Glad to see you, Betty." The Lord had sent an icebreaker, and not a moment too soon.

"Hey, Tim, how're you, I hope I don't have lipstick on my teeth, do I have lipstick on my teeth? I dropped my compact in th' ladies room and busted my mirror, but since I already *had* seven years of bad luck, I hope I'm off th' hook!"

She fastened her gaze on Ernie. "An' you must be th' bigwig of this place, you *look* like you're th' bigwig."

"Why, yes, ma'am, I'm Ernie Fulcher, one an' the same. Have a seat and meet everybody. We're glad to have you."

"I don't suppose ya'll'd have a little drop of diet Pepsi or somethin,' I'm dry as a *bone*! I did th' drivin,' since Ava was busy doin' her nails and takin' her rollers out, an' drivin' always makes me thirsty, does it *you*?"

"Oh, yes, ma'am," said Roanoke, glad to be asked. "When I was haulin' lumber, I sometimes drank a whole case of Cheerwine between Asheville an' Wilmington."

"And you're Junior! I declare, you're better-lookin' than your pictures, don't you think so, Ava? A *whole* lot better-lookin' if you ask me, which nobody did!" Betty whooped with laughter and thumped down at a table, hanging the strap of a largc shoulder bag over the chair back.

Betty patted the tabletop. "Come on, honey," she said to her sister, "sit down a minute and meet all these nice fellas who've been dyin' to see you, then we'll go next door and have a bite to eat, right, Junior?"

"Now, that's what I call a good-lookin' woman . . . ," said Ernie, dazed and staring at the door.

Without glancing up from his duck, Roger nodded in agreement. "But seems like she might be too much for Junior."

Roanoke ground his cigarette out in a bottle cap. "You ain't tellin' us nothin' we don't know."

Roger burned a feather. Lucas yawned. The Dr Pepper clock ticked over the cash register.

"Well," said Father Tim, pushing back from the table, "you all can sit here 'til Judgment Day, but I've got fish to fry."

Ernie looked at him, anxious. "D'you think Junior stands a chance?"

"God only knows," he said, meaning it.

The lowering overcast continued—across the bridge, up the coast, and over the causeway to Dorchester. As he hit the island, the rain began.

He turned the heater on, pondering the fact that he could never think rationally when Morris yelled, but at last he understood that the harsh, repetitive command had little to do with him; in his opinion, it meant something else entirely—out of this body, out of this prison, out of this terrible exile. . . .

There . . . a stop sign, and Little Shell Beach Road. He looked at his watch, checked his odometer, and turned right. One and a half miles to Old Cemetery Road . . .

The lawsuit. It swam into his mind relentlessly. *The Lord is my strength and my shield. . . .*

He'd hold off on saying anything to the Hope House Board of Trustees until he talked again with Walter. The irony, he thought, of a stranger moving into his own house to set up shop to sue him. And why had she moved to Mitford to sue, when she might have done it just as well from Boston? It was the most mind-boggling turn of events imaginable.

He prayed as he slowly moved south on the small island of Dorchester—for Junior, Misty Summers, Cynthia, Jonathan, Janette, Morris Love, Buck and Pauline . . .

Old Cemetery Road. He hooked a right, hearing his tires crunch on gravel.

. . . for Dooley's missing brothers, Dooley's appearance before the judge, Busy Fingers' ability to complete the Lord's Supper needlepoint on time . . .

. . . and Jeffrey Tolson. He didn't want to pray for Jeffrey Tolson, but drew a deep breath and did it anyway. Could he personally forgive Janette's husband, even if the man wasn't repentant for the pain he'd caused?

He wanted to, he was required to, and, yes, he would keep trying to—with God's help.

Ella was looking for him. The moment he hit the porch, she opened the door and he blew into her living room with a gust of rain.

"Oh, mercy," she said, shaking his hand, "you're soaked! But come and stand by the piano. I've got the hair dryer ready."

"The hair dryer?"

"To dry you off!" she said, pleased to be helpful.

He had heard of time warps, and was utterly delighted to be in one. Ella Bridgewater's cottage was as pleasant as anything he'd seen in years. He felt instantly at home. In truth, it appeared as if his own mother might have placed Ella's turn-of-the-century furniture and the numerous family photographs in polished silver frames.

Small flames licked up from a single log in the fireplace, and a stack of wood lay by the hearth, ready for anything.

He inhaled deeply of the glorious aroma in the house, which seemed largely composed of salt air, wood smoke, and sea bass with lemon butter. Sitting by the fire as Ella prepared lunch, the clock ticking on the mantel, he felt as contented as a country squire.

This, he presumed, was the place where antimacassars went when they died—they were in evidence everywhere, and starched to beat the band. His mother had used sugar water to starch her own; as a child he'd had an awful desire to eat the one on the piecrust table; it made his mouth fairly water to see it.

Ella brought a small etched glass and a decanter. "There you are!" she said, clearly delighted to have his company. "That's my plum wine, I hope you like it, it won a blue ribbon in 1978! Lunch in ten minutes. And now you're settled, I'll send Louise in."

She went briskly to an adjoining room, out of which a canary momentarily flew. It made a beeline for the piano, where it perched on the bench and cocked its head at him.

"Louise, do sing for Father Timothy, he's come all the way from Whitecap."

To his astonishment, Louise began to warble with great charm and enthusiasm, and finished her rendition perched on an antimacassar atop the piano.

"Amazing!" he said. "Bring her to St. John's for a solo!" They could do worse than sit and listen to one of God's creatures sing from the depths of an unfettered heart.

The rain increased to gusting, wind-driven sheets that made the small house shudder as they sat at the table.

"Minor and I made plans to marry, and then, two weeks before the ceremony was to take place in our little church down the road, he was ballooning over Nova Scotia, and . . . well . . ."

"I'm sorry," he said.

Ella lifted her glass in a salute, and soldiered on as hostess. "Plums are very hard to find nowadays, unless you buy them in a store, and I'm hardly ever tempted to do that. You know what the problem is?"

"I confess I don't."

"Everyone works away from home these days, they don't keep their fruit trees sprayed or pruned, and the poor things simply fall down in the pasture or the yard or wherever, and that's the end of it."

" 'The world is too much with us; late and soon,' " he said, quoting Wordsworth. " 'Getting and spending, we lay waste our powers;/ little we see in Nature that is ours;/ we have given our hearts away, a sordid boon!' "

"Exactly," she agreed. "Amen!"

He was feeling anxious as they finished their dessert. "Do you have a TV we could watch for weather news?"

Ella sighed. "There hasn't been a TV in this house for years! Do you remember when the Dallas Cowboys beat the Denver Broncos in the Super Bowl?"

"I don't believe I do," he said.

"Mother and I were watching the game, sitting right over there, when the screen went black as pitch. I remember to this day what Mother said, she said, 'Ella, do you think this happened because I bet two dollars on the Cowboys with Joe?' Joe was our postmaster. We tried to have it fixed, but it was dead as a doornail, and we never replaced it."

A clap of thunder broke above them so loudly that he started from his chair. "Just . . . looking for a phone!" he said.

He dialed Dove Cottage as Ella stood by, peering at him anxiously. Her mother had taught her never to use a phone in a storm. She was, in fact, eager to unplug everything electrical, including the lamps, though she supposed that wouldn't be proper during a visit by clergy.

Cynthia reported that things were fine at home, and she was praying for him. While his wife implored him to do nothing reckless in such bad weather, he should, nonetheless, hurry home.

He was wanting out of here fast, though he felt compelled by common courtesy to look at a couple of photographs before leaving. There was Minor standing by a hot-air balloon, quite fit and handsome in a flight suit. Glaring from an oval frame, Mrs. Bridgewater appeared sufficiently formidable to wither the hollyhocks that served as background.

"I just hate this storm. I walked down to church last night and raked Mother's grave and dusted the pews . . . but you'll see it all another day." Ella's rouge was two perfectly circular spots. "And I wanted to show you our live oak. It's the oldest on the island as far as anybody knows. Maybe you can get a peep at it as you leave. It's just a few yards from that side of the porch."

"We'll do the full tour another day. I look forward to it."

"Well, then," she said, slipping a parcel into his hand. "This is a smidgen of my plum wine, and a few morsels of sea bass for your Violet. I'd so love to have a c-a-t, but I *can't* have a c-a-t, you know, as long as Louise is with me."

"Aha. Well, I'm off, and can't thank you enough. I've been happy in your home, Ella, and very much like your idea for next Sunday's anthem."

"Thank you for coming, Father, it was an honor. Now, left out of the driveway and two blocks on the right in the old white two-story, that's Captain Larkin. Remember to look for the blue truck in front and beware the dog, they say he bites."

She opened the door and was struck forcibly by a blast of cold wind and rain.

"I'll pray for you!" she called, as he dashed into the deluge.

He'd been out in a few storms, but this one worried him. As soon as they got back from Mitford, he'd have the blasted car radio fixed so he could find a little weather news when he needed it.

Driving at ten miles an hour, he managed to spot what he presumed to be the captain's house, and pulled up behind the blue truck. Any dog that would take the trouble to bite in weather like this was welcome to try, he thought, as he grabbed the wet umbrella and a leather box containing the home communion set.

He slogged to the concrete steps in a driving wind that threatened to invert the umbrella, and opened the screen door to the porch. A scowling face peered through the glass panels of the front door and quickly vanished.

Lord, bless this time, he prayed as he knocked, *and keep us safe from any harm in this storm. . . .*

He nearly leaped from his sodden loafers as a violent clap of thunder rolled overhead and the door opened. An elderly man with the countenance of an angel peered out.

"Hurry in, Father, hurry in!" said Captain Larkin.

CHAPTER SEVENTEEN

Bread and Wine

He stepped into a large parlor that smelled of fireplace ashes and stale bacon, like country houses he remembered from his Mississippi childhood.

His glance took in an afghan-covered sofa, two worn reclining chairs, a television set on a rolling stand, and a bevy of family portraits lining the white beadboard walls. To his right, a stairway with a curved banister, and closed double doors to what was probably a dining room. The house had once been rather fine, if unpretentious, and he was glad for its refuge.

"Where's your oilskins at, Father?" The captain spoke in a loud voice over the din of rain on the tin roof.

"I'm afraid I'm a mountain man, Captain, with nary an oilskin to my name." He shucked out of his damp jacket and hung it on a peg by the door.

"Brother!" shouted his host. "Bring Father a dishrag, if ye don't object."

He thought Captain Larkin was as lively and quick as any Santa Claus, though he walked with a cane and had a distinct limp. The captain also possessed a combination of the pinkest cheeks and bluest eyes he had ever seen.

The old man hobbled to the sofa and straightened the afghan. "Come sit an' make yourself to home. We'll have ye dried off here in a little."

The man who shuffled into the room looked exactly like the captain, yet his countenance was remarkably different; a scowl appeared permanently etched into his face as if by steel engraving. Light and darkness, observed Father Tim—fire and ice, north pole and south!

"This is Twin Brother," said Captain Larkin. "Brother, this is th' Father from down at St. John's."

" 'Bout time you come," said the old man, glowering at him. "We been lookin' out for you since Brother fell four year ago, he could've killed hisself an' it wouldn've mattered to you none."

"I'm sorry I wasn't around then. I came to St. John's in early July."

"Four month ago," said Brother, glaring at him through filmy eyes. He handed over a rag and Father Tim took it, mopping his head, face, and hands. He felt a chill go along his spine as the thunder crashed again, directly over the roof.

"Bad 'un," said Captain Larkin, shaking his head.

"Will you join us, Brother Larkin?"

"No, sir, I'll not!" snapped Brother, leaving the room. Opening one of the double doors, he turned and shouted, "I don't abide with such foolishness."

Father Tim closed his eyes, took a deep breath, and kept a moment of silence that amplified the sound of the lashing wind and rain. A single light bulb, hanging by a long cord from the ceiling, swayed slightly, causing shadows to dance across the pictures on the wall.

"Peace be to this house and to all who dwell in it. Graciously hear us, O Lord, Holy Father Almighty, everlasting God, and send thy holy angel from heaven to guard, cherish, protect, visit, and defend all who dwell here."

Father Tim saw Brother peering at them from behind the door, as he poured wine from a small cruet into an equally small chalice.

Though he knew he might have stood, the captain chose to kneel. Grasping the arm of his recliner and going to his knees with considerable difficulty, he joined Father Tim in the Lord's Prayer, then cupped his hands to receive the wafer.

"Lord," the captain prayed from memory, "I'm not worthy that Thou should come under my roof, but speak th' word only and my soul shall be healed."

"The Body of our Lord Jesus Christ, which was given for you, my brother."

Tears flowed down the pink cheeks of Captain Larkin as he raised his hands to his mouth and took the wafer.

"The Blood of our Lord Jesus Christ, which was given for you, my brother."

The captain drank and wiped his eyes on his shirtsleeve.

Laying his hands on the captain's head, Father Tim prayed, "The blessing of God Almighty, the Father, the Son, and the Holy Spirit, be upon you and remain with you forever, amen."

"Amen," said the old captain.

Father Tim helped him to his feet and they embraced warmly. The tender spirit of this good man flowed out to him with the smell of liniment and unwashed scalp, of shaving talcum and clothes hung too long in a forgotten closet.

"The Lord be with you, Captain."

"And with thy spirit," replied the supplicant, beaming through his tears.

The wind suddenly roared down the chimney and huffed a shower of ashes into the room. He was in too deep with this storm. It didn't appear to be passing over and seemed to be growing worse, moment by moment. Only a lunatic would go out in . . .

"Captain, may I use your phone?"

"We've not had one in a good while. Too much money for too little talkin' is what Brother calls it."

"Ahh." He went to the front door and stood looking out, agonized. He couldn't see his car or the truck parked in front of the porch, only a gray film as if a heavy curtain had been lowered. He shivered in his knit shirt.

The captain reached up and pulled the chain on the light bulb. "B'lieve I'll just switch this off."

In the odd twilight of the storm-darkened room, the old man eased himself into his recliner and sighed.

"Blowin' a gale," he said.

Father Tim thumped onto the sofa.

He'd wait for a letup—every storm had a letup once in a while—then he'd run for it and drive as far as he could go. One way or another, he'd make it home. . . .

"My great-grandaddy come over from Englan' in a little ship called *Rose of Sharon*. It broke up in a bad storm 'bout this time of year, and him an' five other men was warshed up on Dor'ster. We speculate it was about where this road ends at, down past th' church. Back in those days, th' beaches was littered with shipwreck of ever' stripe an' color, an' so they went to work and knocked together a little shack where they could look out for another ship an' git picked up."

What was this stubborn streak that had made him so all-fired determined to come to Dorchester today as if it were some life-or-death, do-or-die endeavor? Worse, how could he have left his wife saddled with a sick boy and a storm warning? Had he bothered to listen to a weather report and check out the particulars? No, he'd shrugged it all off as if it were nothing. . . .

"They wadn't hardly nobody livin' on these little islands back then 'cept Indians, there's some as thinks it was part of Wanchese's crowd. Story goes, my great-grandaddy wadn't more'n twenty year old when he married a Indian woman off of Whitecap, had a head of hair down to her ankles. I been tol' me'n Brother has th' cheekbones and nose of a Indian, but I don't know, I couldn't say."

Please, God, don't let this storm hit Whitecap and take the bridge out, keep the bridge in good working order, the bridge, that's the crux of the matter. . . .

"I built this house for my wife, Dora, back when I was runnin' trawlers. Dora was nineteen year old when we moved in, an' cheery as any angel out of heaven. Then, when we went down to Whitecap to keep th' light, Brother moved in an' managed things for me. When I quit keepin' th' light, I stayed on in Whitecap 'til Dora died, then come back to Dor'ster where I was born an' raised at."

Two thirty-five. An hour's drive in a storm like this would surely double, maybe triple the driving time, so he'd be home by five-thirty, maybe six o'clock, max. . . .

"I've been foolin' with Canada geese a good while, now, ever' fall I pay a neighbor to sow wheat an' winter rye 'round my pond out yonder. This spring, we seen nests as had four to eight eggs apiece. . . ."

He recognized a growing sense of foreboding . . . something that pressed on his chest and worried his breathing. Maybe he wouldn't wait for a break, he'd take his chances. . . .

He bolted off the sofa. "Captain, I've got a wife and boy to get home to, I'm going to run on, it's been a pleasure meeting you, I know how much they care for you at St. John's, God bless you and keep you, I'll be back before Christmas."

The old man looked at him, dumbfounded. "You ain't goin' out in this, are ye?"

"Yes, sir, I am," he said, running to snatch his damp jacket from the hook.

"Brother!" yelled the Captain. "Come an' say goodbye to th' Father, if ye don't object."

The dining room door opened, and Brother peered out, holding a jar of peanut butter with a spoon in it.

"The Lord bless you, Brother Larkin."

The old man scowled at him. "Goin' out in that, you'd do better to bless y'rself."

As he tossed the drenched umbrella into the backseat and slammed the door, he spied the lasagna sitting on the floor behind the passenger seat. Dadgummit, he'd forgotten to give Ella her present. Cynthia had even tied a bow around the foil-covered dish.

He sat for a moment and considered running it in to the twins. Then, feeling the chill of his sodden clothes, he squelched the notion.

He passed what he thought was Ella's house, but didn't see a light. No, indeed, St. John's organist was snug in her cottage with every plug pulled, as disconnected from civilization as any soul on the Arctic tundra.

A mile and a half to the highway . . .

With no yellow line to guide him, he kept his eyes strictly on the right side of the road, but there were long moments when the wipers were of no effect on the streaming windshield and he lost visibility entirely.

At the end of the gravel lane, he had a moment of sheer panic about pulling out to the highway. Pummeled by gusting sheets of wind and rain, he searched for headlights moving toward him from either direction, but saw nothing.

He eased onto the asphalt, praying.

Was this a hurricane? Surely not, or by now he'd be sitting upside down on the mainland in somebody's tobacco field. Besides, he would have heard if a hurricane was predicted; this was merely a heavy storm with high winds, of which they'd seen more than a few since moving to these parts. The thought consoled him, but a subsequent thought of the sea, roiling and churning not far from the highway, gave his stomach a wrench.

In truth, he had no clue about what he should be doing. To cling on in Dorchester seemed wasteful of precious time, but to push ahead seemed potentially hazardous and plain stupid.

He would push ahead.

Twice, he was tempted to pull into what he thought was a service station, but he seemed to be developing a kind of sixth sense for driving in these conditions, a sense that he didn't want to abandon too hastily.

He remembered what Louella said during their last visit. Something like, "You git in any trouble down there, jus' remember Louella's up here prayin' for you."

"Pray for me, Louella!" he shouted, finding comfort in the sound of his own voice.

On either side of the highway, trucks hunkered down like great beasts, waiting out the storm.

Easing south on what he estimated to be the last half of the coastal highway, the Mustang slammed into something unseen. It was a hard hit, and the motor died instantly.

His heart thundering, he leaped from the car and saw a tree limb fallen across both lanes. He pushed against the wind to get back in the car and switch on the emergency lights—he was a sitting duck out here—then, head down, he dived back into the squall to try to move the limb. Blast. The car had rolled over the limb before the motor died.

In the driver's seat, he turned the key in the ignition. Nothing. Again. Nothing. Flooded.

He tried to think calmly. If he could lift the front of the car backward over the limb, he could then push the Mustang onto the side of the road, out of harm's way. He had never lifted a car. . . .

He got out and walked to the right, checking the shoulder. But there was no shoulder; it was a drop-off to a creek, which was quickly rising to the roadway.

His glasses slid off his nose and he caught them and put them in his pocket, half blind. He was a desperate fool, the worst of fools. The rain was hammering him into the asphalt like a nail.

He saw it as he turned from the creek.

It was the lights of a truck bearing down in his lane.

His heart racing, he ran to the rear of the car and threw up both arms, waving frantically. *Dear Jesus, let him see my lights. . . .*

But what if the driver didn't see his lights? He could be chopped liver between the grille of a tractor-trailer and the bumper of his own car.

"Please!" he shouted over the roar and din of the rain. *"Please!"*

He jumped out of the way as he heard the air brakes applied. The massive vehicle rolled to a stop only inches from the Mustang.

His legs were cooked macaroni, warm Jell-O, sponge cake as he walked to the driver's side of the cab and looked up in utter despair.

The window eased down. "What's your trouble?"

"Limb on the road, motor's flooded."

The driver climbed out of the cab in a flash, wearing an Indiana Jones hat with a chin strap, and a brim that instantly shed water like a downspout.

"I'll take a look." The driver bent into the rain and walked to the front of the car, squatted and peered underneath. "Goin' to need a chain. Get in your car, I'm goin' to haul you over th' limb, then we'll roll it off in Judd's Creek."

Sitting in the car, he heard the chain being attached to his rear bumper, and soon after felt the jerk as the big rig reversed its gears and rolled him backward over the limb. He pulled on the emergency brake and returned to the fray.

Together, they heaved, pushed, and rolled the sodden limb off the road and into the creek.

"Where you headed?" the driver shouted.

"Whitecap!"

"I'm runnin' by Whitecap. Come on an' follow me, but not too close or th' spray'll blind you. Just keep your eyes on my taillights and marker lights."

"Done!"

"I'll pull into that vacant lot by th' Whitecap bridge."

"God be with you!" he shouted.

He followed the truck for roughly half an hour in steadily decreasing rain. About four miles north of Whitecap, the storm had blown over, and he turned his wipers off.

In the vacant lot, rainwater stood in deep pools, and he saw a metal sign blown from Jake's Used Cars leaning against the entrance to the bridge.

But, *hallelujah,* there was no sign claiming the bridge was out.

Dodging the pools, the driver pulled the refrigerated rig into the lot, and Father Tim parked alongside.

Leaving the motor running, the driver swung down and shook his hand with an iron grip.

"Tim Kavanagh. I can't thank you enough."

"Loretta Burgess," said the driver. "Glad to help."

"Loretta?" he said, stunned. "I mean . . ." Well, well. Holy smoke.

Loretta Burgess laughed and removed her sodden hat. A considerable amount of salt-and-pepper hair fell around her broad shoulders. "I don't care what they say, Padre, it ain't totally a man's world."

"You're right about that!"

"I'd show you th' pictures of my grandkids if we had time, but I'm runnin' behind th' clock. You take it easy, now."

As Loretta Burgess pulled onto the highway, he turned to get back in the car. He was standing with his hand on the door handle when he sensed something odd and troubling:

The air was strangely, eerily quiet.

And then he heard the siren.

CHAPTER EIGHTEEN

Simple Graces

Three army trucks blew past the vacant lot, tailed by a mainland ambulance with a wide-open siren.

He scratched onto the slick pavement and followed the procession across the bridge without any memory of doing it.

As he came off the bridge, he was clocking seventy, but had no intention of slowing down. Wherever the rescue squad was needed, he could be needed. Instantly he prayed for the need, whatever it might be, and realized he'd been praying, almost without ceasing, since six o'clock this morning. Surely, days on end had been packed into this single half day.

Water rushed across parts of Tern like bold creeks, carving out sections of asphalt. Whatever the vehicles ahead of him plowed through, he plowed through.

As the cavalcade turned left on Hastings, he saw the tree hanging, as if in a sling, on the sagging power lines. Across from the fallen tree was the gray house on the corner, the one Cynthia always admired—another tree had slammed across the roof, caving it in, and scattering bricks from the chimney into the yard. Next door, a section of picket fence dangled in a tree, and over there, a limb had smashed straight down, like an arrow from above, into the hood of a car.

In the rearview mirror, he saw two more troop trucks behind him and, farther back, another ambulance.

A chilling fear was spreading through him like a virus.

In the sullen afterlight of the storm, he had returned to a place he hardly recognized.

Several houses this side of Dove Cottage appeared to have taken a beating, but without any serious damage.

As his house came into view, his heart was squeezed by a kind of terror he'd never known.

Dove Cottage had no porch.

Its facade was oddly blank, like a staring face. He saw that the porch had been blown into the neighbor's yard, partially intact, the rest in smithereens. Pickets from the fence were scattered everywhere. A few had landed on the roof.

The need he'd prayed for only moments ago was partly his own.

He parked at what had been his front gate, as the stream of vehicles behind him blew past. He fled toward the house and stood looking up to the front door, wondering how to get in.

"Cynthia!"

The back porch . . .

He raced around the house and into the kitchen, where he stepped on fragments of china that crunched like bubble wrap under his feet.

"Cynthia! Barnabas!"

He skidded down the hall, and halted at the living room door, where the entire floor had caved in at the middle, in a deep and perfect V.

Their furnishings lay neatly piled along the crotch of the V, and on top of the pile was his mother's Limoges vase; it appeared unharmed, as if it had rolled down one side of the collapsed flooring and, at the last moment, landed conveniently on a chair cushion.

"Cynthia! *Please!*" He tore along the hall to the bedrooms, which looked as if nothing more than a strong wind had ruffled the bedcovers, as if the porch had not been blown to kingdom come, nor the living room destroyed.

But what if she and Jonathan had been in the living room when . . . ?

He raced out the back door and into the street, thinking he would flag down an ambulance, a neighbor, anybody. But there was no help in sight. Many in the neighborhood worked across, and only a lone pickup truck roared past, the driver refusing to make eye contact.

What had happened? Was it, in fact, a hurricane? Did tornadoes hit the coast? He'd never asked. All his life, he had ignored weather as much as he could, for what could one do about it, anyway?

He would burrow through the furniture like a mole, through the chairs and tables and books and magazines. . . .

Somewhere at the bottom was the rug. If he got to the bottom and found the rug, he'd know she was nowhere in the house. . . .

He called her name unceasingly as he clawed his way through the detritus of their everyday life, terrified that he might find her.

But there was no one, nothing.

And how in heaven's name was he to crawl up the slick, polished floor, from the hole he'd lowered himself into?

"Father! You down there?"

White-faced, Junior Bryson squatted over the threshold of the living room and looked into the pit.

"I'm here, Junior. Have you seen my wife?"

"No, sir, I just drove up from th' Toe an' seen your porch was blowed off. I was goin' to Ernie's. I hear he took a bad hit."

"Can you pull me up?" He'd never been so glad to see a face. He was trembling with feeling and with cold.

"I'm pretty much out of shape, I don't know, but I'll lay down and hook my feet on either side of th' doorway. . . ."

Junior positioned himself and, huffing, reached toward Father Tim.

"OK, you hang on, now, just kind of climb up my arms or whatever."

"This room was built pretty high off the ground, so it's a stretch."

"But don't be pullin' me down in there with you," said Junior, "or we'll both be in a good bit of trouble."

"I can't seem to get any traction with these loafers," he said, breathing hard.

Blast loafers into the next century, he was over loafers.

"It just happened," Junior said, as Father Tim hurriedly changed into dry clothes and pulled warm socks onto his numb feet. "About thirty, forty minutes ago, looks like it tore up th' north end and blew on out to sea, th' rain an' wind just stopped all of a sudden. But we didn't have no damage at th' Toe, not a'tall. Far as I know, 'lectricity's down all over th' island, an' Mr. Bragg's phones went out. How's th' bridge?"

"Still working."

"That's a blessin'," said Junior.

On his way out the back door, he turned and did a final search for Violet, looking under the beds, and hoping she wasn't stranded under the study sofa, which he couldn't get to because of the collapsed living room.

They walked at a trot to the truck and the car.

"Good luck findin' your wife and th' boy. I'm sure they're fine, prob'ly at th' grocery store or post office when it hit."

"Thank you, buddy."

But his wife couldn't have been at the grocery store or the post office; she had no car. She was, he decided, at the church with Jonathan, where she'd gone to work on the Fall Fair. He felt so certain of it, he wanted to shout.

As he drove away from Dove Cottage, he wondered—where was her bicycle? She usually hauled it up the steps and left it on the front porch. Surely she wouldn't have been out on her bicycle. . . .

More cars were on the street now, people coming from across or from the Toe; there was a veritable snake of solid traffic along Hastings, and not a little horn-blowing.

He hated seeing Ernie's. The right wall had crumbled, leaving the framing and a pile of bricks. Glass from the front window was missing as well, and books lay scattered around the parking lot and into the street.

All that unrefrigerated bait, all those books open to the elements, they'd better get a tarp over it, and fast.

But he couldn't think about Ernie's right now.

A camera unit from a mainland TV station blew around him as he wheeled the Mustang into the empty parking lot next to Ernie's, and set off running to St. John's.

"She's leanin' to th' side of my politics, is what it is." Ray Gaskill, who lived in the house closest to St. John's, removed a toothpick from his mouth and surveyed the damage.

Roughly one-third of a live oak had split off and collapsed across the roof of the church, knocking the building askew.

"It's racked to the right," said Leonard Lamb, looking ashen.

"Who was in it?" asked Father Tim.

"Nobody. Sometime after you left for Dor'ster, the women packed up and went over to the Fieldwalkers' to work."

"The organ?"

"It's OK, if we can get a tarp on before it rains again. We can't find Sam, and the phones are down so we can't call Larry to bring a tarp from the ferry docks. Looks like I'll have to go across if th' bridge is working."

"No problem with the bridge."

"Or we could maybe get a tarp from up Dor'ster, maybe at the boat repair."

He felt ridiculously guilty that he hadn't picked up a tarp.

"Trouble is, the plaster's cracked pretty bad and when we set her straight, that'll crack it even worse."

"This ain't nothin' to the' Ash Wednesday storm," said Ray, chewing the toothpick. "Now, that was a storm. This wadn't but prob'ly seventy-five-, maybe eighty-mile-an-hour winds."

He thought St. John's neighbor seemed personally proud of the catastrophe that struck in '62. Though it spared lives, its fury had pretty much battered everything else along five hundred miles of shoreline.

"I've got to find Cynthia," he said. "Do you have any idea . . . ?"

"I don't," said Leonard. "Marjorie's at the Fieldwalkers'. She'd probably be able to say."

Come to think of it, why would Cynthia have taken Jonathan out in a terrible storm, when he was burning with fever and on medication? And she wouldn't have taken Barnabas and Violet to the soiree at the Fieldwalkers'. . . .

His heart was in his throat.

"Looks like some of th' sidin's popped off. That'll expose your studs to water," said Ray.

"What about the basement?" he asked Leonard.

"You don't want to know."

And he didn't. Not until he found Cynthia.

"I'll be back," he said.

When he picked up the Mustang, he spoke with a young police officer in the crowd milling around Ernie's.

"Why is the army in here?" he asked, afraid of the answer.

"They're not any army in here. We use army surplus trucks in storms 'cause saltwater eats up th' brake linin's on our patrol cars. These babies stand way up off th' road."

"Was anyone hurt at Ernie's?"

"No, sir. They think it was all that water in th' ground that did somethin' to part of his foundation, made his wall fall in. Then a big trash can blowed into his front window, an' the' wind scattered books from here to Hatt'ras."

"What about Mona's?"

"One of th' waitresses got her arm burned pretty bad, a deep fryer come off th' stove, fella in a pickup just ran 'er across to ER."

"I've lost my wife," he blurted.

The young man removed his hat. "Gosh," he said.

"I mean, I can't find her," he explained, feeling foolish. Why was he standing here?

Not knowing what else to do, he shook the officer's hand and ran to his car.

Close to tears, he turned the car around in the parking lot and headed onto Hastings, which was covered with water.

He suddenly recalled the time on the beach, only days ago, when she had reached up and stroked his cheek and said she wanted to remember him like this always. Had that been some terrible omen?

With the Whitecap police directing traffic, he made his way back the way he'd come.

The door was not only unlocked at the old Love Cottage, it had been blown open, and most of the furniture overturned. The wind had heaved a rocking chair through a front window; shattered glass was strewn on the sodden floor.

"Cynthia!" There was a basement here, Otis had said so; maybe when the porch had been ripped off their house, she'd come here, fearing worse.

Shaking as with palsy, he searched for the door to the basement, opening closets, finding the water heater, listening for the booming bark of his dog. . . .

"Cynthia! *Please!"*

There! Hidden in the bedroom they'd slept in all those eons ago . . .

He threw open the basement door and peered down into a dark void, unable to switch on a light.

"Cynthia!" he bawled.

Silence.

He turned from the mildewed odor that fumed up at him, and closed the door and put his head in his hands and did what he'd been doing all day.

"Lord," he entreated from the depths of his being, "hear my prayer. . . ."

Maybe there was a note at Dove Cottage.

Maybe there was something on the kitchen counter telling him where they'd gone. If not, he'd drive to the Fieldwalkers' if there were no power lines across the roads. He'd heard that was a problem in some parts of the north end, but so what, he had two feet, and besides, they couldn't have just vanished off the face of the earth. They had to be somewhere. . . .

He parked at the side of Dove Cottage and sprinted across a yard that felt like marsh beneath the soles of his running shoes.

"Father!"

Morris Love . . .

He turned and looked across to the wall. Something odd over there, a blank spot in the sky where a tree had stood. . . .

"They're over here!"

Again, his cognition lapsed, and he wouldn't recall racing from his yard and across the street and through the iron gate, which Morris Love had unlocked and swung back as he dashed onto the familiar turf of Nouvelle Chanson.

"Timothy!"

There had been times of absolute, unfettered joy in his life—his ordination, his wedding, and the day he and Walter stood on a hill in Ireland and looked across to the site of the Kavanagh family castle.

With his wife in his arms, his dog jumping up to lick his face, and Jonathan tugging on his pants leg, he experienced a moment of supreme joy that he felt he may never know again.

"Violet?" he said.

"In the kitchen, having a tin of Mr. Love's sardines."

He regretted that both he and his wife were tearful with happiness, but what could he do?

They saw Morris turn from the reunion in the foyer and stand by the window. There was suffering on his face in profile, something that snatched away the joy in their hearts.

"A nail," said his wife, explaining the bandage on her hand. "Right in the palm."

They sat in the cavernous kitchen lighted by candles in a silver stand, and waited for the teakettle to boil over a can of Sterno. Not seeming to know his kitchen, Morris had been unable to provide anything more than the Sterno and a kettle already filled with water. Cynthia had helped herself to his cabinets and found tea, along with a bag of Fig Newtons, which Morris said belonged to Mamie, but urged them to help themselves. Seeing their reluctance, he ate one himself, out of courtesy.

They all fell to.

"Milk!" said Jonathan. "My mommy, she gives me *milk* and cookies."

"No milk, dear," said Cynthia, hauling the boy onto her lap with one hand. "And no water in the taps, just what we have in the kettle."

"There's apple juice," said Morris.

"I'll get it!" said Father Tim.

"*No*. I'll get it." Morris rose stiffly and went to the refrigerator; he removed a container and poured juice into a glass.

"Say thank you," urged Cynthia.

"Thank you," said Jonathan, gulping it down.

"When the winds became so terrible," she said, "I remembered my bicycle and was afraid it would be blown off the porch like our rockers were last August. So I went out to bring it in the house and it wasn't there, and you know how I love my bicycle. I mean, I could never replace it, it's old as the hills."

"More," said Jonathan.

"More, *please*," counseled his wife.

"More, more, more, please, please, *please*!"

Morris took the glass and got up again, obviously with considerable difficulty, and refilled the glass.

"Thank you," said Jonathan.

Cynthia beamed with pride, and continued her report. "And so, I peered off the porch and saw that my bike had been blown into the side street. I ran down to get it, and all of a sudden, things were flying around in the air, and I realized it was pickets off our fence, they were just showering down, and I raised my hand in front of my face and a picket with a nail in it . . ."

"I'm sorry," he said, taking her bandaged hand.

"Just boom. Nailed. Ugh. Now you finish, Mr. Love."

"Please call me Morris."

"Morris!"

"I had looked out from the music room and seen the tree go over. Fortunately, it fell away from the house, and I had a view of the street. The rain was very heavy and visibility wasn't the best, but I thought I saw your wife, and she appeared to be in distress. I remember you said you were leaving town and I thought she may need . . . help."

"And so he came out to me," said Cynthia, "and at just that moment we saw the porch break off the front of the house. It was awful. I thought—"

Jonathan nodded energetically. "I was, I was *in* th' house!"

"Yes, you were, and so Morris ran to the house with me and we got Jonathan and Violet and Barnabas and he brought us all over here and we stood in his music room, sopping wet, to see if the rest of the house was going, but it didn't, and then Morris saw that I was dripping blood on his carpet. I'm terribly sorry about that, your housekeeper won't be a bit happy—"

"It's a dark Oriental, no one will never know."

"And he washed my wound and put antibiotic cream on it and bandaged me up." His wife beamed at Morris Love, who visibly blanched at the warmth and directness of her feeling.

Father Tim cleared his throat. "Thank you, my friend."

"I was scared," said Jonathan, whose nose was running like a tap. "I was *cryin'*."

He wiped Jonathan's nose and smoothed his hair, feeling a rush of affection. "And what about the bicycle?" he asked his wife.

"Mr. Love—I mean Morris—went back out into that awful storm and retrieved it. It's under his stairwell."

Morris shifted in the chair, looking uneasy.

"There goes the kettle!" said Cynthia. "Now please sit still, Morris, this is my job."

"I'm hungry," said Jonathan.

"I'm starved," said Cynthia.

His own stomach was growling. "We must get home and see what's up, anyway. What do we have in the refrigerator?"

"Nothing. Zip. A salami, a tomato. We're going to Mitford, and so I didn't want to leave anything."

"A salami and a tomato. It's a start," he said, cheerful.

"You're welcome to look here. I don't know, Mamie brings everything. . . ." Morris lifted his hands as if bereft of a solution.

"Bingo!" cried Father Tim.

"Bingo!" repeated Jonathan, slapping the table.

"It just occurred to me, I have just the ticket. Homemade lasagna! Velvety blankets of pasta layered with fresh spinach, fresh ricotta, mozzarella, a thick tomato sauce sweetened with chopped onions, and veal ground from the shank. Precooked, freshly thawed, and ready to roll."

"Mercy!" said his wife. "That sounds like my recipe. Where on earth did it come from?"

"The floor of my car," he replied, feeling as if he'd just hung the moon. "Morris, will you break bread with us?"

"Be thankful for the smallest blessing," Thomas à Kempis had written, "and you will deserve to receive greater. Value the least gifts no less than the greatest, and simple graces as especial favors. If you remember the dignity of the Giver, no gift will seem small or mean, for nothing can be valueless that is given by the most high God."

Father Tim remembered what the old brother had said as he ate his portion of the lasagna with gusto, and set some on the floor for Barnabas.

He thought it was the best thing he ever put in his mouth. His wife, who had always possessed a considerable appetite, was hammering down like a stevedore. Even Morris Love appeared to enjoy her handiwork, and Jonathan ate without prejudice or complaint.

Further, Ella Bridgewater had saved the day. In the packet with the sea bass, which Violet devoured, was the small jar of plum wine, which, to conserve water and washing up, they poured into their empty tea cups and drank with enthusiasm.

They went across the street with Morris Love's flashlight, and into the cold kitchen of Dove Cottage. He thought their house felt as if all life had gone out of it, as if the terrible assault had wounded it in some way that was palpable.

He was walking into the hall when the floorboards creaked and he saw a shadowy figure coming toward him.

"Good heavens, who's there?"

Jonathan let out a howl.

"It's Otis!" said his landlord, beaming his flashlight up. "You're in a bad fix here."

"Tell me about it."

"Looks like that sorry porch wadn't nailed onto th' house for shoot. I can't tell what all's goin' on 'til I get some daylight and a couple of men out here, but I want you and th' family to come stay at my motel. We'll fix you up with a choice room and king-size bed."

"Oh, no, that's fine, we'll just set up camp right here."

"No water here, no power, no heat, an' I don't know what's under these floors that might go next. When th' porch tore off, looks like a rotted floor joist or somethin' gave way in your front room."

Cynthia looked at him. "Otis is right, dear. Jonathan is sick, and the house is a terrible mess. Besides, we need our rest for tomorrow's trip."

"We won't be going to Mitford," he said.

His parish needed him here. God would work out the details.

Holding the sleeping boy in his arms, he stood on the back steps with Otis while Cynthia did some hurried packing with the aid of a flashlight.

"Not a scratch on my place," said Otis, "save for somebody's deck furniture bobbin' around in th' pool. When I heard what was goin' on up here, I run home lookin' for Marlene and couldn't find her. It like to give me a nervous breakdown, she was supposed to be home. Well, in two or three hours, here she comes, paradin' in like th' Queen of

Sheba, complainin' of th' rain ruinin' her hair. She'd been across havin' her roots touched up."

"Aha."

"Where trees blow down, they sometimes take out th' water lines, and course, th' water lines is takin' out th' roads. Thank th' Lord she was drivin' th' four-wheel."

Jonathan stirred in his arms and put the warm palm of his hand on Father Tim's cheek. "What about power?" he asked Otis. "How long to get everything back up?"

"Th' whole island's lost power. That'll prob'ly take four to five days to get goin' again. Water, I don't know, maybe two days. And it'll take a week of hard haulin' to get th' roads graded and asphalted."

He thought the whole thing seemed a dream. "How long 'til we can hold services?"

"The church looks pretty bad. Shingles are poppin' off like corn. But we got tarps on 'er, three of 'em. I had one, Larry brought one, Sam scrounged one. I've got people comin' tomorrow to look it over, see what it's goin' to take, an' how long." Otis heaved a deep sigh. "Th' water runnin' in turns plaster to mush, then when it dries, it turns to powder."

The tenant echoed his landlord's sigh.

"But this'll bring us together," said Otis, adopting a positive view of what lay ahead for the body of St. John's.

Father Tim felt a drop of rain on his cheek. "Oh, boy," he said, stepping onto the back porch.

He heard his parishioner draw a cigar from his pocket and remove the cellophane. There was a moment of silent consideration.

"Dadgum if I ain't goin' to *smoke* this sucker!"

In the flame of a monogrammed lighter, Father Tim saw the face of a happy man.

Cynthia stood inside the door of Number Fourteen at Bragg's Mid-Way Motel and peered at their room, which was lighted by a kerosene lantern.

"Ugh!" she said vehemently. "Shag carpet!"

CHAPTER NINETEEN

Jericho

His wife looked utterly downcast as he dressed the following morning. She sat on the side of the bed in her nightgown, shod in his leather bedroom shoes, refusing to make any direct contact with the carpet.

"You could take me to church and keep the car," he said, desperate to be helpful.

"I can't be dragging Jonathan around in this rain."

They had eaten a breakfast of cheese sandwiches, which Otis had made himself and delivered at six a.m. with scorching coffee in a thermos. The paper sack included a side of bananas, apples, raisins, and oranges, juice and crackers for Jonathan, and packaged brownies from the convenience store.

"I hate to leave you. You can go to the Braggs', you know. Otis invited us."

"Not in a hundred years," she said, setting her mouth in a profoundly straight line. "Make that a thousand!" Marlene Bragg had suggested his wife stop highlighting her own hair and see a professional; further, she proclaimed that fuchsia wasn't becoming to Cynthia's skin color, and recommended another shade of blusher to bring out the blue of her eyes. This had not set well.

"Marjorie and Sam begged us to come." Sam had shown up at the motel last night at eleven, hoping to rescue them.

"But their guest room has a leak in the ceiling and there's no water. Sam says they're using his grandmother's chamber pot."

"There are worse things than chamber pots," he said, trying to console.

"I can't imagine what."

He didn't want to say it, but how about being trapped in a motel room with no power, no phone, and a three-year-old?

He buttoned his shirt, surveying the scene. The kerosene lantern glowed against the dusk of the rainy morning; the oil-fired heater hissed in the corner; Jonathan slept soundly, clutching a pillow; Barnabas snored in the vinyl armchair; Violet snoozed on a mat in the bathroom. Cozy as it all appeared, he would not want to spend the day here. No, indeed.

"How's your hand?"

"Throbbing."

"Do you think you need to see a doctor?"

"I don't think so. Morris poured something on it that was absolutely scalding before he put on the cream. I think it's fine, dearest, don't worry. I'll have a look under the bandage before you come home with lunch. Ugh! Did I say *home*?"

"Home is anywhere you are, Kavanagh."

She fell against the pillows, sighing.

"What do you think of our neighbor?" he asked, putting on his shoes.

"The strangest, yet loveliest sort of man. I feel that underneath his pain is the deepest tenderness. Then again, is it pain, Timothy? I don't know, perhaps it's something more like anger, a terrible, corrosive anger."

"Odd that he would be so adept at home doctoring."

"He said he learned from Mamie."

"Aha. Well. I'll be back around twelve. Maybe the rain will let up and you can drop me at church and take the car."

"Where would I go?" she asked.

"I don't know. The library?"

"The library isn't open today."

"The grocery store?"

"And watch mold grow in the dairy case?"

He had a great idea. "I could bring you some pot holders to finish up for the Fall Fair." There! Just the ticket to keep her mind occupied.

"Pot holders?"

She looked at him as if he were something that had crawled through the pipes and into the kitchen sink.

As phone service was up in other parts of the village, he drove two blocks and stood in a queue to make calls from a pay booth at the rear of Whitecap Drugs.

When the Hope House switchboard answered, he asked for the dining room.

"Pauline . . ."

"Father! We saw on the news you had a bad storm last night."

"Yes. And Pauline . . ." He'd rather be shot than say it. "I . . . can't come. I can't come for the wedding on Sunday. I'm calling to ask if you can . . . cancel, that is, postpone it for two weeks until we get cleaned up here."

There was a moment of silence. The disappointment on the other end was palpable.

"Or," he said, and he really despised hearing these words out of his mouth, "you could get someone else to officiate, someone else to—"

"Well, no, Father, I mean that's fine, we don't want anybody else, you know we were goin' to keep it really simple, anyway, so it's . . . not much trouble to postpone it."

"I'm sorry, I can't tell you how sorry . . ." He was literally nauseous over the whole thing, especially hating that Jessie's, Poo's, and Dooley's glad excitement would have to be put on hold.

"Well, but don't worry," she said. "We'll set another date. We didn't even run it in th' newspaper, but I did tell everybody in the dinin' room, and Miss Louella, she was goin' to come, but . . . they'll all understand."

"What about Buck? How will this affect his plans?"

"Oh, he's not goin' back to Alaska. He's finished up his part. He's goin' to try an' set up his own business in Mitford."

"Hallelujah!"

"So, I understand," said Dooley's mother, "really I do."

But he could hear the sadness in her voice. He was good at hearing sadness in people's voices. . . .

"Two weeks," he said. "No matter what, we'll be there. And we'll talk again in a few days, all right?"

"Yes, sir. How bad is it down there?"

"No lives lost, as far as we know, but power out, and phones down in places, and no water on the north end. The church has taken a hard hit, part of a big tree fell across the roof and . . ."—he felt suddenly close to tears—"and our cottage had some damage."

"I'm sorry," she said, her voice husky with feeling. He knew that she, too, was good at hearing sadness in others.

He was able to reach Buck in Harley's basement apartment; Buck would go with Dooley to court on Monday, and Harley would return Dooley to school, as planned. They would reschedule the wedding for mid-November.

He took a deep breath and went through yet more telephone rigmarole—access code, the number he was calling, his calling card number, his PIN number, then through the switchboard, where, it was declared, there was no answer in the room, and so up to the fourth-floor nurses' station, and down the hall to the sitting room with the cordless. . . .

"Hello?"

"Janette . . ."

"Oh, Father, I'm so glad to hear your voice, I saw about the storm on TV. Is Jonathan . . . ?"

"He's doing great! A bit of a cold, that's all. Our house is torn up for a few days, but everyone's safe. We're at Otis Bragg's motel in the village."

"Thank heaven! And Father, I'm so happy about coming home."

"We'll be over to get you on Tuesday as we discussed. Around two o'clock. Is that still good?"

"Oh, yes. Perfect! I'll be ready."

"If you'd like to call, we're in Room Fourteen at Bragg's Mid-Way Motel. Uh-oh, I forgot. Phones are out over there, but should be up and humming in a day or two."

"I'll be so happy to see my baby. Has he been . . . good?"

"Better than good!"

Her laughter was music to his ears.

"We'll take you home and get you settled in with something hot for your supper. We can bring Jonathan on Thursday," he said, following the doctor's advice. "That will give you a chance to—"

"Oh, no, Father, please bring him Tuesday. I've missed my children so much. I can't wait to have my children home."

"Consider it done, then. And when are Babette and Jason coming?"

"They'll be home Wednesday."

"Good, wonderful," he said.

"Have you . . . seen Jeffrey?"

"Not in some time." Taken by surprise, he chose to be vague without being untruthful.

"Jean Ballenger says there's a pile of work waiting for me."

"Including a blazer for yours truly. I haven't had a blazer in years. Cynthia talked me into it and picked out the buttons."

There was a pause. "I'm . . . so very grateful, Father Timothy. For everything."

"So am I," he said. "So am I."

"Emma," he yelled through a lousy connection, "don't bake a ham!"

"What?"

"Don't bake a ham!"

"Spam? What *about* Spam?"

Rats. "I'll call you back!"

When he called back, the line was busy.

He rang Pauline's small house in the laurels, reluctant to wake Dooley, who had arrived late last night from school.

"Dooley . . ."

"Hey!" Dooley said, hoarse with sleep.

"Hey, yourself, buddy. We've got a problem down here."

He went out into the rain and stood beside his car for a moment, dazed and heartsick, finding that everything was finally sinking in—all at once.

On the way to St. John's, he wheeled into Ernie's, which was swaddled front and side with tarps.

Though Books, Bait & Tackle was down for the count, Mona's half of the building was going full throttle, thanks to a serious stash of bottled water, and a generator that had seen the café through the aftereffects of several storms and a hurricane. He stepped into the warmth of Mona's, smelling dripping coffee and frying bacon, and loving the refuge of it.

Every booth was full. "Over here, Tim!" called Roger Templeton.

"Squeeze in," said Roger, moving over to make room.

"Roanoke, Junior, how's it goin'? How's Ernie?"

"Haulin' books to th' Dumpster," said Junior. "We're just gettin' a bite to eat before we pitch in. I took a day's vacation to help."

"Is there any way he can dry the books out?"

"Nope," said Roanoke. "Dead inventory."

"What about Elmo?"

"Seems fine," said Roger, "but he won't come out from under the cash register."

"Junior, I heard you took somebody to ER yesterday. How'd that go?"

"Good mornin', Reverend, what can I get for you this mornin'?" It was Misty Summers, smiling at him and looking prettier, he thought, than the first time he saw her.

"Why, Misty! Did you break your arm?"

"No, sir, it got burned. Hot grease flew off the stove when Ernie's wall fell down."

"Aha." He glanced at Junior, who was lit up like a Christmas tree. "Well, I'm sorry to hear it and hope it heals soon."

"Thank you. It hurts really bad, but the doctor said it's going to be fine. Let's see, now, that was . . . umm, what did you order, sir? I forgot." For some unknown reason, Misty Summers was blushing like a schoolgirl.

"Coffee, no cream, and orange juice," said Father Tim.

"I'll be right back," she said.

"How bad is it at St. John's?" asked Roger.

"Pretty bad. The force of the tree across the roof racked the building to one side. Otis has a crew coming in. Did a good bit of damage."

"When we get Ernie straightened out," said Roanoke, "we'll be down an' give you a hand."

"Why, thanks," he said, touched by the offer.

Walking across the hall to Ernie's, he asked Roger, "By the way, what happened with Ava?"

"Darned if I know. Just out of the picture, it seems. Junior didn't have much to say about her."

"Well, well."

"Looked like a pretty uneven match, anyway."

"Right," said Father Tim, ducking into Ernie's and not liking what he saw.

In the book room, shelves that weren't anchored to the walls had been knocked sprawling, literally scattering books to the wind. The shelves on the fallen wall had crashed with the bricks, piling books among the debris. The smell of wet paper pulp filled the cold, drafty room, which was only loosely protected by the tarp.

Several of Ernie's fishing buddies were stacking ruined books in wheelbarrows.

He embraced the man who, from the beginning, had taken him in like family. "Sorry, my friend."

Ernie tried hard to produce a characteristic smile, but couldn't.

He was standing under the tent Sam had erected in the churchyard, drinking coffee with Leonard and Otis, peering at the endless rain and waiting for the contractor to arrive.

"You th' Rev'ren' Kavanagh?" An elderly man in a cap and slicker stepped under the tent.

"I am, sir."

"Albert Gragg."

Albert Gragg tipped his cap and shyly extended his hand. "I'm from up Dor'ster, Miss Ella sent me."

"I hope there's no trouble. . . ."

"She couldn't get you on th' phone. She's fell and broke her hip."

"No!" he said, stricken by the news. He hated to hear this. He didn't like this at all.

"A fracture or a break?"

"Clean break. She's in th' hospital and can't play y'r organ a'tall, said she'd call soon as she can get through."

"What happened?"

"In th' storm, said she heard somethin' hit her porch real hard, thought it was a limb offa that tree she thinks so much of, but it was th' neighbor's doghouse that was out there blowin' around. Said when she went runnin' out to check, th' rain had made 'er porch slippery as hog grease an' down she went. She got to th' phone, called me, an' I carried 'er to th' hospital."

"I hate to hear this. You're an old friend, Mr. Gragg?"

"Oh, forty years or more I been lookin' out for Miss Ella and 'er mama, doin' whatnot."

"God bless you for it. Who's her doctor?"

"I don't know, she didn't say."

"Tell her I'll be up as soon as I can, we've got a mess on our hands. Tell her she's in our prayers, and she can count on it."

"Yes, sir," said Albert Gragg, tipping his cap.

"And how's the captain and his brother, do you know?"

"What cap'n?"

"Captain Larkin."

"I can't say. I ain't seen him, he don't get out much. His boy carries his groceries in ever' week or two."

"Well, then," he said, feeling helpless. How many times had he wished there were two of him?

Stanley Harmon stepped under the tent, wiping his bare, bald head with a handkerchief.

"Sorry about this, Tim. Awful sorry."

"Thank you, Stanley. It was a hard hit, all right. Any damage at your place?"

"A few limbs down is all. Y'all are welcome to worship with us on Sunday at eleven, or you could hold your service ahead of ours, at ten o'clock. How'd that be?"

"Terrific. That would be great. Thank you!"

"They say we'll have water by then, so th' commodes'll flush, but far as power goes, bring some candles."

"We'll do it."

"Looks like we won't have power 'til Wednesday. Mildred and I are cookin' on a Coleman stove. Y'all doin' all right over at Mid-Way?"

"Oh, fine, just fine."

"You can come stay with us, and I mean it. Mildred said she'd love to have you. Now the kids are off at school you'd have th' whole basement to yourselves, just y'all and our two dogs, Paul and Silas, they wouldn't hurt a fly."

"Thanks, Stanley, we'll hunker down at Mid-Way for a little while, shouldn't be long."

"What else'll you folks need Sunday?"

"I just learned our organist broke her hip."

"Uh-oh. Well, no problem, we've got a crackerjack organist, and come to think of it, he's played a few Anglican services here and there. I'll talk to him and let you know tomorrow. Run by First Baptist in the morning around eight. I'll show you the ropes, give you a key an' all."

"You'll get a crown for this, Stanley!" he called as his colleague dashed into the rain.

Coleman stove! That was the ticket.

Stanley ducked back under the tent. "Oh, shoot, I forgot we can't have organ music without power."

"True enough. How quickly we forget."

"Well, see you in th' morning."

A cappella, then, and no two ways about it.

Less than half the expected crew had shown up at Dove Cottage and, after hauling furniture out of the pit and stuffing it into the study, were tearing out the living room flooring.

According to Otis, the maverick porch had pulled the front wall away, causing the floor joists to collapse. The wall would have to be winched back before they could replace the flooring, and when that was done a crew would come in to do the refinishing. Bottom line, they were looking at a minimum of two or three weeks to complete the job, and the crew couldn't get to the porch before spring.

Hearing this exceedingly unwelcome news, he thought of Earlene Ferguson, who, lacking a porch at the retirement home, simply "dropped off in the yard like a heathen" when exiting her front door.

"Don't worry," said Otis, "I'll have some of my boys from th' Toe put your porch back on. I ain't scared of drivin' a few nails myself."

Shivering in the raw October air, Sam, Leonard, Otis, and Father Tim waited for the contractor, and surveyed the fallen limbs and debris littering the churchyard.

"We ought to stack th' limbs," said Leonard, impatient to get moving.

"No use stackin' limbs in this weather," said Otis.

Rain drummed on the tent roof.

Sam sighed. "Goodness knows, it's sad to see that old tree half ruined."

"It was probably two hundred years old, maybe more. Marjorie and I've seen any number of people married under that tree." Leonard poured coffee from a thermos. "Did you know there are trees still living since before the time of Christ?"

"Where at?" asked Otis.

Leonard blew on his coffee. "I don't know, I forgot. It was in a magazine."

"I ain't believin' it," said Otis.

When the contractor still hadn't arrived at eleven o'clock, Otis bit the end off a cigar, lit it, and, fuming, blew the smoke out his nostrils.

"I'm goin' to be kickin' some butt from here to Chincoteague," he declared, stomping from the tent.

"How'll we let everybody know where we're holding the service?" Marshall Duncan asked Father Tim. "And how will they know it's at ten, not eleven?"

Ray Gaskill hammered down on his toothpick. "Put a sign at th' post office today, so word gets around. Then put one in th' churchyard, people'll be comin' by to see th' damage."

The road crew roared past St. John's in a parade of heavy equipment, waving at the assembly under the tent.

"You want to see the basement?" Leonard asked Father Tim.

"Is it safe?"

"I wouldn't go down there," said Ray. "No, sir, not me."

"I believe I'll pass. Besides, I've got to run to the motel and take lunch to my wife."

"Where you goin' to get lunch?" asked Ray.

"Mona's."

"Not unless you want to stand in line in th' rain. I just come by there, it ain't a pretty sight. You could go to the grocery store, get you some Vienna sausages in a can, tuna in a can, all kinds of things in a can, and a loaf of bread, some mayonnaise . . ."

"Aha."

"And if I was you," said Ray, "I'd keep th' underside of your Mustang hosed off, you're gonna be eat up with rust."

He said nothing to Cynthia about the predicted duration of the job at Dove Cottage. If the thought of three weeks at the Mid-Way was enough to make him crazy, there was no telling what it might do to his wife.

"There's no way to patch it," said Sewell Joiner. "We're talkin' shore up, tear out, strip off, an' set straight—it's goin' to look a lot worse before it looks better."

"Whatever it takes," said Father Tim.

"We'll have to excavate part of th' basement and tear out and rebuild th' wall. You got a bad crack in th' bed joints of th' masonry—"

"We're more in'erested in th' sanctuary right now," said Otis. "What's it goin' to take to get us back in business?"

"First thing we'll do is get some rollin' scaffold inside and tear off th' plaster that's not already fallen off th' ceilin' joists and studs. We'll be tearin' off some sheathin' an' shingles and replacin' that busted roof joist, then we'll use a come-along to straighten th' whole thing up again an' put on a new roof."

"I'd like you to get your boys started in th' mornin," said Otis.

"Tomorrow's Saturday," said the contractor.

"Go on and get 'em over here, we want to move on this thing. It's depressin' to ever'body not to see some action."

"Fine," said Sewell Joiner. "I can do that."

Otis unwrapped a cigar. "How long to get th' job done?"

"Two, three months if we got th' weather on our side. That'll include gettin' replastered and repainted."

Two or three months? Father Tim's heart sank like a stone.

At three o'clock, a crowd of parishioners had assembled under the tent, looking for a report on the damage, volunteering to help, offering consolation, and fervently commiserating. The rain drew on, shrouding the churchyard in a dusky gloom.

"I've got these little bitty mushrooms growin' between my toes," said Orville Hood, who kept St. John's oil tank filled.

"Let me *see*!" squealed Penny Duncan's youngest.

"I was sittin' in th' livin' room workin' a crossword when I thought th' world was comin' to an end." Maude Proffitt was swaddled in a yellow slicker and rain hat, with only her eyes visible. "Boom, somethin' hit right above my head. Honey, it was the *ceiling*, it just cracked open like a hen egg. Well, don't you know I jumped across th' room, my feet never touched th' floor! Thank th' Lord I didn't stay in that recliner another minute, or I'd've been pushin' up daisies right over yonder."

"Have a brownie," said Marjorie Lamb. "I baked these yesterday before the power went off."

"Law, what I wouldn't give for a cup of coffee to go with this," said Maude, eating the brownie in two bites.

Sue Blankenship's glasses kept trying to slide off her wet nose. "Did you hear th' Father's poor wife was hit by a picket fence?" she asked a baritone in the choir.

"No way! A whole fence?"

"Well, maybe just a picket."

Ann Hartsell, newly arrived from her nursing job across, saw the church and burst into tears. This caused her two youngsters, just fetched from day care, to erupt in a storm of sympathetic weeping.

"Have a brownie!" implored Marjorie, stooping to their level with the plastic tray.

"Th' trouble with this storm," said Ray Gaskill, "is mainly th' trees. It's *trees* that's done th' damage."

" 'Til I moved here, I never knew islands *had* trees," said Edith Johnson, who was an ECW bigwig.

Jean Ballenger shivered in her winter coat. "We nearly got the Last Supper finished, we're just working on the tablecloth. That much white seems to take forever. If you ask me, I don't believe all those men would have *used* a tablecloth."

"Do you think we should still try to have th' Fall Fair?" asked Mildred Harmon, handing around a plate of ham biscuits.

Father Tim turned aside from talking with the contractor. "Yes, *indeed*," he said. "Rain or shine!"

Jean patted her bangs in place. "What a relief! I couldn't bear the thought of all that work lying in a drawer 'til next year."

Early the following morning, the rain stopped.

He drove Cynthia, Jonathan, and Violet to Marion's, popped by First Baptist, and arrived at St. John's at eight-thirty as the five-man work crew blew in, on time and ready to roll.

By eleven o'clock, the sun came out, the temperature rose seven degrees, and a third of the north end regained running water.

"Hallelujah!" shouted Father Tim, tossing his rain hat in the air.

Otis stubbed out his cigar and pocketed the butt. "OK, boys, let's stack limbs."

Father Tim popped into the nave now and again to check the crew's progress. He was over the sick feeling, wanting only to see the work move ahead quickly.

Though pews and pulpit were under tarps, and plaster dust covered everything, the stained-glass window at the rear of the sanctuary was unharmed, with only minor cracking and pulling around the frame. The strong early light illumined the image sharply, casting color onto the white tarps. *Come unto me. . . .* That was sermon enough for this storm, he thought, or for any storm.

Each time he went inside, he glanced nervously at the choir loft, anxious for the safety and protection of the organ.

"No problem," said Sewell, who, Father Tim learned, was known to constituents as Sew, pronounced *Sue.*

He decided to stop worrying. If he couldn't trust a two-hundred-and-fifty-pound man who could kick in the remaining portion of a concrete-block basement wall, who could he trust?

He'd seen smaller crowds show up for Sunday worship.

By noon, more than half the parish had arrived, many with lunch bags from Mona's, some with family picnics. As the ground was too wet to sit on, they sat in parked cars, doors open, calling to one another, ambling through the tent where Sam had set up a folding table and a forty-two-cup coffeepot powered by a portable generator.

"Doughnut holes!" Jean Ballenger plunked down a box from the shop next door to her mainland hairdresser.

"Lookit!" said Ray Gaskill, who didn't want to miss out on the action. He lifted the lid of a bakery box, exposing half a cake, inscribed *HDAY TO RAY* in lime-green icing. "I was sixty-seven last July . . . that's August, September, October, it ain't but four months old and been in th' freezer th' whole time, help yourself."

Penny Duncan arrived with a gallon of sun tea, made before the rains began, and a freezer bag of thawed oatmeal cookies. Mona Fulcher dispatched Junior Bryson with a vast container of hot soup, a pot of chili, and a sack of cups and plastic spoons. Stanley Harmon dropped by with two thawed loaves of homemade bread from the freezer at First Baptist, along with a quart of apple juice he'd nabbed from the Sunday School.

Not knowing that his priest had already asked a blessing, and feeling his own heart so inclined, Sam Fieldwalker offered a fervent psalm of praise and petition.

"A double shot!" remarked someone who had happily bowed for both prayers.

Leonard Lamb popped a doughnut hole in his mouth. "We need a double shot," he said.

At two o'clock, his adreneline still pumping, he drove to the motel to fetch Barnabas for a run along the beach.

The heater had raised the temperature of the room to that of a blast furnace. He turned the heater off, snapped on the leash, and was out of there with a dog so relieved to be rescued that he slammed his forepaws against Father Tim's chest and gave his glasses a proper fogging.

The beach was more littered than usual, but nothing compared to the pictures he'd seen of Whitecap beaches in the aftermath of worse storms.

His brain felt petrified; he could scarcely think. For a man who'd been accused of thinking too much, it was an odd feeling, as if he were living his life in a dream, reacting to, rather than initiating, the circumstances that came his way.

He did know one thing for certain—he had to get his crowd out of the Mid-Way Motel, pronto.

Dodging the detritus of the storm, he ran easily, chuffing south toward the lighthouse and glancing at a sky so blue it might have been fired onto porcelain. The sea beneath was azure and calm, the water lapping gently at the sand.

He saw it, but thought nothing of it. Then, several yards down the beach, he stopped and looked again.

It was a little plane, bright red against the cloudless sky. He thought of his two jaunts into the wild blue yonder with Omer Cunningham, and the time Omer flew him to Virginia so he could attend Dooley's school concert. Blast, he missed the boy terribly. It had been four months since he saw him vanishing around the corner of Wisteria and Main on his bicycle. "*'Bye, Dad . . .*"

Barnabas skidded to a stop and barked furiously as the plane dipped toward the wide beach, then veered out over the water.

Father Tim stood and watched as it gained altitude and headed south. Did he see someone waving at him from the cockpit?

Probably not, but he waved back, just in case.

He was sitting on the bottom step of the walkway through the dunes, tying a shoelace, when he heard it.

Holy smoke, that plane was not only coming this way again, it was coming in low. Very low.

In fact, it was *landing*. . . .

It blew past him, contacted the sand, and bounced lightly along the beach. As it slowed, farther along the strand, the tail came up, then settled again.

He might have been plugged into an electrical outlet the way his scalp was tingling. It couldn't be, he thought, as he saw the doors open. . . .

But it was.

Barking wildly, Barnabas jerked the leash from under his foot and bounded toward the red plane and the people clambering out of it.

"Omer! Dooley!"

No, indeed, he would not bawl like a baby. He wiped his eyes on the sleeve of his jacket as he sprinted behind his dog. Amazing grace! Hallelujah! Unbelievable!

And it wasn't just Omer and Dooley.

"Pauline!" he yelled to the woman running toward him. *"Buck!"*

Dooley reached him first. "Hey," he said, throwing his arms around Father Tim, who hugged back for all he was worth.

"Hey, yourself, buddy, hey, yourself!"

Dooley cackled. "You're breakin' my ribs! Hey, ol' dog, ol' Barn, ol' buddy." Dooley fell onto the sand with Barnabas, as Pauline shyly gave Father Tim a hug, and Buck and Omer pounded him on the back to a fare-thee-well.

"This is my little Stinson Voyager," said Omer. His proud smile revealed teeth large enough to replace the ivories on an upright. "What d'you think?"

"Beautiful! Handsome! A sight for sore eyes!" said Father Tim.

Buck grinned at him, looking pounds lighter and years younger. "We buzzed over here a little bit ago, checkin' out th' beach. We thought it was you we saw."

"Yeah," said Dooley, "how did you know we were coming?"

"I didn't!"

"Cool."

Omer gave the Voyager's rear tire a swift kick. "Tundra tires. Got those special, since I knew I'd be comin' down on a soft field. By th' way, I had my buddy in Raleigh check it out, he said this end of th' beach was church property, so we could land here, no problem.

"Lookit!" Omer dragged him to the open door and pointed to a storage box behind the backseat. Father Tim smelled something wonderful.

"We're carryin' beef stew, we got fried chicken, we got bottled water, an' . . . what else we got?" he asked Pauline.

"The ham Emma baked for tomorrow!" said Pauline, flushed with excitement. "And Miz Bolick's orange marmalade cake."

"Yeah!" said Dooley. "Three layers! Plus stuff that Tony and Mr. Gregory and Anna sent, but it all smells like garlic."

Omer was busy pulling cargo from behind the seat. "Couldn't haul but forty pounds, what with icin' down th' food and carryin' three passengers, but we got more comin' next trip."

"Let me get a wheelbarrow," said Father Tim. "We're covered up with wheelbarrows at church."

Out of the corner of his eye, Father Tim saw several onlookers gathering.

"You probably don't want to leave it here long. Whitecap is full of nice people, but . . ."

"Oh, I ain't goin' to leave it here long a'tall. I'm makin' a run back to Mitford here in a little bit."

"Back to Mitford?"

"See, tomorrow mornin,' I'm haulin' young 'uns."

"Poo and Jessie," said Dooley. "They're comin'."

"Ah," he said, trying to understand.

Dooley adjusted his ball cap. "You better tell 'im, Mama."

"Well," said Pauline. She looked suddenly shy. "Well . . ."

"We tried to call," said Buck, "but we couldn't get through."

"See, what it is," said Dooley, "is Mama and Buck want you to marry 'em tomorrow."

Buck Leeper, who had probably never blushed in his life, turned beet red. "If you don't mind."

"When I heard what was goin' on," said Omer, "I offered to fly 'em down here."

More hand-shaking, back-slapping, and riotous barking as his delirious dog dashed around them in circles.

Hauling a trunk full of food and water, he drove Dooley to the Fieldwalkers', where he let his wife weep the tears he was holding back. That was just one of the many conveniences of marriage, he thought, as Cynthia bawled and clung to Dooley like moss to a log.

On the way to St. John's, he figured Stanley would let him use the sanctuary for the wedding tomorrow afternoon. If that didn't work, surely they'd loan their basement hall. Then, if worse came to worst, there was always the Town Hall—not a pretty sight, but he'd heard of couples getting married there.

Whatever happened would have to happen fast.

Lord, he prayed . . .

They said goodbye to Omer, who was leaving with half the crowd trailing along to see the takeoff.

"What it is," Omer explained as they headed down the lane, "is a complete fabric aircraft. You've got your steel-tube fuselage with a fabric cover . . ."

"Could I go in th' church and look around?" asked Buck.

"Sure, grab a hard hat, I'll go in with you. The crew's packing up to leave. They'll be back on Monday and things will start to get serious around here."

Pauline beamed. "Buck don't have to go far to find a hard hat," she said. "May I come in, too?"

"Come on!" he said. "But watch your step. There's plaster lying forty ways from Sunday."

He called Sew Joiner aside. "Before your men leave, there's something I'd like them to do, if possible. We've just had a very . . . unusual request."

During the impromptu and elaborate meal at the Fieldwalkers', which Marion called a rehearsal dinner, Father Tim proposed a toast to Buck and Pauline. Buck, who was unaccustomed to much society, bobbed his head with awkward appreciation. Pauline smiled and held his hand, saying little, owing to the fullness of a heart overcome with wonder, and what she supposed might even be joy.

Before Tony's tiramisu was passed around, Cynthia and Pauline trundled off to the bedroom with a kerosene lamp to view the wedding frock. Father Tim loved hearing peals of his wife's laughter issuing from the room, as such frivolity had recently been as scarce as hen's teeth.

He put his arm around Dooley, noting that the boy was now a couple of inches taller than himself. He also checked the look on Dooley's face. Was he happy about his mother marrying Buck Leeper? As far as Father Tim could tell, the answer was yes, definitely.

Following an evening made more festive by candles and a crackling fire, Buck and Dooley were dispatched to Room Twenty-two at the Mid-Way. Pauline was invited to bunk in with the Fieldwalkers, who noted that the guest room leak had stopped and another chamber pot had been improvised.

Otis announced that the Kavanaghs would be moving on Tuesday afternoon into the million-dollar home of Martha Talbot, a seasonal resident from Canada who hadn't been in Whitecap for two seasons, due to a series of family weddings from Brazil to Portugal, not to mention Bar Harbor, Maine.

It was all quite breathtaking, thought Father Tim, as he climbed into his pajamas and fell, deeply weary and as deeply grateful, onto the lumpy bed of Room Fourteen.

But he couldn't sleep.

He lay listening to the hiss of the heater and his wife's whiffling snore. Jonathan thrashed and turned, kicking him in the ribs once, then twice.

Numb with exhaustion, he got up and put on his robe and slippers, lit the kerosene lantern, and sat in the worn armchair by the window. A ten o'clock service followed by a one-thirty wedding tomorrow, and here he was at half-past midnight, his eyes as big as the headlights on Loretta Burgess's eighteen-wheeler.

He went to the bathroom and did a glucometer check. Ah, well, no more tiramisu for him for a while; he'd be chopped liver tomorrow.

He took his Bible from the windowsill, opened it in the low light, and closed his eyes and prayed. *Thank you, Lord. . . .*

Let's face it, he could have been fished up from the bottom of Judd's Creek. The nail in the picket could have pierced Cynthia's eye instead of her hand. If Maude Proffitt hadn't jumped when she did, her ceiling would have landed on her head instead of her recliner. The list was endless. St. John's might have been completely demolished, the whole tree could have come down . . .

Jericho.

He jerked awake, realizing he'd dozed off. Out of the blue, a word had come upon his heart.

He saw the word in his mind as if it were inscribed on a blackboard with white chalk, *J E R I C H O.*

"Jericho," he whispered, puzzled. Barnabas stirred at his feet.

Lord, is this of You? Are you telling me something?

He examined his heart, and realized he felt the peace he always required in order to know whether God was in a particular circumstance.

Intrigued, he turned in his Bible to the Old Testament, to the sixth chapter of Joshua, and began to read:

"Now Jericho was securely shut up . . ."

Out of curiosity, Ray Gaskill opened the door of St. John's on Sunday around noon, and gaped at what he saw.

The shattered plaster had been hauled to either side of the nave and covered with tarps. The floor in the middle had been swept perfectly clean, the broken windows covered, and the rolling scaffolds parked neatly at the rear of the nave.

The pulpit had come out from under its tarp and shone with a lustrous coat of lemon wax, as did two pews that were aligned to face the pulpit. Oil-fired heaters, hissing warmth, flanked the pews on either side.

On a table before the altar, which was laid with an embroidered fair cloth and a silver chalice, paten, and candelabra, stood a vase displaying stems of gold leaves and red berries.

Above the wooden cross, the bright autumn noon gave its light through the window where He stood, arms outstretched, waiting.

CHAPTER TWENTY

Dearly Beloved

"Dearly beloved: We have come together in the presence of God, to witness and bless the joining together of this man and this woman in Holy Matrimony."

He knew most of the service by heart, never liking to see a priest's eyes glued to the prayer book instead of the congregation. He spoke the words today with unusually tender feeling.

"The bond and covenant of marriage was established by God in creation, and our Lord Jesus Christ adorned this manner of life by His presence and first miracle at a wedding in Cana of Galilee. It signifies to us the mystery of the union between Christ and His Church, and Holy Scripture commends it to be honored among all people.

"The union of husband and wife in heart, body, and mind is intended by God for their mutual joy; for the help and comfort given one another in prosperity and adversity . . ."

In the front row, Jessie played with the ruffle on her new dress, Poo gave the proceedings his absorbed attention, Dooley looked oddly proud and moved. Cynthia was beaming.

". . . therefore, marriage is not to be entered into unadvisedly or lightly, but reverently, deliberately, and in accordance with the purposes for which it was instituted by God.

"Into this holy union, Pauline Barlowe and Bernard Leeper now come to be joined."

There were enough teeth showing in Omer Cunningham's grin to play the Wedding March.

"Pauline, will you have this man to be your husband; to live together in the covenant of marriage? Will you love him, comfort him, honor and keep him, in sickness and in health; and, forsaking all others, be faithful to him as long as you both shall live?"

Pauline's response was a fervent whisper. "I will!"

Otis Bragg pulled a handkerchief from his plaid sport coat and blew his nose. Marion Fieldwalker dabbed at her eyes; Sam appeared personally pleased, as if the whole lot of Barlowes were, at the very least, first cousins.

"Bernard, will you have this woman to be your wife; to live together in the covenant of marriage? Will you love her, comfort her, honor and keep her, in sickness and in health; and, forsaking all others, be faithful to her as long as you both shall live?"

He saw Buck's eyes mist with tears. Then Buck cleared his throat and spoke in a voice that could be heard to the ceiling joists.

"I will!"

"Will all of you witnessing these promises do all in your power to uphold these two persons in their marriage?"

Dooley spontaneously stood, then sat again, as those assembled chorused in unison, "We *will*!"

He was choking up, himself. He touched his ear, a signal to his wife to pray for him, and step on it.

"Who gives this woman to be married to this man?"

Dooley rose from the pew and came forward, white-faced. Though his heart hammered with anxiety at the responsibility he was about to bear, he felt powerfully certain that this was a good thing; his mother would have someone to care for her, and for the first time ever, his brother and sister would have a real family.

The wedding feast was laid in the basement fellowship hall of First Baptist, where a motley collection of portable generators helped create the welcome aromas of garlic, coffee, hot rolls, and other comestibles, lightly dressed with the scent of gasoline from the generators.

The feast tables were covered with blue paper cloths, and decorated with boughs of red berries purloined from a stand of nandina behind the Sunday School. Votives glimmered on the tables, and along the top of the spinet by the kitchen door.

"Here they come!" someone shouted.

Laughing and excited, St. John's choir, joined by a baritone and soprano from First Baptist, assembled breathlessly in the middle of the room.

As the bride and groom entered, a cheer went up from all who had attended Stanley Harmon's morning service and were thus invited to the feast; then followed the exultant voices of the choir.

"Praise, my soul, the King of heaven
to his feet thy tribute bring;
ransomed, healed, restored, forgiven,
evermore his praises sing:
Alleluia, alleluia!
Praise the everlasting King!"

Pauline Leeper put both hands over her face like an unbelieving schoolgirl, and felt the arm of her husband go around her shoulders. Then she heard the oohs and aahs of her children, who stood beside her. She thought she might never again see, or be blessed with, anything so wondrous.

Following the blessing and subsequent hymn, Father Tim had a moment's thought of Jeffrey Tolson and the earnest choir he had abandoned. His heart felt suddenly moved toward the man; he wondered where he might be, whether he'd escaped harm during the storm, and if he ever longed for his children. Father Tim watched with both sadness and delight as Jeffrey's son made a beeline toward him with an Oreo cookie in each hand, eager to share one. He squatted and proffered the palm of his own hand, eager to receive it.

"Law, where'd this cake *come* from?"

"I don't know, plus, who could bake a cake without electricity? Does anybody know who brought it?"

"I heard it was flown in special."

"I declare, this is th' best cake I ever put in my *mouth*."

"I'd give an arm an' a leg for th' recipe, wouldn't you?"

"If nobody minds, I'm goin' to just scrape off these crumbs that're left and give 'em to Mama—then somebody, meanin' me, can lick th' plate it came on."

He had reserved a piece of the cake, which he wrapped in foil.

He also retrieved a large chunk of lasagna, the drumstick of a baked chicken, four slices of ham, and two biscuits, which he loaded onto a heavy-duty paper plate with a border of irises. He went to the cupboards and found a deluxe-size plastic cup, and stuffed it with potato salad.

Morris Love had been on his mind, and he couldn't shake the thought. He was alone in that dark, rambling house with only candles to light his way, and apparently no clue how to feed himself, unless Mamie was there to do it for him. Even so, she wouldn't have power for cooking, and no Stinson Voyager hauling in victuals.

Aha. A maverick deviled egg. He was tempted to eat it himself, being inordinately fond of deviled eggs, but popped it into a Ziploc sandwich bag. Oh, the infinite resources of a church kitchen . . .

He rummaged around until he found a large, empty jar, took the lid off, and sniffed it. Pickles. He rinsed it out with water from a plastic jug, and filled it with sweet tea.

"I'll be right back," he told his wife. "Looks like this will go on for at least another hour."

"Where on earth . . . ?" she asked, wondering at the bulging plastic grocery bag.

"I'll tell you later." He gave her a jovial kiss, square on the mouth.

Things were different now that the weather had turned cooler. There was no open window to shout to.

At the door, he stood on one foot and then the other, and scratched his head.

Why not ring the bell? That was an original thought!

He pressed the bell, but heard no results from inside. Maybe the bell had a quirk, like most doorbells, and had to be pressed in a certain way. He pressed again. Nothing. What Morris Love needed was a *dog*, for Pete's sake.

When he carved out the chunk of lasagna at church, it was still warm. If he kept standing here, it would be cold.

Hardly believing his audacity, he opened the door and stuck his head into the dim foyer.

"Morris!" he yelled, loudly enough to be heard upstairs. "Morris, it's me, Tim Kavanagh! I've brought your *supper*!"

There, that ought to get a rise out of a man who was, for all he knew, subsisting on Fig Newtons.

"Father . . ."

He nearly jumped out of his skin. Morris Love appeared from behind the stairwell, a ghostly apparition if he'd ever seen one.

"Holy smoke, Morris, sorry I was yelling when you were standing right there."

"Come in," Morris said, not appearing to mean it.

He followed Morris into the cold and cavernous kitchen, illumined only by two small windows above the sink, and set the bag on the table.

"The lasagna is still warm," he said. "I hope you'll eat it soon."

He felt like a mother coaxing a child, and stood back from the table, suddenly awkward.

"Thank you," said Morris, standing with his hands in the pockets of a burgundy bathrobe.

Thank you? A mere *thank you*? He wanted to see the man tear open the bag and dive in!

Father Tim opened the bag and pulled out the heavy plate and set it on the table. "It's on a plate," he said, feeling progressively uneasy. "You can just peel off the aluminum foil. And here's some tea, I put lemon in it. . . ."

Somewhere in the house, a clock chimed three o'clock.

"Well . . . ," he said, not knowing what else to say.

"Your neighborly kindness will, I'm sure, guarantee your place in heaven," said Morris.

Father Tim found his scowling countenance formidable in the dusky light. "Ah, well, it's not kindness that gets us into heaven," he said, feeling himself in quagmire to his knees.

Morris narrowed his eyes. "I would ask you to consider that I have lived alone without the sap of neighborly interaction for most of my life. And yet, over and over again, you would intrude upon the privacy and solitude I find agreeable. This behavior, which I fail entirely to understand, exhibits the most careless disrespect."

"But . . ."

"I am not a novelty, Father, some bizarre experiment to satisfy your prejudices about the essential spirituality of the human heart. I do not need your kindness, nor do I want your salvation."

"It is not my salvation."

"In addition, I do not desire your friendship, nor do I crave your admiration of my pathetic musical skills."

Father Tim felt an alarming weakness in his legs.

"One further thing. Save your breath, Father, and stop praying for me."

He found his ground, and stood it. "Save your own breath, Morris. I shall pray for you until . . ." His mind raced. *Until the Lord comes with his hosts? Until it suits me to stop?*

". . . until the cows come home!" He delivered this fervent declamation straight up and straight out, meaning it from the depths of his being.

He turned from the kitchen and walked quickly across the foyer, hearing the chilling and inevitable words that cut like knives.

"Out! *Out!*"

Closing the front door behind him, he trotted up the driveway in the late afternoon light that slanted through the canopy of trees.

They were crammed into Room Fourteen like sardines in a tin, seven of them, including Violet and Barnabas.

He thought the least they could do was give the Fieldwalkers and Lambs a break. Not only had their good friends pulled off a feast for more than forty people, they'd come in behind the work crew's cleanup and readied the altar and nave for the wedding.

Though a small and certainly impromptu wedding, he noted it was kicking up a considerable swirl of activity.

Buck had reserved a couple of additional rooms, which were in the process of being cleaned, for Omer and the kids, all of which occasioned the hauling of various sacks, pokes, and grips from Room Fourteen into adjacent quarters, with much trailing of vagrant socks and sweaters, and leaving open of the door—a feature his dog particularly relished.

As Omer rambled in the village, and the newlyweds inspected the island in one of Otis's pickup trucks, he and Cynthia put their heads together about dinner. Should they even have dinner, since they'd eaten at two-thirty? Children were always hungry, weren't they? Of course.

But then, Mona's was shut tight as a clam on Sunday, which occasioned searching the yellow pages for what was open across, reminding them of Cap'n Willie's, which seemed the perfect solution; further, he learned that Pauline, Buck, and Jessie were flying home first thing in the morning with Omer, and Harley was arriving this evening to fetch Dooley and Poo back to Mitford early tomorrow, as Omer couldn't do another double airlift, given his need to attend a huge going-away party for his sister-in-law and outgoing mayor, Esther Cunningham, imminently headed west with her husband in the RV.

Breathless, Father Tim reserved a room for Harley, whose reason for an early departure tomorrow morning, according to Dooley, was the emergency overhaul he was doing on the motor in Lew Boyd's wrecker.

The crowd from next door returned, vibrating with energy.

He hated to bring up the unwelcome subject. "I thought you had to be in court tomorrow morning."

"Oh," said Dooley. "I forgot."

"Forgot what?"

"Buster Austin went bawlin' to Chief Underwood and said he was th' one that done it . . . did it . . . not me. He was scared out of his mind about goin' in front of a judge, so they ain't . . . isn't . . . any court. Not for me, anyway. Sorry I forgot to tell you. There was so much goin' on. . . ."

Father Tim sank onto the foot of the bed, feeling as if a great weight had rolled off his shoulders.

"Oh, somethin' else I forgot. Harley said your cousin Walter called, said he couldn't get in touch with you down here, said he had somethin' to tell you about a lawsuit, somethin' really important, said to call him."

The lawsuit!

The weight that had just rolled off, rolled back on and dug in.

"Ahh," he said, wanting nothing more than to seek the opiate of sleep, to put the lawsuit, the storm, the sickening confrontation with Morris Love, out of his mind.

He stood and put on his jacket. "Let's go for a ride," he said to Dooley. "I'll show you around the island."

"Cool," said Dooley. "I'll drive!"

"We want to go, *too*!" shouted Jessie.

Barnabas trotted to the door and sat, looking hopeful.

Poo raced from the bathroom. "Can we go see the lighthouse?"

"I could, I could go, too," said Jonathan, pulling on his hat and grabbing his coat.

Father Tim turned to his wife, who looked decidedly pale around the gills. "Hallelujah," she murmured.

"When we get back to that place we're stayin' at, you can be it," said Jessie.

"It what?" asked Poo.

"Th' husband."

"I don't want to be no husband."

"See, you can marry Jonathan, and I'll say th' words, 'cause I like them words."

"I ain't marryin' no baby," said Poo.

"I'm *not* a baby!" exclaimed Jonathan.

"Well, so Jonathan can be Buck, I can be Mama, and *you* can say th' words, then."

"Say what words?" asked Poo.

"Dearly belove-ud."

"I ain't sayin' that."

Dooley looked into the rearview mirror. "Don't say ain't!" he told his brother.

He lay curled in the fetal position, his back to his wife and Jonathan, feeling a kind of numb pain he couldn't explain or understand. Life was a roller coaster, that simple. Joy and healing here, desperation and demolition there.

With all his heart, he'd desired healing for Morris Love's brokenness, and who was he to think he might give a leg up to such a miracle? There were times when he didn't like being a priest, always on the front line for justice and mercy and forgiveness and redemption; trying to figure out the mind of God; giving the Lord his personal agenda, then standing around waiting for it to be fulfilled. He didn't have an agenda for Morris Love, anymore; he was giving up the entire self-seeking, willful notion. His desperate neighbor belonged to God; it was His responsibility to get the job done. He had schlepped in a paltry sack of victuals when what the man needed was the awesome, thunderstriking power of the Almighty to move in his heart and soul and spirit like a great and consuming fire. . . .

He wiped his eyes on his pajama sleeve.

"So, Lord," he whispered, "just do it."

Though he managed to spend a full half hour with Buck, he had almost no time with Dooley. On Monday morning, he insisted on making the breakfast run to Mona's, and let Dooley drive. They arrived at Mona's as she opened the doors, and waited in the front booth while the kitchen pulled together sacks of sausage biscuits, ham biscuits, fries, Danish, coffee, milk, and Coke for the crowd at Mid-Way.

"How are things with Caroline?" He already knew about Dooley's grades, which were excellent and worthy of all praise. Now he was going for the nitty-gritty.

Dooley reached into the neck of his sweatshirt. Grinning, he pulled forth a small gold ring, set with a single pearl and attached to a chain he was wearing around his neck.

"What does that mean . . . umm, exactly?"

Dooley shrugged. "Just . . . you know."

"Right. Ever see Lace?"

"I ran into her at the drugstore one Saturday. She was in White Chapel with a bunch of girls."

"Did you talk?"

Dooley shrugged again. "Not exactly."

Oh, well. Time would tell.

The boy was becoming handsome, that simple. Father Tim observed sinew gathering on his bones, and noted that his long, slender fingers would be well suited, indeed, to his calling. "Any more thoughts on whether to vet small animals or large?"

"Both," Dooley said with feeling. "I want to vet both."

"Good!" he said. "Good."

"Harley, thanks for making such a long trip. Sorry Omer's plane won't hold but four."

"Don't even think about it, Rev'rend. Hit was good t' git on th' road."

"What do you see of our tenant?"

"Seen 'er twice. She looked kind of hunkered down, like she's scared of 'er own shadow. Somebody said she was lettin' 'er piana students go, an' headin' back up north. She ain't tryin' to run out on th' rent, is she?"

"Oh, no, she's paid up. Well, God be with you, Harley, Poo, Dooley."

" 'Bye, Dad."

" 'Bye, Buddy. See you down here for Christmas, OK?"

"OK!"

"Harley, we want you to come, too."

"Yes, sir, Rev'rend, we'll be here."

"All right, hold her between the ditches."

Feeling a kind of emptiness, he watched the red truck pull out of the motel parking lot and head left on the highway toward Mitford.

"Fella down th' beach said he was sittin' on his deck, said he'd just pulled out his glasses to read th' paper when a book fell in his lap, *whop*."

"No kidding." He had to get out of here fast; he'd only popped by to see how Ernie's reconstruction was coming.

"I'm tellin' you!" said Ernie, who appeared to be more like his old self. "*Th' Mustangs* by Frank Dobie is what it was. That book come right offa my shelf."

"Amazing," he said, wanting to be respectful.

"Bull," said Roanoke.

"Th' storm was Thursday, th' book dropped in 'is lap Sunday.

Must've blowed somewhere to dry off, then was picked up by a stiff wind and sent south."

Roanoke fired a match head under the tabletop and lit a Marlboro. "I ain't believin' that."

"Told me he liked th' book all right, but wouldn't give two cents for th' endin'."

"That's gratitude for you," said Roanoke.

He didn't want to do this, not at all.

"Walter Kavanagh here."

"Walter . . ."

"Timothy! What in blazes happened down there?"

"Storm. Bad. Busy." Sheer dread had reduced his speech to primitive monosyllables.

"Well," said Walter, "I'm afraid you're not going to like this."

"It never once occurred to me that I might like it."

"D'Anjou says a love letter accompanies the holographic will, which makes the old man's personal feelings and legal intentions perfectly clear and in accordance with the will."

"How do we know it's Josiah's Baxter's handwriting and not some forgery?"

"D'Anjou seems to believe that matter is sufficiently demonstrable in court, he didn't say how. Frankly, I think d'Anjou is behind this thing and pushing hard. He's been minding the family's affairs for years. I get a sense of personal greed here. If it were my case, I wouldn't feel so confident—I mean, no one coming forward for fifty years? But he thinks he can convince the jury."

"What about the money Miss Sadie left to Dooley?" Walter and Cynthia were the only other living souls who knew that Miss Sadie had left Dooley more than a million dollars in trust. "That was her mother's money. Surely this legal action couldn't—"

"No, I don't think so. Don't get ahead of things, Timothy. In any case, it looks like we have to go through with this. I'll work with you on the response to the court; we've got three weeks to pull it together. Can you call me Wednesday night? I have some ideas."

Though he knew full well there was no sorrow in heaven, he hoped, nonetheless, that Miss Sadie wouldn't get wind of this deplorable mess. Shortly before her death, she'd learned of an illegitimate half-sister, born to her mother before she married Josiah Baxter. This dark secret, however, had an exceedingly bright side—Miss Sadie ended up with Olivia Harper as her beloved grandniece, which had been, of course, an inarguable benediction.

But another illegitimate half-sister? It seemed like pure fiction; he hated to think what this lawsuit might have done to his old friend and parishioner if she were still living.

In ways he couldn't yet fully understand, he sensed his life would be entwined with Sadie Baxter for the rest of his days.

At one o'clock on Tuesday, he drove to the Mid-Way from a couple of home visits, and helped Cynthia load Jonathan's things into the car. Jonathan talked endlessly.

"I'm goin' home, Cyn'dy."

"I know, dear."

"Will you come an' see me?"

"Of course."

"An' you can see Babette an' Jason, too."

"Will you come and see us?"

"Maybe I could sometime." Jonathan put on his hat.

"We'll bring your movies later. They're at our house that fell down in the front."

"You could, you could watch 'em again before you bring 'em to my house. That would be OK if you want to."

He glanced at his wife as they piled into the car, and felt her suffering as his own.

He was fairly stunned when he saw Martha Talbot's house, sitting quite alone at the end of an oyster-shell lane. A million smackers rising off the undeveloped bank of the Sound was a pretty impressive sight.

"Wow," Cynthia whispered.

"You must be living right, Kavanagh."

They parked in the two-car garage, simply because it was a luxury to have one, and went up the stairs to the front door.

"Here," he said, giving her the key. "You do the honors."

As the door swung open, they stood looking across the sunlit living room and through the wall of windows to the Sound. The water lay as smooth as a lake, glinting in the sun.

His wife gave a small gasp of wonder and delight.

"Now we're talking!" she said.

They prowled through the spacious house like a couple of kids, amazed at their discoveries. Central vacuum system, enormous fireplace in both living room and master suite, glorious views all around, a room with the right light and location for her work, a room with a comfortable and easy spirit for his study, an intercom system, a large kitchen in which they felt decidedly lost, and a media room that, thanks to its dumbfounding technology and wall-size television screen, caused them to shut the door hastily.

They thumped onto one of two sofas in the living room, thinking to build a fire against the chill.

"Well," he said.

"Well," she said.

He wouldn't have mentioned it for the world, but he wished they had Jonathan to put some life in this place.

"Let's unload the car, then. I'll bring Barnabas and Violet up."

"Wouldn't it be marvelous if we had power?" she mused.

"Just in case, try the lamp."

Sixty watts sprang to life at her touch. "Thanks be to God!" they shouted in spontaneous unison.

They leaped up and dashed to the kitchen and turned on the faucet, which spat and chugged and released a brackish stream of water into the sink.

"Try the phone!" she crowed.

A dial tone!

"The heat . . ." They trotted in tandem, searching for a thermostat.

Having located it at the end of the hallway, they grabbed each other and exchanged a fervent hug as the furnace roared into action.

"Priest and deacon die and go to heaven!" he whooped.

Ah, but no million-dollar house on the Sound could ease the sorrow of his wife's heart.

He lay in the strange bed and held her as she wept.

Maybe the bright, three-quarter moon was keeping him awake. . . .

He got up and looked through the French doors that gave onto the upstairs deck. A ribbon of platinum cascaded across the water. Only a mile and a half from Dove Cottage and they were in another world. A miraculous thing.

He closed the draperies over the doors, patted his sleeping dog at the foot of the bed, and lay down again.

He remembered the sleepless exhaustion that had helped crank his diabetes into high gear.

Hadn't Hoppy advised him to find a good doctor when he arrived? Of course. But had he done it? No way.

No more excuses, he promised himself. He would inquire around first thing tomorrow morning. And he must rid his mind of the lawsuit. It was useless to worry and fret about this alarming thing. He and Walter would do what they could; beyond that, he was dependent upon grace alone.

Be anxious for nothing . . .

He began to mentally recite one of the verses he'd tried to live by for a very long time.

. . . but in everything, with prayer and supplication, with thanksgiving, make your requests known unto God, and the peace that passes all understanding will fill your heart and mind through Christ Jesus.

"Ahhh," he sighed.

Jericho.

Not that again.

Lord, I'm no mind-reader. Reveal to me, please, what You're talking about here.

He tried to open his heart and mind to the answer, but dozed off and fell, at last, into a peaceful slumber.

As twilight drew over the Sound, he heard the front bell ring and trotted to the door, wondering who'd be poking around out here.

He saw a car parked in the circle, and a woman standing at the foot of the steps. Before him on the stoop were two small persons in pirate costumes, and a very much smaller person clad in a sheet and extending a plastic pumpkin in his direction.

"Trick or treat!" said Jonathan Tolson.

Feeling oddly distant from one another as they sat in the chairs that flanked the fireplace, they piled onto a sofa. "You know what I'm craving?" she asked.

"I can't begin to know."

"Your mother's pork roast with those lovely angel biscuits."

"My dear Kavanagh, who was it who refused to tote the Dutch oven on our journey into the unknown?"

"I was wrong and I admit it. Can't you make her roast without it?"

"I never have."

"Does that mean you never will?"

"A pork roast in that oven is a guaranteed, hands-down success. Why should I be tempted to veer off on some reckless tangent, like wrapping it in foil or roasting it on a pizza pan or whatever?"

"You're using your pulpit voice," she remonstrated.

"A thousand pardons," he said, getting up to fiddle with the dials on the home entertainment system and trying to make something, *anything,* happen.

"Julia Child didn't require a Dutch oven to make a pork roast," she said, arching one eyebrow.

"And how did you come by this arcane knowledge?"

"I looked it up in her cookbooks in our new kitchen."

"Well," he said, not knowing what else to say.

"Five pounds of flour . . . ," she murmured, making a list. Cynthia Kavanagh was bound and determined to have biscuits on her dinner plate, whate'er betide.

"Do we really want to buy flour, only to haul it back to Dove Cottage?"

"How long do you expect we'll be here?"

"They said the job will probably take three weeks, four at the most."

"Right. Now, double that prediction, thanks to lumber that doesn't arrive on time or is out of stock altogether, and for the crew who decides to go to another job for a whole week, and the rainy weather that makes the floor too tacky for us to move in for ten days, and . . . you get the idea."

"Two months," he said. "Buy the flour."

Cynthia saluted him with her glass. "Here's to Martha Talbot!"

"And here's to Miss Child, bless her heart!"

He wouldn't admit it, of course, but this was as toothsome a pork roast as a man could want, not to mention their first square meal at Sound Doctrine, the name they found engraved on a plaque at the door.

"Three guesses!" said Emma, munching what sounded like popcorn.

"Andrew won by a landslide!"

"Well, he won, all right, but not by a *landslide*, a lot of people who were born in Mitford voted for Coot. Anyway, guess what else."

"Just tell me and get it over with."

"No, you have to guess. Guess what's going to happen to Coot as soon as Andrew's sworn in."

"He'll be the envoy to our sister village of Mitford, England?"

"No, but I love the idea of a sister village! Somebody ought to recommend that to Andrew, he'd pick right up on it. Guess again."

"I give up." After one guess, she usually let him off the hook.

"Andrew's goin' to appoint him to chair a historical committee!"

What he'd always feared might be true, he now knew for a fact—in appointing Coot Hendrick to chair any committee at all, Andrew Gregory had proved to be a man of far greater largesse than himself.

He'd done his utmost to sever the umbilical cord that typically united a parish to a long-term priest, and felt it was at last a done deal. Indeed, he hadn't heard a word from Esther Bolick or anybody else at Lord's Chapel in a month of Sundays. So, the heck with his interim bishop and two-for-a-penny wisdom, he was calling the Bolicks.

"Esther?"

"Who's this?"

"How quickly you forget. It's your old priest."

"Father Hammond?"

"Esther!"

"Just kidding. How in th' world are you? We hadn't heard from you in a coon's age."

"Lots to do in a new parish, but I think about you and Gene and pray for you faithfully. How is he?"

"Better. I've tried to stop worryin' myself sick."

"I'm very glad to hear it. And you may be glad to hear that your fame now extends to Whitecap. In truth, I'm calling with a total of eleven requests for your marmalade cake recipe. I know you don't give it out, but they implored me to ask."

"Eleven?" He didn't know whether she was pleased with the number or disappointed.

"I'm sure as many more are interested, but I've personally received the names of eleven, including that of the Baptist preacher who's renowned for his lemon meringue pie."

"Oh, all right," she said, "I don't see why not. That recipe's been bootlegged forty ways for Sunday, anyhow."

"They'll be thrilled, and not only that, I'll be a hero."

"Cynthia has a copy I told her she could use. She can pass that around."

"Yes, but it's in Mitford. Do you think you could mail me a copy?"

"I declare, that recipe will pester me to my grave. But I'll do it. What's your address?"

"Just send it to St. John's, post office box fourteen." He gave her the zip code. "Bless you, Esther."

"Father Talbot moved into that big house up th' street from the Harpers. He's th' handsomest thing you'd ever want to see, an' th' whitest teeth, oh, mercy. . . ."

He seemed to recall hearing this before.

"We think he bleaches, you know, wears what they call bleach trays, like people on TV."

"So, I'm glad to know Gene is—"

"And *nice*? You wouldn't want to *see* nicer! Crosses th' street to talk to you, waves at you from his car . . . not to mention has been to visit Gene on a house call, and he was just *installed* two days ago!"

"My goodness," he said, quoting Sam.

"And his children—why, they're meek as lambs and smart as whips, plus you should see his wife, she's a regular movie star. And *preach*? Up a *storm*! Why, he brings th' house down! We're goin' to tie his leg to the altar, is what Gene says. This one's too good to let get away."

"Ahhh," he said, exhaling.

He and Walter had talked for more than an hour, but he felt precious little consolation.

What should he do, if anything, about the rumor she was moving back to Boston? Didn't she owe him the courtesy of telling him she was leaving? On the other hand, what did courtesy have to do with anything—under the circumstances?

Walter suggested he lie low on that one, but go ahead and inform the Hope House board of the lawsuit.

He dreaded this like the plague, for more reasons than one. He would wait until after the weekend, when things were . . . calmer. At the moment, St. John's was under exterior scaffolding front to back, a Bobcat was digging out part of the basement, and a backhoe was on the job, doing God knows what. As anyone in their right mind could see, this was no time to call a board and relay bad news.

As he and Cynthia offered their nighttime prayers, he exhorted the Lord with something from "St. Patrick's Hymn at Evening."

" 'May our sleep be deep and soft,' " he whispered, " 'so our work be fresh and hard.' "

His wife, who was again going at her book hammer and tong, liked St. Patrick's way of putting it.

Nonetheless, he still wasn't sleeping soundly.

And he could scarcely believe what he felt God was writing upon his heart.

"You're sure about this?" he asked aloud, standing on the upstairs deck at sunset. A snowy egret flew over the roof and settled into the tall grasses at water's edge.

"I'd hate to get this wrong," he said.

Then again, if he got it wrong, what did he have to lose?

Nothing.

Nothing to lose, and everything to gain.

He spent much of Monday morning speaking with Hoppy Harper and other members of the board. They were shocked, of course. But he was glad he made the calls, because they were rallying together, and he felt the encouragement of it.

They agreed that it was a blow, but if the suit succeeded, they felt they could replace the money via other avenues.

He felt the encouragement, yes, but in the very pit of his stomach was a sick feeling that appeared to be lodged in for the long haul.

"Barnabas and I are going to walk around the old neighborhood, see what's what." Nine o'clock, now, and a meeting at ten with Sewell Joiner at the church. Perfect timing.

"And please do something about cleaning up the car," said Cynthia. "It looks like a farm wagon."

"Consider it done."

"I don't know what you *do* to cars," she muttered.

"We had a storm, remember?"

"But that was days ago, and the rust is going to leap onto the fenders any minute, mark my words."

"Rust . . ."

"It's a living thing, you know. It *grows.* Have you noticed the cars and trucks running around down here? There's hardly anything left but chassis and steering wheel."

"Surely you exaggerate."

"Surely I do, but please—washed and waxed and whatever else it needs; I must have it tomorrow to go up hill and down dale."

"Tomorrow's supposed to be a beautiful day, you could ride your Schwinn."

"Not if it's under Morris Love's stairwell."

"Good point," he said. "See you for lunch."

After checking the progress at Dove Cottage, he began his first march around the wall of Nouvelle Chanson by walking east from the iron gate, hooking a left on Hastings, and praying as he went.

Staying hard by the wall, he trotted north on Hastings and rounded the corner into the lane that dead-ended in front of Ernie's.

He saw the figure up ahead, crossing the lane toward the Love wall. It was someone tall and slender, dark in color, and, though carrying what appeared to be a grocery bag in either arm, moving gracefully.

"Easy," he said to his dog, who was always curious about who and what crossed their path.

Though trying not to stare, he witnessed the sudden collapse of a paper bag, and saw items go spilling onto the sandy lane. Grapefruits rolled hither and yon.

He sprinted ahead.

"Here, let me help!" he said to the woman. "Barnabas, sit!"

Barnabas didn't sit; he reared on his hind legs so he might greet the stranger who stood looking at him with alarm. Grabbing his dog, Father Tim trotted to a small tree growing outside the wall and fastened the leash around it.

"There. I'm sorry. He's harmless." He went to his knees and began collecting grapefruits and bananas, sticks of butter that had burst loose from their package. . . .

"At least there were no eggs," he said, looking up at the elegant, dark-skinned woman who looked down upon him.

"Thank you kindly." Her voice was soft and lilting—genteel, he thought. "That's a big dog," she said simply.

"He is that. Well, now, what shall we put all this in?"

"I'll go back to the house and get my basket," she said. "I almost never carry groceries without my basket, but this mornin' . . . if you'd watch this for me, I'd thank you."

"Be glad to," he said, taking the other bag from her arm.

She walked toward the house at the opposite side of the lane, a house he'd often noticed and admired for its tidy appearance and large, well-tended garden. He'd exchanged greetings with a man working the garden one summer evening, and had occasionally seen a wash hanging on the clothesline. In a world that seldom displayed its wash on a line, the sight always, and happily, took him back to his boyhood.

He stood guarding the small pile of groceries, organized neatly in the middle of the lane, as she left the house and came toward him carrying a large basket. He thought she moved regally for her age, though he couldn't really determine her age.

"Always, always, I use this basket," she said pleasantly, "and this mornin', wouldn't you know . . ."

Together, they stooped down and loaded the basket.

"May I carry it for you?" he asked.

"No, sir," she said, standing. "I'm just goin' right through there." She pointed to an opening in the thick hedge that camouflaged the wall.

"Ah. Morris Love's place."

"Yes, sir."

"You're Mamie," he said, noting her carefully braided hair and the printed scarf tied round like a headband.

"Yes, sir, I'm Mamie. And you're the preacher whose wife sent Mr. Love that nice banana bread."

"I am!" He was as excited as a child. "So pleased to meet you, Miss, Mrs. . . ."

"Just Mamie is all," she said.

"Sure I can't carry that for you? I'd be happy to."

"Thank you, I've been carrying this basket through there for more years than I care to reckon. Well, I hope you'll tell your wife that Mr. Love enjoyed the taste of lemon in her bread."

"Oh, I will. And thank you. Thank you!" A woman with a strong and lively spirit. . . .

Feeling strangely moved and oddly blessed he watched her disappear along a well-worn path through the opening in the wall.

He looked eagerly for her when he circled the wall on the second day, which was Wednesday, but she didn't appear. What he did see was a small wash, neatly arranged on the clothesline and flapping smartly in the November wind.

He received the welcome sight as a sign, a confirmation, and walked on, praying.

He timed his walk around the wall on Thursday for nine-fifteen, which was when they had met, but Mamie was nowhere to be seen. The sight of smoke puffing from her chimney gave him a curious delight, and he wondered why he had such a strong desire to see her again.

He trotted to the end of the lane and then, as he turned left around the wall, the answer came.

It was as if he'd found someone who'd been lost to him for many years.

"Timothy, ring Harley, he's at Lew Boyd's. I wrote the number by the phone."

"How's the book coming?" he called as he popped into his study at Sound Doctrine.

"Great! I've something to show you after dinner!"

It had taken his wife, who was surprisingly shy about her work, a good two years to open up and really share her work with him. So he was always pleased when . . .

"Lew! Tim Kavanagh here. How's it going?"

"Pretty good, soon as we git this wrecker rollin' again."

"Harley's the one for the job, all right. Is he around?"

"Hold on, and come see us, hear?"

He heard the cash register ring; Lew shouted for Harley; someone asked directions to the restroom.

"Harley speakin'."

"Harley! You called?"

"Yes, sir, I did. Let me get on Lew's cordless."

Static, shuffling around, a horn blowing.

"OK, I'm out at th' grease pit, cain't nobody hear."

He didn't want any bad news, no way. . . .

"Hit looks like I've found y'r angel that was stole."

CHAPTER TWENTY-ONE

True Confessions

"An' you'll not believe where at," said Harley.

"Where?"

"You know that ol' car of Miss Pringle's? Well, she brought it in to git th' fluids changed an' said she'd be travelin' in it pretty soon an' was wantin' it to be safe an' whatnot. Lew was up to th' post office so I said, fine, I'll look after it."

"Right, right."

"She walked up th' street an' I got t' checkin' it out, an' seen 'er tars needed rotatin'. See, I had 'er keys an' all, an' a little time t' do it, an' looked like she'd want me to, so I opened up 'er trunk and lifted that panel in there to see if I could find 'er wheel key. Well, see, they's this deep pocket, you might say, on either side under th' panel. I looked in one side an' th' key wadn't in there, an' they was what looked like a sheet stuffed in th' other side."

He was on the edge of his chair.

"So I pulled th' sheet out to look an' Lord help, there was that angel you had on y'r mantelpiece."

He would not jump to conclusions. "About twenty inches high?"

"Yes, sir. An' kind of a dirty gold."

Bronze. "What sort of base?"

"Marble, looked like."

"What color was the marble?"

"Green. An' since she hadn't asked me direct t' do anything but change th' fluids, I didn't do nothin' to 'er tars, or she might figure I found somethin'. When she come back, I jis' said, Miz Pringle, y'r tars need rotatin'."

He sat back in the chair and felt the beating of his heart.

He preferred acting to reacting.

If Hélène Pringle was leaving for Boston, he needed to act fast.

Certainly, he didn't want to focus on this nasty piece of news as he made his fourth trip around the wall. He wanted to keep his mind and heart free of personal anxiety, so he could pray with an unfettered spirit.

God help me, he thought, as he parked the Mustang at the side of Dove Cottage and set off for Hastings with his dog.

Ernie was standing in the parking lot with a couple of fishermen, and hailed him to come in. Without breaking stride, he raised his hand and waved. "I'll be back!" he called.

The glass had been replaced, the side wall was up, and except for some old bricks that hadn't been hauled away, Books, Bait & Tackle was looking fairly normal.

He was only a few yards this side of the passage in the wall when Mamie came through the front door of her house, carrying an empty wicker laundry basket.

"Good morning, Mamie!"

"Good mornin,' Father. How do you like this weather?"

"Oh, I like it. Crisp!"

"My husband built us a good fire again this mornin'. They're calling for frost tomorrow."

As she stepped into the lane with him, he couldn't contain his question another moment. "May I ask where you were educated?"

"Virginia," she said softly. "Mr. Redmon sent me off to a school for young ladies of color. I was sixteen when I left Whitecap, and came home again when I was twenty."

"Ah," he said. Her gentle elegance was balm to his soul.

"Mr. Redmon had his enemies, but he wasn't a bad man, Father, not at all. He gave my mother this house."

"I like your house!" he said, meaning it.

"I remember when Mr. Morris was born, the year before I went to Virginia. I hated to leave him. He couldn't hold his head up 'til he was several months old and couldn't walk 'til he was two and a half. He was . . . special, something told me that."

"His mother . . . ?"

"His mother ran away from her baby. She could never bear to be with him. He had middle-ear infections for the first few years, and used to cry and cry with the pain. Mr. Redmon had all kind of doctors come here, and then Mr. Morris got the base of his skull operated on. There was no end to the suffering, it seemed. No, his mother ran away and stayed most of her life in Europe. Her and Mr. Redmon's other son died in a bad house fire. It was my own mother who took care of Mr. Morris 'til I came home and helped out."

"I see."

"I don't have any idea why I'm standing here talking to you like this, Father, except I believe you to be a kind man. I wouldn't want Mr. Morris to know we talked about such things."

"No, it's between us."

"I've spent many a year trying to help heal the hurt, but there's only One who can heal."

"Yes." He gazed directly into her eyes, finding a kind of refuge he couldn't name. "Morris is blessed to have you."

"I'm blessed to have him. I never dreamed I'd stay on in Whitecap after I saw a little of the world, but I came home and married a good man, and then, when the Lord took Mother . . ."

"Yes?"

". . . I began treading the path through the hedge, just as she'd done for so long."

"Are there any regrets, Mamie?"

"No regrets. Noah and I raised a fine son. He's a doctor in Philadelphia. He looks in on Mr. Morris every time he comes home."

He was happy to hear everything this unusual woman had to tell him, feeling honored, somehow, that she would talk with him at all.

"I see in your face that you understand Mr. Morris, how he's suffered."

He didn't reply. How could he understand?

"He's known a lot of cruelty in this life. Mr. Redmon demanded an awful lot of him. Yet, look at the gift he's been given. Mother was proud of that, and so am I."

"I hope to meet your husband one day. We said hello this summer. And if you ever take a notion to visit St. John's, we'd love to have you."

"Noah and I go across to church. There were never many people of color on Whitecap. Big Daddy Johnson used to take us across in a little fishing boat, then the ferry came, and then the bridge."

"Were you born here?"

"My people washed up on shore like timbers from the old ships. We think our wreck happened sometime around 1860."

"I've kept you far too long, Mamie, forgive me. You're an interesting and gracious lady, and it's a privilege to have this time together."

"I hated that Mr. Morris had nothing to offer when you and your family visited. The next day was grocery day, and what we had on hand, he couldn't heat in the oven."

"By His grace, we had a feast, and food for the soul, as well!"

"I hope we'll meet again," she said, stepping onto the path with her laundry basket.

"The Lord be with you!" he called after her.

She turned and looked back. " 'And with thy spirit!' " she said, quoting the prayer book. "That school I went to in Virginia was an Episcopal school." She smiled, then turned again and vanished along the path.

"You don't know when she's leaving?"

"No."

"Issue a search warrant for her arrest," said his cousin.

"What?"

"Immediately."

"But . . ." Hélène Pringle in *jail*? That meek little woman whose feet didn't touch the floor when she sat down?

"Call your local police chief, that guy you're such buddies with, and describe the angel. Tell him to search her car trunk. If it's not in the car, they'll search the house. You told me the angel has some value?"

"I'm guessing three, maybe even four thousand dollars."

"You can have her arrested for felonious larceny, not to mention felonious breaking and entering. That's a Class H on both counts. If she's convicted, we're talking up to ten years each count. Chances are, she'd get off with three years for each Class H, but for a piano teacher, that's a very long time."

He hung up, stricken over this sordid turn of events.

He and Cynthia would talk and pray about it tonight, and make the decision regarding a search warrant in the morning. He'd never had anyone arrested, and certainly not a woman, but was that the issue here? Wasn't the issue about money being wrongfully gouged out of the Hope House coffers? If it hadn't been for Miss Sadie's meticulous thrift and careful investing, there may not have been any money there at all. Didn't that count for something?

He realized he was once again sitting with his head in his hands.

Whatever the morning's outcome, he could not, would not, miss his fifth walk around the wall.

He called Rodney Underwood at home at eight a.m.

"Rodney, I have a disagreeable piece of business for you."

"I don't guess it's anything as big as th' man in th' attic; prob'ly won't ever get another deal like that." Rodney was talking about the jewel thief who lived in the attic at Lord's Chapel until he turned himself in to local authorities during a Sunday morning worship service.

"I'd like you to take a search warrant to the rectory. I have reason to believe my tenant stole the angel."

The spoken words chilled his blood. He was saying things that couldn't be taken back.

"Unknown to her, Harley Welch found the angel in the trunk of her car while it was at Lew Boyd's."

"You sure it's th' same one? Did he give you a good description?"

"Yes. About twenty inches high, bronze, green marble base."

"You lookin' to search just th' car or you think we ought to have a warrant for the house, too?"

"Both, to be safe."

"It takes a little while to process a search warrant, but I'll personally get right on it."

"What happens if you find the statue?"

"We'll take 'er into custody, take 'er over to th' magistrate in Wesley. He'll prob'ly put an investigative hold on 'er for about twelve hours 'til we get th' statute fingerprinted, get photographs an' all."

"The statue . . ."

"Right, th' statute."

He called Walter. "I didn't like doing it, but it's done."

"Good. When they have the angel in hand, let me know and I'll call her attorney."

In truth, he was only doing what was within the law, but he was literally nauseous over it. So was Cynthia. Oddly, taking legal steps against an unlawful act had made them both feel like criminals.

He didn't want to see Mamie or anyone else this morning. He put his head down and walked quickly, focusing his mind and spirit entirely upon Morris Love and the look on Morris's face as he was ordered from Nouvelle Chanson for what may have been the final time.

He would not exhort God this morning to heal, to bind up, or to transform. He would exhort Him only to bless.

He prayed silently.

Bless the gift You have given him, Lord, to be used to Your glory, bless his spirit which craves You and yet bids You not enter, bless the laughter that is surely there, laughter that has dwelled in him all these years, yearning to be released, longing to spring forth and be a blessing to others. . . .

The laughter of Morris Love—that would be a miracle, he thought, and remembered how he had prayed to hear Dooley Barlowe laugh. That prayer had been answered; he smiled to think of Dooley's riotous cackle.

Thank You for blessing Morris with a quick and lively mind, an inquisitive intellect, and a soul able to form majestic music which ardently glorifies the Giver. Thank You for blessing Morris with Mamie, who, out of all those offered the glad opportunity of loving him, was the only one who came forth to love and serve on Your behalf.

The tears were cold on his face.

Lord, bless him today as he sits at his keyboards, as he breaks bread with Mamie, as he looks out his window onto a world which betrayed him, and which he now betrays. As he lies down to sleep, bless him with Your holy peace. As he rises, bless him with hope. As he thinks, bless him with Your own high thoughts.

Now, Father, I bless You—and praise You and thank You for hearing my prayer, through Christ our Lord who was given to us that we might have new life, Amen.

He walked on.

"It's a done deal," said Rodney, not sounding quite like himself.

"How . . . did it go?"

"We found y'r angel in th' car, like you said, but your tenant broke down pretty bad. . . ." Rodney cleared his throat.

"Broke down?"

"Bawled like I never seen, wrung 'er hands. Me an' th' boys hated to do what we did."

"What did you do?"

"Took her over to th' magistrate an' they're holdin' her 'til everything's nailed down, fingerprints, reports, an' all."

"Then what?" he asked.

"Looks like th' charge'll be felonious breakin' an' enterin', felonious larceny, and felonious possession of stolen property."

He shook his head, hoping to clear it.

"Based on th' evidence, th' magistrate'll issue a warrant for her arrest, an' she'll have to post bond. In two, three weeks, she'll have to show up before a district judge, an' dependin' on how that goes, a grand jury will hear state's evidence which could land 'er in Superior Court."

"What if she leaves and goes to Boston?"

"She can go anywhere she wants to, long as she comes back to court."

"What if she doesn't?" He might as well know the worst-case scenario.

"They'll issue an order for 'er arrest, plus an order of forfeiture on th' bond."

"In other words, she wouldn't want to do that." *Hélène Pringle hunted and pursued . . .*

"Nobody with a lick of sense would want to do that."

Enough. He couldn't go on with this, he was a basket case, let Walter deal with it.

Before services at ten o'clock, he would walk around the wall for the sixth time, and on Monday, seven times consecutively. Then he would have accomplished the thing God had asked him to do.

"I'm a fool for Christ!" he said with St. Paul. Thank heaven nobody had a clue what he was doing; to the world, he was walking his dog, he was getting his exercise, he was increasing his heart rate.

Sunday night on the Sound.

Not a bad life, he thought, sitting on the sofa and holding his wife's hand. He had at last figured out how to work the TV and which of the several remotes it required, and they were watching the Discovery Channel.

"Ugh," said his wife, as a lion bored its head into a carcass, "they're always eating each other."

"That's life," he said as the phone rang.

He muted the sounds of the African plain. "Hello!"

"Father Kavanagh?"

Hélène Pringle. "I am desperate to talk with you."

He thought his hand shook, holding the receiver. "I'd be eager to talk with you, as well, Miss Pringle."

"I cannot go on this way, with so much to confess, so much to make known, it is . . ." She paused. "It is agony."

He heard the great strain in her voice.

"I would give anything to speak with you face-to-face," she said, "but—"

"Just a moment, Miss Pringle." He put his hand over the mouthpiece, as his mind raced over the schedule here—a vestry meeting with Sewell Joiner, Sam would handle it, they could run to Mitford and get back home the morning of the Fall Fair. . . .

"Want to go to Mitford?" he asked his wife.

"Consider us packed!" she said, beaming.

He would walk seven times around the wall tomorrow, first thing—they could be in the car by ten o'clock, and in Mitford by eight on Monday evening. "Miss Pringle, we'll see you at the rectory Tuesday morning at eleven. Will that be convenient?"

Miss Pringle was weeping quietly and, he assumed, unable to speak.

"Take your time," he said. "My time is yours."

He was on his fourth lap when Mamie appeared suddenly on the path from Nouvelle Chanson, startling him.

"Ah, Mamie!"

She laughed easily, her breath making vapor on the air. "I'm just going over home to get mayonnaise. Mr. Morris hardly ever touches it, but this mornin' he has a taste for a little mayonnaise on his grilled cheese."

This seemed to please her very much.

"Mamie, I wonder if I might get my wife's bicycle one day soon. I don't think Morris wants me to come fetch it personally."

Her eyes told him she understood. "I'll roll it down here for you anytime."

"I'll be back around this way in, say . . ."—three and a half laps to go—"twenty, thirty minutes? Would that be good?"

"Fine," she said. "Just fine."

"You could leave it there on the path, where no one can see it. I'd be grateful."

"I used to ride a bicycle—it was a pretty green color with a little bell. I loved my old bicycle."

"Borrow this one anytime," he said.

As they drove into Mitford at eight-fifteen, he felt he was seeing it anew. Though cloaked in fog, the sights he expected to be so familiar seemed fresh and original, almost exotic to his eyes. Lights sparkled in shop windows, street lamps glowed in the heavy mist, the display window of Dora Pugh's Hardware was dressed with pumpkins and shocks of corn stalks.

"I love our town," said his wife, peering out like a kid. Barnabas had his nose flattened against the rear window; even Violet, standing in Cynthia's lap with her paws against the glass, was gazing intently at Main Street.

He realized he was grinning from ear to ear, but when he saw Fancy Skinner's pink neon sign above the Sweet Stuff Bakery, he laughed out loud.

Once they got into the yellow house and turned on the lights and Harley delivered a pan of fudge brownies, it was too late to go visiting in Mitford. Puny, warned of their homecoming, had put roast chicken, potato salad, and tomato aspic in the refrigerator. They fell upon the meal like dock hands.

Afterward, they changed into what he'd been raised to call "nightclothes," and wandered around the house, seeing it all over again, claiming it with their eyes.

"Timothy!" exclaimed his wife. "Doesn't that picture look perfect over the sage-green vase?"

"You must have thought so when you put it there," he said, amused.

"I love our home, Timothy."

"As do I." He thumped down at his desk and idly looked through the drawers.

"What do you think she's going to say tomorrow?"

"I can't imagine, I don't know. I don't think she would have called if she didn't want to make peace. And she spoke of confession. . . ."

"I feel so sorry for Miss Pringle."

He glanced out the study window toward the rectory, where, through the hedge, he saw a light dimly burning in the kitchen.

"As do I," he repeated. "As do I."

Lessons for the Piano, he read on the black and white sign placed in the grass by the front walk, *Inquire Within.*

Hélène Pringle stood in the middle of the rectory living room and looked at him, red-eyed and plaintive. She was dressed simply in a longish dress and worn gray cardigan, and bereft of jewelry or any fanciful adornment. Her hair was swept back severely, as if she'd just dipped her comb in water, and pinned into a chignon.

"I can't tell you how sorry I am . . . and I beg your forgiveness."

He hated that she wrung her hands as she said this. "You are forgiven," he said, meaning it.

"Please sit, Father. I have a long story to relate to you. I pray you aren't in a hurry."

"I'm in no hurry at all." If he did nothing else on this trip, it would be fine with him. Looking around for Barbizon, but failing to spy the outsize mop, he sat in the chair, glad for the ease of it.

"I suppose I should offer you coffee or tea," she said, still standing.

"No, please, Miss Pringle, I have no want of anything. Thank you."

It hurt him, somehow, to witness her terrible anxiety. "Please," he said, smiling.

She sat on the sofa and gazed at her hands in her lap.

"Let me begin, then," she said, "at the beginning."

He was puzzled to realize he scarcely recognized this room, which had been part of his life for more than sixteen years.

"I have two very strong memories of my early childhood," she said, barely speaking above a whisper. "No one ever believed it possible for me to remember the first, for I was still an infant, lying in a pram. I had been rolled outside to the lawn and parked under a tree, and I remember so vividly the color of the leaves above me, almost . . . chartreuse, a delicate and tender shade of green I've seen only once or twice since. I shall never forget the intricate lacework of the leaves, and the sparkle of that wondrous color as they danced in the breeze."

She looked up from gazing at her hands, and he suddenly recognized something vaguely familiar about Hélène Pringle, but he couldn't have said what it was.

"The other early impression that shall remain with me always was when *ma grandmère* looked down upon me as I lay in my little bed in her country home outside Barbizon. I was very sick, and later, as an adult, I thought the whole dreadful episode might have been a feverish dream, but it was not.

"I was perhaps three years old then. She was wearing her lace cap, and the points of the lace appeared to me like the jagged edges of broken glass. I saw every wrinkle in her face; she was suddenly terribly, terribly frightening to me, but I was mesmerized and could not look away. 'You,' she said, 'have no father. I hope you like that piece of news, *ma petite chère*.' " Then she poked me in the chest with her finger, which had a long and hurtful nail, and I wept for the enormous fear I suddenly had of my grandmother, Hélène."

He'd never wanted the ability to feel the pain of others so keenly, but he had it, he had always had it, and there was no help for it. Perhaps it was just as well, for into this empathetic endowment had been lumped the ability to experience his own pain.

"I understand," he said.

She looked at him now with a certain steadiness in her gaze. "At the age of nineteen, my mother, Françoise, went up to Paris to live with her Tante Brigitte. Tante Brigitte was my grandfather's sister, and not a careful person in the least. She was altogether the wrong guardian for my beautiful and innocent mother.

"I think, Father, that aunts and uncles don't always take their roles as seriously as they might."

He saw traces of an old bitterness in her face as she spoke.

"I have always believed that Tante Brigitte conspired to introduce my mother to . . . to . . ." She looked at her hands again.

"Josiah Baxter?"

"Yes. He was a man of wealth, and old enough to be my mother's grandfather."

"Ah," he said.

"It grieves me more than you can know to tell you these things that have lain on my heart for so many years without being spoken."

She wept quietly, placing a handkerchief against her eyes and holding it there.

"Pardon, j'en suis désolée!" she said, at last. "I'm sorry to break down like this."

"Please don't be."

"Mr. Baxter . . . brought many expensive things to the apartment in Paris—paintings, sculpture, beautiful objects . . . my mother has memory of a little hand-carved chair with a needlepoint cushion . . ."

He had seen such a chair in Miss Sadie's bedroom; at the last minute of their negotiations at Fernbank, Andrew Gregory had bought it, along with numerous other pieces of furniture and table linens.

". . . and all those lovely things were shipped to his home in America. The men would come and crate them up, and away they would go across the water, to a place my mother would never know or see.

"I don't mean to imply that he never gave gifts to my mother. He gave her several fine pieces of jewelry which are long vanished, sold to help further my education. And he regularly gave money to Tante Brigitte for the household."

Something about her . . . so familiar . . .

"One day, Mr. Baxter . . ."

He noted that she spoke this name with difficulty, drawing a short breath before she said it.

"... brought the angel to my mother. She told me that he said, 'Here, my dove, is something to watch over you in my absence.'

"Then he pulled a small key from his waistcoat and gave it to her. 'Unlock the little hiding place in the base of the angel,' he said. My mother examined the base very carefully, but could not find a way to insert a key. He took the key from her then, and turned the angel on its side ..."

Hélène Pringle sat for a moment as if made of stone. He sensed that she had heard this story many times; her gaze did not take him in at all, but replayed before her eyes the movie she had made of her mother's memories.

"... and slid out the bottom, which had appeared to be only a piece of felt to keep the statue from marring the furniture. Just inside the lip of the marble base was a very tiny keyhole."

"Ahh," he said.

"Mr. Baxter turned the little key in the hole and the bottom of the base, a thin slab of marble, was released into his hand. 'Now,' he told my mother, 'look inside.'

"She looked inside and found two pieces of paper, folded many times. 'Open this one first,' he told her, and she did. It was his will, written in his own hand and in French, though he spoke and wrote hardly any French at all. He had asked a Paris attorney to translate the wording into the language of my mother, and he had copied it in a very awkward and labored hand. It stated that upon his death he was bequeathing a third of his assets to my mother."

Hélène Pringle drew a deep breath and went on.

"In English, he wrote at the bottom, 'This is a codicil to my final will and testament, which is in the keeping of my solicitor, William Perry, of Philadelphia, Pennsylvania.' It was signed in his handwriting, and dated April 14, 1947. He told her he was traveling back to America with a copy for his solicitor.

"My mother said she felt a strange sort of joy and wonder, yet at the same time a fearful sense of dread. She then withdrew the other folded paper. It was ... a love letter. I hope you might read it one day."

She sat with the handkerchief pressed to her eyes again, making no sound.

"Afterward," she continued, looking at him, "everything was placed back in the marble base, the key was turned in the lock, and the little slab with the felt bottom was put into place.

"Then Mr. Baxter slipped the key into the pocket of my mother's frock and said goodbye until his next visit, which he supposed would be in the summer, in July.

"That afternoon, the men came to crate the pieces he had bought for his home in America, and Tante Brigitte told them what was to be packed and what was to be untouched. Somehow, the angel was packed and taken away and put on the ship to America. . . ."

He saw the stricken look on her face, as if it happened only yesterday, or last week, and was as near to her in reality as this room in which she was sitting.

"Tante Brigitte sent a man to the docks to look for the crate, but the boat had gone."

She rose from the sofa and walked around the room, anxious and alarmed, then stood in front of the windows and drew the sheer panels apart and looked into the street.

He waited, sick with the weight of her distress.

She turned and came again to the sofa and sat down. "He never returned to Paris. You recall that the will was dated the day of his leave-taking, April 14, 1947. I was born December 12, 1947."

The room might have been contained in a timeless, noiseless bubble. He couldn't hear the ticking of a clock or a car moving in the street; he heard only the beating of his heart.

"When he did not come in July, my mother dispatched a letter to his lumberyard near Mitford, and heard nothing in reply. Several weeks after I was born, a letter was sent again. Two months later, it was returned to us unopened, and stamped *Addressee Deceased.*

"Tante Brigitte wrote a letter to the manager of Baxter Lumber Company, believing she could extort money somehow, and it, also, was returned, with *Out of Business* written on the envelope in longhand. Years later, I would pore over those returned envelopes, pondering the words *deceased* and *out of business,* and their tormenting finality.

"My family had lost all hope of any connection with my . . . with the American visitor to the little apartment in Paris.

"My aunt was not entirely poor, Father, but her means were limited, and there was no family friend or legal counsel to fall back upon. She sent my mother home to Barbizon with a seven-month-old child, to live with *ma grandmère.*"

There was a prolonged silence during which Hélène Pringle stared at the piano, as if it might contain an answer long sought.

"Perhaps to compensate for this terrible strait in the family affairs, Grandmère Hélène created a legacy of bitterness and hatred that I hope never to witness again in this life. Bitterness and hatred, Father, are contagious, did you know?"

"I know," he said.

"She infected my mother with this virulent acrimony, and I, too, became horribly contaminated by it. It was as if . . . as if a venomous liturgy were composed among us, and we recited it, day after day, religiously. It became to us larger than the real world. Our entire focus was upon the bitterness and anger felt toward my father and his money and his fine American home named Fernbank and his deceased wife whom he had called beautiful, and his much-adored Sadie and the fact that she had someone called China Mae to serve her and do her laundry and braid her hair.

"My grandmother would begin the recitation with the arrival of her breakfast tray, telling me how my mother never had *le courage, le cran, le culot,* to pursue the matter to its utmost and final outcome, to claim her portion, no matter what the effort, even if it meant going to America and seeking the thing that contained all our future prospects.

"My mother was once a very beautiful woman, but she sacrificed her beauty to bitterness and sorrow. Do you understand?"

"Yes," he said. "I've seen it happen that way."

"I was never . . . beautiful. I wonder how I could have been born to someone so lovely when I was . . ." She looked away.

"When you were what?" he asked.

"Short and plain, like my father."

Just plain Sadie . . . the thought came to him out of the blue. It was the way Miss Sadie had often referred to herself. Just plain Sadie, whose feet, when she sat on the love seat at Fernbank, had never touched the floor. Of course. That was the familiar thing he had recognized in this lost and lonely woman who had come seeking what she believed to be her brightest hope.

"I developed an image of my father over the years, based upon my grandmother's view of his wicked and profligate conduct, his willful neglect of duty, and his great and selfish wealth. He became monstrous to me, yet I can't tell you how I longed to love him a little, if only a little, but I could not."

He didn't like the ashen look on her face.

"Would you care for some water, Miss Pringle?"

"*Non, merci.* But then, yes, that would be—"

"I know just where it is," he said, sprinting toward the kitchen.

He realized he was shaking his head again, as if to clear it and make some sense of all he was hearing. His kitchen seemed strange to him, as if he'd never stepped foot in it before. *Lord,* he prayed, *may Your peace be upon this house. . . .*

He took a glass from the cabinet and ran the spigot for a moment and filled the glass and went along the hall to the rectory parlor. *And bless this woman in ways I can't think to ask. . . .*

"There," he said, as she drank it down. He took the glass from her as if he were a nursemaid and returned to his chair and sat again, holding it.

"Before my grandmother died fourteen years ago, she contended that a trip to Mitford would be a completely sensible thing to do. She believed the angel would be found sitting on someone's mantel, ripe for the picking."

"And so it was," he said gently.

"I determined that I would do this thing for my mother, who, by the way, married Albert Pringle and went to live in Boston about the time I finished college. They were married for seven years before he died of pneumonia. He was a lovely man. I took his name out of gratitude for his kindness. I think he helped relieve my mother of some of the anger. She became almost . . . almost kind again, and every so often, with Albert, I heard her laugh."

"Ahh."

"I always loved my mother, even when her malice removed her from me over and over again. A year ago, when our finances became so . . . strained, I promised her I would come to Mitford. I didn't tell her I would look for the angel, Father, I told her I would come to Mitford and find it."

"I admire confidence, Miss Pringle."

"I could not believe my good fortune when I discovered that you and Miss Sadie had been dear friends, and that your old rectory was for lease, right next door to your home. I believed then with all my heart that I'd been sent on a mission that would . . . would redeem all the hurt, somehow." She looked at her hands again.

"A mission?"

"Yes. I don't know much about God, Father, that is your forte, but I felt somehow that God had a hand in my coming here. I hope you don't think it's impertinent of me."

"No, Miss Pringle, not impertinent in the least."

"I suppose you wondered why I would bring my furnishings and set up a piano practice with only a six-month lease."

"That did cross my mind."

"I wanted . . . let me say that all my life since I was a young child, I've felt the need of a fresh start, a new beginning. I came here to find the angel, but very deep down, I also hoped I wouldn't find it. I came thinking that perhaps Mitford could be . . ." She sighed and shook her head slowly.

"But then, I've spent my life devoted to the desire for retribution—perhaps there are no new beginnings for someone like me."

"New beginnings are always possible," he said. "What of your mother? What are her circumstances?"

"My mother is in a nursing home outside Boston. Her mental faculties are keener than my own, but a series of health problems causes her to require care I cannot give. Albert left us a bit of money and I've gotten on rather well with my piano lessons, but . . ."

He saw the toll this was taking on her, that it would take on almost anyone to recite a legacy of suffering and loss.

"I'm sorry," she said, "I lost my point, somehow."

"Take a deep breath," he said. "Let's rest for a moment, shall we?"

"Rest?"

There! For one fragile instant, he thought he saw Miss Sadie in Hélène Pringle's face.

"Oh, no, Father, I can't rest until I've told you everything."

He nodded.

"I was very bold that day to look into your window. I stacked one cement block on top of another. Can you imagine my great joy and consternation when I peered into your lovely, sunlit room and spied the angel?"

He nodded.

"It was precisely where my grandmother contended it would be found. I was dumbstruck. I hadn't realized I might have to . . . to thieve something that in a sense didn't belong to me, but which, in quite another sense altogether, was mine."

"Yes," he said. A conundrum if ever there was one.

"Perhaps I deceived myself that if I located it, I could buy it, or . . . I suppose I never thought it through. And so, I began to watch your housekeeper come and go, and one afternoon I saw that she failed to lock the door when she departed. At dusk, I slipped to your house and let myself in. I was as quiet as a breath, and it was all done very quickly.

"My good fortune was alarming, Father; to want something so terribly for so many years, and then . . . it was unthinkable! I began to believe that circumstances had been formed just for me, just for this moment, it was a sign that all I was doing was destined. I brought the angel here."

Relief flooded her face. She seemed immediately stronger as she openly confessed the theft to him.

"I drew all the shades and draperies, and placed it on my bed, where I used the little key to unlock the base, and there . . . there were the papers, never once disturbed for more than a half century. I wept like I had never wept before, to hold something of my father's in my hands. I read the letter, and in it, I found a tenderness of feeling which I'd never hoped he might possess. The letter opened its secrets before me like the petals of a flower, and I discovered my father's true affection—and his humanity. I know that his behavior was very wrong, but you see, for all his wrongdoing, I was able at last to love him a little."

Now he heard a clock ticking somewhere, perhaps in the hallway, as if the bubble had been pierced and life was flowing into them again.

"I sent the papers to my mother's attorney in Boston. I was fearful to have them copied, fearful of being seen using the Xerox machine at the post office, and knowing no other way to proceed, I sent the papers by registered mail to Monsieur d'Anjou. He encouraged me in this thing which others might deem merely a bizarre and frivolous gamble.

"After I sent the papers, I became frightened that the angel would be found here, and so I hid it in the trunk of my car.

"I express to you again my sorrow at having done something that grieved you and the trustees at Hope House."

"It is a cloud," he said, "with a silver lining."

"Do you really believe so?" she asked, anxious again.

"I can't know so, but I do believe so."

"Thank you," she said, looking at him directly. "I went up to Hope House before Monsieur d'Anjou served the lawsuit, and looked around. It is . . . a wonderful place, the sort of place I wish for my mother."

"It was all Sadie Baxter's idea," he told her, "every bit of it, from the rooms overlooking the valley to the Scriptures over each doorway . . . the atrium, the fine medical help, the chaplain, all."

"I know the consequences of my actions, Father. I know that I can go to prison for what I have done. Nonetheless, I must tell you that I'm glad I did it. Very, very glad. I took something from you, yet I gained far more than the temporary possession of an angel on a marble base. There's a surprising sense, now, of owning something deeply precious—I don't yet understand what it is. But I know . . . it is in here." She placed her hand over her heart.

"I've grown to feel almost at home in Mitford. I've never known what it is to feel completely at home anywhere, but here, there's a solace I never found before. And so, I have gained even that."

Now it was he who got up and walked to the window and stood with his hands behind his back, peering without seeing through the sheer panels. It was hard to take it all in, to know what to do with all he had heard, but he knew this:

Something must be done with it. For Hélène Pringle; for Sadie Baxter, who, in heaven, would not be judging wrongdoing on anyone's part; and for himself; for his own peace of mind; and certainly for God, who may, indeed, have brought this woman to a crisis of renewal.

"Miss Pringle," he said, turning around, "I'm prepared to drop all charges against you. That may take some doing. I understand I'll have to meet with the district attorney, who may not take kindly to dropping the charges. But that is what I intend to do."

"Father," she said, standing. "I withdraw the lawsuit."

"Thank you," he said. "And the angel is yours."

"*Non! Ce ne serait pas juste!* That would not be fair. . . ."

"It is completely fair. It was the rightful and intended home for the letter and the will. They are all pieces of God's puzzle, and I believe the pieces must be kept together."

She stood by the sofa, awkward and moved; he wanted to go to her and give her a hug, but clergy had been historically advised to avoid such intimate contact, with no one looking on to approve.

"Well," he said, swallowing hard.

"Thank you, thank you, Father. *Mon Dieu, encore des larmes!*" She retrieved the handkerchief from her cardigan pocket and pressed it again to her eyes.

"Miss Pringle," he said, taking a handkerchief from his own pocket, "we are a pair."

He walked across to the rectory before they left for Whitecap, and knocked on the door. He hardly recognized Hélène Pringle. She was holding her shoulders erect; she was looking him in the eye.

"May I have a moment?"

"Please!" she said, opening the door wide.

Aha. There was that blasted cat, curled on the sofa and staring him down. "I won't come in; I just wanted to give you something."

He handed her an ivory envelope.

"Whatever you find inside, please receive it in the spirit in which it is given. Promise me that."

She looked dubious for a moment, then smiled. "Well, then. I shall do it, Father!"

"Good. And Miss Pringle?"

"Yes?"

"We hope you'll stay on in Mitford."

"But . . ."

"I know it's too soon to say, but we trust you'll think about it."

Tears swam in her eyes. *"Oui,"* she said. *"Oui. J'y penserai."*

Passing from the rectory into the bright midday of Mitford, he looked again at the sign in the yard.

He thought it might as easily have read, *Lessons for the Heart, Inquire Within.*

CHAPTER TWENTY-TWO

A New Song

On the morning of the second Sunday of Easter, seven wild ponies trotted through the open gate of the corral near the lighthouse. Cropping grass with seeming contentment, they were spied by a jogger, who managed to close the rusting gate and then ran on, shouting the news along his route to whoever was up and stirring.

The marvelous sight drew Whitecappers of every age and disposition, all gleeful that the ponies from up Dorchester had escaped the government fence that ran into the Sound and, swimming around it, had struck out for Whitecap.

Penny and Marshall Duncan packed up their brood and drove the derelict Subaru to the corral, where they proffered a thank offering of hay and a large scoop of oats purloined from their lean-to barn. On Monday, the *Whitecap Reader* announced that the government would be coming to cart the ponies back where they belonged, so if anybody wanted to observe their brief homecoming, they'd better hop to it.

In the village, merchants prepared for the wave of tourists that would wash over them only two or three weeks hence. They were eager to see an economy that had slowed to a trickle once again surge like the incoming tide: quite a few prices were discreetly raised and the annual flurry of stocking nearly empty shelves began.

The dress shop reordered Whitecap T-shirts printed variously with images of the lighthouse, the historic one-room schoolhouse moved from the Toe to the village green, and the much-photographed St. John's in the Grove; the grocery store manager decided to dramatically expand his usual volume of hush puppy mix, much favored by tourists renting units featuring a kitchen; and Whitecap Flix, the sixty-two-seat theater rehabbed from a bankrupt auto parts store and open from May 15 through October 1, voted to open with *Babe*, convinced it was old enough to bill as a classic. To demonstrate their confidence in the coming season, Flix scheduled a half-page ad to hit on May 15, and included a ten-percent-off coupon for people who could prove it was their birthday.

Hearing of the advertising boom coursing through the business community, Mona elected to run a quarter-page menu once a month for three months, something she'd never done before in her entire career. Plus, she was changing her menu, which always thrilled a paltry few and made the rest hopping mad. She figured to put a damper on any complaints by offering a Friday night all-you-can-eat dinner special of fried catfish for seven ninety-five, sure to pacify everybody. Due to space too small to cuss a cat, she had resisted all-you-can-eat deals ever since she opened in this location, since any all-you-can-eat, especially fried, was bad to back up a kitchen. All-you-can-eat was a two-edged sword, according to Ernie—who could not keep his trap shut about her business, no matter what—because while you could draw a crowd with it, in the end you were bound to lose money on it since people around here chowed down like mules. In the end, all-you-can-eat was what some outfits called a loss leader. Mona did not like the word "loss," it was not in her vocabulary, but she would try the catfish and see how it worked, mainly to draw attention from the fact there was no liver and onions on her new menu, nor would there ever be again in her lifetime, not to mention skillet cornbread which crowded up the oven, cooked cabbage which smelled to high heaven, and pinto beans. Lord knows, she couldn't do everything, this was not New York City, it was Whitecap, and though she'd been born and raised here, it was not where she cared to spend the rest of her life, she was investing money in a condo in Florida, even if Ernie had expressed the hope of retiring to Tennessee. Tennessee! The very thought gave her the shivers. All those log cabins, all those grizzlies stumbling around in the dark, plus moonshine out the kazoo . . . no way.

Sometime in April, a sign appeared in the window of Ernie's Books, Bait & Tackle:

Buy Five Westerns
Any Title, Get a
Free Zane Grey
or Louis L'Amour,
Take Your Pick.

Hardly anyone going in and out of Mona's had ever read Zane Grey, though several had heard of him, and a breakfast regular seemed to remember L'Amour as a prizefighter from Kansas City. Two days after the sign went up, a potato chip rep dropped a hundred and eighty-seven bucks on the special offer and posted Ernie's phone number and address in a chat room devoted to the subject of Old West literature. In the space of eight working days, the book end of the business had blown the bait end in the ditch, and Ernie hired on a couple of high school kids to handle mail orders.

Roanoke Clark was painting one of the big summer houses, and had hired on a helper who, he was surprised to learn, stayed sober as a judge and worked like a horse. He pondered making this a permanent deal, if only for his partner's nearly new pair of telescoping ladders, not to mention late-model Ford truck, an arrangement that would prevent the necessity of renting Chess Doyle's rattletrap Chevy with a homemade flatbed, for which Chess dunned him a flat forty bucks a week.

In the Toe, Bragg's was busy pumping diesel and dispatching tons of gravel and cement to construction sites as far away as Williamston, not to mention an industrial park in Tyrrell County.

At the north end of the small island shaped like a Christmas stocking, St. John's in the Grove was at last divested of its scaffolding. The heavy equipment had vanished, the piles of scrap lumber and roofing had been hauled away, and the errant flapping of loose tarps was heard no more.

Behind this effort had come a parish-wide cleanup. Brooms, rakes, hoes, mattocks and shovels were toted in, along with fresh nursery stock to replace what had been damaged in the general upheaval.

During the windy, day-long workfest, someone discovered that the coreopsis was beginning to bloom, and Father Tim was heard to say that their little church looked ready to withstand another century with dignity and grace.

For months on end, winter weather had delayed work on the reconstruction. He was up to here with plaster dust, drilling, sanding, and sawing. No wonder some of his colleagues resisted the role of "building priest." It probably wasn't the fund-raising they detested, it was the actual putting up and hammering down.

Fortunately, they'd been able to save the old oak, and he was glad for the bonus of increased light that now shone on St. John's.

On a bitterly cold, but bright May morning, he unlocked the front door and stepped across the threshold into a new nave, yet with its old spirit still intact. He sat midway on the gospel side and looked around paternally.

A church, like any other home, had its own singular and individual spirit, and he'd grown to love the unique spirit of St. John's. At Lord's Chapel, he'd felt the bulk and weight of the river stone as a mighty fortress, a sure defense. St. John's, on the other hand, gave him the distinct sense of vulnerability and innocence; it seemed fragile, somehow, as indeed it had been.

Two Sundays hence, the parish would celebrate this glad rebirth with a dinner on the grounds and the first homecoming in more than thirty years. They wouldn't take the long tearing out and putting back for granted, not at all; they would observe it for what it was—a benediction of a high and precious order.

"St. John's in the Grove, Father Kavanagh here."

"Hey, Dad."

"Hey, yourself, buddy!"

"Me and Caroline broke up."

"Ahh. Too bad."

"I'm glad, though. You know what she did?"

"What?"

"Just ran up to me at th' dance and grabbed th' chain around my neck and yanked it so hard, it came apart, and she took her ring back."

"Good grief!" That sounded exactly like something Peggy Cramer might have done.

"Next time, I'm goin' out with somebody more like . . . like . . ."

"Like who?" *Lace Turner!*

"Like, you know, maybe Cynthia."

He could practically feel his chest expand. "Now you're talking!" he said.

"I really liked it down there at Christmas."

"It was great, and we're looking forward to spending the summer together."

"Me, too, and when are we goin' to talk about my Wrangler?"

"I've got Harley checking around for the best deal. We'll get back to you as soon as we find something."

"Not too old," said Dooley, meaning it.

"Right. Not too old. We're looking for mint condition, low mileage, so don't worry about it."

He wasn't going to worry about it, either. This summer, Dooley would be living at the beach with a sharp little ride and a job at Mona's. Father Tim felt the excitement of it as his own.

"So, tell me, why did Caroline do . . . what she did?" Dooley Barlowe seemed to bring out mighty strong feelings in the opposite sex. He remembered the time Lace Turner had nearly knocked Dooley's head off for stealing her hat.

"I don't know, it was weird. Somebody said I was supposed to be dancin' with Caroline, and that I forgot and talked the whole time to Lace, but that's not true, I hardly talked to Lace more than five minutes—I don't know, maybe fifteen."

"Aha. Well." *Well, well, well.*

He sat in his office, mildly addled by the persistent smell of fresh paint and new carpet, and struggled without success to keep his mind on his sermon outline.

Finding Jessie Barlowe had been a fluke, but finding Sammy and Kenny would take a miracle.

There was no way he could trace Kenny via the clues of "thinning hair" and "headed for Oregon."

As for Sammy, Buck had called to say that someone saw Sammy with the road crew who worked on the highway from Holding to New Hampton more than six years ago. The boy's father had once worked on that road crew; maybe Sammy had been taken by his father. It disturbed him that he might one day have to confront Dooley's father; it wasn't a pleasant thought at all, yet he couldn't shut it out of his mind.

When they returned to Mitford, he would have to pursue this fragile thread, this vapor upon the air.

Before lunch, he went down his list of calls.

"If I was going to pass from a broken hip, I'd already have passed," said Ella Bridgewater.

"Absolutely!"

"I'm not ready to be carried down the road in a box just yet!"

"Amen!"

"I am going to the graveyard, though, to plant a little something on Mother's grave. We'll see how this hateful contraption works on gravel."

Ella Bridgewater hobbling down an isolated gravel lane on an aluminum walker? Wearing a long, black dress and toting a spade and a bush?

"I'll come up next week and go with you."

"Now, Father," she said, obviously pleased, "you don't have to do that!"

"I know I don't *have* to, which is another reason I'm happy to."

"You beat all!"

"Worse has been said," he told her.

"Louella!"

"Who that talkin'?"

"Father Kavanagh."

"Honey, how you doin'?"

"I can't complain. But how about you, how's the hip?"

"That hip ain't keepin' me down. This mornin' I rolled to th' kitchen an' made a pan of biscuits."

"Buttermilk?"

"Thass all I use."

"Wish I could have one." He sounded positively wistful. "With plenty of butter and . . . what kind of jam, do you think?"

"Huckleberry!" said Louella.

"Bingo!"

"When you an' Miss Cynthia comin' home?"

"I don't know. Maybe by the end of the year. Soon!"

"Not soon enough. We miss you aroun' here. I go an' pray with Miss Pattie, poor soul. Law, law, that Miss Pattie . . ."

"What's Miss Pattie done now?"

Louella gave forth with her rich, mezzo laughter.

"Miss Pattie have eyes for Mr. Berman, you know he's a mighty handsome man. Now she quit throwin' 'is clothes out th' window, she likes to wear 'is shoes."

"How on earth does she get around in his shoes?"

"Oh, she in a chair, you know, like me; she can't walk a step. She put those shoes on, climb up in that buggy, an' off she go, pleased as punch."

"Aha."

"Mr. Berman is *sweet*, honey, he gave her a pair of alligator loafers, said to Nurse Lola, let 'er have 'em, a man can't wear but one pair of shoes, anyway. Ain't that nice?"

"I'll say!"

She sighed. "Not a soul to sing with up here."

He sighed. "Not a soul to sing with down here."

"You hit one and I'll join in," she said, chuckling.

He didn't think he'd ever sung four verses of anything over the phone before, but when he finished, he was definitely in improved spirits.

His wife set freshly made chicken salad before him, with a hot roll and steaming mug of tea. She stood holding his hand as he asked the blessing.

"What do you think of me coming home for lunch?" he asked. "I've known some who don't take kindly to husbands falling in to be fed." Might as well learn the truth, which his wife seemed generally enthusiastic to deliver.

"I love that you come home for lunch, Timothy, you're my main social contact now that I'm working so hard to finish the book." She set her own plate on the table and kissed the top of his head.

"How's it coming?"

"Peaks, valleys, highs, lows," she said, sitting down.

"Life," he said.

"Oh, gosh, that reminds me, I need the car this afternoon. I'm running over to the Sound to sketch a blue heron."

His wife needed live fodder, flesh and blood; no Polaroids for her, thank you—she was *plein air* all the way. Except for an occasional beach umbrella or background bush that might be lifted from memory, she went looking for the real thing. Violet, who was certainly the real thing, was the fourth or fifth white cat in an unbroken chain of actual Violets adopted by his wife over the years. He had, himself, been recruited to appear as a wise man in her book *The Mouse in the Manger*. He didn't think he'd looked very wise in her watercolor—more idiotic, truth be told—but she'd been pleased.

They'd once gone to the woods together, where he tried to enter her world of absorption as she fixed her gaze on lichen—but his mind had wandered like a free-range chicken, and he ended up thinking through a sermon based on Philippians four-thirteen.

"Oh, and after the Sound, I'm running by Janette's and taking the children out for ice cream."

"Good deal." He thought her eyes were as blue as wild chicory.

"By the way, just before you came in, Roger Templeton called. He said he didn't reach you at church."

"Aha."

"Wants you to give him a ring."

"Will do."

They ate quietly, the clock ticking over the stove.

"Timothy . . ."

"Yes?"

"Don't ever leave me."

Every so often, quite out of nowhere, she asked this plaintive thing, which shook and moved him. He put his fork down and took her hand. "I would never leave you. Never."

"Even when I'm old and covered with crow's-feet?"

"I love your crow's-feet, Kavanagh."

"I thought you once said I didn't have any crow's-feet." He was relieved to see her veer away from the fleeting sadness, and laugh.

"You've nailed me," he said, grinning.

He lifted her hand and kissed her palm and held it to his cheek. "You mean everything to me. How could I ever thank you for what you are, day and night, a gift, a gift. . . ."

She looked at him, smiling. "I love it when you talk like that, dearest. You may come home for lunch whenever you wish."

Roger met him at the church office on Wednesday morning, carrying a paper bag closed with a twist-tie, and looking bashful.

"Face your desk and close your eyes," said Roger.

Father Tim did as he was told, hearing the rustle of the paper bag being opened.

"Okay, you can turn around now."

The green-winged teal in Roger's outstretched hands looked him dead in the eye.

Newly painted in all its subtle and vibrant colors, he found it beautiful, breathtaking, alive. He opened his mouth to speak, but found no words.

"It's yours," said Roger.

"You can't mean that."

"It's yours. It's been yours all along. I saw the look on your face when you watched what I was doing. I know that look; it's yours."

He took it reverently, moved and amazed.

"Turn it over," said Roger, flushing with pleasure.

He turned it over. On the flat bottom was burned the name of the island, today's date, and a message:

Green Winged Teal
For Tim Kavanagh
From Roger Templeton
Fellows in a ship

Clutching the prized possession in his left hand, he embraced Roger Templeton and pounded him on the back.

"Thank you," he said, just this side of croaking.

"I've only given away a few. Ernie has one, and my son and his wife, and . . ." Roger shrugged, awkward and self-conscious.

"I can't thank you enough, my friend. I'll treasure it more than you know."

He set it on his desk and gazed at it again, marveling.

A few months ago, he'd relinquished an angel; today, he'd been given a duck. He'd come out on the long end of the stick, and no two ways about it.

He stood in the sacristy, vested and waiting with the anxious choir, and the eager procession that extended all the way down the steps to the basement.

There was new music this morning, composed by the organist, something wondrous and not so easy to sing, and choir adrenaline was pumping like an oil derrick. Adding voltage to the electricity bouncing off the walls was the fact that the music required congregational response, always capable of injecting an element of surprise, if not downright dismay.

He peered through the glass panels of the sacristy door into the nave, able to see only the gospel side from this vantage point. He spied quite a few faces he'd never laid eyes on, given that today was Homecoming.

Some of the faithful remnant had been beaten to their pews by the homecomers, so he had to search for Otis and Marlene and the Duncan lineup, on the far right. Down front was Janette with Jonathan on her lap, flanked by Babette and Jason, *thank You, Lord.* And two rows back was Sew Joiner, gazing at the work on the walls and ceiling, and generally looking like he'd hung the moon.

At the sound of the steeple bell, the crucifer burst through the door and into the nave with her procession, the organ played its mighty opening notes, and the choir streamed forth as a rolling clap of thunder.

Carried along by the mighty roar and proclamation of the organ, the choir processed up the aisle with vigor.

> *"Sing to the Lord a new song*
> *And His praise from the ends of the earth*
> *Alleluia! Alleluia!*
> *You who go down to the sea, and all that is in it*
> *Alleluia! Alleluia!"*

The congregation joined in the first two alleluias as if waking from a long sleep; at the second pair, they hunkered down and cranked into high gear, swept along by the mighty lead of the choir.

"Let them give glory to the Lord
And declare His praise in the coastlands
Alleluia! Alleluia!"

As the choir passed up the creaking steps to the loft, the organ music soared in the little nave, enlarging it, expanding it, until it might have been o'ercrossed by the fan vaulting of an English cathedral.

Quickly taking their places by the organ, the choir entered again into the fervent acclamations of Isaiah and the psalmist.

"Sing to Him a new song
Play skillfully with a loud and joyful sound
Alleluia!
For the work of the Lord is right
Alleluia!
And all His work is done in faithfulness!
Alleluia!"

A full minute of organ music concluded the first part of the new work, celebrating God's grace to the people of St. John's, and the joyful first homecoming in three decades. Many of the congregants, marveling at the music that poured forth from the loft, turned around in their pews and looked up in wonderment.

"Alleluia! Alleluia!"

In the ascending finale, which was sung a cappella, the soprano reached for the moon and, to the priest's great joy and relief, claimed it for the kingdom.

"When trees and power lines crashed around you, when the very roof gave way above you, when light turned to darkness and water turned to dust, did you call on Him?

"When you called on Him, was He somewhere up there, or was He as near as your very breath?"

He stood in front of the pulpit this morning, looking into the faces of those whom God had given into his hand for this fleeting moment in time.

"What some believers still can't believe is that it is God's passion to be as near to us as our very breath.

"Far more than I want us to have a bigger crowd or a larger parish hall or a more ambitious budget . . . more than anything as your priest, I pray for each and every one of you to sense and know God's presence . . . as near as your breath.

"In short, it has been my prayer since we came here for you to have a personal, one-on-one, day-to-day relationship with Christ.

"I'm talking about something that goes beyond every Sunday service ever created or ever to be created, something you can depend on for the rest of your life, and then forever. I'm talking about the times you cry out in the storm that prevails against you, times when your heart and your flesh fail and you see no way out and no way in, when any prayer you utter to a God you may view as distant and disinterested seems to vanish into thin air.

"There are legions who believe in the existence of a cold and distant God, and on the occasions when they cry out to Him in utter despair and hear nothing in reply, must get up and stumble on, alone.

"Then there are those who know Him personally, who have found that when they cry out, there He is, as near as their breath—one-on-one, heart-to-heart, savior, Lord, partner, friend.

"Some have been in church all their lives and have never known this mighty, marvelous, and yet simple personal relationship. Others believe that while such a relationship may be possible, it's not for them—why would God want to bother with them, except from a very great distance? In reality, it is no bother to God at all. He wants this relationship far, far more than you and I want it, and I pray that you will ponder that marvelous truth.

"But who among us could ever deserve to have such a wondrous and altogether unimaginable thing as a close, personal, day-to-day relationship with Almighty God, creator of the universe?

"It seems unthinkable, and so . . . we are afraid to think it.

"For this fragile time in history, this tender and fleeting moment of our lives, I am your priest; God has called me to lead this flock. As I look out this morning, my heart has a wish list for you. For healed marriages, good jobs, the well-being and safety of your children; for

Eleanor, knees that work; for Toby, ears that hear; for Jessie, good news from her son; for Phillip, good news from his doctor. On and on, there are fervent desires upon my heart for you. But chief among the hopes, the prayers, the petitions is this: *Lord . . . let my people know.* Let them know that the unthinkable is not only real, but available and possible and can be entered into, now, today—though we are, indeed, completely undeserving.

"It can be entered into today, with only a simple prayer that some think not sophisticated enough to bring them into the presence of God, not fancy enough to turn His face to theirs, not long enough, not high enough, not deep enough. . . .

"Yet, this simple prayer makes it possible for you to know Him not only as Savior and Lord, but as a friend. 'No longer do I call you servants,' He said to His followers in the Gospel of John, 'but friends.'

"In the storms of your life, do you long for the consolation of His nearness and His friendship? You can't imagine how He longs for the consolation of yours. It is unimaginable, isn't it, that He would want to be near us—frail as we are, weak as we are, and hopeless as we so often feel. God wants to be *with us.* That, in fact, is His name: Immanuel, God with us. And why is that so hard to imagine, when indeed, He made us for Himself? Please hear that this morning. The One who made us . . . made us for Himself.

"We're reminded in the Book of Revelation that He created all things—for His pleasure. Many of us believe that He created all things, but we forget the very best part—that He created us . . . *for His pleasure.*

"There are some of you who want to be done with seeking Him once a week, and crave, instead, to be with Him day after day, telling him everything, letting it all hang out, just thankful to have such a blessing in your life as a friend who will never, under any circumstances, leave you, and never remove His love from you. Amazing? Yes, it is. It is amazing.

"God knows who is longing to utter that simple prayer this morning. It is a matter between you and Him, and it is a prayer which will usher you into His presence, into life everlasting, and into the intimacy of a friendship in which He is as near . . . as your breath.

"Here's the way this wondrous prayer works—as you ask Him into your heart, He receives you into His. The heart of God! What a place to be, to reside for all eternity.

"As we bow our heads to pray under this new roof and inside these new walls, I ask that He graciously bless each and every one of us today . . . with new hearts."

He bowed his head and clasped his hands together and heard the beating of the blood in his temples. Ella Bridgewater, sitting next to the aisle with her walker handy, looked on approvingly. Captain Larkin, seated to her right, bowed his head in his hands.

"Sense, feel God's presence among us this morning . . ."

He waited.

". . . as those of you who are moved to do so, silently repeat this simple prayer:

"Thank You, God, for loving me . . .

". . . and for sending Your Son to die for my sins.

"I sincerely repent of my sins . . .

". . . and receive Jesus Christ as my personal savior.

"Now, as Your child . . .

". . . I turn my entire life over to You.

"Amen."

He raised his head, but didn't hurry on. Such a prayer was mighty, and, as in music, a rest stop was needed.

The recitation of the Nicene Creed was next in the order of service, and he opened his mouth to say so, but closed it again.

He looked to the epistle side and saw Mamie and Noah; Mamie was smiling and nodding her head. Behind them were Junior Bryson and Misty Summers; he thought Junior's grin was appreciably wider than his tie.

"If you prayed that prayer and would join me at the altar, please come." He hadn't known he would say this; he had utterly surprised himself.

Some would be too shy to come, but that was God's business; he hoped he wouldn't forget and leave out the Creed altogether.

"If you'd like to renew your baptism vows in your heart, please come. If you'd like to express thanksgiving for all that God has fulfilled in your life, please come. If you'd like to make a new beginning, to surrender your life utterly into His care, please come."

Though this part of the service was entirely unplanned, he thought it might be a good time for a little music. His choir, however, was stricken as dumb as wash on a line.

From the epistle side, four people rose and left their pews and walked down the aisle.

On the gospel side, five parishioners and a homecomer stood from the various pews and, excusing themselves, stepped over the feet of several who were furiously embarrassed and looking for the door.

Father Tim opened a vial of oil, knelt for a moment on the sanctuary side of the rail, and prayed silently. One by one, the congregants dropped humbly to their knees, at least two looking stern but determined, others appearing glad of the opportunity to do this reckless thing, to surrender their hearts in an act of wild and holy abandon and begin again.

He dipped his right thumb in the oil and touched the forehead of the first at the rail, making the sign of the cross and saying, "I anoint you, Phillip, in the name of the Father, and of the Son, and of the Holy Spirit . . ."

In the choir loft, the organist rose from the bench, and walked stiffly down the stairs and along the center aisle with the aid of a cane.

Madeleine Duncan scrambled to her knees in the pew and whispered in her mother's ear, "Look, Mommy, it's a little tiny man with a big head."

Observing the penitent who now approached the altar, Leonard Lamb didn't realize he was staring with his mouth open, nor that tears suddenly sprang to his eyes.

Marion Fieldwalker poked Sam in the ribs. "Who's that?"

"Good gracious alive!" Sam whispered, as if to himself.

As Father Tim touched the forehead of the man kneeling before him, it seemed that an electric shock was born from the convergence of their flesh, it arced and flashed along his arm like a bolt.

"I anoint you, Morris, in the name of the Father, and of the Son, and of the Holy Spirit, and beseech the mercy of our Lord Jesus Christ to seal forever what is genuine in your heart. May God be with you always, my brother."

"The Lord drew me up
out of an horrible pit,
out of the miry clay,

Alleluia!
and set my feet upon a rock,
Alleluia!
steadying my steps and
establishing my goings,
Alleluia!
And he has put a new song
in my mouth, a song of praise
to our God!
Alleluia! Alleluia! Amen!"

" 'No one,' " he told Barnabas as they walked down the lane to the beach, " 'appreciates the very special genius of your conversation as the dog does.' "

His dog did not reply.

"Christopher Morley said that."

Barnabas plodded ahead.

"Don't you think there's a certain truth in it?"

What if someone heard him out here talking to his dog? Then again, why couldn't a man talk to his dog whenever he took the notion?

"Ah, my friend, what a sunset this is going to be." He felt positively jaunty, as if spring were luring something out of him that hadn't emerged in a very long while.

He'd asked his wife to come along, but she had a far more important and monumental thing to do than watch a spectacular sunset on a glorious evening; indeed, she was washing her hair.

He'd experienced this feeling of lightness only once before since coming here. It was the day he walked to Ernie's for the first time, free as a bird. Whole hours of freedom had lain before him in a strange new place with secrets yet to be revealed. Why couldn't all of life give one that feeling, the feeling of being on the brink of discovery? Wasn't every moment a revelation? Who ever knew, after all, what lay around the bend?

Ah, well, he'd probably be moping around like the rest of the common horde in a day or two. He'd better sop up this carefree business while he could.

He found himself whistling the organ piece from yesterday's service; difficult though it was, it contained an inner melodic line that he found thoroughly fascinating. What a miracle it had all been; he shook his head with the wonder of it, remembering the stunned delight of his congregation, and Mamie's soulful joy. Indeed, there had been enough gladness in the day to make memories for a month of Sundays.

They left the pavement and went along the boardwalk through the dunes. "Sit," he said, standing on the walk before they trotted down the steps. Watching the color begin to wash over the water, it suddenly occurred to him that St. John's should haul some chairs out here for an early Sunday service.

What a nave, what a sanctuary! And the ceiling beat any fan vaulting he'd ever laid eyes on, hands down. Why on earth they hadn't held this year's sunrise service right here was beyond him; he must be as dumb as a rock.

Well, then, maybe next year. If there was a next year. Very likely, St. John's would call their priest by winter.

They went down the steps and along the beach, not running, not jogging, but strolling. About a quarter of a mile into the walk, he let Barnabas off the leash.

That sunset is smokin', he thought, sitting on the sand to take off his shoes and socks. He remained sitting, looking, wondering.

It had been a joy to see Janette Tolson in church with her children yesterday, her life restored and settled. But it wasn't a joy to see the toll it was taking on her to go it alone, sewing until two in the morning, and rising early to get the children ready for school and Jonathan off to day care.

He dropped by to see her more often than he should, perhaps, but generally stayed only long enough to assure her of his prayers and encourage her in her work. Single parents were a dime a dozen in today's world. Such a thing rolled off the back of modern society like water off a duck; it had become the common run of so-called civilized life.

But it hadn't become common to him, not in the least. It always hurt him to see the damage and confusion and, too often, the utter desperation of those forced to go it alone. In short, it was a hard row to hoe, and fraught with unique assaults by the Enemy.

The last time he visited, she mustered the courage to ask again, "Have you seen him?" He hadn't, nor had anyone else, as far as he knew. "He could be dead," she said, looking across her sewing machine and out the window. "The storm . . ."

It was true. Nobody knew where he was living on the island, or in what sort of circumstances. If the ceiling plaster had narrowly missed Maude Proffitt, who was to say whether the storm had left its fatal mark elsewhere?

But hold on. He was doing the thing he had a made a resolution only yesterday to try to consciously avoid—he was thinking too much. "That young Timothy," an elder in his mother's church once said, "he thinks too much."

He never forgot that offhand remark, though he couldn't have been more than seven or eight years old. How much thinking was too much, he had wondered, and who was to say? Should he quit thinking anything at all once in a while, and go around with an empty mind? He tried to empty his mind and found it completely impossible to do. Or maybe other people could empty their minds and he was the only one who could not. This was disturbing. On the other hand, were there people who thought too little? As an adult, he occasionally considered that he might know a few. . . .

He whistled for his dog, who bounded out of the surf and stood before him, shaking salt water forty ways from Sunday.

"Sit," he said. Barnabas sat.

He remembered the time when the only thing he could get his dog to do was eat. It was years before he sat when asked, or came when called. Old age, that's what it was. Old age and wisdom! If Barnabas had been, say, two years old when he came to the rectory—and that was seven years ago—then in dog years he was . . . sixty-three. About the same age as his master. OK, then, it wasn't old age at all, no indeed, it was merely wisdom.

So thinking, he got up and ran down the beach, his dog loping beside him.

They had turned into the lane when Barnabas stopped and growled low in his throat.

It was dark now; a single street lamp burned just up the road. He saw that someone approached them, thrown into silhouette by the light.

"Who is it?" he asked. "Who's there?"

"Father Kavanagh?"

He recognized the voice at once. "Yes."

"I'm sorry to startle you." Though the figure walked closer, Barnabas stopped growling. In fact, his tail was wagging.

The white shirt gleamed like a pearl. "I've been hoping we could talk."

"I've been hoping that, too."

"If you have time."

Father Tim reached out, extending his hand into the darkness. "My time," he said, "is yours."

Now available from Penguin, the final novel in the beloved Mitford series

Light from Heaven

FATHER TIMOTHY KAVANAGH has never been asked to do the impossible—until now. The retired Episcopal priest takes on the revival of a mountain church that's been closed for forty years. Meanwhile, in Mitford, he's sent on a hunt for hidden treasure, and two beloved friends are called to come up higher. As he meets each new challenge, Father Tim is reminded anew of the most important lesson of all: *It's never too late.*

"Karon saved the best for last." —*The Baltimore Sun*

Includes an excerpt from Jan Karon's next novel, *Home to Holly Springs*, coming from Viking in the fall of 2007

ISBN 0-14-303770-6

For more information about Jan and her books visit
www.mitfordbooks.com

For more works by JAN KARON, look for the

At Home in Mitford
ISBN 0-14-025448-X

A Light in the Window
ISBN 0-14-025454-4

These High, Green Hills
ISBN 0-14-025793-4

Out to Canaan
ISBN 0-14-026568-6

A New Song
ISBN 0-14-027059-0

A Common Life: The Wedding Story
ISBN 0-14-200034-5

In This Mountain
ISBN 0-14-200258-5

Shepherds Abiding
ISBN 0-14-200485-5

Light from Heaven
ISBN 0-14-303770-6

JAN KARON books make perfect holiday gifts.

More Paperbacks from Penguin:

The Mitford Years Boxed Sets
Volume 1–6: 0-14-771779-5
Volume 1–3: 0-14-771203-3
Volume 4–6: 0-14 -771728-0

Patches of Godlight: Father Tim's Favorite Quotes
0-14-200197-X

A Continual Feast 0-14-303656-4

Hardcover books from Viking:

Esther's Gift 0-670-03121-6

The Mitford Snowmen 0-670-03019-8

Christmas in Mitford Gift Set (Esther's Gift and *The Mitford Snowmen)*
0-670-78349-8

The Mitford Cookbook and Kitchen Reader
0-670-03239-5

All of the Mitford books are available in hardcover.

PENGUIN AUDIO: The Mitford Years Audio

At Home in Mitford 0-14-305923-8 (CDs), 0-14-086501-2 (cassettes); *A Light in the Window* 0-14-305926-2 (CDs), 0-14-086596-9 (cassettes); *These High, Green Hills* 0-14-305925-4 (CDs), 0-14-086598-5 (cassettes); *Out to Canaan* 0-14-305924-6 (CDs), 0-14-086597-7 (cassettes); *A New Son* (Abridged) 0-14-086901-8 (cassettes); *A New Song* (Unabridged) 0-14-180013-5 (cassettes); *A Commor Life* 0-14-180274-X (cassettes); *The Mitford Years* Boxed Set 0-14-086813-5 (cassettes); *In This Mountai* (Abridged) 0-14-280004-X (CDs), 0-14-280005-8 (cassettes); *In This Mountain* (Unabridged) 0-14-280006-6 (cassettes); *Shepherds Abiding* 0-14-305821-5 (CDs), 0-14-280033-3 (cassettes); *Light from Heaven* 0-14-305792-8 (CDs), 0-14-305807-X (cassettes)

In bookstores now from Penguin Group (USA)

Visit the Mitford Web site at www.mitfordbooks.com

PENGUIN BOOKS

OUT TO CANAAN

Jan Karon writes "to give readers an extended family, and to applaud the extraordinary beauty of ordinary lives." She is the author of nine Mitford novels, *At Home in Mitford*; *A Light in the Window*; *These High, Green Hills*; *Out to Canaan*; *A New Song*; *A Common Life*; *In This Mountain*; *Shepherds Abiding*; and *Light from Heaven*, all available from Penguin. She is also the author of *The Mitford Bedside Companion*; *Jan Karon's Mitford Cookbook & Kitchen Reader*; *A Continual Feast: Words of Comfort and Celebration, Collected by Father Tim*; *Patches of Godlight: Father Tim's Favorite Quotes*; *The Mitford Snowmen: A Christmas Story*; *Esther's Gift*; and *The Trellis and the Seed*. Her children's books include *Miss Fannie's Hat*; *Jeremy: The Tale of an Honest Bunny*; and *Violet Comes to Stay*. Coming from Viking in fall 2007 is the first Father Tim Novel, *Home to Holly Springs*.

Other Mitford Books by Jan Karon

AT HOME IN MITFORD

A LIGHT IN THE WINDOW

THESE HIGH, GREEN HILLS

A NEW SONG

A COMMON LIFE

Children's Books by Jan Karon

MISS FANNIE'S HAT

JEREMY: THE TALE OF AN HONEST BUNNY

The Mitford Years

Out to Canaan

JAN KARON

PENGUIN BOOKS

PENGUIN BOOKS
Published by the Penguin Group
Penguin Putnam Inc., 375 Hudson Street,
New York, New York 10014, U.S.A.
Penguin Books Ltd, 27 Wrights Lane, London W8 5TZ, England
Penguin Books Australia Ltd, Ringwood, Victoria, Australia
Penguin Books Canada Ltd, 10 Alcorn Avenue,
Toronto, Ontario, Canada M4V 3B2
Penguin Books (N.Z.) Ltd, 182–190 Wairau Road,
Auckland 10, New Zealand

Penguin Books Ltd, Registered Offices:
Harmondsworth, Middlesex, England

First published in the United States of America by Viking Penguin,
a division of Penguin Books USA Inc. 1997
Published in Penguin Books 1998

30 29 28 27 26 25 24 23 22 21

PUBLISHER'S NOTE

This is a work of fiction. Names, characters, places, and incidents either are the product of the author's imagination or are used fictitiously, and any resemblance to actual persons, living or dead, events, or locales is entirely coincidental.

THE LIBRARY OF CONGRESS HAS CATALOGUED THE HARDCOVER AS FOLLOWS:
Karon, Jan, date.
Out to Canaan / Jan Karon.
p. cm.—(The Mitford years)
ISBN 0-670-87485-X (hc.)
ISBN 0 14 02.6568 6 (pbk.)
I. Title. II. Series: Karon, Jan, date. Mitford years.
PS3561.A678078 1997
813'.54—dc21 97-5867

Printed in the United States of America
Set in Adobe Garamond
Designed by Francesca Belanger

Illustrations by Hal Just
Town map by Donna Kae Nelson

For all families
who struggle to forgive
and be forgiven

*"I will restore unto you
the days the locusts
have eaten . . ."*

Joel 2:25

ACKNOWLEDGMENTS

My warmest thanks to:

Candace Freeland; Barry Setzer; Joe Edmisten; Carolyn McNeely; Dr. Margaret Federhart; Fr. Scott Oxford; Jerry Walsh; Blowing Rock BP; Crystal Coffey; Mary Lentz; Jane Hodges; Jim Atkinson; Derald West; Loonis McGlohan; Laura Watts; David Watts; Rev. Gale Cooper and my friends at St. John's; Rev. Jim Trollinger and my friends at Jamestown United Methodist; Fr. Russell Johnson and my friends at St. Paul's; Roald and Marjorie Carlson; W. David Holden; Alex Gabbard; Kay O'Neill; Dr. Richard Chestnutt; Everett Barrineau and all my friends on the Viking Penguin sales force; Aunt Wilma Argo; The Fellowship of Christ, The Saviour; Charles Davant, III; Posie Dauphine; Chuck Meltsner; Kenny Johnson; Fr. Richard Bass; Rev. Richard Holshouser; Christine Hillis; Danilo Ragogna; Dr. Rosemary Horowitz; Helen Horowitz; Susan Weinberg; Sarah Cole; and Tim Knight.

Special thanks to Judy Burns; Jerry Torchia; Dan Blair, a national umpire staff member of the Amateur Softball Association; Flyin' George Ronan of Free Spirit Aviation; Dr. Bunky Davant, Mitford's attending physician; Tony diSanti, Mitford's legal counsel; Alex Hallmark, Mitford's tireless realtor; and all the wonderful readers and booksellers who are helping put the little town with the big heart on the map.

Contents

Out to Canaan

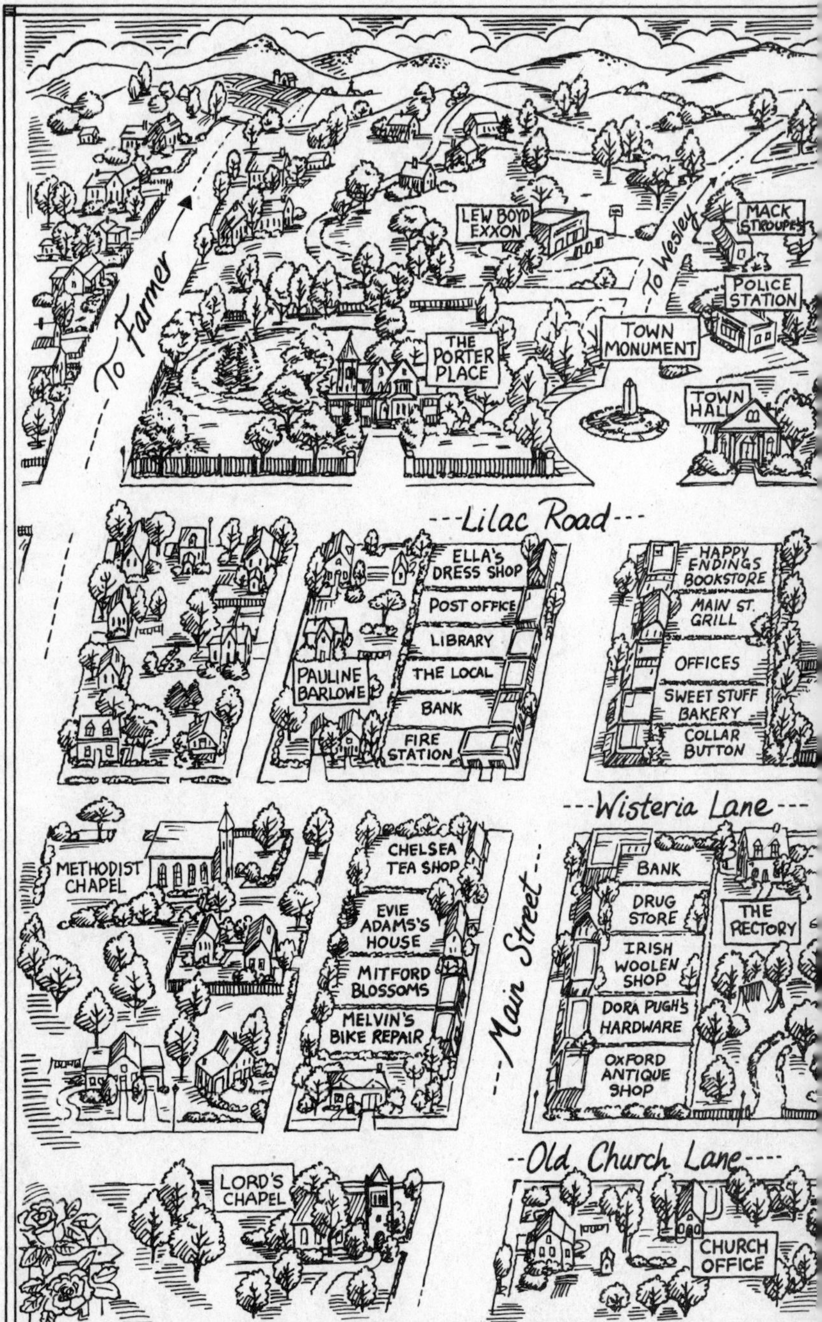

To Farmer
LEW BOYD EXXON
To Wesley
MACK STROUPE'S
POLICE STATION
TOWN MONUMENT
THE PORTER PLACE
TOWN HALL
Lilac Road
ELLA'S DRESS SHOP
POST OFFICE
LIBRARY
THE LOCAL
BANK
FIRE STATION
PAULINE BARLOWE
HAPPY ENDINGS BOOKSTORE
MAIN ST. GRILL
OFFICES
SWEET STUFF BAKERY
COLLAR BUTTON
Wisteria Lane
METHODIST CHAPEL
CHELSEA TEA SHOP
EVIE ADAMS'S HOUSE
MITFORD BLOSSOMS
MELVIN'S BIKE REPAIR
Main Street
BANK
DRUG STORE
IRISH WOOLEN SHOP
DORA PUGH'S HARDWARE
OXFORD ANTIQUE SHOP
THE RECTORY
Old Church Lane
LORD'S CHAPEL
CHURCH OFFICE

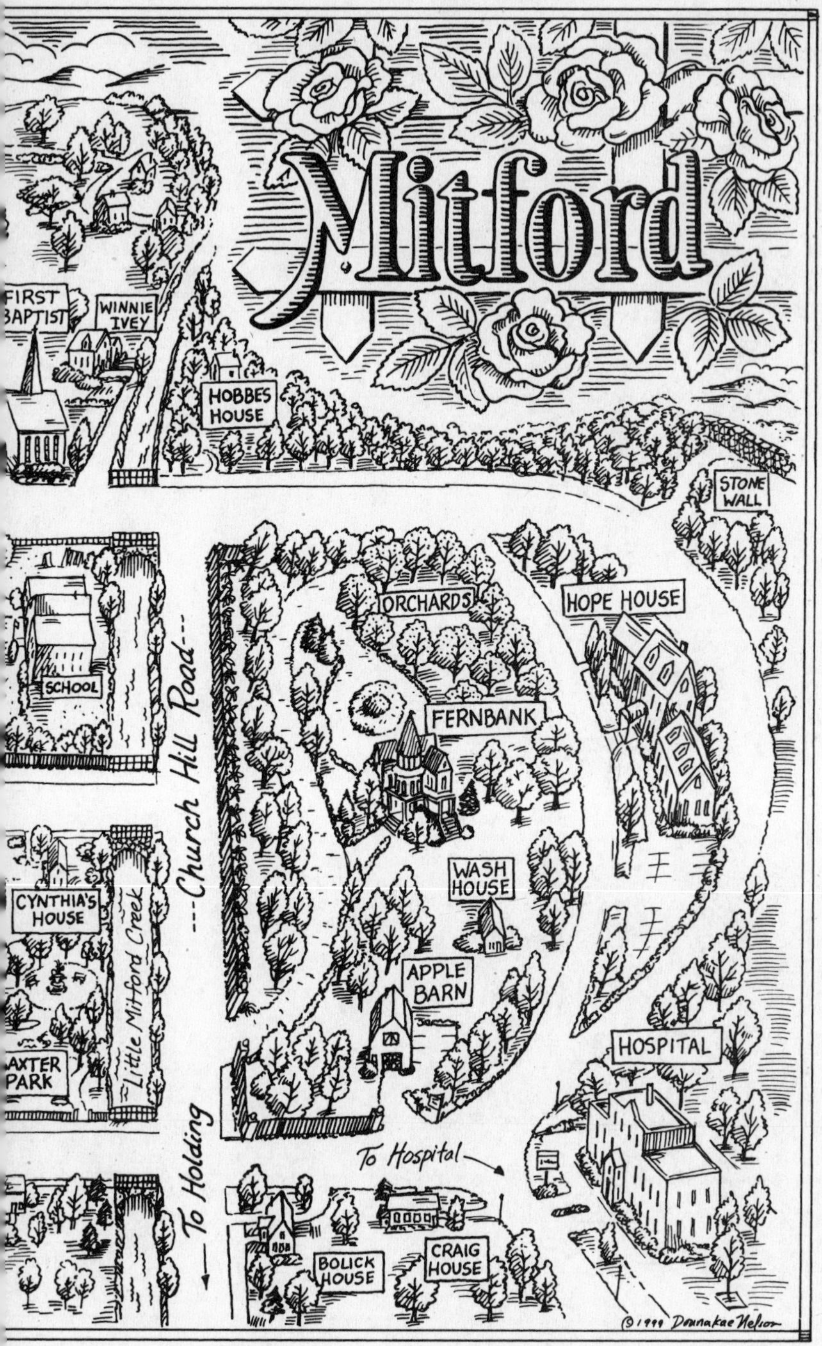
Mitford
FIRST
APTIST
WINNIE IVEY
HOBBES HOUSE
STONE WALL
ORCHARDS
HOPE HOUSE
SCHOOL
FERNBANK
Church Hill Road
WASH HOUSE
CYNTHIA'S HOUSE
Little Mitford Creek
APPLE BARN
HOSPITAL
AXTER PARK
To Holding
To Hospital
BOLICK HOUSE
CRAIG HOUSE
©1999 Donnakae Nelson

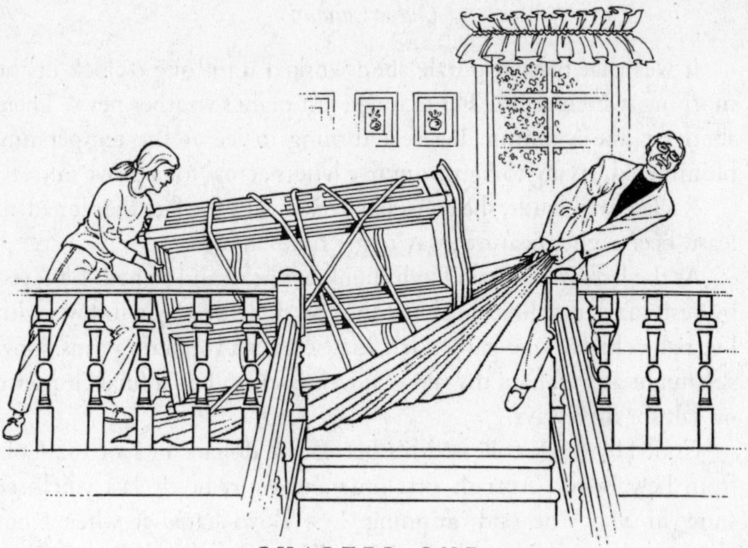

CHAPTER ONE

A Tea and a Half

The indoor plants were among the first to venture outside and breathe the fresh, cold air of Mitford's early spring.

Eager for a dapple of sunlight, starved for the revival of mountain breezes, dozens of begonias and ferns, Easter lilies and Wandering Jews were set out, pot-bound and listless, on porches throughout the village.

As the temperature soared into the low fifties, Winnie Ivey thumped three begonias, a sullen gloxinia, and a Boston fern onto the back steps of the house on Lilac Road, where she was now living. Remembering the shamrock, which was covered with aphids, she fetched it from the kitchen and set it on the railing.

"There!" she said, collecting a lungful of the sharp, pure air. "That ought to fix th' lot of you."

When she opened the back door the following morning, she was stricken at the sight. The carefully wintered plants had been turned to mush by a stark raving freeze and minor snow that also wrenched any notion of early bloom from the lilac bushes.

It was that blasted puzzle she'd worked until one o'clock in the morning, which caused her to forget last night's weather news. There she'd sat like a moron, her feet turning to ice as the temperature plummeted, trying to figure out five letters across for a grove of trees.

Racked with guilt, she consoled herself with the fact that it had, at least, been a chemical-free way to get rid of aphids.

At the hardware, Dora Pugh shook her head and sighed. Betrayed by yesterday's dazzling sunshine, she had done display windows with live baby chicks, wire garden fencing, seeds, and watering cans. Now she might as well haul the snow shovels back and do a final clearance on salt for driveways.

Coot Hendrick collected his bet of five dollars and an RC Cola from Lew Boyd. "Ain't th' first time and won't be th' last you'll see snow in May," he said, grinning. Lew Boyd hated it when Coot grinned, showing his stubs for teeth. He mostly hated it that, concerning weather in Mitford, the skeptics, cynics, and pessimists were usually right.

"Rats!" said Cynthia Kavanagh, who had left a wet scatter rug hanging over the rectory porch rail. Lifting it off the rail, she found it frozen as a popsicle and able to stand perfectly upright.

Father Timothy Kavanagh, rector at the Chapel of our Lord and Savior, had never heard such moaning and groaning about spring's tedious delay, and encountered it even in Happy Endings Bookstore, where, on yet another cold, overcast morning, he picked up a volume entitled *Hummingbirds in the Garden.*

"Hummingbirds?" wailed young Hope Winchester, ringing the sale. "*What* hummingbirds? I suppose you think a hummingbird would dare stick its beak into this arctic tundra, this endless twilight, this . . . this *villatic barbican*?"

"Villatic barbican" was a phrase she had learned only yesterday from a book, and wanted to use it before she forgot it. She knew the rector from Lord's Chapel was somebody she could use such words with—he hadn't flinched when she said "empirical" only last week, and seemed to know exactly what she was talking about.

While everyone else offered lamentations exceeding those of the prophet Jeremiah, the rector felt smugly indifferent to complaints that spring would never come. He had to admit, however, that last

Sunday was one of the few times he'd conducted an Easter service in long johns and ski socks.

Turning up his collar, he leaned into a driving wind and headed toward the office.

Hadn't winter dumped ice, snow, sleet, hail, and rainstorms on the village since late October? Hadn't they been blanketed by fog so thick you could cut it with a dull knife, time and time again?

With all that moisture seeping into the ground for so many long months, didn't this foretell the most glorious springtime in years? And wasn't that, after all, worth the endless assault?

"Absolutely!" he proclaimed aloud, trucking past the Irish Woolen Shop. "No doubt about it!"

"See there?" said Hessie Mayhew, peering out the store window. "It's got Father Tim talking to himself, it's that bad." She sighed. "They say if sunlight doesn't get to your pineal glands for months on end, your sex drive quits."

Minnie Lomax, who was writing sale tags for boiled wool sweaters, looked up and blinked. "What do you know about pineal glands?" She was afraid to ask what Hessie might know about sex drive.

"What does anybody know about pineal glands?" asked Hessie, looking gloomy.

Uncle Billy Watson opened his back door and, without leaving the threshold, lifted the hanging basket off the nail and hauled it inside.

"Look what you've gone and done to that geranium!" snapped his wife of nearly fifty years. "I've petted that thing the winter long, and now it's dead as a doornail."

The old man looked guilt-stricken. "B'fore I hung it out there, hit was already gone south!"

"Shut my mouth? Did you say shut my mouth?" Miss Rose, who refused to wear hearing aids, glared at him.

"I said *gone south*! Dead! Yeller leaves!"

He went to the kitchen radiator and thumped the hanging basket on top. "There!" he said, disgusted with trying to have a garden in a climate like this. "That'll fire it up again."

The rector noted the spears of hosta that had congregated in beds outside the church office. Now, there, as far as spring was concerned, was something you could count on. Hosta was as sturdy a plant as you could put in the ground. Like the postman, neither sleet nor snow could drive it back. Once out of the ground, up it came, fiercely defiant—only, of course, to have its broad leaves shredded like so much Swiss cheese by Mitford's summer hail.

"It's a jungle out there," he sighed, unlocking his office door.

After the snow flurry and freeze came a day of rain followed by a sudden storm of sleet that pecked against the windows like a flock of house sparrows.

His wife, he noted, looked pale. She was sitting at the study window, staring at the infernal weather and chewing her bottom lip. She was also biting the cuticle of her thumb, wrapping a strand of hair around one finger, tapping her foot, and generally amusing herself. He, meanwhile, was reading yet another new book and doing something productive.

A low fire crackled on the hearth.

"Amazing!" he said. "You'd never guess one of the things that attracts butterflies."

"I don't have a clue," said Cynthia, appearing not to want one, either. The sleet gusted against the windowpanes.

"Birdbaths!" he exclaimed. No response. "Ditto with honeysuckle!"

He tried again. "Thinking about the Primrose Tea, are you?"

The second edition of his wife's famous parish-wide tea was coming in less than two weeks. Last year at this time, she was living on a stepladder, frantically repainting the kitchen and dining room, removing his octogenarian drapes, and knocking holes in the plaster to affect an "old Italian villa" look. Now here she was, staring out the window without any visible concern for the countless lemon squares, miniature quiches, vegetable sandwiches, and other items she'd need to feed a hundred and twenty-five women, nearly all of whom would look upon the tea as lunch.

His dog, Barnabas, ambled in and crashed by the hearth, as if drugged.

Cynthia tapped her foot and drummed her fingers on the chair arm. "Hmmm," she said.

"Hmmm what?"

She looked at him. "T.D.A."

"T.D.A.?"

"The Dreaded Armoire, dearest."

His heart pounded. Please, no. Not the armoire. "What about it?" he asked, fearing the answer.

"It's time to move it into our bedroom from the guest room. Remember? We said we were going to do it in the spring!" She smiled at him suddenly, as she was wont to do, and her sapphire-colored eyes gleamed. After a year and a half of marriage, how was it that a certain look from her still made him weak in the knees?

"Aha."

"So!" she said, lifting her hands and looking earnest.

"So? So, it's not spring!" He got up from the sofa and pointed toward the window. "See that? You call that spring? This, Kavanagh, is as far from spring as . . . as . . ."

"As Trieste is from Wesley," she said, helping out, "or the Red Sea from Mitford Creek." He could never get over the way her mind worked. "But do not look at the weather, Timothy, look at the calendar! May third!"

Last fall, they had hauled the enormous armoire down her stairs, down her back steps, through the hedge, up his back steps, along the hall, and finally up the staircase to the guest room, where he had wanted nothing more than to fall prostrate on the rug.

Had she liked it in the guest room, after all that? No, indeed. She had despised the very sight of it sitting there, and instantly came up with a further plan, to be executed in the spring—all of which meant more unloading of drawers and shelves, more lashing the doors closed with a rope, and more hauling—this time across the landing to their bedroom, where, he was convinced, it would tower over them in the night like a five-story parking garage.

"What are you going to do about the tea?" he asked, hoping to distract her.

"Not much at all 'til we get the armoire moved. You know how they are, Timothy, they want to poke into every nook and cranny.

Last year, Hessie Mayhew was down on her very hands and knees, peering into the laundry chute, I saw her with my own eyes. And Georgia Moore opened every cabinet door in the kitchen, she said she was looking for a water glass, when I know for a fact she was seeing if the dishes were stacked to her liking. So, I certainly can't have the armoire standing on that wall in the guest room where it is clearly . . ." she paused and looked at him, "*clearly* out of place."

He was in for it.

He had managed to hold off the move for a full week, but in return for the delay was required to make four pans of brownies (a specialty since seminary), clean out the fireplace, black the andirons, and prune the overgrown forsythia at the dining room windows.

Not bad, considering.

On Saturday morning before the big event the following Friday, he rose early, prayed, studied Paul's first letter to the Corinthians, and sat with his sermon notes; then he ran two miles with Barnabas on his red leash, and returned home fit for anything.

His heart still pounding from the final sprint across Baxter Park, he burst into the kitchen, which smelled of lemons, cinnamon, and freshly brewed coffee. "Let's do it!" he cried.

And get it over with, he thought.

The drawers were out, the shelves were emptied, the doors were lashed shut with a rope. This time, they were dragging it across the floor on a chenille bedspread, left behind by a former rector.

". . . a better way of life!"

Cynthia looked up. "What did you say, dearest?"

"I didn't say anything."

"Mack Stroupe will bring improvement, not change . . ."

They stepped to the open window of the stair landing and looked down to the street. A new blue pickup truck with a public address system was slowly cruising along Wisteria Lane, hauling a sign in the bed. *Mack for Mitford*, it read, *Mitford for Mack.*

". . . improvement, not change. So, think about it, friends and neigh-

bors. And remember—here in Mitford, we already have the good life. With Mack as Mayor, we'll all have a better life!" A loud blast of country music followed: *"If you don't stand for something, you'll fall for anything. . . ."*

She looked at her husband. "Mack Stroupe! Please, no."

He wrinkled his brow and frowned. "This is May. Elections aren't 'til November."

"Starting a mite early."

"I'll say," he agreed, feeling distinctly uneasy.

"He's done broke th' noise ordinance," said Chief Rodney Underwood, hitching up his gun belt.

Rodney had stepped to the back of the Main Street Grill to say hello to the early morning regulars in the rear booth. "Chapter five, section five-two in the Mitford Code of Ordinance lays it out. No PA systems for such a thing as political campaigns."

"Startin' off his public career as a pure criminal," said Mule Skinner.

"Which is th' dadgum law of the land for politicians!" *Mitford Muse* editor J. C. Hogan mopped his brow with a handkerchief.

"Well, no harm done. I slapped a warning on 'im, that ordinance is kind of new. Used to, politicians was haulin' a PA up and down th' street, ever' whichaway."

"What about that truck with the sign?" asked Father Tim.

"He can haul th' sign around all he wants to, but th' truck has to keep movin'. If he parks it on town property, I got 'im. I can run 'im in and he can go to readin' *Southern Livin'*." The local jail was the only detention center the rector ever heard of that kept neat stacks of *Southern Living* magazine in the cells.

"I hate to see a feller make a fool of hisself," said Rodney. "Ain't *no*body can whip Esther Cunningham—an' if you say I said that, I'll say you lied."

"Right," agreed Mule.

"Course, she *has* told it around that one of these days, her an' Ray are takin' off in th' RV and leave th' mayorin' to somebody else."

Mule shook his head. "Fifteen years is a long time to be hog-tied to a thankless job, all right."

"Is that Mack's new truck?" asked Father Tim. As far he knew, Mack never had two cents to rub together, as his hotdog stand across from the gas station didn't seem to rake in much business.

"I don't know whose truck it is, it sure couldn't be Mack's. Well, I ain't got all day to loaf, like you boys." Rodney headed for the register to pick up his breakfast order. "See you in th' funny papers."

J.C. scowled. "I don't know that I'd say nobody can whip Esther. Mack's for improvement, and we're due for a little improvement around here, if you ask me."

"Nobody asked you," said Mule.

Father Tim dialed the number from his office. "Mayor!"

"So it's the preacher, is it? I've been lookin' for you."

"What's going on?"

"If that low-down scum thinks he can run me out of office, he's got another think coming."

"Does this mean you're not going to quit and take off with Ray in the RV?"

"Shoot! That's what I say just to hear my head roar. Listen—you don't think the bum has a chance, do you?"

"To tell the truth, Esther, I believe he does have a chance. . . ."

Esther's voice lowered. "You do?"

"About the same chance as a snowball in July."

She laughed uproariously and then sobered. "Of course, there is *one* way that Mack Stroupe could come in here and sit behind th' mayor's desk."

He was alarmed. "Really?"

"But only one. And that's over my dead body."

Something new was going on at home nearly every day.

On Tuesday evening, he found a large, framed watercolor hanging in the rectory's once-gloomy hallway. It was of Violet, Cynthia's white cat and the heroine of the award-winning children's books created by his unstoppable wife. Violet sat on a brocade cloth, peering into a vase filled with nasturtiums and a single, wide-eyed goldfish.

"Stunning!" he said. "Quite a change."

"Call it an *improvement,*" she said, pleased.

On Wednesday, he found new chintz draperies in the dining room and parlor, which gave the place a dazzling elegance that fairly bowled him over. But—hadn't they agreed that neither would spend more than a hundred bucks without the other's consent?

She read his mind. "So, the draperies cost five hundred, but since the watercolor is worth that and more on the current market, it's a wash."

"Aha."

"I'm also doing one of Barnabas, for your study. Which means," she said, "that the family coffers will respond by allotting new draperies for our bedroom."

"You're a bookkeeping whiz, Kavanagh. But why new draperies when we're retiring in eighteen months?"

"I've had them made so they can go anywhere and fit any kind of windows. If worse comes to worst, I'll remake them into summer dresses, and vestments for my clergyman."

"That's the spirit!"

Why did he feel his wife could get away with anything where he was concerned? Was it because he'd waited sixty-two years, like a stalled ox, to fall in love and marry?

If he and Cynthia had written a detailed petition on a piece of paper and sent it heavenward, the weather couldn't have been more glorious on the day of the talked-about tea.

Much to everyone's relief, the primroses actually bloomed. However, no sooner had the eager blossoms appeared than Hessie Mayhew bore down on them with a vengeance, in yards and hidden nooks everywhere. She knew precisely the location of every cluster of primroses in the village, not to mention the exact whereabouts of each woods violet, lilac bush, and pussy willow.

"It's Hessie!" warned an innocent bystander on Hessie's early morning run the day of the tea. "Stand back!"

Armed with a collection of baskets that she wore on her arms like so many bracelets, Hessie did not allow help from the Episcopal

Church Women, nor any of her own presbyters. She worked alone, she worked fast, and she worked smart.

After going at a trot through neighborhood gardens, huffing up Old Church Lane to a secluded bower of early-blooming shrubs, and combing four miles of country roadside, she showed up at the back door of the rectory at precisely eleven a.m., looking triumphant.

Sodden with morning dew and black dirt, she delivered a vast quantity of flowers, moss, and grapevine into the hands of the rector's house help, Puny Guthrie, then flew home to bathe, dress, and put antibiotic cream on her knees, which were skinned when she leaned over to pick a wild trillium and fell sprawling.

The Episcopal Church Women, who had arrived as one body at ten-thirty, flew into the business of arranging "Hessie's truck," as they called it, while Barnabas snored in the garage and Violet paced in her carrier.

"Are you off?" asked Cynthia, as the rector came at a trot through the hectic kitchen.

"Off and running. I finished polishing the mail slot, tidying the slipcover on the sofa, and trimming the lavender by the front walk. I also beat the sofa pillows for any incipient dust and coughed for a full five minutes."

"Well done!" she said cheerily, giving him a hug.

"I'll be home at one-thirty to help the husbands park cars."

Help the husbands park cars? he thought as he sprinted toward the office. He was a *husband*! After all these months, the thought still occasionally slammed him in the solar plexus and took his breath away.

Nine elderly guests, including the Kavanaghs' friend Louella, arrived in the van from Hope House and were personally escorted up the steps of the rectory and into the hands of the Altar Guild.

Up and down Wisteria Lane, men with armbands stitched with primroses and a Jerusalem cross directed traffic, which quickly grew snarled. At one point, the rector leaped into a stalled Chevrolet and managed to roll it to the curb. Women came in car pools, husbands dropped off spouses, daughters delivered mothers, and all in all, the narrow street was as congested as a carnival in Rio.

"This is th' biggest thing to hit Mitford since th' blizzard two years ago," said Mule Skinner, who was a Baptist, but offered to help out, anyway.

The rector laughed. "That's one way to look at it." Didn't anybody ever *walk* in this town?

"Look here!"

It was Mack Stroupe in that blasted pickup truck, carting his sign around in their tea traffic. Mack rolled by, chewing on a toothpick and looking straight ahead.

"You comin' to the Primrose Tea?" snapped Mule. "If not, get this vehicle out of here, we're tryin' to conduct a church function!"

Four choir members, consisting of a lyric soprano, a mezzo soprano, and two altos, arrived in a convertible, looking windblown and holding on to their hats.

"Hats is a big thing this year," observed Uncle Billy Watson, who stood at the curb with Miss Rose and watched the proceedings. Uncle Billy was the only man who showed up at last year's tea, and now considered his presence at the event to be a tradition.

Uncle Billy walked out to the street with the help of his cane and tapped Father Tim on the shoulder. "Hit's like a Chiney puzzle, don't you know. If you 'uns'd move that'n off to th' side and git that'n to th' curb, hit'd be done with."

"No more parking on Wisteria," Ron Malcolm reported to the rector. "We'll direct the rest of the crowd to the church lot and shoot 'em back here in the Hope House van."

A UPS driver, who had clearly made an unwise turn onto Wisteria, sat in his truck in front of the rectory, stunned by the sight of so much traffic on the usually uneventful Holding/Mitford/Wesley run.

"Hit's what you call a standstill," Uncle Billy told J. C. Hogan, who showed up with his Nikon and six rolls of Tri-X.

As traffic started to flow again, the rector saw Mack Stroupe turn onto Wisteria Lane from Church Hill. Clearly, he was circling the block.

"I'd like to whop him upside th' head with a two-by-four," said

Mule. He glared at Mack, who was reared back in the seat with both windows down, listening to a country music station. Mack waved to several women, who immediately turned their heads.

Mule snorted. "Th' dumb so-and-so! How would you like to have that peckerwood for mayor?"

The rector wiped his perspiring forehead. "Watch your blood pressure, buddyroe."

"He says he's goin' to campaign straight through spring and summer, right up to election in November. Kind of like bein' tortured by a drippin' faucet."

As the truck passed, Emma Newland stomped over. "I ought to climb in that truck and slap his jaws. What's he doin', anyway, trying to sway church people to his way of thinkin'?"

"Let him be," Father Tim cautioned his secretary and on-line computer whiz. After all, give Mack enough rope and . . .

Cynthia was lying in bed, moaning, as he came out of the shower. He went into the bedroom, hastily drying off.

"Why are you moaning?" he asked, alarmed.

"Because it helps relieve exhaustion. I hope the windows are closed so the neighbors can't hear."

"The only neighbor close enough to hear is no longer living in the little yellow house next door. She is, in fact, lying right here, doing the moaning."

She moaned again. "Moaning is good," she told him, her face mashed into the pillow. "You should try it."

"I don't think so," he said.

Warm as a steamed clam from the shower, he put on his pajamas and sat on the side of the bed. "I'm proud of you," he said, rubbing her back. "That was a tea-and-a-half! The best! In fact, words fail. You'll have a time topping that one."

"Don't tell me I'm supposed to *top* it!"

"Yes, well, not to worry. Next year, we can have Omer Cunningham and his pilot buddies do a flyover. That'll give the ladies something to talk about." He'd certainly given all of Mitford something to talk about last May when he flew to Virginia with Omer in his rag-wing taildragger. Four hours in Omer's little plane had gained him more credibility than thirty-six years in the pulpit.

"A little farther down," his wife implored. "Ugh. My lower back is killing me from all the standing and baking."

"I got the reviews as your guests left."

"Only tell me the good ones. I don't want to hear about the cheese straws, which were as limp as linguine."

"'Perfect' was a word they bandied around quite a bit, and the lemon squares, of course, got their usual share of raves. Some wanted me to know how charming they think you are, and others made lavish remarks about your youth and beauty."

He leaned down and kissed her shoulder, inhaling the faintest scent of wisteria. "You are beautiful, Kavanagh."

"Thanks."

"I don't suppose there are any special thanks you'd like to offer the poor rube who helped unsnarl four thousand three hundred and seventy-nine cars, trucks, and vans?"

She rolled over and looked at him, smiling. Then she held her head to one side in that way he couldn't resist, and pulled him to her and kissed him tenderly.

"Now you're talking," he said.

The phone rang.

"Hello?"

"Hey."

Dooley! "Hey, yourself, buddy."

"Is Cynthia sending me a box of stuff she made for that tea? I can't talk long."

"Two boxes. Went off today."

"Man! Thanks!"

"You're welcome. How's school?"

"Great."

Great? Dooley Barlowe was not one to use superlatives. "No kidding?"

"You're going to like my grades."

Was this the little guy he'd struggled to raise for nearly three years?

The Dooley who always shot himself in the foot? The self-assured sound of the boy's voice made his hair fairly stand on end.

"We're going to like you coming home, even better. In just six or seven weeks, you'll be here. . . ."

Silence. Was Dooley dreading to tell him he wanted to spend the summer at Meadowgate Farm? The boy's decision to do that last year had nearly broken his heart, not to mention Cynthia's. They had, of course, gotten over it, as they watched the boy doing what he loved best—learning more about veterinary medicine at the country practice of Hal Owen.

"Of course," said the rector, pushing on, "we want you to go out to Meadowgate, if that's what you'd like to do." He swallowed. This year, he was stronger, he could let go.

"OK," said Dooley, "that's what I'd like to do."

"Fine. No problem. I'll call you tomorrow for our usual phone visit. We love you."

"I love you back."

"Here's Cynthia."

"Hey," she said.

"Hey, yourself." It was their family greeting.

"So, you big galoot, we sent a box for you and one to share with your friends."

"What's in it?"

"Lemon squares."

"I like lemon squares."

"Plus raspberry tarts, pecan truffles, and brownies made by the preacher."

"Thanks."

"Are you OK?"

"Yes."

"No kidding?"

"Yep."

"Good!" said Cynthia. "Lace Turner asked about you the other day."

"That dumb girl that dresses like a guy?"

"She doesn't dress like a guy anymore. Oh, and your friend Jenny was asking about you, too."

"How's Tommy?"

"Missing you. Just as we do. So hurry home, even if you are going to spend the summer at Meadowgate, you big creep."

Dooley cackled.

"We love you."

"I love you back."

Cynthia placed the receiver on the hook, smiling happily.

"Now, you poor rube," she said, "where were we?"

He sat on the study sofa and took the rubber band off the *Mitford Muse.*

Good grief! There he was on the front page, standing bewildered in front of the UPS truck with his nose looking, as usual, like a turnip or a tulip bulb. Why did J. C. Hogan run this odious picture, when he might have photographed his hardworking, good-looking, and thoroughly deserving wife?

Primrose Tee Draws
Stand-Out Crowd

Clearly, Hessie had not written this story, which on first glance appeared to be about golf, but had given her notes to J.C., who forged ahead without checking his spelling.

Good time had by all . . . same time next year . . . a hundred and thirty guests . . . nine gallons of tea, ten dozen lemon squares, eight dozen raspberry tarts . . . traffic jam . . .

The phone gave a sharp blast.

"Hello?"

"Timothy . . ."

"Hal! I've just been thinking of you and Marge."

"Good. And we of you. I've got some . . . hard news, and wanted you to know."

Hal and Marge Owen were two of his closest, most valued friends. He was afraid to know.

"I've just hired a full-time assistant."

"That's the bad news? It sounds good to me, you work like a Trojan."

"Yes, but . . . we won't be able to have Dooley this summer. My assistant is a young fellow, just starting out, and I'll have to give him a lot of time and attention. Also, we're putting him up in Dooley's room until he gets established." Hal sighed.

"But that's terrific. We know Dooley looked forward to being at Meadowgate—however, circumstances alter cases, as my Mississippi kin used to say."

"There's a large riding stable coming in about a mile down the road, they've asked me to vet the horses. That could be a full-time job right there."

"I understand. Of course. Your practice is growing."

"We'll miss the boy, Tim, you know how we feel about him, how Rebecca Jane loves him. But look, we'll have him out to stay the first two weeks he's home from school—if that works for you."

"Absolutely."

"Oh, and Tim . . ."

"Yes?"

"Will you tell him?"

"I will. I'll talk to him about it, get him thinking of what to do this summer. Be good for him."

"So why don't you and Cynthia plan to spend the day when you bring him out? Bring Barnabas, too. Marge will make your favorite."

Deep-dish chicken pie, with a crust like French pastry. "We'll be there!" he said, meaning it.

"Will you tell him?" he asked Cynthia.

"No way," she said.

Nobody wanted to tell Dooley Barlowe that he couldn't spend the summer doing what he loved more than anything on earth.

She opened her eyes and rolled over to find him sitting up in bed.

"Oh, my dear! Oh, my goodness! What happened?"

He loved the look on his wife's face; he wanted to savor it. "It's already turned a few colors," he said, removing his hand from his right temple.

She peered at him as if he were a butterfly on a pin. "Yes! Black . . . and blue and . . . the tiniest bit of yellow."

"My old school colors," he said.

"But what happened?" He never heard such *tsk*ing and gasping.

"T.D.A.," he replied.

"The Dreaded Armoire? What do you mean?"

"I mean that I got up in the middle of the night, in the dark, and went out to the landing and opened the windows to give Barnabas a cool breeze. As I careened through the bedroom on my way to the bathroom, I slammed into the blasted thing."

"Oh, no! Oh, heavens. What can I do? And tomorrow's Sunday!"

"Spousal abuse," he muttered. "In today's TV news climate, my congregation will pick up on it immediately."

"Timothy, dearest, I'm so sorry. I'll get something for you, I don't know what, but something. Just stay right there and don't move."

She put on her slippers and robe and flew downstairs, Barnabas barking at her heels.

T.D.A. might stand for "The *Dreaded* Armoire" as far as his wife was concerned. As far as he was concerned, it stood for something else entirely.

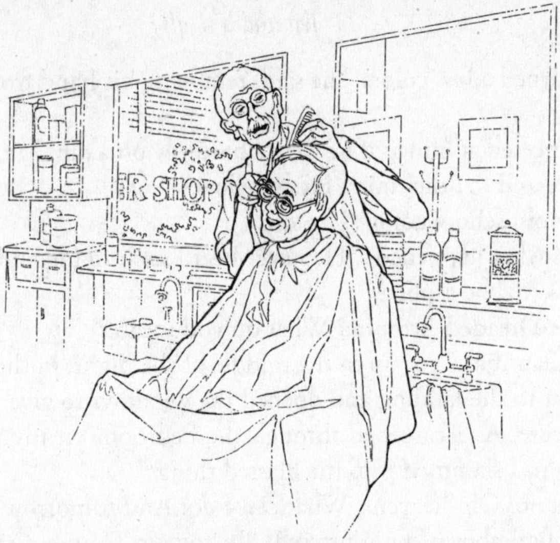

CHAPTER TWO

Step by Step

He was missing her.

How many times had he gone to the phone to call, only to realize she wasn't there to answer?

When Sadie Baxter died last year at the age of ninety, he felt the very rug yanked from under him. She'd been family to him, and a companionable friend; his sister in Christ, and favorite parishioner. In addition, she was Dooley's benefactor and, for more than half a century, the most generous donor in the parish. Not only had she given Hope House, the new five-million-dollar nursing home at the top of Old Church Lane, she had faithfully kept a roof on Lord's Chapel while her own roof went begging.

Sadie Baxter was warbling with the angels, he thought, chuckling at the image. But not because of the money she'd given, no, indeed. Good works, the Scriptures plainly stated, were no passport to heaven. "For by grace are you saved through faith," Paul wrote in his letter to the Ephesians, "and that not of yourselves, it is the gift of God—not of works, lest any man should boast."

The issue of works versus grace was about as popular as the issue of sin. Nonetheless, he was set to preach on Paul's remarks, and soon. The whole works ideology was as insidious as so many termites going after the stairs to the altar.

Emma blew in, literally. As she opened the office door, a gust of cold spring wind snatched it from her hand and sent it crashing against the wall.

"Lord have mercy!" she shouted, trying to snatch it back against a gale that sent his papers flying. She slammed the door and stood panting in front of it, her glasses crooked on her nose.

"Have you *ever*?" she demanded.

"Ever what?"

"Seen a winter that lasted nine months goin' on ten? I said, Harold, why don't we move to Florida? I never thought I'd live to hear such words come out of my mouth."

"And what did Harold say?" he asked, trying to reassemble his papers.

"You know Baptists," she replied, hanging up her coat. "They don't move to Florida; they don't want to be warm! They want to freeze to death on th' way to prayer meetin' and shoot right up to th' pearly gates and get it over with."

The Genghis Khan of church secretaries wagged her finger at him. "It's enough to make me go back to bein' Episcopalian."

"What's Harold done now?"

"Made Snickers sleep in the garage. Can you believe it? Country people don't like dogs in the house, you know."

"I thought Snickers was sleeping in the house."

"He was, 'til he ate a steak off Harold's plate."

"Aha."

"Down th' hatch, neat as a pin. But then, guess what?"

"I can't guess."

"He threw it all up in the closet, on Harold's shoes."

"I can see Harold's point."

"You would," she said stiffly, sitting at her desk.

"I would?"

"Yes. You're a man," she announced, glaring at him. "By the way . . ."

"By the way what?"

"That bump on your head is the worst-lookin' mess I ever saw. Can't you get Cynthia to do somethin' about it?"

Then again, maybe works *could* have an influence. Exercising the patience of a saint while putting up with Emma Newland for fifteen years should be enough to blast him heavenward like a rocket, with no stops along the way.

Emma booted her computer and peered at the screen.

"I nearly ran over Mack Stroupe comin' in this morning, he crossed th' street without lookin'. I didn't know whether to hit th' brakes or the accelerator. You know that hotdog stand of his? He's turnin' it into his campaign headquarters! Campaign headquarters, can you believe it? Who does he think he is, Ross Perot?"

The rector sighed.

"You know that mud slick in front that he called a parkin' lot?" She clicked her mouse. "Well, he's having it paved, the asphalt trucks are all over it like flies. Asphalt!" she muttered. "I hate asphalt. Give me cement, any day."

Yes, indeed. Straight up, right into a personal and highly favorable audience with St. Peter.

"Something has to be done," he said.

"Yes, but what?"

"Blast if I know. If we don't get a new roof on it soon, who can guess what the interior damage might be?"

Father Tim and Cynthia sat at the kitchen table, discussing his second most worrisome problem—what to do with the rambling, three-story Victorian mansion known as Fernbank, and its endless, overgrown grounds.

When Miss Sadie died last year, she left Fernbank to the church, "to cover any future needs of Hope House," and there it sat—buffeted by hilltop winds and scoured by driving hailstorms, with no one even to sweep dead bees from the windowsills.

In Miss Sadie's mind, Fernbank had been a gift; to him, it was an albatross. After all, she had clearly made him responsible for doing the best thing by her aging homeplace.

There had been talk of leasing it to a private school or institution, a notion that lay snarled somewhere in diocesan red tape. On the other hand, should they sell it and invest the money? If so, should they sell it as is, or bite the bullet and repair it at horrendous cost to a parish almost certainly unwilling to gamble in real estate?

"We just got an estimate on the roof," he said.

"How much?"

"Thirty, maybe thirty-five thousand."

"Good heavens!"

They sat in silence, reflecting.

"Poor Fernbank," she said. "Who would buy it, anyway? Certainly no one in Mitford can afford it."

He refilled his coffee cup. Even if they were onto a sour subject, he was happy to be hanging out with his wife. Besides, Cynthia Kavanagh was known for stumbling onto serendipitous solutions for all sorts of woes and tribulations.

"Worse than that," she said, "who could afford to fix it up, assuming they could buy it in the first place?"

"There's the rub."

After staring at the tablecloth for a moment, she looked up. "Then again, why worry about it at all? Miss Sadie didn't give it to *you* . . ."

So why had he worn the thing around his neck for more than ten months?

". . . she gave it to the church. Which, in case you've momentarily forgotten, belongs to God. So, let Him handle it, for Pete's sake."

He could feel the grin spreading across his face. Right! Of course! He felt a weight fly off, if only temporarily. "Who's the preacher around here, anyway?"

"Sometimes you go on sabbatical, dearest."

He stood and cranked open the kitchen window. "When are we going up there and pick out the token or two that Miss Sadie offered us in the letter?"

She sighed. "We don't have a nook, much less a cranny that isn't already stuffed with *things.* My house next door is full, the rectory is brimming, and we're retiring."

She was right. It was a time to be subtracting, not adding.

"What have the others taken?" she wondered.

"Louella took the brooch Miss Sadie's mother painted, and Olivia only wanted a walnut chest and the photographs of Miss Sadie's mother and Willard Porter. The place is virtually untouched."

"Did anyone go sneezing through the attic?"

"Not a soul."

"I absolutely love sneezing through attics! Attics are full of mystery and intrigue. So, yes, let's do it! Let's go up! Besides, we don't have to shop, we can *browse*!"

Her eyes suddenly looked bluer, as they always did when she was excited.

"I love it when you talk like this," he said, relieved.

At least one of the obligations surrounding Fernbank would be settled.

Fernbank was only his second most nagging worry.

What to do about Dooley's scattered siblings had moved to the head of the line.

Over the last few years, Dooley's mother, Pauline Barlowe, had let her children go like so many kittens scattered from a box.

How could he hope to collect what had been blown upon the wind during Pauline's devastating bouts with alcohol? The last that Pauline had heard, her son Kenny was somewhere in Oregon, little Jessie's whereabouts were unknown, and Sammy . . . he didn't want to think about it.

Last year, the rector had gone with Lace Turner into the drug-infested Creek community and brought Dooley's nine-year-old brother out. Poobaw was now living in Betty Craig's cottage with his recovering mother and disabled grandfather, and doing well in Mitford School.

A miracle. But in this case, miracles, like peanuts, were addictive. One would definitely not be enough.

"This news just hit the street," said Mule, sliding into the booth with a cup of coffee. "I got it before J.C."

"Aha," said the rector, trying to decide whether to butter his roll or eat it dry.

"Joe Ivey's hangin' it up."

"No!"

"Goin' to Tennessee to live with his kin, and Winnie Ivey cryin' her eyes out, he's all the family she's got in Mitford."

"Why is he hanging it up?"

"Kidneys."

Velma appeared with her order pad. "We don't have kidneys n'more. We tried kidneys last year and nobody ordered 'em."

"Meat loaf sandwich, then," said Mule. "Wait a minute. What's the Father having?"

"Chicken salad."

"I pass. Make it a BLT on whole wheat."

"Kidneys?" asked the rector as Velma left.

"I don't have to tell you Joe likes a little shooter now and again."

"Umm."

"Lately, he's been drinkin' peach brandy, made fresh weekly in Knox County. The other thing is, varicose veins. Forty-five years of standing on his feet barbering, his legs look like a Georgia road map." Mule blew on his coffee. "He showed 'em to me."

Except for a couple of visits to Fancy Skinner's Hair House, Joe Ivey had been his barber since he came to Mitford. "I hate to hear this."

"We all hate to hear it."

There was a long silence. The rector buttered his roll.

"I despise change," said Mule, looking grim.

"You and me both."

"That's why Mack won't call it change, he calls it improvement. But you and I know exactly what it is. . . ."

"Change," said Father Tim.

"Right. And if Mack has anything to do with it, it won't be change for the better."

What the heck, he opened the container of blackberry jam left from the breakfast crowd and spread that on, too. With diabetes, life may not be long, he thought, but the diet they put you on sure makes it seem that way.

"Have you thought of the bright side of Joe getting out of the business?" asked Father Tim.

"The bright side?"

"All Joe's customers will be running to your wife."

Mule's face lit up. "I'll be dadgum. That's right."

"That ought to amount to, oh, forty people, easy. With haircuts at ten bucks a head these days, you and Fancy can go on that cruise you've been talking about, no problem."

Mule looked grim again. "Yeah, but then Fancy'll be gettin' varicose veins."

"Every calling has an occupational hazard," said the rector. "Look at yours—a real estate market that's traditionally volatile, you never know how much bread you can put on the table, or when."

J.C. threw his bulging briefcase onto the bench and slid into the booth.

"Did you hear what Adele did last night?"

"What?" the realtor and the rector asked in unison.

The editor looked like he'd just won the lottery. "She busted a guy for attempted robbery and probably saved Dot Hamby's life." Adele was not only a Mitford police officer, but J.C.'s wife.

"Your buttons are poppin' off in my coffee," said Mule.

"Where did it happen?"

"Down at the Shoe Barn. She parked her patrol car in back, went in the side door, and was over behind one of the shoe racks, tryin' to find a pair of pumps. Meanwhile, this idiot walks in the front door and asks Dot to change a ten, and when Dot opens the cash register, he whips out a gun and shoves it in her face. Adele heard what was going on, so she slipped up behind the sucker, barefooted, and buried a nine-millimeter in his ribs."

"What did she say?" asked Mule.

"She said what you're supposed to say in a case like that. She said, 'Drop it.'"

Mule raised his eyebrows. "Man!"

J.C. wiped his face with a handkerchief. "His butt is in jail as we speak."

"Readin' casserole recipes out of *Southern Living,*" said Mule. "It's too good for th' low-down snake."

"It's nice to see where my recyclin' is ending up," said the editor, staring at Mule.

"What's that supposed to mean?"

"I just read it takes twenty-six plastic soda bottles to make a polyester suit like that."

"Waste not, want not," said Mule.

J.C. looked for Velma. "You see what Mack's doing up the street?"

"We did."

"A real improvement, he says he's throwing a barbecue soon as the parking lot hardens off. Live music, the whole nine yards. I might give that a front page."

Mule appeared frozen.

"What's the deal with you not liking Mack Stroupe?" asked J.C. "The least you can do is listen to what he has to say."

"I don't listen to double-dealin' cheats," snapped Mule. "They don't have anything to say that I want to hear."

"Come on, that incident was years ago."

"He won't get my vote, let me put it that way."

J.C.'s face flushed. "You want to stick your head in the sand like half the people in this town, go ahead. For my money, it's time we had something new and different around here, a few new businesses, a decent housing development.

"When they staffed Hope House, they hired twenty-seven people from outside Mitford, and where do you think they're living? Wesley! Holding! Working here, but pumping up somebody else's economy, building somebody else's town parks, paying somebody else's taxes."

The rector noticed that Mule's hand was shaking when he picked up his coffee cup. "I'd rather see Mitford throw tax money down a rat hole than put a mealymouthed lowlife in Esther's job."

"For one thing," growled J.C., "you'd better get over the idea it's *Esther's* job."

The regulars in the back booth had disagreed before, but this was disturbingly different.

The roll the rector had eaten suddenly became a rock.

"Just a little off the sides," he said.

"Sides? What sides? Since you slipped off and let Fancy Skinner do your barberin', you ain't got any sides."

What could he say? "We'll miss you around here, Joe. I hate like the dickens to see you go."

"I hate like the dickens to go. But I'm too old to be doin' this."

"How old?"

"Sixty-four."

Good Lord! He was hovering around that age himself. He instantly felt depressed. "That's not old!" he said.

"For this callin', it is. I've tore my legs up over it, and that's enough for me."

"Where are you moving in Tennessee?"

"Memphis. Might do a little part-time security at Graceland, with my cousin. I'll be stayin' with my baby sister—Winnie's th' oldest, you know, we want her to move up, too."

Winnie gone from the Sweet Stuff Bakery? Two familiar faces missing from Mitford, all at once? He didn't like the sound of it, not a bit.

"Here," said Joe, handing him a bottle with an aftershave label. "Take you a little pull on this. It might be your last chance."

"What is it?"

"Homemade peach brandy, you'll never taste better. Go on and take you a snort, I won't tell nobody."

For fifteen years, his barber had offered him a nip of this, a shooter of that, and he had always refused. The rector had preached him a sermon a time or two, years ago, but Joe had told him to mind his own business. Without even thinking, he unscrewed the cap, turned the bottle up, and took a swig. *Holy smoke.*

He passed it back, nearly unable to speak. "That'll do it for me."

"I might have a little taste myself." Joe upended the bottle and polished off half the contents.

"Are you sure you poured out the aftershave before you poured in the brandy?"

Joe cackled. “Listen here,” he said, brushing his customer’s neck, “don’t be lettin’ Mack Stroupe run Esther off.”

“I’ll do my best.”

“Look after Winnie ’til she can sell her bake shop and get up to Memphis.”

“I will. She’s a good one.”

“And take good care of that boy, keep him in a straight line. I never had nobody to keep me in a straight line.”

“You’ve done all right, Joe. You’ve been a good friend to us, and you’ll be missed.” He might have been trying to swallow down a golf ball. He hated goodbyes.

He got out of the chair and reached for his wallet. “I want you to take care of yourself, and let us hear from you.”

Tears stood in Joe’s eyes. “Put that back in your pocket. I’ve barbered you for fifteen years, and this one’s on me.”

He’d never noticed that Joe Ivey seemed so frail-looking and pallid—defenseless, somehow. The rector threw his arms around him in a wordless hug. Then he walked down the stairs to Main Street, his breath smelling like lighter fluid, bawling like a baby.

The date for the Bane and Blessing sale was official, and the annual moaning began.

No show of lilacs, no breathtaking display of dogwoods could alleviate the woe.

Three ECW members suddenly developed chronic back trouble, and an Altar Guild member made reservations to visit her sister in Toledo during the week of the sale. Two Sunday School teachers who had, in a weak moment, volunteered to help trooped up the aisle after Wednesday Eucharist to pray at the altar.

After Esther Bolick agreed to chair the historic church event, she went home and asked her husband, Gene, to have her committed. The Bane and Blessing was known, over the years, for having put two women flat on their backs in bed, nearly broken up a marriage, and chased three families to the Lutherans in Wesley.

Besides, hadn’t she virtually retired from years and years of churchwork, trying to focus, instead, on cake baking? Wasn't baking a ministry in its own right? And didn't she bake an orange marmalade cake at least twice a week for some poor soul who was down and out?

In the first place, she couldn't remember saying she'd *do* the Bane. She had been totally dumbfounded when the meeting ended and everybody rushed over to hug and thank her and tell her how wonderful she was.

In the end, she sighed, determined that it should be done "as unto the Lord and not unto men."

"That's the spirit!" said her rector, doling out a much-needed hug.

He wouldn't have traded places with Esther Bolick for all the tea in China. Esther, however, would do an outstanding job, and no doubt put an unprecedented amount of money in the missions till.

Because it was the most successful fund-raising event in the entire diocese, the women who pulled it off usually got enough local recognition to last a lifetime, or, at the very least, a couple of months.

"October fourth," Esther told Gene.

"Eat your Wheaties," Gene told Esther.

He'd rather be shot. But somebody had to do it.

"Hey," said Dooley, knowing who was on the phone.

"Hey, yourself. What's going on up there?"

"Chorus trip to Washington this weekend. We're singing in a church and a bunch of senators and stuff will be there. I bought a new blazer, my old one got ripped on a nail. How's ol' Barnabas?"

"Sitting right here, licking my shoe, I think I dropped jam on it this morning. There's something I need to talk with you about."

Silence.

"Hal Owen hired an assistant."

He may as well have put a knife in the boy, so keenly could he feel his disappointment.

"That means he'll have help this summer, and the fellow will be . . ."—he especially hated this part—"be staying in your room until he gets situated."

"Fine," said Dooley, his voice cold.

"Hal had to do it, he's been asked to vet a riding stable that's moving in up the road. He's got his hands full and then some."

He couldn't bear Dooley Barlowe's silences; they seemed as deep as wells, as black as mines.

"Hal and Marge want you to come out for two weeks when you get home from school. They'll . . . miss having you for the summer."

"OK."

"You might want to think about a job."

More silence.

"Tommy's going to have a job."

"Where?"

"Pumping gas at Lew's. He'll probably have a uniform with his name on it." It was a weak ploy, but all he could come up with. He pushed on. "Summer will give you time with your brother. Poobaw would like that. And so would your granpaw."

Give him time to think it over. "Listen, buddy. You're going to have a great summer, you'll see. And we love you. Never forget that."

"I don't."

Good! "Good. I'll talk with you Saturday."

"Hey, listen . . ." said Dooley.

"Yes?"

"Nothin'."

"OK. God be with you, son."

He took out his handkerchief and wiped his forehead.

"He who is not impatient is not in love," said an old Italian proverb.

Well, that proved it right there, he thought, leaving his office and hurrying up Main Street toward home.

Why did he feel such excitement about seeing his wife, when he had seen her only this morning? She had brought them coffee in bed at an inhuman hour, and they'd sat up, drinking it, laughing and talking as if it were high noon.

A woman who would get up at five o'clock in order to visit with her husband before his prayer and study time was a saint. Of course, he admitted, she didn't make a habit of it. And didn't that make it all the more welcome?

Cynthia, Cynthia! he thought, looking at the pink dogwood in the yard of the tea room across the street. Like great pink canopies, the trees spread their lacy shade over emerald grass and beds of yellow tulips.

Dear Lord! It was nearly more than a man could bear—spring coming on like thunder, and a woman who had kissed him only hours ago, in a way he'd never, in his bachelor days, had the wits to imagine.

It wouldn't take more than a very short memory to recall the women who'd figured in his life.

Peggy Cramer. That had taught him a thing or two. And when the engagement broke off while he was in seminary, he'd known that it was a good thing.

Then there was Becky. How his parish had worked to pull that one off! She was the woman who thought Wordsworth was a Dallas department store. He hoofed it past Dora Pugh's hardware, laughing out loud.

Ah, but he felt an immense gratitude for his wife's spontaneous laughter, her wisdom, and even her infernal stubborness. He snapped a branch of white lilac from the bush at the corner of the rectory yard.

He raced up his front steps, threw open the door, and bounded down the hall.

"Cynthia!"

As if he had punched a button, a clamor went up. Puny Guthrie's red-haired twins, Sissy and Sassy, began squalling as one.

"Now see what you've done!" said Puny, standing at the ironing board in the kitchen.

"I didn't know you'd still be here," he said lamely.

"An' I just rocked 'em off to sleep! Look, girls, here's your granpaw!"

His house help, for whom he would be eternally grateful, was determined that he be a granpaw to her infants, whether he liked it or not.

"So, looky here, you hold Sissy and I'll jiggle Sassy, I've got another hour to finish all this ironin' from th' tea."

He took Sissy and, as instantly as Sissy had started crying, she stopped and gazed up at him.

"Hey, there," he said, gazing back.

"See? She likes you! She loves 'er granpaw, don't she?"

He could not take his eyes off the wonder in his arms. Because Puny was often gone by the time he arrived home, or was next door at the little yellow house, he hadn't seen much of the twins over the winter. And now here they were, nearly a full year old, and one of them reaching up to pull his lower lip down to his collar.

Puny put Sassy on her hip and jiggled her. "If you'd jis' walk Sissy around or somethin', I'd 'preciate it. Lord, look at th' ironin' that come off of that tea, and all of it antique somethin' or other from a bishop or a pope. . . ."

"Where's Cynthia?"

"I've not seen 'er since lunch. She might be over at her house, workin' on a book."

As far as he knew, his industrious wife was not working on a book these days. She'd decided to take a sabbatical since last year's book on bluebirds.

"I'll just take Sissy and go looking," he said.

"If she cries, jiggle 'er!"

Wanting to be proactive, he started jiggling at once.

He walked through the backyard, ignoring the dandelions that lighted his lawn like so many small, yellow fires. No, indeed, he would not get obsessive over the dandelions this spring, he would not dig them out one by one, as he had done in former years. Dandelions come and dandelions go, and there you have it, he thought, jiggling. Wasn't he a man heading into retirement? Wasn't he a man learning to loosen up and live a little?

Sissy gurgled and squirmed in his arms.

"Timothy!"

It was his wife, trotting through the hedge and looking like a girl.

"You'll never guess what!"

"I can't guess," he said, leaning over to kiss her. He tucked the branch of lilac in her shirt pocket as Sissy socked him on the chin.

"Thank you, dearest! Mule just called to say someone's interested in Fernbank! He tried to ring you at the office, but you'd left. Can you imagine? It's someone from out of town, he said, a corporation or something. Run and call him, and I'll take Sissy!"

Why didn't he feel joyful as he went to the phone in his study? He didn't feel joyful at all. Instead, he felt a strange sense of foreboding.

He lay on his side, propped up on his elbow. "I thought about you today," he said, shy about telling her this simple thing.

She traced his nose and chin with her forefinger. "How very odd! I thought about you today."

"It was the five o'clock coffee that did it," he said, kissing her.

"Is that what it was?" she murmured, kissing him in return.

Perhaps almost anyone could love, he thought; it was the loving back that seemed to count for everything.

He tossed the thing onto a growing pile.

A man who had time to dig dandelions was a man with time to waste, he thought.

While he had no time at all to do something so trivial, he found he couldn't help himself. He'd been lured into the yard like a miner lured to veins of gold.

There were, needless to say, a hundred other things that needed doing more:

The visit to Fernbank's attic, and get cracking now that a possible buyer was on the scene.

Fertilize the roses.

Mulch the beds.

Get up to Hope House and talk to Scott Murphy. . . .

Scott was the young, on-fire chaplain that he and Miss Sadie had hired last year. Ever since he'd come last September, they'd tried to find time to run together, but so far, it hadn't worked. Scott was like the tigers in a favorite childhood story—he was racing around the tree so fast, he was turning into butter.

The new chaplain not only held services every morning, but was making personal rounds to every one of the forty residents, every day.

"It's what I was hired to do," he said, grinning.

In addition, he'd gotten the once-controversial kennel program up and running. In this deal, a Hope House resident could "rent" a cat or a dog for up to two hours a day, simply by placing an advance order for Hector, Barney, Muffin, Lucky, etc. As the rector had seen on his visits to Hope House, this program doled out its own kind of medicine.

Evie Adams's mother, Miss Pattie, who had been literally out of her mind for a decade, had taken a shine to Baxter, a cheerful dachshund, and was, on certain days, nearly lucid.

Every afternoon, the pet wagon rolled along the halls at Hope House, and residents who weren't bedridden got to amuse, and be amused by, their four-legged visitors. There were goldfish for those who couldn't handle the responsibility of a cat or dog, and, for everyone in general, Mitford School kept the walls supplied with bright posters.

"I'll be dadgum if I wouldn't like to move in there," said several villagers who were perfectly able-bodied.

He sat back on his heels and dropped the weed-puller. What about the Creek community? Hadn't he and Scott talked last year about doing something, anything, to bring some healing to that place? It was overwhelming even to think about it, and yet, he constantly thought about it.

And Sammy and Kenny and Jessie . . . there was that other overwhelming, and even more urgent issue, and he had no idea where to begin.

He dug out a burdock and tossed it on the pile.

And now this. A corporation? That didn't sound good. Mule hadn't known any details, he had merely talked on the phone with a real estate company who was making general inquiries about Fernbank.

"Take no thought for the morrow . . ." he muttered, quoting Matthew.

"Don't worry about anything . . ." he said aloud, quoting his all-time standby verse in the fourth chapter of Philippians, "but in everything, by prayer and supplication with thanksgiving, make your requests known unto God, and the peace that passes all understanding will fill your hearts and minds through Christ Jesus."

He'd been doing it all wrong. As usual, he was trying to focus on the big picture.

He glanced at the stepping-stones he and Cynthia had laid together last year, making a path through the hedge. There! Right under his nose.

Step by step. That was the answer.

CHAPTER THREE

Eden

"You know how some people think all we have to do in Mitford is watch paint peel?"

"I do."

Emma snorted with disgust. "Mack Stroupe's house could've held us spellbound for th' last fifteen years."

"I haven't driven by there in a while."

"Looked like a shack on th' Creek 'til guess what?"

"I can't guess."

"Four pickups hauled in there this mornin' with men and step-ladders. Th' first coat was on by noon, I saw it myself when I went to Hessie's for lunch."

"Aha."

"They painted it blue. I hate blue on a house. Somebody said blue is the color of authority—which is why police officers are th' men in blue. They say it's a color that makes you look like you *are* some-body!"

"Well, well . . ."

"An' take pink. What do you think happened when a sheriff in Texas painted his jail cells pink? The men calmed down, no more violence, can you beat that?"

"Hard to beat," he said, gluing the wooden base back onto the bookend. "And Texas, of all places."

"Where do you think Mack Stroupe gets his money?"

"What money?"

"To buy a new truck, to paint his house. I even heard he had a manicure at Fancy Skinner's place."

"A manicure? Mack?"

"A manicure," she said icily.

"Good heavens." This was serious. "He didn't get a mask, too, did he?"

"A mask? Why would he need a mask when he can lie, cheat, and steal without one?"

"Now, Emma, I don't know about the stealing."

"Maybe you don't, but I do." She looked imperious.

Run from gossip! the Scriptures said. It would be hard to put it more plainly than that.

"I'm going up the street a few minutes. It looks like rain, better close the windows before you leave. Give Harold my congratulations on being moved off the route and into sorting."

"Sorting *and* working the window," she said proudly.

"Winnie!" he called, as the bell jingled on the bakeshop door.

Blast if he didn't love the smell of this place. What would happen if the bakery was sold? Anybody could move in here, hawking any manner of goods and wares. Could cards and stationery smell this wonderful, or piece goods, or kitchen wares?

Five years before he arrived on the scene, Winnie had scraped together the money for this storefront, painted it inside and out, installed ovens and secondhand display cases, stenciled *Sweet Stuff Bakery* on the window, and settled into twenty years of unflagging hard work.

Her winning smile and generous spirit had been a hallmark of this street. Hadn't she faithfully fed Miss Rose and Uncle Billy when the old couple tottered by for their daily handout? Yes, and sent something home for the birds, into the bargain.

He found her in the kitchen, sitting on a stool and scribbling on a piece of paper. "Winnie, there you are!"

She beamed at the sight of her visitor. "Have an oatmeal cookie," she said, passing him a tray. "Low-fat."

He was suddenly as happy as a child. "Well, in that case . . ."

He sat on the other stool and munched his cookie. "You know, Winnie, I've been thinking . . ."

Winnie's broad face sobered. She had never known what preachers thought.

"Sweet Stuff isn't a bakery."

"It's not?"

"It's an *institution*! Do you have to go to Tennessee? Can't we keep you?"

"I might be here 'til kingdom come, the way things are lookin'. Not one soul has asked about buyin' it."

"They will, mark my words. God's timing is perfect, even in real estate."

"If I didn't believe that, I'd jump out th' window."

"Wouldn't have far to jump," he said, eyeing the sidewalk through the curtains.

Winnie laughed. He loved it when Winnie laughed. The sound of it had rung in this place far more often than the cash register, but she had done all right, she had come through.

"I'm goin' home in a little bit," she sighed. "I'm not as young as I used to be."

"Who is? I'll be pushing off soon myself, I just came to say hello. How do you like living on Lilac Road?"

"I miss my little cottage by the creek, but that young preacher from Hope House takes good care of it."

"Scott Murphy . . ."

"He washed the windows! Those windows have never been washed! My house sittin' right on th' street and all keeps 'em dirty."

"Well, never much traffic by there to notice."

They sat in silence as he finished his cookie.

"Have another one," she said, wanting him to.

He did. It was soft and chewy, just as he liked cookies to be, and low-fat into the bargain. This was definitely his day. "What do you hear from Joe?"

"Homesick."

"But Tennessee is home."

"Yes, but Mitford's more like home; he's been away from Tennessee fifty years. To tell th' truth, Father, I don't much want to go up there, but here I am with no family left in Mitford, and it seems right for me to go."

Sometimes, what seemed right wasn't so right, after all, but who was he to say?

"Look here," she said, picking up the sheet of paper she'd been scribbling on. "I'm enterin' this contest that's twenty-five words or less. You're educated, would you mind seein' if th' spelling is right?"

He took the paper.

I use Golden Band flour because it's light and easy to work. Also because my mother and grandmother used it. Golden Band! Generation after generation it's the best.

"They sure don't give you much room to rave," he said. "And it looks like you've got twenty-eight words here."

"Oh, law! I counted wrong. What do you think should come out?"

"Let's see. You could take out 'my' and say, 'because Mother and Grandmother used it.'"

"Good! Two to go," she said, sitting on the edge of her stool.

"You could take out 'flour' in the first sentence, since they know it's flour."

"Good! One more to go!"

"This is hard," he said.

"I know it. I been writin' on that thing for four days. But look, they give you a cruise if you win! To the Caribbean! Have you ever been there?"

"Never have."

"Only thing is, it's for two. Who would I go with?"

"Cross that bridge when you get to it," he said. "OK, how about this? 'Generation after generation, Golden Band is best.'"

"How many words?" she asked, holding her breath.

"Twenty-five, right on the money!" He cleared his throat and read aloud. "I use Golden Band because it's light and easy to work. Also because Mother and Grandmother used it. Generation after generation, Golden Band is best."

"Ooh, that sounds good when you read it!" Winnie beamed. "Read it again!"

He read it again, using his pulpit voice. He thought the town's prize baker would fall off the stool with excitement. Why couldn't his congregation be more like Winnie Ivey, for Pete's sake?

As he left the bakery, he saw Mitford's Baptist preacher, Bill Sprouse, coming toward him at a trot.

"Workin' the street, are you?" asked the jovial clergyman, shaking hands.

"And a good day for it!"

"Amen! Wish I could work the south end and we'd meet in the middle for a cup of coffee, but I've got a funeral to preach."

"I, on the other hand, had a baptism this morning."

Bill adjusted the white rose in his lapel. "Coming and going! That's what it's all about in our business!"

"See you at the monument!" said the rector. Since spring arrived, they'd often ended up at the monument at the same time, with their dogs in tow for the evening walk.

He ducked into Happy Endings to see if his order had arrived.

"How do you like your new butterfly book?" asked Hope Winchester, looking fetching, he thought, with her long, chestnut hair pulled back.

"Just the ticket!" he said. "You ought to review it for the *Muse* and first thing you know, half of Mitford would be attracting butterflies."

"That," she said, "is a *very* preponderant idea!"

"Thank you."

"The Butterfly Town! It would bring people from all over."

"I don't think the mayor would much take to that. Unless, of course, they all went home at night."

"Well, Father, progress is going to happen in Mitford, whether our mayor likes it or not. We can't sit here idly, not growing and adapting to the times! And just think. People who like butterflies would be people who like books!"

"Aha. Well, you certainly have a point there."

"Sometimes our mayor can be a bit overweening."

He grinned. "Can't we all? Did my book come in?"

"Let's see," she said, "that was the etymological smorgasbord, I believe."

"'Amo, Amas, Amat,'" he said, nodding.

"I declare!" sniffed Helen Huffman, who owned the place. "Why don't y'all learn to speak English?"

"Father, is this a good time?"

He heard the urgency in Olivia Harper's voice when she rang him at the office.

"It's always a good time for you," he said, meaning it.

"Lace went to the Creek to see her friend Harley. I implored her not to go, Father, I know how dangerous it could be. But she went, and now she's home saying that Harley's sick and she's going back to nurse him. Hoppy's in surgery, and I don't . . . Please. She's packing her things. You're so good at this."

"I'll be right there," he said.

Barnabas leapt into the passenger seat of his Buick and they raced up Old Church Lane.

No, he was not good at this. He was not good at this at all. His years with Dooley Barlowe had been some of the hardest of his life; it had all been done with desperate prayer, flying by the seat of his pants. Who was good at knowing the right parameters for wounded kids? Yet, blast it, it was his job to know about parameters. Being a clergyman, being a Christian, had a great deal to do with parameters, which is why the world often mocked and despised both.

He felt the anxiety of this thing. Lace Turner was a passionately determined girl who had suffered unutterable agony in her thirteen years at the Creek—a bedridden mother whom she had faithfully nursed since early childhood, and a brutalizing father suffering the cumulative effects of drugs, alcohol, and regular unemployment.

Through it all, the toothless, kindhearted Harley Welch had looked after Lace Turner's welfare, shielding her whenever he could from harm. It was Harley's truck that Lace had used to transport Dooley's mother, then another Creek resident, to the hospital last summer.

He shuddered at the memory of Pauline Barlowe, who, burned horribly by a man known as LM, had not only endured the agony of skin grafting and the loss of an ear, but had to live with the bitter truth that she'd given away four of her five children.

Though Lace's father and older brother disappeared last year, no one knew when Cate Turner might return to the Creek, nor what he might do if he found his daughter there.

He made a right turn into the nearly hidden driveway of the Harper's rambling mountain lodge. With its weathered shingles, twin stone chimneys, and broad front porch, it was a welcome sight.

Barnabas leapt out, barking with abandon at the sudden alarm of countless squirrels in the overhead network of trees.

Thanks be to God, Lace was now in the care of the Harpers and doing surprisingly well at Mitford School. Naturally, she continued to use her native dialect, but she had dazzled them all with her reading skills and quick intelligence. He was even more taken, however, by the extraordinary depth of her character.

Another Dooley Barlowe, in a sense—with all of Dooley's hard and thorny spirit, and then some.

He put the leash on his dog and left him secured to the porch railing, then opened the screen door and called. Olivia rushed down the hall and gave him a hug.

"Father, you're always there for us."

"And you for us," he said, hugging back.

"She's in her room, packing. I'm sorry to be so . . . so inept. . . ."

"You're not inept. You're trying to raise a teenager and deal with a broken spirit. Let's pray," he said. He looked into her violet eyes, which he always found remarkable, and saw her frantic concern.

He took Olivia's hands. "Father, this is serious business. Give us your wisdom, we pray, to do what is just, what is healing, what is needed. Give us discernment, also, by the power of your Holy Spirit, and soften our hearts toward one another and toward you. In Jesus' name."

"Amen!" she said.

"Shall we talk to her together?"

"I've said it all, she's heard enough from me, I think. Would you . . . ?"

He found Lace in her room, wearing the filthy hat from her days at the Creek, and zipping up a duffel bag.

She turned and glared at him. "I knowed you'd come. You cain't stop me. Harley's sick and I'm goin'."

"What's the matter with Harley?"

"Pukin' blood. Blood in 'is dump. Cain't eat, got bad cramps, and so weak he cain't git up. But they's somethin' worser."

"What?"

"Somebody stoled 'is dogs."

"Why is that worse?" He'd try to stall her until he collected his wits.

"His dogs bein' gone means anybody could go in there and take th' money he's saved back in 'is bed pillers. I've got t' drive 'is truck out, too, or they'll be stealin' that."

"What do you think the sickness might be?"

"I ain't no doctor!" she said, angry.

"It could be something contagious."

"So? Harley done it f'r me time an' again. I was sick nearly t' dyin' an' he waited on me, even went an' fed my mam when my pap was gone workin'."

She picked up the bag and shoved the hat farther down on her head, and walked to the door.

"I'll go with you," he said. Was he crazy? It was broad daylight. He had gone into the drug-infested Creek with her once before, to bring out Poobaw Barlowe—but that had been under cover of darkness and he'd never felt so terrified in his life.

"You ain't goin' in there with me in th' daylight, a preacher wouldn't be nothin' but trouble. Besides, you couldn't hardly git up th' bank that time, you like t' killed y'rself."

She was right about that. He'd taken one step up and two back, all the way to the top. "What kind of medicine have you got?"

She stopped and looked at him.

"Why go in empty-handed? What can you do, not knowing? Come with me to the hospital, we'll talk to a nurse."

"I ain't goin' t' no hospital.

"Lace. Get smart. You can't do this without help. Drive to the hospital with me, I'll get Nurse Kennedy to come out to the car, if necessary. Tell her what you know, see what she thinks."

Lace looked at the floor, then at him. "Don't try t' trick me," she said.

"I don't think you'd be easy to trick."

God in heaven, he didn't have a clue where this was leading.

Nurse Kennedy leaned down and talked to Lace through the open car window. Lace sat stoically, clutching the duffel bag in her lap.

"It could be a bleeding ulcer," said Kennedy. "Does Harley drink?"

"Harley was bad to drink f'r a long time, but he's sober now."

"Any diarrhea?"

"An awful lot, an' passin' blood in it."

"How's his color?"

"Real white. White as a sheet."

The nurse looked thoughtful. "Vomiting blood, passing blood, pale, weak, cramps, diarrhea. All symptoms of a bleeding ulcer."

At least whatever it was wasn't contagious, thought the rector, feeling relieved. And it was curable.

"What's the prognosis?" he asked.

"I could be wrong of course, but I don't think so. If it's a bleeding ulcer, it can be treated with antibiotics. Diet plays a part, too. The main thing is, he'll need treatment. His hemoglobin will be low, and that's serious."

"We can't thank you enough."

As they drove down the hill, he still didn't know where he was headed or how this would unfold.

He pulled the car to the curb in front of Andrew Gregory's Oxford Antique Shop. "Let's stop and think this through. If you go to the Creek, there's nothing you can do. You heard the nurse, he's got to have treatment. Let me get Chief Underwood to drive us in there, we'll bring Harley out, money, truck, and all."

"Where would you take 'im to? He ain't goin' t' no hospital."

"I don't know. Let me think." Not Betty Craig's, that was for certain. Betty's little house was stuffed to the gills with Russell Jacks, Dooley's disabled grandfather; Dooley's mother, Pauline Barlowe, who was looking for work; and her son, Poobaw. There wasn't a bed available at Hope House, even if Harley could qualify, and the red tape for the county home would be a yard long.

"Blast!" he said.

"Is that some kind of cussin'?" asked Lace.

"In a manner of speaking," he replied.

He was running late for dinner, and he had no idea how he would explain it all to his wife.

Of course, she was vastly understanding about most things, he had to hand her that. So far, she hadn't run him out of the house with a broom or made him sleep in the study.

This, however, could definitely turn the tide in that direction.

She was standing at the back door, looking for him, when he walked up to the stoop with Lace Turner and a weak and failing Harley Welch.

She said only "Good Lord!" and came out to help him.

Hoppy Harper was on his way, possibly the last of that sterling breed of doctors who made house calls.

Heaving Harley up the stairs to the guest room was worse than hauling any armoire along the same route. Though shockingly frail, Harley's limp body seemed to have the weight of a small elephant. It took three of them to get Harley on the bed, where the rector undressed him and bathed him with a cloth, which he dipped in a pan of soapy water.

Harley looked comic in the rector's pajamas, which had to be changed immediately, given Harley's inability to make it to the adjoining bathroom on time. "I didn't go t' do that," said Harley, whose flush of embarrassment returned a bit of color to his face.

What had he gotten into? Father Tim wondered. He didn't know. But when Harley Welch looked at him and smiled weakly, the rector felt the absolute wisdom of this impulsive decision, and smiled back.

He went to bed, exhausted. Lace had gained permission to stay over, sleeping in Dooley's room next to Harley's, and keeping watch.

He reached for his wife, and she took his hand. "Am I dead meat around here?" he asked.

She rolled toward him and kissed him softly on the nearly bare top of his head.

"I married a preacher," she said. "Not a banker, not an exporter, not an industrialist. A preacher. This is what preachers do—if they do it right."

Nobody on the vestry had heard a word from the real estate company that had made inquiries around town.

Oh, well, they'd thrown out the line and there would be another bite at another time. But had they made the bait attractive enough? They couldn't worry about that. They couldn't install additional bathrooms in the hope that Fernbank would lure a bed and breakfast. They couldn't cut up the ground floor into classrooms in the hope it would lure an academy. In the end, they couldn't even afford to paint and roof it, hoping to lure anyone at all.

At eight in the morning he dropped by Town Hall and sat in a Danish modern chair that once occupied the mayor's own family room. He declined the weak coffee in a Styrofoam cup.

"Barbecue?" growled the mayor. "Barbecue? Two can play that game. Ray Cunningham makes the best barbecue in the country—outside the state of Texas, of course."

"I don't know if I'd fight barbecue with barbecue," he said. "I hear Mack's planning to have these things right up 'til election day."

The mayor was just finishing her fast-food sausage biscuit. "Why do anything at all, is what I'd like to know! I don't see how that snake could oust me, even if I was the most triflin' mayor ever put in office."

"Any town in the country would be thrilled to have you running things, Esther. Look at the merchant gardens up and down Main Street, look at our town festival that raised more money than any event in our history. Look at Rose Day, and how you put your shoulder to the wheel and helped turn the old Porter place into a town museum! Look how you rounded up a crew and painted and improved Sophia's little house. . . . The list is endless."

"And look how I don't take any malarkey off the council. You know we've got at least two so-and-sos who'd as soon put a paper plant and a landfill in here as walk up th' street."

"You've never taken your eyes off the target, I'll hand you that."

"So what do you think?" asked Esther, leaning forward. The rector saw that she'd broken out in red splotches, which usually indicated her enthusiasm for a good fight.

"I think I'd wait a while and see how things go in the other camp."

"That's what Ray said."

"In the meantime, I hope you'll have a presence at the town festival. I hear Mack's setting up quite a booth."

"You can count on it! Last year I kissed a pig, this year I'll be kissin' babies. And one of these days, I want to do somethin' for the town, thanking them for their support all these years. Lord, I hope talkin' to you doesn't infringe on any laws of church and state!"

He laughed. "I don't think so. By the way—how about laying off the sausage biscuits for a while? I'd like to see you make it through another couple of terms."

She wadded up the biscuit wrapper and lobbed it into the wastebasket. "You're off duty," she said. "So I'll thank you not to preach."

School would be out in two weeks and Dooley would be home.

Where in the dickens would he find the boy a job, or where would Dooley find one for himself? It would have to be in Mitford, which was no employment capital. He'd talk to Lew Boyd when he filled up his tank, or maybe the fellow who was looking after the church grounds could use a helper. . . .

Another thing. Maybe he and Cynthia could do something he'd never done in his life: take a week at the beach, rent a cottage—his wife would know how to do that. As for their mutual dislike of sand and too much sun, weren't there endless compensations—like time to read, the roar of the ocean, and seafood fresh from the boat?

Dooley would like that, and he could take Tommy. They'd load the car and head out right after Dooley's two weeks at Meadowgate Farm.

A vacation! For a man renowned for his stick-in-the-mudness, this was a great advance.

Whistling, he headed toward home.

Lace Turner was still wearing the battered hat. But her life with the Harpers had revealed a certain beauty. Her once-tangled hair was neatly pulled away from her face, dramatizing the burning determination in her eyes.

"He ain't doin' too good," she said, indicating the pale, small man who lay in the guest room bed.

For someone devoid of a single tooth, Harley Welch's smile was infectious, the rector thought. "I am, too, Rev'rend, don't listen to 'er. She's makin' me walk a chalk line."

"He ain't eat nothin' but baby puddin'."

"Cain't have no black pepper, no red pepper, no coffee, and no choc'late candy," said Harley. "They say it makes you gastric. Without a little taste of candy, I'd as soon be dead."

"You nearly was dead!" said Lace.

"How's your setup?" asked the rector. "Do you have everything you need?"

"Everything a man could want, plus Lace an' your missus an' Puny to look after me. But I feel it's my bounden duty t' tell you I run liquor most of my early days, and I been worryin' whether th' Lord would want me layin' in this bed."

"Seems to me the Lord put you in this bed," said the rector.

Harley's birdlike hands clutched the blanket. "I've not always lived right," he announced, looking the rector in the eye.

"Who has?" asked Father Tim, looking back.

"I pulled y'r shades down," Lace said, "'cause he cain't have no sunshine, he's on this tetra . . . cyline stuff four times a day f'r three weeks. He's got t' take all that's in this other bottle, too, an' look here—Pepto-Bismol he's got t' swaller twice a day."

"I ain't never lived as bad as all that," said Harley.

Father Tim sat on the side of the bed. "Dr. Harper says you're going to be all right. I want you to know we're glad to have you and want you to get strong."

"He has t' eat six times a day. It ain't easy f'r me'n Cynthia t' figure out six snacks f'r somebody with no teeth."

"Teeth never give me nothin' but trouble," said Harley, grinning weakly. "Some rotted out, some was pulled out, and th' rest was knocked out. I've got used t' things th' way they are. Teeth'd just take up a whole lot of room in there."

"I'm comin' after school an' stayin' nights," Lace announced. "Olivia and Cynthia said I could."

"Good, Lace. Glad to have you around. You've got a fine friend, Harley."

Harley grinned. "She's a good 'un, all right. But awful mean to sick people."

"Well, you're lying on your money and your truck's over at Lew Boyd's getting the oil change you mentioned, so you can rest easy."

"I hate that I've let my oil go, but here lately, I've had t' let ever'thing go. I didn't mean f'r you t' do that, Rev'rend, I'm goin' t' do somethin' for you an' th' missus, soon as I'm up an' about."

"Oh, but I wasn't saying—"

"I know you wasn't, but I'm goin' t' do it, I'm layin' here thinkin' about it. Lace tol' me you got a Buick with some age on it, I might like t' overhaul your engine."

Father Tim laughed heartily. "Overhaul my engine?"

"After my liquor days, I was in car racin'."

Was he imagining that good color suddenly returned to Harley Welch's cheeks? "You were a driver?"

"Nossir, I was crew chief f'r Junior Watson."

"Junior Watson! Well, I'll say!"

Harley's grin grew even broader. He didn't think preachers knew about such as that.

That explains it, mused the rector, going downstairs. Yesterday, he had headed Harley's old truck onto Main Street, thinking he'd have to nurse it to Lew Boyd's two blocks away. When he hammered down on the accelerator, he saw he had another think coming. He had roared by Rodney Underwood's patrol car in a blur, as if he'd been shot from a cannon.

He had never gone from Wisteria Lane to the town monument in such record time, except on those occasions when Barnabas felt partial to relieving himself on a favorite monument boxwood.

"Landscaping," announced Emma, her mouth set like the closing on a Ziploc bag.

"Landscaping?" he asked.

"Mack Stroupe."

"Mack Stroupe?"

"Hedges. Shrubs. Bushes." In her fury, his secretary had resorted to telegraphic communications. *"Grass,"* she said with loathing.

He didn't recall ever seeing grass in Mack's yard. Dandelions, maybe . . .

"Plus . . ."

"Plus what?"

Emma looked at him over her half-glasses. "Lucy Stroupe is getting her hair dyed today!"

Manicures, landscaping, dyed hair. He didn't know when his mind had been so boggled by political events, local or otherwise.

He thought he'd never seen his garden look more beautiful. It filled him with an odd sense of longing and joy, all at once.

Surely there had been other times, now forgotten, when the beauty and mystery of this small place, enclosed by house and hedges, had moved him like this. . . .

The morning mist rose from the warm ground and trailed across the garden like a vapor from the moors. Under the transparent wash of gray lay the vibrant emerald of new-mown grass, and the unfurled leaves of the hosta. Over there, in the bed of exuberant astilbe, crept new tendrils of the strawberry plants whose blossoms glowed in the mist like pink fires.

It was a moment of perfection that he would probably not find again this year, and he sat without moving, almost without breathing. There was the upside of a garden, when one was digging and planting, heaving and hauling, and then the downside, when it was all weeding and grooming and watering and sweating. One had to be fleet to catch the moment in the middle, the mountaintop, when perfection was as brief as the visit of a butterfly to an outstretched palm.

For this one rare moment, their garden was all gardens, the finest of gardens, as the wild blackberry he'd found last year had been the finest of blackberries.

He remembered it distinctly, remembered looking at its unusual elongated form, and putting it in his mouth. The blackberry burst with flavor that transported him instantly to his childhood, to his age of innocence and bare feet and chiggers and freedom. The blackberry that fired his mouth with sweetness and his heart with memory was all the blackberry he would need for a very long time, it had done the work of hundreds of summer blackberries.

He gazed at the canopy of pink dogwoods he had planted years ago, at the rhododendron buds, which were as large as old-fashioned Christmas tree lights, and at the canes of his French roses, which were the circumference of his index finger.

Better still, every bed had been dressed with the richest, blackest compost he could find. He had driven to the country where the classic makers of fertilizer resided, and happened upon a farmer who agreed to deliver a truckload of rotted manure to his very door. He'd rather have it than bricks of gold. . . .

He took a deep draught of the clean mountain air, and shut his eyes. Beauty had its limits with him, he could never gaze upon great beauty for long stretches; he had to take rest stops, as in music.

"Praying, are you, dearest?"

His wife appeared and sat beside him, slipping her arm around his waist.

He nuzzled her hair. "There you are."

"I've never seen it so lovely," she whispered.

A chickadee dived into the bushes. A junco flew out.

"Who loves a garden still his Eden keeps," she said, quoting Bronson Alcott.

He had looked upon this Eden, quite alone, for years. The old adage that having someone to love doubles our joy and divides our sorrow was, like most adages, full of plain truth.

He wanted to say something to her, something to let her know that having her beside him meant the world to him, meant everything.

"I'm going to buy us a new frying pan today," he said.

She drew away and looked at him. Then she burst into laughter, which caused the birds to start from the hedge like cannon shots.

He hadn't meant to say that. He hadn't meant to say that at all!

CHAPTER FOUR

A Full House

He put two pounds of livermush and a pack of Kit Kats in a paper sack, and set out walking to Betty Craig's.

Thank heaven his wife wasn't currently working on a book—they'd sat up talking like teenagers until midnight, feeling conspiratorial behind their closed bedroom door, and coming at last to the issue of Dooley's siblings.

"I don't know, Timothy," she said, looking dejected. "I don't know how to find lost children."

Why did he always think his wife had the answers to tough questions? Even he had the sense to believe that milk cartons, though a noble gesture on someone's part, probably weren't the answer.

"You must press Pauline for details," Cynthia told him. "She says she can't remember certain things, but that's because the memories are so painful—she has shut that part of herself down." His wife leaned her head to one side. "I wouldn't have your job, dearest."

People were always telling him that.

He peered through Betty Craig's screen door and called out.

"It's th' Father!" Betty exclaimed, hurrying to let him in.

He gave her a hug and handed over the bag. "The usual," he said, laughing.

"Little Poobaw's taken after livermush like his granpaw! This won't go far," she said, peering at the contents.

Russell Jacks shuffled into the kitchen with a smiling face. "It's th' Father, Pauline! Come an' see!" The old sexton had run down considerably, but there would never be a finer gardener than this one, thought the rector. A regular Capability Brown. . . .

The two men embraced.

"He's buildin' me a little storage cupboard, go and look!" said Betty Craig, pulling at his sleeve.

"I know you b'lieve if a man can build a cupboard, he can keep th' church gardens," said Russell, "but I've not got th' lung power t' plant an' rake an' dig an' all." He looked abashed.

"I understand, I know. And the leaf mold, that's not good for your lungs."

Russell looked relieved as they walked out to the back porch. "See this here? That was a wood box, I'm turnin' it into a cupboard for waterin' cans an' bird seed an' all. Puttin' some handles on it that we took off th' toolshed doors. If I was stout enough to do it, I'd pull that shed down before it falls down."

"Dooley and I might give you a hand with it this summer. He'll be home in two weeks, you know."

"Yessir, and it'll do his mama a world of good. She's not found a job of work nowhere, it's got to 'er a good bit."

"I understand. But something will come through, mark my words."

"Oh, an' I do mark y'r words, Father. I been markin' y'r words a good while, now. About fifteen year, t' be exact."

Poobaw came to the screen door and peered out shyly, his mother standing behind him. "Father?" she said. Tears sprang to her eyes at once and began coursing down her cheeks.

"Oh, law," sighed Russell, looking at the porch floor.

"I don't know," Pauline said. "I don't remember."

Her storm of weeping had passed and she sat quietly with him in the small rear bedroom of Betty Craig's house.

"You've got to remember."

He noticed the patch of skin on the left side of her face, only one of the places where grafting had been done—it was a slightly different color, with a scar running along its boundaries like pale stitching on a quilt. Her long brown hair, tinged with red, covered her missing left ear and hid most of the grafting on her neck. A miracle that she was sitting here. . . .

They sat for a time, wordless. He wouldn't try to chink the cracks of silence with chitchat. He would force her, if he could, to do what she dreaded. But he dreaded it more. He didn't want to force anyone into sorrow. Yet, without this, he couldn't help her do the thing he'd promised when she lay mute and devastated from the horrific burns.

"Holding," she said, turning away from him.

"You were living in Holding?"

"Yes. Mama's second cousin, Rhody, she came and took Jessie. I never told Daddy who done it." She continued to look away from him. "I remember missin' Jessie th' next morning, and there was a note. Rhody said she was taking Jessie for life and for me not to look for her." There was a long silence and Pauline bent her head. "I didn't look. By then, things were so bad . . ."

She was suffering, but without tears.

He waited.

". . . I knew I couldn't take care of her, I might hurt her, I used to lose my temper and throw things. I remember hitting Dooley, it was Christmas. . . ."

She put her head in her hands.

"He'd rode down the mountain on his new bicycle to see me, he was living with you then. I hurt him awful bad when I hit him, and he never said a word back. . . ."

Dooley! He wanted to get in the car and drive to Virginia and find him in his classroom and bring him home and love him, take him fishing, though he didn't have a clue how to fish. He remembered seeing the abandoned boy in overalls for the first time, and his eager, freckled face. . . .

"I remember he rode off on his bicycle and I thought . . . I'll kill myself, I don't deserve to live. And I tried to, Father, I did. I tried to kill myself with drinkin'."

He prayed for her silently.

"I don't know where Rhody is, I wisht I could say she's a good person, but . . . she's not. I think she was glad to see me go down, glad to run off with one of my kids." Pauline took a deep breath. "I've tried to forgive her. Sometimes I can, sometimes I can't. But . . . maybe Jessie was lucky that someone took her."

One thing at a time, his heart seemed to say. This wasn't the day to talk about Sammy and Kenny.

They walked around the sagging toolshed, checking it out.

Why beat around the bush? "Russell, tell me about your wife's cousin Rhody."

The old man looked at him somberly.

"Double-talkin' is what I say. Two-faced. I ain't seed much of 'er since Ida passed."

"How can I find her?"

"Be jinged if I know. Her man run out on 'er, he used t' work at th' post office in Holding, but I don't know what come of 'im. Her mama died, I guess they won't much left in Holding to keep 'er. Seems like th' last I heard, she was off in Florida som'ers."

"Any recollection of where in Florida?"

"Law, I cain't recollect. Seem like it started with a *L.* Los Angelees, maybe."

"Aha," he said.

When he retired from Lord's Chapel and moved out of the rectory, the yellow house next door would be home. And not enough room inside those four walls to skin a cat.

It was time, and then some, he reasoned, to get an architect to tell them how to add a sunroom and study, enlarge the downstairs bath and Cynthia's garage.

Speaking of expansion projects, it was also time to call the president of Buck Leeper's company, the people who'd done such a shining job of constructing Hope House, and see whether he could get in line for Buck as superintendent of the church attic project.

That, and find Dooley a job. And go through Miss Sadie's attic. And figure out what to do with Fernbank before it ran down so badly there'd be nothing to do with it, period.

It was no surprise that he'd never made it up the ladder to bishop; it was all he could do to say grace over being a country parson.

He was hoofing it toward home when Avis Packard stepped out of The Local, wearing his green apron. The screen door slapped shut behind him.

"I don't reckon you'd be havin' a boy who'd like to bag groceries this summer?"

Bingo!

It was different having a full house.

Olivia was in and out, helping Cynthia with the responsibility of a man who wasn't yet able to help himself. Lace arrived after school and did her homework in Harley's room, where she was clearly good medicine for what ailed him.

Violet was spending more time at the rectory, since her mistress wasn't often at the little yellow house, and Barnabas lay in wait for the glorious opportunity of finding Violet on the floor instead of the top of the refrigerator, which she had claimed as permanent headquarters with a potted gloxinia.

"Perfect!" said Cynthia, who set Violet's food up there as nonchalantly as if all cats lived on refrigerators.

With the increased workload of the household, Puny was sometimes still there with the twins when he came home.

Five o'clock in the afternoon might have been ten in the morning, for all he could see. It was not unusual for the washing machine to be running, the vacuum cleaner roaring, the blender turning out nutrition for the toothless and infirm, and the twins jiggling in their canvas seats suspended in the kitchen doorway.

During all this, Barnabas sat patiently in front of the refrigerator, blocking traffic and gazing dolefully at Violet, who scorned his every move.

A madhouse! he thought, grinning. Blast if it wouldn't run most men into the piney woods. But after more than sixty years of being an only child and a bachelor into the bargain, the whole thing seemed marvelous, a veritable circus of laughing and slamming and banging and wailing. He wouldn't wish it on his worst enemy, but for himself, he liked the novelty of it.

"Come in, Rev'rend!" Harley was sitting up in bed, having one of his multiple snacks.

"How're you?" Lace asked, without taking her eyes off the patient.

A civil greeting! Olivia was making headway with her indomitable thirteen-year-old charge. "I'm fine. How about you?"

"I'm OK. Harley, if you hide that banana bread an' don't eat it, I'll knock you in th' head."

Harley grinned. "See there? A feller don't have a chance, she's like a revenue agent lookin' f'r liquor cars, got eyes in th' back of 'er head."

"You're stronger today."

"Yessir, I am. I ain't never laid up in such style as this in m' life, we had it hard when I was comin' up in Wilkes County. We was s' poor, all we had t' play with was a rubber ball, an' th' dog eat half of that."

"Kind of hard to judge which way it would bounce," said the rector.

"Shoot, we was s' poor, I went t' school one time, I was wearin' one shoe. Th' teacher said 'Harley, have you lost a shoe?' an' I said, 'No, ma'm, I found one.'"

"Don't lie," said Lace. "It ain't right."

Harley looked doleful. "I ain't lyin'! Another thing, Rev'rend, I'm gittin' out of this bed tomorrow, sure as you're born. I looked out that back winder and seen y'r yard, you need some rakin' around that hedge."

Lace glared at Harley from beneath her hat brim. "You ain't movin' 'til Doc Harper gives you th' green light."

"Lord have mercy! Git that girl a job of work t' do."

The rector laughed. "She's got a job of work to do! And you leave my hedge alone, buddyroe."

"I hate t' be hangin' on you an' th' missus like a calf on a tit."

"I don't want to hear about it. Eat your banana bread."

"Law, now they's two of 'em," said Harley, taking a bite.

"An' drop y'r crumbs on y'r napkin," said Lace.

"Lace has real beauty."

"But she hides it with that dreadful hat. We let her wear it in the house, of course, but never to school or church."

"Sounds fair," he said.

Cynthia had gone next door for a cake pan, and Olivia was finishing a cup of tea with him.

"It represents something to her," said Olivia. "It's a defense of who she is, I think, of something she doesn't want us to change."

"You're doing a grand job, you and Hoppy, we're seeing a difference."

"We love her. She's quite extraordinary." Olivia stirred her tea, thoughtful. "Perhaps what we want more than anything . . . is for Lace to be able to cry."

"What I wanted more than anything was for Dooley to be able to laugh."

Olivia smiled. "The two things aren't so different, perhaps. Laughter, tears . . . it's all a way of letting something out, letting something go. Forgiveness . . . somehow, I think that's the answer. Did I tell you she's making straight A's?"

"Amazing!"

"She hasn't had much schooling, really, yet she loves to learn, it comes naturally to her. She keeps her nose in a book, with the radio tuned to a country music station."

They sipped their tea.

"She adores Hoppy, of course," Olivia said.

"I'm sure she cares for you, too."

"I don't know. She . . . fights me."

"Ah, well. I know about that."

"I take her to see her mother twice a week."

"What's her mother like?"

Olivia shook her head slowly. "Hard and unkind. I hoped she'd be different. Lace has taken care of her mother all her life, Lila Turner has been ill since Lace was a toddler. I think the only person who ever really cared about Lace, who loved her, is Harley."

"Was Harley ever married? Any children of his own?"

"His wife died years ago, he loved her deeply and never quite got over her death. There weren't any children." Olivia finished her tea. "Well, on to brighter things," she said, smiling. "Our school is out in two weeks. When is Dooley coming home?"

"Next Friday," he said. "He'll come in with a friend's parents. Avis wants him at The Local for the summer."

"Lovely! How does he feel about Meadowgate not being there for him?"

"He'll tough it out. After a couple of weeks at The Local, and hanging around with Tommy, and a few days at the beach . . ." He shrugged, hopeful.

"All the best," she said, her violet eyes bright with feeling.

"All the best to you," he replied, meaning it.

Avis wanted Dooley ASAP, which could mean three days at the farm and four at the beach. Or no days at the beach and a week at the farm. Another thought: Maybe Dooley would like to take Poobaw to the beach and let Tommy fill in for him at The Local before Tommy went to work at Lew Boyd's.

Why did something so simple boggle his mind? Should he call Dooley and tell him he had a job that would place some constraints on the farm? Should he even mention the beach? Should he just wait 'til Dooley came home and deal with it then?

"Lord . . ." he sighed, lifting his hands.

"A billboard," said Emma.

"A billboard?"

"Mack Stroupe."

Mack on a billboard? Is that why Mack had gotten a manicure? He didn't know how these things worked.

"On the highway after you pass Hattie Cloer's market. Right in your face. It's enough to make you jump out of your skin, that thing loomin' up on you. You talk about ugly, his nose takes up half th' board. And those bushy eyebrows, and that egg-suckin' grin . . ." Emma shivered.

"What does it say?"

"It says *Mack for Mitford, Mitford for Mack, Vote Stroupe for Mayor.* I told Harold to stop the car while I puked."

"A billboard. Amazing." Who was repackaging Mack Stroupe?

"Have you seen Lucy since she got her hair dyed? Blond! Can you believe it? Her hair's been the color of a church mouse for a hundred years. You know Mack made her do it. Lucy Stroupe would no more think of dyin' her hair blond than I'd think of runnin' a marathon. But—do you think blond hair will keep Mack Stroupe from cheatin' on his wife with that black-headed hussy in Wesley? I don't think so."

Emma glowered at him as if he were personally responsible for the whole affair. "Are you goin' to his barbecue on Saturday?"

"Dooley's coming in Friday, and we'll be spending the day at Meadowgate on Saturday."

"Good! I hope th' whole town stays away in droves."

"Unfortunately, a lot of people love barbecue."

"You can bet your boots that Harold and I won't be staying more than fifteen minutes."

"You're *going*?"

"Of course we're going, I want to see what the lowlife has to say. How can you knock the opposition when you don't know what they stand for?"

"Aha," he said.

Dooley was home and Barnabas was wild with excitement. The rector wondered if the joy that people seemed so expert at containing somehow transferred to their dogs, who had nothing at all to hide.

"Hey, Barn! Hey, buddy!"

Barnabas licked Dooley on every exposed area with special attention to his left ear. "Say a Scripture!" he yelled.

The rector laughed. "You say a Scripture!"

"Ah . . . the Lord is my shepherd, I shall not want!" Dooley thundered.

Barnabas crashed to the floor and sighed.

"A miracle, if I ever saw it," said Cynthia, of the only dog anyone had ever known whose behavior could be controlled by Scripture recitation.

"Well, you've had your bath," said the rector, putting his arms around the boy in the navy school blazer. "Welcome home!"

"Welcome home, you big lug!" said Cynthia, giving him a warm embrace. "Good heavens, you're tall! You're positively towering!"

"I'm the same as when you saw me the last time," said Dooley.

"Then I guess I've gotten shorter!"

Father Tim hoisted two duffel bags. "I'll help carry your things up. There's someone we'd like you to meet. We have a guest in the guest room."

"Who?"

"Harley Welch," said Cynthia. "He hasn't been well, so he'll be recuperating with us. Put on some old clothes and get comfortable. Dinner will be ready soon. Are you hungry?"

"I'm starved!" said Dooley, meaning it.

Dooley came into the kitchen, glaring at them. "Some girl's stuff is in my room," he said curtly.

Cynthia was taking a roast from the oven. "What kind of stuff?"

"A jacket. A hairbrush. Some . . . hair clips or somethin'."

"Lace Turner has been staying in your room and helping nurse Harley."

He glared at Cynthia. "That's what I thought. My room smells different. She better not come in there again . . . and I mean it!" he said, raising his voice.

Cynthia set the roast on the stove top and took a deep breath. "For the moment, this is a happy, busy, contented household. That is a precious thing for any household to be, and each of us must work to keep it that way.

"It was important for Lace to help with Harley, as I could not do it all myself. She is now out of your room, and you are in it. I will expect you to treat her civilly when you see her, and I expect to be treated civilly, as well. Dinner is nearly ready, it is everything you like best. If your stomach is upset by this incident, which I expect it may be, go to your room and pray about it, then come down and eat like a horse.

"You have," she said, looking at him steadily, "ten minutes."

Dooley stood for a moment, then turned and stomped upstairs.

The rector placed forks, knives, and spoons on the table, trying to be quiet about it. With his wife and Lace Turner running things around here, he and Dooley might be heading for the piney woods, after all.

Dooley Barlowe was indeed taller and, if possible, thinner. For twenty thousand bucks a year, didn't those people at school put food on the table?

And where were his freckles?

"Waiting for the sun to get to them!" exclaimed Cynthia.

What about his cowlick, then? Would they never see that again?

"Not in this lifetime," his wife said.

And his grades—how about those grades? Not bad! Not bad at all! He owed the boy a small fortune. A couple of twenties, at least.

"Would you tell him?" he asked her after dinner.

"What do you think?"

"I think you won't do it," he said, striding into the study and trying to appear casual.

Dooley was waiting for Tommy to come over and fooling with the electric train they kept in the corner by the windows.

"Buddy, I've got good news!" He sounded as phony as a three-dollar bill. "You've got a job for the summer . . . which means, of course, that—"

"I know," said Dooley, looking up.

"You do?"

"Avis told Tommy and Tommy called me up. Avis is hiring Tommy, too."

"I thought Tommy was going to work for Lew Boyd."

"He was, but Lew's nephew turned up for the job. We start Monday."

"Really?"

"Eight o'clock sharp, Avis said."

"Ah, well. We were going to take you to the beach for a few days with Tommy or Poobaw. Stay in a cottage. Swim. Like that." Swim? He couldn't swim a stroke, but Cynthia was a fish. "Eat seafood." Dooley was fooling with the train again. "Have . . . you know, *fun*."

Dooley looked up and suddenly grinned at him. "That's OK. You do stuff for me all the time. It'll be fun working. Me'n Tommy will have a blast."

"Right. Well. Congratulations! We can go out to Meadowgate on Saturday, then. For the day. How's that?"

"Great."

"There!" Cynthia said when he came back to the kitchen. "See how easy it was?"

Easy? Except for the relief of Dooley's grin, he hadn't found it easy at all.

There was, of course, an unexpected compensation.

Now they wouldn't have to get in the car and drive five long hours to the beach. He could stay right here in Mitford like the stick-in-the-mud he was known to be.

Meadowgate.

The very name soothed him, and was, in fact, an apt description.

A broad, green meadow ran for nearly a mile along the front of the Owens' property, sliced in half by a country lane that led through an open farm gate.

He had found solace in this place time and time again over the years, first as a new priest with a brand-new parish.

It had taken months, perhaps even a couple of years, to come to terms with the fact that he'd followed in the footsteps of a canonized saint. Father Townsend had been tall, dynamic, handsome, and at Lord's Chapel for nearly twenty years. Though the parish had called

Timothy Kavanagh after a tough and discriminating search, it had taken all his resources to wean them, at last, from the charismatic Henry Townsend.

He thought back on the pain he'd felt through much of that time, glad, indeed, that he could now laugh about it.

"Dearest, you're laughing!"

"Darn right!" he said, feeling the happiness of driving along a beckoning lane with a comfortable wife, a happy boy, and a dog the size of a haymow.

"Let me drive the rest of the way." Dooley was suddenly breathing on the back of his neck.

"I don't think so."

"Tommy's dad lets him drive. Jack, this guy at school, his dad lets him drive his four-wheel all the time—"

"You can drive when you're sixteen—and believe me, you won't have long to wait."

"You could just let me drive to the house. I know how."

"Since when?"

"Since I went home with Jack and his dad let me drive."

"Aha."

The house came into view and, failing any more intelligent response, he stepped on the accelerator. He'd completely forgotten about the torrid romance between boys and cars.

Marge Owen's French grandmother's chicken pie recipe was a study in contrasts. Its forthright and honest filling, which combined large chunks of white and dark meat, coarsely cut carrots, green peas, celery, and whole shallots, was laced with a dollop of sauterne and crowned by a pastry so light and flaky, it might have won the favor of Louis XIV.

"Bravo!" exclaimed the rector.

"Man!" said Dooley.

"I unashamedly beg you for this recipe," crowed Cynthia.

The new assistant, Blake Eddistoe, scraped his plate with his spoon. "Wonderful, ma'am!"

Hardly anyone ever cooked for diabetes, thought the rector as they trooped out to eat cake in the shade of the pin oak. Apparently it was a disease so innocuous, so bland, and so boring to anyone other than its unwilling victims that it was blithely dismissed by the cooks of the land.

He eyed the chocolate mocha cake that Marge was slicing at the table under the tree. Wasn't that her well-known raspberry filling? From here, it certainly looked like it. . . .

Ah, well. The whole awful business of saying no, which he roundly despised, was left to him. Maybe just a thin slice, however . . . something you could see through. . . .

"He can't have any," said Cynthia.

"I can't believe I forgot!" said Marge, looking stricken. "I'm sorry, Tim! Of course, we have homemade gingersnaps, I know you like those. Rebecca Jane, please fetch the gingersnaps for Father Tim, they're on the bottom shelf."

The four-year-old toddled off, happy with her mission.

Chocolate mocha cake with raspberry filling versus gingersnaps from the bottom shelf. . . .

Clearly, the much-discussed and controversial affliction from which St. Paul had prayed thrice to be delivered had been diabetes.

They were sitting on the porch, working up the energy to pile into the Buick and head back to Mitford.

When in Mitford, it seemed only the small, unhurried village that one loved it for being, with a populace of barely more than a thousand. From out here, however, Mitford seemed a regular metropolis, with traffic, political billboards, and barbecue events staged on slabs of asphalt.

Dooley had been to his room and silently carried out a box of his things.

Thump, thump, thump, thump . . . One of the farm dogs scratched himself vigorously, then licked the irritated flesh.

"Oh, dear," said Marge. "Here we go! It's skin allergy season for Bonemeal."

Hal took his pipe from his pocket. "Every year, he has a hot spot on his right rear flank, where he chews and scratches the skin."

"I can give him a shot of Depo-Medrol," said Blake. He turned to the Kavanaghs. "A long-acting steroid. Goes into the system and lasts up to three months. He'll stop scratching in a couple of hours."

Dooley looked up from the box he was holding between his legs. "I wouldn't do that."

There was a brief silence.

Blake looked awkward. "What would you do?"

"Use a short-acting cortisone, which is easier on his system, and follow it up with tablets and a change of diet . . . medicate his shampoos."

"This is a country practice," said Hal Owen, tamping the tobacco in his pipe. "Not much time to fool with new diets and fancy shampoos."

Dooley stood up with his box. "Right," he said.

They were silent on the way home to Mitford. Maybe it was because of the late afternoon meal and the fresh country air.

"Is Dooley home from school yet?"

It was Jenny, the girl who lived down the street in the house with the red roof. She had shown up at their door, off and on, for the last couple of years, and he knew for a fact that Dooley had once spent hard-earned money on a coffee-table horse book for this girl.

"He is! Won't you come in?"

She came in, looking only slightly less shy than last year.

Barnabas skidded up, wagging his tail and barking. But there was no need to shout a Scripture verse. Jenny looked his dog in the eye and began scratching behind his ears.

He dashed upstairs to Dooley's bedroom, feeling some odd excitement in the air. "There's someone here to see you."

"Who?"

"Jenny."

Aha. He couldn't help but see Dooley's face turning red.

"You missed it," she said archly.

Why did he ever part with fifty cents for a newspaper, when all the news that was fit to print poured unhindered from his secretary?

"Say on."

"You know th' big wooded area behind the Shoe Barn?"

"I do."

"When Mack is elected, that whole sorry-looking scrub pine deal will be a fancy new development called Mitford Woods."

"Mitford Woods?"

"Plus, he said he personally knows of big-money interest in Miss Sadie's old house, which will be revealed shortly."

"Aha." If there was nothing to worry about as far as Mack Stroupe's mayoral win was concerned, why did he feel as if someone had punched him in the solar plexus? "So how was the barbecue?"

"Great. None of that vinegary stuff you sometimes get with politics. Plus, he had a whole raft of country musicians that got half th' crowd to clogging."

He looked at her, but she avoided his eyes. "Hmmm. So what do you think about Mack?"

"Oh . . . time will tell," she said, clicking on her menu. Was this the woman who, barely forty-eight hours ago, had labeled the candidate low-down scum?

"Esther Cunningham has been a great mayor for this town," she said, "but . . ."

He hated to hear it.

". . . but there's always room for improvement."

At the light on Main Street, Rodney Underwood yelled from his patrol car.

"What do you think this is? *Talladega*?"

Could he help it if Harley's truck blew past Rodney like he was standing still? Besides, what business did Rodney have being on Main Street every time he tried to do somebody a favor and take care of their vehicle?

Rodney winked at him. "Don't let it happen ag'in, buddyroe."

He felt the heat above his collar as the truck lunged away from the light and roared south on Main Street.

"What have you got under the hood of that '72 Ford? You nearly got me nailed twice in a row."

The rector thought Harley's toothless grin might meet at the back of his head.

"Lord, I was hopin' you'd ask. Here's what I done. I got rid of th' Ford engine and transmission, took out th' drive train an' rear end, an' dropped a '64 Jagwar XKE engine and transmission in there. Then I bolted in a Jagwar rear end and hooked it up to a new drive shaft. Three hundred and twenty horses! Course, that's all a man needs on a public highway."

He didn't understand a word Harley said, but he knew one thing: He was leaving that truck alone.

"I messed with flathead V-8s most of my life, 'til one day I looked under th' hood of a Jag and seen a steel crank case, twin alumium valve covers, an' a alumium head. Now, you take Junior, he didn't like nothin' foreign, but t' me, hit was th' prettiest thing I ever seen. Well, Rev'rend, when I left th' business, I fell away from flatheads an' ain't never looked back."

"Aha."

"You got t' handle it gentle or it'll jump over th' moon."

Father Tim laid the keys on the dresser. "Tell me about it. I sucked the awnings off every storefront on Main Street."

Harley hooted and cackled 'til the tears streamed from his eyes. If laughter was the medicine the Bible claimed it to be, Harley Welch was a well man.

The patient wiped his eyes on his pajama sleeve. "I thank you ag'in f'r all you an' th' missus do f'r me. Ain't nobody ever treated me s' good, an' I'm goin' t' make it up to you. Doc Harper lets me up tomorrow, said take it easy a day or two an' first thing you know, I'll be ol' Harley ag'in. I'll git me some new dogs an' go back t' my little setup on th' Creek. But not before I do somethin' t' repay y'uns."

"Don't think about it, my friend. Do you have a job to go back to?"

"I had one, but it give out th' same time as I did. I ain't worked in a good while, what with my stomach s' bad off. But I'll git back, I ain't lazy—I like a good job of work."

"We'll see how it goes," said Father Tim. "Has our boy been around this afternoon'

"Heard 'im come in, heard 'im go out is all."

"This was his first day at the store. Where's Lace?"

"After her school lets out tomorrow, she'll be here t' he'p me git up, take me out in th' fresh air an' all."

"Good! I want you to take it easy."

"Yessir, Rev'rend, I will. I want t' be feelin' strong when I go t' work on y'r car engine."

The rector laughed. "You leave my car engine alone," he said, meaning it.

CHAPTER FIVE

Out to Canaan

He peered into the vegetable crisper and took out three zucchini, a yellow onion, two red potatoes, and a few stalks of celery.

Somewhere in here was a beef bone he'd picked up at The Local. Aha. Wrapped in foil, behind the low-fat mayonnaise which he wouldn't touch with a ten-foot pole . . .

He put it all in a brown paper bag with a can of beef broth and a pound of coffee, and set out to Scott Murphy's house next to the bridge over Little Mitford Creek.

They walked along the path by the creek, with Luke and Lizzie straining ahead on their leashes.

It was hot for a June afternoon in the mountains, and he and Scott Murphy were going at a trot. The rector moved the grocery bag to his other arm and took out his handkerchief and wiped his face.

"Father, about your concern for having a Creek ministry . . ."

"Yes?"

"It occurs to me that you have one."

The rector looked at him, puzzled.

"You brought Dooley's kid brother out of there, who's living in the first real home he ever had. You're also providing a home for their mother. . . ."

"But—"

"And look at Lace Turner—last year she was living in the dirt under her house, trying to keep away from an abusive father. Now she's living with one of the most privileged families in town and making straight A's in school."

"Aha."

"And Harley Welch, your race car mechanic . . . you and Mrs. Kavanagh have taken him in, nursed him, maybe even saved his life."

"Yes, well . . ."

Luke stopped to lift his leg at a tree.

"I think we're always looking for the big things," Scott mused. "The big calling, the big challenge. Seems like Bonhoeffer had something to say about that."

"He did," said the rector. "Something like, 'We think we dare not be satisfied with the small measure of spiritual knowledge, experience and love that has been given to us, and that we must constantly be looking forward eagerly for the highest good.'"

"Yes, and I like that he talks about being grateful even where there's no great experience and no discoverable riches, but much weakness, small faith, and difficulty."

The two men pondered this as they walked. It was good to talk shop on a spring day, on a wooded path beside a bold creek.

"Before I came here," said Scott, "I told you I'd go in there and see what can be done. I'm sticking to it."

"Good fellow."

"I've been meaning to tell you we got the garden in at Hope House, fourteen of the residents are able to plant and hoe a little, we have peas coming up."

"You're everything Miss Sadie wanted," said the rector. "You're making Hope House live up to its name."

"Thank you, sir. Mitford is definitely home to me. Maybe I can buy Miss Ivey's little cottage when she sells the bakery and moves to Tennessee—I don't know, I'm praying about it."

They rounded the bend in the footpath and saw Homeless Hobbes sitting on the front step of his small, tidy house, a colorful wash hanging on the line.

"Lord have mercy, if it ain't town people!" Homeless got up and limped toward them on his crutch, laughing his rasping laugh. His mute, brown-and-white spotted dog crouched by the step and snapped its jaws, but no sound escaped. Luke and Lizzie barked furiously.

"Homeless!" The rector was thrilled to see his old friend, the man who'd given up a fast-lane advertising career, returned to his boyhood home, and gone back to "talkin' like he was raised."

"I'm about half wore out lookin' for company! I told Barkless a while ago, I said somebody's comin', my nose is itchin', so I put somethin' extra in th' soup pot!"

The rector embraced Homeless and handed over the bag. "For the pot. And this is Scott Murphy, the chaplain at Hope House. He works sixteen hours a day and still has time to meddle in Creek business."

Homeless looked at the tall, lanky chaplain approvingly. "We need meddlin' in here," he said.

"I'd like to see th' dozers push th' whole caboodle off th' bank, and good riddance!"

Homeless had brought out two aluminum folding chairs that had seen better days, and set them up for his guests. He sat on the step, and the dogs lay panting in a patch of grass.

"They say th' whole thing'll be a shoppin' center in a couple of years. Where all them trailers is parked—Wal-Mart! Where all them burned-out houses is settin'—Lowe's Hardware! Where you could once go in and get shot in th' head, you'll be able t' go in an' get you a flush toilet.

"Still an' all, two years is a good bit of time, and you could do a good bit of work on the Creek, if you handle it right. Now, you take ol' Absalom Greer, he come in here and preached up a storm and some folks got saved and a good many lives were turned around, but Absalom was native and he was old, and they let him be.

"They won't take kindly to a young feller like yourself if you don't give 'em plenty of time to warm up.

"What I think you ought to do is come to my place on Wednesday night when I make soup for whoever shows up, and just set an' talk an' be patient, an' let th' good Lord do a work."

"I'll be here," said Scott.

Homeless grinned. "I wouldn't bring them dogs if I was you. Jack Russells are a mite fancy for my crowd."

"We lost our dining room manager last week," Scott said on the walk back home. "A family problem. Everybody's been pitching in, it's kind of a scramble."

"I like scrambles," said the rector, who was currently living in one.

Sometimes, a thought lodged somewhere in the back of his mind and he couldn't get it out, like a sesame seed stuck between his teeth.

Walking down Old Church Lane the following day, his jacket slung over his shoulder, he tried to focus on the place—was it in his brain?—that had something to tell him, some hidden thing to reveal.

Blast! He hated this. It was like Emma's aggravating game, Three Guesses. He couldn't even begin to guess. . . .

A job. Why did he think it had to do with a job?

We lost our dining room manager last week, Scott had said.

Yes!

Pauline!

Hanging on to his jacket, he started running. He could go to the office and call from there, but no, he'd run across Baxter Park, through his own backyard, and then up the hill and over to Betty Craig's house. Why waste a minute? Jobs were scarce.

He was panting and streaked with sweat when he hit the sidewalk in front of Betty's trim cottage. He stopped for a moment to wipe his face with a handkerchief when Dooley blew by him on his red bicycle.

"Hey!" shouted Dooley.

"Hey, yourself!" he shouted back.

He saw the boy throw the bicycle down by Betty's front steps, fling his helmet in the grass, and race to the door.

"Mama! Mama!" he called through the screen door.

Pauline appeared at the door and let him in as the rector walked up to the porch.

"Mama, there's a job at Hope House! Something in the dining room! I heard it at the store, they need somebody right now."

"Oh." Pauline grew pale and put her hand to the left side of her face. "I . . . don't know."

"You've waited tables, Mama, you can do it! You can do it!"

He saw the look on Dooley's face, and tried to swallow down a knot in his throat. In only a few years, this boy on a bicycle would be worth over a million dollars, maybe two million if the market stayed strong. Dooley wouldn't know this until he was twenty-one, but the rector could see that Sadie Baxter had known exactly what she was doing when she drew up her will.

"Come on, Mama, get dressed and go up there, I've got to get back to The Local or Avis'll kill me, I got five deliveries."

"I'll take you," the rector told Pauline. "I'll go home and get the car, won't be a minute." Hang the meeting in the parish hall at two o'clock.

Pauline looked at him through the screen door, keeping her hand over the left side of her face. "Oh, but . . . I don't have anything to . . . I don't know . . ."

"Don't be afraid," he said.

Tears suddenly filled Pauline's eyes, but she managed to smile. "OK," she said, turning to look at her son. "I can do it."

"Right!" said Dooley. He charged through the door and raced down the steps and was away on his red bicycle, but not before the rector saw the flush of unguarded hope on his face.

"I'll be back," said Father Tim. "Wear that blue skirt and white blouse, why don't you? I thought you looked very . . ."—he wasn't terribly good at this; he searched for a word—"nice . . . in that."

She gazed at him for a long moment, almost smiling, and disappeared down the hall.

An attractive woman, he thought, tall and slender and surprisingly poised, somehow. Her old life was written on her face, as all our lives are written, but something shone through that and transformed it.

In his opinion, Hope House might have done a notch better on their personnel director, Lida Willis.

"How long have you been sober?" asked the stern-looking woman, eyeing Pauline.

"A year and a half."

"What happened to turn you around?"

"I prayed a prayer," said Pauline, looking fully into the director's cool gaze.

"You prayed a prayer?"

Though he sat well across the room, feigning interest in a magazine, Father Tim felt the tension of this encounter. God was calling Pauline Barlowe to come up higher.

"Yes, ma'am."

"Are you in AA?"

"No, ma'am."

"Why not?"

"I don't know. I . . . feel like God has healed me of drinkin'. I don't crave it no more."

"Shoney's fired you for drinking on the job?"

"Yes. But they said that . . . when I was sober, I was the best they ever had."

"Miss Barlowe, what makes you think you might be right for this job?"

"I understand being around food, I get along real well with people, and I'm not afraid of hard work."

The director sat back in her chair and looked at Pauline, but said nothing.

"I need this job and would be really thankful to get it. I know if you call Sam Ward at Sam and Peg's Ham House in Holding, he'll tell you I do good work, I never missed a day at th' Ham House, my station was fourteen tables."

"Were you drinking when you worked there?"

Pauline looked down for a moment, then looked straight at Lida Willis. "Not as bad as . . . later."

"Has your personal injury handicapped you in any way?"

"Sometimes I don't hear as good out of my left ear, but that's all. My arm works wonderful, it's a miracle."

"I appreciate your honesty, Miss Barlowe." She stood up. "Please don't call us. We'll be in touch."

Pauline stood, also. "Yes, ma'am."

Dear God, he wanted this job for Pauline. No, wrong. He wanted this job for Dooley.

He saw Scott Murphy in the hall. "If there's anything you can do," he said under his breath as Pauline drank at the water fountain. "Your dining room manager's job . . ." He never begged anyone for anything, but this was different and he didn't care.

Scott looked at him, knowing.

"She can do it," he told the chaplain.

He was looking something up in his study when he heard a noise in the garage. It sounded like his car engine revving.

Surely Harley wasn't already working on . . .

He went through the kitchen, carrying J. W. Stevenson's rare volume on his ministry in the Scottish highlands.

Dooley was sitting in the Buick, gunning the motor. Barnabas sat on the passenger side, looking straight ahead.

"What's going on?" Father Tim asked through the open car window.

"Nothin'."

"Nothing, is it? Looks like you're gunning that motor pretty good."

"I'm checking it out for Harley."

"Really?"

"He didn't ask me to, but I thought it would help him to know how it sounds."

"Right. Well, you're out of there, buddy. Come on."

Dooley gave him an aloof stare. "Jack's dad lets him—"

"Look. What Jack's dad does is beside the point." Was it, really?

He didn't have a clue. Why would people let fourteen-year-old kids drive a car, two years before they could get a license? Or was that the going thing and he was a stick-in-the mud? "Maybe one day we can drive out to Farmer. . . ."

Dooley turned off the ignition: "Cool," he said. "Your engine's got a knock in it."

At six-thirty, Barnabas was finishing up last week's meat loaf, Violet was sneering down from the refrigerator, Cynthia was running a garlic clove around the salad bowl, Dooley was taking one of his endless showers, and Lace was stuffing a snack down a reluctant Harley Welch.

Father Tim still couldn't get over the fact that only three or four years ago, the rectory had been quiet as a tomb. No dog, no boy, no wife in an apron, no red-haired babies, and hardly ever a soul in the guest room, with the agonizing exception, of course, of his phony Irish cousin and an occasional overnight visit by Stuart Cullen, his seminary friend and current bishop.

"Can I talk t' you som'ers?" Lace wanted to know.

Harley was sitting on the side of the bed, fully dressed, but looking weak. He scraped the last bite from a cup of peach yogurt and wiped his mouth with his sleeve.

"Rev'rend, Lace has got a notion I cain't argue 'er out of. Don't pay no attention to 'er if she talks foolish."

"I don't believe I've ever heard Lace talk foolish," he said. "You look a little peaked today, Harley. How're you feeling?"

"Wore out. We was up an' down an' aroun' ever' whichaway, th' doc said I needed exercise. I been eatin' like a boar hog an' layin' up in this bed 'til I was runnin' t' fat."

"We could go down t' y'r basement," said Lace, tugging at her hat brim.

"My basement?"

"I hate like th' dickens I couldn't talk 'er out of this," said Harley. "She's pigheaded as a mule, always has been since I knowed 'er as a baby."

"What's the deal?" he asked as they trooped down the basement stairs.

"You'll see," she said.

The musty smell of earth came to him, and he remembered the cave he and Cynthia had been lost in only last year. They had wandered in circles for fourteen agonizing hours, until the local police, led by Barnabas, brought them out.

He shuddered and flipped the switch that lit the dark hallway.

There was the bathroom that hadn't been used since he moved here fifteen years ago, and the two bedrooms and the little kitchen—which had served, during the tenures of various rectors, as a mother-in-law apartment, a facility for runaways and later for elderly widows, a home office, an adult Sunday School, a church nursery, and storage space for the detritus of nearly a century of clergy families.

Lace folded her arms across her chest. "This is what I think."

"Shoot."

"When me'n Harley was ramblin' around today outside, we seen y'r basement door. F'r somethin' t' do, I tried t' git th' door open and had t' nearly bust it in."

"Really?"

"But it ain't broke, it was just stuck."

"Good!"

"So we seen how this is a place t' live, with a toilet an' kitchen an' all. An' I got to thinkin' how if Harley goes back to th' Creek, how he ain't goin' t' take care of hisself, an' besides, somethin' bad could happen to 'im."

"Aha."

"So I thought if you was to like th' idea, Harley could live down here and go t' work f'r you an' Cynthia."

He pulled at his chin.

"Harley can work, you ain't never seen 'im work, you just seen 'im laid up sick. Harley can rake, he can saw, he can hammer, he can paint."

"I'll be darned."

"An' he wouldn't charge you a cent to keep you an' Cynthia's cars worked on."

She looked at him steadily under the dim glow of the bulb.

"Well, I don't know. I'd have to think about it, talk to Cynthia about it."

"He wouldn't be no trouble. They wouldn't be no cookin' or nothin' to do for 'im, he could take care of hisself. He could paint this place for you, fix it up, I'd help 'im."

She paused, then said: "You ought t' do it, it'd be good for ever'-body."

Lace Turner had made her case, and rested it.

"Can he draw cats?" asked Cynthia. "He could do my next book."

Uh-oh. "Your next book?"

"I've been meaning to tell you, dearest. I'm starting a new book. You know how I said I'd never do another Violet book?"

"You definitely said that. Several times."

"I lied."

"Aha."

"You won't believe the advance they'll give me to do another Violet book."

It was true. When she told him, he didn't believe it. "Come on. That's four times what they gave you for the bluebird book."

"Well, you see, I refused so fiercely to do another Violet book, they had to make me an offer I couldn't resist."

"You're tough, Kavanagh."

"So kiss me!" she said, laughing.

He kissed her, inhaling the elusive scent of wisteria. "Congratulations! We can build a boat and retire to the Caribbean and spend our lives cruising and fishing."

"Where did you get an idea like that?"

"From Mike Jones at Incarnation in Highlands. He said that's what he wants to do when he retires—the only problem is, he's never mentioned it to his wife."

"The only problem is," she said, "we'll need gobs of money to enlarge my little yellow house to contain a man, an ocean of books, and a dog the size of Esther Bolick's Westinghouse freezer."

"Well, then. What do you think?"

"I think we should let him have the basement and fix it up. I love Harley. He's funny and good-hearted and earnest. And it would be wonderful to have some more help around here. For openers, your garage could use a cleanup and my Mazda needs a new alternator."

"What do you know about alternators?"

"Absolutely nothing. Which means it would be nice to have Harley living in the basement. We'll buy the paint and I'll make his kitchen curtains."

"Done!" he said.

A new book? He knew what that meant. It meant his wife would be working eight hours a day or more, complaining of a chronically stiff neck, staring out the window without speaking, getting headaches from eye strain, and crashing into bed at night as lifeless as a swamp log.

Oh, well. He sighed, trudging up the stairs with his dog to tell Harley the news.

"Goodnight, buddy."

He had left Harley's room and stepped down the hall to sit on the side of Dooley's bed.

"'Night."

"We're praying that your mother gets the job."

"Me, too."

"How about your job? You like it all right?"

"It's neat. But I'm about give out."

When Dooley was tired or angry, Father Tim noted, he often lapsed into the vernacular. He grinned. That prep school varnish hadn't covered the boy's grain entirely. "Are you going to run a booth at the town festival?"

"Yep. Avis wants Tommy and me to do it. Avis'll be the bigwig and take the money."

"Sounds good. What will you do?"

"We'll sell corn and stuff from the valley. Avis has buckets of blackberries and strawberries comin' in from Florida, and peaches from Georgia and syrup from Vermont and all. He's calling it 'A Taste of America.'"

"Great idea! That Avis . . ."

"I'm about half killed."

"Well . . . see you at breakfast."

"What were you doing up at Mama's today? Taking livermush to Granpaw?"

"Just dropped by to say hello, that's all, and check on Poobaw."

"He likes to be called Poo now."

"I'll remember that. I'm glad you heard about the job at Hope House and didn't waste any time."

"Me, too. 'Night."

"Goodnight."

He went downstairs with a heart nearly full to bursting. To borrow a phrase from Dooley's granpaw, blast if he didn't love that boy better than snuff.

In less than a week, the bishop would arrive at Lord's Chapel on his annual confirmation pilgrimage. This year, however, he also had a dirty job to do. It had fallen on him to break the news of Timothy Kavanagh's retirement, just eighteen months away.

Stuart Cullen did not look forward to this bitter task. The parish wouldn't like the news, not even a little. In fact, he was prepared to duck after divulging this woe. Unless he and Martha got out of there immediately after the service, he was in for a virtual cantata of moaning and groaning, not to mention wailing and gnashing.

All that, he knew, would be followed by a series of outraged letters and phone calls to diocesan headquarters, and possibly a small, self-appointed group who would show up on his doorstep, begging him to force Father Tim to remain at Lord's Chapel until he was on a walker or, worse yet, senile and unable to commandeer the pulpit.

The rector, in the meantime, was trying to get himself in shape for an occasion that seemed variously akin to a wedding and then a funeral. His feelings rose and plummeted sharply. Bottom line, he couldn't dismiss the fact that once the words left Stuart's mouth, the deed was done, it was writ on a tablet, he was out of there.

His wife had certainly done everything in her power to help, though nothing seemed to calm his nerves. Certainly not the new suit she ordered from New York and which, he was aghast to find, was double-breasted. Would he look like some Mafia don at the parish brunch, as he struggled to give his stunned parish a look of innocent piety?

And so what if he'd managed to lose a full four pounds six ounces and appear positively trim? The downside was, his stomach stayed so infernally upset, he couldn't eat.

For years, he had feared this whole retirement issue. Even Stuart confessed to dreading it, and had once called retirement "a kind of death."

For himself, however, he had made peace with his fear last year in the cave. He had been able, finally, to forgive his father, to find healing and go on.

In some way he would never fully understand, he'd thought that by preaching into infinity, he could make up for having been unable to save his father's soul. Not that he could have saved it, personally—that was God's job. But he had somehow failed to soften his father's heart or give him ears to hear, and had believed he could never make up for that failing, except to preach until he fell.

Now he knew otherwise, and felt a tremulous excitement about stepping out on faith and finding his Canaan, wherever it may be. Indeed, the fear he now wrestled with was the fear of the unfamiliar. Hadn't he been wrapped in a cocoon for the last sixteen years, the very roof over his head provided?

"By faith, Abraham went out," he often quoted to himself from Hebrews, "not knowing where. . . ."

He knew one thing—he didn't want to leave the priesthood. He was willing to supply other pulpits here, there, anywhere, as an interim. Wouldn't that be an adventure, after all? Cynthia Kavanagh certainly thought so. He suspected she had already packed a bag and stashed it in the closet.

There were only a couple of things left to be done prior to Sunday. One, attend the closed vestry meeting on Friday night and tell them the news before it hit the pulpit. He dreaded it like a toothache. As far as he knew, they didn't have a clue what was coming, and they'd be shocked, stunned. He could stay and take it like a man, or duck out the back door while Buddy Benfield gave the closing prayer.

The list was all downhill from there. Two, book Stuart and Martha's lodging in Wesley, and three, get a haircut.

But hadn't he just had a haircut?

His hair was growing fast, Cynthia said, because of the olive oil in his diet.

Emma said he looked shaggy because Joe Ivey had gotten slack toward the end and hadn't given him his money's worth.

Somebody else declared it was the time of year when hair had a growth spurt like everything else, from ragweed to burdock.

He called Fancy Skinner for an appointment. Today, if possible, and get it over with.

"Oh, law, I don't have an openin' 'til kingdom come! Ever' since Joe Ivey went to Tennessee, I've gone like a house afire! The haircuts he's let loose around here gives me th' shivers, you can spot a Joe Ivey cut a mile away, it's always these little pooches of hair over th' ears, it'll take me a year to get rid of that chipmunk look in this town.

"Let's see . . . Ruth Wallace at eleven for acrylic nails, J. C. Hogan at noon, that's a cut, Beth Lawrence for a perm at twelve-thirty, that'll take two hours, you should see her hair, she calls it fine, I say she's goin' bald. Do you know her, she always wears a hat—if you ask me, wearin' a hat will make you bald, and oh, Lord, look here, at three o'clock I've got Helen Nelson, she will gnaw your ear off talkin', you can't get a word in edgewise, on and on and on, about every old thing from her husband growin' a mustache and how it scratches when he kisses, to th' pig they bought to keep as a house pet. Have you ever heard of keepin' a pig as a house pet? They say they trained it to a litter box!

"I'd rather have a dog any day, which reminds me, did you know one of my poodles ran away and Rodney Underwood found her under the bridge and brought her home in the front seat of his patrol car? Mule took a picture, you should ask to see it.

"How's your wife, how come she don't let me highlight her hair sometime? Does she do it herself? It looks like she does it herself. I bet she uses a cap—honey, foil works better, but don't tell her I said so.

"Let's see, four o'clock, oh, Lord, look here. I've got Marge Beatty's three kids, all at the same time, I should get a war medal. Then at five,

I'm doin' a mask—which reminds me, have I told you about my new product line called Fancy's Face Food? What it is, your face desperately needs nourishment just like your body, did you know that? Most people don't know that.

"First, I do th' Vitamin E Deluxe Re-Charge and Hydration Mask, which is the entrée, followed by a Cucumber Apricot Sesame Soother, which is the dessert, and honey, I'm tellin' you, you will walk out of here lookin' ten years younger, some say fifteen, but I try not to stretch the truth.

"The mask I'm doin' at five takes an hour, so the answer is, no, I couldn't take you today if my life depended on it, how about next Wednesday at ten o'clock?"

Harley removed two twenty-dollar bills from under the guest room mattress and was on his way to the Shoe Barn for new work shoes.

"Harley, be careful. Rodney Underwood has it in for that truck."

"Don't you worry," said Harley. "I'd never let them horses loose in town."

"I don't want to have to haul you out of jail."

"Nossir, Rev'rend, you won't."

So why did he watch that truck like a hawk, all the way to the end of Wisteria, 'til it turned north on Main?

"Miami," said Emma, looking curious.

He lifted the receiver from the phone on his desk.

"Hello?"

"Father, this is Ingrid Swenson with Miami Development Group. I'd like to talk with you about the old Fernbank property, which we understand is owned by your church."

"That's right."

"We're very interested, Father, in viewing this property next week, if that would be convenient."

"Well . . ."

"It is our intention, if everything looks as good as we hope it might, to develop this property as a world-class spa."

"A spa."

"Yes. We've developed similar properties around the country that have gained international clientele."

"Aha."

"How does next Wednesday look to you? Say, around eleven?"

"Ah, well, fine, I think. Yes. I'll have to gather up some of the vestry, and our realtor."

"Good. There'll be two of us."

"We're at the corner of Old Church Lane and Main Street, just as you come into town. Very easy to find."

"You may like to know that Mr. Mack Stroupe has highly recommended this property to us."

"I see."

"We're very grateful for such valued assistance in locating a property as special as Fernbank promises to be. We're told it has seventeen rooms."

"Twenty-one."

"Marvelous!"

"Yes. Well. We'll be looking for you, Miss Swenson."

"Ingrid, Father. And thank you for your time."

He put the phone on the hook.

"You don't look so good," said Emma.

Strange. He didn't feel so good, either. That phone call should have him dancing in the streets, shouting from the rooftops.

If Fernbank was such an albatross, why did he suddenly know he didn't want to lose it?

His heart hadn't pounded like this, even on the day of his ordination. It had pounded, yes, when he preached his first sermon to his first parish in his first small church. But he couldn't remember anything like this. He was glad he was sitting down, and glad he'd been able to persuade Cynthia to trim his hair.

He looked for his lifeline, which was the third pew, gospel side, where his wife sat scratching her nose. That was her signal for "Smile!"

Sitting next to her was Pauline Barlowe, then Poobaw, who was gazing at the ceiling, and Dooley. Russell Jacks anchored the pew at the opposite end.

"I have some good news and some bad news," Stuart told the congregation at the eight o'clock.

Did he have to put it that way? The rector shifted in the carved chair. This was the dress rehearsal for the more formal, well-attended eleven o'clock; whatever happened now would also happen then—except worse. Much worse.

"The good news," said Stuart, smiling the smile that had undoubtedly helped him rise in his calling, "is that Timothy Kavanagh, your beloved priest, generous counselor, and trusted friend . . ."

Get it over with, he thought, gripping the chair arms and closing his eyes. This was like flying with Omer Cunningham in his ragwing taildragger. . . .

". . . is getting ready to . . . *go out to Canaan*!"

How odd that Stuart would have had the same thought, found the same analogy! He noted that most of his congregation didn't seem to know anything about Canaan. Where was Canaan? He saw Esther Bolick glance at Gene and shrug her shoulders. Maybe it was overseas. Or maybe somewhere in Wilkes County, where they had that cheese factory.

"We're told in Genesis that Abram took Sarai his wife, and Lot his brother's son, and all their substance that they had gathered, and they went forth into the land of Canaan . . . a strange land, an alien land.

"God was sending Abram, whom He would later call Abraham, on the greatest journey, the grandest mission, of his life. But what would Canaan be like? Some said giants inhabited the land, and I recall what Billy Sunday once said, 'He said if you want milk and honey on your bread, you must be willing to go into the land of giants!'"

Father Tim felt his hair standing up on his head.

"What," asked Stuart, looking resplendent in embroidered brocade, "did Abraham *feel* when he was called by God to go out into this unfamiliar land, hundreds of miles from home?"

The rector believed he clearly heard the thoughts of half the crowd: *Beats me!*

In fact, Abraham hadn't even made an appearance in this morning's Old Testament reading. Oh, well. Bishops could do whatever they darn well pleased.

Stuart leaned over the pulpit and peered at the assembly, most of whom were admiring his satin mitre.

"Did he, like your faithful friend and priest, feel fearful of this journey into the unknown? Of course! Did he feel sorrow for leaving the familiar behind? Almost certainly! But"—and here Stuart drew himself up to his full height of six feet plus—"given what God had in store for him, didn't he also feel hope and excitement and expectation and *joy*?"

None of the above, thought the rector. What he felt was sheer, holy terror.

With no small amount of admiration, he observed Stuart Cullen getting exactly what he wanted from the congregation, rather like a conductor extracting a great symphony from an orchestra.

Where Stuart wanted tears, he got unashamed tears.

Where he wanted riotous laughter, there it came, pouring forth like a mighty ocean.

By the end of the service, nearly everyone felt as if they'd been called out to a Canaan of their own; that life itself was a type of Canaan.

The rector left the eleven o'clock on legs that felt like cooked macaroni, clinging to the arm of his wife, who was beaming.

"There, now, dearest, this is not a lynching, after all! Cheer up!"

He couldn't believe that his congregation had kissed him, hugged him, pounded him on the back, congratulated him, and wished him well.

Where he had expected faces streaming with tears, he saw only lively concern for his future. Where he had feared stern looks of indignation, he received smiles and laughter and the assurance they'd always love him.

Didn't they *care*?

"Don't kid yourself," said Stuart, as he and Martha dove into the car after the parish hall brunch. "The backlash is yet to come."

As Stuart gunned the Toyota Camry away from the curb, the rector felt brighter. So, maybe his parishioners really would hate to see him go! Right now they were just having a good time—after all, the bishop's visit was always a festive occasion.

CHAPTER SIX

A Small Boom

Emma was right. The billboard of Mack Stroupe's face seemed to loom over the highway. And whoever was responsible for the photo didn't appear to think much of retouching.

Zooming past it in his Buick, he wondered at his feelings about the new candidate, and determined, once and for all, to think the thing through and come to a conclusion he could live with. He was tired of the whole issue crawling around in the back of his mind like so many ants over a sugar bowl.

Why did he feel queasy and uncomfortable about Mack Stroupe being his mayor? J.C. was right—the mayorship wasn't Esther's job, it was the job of anybody who qualified to make the most of the office. But—did Mack qualify?

He couldn't think of a single reason why he should. Was it mere gossip that Mack had carried on a long-term extramarital relationship with a woman in Wesley? People were notorious for giving clergy all manner of information, and apparently the affair wasn't rumor at all, but fact.

While that sort of behavior may be acceptable to some, for him, it wouldn't fly. The whole business spoke of treachery and betrayal, however admissible it might be in the world's view.

He thought of Esther's plank, so well known by everyone in Mitford that first graders could recite it: Mitford Takes Care of Its Own.

Esther had carried out that philosophy in every particular, never wavering.

Wasn't it true that when you take care of what you have, healthy growth follows? Hadn't his trilliums, planted under all the right conditions, spread until they formed a grove? And the lily of the valley, established in the rich, dark soil behind his study, had become a virtual kingdom from only three small plants.

Actually, there had been growth in Mitford; it was no bucolic backwater. The little tea shop next to Mitford Blossoms was flourishing. They were still limited to cakes, cookies, tea, and coffee, but as everyone agreed, you have to crawl before you walk.

Recently, Jena Ivey, their florist, had been forced to add a room to her shop. And take the Irish Woolen Shop. Now, there was a flexible endeavor. In late spring and summer, when temperatures soared, Minnie Lomax removed the word *Woolen* from the store sign, thereby assuring a brisk, year-round trade.

Avis Packard was another example. Avis was a small-town grocer who had done such a terrific job of providing world-class provender that people came from surrounding counties to fill up his rear parking lot and jam the streets, especially when the Silver Queen corn rolled in.

And Happy Endings. When he first came here, there was no such thing as a bookstore; he'd been forced to drive to Wesley and spend his money in another tax jurisdiction. Last summer, there had actually been a queue in front of Happy Endings—he had seen it with his own eyes—when the newest Grisham book arrived by UPS. The UPS man had been astounded when he pulled to the curb and everybody cheered.

Mitford was making it, and without neon signs and factory smoke. So, yes, maybe some well-planned growth would be good, but face it, they were doing something right, and he didn't want to see that mind-set replaced by a mind-set that was only for development and change, whatever the cost.

Another thing. It boggled his mind that Mack Stroupe knew anyone outside the confines of Wesley and Holding. How had Mack engineered contact with what sounded like a large Florida development firm? And this thing about Mitford Woods, and Mack being the ringleader . . .

In the end, what about Mack's platform?

Was Mack really for Mitford?

Or was Mack for Mack?

He found his breakfast cereal tasting exactly like oil-based latex.

Every window was up, three fans were running wide open, and Violet sprawled as if drugged on the top of the refrigerator. Even the gloxinia seemed oppressed by the noxious fumes rising from the basement.

"Let's move!" said Cynthia, meaning it.

"Where?" he asked, liking the idea.

"The little yellow house! I don't even know some of the people I'm meeting in my own hallway!"

"You know Tommy," he said. "He only spent three nights."

"Yes, but—"

"And Harley's friend Cotton, didn't he tell great stories?"

"Of course, but—"

"And certainly Olivia was well meaning when she came down with the women from the hospital auxiliary to bring pots and pans and scatter rugs for Harley's kitchen. I'm sure they didn't mind that you still had curlers in your hair."

"I married a bachelor who led the quietest of lives, and now look!" she exclaimed, eyeing a kitchen sink that contained a roller pan, rollers, and a bevy of brushes.

"The plumbing repairs in the basement," he said lamely, "will be finished tomorrow, and they can wash the brushes down there."

"A likely story!"

"You're beautiful when you're mad," he said.

"I read that line in a pulp novel thirty years ago!"

"So sue me."

She came around the breakfast table and sat in his lap. "I love you, you big lug."

"I love you more," he said, pulling her to him and kissing her hair. "Have you started your book?"

She laughed gaily. "Of course I've started my book! None of this would have happened if I hadn't started my book!"

These days, clergy seldom liked living in rectories. Because they generally preferred to own their own homes, and because the upkeep of the rectory had been considerable over the years, the vestry had long ago voted to sell the old house at the end of his tenure. What with the recent improvement below, the rector suspected they'd get a much better price for it.

Who would have dreamed he'd ever see the grim downstairs hallway come alive under a coat of Peach Soufflé, or a kitchen transformed by Piña Colada and his wife's bright curtains fluttering at the window?

Harley Welch would be living high in this basement.

Before the Miami contingent arrived the following day, he cleaned up some matters at his desk.

Emil Kettner, head honcho of the construction company that built Hope House, regretted that Buck Leeper would be tied up for two years on a project in Virginia.

Perhaps after that, Kettner said, they could send Buck to Mitford for six months, which ought to be enough time to overhaul the church attic. His company never sent Buck on small jobs, but in this case, they'd try to make an exception. Could they wait?

Their Sunday School wasn't yet overflowing, said the rector, but they were getting there.

The conclusion was, Lord's Chapel was willing to wait, as they really wanted Buck for the job.

"He's doing better, I thought you'd like to know that," said Emil.

"A few weekend benders here and there, but nothing daily like it was for years. What happened in Mitford, Father?"

"Buck got rid of something old, so something new could come in."

"You have my personal thanks."

"No thanks to me," said the rector. "Thanks be to God!"

Lace Turner met him at the foot of the basement steps.

"He's done eat a whole bag of choc'late candy!" she said.

Harley, who was a ghastly color, was sitting on the floor of the hallway, clutching his stomach. "Don't be tattlin' on me like I was some young 'un!"

"You act like a young 'un!" said Lace. "That choc'late'll git your ulcer goin' again, just when you was gettin' better!"

"Rev'rend, hit was all that baby puddin' that made me do it. A man needs somethin' he can get 'is teeth into, you might say. But oh, law, I repent, I do, I'm sorry I ever bought that bag of candy, I'll never take another bite long as I live! Nossir!"

"Forty-two pieces, I counted 'em," said Lace. "He wadded up th' wrappers and stuck ever' one under 'is mattress."

"You cain't git by with a thing around this 'un, she's th' worst ol' *po*lice I ever seen." Harley stood up suddenly, looking distraught. "Oh, law! You 'uns better leave!"

He headed for the bathroom at a trot.

What timing. The basement plumbing had been completed barely an hour ago.

He squirmed in his office chair and looked at his watch.

In thirty minutes, he and Ron Malcolm and several others on the vestry were squiring strangers around Sadie Baxter's homeplace. He hated the thought, but he despised himself more for his wishy-washy attitude about the whole situation.

They needed desperately to sell it, get it off the shoulders of the parish; yet, here was a golden opportunity driving up the mountain in a rented car, and he wanted to run in the opposite direction.

Surely it was as simple as his dread of letting Sadie Baxter go entirely. Surely he was trying to hold on to what was vanished and gone, to another way of life that had been vibrantly preserved in Miss Sadie's engrossing stories.

When Fernbank was sold, all that would be left of the old Mitford was three original storefronts on Main Street, Lord's Chapel and the church office, the town library, and the Porter mansion–cum–town museum where Uncle Billy and Miss Rose lived in the little apartment.

Blast! he exhorted himself. Stop being a hick and move on. This is today, this is now!

He glanced at Emma, who was staring at her computer screen. What did people find to stare at on computer screens, anyway? Nothing moved on the screen, yet she was transfixed, as if hearing voices from a heavenly realm.

"I'll be darned," she muttered, clicking her mouse.

He sighed.

"Look here," she said, not taking her eyes off the screen.

He got up and went to her desk and looked.

"What? It looks like a list."

"It is a list. It's a list of everybody in the whole United States, and their addresses. Our computer man sent it to us. See there?"

She moved her pointer to a name. "Albert Wilcox!" he exclaimed. "Good heavens, do you suppose . . ."

"We've been lookin' for Albert Wilcox for how long?"

"Ten years, anyway! Do you think it's *our* Albert Wilcox?"

"We heard he'd moved to Seattle," she said, "and we tried to find him in the phone book, but we never did. This town is somewhere close to Seattle, it's called Oak Harbor."

"Well done! Let's write this Albert Wilcox and see if he's the one whose grandmother's hand-illuminated prayer book turned up in the parish hall storage closet."

"A miracle!" she said. "I remember the day we found it—right behind the plastic poinsettias that had been there a hundred years. How in th' dickens it ended up *there* . . ."

"That book could be worth a fortune. Every page is done in calligraphy and watercolor illustrations—by his own grandfather. When it disappeared out of the exhibition we did for a Bane and Blessing, it broke Albert's heart."

"It was only Rite One, remember, not th' whole thing!"

"Nonetheless . . ."

"And don't forget he was goin' to sue the church 'til Miss Sadie talked him out of it."

Well, that, too.

Ingrid Swenson was fashionably thin, deeply tanned, and expensively dressed.

"Arresting!" she said, as they drove along Fernbank's proud but neglected driveway.

Tendrils of grapevine leapt across the drive and entwined among a row of hemlocks on the other side. To their right, a gigantic mock orange faded from bloom in a tangled thicket of wisteria, star magnolia, and rhododendron.

The house didn't reveal its dilapidation at once, and for that he was relieved. In fact, it stood more grandly than he remembered from his caretaker's visit in March.

He was touched to recall that exactly two years ago there had been the finest of fetes at this house.

On the lawn, young people in tuxedos had served champagne and cups of punch on silver trays, as lively strains of Mozart poured through the tall windows. Inside, the ballroom had been filled with heartfelt joy for Olivia and Hoppy Harper, the glamorous bride and groom, and with awe for the hand-painted ceiling above their heads, which was newly restored to its former glory.

Roberto had flown from Italy to surprise Miss Sadie, and Esther Bolick's orange marmalade cake had stood three tiers high, each tier supported by Corinthian columns of marzipan bedecked with imported calla lilies. It had been, without doubt, the swellest affair since President Woodrow Wilson had attended a ball at Fernbank and given little Sadie Baxter a hard candy wrapped in silver paper.

The man who came with Ingrid Swenson seemed interested only

in biting his nails, speaking in monosyllables, and exploring Fernbank quite on his own. The rector saw him peering into the wash-house and wandering into the orchards, taking notes.

"A little over twelve acres," said Ron Malcolm, a longtime member of Lord's Chapel who kept his broker's license current.

"Excellent," said Ingrid, who took no notes at all. "Twelve acres translates to twenty-four cottages. Town water, I presume?"

"On a well."

"Town sewer, of course. . . ."

"Afraid not," said Ron. "And I must tell you in all fairness that the cost to connect this property to town services will run well above a hundred thousand. The connection is a half mile down the hill and the right-of-ways pose some real problems."

Ingrid looked at him archly. "It could behoove you to make that investment and offer your buyer an upgraded property."

"It behooves us even more," said Ron, "to avoid putting a burden of debt on the parish."

She smiled vaguely. "That is, in any case, a trifle, Mr. Malcolm. But let's consider an issue which is the polar opposite of a trifle, and that's the number of jobs such a facility would bring to your village. An upscale property of twenty-one rooms and twenty-four cottages, including a state-of-the-art health center, would employ well over a hundred people, many of them coming from Europe and the British Isles and requiring satisfactory housing. This, gentlemen, could create a small boom." She paused for effect. "A small boom for a small town!" she said, laughing.

"Yes ma'am," said Ron Malcolm.

"But we'll get to all that later. Now I'd like to start in the attic and work down to the basement."

"Consider it done," said the rector, wanting the whole thing behind them.

§

She would talk it over with her associates, Ingrid told them in the church office. They wouldn't buy an option—they'd take a risk on the property still being available when they returned with an offer in thirty to sixty days.

"Risk," she said, toying with the paperweight on his desk, "has a certain adrenaline, after all."

Their lawyer would begin the title search immediately, and a full topo would be done by a surveyor from Holding. No, they didn't want the window treatments or furnishings, with the possible exception of Miss Sadie's bed, which Ingrid concluded was French, a loveseat and secretary that were almost certainly George II, and a china cabinet that appeared to be made by a native craftsman.

Her people wanted to talk with the town engineer again, and expressed regret that the heating system appeared defunct and the plumbing would have to be completely modernized.

Before leaving, she mentioned the seriousness of the water damage due to years of leakage through a patched roof, and frowned when the subject of the well and sewer emerged again.

He tried to be elated, but was merely thankful that the first phase was over and done with. He made a note to get up to Fernbank with Cynthia and go through the attic, pronto.

Pauline Barlowe had the job and was to report to work on Monday morning at six-thirty.

He called Scott Murphy at once.

"Thank you!" he said. "I can't thank you enough."

"What for, sir?"

"Why, for . . . saying anything that might have helped Pauline Barlowe get the job in your dining room."

"I didn't say a word."

"You didn't?"

"Not a peep out of me. That was our personnel director's idea. She said she knew she might be taking a chance, but she wanted to do it and came to talk to me about it. Lida Willis is tough, she'll watch Mrs. Barlowe like a hawk, but Lida has a soft center; she wants this to work."

"We're thrilled around our place. This means a lot to Dooley as well as his mother. When will you come for dinner? We've got a regular corn shucking going at the rectory; it's just the thing to liven up a bachelor."

"Name the time!" said the chaplain.

"I'll call you," said the rector.

"We're giving a party," announced his wife, flushed with excitement.

"We are?"

"Friday night. In the basement, a housewarming! I'm baking cookies and making a pudding cake for Harley, and Lace is doing the lemonade. I've invited Olivia, Hoppy has a meeting, and oh, I've asked Dooley, but he's not keen on the idea. Who else?"

"Ummm. Scott Murphy!" he wondered

"Perfect. Who else?"

"Tommy. But wait, I think Dooley mentioned that Tommy has a family thing on Friday, and Dooley's going over there later to watch a video."

"OK, that's seven. Terrific! They finished painting today, the place looks wonderful, and it's all aired out and Harley is excited as anything. He raked tons of leaves from under the back hedge, and in the next couple of days he's replacing my alternator."

"Wonderful!" he said

"Harley's so happy, he can't stop grinning, and Lace—she doesn't say so, but she's thrilled by all this."

"It was her idea, and she was bold enough to step forward and ask for it."

"Let us come *boldly* to the throne of grace . . ." said his wife, quoting one of their favorite verses from Hebrews.

". . . that we may obtain mercy and find grace to help in time of need!" he replied.

"Amen!" they cried in unison, laughing.

He frankly relished it when they burst into a chorus of Scripture together. As a boy in his mother's Baptist church, he'd been thumpingly drilled to memorize Scripture verses, which sprang more quickly to memory than something he'd studied yesterday.

"One of the finest exhortations ever delivered, in my opinion," he said. "Well, now, what may I do to help out with the party?"

"Help me move that old sofa from the garage to Harley's parlor, I don't think he's strong enough, then we'll shift that maple wardrobe from the furnace room to his bedroom."

Was there no balm in Gilead?

"Oh, and another thing," she said, smiling innocently. "We need to haul that huge box of books from his parlor to the furnace room."

For his wife's birthday in July, she was getting a back brace whether she wanted it or not. In fact, he'd get one for himself while he was at it.

On his way to Hope House, he stopped at the Sweet Stuff Bakery to buy a treat for Louella.

Winnie Ivey looked at him and burst into tears.

"Winnie! What is it?"

"I heard you're leaving," she said, wiping her eyes with her apron.

"Yes, but not for a year and a half."

"We'll miss you somethin' awful."

"But you'll probably be gone before I will."

"Oh," she said. "I keep forgetting I'm going."

"Besides, we'll still be living in Mitford, in the house next door to the rectory."

"Good!" she said, sniffing. "That's better. Here, have a napoleon, I know you're not supposed to, but . . ."

What the heck, he thought, taking it. At least one person was sorry to hear he was retiring. . . .

When he left the bakery, he looked up the street and saw Uncle Billy sitting in a dinette chair on the grounds of the town museum, watching traffic flow around the monument.

He walked up and joined him. "Uncle Billy! I'm half starved for a joke."

"I cain't git a new joke t' save m' life," said the old man, looking forlorn.

"If you can't get a joke, nobody can."

"My jokes ain't workin' too good. I cain't git Rose t' laugh f'r nothin'."

"Aha."

"See, I test m' jokes on Rose, that's how I know what t' tell an' what t' leave off."

"Try one on me and see what happens."

"Well, sir, two ladies was talkin' about what they'd wear to th' Legion Hall dance, don't you know, an' one said, 'We're supposed t' wear somethin' t' match our husband's hair, so I'll wear black, what'll you wear?' an' th' other one sorta turned pale, don't you know, an' said, 'I don't reckon I'll go.'"

"Aha," said Father Tim.

"See, th' feller married t' that woman that won't goin' was *bald,* don't you know."

The rector grinned.

"It don't work too good, does it?" said Uncle Billy. "How about this 'un? Little Sonny's mama hollered at 'im, said, 'Sonny, did you fall down with y'r new pants on?' An' Sonny said, 'Yes 'um, they won't time t' take 'em off.'"

The rector laughed heartily. "Not bad. Not half bad!"

"See, if I can hear a laugh or two, it gits me goin'."

"About like preaching, if you ask me."

"Speakin' of preachin', me 'n Rose ain't a bit glad about th' news on Sunday. We come home feelin' s' low, we could've crawled under a snake's belly with a hat on. It don't seem right f'r you t' go off like that."

"I'll be living right down the street, same as always. We'll be settling in the yellow house next door to the rectory."

"Me 'n Rose'll try t' git over it, but . . ." Uncle Billy sighed.

Father Tim couldn't remember seeing Bill Watson without a big smile on his face and his gold tooth gleaming.

"See, what Rose 'n me don't like is, when you leave they'll send us somebody we don't know."

"That's the way it usually works."

"I figure by th' time we git t' know th' new man, we'll be dead as doornails, so it ain't no use to take th' trouble, we'll just go back to th' Presbyterians."

"Now, Uncle Billy . . ."

"I hate t' say it, Preacher, but me 'n Rose think you could've waited on this."

The rector made his way down Main Street, staring at the sidewalk. It was the only time in his life he hadn't come away from Bill Watson feeling better than when he went.

At the corner of Main and Wisteria, he saw Gene Bolick coming toward him, and threw up his hand in greeting. It appeared that Gene saw him, but looked away and jaywalked to the other side.

June.

Something about June . . .

What else was happening this month? His birthday!

Dadgum it, he'd just had one.

In fact, the memory of his last birthday rushed back to him with dark force. His wife had brought him coffee in bed and wished him happy birthday, then the phone had rung and he'd raced to the hospital and discovered that a woman who would be irrevocably fixed in his life had been horribly burned by a madman.

He sat back in his swivel chair and closed his eyes. Wrenching, that whole saga of pain and desperation. And days afterward, only doors down the hall from Pauline, Miss Sadie had died.

No wonder he'd come close to forgetting his birthday. When was it, anyway? He looked at the calendar. Blast. Straight ahead.

How old would he be this year? He could never remember.

He called Cynthia at home. "How old will I be this year?"

"Let's see. You're six years older than I am, and I'm fifty-seven. No, fifty-six. So you're sixty-two."

"I can't be sixty-two. I've already been sixty-two, I remember it distinctly."

"Darn!" she said. "Then you're sixty-three?"

"Well, surely I'm not sixty-five, because I'm retiring at sixty-five."

"So you must be sixty-three. Which makes me fifty-seven. Rats."

He realized as he hung up that they could have used their birth years to calculate the answer. What a pair they made! He hoped nobody had tapped his phone line and overheard such nonsense.

"I've been thinking," said Emma.

Please, no.

"I might as well retire when you retire."

"Well!" He was relieved. "Sounds good!"

She looked at him over her half-glasses. "But I wasn't expecting you to give up so soon."

"Give up?"

"I guess you can't take it anymore, the pressure and all—two services every Sunday, the sick and dying . . ."

"It has nothing to do with pressure, and certainly not with the sick and dying. As you know, I've committed to supply pulpits from here to the Azores."

"Yes, well, that's vacation stuff, anybody can go supply somewhere and not get involved."

He felt suddenly furious. Thank God he couldn't speak; he couldn't open his mouth. His face burning, he got up from his desk and left the office, closing the door behind him with some force.

There! he thought. Right there is reason enough to retire.

He deserved a medal for putting up with Emma Newland all these years—which, he realized only this morning, would be a full sixteen in September.

Sixteen years in an office the size of a cigar box, with a woman who made Attila the Hun look sensitive and nurturing?

"A medal!" he exclaimed aloud, going at full trot past the Irish Shop.

"There he goes again, talking to himself," said Hessie Mayhew, who had dropped in to share a bag of caramels with Minnie Lomax.

"What do you think it is?" asked Minnie, who hoped the caramels wouldn't stick to her upper plate.

"Age. Diabetes. And *guilt*," she announced darkly.

"Guilt?"

"Yes, for leaving those poor people in the lurch who've looked after him all these years."

"My goodness," said Minnie, "we don't look after our preacher at all. He looks after himself."

"Yes, but you've got a Baptist preacher. They've been *raised* to look after themselves."

"I declare," said Minnie, who had never considered this possibility.

At The Local, he saw Sophia Burton, who wasn't even a member of Lord's Chapel, and was flabbergasted when she burst into tears by the butcher case.

"I'm sorry," she told him.

"Don't be sorry!" he implored, not knowing what else to say.

"It's just that . . . it's just that you've been so good to us, and . . . and we're *used* to you!"

Didn't he despise change? Didn't he hate it? And here he was, inflicting it on everyone else. If his wife wasn't so excited about the whole adventure of being free, he'd call Stuart up, and . . . no, he wouldn't do any such thing. Actually, he was excited, himself.

"I'm . . . pretty excited, myself," he muttered weakly.

"That's easy for you to say!" Mona Gragg, a former Lord's Chapel Sunday School teacher, strode up to him, clutching a sack of corn and tomatoes. For some reason, Mona looked ten feet tall; she was also mad as a wet hen.

"When I heard that mess on Sunday, I just boiled. Here we've all gotten along just fine all these years, *plus* . . . you're still plenty young, and no reason in the *world* to retire. Did Grandma Moses quit when *she* was sixty-five? Certainly not! She hadn't even gotten *started*! And Abraham, which Bishop Cullen was so quick to yammer about on Sunday . . . he moved to a whole new *country* when he was way up in his *seventies* and didn't even have that *kid* 'til he was a *hundred*!"

Mona stomped away, furious.

"One of my ah, parishioners," he said, flushing.

Sophia wiped her eyes and smiled. "Father, now I can see why you're retiring."

He checked out, liking the sight of Dooley bagging groceries at one of Avis's two counters.

"How's it going, buddy?"

Dooley grinned. "Great! Except for people raisin' heck about you retiring."

"Ah, well." For some reason he didn't completely understand, Dooley seemed to approve of his plans. It wasn't the first time Dooley had stood up for him. A year or so ago, when Buster Austin had called the rector a nerd, Dooley had proceeded to beat the tar out of him.

As he left The Local, he saw Jenny parking her blue bicycle at the lamppost.

He left one end of Main Street feeling like a million bucks, and reached the other end feeling like two cents with a hole in it.

Up and down the street, he was besieged by people who had heard the news and didn't like it, or, on the rarest of occasions, proffered him their sincere best wishes.

Rodney Underwood was shocked and, it seemed, personally insulted.

Lew Boyd shook his head and wouldn't make eye contact. Why in heaven's name his *car mechanic* was piqued was beyond him.

The owner of the Collar Button rushed into the street and extended his deepest regrets. "What a loss!" he muttered darkly, sounding like a delegate from a funeral parlor.

A vestry member called him at the rectory. "This," she announced, "is the worst news since they found somethin' in Lloyd's limp nodes."

He phoned Stuart Cullen.

"Gene Bolick crossed to the other side of the street!" he said, feeling like a ten-year-old whining to a parent.

"Denial! If he doesn't have to talk to you, he doesn't have to acknowledge the truth. He'll get over it. It takes time."

"And some people are mad because I'm retiring so early! I feel like a heel, like I'm running out on them."

"Let them squawk!" Stuart exclaimed. "When people don't express their anger, it turns into depression. So, better this than a parish riddled by resentment and low morale."

"Then," Father Tim said miserably, "there are those who feel it's merely a blasted inconvenience."

"They're right about that," said Stuart. "By the way, your Search Committee is already up and running, but it'll be a long process. So hang in there."

His bishop hadn't been any help at all.

The hasty trim he'd gotten from his reluctant wife had carried him through Stuart's visit, but wouldn't carry him a step further. And blast if Fancy Skinner wasn't booked. That was the way with those unisex shops, he thought, darkly. He made an appointment for a month away, and deceived himself that he could talk Cynthia into an interim deal.

"No, a thousand times no. I can't cut hair! Go to Wesley, where they have the kind of barbershop you like, where men talk trout fishing and politics!"

"I know zero about trout fishing, and even less about politics," he said. "Where did you get that idea?"

"Oh, phoo, darling!" she said, waving him away.

"I'll trim you up!" said Harley, who was getting ready for the party in his basement.

"Oh, I don't—"

"Law, Rev'rend, I've cut hair from here t' west Texas, they ain't nothin' to it, it jis' takes a sharp pair of scissors. Now, th' right scissors is ever'thing. I've cut with a razor, I've cut with a pocketknife, but I like scissors th' best. I ain't got a pair, but I got a good rock I use t' sharpen m' knife, so you git me some scissors, an' we're set. What're you lookin' for—mostly t' git it off y'r collar, I reckon."

"I don't know about this, Harley."

Harley looked at him soberly. "You ought t' let me do it f'r you, Rev'rend. I don't want th' Lord sayin' 'What did you do f'r th' Rev'rend?' an' me have t' tell 'im, 'Nothin', he wouldn't let me do nothin'!' I know what th' Lord'll say, he'll say, 'Harley, that ain't no excuse, you jis' git on down them steps over yonder, I know hit's burnin' hot, but . . .' "

"Oh, for Pete's sake," said the rector. "I'll get the scissors."

There went Harley's grin, meeting behind his head again.

"Ummm," said Cynthia, looking at him as he dressed for Harley's housewarming party.

"Ummm, what?"

"Your hair . . ."

"What about it?"

"It's sort of scalloped in the back."

"Scalloped?"

"Well, yes, up, down, up, down. What did Harley use—pinking shears?"

"Scissors!"

"Not those scissors I cut up chickens with, I fondly hope."

"Absolutely not. He used the scissors from my chest of drawers, which I keep well sharpened."

"You would," she said, looking at him as if he were a beetle on a pin. "Why don't you sit on the commode seat and let me sort of . . . shape it up? You know I hate doing this, but you can't go around with that scalloped look."

Certainly not. He sat on the commode seat, draped with a bath towel, glad he'd soon have the whole dismal business behind him.

Cynthia had done the deed and dashed downstairs. He was putting on a clean shirt when Dooley wandered into the bedroom.

He looked at the boy, fresh from a day's work, and now fresh from the shower. Clean T-shirt, clean jeans; hair combed, shoe laces tied. Upstanding! Getting to look more like a millionaire every day!

The rector might have been a statue in a park, the way Dooley walked around him, staring.

"Man . . ." said Dooley.

"What are you looking at?"

"Your hair."

"What about my hair?" He was beginning to feel positively churlish at any mention of his hair.

"It's cut in a kind of V in the back. I've never seen that before."

"A V? What do you mean, a *V*?"

He stomped to his dresser and, with his wife's hand mirror, looked at the back of his neck in the trifold mirror. It wasn't a V, exactly, it was more like a U. What was the matter with people around here, anyway?

"I'll trim it up for you," said Dooley, "if you'll let me drive your car Saturday."

"Dooley . . ."

"You can drive as far as Farmer, and I can take over at the cutoff."

"This is no time—"

"Anyway, you better let me fix your hair. I know how to do it."

"You're kidding me."

"I'm not kidding you. I've cut Tommy's hair bunches of times."

"A likely story."

"I swear on a stack of Bibles."

"I wouldn't do that. The Bibles you so casually stacked up ask us not to swear."

"That V is hanging down over your collar."

He would drive to Memphis next week, it was only nine or ten hours one way, and see Joe. While he was there, maybe Joe would give him a tour of Graceland. . . .

He sighed deeply. For the third time that day, he got his scissors out of his dresser drawer and handed them over. This time, however, he had the good sense to pray about it.

CHAPTER SEVEN

Housewarming

The showy pudding cake had been reduced to crumbs, the fruit bowl ransacked, the cookies demolished. All that remained in the glass pitcher were two circles of lemon and a few seeds.

In the freshly painted sitting room, Harley opened the last of his housewarming presents.

"Oh, law!" he said, holding up the framed picture of Jesus carrying a sheep. "Hit's th' Lord an' Master, ain't it?"

"Bingo!" said Cynthia, who had given him the print to go over his bed.

"That sheep was lost," Dooley announced. "Tell about it," he said, looking at the rector.

"Why don't you tell about it?"

Dooley scratched his head. "Well, see, it's like . . . if you had a hundred sheep and one of 'em ran off and got lost, you'd go after it, you'd go to the mountains and all, looking for it. And like, when you found it, it would make you feel really good, I mean better than you even feel about the ninety-nine that didn't run off."

"By jing!" said Harley.

Lace sat forward in the chair. "What th' story's about," she said, "is when somebody's lost and Jesus finds 'em an' they give their heart to 'im, it makes 'im feel happier than He feels about all them other'ns that wadn't lost."

Dooley looked at her coldly.

"I reckon that's what th' Lord done with me," said Harley. "Searched through th' mountains lookin' t' find me, an' brought me here." He grinned. "And I ain't lost n'more."

The rector was captivated by an odd confidence—a new maturity, perhaps—in Lace Turner.

"Well, now, I want t' thank ever' one of you'ns," said Harley, tears coming to his eyes. "I ain't never had a Bible with m' name on it, I ain't never had a 'lectric fan that moves to th' left an' right . . ."

He took a paper napkin from his pocket and blew his nose.

". . . I ain't never had a picture t' hang on m' wall 'cept of m' mama as a little young 'un . . . an' Lord *knows,* I ain't never had a . . ." Harley patted Scott's gift, which lay beside him on the sofa. "What d'you call this what you give me?"

"That's an afghan," said the chaplain, grinning. "One of our residents crochets those. They're a big hit on the hill."

"What exactly is it f'r, did you say?"

"It's to keep you warm in winter when you lie on the sofa and watch TV."

"I'll use it, yes, sir, I will, and I thank you, but I ain't goin' t' be layin' on no sofa watchin' TV, I'm goin' t' be workin'."

"Harley's going to change my alternator!" announced Cynthia.

"I'd sure appreciate it if you'd take a look at my brakes," said Scott. "They're sticking."

"Might be y'r calibers."

"I'll pay the going rate."

"Th' only rate goin' for you 'uns is no rate," Harley declared.

Scott Murphy glanced at his watch and stood. "I've got to look in on my folks before they get to sleep. Thanks for inviting me, sir . . . Mrs. Kavanagh—"

"Cynthia!" said Mrs. Kavanagh.

"Cynthia! I had a really good time. Harley, come up and see me at Hope House. And let me know when you can look at my brakes."

Scott left by the basement door, as the rest of the party said their goodbyes to Harley, then trooped up the stairs to the rectory kitchen and along the hall to the front stoop.

"Soon as I get my stuff, I'm going to Tommy's house!" Dooley raced up the steps to his room, Barnabas at his heels. "His dad's waitin' for me, we're going to Wesley to rent a video."

The rector stood on the front walk and talked with Cynthia and Olivia as Lace searched under the bench on the stoop. Then she came down the steps to the yard and peered into the boxwoods near the steps.

"Lace—what is it?" asked Olivia.

"Somebody's stoled my hat," she said. "My hat ain't where I left it at."

"Where did you leave it?" wondered Cynthia.

"I asked her to leave it on the bench," Olivia confessed, looking concerned.

"I'll have a look with you," said the rector, going to the boxwoods. "It probably fell . . ."

"It didn't fall nowhere!" Lace shouted. "It's gone!"

The screen door slammed and Dooley ran down the steps.

"It was you that stoled my hat, won't it? I ought t' bash y'r head in!"

She lunged toward Dooley, and Olivia moved almost as quickly, catching Lace's jumper. There was a ripping sound as the skirt tore from part of the bodice.

"Look what you done t' my new outfit!" Lace struggled to free herself from Olivia. "Let me go, I'm goin' t' knock his head off—"

"Lace! Don't." Cynthia caught her wrist.

"I ought t' kill you, you sorry, redheaded son of a—"

Dooley's face was crimson. "Why would I steal your dirty, stinking, stupid, beat-up hat?"

The rector put his hand on the boy's shoulder. "Easy, son."

"Well, why would I?" he yelled.

"You better give it back and give it back now!" Lace trembled with rage, her own face ashen.

"What would anybody want with your dumb, stupid hat that makes you look so stupid everybody laughs behind your back? Who would even touch your stupid, snotty, dirty hat?"

Lace wrenched away from Cynthia and Olivia and flew at Dooley, who threw his arm in front of his face. She slammed her fist into his left rib, which sent him reeling backward toward the stoop.

Barnabas barked furiously as the rector grabbed Lace by the shoulders. "Stop it *now,*" he said.

Dooley regained his balance and stood without a word. He straightened his shirt. "I've got to go," he said, tight-lipped. "Tommy's dad is waiting for me."

"Go," the rector said quietly.

"If you done it," Lace shouted after Dooley, "I'll stomp your butt 'til you're flatter'n a cow dab."

Cynthia and Olivia walked with Lace to the blue Volvo at the curb, as the rector sat wearily on the top step. Barnabas crashed beside him. He felt shaken by the intensity of Lace Turner's sudden and virulent outburst.

If Dooley Barlowe were, indeed, the culprit, he'd do well to hide in the piney woods 'til this thing blew over.

§

He sat in the chair next to Dooley's desk, reading the Thirty-seventh Psalm, the first two words of which he considered an entire sermon.

He looked up as Dooley raced into the room on the stroke of his curfew.

"Did you do it?"

Dooley stood in the doorway, panting. He hesitated for a moment, peering at his shoes, then faced the rector and said, "Yes, sir."

"Why did you lie about it?"

"I didn't lie. I never told her I didn't do it."

That was true. Dooley had responded to her questions with questions. "Where is it?"

"In my closet."

"Take it to her in the morning and apologize. To Lace *and* Olivia." He would also call Olivia in the morning.

"Do I have to?"

"What do you think?"

Dooley went to the closet and opened the door. He lifted the hat off the floor as if it were something Barnabas had deposited in the backyard. "Man, I hate this stupid hat."

"So do I," said the rector.

"You do?"

"I do. But that hat belongs to someone else, and you were wrong to steal it."

"Yeah." Dooley looked at the hat for a moment, then looked the rector in the eye.

"I'm sorry," he said.

A genuine apology! If this is what that fancy prep school had accomplished, he should be forking over an extra twenty thousand a year, out of the mere goodness of his heart.

"You'll also apologize to Cynthia."

"What for?"

"Helping put a bitter end to Harley's party."

"Lace Turner makes me puke. I could've knocked her stupid head off."

"But you didn't, and I commend you for it."

Dooley sat on the bed, holding his left side. "She'll kill me," he said.

"You might want to apologize to Lace while Olivia is in the room—then run for it."

There was a long silence. A moth beat around the lamp bulb.

"Do something like this again," the rector said, "and I'll . . ." What he needed in closing was a good, hair-raising threat, something like taking the car keys away for a couple of weeks—but Dooley didn't drive.

"And I'll . . ." he said.

Blast. He realized he couldn't come up with a decent threat if his life depended on it.

The mayor asked him to trot to her office—and be quick about it, according to the tone in her voice.

When Esther Cunningham pulled the string, he, like most people, jumped. He hated that about himself, but why not? Esther had kept an unflagging vigil over Mitford, sacrificing years of her time and even her health to keep things on the up and up. They hadn't even had a tax hike in her long tenure. So yes, he came when she called, and glad to do it.

She leaned across the desk, the splotches on her face and neck looking redder than ever.

"Guess what th' low-down jackleg has done now."

"I can't guess."

"He's throwin' one of his free barbecues next Friday—th' very day of the town festival." She looked at him darkly. "See th' strategy?"

He didn't.

"That'll siphon th' crowd down to his place and leave us sittin' under those shade trees at th' town museum like a bunch of flour sacks."

"Aha." The cheese was getting binding.

"Here's what I want you to do," she said, looking at the door and lowering her voice.

He was in for it.

"Sittin' in a booth draped with th' flag won't cut it this election. Times are changin.' I want you to go home and pray about it and come up with somethin'."

"But the town festival is only four days away."

"Somethin'," she said, "that'll blow Mack Stroupe and his barbecue deal clear to Holding."

"You want *me* to do that?"

"And be quick about it," she said, scratching a splotch.

Hadn't his wife arranged countless retreats to help him relax, and cooked dinner on evenings when he wasn't up to the task?

Hadn't she prayed for him faithfully, and overhauled the rectory, and given him a complete set of Charles Dickens, not to mention a lighted world globe?

And wasn't she working on a book nearly eight hours a day?

He would do what the Russians do. Though it was his very own birthday, he would be the host, he would give the dinner.

It would be just the two of them, and afterward, they would dance. He'd put on the CD of the rhumba—or was it the tango she liked?—and positively whirl her around the study. His blood was getting up for it.

And champagne! That was the ticket. Something expensive, of course, that wouldn't give you a blinding headache even as it went down your gullet. Avis would know which label, and didn't Avis mention that a shipment of fresh lamb was expected any day?

Furthermore, weren't his antique French roses blooming like he'd never seen, drenching the air with their intoxicating scent?

By jing!

He examined the back of his head in the mirror again. He'd been fairly butchered in the privacy of his own home.

Best to nip out and get the matter settled, once and for all.

A decent haircut, the new blue sport coat Cynthia had found on sale, dancing with his wife on his birthday—what else could a man want or imagine?

Suddenly he didn't feel a hundred years old in the shade, he was feeling more like—why not say it?—seventeen.

As he looked up Fancy's number, he had to admit he missed Joe Ivey. So what if Joe had never gone to hair conventions to learn the latest thing? Joe was eminently companionable, and never talked your ear off while he barbered your head.

Another thing—Joe hadn't been shy about slapping on the Sea Breeze, an all-time favorite treat for the way it made the scalp tingle. Fancy Skinner, on the other hand, considered the use of Sea Breeze beneath her station.

Ah, well. He sighed, dialing 555-HAIR. Fancy Skinner was the only game in town, and he hoped she could work him in.

"Th' shop's closed today, I'm here givin' Mama a rinse. Mama, she lives in Spruce Pine, but I'm from Newland. If you get over here quick, I'll trim you up because it's you. You might be th' only one I'd do this for, I'm not sure I'd do it for my own preacher, did you see what his wife did to him, it looked like she put a soup bowl on his head and hacked around it with a steak knife. How he had th' nerve to preach a revival lookin' like that is beyond me.

"Oh, Lord, I just remembered, would you mind stoppin' by Th' Local and gettin' me some sugarless gum, I'll pay you th' minute you get here or take it off your bill, either one, I like to have gum in th' shop, I do my best work if I have somethin' in my mouth, at least it's not a cigarette, law, I used to suck down two packs a day, unfiltered, can you believe it?

"Well, if you're comin', come on, tomorrow'll be a zoo, everybody's gettin' ready for the town festival, why anybody would want highlights to eat barbecue in a parkin' lot is beyond me, and if you could pick up a sack of peppermint while you're at it, that'd be great, I like to have it for people with onion breath, doin' hair is close work."

As Fancy draped him with the pink shawl, he sighed resignedly and closed his eyes.

"Prayin', are you? You ought to know by now I won't cut your ear off or poke a hole in your head. Law, I've had too much coffee this mornin', you know I can't drink but two cups or I'm over the moon, how about you, can you still drink caffeine, or are you too old? Course, your wife is young, she probably can do it, I used to drink five or six cups a day . . . and smoke, oh, law, I smoked like a stack! But not anymore, did you know it makes you wrinkle faster? I hate those little lines around my mouth worse than anything, but that wadn't coffee, that was sun, honey, I used to lay out and bake like a chicken.

"Look at this trim! Who did this? I thought Joe Ivey was workin' at Graceland. Mama, come and look at this, this is what I have to put up with. Father, this is Mama, Mama, he's a friend of Mule's, he got married a while back for the first time.

"He preaches at that rock church down the street where they use incense, I declare, Mule and I passed by your church one Sunday, you could smell it comin' out of th' chimney! Lord, my allergies flare up somethin' awful when I smell that stuff, I thought incense was Catholic, anyway, do y'all talk Latin? I had a girlfriend one time, I went to church with her, I couldn't understand a word they said.

"Your hair's growin' like a weed. I hear if you eat a lot of grease, it'll make your hair grow, you shouldn't eat grease, anyway, you've got diabetes.

"Mama! Did you know th' Father has diabetes? My daddy had diabetes. Is that what killed him, Mama, or was it smokin'? Maybe both.

"Look at that! Whoever trimmed your hair, you tell 'em to leave your hair alone. You can call me anytime, I'll work you in. I'm sorry I couldn't take you—when was it?—I think your pope was here, I guess he don't always stay at the Vatican, have you ever been to the Vatican? Law, I haven't even been to Israel, everybody's been to Israel, our preacher is takin' a whole group next year, but I'd rather go on a cruise, do you think that's sacrilegious?

"You ought to let me give you a mask with Fancy's Face Food while we're at it, especially with your wife havin' a birthday, or is it you that's havin' one? Either way, my mask is about as good as a face-lift, not to mention four thousand dollars cheaper. No, I mean it, I'll do it for you, it won't take but an hour. Just *name* a better birthday present than lookin' fifteen years younger, which is more in your *wife's* age group, if I'm not mistaken. OK, lay back, you're stiff as a board, I'm not goin' to claw your eyes out, men are babies, aren't they, Mama? She can't hear for beans, bein' under th' dryer an' all.

"Now, don't try to talk while I'm puttin' this on your face, OK? It'll get hard and you have to lay like this for thirty minutes without sayin' a word or th' whole thing'll crack off and fall on th' floor and that's forty bucks down the tubes. You ought to see this nice green color, it's got mint in it, and cucumber, and I don't know what all, I think there's spinach in here, too, and burdock—my granmaw used to dig burdock for whoopin' cough medicine!

"Don't that feel good, don't you just feel your skin releasin' all those toxins? And those wrinkles on your forehead, I bet you pucker your forehead when you think, you seem like th' type that thinks, well, you can kiss your wrinkles goodbye, honey, 'cause I'm talkin' sayonara, adios, outta here. . . ."

Lying in Fancy's chair had given him a headache, not to mention a crick in his neck that seemed to extend to his upper shoulders and into most of his spinal column. Oh, well. A small price to pay for looking forty-eight on his sixty-third birthday.

Fancy had urged him not to look in the mirror at Hair House. "Why look in the mirror," she asked in what he considered a marvelous burst of philosophy, "when you can see th' real difference by lookin' in her eyes?" She winked at him hugely and blew a bubble, which wasn't easy to do with sugarless spearmint gum.

Not wanting to seem ungrateful, he tipped her five dollars, noting that she hadn't offered a discount for clergy on this particular deal.

He couldn't help himself. The minute he came in the back door, he turned and looked in the mirror.

Good Lord!

His face was . . . *green.*

Unbelievable! Surely not. Was it the dim natural light in the kitchen? He switched on the overhead fixture, fogged his glasses, and looked again.

It wasn't the light.

He dialed 555-HAIR from the kitchen phone, his heart beating dully. No answer.

He raced up the stairs to the bedroom and looked in the mirror he was accustomed to using.

Green.

His watch said five p.m. He'd invited Cynthia to come over at seven.

The birthday dinner, the champagne, the roses . . . the whole deal dashed. Blown on the wind.

He went to the bathroom and lathered his hands with soap and warm water and scrubbed his face.

Who would want to dance the tango with someone whose face was green? And how could he possibly confess that he'd had a facial, something which no other man in the village of Mitford would ever do in a hundred—no, a million—years?

He splashed his face and dried it and looked in the medicine cabinet mirror, which was topped by a 150-watt bulb that never lied.

Green. No two ways about it.

He stood gazing into the mirror, stunned. That's what he got for being a weak-minded sap, unable to say no to a woman in a pair of Capri pants so tight they looked as if they'd been robbed from a toddler.

He wanted to dig a hole and crawl in it.

They had dined, they had danced, they had remarked upon the extraordinary fragrance of the roses. She had raved about his cooking, she had sung a rousing "Happy Birthday," and she'd given him a book about himself and the parish of Mitford, which she had written and illustrated.

He was visibly moved and completely delighted. To have a book in which he saw himself walking down Main Street and standing on the church lawn in his vestments . . . Now he knew how Violet must feel.

He thought it immensely good of her not to comment on anything unusual in his appearance, though he was certain that he saw her staring a time or two, once with her mouth open.

He poured a final glass of champagne.

"This is like . . . like a date!" she said, flushed and happy.

"Which we never had, except for that movie where you ate all my Milk Duds."

"I detest dating!" she said. "I think it should be reserved for marriage."

"Amen!"

He served the poached pears he'd served the first time she came for dinner, drizzling hers with chocolate sauce.

"Dearest," she said, as they lolled on the study sofa, "there's something I've been wanting to say. . . ."

Here it comes, he thought, his heart sinking.

"You aren't looking well at all. You seem . . . a little green around the gills. I'm worried about you, Timothy."

"Aha." He had paid good money to look fifteen years younger, and wound up looking sick and infirm. He would never step foot in

Fancy Skinner's place again, not as long as he lived, so what if the round-trip to Memphis would take eighteen hours' hard driving?

"All that business about your retirement and the worry over Fernbank, and whatever this new, urgent project is for the mayor . . . I think it's time for a retreat."

His wife specialized, actually, in the domestic retreat. It was, to a worn-out clergyman, what retreads were to a tire. Once they'd had a picnic in Baxter Park, once a picnic overlooking the Land of Counterpane, and once she'd carried him off to the little yellow house where they had reclined on her king-size bed like two dissolute Romans, drinking lemonade and listening to the rain.

"Right," he said. "A retreat."

She peered at him again, her brow furrowed.

"Definitely!" she said, looking concerned.

While they partied in the study, Barnabas had stood up to the kitchen counter like a man and polished off what was left of the lamb. He also helped himself to two dinner rolls, half a stick of butter, a bowl of wild rice, and all the mint jelly he could lick off a spoon in the dishwasher.

At two in the morning, the rector felt a large paw on his shoulder. This was major, and no doubt about it.

He hastily pulled on his pants and a shirt, slipped his feet into his loafers, and thumped downstairs behind his desperate dog.

He barely got the leash on before Barnabas was out the back door and across to the hedge.

Barnabas sniffed his turf. Possums, raccoons, hedgehogs, squirrels, and cats had passed this way, not to mention the rector's least favorite of all creatures great and small, the mole. The place was a veritable smorgasbord of smells, apparently causing his dog to forget entirely why he had barreled outside in the middle of the night, dragging his master behind like a ball on a chain.

"Sometime in this century, pal?"

More sniffing.

Suddenly Barnabas had the urge to go around the house . . . then across the yard . . . then out to the sidewalk . . . then up the street.

"Not the monument!" he groaned.

Barnabas strained forward with the muscle and determination of a team of yoked oxen. They were going to the monument.

He trotted behind his dog, noting the peace of their village when no cars were on the street. There seemed an uncommon dignity in the glow of the streetlights tonight and the baskets brimming with flowers that hung from every lamppost.

They had a good life in Mitford, no doubt about it. Visitors were often amazed at its seeming charm and simplicity, wanting it for themselves, seeing in it, perhaps, the life they'd once had, or had missed entirely.

Yet there were Mitfords everywhere. He'd lived in them, preached in them, they were still out there, away from the fray, still containing something of innocence and dreaming, something of the past that other towns had freely let go, or allowed to be taken from them.

How much longer could the Esther Cunninghams of the world hold on? How much longer could common, decent, kind regard hold out against utter disregard?

Like the rest of us, he thought, the mayor may have her blind spots, but I'll take my chances with Esther any day.

He'd almost forgotten what he'd come out here for; he'd been walking as in a dream. Then, thanks be to God, his dog found a spot behind the hedge surrounding the monument.

He stood there as Barnabas did his business, and looked at the summer sky. Cassiopeia . . . the Three Sisters . . . the Bear . . .

He nearly missed seeing the car as it went around the monument and headed down Lilac Road.

Lincoln. New. Black. Quiet.

He felt alarmed, but couldn't figure why. The car seemed to remind him of something or someone. . . .

He had the strange thought that it didn't seem right for a car to be so quiet—it was oddly chilling.

"What's the scoop?" he asked Scott Murphy.

"Interesting. I can't figure it out exactly. When they come to see

Homeless on Wednesday night, they don't have much to say, but they seem to sense something special about being there, as if they're . . . waiting for something."

They are, he thought, suddenly moved. They are.

"I hate to tell you this," he said, glancing at his wife as they weeded the perennial bed next to her garage. The town festival was tomorrow, and all of Mitford was scurrying to look tidy and presentable. Certainly he was looking more presentable. The greenish cast to his skin had disappeared altogether.

A long silence ensued as he pulled knotgrass from among the foxgloves.

"Well? Spit it out, Timothy!"

"I did some simple arithmetic . . ."

"So?"

". . . and I was sixty-four yesterday."

"No!"

"Yes."

"I thought you were sixty-three! This means I'll be fifty-eight, not fifty-seven. Oh, *please*!"

Her moan might have ricocheted off the roof of the town museum two blocks away.

"The neighbors . . ." he said.

"We don't *have* any, remember? Since I moved to the rectory, we don't *have* any neighbors, which means I can wail as loud as I want to."

"Good thinking, Kavanagh."

Sixty-four! He felt like letting go with a lamentation of his own.

"Th' volts was down t' ten," said Harley, wiping his hands on a rag. "Hit was runnin' off the battery. Why don't you take it out and spin it around, I tuned it up some while I was at it."

"We thank you, Harley. This is terrific."

"Hit ought t' go like a scalded dog."

The rector opened the door and Barnabas jumped into the passenger seat, then he got in and backed his wife's Mazda out of the garage.

What a day! he thought as he drove up Main Street, glad to see the bustle of commerce. In a day of shopping malls on bypasses, not every town could boast of a lively business center.

He saw Dooley pedal out of The Local alleyway on his bicycle, wearing his helmet and hauling a full delivery basket. He honked the horn. Dooley grinned and waved.

There was Winnie, putting a tray of something sinful in the window of the Sweet Stuff, and he honked again but was gone before Winnie looked up.

As he approached the monument, he saw Uncle Billy and Miss Rose, stationed in their chrome dinette chairs on the lawn of the town museum, where everybody and his brother had gathered to put up tents, booths, flags, tables, umbrellas, hand-lettered signs, and the much-needed port-a-john, which this year, he observed, appeared to lean to the right instead of the left.

He honked and waved as Uncle Billy waved back and Miss Rose looked scornful.

How in the dickens he could have lived in this town for over fifteen years and still get a kick out of driving up Main Street was beyond him. He'd liked living in his little parish by the sea, too, but the main street hadn't been much to look at, and often, during the hurricane season, their few storefronts had stayed boarded up.

Count your blessings, his grandmother had told him. Count your blessings, his mother had often said.

He eased around the monument and headed west on Lilac Road.

Did anyone really count their blessings, anymore? There was, according to the world's dictum, no time to smell the roses, no time to count blessings. But how much time did it take to recognize that he was, in a sense, driving one around? Hadn't Harley Welch just saved them a hundred bucks, right in his own backyard?

Besides, if there were no time in Mitford, where would there ever be time?

"Ah, Barnabas," he said, reaching over to scratch his dog's ear.

Barnabas stared straight ahead, a behavior he'd always considered appropriate to riding in a car.

He turned on the radio and heard Mozart straining to come across the mountains from the tower in Asheville, and fiddled with the dial until he got a weather report. Sunshine all weekend. Hallelujah!

He realized he was grinning from ear to ear.

How often did he feel as if he didn't have a care in the world? Not often. He'd been equipped, after all, with a nature that could run to the melancholy if he didn't watch it.

"Serious-minded!" a neighbor had said of him as a child, putting on his glasses to get a better look at the tyke who stood before him with a large book under his skinny arm.

He thought of last night, of his vibrant and unstoppable wife sitting up in bed, reading to him, knowing how he loved this simple sacrifice of time and effort. He had put his head in her lap and reached down and held the warm calf of her leg, knowing with all that was in him how extraordinarily rich he was.

He had heard Dooley come in, racing up the stairs on the dot of his curfew, and afterward, the sound of his dog snoring in the hall. . . .

He thought of the old needlepoint sampler his grandmother had done, framed and hanging in the rectory kitchen. He had passed it so often over the years, he had quit seeing it. The patient stitching, embellished with faded cabbage roses, quoted a verse from the Sixty-eighth Psalm.

"Blessed be the Lord," it read, "who daily loadeth us with benefits."

"Loadeth!" he exclaimed aloud. "Daily!"

The car was running like a top, thanks to his live-in mechanic, but he didn't want to turn around and go home; he had a sudden taste for a view of the late-June countryside, maybe a little run out to Farmer, four miles away, then back to help Cynthia bake for the church booth tomorrow.

And while he did the run to Farmer, he would do a seemingly childish thing—he would count his blessings as far as he could.

Quite possibly the list could go on until Wednesday, for he knew a thing or two about blessings and how they were, even in the worst of times, inexhaustible.

It came to him that Patrick Henry Reardon had indirectly spoken of something like this. He had copied it into his sermon notebook only days ago.

"Suppose for a moment," Reardon had said, "that God began taking from us the many things for which we have failed to give thanks. Which of our limbs and faculties would be left? Would I still have my hands and my mind? And what about loved ones? If God were to take from me all those persons and things for which I have not given thanks, who or what would be left of me?"

What would be left of me, indeed? he wondered. The very thought struck him with a force he hadn't recognized when he copied it into his notebook.

He put his hand on his dog's head and hoarsely whispered the beginning of his list:

"Barnabas . . ."

He saw her standing at the corner of Main Street and Wisteria, looking toward the rectory. He had never seen her before in his life, but he knew exactly, precisely, who she was.

He felt himself loving her at once, as she held out her arms and smiled and started running toward him. He tried to run, also, to meet her, but found he moved as if through sand or deep water, and was dumbstruck, unable to call her name.

His wife was shaking him. "Wake up, dearest!"

"What . . . what . . . ?"

"You were dreaming."

He sat up with a pounding heart.

"We have to find Jessie," he said.

CHAPTER EIGHT

Political Barbecue

There was plenty of talk on the street. As early as seven-thirty on the morning of the festival, he couldn't walk from the south end to the north without picking up new funds of information.

Dora Pugh, who was setting flats of borage, chives, and rosemary outside the hardware door, asked if he'd seen the billboards on the highway. They must have been put up in the middle of the night, she said, because when she drove home yesterday, she certainly hadn't noticed Mack Stroupe's ugly mug plastered on three new boards, all the way from Hattie Cloer's market to the Shoe Barn.

"That," she snorted, "is three times more of that cracker than I ever wanted to see." Dora once lived in Georgia, where "cracker" had nothing to do with party snacks.

At the Sweet Stuff, Winnie Ivey hailed him in.

"I'm experimenting," she said, tucking a strand of graying hair under her bandanna. "My license says people can sit down, so I thought I should try fixin' things to where people don't have to stand at th' shelf."

The shelf along the wall had come down, replaced by posters of mountain scenery, and in the long-empty space in front of her display cases stood three tables and a dozen chairs.

"I'm tryin' to do all I can to bring in business. If I'm goin' to sell out, I want my ledgers lookin' good," she said.

"I'm proud of you, Winnie! And to think you've done all this by yourself!"

"I have to do whatever it takes, Father! Of course, it's just coffee and sweets, as usual, except now you get a chair to sit in—but I might add sandwiches next week. And soup in the winter. What do you think?"

"I think you should!"

She brightened. "It helps to have advice."

"Don't I know it!" Weren't his parishioners full of it?

"My husband, Johnny, used to know what to do about things, but he died so many years ago, I can hardly remember his face. Do you think that's bad?"

He could seldom recall his father's face. "No," he said, "it can happen like that. . . ."

"You know, sometimes I . . ." Winnie blushed.

"Sometimes you . . . ?"

"You wouldn't tell this?"

"You have my word."

"Sometimes I think of a man standin' beside me in th' kitchen back there, I don't know who it is because I can't exactly see his face, but it seems like he's tall and dark-headed, and I can tell he has a big heart." She paused, looking shy. "He bakes all th' cakes, and he's always laughin' and sayin' nice things, like how good my cream horns are, and how pretty I glazed the fruit tarts."

He nodded.

"He always has flour on his apron."

"He would."

"It would be nice. . . ." she said, looking at him.

"I know," he said, looking back.

"It might not be right to pray for such as that. . . ."

"I think it would be wrong if we didn't," he said.

§

Apparently, all of merchantdom was up and at it, a full two hours before the festival opened.

The Collar Button man was sweeping the sidewalk, with a sprinkler turned on the handkerchief-sized garden next to his store.

"Good morning, Father! How're you liking the jacket your wife selected for your birthday?"

"Immensely! It brings out the blue of her eyes. How's business?"

"Couldn't be better!" said the Collar Button man, going full tilt with his broom.

When he reached the Grill, he stopped and sniffed the balmy air. The smell of roasting pork drifted on the breeze from Mack Stroupe's campaign headquarters near the monument.

Then he squinted up at the sky.

Blue. Here and there, a few billowing clouds.

Perfect.

He slid into the booth with a mug of coffee

"Where's J.C?"

"Went upstairs to get film out of his refrigerator," said Mule.

"Film was all he had in his refrigerator 'til he married Adele. What's going on with you?"

"Feelin' like somethin' the cat covered up. I can't half sleep 'til Fancy gets to bed, and she was going like a circle saw 'til two o'clock this morning."

"Doing what?"

"Doin' hair."

"Who in the dickens would get their hair done at two o'clock in the morning?"

"You'd be surprised."

"That's true, I would."

"How's your new boarder?" asked the realtor.

"Working on my Buick. I pay for the parts, he insists on doing the labor. He was under the hood at seven o'clock this morning."

J.C. slung his briefcase into the corner and slid in.

"I looked out th' upstairs window and dadgum if th' street ain't *jumpin'*." The editor rubbed his hands together briskly. This was front-page stuff, everything from llamas and political barbecue to a clogging contest and tourists out the kazoo.

"Let me guess," said Velma, arriving at the rear booth in an unusually cheerful frame of mind. "Poached for th' preacher, scrambled for th' realtor—"

"Fried for th' editor," said J.C. "And don't be bringin' me any yogurt or all-bran."

Velma looked him over as if he were a boiled ham. "You're pickin' up weight again."

"I've picked up worse," said J.C.

Mule stirred his coffee. "Just dry toast with mine."

"No grits?" she asked, personally offended.

"Not today."

"What's the matter with Percy's grits?"

"Oh, well, all right. But no butter."

"Grits without butter?" What was wrong with these people?

"Lord, help," sighed Mule. "Just bring me whatever."

"I'll have mine all the way," said J.C., who had lately thrown caution to the wind. "Biscuits, grits, sausage, bacon, and give me a little mustard on the side."

"I'll have the usual," said Father Tim.

Mule looked approving. "That's what I need to do—figure out one thing and stick with it. Same thing every morning, and you don't have to mess with it again."

"Right," said the rector.

"Have you seen Mack's new boards?" asked J.C.

They hadn't.

"They rhyme like those Burma-Shave signs. First one says, '*If Mitford's economy is going to move*' . . . th' second one says, '*we've got to improve.*' Last one says, '*Mack for Mitford, Mack for Mayor.*'"

"Gag me with a forklift," said Mule.

"Esther Cunningham better get off her rear end, because like it or not, Mack Stroupe's eatin' her lunch. She's been lollin' around like this election was some kind of tea party. You're so all-fired thick with the mayor," J.C. said to the rector, "you ought to tell her the facts of life, and the fact is, she's lookin' dead in the water."

"Aha. I thought we agreed not to talk politics."

"Right," said Mule, whose escalating blood pressure had suddenly turned his face beet red.

J.C. looked bored. "So what else is new? Let's see, I was over at the town museum 'til midnight watchin' those turkeys get ready for the festival. Omer Cunningham was draping th' flag on Esther's booth and fell off the ladder and busted his foot."

"Busted his foot?" the rector blurted. "Good Lord! Can he fly?"

"Can he fly? I don't know as he could, with a busted foot."

Mule cackled. "He sure couldn't fly any crazier than when his foot's *not* busted."

"Toast!" said Velma, sliding two orders onto the table.

The rector felt his stomach wrench.

"Biscuits!" said Velma, handing off a plate to J.C.

"May I use your phone?" asked Father Tim.

"You can, if you stay out of Percy's way, you know where it's at."

He went to the red wall phone and dialed, knowing the number by heart. Hadn't he called it two dozen times in the last few days?

No answer.

He hung up and stood by the grill, dazed, his mouth as dry as cotton.

"I just busted th' yolk in one of y'r eggs," said Percy, who despised poaching.

So? Busted feet, busted yolks, busted plans.

He might possibly be looking at the worst day of his life.

His palms were damp, something he'd never appreciated in clergy. Also, his collar felt tight, even though he'd snapped the Velcro at the loosest point.

When he and Cynthia arrived on the lawn of the town museum at 9:35, they had to elbow their way to the Lord's Chapel booth, which was situated, this year, directly across from the llamas and the petting zoo.

"Excellent location!" said his wife, who was known to rely on animals as a drawing card.

They thumped down their cardboard box filled with the results of last night's bake-a-thon in the rectory kitchen. Three Lord's Chapel volunteers, dressed in aprons that said, *Have you hugged an Episcopalian today?* briskly set about unpacking the contents and displaying them in a case cooled by a generator humming at the rear of the tent.

Though the festival didn't officially open until ten o'clock, the yard of the Porter mansion–cum–town museum was jammed with villagers, tourists, and the contents of three buses from neighboring communities. The rear end of a church van from Tennessee displayed a sign, *Mitford or Bust.*

The Presbyterian brass band was already in full throttle on the museum porch, and the sixth grade of Mitford School was marching around the statue of Willard Porter, builder of the impressive Victorian home, with tambourines, drums, and maracas painted in their school colors.

Why was he surprised to see posters on every pole and tree, promoting Mack Stroupe's free barbecue at his campaign headquarters up the street?

His eyes searched the crowd for the mayor, who said she'd be under the elm tree this year, the one that had miraculously escaped the blight.

"I'll be back," he told Cynthia, who was giving him that concerned look. The way things were going, he'd need more than a domestic retreat, he'd need a set of pallbearers.

He saw Uncle Billy next to the lilac bushes, sitting in a hardback chair with a bottomless chair in front of him and a bucket of water at his feet.

"Stop in, Preacher! I'll be a-canin' chairs, don't you know, hit's a demonstration of th' old ways, and I've set out a few of m' birdhouses f'r sale."

"How's your arthur?" asked the rector, concerned.

"Well, sir, last night, I slapped it and said, 'Git on out of there, I ain't havin' nothin' t' do with you!' And m' hands are feelin' some better this mornin', don't you know." He wiggled a couple of fingers to prove his point.

"Where's Miss Rose?"

"She ain't a-comin' out this year, says she don't like s' many people ramblin' around on 'er property."

"Hold that green birdhouse for me, I'll be back!"

He spotted Esther and her husband, Ray, shaking hands by a booth draped with an American flag and a banner hand-lettered with the mayor's longtime political slogan.

"Mayor! Where's Omer?"

"Where's Omer? I thought you'd know where Omer is."

"What about his foot?"

"Broken in two places."

"Right, but what about . . . can he *fly*?"

She glared at him in a way that made Emma Newland look like a vestal virgin. "That's your business," she said, and turned back to the people she'd been shaking hands with.

He headed to the Lord's Chapel booth, his heart hammering. He was afraid to let his wife see his face, since she could obviously read it like a book—but where else could he go?

Dooley! Of course! A Taste of America!

He hung a hard left in the direction of Avis Packard's tent, cutting through the queue to the cotton candy truck, and ran slam into Omer Cunningham on a crutch.

"Good heavens! *Omer*!" He threw his arms around Esther Cunningham's strapping brother-in-law and could easily have kissed his ring, or even his plaster cast.

Heads turned. People stared. He wished he weren't wearing his collar.

Omer's big grin displayed teeth the size of keys on a spinet piano. "We're smokin'," he said, giving a thumbs-up to the rector, who, overcome with joyful relief, thumped down on a folding chair at the Baptists' display of tea towels, aprons, and oven mitts.

"Father!"

It was Andrew Gregory, the tall, handsome proprietor of Oxford Antiques, calling from his booth next to the statue of Willard Porter.

The rector could honestly say he felt a warm affection for the man who once courted Cynthia, escorting her hither and yon in his gray Mercedes, while Father Tim moped at the upstairs window of the rectory. Andrew might be six-four with a closetful of cashmere jackets, but hadn't the five-nine, less stylish country parson won Cynthia?

By jing!

He felt positively lighthearted as he stepped up to the booth and shook hands with the antique dealer, who looked elegant in a linen shirt and trousers.

"Great to see you, my friend!"

"How is it," asked Andrew, "that we seldom meet, though our doors are directly across the street from one another?"

"We've mused on that before," said the rector, "and always to no avail. I've missed you. How are you?"

"Off next week to Italy, to my mother's birthplace, a little town called Lucera."

"I've often visited Italy. . . ."

"You have?"

"In my imagination," confessed the rector.

Andrew smiled. "I'm afraid I've cultivated my paternal English side to the vast neglect of my Italian side. I'll do like you did a couple of years ago—go searching for my roots, sample the local wines, visit cousins."

"Good for the soul! You're selling your fine lemon oil, I see."

"Makes all the difference. Look at this eighteenth-century chest." One side of the late-Georgian walnut chest appeared dark and sullen. The other side shone, revealing the life of the wood.

"I'll take three bottles!" the rector announced.

"I've been wondering," said Andrew, as he bagged the lemon oil, "whether I might give you a price on the contents of Fernbank. If you're interested, I'd like to take a look before I chase off to the old country."

"Well! That's a thought. Let me run it by the vestry." He had certainly dragged his feet on emptying Miss Sadie's house in advance of the possible sale to Miami Development. Why had he tried to put the whole Fernbank issue out of his mind when it clearly needed to be handled—and pronto?

Walking away with his package under his arm, he also questioned why on earth he'd bought three bottles of lemon oil when he hardly had a stick of furniture to call his own. Living in partially furnished rectories since the age of twenty-eight had had its bright side, but it wasn't all it was cracked up to be.

"Father Tim!"

It was Margaret Ann Larkin with five-year old Amy, waving at him from the petting zoo.

He pushed through the crowd.

"Father, we've been looking all over for you. Amy wants to pet the animals, but she's afraid to do it. She wondered if . . . I know this is a strange request, but she wants you to do it for her."

"Aha."

Margaret Ann looked imploring. "She doesn't want me to do it."

Amy handed him a dollar. "You pet," she said soberly.

He knelt beside her, clutching his package. "You could walk inside the fence with me."

"You pet," she said.

He turned his lemon oil over to Margaret Ann and went through the gate, relinquishing the dollar to Jake Greer, a farmer from the valley.

"Pet the goat first," said Amy, looking through the fence.

"Please," instructed Margaret Ann.

"Please!" urged Amy.

He petted the goat, which trotted to the other side of the pen, clearly disgusted.

"Now pet the lamb, please."

He petted the lamb. What a black nose! What soulful eyes!

"Now pet the chickens."

A Dominecker rooster and two Leghorn hens squawked and scattered.

He turned and smiled at Amy. "Now what?"

"Pet the pony!"

He petted the pony, who nuzzled his arm and bared its teeth and flared its nostrils, giving him his money's worth. Having petted the entire assembly, including a small pig named Barney, he withdrew through the gate, laughing.

"That was . . . fun," he said, meaning it.

"Was you afraid?" asked Amy.

"Not a bit. I liked it."

"Was the lamb soft?"

"Very soft."

"Amy, honey, what do you say?"

Amy broke into a dazzling smile. "Thank you!" she said, patting him on the leg.

His wife peered at him again in that odd way. "You look like *you're* having a good time!"

"You mean you're not?" he asked.

"Not since Gene stepped in Esther's cake."

"No!"

"She came in and set the box behind the table, and when Gene came in, he stumbled over it . . ."

"Uh-oh."

". . . then fell on top of it."

"Good grief."

"Mashed flat," she said.

"Orange marmalade?"

"You got it."

"How's Gene?" he inquired, sounding like an undertaker.

"Unhurt but terrified."

"How's Esther?"

"Three guesses."

"That cake was worth some bucks for the Children's Home."

"I think we could still auction it."

"Mashed flat, we could auction it?"

"There was a top on the box when he fell on it. I mean, it's still Esther's orange marmalade cake—some people would be thrilled to eat it out of the box with a *spoon*."

"If you'll auction it, I'll start the bidding," he said, feeling expansive.

He had stopped to pass the time of day with the llamas, who looked at him peaceably through veils of sweeping lashes.

He'd bought a tea towel from the Baptists, a sack of tattered volumes from the Library Ladies, a cookbook from the Presbyterians, and was on his way to see Dooley Barlowe in action.

He paused to check the sky. As he started to look at his watch, he spied them through the queue for popcorn and ducked across.

Olivia kissed him on the cheek. Lace stood looking into the crowd.

He put his arm around Lace's shoulders and found them unyielding. "You ladies are looking lovely—a credit to the town!"

Lace nodded vaguely. "I got to go over yonder a minute."

"Go," said Olivia. "I'll meet you at the llamas in half an hour."

They sat on one of the town museum benches.

"Father, I've had time to think it through and I wanted to say I admire Dooley for the way he handled Lace's outburst. He might have . . . knocked her head off when she attacked him."

"He was asking for it."

"He did a fine job of delivering his apologies. He has character, your boy."

"So does Lace. But character often takes time to show itself. They've both come out of violence and neglect, a matched set. How are you holding up?"

"Better, I think. We're still visiting her mother every week, but it's never a happy visit—her mother is demanding and cold, and her health is deteriorating. Hoppy looked in on her; we're not encouraged."

"We keep you faithfully in our prayers. We're all flying by the seat of our pants." Who would have dreamed he'd be raising a boy? The challenge of it was breathtaking.

"I've read how Lindbergh often flew with the windshield iced over. It's rather like that, don't you think?"

"Indeed. Is she making any friends?"

"Mitford's children have been warned all their lives to avoid anyone from the Creek, so that is very much against her. Then she's smart and she's pretty. Some don't like that, either. They really don't know what to make of her."

"Lord bless you."

"And you, Father."

As they walked away from each other, he turned around and called, "Olivia! Philippians Four-thirteen, for Pete's sake!"

She threw up her hand, smiling at this reminder of the Scripture verse she claimed as a pivot for her life.

It was good to have a comrade in arms, he thought, trotting off to A Taste of America.

Avis Packard's booth was swamped with buyers, eager to tote home sacks of preserves, honey, pies, cakes, and bread from the valley kitchens, not to mention strawberries from California, corn from Georgia, and syrup from Vermont.

Avis stepped out of the booth for a break, while Tommy and Dooley bagged and made change. "I've about bit off more'n I can chew," said Avis, lighting up a Salem. "I've still got a load of new potatoes comin' from Georgia, and lookin' for a crate of asparagus from Florida. Thing is, I don't hardly see how a truck can get down th' street."

"I didn't know you smoked," said the rector, checking his watch.

Avis inhaled deeply. "I don't. I quit two or three years ago. I bummed this offa somebody."

The imported strawberries were selling at a pace, and Avis stepped to the booth and brought back a handful.

"Try one," he said, as proudly as if they'd come from his own patch. "You know how some taste more like straw than berry? Well, sir, these are the finest you'll ever put in your mouth. Juicy, sweet, full of sunshine. What you'd want to do is eat 'em right off th' stem, or slice 'em, marinate in a little sugar and brandy—you don't want to use th' cheap stuff—and serve with cream from the valley, whipped with a hint of fresh ginger."

Avis Packard was a regular poet laureate of grocery fare.

"Is that legal?" asked the rector.

He watched as Dooley passed a bag over the table to a customer. "Hope you like those strawberries!"

He was thrilled to see Dooley Barlowe excited about his work. His freckles, which he and Cynthia had earlier reported missing, seemed to be back with a vengeance.

Avis laughed. "Ain't he a deal?"

"Is he doing right by you?"

"That and then some!"

He noticed Jenny and her mother queuing up at A Taste of America, and saw Dooley glance up at them. Uh-oh. That look on Dooley's face . . .

Was this something he ought to discuss with him, man to man? The very thought made his heart pound.

Ben Sawyer hauled past, carrying a sack of tasseled corn in each arm. "That's a fine boy you got there, Preacher!"

He felt a foolish grin spread across his face, and didn't try to hold it back.

He noticed the crowd was starting to thin out, following the aroma of political barbecue.

In his mind, he saw it on the plate, thickly sliced and served with a dollop of hot sauce, nestled beside a mound of cole slaw and a half dozen hot, crisp hushpuppies. . . .

He shook himself and ate four raisins that had rolled around in his coat pocket since the last committee meeting on evangelism.

At eleven forty-five, Ray and Esther Cunningham strode up to the Lord's Chapel booth with all five of their beautiful daughters, who had populated half of Mitford with Sunday School teachers, deacons, police officers, garbage collectors, tax accountants, secretaries, retail clerks, and UPS drivers.

"Well?" said Esther. The rector thought she would have made an excellent Mafia don.

"Coming right up!" he exclaimed, checking his watch and looking pale.

Cynthia eyed him again. Mood swings, she thought. That seemed to be the key! Definitely a domestic retreat, and definitely soon.

And since the entire town seemed so demanding of her husband, definitely not in Mitford.

Nobody paid much attention to the airplane until it started smoking.

"Look!" somebody yelled. "That plane's on f'ar!"

He was sitting on the rock wall when Omer thumped down beside him. "Right on time!" said the mayor's brother-in-law. "All my flyin' buddies from here t' yonder have jumped on this." The rector thought somebody could have played "Moonlight Sonata" on Omer's ear-to-ear grin.

"OK, that's y'r basic Steerman, got a four-fifty horsepower engine in there. Luke Teeter's flyin' 'er, he's about as good as you can get, now watch this . . ."

The blue and orange airplane roared straight up into the fathomless blue sky, leaving a plume of smoke in its wake. Then it turned sharply and pitched downward at an angle.

"Wow!" somebody said, forgetting to close his mouth.

The plane did another climb into the blue.

Omer punched him in the ribs with an elbow. "She's got a tank in there pumpin' Corvis oil th'ough 'er exhaust system . . . ain't she a sight?"

"Looks like an *N*!" said a boy whose chocolate popsicle was melting down his arm.

The plane plummeted toward the rooftops again, smoke billowing from its exhaust.

"M!" shouted half the festivalgoers, as one.

Esther and Ray and their daughters were joined by assorted grandchildren, great-grandchildren, and in-laws, who formed an impenetrable mass in front of the church booth.

Gene Bolick limped over from the llamas as the perfect *I* appeared above them.

"M . . . I!" shouted the crowd.

"Lookit this!" said Omer, propping his crutch against the stone wall. "Man, oh, man!"

The bolt of blue and orange gunned straight up, leaving a vertical trail, then shut off the exhaust, veered right, and thundered across the top of the trail, forming a straight and unwavering line of smoke.

"M . . . I . . . T!"

The *M* was fading, the *I* was lingering, the *T* was perfect against the sapphire sky.

The crowd thickened again, racing back from Mack Stroupe's campaign headquarters, which was largely overhung by trees, racing back to the grounds of the town museum where the view was open, unobscured, and breathtaking, where something more than barbecue was going on.

"They won't be goin' back to Mack's place anytime soon," said Omer. "Ol' Mack's crowd has done eat an' run!"

"*F!*" they spelled in unison, and then, ". . . *O* . . . *R* . . . *D!*"

Even the tourists were cheering.

J. C. Hogan sank to the ground, rolled over on his back, pointed his Nikon at the sky, and fired off a roll of Tri-X. The *M* and the *I* were fading fast.

Uncle Billy hobbled up and spit into the bushes. "I bet them boys is glad this town ain't called Minneapolis."

"Now, look," said Omer, slapping his knee.

Slowly, but surely, the Steerman's exhaust trail wrote the next word.

T . . . *A* . . . *K* . . . *E* . . . *S* . . . , the smoke said.

Cheers. Hoots. Whistles.

"Lord, my neck's about give out," said Uncle Billy.

"Mine's about broke," said a bystander.

C . . . *A* . . . *R* . . . *E* . . .

"Mitford takes care of its own!" shouted the villagers. The sixth grade trooped around the statue, beating on tambourines, shaking maracas, and chanting something they'd been taught since first grade.

Mitford takes care of its own, its own,
Mitford takes care of its own!

Over the village rooftops, the plane spelled out the rest of the message.

O . . . *F* . . . *I* . . . *T* . . . *S* . . . *O* . . . *W* . . . *N* . . .

TAKES soon faded into puffs of smoke that looked like stray summer clouds. *CARE OF* was on its way out, but *ITS OWN* stood proudly in the sky, seeming to linger.

"If that don't beat all!" exclaimed a woman from Tennessee, who had stood in one spot the entire time, holding a sleep-drugged baby on her hip.

Dogs barked and chickens squawked as people clapped and started drifting away.

Just then, a few festivalgoers saw them coming, the sun glinting on their wings.

They roared in from the east, in formation, two by two.

Red and yellow. Green and blue.

"Four little home-built Pitts specials," said Omer, as proudly as if he'd built them himself. "Two of 'em's from Fayetteville, got one out of Roanoke, and the other one's from Albany, New York. Not much power in y'r little ragwings, they're nice and light, about a hundred and eighty horses, and handle like a dream."

He looked at the sky as if it contained the most beautiful sight he had ever seen, and so did the rector.

"I was goin' to head th' formation, but a man can't fly with a busted foot."

The crowd started lying on the grass. They lay down along the rock wall. They climbed up on the statue of Willard Porter, transfixed, and a young father set a toddler on Willard's left knee.

People pulled chairs out of their booths and sat down, looking up. All commerce ceased.

The little yellow Pitts special rolled over and dived straight for the monument.

"Ahhhhhh!" said the crowd.

As the yellow plane straightened out and up, the blue plane nose-dived and rolled over.

"They're like little young 'uns a-playin'," said Uncle Billy, enthralled.

Miss Rose came out and stood on the back stoop in her frayed chenille robe and looked up, tears coursing down her cheeks for her long-dead brother, Captain Willard Porter, who had flown planes and been killed in the war in France and buried over there, with hardly anything sent home but his medals and a gold ring with the initials SEB and a few faded snapshots from his pockets.

The little planes romped and rolled and soared and glided, like so many bright crayons on a palette of blue, then vanished toward the west, the sun on their wings.

Here and there, a festivalgoer tried getting up from the grass or a chair or the wall, but couldn't. They felt mesmerized, intoxicated. "Blowed away!" someone said.

"OK, buddy, here you go," Omer whispered.

They heard a heavy-duty engine throbbing in the distance and knew at once this was serious business, this was what everyone had been waiting for without even knowing it.

The Cunningham daughters hugged their children, kissed their mother and daddy, wept unashamedly, and hooted and hollered like banshees, but not a soul looked their way, for the crowd was intent on not missing a lick, on seeing it all, and taking the whole thing, blow by blow, home to Johnson City and Elizabethton and Wesley and Holding and Aho and Farmer and Price and Todd and Hemingway and Morristown. . . .

"Got y'r high roller comin' in, now," said Omer. The rector could feel the mayor's brother-in-law shaking like a leaf from pure excitement. "You've had y'r basic smoke writin' and stunt flyin,' now here comes y'r banner towin'!"

A red Piper Super Cub blasted over the treetops from the direction of the highway, shaking drifts of clouds from its path, trembling the heavens in its wake, and towing a banner that streamed across the open sky:

ESTHER . . . RIGHT FOR MITFORD, RIGHT FOR MAYOR.

The Presbyterian brass band hammered down on their horns until the windows of the Porter mansion rattled and shook.

As the plane passed over, a wave of adrenaline shot through the festival grounds like so much electricity and, almost to a man, the crowd scrambled to its feet and shouted and cheered and whistled and whooped and applauded.

A few also waved and jumped up and down, and nearly all of them remembered what Esther had done, after all, putting the roof on old man Mueller's house, and turning the dilapidated wooden bridge over Mitford Creek into one that was safe and good to look at, and sending Ray in their RV to take old people to the grocery store, and jacking up Sophia's house and helping her kids, and making sure they had decent school buses to haul their own kids around in bad weather, and creating that thing at the hospital where you went and held and loved a new baby if its mama from the Creek was on drugs, and never one time raising taxes, and always being there when they had a problem, and actually listening when they talked, and . . .

. . . and taking care of them.

Some who had planned to vote for Mack Stroupe changed their minds, and came over and shook Esther's hand, and the brass band nearly busted a gut to be heard over the commotion.

Right! That was the ticket. Esther was *right* for Mitford. Mack Stroupe might be for change, but Esther would always be for the things that really counted.

Besides—and they'd tried to put it out of their minds time and time again—hadn't Mack Stroupe been known to beat his wife, who was quiet as a mouse and didn't deserve it, and hadn't he slithered over to that woman in Wesley for years, like a common, low-down snake in the grass?

"Law, do y'all vote in th' *summer*?" wondered a visitor. "We vote sometime in th' fall. I can't remember when, exactly, but I nearly always have to wear a coat to the polls."

Omer looked at the rector. The rector looked at Omer.

They shook hands.

It was done.

CHAPTER NINE

Life in the Fast Lane

"What I done was give you thirty more horses under y'r hood."

"Did I *need* thirty more horses?" He had to admit that stomping his gas pedal had been about as exciting as stepping on a fried pie. However . . .

Harley gave him a philosophical look, born from experience. "Rev'rend, I'd hate f'r you t' need 'em and not have 'em."

What could he say?

On Monday morning, he roared to the office, screeching to a halt at the intersection of Old Church Lane, where he let northbound traffic pass, then made a left turn, virtually catapulting into the parking lot.

Holy smoke! Had Harley dropped a Jag engine in his Buick?

Filled with curiosity, he got out and looked under the hood, but realized he wouldn't know a Jag engine from a Mazda alternator.

"Can you believe it?" asked Emma, tight-lipped.

He knew exactly what she was talking about. "Not really."

For a while, he thought they'd lost his secretary's vote to Esther Cunningham's competition. Last week, however, had turned the tide; she'd heard that Mack Stroupe had bought two little houses on the edge of town and jacked up the rent on a widow and a single mother.

"Sittin' in church like he owned th' place, is what I hear. Why th' roof didn't fall in on th' lot of you is beyond me."

"Umm."

"Church!" she snorted. "Is that some kind of new campaign trick, goin' to *church*?"

He believed that particular strategy had been used a time or two, but he didn't comment.

"The next thing you know, he'll be wantin' to *join.* If I were you, I'd run his hide up th' road to th' Presbyterians."

He laughed. "Emma, you're beautiful when you're mad."

She beamed. "Really?"

"Well . . ."

"So, what did he *do,* anyway? Did he kneel? Did he stand? Did he *sing*? Can you imagine a peckerwood like Mack Stroupe singin' those hymns from five hundred years ago, maybe a thousand? Lord, it was all *I* could do to sing th' dern things, which is *one* reason I went back to bein' a Baptist."

She booted her computer, furious.

"I heard Lucy was with him, wouldn't you know it, but that's the way they do, they trot their family out for all the world to see. Was she still blond? What was she wearin'? Esther Bolick said it was a sight the way the crowd ganged up at the museum watchin' the air show, and that barbecue sittin' down the street like so much chicken mash."

She peered intently at her screen.

"Well," she said, clicking her mouse, "has the cat got your tongue? Tell me somethin', *anything*! Were you floored when he showed up at Lord's Chapel, or what?"

"I was. Of course, there's always the possibility that he wants to turn over a new leaf. . . ."

"Right," she said, arching an eyebrow, "and Elvis is livin' at th' Wesley hotel."

As much as he liked mail, and the surprise it was capable of bringing, he let the pile sit on Emma's desk until she came back from lunch.

"No way! I can't believe it!" She held up an envelope, grinning proudly. "Albert Wilcox!"

She opened it. "Listen to this!

" 'Dear one and all, it was a real treat to hear from you after so many years. My grandmother's prayer book that gave us such pain—and delight—sits on my desk as I write to you, waiting to be handed over to the museum in Seattle, which is near my home in Oak Harbor. . . .' "

She read the entire letter, which also contained a great deal of information about Albert's knee replacement, and his felicitations to the rector for having married.

"Have you ever? And all because of modern technology! OK, as soon as I open this other envelope, I've got a little surprise for you. Close your eyes."

He closed his eyes.

"Face the bookcase!" she said.

He faced the bookcase.

He heard fumbling and clicking. Then he heard Beethoven.

The opening strains of the Pastorale fairly lifted him out of his chair.

"OK! You can turn around!"

He didn't see anything unusual, but was swept away by the music, which seemed to come from nowhere, transforming the room.

"CD-ROM!" announced his resident computer expert, as if she'd just hung the moon.

He went home and jiggled Sassy and burped Sissy, as Puny collected an ocean of infant paraphernalia into something the size of a leaf bag.

After a quick trot through the hedge to say hello to his hardworking wife, he and Dooley changed into their old clothes. They were going to tear down Betty Craig's shed and stack the wood. He felt fit for anything.

"Let's see those muscles," he challenged Dooley, who flexed his arm. "Well done!" He wished he had some to show, himself, but thinking and preaching had never been ways to develop muscles.

What with a good job, plenty of sun, and a reasonable amount of home cooking, Dooley Barlowe was looking good. In fact, Dooley Barlowe was getting to be downright handsome, he mused, and tall into the bargain.

Dooley stood against the doorframe as the rector made a mark, then measured. Good heavens!

"I'll be et for a tater if you ain't growed a foot!" he exclaimed in Uncle Billy's vernacular.

Soon, he'd be looking up to the boy who had come to him in dirty overalls, searching for a place to "take a dump."

They were greeted in the backyard by Russell Jacks and Dooley's young brother.

"I've leaned th' ladder ag'inst th' shed for you," said Russell.

"Half done, then!" The rector was happy to see his old sexton.

Poo Barlowe looked up at him. "Hey!"

"Hey, yourself!" he replied, tousling the boy's red hair. "Where were you on Saturday? We missed you at the town festival."

"Mama took me to buy some new clothes." The boy glanced down at his tennis shoes, hoping the rector would notice.

"Man alive! Look at those shoes! Made for leaping tall buildings, it appears."

Poo grinned.

"Want to help us pull that shed down?"

"It ain't hardly worth pullin' down," said Poo, "bein' ready t' fall down."

"Don't say ain't," commanded his older brother.

"Why not?"

"'Cause it ain't good English!" Realizing what he'd just said, Dooley colored furiously.

Father Tim laughed. He'd corrected Dooley's English for three long years. "You're sounding a lot like me, buddy. You might want to watch that."

Betty Craig ran down the back steps.

"Father! Law, this is good of you. I've been standin' at my kitchen window for years, lookin' at that old shed lean to the south. It's aggravated me to death."

"A good kick might be all it takes."

"Pauline's late comin' home, she called to say she'd be right here. Can I fix you and Dooley some lemonade? It's hot as August."

"We'll wait 'til our work is done."

"Let's get going," said Dooley.

Father Tim opened the toolbox and took out a clawhammer and put on his heavy work gloves. He'd never done this sort of thing before. He felt at once fierce and manly, and then again, completely uncertain how to begin.

"What're we going to do?" asked Dooley, pulling on his own pair of gloves.

He looked at the shed. Blast if it wasn't bigger than he'd thought. "We're going to start at the top," he said, as if he knew what he was talking about.

He had removed the rolled asphalt with a clawhammer, pulled off the roofboards, dismantled the rafters, torn off the sideboards with Dooley's help, then pulled nails from the corners of the rotten framework, and shoved what was left into the grass.

Running with sweat, he and Dooley had taken turns driving the rusty nails back and pulling them out of every stick and board so they could be used for winter firewood.

Dooley dropped the nails into a bucket.

"Wouldn't want t' be steppin' on one of them," said Russell, who was supervising.

They paused only briefly, to sit on the porch and devour a steaming portion of chicken pie, hot from Betty's oven, and guzzle a quart of tea that was sweet enough to send him to the emergency room.

Betty apologized. "Hot as it is, your supper ought to be somethin' cold, like chicken salad, but you men are workin' hard, and chicken salad won't stick to your ribs."

"Amen!"

"I want you to come and get your kindlin' off that pile all winter long, you hear?"

"I'll do it."

After they ate, he and Dooley and Poo carried and stacked and heaved and hauled, until it was nearly nine o'clock, and dark setting in.

"You've about killed me," grumbled Dooley.

"I've done sweated a bucket," said Poo.

"I'm give out jis' watchin'," sighed Russell.

As for himself, the rector felt oddly liberated. All that pulling up and yanking off and tearing down and pushing over had been good for him, somehow, creating an exhaustion completely different from the labors surrounding his life as a cleric.

And what better reward than to sit and look across the twilit yard at the mound of wood neatly stacked along the fence, with two boys beside him who had helped make it happen?

Dooley was inspecting Poo's new, if used, bicycle, Russell had shuffled off to bed, and Betty had gone in to watch TV. He sat alone with Pauline.

He didn't see any reason to beat around the bush. "We need to talk about Jessie."

There was a long silence.

"I can do it," she said.

"I need to know everything you can possibly tell me, and the name of the cousin who took her and where you think they might be, and the names of any of your cousin's relatives—everything."

He heard the absolute firmness in his voice and knew this was how it would have to be.

As she talked, he took notes on a piece of paper he had folded and put in his shirt pocket. Afterward, he sat back in the rocker.

"If we find Jessie, can you take care of her?"

"Yes!" she said, and now he heard the firmness in her own voice. "I think about it all the time, how I want to rent a little house and have a tree at Christmas. We never had a tree at Christmas . . . maybe once."

His mind went instantly to all that furniture collecting dust at Fernbank. He and Dooley would load up a truck and . . . But he was putting the cart before the horse.

"There's something we need to look at, Pauline."

"Is it about the drinking?"

"Yes."

"I don't crave it anymore."

"Alcohol is a tough call. Very tough. Do you want help?"

"No," she said. "I want to do this myself. With God's help."

"If you ever want or need help, you've got to have the guts to ask for it. For your sake, for the kids' sake. Can you do that?"

Betty switched the porch light on, and he saw Pauline's face as she turned and looked at him. "Yes," she said.

"Didn't want y'all to be setting out there in the dark," said Betty, going back to her room.

They were silent again. He heard Poo laughing, and faint snatches of music and applause from Betty's TV.

"There's something you need to know," she told him.

He waited.

"I won't make trouble, I won't try to make Dooley come and live with us. He's doing so well . . . you've done so much . . .

"If he wants to, he can come and stay with us anytime he's home, but I want you to be the one who . . . the one who watches over him."

She was giving her boy away again. But this time, he fervently hoped and prayed, it was for all the right reasons.

He kissed her on the cheek as he came into the bedroom.

"Kavanagh . . ." he said, feeling spent.

"Hello, dearest," she said, looking worn.

After he showered, they crawled into bed on their respective sides and were snoring in tandem by ten o'clock.

"Emma, that program on your computer, that thing that helped you find Albert Wilcox . . ."

"What about it?"

"I'd like you to search for these names. I've written down the states I think they could be in."

"Hah!" she said, looking smug. "I knew you'd get to liking computers sooner or later."

Some days were like this. One phone call after another, nonstop.

"Father? Emil Kettner. We met when Buck Leeper—"

"Of course, Emil. Great to hear your voice." Emil Kettner owned the construction company that employed Buck Leeper as their star superintendent.

"I have good news for you, I think, if the timing works for Lord's Chapel."

"Shoot."

"The big job we thought we had fell through, and to tell the truth, I think it's for the best—as far as Buck's concerned. He needs a break, but he'd want to be working, all the same. I wondered if we could send him out to you for the attic job."

He was floored. This was the best news he'd had since . . .

"The way he described it, it sounds like six months, tops. I hate to send him on a job that small, I know you understand, but it's the kind of job he'd find . . . reviving, though he'd never admit it."

"We'd be thrilled to have Buck back in Mitford. We'll look after him, I promise."

"You looked after him before, and it worked wonders. There's been a real change in him, but he still works too hard, too fast, and too much. You won't hear many bosses complaining about that."

They laughed.

"The money's in place if we can keep on budget," said the rector.

"That's what Buck's all about, if you remember."

"I do! Well, I can't say enough for your timing, Emil. Our Sunday

School enrollment is mushrooming, I've had three baptisms this month, and the month's hardly begun. When can we expect to see Buck?"

"A week, maybe ten days. And we can't give him much support on this project, he'll be rounding up locals to do the job. How does that sound?"

"Terrific. The carved millwork in the Hope House chapel is locally done. We've got good people in the area."

"Well, then, Father, I'll be looking in on the project like I did last time. Until then."

"Emil. Thanks."

He'd asked for Buck Leeper to do the attic job, never really believing it could happen, only hoping.

And—bingo.

"Father? Buck Leeper."

"Buck!"

He heard Buck take a drag on his cigarette. "You talked to Emil."

"I did, and we're thrilled."

"You reckon I could get that cottage again?"

That dark, brooding cottage under the trees, where the finest construction superintendent on the East Coast had thrown furniture against the wall and smashed vodka bottles into the fireplace? He didn't think so.

"Let me look around. We'll take care of you."

"Thanks," Buck said, his voice sounding gruff.

And yet, there was something else in his voice, something just under the surface that the rector knew and understood. It was a kind of hope.

"Father. Ingrid Swenson."

Dadgum it, and just when he was having a great day.

"Ingrid."

"We're very close to getting everything in order. I'd like to personally make a proposal to you and your committee on the fifteenth. I'm sure the timing will be good for Lord's Chapel."

He didn't especially care for her almighty presumption about the timing.

"Let me get back to you," he said.

"Father, it's Esther." Esther Bolick didn't sound like herself. "This is th' most awful thing I ever got myself into. . . ."

"What do you mean?"

"I mean I've never heard such bawlin' and squallin' and snipin' and fussin' in my life! I'm about sick of workin' with women, and church women in particular!"

"Aha."

"Why I said I'd do it, I don't know. Th' *Bane*! Of all things to take on, and me sixty-seven my next birthday, can you believe it?" She sighed deeply. "I ought to be sent to Broughton."

"Don't beat yourself up."

"I don't have to, a whole gang of so-called church workers is thrilled to do it for me!"

"You want to come for a cup of coffee? Emma's home today. I'd love to hear more."

"I don't have time to come for a cup of coffee, I don't have time to pee, excuse me, and Gene hadn't had a hot meal in I don't know when!"

Esther Bolick sounded close to tears. "So even if I can't come for a cup of coffee, I wish you'd do your good deed for the day and pray for me. . . ."

"I will. I pray for you, anyway."

You *do*?"

"Of course. The Bane is a cornerstone event for Lord's Chapel, and you've taken on a big job. But you've got a big spirit, Esther, and you can do it. I know it's easy for me to say, but maybe you could stop looking at the big picture, which is always overwhelming, and just take it day by day."

"Day by day is th' problem! Nearly every day, somebody dumps something else in our garage, and mainly it's the worst old clothes and mildewed shoes you ever saw! Mitch Lewis backed his truck up to th' garage, *raked* out whatever it was in th' bed, and drove off. Gene said to me, he said, 'Esther, what's that mound of *stuff* layin' in th' garage?' We couldn't even *identify* it.

"We need *toaster ovens,* we need *framed prints* and *floor lamps* and *plant stands* and such! This sale's got a *reputation* to maintain, but so far, I never saw so much polyester in my *life,* it looks like we'll *never* get rid of polyester, they won't even take it at th' *landfill*!"

He wished he could offer some of the contents of Fernbank, but Miss Sadie hadn't wanted her possessions picked over. One thing was for certain, he wouldn't donate those mildewed loafers from the back of his closet. . . .

"You know the good stuff always comes in," he said, trying to sound upbeat. "It never fails."

"There's always a first time!" she said darkly.

"Let me ask you—are you praying about this, about the goods rolling in and your strength holding out?"

"I hope you don't think th' *Lord* would mess with the *Bane*?"

"I hope you don't think He wouldn't! Tell me again where the funds from the Bane will go."

"Mission fields, as you well know, including a few in our own backyard."

"Exactly! Some of the money will fly medical supplies to a village where people are dying of cholera. Do you think the Lord would mess with that?"

"Well . . ."

"Then there's the four-wheel drive ambulance they need in Landon," he said. "Remember the blizzard we had three years ago?"

"That's when I had to call an ambulance for Gene, who nearly killed himself shoveling snow! I shouted for joy when I saw it turn the corner. If it hadn't been for that ambulance . . ."

"That winter, two children died of burns because nobody could get a vehicle into the coves around Landon."

"I think I know where you're headed with this," she said.

"I don't believe He'll let Esther Bolick—or the Bane—fail."

"Maybe I could ask Hessie Mayhew to help me out, even if she is Presbyterian!" Esther was sounding more like herself.

"I believe it's going to be the best Bane yet. Now, about your volunteers—my guess is, they're moaning and groaning because they need strong leadership, which is why they elected you in the first place! Look," he said, "I have an idea. Why don't I pray for you? Right now."

"On the *phone*?"

"It's as good a place as any. Try taking a deep breath."

"Lately, it's all I can do to get a deep breath."

"I understand."

"You do?"

"I do."

"I didn't know men ever had trouble gettin' their breath."

"Are you sitting down?"

"Standin' up at the kitchen phone, which is where I've been ever since I let myself get roped into this."

"Could you get a chair?"

He heard her drag a kitchen chair from the table, and sit down.

"OK," she said, feeling brighter. "But don't go on and on 'til th' cows come home."

"Fernbank or bust!" cried Cynthia, huffing up Old Church Lane.

"It's only taken us a full year to do this."

"And it's all sitting right there, just as you left it."

He realized why he had put this off, over and over again. He had ducked into Fernbank a few times to check the roof leaks, and ducked out again as if pursued. To see those empty, silent rooms meant she was gone, utterly and eternally, and even now he could hardly bear the fact of it.

"This must be a hard time for Louella, the anniversary of—"

"I'll see her tomorrow," he said, doing some huffing of his own. "Let's have her down to dinner."

"I love that idea. Maybe sometime next week? Oh, for a taste of her fried chicken!"

"We'll have to settle for a taste of my meat loaf. . . ."

They were up to the brow of the hill and turning into the driveway, which was overhung by a thicket of grapevines gone wild. Though Fernbank hadn't been well groomed since the forties, it had still looked imposing and proud during Miss Sadie's lifetime. Now . . .

He saw the house, surrounded by a neglected lawn, and felt the dull beating of his heart.

"Let's buy it!" he croaked. Good Lord! What had he said?

She looked astounded. "Timothy, you don't need a domestic retreat, you need 911. How could you even *think* such a thing?"

And why couldn't he think such a thing? Didn't a man have a right to his own mind?

He felt suddenly peevish and disgruntled and wanted to turn around and run home, but he remembered Andrew Gregory was meeting them on the porch in ten minutes.

Andrew stood in the middle of the parlor and looked up.

That's what everyone did, thought the rector—they stared at the water stains like they were some kind of ominous cloud above their heads. Why couldn't people see the dentil molding, the millwork . . .

"Beautiful millwork!" said Andrew. "I've been here only once before, the day of the wedding reception. I was enchanted by the attention to detail. It's a privilege to see Fernbank again."

"Would you like to see it, stem to stern?"

"Stem to stern!" said Andrew, looking enthused.

Two hours later, they were close to a deal.

"The development firm has unfortunately asked for several of the finest pieces," said Andrew. He referred to notes that he had hastily jotted as they toured the house.

"Nonetheless, I'd be interested in the Federal loveseat in Miss Sadie's bedroom, the Georgian chest of drawers in her dressing room, the three leather trunks in the attic, the chaise in the storage room, which I believe is Louis XIV, the English china dresser, and all the beds in the house, which are exceedingly fine walnut . . . now, let's see . . . the six framed oils we discussed, which appear to be French . . . and the pine farm table in that wonderful kitchen! It must have been made by a local craftsman around the turn of the century."

"Anything else?" asked the rector, feeling like a traitor, a grave robber.

"In truth, I'd like the dining room suite, but it's Victorian, and I never fare well with Victorian. There are two chairs on the landing, however—I'm not certain of their origins, but they're charming. I'll have those chairs, into the bargain . . . and oh, yes, the contents of the linen drawers. I have a customer in Richmond who fancies brocade napery."

"Hardly used!" said Father Tim, knowing that Miss Sadie had certainly never trotted it out for him.

Cynthia roamed around, sounding like a squirrel in the attic, as he went through the miserable ordeal of dismantling someone's life, someone's history.

Miss Sadie's long letter, which was delivered to him after her death, gave very clear instructions: "Do not offer anything for view at a yard sale, or let people pick over the remains. I know you will understand."

Was Andrew picking over the remains? He didn't think so, he was being a four-square gentleman about the whole thing. Besides, something had to be done with the contents of twenty-one rooms and the detritus of nearly a century.

"How about the silver holloware?" asked the rector. He felt like Avis Packard who, after selling and bagging a dozen ears of corn, was trying to get rid of last week's broccoli. "The, ah, flatware, perhaps?"

"Well, and why not?" agreed Andrew, looking jaunty. "Who cares if it's all monogrammed with *B,* I think I'll have it for my own!"

The rector drew a deep breath. This wasn't so hard.

"The rugs! How about the rugs?" After all, every cent he raised would go into the Hope House till. . . .

Andrew smiled gently. "I don't think Miss Sadie's father did his homework on the rugs." He jotted some more and offered a price that nearly floored the rector.

"Done!" he exclaimed.

Feeling vastly relieved, he shook Andrew's hand with undeniable vigor.

"While you and Andrew toured around like big shots, eyeing major pieces, I was burrowing into minor pieces. Look what I found!"

His wife's face was positively beaming.

"An easel! Hand-carved! Isn't it wonderful? And look at this—an ancient wooden box of watercolors, two whole compartments full! The cakes are dried and cracked, of course, but they'll spring back to life in no time at all, with—guess what?—water!"

He hadn't seen Christmas make her so jubilant.

"And look! A boxful of needlepoint chair covers, worked with roses and hydrangeas and pansies, in all my favorite colors! Perfect for our dining room! Oh, Timothy, how could we have neglected this treasure trove for a full year? It's as if we stayed away from a gold mine, content with digging ore!"

She held up a chair cover for him to admire.

"Now it's your turn to find something for yourself, like Miss Sadie asked you to do. She said 'Take anything you like,' those were her very words."

He stood frozen to the spot, suddenly feeling as if he'd burst into tears.

Cynthia quietly put the chair cover down, and came to him and held him.

He found it in the dimly lit attic.

Though the box appeared to be of no special consequence, he felt drawn to it, somehow, and knelt to remove the lid and unwrap the heavy object within.

The figure had the weight of a stone, but a certain lightness about its form, which rested on a sizeable chunk of marble.

Back at the rectory, he set the bronze angel on the living room mantel and stood looking at it.

It was enough. He wanted nothing more.

§

"Mule! What have you got in a little rental house, maybe two bedrooms, something bright and sunny, something spacious and open—and oh, yes, low-maintenance, in a nice part of Mitford, maybe with a fireplace and a washing machine, not too much money, and—"

"Hold it!" exclaimed Mule. "Are you kidding me? You're talkin' like a crazy person. Think about it. If I *had* anything like that, would it be *available*?"

He thought about it. "Guess not," he said.

§

Cynthia's interest was growing. "Let's invite Pauline and Poo!"

They sat in the kitchen, planning the dinner party while their own supper roasted in the oven.

"Terrific idea. Louella, Pauline, Dooley, Poo, Harley, you, and me. Meat loaf for seven!"

"Better make it for ten. Dooley has the appetite of a baseball team."

"Right! Ten, then."

"I'll make lemonade and tea and bake a cobbler," she said.

"Deal."

"In the meantime, dearest, I've planned our retreat."

"Really?"

"Really. Next week, I'm taking you away for two days."

"But Cynthia, I can't go away for two days. I have things to *do*."

"Darling, that's exactly why I'm taking you away!"

"But there's an important vestry meeting, and—"

"Poop on the vestry meeting. Since when does the rector have to attend every vestry meeting as if it were the Nicene Council?"

"Cynthia, Cynthia . . ."

"Timothy, Timothy. Let me remind you of all you've recently done—you've had three baptisms, a death at the hospital, you're working on that project with the bishop which keeps you talking on the phone like schoolgirls, you do two services every Sunday, Holy Eucharist every Wednesday, not to mention your weekly Bible class. *Plus—*"

"There's no way—"

"Plus your hospital visits every morning, and pulling together that huge thing for the mayor, and working on the benefit for the Children's Hospital, and tearing down Betty's shed—not to mention that on your birthday you made a wonderful evening for *me*!"

She took a deep breath. "*Plus—*"

Not that again. "But you see—"

"Plus you still think you haven't done enough."

What was enough? He'd never been able to figure it out.

"Well, dearest, I can see you have no intention of listening to reason, so . . . I shall be forced do what women have been forced to do for millennia."

She marched around the kitchen table and thumped down in his lap. Then she mussed what was left of his hair and kissed him on the top of his head. Next she gave him a lingering kiss on the mouth, and unsnapped his collar, and whispered in his ear.

He blushed. "OK," he said. "I'll do it."

While Cynthia scraped and stacked the dishes, he sat in the kitchen, awaiting his cue to wash, and read the *Muse.*

Violet was perched by the gloxinia, purring; Barnabas lay under the table, snoring.

Four Convicted in Wesley Drug Burst

He roared with laughter. This was one for his cousin Walter, all right! He got up and pulled the scissors from the kitchen drawer and clipped the story. Walter liked nothing better than a few choice headlines from the type fonts of J. C. Hogan.

"Who discovered America?" He heard Lace Turner's voice drifting up the stairs through the open basement door.

"Christopher Columbus!" said Harley.

"Who was America named for?"

"Amerigo Vespucci! Looks like it ought've been named f'r Mr. Columbus, don't it? But see, that's th' way of th' world, you discover somethin' and they don't even notice you f'r doin' it."

Cynthia whispered, "She's been coming over and teaching him for several nights, you've been too busy to notice."

"Who was th' king of England when North Carolina became a royal colony?" Lace Turner sounded emphatic.

"George th' Second!"

"When was th' French and Indian War?"

"Lord, Lace, as long as I've lived, ain't never a soul come up t' me and said, 'Harley, when was th' French and Injun war?'"

"Harley . . ."

"They ain't a bit of use f'r me t' know that, I done told you who discovered America."

"Who defeated George Washington at Great Meadows?"

"Th' dern French."

"Who was th' first state to urge independence from Great Britian?"

"North Carolina!" Harley's voice had a proud ring.

"See, you learn stuff real good, you just act like you don't."

"But you don't teach me nothin' worth knowin'. If we got t' do this aggravation, why don't you read me one of them riddles out of y'r number book?"

"OK, but listen good, Harley, this stuff is hard. You borrow five hundred dollars for one year. Th' rate is twenty percent per year. How much do you pay back by th' end of th' year?"

There was a long silence in the basement.

The rector put his arm around his wife, who had come to sit with him on the top basement step. They looked at each other, wordless.

"Six hundred dollars!" exclaimed Harley.

"Real good!"

"I done that in m' noggin."

"OK, here's another'n—"

"I ain't goin' t' do no more. You git on back home and worry y'r own head."

She pressed forward. "A recipe suggests two an' a half to three pounds of chicken t' serve four people. Karen bought nine-point-five pounds of chicken. Is this enough t' serve twelve people?"

"I told you I ain't goin' t' do it," said Harley. "Let Karen fig'r it out!"

The rector looked at Cynthia, who got up and fled the room, shaking with laughter.

He went to his study and took pen and paper from the desk drawer. Let's see, he thought, if the recipe calls for two and a half to three pounds of chicken to serve four people . . .

CHAPTER TEN

Those Who Are Able

He was changing shirts for a seven p.m. meeting when he heard Harley's truck pull into the driveway. Almost immediately he heard Harley's truck pull out of the driveway.

Harley must have forgotten something, he mused, buttoning a cuff.

When he heard the truck roll into the driveway again, he looked out his bathroom window and saw it backing toward the street. From this vantage point, he could also see through the windshield.

Clearly, it wasn't Harley who was driving Harley's truck.

It was Dooley.

He stood at the bathroom window, buttoning the other cuff, watching. In, out, in, out.

He didn't have five spare minutes to deal with it; he was already cutting the time close since he was the speaker. He'd have to talk to Dooley and Harley about this.

Dadgum it, he thought. He had a car-crazed boy living down the hall and a race-car mechanic in the basement. Was this a good combination? He didn't think so. . . .

Emma looked up from her computer, where she was keying in copy for the pew bulletin.

"I know I'm a Baptist and it's none of my business . . ."

You can take *that* to the bank, he thought.

". . . but it seems to me that people who can't stand shouldn't have to."

"What do you mean?"

"I mean all those people you get in th' summer who don't know an Episcopal service from a hole in the ground, and think they have to do all th' stuff th' pew bulletin tells 'em to do. I mean, some of those people are old as the hills, and what does th' bulletin say? Stand, kneel, sit, stand, bow, stand, kneel, whatever! It's a workout."

"True."

"So why don't we do what they do at this Presbyterian church I heard about?"

"And what's that?" He noticed that his teeth were clenched.

"Put a little line at the bottom of the bulletin that says, 'Those who are *able,* please stand.' "

Who needed the assistance of a curate or a deacon when they had Emma Newland to think through the gritty issues facing the church today?

As he left the office for Mitford Blossoms, Andrew Gregory hailed him from his shop across the street.

"We go three months without laying eyes on each other," said the genteel Andrew, "and now—twice in a row!"

"I prefer this arrangement!"

"Before pushing off to Italy, I have something for your Bane and Blessing. I'll be back in only a month, but what with making room for the Fernbank pieces, I find I've got to move other pieces out. Would you mind having my contribution a dash early?"

"Mind? I should say not. Thrilled would be more like it." He could imagine Esther Bolick's face when she heard she was getting antiques from Andrew Gregory.

Talk about an answer to prayer. . . .

He climbed the hill, slightly out of breath, carrying the purple gloxinia, and stood for a moment gazing at the impressive structure they had named Hope House.

But for Sadie Baxter's generosity, this would be little more than the forlorn site of the original Lord's Chapel, which had long ago burned to the ground. Now that Miss Sadie was gone, he was the only living soul who knew what had happened the night of that terrible fire.

Ah, well. He could muddle on about the fire, or he could look at what had risen from the ashes. Wasn't that the gist of life, after all, making the everyday choice between fire and phoenix?

Louella sat by her sunny window, with its broad sill filled with gloxinias, begonias, philodendron, ivy, and a dozen other plants, including a bewildered amaryllis from Christmas.

Dressed to the nines, she opened her brown arms wide as he came in. "Law, honey! You lookin' like somebody on TV in that blue coat."

He leaned eagerly into her warm hug and returned it with one of his own.

"Have you got room for another gloxinia?"

"This make three gloxinias you done brought me!"

That's what he always took people; he couldn't help it.

"But I ain't never had purple, an' ain't it beautiful! You're good as gold an' that's th' truth!"

He set it on the windowsill and thumped down on the footstool by her chair. "How are you? Are they still treating you right?"

"Treatin' me *right*? They like to worry me to death treatin' me right. Have a stick of candy, eat a little ice cream wit' yo' apple pie, let me turn yo' bed down, slip on these socks to keep yo' feet toasty . . ." She shook her head and laughed in the dark chocolate voice that always made a difference in the singing at Lord's Chapel.

"You're rotten, then," he said, grinning.

"Rotten, honey, and no way 'round it. That little chaplain, too, ain't he a case with them dogs runnin' behind 'im ever' whichaway?"

"Are you still getting Taco every week?"

"Taco done got mange on 'is hip and they tryin' to fix it."

"You could have a cat or something 'til Taco gets fixed."

"A cat? You ain't never seen Louella messin' wit' a *cat.*"

"Are you working in the new garden?"

"You ain't seen me messin' wit' a hoe, neither. Nossir, I done my duty, I sets right here, watches TV, and acts like somebody."

"Well, I've got a question," he said.

Louella, whose salt-and-pepper hair had turned snow-white in the past year, peered at him.

"Will you come to dinner at the rectory next Thursday? Say yes!"

"You talkin' 'bout dinner or supper?"

"Dinner!" he said. "Like in the evening." Louella, he remembered, called lunch "dinner," and the evening meal "supper."

"I doan hardly know 'bout goin' out at *night,*" she said, looking perplexed. "What wit' my other knee needin' t' be operated on . . ."

"I'll hold on to you good and tight," he said, eager for her to accept.

"I doan know, honey. . . ."

"Please," he said.

"Let 'Amazin' Grace' be one of th' hymns this Sunday and I'll do it," she said, grinning. "We ain't sung that in a *month* of Sundays, an' a 'piscopal preacher *wrote* it!"

"Done!" he said, relieved and happy. He had always felt ten years old around Miss Sadie and Louella.

He took the stairs to the second floor to see Lida Willis.

He didn't have to tell her why he'd come.

Lida tapped her desk with a ballpoint pen, still looking stern. "She's doing well. Very well. We couldn't ask for better."

"Glad to hear it," he said, meaning it.

He found Pauline in the dining room, setting tables with the dishes Miss Sadie had paid to have monogrammed with HH. A lifelong miser where her own needs were concerned, she had spared no expense on Hope House.

"Pauline, you look . . . wonderful," he said.

"It's a new apron."

"I believe it's a new Pauline."

She laughed. He didn't think he'd heard her laugh before.

"I have a proposal."

She smiled at him, listening.

"Will you come to dinner next Thursday night and bring Poo? Dooley will be with us, and Harley and Louella."

He could see her pleasure in being asked and her hesitation in accepting.

"Please say yes," he requested. "It's just family, no airs to put on, and we'll all be wearing something comfortable."

"Yes, then. Yes! Thank you. . . ."

"Great!" he said. "Terrific!"

He'd heard people ask, "If you could have anyone, living or dead, come to dinner, who would it be?" Shakespeare's name usually came up at once; he'd also heard Mother Teresa, the Pope, St. Augustine, Thomas Jefferson, Pavarotti, Bach, Charles Schultz . . .

For his money, he couldn't think of anyone he'd rather be having for dinner than the very ones who were coming.

He found Scott Murphy at the kennels.

"That's Harry," said Scott, pointing to a doleful beagle. "He's new."

"Looks like an old bishop I once had."

"That's Taco over there."

"How's his mange?"

"You know everything!"

"I wish."

"I've been thinking," said the chaplain. "I'd like to get my crowd out of here, take them to—I don't know, a baseball game, a softball game, something out in the fresh air where they can hoot and holler and—"

"Eat hotdogs!"

"Right!"

"Great idea. I don't know who's playing around town these days. . . ."

"Maybe you and I could get up our own game? Sometime in August?"

"Well, sure! Before Dooley goes back to school."

"I'll start looking for players."

"Me, too," said the rector.

A softball game!

He felt like tossing his hat in the air. If he had a hat.

"Bingo!" said Emma, handing him the computer printout of names and addresses.

The vestry had said what he thought they'd say, virtually in unison: "Let's get on with it!"

Yes, they wanted Ingrid Swenson and her crew to come on the fifteenth. It was unspoken, but the message was clear—let's unload that white elephant before the roof caves in and we have to get a bank loan to pick up the tab.

He asked Ron Malcolm to call her immediately after the meeting.

There were quite a few R. Davises in the state of Florida, according to the printout, but Lakeland was the only town or city with a Rhody Davis. "Starts with a *L*," Russell Jacks had said of Rhody's dimly recalled whereabouts in Florida.

He was disappointed, but not surprised, that Rhody Davis had an unlisted phone number.

He called Stuart Cullen.

"Who do you know in Lakeland, Florida? Clergy, preferably."

"Let me get back to you."

By noon, he was talking to the rector at a church in Lakeland's inner city. It was an odd request, granted, but the rector said he'd find someone to do it.

The next morning, he got the report.

"Our junior warden drove by at nine o'clock in the morning, and a car was parked by the house. Same at three in the afternoon, and again at eight in the evening. Lights were on in the evening, but no other signs of anyone being around. Maybe this will help—there was a tricycle in the front yard. I used what clout my collar can summon, but no way to get the phone number."

"Ever make it up to our mountains?" asked Father Tim.

"No, but my wife and I have been wanting to. A few of my parish go every summer."

"We've got a guest room. Consider it yours when you come this way."

It was a long shot, but he knew what had to be done.

"I don't want t' worry you, Rev'rend, that's th' last thing I'd want t' do, but th' boy ragged me nearly t' death, an' I done like you'd want me to and told 'im no, then dern if I didn't leave m' key in th' ignition, an' since all he done was back it out and pull it in, I hope you won't lick 'im f'r it, hit's th' way a boy does at his age, hit's natural. . . ."

Harley looked devastated; the rector felt like a heel.

"Maybe you ought t' let me take 'im out to th' country an' put 'im behind th' wheel. In two years, he's goin' t' be runnin' up an' down th' road, anyhow, hit'd be good trainin'. I'd watch 'im like a hawk, Rev'rend, you couldn't git a better trainer than this ol' liquor hauler."

"I don't know, Harley. Let me think on it."

"What's it all about?" he asked his wife, sighing.

"Hormones!" she exclaimed.

Mitford, he noted, was becoming a veritable chatterbox of words and slogans wherever the eye landed.

The mayoral incumbent and her opponent had certainly done their part to litter the front lawns and telephone poles with signage, while the ECW had plastered hand-lettered signs in the churchyard and posters in every shop window.

Even the Library Ladies were putting in their two cents' worth.

14th annual Library Sale
10–4, July 28
Book It!

You Don't Want It? We Do!
34th Annual Bane and Blessing

MACK STROUPE:
Mack For Mitford,
Mack For Mayor

Esther Cunningham:
Right For Mitford
Right For Mayor

Clean Out Attics In Mitford
Help Dig Wells
In Africa!

Cunningham Cares.
Vote Esther Cunningham
For Mayor

YOUR BANE IS OUR BLESSING.
Lord's Chapel, October 4

Mack Stroupe:
I'll Make What's
Good Even Better

He thought he'd seen enough of Mack Stroupe's face to last a lifetime, since it was plastered nearly everywhere he looked. Worse than that, he was struggling with how he felt about seeing Mack's face in his congregation every Sunday morning.

When he dropped by her office at seven o'clock, the mayor was eating her customary sausage biscuit. It wasn't a pretty sight.

Three bites, max, and that sausage biscuit was out of here. But who was he to preach or pontificate? Hadn't he wolfed down a slab of cheesecake last night, looking over his shoulder like a chicken poacher lest his wife catch him in the act?

Oh, well, die young and make a good-looking corpse, his friend Tommy Noles always said.

"If Mack Stroupe's getting money under the table," he said, "isn't there some way—"

"What do you mean *if*? He *is* gettin' money under the table. I checked what it would cost to put up those billboards and—get this—four thousand bucks. I called th' barbecue place in Wesley that helps him commit his little Saturday afternoon crimes—six hundred smackers to run over here and set up and cook from eleven to three. Pitch in a new truck at twenty-five thousand, considering it's got a CD player and leather seats, and what do *you* think's goin' on?"

"Isn't he supposed to fill out a form that tells where his contributions come from? Somebody said that even the media can take a look at that form."

She wadded up the biscuit wrapper and lobbed it into the wastebasket. "You know what I always tell Ray? Preachers are the most innocent critters I've ever known! Do you think th' triflin' scum is goin' to *report* the money he's gettin' under th' table?"

"Maybe he's actually getting enough thousand-dollar contributions legally to pull all this together. It wouldn't hurt to ask."

She scratched a splotch on her neck and leaned toward him. "Who's going to ask?"

"Not me," he said, meaning it.

The screen door of the Grill slapped behind him. "What's going on?" the rector asked Percy.

"All I lack of bein' dead is th' news gettin' out."

"What's the trouble?"

"Velma."

"Aha."

"Wants to drag me off on another cruise. I said we done been on a cruise, and if you've seen one, you've seen 'em all—drink somethin' with a little umbrella in it, dance th' hula, make a fool of yourself, and come home. I ain't goin' again. But she's nagged me 'til I'm blue in th' face."

" 'Til she's blue in the face."

"Whatever."

Velma, who had heard everything, walked over, looking disgusted.

"I hope you've told th' Father that th' cruise you took me on was paid for by our children, and I hope you mentioned that it's the only vacation I've had since I married you forty-three years ago, except for that run over to Wilkes County in th' car durin' which I threw up the entire time, bein' pregnant."

Velma took a deep breath and launched another volley. "And did you tell him about th' varicose veins I've got from stompin' around in this Grill since Teddy Roosevelt was president? Now you take the Father here, I'm sure he's carried *his* wife on *several* nice trips since *he* got married."

Velma tossed her order pad on the counter, stomped off to the toilet, and slammed the door.

Percy looked pained.

The rector looked pained.

If Velma only knew.

§

She would be let down, he thought, maybe even ticked off—and for good reason. After all, she had worked hard to plan something special.

"Listen to me, please," he said. "I can't go on our retreat."

She gazed at him, unwavering, knowing that he meant it.

"I've got to go and look for Jessie Barlowe."

"I'll go with you," she said.

He sat heavily on the side of the bed where she was propped against the pillows with a book. "It's in Florida, a long drive, and I don't know what we'll run into. I also need Pauline to come along. Since she's the birth mother and no papers were signed for Jessie to live with Rhody Davis, Pauline has custody. She can take Jessie legally."

"Would you need . . . police to go in with you? A social worker?"

"It's not required. Only if it looks like a bad situation."

"Does it look bad?"

"I don't know. There's no way to know."

"Do you think you should investigate further, I mean . . ."

"I feel we need to act on this now."

"Will we be back for our dinner next Thursday?"

"Yes," he said.

She leaned against him, and they sat together, silent for a time.

"We need to pray the prayer that never fails."

"Yes," he said again.

He pled Pauline's case with Lida Willis, who gave her dining room manager two days off.

"She'll make it up over Thanksgiving," said Lida. That was when families of Hope House residents would pour into Mitford, straining the reserves of the dining room.

He was vague with Dooley about what was going on and said nothing at all to Emma. He didn't want anyone getting their hopes up. As far as everyone was concerned, he was taking his wife on a small excursion, and Pauline was riding with them to South Carolina and visiting a great aunt. He regretted saying anything to anybody about Florida.

"Florida in July?" asked his secretary, aghast.

"Lord at th' salt they got down there!" said Harley. "Hit'll rust y'r fenders plumb off. Let me git m' stuff together and I'll give you a good wax job."

"You don't have to do that, Harley. Besides, we're leaving early in the morning."

"I'll git to it right now, Rev'rend, don't you worry 'bout a thing. And I'll sweep you out good, too."

It was all coming together so fast, it made his head swim.

"Look after Dooley," he told his resident mechanic as they loaded the car, "and hide your truck keys. Dooley will walk and feed Barnabas, Puny will be in tomorrow, help yourself to the pasta salad in the refrigerator, the car looks terrific, a thousand thanks, we'll bring you something."

Harley grinned. "Somethin' with Mickey on it, Rev'rend! I'd be much obliged."

Hot. He didn't remember being so hot in years, not since his parish by the sea.

And the colors in this part of the world—so vivid, so bright, so . . . different. In the mountains, in his high, green hills, he felt embraced, protected—consoled, somehow.

Here, it was all openness and blue sky and flat land and palm trees. He never ceased to be astonished by the palm tree, which was a staple of the biblical landscape. How did the same One who designed the mighty oak and the gentle mimosa come up with the totally fantastic concept of a palm tree? Extraordinary!

He chuckled.

"Why are you laughing, dearest?"

"I'm laughing at palm trees."

There went that puckered brow and concerned look again. Soon, he really would have to go on a retreat with his wife and act relaxed, so she'd stop looking at him like this.

"You're flying," announced Cynthia, craning her neck to see the speedometer.

Good Lord! Ninety! They'd be arriving in Lakeland in half the anticipated time.

He could feel the toll of the 670-mile one-way trip already grinding on him as they zoomed past Daytona and looped onto the Orlando exit.

The engine might be working in spades, and the wax job glittering like something off the showroom floor, but the air-conditioning performed only slightly better than a church fan at a tent meeting.

He hadn't noticed it at home where the elevation was a lofty five thousand feet, but here, where the sun blazed unhindered, they were all feeling the dismally weak effort of the a/c.

He peered into the rearview mirror, checking on Pauline. She had ridden for hours looking out the window.

He would let Cynthia drive when they got to the rest station in Providence, and once in Lakeland, they'd take a motel and rest before looking for Rhody Davis on Palm Court Way. In order to get Pauline back in time to keep Lida Willis satisfied, they would have only a few short hours to look for Jessie before they hauled back to Mitford on another ten-hour drive.

Maybe he'd been a fool to risk so much on this one grueling trip.

But if not now, when?

He parked the car under a tree by the sidewalk, where the early morning shade still held what fleeting cooler temperature had come in the night.

"That's Rhody's car in the driveway," said Pauline.

"Sit here," he said, "while I check this out. I'll leave the engine running, so you can stay cool."

"Cool!" said his wife. "Ha and double ha. Can't I come with you, Timothy?"

"No," he said.

He had worn his collar, but only after thinking it through. He always wore his collar, he reasoned—why should he not?

His eyes made a quick reconnaissance.

The small yard was nearly barren of grass. Plastic grocery bags were snared in the yucca plants bordering the unsheltered porch. The car was probably twenty years old, a huge thing, the hood almost completely bleached of its original color. A weather-beaten plastic tricycle lay by the steps. No curtains at the windows.

He rang the doorbell, but failed to hear a resulting blast inside, and knocked loudly on the frame of the screen door.

Hearing nothing, he knocked again, louder than before.

Already the perspiration was beginning a slow trickle under his shirt. He might have been a piece of flounder beneath a broiler, and it wasn't even nine a.m.

Had they come so far to find no one home?

He glanced at the bare windows again and saw her face pressed against the glass.

His heart pounded; he might have leaped for joy.

She looked at him soberly, and he looked at her, seeing the reddish blond hair damp against her cheeks, as if she'd been swimming. There was no doubt that this was five-year-old Jessie Barlowe; the resemblance to her brothers was startling.

Not knowing what else to do, he waved.

She lifted a small hand and waved back, eyeing him intently.

He gestured toward the door. "May I come in?" he said, mouthing the words.

She disappeared from the window, and he heard her running across a bare floor.

He knocked again.

This time, she appeared at the window on the left side of the door. She pressed her nose against the glass and stared at him. Perhaps she was in there alone, he thought with some alarm.

She vanished from the window.

Suddenly the door opened a few inches and she peered at him through the screen.

"Who is it?" she asked, frowning. She was barefoot and wearing a pair of filthy shorts. Her toenails were painted bright pink.

"It's Timothy Kavanagh."

"Rhody can't come!" she said, closing the door with force.

He was baking, he was frying, he was grilling.

He mopped his face with a handkerchief and looked toward the street, seeing only the rear end of his Buick sitting in the vanishing point of shade.

"Jessie!" he yelled, pounding again. "Jessie!"

He heard her running across the floor.

She opened the door again, this time wider. "Rhody can't come!" she said, looking stern.

He tried the screen door. It wasn't locked.

He opened it quickly and stepped across the threshold, feeling like a criminal, driven by his need.

The intense and suffocating heat of the small house hit him like a wall. And the smell. Good Lord! His stomach rolled.

He saw a nearly bare living room opening onto a dining area that was randomly filled with half-opened boxes and clothing scattered across the floor

"You ain't 'posed to come in," she said, backing away. "I ain't 'posed to talk to strangers."

"Where is Rhody?"

"Her foot's hurt, she done stepped on a nail." She wiped the sweat from her face with a dirty hand, and put her thumb in her mouth.

"Is she here?"

Jessie glanced down the hall.

"I'd like to talk with her, if I may."

"Rhody talks crazy."

"Can you take me to her?"

She looked at him with that sober expression, and turned and walked into the hall. "Come on!" she said.

The smell. What was it? It intensified as he followed her down the long, dark hallway to the bed where Rhody Davis lay in a nearly empty room. A baby crib stood by the window, containing a bare mattress and a rumpled sheet; a sea of garbage was strewn around the floor.

The woman was close to his own age, naked to the waist, a bulk of a woman with wispy hair and desperate eyes, and he saw instantly what created the odor. Her right foot, which was nearly black, had swollen grotesquely, and streaks of red advanced upward along her bloated leg. The abscesses in the foot were draining freely on the bedclothes.

Her head rolled toward him on the pillow.

"Daddy? Daddy, is that you?" Sweat glistened on her body and poured onto the soaked sheets.

"Rhody—"

"You ain't got no business comin' here lookin' for Thelma."

"What—"

"Thelma's long gone, Daddy, long gone." She moaned and cursed and tossed her head and looked at him again, pleading. "Why'd you bring that dog in here? Git that dog out of here, it'll bite th' baby. . . ." She tried to raise herself, but fell back against the sodden pillow.

"Do you have a phone?" he asked Jessie. He was faint from the heat and the stench and the suffering.

Jessie sucked her thumb and pointed.

It was sitting on the floor by an empty saltine cracker box and a glass of spoiled milk. He tried to open the windows in the room, but found them nailed shut.

Then he dialed the number everyone was taught to dial and went through the agonizing process of giving the name, phone number, street address, and the particular brand of catastrophe.

"Gangrene," he said, knowing.

At the hospital, he got the payoff for wearing his collar. The emergency room doctor not only took time to examine Rhody Davis within an hour of their arrival, but was willing to talk about what he found.

"There was definitely a puncture to the sole of the foot. Blood poisoning resulted in a massive infection, and that led to gangrene."

"Bottom line?" asked the rector.

"There could be a need to amputate—we don't know yet. In the meantime, we're putting her on massive doses of antibiotics."

"What follows?"

"Based on what you've told me, our department of social services will plug her into the system."

"She'll be taken care of?" asked Cynthia.

The amiable doctor chuckled. "Our social services department loves to get their teeth into a tough case. This one looks like it fills that bill, hands down."

"I'll check on her," said Cynthia. "I'm his deacon."

He should have been exhausted, with one long trip behind him and another one ahead. But he wasn't exhausted, he was energized. They all were.

Cynthia chattered, fanning herself with one of the coloring books she'd been optimistic enough to bring. Pauline talked more freely, telling them Miss Pattie stories from Hope House, and holding Jessie on her lap.

Jessie alternately ate cookies, broke in a new box of crayons, and asked questions. What was that white thing around his neck? What was their dog's name? Where were they going? What was wrong with Rhody? Could they get some more french fries? Did they put her monkey in the trunk with her tricycle? Why didn't Cynthia paint her toenails? Why did the skin on Pauline's arm look funny? Could they stop so she could pee again?

Sitting behind the wheel on the first leg of the journey, he glanced often into the rearview mirror.

He saw Jessie touching her mother's face, though the concept of having a mother was not clear to her. "You're pretty," said the child.

"Thank you."

"You don't got no ear."

"It was . . . burned off."

"How'd you burn it off? Did you cry?"

"I'll tell you about it one day. That's why my arm looks funny. It was burned, too."

"Are we goin' back to get Rhody? Are you Rhody's friend?"

"I'm your mother."

Stick in there, he thought, feeling the pain as if part of it belonged to him. He looked at his wife. He knew when she was praying, because she often moved her lips, silently, like a child absorbed in the reading of a book.

As soon as they got around Daytona, they all played cow poker with enthusiasm, using truck-stop diners in place of the nearly nonexistent cows.

He felt as if he'd been hit by a truck, but thanks be to God, he hadn't.

They rolled into Mitford at midnight, dropped Pauline and Jessie at Betty Craig's, and went home and found Dooley's note that said he was spending the night at Tommy's. Crawling into bed on the stroke of one, he looked forward to sleeping in, until Cynthia told him she'd asked Pauline to leave Jessie with them on her way to work. Betty Craig was spending a rare day away from home with a sister, and did it make sense to leave Jessie with her elderly grandfather, who was a total stranger?

He slept until seven, when he heard Jessie come in, shrieking with either delight or fear upon encountering Barnabas. He woke again at eight, when he heard Puny, Sissy, Sassy, and the overloaded red wagon bound over the threshold and clatter down the hall like so much field artillery.

He burrowed under the covers, feeling the guilt of lying abed while the whole household erupted below him.

Someone was bounding up the stairs, and it definitely wasn't his wife.

"Wake up, Mr. Tim!"

Jessie Barlowe, freshly scrubbed, with her hair in a pony tail, trotted into the room. As he opened his eyes, she scrambled onto the bed and peered down at him.

"Time to put your collar on and get my tricycle out of your car!"

§

Actually, it was more like he'd gone a few rounds with Mike Tyson.

Standing helplessly by the coffeepot, he'd fallen prey to Puny's plea that he "watch" the twins while she did the floors upstairs. Cynthia and Jessie had gone next door, out of the fray, and here he was, drinking strong coffee in the study behind closed doors, as Sassy bolted back and forth from the bookcase to the desk, laughing hysterically, and Sissy lurched around the sofa with a string of quacking ducks, occasionally falling over and bawling. Barnabas crawled beneath the leather wing chair, trying desperately to hide.

"Ba!" said Sissy, abandoning the ducks and taking a fancy to him. "Ba!"

"Ba, yourself!" he said.

With the vacuum cleaner roaring above his head on bare hardwood, and Sissy banging his left knee with a rattle, he read Oswald Chambers.

"All your circumstances are in the hand of God," Chambers wrote, "so never think it strange concerning the circumstances you're in."

The fact that this piece of wisdom was the absolute gospel truth did not stop him from laughing out loud.

CHAPTER ELEVEN

Amazing Grace

Pauline and Jessie were sitting at the kitchen table as he cooked dinner.

They heard Dooley coming down the hall.

"It's Dooley," said Pauline, gently pushing Jessie toward her brother as he walked into the kitchen.

Dooley was suddenly pale under his summer tan.

"Jess?"

It had been three years, the rector thought, and for a five-year-old, three years is a long time.

"Jess?" Dooley said again, sinking to his knees on the kitchen floor.

Jessie looked at him soberly. Then, standing only a couple of feet away, she slowly lifted her hand and waved at her brother.

"Hey, Jess."

"Hey," she murmured, beginning to smile.

It came to him during the night.

At seven o'clock on Sunday morning he called Hope House,

knowing she would be sitting by the window, dressed for church and reading her Bible.

"Will you do it?" he asked

"Law, mercy . . . " she said, pondering.

"For Miss Sadie? For all of us?"

Louella took a deep breath. "I'll do it for Jesus!" she said.

Harley Welch was dressed in a dark blue jacket and pants, a dress shirt that Cynthia had plucked out of Bane contributions and washed and ironed, and a tie of his own. It was, in fact, his only tie, worn to his wife's funeral thirteen years ago, and never worn since.

"You look terrific!" exclaimed Cynthia.

"Yeah!" agreed Dooley.

"Here!" said the rector.

Harley took the box and opened what had been hastily purchased at a truck stop in South Carolina.

"Th' law, if it ain't a Mickey watch! I've always wanted a Mickey watch! Rev'rend, if you ain't th' beat!"

There went Harley's grin. . . .

Driving his crew to Lord's Chapel, he thought how it was Harley who was the beat. Harley Welch all rigged up for church and wearing a Mickey Mouse watch was still another amazing grace from an endlessly flowing fountain.

He stood in the pulpit and spoke the simple but profound words with which he always opened the sermon.

"In the name of the Father, and of the Son, and of the Holy Spirit, amen."

Then, he walked over and sat in the chair next to the chalice bearer, leaving the congregation wondering. This morning, someone else would preach the top part of the sermon—an English clergyman, long dead, and one of his own parishioners, very much alive.

In the middle of the nave, on the gospel side, Louella Baxter Marshall rose from her pew and, uttering a silent prayer of supplication, raised the palms of her hands heavenward and began to sing, alone and unaccompanied.

Amazing grace! how sweet the sound
that saved a wretch like me!
I once was lost but now am found
was blind, but now I see.

The power of her bronze voice lifted the hymn of the Reverend John Newton, a converted slave trader, to the rafters.

'Twas grace that taught my heart to fear,
and grace my fears relieved;
how precious did that grace appear
the hour I first believed!

The Lord has promised good to me,
his word my hope secures;
he will my shield and portion be
as long as life endures.

The words filled and somehow enlarged the nave, like yeast rising in a warm place. In more than one pew, hearts swelled with a message they had long known, but had somehow forgotten.

For those who had never known it at all, there was a yearning to know it, an urgent, beating desire to claim a shield and portion for their own lives, to be delivered out of loss into gain.

The rector's eyes roamed his congregation. This is for you, Dooley. And for you, Poo and Jessie, and for you, Pauline, whom the hound of heaven pursued and won. This is for you, Harley, and you, Lace Turner, and even for you, Cynthia, who was given to me so late, yet right on time. . . .

Through many dangers, toils, and snares,
I have already come;
'tis grace that brought me safe thus far,
and grace will lead me home. . . .

Today was the day. He was ready.

Ron Malcolm, who had priced Fernbank at three hundred and fifty thousand, suggested they accept an offer of no less than two ninety-five. Fernbank was not only an architecturally valuable structure, even with its flaws, but the acreage was sizable, chiefly flat, and eminently suited for development. At two hundred and ninety-five thousand, give or take a few dollars, it would be a smart buy as well as a smart sell.

The rector looked toward Fernbank as he walked to the Grill. He couldn't see the house, but he could see the upper portion of the fern-massed bank, and the great grove of trees.

A spa?

As hard as he tried, he couldn't even begin to imagine it.

"Softball?" said Percy. "Are you kiddin' me?"

"I am not kidding you. August tenth, be there or be square."

"Me'n Velma will do hotdogs, but I ain't runnin' around to any bases, I got enough bases to cover in th' food business."

"Fine. You're in. Expect twenty-five from Hope House, twenty or so players . . . and who knows how many in the bleachers?"

Percy scribbled on the back of an order pad. "That's a hundred and fifty beef dogs, max, plus all th' trimmin's, includin' Velma's chili—"

"Wrong!" said Velma. "I'm not standin' over a hot stove stirrin' chili another day of my life! I've decided to go with canned from here out."

"Canned chili?" Percy was unbelieving.

"And how long has it been since you peeled spuds for french fries? Years, that's how long. They come in here frozen as a rock, like they do everywhere else that people don't want to kill theirselves workin'."

"Yeah, but frozen fries is one thing, canned chili is another."

"To you, maybe. But not to me."

Velma stalked away. Percy sighed deeply.

The rector didn't say anything, but he knew darn well their conversation wasn't about chili.

It was about a cruise.

He turned into Happy Endings to see if the rare book search had yielded the John Buchan volume.

Hope Winchester shook her head. "Totally chimerical thus far."

"So be it," he said. "Oh. Know anybody who plays softball?"

Ingrid Swenson was, if possible, more deeply tanned than before. He didn't believe he'd ever seen so much gold jewelry on one person, as his wealthy seasonal parishioners tended to be fairly low-key while summering in Mitford.

She read from the offer-to-purchase document as if, being children, they couldn't read it for themselves. Every word seemed weighted with a kind of doom he couldn't explain, though he noted how happy, even ecstatic, his vestry appeared to be.

"Miami Development, as Buyer, hereby offers to purchase, and The Chapel of Our Lord and Savior, as Seller, upon acceptance of said offer, agrees to sell and convey—all of that plot, piece or parcel of land described below . . . "

While some appeared to savor every word as they would a first course leading to the entrée, he wanted to skip straight to the price and the conditions.

In the interim, they dealt with, and once again agreed upon, the pieces of personal property to be included in the contract.

"The purchase price," she said at last, looking around the table, "is one hundred and ninety-eight thousand dollars, and shall be paid as follows—twenty thousand in earnest money—"

"Excuse me," he said.

She glanced up.

"I don't think I heard the offer correctly."

"One hundred and ninety-eight thousand dollars." He noted the obvious edge of impatience in her voice.

"Thank you," he said, betraying an edge in his own.

Buddy Benfield made coffee, which they all trooped into the kitchen to pour for themselves. Ron brought Ingrid Swenson a china cup, not Styrofoam.

"You do realize," she said, smiling, "that the electrical system violates all state and local ordinances."

Had they realized that?

She withdrew a sheaf of papers from her briefcase. "Let's look at the numbers, which is always an informative place to look.

"The new roof, as you know, is coming in at around forty-five thousand. The plumbing as it stands is corroded cast-iron pipe, all of which must be removed and replaced with copper." She sipped her coffee. "Twenty thousand, minimum. Then, of course, there's the waste-lines replacement and the hookup to city water and sewage at a hundred thousand plus.

"As to the heating system, it is, as you're aware, an oil-fired furnace added several decades ago. Our inspection shows that the firebox is burned through." She sat back in her chair. "I'm sure I needn't remind you how lethal this can be. Estimates, then, for the installation of a forced warm-air system with new returns and ductwork is in excess of ten thousand."

Would this never end?

"Now, before we move to far brighter issues, let's revisit the electrical system."

There was a general shifting around in chairs, accompanied by discreet coughing.

"As you no doubt realize, Mr. Malcolm, Father—the attic has parallel wiring, which fails to pass inspection not merely because it is dangerous, but because it is . . . "—the agent for Miami Development Company gazed around the table—"illegal. Throughout the structure, there is exposed wiring not in conduit, all of which, to make a very long story conveniently shorter, is sufficient to have the structure condemned."

His heart pounded. Condemned.

Ron Malcolm sat forward in his chair. "Miss Swenson, have you stated your case?"

"Not completely, Mr. Malcolm. There are two remarks I'd like to make in closing. One is that the property improvements so far noted will cost the buyer in excess of two hundred and twenty thousand dollars. With that in mind, I believe you'll see the wisdom of selling your . . . distressed property . . . at the very fair price which we're offering.

"Now, to address the brighter side. What we propose to do will bring a vital new economy to Mitford. It will strengthen your tax base by, among other things, raising the value of every property in your village. Mr. Malcolm, I believe that you, for one, live on property contiguous to Fernbank. I don't have to tell you just how great an advantage this will be to your personal assets.

"Surely, all of you realize that nobody in Mitford could afford to take this uninhabitable property off your hands, and I know how grateful you must be to your own Mr. Stroupe for bringing our two parties together. Lacking the local means to reclaim this property, it would be tragic, would it not, to stand by helplessly while Fernbank, the very crown of your village, is torn down?"

The agony he felt was nearly unbearable. He wanted desperately to turn the clock back and have things as they were. He fought an urge to flee the smothering confines of this nightmarish meeting and run into the street.

"In closing, then," she said, looking into the faces of everyone assembled, "we're asking that you respond today, or within a maximum of seven days, to our offer—an offer that is as much designed for the good of Mitford as it is designed to accommodate the interests of Miami Development."

The rector stood, hearing the legs of his chair grate against the bare floor, against the overwhelmed silence of the vestry members.

"We will consider your offer for thirty days," he said evenly.

She paused, but was unruffled. "Thirty days, Father? I assume you understand that, in the volatile business of real estate, seven days is generous."

He saw his vestry's surprised alarm that he'd seized control of a sensitive issue. However, they silently reasoned, he'd been the liaison with Miss Sadie all these years. They probably wouldn't have the property at all if it weren't for the Father.

"And you do realize," Ingrid Swenson continued, "that our legal right to withdraw the offer in view of such a delay puts the sale of your property greatly at risk."

He said to her what she had said to him only weeks before.

"Risk, Miss Swenson, has a certain adrenaline, after all."

She kissed his face tenderly—both cheeks, his forehead, his temples, the bridge of his nose. "There," she said, and trotted off to fetch him a glass of sherry.

He couldn't recall feeling so weary. Somehow, the road miles to Florida and back were still lurking in him, and the meeting . . . he felt as if it had delivered a blow to his very gut.

Ron Malcolm had argued that Miami Development was placing far too much emphasis on the flaws of the structure, and far too little on the valuable and outstanding piece of land that went with it. Though Ron made his case convincingly, even eloquently, Ingrid Swenson was not only unmoved, but in a big hurry to get out of there.

The rector couldn't dismiss some deeply intuitive sense that the whole thing was . . . he couldn't put his finger on what it was. But every time he denied his intuitions, trouble followed. He hadn't turned sixty-three—or was it sixty-four?—without learning a few things, and paying attention to his instincts was one of the precious few things he'd learned.

But how could he reasonably argue for holding on to a property that may, indeed, end up under the wrecking ball? His vestry hadn't said it in so many words, but they wanted the blasted thing behind them—their hands washed, and money in the till.

He put one of the old needlepoint pillows under his head and lay back on the study sofa. His dog sprawled on the rug beside him and licked his hand.

Dear God! If not for this consolation of home and all that now came with it, where or what would he be?

Wandering the waysides, a raving maniac. . . .

"Now that you've rested, dearest . . ."

He knew that look. He knew that look as well as his own face in the mirror.

She leaned her head to one side in the way he'd never been able to resist. "You have rested, haven't you?"

"Well . . . " He didn't know which way to step.

"So here's my idea. You know how formal the dining room is."

"Formal?" The dining room she'd painted that wild, heedless pumpkin color?

"I mean, with the carved walnut highboy from one of the Georges, and those stately chairs with the brocade cushions—"

"Spit it out, Kavanagh."

"I want to move the dining table into the kitchen."

"Are you mad?" he blurted.

"Only for Thursday night," she said, cool as a cucumber. "You see, Pauline and Harley aren't dining room people, and neither is Louella, they'd be stiff as boards in that setting. They know our kitchen, it's like home to them, it's . . . "

He couldn't believe his ears.

" . . . it's what we have to *do,*" she said, looking him in the eye. "Pumpkin walls notwithstanding, the dining room seems filled with the presence of . . . old bishops!"

He had definitely, absolutely heard it all.

Dooley Barlowe was nowhere to be found, and Harley's strengths lay in other areas of endeavor. It was fish or cut bait.

They turned the mahogany table on its side and, by careful engineering, managed to get it through the kitchen door without slashing the inlaid medallion in the center.

He was certain this was a dream; convinced of it, actually.

That there was hardly room to stand at the stove and cook, once the table was in and upright, was no surprise at all. Could he open the oven door?

"Perfect!" she said, obviously elated. "We'll just use that plaid damask cloth of your mother's."

"That old cloth is worn as thin as a moth's wing. Hardly suitable," he said, feeling distinctly grumpy.

"I love old tablecloths!" she exclaimed.

He sighed. "What don't you love?"

"Grits without butter. Dust balls on ceiling fans. Grumpy husbands."

"Aha," he said, going down on his hands and knees to put a matchbook under a table leg.

At breakfast the next morning, he found the much-larger table with the worn cloth looking wonderful in the light that streamed through the open windows. She had filled a basket with roses from the side garden and wrapped the basket with tendrils of ivy. Her cranberry-colored glasses, already set out for the evening meal, caught the light and poured ribbons of warm color across the damask.

Lovely! he mused, careful not to say it aloud.

Finding Jessie had been uncannily simple, he thought, walking to the office with Barnabas on his red leash. He had given thanks for this miracle over and over again. The chase, after all, might have led anywhere—or nowhere. But they'd gone straight to the door and knocked, and she had answered.

He would thank Emma Newland from his very heart, he would do something special for her, but what? Emma loved earrings, the bigger, the better. He would buy her a pair of earrings to end all earrings! No fit compensation for what she had done, but a token, nonetheless, of their appreciation for her inspired and creative thinking.

He pushed open the office door as Snickers rushed past him, snarled hideously into his own dog's face, barked at an octave that could puncture eardrums, and peed on the front step—seemingly all at once.

Barnabas dug in and barked back, grievously insulted and totally astounded. From her desk, Emma shouted over the uproar, "I wouldn't bring him in here if I were you!"

The rector saw that urging his dog over the threshold would result in a savage engagement with this desperately overwrought creature, an engagement in which someone, possibly even himself, could be injured.

Furious, he turned on his heel and stomped toward the Grill, dragging his even more furious dog behind.

He blew past the windows of the Irish Shop, as Minnie Lomax finished dressing a mannequin whose arms, years earlier, had been mistakenly carted off with the trash.

"Can't even get in my own office!" he snorted. "Earrings, indeed!"

"Not again," sighed Minnie, watching him disappear up the street.

Passing the Collar Button, he was hailed by one of his parishioners, one who hadn't been even remotely amused by the announcement that he was going out to Canaan—or anywhere else.

"Father! You're looking well!"

Things were on an even keel again, thanks be to God. After all that uproar, most people seemed to have forgotten he was retiring, and it was business as usual.

He saw Dooley wheel out of the alley across the street and stop, looking both ways. As he glanced toward the monument, Jenny ran down the library steps, carrying a backpack. She saw Dooley and waved, and he pedaled toward her.

He didn't mean to stand there and watch, but he couldn't seem to turn away. Although Dooley's back was to him, he could see Jenny's face very clearly.

She was looking at The Local's summer help as if he had hung the moon.

"It's big doin's," Mule was saying to J.C. as the rector slid into the booth.

"What is?" he asked.

"Th' real estate market in this town. There's Lord's Chapel with that fancy outfit tryin' to hook Fernbank, Edith Mallory's Shoe Barn just went on the block, and I hear major money's lookin' at Sweet Stuff."

"Whose major money?"

"I don't know, Winnie's trying to sell it herself to save the commission, so I don't have a clue who th' prospect is. Meantime, some realtor from Lord knows where is handlin' th' Shoe Barn, Ron Malcolm's brokerin' for Lord's Chapel, and as for yours truly, I can't get a lead, much less a listin'."

"Water, water everywhere, and not a drop to drink," said J.C., hammering down on a vegetable plate with a side of country-style steak.

"Speakin' of th' Shoe Barn, what ever became of that witch on a broom?" asked Mule.

The rector's stomach churned at the mention of Edith Mallory, who owned the large Shoe Barn property. Her focused, unrelenting pursuit of him before he married Cynthia was something he'd finally managed to put out of his mind.

"You're ruinin' his appetite," said Percy, pulling up a stool. Percy had fought his own battle with the woman, who also owned the roof under which they were sitting—she'd tried to jack up the rent and blow him off before his lease expired. That's when the rector discovered that the floor beams of the Grill were rotten and nearly ready to bring the whole building down. Bottom line, Percy walked off with a new lease—on his terms, not hers.

Percy grinned at the rector. "Boys howdy, you fixed her good, you put her high-and-mighty butt through th' *grinder.*"

"Watch your language," said Velma, passing with a tray of ham sandwiches.

"And she ain't been back, neither! No, sirree bob! Hadn't had th' guts to show her face in this town since th' night you whittled her down to size."

J.C. used his favorite epithet for Percy's lessor.

"So when are you closing the deal on Fernbank?" asked Mule.

"I don't know. We'll consider their offer for thirty days."

Mule gave him an astounded look. "You want to sit around for thirty days with that white elephant eatin' out of your pocket?"

He felt suddenly angry, impelled to get up and leave. Chill, he told himself, using advice learned from Dooley Barlowe.

"Do you play softball?" he asked the *Muse* editor, who was busy chewing a mouthful.

"Prezure fum dinnity monce."

"Right. So how about you?" he asked Mule. "Scott Murphy wants to get up a game for the residents at Hope House. August tenth. We need players."

"I ain't too bad a catcher."

"You're on," he said. "Percy, I wouldn't mind having a cheeseburger all the way. With fries!"

Percy scratched his head. "Man! In sixteen years, you prob'ly ordered a cheeseburger twice. And never all the way."

"Life is short," he said, still feeling ticked. "And put a strip of bacon on it."

"How's it coming, buddy?"

"I got Tommy and his dad and Avis. Ol' Avis says he can hit a ball off th' field and clean over our house."

"No kidding? What do you think about Harley? Think he could do it?"

"Harley, don't . . . doesn't have any teeth."

"What do teeth have to do with playing softball?"

Dooley grinned. "We could see if he wants to."

They were setting the table as Cynthia busied herself at the stove. He was leaving in five minutes to pick up Pauline and the kids, and run up the hill for Louella.

He liked setting the table with Dooley. Bit by bit, little by little, Dooley was coming into his own, something was easier in his spirit. Pauline had been part of it, and Poo, and now Jessie. Each brought with them a portion of the healing that was making Dooley whole. He watched the boy place the knife on the left side of the plate, look at it for a moment, then remove it and place it on the right. Good fellow! He saw, too, the smile playing at the corners of Dooley's mouth, as if he were thinking of something that pleased him.

Dooley looked up and caught the rector's gaze. "What are you staring at?"

"You. I'm looking at how you've grown, and taking into account the fine job you're doing for Avis—and feeling how good it is to have you home."

Dooley colored slightly. He thought for a moment, then said, "So let me drive your car this weekend."

Blast if it didn't fly out of his mouth. "Consider it done!"

"Low-fat meat loaf, hot from the oven!" he announced, setting the sizzling platter on the table.

Louella wrinkled her nose. "Low-fat? Pass it on by, honey, you can *skip* this chile!"

"Don't skip this 'un," said Harley.

"He was only kidding," Cynthia declared. "In truth, it contains everything our doctors ever warned us about."

He saw the light in Pauline's face, the softness of expression as she looked upon her scrubbed and freckled children. Thanks be to God! Three out of five. . . .

He sat down, feeling expansive, and shook out one of the linen napkins left behind, he was amused to recall, by an old bishop who once lived here.

He waited until all hands were clasped, linking them together in a circle.

"Our God and our Father, we thank You!" he began.

"Thank You, Jesus!" boomed Louella in happy accord.

"We thank You with full hearts for this family gathered here tonight, and ask Your mercy and blessings upon all those who hunger, not only for sustenance, but for the joy, the peace, and the one true salvation which You, through Your Son, freely offer. . . ."

They had just said "Amen!" when the doorbell rang.

"I'll get it! And for heaven's sake, don't wait for me. Who on earth . . ." Cynthia trotted down the hall to the door.

Father Tim passed the platter to Louella and was starting the potatoes around when he heard Cynthia coming back to the kitchen, a heavy tread in her wake.

"You'll never guess who's here!" said his wife.

Buck Leeper stepped awkwardly into the doorway. In the small, close kitchen, his considerable presence was arresting.

Good Lord! Finding Buck a place to stay had gone completely out of his head. It hadn't entered his mind again since he called Mule. He was mortified.

He stood up, nearly knocking his chair to the floor.

"Good timing, Buck! We'll set another plate, there's more than plenty. Good to see you!" He pumped Buck's large, callused hand. "You remember Louella, Miss Sadie's friend and companion. And Dooley, you remember Dooley."

Buck nodded. "Dooley . . . "

"Hey."

"And this is Harley Welch, Harley lives with us, and there's Pauline, Dooley's mother—as I recall, you brought her a rose when she was in the hospital."

Buck flushed and glanced at the floor.

Rats. He shouldn't have said that. "This is Dooley's brother Poo, and this is Jessie, his sister."

Poobaw grinned at Buck.

"I'm hungry!" said Jessie.

"This is Buck Leeper, everybody, the man who did such a splendid job at Hope House. Can you believe he was born just up the road from me in Mississippi? Keep the potatoes passing, Dooley, there's the gravy. Ah, I see we forgot to set out the butter for the rolls! Buck, I hope you're hungry, we've got enough for an army. Here, take this chair, we're glad to have you back in Mitford! Louella, have you got room over there? Dooley, scoot closer to your sister. . . . "

What a workout. He was exhausted.

"Please sit down, Mr. Leeper," said his smiling wife, taking over.

Dooley had taken Poo and Jessie to his room; Cynthia, Louella, and Pauline were making tea and coffee; and the men had gone into the study.

"What it was," said Harley, "Junior liked t' run on dirt better'n asphalt, which is why they called 'im th' Mud Dobber. One ol' boy said how th' law was tryin' t' jump Junior, said Junior cut out th'ough a cornfield in a '58 Pontiac with th' winders down, said he plowed th'ough about a ten-acre stand of corn 'til he come out th' other side an' looked around an' 'is whole backseat was full of roastin' ears."

Buck laughed the laugh that sounded, to the rector, like a kettle boiling.

"Harley, you ought to tell Buck about your services as a mechanic. There'll be a lot of vehicles on the Lord's Chapel job."

"Yes, sir, I work on most anything with wheels, but I don't touch earth-movin' equipment. Course, I'm goin' t' be tied up pretty good, I'm cleanin' out 'is missus's basement and garage, then startin' on th' attic up yonder." Harley pointed to the ceiling. "Hit ain't been touched since one of them old bishops lived here."

Pauline came to the door of the study. Jessie was right, thought the rector, she's pretty.

"Excuse me . . ."

"Are you ready for us?" he asked.

She smiled. "Yes, sir. Cynthia said please come in."

Buck stood up from the wing chair, gazing at Pauline.

Father Tim saw that he appeared, for a moment, as eager and expectant as a boy.

"I couldn't do that," said Buck.

"Well, you see . . . the truth is, you have to. I looked for a place for you to live and ran into a dead end, and, well, first thing you know, I forgot to keep looking, and there you have it, you're stuck with us—the sheets are clean and the toilet flushes."

Buck laughed. At least he was laughing. . . .

He showed Buck to the guest room at the top of the stairs, where the superintendent's size somehow made the space much smaller. Buck chewed a toothpick, and carefully scanned the room and its adjoining bath.

"I believe you'll be comfortable, and don't worry about a thing. We'll have you out of here in no time, into a place of your own."

"If you're sure . . ."

"More than sure! Oh. By the way—do you play softball?"

Buck took the toothpick out of his mouth. "I've kicked more tail on a softball field than I ever kicked on a construction site. Before I hired on with Emil, I coached softball for a construction outfit in Tucson. The last couple of years I was there, we won every game, two seasons in a row."

Dooley suddenly appeared at the guest room door.

"I'm on his team," he said.

Buck offered to deliver Pauline and the children, while he took Louella to Hope House.

"I had a big time," said Louella, looking misty-eyed. "You and Miss Cynthia, you're family."

"Always will be," he said, meaning it.

At the door of Room Number One, he kissed her goodnight, loving the vaguely cinnamon smell of her cheek that had something of home in it.

Emma looked at him over her half-glasses.

"I guess you're hot about Snickers runnin' you off the other day."

"You might say that."

"How did I know you'd bring Barnabas to work? You never do, anymore. And besides, Snickers has never been here but twice, it seems like he *deserved* a turn. . . ."

"Ummm."

"Emily Hastings called, she said she has an axe to pick with you."

An axe to grind, a bone to pick, what difference did it make?

"Esther Bolick called, said things are looking up, Hessie Mayhew's th' biggest help since Santa's elves."

"Good."

"Hal Owen called, said it's time for Barnabas to get his shots."

"Right."

"Evie Adams called, guess what Miss Pattie's done now?"

"Can't guess," he said curtly, taking the cover off his Royal manual.

"She goes up and down the halls at Hope House, stealing the Jell-O off everybody's trays."

"That's a lot of Jell-O."

"Don't you care?"

"About what?"

"Stealing from old people."

"Miss Pattie is old people."

"So?"

He would like nothing better than to knock his secretary in the head. "So they have a staff of forty-plus at Hope House, I'm sure they can come up with some kind of curtailment of her behavior."

"Some kind of what?"

He didn't answer.

"How can you *use* that old thing?" she asked, glaring at his Royal manual.

He refused to respond.

There was a long silence as she peered at her computer monitor, and he rolled a sheet of paper into the carriage of his machine.

"So when are you going to give me some more names to find?" she inquired at last, trying to make up.

CHAPTER TWELVE

Waiting

"Will you do it?" he asked his wife.

"Of course I won't do it! It's not my job to do it."

"Deacons," he reminded her, "are supposed to do the dirty work."

"You amaze me, Timothy. You bury the dead, counsel the raving, and heedlessly pry into people's souls, yet when it comes to this . . ."

"I can't do it," he said.

"You have to do it."

Of course he had to do it. He knew that all along. He was only seeing how far he could get her to bend.

Not far.

"Dooley . . ."

He picked a piece of lint from his trousers. He stared at his right loafer, which appeared to have been licked by his dog, or possibly the twins, and after he had polished it only yesterday. . . .

"Yessir?"

Barnabas collapsed at his feet and yawned hugely, indicating his extreme boredom. Not a good sign.

"Well, Dooley . . . "

Dooley looked him squarely in the eye.

"It's about Jenny. I mean, it's not about Jenny, *exactly.* It's more indirectly than directly about Jenny, although we could leave her out of it altogether, actually. . . . "

"What about Jenny?"

"Like I said, it's not exactly about Jenny. It's more about . . . "

"About what?"

Had he seen this scenario in a movie? In a cartoon? He was old, he was retiring, he was out of here. He rose from the chair, then forced himself to sit again.

"It's about sex!" Good Lord, had he shouted?

"Sex?" Dooley's eyes were perfectly innocent. They might have been discussing Egyptology.

"Sex. Yes. You know." Hal Owen would have done this for him, Hal had raised a boy, why hadn't he thought of that before?

Dooley looked as if he might go to sleep on the footstool where he was sitting. "What about sex?"

"Well, for openers, what do you *know* about it? If you know anything at all, do you know what you *need* to know? And how do you *know* if you know what you need to know, that is to say, you can never be too *sure* that you know what you need to know, until—"

He actually felt a light spray as Dooley erupted with laughter in his very face. The boy grabbed his sides and threw back his head and hooted. Following that, he fell from the footstool onto the floor, where he rolled around in the fetal position, still clutching his sides and cackling like a hyena.

Father Tim had prayed for years to see Dooley Barlowe break down and really laugh. But this was ridiculous.

"When you're over your hysteria," he said, "we'll continue our discussion."

Not knowing what else to do, he examined his fingernails and tried to retain whatever dignity he'd come in here with.

"Good heavens, Timothy. You look awful! Is it done?"

"It's done."

"What did you tell him?"

"It's more like . . . what he told me."

"Really?" she said, amused. "And what did he tell you?"

"He knows it all."

"Most teenagers do. Figuratively speaking."

"And there's nothing to worry about, he's not even interested in *kissing* a girl."

Cynthia smiled patiently. "Right, darling," she said.

He wouldn't say a word to anybody about the two-thousand-dollar check Mack Stroupe had put in the collection plate on Sunday. He only hoped Emma would keep quiet about it.

On that score, at least, she was pretty dependable, though she'd been the one to tell him about the check. From the beginning, his instructions were, "Don't talk to me about the money, I don't need to know." As he'd often said, he didn't want to look into the faces of his parishioners and see dollar signs.

"Harley, ever played any softball?"

"No, sir, Rev'rend, I ain't been one t' play sports."

"Ah, well."

"I can run as good as th' next 'un, but hittin' and catchin' ain't my call."

The rector was peering into the tank of Harley's toilet, which had lately developed a tendency to run.

"I thank you f'r lookin' into my toilet, hit's bad t' keep me awake at night, settin' on th' other side of th' wall from m' head."

"It's old as Methuselah, but I think I can fix it."

"I want you t' let me fix somethin' f'r you, now, Rev'rend, I'm runnin' behind on that."

"Can't think of anything that needs it," he said, taking a wrench out of his tool kit.

"Maybe it's somethin' that don't need fixin', jis' tendin' to."

"Well, now." Wouldn't Dooley rather get his driving lesson from a bona fide race car mechanic than a preacher? He was sure Harley could make the lesson far more interesting, and even teach Dooley some professional safety tips from the track. Besides, even with the new torque in the Buick, Harley's truck would be a much more compelling vehicle to a fourteen-year-old boy.

"There is something you could do," he said, "if you're going to be around Saturday afternoon."

He could feel the bat in his hands. How many years had it been since he'd slammed a ball over the fence? Too many! He'd better get in shape, he thought, huffing up Old Church Lane in his running gear. Barnabas bounded along in front on the red leash.

Cooler today, but humid. Overcast skies, rain predicted. And didn't the garden need it? He'd worn a hood, just in case.

He wished he could get his wife to run with him, but no way. She was a slave to her drawing board, and lately looking the worse for it. The unofficial job of deacon, the job of organizing their jam-packed household, and the job of children's author/illustrator were wearing on her. And hadn't he helped put another portion on her already full plate by stowing Buck in the guest room?

He was frankly stumped about how to find housing for the superintendent, and with the attic job gearing up, Buck hardly had time to look around for himself. Maybe Scott Murphy would take in a boarder. . . .

He ran up to the low stone wall overlooking what he called the Land of Counterpane, and thumped down with Barnabas, panting.

There was the view that Louella and all the other residents farther along the hill could wake up and see every day of their lives. A feast for the eyes! He didn't get up here much, but when he did . . .

It was here, sitting on this wall, that he had known, at last, he *could* marry her, *must* marry her, and experienced the terrible anxiety of what it could mean to lose her. And it was here that he and Cynthia decided they both wanted to stay in Mitford when he retired.

Was he on time for the train? He looked at his watch. Another few minutes. Perhaps he would wait. Was life so all-fired urgent that he couldn't find five minutes to see a sight that always blessed and delighted him?

He was utterly alone in this place where, for all its singular beauty, few people ever came. It was set steeply above the village, it was off the beaten path, it was . . .

He heard the car below him, on the gravel road that ran along the side of the gorge and was seldom used except by a few local families.

He peered down and saw the black car pull to the shoulder of the road and stop. A man opened the driver's door and leaned out, looking around, then closed the door again. He was wearing a hat, a cap of some kind.

Mighty fine car to be out on Tucker's Mill Road, he thought, glancing again at his watch. Maybe the train would be early.

The pickup truck didn't move so slowly. He saw the plume of dust through the trees, then saw the blue truck screech to a stop beside the black car. A man jumped out, walked around the front of the truck, and stood for a moment by the car. It appeared that he was handed something through the car window.

The driver quickly got back in the truck, gunned the motor, and drove away, leaving a cloud of dust to settle over everything in its wake.

He watched as the car backed onto a narrow turnout, reversed direction, and rolled almost silently along Tucker's Mill.

By George, there was the train; he heard its horn faintly in the distance. Around the track it came, breaking through the trees by the red barn . . .

That scene he had just witnessed—had there been something strangely unsettling about it?

. . . then it huffed along the side of the open fields by the row of tiny houses and disappeared behind the trees.

He hadn't been able to tell from this vantage point what kind of car it was, but then, what difference did it make, anyway?

"Enough!" he said to his dog, and they bounded down the slope toward Baxter Park in the first drops of a misting rain.

Instead of turning into the park, he decided to run to the bottom of the hill and pop into Oxford Antiques. He'd inquire about Andrew and look for a present for Cynthia's birthday. He was barely getting in under the wire, considering that July 20 was two days hence.

Marcie Guthrie, Puny's mother-in-law and one of the mayor's five good-looking deluxe-size daughters, was reading a romance novel behind the cash register. "Father! Bring your dog in, but tell him to watch his tail!"

He tethered Barnabas to the leg of a heavy table. "Marcie, give me a few ideas for my wife's birthday, and I'll give you my eternal thanks."

"Well! Goodness! Let's see."

Cynthia was nearly as simple in her wants as he, thanks be to God. And she always seemed touchingly grateful when he gave her a gift.

"It must be something . . . wonderful," he said.

"I've got it!" she exclaimed. "The very thing! Come over here."

He trotted behind her to a gigantic walnut secretary with beveled glass doors. "There!" she said.

"Oh, no. That's far too large!"

"Not the secretary. The lap desk!"

Aha! Sitting next to the secretary on a Georgian buffet was a lap desk of exquisite proportions. That was it, all right, he knew it at once. A small lap desk with a pen drawer, a built-in inkstand, and a leather writing surface. Perfect!

He was afraid to ask.

"Four hundred and seventy-nine dollars!" she informed him. "It's not that old, just turn-of-the-century."

"Ummm."

"But for you, only four hundred. Andrew said whenever you come in to buy, to give you a special discount."

"Done!" he said, feeling a combination of vast relief, excitement over such a find, and momentary guilt for shelling out four hundred bucks. "I'll bring you a check in the morning. Will you wrap it?"

"Of course, and look at this little drawer. Lined with old Chinese tea paper, and here's one of the original pen nibs."

His guilt vanished at once.

"Have you heard about Andrew?" she asked.

"How is he, when is he coming home?"

"He doesn't know. It all sounds mysterious to me. He usually never stays away so long. But of course, it is his mama's hometown and he's probably visitin' cousins an' all. . . ."

"Probably. I seldom see him, but when he's not here, I miss him."

"He's called twice to see how business is. He sounds . . . different."

"Oh? How do you mean, different?"

"I mean, well, really *happy* or somethin'."

"Cousins can do that for you," he said, grinning. He suddenly realized he missed his own cousin, the only blood kin he had on the face of the earth. He'd call Walter tonight.

He put his hood up and sprinted along Main Street with his dog. May as well make one more stop, then head for home.

"Winnie?"

He parked Barnabas by the door and peered over the bakery counter.

"I'm comin'!" she said, breezing through the curtains that hid the bakery kitchen. "Father, I'm glad it's you!"

"I hear you got a bite!"

"Maybe a nibble, I don't know."

"What's the scoop?"

"Well, this real estate agency wants to know everything, so I sent 'em all the information, but nobody's turned up to see it yet."

"Terrific!" He didn't really think it was terrific, but what else could he say? "Who's the realtor?"

"Somebody named H. Tide Realty from—I forget, maybe Florida."

Florida again. "How do you feel about it?"

"After waitin' for somebody to be interested, when this finally happened, it kind of . . ."

"Kind of what?"

"Made me sick."

"I understand."

"You do?"

"Definitely."

She looked uncertain.

"You know we want you to stay. But if you decide to go, remember we'll stand behind that, too."

Winnie looked relieved. "Good! I don't know why, but I always feel better when I talk to you."

"Maybe it's the collar."

"Have a napoleon!" she urged, in her usual burst of generosity.

"Get thee behind me, absolutely not. But tell you what—I've got a houseful, so bag me a dozen donuts, Dooley will love that, and Harley, too, and let's see, a dozen oatmeal cookies . . . "

"Low-fat!" she said.

"Great. Now, what about that pie on the right? The one with the lattice top?"

"Cherry!"

"My favorite. Box it up!" Spending four hundred dollars had made him feel so good, he was trying to do it all over again.

Rhody Davis's leg was being amputated today.

He was praying for her this morning at first light, soon after reading Blaise Pascal. A young man who lived in the seventeenth century knew what Rhody Davis and several others on his current prayer list needed more than anything else.

"There is a God-shaped vacuum in the heart of every person," Pascal wrote. "And it can never be filled by any created thing. It can only be filled by God, made known through Jesus Christ."

Pascal had dazzled Europe with his sophisticated mathematical equations when he was only sixteen, and written about the God-shaped vacuum when he wasn't much older.

Nearly every day of his priesthood, Father Tim had seen what happened when people tried filling that vacuum with any created thing. Pauline had tried to fill it with alcohol. Rhody Davis had tried to fill it with someone else's child. . . .

He closed his eyes and prayed for all those who turn to the created thing, expecting much and receiving nothing.

The talk on the street was that Mack Stroupe was responsible for hooking the Fernbank sale, which would do wonders for Mitford's economy. Not only would such an enterprise draw people from other parts of the country, maybe even the world, but a major part of the staff would be locals. All that landscaping, all that maintenance, all that ocean of roofing and plumbing—and all that money flowing into Mitford pockets.

According to several reports, Fernbank was already sold, it was a done deal.

Mack Stroupe was looking good.

He called the mayor's office.

"She's not in," said the painfully shy Ernestine Ivory, who gave the mayor a hand two days a week.

"May I ask where she is?"

"Down at the school. She's doing a special program for the children."

"Children can't vote," he said.

"Yes, Father, that's true. But their parents can."

Bingo. "Tell her I called."

Harley nodded, looking sober.

"Don't let him talk you into anything you don't think is right . . . "

"Yes, sir."

" . . . or safe. Especially safe!"

"No, sir, I wouldn't."

The rector sighed and moved closer to Harley's oscillating fan.

"Now, don't you worry, Rev'rend. I'll watch after 'im like m' own young 'un."

"I know you will."

"Hit'll work some of th' juice out of 'im."

"Right."

"While I've got a educated man settin' here, I'd be beholden if you'd give me a little help with m' homework an' all."

"Your homework?"

"Lace has it in 'er head t' educate me, she's givin' me a test in a day or two."

"How do you feel about getting educated?"

"I've a good mind t' quit, but she's got 'er heart set on learnin' me somethin'. Lace has had a good bit of hard knocks, I don't want t' let 'er down."

"That's right. How can I help you?"

"Well, looky here. Sixty seventh-grade students toured th' Statue of Liberty in New York City. Two-thirds of 'em climbed to th' halfway point, and one-fourth of 'em was able t' climb all th' way to th' top. Now, th' remainin' group, they stayed down on th' base of th' pedestal, it says here. How many students didn't climb th' steps? I can't figger it t' save m' neck."

The rector mopped his brow. "Oh, boy."

"Here's another'n, this 'uns easier. The torch of th' Statue of Liberty is three hundred an' five foot from th' bottom of th' base. If th' pedestal on which th' statue rests is eighty-nine foot high, how high is th' base?"

"Let me go get a drink of water and I'll come back and see what I can do."

As he drank a glass of water at Harley's kitchen sink, he heard him muttering in the next room, "Elton washes winders at a office buildin'. Some offices has four winders and some has six . . . "

How did he get himself into these scrapes, anyway?

He kissed the nape of her neck, just under the ponytail she'd lately taken to sporting.

"Is there anything special you'd like to do for your birthday?" Please, Lord, don't let her say a domestic retreat. I don't have time, she doesn't have time, it can't happen.

She sighed. "We're both exhausted, dearest. Let's don't do any fancy dinners or tangos, let's get Chinese take-out from Wesley, lock our bedroom door, and just *be.*"

And what would their teeming household think about such a thing? Oh, well.

"I can handle that," he said, drawing her close.

"Ron, was there ever any discussion with Miami Development about Fernbank's apple orchard? There are a hundred and sixty-two trees up there, and all are still bearing."

"She mentioned the orchard the first time she was here. They'd tear it out. That's where most of the cottages will be built."

A small point, but it stung him. Those trees had dropped their fruit into any hand that passed, for years. They had filled Mitford's freezers with pies and cobblers, and crowded endless pantry shelves with sauce and jelly.

An even smaller point, perhaps, but he noticed that Ron had said "*will* be built."

A new day-care program was getting under way at Lord's Chapel as Buck Leeper's crew began their invasion of the attic.

Given that the only access to the attic was through the trapdoor over the pulpit, merely getting into the attic was a project.

Under Buck's supervision, the crew removed stones from the east wall, cut through studs, sheeting, and insulation, installed a new header and a sill, and created a double-door entrance. Until the outside steps could be built, ladders and scaffolding permitted the crew to haul up endless feet of lumber for classroom partitions and a restroom.

It was all going forward exactly as he expected: his very hair, what was left of it, was filled with a fine dust, as were the pews and all that lay below. Kneelers got their share, so that when parishioners wearing black arose from prayer, the fronts of skirts and trousers displayed a clear mark of piety.

Anybody else, he thought, would have retired and left the attic project to the next poor fellow, but he had celebrated and preached beneath the vast, empty loft for sixteen years, dreaming of the day they could fill it with children.

Yes, there'd be the patter of little feet above the heads of the congregation, though measures would be taken to muffle the sound considerably. In any case, it was a sound he'd be glad to hear.

Puny met him at the front door with Sissy on one hip and Sassy on the other.

"Father, I jis' don't think I can keep bringin' th' girls to work with me, even though I know how much it means to you to have 'em here." She looked unusually distressed.

He took Sissy and walked down the hall behind his house help.

"Ba!" said the happy twin, bashing him on the head with a plastic frying pan. "Ba!"

"That's what she calls you, did you know that?"

"Really?"

"That's your name. When I show her your wedding picture at home, she always says Ba!"

He felt honored. Ba! He'd never had another name before, except Father.

He sat down at the kitchen table and took a twin on either knee, which he immediately geared to the jiggling mode. "I know it's hard for you trying to work with two little ones. . . ."

"I cain't hardly get my work done anymore, but I hated to put 'em out to day care, they'll only be babies once, and I didn't want . . . " Puny looked close to tears. "I didn't want to miss that!"

"Of course not! I know it's a strain for you, but we'll work with you on it. We're pleased with all you do, Puny. You're the best, and always have been."

Her face brightened. He loved the look of the red-haired, freckle-faced Puny Guthrie, who was like blood kin, the closest thing to a daughter he'd ever have. Besides, who else would clean the mildew off his shoes, wipe *behind* the picture frames, mend his shirts, bake cornbread deserving of a blue ribbon, and keep the clothes closets looking like racks at a department store? What she was able to do, even with two toddlers in tow, was more than anyone else *would* do, he was sure of it.

"The church day care will be open next week. Hang on, and if you'd like to put them in for a day or two to see how it goes, well . . . "

"Thank you, Father! You're a wonderful granpaw. Would you mind holdin' 'em a minute while I run up and bring th' laundry down?"

"Mama, Mama!" yelled Sassy.

"Ba!" sighed Sissy, snuggling against him.

He nuzzled the two heads of tousled hair and thought that, all things considered, he was a very fortunate man. He needed challenges in his life . . . But wait a minute, did he need that warm, wet feeling spreading over his left knee?

He had showered, she had bathed in a tubful of scented bubbles; she had laid out his clean robe, he had plumped up the pillows behind her head; they had devoured their chicken with almonds, shrimp with lobster sauce, and two spring rolls.

"What's your fortune?" she asked, looking discontented with her own.

"I will uncover a surprise and receive great recognition."

"Poop, darling, you're always receiving great recognition. Everyone loves you, it's like being married to the Pope. Here's mine. 'Prepare for victory ahead!' Who writes this stuff?"

"Now," he urged.

"OK!"

"Close your eyes."

"I love this part," she said, putting her hands over her eyes. "Don't you want me to guess?"

"Absolutely not. We're going straight to the punch line."

He trotted to the closet, retrieved the box which Marcie had wrapped in the signature brown paper of Oxford Antiques, and thumped it on the bed next to his wife.

"OK. You can look."

"A box! I love boxes!"

"Heave to, Kavanagh."

She tore the raffia bow off, and the paper, and pulled back the tape on top of the box.

He helped remove the writing desk and set it on her lap.

"Timothy!" she whispered, unbelieving.

"Happy birthday, my love."

No two ways about it, he had hit a home run.

They lay in bed, holding each other, the room warmed by the glow of her bedside lamp.

"You're wonderful," he said, meaning it.

She smiled. "But I'm old!"

"Old? You? Never!"

"Just look at these crow's feet. . . ."

"I don't see any crow's feet," he said, kissing her crow's feet.

"Father, this is Lottie Greer."

Lottie Greer—the spinster sister of Absalom Greer, the elderly revival preacher who had loved Sadie Baxter . . .

"It's Absalom." He heard the fear in her voice.

"What is it?"

"It's pneumonia. He wants you to pray."

"I will, Miss Lottie, and others with me. Shall I come?"

"He said to just pray. There's fluid in his lungs."

He told her he was available anytime, that she should let him know what he could do. Then he called Cynthia and the all-church prayer chain.

He had come to love Absalom Greer. The eloquent, unschooled preacher had been a force in his life and those of countless others, including Pauline and Lace. He was among the last of the old warriors who fearlessly confronted the issue of sin, preached repentence and salvation, and pulled no punches when it came to the Gospel of Jesus Christ.

Bottom line, the old man was his brother. He would go out on Sunday.

What was he waiting for?

The question was unspoken, but every time he ran into a member of the vestry, he felt the weight of it. Thirty days? For what? Ingrid Swenson didn't look like somebody who could be bluffed into coughing up two ninety-five after she offered one ninety-eight. But the point was, the property was fully worth two ninety-five, and in his opinion, Miami Development was trying to steal it. To be bluffed themselves was a humiliation not to be suffered lightly.

The answer was, he didn't know what he was waiting for. He only knew that selling Fernbank to Miami Development was something that didn't feel right. Maybe it would feel right later—then again, later could be too late.

He hated this, he hated it.

He tried to act nonchalant by puttering in the side garden as they backed out of the driveway. Dooley was lit up like downtown Holding at Christmas, and Harley was generating a few kilowatts himself.

He looked up and waved, and they waved back.

Four-thirty. Dooley had left work a half hour early, and they had promised to be back at the rectory around six.

He looked through the hedge to the little yellow house. A window box needed fixing, the bolt had come loose and the box was hanging whomper-jawed under the studio window.

Too bad that little house didn't get more use. But one day . . .

He'd better get cracking and have Buck look it over, tell them what to do, help them get started with the additions and renovations. If there was ever a perfect opportunity to get top-drawer input, Buck Leeper was providing it.

He turned to go inside, then stopped and looked at the yellow house again.

By jing!

"But he'll never be there when you're there, because when you're working, he'll be working."

"That great big man in work boots and chinos stomping around and picking his teeth? In my *house*? Goodness, Timothy . . ."

"His company will pay the rent."

"Do you really think it would be all right?"

"Of course it would be all right. With Buck living there, he'd get to know exactly what we need and how to pull it off, and we wouldn't have to hire an architect, he can draw it up—*and* hire the crew."

She wrinkled her brow. "I don't know. . . ."

"It's a great opportunity."

"Consider it done, then," she said, quoting her priest.

At a quarter 'til six, he was standing at the front door, searching the street. Then he walked out and sat on the top step of the front porch.

"Come out with me," he called to Cynthia.

She came and sat with him and took his hand.

"I've been thinking," she said.

"Uh-oh."

"I want to play in that softball game."

"You do?"

"Yes. I can hit a ball. I can run. I can—"

"You can whistle."

She put her fingers to her mouth and blew out the windows.

"You're good, Kavanagh."

"So hire me."

"You're the only female."

"So far," she said. "I hear Adele Hogan wants to play."

"The police officer? J.C.'s wife?"

"She's the baddest softball player you ever want to see. At least, that's what she said."

"J.C. didn't mention that."

"He probably thought it was a guy's game."

"Well," he said, "it was. . . ."

At seven o'clock, he was ready to make a search of Farmer, which he and Harley had judged a perfect location for the driving lesson.

But maybe he should call the hospital first. He went to the study to find his cordless.

Cynthia wasn't worried at all. "Give them another fifteen minutes. It's a beautiful summer evening. . . ."

"Yes, but Harley knew the curfew, he wouldn't do this. I'm calling the police."

Barnabas let out a loud series of barks. As the rector raced up the front hall, he saw Harley standing on the porch. He looked like he'd gone a few rounds with a grizzly.

"Now, Rev'rend, I wouldn't want you t' worry. . . ."

He pushed open the screen door. "Where's Dooley? What happened?"

"Th' last thing I'd want t' do is cause you an' th' missus t' worry. . . ."

"Tell me, Harley."

"No, sir, worry's not what I'd ever want to' bring in y'r house. . . ."

"Dadgum it, Harley, I am worried, and will be 'til you tell me what the dickens went on."

"Well, sir, y'r boy's fine."

"Thank God."

"We crashed m' truck."

"No!"

"We did."

"Who did?"

"Now, I don't want you t' worry. . . ."

"Harley . . ."

"Y'r boy did."

"Good Lord!"

"But hit 'us my fault."

"You're sure he wasn't hurt? Where is he?"

"No, sir, he won't hurt, but m' truck was."

"How bad?"

"Tore up th' front an' all."

"Any damage to your engine?"

"Good as new."

"How'd you get home?"

"You mean after we hauled it out'n th' ditch?"

"Yes."

"You mean after we hauled it out'n th' ditch an' had t' help th' farmer chase 'is cow back to th' pasture?"

"What about a cow?"

"That's what come high-tailin' 'cross th' road an' made th' boy hit 'is brakes an' land in th' ditch."

"I see."

The rector glanced toward the driveway and saw Dooley peering at him around a bush.

"I'd sure hate f'r you t' worry. . . ."

Ha. Worry had just become his middle name—at least until Dooley Barlowe went back to school where somebody else could do the worrying.

CHAPTER THIRTEEN

The Fields Are White

He unlocked the office and went in, feeling an odd foreboding as he raised the windows and turned on the fan. Today's temperature was nearly what they'd had in Florida.

He heard the bathroom door creak on its hinges and wheeled around. Edith Mallory was standing there in something like a bathrobe.

"Edith . . . "

She smiled and moved toward him, smelling of the dark cigarettes she smoked, untying the sash. . . .

"Timothy!"

He opened his eyes and looked into the face of his anxious wife. "Thank God!" he said, sitting up.

"These dreams you've been having . . . it's scary. What was it this time?"

"I can't remember," he lied. Bathed with perspiration, he reached to the bedside table and turned the fan on high.

"That's better," she said. "Are you all right?"

"Yes. Sorry I woke you."

"Don't be. I remember the times I used to wake in the night with bad dreams and there was no one to turn to."

She switched off her bedside lamp and rolled over to him and held his hand.

Soon she was sleeping again, but he was not.

This wasn't the first dream he'd had of Edith Mallory. He distinctly remembered the one in which he was locked with her in the parish hall coat closet, pounding on the door for help.

While he was in Ireland a couple of years ago, her husband, Pat, had died of a heart attack. When the rector returned home, she had tried every strategy imaginable to seduce and dominate him. Always seeking to entice, always looking at him in a way that made him want to run for the hills, once detaining him overnight at Clear Day, her house on the highest ridge above Mitford.

He recalled the visit to Children's Hospital, where she gave $15,000 as imperiously as if it were a quarter million, and afterward being trapped in the backseat of her car while she stroked his leg. He had demanded that Ed Coffey, her chauffeur, stop the car, and had jumped from the Lincoln while it was still rolling.

After the miserable wrestling match over the Grill, which she had thumpingly lost, she had gone to Spain and, as far as he knew, hadn't returned—nor had she sent her annual contribution to Lord's Chapel. Fine. So be it. It was money he didn't want, though the finance chairman was certainly anxious about it.

He'd been able to put her out of his mind until someone at the Grill had brought up her name.

Suddenly he was feeling the old contamination he'd felt for years as her eyes roved over him in the pulpit. . . .

Blast.

He rolled on his side and tried to imagine the breeze from the fan was an island trade wind somewhere in the Indian Ocean.

"My wife's house is nonsmoking. Will that be a problem?" Buck Leeper was known for sucking down two packs of unfiltered Lucky Strikes a day.

"No problem. I've cut back, anyhow."

They walked into Cynthia's kitchen, where a faint breeze stirred through the open windows.

"The house is small, but—"

"There's something I've been wanting to tell you," said the superintendent.

There was a brief silence while Buck looked at his work boots, then directly at Father Tim.

"I appreciate what you did for me."

The rector nodded, silent.

"I could have killed you, slingin' th' furniture around like that."

He remembered Buck's drunken violence at Tanner Cottage during the construction of Hope House. Unable to flee, he had sat, praying, as Buck's torrential anger poured forth for hours.

"Sorry," Buck said, hoarse with feeling.

"Don't even think about it." He hadn't expected an apology for that long-ago night, but it felt better to have it, somehow. He knew instinctively that Buck didn't want to say anything more.

"Well . . . you can see how cramped the house is. Built for one, really."

"What are you lookin' to do?"

"We'd like to knock out this rear wall and add a large studio with a bank of windows, maybe French doors leading to a patio, perhaps connecting with a two-car garage and extra storage. I know you can help us figure it out.

"Also, we thought it would be good to have a fireplace at that end, possibly of native stone, with bookshelves on either side. Oh, and hardwood floors, of course, with another bathroom adjoining the studio. The only bathroom is upstairs, which reminds me . . . "

This was exciting. His blood was up for it.

". . . we're thinking of widening the stairway, if possible, and building storage closets on the landing, but I'm getting ahead of myself. Since we're in the kitchen, what would you think about a cooking island, and bay windows looking out to the hedge?"

Buck took the toothpick from his mouth and stared around the small room. "You want to live in it a year from now?"

"Right!"

"You'll have to haul ass," he said.

Mack Struope
Already Working For
Improved Economy

"I'm not going to wait til I'm elected to work hard for Mitford," says mahoral candidate MackStrouope at his downtown campaign headquarters. "I'm already working hard to bring in new growth and development.

"For example, I recommended the fine property of Sweet Stuff Bakery to one real estate company, and was able to get another realtor to look at Fernbank. When the Fernbank deal goes through, it will put big dollars in everybody's pockets.

"I'm not one to say if it ain't broke, don't fix it. I say let's make a good thing better."

Strouple is running against mayoral incumbent, Esther Cunninghanm, who has seen eight terms in local office, with three of those terms unopposed.

Stroupe's free Saturday barbecues will be held until election week at his campaign headquarters on Main Street.

ThisSaturdzy will feature the live country music of everybody's favorit, the Wesley Washtub Band. All are invited.

He hadn't missed Mack's terminology, "*when* the Fernbank deal goes through . . ."

Part of Miss Sadie's letter had been running through his mind like a chanted refrain.

"I leave Fernbank to supply any requirements of Hope House," she had written. "Do with it what you will, but please treat it kindly."

Treat it kindly.

Was selling it for half its worth treating it kindly? All her adult life, Sadie Baxter had done without, so that her mother's and father's money could be invested wisely. Hadn't her penury and smart management provided a five-million-dollar budget for Hope House, and a home for forty people who needed one?

Who was he to swallow down an arrogant offer that robbed the coffers of a deserving institution?

But then, what was the alternative?

Back and forth, back and forth—always the same questions, and never any answers. At least, not as far as he was concerned.

He couldn't deal with this any longer.

He got up from the sofa and knelt by his desk in the quiet study.

"Lord, Miss Sadie's house belongs to You, she told me that several times. You know I've got a real problem here."

He paused. "Actually, You've got it, because I'm giving it to You right now, free and clear. I'll do my part, just show me what it is. In Jesus' name, amen."

"Poached, whole wheat, no grits," he told Velma, as he walked to the rear booth and slid in.

"J.C., I've got a story idea for you."

"Don't give me any small-town, feel-good stuff," snapped the editor. "I've had enough of that to choke a horse."

"I hear political candidates have to fill out a form that discloses the amount of a campaign contribution and who made it. I'm also told that anyone, including media, can ask to see that form."

He could tell J.C. was getting the message, and didn't particularly like it, either. "So why don't you get Mack to show it to you?" asked the editor.

"So why don't *you*?" asked the rector.

"Father?"

It was Lottie Greer. Years of experience told him all he needed to know.

"I'm on my way," he said.

He parked behind a long line of cars and pickup trucks on the country road, and walked to Greer's Store.

Men were congregated on the porch, dressed in overalls and work clothes; many were smoking, and all talked in undertones.

They nodded to him as he came up the steps. He heard the faint singing inside.

"How is he?" he asked an elderly man sitting on a bench.

"Bad off, Preacher."

He opened the fragile screen door that had slapped behind him on happier occasions, and entered the store that resembled a room in a Rembrandt canvas. The aged floors and burnished wood, the low wattage in the bulbs, the fading afternoon light through the windows—it was beautiful; saintly, somehow, more a church than a store. But then, hadn't Absalom Greer preached the gospel in this place for nearly seventy years?

Several women sat around the cold summer stove, talking in low voices. One sang softly with the chorus inside. ". . . *that calls me from a world of care, and bids me at my Father's throne, make all my wants and wishes known . . .*"

Three men in ill-fitting dark suits met him at the door of the rooms where Absalom lived with his sister, Lottie. All were clutching Bibles, and all spoke or nodded as if they knew him.

Lottie Greer sat in the chair by the fireplace, where she always implored him to sit when he visited.

"Miss Lottie . . ."

She looked up, gaunt and shockingly frail, her cane across her knees. "He said yesterday he wanted to see you, Father. He asked to die at home, the old way."

He put his hand on her shoulder.

"He's lingered on," she murmured, lowering her head. "It's been hard."

"Yes," he said. "I understand." And he did. His mother had lingered, fighting the good fight.

Seven or eight men were gathered outside Absalom's open bedroom door, and quietly, but forcefully, singing the old hymn the rector had known since a child.

"He wanted us to sing his favorites," said one of the men with a Bible. "Join in, if you take a notion. Th' doctor's with 'im right now, looks like he's in an' out of knowin' where he's at."

"Lena, get the Father something," said Lottie.

"I've just poured him a glass of tea, Miss Lottie. I hope you like it sweet," she said, placing the icy glass in his hand.

"Oh, I do. Thank you."

"And some cake, you'll want some cake," she said, eager to please.

"Thank you, not now."

"You help yourself, then, anytime," she said, pointing to the kitchen table, which was laden with food. "It's to eat, not throw out." She colored slightly, and made a faint curtsy. "I hope you'll try my pineapple upside down, it's over by the sink."

"Sing up!" said one of the chorus. "Brother Greer likes it loud."

"Jesus, lover of my soul . . . " they began, limning the words of Charles Wesley.

He joined in.

. . . Let me to Thy bosom fly,
While the nearer waters roll,
While the tempest still is high:
Hide me, O my Savior hide,
Till the storm of life is past;
Safe into the haven guide,
O receive my soul at last.

Other refuge have I none;
Hangs my helpless soul on Thee;
Leave, O leave me not alone,
Still support and comfort me . . .

He felt as if he were a child again, in his mother's Mississippi Baptist church, where his own grandfather once preached. A kind of joy was rising in him, but how could it not? Absalom Greer would soon pass safely into the haven. . . .

Someone who appeared to be the doctor stepped out of Absalom's room. "Go in, Father," he said. "He's asked for you."

The bed on the other side of the spartan room seemed far away. It was as if he treaded water to reach it.

He heard the dense rattle in Absalom's chest.

"Brother Timothy, is that you?" The old man kept his filmy blue eyes fixed on the ceiling.

"It is."

"I've been lookin' for you."

Over the years, he'd seen it—as death drew near, the skin had a way of connecting with the bones, of fusing into a kind of cold marble that was at once terrible and beautiful.

"The Lord's given me a truth for you," said Absalom. It was as if each word were delicately formed, so it would move through the maze of the rattle and come forth whole and lucid.

Father Tim bent closer. "I'm listening, my Brother."

"The fields are white. . . . "

Jesus had said it to the disciples. . . .

Then Absalom turned his head and looked past him, his face growing suffused with a kind of joy. "Glory, glory . . . there they are . . . I knew they'd come again. . . . "

The rector's heart raced with feeling—he knew instinctively that Absalom Greer was seeing the angels, the angels he'd once seen as a young boy, swarming around his mother and baby sister in the next room.

The old preacher lifted his trembling hands above the coverlet, issuing a last pastoral command.

The men stopped singing. The talking in the kitchen ceased.

Lottie came into the room, leaning on her cane. "Is it his angels?" she whispered.

"I believe so," he said.

He took the back roads, wanting to see pastures and open fields, wanting a span of silence between dying and living.

Perhaps Sadie Baxter had been among the first to greet Absalom, to bestow some heavenly welcome upon one to whom God would surely say, "Well done, good and faithful servant."

He would miss Absalom Greer. It had been a privilege to know him. He was the last of a breed, willing, like Saint Paul, to be "a fool for Christ."

In the fields, Queen of the Meadow towered over goldenrod and fleabane, over milkweed and wild blue aster. Beautiful, but dry. They needed rain. He wished he had his dog with him, licking up the windows to a fare-thee-well.

He made a turn onto the state highway and spoke it aloud: "The fields are white. . . ."

"Lift up your eyes, and look on the fields," Jesus had said to his disciples, "for they are white already to harvest."

The standing fields were the legions who hadn't filled their God-vacuum with the One who was born to fill it; the standing fields were those who waited for someone to reach out and speak the truth, and tell them how they might be saved.

He had received Absalom's message as a reminder, and did not take it lightly.

He glanced at the gas gauge. Nearly empty.

There was a little grocery store and service station up the road. He'd once stopped there for a pack of Nabs and a Cheerwine.

It came up sooner than he expected. He wheeled in and parked beside the building, then got the key from the store owner and walked around and unlocked the restroom. First things first.

Coming out of the restroom, he saw the black Lincoln pull off the road and ease past the gas pumps.

He stepped back instinctively, and watched Ed Coffey get out of the Lincoln and go into the station.

Ed Coffey. Edith Mallory's chauffeur. The one who was driving when he leaped from the moving car in the Shoe Barn parking lot, the one who'd driven him home after the gruesome, rain-drenched night at Clear Day.

Ed wasn't wearing his uniform. The rector didn't think he'd ever seen Ed out of uniform since Pat Mallory died.

He stood by the building, wondering why he didn't step forward and speak to the man, a Mitford native who had always seemed a decent fellow, though clearly snared by the lure of Mallory money. Hadn't Ed looked at him a couple of times as if to say, I don't want to do this, I know better, but it's too late?

Ed left the station with a bulging paper sack in his arm, which he put in the trunk. Then he got in the car and quietly pulled onto the road, headed south.

A new Lincoln, clearly, not the old model Edith had kept around after Pat's death. And this one had dark windows. He despised dark windows in a car. . . .

So Edith was back in Mitford. He could probably expect to see her at Lord's Chapel. Edith on the gospel side, Mack Stroupe on the epistle side.

What happened when clergy looked into their congregations, only to see a growing number of people whose motives they distrusted, and whose spirits made their own feel anxious and uneasy?

He noticed that a new battery of yard signs had gone up, along with the general clutter.

We're stickin' with Esther
BILL AND ARLENE

We're stickin' with Esther
Ralph And Fay Lewis

OUR BANE WILL
BE YOUR BLESSING
Best Sale Ever!
Oct. 4, from 10 a.m.
After Work Supper
6:00 p.m.

MACK MEANS
MONEY IN
MITFORD POCKETS.
$Mack for Mayor$

VOTE YOUR VALUES
Esther for Mayor

Play Ball!
Come one, come all
Baxter Field, August 10
HOTDOGS $1

"Seventy-five bucks from the glove factory, a thousand from Lee-land Mining Company—which should be no surprise, that's his fourth cousin. Five hundred from the canning plant, who'd also like to see some more development in these parts, ten bucks from Lew Boyd's cousin, fifteen from Henry Watts, blah, blah, blah—exactly what you'd expect." J.C. looked pleased with himself. "You can get off your high horse, buddyroe."

Why pursue it? "So, tell me, have you seen Ed Coffey around lately?"

"Ed Coffey? If he's around, so's your old girlfriend."

He felt as if he'd been dashed with cold water. "You might rephrase that," he said.

"You're plenty touchy," snapped the editor.

"I learned it from you," he replied.

Lace Turner was visiting Harley and had come up to the kitchen to have a piece of cake with Cynthia. He was taking the pitcher of tea out of the refrigerator when they heard a light knock at the door.

Jenny stood outside, peering through the screen. "Hello! Is Dooley home?"

Barnabas skidded into the kitchen, barking.

"He ain't here!" Lace said.

"Why, Lace!" said Cynthia. "He *is* here. Won't you come in, Jenny?"

"No ma'am. I just brought Dooley this."

Cynthia opened the screen door and took the parcel. "We're having cake, it's chocolate—"

"No, ma'am, I can't. Thank you." She ran down the steps and across the yard.

Cynthia looked at Lace. "Why did you lie?"

"I didn't know he was here."

"But you did. You saw him come in ten minutes ago. So, that's two lies." His wife never pulled punches.

Lace shrugged.

"I'm not going to preach you a sermon," said Cynthia, "but I want you to know something. I'm disappointed that you'd lie to her and to me. You're better than that."

Lace stared at the half-eaten cake on her plate. "I hate that girl."

"Why?"

"She thinks she's so smart, so pretty, so . . . *fine.*" Lace spit the word.

"Lace, look at me, please." Lace looked at her. "You're smart. You're pretty. You're—"

"I ain't! I ain't nothin'!" She stood up from the table, weeping, and ran down the basement stairs.

"So," said his wife, looking grim. "She's crying—it's what Olivia's been hoping for."

"That's good news," he said, putting his arm around her shoulders.

She smiled weakly. "Yes, but sometimes even good news feels bad."

Esther Bolick picked up on the first ring.

"So, Esther, how's it coming?"

"You'll never believe it—we got an armoire from Marie Sanders!"

If he had anything to do with it, Esther would have two armoires. "How's Hessie working out for you?"

"A saint, Hessie's a saint. She's heading up the After Work Sale, includin' th' supper."

"Wow."

"Did you know Hessie and I are wearin' beepers? I feel like Dick Tracy."

"I've heard everything."

"Course, th' polyester and double-knit is still pourin' in."

"Find me an orange leisure suit with stitched lapels, I'll pay big money."

"Too late, Mule Skinner already spoke for it."

"Oh, well."

"But the quality's picking up, we just got a Hoover vacuum cleaner and a whole set of Hummel figurines. Oh, and a mink jacket, th' hole's where you can't even see it."

"How's Gene?"

"Suing for divorce."

"It could be worse," he said.

Esther laughed heartily. How he loved hearing a Bane chairperson laugh. A minor miracle!

He was putting the receiver on the hook when it came to him out of left field.

Land of Counterpane. Black car, blue pickup.

Surely not . . .

And the black car that had eased around the monument at two in the morning, so quiet he scarcely heard the engine . . .

But that was weeks ago. That was the evening of his birthday, which was well over a month back, maybe five or six weeks. If Edith was around, why hadn't anyone seen her?

Was Ed Coffey steering clear of Mitford, buying their groceries at country stores, keeping to the back roads, going ununiformed to attract less attention?

He'd drive by Clear Day and see what was going on, but there wasn't any way to spot the house, since it sat a half mile beyond a locked electronic gate. That gate had been locked even on evenings when Edith invited the vestry to meet at her house. Guests were required to punch a password into a black box at the entrance.

There was a churning sensation in his stomach.

Not knowing what else to do, he went into the office bathroom and stuck his finger for a glucometer check. In his opinion, the glucometer was a decided improvement over peeing on a strip to check his sugar.

One twenty-four. Not bad.

He made a call from the office, still knowing the number by heart, and went home and got his old gardening hat from the closet shelf.

Rifling through the chest of drawers, he found the sunglasses he seldom wore because someone said they made him look like a housefly.

He put on the hat and glasses as he went down the stairs, thinking he'd check himself out in the kitchen mirror.

"Lord God!" shrieked Puny, standing frozen at the foot of the stairs. "You like to scared me to death!"

Hearing their mother's alarm, both babies set up an earsplitting wail in the kitchen.

He tried bouncing their car seats, squeaking a rubber duck, making a face, and barking like a dog, but they were inconsolable, and he was out of there.

"This Cessna 152 don't make as much noise as m' little ragwing," shouted Omer.

The rector was holding up pretty well, all things considered. He had skipped lunch, knowing he'd be airborne, had driven twenty-five miles to the airstrip, and here he was, skimming above the treetops with the mayor's brother-in-law in a borrowed plane, wearing a decrepit garden hat and shades.

Father Roland, who occasionally wrote from the wilds of Canada, was totally wrong to think he was having all the fun, celebrating the Eucharist in crude forest huts and being chased by a bull moose. Mitford had its grand adventures, too. You just had to go looking for—

"Holy smoke, Omer!"

Omer flashed his piano-key grin at the rector, who was only momentarily hanging upside down.

"That's what you call a one-G maneuver."

"No more, thanks!" His face had been green twice in only a few weeks.

"OK, I'll fly steady," yelled his pilot. "How low d'you think you'll want to go?"

"Low enough to see what's going on."

"I can take you down to two hundred feet, how's that?"

He swallowed hard. "Fine."

"You sure don't look like yourself in that getup," Omer shouted.

"Good!" he shouted back.

They saw the ridge looming ahead, the ridge from which Clear Day could see forever, but could not be seen.

"Here she comes!" Omer said. Father Tim pulled the brim of the hat farther down and adjusted the glasses.

What could have been a small landing strip emerged from the trees. It was the shake roof that covered the much-talked-about eight thousand square feet of living space, with its vast expanse of driveway and parking area to the left.

Bingo.

A blue pickup truck was parked next to a black car. And there, on the uncovered terrace, standing by the striped umbrellas, were two people.

"Circle back!" he shouted to his pilot.

He wanted to be dead sure.

Omer circled back and buzzed the house. The man and woman on the terrace looked up angrily as he looked down.

Then the blue Cessna roared over the quaking treetops and across the gorge.

Omer glanced at him and winked.

Edith Mallory was not touring Spain or France or Malaysia or any of her other haunts, and neither was she living in her sprawling home in Florida.

She was living in Mitford, at Clear Day, and masterminding the political career of Mack Stroupe.

CHAPTER FOURTEEN

Play Ball

On the morning of the game at Baxter Field, Velma Mosely had a change of heart and started chopping onions.

This, she told herself, would absolutely, positively be her last pot of homemade chili.

❧

"Listen up!"

Buck Leeper looked ten feet tall as he stood in the dugout before the Mitford Reds.

"We're not here to fool around," said the team manager, "we're here to win. Got it?"

"Got it!" said his players, who were wearing red-dyed T-shirts and ball caps advertising The Local.

It was twenty minutes before game time, and the rector felt his adrenaline pumping like oil through a Texas derrick.

"Father, you're th' team captain, and I'm lookin' to you to be th' coach on th' field. Keep 'em pepped up and give 'em advice when they need it—your job is to call the shots." Buck looked him in the eye. "I know you can do it."

Could he do it? He had prayed about this softball game as if it were life or death, instead of good, clean fun on a Saturday afternoon. Surely the three practice games, which had gone pretty well, would count for something.

Buck took a Lucky Strike out of his shirt pocket and paced in front of them. "Dooley, you're my first batter. I've watched you get ready for today's game, and you're always hustlin', always quick on your feet. I want you to wait on the pitch that's yours, got it?"

"Got it," said Dooley.

"We want you on that base."

"Yes, sir."

"Adele, you're plenty quick and sure-handed, you'll play first base. I'm hittin' you in th' second slot. When Dooley gets on, advance th' runner at any cost. We've got to get somebody in scoring position."

Adele socked her right fist into her glove.

Buck laughed his water-boiling-in-a-kettle laugh. "We want those turkeys to play with their backs to the wall. Right?"

"Right!" said his team.

"Avis, you're my first power hitter. I want you to slam it clear to Wesley. Father, you're my cleanup batter—stay strong and quick, and remember to keep your shoulders straight."

Buck might have been commandeering a crew of backhoe operators in a thirty-foot excavation.

"Mrs. Kavanagh—"

"Cynthia," she said.

"Cynthia, you're battin' in my number five spot. I want you to dig in and crush that ball. As the catcher, I want you to call our pitches—look at how they're standin', check out their feet. Bottom line, be alert at all times."

"You got it, Coach."

Buck completed the lineup with Hal Owen as second baseman and Mule Skinner, Jena Ivey, Pauline Barlowe, and Lew Boyd in the outfield.

"I've been watchin' th' other team," said Buck, "and we're better than they are. We can do the job. I want you to give it a hundred percent, understand? Not eighty-five, not ninety-five—a *hundred.*"

He looked at every earnest face, rolling the unlit cigarette between his fingers. "Father, you want to pray?"

"He wants to!" said Dooley.

After the prayer, they scrambled to their feet and trooped past the concession stand. At that moment, the rector was certain he experienced a brief out-of-body reverie. He saw their team charging out on the field, and there he was in the middle of the fray, wearing, for Pete's sake, his green Pentecost vestments.

"Man!" exclaimed Dooley.

The stands were full, people were sitting on the grass, and the smell of hotdogs and chili wafted through the humid summer air.

Tommy's dad, who was the plate umpire, looked at the coin he'd just flipped. The Mitford Reds were the home team.

The rector scanned the crowd, just as he always did at Lord's Chapel.

The residents of Hope House were lined up in wheelchairs and seated on the front bleachers, looking expectant.

There was Mack Stroupe, standing with one foot on a bleacher and a cigarette in his mouth, and over to the right, Harley and Lace. He spotted Fancy Skinner and Uncle Billy and Miss Rose and Coot and Omer, and about midway up, Tommy, who had hurt his leg and couldn't play. He noted that quite a few sported a strawberry sucker stuck in their jaw, evidence that the mayor had doled out her customary campaign favors.

From the front row, where she sat with Russell Jacks and Betty Craig, Jessie waved to the field with both hands.

"Ladies and gentlemen," announced town councilman, Linder Hayes, "it is my immense privilege to introduce Esther Cunningham, our beloved mayor, who for sixteen years and eight great terms in office has diligently helped Mitford take care of its own! Your Honor, you are hereby officially invited to . . . *throw out the first ball.*"

"Burn it in, Esther!" somebody yelled.

The other umpire ran a ball to the mayor, who stood proudly in the dignitaries section, cheek by jowl with the county sheriff.

At this, the *Muse* editor bounded from the concession stand to the bleachers and skidded to a stop about a yard from the mayor. He dropped to his knees and pointed the Nikon upward.

"Dadgum it," hissed the mayor, "don't shoot from down there, it gives me three double chins!"

"And behind the plate," boomed Linder Hayes, "our esteemed police chief and vigilant overseer of law and order, Mr. Rodney Underwood!"

Applause. Hoots. Whistles. Rodney adjusted his holster belt and waved to the crowd with a gloved hand.

"Hey, Esther, smoke it in there!"

The mayor threw back her head, circled her arm like a prop on a P-51, and let the ball fly.

"*Stee-rike* one!" said the umpire.

"Oh, *please,*" said Cynthia, who was perspiring from infield practice.

"What is it?" whispered the rector.

"I have to use the port-a-john."

"It's your nerves," declared her husband, who appeared to know.

"Take the field!" yelled Buck.

The players sprinted to their positions. Then, the home-plate ump took a deep breath, pointed at the pitcher, and shouted what they'd all been waiting to hear.

"Play ball!"

The Reds' batboy, Poo Barlowe, passed his brother a bat which he had personally inscribed with the name *Dools* and a zigzag flash of lightning. He had rendered this personal I.D. with a red ballpoint pen, bearing down hard and repeatedly until it appeared etched into the wood.

Dooley took a couple of warm-up swings, then stepped into the batter's box. He gripped the bat, positioned his feet, and waited for the pitch.

A high, looping pitch barely missed the strike zone.

"Ball one!"

The second pitch came in chest-high, as Dooley tightened his grip, took a hefty swing, and connected. *Crack!* It was the first ball hitting the bat for the newly formed Mitford Reds; the sound seemed to reverberate into the stands.

"Go, buddy!"

Dooley streaked to first base, his long legs eating the distance, and blew past it to second as the crowd cheered. He slid into second a heartbeat ahead of the ball that socked into Scott Murphy's glove.

"Ride 'em, cowboy!" warbled Miss Pattie, who believed herself to be at a rodeo.

The game was definitely off to a good start.

"Mama!"

Fancy Skinner waved to her mother, who was shading her eyes and peering into the stands. "I'm up here!"

Fancy was wearing shocking pink tights and a matching tunic, and stood out so vividly from the crowd that her mother recognized her at once and made the climb to the fifth row, carrying a knitting bag with the beginnings of an afghan.

"I declare," said Fancy, "I hardly knew that was you, don't you just love bein' blond, didn't I tell you it would be more fun? I mean, look at you, out at a softball game instead of sittin' home watchin' th' Wheel or whatever. And oh, my lord, what're you wearin', I can't believe it, a Dale Jarrett T-shirt, aren't you th' cat's pajamas, you look a hundred years younger!

"Next, you might want to lose some weight, if you don't mind my sayin' so, around forty pounds seems right to me, it would take a strain off your heart. Lord have mercy, would you look at that, he backed th' right fielder clean to th' fence. *Hey, ump, open your eyes, I thought only horses went to sleep standin' up!*

"Oh, shoot, I forgot about your hearin' aid bein' so sensitive, was that me that made it go off? It sounds like a burglar alarm, I thought th' old one was better, here, have some gum, it's sugarless. Look! There he is, there's Mule, mama, see? Th' one in the grass over yonder, idn't he cute, *Mule, honey, we're up here, look up here, sweetie,* oh mercy, the ball like to knocked his head off. *Pay attention to what you're doin', Mule!*

"Mama, you want a hotdog? I'll get us one at th' end of fifth innin', Velma made th' chili. I didn't say it's chilly, I said Velma—mama, are you sure that hearin' aid works right, it seems like th' old one did better, and look at what you paid for it, an arm and a leg, you want relish? I can't hardly eat relish, it gives me sour stomach.

"How in th' world you can knit and watch a ballgame is beyond me, I have to concentrate. See there, that's th' preacher Mule hangs out with at the Grill, th' one I gave a mask to th' day you got a perm, you remember, I can't tell whether he tries to hit a ball or club it to death. That's his wife on third base, I think she bleaches with a cap, I never heard of a preacher's wife playin' softball, times sure have changed, our preacher's wife leads th' choir and volunteers at th' hospital.

"Go get 'em, Avis! Hit it outta there! I wonder why Avis idn't married, I think he likes summer squash better than women, but it's important to really like your work. Lord, he sent that ball to th' moon! Look, Mama, right over yonder, see that man eyeballin' you? So what if he's younger, that's th' goin' thing these days, I told you blondes have more fun. Whoa, did you see that, he winked at you, well, maybe he got somethin' in his eye. *Hey, ump, pitcher's off th' plate, how thick are your glasses?*

"That red-headed kid, that's Dooley, he's sort of th' preacher's boy, he's a real slugger and he can run, too. Was that a spitball, Mama, did it look like a spitball to you? *Spitball! Spitball!* Who is that umpire, anyway, he's blind as a bat and deaf as a tater, oops, I better go down an' get in line, did you say you want relish?"

Ben Isaac Berman, whose family had brought him to Hope House all the way from Decatur, Illinois, was liking this ball game better than anything he'd done since coming to Mitford in July.

He liked the fresh air, the shouting, the tumult—even the heat was a *makhyeh*—though he didn't like the way his hotdog had landed in his lap, requiring two Hope House attendants to clean it up. What he couldn't figure was how chili had somehow made its way into one of his pants cuffs.

He felt like a *shlimazel* for not having better control of his limbs. But then, there was Miss Pattie sitting right next to him, who couldn't control a thought in her head, God forbid it should happen to him.

He also liked the game because it reminded him of his boyhood, which was as vivid in his recall as if he had lived it last week.

Take that boy at second base, that red-haired kid who could run like the wind. That was the kind of kid he'd been, that was the kind of kid he still was, deep down where nobody else had ever seen or ever would, not even his wife, blessed be her memory. Even he forgot about the kid living inside him, until he came out to a game like this and smelled the mountain air and heard the crack of the bat—that was when he began to feel his own legs churning, flying around to the bases and tearing up the dirt as he slid into home. . . .

At the bottom of the seventh inning, the score was 10–10.

"It's our bat and we've got three outs," said the rector. "We don't want any extra innings, so let's finish now and go home winners."

His shirt was sticking to him. He felt like he'd been rode hard and put up wet, as Tommy Noles used to say.

He watched as Mule Skinner stepped up to bat.

The ball came in high.

"Ball one!"

Mule swung at the next pitch and cracked it over second base into center field. The rector was amazed at Mule's speed as he sprinted to first. This game would be fodder for the Grill regulars 'til kingdom come.

After Jena Ivey made the first out of the inning, it was Pauline Barlowe's turn to bat.

She looked confident, he thought. In fact, she'd made a pretty good showing all afternoon, but had a tendency to waffle, to be strong one minute and lose it the next.

She took a couple of pitches, and slammed a hit to second base. Dadgum, a double play! But the second baseman kicked the ball, and all runners were safe.

"Time out!" yelled Buck, striding onto the field.

"OK, Pitch," he said to Lew Boyd, "you've been a defensive star all day, I want you to use that bat and get the big hit. Or give me a fly ball to the outfield to advance the runners."

"I'm gonna give you premium unleaded on this 'un."

The first pitch came down the middle.

"Strike one!"

Lew hit the next pitch into right field, where the outfielder nailed it and threw it to third. The runners held.

Two outs.

Dooley hurried into the batter's box and scratched the loose dirt to get a strong foothold.

Buck yelled, "You've got to get on base. Can you do it?"

"I can do it!"

Poobaw Barlowe squeezed his eyes shut and prayed, *Jesus, God, and ever'body . . .*

The rector was holding his breath. Dooley had been on base every time he came to bat today. He saw the determined look on the boy's face as he waited for the pitch.

Realizing her feet were swelling, Fancy Skinner removed her high heel shoes and put them in her mother's knitting bag.

Coot Hendrick hoped to the good Lord he would not lose the twenty-five dollars he had bet on the Reds. He had borrowed it out of the sugar bowl, leaving only a few packages of NutraSweet and three dimes. He squirmed with anxiety. His mama might be old, but she could still whip his head.

Crack!

Dooley connected on a line shot into the outfield, which was hit so sharply that Father Tim stopped Mule at third.

"Way to go, buddy, way to do it, great job!" he yelled.

Dooley punched his fist into the air and pumped it, as the crowd hooted and cheered.

With two outs and the bases loaded, it was Adele Hogan's turn at bat.

"OK, Adele, let's get 'em, let's go, you can do it!" For tomorrow's services, he would sound like a bullfrog with laryngitis.

"Ball one!"

The second ball came in on the outside.

"Ball two!"

She swung at the next pitch.

"Strike one!"

The stands were going crazy. "Hey, ump," somebody yelled. "Wake up, you're missin' a great game!"

The ball came down the middle.

"Strike two!"

Two balls, two strikes. Adele stooped down, grabbed some dirt and rubbed it in her hands, then took the bat and gripped it hard. The rector thought he could see white knuckles as she rocked slightly on her feet and watched the pitch.

She caught the ball on the inside of her bat, away from the heavy part, sending it into short left center field.

Nobody called for the ball.

The outfielders all moved at once, collided, and stumbled over each other as the ball fell in. Adele Hogan ran for her life and reached first base as Mule scored.

The game was over.

The crowd was wild.

The score was 11–10.

Ray Cunningham huffed to the field with the mayor's ball and asked Adele to sign it. Unable to restrain himself, he pounded her on the back and gave her a big hug, wondering how in the world J. C. Hogan had ever gotten so lucky.

Ben Isaac Berman pulled himself up on his aluminum walker and waved to the red-haired kid on the field. He squinted into the sun, almost certain that the boy waved back.

The *Muse* editor, who had been sitting under a shade tree, panted to first base and cranked off a roll of Tri-X. All the frames featured his wife, who, as far as he was concerned, looked dynamite even with sweat running down her face. He wondered something that had never occurred to him before; he wondered how he'd ever gotten so lucky, and decided he would tell her that very thing—tonight.

Well, maybe tomorrow.

Soon, anyway.

CHAPTER FIFTEEN

Day into Night

"You know how I respect your judgment, I don't fight you on much."

"That's true, you don't."

Ron Malcolm had come to the rectory, and they'd taken refuge behind the closed door of the study.

His senior warden looked pained, but firm. "The time to sit on this thing is over. We've got to make a decision, and the only decision to make is to sell it to Miami Development. You know why, I know why. We can't afford to do otherwise."

Father Tim sat back in the chair. He was exhausted from the ordeal of it, from the conflict between hard-nosed reality and his own intuitions, however vague. He had prayed, he had stalled, he had wrestled, he had hoped—all the avenues open to most mortals—and like it or not, there was nothing else he could do.

"All right," he said.

At the front door, they shook hands on what had been agreed, and Ron went down the walk to his car.

The rector stood there, looking through the screen into the dusk. *Treat it kindly. . . .*

"Now, Miss Sadie," he said aloud, "don't be wagging your cane at me. I did the best I could."

He was running late for the meeting, having just fled one at First Baptist, and stopped at the water fountain in the parish hall corridor.

Around the bend to the right, he heard footsteps on the tile floor, and someone talking.

"The old woman was lucky to die a natural death, the furnace in that dump could have blown her head off."

Ingrid Swenson. Then he heard the murmured assent of her nail-biting crony, and their mutual laughter as they passed through the door into the parish hall.

The voices around the table droned on. He tried to pay attention, but couldn't. It was all done but the signing of the contract. There was hardly any reason for him to be here.

His gaze roamed the assembly. Buddy Benfield was grinning from ear to ear. Ron Malcolm was facing down Ingrid Swenson in a last contest of wills concerning the crumbling pavement of the Fernbank driveway. Mamie Gordon, who had a new job at the Collar Button, was looking anxiously at her watch. Sandra Harris was trying to figure how she could pop outside for a smoke. Clarence Daly was trooping in with a tray of cups and a pot of coffee.

The phone rang in the parish kitchen, but no one moved to answer it.

Sandra drummed her nails on the table, impatient. "We look forward to seeing Fernbank turned into a spa," she said to Ingrid, "but I hope you don't try to push body wraps and mud, I don't think anybody around here would go for that."

The phone continued to ring.

"So," said Ron, "even though our attorneys have gone over the contract thoroughly, let's take one last look before we sign, to the advantage of all concerned."

"I can't imagine what purpose that will serve."

Ron smiled. "Won't take but a couple of minutes."

The phone persisted.

"Here you go," said Clarence, setting cups before Ingrid and her associate. "Fresh out of th' pot."

"Oh, for Pete's *sake,*" said Sandra, "why doesn't somebody answer the phone?"

Nobody moved.

"Who would let a phone ring like that, anyway?" Scowling, she marched to the kitchen.

Ron glanced at Ingrid. "I've struck through and initialed your clause about the driveway repairs being a responsibility of Lord's Chapel."

She gave him a cold look and pushed the coffee away.

"Father! It's Andrew Gregory on the phone!"

"Tell him—"

"He's calling all the way from Italy. Says it's *important*!"

"Excuse me," he said, leaving the table.

Sandra handed him the receiver with a look of rekindled interest in the morning's proceedings. The most exotic call she'd ever had was from Billings, Montana.

"Andrew?"

"Father, Emma told me I could find you in the parish hall. Sorry to disturb you, but something . . . terribly important has just happened. Is the Fernbank property still available?"

"Well . . . " For about five minutes, maximum.

"I'd like to make an offer. I'll wire earnest money at once."

Had he heard right? Was he dreaming this?

"Two hundred and ninety-five thousand, Father." Andrew took a deep breath. "As is."

He felt a sudden, intense warmth throughout his body, as if he were melting in a spring thaw.

"Andrew?"

"Yes?"

"Consider it done!"

He didn't think he'd ever confess to anyone, not even his wife, how thrilled he'd been to see the look on Ingrid Swenson's face.

No. *Ecstatic* was the word. He'd been forced to restrain himself from leaping into the air, clicking his heels together, and whooping.

Upon being told that Fernbank would in fact be sold, but not to Miami Development, Ingrid Swenson had used language that, as far as he knew, had never been spoken on the grounds of Lord's Chapel. Mamie Gordon had actually put her hands over her ears, her mouth forming a perfect O.

When he saw Andrew, he would kiss his ring, the very cuff of his trousers! He would sweep his chimney, wash his windows, put him at the head of the Christmas parade in Tommy Ledbetter's yellow Mustang convertible . . . the possibilities for thanking Andrew Gregory were unlimited.

Hallelujah!

"I'm jealous," said his wife, rejoicing with him.

"Whatever for?"

"You weren't this happy on our wedding day!"

"How quickly you forget. Let's dance!"

"But there's no music."

"No problem!" he said, doing a jig step. "I'll hum!"

Happy Endings was having a twenty-percent-off sale on any book title starting with A, to commemorate August.

"What about Jane Austen, can I get twenty percent off?" asked Hessie Mayhew, who didn't have time to read a book in the first place.

"Sorry, no authors starting with A, just book titles," said Hope Winchester.

He staggered to the counter with *A Guide to Fragrance in the Garden, Andersonville: Men and Myth* (Walter's Christmas present), *A Reunion of Trees, A Grief Observed, Alone* by Admiral Byrd, *Anchor Book of Latin Quotations,* and *A Child's Garden of Verses.*

"A very perspicacious selection!" said Hope.

"Thank you. My wife will not be thrilled, however, as we have no place to put them."

"As long as you have any floor space at all, you have room for books! Just make two stacks of books the same height, place them three or four feet apart, lay a board across them, and repeat. Violà! Bookshelves!"

"I'll be darned."

He nearly always learned something new on Main Street.

The nave of Lord's Chapel became a deep chiaroscuro shadow as dusk settled over Mitford. Candles burned on the sills of the stained-glass windows to light the way of the remnant who came for the evening worship on Thursday, scheduled unexpectedly by the rector.

Winnie Ivey had donated tarts and cookies for a bit of refreshment afterward, and the rector's wife had made pitchers of lemonade from scratch, not frozen. Hearing of this, Uncle Billy and Miss Rose Watson, not much used to being out after dark, arrived in good spirits.

Esther Bolick, weary in every bone, trudged down the aisle with Gene to what had long ago become their pew on the gospel side. Several Bane volunteers, already feeling the numbing effects of pulling together the largest fund-raiser in the diocese, slipped in quietly, glad for the peace, for the sweetness of every shadow, and for the familiar, mingled smells of incense and flowers, lemon wax and burning wick.

Most of the vestry turned out, some with the lingering apprehension that they'd robbed Mitford of a thriving new business, others completely satisfied with a job well done.

Hope Winchester, invited by the rector and deeply relieved that the A sale was successful, stood inside the door and looked around awkwardly. She found it daunting to be here, since she hadn't been raised in church, but Father Tim was one of their good customers and never pushy about God, so she figured she had nothing to lose.

She slid into the rear pew, in case she needed to make a quick exit, and lowered her head at once. It was a perfect time to think about the S sale, coming in September, and how they ought to feature *Sea of Grass* by Conrad Richter, which nobody ever seemed to know about, but certainly should.

The *Muse* editor and his wife, Adele, slid into the rear pew across the aisle, and wondered what they would do when everybody got down on their knees. They both had Baptist backgrounds and felt deeply that kneeling in public, even if it was in church, was too in-your-face, like those people who prayed loud enough for everybody in the temple to hear.

Sophia Burton, who had seen the rector on the street that morning, had been glad to come and bring Liza, glad to get away from the little house with the TV set she knew she should turn off sometimes, but couldn't, glad to get away from thinking about her job at the canning plant, and the supervisor who made her do things nobody else had to do. Not wanting her own church, which was First Baptist, to think she was defecting, she had invited a member of her Sunday School class so it would look more like a social outing than something religious.

Farther forward on the gospel side, Lace Turner sat with Olivia and Hoppy Harper, and Nurse Kennedy, who had been at the hospital long before Dr. Harper arrived and was known to be the glue that held the place together.

And there, noted the rector, as he stood waiting at the rear of the nave, were his own, Cynthia and Dooley, and next to them, Pauline and Jessie and Poo and . . . amazing! Buck Leeper.

The rector might have come to the church alone and given thanks on his knees in the empty nave. But he'd delighted in inviting one and all to a service that would express his own private thanksgiving—for the outcome of Fernbank, for Jessie, for this life, for so much.

He came briskly down the aisle in his robe, and, in front of the steps to the altar, turned eagerly to face his people.

"Grace to you and peace from God our Father and from the Lord Jesus Christ!" he quoted from Philippians.

"I will bless the Lord who gives me counsel," he said with the psalmist, "my heart teaches me, night after night. I have set the Lord always before me; because He is at my right hand, I shall not fall."

He spoke the ancient words of the sheep farmer, Amos: "Seek Him who made the Pleiades and Orion, and turns deep darkness into the morning, and darkens the day into night; who calls for the waters of the sea and pours them out upon the surface of the earth: the Lord is His name!"

There it was, the smile he was seeking from his wife. And lo, not one but two, because Dooley was giving him a grin into the bargain.

"Dear friends in Christ, here in the presence of Almighty God, let us kneel in silence, and with patient and obedient hearts confess our sins, so that we may obtain forgiveness by His infinite goodness and mercy."

Here it comes, thought Adele Hogan, who, astonishing herself, slid off the worn oak pew onto the kneeler.

Hope Winchester couldn't do it; she was as frozen as a mullet, and felt her heart pounding like she'd drunk a gallon of coffee. Her mouth felt dry, too. Maybe she'd leave, who would notice anyway, with their heads bowed, but the thing was, there was always somebody who probably wasn't keeping his eyes closed, and would see her dart away like a convict. . . .

"Most merciful God," Esther Bolick prayed aloud and in unison with the others from the Book of Common Prayer, "we confess that we have sinned against You in thought, word, and deed . . ."

She felt the words enter her aching bones like balm.

" . . . by what we have done," prayed Gene, "and by what we have left undone."

"We have not loved You with our whole heart," intoned Uncle Billy Watson, squinting through a magnifying glass to see the words in the prayer book, "we have not loved our neighbors as ourselves."

He found the words of the prayer beautiful. They made him feel hopeful and closer to the Lord, and maybe it was true that he hadn't always done right by his neighbors, but he would try to do better, he would start before he hit the street this very night. He quickly offered a silent thanks that somebody would be driving them home afterward, since it was pitch-dark out there, and still hot as a depot stove into the bargain.

"We are truly sorry and we humbly repent," prayed Pauline Barlowe, unable to keep the tears back, not wanting to look at the big, powerful man beside her. Though plainly reluctant to be there, he nonetheless held the hand of her daughter, who was sucking her thumb and gazing at the motion of the ceiling fans.

"For the sake of Your Son Jesus Christ, have mercy on us and forgive us," prayed Cynthia Kavanagh, amazed all over again at how she'd come to be kneeling in this place, and hoping that the stress she'd recently seen in her husband was past, and that this service would mark the beginning of renewal and refreshment.

" . . . that we may delight in Your will, and walk in Your ways," prayed Sophia Burton, wishing with all her heart that she could do that very thing every day of her life, really do it and not just pray it—but then, maybe she could, she was beginning to feel like she could . . . maybe.

" . . . to the glory of Your Name!" prayed the rector, feeling his spirit moved toward all who had gathered in this place.

"Amen!" they said in unison.

It wasn't that it didn't trouble him; in fact, it made him a little crazy whenever the thought crossed his mind. But what could he do? What could he prove?

He couldn't talk about it around town—it would seem like the worst sort of rumor-mongering and political meddling; he certainly wouldn't mention it at the Grill, and didn't think it wise to tell his wife, either. The new Violet book was wearing on her, and why clutter her mind with what appeared to be a very nasty piece of business?

Omer had sworn he'd keep quiet, at least for the time being. What could talk like that do, after all, except give his sister-in-law a stroke? And who could prove anything, anyway?

The rector took some comfort in the fact that election day was more than a couple of months away. Surely by that time Mack would show his hand, somebody would stumble, something . . .

The attic job was the current local recreation for those who had nothing better to do. Uncle Billy shambled down the street on his cane and gave all manner of directions to the crew, occasionally sharing the lunches they carried in bags from home or raced to the highway to pick up from Hardee's. So far, he had wheedled french fries from two stonecutters and a joiner.

Coot Hendrick pulled his rusted pickup truck to the curb every morning around eleven, scooted over to the passenger side, rolled the window down, and watched the whole show in the privacy and comfort of his vehicle. While the crew mixed mortar, sawed lumber, and in general tore up large expanses of grass and two perennial beds, he ate Nabs, shucked peanuts, and drank Cheerwine until three o'clock. He then drove to Lew Boyd's Esso, where he played checkers until five, after which he went home to his elderly mother and fixed her supper, usually a small cake of cornbread accompanied by a bowl of lettuce and onions, which he wilted with a blast of sizzling bacon grease and cider vinegar.

Beneath the attic, yet another church project was going at a trot.

While the preschool crowd gave new life to the old verger's quarters, the kindergarten had stationed itself in the largest of the Sunday School rooms, where all manner of shrieking, cackling, giggling, and wailing could be heard emanating from its walls.

The rector loved walking into a room that was completely alien to the adult world—filled with fat plastic tricycles and huge vinyl balls that could be knocked around without smashing the windows. He especially liked the rocking horses, which, upon each visit, were going at a frantic pace with astonished babies hanging on for dear life.

Sissy and Sassy had taken to the fray like fish to water. After a full day of howling for their mother, they had settled down to a new life and hardly noticed the guilt-stricken Puny when he went with her to see them at lunchtime.

"Sassy, it's Mama, come to Mama, *please*!" Sassy turned her head and chewed on a string of rubber clowns, recently chewed by a toddler who had poured a cup of juice on his head.

Sissy pulled up on a wooden table and tottered toward him at full throttle. "Ba!" she shouted. "Ba!"

"Ba, yourself!" He fell to his knees and held out his arms. "Come to granpaw, you little punkinhead!"

"I didn't know he was a granpaw," said Marsha Hunt, who was in charge of the mayhem.

Puny looked suddenly cheerful. "Oh, yes!" she declared. "And it's the best thing that ever happened to him!"

After the eleven o'clock, Mack Stroupe positioned himself a couple of yards to the left of the rector and pumped hands enthusiastically as the crowd flowed through the door. Anyone driving by, thought Father Tim, wouldn't have known which was the priest if one of them hadn't worn vestments.

As she tallied the collection on Monday morning, Emma couldn't wait to tell him:

Mack Stroupe had dropped a thousand bucks in the plate.

Rain. Torrents of rain. Rain that washed driveways, devastated what was left of the gardens, and hammered its way through roofs all over Mitford. The little yellow house had its first known leak, which Buck fixed by climbing around on the slate in a late afternoon downpour.

The rector drove up to check the leak problem at Fernbank and arrived in the nick of time. The turkey roaster and other assorted pots and pans were only moments before overflowing. He dutifully dumped each potful down the toilet, giving Fernbank a free flush, an economy which Miss Sadie had often employed.

He had tried to be completely candid with Andrew in a subsequent phone conversation, giving him the hair-raising truth about everything from roof to furnace. Oddly, Andrew had seemed jubilant about the whole prospect.

The wire for the earnest money had arrived at the bank and was deposited, the papers were being drawn up, and all was on go. Andrew would return to Mitford in a few weeks, anxious to begin work on the house before winter.

Father Tim stood in the vast, empty kitchen, looking out to sheets of rain lashing the windows. Even on a day like this, he hadn't felt so good about Fernbank in a very long time.

Everywhere he went, he made known that he was on the incumbent's side—without, he hoped, seeming preachy. Local politics was a fine line to walk for anybody, much less clergy.

What else could he do?

"You've already *done*!" said Cynthia. "An air show with banners and barrel rolls!"

"Yesterday's barrel rolls can't compete with today's barbecue."

"You've got a point there," she said.

He watched as his wife furrowed her brow, looking thoughtful. Maybe *she'd* be able to come up with something.

"Tell me how things are, Betty."

He'd gone to sit on the porch with Betty Craig, who heaved a sigh at his question.

"Well, Father, Jessie wets the bed and has awful bad dreams."

"I'm sorry, but not surprised."

"And poor Pauline, she's just tryin' ever' whichaway to be a good mama, but I don't think anybody ever showed her how."

"I'm hoping preschool will help Jessie. I doubt if she's been with other children very much."

"She came home cryin' her heart out yesterday, sayin' she didn't want to go back. But of course she seemed all right about it this morning when I took her to day care at Lord's Chapel. I take her, you know, because Pauline goes to work so early."

"Can you handle all this crowd in your house?"

"Oh, yes! It's good to have a crowd, but I don't think we could stuff another one in, unless they set on their fist and lean back on their thumb. You won't be . . . sendin' any more?"

"I believe Pauline will be looking for a little house soon."

Betty was quiet, rocking. "You know, Mr. Leeper's coming around."

"What do you think of that?" he asked, trusting her judgment.

"Oh, I like Mr. Leeper, and he's good to th' children, too. But with her tryin' to stay off alcohol . . . and I hear he's still drinkin' some . . . I don't know if it's the best thing."

He'd thought the same, but hadn't wanted to admit it to himself.

"I'd like to see," he said, feeling shy as a schoolboy.

"Are you sure?" she asked.

"Of course! I've been wanting to do it for weeks."

They trooped through the hedge to her workroom, where she showed him the growing stack of large watercolor illustrations for *Violet Goes Back to School.* He sat on her minuscule love seat and she displayed the results of her labors, revealing at the same time a shyness of her own.

He was dazzled by his wife's gift. It knocked his socks off. "It's wonderful, absolutely wonderful. The best yet!"

"Thank you! That means so much."

"And Violet—in this one, she looks so, what shall I say? Happy!"

"Yes! You see, Violet likes going to school."

"Aha."

"Which reminds me—I've been wanting to tell you something, dearest."

"Tell me," he said, loving the earnest look of her in a bandanna and denim jumper.

"I'll be traveling for several weeks after the book is released, going to schools and libraries. I know how you feel about that."

He hated it, actually. He remembered how pathetically lost he felt when she traveled a couple of times last year. Worse, he'd gotten the most bizarre notions—that she might miss the bridge and drive into the river, or be mugged in the school parking lot, or that her crankcase was leaking oil. And what if she were stranded on the side of the road? Did she realize that people had been murdered doing that very thing?

He said what he always said. "Do you have to?"

And she said what she always said. "Yes."

Ron removed his cap and jacket and shook the rain onto the rug at the office door.

"Feast or famine," he said. "Drought or flood."

"Are you talking about life or the weather?" queried Father Tim.

"Life *and* the weather," said Ron. "We're currently seeing a flood of real estate activity."

"Now what?" He was sick of real estate activity.

"We've got a prospective buyer for the rectory."

His blood chilled. "Already?"

Ron sat on the visitor's bench. "They're very interested, and said they'd like to see it next week."

"Who is they?" Why did he feel so defensive, even angry?

"H. Tide. Out of Orlando."

"That's who's looking at Sweet Stuff." And if that's who's looking at Sweet Stuff, then Mack Stroupe was involved. Hadn't Mack taken credit in the newspaper article for sending Winnie a realtor who was, in fact, H. Tide?

He'd never been able to bear the brunt of bad news in his head, in his intellect; he felt it instead in his body—in his chest, in his stomach, in his throat.

"Sorry," said Ron, seeing the look on his face. "If they want it right away, we'll do all we can to help you find whatever situation you need. Ideally, we'll try to work something out that lets you stay in the rectory 'til you retire."

"You'll *try* to work something out?"

"Well . . . " Ron looked embarrassed and uneasy.

"Keep me posted," he said, hearing the cold anger in his voice. He hadn't meant to sound that way, but he couldn't help it, couldn't mask it.

He felt strangely frightened and alone.

Walking home, he concluded that he wouldn't mention this to Cynthia, not until he had to. After all, nothing was written in stone.

Here was yet another circumstance he'd be withholding from his wife, and he knew instinctively this wasn't a good tactic—the most fundamental counseling book would tell him that.

Disrupting the household . . . where would they go? Buck had a crew starting next door in September, in only a couple of weeks, and Cynthia would be moving her drawing board and library into his study. He had never liked change, and here he was, facing the biggest change of his life, combined with a possible change of address at the most inconvenient time imaginable.

His retirement had all looked so smooth, so easy, so . . . reviving when he made the decision last year. Now it looked as if he could be set out on the sidewalk like so much rubbish.

But he was being hasty. Premature. He was overreacting.

He sucked in a draught of fresh air and turned the corner onto Wisteria. He dreaded facing Cynthia Kavanagh, who could look in his eyes and know instantly that something was wrong.

For two cents, he'd get in the car and drive.

And keep going.

CHAPTER SIXTEEN

Bookends

Going at a clip toward the Grill, they met Uncle Billy tottering homeward from the construction site at Lord's Chapel.

"I'll be et f'r a tater if y'r boy ain't growed a foot!"

Dooley cackled, looking at his feet. "Where's it at?"

The rector noted that Dooley was slipping back into the vernacular, which, frankly, he had rather missed. Any wild departure from the King's English, of course, would be remedied just ten days hence. Blast, he hated the thought of driving Dooley to Virginia and depositing him in that place, even if it was helping him learn and grow and expand his horizons.

Percy turned from the grill and beamed. "Lookit th' big ball player. You ought t' be traded to th' Yankees and that's a fact."

"Dodgers," said Dooley, laughing again.

The rector had seen more laughter in his boy this summer than ever before. And why not? He had a steady paycheck, a girl who was crazy about him, a best friend, a family that was pulling itself together, and, generally, a swarm of people who loved him. Not to mention, of course, an education that was annually the cost of a new car—with leather and airbags.

"Hey, buddyroe," said J.C., cracking one of his biennial grins.

"Hey," said Dooley, sliding into the rear booth. This was his first time hanging with these old guys, and he wasn't too sure about it. He could have been scarfing down a pizza with Tommy over on the highway.

"Hey, slugger!" said Mule. "Let's see that arm!"

Dooley flexed the muscle in his upper right arm, and everybody helped themselves to squeezing it.

"A rock," said J.C., approving.

Mule nodded soberly.

"Killer!" said the rector.

J.C. pulled out a handkerchief and mopped his face. "I'll treat!"

"There it is again," said Mule. "The feelin' I'm goin' deaf as a doorknob."

"I mean I'll treat Dooley, not th' whole bloomin' booth."

"You better have some deep pockets if you're feeding Dooley Barlowe," said Father Tim, as proud as if the boy had an appetite for Aristotle.

"I'll have a large Coke, large fries, and two hotdogs all th' way," announced the editor's guest.

"All th' way?" Mule raised his eyebrows. "I thought you had a girlfriend, you don't want to be eatin' onions."

"Don't listen to these turkeys," said J.C., "they tried to run my . . . my, ah . . . thing with Adele and like to ruined my life. Anything you want to know about women, you ask me."

Mule nearly fell out of the booth laughing.

"What's goin' on over here?" asked Velma, who couldn't bear to hear laughter unless she knew what it was about.

"You don't want to know," said Father Tim.

"I certainly do want to know!" She put her hands on her hips and squinted at them over her glasses.

"Oh, shoot," said Mule. "Can't a bunch of men have a little joke without women wantin' to know what it's about?"

"No," said Velma. "So what's it about?"

"We're teachin' Dooley about the opposite sex," said Mule.

"Oh, Lord, help!" Velma looked thoroughly disgusted.

"I wish y'all would quit," said Dooley. "I don't need to know anything about girls, I already know it."

"See?" said Velma. "Now, let 'im alone. Dooley, if you ever want to know anything about th' opposite sex, you come and ask me or Percy, you hear? We'll tell you th' blessed truth."

"Dadgum!" Mule covered his face with his hands. "He'll be glad to get back to school after listenin' to this mess. . . ."

"Right!" said Dooley.

Ron Malcolm called to say that he'd be at the rectory Wednesday at noon, with the people from H. Tide.

Father Tim decided he'd be in the piney woods, as far from that miserable experience as he could get.

When he finally got the nerve to tell Cynthia, she looked at him blankly.

"Why are they showing it now if they're not going to sell it until we move?"

"The truth is, if they get the right offer and the buyer's anxious to move in, they'll sell it now and find us something. . . ."

He could tell she didn't believe her ears. "Find us something . . . ?"

He looked away. "The real estate scene in Mitford, as you know, is historically sluggish. The vestry feels they can't afford to pass up the offer, if it's right. People have known for two or three years that it would be on the market, and nobody's spoken up for it."

"The real estate market is historically sluggish because development in Mitford goes at a snail's pace." She turned away, and he saw a muscle moving in her cheek. "It's almost enough to make me vote for Mack Stroupe."

"I can't believe you said that."

"I was only kidding, for Pete's sake, you don't have to bite my head off."

"I didn't bite your head off."

"You most certainly did. And furthermore, your nerves stay absolutely frazzled these days. You tote every barge and lift every bale in Mitford, with nothing left over for yourself. And now you tell me we could be run out of our home, thanks to a parish you have faithfully served for sixteen years? If that's the way your vestry thinks, Timothy, then I would ask you to do me the favor of lining them up, one by one, and enjoining them to bend over. I will then go down the row and give every distinguished member exactly what they deserve, which is, need I say it, a good, swift kick!"

She turned and left the study, and he heard her charging up the stairs. Their bedroom door, which was rarely closed, slammed.

He felt as if he'd been dashed with ice water. All the feelings he'd lately had, the heaviness on his chest, the pounding of blood in his temples, the wrenching in his stomach . . . all rushed in again, except worse.

He sat at the kitchen table, stricken. They'd never before had words like that. They were both overworked, overstressed, and who wanted to be told they might be dumped on the street?

He was grieved that this was even a consideration by his own church officers.

Also, he was humiliated for Ron Malcolm, one of the finest men he'd ever known, and a personal friend into the bargain. Ron Malcolm was behaving like . . . like Ed Coffey, doing whatever it took, and all because of money.

Money!

He was glad he didn't have enough money to matter, glad he'd given most of it away in this fleeting life. Dear God, to see what some people would do for a dollar was enough to make him call his broker and have the whole lot transferred to the coffers of Children's Hospital.

What was the amount, anyway, that was left of his mother's estate? A hundred and forty thousand or so, which he'd been growing for years. Even though he'd dipped into it heavily every time the Children's Hospital had a need, smart investing had maintained most of the original two hundred thousand.

Actually, it hadn't been smart investing, it had been safe investing. He was as timid as a hare when it came to flinging assets around. He wished he'd asked Miss Sadie her investing strategies. There were a thousand things he'd thought of asking after she died, and now it was too late to find out how she'd come up with more than a million bucks for Dooley, even after spending five million on Hope House.

Should he go upstairs and talk to Cynthia? What would he say?

He couldn't remember feeling so weary, so . . . He searched for the word that would express how he felt, but couldn't find it.

He didn't have the energy to say he was sorry. Actually, he didn't know if he was sorry. What had he said, after all? He couldn't remember, but it all had something to do with Mack Stroupe.

Blast Mack Stroupe to the lowest regions of the earth. He was sick of Mack Stroupe.

So what if he shouldn't have a napoleon? Hadn't he waited more than a decade to eat a measly cheeseburger the other day?

He was no ascetic living in the desert, he was a busy, active clergyman in need of proper nourishment.

He did the glucometer check and marched to Winnie Ivey's, blowing past several people who greeted him, but to whom he merely lifted a hand. They stared after him, dumbfounded. They'd never seen the local priest scowling like that. It was completely unlike him.

The bell on the Sweet Stuff door jingled, which turned the heads of four customers sitting at a table. It was fifth- and sixth-grade teachers from Mitford School, having tea. He could tell at once they wanted to talk, and he turned to leave.

"Father?" said Winnie, coming through the curtains behind the bake cases. "Can you stay a minute?"

Good heavens, Winnie Ivey looked as glum and pressed to the wall as he felt. What was wrong with people these days?

She set out another pot of hot water for the teachers, who were peering at him oddly, and caught his sleeve. "I need to talk to you about something," she said, whispering.

They went to the kitchen, which, as always, smelled like a child's version of paradise—cinnamon, rising dough, baking cookies. Somebody should put the aroma in an aerosol container. It was so soothing that he immediately felt more relaxed.

"You look terrible," she said.

"Oh, well." If Winnie Ivey didn't tell him so, Emma Newland certainly would, or, for that matter, any number of others.

"Father, the most awful thing . . . "

If it wasn't one awful thing these days, it was two.

"That real estate company wants to buy my business."

"They do?"

"And I can't get a minute's peace about selling it. After runnin' ads and prayin' my head off, here's my big chance and I feel awful about it."

"If you've prayed and there's no peace about a decision, then wait. That's one rule I stick with."

"But they want to buy it right away."

"Will they give you your asking price?"

"Not exactly. Mr. Skinner believes it's worth seventy-five thousand, but I'm asking sixty, and they want to give me forty-five."

"Forty-five thousand for twenty years' work," he said, musing. "That's not much more than two thousand a year."

"Oh," she said, stricken.

He was feeling worse by the minute. Any longing for a napoleon had flown out the window.

"I'd really like your advice, Father, I trust what you say."

He didn't like being anyone's Providence, but she'd asked for help and he'd give her his best shot. He said what he was becoming known for saying in all real estate matters these days.

"Tell them you'd like to think about it for thirty days."

She looked alarmed. "I don't believe they'd like that."

"They probably wouldn't. That's true."

"And I might not get another offer."

"That's true, too. However, consider this: You're the only game in town. There's not another business currently for sale on Main Street, and this is highly desirable property. I think you're holding the ace."

She hugged herself, furrowing her brow and thinking. "Well, I *might* do that. But . . . it's risky."

He wouldn't tell her that risk had a certain adrenaline.

Didn't he have a bishop? An advocate? He wasn't hanging out there in space, all alone. Stuart Cullen would go to bat for him. That's what bishops were for, wasn't it?

But Stuart wasn't in the office and wouldn't be in for two long weeks, as his wife, according to Stuart's secretary, had forced the bishop to go away to—she wasn't sure where, but she thought it was southern France, or at least someplace where they spoke another language and wore bikinis on the beach.

Dooley, whose job had ended day before yesterday, showed up at the church office with a letter in his hand.

He sat on the visitor's bench and examined his tennis shoes, whistled, jiggled his leg, and stared into space while the rector opened it and read:

My dearest husband,

I regret that I snapped at you this morning. You snapped, I snapped. And for what? As you left, looking hurt, I wanted to run after you and hold you, but I could not move. I stood upstairs on the landing and moped at the window like a schoolgirl, watching as you went along the sidewalk.

I saw you stop for a moment and look around, as if you wanted to turn back. You seemed forlorn, and I was overcome with sorrow for anything I might ever do to give you pain. My darling Timothy, who means all the world to me—forgive me.

It was the slightest thing between us, something that would hardly matter to anyone else, I think. We are both so sensitive, so alike in that region of the heart which fears rejection and resists chastisement.

As I looked down upon you, I received your hurt as my own, and so have had a double measure all these hours.

Hurry home, dearest husband!

Come and kiss me and let us hold one another in that way which God has set aside for us. You are precious to me, more than breath.

Ever thine,

Cynthia

(still your bookend?)

PS *I know it is a pitiable gesture, but I shall roast something savoury for your supper and make your favorite oven-browned potatoes.*

Truce?

Dooley looked at the ceiling, got up, peered out the window, sat down again, then found some gum on the sole of his left shoe and painstakingly peeled it off. "You an' Cynthia had a fuss?"

"Yes."

"I understand."

"You do?" He was thrilled to hear those words out of Dooley Barlowe. *I understand.* A mature thing for anyone, much less a fourteen-year-old boy, to utter.

"Jenny and I had a fuss. She blamed me for somethin' I didn't do."

"Aha."

"She said I paid too much attention to Lace Turner the other day."

"No kidding. . . ."

"I didn't."

"I'm sure."

"Lace wanted to talk about American history, is all, and I talked back." He shrugged.

"Right. What did you talk about—I mean, concerning American history?"

"About going west in a wagon train. I'd like to do that. Lace said she'd like to." His freckles were showing. "That's all."

"I'm amazed every day," said the rector, "how people can misunderstand each other about the simplest things."

"Lace is writing a story about going west on a wagon train from Springfield, Illinois, where the Donner party started out. In her story, the leader gets killed and a woman has to lead the train."

"Wow."

"She got A's for her stories last year."

"Well done."

"She quit wearin' that stupid hat."

"I noticed."

"So, look, I don't have all day. Are you goin' to write Cynthia back?"

"You bet."

"I've got to go see Poo and Jessie. You goin' to type or write by hand?"

"Type. I'll hurry."

He took the cover off the Royal manual and rolled in a sheet of paper.

Bookend—

dooley has delivered your letter and is waiting for me to respond. ii have suffered, you have suffered.

Enough!

You are dear to me beyond measure. That God allowed us to have thiis union at all stuns me daily/

"Bright star, would I were stedfast as thou art—"

love, timothy—who, barely two years ago, you may recall, vowed to cherish you always, no matter what

Truce.

ps. ii will gladly wash the dishes and barnabas will dry.

He had to do something for Esther.

More billboards on the highway wouldn't cut it. Esther's campaign needed one-on-one, it needed looking into people's eyes and talking about her record. It needed . . . a coffee in someone's home.

But not in his home. No, indeed. For a priest to dip his spoon into mayoral coffee was not politically correct. He would have to talk someone else into doing it.

Esther Bolick laughed in his face. "Are you kidding me?" she said. He should have known better than to call Esther. What a dumb notion; he felt like an idiot. So why did he pick up the phone and call Hessie?

"You must have the wrong number," said Hessie Mayhew, and hung up.

He called the president of ECW, thinking she might be interested in having the mayor do a program at the next monthly meeting.

"She did a program last year," said Erlene Douglas, "and we never repeat a speaker unless it's the bishop or a bigwig."

"Put a sign in your window," he implored Percy, "one of those that says, 'We're stickin' with Esther.'"

"No way," said Percy. "I run a business. I'm not campaignin' for anybody. Let 'em tough it out whichever way they can."

"Olivia," he said in his best pulpit voice, "I was wondering if . . ."

But Olivia, Hoppy, and Lace were going to the coast for the last couple of days before school started, which, except for their honeymoon, would be the first vacation her husband had had in ten years.

He sat staring at his office bookshelves, drumming his fingers on the desk. Maybe Esther could visit the police station and hand around donuts one morning. Better still, what about giving out balloons at Hattie Cloer's market on the highway? He was running on fumes with this thing.

He called Esther's office, noting that she sounded depressed.

"I don't know," she said, sighing heavily. "Who needs this aggravation? Th' low-down egg sucker has been campaignin' practically since Easter, it's more politics than I can stomach."

"But you can't give up now!"

"Who says I can't?" demanded the mayor.

"Mr. Tim!"

On his livermush delivery to Betty Craig's, Jessie met him at the door, carrying a coloring book. "Look!" she said, holding it up for his close inspection.

"Outstanding!" he said squatting down.

"Them's camels. Camels stores water in their humps."

"Right. Amazing!"

"Can I sit on your lap?"

"Absolutely."

He set the bag of livermush down and sought out the slipcovered armchair in the living room. Jessie crawled into his lap and clung to him, sucking her thumb.

"I thought you were going to try and quit sucking your thumb," he said, cradling her in his arm.

"Betty put pepper on it, but I washed it off."

He didn't know much about thumb-sucking, but he knew the cure. It was the thing that cured every other ill in this world, and of which there was far too little in general supply.

After talking with Pauline, he put another list, however brief, on Emma's desk.

But this time, Emma found nothing. Nothing at all.

The realtors from Orlando had made an offer. A hundred and five thousand, cash. Which was, to a penny, the asking price.

He hadn't heard of anybody meeting an asking price lately.

When he spoke to Ron about it, he felt as if his jaws were frozen, or partially wired shut. "When do they want occupancy?"

"October fifteenth."

"Who's buying it?"

"They didn't specify. Whoever it is may be renting it."

"I'd like you to wait on this."

"They made it clear they don't want to drag their feet. They were ready to shell out the cash today, but I won't sign anything of course, 'til I run all this by the vestry."

"I'm going to ask you to do something."

"You know I want to help, Father."

Did he know that? "I want you to wait on this for ten days. Don't do anything for ten days." He didn't think his now-customary thirty days would wash, but he had to have some time to adjust to this. The thought of the deal being done immediately made him feel trapped, helpless.

Ron pulled at his chin. "They've already said they want me to get back to them by the end of the week. If we make them wait, they could withdraw the offer."

"Look. If you think we feel good about being swept out of our house like this, you've got another think coming. I've got to tell you that I don't appreciate it, and if you have in mind some early retirement plan I don't know about, then let's lay the cards on the table."

His heart wasn't pounding, his brow wasn't perspiring. He was as cool as a cucumber.

Ron tried to smile, but couldn't. "Early retirement? Father, we'd keep you forever, if you'd let us. Retirement wasn't our idea, it was yours."

"And it's my idea to have ten days to digest all this. Sixteen years in this parish has earned me ten days." Period.

He wasn't taking no for an answer, and Ron knew it.

"Father! Stop! Wait!"

It was Winnie Ivey in her apron, running up Main Street behind him.

"I saw you pass, but I was on th' phone. Oh, you won't believe this! You won't believe it!"

"I'll believe it!" he said, laughing at her excitement.

"I won that cruise! I won it! A cruise to a whole bunch of islands!"

"Hallelujah!" he said, taking her hands as she jumped up and down. Her bandanna slipped back from her forehead, and graying curls sprung loose.

"I've never won anything, not even a stuffed animal in a shootin' gallery!"

"First time for everything!" he said, rejoicing with her.

"Golden Band said I could go anytime, starting in October! They were the nicest people, they said my entry was just perfect, they said it hit th' nail on th' head! I thank you for helpin' me with it, Father, stop by for a napoleon anytime! Well, gosh, I better get back, I've got two customers havin' donuts and coffee."

He watched her dash down the street, thinking he might see her leap off the pavement and fly.

In two short days, Harley had hauled away three barrows of trash from Cynthia's garage, washed and waxed her car, mowed the grass at both houses, removed the dead and dying stems of the hosta, and weeded the flower beds.

"Harley, you'd better slow down," said the rector, taking a turn at the weeding himself.

"No, sir, I ain't goin' to, I'm glad t' be workin', it's th' best fix I've been in and I thank th' Lord 'n Master f'r it."

Right there, he thought, was another consideration. Any interim living arrangement the vestry might provide may not accommodate Harley Welch.

Father Tim squatted by the perennial bed and watched the dappled light play over the grass. He and Cynthia had prayed the prayer that never fails, and besides that, what else could they do?

He pondered the sudden, unexpected idea he'd had this morning as he ran. It had come to him out of the blue and slowed him to a walk. Of course, he'd never done anything like that before. But was that any reason not to do it now? Cynthia would know the answer.

The rotten thing about this new development with the rectory was that every time he turned around these days, he was standing under an ax waiting to fall. Thirty days here, ten days there, it seemed endless.

There was an upside, however. Going out to Canaan didn't look so ominous anymore. It looked like a blasted good way to introduce a little peace into his life.

He thought they might have to talk about it until the wee hours. But it was coming together very quickly.

"I think we should do it," he told his wife.

"I think we should, too," she said, looking intrigued.

She reached out to him, put her warm palm to his cheek, and smiled. "It would solve everything," she said.

CHAPTER SEVENTEEN

Deep Blue Sea

The following morning, he reached the office earlier than usual and found a message on his machine.

"Father? Ron here. I talked with H. Tide and they want to do the deal now—or never." Ron cleared his throat. "Ah, also, they're saying they don't want to rent to us, they'd like to take possession by October fifteenth."

There was a moment of uneven breathing. "Don't worry about a thing, Father, we'll take care of you."

Wilma Malcolm's voice sounded in the background. "The Randall house!"

"Wilma heard the Randall house is available, and I'm sure we could work something out. Well, listen, we're headed to see the grandkids for a couple of days, I'll get back to you." The machine clicked, whirred, and clicked again.

He sat at his desk, frozen.

In all his years as a priest. . . .

He didn't move for what seemed a long time.

Then he got up, hit the erase button on the machine, and walked out the door.

He went home to oversee Dooley's packing for the trip to Virginia in the morning.

He didn't know how he could face anybody right now, much less Dooley Barlowe. Would he break down and bawl like a baby? Or worse, reach for some heavy object and slam it through a window?

He made an effort to remember how Ron had stood by him the night they faced down Edith Mallory. It had happened a few years ago at Clear Day.

After confronting her with the rotten floor beams that they discovered under the Grill, Edith was persuaded to repair the damage and extend Percy's lease for five years, at a fraction of the rent hike she'd originally hit him with—the rent hike that had, in fact, been designed to put the Grill out of business.

Edith Mallory hated his guts, no two ways about it. She had revealed her rage toward him that night in a way he didn't care to recall.

He and Ron had left Clear Day, triumphant and ecstatic, brothers in a victory that had less to do with winning than with maintaining something central to the core and spirit of the village. While the sense of connectedness was vanishing in small towns everywhere, he and Ron had fought for something vital, and won.

Before he let this thing with the rectory eat him alive, he'd better forgive Ron Malcolm. By God's grace, maybe he could actually do it. So what if he might have to start all over again every five minutes?

The point was to start.

"You home?" yelled Dooley from the landing.

"I'm home. Give me a half hour." He stopped in the kitchen to drink a glass of ice water.

Cynthia was shopping in Wesley, and Lace, who was leaving for the beach tomorrow, was baking cookies in Harley's kitchen. The fragrance drifted up the stairs like a sylph.

He went to his bedroom with Barnabas at his heels and sat in the wing chair, taking a few deep breaths to quiet the turmoil that had moved from his head and invaded his heart.

He and Cynthia had already prayed the prayer that never fails regarding the rectory, but he felt the need to pray it again.

Barnabas laid his head on his master's foot.

"Ah, fella," he sighed, nudging his good dog's neck with the toe of his loafer.

The sound came through the open bedroom windows—a terrible screeching noise, a loud thud, the high-pitched yelping of a dog. Dooley was shouting.

He bolted to the front window and looked down on Wisteria Lane.

Good God! Barnabas lay in the street with Dooley bending over him.

He didn't remember racing down the stairs, but seemed to be instantly in the street with Dooley, crouching over Barnabas, hearing the horrific sound that welled up from his own gut like a long moan.

Blood ran from his dog's chest, staining the asphalt, and he reached out. . . .

"Don't touch 'im!" shouted Dooley. "He'll bite. We got t' muzzle 'im! Git Lace! Git Lace!"

The rector was on his feet and running for the house, calling, shouting. "And git me some towels!" yelled Dooley. "He's got a flail chest, I got t' have towels!"

His heart was pounding into his throat. Dear God, don't take my dog, don't take this good creature, have mercy!

Lace flew through the door. "Help Dooley!" he said, running toward the guest bathroom, where he picked up an armload of towels, then turned and sprinted up the hall and down the steps and into the street in a nightmarish eternity of slow motion.

"Give me that thing on your head," Dooley told Lace, "and help me hold 'im! We got to muzzle 'im or he'll bite, look, do it this way, hold 'im right here."

Father Tim could hardly bear the look of his dog, suffering, whimpering, thrashing on the asphalt, as fresh blood poured from the wound in his chest.

Dooley tied the bandanna around the dog's nose and mouth, and knotted it. "Okay," he said, taking off his T-shirt. "Don't look, you can see 'is lungs workin' in there." He pressed the balled-up shirt partially into the gaping wound; immediately, the dark stain of blood seeped into the white cotton.

"Give me a towel," Dooley said, clenching his jaw. He took the towel and wrapped the heaving chest, making a bandage. "Another one," said Dooley, working quickly. "And git me a blanket, we got t' git 'im to Doc Owen. He could die."

The rector ran into the house, praying, sweat streaming from him, and opened the storage closet in the hall. No blankets. The armoire! *He could die.*

Christ, have mercy. He dashed up the stairs and flung open the door of the armoire and grabbed two blankets and ran down again, breathless, swept out of himself with fear.

Cynthia, come home . . . *he could die.*

"Spread 'em down right there," Dooley told the rector. "Help 'im," he said to Lace.

They spread the blankets, one on top of the other, next to Barnabas, as a car slowed down and stopped. "Can we help?" someone called.

"You can pray!" shouted Lace, waving the car around them.

Together, they managed to move Barnabas onto the blankets. "Careful," said Dooley, "careful. He's in awful pain, and his leg's broke, too, but they ain't nothin' I can do about it now, we got to hurry. Where's Harley?"

"He walked t' town," said Lace, her face white.

"Git his keys, they're hangin' on th' nail. Back 'is truck out here, we'll put Barnabas in th' back, an' you'n me'll ride with 'im."

She raced to the house as Dooley, naked to the waist, crouched over Barnabas and put his hand on the dog's head. "It's OK, boy, it's OK, you're goin' t' be fine."

"Thank You, Jesus, for Your presence in this," the rector prayed. "Give us your healing hands. . . ."

They heard Lace gun the truck motor and back out of the driveway. She hauled up beside them and screeched to a stop, the motor running.

"Let down th' tailgate," said Dooley. Lace jumped out of the truck and let it down.

"Grab this corner of th' blanket with me," he said to Lace. "Dad, you haul up that end. Take it easy. Easy!"

The dog's weight seemed enormous as they lifted him into the truck bed. "OK, boy, we're layin' you down, now."

Lace and Dooley climbed up with Barnabas and gently positioned the whimpering dog in the center of the bed. Then Dooley slammed the tailgate and looked at the rector.

"Hurry," he said.

They blew past Harley, who was walking home on Main Street. He turned to look after them, bewildered.

In twenty-five minutes, Barnabas was on the table at Meadowgate, and Hal Owen and Blake Eddistoe were at work. "You'd better not come in," said Dooley, closing the door to the surgery.

The rector sat with Lace in the small waiting room. A fan droned overhead. The front door stood open to a yard where four chickens scratched in the grass.

His legs had turned to rubber when he got out of the truck a few minutes ago. He had driven like the wind, praying without ceasing, making the half-hour run in twenty minutes. Twice, he glanced behind him, through the window of the cab, to see Dooley give him the high sign.

Lace looked firm. "I believe he's goin' to make it."

"I believe that with you," he said, taking her hand. "You were wonderful."

"I like your dog," she said.

Barnabas would stay at Meadowgate for a couple of weeks, recovering. The leg would mend; it was a clean break. But the chest wound, apparently caused by the violent assault of the chassis when the vehicle ran over him, would take longer, and could even open the door to pneumonia.

Bottom line, it would be a while before Barnabas would go jogging with his master.

The rector went into the surgery, where Hal had made a comfortable bed on the floor, and looked at Barnabas sleeping, his chest swaddled in bandages, his left leg stiff in the splint. He watched for his breathing, then knelt and put his hand on his forepaws, which were curled together peacefully.

He wept, tasting the salt in his mouth.

Afterward, they sat in Hal's office, drinking Marge Owen's iced tea, trying to reconstruct the chain of events.

He supposed he had fallen asleep in the chair in the bedroom, with Barnabas lying at his feet. When Barnabas heard Dooley go downstairs, he followed, and at the moment Dooley opened the front door to look for Tommy, Barnabas saw a squirrel on the lawn.

"I didn't even know he was standin' there," said Dooley, "and then he was through the door so fast I couldn't have stopped him." Dooley, sitting bare-chested in his jeans and tennis shoes, dropped his head.

"Don't blame yourself," said Father Tim. "A dog is a dog. He saw the squirrel and did what dogs do. It could have happened with me just as easily."

"Right," said Hal. "The issue isn't that you opened the door, it's that you saved his life."

"I agree," said Lace, her amber eyes intense.

"I don't want to go back to school," said Dooley. "I want to stay here and look after Barn."

Hal leaned against the wall, lighting his pipe. "You can trust me to do that, pal. I'll even give you a report once a week. How's that?"

"No kidding? You will?"

"You bet. Leave me your new phone number at school. Just write it on the wall over there, everybody else does."

"What I don't understand," said Lace, "is why the person who hit 'im didn't stop."

Dooley shrugged. "It happened so fast. . . . I saw Barnabas run after the squirrel, and then the car . . . I don't know what kind of car it was. Maybe brown, I think it was brown."

Father Tim phoned Cynthia, who was frantic. A neighbor across the street told her Barnabas had been hurt and the preacher had taken him to the hospital. Harley reported he'd seen his truck roaring up Main Street, but didn't have any idea what was going on.

"He's going to be fine, Timothy," said Hal. "I'll watch him carefully for any signs of pneumonia. You know we love Barnabas like family. We won't let him suffer."

Marge nodded. "It's true, Tim. And Blake and Rebecca and I will also look after him."

Still, he felt like a heel for leaving his dog.

Blake Eddistoe walked into the yard with them and shook hands with Dooley. "Well done," he said.

At the truck, Dooley suddenly turned and said, "You ought to let me drive."

When it came to persistence, the kid was a regular Churchill. He tossed him the keys.

Dooley's eyes grew bigger. "You mean it?"

"All the way to the highway."

Dooley, now wearing one of Hal's shirts, opened the driver's door. "Get in," he said to Lace. "You can ride in th' middle."

He was glad the Meadowgate road to the highway seemed a little longer than he remembered, glad for the boy's sake. He wished the road could go all the way to Canada before it reached the highway.

He was home and in the shower before it hit him.

Today, for the first time, Dooley Barlowe had called him "Dad."

Driving to Virginia, part of Miss Sadie's letter ran through his mind.

> *. . . the money is his when he reaches the age of twenty-one. (I am old-fashioned and believe that eighteen is far too young to receive an inheritance.)*
>
> *I have put one and a quarter million dollars where it will grow,*

and have made provisions to complete his preparatory education. When he is eighteen, the income from the trust will help send him through college.

I am depending on you never to mention this to him until he is old enough to bear it with dignity. I am also depending on you to stick with him, Father, through thick and thin, just as you've done all along.

The question of sticking with Dooley had been answered nearly four years ago; he was in for the long haul. The question of when the boy might bear such information with dignity was another matter.

In truth, if he'd ever seen dignity, he'd seen it yesterday in the street. Dooley had acted with the utmost precision, wisdom, and grace.

Even so, something cautioned him about speaking of the inheritance. Soon before they reached the school, he knew the answer, and the answer was, "Wait."

"Buddy?"

"Yes, sir?"

"When you come home at Christmas, I'll loan you the keys to the Buick."

Ah, the bright hope that leapt into the boy's face. . . .

"There's only one problem."

The bright hope dimmed.

"You'll have to do your driving on back roads, and I'll have to ride in the backseat."

Dooley munched one of the cookies Lace had sent along. "OK," he said, grinning, "but try and hunker down so nobody can see you."

He rang Buddy Benfield to ask when the contract would be signed. "Whenever Ron gets back," said the junior warden, clearly uncomfortable to be talking to a man who would soon be evicted.

"Timothy."

His wife was sitting on the back stoop, having her morning coffee and looking determined about something.

"I want you to call Father Douglas to lead the service for you on Sunday."

"Whatever for?" he asked.

"Because you're exhausted."

She didn't argue, she didn't nag. She just stated the fact, and looked at him with her cornflower-blue eyes, meaning business.

"All right," he said.

She was clearly surprised. "I suppose I should quit while I'm ahead . . ."

"Probably."

" . . . but I'd also like you to plan to sleep late on Sunday morning. None of that padding around in your slippers at five a.m., like a Christmas elf."

"Keep talking," he said.

"You mean you'll actually *do* it?"

"Whatever you say," he assured her. "Just don't ask me to go to any beaches wearing a bikini."

What had Velma done to herself? She was sporting some gaudy garland of colored paper around her neck, and earrings that appeared to be small bananas. He wouldn't say so, but it looked like she'd dressed herself out of Emma Newland's closet.

"What's that?" he asked.

"A lei. Didn't you hear?"

"Hear what?"

"She's goin' on that cruise with Winnie!" said Percy, looking relieved. "Sailin' over th' deep blue sea to five ports, an' eatin' eight meals a day, includin' a midnight buffet!"

"No kidding! That's perfect! Fantastic!"

Velma put her hands over her head and wiggled her hips, which wasn't a pretty sight.

"Course, I don't know if they do the hula in St. Thomas."

"I don't think they do," said the rector. "I believe that's more of a limbo kind of place."

"Stand still," said J.C. "I'll take your picture." He raised the Nikon and banged off four shots of Velma standing at the cash register. "Won't be front page, but I think I can work it in next to 'Home Gardenin' Tips.' "

Coot Hendrick put in his two cents' worth from the counter. "You ought to have waited and took a snap of Winnie standin' next to Velma."

"You got to jump on news where you find it," said J.C. "I'm headin' to th' booth, I'm starved!"

"*You're* starved?" said Coot. "I've done had to eat a table leg to keep my strength." He despaired that Velma would ever get back to work and bring his regular order of Breakfast Number One with a fountain Pepsi.

Mule looked worried. "How's Barnabas?"

"If pneumonia doesn't set in, he'll be fine, thanks for asking. It was bad. Dooley saved his life."

"Fancy says to tell you she's sorry about what happened."

"Adele says the same."

"Thanks. I'll go out and see him tomorrow."

"Fancy said to ask why you haven't been around, said to call her anytime, she'll work you in." Mule eyed the rector's head as if searching for chicken mites. "Lookin' a little scraggly around the collar."

So be it. He didn't care if he looked like John the Baptist on a bad day, he was never setting foot—

"Th' Randall place is empty, they moved to California to be with their kids," said Mule, dispensing a round of late-breaking real estate news. "Winnie's buyer is breathin' on her pretty heavy, and Shoe Barn sold this week."

"Who to?" asked J.C., spooning yogurt onto half a cling peach.

"Who else? H. Tide."

The editor looked disgusted. "What are they tryin' to do, anyway, make Mitford a colony of Orlando?"

"I've been wondering," said the rector, "what H. Tide stands for."

"Beats me," said Mule. "Maybe High Tide. Or Henry Tide, somethin' like that. Did I hear your deacons got an offer on your house?"

"They're not deacons, they're vestry. And it's not my house."

"They'll sell it out from under you, I reckon, if they get the right price."

"Who knows?" he asked, appearing casual.

"Lookit," said J.C., pulling the *Muse* out of his briefcase. "Hot off th' press, get your own copy on th' street." He turned a couple of pages, folded the paper face out, and laid it on the table.

An entire page of small-space ads . . .

We're stickin' with Esther. Love, Esther and Gene Bolick

We're stickin' with Esther. Hope you do the same.
Tucker, Ginny, and Sue

We're stickin with Esther. She's the best. Sophia and Liza Burton

We're stickin' with Esther. Vote your conscience! The Simpson family

We're stickin' with Esther. She does what it talks about
in Psalm 72:12. A supporter

The rector slapped the table. "This is terrific! Terrific! How much do the ads cost?"

"Forty bucks," said J.C., pleased with himself.

"Where did Sophia get forty bucks?"

J.C. looked uncomfortable. "Don't ask."

"She doesn't have forty bucks."

"So? She wanted to stick up for Esther but didn't have the money. Big deal, I gave 'er the ad free, but if you tell anybody I said that . . . "

Mule gave J.C. a thumbs-up. "I don't care what people say about you, buddyroe, you're all right."

"Look here." J.C. pointed to a couple of the ads.

We're stickin' with Esther. Minnie Lomax, The Irish Woolen Shop

We're stickin' with Esther. Dora Pugh, Mitford Hardware

"Two businesses that aren't afraid to show their politics in front of God an' everybody!" said the editor, approving.

The rector drew a deep breath. Maybe this cloud had a silver lining, after all. He'd certainly drop by and congratulate Minnie and Dora. "You get around town," he said to J.C. "From where you stand, how's the election looking?"

"From where I stand?" J.C. scowled and pushed the yogurt away.

"I'd say that once this edition gets out to th' readers, it'll be runnin' about fifty-fifty."

Something or somebody would have to tip the numbers in Esther's favor, or Edith Mallory would have her claws all over Mitford. This was September fifth, and the election would be hitting the fan less than two months hence. Surely on Sunday he could offer a special prayer, or dedicate the communion service to those who unflaggingly devote themselves to the nobler welfare of the community. And speaking of Psalms, didn't the reading for Sunday say that "the mouth of them that speak lies shall be stopped"?

Ah, well. He remembered that he wouldn't be in the pulpit on Sunday, he'd be sleeping 'til noon, according to his wife's plan, and waking up strong, renewed, and altogether carefree.

"Here," he said, giving J.C. two tens and a twenty. "Run one for me next week and sign it, 'A Friend.' "

They stopped at The Local on their way to Meadowgate, to pick up a brisket for Marge Owen. While Cynthia paid their monthly bill, he inspected the contents of the butcher's case.

"Father!" It was Winnie Ivey, carrying a ten-pound bag of flour.

"I'm glad I ran into you, I've made a decision! I decided to go on th' cruise with Velma and not do anything about sellin' 'til I get back. I told the real estate people to wait, just like you said, and I feel like a different person!"

She flushed. "Can you believe I did that?"

"I can! Well done!"

"They didn't like it, they tried to push me, they said I might not get another chance. But then, guess what?"

"What?"

"They offered me another three thousand, but I said no, I'm goin' to wait, and that's that. Besides, thank th' Lord, I'm up seven percent over this time last year!"

"You don't mean it!"

"I do!" He thought Winnie Ivey looked ten years younger, all of which made him feel immeasurably better into the bargain.

"You know what?"

"What?" he asked.

"I'm gettin' to where I don't hardly want to go to Tennessee n'more. Joe said he thought he could get me a job at Graceland, but to tell th' truth, Father, I never cared much for rock an' roll."

He didn't have to be George Burns to know that timing was everything.

According to Buddy Benfield, the Malcolms would be getting back to Mitford around eleven o'clock.

He was waiting in front of their house when they pulled into the driveway.

Saturday night, and he was looking at a clean slate. No services tomorrow, no arriving early to unlock the church. . . .

Thank God he could rest in the morning. Why did he never know he needed refreshment 'til somebody hit him over the head with a two-by-four?

He ached all over with a weariness he felt even in his teeth.

Yet, how could he lie here like a hog in slop, when there was so much to be thankful for? He ought to be up and shouting and clicking his heels.

"How does it feel?" asked his beaming wife, sitting in bed against a stack of pillows.

"Wonderful. Amazing. *Powerful!*"

"Exactly how I felt!"

"I should have done something like this years ago," he said.

"Maybe. But God's timing is perfect."

"Do you really think we should go ahead with . . . ?"

She nodded. "I think so. It's a nuisance now, but it will pay off down the road."

"Maybe a breezeway someday."

"Maybe. But I'd miss popping back and forth through the hedge, wouldn't you?"

"Ah, the hedge. Where I first laid eyes on my attractive new neighbor."

She laughed happily. "Your doom was sealed."

He sat up and took her in his arms and brushed her cheek with his. "Thank you," he murmured.

"For what?"

"For being the woman you are, for putting up with me, for looking after me."

"You mean you don't think I'm a bossy dame?"

"Sometimes."

"You know what tomorrow is," she said.

"I do. Two years."

"Two *long* years?"

"Not so long," he said, kissing her ear. "But alas, I haven't had a chance to buy—"

"Don't buy me anything," she said, leaning against him. "Don't give me anything you have to wrap."

"You can count on it," he said, feeling the softness of her shoulders, the blue satin gown. . . .

She pulled away, laughing. "Maybe we should try to get some sleep, darling. It's been a long day, a whole string of long days, and besides, now that you're a home owner, you need to save your strength for all those little chores that crop up—like fixing the foundation where it's crumbling, and mending the leak over Dooley's room."

"Aha. The vestry won't be having that done anymore, will they?"

"That's right," she said, kissing him goodnight. "It's just you and me."

"And Harley," he said, brightening.

She turned out the light and rolled on her side, and for a time, he listened for her light, whiffling snore.

He missed his dog and prayed for him, thankful he was mending. He wondered about Dooley, and thought they should call him at school tomorrow, though it might be a trifle soon.

What's more, he was concerned that Father Douglas would leave out The Peace—which he was known, on occasion and for no good reason, to do.

And how would he fix the foundation, anyway? He supposed Harley would know, but what if he didn't? Probably a little mortar; and some new stones where the old had crumbled and fallen out. . . .

He rolled on his back and looked at the ceiling—his ceiling, their ceiling, the first ceiling he had ever owned, as soon as the papers were signed. Now she had a house and he had a house. Bookends. After the work on hers was finished, they would live there and rent this. "To someone with children!" Cynthia hoped.

He had liked handing Ron the check for a hundred and five thousand dollars, though it had taken his breath away to write it. . . .

"Timothy?" she said.

"Yes?"

"You're thinking."

"Right."

"Stop it at once, dearest."

He chuckled. "OK," he said.

He knew the truth, now, of what Stuart Cullen had written to him several years ago:

> *Martha has come in to tell me it is bedtime. I cannot express how wonderful it is to be sometimes told, rather than always doing the telling. . . . There she is again, my friend, and believe me, my wife does not enjoy reminding me twice. That she monitors my energy is a good thing. Otherwise, I would spill it all for Him and have nothing left with which to get out of bed in the mornings. . . .*

He reached for her, and she turned to him, eagerly, smiling in the darkness.

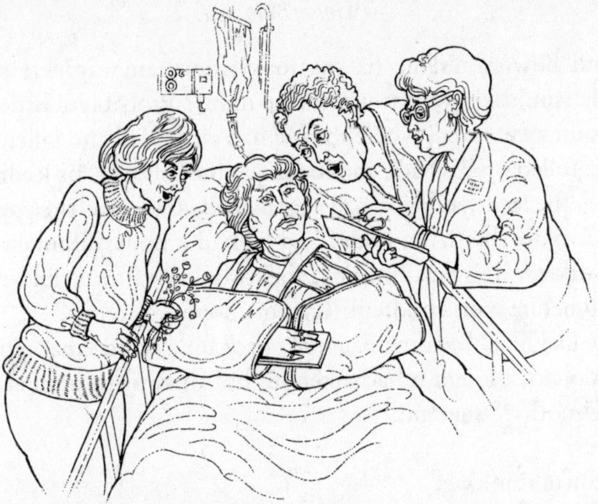

CHAPTER EIGHTEEN

A Cup of Kindness

An early October hurricane gathered its forces in the Caribbean, roared north along the eastern seaboard, and veered inland off Cape Hatteras. In a few short hours, it reached the mountains at the western end of the state, where it pounded Mitford with alarming force.

Rain lashed Lord's Chapel in gusting sheets, rattled the latched shutters of the bell tower, blew the tarps off lumber stacked on the construction site, and crashed a wheelbarrow into a rose bed.

The tin roof of Omer Cunningham's shed, formerly a hangar for his antique ragwing, was hurled toward Luther Green's pasture, where the sight of it, gleaming and rattling and banging through the air, made the cows bawl with trepidation.

Coot Hendrick's flock of three Rhode Island Reds took cover on the back porch after nearly drowning in a pothole in the yard, and Lew Boyd, who was pumping a tank of premium unleaded into an out-of-town Mustang, reported that his hat was whipped off his head and flung into a boxwood at the town monument, nearly a block away.

Phone lines went out; a mudslide slalomed down a deforested

ridge near Farmer, burying a Dodge van; and a metal Coca-Cola sign from Hattie Cloer's market on the highway landed in Hessie Mayhew's porch swing.

At the edge of the village, Old Man Mueller sat in his kitchen, trying to repair the mantel clock his wife asked him to fix several years before her death. He happened to glance out the window in time to see his ancient barn collapse to the ground. He noted that it swayed slightly before it fell, and when it fell, it went fast.

"Hot ding!" he muttered aloud, glad to be spared the aggravation of taking it down himself. "Now," he said to the furious roar outside, "if you'd stack th' boards, I'd be much obliged."

The villagers emerged into the sunshine that followed, dazzled by the spectacular beauty of the storm's aftermath, which seemed in direct proportion to its violence.

The mountain ridges appeared etched in glass, set against clear, perfectly blue skies from horizon to horizon.

At Fernbank, a bumper crop of crisp, tart cooking apples lay on the orchard floor, ready to be gathered into local sacks. The storm had done the picking, and not a single ladder would be needed for the job.

"You see," said Jena Ivey, "there's always two sides to everything!" Jena had closed Mitford Blossoms to run up to Fernbank and gather apples, having promised to bake pies for the Bane just three days hence.

"But," said another apple gatherer, "the autumn color won't be worth two cents. The storm took all the leaves!"

"Whatever," sighed Jena, who thought some people were mighty hard to please.

Balmy. Like spring. It was that glad fifth season called Indian summer, which came only on the rarest occasions.

He was doing his duties, he was going his rounds, he was poking his nose into everybody's business. How else could a priest know what was happening?

He rang the Bolicks. "Esther? How's it going?"

"I'd kill Gene Bolick if I could catch him, that's how it's goin'!"

"What now?"

"Haven't I been bakin' since the bloomin' Boer War, tryin' to get ready for Friday? And didn't I tell him, I said, 'Gene, don't you mess with these cookies, there's three hundred cookies I just baked, and I'm puttin' 'em in these two-gallon freezer bags this minute, so you'll keep your paws off.' Well, I zipped up those bags and stacked 'em in th' freezer and first thing you know, I came home last night and *who* was sittin' at the table with his head stuck in one of those two-gallon bags, goin' at it like a fox in a henhouse? I ask you!"

"You don't mean it!"

"Frozen hard as bricks and him hammerin' down on those cookies like they'd just come out of th' oven."

"Aha."

"It's a desperate man who'll do a trick like that."

"I agree. But try to forgive him," he said, knowing that Gene Bolick had not had a cookie to call his own since this whole event began brewing several months ago.

He rang off, assuring her that he'd do his part on Friday, down in the trenches with the rest of the troops.

He flipped quickly through the *Muse,* looking for another batch of *Stickin'* ads.

"Looks like Esther's pullin' ahead," said J.C., totally convinced that his small-space ad idea had done the trick. It was generally agreed that the full page of Mack Stroupe's face had been a dire mistake by the other camp. It was one thing to look at Mack's mug on a billboard, but somehow seeing it right under your nose had been a definite turnoff, according to the buzz around town.

Along with a growing number of others, the rector was beginning to feel upbeat about the outcome of the election just one month away. The wife of a deacon at First Baptist had planned a preelection Stickin' With Esther tea, and the mayor would also be riding down Main Street in a fire truck during a parade for Fire Awareness Day.

Things were definitely looking up.

Coming into the kitchen to make a pot of tea, he noted that Violet had descended from her penthouse atop the refrigerator and was curled up on his dog's bed under the table.

Thank God Barnabas was coming home on Saturday, the day after the Bane. Hal had kept him at Meadowgate nearly a month, just in case.

He'd still have the splint on for a couple of weeks, but the chest wrap had come off. The job of healing could be finished up neatly by close confinement for five or six months, with no running, chasing, or stick-fetching.

"There's certainly a lot of hilarity going on in my house," said Cynthia. She stood at the kitchen door, her head cocked to one side.

"What do you mean?"

She listened intently, as if to the music of the spheres. "Somebody's laughing!"

"What's wrong with laughter?"

She didn't answer, but came and stood by the stove, her brow furrowed, as he put the kettle on.

"Elton used six blocks t' build a model of a staircase that has three steps . . ." Harley's voice drifted up to the kitchen.

"Poor Harley," said Cynthia. "I hope he makes an A this time."

"That B-minus cut him to the quick."

"I think Lace is too hard on him."

"And you're too soft! Delivering his breakfast downstairs on a *tray*, for Pete's sake."

"You're jealous because I don't deliver yours, much less on a tray, but then, dear fellow, you have never, ever once cleaned out and organized my attic so that it looks better than my studio!"

"True."

"Nor have you ever hauled the detritus from said cleanup to the Bane, and brought me back a form which makes it all tax deductible." She turned and went quickly to the door.

"Good Lord, Timothy! Listen!"

He heard a woman's hysterical laughter coming from the little house next door.

They went out to the back stoop. The high-pitched laughter continued, followed by a crash that sounded like breaking glass.

"What on earth?" she asked. Her alarm was evident.

"I'll go and see." He didn't want to go and see; he didn't want anything out of the ordinary to be going on next door.

He darted through the hedge and up the dark steps to the screen door. He looked into Cynthia's kitchen and saw Pauline Barlowe standing at the sink. She was throwing up.

"Pauline," he said.

She retched into the sink again, then turned and stared toward the door, her eyes swollen, wiping her mouth.

"What?" she said. Her voice was cold, coarse; the stench of warm bile and alcohol permeated the room.

He opened the door and went in. "What's going on?" He tried to keep his voice free of anger, tried to make it a simple question, but failed.

"Ask y'r big high an' mighty in there what's goin' on, and if you find out, let me know, that's what *I've* been tryin' to do, is figure out what's goin' on."

She laughed suddenly and sank to the floor, leaning against the cabinets.

He walked down the hall and into the living room, where Buck Leeper sat in a Queen Anne chair, asleep and snoring, an empty vodka bottle on the lamp table and a glass on the floor at his feet.

He cleaned the kitchen and swept up a broken glass on the back stoop, while Pauline sat in a chair with her head in her hands. He sensed that she was crying, though she made no sound. Then he turned off the downstairs lights, except for the lamp in the living room and the light in the hallway. Buck didn't stir and he didn't wake him. He would deal with this tomorrow.

He drove Pauline home and they sat in the car in front of the house where her father, son, and daughter were sleeping.

The hilarity and weeping had passed; she was silent as a stone, her face turned away from him.

"We need to talk," he said.

She nodded.

"Sunday afternoon, if you can."

She nodded again. "I'm so sorry," she whispered.

He got out of the car and opened her door and helped her up the sidewalk. The temperature had dropped considerably and she was shivering in a sleeveless dress. "Will you wake anyone?"

"Don't worry," she said, still avoiding his gaze. "I won't let nobody see me like this."

When he came in from the garage, Cynthia met him in the hallway.

"It's Esther!" she said. "She had an accident, and they say it looks bad. They want you to come to the hospital at once!"

Esther! He raced to the bathroom, splashed water on his face, took his jacket off the hook in the kitchen, and once again backed the Buick out of the garage, tires screeching.

There were many ways to lose an election. He prayed to God this wasn't one of them.

"What happened?" he asked Nurse Kennedy in the hospital corridor.

"She fell off a ladder, broke her left wrist, broke the right elbow, and . . ." Nurse Kennedy shook her head.

"And what?"

"Fractured her jaw. Dr. Harper is wiring her mouth shut as we speak."

"Good Lord!"

"But she'll be fine."

"Be *fine*? How could anybody be fine with two broken limbs and her mouth wired shut?"

"It happens, Father." Nurse Kennedy sighed and continued down the hall.

He wound his way along the corridor to the waiting room, where Gene Bolick sat on a Danish modern sofa in shock.

"Where's Ray?" he asked Gene. Why wasn't Ray Cunningham here? Didn't he know his wife had had a terrible accident?

"Ray who?" queried Genc, looking stupefied.

"Esther's husband!"

"I'm Esther's husband," said Gene, as plainly as he knew how.

"You mean . . . you mean, the mayor didn't fall off a ladder?"

"I don't know about th' mayor, but Esther sure did, and it busted her up pretty bad." He appeared disconsolate.

"Good heavens, Gene, I'm sorry. Terribly sorry." He sat beside his parishioner on the sofa. "How is she?"

"Not so good, if you ask me. She was down at th' parish hall on a ladder, puttin' up signs—you know, *Kitchen Goods, Clothing Items,* such as that, and went to step down and . . ." Gene lifted his hands. "And crashed."

"Where is everybody?" Usually, when someone was rushed to the hospital in Mitford, a whole gaggle of friends and family showed up to pray, make a run on the vending machines, and rip recipes from outdated issues of *Southern Living.*

"They're down at th' parish hall, I reckon, where they've been for th' last forty-eight hours."

"I'll get the prayer chain going," said the rector. He sped along the hall to the phone, where he called his wife to put the chain in motion. "How bad is it?" asked Cynthia.

"There's a break in both arms, and they're wiring her jaws shut."

She gasped. "Good heavens!"

"I'll be here for a while."

"Poor Esther. How awful. Please tell Gene I'm sorry, I'll go see Esther tomorrow, and I'll call the chain right now. Love you, dearest."

"Love you. Keep my place warm."

Hurrying down the hall, he stopped briefly at a vending machine for a pack of Nabs and a Sprite.

He'd just finished praying with Gene for Esther to be knit back together as good as new when Hessie Mayhew rushed into the waiting room. He looked at his watch. Eleven o'clock. Hardly anyone in this town stayed up 'til eleven o'clock.

"How is she?" asked Hessie.

"Doped up," said Gene.

"I've got to see her," insisted the Bane co-chair. Given her wide eyes and frazzled hair, Hessie looked as if she'd been plugged into an electrical outlet.

"You can't see 'er," said Gene. "Just me an' th' Father can go in."

"Do you realize that at seven in the morning, the Food Committee's gettin' together at my house to bake twelve two-layer orange marmalades, and we don't even have th' *recipe*?"

Gene slapped his forehead. "Oh, Lord help!"

"I'm sure it's written down somewhere," suggested the rector.

"Nope, it's not," said Gene.

"That's right. It's not." Hessie pursed her lips. "If I've told her once, I've told her a thousand times to write her recipes down, *especially* the orange marmalade, for heaven's sake."

"It's in her head," said Gene, defending his wife.

"Well," announced the co-chair, looking determined, "we'll have to find a way to get it out!"

He arrived at the office the next morning, feeling the exhaustion of half a night at the hospital.

At two a.m., he'd left Esther resting, one arm in a cast, the other in a cast and a sling, and unable to speak a word even if she wanted to. Gene slept by her bed on a hospital cot.

How on earth anybody was going to get a cake recipe out of Esther Bolick was beyond him. In any case, Hessie had postponed the baking session until Thursday afternoon, which meant the cakes would be squeaking in under the wire—if at all.

"We *have* to have Esther's orange marmalades," she had said flatly. "People *expect* Esther's marmalades. At twenty dollars per cake times twelve, that's two hundred and forty dollars, which is nothing to sneeze at."

He yawned and sat wearily at his desk.

He was rubbing his eyes as Buck Leeper opened the door and walked in, taking off his hard hat.

"Good morning," said the rector.

Buck stood in the doorway, uneasy. "I need to talk."

"Sit down."

"I can't stay. I came to tell you I'm . . ." Buck looked at the floor, then met the rector's gaze. "I'm sorry. That was bad, what happened. I took a drink, I offered her one, and it went from there."

"Did you know she's an alcoholic? An addict?"

"Yes." Buck's voice was hoarse. "I got to tell you, I talked her into it, I shouldn't have done it, I'm sick to my gut about it."

"There's help, Buck."

The superintendent scraped his work boot on the floor, looking down. "No. I can beat this, I've been beatin' it, this is th' first time in . . . in a while. I wanted to tell you I'm movin' out, one of the crew knows a house for sale, but thinks they'll rent."

"Before we talk about that, let's name the problem. It has a name. It's your alcoholism. Your addiction."

Buck stiffened and turned away, but didn't walk to the door.

"How long have you been drinking, seriously drinking?"

"I was thirteen when my old man started pourin' it down my gullet. The first time, he made me drink 'til I puked." He faced the rector. "Bourbon. Sour mash. He liked it when I got to where I could drink him under the table, not many people could. When he died, I swore I'd never touch th' stuff again."

"But you did, and now you're suffering on your own account as well as Pauline's. Do you care for Pauline?"

"Yeah. I care for her."

"Why?"

"I respect what she's been able to do, to come back like that, out of her hell, and find faith. God, I hate what I did."

"You did it together. It takes two."

"And her kids. They're great kids. Who deserves kids like that? Nobody, not even people who have it all together, who never took a drink! I thought that maybe I could . . . maybe we could . . ."

"You can."

"No." His voice was hard. "It's too late for me."

"What if you had somebody in this thing with you, somebody who'd stick closer than a brother, somebody who'd go to bat for you, help you through it—help you over it?"

"Oh, Jesus Christ!" Buck said with disgust, moving toward the door.

"That's who I had in mind, actually."

Buck's face colored. "That crap don't work for me."

"How long have you hauled the pain of your dead brother in your gut? And how much longer do you want to haul it? Stop, friend. Stop and look at this thing that cheats you out of all that's valuable, all that's precious."

The superintendent turned and stared out the window, his back to the rector.

"You can't beat this alone, Buck. You've tried for years and it never worked. Bottom line, we're not created to go it alone, we're made to hammer out our lives with God as our defender. Going it alone may work for a while, but it never has and never will go the mile."

Buck shrugged his shoulders, still looking out the window. "Pauline knows about God and she couldn't make it."

"No, but she's going to. In any case, we don't come to God to attain perfection, we come to be saved."

"You remember my grandaddy was a preacher. There's no way I could be good enough to get saved or whatever you call it. No way."

"It isn't about being good enough."

Buck turned to him, furious. "So what is it about, for Christ's sake?"

"It's about letting Him into our lives in a personal way. You can do that with a simple prayer you can repeat with me. When we let Him in, He guarantees that we become new creatures."

"New creatures?" Buck laughed bitterly. "Who wants to be a new creature when you can't even get the old one to work?"

"New creatures make mistakes, too, they stumble around and fall in a ditch. But once the commitment is made with the heart, He takes it from there."

"It always sounded like a lot of bull to me."

Father Tim got up and stood beside his desk. "I could tell you all day what you'd gain by making that commitment—but look at it another way: What do you have to lose?"

For a time, the only sound was the ticking of the clock on the bookshelf.

"Listen," said Buck, "I'll be out of the house in a couple of days."

He moved suddenly to the door and opened it, then went down the walk to his truck, not looking back.

"The fields are white . . ."

"Buck!" said the rector. "Wait . . ."

But he didn't wait.

"They want to buy me out and let me run it," said Winnie, looking anxious. "What do you think?"

If he ever had to mess with another real estate deal . . .

"What do *you* think?" he asked.

"It sounds like a good idea. I mean, I do the work and get a regular paycheck, and they have all th' headaches." She sighed. "That might be refreshin'."

"Weren't you going to wait 'til after the cruise to make a decision?"

"They want an answer right away. Soon." She wrung her hands. "At once!"

He didn't feel he had the credentials to counsel Winnie on what amounted to the next few years of her life. "What's God saying to you about all this?"

"I still have that stuck feelin', like I don't know which way to turn."

Definitely not a good sign, but what more could he say?

"Your hair . . ." said Emma.

"What about it?" he snapped.

"Dearest," said Cynthia, "about your hair . . ."

"Don't touch it!" he said. So what if he had hacked on it himself? At least it wasn't draping over his collar like so much seaweed.

"Man!" exclaimed Mule, eyeing him with interest.

"You don't *like* it?" he asked. "I never say anything about *your* hair, I never even *notice* your hair, why you can't do the same for *me* is beyond all *imagining*—"

"Gee whiz," said Mule, looking perplexed. "I was just goin' to ask where you got that blue shirt."

When he walked into Esther's hospital room on Thursday morning, her bed was surrounded by Bane volunteers. One of them held a notepad at the ready, and he felt a definite tension in the air.

They didn't even look up as he came in.

Hessie leaned over Esther, speaking as if the patient's hearing had been severely impaired by the fall.

"Esther!" she shouted. "You've got to cooperate! The doctor said he'd give us twenty minutes and not a second more!"

"Ummaummhhhh," said Esther, desperately trying to speak through clamped jaws.

"Why couldn't she write something?" asked Vanita Bentley. "I see two fingers sticking out of her cast."

"Uhnuhhh," said Esther.

"You can't write with two fingers. Have you ever tried writing with two fingers?"

"Oh, Lord," said Vanita. "Then *you* think of something! We've got to hurry!"

"We need an alphabet board!" Hessie declared.

"Who has time to go lookin' for an alphabet board? Where would we find one, anyway?"

"Make one!" instructed the co-chair. "Write down the alphabet on your notepad and let her point 'til she spells it out."

"Ummuhuhnuh," said Esther.

"She can't move her arm to point!"

"So? We can move the notepad!"

Esther raised the forefinger of her right hand.

"One finger. *One!* Right, Esther? If it's yes, blink once, if it's no, blink twice."

"She blinked once, so it's yes. *One!* One what, Esther? Cup? Teaspoon? Vanita, are you writin' this down?"

"Two blinks," said Marge Crowder. "So, it's not a cup and it's not a teaspoon."

"Butter!" said somebody. "Is it one stick of butter?"

"She blinked twice, that's no. Try again. One *teaspoon*? Oh, thank God! Vanita, one teaspoon."

"Right. But one teaspoon of what? Salt?"

"Oh, please, you wouldn't use a teaspoon of *salt* in a *cake*!"

"Excuse me for living," said Vanita.

"Maybe cinnamon? Look! One blink. One teaspoon of cinnamon!"

"Hallelujah!" they chorused.

Esther wagged her finger.

"One, two, three, four, five . . ." someone counted.

"Five what?" asked Vanita. "Cups? No. Teaspoons? No. *Tablespoons?*"

"One blink, it's tablespoons! *Five tablespoons!*"

"Oh, mercy, I'm glad I took my heart pill this morning," said Hessie. "Is it of butter? I just have a feelin' it's butter. Look! One blink!"

"Five tablespoons of butter!" shouted the crowd, in unison.

"OK, in cakes, you'd have to have baking powder. How much baking powder, Esther?"

Esther held up one finger.

"One teaspoon?"

"Uhnuhhh," said Esther, looking desperate.

"One *tablespoon*?" asked Vanita.

"You wouldn't use a *tablespoon* of baking powder in a cake!" sniffed Marge Crowder.

"Look," said Vanita, "I'm helpin' y'all just to be nice. My husband personally thinks I am a great cook, but I don't do cakes, OK, so if you'd like somebody else to take these notes, just step right up and help yourself, thank you!"

"You're doin' great, honey, keep goin'," said Hessie.

"Look at that!" exclaimed Vanita. "She's got one finger out straight and the other one bent back! Is that one and a half? It *is,* she blinked once! I declare, that is the cleverest thing I ever saw. OK, one and a half teaspoons of bakin' powder!"

Everyone applauded.

"This is a killer," said Vanita, fanning herself with the notebook. "Don't you think we could sell two-layer triple chocolates just as easy?"

"Ummunnuhhh," said Esther, her eyes burning with disapproval.

Hessie snorted. "This could take 'til kingdom come. How much time have we got left?"

"Ten minutes, maybe eleven!"

"Eleven minutes? Are you kidding me? We'll never finish this in eleven minutes."

"I think she told me she uses buttermilk in this recipe," said Marge Crowder. "Esther," she shouted, "how much buttermilk?"

Esther made the finger and a half gesture.

"One and a half cups, right? Great! Now we're cookin'!"

More applause.

"OK," commanded the co-chair, "what have we got so far?"

Vanita, being excessively near-sighted, held the notepad up for close inspection. "One teaspoon of cinnamon, five tablespoons of butter, one and a half teaspoons of baking powder, and one and a half cups of buttermilk."

"I've got to sit down," said the head of the Food Committee, pressing her temples.

"It looks like Esther's droppin' off to sleep, oh, Lord, Esther, honey, don't go to sleep, you can sleep tonight!"

"Could somebody ask th' nurse for a stress tab?" wondered Vanita. "Do you think they'd mind, I've written checks to th' hospital fund for nine years, goin' on ten!"

"By the way," asked Marge Crowder, "is this recipe for one layer or two?"

He decided to step into the hall for a breath of fresh air.

Hammer and tong. That's how one Bane worker said they went at it on Friday.

The weather was glorious, the parish hall was full to overflowing with both goods and people, the lawn was adorned with three white tents, sheltering from any possible bad weather everything from fine antiques and children's toys to hot meals and homemade desserts. Three tour buses stood parked at the curb, signaling the penultimate event of the year.

Parkers filled the two church lots first, then sent traffic up the hill to satellite hospital parking, and down a side street to the Methodists. A stream of cars and pickups also flowed into lots behind the Collar Button, the Irish Woolen Shop, and the Sweet Stuff Bakery.

Mitford Blossoms kicked in ten parking spaces while several Main Street residents, including Evie Adams, earned good money renting their private driveways.

For the Bane workers, it was down in the trenches, and no two ways about it.

For eleven hours running, the rector made change, sorted through plunder for eager customers, dished up chili and spaghetti, boxed cakes, bagged cookies, carried trash bags to Gene Bolick's pickup, made coffee, hauled ice, picked up debris, found Band-Aids and patched a skinned knee, demonstrated a Hoover vacuum cleaner, took several cash contributions for the dig-a-well fund, told the story of the stained-glass windows, and mopped up a spilled soft drink in the parish hall corridor.

Uncle Billy came to supervise, armed with three new jokes collected especially for the occasion.

After five o'clock, vans from area companies and organizations hauled in and out like clockwork, carrying employees who proceeded to eat heartily and shop heavily.

By eight o'clock, the cleaning crew came on with a vengeance, and at eight-fifteen, a small but faithful remnant, despite weariness in every bone, arrived at the hospital, where they gathered around Esther Bolick's bed and sang, "For she's a jolly good fellow."

The marmalades, they reported, had been among the first items to go, with some anonymous donor kicking in sixty bucks—thereby bringing the total to three hundred dollars, or ten feet of well-digging.

It had been the most successful Bane in anyone's memory, and had raised the phenomenal sum of twenty-two thousand dollars. This total not only defeated the Bane's previous record by several thousand, it clearly put every other church fund-raiser, possibly in the entire world, to utter vexation and shame.

Pauline came to his office in the afternoon and sat on the visitor's bench, looking proud and strong.

"I'm goin' to AA," she said, "and I'm not seein' Buck anymore. That's the best I can do, Father, and I want to do it, and I'm askin' God to give me strength to do it." She looked at him earnestly. "Will you pray that I can?"

It was the longest speech he'd ever heard her make.

He walked home with Pauline, loving the crisp air, the blue skies.

"Whenever you think you'd like to move into your own place, I'll give you a hand, and so will Harley."

"Thank you. But I don't deserve—"

"Pauline, you've given me one of the richest gifts of this life—the chance to know Dooley Barlowe. I don't deserve that. So, let's not talk about deserving, OK?"

She looked at him and smiled. And then she laughed.

"Mr. Tim!" Jessie ran up the hall and grabbed him around the legs. "I ain't suckin' my thumb n'more. Looky there!" She held her thumb aloft and he inspected it closely.

"Buck got me to quit," she said, grinning up at him. "He give me a baby doll with hair to comb, you want to see it?"

"I do!" he said.

Jessie darted into the living room and returned with the doll. "See how 'er hair's th' color of mine, Buck said he looked at a whole *bunch* of baby dolls 'til he found this 'un. You want to hold it? Her name's Mollie, she don't wet or nothin'." She took him by the hand. "Come and sit down if you're goin' to hold 'er. Buck holds 'er a lot, but he cain't come n'more, Pauline said he cain't."

Jessie popped her thumb in her mouth, then took it out again.

Pauline glanced at the rector and shrugged and turned away, but he'd seen the sorrow in her eyes.

Bane is a Blessing To Thousands

Last Friday, Lord's Chapel gave their annual Bane and Blessing sale, which netted the record-braking sum of $22,000.

According to Bane co-chair Hessie Mayhew, major funding will be provided to dig wells in east Africa, and buy an ambulance for a hospital in Landon county. Other recipients of Bane funds include mission fields in Bosnia, Croatia, Ruwanda, Harlan County, Kentucky, and food banks throughout our local area.

Mrs. Mayhew said that special thanks are due to co-chai, Esther Bolck, who demanded the best from all volunteers and got it.

A list of volunteers is printed on the back page of today's edition. As Mrs. Bolik is sadly laid up in the hospital with two broken arms and a fractured jaw, you may send a card to room 107, but please, no visits until next Wednesday, doctor's orders. She is allergic to lilies, which kill her sinuses, but likes everything else.

A photograph of a large, fake check for twenty-two thousand dollars was included in the story.

"Who *wrote* this?" asked Father Tim.

"I've hired help," said J.C., looking expansive. "Vanita Bentley!"

"Who keyed it in?"

"I did, Vanita only does longhand. She'll be writin' a special 'Around Town' column every week from here out."

"Congratulations!" said the rector. So what if the *Muse* would never win a Pulitzer? It wasn't like it was *The New York Times*, for Pete's sake.

"*Buon giorno,* Father! Andrew Gregory, home at last!"

"Andrew! By George, you've been missed!"

Andrew laughed. The rector didn't think he'd ever heard his friend sounding quite so . . .

"Fernbank has been my fervent contemplation since we last talked," said Andrew. "I'm eager to go up and have a look. How's it faring?"

"Well, for one thing, you have an orchard full of apples, and the roof is holding its own."

"Splendid! Can you let me in to have a look around?"

"Absolutely. What's good for you? How about . . . fifteen minutes?"

"Perfect!" said Andrew, sounding . . . how *was* Andrew sounding, anyway? Was it carefree? Boyish? Relaxed?

Come to think of it, who wouldn't be relaxed after three months of visiting cousins in Italy?

When Father Tim arrived at Fernbank, Andrew's gray Mercedes was already parked in the drive, and Andrew stood waiting on the porch with a man and woman.

As he trotted up the steps, he couldn't help but notice that the woman was exceedingly attractive, nearly as tall as the tall Andrew, and with a striking figure. He blinked into the dazzling warmth of her smile, hardly noticing the dark-haired man standing with them.

"Father!"

"Welcome home, my friend!"

They embraced, and Andrew kissed the rector, European-style, on both cheeks.

"Father, first I'd like to introduce you to Anna, my cousin . . ."

Good heavens, this was a *cousin*?

". . . and my wife," said the beaming Andrew.

CHAPTER NINETEEN

Fernbank

Surprised, if not stunned, by joy, the rector could scarcely speak. "Congratulations!" he blurted. "*Mazel tov!* Ah, *felicitaziones!*"

Andrew pumped his hand. "Well done, Father! And this is Anna's brother, Antonio Nocelli."

"Call me Tony!" said Antonio, embracing the rector and kissing him on either cheek. "I have heard much about you, Father."

"While I have heard nothing at all about you and Anna!"

Anna laughed, throwing her head back. "Let me say, Father, that Andrew is our *fourth* cousin, so you must not alarm."

"Yes, for heaven's sake, don't alarm!" said Andrew, chuckling.

Anna shrugged and smiled. "My English? Not perfect."

"Whose is?" asked the rector. "Well, shall we go in? Would you like to take them in while I wait outside?"

"Heavens, no, you must come in, also," said Andrew. The rector thought he'd never seen his friend so tanned, so boyish, so eager.

"Here's the key, then. Fernbank will be yours soon enough, why don't you unlock the door?"

"I am very excited," Anna told her husband.

Tony agreed. "We could not sleep for thinking of the house Andrew has taken into his heart."

Andrew swung the double doors open, and they walked in. There was a moment of hushed silence.

"Ahh, *bella . . .*" said Tony. *"Molto bella!"*

Anna opened her arms to the room. "It is beautiful! Just as you said!"

"A bit damp, my dear, but—"

"But, *amore mio,* sunlight can fix!"

"Anna believes sunlight can fix everything," Andrew told the rector, pleased.

They strolled through the house, savoring each room.

Anna touched the walls, the banisters, the furnishings, often murmuring, "Fernbank . . ."

In the ballroom, he told the story of the painted ceiling and two other Italians, a father and son, who had come all the way to Mitford to paint it, living with Miss Sadie's family for nearly three years.

As angels soared above them among rose-tinted clouds, he felt oddly proud, like a father proud of a child, eagerly savoring the cries of delight.

Someone to love Fernbank! Thanks be to God!

Indian summer had drawn on, offering a final moment of glad weather.

They sat on Miss Sadie's frail porch furniture, which the rector had dusted off. Andrew and Anna took the wicker love seat.

"Now!" said Andrew. "We will tell you everything."

Father Tim laughed. "Easy. I can't handle much more excitement."

"Tony and Anna owned a wonderful little restaurant in Lucera, only a few steps from my *penzione.* The food was outstanding, perhaps the best I've had in my travels around the Mediterranean. I began to go there every day for lunch."

"Soon," said Anna, looking boldly at Andrew, "he came also for dinner."

"Tony cooked, Anna served, we discovered we were cousins, and, well . . ." Andrew smiled, suddenly speechless.

"Shy," said the rector, nodding to the others.

Anna made a wickedly funny face. "He is not shy, Father, he is English!" She put her arms stiffly by her sides, pretending to be a board. "But that is outside! Inside, he is Italian, tender as fresh *ravioli*! If not this, I could not marry him and come so far from home!" She laughed with pleasure, and brushed Andrew's cheek with her hand.

"The building that contained the restaurant was being rezoned," said Andrew, "and Mrs. Nocelli died last year . . ."

Anna and Tony crossed themselves.

"The cousins had moved away, some to Rome, others to Verona; the vineyard had sold out of the family, so there were almost no ties left. Yet, when I asked Anna to marry me, I feared she wouldn't leave Italy."

Anna patted her husband's knee. "Timing is good, Father."

"Don't I know it?"

Andrew smiled easily. "The Nocellis are an old wine-making family in Lucera. We were married by their priest of many years. Fortunately, I was able to squeak in under the wire because of my Catholic boyhood."

"Your children," said the rector, "do they know?"

"Oh, yes. They came to Lucera for the wedding. They are very happy for us."

"Any children for you, Anna?"

"I never had children, Father, and my husband was killed ten years behind by a crazy person in a fast car."

"And so at Fernbank," Andrew said, "Anna and Tony and I will have our home and open a very small restaurant."

"Very small!" exclaimed Anna.

"And very good!" said Tony, giving a thumbs-up. The rector thought Tony was nearly as good-looking—and good-natured—as his sister.

Unable to sit still another moment, Andrew rose and made a proclamation. "We will call the restaurant Lucera, in honor of their lovely village and my mother's girlhood home—and the wine for the restaurant will come from one of the many old vineyards which have produced there since the tenth century."

"*Brava,* Lucera!" said Tony. "*Brava,* Mitford!"

"Good heavens!" The rector felt the wonder of it. "An Italian restaurant in Mitford, wine from old vineyards, and handsome people to live in this grand house! Miss Sadie would be dazzled. We shall all be dazzled!"

Anna stood, nearly dancing with expectation. "I am longing to visit the apples!"

"In those shoes, my dear?" asked Andrew.

"I shall take them off at once!" she said, and did so.

As he walked up Wisteria toward the rectory, he looked at his house in the growing darkness, trying to find the sense of ownership he expected to feel. Oh, well, he thought, that will come when the pipes burst in a hard winter and I'm the one to pick up the tab.

He patted his coat pocket. In it was a check for fifteen thousand dollars, given him at this evening's vestry meeting.

Ron Malcolm had presented it with some ceremony. "Father, we priced the house to allow for a little negotiation. H. Tide wanted it so badly, they didn't try to negotiate, so you paid top price. We all feel that ninety thousand is fair to you and to us, and . . . we thank you for your business!"

Warm applause all around.

He was feeling positively over the top. A two-story residence of native stone, all paid for, and fifteen thousand bucks in his pocket. Not bad for an old guy.

He whistled a few bars from the Pastorale as he ran up the front steps to tell his wife the good news.

He didn't know where Buck had moved, and though he saw the superintendent on the job site, nothing was mentioned of his new whereabouts.

Buck had left the yellow house spotless. This, however, hardly mattered, since the late-starting conversion would be getting under way next week. It would be all sawdust and sawhorses for longer than he cared to think, and Buck would probably leave it in someone else's hands as soon as the attic job was finished.

He didn't want to lose Buck Leeper. In some way he couldn't explain, Buck was part of Mitford now.

§

"Timothy!"

"Stuart! I was just thinking of you."

"Good, I hope?"

"I wouldn't go that far," said the rector, chuckling. "What's up, old friend?"

"*Old* friend. How odd you'd say that. I'm feeling a hundred and four."

"Whatever for? You've just been where people wear bikinis."

Stuart groaned. "Yes, and where I held my stomach in for two long weeks."

"Holding your stomach in is no vacation," said the rector.

"Look, I'm over on the highway, headed to a meeting in South Carolina. Can we meet for coffee?"

"Coffee. Hmmm. How about the Grill? It's close to lunchtime. I'll treat."

"Terrific. Main Street, as I recall?"

"North of The Local, green awning, name on the window. When?"

"Five minutes," said the bishop, sounding brighter.

§

"This," he said, introducing his still-youthful seminary friend, "is my bishop, the Right Reverend Stuart Cullen."

"Right Reverend . . ." said Percy, pondering. "I guess you wouldn't hardly talk about it if you was th' Wrong Reverend."

"Percy!" said Velma.

"Oh, for heaven's sake, don't listen to Timothy, call me Stuart." Stuart shook hands all around, and the rector watched him charm the entire assembly.

"Hold it right there!" J.C. hunkered over his Nikon and cranked off six shots in rapid succession.

"I ain't never seen a pope," said Coot Hendrick, wide-eyed.

"Not a pope, a bishop," said Mule.

Percy looked puzzled. "I thought you said he was a reverend."

"Call me Stuart and get it over with," pleaded the bishop, hastening to a booth with Father Tim.

Stuart poured cream in his coffee. "By the way, someone told me that Abraham's route to Canaan now requires four visas."

"Not surprising, since it's a six-hundred-mile trip. I wouldn't mind seeing the real thing one day. I was just remembering from a study we did in seminary that Canaan is the birthplace of the word *Bible.*"

"Not to mention the birthplace of our alphabet. So, how would you like a stint on the Outer Banks at some point? I fancy it might be your Plain of Jezreel, at the very least."

"Tell me more."

"Wonderful parish, small Carpenter Gothic church, historic cemetery, gorgeous setting . . ."

"Keep talking."

"There's a rector down there who'd like nothing better than a mountain church. I have just the church, and Bill Harvey, who's the bishop in that diocese, thinks we might work out a trade—you could go down as an interim . . . the summer after you retire."

"I'll mention it to Cynthia. Let me know more. So when are *you* going out to Canaan, my friend?"

"I knew you'd ask, but I don't know. I'm still terrified, just as you were."

"How did I get smarter than you?"

"You're older," said Stuart, grinning. "Much older."

"Remember Edith Mallory?"

"The vulture who tried to get her talons in your hide."

"We have an election coming up, and I feel certain she's been funneling big money to the opposition."

"Who's the opposition?" asked Stuart, taking a bite of his grilled cheese sandwich.

"Not known as the sort who'd be good for this town."

"If I know where you're going with this, the best policy is hands off."

"I agree. Especially since I have no proof."

"Poisonous business. But you know the antidote."

"Prayer."

"Exactly. How's your Search Committee coming along? I haven't had a report recently."

"I'm pretty much out of the loop," said the rector, "but they seem excited. We surveyed the parish, and the consensus is for a young priest with children."

"They can save all of us some heartache by asking the candidates a central question."

"Which is?"

"'Do you believe Jesus is God?'"

"Right. I've talked about that with the committee. Sad state of affairs when we have to point such a question at candidates who took the ordination vows . . ."

The bishop sighed. "Paul said in the second epistle to the good chap you were named after, 'The time is coming when people will not put up with sound doctrine . . . they will accumulate for themselves teachers to suit their own desires, and will turn from the truth and wander away to myths.' Ah, Timothy . . ."

"Eat up, my friend. You've got a long haul ahead of you. Why aren't you flying?"

"I'm driving because I need time to think, I need some time alone."

"A man has to get in a car and hurtle down the interstate to get time alone? Ah, Stuart . . ."

Stuart chuckled. "Two weeks at the beach doesn't solve everything."

"Especially not when you're holding your stomach in," said the rector.

"I've done it," Winnie announced.

He couldn't tell whether she was going to laugh or cry.

"Would you take this copy of the contract home and look it over?" she asked. "I had a lawyer look it over, but I don't know how good he is, maybe if you're not too busy, you could do it, I should have asked you before. Course I guess it's too late now, since it's mailed, but still, if you would . . ."

"I don't know what help I can be, but yes, I'll look it over." Dadgum it, why didn't he just go study for a broker's license? He seemed to be spending as much time in real estate as in the priesthood.

"They've about ragged me to death, Father. I guess I'll stay on and run it." She looked white as a sheet, he thought.

"I'm thrilled to hear you'll stay in Mitford. Your business is thriving, you have a legion of friends here—"

"But my family's up there—a brother and sister and two nieces and a nephew."

"I know. But aren't we family? Don't we love you?" Shame on him, trying to win her heart from her own blood kin.

"I'll be glad to go on that cruise next week," she said, not looking glad about anything.

Lace was sitting at the kitchen table doing her history homework when Dooley called from school. Father Tim answered the wall phone by the sink. "Rectory . . ."

"I'm on my way to study hall."

"Hey, buddy!"

"Hey, yourself," said Dooley. "What's going on?"

"Not much. What about you?"

"We're having our fall mixer tomorrow night. Man!"

"Man, what?"

"Four busloads of girls are coming, maybe five."

"Man!" He agreed that seemed to say it all.

"How's Barn?"

"Looking good. Eating well. Sleeping a lot."

"I sort of miss him."

"He misses you more. So, what kind of mixer is it?"

"We're having a band, it's gong to be in the field house. I helped decorate."

"Aha."

"We hung a lot of sheets with wires and turned it into a huge tent. It's neat, you should see it."

"When are we coming up for a visit?"

"I'll let you know. I gotta go."

"Want to say a quick hello to Lace? She's here."

"Sure."

He handed the phone to Lace. "Dr. Barlowe."

Her smile, which he had seldom seen, was so spontaneous and unguarded, he blushed and left the room.

They were sitting at the table having a cup of tea as Lace organized her books and papers to go home.

"What's interesting in school these days?" Cynthia wanted to know.

"I just found out about palindromes, I'm always lookin' for 'em," she said.

"Like Bob, right?"

"Right. Words that're the same spelled forwards or backwards. Like that," she said, pointing to the contract he'd left lying on the table, "isn't a palindrome, it says H. Tide readin' forwards, and Edith if you read it backwards. But guess what, you can also make a palindrome with whole sentences, like 'Poor Dan is in a droop.'"

"Neat!" said Cynthia.

"See you later," she said, going to the basement door. "'Bye, Harley! Read your book I left on the sink!"

"What did you leave on the sink?" inquired the rector, filled with curiosity.

"Silas Marner."

"Aha. Well, come back, Lace."

"Anytime," said Cynthia.

"OK!"

He pulled the contract toward him.

EdiT .H

His blood pounded in his temples. Edith? Could H. Tide be owned by Edith Mallory?

Is that why H. Tide wanted the rectory so urgently? Edith knew he and Cynthia would be living in the yellow house. Did she want to control the house next door to him in some morbid, devious way?

"What is it, Timothy?"

"Nothing. Just thinking." He took the contract into the study and sat at his desk, looking out the window at the deepening shadows of Baxter Park.

Mack Stroupe. H. Tide. Edith Mallory.

If what Lace just prompted him to think was true, Edith was now trying to get her hands on another piece of Main Street property. The way she had treated Percy wasn't something he'd like to see happen to anyone else, especially Winnie. And what might Edith be trying to gouge from Winnie, who was selling her business without the aid of a realtor?

He glanced at the contract—it was right up there with cave-wall hieroglyphs—and called his attorney cousin, Walter. "You've reached Walter and Katherine, please leave a message at the sound of the beep. We'll return your call with haste."

Wasn't a signed contract legal and binding?

He paced the floor.

Edith Mallory had always held a lot of real estate. But why would she sell the Shoe Barn to her own company? He didn't understand this. Was he making too much of a name spelled backward?

Then again, why had Mack Stroupe swaggered around town, boasting of his influence on H. Tide's buying missions?

Another thing. Could Miami Development have anything to do with all this? Or was that merely a fluke?

He didn't know what the deal was, but he knew something was much worse than he had originally believed.

He knew it because the feeling in the pit of his stomach told him so.

Walter rang back.

"Cousin! What transpires in the hinterlands?"

"More than you want to know. Legal question."

"Shoot," said his cousin and lifelong best friend.

After talking with Walter, he rang an old acquaintance who worked at the state capitol. So what if it was nine-thirty in the evening and he hadn't seen Dewey Morgan in twelve years? Maybe Dewey didn't even work at the state capitol anymore.

"No problem," said Dewey, who'd received quite a bureaucratic leg up in the intervening years. "I'll call you tomorrow."

"As quickly as possible, if you'd be so kind. And if you're ever in Mitford, our guest room is yours."

"I may take you up on it. Arlene has always wanted to see Mitford."

If all the people he'd invited to use the guest room ever cashed in their invitations . . .

At ten o'clock, the phone rang at the church office.

"Tim? Dewey. I looked up the name of the undisclosed partner in H. Tide of Orlando, right? And also Miami Development. It says here Edith A. Mallory—both companies. Hope that's what you're looking for."

"Oh, yes," he said. "Exactly!"

He'd been looking for it, all right, but he hated finding it.

He pushed through the curtains to the bakery kitchen without announcing himself from the other side.

"Winnie, I've got to tell you something."

"What is it, Father? Sit down, you don't look so good."

"H. Tide is owned by someone who may not treat you very well, I won't go into the details. The truth is, you probably don't want to sell to these people and be under their management."

"Oh, no!"

"You'd be in the hands of Percy's landlord. I think you should talk to Percy."

"But I've already signed the contract and sent it off."

"And I've just talked with my cousin who's an attorney. Please.

Talk with Percy about his landlord. And if you don't like what you hear, we need to move fast."

She wiped her hands and straightened her bandanna. "Whatever you say, Father."

"Don't get 'is blood pressure up 'til we've served th' lunch crowd," said Velma.

She turned to Winnie. "I'm takin' three pairs of shorts, not short short, just medium, three tops, and two sleeveless dresses with my white sweater. Are you takin' a formal for Captain's Night?"

"Oh, law," said Winnie, looking addled, "I don't even have time to think about it, I don't know what I'm takin', I don't have a formal."

"Well, be sure and take a pair of shoes with rubber soles so you don't slip around on deck." Velma had been on a cruise sponsored by her children, and knew what was what.

"Velma," urged the rector, "we need to move quickly. May I ask Percy just one question? How high can his blood pressure shoot if we ask just one question?"

"Oh, all right, but don't go on and on."

Coot Hendrick banged a spoon against his water glass. Ever since Velma got invited on that cruise, she hadn't once refilled his coffee cup unless he asked for it outright.

The rector motioned to the proprietor. "Percy, give us a second, if you can."

Percy stepped away from the grill, slapping a towel over his shoulder, and came to the counter.

Why was he always putting himself in the middle of some unpleasant circumstance? Had he become the worst thing a clergyman could possibly become—a meddler?

"Percy, now, take it easy. Don't get upset. I just need you to tell Winnie about . . ."

"About what?"

"Your landlord."

The color surged into Percy's face. Two hundred and forty volts, minimum.

"Just a sentence or two," he said lamely.

He marched down to Sweet Stuff with Winnie, who called H. Tide to say she was withdrawing the contract. She held the phone out for him to hear the general babble that erupted on the other end.

According to Walter, until the contract had been delivered back to the seller by the buyer, either by hand or U.S. mail, it was unenforceable.

When she hung up, he went to a table out front and thumped down in a chair. His own blood pressure wasn't exactly one-twenty over eighty.

"Earl Grey!" he said to Winnie. "Straight up, and make it a double."

Once again, the candy had been snatched from Edith Mallory's hand. She'd lost Fernbank. She'd lost the rectory. And now she'd lost a prime property on Main Street.

In truth, the only property she'd been able to buy was one she already owned.

He was certain she'd make every effort not to lose Mack Stroupe.

Winnie served his tea, looking buoyant. "Lord help, I feel like a truck's just rolled off of me. Now I'm right back where I started—and glad to be there!"

"I have a verse for you, Winnie, from the prophet Jeremiah. 'The Lord is good to those whose hope is in Him, to the one who seeks Him; His compassions never fail. They are new every morning; great is His faithfulness.'"

"Have a piece of chocolate cake!" said Winnie, beaming. "Or would you like a low-fat cookie?"

Esther Bolick was at home and mending, Barnabas was gaining strength, the yellow house was full of sawing and sanding, Cynthia's book was finished, and Winnie and Velma had sent postcards back to Mitford.

Percy taped Velma's to the cash register.

Dear Everybody, Wish you were here, you wouldn't believe the colors of the fish, their like neon. Winnie is sunburnt. If you include the ice

cream sundae party and early bird breakfast on deck, you can eat 11 times a day. I am keeping it to 9 or 10. Ha ha.
Velma

Winnie had left a sign in her window:

Gone cruisin.' Back on October 30

Percy trotted down the street and taped her postcard next to the sign.

Hi, folks, sorry I can't be here to serve you, but I am in the Caribean soaking up some sun. The Golden Band people had a fruit basket in our cabin and champagne which gave Velma a rash. Gosh, its beautiful down here, some places there are pigs in the road, though. Well, you keep it in the road til I get back, I will have you a big surprise in the bake case. Winnie

"Father? Scott Murphy!"

He could hear it in Scott's voice. "When? Who?" he asked.

"Last night! Two men who've been showing up every Wednesday, one with his kids. They said they wanted to know more about God's plan for their lives, and we talked, and they prayed and it was a wondrous thing, marvelous. Homeless is beside himself. He thinks that next summer we may be able to do what Absalom Greer did, have weekly services on the creek bank."

"You must tell me every detail," said the rector. "Want to run together tomorrow morning?"

"Six-thirty, starting from my place?"

"You got it."

Scott laughed, exultant. "Eat your Wheaties," he said.

Andrew rang to find out if Buck Leeper might be available for the renovation of Fernbank. "I don't think so, but I'll ask him," he said.

"I'll also be looking for a good nursery. I'd like to replace some of the shrubs and trees."

"I know a splendid nursery, though their trees are fairly small."

"At my age, Father, one doesn't permit oneself two things—young wine and small trees."

The rector laughed.

"I'd give credit to the fellow who said that, but I can't remember who it was—another distinguishing mark of advancing years."

"Come, come, Andrew. You're looking like a lad, thanks to your beautiful bride! I'm smitten with Anna, as everyone else will be. Thanks for bringing Anna and Tony to Mitford. I know they'll make a wonderful difference."

"Thank you, Father, we're anxious to get started on the hill. Anna would like to have a couple of rooms finished by Christmas, though it could take a year to do the whole job properly, given our weather."

"Let me step down to the church and see what's up. If Buck is interested, I'll have him ring you."

He left the office, zipping his jacket, eager to be in the cold, snapping air, and on a construction site where the real stuff of life was going on.

"Early December, I'm out of here," said Buck, stomping the mud off his work boots. "Your house is in good hands and I'll keep in touch, I'll check on it."

"Well, you see, there's another job for you up the hill at Fernbank. I know Andrew Gregory would be a fine person to work with, and certainly Miss Sadie would be thrilled, she was so pleased with what you did at Hope House—"

"I've laid out long enough," Buck said curtly.

Father Tim pressed on. "I believe if you stayed in Mitford, there'd be plenty of work for you. You could grow your own business."

"No way. There's nothing here for me."

He thought of Jessie and the doll . . .

"Well, then," he said, feeling a kind of despair.

"I brought you somethin'!" said Velma.

"Me? You brought *me* something?"

"Lookit," said Velma, taking a tissue-wrapped item from a bag.

She held up a shirt with orange, red, and green monkeys leaping around in palm trees.

"Aha. Well. That's mighty generous . . ."

"You helped Winnie win th' contest, and I got to go free, so . . ."

"I'll wear it!" he said, getting up for the idea.

"Have you seen what Winnie brought home?" asked Percy.

"Can't imagine."

"And don't you tell 'im, either," said Velma. "He gets to find that out for hisself. Go on down there and look and I'll start your order. But hop to it."

Tanned people returning from exotic places seemed to bring new energy home with them. He fairly skipped to the bake shop.

He inhaled deeply as he went in. The very gates of heaven! "Winnie!" he bellowed.

She came through the curtains. Or was that Winnie?

"Winnie?" he said, taking off his glasses. He fogged them and wiped them with his handkerchief. "Is that you?"

"Course it's me!" she said. Winnie was looking ten years younger, maybe twenty, and tanned to the gills.

"Velma said you brought something back."

"Come on," she said, laughing. "I'll show you."

He passed through the curtains and there, standing beside the ovens, was a tall, very large fellow with full, dark hair and twinkling eyes, wearing an apron dusted with flour.

"This is *him*!" crowed Winnie, looking radiant.

"Him?"

"You know, the one I always dreamed about standin' beside me in th' kitchen. Father Kavanagh, this is Thomas Kendall from Topeka, Kansas."

"What . . . where . . . ?"

"I met him on th' ship!"

"In the kitchen, actually," said Thomas, extending a large hand and grinning from ear to ear. "I'm a pastry chef, Father."

"You stole the ship's pastry chef? Winnie!"

They all laughed. "No," said Winnie, "it was his last week on the job, he was going back to Kansas and decided he'd come home with me first. He's stayin' with Velma and Percy."

No doubt about it, he was dumbfounded. First Andrew, now Winnie . . .

"He likes my cream horns," she said, suddenly shy.

"Who doesn't?"

Thomas put his arm around Winnie and looked down at her, obviously proud. "I'm mighty glad to be in Mitford," he said simply.

"By jing, we're mighty glad to have you," replied the rector, meaning it.

Esther Cunningham released a special news story to the *Mitford Muse,* which ran the morning before the election.

"When I'm re-elected," she was quoted as saying, "I'll give you something we've all been waiting for—new Christmas decorations!" The single ropes of lights up and down Main Street had caused squawking and grumbling for over a decade. So what if this solution had been forced by economic considerations, when it made the town look like a commuter landing strip?

"Stick with the platform that sticks by the people," said the mayor, "and I'll give you angels on Main Street!"

He was among the first at the polls on Tuesday morning. He didn't have to wonder about Mule's and Percy's vote, but he was plenty skeptical about J.C.'s. Had J.C. avoided looking him in the eye when they saw each other in front of Town Hall?

His eyes scanned the crowd.

The Perkinses, they were big Esther fans. And there were Ron and Wilma . . . surely the Malcolms were voting for Esther. Based on the crowd standing near the door, he figured eight or nine out of ten were good, solid, dependable *Stickin'* votes.

So what was there to worry about?

Mack's last hoorah had been another billboard, which definitely hadn't gone over well, as far as the rector could determine.

"Did you see th' pores in his face?" asked Emma, who appeared completely disgusted. They looked like craters on th' moon. If I never set eyes on Mack Stroupe again, it'll be too soon!"

From the corner of his eye, he watched her boot the computer and check her E-mail from an old schoolmate in Atlanta, a prayer chain in Uruguay, and a church in northern England. Emma Newland in cyberspace. He wouldn't have believed he'd live to see the day.

He walked up the street after lunch, leaning into a bitter wind. As Esther Bolick still wasn't going out, he hoped Gene had seen to turning in her proxy vote.

"Good crowd?" he asked at the polls.

"Oh, yes, Father. Real good. Bigger than in a long while."

He adjusted his *Stickin'* button and stood outside, greeting voters, for as long as he could bear the knifing wind.

He hoped his bishop didn't drive by.

"You and Cynthia come on over and bring that little fella who lives in your basement," said the mayor.

"Harley."

"Right. I'd like to get him workin' on our RV. Anyway, we're havin' a big rib feast while they count th' votes, Ray's cookin'."

"What time?" he asked, thrilled that his carefully watched food exchange would actually permit such an indulgence.

"Th' polls close at seven-thirty, be at my office at seven thirty-five."

"Done!" he said. He could just see the red splotches breaking out on the mayor.

Uncle Billy and Miss Rose were there when he arrived with Cynthia and Harley. Cynthia zoomed over to help Ray finish setting up the food table.

"I've done got a joke t' tell you, Preacher."

"Shoot!" he said. "And tell Harley, while you're at it."

Miss Rose sniffed and stomped away.

"Rose don't like this 'un," said Uncle Billy. "Well, sir, a feller died who had lived a mighty sinful life, don't you know. Th' minute he got down t' hell, he commenced t' bossin' around th' imps an' all, a-sayin' do this, do that, and jump to it. Well, sir, he got so dominatin' that th' little devils reported 'im to th' head devil who called th' feller in, said, 'How come you act like you own this place?'

"Feller said, 'I do own it, my wife give it to me when I was livin'.'"

Harley bent over and slapped his leg, cackling. Father Tim laughed happily. Oh, the delight of an Uncle Billy joke.

"Seein' as you like that 'un, I'll tell you 'uns another'n after we've eat."

"I'll keep up with you," promised the rector.

Aha, there was a fellow clergyman, heedlessly exposing his political views. Bill Sprouse of First Baptist bowled over with his dog, Sparky, on a leash. "Sparky and I were out walking, Esther hailed us in."

"You stuck with Esther at the polls, I devoutly hope."

"Is the Pope a Catholic?"

"You bet," said the rector, shaking his colleague's hand. "Reverend Sprouse, Harley Welch."

"Pleased to meet you, Harley. I heard you're mighty good with automobiles. Here lately, my car's been actin' funny, don't know what th' trouble is, makes a real peculiar sound. Kind of like *ooahooojigjigooump*. Like that."

Harley nodded, listening intently. "Might be y'r fan belt."

Ray Cunningham strode up, wiping his hands on a tea towel. "Got you boys some ribs laid on back there, I want you to eat up. Harley, be sure and get with me before you leave. I got a awful knock in my RV engine."

"What time do you think we'll know somethin'?" wondered Bill Sprouse.

"Oh, 'bout nine," said Ray, who, after eight elections, considered himself heavily clued in.

The rector backed away from Sparky, who seemed intent on raising his leg on his loafer.

"For th' Lord's sake, Sparky!" the preacher hastily picked up his dog, whereupon Sparky draped himself over his master's arm, looking doleful.

"Esther's got Ernestine Ivory up at th' polls where the countin's goin' on," said Ray. "She'll run down here when it's all over, shoutin' th' good news. Well, come on, boys, and don't hold back, I been standin' over a hot stove all day."

Omer rolled in, flashing a fugue in G major. "Ninth term comin' up!" he said to his sister-in-law, giving her a good pounding on the back.

Uncle Billy yawned hugely. "Hit's way after m' bedtime," he said as the clock struck nine. Miss Rose, who even in her sleep looked fierce, was snoring in a blue armchair transported years ago from the mayor's family room. In her hands, Miss Rose clutched several tightly sealed baggies of take-outs.

"Won't be long," announced Ray. "Doll, does Ernestine have the cell phone? She ought to at least be callin' in with a status report."

The phone rang as if on cue, making several people jump.

"Speak of th' devil," said Bill Sprouse, who often did.

The mayor bounded across the room to her desk. "Hello? Ernestine? Right. Right."

Every eye in the room was on Esther Cunningham, as the color drained slowly from her face.

"You don't mean that, Ernestine," she said in a low voice.

Everybody looked at everybody else, wondering, aghast.

Esther slowly hung up the phone.

"Mack Stroupe," she said, unbelieving, "is th' mayor of Mitford."

CHAPTER TWENTY

New Every Morning

In the stunned silence that followed the announcement of Mack Stroupe's win, Ernestine Ivory delivered yet another confounding report:

He had won by one vote.

Esther Cunningham's various red splotches congregated as a single flame as she dialed the Board of Elections bigwig at home and demanded a recount on the following Thursday.

No problem, he said.

Feeling Ray's supper turned to stone in their alarmed digestive systems, and not knowing what else to say or do, nearly everyone fled for home.

Looking ashen, Uncle Billy shook Miss Rose awake. "Esther's lost," he said.

"Esther's *boss*?" shouted Miss Rose. "She's always been boss, and always will be, so what's the commotion?"

As the Lord's Chapel bells tolled seven a.m., he left home with Barnabas and turned north on Main Street. Following Hal's orders, they could now cover a couple of blocks of their running route, but only at normal walking speed.

As they passed Sweet Stuff, he saw Thomas, attired in an apron and baker's hat, putting a tray of something illegal in the window. The big, dark-haired fellow looked up and smiled, waving.

This was only the second time he'd laid eyes on Thomas Kendall, yet it seemed as if the jovial baker had always been there. His face was utterly comfortable and familiar.

"Father!"

He was hoofing past the office building and closing in on the Grill when he turned around and saw Winnie. She waved furiously. "Can you come back a minute?"

Barnabas yanked the leash from his hand and galloped toward Winnie, who always smelled like something good to eat. Before she could duck, he lunged up to give her face a proper licking.

"Oh, no!" she whooped.

"The Lord is good to those whose hope is in Him," bellowed the rector, "His compassions never fail!"

Barnabas sprawled on the sidewalk, obedient. He could not, however, resist licking the powdered sugar off Winnie's shoes.

"They are new every morning! Great is his faithfulness!"

Barnabas sighed, desisted, and rolled over on his back.

"Amen!" shouted Winnie. "You said my verse!"

"What's up with you on this glorious day?"

"Can you come in a minute, Father? We were going to call you today, we have somethin' special to tell you." He thought she might begin jumping up and down.

They trooped into the bakery, as Thomas came through the curtains with yet another tray from the kitchen.

"Good morning, Father! Top of the day! It's baclava!" The rector felt his knees grow weak as Thomas displayed the tray of honey-drenched morsels under his very nose; Barnabas salivated.

"Please have one," urged Winnie. "I never made baclava in my life, but Thomas is an expert."

Thomas decided they should all thump down and have a diamond-shaped piece of the flaky baclava. This moment's indiscretion would cramp his food exchanges for a week, mused the rector. How could he be such a reckless gambler when he appeared so altogether conservative?

"Guess what?" said Winnie, unable to wait any longer.

"I can't guess," he replied, although, in truth, he thought he might be able to.

"Thomas isn't going back to Kansas City."

"Aha."

"Not to live, anyway."

"Father," said Thomas, "I'd like to ask you for Winnie's hand in marriage."

"Aha!" Was Thomas Kendall a man of character? Would he be good for Winnie? He'd simply have to trust his instincts, which, as far as he could tell, had no reservations at all.

"He's th' one, Father," Winnie said with conviction. "God sent him."

"Well, then!"

The men laughed, then stood and embraced, slapping each other on the back. The rector pulled out a handkerchief and blew his nose.

"Oh, for gosh sake!" said Winnie, dabbing her eyes with the hem of her apron.

"I'll be gladder than glad to give you her hand in marriage, Thomas, but Winnie, what about your brother? Shouldn't he have the say in this?"

Winnie beamed. "Joe told us to ask you. He said whatever you say is fine with him." She looked proudly at the gentle man beside her.

"Would you perform the ceremony, Father? Sometime in early January? I need to run back to Kansas to see my mother and pack up a few boxes. I've lived on and off a cruise ship for fifteen years, so I haven't accumulated much." Thomas's large hand covered Winnie's.

"Velma will be matron of honor," Winnie said, barely able to contain her joy.

The rector took Winnie's other hand.

"May the Lord bless you both!" he said, meaning it.

"Hello, Father Kavanagh here—"

"Town Hall, tomorrow at four o'clock," said Esther Cunningham darkly. "I told th' Lord I'd give up sausage biscuits. *Pray!*"

"I *am* praying!" he exclaimed.

"Timothy?" Cynthia looked thoughtful. "About your hair . . ."

Not again.

"You could drive to Charlotte."

"Not in this lifetime."

"You could forgive Fancy Skinner, and—"

"I have forgiven Fancy Skinner, which has nothing to do with the fact that I will never set foot in her chair again."

She eyed him. "That's one way to put it."

"Never," he said, eyeing her back.

He was there at three forty-five, as was nearly everyone else, as far as he could see. Even Esther Bolick turned up, with Gene, who looked worried.

Mack Stroupe stood near the door, shaking hands as if the event were in his honor. He frequently stepped outside to smoke, where he flipped the butts into the pansy bed.

Esther Cunningham steamed in with Ray, their five beautiful daughters, and a mixture of grandchildren and great-grandchildren, including Sissy and Sassy, who had come in tow with Puny, straight from day care. He lifted Sissy into his arms and sat next to Puny in the block of seats occupied by the Cunningham contingent.

"This is the most aggravation in th' world," announced his house help. "I had to let your toilets go to come over here and mess with this foolishness."

"You can let my toilets go anytime," he said, jiggling Sissy.

She glared at Mack Stroupe, who was laughing his loud, whinnying laugh and talking with a band of supporters. "If I wadn't a Christian, I'd march over there an' scratch his eyes out!" She examined her nails, as if she might really consider doing such a thing.

Joe Joe Guthrie, Puny's husband and the Cunninghams' grandson, slipped in next to them. "What do you think, Father?"

Joe Joe looked at him the way so many had looked at him over the years, as if he could prophesy exactly how things would turn out. It was not one of the ways he enjoyed being looked at.

The recounting was labored, taking nearly three hours. People milled around, going in and out, smoking, muttering, laughing. Some of those accustomed to an early dinner drove over to the highway, wolfed down a pizza, and returned smelling of pepperoni.

Others stayed glued to their seats, counting every vote with the three Board of Elections officials. Sassy fell asleep, while Sissy tore around the hall as if on wheels.

At a little before seven, he moved across the aisle to sit with the Bolicks. "The end is near," said Gene, looking worn.

The votes were running neck and neck. Mack or Esther would pull ahead in the counting, and then the other would catch up and move ahead.

As the stack of ballots slowly dwindled, the laughing and muttering, hooting and yelping died down.

Something had better happen here pretty quick, he thought, as the last three ballots were held up and counted.

"Ladies and gentlemen!" exclaimed the Board of Elections official, "according to the recount, which ya'll have witnessed here with your own eyes . . . it's a tie."

A communal gasp resounded through the hall, followed by murmurs and shouts.

"What we do . . ." the elections official said, trying to speak over the hubbub. The hubbub escalated wildly.

He pounded the mayor's podium with the gavel. "According to th' by-laws, what we do in such a case is . . . we flip a coin."

The rector leaned forward in his chair. Flip a coin? You determine the well-being of a whole town by flipping a coin?

"God help us," said Esther Bolick.

He saw that Esther Cunningham had turned deathly pale. Where were the fiery splotches, the indomitable spirit? Come on, Esther . . .

He prayed the prayer that never fails.

"Ladies first," said the elections official. "Heads . . . or tails?"

Breathless silence.

Esther Cunningham stood and peered into the crowd as if she were about to deliver the Gettysburg Address.

"Heads!" she said in a voice that thundered beyond the back row and bounced off the wall.

The elections official looked toward the door. "Mr. Stroupe?"

Mack Stroupe shrugged.

The official put his hand into his pocket and brought it out again, looking embarrassed. "Ah, anybody got a nickel or a dime?"

Someone rushed to give him a quarter, as the other two officials drew near, ready to verify the outcome.

He took a deep breath, cleared his throat, and bowed slightly over the coin. Then, working his mouth silently as if uttering an official oath, he flipped it.

Around Town
—by Vanita Bentley

Last night, in the parish hole of Lord's Chapel, Bane and Blessing co-chairs Esther Bolick and Hessie Mayhe, were feted at a supper in their honor.

Along with nearly eighty volunteears, some from other Mitford churches, Bolck and Mayhew raised $22,000 and were praised for their "heroic endeavor" by Father Timothy Kavanagh.

"Hero simply means someone who models the ideal" said Rev. Kavanagh, "and these volunteears have done this for all of us.

"Also, a hero can be someone who saves lives in a valiant way and these volunteears have almost certainly done that, as well."

The reverend said Bane proceeds have been used for food

and medical supplys to Zaiear, pure well water in several east African villages, and a ambulance for Landon, where two children died last yr for lack of medical ade.

"The Bane has always been a blessing to others," he said. "But this year, thanks to the outstanding organizational skills of two women and their willingness to serve as unto the Lord, we may all celebrate a special triumph for His kingdom."

Bolk and Mayew were presented with plaques and other volunteers were each given a bag of goodies by local merchants.

Mrs. Bvolk whose jaws were wired shut due an accident reported here previously got to request a special dinner of mashed potatoes and gravey to celebrate being able to eat real food again.

If time does, indeed, fly, it was the season when it became a Concorde jet, as far as the rector was concerned.

Following the annual All-Church Thanksgiving Feast, which, thankfully, was held this year at First Baptist, events went into overdrive.

Cynthia drove Dooley back to school on St. Andrew's Day, while the rector prepared the sermon for the first Sunday of Advent and began the serious business of trying to juggle the innumerable Advent activities, not the least of which was Lessons and Carols, to be performed this year on a grand scale with the addition of a visiting choir and an organist from Cambridge, England, all of whom would stay over in parish homes for five days and participate in the Advent Walk on December 15, after which everyone would come to the rectory for a light supper in front of the fire.

"Light supper, heavy dessert," said Cynthia, paging frantically through their cookbooks.

He panted just thinking about it all, and so did his wife, who was making something for everyone on her list, and running behind.

"Whatever you do," she told him at least three times, "don't look in *there.*" Upon saying this, she would point to the armoire, which he always stayed as far away from as possible.

Then, of course, there was the annual trek into the woods at the north end of the Fernbank property, to hew down a Fraser fir with the Youth Group, which would become the Jesse tree in front of the altar, followed by a visit to the Sunday School to discuss the meaning of the ornaments the children would be making for the tree, and the courtesy call on the Christmas pageant rehearsal, which this year, much to the shock of the parents and the dismay of at least two teachers, would be done in modern dress, inspired by the recent success of the movie *Hamlet* in which Hamlet had worn blue jeans with what appeared to be a golf shirt.

"What will we do with all these *wings*?" wailed a teacher who had voted for traditional costumes, and lost.

He made himself scarce whenever the wrangling over the pageant issue erupted, and gave himself to the more rewarding annual task of negotiating with Jena Ivey for forty-five white poinsettias and the cartload of boxwood, balsam, fir, and gypsophila to be used on Christmas Eve for the greening of the church.

"Why can't you do the negotiating?" he once asked a member of the Altar Guild.

"Because she likes you better and you get a better price," he was told. This notion of improved economics had engraved the mission in stone and caused it to belong, forever, to him.

He had to remember to order the Belgian chocolates for the nurses at the hospital, and meet with the organist and choir director to thrash through the music for the Christmas Eve services, and put in his two cents' worth about the furniture being ordered for the new upstairs Sunday School rooms, and call Dooley's schoolmate's parents to see if they'd bring him to Mitford on their way to Holding, and check to see if anybody was going to visit Homeless Hobbes and sing carols with him this year, and go through what Andrew Gregory didn't want at Fernbank and help Harley haul it to Pauline's tiny house behind the post office so it would look like a home in time for . . .

"We've done it again," proclaimed his wife, shaking her head.

They gazed at each other, spent and pale.

"Next year," she said, relieved, "it will be different."

Next year, he would not be running around like a chicken with its head cut off, because next year, he would not have a parish.

Suddenly his eyes misted, just thinking about it.

Less than twelve months hence, his parishioners would be standing around him in the parish hall, singing "For he's a jolly good fellow," and giving him money, and a plaque of some sort, and tins of mixed nuts.

§

After the wedding, Winnie and Thomas planned to move into her cottage by the creek, while Scott Murphy would move his wok and precious few other possessions into Winnie's present quarters, once the home of Olivia Harper's socialite mother.

"Musical chairs!" said Cynthia.

§

It was the season of good news and glad tidings, in every way. Joe Ivey was moving back to Mitford.

"Hallelujah!" Father Tim said.

Winnie looked pleased as punch. "He said people kept askin' if Elvis was really dead, and he just couldn't take it anymore. He'll barber in that little room behind th' Sweet Stuff kitchen."

"Baking and barbering!" said the jubilant rector. "I like it!" A little off the sides and a fruit tart to go.

§

"Look!" said Jessie. "A baby in a box."

She stood on tiptoes, holding her doll, and gazed into the crèche that had belonged to his grandmother.

He realized she didn't know about the Babe, and wondered how his life could be so sheltered that he should be surprised.

He glanced at his watch and picked her up and stood looking down upon the crèche with her. Standing there in the lamplit study, he told her about the Babe and why He came, as she sucked her thumb and patted his shoulder and listened intently.

Four days before Christmas, and he was running ragged like the rest of crazed humanity. He resisted glancing at his watch again, and set her down gently as the front doorbell gave a blast.

If that wasn't a fruitcake from the ECW, he'd eat his hat. Or, more likely, it was the annual oranges from Walter.

"I came to say . . . so long." Buck Leeper stood in the stinging cold, bareheaded.

He had dreaded this moment. "Come in, Buck!"

"I can't, I'm on my way to Mississippi, I just—"

"Buck!" Jessie came trotting down the hall and grabbed the superintendent around the legs, as Barnabas raced in from the kitchen, barking.

"Please," said the rector, standing back for Buck to come in. "We're keeping Jessie while Pauline shops for pots and pans. Come on back, we'll scare up something hot for the road."

"Well," Buck said, awkward, then stooped and picked Jessie up in his arms.

They walked down the hall and into the study, where a fire simmered on the hearth. Buck stood in the doorway as if in a trance, taking in the tree ablaze with tiny lights and the train running around its base.

Suddenly the rector saw the room with new eyes, also—the freshly pungent garlands over the mantel and the candles burning on his desk, reflected in the window. He had been passing in and out of this room for days, scarcely noticing, enjoying it with his head instead of his heart.

Buck abruptly set Jessie down and squatted beside her on one knee. "Look, you have a good Christmas," he said, speaking with some difficulty.

Her eyes filled with tears. "Buck, please don't go off nowhere!"

"I've got to," he said.

She threw her arms around his neck, sobbing. "Me an' Poo wanted you to live with us!"

Buck held her close and covered his eyes with his hand.

"Don't cry," said Jessie, clinging to him and patting his shoulder. "Please don't cry, Buck."

He stood and wiped his eyes on the sleeve of his jacket. "Thanks for . . . everything. Your job is in good hands. I'll let myself out."

Buck stalked out of the study and up the hall, closing the front door behind him. The rector had been oddly frozen in place, unable to move; Jessie stood at the study door, crying, holding her doll.

The clock ticked, the train whistled and clacked, the fire hissed.

He walked over to her with a heavy heart and touched her shoulder.

She looked up at him, stricken. "Buck shouldn't of done that," she said.

Seven-thirty a.m., and he'd already gone through yesterday's mail, typed two letters, and been to see Louella.

Surely he could take ten minutes . . .

He walked to the end of the corridor and opened the door without knocking, just as he'd always done.

"Oh, rats, I might have known that was you," said Esther Cunningham, using both hands to hide something on her desk.

"What's the deal? What're you hiding? Aha! A sausage biscuit!"

"It's no such thing, it's a *ham* biscuit!"

"Sausage, ham, what's the difference?"

"I specifically spoke to th' Lord about *sausage,*" she said, her eyes snapping, "so lay off."

"Esther, Esther."

He sat down and put his feet up on the Danish modern coffee table, grinning.

She grinned in return, gave him a thumbs-up, then threw back her head and roared with laughter.

Ah, but it was good to hear the mayor laughing again.

As a bachelor, he had wondered every year what to do on Christmas eve. With both a five o'clock and a midnight service, he struggled to figure out when or what to eat, whether to open a few presents after he returned home at nearly one a.m. on Christmas morning, or wait and do the whole thing on Christmas afternoon while he was still exhausted from the night before.

Now it was all put into perspective and, like his bishop who loved being told what to do for a change, he listened eagerly to his wife.

"We're having a sit-down dinner at two o'clock on Christmas Eve, and we'll open one present each before we go to the midnight service. We will open our presents from Dooley on Christmas morning, because he can't wait around 'til us old people get the stiffness out of our joints, and after brunch at precisely one o'clock, we'll open the whole shebang."

She put her hands on her hips and continued to dish out the battle plan.

"For brunch, of course, we'll invite Harley upstairs. The menu will include roasted chicken and oyster pie, which I'll do while you squeeze the juice and bake the asparagus puffs."

All she needed was a few military epaulets.

"After that, Dooley will go to Pauline's and spend the night, and our Christmas dinner will be served in front of the fire, and we shall both wear our robes and slippers!"

She took a deep breath and smiled like a schoolgirl. "How's that?"

How was that? It was better than good, it was wonderful, it was fabulous. He gave her a grunting bear hug and made her laugh, which was a sound he courted from his overworked wife these days.

He reached up to the closet shelf for the camera and touched the box of his mother's things—the handkerchiefs, her wedding ring, an evening purse, buttons . . .

He stood there, not seeing the box with his eyes, but in his memory. It was covered with wallpaper from their dining room in Holly Springs a half century, an eon, ago. Cream colored roses with pale green leaves . . .

He would not take it down, but it had somehow released memories of his mother's Christmases, and the scent of chickory coffee and steaming puddings and cookies baking on great sheets; his friends from seminary gathering 'round her table; and the guest room with its swirl of gifts and carefully selected surprises, tied with the signature white satin ribbon.

He stood there, still touching the box, recalling what C. S. Lewis had said. It was something which, long ago, had expressed his own feelings so clearly.

"With my mother's death," Lewis wrote, "all settled happiness, all that was tranquil and reliable, disappeared from my life. There was to be much fun, many pleasures, many stabs of Joy; but no more of the old security. It was sea and islands now; the great continent had sunk like Atlantis. . . ."

"Mother . . ." he whispered into the darkened warmth of the closet. "I remember. . . ."

He wasn't surprised that he hadn't seen Mack Stroupe again at Lord's Chapel. It appeared that even his hotdog stand was closed—perhaps for the holidays, he thought.

He didn't want to consider whether he'd ever see Edith Mallory again.

"I do this every year!" said Cynthia, looking alarmed.

"Do what?"

"Forget the cream for tomorrow's oyster pie. And of course no one will be open tomorrow."

It was that lovely lull between the five o'clock and midnight services of Christmas Eve, and he was sitting by the fire in a state of contentment that he hadn't felt in some time. Tonight, after the simplicity of the five o'clock, which was always held without the choir and the lush profusion of garlands and greenery, would come the swelling rush of voices and organ, and the breathtaking spectacle of the nave bedecked, as if by grace, with balsam, fir, and the flickering lights of candles.

He roused himself as from a dream. "I'll run out and find some. I think Hattie Cloer is open 'til eight."

"I'm so sorry."

"Don't be. You cook, I fetch. I get a much better deal." He took her face in his hands and kissed her on the forehead, then went to the kitchen peg for his jacket.

"Man! What's that terrific smell?" He sniffed the air, homing in on the oven.

"Esther's orange marmalade cake! Vanita Bentley gave me a bootleg copy of her recipe. She ran off dozens on her husband's Xerox."

"Where's your conscience, Kavanagh?"

"Don't worry, this is legal. I called Esther and she gave me permission to use it. Have at it! she said."

"Oh, well," he sighed, feeling diabetic and out of the loop.

"You can have the tiniest sliver, dearest. I'm sure your food exchange will allow it."

If she only knew. "Harley!" he called down the basement stairs. "Want to run to the highway?"

"Yessir, Rev'rend, I do, I'm about t' gag on this book about that feller hoardin' 'is gold."

He heard Dooley and Barnabas clambering down from above. "Where're you going?" asked Dooley.

"To the store. Want to come?"

"Sure. Can I drive?"

"Well . . ."

"You said I could when I came home for Christmas."

"Right. Consider it done, then!" Perfect timing! It was just getting dark, and hardly a soul would be out on a cold Yuletide eve.

Harley came up the stairs, wearing a fleece-lined jacket that he'd found, good as new, at the Bane. "I was hopin' f'r a excuse t' lay that book down. It ain't even got a picture in it!"

Barnabas stood in the fray, wagging his tail and hoping to be invited, as the doorbell gave a sharp blast.

"I'll get it!" said the rector, hurrying along the hall.

It was Buck Leeper, standing in the pale glow of the porch light.

"I got as far as Alabama and turned around," he said. "I'm willing to do whatever it takes."

CHAPTER TWENTY-ONE

Lion and Lamb

Buck was shaking as they went into the study. Though the rector knew it wasn't from the cold, he asked him to sit by the fire.

There was a long silence as Buck waited for the trembling to pass; he sat with his head down, looking at the floor. The rector remembered the times of his own trembling, when his very teeth chattered as from ague.

"Does Pauline know you're back in Mitford?"

"No. I came for . . . I came for this." He looked up. "I didn't want to come back."

"I know."

"It was sucking the life out of me all the way. I was driving into Huntsville when I knew I couldn't keep going . . ."

He was shaking again, and closed his eyes. Father Tim could see a muscle flexing in his jaw.

"God a'mighty," said Buck.

Father Tim looked at him, praying. The man who had controlled some of the biggest construction jobs in the Southeast and some of the most powerful machinery in the business couldn't, at this moment, control the shaking.

"I pulled into an Arby's parkin' lot and sat in the car and tried to pray. The only thing that came was somethin' I'd heard all those years in my grandaddy's church." Buck looked into the fire. "I said, Thy will be done."

"That's the prayer that never fails."

The clock ticked.

"He can be for your life what the foundation is for a building."

Buck met his gaze. "I want to do whatever it takes, Father."

"In the beginning, it takes only a simple prayer. Some think it's too simple, but if you pray it with your heart, it can change everything. Will you pray it with me?"

"I don't know if I can live up to . . . whatever."

"You can't, of course. No one can be completely good. The point is to surrender it all to him, all the garbage, all the possibilities. All."

"What will happen when . . . I pray this prayer?"

"You mean what will happen now, tonight, in this room?"

"Yes."

"Something extraordinary could happen. Or it could be so subtle, so gradual, you'll never know the exact moment He comes in."

"Right," said Buck, whispering.

The rector held out his hand to a man he'd come to love, and they stood before the fire and bowed their heads.

"Thank You, God, for loving me . . ."

"Thank You, God . . ." Buck hesitated and went on, "for loving me."

". . . and for sending Your Son to die for my sins. I sincerely repent of my sins, and receive Christ as my personal savior."

The superintendent repeated the words slowly, carefully.

"Now, as Your child, I turn my entire life over to You."

". . . as Your child," said Buck, weeping quietly, "I turn my entire life over to You."

"Amen."

"Amen."

He didn't know how long they stood before the fire, embracing as brothers—two men from Mississippi; two men who had never known the kindness of earthly fathers; two men who had determined to put their lives into the hands of yet another Father, one believing—and one hoping—that He was kindness, Itself.

In the kitchen, Cynthia said, "You won't believe this! Look!"

She pointed under the kitchen table, where Barnabas and Violet were sleeping together. The white cat was curled against the black mass of the dog's fur, against his chest, against the healing wound.

Father Tim sank to his knees, astounded, peering under the table with unbelieving eyes.

"It's a miracle," Cynthia told Buck. "They've been mortal enemies for years. You can't imagine how he's chased her, and how she's despised him."

Barnabas opened one eye and peered at the rector, then closed it.

"The lion shall lie down with the lamb!" crowed Cynthia.

"Merry Christmas, one and all!" whooped the rector.

"Merry Christmas!" exclaimed his wife.

"Right," said Buck. "You, too."

"I thought you'd never get finished." Dooley came up the basement steps with Harley. "Hey, Buck, I thought you'd left for Mississippi. How's it goin'?"

"Real good, what are you up to?"

Dooley pulled a pair of gloves out of his jacket pocket. "I'm drivin' to the store! Let's bust out of here, I'm ready."

"Settin' on high idle, is what he is," said Harley.

They trooped to the garage and pushed the button that opened the automatic door. It rose slowly, like a stage curtain, on a scene that stopped them in their tracks.

"Snow!" Dooley shouted.

It was swirling down in large, thick flakes and already lay like a frosting of sugar on the silent lawn.

"Maybe you'd better let me drive," said the rector.

"I can drive in snow! Besides, I won't go fast, I'll go really slow."

"I don't reckon they's any cows out plunderin' around in this, Rev'rend."

Buck and Harley climbed into the backseat, and he slid in beside Dooley. "This isn't Harley's truck, buddy, so there's no clutch. Remember to keep your left foot—"

"I know how," said Dooley.

As they turned right on Main Street, there they were, on every lamppost—angels formed of sparkling lights, keeping watch over the snow-covered streets.

"By jing," said Harley, "hit's another world!"

"Glorious!" said the rector. The Buick seemed to be floating through a wonderland, lighter than air. He turned the radio to his favorite music station. *Hark the herald angels . . .*

"Buck, where are you staying?"

"I'll bunk in with one of my crew for a couple days, then head back. Emil's got me on a big job in Texas startin' January."

"Why don't you bunk in with us? Harley, would you let Buck use your sofa bed? Cynthia's using the guest room as a gift-wrapping station."

"Hit'd be a treat. I sleep s' far down th' hall, I don't reckon I'd keep you awake with m' snorin'."

"And you'll have brunch with us tomorrow, if that suits."

"I'd like that," said Buck. "Thank you."

Dooley braked at the corner. "Let's ride by Mama's, want to?"

"I'll go anywhere you 'uns say," declared Harley.

"We'll just ride by and honk th' horn," said Dooley, "then let's ride by some more places before we go to the store, OK?"

The rector grinned. "Whatever you say, buddy. You're driving."

Dooley turned left at the corner and made a right into the alley. Pauline's small house, nestled into a grove of laurels, was a cheerful sight, with the lights of a tree sparkling behind its front windows and the snow swirling like moths around the porch light.

Dooley hammered on the horn, and the rector cranked his window down as Pauline, Poo, and Jessie appeared at the door.

"Look, Mama, I'm drivin'!"

"Dooley! Father! Can you come in?" She peered at the rear window, but was unable to see anyone in the darkened backseat.

"We're on a mission to the store, but we'll see you tomorrow. Merry Christmas! Stay warm!"

"Merry Christmas, Mama, Jessie, Poo! See you tomorrow!"

"Merry Christmas! We're bakin' the ham you sent, Father, be careful, Dooley!"

"Merry Christmas, Mr. Tim!"

Sammy and Kenny, thought the rector. He hoped he would live to see the day . . .

Dooley put the Buick in low gear and glided off.

"Burn rubber!" yelled Poo.

At the end of the alley, Buck leaned forward, urgent. "Father, I can't . . . I'd like to go back and see Pauline and the kids. Do you think it would be all right?"

Dooley spoke at once. "I think it would."

"Go," said the rector.

In the side mirror, he saw Buck running along the alley, running toward the light that spilled onto the snow from the house in the laurels.

"The last time we had snow at Christmas, we burned the furniture, remember that?" he asked, as Dooley turned onto Main Street. It was, in fact, the blizzard the media had called the Storm of the Century.

Dooley cackled. "We were bustin' up that ol' chair and throwin' it in th' fireplace, and fryin' baloney . . ."

"Those were the good old days," sighed the rector, who certainly hadn't thought so at the time.

Dashing through the snow . . .

He was losing track of time, happy out here in this strange and magical land where hardly a soul marred the snow with footprints, where Dooley sang along with the radio, and Harley looked as wide-eyed as a child. . . .

And there was Fernbank, ablaze with lights through the leafless winter trees, crowning the hill with some marvelous presence he'd never seen before. He wanted suddenly to see it up close, feel its warmth, discover whether it was real, after all, or a fanciful dream come to please him at Christmas.

"Want to run by Jenny's?" he asked. "It's on the way to the store."

"Nope," said Dooley. "Let's go by Lace's."

"Excellent! Then we can run over to Fernbank while we're at it."

"And by Tommy's! He'll hate my guts."

"Anywhere you want to run, Harley?"

"No, sir, I've done run to where I want t' go, hit's right here with you 'uns."

They should have brought presents—fruitcakes, candy, tangerines! He was wanting to hand something out, give something away, make someone's face light up . . .

Bells on bobtail ring, making spirits bright, what fun it is to ride and sing a sleighing song tonight! Hey! . . .

They honked the horn in the Harper driveway and shouted their season's greetings, then drove up the long, winding lane to Fernbank, where he would have been contented merely to sit in the car and look at its lighted rooms with a candle in every window.

They circled around to the front steps and honked, as Andrew and Anna came to the door and opened it and waved, calling out felicitations of their own. "Don't mention this to Rodney Underwood!" he said to the couple on the porch.

Andrew laughed. "Our lips are sealed! *Joyeux noël!*"

"Ciao!" cried Anna. "Come soon again!"

They eased down the Fernbank drive and saw the town lying at the foot of the steep hill like a make-believe village under a tree. There was the huge fir at Town Hall with its ropes of colored lights, and the glittering ribbon of Main Street, and the shining houses.

An English writer, coincidentally named Mitford, had said it so well, he could recite it like a schoolboy.

She had called her village "a world of our own, close-packed and insulated like . . . bees in a hive or sheep in a fold or nuns in a convent or sailors in a ship, where we know everyone, and are authorized to hope that everyone feels an interest in us."

Go tell it on the mountain, over the hills and everywhere . . .

After a stop by Tommy's and then by Hattie Cloer's, they headed home.

"Harley, want to have a cup of tea with us before tonight's service?"

"No, sir, Rev'rend, I'm tryin' t' fool with a batch of fudge brownies to bring upstairs tomorrow."

Temptation on every side, and no hope for it.

"Say, Dad, want to watch a video before church? Tommy loaned me his VCR. It's a baseball movie, you'll like it."

If there were a tax on joy on this night of nights, he'd be dead broke.

"Consider it done!" he said.

He sat clutching the pint of cream in a bag, feeling they'd gone forth and captured some valuable trophy or prize, as they rode slowly between the ranks of angels on high and turned onto their trackless street.

Visit America's favorite small town—
one book at a time

Welcome to the next book,

A New Song

CHAPTER ONE

Angel of Light

Dappled by its movement among the branches of a Japanese cherry, the afternoon light entered the study unhindered by draperies or shades.

It spilled through the long bank of windows behind the newly slipcovered sofa, warming the oak floor and quickening the air with the scent of freshly milled wood.

Under the spell of the June light, a certain luster and radiance appeared to emerge from every surface.

The tall chest, once belonging to Father Tim's clergyman great-grandfather, had undergone a kind of rebirth. Beneath a sheen of lemon oil, the dense grain of old walnut, long invisible in the dark rectory hallway next door, became sharply defined. Even the awkward inscription of the letter M, carved by a pocketknife, could now be discovered near one of the original drawer pulls.

But it was the movement and play of the light, beyond its searching incandescence, that caused Father Tim to anticipate its daily arrival as others might look for a sunrise or sunset.

He came eagerly to this large, new room, as if long deprived of light or air, still incredulous that such a bright space might exist, and especially that it might exist for his own pursuits since retiring six months ago from Lord's Chapel.

As the rector of Mitford's Episcopal parish, he had lived next door in the former rectory for sixteen years. Now he was a rector no more, yet he owned the rectory; it had been bought and paid for with cash from his mother's estate, and he and Cynthia were living in the little yellow house.

Of course—he kept forgetting—this house wasn't so little anymore; he and his visionary wife had added 1,270 square feet to its diminutive proportions.

Only one thing remained constant. The house was still yellow, though freshly painted with Cynthia's longtime favorite, Wild Forsythia, and trimmed with a glossy coat of the dark green Highland Hemlock.

"Cheers!" said his wife, appearing in jeans and a denim shirt, toting glasses of lemonade on a tray. They had recently made it a ritual to meet here every afternoon, for what they called the Changing of the Light.

He chuckled. "We mustn't tell anyone what we do for fun."

"You can count on it! Besides, who'd ever believe that we sit around watching the light change?" She set the tray on the table, next to a packet of mail.

"We could do worse."

They thumped onto the sofa, which had been carted through the hedge from the rectory.

"One more week," he said, disbelieving.

"Ugh. Heaven help us!" She put her head back and closed her eyes. "How daunting to move to a place we've never seen . . . for an unknown length of time . . . behind a priest who's got them used to the guitar!"

He took her hand, laughing. "If anyone can do it, you can. How many cartons of books are we shipping down there, anyway?"

"Fourteen, so far."

"And not a shelf to put them on."

"We're mad as hatters!" she said with feeling. During the past week, his wife had worked like a Trojan to close up the yellow house, do most of the packing, and leave their financial affairs in order. He, on the other hand, had been allowed to troop around town saying his goodbyes, sipping tea like a country squire and trying to keep his mitts off the cookies and cakes that were proffered at every turn.

He had even dropped into Happy Endings Bookstore and bought two new books to take to Whitecap, a fact that he would never, even on penalty of death, reveal to Cynthia Kavanagh.

She looked at him and smiled. "I've prayed to see you sit and relax like this, without rushing to beat out a thousand fires. Just think how the refreshment of the last few weeks will help you, dearest, when we do the interim on the island. Who knows, after all, what lies ahead and what strength you may need?"

He gulped his lemonade. Who knew, indeed?

"The jig, however, is definitely up," she said, meaning it. "Next week . . ."

"I know. Change the furnace filter next door, weed the perennial beds, fix the basement step, pack my clothes . . . I've got the entire, unexpurgated list written down."

"Have your suit pressed," she said, "buy two knit shirts—nothing with an alligator, I fervently hope—and find the bicycle pump for Dooley."

"Right!" He was actually looking forward to the adrenaline of their last week in Mitford.

"By the way," she said, "I've been thinking. Instead of loading the car in bits and pieces, just pile everything by the garage door. That way, I can check it twice, and we'll load at the last minute."

"But it would be simpler to—"

"Trust me," she said, smiling.

Barnabas would occupy the rear seat, with Violet's cage on the floor, left side. They'd load the right side with linens and towels, the trunk would be filled to the max, and they'd lash on top whatever remained.

"Oh, yes, Timothy, one more thing . . . stay out of the bookstore!"

She peered at him with that no-nonsense gleam in her sapphire eyes, a gleam that, for all its supposed authority, stirred a fire in him. As a man with a decidedly old-shoe nature, he had looked forward to the old-shoe stage of their marriage. So far, however, it hadn't arrived. His blond and sensible wife had an unpredictable streak that kept the issues of life from settling into humdrum patterns.

"Anything wonderful in the mail?" she asked.

"I don't know, I just fetched it in. Why don't you have a look?"

His wife's fascination with mail was greater even than his own, which was considerable. William James, in his opinion, had hit the nail on the head. "As long as there are postmen," James declared, "life will have zest."

"Oh, look! Lovely! A letter from Whitecap, and it's to *me*!"

He watched her rip open the envelope.

"My goodness, listen to this. . . .

" '*Dear Mrs. Kavanagh, We are looking forward with great enthusiasm to your interim stay in our small island parish, and trust that all is going smoothly as you prepare to join us at the end of June.*

" '*Our ECW has been very busy readying Dove Cottage for your stay at Whitecap, and all you need to bring is bed linens for the two bedrooms, as we discussed, and any towels and pillows which will make you feel at home.*

" '*We have supplied the kitchen cupboards with new pots, and several of us have lent things of our own, so that you and Father Kavanagh may come without much disruption to your household in Mitford. Sam has fixed the electric can opener, but I hear you are a fine cook and probably won't need it, ha ha.*

" '*Oh, yes. Marjorie Lamb and I have done a bit of work in the cottage gardens, which were looking woefully forlorn after years of neglect. We found a dear old-fashioned rose, which I hear your husband enjoys, and liberated it from the brambles. It is now climbing up your trellis instead of running into the street! We expect the hydrangeas and crepe myrtle to be in full glory for your arrival, though the magnolias in the churchyard will, alas, be out of bloom.*

" '*Complete directions are enclosed, which Marjorie's husband, Leonard, assures me should take you from Mitford straight to the door of Dove Cottage without a snare. (Leonard once traveled on the road selling plumbing supplies.)*

" '*Please notice the red arrow I have drawn on the map. You must be very careful at this point to watch for the street sign, as it is hidden by a dreadful hedge which the property owner refuses to trim. I have thought of trimming it myself, but Sam says that would be meddling.*

" '*We hope you will not object to a rather gregarious greeting committee, who are bent on giving you a parish-wide luau the day following your arrival. I believe I have talked them out of wearing grass skirts, but that embarrassing notion could possibly break forth again.*

" '*When Father Morgan joined us several years ago, he, too, came in the summer and was expecting a nice holiday at the beach. I'm sure you've been warned that summer is our busiest time, what with the tourists who swell our little church to bursting and push us to two services! We all take our rest in the winter when one must hunker down and live off the nuts we've gathered!*

" '*Bishop Harvey was thrilled to learn from Bishop Cullen how greatly you and Father Kavanagh were appreciated by your parish in Mitford! We shall all do our utmost to make you feel as welcome as the flowers in May, as my dear mother used to say.*

" '*Goodness! I hope you'll forgive the length of this letter! Since childhood, I have loved the feel of a pen flowing over paper, and often get carried away.*

" '*We wish you and Father Timothy safe travel.*

" '*Yours sincerely,*

" '*Marion Fieldwalker, vestry member of St. John's in the Grove, and Pres. Episcopal Church Women*

" '*P.S. I am the librarian of Whitecap Island Community Library (35 years) and do pray you might be willing to give a reading this fall from one of your famous Violet books. Your little books stay checked out, and I believe every child on the island has read them at least twice!*' "

His wife flushed with approval. "There! How uplifting! Marion sounds lovely! And just think, dearest—trellises and old roses!"

"Not to mention new saucepans," he said, admiring the effort of his future parishioners.

She drank from her perspiring glass and continued to sort through the pile. "Timothy, look at his handwriting. He's finally stopped printing and gone to cursive!"

"Let me see. . . ."

Definitely a new look in the handwriting department, and a distinct credit to Dooley Barlowe's Virginia prep schooling. Miss Sadie's big bucks, forked over annually, albeit posthumously, were continuing to put spit and polish on the red-haired mountain boy who'd come to live with him at the rectory five years ago.

" '*Hey,*' " he read aloud from Dooley's letter, " '*I have thought about it a lot and I would like to stay in Mitford and work for Avis this summer and make money to get a car and play softball with the Reds.*

" '*I don't want to go to the beach.*

" '*Don't be mad or upset or anything. I can live in the basement with*

Harley like you said, and we will be fine. Puny could maybe come and do the laundry or we could do stuff ourselves and eat in Wesley or at the Grill or Harley could cook.

" '*I will come down to that island for either Thanksgiving or Christmas like we talked about.*

" '*Thanks for letting me go home from school with Jimmy Duncan, I am having a great time, he drives a Wrangler. His mom drives a Range Rover and his dad has a BMW 850. That's what I would like to have. A Wrangler, I mean. I'll get home before you leave, Mr. Duncan is driving me on his way to a big meeting. Say hey to Barnabas and Violet. Thanks for the money. Love, Dooley.*' "

"Oh, well," said his wife, looking disappointed. "I'm sure he wanted to be close to his friends. . . ."

"Right. And his brother and sister. . . ."

She sighed. "Pretty much what we expected."

He felt disappointed, himself, that the boy wouldn't be coming to Whitecap for the summer, but they'd given him a choice and the choice had been made. Besides, he learned a couple of years ago not to let Dooley Barlowe's summer pursuits wreck his own enjoyment of that fleeting season.

It was the business about cars that concerned him. . . . Dooley had turned sixteen last February, and would hit Mitford in less than three days, packing a bona fide driver's license.

"Knock, knock!" Emma Newland blew down the hall and into the study. "Don't get up," she said, commandeering the room. "You'll never believe this!"

His former part-time church secretary, who had retired when he retired, had clearly been unable to let go of her old job. She made it her business to visit twice a week and help out for a couple of hours, whether he needed it or not.

"I do it for th' Lord," she had stated flatly, refusing any thanks. Though Cynthia usually fled the room when she arrived, he rather looked forward to Emma's visits, and to the link she represented to Lord's Chapel, which was now under the leadership of its own interim priest.

Emma stood with her hands on her hips and peered over her glasses. "Y'all won't believe what I found on th' Internet. Three guesses!"

"Excuse me!" said Cynthia, bolting from the sofa. "I'll just bring you a lemonade, Emma, and get back to work. I've *gobs* of books to pack."

"Guess!" Emma insisted, playing a game that he found both mindless and desperately aggravating.

"A recipe for mixing your own house paint?"

"Oh, *please,*" she said, looking disgusted. "You're not trying."

"The complete works of Fulgentius of Ruspe!"

"Who?"

"I give up," he said, meaning it.

"I found another Mitford! It's in England, and it has a church as old as mud, not to mention a castle!" She looked triumphant, as if she'd just squelched an invasion of Moors.

"Really? Terrific! I suppose it's where those writing Mitfords came from—"

"No connection. They were from th' Cotswolds, this place is up north somewhere. I had a stack of stuff I printed out, but Snickers sat on th' whole bloomin' mess after playin' in the creek, and I have to print it out again."

"Aha."

"OK, guess what else!"

"Dadgummit, Emma. You know I hate this."

She said what she always said. "It's good for you, keeps your brain active."

As far as she was concerned, he'd gone soft in the head since retiring six months ago.

"Just tell me and get it over with."

"Oh, come on! Try at least one guess. Here's a clue. It's about the election in November."

"Esther's stepping down and Andrew Gregory's going to run."

She frowned. "How'd you know that?"

"I haven't gone deaf and blind, for Pete's sake. I do get around."

"I suppose you also know," said Emma, hoping he didn't, "that the restaurant at Fernbank is openin' the night before you leave."

"Right. We've been invited."

She thumped into the slipcovered wing chair and peered at him as if he were a beetle on a pin. Though she'd certainly never say such a thing, she believed he was existing in a kind of purgatory between the inarguable heaven of Lord's Chapel and the hell of a strange parish in a strange place where the temperature was a hundred and five in the shade.

"Will you have a secretary down there?" she asked, suspicious.

"I don't think so. Small parish, you know."

"How small can it be?"

"Oh, fifty, sixty people."

"I thought Bishop Cullen was your *friend*," she sniffed. She'd never say so, but in her heart of hearts, she had hoped her boss of sixteen years would be given a big church in a big city, and make a comeback for himself. As it was, he trotted up the hill to Hope House and the hospital every livelong morning, appearing so cheerful about the whole thing that she recognized it at once as a cover-up.

Cynthia returned with a glass of lemonade and a plate of shortbread, which she put on the table next to Emma. "I'll be in the studio if anyone needs me. With all the books we're taking, we may sink the island!"

"A regular Atlantis," said Father Tim.

"Speakin' of books," Emma said to his wife, "are you doin' a new one?"

"Not if I can help it!"

He laughed as Cynthia trotted down the hall. "She usually can't help it." He expected a new children's book to break forth from his energetic wife any day now. Indeed, didn't she have a history of starting one when life was upside down and backward?

Emma munched on a piece of shortbread, showering crumbs in her lap. "Do you have those letters ready for me to do on th' computer?"

"Not quite. I wasn't expecting you 'til in the morning."

"I'm coming in th' morning, I just wanted to run by and tell you all th' late-breakin' news. But," she said, arching one eyebrow, "I haven't told you everything, I saved th' best 'til last."

His dog wandered into the study and crashed at his master's feet, panting.

"If you say you already know this, I'll never tell you another thing as long as I live. On my way here, I saw Mule Skinner, he said he's finally rented your house."

She drew herself up, pleased, and gulped the lemonade.

"Terrific! Great timing!" He might have done a jig.

"He said there hadn't been time to call you, he'll call you tonight, but it's not a family with kids like Cynthia wanted."

"Oh, well . . ." He was thrilled that someone had finally stepped forward to occupy the rectory. He and Harley had worked hard over the last few months to make it a strong rental property, putting new vinyl flooring in the kitchen, replacing the stair runners, installing a new toilet in the master bath and a new threshold at the front door . . . the list had been endless. And costly.

"It's a woman."

"I can't imagine what one person would want with all that house to rattle around in."

"How quickly you forget! *You* certainly rattled around in there for a hundred years."

"True. Well. I'll get the whole story from Mule."

"He said she didn't mind a bit that Harley would be livin' in the basement, she just wanted to know if he plays loud rock music."

Emma rattled the ice in her glass, gulped the last draught, and got up to leave. "Before I forget, you won't believe what else I found on th' Internet—church bulletins! You ought to read some of th' foolishness they put out there for God an' everybody to see."

She fished a piece of paper from her handbag. " 'Next Sunday,' " she read, " 'a special collection will be taken to defray the cost of a new carpet. All those wishin' to do somethin' on the new carpet will come forward and do so.' "

He hooted with laughter.

"How 'bout this number: 'Don't let worry kill you, let th' church help.' "

He threw his head back and laughed some more. Emma's life in cyberspace definitely had an upside.

"By th' way, are you takin' Barnabas down there?" She enunciated "down there" as if it were a region beneath the crust of the earth.

"We are."

"I don't know how you could do that to an animal. Look at all that fur, enough to stuff a mattress."

Barnabas yawned hugely and thumped his tail on the floor.

"You won't even be able to *see* those horrible sandspurs that will jump in there by th' hundreds, not to mention *lodge in his paws.*"

Emma waited for an argument, a rationale—something. Did he have no conscience? "And th' *heat* down there, you'll have to shave 'im bald."

Father Tim strolled across the room to walk her to the door.

"Thanks for coming, Emma. Tell Harold hello. I'll see you in the morning."

His unofficial secretary stumped down the hallway and he followed.

He was holding the front door open and biting his tongue when she turned and looked at him. Her eyes were suddenly red and filled with tears.

"I'll miss you!" she blurted.

"You *will*?"

She hurried down the front steps, sniffing, searching her bag for a Hardee's napkin she knew was in there someplace.

He felt stricken. "Emma! We'll . . . we'll have jelly doughnuts in the morning!"

"*I'll* have jelly doughnuts, *you'll* have dry toast! We don't want to ship you down there in a coma!"

She got in her car at the curb, slammed the door, gunned the motor, and roared up Wisteria Lane.

For one fleeting moment, he'd completely forgotten his blasted diabetes.

PENGUIN BOOKS

THESE HIGH, GREEN HILLS

Jan Karon writes "to give readers an extended family, and to applaud the extraordinary beauty of ordinary lives." She is the author of nine Mitford novels, *At Home in Mitford*; *A Light in the Window*; *These High, Green Hills*; *Out to Canaan*; *A New Song*; *A Common Life*; *In This Mountain*; *Shepherds Abiding*; and *Light from Heaven*, all available from Penguin. She is also the author of *The Mitford Bedside Companion*; *Jan Karon's Mitford Cookbook & Kitchen Reader*; *A Continual Feast: Words of Comfort and Celebration, Collected by Father Tim*; *Patches of Godlight: Father Tim's Favorite Quotes*; *The Mitford Snowmen: A Christmas Story*; *Esther's Gift*; and *The Trellis and the Seed*. Her children's books include *Miss Fannie's Hat*; *Jeremy: The Tale of an Honest Bunny*; and *Violet Comes to Stay*. Coming from Viking in fall 2007 is the first Father Tim Novel, *Home to Holly Springs*.

The Mitford Years

These High, Green Hills

JAN KARON

PENGUIN BOOKS

PENGUIN BOOKS
Published by the Penguin Group
Penguin Books USA Inc., 375 Hudson Street, New York, New York 10014, U.S.A.
Penguin Books Ltd, 27 Wrights Lane, London W8 5TZ, England
Penguin Books Australia Ltd, Ringwood, Victoria, Australia
Penguin Books Canada Ltd, 10 Alcorn Avenue, Toronto, Ontario, Canada M4V 3B2
Penguin Books (N.Z.) Ltd, 182–190 Wairau Road, Auckland 10, New Zealand

Penguin Books Ltd, Registered Offices: Harmondsworth, Middlesex, England

First published in the United States of America by Viking Penguin,
a division of Penguin Books USA Inc. 1996
Published in Penguin Books 1997

31 32 33 34 35 36 37 38 39 40

Illustrations by Donna Kae Nelson

Grateful acknowledgment is made for permission to reprint an excerpt from *Life Together* by Dietrich Bonhoeffer. English translation copyright © 1954 by Harper and Brothers. Copyright renewed 1982 by Helen S. Doberstein. Reprinted by permission of HarperCollins Publishers Inc.

PUBLISHER'S NOTE

This is a work of fiction. Names, characters, places, and incidents either are the product of the author's imagination or are used fictitiously, and any resemblance to actual persons, living or dead, events, or locales is entirely coincidental.

THE LIBRARY OF CONGRESS HAS CATALOGUED THE HARDCOVER AS FOLLOWS:
Karon, Jan, date.
These high, green hills/Jan Karon.
p. cm.—(The Mitford years)
ISBN 0-670-86934-1 (hc.)
ISBN 0 14 02.5793 4 (pbk.)
1. City and town life—United States—Fiction. I. Title. II. Series: Karon, Jan, date Mitford years.
PS3561.A678T48 1996
813'.54—dc20 96–11933

Printed in the United States of America
Set in Adobe Garamond
Designed by Francesca Belanger

For my precious grandmother,
Fannie Belle Bush Cloer,
Mama, Redwing, The Storyteller.
1893–1993

With sincere thanks to:

Miss Read (Dora Saint); Rev. Rocky Ward; Marrion Ward; Dr. Greg Adams; Dr. "Bunky" Davant; Dr. Greg Hawthorne; Flyin' George Ronan; Jim Atkinson; Dr. John C. Wolff, Jr.; Billy Wilson; Dr. Buck Henson; Dr. Cara Roten-Henson; David Watts; Tony di Santi; Dr. Ken McKinney; Fr. James Harris; Ruth Bell Graham; Earl and Nancy Trexler; Sonny Klutz; Richard J. Foster; Dr. William Standish Reed; Jim Barber; Diane Grymes; Steve Sudderth; Bear Green; Bob Moody; Fr. Chuck Blanck; Fr. Rick Lawler; Fr. Russell Johnson; Raney MacArthur-Ratchford; Maribelle Freeland; Julie Q. Hayes, R.N. BSN, Blowing Rock Hospital; Pam Collette, R.N. BSN, Clinical Nurse Mgr., Donna Joyner, Assistant Clinical Nurse Mgr., and Pamela Thomas, R.N. BSN, of the Burn Center, North Carolina Baptist Hospitals, Inc., Winston-Salem; Dana Watkins, R.N. BSN, Sanger Clinic, Charlotte; Rev. James Stuart; Fr. Kale King; Dr. Ross Rhoads; Doug Galke; Shirlee Gaines Edwards; Bertie Beam; Nancy Olson of Quail Ridge Books; Shirley Sprinkle of The Muses; my friends at Gideon Ridge Inn; Liz Darhansoff, my gifted and indefatigable agent, and Carolyn Carlson, my visionary Viking Penguin editor and friend; Jerry Burns, the small-town newspaperman with the big heart; and the vanishing breed of old-time Gospel preachers (especially the late Vance Havner and the still-present Arndt Greer), who brought conviction to their calling and color to the language.

Last but never least, thanks to the wonderful booksellers who have enthusiastically spread the word, and to the many readers who have cheered me on, given my books to family and friends, and come to feel comfortably at home in Mitford.

Contents

These High, Green Hills

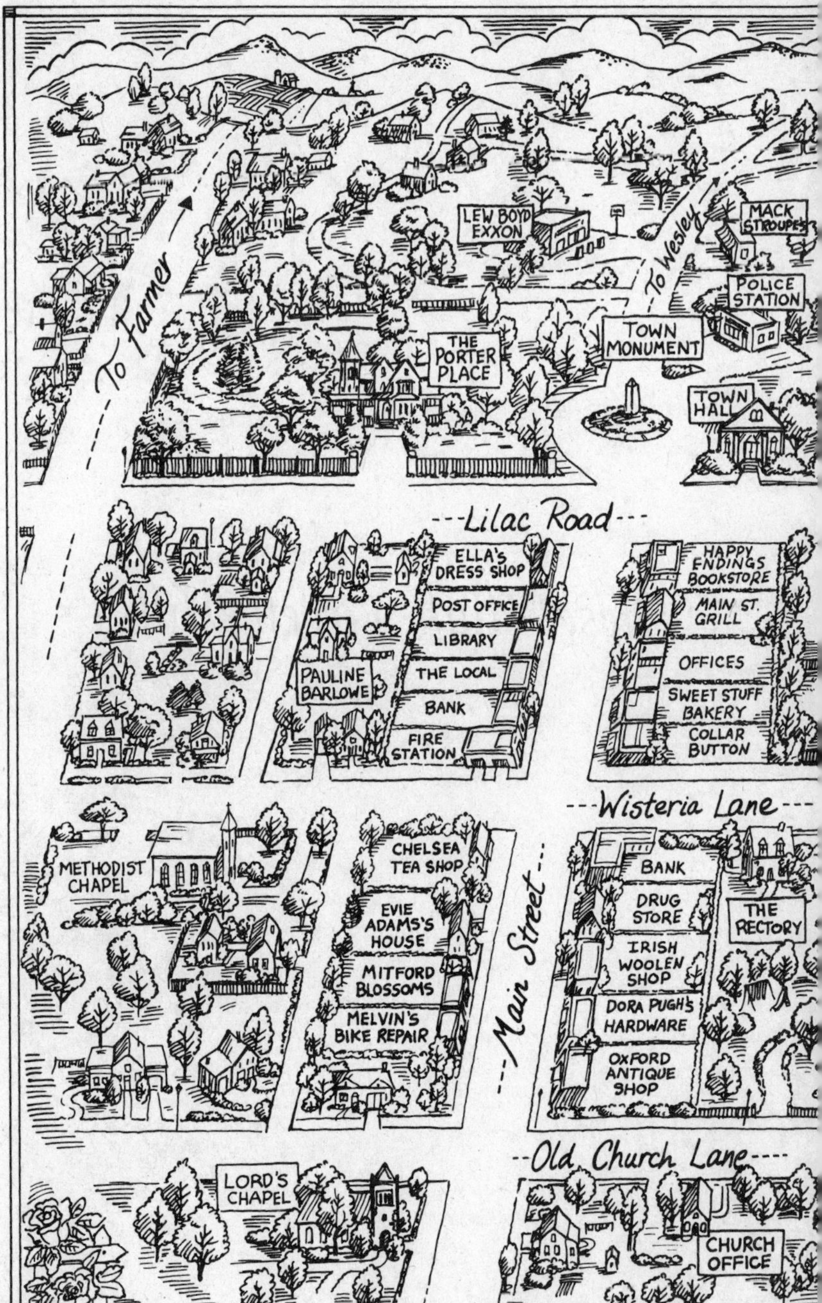
LEW BOYD EXXON
MACK STROUPE'S
POLICE STATION
To Farmer
To Wesley
THE PORTER PLACE
TOWN MONUMENT
TOWN HALL
Lilac Road
ELLA'S DRESS SHOP
POST OFFICE
LIBRARY
THE LOCAL
BANK
FIRE STATION
PAULINE BARLOWE
HAPPY ENDINGS BOOKSTORE
MAIN ST. GRILL
OFFICES
SWEET STUFF BAKERY
COLLAR BUTTON
Wisteria Lane
METHODIST CHAPEL
CHELSEA TEA SHOP
EVIE ADAMS'S HOUSE
MITFORD BLOSSOMS
MELVIN'S BIKE REPAIR
Main Street
BANK
DRUG STORE
IRISH WOOLEN SHOP
DORA PUGH'S HARDWARE
OXFORD ANTIQUE SHOP
THE RECTORY
Old Church Lane
LORD'S CHAPEL
CHURCH OFFICE

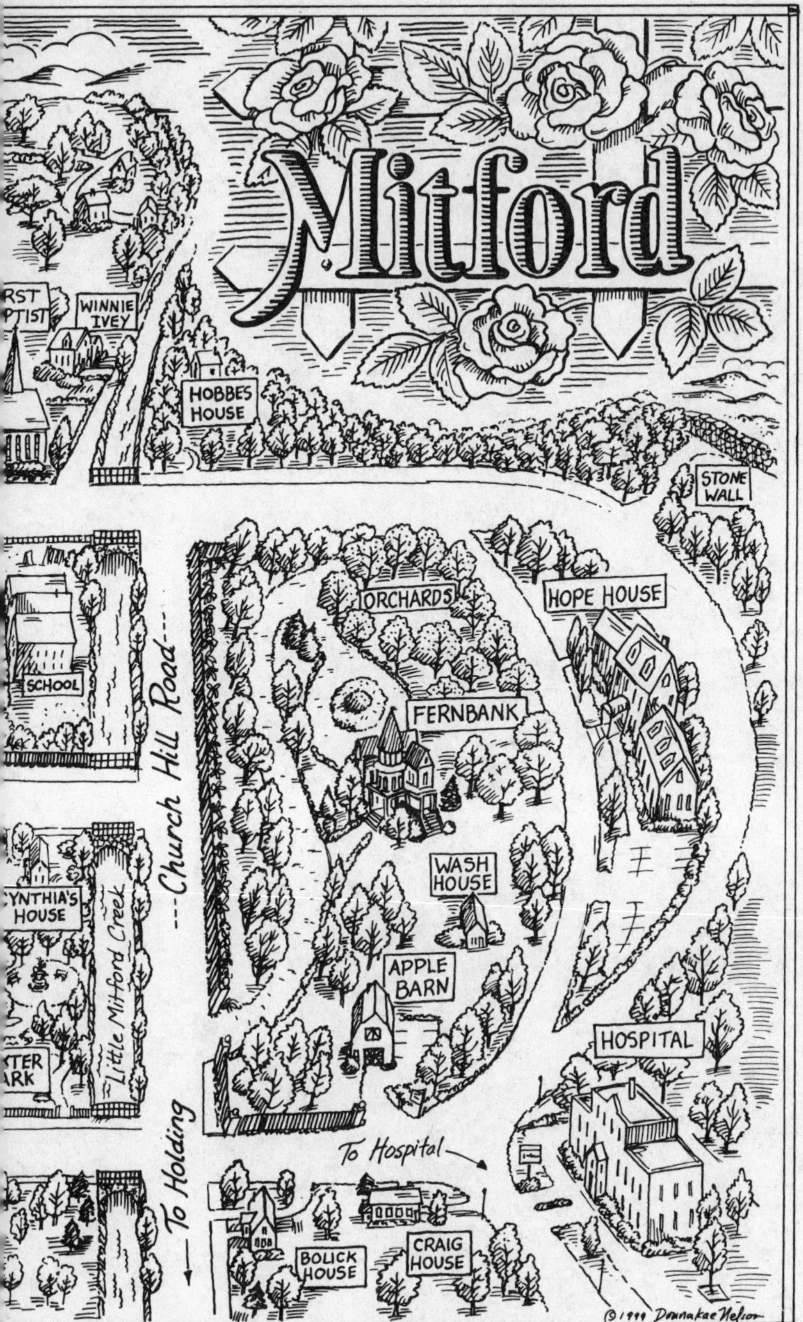

Mitford
WINNIE IVEY
HOBBES HOUSE
STONE WALL
ORCHARDS
HOPE HOUSE
SCHOOL
Church Hill Road
FERNBANK
WASH HOUSE
Little Mitford Creek
APPLE BARN
HOSPITAL
To Holding
To Hospital
BOLICK HOUSE
CRAIG HOUSE

CHAPTER ONE

Through the Hedge

HE STOOD at the kitchen window and watched her coming through the hedge.

What was she lugging this time? It appeared to be a bowl and pitcher. Or was it a stack of books topped by a vase?

The rector took off his glasses, fogged them, and wiped them with his handkerchief. It was a bowl and pitcher, all right. How the little yellow house next door had contained all the stuff they'd recently muscled into the rectory was beyond him.

"For your dresser," she said, as he held the door open.

"Aha!"

The last thing he wanted was a bowl and pitcher on his dresser. The top of his dresser was his touchstone, his home base, his rock in a sea of change. That was where his car keys resided, his loose coins, his several crosses, his cuff links, his wallet, his checkbook, his school ring, and a small jar of buttons with a needle and thread.

It was also where he kept the mirror in which he occasionally examined the top of his head. Was his hair still thinning, or, by some mysterious and hoped-for reversal, growing in again?

"Cynthia," he said, going upstairs in the wake of his blond and shapely wife, "about that bowl and pitcher . . ."

"The color is wonderful. Look at the blues. It will relieve all your burgundy and brown!"

He did not want his burgundy and brown relieved.

He saw it coming.

Ever since their marriage on September seventh, she had plotted to lug that blasted armoire over for the rectory guest room.

The lugging over was one thing; it was the lugging back that he dreaded. They had, for example, lugged over an oriental rug that was stored in her basement. "Ten by twelve!" she announced, declaring it perfect for the bare floor of the rectory dining room.

After wrestling the table and chairs into the hall, they had unrolled the rug and unrolled the rug—to kingdom come. It might have gone up the walls on all four sides and met at the chandelier over the table.

"This is a rug for a school gym!" he said, wiping the pouring sweat from his brow.

She seemed dumbfounded that it didn't fit, and there they had gone, like pack mules, carting it through the hedge again.

The decision to keep and use both houses had been brilliant, of course. The light in the rectory would never equal that of her studio next door, where she was already set up with books and paints and drawing board. This meant his study could remain unchanged—his books could occupy the same shelves, and his vast store of sermon notebooks in the built-in cabinets could hold their place.

Marrying for the first time at the age of sixtysomething was change enough. It was a blessed luxury to live with so few rearrangements in the scheme of things, and life flowing on as usual. The only real change was the welcome sharing of bed and board.

Over breakfast one morning, he dared to discuss his interest in getting the furniture settled.

"Why can't we keep things as they were . . . in their existing state? It seemed to work. . . ."

"Yes, well, I like that our houses are separate, but I also want them to be the same—sort of an organic whole."

"No organic whole will come of dragging that armoire back and forth through the hedge. It looks like a herd of elephants has passed through there already."

"Oh, Timothy! Stop being stuffy! Your place needs fluffing up, and mine needs a bit more reserve. For example, your Chippendale chairs would give a certain sobriety to my dining table."

"Your dining table is the size of something in our nursery school. My chairs would look gigantic."

She said exactly what he thought she would say. "We could try it and see."

"Cynthia, trust me on this. My chairs will not look right with your table, and neither will that hand-painted magazine rack do anything for my armchair."

"Well, what was the use of getting married, then?"

"I beg your pardon?"

"I mean, if no one is going to change on either side, if we're both just going to be our regular, lifetime selves, what's the use?"

"I think I see what you're getting at. Will nothing do, then, but to cart those chairs to your house? And what about my own table? It will be bereft of chairs. I hardly see the point." He felt like jumping through the window and going at a dead run toward the state line.

"One thing at a time," she said happily. "It's all going to work out perfectly."

deAr stuart,

thanx for your note re: diocesan mtg, and thank martha for the invitation to put my feet under yr table afterward. however, I must leave for home at once, following the mtg—hope you'll understand.

while i'm at it, let me ask you:

why are women always moving things around? at Sunday School, jena iivey just had the youth group move the kindergarten bookcAses to a facing wall.

on the homefront, my househelp has moved a ladderback chair from my bedroom into the hall, never once considering that i hung my trousers over it for 14 years, and put my shoes on the seat so they could be found in an emergency.

last but certainly not least, if C could lift me in my armchair and put it by the window while i'm dozing, she would do it.

without a doubt, you have weightier things to consider, but tell me, how docs one deal with this?

i hasten to add that ii've never been happier in my life. to tell the truth, i am confounded that such happiness—in such measure—even exists.

He signed the note, typed on his Royal manual, thankful that Stuart Cullen was not merely his bishop, but his closest personal friend since the halcyon days of seminary.

Fr Timothy Kavanaugh,
The Chapel of Our Lord and Savior
Old Church Lane, Mitford, N.C.

Dear Timothy:

In truth, it is disconcerting when one's househelp, SS supervisor, and wife do this sort of thing all at once.

My advice is: do not fight it. It will wear off.

In His peace,
Stuart

P.S. Martha would add a note, but she is busy moving my chest of drawers to the far side of our bedroom. As I am dealing with an urgent matter with the House of Bishops, I could not be browbeaten to help, and so she has maneuvered it, at last, onto an old bedspread, and I can hear her hauling the whole thing across the floor above me. This particular behavior had lain dormant in her for nearly seven years, and has suddenly broken forth again.

Perhaps it is something in the water.

He could see, early on, that beds were a problem that needed working out.

They had spent their wedding night in his bed at the rectory, where they had rolled down their respective sides and crashed together in the middle.

"What is this *trough* doing in your bed?" she asked.

"It's where I sleep," he said, feeling sheepish.

They had been squeezed together like sardines the livelong night, which he had profoundly enjoyed, but she had not. "Do you think this is what's meant by 'the two shall be one flesh'?" she murmured, her cheek smashed against his.

The following night, he trooped through the hedge with his pajamas and toothpaste in a grocery bag from The Local.

Her bed was a super-king-size, and the largest piece of furniture in her minuscule house.

He found it similar in breadth to the state of Texas, or possibly the province of Saskatchewan. Was that a herd of buffalo racing toward him in the distance, or a team of sled dogs? "Cynthia!" he shouted across the vast expanse, and waited for the echo.

They had ordered a new mattress for the rectory immediately after returning from their honeymoon in Stuart Cullen's summer house. There, on the rocky coast of Maine, they had spent time listening to the cry of the loons, holding hands, walking along the shore, and talking until the small hours of the morning. The sun turned her fair skin a pale toast color that he found fascinating and remarkable; and he watched three freckles emerge on the bridge of her nose, like stars coming out. Whatever simple thing they did together, they knew they were happier than ever before in their lives.

One evening, soon after the new mattress and springs were installed at the rectory, he found her sitting up in bed as he came out of the shower.

"I've had a wonderful idea, Timothy! A fireplace! Right over there where the dresser is."

"What would I do with my dresser?"

She looked at him as if he had toddled in from the church nursery. "Put it in the alcove, of course."

"Then I couldn't see out the window."

"But how much time do you spend staring out the alcove window?"

"When you were parading about with Andrew Gregory, a great deal of time." His face burned to admit it, but yes, he'd been jealous of the handsome antique dealer who had squired her around for several months.

She smiled, leaning her head to one side in that way he could barely resist. "A fireplace would be so romantic."

"Ummm."

"Why must I be the romantic in the family while you hold up the conservative, let's-don't-make-any-changes end?"

He sat down beside her. "How quickly you forget. When we were going steady, you said I was wildly romantic."

She laughed and kissed him on the cheek. "And I was right, of course. I'm sorry, old dearest."

He regretted being anyone's *old* dearest.

"Old dearest, yourself," he said grumpily. "I am, after all, only six years your senior."

"By the calendar," she said imperiously, referring, he supposed, to something decrepit in his overall attitude about life.

In any case, the fireplace issue did not come up again.

In truth, he had no words for his happiness. It grew deeper every day, like the digging of a well, and astounded him by its warmth and power. He seemed to lose control of his very face, which, according to the regulars at the Main Street Grill, displayed a foolish and perpetual grin.

"I love you . . . terribly," he said, struggling to express it.

"I love you terribly, also. It's scary. What if it should end?"

"Cynthia, good grief . . ."

"I know I shouldn't talk of endings when this is a blessed beginning."

"Don't then," he said, meaning it.

That Barnabas had so willingly given up the foot of his master's bed to sleep on a rug in the hall was a gesture he would never forget. Not only did his dog enjoy eighteenth-century poets and submit to his weekly bath without rancor, his dog was a gentleman.

The decisions were made, and both parties were in amicable accord.

They would sleep at the rectory primarily, and on occasion at the little yellow house. Though she would work there, as always, they would treat it much as a second home, using it for refreshment and private retreat.

He promised to have his sermon well under control each Saturday afternoon, with time to relax with her on Saturday evening, and he would continue to make breakfast on Sunday morning.

He showed her where his will was, and promised to have it rewritten. She confessed she didn't have a will, and promised to have one drawn up.

If they should ever, God forbid, have a misunderstanding, neither would dash off to the other house to sulk.

He would continue to have the cheerful and enterprising Puny Guthrie, née Bradshaw, clean the rectory three days a week, and Cynthia would use her services on a fourth day, next door.

They would go on with their separate checking accounts, make some mutual investments, counsel with the other about gift offerings, and never spend more than a certain fixed sum without the other's prior agreement.

He suggested fifty dollars as the fixed sum.

"One hundred!" she countered.

He was glad he had opened the bidding low. "One hundred, then, and I keep that old jacket you earmarked for the Bane and Blessing sale."

"Done!"

They laughed.

They shook hands.

They felt relieved.

Getting a marriage off on the right foot was no small matter.

"I reckon you're gone with th' wind," said Percy Mosely, who rang up his lunch tab at the Main Street Grill.

"How's that?" asked the rector.

"Married an' all, you'll not be comin' in regular, I take it." The proprietor of the Grill felt hurt and betrayed, he could tell.

"You've got that wrong, my friend."

"I do?" said Percy, brightening.

"I'll be coming in as regular as any man could. My wife has a working life of her own, being a well-known children's book writer and illustrator. She will not be trotting out hot vittles for my lunch every day—not by a long shot."

Percy looked suspicious. "What about breakfast?"

"That," said the rector, pocketing the change, "is another matter entirely."

Percy frowned. He liked his regulars to be married to his place of business.

He looked up from his chair in the study. Curlers, again.

"I have to wear curlers," she said, as if reading his mind. "I'm going to Lowell tomorrow."

"Lowell? Whatever for?"

"A school thing. They want me to read *Violet Goes to France* to their French class, and then do a program in the auditorium."

"Must you?"

"Must I what? Read *Violet Goes to France*? That's what they asked me to read."

"No, must you go to Lowell?"

"Well, yes."

He didn't want to say anything so idiotic, but he would miss her, as if she were being dropped off the end of the earth.

A long silence ensued as she curled up on the sofa and opened a magazine. He tried to read, but couldn't concentrate.

He hadn't once thought of her traveling with her work. Uneasy, he tried to let the news sink in. Lowell. Somebody there had been shot on the street in broad daylight.

And another thing—Lowell was a full hundred miles away. Did she have good brakes? Plenty of gas? When had she changed her oil?

"How's your oil?" he asked soberly.

She laughed as if he'd said something hilariously funny. Then she left the sofa and came to him and kissed him on the forehead. He was instantly zapped by the scent of wisteria, and went weak in the knees.

She looked him in the eye. "I love it when you talk like that. My oil is fine, how's yours?"

"Cynthia, Cynthia," he said, pulling her into his lap.

"Guess what?" said Emma, who was taping a photo of her new grandchild on the wall next to her desk.

This was his secretary's favorite game, and one he frankly despised. "What?"

"Guess!"

"Let's see. You're going to quit working for the Episcopalians and go to work for the Baptists." He wished.

"I wish," she said, rolling her eyes. "Try again."

"Blast, Emma, I hate this game."

"It's good for you, it exercises the brain."

"Esther Bolick's orange marmalade cake recipe is coming out in the *New York Times* food section."

"See? You don't even try. You're just talking to hear your head roar. One more guess."

"Give me a clue."

"It has to do with somebody being mad."

"The vestry. It must have something to do with the vestry."

"Wrong. Do you want me to tell you?"

"I beg you."

"Marge Wheeler left her best basket in the kitchen after the bishop's brunch last June, and Flora Lou Wilcox put it in the Bane and Blessing sale. Somebody walked off with it for a hundred dollars! Can you believe a hundred dollars for a basket with a loose handle? Marge is mad as a wet hen, she threatened to sue. But Flora Lou said she doesn't have a leg to stand on, since you're always running notices in the pew bulletin to pick up stuff left in th' kitchen."

"Ummm. Keep me posted."

"It's been four months since the brunch, so I can see Flora Lou's point that Marge should have picked it up and carted it home. Anyway, how could Flora Lou know it was handmade by Navajo Indians in 1920?" Emma sighed. "Of course, I can see Marge's point, too, can't you?"

He could, but he knew better than to intervene unless asked. His job, after all, was Sales and Service.

He rifled through the mail. A note from his cousin, Walter, and wife, Katherine, who had done the Ireland jaunt with him last year.

Dear Timothy,

Since Ireland is now old stomping grounds, why don't you and Cynthia plan to go with us next summer? Thought we'd plant the seed, so it can sprout over the winter.

We shall never forget how handsome you looked on the other side of the pulpit, standing with your beautiful bride. We love her as much as we love you, which is pecks and bushels, as ever,

Katherine

PS, Pls advise if canna and lily bulbs should be separated in the fall, I'm trying to find a hobby that has nothing to do with a pasta machine

Yrs, Walter

He rummaged toward the bottom of the mail stack.

Aha!

A note from Dooley Barlowe, in that fancy prep school for which his eldest parishioner, Miss Sadie Baxter, was shelling out serious bucks.

Hey. I don't like it here. That brain in a jar that we saw is from a medical school. I still don't know whose brain it is. When are you coming back? Bring Barnbus and granpaw and Cynthia. I culd probly use a twenty. Dooley

There! Not one 'ain't,' and complete sentences throughout. Hallelujah!

Who could have imagined that this boy, once barely able to speak the King's English, would end up in a prestigious school in Virginia?

He gazed at the note, shaking his head.

Scarcely more than two years ago, Dooley Barlowe had arrived at the church office, dirty, ragged, and barefoot, looking for a place to "take a dump." His grandfather had been too ill to care for the boy, who was abandoned by a runaway father and alcoholic mother, and Dooley had ended up at the rectory. By grace alone, he and Dooley had managed to live through those perilous times.

"I've been wondering," said Emma, peering at him over her glasses. "Is Cynthia goin' to pitch in and help around the church?"

"She's free to do as much or as little as she pleases."

"I've always thought a preacher's wife should pitch in." She set her mouth in that way he deplored. "If you ask me, which you didn't, the parish will expect it."

Yes, indeed, if he could get the Baptists to take Emma Newland off his hands, he would be a happy man.

"Miss Sadie," he said when she answered the phone at Fernbank, "I've had a note from Dooley. He says he doesn't like it in that fancy school."

"He can like it or lump it," she said pleasantly.

"When you're dishing out twenty thousand a year, you sure can be tough, Miss Sadie."

"If I couldn't be tough, Father, I wouldn't have twenty thousand to dish out."

"You'll be glad to know the headmaster says he's doing all right. A little slow on the uptake, but holding his own with those rich kids. In fact, they're not all rich. Several are there on scholarship, with no more assets than our Dooley."

"Good! You mark my words, he'll be better for it. And don't you go soft on me, Father, and let him talk you into bailing him out in the middle of the night."

"You can count on it," he said.

"Louella and I have nearly recovered from all the doings in June. . . ."

"June was a whopper, all right."

"We're no spring chickens, you know."

"You could have fooled me."

"I'll be ninety my next birthday, but Louella doesn't tell her age. Anyway, we're going to have you and Cynthia up for supper. What did we say we'd have, Louella?"

He heard Louella's mezzo voice boom from a corner of the big kitchen, "Fried chicken, mashed potatoes, gravy, an' cole slaw!"

"Man!" he exclaimed, quoting Dooley.

The announcement rolled on. "Hot biscuits, cooked apples, deviled eggs, bread and butter pickles . . ."

Good Lord! The flare-up from his diabetes would have him in the emergency room before the rest of them pushed back from the table.

"And what did we say for dessert?" Miss Sadie warbled into the distance.

"Homemade coconut cake!"

Ah, well, that was a full coma right there. Hardly any of his parishioners could remember he had this blasted disease. The information seemed to go in one ear and out the other.

"Ask Louella if she'll marry me," he said.

"Louella, the Father wants to know if you'll marry him."

"Tell 'im he got a short mem'ry, he done married Miss Cynthia."

He laughed, contented with the sweetness of this old friendship. "Just name the time," he said. "We'll be there."

Autumn drew on in the mountains.

Here, it set red maples on fire; there, it turned oaks russet and yellow. Fat persimmons became the color of melted gold, waiting for frost to turn their bitter flesh to honey. Sassafras, dogwoods, poplars, redbud—all were torched by autumn's brazen fire, displaying their colorful tapestry along every ridge and hogback, in every cove and gorge.

The line of maples that marched by First Baptist to Winnie Ivey's cottage on Little Mitford Creek was fully ablaze by the eleventh of October.

"The best ever!" said several villagers, who ran with their cameras to document the show.

The local newspaper editor, J. C. Hogan, shot an extravagant total of six rolls of film. For the first time since the nation's bicentennial, readers saw a four-color photograph on the front page of the *Mitford Muse.*

Everywhere, the pace was quickened by the dazzling light that now slanted from the direction of Gabriel Mountain, and the sounds of football practice in the schoolyard.

Avis Packard put a banner over the green awning of The Local: *Fresh Valley Hams Now, Collards Coming.*

Dora Pugh laid on a new window at the hardware store featuring leaf rakes, bicycle pumps, live rabbits, and iron skillets. "What's th' theme of your window?" someone asked. "Life," replied Dora.

The library introduced its fall reading program and invited the author of the *Violet* books to talk about where she got her ideas. "I have no idea where I get my ideas," she told Avette Harris, the librarian. "They just come." "Well, then," said Avette, "do you have any ideas for another topic?"

The village churches agreed to have this year's All-Church Thanksgiving Feast with the Episcopalians, and to get their youth choirs together for a Christmas performance at First Presbyterian.

At Lord's Chapel, the arrangements on the altar became gourds and pumpkins, accented by branches of the fiery red maple. At this time of year, the rector himself liked doing the floral offerings. He admitted it was a favorite season, and his preaching, someone remarked, grew as electrified as the sharp, clean air.

"Take them," he said one Sunday morning, lifting the cup and the Host toward the people, "in remembrance that Christ died for you, and feed on Him in your hearts by faith, with thanksgiving."

Giving his own wife the Host was an act that might never cease to move and amaze him. More than sixty years a bachelor, and now this—seeing her face looking up expectantly, and feeling the warmth of her hand as he placed the bread in her palm. "The body of our Lord Jesus Christ, which was given for you, Cynthia."

He couldn't help but see the patch of colored light that fell on her hair through the stained-glass window by the rail, as if she were being appointed to something divine. Surely there could be no divinity in having to live the rest of her life with him, with his set-in-concrete ways and infernal diabetes.

They walked home together after church, hand in hand, his sermon notebook tucked under his arm. He felt as free as a schoolboy, as light as air. How could he ever have earned God's love, and hers into the bargain?

The point was, he couldn't. It was all grace, and grace alone.

He was sitting in his armchair by the fireplace, reading the newspaper. Barnabas ambled in from the kitchen and sprawled at his feet.

Cynthia, barefoot and in her favorite robe, sat on the sofa and scribbled in a notebook. One of his antiquated towels was wrapped around her damp hair. He still couldn't get over the sight of her on his sofa, looking as comfortable as if she lived here—which, he was often amazed to realize, she did.

"Wasn't it wonderful?" she asked.

"Wasn't what wonderful?"

"Our wedding."

"It was!" She brought the subject up fairly often, and he realized he'd run out of anything new to say about it.

"I love thinking about it," she said, plumping up a needlepoint pillow and putting it behind her head. "A tuxedo and a tab collar are a terrific combination."

"No kidding?" He would remember that.

"I think you should dress that way again at the first possible opportunity."

He laughed. "It doesn't take much for you."

"That's true, dearest, except in the area of my new husband. There, it took quite a lot."

He felt that ridiculous, uncontrollable grin spreading across his face.

"It was a wonderful idea to ask Dooley to sing. He was absolutely masterful. And thank goodness for Ray Cunningham's video camera. I love the frames of you and Stuart in his bishop's regalia, standing in the churchyard . . . and the part where Miss Sadie and Preacher Greer are laughing together."

"Another case of two hearts beating as one."

"Would you like to see it again? I'll make popcorn."

"Maybe in a day or two." Hadn't they watched it only last week?

"It was very sweet and charming, the way you insisted on baking a ham for our reception."

"I always bake a ham for wedding receptions at Lord's Chapel," he said. "I'm stuck in that mode."

"Tell me something . . . ?"

"Anything!" Would he really tell her anything?

"How did you unstick your mode long enough to propose to me? What happened?"

"I realized . . . that is, I . . ." He paused thoughtfully and rubbed his chin. "To tell the truth, I couldn't help myself."

"Ummm," she said, smiling at him across the room. "You know I love that you knelt on one knee."

"Actually, I was prepared to go down on both knees. As soon as I dropped to one, however, you saw what was coming, and seemed so happy about it, I didn't bother to advance to the full kneel."

She laughed uproariously, and held her arms out to him. "Please come over here, dearest. You're so far away over there!"

The evening news was just coming on when the phone rang. It was his doctor and friend, Hoppy Harper, calling from the hospital.

"How fast can you get here?"

"Well . . ."

"I'll explain later. Just get here."

He was out the door in thirty seconds.

CHAPTER TWO

Bread of Angels

"DR. HARPER's in the operating room, Father, he can't come out. He said put you in his office."

Nurse Kennedy opened a door and firmly pushed him inside.

"He said for you to pray and pray hard, and don't stop till he comes in here. Pray for Angie Burton, she's seven. Dr. Harper says it's a ruptured appendix, septic shock. We're all praying—except Dr. Wilson."

Nurse Kennedy, who generally looked cheerful, looked strained as she closed the door.

In Hoppy's cluttered office, only a lamp burned.

Angie Burton. That would be Sophia Burton's youngest. He thought of Sophia, who was well known for taking her two girls to First Baptist every Sunday morning, rain or shine, and for teaching them the Twenty-third Psalm as soon as they could talk. Working in the canning plant in Wesley, she kept bravely on in the wake of a husband who had totaled their car, tried to burn down their house, and disappeared into Tennessee only yards ahead of the law.

He phoned home and asked Cynthia to pray, then fell to his knees by Hoppy's desk.

"God of all comfort, our only help in time of need, be present in Your goodness with Angie. . . ."

It was nearly midnight when Hoppy opened the door. "I owe you an apology," he said. "I could have asked you to pray at home, but all I could think of was having you here—on the premises."

The rector had seen that look on his friend's face before. It was utter exhaustion. "How did it go?"

There was a long pause. Hoppy looked up and shook his head. "We did everything we could."

He sank wearily into the chair at his desk. "Ever since we prayed for Olivia's transplant and I saw the miracles that happened, I've been praying for my patients. One day, I asked Kennedy if she would pray. Then she told Baker, and soon we discovered that the whole operating room was praying.

"I never talked to you about it, I kept thinking I would. . . . Anyway, we've seen some turnarounds. No miracles, maybe, but turnarounds. We felt something powerful was going on here, something we wanted to explore."

Hoppy took off his glasses and rubbed his eyes. "The bottom line is, we prayed, you prayed, and Angie Burton didn't make it."

What could he say, after all?

Angie Burton's death was something the village could hardly bear.

Winnie Ivey was grief-stricken—Angie and her sister, Liza, often visited the Sweet Stuff Bakery after school. To them, she was Granny Ivey, who hung their school drawings on the wall in the Sweet Stuff kitchen.

The editor of the *Mitford Muse*, who scarcely ever spoke to or acknowledged a child, was moved to sudden tears over breakfast at the Grill and excused himself from the booth.

Coot Hendrick went to Sophia's house with a pie his elderly mother had baked, but, not knowing what to say, ran before anyone answered the door.

The members of First Baptist mourned the loss. So many of them had been involved in Angie's life; had held her as a baby, taught her in

Sunday School, and made certain that she and Liza regularly got a box of decent clothes. In recent years, some had quietly paid the drugstore bill when the girls were sick with flu.

After the funeral, the rector went with his wife to the rented house behind Lew Boyd's Exxon station, still known to most villagers as the Esso.

He didn't say much, but sat on the sofa and held Sophia's hand, against a background murmur of neighbors bringing food into the kitchen.

Next to him, Cynthia cradled Liza on her lap, caressing the damp cheek that lay against her shoulder.

When Liza began to sob, Cynthia began to quietly weep with her. Then, somehow, they were all weeping and clinging to each other, huddled together on the sofa.

It was at once a terrible and a wondrous thing. He didn't care that he suddenly had no control, that he had lost it, that his grief was freely pouring forth, apart from his will.

They held each other until the wave of their sorrow passed and he was able to pray. They all knew that he had no answers, though they had hoped he might.

Afterward, he and Cynthia walked down the path to their car.

"Blast," he said, clenching his jaw.

She looked at him, at the way this death had moved and stricken him. In the car, she took his hand and drew it to her cheek. "Thank you for being a loving priest."

He didn't feel loving. He felt helpless and poured out.

"Upside down and backwards," the new Baptist preacher had assured him yesterday.

The usually cheerful preacher looked as if he'd swallowed a dose of castor oil. "Plan to spend the first six months in misery and confusion, and the next six months merely in confusion."

For someone who could barely heat coffee in a microwave, the thought of what lay ahead was mind-boggling. Yet, for all the gloom and doom he had heard on the subject, he knew his vestry was right—it had to be done. Death, taxes, and computer systems. This was the law of the land, and no getting around it.

"Emma, I don't know how to tell you this. But the vestry wants us to go on computer."

She looked at him over her glasses. "What? What did you say?"

"I said the vestry wants us to go on computer. The bishop thinks it will bring some consistency to the affairs of the diocese. And chances are, it will do as much for the affairs of Lord's Chapel. You'll think so, too, once we get the hang of it."

"No way, José!"

She rose from her chair, doing that thing with her mouth that made her look like Genghis Khan with earrings.

"No one hates it more than I do," he said. "But it's going to happen."

"I work here fourteen years, day in and day out, and this is the thanks I get? I labor over these books like a slave, watching every penny, checking every total, and how many mistakes have I made?"

"Well," he said, "there was that pledge report five years ago . . ."

"Big deal! As if a measly fourteen thousand dollars was something to get upset about."

". . . and the incident with Sam McGee . . ."

"Sam McGee! That skinflint! Anybody can say they put a thousand dollars in the plate and the check was lost by the church secretary! I hope you're not telling me a *computer* could have found that stupid check he probably never wrote in the first place!"

"Ah, well . . ."

"So!" she said, inhaling deeply. "Go and find some young thing with her skirt up to here, and pay her out th' kazoo. Does the vestry take into consideration the kind of money they'll be shellin' out for her, while the money they save on *me* goes to Sunday School literature and soup kitchens? Ha! Never entered their minds, is my guess!"

He had expected Mount Vesuvius—and he was getting it.

They were in bed at the rectory, propped against the huge pillows she had carted from her house in leaf bags. He had to admit it was a comfort, all that goose down squashing around back there. He could hardly get past the first page of his book without nodding off.

"Timothy, do I snore?"

He liked the way her questions sometimes bolted in from the blue, contained within no particular context that he could see. Good practice for a clergyman.

He removed his glasses and looked at his wife. "Snore? My dear, I don't know how to tell you this, but you positively rattle the windows. I think it could be overcome, however, if you would sleep with your mouth closed . . . which might also eliminate the drooling problem."

"Timothy!"

"See how it feels? You told me I mutter in my sleep and grind my teeth. So, tit for tat."

"*Please* tell me you're kidding. I don't really snore, do I?"

"To tell the truth, no. You never snore. Maybe a whiffle now and again, but nothing serious."

"And no drooling?"

"Not that I've witnessed."

She looked smug. "You really do mutter in your sleep, you know."

"Worse has been said."

He never failed to wonder how all this had come about. If he had known that being together was so consoling, he would have capitulated sooner. Why had he been so terrified of marriage, of intimacy, of loving?

He had read again this morning about the wilderness trek of the Israelites and the way God miraculously provided their needs. Manna every day, and all they had to do was gather it.

"Men ate the bread of angels," was how the psalmist described it.

That appeared, somehow, to illustrate his marriage. Every day, with what seemed to be no effort at all on his part, he received God's extraordinary provision of contentment—there it was, waiting for him at every dawn; all he had to do was gather it in.

". . . bread of angels," he mused under his breath.

"See! You mutter even when you're not sleeping!"

"I hardly ever knew what I was doing 'til you and Dooley Barlowe came along and started telling me."

She leaned against him in her striped pajamas and yawned happily.

"You're so comforting, Timothy. I never dreamed I would find anyone like you—sometimes, I hardly know where I end and you begin."

It was true for him, as well, but he said nothing.

"I think our love fits into the miracle category," she said.

"Right up there with the Red Sea incident, in my opinion."

"Do you think the people who love you are happy about us? Isn't some of the parish feeling a bit . . . betrayed?"

"Never. They're glad to have someone look after me, so they don't have to. Of course, they never had to, but bachelor priests are thought to require extra attention."

He put his arm around her shoulder and pulled her close.

She kissed his chin. "Dearest?"

"Ummm?"

"Shall we bring the armoire over this Saturday?"

Out of the blue, again! He had to be quick. "This Saturday, I'm taking you for a little . . . recreation."

"I love recreation! What are we going to do?"

In all his life, he had never been able to figure out what to do for recreation. As a bachelor, he was forever dumbfounded by the way people planned ahead for this very thing. "What are you doing this weekend?" someone might ask, and the respondent would roll off a daunting list of activities—a ball game, a movie, dinner out, a play, hiking, a picnic, and God knows what else. If he were asked such a question, he always wound up scratching his head, speechless. He never knew what he might do until he did it.

"It'll be a surprise," he announced.

"Good! I love surprises!"

"Cynthia, Cynthia. What don't you love?"

"Exhaust fumes, movies made for TV, and cakes baked from mix."

"I'm all for a woman who knows what she likes—and doesn't like." He cleared his throat. "As for me, I like this."

"This what?"

"This . . . living with you."

"Then why did you fight me tooth and nail for longer than it took to build the Brooklyn Bridge?"

"No vision," he admitted. "No imagination. No—"

"No earthly idea of heaven!"

"You said it."

"Well, then . . ."

He leaned over and kissed her mouth, lingering.

"Oh, my goodness," she murmured at last. "Who would ever have thought . . . ?"

"Barnabas!" he called, coming in the kitchen door.

It was time for recreation, and he'd better hop to it. Otherwise, he'd have to leg it to the hardware to rent a back brace for the lugging over.

Barnabas raced from the study, skidded through the kitchen on a rag rug, and leaped up to give his master a lavish bath around the left ear.

"If we confess our sins," the rector quoted hastily from First John, "He is faithful and just to forgive us our sins, and to cleanse us from all unrighteousness!"

Barnabas retreated on his hind legs, lay down, sighed, and gazed up at his master.

His was the only dog in creation who was unfailingly disciplined by the hearing of God's Word. Now, if all of humankind would respond in the same vein . . .

"I'm ready!" she said, appearing from the study. She was dressed in blue jeans and a sweatshirt, tennis shoes and a parka, looking like a girl.

"Ready for what?" he inquired, grinning.

"What you said. . . ."

He was as excited as a boy, and no help for it.

"Here we go," he announced, offering his arm.

Barnabas lay in the high grass, his tongue hanging out from the long climb uphill.

They had walked around Mitford Lake twice, their cheeks red with the sting in the air, eaten lunch from a paper bag, sat on a log and laughed, and then headed up Old Church Lane to rest on the stone wall overlooking what he called the Land of Counterpane.

In the valley, with its church steeples and croplands, tiny houses and gleaming river, they saw the retreat of autumn. Only the barest hint of color remained in the trees.

"I have a great idea," he said.

"Shoot!"

"Why don't we do something like this every week? Both of us can get bogged down with work, and maybe this would be a way around it. Even for a few hours, let's plan to get away." He was learning something new, he could just feel it. Who said you can't teach an old dog new tricks?

"Lovely!"

He pressed on with mounting enthusiasm. "Even in the dead of winter!"

"Wonderful! I couldn't agree more."

There. Since all the stuff about checking accounts, where to sleep, and how much to spend without the other's consent, this was their first important pact.

"Shake," she said.

They sat on the wall until a stinging wind blew in from the north, then walked briskly down Old Church Lane and through Baxter Park.

"Look," he said, "there's our bench."

"Where we were sitting when the rain came . . . where you said you felt like thin soup, and invited me to go with you to see the bishop."

He was impressed with his wife's memory, as he didn't recall saying anything about thin soup.

"By the way," he wondered, "who's supposed to cook dinner this evening?"

"I can't remember," she said, wrinkling her brow.

Percy shuffled to the back booth and poured coffee for the rector, who had come in for an early lunch. "How d' you like it?"

"Same as ever. Black."

"That ain't what I'm talkin' about."

"So what are you talking about?"

"How do you like bein' married?"

"I like it."

This was the first time since he'd returned from the honeymoon that any of the crowd at the Grill had really questioned his new circumstances. He had strolled in one day during Percy's beef stew special, looking tanned and thinner, fresh from Maine, and not one word had Percy Mosely, Mule Skinner, or J. C. Hogan said about it.

All he could figure was, they were ticked off at knowing somebody for nearly fifteen years who suddenly upped and married. It required a certain change of mind, which, as Emerson had pointed out, was a blasted inconvenience.

"If I had it t' do over, I wonder if I'd do it," said Percy.

"You know you would. Where else would you get those terrific grandkids?"

"Oh, yeah," said the Grill owner, brightening.

"I'd do it over in a heartbeat," said Mule, sliding into the booth. "Fancy's better lookin' today than she was when I married her."

J.C. slid in on the other side. "I wouldn't touch it with a ten-foot pole. You couldn't get me to do it for a million dang dollars."

"Before or after taxes?" Mule wanted to know.

J.C. mopped his face with what appeared to be a section of paper towel. "Once was one time too many. I'd rather be shot by a firin' squad."

"Is that caf or decaf?" Mule asked Percy. "Fancy's got me on decaf, I been stumblin' around for two days tryin' to get awake. Hit me with a little shooter of both."

J.C. held his cup out to Percy. "I tried decaf for a week, and it was all I could do to get th' paper printed. We whittled that sucker down to four pages, I couldn't paste up an ad without droppin' to the floor to take a nap." He blew on the steaming coffee. "Nossir, I wouldn't be married for all the tea in China, women want to run your business—they put you on fiber, take you off bacon, put you on margarine, take you off caffeine."

"You're mighty talkative today," said Mule.

"I was up half the night with the fire department. Omer Cunningham's old hay barn caught fire and the sparks jumped over and started on the shed where he stores that antique airplane. The fire engine came, and it was fish or cut bait 'til three in the mornin'."

"I thought I might go into newspaper work," said Mule, "but I got over it."

"If that airplane had caught, you might've found a landin' gear on your front porch."

"Had gas in it, did he?"

"You know Omer, he's always ready to fly. All he needs is a cornfield that hasn't been plowed. He said he's moving it to a hangar at the airstrip."

Mule stirred cream into his coffee. "Somebody told me Mack Stroupe's going to run in the next mayor's race."

"Mack's for change," said J.C. "Development, progress, and change—that's his platform."

"I like the platform we've got," said the rector. " 'Mitford takes care of its own'!" he recited in unison with Mule.

Everybody in Mitford knew Mayor Esther Cunningham's platform, including the students at Mitford School, who had painted it on a nylon banner that was annually carried in the Independence Day parade up Main Street.

"You know how he built on to his hot-dog stand when he thought Percy was goin' out of business? He's goin' to use that side of th' building for his campaign headquarters."

"Right," said J.C. "And I'm the Pope. You couldn't get this town to vote for anybody but Esther Cunningham if you paid 'em cash money. They'll carry her out of office in a coffin."

"He'll never run," said the rector, "so we might as well forget it. Mack's no genius, but he's not stupid, either."

Mule leaned out of the booth, searching for Velma. "Are we goin' to order, or did I come in here for my health?"

"You definitely didn't come in here for your health," said J.C.

Percy's wife, Velma, magically appeared with her order pad. "Order th' special."

"What is it?" asked the rector.

"Ground beef patty with a side of Hi-waiian pineapple."

"How's the' pineapple cut up?" Mule inquired. "I like slices, not chunks."

Velma frowned. "It's chunks."

"I'll have a grilled cheese, then. No, wait." Mule drummed the tabletop with his fingers. "Give me bowl of soup and a hot dog all the way. Fancy's got me off cheese."

"I'll take a double cheeseburger all the way, plenty of mustard and mayonnaise, and large fries." J.C. gave his order louder than usual, to make it clear he was a free man.

"You don't have to bust my eardrums," said Velma.

Mule sighed. "On second thought, hold th' onions on my hot dog, they give me indigestion."

Velma eyed the rector, who was inspired by the sting he felt in the late October air. "Beef stew!" he announced.

"Cup or bowl?"

"Bowl."

"Roll or crackers?"

"Crackers."

"Change my order and bring me th' beef stew," said Mule. "I always like what he orders. But no crackers for me, I'll take the roll. And skip th' butter."

"I never heard of a *cup* of beef stew," said J.C.

"Crackers are for sick people," said Mule.

"Lord!" Velma ripped the order off her pad and delivered it to Percy.

Mule turned to the rector. "One thing I've been wondering . . ."

"What's that?"

"How do your dog and her cat get along?"

"Violet lives in the house next door, and Barnabas keeps to himself at the rectory."

Actually, Cynthia fed Violet her evening meal at five, then popped through the hedge to the rectory, after which Violet curled up on Cynthia's love seat and slept until her mistress returned to work the following morning and opened one of those canned items whose odor could knock a man winding at fifty paces.

"A cat with a house," said J.C. "That's some deal."

"So her cat and your dog don't cross?"

"Not if we can help it."

"One time you told me Barnabas slept on your bed."

"Now he sleeps in the hall."

There was a reflective silence.

"Anybody been up on the hill?" asked the rector.

He had just come from the site of Hope House, the five-million-dollar nursing home that Sadie Baxter had given as a memorial gift to Lord's Chapel. By the look of things, it would be a year before it was up and running with staff.

"I shot two rolls up there Wednesday. Doin' a feature page next week."

"That's going to be some deal," said Mule. "I wouldn't mind movin' in there myself. I hear there's goin' to be a fountain in the lobby."

"And an aviary in the dining room," the rector announced proudly.

Mule scratched his head. "Did I hear it'll have its own church?"

"A chapel. A small chapel. Local millwork, a rose window. First-rate."

Velma carried two lunch plates on her left arm, and a third in her right hand.

Mule looked on with approval. "That's a trick I always thought highly of."

"Beef stew with crackers. Beef stew with roll, no butter. Double cheesburger all the way, with large fries." Velma set the plates down in no particular order and stalked off.

The men dropped their heads as the rector asked a blessing.

"Amen," said Mule, rubbing his hands together.

"How's your boy?" asked J.C., who was busy pouring salt on his burger and fries.

"Great. Couldn't be better. He'll be home for Thanksgiving."

"He's not gettin' the big head in that fancy school, is he?"

"Nope. Dooley Barlowe might get a lot of things, but the big head won't be one of them."

"Did you read my story on Rodney hirin' a woman?" J.C. was not a pretty sight when he talked with his mouth full.

"You don't mean it."

"I bloomin' well do mean it. She starts the middle of November. A woman in a police uniform. . . . I can't see it."

"Why not? It's the law, no pun intended."

"Would you want a woman preachin' in your pulpit?" asked J.C., spilling coffee on his tie.

"Depends on the woman."

"I can't see a woman carrying a pistol."

"How come you don't like women?" asked Mule. "I like women."

"I told you. They're in the overhauling business."

"Maybe you could use a little overhaulin'."

"I *been* overhauled, buddyroe. Dropped fifty pounds, quit

cigarettes, gave up red meat, and quit readin' trashy books. Oh, yeah. I even got shots for smelly feet. Was that good enough? No way. She was outta there the year the Dallas Cowboys defeated the Denver Broncos twenty-seven to ten."

"Big year," said Mule. "The Yankees won the World Series."

"Not to mention the Chicago *Daily News* went belly-up."

None of this information gave the rector a clue as to what year they were talking about, and he had no intention of asking.

"So," said Mule, "did the shot work, or have you still got smelly feet?"

Lunch at the Grill, thought Father Tim, was what kept life real. He had to confess, however, that he could hardly wait to get back to the office and finish the C. S. Lewis essay entitled "Thought, Imagination, Language."

Cynthia gave him a hug as he came in the back door. "We've been invited to Miss Rose's and Uncle Billy's for banana pudding this evening."

"Oh, no! Please, no!"

"Dearest, don't be stuffy."

"Stuffy? Miss Rose has been hospitalized with ptomaine poisoning twice—and nearly sent a Presbyterian parishioner to her reward. You're the only person in town who'd put your feet under her table."

"So, pray for protection and let's go," she said, looking eager.

It didn't take much to delight Cynthia Kavanagh. No, indeed, it hardly took anything at all. What's more, she loved flying in the face of mortal danger.

"Besides, they've invited us for banana pudding practically since the day I moved here, so we can't disappoint them."

"Of course not."

"Next Wednesday," she said, "Miss Sadie and Louella are having us up for supper."

"Right."

"Fried chicken and mashed potatoes."

"We'll be there."

"And homemade coconut cake!"

"I've made a reservation in the emergency room," he declared, sitting down at the kitchen table.

"Don't worry, I'll watch you every minute. You mustn't have the gravy or the cake, and only the tiniest portion of potatoes, they'll be loaded with butter and cream."

He was glad J. C. Hogan wasn't around to hear this.

"Then," she said, adjusting her half-glasses to read from a list, "Ron and Wilma invited us for Friday evening."

"Ummm."

"Hal and Marge want us for dinner at the farm, the first Sunday of November."

"Aha."

"And the mayor has asked us for a family barbecue the following Sunday. What do you think?"

"Book it."

She looked faintly worn. "So much social activity! I thought you led a quiet life."

"I did," he said, "until I got married."

"Oh."

"Everybody wants a look at you."

"But they've seen me for ages!"

"Not in your new circumstances."

She sighed. "And then there's Thanksgiving!"

"And the All-Church Feast, which we must attend, and Dooley and Russell Jacks and Betty Craig for turkey here the day after, and . . . You look all in, what's up?"

She sighed again. "I've started a new book, and it has a crushing deadline."

All or nothing at all. That's what he liked about this new life.

They walked to the Porter place–cum–town museum, holding hands. A Canadian cold front had moved in, inspiring them to wrap like mummies.

"I went to see Miss Pattie this morning," she announced, her breath sending puffs of steam into the frigid air.

"You did?"

"I gave Evie two hours off."

"God knows when Evie's had two hours off. You're a saint."

"I'm no such thing. We played Scrabble."

"Scrabble? With Miss Pattie?" Evie Adams's mother hadn't been in her right mind for a decade, causing Evie to call the church office with some frequency, in tears of frustration.

"She spelled one word—'go'—and declared herself the winner. Then we had an imaginary lunch and she showed me her imaginary doll."

"Knowing you, you can describe that doll in detail."

She laughed. "Dimples. Blue eyes—one won't shut. It had lost its socks and shoes, and I think its toes were once chewed by a puppy. I told Evie I'd come again."

He stopped and put his arms around her. "I've always wanted a deacon. You're hired." He kissed her on both cheeks and then on the mouth.

"Dearest . . . everyone will talk."

"It's time I gave them something to talk about," he said, meaning it.

"I'll be et for a tater if it ain't th' preacher! Rose, come and look, he's got 'is missus with 'im."

They stood at the back door of the museum that led to the apartment the town had remodeled for Miss Rose and Uncle Billy Watson.

The old man's schizophrenic wife of nearly fifty years peered around the door. The rector thought she looked fiercer than ever.

"What do they want?" she demanded, staring directly at the shivering couple on the steps.

Uncle Billy appeared bewildered.

"You invited us for banana pudding!" said Cynthia. "Yesterday, when I saw you on the street."

"I did?" Miss Rose put her hands on her hips and gave them a withering look. "Well, I don't have any banana pudding!"

"Oh, law," said Uncle Billy, "did you go an' forget you invited th' preacher and 'is missus?"

"I certainly did not forget. It's too close to Thanksgiving to make banana pudding. I would never have had such an idea."

Uncle Billy looked anguished. "You 'uns come on in, anyway, and set where it's warm. I've got somethin' for you, Preacher, hit's nearly burnt a hole in m' pocket."

"That's all right, Uncle Billy, we'll come another time." Talk about a life-saving turn of events.

"Nossir, I need t' give you this. It's somethin' that belongs to th' Lord, don't you know."

They trooped in as Miss Rose eyed them with suspicion.

The rector observed that she was still dressing out of her long-dead brother's military wardrobe. Under a worn housecoat whose belt dragged the floor, she was wearing Army pants and a World War II field jacket. He was almost comforted by the sight of her unlaced saddle oxfords, which were her all-time favorite footwear.

"I cain't set down, cain't lay down, an' cain't hardly stand up," said Uncle Billy, who was leaning on a cane. "Ol' arthur's got me, don't you know."

They hovered timidly by the kitchen table while Miss Rose stood at the stove and gave them a thorough looking-over.

"Preacher, could you step in here a minute?" Uncle Billy opened the door to the unheated part of the house, admitting a blast of arctic air, and led the way. As the door closed behind them, the rector looked back at his wife, who was trying to appear brave.

"I put it over yonder," said Uncle Billy, turning on a light in a room stacked with old newspapers. "I've kep' it hid from Rose—she wouldn't take t' me doin' this, don't you know."

He felt thoroughly refrigerated by the time the old man located the stack of yellowed papers and withdrew an envelope. With a trembling hand, he gave it to the rector.

"It's m' tithe," he said, his voice breaking. "Th' Lord give me that money for my pen an' ink drawin's that Miss Cynthia sold, and I'm givin' His part back."

The rector was so moved, he could barely speak. "May the Lord bless you, Bill!"

"Oh, an' He does. Ever' day, don't you know."

"I'm glad we went," he said, buttoning his pajama top.

"Me, too. Even if Miss Rose does scare me half to death!"

She put her hands on her hips and said fiercely, "I don't *have* any banana pudding!"

"Thanks be to God!" he shouted, as they collapsed on the bed with laughter.

CHAPTER THREE

Gathered In

"YOU LOOKIN' at th' las' supper," said Louella.

As Fernbank's dining room was closed off for winter, they were sitting at the kitchen table.

"Louella's having her knee operation on Thursday," Miss Sadie reminded her guests. "She won't be able to cook like this again for a long time." His hostess, who was also his oldest, not to mention favorite, parishioner, appeared wistful.

"Who's driving you to Winston-Salem?" asked Cynthia, who had offered to do it a month earlier.

"Ed Malcolm. I don't know how Mr. Leeper heard about it, but somehow he did, and gave Ed the day off so he can drive us. Have you ever?"

"Extraordinary," said the rector. Buck Leeper, the abrasive, profane, don't-tread-on-me supervisor of the Hope House project . . .

Cynthia helped herself to another deviled egg. "How long will you be there?"

"Five days, we think," said Miss Sadie.

"What will you do down there for five days? And where will you stay?"

"I'll have a cot in Louella's room!"

"She goan baby me," said Louella, looking sunny. Miss Sadie had babied Louella, who had been born at Fernbank, since they were children. In recent years, however, circumstances had begotten the reverse.

Five nights on a hospital cot? he thought. Not good.

"Louella would do the same for me."

"Amen!" pronounced Louella, passing the mashed potatoes. "Y'all eat these up. We don't have no puppy dogs t' feed 'em to."

He could tell that his wife was in seventh heaven, eating like a trencherman and happy as a child. She looked at him and smiled. "Keep your eyes off the gravy, dearest."

Lord knows, he was trying. "What will you do when you come back? Surely the stairs . . ."

Louella will sleep down here in the kitchen."

"For how long?"

"The doctor said no stairs for three months."

"We ain't tol' him our stairs go almos' to th' Pearly Gates. How many we got, Miss Sadie?"

"Twenty-nine! Papa wanted thirty, but it didn't work out."

Sadie Baxter alone at night on that cavernous second floor? And what if Louella were to take a tumble on this cracked and broken linoleum? He didn't like the sound of the plan, not at all.

"When we go up at night, we go together," said Louella. "But sometime, it's more settin' down than goin' up."

"That's right. Sometimes it takes so long to get to the top, it's nearly time to start back to the bottom!"

"Me an' Miss Sadie, we sing our way up. I say, Do you remember 'To You before the close of day . . .'? She say, Sho' I do, you start and I'll jump in. We set there and sing a verse, then we climb up another little step or two. Sometime, we go through two or three hymns jus' to lay our bones down."

"And *sometimes,*" said Miss Sadie, inspired by the excitement of revelation, "we don't come *downstairs* at all."

"Miss Sadie, she keep candy in her vanity, an' I keeps Spam and loaf bread in my bureau. We watch th' soaps and th' news."

"We play checkers, or go ramble in the attic. I love to ramble in the attic. It keeps me young to remember old times."

"Many a day," said Louella, "we read th' Bible out loud, or Miss Sadie jus' sleep 'til dark."

"Louella, you don't need to tell that!"

"It's th' gospel truth."

Miss Sadie looked suddenly tired. "This old house . . ." she murmured. "I don't know. . . ."

You can learn a lot over a platter of fried chicken, he thought. Why had Miss Sadie never told him any of this? She always made everything seem bright and shining. They had no business rattling around in this clapboard coliseum alone. But what could be done? Hope House wouldn't be finished and staffed for another year. Maybe good help was the solution, someone to come in at night.

Or . . . well, now. That was a thought. Why hadn't it occurred to him before? The fine old house on Lilac Road, bequeathed to Olivia Davenport by her mother . . . perfect!

Only months ago, Miss Sadie had found something she never knew she had—blood kin. The beautiful Olivia was her great-niece, a surprising revelation that had thrilled both women. It was, however, a revelation they chose to keep secret, as it pointed to an illegitimate child by Miss Sadie's own mother.

Now, Olivia was married to Hoppy Harper, who had engineered her miraculous heart transplant. As they were living happily in the doctor's rambling mountain lodge, Olivia's house on Lilac Road sat quite empty. And didn't it have a brand-new furnace, wall-to-wall carpet, and every imaginable convenience, all on one floor?

He wouldn't introduce the idea just now, however. He'd make his move on Monday.

The shrill ring of the phone sounded in the hallway.

"I'll get it!" said Cynthia.

He would ask Olivia if there were any plans to sell her house. If not, he'd work on breaking down Miss Sadie's resistance to the idea of leaving Fernbank. She had lived in the house her father built since she was nine years old—more than eighty years. One didn't casually walk away from such a bond.

"Miss Sadie, it's Olivia."

As Miss Sadie left the room with her cane, Louella leaned over and whispered, "Honey, this ol' house killin' me and it killin' her, don't let her fool you. 'Sides that, when I say Miss Sadie, you 'member this hymn, she say she do, but she don't. Miss Sadie doan want you to think she doan remember. And ramblin' in th' attic?' She could stay up there 'til Jesus comes, kickin' up all that dust."

"I don't like the thought of you two being twenty-nine stair steps apart at night," he said.

"An' I don't like th' idea of Miss Sadie doin' th' cookin' aroun' here! Fact is, she don't cook—she sets out. She sets out mustard, she sets out baloney, she sets out light bread. Bless th' Lord, we in a pickle!"

Cynthia put on Louella's apron and announced she was washing the dishes. She handed her husband a drying towel.

Miss Sadie came back to the kitchen and closed the door. "I declare, if it's not one thing to muddle over, it's two. You'll never guess what that was all about."

"I could never guess," Cynthia admitted.

"Olivia said, Aunt Sadie, I want you to come and live in Mother's house, we're worried about you and Louella."

"Thanks be to God!" said the rector.

"Praise Jesus!" boomed Louella.

"Bingo!" exclaimed Cynthia. "And what did *you* say?"

Miss Sadie sat down and met each pair of eyes. "I said I'd have to think about it."

Cynthia spoke up at once. "I hope you'll think about the fact that it's all on one floor."

"And think about the heating system," he added, "and the insulation, and those good, tight windows, all brand-new. Warm as toast!"

"Think 'bout where it is!" crowed Louella. "One block from th' grocery! Aroun' the corner from th' post office!"

"You all don't have to preach me a sermon!"

After a respectful silence, he plunged in again. "Twenty-nine steps and nobody to sit and sing a hymn with. I wouldn't want to do it."

Miss Sadie looked at him coolly.

"I'll be sleepin' in th' kitchen, listenin' to th' roof leakin' in th' buckets," moaned Louella.

"Is the roof leaking again?" he asked. "I thought it was fixed."

"I thought it was fixed, Miss Sadie thought it was fixed. But it ain't fixed."

"It's fixed everywhere except the entrance hall!" said Miss Sadie, looking stern.

"Yas 'um," Louella muttered. "An' when it rains, it take a soup pot, a Dutch oven, an' a turkey roaster t' catch it!"

Miss Sadie thumped the floor with her cane. In all his years of knowing her, he'd never seen her do such a thing. "Shush!" she commanded. "I said I had to *think* about it. I didn't say how *long* I had to think about it. Coming down the hall, I thought about it."

Nobody said a word.

"And I have every intention of doing it!"

"Save us from troubled, restless sleep," he sang softly in the darkened room, "from all ill dreams Your children keep . . ."

"How lovely," she murmured, lying beside him. "What are you singing?"

"A verse from Louella's hymn, 'To You before the close of day . . .' "

He sang again, ". . . so calm our minds that fears may cease, and rested bodies wake in peace."

"Amen," she whispered, taking his hand.

The crowd at St. Andrews in Canton had hammered out a description of what every parish was looking for, and sent him a copy.

> The perfect pastor preaches exactly ten minutes. He condemns sin, but never hurts anybody's feelings. He works from eight in the morning until midnight and is also the church janitor. He is twenty-nine years old and has forty years experience. He makes fifteen house calls a day and is always in the office.

Right up there with what's currently expected of Cynthia Kavanagh, he thought.

"They asked me to be president of the ECW," she said, looking pale.

"What did you say?"

"I said I have full-time work and that it wouldn't be fair to be president of anything, for I would surely have to shirk my duty."

"Well put."

"And so they invited me to head up the Altar Guild."

They had discussed this very thing, long before he proposed to her on the night of his birthday last June.

"Of course I said no, thank you. That's when they asked me to chair that awful Bane and Blessing sale, which has put at least two women flat on their backs in bed."

"True."

"When they got to a nomination for program chairman, every eye turned to me. I excused myself and went to the ladies' room. It was awful."

She sighed. "Well, dearest, I turned down six things in a row—they were all positively glaring at me. It took enormous courage."

"I'm certain of that." Where the Episcopal Church Women were concerned, he personally wouldn't have the guts to turn down six things—in a row or otherwise.

She took a deep breath. "That's when I announced that I'm reserving my energies to give a parish-wide tea in the spring."

Aha! He knew the fondness of his parish for a roaring good tea.

"I was off the hook in a flash. You should have seen the look of forgiveness in their eyes! Now, guess what."

"What?"

"Now I have to do it!" she wailed.

The Hope House Board of Directors was searching for an administrator.

According to Hoppy, all was going well. As a graduate of Harvard Medical School, and the personal friend of a distinguished heart man at Mass General, his contacts had already turned up the names of several promising candidates.

It would take something like fifty people to run the two-story, forty-bed nursing home, and Miss Sadie had insisted on a full-time chaplain into the bargain. Finding the right candidate, the rector learned, was his job.

There would be RNs, LPNs, nurses' aides, business staff . . . the list went on and on, and most would have to be hired from outside the area. All of which would give a boost to merchants up and down Main Street and beyond.

No doubt about it, Hope House would be a shot in the arm for Mitford's economy.

"Who needs a canning factory?" asked a jubilant Mayor Cunningham at a town meeting.

Puny had been looking a bit peaked, in his opinion. Somehow, she wasn't the same girl he had escorted down the aisle in June and given in marriage to the mayor's grandson.

"Do you have to scrub the floor like this?" he asked his house help on Monday. Seeing Puny on her hands and knees on his kitchen floor always distressed him. "You know I'll buy you a mop."

"You always say that. When I scrub on my hands and knees, I wisht you'd look th' other way. I don't know why it makes you s' mournful, it's the same as my granmaw did it, and my mama, too, and it's th' way I'm goin' to do it."

She seemed to scrub the worn kitchen tiles even harder. "Some gloves, then!" he said. "Rubber gloves!" He had taken to worrying about the freckle-faced, red-haired Puny Guthrie as if she were his own blood.

"Ooooh, I jis' hate it when you preach!" she said.

"Preach? If you think that's preaching, wait 'til you hear the real thing, young lady."

She looked at him and smiled, and pushed her hair from her eyes. "I kind of like it when you boss me."

"I'm not bossing you, and you know it. But you look a little . . . pale, somehow. Are you feeling your usual self?"

"Well," she said, sitting back on her heels, "if you're goin' to hound it out of me, th' truth is, I ain't. I'm give out, sort of. I don't know what it is."

"You want a few days off? We can push along."

"Nossir, I don't want a few days off! Me an' Joe Joe are addin' a bathroom on our house an' puttin' on a new roof. I sure don't need to be takin' days off, with roofin' at twenty dollars a square."

Since she walked in and took over his house two years ago, Puny had been like a candle against the darkness—he wouldn't take the world for her cheerfulness, her vigor, her adamant faith, and the life she had brought to his household. Joe Joe Guthrie had won himself a pearl beyond price.

"OK, I'll hush."

"Good!" she said, grinning up at him.

He woke in the middle of the night, searching for the glass of water on the nightstand. He took a swallow and lay there listening to her breathe. He was confounded over and over again that she was lying beside him. He hadn't known what to expect, after all, when it came to sleeping with someone.

Would he feel hemmed in? Invaded?

But he had never felt hemmed in or invaded, not once. He felt, instead, a kind of awe that made him lie very still, scarcely breathing. How this could have happened, he couldn't imagine. During the day, he could imagine it, and muse over the slow and gradual process that had brought them to this place. But at night, it seemed a miracle, defying reason.

Oddly, he could feel himself becoming something more, as one might discover new rooms in a house he had lived in all his life. Doors had opened, shutters had been cranked back to let in new light. When he lay there and simply let the wonder of it sink in, he was suffused with a kind of joy he'd never known before.

This joy was different from what he felt when the Holy Spirit broke down his defenses and circumcised his heart. But both these joys produced in him a tenderness that was nearly unbearable.

"Thank you, Lord," he whispered.

"Hmmm?" Cynthia said, sleepily. "What did you say, dearest?"

"I said . . . thank you," he croaked.

"You're welcome," she sighed, falling back to sleep.

He walked to the Grill with Barnabas on his red leash, feeling the keen, pure cold of the day. Overhead, he heard the drone of a small airplane and looked up. Omer Cunningham, he supposed, who had nothing better to do than dip and soar in the wild blue yonder, while the rest of them had to fetch and carry like so many ants on a hill.

He reflected on Dooley's call last night—not once had he said "ain't," a piece of grammatical mayhem that Cynthia particularly disliked. That boy was a quick learner, he could say that for him. But there was something held-back in him, also—something cautious and wary like the old Dooley, yet more severe.

"How's Tommy?" Dooley had asked.

"Missing you, I think. Doing fairly well on his crutch. Dr. Harper is hopeful there won't be a limp." The friend who had fallen from a collapsing pile of lumber had survived a terrible wound to the head and a leg slashed to the bone.

"Can he talk right?"

"Nearly as well as the rest of us, I'd say."

Silence.

"How are you? How's your science class?"

"All right."

"And math? You're killing them, I take it."

"It's OK."

"The chorus is coming along—you're singing?"

"Uh-huh."

If only he could see his face. "We're wanting to see your face, pal. In just ten days, you'll be home."

"Yeah."

Was the "yes, sir" he'd once managed to gouge out of Dooley now gone with the wind? He felt an inexpressible love for the boy who had changed his life, who had turned it upside down and backward, and had come to be like his own son. They had toughed it out, they had made it through.

Or had they? "Are you OK?"

"Yeah."

Blast it, he was not OK, but there was nothing he could do about it on the phone. In no time at all, he and Cynthia would fetch him home from school, and everything would be fine. All Dooley Barlowe needed, after all, was a good dose of family and friends and somebody to catch up his laundry.

Hoppy Harper had called the church office earlier, saying merely, "I need to bust out of here, and I need to talk. What about lunch?"

His friend was already in the front booth, looking, as Emma once remarked, "like a young Walter Pidgeon."

"Track me on this," said Hoppy. After years of exhausting himself as the only doctor in town, he had learned the economy of never mincing words.

"Hippocrates said that in the body, there's no beginning—in a described circle, no beginning can be found. He believed that if the smallest part of the body suffers, it imparts suffering to the whole frame."

The rector nodded. If the smallest part of the spirit suffers, it imparts suffering to the whole being. He'd seen this principle at work too often. "Keep going."

Velma appeared with her order pad. "What're you havin'?"

"What's the Father having?" asked the doctor. "Give me the same."

"Chicken salad on whole wheat, no mayonnaise," said the rector, "with a cup of vegetable soup." Why did people always want to order what he ordered? Did they think he had some special sign from Providence about what to order for lunch?

Hoppy leaned toward him, his brow furrowed. "So, nothing happens to any part of the envelope that affects us in an isolated area. And part of the envelope is the spirit—right in there with the lymphatic and enzymatic and neurological and circulatory factors.

"Even Socrates jumped on this. He said the cure of a lot of diseases was unknown, because physicians were ignorant of the whole. His bottom line was, the part can never be well unless the whole is well."

"I'm with you," said the rector.

"For the first few months, the staff and I prayed silently before operating, and that was good. It got us up for the job ahead in a whole new way. Now we usually ask the patient if we can pray aloud before we begin the surgical procedure.

"It works for me, it works for the staff. That alone has to be of some benefit. But it's working for the patients, too. I think it helps them go under the anesthetic as a complete entity, not merely a diseased bladder or a ruptured appendix."

"Makes complete sense."

"Besides, wouldn't God care as much about our bodies as our souls? Isn't redemption total? Doesn't it involve body, soul, mind—all?"

"Absolutely all."

"By the way, Olivia read that in certain primitive cultures, the doctor and the priest are one and the same person."

"Quite a packaging concept."

He had never before seen his friend so passionate about anything—except, perhaps, securing the miraculous heart transplant that saved the life of the woman he married last June.

Hoppy ran his hand through his disheveled hair. "As I said, there's nothing in this you can print out, nothing you can prove. Yet I know it's real, it's right, it works—even though we see through a glass darkly."

They didn't notice that Velma had set their orders on the table, until Percy dropped by to refill their cups.

"Your soup's gettin' cold," he snapped. "And your san'wiches are dryin' out."

Percy Mosely did not like his customers to be indifferent to his fare. No, indeed.

The annual All-Church Feast, convening this Thanksgiving Day at Lord's Chapel, was drawing its largest crowd in years. Villagers trooped across the churchyard hooting and laughing, as if to a long-awaited family reunion.

It was one of his favorite times of the year, hands down.

People he saw only at the post office or The Local were, on this day, eager to give him the details of their gallbladder operation, inquire how he liked married life, boast of their grandchildren, and debate the virtues of pan dressing over stuffing.

This year, the Presbyterians were kicking in the turkeys, which were, by one account, "three whoppers."

Esther Bolick had made two towering orange marmalade cakes, to the vast relief of all who had heard she'd given up baking and was crocheting afghans.

"*Afghans?*" said Esther with disgust. "I don't know who started such a tale as that. I crocheted some pot holders for Christmas, but that's a far cry from *afghans.*"

Miss Rose Watson marched into the parish hall and marked her place at a table by plunking her pocketbook in a chair. She then placed a half dozen large Ziploc plastic containers on the table, which announced her intent to do doggie bags again this year.

Ray Cunningham came in with a ham that he had personally smoked with hickory chips, and the mayor, who had renounced cooking years ago, contributed a sack of Winesaps.

Every table in the Lord's Chapel storage closets had been set up, and the Presbyterians had trucked in four dozen extra chairs. The only way to walk through the room, everyone discovered, was sideways.

Cynthia Kavanagh appeared with two pumpkin chiffon pies in a carrier, Dooley Barlowe followed with a tray of yeast rolls still hot from the oven, and the rector brought up the rear with a pan of sausage dressing and a bowl of cranberry relish.

Sophia and Liza arrived with a dish of cinnamon stickies that Liza had baked on her own. Handing them off to her mother, she ran to catch Rebecca Jane Owen, who had grown three new teeth and was toddling headlong toward the back door, which was propped open with a broom handle.

Evie Adams helped her mother, Miss Pattie, up the parish hall steps, while lugging a gallon jar of green beans in the other arm.

Mule and Fancy Skinner, part of the Baptist contingent, came in with a sheet cake from the Sweet Stuff Bakery.

And Dora Pugh, of Pugh's Hardware, brought a pot of stewed apples, picked in August from her own tree. "Get a blast of that," she said, lifting the lid. The aroma of cinnamon and allspice permeated the air like so much incense from a thurible.

In the commotion, George Hollifield's grandchildren raced from table to table, plunking nuts and apples in the center of each, as Wanda Hollifield came behind with orange candles in glass holders.

In his long memory of Mitford's All-Church Feasts, the rector thought he'd never seen such bounty. He thought he'd never seen so many beaming faces, either—or was that merely the flush from the village ovens that had been cranked on 350 since daybreak?

The face he was keeping his eye on, however, was Dooley Barlowe's.

Following the regimental trooping to the dessert table, someone rattled a spoon against a water glass. No one paid the slightest attention.

Somebody shouted "Quiet, please!" but the plea was lost in the din of voices.

Esther Bolick stepped to the parish hall piano, sat down, and played the opening bars of a ragtime favorite at an intense volume.

A hush settled over the assembly, except for the kitchen crew, who was lamenting a spinach casserole somebody forgot to set out.

"Hymn two-ninety!" announced the rector, as the youth group finished passing out song sheets. "And let me hear those calories *burn*!"

Esther gave a mighty intro, and everyone stood and sang lustily.

Come, ye thankful people, come
Raise the song of harvest home
All is safely gathered in
Ere the winter storms begin
God, our Maker, doth provide
For our wants to be supplied
Come to God's own temple, come
Raise the song of harvest home.

Baptists warbled with Anglicans, Presbyterians harmonized with Methodists, and the Lutherans who had trickled in from Wesley gave a hand with the high notes.

The adults soldiered on through two more hymns, followed by the Youth Choir, who fairly blew out the windows with three numbers in rapid succession. The grand finale was a solo from Dooley Barlowe, whose voice carried all the way to the back of the room and moved several of the women to tears.

"He ain't got th' big head no more'n you or me," said Dora Pugh.

It was some time before anyone could move to help clear the tables.

"Let's just lay down right here," said Mule Skinner, pointing to the floor.

"You 'uns cain't be alayin' down," said Uncle Billy. "You've got baskets to take around, don't you know."

Somebody groaned. "Tell us a joke, Uncle Billy!"

"Well, sir, this feller had a aunt who'd jis' passed on, an' his buddy said, 'Why are you acryin'? You never did like that ol' woman.' And th' feller said, 'That's right, but hit was me as kept her in th' insane asylum. Now she's left me all 'er money an' I have t' prove she was in 'er right mind.' "

Groans and laughter all around. "Hit us again, Uncle Billy!"

"Well, sir, this feller was sent off to Alaska to do 'is work, and he was gone f'r a long time, don't you know, and he got this letter from his wife, and he looked real worried an' all. His buddy said, 'What's th' matter, you got trouble at home?' An' he said, 'Oh, law, looks like we got a freak in th' family. My wife says I won't recognize little Billy when I git home, he's growed another foot.' "

Miss Rose Watson sat silent as a stone, concerned that the Ziploc bags of turkey and dressing would shift under her coat.

Goodbyes were said, hugs were given out, and everyone shook the hand of the rector and his new wife, thanking them for a fine Feast. Several inspected Dooley's school blazer and commented that he'd shot up like a weed.

The contingent organized to deliver baskets waited impatiently as the packers worked to fulfill a list of sixteen recipients. These included Miss Sadie and Louella, Homeless Hobbes, and Winnie Ivey, who had shingles.

"You doin' a basket run?" Mule asked the rector.

He nodded. "Over to Miss Sadie's new digs on Lilac Road, then back here to help clean up. What about you?"

"Headed to Coot Hendrick's place. His mama's weak as pond water since th' flu."

"I thought J.C. was coming to the Feast this year."

"He probably boiled off a can of mushroom soup and ate what he didn't scorch."

"It's a miracle he's alive."

"Ain't that th' truth?" Mule agreed.

"There's nothin' wrong with J.C. that a good woman couldn't cure," said Fancy, who was dressed for today's occasion in fuchsia hot pants, spike heels, V-neck sweater, and a belt made of sea shells sprayed with gold paint.

"Don't hold your breath on that deal," said Mule.

Sophia came over and hugged the rector around the neck, as Liza clasped his waist and clung for a moment. "We love you, Father," said Sophia. He leaned down and kissed Liza on the forehead.

"Lord have mercy," said Mule, as Liza and Sophia left. "I don't know what these people will do when you retire. I hate t' think about it."

"Then don't," snapped the rector.

He saw the surprised look on his friend's face. He hadn't meant to use that tone of voice.

"Line up and collect your baskets," hollered Esther Cunningham, "and hot foot it out of here! This is not a cold-cut dinner you're deliverin'."

The delivery squad obediently queued up at the kitchen door.

"If you could knock th' Baptists out of this deal," said Charlie Tucker, "we'd have somethin' left to go *in* these baskets. Baptists eat like they're bein' raptured before dark."

"It wasn't the *Baptists* who gobbled up the turkey," said Esther Bolick, appearing to know.

"Well, it sure wasn't the Methodists," retorted Jena Ivey, taking it personally. "We like fried chicken!"

"It was the dadgum Lutherans!" announced Mule, picking up the basket for Coot Hendrick's mother. "Outlanders from Wesley!"

Everyone howled with laughter, including the Lutherans, who had personally observed the Episcopalians eating enough turkey to sink an oil freighter.

Abner Hickman came in the back door of the parish hall, returned from taking his kids home.

"Y'all want to see a *sunset*?"

A little murmur of excitement ran through the cleanup crew. Mitford was a place where showy sunsets were valued.

"Better get up to th' wall," declared Abner, "and step on it."

Esther Bolick parked her carpet sweeper in a corner. "Drop everything and let's go! Life is short."

They piled into vans and cars and screeched out of the parking lot, gunning their engines all the way to the steep crest of Old Church Lane, where they tumbled out and raced to the stone wall that overlooked the Land of Counterpane.

"Good heavens!"

"That's a big 'un, all right."

Little by little, the sharp intakes of breath and the murmurs and whooping subsided, and they stood there, lined up along the wall, gazing at the wonder of a sunset that blazed across the heavens. Where the sun was sinking, the skies ran with molten crimson that spread above the mountains like watercolor, changing to orange and pink, lavender and gold. A cool fire of platinum rimmed the profile of Gabriel Mountain and the dark, swelling ridges on either side.

He put one arm around Dooley's shoulders and the other around Cynthia's waist. The fullness of his heart was inexpressible.

All is safely gathered in . . .

He knew it could not always be this way. No, nothing ever remained the same. If he had learned anything in life, he had learned that such moments were fragile beyond knowing.

Ere the winter storms begin . . .

CHAPTER FOUR

Passing the Torch

THE LIGHT from the street lamp in front of the rectory shone through the hall window, reflected into the mirror at the top of his dresser, and bounced softly onto the bedroom ceiling.

Because a mimosa tree had grown up beside the old street lamp, the light gleamed through its leaves, casting shadows overhead. He could tell when a breeze was up, as the shadow of the leaves danced above him.

"Timothy?"

"Hmmm?"

Cynthia turned over and lay facing him. "I can feel you lying there stiff as a board. Something's on your mind, I just know it. Can't you tell me?"

He didn't want to say it to himself, much less to anyone else. "It's Dooley."

"Yes."

"What's happened to him?"

"I've been wondering that, too."

"He's different. Was I so wrong to send him away to school?"

"I don't know." She sighed. "At least he isn't saying 'ain't.' But that's no consolation."

"God's truth, as much as I fought him on it, I miss hearing him say it."

Cynthia turned and lay on her back. "The wind is up," she said, looking at the ceiling.

"I sense something hard in him, something harder than before."

"He hates that school."

"I can't help but wonder if I should bail him out. Or trust the old adage that time heals all wounds. Maybe it's just a matter of time until he puts down roots where he is. He put roots down here—his very first—then I hauled him off to Virginia. Transplanting is always risky business."

"Look what happened," she said, "when I moved my white lilac in the middle of summer. How did I know it should be moved in early spring?"

"Yes. Maybe it was timing, maybe we should have waited a year to send him away."

"Have you talked to him?"

"He won't talk. He's hard as stone—face, heart, spirit."

"He needs to spend time with Tommy," she said. "He's avoiding his best friend."

He despised losing sleep over any issue. Broad daylight was the time for fretting and wrestling—if it had to be done at all. "Don't worry about anything," Paul had written to the church at Philippi, "but in everything, by prayer and supplication, make your requests known unto God. And the peace that passes all understanding will fill your hearts and minds through Christ Jesus." In the last hour, he had twice given his concerns to God and then snatched them back, only to lie here staring at the ceiling, worried.

"What were you like when you were thirteen? What was going on in your life? Maybe that will help us."

"My best friend was named Tommy, also. We did everything together. My father despised him."

"Your father. What was it, Timothy, that made him so cold? Did you ever do anything that pleased him?"

He thought about it. No. He really couldn't remember doing anything that pleased his father. His grades had been very good, but never good enough. There was the incident with the bicycle, but he didn't want to remember that. He didn't want to talk about his father. It was the middle of the night and he suddenly felt the weight lying on his chest.

"Let me rub your neck," he said, turning to her. "I know you had a long day over the drawing board."

"But, dearest—"

"There. How's that?"

"Lovely," she murmured.

The softness of her skin, the warmth of the down comforter, the leaves moving softly above them . . .

He was asleep in two minutes.

He drove to the country to see the ninety-year-old preacher he'd hooked up with Homeless Hobbes and the residents of Little Mitford Creek.

Every Wednesday night, in clement weather, Homeless cooked a vast pot of soup and fed any who would come to his one-room shack on the creek bank. Homeless's broader concern for their spiritual feeding had moved the rector to ask Absalom Greer to preach a summer meeting, his last call before retiring from his "little handfuls" at three mountain churches.

The old parson had willingly gone into the desperately impoverished area, where alcohol, drugs, and violence had eaten into the Creek like cancer.

"I quit!" said Absalom Greer, opening a cold bottle of Orange Crush and passing it to the rector.

"I hate to hear it," said Father Tim.

"Every time I try to get loose of preachin', there's somebody who hates to hear it, and so I fall to doing it again, goin' like a circle saw. But this is it, my brother, as far as churches and camp meets go. The Lord paid me off, showed me the gate, and told me to trot."

The two men sat by the ancient soft-drink box in Absalom Greer's country store, twelve miles from Mitford. Among the comforts of this life, the rector once said, was sitting in Greer's Store in the late afternoon, with the winter sun slanting across heart-of-pine floors laid nearly a century ago.

"I'll do my preaching from the drink box, from here on out.

There's many a lost soul comes down that road looking to quench their thirst, thinkin' they can do it with a Pepsi."

The rector nodded.

"Used to, I could give 'em a soft drink and a sermon for a nickle. Now the drink companies gouge a man for the best part of a dollar." The preacher's pale blue eyes twinkled. "Some days, it's hard to come up with a dollar's worth of preaching."

"Amen!"

The rector gazed with affection on the man who, more than sixty years ago, tried to win the hand of Sadie Baxter, and lost—the self-educated man who, to the horror and delight of his parishioners, had supplied the pulpit at Lord's Chapel while Father Tim hustled off to Ireland last year. What was more extraordinary was that Absalom Greer had packed them in—after the initial shock wore off.

"Tell me about your stint on the Creek. Homeless said wonderful things happened."

"My brother, they were a rough bunch—a handful and a half! I was preaching on sin, and they didn't like it a bit—same as the fancy churches, where the very mention of sin empties the pews.

"But a man has to start somewhere, and that's where the Lord told me to start—with sin and repentance.

"Folks like to think sin is what everybody else is doing, but the mighty book of Romans lays it out plain and simple—'For all have sinned and come short of the glory of God.'

"I didn't go on about drinking and fornicating, or backbiting and stealing. Nossir, I jumped right to the heart of the matter and preached the taproot of sin, which is found in the middle of the word, itself—*I*! I want this, I want that, and I want it right now. I want to run things, I want to call the shots, I want be in charge. . . .

"When we turn from our sin, and have the blessed forgiveness of the Almighty, then we can ask Him to run things, and let Him be in charge. But boys howdy, folks don't want to hear that, either.

"Nossir, they like to keep control, even if their little boat's pitchin' around in the storm and takin' on water and about to be swamped."

Preacher Greer took a long swallow of his cold drink.

"I got to chasing rabbits there for a minute. You asked how it went.

"Wellsir, you know how you stick a seed in the ground and you squat down and look where you planted it, and you get up and walk around a little bit, waiting for something to happen, and the rain falls and the sun shines, and you water that seed some more . . . and still nothing pokes up. So after a while, you're tempted to go off and lay down under a tree, and plumb quit on that seed.

"Week after week, I was preaching the living redemption of our Savior, and I look out and see dead faces and stony hearts. A rough life had killed back their feelin's like a hard freeze on a peach crop.

"Some nights I'd go home and cry like a baby for the way they were hangin' on to their hurt.

"But I plowed on. One evenin', we preached the Word where it tells us the wages of sin is death, but the gift of God is eternal life through Jesus Christ.

"We told how Christ died for us out of love, which is mighty hard to understand, saved or unsaved.

"Then, we preached that noble verse from Revelation that makes me shiver to hear it—'Behold, I stand at the door and knock! If any man hears my voice and opens the door, I'll come in to him, and will sup with him, and he with me.'

"I said the Lord Jesus will knock and keep knocking 'til you let Him come in and make you a new creature. He'll never break down the door. Nossir, the Lord is a gentleman. He waits to be *invited.*"

The bell jingled, and a customer walked in. "Brother Greer, I need a box of oatmeal!"

"Comin' up," said Absalom, leaving his guest.

The rector noted the slowness of the old man's gait as he walked toward the shelves. He hadn't seen that last year and felt troubled by it. Deep down, he expected the people he loved to live forever, no matter how many funerals he had performed during his years as a priest.

Absalom rejoined the rector and sat again.

"My brother, I was in deep prayer as I preached, that the Holy Ghost would knock through the crust on every heart along that creek—but I have to tell you, my own heart was sinking, for it looked like the vineyard wasn't givin' off a single grape."

"I hear you."

"That's the way it was goin' when I noticed a young girl sitting on a limb of that big tree by the water.

"Usually, a good many young 'uns would sit up there for the preaching, but somebody had put a board across some rocks that evenin', and all the young 'uns but her was sitting on the board. I pay a good bit of attention to young 'uns, having been one myself, but I'd never spotted Lacey Turner before.

"You talk about listening! Her eyes like to bored a hole in me. If a preacher had a congregation to sit up and take notice like that, he'd be a happy man. It seemed like every word the Holy Ghost put in my mouth was something she craved to hear. I got the feeling my words were like arrows, shooting straight at that long-legged, barefooted girl, but still missing the souls on the ground.

"Wellsir, that young 'un slid off that limb and landed on her feet right in front of me, blam!

"Strikin' the ground like that kicked the dust up around her feet. I looked at that dust and looked at that girl, and I knew the Lord was about to do a work.

"She said, 'I'm sorry for th' bad I've done, and I want to git saved.' It was as matter-of-fact a thing as you'd ever want to hear.

"Well, the young 'uns on the board, they started in laughing, but that girl, she stood there like a rock, you should have seen her face! She was meaning business.

"I said, 'What would you be repenting of?' And she said, 'Bein' generally mean and hatin' ever'body.' "

"My brother, that's as strong an answer as you're likely to get from anybody, anywhere.

"I said, 'Do you want to be forgiven of meanness and hatred?' and she squared back her shoulders and said, 'That's what I jumped down here for.'

"I said, 'Well, jump in here and say a prayer with me and turn your heart over to Jesus.' And we both went down on our knees right there by the water, saying those words that's changed the lives of so many lost and hurting souls.

" 'Lord Jesus,' she prayed in behind me, 'I know I'm a sinner. I believe You died for my sins. Right now, I turn from my sins and receive You as my personal Lord and Savior. Amen.'

"Wellsir, I looked up and half the crowd had moved over to that big tree and was going down on their knees, one by one, and oh, law, the Holy Ghost got to working like you never saw, softening hearts and convicting souls 'til it nearly snatched the hair off my head.

"We stayed kneeling right there, and I led first one and then another in that little prayer, and before you know it, brand-new people were getting up off their knees and leaping for joy!

"Oh, you know the lightness that comes with having your sins forgiven! It's a lightness that fills you from one end to the other and runs through your soul like healing balm."

The rector could feel the smile stretching across his face.

"My brother, I scrambled down the bank to that creek, and that little handful swarmed down over rocks and roots, some crying, some whooping for joy, and we baptized in the name of the Father and the Son and the Holy Ghost 'til I was sopping wet from head to toe."

The old preacher was silent, then he smiled. "I've never seen anything to top it."

"Nor I," said the rector.

Absalom got up and set his empty bottle in a crate.

"You can baptize anywhere you've got water," he said, "but to my way of thinking, you can't beat a creek. It's the way ol' John did it—out in the open, plain and simple.

"Only one thing nags me," he told the rector. "Who's goin' to disciple those children of God?

"What's goin' to become of Lacey Turner, as pert and smart a young 'un as you'll ever see, with a daddy that's beat her all her life, and a mama sick to death with a blood ailment?

"I can't keep goin' back in there. My arthritis won't hardly let me get down the bank from the main road."

The old man shook his head. "It grieves me, brother, it grieves me."

The knot in the rector's throat was sizable. "I don't know right now what we can do," he said, "but we'll do something. You can count on it."

They walked out to the porch and looked across the pasture and up to the hills. The sun was disappearing behind a ridge.

"How's Sadie?" asked Absalom.

"Never better, I think. She has a heart like yours."

"Well . . ." said the old preacher, gazing at the hills. They stood on the porch for a moment, silent.

Absalom Greer had passed a torch, and Father Tim had taken it. The only problem was, he had no idea what to do with it.

He was fixing dinner as Dooley stood at the kitchen door, staring into the yard. Cynthia looked up from setting the table and walked over and put her hand on his shoulder. He shrugged it off.

"What is it, Dools?"

"Nothin'."

"Why won't you talk to us, be with your family for the two days you've got left of your school break?"

Dooley turned around and they saw that his face was white with anger. "You're not my family. I don't have a family."

He stalked from the kitchen, slamming the door behind him.

On Saturday, Cynthia popped through the hedge for an early call from her editor, so he hot-footed it to the Grill, with Barnabas on the red leash. Advent was coming up, and still no snow, or promise of snow. Perhaps they would have a white Christmas—but, God forbid, not a blizzard like the one that paralyzed them last winter.

He took his cup off the hook at the counter and poured his own coffee. "Poached," he said to Percy, who was flipping bacon on the grill. Percy frowned. He had never liked doing poached, which he considered too time-consuming.

In the rear booth, Mule was reading the paper, printed on the *Muse* presses overhead. "How'd we get th' pleasure of your company this morning?"

"I lost the pleasure of my wife's company," said the rector.

"I know th' feelin'. Fancy was up doin' highlights and a perm at six-thirty." He folded the *Muse* and laid it on the table. "You see J.C.'s story?"

" 'Getting to Know Your MPD,' I think he called it."

"He drove around in a squad car for a couple of days, gathering material."

"Very readable," said the rector. "Well done. Anybody seen the new police officer?"

"You mean th' woman?"

"Right."

"Fills out 'er uniform pretty good. She was in here before you, picked up a coffee with cream and sugar. Forty, if she's a day. Name's Adele Lynwood."

"Where's J.C.?" wondered Father Tim.

"Gettin' barbered. I saw him leggin' it up th' steps to Joe Ivey an hour ago. Speakin' of which, you're lookin' a little lank around th' collar."

"Always drumming up business for Fancy. If she did as much for your real estate interests, you'd be rolling in dough."

"I call it like I see it, and you could use a trim."

"Man!" said J.C., sliding into the booth. "He shaved me for boot camp."

"That's Joe's deal," said Mule. "Take it all off at one whack. Fancy's of the new school. She believes in trimmin' a little at a time. More natural."

"And more money," said J.C., wiping his face with a paper napkin. "Six bucks here, six bucks there. Joe gives you fifteen dollars' worth for five."

"And sends you out needin' a hat to keep your head warm," said Mule.

Given the surprised, newly hatched look of J. C. Hogan, the rector thought he might dodge Joe Ivey this time and step over to Fancy's himself.

"Good story," said the rector. "One of the best in some time. I didn't know the chief played minor league baseball."

"Nobody else did, except his mama and daddy, and maybe his wife."

"Journalism at its best!" announced Mule.

Percy poured a round of coffee and eyed J.C. "What'll it be?"

"Give me a bowl of Wheaties, skim milk, a cup of yogurt, and dry toast . . . whole wheat."

There was a stunned silence. "Call nine-one-one!" said Mule.

Percy dug a finger in his ear. "Am I goin' deef?"

"And snap to it," said J.C. "I could eat a horse."

Mule blew on his coffee. "You'll have to drink a saucer of grease to let your stomach know it's you."

"Why didn't you come to the Feast?" asked the rector.

"Too much carryin' on."

"You could use a little carrying on, if you ask me."

"I didn't ask you," said J.C.

One thing he could say for his collar—it never earned him any respect at the Grill.

After breakfast, he walked out with Mule and untied Barnabas from the bench.

"I don't get it," said the Realtor. "Clean tie. Haircut . . ."

"Dry toast. Skim milk . . ." mused the rector, shaking his head.

"I just thought . . . we've been wondering . . . is anything going on at school that we should know about? Dooley's not himself, not at all."

"Glad you asked," said the headmaster, who promised he didn't mind being rung up on a holiday. "I thought the trip home might do him good, so I didn't say anything."

"Say anything about what?" He was afraid to know.

"About what happened. He made friends with one of the boys, one of the . . . disadvantaged boys, if you will, and he talked to him about his family, about his mother and what happened to his brothers and sisters. I think it was hard for him to talk to someone about this. I think it plagues him a good deal. The bottom line is, Dooley spilled his guts to the boy, and the boy betrayed him. He told it around school."

Dear God. So that was what had chilled Dooley to the bone and hardened his heart all over again.

"While we're at it," said the headmaster, "Dooley was caught smoking on the grounds. This put his name on a roster that's posted in the hall for all to see. He's also skipped chapel a couple of times. Not a good start. He mustn't think that's a way to make a name for himself around here. I've spent a bit of time with him, Father, he's got strong potential. But there may be equally strong liabilities."

"What can I do?"

"Well, for one thing, you can increase his allowance, if it seems appropriate. Even with the few students from lower economic backgrounds, this is a school for the privileged, and there's no getting around it. He sees the boys buy expensive school sweatshirts or take off on weekend field trips to Washington, and his allowance doesn't stretch that far. Perhaps the generous woman who's sending him here would—"

"What kind of money are we talking about?"

"A hundred and fifty dollars a month. I think that's fair."

"Consider it done," he said.

After the phone conversation, he stared out his office window. He had to hand it to Dooley Barlowe. The boy had never once complained about his allowance, and only once had he asked for money.

He took his checkbook out of his jacket and sighed. Then he called home. Dooley answered.

"I'm taking you to Wesley for a cheeseburger," he said.

"I don't want a cheeseburger."

"I'll pick you up in ten minutes. Flat."

Shelling out a hundred and fifty bucks a month did not put him in the mood to mince words.

Sitting in the fast-food restaurant, he laid the check on the table and went over the program.

"Get caught smoking again, and you're back to what you've been getting. Got it?"

No answer.

"Got it?"

"Yeah."

"No yeah."

"Yes, sir."

"Another thing. Skip chapel again and you blow off seventy-five bucks a month. Period."

Dooley looked at him.

"I've talked with Dr. Fleming and I know what happened. Hear me on this. Your friends *will* betray you. Not all your friends, but some of your friends. That's life. Let it teach you this: *You* mustn't betray *your* friends. Ever."

"I could kick his guts out."

"You could. But for what?"

Dooley stared out the window.

"You can make it or break it in that school. You can stick in there and obey the rules and suck it up and learn something, or you can come crawling home for the world to know you couldn't hack it up there with the big guys.

"Listen, pal, life is tough. School's no picnic. But you'll be home again at Christmas. That's not far away. Take it a little at a time. A little at a time. You're going to be OK up there. I promise."

Dooley wadded his burger wrapper into a ball and lobbed it into a trash can.

"You said the other day you don't have a family. That hurt. It made us feel rotten. I want you to know that. The truth is, you do have a family, because we love you and care for you and we're sticking with you, no matter what. That's family."

Dooley dropped his gaze. "I didn't mean it," he said.

"I know you didn't. Go call Tommy and ask if he wants us to bring him a cheeseburger, and does he want waffle fries or seasoned."

It was only there for a moment, but he saw it—Dooley Barlowe couldn't fool him. It was an instant of happiness in the boy's eyes, something like hope or relief.

He'd pop a load of Dooley's laundry in the machine, then swing by Winnie Ivey's for a sack of donuts to take on the trip back to school tomorrow. A bitterly cold wind was gusting through the village.

"I wish I could go with you to take Dooley," Cynthia said. "I hate to see him leave."

"Ummm."

"Did you hear me?" she asked, peering at him.

"What's that?"

"Sometimes you're a thousand miles away."

He grinned. "The rest of me is a stick-in-the-mud, but my mind has always liked to wander. Living alone so many years didn't help matters any."

"A likely story."

"I'll try to do better, I promise. What are you up to today?" His wife, he knew, was always up to something.

"I'm mending two of Dooley's shirts and then working on an illustration of bluebirds in a nest."

"Your new book is about bluebirds?" Things had been so frantic, they hadn't found a chance to discuss her book.

"I think so," she said, "but I'm not sure, yet. I feel it should *open* with bluebirds, but I don't know if it's *about* bluebirds."

Sounded like the way he wrote his sermons.

"I've always wondered what it's like to be a bird—soaring around in the clouds, sleeping in trees. I think children would want to know that. All we see from the ground is that lovely, winged freedom. But they must have perils and scrambles like the rest of us, don't you think?" She peered at him over her glasses.

"I'm inclined to think so, yes."

"I can hardly wait 'til spring to go out with my sketchbook," she said, getting that abstracted look in her eyes.

"Ummm."

"I hope you'll come with me! You can exegete Jeremiah while I draw birds."

"I'd rather draw a bird any day than exegete Jeremiah!" he said with feeling.

"By the way, dearest, what's blooming around the rectory in May?"

"Let's see. A fine grove of white mountain trillium, a border of primroses which are pretty showy . . . and there's lily of the valley, of course, a side yard full."

"Perfect!"

As he kissed her goodbye, he was struck again by the endlessly compelling blue of her eyes. Would he one day take them for granted, or would they always draw him in like this?

He was unplugging the coffeepot on Monday morning when he heard Puny let herself in the front door.

She came down the hall at a trot and disappeared into the downstairs bathroom, where she remained for some time. When she came out, he was leaving for the hospital.

He couldn't help seeing that she was an odd green color—something in the mint family, to be precise.

"Good heavens, Puny, what is it?"

She sighed. "Remember I said Joe Joe and me won't be in any hurry to have babies?"

"Yes. I remember that."

"Well, *we* forgot to remember," she said, looking ghastly.

CHAPTER FIVE

A Close Call

IT MIGHT HAVE BEEN a nest of copperheads, for the cold dread he felt when seeing the boxes left by UPS on Emma's desk.

"Get it off my desk," she said, her shoulders rigid.

"Where would we put it? The shower stall is filled with everything from 1928 prayer books to the office Christmas wreath."

"Set it on the visitor's bench."

"But we usually have visitors." Why couldn't the people it came from have kept the blasted thing 'til they were ready to install it?

She turned and eyed his desk, a cue that he ignored.

"Put it on the floor, then," she said with disgust. "In front of your bookcase."

"Then we can't open the front door all the way."

"You ought to see the nice preacher's office at First Baptist," she said, glaring around their nine-by-ten-foot confinement. "Enough room for a bowling alley!"

He saw it coming—the Baptist preacher's office would grow into a stadium, a coliseum, the Parthenon.

"Emma," he said, "why don't you take the day off?"

He was sure someone would be around tomorrow to plug it in.

Or whatever.

But nobody came on the morrow.

Reluctantly, he read what was printed on the boxes: 420 drive megabytes. Eight megabytes of ram. PCI architecture. He might have been reading Serbian. If you couldn't make sense of the box, he reasoned, what sense could you make of its contents?

"Put it in your car," said Emma. "You could put it in mine, but Harold's storing hay in the backseat."

"Hay?"

"It's wrapped up with old blankets to keep from makin' a mess, you can't tell it's hay. He wanted to keep it dry and didn't have any room left in that little barn he built."

"Aha."

"Just stick it in your trunk, if it'll fit."

He had to hand it to her—Emma Newland could come up with a really good idea once in a while.

"Don't worry," he told her as he hauled the largest box out the door, "somebody said a child could operate it."

He knew he was repeating a barefaced lie, told by someone who foolishly believed clergy to be ignorant of reality and bereft of common sense.

"Hello, Rodney!"

He hadn't had a call from the Mitford police chief in quite a while, not since they'd done all that business together before his trip to Ireland.

During the dognapping of Barnabas that had led to the drug bust, and the drama of the jewel thief who had lived in the church attic and turned himself in during a Sunday service, he'd seen Rodney Underwood nearly every day for a couple of months.

"Father, I need to talk to you about somethin'. We could meet at the Grill—or how about me comin' by your office?" Rodney sounded worried.

"Why don't I come by your office? I haven't been there in a while. Got anybody I can visit, while I'm at it?"

"Not a soul. I released a DUI this mornin'. We've done cleaned th' cell and mopped th' floor." Rodney was the only police chief he'd ever heard of who kept house like a barracks sergeant and provided back issues of *Southern Living* for inmates.

At the station, Rodney met him at the door. "Looks like marriage is treatin' you right."

"It is, thank you."

"How's Dooley? I been meanin' to ask."

"Fine. Doing great."

"Not gettin' the big head, is he?"

If there was anything the village didn't want Dooley to get, it was the big head. "Let that be the least of your concerns."

Rodney took him into his office and closed the door. "It's Miss Sadie," he said, hitching up his gun belt.

He distinctly felt his heart skip a beat. "What happened?"

Rodney sat on the corner of his desk and invited the rector to take a chair. "She's done run that Plymouth up on the sidewalk one time too many.

"You know I've closed my eyes and looked the other way ever since I stepped into this job—but only where Miss Sadie's concerned. She's th' only one I'd look th' other way for."

The rector nodded. If there was ever an honest man, it was Rodney Underwood.

"Drivin' up on th' sidewalk ain't goin' to hack it from here out. This mornin', she hauled up in front of The Local so close you'd bust out the store window if you opened the passenger door. I mean, we got new people movin' in here, it's not just homefolks anymore. These are modern times. Why, there's somebody from Los Angelees, California, livin' on Grassy Creek Road."

"I'll be darned."

"The way I figure it, that car rolled off the line when Eisenhower was in office. If it hit a Toyota, it'd send it all the way to Wesley—air express. Another thing. She hugs th' yellow line like it was laid out for her to personally run on. People scatter like chickens when they see her comin' in that Sherman tank."

The police chief looked closely at the rector, to be sure he was getting the point. Clearly, he wasn't. "What I'm sayin' is, she's got to do better or we got to get her off th' street."

"Aha." He didn't want to hear this, no indeed, he liked things to go along smoothly, business as usual. Sadie Baxter had been driving up on the sidewalk for years. What was the big deal?

"My men have spoke to her twice, but it ain't sinkin' in. Next time, we're givin' her a citation. And if she don't do better then, I'm turnin' her in to th' MVB for reevaluation."

"Can *you* discuss it with her?" asked the rector, knowing the answer already.

"That's what I'd like you to do, Father."

"I hate to meddle," he said, knowing full well that he would have to do it, anyway. Actually, someone once told him that meddling was his job. Godly meddling, they'd called it, though it hardly ever felt godly to him.

"I don't call it meddlin' when you might be savin' somebody's life, not to mention hers. How she even sees over the dashboard is more than I can figure, low as she is."

"Ah, well," he said weakly. He had rather be horsewhipped than tell Sadie Baxter she'd have to park at the curb like everybody else and stick to her own lane. He had seen the stern way she rapped the floor with her cane before Louella's operation. To tell the truth, he might be a little afraid of Sadie Baxter.

Maybe Cynthia would do this uncomfortable deed, and let him out of it altogether.

He had shaved and showered, and was about to walk into the bedroom when he realized his wife would be there.

He shook his head as if to return some sense to it. His *wife.* He more than relished the company of his wife; there were times he could hardly wait to see her. But when would his heart stop this foolish pounding on nearly every encounter? When would the comfort of merely being two old shoes kick in?

She was sitting up in bed in something blue, with Barnabas on the floor beside her. "I gave Evie a little break today."

"You're wonderful."

"Never! What do you think Miss Pattie and I did?"

"I can't even begin—"

"We danced."

"No!"

"Yes."

"The rumba? The fox-trot?"

"Free-form."

"You had . . . music?"

"She turned on the radio. It was something about calling the wind Mariah."

"Aha."

"When Evie came home and saw her little mother dancing, she cried."

"Evie always cries."

He loved the open expectancy that so often lit her face. He sat on the bed next to her. "It all sounds amusing, but I know it isn't, really. You're brave and good to let Miss Pattie express something of her spirit."

"I'm not good, dearest, and I'm certainly not brave. I really don't like going over there at all. It's hard. But when I think how hard it is for Evie . . . "

He took her hand, grateful.

"There's something terribly winsome and sweet about Miss Pattie," Cynthia said. "She looks rather like the Pillsbury Dough Boy in a dress, don't you think?"

"Exactly!" He wouldn't talk to her about Miss Sadie tonight.

"I thought I might take her to ride one day. Rodney Underwood used to take her to ride in his squad car, but he's too busy now. Do you think a Mazda would do just as well?"

Yes, indeed, he thought, angels were very real. Miss Pattie and Evie Adams had been given one of their own, in the flesh. As had he.

"Ah, Father!" It was Hope Justice, appearing out of the fog as the rector jogged his final lap up Main Street.

He stopped, panting. He always liked seeing her face. And since she worked the night shift and slept most of the day, he didn't see it often.

"I wanted to thank you and the missus for what you did for our Benjamin and all. It was mighty big of you in every way. We just appreciate it, Father." He saw tears welling up in Hope's brown eyes.

"Why, think nothing of it!"

"It helped more than you know," said Hope, pulling out a handkerchief.

Jogging away in the damp December cold, he couldn't help but wonder what he had done for Hope Justice. He didn't want to seem dense, but the last time he could remember doing anything was years ago, when her husband was laid off from the glove factory.

Puny Bradshaw Guthrie was getting back to her old self. In fact, he'd never seen her look better.

"Stop starin' at my belly!" she said, giggling. "I can jis' feel you starin' down there to see what's what. I prob'ly won't even show for another month or two!"

He felt that uncontrollable grin spreading across his face. His Puny, with the red hair and freckles and the soul of a saint. . . . "And what docs your mother-in-law, the mayor, think?"

"She's excited as anything. This'll be her eighth great-gran."

"And twenty-five grans, I believe?"

"Twenty-six, countin' her youngest girl's little boy that popped out last week."

"I got you something and don't sass me for doing it." He went to the pantry and took out the mop.

"It's a squeegee with a flexible handle, and look here, you don't ever have to bend over again, just work this lever. . . . "

She eyed the demonstration with suspicion.

"And another thing," he said. "I want you to eat a good lunch and stop pecking around here like a bird."

She laughed and saluted him. "Yes, sir!"

He sighed. "I don't know what I'll do without you when—"

"You don't have to do without me! I'll bring it to work with me!"

"You . . . you will?"

"I sure will! And I won't mind a bit if you play with it!"

"You won't?"

"That little train you set up at Christmas, you could run that an' all. That would be entertainin'."

There was a thought, he mused, scratching his head.

Out of sight, out of mind.

He had forgotten the three boxes shifting around in his car trunk, until the computer company called to say they'd be heading up the mountain "real soon."

While he had them on the line, he said, maybe they could tell him what to expect. No problem, said the caller. They would come and install the computer, the monitor, the printer, and the bookkeeping system, and give a two-hour introduction. Then they'd come back every week or so for a couple of hours until the church office could handle it on their own.

How long, he wondered, would it take for his office to . . . handle it? About a year, no problem, piece of cake, said the caller. Father Tim felt his stomach wrench. As for scheduling, they'd install it the week after Christmas, if that was all right with him.

All right? He couldn't thank them enough for their inexcusable, unprofessional delay in getting the blasted job done.

When she heard the news, it seemed to him that Emma was her old self again. Not that this was any improvement.

"Lord!" she said. "What I wouldn't give for a chocolate Little Debbie, to celebrate!"

Emma had given up Little Debbies for Lent three years ago, a sacrifice he deeply appreciated. Being in the same room with a Little Debbie of any variety was more temptation than he could handle.

Emma eyed him. "She's watching your diet, I suppose?"

"Somebody has to."

There was a prickly silence.

"I hear the ECW wanted her to be president."

"They did."

"I hear she wouldn't be program chairman, either."

"You heard right."

"My, my," said Emma, twisting her mouth in that way he so thoroughly disliked.

He stopped by Mitford Blossoms only a hair before closing time and bought three roses of good breeding, along with several stems of freesia. Jena Ivey wrapped the bouquet in crackling green florist paper and tied it with satin ribbon—an extra business expense she willingly assumed for the fine presentation it made.

"Special occasion, Father?" Jena liked to know what was up with her customers, and would look a man straight in the eye until she got the answer.

He said it all together, as one word, "Marriedthreemonths."

On the back stoop of the rectory, he straightened his collar, held the bouquet behind his back, and marched into the kitchen.

"Cynthia!"

Barnabas came bounding down the stairs, sailed toward him, airborne, and gave his face a fine licking before he could summon a scripture. "You got me that time," he said, wiping up the damage with his coat sleeve. The excited barking of his good dog filled the rectory like the bass of the Lord's Chapel organ filled the nave.

It was a wonderful thing, to be greeted as if you were the very Pope, but where was the woman who had moved in with him and shared his bed and left hilarious notes in his sock drawer?

"Cynthia!"

Maybe she was late coming home from work, from the little yellow house next door.

He ran some water in a vase and put the roses and freesia in it. The barest whiff of scent came to him.

He stood in the middle of the kitchen floor, holding the vase, and listened for her footsteps on the back stoop. Barnabas sat at his feet, staring up at him.

"Come, then, old fellow, we'll go for a walk." Barnabas danced on his hind legs, barking.

Cynthia would be home by the time they got back from the monument, and he'd take her to dinner in Wesley. Why not? He had done it once before, and she seemed to enjoy it immensely. He set the roses in the center of the kitchen table, wrote a hasty note on the back of the electric bill, and propped it by the vase.

Gone to the monument. Back in a trice. Taking you to dinner.
Love, Timothy

He loved the soft shine of the street lamps in their first hour of winter dark. And now, Christmas lights added to the glow. Up and down Main Street the tiny lights burned, looping around every street lamp with its necklace of fresh balsam and holly.

If he never left Mitford at all, it would suit him. He had been happier here than in any parish of his career. To tell the truth, there wasn't even a close second, except, perhaps, for the little mission of fifty souls where he had served at the age of twenty-seven. They had taken him under their wing and loved him, but refused to protect him from sorrow and hardship. Indeed, there had been plenty of both, and that little Arkansas handful had made a man and a priest of him, all at once.

He looked up to see clouds racing across the moon, as Barnabas lifted his leg on a fire hydrant.

A line came to him, written by a fellow named Burns, who put out the newspaper in a neighboring village.

Big cities never sleep, but little towns do.

At barely six o'clock, Mitford was already tuckered out and tucked in, poking up the fires that sent wafts of scented smoke on the December wind. He drew the muffler close around his neck.

"Father!"

It was Bill Sprouse, the new preacher at First Baptist, bounding along behind something that looked like a tumbleweed on a leash. Barnabas growled.

"Good evening, Reverend!" He was glad to see the jolly face of the man who was working wonders at First Baptist and was liked by the entire community. Last summer, he and Bill and two other Mitford clergymen had pushed peanuts down Main Street with their noses to raise funds for the town museum. If nothing else had come of that miserable experience, it had bonded the local clergy for all time.

"That's Sparky," said Bill Sprouse, with evident pride.

The two dogs sniffed each other.

"What breed?"

"Beats me. We think it was a rag mop that mated with a feather duster. He was left on our doorstep in a cracker box twelve years ago. Rachel and I are foolish about the little so-and-so."

"I know the feeling."

"How's the computer coming? Learned your way around a menu yet?"

"A menu?"

Bill Sprouse laughed. "Do you have Windows? CD-ROM?"

He didn't even pretend to know what Bill was talking about. "It hasn't been installed yet. Right after Christmas, they say. My secretary has threatened to quit."

"I lost two secretaries in the start-up at my old church. To get a computer system going in a church office takes youth, stamina, and the faith of an early martyr." Bill Sprouse grinned knowingly.

"Aha."

"I guess I'd liken it to having all your wisdom teeth pulled, with no gas to knock you out." The two dogs continued in a circle, sniffing. "No, wait, that's too mild. It's more like . . . "

The rector stepped back, ready to turn and run.

" . . . having a frontal lobotomy. Yes! That's it!"

"Bill, good seeing you. My best to Rachel. So long, Sparky."

As he hurried toward the monument, did he hear Bill Sprouse guffawing, or was it the wind? He bitterly resented the thought of wrecking the peace of his workplace—not to mention the infernal aggravation of reworking the budget to accommodate the cost of the system.

He saw the squad car coming, but noted that the passenger in the front seat didn't see him. J.C. was too busy laughing. J.C. laughing? He turned his head to get another look, but the car disappeared around the corner.

He quickened his steps toward home.

Cynthia would be waiting.

But Cynthia wasn't waiting.

He shouted through the rectory, finding it empty as a tomb. Then he dialed the house next door. No answer.

Still in his coat and muffler, he popped through the hedge, noting with dread that the only light shining against the darkness was the one over the back stoop.

"Cynthia!"

He walked into the dark kitchen, turning on a light, and raced to her small studio. He was alarmed at what he might . . .

But she was not there, which gave him an ironic mixture of dread and relief.

"Cynthia!" He turned on the hall light and bounded up the stairs and into her bedroom. What was that on the bed . . .

Good Lord!

But it was only a pile of clothes she had stacked there for the Bane and Blessing sale.

He went in the bathroom and drew back the shower curtain.

Would she have driven to The Local for groceries? But they shopped only yesterday. Had she gone out to the FedEx drop on the highway to Wesley? But why wouldn't she have told him or left a note? She had never before caused him to wonder at her whereabouts.

He looked at his watch. Six-thirty. She was always home by five-fifteen, sometimes earlier. He must not panic, no indeed. His wife was a grown woman, fully capable of taking care of herself and having plenty of common sense into the bargain.

He found he was pacing the bedroom floor.

Should he call Rodney Underwood? That was a dark thought. Rodney would have his force swarming over the town and fanning out into the woods, not to mention taking fingerprints in both houses and talking over a radio crackling with static. He hated even thinking of it.

Violet! He realized there was no Violet trooping along at his heels, trying to scratch him on the ankle.

He could just feel it—Violet was definitely not in the house, or she would have made herself present at once.

He went back to the kitchen and looked under the shelves in the pantry. The cat carrier was gone.

The serenity of the little house was maddening—it revealed absolutely nothing. Everything was the same, yet everything was disturbingly different.

He went to the sink and leaned against it and prayed.

"Look here, Father, this is serious business. Protect Cynthia wherever she is, bring an end to the fear I'm feeling, and give me wisdom. Show me precisely what to do, through Christ our Lord, Amen." Direct and specific. Plain and simple. Any tendency he had to pray like a Philistine fled before such confused anxiety as this.

Her car was, of course, gone from the garage.

He sat on the study sofa at the rectory, where he had often sat to figure things out. But he could not figure this. It was past seven o'clock and his wife was two hours late arriving home on a cold, dark, and windy night in December.

He would call his cousin, Walter, in New Jersey. But what would he say? Katherine would get on the phone and insist he call the police at once.

Well, then, he would call Marge Owen, his friend ever since coming to Mitford, and the wife of the finest senior warden he'd ever had. She would know what to do.

But he couldn't make the call. He went out to the back stoop of the rectory and waited for Cynthia's car lights to come down the driveway on the other side of the hedge.

The wind was blustering, now, lashing the trees in Baxter Park.

He couldn't bear the torment any longer, and he wouldn't consider the consequences. At eight o'clock, he went to his kitchen phone and called Rodney Underwood at home.

"Hello, Rodney?" His voice sounded like the croaking of a frog. "Tim Kavanagh here."

Did he hear something outside? "Excuse me a moment . . . "

He raced to the stoop and saw her car, parked in the driveway next door with its lights on. "Hello, dearest!" she called through the hedge.

He sprinted back to the phone.

"Rodney! About that talk we had yesterday. Just wanted you to know I'm working on it, consider it done. Goodbye!"

He couldn't hold her close enough.

"Timothy, you're smashing *by doze,*" she said, coming up for air.

"Cynthia . . . "

"I know you were frantic, and I don't blame you. I should have told you again this morning, but you see, even *I* forgot! I didn't remember my one o'clock at Trent School until nine-thirty, and it's a four-hour drive! I flew down the highway. I'm telling you, if they had nailed me for speeding, I would be on bread and water in solitary confinement in some little town that's not even on the map!

"I screeched to the door practically on the dot of one, and you should have seen the children, Timothy! They brought flowers, they'd made posters, one little girl brought apple jelly from her grandmother's tree and wrote a poem for the lady author. Nearly everyone had drawn pictures of Violet. I can't wait for you to see them, some are better than mine!

"If I hadn't shown up, it would have been terrible, they had looked forward to it so much. We sat on the floor and read and talked and had a wonderful time for two whole hours, and Violet was her best-behaved in years.

"And then I had to start home and I was famished because I'd gone without lunch, and when I stopped for a hamburger, I took a wrong turn and drove an hour in the opposite direction.

"It was horrible, horrid, I can't tell you. I wanted to stop and call you, but I thought it would be best to spend time driving, because I *told* you I'd be late. Finally, I did stop and call—it was six-thirty—but there was no answer."

"I was combing your house and trying to keep myself calm," he said.

"I'm so sorry, darling, but I did tell you I was going. I did! I was very specific. We were sitting at the kitchen table when I told you just the other morning . . . but Timothy, you must not have been listening."

So that was the penalty for not listening—mortal terror.

Actually, he seemed to recall that she'd mentioned Trent School, but beyond that, he drew a blank. "Must you do this again, these school visits?"

"Yes." There was a note of finality in her voice, and he didn't press the issue.

But even if she *had* told him, she owed him one, he could say that. Tomorrow, he would ask her to talk to Sadie Baxter.

"No way," said Cynthia.

"Please."

"You're the priest, Timothy, I'm merely the deacon. This is a job for the top dog."

You owe me, he wanted to say, but didn't. "I can't do it," he said flatly.

"You're scared."

"You're right."

"So who can we get to do it?"

"If I had an answer to that, I wouldn't be here practically begging on my knees."

"You're cute when you're desperate."

"You're so good at this sort of thing . . ."

"At what? Asking people to change their ways, give up familiar habits?"

"Habits maintained at the possible expense of human life?"

Cynthia frowned. He had her there, he could tell.

"Oh, poop," she said. "I'll do it."

He sat down, immeasurably relieved.

"But you owe me," she said, narrowing her blue eyes in that way he'd come to know as meaning business.

It happened on the fourteenth day of Advent, the date marked on the calendar to take his Buick to Lew Boyd for a tune-up and muffler. Nor was it a day to be walking around without a car. He might have stopped by the house and borrowed Cynthia's, but no, he had pressed toward the office from the service station, his head bent into the first falling snow of the season.

Ron Malcolm slowed down, pulled to the curb, and lowered his window. "Father! Good morning. Been wanting to ask when our computer system's going in."

"After Christmas!" he snapped.

Ron blanched. "Want a ride?"

No, he did not want a ride. If he had wanted a ride, he would *have* a ride.

He looked into the face of one of the most loyal parishioners on earth, suddenly feeling like two cents with a hole in it. "Sorry, my friend. The very mention of that computer system is like gall in a wound. I need to grow up, get with it."

"I understand. We hooked one up in my construction company right before I retired. Actually, that's why I retired."

"That bad, huh?"

"Something like getting gored by a bull, in slow motion."

The snow was melting on his hatless head. "Got time for a cup of coffee at the Grill?" He went around the car and opened the door, and slid in with his Hope House building committee chairman.

"Speaking of retiring," said Ron, as he pulled away from the curb, "I guess that's something you're thinking about."

"It certainly isn't. I never think about it." The unbidden coldness came into his voice again. If he couldn't control his peevish tongue, who could?

They drove in silence until Ron found a parking place across the street from the Grill.

"Thinking about it isn't so bad . . ." said Ron, turning off the ignition, "once you get the habit of doing it."

"Maybe." Why should his retirement be anyone's concern? If Lord's Chapel wanted him to leave, that was one thing. But retiring was his own blasted business.

Hadn't Churchill begun writing *A History of the English-Speaking Peoples* while in his eighties? Hadn't Eamon de Valera served as Ireland's president when he was ninety-one? It was a litany he often recited to himself. And George Abbott, the Broadway legend—Good Lord, the man had married again at the age of ninety-six! What was all the blather about retirement? He despised the very word.

"Coffee straight up," said Ron to Percy, "and make his a double."

Just before noon, the phone rang. Emma handed him the receiver with patent distaste. It was the computer company.

"Father, we've had some schedule changes. Would it be all right if we come at two o'clock today and get you up and running?"

He was sick of the whole affair. "Perfect!" he said, without consulting his secretary. "Come ahead!"

Emma winced when he told her. "No use to fret," he declared. "We might as well get it behind us and enjoy the Christmas season."

"And you might as well bring the dern thing in and have it ready when they get here."

There was only one problem. The dern thing was in the trunk of his car.

He dialed Lew Boyd, but the line was busy. He was still getting a busy signal when Emma unwrapped her sandwich at the noon hour.

"Why don't you take my car and run up there?" she asked. "It's still got hay in it, but at least you could go and tell Lew to bring those boxes over here in his truck."

Emma was a clear thinker, all right.

The wall clock said twelve-thirty when he arrived at the station, where Lew and Bailey Coffey were playing checkers with the phone off the hook.

"I've got to get something out of the trunk of my car," he told Lew. "It's three boxes, and I'd appreciate it if you could run them down to my office in your truck before two o'clock. I'd take them in that big Olds out there, but it's, ah, full of hay."

Lew looked sheepish. "I hate to tell you, but I just sent Coot t' Wesley to pick up your muffler—in your Buick. Th' rear end's been lockin' up in my truck, and I can't drive it 'til it's fixed. Sendin' Coot in your car was th' only way to get your part in here today."

"Aha. What time will Coot be back?"

"I'd give 'im a half hour if I was you," said Bailey Coffey. "He hain't been gone more'n ten minutes. Take a load off your feet."

"Don't mind if I do," said the rector, perching on a vinyl-covered dinette chair and peering at the checkerboard.

Beyond the unwashed windows of the service station, the flakes spiraled down as in a snow globe.

He had given Coot thirty minutes, then forty-five. "Stopped off for a burrito, is my guess," said Lew.

It was nearly two o'clock when the phone rang. Lew Boyd turned white as a sheet.

"You're lyin'! You ain't lyin'. . . . Call Bud and get 'im to tow it in."

Lew stared at the rector, who was checking the wall clock with mounting aggravation. "It's your Buick," said Lew, looking stricken.

"What about it?"

"Somebody rear-ended Coot after he pulled out of the parts place. Plowed right into 'im."

"Good grief!"

"I don't know how t' tell you this, but them boxes in the trunk of your car . . . "

He stood rooted to the spot.

" . . . they're tore up pretty bad. He looked in there, said he couldn't tell from jig what it was in 'em, but said whatever it was is history."

"Hallelujah!" He was shocked at what flew out of his mouth.

"What's that?" said Lew.

"I said thank you!" He grabbed Lew's hand and shook it. "Thank you, thank you!"

"I'm awful sorry, I cain't tell you how—"

"No problem. Quite all right. Good. Fine. Excellent!" Knowing some insurance companies, it could take weeks on end, even months, to put things straight. His neck was out of the noose. Goodbye and good riddance!

The two men watched the rector roar out of the station in the lavender Oldsmobile.

Bailey Coffey shook his head. "Seem like he wanted to hug your neck for gettin' his car tore up."

"Th' man is a saint," said Lew, meaning it.

CHAPTER SIX

Love Came Down

HE WAS WITHOUT a car again, but so what?

Hadn't he once given up his car for Lent and, liking the idea, gone without it for eight years? He could always use Cynthia's car, or, if push came to shove, haul his motor scooter out of mothballs.

After all, their winter weather was nearly like spring. They'd been given a couple of snow flurries and a few bitter winds, but beyond that, temperatures had been unseasonably mild.

He would think all of Mitford would leap for joy about this weather. But no.

"You talk about a flea problem this summer!" Dora Pugh grumbled to him at the hardware. "With no cold weather to kill 'em off, they'll be swarmin' over your dog like ants over jam. An' wait'll you see th' Japanese beetles. Your roses'll look like Swiss cheese."

The Collar Button man was complaining that he couldn't sell his winter topcoats and practically had to give them away, the Irish Woolen Shop was stuck with a load of boiled-wool sweaters from the British Isles, and Percy Mosely railed that his ice-cream business had cranked up again, which tended to overwork his wintertime "skeletal crew."

Those who slogged through last year's blizzard, saying they never wanted to see snow again, grumbled about not having any. And Bud Bradley made it known that without rotten weather to send people crashing into ditches, his tow truck business was suffering.

On the bright side, Father Tim called Dooley and learned the school had just gotten a fine snowfall.

"Went sledding, did you?"

"Yep. Me'n Harvey Upton crashed."

"Into a tree?" That's what he'd always crashed into when he went sledding.

"Into one another."

"Anybody hurt?"

"Ol' Harvey busted his hands when he run in the back of me."

"You OK?"

"He sent me windin', but I rolled down th' hill."

"How's your computer stuff coming along?"

"I been on th' Internet."

"You what?"

"You wouldn't understand."

"Truer words were never spoken, thanks be to God. What did you learn on the, ah . . ."

"Internet."

"Right."

"Learned about Labrador retrievers. When I get out of this school, I want one."

"Fine. You got it."

"They eat th' furniture and rugs an' all."

"Ummm."

"But they get over it."

"How long does it take them to get over it?"

" 'Bout three years."

"Aha. Well, listen, son, we miss you."

Silence.

"Christmas break will be here soon. We're coming to get you, save up your laundry. You'll see your granpaw, he's been asking about you, and you'll see Tommy. He can spend the night anytime you like."

Silence.

"Shoot straight with me, buddy. Are you OK?"

Dooley hesitated, but only for a moment. "Yeah."

He heard the ache in the boy's voice. It was something no one else would hear, he supposed, but he had gotten to know Dooley Barlowe, gotten to love. . . .

Dooley was in his prayers throughout the day, and as he prayed with Cynthia in the evening, which gave him the confidence to watch and wait.

He decided not to consult with the headmaster again until after the Christmas holy days.

"It's done," said Cynthia, looking gloomy.

"It is?"

"But I didn't do it."

"You didn't?"

"Miss Sadie did the thing herself."

"Aha."

"When Miss Sadie tried to raise one of Olivia's silk shades, it flew up and wrapped itself around the roller, so Miss Sadie climbed on the divan, as she calls it, and tried to pull the shade down and lost her balance."

A broken hip! Ninety years old . . . months in a wheelchair, or worse, in bed. . . .

"She fell off the sofa," said Cynthia, "and broke her wrist."

"Thanks be to God!"

"Timothy! How could you?"

"I mean I'm thankful that it was only her wrist that was broken. Think what could have happened."

"I know. She was very brave about it . . . wanted to set it herself to save a doctor bill. But Louella called Hoppy and they sent the ambulance, which made Miss Sadie furious because it cost a fortune. Of course, it went through town blasting the siren, which she really didn't like, and now her arm is in a sling."

"I'm having what's called mixed emotions."

"Me, too. Now Louella and Miss Sadie are both down for the count. But Olivia will visit every day and I'll check on them faithfully, plus The Local delivers, and there's a mail slot in their front door, so . . ."

"So, all's well that ends well," he said.

"For now," she replied, looking concerned.

J. C. Hogan must be hitting the skim milk pretty hard, he thought, as he saw the editor hiking along the other side of the street, toting his briefcase in one hand and hitching up his pants with the other.

They were hurtling toward Christmas, which left little time for lunch at the Grill.

There were multiple meetings with the choir director, the Hope House building committee, the vestry, the new Evangelism Committee, and the Sunday School supervisor, not to mention his involvement in the mayor's projects to repair and paint Sophia Burton's house, and a Lord's Chapel Christmas party at Children's Hospital.

He also felt led to attend an overnight with the youth group, during which they made tree ornaments, wolfed pizza, and listened to loud music until he went home at two a.m., wildly energized by teenage adrenaline.

Woven into the fabric of this seasonal tapestry were his daily hospital visits and a desperate jog up Old Church Lane four afternoons a week.

Seizing the moment on Wednesday, he dashed from the office to the Grill and slid into the rear booth on the stroke of noon, literally panting.

"We thought you'd died and gone to heaven," declared Mule.

"I'm working on it."

"Still haven't had your neck cleaned up."

"My neck has been in the noose," he said testily. "Where's J.C.?"

"Probably blown away by a strong wind. Have you seen him? He's droppin' off to a stick."

"Yeah," said Percy, pouring coffee, "if he don't watch it, he'll walk out of his britches right on Main Street."

"That," said the Realtor, "would be a sight for sore eyes. What'll it be?"

"Soup du jour!' said Father Tim. "A bowl and a roll."

"You'll like the soup," Percy announced. "It's got fresh broccoli in it."

"I don't like broccoli," said the rector.

"I don't have time t' argue about it. Have th' soup," said Percy.

"Fine," he sighed, too exhausted to care.

Mule leaned toward his lunch companion. "So, what do you think is goin' on with J.C.?"

"Beats me. I guess we finally talked some sense into his hard head before he fell out with a stroke."

"I don't think it's got anything to do with health. Do you think he's interviewin' for a job and wants to look sharp?"

"What kind of job would he interview for? The Wesley paper is against his politics."

J.C. slammed his briefcase onto the bench and slid into the booth, "Been hangin' around the hospital for three dern hours."

Mule eyed him suspiciously. "You're not gettin' shots for smelly feet, are you?"

"I got a dadgum physical to the tune of two hundred bucks," snapped the *Muse* editor.

"It didn't improve your disposition any," said Mule.

"Turns out I've lowered my cholesterol, brought my blood pressure down, and passed the treadmill test—"

"That's worth two hundred right there," said the rector.

"You did all that with yogurt?" asked Mule.

"Lookit," said J.C., grabbing the waistband of his pants and pulling it away from his stomach a full two inches.

After lunch, the rector stood and talked with the Realtor in front of the Grill.

Mule furrowed his brow. "Did you notice his shoes were shined?"

"Did you notice he was carrying a handkerchief instead of a paper towel?"

They eyed each other.

"And the handkerchief was clean."

They went their separate ways, deep in thought.

"Puce," said Cynthia, staring at the walls of the rectory dining room.

"I beg your pardon?"

"Puce. Your dining room color. I just figured it out."

"Spell it," he said.

"P-u-c-e. I loathe puce. Besides, who wants a brown dining room?"

Nobody, if her wrinkled nose was any indication.

"Dearest, I've been thinking. We've set the date of the parish-wide tea for May fifteenth. It should be a happy time, definitely not a time for brown—especially not ancient brown. This paper must have been on these walls since Lord's Chapel was a mission church!"

"The turn of the century, then."

"Look at this stuff!" She waved her hand at the walls he'd never fully seen, somehow, until now. They were brown, all right. With a tint of muddy purple.

"I agree."

"Agree with what?"

"That you can have it repapered."

"That's not what I had in mind, exactly."

"Aha."

"Close your eyes and imagine this. We steam off the paper. Put on a coat of primer. Paint over that with a wonderfully soft, rich pumpkin. And then use a creamy bisque color to rag it."

"What it?"

"Rag it. Go over it with a rag and make it look like the walls of an old Italian villa. What do you think?"

"But it's not an old Italian villa."

"Timothy."

"Well," he said, "it isn't."

"Lord's Chapel has a Norman tower, and the church isn't in England. Not only that, but your gardens are full of French and German roses and this—must I remind you?—is Mitford!"

No two ways about it, his wife was a quick thinker.

"Go for it!" he said, with feeling.

Placing the phone on the hook, he sank into a chair at the kitchen table as Cynthia walked in from next door.

"Timothy! What is it?"

"You won't believe this."

"Tell me!"

"Dooley isn't coming home for Christmas."

"But why? What's wrong? Is he—"

"He's going to Europe."

"Europe?"

"To sing. In the school chorus. They're leaving next week. They'll be gone fourteen days."

She sat down, too.

"A boy has pneumonia, and Dr. Fleming said the choirmaster pulled Dooley off the bench, as it were. All expenses paid. It's part of a grant."

"Why, I'm . . . it's . . . I'm speechless. It's too wonderful for words!"

"I was just going to bring the electric train down from the attic," he said, looking dazed and forlorn.

She reached over and took his hand. "Don't worry, dearest. We'll get it down, anyway. I love electric trains."

A hastily scrawled note from Dooley:

> Here's ten dollars to get a present for Tommy. Merry Christmas.
> P.S. If I could I would buy you a world globe with a light in it.

A world globe with a light in it! Merely the present he'd wanted all his life. Amazing that the boy recalled something he'd mentioned only once, a very long time ago.

He had found a few precious moments to make notes in his sermon notebook, while a fire blazed on the hearth, the Christmas tree lights glimmered, and Cynthia made dinner.

It was a type of grace, this small hour he'd been given during the haste and hurry of Advent. He gazed away from the notebook, giving thanks for small things.

"We look for visions of heaven," Oswald Chambers had written, "and we never dream that all the time God is in the commonplace things and people around us."

He went to his bookshelf and took down a volume. He was thankful merely for the time to go to his bookshelf and look with leisure for a reference.

He thumbed the pages. Dietrich Bonhoeffer had talked of the small things, too, saying in *Life Together:*

> We prevent God from giving us the great spiritual gifts He has in store for us, because we do not give thanks for daily gifts.
>
> We think we dare not be satisfied with the small measure of spiritual knowledge, experience, and love that has been given to us, and that we must constantly be looking forward eagerly for the highest good. Then we deplore the fact that we lack the deep certainty, the strong faith, and the rich experience that God has given to others, and we consider this lament to be pious. . . .
>
> Only he who gives thanks for little things receives the big things.

Cynthia came in quietly and set a cup of tea before him. He kissed her hand, inexpressibly grateful, and she went back to the kitchen.

When we view the little things with thanksgiving, he thought, even they become big things.

Where his hair was concerned, it was fish or cut bait. Some of the youth group mentioned it, asking when he was getting an earring.

He'd been to Fancy Skinner only twice. On both occasions, his longtime barber, Joe Ivey, was either down with the flu or in Tennessee with relatives. Whatever Fancy had done, he'd liked it, noting both times that he looked suddenly thinner—a look he could currently use, if the tightness of his collar was any indication.

Joe Ivey, however, was in town and healthy as a horse, and he couldn't figure out how to give his business to Joe's competition without being found out.

"When are you gettin' your neck cleaned up?" asked Emma. She considered it her business to remind him about haircuts, shoe shines, and a variety of other personal services.

"Ah . . ."

"Christmas is on top of us and you look like a wise man who's been travelin' from afar." She peered at him over her glasses. "They traveled two years, you know."

Whatever that was supposed to mean.

"I'm surprised Cynthia hasn't made you get a haircut."

In his secretary's view, his wife was doing nothing for the church, much less ministering to the needs of her husband.

"Anyway," she said, "if I were you, I'd try Fancy Skinner. Joe Ivey makes you look like a chipmunk."

Permission! Is that what he'd been waiting for like a schoolboy? He was out the door in a flash.

"Lord!" said Fancy, who had worked him in between her eleven-thirty trim and twelve o'clock perm. "Look at this mess, it's cut in three different lengths. I hate to say it, but I hear Joe Ivey gets in th' brandy, and if your hair's any proof, his liver's not long for this world.

"How's your wife? I'm glad you married her, she's cute as anything and really young. How much younger is she than you, anyway? Lord, I know I shouldn't ask that, but ten years is my guess.

"So, what are you givin' Cynthia for Christmas? Mule's givin' me a fur coat, I have always wanted a fur coat, I said, 'Honey, if you buy me a fur coat at a yard sale, do not come home, you can sleep at your office 'til kingdom come.' I know it's not right to wear fur, think of the animals and how they feel about it, but it gets so dern *cold* up here in th' winter. Of course, it's not been cold *this* winter, they say th' fleas will be killer this summer.

"D'you want some gum, have some gum, it's sugarless.

"Speakin' of sugar, I hear you're diabetic, how does that affect you? I hear it makes some people's legs swell or is it their feet? Lord, your scalp is tight as a drum, as usual—you ought to be more relaxed now that you're married, but of course, some people get more uptight when they tie th' knot. I bet married people come bawlin' to you all th' time, I don't know how you have a minute to yourself, bein' clergy.

"My great uncle is clergy, they handle snakes at his church. Mule says for God's sake, Fancy, don't tell that your uncle handles snakes, so don't say I mentioned it. Have you ever seen anybody handle snakes, it's in th' Bible about handlin' snakes, but if you have to do that to prove you love th' Lord, I'm goin' to hell in a hand basket.

"Oops, I like to poked a hole in you with that fingernail, it's acrylic.

"How's Dooley, I hope he don't get th' big head in that fancy school. I've never been to Virginia, I hear seven presidents were born in that state, I think we had one president from our state, maybe two, but I can't remember who it was, maybe Hoover, do you think he had anything to do with th' vacuum cleaner, I've always wondered that. Speakin' of school, they asked me to come to Mitford School and talk about bein' a hairdresser for Occupation Day, I think I'll do a make-over, wouldn't that be somethin'? I'd like to make over th' principal, that is the meanest school principal in the world! I'd dye her hair blue in a heartbeat, then swing her around in this chair and say, 'Look at that, Miss Hayes, honey, don't you just love it, it's *you*!'

"See there? Aren't you some kind of handsome with all that glop cut from over your ears? You looked like you were wearing earmuffs. Oooh, yes! Cute! I'll just swivel you around so you can look at the back, your wife'll eat you with a spoon. . . ."

He paid Fancy and reeled out of her shop, his ears ringing. By dodging the Skinners' driveway and taking the footpath, he was able to avoid the next customer, who merely glimpsed his back as he fled the premises.

Not only was he at a loss about what to give Cynthia, he couldn't figure out what to buy Tommy with Dooley's ten bucks.

It came to him while he was walking home from Fancy's. Just go by the bank and exchange it for ten silver dollars. A great idea! His new haircut clearly helped him think better. He felt as if he'd just hatched out of an egg for the lightness of spirit that overcame him.

And what the heck would he get Dooley? He'd better knuckle down and come up with something pronto. Maybe a parka. But he already had one, and besides, Dooley Barlowe did not consider clothing items to be gifts.

Tommy's mother welcomed him with a hug.

"We're so glad to see you, Father. Tommy is doing better each day. He'll be back in school after Christmas, Dr. Harper said."

"Wonderful news!"

"Come down the hall and see him. He's reading a new book. It's been awful hard to keep up with his schooling. I can't help him a bit with his math, and his daddy says he never even heard of diagramming a sentence."

"What a grand tree!" he said, stopping to look at the bedecked Fraser fir that stood in the corner. A veritable sea of gifts lay under its branches.

"See those three big packages by the sofa? They're from Mr. Leeper! He's been wonderful, Father. Thank you for asking him to look in on Tommy."

"Oh, but I didn't have a thing to do with it. It was all Mr. Leeper's idea."

"I've heard he's not a very nice person, but I disagree, don't you?"

He looked at the gifts, given by a man who was also healing—not from a terrible accident, but from other, far deeper, wounds. He would go and see Buck Leeper over Christmas and sit with him in the room where the drunken Hope House supervisor had hurled and smashed a bottle and a chair around his head, venting a black rage that lasted for hours. He would never forget that night, and his inability to get up and walk out on the pain that was forged by a brutal father, years of alcoholism, and Buck's part in the death of his younger brother.

He smiled at Tommy's soft-spoken mother. Seeing the three large presents under the tree was somehow a gift to him, as well.

A collect call from France? He couldn't imagine who . . .

Yes, of course, he would accept the charges, if only out of curiosity.

"Bonejure, messure!" said a strange voice through a crackling phone line.

"Ah . . . *bonjour.* Who's calling, please?"

Dooley Barlowe laughed like a hyena.

"Dooley?"

"Oui, messure! Come on talley voo."

"Unbelievable! I'm thrilled you called."

"They made us do it. Everybody had to call home."

Home! If Dooley Barlowe had used that word before, Father Tim hadn't heard it. "Merry Christmas, pal! Where are you?"

"Paris, France. We been lookin' at statues and paintin's and I don't know what all, and we're singin' tonight in a big church, a cathedral. Man, it's huge."

"You know all those songs?"

"I'm learnin' quick as I can. Ol' Mr. Pruitt, he'll knock you in the head if you don't get it right."

Good old Mr. Pruitt. "I've never talked to anybody in Paris, France, before. How's the tour going?"

"Great. We're singin' in Austria or somewhere tomorrow night. I'm about wore out."

"We miss you, buddy."

Expensive silence.

"We put the train under the tree."

"I bet ol' Cynthia likes that train."

"How did you know?"

"She likes everything."

"I'll get a present off to you when you're back at school."

"That's OK. You give me a lot of money an' all."

He felt a mild lump in his throat. "Will you send Miss Sadie and Louella a card, like I asked? You wouldn't be in Paris, France, if it weren't for Miss Sadie."

"I already done—did it. It had th' Eiffel Tower on it. Did you take Tommy his present?"

"Ten silver dollars!"

"Cool."

Thank goodness he'd done that right. He wished Cynthia was here to say hello. It would do her good to hear Dooley's unconcealed excitement.

"Tell ol' Cynthia I said hey. And ol' Barnabas. Well, I got to go. 'Bye."

"Dooley? Dooley!"

But Dooley was gone.

With the jam-packed schedule of the holy days, he'd never been able to settle on a good plan for opening gifts.

To do it on Christmas Eve meant doing it in broad daylight before the five o'clock and midnight masses. That didn't seem quite the ticket.

To do it after arriving home at one-thirty in the morning never had much appeal.

To do it on Christmas morning meant stumbling around in the dark at five a.m., mindlessly racing through the gift opening, then sprinting to church for two services.

To do it on Christmas day, after the high moments of His birth, seemed paltry, somehow.

Consequently, he had done it differently every year, by the seat of his pants, with a mild semblance of tradition kicking in only when Dooley Barlowe came under his roof.

Now he had a wife who would tell him how to do it.

When his flock thronged into the midnight service, there was wonder on every face at the newly hung greens and the softly flickering candles on each windowsill. To the simple beauty of the historic church was added fresh, green hope, the lush scent of flowers in winter, and candle flame that cast its flickering shadows over the congregation like a shawl.

Holy, holy, holy . . .
Joyful, joyful, we adore Thee . . .

The choir packed their creaking stall, and leaving the exertion of the eternal crush behind, their voices carried from behind closed doors onto the soft December air.

Lord's Chapel could not, on that night, contain the joy.

"Listen!" murmured the elderly widow who lived next door to the church. "It sounds like angels!" In the hushed and sleep-drugged village, voices stole upon the midnight air, blessing the Lord of Hosts and praising His holy name.

To every weary and overworked soul came some new energy that flowed through the nave like a current.

Unto us a child is born, unto us a Savior is given . . .
Alleluia! Alleluia!
Come let us adore Him . . .

New life to replace the old, the old one that so often disappoints us and lures us into forgetting the Birth, sending us into despair.

It was no surprise that with the joy came tears for those whose hearts felt a crust falling away. . . .

Cynthia had gone through it with him like a trouper. Up and out to nearly every service, making his breakfast, preparing the early dinners he had no appetite for, praying for his stamina, rubbing his shoulders. . . .

"I can't let you do this," he said, loving the feel of her hands on his tense muscles.

"But why not?"

He had no answer. Why not, indeed? "I'll do something for you."

"You're always doing something for me."

"I am?" Why did she think that? His wife had a certain innocence.

"Timothy, dearest, you have an innocence that amazes me."

He allowed the resistance to go out of his body.

"That's better. Sometimes you make it hard to do anything for you, because you've been so . . . self-sufficient."

"Ummm," he said, his face smashed into the pillow.

She had suggested they open their gifts on Christmas evening in front of the fire, dressed in their favorite robes. Thank heaven her gift had arrived—and already wrapped, into the bargain. He'd had it delivered to Dora Pugh at the hardware, in case he couldn't be found at his office to sign for it.

It was all too easy, he thought. Just call toll-free and talk to someone solicitous and give them a credit card number. It seemed a man should suffer a bit over what to give his beloved. Next year, he would do better.

"Are you crying?" he asked, as she stared into the small box.

"Definitely!" she said, the tears coursing down her cheeks.

"It's to go with your wedding band. I hope . . . I do hope . . . you don't think it . . ." Gaudy, he wanted to say, or tacky. The emeralds glimmered in the firelight.

She threw her arms around his neck, weeping. Nothing discreet about Cynthia Kavanagh's tears—they were honest and forthright. He patted her fondly on the back. He wished she wouldn't do this . . . yet, there was something touching about so much carrying on.

"I love emeralds!" she pronounced, pulling away from him to wipe her tears on the hem of her robe. "I'm so glad you didn't give me sapphires to *go with my eyes. . . .*"

Like her former husband, who had been cruelly unfaithful, he thought.

"It's beautiful, and I'm so proud of it. Thank you, my darling. Is all this a lovely dream?"

He kissed her.

"Well, is it?"

"I think we'll get used to it, somehow."

"You mean we'll become old shoes, and all that?"

"Very likely. They say it happens."

"I can't imagine it happening. I think you're the most delicious, attractive, fascinating man in the world."

"Cynthia, Cynthia . . ." he said, touching her face. "I'm only a country parson, foolishly in love with his wife. Nothing more."

"Shall I go fetch what I have for you?"

"Wait," he said, holding her close to him. "Wait."

She had turned the Christmas music on and gone off to the garage. He heard it creaking across the kitchen linoleum, then over the hardwood floor and onto the rug of the study.

"Don't open your eyes yet," she insisted.

Whatever it was, she had rolled it next to the crackling fire, then he heard something that sounded like a cord being plugged into the socket at his desk.

"Now," she said, almost shyly.

He saw it, but could hardly believe what he was seeing. It was a magnificent world globe, lit from within and bathed in the glow of the firelight.

He got up slowly and went to it and gazed at it, and was speechless.

"Dooley told me you've always wanted one," she said, slipping her arm around his waist.

He spread his hands over the parchment seas and continents, as if some inner warmth were coming from inside. There was the seductive blue of the Gulf of Bothnia, and, as he twirled the globe, the vastness of Arabia, and the emerald masses of the Angola and Argentine Basins.

"I love you, my dearest husband."

"And I love you," he said, resting his cheek against the top of her head. Grace, and grace alone.

The music was only a flute, and a clear, simple voice singing what Christina Rossetti had written.

Love came down at Christmas
Love all lovely, love divine
Love was born at Christmas
Star and angels gave the sign.
Love shall be our token
Love be yours and love be mine . . .
Love was born at Christmas . . .
Love incarnate, love divine . . .

CHAPTER SEVEN

Flying High

Lady Spring's Grand Surprise

—by Mitford Muse *reporter, Hessie Mayhew*

Lady Spring has surprised us yet again.

Arriving in our lofty Citadel prematurely this year, she caught us looking to the mending of our winter mittens. As early as mid-April, the first bloom of the lilac peeked out, whilst in years past, not one of us had caught its virtuous scent until May. Last April at this time, you may recall, we were shivering in our coats as white icing lay upon the bosom of our Village as upon a wedding cake.

In any case, Lady Spring has left her calling card in our expectant Garden—this little Niche where, upon the margin of a rushing streamlet, the woods violet first revealed its innocent face on yesterday morn.

Those with an eye for fashion will wonder what fanciful attire our Lady is wearing this year. I have as yet glimpsed her only briefly, and cannot be certain of every detail, but she appears to have arrayed herself in lacy ferns from her maiden

Breast to her unshod feet, and crowned her fickle head with trumpet vines and moss.

At any moment, she will make her couch upon the banks of Miss Sadie Baxter's hillside orchard, so that every rude Cottage and stately pile might have a view of Heaven come down to earth.

Gentle Reader, may fragrant breezes fan thy brow this Spring, and whether you meet our Lady upon the wild summit or in the sylvan glade, please remember:

DO NOT PLANT UNTIL MAY 15.

He dropped the newspaper beside his wing chair, laughing.

Hessie Mayhew had been reading Wordsworth, again, while combing the village environs with looking-glass and flower press.

Rude cottages and stately piles, wild summits and sylvan glades! Only in the *Mitford Muse*, he thought, unashamedly proud of a newspaper whose most alarming headline in recent months had been "Man Convicted of Wreckless Driving."

Though Hessie had given him a good laugh, he realized he hadn't been much amused lately.

The rectory dining room and kitchen were upside down and backward, and the plunder from the two rooms had been scattered throughout the parlor and along the hallway, not to mention dumped on either side of the steps all the way to the landing.

On Easter Monday, his dining chairs and china dresser had been hauled to the foyer, along with a stack of pots, pans, dishes, and nine boxes of oatmeal. As he hadn't cooked oatmeal in two or three years, he had no idea where it came from, and was afraid to ask.

He saw his wife on occasion, but hardly recognized her, smeared as she was with pumpkin-colored paint, and her hair tied back with a rag.

"Cynthia?" he said, peering into the dining room. He might have stuck his head inside a cantaloupe, for all the brazen new color on his walls.

She looked down from the top rung of a ladder. "H'lo, dearest. What do you think?"

He honestly didn't know what he thought.

What he wondered was how much longer they'd be dodging

around paint buckets and ladders, not to mention that he'd stepped in a skillet last night as he went up to bed. His study was the only place on the ground floor that hadn't been invaded by the haste to transform the rectory into an old Italian villa before May fifteenth.

The kitchen, which certainly hadn't been painted in his fourteen-year tenure, was becoming the color of "clotted Devon cream," according to Cynthia. She was also doing something with a hammer and sponge that made the walls look positively ancient.

If anything, shouldn't they be trying to make the place look more up-to-date?

As worthless as guilt was known to be, he couldn't help feeling it, seeing his wife work herself to exhaustion for a parish tea that would last only two hours.

"Yes," said their friend Marge Owen, "but they'll talk about it for two years!"

He tried once to help her, but he'd never held a paintbrush in his life.

"You bake," she finally said, exasperated, "and I'll paint. For starters, I need ten dozen lemon squares—they freeze beautifully. When you're through with those, I need ten dozen raspberry tarts and fourteen dozen cookies, assorted . . ."

She rattled off a baking list that sounded like the quarterly output of Pepperidge Farm.

Why couldn't they just do vegetable sandwiches and strawberries dipped in chocolate . . . or something?

"We're also doing those, but not until the last minute," she said, peering down at him from a ladder. She was always on a ladder. Except, of course, for the times she popped through the hedge to work on her book, which had an ominous deadline.

"I can't even *think* about the deadline," she wailed. "I can't even *think* about it!"

At night, she rolled over and expired, while he stared at dancing shadows on the ceiling and listened to Barnabas snore in the hall.

"We're thrilled," said Esther Bolick. "I can't remember when something this big has happened and I didn't have to bake a cake for it!"

"You're not hurt that we didn't ask you to bake?"

"Hurt? I should say not!"

He could tell, however, that Esther wouldn't have minded doing a two-layer orange marmalade.

He was relieved to see that Emma was softening toward the coming event. But she made it clear to him that Cynthia should at least get involved in Sunday School and chair the parish brunches.

The ECW called to offer help in serving and pouring, and promised to line up four or five husbands to keep the tea traffic untangled on the street in front of the rectory.

Hessie Mayhew stopped by, wanting an interview, just as Father Tim trekked home to pick up his sermon notebook.

"Talk to my wife," he said, "it's all her doing." He hoped that Hessie would not read any Coleridge before she wrote the story.

Clutching her note pad, Hessie grilled Cynthia, who was painting dentil molding from the top rung of a ladder. "What are you serving? How many people? What time of day? Any special colors? Do you have a theme?"

He ran from the room.

Going out the back door five minutes later, he heard Cynthia announce that the event would be called the "First Annual Primrose Tea."

Hessie gave a squeal of delight, which was definitely a good sign.

He had talked to local clergy over the winter, but wasn't encouraged. Bottom line, Creek people were not known to welcome meddling preachers, and especially not meddling town preachers.

When he reminded them that Absalom Greer had gone in there every week for an entire summer, they reminded him that not only was Greer elderly, which generally translates to nonthreatening, but he was a native—always an advantage.

"From what I've heard," said Bill Sprouse, "I wouldn't mess around in there. I hear they'd as soon shoot you as look at you, and there's no question that drugs and alcohol are serious problems."

"Isn't something being done through social services?"

"When it comes to the Creek, I don't think much gets done one way or the other."

"Tell me what else you've heard."

"The usual intermarrying, as you might guess. Used to be a nest of bootleggers in there, and before that the Creek was where they made corn whiskey. A lot of poverty. Houses where you can see through the walls, kerosene stoves in winter, a fair amount of families get burned out."

"Where do they go when that happens?"

"They don't usually come into Mitford or Wesley. They stay with their own. Of course, once in a while you'll see some of the older kids hanging around town, but not often. The Creek buys its groceries and gets doctored over the county line, in Ipswich—that's where they get their schooling, too, if they get any. I think the county line runs along the creek bank for several miles."

"Go in there with me," he said. That was radical, but was anything worthwhile ever accomplished without radical action? Preaching the Gospel was radical, forming the church had been radical. Heaven knows, marrying Cynthia—at his age—had been radical.

"Brother, I've got all the sick and hurting I can say grace over. I don't have to go to the Creek to find suffering. My organist is dying of a brain tumor, and one of my finest deacons is too depressed to get out of bed in the mornings." The usually jovial preacher looked solemn.

"Yes, well . . ."

"Not to mention that Rachel's old mother just passed and me and Sparky are on our own while she's in Springfield cleaning out the home place."

"My condolences to Rachel."

"I keep on a tight string with what the Lord's laid at my own back door," said Bill.

Yes, but if they didn't do something, who would?

"Tell you what," said Bill, looking jovial again, "I'll commit to pray about it."

Father Tim felt strangely restless and annoyed. Certainly he had prayed about it and would continue to pray about it, but he was moved to act, as well. Somehow, he could see the girl who had jumped out of the tree; he could see her as plainly as if she'd landed at his own feet.

"Big doin's comin' up at your place," said J.C. "A real front-pager." He slid into the rear booth, protecting a bandaged hand.

"Why don't you run your story *after* the fact?" queried the rector. "You know, one of those good-time-was-had-by-all deals."

"We're running a story before *and* after," said the editor, looking as if he owned the world.

"Aha."

Mule stirred cream into his coffee. "Your wife's tea party is sure rackin' up business for Fancy. She's booked solid through the morning of the fifteenth for perms and color, not to mention acrylic nails."

He had never thought that a rectory tea might boost the local economy. "What happened to your hand?" he asked the editor.

"Jabbed a knife in it."

"How come?"

"Tryin' to punch another hole in my belt. The knife slipped and I punched a hole in myself."

"That's a mighty neat-looking bandage. Did you do that?"

"Not exactly," said J.C.

"You better get some nourishment. You look like you've been sent for and couldn't go," Mule told him.

"Ten more pounds and I'm home free."

"You'll need a whole new set of clothes. That'll hit you up for a bundle."

J.C. mopped his face with his handkerchief. "I'll shop yard sales like some people I know, and dress myself with pocket change."

"Who's shakin' the sheets to find you of a mornin'?" Velma asked the editor as she poured coffee.

J.C. grinned hugely. "That's for me to know and you to find out. And by the way, I'll take the check for this booth."

"My hearin' just went bad," said Mule. "What'd you say?"

"I said I'm pickin' up the check."

"Why?" asked the rector.

"It's spring!" said J.C., still grinning.

"Miss Sadie's sleepin'," Louella whispered, answering his knock on the door. "Come in an' drink a glass of tea. I ain't put th' sugar in yet."

Louella led him into the kitchen on tiptoe and closed the door. "Now!" she said. "You can talk yo' head off and Miss Sadie can't hear nothin'!"

"How's your knee doing?"

"Stiff, honey, but perkin'."

"Are you cooking?"

"One time a day. I said Miss Sadie, pick yo' time, she said lunch! So, I cooks lunch, then we put them dishes in th' dishwasher and set back and listen to it go. It's a treat an' a half to have a dishwasher!"

"I wouldn't know," he said. "I've never had one."

"Father, you ought t' get more modern, now you're a married man."

"Right. How's Miss Sadie's wrist?"

"Oh, law. Law, law, law!" Louella shook her head. "Gittin' better."

"That's not good?"

"Soon's that little bone git strong, Miss Sadie goan be drivin' that car hard as she can go! You see this pore ol' gray head? Thass not ol' age, honey, thass Miss Sadie's drivin'."

"Ummm."

"When she break her wrist, I said, 'Thank you, Jesus, now we both goan live longer!' I hate to cross over Jordan meetin' head-on with a truck. I'd 'preciate crossin' in my sleep with a smile on my face!"

"She'll be ninety in June. Won't she have to take another test?"

"She don't have t' test again 'til she hit ninety-two. And Miss Sadie, she test good. She test real good."

They sat in silence for a moment, sipping their tea.

"I don't know what to do," he said, meaning it. "But I'll do something."

Why was he always offering to do something he had no earthly idea how to do? Was his ego so twisted that he had to seize control over outcomes? No, it was almost worse than that. He was driven to console people, to bind them up, to protect them from the worst—an ambition that often got in the way of the Holy Spirit's ministrations.

"This boy," the old bishop of Mississippi had said to Tim's mother, "will make the sort of priest God can use around His house. Timothy will pay attention to his flock in the small particulars, and most of all . . . he'll love them."

He didn't know if it was so loving to protect people. Perhaps really loving meant not protecting them.

He certainly hadn't protected Dooley Barlowe. Sending him off to school with those fancy rich kids was like throwing red meat to wolves. But hadn't the boy turned up in Paris, France, singing in a cathedral?

"I never thought I'd live to see the day . . ." said Cynthia, lying prostrate in bed.

"Which day?"

"The day I'd be in bed at eight-thirty."

"You've become a true Mitfordian. The mountain air has finally gotten the best of your big-city habits."

"Did I clean my face? I forgot. Could you look? I hope I did, because I can't get up, I'm sore all over."

"I've been meaning to ask . . . why are you giving one colossal, backbreaking tea when you might, say, give a couple of medium-size teas?"

"Medium-size does not hack it in today's world, dearest. Medium, tedium. The idea is to kill yourself once a year and keep them talking, and then I don't have to be president or chairman of anything, and everybody still speaks to me and respects my husband."

"Aha."

"Do you really like the dining room?"

"I really do. Very much. It's wonderful. But I was wondering . . ."

"Ummm . . ."

"What happened to the drapes."

"I unhooked them from the rod and Puny wore a mask and caught them in a laundry basket and took them to the Dumpster. We would have burned them in the backyard, but there's a law."

"That bad, huh?"

"Historic."

He looked at the ceiling. No wind or breezes tonight. "Sorry I messed up that batch of lemon squares."

She yawned hugely. "It's OK. Puny and I are baking all day tomorrow. I know I could have accepted help or called on the ECW, but those women already work like slaves, and I want to give everyone a lovely break. I want them to feel honored and special.

"I don't mind all this work, really I don't. It's my own fault that I decided to redecorate, but it had to be done, you know, it was like a cave down there. Next year will be a breeze. Oh. Can you help me with the vegetable sandwiches Wednesday morning, and melt the chocolate and dip the strawberries?"

"My pleasure," he said, meaning it.

"I need your moral support more than you imagine. To tell the truth, it will mean everything. It's the first time out for the rector's new wife, you know."

He took her hand. "Mark my words, it's going to be the grandest event since the unveiling of the statue at the town museum."

"Just one more day to go," she said, "and then boom, a hundred and twenty women all talking at once! I have a feeling Uncle Billy will come with Miss Rose, don't you?"

"I'd be surprised if he doesn't."

"I hope he does. It will add an air of intrigue."

Uncle Billy? Intrigue?

"Do you really like the kitchen, Timothy?"

"Greatly. I think it's . . . interesting . . . that you knocked the plaster off the wall in forty-seven places."

"It's that wonderful ruined look. Are you laughing?"

"I am not."

"I see your stomach jiggling."

"The kitchen might go over a few heads on Wednesday."

"When we leave, I'll replaster," she said.

There was a long silence.

She looked at him. "We never talk about when you—we—might . . . leave."

"That's because I don't have the faintest idea," he snapped.

Why had he snapped at her? Because Stuart Cullen was always pushing him to consider his retirement—what he was going to do and when he was going to do it. He wouldn't know until he did it, and that should be enough for anybody.

The phone by the bed gave a sharp blast.

"Father? Richard Fleming."

"Yes?" he said cautiously.

"I'm very embarrassed about something. Do you have a moment?"

"I do." He sat straight up.

"Nearly four weeks ago, we sent a hand-addressed mailing to all parents, an invitation to a special choral concert here at the school. I walked over to the office tonight and saw that yours has just come back. Where it has languished for so long, I can't say, but it was marked Return to Sender."

"Aha."

"We'd made the regrettable mistake of addressing it to Milford, a slip of the pen, as it were, though you're in our computer correctly.

"What I'm getting around to is, this concert is the most ambitious thing we've done all year. Very important. I wondered why you hadn't responded, and Dooley was very concerned that we had no reply from you.

"I must tell you this means a great deal to him. The parents are turning out in enthusiastic numbers, and, well, I'm dreadfully sorry about the mix-up. . . ."

"Quite all right," said the rector. "I'm sure we can make arrangements. Whatever it takes, I'll be there. You have my word."

"Excellent! A great relief!"

"When is it . . . exactly?"

"Wednesday morning—the day after tomorrow—at eleven o'clock. It's followed by a luncheon at one. We had a conflict at the weekend and were forced to schedule a weekday, but the parents have been very accommodating. Well, then, this is lovely. Shall I jot you down for two Kavanaghs?"

He looked at his wife, feeling stricken. He had given Richard Fleming his word.

"No," he said hoarsely. "Just one."

To be there at eleven, he would have to leave Mitford no later than six a.m., maybe six-fifteen, after melting the chocolate and dipping a hundred and fifty strawberries. Puny had agreed to come early and do the vegetable sandwiches.

Cynthia had been gravely disappointed, but tried hard not to show it. His wife, however, had the complete inability to hide her feelings. They were right out there for all to see, as accurate as a top-of-the-line wall barometer.

"Of course you must go," she said. "Dooley would be heartbroken if you didn't. I'll pack him a box of treats, and you don't have to do the strawberries, it's too much—"

"It's no such thing. I'll do them and that's that."

She sighed. "Puny will be here all day, and Hessie Mayhew is collecting primroses from every garden and insists on helping clean up, and Marge Owen wants to help, too, so—"

"So I'll be back around six-thirty, and anything that's left to clean up, I'll do it."

"I love you madly," she said, looking brave.

He finished setting out squares of chocolate and a double boiler for the morning. Then he turned and drew her to him and took her face in his hands. "In truth," he said, "it's the other way around."

He was thirty miles out of Mitford when, without warning, his engine quit.

He managed to steer his car onto the shoulder of the road, where it sat at the edge of a ditch. He tried the ignition several times, to the sound of nothing but a click. The engine, the battery, whatever, was as dead as a doornail.

"Blast!"

Agitated, he got out of the car and looked up and down the road. He had thoroughly enjoyed the eight years he traveled by foot. Not once had he been forced to put up with the aggravation and expense of car trouble.

He saw a house situated at the end of a pasture. In the other direction, some kind of low building set back from the road, with a sign out front.

He walked toward it quickly, feeling the cold sting of the clear spring morning. Seven-fifteen. He had three and a half hours or so to drive the network of time-saving back roads that led to Dooley's school.

The sign had rusted, but was still readable.

Beaumont Aviation
Charters and Instruction
Have a nice day

If he could get to a phone and call Lew Boyd, Lew could call and ask Cynthia to follow Lew's tow truck. He could use her car, though he'd definitely be late.

He didn't see anybody when he opened the door. "Hello!" he shouted.

Silence.

"Hello! Anybody here?"

He spied a phone on a table. Knowing Lew's number by heart, he dialed it. Busy.

Dadgum it, if Lew Boyd was sitting around playing checkers this time of morning . . .

He glanced out the window and saw somebody tinkering with a little plane on the grass landing strip.

He dialed Lew again. Still busy.

One problem. If Lew called Cynthia, what could she do, after all? And what a rotten thing it would be to have her drive a half hour from home on a morning when every moment was vital to her.

He'd stick it out for Lew, however.

Still busy.

Lord, show me where to step here. We've got a boy who's looking for a familiar face in the crowd. We can't let him down.

He paced the floor. If Mule Skinner drove out to loan him his car, how would Mule get home? He certainly couldn't ask the man to drive all the way to Dooley's school and back, as if he had nothing better to do.

Ron Malcolm! He didn't know how Ron could help, but Ron had a solution for everything. Wilma's voice on the machine said, "We're out of town. If you're Tommy, Rachel, or Nell, please call us in Boca Raton at—"

He hung up, took a dollar from his billfold, and laid it next to the phone.

"Mornin'," said a man coming in the door. He wiped his hands on a rag.

"Good morning. I just made a phone call to Mitford. I left a dollar on the table."

"Can I help you?"

"I wish you could. My car broke down. I think the engine quit."

"Could be a timing belt," said the man, still wiping. "Maybe your ignition switch."

"Could you take a look at it?"

"I'm not much good around automobiles. Coffee?"

Outside, he heard a car screech onto the gravel and park near the door.

"No, thanks. I've got to be at my boy's school in Virginia at eleven o'clock, come hell or high water."

Omer Cunningham strode in, wearing a leather flying jacket and a grin. "Hey, Preacher, I thought I seen your car out there. You here to charter or take lessons?"

"Omer!" He felt like a man in a foreign country who sees a face from home. "My car broke down and I've got to get to Virginia, Dooley's singing in a concert, and Lew Boyd won't answer the blasted phone, and . . . can you drive me into town? I could pick up my wife's car." This would put him at the school a little past noon. He felt sick with regret.

"Where you goin' in Virginia?"

"White Chapel, and running late."

"I'll fly you," said Omer.

"Oh, I don't think—"

"When you got to be there?"

"Eleven o'clock."

"It's goin' on eight. You'll never make it runnin' home t' Mitford."

He felt the blood drain from his face. *Lord, if this is an answer to prayer, I don't believe I can take You up on it.*

"I've flew in and out of White Chapel many's th' time. We could borrow a pickup at the airstrip and whip you over to that fancy school in ten minutes. I know where it's at."

"You could?"

"I'll take you in m' little rag-wing tail dragger!" Omer's face lit up like a Christmas tree.

"Your . . . what?"

"Rag-wing tail dragger. She's a honey, a little J-3 Cub. Fabric stretched over a few tubes of steel, wheel under th' tail. You don't see 'em much anymore."

Fabric stretched over a few tubes . . . ?

"Better built than anything out there today. Get your plunder, and let's go. You'll be there ten-thirty sharp, with time to spare."

"Is, ah, your pilot's license current?"

"Omer's license is always current," said the man, grinning.

Father Tim hobbled to his car, his knees nearly giving out. When he reached for his jacket, he saw that his hand was visibly shaking.

He couldn't do this.

His aversion to flying had kept him stuck to Mitford like moss on a log for fourteen years—except for that witless sojourn to New York, which his heart had forced him to make, and the long-ago jaunt to write the paper on C. S. Lewis. As for the trip across the pond to Ireland, that had been his bishop's idea. He had flown six interminable hours with his jaw set like a stone.

Lord, if this is Your answer, then You've got to help me do this thing. I know how You feel about fear, and I agree. But I'm scared stiff and You know it, and I'm needing a generous hand-out of grace.

The little yellow plane looked like a toy sitting on the green airstrip. While merely walking to it was a problem, climbing into the thing was worse. His knees were Silly Putty, his breathing labored, his palms drenched.

Omer settled in and pulled on a cap. "I don't reckon you'd want t' fly with th' doors off?"

"I don't . . . reckon so."

"Yessir," said Omer, displaying a mouthful of teeth the size of piano keys, "flyin' my little tail dragger is th' most fun you can have with y'r clothes on."

"Hang tight!" yelled Omer.

He felt as if he were lashed to a jackhammer as they tore along the grass strip for what seemed an eternity.

At last the little plane nosed up, up, up into the blue. His stomach crawled under his lung cage. Perspiration dampened his forehead like summer fog. The racking vibration in the cockpit bounced his glasses on his nose.

Flying with Omer Cunningham, he suspected, was aviation's equivalent of eating Rose Watson's cooking. Wasn't he the guy who, years ago, flew so low over a pasture that he soured the milk in a farmer's cows? The farmer had sued—and won.

Omer leaned toward him and shouted at the top of his lungs, "Beautiful day for flyin', ain't it?"

He ran his tongue around the inside of his teeth, to make sure he wasn't losing any. "Yes, indeed!" he yelled back.

He regretted even the few strawberries he'd eaten for breakfast. *Lord, please don't let me make a mess of this man's airplane.*

Clearly, he was gaining a whole new perspective on St. Paul's admonition to pray without ceasing.

"Dooley, this is Mr. Omer Cunningham, my pilot."

"Your *pilot*?"

"He flew me up here."

"You *flew*?"

He held his thumb and forefinger about three inches apart. "In a little yellow plane about this big."

"Man!"

He shook Dooley's hand. "You were great, son. Words fail me. It was a thrilling experience."

"Real good," said Omer, with feeling.

While Omer smoked a cigarette by the pickup truck, he and Dooley walked to the school green and sat under a tree.

"I'm glad you could come. I wish ol' Cynthia could've come."

He handed over the samples from the First Annual Primrose Tea. "She sent you a box of stuff that will melt in your mouth."

"I want t' open it now."

"Go to it."

Dooley opened the box, popped an entire lemon square into his mouth, and reached for a cookie.

"Chew before you swallow is my advice."

He looked at the place where Dooley's cowlick used to spout up like a geyser, and wondered how it had mysteriously vanished. He looked at his tennis shoes, which were size eleven, and the long legs, which had grown longer just since Thanksgiving.

It seemed only yesterday that he'd been chosen as the one to take the boy in, and already Dooley was gone—growing up, finding his own way. Why did time seem so short, so fleeting?

"How're you doing, buddy?"

"All right."

"Really and truly?"

"Yep."

"No kidding?"

"Yep."

"You going to make it up here?"

"Yes, sir."

"You're sticking with it?"

"Yep."

"That concert was as fine as anything I've heard anywhere. A lot of hard work in that."

"Yes, sir."

He put his arm around the boy. "I love you, pal."

"Looky here," said Omer, walking over to the tree. "Don't you want me t' take th' boy up for a little spin?"

"Well . . ."

"Man!" said Dooley, jumping to his feet.

Walking to the office to get the headmaster's permission, he reflected that there was a full lunch, two lemon squares, and three cookies in that boy. He was thrilled there was only one passenger seat in the little plane, which meant he'd be forced to stick it out on the ground during this particular joy ride.

When they dropped Dooley back at school, he hugged him, and got a good, hard hug in return.

That was worth the trip right there, he thought, choking up.

"Boneswar, Messure!" Dooley yelled after him.

They vibrated toward Mitford, having altered their return course so Omer could give his passenger an aerial view of the rectory.

"Where's the Creek?" he shouted. "Do we fly over the Creek?"

"If you want to, we do!" Omer shouted back. The rector thought he could count thirty-two piano keys in his pilot's grin. "But it ain't scenic."

"I'm not looking for scenic!"

Omer veered to the right and dipped, only slightly ahead of the rector's stomach.

"Over yonder, see that power station?"

"I see it!"

"Th' Creek's on th' other side. Comin' up!"

After roaring over the power station and a patch of woods, he saw a ribbon of water gleaming in the sunlight. Then he saw the open sore on the breast of the creek bank—ramshackle, unpainted houses, tin-roofed sheds, houses that had burned and stood in their rubble, rusted trailers and vehicles abandoned in the weeds or sitting on blocks. A few hens pecked at the ground, which appeared to be hard, baked clay.

Dogs ran out and barked at the sky. A few people stood, shading their eyes, looking up. Near the woods, piles of abandoned stoves, refrigerators, tires, and other debris flowed down the bank to the water's edge.

"It ain't Dollywood!" shouted Omer, as they roared over the treetops and gained altitude.

"I'm buzzin' Lew's place first!"

Man alive, he thought, seeing the station sign come closer. *EXXON*. Coot Hendrick stood at the gas pumps, gawking and waving.

"OK! Here comes your house!"

The trees were so close, he might have stripped the leaves off a maple.

"Isn't this against the law?" he yelled.

"I cain't hear you!" shouted Omer.

"I don't see the rectory!"

"Yank up y'r floor mat and I'll spot 'er for you!"

He peeled back the mat, revealing a sizable hole, as Omer careened to the left and dipped.

He recognized the monument, then the school and First Baptist—and, by George, there was the Grill! Somebody stepped out to the sidewalk and looked up, but Omer roared on before he could tell who it was.

"There you go!" hollered his pilot.

Just below, tucked beside the little yellow house with the tile roof, was the place where a hundred and twenty women had devoured as many lemon squares this very day. He could see the pink and white trilliums blooming in the backyard. He could number the slates on his roof.

If he looked through that hole another minute, he would deposit his calling card all over Wisteria Lane. He slapped the mat back in place.

"What else you want t' see?" hollered Omer, nosing them straight up. Omer was getting a second wind.

"That'll do it!" he shouted. "Just take me to my car!"

Please!

He drove to Mitford with Omer.

"What do I owe you?" he asked Mayor Cunningham's brother-in-law.

"Oh, about three or four hundred! But seein' as I owe *you* for th' pleasure of doin' it, you can give me fifty."

"Fifty? Surely—"

"I ain't licensed to charge commercial. I can only charge gas, and that's fifty on th' button. Besides, you're clergy."

He peeled off two twenties and a ten. Here he was, a small-town priest flying around in a chartered plane, shelling out bucks like an oil field executive.

His legs were still wobbly, but he managed to give Omer Cunningham an invigorating slap on the back, as Omer put the money in his pocket and grinned hugely.

"That was a ride I won't forget," said the rector, meaning it.

Cynthia was in bed, her face mashed into the pillow.

"I never thought I'd see the day."

"H'lo, dearest," she murmured. "What day?"

"The day my wife would hit the hay while it's still daylight." It was, in fact, only a little after seven o'clock.

She moaned.

"That bad, huh?"

"They had a wonderful time. I'm a heroine, Timothy. Your good name is untarnished. But I can't move."

"The house looks wonderful. I can't tell anybody's been here. How did the food hold out?"

"You'd think they hadn't eaten in days. There's nothing left but a couple of hazelnuts, which rolled under the primroses."

"Off the hook for another year, are you?"

She moaned again.

"Speak," he said, sitting on the bed and rubbing her back.

"They thought the tea was so fabulous, they asked me to do the bishop's brunch in June."

"No rest for the wicked, and th' righteous don't need none," he quoted Uncle Billy.

"You'll be glad to know I flatly refused."

"Well done!"

"Now it's your turn. Tell me everything about our Dools." She rolled over and looked at him. "Why, Timothy! You're beaming like a light tower! An eight-hour drive and up before dawn, and you look positively . . . wonderful!"

"Dooley's the one who was wonderful. The whole choral presentation was outstanding. You would have been proud. He missed you."

She took his hand. "I miss him every day. Is he going to make it?"

"He's going to make it," he said.

"I knew he would."

"Well . . . we both have lots to tell."

She leaned up and kissed him. "I want to hear everything. There's supper in the oven."

"Thanks, maybe later."

"Then take your shower, why don't you? I'll be here waiting, and we can have our prayers."

She was there waiting, all right, but dead asleep doing it.

He snuggled up to her back, conforming to her soft contours. "Spoons" is what this marital position was called in their part of the South.

He lay there, comforted by his bed and his room and his house and his wife, and thanked God silently.

He didn't realize it until after he prayed, but blast if he hadn't had a good time today in that little yellow tail dragger.

CHAPTER EIGHT

Serious About Fun

J.C. HAD BEEN to the dentist and was sucking tea through a straw. "That crazy Omer Cunningham was flyin' so low yesterday, he could have picked my pocket."

"No kidding?" said the rector.

Mule whistled. "I wouldn't go up in that plane for a million bucks before taxes. What is it but a bed sheet wrapped around a bale of chicken wire?"

J.C. sucked his tea to the bottom of the glass. "I've personally never met the fool who'd fly with Omer Cunningham."

"What're you grinnin' about?" Mule asked the rector.

"Grinning?" he said. "I didn't know I was grinning."

He was in Wesley buying a new shaving kit, when he happened to glance out the shop window into the mall. He saw J.C. walking with a police officer. When they stopped for a moment, the rector threw up his hand and waved, but J.C. didn't see him. It appeared that J.C. glanced around to see if anybody was looking, then he hugged the police officer and the officer hugged him back.

He fogged his glasses and wiped them with his handkerchief and looked again. The two parted and went in opposite directions.

Aha. That was no police officer J.C. had hugged. It was a woman.

He pressed his nose to the shop window.

Actually, it was a woman police officer.

After Omer Cunningham told Lew Boyd at the Esso on North Main, word spread to the end of South Main with the speed of a brush fire.

The rector noticed that people dropped what they were doing and nodded respectfully when he walked by. The postmaster pitched in a nickel when he ran out of change for a stamp. Uncle Billy gave him a strawberry-flavored sucker as a token of admiration. The following Sunday, his congregation proffered their rapt and undivided attention throughout the sermon.

Four hours in an airplane had given him more credibility than thirty-six years in the pulpit.

He wasn't seeing much of his wife.

What with working on her book, visiting schools, turning the rectory into a villa, and giving a tea for a hundred and twenty women, which, at the last minute, had numbered a hundred and thirty-one, she hardly had time to roll her hair, much less sit and talk at the breakfast table.

At the office, he uncovered his Royal manual, bent on giving a hundred percent to his sermon, which was largely inspired by a saintly challenge. "Preach the Gospel at all times," St. Francis had said. "If necessary, use words."

"Guess what?" asked his secretary.

"What?" he snapped.

"Oooh. Touchy."

"Try again."

"It's something we just got. Three guesses."

Defend us, deliver us . . .

"Come on!" Emma said. "Be a sport, for Pete's sake."

"Would it be asking too much for you to give me a clue?"

"It's brown."

"Ah. That's helpful. A new suit for Harold."

"You know he hates to wear a suit."

"Runoff from the Clark River."

"Please."

"I give up."

"You always give up. OK, it's a dog."

He had never seen Emma Newland beam. Smile, maybe. Laugh, certainly. But not beam.

"You? Harold? A *dog*?"

"A brown poodle named Snickers."

"A poodle! What does Harold think of that?"

"He thinks all dogs should live outside. He was raised in the country, you know, and that's how country people think."

"So, where's Snickers going to live?" he inquired.

"Inside!" she said, looking determined.

He walked up to Fernbank after he left the office, to check on Miss Sadie's house. He could sense the worry when he talked with her on the phone. Had that dead tree crashed onto the porch during a recent storm? And what about the old washhouse—could rain have come in where the handmade bricks had fallen out of the chimney, and ruined the pine table that belonged to her mother?

"I'll go," he said.

"Oh, Father, I promise I wasn't asking you to run up there. I was just thinking out loud."

"Glad to do it," he said, meaning it.

He veered off Church Hill Road along a path through the ferns on the steeply pitched bank. The path, which led from the road to the orchard, had been worn by locals over the past few years, owing to Miss Sadie's invitation to the town. "Come and get them!" she said annually, unable to have the apples picked.

He was halfway up the bank and had stopped to rest by a huge oak when he saw movement ahead, among the ferns. It looked like a young boy, who was facing away from him and digging.

He watched intently. The boy was digging ferns with their root balls, and putting them into a sack, looking constantly to the left and right, but not behind. Clearly, he thought he was well-protected from behind by the tree.

Certain people, he recalled, often dug ferns and rhododendron on someone else's property and sold them to nurseries who looked the other way. He knew, too, about the flourishing traffic in galax leaves, and local moss, which was peeled off the ground or pulled from logs in large, unbroken sheets and sold to florists.

The ways and means of making a living in these mountains had never been easy, he knew that, but let an incident like this go by, and Fernbank could be stripped of the very resource that inspired its name.

As he started to move away from the tree, he saw the boy take off his hat. Long hair spilled down and fell over his shoulders. Actually, it appeared to be a girl, a girl wearing boy's clothes, or even a man's clothes, given the way they hung on her. She had sashed the oversized shirt with vines.

"Hello," he called.

She whirled around, letting the mattock drop. He saw the fear in her eyes, then the anger.

"I ain't done nothin'," she said harshly, standing her ground as he walked toward her. He saw that she noted his clerical collar.

The point was to speak kindly, he thought. She might have been a wild rabbit for the look in her eyes and the fierce way she glared at him. He knew a thing or two about rabbits, having raised them as a boy. They didn't like sudden moves.

"These ferns are pretty special."

"I don't care nothin' about 'em."

She backed away from him and put her foot on the mattock handle.

He stopped about a yard from her and glanced toward the sack.

"I'll knock you in th' head if you lay hands on my sack. I don't care if you are a preacher."

"Miss Sadie Baxter's ferns are a town treasure." He spoke as if he had all the time in the world. If he had a stick, he would have whittled it with his pocket knife. "These banks have been covered with the wild cinnamon fern for many years—there's not another stand like it anywhere, I hear."

"Don't mean nothin' t' me," she said, edging toward the sack.

"Ferns grow in families, like most other kinds of plants. Actually, there are four different fern families . . . and look at this. See how the leaves curl at the tip of the stem and curve around? That's called a fiddlehead."

She was going to grab the mattock and sack and run for it, he could tell by the language of her movements.

"I'd personally appreciate if it you'd replant everything you just dug," he said kindly. "In fact, I'll help you do it. And I won't say anything to anybody about it, unless I see you here again."

She reached down and grabbed the mattock and dived toward the sack. Quick as lightning, she threw it over her shoulder and was away, racing down the bank like a hare.

He saw that she was barefoot and that she'd left her hat lying at his feet.

Had he done or said the right thing? He didn't know. He had never liked the pressure to do and say the right thing because he was a preacher. He was also a human being, blast it, and he stumbled along like the rest of humankind.

He squinted his eyes and watched her disappear over the curve of the green bank.

She had not looked back.

What they needed, he thought, was an adventure, some recreation. Hadn't they agreed on that very thing not long after their honeymoon? He had boldly declared they'd do something interesting every weekend, even in the dead of winter. In fact, they'd shaken hands on it.

But what were they doing? Why, working, of course. And falling into bed like two logs, with scarcely a fare-thee-well.

Once again, he'd let the puzzling mystery of recreation hold him back. What was fun, after all? And how did one go about having it?

He'd been so fired up the day they shook hands; the possibilities had seemed endless. Now, all he could think of was going out to dinner in Wesley. But they'd done that twice. Besides, anybody could go out to dinner. What was needed here was something fresh and new, something unexpected, to captivate the imagination of his highly imaginative wife.

Then again, if she was so highly imaginative, why not ask her to think of something?

He would not. It was his own bounden duty to come up with a solution.

He walked around his rosebushes. He pulled a wild burdock out of the daylilies. He sat on the stone bench and stared at a tree. Maybe he should ask somebody for an idea. But who?

Not Emma Newland, who thought fun was watching TV game shows and nagging Harold to eat his vegetables.

Not Mule Skinner, who thought fun was clipping cents-off coupons and going to yard sales.

Not Ron and Wilma Malcolm, who thought fun was packing their car to the roof and driving nonstop to Boca Raton, where the temperatures would roast a pork loin.

Come to think of it, he didn't know anybody who was good at having fun, except, of course, Omer Cunningham, who clearly knew how to have a good time—and all for the price of a few gallons of gas.

Oh, well. He would think about it. He would make some notes. He might go to the library. In the meantime, he knew he couldn't count on reading Wordsworth aloud forever. Somehow, that had been just dandy while they were going steady, but now it didn't go over so well. Cynthia's gaze wandered around the room, she fidgeted, she got up and made notes that had absolutely nothing to do with Wordsworth.

Even Barnabas, once so attracted to the romantic poets, went to sleep before the end of an opening stanza.

There was nothing for it but to come up with a whole new ball game in the area of recreation.

He stopped by the rectory for his checkbook, in transit to the Children's Hospital in Wesley.

Puny Guthrie looked exceedingly plump, not to mention smug and self-satisfied. Everything about her had gained a certain largesse—her hair seemed redder and curlier, her freckles bigger, her eyes greener.

"Guess what?" she said, turning from the sink where she was peeling potatoes.

"I promise I can't guess," he said.

"Remember you said you'd play with it, an' all, when I brought it to work with me?"

"Now, Puny . . ."

"Well, th' only thing is—it's not an it."

"It's not?"

"It's *twins*!"

"No!"

"Yes!" she exclaimed, looking joyful.

He thumped down into a chair at the kitchen table.

She rubbed her stomach, giggling. "You'll have two t' play with! Don't that beat all?"

"You can say that again," he replied, loosening his collar.

"Dearest," she said, before popping through the hedge to her drawing board, "why don't you come with me to Hastings School tomorrow? You never take a real day off, and besides, it would be *fun*!"

Fun? "Sure!" he said without hesitation.

Emma could cover for him. They also had an office answering machine, didn't they? Besides, it was true—he hardly ever took a real day off.

"I'll be reading *Violet Visits the Queen.* Oh—I just thought of something!—you could read the part of the palace guard!"

He looked dazed.

"Just say yes!" she implored. "Remember the first time you took me to visit Miss Pattie, and let me see into *your* work? This way, you can see into mine. That will be the most fun of all!"

To hear her tell it, this sojourn would be loaded with the very thing he'd been trying so hard to get a bead on.

"I'll tell you how the sun rose . . ." she said, zooming down the road in her Mazda.

"Tell me!" he said.

"A ribbon at a time—
The Steeples swam in Amethyst—
The news, like Squirrels, ran—
The Hills untied their Bonnets—
The Bobolinks—begun—
Then I said softly to myself—

That must have been the Sun!"

"Mark Twain!" he said recklessly, leaving all care behind.

"Timothy, you're not trying! Guess again."

Women wanted you to guess something every time you turned around. "Christina Rossetti?"

"No, but you're close. One more guess. Listen—steeples, amethyst, bobolinks. Who writes like that?"

"Hessie Mayhew!"

She laughed uproariously. It didn't take much for his agreeable wife. Give her an inch of amusement and she'd convert it to a mile's worth.

"Emily Dickinson, for Pete's sake. Now it's your turn."

"Can't we play cow poker?" he wondered, gazing out the window for a pasture.

"I can't be mooning into ditches counting cows while I'm driving. No, you have to do a poem or something. And not Wordsworth."

"Blast! A man can't take a day off . . ."

She whipped around a truck. "Something from the eighteenth century would be nice."

After yowling from Mitford to Holding, Violet had finally curled up and gone to sleep in her carrier. Now, at least, he could think straight.

"Ye fearful saints, fresh courage take
The clouds ye so much dread
Are big with mercy, and shall break
In blessings on your head.
His purposes will ripen fast
Unfolding every hour
The bud may have a bitter taste
But sweet will be the flower."

"Are you sure that's not Wordsworth?" she asked, slowing down for an intersection.

"Positive," he said. "One of his friends, however."

"Cowper, then."

"Yes, from the hymn that opens with 'God moves in a mysterious way, His wonders to perform.' Most people think that line is from Scripture."

" 'The bud may have a bitter taste, but sweet will be the flower.' "

She laughed, looking happy. "That's our courtship and marriage he was writing about!"

It was grand to be on the road with a comfortable companion.

"And this is Miss Coppersmith's husband, Mr. Coppersmith."

The students applauded.

"And they're both going to read about one of your favorite friends."

"Violet!" shouted the class in unison.

"Let's sit on the floor with the children," Cynthia whispered.

He looked at the half-circle of bright faces, hoping his knees didn't creak like a garden gate when he sat down. Could he get up? He would cross that bridge when he came to it.

"Miss Coppersmith is very, very famous. She has won a medal for one of her books. I know Mr. Coppersmith must be very proud."

"Actually," said Cynthia, "my husband's name is not Coppersmith. It's Kavanagh."

"Oh," said the teacher. "How modern!"

"Actually, we both have the same name. Coppersmith is my writing name. OK, everybody! This is Father Kavanagh. And this is Violet!" They sat down in front of the children, with Violet's carrier. The kids scrambled close and peered inside.

"I never seen a cat that's in books," somebody said.

"Does she live in there?"

"What does she do all day?"

"Where are her kittens?"

Violet blinked imperiously from her carrier.

"I have a cat!" announced a girl. "Its name is Perry Winkle!"

"I have two dogs!" said a boy, raising his hand and flapping it. "One throws up if he eats spaghetti."

"My mom knows somebody who has a pig!" offered another. "They let it live in the house. Yuck! A pig in the house! I wonder where it goes to the bathroom."

The pupils guffawed.

"Children!" said the teacher.

"A pig in the house is no big deal," said Cynthia. "When I was your age, I had an alligator that lived in my bathtub."

"Wow!"

"Neat!"

"How did you take a bath?" More hysterical laughter.

"I didn't," said Cynthia. "I didn't take a bath for a whole month. Maybe two whole months!"

"Cool," someone murmured in heartfelt awe.

"Neat-o!"

"I took showers at my friend's house!" said Cynthia.

Groans, moans.

"How can your husband be married to you if he's your father?" inquired the boy whose dog couldn't tolerate spaghetti.

"Well, you see, he's a priest. And we call a priest 'Father.' Now, settle down, and I don't mean maybe, because we're going to read a story. Anybody who doesn't listen, or who talks or whispers, gets to come up here and read my part—in *French.*"

He thought they'd never get to the section with the palace guard, but when they did, he hoped he wouldn't mess up.

"The palace guard," Cynthia read at last, "looked down upon Violet and said . . ."

He gave the line a wicked snarl. *"Aha, my fine feline, thought you'd pull the wool over my eyes, did you?"*

"Violet was very frightened," continued Cynthia. "She didn't know what to do. As the palace guard's big hand moved to catch her by the neck, she darted between his legs.

"She ran down the long corridor as fast as she could go.

"She looked behind her and saw the big, black boots of the guard. Then, other people were running behind her and shouting, 'Stop that cat!'

"As she ran, Violet's heart beat very fast. She could hardly get her breath. Boots and slippers and mops and brooms followed in hot pursuit."

He jumped on his line in the nick of time. *"We must stop that cat! The Queen hates cats!"*

"Violet rounded the corner at a very great speed, and skidded into a large room. It was bright and beautiful. The sun shone in on a polished marble floor. And there, sitting on a throne, was . . . the *Queen.*"

He heard a gasp or two. Large eyes fixed on Cynthia.

"Violet tried to stop, but the marble floor wouldn't let her. She slid right up to the hem of the Queen's royal gown. And then . . . she *bowed.*

"That's when she felt the fearsome hand on the scruff of her neck.

"Suddenly, she was lifted up, up, up—and then down, down, down as the palace guard bowed, also.

"What is *that?*" the Queen demanded.

"Your Majesty, that *is a cat!"*

"I'm supposed to hate cats!" said the Queen.

"Yes, Your Majesty."

"But *why* am I supposed to hate cats?" asked the Queen.

"Because your father, the King, hated cats, Your Majesty."

"Hmmm," said the Queen. "It looks soft. Let me hold it."

"But Your Majesty, I couldn't—"

"Of course you could, because I am the *Queen!*"

At that high moment, Cynthia looked up to see Violet suddenly bolt from her carrier and, leaping over laps and darting past grasping hands, race through the open classroom door to the shrieks of the entire assembly.

"Oh, no!" cried Cynthia, unbelieving.

The catch on Violet's decrepit carrier had jiggled loose again.

Cynthia sprinted toward the door.

"Stop that cat!" she shouted.

Half the classroom emptied before the rector could get up.

He sat down again quickly, however, as both legs had gone completely to sleep.

"You were a wonderful palace guard," she said, smiling over at him. "So fierce!"

He zoomed around an RV with a sign that read *Dollywood Or Bust.* "It was a new and different experience, all right."

"I thought it was great fun!"

"Which part? When we read the story together, or when Violet leaped through the window and was caught in midair by the assistant principal?"

"All of it!" she said, laughing.

"I've always heard that truth is stranger than fiction." He looked at Violet, who was sleeping in Cynthia's lap, the very picture of innocence.

His wife furrowed her brow. "Maybe it *is* time for a new carrier," she said.

The summer people were slowly making their annual come-back to Mitford. Attendance was building every Sunday, and the Wednesday Eucharist was definitely up in numbers.

Four buildings on Main Street installed new green awnings, including The Local, which inscribed theirs with white lettering: *Fresh Meats and Produce Since 1957, Avis Packard, Grocer.*

Dora Pugh gave a sidewalk sale and moved forty-five flats of pansies in a record two hours and nine minutes. The candy tuft did not do as well. Lank Pitts drove a pickup load of rotted manure into town and parked it in front of Dora's hardware, where he sold it by the pound in garbage bags.

"Most people give that away," grumbled a customer, who nonetheless purchased two sacks full. "I pay f'r th' feed that goes in m' horses," said Lank. "Seems fair t' charge f'r what comes out."

Evie Adams, whose family home faced Main Street, received a check from an uncle and replaced the rusted porch glider, a longtime village eyesore, with two green rocking chairs. New window screens also went up, but only on the front of the house. Uncle Billy looped a hanging basket of geraniums over a nail beside his back door, where they'd be easy to bring in, in case of frost.

In all, the days were longer, the air warmer, and the Lord's Chapel youth group more restless.

"You've promised two or three times," said Larry Johnson, the group leader.

"Could I help it I had the flu the first time you went camping, and the next time you asked, I got married?"

"You better do it this time," said Larry, "or I don't know what dark revenge the kids might come up with. They really want you to go. Besides, it will be fun."

Suddenly, everybody knew how to have fun. Why bother to come up with ideas of his own?

"Oh, and they want you to bring Cynthia," said Larry.

Cynthia camping? He didn't know about that. However, a girl who'd kept an alligator in her bathtub might possibly be up for it.

"How would you like to go camping weekend after next?"

"Camping?" He might have asked her how she'd like to go bungee jumping.

"With the youth group. They like you, said you'd be a blast to go camping with."

"A blast?"

"That's what they said."

"How do you go camping? What do you do?"

"You take a bedroll and a tent and a frying pan, and saunter forth," he said.

"Have you ever done it?"

"Hundreds of times!" As good as that sounded, he couldn't tell a lie. "Five or six, anyway. I've been promising the kids I'd do it, and the jig is up."

"Snakes," she said. "I hate snakes."

"Snakes hate you even more. Watch your step and you'll be fine."

"What about bugs?"

"Cynthia, Cynthia . . ."

"And how do you . . . I mean . . . what do you do about . . . ?"

"The woods."

"Oh."

"Take sketch pads and pencils—you could see a deer or wild turkeys, even beavers. It's just your dish of tea. I'll teach you to throw a line in the water, and who knows, we could catch dinner for the whole crowd, and be heroes."

"Do you have a tent?"

"Sort of," he said.

"Sort of?"

He could tell she smelled a rat. "A few poles and a blanket."

"I don't think so."

"Come on," he said, kissing her. "We'll have a blast."

She looked at him, leaning her head to one side in that way he couldn't resist. He realized he didn't want to go without her.

"Sleeping under the stars, singing around the campfire, roasting marshmallows . . ." He searched her face for some sign of interest. Blank.

"Walking in the woods, listening to the creek rush boldly over the rocks . . ." He was giving it everything he had.

"Searching yourself for ticks . . ." she put in.

"Didn't you say you wanted to study different kinds of moss, draw birds, go out into nature? That's where you find nature—*in the woods*!"

"Yes, but . . . camping?"

"Cynthia, it'll be *fun*!" he said, desperate for a merchandising tactic.

She looked at him soberly, then grinned. "OK. But just this once."

"You remember that dictionary I found in th' Dumpster?" Uncle Billy asked him when they met on the street.

"I do."

"I cain't hardly enjoy readin' it n' more."

"Is that right?"

"Yessir, it's one thing here and another thing there—they're always changin' th' subject, don't you know."

The rector rolled his eyes and chuckled.

"That's m' new joke, but it's not m' main joke. I'm workin' out m' main joke for spring. By th' almanac, spring comes official on June twenty-one."

"Well, then, you've got a little time," he said. "Let me treat you to a cheeseburger."

Uncle Billy grinned, his gold tooth gleaming. "I'd be beholden to you, Preacher. An' I wouldn't mind a bit if you'd tip in some fries."

He put his arm around the old man's shoulders as they walked toward the Grill. He'd be et for a tater if he didn't love Bill Watson like blood kin.

He sat in the living room on Lilac Road, where Miss Sadie had come to look perfectly at home.

He wanted to get the thing accomplished. He was actually losing sleep over it. What if she really did hurt someone, or herself, or both? The last time he was told to deliver a warning to another party, he didn't deliver it—and Dooley's best friend was nearly killed.

"Have you looked into getting a chaplain yet?" asked Miss Sadie.

"No, ma'am, I haven't." He suddenly felt about nine years old.

"Well . . ." she said, sounding a trifle stern. She'd had to keep after him with a stick to find a school for Dooley.

"But I'll get to it. We've months to go yet."

"What have you got on your mind, Father? When you have something on your mind, it shows."

Dive in, and pray there's water in the pool. "Miss Sadie, I know your wrist is healing."

"Look there!" She jiggled her hand as a demonstration.

"Planning to drive soon?"

"I certainly am! I've nearly turned to a fossil sitting around here, and it's made me grumpy as all get-out. You know I've never been grumpy."

"No, indeed."

"It's not my nature."

"I agree completely."

"But there's a first time for everything," she declared.

"Miss Sadie, Rodney Underwood is going to give you a citation the next time you drive up on the sidewalk."

She looked at him. "Did he tell you that?"

"He did."

"Did he send you to tell me that?"

"Yes ma'am." Seven years old.

"Well, you tell Chief Underwood that he can march over here himself and do his business like a man. Sending my priest to do his dirty work is something I don't cotton to, and I don't mean maybe."

"He said his men had spoken to you before. . . ."

"Yes, indeed, they did, and I took no notice of it. He certainly likes to send people around to do his job! Is he so overworked he can't take care of important matters himself? You and I pay his salary, Father, need I remind you?"

Sadie Baxter was in a huff, and grumpy wasn't the word for it. He wanted to sprint to the door and head for the city limits. She had fussed at him before, but he'd never been around when she unloaded both barrels.

He saw Louella peering through the doorway.

"As if you didn't have enough on your hands, Father, with the sick and hurting all around us. You know what I'd like to do?" Miss Sadie looked fierce.

"No, what?"

"I'd like to yank a knot in Chief Underwood's tail!" she said, meaning it.

He thought he'd never seen her look so young and spunky. Maybe being grumpy had done her good. In any case, he was quitting while he was ahead.

He stood up. "The construction at Hope House is moving along at a pace, everything looks terrific, and I'd like to take you up there any day you want to go. Oh. I nearly forgot." He pulled the paper sack from his jacket pocket and handed it to her.

"Donut holes!" he said. They were her hands-down favorite.

She looked at the bag and then at him. "Were these supposed to soften me up?"

"They were," he said. Why beat around the bush?

She threw her head back and laughed merrily. There was the Sadie Baxter he knew, thanks be to God.

Taking the bag, she said, "You tell Chief Underwood to pay me a call in person and stop sending his henchmen to tell me what it's his job to say."

"I will."

Miss Sadie rose from the chair, taking her cane. "And tell him to call first, so I'll be dressed."

"I'll do that."

She laughed again. "I declare, it's kind of fun to be grumpy. People jump when I speak. I never noticed people doing that before."

He put his arm around her as they walked to the door. "Cynthia and I will come and take you for a spin, drive you up to Fernbank. Maybe you've got a little cabin fever."

"I'd like that. And Father?"

"Yes?"

"You know we love you. But you're not suited to meddling."

"Hessie's story on your Primrose Tea was a whopper," said J.C.

"A prize-winner," said the rector. "Cynthia had a copy laminated."

"If I paid that woman by the word, I'd be in deep manure."

Mule slid in beside the rector, wearing a chartreuse jacket. "I just did a closing that will set me up for a month of Sundays."

"Maybe now you can dump your polyester in a landfill and get you a new wardrobe," said the editor, finishing his house salad.

"Congratulations!" put in the rector.

"I just dropped a bundle at the Presbyterian parking lot sale. Two suits, a brand-new sweater, and a runnin' suit."

"You don't run," J.C. said.

"So, I'll protect my investment and start," Mule replied. "What's that smell?"

The rector didn't mention that he'd smelled something peculiar ever since J.C. sat down. So far, it had killed off all cooking odors from the grill, driven his sinuses haywire, and made the inside of his mouth feel funny.

"What smell?" asked the editor.

"Somethin' foul. Man! Stinks like cat musk." Mule sniffed the air like a beagle. "No offense," he told J.C., "but it's comin' from your direction."

"It's your upper lip," snapped the editor, grabbing his briefcase. "I'll just leave you boys to figure it out. I got to get over to th' mayor's office. *Hasta la vista.*"

J.C. left a heavy blast of scent in his wake. The two men looked at each other.

"Cologne," said the rector.

Understanding slowly dawned on Mule's face. He broke into one of his cackling laughs. "So that's it! Well, I'll be dadgum. Ol' J.C., he's . . . he's . . ."

"Getting overhauled," said the rector.

CHAPTER NINE

Locked Gates

IF SPRING had blown in like a zephyr, its mood soon changed.

Gentle rains became wind-lashed torrents, washing seeds from furrows and carving deep gullies in driveways and lawns. Power blinked off and surged on again, those with computers kept them unplugged, and TVs went down before the lightning like so many ducks in a shooting gallery.

Sudden, startling downpours of hail unleashed themselves on the village, leaving holes the size of dimes in the burgeoning hosta, and flattening whole groves of trillium and Solomon's seal. Seedlings keeled over in the mud, and Winnie Ivey's hens and chicks scattered for high ground.

Mitford was driven indoors for three days running, to watch the mildew make its annual invasion of basements, bathrooms, and closets.

It was Tuesday morning before the village awoke to a dazzling sunrise, clear skies, and balmy temperatures. The foul weather, however, lingered on in his secretary.

"If I ever read another word about Hessie Mayhew's Lady Spring, I'll *puke,*" Emma said.

"Did Harold get his potatoes in?"

"Got 'em in, watched 'em slide off the side of the mountain. Along with his peas, beans, squash, and onions."

"A regular blue plate special."

"I haven't heard you talk about a garden this year. Too busy, I suppose." Emma gave him one of her unmistakable looks-with-a-message.

"Not at all. We're filling out a couple of beds with purple foxglove, lupine, cosmos . . . let's see, delphinium, Canterbury bells, a dozen astilbe . . ."

"Humph. Astilbe. Too feathery for me. I'll take a good, hardy marigold any day."

"To each his own," he said mildly.

"That was some shindig at your place."

He had wondered when she would at last bring up the social event that was still the talk of the town. "So I hear."

"Cynthia did a good job."

"Thank you. I hear that, too."

"A little too much sugar in the lemon squares."

"I see it failed to sweeten your disposition."

"Ha ha. What do you think about your kitchen walls being banged up with a hammer?"

"The best thing to happen to the rectory since Father Hanes installed a fireplace in the study."

"I didn't think you'd go much for that deal."

"I hope you know the ruined look is the very thing to give mundane surfaces a mellow, weathered appeal. Take your old villas in Italy, for example, where the plaster is put on thickly, without superficial concern for perfection, where the surfaces ripple and change like . . . like life itself . . ."

She peered at him over her glasses.

". . . where buildings shift and settle with the passage of years, where a century is but a fleeting moment in time . . ."

"I get it!" she said, wanting him to stop at once.

". . . where decades of smoking olive oil and burning wood wash the walls with a palette of color as subtle as the nuances of old stone or ancient marble—where, indeed, the very movement of light and shadow are captured in the golden glow of the walls, grown as redolent with history as trade routes worn by ancient Romans. . . ." He had no idea what he was saying, but he was enjoying it immensely.

She stared at him with her mouth slightly agape.

That ought to fix her.

When Cynthia wasn't bending over the drawing board with her elaborate wooden box of watercolors, she was laying a flagstone walkway through the hedge. This time, he couldn't claim ineptitude. It was down in the dirt with his wife, or else.

She was wearing one of Dooley's baseball caps, a T-shirt, blue jeans, and out-at-the-seams tennis shoes. Given how youthful she was looking and what he was thinking, he could be jailed for a violation of the Mann Act.

"I'm packing for your camping trip," she said, huffing a heavy flagstone into the hollow he'd just dug with a shovel and edger. He would have huffed it in himself, but she preferred her way of placing the stones.

"So it's my camping trip, is it?"

"Well, yes, I would never in a hundred years do this on my own."

"What are you packing?"

"Colored pencils, Snickers bars, and a change of socks and underwear."

"That ought to do it," he said, trying not to laugh.

"What are you packing?"

"They're bringing the food, so we're traveling light. Tent, flashlight, emergency candles, matches, bottled water, a Swiss army knife, an iron skillet, a coffeepot, coffee, fire starter . . . ah, let's see . . . inflatable pillows, ground cover, lantern, sleeping bags, bandages, toilet paper, dried fruit and nuts . . . what else? A canteen, fishing poles, bait, talcum powder, mosquito repellent, Band-Aids, sunscreen, and, oh, yes . . . a bucket to put the fish in. Ah, I just remembered—an egg turner to flip the fish in the skillet. And cornmeal, of course. Can't fry fish without cornmeal."

"We'll need a U-Haul," she said, muscling the stone around until it pleased her.

"We're going to pack it in to the campsite."

"You do have someone meeting us there with *a team of mules*?"

"You're looking at the team," he said, pleased with himself.

"Do we really need all that for one night?"

"They've asked us to stay two nights."

"Timothy!"

He rolled his eyes and shrugged.

"Oh, well," she said, wiping her forehead with the back of her garden glove. "Dig this one a little bigger. See that stone? It needs to go in next, I think. What do you think?" She sat back on her heels.

"Perfect."

"It will be lovely not to get mud on our shoes when we pop through the hedge."

"I'll say."

"Timothy, dearest, do you like being married?"

"Married to you, or married in general?"

"In general," she said, watching intently as he dug the hollow.

"I do. Very . . ." he searched for the right word, "consoling."

"Lovely! Now, do you like being married to me?" He looked down upon her sapphire gaze under the bill of the baseball cap and squatted beside her.

"Words fail," he said, meaning it. The scent of wisteria floated out from her like scent from a bush in an old garden.

"I want to be your best friend," she said.

"You are my best friend."

"You can speak your heart to your best friend," she said.

"What is it you want me to say?"

"I want us to talk about our future. It really doesn't matter if you don't know what you want to do, or when. It would be lovely just to talk, to have it out in the open. I can't bear that closed place in you. It's like coming up to a gate that's been locked, and the key thrown away."

"Perhaps we all contain gates that have been locked."

"Perhaps," she said.

He wanted to stand up again and turn away from her and go on with their work. Wasn't that what they'd come out here to do? But he sat down in the grass and looked at her across the half-finished walkway. He was grateful for the shade because he felt warm, and suddenly peevish.

Katherine had taken it upon herself to counsel him before he got married, whether he needed it or not. "First and foremost," she had said in her salty way, "communicate! If Cynthia wants to talk, Teds, you'd better hop to it. Communicating is everything, painful as it may be. Trust me on this."

So far, so good. But he wanted to draw the line somewhere. He wanted to draw it right here and right now—but he sat and faced her, making the effort.

"I don't want to talk about it," he said, finally.

"I know." She sat, too, and took off her work gloves.

There was a long silence, filled with the chatter and song of birds. A junco dipped through the air and vanished into the hedge. They heard a neighbor's phone ring.

A nap, he thought. A nap would be the very thing. Why this Puritan work ethic pumping through them like so much adrenaline? Hadn't they come and gone through the hedge with perfect ease for the last two years? So what if they got their shoes muddy once in a blasted blue moon?

"You're angry," she said.

Yes, he was. And he didn't like it. "What good can it do, talking of something I don't know anything about? We came out here to work, why not work?"

"Lord," she prayed aloud, "will You please help us through this?"

His heart was hard toward her, something he hadn't experienced since they married, and wanted never to experience. It felt like the time she had mentioned marriage—only mentioned it. His heart had turned to stone, and remained stone for weeks on end.

"There's your gate," she said. "I'm right up against it, and it's still locked."

More birdsong. A car passing on Wisteria Lane.

"You'll have to do the talking," he said, "because I don't know what to say. I don't have a clue."

She looked at her hands, a little furrow between her brows. He thought she was weighing whether it was worth it to try and figure out their future.

"All that really matters about our future," she said, "is that we're together. I mean that with all my heart. I feel so puzzled about why you shut down like this—why does this wave of coldness seep out from you when there's any mention of your retirement? Oh, rats, Timothy, why does it have to be complicated? All I want to know is . . .

"... are you going to preach 'til you keel over? Will we someday have our own home? Have you thought where we might live?"

"I mean," she said, waving her arm toward the new flower bed, "should we be planting all these *perennials*?"

He stared at the row of astilbe. "I don't know. Why do I have to know?"

"Ummm," she said, looking at him. "This is going nowhere."

"So let's get back to work." He got to his feet and picked up the shovel.

What had happened? They had been working together as one flesh and one spirit, laying one flagstone walkway to link two houses. And then it had all come apart.

They were silent as they placed the remaining stones.

He felt oddly embarrassed at his hardheaded behavior, behavior that even he didn't truly understand.

They were an hour out of Mitford, headed north to the campsite, when a drumming rain began. It transformed the overloaded van into an odorous cocoon on wheels. A radio report guaranteed the downpour would last through the morning and well into the afternoon.

Turning around and going back was loudly argued among eight teenagers.

Bo Derbin, who had a surging, but nonetheless repressed, attraction to Lila Shuford, would have none of turning back. He imagined himself swinging on a vine across a broad creek or tributary, to rescue her from a human savage raised by wolves.

Avoiding eye contact with his wife, the rector voted to press on. Larry declared he had no intention of doing otherwise.

They pressed on.

Eight teenagers with lower lips they might have tripped over was not a pretty sight.

"Oh, pipe down!" yelled Larry, clipping along at the front of the line as they hiked into the woods in a persistent drizzle. Though known for not taking any flack from the youth group, he was nonetheless their hands-down favorite leader, not to mention an Eagle Scout, an Orvis fly-casting school graduate, and onetime wrestler of a grizzly bear.

"When we get there," shouted Larry, "the sun will be shining, the fish will be biting—"

"And the ground will be sopping!" he heard Cynthia mutter.

Sopping was right. The ground at the campsite was like okra that had been boiled and mashed.

He had never seen his wife look so pathetic, though she didn't utter a word of complaint. The kids, on the other hand, howled and grumbled. They wanted Nintendos, they wanted TV, they wanted a bathroom with a lock on the door.

But they hadn't come two miles from civilization and forty miles from Mitford to coddle themselves.

"Strip bark!" commanded Larry Johnson, who was humiliated to find he'd forgotten the Coleman stove.

"Strip . . . *bark*?" said Cynthia.

In the rector's opinion, that was where the whole thing began to slide downhill.

He knelt by the sleeping bag, which, like a bicycle, was built for two.

He had endured some discomfort with the salesperson when he bought the thing in Holding, but spreading it on the ground in front of God and everybody had been worse.

The kids had snickered, Larry Johnson had cocked his eyebrow like some two-bit actor, and Cynthia had been bashful as a girl. The heck with it, he thought, unzipping his side at a little after ten o'clock on Friday night.

So what if he had forgotten the tent poles and they had no earthly cover from whatever the weather might bring? So what if they were lying out in the open like so much carrion for wolves, bears, or worse, wild boar?

He glanced around the campsite, making certain no one watched as he slithered in beside his slumbering wife. Clearly, no one cared.

Larry Johnson was playing a final tune on his guitar, which, thanks to the dense humidity that followed the rain, sounded precisely like rubber bands stretched over a cigar box.

Cynthia had almost completely enveloped herself in the bag, leaving only her nose in view. The thought of sleeping on the ground with but a thin cover under them and nothing above them had stunned her—no two ways about it. It had put a positive curl in her lip that he didn't believe he'd ever seen before.

In the end, however, the fresh air worked wonders. After crawling into the bag a little before eight-thirty, she had gone out like a light.

He drew her close, feeling how much she meant to him, and how like his own body her sleeping form seemed to be. One flesh! There were miracles in that phrase, in that unfathomable concept. He realized he sometimes felt attached to her like a Siamese twin, joined at the heart or the groin, the shoulder or the spleen.

How had he lived so long without this vital connection in his life? Where had he been all these years? How had he gotten by before he was married?

He couldn't reckon how it had been before. It was as if he'd always lain with her in this sleeping bag built for two, spooning like a farmhand, inhaling her warmth. What power it must have taken to draw him out of himself, he thought with wonder, out of his endless surmise, out of his inward-seeing self, into such a union as this.

"How lucky you are!" people continually said to him. But, no. There was never any time he thought of it as luck. Luck! What was that, after all, but so much random good fortune? It was grace, and grace alone that brought Cynthia's body close to his, made them this single mystical flesh that, once laced together like brandy in coffee, could not be riven apart—even by the world and its unending pressures.

He closed his eyes and thanked God for the crucible of peace and laughter and love that lay beside him, snoring with the galvanized precision of a chain saw.

"Lila Shuford!" yelled Larry Johnson, beating on a skillet with an egg turner. A pitiful fire crackled in a ring of rocks.

"Here!"

"Lee Lookabill!" More beating.

"Here!"

Murky sunshine. Birdsong.

"Luke Burnett!"

He sat up in the sleeping bag and looked at his watch. Five after six. He hadn't slept this late since his honeymoon. Cynthia rolled over and peered at him as if he were a Canadian moose who had stumbled into camp.

"Cynthia Kavanagh!"

"Ugh!" muttered Cynthia, sitting up in a T-shirt from The Local, which was printed with a huge yellow squash. "Here, for Pete's sake!"

He reached for the camera in his duffel bag, but not before she slammed his wrist with a karate chop.

"Do it and die," she said, meaning it.

"Rats. I was going to put it on the parish hall bulletin board. Enlarged."

She grinned, surprising him entirely. "Actually, that wasn't so bad," she said, stretching. "Except I feel bruised all over. Were we sleeping on a *rock*?"

"You *slept* like a rock, I know that."

"I remember when you crawled in here with me, but I played like I was asleep. I was furious. But I'm over it."

"You knew nothing when I got in here with you. You were snoring with the might of a top-of-the-line fellerbuncher."

"What in heaven's name is that?"

"You don't want to know," he said, slithering out of the bag.

"Clarence Austin!"

Birdsong.

"Clarence! Rise and shine!"

"Clarence ain't here," said Lee Lookabill.

"Where is he?"

"I ain't seen 'im."

"Take Henry Morgan and find him," said Larry. "Bo Derbin!"

Muted laughter from the three girls who had slept under a quilt tied to four poles.

"Bo! Snap to!"

"Bo's not here," said Lila Shuford.

"Where is he?"

"He slipped off, we saw him. He went with Clarence. They've been gone a really long time."

"Prob'ly takin' a leak," said Lee Lookabill, trying to be helpful.

"Move it," Larry told the search party, "and while you're at it, strip more bark. We've got grub to cook." The rector thought Larry looked like he'd just wrestled with yet another grizzly.

"Gross to the max," muttered Cynthia, remembering last night's chicken à la king, which had come packaged in industrial-strength brown plastic.

"You're losing your vocabulary out here in the woods. Didn't you like your peach bar?"

"I hated it. I was too hungry to wait while it soaked in water, so I ate it dry. It's still reconstituting in my stomach."

"And the peanut butter. I thought you loved peanut butter."

"Can you imagine having to *knead* your peanut butter in the package before opening it? And what was that they gave you to spread it on, a flagstone for the path through our hedge? I'm so starved, I could eat a helping of moss. What's in that package you had left?"

He picked it up and squinted at it. "Sugar, salt, chewing gum, matches, and toilet tissue."

"Yum," she said, slithering out into the chill morning air. "Let's save that for afternoon tea."

Lee Lookabill lost his glasses while stripping bark, and Henry Morgan returned with a report.

"We cain't find Bo 'n Clarence, and Lee's done lost 'is glasses and cain't hardly see to walk back. I thought I stepped on 'em, somethin' crunched, but it was a stick."

"Fine!" snapped Larry. "Luke, go back with Henry and help Lee find his glasses. Tim, Cynthia, look for Bo and Clarence. They can't be far. Tell 'em I said they're in deep manure. And remember—step *on* a log, not over it."

Larry squatted over the smoking fire with a skillet, trying to dignify a cement-colored block of hash browns, as the rector and his wife vanished into a thicket.

Cynthia pulled on blue jeans and a denim shirt. He got into jeans, also, and hiking boots, leaving on the turtleneck he'd slept in, and adding a corduroy shirt. The air was damp and cool from yesterday's rain, and the skies again appeared overcast.

"I'll take my day pack. We might see something worth drawing." She pulled her blond hair back and whipped a rubber band around it.

"I don't think this is a drawing trip."

"You never know," she said brightly. "Besides, I think it has two candy bars in it."

"Ummm. No substitute for Percy's poached eggs with a side of grits."

"Dearest," she said, looking at him sternly, "we didn't come on this trip to coddle ourselves."

Give his wife a little time and a good night's rest, and she could bounce back with the best of them, he thought with pride.

"Bo!" he called as they stepped into a clearing in the woods. "Clarence! Give us a shout!"

"You want me to whistle?" asked Cynthia.

"Whistle?"

"Like this," she said, piercing the air with a note so high and shrill, it might have dropped the Chicago Bulls in their tracks.

"Good Lord!" he said, holding his ears. "Where did you learn to do that?"

"When I was eleven. I was in a girls' club and we all learned to do something boys did. Phyllis Pringle learned to shoot marbles, Alice Jacobs took up the slingshot, and I learned to whistle."

"Aha."

"Want me to do it again?"

"Well . . ."

She did it again.

"You're strong stuff, Kavanagh," he said with admiration.

They heard the answering whistle reverberate in the woods.

"Listen!" she exclaimed.

"Sounds like it came from over there."

They sprinted into the clearing and were nearly across when they saw Bo and Clarence emerge from the woods.

"Man!" shouted Bo. "You won't believe this!"

"It better be good," said the rector, meaning it.

Clarence pointed toward the trees. "There's a big cave in there!"

"Huge!" announced Bo. "And scary, too. Clarence was too chicken to go in, but I did, and you won't believe it!"

"You can believe Larry Johnson will strip your hide for leaving camp like this."

"Let's go see it," said Cynthia.

"No way," said the rector, herding the boys toward the clearing.

"Oh, please, Timothy! Where is it, Bo? Is it far?"

"It's just right in there. I was coming out when I heard you whistle. Clarence can't whistle—it was me who whistled back."

"I can too whistle!" said Clarence.

"It's right through there," said Bo, "behind that big rock. Just go in behind that rock and you'll see this *hole* in the side of the hill, kind of covered up with bushes and stuff."

"Did you see any bats?" asked Cynthia.

"Nope. Just heard water dripping, and saw all those weird things sticking up."

"Stalactites," said the rector. "Or is it stalagmites?"

"Timothy, dearest, just five minutes? The boys can go back and we'll follow right behind. I've never seen a cave. Five minutes, I promise!" She looked imploring.

"Well . . ." he said.

"Wonderful!"

"Straight across the clearing, hit the trail to the left, and be quick about it," the rector told the boys.

Clarence looked disconsolate. "Larry's prob'ly goin' to whip our head."

"*C'est la vie.* Get moving."

"We're right behind you!" called Cynthia as the boys sprinted away.

Father Tim cupped his hands to his mouth. "And stay together!" he shouted.

It was a word of caution he'd soon have to reckon with himself.

"Uh-oh," said Cynthia, staring at the nearly hidden opening in the side of the hill.

"What do you mean?"

"That hole! I can't go through that hole like some rabbit into a burrow."

"But you love rabbits."

"Rabbits, yes, but not burrows."

He had once seen her crawl on her hands and knees into Miss Rose Watson's minuscule play hole in the attic of the old Porter place, entirely without a qualm.

"So let's head back," he said. "I'm famished."

"Well . . . but I've never seen a cave. Let's at least have a look."

She climbed the short ascent to the hole, swept aside the weeds and brush, and peered in. "It drops straight down and then flattens out. I can't really see anything."

Personally, he didn't want to see anything. He had no interest in disappearing into a hole in the ground that was hardly bigger around than he was.

His stomach growled. "Remember what happened to Alice in Wonderland. . . ."

"Ummm," she said, sticking her head in the opening. "Ummm."

Which was it, anyway? Did stalactites go up or down? Tite. Tight. Tight to the ceiling! That's what his seventh-grade teacher, Mrs. Jarvis, had said when they studied Mississippi caves, and then actually took a bus trip to a local cave. Stalactites hang down, mites stick up! Anita Jarvis. Now, there was a force to reckon with. . . .

"The tites hang down!" he said aloud, looking up as Cynthia's head disappeared into the hole.

He scrambled after her. "Cynthia!"

"Slide in feet first, Timothy. That's the way to do it!"

He did it.

He might have been dropping into a tomb, for all he knew. What if there should be a landslide, a mudslide, any sort of shift in the terrain? The hole would be blocked until kingdom come. He felt his heart pound and his breath constrict.

He slid along the muddy entrance shaft on his backside and landed on his feet behind his wife. Enough light streamed into the mouth of the cave to illumine part of the large chamber in which they stood. It resembled a subway tunnel, long and rather narrow, and he was able to breathe easily again, sensing the space that opened up around them.

Odd, how the air was different. He could tell it at once. He felt the moisture in it, and smelled the earth. Like his grandmother's basement, except better.

"Are you OK?" he asked, noting the absence of an expected echo.

"Wonderful! This is too good for words! A glorious opportunity! I've got a flashlight in here somewhere." She fished in her day pack. "There!"

The beam from the flashlight snaked up the wall. "Good heavens! Look, dearest! It's a whole rank of organ pipes!"

"Limestone. Limestone does this." The vast wall might have been formed of poured marble, richly tinted with rose and blue, and glistening with an omnipresent sheen of moisture. He had never before observed what God was up to in the unseen places. A fine chill ran along his right leg.

The beam of light inched up the wall, shining palely on formations that appeared to be folds of draperies with fringed cornices, overhanging an outcropping of limestone as smooth as alabaster.

"Heavens!" gasped Cynthia. He slipped his forefinger into the band of her jeans as they inched along the chamber wall, looking up.

"Look!" she said. "There's just enough light to see how the ceiling of this thing soars—it's like a cathedral.

"Can you believe we're under the crust of the earth, possibly where no one has ever been before, except Indians? And who knows how old this cave is? It could be millions of years old, maybe billions. . . ."

"Hold the light close to your face for a minute," he said.

"You're interested in seeing another ancient formation, I presume?"

"Your breath is vaporizing on the air."

She turned around and shone the light toward him. "And so is yours! But it doesn't feel cold in here."

"Not cold. But different."

Cynthia strode forth again, at a gallop.

"Hey! Are you going to a fire, Mrs. Kavanagh? Slow down."

"But we only have five minutes. . . . Yuck! Mud. These shoes will be history. I never have the right shoes for anything. When I was in New York last year in the blizzard, I only had *pumps*—"

"What's that?" They stopped, and he turned and listened. It sounded like water dripping. Here. There. At random. Everywhere. Water falling on water. Plink. Plink. Plinkplink.

"Obviously, there's water in here," he said. "Watch your step. Maybe we shouldn't be going in so far."

"Just two more minutes," she said, shining the light on the wall that curved ahead of them. "There! See that? Doesn't it look just like the rib cage of a dinosaur?"

"Spoken like the woman who once spotted Andrew Jackson in a cumulus cloud."

She placed her hand on the limestone wall that rippled with smooth, undulating forms. "Feel it, Timothy. It's so strange to the touch. Slick. Wet. But friendly, somehow, don't you think?"

"Ummm." Larry Johnson would have that slab of potatoes browning to a fare-thee-well. A little green onion in the mix wouldn't be bad, either, not to mention a sprinkle of the Romano cheese he'd carried along in a sandwich bag. It didn't take Ecclesiastes to know there was a time to seek nourishment and a time to explore caves.

"Time to go," he said firmly.

"There at the end of the passage, dearest. See? It looks like a huge urn, doesn't it, sitting in that vault? How extraordinary, all these wonders that remind us of things on top of the earth—and yet, surely all this came long before cathedrals and urns."

"Listen, people are depending on us. We've run off exactly like Bo and Clarence did, and Larry will not like this one bit. You talk about getting our head whipped . . ." He took her arm.

"What are you doing?"

"We're turning around and going back the way we came."

She sighed. "You're right, of course." They turned and began walking. "I was going to sketch something while you held the light, but I suppose there's not time."

"Darn right. How's the battery in that thing? It looks weak."

"It's just that this place is so huge and so dark, it absorbs the light."

"Let's hope so."

"I guess I'm ready to get out of here, too. I'm starved, not to mention freezing. Are you freezing? Suddenly, it's . . . like a grave in here."

"Kindly rephrase that."

They walked in silence, shining the light along the walls on either side. He had no memory of the little cave in Mississippi looking anything like this; in fact, he remembered being pretty bored with that field trip. The most vivid memory of it was the picture someone took of him with Anita Jarvis, who was nearly as wide as the bus. He had tried to flee the camera, but she grabbed him by the ear and yanked him back, while everyone laughed their heads off. He had wanted to tear the resulting snapshot in a hundred pieces, but was so entranced with having a picture of himself, even with Anita Jarvis, that he couldn't do it.

"I've got an idea," she said. "Why don't we stop and turn the light off? I'd love to see how dark it really is in here."

"Cynthia, Cynthia . . ."

"It will only take a minute. Then we'll go, I promise."

"Well . . ."

Bright, unidentifiable images swam before his eyes, then gradually faded, leaving a velvet and permeating darkness.

He thought he heard her teeth chattering. "Maybe I should turn the light back on."

"Wait," he said, touching her arm. "Our eyes are just starting to get adjusted." They stood together in silence. "I think this place is totally devoid of light," he said at last. "We're in complete and utter darkness. Amazing."

"Scary."

"Don't be scared. I've got you." He put his arm around her shoulders, noting that the musical sounds of water-on-water seemed louder than before.

"I'm glad you're here," she whispered.

"I'll always be here."

"You will? Do you mean that?"

"Of course I mean that. I took a vow on it, for one thing."

Some fragment of a poem came swimming to him, something, he thought, by Wendell Berry: ". . . and find that the dark, too, blooms and sings." What was it about this darkness, the particular, nearly tangible density of it, and the odd sense that he was somehow blending into it?

"Why can't we see light from the mouth of the cave?" Cynthia asked.

"I don't know. We were standing in the light only a minute ago."

"We can't have walked completely away from the light that was coming through the hole." She switched on the flashlight, which glimmered on columns of roseate limestone.

"This isn't the way we came," she said. "We haven't seen these before."

"We must have missed a turn." He puzzled for a moment, rubbing his forehead and feeling disoriented. "You were hauling along there pretty good."

"You get in front and haul, then," she said testily.

"OK, let's retrace our steps and watch where we're going." But they had just retraced their steps. . . .

In less time than it might have taken to recite the Comfortable Words, they'd been thrown off kilter. He felt for a moment as if his mind had walked out on him.

They had begun to move in the opposite direction when the light faded, glimmered weakly, and failed.

"No," she said, as the darkness overtook them. "Please, no."

CHAPTER TEN

The Cave

"PRAY, Timothy!"

"I am praying. Keep moving. We're bound to come back to the light from the entrance."

"Are you sure?"

"Positive."

"It's so terribly dark. Don't you have some matches in your shirt pocket? I thought campers always took matches."

"No matches."

"Don't lose me, Timothy."

"I won't lose you. Hang on to my belt; we're doing fine. The wall is leading us."

"The flashlight battery . . . I haven't used that flashlight since I moved next door and the electricity went off. I'm a terrible partner."

"Careful. Slippery here. Feels like . . ."

"Water," she said. "We're stepping in water. It's soaking through my tennis shoes."

He stopped. They hadn't come through water before. His heart pumped like an oil derrick. It wasn't the darkness, exactly, that was disconcerting. It wasn't the sense of being hemmed in by walls of limestone on either side. No, the worst of it was the sudden sense of being turned around, of having no idea at all which way was north, east, south, or west. It was as if the beaters of a mixing machine had been lowered into his brain and turned on high.

"I'm terrified," she said, clinging to his back. Whatever he did, he must not let her sense his own fear.

Something like light flickered at the periphery of his vision.

"Light!" he said. "I saw light."

"Where? Thank God!"

He blinked. Then blinked again. But it wasn't light at all. He realized his nervous system was generating neural impulses that resulted in the strange, luminous flickers.

"Wrong," he said. "Something's going on with our vision. It's still adjusting."

"Poop!" she said with feeling.

The sound of dripping water was random, but constant, and now he realized it was dripping nearby.

Were they standing in a puddle they had stepped through before without noticing, or something they had walked around and missed entirely? "Wait here," he said. "I'm going to see if this stuff gets deeper."

"Don't leave me!"

"I'll be only inches away. Let me check it out."

"I'll come with you." She dug both hands under his belt and hung on.

The water definitely got deeper as they stepped forward. Then the wall on either side ended, and his hands were suddenly groping thin air. He sensed they might be entering a large chamber at the end of the passage.

"We're turning back," he said evenly.

"We keep turning back—and turning around! I'm so confused."

"Hang on." Dear God, what was a complete turn when you could see nothing? Had he been misjudging their turns? Had he been making half turns that sent them off along some other route? Why hadn't they crashed into something?

They turned slowly, as one, and began walking. He kept his hands out, feeling for the wall that had been within reach only moments ago.

There! He felt the sweat pour from his body, followed by a stinging chill as it met the cool air of the cave.

"Keep your left hand in my belt and put your right hand on the wall, and don't take it off, even for a moment. We'll come back to the light, I promise. There's no way we can't." His voice was about to gear down into the croaking mode, and he mustn't let her hear that. In him, croaking was a sure sign of depression, anger, or fear, and she knew it.

They hadn't been in here long enough for Larry Johnson to be worried. Knowing Larry, he probably thought the newlyweds were off doing a little hand holding, and he'd give them plenty of time to enjoy it.

"I'm thirsty," she said. "Stop and let me take the day pack off. I think I've got a bottle of water."

They stood with their backs to the damp wall, and she found the bottle and shook it. "There's not much left. The flashlight . . . the water. I can't do anything right."

"So, what did I come off with? Nothing. You get extra points."

She unscrewed the cap and reached for his hand and gave him the bottle.

"No," he said. "You first."

"I think you should be first. You're the leader."

"Drink," he said. She took the bottle and drank, and passed it back to him. There wasn't much left, but he drained the bottle and felt revived.

"Why don't I scream for help?"

"Not yet. We can find our way out." Who would hear them if they yelled their heads off?

"I forgot you're one of those men who won't stop at a service station and ask directions."

"There are no service stations anymore," he said unreasonably. "Just places to buy hot dogs and T-shirts and pump your own."

"We should be screaming our heads off. Someone will be looking for us, Timothy. They'll hear us."

He stuffed the empty bottle into her pack. "Save your breath. We've only been in here ten minutes." Had it been ten minutes? Twenty? An hour? He couldn't see his watch. He had never bought a watch with an illuminated dial, thinking it an unnecessary expense. After all, who needed to know what time it was in the dark, except when one was in bed? For that, there was the illuminated face of the clock on his nightstand.

"I hate this," she said, whispering. "It's horrid. We're sopping wet all over."

His unspoken prayers had been scrambled, frantic. He needed to stop, take a deep breath, and state it plainly. He put his arms around her and she instantly recognized the meaning of his touch and bowed her head against his.

"Father, Your children have stumbled into a bit of trouble here, and we're confused. You know the way out. Please show it to us. In Jesus' name."

"Amen!" she said, squeezing his arm.

"That's the ticket."

He wanted to stand there for a moment, collect his thoughts, get a real sense of the place. Maybe that would help, maybe that would give them some idea of what to do next. They had raced into this place, after all, like two heedless children, then panicked and gotten wildly confused.

Stop. Slow down. That was definitely the answer.

He drew a deep breath. "Actually, this is the way a lot of people live their lives."

"What do you mean?"

"Never knowing, in the dark, constantly guessing. It's the guessing that's the worst."

"Always working, dearest."

"Sermons are everywhere," he said.

"Speaking of guessing—you've been guessing, haven't you, about the way to get back to the entrance?"

Why lie? "Yes."

She was silent for a time. "We can't possibly be far. It seemed so simple when we came in, just a long room with that vault thing and the urn."

"Right," he said. "We can't be more than a few yards from the entrance. If it were a snake, it would bite us."

"Did we turn right or left at that vault thing?"

"Right. We went around the corner, and there were the dinosaur ribs. . . ."

"The dinosaur ribs came before the vault."

He made a conscious effort not to sigh, and put his arm around her shoulders. "Let's chill to the next episode, dude."

"What kind of talk is that?"

"That's Dooley's new foreign language, in addition to French. Let's take a couple of deep breaths and go from there."

"I feel as if every crawling thing ever created is lurking in here."

"Anything lurking in here is blind—if that's any comfort."

"Blind?"

"All creatures who live in caves are blind."

"That makes sense, I suppose. I mean, what good would it do them to see?"

"I learned that in the seventh grade when we went on a bus trip to a local cave. I wanted to hold Justine Ivory's hand while we were standing by the blind trout pool, but I didn't have the guts."

"In the seventh grade, you wanted to hold hands?"

"Didn't you?"

"Absolutely not. I fell in love with Russell Lowell in the fifth grade, got my heart broken, and didn't even think of boys again until high school."

"Different strokes . . ."

He visualized Larry running this way right now, with the entire pack at his heels. Hadn't Bo said the cave was scary? And big? And the opening half-covered by brush? That wouldn't sound good to Larry Johnson, who was pretty savvy about things of the woods.

On the other hand, what if the boys couldn't find their way back to the cave?

"Oh, Lord, Timothy! Gross! Vile! Get it off me!"

"What?" he said, his heart thundering.

"Something fell on my head, oh, please, oh, no, it's running down my neck, oh, get it off . . . !"

"Water," he said stoically, feeling a large drop crash onto his own head and roll down his back.

"Are you sure? Run your hand down my back."

It had hit with such force, it must have come from a great distance. "Water," he said again, smoothing her damp shirt.

"Timothy, we've got to get out of here. We can't just stand around talking about the seventh grade!"

"Did you say you have candy bars in your day pack?"

"Snickers. Two." She turned her back to him and he reached into the pack and felt around among the colored pencils and the sketchbook and the dead flashlight and socks, and found them rolled up in her underwear.

He didn't know why it swam to the surface at just that moment, but he remembered Miss Sadie's story of falling in the well, of the darkness and her terrible fear, and the long night when no one seemed destined to find her because of the rain. The rain had destroyed the scent for the bloodhounds. What if it were raining out there again, erasing their scent?

But he was making mountains out of molehills. Good Lord, they'd been fumbling around in here for only ten or fifteen minutes, and already he was calling in the bloodhounds.

His adrenaline had stopped pumping, and he felt exhausted, as if he wanted nothing more than to lie down and sleep. He ate two bites of the candy, wondering at its astonishing sweetness, its texture and form, the intricate crackle of the paper, and the way the smell of chocolate intensified in the darkness.

"Please don't eat the whole thing." She had seen him in a diabetic coma once, which had been once too often.

He put the rest of the bar in her day pack, realizing he felt completely befuddled. He didn't want to press on until the sugar hit his bloodstream.

"I'm going to start walking," she said impatiently.

"Which way?"

"To my right. That's the way we were going when we stopped to reflect on our early love interests."

"We were going to your left. I was ahead of you, remember?"

"I thought I was ahead of you. No, wait. That was before."

"Trust me. We go this way. Grab my belt and hold on."

"I think it's time to scream. In fact, I think we should scream now and walk ten paces and scream again, and so on until someone comes or we see the light."

"Have at it," he said tersely.

She swallowed the last bite of her Snickers, then bellowed out a sound that would have shattered the crystal in their own cabinets, forty miles distant.

"How was that?" she wanted to know.

"You definitely get the job of screaming, if further screaming is required."

"Every ten paces," she said, feeling encouraged. "You pray and I'll scream."

"A fair division of labor." He was feeling the numbing cold, now, and the dampness of his clothes. Didn't the French keep wine in caves because of a mean temperature in the fifties? This felt like thirty degrees and dropping.

"Five, six, seven . . ." said Cynthia.

His foot met thin air. He pitched wildly to the left, banging his head on a sharp object, and fell sprawling.

Was it blood, or mud, or the moisture that covered everything in this blasted place?

Blood. Definitely. He felt the sharp sting as he rubbed his fingers over the gash.

"Are you all right?" He heard the fear in her voice.

"I'm OK. Just a knock on the head." He was struggling to find the breath that had failed him.

"Let me help."

"Don't move!"

Her voice seemed to come from somewhere above him. He reached up, feeling nothing but air, then touched a flat rock. He inched his hand along the edge, and found the tip of her shoe. "You're standing on some kind of ledge. Back up a little, and take it easy."

"Timothy . . ."

"Don't panic. I'm fine. I'm telling you, we've got to be right at the entrance. We'll be out of here in no time. Stay calm."

"Let me give you a hand."

"Back up and stay put."

He grabbed the ledge and hauled himself up. He had fallen only a couple of feet, thanks be to God.

Lord, You know I'm completely in the dark, in more ways than one. I don't have a clue where we are or what to do. I know You're there, I know You'll answer, give me some supernatural understanding here. . . .

He stood up and leaned against the wall, and reached for her, and found her sleeve and took her hand. He had lost all sense of time. *A thousand years in Thy sight are but as yesterday when it is past, and as a watch in the night. . . .* Was he being introduced to something like God's own sense of time?

"I'm going to scream again."

"Don't," he said, meaning it.

"Why not, Timothy? People will be looking for us. We'll never get out of here."

"Turn around."

"Turn around? Again? We're so turned around now we can't think straight. We've turned around and turned around, 'til we're fairly churned to butter!"

"Clearly, this is not the way. It vanishes into thin air."

He stepped around Cynthia, and she tucked her hands into his belt.

The sugar was beginning to work. He felt suddenly victorious as he moved along the wall, his wife attached to his belt like a boxcar to an engine.

He walked more quickly now, his hands never leaving the wet surfaces on either side. There. That felt better. His adrenaline was definitely up and pumping.

"We're out of here!" he whooped. He reached up and brushed away the blood that was running into his left eye. A handkerchief. In his pocket. He took it out, still walking, and patted it to his forehead.

When he put it in his pocket and reached for the wall on his left, he groped air.

"Why did you stop?" she said.

"The wall just ran out on the left. Maybe that's another passage. Maybe that's the way we came before I crashed. Hold on, we're backing up."

He took two steps backward and found the wall on the left, and examined it with his hand. Did it end abruptly or did it curve around?

It curved around. A fairly gentle curve. If they had come through this passage to where they were standing now, they might easily have continued around the curve to their right, which had pitched him off the ledge.

What if he left her here and explored the passage? Perhaps just around the turn, he would see light from the entrance. Or what if they both explored that passage? But they could be stumbling along passages until kingdom come. Who would have thought that an innocent-looking hole in the side of a hill might lead to such unutterable complexity?

Mush. His mind was mush.

"We need to stop again," he said.

"Why stop again? You said we were going out of here."

"We are. But we need to stop and think, right here where these two passages converge. We've got to think."

They sat with their backs to the wall, and he put his arm around her to warm her, and pulled her to him. He felt the cool slime of mud under them, but he didn't care.

In his life, he had never confronted anything like this. He had never been to war, he had never been in peril, he had never even gone to the woods and lived on berries like Father Roland once boasted of doing. No, he had lived a sheltered life, a life of the soul, of the mind, and what had it gained him in the real circumstances of day-to-day living?

He had spent nearly forty years telling other people how to live in the light, and here he was, lost in a complex maze in the bowels of the earth, in total, devastating darkness.

For no reason he could have explained, he thought of his father calling him into the house that summer night, the night the chain had broken and he had walked his bicycle home from Tommy's house.

"Timothy." The kitchen light was behind his father, throwing him into silhouette at the screen door. He had looked up and been frightened instantly. The silhouette of his father was somehow larger than life, immense.

"Yes, sir?"

"Come in and tell me why."

Come in and tell me why. He would never forget that remark. What did it mean? He knew it had something to do with why he could never do anything right. He had stood there, unable to go in, frozen.

His father had opened the screen door and held it, and he walked inside.

He saw the look on his mother's face. "Don't hurt him, Matthew."

"You're crying," Cynthia whispered, wiping the tears from his cheek. He hadn't known he was weeping until she touched his face. It was as if he stood nearby, watching two people sitting on the floor of the cave, holding each other.

"Dearest . . ." Cynthia whispered, stroking his arm.

The self who stood was humiliated that the priest had broken down and broken apart. The priest who would do this under pressure was a priest who could not get it right.

"I can't get it right," he managed to say, as if repeating some unwritten liturgy.

Unwritten liturgy. All these years, he had spoken the written liturgy, while underneath . . .

"Almighty God, to You all hearts are open, all desires known, and from You no secrets are hid. . . ."

I can't get it right.

"Holy and gracious Father, in Your infinite love You made us for Yourself. . . ."

I can't get it right.

"It's all my fault," she said. "I was the one who insisted we come in here. I led us on a merry chase and brought that no-good flashlight. . . . You mustn't blame yourself."

He didn't want to weep like this, but there was nothing he could do about it; he felt as if he'd broken open like a geode.

"I'm sorry," she said. "Please forgive me."

"He couldn't tolerate anything that wasn't perfect."

"Who, dearest? What . . . ?"

"That's why he was enraged when something broke. It had to be fixed at once—or thrown away. There was a terrible pressure to keep things from breaking, to keep them like new. Mr. Burton's tractor broke down along the road from our house. . . . Mr. Burton pushed it off the road and left it in the field for days. My father never passed that tractor without lambasting the owner's incompetence."

"Ah," she said, quietly.

"I can't retire," he told her. Why had he said that? . . . like a geode.

"Tell me why."

"The way things are, they're running smoothly, most of the bases are covered. I'm trying to get it right, Cynthia. I can't stop now."

"But you have got it right, Timothy."

He didn't want to be placated and mollycoddled. He drew away from her, and she sat in silence.

He was hurting her, he could feel it, but here in this total, mind-numbing darkness, he could not summon what it might take to care. Out there in the light, out there where his ministry was, he could always summon what it took to care.

"Listen to me, dearest, and listen well." He had heard knives in her voice once before, when he'd drawn away from her prior to their marriage. It was knives he heard again, but they were sheathed, and he leaned his head against the cold wall and closed his eyes.

"I lived with Elliott for seventeen years, always trying to get it right. When I tried to kill myself and it didn't work, I remember thinking, I can't even get this right. Elliott was never there for me, not once—he was out making babies with other women, trying in his *own* confused way to get it right. During those long months when I was recovering in a friend's house in the country, God spoke to my heart in a way He hadn't spoken before. No. Erase that. He made me able to listen in a way I couldn't listen before.

"He let me know that trying to get it right is a dangerous thing, Timothy, and He does not like it."

His head pounded where the blood had congealed. "What do you mean?"

"I mean that getting it absolutely right is God's job."

The cold was seeping into him. He was beginning to feel it in his very marrow. He also felt the loss of her living warmth, though she was right beside him. He drew her to him and took her hands and put them inside his shirt and held her. She was shaking.

"Must I remind you that your future belongs to God, and not to you? Please unlock your gate, Timothy. Leave it swinging on the hinges, if you will. This thing about our future must go totally out of our hands. We cannot hold on to it for another moment."

He smiled in the darkness. "Don't preach me a sermon, Mrs. Kavanagh." The weeping had stopped, but the geode lay open. He felt a raw place in himself that seemed infantile, newly hatched.

He stood up and helped her to her feet. He was stiff in every joint, but stronger.

"I think I should take this passage and check it out. I won't go beyond the range of your voice, I promise. Maybe I can see light, maybe this is the way."

"Don't leave me, Timothy."

"I promise I won't go beyond the range . . ."

"I'll come with you."

"I feel you need to stay here and be the compass. If I don't turn anything up, I'll pop right back. We're not far from the opening. We can't be. Besides, I know Larry, and he's starting to get worried, maybe even ticked off, for Pete's sake. One way or the other—"

"Timothy . . ."

"Yes?"

"You have your fears, I have mine. Don't leave me." Her own geode had come apart; he heard her panic.

"But I don't know what's along that passage. Why should we both take the risk?"

"You could go pitching headfirst into God knows what, you might not . . ."

"Might not what?"

"Might not come back."

"Of course I'll come back. I'll test every step I take."

"The buddy system—they say to always use the buddy system. We're stronger together, smarter. If we only had something to scatter as we go, like bread crumbs. But then, we couldn't see them. . . ."

Why hadn't they left something at the entrance of the cave, some sign that they'd gone in, like the nearly empty water bottle or a candy wrapper? It might have said, *If you find this, we're still in here. Start the search.*

Stay calm was still the directive. They couldn't go blasting down every passageway that presented itself. Light! If only he had the tiniest flame, the barest flicker of illumination, he would fall to his knees in thanksgiving.

In Him was life; and the life was the light of men. And the light shineth in the darkness; and the darkness overcame it not. . . .

He refused to fear this thick, palpable darkness. As far as he knew, God had not drawn the line on caves. He hadn't said, *I'll stick by you as long as you don't do some fool thing like get lost in a cave, you poor sap.* What He had said was, *I will never leave you. Period.*

"Trust God!" he blurted to his wife.

"Don't preach me a sermon, Father Kavanagh. I am trusting Him, for Pete's sake. It's you I can't get a bead on. Are we going or coming?"

"Definitely going. Let's tuck along this passageway for a bit. I won't take a step I haven't tested first. I'll keep my left hand on the wall and my right hand in front of me. Hang on. And no backseat driving, thank you."

They moved carefully around the curving limestone wall with its thrusting formations.

" 'I cannot see what flowers are at my feet,' " she murmured, " 'nor what soft incense hangs upon the boughs, but, in embalmed darkness, guess each sweet wherewith the seasonable month endows.' Who said that?"

"Will Rogers!"

She laughed. "One more guess."

"Joe DiMaggio?"

"Keats!"

"Aha."

"How's it going up there?"

"Ummm. Same old, same old. But no mud. Feels like we're walking on dry clay. Does that ring any bells as to our previous sojourn?"

"I can't remember," she said. "Our sojourns all run together like so much goulash."

He was feeling more closed in than he had before, when his hand suddenly struck something in front of him. It was a wall of sheer limestone with—he moved his cold hand over it as someone blind might examine a sculpture—with a swollen formation attached to its surface.

It was another of those columns, perhaps, something like a great elephant trunk. He turned slowly to the right, reading the wall with his hands. More columns.

The columned wall, he found, continued around in a U curve.

It was a moment before he told her what neither wanted to know.

They had reached a complete dead end.

CHAPTER ELEVEN

Darkness into Light

HE FELT as if the circuits had gone down in his brain.

No logic, no reason, no common sense had worked to lead them to the opening. Every turn had been a wrong turn. Every decision had been fruitless. It was maddening.

Dear God! Now what?

The darkness seemed to fall like a heavy curtain over his mind.

"If we go back the way we came," he said, forcing himself to think rationally, "we'll come to where we were sitting. We know that turning right isn't the way; that's where I fell off the ledge. So, let's retrace our steps and turn left."

She was trembling as he put his arm around her shoulders.

"We can't be far from the opening," he said. "We're going to find it, I promise. Besides, Larry won't let this go on much longer. Hang on."

She tucked her hands into his belt and they began the return trek.

He was blasted sick and tired of this everlasting fumbling around in the dark. Where in God's name was Larry, anyway? Putting a fly in the water and showing off the cast he learned from his Orvis seminar?

His thirst was becoming hard to ignore, and he realized how seductive the dripping water sounded. He saw them down on their hands and knees, lapping at a puddle like Barnabas and Violet. But what might the water contain, what could limestone do to the human system, what algae or larvae might be lurking in it?

"I'm so thirsty," she said, as if reading his mind. "Are we almost there?"

"The wall is beginning to curve a little, I think." Would they recognize the curve, the place where they'd been sitting, or go careening around to the right until he fell off the ledge again? Good Lord, why hadn't they marked the place they'd sat, left something there as a touchstone?

"Here. I think we're here." That was the thin slime of mud they'd been sitting on, wasn't it? Something was squishing under his shoes. It might have been a light in a window, for the moment of warm familiarity it kindled in him.

"How are your feet?"

"Frozen," she said.

"We're turning left. Hang on."

"You're sure? You're positive this is the way?"

"Positive." He wasn't positive.

Except for the time they had sat by the wall . . . when? How long ago? Twenty minutes ago? Except for that time, they had been constantly on the move, battling their fear, struggling to make sense of this mind-altering confusion. His knees felt weak—or was it the numbing cold and dampness that was seeping into their very bones and slowing them down?

Now. They were back to a passage he could touch on either side, thanks be to God!

"Soon," he said, hearing the despair in his voice, "we'll be at the opening. We just took a couple of wrong turns."

"Right."

He heard the echoing despair in her own voice.

He didn't try to imagine how much time had passed.

He leaned against the day pack, using it as insulation between his back and the damp cold of the wall, and held her tightly between his legs.

They had groped along an endless passage strewn with boulders and low shelves of limestone, which banged up their knees and twice sent him sprawling. At a pool of water, they stopped and made the decision to go no farther.

"I think we should wait it out," he said, edging back from the pool. "We need to stop moving, and let them find us." How much deeper had they gone in, struggling to find their way out?

She didn't speak.

Exhausted, they sat away from the water, under a ledge, and prayed silently.

He felt as if they had become part of the cave. The damp cold had made such a thorough invasion of their bodies that their nervous systems had slowed to a crawl. It wasn't cold enough to freeze them to death, he reasoned, but it was blasted cold and dark and still enough to numb every limb, not to mention the mind.

Leaning with her back against his chest, she rubbed his legs and ankles, and he rubbed her arms and shoulders for warmth.

His throat was as parched as if they'd wandered the desert. Couldn't he scoop up the water in one hand, and with the other examine it for living things? He did not want to gulp down an eel or a worm or whatever else might live in these waters, and though his wife had remained substantially calm until now, straining a wriggling organism through her teeth would not improve matters.

What was going on out there in the world, anyway, where people were free to move around and look at trees and hear the call of other human voices? The kids couldn't find the cave, he was convinced of it. Furthermore, it was almost certainly raining, and no trace of their scent remained on the ground.

Drops of moisture hit the pools, plink*plink*plink. He felt a sudden shortness of breath and a racking, intense thirst.

He sat up and pulled the bag to his side and reached in and found the bottle. He also found the two soft bundles she had tucked next to her pencil case. Socks!

"Put these on," he said, handing her a pair.

It was difficult to draw his feet from his shoes, as most of the feeling had gone. The good news was, his socks were still dry, thanks to the investment he'd made in the boots. Her socks, however, were sopping. "Put on both pairs," he said.

"No, dearest. You—"

"Please mind your priest."

She pulled his feet into her lap and massaged them briskly, and put his socks on again. Then she rubbed her own feet and pulled on the dry socks. "Heaven," she murmured.

"I'm going to get water," he said.

"But—"

"How bad can it be?"

She thought a moment. "Maybe we could scoop some into our hand and feel if there's anything in it."

"Whatever."

"Don't leave me!"

"It's just over there, for Pete's sake."

"Just over there? Where is just over there? We thought the opening was just over there."

"Cynthia . . ."

"I'm coming with you."

"Hitch on, then."

They crawled the short distance to the pool, feeling their way, the smell of damp earth in their nostrils.

"It smells clean," he said. "That's one thing I can say for this place. And the air . . . no sneezing, no sinus drainage."

"No exhaust fumes, no pollen!" she said, catching the spirit.

He splashed his hand into the edge of the pool. Then, pushing up his muddy sleeve, he slid his hand into the water and tested the depth. It dropped off steeply. Thank God they hadn't bungled their way into it.

"Do you feel anything moving?"

He didn't. He scooped water into his cupped hands and recklessly drank it. Good Lord! Sweet. Sweet as sugar! It went down his throat in a great, healing stream. He scooped some more and drank.

"It's OK, you can drink it! Move up to the edge, but be careful. This pool could be pretty deep."

He splashed water into his mouth with the palm of his hand. Then he bent his head to the pool and drank freely, feeling the mentholated coolness of the water against his face, and the drops from above splatter on his back.

"Oh," she said, simply, weeping with relief as she drank.

It was as if God had touched them, instilling a new, raw hope.

They crawled back to the dry pack, and he fetched the bottle to the pool and filled it and put the cap on, and returned to where she sat under the ledge.

"Why don't I start screaming?"

"Give you a little refreshment and you're off again," he said.

"I mean it, Timothy. It would be such a help to whoever is looking for us."

"Well . . ."

He held his ears, and she screamed.

"Well done!"

"I'm going back to the screaming program. I don't care what you say."

"So be it," he said. "Let's get warm."

She crawled into the embrace of his legs and arms, and pulled her own legs under her chin.

"Thank God Sophia and Liza are looking in on Barnabas," he mused. "He's probably dragging them around the town monument as we speak."

"And Liza's loving it!"

"I like the way you smell," he said, burying his face in her hair. Even in this dark, damp place that reeked only of earth, he inhaled the faintest scent of wisteria.

"Tell me something."

"What?" she asked.

"Why are you especially afraid of being left?"

There was a long silence. He listened to the musical drip, dripping of the water, calling upon every discipline to avoid the sheer panic that lay beneath the surface of his outward calm. They should be finding their way out of here, executing some rationale that he couldn't seem to get a fix on. But no, stumbling around hadn't worked, he had to fight the fear with everything in him and stay exactly where they were until help came.

"Because I was always being left by someone. My mother and father . . . and then Elliott."

"Tell me about it."

"Well, you see . . ." She hesitated, then went on. "I remember when I was in fourth grade and Mother and Daddy were to pick me up from school. Except . . . they never came."

"Never?"

"I waited out front until all the buses had left, and Miss Phillips stayed with me. Then everyone left, and we went back inside and stood by the windows in my classroom and watched for them to drive up."

She trembled slightly.

"They . . . never did come. Miss Phillips called our house over and over, but there was no answer, so she took me home with her."

He kissed her hair.

"Miss Phillips kept calling, but there was no answer, and I remember she made grilled cheese sandwiches and hot cocoa, and finally I did my homework and we went to bed. I slept on her sofa and her cat curled up beside me—his name was Alexander, as in Alexander the Great. We got up the next morning and I put my clothes back on and we went to school, and I was afraid people would know that I hadn't been home, that Mother and Daddy . . . At recess, Miss Phillips said Mother called to say they'd been . . ."

He waited.

". . . detained."

The water dripped all around them, and he was glad for the ledge that kept them dry.

"I don't know why I remember that particular thing."

"I'll never leave you," he said, holding her.

"Not even to explore a passage?"

"Not even for that," he said.

She had fallen asleep in his arms, and he sat with his eyes open, staring ahead, not wanting to miss the light when it came.

The feeling of panic had wondrously left him, and in its place had come an odd and surprising peace. Somehow, he wasn't afraid of this place anymore. He could wait.

A line from Roethke surfaced in his mind: *In a dark time, the eye begins to see.*

It was as if he were drifting through space, and every care he had was reduced to nothing. What were his cares, anyway? They were few. So few. Who cared where they put the linen closets in Hope House? He had cared very much out there in the light, just as he had cared about Sadie Baxter hanging up her car keys, and Buck Leeper coming to terms with his Creator, and Dooley Barlowe growing up and having a life that no one could take from him, no matter what.

He had cared that Lord's Chapel was running several thousand dollars behind budget, and that two of his favorite families had gone over to the Presbyterians for no reason he could understand. It was his job to care, but what he was beginning to understand, sitting here in this unspeakable darkness, was that God cared more.

Whether Tim Kavanagh cared wasn't the point, after all, and whether Tim Kavanagh was in control didn't matter in the least. God was fully in control—firmly and finally and awfully—and he knew it for the first time in his heart, instead of in his head.

He felt himself smiling, and wondered at the laughter welling up in him, like a spring seeping into a field where the plow had passed.

But he wouldn't wake her, not for anything, and he pushed the laughter back, and felt its warmth spreading through him like the glowing of a coal.

"Father?" he whispered.

Come in and tell me why. . . .

"I love you," he heard himself saying. "I forgive you. It's all right."

Cynthia murmured in her sleep, and the surge of inexpressible tenderness that stirred in him was unlike anything he'd known before.

He sensed that everything was possible—yet he had no idea what that meant, nor what everything might be.

Maybe he, too, had fallen asleep and was dreaming.

But he wasn't dreaming.

He heard it again—a kind of woofing or huffing. He sat, frozen, afraid he had imagined it.

Woof, woof!

"It's Barnabas!" he shouted. It was the mighty voice of a Wurlitzer, it was the voice of angels on high, it was his dog!

He heard himself yelling in odd harmony with Cynthia's ear-splitting scream, their voices raised in a single, joyful invective against the primordial dark.

The miner's lamp attached to his collar wildly illuminated the walls as Barnabas licked every exposed part of their bodies, pausing only to bark for the rescue team.

The faces of Larry Johnson and Joe Joe Guthrie finally bobbed toward them under hats with miner's lamps.

"Lord have mercy, are y'all OK?" yelled Joe Joe, tripping over the long rope leash they'd anchored to Barnabas.

"Fine! Wonderful!" shouted the rector.

"I ought to kick your butt," said Larry Johnson, meaning it.

They stumbled out of the opening into the light, which issued from a ring of lanterns and the flash of J. C. Hogan's Nikon.

J.C. walked backward as they advanced from the cave, shooting at close range, and crashed into the underbrush.

Cynthia, who was covered with mud from head to toe, embraced various members of the exultant youth group and shouted, "Hallelujah!"

"What time is it?" asked the rector.

"Ten o'clock!" announced Bo Derbin, proud to be asked. "We thought Indians were living in that cave and had scalped you or made you their slaves."

Mule Skinner appeared, carrying a lantern. "Lord help, look at that gash on your head! I hope you're up to walkin' th' two miles out of here. We got to get you to th' hospital."

"We're fine," he said. "No harm done!"

"We was goin' to radio for a helicopter in case you was in *real* bad shape," said a police officer, who appeared disappointed.

Father Tim felt positively humiliated by all this ruckus. Not only had he and Cynthia spoiled the camping trip, they'd brought out the police and the press, who, worse yet, had to hump it on foot across two miles of rough terrain.

"Cave!" said Larry Johnson. "That's all I had to hear. I gave you an hour and we started looking. We called and hollered, then went a little ways in and poked around, but couldn't see for squat, even with a lantern and flashlight. I walked out to the van, drove to the nearest phone, and called Rodney."

"I was down at th' station chewin' th' fat when Larry called," said Mule. "I told 'em how my daddy was lost in a cave in Kentucky, and they like to never found 'im 'til they sent in his Blue Tick hound. So Rodney collected th' boys and went to your house and got Barnabas."

"A stroke of genius."

Larry leaned close to the rector's ear. "I hate to tell you that Rodney took a wrong turn outside Farmer and every one of 'em were lost as the tribes of Israel for two hours."

"We followed Barnabas as hard as we could go," said Joe Joe. "The way he tracked you, y'all must've been runnin' around in there like chickens with their heads cut off."

"Tell me about it," said the rector.

"Actually," Cynthia informed J.C., "it was a very *interesting* experience. So sorry we alarmed everybody."

"Want my last package of peanut butter?" Lee Lookabill asked Cynthia.

"If you'll *knead* it first, I'll eat it," she said. "I never thought it would come to this."

Rodney Underwood looked at the rector sternly and hitched up his holster belt. "I don't know when I've had to fool with a man who was lost in a cave. I just radio'd th' county sheriff. He says this cave is totally unexplored."

"Not anymore it ain't," said Mule, grinning proudly.

Emma Newland was making her pronouncement.

"Anybody who'd step *foot* in a cave *deserves* to get lost!"

"It was a very interesting experience," he said, quoting his wife.

"Interesting? With *bats* swarmin' around your head, and steppin' in water out th' *kazoo*?"

"We never saw a bat, actually."

"Never *saw* a bat? That's where bats *live*—in *caves*!"

"So sue me," he said.

Merely walking out the door of the rectory was invigorating. It was as if he'd come back from the grave, given the dazzling, living energy of every green thing he saw.

He had escaped the tomb, and felt his spirit quicken in response. In a way, it was his own Eastertide.

"Lost in a cave?" said Bill Sprouse, who passed him on the way to the Grill. "That'll preach, Brother, that'll preach!"

"For you," said Percy, "a dollar off th' special."

"Why a dollar off?" He was leery of Percy's specials.

"You been lost in a cave! You're a big gun!"

He grinned. "Big gun, is it? Well, then, bring on the special."

"Velma," Percy called to his wife, "th' Father'll have th' special! Coffee's on th' house."

"What, ah, is the special?" he inquired.

"Grilled horned toad on a bed of fresh mustard greens," said Percy, looking solemn.

"Give me a side of salsa with that," replied the rector.

Percy doubled over with laughter, slapping his leg. Clearly, the week that Percy and Velma had spent in Hawaii last summer was still working wonders with the proprietor's sense of humor.

"You got lost in a dern *cave*?" Dooley yelled into the phone.

"Totally!" Where Dooley Barlowe was concerned, only the bald truth would do. "Completely!"

"Totally, completely lost? Man!"

"Want to do it sometime?"

"What? Get lost in a cave? No way."

"You don't know what you're missing," he said.

"Did ol' Cynthia get scared?"

"Terrified."

Dooley cackled. "Did you get scared?"

"What do you think?"

"I think it scared th' poop outta you, is what I think."

"You hit the nail on the head, buddy."

Dooley Barlowe sounded as if he were rolling on the floor. Maybe, just maybe, hearing Dooley laugh was the payoff for that miserable experience.

A dollar off a horned toad that turned out to be tuna salad, and a ripping good laugh out of Dooley Barlowe. . . .

So far, so good, for a couple of hours spent stumbling around in the dark.

When he arrived home at five-thirty, he thought he had never smelled such a seductive aroma in his life, though something in his stomach was definitely off.

"Leg of lamb!" exclaimed Cynthia.

"Man!" Sometimes there was nothing else to do but quote Dooley Barlowe.

"And glazed carrots, and roasted potatoes with rosemary."

"The very gates of heaven."

"Dearest," she said, putting her arms around his neck, "there's something different about you. . . ."

"What? Exhaustion, maybe, from only four hours of sleep."

She kissed his chin. "No. Something deeper. I don't know what it is."

"Something good, I fondly hope."

"Yes. Very good. I can't put my finger on it, exactly. Oh. I forgot—and a salad with oranges and scallions, and your favorite dressing."

"But why all this?"

"Because you were so brave when we were lost in that horrible cave."

The payoff was definitely improving. He brushed her hair back and kissed her forehead. "It wasn't so horrible."

"Timothy . . ."

"OK," he said, "I was scared out of my wits."

She laughed. "I knew that!"

"You did not."

"Did so."

"Did not."

"Are y'uns havin' a fuss?" Uncle Billy peered through the screen door.

"Not yet," said the rector. "Come in and sit!"

"I cain't. I dragged m'self down here t' give you m' tithe, as Rose is on to me akeepin' it in th' newspapers. She's done gone through a big stack alookin' for it, don't you know. It's a scandal what a man with a little cash money has t' put up with, ain't it?"

"I don't have a clue, Uncle Billy. I never had much cash money."

"I hear you'n th' missus was lost in a cave. I got lost in a cave when I was a boy. Hit's somethin' you don't never forget. Them red Inyuns that roamed these mountains, they knowed caves like th' back of their hands, but th' white feller cain't hardly go a step without broad daylight in 'is face."

"That's a fact," he said.

"I hear your dog pulled you out, or y'uns might've been in there 'til Christmas."

Barnabas, who was lying under the kitchen table, thumped his tail on the floor.

"He's the man of the hour, all right," said the rector, stepping outside. "They say he led them straight to us, nearly a quarter of a mile in. We got to bed about three o'clock this morning."

"I hope y'uns didn't drink no water while you was in there."

"Why's that?"

"Oh, law, that cave water can send you high-steppin', don't you know. It don't hit you right off, might take a while, but let them cave germs git t' workin', and first thing you know . . ." The old man shook his head, grinning.

"Uncle Billy, would you do us a favor?" Cynthia asked through the screen door.

"If they was anybody I'd do a favor, hit'd be you 'uns."

"Would you take the nice, fresh chocolate cake Esther brought today? We can't touch a bite. We'd just have to throw it out."

"Oh, law!" said Uncle Billy, stricken at the thought. "Me an' Rose'll be glad to take it off y'r hands if hit'll help y'uns out."

"Thanks be to God!" she said when Uncle Billy left with his foil-wrapped parcel. "If he hadn't taken it, I would have eaten the whole thing! I would have absolutely stuffed it in my ears."

"Dodged a bullet," he said, feeling his stomach wrench.

She sat down suddenly in a kitchen chair.

"What is it? You're white as a bed sheet."

"I don't know. Oh, dear. Oh, no!" She bounded from the chair and sprinted down the hall to the guest bathroom, clutching her stomach.

His own stomach gave a loud, empathetic gurgle, signaling what he recognized as a dire emergency.

"Cave germs!" he shouted, racing upstairs.

Dog Rescues Rector and Wife

Lost Fourteen Hours

In Hidden Cave

He peered at the latest edition of the *Muse.*

That Cynthia Kavanagh looked terrific, even when smeared with mud from head to toe, was no surprise.

As for himself, his face looked oddly like a turnip that had just been yanked from the ground. Worse yet, the photo of them staggering out of the cave was shot at such close range, he could see the whites of his own eyes. Not a pretty sight.

The photo of Barnabas, on the other hand, was snapped from such a great distance that it appeared to be a ground squirrel that had led the rescue team.

He fogged his glasses, wiped them on the lapel of his old burgundy bathrobe, and scanned the story.

He had *not* said they found the fossil remains of a dinosaur, much less discovered a *vase* in a vault.

And he certainly didn't care for J.C.'s insinuation that all they'd done was sit around eating candy, waiting to be rescued.

In any case, he made a mental note to pick up extra copies of the paper for Walter and Katherine, and one for Father Roland in Canada, all of whom were patently wrong to believe he led a rustic and uneventful life.

The mayor called at five a.m. and asked him to hotfoot it to the hospital, where Puny's labor was intense, and they were worried.

He had barely skidded into the deserted hallway when Nurse Herman found him and steered him toward the delivery room.

"I can't go in there," he said.

"Why not?" demanded Nurse Herman. "Everybody else does. It's the latest thing to watch the birth."

What could people be thinking, to stand around and watch babies being born, as if the whole affair were some daytime TV show? Didn't they have anything else to do, like mow their lawns or work for a living?

"Besides, th' mayor wants you to pray," said Nurse Herman.

He ran a finger around his collar, which suddenly seemed constricting. "I can do that standing in the hall!"

Esther Cunningham opened the door and poked her head into the hallway. "There you are!" she snapped, as if he had taken hours to arrive. "One just popped out, it's a girl, we're on a roll."

Nurse Herman shoved him into the room, where he saw Joe Joe sitting by Puny, her sweat-drenched red hair spread over the pillow. Joe Joe's mother, Marcie Guthrie, stood across the room covering her face with her hands, but observing the proceedings through her fingers. At the sink, a nurse cleaned up a red-haired infant, who was crying lustily.

"Bear down!" said Joe Joe.

"Pray!" said the mayor.

"Breathe!" said Dr. Wilson.

"Oh, *Lord*!" said Marcie Guthrie.

The mayor's husband, Ray, leaned unsteadily on a chair, wearing a look of mortified horror.

"Ray's not up to this," said the mayor, "but it's the latest thing to do, and he likes to keep current."

The rector thought the whole event was closely akin to a political barbecue.

"Here it comes!" shouted Esther.

"Hallelujah!" whooped Marcie.

"It's a girl!" announced the doctor.

"Catch him!" cried Nurse Herman, as the rector toppled toward the floor.

"Sissy and Sassy?" he inquired.

"It's really Kaitlin and Kirsten," said Puny, smiling hugely. "But we decided to call 'em Sissy and Sassy." She was holding one infant on either side. The whole lot had mops of red hair like he'd never seen before in his life.

"Which is, ah, Sissy and which is . . . ?"

"This," said Puny, shrugging her right shoulder, "is Sissy. And this," she said, shrugging her left shoulder, "is Sassy. You'll get to know 'em apart when they come to work with me."

"Take your time on that," he said, meaning it. "No hurry. Why not take a month? Or take two—we can manage!"

Puny looked at him, wide-eyed. "We'd never pay our bills if I laid out for a month or two! You know that bathroom we added on, our *own* self? It cost four thousand dollars, and that's without a toilet! Lord only knows when we can git a toilet!"

"Aha."

"They say you fainted when Sassy popped out!"

"Went black," he said, grinning. If Nurse Herman hadn't snatched him up, he might have cracked his skull on the tile floor.

"Don't y'all worry about a thing," Puny assured him. "I'll be back in two weeks, good as new."

He gazed at the new mother and her little brood, feeling a glad delight for the young woman who had taken over his home and his heart, all to his very great relief.

"You're the best, Puny Guthrie."

"I'll bake you a cake of cornbread first thing," she said, smiling happily.

He had never bought a toilet before, but after some discussion about a wooden, plastic, or soft seat, and the new, economical tank capacity, he decided on a standard model and, to save the delivery fee, had it put in his trunk in two boxes and drove it to the Guthries' little cottage, where, with no small difficulty, he wrestled the boxes out of the car and onto the porch, and assembled the thing on the spot with the aid of his auto repair kit.

He couldn't help but observe, as he drove away, that it had a certain panache sitting there.

He sat up in bed and listened. Was it the wind? The shadows on the ceiling weren't moving.

In the hall, Barnabas growled.

"What is it?" Cynthia asked.

"I heard something."

She sat up with him.

Someone was knocking at the door. Barnabas raced down the stairs and stood barking in the foyer.

When he reached the foyer, he turned on the porch light, grabbed his dog by the collar, and opened the door.

As long as he lived, he would never forget what he saw.

It was a girl, he knew that from the long blond hair that fell over her shoulders, but she had been beaten so brutally that her face made little sense to him.

"Good God!" he said.

She fell toward him, and he saw the smear of blood in her hair.

"Lace Turner," she murmured.

It was the girl who had jumped from the tree and landed at Absalom's feet, the girl who had stolen the ferns and run.

CHAPTER TWELVE

Lace

BARNABAS BARKED wildly as the girl leaned against Father Tim to steady herself. "I got t' lay down som'ers."

He gripped her arms and drew her into the hallway. "You're OK," he said, his heart thundering. "I've got you."

"Git that dog away from me."

Cynthia appeared on the stairs. "Who is it?"

"It's a girl. She's badly hurt. Put Barnabas in the garage."

"Dear God!"

"I'll take her to the study."

Her knees gave way, and he moved to pick her up. "Don't touch m' back!" she cried. "Git me laid down." The look of appeal on her face was crucifying.

"Put your arm over my shoulder," he said. "I'll help you walk."

"I cain't. It pulls m' back."

Together, he and Cynthia eased her along the hall and into the study. "Quit . . . jigglin' me," Lacey murmured through bruised lips.

As his wife hurriedly spread an old blanket over the sofa, he became aware of the strong scent of blood and body odor, and something unidentifiable that wrenched his stomach. He sensed that it was, somehow, the smell of violence itself.

"Lay me down easy."

"Right. Easy does it."

She cursed as they helped her down. "Not on m' back!" she said. "On m' side."

The blood on her arms had crusted, but fresh blood appeared to be coming from her head, staining her hair at the crown.

"I'll call Hoppy," he said. "She needs a doctor."

"Don't call no doctor!" yelled Lacey, trying to raise her head. "Don't call no doctor, I don't need no doctor—"

"You're badly hurt."

"I been hurt worser. I ain't killed."

"You could be hurt internally."

"I ain't, I know m'self. If you call a doctor, I'm leavin'. Wash me off, git some salve on m' back."

"Can you do that?" he asked his wife.

"Yes," she said, looking pale. "Get hot water and soap and clean rags—those old diapers I use to clean silver. And bring the peroxide—and the bandages."

"Done," he said, going from the room, shaken.

They sat in the study with a single lamp burning against the dark.

Cynthia had bathed Lacey's wounds and patiently worked the fibers of her shirt from the raw flesh on her back. She had cried out only once when the peroxide was swabbed into the swelling lesions, and said nothing as Cynthia applied an antibiotic ointment and bandages.

He made a strong, dark tea with sugar and lemon, and Cynthia spooned it onto Lacey's tongue, avoiding her swollen lips, then helped her lie again on her side, covered with a light blanket. She was silent, except for occasional sharp intakes of breath through her teeth.

He looked at his wife, sitting on a footstool drawn close to the sofa, and saw the suffering in her own face. She was moved to tears or laughter with nearly anyone at all, being as open as a door to the feelings of others.

"You're safe here," she told Lacey. "I want you to know that."

The girl nodded.

"How did you come to us?"

"Ol' Preacher Greer. I met 'im in th' road here lately. He said if I was ever to git bad hurt, run to th' preacher in th' collar, he takes in young 'uns."

"Did you know," asked the rector, "that the preacher in the collar was the same person you saw in the ferns?"

"I tol' Preacher Greer I couldn't run t' you, you'd done caught me stealin'. He said go on, anyway, he'll he'p you."

"You were brave to come to a strange house in the night," said Cynthia.

"I was s' skeered of Pap, it didn't make no mind t' me where I hid at. Preacher Greer wouldn't tell me wrong, so I come. Always before, I run t' Widder Fox, but she went off to th' ol' people's home. You cain't tell nobody I come here, or Pap'll lick me worse'n this."

"Why did your pap lick you, Lacey?"

"I don't go by Lacey, I go by Lace."

"Lace, then," said Cynthia. "Why did your pap lick you?"

" 'Cause he was drunk and you cain't say nothin' to 'im if he's drunk. I knowed better, I should've hid under th' house or som'ers, but he come in th' house s' quick, I couldn't do nothin'. I quit diggin' ferns and rhodos, is what it was, an' he seen m' sack was empty. Two or three times, I repented of stealin' an' quit, and ever' time, he licked me bad.

"Me'n Jess is got t' dig twenty-five fern and sixteen rhodo a week when th' weather's good, and I ain't dug my half n'r nowhere near. So he said he was goin' to knock m' teeth out to where I couldn't eat nothin', as I wadn't doin' my part t' earn nothin' t' eat, then he took off 'is belt and got me with th' buckle. He was goin' to beat m' head in, but I give 'im m' back or he'd of killed me."

"Your mother . . . can't she do something?"

"M' mam's got a blood ailment and cain't git outta th' bed. She lays there and hollers f'r 'im t' quit, but he don't."

His heart weighed in him like a stone. "Are you hungry?" he asked.

"I ain't eat, but I ain't hungry, neither. M' head's asplittin'."

"The capsules I gave you should help," said Cynthia. "Lace—please let us take you to the doctor, we'll pay for it, and there's no need for your father to know—"

"I ain't goin' t' no doctor—no way, nohow," she said, and sucked in her breath.

"The guest room . . ." said the rector. "We could put her in bed so she can sleep."

"I cain't sleep. I got t' git back by daylight."

"You mustn't go back. You're in no condition—"

"I got t' feed m' mam. She won't eat a bite f'r nobody but me. M' pap, he'll be sleepin', an' Jess won't do nothin'. My mam'll die 'ithout me, she said she would."

"I don't think you should get up and go anywhere," said Cynthia. "There must be someone who can take care of your mother while you—"

"They ain't nobody, an' I ain't stayin'!" Lace said vehemently. "Leave me be 'til I can git up an' go, an' I don't aim t' argue about it, neither. I hate town people. I hate th' guts of town people. You talk stupid." She cursed again, with the same feeling he had heard in Buck Leeper.

"We'll sit with you," Cynthia told her.

Like he had sat with Buck Leeper last year, through Buck's suffering. Unable to walk away, he had stuck with Buck's rage and lasted it out.

The clock ticked in the silent room as the hands moved slowly toward one in the morning.

Lord have mercy, he prayed silently, *Christ have mercy . . .*

He dozed in the chair until five-thirty, when he heard Cynthia in the kitchen and went in and called Rodney Underwood at home.

Lace had slept fitfully, occasionally talking in her sleep or waking and asking for water. At a little past six, he helped her up, and she sat on the edge of the sofa.

He placed his hands on her head gently, over the place that had bled, and prayed for her. It was madness to let her leave, but her determination to go to her mother was final and complete; he felt the sheer, unswerving power of it.

Cynthia wiped the girl's face with a damp cloth, helped her swallow hot cocoa from a spoon, then knelt to put her shoes on.

"I've brought you some socks," Cynthia said.

"I don't want no socks. Pap'll be wantin' t' know where they come from."

"You'll need peroxide and ointment on your back every day for a while. Can you come and let me treat you?"

"They ain't no way."

"Will your father be up when you get home?"

"He'll lay asleep 'til up in th' day, but my mam, she'll be needin' me. She'll want 'er egg and coffee, she cain't go 'ithout it."

"Your school . . . is it over yet?"

"I don't go t' no school. I laid out s' long, they come lookin' f'r me, but Pap told 'em I'd went t' Tennessee t' live with 'is kin people."

He saw the pain in Cynthia's face as she tied the laces of the battered work shoes. "I've packed your breakfast. There's hardboiled eggs and rolls and bacon and fruit and cheese. You must eat, Lace, and keep your strength."

"If I git a notion. . . ."

They helped her up and led her through the kitchen, where he opened the screen door and held it. "What can we do?" he asked, hoarse with feeling.

"Nothin'. I thank you f'r washin' me an' all."

Cynthia touched the girl's hand. "Come back, Lace," she said.

"Anytime," he added.

They watched her go across the yard, walking as if bent with age. She passed through the hedge that gave way to Baxter Park, and vanished in the cool morning mist.

They stood silent, then turned back to the kitchen, where they poured coffee and sat at the table.

Cynthia put her head in her hands. "We lead a sheltered life, Timothy . . . out of the fray."

"The fray," he said, "has come to us."

According to Rodney, he'd have to go to social services and file a statement that Lacey Turner said she was being battered. A law enforcement officer could go along to investigate, but that was up to social services.

When he finally found the right office in Wesley and told what he knew, the social worker said matter-of-factly, "It happens all the time."

"How long will it take you to investigate and get back to me?"

"I'll put the report in today. Depends. Five days, a week at the most."

A week. Someone could be killed in a week.

He felt useless, impotent—stupid, somehow, like Lace Turner had said.

Dooley would be home from school in a matter of days. He'd ride down with a boy and his family on their way to Holding, and be delivered to the rectory. A blessed relief, given the demands of Cynthia's new book and his own commitments, which included plans for a surprise celebration of Miss Sadie's ninetieth birthday, to be held in the parish hall Sunday after next.

There was no question in his mind that a blowout was in order.

Hadn't Sadie Baxter given five million dollars to Lord's Chapel, to build one of the finest nursing homes in the state? And hadn't her father, and then Miss Sadie herself, kept a roof on the church building throughout its long history?

He called the bishop, to ask whether he could attend, but Stuart Cullen had no fewer than four events on the Sunday in question, all of them miles from Mitford.

"Emma," he said, "call the entire parish and tell them they're invited."

Emma's lip curled. "Call th' whole bloomin' mailin' list?"

"The whole blooming list," he said, his excitement mounting.

"That's a hundred and twenty households, you know."

"Oh, I know." He was pleased with the number, especially as it had risen by seven percent in two years, even with the recent loss to the Presbyterian camp.

"I suppose you realize that nobody's ever home anymore, to *answer* the phone."

He couldn't argue that point. "So have cards done at QuikCopy. But you'll have to get them in the mail no later than tomorrow. Oh. And remember to say it's a surprise."

"It's certainly a surprise to me."

"When we get our computer," he said jauntily, "it'll knock the labels out in no time. Until then . . ."

She glared at him darkly. "I'll have to address every blasted one by hand."

"Every blasted one," he said, swiveling around in his chair and dialing Esther Bolick. This was an occasion for a three-tier orange marmalade cake, and no two ways about it.

"Have you found out anything?" he asked the social worker. It had been only four days since he had filed the complaint, but it didn't hurt to ask.

"I can't say. I haven't seen anything on it."

"Have you investigated?"

"The person responsible for the investigation isn't in today. You'll be advised as soon as possible."

"I'll call back," he said.

Cynthia agreed to buy the birthday present in Wesley when she went to get new towels and washcloths for the rectory. She thought it should be a cardigan sweater, a blend of wool and cotton, even silk.

"Spare no expense!" he said, feeling a warm largesse toward his all-time favorite parishioner.

Emma softened and bought a silver-plated letter opener, as Miss Sadie had lost hers and was using a kitchen knife with a serrated edge. "She goan cut her han' off jus' openin' th' 'lectric bill," Louella said. "An' th' 'lectric company already takin' a arm an' a leg."

He called Katherine in New Jersey, thinking she might like to drop a card to the lady who'd been kind to her on a long-ago visit to Mitford.

Katherine proceeded to give yet another of her sermons on why he and Cynthia should go to Ireland with them in August, and he responded with yet another sermon on why they could not, the chief reason being that Dooley Barlowe would still be home from school, and he wanted to spend every possible moment with the boy.

"Oh, well," said his cousin's wife, "I'll keep trying. In the meantime, I'll send Miss Sadie two of the pot holders I'm making for our church bazaar."

He didn't mention that the pot holders she once sent him had unraveled to the size of petits fours, and faded in the wash on his underwear.

The Sweet Stuff Bakery volunteered to make vegetable sandwiches, and the ECW promised to round up trays of lemon squares, brownies, and ham biscuits, not to mention a heap of Miss Sadie's favorite party food, which was peanut butter and jelly on triangles of white bread without crusts.

He jogged up Old Church Lane to the Hope House site to render an invitation to Buck Leeper, and marveled at the way construction was humming along. The windows, at last set in place, reflected the afternoon sun like so many squares of gold. Dazzling!

Buck would, indeed, come to the party, though the fact that it was being held in a church building did not appear to increase his eagerness.

Father Tim ordered ice cream, and plenty of it, vanilla *and* chocolate, and rummaged through drawers in the parish hall kitchen for birthday candles. He came up with fewer than twenty-one pink candles, and made a note to pick up more at the drugstore, along with a container of rouge called Wild Coral, which Miss Sadie once said she liked.

Esther Bolick would play the piano, Mayor Cunningham would deliver a speech, and Dooley Barlowe, he felt certain, would sing.

In advance of the occasion, Cynthia brushed his best dark suit and picked one of two silk squares for his jacket pocket. He shined his shoes and wrote, in longhand, a poem that he would read aloud. He rifled through his study library to find any references to "birthday" that might be funny, wise, thought-provoking, or all of the above.

He supposed he should let Louella in on it, and popped over to Lilac Road during Miss Sadie's nap time.

"You ain't!" said Louella. "You ain't gone an' done all that!"

"I certainly have," he said, suspicious of her frown.

"Miss Sadie don't want no big doin's for her birthday, she done tol' me that."

"What do you mean?"

"She say, 'Louella, don't you let nobody be singin' and jumpin' aroun'.' "

"But Miss Sadie likes singing and jumping around!"

"Not this time, she don't. She ain't feelin' herself. Ever since she fell off th' sofa and broke her wris' bone, she been grumpy as you ever seen." Louella shook her head. "I don' know. She ain't sick, she ain't ailin', she jus' ain't th' same Miss Sadie."

"Let me have a word with her." Sadie Baxter was not a grumpy person. She was sunshine itself. Maybe he should tell her about the party, how excited people were. That would fix everything, no problem.

"Come eat with us Wednesday, after Holy Euc'ris'," said Louella. "I'll have a pot of snap beans an' a cake of cornbread. It puts her in a good mood t' have comp'ny."

"Done!" he said, feeling encouraged.

It was the last thing he needed in his life, the very last thing he needed on the whole of this earth. The prospect made a series of root canals seem nothing at all, a picnic.

"We'll be there tomorrow," said the computer technician.

He went to the Grill for breakfast, as Cynthia had been up since four-thirty working on an illustration due in New York, pronto.

Sliding into the booth, he felt as if breakfast were his last supper.

"Business has fell off," said Percy, looking gloomy.

"Looks th' same to me," said Mule, eyeing the room. "An empty stool or two . . ."

"I cain't afford a empty stool or two, especially with th' new help I've got on th' breakfast shift. Th' doc said, 'Percy, take a load off your feet,' so here I set, swillin' coffee like th' rest of th' loafers."

"You'll catch up," said J.C., unusually consoling.

"I cain't see how. Th' price of cookin' oil is up, th' price of eggs is up, even bread has went up. I need to expand my customer base."

"You've got us," said Mule. "We come in regular as clockwork. That ought to count for something."

"I cain't make a livin' off a preacher, a part-time Realtor, and a jack-leg newspaper man. I got to advertise."

"I can't believe you used that dirty word," said J.C., chewing a combination mouthful of sausage, eggs, toast, and grits. "You've fought advertisin' like a chicken fights a hawk."

"I'm not talkin' ordinary, run of th' mill advertisin' like newspapers and such."

"Thanks a lot."

"I'm talkin' a banner to hang over my awnin'."

"A banner," said J.C., obviously bored with the conversation.

"Happy Endings uses banners, th' Collar Button puts up two banners a year at sale time . . . an' remember how they lined up when Th' Local did a banner on fresh collards last October?"

"Who can keep up with such as that?" asked Velma, refilling their cups. "Lord, I hardly know where I was yesterday, much less who lined up for collards last October."

"You was here yesterday," Percy said helpfully. "From ten t' two. I needed you from eight t' two, but you was havin' your hair dyed."

"Put that on a banner," Velma snapped. "Most people think this is my natural color."

"What do you want the banner to say?" asked the rector.

"Dern if I know, I just this mornin' decided to do it."

"How much does a banner cost?" Mule asked.

"Two hundred dollars."

Mule blew on his coffee. "What it says better be good, then."

"Memorable," suggested the rector.

"Right," said Mule.

Percy looked at Father Tim. "What do you think it ought to say? You write sermons and put those snappy little notions on your wayside pulpit. And here sets th' editor of th' local paper, a scribbler and a half, to my mind. Seems like between th' two of you, you could come up with what to say."

"How many words?" asked J.C.

"No more'n ten. More'n ten, th' price goes up and readership goes down. That's th' rule for billboards same as banners, is what th' banner man says."

"Homeless Hobbes," said the rector. "He's your man. He was in advertising. Did cereal, automotive, and toothpaste."

"I don't have time to go stumblin' around th' Creek, gettin' my head shot off by one of them hillbillies. I got to get right on this thing."

"When it comes to advertising," said J.C., "there's always some big deadline deal. You waited this long, why can't you give a man a day or two to come up with the copy?"

"If I call it in today, th' paint dries Thursday, an' it's delivered Friday. That way, I get drive-by recognition all weekend, and when I open th' door on Monday mornin'—full house!" It was a rare occasion when Percy Mosely smiled.

J.C. sopped his toast around his plate and handed the plate to Velma as she walked by. "No need to wash that." He took out a handkerchief and mopped his face. "So why don't we come up with a line right now?"

"Right now?"

"Why not? I can't be laborin' over a dadblame banner like I got nothing else to do."

"I'll throw in a free breakfast, two mornin's," said Percy.

"Two mornings?"

"Three."

"With sausage?"

"Links or patties, your call."

"Deal," said J.C., taking a legal pad from his bulging briefcase and a pencil from his shirt pocket. "OK, what's the occasion? Free refills on coffee? Twenty percent off for senior citizens?"

"Just general."

"General? You can't write great advertising about general. You got to have particular. In fact, outstanding particular. The finest pies, the cheapest breakfasts, the biggest salad bar. Like that."

"I got one," said Mule. *"This is the best place to eat in town."*

J.C. rolled his eyes. "This is the only place to eat in town."

"Scratch that," said Mule.

The rector smoothed his paper napkin and took out the pen he won in an American Legion raffle. "Since this is the only place, being better than somebody else won't hack it. Maybe you need to give something away."

"Balloons!" said Mule. "Bumper stickers! Mugs!" He looked around the table. "How about refrigerator magnets?"

Percy wagged his head vigorously. "I ain't givin' nothin' away. Look what I'm givin' away now—breakfast, two ninety-nine; cheeseburgers a buck-fifty; BLTs a buck-eighty when I ought t' be haulin' down two dollars . . . nossir, I ain't givin' nothin' else away."

"Right," said Velma.

"Th' deal," Percy said, "is to pull in some new people, people that could be stoppin' by on their way to work in Wesley or Holding, like that. Or people that's packin' their lunch and could be eatin' right here just as cheap."

"OK," said Father Tim, "what about a line . . . something like . . . these aren't the words, just the gist of it . . . something like, check us out and you'll come back again and again. I don't know. This is hard."

"That doesn't have any spin on it," said J.C., chewing the pencil.

"Spin?" said Percy. "What's that?"

"What time is it?" asked the rector, checking his watch. "Good Lord! I'm out of here."

"What's th' hurry?" said Mule. "The fun's just beginnin'."

That, thought the rector as he raced to the office, was not how he would describe things, at all.

"There you go," said the technician, slapping a manual on his desk.

The rector picked it up and stared at it. It was heavier than his study edition of the Old Testament, something close to the weight of a truck tire.

He thumbed through to the back as the technician plugged in the keyboard. Eight hundred and twenty-nine pages! If this didn't turn out to be the worst experience of his life, he'd eat the index—a mere ten pages, including appendixes.

Emma had scarcely moved since he arrived at the office. She sat at her desk, as frozen as a halibut, and deathly pale under two spots of rouge. He could not come up with one word of consolation.

"Before we go into your spreadsheet application," said the technician, whose name was Dave, "let's take a look at your word processing toolbars."

"Aha."

"Would you like to hide your toolbars or display them?"

Honesty was the best policy. "I don't have a clue."

"OK, so let's get basic."

"Right."

"Let's start with your mouse, and practice pointing, clicking, and dragging."

Emma didn't move her head, but rolled her eyes around to watch the demonstration.

"OK, put your hand on your mouse like this. . . ." Dave demonstrated. "Click it. Fun, right? You're off and running. Now, let's choose a menu option. Or would you rather use a keyboard shortcut?"

"What do you, ah, recommend?" he asked.

"Hey, I bet you'd like choosing a keyboard shortcut."

"I'm a shortcut kind of guy," he said.

Emma rolled her eyes, but still didn't move her head.

"OK, great. Position the insertion point in the text . . . oops, hey, no problem. OK, click your mouse button. Right. Very good. And press this key. No, the other one. Lost that.

"OK. Here we are in Dialog Boxes. You'll really like Dialog Boxes. Hey, there are your Fonts! And look, there's Roman. Being Catholic, you'll probably go for that, ha ha, just kidding. I'll be darned. Never seen that before. Things change so fast in this business, you can't keep up. I was in chicken feed before I got into computers.

"Man, look at this, you'll love this, it's a zoom box . . . right there on your standard toolbar. Just click the down arrow to select the percentage you want . . . right . . . hey, two hundred percent, you're a high roller. Terrific.

"Actually," said Dave, looking suddenly profound, "I should probably show you how to create a document . . . or would you rather learn to save one?"

"With the, ah, little I know about it, it seems you can't save something you haven't created."

"Great line. A little religion there, right? OK. Creating a document. Click your New button on your standard toolbar. Hey. Very good. First thing you know, we'll be into typing, editing, opening, and saving."

Emma lunged from her chair and ran into the bathroom, slamming the door.

He went home early.

Parked outside his back stoop was a baby carriage. A double baby carriage, with a cheerful striped awning. Standing at the screen door, he heard a lively combination of sounds, including his dryer set on spin, his washing machine in the rinse cycle, his vacuum cleaner going full throttle, and something like rusty gate hinges moving back and forth.

Stepping inside, he discovered the gate hinges were squeals of joy and shrieks of delight. There on the kitchen floor in front of his stove were Sissy and Sassy, belted into small recliners that appeared to be rocking or jiggling.

Their attention was riveted on something hanging above them, which was attached to the light fixture. It was a gaggle of geese, and not only were they moving in a circle, but they were bobbing their heads and quacking.

"Well, well, well," he said, peering down at two happy faces.

"Father!" said Puny, coming down the hall at a trot. "We're glad as anything to see you! Th' girls are jus' dyin' to git t' know you! Looky here, Sassy it's th' Father, and Sissy, honey, you are soppin'! Father, wouldn't you like t' play with Sassy while I change Sissy? Then you can hold Sissy while I feed Sassy! Won't that be fun?"

Cynthia breezed in the back door at six o'clock, carrying a pink rattle she had found in the yard. "Hello, darling! Aren't those twins adorable?"

She laid the rattle on the table and peered at him. "Oh, dear, you don't look so good."

"You never mince words, Mrs. Kavanagh."

"Well, but dearest, you don't. Are you all right?"

"Oh . . ." He shrugged, speechless.

"And what's that on your shoulder? It looks like pigeon poop."

"Really?"

"And your hair. It's standing up funny on both sides."

"No kidding."

"Your eyes . . ." she said, unrelenting, "they're sort of . . . glazed over."

"I'll be darned."

"If you were a drinking man, I'd offer you a double scotch."

"If I were a drinking man," he said, "I'd take it."

CHAPTER THIRTEEN

Homecoming

He checked his calendar.

Following Holy Eucharist at eleven, he was having lunch with Miss Sadie and Louella, then racing home to put the new spread on Dooley's bed, which he'd buy in Wesley following a nine o'clock meeting at the Children's Hospital, during which he would try to wrestle money from a donor—a job he hated more than anything on earth.

Dooley was arriving at the rectory at two-thirty, and they'd promised to give his friend's parents a quick refreshment before they continued down the mountain to Holding.

Cheese and crackers . . .

He was supposed to pick up cheese and crackers right after the meeting at the hospital—and don't forget livermush. Russell Jacks was primed for livermush, and no two ways about it. The rector determined to buy six pounds and freeze four, and let Dooley make a delivery to his grandfather tomorrow morning. A fine boy in clean clothes, talking like a scholar and bearing two pounds of livermush? It was enough to make a man's heart fairly burst with pride—his own as well as Russell's.

He could hardly wait to see Dooley Barlowe, and Cynthia was preoccupied with her own excitement. She had cleaned the boy's room to a fare-thee-well, hung new curtains, and bought a remote for his TV set.

After showing him her handiwork, they had passed the guest room and paused to look in.

"Next fall," she said, eyeing the bare wall at the foot of the bed, "the armoire."

"Next fall—the armoire," he repeated.

"Right there," she said, staring at the wall. "Perfect."

"Next fall," he said. "Perfect."

Miss Sadie was wearing a blue dress with an ecru lace collar and one of her mother's hand-painted brooches. He didn't think he'd ever seen her looking finer. Her wrist appeared almost normal, and the car key was hanging on a hook in the kitchen, untouched in recent months, thanks be to God!

They sat down to green beans and cornbread, with glasses of cold milk all around, and held hands as he asked the blessing.

"Lord, we thank You for the richness of this life and our friendship, and for this hot, golden-crusted cornbread. Please bless the hands that prepared it, and make us ever mindful of the needs of others."

They had hardly said "Amen" when Miss Sadie shook out her paper napkin as if it were starched damask and peered at him.

"I hear," she said sternly, "that you're fixing up a surprise party for my birthday."

He glanced at Louella.

"Don' look at me, honey, I didn' say nothin'."

"Esther Cunningham slipped and told me without meaning to." Miss Sadie looked disgusted. "She went red as a turkey gobbler, and said she ought to slap her own face for doing that."

"Th' mayor done blabbed it," Louella said, in case he hadn't heard right.

"I thought you liked parties," he said. There it was again, the feeling that he was twelve years old.

"I do like parties."

"Well, then?"

"I don't want a party on an even year. It's bad luck, and everybody in creation knows it."

"I never heard that in my whole life," he said, and he hadn't. He yearned to light into his cornbread, but waited for Miss Sadie to pick up her fork.

"You should have had a party last year when I was eighty-nine," his hostess told him, as if he didn't possess enough sense to get in out of the rain. "Now it's too late."

"Too late?" he said, offended. "Miss Sadie, need I remind you that it's never too late?" He didn't have time to stand on ceremony. He buttered his cornbread and broke it and took a bite. Man alive! Crunchy on the outside, soft and steaming on the inside. Had he died on the way up Old Church Lane and gone to heaven?

Miss Sadie forked a bean and looked at it.

"You didn' say nothin' to th' Lord 'bout my beans," Louella reminded him.

"I didn't?"

"Jus' th' cornbread," she said darkly.

What was the matter with people around here, anyway? Fernbank had been a place where the sun shone, birds sang, and flowers bloomed in the dead of winter. And now look. Louella once told him that if Miss Sadie cried, she cried, and if Miss Sadie laughed, she laughed. She said her joints ached when Miss Sadie's did, and their necks got stiff at the same time. There you have it, he thought. Miss Sadie was the culprit, and he was going to fix the problem or bust.

"Miss Sadie, I think you owe it to everybody to let them give you a surprise birthday party."

"Who is everybody?"

"Why, the entire parish! One hundred and twenty families! People who know you and care about you."

That got her, he could tell. But he'd have to step on it if he wanted to build any kind of momentum. "Besides, Sunday after next, you won't even *be* ninety."

"I won't?"

"Certainly not. Your birthday falls on Saturday, so guess what?"

"What?"

"On Sunday, you'll already be in your ninety-first year." Smoke that over, he thought, pleased with himself.

"Thass right," said Louella, crumbling the cornbread and dumping it in her milk.

Two against one, he observed. He helped himself to another piece of cornbread and laid on the butter. If his wife knew he was doing this . . .

"I'm too old to be jumping around at a birthday party," his hostess declared.

"Nonsense!" he said, with feeling. "Nonsense!"

He had never spoken to Sadie Baxter like that in his life. Lightning might strike at any moment. He was ready to duck.

"You've certainly gotten cheeky in your old age, Father!" She sat back in her chair and looked at him imperiously.

Louella tried to suppress a laugh, but failed, and clapped her hand over her mouth.

Miss Sadie glared at her and then at him. He was ready to duck, all right.

Then she began to laugh. She laughed and laughed some more. So did he. So did Louella. They roared, they rocked in their chairs, they slapped the table.

He hauled out his handkerchief, Miss Sadie used her napkin, and Louella fetched a paper towel from over the sink.

They wiped their eyes. They blew their noses.

"Two o'clock in the parish hall, Sunday the fourteenth!" he announced. "Be there or be square!"

A little depression, he mused, as he drove toward the rectory. That's what had gotten into Sadie Baxter. Too much sitting around. Not enough hurtling through the streets in her green 1958 Plymouth. And no rummaging through the attic at Fernbank, which had been one of her favorite pastimes.

He'd had a call or two from prospective chaplains for Hope House, and needed to respond to at least five letters of inquiry. As soon as the search process was seriously under way, he'd ask Miss Sadie to look over the applications with him. That might help her spirits. In the meantime . . .

He had received a letter this morning from social services. The letter, which he suspected of being a form letter, said they were continuing the investigation and would advise him further.

He glanced at the copy of the New Testament on the front seat of his car as he parked in the garage. How he wished he had given it to Lacey Turner. Could she read? He thought he might call the social worker again, in case they had learned something. . . .

Barnabas leaped up as he came into the kitchen, barking to beat thunder. He didn't bother to haul forth a Scripture verse; he took the lavish licking on both ears and was darned glad to get it. Today was the day! Today, Dooley Barlowe was coming home.

"Where's your wife at?"

He turned and saw Lacey Turner on the other side of the screen door.

"Lace!" She was filthy. The sight of her pierced his heart. Blond hair spilled from under the old hat she'd left behind in the fern grove.

"Come in!" He held the door open as she stared at his dog.

"Not 'til you put that dog som'ers else."

"This dog," he said, holding Barnabas by the collar and propping the door open with his foot, "is harmless. Look." He stroked his dog's head to prove his point.

"I don't trust dogs."

"Barnabas would protect you, not hurt you."

"My back's itchin' s' bad I cain't hardly stand it. I cain't reach back there, an' Pauline ain't home an' my mama cain't do nothin'. Where's your wife at?"

"She's next door. I'll get her. Look, come in. Barnabas will lie down right there, don't worry." He instructed his dog to lie on the rug by his water bowl, which he did at once. "We'll get your bandages changed. Sounds like the itching means you're healing up."

"Pap tried t' git me agin las' night, but I dodged 'im an' hid under th' house. Some ol' car oil was under there." Frowning, she brushed at her shirtsleeve as if to remove the dark stain.

"Sit here," he said, pulling out a kitchen chair. "And look, how about a glass of milk and"—of course!—"a bologna sandwich?" This household was ready for Dooley Barlowe, all right. They'd bought a deluxe family pack of his favorite lunch meat only yesterday.

"Don' put nothin' on it, I like t' died from eatin' mayonnaise onc't."

The rector dialed the little yellow house as Barnabas lay with his head on his paws, blinking at the girl.

"Lace is here. Yes. She's going to eat a bite. Her back is itching, and she's asking for you. Right."

"She's on her way," he said. What a good thing to have a wife to call at a time like this. He put two slices of bologna between two slices of bread and added chips to the plate.

"I cain't eat no pickles," she said, watching him take the jar from the refrigerator. "They sour m' stomach."

He looked at her hands. Not a pretty sight. "Want to wash up?"

"I done washed."

He set the sandwich before her and turned to pour a glass of milk. When he turned again, the sandwich had vanished.

"I'll fix you another one," he said, oddly happy.

"No more bread, jis' meat." The hat sat so low on her head, he could barely see her hazel eyes.

He was putting slices of bologna on her plate when he heard the front door open, and voices in the hallway.

"Lovely!" said a woman. "So old and charming! My grandfather was a minister."

"He gets his house from the church," said a man's voice. But it wasn't a man's voice, it was . . .

His heart pounded for joy. Dooley Barlowe was home!

He handed the plate to Lace. "I'll be back!" he said, and bounded down the hall with Barnabas, who made a beeline for the woman and backed her into a corner by the door.

"Take no thought for the morrow!" the rector quoted loudly from Matthew. "For the morrow will take thought for the things of itself! Sufficient unto the day . . ."

Barnabas collapsed obediently, as Dooley Barlowe came toward him, grinning. It was a sight he wanted never to forget. "Dooley!" he said, hugging the boy in the school blazer.

"Hey," said Dooley.

"Hey, yourself!"

Dooley stooped to scratch Barnabas under a floppy ear. "How's this ol' dog?"

"Father? Vince Barnhardt. I'm afraid we're a bit early." A portly man extended a hand.

"And I'm Susan Barnhardt," announced the smartly dressed woman, grabbing his hand and shaking it.

"Sorry about my dog," he said, shaking back.

Another hand came his way. "Joseph, sir. How do you do?"

He felt enough energy pumping through the rectory to light up downtown Wesley.

"Hello!" said Cynthia, coming along the hall and embracing Dooley. "Why, you big lug, look how you've grown, I can't bear it. Squeeze down a couple of inches this minute!" She gave Dooley a resounding kiss on the cheek, which caused his face to turn red.

"Isn't it amazing how they grow in school?" asked Susan, who was now shaking Cynthia's hand.

"Amazing! Come into the dining room," said his wife. "I've set out lemonade and cookies, and cheese and crackers, and I'm just popping back to the kitchen a moment. Please excuse me."

Cynthia slid away, leaving him with what seemed a swarm of people, who were noting everything from his grandmother's silver service to the "unusual" color of the dining room walls to the size of his dog and the generous platter of walnut cookies.

He had entertained to a fare-thee-well as a bachelor, but now, let his wife leave it up to him for five minutes, and he was dashed if he could remember how to pull it off.

"How was your drive down?" he asked, pouring lemonade into glasses.

"Wonderful!" said Susan Barnhardt. "Dooley kept us entertained the whole way."

Dooley? Kept them entertained? A new thought.

"I want some milk," said Dooley, going off to the kitchen.

"I can't eat nuts," announced Joseph, peering at the cookies. "I have braces."

"I can eat nuts," said his father. After piling several cookies on a plate, he turned to the rector. "I've always wondered—what's it like to be a preacher?"

"Have a seat in the living room," said the rector, "and I'll try to answer that."

When everyone was seated with glasses and coasters and cookies and cheese and crackers and napkins, he sat on the piano bench and tried to address the question. How did he know what it was like to be a preacher? He never considered what it was like. He just did it, and that was that.

"Well," he said, wishing for his wife. "Let's see . . ."

"It must be interesting," said Vince.

"Oh, it is."

"Busy?"

"Absolutely. Keeps me hopping."

"Has its stresses, I suppose."

"Definitely. Definitely. What's your calling, Vince?"

"Prosthetics," said Vince.

"Aha. And what's it like to be in prosthetics?" By George . . .

Dooley walked in with a plate of cookies and a glass of milk. "Cynthia said she'll be here in a minute. Who's that in the kitchen?"

"That's Lacey Turner."

"Gross," said Dooley, with obvious distaste.

"Don't go to your room yet," he told Dooley. He had left the new spread on the backseat of his car and wanted to put it on the bed before Dooley saw his renovated room.

"I already went," said Dooley. "I took Joseph up there while you all talked about artificial legs."

"Arms. I bought you a new bedspread. It looks like an Indian blanket."

"Neat. I like my remote. But you still get the same old three channels. At school, we get fifty-four."

"Fifty-four? Amazing."

"It's not amazing, it's cable. You could get cable."

He had once entertained the idea, but decided to send the twenty dollars a month to the Children's Hospital. What did he need with the native dances of Malaysia, anyway, much less all the sports he could watch, when he never watched sports?

"You'll be too busy to lie around this summer watching fifty-four channels. Tommy wants you to go to his grandmother's place in Arkansas for two weeks, there's the town festival where you said you'd like to have a cold-drink stand, and I know Hal and Marge want you to come and visit—"

"I'm going out there to stay," said Dooley.

"What's that?"

"I'm going to spend the summer at Meadowgate Farm, helping out Doc Owen."

He felt his throat tighten. Had he heard wrong? "What do you mean, spend the summer at Meadowgate? We never talked about that."

"I wrote Miz Owen and asked her and she wrote back and said if it was all right with you, I could do it."

He felt an odd chill. "But I never said . . . we never talked about . . ."

"I knew you wouldn't care."

"But I do care. And Cynthia cares. We've been looking forward to seeing you, to having you home." He felt a kind of anguish, as if he would burst into tears. Then he felt the anger.

Dooley looked at him and shrugged.

Hot.

He got up and took off his pajamas, and padded to the bathroom.

All the windows were open, but no breeze was stirring.

He went to the closet and, as quietly as he could, took the fan off the shelf without turning on the light. He removed the clock from the night table, set the fan in its place, and plugged the cord into the socket by the bed.

"Timothy, what in heaven's name are you doing? You sound like the charge of the light brigade."

"Plugging in the fan."

"With a large crew of helpers, I take it."

"Sorry," he said. "It's hot."

"Like a sauna."

He aimed the fan at the bed, turned it on high, and climbed in beside her.

"Wonderful," she said. "Well done."

They lay there, looking at the shadow of leaves on the ceiling.

"What is it?" she asked, finding his hand and holding it.

"What do you mean?"

"What's on your mind? I always know, you know."

Marriage had many benefits. But a wife who could read your mind didn't seem, at the moment, to be one of them.

"Dooley," he said.

She waited.

"He wants to go to Meadowgate for the summer."

"No!"

"Yes. And determined to do it, too."

"But why? Why not just a visit?"

"He wants to work with Hal, said he wrote Marge and she said he could do it if we agreed."

"Do we agree?"

"No! No, blast it."

"I hate this," she whispered. "We thought he'd be glad to come home."

"The truth is," he said, bitterly, "only we were glad. It was a one-way street."

"Why hasn't Marge mentioned this to us?"

"I don't know." Marge Owen was his oldest friend in Mitford, the first friend he had made here, fifteen years ago. He and Hal and Marge had been as thick as thieves until Dooley came to the rectory and Rebecca Jane was born to Meadowgate. Then they had drifted apart, but never, he thought, in their affections. They knew very well how he cherished the boy, but they cherished him, too, had grown close to him. . . .

"Let me talk to Marge," said Cynthia.

"No, leave it. He wants to go. That's the whole point, after all. Not whether they somehow instigated this or how we feel about losing him. The point is, he wants to go."

Devastated. That's how he felt. Empty, yet filled with heaviness.

He occasionally thought about the cave, how frightened they had been, and about the peace he had felt toward the end. He had learned something in there, but he didn't know what. Perhaps he didn't know what because he hadn't allowed himself to think about it, to chew over it. Things had been so busy, after all, there was no time for reflection.

Feast or famine, he mused, walking from the office toward the church. As a bachelor, he had nothing but time in the evenings. This was a different life, all right, and he was glad of it. Having his wife sit on his lap and muss what was left of his hair, waking up to a kiss that sent him reeling, spending hours with someone whose company he relished, who made his conversation seem witty when clearly it wasn't . . .

Once again, mice had been gnawing at the retable, that venerable shelf to the left of the altar. According to the junior warden, they may need to replace the side paneling, would he have a look? Mice had always been attracted to that particular spot, as if the wood were infused with Vermont cheddar.

While he was there, Emma said, he should check whether the coffeepot was left on from the lay readers' meeting in the parish hall last night. According to her, lay readers loved to leave the pot on 'til the contents turned to mud. Lay readers were, in her opinion, at the bottom of the church ladder, having no candles to light, no wine to dispense, no cross to carry, no linen to wash and iron, no sacramental bread to bake, no flowers to arrange, no music to learn—all they had to do was stand up there and read from a *book*.

He regretted not having time to spend with Lacey. She had gone before he could get away from the Barnhardts. He wanted to learn how her prayer on the creek bank had affected her heart and her spirit, what it had meant to her. What had it meant to the other people who flowed down the bank into the water, to be baptized in the name of the Father, the Son, and the Holy Ghost? What had changed back there on the Creek, that place where even angels feared to tread?

He unlocked the door to the narthex and went in, feeling at once his gladness to be there.

He was seldom alone in the church anymore—the parish was growing, and more and more often, someone was puttering about or having a meeting, or the tourists were trying to get in and see the ancient Mortlake tapestry, which was insured to the hilt.

He bowed before the altar and sat down in the second pew on the Gospel side, and kicked his shoes off.

This was home.

He didn't much care about the mice, who were not, at least for the moment, dining on the retable. He wanted merely to sit and let the peace soak in, and the fragrace of the chestnut walls, and the years of incense and dried hydrangeas and fresh flowers and beeswax and lemon oil.

He had loved the smell of his churches over the years, perhaps especially the little mission church by the sea. With the windows cranked open to the fresh salt breezes, and the incense wafting about on high holy days, it was enough to send a man to the moon. The Protestants didn't think much of incense, and the culture of the sixties hadn't done anything for its reputation, either, but he was all for it.

When the Lord was laying out the plan for the Tent of Meeting to Moses, He was pretty clear about it. He asked that Aaron "burn sweet spices every morning" when he trimmed and filled the lamps, and to burn them again in the evening. Bottom line, there was to be "a perpetual incense before the Lord, throughout the generations."

Ah, well, it wasn't worth wrangling over, incense. In the end, it was just one more snare of church politics.

Why are church politics so bitter? someone recently asked. Because the stakes are so small, was the answer.

He chuckled.

Lord's Chapel had had its share of political squabbles, but thanks be to God, not in the last three or four years. No, things had gone smoothly enough, and he was grateful.

But why was he musing on politics, when the church was so sweetly hushed and somehow expectant? The light poured through the stained-glass depiction of the boy preaching in the temple, through purple and scarlet and gold, and the azure of the boy's robe as He stood before the elders. That was one smart, courageous kid, he thought. I'm glad I know Him.

"Rest. Rest. Rest in God's love," Madame Guyon had written. "The only work you are required now to do is to give your most intense attention to His still, small voice within."

He sighed and moved forward in the worn pew, and fell to his knees on the cushion.

"Lord," he said aloud, "I'm not going to pray, I only want to listen. Why does Dooley turn away from us?

"And what was the lesson of the cave?"

Cynthia wasn't interested in pulling punches.

"I don't want to make Dooley feel guilty, that's not the point. What I want is for him to know how I feel. That's fair. And besides, why didn't he let us know?"

His style was to give the issue to God and haul it back again, ad infinitum, 'til the cows came home, until the thing finally wore itself out in him. His wife, however, had her own style.

"Dooley," she said over dinner at the kitchen table, "we were looking forward to your homecoming."

Dooley nodded.

"We love you, and we've been excited about having you home for the summer."

Dooley stared at the wall.

"It makes us sad that you're choosing to go to the farm."

Dooley took a mouthful of lasagna.

"We wanted to spend time together, but we respect your choice and want you to have a good summer and learn a lot from Dr. Owen."

Dooley nodded.

"But that's only part of how I feel. Here's the other part." She made eye contact with Dooley and held it. "You have hurt my feelings and made me mad as heck. Sometimes, I think you act like a creep."

Dooley gulped.

So did the rector.

So be it.

"Did you see it?" asked Percy.

"See what?"

"Th' banner."

"Aha! Got it up, did you?"

Percy looked grim. "Went up this mornin' at ten o'clock. Caused a stir."

"It's hard to see a banner when it's on an awning over your head. I'll step across the street and take a look."

"They left a letter out of th' dadgum thing."

"You don't mean it."

"But they knocked fifty bucks off th' price."

"The least they could do."

"I started to tell 'em to jus' shove th' whole business, but . . ." Percy shrugged, despondent.

"Go ahead and make me a tuna melt. I've got some leeway in my diet today. Be right back."

He jaywalked toward the other side of the street, barely dodging Esther Bolick in her husband's pickup truck. Esther screeched to a halt and leaned out the window. "I hear th' mayor leaked the news to Miss Sadie."

"We're forging ahead."

"I'm not doing orange marmalade," said Esther. "I'm doing peanut butter. Three layers, with jelly in between. Apple or grape?"

"Grape!"

"For gosh sake, get out of the street before somebody nails you," she said, roaring off.

Safely on the other side, he turned and peered at the banner over Percy's awning.

Eat Here Once, And You'll Be Regular

He guffawed, slapping his leg.

But whoa. He couldn't stand here laughing. What if Percy looked out the window and saw him?

He turned his back to the Grill as if he were examining the brick-work in the post office, and hooted. The postmaster stuck his head out the door and pointed to the banner, grinning. "I've also known it to be otherwise," he reported.

He trotted across the street. "Percy," he said, soberly, "I'd give the banner company their fifty dollars back."

"What do you mean?"

"I mean that banner is going to be the talk of the town."

Percy brightened. "You think so?"

"That's what advertising is all about, isn't it?"

"Well . . ." said Percy.

"Trust me on this," said the rector.

Cynthia put her arm around his waist. "You want me to do it?"

"I'll do it," he said.

He went to the study and sat at his desk and dialed the Owens. Barnabas followed and lay down at his feet.

"Hello? Meadowgate here."

"Marge? Timothy."

"Timothy!"

"I won't keep you . . ."

"That's OK, Rebecca is sleeping and Hal is at a Grange meeting. How are you?"

"Good. Dooley says he's coming out to you for the summer."

"Is he? I . . . I didn't know, exactly. I said if you all agreed . . ."

"It's what he wants to do. Just wanted you to know that I'll need him here until Miss Sadie's party on Sunday the fourteenth."

"Of course! Well . . . yes. Miss Sadie's party. We're looking forward to it."

"He's singing, you see."

"I see."

Long pause.

"Well, Marge. Thanks for everything. When shall we have him out there?"

"Oh . . . anytime. Just anytime that suits. Perhaps you could . . . send him home with us after the party?"

"Good. All the best to Hal, then."

"Yes, and to Cynthia."

He hung up, feeling his stomach wrench. He had never before been uncomfortable with Marge Owen; she had, in fact, been the one who had made him most comfortable from the very beginning. How often had he put his feet under their table, in the peace of the old farmhouse, while the duties of a new and difficult parish kept him spinning?

Another thing. It was clear that Dooley Barlowe hadn't exercised the good sense or common courtesy even to tell them he was definitely coming.

He hated this. He hated it.

"I'm excited, Father, I just wanted you to know it." It was Sadie Baxter, and the old zing was back in her voice.

"That's what I like to hear. We're excited, too. It's mighty hard to dig up a brass band these days, but we're trying."

"Don't you go to any trouble, now!"

"Trouble? Why, Miss Sadie, trouble is what it's all about! If nobody went to any trouble in this world, the church would never have a roof. Cornbread would never get baked. Boys would never go to school."

She laughed. "Cynthia says Dooley is coming to visit us today."

"Around two o'clock, I think. You'll be looking at a new boy."

"Not so new he won't be hungry. You tell him not to stand on ceremony. Louella is fixing lemonade and cinnamon stickies just like Mama used to make."

"I'm jealous."

"You're a case is what you are!"

"Worse has been said," he assured her.

He woke up with it on his mind, and went downstairs to his study, padding as quietly as he could through the bedroom.

Five o'clock.

He had been getting up at five a.m. for years. It had become his appointed hour, even if he'd gone to sleep wretchedly late.

He leaned against the mantel and stretched, breathing the prayer he learned from his grandmother: *Lord, make me a blessing to someone today.*

Good. So good to stretch, to come alive, he thought, pushing up on the balls of his feet.

He would make coffee, he would read the Morning Office and pray, he would sit quietly for twenty minutes; then he'd go to the hospital, a round he made every morning, with rare exceptions.

Visiting the sick continued to be good medicine, as far as he was concerned. If he was having a rough go of it, all he had to do was pop up the hill to the hospital and self-concern went out the window.

When he retired, he intended to keep at that very thing. . . .

When he retired?

He let the tension go from his arms and stood holding the mantel.

When he *retired.* Where had that come from?

He went to the kitchen and ground the beans and brewed the coffee, feeling an odd blessing in this simple daily ritual. A ritual of well-being, of safekeeping, in the still and slumbering house.

He took the steaming cup and set it next to his wing chair, then turned on the lamp and picked up his worn prayerbook.

This was the time to fill the tank for the day's ride. He could put in a quarter of a tank and, later, get stranded on the road, or he could pump in a full measure now and go the distance.

But something was pushing ahead of the Morning Office.

Why haven't You answered those questions? he asked silently.

He had received nothing in that hour at the church but a sense of calm. That in itself was an answer, but not the one he was looking for.

Forgiveness.

He felt the word slowly inscribe itself on his heart, and knew at once. This simple thing was the answer.

"Forgiveness," he said aloud. "Forgiveness is the lesson of the cave. . . ."

He sat still, and waited.

"And what about Dooley, Lord? Why does Dooley pull away from us?"

Again, a kind of inscription.

Ditto.

He shook his head. Ditto? God didn't talk like that; God didn't say ditto. He laughed out loud. Ditto?

He felt his spirit lifting.

Ditto! Of course God talks like that, if He wants to.

He got up and walked to the window and looked out at the new dawn.

He would have to forgive Dooley Barlowe and Marge and Hal Owen, whether he liked it or not.

CHAPTER FOURTEEN

The One for the Job

Coot Hendrick passed the rear booth on his way to the men's room. "I bin eatin' here thirty years," he said, "an' I ain't regular yet."

"Percy'll give you a dish of prunes," said Mule. Mule looked at the rector and dropped his voice. "Did you see who came in behind you?"

"Who?"

"Officer Lynwood. She's sittin' at th' counter."

"Aha."

Mule whistled. "Man . . ."

"Man what?"

"What makes J.C. think he can handle that? She's packin' a nine-millimeter."

The rector laughed.

"Yogurt and dry toast won't hack that, in my opinion."

"J.C.'s not interested in your opinion."

"No kidding. What's your boy doin' this summer?"

"He's going to Meadowgate to help Hal Owen."

"I thought you were planning some big surprise camping trip, just you and him."

"I was planning that, but I've recently had enough surprise camping, thank you."

"There's J.C. comin' in. Well, I'll be . . . he nodded to her like he never saw her before in his life."

"That's standard."

"It is?"

"When you're in love, sometimes you act like you don't know the other person."

"Is that a fact? I never acted like that. Did you?"

"Over and over again," said the rector.

"Why?"

"Beats me."

"Whoa, he's sittin' down right next to her. But he's not even lookin' her way."

"That's a sure sign."

"Of what?"

"Of something serious."

A long silence ensued while Mule peered toward the counter.

"Seems like he'd at least step back here and speak to his friends. After all, we've been meetin' in this booth for fifteen years. Maybe he's just chewin' the fat with Percy, maybe he'll walk on back in a minute or two. Dadgum. Percy just handed him a cup of coffee and some silverware. I can't believe it—th' blame fool is goin' to eat at the counter."

"He's outta here," said the rector.

"What'll y'all have?" asked Velma.

"Who cares?" sighed Mule, looking despondent.

It took innumerable phone calls and the repeated qualifier that he was clergy. When he finally received a return call from the social services investigator, he felt as if he'd gotten through to the Pentagon.

"According to all we can learn, it's true that Lacey Turner doesn't live in the Creek community. One neighbor said West Virginia, another said Tennessee. No one came to the door at the Turner house. We left a note for the family to contact us, but we don't have much hope of that happening."

"The girl is living there. I know it for a fact."

"We've had a confidential source on the Creek for some years, but she's gone to a county nursing home. Until we can locate another source of reliable information, we're forced to deal with the information at hand."

"You've got to do something. I'm telling you, this is an urgent situation."

"We can go in with a law enforcement officer, but that puts a different cast on it. The Creek shuts up like a clam when they see a uniform. . . . They shot three deputies in there in the last twelve, thirteen years. I don't think that's the way to go."

"What is the way to go?" He regretted the coldness in his voice.

"We could use a court order. That gets us inside the house to check, and might at least produce the girl."

"What would you do with the girl if you found her?"

"If things are like you say, she'd be removed from the home. But first we'd do a medical exam, check for any evidence of abuse."

"Removed from the home to where?"

"We'd look for a suitable relative, and if that didn't work—foster care."

"What excuse would you use for the court order?" he asked.

"The truth. A complaint of child abuse."

"What if you can't find the girl?"

"We're required by law to try and substantiate your report. Ideally, we substantiate it by locating the abuse victim and doing a medical exam. If we can't find her, we can use your report as substantiation, along with another witness who's seen her bruises. In this case, that could be your wife."

"Then?"

"Then it's turned over to the district attorney's office. They'll do a complete and thorough search to locate Lacey."

He felt shaken.

"You need to know," said the investigator, "that she probably doesn't want to leave the home. It may be a violent situation, but it's a known situation. However, a minor doesn't have the right to refuse help, and we'd be required to take her out of there."

"The mother . . . she's an invalid. If Lacey leaves . . ."

"If she's a mentally competent adult, she has a right to choose between leaving or staying. The odds are, she won't leave."

He was silent.

"There's something you ought to know, Father. In cases like this, there are very few happy endings."

"What," he asked, "is the bottom line here?"

"You did what the law requires you to do—you reported it. Bottom line, we have to do what the law requires us to do, which is try and locate the girl. We'll pursue a few other avenues, and if those fail, we'll use your report as substantiation—and the DA's office steps in."

He hung up the phone, distraught. If they found Lacey, they would take her away from her mother, which would be devastating to both. If Lacey managed to hide, God knows what her father might do to retaliate for the investigation.

He felt a weight unlike anything he'd known in years.

Who was he to cause more breakage in lives already broken?

He turned left at Winnie Ivey's cottage and headed along the creek to visit his old friend.

Homeless Hobbes knew the Creek community like the back of his hand—didn't he live on the edge of it, and feed half the neighborhood every Wednesday night from his big soup pot?

As he approached the minuscule house on the bank of Little Mitford Creek, he saw Homeless sitting on the front step reading, and Barkless trying unsuccessfully to bark.

"I'm seein' things," said Homeless, dropping the book and rubbing his eyes. "It's a vision of John th' Baptist, or is it one of th' old prophets wanderin' th' wilderness? Where you been?"

"Married, my friend, married. The days fly by, and the first thing you know . . ."

"You've fell off to a total stranger. Come and get you some lemonade before you have a heat stroke."

He followed Homeless and Barkless into the house, which, even with its thin walls, seemed sweetly cool inside the oven of summer.

He saw that his friend, who often boasted of owning only one pair of britches, was clad in a fine pair of corduroy trousers with leather braces.

"Homeless, you're looking natty."

"Found these in th' Dumpster off Kildale Road, same as Miss Rose Watson used to plunder when she could hitch a ride that way. These come from a widder woman whose husband kicked. They say she didn't give a plugged nickel for th' fella, jus' loaded all he had in her yard man's pickup an' sent it out to Kildale. I was standin' there like I knowed he was comin.' There was a watch in th' pocket of these britches. I sold it to Avis Packard for sixty dollars and give th' rest of th' stuff away."

"Well done!"

"Have a seat right here," said his host, offering the only chair in the house. "That money paid for a crib mattress and blankets for Sis Thompson's granbaby. It was sleepin' on sacks." Homeless eyed his braces ruefully. "I don't know if I'll keep this getup or not. I might get stuck on m'self."

After thoroughly sniffing the rector's shoes and pants, Barkless leaped into the rector's lap and settled down contentedly.

"Ain't he a sight?" Homeless said. "That's th' most comfort a man could ever want, rolled up in nine pounds of brown an' white spots. How's ol' Barnabas? I hear he bailed you out of that cave."

"He did, and deserves a medal for it. My advice is, stay out of holes in the side of a hill."

"I ain't foolin' with nothin' I can't go in standin' up."

The rector rubbed the dog's ears. "I wanted to ask you about that night at camp meeting. . . ."

"The night so many got saved? To my way of thinkin', it was somethin' only a few see in a lifetime."

"There was a young girl. . . ."

"Lace Turner."

"Tell me everything you know about her."

"Hard life, that 'un. They live across th' creek and up th' hill, I'm kind of divided from that hardscrabble section, but I hear this 'n that. She's smart, and can read like a son of a gun. She's got a quick hand, too, with stealin'. Her daddy beats her bad, and her mama's an invalid. Last news was, Lace picked up and went to live somewhere else."

"She's still living at home. We want to help get her out of there if we can."

"You'll have to get her mama out before you'll get her out, is my guess. Her daddy's threatened to hurt her mama if Lace talks to anybody about what's goin' on."

"Tell me about her father."

"Name's Cate—he's bad business, people cut a wide circle around 'im. I've seen 'im a time or two, and that's enough for me. You don't mix a hair trigger temper with rotgut alcohol."

"Job?"

"Off an' on, I take it. Worked on that new bridge over th' Shantee River, but that's been built a good while."

"I believe there's a brother."

"Jess. Eighteen, twenty years old. His elevator don't go all th' way to th' top, th' way I see it."

The rector pondered this as he stroked the dog's ears. "What did the camp meeting do to the Creek? Have any lives been changed?"

"Oh, they have. Sis Thompson's one of 'em. Sis had a mouth on 'er like you'd never want to hear. She didn't drink, but she was mean and carried a knife. Sis ain't th' same woman, I can vouch for that. Th' Lord's give her as tender a heart as you'll ever see."

"Anybody else?"

"Slap Jones. There's a changed man. Slap runs me to town to pick up what your grocery throws out, carries me around to th' Dumpsters, helps run soup to th' sick. I read th' Bible to 'im now and again, he's comin' along in th' Lord." Homeless paused and looked at the rector. "Slap did time for killin' his brother."

"You need somebody back here, a young Absalom Greer."

"Yessir, we do. Sometimes a changed life stays changed, sometimes it falls right back into meanness. Meanness is awful easy to fall back into, as I recollect."

"I don't know what to do, Homeless. Mitford clergy is uneasy about coming in here; it's out of our police jurisdiction, it's a whole other school district and a different social services department. . . ."

"I'd go to preachin' myself, but th' Lord won't call me."

"He's already called you. You've got a ministry."

"Th' way I see it, soup ain't much of a ministry."

"That may be the first thing we ever disagreed on. In truth, I disagree strongly."

"Have some lemonade, then, and we'll square off about it," said Homeless, sounding his rasping laugh.

He opened the door of the ancient refrigerator and removed an ice tray. "You were askin' about changed lives. Another one comes to mind is Pauline Barlowe. Boys, there was as bad a case of alcohol as you'd ever want to see. An' I ought to know, as I was a five-star sot for thirty years."

"Pauline . . . ?"

"Barlowe. Right good-lookin' woman, got a young 'un, moved up there a while back with some low-down jack-leg that uses th' butt end of a shotgun to keep 'er in line."

He felt sick to his stomach.

"She was one that jumped out an' prayed with Brother Greer. She's turned around since then, kind of an inspiration to some folks, I hear. Time will tell."

Homeless continued to talk, but the rector couldn't concentrate on what he was saying.

Pauline Barlowe was Dooley's missing mother.

There was still no breeze in the warm June night, except for the steady flow of air coming from their bedside fan.

"What are we going to do?" he asked, suffering.

"I don't feel we should do anything at all. She left Dooley in the care of his grandfather, and there, in a sense, he remains. Through you, through us, his grandfather is taking care of him. She hasn't come forward to change that. It's a precarious time in Dooley's life—look how he's growing, Timothy. Yes, he hurt us, but consider why—he wants to spend the summer learning more about what may be his life's work.

"Think of it! A boy who came to you in ragged overalls, with no knowledge that anyone could even *have* a life's work . . ."

He took her hand.

"She may not know he's here. And there's no reason for him to know she's there. No reason at all," she said with feeling. "Put this out of your mind. We'll pray that his mother is healing, as Dooley is healing. Leave it alone. Let God handle it."

"Thank you," he said. "I needed to hear that."

But what if Pauline Barlowe came for Dooley and demanded him back?

Even in the close, humid heat, he felt a sudden chill.

"Then there's Lace," he said. Cut from the same rough bolt of cloth as Dooley Barlowe.

Why had God sent her on Dooley's very heels? Maybe he hadn't gotten it right the first time and was being given another chance.

He turned on his side and Cynthia drew close, putting her arm around him.

"Mind your deacon, dearest, and go to sleep."

He tried to mind her, but couldn't.

He was sitting at his desk when the door opened and a tall, slender young man walked into the office.

"Father Kavanagh? Scott Murphy."

He looked into the pleasant face of someone he might have known for years, but had never seen before in his life.

"Come in, Scott! Have a seat."

Scott Murphy adjusted his glasses. "I hear you're looking for a chaplain, sir, for Hope House. I'm here to say . . . I believe I'm your man."

The rector stood and shook his hand, laughing. Scott Murphy had made that statement as if he believed it utterly.

"I like that," he said, sitting again. "Tell me why you think so." This was certainly not going to be the morning he'd expected.

"Well, Father, I'm willing to work hard, that's the first thing. I would give myself freely—not to the job, but to the patients. I've got the background, but more than that, I like being with the elderly. I care about them very much." The young man stopped and smiled.

"Anything else?"

Scott Murphy sat on the visitor's bench. "No, sir. That's it."

Disarmed. Caught off guard. It had a certain charm, after all. "Well, Scott, if that's true, I want to hear more. Who sent you?"

"I had a dream. It may be hard to believe, Father. All I can say is, you'll have to go with me on this."

"I'll go with you," he said, intrigued. "Will you have a cup of coffee?"

"No, sir. Coffee makes me jump."

"A sight I'd like to see sometime."

They laughed together easily.

"Father, when I was nine years old, a terrible thing happened to us, to our family." Scott took a deep breath and leaned against the wall behind the bench.

"My father's and mother's parents were good friends. They lived in the same little town, Redwing, Kansas, not far from where we lived. My two sets of grandparents shared their garden produce and took a lot of their meals together, and went to the same church.

"Every summer, I could hardly wait for school to let out. I'd get on a bus to Redwing, and there I'd stay for three months, going back and forth from Granma and Granpa Murphy's house to Granma and Granpa Lewis's farm.

"Being with them was a wonderful experience. There was love coming at me from all four directions, and all at the same time. It was as concentrated and direct as a laser beam."

Scott Murphy adjusted his glasses and grinned.

"They took me to the zoo, they gave me a pony, they built me a tree house, they let me work my own garden—they did everything anybody could ever do to make a kid feel great about life in general.

"But it wasn't stuff like the pony or the tree house that made the difference, sir. What made the difference was their love. It had a force to it, and it stayed with me all the time. Looking back, I'd say it made me feel . . . invincible."

The rector nodded.

"One night, it was in the winter, all four of my grandparents piled into Granpa Murphy's new Chevrolet Caprice and drove to the next town to see a Disney movie. Granma Murphy loved Walt Disney. On the way home . . ."

Scott lowered his eyes for a moment, then looked at Father Tim.

"On the way home, they were hit head-on by a truck."

The bookshelf clock ticked against the brief silence.

"Granma and Granpa Lewis were killed instantly, and so was Granpa Murphy. Granma Murphy was still alive when the ambulance reached the hospital, but she was in a deep coma."

Over the years, how many tales that went beyond bearing, even beyond repeating outside these walls, had been poured out in this one small room?

"I can't remember anything from then until I was about twelve or thirteen. There's a blank there, like I was hit on the head and didn't come to for a long time.

"You might say that accident left no survivors. Mom and Dad . . . we couldn't seem to get over it, to go on." Scott shook his head. "You'd think that all the love I felt from my grandparents would stay with me like some kind of armor plating. Instead, I felt it had been stripped away. Whatever they'd given me, I lost it."

"I understand."

"Can you understand that whatever faith I had in God was lost, too?"

"Yes. It can happen like that."

"We pretty much stayed away from the nursing home where Granma Murphy lived—if you could call it living. One reason we didn't go was because she never knew who we were.

"Something about that bothered me, the staying away because she didn't recognize us. But I was in school, and ever since the accident, school had been hard for me. There was a while when I didn't think I'd make it to my senior year. I had plenty on my mind, so not going to see her didn't trouble me too much. But something kept gnawing at me.

"One day, I was out on my bike, and I stopped by a picnic area and I looked at those tables sitting there with no one around, and I thought of all the picnics my grandparents had taken me on, and I was overwhelmed with . . . with grief, with something I had never allowed myself to feel. I thought I would die from the pain."

He let out a deep breath. "That was the best thing that could have happened to me, that I stopped and felt the pain.

"I knew right then that I had to go see Granma Murphy, really go see her, look at her, touch her, tell her I loved her. I can't tell you the urgency I felt.

"We had put her in a nursing home about twenty miles away. I hardly remember that bike ride—twenty miles and I hardly remember it, something else was pumping those pedals. It was like I was divinely guided, given wings."

Scott Murphy's face was beaming. "I slammed my bike down outside the door and ran down the hall and found Granma. . . ."

Tears streamed down the young man's face, and he took off his glasses and wiped his eyes, but he was still smiling. "And I kissed her face and her hands and told her I loved her, and that I would always love her.

"I also told her I'd be back.

"I could see she didn't know me. And Father . . . it was OK that she didn't know me. A lot of people stop going to see someone they love because that person doesn't recognize them. Right then, I thought, who cares if she doesn't recognize me? One out of two people in this room knows their identity, and those odds are good enough for me."

"Yes!"

"I went back twice a week, it was like the old days, like the beginning of summer—I couldn't wait to go see Granma. I just believed that somewhere in there, behind the eyes that didn't appear to see, and the ears that didn't seem to hear, was a heart still full of love, a heart that still wanted to give and still wanted to receive.

"You can imagine that I've told this story a few times in my work, and once in a while, people ask how some teenage kid knew to think like that.

"I've got to tell you, I didn't know how to think like that. I was just a tall, gangly, mixed-up kid like a lot of other kids that age. Something else was at work in me.

"My parents started going, too. And somehow, we just began pouring love into my Granma, and talking to her as if she understood everything we said. My dad would tell her jokes, she always loved jokes, and we believed she could hear and was laughing somewhere inside. We just stopped doubting that she knew us and could hear us."

Scott paused and grinned.

"Go on!" said the rector.

"Today, my Granma is one of the activity leaders in her nursing home."

"Hallelujah!" he nearly shouted.

Scott looked at his watch. "Two-thirty. She's in crafts class right now. They're painting canister sets for their children and grandchildren."

The rector burst into laughter. Painting canister sets! How ordinary and insignificant that would seem to the world. He wanted to clap and shout.

"Some people," said Scott, "ask if I prayed while she was in that coma. Once in a while, I'd say something like, 'God, I'm really mad at

You, but I still believe You're God and You can do anything You want to, and I want You to heal Granma. Period.' "

"What do you think happened?"

"I think He healed Granma, just like I asked Him to. I think He did it with love, and He used us to help. He could have used anybody—a nurse, an old friend, maybe—but it was us, and I'm grateful.

"I came away from that time in my life with a special sense of a couple of verses in second Corinthians:

" 'For our light affliction, which is but for a moment, works for us a far more exceeding and eternal weight of glory; while we look not at the things which are seen, but at the things which are not seen: for the things which are seen are temporal; but the things which are not seen are eternal.'

"In my ministry as a chaplain, I try to look for the things which aren't seen."

"Well done."

Scott stood up and stretched. "Excuse me, sir, but I haven't been running in a while, and I can feel it."

"I've slacked off, too, in the last few days. How long are you going to be around?"

"I don't know. Maybe I should tell you the rest of the story. . . ."

"Please."

Scott Murphy sat back down and leaned against the wall behind the bench.

"I think I got my calling to be a chaplain during the time we were visiting Granma. And so, when college came around, it just seemed the natural thing to do to go to Fuller, where a couple of uncles had gone. I got my M. Div. there, and did a C.P.E. year in a hospital working with geriatric patients.

"Then I was hired as chaplain at a large eldercare center in Boston. It's all in my résumé, sir, and I have several letters of recommendation."

"I look forward to seeing them."

"I've been at the center for three years, and I've worked hard and I've learned a lot, but somehow, it's time to move on. All I can say is, I've been feeling restless, and I haven't really known why.

"I've done a lot of praying about where I'm supposed to be, and two or three months ago, I had a dream. In the Old Testament, God does some pretty incredible stuff with dreams."

"You can say that again."

"In the dream, this black curtain came down in my mind, with a word on it. The letters were white, and they were big and they were printed. 'Mitford' was the word.

"Somehow, I felt this was the answer, but it sure didn't come with any instruction manual. I didn't have a clue what to do about dealing with this answer. So I went to the little neighborhood library down the street and cross-referenced that word 'til it was chopped liver. Geriatric centers, military schools, you name it. Nothing. Then, I was looking through an atlas, because I like maps a lot, and it hit me—maybe Mitford was a place."

"Good shot!"

"I found a lot of Milfords. They're everywhere. But there's only one Mitford in the whole country.

"I did some research on the Web, and learned you're building a five-million-dollar nursing home here."

Scott looked at the computer sitting on Emma's desk. "Are you on the Web?"

"You don't want to know," said the rector, grimacing.

Scott Murphy laughed. "So, I waited for a four-day break, and I got in my car and I drove down here.

"I won't ask if that sounds crazy, sir, because I know it does. I spent last night in Wesley, and I've been walking around your town all morning, and I've just been up to see Hope House. It's an outstanding facility, sir, the best I've ever seen. The space is filled with light . . . everything about it lives up to its name.

"I like your town a lot. People have been very friendly to us all morning, especially to Luke and Lizzie."

"Luke and Lizzie?"

"My Jack Russells, sir. They're two years old. You might say they work with me."

"Aha."

"The elderly love dogs, and Luke and Lizzie love them. So, we're a team, sir." Scott smiled. "Hope House, your town, the people . . . it all seems right to me, Father. It all seems very right. I just lay it out to you like it is, with no window dressing."

Scott Murphy stood up from the visitor's bench and put his hands behind his back like a schoolboy about to deliver a review of *War and Peace.*

"There's only one more thing I want to say, Father. And that is, I'd like very much to have this job."

The rector got up and walked over to Scott Murphy. He looked into the young man's urgent brown eyes and shook his hand.

"You're hired," he said.

Good Lord! He had hired a man who should have been reviewed by the vestry, not to mention Hoppy Harper, and—last, but definitely, absolutely not least—Sadie Baxter.

If Sadie Baxter, who was footing the bill, didn't approve of Scott Murphy, Timothy Kavanagh was dead meat.

"Scott, I want you to visit Miss Sadie Baxter for a half hour or so, and please don't mention that I just hired you."

Scott laid his résumé folder on the rector's desk. "Yes, sir."

He dialed the number on Lilac Road.

"Miss Sadie, if it's convenient, I'm sending over a candidate for chaplain. I hope you'll give him a few minutes of your time."

"What do you think of him, Father?"

He was tempted to say he thought Scott Murphy uniquely suited to the job. But, no. Something held him back.

"Qualified. Good fellow," he said, trying to sound casual. "Call me when you can."

If this didn't work, he didn't even want to guess the outcome. Bottom line, he would be retired long before his time.

Two hours passed, then three, when the phone rang.

"Father?" said Miss Sadie. "I think Scott Murphy is the one for the job. Hire him!"

"Consider it done," he said.

CHAPTER FIFTEEN

And Many More

FOXGLOVES HAD TO BE staked earlier than usual, and the hosta, growing in lush groves throughout the village, produced rows of tight, urgent buds along erect stems.

Cream-colored bank roses bloomed along Old Church Lane, forming billowy clouds over the emerald grass. Pink and fuchsia climbers massed themselves on trellises, and in one yard, a vast stand of old shrub roses cast their rich, heady perfume on the air.

The scoop on June was captured by Winnie Ivey, who was never much on words:

"It's a dazzler!" she was quoted as saying in Hessie Mayhew's column.

He could scarcely appreciate the dazzle, given the fact that another computer session awaited him at the office.

He could, of course, fail to show up and let Emma take the heat. He could call in sick with the flu. He could fall in a ditch while jogging—heaven knows he had once done that very thing, and banged up his leg pretty badly.

He knew Stuart Cullen wasn't sitting over there at diocesan

headquarters pushing a mouse around. No indeed, Stuart could dish it out, but . . .

Dave was waiting in front of the church office.

"Hey, big guy! How's it going?"

"I'm over toolbars," replied the rector, unlocking the door. "What's the agenda for today?"

"Typing and Revising, Finding and Replacing," said Dave, obviously excited, "with a smidgen of Editing and Proofing."

If he were anything other than the responsible stick-in-the-mud that everyone knew him to be, he would get in his car and head for the county line.

He had loaded a font, he had formatted a paragraph, he had bulleted a list, he had selected a font, he had embedded a graph, he had kerned a headline, he had set margins, and he was exhausted.

He went home early, and did something he hadn't done since he was a boy.

With a cool spring rain drumming on the roof, he got between the covers without removing his clothes, where he slept until Cynthia arrived, looking pale from hours of labor over a drawing board.

"Good idea," she said, crawling in beside him and falling sound asleep.

A fine pair they made, and newlywed into the bargain.

They were getting dressed for Miss Sadie's party, and Dooley was presenting himself to them in blue jeans, a starched shirt, and his navy school blazer.

"Stunning!" said Cynthia. "Where's the camera?"

"Top shelf in the closet," said the rector.

"We'll get someone to shoot us at church," she said, taking it off the shelf and putting it in her handbag.

"Can I take my TV to the farm?" asked Dooley.

Were the boy's loafers newly shined, or was he imagining things? "Well, sure."

"Thanks," said Dooley, leaving the room.

"He told me he's helping Hal with a sick calf tonight," said Cynthia. "He is compassionate, Timothy."

"Compassion for animals does not make up for being indifferent to humans."

She was silent for a moment. "This is a pressing day for you, dearest—two services, adult Sunday School, a major party, and Evensong—I'm making dinner at my house tonight and giving us a retreat."

He smiled at his wife, who was putting on something the color of his favorite clematis. "Terrific. When I retire, I hope we'll have many retreats."

"When you . . . what?"

"When I . . . retire." He had said it; it had slipped forth without his knowing.

Cynthia's eyes shone. "Well, I'll be et for a tater!"

"We'll . . . talk about it sometime," he said, coloring.

"Good! I love to talk about the future."

"Cynthia, Cynthia," he said, putting on a fresh tab collar, "what don't you love?"

"Daytime TV, pickled onions, and cheap ballpoint pens."

He laughed easily. A retreat at the little yellow house. It might have been the south of France for the odd pleasure he took in thinking of it.

Sadie Baxter had been a member of Lord's Chapel for eighty years. Hardly anyone ever did anything, he mused, for eighty years. This was a blessing not to be taken lightly.

The children lined up and stationed themselves behind Ray Cunningham, who stood at the open door of the parish hall with a video camera on his shoulder.

The rector gazed at the eager faces of thirteen children, ranging in ages from four and a half to twelve years, all with their own excitement over the event.

In today's world, how many children got to mix with the elderly? How did one ever "learn" what it meant to grow old?

In his time, all that had been in place, there were models for aging everywhere—up and down the street, talking on porches, working in the yard, sitting on benches—visible, out there.

"Here she comes!" shouted Ray.

Esther Bolick banged on a dishpan with a wooden spoon. "Quiet, get ready, here she comes!" Esther threw down the dishpan and took her place at the piano.

"I hope I don't break your camera!" said Miss Sadie, arriving with Louella and Ron Malcolm, and her best silver-tipped cane.

"Hit it!" shouted Esther.

Happy Birthday to you!
Happy Birthday to you!
Happy Birthday, Miss Sadie,
Happy birthday to you!
And many mo-oh-ore!

"Happy Birthday, Miss Sadie!" chorused the children, holding up posters they had made for the occasion.

The entire room burst into hoots, cheers, and applause as he offered his arm and led the guest of honor to a chair in front of the fireplace.

"I'd better sit down before I fall down!" she warbled.

Laughter all around.

"Please come and pay your respects to our precious friend on the occasion of her ninetieth birthday," said the rector. "Help yourself to the refreshments, and save room for cake and ice cream after the mayor's speech. But first, let's pray!"

Much shuffling around and grabbing of loose toddlers.

"Our Father, we thank You profoundly for this day, that we might gather to celebrate ninety years of a life well-lived, of time well-spent in your service.

"We thank You for the roof on this house which was given by Your child, Sadie Baxter, and for all the gifts she freely shares from what You graciously provide.

"We thank You for her good health, her strong spirits, her bright hope, and her laughter. We thank You for Louella, who brings the zestful seasoning of love into our lives. And we thank You, Lord, for the food You've bestowed on this celebration, and regard with thanksgiving how blessed we are in all things. Continue to go with Sadie, we pray, and keep her as the apple of Your eye. We ask this in Jesus' name."

"Amen!" chorused the assembly, who either broke into a stampede to the food table or queued up to deliver felicitations to the honored guest.

He saw Buck Leeper, the job superintendent of Hope House, bow awkwardly in front of Miss Sadie and move quickly toward the door.

He was enthralled to see the children approach her one by one, each with a small, wrapped box—all of which contained, he was told on good authority, peanut butter candy.

Mostly, he loved the sight of Absalom Greer, who, to pay his earnest respects, and regardless of advanced arthritis, knelt by Miss Sadie's chair on one knee.

And many more! he thought, smiling. And many more, indeed.

They walked home from church, Cynthia carrying a wrapped parcel of the peanut butter and jelly birthday cake, which had been a dubious hit.

"Dooley," she said, "you sang so beautifully, the top of my head tingled."

The rector put his arm around the boy's shoulders. "And I got cold chills."

"Miz Bolick hammered down on that piano pretty good. You ought to get it tuned."

"We'll see to it," promised the rector. "Run in and finish getting your things together. Marge and Hal will be along in a few minutes."

"I want to take that cage Jack used to stay in, in case I find a rabbit or anything hurt."

"Take it."

Dooley dashed into the rectory ahead of them, and they paused on the stoop.

"How are you?" asked Cynthia.

"Struggling."

She put her hand on his arm. "Nobody knew it. The party was a huge success! Miss Sadie wept when Dooley sang, and everyone loved your poem."

"Ummm."

"Do you think we'd have celebrated Miss Sadie like that if she hadn't put the roof on and given the nursing home?"

"Definitely! Absolutely!"

"Good." She started inside as Dooley came along the hallway.

"That girl's here again," he said, looking coldly at them.

"Lacey . . ."

"In the kitchen. Man, she stinks."

"Get your things," said the rector, and turned to his wife. "Would you see if he's rounded up what he needs? I'll look in on Lacey."

He found her slumped in a chair at the kitchen table, her hair pushed under the battered hat.

"Y'r door won't locked, so I come in."

He sat opposite her. "How are you?"

"M' pap's gone t' Tennessee t' work on th' bridge."

"Wonderful!" he said.

"He'll come home Fridays. They ain't nothin' t' eat in th' house, he done cleaned out what we had and took it."

"We'll handle that. How's your mother?"

"Bad off."

He heard the emptiness in her voice. "I'm sorry, Lacey."

She looked at him coolly. "I said t' call me Lace."

"Yes. Has your mother got her medicine?"

"Yeah."

"What about a hot bath? It'll be good for you, and good for your back, and we'll fix you something to eat."

"I don't need no bath."

Dooley and Cynthia came into the kitchen. "Lace! We're glad you're here! Dooley Barlowe, Lace Turner."

Dooley glared at the girl, and she glared back.

"Everything's at the front door," said Cynthia, unwrapping the cake. "I'm just going to cut some of this to send to the farm."

"I'd eat a piece of that if you was t' give it t' me," said Lace.

"I'm taking it with me," Dooley announced. "It's mine."

"Actually, it's ours," Cynthia said. "And she may have a piece."

Dooley gave the girl a withering look. "Where'd you come from?"

"None of y'r business."

The phone rang, and Dooley bolted for it. "Hello!" He listened intently. "Yes, ma'am. I liked doing it. I hope you have a real good birthday and . . . many more. Thank you for doing stuff for me. Yes ma'am. I will. 'Bye."

"Miss Sadie?" queried Cynthia.

"She said she appreciated that I sang her favorite hymn. I hated to make her cry."

"Oh, but it was a good cry!" said Cynthia, giving Lace a piece of cake. Lace took it from the plate with both hands and devoured it.

Dooley glowered at her. "You ought to say thank you."

Lace licked her fingers and gave him an insolent look. "You ain't my boss."

"Step out front with me, son," said the rector, "and we'll visit 'til Marge and Hal get here."

They carried the bags to the front porch, where Dooley thumped down on the top step. "If she wasn't a girl, I'd knock her head off."

"What would that accomplish?" the rector asked.

"She'd know who she was talkin' to, that's what."

"Who would she be talking to?"

"I bet you're lettin' her move in here, lettin' her eat here and everything. She sure as heck better stay out of my room—and why's she tryin' to look like a guy, anyway? Gag. Puke."

He noticed that Dooley's prep school varnish was peeling off pretty fast. "Calm down," he said. "If you knew her circumstances . . . "

Hal Owen pulled his red pickup to the curb, and Rebecca Jane leaned out the window. "Uncle Dools!"

Dooley grabbed a heavy bag in each hand, and the rector hoisted the duffle and the rabbit cage.

His heart beat dully. It seemed they had welcomed him home only yesterday, and now . . .

Swallow it down, he thought, going to the curb. Swallow it down.

Hal got out and came around to help. "We'll just put your stuff in the back. Everything zipped up tight?"

"Yes, sir," said Dooley.

Marge opened the door and pulled Rebecca Jane onto her lap. "Climb in," she said.

"Marge . . . " He didn't know what else to say.

"Timothy, I . . . " She lifted her hands and let them fall.

Hal slapped the rector on the back. "We'll take care of him, and you and Cynthia come out anytime. We mean it."

"Anytime," said Marge, nearly whispering.

He reached in and patted Rebecca Jane, who displayed teeth like seed corn when she smiled. "Come with us!" she said.

The rector managed to smile back. "Not today."

Cynthia ran down the walk with the bag. "Wait! Esther's cake!"

Cynthia stuck her head in the truck cab and gave Rebecca Jane a kiss. "Take care of Uncle Dools for us."

"We will," said the little girl, nodding soberly.

She kissed Dooley. "Call us."

"OK."

"We love you, buddy," he said, suffering. He looked into the boy's eyes. Would the pain he saw there never go away?

"Mam says if you wash an' go outside, y'r pores'll be open an' y'll git sick."

Cynthia passed her another piece of roast chicken. "This is June, though, Lace, and that's not likely to happen. Washing and going out in winter is probably what she meant. In any case, I want to look at your back."

Lace thought for a moment. "I thank y'uns, but I ain't goin' t' take no bath."

"Fine. How do you like the chicken?"

"I like chicken, it's m' favorite."

"Mine, too," said Cynthia.

"I'd like it better if it was fried."

There was a long silence as they ate their hastily prepared dinner.

"Lace . . . " said Cynthia.

"Huh?"

"How do you feel about your father?"

"I hate 'im." More silence. "But I used t' like 'im."

"What did you like about him?"

"He was good t' me when I was a baby. They said I was s' little, I slep' in Pap's beard 'til I growed out of it. He used t' be nice t' me, bring me candy an' all, then liquor got 'im and he went down."

"Went down," said the rector.

"Yeah."

"Has he actually threatened to kill you?"

"Lots of times. An' he said if I tol' anybody anything, or let th' school people catch me, he'd hit Mam a lick she wouldn't forgit."

"I hear," he said, "that a woman named Pauline Barlowe lives at the Creek. Do you know her?"

"Yeah."

"What do you know about her?"

"She's nice, she's good. She he'ps me sometimes, but 'er man don't like her doin' it."

"What's nice about her?"

"She prayed that prayer I prayed, an' it made 'er different, she smiles an' all, an' does things f'r people."

"I heard she has a child."

"She's got Poobaw, he's ten."

"That prayer you prayed, Lace . . . did it make you different?"

The girl shrugged. "Made me want t' quit stealin'. I know it ain't right, m' mam knows it ain't right."

"Anything else?"

She stared at them coldly. "Y'uns ask a lot of questions."

He didn't know why, but that struck him as funny, and he burst into laughter, liking the feeling. Cynthia laughed, too.

And then, so did Lace.

She paused at the back door, clutching the parcel of food. "I'll be back, now an' agin."

"If I were to give you this," he said, holding a twenty-dollar bill, "what would you do with it?"

"I'd buy Mam some goobers, she loves goobers, an' I'd spend th' rest on somethin' t' eat, like ham an' all."

"Do you go to the store?"

"I don't go t' no stores n'r anywhere th' school people can catch me. I dress like a boy, an' know how t' duck around so people cain't see me. Like when I come here, I come th' back way—down th' creek and th'ough th' apple trees an' acrost th' park."

"Who goes to the store for you, then?"

"Pauline, most of th' time."

"She's honest?"

"Yeah. Honester'n anybody 'cept Mam."

He handed her the money. "Take it. And I'd also like you to take this. I know you have a place to hide it, if you need to." He pulled a small edition of the New Testament from his pocket and gave it to her.

She looked at it without comment and dropped it inside the bag of food.

"When you send to the store," said Cynthia, "please get a bar of soap and wash yourself." He thought his wife sounded as if she meant it.

"I might," said Lace. "If I take a notion."

As they watched her pass through the hedge, he remembered that social services was looking for her. The very thought horrified him one moment, and gave him relief the next.

At Cynthia's house, a cool breeze blew through the open kitchen window, and another from the living room met it in the hallway. In the bedroom upstairs, he found she had turned the covers back, and a vase of flowers sat on the small table she kept before the fireplace.

Violet lay curled on the vanity seat, and a breeze puffed the curtains out.

"Thank God!" he exclaimed, surveying the peace of it.

"Undress, dearest. I've got your robe hanging on the bathroom door."

He turned and kissed her on the forehead. "I'm dashed if I have a clue how I ever made it without you."

"Don't try and figure it out," she said gently. "Don't try and figure anything out. This is a retreat!"

They were sprawled in bed, listening to the patter of a summer rain. The crumbs of a shared piece of cake sat in a plate on the nightstand, and glasses of lemonade perspired on coasters.

"It's like going on holiday," he said, yawning hugely.

"What do you know about going on holiday, you big lug? You never go on holiday unless forced by a direct command from the bishop."

"True enough. But that's going to change."

"It is?" she said, looking hopeful.

"Absolutely."

"That's wonderful news, darling! Someone said that people who can't find time for recreation are obliged sooner or later to find time to be sick."

"I don't doubt it. Where do you want to go this summer? August is a good time for me to get away. How about you?"

"Perfect. The book will be out of my hands, and I'll be able to kick up my heels. What about . . . " she threw her arms open wide, "northern Italy?"

"I was thinking of something more . . . within driving distance."

"Of course. You didn't say you were going to get over your fear of flying, just your fear of having fun."

"Right."

"How about Mississippi? You could show me where you lived when you raised rabbits!"

"Mississippi in August? I don't think so."

"How about Massachusetts, then, and I'll show you where I lived when I learned to whistle."

"You may be on to something, Kavanagh. And while we're at it, I've been meaning to ask you another question."

"What's that?"

He cleared his throat. Could he actually talk about this? Yes. Yes, he could. In fact, he felt a small tremor of excitement. "Where would you like to live when we . . . retire?"

The faint ticking of the clock merged with the sound of the rain.

"Goodness! I've steeled myself not to think about it, so now I don't have a clue," she said. "Somewhere warm in winter?"

"That's for sissies."

She peered at him. "So you like having your face blistered by the wind, and your feet go numb on the short walk between our house and The Local?"

"Crazy about it."

"So am I, actually."

He laughed. "So we're both keen on four distinct seasons. . . . "

"Quite."

"Possibly somewhere near water?" he mused.

"Possibly."

"But nothing flat."

"No! Absolutely nothing flat."

They listened to the rain for a time, and felt the ravishing coolness of the breeze on their faces.

"Something rather small," she said happily.

"Right. Fine. But with a big yard."

"Small house, big yard. OK. I plant, you mow."

"No way. We plant, we mow."

They shook hands, grinning.

"Well," he said, "we have lots of time to think about it."

"Really?" she inquired. "How *much* time, do you imagine? Just asking, of course."

"Oh. Maybe a couple of years."

"Ummm. Yes. A couple of years sounds perfect to me."

"Good! Then it's settled."

"What's settled?"

"It's settled that we have a future," he said. "Don't you like having a future?"

"Like it?" she exclaimed. "I love it!"

Holding her close, he drifted into sleep as peacefully as a child.

The cave had been about forgiveness. And because of that, it had also been about freedom.

He glanced at the clock when the phone rang. Three in the morning. "Hello?" he answered, dreading the news.

"Miss Sadie done fell ag'in," moaned Louella. "Come quick."

He increased the speed of the windshield wipers.

Thank heaven they'd given the party, and not a moment too soon. But if God's timing had been perfect for the party, he had to believe it had been perfect, as well, for allowing this hard thing. Like it or lump it, nothing happened to a child of God by accident, and scripture inarguably proved that out.

"For all things work together for good . . . " he murmured, quoting from the book of Romans. "Use this for good," he prayed.

As he turned onto Lilac Road, he saw the attendants carrying the stretcher to the ambulance. He heard his heart beating as they closed the doors, and he followed them up the hill in the rain.

How many times had he received grim news from Hoppy Harper?

"Bad break," said the doctor, shaking his head. "Very bad. We're taking her into surgery, but . . ." He paused and ran his fingers through disheveled hair. "I didn't want to tell you this."

"I didn't want to hear it."

Sadie Baxter would be among the first to need the nursing home she was building.

During surgery, he sat in Hoppy's lamp-lit office with Louella and Cynthia and Olivia Harper.

"She say she spill a little drinkin' water goin' out of her bathroom to her bedroom, an' when she went to th' toilet in th' night, her foot hit that little patch of water and she went down."

Miss Sadie's friend and companion since childhood hugged herself as if she felt a chill. "This is a bad thing, honey, a bad thing. I can feel it in m' bones."

Olivia put her arm around Louella. "This strikes us all at the marrow," she said, trying to appear calm. Not long ago, Olivia had discovered Miss Sadie to be her great-aunt and only living relative. The bond had been, for both of them, one of the great joys of their lives.

They held hands and took turns praying as the clock ticked toward daylight.

He swallowed hard before he went into Intensive Care, and could scarcely believe what he saw. It was Sadie Baxter with the light gone from her countenance; it was someone gray and suffering and very, very old.

He had to force down the cry that welled up in him, a cry that said, *This can't be, I can't accept this, this is wrong.*

He stood at the study window and looked out to a drenching rain that made the rhododendron leaves glisten and dance. Beyond the hedge lay Baxter Park, a green pool of quiet and solitude in the summer dusk.

Cynthia came to him and put her arm around his waist. "What is it, my dearest?"

He clenched his jaw and spoke hoarsely. "It's Dooley. And Lace. And Sadie Baxter. And Sophia and Liza. And all the others."

"I'll go to the hospital tonight. You've had only three or four hours sleep."

"Thanks, but—"

"I'm your deacon, Timothy, you said so. Give me a chance to do my job."

He wanted to weep, he wanted to wail, he heard sounds forming somewhere in him that were unrecognizable, sounds of grieving he could never express.

"We'll go together," he said.

She went off to the kitchen. "I'll make us a cup of tea."

Sadie Baxter was tough, she was resilient, she was made of strong stuff, and last but not least, her faith was up to the job. She could live to be a hundred. Still, he could not shake the dread he felt.

"And many more," he whispered urgently into the gathering dusk outside the window.

CHAPTER SIXTEEN

Loving Back

"OK," SAID PUNY, giving him a mischievous look, "which one is Sissy and which one is Sassy?"

"Now, Puny . . . "

"Oh, jis' try!"

He didn't have a clue, but figured the odds were pretty good. "This one is Sissy!"

"Wrong! That's Sassy!"

He was resting on the study sofa, under what he felt to be a veritable pile of fat, squirming babies, stuffed ducks, squashy monkeys, a rubber pig that squealed when he sat on it, and a stack of folded diapers.

"Blast," he said. "How do you tell?" As far as he could see, both had red hair, both had the same eye color, both were the same size, and they smelled exactly alike.

"See this?" said Puny, pointing to a fat cheek. "Sissy has a dimple on the left side, Sassy has a dimple on the right side."

Sissy, Sassy, left, right. He could hardly wait until they were walking and talking, at which time he would simply speak a name, and whoever came running, well, that's how he would know which was which.

"Would you like t' hold Sissy while I change Sassy? It won't take a minute. Or—*you* could change Sissy while *I* hold Sassy!"

She looked so excited and pleased about the prospect of either that he could hardly refuse. "The first thing you said," he mumbled.

"OK, here she is. Uh-oh. I need to change Sissy worse'n I need t' change Sassy!"

"If it's not one thing, it's two," he said, quoting a former bishop.

She hauled Sissy to his wing chair, plopped her in the seat, and did what she had to do. "Now!" she said, snapping the diaper in place. "Come and sit on your granpaw's lap!"

Granpaw! Granpaw? He'd better nip this thing in the bud while the nipping was good. "Ah . . . Puny."

"Yes, sir?" She turned around with the baby in her arms, and he saw the prettiest sight this side of heaven—his one and only Puny, who had lit up the gloomy rectory with the glow of a thousand candles. Could he refuse her anything at all?

"Bring her on!" he said, holding out his arms, as Sassy landed him a swift kick.

He had jogged, Puny had scooped up the babies and their ocean of paraphernalia and gone home, and Cynthia was arriving any minute. It was his night to cook dinner, and he was running behind.

Did he dare fix the boring and economical Parson's Meatloaf for a woman who had been his bride only a few months? He had spoiled her rotten with roasted this and glazed that, not to mention his barbecued ribs specialty, which she craved, plus a fairly deft output of everything from grilled quail and oyster stuffing to broiled mountain flounder with pecan sauce.

Was the honeymoon over? He bowled ahead with the meatloaf, fervently hoping not.

He heard tapping at the back door and turned to see Olivia Harper peering through the screen. "Hello!" she said.

"Olivia! Hello, yourself! Come in!"

He held the screen door open and was dazzled, as was everyone, by the striking beauty of Sadie Baxter's great-niece. "This is a grand surprise. Cynthia's on her way any minute, and I've got kitchen duty tonight. Have you been up with Miss Sadie?"

"Yes," she said, sitting down at the table, "and she's in terrible pain, Father."

"I know."

"The bedpan is impossible with the kind of break she had, and getting up to use the potty chair is nearly more than she can bear. It hurts me so to see her suffer like this, and Hoppy says there's nothing we can do."

"I know. She's too small and too frail to medicate more heavily."

"I didn't want to come bringing doom and gloom," said Olivia.

He saw the grim concern that shaded her extraordinary violet eyes. "And you didn't," he assured her.

"I suppose I'm thinking of the future."

"Of sending her away to a rehab center," he said. "Then nurses around the clock when she comes home. . . . "

"And possibly confined to bed for . . . a long time."

"You know Cynthia and I will do whatever it takes. You're not in this alone. How is Louella today? I didn't see her when I went at three."

"Suffering, Father. This thing has aged them both at once."

" . . . the Lord do so to me, and more also," he quoted from the Book of Ruth.

" . . . if ought but death part thee and me," she said, finishing the verse.

Cynthia and Lace came up the back steps and into the kitchen.

"Olivia!"

The two women embraced warmly. "Olivia, meet Lace Turner. Lace, this is Mrs. Olivia Daven . . . oops, Harper."

Olivia extended her beautifully manicured hand to Lace, who looked at it for a fleeting moment, then awkwardly took it.

"I'm very pleased to meet you, Lace."

The girl dropped her head.

"Oh, Timothy," said Cynthia, "I'm so glad it's your night in the barrel. I thought it was mine, and I didn't have a clue what to fix. Maybe meatloaf, or something consoling."

"Meatloaf!" he said. "Just the ticket!" Great minds think alike.

"Lace came to see me," Cynthia said, "and I've been showing her my watercolors."

"She c'n draw!" Lace announced, sitting down and pushing her hat back on her head. "Looky here, she gave me these books." She hauled two *Violet* books from the belt of her workpants, and passed them to Olivia. He saw a sparkle in her eyes that he'd never seen before.

"I've seen them," said Olivia, "and they're grand! I can't draw a straight line, can you?"

"I can draw some." Lace rested her chin on her dirty hand and stared at Olivia. "You're real purty," she said.

"So are you, Lace."

"No, I ain't! You don't have t' tell me that 'cause I said it t' you."

"I didn't say it because you said it to me. I said it because it's true. You're a very pretty girl, with beautiful features and wonderful hazel eyes."

Lace blushed and pulled the hat down, nearly covering her eyes.

"I see you like hats," Olivia said. "I like hats, too."

"I can't wear a hat," said Cynthia, thumping into a chair at the table. "I look ridiculous."

The rector turned from dicing onions. "Don't be so modest. You look fetching in a baseball cap!"

Olivia laughed. "If you'd ever like to see my hats, Lace, I'd like to show them to you. I have hats that were made at the turn of the century, with glorious feathers and pins and veils. They came from someone in my family."

"This was m' pap's hat."

"Where do you go to school?"

"I don't go t' no school. I lay out."

"I see."

"M' pap won't let me go t' school. They'd land him in jail f'r whippin' me." She pulled up her shirtsleeve and showed Olivia the healing bruises, then suddenly yanked the sleeve down and stood up from the table.

"I got t' git home. Pap's comin' tonight." She collected the books and stuffed them under her belt.

"Wait, don't go just yet!" Cynthia went to the refrigerator, found cheese and tomatoes, and removed a loaf of bread from the freezer. She quickly put a jar of mayonnaise into a bag with a jar of pickles, cans of soup and baked beans, and two apples.

"There," she said, nearly out of breath. "Run home quickly, then, and hide it if you have to. You're in our prayers, all of you. Be safe, be careful—don't cross your father, and come back when you can."

Lace nodded and backed toward the door, clutching the bag. "Thank y'uns f'r th' stuff. I'll see y'uns now an' ag'in."

He stepped to the door and watched her walk toward Baxter Park. Today, he had seen the child in her, if only for a moment; he thought she nearly skipped through the hedge.

He was getting ready to go to the hospital when the phone rang.

"Timothy?"

"Yes, Marge?"

"I . . . we need to talk. Is this a good time?"

"I was just stepping out the door to see Miss Sadie."

"Shall I call you tomorrow?"

"No. Let's talk now." He took the cordless into the study and sat in his wing chair.

"Timothy, there's a hard thing between us."

He didn't know what to say.

"Let me tell you how I feel. I feel . . . caught in the middle. You see, Dooley wrote and asked if he could come for the summer and, of course, I said he could, if that's what all of you wanted and agreed on. I thought he would talk to you about it, and you would talk to me. I'm so sorry it came as a surprise to you."

"We were both surprised, then."

"Yes. You know I treasure your friendship, and I love Dooley. Nothing can change that. Whatever I've done to hurt you, Timothy, please forgive me."

He thought he had forgiven her, but he hadn't. He felt the bile of it in him yet.

"I'm sorry, Marge. I'm sorry for being so . . . " What had he been? Possessive? Selfish?

"Then you forgive me?"

He heard the concern in her voice, and his heart softened. "Yes," he said eagerly. "Yes. There's nothing to forgive, nothing at all."

"I think I've had an insight about Dooley. When he helps Hal with a sick or wounded animal, I believe it's his way of loving his brothers and his little sister. Perhaps that's why he runs to the opportunity to help an animal, which makes it look like he's running from you and Cynthia."

"Yes," he said softly.

"I believe he hated to leave you the other day, that he was conflicted about it, but he sucked up and did it."

"Thank you, Marge, for talking this over. I'm ashamed of—"

"Don't be ashamed, old friend. Life is too short."

He chuckled. How good to have the weight off their hearts.

"Please come on Sunday afternoon and visit, you and Cynthia. Bring Barnabas, too. I'll give you chicken pie, your old favorite."

He felt a grin spreading across his face. "Consider it done. And thank you. Thank you."

"You know, Timothy, it's not having someone to love us that's so important—but having someone to love, don't you think?"

"Yes!" he said, knowing. "Oh, yes."

"I pray he'll be reunited with his family. Do you think that's possible?"

He was silent for a moment. "I don't know, Marge. With God, all things are possible. So, yes. The answer is yes."

Miss Sadie was reported to have made a good turn, and was gathering strength. Before he reached the hospital on Wednesday morning to give her the Holy Eucharist, she sat up, according to the nurses, and sang the opening verse of "Love Divine, All Loves Excelling."

"It was a little squeaky," said Nurse Kennedy, "but she did it and we're thrilled!"

He sang it himself, barreling down the hill in his Buick to the noon service—shouted it, in fact, to whoever might be listening.

Love divine, all loves excelling,
joy of heaven, to earth come down,
fix in us Thy humble dwelling,
all Thy faithful mercies crown.
Jesus, Thou art all compassion,

pure, unbounded love Thou art;
visit us with Thy salvation,
enter every trembling heart.

Sometimes, being elated drained him more than feeling despondent. His high at Miss Sadie's turnaround left him limp on Wednesday night.

His wife was propped up in bed, scribbling in a sketchbook, while he examined himself in the dresser mirror.

"You're tired, dearest?" she asked.

"A dash."

"More than a dash, I think. You know you can't shine if you don't fill your lamp."

"Where did you dig up that old platitude, Kavanagh?"

"Ummm. I can't remember."

He peered into the mirror, lamenting the new gray in what was left of his hair.

"Darling," she said, "I think your gray hair is wonderful. Very distinguished, in fact!"

He gave her a wicked sidelong glance. "Yes, and just because there's snow on the roof doesn't mean there's no fire in the furnace."

She went into gales of laughter. "Timothy! I can't believe you said such a thing."

"That may be only the first of the things you can't believe I said."

"Whatever do you mean?"

"I mean . . . what do I mean? I mean, let's drive to Holding for dinner tomorrow evening, for starters. There's a new place, and it's foolishly expensive."

"I can't believe it!"

"You see? And another thing: Let's take in a movie. You can eat all my Milk Duds."

"Timothy! What is happening to you? If you don't watch out, you're going to be positively *fun.*"

"I wouldn't go that far," he said, grinning.

"I'd love to do all of that! And now that Miss Sadie is feeling better, I can talk to you about something I've been thinking."

"And what's that?" he asked, coming to sit on the side of the bed.

"Having my will made last week reminded me . . . if I keel over before I get my roots touched up, don't let Fancy Skinner lay a hand on me, do you hear?"

He stared at her, blankly.

"You must send for a hairdresser in Charlotte, and I definitely want foil, not a cap. Understand?"

"I beg your pardon?"

"Foil! Not a cap! Oh, phoo, I'll write it down and put it in the envelope with the will. I did tell you where I put the will, didn't I?"

"I don't recall that you did." Good Lord, she sounded as if it were all coming down the pike tomorrow.

"In the top drawer of your desk in the study. Under the ledger."

"Right. So why are you concerned about your hair if you're going to be cremated?" Episcopalians were historically fond of ending up in an urn, which surely didn't require getting their roots touched up, much less by out-of-towners.

"I'm not going to be cremated! Just plopped in the old-fashioned casket that takes up all that room underground and is now politically incorrect from here to the Azores."

"Aha."

"I'll leave you a note about what I'm going to wear. I think it should be that plum-colored suit you like so much." She stopped and pondered. "Unless, of course, I keel over in the summer, which means that little piqué dress with the blue piping."

"Could we talk about something else?" he asked. When it came to discussing the future, he was far and away better at it than his wife, and he'd only recently begun.

Sunday was all the perfection of June rolled into one fragile span of time, a golden day that no one would have end.

They feasted on Marge's chicken pie and raved over the flaky crust, and drank an entire pitcher of iced tea. Dooley rode Goosedown Owen around the barnyard, holding tightly to Rebecca Jane, who shared the saddle. Barnabas caroused with several of the Meadowgate dogs, and returned with a coat full of burrs, twigs, dead leaves, and other cast-offs of nature.

The rector headed for the woods with his wife and her sketchbook, where they found a cushion of moss along the sunlit path.

"Dearest," she said, opening her box of colored pencils, "maybe we should buy a farm when you retire."

"That's a thought."

"I'd love to pick wildflowers and put them in Mason jars on a windowsill!" She peered at a grove of Indian pipes that had pushed through a layer of leaf mold, and sketched quickly. "And I'd love making deep-dish blackberry pies. Would you do the picking?"

"No way," he said.

"Why not?"

"The last time I picked blackberries, I was so covered with chigger bites, I was nearly unrecognizable."

"When was that?"

"Oh, when I was ten or eleven."

"And it put you off blackberry picking for life?"

"Absolutely."

"Maybe we'd better not buy a farm."

"Maybe not," he said laughing.

Dooley and Barnabas came crashing along the wooded path, followed by Bonemeal, one of Meadowgate's numerous canine residents.

"Hey!" said Dooley.

"Hey, yourself!" they replied in unison.

"I'm through watering the horses."

"Great. Come and sit while Cynthia draws."

Dooley thumped down on the moss as Barnabas sprawled on the Indian pipes.

"Get up, you big oaf!" cried Cynthia.

"Barnabas, old fellow, over here!" Barnabas lumbered over and lay next to his master, panting.

"Mashed pipes," said Cynthia. "Oh, well, Dooley, I'll draw you."

"Don't draw me," he said. "I ain't . . . I'm not . . . my hair's not combed and all."

"Perfect! It'll be a candid portrait."

Dooley covered his face with his hands.

"Uncover your funny face this minute!" said Cynthia, charcoal pencil at the ready.

Dooley kept his face covered, cackling with laughter.

"Nobody minds me," she sighed. "Timothy won't pick blackberries, Barnabas squashes my subject matter, and you hide your face. Rats, I'll just take a nap." She crashed back onto the moss.

"No, don't take a nap!" said Dooley. "You can draw me."

"Great!" she said springing up. "OK, hold still and look this way. Actually . . . look that way. Now, drop your chin. I love your freckles. Don't squint your eyes. Is that a cut on your forehead? What happened?" She sketched hurriedly. "Don't mash down your hair, it looks wonderful that way. Ummm, raise your chin a little. Just a tish. No, that's too much—"

"I hate this," said Dooley, as the rector shook with laughter.

"Why," asked Father Tim, "should you do all the drawing in the family, anyway? We'll draw you."

"No, no, a thousand times no, you will make my nose look like a squash."

"Tough," said Dooley.

"Yeah!" said the rector.

"Have a go, then," she said, finishing the drawing and giving Dooley her pencil and sketchbook.

"Look this way!" urged the rector.

"No, look that way!" said Dooley. "And get your hair out of your face!"

"Amazing!" said Father Tim, peering at the hastily completed sketch. "Your nose doesn't look like a squash at all. It looks like a gourd."

Dooley and the rector rolled with laughter, as Cynthia peered at them with stunning disdain.

"It certainly doesn't take much for you turkeys."

Dooley picked up the sketch she'd done of him and examined it carefully. "Man!" he said. "That's me all right."

The rector looked into the boy's eager eyes. "You like it out here, buddy?"

"Yep."

"I'm glad you were such a big help with the calf."

"That calf is jumping around like new. Doc Owen said he couldn't have done it without me."

There were a few things that he, too, couldn't have done without Dooley Barlowe.

Smiling, he made a fist and scrubbed the top of Dooley's head. "We love you, big guy."

Dooley looked away, and said something. It was barely audible, but they heard it clearly. He said, "I love you back."

"Where are Sissy and Sassy?" he asked, popping home for a meatloaf sandwich and a couple of books from his study shelves.

"Shhh," said Puny. "They're asleep in your study. You ought to see 'em, they've growed a foot!"

"I have to get a couple of books out of there," he said, keeping his voice low.

"I'll git 'em for you. You'd wake 'em up and oh, law, they didn't sleep five minutes straight last night. What d'you need?"

He scratched his head, trying to imagine the books on their particular shelves. "I need *Pilgrim's Progress*—I'm referring to it in a sermon—and a book called *In the Wake of Recovery.*"

"Where're they at?" she whispered.

"Let's see. *Pilgrim's Progress* should be on the third or fourth shelf down, right-hand side, blue leather cover. The other one should be on the left-hand side, maybe the bottom shelf, I don't know what color the cover is."

"Third or fourth shelf, right side, blue cover, and left side, bottom shelf—what's th' name again?"

"In the Wake of Recovery."

"Shhh. OK, I'll be right back. Try not to rattle anything."

He opened the refrigerator door quietly, removed the meatloaf, and carefully pushed the door shut. He took the bread from the breadbox, and nearly jumped out of his skin when the round box lid crashed onto the floor, rolled under the table, and came to a window-rattling stop.

Crawling under the table after it, he decided to go next door to the little yellow house, where he could occasionally find crackers and cheese.

Puny returned to the kitchen, closing the door behind her. "Lord help!" she whispered. "What did you drop in here, your teeth? I cain't find nothin' with any pilgrims on th' cover. And this . . . is this what you were talkin' about on the bottom shelf?"

"It is, thank you. Well done! But I have to have *Pilgrim's Progress*, too."

"Does the cover have pilgrims with black hats and those funny shoe buckles and all?"

"No, there's no drawing or anything, just a plain blue cover and the title and the author's name, John Bunyan."

"That huge man that cut down trees? What do you need him for in a sermon? Or was that Davy Crockett?"

"Let me go in. I won't wake them up, I'll tiptoe."

"Men don't know how to tiptoe. You should hear Joe Joe tiptoe-ing—clunkety, clunk, slam, bam—"

"Puny . . . "

"Oh, all right," she said, reluctant.

He took off his shoes and eased into the study like a burglar, dodging the floorboards that usually groaned when he passed. At the bookcase, he searched the right-hand shelves. . . . Where in blast was it, anyway?

He heard a squeal behind him and turned to look at the twins, who were bedded down in tandem on his sofa. One of them slept peacefully, while one gazed at him with wide, solemn eyes.

He made another frantic search of the shelf and fled the room, empty-handed.

Sliding into his loafers, he whispered to Puny, "One of the girls is awake, I saw her eyes—and trust me, I didn't do it!"

"Which one is awake?" inquired the concerned mother.

"Sassy!" he said, gambling. A great howl issued from the study.

He snatched the recovery book from the table and made a run for it.

"I thought you'd want to know," said Hoppy, calling early.

"I do."

"I was listening to her heartbeat this morning and something doesn't sound right. There's swelling in her ankles, looks like edema. My guess is early congestive heart failure."

"What can you do?"

"Medication. Some respond, some don't."

He was silent for a moment. "It's hard to get good news out of you, pal."

The doctor sighed. "Right. Let's just say I owe you one."

When he arrived at the Grill for breakfast, he found Mule looking puzzled.

"So why do you think J.C. won't tell us about Adele Lynwood?"

"I think," said the rector, "that he doesn't want anybody to know he's getting overhauled. After what he's said about women to half the population in this town, he's probably trying to save face."

"I think he ought to come out with it and go on about his business. It looks like she's good for him, don't you think?"

"Considering he's dropped twenty-nine pounds, lowered his cholesterol, and carries a clean handkerchief, yes, I think so."

"Fancy Skinner's the best thing that ever happened to me," Mule said proudly.

"Is that right?"

"Yessir, I was rough as a cob when I met her. I'd never taken a drink in my life, but I was about to jump on some Beefeater gin my buddies had lifted off a transfer truck."

"No kidding."

"I was saved by the bell. Her daddy told me, he said, 'Mule, if I ever hear of you takin' a drink, I will personally whip your head to a very bad degree. My lips have never touched liquor,' he said, 'and lips that touch liquor will never touch Fancy's.' Buddy, he stood there in front of me, he was big as a house, her daddy, and I told him I wouldn't—and I didn't."

"Excellent."

"He bought us our first little home."

"Good fellow."

"Three rooms. Neat as a pin. I was sellin' Collier's encyclopedias."

"I didn't know that."

Velma set poached eggs and toast in front of the rector and gave the Realtor a box of Wheaties and a bowl.

"Thank you," said Mule, responding to Velma's recent lament that customers seldom said thank you, much less left decent tips. "So is bein' married good for you?"

"Absolutely."

"You never look back?"

"Never. It's the best thing I ever did. Cynthia keeps me . . . real," he said, meaning it. He pushed the butter aside and took a bite of the dry whole wheat toast his wife insisted was good for him.

Mule stared into his empty bowl. "Velma didn't bring me any milk. No wonder nobody around here says thank you. How can you eat cereal without milk?"

"You can't," said the rector.

Mule looked up, brightening. "Well, I'll be dadgum! Here comes J.C., he's comin' back here straight as a shot. I declare! Speak of th' devil!"

J.C. threw his bulging briefcase under the table and slid in beside Mule, glowering.

Mule slapped him on the back. "Where you been, buddyroe?"

J.C. ignored the question and gave his order to Velma, who had followed him with her order pad. "I'll take two sausage patties, a double order of grits, two buttered biscuits, two eggs over well, and I wouldn't mind if you'd slip a piece of country ham in there."

J.C. removed a section of paper towel from his shirt pocket and mopped his face.

The rector and the Realtor turned their heads and looked at each other, blinking.

He pulled the chair close to her bed and sat down and took her hand. Oh, how small it was, and delicate and cool, with the blue veins shining through. He wanted the warmth of his own hand to radiate heat to hers, for his own vitality to flow out like a spring and emerge in her, so she could raise her head and sit up and tell him a story.

"Miss Sadie . . . "

"Father."

They were quiet for a time.

"I need you," he said, but that was not at all what he meant to say. "I need you . . . to tell me a story."

"Oh, Father. My stories are done."

That was what he had feared most. He could not bear to hear it.

"I don't want to believe that, so I . . . I'll just go on believing there are stories yet to be told. Will you promise me one?" He would have to be positive in the face of this thing.

She smiled faintly. "You're a bother."

"I know it!" he said, encouraged. "I am!"

"Let me gather my strength," she said, and turned her head on the pillow to look at him. "And then, perhaps then . . . "

"I'll appreciate it," he said, swallowing hard.

He kissed her hand and gently lowered her arm by her side. "There was the story of the 1916 flood you once mentioned."

"Ah. So long ago. . . . "

"And the story of the dentist who pulled the wrong tooth when you were a little girl. You never told me that from start to finish."

She closed her eyes and smiled. "I'm glad we hired Scott Murphy," she said.

"Yes, ma'am. That was a good thing."

"Go home, now, Father, and rest. If I'm going to tell you a story, I must have time to think which one."

He leaned down and kissed her cool cheek, not wanting to go.

At the door, he paused and looked back, thinking he would say something more, or wave, perhaps, but she had turned her head toward the window.

CHAPTER SEVENTEEN

Sing On!

When he dropped by to see Uncle Bill Watson, the old man welcomed him happily. "Preacher, come set in th' yard an' we'll watch th' traffic."

They walked across the grass, which had been recently mowed and watered by the town crew, and thumped down in chrome dinette chairs stationed by the sign that identified the Porter place as Mitford's Town Museum.

Uncle Billy spit in the bushes and drew his hand across his mouth. "Sadie Baxter ain't doin' too good, is she?"

"She sat up and sang a hymn the other day, but I don't know, Uncle Billy—she's weak."

"She's old!" said Uncle Billy. "That's what it is. Now you take Rose—Rose is startin' t' git s' old, she's losin' her hearin'. Yessir, cain't hardly understand a word I say and won't git aids."

The rector nodded.

"Like th' other day, Rose said t' me, 'Billy, I ain't got a dadblame thing t' do,' an' I said, 'Rose, you ought t' go in there an' start readin'.' Well, she like to had a fit. 'I ought t' go in there an' stop breathin'?' she said. 'You're tellin' me I ought t' go in there an' stop breathin'?' I said,

'Rose, I didn't say no such thing. I said you ought t' go in there an' start readin'.' "

He roared with laughter. "Uncle Billy, I'm sorry to laugh . . . "

"Oh, don't think nothin' of it, that's th' way I do—I keep laughin', don't you know."

"You're a good one."

"Nossir, I ain't. I lose heart, now'n ag'in."

They watched the traffic circle the monument. Coot Hendrick rattled by in his rusted pickup truck, waving, and they waved back. Ron Malcolm circled in his Cadillac and threw up a hand.

"Preacher, did you hear about th' deputy sheriff who caught a tourist drivin' too fast?"

"Don't believe I did."

"Well, sir, he pulled that tourist over and said, 'Where you from?' An' th' tourist said, 'Chicago.' 'Don't try pullin' that stuff on me,' said th' deputy. 'Your license plate says Illinoise.' "

The rector threw back his head and laughed.

"Did y' hear that 'un about th' feller whose driver's license said he had t' wear glasses when drivin'? Well, th' sheriff stopped 'im, don't you know, an' said, 'Buddy, you're agoin' t' jail for drivin' without glasses.' Th' feller said, 'But Sheriff, I have contacts.' An' th' sheriff said, 'I don't care who you know, you're agoin' t' jail.' "

"Bill Watson, you're good medicine!"

"One more an' I'll walk down th' street with you," said Uncle Billy. "Did y' hear about th' feller hit 'is first golf ball and made a hole in one? Well, sir, he th'owed 'is club down an' stomped off, said, 'Shoot, they ain't nothin' to this game. I quit.' "

He ought to be paying good money for this. "I've got to get down to my office," he said. "Come and walk with me."

Ray Cunningham roared around the monument in his RV and hammered down on the horn. They waved.

"Let me tell Rose I'm agoin' with th' preacher. She don't like me disappearin', don't you know." Uncle Billy creaked out of the chair, and they walked slowly across the yard and around to the side of the house.

"Rose!" called the old man, pounding on the screen door. "Rose, I'm agoin' off with th' preacher. I'll be back."

Miss Rose appeared in a chenille robe, argyle socks, and a shower cap. "You're going to see *Jack*?"

"Said I'll be back!"

"Be back by four o'clock, and I don't mean maybe!"

"See what I'm tellin' you?" said Uncle Billy as they made their way to the sidewalk. "Old age is settin' in t' ever'body! Rose cain't hear and I cain't half remember. What time did she say she wanted me back?"

Winnie Ivey, bless her soul, was spending nights with Louella, who had seldom spent a night alone in her seventy-nine years.

He picked Winnie up and when she closed the Sweet Stuff bakery at five-thirty, and, since her car was in the garage and her bunions didn't permit much walking, he drove her to her little house by the bridge, where she fed her cat before going to Louella's.

He sat in Winnie's porch swing and looked across Little Mitford Creek to the green woods. Somewhere in there, quite out of view from this peaceful place, was the community hardly anyone wanted to acknowledge.

Out of sight, out of mind. . . .

When he arrived home at nearly six o'clock, Cynthia was drinking a cup of tea at the kitchen table, with Barnabas at her feet. He saw his wife's face and knew something was wrong.

"Timothy . . . "

He pulled out a chair and sat down. "What is it?"

"They want me to sign a paper saying I've seen Lace's bruises, that I know she's been beaten. Then they'll get the district attorney's office involved, and they fully expect to find her and take her out of the home. This is too hard. . . . "

"I know."

"It was one thing to want her out of there, but this is quite another. How can I be the one to sign the paper, to make a decision that will take her away from her mother? And yet, how can I not?"

"They'll give her mother the choice of staying or leaving."

"Yes, but they say she probably won't leave. I asked what might happen, and apparently people often choose the horror over help."

"We haven't seen Lace since her father came home. I wish we knew what's going on. I'd like to think that having work will help his drinking problem, but . . . "

"But you don't think so."

"No, I don't think so. What did you tell them?"

"I said I'd let them know by Wednesday. If we do this thing and she's taken away, where will they send her?"

"They'll try to place her with a relative. Failing that, she'll be placed in foster care."

"What if . . . that is . . . should we consider being her foster care?"

"I have no idea how that works."

She was silent for a time before she spoke again. "I wish I could go to the Creek and see things for myself."

"What possible good would that do? What would that solve?"

"I don't know," she said vaguely. "I don't know."

If there was anything a church had, it was lists, and in no time flat, according to Dave, they would have their lists formatted, bulleted, and numbered, not to mention sorted. Before Dave arrived, he hoisted the manual and read the following:

> To change text appearing next to a number in the list, enter text in the Text Before box or the Text After box. To alter a number format or the bullet, select a number or bullet format under Number Format, Bullet Character, or Number or Bullet.
>
> To change the indentation between sections of the list, enter a measurement in the Distance From Indent To Text box.

He noted that, to include hanging indents, he was to select the Hanging Indent box. He would not know a hanging indent if he met it in the street.

He looked with longing at his Royal manual, which sat mutely under its ancient black cover.

"There's only one problem with doin' lists today," Emma announced.

"More than one, to my mind."

"I can't find the folder with the lists in it. The ones we're supposed to key in this morning."

"It was right there on your desk two weeks ago, as I recall."

"Not anymore. I've searched high and low. Did you move it?"

"I never touch your desk." It might have been ringed with barbed wire for all the touching he ever did of her desk. "Which lists did it contain?"

"All the lists. Current membership, Sunday School roll with names, addresses, and phone numbers, lists of pledgers and nonpledgers, lists of people who've made special contributions and memorial gifts . . . lists of people who worked on the roof since who-shot-Lizzie . . . and oh, a list of all the costs to date on Hope House, and the projected expenses for next year's budget."

"Certainly those lists weren't the originals?" He didn't want to know the answer.

"Well, of course they were the *originals*; they were what I typed directly from all those messy notes you've been giving me since kingdom come. Plus, how was I going to make copies when the copier at the post office stays broken down half the time, and the one at the library's so little you can hardly get a postcard on it? Besides, we've been out of carbon paper practically since I went back to bein' a Baptist."

"We've got to find those lists."

"Fine," she said. "You look."

"Who else has been in here?"

"In the last two weeks? How am I supposed to remember? That chaplain you hired. . . ." She looked at him as if Scott Murphy were the culprit, there was the answer right there.

"Emma . . . "

"I know you're mad as a wet hen. But when things get so bad you can't leave a file folder on your own desk without somebody helping themselves, what do you expect?"

"For God has not given us the spirit of fear, but of power, and of love, and of a sound mind," he read aloud from Paul's second letter to Timothy.

He remembered Katherine's passionate counsel on the phone last year before he proposed to Cynthia. He had been sorely afraid of letting go, and Katherine had reminded him in no uncertain terms where fear comes from. If, she reasoned, it doesn't come from God, there's only one other source to consider. "Teds," she said, "fear is of the Enemy." And she was right.

As a young seminarian, he had wanted to believe the letters were, in some supernatural way, written directly to him. There were oddly personal links throughout the letters, not the least of which was Paul's reference to Timothy's mother and grandmother as women of "unfeigned faith." No better description could have been rendered of his own mother and grandmother.

It was a long-standing tradition to read the letters on or near his birthday. Of course, there had been several years when he didn't have a clue that his birthday had come and gone, but this year was different. Now, there was more to celebrate about June 28, only days away, than his nativity in Holly Springs, Mississippi. Now it was also the date on which he'd proposed to his next-door neighbor.

He adjusted his glasses and read toward a favorite passage, a passage that, every year, seemed to stand apart for him.

"Continue in the things which you've learned and have been assured of, knowing of whom you learned them, and that from a child you've known the holy scriptures, which are able to make you wise unto salvation through faith in Christ Jesus."

He read on, toward the end of the second letter, where the chief apostle made a request. "The cloak that I left at Troas . . . , when you come, bring it with you. . . ." Because Paul was then almost certainly ill and dying, those few lines never failed to move him.

"Do thy diligence to come before winter," the letter said in closing. In other words, Hurry! Don't let me down. Soon, it will be bitterly cold.

In the end, would he be able to say with Paul, *I have fought a good fight! I have finished the course! I have kept the faith!*

Time, which tells everything, would tell that, also.

He was running late and no help for it.

Opening the office door, he was about to say good morning to his secretary when something brown dashed from nowhere and attached itself to his right ankle, growling.

"What in the dickens?"

Emma lunged from her desk. "Snickers! Come here this minute!"

"Good heavens," he said, trying to shake his ankle free. The teeth weren't actually puncturing the skin, but if he made a wrong move . . .

"Don't mind him," said Emma.

Don't *mind* him? This dog was determined to attach itself to his leg permanently.

"Don't pay any attention and he'll stop doing it."

"Oh." He walked to his desk, dragging the dog with him, as if it didn't exist.

"That's Snickers," said Emma. "Since you've pretty much quit bringing Barnabas to work, I thought I'd bring Snickers once in a while."

Was there *any* balm in Gilead?

"I suppose I could just leave my ankle in his mouth until he falls asleep," said the rector, taking the cover off his Royal manual.

Emma peered at him over her glasses. "You don't like my dog?"

"Well . . . "

"He certainly likes you," she said, offended.

He had wired Roberto in Florence, asking if his grandfather might write a letter to Miss Sadie.

It would be good medicine to have word from her childhood friend, Leonardo. As a young boy, Leonardo had lived at Fernbank with his artist father for three years, transforming the ballroom ceiling into a heavenly dome alive with a host of angels.

When the letter arrived at the church office, carefully translated into English, he took it to the hospital at once.

"May I read it to you?" he asked, sitting by her bed.

She nodded, and he noticed how transparent her skin seemed. He had never noticed that before.

My dearest Sadie,

Time continues to be money, my cherished friend, but I no longer care about such things.

What do I care about, then, and what moves me, still? Hearing Roberto sing your praises, and tell of the journey he made last June into the bosom of your family and friends, and of the grand occasion held in your ballroom, that same lovely room in which my father and I labored so happily.

I delight to listen again and again to Roberto's description of the ceiling, which had grown faded in memory, but which he has made vividly fresh and beautiful to me once more.

I care, Sadie, that I have lived my life doing what I loved most passionately—painting.That is all I ever wanted to do, I never once thought of being a banker, or pondered the lure of exporting, I was able to do what I loved! I consider this a most extraordinary miracle in a world which conspires to rob us of our dreams, and even of our passion.

Your priest tells us that you have fallen, but that your spirits are strong and you are singing in your bed! That is the Sadie Baxter who met us at the door so many years ago and said, Tempo e denaro! Time is money! Did you know that my father often pressed me to quicken my brushstrokes, in remembrance of what you said to us in greeting? He thought your father had asked you to say it, being too much a gentleman to press us himself.

I, also, lie in bed these days, and am not often up. My old enemy, arthritis, afflicts me savagely. Yet I, too, sing in my bed, Sadie, the old music from La Traviata. I have no voice left, it is my spirit which sings.

My dear friend, across half the world, I challenge you:

Sing on! Sing on!

You live forever in my soul.

Yours faithfully,

Leonardo Francesca

Miss Sadie nodded, which told him she had heard and was pleased.

"Where is Louella?" she asked, looking out the window.

"I'm going to get her at nine o'clock and bring her to see you."

"Oh, Father," she said slowly, "you don't have time to be ferrying people around."

"It's my job to ferry people around, if it has anything to do with you."

She turned her gaze to him. "I wasn't going to tell you this, Father, for it might give you the big head . . . "

"Tell me!" he said, urgent. "Whatever it is, I promise I won't get the big head."

"We've had seven priests in my eighty years at Lord's Chapel, and you . . . you are the one who has loved us best."

He swallowed hard. Whatever he did, he must seize the moment. "And the thanks I get from you is no more stories?"

She closed her eyes and smiled. "When you come again," she said. "But I hope you won't expect too much, Father. I think I've spoiled you with stories of angels and painted ceilings, and broken hearts that never mended."

"Miss Sadie, you can tell me anything. You can read me the phone book, for all I care! Just keep . . . "

She looked at him.

"Just keep being Miss Sadie."

She closed her eyes again and he bent down and kissed her forehead. "Would you like me to bring you a bag of donut holes?" Please say yes, he thought.

"Oh, no. No."

He tried to sing "Love Divine, All Loves Excelling" as he drove down the hill, but he could not.

"Happy birthday!" crowed his wife, kissing his face.

"What in the world?"

"Wake up, sleepyhead, it's your birthday! You're now a full seven years older than me, and I'm thrilled!"

"Being seven years older than you will last less than a month, so enjoy it while you can."

"Oh, I will, I will! Now sit up, I've brought your coffee."

"I've never had coffee in bed in my life, except for a cup Dooley brewed when I had the flu. What time is it, anyway? Good Lord, Kavanagh, it's not even daylight."

"I had to do it now because if I didn't, you'd be careening down Main Street in that funny jogging suit, or in your study doing the Morning Office."

"What is this?" he asked suspiciously, taking the tray on his lap and looking at something discreetly covered with a napkin.

"First, drink your coffee. Then I have a little present for you."

"A present? At five'clock in the morning? This is earlier than I ever got up for Santa Claus when I was a kid."

"Isn't it fun?" she asked, sitting cross-legged on the bed.

"For you, maybe. I have my hospital visits, two meetings before noon, Winnie Ivey to fetch back to the bakery, and a sermon to finish so I can squire you out to dinner Saturday evening. Not to mention another round with the computer technician."

"Oh, dear. Dave?"

"Dave."

"Ummm. Drink your coffee, dearest."

"By the way," he said, "happy anniversary of . . . well, you know."

"Say it, you big lug."

"Of the night I hauled myself down on one knee and recklessly abandoned my freedom, my liberty—"

"Your boring existence as a dry old crust . . . "

"Exactly."

He had taken his first sip of coffee from his favorite mug when the phone rang. No, he thought. Please, not that. . . .

It was Nurse Kennedy. Someone had been critically burned. Would he come and pray at the hospital, or did he want to do it at home?

"Pray," he told Cynthia as he hurriedly dressed. "A burn victim."

All he could think as he drove up the hill was, Why, God?

"They don't know who it is, Father. It's somebody from the Creek, that's all I can tell you. Dr. Harper's having a trauma surgeon fly in who knows more about what to do. He and Dr. Wilson are both working in there. He says to pray like you've never prayed before."

"It's bad?"

"It's very bad."

Bill Sprouse had talked about families who got burned out at the Creek, but that was in winter, when kerosene stoves and open fireplaces posed a threat.

He didn't dare think. . . .

He ran after the retreating nurse, his heart pounding. "Kennedy! Is it a girl?"

"I don't think so, Father. Is it important to know?"

"Yes!" he said. "Very!"

"I'll find out as soon as I can." She walked away quickly, the soles of her shoes making loud squishing noises along the empty hallway.

Kennedy knocked lightly and opened Hoppy's office door. "One of the nurses says it's not a girl. It's an adult female."

"Do you know who it is, then?"

"No, sir. Nurse Gilbert says the patient can't talk, and whoever brought the patient didn't stay."

"No idea who she is?"

"They said she's wearing a bracelet with the initials LM. I think Dr. Harper wants you with her when she goes to isolation, that's what I heard—but he hasn't come and said anything to me."

"Whatever," he said, meaning it.

There were two choices, Hoppy once told him. A doctor could believe the patient was going to live, or that the patient was going to die. He had referred to something a patient told him about her former physician. She said he hadn't believed she was going to live. In fact, she went on to say she felt like the doctor's attitude was killing her.

Nurse Kennedy rapped on the door and peered in.

"Father, Dr. Harper wants you in isolation in ten minutes. He asked me to give you a run-down.

"It's a forty percent burn, primarily on the left side of the body and mostly third-degree. No eye injury, but a lot of grafting will be necessary. They've put the patient on a respirator, to keep the airway open. It was a flash burn with kerosene, there was some inhalation injury, and swelling was occluding the airway. She can't talk, even without the endotracheal tube, and probably won't be able to for several days."

"Grafting . . ." he said, remembering a seminary friend who was in a car accident.

"Yes, sir. They've just washed off the debris and given her another shot of morphine for the pain, but there's a lot of pain that can't be controlled. The trauma surgeon said to talk to her, it will calm her. We hope you don't mind doing it. You're so good at it."

"Of course I don't mind. Anything else I should know?"

"Dr. Harper will tell you anything else. They've admitted her as LM, for the time being. Want some coffee?"

If he had passed out when Sassy Guthrie came into the world, what might he do in the face of this hellish thing?

Isolation.

As he opened the door to the gray room, he felt he was stepping into a place removed, out of time. And the smell. There was always the alien smell of fluids that didn't belong to the human frame, but could, nonetheless, sustain it.

The suffering beneath the mound of wet dressing was palpable. He felt the impact of it like a blow.

He walked to the bed and looked hard at what he could see of the patient. Only a small portion of the right side of her face was visible, distorted by the large tube that entered her mouth. The smell of saline, which permeated the dressings, came to him like a sour wind from the sea. Dear God. Could he speak?

The patient opened her eye and gazed into his, and he suddenly felt the power to do this thing surge through him.

"You're not alone. I'm with you."

Tears coursed from her eye onto the pillow, and he took a tissue from the box by the bed. He started to wipe her tears, but instinctively drew back, afraid of inflicting pain with his touch.

"I've asked the Holy Spirit to be with us, also."

He had seen eyes that beseeched him from the very soul, but he hadn't seen anything like this in his life as a priest.

He had no idea where the thought came from—it seemed to come from a place in him as deep as the patient's desperation. "I'm asking God to give me some of your pain," he said, hoarse with feeling. "I'll share this thing with you."

She looked at him again and closed her eye.

He brought the chair from the corner of the gray room and placed it next to her bed, and sat down.

Lord, give me power and grace to do what I just said I'd do. Whatever it takes.

He called the little yellow house and told Cynthia what he knew.

"The decision has been made, then," she said.

"What do you mean?"

"The burn victim from the Creek—I was praying for a sign, something certain, and this is it. Lace must be taken out of that hell."

"Yes," he said.

"I can't imagine what's going on, why we haven't seen her. I'll call social services and find out if they've learned anything. Then I'll go and sign the papers."

"Let me know. I'll be home . . . sometime. Probably before dinner. I have the distinct sense I'm to stick here."

"I'll bring Louella to see Miss Sadie at eleven, and I'll fetch Winnie this evening. Against everything that strives to make it otherwise, I shall say it anyway—happy birthday, dearest love."

"You're precious to me, Kavanagh."

His wife gulped and hung up.

He had missed Dave, the computer technician, but Emma had not. She'd been there, alone, for a two-hour session he presumed would put her over the edge.

The least he could do was call. "How was it?" he asked cautiously.

"It was terrific! It was fabulous!"

"It was?" Had his hearing failed utterly?

"Dave brought lunch, it was cheeseburgers all the way and fries with milkshakes. We ate ours and split yours."

"Glad to be of service." He dreaded the rest of the conversation.

"Finally, I don't know how it happened, but I just got . . . I don't know, it started coming together. You won't believe this . . . "

"Try me."

"I did the first page of the newsletter."

"No!"

"All the margins, a bulleted list, your message of the month, and the masthead."

"Fantastic!"

"Not to mention a border. And not just a bunch of those dumb rule lines, either."

"Really?"

"Greek keys," she said with feeling. "Dave brought me a free solitaire program, and you get *Learning the Books of the Bible.*"

"I'll be darned."

"You won't have to hire some young thing with her skirt up to here, after all," she crowed.

"Aha."

"But you will have to give me a raise."

"Well . . . "

"And I don't mean maybe!"

He viewed this turn of events as the best birthday present, bar none, since Cynthia Coppersmith accepted his marriage proposal. If Emma Newland would take on the infernal nuisance of the whole thing, including hanging indents, he wouldn't oppose her raise for all the tea in China.

"By the way," said Emma, "I found the file folder with the lists in it."

"Where?"

"Under the seat cushion of Harold's recliner next to the TV in our sunroom."

He didn't inquire, because he didn't want to know.

Hoppy creaked back in his desk chair, exhausted.

"What's the worst that can happen?" he asked, exhausted himself.

"Infection. Pneumonia. Setbacks. If we don't have one or all of these, it will be a minor miracle."

"Tell me everything."

"The burns are of mixed depths—some partial, but mostly full-thickness burns. I don't think there'll be any grafting to fat, but I won't know until Cornell Wyatt gets here. He'll fly in tomorrow with his burn nurse, and we expect to harvest the donor sites the following day."

"What areas will need new skin?"

"The left side of her face—we'll probably harvest the graft from behind the ear and neck on the right side. Her neck, shoulder, arm, upper body, and portion of the upper hip will also be recipient sites. It looks like an explosion, maybe the kerosene ignited in front of her and exploded as she turned away."

"I have a special feeling for this patient."

"Why?"

"I don't have a clue," he said. "Maybe it's the praying. I think when we pray for others, even total strangers, it bonds us in ways we can't understand."

"We're pulling this thing together by the seat of our pants. I've never had serious burn experience. Cornell owes me a big one, and this is a big one. By the way, LM lost her left ear."

"Blast."

"We'll be changing her dressings twice a day until the grafts are done, and no amount of morphine can kill the pain that comes with that. I'd like you to be with her after the dressing changes, whenever you can, around nine in the morning and eight at night. I know you're busy, this is not your job . . . "

"Actually, it is my job."

"LM," said Hoppy, abstractedly looking at the wall. "Cornell said if we could call her by her first name, it would help."

"What's the best that can happen?"

"With no pneumonia, no infection, no setbacks, she'll be here two, maybe three weeks, then to Winston-Salem for some very aggressive physical therapy. Best scenario, a long recovery and pronounced scarring."

"How is the grafting done?"

"You don't want to know."

"I do want to know."

"Picture a machine like an electric cheese slicer. You adjust the calibration to the desired thickness and width of the graft you need to harvest. I've heard burn patients say the sound of it gave them nightmares for years.

"In any case, it generally gives you a nice sheet of skin from the buttocks, which can be used for trunk and arm injuries. Bottom line, grafting is a big slice of hell for everybody—doctors, staff, and patient alike."

"I wouldn't have your job, pal."

"I wouldn't have yours."

"So, it's a wash," said the rector, managing a smile. "I'm going in to talk with LM a few minutes, then I'll step down the hall to Miss Sadie. How is she?"

Hoppy ran his fingers through his graying hair. He started to speak, then changed his mind.

If Hoppy was short on burn experience, so was he. They were all flying by the seat of their pants.

He stood by her bed and held the rail, and watched the random flickering of the lid over her closed eye. Sleeping, perhaps, or lost in the mist produced by morphine. The air in the tube that formed her breath sounded harsh against the constant hiss and gurgle of the IV drips.

He prayed aloud, but kept his voice quiet. "Our Father, thank You for being with us, for we can't bear this alone. Cool and soothe, heal and restore, love and protect. Comfort and unite those who're concerned for her, and keep them in Your care. We're asking for Your best here, Lord, we're expecting it. In Jesus' name."

She opened her eye after a moment and he looked into the deep well of it, feeling a strangely familiar connection.

"Hey, there," he said, smiling foolishly.

CHAPTER EIGHTEEN

Every Trembling Heart

SADIE ELEANOR BAXTER died peacefully in her sleep on June 30, in the early hours of the morning.

When the rector of Lord's Chapel received the phone call, he went at once to the hospital room, where he took Miss Sadie's cold hand and knelt and prayed by her bedside.

He then drove to the church, climbed the stairs to the attic, and tolled the death bell twenty times. The mournful notes pealed out on the light summer air, waking the villagers to confusion, alarm, or a certain knowing.

"It's old Sadie Baxter," said Coot Hendrick's mother, sitting up in bed in a stocking cap. Coot, who was feeding a boxful of biddies he had bought to raise for fryers, called from the kitchen, "Lay back down, Mama!"

Mule Skinner turned over and listened, but didn't wake Fancy, who could have slept through the bombing of London. "There went Miss Baxter," he whispered to the darkened room.

J. C. Hogan heard the bells in his sleep and worked them into a dream of someone hammering spikes on a railroad being laid to Tulsa, Oklahoma. *Bong, bong, bong, John Henry was a steel drivin' man . . .*

Cynthia Kavanagh got up and prayed for her husband, whose pain she felt as if it were her own, and went to the kitchen and made coffee, and sat at the table in her robe, waiting until a reasonable hour to call Meadowgate Farm and all the others who'd want to know.

Winnie Ivey, awake since four-thirty, stopped in the middle of the kitchen on Lilac Road, where a dim light burned in the hood of the stove, and prayed, thanking God for the life of one who had cared about people and stood for something, and who, as far as she was concerned, would never be forgotten.

Louella Baxter Marshall had not been asleep when she heard the bells toll; she had been praying on and off throughout the night, and weeping and talking aloud to Miss Sadie and the Lord. When the tolling came, she sat up, and, without meaning to, exactly, exclaimed, "Thank you, Jesus! Thank you for takin' her home!"

Lew Boyd heard the bells and woke up and looked at his watch, which he never took off except in the shower, and saw the long line of automobiles snaking up to his gas pumps and buying his candy and cigarettes and canned drinks. Sadie Baxter's funeral would draw a crowd, he could count on it. He sighed and went back to sleep until his watch beeped.

Jena Ivey, who was up and entering figures in her ledger for Mitford Blossoms, shivered. She would have to hire on help to do the wreaths and sprays for this one. This would be bigger than old Parrish Guthrie's had ever hoped to be, the old so-and-so, and so what if Miss Sadie had never bought so much as a gloxinia from Mitford Blossoms, Sadie Baxter had been a lady and she had loved this town and done more for it than anybody else ever would, God rest her soul in peace.

Esther Bolick punched Gene and woke him up.

"Sadie Baxter's gone," she said.

"How d'you know?"

"The bells are tolling."

"Maybe it's th' president or somebody like that," said Gene, who remembered the hoopla over Roosevelt's passing.

"I don't think so," said his wife. "I saw the president on TV yesterday and he looked fit as a fiddle."

Percy Mosely was leaving his house at the edge of town when he heard the first tolling. He removed his hat and placed it over his heart and was surprised to feel a tear coursing down his cheek for someone he'd hardly ever exchanged five words with in his life, but whose presence above the town, at the crest of the steep fern bank, had been a consolation for as long as he could remember.

After tolling the bell, the rector went to Lilac Road and sat with Louella and prayed the ancient prayer of commendation: "Acknowledge, we humbly beseech You, a sheep of Your own fold, a lamb of Your own flock. . . . Receive her into the arms of Your mercy, into the blessed rest of everlasting peace, and into the glorious company of the saints. . . ."

Then he did what others after him would do with Sadie Baxter's lifelong friend. He sat and wept with her, sobbing like a child.

He dialed the number and listened to the odd, buzzing ring of a rural telephone.

"Brother Greer . . ." he said.

"Is it Sadie?" asked the old man.

"It is."

"I'll come, then," said Absalom.

He had done this for thirty-eight years—arranging the funeral, delivering the service, consoling the family. But now he was the family, and there was no consolation anywhere. It was as if a part of his own life had been suddenly lost, and there was no getting it back again.

He signed the papers that allowed her body to be taken to Holding and cremated, and was wondering what to do about a marker and urn when the phone rang.

"Father Kavanagh? Lewis Cromwell of Cromwell, Cromwell and Lessing, in Wesley. We've been the Baxter family law firm since the turn of the century."

"Of course. Miss Sadie often spoke of you and your father and grandfather."

"I've just learned of her passing; Louella called this morning. I wanted you to know there's a letter here, and it was Miss Baxter's express wish that you have it immediately following her death."

"How shall I get it?"

"We'll send it over to you. I have a young assistant who must come that way to pick up produce at your local grocery store. You know how fond we Wesleyans are of your fine grocer."

"Avis Packard is almost as famous as his advertising professes."

"I know you were important to Miss Baxter, and we'd like to express our condolences to you, sir."

"Thank you."

"It's the end of an era," said Lewis Cromwell.

It was delivered to the office as he was leaving for home.

He hardly knew what to do with it. Perhaps he should sit with it awhile before he opened it. She had inscribed his name on the front of the fat envelope in her spidery scrawl, and sealed it with Scotch tape that looked nearly fresh.

When he arrived home, he thumped down at the kitchen table, holding it in his hand.

"Take it to your study," said Cynthia, "and I'll bring you a pot of tea."

He didn't want tea. He didn't want to go to his study. He felt desperately worn and addled, as if he had overused his mind for something he couldn't even call to memory.

He wanted to lie down, that's what he wanted. But somehow, that was no way to read a letter, especially a letter from the departed. That seemed to warrant sitting up in a straight-back chair.

"Blast," he said to nothing and no one in particular.

"Then take it over to my house," she said, reading his mind. "Sit on my loveseat in the studio. That's what I do when I need consolation."

He didn't want to go over to her small, empty house and sit on that small loveseat in that small room.

"Why don't I just sit here and read it?" he asked, looking forlorn.

"Wonderful! Do you mind if I make dinner while you sit there?"

Mind? He couldn't think of anything he'd like better. He suddenly felt protected by his wife's close presence, the familiarity of the cooking ritual, the ordinariness of it all.

Brightening, he opened the letter with a table knife.

The date was September seventh of the previous year.

Dear Father,

We have just come home from your lovely wedding ceremony, and I don't know when our hearts have felt so refreshed. The joy of it makes my pen fairly fly over the page.

To see you taking a bride, even after so many years, seemed like the most natural thing in the world. Certainly no one can ever say that you married in haste to repent at leisure!

Long years ago when I loved Willard so dearly and hoped against hope that we might marry, I wrote down something Martin Luther said. He said, there is no more lovely, friendly and charming relationship, communion, or company than a good marriage.

May God bless you and Cynthia to enjoy a good marriage, and a long and happy life together.

As you know, I have given a lot of money to human institutions, and I would like to give something to a human individual for a change.

I have prayed about this and so has Louella and God has given us the go ahead.

I am leaving Mama's money to Dooley.

We think he has what it takes to be somebody. You know that Papa was never educated, and look what he became with no help at all. And Willard—look what he made of himself without any help from another soul.

Father, having no help can be a good thing. But having help can be even better—if the character is strong. I believe you are helping Dooley develop the kind of character that will go far in this world, and so the money is his when he reaches the age of twenty one.

(I am old fashioned and believe that eighteen is far too young to receive an inheritance.)

I have put one and a quarter million dollars where it will grow, and have made provisions to complete his preparatory education. When he is eighteen, the income from the trust will help send him through college.

I am depending on you never to mention this to him until he is old enough to bear it with dignity. I am also depending on you to stick with him, Father, through thick and thin, just as you've done all along.

When you receive this letter, there are two things you will need to know at once. First, the urn for my ashes is in the attic at Fernbank. When you go up the stairs, turn to the right and go all the way to the back. I have left it there on a little table, it is from czarist Russia, which Papa once visited. Don't scatter me among any rose bushes, Father, I know how you think. Just stick the urn in the ground as far away from Parrish Guthrie as you can, cover it with enough dirt to support a tuft of moss, and add my little marker.

The other thing you need to know at once is that my marker is with Mr. Charles Hartley of Hartley's Monument Company in Holding. It is paid for. You might say it is on hold in Holding, ha ha. I think it is foolish nonsense to choose one's own epitaph, it makes one either overly modest or overly boastful. I leave this task to you, and trust you not to have anything fancy or high-toned engraved thereon, for I am now and always will be just plain Sadie.

I am going to lay down my pen and rest, but will take it up again this evening. It is so good to write this letter, which has been composing in my head for years! It was your wedding today which made me understand that one must get on with one's life, and that always includes the solemn consideration of one's death.

He looked up to see his wife rubbing a chicken with olive oil, and humming quietly to herself. An extraordinary sight, somehow, in view of this even more extraordinary letter.

He noted the renewed strength of Miss Sadie's handwriting as the letter resumed.

We are going to watch TV this evening and pop some corn, so I will make it snappy.

As for Fernbank, I ask you to go through the attic with Olivia and Cynthia and take whatever you like. Take anything that suits you from the house, also. I can't imagine what it might be, but I would like you to select something for Mr. Buck Leeper, who is doing such a lovely job with Hope House. Perhaps something of Papa's would be in order.

Whatever is left, please give it to the needy, or to your Children's Hospital. Do not offer anything for view at a yard sale or let people pick over the remains. I know you will understand.

I leave Fernbank to supply any future requirements of Hope House. Do with my homeplace what you will, but please treat it kindly. If I should pass before Louella, she has a home for life at Hope House, and provision to cover any special needs. I know you will do all in your power to look after her, she is my sister and beloved friend.

It would be grand if I could live to be a hundred, and go Home with a smile on my face. I believe I will! But if not, I have put all the buttons on my affairs, and feel a light spirit for whatever God has in store for me.

May our Lord continue to bless you, Father, you mean the world to

yours truly,
Sadie Eleanor Baxter

He looked up and met Cynthia's concerned gaze.

"What is it, dearest?"

"You mustn't speak this to another soul," he said.

"I won't. I promise."

"Sit down," he said. She sat.

"Dooley Barlowe," he told her, "is a millionaire."

"No one ever thinks the preacher might be sad at a funeral," said Absalom Greer, who had come to the rector's office.

"You're right about that."

"They don't know we suffer, too."

The two men grew silent for a moment, drinking their coffee.

"How did you get here?" asked the rector.

"Th' man that keeps my orchard, he brought me in his truck. He'll bring me back for the memorial service."

"After the service, we'll take the urn to the churchyard. There'll be just a few of us for that. Will you come?"

"Oh, I will," said the old man. "I once told Sadie Baxter I'd love her to her grave, and I'm a man of my word." His blue eyes twinkled. "Lottie told me this morning, she said, 'Absalom, I forgive Sadie.' It was all I could do to keep from saying, 'This is a fine time to do it, after she's dead and gone.' If I was the Lord, I'd say that dog won't hunt."

"Thank heaven you're not the Lord," said the rector.

They laughed easily.

"I wonder who she left her money to," wondered Absalom. "The church, I'd say."

"That's a good guess."

"Sadie's life will preach up a storm. You'll have a fine subject and a big crowd. What do you want me to do?"

"I'd like you to sit with Louella and Olivia and Hoppy, as family."

"I will, and glad to."

"You sent Lacey Turner to see me," said the rector.

"I knew you'd help her, if you could."

"I want you to know we care about her. I reported the abuse, and the DA's office is looking for her. They'll put her in foster care if they can't locate a relative."

The old preacher nodded. "It's a hard case, Brother, a hard case. God help you to do what you can."

Louella would sing a hymn in her throaty mezzo soprano, which was as consoling as raisins in warm bread. No, she wouldn't break down, she was wanting to do it! Hadn't she sung with Miss Sadie since they were both little children?

The choir director, who was known for inventiveness, suggested Dooley sing with Louella, but no one thought he would. The rector called the boy, anyway.

"What're we singing?" Dooley asked, already persuaded.

" 'Love Divine, All Loves Excelling.' "

"No problem. What instruments?"

"Organ and trumpets."

"I can't sing over trumpets," said Dooley.

"You don't have to sing when the trumpets are playing."

"When is rehearsal?"

"Tomorrow at three o'clock. I'll see you at Meadowgate around two."

"I'm sorry she died," he said. "It seemed like she'd live a long time."

That, he thought, is the way it always seems with someone we love.

He raced to the hospital to see LM. Who had sat with her after the last dressing change? How was the morphine doing? Any signs of infection? A few hours away from a desperate situation could seem interminable; he felt out of the loop.

"So far, so good," said Nurse Gilbert. "They start grafting in the morning. Dr. Wyatt got in last night with his nurse."

He let himself into the room and stood by her bed.

"Hey, there," he said, softly.

It appeared she had not moved since he first saw her. Still the great, swollen mass of wet dressings and the odor that stung the nostrils. Still the eye looking desperately into his, and the air pumping mechanically from the respirator into the green tube.

He didn't know why, but as he looked down at her, something in him connected with a new reality. It suddenly became real to him that Sadie Baxter was where the gospel had promised a redeemed soul would be—in Paradise. If he believed that so fully and completely, why was he grieving? Because it had taken time for such supernal knowledge to make its way from his heart to his head. Or was it from his head to his heart?

He realized that he was smiling uncontrollably, as he had smiled in those first months of his marriage. Tears sprang to his eyes, tears of joy, and he felt he should turn away from the woman lying there who felt no joy, whose tears were born of an agony he couldn't possibly know. But he couldn't turn away. He felt riveted there, beaming, as if his face were not his own.

He reached out to touch her right hand, the one that was completely and wholly well, and saw that he took it, and held it, and wept and did not turn away.

"Father! It's Scott Murphy!"

"I needed to hear your voice, my friend."

"I'm excited about coming to Hope House, sir. September is only two months away, and I've already given my notice. How are things in Mitford?"

"Sadie Baxter has died. The memorial service is tomorrow." That was precisely how things were in Mitford—that one event had, for him, obscured all others.

"Miss Baxter? She died? She was . . . so alive when I saw her!"

"She fell, and couldn't recover from the shock of what came with it. I want you to know how heartily she approved of you."

"I'll do my best to honor that, sir."

There was a comfortable silence.

"I'd like you to know what I've been thinking, Father, if it's not too premature to talk about it."

"Never too soon."

"I was wondering . . . I've seen how positively the elderly respond to animals—rabbits, dogs, kittens, I've even worked with ponies. I was just wondering, sir, if there might be anything left in the Hope House budget to build a small . . . kennel."

"A *kennel*?"

"Too rash?" asked Scott, concerned.

"You must admit it's not the ordinary line of thinking."

"But that's just it, Father. Ordinary lines of thinking don't extend far enough when reaching into the lives of people who're often losing touch."

"Keep talking."

"Only a small kennel, so the animals could visit on a regular basis. It's awkward to round up people who'll bring their dogs and cats in. As I recall, that area behind the parking garage might work for a kennel and a run. But it's just a thought, sir, only a thought. Actually, we have the greatest resource of all, right down the street from Hope House."

"We do?"

"At Lord's Chapel. The children, sir."

"Aha."

"I don't have to tell you what a positive influence children and old people can have on each other."

Where had his own enthusiasm gone? Had it flown with his youth?

"I'm also thinking of a garden. There's a plot behind the dining hall that would be perfect for the residents because it's easy to get to. A little digging in the dirt can be good for the soul."

"Absolutely!"

"Anyway, Father, I just wanted you to know that I'm very excited about my future in Mitford, and I thank you—and Miss Baxter—for asking me to come."

"It will be a fine thing, Scott, I know it in my bones."

"Speaking of bones, Luke and Lizzie send their regards."

He laughed when he hung up. Scott Murphy's new blood would be good, indeed, for this old rector, not to mention the forty residents of Hope House who, whether they liked it or not, would be forced to enjoy their last years.

On his way down Main Street from Lew Boyd's, he saw the Independence Day parade forming behind the police station.

The Mitford School Chorus was at the front, as always, carrying the banner inscribed with the mayor's longtime political platform. *Mitford Takes Care of Its Own.*

Next came Coot Hendrick's truck, loaded with hay, and kids waving American flags.

The truck was followed by Fancy Skinner's pink Cadillac, with Mule's real estate sign on the hood and a Hair House sign on the rear. He saw Fancy, dressed in a pink sweater and Capri pants, polishing the hood ornament with a rag.

Still jockeying for position, it appeared, was a woman in a cowboy hat, leading two llamas. He heard the Presbyterian brass band strike up somewhere, and caught a glimpse of a drum majorette who, he presumed, was borrowed from Wesley.

As he drove down Main Street, already lined with spectators, he saw cars turning into the Lord's Chapel parking lot.

To other eyes, perhaps, the north end of Main was getting ready to celebrate while the south end was in mourning.

But he didn't see it that way. Not at all.

While the trumpets sounded the good news of Sadie Baxter's presence in a glorious Heaven, the electric cheese slicer would sound LM's entry into a living Hell.

"Pray for LM," he said to Marge and Olivia before the memorial service.

Ron Malcolm overhead the request. "I'll pray, too," he said.

A priest was thankful for people who didn't need all the details, but took the smallest request to heart, and acted.

"The people have gathered, the trumpets have sounded!" he exclaimed. "Sadie Eleanor Baxter is at home and at peace, and I charge us all to be filled with the joy of this simple, yet wondrous fact."

How often had people heard that, for a Christian, death is but the ultimate triumph, a thing to celebrate? The hope was that it cease being a fact merely believed with the head, and become a fact to know with the heart, as he now knew it.

He looked out to the congregation who packed the nave to bursting, and saw that they knew it too. They had caught the spark. A kind of warming fire ran through the place, kindled with excitement and wonder.

When Louella sang, her voice was steady as a rock, mingling sweetly, yet powerfully, with the boy's. Their music flooded the church with a high consolation.

Jesus, Thou art all compassion
Pure, unbounded love Thou art
Visit us with Thy salvation
Enter every trembling heart . . .

Into the silence that followed the music, and true to his Baptist roots, Absalom Greer raised a heartfelt "Amen!"

The rector looked to the pew where Sadie Baxter had sat for the fifteen years he had been in this pulpit, and saw Olivia and Hoppy, Louella and Absalom holding hands. Those left behind. . . .

"We don't know," he said, in closing, "who among us will be the next to go, whether the oldest or the youngest. We pray that he or she will be gently embraced by death, have a peaceful end, and a glorious resurrection in Christ.

"But for now, let us go in peace—to love and serve the Lord."

"Thanks be to God!" said the congregation, meaning it.

The trumpets blew mightily, and the people moved to the church lawn, where Esther Bolick's three-tiered cake sat on a fancy table, where the ECW had stationed jars of icy lemonade, and where, as any passerby could see, a grand celebration was under way.

"There," he said, placing the small, engraved stone over the fresh earth. *Sadie Eleanor Baxter,* it read. *Beloved.*

She didn't open her eyes at all. He had no way of knowing whether she realized he had come, or even cared.

He pulled the chair close to her bed and sat down. Today, they had taken sheets of skin from the back of her neck, her buttocks, and abdomen, and done all the grafting in one long ordeal which he saw reflected in the face of every nurse he encountered in the hallway.

All of it was beyond words, but he did the best he could.

"Hey, there," he said.

"Timothy!" It was Marge Owen.

"I thought you'd like to know that Dooley delivered twin calves this evening! Hal had gone to a Grange meeting, and Mr. Shuford called and said his prize heifer was having a bad time. I drove Dooley to his farm and . . . he did it!"

He gulped.

"Maybe it wasn't strictly ethical, but . . ."

"Someone had to do it!" he said, heady with pride. "Put him on if he's around."

He heard Marge calling, "Dooley! Dooley?"

Dooley.

"Hey," Dooley said in his grown-up voice.

"Hey, yourself. Tell me everything. Twins, was it?" Sissy and Sassy had started a trend.

"It was Mr. Shuford's best heifer, and Miz Shuford was out in the barn having a fit. She said that heifer was her best friend. I never heard of such a thing, but I knew I better get it right."

He laughed.

"The heifer was in dystocia. If somebody hadn't been there, she could have died. I saw these feet sticking out, one front hoof and one back hoof, and when I reached in there, I could tell there was two calves. I like to died. I figured I had to match up the hooves before I started pulling or I could have strangled one of the calves or something.

"So I run my arm in there and found the front hoof that went with the back hoof that was sticking out, and started pulling, and pretty soon, we had two calves lying in the straw."

Dooley took a deep breath. "I can't exactly remember everything."

"What did Mrs. Shuford say?"

"She gave me a big hug and all, and Mr. Shuford, he gave me a twenty-dollar bill and said it was mine to keep."

"Phew! What a story. I'm proud as heck."

"Yeah," said Dooley. The rector could almost hear the grin spreading over the boy's face.

"I'd like you to tell Cynthia, but she's taking a bath. Can she call you in the morning?"

"She better call before seven. I'm going with Doc Owen to Asheville, to a vet meeting or something."

"Big doings, pal. Well, listen—we love you."

"I love you back!" said Dooley.

He literally jumped around the room, shouting.

"Yee hah!" he yelled. "Yee hah!"

There was no need to hurry back to Fernbank to go through her possessions. That could wait until things slowed down, when it would be a pleasure and not a burden.

He had checked the house carefully when he went for the urn. The roof was still leaking, but not enough to pose a problem as long as he left the pots where they were.

Winnie Ivey had agreed to spend her nights with Louella until Hope House opened in the fall. Winnie appreciated the extra money, but better than that, she and Louella liked each other's company.

All he had to do was go to the law office in Wesley and sign a few papers, which he'd take care of next week.

He mused that he might drive Cynthia to Meadowgate on Sunday, and they'd all troop over to the Shufords and see the twins. It made him grin, just thinking about it.

Cynthia offered to sit with LM in the evening; in fact, she insisted on it.

"Can you handle it?" he asked. "It's not . . . easy, exactly."

"Of course I can handle it. I'm your deacon."

She brought his supper on a tray, and did everything but feed him with a spoon. "Now, rest," she told him, stern as any school principal, "and I don't mean maybe."

Which was worse? Emma Newland or his own wife?

"Yes, ma'am," he said, lying on the sofa and stuffing a pillow under his head. Barnabas leaped up and crashed on top of him, sighing. What more could he ask of life, after all?

He had just fallen asleep when the phone rang.

"Timothy? She wants you."

"Who?" he said, feeling groggy.

"LM. They say she's looking around the room for you, and seems agitated. I wasn't going to disturb you, no matter what, but . . . even I feel this desperation in her. They're taking the breathing tube out in a little while. Can you come?"

"I'll be right up."

The questions he'd been storing were endless.

Who are you? Why hasn't your family been here? How did this happen? What does LM stand for? He had thought Lillian, perhaps, for no sensible reason. How old are you? What do you do? What can I do?

When he arrived at the hospital, Cynthia went home to work on her book, which was due at the publisher in only four weeks.

"Stop at my house as soon as you get home," she said, looking anguished. "I want to know."

In the hallway, he met Hoppy, who grinned at him with relief.

"You can come in while we take out the breathing tube. We're so used to you, it's like you work here."

He waited until the thing was finished, the tube out, and went and stood by the bed. "You probably can't say much for a day or two," Hoppy told his patient. "This thing was inserted between your vocal cords, which means your throat will be sore, and talking won't feel so good. Go easy."

He knew Hoppy was also curious to know more about his patient, but respectfully let the rector have the first round while he took a much-needed break down the hall.

The doctor and the nurse closed the door as they left.

She was swathed in fresh dressings over the grafts. "You're looking good," he said.

She whispered something that was barely audible, and he leaned down to hear it again. "My . . . kids."

"Tell me what I can do."

She only looked at him and shook her head slowly.

What was her name? Was it Lillian? He didn't think he could wait any longer. "What is your name?"

She struggled to swallow.

"What does LM stand for?"

She shook her head. No. "That's . . . th' name of . . ." the tears began, "th' man who . . ."

"Who did this to you?" he said, suddenly knowing.

She nodded her head. Yes.

"Can you tell me your name?" She would like to hear her own name spoken; according to Wyatt, it would be a consolation.

The tears came freely, now, and she worked to open her mouth and speak. "Pauline," she whispered.

"Barlowe," he said, his heart pounding.

She looked at him for what seemed a long time, then nodded her head.

Yes.

CHAPTER NINETEEN

Starting Over

"POOBAW," she whispered.

"Your son." Dooley's little brother, now ten years old.

"Where . . . ?" She swallowed and grimaced. "How is he?"

He knew at once that he would lie. "Fine. Don't worry." What if it was, in fact, a lie? Could LM have done something as sinister to the boy? He would face that later.

"Who . . . has him?"

"He's in good hands."

The tears continued. "So much . . . to tell you," she managed to say.

"I want to hear."

"Th' pain . . . "

"Yes." They had given her a shot only minutes before.

"I want you to know . . . " Her eye closed, and she began to breathe quietly.

"Yes?" he said.

"That I can bear it."

"I can do all things through Christ . . . ," he said, quoting the first part of Olivia's favorite verse from Philippians. He could scarcely hear her response.

" . . . who strengthens me," she whispered.

"What're you havin'?" asked Velma, as J.C. slid into the booth.

"Wheaties and skim milk."

Velma raised her eyebrows. "No coffee?"

"I'm off coffee."

Mule sighed. "Here we go again," he said, as Velma moved to the next booth.

"What's that supposed to mean?" glowered the editor.

"I mean, why don't you marry th' woman and get it over with?"

"What woman?"

"Adele Lynwood! Who else would I be talkin' about?"

The rector blew on his steaming coffee, ready to duck. It was clear that Mule Skinner was tired of intrigue and cover-up. He wanted to see cards on the table.

J.C. sat back in the booth, looking exhausted, and wiped his face with a handkerchief. "Dadblame it," he said.

"Dadblame what?" queried Mule, pressing on.

"I guess you know about Adele."

"Any ninny can see you're sweet on her. What we don't know is—what in th' dickens is goin' on?"

"Dern if I can figure it out," said J.C. "One minute it's on, the next minute it's off."

"One minute it's Wheaties, the next minute it's grits," said the rector.

"Right," said Mule.

The rector swigged his coffee. "Sounds pretty typical to me."

J.C. leaned forward. "It does?"

"Sure. One day you know, one day you don't. Pretty soon, if it's right, you *really* know."

"Oh."

"But how do you know if you really know?" asked Mule.

The rector looked slightly dazed. "I don't know," he said, meaning it.

Mule sighed. "We're kind of rusty at this."

"How come she wants me to get off coffee and axe the fat and lower my cholesterol if she wouldn't go out with me last night? I mean, what's th' deal?"

"Maybe she had to work," said Mule, wanting to help.

"No way. She was home cleanin' her gun."

"How do you know?"

"Because I called her up and that's what she said she was doing."

"Where had you offered to take her?" asked the rector.

"To Brendle's, they were having a sale on Tri-X film."

"No wonder she stayed home to clean a gun," said Mule.

"Have you sent her flowers?" asked Father Tim. "That's a good thing to do."

"Flowers? To a woman who carries a nine-millimeter?"

"Whoa, buddy," said Mule. "You're soundin't mighty macho there. It's th' woman's *job* to carry a gun."

"Women like flowers," said the rector. "It's that simple. Maybe she's trying to look after your best interests, and you're not looking after hers."

J.C. scratched his head. "I don't think that's it. I sent my first wife flowers once, and look what happened."

"Once won't cut it," said the rector.

"Right," said Mule.

"Do you care about her?" asked Father Tim.

J.C. turned red. "Yeah. I care about her. We go out. We do stuff."

"What stuff?"

"Oh, this and that. She cooks at her place pretty often, I took pork chops once."

Mule looked at the rector.

"Sounds like there's a whole lot of *once* in the way you operate," said Father Tim. "Once you sent flowers, once you took pork chops."

"Yeah," said Mule.

"There's the problem," said the rector.

"So? So I'm supposed to go crawling on my belly like a snake to get this woman interested in me again?"

"Sending flowers is not crawling on your belly."

"And why take pork chops," asked Mule, "if she's tryin' to get you off fat and cholesterol? You ought to take . . . let's see . . . "

"Tofu," said the rector.

"Man!" said J.C., mopping his face. "If I listen to you turkeys, I'll be in up to my neck."

Mule leaned back for Velma to set his plate down. "You're in so deep now, you need a bloomin' shovel. And why not listen to us? We've got credentials."

"Right," said the rector. "We're married."

"By th' dern grace of God, if you ask me," said J.C.

"Right again," agreed Father Tim.

"OK, I'll listen," sighed the editor. "But just this once."

He could hardly wait to leave the office and get to the hospital, where, according to Nurse Kennedy, Pauline Barlowe had been up to the bathroom and was drinking juice.

We're still praying, Kennedy had said, pneumonia is a possibility, infection is a likelihood—we're not out of the woods by a long shot.

He was finishing his sermon notes, which Emma, God love her, had offered to key into the computer, when he heard a knock on the door.

"Father?"

Olivia Harper stuck her head in the office and smiled. "Is this a good time?"

He got up and went to greet her. "It's always a good time for you."

"I just wanted to talk to you about something at Aunt Sadie's."

"Sit in Emma's chair. Want some bubble gum?"

She took a piece. "What in the world are you doing with bubble gum?"

"Amy Larkin keeps me supplied."

She laughed. "Who doesn't love you?"

"Don't tell me that. I'll get the big head."

"You know we were thrilled with Aunt Sadie's memorial service. Thank you for talking about who she was and what she stood for."

"It's important to do that in a small community, important to talk about the loved one. It departs a bit from the traditional Anglican burial service, but . . . "

"But this is the *South*!" she said, laughing.

He grinned. "What's up?"

"There's a mahogany chest of drawers at Fernbank, which Louella says I should have. I just wanted to check with you before I go rifling through."

"My dear, you don't have to check with me. Take whatever you want, and after Louella's gone through, Cynthia and I will go through. Miss Sadie would have wanted it that way, she just assumed we'd know that. After all, you're blood kin."

"I had my great-aunt for such a short time."

"That you had her at all was supernatural."

"You're so right," she said, as the phone rang.

"Lord's Chapel, Father Kavanagh speaking."

"Father Kavanagh, Doug Wyeth at social services in Wesley. We thought you'd like to know the DA's office was successful."

"They were?"

"We have Lacey."

He felt caught off guard.

"We're looking for a foster home, but so far nothing has worked out. We've established there are no other relatives, at least none that we can locate."

"What will you do, then?" he asked.

"If we can't work out the foster care, she'll have to go down the mountain to an emergency shelter."

That didn't sound good.

"I know your interest in this case, Father. Would you be open to taking her on a temporary basis? You're not licensed for foster care, but we could get you authorized temporarily."

"Let me . . . think about it," he said. "I'd have to . . . Let me call you back in, what, half an hour?"

"Fine. You have my number."

"How is Lace?"

"Angry," said Doug Wyeth.

He put the phone down and shook his head.

"Lace?" asked Olivia.

"The district attorney's office. They found her—she's with social services. They're trying to get her in foster care, but haven't been successful yet."

Olivia sat forward in the chair. "Let us take her, Father."

"Good Lord, Olivia! You can't know what you're saying."

"But I do. Hoppy and I, we've talked about taking someone in. We thought it would be Louella until Hope House opens, but it worked out so beautifully for Winnie to keep Louella company. I liked Lace. We can do it."

"But surely it would be too much. . . ." The idea seemed wildly improbable.

"Father, God spared my life! Against impossible odds, he gave me a new heart. I believe to this day it was yours and Hoppy's prayers that opened the gates of heaven and worked miracles with my transplant. All that for what?" she asked, her violet eyes dark with feeling.

"To be the happy wife of a wonderful man? I need to give something back. I may not do it well, but I shall give it everything I've got. Let us take Lace."

Why shouldn't he grant this request to the woman whose lifetime verse was one he'd just quoted to Pauline Barlowe?

"Besides," she said, pressing on, "look what you've done with Dooley."

Surely, as clergy, his word could help get the Harpers authorized.

"Call them back," she urged, meaning it.

She was hoarse, still, and could only whisper. "When you looked at me . . . " she said, trying to swallow.

He waited.

" . . . and cried, I felt some of the pain leave me."

"Really?" He was croaking like a frog. Who could tell which one of them had had a tube shoved down their trachea? "I'm glad."

"I think I always know when you come, no matter how much morphine."

"Yes. Good."

"Why?" she asked.

"Why what?"

"Why do you care?"

"Because . . . " What could he say, after all? Because I love your son with all my heart? Because any mother of his is a friend of mine? Because you were sufferering and that was enough for me? Who knows why? The truth was, he had come because they called him, and then he started caring and couldn't stop.

"I've done . . . terrible things."

"Haven't we all?" he asked with feeling.

Her tears came freely. "Terrible," she said again.

He stood with her and waited.

"My children. I gave 'em away."

He nodded, understanding that the tears would swell her eyes and cause more pain and discomfort. Pain, and endless pain, he thought.

"What . . . is your name?" she asked.

"Timothy Kavanagh. Father Kavanagh."

"You're the one who has Dooley."

"Yes."

"I knew you had him. They said . . . "

"What did they say?" he asked gently.

"They said you sent him . . . to school."

"A friend sent him. It's helping. He's healing."

"Healing." She closed her eye, and the tears continued to flow. She was silent for a long time. "I wanted to see him. . . . I sat in front of your house twice, hoping to see him. But I heard you were good to him, and so . . . I let him be."

He nodded.

"A while back, I said a prayer . . . with old Preacher Greer . . . "

He waited.

"When I done that, I seen what a mess I'd made of my life . . . an' th' pain was . . . so big, so terrible."

She swallowed and looked at him. "But for the first time . . . "

"Yes?"

"I had the strength to bear it."

"It often happens that way."

"Th' reason I used to drink whiskey and anything I could lay my hands on was because . . . I couldn't bear it."

He nodded.

"I lost my ear," she whispered.

"Yes. I'm sorry." He realized he'd been whispering, too.

"I've asked God to help me forgive Lester Marshall. I knowed it was wrong to go on livin' with him, but . . . " She moved her right hand toward the rector. "Pray for me," she implored, "to get my children back."

He stood there, frozen, and saw her hand move toward his as if in slow motion.

Pray for her to take Dooley? Ask God to let the unthinkable happen?

The recent events of his life had forced more than one truth to the surface, and now another came.

Dooley did not belong to Pauline Barlowe. Nor did he belong to him. Dooley belonged to God. Period. Dooley was not his to give back.

"I been drivin' Harley Welch's ol' truck since I was twelve. I can haul butt."

Lacey sat on a high stool in the small office, swinging her leg and chewing gum. She was wearing the hat, and her clothes were caked with engine oil and mud.

"So when I heard Pauline hollerin', I run down there and th' son of a—" She stopped and looked at the rector. "Th' son of a gun was tryin' to burn 'er up. He run out of th' house, and I th'owed a blanket around 'er and hauled 'er out to th' porch. I went an' got Harley's truck and we put 'er in it, and I took 'er to th' hospital. I left th' hospital before they knowed anything, 'cause I heard police was lookin' for me."

"Where's Poobaw?" asked the rector.

"I ain't tellin' that."

"No harm will come to him or you, Lace."

"I still ain't tellin'."

"His mother would like to know. Is he safe?"

She shrugged. "I don't know, how do I know? I was th' one lookin' out for 'im. Now y'll done ruint that."

"We're going to be placing you in foster care," said Doug Wyeth. "We'll just need—"

She jumped off the stool. "You ain't doin' any such thing!" she shouted. "I thought you brung me in here 'cause of drivin' without a license."

Cursing, she made a run for the door. It took two social workers to stop her and hold her.

If Olivia Harper could handle this, he thought, she could become a canonized saint.

They lay in bed, looking at the ceiling. Rain had pounded the village all day, and shadows cast by the tossing leaves danced above them.

"It's not a question of if, but when," he said.

"I feel we should let him see her right away. He can handle it. Surely she can't take him out of school or even away from Meadowgate, because she has no place to live. Also, she's facing months of physical therapy."

"I'll call him. What time is it?"

"Eight-thirty. Good heavens, don't ever tell anybody we're in bed this early. We'd be the laughingstock."

"If you only knew how many people are sawing wood in this town, even as we speak."

"I've become a rustic," she sighed.

"And no help for it."

Why think about it and ponder it and try to make up the right thing to say? He'd just say it simply, and go on, believing the best. He was reaching for the phone when it rang.

"Hey," said Dooley.

"Hey, yourself, buddy."

"Miz Shuford asked me to name them calves."

"That's terrific. And what did you name them?"

"Jessie and Kenny."

"Ah. Good. That's good." The names of his little sister and younger brother.

"I was going to name them Lillie and Willie."

"I like Jessie and Kenny."

"How's ol' Cynthia?"

"Couldn't be better. Want to say hello?"

"Yeah."

"Dooley, you big lug. How are you?"

"I named the calves Jessie and Kenny."

"Dr. Dooley Barlowe, full-service vet. I heal, I deliver, I name. You're great!"

"You coming out Sunday?"

"Yes, we want to see Jessie and Kenny."

"Good. They're real healthy. You'll like 'em."

"I like you!"

"I like you back."

She reached across him and hung up the phone.

"I couldn't do it," she said.

"I couldn't, either."

"We're letting him have two more days of innocent boyhood," she said. "We can tell him on Sunday."

"Right. I'll tell Pauline he's coming to see her."

They were silent for a long time, holding hands.

"Are you ever sorry you married a parson?"

"Why should I be?"

"I can't leave my work at the office."

"Of course you can't. Your job isn't nine to five, it's noon to noon. I knew that, dearest. Besides, I love your work, too. Remember, I'm your deacon."

He rolled over and kissed her and felt the softness of her body against his. "Such a deal," he murmured. "Every clergyman in the nation would be wildly jealous."

It was ponytail time again, if he didn't act soon.

Hadn't he just had his hair cut? What a blasted aggravation that, while no hair ever grew on top, the rest of his head appeared to be fertilized with Miracle-Gro.

Another aggravation was whether to slip around behind Joe Ivey's back and see Fancy, or be loyal, as was his bent, and force himself up the stairs to Joe's chair, where, according to Fancy, those chipmunk puffs over his ears were made to prosper and flourish.

Dadgum it, it seemed a man should at least be able to get a haircut without a hassle.

"Six hundred and thirty-two," said Emma, keying in the previous week's collections. "No, six hundred and seventy-five. You need a haircut."

"Where should I get it?" he asked, thrilled to pass on the responsibility of a decision.

"Go to Fancy. Joe makes you look like a chipmunk," she said without looking away from the computer screen.

He was liking Emma Newland better every day.

"Has your raise come through yet?" he asked.

"Not unless Harold's goat ate it out of th' mailbox."

"I'll take care of it," he said, glad to be of service.

"We're bringing Dooley to see you," he said. "Either Sunday evening or Monday."

"I don't deserve it."

"God's grace isn't about deserving," he said, taking her hand.

She smiled. It was the first time he had seen her smile.

"May I . . . call you Father?"

"Please. And would you like to see your own father? He's well and well cared for. It will give him joy."

She nodded yes.

"I've been . . . thinking, Father."

"Tell me."

"You should keep Dooley 'til he's out of school. School is a good thing—my mother tried to tell me that. Then he can do whatever God wants him to do. I won't try . . . to take him back."

"Good," he said. "That's best."

"But my other kids . . . "

"Where are they?"

"After I prayed that prayer, I tried to find them."

He was used to her tears. They were a kind of language that needed expression.

"Kenny, I gave him to . . ."

He sat in the chair by her bed and waited.

"To . . . "

"It's all right."

" . . . somebody for a gallon of whiskey an' . . . a hundred dollars."

He really didn't know if he could deal with this. He was only human, after all. Being clergy didn't equip him with some shield and suit of armor. No, this was too blasted much. He needed reinforcement. He didn't even want to hear any more.

"It hurts me to hear it," he said. Why beat around the bush?

She looked at him, imploring.

"Can we find Kenny?" he asked.

"He was in Oregon th' last time I knowed."

There was a long silence, which he didn't try to break.

"Poobaw," she said. "We call him that because he liked to tote around a pool ball I brought home, an' that's what he called it. He's ten, he's such a good boy, Father, always happy. . . . "

"And Jessie?"

"She's four. So . . . little. So . . . pretty." She sobbed brokenly, and he wanted to turn away, to run out the door and not come back.

"Father . . . I want so much . . . to start over. Do you think God . . . will let me start over?"

"That," he said, meaning it, "is what God is all about."

Nurse Gilbert's uniform rustled cripsly as she walked in with a needle. "This will help," she said, going to Pauline.

If only it could, he thought.

"Lord help! Look at this! Are you practicin' to be John the Baptist in a church play? Remember what happened to him, honey, his hair was so bad-lookin', they cut his head off.

"How's your wife, I saw her the other day, she was at the food bank givin' a ton of stuff, all I took was sweet potatoes and cream of mushroom soup, do you think that's OK? Do you know what all you can *do* with cream of mushroom soup? It's more versatile than Cheez Whiz, you can pour it over chicken and bake it covered, and Lord, it is the best thing you ever put in your mouth, Mule loves it, do you ever use it? Well, you should, you can also pour it over a roast, but you have to wrap that thing like a mummy for it to work, at least two sheets of foil, and let it go on three fifty for two hours.

"Speakin' of foil, I'm learning to highlight with foil, I used to use a cap, but that is outdated, nobody does that anymore who's up to the minute. Do you know what it costs to be up to the minute in this business? I went to a convention in Charlotte, you wouldn't believe the hotel rooms down there, they cost an arm and a leg and you open your curtains and all you see is a brick wall.

"Speakin' of walls, I hear Cynthia knocked holes in your kitchen, I said, 'Mule, what is that *about*?' Is that the latest thing, to knock holes in your wall? He said, 'Fancy, if you knock holes in our walls, I will personally knock your head off,' ha, ha. I'm sure she had a reason, she's so smart, we all like her, I think you did really great to get her.

"Oops, there I go, pokin' you with these nails, they're acrylic, mine won't grow because I never drank milk as a kid, don't you think it's awful the things you do when you're young and have to pay for down the road? Like layin' in th' sun. Look at these wrinkles around my mouth, see that? Sun! Too much sun. But I say, why quit now, if it's goin' to kill me, I've already had enough to keel me over two or three times.

"Speakin' of keelin' over, I hated to hear about ol' Miss Baxter, was she a friend of yours, I hope she left you some of that money she's been hoardin' back all these years. Whoa, baby, wouldn't it be a deal for a preacher to have big bucks? What would you do, probably go to the Caribbean on a cruise, I have always wanted to go on a cruise, Mule says next year. Have you ever been on a cruise? Do you think you would throw up? I might throw up. I hear that is the worst sick anybody can get, but the food, they say you eat twelve or fourteen times a day, which is enough right there to make you throw up.

"Sit still! I declare, men squirm like babies in this chair, I don't understand it. Did you know Buck Leeper had th' guts to come back and set down where you're settin' and was nice as anything you'd ever want to see? Remember I nearly scratched his eyes out th' last time because he sassed me so bad?

"Do you know who else comes in here? Adele Lynwood. Have you heard she goes out with J. C. Hogan? Can you believe it? Who would go out with J. C. Hogan? She's really nice. You ought to talk to her sometime, she has a son who's a cop in Deerfield—is that Connecticut or Massachusetts? And two of the cutest little granbabies you'll ever lay eyes on. Seriously, what do you think she sees in him? It is *beyond* me.

"Lord! Look at this stuff, I need a hay baler and a combine to clean up after you.

"But let me tell you, honey, it is lookin' *good*, your wife will eat you with a spoon! And I *am* talkin' a *spoon*!

"See there? What do you think? That'll be six dollars, you're clergy."

"Any infection?" he asked Hoppy.

"Nothing. No setback, no pneumonia, no infection."

"An answer to prayer?"

"I don't know. There's no way to know. But I have my opinion, and it's yes."

"So is this a miracle?"

Hoppy ran his fingers through his unruly hair. "Definitely untypical. Definitely a minor miracle."

The rector grinned. "So why split hairs?" he asked.

He called Olivia. "How's it going?"

She laughed.

"Thank God you're laughing."

"One must, Father, don't you think?"

"Yes, and I need desperately to remember that. Tell me everything. How is she?"

"Very solemn. Did you know her mother has agreed to come out? They'll be putting her in a women's shelter in Wesley on Tuesday."

"Excellent! I'm relieved to hear that."

"I only hope this removes the impulse for Lace to run away. She's quite a character, I must say, but more than that, she has character."

"Yes. I think so, as well."

"She likes Hoppy enormously! Oh, and I've cleaned her up and she looks wonderful in a dress, but I don't think she likes it. Actually, I know she doesn't like it, so we've washed and ironed all her old clothes and will keep them in her closet."

"Sounds like you've got a handle on it."

"I don't know, Father, I think we mustn't try and remove all her identity at once. The way she dresses seems rude and unworthy to us, perhaps, but it's who she is, and we must let her grow up into a new creature without much forcing."

"I like your style."

"That hat, though . . . "

He laughed. "A test, Olivia, a test."

"Mercy . . . "

"I'll be up to look in on you. Does she think I had anything to do with what happened?"

"She's generally distrustful of us all. I'm only hoping she doesn't run away. But I don't think there's anywhere to run, now that her mother is leaving the Creek."

"I hope you're right. Has she mentioned Poobaw?"

"She said he was living under the house with her. They slept on a pile of blankets under the house, right under her mother's bed. She said she could remove the floorboards and go in and out of the house without being seen. She knew they were looking for her, and thought they'd be looking for the boy, too. She was protecting him. She said it was the only child Pauline had left."

"Where is he now?"

"She left him under the house when she went out to get food, and that's when she was picked up."

Please, God, give us a break here.

He wanted to move to Nova Scotia, one of the few places left that had home milk delivery, and be a milkman. It was not a high ambition, but the thought had always consoled him in times like these.

"I like your hair," said Puny, who was peeling potatoes at the sink.

"I like yours."

She laughed.

"Where are Luke and Lizzie today?"

"Who?" She turned around and stared at him, blankly.

"Uh-oh." Luke and Lizzie, Sissy and Sassy, Jessie and Kenny . . . how he'd ever keep them all sorted out was a blasted mystery.

He went to the phone to call Miss Sadie and tell her that Dooley's mother was improving. He had his hand on the receiver when he stopped and shook his head, realizing all over again that Miss Sadie was not there.

"Father," said Nurse Kennedy, "someone was here to see you about Miss Barlowe, but he didn't stay."

"Who was it?"

"Mr. Leeper—he's the supervisor at Hope House. He said he heard Dooley's mother was in here and he was sorry."

He was dumbfounded. Buck Leeper?

"He left this for Miss Barlowe."

Nurse Kennedy handed him a rose in a vase.

The man who had smashed furniture against his walls had left a rose in a vase?

He shook his head with a kind of wonder.

"There's something I've been wanting to ask you, Father," said Nurse Kennedy, walking with him along the hall.

"Shoot."

"Why is it God so often breaks our hearts?"

"Well. Sometimes He does it to increase our faith. That's the way He stretches us. But there's another reason, I think, why our hearts get broken."

She looked at him.

"Usually," he said, "what breaks is what's brittle."

She nodded thoughtfully. "So we have to be careful of getting hard-hearted?"

"Bingo," he said, putting his arm around her shoulders as they walked to the end of the hall.

CHAPTER TWENTY

Send Me

"It's our retreat for the month," Cynthia announced, "and you have to come."

"No problem," he said, happy to mind his wife.

At twilight, they trooped through the backyard and out to Baxter Park, carrying a blanket.

She brought a little sackful of things and began setting them out. There were small candles in holders, which she lit with a match, then placed in the grass like so many fireflies caught in jars.

Two ripe peaches. A bottle of champagne. Crystal stemware. Two damask napkins.

"There!" she said, pleased with herself.

He fell back on the blanket, quietly intoxicated with an idea he couldn't have come up with in a hundred years. Tree frogs called, crickets whirred, a night bird swooped from the hedge and rushed over them.

"Ahhhh," said his wife, letting out her breath.

"What did you do today?" he asked, feeling a sudden tenderness for his wife's good instincts.

"The usual, of course. And I sat with Miss Pattie for an hour and a half."

He loved the familiarity of the question everyone asked of Evie Adams's elderly mother. "What's Miss Pattie done now?"

"Nothing much, actually. We were sitting on the sofa playing Who's Got the Button, that's her favorite, when she went sound asleep. She just sort of fell over on my shoulder and snored for ages."

"And what did you do?"

"I didn't want to move and wake her up, of course, so I just sat there and prayed for Pauline and Evie and Miss Pattie, then I made out our grocery list in my head, and figured out how to mix two blues together with a dash of green, for some feathers I'm painting."

He smiled. "Good work, Deacon. How's your book?"

"Wonderful! Just two more pages to go. Do you know I absolutely love painting birds?"

"What don't you love?"

"Three things. Stress, stress, and stress."

"We've certainly had all three lately. And all for good reason, of course, but . . . "

"We shouldn't even have to *talk* about stress, much less *have* it. After all, we live in Mitford!"

"Right. A quaint little town where people value each other and nothing bad ever happens to anybody."

"Poop!" she said, with feeling.

"Where are we going to live when we retire?" he asked, seeing a star appear. "And where are we going in August, which is only next month? To the coast?"

"I can't swim!" she said.

"I can't tolerate sun," he confessed.

"I hate sand!"

"So that's out," he declared. "Let's open the champagne." They hadn't had champagne since . . .

"We haven't had champagne since our wedding," she said, handing him the bottle. "And please be careful. My nephew, David, drew out the cork one evening and looked in to see why it hadn't all come out."

"Uh-oh."

"That's when it came out! He wore the eyepatch for two months."

He drew out the cork and they heard it pop across the grass and into the rhododendron.

"Bingo!" exclaimed his wife.

They raised their glasses. "How did I ever find you?" he asked.

"You were poking around in the hedge, and there I was!"

"In your curlers," he said, grinning.

"To curlers!" she crowed. "Let's figure out August later, and dream of the other, now. We can paint retirement with a much bigger brush!"

"How about if I supply in Canada?" he asked, lying back and holding the glass on his chest.

"We could live in the wilds!"

"Wherever I'm called."

"I could do that," she said.

"Or England. We could live in England. We know the language. Roughly speaking, of course."

"I could do almost anything, dearest. And just think—I can work anywhere, as long as I have paints and a brush. By the way, I hear there's a little church at the coast with an apartment in the rear, and clergy from different denominations supply it every week or so. Of course we'd hate the sand, but we'd love the seafood. That might be fun."

"Maybe . . . " he said, smiling.

The champagne was going straight to his head. He saw himself wearing shoes with treads that might have been spliced from tractor tires. He would be a veritable globe-trotter; he would go here, he would go there . . .

"Timothy, dear?" She nudged him in the side. "Are you dropping off?"

He sat upright at once. "Who, me? Dropping off? Of course not!"

Good Lord! Where would he get the energy to go farther than his own backyard?

Dooley came from his mother's hospital room, looking drawn and silent.

They drove slowly down Old Church Lane in a downpour, the windshield wipers turned on high.

"Your mother is going to be all right."

"She ain't got but one ear."

It was the old Dooley talking, the boy who still lived under the emblem on his prep school blazer.

"Do you want to stay with us awhile, and go see her every day?"

Dooley was quiet. Then he said, "I want t' go back to th' farm. I've got stuff t' do."

Two steps forward, one step back.

On Main Street, they passed Olivia Harper in the blue Volvo, who blew the horn and waved. He saw Lace sitting beside her, unsmiling, the old hat jammed on her head.

One for you and one for me, he thought, waving back.

The Hope House project was booming along, even with the heavy rains. Buck Leeper was driving his crew to finish on time, and unbelievable as it seemed in today's world, he was still committed to bringing it in on budget.

"He'll kill himself one day," said Ron Malcolm. "He'll just fall over in an excavation and they'll throw the dirt over him. Or, he's going to blow like a volcano." Ron shook his head. "It's not worth it."

"Amen."

"How's the computer? And don't bite my head off for asking."

"My friend, I am a happy man. By some miracle I'll never understand, Emma likes the blasted thing, and has taken to it like a bee to clover. Go figure!"

Ron laughed. "Hope House is going to be a dazzler."

"Indeed. Have you found an administrator? I missed the last meeting."

"It looks like Hoppy has one," said Ron. "We'll be in the interview process in the next week or two. I hear she's tough."

"You'd have to be tough to run a forty-bed nursing home and make it go like clockwork."

"What do you know about tough?" Ron asked fondly.

"What do I know about tough? Plenty. More than I'd like to know."

"You've been looking all in, if you ask me. Are you taking care of your Big D?"

"Pretty well. I'm off my running schedule, but Scott Murphy will be here in September, we're going to try and run together. That'll get me going again."

Ron looked concerned. "I wouldn't wait for Scott Murphy to get you going."

"So?" said Mule, as a rain-soaked J.C. slammed into the booth.

"So what?" snapped J.C.

"Oh, no. Don't tell me . . . "

"I don't have any intention of telling you. It's none of your dadgum business."

"After all we did to help you, it's none of our business?" asked the rector.

"You didn't send the flowers," said Mule, looking depressed.

"I sent the bloomin' flowers."

"You forgot the reservation at the restaurant and they wouldn't seat you and you had to go to Hardee's," surmised the rector.

"I not only remembered the reservation, I shelled out sixty bucks for something on a lettuce leaf the size of snail droppings."

"Oh, law!" said Mule. "We told you not to go to that French place."

"Maybe it *was* snail droppings," said the rector, trying not to laugh.

"So, did you propose?"

"Propose? We never talked about me proposing."

"We didn't think we had to talk about it, we thought you got the drift. Did you at least tell her you love her?" asked Mule.

"Sort of."

The rector looked at the editor over his glasses. "What do you mean, sort of?"

"I said . . . well, you know."

"No, we don't know. And if we don't know, chances are she doesn't know, either. Have you ever thought of that? Read my lips," said the rector. "You have to say it outright, I l-o-v-e y-o-u. Get it?"

"I said something kind of like that."

"What was it?" asked Mule.

"I told her I really like the way she keeps her squad car clean."

Mule slapped himself on the forehead. "No way, no way, no way! You're hopeless." He turned to the rector. "We're wasting our time."

"Go back and try again," said Father Tim. "Send the flowers. Take her to dinner. Tell her you love her."

"Then give her a ring," said Mule. "Don't you know *anything* about th' birds and bees?"

"I might tell her I love her, but I'm not doin' flowers and snail stuff again."

The rector peered at J.C. "There's that one-time deal rearing its ugly head. Flowers one time, a fancy dinner one time. You're getting off the train before you get to the station, buddyroe."

"Whatever that's supposed to mean."

"Go back and start over," said Mule, looking grouchy.

J.C. gave a shuddering sigh and wiped his face with a Scot towel.

"See? Look at that? A paper towel. You're in such sorry shape, I can't believe it. If you're ever going to get a woman to look after you, the time is now, before you're too far gone."

"Right!" said the rector.

J.C. shambled out of the booth, dragging his bulging briefcase.

"Call her up!" said Mule.

"Right now!" instructed the rector.

"Lord have mercy," groaned J.C., heading for the door.

Mule blew on his coffee. "You don't think we were too hard on him, do you?"

"Stuart? Tim Kavanagh."

"I'll be hanged, I was just thinking about you," said his bishop and seminary friend.

"What were you thinking?" asked the rector. "Do I want to know?"

"I was thinking that I hadn't heard from you in far too long. I'm curious about something."

"You're always curious about something. Nosy was what we called it when I was coming up."

"I admit, I'm nosy. Anyway, I want to know how you like being married."

"I like it greatly, as a matter of fact."

"Excellent! Not too much for you, then?"

"What do you mean, too much for me?"

"Cynthia's a live wire."

"So am I," he said.

"You? A live wire? Since when?"

"Since I decided to retire, which is why I'm calling."

"What?"

"What, indeed, my friend. I would have written you, but I can't find the time." He hoped that didn't sound cocky, but why worry about it when there were larger issues to occupy his mind?

"Keep talking."

"I've decided to retire in two years, and thought I'd go ahead and let you know now. I'll be sixty-five then, that's my cutoff date. I'm thinking that I definitely want to remain active, which means I'd like to supply. You can give us something in this diocese, of course, but not necessarily. I'm ready for some adventure in my life."

"Excuse me, is this Father *Timothy* Kavanagh?"

"One and the same."

"Being married has clearly loosened you up, Timothy! There's a new . . . tone in your voice."

"That's determination you hear, Stuart, determination. I'm determined to have a new life, which is not to say I don't like the one I've got. Actually, I like it vastly."

"I knew Cynthia would be good for you!"

"Cynthia is good for me, you're perfectly right. But she can't take all the credit."

"Really? How's that?"

"I foolishly—or wisely, as the case may be—dropped through a hole in the ground like the White Rabbit, and was lost in a cave. It gave me something to think about."

"You old stick-in-the-mud!" Stuart said fondly.

"I'm convinced that every stick-in-the-mud should get stuck in a hole in the ground."

Stuart laughed. "What did you learn down there?"

"For one thing, I learned something about my father and about my feelings. I've been chewing over it for weeks, and it strikes me that one reason I went into the priesthood was to minister to my father. I wanted his soul to be saved, but as far as I know, that never happened.

I believed that if I kept going and never stopped, I could reach people like my father, and make up, somehow, for failing to reach him for Christ. I still feel the urgency to reach people, but bottom line, I don't feel the bondage anymore. I feel . . . the liberty."

Stuart was quiet. "Maybe I need to fall in a hole."

"Maybe," he said, boldly.

His bishop sighed. "There are a few old wounds I've kept licking over the years, but conveniently, I've kept too busy to deal with them."

"Fall in a hole and the only busy you'll be is trying to haul your tail out of there."

They laughed.

"I don't know when I've liked a phone call better," said Stuart. "So. You want to supply, and I can trade you around like a fancy baseball player to other bishops?"

"Something in the Caribbean, maybe."

"You dog."

"Seriously, Canada would be of interest to us, or England. Ireland, possibly. Virginia? Vermont? I don't know. I have the providence of a wife who finds all of life an adventure. And I think there's definitely something in me that needs airing out, so there you have it. Should I put it in writing to make it official?"

"Consider it official. Write me when you get around to it, just for the records. In the fullness of time, we'll get the search process started at Lord's Chapel. It can take up to a year and a half to put a new priest in place, given the tough parameters we're now using."

"Keep it quiet until we have to make it public. My parish is—"

"Your parish is devoted to you! I hope I'm in farthest Africa when the word gets out that I've allowed you to go."

"You're kind."

"I'm your friend."

"How many years?" asked the rector. "Thirty-six, thirty-seven?"

"Thirty-nine."

"Sorry I asked. How's Martha?"

"Trying to get me to slow down. . . ."

"And having no success," he said.

"I see slowing down as a kind of death."

"You think slowing down to take your two adopted grandkids to the zoo or out to lunch is death? My friend, that is life."

"Don't preach me a sermon, Timothy."

"You've certainly been known to preach me one, Bishop."

"Go fly a kite," said Stuart, chuckling.

"Go step in a hole," said the rector, meaning it.

Uncle Billy's arthur was so bad after the rain that he asked Father Tim to come fetch his tithe.

The rector arrived just before lunch, and went around to the back stoop. He should have sent his beautiful deacon, he thought, but the moment the old man opened the door, he was glad he'd come. If there was ever a face to give a preacher a lift, it was Bill Watson's.

"Come in an' take a load off y'r feet, hit's hot as blazes and Rose made us a pitcher of tea."

What the heck? He'd resisted Rose Watson's suspect refreshments for years on end, but maybe he'd loosen up, for once, and do the thing.

"Rose! Hit's th' preacher come t' have a glass of tea."

"Pour it yourself," she snapped, glaring at them from the hallway.

"Oh, law," said the old man, embarrassed, "hit's th' heat, she don't like it."

Miss Rose came and stood in the doorway and watched her husband pour tea for their guest. She was wearing a calf-length chenille bathrobe, the sling-back pumps Uncle Billy had ordered last year from an almanac, and the hat from Esther Cunningham's Waves uniform.

Uncle Billy passed him the glass of tea with a trembling hand. "That was some rain, won't it, Preacher?"

"Either that or a colossal dew!"

"Possum stew?" demanded Miss Rose. "What're you saying about possum stew?"

Where was his deacon?

"I'd never eat a bite of anything made with possum," said the old woman, "and I wouldn't think you would, either, being a preacher!"

"Yes ma'am," he said, cowering in the corner.

He dearly loved his parishioners, but collections had never been his long suit.

"Father? Scott Murphy! I hope I'm not making a pest of myself."

He instantly felt the grin spreading across his face. "Quite the reverse! How are you?"

"Great, sir. I'm back to running. How about you?"

"Off my schedule and no help for it."

"Go out there and do it, sir, and get in shape for September. I'm not going to hang back for you."

He laughed with delight. Here was someone who'd give him a run for his money, all right. "Consider it done. What's up?"

"I just called your friend, Mr. Skinner, about places for rent, and he said a Miss Winnie Ivey's cottage might be coming up."

"That's right." Olivia had invited Winnie to stay on in her home on Lilac Road, and graciously included Winnie's two elderly cats in the bargain. "I know that cottage well. It sits on a creek. Has a porch, a nice view, and it's private. Winnie runs the bakery here."

"Yes, I stopped in there and had a Napoleon."

"She's kept her little place as clean as a pin. And it's only a short run to Hope House, up the hill and past the orchards."

"Sounds too good to be true. I'll call Mr. Skinner back and tell him I'll take it. What's going on in your parish, Father?"

"I've had a boy with me for a couple of years, and his mother's just been terribly burned, but we're sorting that out. And there's a girl, thirteen . . . we've just had her removed from a very bitter and violent situation in a blighted community we call the Creek."

"Poverty? Inbreeding? Drugs?"

"All that. It's said to be dangerous in there for law enforcement and clergy, and the upshot is—nobody does much about it, including myself, I'm ashamed to admit."

There was a thoughtful pause.

"I'll go in there, Father. When I come to Mitford, send me."

Send me. The words spoken by the prophet Isaiah, when God had a rotten job to get done.

"I don't know, Scott, maybe you need to . . . look into it first."

"Well, sir, I believe the only way to look into something is to go in and look."

That wasn't an impertinence. What it was, was the truth.

"Remember how I said I felt invincible because of my grandparents' love?"

"I remember."

"Because I know so surely that God loves me, I feel that invincibility all over again," said Scott. "When I come, let's talk about it. I'll go in there and see what I can do. There has to be a way."

Scott was right, of course. There has to be a way. The rector felt suddenly encouraged about something that had discouraged him for months.

Was Scott Murphy's bravado just a lot of smoke and youthful optimism? Time, which tells everything, would also tell this, he reasoned.

What could be done about Poobaw? Father Tim hadn't said a word to Dooley about his little brother, and apparently Pauline hadn't, either.

He went up to the Harpers' rambling mountain lodge and found Olivia cutting out a dress for Lace on the dining room table.

She looked peaked, to say the least.

"I'm not exactly wringing my hands yet, but I don't do very well at . . . reaching her."

"That's to be expected," he said, grinning. "What you're talking about takes two or three hundred years to accomplish."

"Oh," said Olivia, laughing. "I thought I was supposed to do it in two or three days."

"It's hard to reach someone who's been betrayed by everyone she's ever known, including her mother."

"What do you mean?"

"I mean her mother's inability to look after herself and her daughter has cost Lace great heartache. I know her mother is an invalid, but even that has something of betrayal in it, since Lace has had to be the mother."

Olivia sighed. "It's not that we haven't made any progress at all. So far, she's taken two baths and even let me scrub her hands and nails. Oh, and she allowed me to brush the tangles out of her hair, which is a miracle. I don't think anyone had ever done that for her."

"What does she like about living here, so far?"

"My makeup. Hoppy. Breakfast, lunch, and dinner. My hats."

"Terrific. You know you can be a lifelong blessing to her."

"If I hold up," said Olivia, who gave him a dazzling smile.

"If you can't hold up, nobody can. I need to talk with Lace. May I?"

Olivia brought Lace into the living room, and he found that he hardly recognized her in a skirt and blouse, with her hair tied back. He was, in fact, shocked at her surprising beauty.

"You look wonderful. Absolutely wonderful!" he said.

Lace glanced at him, then looked at the wall.

"I have a report on your mother. You can visit her tomorrow. She's doing very well and seems to feel stronger." Just in case she didn't get it, he drew the bottom line. "This is good news."

"Yeah," said Lace.

"I need to know everything you can tell me about Poobaw, and I need you to tell me now." He spoke gently, but he meant it and she knew it. "Let's sit down."

She sat in a chair, looking suddenly awkward in her new clothes. Odd, but he'd gotten used to the rags she'd worn.

"Pauline Barlowe is going to improve, but soon she'll go away for a long stay to a place where she'll learn to use her arm again and care for herself. She's just seen her oldest son, Dooley—you met him."

"He's a creep. I hate redheads."

"Some of my best friends are redheads, so I'll thank you to be kind. What she needs now is to see Poobaw, to know he's safe and taken care of." He let that sink in. "So tell me. Where is he? How can we find him?"

She looked at him.

"Listen to me, Lace. You don't trust me, and I don't blame you because you don't know me. But you've got to believe that no harm will come to Poobaw. We need to locate him and take him out of that place, and find someone for him to live with until Pauline is well and can take care of him herself."

She shrugged. "I told 'im t' go t' Harley's trailer if I didn't come back from gittin' us somethin' t' eat."

"Who is Harley?"

"Harley's crazy, but he's all right. He wouldn't tell nobody that Poobaw was there, an' if they come lookin' for Poobaw, I told Harley t' shoot their brains out, it's th' only kid Pauline had left. I didn't know about Dewey, or whatever 'is name is."

"Where does Harley live?"

"Down there where people dump stuff off th' side of th' hill. He's got a blue trailer and three dogs that'll eat your butt up, so you better step easy if you mess around there."

He was going to need Scott Murphy before September . . . way before September.

Why did she have to tell Harley to shoot somebody's brains out if they came looking for Poobaw?

Every time he raised the courage to go get the boy himself, he thought about Harley and sank back. Blast, he hated cowardice. He had nearly lost Cynthia through a type of cowardice, and here he was a grown man in a free country, perspiring—no, sweating like a field hand—at the thought of stepping up to a door and knocking on it.

Rodney Underwood would be of no use—it wasn't his county. And social services, by their own admission, could take days to get the wheels turning.

Right. But better them than him staring down the barrel of what had, in his mind, become crazy Harley Welch's twelve-gauge shotgun.

The urge to do something would not let him alone; it was now on his heart constantly. This morning, Pauline had searched his face as she asked again, "Poobaw? Is he all right?"

Worse still, he recalled the anguish on Dooley's face, the kind of anguish he'd believed time would erase, and remembered how he and Dooley, long ago, had held hands and prayed for his sister and brothers, with a special sense of concern for Poobaw.

Why couldn't they call Harley and ask him to drive the boy to the hospital in his truck, for Pete's sake? He and Cynthia would take it from there.

He rang Olivia and asked to speak with Lace.

"Harley ain't got a phone. He ain't even got a toilet."

Was there any way she could get a message to Harley?

"Th' only way is to go up there."

"Up there?"

"Acrost th' creek and up th' bank. Hit's steep but I been up it a million times, don't anybody use that trail but me an' Granny Sykes."

"What about the dogs?"

"They know me pretty good, but anybody else goin' in there better tote a sack of meat."

When he hung up, he realized he was perspiring again. He thought he had hidden the idea from his conscious mind, but he had not.

He suddenly knew very clearly that he was going in there to get Poobaw.

"We can't leave that boy in these circumstances," he told Olivia. "I know it's a crazy idea and there could be tremendous risk, but I feel we must do it. Would you agree?"

She didn't hesitate. "Yes," she said, her violet eyes dark with concern.

"How many you feedin'?" asked Avis Packard at the meat counter of The Local.

"Three," he said. "But they're plenty hungry."

"Three pounds ought to do it, then."

"Better make it six pounds," he said, wiping his forehead with a handkerchief. "And it doesn't have to be your best."

Avis winked. "Must be entertainin' your vestry."

He laughed. "I'm not entertaining at all. This is . . . " Should he tell? Why not? It wouldn't reveal anything. "This is for dogs," he said.

"Six pounds of beef for three dogs. Must be some dogs."

"Oh, they are, they are."

The large, wrapped parcel seemed so conspicuous as he hit the sidewalk, he wanted to shove it under his coat.

Be back soon, he wrote. Should he say, "Don't worry?" Of course not. That would make her worry. *Important meeting.* Wasn't that the truth? *Love, Timothy.*

He kept the beam of the flashlight low to the ground.

"You better catch on right here if you don't want to bust your butt." Lace had gone up the muddy bank ahead of him, as nimbly as a squirrel.

"Slow down!" he whispered. The shoe treads he had envisioned the other night would sure come in handy. . . .

"You don't want t' lose y'r step along here or you'll end up some'ers around Leesville."

His heart was pounding—thundering, in fact. If somebody named Granny could negotiate this bank, so could he. However, somebody named Granny was not likely to have six pounds of red meat swinging in a sack lashed to her back.

"Git m' hat!" said Lace, keeping her voice low. "That bush knocked it off."

"Keep going," he said. "I've got it."

He jammed it on his head and hauled himself up by grabbing onto the exposed root of a tree.

What was he doing out here in the dark of the night, scrambling up a bank like some chicken-poaching thief? He had put Lace Turner and himself at senseless risk, and in a foolish and impetuous way, to boot. What if her father saw her? What if Lester Marshall was hanging around Harley's trailer? Not a living soul would be likely to forgive the local rector if anything happened.

However, if God's love had made Scott Murphy invincible, why wouldn't it do the same for him and for her? When it came to loving His children, God didn't pick favorites.

"We're gittin' there," she said. "You OK?"

"I'm hangin' in." He was so out of breath, he might have run a 10k. If he could only rest a minute. . . .

"Don't be settin' down," she hissed. "I can see ol' Harley's TV shinin' th'ough th' winder."

The stench of garbage and mold had assaulted his nostrils all the way up the bank. In the moonlight, lining the trail to their left, he saw the pale, abandoned hulks of refrigerators and stoves, half-exposed in mounds of rain-soaked debris. That day in Omer's plane, he had looked down on this very place, never dreaming—

He heard skittering noises in the dump, and shivered.

They reached the top of the bank, where the ground leveled off. "Set!" she whispered. "Git that sack out an' give it t' me."

He did, noting that his hands shook.

"They ain't nothin' t' be skeered of," she said. "I done this a million times. When we git beyond here, th' dogs'll start up. I'll th'ow down th' meat and you hit Harley's winder with these little rocks. Here." She handed him two pieces of gravel she had picked up from the creek. "That's m' signal f'r 'im t' let me in."

"What if he's sleeping?"

"He don't sleep 'til 'way up in th' night."

"What if he can't hear it hit the window?"

"He'll hear th' dogs start up an' listen f'r th' rocks."

He hoped her plan worked as well as she seemed to think it would. Six pounds of meat wouldn't last six minutes. If Barnabas Kavanagh was any indication, three seconds, maximum, was what they could count on.

"What about the dogs when we leave?" he whispered urgently. The sack of meat might work up front, but what strategy would they use to protect the rear?

"He'll call 'em off," she said. "You ready?"

"Ready." An outright lie.

"Lord, if it ain't Lace," said Harley Welch, grinning. They were in the trailer with the door slammed behind them and three dogs pounding on it like jackhammers. He was breathing hard.

"You won't have t' feed them dogs f'r a couple of days," said Lace.

Harley shook his hand, still grinning. If there was a tooth in Harley's head, the rector didn't see it. He instantly liked this whiskered man whose eyes revealed genuine kindness.

"You 'uns come in. Th' boy's sleepin' an' I'm jis' havin' me a little snack." Harley held up a spoon.

The rector saw a cracked green vinyl sofa with an open food can sitting on one of the cushions. A lamp with a bare light bulb illuminated the corner of the room, and newspapers were taped over the windows.

"You 'uns want a bite?"

"I done eat," said Lace.

"Me, too," said the rector.

"I like y'r hat." Harley pointed to his head. "Ol' Lace has a hat jis' like it, 'cept I think your'n's in worser shape."

Lace sat on the arm of the sofa. "We come t' git Poobaw. Pauline's still half burned up in th' hospital."

"Yeah," said Harley, "an' th' law's done got 'er man."

There was some good news in this world, the rector thought.

"Better wake 'im up and git 'im started," she said. "Are they any of 'is clothes over here?"

"Ain't but what he had on," said Harley, still grinning. He picked up the can and rattled the spoon around in it. "Boys, if them beans didn't walk right out of there." He looked at the rector and said mischievously, "Ol' dump rat got 'em."

"Oh, hush, Harley, they ain't any rats in here. Rats stay as far away from you as they can git."

He cackled. "Ain't she a bird? I knowed 'er since she was knee high to a duck. Lace, your pap's done left, he raked ever'thing out and hauled it off."

Father Tim saw her face, and thought he could not bear to see another hurting soul in this world.

"Took y'r brother with 'im." Harley laughed. "Good riddance t' bad rubbish."

"There's ol' Poobaw," she said. The boy came into the room, rubbing his eyes.

"Hey," he murmured sleepily, smiling up at her.

Hey, yourself, he almost said, feeling his heart swell with a nameless joy.

They were down the bank. They were across the creek. They were walking over the little bridge.

There was Winnie Ivey's small cottage, with the glow of a lamp in the window. And above them sailed a great orb of moon that washed the whole scene with a silvery light.

He felt the boy's hand in his and saw Lace walking ahead of them, her shoulders squared under the old coat she'd worn again for tonight.

He felt touched by something that, in all his years as a priest, he had never known and, for the moment, didn't even wish to understand or define.

"Cynthia," he said, coming through the back door, "there's someone I'd like you to meet. . . ."

The boy walked in, blinking in the bright light of the kitchen.

"Poobaw Barlowe!" the rector said.

If he thought he was thrilled, it was nothing compared to what he saw expressed in the face of his jubilant wife.

"Pauline, there's someone here to see you."

He backed out the door as Poobaw went in.

"Mama?" said the boy, and ran to her bed.

He was closing the door as he saw Poobaw lift his hand and tenderly pat the right side of his mother's beaming face.

"Dooley," he shouted, hailing him between the Meadowgate farmhouse and the barn, "there's someone here to see you. They're waiting on the porch!"

CHAPTER TWENTY-ONE

These High, Green Hills

FIELDS OF BROOM SEDGE turned overnight into lakes of gold, and the scented vines of Lady's Mantle crept into hedges everywhere, as the sun moved and the light changed, and the brisk, clean days grew shorter.

"You always say this is the best fall we've ever had," Dora Pugh scolded a customer at the hardware. "How can every year be the best?"

Avis Packard put up a banner, Percy Mosely at last took his down, and the Collar Button was having its annual fall sale. The latter encouraged the rector to make a few purchases for Dooley Barlowe, now back at school, which included three pairs of khakis, four pairs of socks, and a couple of handkerchiefs that Dooley would never use for their intended purpose.

Pauline Barlowe was two hours away in a burn therapy center, Lace Turner was enrolled in seventh grade at Mitford School, and Poobaw—living with his grandfather, Russell Jacks, at the home of practical nurse Betty Craig—was enrolled in fourth grade.

Louella was pushing along with Winnie Ivey, Scott Murphy had moved into the cottage on the creek with Luke, Lizzie, a bed, three chairs, and a wok, and J. C. Hogan had, only days ago, announced his news.

"I thought for a while there," said Mule," that we'd have to do it for you—like that feller with th' big nose."

"Do what for me, and what big nose?" asked J.C.

"You know . . . " Mule looked to the rector for help.

"Cyrano de Bergerac. He proposed to Roxane as proxy for Christian de Neuvillette."

"Never heard of him. Anyway, I pulled it it off myself, thank you."

"How'd you feel about proposing?" Mule asked.

"I threw up right after."

"I bet that was attractive. How'd you do it?"

"Just bent over the toilet and up it came."

"That," said Mule, "is not what I was askin'. How did you propose? I hope you didn't do one of those dumb tricks like put th' ring in a piece of cake."

J.C. looked surprised. "How'd you know? I was over at her place and she'd baked a cake for my birthday and while she was in the kitchen, I mashed the ring down in her piece—in the icing part."

"What if she'd bitten into it?" asked the rector.

"What if she'd swallowed it?" asked the Realtor.

J.C. mopped his face with a handkerchief. "Bein' a working woman, she eats fast, and before you know it, she was bearin' down on that ring pretty hard, so I looked over and said, 'What in the dickens is that in your cake?' and she said, 'Well, I never, it's a ring.' "

"Then what did you say?" asked Mule.

"Y'all are worse'n a bunch of old women."

"It's true," admitted the rector.

"I said, 'Want to do it?' and she said, 'OK.' "

Mule rolled his eyes. "*Want to do it?* You said *that*?"

"If it was good enough for Officer Adele Lynwood," snapped J.C., "it ought to be good enough for you, buddyroe."

Mule peered across the table. "Did you get down on your knees or anything?"

"Are you kidding me?"

"So you proposed on your birthday!" exclaimed the rector.

"Right."

"That's what I did, you know."

Mule cackled. "You don't mean it. I didn't know that. I declare."

"It's a dadblame epidemic," said the editor, grinning.

Velma skidded up to the booth and glared at J.C. "OK, what'll you have, and don't take all day."

The rector and the Realtor looked expectantly at J.C. "Low-fat yogurt and grapefruit juice . . . "

"Here we go again," sighed Mule.

"With a side of sausage and grits," said the editor.

"When it boots," Emma told him, "I have the configuration file install all the device drivers I'll need all day."

"Great!" he said, oiling the roller on his Royal manual.

"Can you believe the object linking and embedding capabilities allow me to make all my applications interactive?"

"I'll be darned," he said.

"Not only that, I can append to th' database, paste from th' clipboard, or drag and drop anywhere . . . "

"No kidding!"

" . . . within seconds," she said, looking triumphant.

On what Emma called their now bimonthly "Tech Day," she hauled in everything from roast beef and green beans to macaroni and cheese, which she fed Dave in huge quantities. Over lunch at the rector's desk, which resembled a neighborhood cafeteria, they blithely spoke a language as foreign to him as Croatian.

On Tech Day, one thing was for certain:

He was out of there.

Whenever he met Bill Sprouse, who always wanted to know how it was going, he answered from an assortment of enthusiastic responses, including "Terrific!" "Couldn't be better!" and his increasing favorite, "No problem!" With Emma Newland having taken to advanced technology like a duck to water, wasn't every word of that the everlasting truth?

Never say you can't teach an old dog new tricks, he thought, hoofing it to the Grill before Dave roared in at eleven-thirty.

He had dropped the Fernbank key in his pocket when he dressed to go running, and was standing in the middle of Miss Sadie's attic, trying to find the right thing. In a way, it was like shopping, without the blasted aggravation of a mall.

Hat boxes, trunks, rocking chairs, a rolltop desk. Old newspapers, neatly piled and the stacks numbered. Dozens of umbrellas, both Chinese paper and crumbling silk, lamp bases, a magnificent chair with wheels, piles of folded draperies covered with sheets, a child's rocker, a child's table and chairs, headboards, footboards, rusting bedsprings.

It was overwhelming, and only a little light fell in through the window.

There. A large trunk with the initials JB. Josiah Baxter.

A cracked leather chair, a floor lamp with a hand-painted parchment shade. Books, books, and more books. A series of boxes stacked on a Jacobean table.

He looked at the boxes, one by one, until he came to the traveling case fitted with a comb and brushes, a shoehorn, talcum powder, and empty, cut-crystal bottles for cologne.

He picked it up and brushed away the dust with his handkerchief. *JB,* read the dim monogram on the leather.

"Something of Papa's," Miss Sadie had said.

It was a little fancy for a man like Buck Leeper, but it would certainly do.

"Retreat time!" she announced as he came in the back door, ready to do another few hours' work at home.

"Didn't we just have one?" he asked, scratching his head.

"Timothy, that was July! This is October."

"Oh," he said.

"I'm just packing up this hamper and we'll be off. The sunset should be glorious tonight; there was a red sky this morning!"

"Doesn't red sky in morning mean sailor take warning?"

"Whatever," she said happily, stuffing in a wedge of cheese.

Barnabas trudged with them up the hill, where, panting furiously, they all arrived at the stone wall.

"Don't really look at the view just yet, dearest. Let's save it until we finish setting up our picnic, shall we?"

He spread the old fringed cloth, which had belonged to a bishop's wife in the late forties, over the wall, and Cynthia began unpacking what she'd just packed.

Why was he up here on the hill, lolling about like some gigolo, when he had a nursing home to officially open one week hence, and a thousand details to be ironed out, only two of which had kept him up until one o'clock in the morning? But no, let his wife finish a book and she went instantly into the lolling mode. Perhaps it was this very lolling mode of the last two months that had given her countenance the beatific look he'd lately noticed.

"The domestic retreat," she said, setting out a plate of crackers, "is an idea which could literally save the institution of marriage. Do you know that studies say husbands and wives speak to each other a total of only seventeen minutes a week?"

"We're so far over that quota, we've landed in another study."

"I'll say. Roasted garlic. Ripe pears. Toasted pecans. Saga bleu."

She pulled out napkins and two glasses and poured a round of raspberry tea.

"There!" she said. "Now we can look!"

The Land of Counterpane stretched beneath their feet, a wide panorama of rich Flemish colors under a perfectly blue and cloudless sky.

Church steeples poked up from groves of trees.

Plowed farmland appeared like velveteen scraps on a quilt, featherstitched with hedgerows.

There, puffs of chimney smoke billowed heavenward, and over there, light gleamed on a pond that regularly supplied fresh trout to Avis Packard's Local.

"Look, dearest! Look at our high, green hills."

He gazed across the little valley and up, up to the green hills, where groves of blazing hardwoods topped the ridges, and fences laced the broad, uneven meadows.

"Aren't they beautiful in this light?"

"They are!" he said, meaning it.

"Where's the train?"

He peered at his watch. "Ten minutes!" The little train would come winding through the valley, over the trestle that spanned the gorge, and just as it broke through the trees by the red barn and the silo, they would see it. If providence were with them, they would also hear the long, mournful blast of its horn.

Away to the east, he thought he saw a speck of some kind, a bird perhaps. But birds didn't gleam. Aha! It was a little plane. It was a little yellow plane. By jing, it was Omer Cunningham. Dipping, rolling, gliding, soaring. Omer! He stood up on the wall and waved.

"What in the world . . . ?" asked his wife.

"That's Omer," he said, gleeful.

"Who is Omer?"

He waved some more and thought he could see Omer waving back as the little plane dipped its right wing and roared into the blue.

"Omer. I declare." He felt a silly grin stretching all the way across his face.

"You know absolutely everybody," she said, impressed.

He sat back down and gazed around and gulped his tea. "Ah, well, we won't be doing this forever," he said.

"I know!" She raised her glass to his. "We'll be living in some far-off land filled with adventure!"

"Right."

She sighed.

"Why are you sighing?"

"Was I sighing? I didn't know I was sighing."

"Sighing often goes unnoticed by the sigher," he said.

"Ummm. What did we agree we wanted in the place where we'll retire?" she asked.

"Oh, as I recall, four distinct seasons . . ."

"Absolutely!" she said.

"A small house and a big yard."

"Oh, yes. Now I remember. We plant, we mow."

"You got it. And nothing flat, we said."

"Flat is so . . ." She paused, looking for words.

"Flat," he remarked.

"Right!" she agreed.

"Didn't we say something about liking winters that freeze our glasses to our noses?"

"Definitely."

"Listen!" He cupped his hands to his ears. "Here it comes!"

A freight train broke into view at the red barn, blowing its horn as it rushed past a field, disappeared into the trees, and appeared again along a row of tiny houses.

She applauded, and turned to him, laughing. No, indeed, it didn't take much for his wife. . . .

They tried the roasted garlic and spread the Saga bleu on crackers and munched the pecans and emptied the tea container and watched the sky blush with pink, then fuchsia.

"You're sighing again," he announced.

"I can't think why."

"You can't fool me. If anybody can think why they do something, it's you, Kavanagh."

"OK. I think I'll miss Mitford."

"Aha. So will I."

A bird called. Barnabas rolled over at his master's feet and yawned, and the rector leaned down to scratch the pink belly that was offered.

"So . . . " she said, pausing thoughtfully.

"So?"

"It occurs to me that we've found a place that meets all our strict requirements."

"Hmmm. Small house, big yard," he mused.

"Winters that freeze our glasses to our noses . . . "

"Nothing flat, lots of hills . . . "

"No sand," she said.

They turned to each other and smiled. Then they laughed.

Neither said anything more as they packed up the hamper and folded up the cloth and went down the hill with their dog at their heels.

Next year, they agreed, they'd be adding a large room to the back of the little yellow house. With lots of windows, said the rector. With gleaming hardwood floors, said his wife.

" 'There are two things to aim at in life,' " he quoted from Logan Pearsall Smith. " 'First, to get what you want, and after that, to enjoy it.' "

"There's the rub!" she said.

Using a Magic Marker, she inscribed the wisdom on the wall above her drawing board, relishing the freedom to do it, loving the notion of making the little yellow house larger, and living there forever.

There was so much to do and so much to think about, they had trouble sleeping at night. He'd even talked the vestry into building the kennel and dog run, and two men from Farmer had been working around the clock to complete the job.

The ECW was out in force, canvassing every garden and meadow for autumn flowers, dried herbs, pumpkins, and gourds to decorate the public rooms at Hope House. Cynthia volunteered to round up vases, buckets, and mounds of oasis from the florist, not to mention bake six dozen lemon squares for the reception.

J. C. Hogan's wedding was coming straight up, in the middle of the week after the grand opening, and the rector would not only officiate, but had offered to bake a ham.

Immediately following the police station wedding at which Mule Skinner would be best man, they would troop to the Skinner household, where Fancy was giving a reception on the premises of Hair House, owing to the fact that their living quarters were being repainted.

For this affair, Cynthia had been asked to contribute four dozen vegetable sandwiches, four dozen lemon squares, and as many barbecued chicken drumettes as she could manage.

"I will not make drumettes, barbecued or otherwise," she told her husband. "There are two cardinal rules from which I will not depart—I will not cook with Cheez Whiz and I will not do drumettes. I will substitute meat balls in sauce."

Scott Murphy was collecting animals, large and small, having them vetted by Hal Owen, and installing them in the brand-new Hope House kennels, which were complete except for fencing in the runs.

The Presbyterian brass band was busy rehearsing three nights a week and could be heard through half the village. The Lord's Chapel Youth Choir was holding rehearsals in Jena Ivey's florist shop because the Sunday School rooms were overtaken by the ECW, who had twenty-seven major floral arrangements to pull together.

"Raffia!" cried the frantic Hope House chairperson for opening day events. "We need raffia!"

"What's raffia?" several volunteers wanted to know.

"Don't use raffia," said Jena Ivey. "The last I got had bugs in it."

Someone said Buck Leeper had bought a suit at the Collar Button that wasn't even on sale, and J. C. Hogan was seen leaving the Collar Button with a box the size of a small garage. He was reported to have been with Officer Lynwood, who was out of uniform and looking good in a pants suit.

Percy Mosely was running a special on a vegetable plate: collards, black-eyed peas, candied yams, cornbread, and banana pudding for two-fifty, during the week of the Hope House grand opening, only. After that, three bucks.

Happy Endings Bookstore was giving twenty percent off every title starting with H. "Does that include th' Holy Bible?" asked Uncle Billy Watson, who, when assured that it did, shelled out fourteen dollars on the spot, plus three-fifty for a magnifying glass.

Hardly anyone in the village was untouched by the excitement of the great glass and brick building at the crest of the hill, which stood where the town's first Episcopal church had burned to the ground in a tragic fire. Only one living person knew the full truth about that fire, thought the rector, and he was the one.

Sadie Baxter's attempt to right a wrong was a better thing than he could now imagine. Good things would come of Hope House; he could feel it in his bones.

"I'm here," said Scott Murphy, "because God brought me here. And so are you."

Clearly, the chaplain's message was directed at the forty new residents of Hope House, most of whom were present, and all of whom were in unfamiliar circumstances.

"Because God has brought us here, we're going to honor Him by having fun, and enjoying this wonderful and remarkable place.

"You need to know that I do not now, nor will I ever, consider this a nursing home, though some of you will need nursing. Good nursing care is vital, but it isn't everything."

The mayor looked at the rector and nodded.

Ron Malcolm sat back and relaxed.

A muscle jumped in Buck Leeper's jaw.

"We're going to sing here," said Scott Murphy, stepping from behind the pulpit and walking into the aisle. "We're going to dance here. We're going to pray here. We're going to laugh here, and love here. And we're going to do all that by sustaining the powerful, eternal, and life-giving spirit of hope through Jesus, the Christ.

"As your chaplain, I will not be working alone. That's because I come to you not as an individual, but as part of a team.

"Luke!"

A Jack Russell terrier trotted out from the behind the pulpit, wagged its tail, and sat down.

The audience laughed with surprise.

"Lizzie!"

Another Jack Russell, nearly identical, shyly poked its head around the side of the pulpit, then walked out and sat down next to Luke.

The audience applauded wildly, glad for laughter after the formality of a ribbon-cutting in a whipping October wind, a lengthy dedication with choral music, and a bombastic mayoral speech.

"You hit a home run with the chaplain," whispered the mayor to the rector.

"I wasn't the one who hit it," whispered the rector to the mayor.

After the grand reception, held around the splashing fountain in the atrium, forty residents, many in wheelchairs, took occupancy of their new quarters.

Louella Baxter Marshall was escorted to Room Number One by Olivia and Hoppy Harper, Lacey Turner, Cynthia and Timothy Kavanagh, and Dooley Barlowe. Miss Pattie was led to Room Thirty-four by Evie Adams, who was weeping with gratitude and relief.

Up and down the corridors, families helped loved ones settle in, meeting nurses, talking with doctors, and admiring the lavish display of flowers that filled rooms and nursing stations.

"I'm movin' in here as soon as Gene kicks," said Esther Bolick.

"But you're not sick!" said Fancy Skinner.

"No, but I'm workin' on it," declared Esther, looking around at the rose-colored carpet, Palladian windows, and crystal chandeliers.

"Buck," said the rector, shaking the superintendent's rough hand, "this is as fine a job as I've ever seen done. Personally, I can't thank you enough, nor can Lord's Chapel."

Buck nodded, and the rector was suddenly moved by the reality of thousands of hours of labor, and a promise that, at great personal sacrifice, had been kept. He threw his arms around the man and hugged him. "May God bless you for this, Buck."

"No problem," said Buck Leeper, turning to walk away.

"Wait! When are you leaving?"

"I'll be pulling out tomorrow." The nerve twitched in his jaw.

He didn't want to see Buck Leeper go. No, he didn't want that at all.

"The church attic—all that space Miss Sadie's father wanted to turn into Sunday School rooms—is that job big enough for you? Could we get you back for that?"

Buck shrugged. "Maybe."

"Could you—would you come over for supper tonight? We'd love to have you."

"I've got a lot to pull together," said Buck Leeper, looking awkward.

The rector tried to smile. "Maybe another time."

He felt deflated as he and Cynthia drove home with Dooley. He was glad they'd had the plaque made, honoring Buck.

"What is it?" she asked, always knowing his heart.

He couldn't find the words, exactly. Tomorrow he'd start looking into the attic project, and how they might initiate fund-raising; he would call Buck's boss, whom he'd met at the country club, and put in a special request for his star superintendent.

Something told him very clearly that Buck Leeper was not finished in Mitford.

Not by a long shot.

"Well, buddy."

Fall break was over and they had delivered Dooley back to school, taking Poobaw along for the ride.

"You know we love you," said the rector, giving the boy a hug. With the obvious exception of Miss Sadie, he couldn't remember ever hugging a millionaire before.

Cynthia kissed him on the cheek. "Yes, you big lug, we love you."

"I love you back," Dooley said, meeting their gaze.

Dooley squatted on one knee and put his hands on Poobaw's shoulders. "Stay cool, Poo."

"I will," said Poobaw, nodding and smiling. "I'll see y'uns later."

"Don't say y'uns," his brother admonished.

"What should I say?"

"Get them to tell you what to say." Dooley stood up and smiled, then turned around and was gone along the hallway.

"Today's the day!" announced his wife, looking infernally pleased with herself.

"Today," he murmured, trying to accept the inevitable.

"It will be over in no time!" she said, beaming.

"Over in no time. Of course."

"So, let's roll up our sleeves and begin!"

He began rolling. " 'He has half the deed done who has made a beginning.' "

"Plato!" crowed his wife.

"Horace!" he snapped.

Cynthia brushed her hair from her eyes and peered at him with cool disdain. "My escort to the junior prom, as I recall. I didn't realize you'd met."

They emptied everything onto the floor in a pile that, he surmised, was altogether large enough to fill an eighteen-wheeler.

After removing the drawers and roping the doors shut, they muscled the thing down the stairs and through the hallway, out to the stoop and down the steps, then across the side yard and through the hedge, where they set it on the flagstones.

He mopped his face.

She panted and moaned.

He squatted on his heels and looked at the ground.

She leaned against a tree and stared at the sky.

A bird called. An airplane roared over.

"Ready?" she inquired.

"Ready," he replied.

"Didn't I tell you we could do it?"

"You did."

"OK," she shouted, "one, two, three, lift!"

Off they bolted like two pack mules, across the side yard of the rectory, up the steps, and over the threshold, where the door was propped open with a broom handle.

Safely inside, they set their cargo down and fell exhausted into chairs at the table.

"Lemonade?" she asked after a labored pause.

"And step on it," he said, mopping again.

He looked at the alien thing sitting in his kitchen. A three-bedroom condo, at the very least. A shipping crate for a Canadian moose. . . .

"There!" she said, handing him the lemonade and gulping hers.

If this wasn't the last blasted piece of decorating business on his wife's agenda, he was going to build a brick wall across the path through the hedge and be done with it.

"You might have waited for Puny to give us a hand," he said.

"I can't ask a new mother to be hauling heavy furniture."

"Heavy? Did I hear you say heavy? You've insisted for a year that this thing is light as a feather!"

"Oh, poop," she said darkly, "you know what I mean."

He downed his lemonade and stood up to take his medicine like a man. "Ready?"

"'Ready," she said, eyeing him. "And don't scratch the hall floors. They've just been waxed."

Waxed, was it? He could see them taking one wrong step, skating up the hall, bursting through the front door, and landing in the street with the blooming thing on top of them. Bachelors didn't rearrange the decor, no, indeed. In fifteen years, he had scarcely moved a side chair from one place to another.

He sighed deeply.

"You're sighing," she said.

"A penetrating observation."

"One, two, three, lift!"

Away they went, lumbering down the hall. He tried to grip the slick floor with his toes, but they were imprisoned in his loafers.

"There!" she said happily, stepping back from the guest room wall to take a look. "What do you think, darling?"

"It's wonderful!" he said, meaning it. "It belongs there. You were right all along, Kavanagh."

"We'll have so much more room for towels and linens . . . "

"Exactly!" he said, mopping his face. "Absolutely." What was that zapping pain that raced up his right leg? Or was it coming from his lower back?

" . . . and wonderful storage for sheets and pillowcases!"

"Well done," he said, ready to crash on the study sofa, next to the electric fan.

"However . . . " She stood still farther from the wall and peered over her glasses. She folded her arms across her chest and frowned.

"However, what?"

"When you consider the way the windows are situated in this room, it looks out of proportion to the wall. Rats! Do you see what I mean?"

He recognized the faraway look she often got when thinking up a book. "Not at all," he said. "I don't see that at all, it's wonderful right where it is, we should have done this ages ago." He regretted sounding desperate.

"In fact, Timothy, do you know where it would really look grand? In our bedroom! On the wall to the right as you go in the door, just where your family chest is. We could move the chest in here—it would look terrific. All *that* old, dark wood with all *this* old, dark wood. I think that's the answer."

He backed from the room, looking pale.

"But not today, dearest!" she said, coming after him and planting a kiss on his cheek. "More like . . . in the spring."

"Of course!" he said, feeling brighter. "In the spring!"

They walked across the hall and into their bedroom. "Right there!" she said, pointing at the wall behind the family chest. "Perfect!"

He took a deep breath.

"In the spring," he said, smiling at his determined wife. "Perfect!"

Visit America's favorite small town—
one book at a time

Welcome to the next book,

Out to Canaan

CHAPTER ONE

A Tea and a Half

THE INDOOR PLANTS were among the first to venture outside and breathe the fresh, cold air of Mitford's early spring.

Eager for a dapple of sunlight, starved for the revival of mountain breezes, dozens of begonias and ferns, snake plants, Easter lilies, and wandering Jew were set out, pot-bound and listless, on porches throughout the village.

As the temperature soared into the low fifties, Winnie Ivey thumped three begonias, a sullen gloxinia, and a Boston fern onto the back steps of the house on Lilac Road, where she was now living. Remembering the shamrock, which was covered with aphids, she went back and fetched it out and set it on the railing.

"There!" she said, collecting a lungful of the sharp, pure air. "That ought to fix th' lot of you."

When she opened the back door the following morning, she was stricken at the sight. The carefully wintered plants had been turned to mush by a stark raving freeze and minor snow that also wrenched any notion of early bloom from the lilac bushes.

It was that blasted puzzle she'd worked until one o'clock in the morning, which caused her to forget last night's weather news. There she'd sat like a moron, her feet turning to ice as the temperature plummeted, trying to figure out five letters across for a grove of trees.

Racked with guilt, she consoled herself with the fact that it had, at least, been a chemical-free way to get rid of aphids.

At the hardware, Dora Pugh shook her head and sighed. Betrayed by yesterday's dazzling sunshine, she had done display windows with live baby chicks, wire garden fencing, seeds, and watering cans. Now, she might as well haul the snow shovels back and do a final clearance on salt for driveways.

Coot Hendrick collected his bet of five dollars and an RC cola from Lew Boyd. "Ain't th' first time and won't be th' last you'll see snow in May," he said, grinning. Lew Boyd hated it when Coot grinned, showing his stubs for teeth. He mostly hated it that, concerning weather in Mitford, the skeptics, cynics, and pessimists were usually right.

"Rats!" said Cynthia Kavanagh, who had left a wet scatter rug hanging over the rectory porch rail. Lifting it off the rail, she found it frozen as a Popsicle and able to stand perfectly upright.

Father Timothy Kavanagh, the local rector, had never heard such moaning and groaning about spring's tedious delay, and encountered it even in Happy Endings bookstore, where, on yet another cold, overcast morning, he picked up a volume entitled *Hummingbirds in the Garden.*

"Hummingbirds?" wailed young Hope Winchester, ringing the sale. "*What* hummingbirds? I suppose you think a hummingbird would dare stick its beak into this arctic tundra, this endless twilight, this . . . this *villatic barbican*?"

Villatic barbican was a phrase she had learned just yesterday from a book, and wanted to use it before she forgot it. She knew the rector from Lord's Chapel was somebody she could use such words with—he hadn't flinched when she said "empiric" only last week, and seemed to know exactly what she was talking about.

While everyone else offered lamentations exceeding those of the prophet Jeremiah, the rector felt smugly indifferent to complaints that spring would never come. Turning up his collar, he leaned into a driving wind and headed toward the office.

Hadn't winter dumped ice, snow, sleet, hail, and rain storms on the village since late October? Hadn't they been blanketed by fog so thick you could cut it with a dull knife, time and time again? With all that moisture seeping into the ground for so many long months, didn't it foretell the most glorious springtime in years? And wouldn't that be, after all, worth the endless assault?

"Absolutely!" he proclaimed aloud, trucking past the Irish Woolen Shop. "No doubt about it!"

"See there?" said Hessie Mayhew, peering out the store window. "It's got Father Tim talking to himself, it's that bad." She sighed. "They say if sunlight doesn't get to your pineal glands for months on end, your sex drive quits."

Minnie Lomax, who was writing sale tags for boiled wool sweaters, looked up and blinked. "What do you know about pineal glands?" She was afraid to ask what Hessie might know about sex drive.

"What does anybody know about pineal glands?" asked Hessie, looking gloomy.

Uncle Billy Watson opened his back door and, without leaving the threshold, lifted the hanging basket off the nail and hauled it inside.

"Look what you've gone and done to that geranium!" snapped his wife of nearly fifty years. "I've petted that thing the winter long, and now it's dead as a doornail."

The old man looked guilt stricken. "B'fore I hung it out there, hit was already gone south!"

"Shut my mouth? Did you say shut my mouth?" Miss Rose, who refused to wear hearing aids, glared at him.

"I said *gone south*! Dead! Yeller leaves!"

He went to the kitchen radiator and thumped the hanging basket on top. "There," he said, disgusted with trying to have a garden in a climate like this, "that'll fire it up again."

The rector noted the spears of hosta that had congregated in beds outside the office door. Now, there, as far as spring was concerned, was something you could count on. Hosta was as sturdy a plant as you could put in the ground. Like the postman, neither sleet nor snow could drive it back. Once it emerged from the dirt, up it came, fiercely defiant—only, of course, to have its broad leaves shredded like so much Swiss cheese by Mitford's summer hail.

"It's a jungle out there," he sighed, unlocking his office door.

After the snow flurry and freeze came a day of rain, followed by a sudden storm of sleet that pecked against the windows like a flock of house sparrows.

His wife, he noted, looked pale. She was sitting at the study window, staring at the infernal weather and chewing her bottom lip. She was also biting the cuticle of her thumb, wrapping a strand of hair around one finger, tapping her foot, and generally amusing herself. He, meanwhile, was reading his new book, and doing something productive.

A low fire crackled on the hearth.

"Amazing!" he said. "You'd never guess one of the things that attracts butterflies."

"I don't have a clue," said Cynthia, appearing not to want one, either. The sleet gusted against the window panes.

"Birdbaths!" he exclaimed. No response. "Thinking about the Primrose Tea, are you?"

The second edition of his wife's famous parish-wide tea was coming in less than two weeks. Last year at this time, she was living on a stepladder, frantically repainting the kitchen and dining room, removing his octogenarian drapes, and knocking holes in the plaster to affect an "old Italian villa look." Now here she was, staring out the window without any visible concern for the countless lemon squares, miniature quiches, vegetable sandwiches, and other items she'd need to feed a hundred and twenty-five women, nearly all of whom would look upon the tea as lunch.

His dog, Barnabas, ambled in and crashed by the hearth, as if drugged.

Cynthia tapped her foot and drummed her fingers on the chair arm. "Hmmm," she said.

"Hmmm what?"

She looked at him. "T. D. A."

"T. D. A.?"

"The Dreaded Armoire, dearest."

His heart pounded. Please, no. Not the armoire. "What about it?" he asked, fearing the answer.

"It's time to move it into our bedroom from the guest room. Remember? We said we were going to do it in the spring!" She smiled at him suddenly, as she was wont to do, and her sapphire-colored eyes gleamed. After a year and a half of marriage, how was it that a certain look from her still made him weak in the knees?

"Aha."

"So!" she said, lifting her hands and looking earnest.

"So? So, it's not spring!" He got up from the sofa and pointed toward the window. "See that? You call that spring? This, Kavanagh, is as far from spring as . . . as . . ."

"As Trieste is from Wesley," she said, helping out, "or the Red Sea from Mitford Creek." He could never get over the way her mind worked. "But do not look at the weather, Timothy, look at the calendar! May third!"

Last fall, they had hauled the enormous armoire down her stairs, down her back steps, through the hedge, up his back steps, along the hall, and finally, up the staircase to the guest room, where he had wanted nothing more than to fall prostrate on the rug.

Had she liked it in the guest room, after all that? No, indeed. She had despised the very sight of it sitting there, and instantly came up with a further plan, to be executed in the spring; all of which meant more unloading of drawers and shelves, more lashing the doors closed with a rope, and more hauling—this time across the landing to their bedroom, where, he was convinced, it would tower over them in the night like a five-story parking garage.

"What are you going to do about the tea?" he asked, hoping to distract her.

"Not much at all 'til we get the armoire moved. You know how they are, Timothy, they want to poke into every nook and cranny. Last year, Hessie Mayhew was down on her very hands and knees, peering into the laundry chute, I saw her with my own eyes. And Georgia Moore opened every cabinet door in the kitchen, she said she was looking for a water glass, when I know for a fact she was seeing if the dishes were stacked to her liking. So, I certainly can't have the armoire standing on that wall in the guest room where it is clearly"—she paused and looked at him—"*clearly* out of place."

He was in for it.

He had managed to hold off the move for a full week, but, in return for the delay, was required to make four pans of brownies (a specialty since seminary), clean out the fireplace, black the andirons, and prune the overgrown forsythia at the dining room windows.

Not bad, considering.

On Saturday morning before the big event the following Friday, he rose early, prayed, studied Paul's first letter to the Corinthians, and sat with his sermon notes; then he ran two miles with Barnabas on his red leash, and returned home fit for anything.

His heart still pounding from the final sprint across Baxter Park, he burst into the kitchen, which smelled of lemons, cinnamon, and freshly brewed coffee. "Let's do it!" he cried. *And get it over with,* he thought.

The drawers were out, the shelves were emptied, the doors were lashed shut with a rope. This time, they were dragging it across the floor on a chenille bedspread, left behind by a former rector.

". . . a better way of life!"

Cynthia looked up. "What did you say, dearest?"

"I didn't say anything."

"Mack Stroupe will bring improvement, not change . . ."

They stepped to the open window of the stair landing and looked down to the street. A new blue pickup truck with a public address system was slowly cruising along Wisteria Lane, hauling a sign in the bed. *Mack for Mitford,* it read; *Mitford for Mack.*

". . . improvement, not change. So, think about it, friends and neighbors. And remember—here in Mitford, we already have the good life. With Mack as mayor, we'll all have a better life!" A loud blast of country music followed: *"If you don't stand for something, you'll fall for anything . . ."*

She looked at him. "Mack Stroupe! Please, no."

He wrinkled his brow and frowned. "This is May. Elections aren't 'til November."

"Starting a mite early."

"I'll say," he agreed, feeling distinctly uneasy.

"He's done broke th' noise ordinance," said Chief Rodney Underwood, hitching up his gun belt.

Rodney had stepped to the back of the Main Street Grill to say hello to the early morning regulars in the rear booth. "Chapter five, section five-two in the Mitford Code of Ordinance lays it out. No PA systems for such a thing as political campaigns."

"Startin' off his public career as a pure criminal," said Mule Skinner.

"Which is th' dadgum law of the land for politicians!" The *Mitford Muse* editor, J. C. Hogan, mopped his brow with a handkerchief.

"Well, no harm done. I slapped a warning on 'im, that ordinance is kind of new. Used to, politicians was haulin' a PA up and down th' street, ever' whichaway."

"What about that truck with the sign?" asked Father Tim.

"He can haul th' sign around all he wants to, but th' truck has to keep movin.' If he parks it on town property, I got 'im. I can run 'im in and he can go to readin' *Southern Livin'*." The local jail was the only detention center the rector ever heard of that kept neat stacks of *Southern Living* magazine in the cells.

"I hate to see a feller make a fool of hisself," said Rodney. "Ain't *no*body can whip Esther Cunningham—an' if you say I said that, I'll say you lied."

"Right," agreed Mule.

" 'Course, she *has* told it around that one of these days, her an' Ray are takin' off in th' RV and leave th' mayorin' to somebody else."

Mule shook his head. "Fifteen years is a long time to be hog-tied to a thankless job, all right."

"Is that Mack's new truck?" asked Father Tim. As far he knew, Mack never had two cents to rub together, as his hot-dog stand by the Exxon station never seemed to rake in much business.

"I don't know whose truck it is, it sure couldn't be Mack's. Well, I ain't got all day to loaf, like you boys." Rodney headed for the register to pick up his breakfast order. "See you in th' funny papers."

J.C. scowled. "I don't know that I'd say nobody can whip Esther. Mack's for improvement, and we're due for a little improvement around here, if you ask me."

"Nobody asked you," said Mule.

He dialed the number from his office. "Mayor!"

"So it's the preacher, is it? I've been lookin' for you."

"What's going on?"

"If that low-down scum thinks he can run me out of office, he's got another think coming."

"Does this mean you're not going to quit and take off with Ray in the RV?"

"Shoot! That's what I say just to hear my head roar. Listen—you don't think the bum has a chance, do you?"

"To tell the truth, Esther, I believe he does have a chance. . . ."

Esther's voice lowered. "You do?"

"About the same chance as a snowball in July."

She laughed uproariously, and then sobered. "Of course, there is *one* way that Mack Stroupe could come in here and sit behind th' mayor's desk."

He was alarmed. "Really?"

"But only one. And that's over my dead body."

Something new was going on at home nearly every day.

On Tuesday evening, he found a large, framed watercolor hanging in the rectory's once-gloomy hallway. It was of Violet, Cynthia's white cat and the heroine of the award-winning children's books created by his unstoppable wife. Violet sat on a brocade cloth, peering into a vase filled with nasturtiums and a single, wide-eyed goldfish.

"Stunning!" he said. "Quite a change."

"Call it an *improvement*," she said, pleased.

On Wednesday, he found new chintz draperies in the dining room and parlor, which gave the place a dazzling elegance that fairly bowled him over. But—hadn't they agreed that neither would spend more than a hundred bucks without the other's consent?

She read his mind. "So, the draperies cost five hundred, but since the watercolor is worth that and more on the current market, it's a wash."

"Aha."

"I'm also doing one of Barnabas, for your study. Which means," she said, "that the family coffers will respond by allotting new draperies for our bedroom."

"You're a bookkeeping whiz, Kavanagh. But why new draperies when we're retiring in eighteen months?"

"I've had them made so they can go anywhere, and fit any kind of windows. If worse comes to worst, I'll remake them into summer dresses, and vestments for my clergyman."

"That's the spirit!"

Why did he feel his wife could get away with anything where he was concerned? Was it because he'd waited sixty-two years, like a stalled ox, to fall in love and marry?

If he and Cynthia had written a detailed petition on a piece of paper and sent it heavenward, the weather couldn't have been more glorious on the day of the talked-about tea.

Much to everyone's relief, the primroses actually bloomed. However, no sooner had the eager blossoms appeared than Hessie Mayhew bore down on them with a vengeance, in yards and hidden nooks everywhere. She knew precisely the location of every cluster of primroses in the village, not to mention the exact whereabouts of each woods violet, lilac bush, and pussy willow.

"It's Hessie!" warned an innocent bystander on Hessie's early morning run the day of the tea. "Stand back!"

Furnished with a collection of baskets, which she wore on her arms like so many bracelets, Hessie did not allow help from the Episcopal Church Women, or any of her own presbyters. She worked alone, she worked fast, and she worked smart.

After going at a trot through neighborhood gardens, huffing up Old Church Lane to a secluded bower of early-blooming shrubs, and combing four miles of country roadside, she showed up at the back door of the rectory at precisely eleven a.m., looking triumphant.

Sodden with morning dew and black dirt, she delivered a vast quantity of flowers, moss, and grapevine into the hands of the rector's househelp, Puny Guthrie, then flew home to bathe, dress, and put antibiotic cream on her knees, which were skinned when she leaned over to pick a wild trillium and fell sprawling.

The Episcopal Church Women, who had arrived as one body at ten-thirty, flew into the business of arranging "Hessie's truck," as they called it, while Barnabas snored in the garage and Violet paced in her carrier.

"Are you off?" asked Cynthia, as the rector came at a trot through the hectic kitchen.

"Off and running. I finished polishing the mail slot, tidying the slipcover on the sofa, and trimming the lavender by the front walk. I also beat the sofa pillows for any incipient dust, and coughed for a full five minutes."

"Well done!" she said, cheerily, giving him a hug.

"I'll be home at one-thirty to help the husbands park cars."

Help the husbands park cars? he thought as he sprinted toward the office. He was a *husband*! After all these months, the thought still occasionally slammed him in the solar plexus and took his breath away.

Nine elderly guests, including the Kavanaghs' friend, Louella, arrived in the van from Hope House and were personally escorted up the steps of the rectory and into the hands of the Altar Guild.

Up and down Wisteria Lane, men with armbands stitched with primroses and a cross directed traffic, which quickly grew snarled. At one point, the rector leaped into a stalled Chevrolet and managed to roll it to the curb. Women came in car pools, husbands dropped off spouses, daughters delivered mothers, and all in all, the narrow street was as congested as a carnival in Rio.

"This is th' biggest thing to hit Mitford since th' blizzard two years ago," said Mule Skinner, who was a Baptist, but offered to help out, anyway.

The rector laughed. "That's one way to look at it." Didn't anybody ever *walk* in this town?

"Look here!"

It was Mack Stroupe in that blasted pickup truck, carting his sign around in their tea traffic. Mack rolled by, chewing on a toothpick and looking straight ahead.

"You comin' to the Primrose Tea?" snapped Mule. "If not, get this vehicle out of here, we're tryin' to conduct a church function!"

Four choir members, consisting of a lyric soprano, a mezzo-soprano, and two altos, arrived in a convertible, looking windblown and holding on to their hats.

"Hats is a big thing this year," observed Uncle Billy Watson, who stood at the curb with Miss Rose and watched the proceedings. Uncle Billy was the only man who showed up at last year's tea, and now considered his presence at the event to be a tradition.

Uncle Billy walked out on the street with the help of his cane and tapped Father Tim on the shoulder. "Hit's like a Chiney puzzle, don't you know. If you 'uns'd move that'n off to th' side and git that'n to th' curb, hit'd be done with."

"No more parking on Wisteria," Ron Malcolm reported to the rector. "We'll direct the rest of the crowd to the church lot and shoot 'em back here in the Hope House van."

A UPS driver, who had clearly made an unwise turn onto Wisteria, sat in his truck in front of the rectory, stunned by the sight of so much traffic on the usually uneventful Holding-Mitford-Wesley run.

"Hit's what you call a standstill," Uncle Billy told J. C. Hogan, who showed up with his Nikon and six rolls of Tri-X.

As traffic started to flow again, the rector saw Mack Stroupe turn onto Wisteria Lane from Church Hill. Clearly, he was circling the block.

"I'd like to whop him upside th' head with a two-by-four," said Mule. He glared at Mack, who was reared back in the seat with both windows down, listening to a country music station. Mack waved to several women, who immediately turned their heads.

Mule snorted. "Th' dumb so-and-so! How would you like to have that peckerwood for mayor?"

The rector wiped his perspiring forehead. "Watch your blood pressure, buddyroe."

"He says he's goin' to campaign straight through spring and summer, right up to election in November. Kind of like bein' tortured by a drippin' faucet."

As the truck passed, Emma Newland stomped over. "I ought to climb in that truck and slap his jaws. What's he doin', anyway, trying to sway church people to his way of thinkin'?"

"Let him be," he cautioned his secretary and on-line computer whiz. After all, give Mack enough rope and . . .

Cynthia was lying in bed, moaning, as he came out of the shower. He went into the bedroom, hastily drying off.

"Why are you moaning?" he asked, alarmed.

"Because it helps relieve exhaustion. I hope the windows are closed so the neighbors can't hear."

"The only neighbor close enough to hear is no longer living in the little yellow house next door. She is, in fact, lying right here, doing the moaning."

She moaned again. "Moaning is good," she told him, her face mashed into the pillow. "You should try it."

"I don't think so," he said.

Warm as a steamed clam from the shower, he put on his pajamas and sat on the side of the bed. "I'm proud of you," he said, rubbing her back. "That was a tea and a half! The best! In fact, words fail. You'll have a time topping that one."

"Don't tell me I'm supposed to top it!"

"Yes, well, not to worry. Next year, we can have Omer Cunningham and his pilot buddies do a fly-over. That'll give the ladies something to talk about."

"A little further down," she implored. "It's my lower back. Ugh. It's killing me from all the standing and baking."

"I got the reviews as your guests left."

"Only tell me the good ones, I don't want to hear about the cheese straws, which were as limp as linguine."

" 'Perfect' was a word they bandied around quite a bit, and the lemon squares, of course, got their usual share of raves. Some wanted me to know how charming they think you are, and others made lavish remarks about your youth and beauty."

He leaned down and kissed her on the cheek, inhaling the faintest scent of wisteria. "You are beautiful, Kavanagh."

"Thanks."

"I don't suppose there are any special thanks you'd like to offer the poor rube who helped unsnarl four thousand three hundred and seventy-nine cars, trucks, and vans?"

She rolled over and looked at him, smiling. Then she held her head to one side in that way he couldn't resist, and pulled him to her and kissed him tenderly.

"Now you're talking," he said.

The phone rang.

"Hello?"

"Hey."

Dooley! "Hey, yourself, buddy."

"Is Cynthia sending me a box of stuff she made for that tea? I can't talk long."

"Two boxes. Went off today."

"Man! Thanks!"

"You're welcome. How's school?"

"Great."

Great? Dooley Barlowe was not one to use superlatives. "No kidding?"

"You're going to like my grades."

Was this the little guy he'd struggled to raise for nearly three years? The Dooley who always shot himself in the foot? The self-assured sound of the boy's voice made his hair fairly stand on end.

"We're going to like you coming home, that's what. In just six or seven weeks, you'll be here. . . ."

Silence. Was Dooley dreading to tell him he wanted to spend the summer at Meadowgate Farm? The boy's decision to do that last year had nearly broken his heart, not to mention Cynthia's. They had, of course, gotten over it, as they watched the boy doing what he loved—learning more about veterinary medicine at the country practice of Hal Owen.

"Of course," said the rector, pushing on, "we want you to go out to Meadowgate, if that's what you'd like to do." He swallowed. This year, he was stronger, he could let go.

"OK," said Dooley, "that's what I'd like to do."

"Fine. No problem. I'll call you tomorrow for our usual phone visit. We love you."

"I love you back."

"Here's Cynthia."

"Hey," she said.

"Hey, yourself." It was their family greeting.

"So, you big galoot, we sent a box for you and one to share with your friends."

"What's in it?"

"Lemon squares."

"I like lemon squares."

"Plus raspberry tarts, pecan truffles, and brownies made by the preacher."

"Thanks."

"Are you OK?"

"Yes."

"No kidding?"

"Yep."

"Good!" said Cynthia. "Lace Turner asked about you the other day."

"That dumb girl that dresses like a guy?"

"She doesn't dress like a guy anymore. Oh, and Jenny was asking about you, too."

"How's Tommy?"

"Missing you. Just as we do. So hurry home, even if you are going to spend the summer at Meadowgate, you big creep."

Dooley cackled.

"We love you."

"I love you back."

Cynthia placed the receiver on the hook, smiling happily.

"Now, you poor rube," she said, "where were we?"

He sat on the study sofa and took the rubber band off the *Mitford Muse.*

Good grief! There he was on the front page, standing bewildered in front of the UPS truck with his nose looking, as usual, like a turnip or a tulip bulb. Why did J. C. Hogan run this odious picture, when he might have photographed his hardworking, good-looking, and thoroughly deserving wife?

Primrose Tee Draws
Stand-Out Crowd

Clearly, Hessie had not written this story, but had given her notes to J.C., who had forged ahead without checking his spelling.

Good time had by all . . . same time next year . . . a hundred and thirty guests . . . nine gallons of tea, ten dozen lemon squares, eight dozen raspberry tarts . . . traffic jam . . .

The phone gave a sharp blast.

"Hello?"

"Timothy . . ."

"Hal! I've just been thinking of you and Marge."

"Good. And we of you. I've got some . . . hard news, and wanted you to know."

Hal and Marge Owen were two of his closest, most valued friends. He was afraid to know.

"I've just hired a full-time assistant."

"That's the bad news? It sounds good to me, you work like a Trojan."

"Yes, but . . . we won't be able to have Dooley this summer. My assistant is a young fellow, just starting out, and I'll have to give him a lot of time and attention. Also, we're putting him up in Dooley's room until he gets established." Hal sighed.

"But that's terrific. You know Dooley's looking forward to being there—however, circumstances alter cases, as my Mississippi kin used to say."

"There's a large riding stable coming in about a mile down the road, they've asked me to vet the horses. That could be a full-time job, right there."

"I understand. Of course. Your practice is growing."

"We'll miss the boy, Tim, you know how we feel about him, how Rebecca Jane loves him. But look, we'll have him out the first two weeks he's home from school, if that works for you."

"Absolutely."

"Ah . . ."

"Yes?"

"Will you tell him?"

"I will. I'll talk to him in the next couple of days, get him thinking of what to do this summer. Be good for him."

"So why don't you and Cynthia plan to bring him out and spend the day? Bring Barnabas, too. Marge will make your favorite."

Deep-dish chicken pie, with a crust like French pastry. "We'll be there!" he said, meaning it.

"Will you tell him?" he asked Cynthia.

"No way," she said.

Nobody wanted to tell Dooley Barlowe that he couldn't spend the summer doing what he loved more than anything on earth.

She opened her eyes and rolled over to find him sitting up in bed.

"Oh, my dear! Oh, my goodness! What happened?"

He loved the look on his wife's face, he wanted to savor it. "It's already turned a few colors," he said, removing his hand from his right temple.

She peered at him as if he were a butterfly on a pin. "Yes! Black . . . and blue and . . . the tiniest bit of yellow."

"My old school colors," he said.

"But what happened?" He never heard such tssking and gasping.

"T. D. A," he replied.

"The dreaded armoire? What do you mean?"

"I mean that I got up in the middle of the night, in the dark, and went out to the landing, and opened the windows to give Barnabas a cool breeze. As I careened through the bedroom on my way to the bathroom, I slammed into the blasted thing."

"Oh, no. Oh, heavens. What can I do? And tomorrow's Sunday!"

"Spousal abuse," he muttered. "In today's TV news climate, my congregation will pick up on it immediately."

"Timothy, dearest, I'm so sorry. I'll get something for you, I don't know what, but something. Just stay right there and don't move."

She put on her slippers and robe and flew downstairs, Barnabas barking at her heels.

T. D. A. might stand for "The *Dreaded* Armoire" as far as his wife was concerned. As far as *he* was concerned, it stood for something else entirely.